GIOVANNI BOCCACCIO

Mrs Rosie and the Priest

Translated by
Peter Hainsworth

PENGUIN BOOKS

PENGUIN CLASSICS

UK | USA | Canada | Ireland | Australia
India | New Zealand | South Africa

Penguin Books is part of the Penguin Random House group of companies
whose addresses can be found at global.penguinrandomhouse.com.

This selection published in Penguin Classics 2015

008

Translation copyright © Peter Hainsworth, 2015

The moral right of the translator has been asserted

Set in 9.5/13 pt Baskerville 10 Pro
Typeset by Jouve (UK), Milton Keynes
Printed in Great Britain by Clays Ltd, Elcograf S.p.A.

A CIP catalogue record for this book is available from the British Library

ISBN: 978–0–141–39782–5

www.greenpenguin.co.uk

| MIX
Paper from
responsible sources
FSC® C018179

Penguin Random House is committed to a
sustainable future for our business, our readers
and our planet. This book is made from Forest
Stewardship Council® certified paper.

'When the men were off somewhere, he would come visiting their wives more solicitously than any priest they'd had before . . .'

GIOVANNI BOCCACCIO
Born 1313, Tuscany
Died 1375, Tuscany

Selection taken from Boccaccio's *Decameron*,
translated by Peter Hainsworth.

BOCCACCIO IN PENGUIN CLASSICS
The Decameron
Tales from the Decameron

Contents

Andreuccio's da Perugia's Neapolitan
    adventures   1

Ricciardo da Chinzica loses
    his wife   21

Mrs Rosie and the Priest   31

Patient Griselda   39

Andreuccio da Perugia's Neapolitan adventures

I was told some time ago about a young man from Perugia called Andreuccio, the son of a certain Pietro and a horse-dealer by trade. Having heard that horses were trading well in Naples, he put five-hundred gold florins in his bag and went off there with some other merchants, never having previously been away from home. He arrived on a Sunday evening, about vesper time, got the necessary information from his innkeeper and was in the market square early the next morning. He saw a lot of horses, many of which met with his approval, and did a good deal of bargaining without being able to agree a price for any of them. But he was keen to show that he was there to do some buying and naively and imprudently pulled out his bag of florins several times before the eyes of people coming and going past him. It was while he was negotiating, with his bag in full view, that a young Sicilian woman walked past. She was very beautiful, but ready to give any man what he wanted for a small payment. He didn't see her, but she saw his bag and immediately said to herself, 'Wouldn't I be a lucky one if that money were mine?' Then she went on her way.

There was old woman with her who was also Sicilian. As soon as she saw Andreuccio, she let the girl go on and hurried over to give him an affectionate hug. The young woman noticed and, without saying anything, stopped and waited for her on one side. Andreuccio, who had turned round and recognized the old woman, greeted her with great warmth. She promised to come and see him at his inn, but didn't keep him talking for too long just then and soon left. Andreuccio went back to his bargaining, though he made no purchases that morning. After seeing first the bag and then the intimacy with the old servant, the young woman began to wonder if she might get hold of some or all of the money. She asked a few cautious questions about who the young man was, where he was from, what he was doing there and how she came to know him. The old servant gave her all the information she wanted, almost in as much detail as Andreuccio might have supplied himself, being able to do this because she had spent a long time with his father first in Sicily and then in Perugia. She likewise told her where he was lodging and why he had come to Naples.

Once the young woman was fully informed about his family and their names, she had the basis for playing a clever trick that would bring her what she wanted. Back at her house she made sure that the old woman was busy all day so that she couldn't go and see Andreuccio. She had a much younger servant-girl to whom she had given a very good training in the sort of work she had in mind, and towards evening she sent her to the inn where Andreuccio was staying. When she arrived, she found him by chance standing alone in the doorway. She asked for Andreuccio and he said that he was the very man. At which she drew him to one side.

'Sir,' she said, 'there is a noble lady in this town who would appreciate a conversation with you, if you were so inclined.'

Andreuccio thought carefully for a moment when he heard this. He decided that he was a good-looking lad and deduced that this lady must have fallen for him, as if there were no other fine young men in Naples just then apart from himself. He quickly said that he was up for it, and asked where and when this lady wanted to have a talk with him.

The young servant-girl replied, 'She's waiting for you in her house, sir, whenever you feel like coming along.'

'Well, you lead the way and I'll follow on,' said Andreuccio immediately, with no thought of letting anyone in the inn know.

So the girl led him to the Sicilian woman's house, which was in a district called Malpertugio, a name meaning Bad Passage, which gives a clear idea of just how respectable a district it was. But Andreuccio, knowing nothing of this and quite unsuspecting, thought he was going to a most respectable house to see a lady of some standing, and confidently followed the girl into the house. As they were climbing the stairs, she called out to her mistress, 'Here's Andreuccio', and he saw her appear at the top, waiting for him.

She was still young, with a full figure and a lovely face, and her clothes and jewellery were tastefully ornate. When Andreuccio was closer, she came down three steps towards him, her arms wide, and, flinging them round his neck, stayed like that for a while without saying a word, as if too overcome to speak. Then she tearfully kissed his forehead and said in a broken voice, 'O my precious Andreuccio, welcome to my house!'

Such a heartfelt reception amazed Andreuccio, and he replied quite dazed, 'Well, it's wonderful to meet you, my lady!'

After this she took him by the hand and led him into the main room, and from there, without saying another word, into her private chamber, which was redolent with the scents of roses, orange blossom and other flowers. Andreuccio noticed a splendid curtained bed, and an abundance of beautiful dresses arranged on hangers in the south Italian way, and many other fine and costly items. In his inexperience he was fully convinced by all this that the woman could be nothing but a great lady. Once they were seated together on a chest that was at the foot of her bed, she embarked on the following speech.

'I am quite certain, Andreuccio, that you are startled at being embraced and wept over by me in this way. After

Andreuccio da Perugia's Neapolitan adventures

all, you don't know me and may never have heard my name mentioned. But in a moment you are going to hear something which will perhaps amaze you even more. The fact is, I am your sister. And I can tell you that, since God has granted me the enormous grace of letting me see one of my brothers before I die – though of course I want to see all of you – I shall not die unconsoled. Perhaps you have never heard a word of this. So I shall happily tell you all about it.

'As I think you may have been told, Pietro – that is, your father and mine – lived for a long time in Palermo. Thanks to his native goodness and appealing character he gained the affections of those who came to know him and still has a place in their hearts. But, among those most attached to him, there was someone who loved him more than anyone else, and that was my mother, who was a noble lady and recently widowed. She loved him so much that she put aside all fears of her father and brothers and any concern for her honour, and entered into intimate relations with him. As a result I was born into the world and am now the person you see before you.

'A little later, when a reason arose for Pietro to return to Perugia, he left me, still a very little girl, with my mother. From everything I heard, he never gave me or her another thought. If he had not been my father, I would be very critical of him, considering the ingratitude he showed to my mother – and let's leave aside the love he should have felt for me his daughter, and not by a servant-girl or some woman of easy virtue either. My mother was inspired by the truest form of love when, knowing nothing of who he was, she put herself and everything she had in his hands. But there you are. Wrongs of long ago are more easily criticized than put right.

'So he left me a little girl in Palermo. When I had grown into more or less the woman you see before you, my mother, who was a rich lady, married me to a man from Agrigento, an upstanding man of noble rank. Out of love for myself and my mother he moved to Palermo, and there, being very much on the Guelf side, he became involved in plotting with our King Charles. King Frederick got wind of the plot before any of our plans could be acted on, and so we had to flee Sicily just at the moment when I was expecting to become the finest lady there had ever been on the island. We took with us what few things we could – I mean few in comparison to all the possessions we had – and, leaving our lands and mansions behind, escaped to this city. We found King Charles very grateful. He partially compensated us for the losses we had suffered on his behalf. He gave us lands and houses, and he still gives my husband, your brother-in-law, a substantial pension, as you'll soon be able to see. So that is how I came to be here, and how, thanks to God's grace, though not at all to you, I now see you before me, my sweet brother.'

With this she clasped him to her again and kissed his forehead, still weeping tenderly.

She told her cock-and-bull story in a supremely coherent and convincing way, with not a hesitation or stutter. Andreuccio recalled that his father really had been in Palermo and he knew from his own experience what young men are like, and how prone they are to falling in love. What with the tender tears, embraces and decidedly unamorous kisses, he was convinced that what she said was more than true. When she finished, he made the following reply.

'My lady, you must not be shocked by my own amazement. To be candid, either my father for some reason of his own never spoke about you and your mother, or if he did speak of you, not a whisper reached my ears. So I had no more knowledge of you than if you had never existed. But it's all the more precious to me to have found you, my sister, in this place, because I'm here all alone and this was the thing I least expected. And to tell the truth, I can't imagine your not being precious to the grandest businessman I can think of, let alone to a small-scale merchant like myself. But please, explain one thing for me. How did you come to know I was here?'

'I was told this morning,' she replied. 'And the person who told me is a poor woman who spends a lot of time here with me, the reason being that, from what she says, she was with our father for a long time in both Palermo and Perugia. If it hadn't seemed to me more honourable for you to come here to what is your house than for me to come and see you at someone else's, I would have been with you ages ago.'

After this she started putting precise questions to him about his relatives, identifying each one by name. Andreuccio told her about them all, becoming more and more willing to believe what he should not have believed at all.

Since they kept on talking for a long time and it was very hot, she called for white wine and sweetmeats, and ensured that Andreuccio was duly served. He made to leave after this since it was now dinnertime, but she wouldn't allow it. Looking deeply distressed, she flung her arms round him, saying, 'Oh, poor me, I can tell I don't really matter to you! To think that you're here with a sister you've never seen before, in her house, where you should have come and stayed when you arrived, and you want to go off and have your dinner in an inn. No, you'll dine with me, and though my husband is not here, I'm very sorry to say, I'll do what little a lady is capable of to see you are treated with some degree of honour.'

Andreuccio could only come up with one reply.

'You do matter to me,' he said, 'as much as any sister should. But if I don't go, I shall keep them waiting for me for dinner all evening, which would be really churlish.'

'Lord in heaven,' she said, 'do you think I've nobody

in the house I can send to tell them not to expect you? Though you would be doing a finer thing, not to say your duty, if you sent a message to your friends inviting them to come and dine here. Then afterwards, if you were set on leaving, you and all the rest could go off in one big party.'

Andreuccio replied that he had no wish to see his friends that evening, and that, if this was how she felt, she should treat him as she pleased. She then made a show of sending a message to the inn telling them not to expect him for dinner. After this they talked on for a long time before sitting down to eat. They were served in a splendid fashion with a series of dishes, the woman cunningly prolonging the dinner well into the night. When they got up from the table, and Andreuccio expressed a desire to leave, she said that she could not possibly allow it. Naples was not a city for anyone to walk through at night, especially a stranger. She had sent a message to say he should not be expected for dinner and then she had sent another regarding where he was staying. He believed everything she said, and was delighted, in his deluded state, to stay on.

At her instigation conversation after dinner was prolonged and varied. Late into the night she left Andreuccio in her own chamber, with a young servant-boy to show him anything he needed, while she herself went off to another room with her maids.

It was very hot and as soon as he saw he was alone

Andreuccio removed his jacket and peeled off his leggings, which he left over the bedhead. Feeling nature calling him to lighten his stomach of the excess weight within it, he asked the servant where one did that sort of thing. The boy pointed to a door in a corner of the room.

'Go in there,' he said.

Andreuccio went insouciantly through the door. By chance he brought one of his feet down on a board, the other end of which was no longer attached to the joist on which it was resting. The result was that the board swung up in the air and then crashed downwards, taking Andreuccio with it. God was kind to him and he did himself no harm in the tumble, although he fell from a considerable height, but he was thoroughly covered in the horrible filth that the place was full of. To explain the arrangement in order to give you a clearer picture of what I've just said and what follows, two narrow beams had been fixed over the sort of narrow alleyway we often see separating two houses, with some boards nailed to them and a place to sit on fitted. It was one of these boards which had fallen with Andreuccio.

When he found himself down below in the alleyway, he was extremely upset at what had happened and began calling out to the boy. But, as soon as he had heard him fall, the boy had rushed to tell his mistress. She in her turn rushed into the bedroom, quickly looked to see if his clothes were there and found them. With them was the money, which, crazily, the ever suspicious Andreuccio

Andreuccio da Perugia's Neapolitan adventures

always carried on his person. The Palermo tart, who now had what she had schemed for by turning into the sister of the visitor from Perugia, couldn't care less any more about Andreuccio. She went promptly over to the door which Andreuccio had passed through when he fell, and closed it.

When the boy didn't reply, Andreuccio started calling more loudly, but to no avail. He was now becoming suspicious and beginning, somewhat late in the day, to have an inkling of the trickery. He climbed on to the low wall separating the alleyway from the street and, once down on the other side, found his way to the door of the house, which he easily recognized. He stood there for a long time, vainly calling out and shaking and banging on the door. He could now see the full extent of his misfortune quite clearly, which reduced him to tears.

'Oh, poor me,' he began saying. 'How little time it's taken for me to lose five-hundred florins and a sister too!'

After a lot more of this he began again beating on the door and calling out. The result was that many people living nearby woke up and then, when the din became unbearable, got themselves out of bed. One of the lady's female servants appeared at a window, looking all sleepy, and called out in an irritated voice, 'Who's banging away down there?'

'Oh, don't you know me?' said Andreuccio. 'I'm Andreuccio, the brother of Lady Fiordiliso.'

The servant replied, 'My good man, if you've had too

much to drink, go and sleep it off and come back in the morning. I don't know anything about any Andreuccio or anything else you're gabbling on about. Do us a favour, please go away and let us get some sleep.'

'What?' said Andreuccio. 'Don't you really know what I'm saying? Oh, you must do. But if family relations in Sicily are like that and get forgotten as quickly as this, at least let me have back the clothes I left with you and I'll be glad to go on my way with only the Lord for company.'

The servant almost broke out laughing.

'Good man,' she said, 'I think you're dreaming.'

And even before she finished speaking, she was back inside with the window shut.

Andreuccio was now fully aware of his losses and the pain of the realization made him so angry it almost drove him wild. He could not recover what he had lost through words and he resorted to physical violence. He picked up a big stone and began savagely beating at the door again, only now with much more force. At this many of the neighbours who had been woken up and were out of their beds started thinking that he was some no-gooder who was inventing the whole palaver to bother the good woman. When the banging got too much for them, they started calling out from their windows, as if they were the neighbourhood dogs barking all together at some stray intruder.

'It's an outrage,' they said, 'coming at this hour of night to respectable women's houses with all this claptrap. Oh, go away, for God's sake, and please let us sleep. If you have anything to sort out with her, you can come back tomorrow. Just don't be such a blasted nuisance tonight.'

What they were saying perhaps encouraged the good Sicilian woman's pimp, who was inside the house, though he had not been seen or heard till now by Andreuccio. He came to the window and in his best horrible and savage voice called out loudly, 'Who's that down there?'

Andreuccio looked up when he heard this and saw someone who, so far as he could tell (which was not much), had the air of a man to be taken seriously. He had a thick black beard and was yawning and rubbing his eyes, as if he'd just awoken from deep sleep.

'I'm a brother of the lady of the house,' replied Andreuccio nervously.

The man did not wait for him to go on.

'I can't think,' he said in an even more intimidating voice than before, 'why I'm stopping myself from coming down there and giving you such a thrashing you won't ever move again. An irritating drunk of a donkey, that's what you must be, not letting anyone round here get any sleep tonight.'

With that he turned back inside and bolted the window.

Some of the neighbours knew what sort of a man he

was and whispered a few fearful words of advice to Andreuccio.

'For God's sake,' they said, 'go away, good man, don't get yourself murdered down there. Go away for your own good.'

Being already terrified by the ruffian's voice and appearance, Andreuccio saw every reason for accepting this advice, which he felt was motivated by simple goodwill. He was now as dejected as anyone could be and despaired of recovering his money. He set off towards the part of the city he had come from following the servant-girl earlier that day, aiming to get back to his inn, but with no idea of the way. Then, since the stench he could smell coming from him was disgusting, he decided to go towards the sea in order to wash himself down. But he turned leftwards and headed up a street called the Ruga Catalana, or Catalan Way. This was taking him to the higher part of the city, when he happened to see in front two figures coming towards him with a lantern. He was afraid they might be part of the official watch, or else just up to no good. He noticed an open building nearby and quietly crept in to try to avoid them. But it was as if they had been directed precisely to that spot. They too entered the building. One was carrying various tools round his neck, which he unloaded, and the two of them began looking the tools over and commenting on them.

At a certain point in their conversation, one of them said, 'What can it be? I can smell the worst stink I've ever smelt.' And then, lifting up the lantern a bit, they saw the miserable Andreuccio.

'Who's that there?' they asked, astounded.

When Andreuccio said nothing, they came over to him with the light and asked him what he was doing there in such a repulsive state. Andreuccio told them the whole story of what had happened to him. They guessed where it could have been and said to each other, 'It must have all happened at that villain Buttafuoco's.'

'My good lad,' said one of them, turning to Andreuccio, 'you might have lost your money, but you have plenty reason for praising the Lord that you happened to have that fall and then couldn't get back into the house. If you hadn't fallen, you can be sure that you'd have been murdered as soon as you dropped off to sleep, and then you'd have lost your life as well as your money. But what's the point of crying over it at this stage? You've as much chance of getting a penny back as of picking stars from the sky. You're likely to end up dead if that villain hears you've been blabbing away.'

Then, after some conferring together, they put a proposal to him.

'Look, we feel sorry for you,' they said. 'So, if you want to join us in a certain project we are en route to perform, we are of the definite opinion that your share of the profits will amount to much more than what you have lost.'

Andreuccio, in his desperate state, replied that he was ready and willing.

That day had seen the burial of a certain Archbishop of Naples called Messer Filippo Minutolo. He had been buried in elaborate finery with a ruby ring on his finger worth over five-hundred gold florins. The two of them had in mind to detach it. They explained the scheme to Andreuccio, who let greed override good sense, and the three of them set off.

Andreuccio was still giving off a strong smell as they proceeded towards the cathedral.

'Can't we find a way,' said one of the two at a certain point, 'for this companion of ours to have a wash somewhere to stop him stinking so horribly?'

'Yes,' said the other, 'we're near to a well now. It's always had a pulley and a big bucket. Let's go over and give him a quick wash.'

When they reached the well, they found the rope was there but the bucket had been removed. So they decided to tie Andreuccio to the rope and lower him into the well. Once at the bottom, he would wash himself, and then, when he had done, he would give the rope a shake and they would pull him up.

So they moved into action and lowered Andreuccio into the well. But it so happened that some of the night watch were feeling thirsty because of the heat and also because they had been chasing after someone. They were coming towards the well to get a drink when the other two saw them, and at once took to their heels, without any of the company coming after water seeing them.

Andreuccio da Perugia's Neapolitan adventures

Down in the well, Andreuccio, having finished washing, shook the rope a few times. The thirsty watchmen, who had now unstrapped their bucklers, their weapons and their surcoats, began pulling on the rope, believing that it was attached to a big bucketful of water.

As soon as Andreuccio saw he was near the rim of the well, he let go of the rope and grabbed hold of the rim in his hands. The sight was enough to terrify the watchmen, who immediately, without a word, let go of the rope and ran off as fast as they could. Andreuccio was profoundly startled. If he had not kept a firm hold, he would have fallen back into the well and perhaps have hurt himself badly, or even finished up dead. Once he was finally out of the well, he found the abandoned weaponry, which he knew his companions had not been carrying, and was even more amazed. Nervous, unclear what was going on, bemoaning his misfortune, he decided to take himself off without touching anything and wandered away with no idea of where he was heading. He was going along like this when he bumped into his two companions, who were coming back to pull him up out of the well. They were astonished and asked him who had actually done that. Andreuccio replied that he did not know, but gave them a full account of what had occurred and of what he had found by the well.

His companions realized what had happened and explained, laughing, why they had run away and who the people were who had pulled him up. Then, without wasting any more words since it was already midnight, they all went off to the cathedral. They got in quite easily and reached the tomb, which was marble and very large. They used their irons to lift the cover, which was enormously heavy, raising it just enough for a single man to get inside, and then they propped it up.

When this was done, one of them asked, 'Who's going to go inside?'

'Not me,' said the other.

'Nor me either,' said the first. 'But let Andreuccio go in.'

'I'm not doing that,' said Andreuccio.

Both of them turned on him.

'What do you mean you won't go in?' they said. 'By God, if you don't go in, we'll give you a bashing round the head with one of these iron poles and that'll be the end of you.'

This put the wind up Andreuccio. He went inside, thinking to himself as he did so, 'These two are making me enter the tomb in order to trick me. When I've passed them everything and am getting myself out again, they'll be off and I'll be left with nothing.'

He decided first and foremost to pocket his own share. He remembered the precious ring he had heard them discussing and, as soon as he was in the tomb, he took it off the Archbishop's finger and put it on his own. Then he passed them the crozier, the mitre and the gloves and stripped the body down to the shirt, passing them each item, saying that was all there was. They protested that

Andreuccio da Perugia's Neapolitan adventures

the ring must be somewhere and told him to look everywhere. He replied that he couldn't find it and pretended to go on looking, keeping them waiting for some time. But they were as canny as he was. They continued telling him to keep looking and then, picking their moment, they pulled away the prop supporting the lid of the tomb and ran off, leaving Andreuccio enclosed within. Anyone can guess how Andreuccio felt when he heard the lid fall.

He tried many times to push up the lid with his head and shoulders, but his efforts were useless. He was so overcome with the anguish of it all that he passed out, collapsing on the Archbishop's dead body. And anyone who had seen the two of them would have had difficulty deciding which was the more lifeless, the Archbishop or Andreuccio. When he came to his senses, he broke into a flood of tears, foreseeing that he could not avoid one of two ends. If no one came to open the tomb, he was doomed to die of hunger and the stink among the worms from the corpse. Or else, if people came and found him inside the tomb, he would be hung as a thief.

With these bleakly distressing thoughts going round in his head, he heard movement in the church and many people talking. They were, he gathered, going to do what he and his companions had already done. This sharply increased his terror. But when they had opened the tomb and propped up the lid, they began to argue about who should go inside, which none of them wanted to do. At last, after much dispute, a priest said, 'What are you frightened of? Do you think he's going to eat you? The dead don't eat people. I'll be the one to go in.' With this he leaned over the edge of the tomb, turned his head outwards and swung his legs inside in order to lower himself down. Andreuccio saw what was going on, jumped up and seized the priest by one of his legs and made as if to pull him down inside. When the priest felt himself being pulled, he let out an enormous shriek and scrambled out of the tomb as fast as he could. This terrified the rest of them. Leaving the tomb open, they took off as if they were being chased by a hundred thousand devils.

Seeing them go, Andreuccio clambered out of the tomb, happier than he could have hoped, and left the church by the way he had come in. It was almost daylight as he walked off, trusting to luck, with the ring on his finger. But he reached the seafront and finished up somehow at his inn, where he discovered that the merchants he had come with and the innkeeper had been worrying about him all night. He told them what had happened to him and they all opined that he should take the innkeeper's advice and leave Naples immediately. He quickly did so and returned to Perugia, with his funds now invested in a ring, after having set out to do some horse-trading.

Ricciardo da Chinzica loses his wife

There was once a judge in Pisa with more brains than muscle called Messer Ricciardo da Chinzica, who may have thought that what worked well with his studies would satisfy a wife too. Being very rich, he was able to devote considerable time and effort to searching for a good-looking young lady to marry, whereas, if he had been able to give himself the sort of professional counsel he gave to others, good looks and youth were just what he should have run away from. And he managed it: Ser Lotto Gualandi gave him one of his daughters in marriage. She was called Bartolommea and she was one of the best-looking and most fanciable girls in Pisa, though admittedly there aren't many there who don't look like hairy spiders. The judge took her home with great razzmatazz, and the marriage-feast was magnificent.

When he finally geared himself up for the actual consummation, he just about brought it off. But being scrawny, wizened and not exactly spunky, next morning he had to have a glass of fortified wine, some sweet biscuits and other pick-me-ups before he could re-enter the world of the living. The experience gave the judge a better idea of his capabilities than he had had before, and he began teaching his wife a calendar of saints' days of the kind that schoolboys pore over looking for holidays which might have been made in Ravenna. As he now showed her, there wasn't a day that wasn't a saint's day, or rather every day had a multitude of them. Reverence for these demanded, as he demonstrated on various grounds, that man and woman should abstain from acts of congress. Then he threw in fasts, the four Ember days, evening vigils for the Apostles and hundreds of other saints, Fridays, Saturdays, the Lord's Day, the whole of Lent, certain phases of the moon and endless other special cases, no doubt assuming that the breaks from court-work he enjoyed from time to time applied just as much to women in bed. So this was how he managed things for a long time, with his wife becoming seriously depressed from being given at best a monthly treat, while he always kept a watchful eye on her just in case someone else gave her lessons about working days like the ones he had given her about saints' days.

Since the next summer was very hot, Messer Ricciardo found himself wanting to go off to a beautiful property he had near Monte Nero, where he could relax and enjoy the air for a few days. With him he took his lovely wife. To give her some entertainment while they were there, one day he organized a fishing trip. The two of them sailed out on small boats to watch the spectacle, he on

Ricciardo da Chinzica loses his wife

one with the fishermen, she on the other with some ladies. They were so captivated that they drifted several miles along the coast almost without realizing it. But while they were gazing in rapt attention, a sloop suddenly came on the scene, belonging to Paganino da Mare, a celebrated corsair of the time. Once it sighted the boats, it set a course straight for them. They were unable to get away fast enough and Paganino caught up with the boat with the ladies in it. As soon as he laid eyes on Messer Ricciardo's beautiful wife, he stopped wanting any other booty, and whisked her into his sloop under the eyes of her husband, who was now on shore, and sailed away.

It doesn't take much to imagine how upset the judge was by the sight, given that he was so jealous he was fearful of the very air she breathed. In Pisa and elsewhere, he started fruitlessly complaining about the criminal behaviour of corsairs, but without discovering who had carried off his wife, or where they had taken her.

When Paganino took in how beautiful she was, he felt that he was on to a good thing. Not having a wife, he thought he might hang on to her permanently and began gently soothing her tears, which were copious. He had long ago thrown away saints' calendars and forgotten all about feast-days and holidays. That night he consoled her with some action, on the grounds that words had not helped much during the day. His consolations were so effective that the judge and his rules had gone entirely out of her head before they reached Monaco, and she began to have the time of her life with Paganino. And once he had got her there, he not only consoled her day and night, but honoured her as his wife.

After a while Messer Ricciardo got wind of the whereabouts of his good lady. Ardently desiring to do something and believing that no one else could manage to do what needed to be done, he made up his mind to go and get her himself, being prepared to pay out any amount of money to recover her. So he set to sea and sailed to Monaco. Once there he caught sight of his wife, and she caught sight of him, as she reported back to Paganino that evening, also informing him what his intentions were. When Messer Ricciardo saw Paganino the next morning, he went up to him and quickly started an easy, friendly conversation with him, while Paganino pretended all the while not to recognize him and waited for him to get to the point. When he judged the moment had arrived, deploying his best abilities in the most ingratiating way possible, Messer Ricciardo disclosed the reason why he had come to Monaco, begging Paganino to take as much money as he wanted and give him back the lady.

'Sir,' replied Paganino with a cheerful expression on his face, 'you are very welcome here. My reply in brief is as follows: it is true I have a young woman in my house, though I don't know whether she's your wife or someone else's. I don't know anything about her except what I've gathered from her during her stay with me. If you are her husband as you say, I'll take you to her since you seem

Ricciardo da Chinzica loses his wife

to me a likeable gentleman and I'm sure she'll recognize you very well. If she says that the situation is as you say and wishes to go away with you, then, since I do love a likeable man such as you, you can give me the amount you yourself decide on for a ransom. But if the situation should be different, it would be indecent for you to try to take her from me, since I've got youth on my side and can hold a woman in my arms as well as any man, particularly one who is more attractive than any other girl I've ever seen.'

'She certainly is my wife,' said Messer Ricciardo, 'as you'll soon see if you take me to where she is. She'll fling her arms round my neck straight away. So I won't ask for the terms to be different from those you've thought up yourself.'

'Let's go then,' said Paganino.

So they walked off to Paganino's house and went into a reception-room, from where Paganino sent for her. She appeared from a chamber properly and neatly dressed and went over where Messer Ricciardo was waiting with Paganino. There she addressed only the sort of remarks to Messer Ricciardo that she might have made to any other stranger who had come with Paganino to his house. The judge, who was expecting to be given a rapturous welcome, was amazed.

'Could it be,' he began to wonder, 'that depression and my protracted sufferings ever since I lost her have altered me so much that she doesn't recognize me?'

'Lady,' he said, 'taking you fishing has cost me dear. No one has suffered as much as I have since I lost you, and here you are seeming not to recognize me, given the unfriendly way you're talking. Can't you see that I'm your Messer Ricciardo, who's come here to pay whatever sum is demanded by this fine gentleman in whose house we find ourselves, so that I can have you back and take you away from here? He's being kind enough to restore you to me for a sum of my own choosing.'

The lady turned to him and gave him a faint smile.

'Are you addressing me, sir?' she asked. 'You should check you've not mistaken me for somebody else. As far as I'm concerned, I don't recall ever seeing you before.'

'It's you who should check what you're saying,' said Messer Ricciardo. 'Look at me properly. If you're willing to do a little serious recalling, you're bound to see that I'm your very own Ricciardo da Chinzica.'

'Sir, you'll forgive me,' said the lady, 'but it's not as right and proper as you imagine for me to give you a lengthy looking-over. All the same, I've looked at you enough to know that I've never seen you before.'

Messer Ricciardo imagined that she was acting in this way out of fear of Paganino and did not want to admit to knowing him in his presence. So, after a few moments, he asked Paganino if he would be so kind as to let him speak with the lady alone in her chamber. Paganino said that he was happy to do so, on condition that he didn't start kissing her against her will. Then he told the lady

Ricciardo da Chinzica loses his wife

to go with him into the chamber, listen to what he wanted to say and give him whatever reply she felt like.

Once the lady and Messer Ricciardo were in the chamber by themselves and had sat down, Messer Ricciardo began entreating her. 'Oh, heart of my life, my own sweet soul, my one hope, don't you recognize your Ricciardo, who loves you more than he loves himself? How can it be? Have I altered so much? Oh, lovely darling girl, at least give me a little look.'

The lady broke out laughing and wouldn't let him go on. 'You are very well aware,' she said, 'that I've not such a bad memory that I don't know you are Messer Ricciardo da Chinzica, my husband. But you made a poor show of knowing me as long as I was with you. You're not as wise as you want people to think you are, and you never were. If you had been, you really should have had the wit to see that I was young, fresh and frisky, and then have consequently acknowledged that young ladies require something else apart from food and clothing, though modesty forbids them to spell it out. But you know how you managed all that.

'You shouldn't have married, if you liked studying law more than studying your wife. Not that I thought you were much of a judge. You seemed more like a crier calling out holy days and feast-days, you knew them so well, not to mention fast-days and overnight vigils. Let me tell you that if you had given as many days off to the labourers working your lands as you did to the one who should have been working my little plot, you'd not have harvested one grain of corn. By chance I've met with this man here, chosen by God, because he shows a compassionate concern for my young age. And I stay with him in this chamber, where no one knows what a feast-day is. I mean those feast-days that you celebrated one after another, piously serving the Lord in preference to the ladies. Saturdays don't pass through that door, neither do Fridays, vigils, Ember days or Lent, which just goes on and on. No, it's all work, day and night, banging away all the time. As soon as the bell rang for matins this morning, there we were back at it, doing the same job again and again, as I know very well. So I intend to stay and work with him while I'm young, and keep feast-days and penances and fasts for when I'm old. Get out of here as soon as you can and good luck to you. Go and keep your saints' days as much as you like without me.'

Messer Ricciardo's distress at hearing her speak like this was unbearable.

'Oh, sweet soul of mine,' he said, when he realized she had finished, 'what are you saying? Aren't you bothered at all about your family's honour or your own? Do you want to stay here as this fellow's tart, living in mortal sin, rather than be my wife in Pisa? He'll get fed up with you and throw you out in total disgrace. But I'll always hold you dear and you'll always be the lawful mistress of my house, even if I didn't want to be your husband. Oh, please listen. Are you going to let this unbridled, immoral

Ricciardo da Chinzica loses his wife

lust make you forget your honour and forget me, when I love you more than my very life? Please, my dear love, don't say things like that any more, just come away with me. Now that I know what you want, I'll really make an effort from now on. So, sweetheart, change your mind, come away with me. I've been so miserable since you were carried off.'

'Now that there's nothing to be done about it,' said the lady, 'I don't see how anyone apart from me can be squeamish over my honour. I just wish my family had been a bit more squeamish when they gave me to you! But since they didn't bother about my honour then, I don't intend to bother about theirs now. If my sin's a mortar one, I'll stay stuck in it like a pestle. So don't you worry about me. And what's more, let me tell you that I feel like Paganino's wife here, while I felt like your tart in Pisa, what with lunar charts and geometric squarings having to align your planet and mine, while here Paganino has me in his arms all night, squeezing me, biting me, and the state he leaves me in God alone can tell you. Then you say you'll make an effort. Doing what? Waiting for something to happen? Straightening it by hand? I can tell you've turned into a redoutable knight since I saw you last! Go on, do your best to come to life. But you can't manage it. I don't think you belong in this world, you look such a wasted, miserable little wimp. And another thing. If he leaves me – which I don't think he's inclined to do as long I want to stay with him – I've no

Boccaccio

intention of ever coming back to you. Squeeze you till you squeaked, and you still wouldn't produce a spoonful of sauce. That meant that when I was with you I just lost out and paid out. I'm after better returns somewhere else. To go back to where I started, I tell you there are no feast-days and no vigils here, where I intend to stay. So leave as quickly as you can, and the Lord be with you. If you don't, I'll start shouting that you're forcing yourself on me.'

Messer Ricciardo saw that the game was up, recognizing there and then the folly in marrying a young wife without the appropriate wherewithal. He left the chamber in a saddened, suffering state and spoke a lot of waffle to Paganino, which got him nowhere. In the end, he left the lady and returned empty-handed to Pisa. The blow affected his mind and, when he was walking around the city, if someone greeted him or asked him a question, he would only reply, 'A horrid hole hates a holy day.'

It wasn't long before he died. When Paganino heard, knowing how much the lady loved him, he took her as his lawful wedded wife. Thereafter, with no thought for holy days or vigils or Lent, they worked their patch as much as their limbs would let them, and had a wonderful time together.

Mrs Rosie and the Priest

So, to begin, there's a village not far from here called Varlungo, as every one of you knows or will have heard from other people. It had once a valiant priest, a fine figure of a man who served the ladies well. He was not much of a reader, but every Sunday he would spout wholesome holy verbiage beneath the churchyard elm to refresh the spirits of his parishioners. When the men were off somewhere, he would come visiting their wives more solicitously than any priest they'd had before, sometimes bringing religious bits and pieces, holy water or candle-ends into their houses, and giving them his blessing.

Now among the women of the parish he took a fancy to, there was one he particularly liked, called Mrs Rosie Hues. She was the wife of a labourer by the name of Willy Welcome, and she really was a lovely ripe country-girl, tanned, sturdy, with lots of grinding potential. She was also better than any girl around at playing the tambourine, singing songs like 'The water's running down my river', and dancing reels and jigs, when she had to, waving a pretty little kerchief in her hand. With all these talents, she reduced the good priest to a quivering wreck. He would wander round the village all day trying to catch sight of her. When he realized she was in church on a Sunday morning, he would launch into a Kyrie or a Sanctus and struggle to come over as a virtuoso singer, though he sounded more like an ass braying, whereas, when he didn't see her there, he barely bothered to sing at all. All the same, he was clever enough not to arouse the suspicions of Willy Welcome or any neighbours of his.

From time to time, he would send Mrs Rosie presents in an effort to win her over. Sometimes it was a bunch of fresh garlic, since he grew the best in the region in a vegetable garden he worked with his own hands, sometimes it was a basket of berries, and now and then a bunch of shallots or spring onions. When he saw his chance, he would give her a hurt look and mutter a few gentle reproaches, while she acted cold, pretending not to notice, and looking all supercilious. So the estimable priest was left getting nowhere.

Now it happened one day that the priest was kicking his heels in the noontime heat out in the countryside with nothing much to do, when he bumped into Willy Welcome driving an ass loaded up with a pile of things on its back. He greeted him and asked him where he was going.

'To tell the truth, Father sir,' replied Willy, 'I'm off to town on a bit of business. I'm transporting these materials to Mr Notary Bonaccorri da Ginestreto to get him to aid and assist with a fiddle-faddle on the legal side that the

Mrs Rosie and the Priest

assessor is officializing to put the whole house in order at last.'

'That, my son, is a good thing to do,' said the priest, full of glee. 'Go with my blessing and come back soon. And if you should happen to see Lapuccio or Naldino, don't let it slip your mind to tell them to bring me those straps for my threshing flails.'

Willy said he would do that and went off towards Florence, while the priest decided the time had come for him to go and try his luck with Rosie. He strode out vigorously and did not stop until he reached her house. He went in, calling out, 'God be with us! Is anyone here?'

Rosie was up at the top of the house. Hearing him, she shouted, 'Father, you're very welcome. What are you doing all fancy free in this heat?'

'God help me,' said the priest, ' I've come to spend a little time with you, having just met your man on his way to town.'

Rosie was downstairs by now. She sat and began cleaning some cabbage seeds her husband had sifted out a short time before.

'Well, Rosie,' said the priest, 'must you go on being the death of me like this?'

Rosie began to laugh.

'Well, what am I doing to you?' she said.

'You're not doing anything to me,' said the priest, 'but you don't let me do what I'd like to do to you, which is love my neighbour as God commanded.'

'Oh, get on with you,' said Rosie. 'Do priests do things of that sort?'

'Yes,' said the priest, 'and better than other men. And why shouldn't we? I tell you, we do a much, much better job. And do you know why? It's because we let the pond fill up before the mill starts grinding. And truly I can give you just what you need, if you'll only stay quiet and let me do the business.'

'What do you mean, just what I need?' said Rosie. 'You priests are all tighter-fisted than the devil himself.'

'I don't know,' said the priest. 'Just ask me. Maybe you want a nice little pair of shoes, or a headscarf, or a pretty woollen waistband, or maybe something else.'

'That's all very well, Brother Priest,' said Rosie. 'I've enough of that stuff. But if you're that keen on me, you can do me a particular favour, and then I'll do what you want.'

'Tell me what you're after and I'll be glad to do it,' said the priest.

'I have to go to Florence on Saturday,' said Rosie, 'to give in the wool I've been spinning and get my spinning wheel mended. If you let me have five pounds (which I know you've got), I'll get the pawnbroker to give me back my purple skirt and the decorated Sunday belt I wore when I got married. You know not having it has meant I can't go to church or anywhere respectable. And after that I'll be up for what you want for evermore.'

'God help me,' said the priest, 'I haven't the money on

Mrs Rosie and the Priest

me. But trust me, I'll make sure you have it before Saturday.'

'Oh yes,' said Rosie, 'you're all great at making promises. And then you don't keep any of them. Do you think you can treat me the way you treated Nell the Belle, who was left with just a big bass tum to play with? You're not going to do the same to me, by God. She ended up on the game because of you. If you haven't got it here, go and get it.'

'Oh, please,' said the priest, 'don't make me go all the way back to the house. You can tell my luck is up, and there's no one about. It could be that when I came back someone would be here to get in our way. I don't know when it might next stand up as well as it's standing up now.'

'That's all very fine,' she said, 'but if you're willing to go, go. If not, you'll just have to manage.'

He saw that she was only going to agree to his wishes when a contract was signed and delivered, whereas he was hoping for a bit of free access.

'Look,' he said, 'you don't believe I'll bring you the money. What about if I leave you this blue cape of mine as a guarantee? It's a good one.'

Rosie gave him a haughty look.

'This cape,' she said, 'how much is it worth?'

'What do you mean, how much is it worth?' said the priest. 'Let me tell you it's Douai cloth, double ply, maybe triple ply, and there are even people here who say it's got some foreplay in it. I paid seven pounds at Lotto's second-hand clothes shop less than two weeks ago. It had five shillings knocked off, so it was a bargain, according to Bulietto d'Alberto, who you know is a bit of an expert in blue cloths.'

'Oh yes?' said Rosie. 'God help me, I'd never have believed it. But give it to me first.'

The good priest, who was feeling hard-pressed by his loaded weapon, unfastened his cape and passed it over.

'Well, Mr Priest,' she said, when she'd put it away, 'let's go down here to the shed. It doesn't get visitors.'

So off they went. And there he covered her in the sloppiest kisses in the world, introduced her to God's holy bliss and enjoyed himself generally with her for a good while. He finally left in the uncaped state priests normally appear in only at weddings and went back to the church.

There he reflected how all the candle-ends he picked up from his parishioners in the course of a year weren't worth half a fiver, and felt he had made a mistake. Now regretting leaving the cape behind, he started thinking about how to get it back at no cost to himself. Since he was quite crafty-minded, he figured out a good way of doing so. And it worked.

The next day being a feast-day, he sent the son of a neighbour of his to Rosie Hues's house, with a request for her to be so kind as to lend him her stone mortar, since Binguccio del Poggio and Nuto Buglietti were dining with him that morning and he wanted to make a

Mrs Rosie and the Priest

sauce. Rosie sent it back with the boy. When it got to round lunchtime, the priest guessed Willy Welcome and Rosie Hues would be eating. He called his curate and said to him, 'Pick up that mortar and take it back to Mrs Rosie. Tell her, "The Father is immensely grateful and would like to have back the cape the boy left with you as a guarantee."'

The curate went to Rosie's house with the mortar and found her with Willy at the table eating their meal. He set down the mortar and gave them the priest's message.

Rosie was all set to give her reply to this request for the cape. But Willy's brow darkened.

'So you need guarantees from our estimated father, do you?' he said. 'I swear to Christ, I could really give you a clout up the bracket. Go and fetch it right now, and get yourself cancered while you're at it. And watch out for him wanting anything else of ours. He'd better not be told no, whatever it is. Even if it's our donkey, our donkey he gets.'

Rosie got up grumbling to herself and went over to the linen-chest. She took out the cape and passed it to the curate.

'You must give that priest a message from me,' she said, 'Say, "Rosie Hues vows to God that you'll never again be sauce-pounding in her mortar. That last time you didn't do yourself any credit."'

The curate went off with the cape and relayed Rosie's message to the priest, who burst out laughing.

'You can tell her next time you see her,' he told him, 'that if she won't lend out the mortar, I won't lend her the pestle. The one goes with the other.'

Willy believed that his wife had spoken as she did because he had told her off and gave the matter no further thought. But coming off worst made Rosie fall out with the priest, and she refused to speak to him until the grape-harvest, when he terrified her by threatening to have her stuffed into the mouth of the biggest devil in hell. She made her peace with him over fermenting must and roasting chestnuts, and after that the two of them had a good guzzle together on various occasions. To make up for the five pounds, the priest had her tambourine re-covered and a dinky little bell attached, which made her very happy.

Patient Griselda

Years ago a young man called Gualtieri inherited the marquisate of Saluzzo as the eldest son of the family. Being unmarried and childless, he spent all his time hunting birds and beasts, without giving a thought to marriage or future offspring. He should have been considered a very wise man, but his subjects disapproved. They kept begging him to get himself a wife so that he should not die without an heir and they should not be left without a lord. They kept offering to find him one with a suitable father and mother, who would satisfy their hopes and who would make him very happy.

Gualtieri's response was as follows: 'My friends, you are forcing me into something I had been completely set on never ever doing, given how difficult it is to find someone with the right character and habits, how plentiful are the inappropriate candidates, and how hard life becomes for the man who ends up with someone he doesn't get on with. You claim you can tell the daughters' characters from how the fathers and mothers behave, and argue on that basis that you can provide me with a wife I'll be pleased with. That is rubbish. I don't see how you can know the fathers properly, or the mothers' secrets for that matter. Besides, even if you could, daughters are very often unlike their fathers and their mothers. But since you like the idea of tying me up in these chains, I'll try to satisfy you, and, in order not to end up blaming anyone but myself if things should go wrong, I want to do the finding myself. But I tell you that if you don't honour and respect whoever I choose, you'll learn to your cost how hard it's been for me to take a wife against my will, just because you begged me to.'

His valiant subjects replied that they would be happy just so long as he could bring himself to get married.

Gualtieri had been impressed for a good while by the behaviour of a poverty-stricken young woman from a village near his family home. Since he also judged her to be beautiful, he calculated that life with her could be very pleasant. He looked no further and made up his mind to marry her. He had the father summoned and entered into an agreement with this complete pauper to take the girl as his wife.

That done, he called together all his friends in the area he ruled.

'My friends,' he said to them, 'you have been eager for me to make my mind up about a wife for some time. Well, I have made a decision, more out of wanting to comply with your wishes than from any desire to be married on my part. You know what you promised me – that is, to

Patient Griselda

be content with the woman I chose, whoever she was, and to honour her as your lady. The time has come when I am about to keep my promise to you, and when I expect you to keep yours to me. I have found very near here a young woman after my heart. I intend to make her my wife and to bring her into my house in a few days. So arrange for the marriage-feast to be a fine one and to give her an honourable welcome. In that way I shall be able to say I am happy with how you have fulfilled your promise, and you will be able to say the same about me.'

His trusty subjects all replied that they were happy with this and that, no matter who she was, they would treat her as their lady and would honour her as such in every way. Then they all set about organizing a suitably grand and joyous celebration. And Gualtieri did his part too, arranging for a sumptuous and splendid marriage-feast, to which he invited a multitude of friends, relations, great nobles and other people from the surrounding area. In addition he had beautiful, expensive dresses made to fit a young woman who, he judged, had the same measurements as the girl he had decided to marry. Not only that, but he ordered belts, rings and a lovely, costly tiara, plus everything else a new bride should have.

Soon after sunrise on the day appointed for the wedding, Gualtieri mounted his horse, and all those who had come to honour him did the same. Everything needed was now in order, and he called out, 'Gentlemen, it is time to go for the new bride.'

After which he set off along the road to the village with the whole company. When they reached the girl's father's cottage, they found her hurrying back from the spring with some other women in the hope of catching sight of Gualtieri's bride. When he saw her, he called out to her by her name – that is, Griselda – and asked her where her father was.

'My lord,' she replied bashfully, 'he is in the house.'

Gualtieri dismounted and, telling everyone to wait, entered the poor cottage. Inside he found the father, a man called Giannucolo, to whom he said, 'I have come to make your Griselda my wife, but first I want to learn something from her own lips in your presence.'

What he asked her was whether, when he took her as his wife, she would do everything she could to please him, would not be upset by anything he might say or do, and would be obedient, together with many other questions of this sort. She replied yes to everything. Then Gualtieri took her by the hand and led her outside, where, in the presence of his whole company and everyone else, he had her stripped naked. He ordered the clothing he had had made to be brought and immediately had her dressed, and shoes put on her, and a tiara placed on her hair, unkempt though it was. Everyone was amazed.

'Gentlemen,' he said, 'this is the person I intend should be my wife, if she wishes to have me for her husband.'

Then he turned to her, standing there bashful and

Patient Griselda

awkward, and said, 'Griselda, do you want me for your husband?'

'Yes, my lord,' she replied.

'And I want you for my wife,' he said.

With that, before everyone present, he formally married her. Then he had her set on a charger, with attendants to do her honour, and took her home. The marriage-feast was grand and fine, and the festivities no different from what they would have been if he had married the daughter of the king of France.

The young wife's character and behaviour seemed to change with her change of clothing. As I said earlier, she had a lovely face and figure. And now to her natural good looks she added enough charm, attraction and refinement to make you think she could not possibly have been Giannucolo's daughter and a shepherd-girl, but the daughter of some noble lord. Everyone who had known her before was astounded. What is more, she was so ready to obey and serve her husband that he considered himself the most contented and satisfied man in the world. She was similarly so gracious and kindly towards her husband's subjects that every one of them loved her wholeheartedly and spontaneously honoured her in every way, asking God in their prayers to give her health, prosperity and greater glory still. If they used to say that Gualtieri had acted ill-advisedly in taking such a wife, now they said he was a paragon of wisdom and insight, arguing that no one else could have perceived the exceptional virtues concealed beneath the poverty of her peasant dress. All in all, before much time had passed, she had people speaking of her good qualities and virtuous deeds throughout the marquisate and beyond, and completely turning round any negative comments about her husband that had been made when he married her.

She had not been with Gualtieri very long when she became pregnant, and in due course she gave birth to a little girl, much to Gualtieri's delight. But a little later a strange idea came into his head. He felt a need to test her patience by inflicting unbearable torments on her over a prolonged period of time. First of all he made cutting remarks, and gave an impression of being angry with her. He said that his men were badly put out by her low-class origins, all the more now that she was having children. The girl-child was a particular source of resentment, and they wouldn't stop muttering about her.

When his lady heard this, she kept her composure and gave no sign of being thrown off the virtuous course she had set herself.

'My lord,' she said, 'treat me in the way that most accords with your honour and your happiness. I shall be content with anything. I am aware I'm less than they are and that I didn't deserve the honour you have had the generosity to bestow on me.'

Her response was warmly received by Gualtieri, who recognized that any honour that he or anyone else had

Patient Griselda

paid her had not made her feel in the slightest bit superior.

A little while later, after giving his wife the general impression that his subjects couldn't stand the little girl she had borne him, he had a word with one of the household staff and sent him to her. The man addressed her with a distressed air.

'My lady,' he said, 'I am obliged to do something my lord commands me to do, if I do not wish to die. He has ordered me to take this daughter of yours and . . .'

He stopped there. Hearing his words and seeing his face, the lady recalled what her husband had been saying and deduced that he had orders to kill the child. She quickly took her from her cradle, kissed her and blessed her. For all the immense pain in her heart, she again kept her composure and put the child in the man's arms.

'Take her,' she said, 'and carry out to the letter what your lord and mine has ordered you to do. Only do not leave her for animals and birds to devour, unless he told you to.'

The servant took the child away and passed on what his wife had said to Gualtieri, who was astounded by her constancy. He then sent the servant off with the child to a female relative of his in Bologna, with a request to bring her up and educate her with the utmost care, but not to let anyone know whose daughter she was.

The next thing to happen was that the lady became pregnant again. In due course she gave birth to a male child, which pleased Gualtieri immensely. But what he had done already was not enough for him. His criticisms became sharper and sharper, and one day, his face contorted with rage, he said this to her:

'My lady, ever since you had this boy child, I haven't been able to live with these men of mine. They are bitterly against some grandson of Giannucolo ending up their lord after me. If I don't want to be hounded out of here, I'm afraid I'm going to have to do what I did the other time, and then in the end I'm going to have to leave you and take another wife.'

The lady heard him out without flinching.

'My lord,' was all she replied, 'think only of contenting yourself and following your own inclinations, and don't worry at all about me. Nothing matters to me except whatever I see pleases you.'

A few days later Gualtieri sent someone for his son, much as he had done as regards his daughter. After a similar show of having him murdered, he dispatched him to Bologna to be brought up there, like the little girl. What the lady said and showed in her face was no different from before, which stunned Gualtieri. He declared to himself that there wasn't a woman anywhere capable of behaving like that. If he hadn't seen her visceral attachment to the children as long as she had his approval, he would have thought she was glad to see the back of them, but he knew that there was sense and wisdom in her.

His subjects, believing he had had his children killed, strongly condemned him for his cruelty and felt nothing

Patient Griselda

but compassion for the lady. When other ladies sympathized with her for having lost her children in this way, she said only that what pleased her was precisely what pleased the man who had fathered them.

Some years after the little girl's birth, Gualtieri decided it was time to put her capacity for endurance to the ultimate test. He told many of his men that he just could not bear Griselda being his wife any more, and that it was clear to him that marrying her had been a bad juvenile error; he was now going to do all he could to obtain special dispensation from the Pope to take another wife and leave Griselda. Quite a few of his better men took him to task, but he only replied that that was how things had to be. When his lady heard the news, she found herself having to face the idea of going back to her father's house, and perhaps tending the sheep as she had done in the past, with the added prospect of some other lady taking possession of the man to whom she had given all the love she had. She was devastated. But she had borne all the other wrongs that fortune had done her, and she set herself to bear this one with similar fortitude.

A little later Gualtieri arranged for some counterfeit letters to be sent from Rome and gave his subjects to believe that in these the Pope had given him dispensation to marry again and leave Griselda. He had her summoned and addressed her before a crowd of onlookers.

'My lady,' he said, 'thanks to a special concession granted me by the Pope, I can take another wife and let you go. Since my ancestors were from the high nobility and the lords of these lands, whereas yours have always been labourers, I intend that you should no longer be my wife and should go back to Giannucolo's house with the dowry you brought me. After that I shall marry someone I've found who will be appropriate for my station.'

Hearing this, the lady had to make an immense effort, one beyond women's natural capacities, in order to keep back her tears.

'My lord,' she replied, 'I always knew my lowly origins in no way accorded with your own nobility. I was glad to attribute to God and to yourself the position I have enjoyed with you. I have never thought it something I had been given, or treated it as anything more than a loan. Your wish is to recover it. I must make it my wish to let you have it, and I am happy to do so. Here is the ring with which you married me. Take it. You order me to carry away with me the dowry I brought you. That's not something for which you'll need a banker, or for which I'll need a bag or a packhorse. It does not escape me that you took me in naked. If you consider it decent for that body in which I carried the children you fathered to be seen by all and sundry, I shall go away naked. But I beg you that you let me have some payment for the virginity that I brought here and do not take away again by allowing me, over and above my dowry, to have a single shift to wear.'

Patient Griselda

Gualtieri wanted to weep more than anything else. But his face stayed as hard as ever.

'So you go off with a shift then,' he said.

Everyone round him begged him to make her the gift of a robe, and not let the woman who had been his wife for thirteen years or more be seen leaving his house penniless and utterly humiliated, which was what leaving in just a shift would mean. But their requests came to nothing. So it was in a shift, barefoot and bareheaded, that the lady commended them to God's care, and walked out of her husband's house and back to her father's, amid the weeping and wailing of all who saw her.

Giannucolo had never been able to believe that Gualtieri really wanted his daughter as his wife, expecting every day something like this to happen, and had kept the clothes she was wearing on the morning Gualtieri married her. He brought them out and she put them on. Then she gave herself over to the menial tasks around her father's house that she used to do in the past, valiantly bearing the savage assault that hostile fortune had inflicted on her.

Gualtieri's next step was to pretend to his subjects that he had got himself a daughter of one of the Counts of Panago. In the course of the grandiose preparations for the marriage ceremony, he sent for Griselda to come and see him.

'I'm bringing here as my bride,' he said to her when she arrived, 'this lady I've very recently promised to marry. My intention is to receive her with due honour when she comes here for the first time. You're aware that I don't have ladies in the house who can spruce up the rooms and do all the things required for a festive occasion of this sort. Since you know better than anyone else how this house works, sort out what needs to be done, and also invite a welcome party of ladies you think suitable, and receive them as if you were the lady in charge. Then once the marriage-feast is over, you can go back to your own house.'

His words were so many knives in Griselda's heart. She had never been able to abandon the love she felt for him in the way she had let go of her good fortune.

'My lord, I am willing and ready,' she said.

And so, in a makeshift dress of thick, rough cloth, she went back into the house she had left in just her shift not long before, and began sweeping the chambers and tidying them up, fixing hangings and drapes in the halls, and getting the kitchen ready, doing every single thing with her own hands as if she were nothing but a mere servant-girl. Nor did she stop till she had everything as neat and orderly as the occasion required.

Once she had had invitations sent out on Gualtieri's behalf to all the ladies in the area, the only thing left for her to do was to await the coming festivities. When the day of the wedding-feast arrived, in spite of the poor clothes she had on, she gave every one of the ladies who came a joyful and dignified welcome.

Gualtieri had taken care the children should be properly

brought up in Bologna by his female relative, who had married into the house of the Counts of Panago. The girl was now twelve and the prettiest creature ever, and the boy was six. Gualtieri had written to the relative's husband, asking him to be so good as to bring his daughter and son to Saluzzo, accompanied by an appropriate guard of honour, and to tell everyone that he was bringing the girl to be Gualtieri's wife, with no hint to anyone of who she really was.

This gentleman did as the Marquis asked and set off with the girl, her brother and the guard of honour. After some days, around the time of the morning meal, they arrived in Saluzzo, where they found all the local people and many others from round about waiting for this new bride of Gualtieri. The girl was greeted by the ladies and entered the hall where the tables were laid out. Griselda, dressed just as she was, went towards her happily enough, saying, 'My lady is welcome.'

The other ladies, who had repeatedly but fruitlessly begged Gualtieri either to let Griselda stay in one of the chambers or to lend her one of the robes that were once hers, so that she would not appear before the visitors looking as she did, were now assigned their places at the tables and began to be served. The girl was the object of everybody's attention and the general view was that Gualtieri had made a good exchange. One of those who was most lavish with her praises, both of the girl and of her little brother, was Griselda.

Gualtieri thought he had now had all the proof he could want of the patience of his lady. He could tell that it was not at all affected by events, no matter how bizarre they were, and, given the wisdom he knew was in her, he was sure that dullness of mind was not a factor. He decided it was time to release her from the tortures he judged she must be suffering beneath her calm and steady exterior. He had her come forward and, before everyone who was there, gave her a smile and asked:

'What do you think of our bride?'

'My lord,' replied Griselda, 'I can only think very well of her. If her good sense is equal to her beauty, as I believe it must be, I have no doubt that living with her will make you the most most contented lord in the world. But I beg you with all my heart not to inflict on her the sort of wounds you inflicted on the other one, the one who was your wife before. I can't really believe that she could stand it. She's younger, and what's more she's been brought up in luxury, whereas the other had spent her childhood doing hard physical work.'

Gualtieri could see that she firmly believed that the girl was going to be his wife and yet still said nothing he could disapprove of. He sat her down at his side and then spoke.

'Griselda,' he said, 'it is now time for you to taste the fruit of your steadfast patience and for those who judged me cruel, unjust and inhuman to acknowledge that what I did had a deliberate purpose. I wanted to teach you to be a wife, to teach my critics how to take a wife and to

Patient Griselda

keep one, and to bring about for myself unbroken peace and quiet for as long as my life with you might last. This was something I was very afraid wouldn't happen when I first took a wife. It was to test if it were possible that I inflicted on you the wounds and torments you are all too aware of.

'Since I have never perceived you going against my wishes in anything you have said or done, I judge that I do indeed have from you the contentment I desired. I therefore intend to restore to you in one single moment what I took from you over the years, and to apply the sweetest possible medicine to the wounds I inflicted. So now, with joy in your heart, receive this girl you think is my bride, and her brother too. These are our children that you and many others have long thought I had brutally murdered. And I myself am your husband, who loves you more than anything else. I think I can rightly and honestly boast that no other man alive can be as happy with his wife as I am.'

After this speech he put his arms round her and kissed her. He then raised her to her feet and led her, weeping for joy, over to where their daughter was sitting, astounded by what she was hearing. They tenderly embraced the two children, and then told the girl and many other people there the truth of the situation. The ladies were delighted to get up from the tables and go with Griselda into one of the chambers. Expressing hopes of a better outcome this time, they helped her out of her rough clothing and dressed her in one of her noble robes. Then they led her back into the hall a courtly lady, which even in her rags she had retained the air of being. There followed a moment of marvellous celebration with the children, and everyone showed their joy at the way things had turned out. Then they plunged into fun and merrymaking, which went on for days.

Everyone judged Gualtieri to have shown great wisdom, though they judged the tests inflicted on his lady to have been too severe, indeed intolerable. Griselda they held to have shown more wisdom than anyone.

After some days the Count of Panago returned to Bologna and Gualtieri took Giannucolo away from his work. From then he was treated as a proper father-in-law, and lived very happily and much respected until a ripe old age. After finding a noble husband for his daughter, Gualtieri himself lived a long and happy life with Griselda, and treated her with all possible honour.

What can be said here except that divine spirits descend from heaven even into poor houses and into royal houses come spirits which deserve more to look after pigs than be lords over men? Who else but Griselda could have borne the callous, unprecedented tests Gualtieri subjected her to, not just without tears but with what looked like cheerfulness? Perhaps it would have served him right if the woman he happened to pick had let another man shake her muff when she was driven from home in her shift, and that way got herself a decent dress.

1. BOCCACCIO · *Mrs Rosie and the Priest*
2. GERARD MANLEY HOPKINS · *As kingfishers catch fire*
3. *The Saga of Gunnlaug Serpent-tongue*
4. THOMAS DE QUINCEY · *On Murder Considered as One of the Fine Arts*
5. FRIEDRICH NIETZSCHE · *Aphorisms on Love and Hate*
6. JOHN RUSKIN · *Traffic*
7. PU SONGLING · *Wailing Ghosts*
8. JONATHAN SWIFT · *A Modest Proposal*
9. *Three Tang Dynasty Poets*
10. WALT WHITMAN · *On the Beach at Night Alone*
11. KENKŌ · *A Cup of Sake Beneath the Cherry Trees*
12. BALTASAR GRACIÁN · *How to Use Your Enemies*
13. JOHN KEATS · *The Eve of St Agnes*
14. THOMAS HARDY · *Woman much missed*
15. GUY DE MAUPASSANT · *Femme Fatale*
16. MARCO POLO · *Travels in the Land of Serpents and Pearls*
17. SUETONIUS · *Caligula*
18. APOLLONIUS OF RHODES · *Jason and Medea*
19. ROBERT LOUIS STEVENSON · *Olalla*
20. KARL MARX AND FRIEDRICH ENGELS · *The Communist Manifesto*
21. PETRONIUS · *Trimalchio's Feast*
22. JOHANN PETER HEBEL · *How a Ghastly Story Was Brought to Light by a Common or Garden Butcher's Dog*
23. HANS CHRISTIAN ANDERSEN · *The Tinder Box*
24. RUDYARD KIPLING · *The Gate of the Hundred Sorrows*
25. DANTE · *Circles of Hell*
26. HENRY MAYHEW · *Of Street Piemen*
27. HAFEZ · *The nightingales are drunk*
28. GEOFFREY CHAUCER · *The Wife of Bath*
29. MICHEL DE MONTAIGNE · *How We Weep and Laugh at the Same Thing*
30. THOMAS NASHE · *The Terrors of the Night*
31. EDGAR ALLAN POE · *The Tell-Tale Heart*
32. MARY KINGSLEY · *A Hippo Banquet*
33. JANE AUSTEN · *The Beautifull Cassandra*
34. ANTON CHEKHOV · *Gooseberries*
35. SAMUEL TAYLOR COLERIDGE · *Well, they are gone, and here must I remain*
36. JOHANN WOLFGANG VON GOETHE · *Sketchy, Doubtful, Incomplete Jottings*
37. CHARLES DICKENS · *The Great Winglebury Duel*
38. HERMAN MELVILLE · *The Maldive Shark*
39. ELIZABETH GASKELL · *The Old Nurse's Story*
40. NIKOLAY LESKOV · *The Steel Flea*

41. HONORÉ DE BALZAC · *The Atheist's Mass*
42. CHARLOTTE PERKINS GILMAN · *The Yellow Wall-Paper*
43. C.P. CAVAFY · *Remember, Body . . .*
44. FYODOR DOSTOEVSKY · *The Meek One*
45. GUSTAVE FLAUBERT · *A Simple Heart*
46. NIKOLAI GOGOL · *The Nose*
47. SAMUEL PEPYS · *The Great Fire of London*
48. EDITH WHARTON · *The Reckoning*
49. HENRY JAMES · *The Figure in the Carpet*
50. WILFRED OWEN · *Anthem For Doomed Youth*
51. WOLFGANG AMADEUS MOZART · *My Dearest Father*
52. PLATO · *Socrates' Defence*
53. CHRISTINA ROSSETTI · *Goblin Market*
54. *Sindbad the Sailor*
55. SOPHOCLES · *Antigone*
56. RYŪNOSUKE AKUTAGAWA · *The Life of a Stupid Man*
57. LEO TOLSTOY · *How Much Land Does A Man Need?*
58. GIORGIO VASARI · *Leonardo da Vinci*
59. OSCAR WILDE · *Lord Arthur Savile's Crime*
60. SHEN FU · *The Old Man of the Moon*
61. AESOP · *The Dolphins, the Whales and the Gudgeon*
62. MATSUO BASHŌ · *Lips too Chilled*
63. EMILY BRONTË · *The Night is Darkening Round Me*
64. JOSEPH CONRAD · *To-morrow*
65. RICHARD HAKLUYT · *The Voyage of Sir Francis Drake Around the Whole Globe*
66. KATE CHOPIN · *A Pair of Silk Stockings*
67. CHARLES DARWIN · *It was snowing butterflies*
68. BROTHERS GRIMM · *The Robber Bridegroom*
69. CATULLUS · *I Hate and I Love*
70. HOMER · *Circe and the Cyclops*
71. D. H. LAWRENCE · *Il Duro*
72. KATHERINE MANSFIELD · *Miss Brill*
73. OVID · *The Fall of Icarus*
74. SAPPHO · *Come Close*
75. IVAN TURGENEV · *Kasyan from the Beautiful Lands*
76. VIRGIL · *O Cruel Alexis*
77. H. G. WELLS · *A Slip under the Microscope*
78. HERODOTUS · *The Madness of Cambyses*
79. *Speaking of Siva*
80. *The Dhammapada*

'O let them be left, wildness and wet . . .'

GERARD MANLEY HOPKINS
Born 1844, Essex, England
Died 1889, Dublin, Ireland

Hopkins's poems were first published posthumously in 1918, in a volume edited by his friend, the poet Robert Bridges.

HOPKINS IN PENGUIN CLASSICS
Poems and Prose

GERARD MANLEY HOPKINS

As kingfishers catch fire

PENGUIN BOOKS

PENGUIN CLASSICS

UK | USA | Canada | Ireland | Australia
India | New Zealand | South Africa

Penguin Books is part of the Penguin Random House group of companies whose addresses can be found at global.penguinrandomhouse.com.

This selection published in Penguin Classics 2015

009

Set in 9.5/13 pt Baskerville 10 Pro
Typeset by Jouve (UK), Milton Keynes
Printed and bound in Great Britain by Clays Ltd, Elcograf S.p.A.

A CIP catalogue record for this book is available from the British Library

ISBN: 978–0–141–39784–9

www.greenpenguin.co.uk

Penguin Random House is committed to a sustainable future for our business, our readers and our planet. This book is made from Forest Stewardship Council® certified paper.

Contents

God's Grandeur	1
The Starlight Night	2
'As kingfishers catch fire, dragonflies draw flame'	3
Spring	4
The Lantern Out of Doors	5
The Sea and the Skylark	6
The Windhover	7
Pied Beauty	8
Hurrahing in Harvest	9
The Caged Skylark	10
In the Valley of the Elwy	11
Binsey Poplars	12
Duns Scotus's Oxford	14
Peace	15
The Candle Indoors	16

At the Wedding March	17
Felix Randal	18
Spring and Fall	20
Inversnaid	21
The Leaden Echo and the Golden Echo	22
'To seem the stranger lies my lot, my life'	26
'I wake and feel the fell of dark, not day'	27
'No worst, there is none. Pitched past pitch of grief'	28
(Carrion Comfort)	29
'Patience, hard thing! the hard thing but to pray'	31
'My own heart let me more have pity on; let'	32
Spelt from Sibyl's Leaves	33
That Nature is a Heraclitean Fire and of the Comfort of the Resurrection	35
In honour of St Alphonsus Rodriguez	37

'Thou art indeed just, Lord,
   if I contend'   38

To R. B.   39

'Stars twiring brilliantly': Extracts
   from Hopkins's Journals   40

God's Grandeur

The world is charged with the grandeur of God.
    It will flame out, like shining from shook foil;
    It gathers to a greatness, like the ooze of oil
Crushed. Why do men then now not reck his rod?
Generations have trod, have trod, have trod;
    And all is seared with trade; bleared, smeared with
        toil;
    And wears man's smudge and shares man's smell:
        the soil
Is bare now, nor can foot feel, being shod.

And for all this, nature is never spent;
    There lives the dearest freshness deep down things;
And though the last lights off the black West went
    Oh, morning, at the brown brink eastward, springs –
Because the Holy Ghost over the bent
    World broods with warm breast and with ah! bright
        wings.

The Starlight Night

Look at the stars! look, look up at the skies!
   O look at all the fire-folk sitting in the air!
   The bright boroughs, the circle-citadels there!
Down in dim woods the diamond delves! the
   elves'-eyes!
The grey lawns cold where gold, where quickgold lies!
   Wind-beat whitebeam! airy abeles set on a flare!
   Flake-doves sent floating forth at a farmyard scare!
Ah well! it is all a purchase, all is a prize.

Buy then! bid then! – What? Prayer, patience, alms,
   vows.
Look, look: a May-mess, like on orchard boughs!
   Look! March-bloom, like on mealed-with-yellow
   sallows!
These are indeed the barn; withindoors house
The shocks. This piece-bright paling shuts the spouse
   Christ home, Christ and his mother and all his
   hallows.

'As kingfishers catch fire'

As kingfishers catch fire, dragonflies draw flame;
As tumbled over rim in roundy wells
Stones ring; like each tucked string tells, each hung bell's
Bow swung finds tongue to fling out broad its name;
Each mortal thing does one thing and the same:
Deals out that being indoors each one dwells;
Selves – goes itself; *myself* it speaks and spells,
Crying *Whát I dó is me: for that I came.*

I say móre: the just man justices;
Keeps gráce: thát keeps all his goings graces;
Acts in God's eye what in God's eye he is –
Chríst – for Christ plays in ten thousand places,
Lovely in limbs, and lovely in eyes not his
To the Father through the features of men's faces.

Spring

Nothing is so beautiful as Spring –
  When weeds, in wheels, shoot long and lovely and
    lush;
  Thrush's eggs look little low heavens, and thrush
Through the echoing timber does so rinse and wring
The ear, it strikes like lightnings to hear him sing;
  The glassy peartree leaves and blooms, they brush
  The descending blue; that blue is all in a rush
With richness; the racing lambs too have fair their fling.

What is all this juice and all this joy?
  A strain of the earth's sweet being in the beginning
In Eden garden. – Have, get, before it cloy,
  Before it cloud, Christ, lord, and sour with sinning,
Innocent mind and Mayday in girl and boy,
  Most, O maid's child, thy choice and worthy the
    winning.

The Lantern Out of Doors

Sometimes a lantern moves along the night,
    That interests our eyes. And who goes there?
    I think; where from and bound, I wonder, where,
With, all down darkness wide, his wading light?

Men go by me whom either beauty bright
    In mould or mind or what not else makes rare:
    They rain against our much-thick and marsh air
Rich beams, till death or distance buys them quite.

Death or distance soon consumes them: wind
    What most I may eye after, be in at the end
I cannot, and out of sight is out of mind.

Christ minds: Christ's interest, what to avow or amend
    There, éyes them, heart wánts, care haúnts, foot fóllows kínd,
Their ránsom, théir rescue, ánd first, fást, last friénd.

The Sea and the Skylark

On ear and ear two noises too old to end
    Trench – right, the tide that ramps against the shore;
    With a flood or a fall, low lull-off or all roar,
Frequenting there while moon shall wear and wend.

Left hand, off land, I hear the lark ascend,
    His rash-fresh re-winded new-skeinèd score
    In crisps of curl off wild winch whirl, and pour
And pelt music, till none's to spill nor spend.

How these two shame this shallow and frail town!
    How ring right out our sordid turbid time,
Being pure! We, life's pride and cared-for crown,

    Have lost that cheer and charm of earth's past prime:
Our make and making break, are breaking, down
    To man's last dust, drain fast towards man's first
        slime.

The Windhover

to Christ our Lord

I caught this morning morning's minion, king-dom of
>daylight's dauphin, dapple-dawn-drawn Falcon,
>in his riding
>>Of the rolling level underneath him steady air, and
>>striding
>
>High there, how he rung upon the rein of a wimpling
>wing
>In his ecstasy! then off, off forth on swing,
>>As a skate's heel sweeps smooth on a bow-bend:
>>the hurl and gliding
>>Rebuffed the big wind. My heart in hiding
>
>Stirred for a bird, – the achieve of, the mastery of the
>thing!

Brute beauty and valour and act, oh, air, pride, plume,
>here
>>Buckle! AND the fire that breaks from thee then, a
>>billion
>
>Times told lovelier, more dangerous. O my chevalier!

>>No wonder of it: shéer plód makes plough down
>>sillion
>
>Shine, and blue-bleak embers, ah my dear,
>>Fall, gall themselves, and gash gold-vermilion.

Pied Beauty

Glory be to God for dappled things –
    For skies of couple-colour as a brinded cow;
        For rose-moles in all stipple upon trout that swim;
Fresh-firecoal chestnut-falls; finches' wings;
    Landscape plotted and pieced – fold, fallow, and
        plough;
        And áll trádes, their gear and tackle and trim.

All things counter, original, spare, strange;
    Whatever is fickle, freckled (who knows how?)
        With swift, slow; sweet, sour; adazzle, dim;
He fathers-forth whose beauty is past change:
        Praise him.

Hurrahing in Harvest

Summer ends now; now, barbarous in beauty, the
    stooks rise
    Around; up above, what wind-walks! what lovely
        behaviour
    Of silk-sack clouds! has wilder, wilful-wavier
Meal-drift moulded ever and melted across skies?

I walk, I lift up, I lift up heart, eyes,
    Down all that glory in the heavens to glean our
        Saviour;
    And, éyes, heárt, what looks, what lips yet gave you a
Rapturous love's greeting of realer, of rounder replies?

And the azurous hung hills are his world-wielding
    shoulder
    Majestic – as a stallion stalwart, very-violet-sweet! –
These things, these things were here and but the beholder
    Wanting; which two when they once meet,
The heart réars wíngs bold and bolder
    And hurls for him, O half hurls earth for him off
        under his feet.

The Caged Skylark

As a dare-gale skylark scanted in a dull cage
    Man's mounting spirit in his bone-house, mean
        house, dwells –
   That bird beyond the remembering his free fells;
This in drudgery, day-labouring-out life's age.

Though aloft on turf or perch or poor low stage,
    Both sing sometímes the sweetest, sweetest spells,
    Yet both droop deadly sómetimes in their cells
Or wring their barriers in bursts of fear or rage.

Not that the sweet-fowl, song-fowl, needs no rest –
Why, hear him, hear him babble and drop down to
    his nest,
   But his own nest, wild nest, no prison.

Man's spirit will be flesh-bound when found at best,
But uncumberèd: meadow-down is not distressed
   For a rainbow footing it nor he for his bónes rísen.

In the Valley of the Elwy

I remember a house where all were good
    To me, God knows, deserving no such thing:
    Comforting smell breathed at very entering,
Fetched fresh, as I suppose, off some sweet wood.
That cordial air made those kind people a hood
    All over, as a bevy of eggs the mothering wing
    Will, or mild nights the new morsels of Spring:
Why, it seemed of course; seemed of right it should.

Lovely the woods, waters, meadows, combes, vales,
All the air things wear that build this world of Wales;
    Only the inmate does not correspond:
God, lover of souls, swaying considerate scales,
Complete thy creature dear O where it fails,
    Being mighty a master, being a father and fond.

Binsey Poplars

felled 1879

My aspens dear, whose airy cages quelled,
Quelled or quenched in leaves the leaping sun,
All felled, felled, are all felled;
    Of a fresh and following folded rank
        Not spared, not one
       That dandled a sandalled
     Shadow that swam or sank
On meadow and river and wind-wandering weed-
    winding bank.

O if we but knew what we do
     When we delve or hew –
   Hack and rack the growing green!
    Since country is so tender
  To touch, her being só slender,
That, like this sleek and seeing ball
But a prick will make no eye at all,
Where we, even where we mean

Binsey Poplars

    To mend her we end her,
     When we hew or delve:
After-comers cannot guess the beauty been.
   Ten or twelve, only ten or twelve
     Strokes of havoc únselve
      The sweet especial scene,
    Rural scene, a rural scene,
    Sweet especial rural scene.

Duns Scotus's Oxford

Towery city and branchy between towers;
Cuckoo-echoing, bell-swarmèd, lark-charmèd,
    rook-racked, river-rounded;
The dapple-eared lily below thee; that country and
    town did
Once encounter in, here coped and poisèd powers;

Thou hast a base and brickish skirt there, sours
That neighbour-nature thy grey beauty is grounded
Best in; graceless growth, thou hast confounded
Rural rural keeping – folk, flocks, and flowers.

Yet ah! this air I gather and I release
He lived on; these weeds and waters, these walls are
    what
He haunted who of all men most sways my spirits to
    peace;

Of realty the rarest-veinèd unraveller; a not
Rivalled insight, be rival Italy or Greece;
Who fired France for Mary without spot.

Peace

When will you ever, Peace, wild wooddove, shy wings shut,
Your round me roaming end, and under be my boughs?
When, when, Peace, will you, Peace? I'll not play hypocrite
To own my heart: I yield you do come sometimes; but
That piecemeal peace is poor peace. What pure peace allows
Alarms of wars, the daunting wars, the death of it?

O surely, reaving Peace, my Lord should leave in lieu
Some good! And so he does leave Patience exquisite,
That plumes to Peace thereafter. And when Peace here does house
He comes with work to do, he does not come to coo,
              He comes to brood and sit.

The Candle Indoors

Some candle clear burns somewhere I come by.
I muse at how its being puts blissful back
With yellowy moisture mild night's blear-all black,
Or to-fro tender trambeams truckle at the eye.
By that window what task what fingers ply,
I plod wondering, a-wanting, just for lack
Of answer the eagerer a-wanting Jessy or Jack
There / God to aggrándise, God to glorify. –

Come you indoors, come home; your fading fire
Mend first and vital candle in close heart's vault:
You there are master, do your own desire;
What hinders? Are you beam-blind, yet to a fault
In a neighbour deft-handed? are you that liar
And, cast by conscience out, spendsavour salt?

At the Wedding March

God with honour hang your head,
Groom, and grace you, bride, your bed
With lissome scions, sweet scions,
Out of hallowed bodies bred.

Each be other's comfort kind:
Déep, déeper than divined,
Divine charity, dear charity,
Fast you ever, fast bind.

Then let the March tread our ears:
I to him turn with tears
Who to wedlock, his wonder wedlock,
Déals tríumph and immortal years.

Felix Randal

Felix Randal the farrier, O is he dead then? my duty all ended,
Who have watched his mould of man, big-boned and hardy-handsome
Pining, pining, till time when reason rambled in it and some
Fatal four disorders, fleshed there, all contended?

Sickness broke him. Impatient, he cursed at first, but mended
Being anointed and all; though a heavenlier heart began some
Months earlier, since I had our sweet reprieve and ransom
Tendered to him. Ah well, God rest him all road ever he offended!

This seeing the sick endears them to us, us too it endears.
My tongue had taught thee comfort, touch had quenched thy tears,
Thy tears that touched my heart, child, Felix, poor Felix Randal;

How far from then forethought of, all thy more
    boisterous years,
When thou at the random grim forge, powerful amidst
    peers,
Didst fettle for the great grey drayhorse his bright and
    battering sandal!

Spring and Fall

to a young child

Márgarét, áre you gríeving
Over Goldengrove unleaving?
Leáves líke the things of man, you
With your fresh thoughts care for, can you?
Ah! ás the heart grows older
It will come to such sights colder
By and by, nor spare a sigh
Though worlds of wanwood leafmeal lie;
And yet you will weep and know why.
Now no matter, child, the name:
Sórrow's spríngs áre the same.
Nor mouth had, no nor mind, expressed
What heart heard of, ghost guessed:
It ís the blight man was born for,
It is Margaret you mourn for.

Inversnaid

This darksome burn, horseback brown,
His rollrock highroad roaring down,
In coop and in comb the fleece of his foam
Flutes and low to the lake falls home.

A windpuff-bonnet of fáwn-fróth
Turns and twindles over the broth
Of a pool so pitchblack, féll-frówning,
It rounds and rounds Despair to drowning.

Degged with dew, dappled with dew
Are the groins of the braes that the brook treads
    through,
Wiry heathpacks, flitches of fern,
And the beadbonny ash that sits over the burn.

What would the world be, once bereft
Of wet and of wilderness? Let them be left,
O let them be left, wildness and wet;
Long live the weeds and the wilderness yet.

The Leaden Echo and the Golden Echo

(Maiden's song from St Winefred's Well)

THE LEADEN ECHO

How to kéep – is there ány any, is there none such, nowhere known some, bow or brooch or braid or brace, láce, latch or catch or key to keep
Back beauty, keep it, beauty, beauty, beauty, . . . from vanishing away?
Ó is there no frowning of these wrinkles, rankèd wrinkles deep,
Dówn? no waving off of these most mournful messengers, still messengers, sad and stealing messengers of grey?
No there's none, there's none, O no there's none,
Nor can you long be, what you now are, called fair,
Do what you may do, what, do what you may,
And wisdom is early to despair:
Be beginning; since, no, nothing can be done
To keep at bay
Age and age's evils, hoar hair,
Ruck and wrinkle, drooping, dying, death's worst, winding sheets, tombs and worms and tumbling to decay;

So be beginning, be beginning to despair.
O there's none; no no no there's none:
Be beginning to despair, to despair,
Despair, despair, despair, despair.

THE GOLDEN ECHO

    Spare!
There ís one, yes I have one (Hush there!);
Only not within seeing of the sun,
Not within the singeing of the strong sun,
Tall sun's tingeing, or treacherous the tainting of the earth's air,
Somewhere elsewhere there is ah well where! one,
Ońe. Yes I cán tell such a key, I dó know such a place,
Where whatever's prized and passes of us, everything that's fresh and fast flying of us, seems to us sweet of us and swiftly away with, done away with, undone,
Úndone, done with, soon done with, and yet dearly and dangerously sweet
Of us, the wimpled-water-dimpled, not-by-morning-matchèd face,
The flower of beauty, fleece of beauty, too too apt to, ah! to fleet,
Never fleets móre, fastened with the tenderest truth

To its own best being and its loveliness of youth: it is an
 everlastingness of, O it is an all youth!
Come then, your ways and airs and looks, locks, maiden
 gear, gallantry and gaiety and grace,
Winning ways, airs innocent, maiden manners, sweet
 looks, loose locks, long locks, lovelocks, gaygear,
 going gallant, girlgrace –
Resign them, sign them, seal them, send them, motion
 them with breath,
And with sighs soaring, soaring síghs deliver
Them; beauty-in-the-ghost, deliver it, early now, long
 before death
Give beauty back, beauty, beauty, beauty, back to God,
 beauty's self and beauty's giver.
See; not a hair is, not an eyelash, not the least lash lost;
 every hair
Is, hair of the head, numbered.
Nay, what we had lighthanded left in surly the mere
 mould
Will have waked and have waxed and have walked with
 the wind what while we slept,
This side, that side hurling a heavyheaded hundredfold
What while we, while we slumbered.
O then, weary then whý should we tread? O why are we
 so haggard at the heart, so care-coiled, care-killed, so
 fagged, so fashed, so cogged, so cumbered,
When the thing we freely fórfeit is kept with fonder a care,
Fonder a care kept than we could have kept it, kept

Far with fonder a care (and we, we should have lost it)
    finer, fonder
A care kept. – Where kept? Do but tell us where kept, where. –
Yonder. – What high as that! We follow, now we follow. –
    Yonder, yes yonder, yonder,
Yonder.

'To seem the stranger'

To seem the stranger lies my lot, my life
Among strangers. Father and mother dear,
Brothers and sisters are in Christ not near
And he my peace/my parting, sword and strife.
    England, whose honour O all my heart woos, wife
To my creating thought, would neither hear
Me, were I pleading, plead nor do I: I wear-
y of idle a being but by where wars are rife.

    I am in Ireland now; now I am at a thírd
Remove. Not but in all removes I can
Kind love both give and get. Only what word
Wisest my heart breeds dark heaven's baffling ban
Bars or hell's spell thwarts. This to hoard unheard,
Heard unheeded, leaves me a lonely began.

'I wake and feel'

I wake and feel the fell of dark, not day.
What hours, O what black hours we have spent
This night! what sights you, heart, saw; ways you went!
And more must, in yet longer light's delay.
   With witness I speak this. But where I say
Hours I mean years, mean life. And my lament
Is cries countless, cries like dead letters sent
To dearest him that lives alas! away.

    I am gall, I am heartburn. God's most deep decree
Bitter would have me taste: my taste was me;
Bones built in me, flesh filled, blood brimmed the curse.
    Selfyeast of spirit a dull dough sours. I see
The lost are like this, and their scourge to be
As I am mine, their sweating selves; but worse.

'No worst'

No worst, there is none. Pitched past pitch of grief,
More pangs will, schooled at forepangs, wilder wring.
Comforter, where, where is your comforting?
Mary, mother of us, where is your relief?
My cries heave, herds-long; huddle in a main, a chief
Woe, wórld-sorrow; on an áge-old anvil wince and sing –
Then lull, then leave off. Fury had shrieked 'No lingering! Let me be fell: force I must be brief'.

    O the mind, mind has mountains; cliffs of fall
Frightful, sheer, no-man-fathomed. Hold them cheap
May who ne'er hung there. Nor does long our small
Durance deal with that steep or deep. Here! creep,
Wretch, under a comfort serves in a whirlwind: all
Life death does end and each day dies with sleep.

(Carrion Comfort)

Not, I'll not, carrion comfort, Despair, not feast on thee;
Not untwist – slack they may be – these last strands
    of man
In me ór, most weary, cry *I can no more.* I can;
Can something, hope, wish day come, not choose
    not to be.
But ah, but O thou terrible, why wouldst thou rude
    on me
Thy wring-world right foot rock? lay a lionlimb against
    me? scan
With darksome devouring eyes my bruisèd bones?
    and fan,
O in turns of tempest, me heaped there; me frantic to
    avoid thee and flee?

   Why? That my chaff might fly; my grain lie, sheer
    and clear.
Nay in all that toil, that coil, since (seems) I kissed
    the rod,
Hand rather, my heart lo! lapped strength, stole joy,
    would laugh, chéer.
Cheer whom though? the hero whose heaven-handling
    flung me, fóot tród

Me? or me that fought him? O which one? is it each
 one? That night, that year
Of now done darkness I wretch lay wrestling with
 (my God!) my God.

'Patience, hard thing'

Patience, hard thing! the hard thing but to pray,
But bid for, Patience is! Patience who asks
Wants war, wants wounds; weary his times, his tasks;
To do without, take tosses, and obey.
   Rare patience roots in these, and, these away,
Nowhere. Natural heart's ivy, Patience masks
Our ruins of wrecked past purpose. There she basks
Purple eyes and seas of liquid leaves all day.

   We hear our hearts grate on themselves: it kills
To bruise them dearer. Yet the rebellious wills
Of us we do bid God bend to him even so.
   And where is he who more and more distils
Delicious kindness? – He is patient. Patience fills
His crisp combs, and that comes those ways we know.

'My own heart'

My own heart let me more have pity on; let
Me live to my sad self hereafter kind,
Charitable; not live this tormented mind
With this tormented mind tormenting yet.
    I cast for comfort I can no more get
By groping round my comfortless, than blind
Eyes in their dark can day or thirst can find
Thirst's all-in-all in all a world of wet.

Soul, self; come, poor Jackself, I do advise
You, jaded, let be; call off thoughts awhile
Elsewhere; leave comfort root-room; let joy size
At God knows when to God knows what; whose smile
's not wrung, see you; unforeseen times rather – as skies
Betweenpie mountains – lights a lovely mile.

Spelt from Sibyl's Leaves

Earnest, earthless, equal, attuneable, ' vaulty, voluminous, . . . stupendous
Evening strains to be time's vást, ' womb-of-all, home-of-all, hearse-of-all night.
Her fond yellow hornlight wound to the west, ' her wild hollow hoarlight hung to the height
Waste; her earliest stars, earl-stars, ' stárs principal, overbend us,
Fíre-féaturing heaven. For earth ' her being has unbound, her dapple is at an end, as-
tray or aswarm, all throughther, in throngs; ' self ín self steepèd and páshed – qúite
Disremembering, dísmémbering ' áll now. Heart, you round me right
With: Óur évening is over us; óur night ' whélms, whélms, ánd will end us.
Only the beak-leaved boughs dragonish ' damask the tool-smooth bleak light; black,
Ever so black on it. Óur tale, O óur oracle! ' Lét life, wáned, ah lét life wind
Off hér once skéined stained véined varíety ' upon, áll on twó spools; párt, pen, páck
Now her áll in twó flocks, twó folds – black, white; ' right, wrong; reckon but, reck but, mind

But thése two; wáre of a wórld where bút these ' twó
 tell, each off the óther; of a rack
Where, selfwrung, selfstrung, sheathe- and shelterless, '
 thóughts agaínst thoughts ín groans grínd.

That Nature is a Heraclitean Fire and of the Comfort of the Resurrection

Cloud-puffball, torn tufts, tossed pillows ' flaunt forth,
    then chevy on an air-
built thoroughfare: heaven-roysterers, in gay-gangs '
    they throng; they glitter in marches.
Down roughcast, down dazzling whitewash, ' wherever
    an elm arches,
Shivelights and shadowtackle in long ' lashes lace,
    lance, and pair.
Delightfully the bright wind boisterous ' ropes,
    wrestles, beats earth bare
Of yestertempest's creases; ' in pool and rut peel
    parches
Squandering ooze to squeezed ' dough, crust, dust;
    stanches, starches
Squadroned masks and manmarks ' treadmire toil there
Footfretted in it. Million-fuelèd, ' nature's bonfire
    burns on.
But quench her bonniest, dearest ' to her, her clearest-
    selvèd spark
Man, how fast his firedint, ' his mark on mind, is gone!
Both are in an unfathomable, all is in an enormous dark
Drowned. O pity and indig ' nation! Manshape, that
    shone

Sheer off, disseveral, a star, ' death blots black out; nor mark
                      Is any of him at all so stark
But vastness blurs and time ' beats level. Enough! the Resurrection,
A heart's-clarion! Away grief's gasping, ' joyless days, dejection.
                      Across my foundering deck shone
A beacon, an eternal beam. ' Flesh fade, and mortal trash
Fall to the residuary worm; ' world's wildfire, leave but ash:
                      In a flash, at a trumpet crash,
I am all at once what Christ is, ' since he was what I am, and
This Jack, joke, poor potsherd, ' patch, matchwood, immortal diamond,
                      Is immortal diamond.

in honour of

St Alphonsus Rodriguez

laybrother of the Society of Jesus

Honour is flashed off exploit, so we say;
And those strokes once that gashed flesh or galled shield
Should tongue that time now, trumpet now that field,
And, on the fighter, forge his glorious day.
On Christ they do and on the martyr may;
But be the war within, the brand we wield
Unseen, the heroic breast not outward-steeled,
Earth hears no hurtle then from fiercest fray.

   Yet God (that hews mountain and continent,
Earth, all, out; who, with trickling increment,
Veins violets and tall trees makes more and more)
Could crowd career with conquest while there went
Those years and years by of world without event
That in Majorca Alfonso watched the door.

'Thou art indeed just, Lord'

Justus quidem tu es, Domine, si disputem tecum; verumtamen justa loquar ad te: Quare via impiorum prosperatur? &c.

Thou art indeed just, Lord, if I contend
With thee; but, sir, so what I plead is just.
Why do sinners' ways prosper? and why must
Disappointment all I endeavour end?

    Wert thou my enemy, O thou my friend,
How wouldst thou worse, I wonder, than thou dost
Defeat, thwart me? Oh, the sots and thralls of lust
Do in spare hours more thrive than I that spend,
Sir, life upon thy cause. See, banks and brakes
Now, leavèd how thick! lacèd they are again
With fretty chervil, look, and fresh wind shakes
Them; birds build – but not I build; no, but strain,
Time's eunuch, and not breed one work that wakes.
Mine, O thou lord of life, send my roots rain.

To R. B.

The fine delight that fathers thought; the strong
Spur, live and lancing like the blowpipe flame,
Breathes once and, quenchèd faster than it came,
Leaves yet the mind a mother of immortal song.
Nine months she then, nay years, nine years she long
Within her wears, bears, cares and combs the same:
The widow of an insight lost she lives, with aim
Now known and hand at work now never wrong.

    Sweet fire the sire of muse, my soul needs this;
I want the one rapture of an inspiration.
O then if in my lagging lines you miss
The roll, the rise, the carol, the creation,
My winter world, that scarcely breathes that bliss
Now, yields you, with some sighs, our explanation.

'Stars twiring brilliantly':
Extracts from Hopkins's Journals

May 3, 1866. Cold. Morning raw and wet, afternoon fine. Walked then with Addis, crossing Bablock Hythe, round by Skinner's Weir through many fields into the Witney Road. Sky sleepy blue without liquidity. Fr. Cumnor Hill saw St Philip's and the other spires through blue haze rising pale in a pink light. On further side of the Witney road hills, just fleeced with grain or other green growth, by their dips and waves foreshortened here and there and so differenced in brightness and opacity the green on them, with delicate effect. On left, brow of the near hill glistening with very bright newly turned sods and a scarf of vivid green slanting away beyond the skyline, agst. which the clouds shewed the slightest tinge of rose or purple. Copses in grey-red or grey-yellow – the tinges immediately forerunning the opening of full leaf. Meadows skirting Seven-bridge road voluptuous green. Some oaks are out in small leaf. Ashes not out, only tufted with their fringy blooms. Hedges springing richly. Elms in small leaf, with more or less opacity. White poplars most beautiful in small grey crisp spray-like leaf. Cowslips capriciously colouring meadows in creamy drifts. Bluebells, purple orchis. Over the green water of the river passing the slums of the town and under its bridges swallows shooting, blue and purple above and shewing their amber-tinged breasts reflected in the water, their flight unsteady with wagging wings and leaning first to one side then the other. Peewits flying. Towards sunset the sky partly swept, as often, with moist white cloud, tailing off across which are morsels of grey-black woolly clouds. Sun seemed to make a bright liquid hole in this, its texture had an upward northerly sweep or drift fr. the W. marked softly in grey. Dog violets. Eastward after sunset range of clouds rising in bulky heads moulded softly in tufts or bunches of snow – so it looks – and membered somewhat elaborately, rose-coloured. Notice often imperfect fairy rings. Apple and other fruit trees blossomed beautifully.

June 30. Thunderstorms all day, great claps and lightning running up and down. When it was bright betweentimes great towering clouds behind which the sun put out his shaded horns very clearly and a longish way. Level curds and whey sky after sunset. – Graceful growth of Etzkoltzias or however those unhappy flowers are spelt. Yews and evergreen trees now very thin and putting out their young pale shoots.

July 1. Sharp showers, bright between. Late in the afternoon, the light and shade being brilliant, snowy blocks of cloud were filing over the sky, and under the sun hanging above and along the earth-line were those multitudinous up-and-down crispy sparkling chains with pearly shadows up to the edges. At sunset, wh. was in a grey bank with moist gold dabs and racks, the whole round of skyline had level clouds naturally lead-colour but the upper parts ruddled, some more, some less, rosy. Spits or beams braided or built in with slanting pellet flakes made their way. Through such clouds anvil-shaped pink ones and up-blown fleece-of-wool flat-topped dangerous-looking pieces.

July 18. Bright. Sunset over oaks a dapple of rosy clouds blotted with purple, sky round confused pale green and blue with faint horned rays, crimson sparkles through the leaves below . . .

Aug. 30, 1867. Fair; in afternoon fine; the clouds had a good deal of crisping and mottling. – A round by Plumley. – Stands of ash in a copse: they consisted of two or three rods most gracefully leaved, for each wing or comb finally curled inwards, that is upwards. – Putting my hand up against the sky whilst we lay on the grass I saw more richness and beauty in the blue than I had known of before, not brilliance but glow and colour. It was not transparent and sapphire-like, but turquoise-like, swarming and blushing round the edge of the hand and in the pieces clipped in by the fingers, the flesh being sometimes sunlit, sometimes glassy with reflected light, sometimes lightly shadowed in that violet one makes with cobalt and Indian red.

July 3, 1868 . . . Started with Ed. Bond for Switzerland. We went by Dover and Ostende to Brussels . . .

July 9. Before sunrise looking out of window saw a noble scape of stars – the Plough all golden falling, Cassiopeïa on end with her bright quains pointing to the right, the graceful bends of Perseus underneath her, and some great star whether Capella or not I am not sure risen over the brow of the mountain. Sunrise we saw well: the north landscape was blighty but the south, the important one, with the Alps, clear; lower down all was mist and flue of white cloud, wh. grew thicker as the day went on and like a junket lay scattered on the lakes. The sun lit up the bright acres of the snows at first with pink but afterwards clear white: the snow of the Bernese Highland remained from its distance pinkish all day. – The mountain ranges, as any series or body of inanimate like things not often seen, have the air of persons and of interrupted activity; they are multitudinous too, and also they express a second level with an upper world or shires of snow. – In going down betw. Pilatus and a long streak of cloud the blue sky was greenish. Since I have found this colour is seen in looking fr. the snow to the sky but why I do not understand: can there possibly be a rose hue suppressed in the white (– *purpurea candidior nive*)?

July 11. Fine. We took a guide up the Wylerhorn but the top being clouded dismissed him and stayed up the mountain, lunching by a waterfall. Presently after long climbing – for there was a good chance of a clearance – we nearly reached the top, when a cloud coming on thick frightened me back: had we gone on we shd. have had the view, for it cleared quite. Still we saw the neighbouring mountains well. The snow is often cross-harrowed and lies too in the straightest paths as though artificial, wh. again comes fr. the planing. In the sheet it glistens yellow to the sun. How fond of and warped to the mountains it wd. be easy to become! For every cliff and limb and edge and jutty has its own nobility. – Two boys came down the mountain yodelling. – We saw the snow in the hollows for the first time. In one the surface was crisped across the direction of the cleft and the other way, that is across the broader crisping and down the stream, combed: the stream ran below and smoke came fr. the hollow: the edge of the snow hewn in curves as if by moulding planes. – Crowd of mountain flowers – gentians; gentianellas; blood-red lucerne; a deep blue glossy spiked flower like plantain, flowering gradually up the spike, so that at the top it looks like clover or honeysuckle; rich big harebells glistening black like the cases of our veins when dry and heated fr. without; and others. All the herbage enthronged with every fingered or fretted leaf. – Firs very tall, with the swell of the branching on the outer side of the slope so that the peaks seem to point inwards to the mountain peak, like the lines of the Parthenon, and the outline melodious and moving on many focuses. – I wore my pagharee and turned it with harebells below and gentians in two rows above like double pan-pipes. – In coming down we lost our way and each had a dangerous slide down the long wet grass of a steep slope.

Waterfalls not only skeined but silky too – one saw it fr. the inn across the meadows: at one quain of the rock the water glistened above and took shadow below, and the rock was reddened a little way each side with the wet, wh. sets off the silkiness . . .

July 19 [. . .] We saw Handeck waterfall. It is in fact the meeting of two waters, the right the Aar sallow and jade-coloured, the left a smaller stream of clear lilac foam. It is the greatest fall we have seen. The lower half is hidden in spray. I watched the great bushes of foam-water, the texture of branchings and water-spandrils which makes them up. At their outsides nearest the rock they gave off showers of drops strung together into little quills which sprang out in fans.

On crossing the Aar again there was as good a fall as some we have paid to see, all in jostling foam-bags.

Across the valley too we saw the fall of the Gelmer – like milk chasing round blocks of coal; or a girdle or long purse of white weighted with irregular black rubies, carelessly thrown aside and lying in jutty bends, with a black clasp of the same stone at the top – for those were the biggest blocks, squared, and built up, as it happened, in lessening stories, and the cascade enclosed them on the right and left hand with its foam; or once more like the skin of a white snake square-pied with black.

Gerard Manley Hopkins

July 20. Fine.

Walked down to the Rhone glacier. It has three stages – first a smoothly-moulded bed in a pan or theatre of thorny peaks, swells of ice rising through the snow-sheet and the snow itself tossing and fretting into the sides of the rock walls in spray-like points: this is the first stage of the glaciers generally; it is like bright-plucked water swaying in a pail –; second, after a slope nearly covered with landslips of moraine, was a ruck of horned waves steep and narrow in the gut: now in the upper Grindelwald glacier between the bed or highest stage was a descending limb which was like the rude and knotty bossings of a strombus shell –; third the foot, a broad limb opening out and reaching the plain, shaped like the fan-fin of a dolphin or a great bivalve shell turned on its face, the flutings in either case being suggested by the crevasses and the ribs by the risings between them, these being swerved and inscaped strictly to the motion of the mass. Or you may compare the three stages to the heel, instep, and ball or toes of a foot. – The second stage looked at from nearer appeared like a box of plaster of Paris or starch or tooth-powder a little moist, tilted up and then struck and jarred so that the powder broke and tumbled in shapes and rifts.

We went into the grotto and also the vault from which the Rhone flows. It looked like a blue tent and as you went further in changed to lilac. As you come out the daylight glazes the groins with gleaming rosecolour. The ice inside has a branchy wire texture. The man shewed us the odd way in which a little piece of ice will stick against the walls – as if drawn by a magnet.

Standing on the glacier saw the prismatic colours in the clouds, and worth saying what sort of clouds: it was fine shapeless skins of fretted make, full of eyebrows or like linings of curled leaves which one finds in shelved corners of a wood.

I had a trudge over the glacier and a tumble over the side moraine, which was one landslip of limestone. It was neighboured however by hot sweet smells and many flowers – small crimson pinks, the brown tulip-like flower we have seen so often, another which we first saw yesterday like Solomon's seal but rather coarser with a spike of greenish veiny-leaved blossom, etc.

July 24. Bright.

E. B. started in the night for the Cima di Jazzi; I stayed behind being ill.

At sunset great bulks of brassy cloud hanging round, which changed their colour to bright reds over the sundown and to fruittree-blossom colour opposite: later a honey-brown edged the Dent Blanche and Weisshorn ridge.

Note that a slender race of fine flue cloud inscaped in continuous eyebrow curves hitched on the Weisshorn peak as it passed: this shews the height of this kind of cloud, from its want of shadow etc. not otherwise discoverable.

July 25. But too bright.

Up at two to ascend the Breithorn. Stars twiring brilliantly. Taurus up, a pale light stressily edging the eastern skyline, and lighting mingled with the dawn. In the twilight we tumbled over the moraine and glacier until the sunrise brightly fleshed the snow of the Breithorn before us and then the colour changing through metallic shades of yellow recovered to white.

We were accompanied by a young Mr Pease of Darlington, his guide Gasser, and ours, Welchen.

From the summit the view on the Italian side was broken by endless ranges of part-vertical dancing cloud, the highest and furthest flaked or foiled like fungus and coloured pink. But, as the Interlaken Frenchman said, the mountain summits are not the places for mountain views, the things do not look high when you are as high as they are; besides Monte Rosa, the Lyskamm, etc. did not make themselves; shape as well as size went: then the cold feet, the spectacles, the talk, and the lunching came in. Even with one companion ecstasy is almost banished: you want to be alone and to feel that, and leisure – all pressure taken off.

March 12, 1870. A fine sunset: the higher sky dead clear blue bridged by a broad slant causeway rising from right

Extracts from Hopkins's Journals

to left of wisped or grass cloud, the wisps lying across; the sundown yellow, moist with light but ending at the top in a foam of delicate white pearling and spotted with big tufts of cloud in colour russet between brown and purple but edged with brassy light. But what I note it all for is this: before I had always taken the sunset and the sun as quite out of gauge with each other, as indeed physically they are, for the eye after looking at the sun is blunted to everything else and if you look at the rest of the sunset you must cover the sun, but today I inscaped them together and made the sun the true eye and ace of the whole, as it is. It was all active and tossing out light and started as strongly forward from the field as a long stone or a boss in the knop of the chalice-stem: it is indeed by stalling it so that it falls into scape with the sky.

The next morning a heavy fall of snow. It tufted and toed the firs and yews and went on to load them till they were taxed beyond their spring. The limes, elms, and Turkey-oaks it crisped beautifully as with young leaf. Looking at the elms from underneath you saw every wave in every twig (become by this the wire-like stem to a finger of snow) and to the hangers and flying sprays it restored, to the eye, the inscapes they had lost. They were beautifully brought out against the sky, which was on one side dead blue, on the other washed with gold.

Sept. 24. First saw the Northern Lights. My eye was caught by beams of light and dark very like the crown of horny rays the sun makes behind a cloud. At first I thought of silvery cloud until I saw that these were more luminous and did not dim the clearness of the stars in the Bear. They rose slightly radiating thrown out from the earthline. Then I saw soft pulses of light one after another rise and pass upwards arched in shape but waveringly and with the arch broken. They seemed to float, not following the warp of the sphere as falling stars look to do but free though concentrical with it. This busy working of nature wholly independent of the earth and seeming to go on in a strain of time not reckoned by our reckoning of days and years but simpler and as if correcting the preoccupation of the world by being preoccupied with and appealing to and dated to the day of judgement was like a new witness to God and filled me with delightful fear

April 22, 1871. But such a lovely damasking in the sky as today I never felt before. The blue was charged with simple instress, the higher, zenith sky earnest and frowning, lower more light and sweet. High up again, breathing through woolly coats of cloud or on the quains and branches of the flying pieces it was the true exchange of crimson, nearer the earth/ against the sun/ it was turquoise, and in the opposite south-western bay below the sun it was like clear oil but just as full of colour, shaken over with slanted flashing 'travellers', all in flight, stepping one behind the other, their edges tossed with bright ravelling, as if white napkins were thrown up in the sun but not quite at the same moment so that they were all in a scale down the air falling one after the other to the ground

May 9 . . . This day and May 11 the bluebells in the little wood between the College and the highroad and in one of the Hurst Green cloughs. In the little wood/ opposite the light/ they stood in blackish spreads or sheddings like the spots on a snake. The heads are then like thongs and solemn in grain and grape-colour. But in the clough/ through the light/ they came in falls of sky-colour washing the brows and slacks of the ground with vein-blue, thickening at the double, vertical themselves and the young grass and brake fern combed vertical, but the brake struck the upright of all this with light winged transomes. It was a lovely sight. – The bluebells in your hand baffle you with their inscape, made to every sense: if you draw your fingers through them they are lodged and struggle/ with a shock of wet heads; the long stalks rub and click and flatten to a fan on one another like your fingers themselves would when you passed the palms hard across one another, making a brittle rub and jostle like the noise of a hurdle strained by leaning against; then there is the faint honey smell and in the mouth the sweet gum when you bite them. But this is easy, it is the eye they baffle. They give one a fancy of pan-pipes and of some wind instrument with stops – a trombone perhaps. The overhung necks – for growing they are little more than a staff with a simple crook but in water, where they stiffen, they take stronger turns, in the head like sheephooks or, when more waved throughout, like the waves riding through a whip that is being smacked – what with these overhung necks and what with the crisped ruffled bells dropping mostly on one side and the gloss these have at their footstalks they have an air of the knights at chess. Then the knot or 'knoop' of buds some shut, some just gaping, which makes the pencil of the whole spike, should be noticed: the inscape of the flower most finely carried out in the siding of the axes, each striking a greater and greater slant, is finished in these clustered buds, which for the most part are not straightened but rise to the end like a tongue and this and their tapering and a little flattening they have make them look like the heads of snakes.

Feb. 24, 1873. In the snow flat-topped hillocks and shoulders outlined with wavy edges, ridge below ridge, very like the grain of wood in line and in projection like relief maps. These the wind makes I think and of course drifts, which are in fact snow waves. The sharp nape of a drift is sometimes broken by slant flutes or channels. I think this must be when the wind after shaping the drift first has changed and cast waves in the body of the wave itself. All the world is full of inscape and chance left free to act falls into an order as well as purpose: looking out of my window I caught it in the random clods and broken heaps of snow made by the cast of a broom. The same of the path trenched by footsteps in ankledeep snow across the fields leading to Hodder wood through which we went to see the river. The sun was bright, the broken brambles and all boughs and banks limed and cloyed with white, the brook down the clough pulling its way by drops and by bubbles in turn under a shell of ice

In March there was much snow

April 8. The ashtree growing in the corner of the garden was felled. It was lopped first: I heard the sound and looking out and seeing it maimed there came at that moment a great pang and I wished to die and not to see the inscapes of the world destroyed any more

1. BOCCACCIO · *Mrs Rosie and the Priest*
2. GERARD MANLEY HOPKINS · *As kingfishers catch fire*
3. *The Saga of Gunnlaug Serpent-tongue*
4. THOMAS DE QUINCEY · *On Murder Considered as One of the Fine Arts*
5. FRIEDRICH NIETZSCHE · *Aphorisms on Love and Hate*
6. JOHN RUSKIN · *Traffic*
7. PU SONGLING · *Wailing Ghosts*
8. JONATHAN SWIFT · *A Modest Proposal*
9. *Three Tang Dynasty Poets*
10. WALT WHITMAN · *On the Beach at Night Alone*
11. KENKŌ · *A Cup of Sake Beneath the Cherry Trees*
12. BALTASAR GRACIÁN · *How to Use Your Enemies*
13. JOHN KEATS · *The Eve of St Agnes*
14. THOMAS HARDY · *Woman much missed*
15. GUY DE MAUPASSANT · *Femme Fatale*
16. MARCO POLO · *Travels in the Land of Serpents and Pearls*
17. SUETONIUS · *Caligula*
18. APOLLONIUS OF RHODES · *Jason and Medea*
19. ROBERT LOUIS STEVENSON · *Olalla*
20. KARL MARX AND FRIEDRICH ENGELS · *The Communist Manifesto*
21. PETRONIUS · *Trimalchio's Feast*
22. JOHANN PETER HEBEL · *How a Ghastly Story Was Brought to Light by a Common or Garden Butcher's Dog*
23. HANS CHRISTIAN ANDERSEN · *The Tinder Box*
24. RUDYARD KIPLING · *The Gate of the Hundred Sorrows*
25. DANTE · *Circles of Hell*
26. HENRY MAYHEW · *Of Street Piemen*
27. HAFEZ · *The nightingales are drunk*
28. GEOFFREY CHAUCER · *The Wife of Bath*
29. MICHEL DE MONTAIGNE · *How We Weep and Laugh at the Same Thing*
30. THOMAS NASHE · *The Terrors of the Night*
31. EDGAR ALLAN POE · *The Tell-Tale Heart*
32. MARY KINGSLEY · *A Hippo Banquet*
33. JANE AUSTEN · *The Beautifull Cassandra*
34. ANTON CHEKHOV · *Gooseberries*
35. SAMUEL TAYLOR COLERIDGE · *Well, they are gone, and here must I remain*
36. JOHANN WOLFGANG VON GOETHE · *Sketchy, Doubtful, Incomplete Jottings*
37. CHARLES DICKENS · *The Great Winglebury Duel*
38. HERMAN MELVILLE · *The Maldive Shark*
39. ELIZABETH GASKELL · *The Old Nurse's Story*
40. NIKOLAY LESKOV · *The Steel Flea*

41. HONORÉ DE BALZAC · *The Atheist's Mass*
42. CHARLOTTE PERKINS GILMAN · *The Yellow Wall-Paper*
43. C.P. CAVAFY · *Remember, Body . . .*
44. FYODOR DOSTOEVSKY · *The Meek One*
45. GUSTAVE FLAUBERT · *A Simple Heart*
46. NIKOLAI GOGOL · *The Nose*
47. SAMUEL PEPYS · *The Great Fire of London*
48. EDITH WHARTON · *The Reckoning*
49. HENRY JAMES · *The Figure in the Carpet*
50. WILFRED OWEN · *Anthem For Doomed Youth*
51. WOLFGANG AMADEUS MOZART · *My Dearest Father*
52. PLATO · *Socrates' Defence*
53. CHRISTINA ROSSETTI · *Goblin Market*
54. *Sindbad the Sailor*
55. SOPHOCLES · *Antigone*
56. RYŪNOSUKE AKUTAGAWA · *The Life of a Stupid Man*
57. LEO TOLSTOY · *How Much Land Does A Man Need?*
58. GIORGIO VASARI · *Leonardo da Vinci*
59. OSCAR WILDE · *Lord Arthur Savile's Crime*
60. SHEN FU · *The Old Man of the Moon*
61. AESOP · *The Dolphins, the Whales and the Gudgeon*
62. MATSUO BASHŌ · *Lips too Chilled*
63. EMILY BRONTË · *The Night is Darkening Round Me*
64. JOSEPH CONRAD · *To-morrow*
65. RICHARD HAKLUYT · *The Voyage of Sir Francis Drake Around the Whole Globe*
66. KATE CHOPIN · *A Pair of Silk Stockings*
67. CHARLES DARWIN · *It was snowing butterflies*
68. BROTHERS GRIMM · *The Robber Bridegroom*
69. CATULLUS · *I Hate and I Love*
70. HOMER · *Circe and the Cyclops*
71. D. H. LAWRENCE · *Il Duro*
72. KATHERINE MANSFIELD · *Miss Brill*
73. OVID · *The Fall of Icarus*
74. SAPPHO · *Come Close*
75. IVAN TURGENEV · *Kasyan from the Beautiful Lands*
76. VIRGIL · *O Cruel Alexis*
77. H. G. WELLS · *A Slip under the Microscope*
78. HERODOTUS · *The Madness of Cambyses*
79. *Speaking of Siva*
80. *The Dhammapada*

'Into two I'll slice
the hair-seat
of Helga's
kiss-gulper...'

The Saga of Gunnlaug Serpent-tongue was written down in Iceland around 1270–1300, although it would have circulated much earlier in oral form. The action is set 990–1010. This translation is taken from *Sagas of Warrior-Poets*, published in Penguin Classics in 2002.

ICELANDIC SAGAS IN PENGUIN CLASSICS
Comic Sagas and Tales from Iceland
Egil's Saga
Gisli Sursson's Saga and The Saga of the People of Eyri
Hrafnkel's Saga and Other Icelandic Stories
Njal's Saga
The Orkneyinga Saga
Sagas of Warrior-Poets
The Saga Of Grettir the Strong
The Saga of the People of Laxardal and Bolli Bollason's Tale
The Saga of the Volsungs
The Vinland Sagas

The Saga of Gunnlaug
Serpent-tongue

Translated by
Katrina C. Attwood

PENGUIN BOOKS

PENGUIN CLASSICS

UK | USA | Canada | Ireland | Australia
India | New Zealand | South Africa

Penguin Books is part of the Penguin Random House group of companies
whose addresses can be found at global.penguinrandomhouse.com.

This edition published in Penguin Classics 2015

009

Translation copyright © Leifur Eiríksson Publishing Ltd, 1997

The moral right of the translator has been asserted

Set in 9/12.4 pt Baskerville 10 Pro
Typeset by Jouve (UK), Milton Keynes

Printed and bound in Great Britain by Clays Ltd, Elcograf S.p.A.

A CIP catalogue record for this book is available from the British Library

ISBN: 978-0-141-39786-3

www.greenpenguin.co.uk

Penguin Random House is committed to a
sustainable future for our business, our readers
and our planet. This book is made from Forest
Stewardship Council® certified paper.

This is the saga of Hrafn and of Gunnlaug Serpent-tongue, as told by the priest Ari Thorgilsson the Learned, who was the most knowledgeable of stories of the settlement and other ancient lore of anyone who has lived in Iceland.

1 There was a man named Thorstein. He was the son of Egil, the son of Skallagrim, the son of the hersir Kveldulf from Norway. Thorstein's mother was named Asgerd. She was Bjorn's daughter. Thorstein lived at Borg in Borgarfjord. He was rich and a powerful chieftain, wise, tolerant and just in all things. He was no great prodigy of either size or strength, as his father, Egil, had been. Learned men say that Egil was the greatest champion and duellist Iceland has ever known and the most promising of all the farmers' sons, as well as a great scholar and the wisest of men. Thorstein, too, was a great man and was popular with everyone. He was a handsome man with white-blond hair and fine, piercing eyes.

Scholars say that the Myrar folk – the family descended from Egil – were rather a mixed lot. Some of them were exceptionally good-looking men, whereas others are said to have been very ugly. Many members of the family, such as Kjartan Olafsson, Killer-Bardi and Skuli Thorsteinsson were particularly talented in various ways. Some of them were also great poets, like Bjorn, the Champion of the Hitardal people, the priest Einar Skulason, Snorri Sturluson and many others.

Thorstein married Jofrid, the daughter of Gunnar Hlifarson. Gunnar was the best fighter and athlete among the farmers in Iceland at that time. The second best was Gunnar of Hlidarendi, and Steinthor from Eyri was the third. Jofrid was eighteen years old when Thorstein married her. She was a widow, having previously been married to Thorodd, the son of Tunga-Odd. It was their daughter, Hungerd, who was being brought up at Borg by Thorstein. Jofrid was an independent woman. She and Thorstein had several children, although only a few of them appear in this saga. Their eldest son was named Skuli, the next Kollsvein and the third Egil.

2 It is said that, one summer, a ship came ashore in the Gufua estuary. The skipper was a Norwegian named Bergfinn, who was rich and getting on in years. He was a wise man. Farmer Thorstein rode down to the ship. He usually had the greatest say in fixing the prices at the market, and that was the case this time. The Norwegians found themselves lodgings, and Thorstein himself took the skipper in, since Bergfinn asked him if he could stay at his house. Bergfinn was rather withdrawn all winter, but Thorstein was very hospitable to him. The Norwegian was very interested in dreams.

One spring day, Thorstein asked Bergfinn if he wanted to ride with him up to Valfell. The Borgarfjord people held their local assembly there in those days, and Thorstein had been told that the walls of his booth had fallen in. The Norwegian replied that he would indeed like to go, and they set out later that day, taking a servant of Thorstein's with them. They rode until they arrived at Grenjar farm, which was near Valfell. A poor man named Atli, a tenant of Thorstein's, lived there. Thorstein asked him to come and help them with their work, and to bring with him a turf-cutting spade and a shovel. He did so, and when they arrived at the place where the booths were they all set to work digging out the walls.

It was a hot, sunny day, and when they had finished digging out the walls, Thorstein and the Norwegian sat down inside the booth. Thorstein dozed off, but his sleep was rather fitful. The Norwegian was sitting beside him and let him finish his dream undisturbed. When Thorstein woke up, he was in considerable distress. The Norwegian asked him what he had been dreaming about, since he slept so badly.

'Dreams don't mean anything,' Thorstein answered.

Now when they were riding home that evening, the Norwegian again asked what Thorstein had been dreaming about.

'If I tell you the dream,' Thorstein replied, 'you must explain it as it really is.' The Norwegian said that he would take that risk.

Then Thorstein said, 'I seemed to be back home at Borg, standing outside the main doorway, and I looked up at the buildings, and saw a fine, beautiful swan up on the roof-ridge. I thought that I owned her, and I was very pleased with her. Then I saw a huge eagle fly down from the mountains. He flew towards Borg and perched next to the swan and chattered to her happily. She seemed to be well pleased with that. Then I noticed that the eagle had black eyes and claws of iron; he looked like a gallant fellow.

'Next, I saw another bird fly from the south. He flew here to Borg, settled on the house next to the swan and tried to court her. It was a huge eagle too. As soon as the second eagle arrived, the first one seemed to become rather ruffled, and they fought fiercely for a long time, and I saw that they were both bleeding. The fight ended with each of them falling off the roof-ridge, one on each side. They were both dead. The swan remained sitting there, grief-stricken and dejected.

'And then I saw another bird fly from the west. It was a hawk. It perched next to the swan and was gentle with her, and later they flew off in the same direction. Then I woke up. Now this dream is nothing much,' he concluded, 'and must be to do with the winds, which will meet in the sky, blowing from the directions that the birds appeared to be flying from.'

'I don't think that's what it's about,' said the Norwegian.

'Interpret the dream as seems most likely to you,' Thorstein told him, 'and let me hear that.'

'These birds must be the fetches of important people,' said the Norwegian. 'Now, your wife is pregnant and will give birth to a pretty baby girl, and you will love her dearly. Noble men will come from the directions that the eagles in your dream seemed to fly from, and will ask for your daughter's hand. They will love her more strongly than is reasonable and will fight over her, and both of them will die as a result. And then a third man, coming from the direction from which the hawk flew, will ask for her hand, and she will marry him. Now I have interpreted your dream for you. I think things will turn out like that.'

'Your explanation is wicked and unfriendly,' Thorstein replied. 'You can't possibly know how to interpret dreams.'

'You'll see how it turns out,' the Norwegian retorted.

After this, Thorstein began to dislike the Norwegian, who went away that summer. He is now out of the saga.

3   Later in the summer, Thorstein got ready to go to the Althing. Before he left, he said to his wife, Jofrid, 'As matters stand, you are soon going to have a baby. Now if you have a girl, it must be left out to die, but if it is a boy, it will be brought up.'

When the country was completely heathen, it was something of a custom for poor men with many dependants in their families to have their children exposed. Even so, it was always considered a bad thing to do.

When Thorstein had said this, Jofrid replied, 'It is most unworthy for a man of your calibre to talk like that, and it cannot seem right to you to have such a thing done.'

'You know what my temper is like,' Thorstein replied. 'It will not do for anyone to go against my command.'

Then he rode off to the Althing, and Jofrid gave birth to an extremely pretty baby girl. The women wanted to take the child to Jofrid, but she said that there was little point in that, and had her shepherd, whose name was Thorvard, brought to her.

'You are to take my horse and saddle it,' Jofrid told him, 'and take this child west to Egil's daughter Thorgerd at Hjardarholt. Ask her to bring the child up in secret, so that Thorstein never finds out about it. For I look upon the child with such love that I really have no heart to have it left out to die. Now, here are three marks of silver which you are to keep as your reward. Thorgerd will procure a passage abroad for you out there in the west, and will give you whatever you need for your voyage overseas.'

Thorvard did as she said. He rode west to Hjardarholt with the child and gave it to Thorgerd. She had it brought up by some of her tenants who lived at Leysingjastadir on Hvammsfjord. She also secured a passage for Thorvard on a ship berthed at Skeljavik in Steingrimsfjord in the north, and made provision for his voyage. Thorvard sailed abroad from there, and is now out of this saga.

Now when Thorstein came back from the Althing, Jofrid told him that the child had been exposed – just as he said it should be – and that the shepherd had run away, taking her horse with him. Thorstein said she had done well, and found himself another shepherd.

Six years passed without this coming out. Then one day Thorstein rode west to Hjardarholt, to a feast given by his brother-in-law Olaf Peacock, who was then the most respected of all the chieftains in the west country. Thorstein was warmly welcomed at Hjardarholt, as might be expected.

Now it is said that, one day during the feast, Thorgerd was

sitting in the high seat talking to her brother Thorstein, while Olaf was making conversation with other men. Three girls were sitting on the bench opposite them.

Then Thorgerd said, 'Brother, how do you like the look of those girls sitting opposite us?'

'Very well,' he replied, 'though one of them is by far the prettiest, and she has Olaf's good looks, as well as the fair complexion and features we men of Myrar have.'

'You are certainly right, brother, when you say that she has the complexion and features of the Myrar men,' Thorgerd said, 'but she has none of Olaf Peacock's looks, since she is not his daughter.'

'How can that be,' Thorstein asked, 'since she's your daughter?'

'Kinsman,' she answered, 'to tell you the truth, this beautiful girl is your daughter, not mine.' Then she told him everything that had happened, and begged him to forgive both her and his wife for this wrong.

'I cannot blame you for this,' Thorstein said. 'In most cases, what will be will be, and you two have smoothed over my own stupidity well enough. I'm so pleased with this girl that I count myself very lucky to have such a beautiful child. But what's her name?'

'She's named Helga,' Thorgerd replied.

'Helga the Fair,' mused Thorstein. 'Now you must get her ready to come home with me.'

And so she did. When he left, Thorstein was given splendid gifts, and Helga rode home to Borg with him and was brought up there, loved and cherished by her father and mother and all her relatives.

4 In those days, Illugi the Black, the son of Hallkel Hrosskelsson, lived at Gilsbakki in Hvitarsida. Illugi's mother was Thurid Dylla, the daughter of Gunnlaug Serpent-tongue. Illugi was the second greatest chieftain in Borgarfjord, after Thorstein Egilsson. He was a great landowner, very strong-willed, and he stood by his friends. He was married to Ingibjorg, the daughter of Asbjorn Hardarson from Ornolfsdal. Ingibjorg's mother was Thorgerd, the daughter of Skeggi from Midfjord. Ingibjorg and Illugi had many children, but only a few of them appear in this saga. One of their sons was named Hermund and another Gunnlaug. They were both promising fellows, and were then in their prime.

It is said that Gunnlaug was somewhat precocious, big and strong, with light chestnut hair, which suited him, dark eyes and a rather ugly nose. He had a pleasant face, a slender waist and broad shoulders. He was very manly, an impetuous fellow by nature, ambitious even in his youth, stubborn in all situations and ruthless. He was a gifted poet, albeit a somewhat abusive one, and was also called Gunnlaug Serpent-tongue. Hermund was the more popular of the two brothers and had the stamp of a chieftain about him.

When Gunnlaug was twelve years old, he asked his father for some wares to cover his travelling expenses, saying that he wanted to go abroad and see how other people lived. Illugi was reluctant to agree to this. He said that people in other countries would not think highly of Gunnlaug when he himself found that he could scarcely manage him as he would wish to at home.

Soon after this, Illugi went out early one morning and saw

that his outhouse was open and that half a dozen sacks of wares had been laid out in the yard, with some saddle-pads. He was very surprised at this. Then someone came along leading four horses; it was his son Gunnlaug.

'I put the sacks there,' he said. Illugi asked why he had done so. He said they would do to help cover his travelling expenses.

'You will not undermine my authority,' said Illugi, 'nor are you going anywhere until I see fit.' And he dragged the sacks back inside.

Then Gunnlaug rode off and arrived down at Borg that evening. Farmer Thorstein invited him to stay and he accepted. Gunnlaug told Thorstein what had happened between him and his father. Thorstein said he could stay as long as he liked, and he was there for a year. He studied law with Thorstein and everyone there thought well of him.

Gunnlaug and Helga often amused themselves by playing board games with each other. They quickly took a liking to each other, as events later bore out. They were pretty much the same age. Helga was so beautiful that learned men say that she was the most beautiful woman there has ever been in Iceland. She had such long hair that it could cover her completely, and it was radiant as beaten gold. It was thought that there was no equal to Helga the Fair throughout Borgarfjord or in places further afield.

Now one day, when people were sitting around in the main room at Borg, Gunnlaug said to Thorstein, 'There is still one point of law that you haven't taught me – how to betroth myself to a woman.'

'That's a small matter,' Thorstein replied, and he taught Gunnlaug the procedure.

Then Gunnlaug said, 'Now you should check whether I've understood properly. I'll take you by the hand and act as though I'm betrothing myself to your daughter Helga.'

'I don't see any need for that,' Thorstein said.

Then Gunnlaug grabbed his hand. 'Do this for me,' he said.

'Do what you like,' Thorstein said, 'but let those present here know that it will be as if this had not been said, and there must be no hidden meaning to it.'

Then Gunnlaug named his witnesses and betrothed himself to Helga. Afterwards, he asked whether that would do. Thorstein said that it would, and everyone there thought it was great fun.

5   There was a man named Onund who lived to the south at Mosfell. He was a very wealthy man, and held the godord for the headlands to the south. He was married, and his wife was named Geirny. She was the daughter of Gnup, the son of Molda-Gnup who settled at Grindavik in the south. Their sons were Hrafn, Thorarin and Eindridi. They were all promising men, but Hrafn was the most accomplished of them in everything. He was a big, strong man, well worth looking at, and a good poet. When he was more or less grown up, he travelled about from country to country and was well respected wherever he went.

Thorodd Eyvindarson the Wise and his son Skafti lived at Hjalli in Olfus in those days. Skafti was Lawspeaker in Iceland at that time. His mother was Rannveig, the daughter of Gnup Molda-Gnupsson, and so Skafti and the sons of Onund were cousins. There was great friendship between them, as well as this blood tie.

Thorfinn Seal-Thorisson was then living out at Raudamel. He had seven sons, and they were all promising men. Their names were Thorgils, Eyjolf and Thorir, and they were the leading men in that district.*

All the men who have been mentioned were living at the same time, and it was about this time that the best thing ever to have happened in Iceland occurred: the whole country became Christian and the entire population abandoned the old faith.

For six years now, Gunnlaug Serpent-tongue, who was mentioned earlier, had been living partly at Borg with Thorstein and partly at Gilsbakki with his father Illugi. By now, he was eighteen years old, and he and his father were getting on much better.

There was a man named Thorkel the Black. He was a member of Illugi's household and a close relative of his, and had grown up at Gilsbakki. He came into an inheritance at As in Vatnsdal up in the north, and asked Gunnlaug to go with him to collect it, which he did. They rode north to As together and, thanks to Gunnlaug's assistance, the men who had Thorkel's money handed it over to them.

On their way home from the north, they stayed overnight at Grimstungur with a wealthy farmer who was living there. In the morning, a shepherd took Gunnlaug's horse, which

---

* The copyist has presumably skipped a section in his exemplar, where the names of Thorfinn's four remaining sons were recorded.

was covered in sweat when they got it back. Gunnlaug knocked the shepherd senseless. The farmer would not leave it at that, and demanded compensation for the blow. Gunnlaug offered to pay him a mark, but the farmer thought that was too little. Then Gunnlaug spoke a verse:

1. A mark to the middle-strong man,
    lodgings-lord, I held out in my hand;   *lodgings-lord*: man
    you'll receive a fine silver-grey wire   *silver-grey wire*:
    for the one who spits flame from   piece of silver
       his gums.   *flame*: blood
    It will cause you regret
    if you knowingly let
    the sea-serpent's couch   *sea-serpent's couch*: gold
    slip out of your pouch.

They arranged that Gunnlaug's offer should be accepted, and when the matter was settled Gunnlaug and Thorkel rode home.

A little while later, Gunnlaug asked his father a second time for wares, so that he could travel abroad.

'Now you may have your own way,' Illugi replied, 'since you are better behaved than you used to be.'

Illugi rode off at once and bought Gunnlaug a half-share in a ship from Audun Halter-dog. The ship was beached in the Gufua estuary. This was the same Audun who, according to *The Saga of the People of Laxardal*, would not take the sons of Osvif the Wise abroad after the killing of Kjartan Olafsson, though that happened later than this.

When Illugi came home, Gunnlaug thanked him

profusely. Thorkel the Black went along with Gunnlaug, and their wares were loaded on to the ship. While the others were getting ready, Gunnlaug was at Borg, and he thought it was nicer to talk to Helga than to work with the traders.

One day, Thorstein asked Gunnlaug if he would like to ride up to his horses in Langavatnsdal with him. Gunnlaug said that he would, and they rode together until they arrived at Thorstein's shielings, which were at a place called Thorgilsstadir. Thorstein had a stud of four chestnut horses there. The stallion was a splendid creature, but was not an experienced fighter. Thorstein offered to give the horses to Gunnlaug, but he said that he did not need them, since he intended to go abroad. Then they rode over to another stud of horses. There was a grey stallion there with four mares; he was the best horse in Borgarfjord. Thorstein offered to give him to Gunnlaug.

'I don't want this horse any more than I wanted the others,' Gunnlaug answered. 'But why don't you offer me something I will accept?'

'What's that?' Thorstein asked.

'Your daughter, Helga the Fair,' Gunnlaug replied.

'That will not be arranged so swiftly,' he said, and changed the subject.

They rode home, down along the Langa river.

Then Gunnlaug spoke: 'I want to know how you will respond to my proposal.'

'I'm not taking any notice of your nonsense,' Thorstein replied.

'This is quite serious, and not nonsense,' Gunnlaug said. 'You should have worked out what you wanted in the first place,' Thorstein countered. 'Haven't you decided to go abroad? And yet you're carrying on as if you want to get married. It wouldn't be suitable for you and Helga to marry while you are so undecided. I'm not prepared to consider it.'

'Where do you expect to find a match for your daughter if you won't marry her to Illugi the Black's son?' Gunnlaug asked. 'Where in Borgarfjord are there more important people than my father?'

'I don't go in for drawing comparisons between men,' Thorstein parried, 'but if you were such a man as he is you wouldn't be turned away.'

'To whom would you rather marry your daughter than me?' Gunnlaug asked.

'There's a lot of good men around here to choose from,' Thorstein replied. 'Thorfinn at Raudamel has seven sons, all of them very manly.'

'Neither Onund nor Thorfinn can compare with my father,' Gunnlaug answered, 'considering that even you clearly fall short of his mark. What have you done to compare with the time when he took on Thorgrim Kjallaksson the Godi and his sons at the Thorsnes Assembly by himself and came away with everything there was to be had?'

'I drove away Steinar, the son of Ogmund Sjoni – and that was considered quite an achievement,' Thorstein replied.

'You had your father, Egil, to help you then,' Gunnlaug retorted. 'Even so, there aren't many farmers who would be safe if they turned down a marriage bond with me.'

'You save your bullying for the people up in the hills,'

Thorstein replied. 'It won't count for much down here in the marshes.'

They arrived home later that evening, and the following morning Gunnlaug rode up to Gilsbakki and asked his father to ride back to Borg with him to make a marriage proposal.

'You are an unsettled fellow,' Illugi replied. 'You've already planned to go abroad, yet now you claim that you have to occupy yourself chasing after women. I know that Thorstein doesn't approve of such behaviour.'

'Nevertheless,' Gunnlaug replied, 'while I still intend to go abroad, nothing will please me unless you support me in this.'

Then Illugi rode down from Gilsbakki to Borg, taking eleven men with him. Thorstein gave them a warm welcome.

Early the next morning, Illugi said to Thorstein: 'I want to talk to you.'

'Let's go up on to the Borg* and talk there,' Thorstein suggested.

They did so, and Gunnlaug went along too.

Illugi spoke first: 'My kinsman Gunnlaug says that he has already spoken of this matter on his own behalf; he wants to ask for the hand of your daughter Helga. Now I want to know what is going to come of this. You know all about his breeding and our family's wealth. For our part, we will not

---

* The *Borg* is a high rocky outcrop immediately behind the site of Borg farm from which the farm takes its name.

neglect to provide either a farm or a godord, if that will help bring it about.'

'The only problem I have with Gunnlaug is that he seems so unsettled,' Thorstein replied. 'But if he were more like you, I shouldn't put it off.'

'If you deny that this would be an equal match for both our families, it will bring an end to our friendship,' Illugi warned.

'For our friendship's sake and because of what you've been saying, Helga will be promised to Gunnlaug, but not formally betrothed to him, and she will wait three years for him. And Gunnlaug must go abroad and follow the example of good men, and I will be free of any obligation if he doesn't come back as required, or if I don't like the way he turns out.'

With that, they parted. Illugi rode home and Gunnlaug rode off to his ship, and the merchants put to sea as soon as they got a fair wind. They sailed to the north of Norway, and then sailed in past Trondheim to Nidaros, where they berthed the ship and unloaded.

6   Earl Eirik Hakonarson and his brother Svein were ruling Norway in those days. Earl Eirik was staying on his family's estate at Lade, and was a powerful chieftain. Skuli Thorsteinsson was there with him: he was one of the earl's followers and was well thought of.

It is said that Gunnlaug and Audun Halter-dog went to Lade with ten other men. Gunnlaug was dressed in a grey tunic and white breeches. He had a boil on his foot, right on the instep, and blood and pus oozed out of it when he walked. In this state, he went before the earl with Audun and the others and greeted him politely. The earl recognized Audun, and asked him for news from Iceland, and Audun told him all there was. Then the earl asked Gunnlaug who he was, and Gunnlaug told him his name and what family he came from.

'Skuli Thorsteinsson,' the earl asked, 'what family does this fellow come from in Iceland?'

'My lord,' he replied, 'give him a good welcome. He is the son of the best man in Iceland, Illugi the Black from Gilsbakki, and, what's more, he's my foster-brother.'

'What's the matter with your foot, Icelander?' the earl asked.

'I've got a boil on it, my lord,' he replied.

'But you weren't limping?'

'One mustn't limp while both legs are the same length,' Gunnlaug replied.

Then a man named Thorir, who was one of the earl's followers, spoke: 'The Icelander is rather cocky. We should test him a bit.'

Gunnlaug looked at him, and spoke:

2. A certain follower's
especially horrible;
be wary of trusting him:
he's evil and black.

Then Thorir made as if to grab his axe.

'Leave it be,' said the earl. 'Real men don't pay any attention to things like that. How old are you, Icelander?'

'Just turned eighteen,' Gunnlaug replied.

'I swear that you'll not survive another eighteen,' the earl declared.

'Don't you call curses down on me,' Gunnlaug muttered quite softly, 'but rather pray for yourself.'

'What did you just say, Icelander?' the earl asked.

'I said what I thought fit,' Gunnlaug replied, 'that you should not call curses down on me, but should pray more effective prayers for yourself.'

'What should I pray for then?' asked the earl.

'That you don't meet your death in the same way as your father Earl Hakon did.'*

The earl turned as red as blood, and ordered that the fool be arrested at once.

Then Skuli went to the earl and said, 'My lord, do as I ask: pardon the man and let him get out of here as quickly as he can.'

'Let him clear off as fast as he can if he wants quarter,' the earl commanded, 'and never set foot in my kingdom again.'

Then Skuli took Gunnlaug outside and down to the quay, where there was a ship all ready for its voyage to England. Skuli procured a passage in it for Gunnlaug and his kinsman Thorkel, and Gunnlaug entrusted his ship and the other belongings he did not need to keep with him to Audun for safe-keeping. Gunnlaug and Thorkel sailed off into the

---

* Earl Hakon Sigurdsson was murdered by his servant Kark, while hiding from his enemy Olaf Tryggvason in a pigsty.

North Sea, and arrived in the autumn at the port of London, where they drew the ship up on to its rollers.

7 King Ethelred, the son of Edgar, was ruling England at that time. He was a good ruler, and was spending that winter in London. In those days, the language in England was the same as that spoken in Norway and Denmark, but there was a change of language when William the Bastard conquered England. Since William was of French descent, the French language was used in England from then on.

As soon as he arrived in London, Gunnlaug went before the king and greeted him politely and respectfully. The king asked what country he was from. Gunnlaug told him – 'and I have come to you, my lord, because I have composed a poem about you, and I should like you to hear it'.

The king said that he would. Gunnlaug recited the poem expressively and confidently. The refrain goes like this:

3. All the army's in awe and agog
at England's good prince, as at God:
everyone lauds Ethelred the King,
both the warlike king's race and men's kin.

The king thanked him for the poem and, as a reward, gave him a cloak of scarlet lined with the finest furs and with an embroidered band stretching down to the hem. He also made him one of his followers. Gunnlaug stayed with the king all winter and was well thought of.

Early one morning, Gunnlaug met three men in a street.

Their leader was named Thororm. He was big and strong, and rather obstreperous.

'Northerner,' he said, 'lend me some money.'

'It's not a good idea to lend money to strangers,' Gunnlaug replied.

'I'll pay you back on the date we agree between us,' he promised.

'I'll risk it then,' said Gunnlaug, giving Thororm the money.

A little while later, Gunnlaug met the king and told him about the loan.

'Now things have taken a turn for the worse,' the king replied. 'That fellow is the most notorious robber and thug. Have nothing more to do with him, and I will give you the same amount of money.'

'Then your followers are a pretty pathetic lot,' Gunnlaug answered. 'We trample all over innocent men, but let thugs like him walk all over us! That will never happen.'

Shortly afterwards, Gunnlaug met Thororm and demanded his money back, but Thororm said that he would not pay up. Then Gunnlaug spoke this verse:

4. O god of the sword-spell, you're unwise to withhold your wealth from me; you've deceived the sword-point's reddener. I've something else to explain – 'Serpent-tongue' as a child was my name. Now again here's my chance to prove why.	*sword-spell*: battle; its *god*: warrior *sword-point's reddener*: warrior, who reddens the sword's point with blood

'Now I'll give you the choice the law provides for,' said Gunnlaug. 'Either you pay me my money or fight a duel with me in three days' time.'

The thug laughed and said, 'Many people have suffered badly at my hands, and no one has ever challenged me to a duel before. I'm quite ready for it!'

With that, Gunnlaug and Thororm parted for the time being. Gunnlaug told the king how things stood.

'Now we really are in a fix,' he said. 'This man can blunt any weapon just by looking at it. You must do exactly as I tell you. I am going to give you this sword, and you are to fight him with it, but make sure that you show him a different one.'

Gunnlaug thanked the king warmly.

When they were ready for the duel, Thororm asked Gunnlaug what kind of sword he happened to have. Gunnlaug showed him and drew the sword, but he had fastened a loop of rope around the hilt of King's Gift and he slipped it over his wrist.

As soon as he saw the sword, the berserk said, 'I'm not afraid of that sword.'

He struck at Gunnlaug with his sword, and chopped off most of his shield. Then Gunnlaug struck back with his sword King's Gift. The berserk left himself exposed, because he thought Gunnlaug was using the same weapon as he had shown him. Gunnlaug dealt him his death-blow there and then. The king thanked him for this service, and Gunnlaug won great fame for it in England and beyond.

In the spring, when ships were sailing from country to country, Gunnlaug asked Ethelred for permission to do some travelling. The king asked him what he wanted to do.

'I should like to fulfil a vow I have made,' Gunnlaug answered, and spoke this verse:

5. I will most surely visit
   three shapers of war   *shapers of war*: kings
   and two earls of lands,
   as I promised worthy men.
   I will not be back
   before the point-goddess's son   *point-goddess*: valkyrie; her *son*:
   summons me; he gives me   Ethelred
   a red serpent's bed to wear.   *serpent's bed*: gold

'And so it will be, poet,' said the king, giving him a gold arm ring weighing six ounces. 'But,' he continued, 'you must promise to come back to me next autumn, because I don't want to lose such an accomplished man as you.'

8

Then Gunnlaug sailed north to Dublin with some merchants. At that time, Ireland was ruled by King Sigtrygg Silk-beard, the son of Olaf Kvaran and Queen Kormlod. He had only been king for a short while. Straight away, Gunnlaug went before the king and greeted him politely and respectfully. The king gave him an honourable welcome.

'I have composed a poem about you,' Gunnlaug said, 'and I should like it to have a hearing.'

'No one has ever deigned to bring me a poem before,' the king replied. 'Of course I will listen to it.'

Gunnlaug recited the drapa, and the refrain goes like this:

6. To the sorceress's steed   *sorceress's steed*: wolf
   Sigtrygg corpses feeds.

And it contains these lines as well:

7. I know which offspring,
   descendant of kings,
   I want to proclaim
   – Kvaran's son is his name;
   it is his habit
   to be quite lavish:
   the poet's ring of gold
   he surely won't withhold.

8. The flinger of Frodi's flame   *Frodi's* (sea-king's) *flame*: gold; its
   should eloquently explain   *flinger*: generous man (Sigtrygg)
   if he's found phrasing neater
   than mine, in drapa metre.

The king thanked Gunnlaug for the poem, and summoned his treasurer.

'How should I reward the poem?' he asked.

'How would you like to, my lord?' the treasurer said.

'What kind of reward would it be if I gave him a pair of knorrs?' the king asked.

'That is too much, my lord,' he replied. 'Other kings give fine treasures – good swords or splendid gold bracelets – as rewards for poems.'

The king gave Gunnlaug his own new suit of scarlet

clothes, an embroidered tunic, a cloak lined with exquisite furs and a gold bracelet which weighed a mark. Gunnlaug thanked him profusely and stayed there for a short while. He went on from there to the Orkney Islands.

In those days, the Orkney Islands were ruled by Earl Sigurd Hlodvesson. He thought highly of Icelanders. Gunnlaug greeted the earl politely and said that he had a poem to present to him. The earl said that he would indeed listen to Gunnlaug's poem, since he was from such an important family in Iceland. Gunnlaug recited the poem, which was a well-constructed flokk. As a reward, the earl gave him a broad axe, decorated all over with silver inlay, and invited Gunnlaug to stay with him.

Gunnlaug thanked him for the gift, and for the invitation, too, but said that he had to travel east to Sweden. Then he took passage with some merchants who were sailing to Norway, and that autumn they arrived at Kungalf in the east. As always, Gunnlaug's kinsman, Thorkel, was still with him. They took a guide from Kungalf up into Vastergotland and so arrived at the market town named Skarar. An earl named Sigurd, who was rather old, was ruling there. Gunnlaug went before him and greeted him politely, saying that he had composed a poem about him. The earl listened carefully as Gunnlaug recited the poem, which was a flokk. Afterwards, the earl thanked Gunnlaug, rewarded him generously and asked him to stay with him over the winter.

Earl Sigurd held a great Yule feast during the winter. Messengers from Earl Eirik arrived on Yule eve. They had travelled down from Norway. There were twelve of them in all, and they were bearing gifts for Earl Sigurd. The earl gave them a warm welcome and seated them next to Gunnlaug for the Yule festival. There was a great deal of merriment. The people of Vastergotland declared that there was no better or more famous earl than Sigurd; the Norwegians thought that Earl Eirik was much better. They argued about this and, in the end, both sides called upon Gunnlaug to settle the matter. It was then that Gunnlaug spoke this verse:

9. Staves of the spear-sister,   *spear-sister*: valkyrie; her *staves*:
   you speak of the earl: warriors
   this old man is hoary-haired,
   but has looked on tall waves.
   Before his billow-steed   *billow-steed*: ship
   battle-bush Eirik, tossed   *battle-bush*: warrior
   by the tempest, has seen
more blue breakers back in the east.

Both sides, but particularly the Norwegians, were pleased with this assessment. After Yule, the messengers left with splendid gifts from Earl Sigurd to Earl Eirik. They told Earl Eirik about Gunnlaug's assessment. The earl thought that Gunnlaug had shown him both fairness and friendliness, and spread the word that Gunnlaug would find a safe haven in his domain. Gunnlaug later heard what the earl had had to say about the matter. Gunnlaug had asked Earl Sigurd for a guide to take him east into Tiundaland in Sweden, and the earl found him one.

9 In those days, Sweden was ruled by King Olaf the Swede, the son of King Eirik the Victorious and Sigrid the Ambitious, daughter of Tosti the Warlike. He was a powerful and illustrious king, and was very keen to make his mark.

Gunnlaug arrived in Uppsala around the time of the Swedes' Spring Assembly. When he managed to get an audience, he greeted the king, who welcomed him warmly and asked him who he was. He said that he was an Icelander. Now Hrafn Onundarson was with the king at the time.

'Hrafn,' the king said, 'what family does this fellow come from in Iceland?'

A big, dashing man stood up from the lower bench, came before the king and said, 'My lord, he comes from the finest of families and is the noblest of men in his own right.'

'Then let him go and sit next to you,' the king said.

'I have a poem to present to you,' Gunnlaug said, 'and I should like you to listen to it properly.'

'First go and sit yourselves down,' the king commanded. 'There is no time now to sit and listen to poems.'

And so they did. Gunnlaug and Hrafn started to chat, telling one another about their travels. Hrafn said that he had left Iceland for Norway the previous summer, and had come east to Sweden early that winter. They were soon good friends.

One day when the assembly was over, Hrafn and Gunnlaug were both there with the king.

'Now, my lord,' Gunnlaug said, 'I should like you to hear my poem.'

'I could do that now,' the king replied.

'I want to recite my poem now, my lord,' Hrafn said.

'I could listen to that, too,' he replied.

'I want to recite my poem first,' Gunnlaug said, 'if you please.'

'I should go first, my lord,' Hrafn said, 'since I came to your court first.'

'Where did our ancestors ever go with mine trailing in the wake of yours?' Gunnlaug asked. 'Nowhere, that's where! And that's how it's going to be with us, too!'

'Let's be polite enough not to fight over this,' Hrafn replied. 'Let's ask the king to decide.'

'Gunnlaug had better recite his poem first,' the king declared, 'since he takes it badly if he doesn't get his own way.'

Then Gunnlaug recited the drapa he had composed about King Olaf, and when he had finished, the king said, 'How well is the poem composed, Hrafn?'

'Quite well, my lord,' he answered. 'It is an ostentatious poem, but is ungainly and rather stilted, just like Gunnlaug himself is in temperament.'

'Now you must recite your poem, Hrafn,' the king said.

He did so, and when he had finished, the king asked: 'How well is the poem put together, Gunnlaug?'

'Quite well, my lord,' he replied. 'It is a handsome poem, just like Hrafn himself is, but there's not much to either of them. And,' he continued, 'why did you compose only a flokk for the king, Hrafn? Did you not think he merited a drapa?'

'Let's not talk about this any farther,' Hrafn said. 'It might well crop up again later.' And with that they parted.

A little while later, Hrafn was made one of King Olaf's followers. He asked for permission to leave, which the king granted.

Now when Hrafn was ready to leave, he said to Gunnlaug, 'From now on, our friendship is over, since you tried to do me down in front of the court. Sometime soon, I will cause you no less shame than you tried to heap on me here.'

'Your threats don't scare me,' Gunnlaug replied, 'and I won't be thought a lesser man than you anywhere.'

King Olaf gave Hrafn valuable gifts when they parted, and then Hrafn went away.

Hrafn left the east that spring and went to Trondheim, where he fitted out his ship. He sailed to Iceland during the summer, and brought his ship into Leiruvog, south of Mosfell heath. His family and friends were glad to see him, and he stayed at home with his father over the winter.

Now at the Althing that summer, Hrafn the Poet met his kinsman Skafti the Lawspeaker.

'I should like you to help me ask Thorstein Egilsson for permission to marry his daughter Helga,' Hrafn said.

'Hasn't she already been promised to Gunnlaug Serpent-tongue?' Skafti answered.

'Hasn't the time they agreed passed by now?' Hrafn countered. 'Besides, Gunnlaug's so proud these days that he won't take any notice of this or care about it all.'

'We'll do as you please,' Skafti replied.

Then they went over to Thorstein Egilsson's booth with several other men. Thorstein gave them a warm welcome.

'My kinsman Hrafn wants to ask for the hand of your daughter Helga,' Skafti explained. 'You know about his family background, his wealth and good breeding, and that he has numerous relatives and friends.'

'She is already promised to Gunnlaug,' Thorstein answered, 'and I want to stick to every detail of the agreement I made with him.'

'Haven't the three winters you agreed between yourselves passed by now?' Skafti asked.

'Yes,' said Thorstein, 'but the summer isn't gone, and he might yet come back during the summer.'

'But if he hasn't come back at the end of the summer, then what hope will we have in the matter?' Skafti asked.

'We'll all come back here next summer,' Thorstein replied, 'and then we'll be able to see what seems to be the best way forward, but there's no point in talking about it any more at the moment.'

With that they parted, and people rode home from the Althing. It was no secret that Hrafn had asked for Helga's hand.

Gunnlaug did not return that summer. At the Althing the next summer, Skafti and Hrafn argued their case vehemently, saying that Thorstein was now free of all his obligations to Gunnlaug.

'I don't have many daughters to look after,' Thorstein said, 'and I'm anxious that no one be provoked to violence on their account. Now I want to see Illugi the Black first.'

And so he did.

When Illugi and Thorstein met, Thorstein asked, 'Do you

consider me to be free of all obligation to your son Gunnlaug?'

'Certainly,' Illugi replied, 'if that's how you want it. I cannot add much to this now, because I don't altogether know what Gunnlaug's circumstances are.'

Then Thorstein went back to Skafti. They settled matters by deciding that, if Gunnlaug did not come back that summer, Hrafn and Helga's marriage should take place at Borg at the Winter Nights, but that Thorstein should be without obligation to Hrafn if Gunnlaug were to come back and go through with the wedding. After that, people rode home from the Althing. Gunnlaug's return was still delayed, and Helga did not like the arrangement at all.

10 Now we return to Gunnlaug, who left Sweden for England in the same summer as Hrafn went back to Iceland. He received valuable gifts from King Olaf when he left. King Ethelred gave Gunnlaug a very warm welcome. He stayed with the king all winter, and was thought well of.

In those days, the ruler of Denmark was Canute the Great, the son of Svein. He had recently come into his inheritance, and was continually threatening to lead an army against England, since his father, Svein, had gained considerable power in England before his death there in the west. Furthermore, there was a huge army of Danes in Britain at that time. Its leader was Heming, the son of Earl Strut-Harald and the brother of Earl Sigvaldi. Under King Canute, Heming was in charge of the territory which King Svein had previously won.

During the spring, Gunnlaug asked King Ethelred for permission to leave.

'Since you are my follower,' he replied, 'it is not appropriate for you to leave me when such a war threatens England.'

'That is for you to decide, my lord,' Gunnlaug replied. 'But give me permission to leave next summer, if the Danes don't come.'

'We'll see about it then,' the king answered.

Now that summer and the following winter passed, and the Danes did not come. After midsummer, Gunnlaug obtained the king's permission to leave, went east to Norway and visited Earl Eirik at Lade in Trondheim. The earl gave him a warm welcome this time, and invited him to stay with him. Gunnlaug thanked him for the offer, but said that he wanted to go back to Iceland first, to visit his intended.

'All the ships prepared for Iceland are gone now,' said the earl.

Then a follower said, 'Hallfred the Troublesome Poet was still anchored out under Agdenes yesterday.'

'That might still be the case,' the earl replied. 'He sailed from here five nights ago.'

Then Earl Eirik had Gunnlaug taken out to Hallfred, who was glad to see him. An offshore breeze began to blow, and they were very cheerful. It was late summer.

'Have you heard about Hrafn Onundarson's asking for permission to marry Helga the Fair?' Hallfred asked Gunnlaug.

Gunnlaug said that he had heard about it, but that he did not know the full story. Hallfred told him everything he knew about it, and added that many people said that Hrafn might well prove to be no less brave than Gunnlaug was. Then Gunnlaug spoke this verse:

10. Though the east wind has toyed
 with the shore-ski this week   *shore-ski*: ship
 I weigh that but little –
 the weather's weaker now.
 I fear more being felt
 to fall short of Hrafn in courage
 than living on to become
 a grey-haired gold-breaker.   *gold-breaker*: man

Then Hallfred said, 'You will need to have better dealings with Hrafn than I did. A few years ago, I brought my ship into Leiruvog, south of Mosfell heath. I ought to have paid Hrafn's farmhand half a mark of silver, but I didn't give it to him. Hrafn rode over to us with sixty men and cut our mooring ropes, and the ship drifted up on to the mud flats and looked as if it would be wrecked. I ended up granting Hrafn self-judgement, and paid him a mark. That is all I have to say about him.'

From then on, they talked only about Helga. Hallfred heaped much praise on her beauty. Then Gunnlaug spoke:

11. The slander-wary god
    of the sword-storm's spark   *sword-storm*: battle; *its spark*:
                                                        sword; *god*
mustn't court the cape of the earth   *of the sword*: warrior(Hrafn)
with her cover of linen like snow.
For when I was a lad,   *forearm's fire*: ring; its
I played on the headlands   *headlands*: fingers;
of the forearm's fire   *played* on the fingers: was
with that land-fishes' bed-land.   her favourite
                                                        (*or* caressed her)
                                                        land-fishes: snakes; their *beds*:
                                                        gold; gold-*land*: woman

'That is well composed,' Hallfred said.

They came ashore at Hraunhofn on Melrakkasletta a fortnight before winter, and unloaded the ship.

There was a man named Thord, who was the son of the farmer on Melrakkasletta. He was always challenging the merchants at wrestling, and they generally came off worse against him. Then a bout was arranged between him and Gunnlaug, and the night before, Thord called upon Thor to bring him victory. When they met the next day, they began to wrestle. Gunnlaug swept both Thord's legs out from under him, and his opponent fell down hard, but Gunnlaug twisted his own ankle out of joint when he put his weight on that leg, and he fell down with Thord.

'Maybe your next fight won't go any better,' Thord said.

'What do you mean?' Gunnlaug asked.

'I'm talking about the quarrel you'll be having with Hrafn

when he marries Helga the Fair at the Winter Nights. I was there when it was arranged at the Althing this summer.'

Gunnlaug did not reply. Then his foot was bandaged and the joint reset. It was badly swollen.

Hallfred and Gunnlaug rode south with ten other men, and arrived at Gilsbakki in Borgarfjord on the same Saturday evening that the others were sitting down to the wedding feast at Borg. Illugi was glad to see his son Gunnlaug and his companions. Gunnlaug said that he wanted to ride down to Borg there and then, but Illugi said that this was not wise. Everyone else thought so too, except Gunnlaug, but he was incapacitated by his foot – although he did not let it show – and so the journey did not take place. In the morning, Hallfred rode home to Hreduvatn in Nordurardal. His brother Galti, who was a splendid fellow, was looking after their property there.

11 Now we turn to Hrafn, who was sitting down to his wedding feast at Borg. Most people say that the bride was rather gloomy. It is true that, as the saying goes, 'things learned young last longest', and that was certainly the case with her just then.

It so happened that a man named Sverting, who was the son of Goat-Bjorn, the son of Molda-Gnup, asked for the hand of Hungerd, the daughter of Thorodd and Jofrid. The wedding was to take place up at Skaney later in the winter, after Yule. A relative of Hungerd's, Thorkel the son of Torfi Valbrandsson, lived at Skaney. Torfi's mother was Thorodda, the sister of Tunga-Odd.

Hrafn went home to Mosfell with his wife Helga. One morning, when they had been living there for a little while,

Helga was lying awake before they got up, but Hrafn was still sleeping. His sleep was rather fitful, and when he woke up, Helga asked him what he had been dreaming about. Then Hrafn spoke this verse:

12. I thought I'd been stabbed
　　by a yew of serpent's dew
　　and with my blood, O my bride,
　　your bed was stained red.
　　Beer-bowl's goddess, you weren't
　　able to bind up the damage
　　that the drubbing-thorn dealt to Hrafn:
　　linden of herbs, that might please you.

serpent's dew: blood;
its *yew* (twig): sword

beer-bowl's goddess:
woman (Helga)

drubbing-thorn: sword
linden (tree) *of herbs*:
woman

'I will never weep over that,' Helga said. 'You have all tricked me wickedly. Gunnlaug must have come back.' And then Helga wept bitterly.

Indeed, a little while later news came of Gunnlaug's return. After this, Helga grew so intractable towards Hrafn that he could not keep her at home, and so they went back to Borg. Hrafn did not enjoy much intimacy with her.

Now people were making plans for the winter's other wedding. Thorkel from Skaney invited Illugi the Black and his sons. But while Illugi was getting ready, Gunnlaug sat in the main room and did not make any move towards getting ready himself.

Illugi went up to him and said, 'Why aren't you getting ready, son?'

'I don't intend to go,' Gunnlaug replied.

'Of course you will go, son,' Illugi said. 'And don't set so much store by yearning for just one woman. Behave as though you haven't noticed, and you'll never be short of women.'

Gunnlaug did as his father said, and they went to the feast. Illugi and his sons were given one high seat, and Thorstein Egilsson, his son-in-law Hrafn and the bridegroom's group had the other one, opposite Illugi. The women were sitting on the cross-bench, and Helga the Fair was next to the bride. She often cast her eyes in Gunnlaug's direction, and so it was proved that, as the saying goes, 'if a woman loves a man, her eyes won't hide it'. Gunnlaug was well turned out, and had on the splendid clothes which King Sigtrygg had given him. He seemed far superior to other men for many reasons, what with his strength, his looks and his figure.

People did not particularly enjoy the wedding feast. On the same day as the men were getting ready to leave, the women started to break up their party, too, and began getting themselves ready for the journey home. Gunnlaug went to talk to Helga, and they chatted for a long time. Then Gunnlaug spoke this verse:

13. For Serpent-tongue no full day
    under mountains' hall was easy *mountains' hall*: sky
    since Helga the Fair
    took the name of Hrafn's Wife.
    But her father, white-faced
    wielder of whizzing spears,
    took no heed of my tongue.
    – the goddess was married for money.

And he spoke another one, too:

14. Fair wine-goddess, I must reward
    your father for the worst wound –
    the land of the flood-flame steals joy
    from this poet – and also your mother.
    For beneath bedclothes they both
    made a band-goddess so beautiful:
    the devil take the handiwork
    of that bold man and woman!

wine-goddess: woman (Helga)
flood-flame: gold; its *land*: woman

band-goddess: woman wearing garments of woven bands (Helga)

And then Gunnlaug gave Helga the cloak Ethelred had given him, which was very splendid. She thanked him sincerely for the gift.

Then Gunnlaug went outside. By now, mares and stallions – many of them fine animals – had been led into the yard, saddled up and tethered there. Gunnlaug leapt on to one of the stallions and rode at a gallop across the hayfield to where Hrafn was standing. Hrafn had to duck out of his way.

'There's no need to duck, Hrafn,' Gunnlaug said, 'because I don't mean to do you any harm at the moment, though you know what you deserve.'

Hrafn answered with this verse:

15. Glorifier of battle-goddess,   *battle-goddess*: valkyrie; her
    god of the quick-flying weapon,   *glorifier*: warrior;
    it's not fitting for us to fight   *god of the . . . weapon*: warrior
    over one fair tunic-goddess.   *tunic-goddess*: woman
    Slaughter-tree, south over sea   *Slaughter-tree*: warrior
    there are many such women,
    you will rest assured of that.
    I set my wave-steed to sail.   *wave-steed*: ship

'There may well be a lot of women,' Gunnlaug replied, 'but it doesn't look that way to me.'

Then Illugi and Thorstein ran over to them, and would not let them fight each other. Gunnlaug spoke a verse:

16. The fresh-faced goddess
    of the serpent's day   *serpent's day* (i.e.
    was handed to Hrafn for pay –   brightness): gold;
    he's equal to me, people say –   its *goddess*: woman
    while in the pounding of steel   *pounding of steel*: battle
    peerless Ethelred delayed
    my journey from the east – that's why
    the jewel-foe's less greedy for words.   *jewel-foe*: generous
                                                                                 man (Gunnlaug)

After that, both parties went home, and nothing worth mentioning happened all winter. Hrafn never again enjoyed intimacy with Helga after she and Gunnlaug had met once more.

That summer, people made their way to the Althing in large groups: Illugi the Black took his sons Gunnlaug and

Hermund with him; Thorstein Egilsson took his son Kollsvein; Onund from Mosfell took all his sons; and Sverting the son of Goat-Bjorn also went. Skafti was still Lawspeaker then.

One day during the Althing, when people were thronging to the Law Rock and the legal business was done, Gunnlaug demanded a hearing and said, 'Is Hrafn Onundarson here?'

Hrafn said that he was.

Then Gunnlaug Serpent-tongue said, 'You know that you have married my intended and have drawn yourself into enmity with me because of it. Now I challenge you to a duel to take place here at the Althing in three days' time on Oxararholm (Axe River Island).'

'That's a fine-sounding challenge,' Hrafn replied, 'as might be expected from you. Whenever you like – I'm quite ready for it!'

Both sets of relatives were upset by this, but, in those days, the law said that anyone who felt he'd received underhand treatment from someone else could challenge him to a duel.

Now when the three days were up, they got themselves ready for the duel. Illugi the Black went to the island with his son, along with a large body of men; and Skafti the Lawspeaker went with Hrafn, as did his father and other relatives. Before Gunnlaug went out on to the island, he spoke this verse:

17. I'm ready to tread the isle
    where combat is tried
    – God grant the poet victory –
    a drawn sword in my hand;
    into two I'll slice the hair-seat   *hair-seat*: head
    of Helga's kiss-gulper;   *Helga's kiss-gulper*: her lover,
    finally, with my bright sword,   Hrafn
    I'll unscrew his head from his neck.

Hrafn replied with this one:

18. The poet doesn't know
    which poet will rejoice –
    wound-sickles are drawn,   *wound-sickles*: swords
    the edge fit to bite leg.
    Both single and a widow,
    from the Thing the thorn-tray will hear   *thorns*: brooch-pins,
    – though bloodied I might be –   its *tray*: woman
    tales of her man's bravery.

Hermund held his brother Gunnlaug's shield for him; and Sverting, Goat-Bjorn's son, held Hrafn's. Whoever was wounded was to pay three marks of silver to release himself from the duel. Hrafn was to strike the first blow, since he had been challenged. He hacked at the top of Gunnlaug's shield, and the blow was so mightily struck that the sword promptly broke off below the hilt. The point of the sword glanced up and caught Gunnlaug on the cheek, scratching him slightly. Straight away, their fathers, along with several other people, ran between them.

Then Gunnlaug said, 'I submit that Hrafn is defeated, because he is weaponless.'

'And I submit that you are defeated,' Hrafn replied, 'because you have been wounded.'

Gunnlaug got very angry and said, all in a rage, that the matter had not been resolved. Then his father, Illugi, said that there should not be any more resolving for the moment.

'Next time Hrafn and I meet, Father,' Gunnlaug said, 'I should like you to be too far away to separate us.'

With that they parted for the time being, and everyone went back to their booths.

Now the following day, it was laid down as law by the Law Council that all duelling should be permanently abolished. This was done on the advice of all the wisest men at the Althing, and all the wisest men in Iceland were there. Thus the duel which Hrafn and Gunnlaug fought was the last one ever to take place in Iceland. This was one of the three most-crowded Althings of all time, the others being the one after the burning of Njal and the one following the Slayings on the Heath.

One morning, when the brothers Hermund and Gunnlaug were on their way to the Oxara river to wash themselves, several women were going to its opposite bank. Helga the Fair was one of them.

Then Hermund asked Gunnlaug, 'Can you see your girlfriend Helga on the other side of the river?'

'Of course I can see her,' Gunnlaug replied. And then he spoke this verse:

19. The woman was born to bring war
    between men – the tree of the valkyrie   *tree of the valkyrie*:
    started it all; I wanted her   warrior (perhaps
    sorely, that log of rare silver.   Hrafn, but more
    Henceforward, my black eyes   probably Thorstein)
    are scarcely of use to glance   *log of silver*: woman
    at the ring-land's light-goddess,   *ring-land*: hand; its
    splendid as a swan.   *light*: ring;
      goddess of the ring:
      woman

Then they went across the river, and Helga and Gunnlaug chatted for a while. When they went back eastwards across the river, Helga stood and stared at Gunnlaug for a long time. Then Gunnlaug looked back across the river and spoke this verse:

20. The moon of her eyelash – that valkyrie   *moon*: eye
    adorned with linen, server of herb-surf,   *herb-surf*: ale; its
    shone hawk-sharp upon me   *server*: woman
    beneath her brow's bright sky;   *brow's sky*: forehead
    but that beam from the eyelid-moon   *beam*: gaze
    of the goddess of the golden torque   *goddess of the golden*
    will later bring trouble to me   *torque*: woman
    and to the ring-goddess herself.   *ring-goddess*: woman

After this had happened, everyone rode home from the Althing, and Gunnlaug settled down at home at Gilsbakki. One morning, when he woke up, everyone was up and about except him. He slept in a bed closet further into the hall than were the benches. Then twelve men, all armed to the teeth, came into the hall: Hrafn Onundarson had arrived. Gunnlaug leapt up with a start, and managed to grab his weapons.

'You're not in any danger,' Hrafn said, 'and you'll hear what brings me here right now. You challenged me to a duel at the Althing last summer, and you thought that the matter was not fully resolved. Now I want to suggest that we both leave Iceland this summer and travel to Norway and fight a duel over there. Our relatives won't be able to stand between us there.'

'Well spoken, man!' Gunnlaug replied. 'I accept your proposal with pleasure. And now, Hrafn, you may have whatever hospitality you would like here.'

'That is a kind offer,' Hrafn replied, 'but, for the moment, we must ride on our way.'

And with that they parted. Both sets of relatives were very upset about this, but, because of their own anger, they could do nothing about it. But what fate decreed must come to pass.

12 Now we return to Hrafn. He fitted out his ship in Leiruvog. The names of two men who travelled with him are known: they were the sons of his father Onund's sister, one named Grim and the other Olaf. They were both worthy men. All Hrafn's relatives thought it was a great blow when he went away, but he explained that he had challenged Gunnlaug to a duel because he was not getting anywhere with Helga; one of them, he said, would have to perish at the hands of the other.

Hrafn set sail when he got a fair breeze, and they brought the ship to Trondheim, where he spent the winter. He received no news of Gunnlaug that winter, and so he waited there for him all summer, and then spent yet another winter in Trondheim at a place named Levanger.

Gunnlaug Serpent-tongue sailed from Melrakkasletta in the north with Hallfred the Troublesome Poet. They left their preparations very late, and put to sea as soon as they got a fair breeze, arriving in the Orkney Islands shortly before winter.

The islands were ruled by Earl Sigurd Hlodvesson at that time, and Gunnlaug went to him and spent the winter there. He was well respected. During the spring, the earl got ready to go plundering. Gunnlaug made preparations to go with him, and they spent the summer plundering over a large part of the Hebrides and the Scottish firths and fought many battles. Wherever they went, Gunnlaug proved himself to be a very brave and valiant fellow, and very manly. Earl Sigurd turned back in the early part of the summer, and then Gunnlaug took passage with some merchants who were sailing to Norway. Gunnlaug and Earl Sigurd parted on very friendly terms.

Gunnlaug went north to Lade in Trondheim to visit Earl Eirik, arriving at the beginning of winter. The earl gave him a warm welcome, and invited him to stay with him. Gunnlaug accepted the invitation. The earl had already heard about the goings-on between Gunnlaug and Hrafn, and he told Gunnlaug that he would not allow them to fight in his realm. Gunnlaug said that such matters were for the earl to decide. He stayed there that winter, and was always rather withdrawn.

Now one day that spring, Gunnlaug and his kinsman Thorkel went out for a walk. They headed away from the town, and in the fields in front of them was a ring of men. Inside the ring, two armed men were fencing. One had been given the name Gunnlaug, and the other one Hrafn. The bystanders said that Icelanders struck out with mincing blows and were slow to remember their promises. Gunnlaug realized that there was a great deal of contempt in this, that it was a focus for mockery, and he went away in silence.

A little while after this, Gunnlaug told the earl that he did not feel inclined to put up with his followers' contempt and mockery concerning the goings-on between himself and Hrafn any longer. He asked the earl to provide him with guides to Levanger. The earl had already been told that Hrafn had left Levanger and gone across into Sweden, and he therefore gave Gunnlaug permission to go, and found him two guides for the journey.

Then Gunnlaug left Lade with six other men, and went to Levanger. He arrived during the evening, but Hrafn had departed from there with four men the same morning. Gunnlaug went from there into Veradal, always arriving in the evening at the place where Hrafn had been the night before. Gunnlaug pressed on until he reached the innermost farm in the valley, which was named Sula, but Hrafn had left there that morning. Gunnlaug did not break his journey there, however, but pressed on through the night, and they caught sight of each other at sunrise the next day. Hrafn had reached a place where there were two lakes, with a stretch of flat land between them. This area was named Gleipnisvellir (Gleipnir's Plains). A small headland called Dingenes jutted out into one of the lakes. Hrafn's party, which was five strong, took up position on the headland. His kinsmen, Grim and Olaf, were with him.

When they met, Gunnlaug said, 'It's good that we have met now.'

Hrafn said that he had no problem with it himself – 'and now you must choose which you prefer,' he said. 'Either we will all fight, or just the two of us, but both sides must be equal.'

Gunnlaug said that he would be quite happy with either arrangement. Then Hrafn's kinsmen, Grim and Olaf, said that they would not stand by while Gunnlaug and Hrafn fought. Thorkel the Black, Gunnlaug's kinsman, said the same.

Then Gunnlaug told the earl's guides: 'You must sit by and help neither side, and be there to tell the story of our encounter.' And so they did.

Then they fell to, and everyone fought bravely. Grim and Olaf together attacked Gunnlaug alone, and the business between them ended in his killing them both, though he was not himself hurt. Thord Kolbeinsson confirms this in the poem he composed about Gunnlaug Serpent-tongue:

21. Before reaching Hrafn,
　　Gunnlaug hacked down Grim
　　and Olaf, men pleased
　　with the valkyrie's warm wind;　　*valkyrie's warm wind*: battle
　　blood-bespattered, the brave one
　　was the bane of three bold men;
　　the god of the wave-charger　　*wave-charger*: ship; its *god*:
　　dealt death out to men.　　　　　　seafarer, man

Meanwhile, Hrafn and Thorkel the Black, Gunnlaug's kinsman, were fighting. Thorkel succumbed to Hrafn, and lost his life. In the end, all their companions fell. Then the two of them, Hrafn and Gunnlaug, fought on, setting about each other remorselessly with heavy blows and fearless counterattacks. Gunnlaug was using the sword which Ethelred had given him, and it was a formidable weapon. In the end, he hacked at Hrafn with a mighty blow, and chopped off his leg. Yet Hrafn did not collapse completely, but dropped back to a tree stump and rested the stump of his leg on it.

'Now you're past fighting,' Gunnlaug said, 'and I will not fight with you, a wounded man, any longer.'

'It is true that things have turned against me, rather,' Hrafn replied, 'but I should be able to hold out all right if I could get something to drink.'

'Don't trick me then,' Gunnlaug replied, 'if I bring you water in my helmet.'

'I won't trick you,' Hrafn said.

Then Gunnlaug went to a brook, fetched some water in his helmet and took it to Hrafn. But as Hrafn reached out his left hand for it, he hacked at Gunnlaug's head with the sword in his right hand, causing a hideous wound.

'Now you have cruelly deceived me,' Gunnlaug said, 'and you have behaved in an unmanly way, since I trusted you.'

'That is true,' Hrafn replied, 'and I did it because I would not have you receive the embrace of Helga the Fair.'

Then they fought fiercely again, and it finished in Gunnlaug's over-powering Hrafn, and Hrafn lost his life right there. Then the earl's guides went over and bound Gunnlaug's head wound. He sat still throughout and spoke this verse:

22. Hrafn, that bold sword-swinger,
    splendid sword-meeting's tree,
    in the harsh storm of stingers
    advanced bravely against me.
    This morning, many metal-flights
    howled round Gunnlaug's head
    on Dingenes, O ring-birch
    and protector of ranks.

sword-meeting: battle; its *tree*: warrior
stingers: spears; *spears' storm*: battle
metal-flights: thrown weapons
ring-birch: man
protector of ranks: leader of an army, warrior

Then they saw to the dead men, and afterwards they put Gunnlaug on his horse and brought him down into Levanger. There he lay for three nights, and received the full rites from a priest before he died. He was buried in the church there. Everyone thought the deaths of both Gunnlaug and Hrafn in such circumstances were a great loss.

13 That summer, before this news had been heard out here in Iceland, Illugi the Black had a dream. He was at home at Gilsbakki at the time. He dreamed that Gunnlaug appeared to him, covered in blood, and spoke this verse to him. Illugi remembered the poem when he woke up, and later recited it to other people:

23. I know that Hrafn hit me
   with the hilt-finned fish
   that hammers on mail,
   but my sharp edge bit his leg
   when the eagle, corpse-scorer,
   drank the mead of warm wounds.
   The war-twig of valkyrie's thorns
   split Gunnlaug's skull.

fish: sword (with a hilt for fins)
corpse-scorer: eagle, which carves up corpses with its beak
mead of wounds: blood
valkyrie's thorns: warriors; their *war-twig*: sword

On the same night, at Mosfell in the south, it happened that Onund dreamed that Hrafn came to him. He was all covered in blood, and spoke this verse:

24. My sword was stained with gore,
   but the Odin of swords
   sword-swiped me too; on shields
   shield-giants were tried overseas.
   I think there stood blood-stained
   blood-goslings in blood round my brain.
   Once more the wound-eager wound-raven
   wound-river is fated to wade.

Odin (god) *of swords*: warrior (Gunnlaug)
shield-giants: enemies of shields, i.e. swords
blood-goslings: ravens
wound-river: blood

At the Althing the following summer, Illugi the Black spoke to Onund at the Law Rock.

'How are you going to compensate me for my son,' he asked, 'since your son Hrafn tricked him when they had declared a truce?'

'I don't think there's any onus on me to pay compensation for him,' Onund replied, 'since I've been so sorely wounded by their encounter myself. But I won't ask you for any compensation for my son, either.'

'Then some of your family and friends will suffer for it,' Illugi answered. And all summer, after the Althing, Illugi was very depressed.

People say that during the autumn, Illugi rode off from Gilsbakki with about thirty men, and arrived at Mosfell early in the morning. Onund and his sons rushed into the church, but Illugi captured two of Onund's kinsmen. One of them was named Bjorn and the other Thorgrim. Illugi had Bjorn killed and Thorgrim's foot cut off. After that, Illugi rode home, and Onund sought no reprisals for this act. Hermund Illugason was very upset about his brother's death, and thought that, even though this had been done, Gunnlaug had not been properly avenged.

There was a man named Hrafn, who was a nephew of Onund of Mosfell's. He was an important merchant, and owned a ship which was moored in Hrutafjord.

That spring, Hermund Illugason rode out from home on his own. He went north over Holtavarda heath, across to Hrutafjord and then over to the merchants' ship at Bordeyri. The merchants were almost ready to leave. Skipper Hrafn was ashore, with several other people. Hermund rode up to him, drove his spear through him and then rode away. Hrafn's colleagues were all caught off-guard by Hermund. No compensation was forthcoming for this killing, and with it the feuding between Illugi the Black and Onund was at an end.

Some time later, Thorstein Egilsson married his daughter Helga to a man named Thorkel, the son of Hallkel. He lived out in Hraunsdal, and Helga went back home with him, although she did not really love him. She could never get Gunnlaug out of her mind, even though he was dead. Still, Thorkel was a decent man, rich and a good poet. They had a fair number of children. One of their sons was named Thorarin, another Thorstein, and they had more children besides.

Helga's greatest pleasure was to unfold the cloak which Gunnlaug had given her and stare at it for a long time. Now there was a time when Thorkel and Helga's household was afflicted with a terrible illness, and many people suffered a long time with it. Helga, too, became ill but did not take to her bed. One Saturday evening, Helga sat in the fire-room, resting her head in her husband Thorkel's lap. She sent for the cloak Gunnlaug's Gift, and when it arrived, she sat up and spread it out in front of her. She stared at it for a while. Then she fell back into her husband's arms, dead. Thorkel spoke this verse:

25. My Helga, good arm-serpent's staff, *arm-serpent*: gold
    dead in my arms I did clasp. bracelet; its *staff*:
    God carried off the life woman
    of the linen-Lofn, my wife. *linen-Lofn* (goddess):
    But for me, the river-flash's poor craver, woman
    it is heavier to be yet living. *river-flash*: gold; its
    craver: man

Helga was taken to the church, but Thorkel carried on living in Hraunsdal. As one might expect, he found Helga's death extremely hard to bear.

And this is the end of the saga.

Glossary

Althing – Iceland's general assembly; also called the 'Thing'. At the annual Althing, the thirty-nine *godis* (local chieftains) reviewed and made new laws, and set fines and punishments.

beserk – a man who worked himself into an animal-like frenzy to increase his strength and make himself immune to blows from weapons.

drapa – a heroic poem in a complicated metre, usually composed in honour of kings, earls and other prominent people, or in memory of a loved one.

fetch – a personal spirit that often symbolized a person's fate or signalled impending doom. It could take various forms, sometimes appearing in the shape of an animal.

flokk – a short poem.

hersir – a local leader in western and northern Norway.

knorr – an ocean-going cargo vessel.

shieling – a hut in the highland grazing pastures away from the farm, where shepherds and cowherds lived in summer.

Winter Nights – the period of two days when winter began, around the middle of October. It was a particularly holy time of year, when sacrifices and social activities such as weddings took place.

1. BOCCACCIO · *Mrs Rosie and the Priest*
2. GERARD MANLEY HOPKINS · *As kingfishers catch fire*
3. *The Saga of Gunnlaug Serpent-tongue*
4. THOMAS DE QUINCEY · *On Murder Considered as One of the Fine Arts*
5. FRIEDRICH NIETZSCHE · *Aphorisms on Love and Hate*
6. JOHN RUSKIN · *Traffic*
7. PU SONGLING · *Wailing Ghosts*
8. JONATHAN SWIFT · *A Modest Proposal*
9. *Three Tang Dynasty Poets*
10. WALT WHITMAN · *On the Beach at Night Alone*
11. KENKŌ · *A Cup of Sake Beneath the Cherry Trees*
12. BALTASAR GRACIÁN · *How to Use Your Enemies*
13. JOHN KEATS · *The Eve of St Agnes*
14. THOMAS HARDY · *Woman much missed*
15. GUY DE MAUPASSANT · *Femme Fatale*
16. MARCO POLO · *Travels in the Land of Serpents and Pearls*
17. SUETONIUS · *Caligula*
18. APOLLONIUS OF RHODES · *Jason and Medea*
19. ROBERT LOUIS STEVENSON · *Olalla*
20. KARL MARX AND FRIEDRICH ENGELS · *The Communist Manifesto*
21. PETRONIUS · *Trimalchio's Feast*
22. JOHANN PETER HEBEL · *How a Ghastly Story Was Brought to Light by a Common or Garden Butcher's Dog*
23. HANS CHRISTIAN ANDERSEN · *The Tinder Box*
24. RUDYARD KIPLING · *The Gate of the Hundred Sorrows*
25. DANTE · *Circles of Hell*
26. HENRY MAYHEW · *Of Street Piemen*
27. HAFEZ · *The nightingales are drunk*
28. GEOFFREY CHAUCER · *The Wife of Bath*
29. MICHEL DE MONTAIGNE · *How We Weep and Laugh at the Same Thing*
30. THOMAS NASHE · *The Terrors of the Night*
31. EDGAR ALLAN POE · *The Tell-Tale Heart*
32. MARY KINGSLEY · *A Hippo Banquet*
33. JANE AUSTEN · *The Beautifull Cassandra*
34. ANTON CHEKHOV · *Gooseberries*
35. SAMUEL TAYLOR COLERIDGE · *Well, they are gone, and here must I remain*
36. JOHANN WOLFGANG VON GOETHE · *Sketchy, Doubtful, Incomplete Jottings*
37. CHARLES DICKENS · *The Great Winglebury Duel*
38. HERMAN MELVILLE · *The Maldive Shark*
39. ELIZABETH GASKELL · *The Old Nurse's Story*
40. NIKOLAY LESKOV · *The Steel Flea*

41. HONORÉ DE BALZAC · *The Atheist's Mass*
42. CHARLOTTE PERKINS GILMAN · *The Yellow Wall-Paper*
43. C.P. CAVAFY · *Remember, Body . . .*
44. FYODOR DOSTOEVSKY · *The Meek One*
45. GUSTAVE FLAUBERT · *A Simple Heart*
46. NIKOLAI GOGOL · *The Nose*
47. SAMUEL PEPYS · *The Great Fire of London*
48. EDITH WHARTON · *The Reckoning*
49. HENRY JAMES · *The Figure in the Carpet*
50. WILFRED OWEN · *Anthem For Doomed Youth*
51. WOLFGANG AMADEUS MOZART · *My Dearest Father*
52. PLATO · *Socrates' Defence*
53. CHRISTINA ROSSETTI · *Goblin Market*
54. *Sindbad the Sailor*
55. SOPHOCLES · *Antigone*
56. RYŪNOSUKE AKUTAGAWA · *The Life of a Stupid Man*
57. LEO TOLSTOY · *How Much Land Does A Man Need?*
58. GIORGIO VASARI · *Leonardo da Vinci*
59. OSCAR WILDE · *Lord Arthur Savile's Crime*
60. SHEN FU · *The Old Man of the Moon*
61. AESOP · *The Dolphins, the Whales and the Gudgeon*
62. MATSUO BASHŌ · *Lips too Chilled*
63. EMILY BRONTË · *The Night is Darkening Round Me*
64. JOSEPH CONRAD · *To-morrow*
65. RICHARD HAKLUYT · *The Voyage of Sir Francis Drake Around the Whole Globe*
66. KATE CHOPIN · *A Pair of Silk Stockings*
67. CHARLES DARWIN · *It was snowing butterflies*
68. BROTHERS GRIMM · *The Robber Bridegroom*
69. CATULLUS · *I Hate and I Love*
70. HOMER · *Circe and the Cyclops*
71. D. H. LAWRENCE · *Il Duro*
72. KATHERINE MANSFIELD · *Miss Brill*
73. OVID · *The Fall of Icarus*
74. SAPPHO · *Come Close*
75. IVAN TURGENEV · *Kasyan from the Beautiful Lands*
76. VIRGIL · *O Cruel Alexis*
77. H. G. WELLS · *A Slip under the Microscope*
78. HERODOTUS · *The Madness of Cambyses*
79. *Speaking of Siva*
80. *The Dhammapada*

'People begin to see that something more goes to the composition of a fine murder than two blockheads to kill and be killed – a knife – a purse – and a dark lane . . .'

THOMAS DE QUINCEY
Born 1785, Manchester, England
Died 1859, Edinburgh, Scotland

In December 1811, a series of brutal murders was carried out in Ratcliffe Highway, in London's East End. The presumed murderer, John Williams, was arrested on 22 December and found hanged in his cell a few days later. De Quincey was haunted by the crime, and returned to it many times in his writing over the next thirty years. This essay first appeared in *Blackwood's Magazine* in February 1827.

DE QUINCEY IN PENGUIN CLASSICS
Confessions of an English Opium-Eater and Other Writings

THOMAS DE QUINCEY

*On Murder Considered as
One of the Fine Arts*

PENGUIN BOOKS

PENGUIN CLASSICS

UK | USA | Canada | Ireland | Australia
India | New Zealand | South Africa

Penguin Books is part of the Penguin Random House group of companies whose addresses can be found at global.penguinrandomhouse.com.

This selection published in Penguin Classics 2015

010

Set in 10/14.5 pt Baskerville 10 Pro
Typeset by Jouve (UK), Milton Keynes
Printed and bound in Great Britain by Clays Ltd, Elcograf S.p.A.

A CIP catalogue record for this book is available from the British Library

ISBN: 978–0–141–39788–7

www.greenpenguin.co.uk

Penguin Random House is committed to a sustainable future for our business, our readers and our planet. This book is made from Forest Stewardship Council® certified paper.

TO THE EDITOR OF BLACKWOOD'S MAGAZINE

Sir,
We have all heard of a Society for the Promotion of Vice, of the Hell-Fire Club, &c. At Brighton I think it was that a Society was formed for the Suppression of Virtue. That Society was itself suppressed – but I am sorry to say that another exists in London, of a character still more atrocious. In tendency, it may be denominated a Society for the Encouragement of Murder; but, according to their own delicate ευφημισμὸς [euphemism], it is styled – The Society of Connoisseurs in Murder. They profess to be curious in homicide; amateurs and dilettanti in the various modes of bloodshed; and, in short, Murder-Fanciers. Every fresh atrocity of that class, which the police annals of Europe bring up, they meet and criticise as they would a

picture, statue, or other work of art. But I need not trouble myself with any attempt to describe the spirit of their proceedings, as you will collect *that* much better from one of the Monthly Lectures read before the Society last year. This has fallen into my hands accidentally, in spite of all the vigilance exercised to keep their transactions from the public eye. The publication of it will alarm them; and my purpose is that it should. For I would much rather put them down quietly, by an appeal to public opinion through you, than by such an exposure of names as would follow an appeal to Bow-street; which last appeal, however, if this should fail, I must positively resort to. For it is scandalous that such things should go on in a Christian land. Even in a heathen land, the public toleration of murder was felt by a Christian writer to be the most crying reproach of the public morals. This writer was Lactantius; and with his words, as singularly applicable to the present occasion, I shall conclude: – 'Quid tam horribile,' says he, 'tam tetrum, quam hominis trucidatio? Ideo severissimis legibus vita nostra munitur; ideo bella execrabilia sunt. Invenit tamen consuetudo quatenus homicidium sine bello ac sine legibus faciat: et hoc sibi voluptas quod scelus vindicavit. Quod si interesse homicidio sceleris conscientia est, – et eidem facinori spectator obstrictus est cui et admissor; ergo et in his gladiatorum caedibus non minus cruore profunditur qui spectat, quam ille qui facit: nec potest esse immunis à sanguine qui voluit effundi; aut videri non interfecisse, qui interfectori et favit et proemium postulavit.' 'Human life,' says he, 'is guarded by laws of the uttermost rigour, yet custom has devised a mode of evading them in behalf of murder; and the demands of taste (*voluptas*) are now become the same as those of abandoned guilt.' Let the Society of Gentlemen Amateurs consider this; and let me call their especial attention to the last sentence, which is so weighty, that I shall attempt to convey it in English: – 'Now, if merely to be present at a murder fastens on a man the character of an accomplice, – if barely to be a spectator involves us in one common guilt with the perpetrator; it follows of necessity, that, in these murders of the amphitheatre, the hand which inflicts the fatal blow is not more deeply imbrued in blood than his who sits and looks on; neither can *he* be clear of blood who has countenanced its shedding; nor that man seem other than a participator in murder who gives his applause to the murderer, and calls for prizes in his behalf.' The '*proemia postulavit*' ['call for prizes'] I have not yet heard charged upon the Gentlemen Amateurs of London, though undoubtedly their proceedings tend to that; but the '*interfectori favit*' ['applause to the murderer'] is implied in the very title of this association, and expressed in every line of the lecture which I send you. – I am, &c.

X.Y.Z.

(*Note of the Editor*. – We thank our correspondent for his communication, and also for the quotation from Lactantius, which is very pertinent to *his* view of the case; our own, we confess, is different. We cannot suppose the lecturer to be in earnest, any more than Erasmus in his Praise of Folly, or Dean Swift in his proposal for eating children. However, either on his view or on ours, it is equally fit that the lecture should be made public.)

LECTURE

Gentlemen, – I have had the honour to be appointed by your committee to the trying task of reading the

Williams' Lecture on Murder, considered as one of the Fine Arts – a task which might be easy enough three or four centuries ago, when the art was little understood, and few great models had been exhibited; but in this age, when masterpieces of excellence have been executed by professional men, it must be evident, that in the style of criticism applied to them, the public will look for something of a corresponding improvement. Practice and theory must advance *pari passu* ['with an equal step']. People begin to see that something more goes to the composition of a fine murder than two blockheads to kill and be killed – a knife – a purse – and a dark lane. Design, gentlemen, grouping, light and shade, poetry, sentiment, are now deemed indispensable to attempts of this nature. Mr Williams has exalted the ideal of murder to all of us; and to me, therefore, in particular, has deepened the arduousness of my task. Like Aeschylus or Milton in poetry, like Michael Angelo in painting, he has carried his art to a point of colossal sublimity; and, as Mr Wordsworth observes, has in a manner 'created the taste by which he is to be enjoyed.' To sketch the history of the art, and to examine its principles critically, now remains as a duty for the connoisseur, and for judges of quite another stamp from his Majesty's Judges of Assize.

Before I begin, let me say a word or two to certain prigs, who affect to speak of our society as if it were in some degree immoral in its tendency. Immoral! – God bless my soul, gentlemen, what is it that people mean? I am for morality, and always shall be, and for virtue and all that; and I do affirm, and always shall, (let what will come of it,) that murder is an improper line of conduct – highly improper; and I do not stick to assert, that any man who deals in murder, must have very incorrect ways of thinking, and truly inaccurate principles; and so far from aiding and abetting him by pointing out his victim's hiding-place, as a great moralist* of Germany declared it to be every good man's duty to do, I would subscribe one shilling

---

* Kant – who carried his demands of unconditional veracity to so extravagant a length as to affirm, that, if a man were to see an innocent person escape from a murderer, it would be his duty, on being questioned by the murderer, to tell the truth, and to point out the retreat of the innocent person, under any certainty of causing murder. Lest this doctrine should be supposed to have escaped him in any heat of dispute, on being taxed with it by a celebrated French writer, he solemnly reaffirmed it, with his reasons.

and sixpence to have him apprehended, which is more by eighteen-pence than the most eminent moralists have subscribed for that purpose. But what then? Everything in this world has two handles. Murder, for instance, may be laid hold of by its moral handle, (as it generally is in the pulpit, and at the Old Bailey;) and *that*, I confess, is its weak side; or it may also be treated *aesthetically*, as the Germans call it, that is, in relation to good taste.

To illustrate this, I will urge the authority of three eminent persons, viz. S. T. Coleridge, Aristotle, and Mr Howship the surgeon. To begin with S.T.C. – One night, many years ago, I was drinking tea with him in Berners' Street, (which, by the way, for a short street, has been uncommonly fruitful in men of genius.) Others were there besides myself; and amidst some carnal considerations of tea and toast, we were all imbibing a dissertation on Plotinus from the attic lips of S.T.C. Suddenly a cry arose of '*Fire – fire!*' – upon which all of us, master and disciples, Plato and οἱ περί τον Πλάτωνα ['those around Plato'], rushed out, eager, for the spectacle. The fire was in Oxford Street, at a piano-forte maker's; and, as it promised to be a conflagration of merit, I was sorry that my engagements forced me away from Mr Coleridge's party before matters were come to a crisis. Some days after, meeting with my Platonic host, I reminded him of the case, and begged to know how that very promising exhibition had terminated. 'Oh, sir,' said he, 'it turned out so ill, that we damned it unanimously.' Now, does any man suppose that Mr Coleridge, – who, for all he is too fat to be a person of active virtue, is undoubtedly a worthy Christian, – that this good S.T.C., I say, was an incendiary, or capable of wishing any ill to the poor man and his piano-fortes (many of them, doubtless, with the additional keys)? On the contrary, I know him to be that sort of man that I durst stake my life upon it he would have worked an engine in a case of necessity, although rather of the fattest for such fiery trials of his virtue. But how stood the case? Virtue was in no request. On the arrival of the fire-engines, morality had devolved wholly on the insurance office. This being the case, he had a right to gratify his taste. He had left his tea. Was he to have nothing in return?

I contend that the most virtuous man, under the premises stated, was entitled to make a luxury of the fire, and to hiss it, as he would any other performance that raised expectations in the public mind, which afterwards it disappointed. Again, to cite another great authority, what says the Stagyrite? He (in the Fifth Book, I think it is, of his Metaphysics,) describes what he calls κλεπτὴν τέλειον, i.e. *a perfect thief*; and, as to Mr Howship, in a work of his on Indigestion, he makes no scruple to talk with admiration of a certain ulcer which he had seen, and which he styles 'a beautiful ulcer.' Now will any man pretend, that, abstractedly considered, a thief could appear to Aristotle a perfect character, or that Mr Howship could be enamoured of an ulcer? Aristotle, it is well known, was himself so very moral a character, that, not content with writing his Nichomachean Ethics, in one volume octavo, he also wrote another system, called *Magna Moralia*, or Big Ethics. Now, it is impossible that a man who composes any ethics at all, big or little, should admire a thief *per se*, and, as to Mr Howship, it is well known that he makes war upon all ulcers; and, without suffering himself to be seduced by their charms, endeavours to banish them from the county of Middlesex. But the truth is, that, however objectionable *per se*, yet, relatively to others of their class, both a thief and an ulcer may have infinite degrees of merit. They are both imperfections, it is true; but to be imperfect being their essence, the very greatness of their imperfection becomes their perfection. *Spartam nactus es, hanc exorna* ['Sparta is yours: adorn it!']. A thief like Autolycus or Mr Barrington, and a grim phagedaenic ulcer, superbly defined, and running regularly through all its natural stages, may no less justly be regarded as ideals after *their* kind, than the most faultless moss-rose amongst flowers, in its progress from bud to 'bright consummate flower;' or, amongst human flowers, the most magnificent young female, apparelled in the pomp of womanhood. And thus not only the ideal of an inkstand may be imagined, (as Mr Coleridge demonstrated in his celebrated correspondence with Mr Blackwood,) in which, by the way, there is not so much, because an inkstand is a laudable sort of thing, and a valuable member of society; but even imperfection itself may have its ideal or perfect state.

Really, gentlemen, I beg pardon for so much philosophy at one time, and now, let me apply it. When a murder is in the paulo-post-futurum tense, and a rumour of it comes to our ears, by all means let us treat it morally. But suppose it over and done, and that you can say of it, Τετέλεσαι ['it is completed'] or (in that adamantine molossus of Medea) εἴργασαι ['it is done']; Suppose the poor murdered man to be out of his pain, and the rascal that did it off like a shot, nobody knows whither; suppose, lastly, that we have done our best, by putting out our legs to trip up the fellow in his flight, but all to no purpose – 'abiit, evasit' ['he has left, escaped'], &c. – why, then, I say, what's the use of any more virtue? Enough has been given to morality; now comes the turn of Taste and the Fine Arts. A sad thing it was, no doubt, very sad; but *we* can't mend it. Therefore let us make the best of a bad matter; and, as it is impossible to hammer anything out of it for moral purposes, let us treat it aesthetically, and see if it will turn to account in that way. Such is the logic of a sensible man, and what follows? We dry up our tears, and have the satisfaction perhaps to discover, that a transaction, which, morally considered, was shocking, and without a leg to stand upon, when tried by principles of Taste, turns out to be a very meritorious performance. Thus all the world is pleased; the old proverb is justified, that it is an ill wind which blows nobody good; the amateur, from looking bilious and sulky, by too close an attention to virtue, begins to pick up his crumbs, and general hilarity prevails. Virtue has had her day; and henceforward, *Vertu* and Connoisseurship have leave to provide for themselves. Upon this principle, gentlemen, I propose to guide your studies, from Cain to Mr Thurtell. Through this great gallery of murder, therefore, together let us wander hand in hand, in delighted admiration, while I endeavour to point your attention to the objects of profitable criticism.

The first murder is familiar to you all. As the inventor of murder, and the father of the art, Cain must have been a man of first-rate genius. All the Cains were men of genius. Tubal Cain invented tubes, I think, or some such thing. But, whatever were the originality and genius of the artist, every art was then in its infancy; and the works must be criticised with a recollection of that fact. Even Tubal's work would probably be little approved at this day in Sheffield; and therefore of Cain (Cain senior, I mean,) it is no disparagement to say, that his performance was but so so. Milton, however, is supposed to have thought differently. By his way of relating the case, it should seem to have been rather a pet murder with him, for he retouches it with an apparent anxiety for its picturesque effect: –

> Whereat he inly raged; and, as they talk'd,
> Smote him into the midriff with a stone
> That beat out life: he fell; and, deadly pale,
> Groan'd out his soul *with gushing blood effus'd*.
> *Par. Lost, B. XI*.

Upon this, Richardson the painter, who had an eye for effect, remarks as follows, in his Notes on Paradise Lost, p. 497: – 'It has been thought,' says he, 'that Cain beat (as the common saying is,) the breath out of his brother's body with a great stone; Milton gives in to this, with the addition, however, of a large wound.' In this place it was a judicious addition; for the rudeness of the weapon, unless raised and enriched by a warm, sanguinary colouring, has too much of the naked air of the savage school; as if the deed were perpetrated by a Polypheme without science, premeditation, or anything but a mutton bone. However, I am chiefly pleased with the improvement, as it implies that Milton was an amateur. As to Shakspeare, there never was a better; as his description of the murdered Duke of Gloucester, in Henry VI., of Duncan's, Banquo's, &c. sufficiently proves.

The foundation of the art having been once laid, it is pitiable to see how it slumbered without improvement for ages. In fact, I shall now be obliged to leap over all murders, sacred and profane, as utterly unworthy of notice, until long after the Christian era. Greece, even in the age of Pericles, produced no murder of the slightest merit; and Rome had too little originality of genius in any of the arts to succeed, where her model failed her. In fact, the Latin language sinks under the very idea of murder. 'The man was murdered;' – how will this sound in Latin? *Interfectus est, interemptus est* [he was killed, he was destroyed] – which simply expresses a homicide; and hence the Christian Latinity of the middle ages was obliged to introduce a new word, such as the feebleness of classic conceptions never ascended to. *Murdratus est*, says the sublimer dialect of Gothic ages. Meantime, the Jewish school of murder kept alive whatever was yet known in the art, and gradually transferred it to the Western World. Indeed the Jewish school was always respectable, even in the dark ages, as the case of Hugh of Lincoln shows, which was honoured with the approbation of Chaucer, on occasion of another performance from the same school, which he puts into the mouth of the Lady Abbess.

Recurring, however, for one moment to classical antiquity, I cannot but think that Catiline, Clodius, and some of that coterie, would have made first-rate artists; and it is on all accounts to be regretted, that the priggism of Cicero robbed his country of the only chance she had for distinction in this line. As the *subject* of a murder, no person could have answered better than himself. Lord! how he would have howled with panic, if he had heard Cethegus under his bed. It would have been truly diverting to have listened to him; and satisfied I am, gentlemen, that he would have preferred the *utile* [expediency] of creeping into a closet, or even into a *cloaca* [sewer], to the *honestum* [honourable thing] of facing the bold artist.

To come now to the dark ages – (by which we, that speak with precision, mean, *par excellence*, the tenth century, and the times immediately before and after) – these ages ought naturally to be favourable to the art of murder, as they were to church-architecture, to stained-glass, &c.; and, accordingly, about the latter end of this period, there arose a great character in our art, I mean the Old Man of the Mountains. He was a shining light, indeed, and I need not tell you, that the very word 'assassin' is deduced from him. So keen an amateur was he, that on one occasion, when his own life was attempted by a favourite assassin, he was so much pleased with the talent shown, that notwithstanding the failure of the artist, he created him a Duke upon the spot, with remainder to the female line, and settled a pension on him for three lives. Assassination is a branch of the art which demands a separate notice; and I shall devote an entire lecture to it. Meantime, I shall only observe how odd it is, that this branch of the art has flourished by fits. It never rains, but it pours. Our own age can boast of some fine specimens; and, about two centuries ago, there was a most brilliant constellation of murders in this class. I need hardly say, that I allude especially to those five splendid works, – the assassinations of William I. of Orange, of Henry IV. of France, of the Duke of Buckingham, (which you will find excellently described in the letters published by Mr Ellis, of the British Museum,) of Gustavus Adolphus, and of Wallenstein. The King of Sweden's assassination, by the by, is doubted by many writers, Harte amongst others; but they are wrong. He was murdered; and I consider his murder unique in its excellence; for he was murdered at noon-day, and on the field of battle, – a feature of original conception, which occurs in no other work of art that I remember. Indeed, all of these assassinations may be studied with profit by the advanced connoisseur. They are all of them *exemplaria*, of which one may say, –

> Nocturnâ versatâ manu, versate diurne;
> ['Let these be your models by day and by night']

Especially *nocturnâ*.

In these assassinations of princes and statesmen, there is nothing to excite our wonder: important changes often depend on their deaths; and, from the eminence on which they stand, they are peculiarly exposed to the aim of every artist who happens to be possessed by the craving for scenical effect. But there is another class of assassinations, which has prevailed from an early period of the seventeenth century, that really *does* surprise me; I mean the assassination of philosophers. For, gentlemen, it is a fact, that every philosopher of eminence for the two last centuries has either been murdered, or, at the least, been very near it; insomuch, that if a man calls himself a philosopher, and never had his life attempted, rest assured there is nothing in him; and against Locke's philosophy in particular, I think it an unanswerable objection, (if we needed any) that, although he carried his throat about with him in this world for seventy-two years, no man ever condescended to cut it. As these cases of philosophers are not much known, and are generally good and well composed in their circumstances, I shall here read an excursus on that subject, chiefly by way of showing my own learning.

The first great philosopher of the seventeenth century (if we except Galileo,) was Des Cartes; and if ever one could say of a man that he was all *but* murdered – murdered within an inch, one must say it of him. The case was this, as reported by Baillet in his *Vie De M. Des Cartes*, tom. I. pp. 102–3. In the year 1621, when Des Cartes might be about twenty-six years old, he was touring about as usual, (for he was as restless as a hyaena,) and, coming to the Elbe, either at Gluckstadt or at Hamburg, he took shipping for East Friezland: what he could want in East Friezland no man has ever discovered; and perhaps he took this into consideration himself; for, on reaching Embden, he resolved to sail instantly for *West* Friezland; and being very impatient of delay, he hired a bark, with a few mariners to navigate it. No sooner had he got out to sea than he made a pleasing discovery, viz. that he had shut himself up in a den of murderers. His crew, says M. Baillet, he soon found out to be 'des scélérats,' – not *amateurs*, gentlemen, as we are, but professional men – the height of whose ambition at that moment was to cut his throat. But the story is too pleasing to be abridged – I shall give it, therefore, accurately, from the French of his biographer: 'M. Des Cartes had no company but that of his servant, with whom he was conversing in French. The sailors, who took him for a foreign merchant, rather than a cavalier, concluded that he must have money about him. Accordingly they came to a resolution by no means advantageous to his purse. There is this difference, however, between sea-robbers and the robbers in forests, that the latter may, without hazard, spare the lives of their victims; whereas the other cannot put a passenger on shore in such a case without running the risk of being apprehended. The crew of M. Des Cartes arranged their measures with a view to evade any danger of that sort. They observed that he was a stranger from a distance, without acquaintance in the country, and that nobody would take any trouble to inquire about him, in case he should never come to hand, (*quand il viendroit à manquer*.)' Think, gentlemen, of these Friezland dogs discussing a philosopher as if he were a puncheon of rum. 'His temper, they remarked, was very mild and patient; and, judging from the gentleness of his deportment, and the courtesy with which he treated themselves, that he could be nothing more than some green young man, they concluded that they should have all the easier task in disposing of his life. They made no scruple to discuss the whole matter in his presence, as not supposing that he understood any other language than that in which he conversed with his servant; and the amount of their deliberation was – to murder him, then to throw him into the sea, and to divide his spoils.'

Excuse my laughing, gentlemen, but the fact is, I always *do* laugh when I think of this case – two things about it seem so droll. One is, the horrid panic or 'funk,' (as the men of Eton call it,) in which Des Cartes must have found himself upon hearing this regular drama sketched for his own death – funeral – succession and administration to his effects. But another thing, which seems to me still more funny about this affair is, that if these Friezland hounds had been 'game,' we should have no Cartesian philosophy; and how we could have done without *that*, considering the worlds of books it has produced, I leave to any respectable trunk-maker to declare.

However, to go on; spite of his enormous funk, Des Cartes showed fight, and by that means awed these Anti-Cartesian rascals. 'Finding,' says M. Baillet, 'that the matter was no joke, M. Des Cartes leaped upon his feet in a trice, assumed a stern countenance that these cravens had never looked for, and addressing them in their own language, threatened to run them through on the spot if they dared to offer him any insult.' Certainly, gentlemen, this would have been an honour far above the merits of such inconsiderable rascals – to be spitted like larks upon a Cartesian sword; and therefore I am glad M. Des Cartes did not rob the gallows by executing his threat, especially as he could not possibly have brought his vessel to port, after he had murdered his crew; so that he must have continued to cruise for ever in the

Zuyder Zee, and would probably have been mistaken by sailors for the *Flying Dutchman*, homeward-bound. 'The spirit which M. Des Cartes manifested,' says his biographer, 'had the effect of magic on these wretches. The suddenness of their consternation struck their minds with a confusion which blinded them to their advantage, and they conveyed him to his destination as peaceably as he could desire.'

Possibly, gentlemen, you may fancy that, on the model of Caesar's address to his poor ferryman, – '*Caesarem vehis et fortunas ejus*,' ['You carry Caesar and his fortunes'] – M. Des Cartes needed only to have said, – 'Dogs, you cannot cut my throat, for you carry Des Cartes and his philosophy,' and might safely have defied them to do their worst. A German emperor had the same notion, when, being cautioned to keep out of the way of a cannonading, he replied, 'Tut! man. Did you ever hear of a cannon-ball that killed an emperor?' As to an emperor I cannot say, but a less thing has sufficed to smash a philosopher; and the next great philosopher of Europe undoubtedly *was* murdered. This was Spinosa.

I know very well the common opinion about him is, that he died in his bed. Perhaps he did, but he was murdered for all that; and this I shall prove by a book published at Brussels, in the year 1731, entitled, *La Via de Spinosa; par M. Jean Colerus*, with many additions, from a MS. life, by one of his friends. Spinosa died on the 21st February 1677, being then little more than forty-four years old. This of itself looks suspicious; and M. Jean admits, that a certain expression in the MS. life of him would warrant the conclusion, 'que sa mort n'a pas été tout-à-fait naturelle.' Living in a damp country, and a sailor's country, like Holland, he may be thought to have indulged a good deal in grog, especially in punch,* which was then newly discovered. Undoubtedly he might have done so; but the fact is that he did not. M. Jean calls him 'extrêmement sobre en son boire et en son manger.' And though some wild stories were afloat about his

---

* 'June 1, 1675. – Drinke part of 3 boules of punch, (a liquor very strainge to me,)' says the Rev. Mr Henry Teonge, in his Diary lately published. In a note on this passage, a reference is made to Fryer's Travels to the East Indies, 1672, who speaks of 'that enervating liquor called *Paunch*, (which is Indostan for five,) from five ingredients.' Made thus, it seems the medical men called it Diapente; if with four only, Diatessaron. No doubt, it was its Evangelical name that recommended it to the Rev. Mr Teonge.

using the juice of mandragora (p. 140,) and opium, (p. 144,) yet neither of these articles appeared in his druggist's bill. Living, therefore, with such sobriety, how was it possible that he should die a natural death at forty-four? Hear his biographer's account: – 'Sunday morning the 21st of February, before it was church-time, Spinosa came down stairs and conversed with the master and mistress of the house.' At this time, therefore, perhaps ten o'clock on Sunday morning, you see that Spinosa was alive, and pretty well. But it seems 'he had summoned from Amsterdam a certain physician, whom,' says the biographer, 'I shall not otherwise point out to notice than by these two letters, L. M. This L. M. had directed the people of the house to purchase an ancient cock, and to have him boiled forthwith, in order that Spinosa might take some broth about noon, which in fact he did, and ate some of the *old cock* with a good appetite, after the landlord and his wife had returned from church.'

'In the afternoon, L. M. staid alone with Spinosa, the people of the house having returned to church; on coming out from which they learnt, with much surprise, that Spinosa had died about three o'clock, in the presence of L. M., who took his departure for Amsterdam the same evening, by the night-boat, without paying the least attention to the deceased. No doubt he was the readier to dispense with these duties, as he had possessed himself of a ducatoon and a small quantity of silver, together with a silver-hafted knife, and had absconded with his pillage.' Here you see, gentlemen, the murder is plain, and the manner of it. It was L. M. who murdered Spinosa for his money. Poor S. was an invalid, meagre, and weak: as no blood was observed, L. M., no doubt, threw him down and smothered him with pillows, – the poor man being already half suffocated by his infernal dinner. – But who was L. M.? It surely never could be Lindley Murray; for I saw him at York in 1825; and besides, I do not think he would do such a thing; at least, not to a brother grammarian: for you know, gentlemen, that Spinosa wrote a very respectable Hebrew grammar.

Hobbes, but why, or on what principle, I never could understand, was not murdered. This was a capital oversight of the professional men in the seventeenth century; because in every light he was a fine subject for murder, except, indeed, that he was lean and skinny; for I can prove that he had money, and (what is very funny,) he had no right to make the least resistance; for, according to himself, irresistible power creates the very highest species of right, so that it is rebellion of the blackest die to refuse to be murdered, when a competent force appears to murder you. However, gentlemen, though he was not murdered, I am happy to assure you that (by his own account,) he was three times very near being murdered. – The first time was in the spring of 1640, when he pretends to have circulated a little MS. on the king's behalf, against the Parliament; he never could produce this MS., by the by; but he says that, 'had not his Majesty dissolved the Parliament,' (in May,) 'it had brought him into danger of his life.' Dissolving the Parliament, however, was of no use; for, in November of the same year, the Long Parliament assembled, and Hobbes, a second time, fearing he should be murdered, ran away to France. This looks like the madness of John Dennis, who thought that Louis XIV. would never make peace with Queen Anne, unless he were given up to his vengeance; and actually ran away from the sea-coast in that belief. In France, Hobbes managed to take care of his throat pretty well for ten years; but at the end of that time, by way of paying court to Cromwell, he published his Leviathan. The old coward now began to 'funk' horribly for the third time; he fancied the swords of the cavaliers were constantly at his throat, recollecting how they had served the Parliament ambassadors at the Hague and Madrid. 'Tum,' says he, in his dog-Latin life of himself,

> Tum venit in mentem mihi Dorislaus et Ascham;
> Tanquam proscripto terror ubique aderat.
> ['Then I began thinking about Dorislaus and Ascham
> Terror was all around, as for someone condemned
> to death']

And accordingly he ran home to England. Now, certainly, it is very true that a man deserved a cudgelling for writing Leviathan; and two or three cudgellings for writing a pentameter ending so villainously as – 'terror ubique aderat!' But no man ever thought him worthy of any thing beyond cudgelling. And, in fact, the whole story is a bounce of his own. For, in a most abusive letter which he wrote 'to a learned person,' (meaning Wallis the mathematician,) he gives quite another account of the matter, and says

(p. 8.), he ran home 'because he would not trust his safety with the French clergy;' insinuating that he was likely to be murdered for his religion, which would have been a high joke indeed – Tom's being brought to the stake for religion.

Bounce or not bounce, however, certain it is, that Hobbes, to the end of his life, feared that somebody would murder him. This is proved by the story I am going to tell you: it is not from a manuscript, but, (as Mr Coleridge says), it is as good as manuscript; for it comes from a book now entirely forgotten, viz. – 'The Creed of Mr Hobbes Examined; in a Conference between him and a Student in Divinity,' (published about ten years before Hobbes's death.) The book is anonymous, but it was written by Tennison, the same who, about thirty years after, succeeded Tillotson as Archbishop of Canterbury. The introductory anecdote is as follows: – 'A certain divine, it seems, (no doubt Tennison himself,) took an annual tour of one month to different parts of the island. In one of these excursions (1670) he visited the Peak in Derbyshire, partly in consequence of Hobbes's description of it. Being in that neighbourhood, he could not but pay a visit to Buxton; and at the very moment of his arrival, he was fortunate enough to find a party of gentlemen dismounting at the inn door, amongst whom was a long thin fellow, who turned out to be no less a person than Mr Hobbes, who probably had ridden over from Chattsworth. Meeting so great a lion, – a tourist, in search of the picturesque, could do no less than present himself in the character of bore. And luckily for this scheme, two of Mr Hobbes's companions were suddenly summoned away by express; so that, for the rest of his stay at Buxton, he had Leviathan entirely to himself, and had the honour of bowsing with him in the evening. Hobbes, it seems, at first showed a good deal of stiffness, for he was shy of divines; but this wore off, and he became very sociable and funny, and they agreed to go into the bath together.' How Tennison could venture to gambol in the same water with Leviathan, I cannot explain; but so it was: they frolicked about like two dolphins, though Hobbes must have been as old as the hills; and 'in those intervals wherein they abstained from swimming and plunging themselves,' (i.e. diving) 'they discoursed of many things relating to the Baths of the Ancients, and the Origine of Springs. When they had in this manner passed away an hour, they stepped out of the bath; and, having dried and cloathed themselves, they sate down in expectation of such a supper as the place afforded; designing to refresh themselves like the *Deipnosophilae*, and rather to reason than to drink profoundly. But in this innocent intention they were interrupted by the disturbance arising from a little quarrel, in which some of the ruder people in the house were for a short time engaged. At this Mr Hobbes seemed much concerned, though he was at some distance from the persons.' – And why was he concerned, gentlemen? No doubt you fancy, from some benign and disinterested love of peace and harmony, worthy of an old man and a philosopher. But listen – 'For a while he was not composed, but related it once or twice as to himself, with a low and careful tone, how Sextus Roscius was murthered after supper by the Balneae Palatinae. Of such general extent is that remark of Cicero, in relation to Epicurus the Atheist, of whom he observed that he of all men dreaded most those things which he contemned – Death and the Gods.' – Merely because it was supper-time, and in the neighbourhood of a bath, Mr Hobbes must have the fate of Sextus Roscius. What logic was there in

On Murder Considered as One of the Fine Arts

this, unless to a man who was always dreaming of murder? – Here was Leviathan, no longer afraid of the daggers of English cavaliers or French clergy, but 'frightened from his propriety' by a row in an ale-house between some honest clod-hoppers of Derbyshire, whom his own gaunt scare-crow of a person that belonged to quite another century, would have frightened out of their wits.

Malebranche, it will give you pleasure to hear, was murdered. The man who murdered him is well known: it was Bishop Berkeley. The story is familiar, though hitherto not put in a proper light. Berkeley, when a young man, went to Paris and called on Père Malebranche. He found him in his cell cooking. Cooks have ever been a *genus irritabile*; authors still more so: Malebranche was both: a dispute arose; the old Father, warm already, became warmer; culinary and metaphysical irritations united to derange his liver: he took to his bed, and died. Such is the common version of the story: 'So the whole ear of Denmark is abused.' – The fact is, that the matter was hushed up, out of consideration for Berkeley, who (as Pope remarked) had 'every virtue under heaven:' else it was well known that Berkeley, feeling himself nettled by the waspishness of the old Frenchman, squared at him; a *turn-up* was the consequence: Malebranche was floored in the first round; the conceit was wholly taken out of him; and he would perhaps have given in; but Berkeley's blood was now up, and he insisted on the old Frenchman's retracting his doctrine of Occasional Causes. The vanity of the man was too great for this; and he fell a sacrifice to the impetuosity of Irish youth, combined with his own absurd obstinacy.

Leibnitz, being every way superior to Malebranche, one might, *a fortiori*, have counted on *his* being murdered; which, however, was not the case. I believe he was nettled at this neglect, and felt himself insulted by the security in which he passed his days. In no other way can I explain his conduct at the latter end of his life, when he chose to grow very avaricious, and to hoard up large sums of gold, which he kept in his own house. This was at Vienna, where he died; and letters are still in existence, describing the immeasurable anxiety which he entertained for his throat. Still his ambition, for being *attempted* at least, was so great, that he would not forego the danger. A late English pedagogue, of Birmingham manufacture, viz. Dr Parr, took a more selfish course, under the same circumstances. He had amassed a considerable quantity of gold and silver plate, which was for some time deposited in his bed-room at his parsonage house, Hatton. But growing every day more afraid of being murdered, which he knew that he could not stand, (and to which, indeed, he never had the slightest pretension,) he transferred the whole to the Hatton blacksmith; conceiving, no doubt, that the murder of a blacksmith would fall more lightly on the *salus reipublicae* [the safety of the republic], than that of a pedagogue. But I have heard this greatly disputed; and it seems now generally agreed, that one good horse-shoe is worth about 2¼ Spital sermons.

As Leibnitz, though not murdered, may be said to have died, partly of the fear that he should be murdered, and partly of vexation that he was not, – Kant, on the other hand – who had no ambition in that way – had a narrower escape from a murderer than any man we read of, except Des Cartes. So absurdly does Fortune throw about her favours! The case is told, I think, in an anonymous life of this very great man. For health's sake, Kant imposed upon himself, at one time, a walk of six miles every day along a highroad. This fact becoming known to a man who had his private reasons for committing murder, at the third milestone from Königsberg, he waited for his 'intended,' who came up to time as duly as a mail-coach. But for an accident, Kant was a dead man. However, on considerations of 'morality,' it happened that the murderer preferred a little child, whom he saw playing in the road, to the old transcendentalist: this child he murdered; and thus it happened that Kant escaped. Such is the German account of the matter; but my opinion is – that the murderer was an amateur, who felt how little would be gained to the cause of good taste by murdering an old, arid, and adust metaphysician; there was no room for display, as the man could not possibly look more like a mummy when dead, than he had done alive.

Thus, gentlemen, I have traced the connexion between philosophy and our art, until insensibly I find that I have wandered into our own era. This I shall not take any pains to characterise apart from that which preceded it, for, in fact, they have no distinct character. The 17th and 18th centuries, together with so much of the 19th as we have yet seen, jointly compose the Augustan age of murder. The finest work of the 17th century is, unquestionably, the murder of Sir Edmondbury Godfrey, which has my entire approbation. At the same time, it must be observed, that the quantity of murder was not great in this century, at least amongst our own artists; which, perhaps, is attributable to the want of enlightened patronage. *Sint Maecenates, non deerunt, Flacce, Marones* ['Let there be a patron like Maecenus, Flaccus, and your lands will give you a poet like Virgil.'] Consulting Grant's 'Observations on the Bills of Mortality,' (4th edition, Oxford, 1665,) I find, that out of 229,250, who died in London during one period of twenty years in the 17th century, not more than eighty-six were murdered; that is, about 4 three-tenths per annum. A small number this, gentlemen, to found an academy upon; and certainly, where the quantity is so small, we have a right to expect that the quality should be first-rate. Perhaps it was; yet, still I am of opinion that the best artist in this century was not equal to the best in that which followed. For instance, however praiseworthy the case of Sir Edmondbury Godfrey may be (and nobody can be more sensible of its merits than I am,) still I cannot consent to place it on a level with that Mrs Ruscombe of Bristol, either as to originality of design, or boldness and breadth of style. This good lady's murder took place early in the reign of George III. – a reign which was notoriously favourable to the arts generally. She lived in College Green, with a single maid-servant, neither of them having any pretension to the notice of history but what they derived from the great artist whose workmanship I am recording. One fine morning, when all Bristol was alive and in motion, some suspicion arising, the neighbours forced an entrance into the house, and found Mrs Ruscombe murdered in her bed-room, and the servant murdered on the stairs: this was at noon; and, not more than two hours before, both mistress and servant had been seen alive. To the best of my remembrance, this was in 1764; upwards of sixty years, therefore, have now elapsed, and yet the artist is still undiscovered. The suspicions of posterity have settled upon two pretenders – a baker and a chimney-sweeper. But posterity is wrong; no unpractised artist could have conceived so bold an idea as that of a noon-day murder in the heart of a great city. It was no obscure baker, gentlemen, or anonymous chimney-sweeper, be assured, that executed this work. I know who it was. (*Here there was a general buzz, which at length broke out into open applause; upon which the lecturer blushed, and went on with much earnestness.*) For Heaven's sake, gentlemen, do not mistake me; it was not I that did it. I have not the vanity to think myself equal to any such achievement; be assured that you greatly overrate my poor talents; Mrs Ruscombe's affair was far beyond my slender abilities. But I came to know who the artist was, from a celebrated surgeon, who assisted at his dissection. This gentleman had a private museum in the way of his profession, one corner of which was occupied by a cast from a man of remarkably fine proportions.

'That,' said the surgeon, 'is a cast from the celebrated Lancashire highwayman, who concealed his profession for some time from his neighbours, by drawing woollen stockings over his horse's legs, and in that way muffling the clatter which he must else have made in riding up a flagged alley that led to his stable. At the time of his execution for highway robbery, I was studying under Cruickshank: and the man's figure was so uncommonly fine, that no money or exertion was spared to get into possession of him with the least possible delay. By the connivance of the under-sheriff he was cut down within the legal time, and instantly put into a chaise and four; so that, when he reached Cruickshank's, he was positively not dead. Mr —, a young student at that time, had the honour of giving him the *coup de grace* – and finishing the sentence of the law.' This remarkable anecdote, which seemed to imply that all the gentlemen in the dissecting-room were amateurs of our class, struck me a good deal; and I was repeating it one day to a Lancashire lady, who thereupon informed me, that she had herself lived in the neighbourhood of that highwayman, and well remembered two circumstances, which combined in the opinion of all his neighbours, to fix upon him the credit of Mrs Ruscombe's affair. One was, the fact of his absence for a whole fortnight at the period of that murder: the other, that, within a very little time after, the neighbourhood of this highwayman was deluged with dollars: now Mrs Ruscombe was known to have hoarded about two thousand of that coin. Be the artist, however, who he might, the affair remains a durable monument of his genius; for such was the impression of awe, and the sense of power left behind, by the strength of conception manifested in this murder, that no tenant (as I was told in 1810) had been found up to that time for Mrs Ruscombe's house.

But, whilst I thus eulogize the Ruscombian case, let me not be supposed to overlook the many other specimens of extraordinary merit spread over the face of this century. Such cases, indeed, as that of Miss Bland, or of Captain Donnellan, and Sir Theophilus Boughton, shall never have any countenance from me. Fie on these dealers in poison, say I: can they not keep to the old honest way of cutting throats, without introducing such abominable innovations from Italy? I consider all these poisoning cases, compared with the legitimate style, as no better than wax-work by the side of sculpture, or a lithographic print by the side of a fine Volpato. But, dismissing these, there remain many excellent works of art in a pure style, such as nobody need be ashamed to own, as every candid connoisseur will admit. *Candid*, observe, I say; for great allowances must be made in these cases; no artist can ever be sure of carrying through his own fine preconception. Awkward disturbances will arise; people will not submit to have their throats cut quietly; they will run, they will kick, they will bite;

and, whilst the portrait painter often has to complain of too much torpor in his subject, the artist, in our line, is generally embarrassed by too much animation. At the same time, however disagreeable to the artist, this tendency in murder to excite and irritate the subject, is certainly one of its advantages to the world in general, which we ought not to overlook, since it favours the developement of latent talent. Jeremy Taylor notices with admiration, the extraordinary leaps which people will take under the influence of fear. There was a striking instance of this in the recent case of the M'Keands; the boy cleared a height, such as he will never clear again to his dying day. Talents also of the most brilliant description for thumping, and indeed for all the gymnastic exercises, have sometimes been developed by the panic which accompanies our artists; talents else buried and hid under a bushel to the possessors, as much as to their friends. I remember an interesting illustration of this fact, in a case which I learned in Germany.

Riding one day in the neighbourhood of Munich, I overtook a distinguished amateur of our society, whose name I shall conceal. This gentleman informed me that, finding himself wearied with the frigid pleasures (so he called them) of mere amateurship, he had quitted England for the continent – meaning to practise a little professionally. For this purpose he resorted to Germany, conceiving the police in that part of Europe to be more heavy and drowsy than elsewhere. His *debut* as a practitioner took place at Mannheim; and, knowing me to be a brother amateur, he freely communicated the whole of his maiden adventure. 'Opposite to my lodging,' said he, 'lived a baker: he was somewhat of a miser, and lived quite alone. Whether it were his great expanse of chalky face, or what else, I know not – but the fact was, I "fancied" him, and resolved to commence business upon his throat, which by the way he always carried bare – a fashion which is very irritating to my desires. Precisely at eight o'clock in the evening, I observed that he regularly shut up his windows. One night I watched him when thus engaged – bolted in after him – locked the door – and, addressing him with great suavity, acquainted him with the nature of my errand; at the same time advising him to make no resistance, which would be mutually unpleasant. So saying, I drew out my tools; and was proceeding to operate. But at this spectacle, the baker, who seemed to have been struck by catalepsy at my first announce, awoke into tremendous agitation. "I will *not* be murdered!" he shrieked aloud; "what for will I lose my precious throat?" – "What for?" said I; "if for no other reason, for this – that you put alum into your bread. But no matter, alum or no alum, (for I was resolved to forestall any argument on that point) know that I am a virtuoso in the art of murder – am desirous of improving myself in its details – and am enamoured of your vast surface of throat, to which I am determined to be a customer." "Is it so?" said he, "but I'll find you custom in another line;" and so saying, he threw himself into a boxing attitude. The very idea of his boxing struck me as ludicrous. It is true, a London baker had distinguished himself in the ring, and became known to fame under the title of the Master of the Rolls; but he was young and unspoiled: whereas this man was a monstrous feather-bed in person, fifty years old, and totally out of condition. Spite of all this, however, and contending against me, who am a master in the art, he made so desperate a defence, that many times I feared he might turn the tables upon me; and that I, an amateur, might be murdered by a rascally baker. What a situation!

Minds of sensibility will sympathize with my anxiety. How severe it was, you may understand by this, that for the first 13 rounds the baker had the advantage. Round the 14th, I received a blow on the right eye, which closed it up; in the end, I believe, this was my salvation: for the anger it roused in me was so great that, in this and every one of the three following rounds, I floored the baker.

'Round 18th. The baker came up piping, and manifestly the worse for wear. His geometrical exploits in the four last rounds had done him no good. However, he showed some skill in stopping a message which I was sending to his cadaverous mug; in delivering which, my foot slipped, and I went down.

'Round 19th. Surveying the baker, I became ashamed of having been so much bothered by a shapeless mass of dough; and I went in fiercely, and administered some severe punishment. A rally took place – both went down – Baker undermost – ten to three on Amateur.

'Round 20th. – The baker jumped up with surprising agility; indeed, he managed his pins capitally, and fought wonderfully, considering that he was drenched in perspiration; but the shine was now taken out of him, and his game was the mere effect of panic. It was now clear that he could not last much longer. In the course of this round we tried the weaving system, in which I had greatly the advantage, and hit him repeatedly on the conk. My reason for this was, that his conk was covered with carbuncles; and I thought I should vex him by taking such liberties with his conk, which in fact I did.

'The three next rounds, the master of the rolls staggered about like a cow on the ice. Seeing how matters stood, in round 24th I whispered something into his ear, which sent him down like a shot. It was nothing more than my private opinion of the value of his throat at an annuity office. This little confidential whisper affected him greatly; the very perspiration was frozen on his face, and for the next two rounds I had it all my own way. And when I called *time* for the twenty-seventh round, he lay like a log on the floor.'

After which, said I to the amateur, 'It may be presumed that you accomplished your purpose.' – 'You are right,' said he mildly, 'I did; and a great satisfaction, you know, it was to my mind, for by this means I killed two birds with one stone;' meaning that he had both thumped the baker and murdered him. Now, for the life of me, I could not see *that*; for, on the contrary, to my mind it appeared that he had taken two stones to kill one bird, having been obliged to take the conceit out of him first with his fists, and then with his tools. But no matter for his logic. The moral of his story was good, for it showed what an astonishing stimulus to latent talent is contained in any reasonable prospect of being murdered. A pursy, unwieldy, half cataleptic baker of Mannheim had absolutely fought six-and-twenty rounds with an accomplished English boxer merely upon this inspiration; so greatly was natural genius exalted and sublimed by the genial presence of his murderer.

Really, gentlemen, when one hears of such things as these, it becomes a duty, perhaps, a little to soften that extreme asperity with which most men speak of murder. To hear people talk, you would suppose that all the disadvantages and inconveniences were on the side of being murdered, and that there were none at all in *not* being murdered. But considerate men think otherwise. 'Certainly,' says Jer. Taylor, 'it is a less temporal evil to fall by the rudeness of a sword than the violence of a fever: and the axe' (to which he might have added the ship-carpenter's mallet and the crow-bar) 'a much less affliction than a strangury.' Very true; the Bishop talks like a wise man and an amateur, as he is; and another great philosopher, Marcus Aurelius, was equally above the vulgar prejudices on this subject. He declares it to be one of 'the noblest functions of reason to know whether it is time to walk out of the world or not.' (Book III. Collers' Translation.) No sort of knowledge being rarer than this, surely *that* man must be a most philanthropic character, who undertakes to instruct people in this branch of knowledge gratis, and at no little hazard to himself. All this, however, I throw out only in the way of speculation to future moralists; declaring in the meantime my own private conviction, that very few men commit murder upon philanthropic or patriotic principles, and repeating what I have already said once at least – that, as to the majority of murderers, they are very incorrect characters.

With respect to Williams's murders, the sublimest and most entire in their excellence that ever were committed, I shall not allow myself to speak incidentally. Nothing less than an entire lecture, or even an entire course of lectures, would suffice to expound their merits. But one curious fact, connected with his case, I shall mention, because it seems to imply that the blaze of his genius absolutely dazzled the eye of criminal justice. You all remember, I doubt not, that the instruments with which he executed his first great work (the murder of the Marrs), were a ship-carpenter's mallet and a knife. Now the mallet belonged to an old Swede, one John Petersen, and bore his initials. This instrument Williams left behind him, in Marr's house, and it fell into the hands of the Magistrates. Now, gentlemen, it is a fact that the publication of this circumstance of the initials led immediately to the apprehension of Williams, and, if made earlier, would have prevented his second great work, (the murder of the Williamsons,) which took place precisely twelve days after. But the Magistrates kept back this fact from the public for the entire twelve days, and until that second work was accomplished. That finished, they published it, apparently feeling that Williams had now done enough for his fame, and that his glory was at length placed beyond the reach of accident.

As to Mr Thurtell's case, I know not what to say. Naturally, I have every disposition to think highly of my predecessor in the chair of this society; and I acknowledge that his lectures were unexceptionable. But, speaking ingenuously, I do really think that his principal performance, as an artist, has been much overrated. I admit that at first I was myself carried away by the general enthusiasm. On the morning when the murder was made known in London, there was the fullest meeting of amateurs that I have ever known since the days of Williams; old bed-ridden connoisseurs, who had got into a peevish way of sneering and complaining 'that there was nothing doing,' now hobbled down to our club-room: such hilarity, such benign expression of general satisfaction, I have rarely witnessed. On every side you saw people shaking hands, congratulating each other, and forming dinner-parties for the evening; and nothing was to be heard but triumphant challenges of – 'Well! will *this* do?' 'Is *this* the right thing?' 'Are you satisfied at last?' But, in the midst of this, I remember we all grew silent on hearing the old cynical amateur, L. S——, that *laudator temporis acti* [a praiser of time past], stumping along with his wooden leg; he entered the room with his usual scowl, and, as he advanced, he continued to growl and stutter the whole way – 'Not an original idea in the whole piece – mere plagiarism, – base plagiarism from hints that I threw out! Besides, his style is as hard as Albert Durer, and as coarse as Fuseli.' Many thought that this was mere jealousy, and general waspishness; but I confess that, when the first glow of enthusiasm had subsided, I have found most judicious critics to agree that there was something *falsetto* in the style of Thurtell. The fact is, he was a member of our society, which naturally gave a friendly bias to our judgments; and his person was universally familiar to the cockneys, which gave him, with the whole London public, a temporary popularity, that his pretensions are not capable of supporting; for *opinionum commenta delet dies, naturae judicia confirmat* ['Time erases the fictions of opinion, but it confirms the judgements of nature']. – There was, however, an unfinished design of Thurtell's for the murder of a man with a pair of dumb-bells, which I admired greatly; it was a mere outline, that he never completed; but to my mind it seemed every way superior to his chief work. I remember that there was great regret expressed by some amateurs that this sketch should have been left in an unfinished state: but there I cannot agree with them; for the fragments and first bold outlines of original artists have often a felicity about them which is apt to vanish in the management of the details.

The case of the M'Keands I consider far beyond the vaunted performance of Thurtell, – indeed above all praise; and bearing that relation, in fact, to the immortal works of Williams, which the Aeneid bears to the Iliad.

But it is now time that I should say a few words about the principles of murder, not with a view to regulate your practice, but your judgment: as to old women, and the mob of newspaper readers, they are pleased with anything, provided it is bloody enough. But the mind of sensibility requires something more. *First*, then, let us speak of the kind of person who is adapted to the purpose of the murderer; *secondly*, of the place where; *thirdly*, of the time when, and other little circumstances.

As to the person, I suppose it is evident that he ought to be a good man; because, if he were not, he might himself, by possibility, be contemplating murder at the very time; and such 'diamond-cut-diamond' tussles, though pleasant enough where nothing better is stirring, are really not what a critic can allow himself to call murders. I could mention some people (I name no names) who have been murdered by other people in a dark lane; and so far all seemed correct enough; but, on looking farther into the matter, the public have become aware that the murdered party was himself, at the moment, planning to rob his murderer, at the least, and possibly to murder him, if he had been strong enough. Whenever that is the case, or may be thought to be the case, farewell to all the genuine effects of the art. For the final purpose of murder, considered as a fine art, is precisely the same as that of Tragedy, in Aristotle's account of it, viz. 'to cleanse the heart by means of pity and terror.' Now, terror there may be, but how can there be any pity for one tiger destroyed by another tiger?

It is also evident that the person selected ought not to be a public character. For instance, no judicious artist would have attempted to murder Abraham Newland. For the case was this: everybody read so much about Abraham Newland, and so few people ever saw him, that there was a fixed belief that he was an abstract idea. And I remember that once, when

I happened to mention that I had dined at a coffee-house in company with Abraham Newland, everybody looked scornfully at me, as though I had pretended to have played at billiards with Prester John, or to have had an affair of honour with the Pope. And, by the way, the Pope would be a very improper person to murder: for he has such a virtual ubiquity as the Father of Christendom, and, like the cuckoo, is so often heard but never seen, that I suspect most people regard *him* also as an abstract idea. Where, indeed, a public character is in the habit of giving dinners, 'with every delicacy of the season,' the case is very different: every person is satisfied that *he* is no abstract idea; and, therefore, there can be no impropriety in murdering him; only that his murder will fall into the class of assassinations, which I have not yet treated.

Thirdly, The subject chosen ought to be in good health: for it is absolutely barbarous to murder a sick person, who is usually quite unable to bear it. On this principle, no Cockney ought to be chosen who is above twenty-five, for after that age he is sure to be dyspeptic. Or at least, if a man will hunt in that warren, he ought to murder a couple at one time; if the Cockneys chosen should be tailors, he will of course think it his duty, on the old established equation, to murder eighteen – And, here, in this attention to the comfort of sick people, you will observe the usual effect of a fine art to soften and refine the feelings. The world in general, gentlemen, are very bloody-minded; and all they want in a murder is a copious effusion of blood; gaudy display in this point is enough for *them*. But the enlightened connoisseur is more refined in his taste; and from our art, as from all the other liberal arts when thoroughly cultivated, the result is – to improve and to humanize the heart; so true is it, that –

> – Ingenuas didicisse fideliter artes,
> Emollit mores, nec sinit esse feros.
> ['A careful study of the liberal arts refines
> manners and prevents them from being savage']

A philosophic friend, well-known for his philanthropy and general benignity, suggests that the subject chosen ought also to have a family of young children wholly dependent on his exertions, by way of deepening the pathos. And, undoubtedly, this is a judicious caution. Yet I would not insist too keenly on this condition. Severe good taste unquestionably demands it; but still, where the man was otherwise unobjectionable in point of morals and health, I would not look with too curious a jealousy to a restriction which might have the effect of narrowing the artist's sphere.

So much for the person. As to the time, the place, and the tools, I have many things to say, which at present I have no room for. The good sense of the practitioner has usually directed him to night and privacy. Yet there have not been wanting cases where this rule was departed from with excellent effect. In respect to time, Mrs Ruscombe's case is a beautiful exception, which I have already noticed; and in respect both to time and place, there is a fine exception in the Annals of Edinburgh, (year 1805), familiar to every child in Edinburgh, but which has unaccountably been defrauded of its due portion of fame amongst English amateurs. The case I mean is that of a porter to one of the Banks, who was murdered whilst carrying a bag of money, in broad daylight, on turning out of the High Street, one of the most public streets in Europe, and the murderer is to this hour undiscovered.

> Sed fugit interea, fugit irreparabile tempus,
> Singula dum capti circumvectamur amore.
> ['But meanwhile time is flying, flying beyond recall,
> while we linger, captivated by our love of detail']

And now, gentlemen, in conclusion, let me again solemnly disclaim all pretensions on my own part to the character of a professional man. I never attempted any murder in my life, except in the year 1801, upon the body of a tom-cat; and *that* turned out differently from my intention. My purpose, I own, was downright murder. 'Semper ego auditor tantum?' said I, 'nunquamne reponam?' ['Am I always to be a listener? And never get a word in?'] And I went down stairs in search of Tom at one o'clock on a dark night, with the 'animus,' and no doubt with the fiendish looks, of a murderer. But when I found him, he was in the act of plundering the pantry of bread and other things. Now this gave a new turn to the affair; for the time being one of general scarcity, when even Christians were reduced to the use of potato-bread, rice-bread, and all sorts of things, it was downright treason in a tom-cat to be wasting good wheaten-bread in the way he was doing. It instantly became a patriotic duty to put him to death; and as I raised aloft and shook the glittering steel, I fancied myself rising like Brutus, effulgent from a crowd of patriots, and, as I stabbed him, I

> called aloud on Tully's name,
> And bade the father of his country hail!

Since then, what wandering thoughts I may have had of attempting the life of an ancient ewe, of a superannuated hen, and such 'small deer,' are locked up in the secrets of my own breast; but for the higher departments of the art, I confess myself to be utterly unfit. My ambition does not rise so high. No, gentlemen, in the words of Horace,

> ——fungar vice cotis, acutum
> Reddere quae ferrum valet, exsors ipsa secandi.
> ['I'll play the part of a whetstone, which sharpens iron, but is itself unable to cut.']

1. BOCCACCIO · *Mrs Rosie and the Priest*
2. GERARD MANLEY HOPKINS · *As kingfishers catch fire*
3. *The Saga of Gunnlaug Serpent-tongue*
4. THOMAS DE QUINCEY · *On Murder Considered as One of the Fine Arts*
5. FRIEDRICH NIETZSCHE · *Aphorisms on Love and Hate*
6. JOHN RUSKIN · *Traffic*
7. PU SONGLING · *Wailing Ghosts*
8. JONATHAN SWIFT · *A Modest Proposal*
9. *Three Tang Dynasty Poets*
10. WALT WHITMAN · *On the Beach at Night Alone*
11. KENKŌ · *A Cup of Sake Beneath the Cherry Trees*
12. BALTASAR GRACIÁN · *How to Use Your Enemies*
13. JOHN KEATS · *The Eve of St Agnes*
14. THOMAS HARDY · *Woman much missed*
15. GUY DE MAUPASSANT · *Femme Fatale*
16. MARCO POLO · *Travels in the Land of Serpents and Pearls*
17. SUETONIUS · *Caligula*
18. APOLLONIUS OF RHODES · *Jason and Medea*
19. ROBERT LOUIS STEVENSON · *Olalla*
20. KARL MARX AND FRIEDRICH ENGELS · *The Communist Manifesto*
21. PETRONIUS · *Trimalchio's Feast*
22. JOHANN PETER HEBEL · *How a Ghastly Story Was Brought to Light by a Common or Garden Butcher's Dog*
23. HANS CHRISTIAN ANDERSEN · *The Tinder Box*
24. RUDYARD KIPLING · *The Gate of the Hundred Sorrows*
25. DANTE · *Circles of Hell*
26. HENRY MAYHEW · *Of Street Piemen*
27. HAFEZ · *The nightingales are drunk*
28. GEOFFREY CHAUCER · *The Wife of Bath*
29. MICHEL DE MONTAIGNE · *How We Weep and Laugh at the Same Thing*
30. THOMAS NASHE · *The Terrors of the Night*
31. EDGAR ALLAN POE · *The Tell-Tale Heart*
32. MARY KINGSLEY · *A Hippo Banquet*
33. JANE AUSTEN · *The Beautifull Cassandra*
34. ANTON CHEKHOV · *Gooseberries*
35. SAMUEL TAYLOR COLERIDGE · *Well, they are gone, and here must I remain*
36. JOHANN WOLFGANG VON GOETHE · *Sketchy, Doubtful, Incomplete Jottings*
37. CHARLES DICKENS · *The Great Winglebury Duel*
38. HERMAN MELVILLE · *The Maldive Shark*
39. ELIZABETH GASKELL · *The Old Nurse's Story*
40. NIKOLAY LESKOV · *The Steel Flea*

41. HONORÉ DE BALZAC · *The Atheist's Mass*
42. CHARLOTTE PERKINS GILMAN · *The Yellow Wall-Paper*
43. C.P. CAVAFY · *Remember, Body...*
44. FYODOR DOSTOEVSKY · *The Meek One*
45. GUSTAVE FLAUBERT · *A Simple Heart*
46. NIKOLAI GOGOL · *The Nose*
47. SAMUEL PEPYS · *The Great Fire of London*
48. EDITH WHARTON · *The Reckoning*
49. HENRY JAMES · *The Figure in the Carpet*
50. WILFRED OWEN · *Anthem For Doomed Youth*
51. WOLFGANG AMADEUS MOZART · *My Dearest Father*
52. PLATO · *Socrates' Defence*
53. CHRISTINA ROSSETTI · *Goblin Market*
54. *Sindbad the Sailor*
55. SOPHOCLES · *Antigone*
56. RYŪNOSUKE AKUTAGAWA · *The Life of a Stupid Man*
57. LEO TOLSTOY · *How Much Land Does A Man Need?*
58. GIORGIO VASARI · *Leonardo da Vinci*
59. OSCAR WILDE · *Lord Arthur Savile's Crime*
60. SHEN FU · *The Old Man of the Moon*
61. AESOP · *The Dolphins, the Whales and the Gudgeon*
62. MATSUO BASHŌ · *Lips too Chilled*
63. EMILY BRONTË · *The Night is Darkening Round Me*
64. JOSEPH CONRAD · *To-morrow*
65. RICHARD HAKLUYT · *The Voyage of Sir Francis Drake Around the Whole Globe*
66. KATE CHOPIN · *A Pair of Silk Stockings*
67. CHARLES DARWIN · *It was snowing butterflies*
68. BROTHERS GRIMM · *The Robber Bridegroom*
69. CATULLUS · *I Hate and I Love*
70. HOMER · *Circe and the Cyclops*
71. D. H. LAWRENCE · *Il Duro*
72. KATHERINE MANSFIELD · *Miss Brill*
73. OVID · *The Fall of Icarus*
74. SAPPHO · *Come Close*
75. IVAN TURGENEV · *Kasyan from the Beautiful Lands*
76. VIRGIL · *O Cruel Alexis*
77. H. G. WELLS · *A Slip under the Microscope*
78. HERODOTUS · *The Madness of Cambyses*
79. *Speaking of Siva*
80. *The Dhammapada*

'We must learn to love, learn to be kind, and this from earliest youth . . . Likewise, hatred must be learned and nurtured, if one wishes to become a proficient hater.'

FRIEDRICH NIETZSCHE
Born 1844, Röcken, Germany
Died 1900, Weimar, Germany

Selection taken from *Human, All Too Human*,
first published in 1878.

NIETZSCHE IN PENGUIN CLASSICS
A Nietzsche Reader
Beyond Good and Evil
Ecce Homo
Human, All Too Human
On the Genealogy of Morals
The Birth of Tragedy
The Portable Nietzsche
Thus Spoke Zarathustra
Twilight of Idols and *Anti-Christ*

FRIEDRICH NIETZSCHE

Aphorisms on Love and Hate

Translated by
Marion Faber and Stephen Lehmann

PENGUIN BOOKS

PENGUIN CLASSICS

UK | USA | Canada | Ireland | Australia
India | New Zealand | South Africa

Penguin Books is part of the Penguin Random House group of companies whose addresses can be found at global.penguinrandomhouse.com.

This selection published in Penguin Classics 2015

018

Translation copyright © Marion Faber, 1984

The moral right of the translator has been asserted

Set in 9.5/13 pt Baskerville 10 Pro
Typeset by Jouve (UK), Milton Keynes
Printed and bound in Great Britain by Clays Ltd, Elcograf S.p.A.

A CIP catalogue record for this book is available from the British Library

ISBN: 978–0–141–39790–0

www.greenpenguin.co.uk

Penguin Random House is committed to a sustainable future for our business, our readers and our planet. This book is made from Forest Stewardship Council® certified paper.

The advantages of psychological observation. That meditating on things human, all too human (or, as the learned phrase goes, 'psychological observation') is one of the means by which man can ease life's burden; that by exercising this art, one can secure presence of mind in difficult situations and entertainment amid boring surroundings; indeed, that from the thorniest and unhappiest phases of one's own life one can pluck maxims and feel a bit better thereby: this was believed, known – in earlier centuries. Why has it been forgotten in this century, when many signs point, in Germany at least, if not throughout Europe, to the dearth of psychological observation? Not particularly in novels, short stories, and philosophical meditations, for these are the work of exceptional men; but more in the judging of public events and personalities; most of all we lack the art of psychological dissection and calculation in all classes of society, where one hears a lot of talk about men, but none at all *about man*. Why do people let the richest and most harmless source of entertainment get away from them? Why do they not even read the great masters of the psychological maxim any more? For it is no exaggeration to say that it is hard to find the cultured European who has read La Rochefoucauld and his spiritual and artistic cousins. Even more uncommon is the man who knows them and does not despise them. But even this unusual reader will probably find much less delight in those artists than their form ought to give him; for not even the finest mind is capable of adequate appreciation of the art of the polished maxim if he has not been educated to it, has not been challenged by it himself. Without such practical learning one takes this form of creating and forming to be easier than it is; one is not acute enough in discerning what is successful and attractive. For that reason present-day readers of maxims take a relatively insignificant delight in them, scarcely a mouthful of pleasure; they react like typical viewers of cameos, praising them because they cannot love them, and quick to admire but even quicker to run away.

*

Objection. Or might there be a counterargument to the thesis that psychological observation is one of life's best stimulants, remedies, and palliatives? Might one be so persuaded of the unpleasant consequences of this art as to intentionally divert the student's gaze from it? Indeed, a certain blind faith in the goodness of human nature, an inculcated aversion to dissecting human behavior, a kind of shame with respect to the naked soul, may really be more desirable for a man's overall happiness than the trait of psychological sharpsightedness, which is helpful in isolated instances. And perhaps the belief in goodness, in virtuous men and actions, in an abundance of impersonal goodwill in the world has made men better, in that it has made them less distrustful. If one imitates Plutarch's heroes with enthusiasm and feels an aversion toward tracing skeptically the motives for their actions, then the welfare of human society has benefited (even if the truth of human society has not). Psychological error, and dullness in this area generally, help humanity forward; but knowledge of the truth might gain more from the stimulating power of an hypothesis like the one La Rochefoucauld places at the beginning of the first edition of his *Sentences et maximes morales:* 'Ce que le monde nomme vertu n'est d'ordinaire qu'un fantôme formé par nos passions, à qui on donne un nom honnête pour faire impunément ce qu'on veut.'* La Rochefoucauld and those other French masters of soul searching (whose company a German, the author of *Psychological Observations*, has recently joined) are like accurately aimed arrows, which hit the mark again and again, the black mark of man's nature. Their skill inspires amazement, but the spectator

---

* 'That which men call virtue is usually no more than a phantom formed by our passions, to which one gives an honest name in order to do with impunity whatever one wishes.'

who is guided not by the scientific spirit, but by the humane spirit, will eventually curse an art which seems to implant in the souls of men a predilection for belittling and doubt.

*

Nevertheless. However the argument and counterargument stand, the present condition of one certain, single science has made necessary the awakening of moral observation, and mankind cannot be spared the horrible sight of the psychological operating table, with its knives and forceps. For now that science rules which asks after the origin and history of moral feelings and which tries as it progresses to pose and solve the complicated sociological problems; the old philosophy doesn't even acknowledge such problems and has always used meager excuses to avoid investigating the origin and history of moral feelings. We can survey the consequences very clearly, many examples having proven how the errors of the greatest philosophers usually start from a false explanation of certain human actions and feelings, how an erroneous analysis of so-called selfless behavior, for example, can be the basis for false ethics, for whose sake religion and mythological confusion are then drawn in, and finally how the shadows of these sad spirits also fall upon physics and the entire contemplation of the world. But if it is a fact that the superficiality of psychological observation has laid the most dangerous traps for human judgment and conclusions, and continues to lay them anew, then what we need now is a persistence in work that does not tire of piling stone upon stone, pebble upon pebble; we need a sober courage to do such humble work without shame and to defy any who disdain it. It is true that countless individual remarks about things human and all too human were first detected and stated in those social circles which would make every sort of sacrifice not for scientific knowledge, but for a witty coquetry. And because the scent of that old homeland (a very seductive scent) has attached itself almost inextricably to the whole genre of the moral maxim, the scientific man instinctively shows some suspicion towards this genre and its seriousness. But it suffices to point to the outcome: already it is becoming clear that the most serious results grow up from the ground of psychological observation. Which principle did one of the keenest and coolest thinkers, the author of the book *On the Origin of Moral Feelings*, arrive at through his incisive and piercing analysis of human actions? 'The moral man,' he says, 'stands no nearer to the intelligible (metaphysical) world than does the physical man.' Perhaps at some point in the future this principle, grown hard and sharp by the hammerblow of historical knowledge, can serve as the axe laid to the root of men's 'metaphysical need' (whether *more* as a blessing than as a curse for the general welfare, who can say?). In any event, it is a tenet with the most weighty consequences, fruitful and frightful at the same time, and seeing into the world with that double vision which all great insights have.

*

Morality and the ordering of the good. The accepted hierarchy of the good, based on how a low, higher, or a most high egoism desires that thing or the other, decides today about morality or immorality. To prefer a low good (sensual pleasure, for example) to one esteemed higher (health, for example) is taken for immoral, likewise to prefer comfort to freedom. The hierarchy of the good, however, is not fixed and identical at all times. If someone prefers revenge to justice, he is moral by the standard of an earlier culture, yet by the standard of the present culture he is immoral. 'Immoral' then indicates that someone has not felt, or not felt strongly enough, the higher, finer, more spiritual motives which the new culture of the time has brought with it. It indicates a backward nature, but only in degree.

The hierarchy itself is not established or changed from the point of view of morality; nevertheless an action is judged moral or immoral according to the prevailing determination.

*

Cruel men as backward. We must think of men who are cruel today as stages of *earlier cultures*, which have been left over; in their case, the mountain range of humanity shows openly its deeper formations, which otherwise lie hidden. They are backward men whose brains, because of various possible accidents of heredity, have not yet developed much delicacy or versatility. They show us what we *all* were, and frighten us. But they themselves are as little responsible as a piece of granite for being granite. In our brain, too, there must be grooves and bends which correspond to that state of mind, just as there are said to be reminders of the fish state in the form of certain human organs. But these grooves and bends are no longer the bed in which the river of our feeling courses.

*

Gratitude and revenge. The powerful man feels gratitude for the following reason: through his good deed, his benefactor has, as it were, violated the powerful man's sphere and penetrated it. Now through his act of gratitude the powerful man requites himself by violating the sphere of the benefactor. It is a milder form of revenge. Without the satisfaction of gratitude, the powerful man would have shown himself to be unpowerful and henceforth would be considered such. For that reason, every society of good men (that is, originally, of powerful men) places gratitude among its first duties.

Swift remarked that men are grateful in the same proportion as they cherish revenge.

*

Double prehistory of good and evil. The concept of good and evil has a double prehistory: namely, first of all, in the soul of the ruling clans and castes. The man who has the power to requite goodness with goodness, evil with evil, and really does practice requital by being grateful and vengeful, is called 'good'. The man who is unpowerful and cannot requite is taken for bad. As a good man, one belongs to the 'good', a community that has a communal feeling, because all the individuals are entwined together by their feeling for requital. As a bad man, one belongs to the 'bad', to a mass of abject, powerless men who have no communal feeling. The good men are a caste; the bad men are a multitude, like particles of dust. Good and bad are for a time equivalent to noble and base, master and slave. Conversely, one does not regard the enemy as evil: he can requite. In Homer, both the Trojan and the Greek are good. Not the man who inflicts harm on us, but the man who is contemptible, is bad. In the community of the good, goodness is hereditary; it is impossible for a bad man to grow out of such good soil. Should one of the good men nevertheless do something unworthy of good men, one resorts to excuses; one blames God, for example, saying that he struck the good man with blindness and madness.

Then, in the souls of oppressed, powerless men, every *other* man is taken for hostile, inconsiderate, exploitative, cruel, sly, whether he be noble or base. Evil is their epithet for man, indeed for every possible living being, even, for example, for a god; 'human', 'divine' mean the same as 'devilish', 'evil'. Signs of goodness, helpfulness, pity are taken anxiously for malice, the prelude to a terrible outcome, bewilderment, and deception, in short, for refined evil. With such a state of mind in the individual, a community can scarcely come about at all – or at most in the crudest form; so that wherever this concept of good and evil predominates, the downfall of individuals, their clans and races, is near at hand.

Our present morality has grown up on the ground of the *ruling* clans and castes.

*

Pity more intense than suffering. There are cases where pity is more intense than actual suffering. When one of our friends is guilty of something ignominious, for example, we feel it more painfully than when we ourselves do it. For we believe in the purity of his character more than he does. Thus our love for him (probably because of this very belief) is more intense than his own love for himself. Even if his egoism suffers more than our egoism, in that he has to feel the bad consequences of his fault more intensely, our selflessness (this word must never be taken literally, but only as a euphemism) is touched more intensely by his guilt than is his selflessness.

*

Economy of kindness. Kindness and love, the most curative herbs and agents in human intercourse, are such precious finds that one would hope these balsamlike remedies would be used as economically as possible; but this is impossible. Only the boldest Utopians would dream of the economy of kindness.

*

Goodwill. Among the small but endlessly abundant and therefore very effective things that science ought to heed more than the great, rare things, is goodwill. I mean those expressions of a friendly disposition in interactions, that smile of the eye, those handclasps, that ease which usually envelops nearly all human actions. Every teacher, every official brings this ingredient to what he considers his duty. It is the continual manifestation of our humanity, its rays of light, so to speak, in which everything grows. Especially within the narrowest circle, in the family, life sprouts and blossoms only by this goodwill. Good nature, friendliness, and courtesy of the heart are ever-flowing tributaries of the selfless drive and have made much greater contributions to culture than those much more

Aphorisms on Love and Hate

famous expressions of this drive, called pity, charity, and self-sacrifice. But we tend to underestimate them, and in fact there really is not much about them that is selfless. The *sum* of these small doses is nevertheless mighty; its cumulative force is among the strongest of forces.

Similarly, there is much more happiness to be found in the world than dim eyes can see, if one calculates correctly and does not forget all those moments of ease which are so plentiful in every day of every human life, even the most oppressed.

*

Desire to arouse pity. In the most noteworthy passage of his self-portrait (first published in 1658), La Rochefoucauld certainly hits the mark when he warns all reasonable men against pity, when he advises them to leave it to those common people who need passions (because they are not directed by reason) to bring them to the point of helping the sufferer and intervening energetically in a misfortune. For pity, in his (and Plato's) judgment, weakens the soul. Of course one ought to *express* pity, but one ought to guard against *having* it; for unfortunate people are so *stupid* that they count the expression of pity as the greatest good on earth.

Perhaps one can warn even more strongly against having pity for the unfortunate if one does not think of their need for pity as stupidity and intellectual deficiency, a kind of mental disorder resulting from their misfortune (this is how La Rochefoucauld seems to regard it), but rather as something quite different and more dubious. Observe how children weep and cry, *so that* they will be pitied, how they wait for the moment when their condition will be noticed. Or live among the ill and depressed, and question whether their eloquent laments and whimpering, the spectacle of their misfortune, is not basically aimed at *hurting* those present. The pity that the spectators then express consoles the weak and suffering, inasmuch as they see that, despite all their weakness, they still *have* at least one *power: the power to hurt*. When expressions of pity make the unfortunate man aware of this feeling of superiority, he gets a kind of pleasure from it; his self-image revives; he is still important enough to inflict pain on the world. Thus the thirst for pity is a thirst for self-enjoyment, and at the expense of one's fellow men. It reveals man in the complete inconsideration of his most intimate dear self, but not precisely in his 'stupidity,' as La Rochefoucauld thinks.

In social dialogue, three-quarters of all questions and answers are framed in order to hurt the participants a little bit; this is why many men thirst after society so much: it gives them a feeling of their strength. In these countless, but very small doses, malevolence takes effect as one of life's powerful stimulants, just as goodwill, dispensed in the same way throughout the human world, is the perennially ready cure.

But will there be many people honest enough to admit that it is a pleasure to inflict pain? That not infrequently one amuses himself (and well) by offending other men (at least in his thoughts) and by shooting pellets of petty malice at them? Most people are too dishonest, and a few men are too good, to know anything about this source of shame. So they may try to deny that Prosper Merimée is right when he says, 'Sachez aussi qu'il n'y a rien de plus commun que de faire le mal pour le plaisir de le faire.'*

*

How seeming becomes being. Ultimately, not even the deepest pain can keep the actor from thinking of the impression of his part and the overall theatrical effect, not even, for example, at his child's funeral. He will be his own audience, and cry about his own pain as he expresses it. The hypocrite who always plays one and the same role finally ceases to be a hypocrite. Priests, for example, who are usually conscious or unconscious hypocrites when they are young men, finally end by becoming natural, and then they really are priests, with no affectation. Or if the father does not get that far, perhaps the son, using his father's headway, inherits the habit. If someone wants to *seem* to be something, stubbornly and for a long time, he

---

* 'Know that nothing is more common than to do harm for the pleasure of doing it.'

eventually finds it hard to *be* anything else. The profession of almost every man, even the artist, begins with hypocrisy, as he imitates from the outside, copies what is effective. The man who always wears the mask of a friendly countenance eventually has to gain power over benevolent moods without which the expression of friendliness cannot be forced – and eventually then these moods gain power over him, and he *is* benevolent.

*

Triumph of knowledge over radical evil. The man who wants to gain wisdom profits greatly from having thought for a time that man is basically evil and degenerate: this idea is wrong, like its opposite, but for whole periods of time it was predominant and its roots have sunk deep into us and into our world. To understand ourselves we must understand *it;* but to climb higher, we must then climb over and beyond it. We recognize that there are no sins in the metaphysical sense; but, in the same sense, neither are there any virtues; we recognize that this entire realm of moral ideas is in a continual state of fluctuation, that there are higher and deeper concepts of good and evil, moral and immoral. A man who desires no more from things than to understand them easily makes peace with his soul and will err (or 'sin', as the world calls it) at the most out of ignorance, but hardly out of desire. He will no longer want to condemn and root out his desires; but his single goal, governing him completely, to *understand* as well as he can at all times, will cool him down and soften all the wildness in his disposition. In addition, he has rid himself of a number of tormenting ideas; he no longer feels anything at the words 'pains of hell', 'sinfulness', 'incapacity for the good': for him they are only the evanescent silhouettes of erroneous thoughts about life and the world.

*

Morality as man's dividing himself. A good author, who really cares about his subject, wishes that someone would come and destroy him by representing the same subject more clearly and by answering every last question contained in it. The girl in love wishes that she might prove the devoted faithfulness of her love through her lover's faithlessness. The soldier wishes that he might fall on the battlefield for his victorious fatherland, for in the victory of his fatherland his greatest desire is also victorious. The mother gives the child what she takes from herself: sleep, the best food, in some instances even her health, her wealth.

Are all these really selfless states, however? Are these acts of morality *miracles* because they are, to use Schopenhauer's phrase, 'impossible and yet real'? Isn't it clear that, in all these cases, man is loving *something of himself*, a thought, a longing, an offspring, more than *something else of himself;* that he is thus *dividing up* his being and sacrificing one part for the other? Is it something *essentially* different when a pigheaded man says, 'I would rather be shot at once than move an inch to get out of that man's way'?

The *inclination towards something* (a wish, a drive, a longing) is present in all the above-mentioned cases; to yield to it, with all its consequences, is in any case not 'selfless'. In morality, man treats himself not as an 'individuum', but as a 'dividuum'.

*

What one can promise. One can promise actions, but not feelings, for the latter are involuntary. He who promises to love forever or hate forever or be forever faithful to someone is promising something that is not in his power. He can, however, promise those actions that are usually the consequence of love, hatred, or faithfulness, but that can also spring from other motives: for there are several paths and motives to an action. A promise to love someone forever, then, means, 'As long as I love you I will render unto you the actions of love; if I no longer love you, you will continue to receive the same actions from me, if for other motives.' Thus the illusion remains in the minds of one's fellow men that the love is unchanged and still the same.

One is promising that the semblance of love will

endure, then, when without self-deception one vows everlasting love.

*

Intellect and morality. One must have a good memory to be able to keep the promises one has given. One must have strong powers of imagination to be able to have pity. So closely is morality bound to the quality of the intellect.

*

Desire to avenge and vengeance. To have thoughts of revenge and execute them means to be struck with a violent – but temporary – fever. But to have thoughts of revenge without the strength or courage to execute them means to endure a chronic suffering, a poisoning of body and soul. A morality that notes only the intentions assesses both cases equally; usually the first case is assessed as worse (because of the evil consequences that the act of revenge may produce). Both evaluations are short-sighted.

*

The ability to wait. Being able to wait is so hard that the greatest poets did not disdain to make the inability to wait the theme of their poetry. Thus Shakespeare in his

Othello, Sophocles in his Ajax, who, as the oracle suggests, might not have thought his suicide necessary, if only he had been able to let his feeling cool for one day more. He probably would have outfoxed the terrible promptings of his wounded vanity and said to himself: 'Who, in my situation, has never once taken a sheep for a warrior? Is that so monstrous? On the contrary, it is something universally human.' Ajax might have consoled himself thus.

Passion will not wait. The tragedy in the lives of great men often lies not in their conflict with the times and the baseness of their fellow men, but rather in their inability to postpone their work for a year or two. They cannot wait.

In every duel, the advising friends have to determine whether the parties involved might be able to wait a while longer. If they cannot, then a duel is reasonable, since each of the parties says to himself: 'Either I continue to live, and the other must die at once, or vice versa.' In that case, to wait would be to continue suffering the horrible torture of offended honor in the presence of the offender. And this can be more suffering than life is worth.

*

Reveling in revenge. Crude men who feel themselves insulted tend to assess the degree of insult as high as possible, and talk about the offense in greatly exaggerated language, only so they can revel to their heart's content in the aroused feelings of hatred and revenge.

*

Those who flare up. We must beware of the man who flares up at us as of someone who has once made an attempt upon our life. For *that* we are still alive is due to his lacking the power to kill. If looks could kill, we would long ago have been done for. It is an act of primitive culture to bring someone to silence by making physical savageness visible, by inciting fear.

In the same way, the cold glance which elegant people use with their servants is a vestige from those castelike distinctions between man and man, an act of primitive antiquity. Women, the guardians of that which is old, have also been more faithful in preserving this cultural remnant.

*

Love and justice. Why do we overestimate love to the disadvantage of justice, saying the nicest things about it, as if it were a far higher essence than justice? Isn't love obviously more foolish? Of course, but for just that reason so much more pleasant for everyone. Love is foolish, and possesses a rich horn of plenty; from it she dispenses her gifts to everyone, even if he does not deserve them, indeed, even if he does not thank her for them. She is as nonpartisan as rain, which (according to the Bible and to experience) rains not only upon the unjust, but sometimes soaks the just man to the skin, too.

*

Degree of moral inflammability unknown. Whether or not our passions reach the point of red heat and guide our whole life depends on whether or not we have been exposed to certain shocking sights or impressions – for example a father falsely executed, killed or tortured; an unfaithful wife; a cruel ambush by an enemy. No one knows how far circumstances, pity, or indignation may drive him; he does not know the degree of his inflammability. Miserable, mean conditions make one miserable; it is usually not the quality of the experiences but rather the quantity that determines the lower and the higher man, in good and in evil.

*

The honor of the person applied to the cause. We universally honor acts of love and sacrifice for the sake of one's neighbor, wherever we find them. In this way we heighten the *value of the things* loved in that way, or for which sacrifices are made, even though they are in themselves perhaps not worth much. A valiant army convinces us about the cause for which it is fighting.

*

Misunderstanding between the sufferer and the perpetrator. When a rich man takes a possession from a poor man (for example, when a prince robs a plebeian of his sweetheart), the poor man misunderstands. He thinks that the rich man must be a villain to take from him the little he has. But the rich man does not feel the value of a *particular* possession so deeply because he is accustomed to having many. So he cannot put himself in the place of the poor man, and he is by no means doing as great an injustice as the poor man believes. Each has a false idea of the other. The injustice of the mighty, which enrages us most in history, is by no means as great as it appears. Simply the inherited feeling of being a higher being, with higher pretensions, makes one rather cold, and leaves the conscience at peace. Indeed, none of us feels anything like injustice when there is a great difference between ourselves and some other being, and we kill a gnat, for example, without any twinge of conscience. So it is no sign of wickedness in Xerxes (whom even all the Greeks portray as exceptionally noble) when he takes a son from his father and has him cut to pieces, because the father had expressed an anxious and doubtful distrust of their entire campaign. In this case the individual man is eliminated like an unpleasant insect; he stands too low to be allowed to keep on arousing bothersome feelings in a world ruler. Indeed, no cruel man is cruel to the extent that the mistreated man believes. The idea of pain is not the same as the suffering of it. It is the same with an unjust judge, with a journalist who misleads public opinion by little dishonesties. In each of these cases, cause and effect are experienced in quite different categories of thought and feeling; nevertheless, it is automatically assumed that the perpetrator and sufferer think and feel the same, and the guilt of the one is therefore measured by the pain of the other.

*

Malice is rare. Most men are much too concerned with themselves to be malicious.

*

Limit of human love. Any man who has once declared the other man to be a fool, a bad fellow, is annoyed when that man ends by showing that he is not.

*

Mores and morality. To be moral, correct, ethical means to obey an age-old law or tradition. Whether one submits

Aphorisms on Love and Hate

to it gladly or with difficulty makes no difference; enough that one submits. We call 'good' the man who does the moral thing as if by nature, after a long history of inheritance – that is, easily, and gladly, whatever it is (he will, for example, practice revenge when that is considered moral, as in the older Greek culture). He is called good because he is good 'for' something. But because, as mores changed, goodwill, pity, and the like were always felt to be 'good for' something, useful, it is primarily the man of goodwill, the helpful man, who is called 'good'. To be evil is to be 'not moral' (immoral), to practice bad habits, go against tradition, however reasonable or stupid it may be. To harm one's fellow, however, has been felt primarily as injurious in all moral codes of different times, so that when we hear the word 'bad' now, we think particularly of voluntary injury to one's fellow. When men determine between moral and immoral, good and evil, the basic opposition is not 'egoism' and 'selflessness', but rather adherence to a tradition or law, and release from it. The *origin* of the tradition makes no difference, at least concerning good and evil, or an immanent categorical imperative; but is rather above all for the purpose of maintaining *a community*, a people. Every superstitious custom, originating in a coincidence that is interpreted falsely, forces a tradition that it is moral to follow. To release oneself from it is dangerous, even more injurious for the *community* than for the individual (because the divinity punishes the whole community for sacrilege and violation of its rights, and the individual only as a part of that community). Now, each tradition grows more venerable the farther its origin lies in the past, the more it is forgotten; the respect paid to the tradition accumulates from generation to generation; finally the origin becomes sacred and awakens awe; and thus the morality of piety is in any case much older than that morality which requires selfless acts.

*

Pleasure in custom. An important type of pleasure, and thus an important source of morality, grows out of habit. One does habitual things more easily, skillfully, gladly; one feels a pleasure at them, knowing from experience that the habit has stood the test and is useful. A morality one can live with has been proved salutary, effective, in contrast to all the as yet unproven new experiments. Accordingly, custom is the union of the pleasant and the useful; in addition, it requires no thought. As soon as man can exercise force, he exercises it to introduce and enforce his mores, for to him they represent proven wisdom. Likewise, a community will force each individual in it to the same mores. Here is the error: because one feels good with one custom, or at least because he lives his life by means of it, this custom is necessary, for he holds it to be the *only* possibility by which one can feel good; the enjoyment of life seems to grow out of it alone.

This idea of habit as a condition of existence is carried right into the smallest details of custom: since lower peoples and cultures have only very slight insight into the real causality, they make sure, with superstitious fear, that everything take the same course; even where a custom is difficult, harsh, burdensome, it is preserved because it seems to be highly useful. They do not know that the same degree of comfort can also exist with other customs and that even higher degrees of comfort can be attained. But they do perceive that all customs, even the harshest, become more pleasant and mild with time, and that even the severest way of life can become a habit and thus a pleasure.

*

Pleasure and social instinct. From his relationship to other men, man gains a new kind of pleasure, in addition to those pleasurable feelings which he gets from himself. In this way he widens significantly the scope of his pleasurable feelings. Perhaps some of these feelings have come down to him from the animals, who visibly feel pleasure when playing with each other, particularly mothers playing with their young. Next one might think of sexual relations, which make virtually every lass seem interesting to every lad (and vice versa) in view of potential pleasure. Pleasurable feeling based on human relations generally makes man better; shared joy, pleasure taken together, heightens this feeling; it gives the individual security, makes him better-natured, dissolves distrust and envy: one feels good oneself and can see the other man feel good in the same way. *Analogous expressions of pleasure* awaken the fantasy of empathy, the feeling of being alike. Shared sorrows do it, too: the same storms, dangers, enemies. Upon this basis man has built the oldest covenant, whose purpose is to eliminate and resist communally any threatening unpleasure, for the good of each individual. And thus social instinct grows out of pleasure.

*

Innocence of so-called evil actions. All 'evil' actions are motivated by the drive for preservation, or, more exactly, by the individual's intention to gain pleasure and avoid unpleasure; thus they are motivated, but they are not evil. 'Giving pain in and of itself' *does not exist*, except in the brain of philosophers, nor does 'giving pleasure in and of itself' (pity, in the Schopenhauerian sense). In conditions *preceding* organized states, we kill any being, be it ape or man, that wants to take a fruit off a tree before we do, just when we are hungry and running up to the tree. We would treat the animal the same way today, if we were hiking through inhospitable territory.

Those evil actions which outrage us most today are based on the error that that man who harms us has free

Aphorisms on Love and Hate

will, that is, that he had the *choice* not to do this bad thing to us. This belief in his choice arouses hatred, thirst for revenge, spite, the whole deterioration of our imagination; whereas we get much less angry at an animal because we consider it irresponsible. To do harm not out of a drive for preservation, but for requital – that is the result of an erroneous judgment, and is therefore likewise innocent. The individual can, in conditions preceding the organized state, treat others harshly and cruelly to *intimidate* them, to secure his existence through such intimidating demonstrations of his power. This is how the brutal, powerful man acts, the original founder of a state, who subjects to himself those who are weaker. He has the right to do it, just as the state now takes the right. Or rather, there is no right that can prevent it. The ground for all morality can only be prepared when a greater individual or collective-individual, as, for example, society or the state, subjects the individuals in it, that is, when it draws them out of their isolatedness and integrates them into a union. *Force* precedes morality; indeed, for a time morality itself is force, to which others acquiesce to avoid unpleasure. Later it becomes custom, and still later free obedience, and finally almost instinct: then it is coupled to pleasure, like all habitual and natural things, and is now called *virtue*.

*

Judge not. When we consider earlier periods, we must be careful not to fall into unjust abuse. The injustice of slavery, the cruelty in subjugating persons and peoples, cannot be measured by our standards. For the instinct for justice was not so widely developed then. Who has the right to reproach Calvin of Geneva for burning Dr Servet? His was a consistent act, flowing out of his convictions, and the Inquisition likewise had its reasons; it is just that the views dominant then were wrong and resulted in a consistency that we find harsh, because we now find those views so alien. Besides, what is the burning of one man compared to the eternal pains of hell for nearly everyone! And yet this much more terrible idea used to dominate the whole world without doing any essential damage to the idea of a god. In our own time, we treat political heretics harshly and cruelly, but because we have learned to believe in the necessity of the state we are not as sensitive to this cruelty as we are to that cruelty whose justification we reject. Cruelty to animals, by children and Italians, stems from ignorance; namely, in the interests of its teachings, the church has placed the animal too far beneath man.

Likewise, in history much that is frightful and inhuman, which one would almost like not to believe, is mitigated by the observation that the commander and the executor are different people: the former does not witness his cruelty and therefore has no strong impression of it in his imagination; the latter is obeying a superior and feels no responsibility. Because of a lack of imagination, most princes and military leaders can easily appear to be harsh and cruel, without being so.

Egoism is not evil, for the idea of one's 'neighbor' (the word has a Christian origin and does not reflect the truth) is very weak in us; and we feel toward him almost as free and irresponsible as toward plants and stones. That the other suffers *must be learned;* and it can never be learned completely.

*

Harmlessness of malice. Malice does not aim at the suffering of the other in and of itself, but rather at our own enjoyment, for example, a feeling of revenge or a strong nervous excitement. Every instance of teasing shows that it gives us pleasure to release our power on the other person and experience an enjoyable feeling of superiority. Is the *immoral* thing about it, then, to have *pleasure on the basis of other people's unpleasure?* Is Schadenfreude devilish, as Schopenhauer says? Now, in nature, we take pleasure in breaking up twigs, loosening stones, fighting with wild animals, in order to gain awareness of our own strength. Is the *knowledge*, then, that another person is suffering because of us supposed to make immoral the same thing about which we otherwise feel no responsibility? But if one did not have this knowledge, one would not have that pleasure in his own superiority, which can *be discovered* only in the suffering of the other, in teasing, for example. All joy in oneself is neither good nor bad; where should the determination come from that to have pleasure in oneself one may not cause unpleasure in others? Solely from the point of view of advantage, that is, from consideration of the *consequences*, of possible unpleasure, when the injured party or the state representing him leads us to expect requital and revenge; this alone can have been the original basis for denying oneself these actions.

Pity does not aim at the pleasure of others any more than malice (as we said above) aims at the pain of others, per se. For in pity at least two (maybe many more) elements of personal pleasure are contained, and it is to that extent self-enjoyment: first of all, it is the pleasure of the emotion (the kind of pity we find in tragedy) and second, when it drives us to act, it is the pleasure of our satisfaction in the exercise of power. If, in addition, a suffering person is very close to us, we reduce our own suffering by our acts of pity.

Aside from a few philosophers, men have always placed pity rather low in the hierarchy of moral feelings – and rightly so.

*

Self-defense. If we accept self-defense as moral, then we must also accept nearly all expressions of so-called immoral egoism; we inflict harm, rob or kill, to preserve or protect ourselves, to prevent personal disaster; where cunning and dissimulation are the correct means of self-preservation, we lie. *To do injury intentionally*, when it is a matter of our existence or security (preservation of our well-being) is conceded to be moral; the state itself injures from this point of view when it imposes punishment. Of course, there can be no immorality in unintentional injury; there coincidence governs. Can there be a kind of intentional injury where it is *not* a matter of our existence, the preservation of our well-being? Can there be an injury out of pure *malice*, in cruelty, for example? If one does not know how painful an action is, it cannot be malicious; thus the child is not malicious or evil to an animal: he examines and destroys it like a toy. But do we ever completely *know* how painful an action is to the other person? As far as our nervous system extends, we protect ourselves from pain; if it extended further, right into our fellow men, we would not do harm to anyone (except in such cases where we do it to ourselves, that is, where we cut ourselves in order to cure ourselves, exert and strain ourselves to be healthy). We *conclude* by analogy that something hurts another, and through our memory and power of imagination we ourselves can feel ill at such a thought. But what difference remains between a toothache and the ache (pity) evoked by the sight of a toothache? That is, when we injure out of so-called malice, the *degree* of pain produced is in any case unknown to us; but in that we feel *pleasure* in the action (feeling of our own power, our own strong excitement) the action takes place to preserve the well-being of the individual and thus falls within a point of view similar to that of self-defence or a white lie. No life without pleasure; the struggle for pleasure is the struggle for life. Whether the individual fights this battle in ways such that men call him *good* or such that they call him *evil* is determined by the measure and makeup of his intellect.

*

Censor vitae.* For a long time, the inner state of a man who wants to become free in his judgments about life will be characterized by an alternation between love and hatred; he does not forget, and resents everything, good as well as evil. Finally, when the whole tablet of his soul is written full with experiences, he will neither despise and hate existence nor love it, but rather lie above it, now with a joyful eye, now with a sorrowful eye, and, like nature, be now of a summery, now of an autumnal disposition.

*

Secondary result. Whoever seriously wants to become free, will in the process also lose, uncoerced, the inclination

*   *Censor vitae:* critic of life.

Aphorisms on Love and Hate

to faults and vices; he will also be prey ever more rarely to annoyance and irritation. For his will desires nothing more urgently than knowledge, and the means to it – that is, the enduring condition in which he is best able to engage in knowledge.

*

Caution of free spirits. Free-spirited people, living for knowledge alone, will soon find they have achieved their external goal in life, their ultimate position vis à vis society and the state, and gladly be satisfied, for example, with a minor position or a fortune that just meets their needs; for they will set themselves up to live in such a way that a great change in economic conditions, even a revolution in political structures, will not overturn their life with it. They expend as little energy as possible on all these things, so that they can plunge with all their assembled energy, as if taking a deep breath, into the element of knowledge. They can then hope to dive deep, and also get a look at the bottom.

Such a spirit will be happy to take only the corner of an experience; he does not love things in the whole breadth and prolixity of their folds; for he does not want to get wrapped up in them.

He, too, knows the week-days of bondage, dependence, and service. But from time to time he must get a Sunday of freedom, or else he will not endure life.

It is probable that even his love of men will be cautious and somewhat shortwinded, for he wants to engage himself with the world of inclination and blindness only as far as is necessary for the sake of knowledge. He must trust that the genius of justice will say something on behalf of its disciple and protégé, should accusatory voices call him poor in love.

In his way of living and thinking, there is a *refined heroism;* he scorns to offer himself to mass worship, as his cruder brother does, and is used to going quietly through the world and out of the world. Whatever labyrinths he may wander through, among whatever rocks his river may at times have forced its tortured course – once he gets to the light, he goes his way brightly, lightly, and almost soundlessly, and lets the sunshine play down to his depths.

*

Lack of intimacy. Lack of intimacy among friends is a mistake that cannot be censured without becoming irreparable.

*

Twofold kind of equality. The craving for equality can be expressed either by the wish to draw all others down to one's level (by belittling, excluding, tripping them up)

Aphorisms on Love and Hate

or by the wish to draw oneself up with everyone else (by appreciating, helping, taking pleasure in others' success).

*

Trust and intimacy If someone assiduously seeks to force intimacy with another person, he usually is not sure whether he possesses that person's trust. If someone is sure of being trusted, he places little value on intimacy.

*

Balance of friendship. Sometimes in our relationship to another person, the right balance of friendship is restored when we put a few grains of injustice on our own side of the scale.

*

Making them wait. A sure way to provoke people and to put evil thoughts into their heads is to make them wait a long time. This gives rise to immorality.

*

Means of compensation. If we have injured someone, giving him the opportunity to make a joke about us is often enough to provide him personal satisfaction, or even to win his good will.

*

Motive for attack. We attack not only to hurt a person, to conquer him, but also, perhaps, simply to become aware of our own strength.

*

The sympathetic. Sympathetic natures, always helpful in a misfortune, are rarely the same ones who share our joy: when others are happy, they have nothing to do, become superfluous, do not feel in possession of their superiority, and therefore easily show dissatisfaction.

*

Silence. For both parties, the most disagreeable way of responding to a polemic is to be angry and keep silent: for the aggressor usually takes the silence as a sign of disdain.

*

The friend's secret. There will be but few people who, when at a loss for topics of conversation, will not reveal the more secret affairs of their friends.

*

Vexation at the goodwill of others. We are wrong about the degree to which we believe ourselves hated or feared; for we ourselves know well the degree of our divergence from a person, a direction, or a party, but those others know us only very superficially, and therefore also hate us only superficially. Often we encounter goodwill which we cannot explain; but if we understand it, it offends us, for it shows that one doesn't take us seriously or importantly enough.

*

Traitor's tour-de-force. To express to your fellow conspirator the hurtful suspicion that he might be betraying you, and this at the very moment when you are yourself engaged in betraying him, is a tour-de-force of malice, because it makes the other person aware of himself and forces him to behave very unsuspiciously and openly for a time, giving you, the true traitor, a free hand.

*

To offend and be offended. It is much more agreeable to offend and later ask forgiveness than to be offended and grant forgiveness. The one who does the former demonstrates his power and then his goodness. The other, if he does not want to be thought inhuman, *must* forgive; because of this coercion, pleasure in the other's humiliation is slight.

*

The talent for friendship. Among men who have a particular gift for friendship, two types stand out. The one man is in a continual state of ascent, and finds an exactly appropriate friend for each phase of his development. The series of friends that he acquires in this way is only rarely interconnected, and sometimes discordant and contradictory, quite in accordance with the fact that the later phases in his development invalidate or compromise the earlier phases. Such a man may jokingly be called a *ladder*.

The other type is represented by the man who exercises his powers of attraction on very different characters and talents, thereby winning a whole circle of friends; and these come into friendly contact with one another through him, despite all their diversity. Such a man can be called a *circle;* for in him, that intimate connection of so many different temperaments and natures must somehow be prefigured.

In many people, incidentally, the gift of having good friends is much greater than the gift of being a good friend.

*

About friends. Just think to yourself some time how different are the feelings, how divided the opinions, even among the closest acquaintances; how even the same opinions have quite a different place or intensity in the heads of your friends than in your own; how many hundreds of times there is occasion for misunderstanding or hostile flight. After all that, you will say to yourself: 'How unsure is the ground on which all our bonds and friendships rest; how near we are to cold downpours or ill weather; how lonely is every man!' If someone understands this, and also that all his fellow men's opinions, their kind and intensity, are as inevitable and irresponsible as their actions; if he learns to perceive that there is this inner inevitability of opinions, due to the indissoluble interweaving of character, occupation, talent, and environment – then he will perhaps be rid of the bitterness and sharpness of that feeling with which the wise man called out: 'Friends, there are no friends!' Rather, he will admit to himself that there are, indeed, friends, but they were brought to you by error and deception about yourself; and they must have learned to be silent in order to remain your friend; for almost always, such human relationships rest on the fact that a certain few things are never said, indeed that they are never touched upon; and once these pebbles are set rolling, the friendship follows after, and falls apart. Are there men who cannot be fatally wounded, were they to learn what their most intimate friends really know about them?

By knowing ourselves and regarding our nature itself as a changing sphere of opinions and moods, thus learning to despise it a bit, we bring ourselves into balance with others again. It is true, we have good reason to despise each of our acquaintances, even the greatest; but we have just as good reason to turn this feeling against ourselves.

And so let us bear with each other, since we do in fact bear with ourselves; and perhaps each man will some day know the more joyful hour in which he says:

'Friends, there are no friends!' the dying wise man shouted.

'Enemies, there is no enemy!' shout I, the living fool.

*

Friendship and marriage. The best friend will probably get the best wife, because a good marriage is based on a talent for friendship.

*

From the mother. Everyone carries within him an image of woman that he gets from his mother; that determines whether he will honor women in general, or despise them, or be generally indifferent to them.

*

A kind of jealousy. Mothers are easily jealous of their sons' friends if they are exceptionally successful. Usually a mother loves *herself* in her son more than she loves the son himself.

*

Different sighs. A few men have sighed because their women were abducted; most, because no one wanted to abduct them.

*

Love matches. Marriages that are made for love (so-called love matches) have Error as their father and Necessity (need) as their mother.

*

Women's friendship. Women can very well enter into a friendship with a man, but to maintain it – a little physical antipathy must help out.

*

Unity of place, and drama. If spouses did not live together, good marriages would be more frequent.

*

To want to be in love. Fiancés who have been brought together by convenience often try to *be* in love in order to overcome the reproach of cold, calculating advantage. Likewise, those who turn to Christianity for their advantage try to become truly pious, for in that way the religious pantomime is easier for them.

*

No standstill in love. A musician who *loves* the slow tempo will take the same pieces slower and slower. Thus there is no standstill in any love.

*

Proteus nature. For the sake of love, women wholly become what they are in the imagination of the men who love them.

*

Loving and possessing. Women usually love an important man in such a way that they want to have him to themselves. They would gladly put him under lock and key, if their vanity, which wants him to appear important in front of others, too, did not advise against it.

Aphorisms on Love and Hate

*

Masks. There are women who have no inner life wherever one looks for it, being nothing but masks. That man is to be pitied who lets himself in with such ghostly, necessarily unsatisfying creatures; but just these women are able to stimulate man's desire most intensely: he searches for their souls – and searches on and on.

*

Marriage as a long conversation. When entering a marriage, one should ask the question: do you think you will be able to have good conversations with this woman right into old age? Everything else in marriage is transitory, but most of the time in interaction is spent in conversation.

*

The female intellect. Women's intellect is manifested as perfect control, presence of mind, and utilization of all advantages. They bequeath it as their fundamental character to their children, and the father furnishes the darker background of will. His influence determines the rhythm and harmony, so to speak, to which the new life is to be played out; but its melody comes from the woman.

To say it for those who know how to explain a thing: women have the intelligence, men the heart and passion.

This is not contradicted by the fact that men actually get so much farther with their intelligence: they have the deeper, more powerful drives; these take their intelligence, which is in itself something passive, forward. Women are often privately amazed at the great honor men pay to their hearts. When men look especially for a profound, warm-hearted being, in choosing their spouse, and women for a clever, alert, and brilliant being, one sees very clearly how a man is looking for an idealized man, and a woman for an idealized woman – that is, not for a complement, but for the perfection of their own merits.

*

Short-sighted people are amorous. Sometimes just a stronger pair of glasses will cure an amorous man; and if someone had the power to imagine a face or form twenty years older, he might go through life quite undisturbed.

*

Love. The idolatry that women practice when it comes to love is fundamentally and originally a clever device, in that all those idealizations of love heighten their own power and portray them as ever more desirable in the eyes of men. But because they have grown accustomed over the centuries to this exaggerated estimation of love, it has happened that they have run into their own net and forgotten the reason behind it. They themselves are now more deceived than men, and suffer more, therefore, from the disappointment that almost inevitably enters the life of every woman – to the extent that she even has enough fantasy and sense to be able to be deceived and disappointed.

*

Letting oneself be loved. Because one of the two loving people is usually the lover, the other the beloved, the belief has arisen that in every love affair the amount of love is constant: the more of it one of the two grabs to himself, the less remains for the other person. Sometimes, exceptionally, it happens that vanity convinces each of the two people that *he* is the one who has to be loved, so that both want to let themselves be loved: in marriage, especially, this results in some half-droll, half-absurd scenes.

*

Who suffers more? After a personal disagreement and quarrel between a woman and a man, the one party suffers most at the thought of having hurt the other; while that other party suffers most at the thought of not having hurt the first enough; for which reason it tries by tears, sobs, and contorted features, to weigh down the other person's heart, even afterwards.

*

Opportunity for female generosity. Once a man's thoughts have gone beyond the demands of custom, he might consider whether nature and reason do not dictate that he marry several times in succession, so that first, aged twenty-two years, he marry an older girl who is spiritually and morally superior to him and can guide him through the dangers of his twenties (ambition, hatred, self-contempt, passions of all kinds). This woman's love would later be completely transformed into maternal feeling, and she would not only tolerate it, but promote it in the most salutary way, if the man in his thirties made an alliance with a quite young girl, whose education he himself would take in hand.

For one's twenties, marriage is a necessary institution; for one's thirties, it is useful, but not necessary; for later life, it often becomes harmful and promotes a husband's spiritual regression.

*

Tragedy of childhood. Not infrequently, noble-minded and ambitious men have to endure their harshest struggle in childhood, perhaps by having to assert their characters

Aphorisms on Love and Hate

against a low-minded father, who is devoted to pretense and mendacity, or by living, like Lord Byron, in continual struggle with a childish and wrathful mother. If one has experienced such struggles, for the rest of his life he will never get over knowing who has been in reality his greatest and most dangerous enemy.

*

From the future of marriage. Those noble, free-minded women who set themselves the task of educating and elevating the female sex should not overlook one factor: marriage, conceived of in its higher interpretation, the spiritual friendship of two people of opposite sexes, that is, marriage as hoped for by the future, entered into for the purpose of begetting and raising a new generation. Such a marriage, which uses sensuality as if it were only a rare, occasional means for a higher end, probably requires and must be provided with a natural aid: *concubinage*. For if, for reasons of the man's health, his wife is also to serve for the sole satisfaction of his sexual need, a false point of view, counter to the goals we have indicated, will be decisive in choosing a wife. Posterity becomes a coincidental objective; its successful education, highly improbable. A good wife, who should be friend, helpmate, child-bearer, mother, head of the family, manager, indeed, who perhaps has to run her own business or office separate from her husband, cannot be a concubine at the same time: it would usually be asking too much of her. Thus, the opposite of what happened in Pericles' times in Athens could occur in the future: men, whose wives were not much more than concubines then, turned to Aspasias as well, because they desired the delights of a mentally and emotionally liberating sociability, which only the grace and spiritual flexibility of women can provide. All human institutions, like marriage, permit only a moderate degree of practical idealization, failing which, crude measures immediately become necessary.

*

Happiness of marriage. Everything habitual draws an ever tighter net of spiderwebs around us; then we notice that the fibres have become traps, and that we ourselves are sitting in the middle, like a spider that got caught there and must feed on its own blood. That is why the free spirit hates all habits and rules, everything enduring and definitive; that is why, again and again, he painfully tears apart the net around him, even though he will suffer as a consequence from countless large and small wounds – for he must tear those fibres *away from himself*, from his body, his soul. He must learn to love where he used to hate, and vice versa. Indeed, nothing may be impossible for him, not even to sow dragons' teeth on the same field where he previously emptied the cornucopias of his kindness.

Aphorisms on Love and Hate

From this one can judge whether he is cut out for the happiness of marriage.

*

Too close. If we live in too close proximity to a person, it is as if we kept touching a good etching with our bare fingers; one day we have poor, dirty paper in our hands and nothing more. A human being's soul is likewise worn down by continual touching; at least it finally *appears* that way to us – we never see its original design and beauty again.

One always loses by all-too-intimate association with women and friends; and sometimes one loses the pearl of his life in the process.

*

Voluntary sacrificial animal. Significant women bring relief to the lives of their husbands, if the latter are famous and great, by nothing so much as by becoming a vessel, so to speak, for other people's general ill-will and occasional bad humor. Contemporaries tend to overlook their great men's many mistakes and follies, even gross injustices, if only they can find someone whom they may abuse and slaughter as a veritable sacrificial animal to relieve their feelings. Not infrequently a woman finds in herself the ambition to offer herself for this sacrifice, and then the man can of course be very contented – in the case that he is egoist enough to tolerate in his vicinity such a voluntary conductor of lightning, storm, and rain.

*

Ceterum censeo.* It is ludicrous when a have-not society declares the abolition of inheritance rights, and no less ludicrous when childless people work on the practical laws of a country: they do not have enough ballast in their ship to be able to sail surely into the ocean of the future. But it seems just as nonsensical if a man who has chosen as his task the acquisition of the most general knowledge and the evaluation of the whole of existence weighs himself down with personal considerations of a family, a livelihood, security, respect of his wife and child; he is spreading out over his telescope a thick veil, which scarcely any rays from the distant heavens are able to penetrate. So I, too, come to the tenet that in questions of the highest philosophical kind, all married people are suspect.

*

Passion for things. He who directs his passion to things (the sciences, the national good, cultural interests, the arts)

---

* 'Incidentally, I am of the opinion.'

takes much of the fire out of his passion for people (even when they represent those things, as statesmen, philosophers, and artists represent their creations).

*

The right profession. Men seldom endure a profession if they do not believe or persuade themselves that it is basically more important than all others. Women do the same with their lovers.

*

Friend. Shared joy, not compassion, makes a friend.

*

More troublesome than enemies. When some reason (e.g., gratitude) obliges us to maintain the appearance of unqualified congeniality with people about whose own congenial behavior we are not entirely convinced, these people torment our imagination much more than do our enemies.

*

Wanting to be loved. The demand to be loved is the greatest kind of arrogance.

Contempt for people. The least ambiguous sign of a disdain for people is this: that one tolerates everyone else only as a means to *his* end, or not at all.

*

The life of the enemy. Whoever lives for the sake of combating an enemy has an interest in the enemy's staying alive.

*

Want of friends. A want of friends points to envy or arrogance. Many a man owes his friends simply to the fortunate circumstance that he has no cause for envy.

*

Love and hatred. Love and hatred are not blind, but are blinded by the fire they themselves carry with them.

*

Punctum saliens* of passion. He who is about to fall into a state of anger or violent love reaches a point where his

---

* *the salient point*

soul is full like a vessel; but it needs one more drop of water: the good will to passion (which is generally also called the bad will). Only this little point is necessary; then the vessel runs over.

*

The hour-hand of life. Life consists of rare, isolated moments of the greatest significance, and of innumerably many intervals, during which at best the silhouettes of those moments hover about us. Love, springtime, every beautiful melody, mountains, the moon, the sea – all these speak completely to the heart but once, if in fact they ever do get a chance to speak completely. For many men do not have those moments at all, and are themselves intervals and intermissions in the symphony of real life.

*

Learning to love. We must learn to love, learn to be kind, and this from earliest youth; if education or chance give us no opportunity to practice these feelings, our soul becomes dry and unsuited even to understanding the tender inventions of loving people. Likewise, hatred must be learned and nurtured, if one wishes to become a proficient hater: otherwise the germ for that, too, will gradually wither.

*

Love and respect. Love desires; fear avoids. That is why it is impossible, at least in the same time span, to be loved and respected by the same person. For the man who respects another, acknowledges his power; that is, he fears it: his condition is one of awe. But love acknowledges no power, nothing that separates, differentiates, ranks higher or subordinates. Because the state of being loved carries with it no respect, ambitious men secretly or openly balk against it.

*

Love as a device. Whoever wants really to get to *know* something new (be it a person, an event, or a book) does well to take up this new thing with all possible love, to avert his eye quickly from, even to forget, everything about it that he finds inimical, objectionable, or false. So, for example, we give the author of a book the greatest possible head start, and, as if at a race, virtually yearn with a pounding heart for him to reach his goal. By doing this, we penetrate into the heart of the new thing, into its motive centre: and this is what it means to get to know it. Once we have got that far, reason then sets its limits; that overestimation, that occasional unhinging of the critical pendulum, was just a device to entice the soul of a matter out into the open.

Aphorisms on Love and Hate

*

Seriousness in play. At sunset in Genoa, I heard from a tower a long chiming of bells: it kept on and on, and over the noise of the backstreets, as if insatiable for itself, it rang out into the evening sky and the sea air, so terrible and so childish at the same time, so melancholy. Then I thought of Plato's words and felt them suddenly in my heart: *all in all, nothing human is worth taking very seriously; nevertheless . . .*

1. BOCCACCIO · *Mrs Rosie and the Priest*
2. GERARD MANLEY HOPKINS · *As kingfishers catch fire*
3. *The Saga of Gunnlaug Serpent-tongue*
4. THOMAS DE QUINCEY · *On Murder Considered as One of the Fine Arts*
5. FRIEDRICH NIETZSCHE · *Aphorisms on Love and Hate*
6. JOHN RUSKIN · *Traffic*
7. PU SONGLING · *Wailing Ghosts*
8. JONATHAN SWIFT · *A Modest Proposal*
9. *Three Tang Dynasty Poets*
10. WALT WHITMAN · *On the Beach at Night Alone*
11. KENKŌ · *A Cup of Sake Beneath the Cherry Trees*
12. BALTASAR GRACIÁN · *How to Use Your Enemies*
13. JOHN KEATS · *The Eve of St Agnes*
14. THOMAS HARDY · *Woman much missed*
15. GUY DE MAUPASSANT · *Femme Fatale*
16. MARCO POLO · *Travels in the Land of Serpents and Pearls*
17. SUETONIUS · *Caligula*
18. APOLLONIUS OF RHODES · *Jason and Medea*
19. ROBERT LOUIS STEVENSON · *Olalla*
20. KARL MARX AND FRIEDRICH ENGELS · *The Communist Manifesto*
21. PETRONIUS · *Trimalchio's Feast*
22. JOHANN PETER HEBEL · *How a Ghastly Story Was Brought to Light by a Common or Garden Butcher's Dog*
23. HANS CHRISTIAN ANDERSEN · *The Tinder Box*
24. RUDYARD KIPLING · *The Gate of the Hundred Sorrows*
25. DANTE · *Circles of Hell*
26. HENRY MAYHEW · *Of Street Piemen*
27. HAFEZ · *The nightingales are drunk*
28. GEOFFREY CHAUCER · *The Wife of Bath*
29. MICHEL DE MONTAIGNE · *How We Weep and Laugh at the Same Thing*
30. THOMAS NASHE · *The Terrors of the Night*
31. EDGAR ALLAN POE · *The Tell-Tale Heart*
32. MARY KINGSLEY · *A Hippo Banquet*
33. JANE AUSTEN · *The Beautifull Cassandra*
34. ANTON CHEKHOV · *Gooseberries*
35. SAMUEL TAYLOR COLERIDGE · *Well, they are gone, and here must I remain*
36. JOHANN WOLFGANG VON GOETHE · *Sketchy, Doubtful, Incomplete Jottings*
37. CHARLES DICKENS · *The Great Winglebury Duel*
38. HERMAN MELVILLE · *The Maldive Shark*
39. ELIZABETH GASKELL · *The Old Nurse's Story*
40. NIKOLAY LESKOV · *The Steel Flea*

41. HONORÉ DE BALZAC · *The Atheist's Mass*
42. CHARLOTTE PERKINS GILMAN · *The Yellow Wall-Paper*
43. C.P. CAVAFY · *Remember, Body . . .*
44. FYODOR DOSTOYEVSKY · *The Meek One*
45. GUSTAVE FLAUBERT · *A Simple Heart*
46. NIKOLAI GOGOL · *The Nose*
47. SAMUEL PEPYS · *The Great Fire of London*
48. EDITH WHARTON · *The Reckoning*
49. HENRY JAMES · *The Figure in the Carpet*
50. WILFRED OWEN · *Anthem For Doomed Youth*
51. WOLFGANG AMADEUS MOZART · *My Dearest Father*
52. PLATO · *Socrates' Defence*
53. CHRISTINA ROSSETTI · *Goblin Market*
54. *Sindbad the Sailor*
55. SOPHOCLES · *Antigone*
56. RYŪNOSUKE AKUTAGAWA · *The Life of a Stupid Man*
57. LEO TOLSTOY · *How Much Land Does A Man Need?*
58. GIORGIO VASARI · *Leonardo da Vinci*
59. OSCAR WILDE · *Lord Arthur Savile's Crime*
60. SHEN FU · *The Old Man of the Moon*
61. AESOP · *The Dolphins, the Whales and the Gudgeon*
62. MATSUO BASHŌ · *Lips too Chilled*
63. EMILY BRONTË · *The Night is Darkening Round Me*
64. JOSEPH CONRAD · *To-morrow*
65. RICHARD HAKLUYT · *The Voyage of Sir Francis Drake Around the Whole Globe*
66. KATE CHOPIN · *A Pair of Silk Stockings*
67. CHARLES DARWIN · *It was snowing butterflies*
68. BROTHERS GRIMM · *The Robber Bridegroom*
69. CATULLUS · *I Hate and I Love*
70. HOMER · *Circe and the Cyclops*
71. D. H. LAWRENCE · *Il Duro*
72. KATHERINE MANSFIELD · *Miss Brill*
73. OVID · *The Fall of Icarus*
74. SAPPHO · *Come Close*
75. IVAN TURGENEV · *Kasyan from the Beautiful Lands*
76. VIRGIL · *O Cruel Alexis*
77. H. G. WELLS · *A Slip under the Microscope*
78. HERODOTUS · *The Madness of Cambyses*
79. *Speaking of Siva*
80. *The Dhammapada*

'You shall have thousands of gold pieces; – thousands of thousands – millions – mountains, of gold: where will you keep them?'

JOHN RUSKIN
Born 1819, London
Died 1900, Coniston, England

'Traffic' was originally a lecture and was published in written form in *The Crown of Wild Olive* (1866). 'The Roots of Honour' is the opening essay in *Unto This Last* (1862).

RUSKIN IN PENGUIN CLASSICS
Unto This Last and Other Writings

JOHN RUSKIN

Traffic

PENGUIN BOOKS

PENGUIN CLASSICS

UK | USA | Canada | Ireland | Australia
India | New Zealand | South Africa

Penguin Books is part of the Penguin Random House group of companies whose addresses can be found at global.penguinrandomhouse.com.

This edition published in Penguin Classics 2015

011

Set in 9.5/13 pt Baskerville 10 Pro
Typeset by Jouve (UK), Milton Keynes
Printed and bound in Great Britain by Clays Ltd, Elcograf S.p.A.

A CIP catalogue record for this book is available from the British Library

ISBN: 978–0–141–39814–3

www.greenpenguin.co.uk

Penguin Random House is committed to a sustainable future for our business, our readers and our planet. This book is made from Forest Stewardship Council® certified paper.

Contents

Traffic 1

The Roots of Honour 33

Traffic

DELIVERED IN THE TOWN HALL, BRADFORD [APRIL 21, 1864]

My good Yorkshire friends, you asked me down here among your hills that I might talk to you about this Exchange you are going to build: but, earnestly and seriously asking you to pardon me, I am going to do nothing of the kind. I cannot talk, or at least can say very little, about this same Exchange. I must talk of quite other things, though not willingly; – I could not deserve your pardon, if, when you invited me to speak on one subject, I *wilfully* spoke on another. But I cannot speak, to purpose, of anything about which I do not care; and most simply and sorrowfully I have to tell you, in the outset, that I do *not* care about this Exchange of yours.

If, however, when you sent me your invitation, I had answered, 'I won't come, I don't care about the Exchange of Bradford,' you would have been justly offended with me, not knowing the reasons of so blunt a carelessness. So I have come down, hoping that you will patiently let me tell you why, on this, and many other such occasions, I now remain silent, when formerly I should have caught at the opportunity of speaking to a gracious audience.

In a word, then, I do not care about this Exchange – because *you* don't; and because you know perfectly well I cannot make you. Look at the essential conditions of the case, which you, as business men, know perfectly well, though perhaps you think I forget them. You are going to spend £30,000, which to you, collectively, is nothing; the buying a new coat is, as to the cost of it, a much more important matter of consideration to me, than building a new Exchange is to you. But you think you may as well have the right thing for your money. You know there are a great many odd styles of architecture about; you don't want to do anything ridiculous; you hear of me, among others, as a respectable architectural man-milliner; and you send for me, that I may tell you the leading fashion; and what is, in our shops, for the moment, the newest and sweetest thing in pinnacles.

Now, pardon me for telling you frankly, you cannot have good architecture merely by asking people's advice on occasion. All good architecture is the expression of national life and character; and it is produced by a prevalent and eager national taste, or desire for beauty. And I want you to think a little of the deep significance of this word 'taste'; for no statement of mine has been more earnestly or oftener controverted than that good taste is essentially a moral quality. 'No,' say many of my antagonists, 'taste is one thing, morality is another. Tell us what is pretty: we shall be glad to know that; but we need no sermons – even were you able to preach them, which may be doubted.'

Permit me, therefore, to fortify this old dogma of mine somewhat. Taste is not only a part and an index of morality; – it is the ONLY morality. The first, and last, and closest trial question to any living creature is, 'What do you like?' Tell me what you like, and I'll tell you what you are. Go out into the street, and ask the first man or woman you meet, what their 'taste' is; and if they answer candidly, you know them, body and soul. 'You, my friend in the rags, with the unsteady gait, what do *you* like?' 'A pipe, and a quartern of gin.' I know you. 'You, good woman, with the quick step and tidy bonnet, what do you like?' 'A swept hearth, and a clean tea-table; and my husband opposite me, and a baby at my breast.' Good, I know you also. 'You, little girl with the golden hair and the soft eyes, what do you like?' 'My canary, and a run among the wood hyacinths.' 'You, little boy with the dirty hands, and the low forehead, what do you like?' 'A shy at the sparrows, and a game at pitch farthing.' Good; we know them all now. What more need we ask?

'Nay,' perhaps you answer; 'we need rather to ask what these people and children do, than what they like. If they *do* right, it is no matter that they like what is wrong; and if they *do* wrong, it is no matter that they like what is right. Doing is the great thing; and it does not matter that the man likes drinking, so that he does not drink; nor that the little girl likes to be kind to her canary, if she will not learn her lessons; nor that the little boy likes throwing stones at the sparrows, if he goes to the Sunday school.' Indeed, for a short time, and in a provisional sense, this is true. For if, resolutely, people do what is right, in time to come they like doing it. But they only are in a right moral state when they *have* come to like doing it; and as long as they don't like it, they are still in a vicious state. The man is not in health of body who is always thinking of the bottle in the cupboard, though he bravely bears his thirst; but the man is who heartily enjoys water in the morning, and wine in the evening, each in its proper quantity and time. And the entire object of true education is to make people not merely *do* the right things, but *enjoy* the right things: – not merely industrious, but to love industry – not merely learned, but to love knowledge – not merely pure, but to love purity – not merely just, but to hunger and thirst after justice.

But you may answer or think, 'Is the liking for outside ornaments, – for pictures, or statues, or furniture, or architecture, a moral quality?' Yes, most surely, if a rightly set liking. Taste for *any* pictures or statues is not a moral quality, but taste for good ones is. Only here again we have to define the word 'good.' I don't mean by 'good,' clever – or learned – or difficult in the doing. Take a picture by Teniers, of sots quarrelling over their dice; it is an entirely clever picture; so clever that nothing in its kind has ever been done equal to it; but it is also an entirely base and evil picture. It is an expression of delight in the prolonged contemplation of a vile thing, and delight in that is an 'unmannered,' or 'immoral' quality. It is 'bad taste' in the profoundest sense – it is the taste of the devils. On the other hand, a picture of Titian's, or a Greek statue, or a Greek coin, or a Turner landscape, expresses delight in the perpetual contemplation of a good and perfect thing. That is an entirely moral quality – it is the taste of the angels. And all delight in fine art, and all love of it, resolve themselves into simple love of that which deserves love. That deserving is the quality which we call 'loveliness' – (we ought to have an opposite word, hateliness, to be said of the things which deserve to be hated); and it is not an indifferent nor optional thing whether we love this or that; but it is just the vital function of all our being. What we *like* determines what we *are*, and is the sign of what we are; and to teach taste is inevitably to form character.

As I was thinking over this, in walking up Fleet Street the other day, my eye caught the title of a book standing open in a bookseller's window. It was – *On the necessity of the diffusion of taste among all classes*. 'Ah,' I thought to myself, 'my classifying friend, when you have diffused your taste, where will your classes be? The man who likes what you like, belongs to the same class with you, I think. Inevitably so. You may put him to other work if you choose; but, by the condition you have brought him into, he will dislike the work as much as you would yourself. You get hold of a scavenger or a costermonger, who enjoyed the Newgate Calendar for literature, and "Pop goes the Weasel" for music. You think you can make him like Dante and Beethoven? I wish you joy of your lessons; but if you do, you have made a gentleman of him: – he won't like to go back to his costermongering.'

And so completely and unexceptionally is this so, that, if I had time to-night, I could show you that a nation cannot be affected by any vice, or weakness, without expressing it, legibly, and for ever, either in bad art, or by want of art; and that there is no national virtue, small or great, which is not manifestly expressed in all the art which circumstances enable the people possessing that virtue to produce. Take, for instance, your great English virtue of enduring and patient courage. You have at present in England only one art of any consequence – that is, iron-working. You know thoroughly well how to cast and hammer iron. Now, do you think, in those masses of lava which you build volcanic cones to melt, and which you forge at the mouths of the Infernos you have created; do you think, on those iron plates, your courage and endurance are not written for ever, – not merely with an iron pen, but on iron parchment? And take also your great English vice – European vice – vice of all the world – vice of all other worlds that roll or shine in heaven, bearing with them yet the atmosphere of hell – the vice of jealousy, which brings competition into your commerce, treachery into your councils, and dishonour into your wars – that vice which has rendered for you, and for your next neighbouring nation, the daily occupations of existence no longer possible, but with the mail upon your breasts and the sword loose in its sheath; so that at last, you have realised for all the multitudes of the two great peoples who lead the so-called civilization of the earth, – you have realised for them all, I say, in person and in policy, what was once true only of the rough Border riders of your Cheviot hills –

> 'They carved at the meal
> With gloves of steel,
> And they drank the red wine through the
>   helmet barr'd;' –

do you think that this national shame and dastardliness of heart are not written as legibly on every rivet of your iron armour as the strength of the right hands that forged it?

Friends, I know not whether this thing be the more ludicrous or the more melancholy. It is quite unspeakably both. Suppose, instead of being now sent for by you, I had been sent for by some private gentleman, living in a suburban house, with his garden separated only by a fruit wall from his next door neighbour's; and he had called me to consult with him on the furnishing of his drawing-room. I begin looking about me, and find the walls rather bare; I think such and such a paper might be desirable – perhaps a little fresco here and there on the ceiling – a damask curtain or so at the windows. 'Ah,' says my employer, 'damask curtains, indeed! That's all very fine, but you know I can't afford that kind of thing just now!' 'Yet the world credits you with a splendid income!' 'Ah, yes,' says my friend, 'but do you know, at present I am obliged to spend it nearly all in steel-traps?' 'Steel-traps! for whom?' 'Why, for that fellow on the other side the wall, you know: we're very good friends, capital friends; but we are obliged to keep our traps set on both sides of the wall; we could not possibly keep on friendly terms without them, and our spring guns. The worst of it is, we are both clever fellows enough; and there's never a day passes that we don't find out a new trap, or a new gun-barrel, or something; we spend about fifteen millions a year each in our traps, take it altogether; and I don't see how we're to do with less.' A highly comic state of life for two private gentlemen! but for two nations, it seems to me, not wholly comic. Bedlam would be comic, perhaps, if there were only one madman in it; and your Christmas pantomime is comic, when there is only one clown in it; but when the whole world turns clown, and paints itself red with its own heart's blood instead of vermilion, it is something else than comic, I think.

Mind, I know a great deal of this is play, and willingly allow for that. You don't know what to do with yourselves for a sensation: fox-hunting and cricketing will not carry you through the whole of this unendurably long mortal life: you liked pop-guns when you were schoolboys, and rifles and Armstrongs are only the same things better made: but then the worst of it is, that what was play to you when boys, was not play to the sparrows; and what is play to you now, is not play to the small birds of State neither; and for the black eagles, you are somewhat shy of taking shots at them, if I mistake not.

I must get back to the matter in hand, however. Believe me, without farther instance, I could show you, in all time, that every nation's vice, or virtue, was written in its art: the soldiership of early Greece; the sensuality of late Italy; the visionary religion of Tuscany; the splendid human energy of Venice. I have no time to do this to-night (I have done it elsewhere before now); but I proceed to apply the principle to ourselves in a more searching manner.

I notice that among all the new buildings which cover your once wild hills, churches and schools are mixed in due, that is to say, in large proportion, with your mills and mansions; and I notice also that the churches and schools are almost always Gothic, and the mansions and mills are never Gothic. May I ask the meaning of this? for, remember, it is peculiarly a modern phenomenon. When Gothic was invented, houses were Gothic as well as churches; and when the Italian style superseded the Gothic, churches were Italian as well as houses. If there is a Gothic spire to the cathedral of Antwerp, there is a

Gothic belfry to the Hôtel de Ville at Brussels; if Inigo Jones builds an Italian Whitehall, Sir Christopher Wren builds an Italian St Paul's. But now you live under one school of architecture, and worship under another. What do you mean by doing this? Am I to understand that you are thinking of changing your architecture back to Gothic; and that you treat your churches experimentally, because it does not matter what mistakes you make in a church? Or am I to understand that you consider Gothic a pre-eminently sacred and beautiful mode of building, which you think, like the fine frankincense, should be mixed for the tabernacle only, and reserved for your religious services? For if this be the feeling, though it may seem at first as if it were graceful and reverent, at the root of the matter, it signifies neither more nor less than that you have separated your religion from your life.

For consider what a wide significance this fact has; and remember that it is not you only, but all the people of England, who are behaving thus, just now.

You have all got into the habit of calling the church 'the house of God.' I have seen, over the doors of many churches, the legend actually carved, '*This* is the house of God and this is the gate of heaven.' Now, note where that legend comes from, and of what place it was first spoken. A boy leaves his father's house to go on a long journey on foot, to visit his uncle: he has to cross a wild hill-desert; just as if one of your own boys had to cross the wolds to visit an uncle at Carlisle. The second or third day your

Traffic

boy finds himself somewhere between Hawes and Brough, in the midst of the moors, at sunset. It is stony ground, and boggy; he cannot go one foot farther that night. Down he lies, to sleep, on Wharnside, where best he may, gathering a few of the stones together to put under his head; – so wild the place is, he cannot get anything but stones. And there, lying under the broad night, he has a dream; and he sees a ladder set up on the earth, and the top of it reaches to heaven, and the angels of God are seen ascending and descending upon it. And when he wakes out of his sleep, he says, 'How dreadful is this place; surely this is none other than the house of God, and this is the gate of heaven.' This PLACE, observe; not this church; not this city; not this stone, even, which he puts up for a memorial – the piece of flint on which his head was lain. But this *place*; this windy slope of Wharnside; this moorland hollow, torrent-bitten, snow-blighted! this *any* place where God lets down the ladder. And how are you to know where that will be? or how are you to determine where it may be, but by being ready for it always? Do you know where the lightning is to fall next? You *do* know that, partly; you can guide the lightning; but you cannot guide the going forth of the Spirit, which is as that lightning when it shines from the east to the west.

But the perpetual and insolent warping of that strong verse to serve a merely ecclesiastical purpose, is only one of the thousand instances in which we sink back into gross Judaism. We call our churches 'temples.' Now, you know perfectly well they are *not* temples. They have never had, never can have, anything whatever to do with temples. They are 'synagogues' – 'gathering places' – where you gather yourselves together as an assembly; and by not calling them so, you again miss the force of another mighty text – 'Thou, when thou prayest, shalt not be as the hypocrites are; for they love to pray standing in the *churches*' [we should translate it], 'that they may be seen of men. But thou, when thou prayest, enter into thy closet, and when thou hast shut thy door, pray to thy Father,' – which is, not in chancel nor in aisle, but 'in secret.'

Now, you feel, as I say this to you – I know you feel – as if I were trying to take away the honour of your churches. Not so; I am trying to prove to you the honour of your houses and your hills; not that the Church is not sacred – but that the whole Earth is. I would have you feel what careless, what constant, what infectious sin there is in all modes of thought, whereby, in calling your churches only 'holy,' you call your hearths and homes 'profane'; and have separated yourselves from the heathen by casting all your household gods to the ground, instead of recognizing, in the places of their many and feeble Lares, the presence of your One and Mighty Lord and Lar.

'But what has all this to do with our Exchange?' you ask me, impatiently. My dear friends, it has just everything to do with it; on these inner and great questions depend all the outer and little ones; and if you have asked me down here to speak to you, because you had before been interested in anything I have written, you must know that all I have yet said about architecture was to show this. The book I called *The Seven Lamps* was to show that certain right states of temper and moral feeling were the magic powers by which all good architecture, without exception, had been produced. *The Stones of Venice* had, from beginning to end, no other aim than to show that the Gothic architecture of Venice had arisen out of, and indicated in all its features, a state of pure national faith, and of domestic virtue; and that its Renaissance architecture had arisen out of, and in all its features indicated, a state of concealed national infidelity, and of domestic corruption. And now, you ask me what style is best to build in, and how can I answer, knowing the meaning of the two styles, but by another question – do you mean to build as Christians or as infidels? And still more – do you mean to build as honest Christians or as honest infidels? as thoroughly and confessedly either one or the other? You don't like to be asked such rude questions. I cannot help it; they are of much more importance than this Exchange business; and if they can be at once answered, the Exchange business settles itself in a moment. But before I press them farther, I must ask leave to explain one point clearly.

In all my past work, my endeavour has been to show that good architecture is essentially religious – the production of a faithful and virtuous, not of an infidel and corrupted people. But in the course of doing this, I have had also to show that good architecture is not *ecclesiastical*. People are so apt to look upon religion as the business of the clergy, not their own, that the moment they hear of anything depending on 'religion,' they think it must also have depended on the priesthood; and I have had to take what place was to be occupied between these two errors, and fight both, often with seeming contradiction. Good architecture is the work of good and believing men; therefore, you say, at least some people say, 'Good architecture must essentially have been the work of the clergy, not of the laity.' No – a thousand times no; good architecture has always been the work of the commonalty, *not* of the clergy. 'What,' you say, 'those glorious cathedrals – the pride of Europe – did their builders not form Gothic architecture?' No; they corrupted Gothic architecture. Gothic was formed in the baron's castle, and the burgher's street. It was formed by the thoughts, and hands, and powers of labouring citizens and warrior kings. By the monk it was used as an instrument for the aid of his superstition: when that superstition became a beautiful madness, and the best hearts of Europe vainly dreamed and pined in the cloister, and vainly raged and perished in the crusade, – through that fury of perverted faith and wasted war, the Gothic rose also to its loveliest, most fantastic, and, finally, most foolish dreams; and in those dreams was lost.

Traffic

I hope, now, that there is no risk of your misunderstanding me when I come to the gist of what I want to say to-night; – when I repeat, that every great national architecture has been the result and exponent of a great national religion. You can't have bits of it here, bits there – you must have it everywhere or nowhere. It is not the monopoly of a clerical company – it is not the exponent of a theological dogma – it is not the hieroglyphic writing of an initiated priesthood; it is the manly language of a people inspired by resolute and common purpose, and rendering resolute and common fidelity to the legible laws of an undoubted God.

Now there have as yet been three distinct schools of European architecture. I say, European, because Asiatic and African architectures belong so entirely to other races and climates, that there is no question of them here; only, in passing, I will simply assure you that whatever is good or great in Egypt, and Syria, and India, is just good or great for the same reasons as the buildings on our side of the Bosphorus. We Europeans, then, have had three great religions: the Greek, which was the worship of the God of Wisdom and Power; the Mediæval, which was the worship of the God of Judgment and Consolation; the Renaissance, which was the worship of the God of Pride and Beauty: these three we have had – they are past, – and now, at last, we English have got a fourth religion, and a God of our own, about which I want to ask you. But I must explain these three old ones first.

John Ruskin

I repeat, first, the Greeks essentially worshipped the God of Wisdom; so that whatever contended against their religion, – to the Jews a stumbling-block, – was, to the Greeks – *Foolishness*.

The first Greek idea of deity was that expressed in the word, of which we keep the remnant in our words '*Di*-urnal' and '*Di*-vine' – the god of *Day*, Jupiter the revealer. Athena is his daughter, but especially daughter of the Intellect, springing armed from the head. We are only with the help of recent investigation beginning to penetrate the depth of meaning couched under the Athenaic symbols: but I may note rapidly, that her ægis, the mantle with the serpent fringes, in which she often, in the best statues, is represented as folding up her left hand, for better guard; and the Gorgon, on her shield, are both representative mainly of the chilling horror and sadness (turning men to stone, as it were,) of the outmost and superficial spheres of knowledge – that knowledge which separates, in bitterness, hardness, and sorrow, the heart of the full-grown man from the heart of the child. For out of imperfect knowledge spring terror, dissension, danger, and disdain; but from perfect knowledge, given by the full-revealed Athena, strength and peace, in sign of which she is crowned with the olive spray, and bears the resistless spear.

This, then, was the Greek conception of purest Deity; and every habit of life, and every form of his art developed themselves from the seeking this bright, serene, resistless wisdom; and setting himself, as a man, to do things evermore rightly and strongly;* not with any ardent affection or ultimate hope; but with a resolute and continent energy of will, as knowing that for failure there was no consolation, and for sin there was no remission. And the Greek architecture rose unerring, bright, clearly defined, and self-contained.

Next followed in Europe the great Christian faith, which was essentially the religion of Comfort. Its great doctrine is the remission of sins; for which cause, it happens, too often, in certain phases of Christianity, that sin and sickness themselves are partly glorified, as if, the more you had to be healed of, the more divine was the healing. The practical result of this doctrine, in art, is a continual contemplation of sin and disease, and of imaginary states of purification from them; thus we have an architecture conceived in a mingled sentiment of melancholy and aspiration, partly severe, partly luxuriant, which will bend itself to every one of our needs, and every one of our

---

* It is an error to suppose that the Greek worship, or seeking, was chiefly of Beauty. It was essentially of rightness and strength, founded on Forethought: the principal character of Greek art is not beauty, but design: and the Dorian Apollo-worship and Athenian Virgin-worship are both expressions of adoration of divine wisdom and purity. Next to these great deities, rank, in power over the national mind, Dionysus and Ceres, the givers of human strength and life; then, for heroic examples, Hercules. There is no Venus-worship among the Greeks in the great times: and the Muses are essentially teachers of Truth, and of its harmonies.

fancies, and be strong or weak with us, as we are strong or weak ourselves. It is, of all architecture, the basest, when base people build it – of all, the noblest, when built by the noble.

And now note that both these religions – Greek and Mediæval – perished by falsehood in their own main purpose. The Greek religion of Wisdom perished in a false philosophy – 'Oppositions of science, falsely so called.' The Mediæval religion of Consolation perished in false comfort; in remission of sins given lyingly. It was the selling of absolution that ended the Mediæval faith; and I can tell you more, it is the selling of absolution which, to the end of time, will mark false Christianity. Pure Christianity gives her remission of sins only by *ending* them; but false Christianity gets her remission of sins by *compounding for* them. And there are many ways of compounding for them. We English have beautiful little quiet ways of buying absolution, whether in low Church or high, far more cunning than any of Tetzel's trading.

Then, thirdly, there followed the religion of Pleasure, in which all Europe gave itself to luxury, ending in death. First, *bals masqués* in every saloon, and then guillotines in every square. And all these three worships issue in vast temple building. Your Greek worshipped Wisdom, and built you the Parthenon – the Virgin's temple. The Mediæval worshipped Consolation, and built you Virgin temples also – but to our Lady of Salvation. Then the Revivalist worshipped beauty, of a sort, and built you

Traffic

Versailles and the Vatican. Now, lastly, will you tell me what *we* worship, and what *we* build?

You know we are speaking always of the real, active, continual, national worship; that by which men act, while they live; not that which they talk of, when they die. Now, we have, indeed, a nominal religion, to which we pay tithes of property and sevenths of time; but we have also a practical and earnest religion, to which we devote nine-tenths of our property, and six-sevenths of our time. And we dispute a great deal about the nominal religion: but we are all unanimous about this practical one; of which I think you will admit that the ruling goddess may be best generally described as the 'Goddess of Getting-on,' or 'Britannia of the Market.' The Athenians had an 'Athena Agoraia,' or Athena of the Market; but she was a subordinate type of their goddess, while our Britannia Agoraia is the principal type of ours. And all your great architectural works are, of course, built to her. It is long since you built a great cathedral; and how you would laugh at me if I proposed building a cathedral on the top of one of these hills of yours, to make it an Acropolis! But your railroad mounds, vaster than the walls of Babylon; your railroad stations, vaster than the temple of Ephesus, and innumerable; your chimneys, how much more mighty and costly than cathedral spires! your harbour-piers; your warehouses; your exchanges! – all these are built to your great Goddess of 'Getting-on'; and she has formed, and will continue to form, your architecture, as long as you worship her; and it is quite vain to ask me to tell you how to build to *her*; you know far better than I.

There might, indeed, on some theories, be a conceivably good architecture for Exchanges – that is to say, if there were any heroism in the fact or deed of exchange, which might be typically carved on the outside of your building. For, you know, all beautiful architecture must be adorned with sculpture or painting; and for sculpture or painting, you must have a subject. And hitherto it has been a received opinion among the nations of the world that the only right subjects for either, were *heroisms* of some sort. Even on his pots and his flagons, the Greek put a Hercules slaying lions, or an Apollo slaying serpents, or Bacchus slaying melancholy giants, and earthborn despondencies. On his temples, the Greek put contests of great warriors in founding states, or of gods with evil spirits. On his houses and temples alike, the Christian put carvings of angels conquering devils; or of hero-martyrs exchanging this world for another: subject inappropriate, I think, to our direction of exchange here. And the Master of Christians not only left His followers without any orders as to the sculpture of affairs of exchange on the outside of buildings, but gave some strong evidence of His dislike of affairs of exchange within them. And yet there might surely be a heroism in such affairs; and all commerce become a kind of selling of doves, not impious. The wonder has always been great to me, that heroism has never been supposed to be in anywise consistent with the practice of supplying people with food, or clothes; but rather with that of quartering one's self upon them for food, and stripping them of their clothes. Spoiling of armour is an heroic deed in all ages; but the selling of clothes, old, or new, has never taken any colour of magnanimity. Yet one does not see why feeding the hungry and clothing the naked should ever become base businesses, even when engaged in on a large scale. If one could contrive to attach the notion of conquest to them anyhow! so that, supposing there were anywhere an obstinate race, who refused to be comforted, one might take some pride in giving them compulsory comfort!* and, as it were, '*occupying* a country' with one's gifts, instead of one's armies? If one could only consider it as much a victory to get a barren field sown, as to get an eared field stripped; and contend who should build villages, instead of who should 'carry' them! Are not all forms of heroism conceivable in doing these serviceable deeds? You doubt who is strongest? It might be ascertained by push of spade, as well as push of sword. Who is wisest? There are witty things to be thought of in planning other business than campaigns. Who is bravest? There are always the elements to fight with, stronger than men; and nearly as merciless.

The only absolutely and unapproachably heroic

---

*   Quite serious, all this, though it reads like jest.

element in the soldier's work seems to be – that he is paid little for it – and regularly: while you traffickers, and exchangers, and others occupied in presumably benevolent business, like to be paid much for it – and by chance. I never can make out how it is that a *knight*-errant does not expect to be paid for his trouble, but a *pedlar*-errant always does; – that people are willing to take hard knocks for nothing, but never to sell ribands cheap; that they are ready to go on fervent crusades, to recover the tomb of a buried God, but never on any travels to fulfil the orders of a living one; – that they will go anywhere barefoot to preach their faith, but must be well bribed to practise it, and are perfectly ready to give the Gospel gratis, but never the loaves and fishes.*

If you chose to take the matter up on any such soldierly principle; to do your commerce, and your feeding of nations, for fixed salaries; and to be as particular about giving people the best food, and the best cloth, as soldiers are about giving them the best gunpowder, I could carve something for you on your exchange worth looking at. But I can only at present suggest decorating its frieze with pendant purses; and making its pillars broad at the base, for the sticking of bills. And in the innermost chambers of it there might be a statue of Britannia of the Market, who may have, perhaps advisably, a partridge

---

* Please think over this paragraph, too briefly and antithetically put, but one of those which I am happiest in having written.

Traffic

for her crest, typical at once of her courage in fighting for noble ideas, and of her interest in game; and round its neck, the inscription in golden letters, 'Perdix fovit quæ non peperit.'* Then, for her spear, she might have a weaver's beam; and on her shield, instead of St George's Cross, the Milanese boar, semi-fleeced, with the town of Gennesaret proper, in the field; and the legend, 'In the best market,'† and her corslet, of leather, folded over her heart in the shape of a purse, with thirty slits in it, for a piece of money to go in at, on each day of the month. And I doubt not but that people would come to see your exchange, and its goddess, with applause.

Nevertheless, I want to point out to you certain strange characters in this goddess of yours. She differs from the great Greek and Mediæval deities essentially in two things — first, as to the continuance of her presumed power; secondly, as to the extent of it.

1st, as to the Continuance.

The Greek Goddess of Wisdom gave continual increase of wisdom, as the Christian Spirit of Comfort (or Comforter) continual increase of comfort. There was no question, with these, of any limit or cessation of function. But with your Agora Goddess, that is just the most

---

* Jerem. xvii. 11 (best in Septuagint and Vulgate). 'As the partridge, fostering what she brought not forth, so he that getteth riches, not by right, shall leave them in the midst of his days, and at his end shall be a fool.'
† Meaning, fully, 'We have brought our pigs to it.'

John Ruskin

important question. Getting on – but where to? Gathering together – but how much? Do you mean to gather always – never to spend? If so, I wish you joy of your goddess, for I am just as well off as you, without the trouble of worshipping her at all. But if you do not spend, somebody else will – somebody else must. And it is because of this (among many other such errors) that I have fearlessly declared your so-called science of Political Economy to be no science; because, namely, it has omitted the study of exactly the most important branch of the business – the study of *spending*. For spend you must, and as much as you make, ultimately. You gather corn: – will you bury England under a heap of grain; or will you, when you have gathered, finally eat? You gather gold: – will you make your house-roofs of it, or pave your streets with it? That is still one way of spending it. But if you keep it, that you may get more, I'll give you more; I'll give you all the gold you want – all you can imagine – if you can tell me what you'll do with it. You shall have thousands of gold pieces; – thousands of thousands – millions – mountains, of gold: where will you keep them? Will you put an Olympus of silver upon a golden Pelion – make Ossa like a wart? Do you think the rain and dew would then come down to you, in the streams from such mountains, more blessedly than they will down the mountains which God has made for you, of moss and whinstone? But it is not gold that you want to gather! What is it? greenbacks? No; not those neither. What is it

Traffic

then – is it ciphers after a capital I? Cannot you practise writing ciphers, and write as many as you want! Write ciphers for an hour every morning, in a big book, and say every evening, I am worth all those noughts more than I was yesterday. Won't that do? Well, what in the name of Plutus is it you want? Not gold, not greenbacks, not ciphers after a capital I? You will have to answer, after all, 'No; we want, somehow or other, money's *worth*.' Well, what is that? Let your Goddess of Getting-on discover it, and let her learn to stay therein.

II. But there is yet another question to be asked respecting this Goddess of Getting-on. The first was of the continuance of her power; the second is of its extent.

Pallas and the Madonna were supposed to be all the world's Pallas, and all the world's Madonna. They could teach all men, and they could comfort all men. But, look strictly into the nature of the power of your Goddess of Getting-on; and you will find she is the Goddess – not of everybody's getting on – but only of somebody's getting on. This is a vital, or rather deathful, distinction. Examine it in your own ideal of the state of national life which this Goddess is to evoke and maintain. I asked you what it was, when I was last here; – you have never told me. Now, shall I try to tell you?

Your ideal of human life then is, I think, that it should be passed in a pleasant undulating world, with iron and coal everywhere underneath it. On each pleasant bank of this world is to be a beautiful mansion, with two wings;

John Ruskin

and stables, and coach-houses; a moderately-sized park; a large garden and hot-houses; and pleasant carriage drives through the shrubberies. In this mansion are to live the favoured votaries of the Goddess; the English gentleman, with his gracious wife, and his beautiful family; he always able to have the boudoir and the jewels for the wife, and the beautiful ball dresses for the daughters, and hunters for the sons, and a shooting in the Highlands for himself. At the bottom of the bank, is to be the mill; not less than a quarter of a mile long, with one steam engine at each end, and two in the middle, and a chimney three hundred feet high. In this mill are to be in constant employment from eight hundred to a thousand workers, who never drink, never strike, always go to church on Sunday, and always express themselves in respectful language.

Is not that, broadly, and in the main features, the kind of thing you propose to yourselves? It is very pretty indeed, seen from above; not at all so pretty, seen from below. For, observe, while to one family this deity is indeed the Goddess of Getting-on, to a thousand families she is the Goddess of *not* Getting-on. 'Nay,' you say, 'they have all their chance.' Yes, so has every one in a lottery, but there must always be the same number of blanks. 'Ah! but in a lottery it is not skill and intelligence which take the lead, but blind chance.' What then! do you think the old practice, that 'they should take who have the power, and they should keep who can,' is less iniquitous, when the power has become power of brains instead of fist? and that, though we may not take advantage of a child's or a woman's weakness, we may of a man's foolishness? 'Nay, but finally, work must be done, and some one must be at the top, some one at the bottom.' Granted, my friends. Work must always be, and captains of work must always be; and if you in the least remember the tone of any of my writings, you must know that they are thought unfit for this age, because they are always insisting on need of government, and speaking with scorn of liberty. But I beg you to observe that there is a wide difference between being captains or governors of work, and taking the profits of it. It does not follow, because you are general of an army, that you are to take all the treasure, or land, it wins; (if it fight for treasure or land;) neither, because you are king of a nation, that you are to consume all the profits of the nation's work. Real kings, on the contrary, are known invariably by their doing quite the reverse of this, – by their taking the least possible quantity of the nation's work for themselves. There is no test of real kinghood so infallible as that. Does the crowned creature live simply, bravely, unostentatiously? probably he *is* a King. Does he cover his body with jewels, and his table with delicates? in all probability he is *not* a King. It is possible he may be, as Solomon was; but that is when the nation shares his splendour with him. Solomon made gold, not only to be in his own palace as stones, but to be in Jerusalem as stones. But, even so, for the most part, these splendid kinghoods expire in ruin, and only the true kinghoods live, which are of royal labourers governing loyal labourers; who, both leading rough lives, establish the true dynasties. Conclusively you will find that because you are king of a nation, it does not follow that you are to gather for yourself all the wealth of that nation; neither, because you are king of a small part of the nation, and lord over the means of its maintenance – over field, or mill, or mine, – are you to take all the produce of that piece of the foundation of national existence for yourself.

You will tell me I need not preach against these things, for I cannot mend them. No, good friends, I cannot; but you can, and you will; or something else can and will. Even good things have no abiding power – and shall these evil things persist in victorious evil? All history shows, on the contrary, that to be the exact thing they never can do. Change *must* come; but it is ours to determine whether change of growth, or change of death. Shall the Parthenon be in ruins on its rock, and Bolton priory in its meadow, but these mills of yours be the consummation of the buildings of the earth, and their wheels be as the wheels of eternity? Think you that 'men may come, and men may go,' but – mills – go on for ever? Not so; out of these, better or worse shall come; and it is for you to choose which.

I know that none of this wrong is done with deliberate purpose. I know, on the contrary, that you wish your workmen well; that you do much for them, and that you desire to do more for them, if you saw your way to such benevolence safely. I know that even all this wrong and misery are brought about by a warped sense of duty, each of you striving to do his best; but, unhappily, not knowing for whom this best should be done. And all our hearts have been betrayed by the plausible impiety of the modern economist, telling us that, 'To do the best for ourselves, is finally to do the best for others.' Friends, our great Master said not so; and most absolutely we shall find this world is not made so. Indeed, to do the best for others, is finally to do the best for ourselves; but it will not do to have our eyes fixed on that issue. The Pagans had got beyond that. Hear what a Pagan says of this matter; hear what were, perhaps, the last written words of Plato, – if not the last actually written (for this we cannot know), yet assuredly in fact and power his parting words – in which, endeavouring to give full crowning and harmonious close to all his thoughts, and to speak the sum of them by the imagined sentence of the Great Spirit, his strength and his heart fail him, and the words cease, broken off for ever.

They are at the close of the dialogue called *Critias*, in which he describes, partly from real tradition, partly in ideal dream, the early state of Athens; and the genesis, and order, and religion, of the fabled isle of Atlantis; in which genesis he conceives the same first perfection and final degeneracy of man, which in our own Scriptural tradition is expressed by saying that the Sons of God inter-married with the daughters of men, for he supposes the earliest race to have been indeed the children of God; and to have corrupted themselves, until 'their spot was not the spot of his children.' And this, he says, was the end; that indeed 'through many generations, so long as the God's nature in them yet was full, they were submissive to the sacred laws, and carried themselves lovingly to all that had kindred with them in divineness; for their uttermost spirit was faithful and true, and in every wise great; so that, in *all meekness of wisdom, they dealt with each other*, and took all the chances of life; and despising all things except virtue, they cared little what happened day by day, and *bore lightly the burden* of gold and of possessions; for they saw that, if *only their common love and virtue increased, all these things would be increased together with them*; but to set their esteem and ardent pursuit upon material possession would be to lose that first, and their virtue and affection together with it. And by such reasoning, and what of the divine nature remained in them, they gained all this greatness of which we have already told; but when the God's part of them faded and became extinct, being mixed again and again, and effaced by the prevalent mortality; and the human nature at last exceeded, they then became unable to endure the courses of fortune; and fell into shapelessness of life, and baseness in the sight of him who could see, having lost everything that was fairest of their honour; while to the blind hearts

Traffic

which could not discern the true life, tending to happiness, it seemed that they were then chiefly noble and happy, being filled with all iniquity of inordinate possession and power. Whereupon, the God of Gods, whose Kinghood is in laws, beholding a once just nation thus cast into misery, and desiring to lay such punishment upon them as might make them repent into restraining, gathered together all the gods into his dwelling place, which from heaven's centre overlooks whatever has part in creation; and having assembled them, he said'—

The rest is silence. Last words of the chief wisdom of the heathen, spoken of this idol of riches; this idol of yours; this golden image, high by measureless cubits, set up where your green fields of England are furnace-burnt into the likeness of the plain of Dura: this idol, forbidden to us, first of all idols, by our own Master and faith; forbidden to us also by every human lip that has ever, in any age or people, been accounted of as able to speak according to the purposes of God. Continue to make that forbidden deity your principal one, and soon no more art, no more science, no more pleasure will be possible. Catastrophe will come; or, worse than catastrophe, slow mouldering and withering into Hades. But if you can fix some conception of a true human state of life to be striven for – life, good for all men, as for yourselves; if you can determine some honest and simple order of existence; following those trodden ways of wisdom, which are pleasantness, and seeking her quiet and withdrawn paths, which are peace;* – then, and so sanctifying wealth into 'commonwealth,' all your art, your literature, your daily labours, your domestic affection, and citizen's duty, will join and increase into one magnificent harmony. You will know then how to build, well enough; you will build with stone well, but with flesh better; temples not made with hands, but riveted of hearts; and that kind of marble, crimson-veined, is indeed eternal.

---

*   I imagine the Hebrew chant merely intends passionate repetition, and not a distinction of this somewhat fanciful kind; yet we may profitably make it in reading the English.

The Roots of Honour

Among the delusions which at different periods have possessed themselves of the minds of large masses of the human race, perhaps the most curious – certainly the least creditable – is the modern *soi-disant* science of political economy, based on the idea that an advantageous code of social action may be determined irrespectively of the influence of social affection.

Of course, as in the instances of alchemy, astrology, witchcraft, and other such popular creeds, political economy has a plausible idea at the root of it. 'The social affections,' says the economist, 'are accidental and disturbing elements in human nature; but avarice and the desire of progress are constant elements. Let us eliminate the inconstants, and, considering the human being merely as a covetous machine, examine by what laws of labour, purchase, and sale, the greatest accumulative result in wealth is obtainable. Those laws once determined, it will be for each individual afterwards to introduce as much of the disturbing affectionate element as he chooses, and to determine for himself the result on the new conditions supposed.'

John Ruskin

This would be a perfectly logical and successful method of analysis, if the accidentals afterwards to be introduced were of the same nature as the powers first examined. Supposing a body in motion to be influenced by constant and inconstant forces, it is usually the simplest way of examining its course to trace it first under the persistent conditions, and afterwards introduce the causes of variation. But the disturbing elements in the social problem are not of the same nature as the constant ones: they alter the essence of the creature under examination the moment they are added; they operate, not mathematically, but chemically, introducing conditions which render all our previous knowledge unavailable. We made learned experiments upon pure nitrogen, and have convinced ourselves that it is a very manageable gas: but, behold! the thing which we have practically to deal with is its chloride; and this, the moment we touch it on our established principles, sends us and our apparatus through the ceiling.

Observe, I neither impugn nor doubt the conclusion of the science if its terms are accepted. I am simply uninterested in them, as I should be in those of a science of gymnastics which assumed that men had no skeletons. It might be shown, on that supposition, that it would be advantageous to roll the students up into pellets, flatten them into cakes, or stretch them into cables; and that when these results were effected, the re-insertion of the skeleton would be attended with various inconveniences to their constitution. The reasoning might be admirable, the conclusions true, and the science deficient only in applicability. Modern political economy stands on a precisely similar basis. Assuming, not that the human being has no skeleton, but that it is all skeleton, it founds an ossifiant theory of progress on this negation of a soul; and having shown the utmost that may be made of bones, and constructed a number of interesting geometrical figures with death's-head and humeri, successfully proves the inconvenience of the reappearance of a soul among these corpuscular structures. I do not deny the truth of this theory: I simply deny its applicability to the present phase of the world.

This inapplicability has been curiously manifested during the embarrassment caused by the late strikes of our workmen. Here occurs one of the simplest cases, in a pertinent and positive form, of the first vital problem which political economy has to deal with (the relation between employer and employed); and, at a severe crisis, when lives in multitudes and wealth in masses are at stake, the political economists are helpless – practically mute: no demonstrable solution of the difficulty can be given by them, such as may convince or calm the opposing parties. Obstinately the masters take one view of the matter; obstinately the operatives another; and no political science can set them at one.

It would be strange if it could, it being not by 'science' of any kind that men were ever intended to be set at one. Disputant after disputant vainly strives to show that the interests of the masters are, or are not, antagonistic to those of the men: none of the pleaders ever seeming to remember that it does not absolutely or always follow that the persons must be antagonistic because their interests are. If there is only a crust of bread in the house, and mother and children are starving, their interests are not the same. If the mother eats it, the children want it; if the children eat it, the mother must go hungry to her work. Yet it does not necessarily follow that there will be 'antagonism' between them, that they will fight for the crust, and that the mother, being strongest, will get it, and eat it. Neither, in any other case, whatever the relations of the persons may be, can it be assumed for certain that, because their interests are diverse, they must necessarily regard each other with hostility, and use violence or cunning to obtain the advantage.

Even if this were so, and it were as just as it is convenient to consider men as actuated by no other moral influences than those which affect rats or swine, the logical conditions of the question are still indeterminable. It can never be shown generally either that the interests of master and labourer are alike, or that they are opposed; for, according to circumstances, they may be either. It is, indeed, always the interest of both that the work should be rightly done, and a just price obtained for it; but, in the division of profits, the gain of the one may or may not be the loss of the other. It is not the master's interest to pay wages so low as to leave the men sickly and depressed, nor the workman's interest to be paid high wages if the smallness of the master's profit hinders him from enlarging

The Roots of Honour

his business, or conducting it in a safe and liberal way. A stoker ought not to desire high pay if the company is too poor to keep the engine-wheels in repair.

And the varieties of circumstance which influence these reciprocal interests are so endless, that all endeavour to deduce rules of action from balance of expediency is in vain. And it is meant to be in vain. For no human actions ever were intended by the Maker of men to be guided by balances of expediency, but by balances of justice. He has therefore rendered all endeavours to determine expediency futile for evermore. No man ever knew, or can know, what will be the ultimate result to himself, or to others, of any given line of conduct. But every man may know, and most of us do know, what is a just and unjust act. And all of us may know also, that the consequences of justice will be ultimately the best possible, both to others and ourselves, though we can neither say what *is* best, or how it is likely to come to pass.

I have said balances of justice, meaning, in the term justice, to include affection, – such affection as one man *owes* to another. All right relations between master and operative, and all their best interests, ultimately depend on these.

We shall find the best and simplest illustration of the relations of master and operative in the position of domestic servants.

We will suppose that the master of a household desires only to get as much work out of his servants as he can, at the rate of wages he gives. He never allows them to be idle;

feeds them as poorly and lodges them as ill as they will endure, and in all things pushes his requirements to the exact point beyond which he cannot go without forcing the servant to leave him. In doing this, there is no violation on his part of what is commonly called 'justice.' He agrees with the domestic for his whole time and service, and takes them; – the limits of hardship in treatment being fixed by the practice of other masters in his neighbourhood; that is to say, by the current rate of wages for domestic labour. If the servant can get a better place, he is free to take one, and the master can only tell what is the real market value of his labour, by requiring as much as he will give.

This is the politico-economical view of the case, according to the doctors of that science; who assert that by this procedure the greatest average of work will be obtained from the servant, and therefore the greatest benefit to the community, and through the community, by reversion, to the servant himself.

That, however, is not so. It would be so if the servant were an engine of which the motive power was steam, magnetism, gravitation, or any other agent of calculable force. But he being, on the contrary, an engine whose motive power is a Soul, the force of this very peculiar agent, as an unknown quantity, enters into all the political economist's equations, without his knowledge, and falsifies every one of their results. The largest quantity of work will not be done by this curious engine for pay, or under pressure, or by help of any kind of fuel which may be supplied by the chaldron. It will

The Roots of Honour

be done only when the motive force, that is to say, the will or spirit of the creature, is brought to its greatest strength by its own proper fuel: namely, by the affections.

It may indeed happen, and does happen often, that if the master is a man of sense and energy, a large quantity of material work may be done under mechanical pressure, enforced by strong will and guided by wise method; also it may happen, and does happen often, that if the master is indolent and weak (however good-natured), a very small quantity of work, and that bad, may be produced by the servant's undirected strength, and contemptuous gratitude. But the universal law of the matter is that, assuming any given quantity of energy and sense in master and servant, the greatest material result obtainable by them will be, not through antagonism to each other, but through affection for each other; and that, if the master, instead of endeavouring to get as much work as possible from the servant, seeks rather to render his appointed and necessary work beneficial to him, and to forward his interests in all just and wholesome ways, the real amount of work ultimately done, or of good rendered, by the person so cared for, will indeed be the greatest possible.

Observe, I say, 'of good rendered,' for a servant's work is not necessarily or always the best thing he can give his master. But good of all kinds, whether in material service, in protective watchfulness of his master's interest and credit, or in joyful readiness to seize unexpected and irregular occasions of help.

John Ruskin

Nor is this one whit less generally true because indulgence will be frequently abused, and kindness met with ingratitude. For the servant who, gently treated, is ungrateful, treated ungently, will be revengeful; and the man who is dishonest to a liberal master will be injurious to an unjust one.

In any case, and with any person, this unselfish treatment will produce the most effective return. Observe, I am here considering the affections wholly as a motive power; not at all as things in themselves desirable or noble, or in any other way abstractedly good. I look at them simply as an anomalous force, rendering every one of the ordinary political economist's calculations nugatory; while, even if he desired to introduce this new element into his estimates, he has no power of dealing with it; for the affections only become a true motive power when they ignore every other motive and condition of political economy. Treat the servant kindly, with the idea of turning his gratitude to account, and you will get, as you deserve, no gratitude, nor any value for your kindness; but treat him kindly without any economical purpose, and all economical purposes will be answered; in this, as in all other matters, whosoever will save his life shall lose it, whoso loses it shall find it.*

---

* The difference between the two modes of treatment, and between their effective material results, may be seen very accurately by a comparison of the relations of Esther and Charlie in *Bleak House*

The Roots of Honour

The next clearest and simplest example of relation between master and operative is that which exists between the commander of a regiment and his men.

Supposing the officer only desires to apply the rules of discipline so as, with least trouble to himself, to make the regiment most effective, he will not be able, by any rules or administration of rules, on this selfish principle, to

---

with those of Miss Brass and the Marchioness in *Master Humphrey's Clock*.

The essential value and truth of Dickens's writings have been unwisely lost sight of by many thoughtful persons, merely because he presents his truth with some colour of caricature. Unwisely, because Dickens's caricature, though often gross, is never mistaken. Allowing for his manner of telling them, the things he tells us are always true. I wish that he could think it right to limit his brilliant exaggeration to works written only for public amusement; and when he takes up a subject of high national importance, such as that which he handled in *Hard Times*, that he would use severer and more accurate analysis. The usefulness of that work (to my mind, in several respects the greatest he has written) is with many persons seriously diminished because Mr Bounderby is a dramatic monster, instead of a characteristic example of a worldly master; and Stephen Blackpool a dramatic perfection, instead of a characteristic example of an honest workman. But let us not lose the use of Dickens's wit and insight, because he chooses to speak in a circle of stage fire. He is entirely right in his main drift and purpose in every book he has written; and all of them, but especially *Hard Times*, should be studied with close and earnest care by persons interested in social questions. They will find much that is partial, and, because partial, apparently unjust; but if they examine all the evidence on the other side, which Dickens seems to overlook, it will appear, after all their trouble, that his view was the finally right one, grossly and sharply told.

develop the full strength of his subordinates. If a man of sense and firmness, he may, as in the former instance, produce a better result than would be obtained by the irregular kindness of a weak officer; but let the sense and firmness be the same in both cases, and assuredly the officer who has the most direct personal relations with his men, the most care for their interests, and the most value for their lives, will develop their effective strength, through their affection for his own person, and trust in his character, to a degree wholly unattainable by other means. This law applies still more stringently as the numbers concerned are larger: a charge may often be successful, though the men dislike their officers; a battle has rarely been won, unless they loved their general.

Passing from these simple examples to the more complicated relations existing between a manufacturer and his workmen, we are met first by certain curious difficulties, resulting, apparently, from a harder and colder state of moral elements. It is easy to imagine an enthusiastic affection existing among soldiers for the colonel. Not so easy to imagine an enthusiastic affection among cotton-spinners for the proprietor of the mill. A body of men associated for purposes of robbery (as a Highland clan in ancient times) shall be animated by perfect affection, and every member of it be ready to lay down his life for the life of his chief. But a band of men associated for purposes of legal production and accumulation is usually animated, it appears, by no such emotions, and none of

The Roots of Honour

them are in any wise willing to give his life for the life of his chief. Not only are we met by this apparent anomaly, in moral matters, but by others connected with it, in administration of system. For a servant or a soldier is engaged at a definite rate of wages, for a definite period; but a workman at a rate of wages variable according to the demand for labour, and with the risk of being at any time thrown out of his situation by chances of trade. Now, as, under these contingencies, no action of the affections can take place, but only an explosive action of *dis*affections, two points offer themselves for consideration in the matter.

The first – How far the rate of wages may be so regulated as not to vary with the demand for labour.

The second – How far it is possible that bodies of workmen may be engaged and maintained at such fixed rate of wages (whatever the state of trade may be), without enlarging or diminishing their number, so as to give them permanent interest in the establishment with which they are connected, like that of the domestic servants in an old family, or an *esprit de corps*, like that of the soldiers in a crack regiment.

The first question is, I say, how far it may be possible to fix the rate of wages, irrespectively of the demand for labour.

Perhaps one of the most curious facts in the history of human error is the denial by the common political economist of the possibility of thus regulating wages; while, for all the important, and much of the unimportant, labour, on the earth, wages are already so regulated.

We do not sell our prime-ministership by Dutch auction; nor, on the decease of a bishop, whatever may be the general advantages of simony, do we (yet) offer his diocese to the clergyman who will take the episcopacy at the lowest contract. We (with exquisite sagacity of political economy!) do indeed sell commissions; but not openly, generalships: sick, we do not inquire for a physician who takes less than a guinea; litigious, we never think of reducing six-and-eightpence to four-and-sixpence; caught in a shower, we do not canvass the cabmen, to find one who values his driving at less than sixpence a mile.

It is true that in all these cases there is, and in every conceivable case there must be, ultimate reference to the presumed difficulty of the work, or number of candidates for the office. If it were thought that the labour necessary to make a good physician would be gone through by a sufficient number of students with the prospect of only half-guinea fees, public consent would soon withdraw the unnecessary half-guinea. In this ultimate sense, the price of labour is indeed always regulated by the demand for it; but, so far as the practical and immediate administration of the matter is regarded, the best labour always has been, and is, as *all* labour ought to be, paid by an invariable standard.

'What!' the reader perhaps answers amazedly: 'pay good and bad workmen alike?'

The Roots of Honour

Certainly. The difference between one prelate's sermons and his successor's – or between one physician's opinion and another's, – is far greater, as respects the qualities of mind involved, and far more important in result to you personally, than the difference between good and bad laying of bricks (though that is greater than most people suppose). Yet you pay with equal fee, contentedly, the good and bad workmen upon your soul, and the good and bad workmen upon your body; much more may you pay, contentedly, with equal fees, the good and bad workmen upon your house.

'Nay, but I choose my physician, and (?) my clergyman, thus indicating my sense of the quality of their work.' By all means, also, choose your bricklayer; that is the proper reward of the good workman, to be 'chosen.' The natural and right system respecting all labour is, that it should be paid at a fixed rate, but the good workman employed, and the bad workman unemployed. The false, unnatural, and destructive system is when the bad workman is allowed to offer his work at half-price, and either take the place of the good, or force him by his competition to work for an inadequate sum.

This equality of wages, then, being the first object towards which we have to discover the directest available road, the second is, as above stated, that of maintaining constant numbers of workmen in employment, whatever may be the accidental demand for the article they produce.

John Ruskin

I believe the sudden and extensive inequalities of demand, which necessarily arise in the mercantile operations of an active nation, constitute the only essential difficulty which has to be overcome in a just organization of labour.

The subject opens into too many branches to admit of being investigated in a paper of this kind; but the following general facts bearing on it may be noted.

The wages which enable any workman to live are necessarily higher, if his work is liable to intermission, than if it is assured and continuous; and however severe the struggle for work may become, the general law will always hold, that men must get more daily pay if, on the average, they can only calculate on work three days a week than they would require if they were sure of work six days a week. Supposing that a man cannot live on less than a shilling a day, his seven shillings he must get, either for three days' violent work, or six days' deliberate work. The tendency of all modern mercantile operations is to throw both wages and trade into the form of a lottery, and to make the workman's pay depend on intermittent exertion, and the principal's profit on dexterously used chance.

In what partial degree, I repeat, this may be necessary in consequence of the activities of modern trade, I do not here investigate; contenting myself with the fact that in its fatallest aspects it is assuredly unnecessary, and results merely from love of gambling on the part of the masters, and from ignorance and sensuality in the men. The masters cannot bear to let any opportunity of gain escape them, and frantically rush at every gap and breach in the walls of Fortune, raging to be rich, and affronting, with impatient covetousness, every risk of ruin, while the men prefer three days of violent labour, and three days of drunkenness, to six days of moderate work and wise rest. There is no way in which a principal, who really desires to help his workmen, may do it more effectually than by checking these disorderly habits both in himself and them; keeping his own business operations on a scale which will enable him to pursue them securely, not yielding to temptations of precarious gain; and at the same time, leading his workmen into regular habits of labour and life, either by inducing them rather to take low wages, in the form of a fixed salary, than high wages, subject to the chance of their being thrown out of work; or, if this be impossible, by discouraging the system of violent exertion for nominally high day wages, and leading the men to take lower pay for more regular labour.

In effecting any radical changes of this kind, doubtless there would be great inconvenience and loss incurred by all the originators of the movement. That which can be done with perfect convenience and without loss, is not always the thing that most needs to be done, or which we are most imperatively required to do.

I have already alluded to the difference hitherto existing between regiments of men associated for purposes of violence, and for purposes of manufacture; in that the former appear capable of self-sacrifice – the latter, not; which singular fact is the real reason of the general lowness of estimate in which the profession of commerce is held, as compared with that of arms. Philosophically, it does not, at first sight, appear reasonable (many writers have endeavoured to prove it unreasonable) that a peaceable and rational person, whose trade is buying and selling, should be held in less honour than an unpeaceable and often irrational person, whose trade is slaying. Nevertheless, the consent of mankind has always, in spite of the philosophers, given precedence to the soldier.

And this is right.

For the soldier's trade, verily and essentially, is not slaying, but being slain. This, without well knowing its own meaning, the world honours it for. A bravo's trade is slaying; but the world has never respected bravos more than merchants: the reason it honours the soldier is, because he holds his life at the service of the State. Reckless he may be – fond of pleasure or of adventure – all kinds of bye-motives and mean impulses may have determined the choice of his profession, and may affect (to all appearance exclusively) his daily conduct in it; but our estimate of him is based on this ultimate fact – of which we are well assured – that put him in a fortress breach, with all the pleasures of the world behind him, and only death and his duty in front of him, he will keep his face to the front; and he knows that his choice may be put to him at any

The Roots of Honour

moment – and has beforehand taken his part – virtually takes such part continually – does, in reality, die daily.

Not less is the respect we pay to the lawyer and physician, founded ultimately on their self-sacrifice. Whatever the learning or acuteness of a great lawyer, our chief respect for him depends on our belief that, set in a judge's seat, he will strive to judge justly, come of it what may. Could we suppose that he would take bribes, and use his acuteness and legal knowledge to give plausibility to iniquitous decisions, no degree of intellect would win for him our respect. Nothing will win it, short of our tacit conviction, that in all important acts of his life justice is first with him; his own interest, second.

In the case of a physician, the ground of the honour we render him is clearer still. Whatever his science, we would shrink from him in horror if we found him regard his patients merely as subjects to experiment upon; much more, if we found that, receiving bribes from persons interested in their deaths, he was using his best skill to give poison in the mask of medicine.

Finally, the principle holds with utmost clearness as it respects clergymen. No goodness of disposition will excuse want of science in a physician, or of shrewdness in an advocate; but a clergyman, even though his power of intellect be small, is respected on the presumed ground of his unselfishness and serviceableness.

Now, there can be no question but that the tact,

foresight, decision, and other mental powers, required for the successful management of a large mercantile concern, if not such as could be compared with those of a great lawyer, general, or divine, would at least match the general conditions of mind required in the subordinate officers of a ship, or of a regiment, or in the curate of a country parish. If, therefore, all the efficient members of the so-called liberal professions are still, somehow, in public estimate of honour, preferred before the head of a commercial firm, the reason must lie deeper than in the measurement of their several powers of mind.

And the essential reason for such preference will be found to lie in the fact that the merchant is presumed to act always selfishly. His work may be very necessary to the community; but the motive of it is understood to be wholly personal. The merchant's first object in all his dealings must be (the public believe) to get as much for himself, and leave as little to his neighbour (or customer) as possible. Enforcing this upon him, by political statute, as the necessary principle of his action; recommending it to him on all occasions, and themselves reciprocally adopting it, proclaiming vociferously, for law of the universe, that a buyer's function is to cheapen, and a seller's to cheat, – the public, nevertheless, involuntarily condemn the man of commerce for his compliance with their own statement, and stamp him for ever as belonging to an inferior grade of human personality.

This they will find, eventually, they must give up doing.

They must not cease to condemn selfishness; but they will have to discover a kind of commerce which is not exclusively selfish. Or, rather, they will have to discover that there never was, or can be, any other kind of commerce; that this which they have called commerce was not commerce at all, but cozening; and that a true merchant differs as much from a merchant according to laws of modern political economy, as the hero of the *Excursion* from Autolycus. They will find that commerce is an occupation which gentlemen will every day see more need to engage in, rather than in the businesses of talking to men, or slaying them; that, in true commerce, as in true preaching, or true fighting, it is necessary to admit the idea of occasional voluntary loss; – that sixpences have to be lost, as well as lives, under a sense of duty; that the market may have its martyrdoms as well as the pulpit; and trade its heroisms as well as war.

May have – in the final issue, must have – and only has not had yet, because men of heroic temper have always been misguided in their youth into other fields; not recognizing what is in our days, perhaps, the most important of all fields; so that, while many a zealous person loses his life in trying to teach the form of a gospel, very few will lose a hundred pounds in showing the practice of one.

The fact is, that people never have had clearly explained to them the true functions of a merchant with respect to other people. I should like the reader to be very clear about this.

John Ruskin

Five great intellectual professions, relating to daily necessities of life, have hitherto existed – three exist necessarily, in every civilized nation:

The Soldier's profession is to *defend* it.

The Pastor's to *teach* it.

The Physician's to *keep it in health*.

The Lawyer's to *enforce justice* in it.

The Merchant's to *provide* for it.

And the duty of all these men is, on due occasion, to *die* for it.

'On due occasion,' namely: –

The Soldier, rather than leave his post in battle.

The Physician, rather than leave his post in plague.

The Pastor, rather than teach Falsehood.

The Lawyer, rather than countenance Injustice.

The Merchant – what is *his* 'due occasion' of death?

It is the main question for the merchant, as for all of us. For, truly, the man who does not know when to die, does not know how to live.

Observe, the merchant's function (or manufacturer's, for in the broad sense in which it is here used the word must be understood to include both) is to provide for the nation. It is no more his function to get profit for himself out of that provision than it is a clergyman's function to get his stipend. This stipend is a due and necessary adjunct, but not the object of his life, if he be a true clergyman, any more than his fee (or honorarium) is the object of life to a true physician. Neither is his fee the object of life to a true merchant. All three, if true men, have a work to be done irrespective of fee – to be done even at any cost, or for quite the contrary of fee; the pastor's function being to teach, the physician's to heal, and the merchant's, as I have said, to provide. That is to say, he has to understand to their very root the qualities of the thing he deals in, and the means of obtaining or producing it; and he has to apply all his sagacity and energy to the producing or obtaining it in perfect state, and distributing it at the cheapest possible price where it is most needed.

And because the production or obtaining of any commodity involves necessarily the agency of many lives and hands, the merchant becomes in the course of his business the master and governor of large masses of men in a more direct, though less confessed way, than a military officer or pastor; so that on him falls, in great part, the responsibility for the kind of life they lead: and it becomes his duty, not only to be always considering how to produce what he sells, in the purest and cheapest forms, but how to make the various employments involved in the production, or transference of it, most beneficial to the men employed.

And as into these two functions, requiring for their right exercise the highest intelligence, as well as patience, kindness, and tact, the merchant is bound to put all his energy, so for their just discharge he is bound, as soldier or physician is bound, to give up, if need be, his life, in such way as it may be demanded of him. Two main points he has in his providing function to maintain: first, his engagements (faithfulness to engagements being the real root of all possibilities, in commerce); and, secondly, the perfectness and purity of the thing provided; so that, rather than fail in any engagement, or consent to any deterioration, adulteration, or unjust and exorbitant price of that which he provides, he is bound to meet fearlessly any form of distress, poverty, or labour, which may, through maintenance of these points, come upon him.

Again: in his office as governor of the men employed by him, the merchant or manufacturer is invested with a distinctly paternal authority and responsibility. In most cases, a youth entering a commercial establishment is withdrawn altogether from home influence; his master must become his father, else he has, for practical and constant help, no father at hand: in all cases the master's authority, together with the general tone and atmosphere of his business, and the character of the men with whom the youth is compelled in the course of it to associate, have more immediate and pressing weight than the home influence, and will usually neutralize it either for good or evil; so that the only means which the master has of doing justice to the men employed by him is to ask himself sternly whether he is dealing with such subordinate as he would with his own son, if compelled by circumstances to take such a position.

The Roots of Honour

Supposing the captain of a frigate saw it right, or were by any chance obliged, to place his own son in the position of a common sailor: as he would then treat his son, he is bound always to treat every one of the men under him. So, also, supposing the master of a manufactory saw it right, or were by any chance obliged, to place his own son in the position of an ordinary workman; as he would then treat his son, he is bound always to treat every one of his men. This is the only effective, true, or practical RULE which can be given on this point of political economy.

And as the captain of a ship is bound to be the last man to leave his ship in case of wreck, and to share his last crust with the sailors in case of famine, so the manufacturer, in any commercial crisis or distress, is bound to take the suffering of it with his men, and even to take more of it for himself than he allows his men to feel; as a father would in a famine, shipwreck, or battle, sacrifice himself for his son.

All which sounds very strange: the only real strangeness in the matter being, nevertheless, that it should so sound. For all this is true, and that not partially nor theoretically, but everlastingly and practically: all other doctrine than this respecting matters political being false in premises, absurd in deduction, and impossible in practice, consistently with any progressive state of national life; all the life which we now possess as a nation showing itself in the resolute denial and scorn, by a few strong minds and faithful hearts, of the economic principles taught to our multitudes, which principles, so far as accepted, lead straight to national destruction. Respecting the modes and forms of destruction to which they lead, and, on the other hand, respecting the farther practical working of true polity, I hope to reason farther in a following paper.

1. BOCCACCIO · *Mrs Rosie and the Priest*
2. GERARD MANLEY HOPKINS · *As kingfishers catch fire*
3. *The Saga of Gunnlaug Serpent-tongue*
4. THOMAS DE QUINCEY · *On Murder Considered as One of the Fine Arts*
5. FRIEDRICH NIETZSCHE · *Aphorisms on Love and Hate*
6. JOHN RUSKIN · *Traffic*
7. PU SONGLING · *Wailing Ghosts*
8. JONATHAN SWIFT · *A Modest Proposal*
9. *Three Tang Dynasty Poets*
10. WALT WHITMAN · *On the Beach at Night Alone*
11. KENKŌ · *A Cup of Sake Beneath the Cherry Trees*
12. BALTASAR GRACIÁN · *How to Use Your Enemies*
13. JOHN KEATS · *The Eve of St Agnes*
14. THOMAS HARDY · *Woman much missed*
15. GUY DE MAUPASSANT · *Femme Fatale*
16. MARCO POLO · *Travels in the Land of Serpents and Pearls*
17. SUETONIUS · *Caligula*
18. APOLLONIUS OF RHODES · *Jason and Medea*
19. ROBERT LOUIS STEVENSON · *Olalla*
20. KARL MARX AND FRIEDRICH ENGELS · *The Communist Manifesto*
21. PETRONIUS · *Trimalchio's Feast*
22. JOHANN PETER HEBEL · *How a Ghastly Story Was Brought to Light by a Common or Garden Butcher's Dog*
23. HANS CHRISTIAN ANDERSEN · *The Tinder Box*
24. RUDYARD KIPLING · *The Gate of the Hundred Sorrows*
25. DANTE · *Circles of Hell*
26. HENRY MAYHEW · *Of Street Piemen*
27. HAFEZ · *The nightingales are drunk*
28. GEOFFREY CHAUCER · *The Wife of Bath*
29. MICHEL DE MONTAIGNE · *How We Weep and Laugh at the Same Thing*
30. THOMAS NASHE · *The Terrors of the Night*
31. EDGAR ALLAN POE · *The Tell-Tale Heart*
32. MARY KINGSLEY · *A Hippo Banquet*
33. JANE AUSTEN · *The Beautifull Cassandra*
34. ANTON CHEKHOV · *Gooseberries*
35. SAMUEL TAYLOR COLERIDGE · *Well, they are gone, and here must I remain*
36. JOHANN WOLFGANG VON GOETHE · *Sketchy, Doubtful, Incomplete Jottings*
37. CHARLES DICKENS · *The Great Winglebury Duel*
38. HERMAN MELVILLE · *The Maldive Shark*
39. ELIZABETH GASKELL · *The Old Nurse's Story*
40. NIKOLAY LESKOV · *The Steel Flea*

41. HONORÉ DE BALZAC · *The Atheist's Mass*
42. CHARLOTTE PERKINS GILMAN · *The Yellow Wall-Paper*
43. C.P. CAVAFY · *Remember, Body . . .*
44. FYODOR DOSTOEVSKY · *The Meek One*
45. GUSTAVE FLAUBERT · *A Simple Heart*
46. NIKOLAI GOGOL · *The Nose*
47. SAMUEL PEPYS · *The Great Fire of London*
48. EDITH WHARTON · *The Reckoning*
49. HENRY JAMES · *The Figure in the Carpet*
50. WILFRED OWEN · *Anthem For Doomed Youth*
51. WOLFGANG AMADEUS MOZART · *My Dearest Father*
52. PLATO · *Socrates' Defence*
53. CHRISTINA ROSSETTI · *Goblin Market*
54. *Sindbad the Sailor*
55. SOPHOCLES · *Antigone*
56. RYŪNOSUKE AKUTAGAWA · *The Life of a Stupid Man*
57. LEO TOLSTOY · *How Much Land Does A Man Need?*
58. GIORGIO VASARI · *Leonardo da Vinci*
59. OSCAR WILDE · *Lord Arthur Savile's Crime*
60. SHEN FU · *The Old Man of the Moon*
61. AESOP · *The Dolphins, the Whales and the Gudgeon*
62. MATSUO BASHŌ · *Lips too Chilled*
63. EMILY BRONTË · *The Night is Darkening Round Me*
64. JOSEPH CONRAD · *To-morrow*
65. RICHARD HAKLUYT · *The Voyage of Sir Francis Drake Around the Whole Globe*
66. KATE CHOPIN · *A Pair of Silk Stockings*
67. CHARLES DARWIN · *It was snowing butterflies*
68. BROTHERS GRIMM · *The Robber Bridegroom*
69. CATULLUS · *I Hate and I Love*
70. HOMER · *Circe and the Cyclops*
71. D. H. LAWRENCE · *Il Duro*
72. KATHERINE MANSFIELD · *Miss Brill*
73. OVID · *The Fall of Icarus*
74. SAPPHO · *Come Close*
75. IVAN TURGENEV · *Kasyan from the Beautiful Lands*
76. VIRGIL · *O Cruel Alexis*
77. H. G. WELLS · *A Slip under the Microscope*
78. HERODOTUS · *The Madness of Cambyses*
79. *Speaking of Siva*
80. *The Dhammapada*

'. . . revealing great shining fangs more than three inches long.'

PU SONGLING
Born 1640, Zibo, China
Died 1715, Zibo, China

PU IN PENGUIN CLASSICS
Strange Tales from a Chinese Studio

PU SONGLING

Wailing Ghosts

Translated by
John Minford

PENGUIN BOOKS

PENGUIN CLASSICS

UK | USA | Canada | Ireland | Australia
India | New Zealand | South Africa

Penguin Books is part of the Penguin Random House group of companies
whose addresses can be found at global.penguinrandomhouse.com.

This selection published in Penguin Classics 2015
008

Translation copyright © John Minford, 2006

The moral right of the translator has been asserted

Set in 9.5/13 pt Baskerville 10 Pro
Typeset by Jouve (UK), Milton Keynes

Printed and bound in Great Britain by Clays Ltd, Elcograf S.p.A.

A CIP catalogue record for this book is available from the British Library

ISBN: 978-0-141-39816-7

www.greenpenguin.co.uk

Penguin Random House is committed to a sustainable future for our business, our readers and our planet. This book is made from Forest Stewardship Council® certified paper.

Contents

The Troll	1
The Monster in the Buckwheat	4
Stealing a Peach	7
Growing Pears	12
The Golden Goblet	16
Wailing Ghosts	23
Scorched Moth the Taoist	25
The Giant Turtle	28
A Fatal Joke	30
A Prank	32
King of the Nine Mountains	34
Butterfly	41
The Black Beast	49
The Stone Bowl	51

The Troll

Sun Taibo told me this story.

His great-grandfather, also named Sun, had been studying at Willow Gully Temple on South Mountain, and came home for the autumn wheat harvest. He only stayed at home for ten days, but when he returned to the temple and opened the door of his lodgings, he saw that the table was thick with dust and the windows laced with cobwebs. He ordered his servant to clean the place, and by evening it was in sufficiently good order for him to be able to install himself comfortably again. He dusted off the bed, spread out his quilt, closed the door and lay his head down on the pillow. Moonlight came flooding in at the window.

He tossed and turned a long while, as silence descended on the temple. Then suddenly a wind got up and he heard the main temple door flapping noisily. Thinking to himself that one of the monks must have forgotten to close it, he lay there a while in some anxiety. The wind seemed to be coming closer and closer in the direction of his quarters, and the next thing he knew the door leading into his room blew open. He was now seriously alarmed, and quite unable to compose himself. His room filled with the roaring of the wind, and he heard the sound of clomping boots gradually approaching the alcove in which his bed was situated. By now he was utterly terrified. Then the door of the alcove itself flew open, and there it was, a great troll, stooping down at first as it approached, then suddenly looming up over his bed, its head grazing the ceiling, its face dark and blotchy like an old melon rind. Its blazing eyes scanned the room, and its cavernous mouth lolled open, revealing great shining fangs more than three inches long. Its tongue flickered from side to side, and from its throat there issued a terrible rasping sound that reverberated through the room.

Sun quaked in sheer terror. Thinking quickly to himself that the beast was already too close for him to have any chance of escape and that his only hope now lay in trying to kill it, he secretly drew his dagger from beneath his pillow, concealed it in his sleeve, then swiftly drew it out and stabbed the creature in the belly. The blade made a dull thud on impact, as if it had struck a stone mortar. The enraged troll flailed out at him with its huge claws, but Sun shrank back from it. The troll only succeeded in tearing at the bedcover, and pulled it down on to the ground as it stormed out.

Sun had been dragged to the ground with the bedcover, and he lay there howling. His servant came running with a lantern, and, finding the door locked, as it usually was during the night, he broke open the window and climbed in. Appalled at the state his master was in, he helped him back to bed and heard his tale. Afterwards they examined the room together and saw that the bedcover was still caught tight between the door and the door frame. As soon as they opened the door and the cover fell free, they saw great holes in the fabric, where the beast's claws had torn at it.

When dawn broke the next morning, they dared not stay there a moment longer but packed their things and returned home. On a subsequent occasion they questioned the resident monks, but there had been no further apparition.

The Monster in the Buckwheat

An old gentleman of Changshan County, by the name of An, enjoyed working on his land. One autumn, when his buckwheat was ripe, he went to supervise the harvest, cutting it and laying it out in stacks along the sides of the fields. At that time, someone was stealing the crops in the neighbouring village, so the old gentleman asked his men to load the cut buckwheat on to a cart that very night and push it to the threshing ground by the light of the moon. He himself stayed behind to keep watch over his remaining crops, lying in the open field with spear at hand as he waited for them to return. He had just begun to doze off, when he heard the sound of feet trampling on the buckwheat stalks, making a terrific crunching noise, and suspected that it might be the thief. But when he looked up, he saw a huge monster bearing down upon him, more than ten feet tall, with red hair and a big bushy beard. Leaping up in terror, he struck out at it with all his might, and the monster gave a great howl of pain and fled into the night.

Afraid that it might reappear at any moment, An

The Monster in the Buckwheat

shouldered his spear and headed home, telling his labourers, when he met them on the road, what he had seen, and warning them not to proceed any further. They were reluctant to believe him.

The next day, they were spreading out the buckwheat in the sun when suddenly they heard a strange sound in the air.

'It's the monster again!' cried old An in terror, and fled, as did all the others.

A little later that day, they gathered together again and An told them to arm themselves with bows and lie in wait. The following morning, sure enough, the monster returned a third time. They each shot several arrows at it, and it fled in fear. Then for two or three days it did not return. By now all the threshed buckwheat was safely stored in the granary, but the stalks of straw still lay higgledy-piggledy on the threshing floor. Old An gave orders for the straw to be bound together and piled into a rick, then he himself climbed up on to the rick, which was several feet high. He was treading it down firmly when suddenly he saw something in the distance.

'The monster is coming again!' he cried aghast.

Before his men could get to their bows, the creature had already jumped at him, and knocked him back on to the rick. It took a bite out of his forehead and went away again. The men climbed up and saw that a whole chunk of the old man's forehead, a piece the size of a man's palm, had been bitten off, bone and all. He had already lost consciousness, and they carried him home, where he died.

The monster was never seen again. Nobody could even agree on what sort of creature it was.

Stealing a Peach

When I was a boy, I went up to the prefectural city of Ji'nan to take an examination. It was the time of the Spring Festival, and, according to custom, on the day before the festival all the merchants of the place processed with decorated banners and drums to the provincial yamen. This procession was called Bringing in the Spring. I went with a friend to watch the fun. There was a huge crowd milling about, and ahead of us, facing each other to the right and left of the raised hall, sat four mandarins in their crimson robes. I was too young at the time to know who they were. All I was aware of was the hum of voices and the crashing noise of the drums and other instruments.

In the middle of it all, a man led a boy with long unplaited hair into the space in front of the dais and knelt on the ground. The man had two baskets suspended from a carrying pole on his shoulders and seemed to be saying something, which I could not distinguish for the din of the crowd. I only saw the mandarins smile, and immediately afterwards an attendant came down and in a loud voice ordered the man to give his performance.

'What shall I perform?' said the man, rising to his feet.

The mandarins on the dais consulted among themselves, and then the attendant inquired of the man what he could do best.

'I can make the seasons go backwards, and turn the order of nature upside down.'

The attendant reported back to the mandarins, and after a moment returned and ordered the man to produce a peach. The man assented, taking off his coat and laying it on one of his baskets, at the same time complaining loudly that they had set him a very hard task.

'The winter frost has not melted – how can I possibly produce a peach? But if I fail, their worships will surely be angry with me. Alas! Woe is me!'

The boy, who was evidently his son, reminded him that he had already agreed to perform and was under an obligation to continue. After fretting and grumbling a while, the father cried out, 'I know what we must do! Here it is still early spring and there is snow on the ground – we shall never get a peach *here*. But up in heaven, in the garden of the Queen Mother of the West, they have peaches all the year round. *There* it is eternal summer! It is *there* we must try!'

'But how are we to get up there?' asked the boy.

'I have the means,' replied his father, and immediately proceeded to take from one of his baskets a cord some

Stealing a Peach

dozens of feet in length. He coiled it carefully and then threw one end of it high up into the air, where it remained suspended, as if somehow caught. He continued to pay out the rope, which kept rising higher and higher until the top end of it disappeared altogether into the clouds, while the other end remained in his hands.

'Come here, boy!' he called to his son. 'I am getting too old for this sort of thing, and anyway I am too heavy, I wouldn't be able to do it. It will have to be you.'

He handed the rope to the boy.

'Climb up on this.'

The boy took the rope, but as he did so he pulled a face. 'Father, have you gone mad?' he protested. 'You want me to climb all the way up into the sky on this flimsy thing? Suppose it breaks and I fall – I'll be killed!'

'I have given these gentlemen my word,' his father pleaded, 'and there's no backing out now. Please do this, I beg of you. Bring me a peach, and I am sure we will be rewarded with a hundred taels of silver. Then I promise to get you a pretty wife.'

So his son took hold of the rope and went scrambling up it, hand over foot, like a spider running up a thread, finally disappearing out of sight and into the clouds.

There was a long interval, and then down fell a large peach, the size of a soup bowl. The delighted father presented it to the gentlemen on the dais, who passed it around and studied it carefully, unable to tell at first glance whether it was genuine or a fake. Then suddenly the rope came tumbling to the ground.

'The poor boy!' cried the father in alarm. 'He is done for! Someone up there must have cut my rope!'

The next moment something else fell to the ground, an object which was found on closer examination to be the boy's head. 'Ah me!' cried the father, weeping bitterly and holding the head up in both his hands. 'The heavenly watchman caught him stealing the peach! My son is no more!'

After that, one by one, the boy's feet, his arms and legs, and every single remaining part of his anatomy came tumbling down in a similar manner. The distraught father gathered all the pieces up and put them in one of his baskets, saying, 'This was my only son! He went with me everywhere I went. And now, at his own father's orders, he has met with this cruel fate. I must away and bury him.'

He approached the dais.

'Your peach, gentlemen,' he said, falling to his knees, 'was obtained at the cost of my boy's life. Help me, I beg you, to pay for his funeral expenses, and I will be ever grateful to you for your kindness.'

The mandarins, who had been watching the scene in utter horror and amazement, immediately collected a good purse for him. When the father had received the money and put it in his belt, he rapped on the basket.

'*Babar!*' he called out. 'Out you come now and thank the gentlemen! What are you waiting for?'

He had no sooner said this than there was a knock from within and a tousled head emerged from the basket. Out jumped the boy, and bowed to the dais. It was his son.

To this very day I have never forgotten this extraordinary performance. I later learned that this 'rope trick' was a speciality of the White Lotus sect. Surely this man must have learned it from them.

Growing Pears

A peasant was selling pears in the market. Sweet they were and fragrant – and exceedingly expensive. A Taoist monk in a tattered cap and robe came begging by the pear vendor's cart, and the man told him to be gone. When the monk lingered, the vendor began to abuse him angrily.

'But you have hundreds of pears in your cart,' returned the monk, 'and I am only asking for one. You would hardly notice it, sir. Why are you getting so angry?'

Onlookers urged the vendor to give the monk one of his less succulent pears, just to be rid of him, but the man obstinately refused. A waiter who was serving the customers at a nearby wine-stall, seeing that the scene was threatening to grow ugly, bought a pear and gave it to the monk, who bowed in thanks and turned to the assembled crowd.

'Meanness,' he declared, 'is something we monks find impossible to understand. I have some very fine pears of my own, which I should like to give you.'

'If you have such fine pears,' said one of the crowd,

Growing Pears

'then why did you not eat them yourself? Why did you need to go begging?'

'I needed this one for the seed,' was the monk's reply.

So saying, he held the pear out in front of him and began munching it until all he had left was a single seed from its core, which he held in one hand while taking down a hoe from his shoulder and making a little hole in the ground. Here he placed the seed and covered it with earth. He now asked for some hot water to sprinkle on it, and one of the more enterprising members of the crowd went off and fetched him some from a roadside tavern. The water was scalding hot, but the monk proceeded to pour it on the ground over his seed. The crowd watched riveted, as a tiny sprout began pushing its way up through the soil, growing and growing until soon it was a fully fledged tree, complete with branches and leaves. And then it flowered and bore fruit, great big, fragrant pears. Every branch was laden with them. The monk now climbed up into the tree and began picking the pears, handing them down to the crowd as he did so. Soon every single pear on the tree had been given away. When this was done, he started hacking at the tree with his hoe, and had soon felled it. Then, shouldering the tree, branches, leaves and all, he sauntered casually off.

Now, from the very beginning of this performance, the pear vendor had been standing in the crowd, straining his neck to see what the others were seeing, quite forgetting his trade and what he had come to market for. Only

The water was scalding hot.

when the monk had gone did he turn and see that his own cart was empty. Then he knew that the pears the monk had just been handing out were all from his cart. And he noticed that his cart was missing one of its handles; it had been newly hacked away. The peasant flew into a rage and went in hot pursuit of the monk, following him the length of a wall, round a corner, and there was his cart-handle lying discarded on the ground. He knew at once that it had served as the monk's pear tree. As for the monk himself, he had vanished without trace, to the great amazement of the crowd.

The Golden Goblet

Yin Shidan, who rose to be President of the Board of Civil Office, was a native of Licheng who grew up in circumstances of great poverty and had shown himself to be a young man of courage and resourcefulness.

In his home town there was a large estate that had once belonged to a long-established family, a rambling property consisting of a series of pavilions and other buildings that extended over several acres. Strange apparitions had often been witnessed on the estate, with the result that it had been abandoned and allowed to go to ruin. No one was willing to live there. With time the place grew so overgrown and desolate that no one would so much as enter it even in broad daylight.

One day, Yin was drinking with some young friends of his when one of them had a bright idea.

'If one of us dares to spend a night in that haunted place,' he proposed jokingly, 'let's all stand him a dinner!'

Yin leaped up at once. 'Why, what could be easier!'

And so saying he took his sleeping mat with him and

went to the place, the others accompanying him as far as the entrance.

'We will wait here outside,' they said, smiling nervously. 'If you see anything out of the ordinary, be sure to raise the alarm.'

Yin laughed. 'If I find any ghosts or foxes, I'll catch one to show you.' And in he went.

The paths were overgrown with long grass and tangled weeds. It was the first quarter of the month, and the crescent moon gave off just enough light for him to make out the gateways and doors. He groped his way forwards until he found himself standing before the building that stood at the rear of the main compound. He climbed on to the terrace and thought it seemed a delightful place to take a little nap. The slender arc of the moon shining in the western sky seemed to hold the hills in its mouth. He sat there a long while without observing anything unusual, and began to smile to himself at the foolish rumours about the place being haunted. Spreading his mat, and choosing a stone for a pillow, he lay there gazing up at the constellations of the Cowherd and the Spinning Maid in the night sky.

By the end of the first watch, he was just beginning to doze off when he heard the patter of footsteps from below, and a servant-girl appeared, carrying a lotus-shaped lantern. The sight of Yin seemed to startle her and she made as if to flee, calling out to someone behind her, 'There's a strange-looking man here!'

'Who is it?' replied a voice.

'I don't know.'

Presently an old gentleman appeared and, approaching Yin, scrutinized him.

'Why, that is the future President Yin! He is fast asleep. We can carry on as planned. He is a broad-minded fellow and will not take offence.'

The old man led the maid on into the building, where they threw open all the doors. After a while a great many guests started arriving, and the upper rooms were as brightly lit as if it had been broad daylight.

Yin tossed and turned on the terrace where he lay. Then he sneezed. The old man, hearing that he was awake, came out and knelt down by his side.

'My daughter, sir, is being given in marriage tonight. I had no idea that Your Excellency would be here, and crave your indulgence.'

Yin rose to his feet and made the old man do likewise.
'I was not aware that a wedding was taking place tonight. I regret I have brought no gift with me.'

'Your very presence is gift enough,' replied the old man graciously, 'and will help to ward off noxious influences. Would you be so kind as to honour us further with your company now?'

Yin assented. Entering the building, he looked around him at the splendid feast that had been prepared. A woman of about forty, whom the old gentleman introduced as his wife, came out to welcome him, and Yin made her a bow. Then the sound of festive pipes was heard, and someone came rushing in, crying, 'He has arrived!'

The old man hurried out to receive his future son-in-law, and Yin remained standing where he was in expectation. After a little while, a bevy of servants bearing gauze lanterns ushered in the groom, a handsome young man of seventeen or eighteen, of a most distinguished appearance and prepossessing bearing. The old gentleman bade him pay his respects to the guest of honour, and the young man turned to Yin, whom he took to be some sort of Master of Ceremonies, and bowed to him in the appropriate fashion. Then the old man and the groom exchanged formal courtesies, and when these were completed, they took their seats. Presently a throng of finely attired serving-maids came forward, with choice wines and steaming dishes of meat. Jade bowls and golden goblets glistened on the tables. When the wine had been round several times, the old gentleman dispatched one of the maids to summon the bride. The maid departed on her errand, but when she had been gone a long while and still there was no sign of his daughter, the old man himself eventually rose from his seat and, lifting the portière, went into the inner apartments to chivvy her along. At last several maids and serving-women ushered in the bride, to the sound of tinkling jade pendants, and the scent of musk and orchid wafted through the room. Obedient to her father's instructions, she curtseyed to the senior guests and then took her seat by her mother's side. Yin could see from a glance that beneath the kingfisher-feather ornaments she was a young woman of extraordinary beauty.

They were drinking from large goblets of solid gold, each of which held well over a pint, and Yin thought to himself that one of these would be an ideal proof of his adventure that night. So he hid one in his sleeve, to show his friends on his return, then slumped across the table, pretending to have been overpowered by the wine.

'His Excellency is drunk,' they remarked.

A little later, Yin heard the groom take his leave, and as the pipes started up again, all the guests began trooping downstairs.

The old gentleman came to gather up his golden goblets, and noticed that one of them was missing. He searched for it to no avail. Someone suggested their sleeping guest as the culprit, but the old gentleman promptly bid him be silent, for fear that Yin might hear.

After a while, when all was still within and without, Yin rose from the table. The lamps had all been extinguished and it was dark, but the aroma of the food and the fumes of wine still lingered in the hall. As he made his way slowly out of the building, and felt inside his sleeve for the golden goblet, which was still safely hidden, the first light of dawn glimmered in the eastern sky.

He reached the entrance of the estate to find his friends still waiting outside. They had stayed there all night, in case he should try to trick them by coming out and going

The Golden Goblet

back in again early in the morning. He took the goblet from his sleeve and showed it to them. In utter amazement they asked him how he had come by it, whereupon he told them the whole story. They knew how poor he was, and that he was most unlikely to have owned such a valuable object himself, and so were obliged to believe him.

Some years later, Yin passed his final examination and obtained the degree of Doctor or *jinshi*, after which he was appointed to a post in Feiqiu. A wealthy gentleman of the district by the name of Zhu gave a banquet in his honour, and ordered his large golden goblets to be brought out for the occasion. They were a long time coming, and as the company waited a young servant came up and whispered something to the master of the household, who instantly flew into a rage. Presently the goblets were brought in, and Zhu urged his guests to drink. To his astonishment, Yin at once recognized the shape and pattern of the goblets as being identical with the one he had 'kept' from the fox wedding. He asked his host where they had been made.

'I had eight of them,' was the reply. 'An ancestor of mine was a high-ranking mandarin in Peking and had them made by a master goldsmith of the time. They have been in my family for generations, but it is a long while since I last had them taken out of storage. When I knew we would have the honour of your company today, I told my man to open the box, and it turns out there are only seven left! I would have suspected one of my household of stealing it, but apparently there was ten years' dust on the seals and the box was untampered with. It baffles me how this can have happened.'

'The thing must have grown wings and flown away of its own accord!' quipped Yin with a laugh. 'But seeing that you have lost an heirloom, I feel I must help you replace it. I myself have a goblet, sir, very similar to this set of yours. Allow me to make you a present of it.'

When the meal was over, he returned to his official residence, and taking out his own goblet, sent it round straightaway to Zhu's house. When he inspected it, Zhu was absolutely amazed. He went to thank Yin in person, and when he asked him where he had acquired the goblet, Yin told him the whole story.

Which all goes to show that although foxes may be capable of getting hold of objects from a very long way away, they do not hold on to them for ever.

Wailing Ghosts

At the time of the Xie Qian troubles in Shandong, the great residences of the nobility were all commandeered by the rebels. The mansion of Education Commissioner Wang Qixiang accommodated a particularly large number of them. When the government troops eventually retook the town and massacred the rebels, every porch was strewn with corpses. Blood flowed from every doorway.

When Commissioner Wang returned, he gave orders that all the corpses were to be removed from his home and the blood washed away, so that he could once more take up residence. In the days that followed, he frequently saw ghosts in broad daylight, and during the night ghostly will-o'-the-wisp flickerings of light beneath his bed. He heard the voices of ghosts wailing in various corners of the house.

One day, a young gentleman by the name of Wang Gaodi who had come to stay with the Commissioner heard a little voice crying beneath his bed, 'Gaodi! Gaodi!'

Then the voice grew louder. 'I died a cruel death!'

The voice began sobbing, and was soon joined by ghosts throughout the house.

The Commissioner himself heard it and came with his sword.

'Do you not know who I am?' he declared loudly. 'I am Education Commissioner Wang.'

The ghostly voices merely sneered at this and laughed through their noses, whereupon the Commissioner gave orders for a lengthy ritual to be immediately performed for all departed souls on land and sea, in the course of which Buddhist bonzes and Taoist priests prayed for the liberation of his supernatural tenants from their torments. That night they put out food for the ghosts, and will-o'-the-wisp lights could be seen flickering across the ground.

Now before any of these events, a gate-man, also named Wang, had fallen gravely ill, and had been lying unconscious for several days. The night of the ritual he suddenly seemed to regain consciousness, and stretched his limbs. When his wife brought him some food, he said to her, 'The Master put some food out in the courtyard – I've no idea why! Anyway I was out there eating with the others, and I've only just finished, so I'm not that hungry.'

From that day, the hauntings ceased.

Does this mean that the banging of cymbals and gongs, the beating of bells and drums, and other esoteric practices for the release of wandering souls are necessarily efficacious?

Scorched Moth the Taoist

The household of Hanlin Academician Dong was troubled by fox-spirits. Tiles, pebbles and brick shards were liable to fly around the house like hailstones at any moment, and his family and household were forever having to take shelter and wait for the disturbances to abate before they dared carry on with their daily duties. Dong himself was so affected by this state of affairs that he rented a residence belonging to Under-Secretary Sun, and moved there to avoid his troubles. But the fox-spirits merely followed him.

One day when he was on duty at court and described this strange phenomenon to his colleagues, a senior minister mentioned a certain Taoist master from the north-east by the name of Jiao Ming – Scorched Moth – who lived in the Inner Manchu City and issued exorcist spells and talismans reputed for their efficacy. Dong paid the man a personal call and requested his aid, whereupon the Master wrote out some charms in cinnabar-red ink and told Dong to paste them on his wall. The foxes were unperturbed by these measures, however, and continued to hurl things around with greater vigour than ever. Dong reported back to the Taoist, who was angered by this apparent failure of his charms and came in person to Dong's house, where he set up an altar and performed a full rite of exorcism. Suddenly they beheld a huge fox crouching on the ground before the altar. Dong's household had suffered long from this creature's antics, and the servants felt a deep-seated sense of grievance towards it. One of the maids went up to it to deal it a blow, only to fall dead to the ground.

'This is a vicious beast!' exclaimed the Taoist. 'Even I could not subdue it! This girl was very foolish to provoke it.' He continued, 'Nonetheless, we can now use *her* to question the fox.'

Pointing his index finger and middle finger at the maid, he pronounced certain spells, and suddenly she rose from the ground and knelt before him. The Taoist asked her where she hailed from.

'I come from the Western Regions,' replied the maid, in a voice that was clearly not her own but that of the fox. 'We have been here in the capital for eighteen generations.'

'How dare creatures such as you dwell in the proximity of His Imperial Majesty? Off with you at once!'

The fox-voice was silent, and the Taoist thumped the altar-table angrily. 'How dare you disobey my orders? Delay a moment longer, and my magic powers will work on you harshly!'

Scorched Moth the Taoist

The fox shrank back fearfully, indicating his submission, and the Taoist urged him once more to be gone. Meanwhile the maid had fallen to the ground again, dead to the world. It was a long while before she regained consciousness.

All of a sudden they saw four or five white lumps of some strange substance go bouncing like balls one after the other along the eaves of the building, until they were all gone. Then peace finally reigned in the Dong household.

The Giant Turtle

An elderly gentleman called Zhang, a native of the western region of Jin, was about to give away his daughter in marriage, and took his family with him by boat on a trip to the South, having decided to purchase there all that was necessary for her trousseau. When the boat arrived at Gold Mountain, he went ahead across the river, leaving his family on board and warning them not to fry any strong-smelling meat during his absence, for fear of provoking the turtle-demon that lurked in the river. This vicious creature would be sure to come out if it smelled meat cooking, and would destroy the boat and eat alive anyone on board. It had been wreaking havoc in the area for a long while.

Once the old man had left, his family quite forgot his words of caution, lit a fire on deck and began to cook meat on it. All of a sudden a great wave arose, overturning their boat and drowning both Zhang's wife and daughter. When Zhang returned, he was grief-stricken at their deaths. He climbed up to the monastery on Gold Mountain and called on the monks there, asking them for

The Giant Turtle

information about the turtle's strange ways, so that he could plan his revenge. The monks were appalled at his intentions.

'We live with the turtle every day, in constant fear of the devastation it is capable of causing. All we can do is worship it and pray to it not to fly into a rage. From time to time we slaughter animals, cut them in half and throw them into the river. The turtle jumps out of the water, gulps them down and disappears. No one would be so crazy as to try to seek revenge!'

As he listened to the monks' words, Zhang was already forming his plan. He recruited a local blacksmith, who set up a furnace on the hillside above the river and smelted a large lump of iron, over a hundred catties in weight. Zhang then ascertained the turtle's exact hiding place and hired a number of strong men to lift up the red-hot molten iron with a great pair of tongs and hurl it into the river. True to form, the turtle leaped out of the water, gulped down the molten metal and plunged back into the river. Minutes later, mountainous waves came boiling to the water's surface. Then, in an instant, the river became calm and the turtle could be seen floating dead on the water.

Travellers and monks alike rejoiced at the turtle's death. They built a temple to old man Zhang, erected a statue of him inside it and worshipped him as a water god. When they prayed to him, their wishes were always fulfilled.

A Fatal Joke

The schoolmaster Sun Jingxia once told this story.

A certain fellow of the locality, let us call him 'X', was killed by bandits during one of their raids. His head flopped down on to his chest. When the bandits had gone and the family came to recover the corpse for burial, they detected the faintest trace of breathing, and on closer examination saw that the man's windpipe was not quite severed. A finger's breadth remained. So they carried him home, supporting the head carefully, and after a day and a night, he began to make a moaning noise. They fed him minute quantities of food with a spoon and chopsticks, and after six months he was fully recovered.

Ten years later, he was sitting talking with two or three of his friends when one of them cracked a hilarious joke and they all burst out laughing. 'X' was rocking backwards and forwards in a fit of hysterical laughter, when suddenly the old sword-wound burst open and his head fell to the ground in a pool of blood. His friends examined him, and this time he was well and truly dead.

A Fatal Joke

His father decided to bring charges against the man who had told the joke. But the joker's friends collected some money together and succeeded in buying him off. The father buried his son and dropped the charges.

A Prank

A certain fellow of my home district, a well-known prankster and libertine, was out one day strolling in the countryside when he saw a young girl approaching on a pony.

'I'll get a laugh out of her, see if I don't!' he called out to his companions.

They were sceptical of his chances of success and wagered a banquet on it, even as he hurried forward in front of the girl's pony and cried out loudly, 'I want to die! I want to die . . .'

He took hold of a tall millet stalk that was growing over a nearby wall and, bending it so that it projected a foot into the road, untied the sash of his gown and threw it over the stalk, making a noose in it and slipping it round his neck, as if to hang himself. As she came closer, the girl laughed at him, and by now his friends were also in fits. The girl then rode on into the distance, but the man still did not move, which caused his friends to laugh all the more. Presently they went up and looked at him: his tongue was protruding from his mouth, his eyes were closed. He was quite lifeless.

Strange that a man could succeed in hanging himself from a millet stalk. Let this be a warning to libertines and pranksters.

King of the Nine Mountains

There was a certain gentleman by the name of Li from the town of Caozhou, an official scholar of the town, whose family had always been well off, though their residence had never been extensive. The garden behind their house, of an acre or two, had been largely abandoned.

One day, an old man arrived at the house, inquiring about a place to rent. He said he was willing to spend as much as a hundred taels, but Li declined, arguing that he had insufficient space.

'Please accept my offer,' pleaded the old man. 'I will cause you no trouble whatsoever.'

Li did not quite understand what he meant by this, but finally agreed to accept the money and see what happened.

A day later, the local people saw carriages and horses and a throng of people streaming into the garden behind Li's residence. They found it hard to believe that the place could accommodate so many, and asked Li what was going on. He himself was quite at a loss to explain, and hurried in to investigate, but found no trace of anything.

King of the Nine Mountains

A few days later, the old man called on him again.

'I have enjoyed your hospitality already for several days and nights,' he said. 'Things have been very hectic. We have been so busy settling in, I am afraid we simply have not had time to entertain you as we should have done. Today I have asked my daughters to prepare a little meal, and I hope you will honour us with your presence.'

Li accepted the invitation and followed the old man into the garden, where this time he beheld a newly constructed range of most splendid and imposing buildings. They entered one of these, the interior of which was most elegantly appointed. Wine was being heated in a cauldron out on the verandah, while the delicate aroma of tea emanated from the kitchen. Presently wine and food were served, all of the finest quality and savour. Li could hear and see countless young people coming and going in the courtyard, and he heard the voices of girls chattering and laughing behind gauze curtains. Altogether he estimated that, including family and servants, there must have been over a thousand people living in the garden.

Li knew they must all be foxes. When the meal was finished, he returned home and secretly resolved to find a way of killing them. Every time he went to market he bought a quantity of saltpetre, until he had accumulated several hundred catties of the stuff, which he put down everywhere in the garden. He set light to it, and the flames leaped up into the night sky, spreading a cloud of smoke like a great black mushroom. The pungent odour of the smoke and the choking particles of burning soot prevented anyone from getting close, and all that could be heard was the deafening din of a thousand screaming voices. When the fire had finally burned itself out and Li went into the garden, he saw the bodies of dead foxes lying everywhere, countless numbers of them, charred beyond recognition. He was still gazing at them when the old man came in from outside, an expression of utter devastation and grief on his face.

'What harm did we ever do you?' he reproached Li. 'We paid you a hundred taels – far more than it was worth – to rent your ruin of a garden. How could you be so cruel as to destroy every last member of my family? It is a terrible thing that you have done, and we will most certainly be revenged!'

And with those bitter words of anger, he took his leave.

Li was concerned that he would cause trouble. But a year went by without any strange or untoward occurrence.

It was the first year of the reign of the Manchu Emperor Shunzhi. There were hordes of bandits up in the hills, who formed huge roving companies which the authorities were quite powerless to apprehend. Li had numerous dependants and was especially concerned at the disturbances.

Then, one day, a fortune-teller arrived in the town, calling himself the Old Man of the Southern Mountain. He claimed to be able to see into the future with the utmost accuracy, and soon became something of a local

'What harm did we ever do you?'

celebrity. Li sent for him and asked him to read his Eight Astrological Signs. The old man did so, and then rose hurriedly to his feet with a gesture of reverence.

'You, sir, are a true lord, an emperor among men!'

Li was flabbergasted and thought that perhaps the old man was making it all up. But he insisted that he was telling the truth, and Li was almost tempted to believe it himself.

'But I am a nobody,' he said. 'Tell me: when did a man ever receive the Mandate of Heaven and become Emperor in this way – with his own bare hands?'

'Why,' declared the old man, 'throughout history! Our Emperors have always come from the ranks of the common people. Which founder of a dynasty was ever *born* Son of Heaven?'

Now Li, who was beginning to get carried away, drew close to the fortune-teller and asked him for further guidance. The old man declared that he himself would be willing to serve as Li's Chief Marshal, just as the great wizard and strategist Zhuge Liang had once served the Pretender Liu Bei in the time of the Three Kingdoms. Li was to make ready large quantities of suits of armour and bows and crossbows. When Li expressed doubts that anyone would rally to his side, the old man replied, 'Allow me to work for you in the hills, sir. Let me forge links and win men over. Once word is out that you are indeed the true Son of Heaven, have no fear, the fighters of the hills will flock to you.'

King of the Nine Mountains

Li was overjoyed, and instructed the old man to do as he proposed. He took out all the gold he had and gave orders for the necessary quantity of suits of armour to be made. Several days later, the old man was back.

'Thanks principally to Your Majesty's great aura of blessing, and in some negligible part to my own paltry abilities as an orator, on every hill the men are now thronging to join your cause and rallying to your banner.'

Sure enough, ten days later, a large body of men came in person to swear their allegiance to the new Son of Heaven and to the Old Man of the Southern Mountain whom they acknowledged as their Supreme Marshal. They set up a great standard, with a forest of brightly coloured pennants fluttering in the breeze, and from their stockade on one of the hills they lorded it over the region.

The District Magistrate led out a force to quell this rebellion, and the rebels under the command of the old fortune-teller inflicted a crushing defeat on the government troops. The Magistrate took fright and sent for urgent reinforcements from the Prefect. The Old Marshal harassed these fresh troops, ambushing and overwhelming them, killing large numbers, including several of their commanding officers. The rebels were now more widely feared than ever. They numbered ten thousand, and Li formally proclaimed himself the King of the Nine Mountains, while his Marshal was given the honorific title of Lord Marshal Protector of the Realm. The old man now reckoned his troops were short of horses, and since it so happened that the authorities in the capital were sending some horses under escort to the south, he dispatched some men to intercept the convoy and seize the horses. The success of this operation increased the prestige of the King of the Nine Mountains still further. He took his ease in his mountain lair, well satisfied with himself and considering it now merely a matter of time before he was officially installed on the Dragon Throne.

The Governor of Shandong Province now decided, mainly on account of the seizure of the horses, to launch a large-scale expedition to quell the rebellion once and for all. He received a report from the Prefect of Yanzhou, and sent large numbers of crack troops, who were to co-ordinate with detachments from the six local circuits and converge on the rebel stronghold from all sides. The King of the Nine Mountains became alarmed and summoned his Marshal for a strategic consultation, only to find that the old man had vanished. The 'King' was truly at his wits' end. He climbed to the top of one of the mountains of his 'domain' and looked down on the government forces and their standards, which stretched along every valley and on every hilltop.

'Now I see,' he declared sombrely, 'how great is the might of the Emperor's court!'

His stronghold was destroyed, the King himself was captured, his wife and entire family were executed. Only then did Li understand that the Marshal was the old fox, taking his revenge for the destruction of his own fox-family.

Butterfly

Luo Zifu was born in Bin County, and lost both his parents at an early age. When he was eight or nine years old he went to live with his Uncle Daye, a high official in the Imperial College and an immensely wealthy man. Daye had no sons of his own and came to love Luo as if he were his own child.

When the boy was fourteen, he fell in with bad company and became a regular frequenter of the local pleasure-houses. A famous Nanking courtesan happened to be in Bin County at the time, and the young Luo became hopelessly infatuated with her. When she returned to Nanking, he ran away with her and lived with her there in her establishment for a good six months – by which time his money was all gone and the other girls had begun to mock him mercilessly, though they still tolerated his presence.

Then he contracted syphilis and broke out in suppurating sores, which left stains on the bedding, and they finally drove him from the house. He took to begging in the streets, where the passers-by shunned him. He began to dread the thought of dying so far from home, and one day set off begging his way back to Shaanxi, covering ten or so miles a day, until eventually he came to the borders of Bin County. His filthy rags and foul, pus-covered body made him too ashamed to go any further into his old neighbourhood, and instead he hobbled about on the outskirts of town.

Towards evening, he was stumbling towards a temple in the hills, seeking shelter for the night, when he encountered a young woman of a quite unearthly beauty, who came up to him and asked him where he was going. He told her his whole story.

'I myself have renounced the world,' was her response. 'I live here in a cave in the hills. You are welcome to stay with me. Here at least you will be safe from tigers and wolves.'

Luo followed her joyfully, and together they walked deeper into the hills. Presently he found himself at the entrance to a grotto, inside which flowed a stream, with a stone bridge leading over it. A few steps further and they came to two chambers hollowed out of the rock, both of them brightly lit, but with no sign anywhere of either candle or lamp. The girl bid Luo remove his rags and bathe in the waters of the stream.

'Wash,' she said, 'and your sores will all be healed.'

She drew apart the bed-curtains and made up a bed for him, dusting off the quilt.

'Sleep now,' she said, 'and I will make you a pair of trousers.'

Butterfly

She brought in what looked like a large plantain leaf and began cutting it to shape. He lay there watching her, and in a very short while the trousers were made and placed folded on the bed.

'You can wear these in the morning.'

She lay down on a couch opposite.

After bathing in the stream, Luo felt all the pain go out of his sores, and when he awoke during the night and touched them, they had already dried and hardened into thick scabs. In the morning he rose, wondering if he would truly be able to wear the plantain-leaf trousers. When he took them in his hands, he found that they were wonderfully smooth, like green satin.

In a little while, breakfast was prepared. The young woman brought more leaves from the mountainside. She said that they were pancakes, and they ate them, and sure enough they were pancakes. She cut the shapes of poultry and fish from the leaves and cooked them, and they made a delicious meal. In the corner of the room stood a vat filled with fine wine, from which they drank, and when the supply ran out she merely replenished it with water from the stream.

In a few days, when all his sores and scabs were gone, he went up to her and begged her to share his bed.

'Silly boy!' she cried. 'No sooner cured than you go losing your head again!'

'I only want to repay your kindness . . .'

They had much pleasure together that night.

Time passed, and one day another young woman came into the grotto and greeted them with a broad grin.

'Why, my dear wicked little Butterfly!' (for such was the girl's name). 'You *do* seem to be having a good time! And when did this cosy little idyll of yours begin, pray?'

'It's been such an age since you last visited, dearest Sister Flower!' returned Butterfly, with a teasing smile. 'What Fair Wind of Love blows you here today? And have you had your little baby boy yet?'

'Actually I had a girl . . .'

'What a doll factory you are!' quipped Butterfly. 'Didn't you bring her with you?'

'She's only just this minute stopped crying and fallen asleep.'

Flower sat down with them and drank her fill of wine.

'This young man must have burned some very special incense to be so lucky,' she remarked, looking at Luo. He in turn studied her. She was a beautiful young woman in her early twenties, and the susceptible young man was instantly smitten. He peeled a fruit and 'accidentally' dropped it under the table. Bending down to retrieve it, he gave the tip of one of her tiny embroidered slippers a little pinch. She turned away and smiled, pretending not to have noticed. Luo, who was now totally entranced and more than a little aroused, noticed all of a sudden that his gown and trousers were growing cold, and when he looked down at them they had turned into withered leaves. Horrified, he sat primly upright for a moment, and slowly they reverted to their former soft, silken appearance. He was secretly relieved that neither of the girls seemed to have noticed anything.

A little later, they were still drinking together when he let his finger stray to the palm of Flower's dainty little hand. Flower carried on laughing and smiling, as if nothing had happened. And then suddenly, to his horror, it happened a second time: silk was transformed to leaf, and leaf back to silk. He had learned his lesson this time, and resolved to behave himself.

'Your young man is rather naughty!' said Flower, with a smile. 'If you weren't such a jealous jar of vinegar, he'd be roaming all over the place!'

'You faithless boy!' quipped Butterfly. 'You deserve to freeze to death!'

She and Flower both laughed and clapped their hands.

'My little girl's awake again,' said Flower, rising from her seat. 'She'll hurt herself crying like that.'

'Hark at you,' said Butterfly, 'leading strange men astray and neglecting your own child!' Flower left them, and Luo was afraid he would be subjected to mockery and recrimination from Butterfly. But she was as delightful as ever.

The days passed, and, as autumn turned to winter, the cold wind and frost stripped the trees bare. Butterfly gathered the fallen leaves and began storing them for food to see them through the winter. She noticed Luo shivering, and went to the entrance of the grotto, where she gathered white clouds with which to line a padded gown for him. When it was made, it was warm as silk, and the padding was light and soft as fresh cotton floss.

A year later, she gave birth to a son, a clever, handsome child with whom Luo loved to pass the days playing in the grotto. But, as time went by, he began to pine for home and begged Butterfly to return with him.

'I cannot go,' she told him. 'But you go if you must.'

A further two or three years went by. The boy grew, and they betrothed him to Flower's little daughter. Luo was now constantly thinking of his old uncle, Daye.

'The old man is strong and well,' Butterfly assured him. 'You do not need to worry on his behalf. Wait until your boy is married. Then you can go.'

She would sit in the grotto and write lessons on leaves for their son, who mastered them at a single glance.

'Our son has a happy destiny,' she said to Luo. 'If he goes into the human world, he will certainly rise to great heights.'

When the boy was fourteen, Flower came with her daughter, dressed in all her finery. She had grown into a radiantly beautiful young woman. She and Butterfly's son were very happy to be married, and the whole family held a feast to celebrate their union. Butterfly sang a song, tapping out the rhythm with her hairpin:

> A fine son have I,
> Why should I yearn

> For pomp and splendour?
> A fine daughter is mine,
> Why should I long
> For silken luxury?
> Tonight we are gathered
> To sing and be merry.
> For you, dear lad, a parting cup!
> For you, a plate of food!

Flower took her leave. The young couple made their home in the stone chamber opposite, and the young bride waited dutifully on Butterfly as if she were her own mother.

It was not long before Luo started talking again of returning home.

'You will always be a mortal,' said Butterfly. 'It is in your bones, and in our son's. He, too, belongs in the world of men. Take him with you. I do not wish to blight his days.'

The young bride wanted to say a last farewell to her mother, and Flower came to visit them. Both she and her husband were loth to leave their mothers, and their eyes brimmed with tears.

'Go for a while,' said the women, by way of comforting them. 'You can always come back later.'

Butterfly cut out a leaf and made a donkey, and the three of them, Luo and the young couple, climbed on to the beast and rode away upon it.

Luo's uncle, Daye, was by now an old man and retired from public life. He thought that his adopted son had died. And now, out of the blue, there he was, with a son of his own and a beautiful daughter-in-law! He rejoiced as if he had come upon some precious treasure. The moment they entered his house, their silken clothes all turned once more into crumbling plantain leaves, while the 'cotton padding' drifted up into the sky. They dressed themselves in new, more ordinary clothes.

As time went by, Luo pined for Butterfly, and he went in search of her with his son. But the path through the hills was strewn with yellow leaves, and the entrance to the grotto was lost in the mist. The two of them returned weeping from their quest.

The Black Beast

My friend's grandfather Li Jingyi once told the following story.

A certain gentleman was picnicking on a mountainside near the city of Shenyang when he looked down and saw a tiger come walking by, carrying something in its mouth. The tiger dug a hole and buried whatever it was in the ground. When he had gone, the gentleman told his men to find out what it was the tiger had buried. They came back to inform him that it was a deer, and he bade them retrieve the dead animal and fill up the hole.

Later the tiger returned, followed this time by a shaggy black beast. The tiger went in front as if it were politely escorting an esteemed guest. When the two animals reached the hole, the black beast squatted to one side and watched intently while the tiger felt in the earth with his paws, only to discover that the deer was no longer there. The tiger lay there prostrate and trembling, not daring to move. The black beast, thinking that the tiger had told a lie, flew into a fury and struck the tiger on the forehead with its paw. The tiger died immediately, and the black beast went away.

The tiger returned, followed by a shaggy black beast.

The Stone Bowl

A certain gentleman by the name of Yin Tu'nan, of Wuchang, possessed a villa that he rented out to a young scholar. Half a year passed and he never once had occasion to call on this young tenant of his. Then one day he chanced to see him outside the entrance to the compound, and observing that, despite the tenant's evident youth, he had the fastidious manner and elegant accoutrements of a person of refinement, Yin approached him and engaged him in conversation. He found him indeed to be a most charming and cultivated person. Clearly this was no ordinary lodger.

Returning home, Yin mentioned the encounter to his wife, who sent over one of her own maids to spy out the land, on the pretext of delivering a gift. The maid discovered a young lady in the young man's apartment, of a breathtaking beauty that surpassed (as she put it) that of a fairy, while the living quarters, she observed to her mistress, were furnished with an extraordinary variety of plants, ornamental stones, rare clothes and assorted curios, things such as she had never before set eyes on.

Yin was intrigued to find out exactly what sort of person this young man could be, and went himself to the villa to pay him a visit. It so happened the man was out, but the following day he returned Yin's visit and presented his name card. Yin read on the card that his name was Yu De, but when Yin pressed Yu De for further details of his background, he became extremely vague.

'I am happy to make your acquaintance, sir. Trust me, I am no robber, nor am I a fugitive from justice. But beyond that, I am surely not obliged to divulge further particulars of my identity.'

Yin apologized for his incivility and set wine and food before his guest, whereupon they dined together in a most convivial manner until late in the evening, when two dark-skinned servants came with horses and lanterns to fetch their young master home.

The following day, he sent Yin a note inviting him over to the villa for a return visit. When Yin arrived, he observed that the walls of the room in which he was received were lined with a glossy paper that shone like the surface of a mirror, while fumes of some exotic incense smouldered from a golden censer fashioned in the shape of a lion. Beside the censer stood a vase of dark-green jade containing four feathers – two phoenix feathers, two peacock – each of them over two feet in length. In another vase, made of pure crystal, was a branch of some flowering tree which he could not identify, also about two feet long, covered with pink blossoms and trailing down over

The Stone Bowl

the edge of the little table on which it stood. The densely clustered flowers, still in bud, were admirably set off by the sparsity of leaves. They resembled butterflies moistened by the morning dew, resting with closed wings on the branch, to which they were attached by delicate antenna-like tendrils.

The dinner served consisted of eight dishes, each one a gastronomic delicacy. After dinner, the host ordered his servant to 'sound the drum for the flowers' and to commence the drinking game. The drum duly sounded, and as it did so the flowers on the branch began to open tremulously, spreading their 'butterfly wings' very slowly one by one. And then as the drumming ceased, on the final solemn beat, the tendrils of one flower detached themselves from the branch and became a butterfly, fluttering through the air and alighting on Yin's gown. With a laugh, Yu poured his guest a large goblet of wine, and when Yin had drained the goblet dry, the butterfly flew away. An instant later the drumming recommenced, and this time when it ceased two butterflies flew up into the air and settled on Yu's cap. He laughed again.

'Serves me right! I must drink a double sconce myself!'

And he downed two goblets. At the third drumming, a veritable shower of butterfly-flowers began to fall through the air, fluttering here and there and eventually settling in large numbers on the gowns of both men. The pageboy drummer smiled and thrust out his fingers twice, in the manner of drinking games: once for Yin, and it came to nine fingers; once for Yu, and it came to four. Yin was already somewhat the worse for drink and was unable to down his quota. He managed to knock back three goblets, and then got down from the table, excused himself and stumbled home. His evening's entertainment had only served to intensify his curiosity. There was indeed something very unusual about his lodger.

Yu seldom socialized, and spent most of his time shut up at home in the villa, never going out into society even for occasions such as funerals or weddings. Yin told his friends of his own strange experience and word soon got around, with the result that many of them competed to make Yu's acquaintance, and the carriages of the local nobility were often to be seen at the doors of the villa. Yu found this attention more and more irksome, and one day he suddenly took his leave of Yin and went away altogether. After his departure, Yin inspected the villa and found the interior of the building quite empty. It had been left spotlessly clean and tidy. Outside, at the foot of the stone steps leading up to the terrace, was a pile of 'candle tears', the waxen accumulation, no doubt, of the revels of many evenings. Tattered curtains still hung in the windows, and there seemed to be the marks of fingers still visible on the fabric. Behind the villa, Yin found a white stone bowl, about a gallon in capacity, which he took home with him, filled with water and used for his goldfish. A year later, he was surprised to see that the water in the bowl was still as clear as it had been on the very first day. Then, one day, a servant was moving a rock and accidentally broke a piece out of the rim of the bowl. But somehow, despite the break, the water stayed intact within the bowl, and when Yin examined it, it seemed to all intents and purposes whole. He passed his hand along the edge of the break, which felt strangely soft. When he put his hand inside the bowl, water came trickling out along the crack, but when he withdrew his hand, water filled the bowl as before.

Throughout the winter months, the water in the bowl never froze. And then one night it turned into a solid block of crystal. But the fish could still be seen swimming around inside it.

Yin was afraid that others might get to know of this strange bowl, and he kept it in a secret room, telling only his own children and their husbands and wives. But, with time, word got out and everyone was at his door wanting to see and touch this marvel.

The night before the festival of the winter solstice, the crystal block suddenly melted and water leaked from the bowl, leaving a large dark stain on the floor. Of the goldfish there was no sign whatsoever. Only the fragments of the broken bowl remained.

One day, a Taoist came knocking at the door and asked to see the bowl. Yin brought out the broken pieces to show him.

'This,' said the Taoist, 'was once a water vessel from the Dragon King's Underwater Palace.'

Yin told him how it had been broken, and how it had continued to hold water.

'That is the spirit of the bowl at work,' commented the Taoist, entreating Yin to give him a piece of it. Yin asked him why he wanted it.

'By pounding such a fragment into a powder,' he replied, 'I can make a drug that will give everlasting life.'

Yin gave him a piece, and the Taoist thanked him and went on his way.

1. BOCCACCIO · *Mrs Rosie and the Priest*
2. GERARD MANLEY HOPKINS · *As kingfishers catch fire*
3. *The Saga of Gunnlaug Serpent-tongue*
4. THOMAS DE QUINCEY · *On Murder Considered as One of the Fine Arts*
5. FRIEDRICH NIETZSCHE · *Aphorisms on Love and Hate*
6. JOHN RUSKIN · *Traffic*
7. PU SONGLING · *Wailing Ghosts*
8. JONATHAN SWIFT · *A Modest Proposal*
9. *Three Tang Dynasty Poets*
10. WALT WHITMAN · *On the Beach at Night Alone*
11. KENKŌ · *A Cup of Sake Beneath the Cherry Trees*
12. BALTASAR GRACIÁN · *How to Use Your Enemies*
13. JOHN KEATS · *The Eve of St Agnes*
14. THOMAS HARDY · *Woman much missed*
15. GUY DE MAUPASSANT · *Femme Fatale*
16. MARCO POLO · *Travels in the Land of Serpents and Pearls*
17. SUETONIUS · *Caligula*
18. APOLLONIUS OF RHODES · *Jason and Medea*
19. ROBERT LOUIS STEVENSON · *Olalla*
20. KARL MARX AND FRIEDRICH ENGELS · *The Communist Manifesto*
21. PETRONIUS · *Trimalchio's Feast*
22. JOHANN PETER HEBEL · *How a Ghastly Story Was Brought to Light by a Common or Garden Butcher's Dog*
23. HANS CHRISTIAN ANDERSEN · *The Tinder Box*
24. RUDYARD KIPLING · *The Gate of the Hundred Sorrows*
25. DANTE · *Circles of Hell*
26. HENRY MAYHEW · *Of Street Piemen*
27. HAFEZ · *The nightingales are drunk*
28. GEOFFREY CHAUCER · *The Wife of Bath*
29. MICHEL DE MONTAIGNE · *How We Weep and Laugh at the Same Thing*
30. THOMAS NASHE · *The Terrors of the Night*
31. EDGAR ALLAN POE · *The Tell-Tale Heart*
32. MARY KINGSLEY · *A Hippo Banquet*
33. JANE AUSTEN · *The Beautifull Cassandra*
34. ANTON CHEKHOV · *Gooseberries*
35. SAMUEL TAYLOR COLERIDGE · *Well, they are gone, and here must I remain*
36. JOHANN WOLFGANG VON GOETHE · *Sketchy, Doubtful, Incomplete Jottings*
37. CHARLES DICKENS · *The Great Winglebury Duel*
38. HERMAN MELVILLE · *The Maldive Shark*
39. ELIZABETH GASKELL · *The Old Nurse's Story*
40. NIKOLAY LESKOV · *The Steel Flea*

41. HONORÉ DE BALZAC · *The Atheist's Mass*
42. CHARLOTTE PERKINS GILMAN · *The Yellow Wall-Paper*
43. C.P. CAVAFY · *Remember, Body . . .*
44. FYODOR DOSTOEVSKY · *The Meek One*
45. GUSTAVE FLAUBERT · *A Simple Heart*
46. NIKOLAI GOGOL · *The Nose*
47. SAMUEL PEPYS · *The Great Fire of London*
48. EDITH WHARTON · *The Reckoning*
49. HENRY JAMES · *The Figure in the Carpet*
50. WILFRED OWEN · *Anthem For Doomed Youth*
51. WOLFGANG AMADEUS MOZART · *My Dearest Father*
52. PLATO · *Socrates' Defence*
53. CHRISTINA ROSSETTI · *Goblin Market*
54. *Sindbad the Sailor*
55. SOPHOCLES · *Antigone*
56. RYŪNOSUKE AKUTAGAWA · *The Life of a Stupid Man*
57. LEO TOLSTOY · *How Much Land Does A Man Need?*
58. GIORGIO VASARI · *Leonardo da Vinci*
59. OSCAR WILDE · *Lord Arthur Savile's Crime*
60. SHEN FU · *The Old Man of the Moon*
61. AESOP · *The Dolphins, the Whales and the Gudgeon*
62. MATSUO BASHŌ · *Lips too Chilled*
63. EMILY BRONTË · *The Night is Darkening Round Me*
64. JOSEPH CONRAD · *To-morrow*
65. RICHARD HAKLUYT · *The Voyage of Sir Francis Drake Around the Whole Globe*
66. KATE CHOPIN · *A Pair of Silk Stockings*
67. CHARLES DARWIN · *It was snowing butterflies*
68. BROTHERS GRIMM · *The Robber Bridegroom*
69. CATULLUS · *I Hate and I Love*
70. HOMER · *Circe and the Cyclops*
71. D. H. LAWRENCE · *Il Duro*
72. KATHERINE MANSFIELD · *Miss Brill*
73. OVID · *The Fall of Icarus*
74. SAPPHO · *Come Close*
75. IVAN TURGENEV · *Kasyan from the Beautiful Lands*
76. VIRGIL · *O Cruel Alexis*
77. H. G. WELLS · *A Slip under the Microscope*
78. HERODOTUS · *The Madness of Cambyses*
79. *Speaking of Siva*
80. *The Dhammapada*

'For hate is not conquered by hate: hate is conquered by love. This is a law eternal.'

Taken from Juan Mascaró's translation and edition of
The Dhammapada, first published in 1973.

The Dhammapada

Translated by
Juan Mascaró

PENGUIN BOOKS

PENGUIN CLASSICS

UK | USA | Canada | Ireland | Australia
India | New Zealand | South Africa

Penguin Books is part of the Penguin Random House group of companies
whose addresses can be found at global.penguinrandomhouse.com.

This selection published in Penguin Classics 2015

012

Translation copyright © Juan Mascaró 1973

The moral right of the translator has been asserted

Set in 9/12.4 pt Baskerville 10 Pro
Typeset by Jouve (UK), Milton Keynes
Printed in Great Britain by Clays Ltd, Elcograf S.p.A.

A CIP catalogue record for this book is available from the British Library

ISBN: 978-0-141-39881-5

www.greenpenguin.co.uk

MIX
Paper from
responsible sources
FSC® C018179

Penguin Random House is committed to a sustainable future for our business, our readers and our planet. This book is made from Forest Stewardship Council® certified paper.

1

Contrary Ways

1. What we are today comes from our thoughts of yesterday, and our present thoughts build our life of tomorrow: our life is the creation of our mind.

   If a man speaks or acts with an impure mind, suffering follows him as the wheel of the cart follows the beast that draws the cart.

2. What we are today comes from our thoughts of yesterday, and our present thoughts build our life of tomorrow: our life is the creation of our mind.

   If a man speaks or acts with a pure mind, joy follows him as his own shadow.

3. 'He insulted me, he hurt me, he defeated me, he robbed me.' Those who think such thoughts will not be free from hate.

4. 'He insulted me, he hurt me, he defeated me, he robbed me.' Those who think not such thoughts will be free from hate.

5. For hate is not conquered by hate: hate is conquered by love. This is a law eternal.

6. Many do not know that we are here in this world to live in harmony. Those who know this do not fight against each other.

7. He who lives only for pleasures, and whose soul is not in harmony, who considers not the food he eats, is idle and

has not the power of virtue – such a man is moved by MARA, is moved by selfish temptations, even as a weak tree is shaken by the wind.

8 But he who lives not for pleasures, and whose soul is in self-harmony, who eats or fasts with moderation, and has faith and the power of virtue – this man is not moved by temptations, as a great rock is not shaken by the wind.

9 If a man puts on the pure yellow robe with a soul which is impure, without self-harmony and truth, he is not worthy of the holy robe.

10 But he who is pure from sin and whose soul is strong in virtue, who has self-harmony and truth, he is worthy of the holy robe.

11 Those who think the unreal is, and think the Real is not, they shall never reach the Truth, lost in the path of wrong thought.

12 But those who know the Real is, and know the unreal is not, they shall indeed reach the Truth, safe on the path of right thought.

13 Even as rain breaks through an ill-thatched house, passions will break through an ill-guarded mind.

14 But even as rain breaks not through a well-thatched house, passions break not through a well-guarded mind.

15 He suffers in this world, and he suffers in the next world: the man who does evil suffers in both worlds. He suffers, he suffers and mourns when he sees the wrong he has done.

16 He is happy in this world and he is happy in the next world: the man who does good is happy in both worlds.

He is glad, he feels great gladness when he sees the good he has done.

17 He sorrows in this world, and he sorrows in the next world: the man who does evil sorrows in both worlds. 'I have done evil', thus he laments, and more he laments on the path of sorrow.

18 He rejoices in this world, and he rejoices in the next world: the man who does good rejoices in both worlds. 'I have done good', thus he rejoices, and more he rejoices on the path of joy.

19 If a man speaks many holy words but he speaks and does not, this thoughtless man cannot enjoy the life of holiness: he is like a cowherd who counts the cows of his master.

20 Whereas if a man speaks but a few holy words and yet he lives the life of those words, free from passion and hate and illusion – with right vision and a mind free, craving for nothing both now and hereafter – the life of this man is a life of holiness.

2

Watchfulness

21 Watchfulness is the path of immortality: unwatchfulness is the path of death. Those who are watchful never die: those who do not watch are already as dead.

22 Those who with a clear mind have seen this truth, those

who are wise and ever-watchful, they feel the joy of watchfulness, the joy of the path of the Great.

23 And those who in high thought and in deep contemplation with ever-living power advance on the path, they in the end reach NIRVANA, the peace supreme and infinite joy.

24 The man who arises in faith, who ever remembers his high purpose, whose work is pure, and who carefully considers his work, who in self-possession lives the life of perfection, and who ever, for ever, is watchful, that man shall arise in glory.

25 By arising in faith and watchfulness, by self-possession and self-harmony, the wise man makes an island for his soul which many waters cannot overflow.

26 Men who are foolish and ignorant are careless and never watchful; but the man who lives in watchfulness considers it his greatest treasure.

27 Never surrender to carelessness; never sink into weak pleasures and lust. Those who are watchful, in deep contemplation, reach in the end the joy supreme.

28 The wise man who by watchfulness conquers thoughtlessness is as one who free from sorrows ascends the palace of wisdom and there, from its high terrace, sees those in sorrow below; even as a wise strong man on the holy mountain might behold the many unwise far down below on the plain.

29 Watchful amongst the unwatchful, awake amongst those who sleep, the wise man like a swift horse runs his race, outrunning those who are slow.

30 It was by watchfulness that Indra became the chief of the

gods, and thus the gods praise the watchful, and thoughtlessness is ever despised.

31 The monk who has the joy of watchfulness and who looks with fear on thoughtlessness, he goes on his path like a fire, burning all obstacles both great and small.

32 The monk who has the joy of watchfulness, and who looks with fear on thoughtlessness, he can never be deprived of his victory and he is near NIRVANA.

3

The Mind

33 The mind is wavering and restless, difficult to guard and restrain: let the wise man straighten his mind as a maker of arrows makes his arrows straight.

34 Like a fish which is thrown on dry land, taken from his home in the waters, the mind strives and struggles to get free from the power of Death.

35 The mind is fickle and flighty, it flies after fancies wherever it likes: it is difficult indeed to restrain. But it is a great good to control the mind; a mind self-controlled is a source of great joy.

36 Invisible and subtle is the mind, and it flies after fancies wherever it likes; but let the wise man guard well his mind, for a mind well guarded is a source of great joy.

37 Hidden in the mystery of consciousness, the mind, incorporeal, flies alone far away. Those who set their mind in harmony become free from the bonds of death.

38 He whose mind is unsteady, who knows not the path of Truth, whose faith and peace are ever wavering, he shall never reach fullness of wisdom.

39 But he whose mind in calm self-control is free from the lust of desires, who has risen above good and evil, he is awake and has no fear.

40 Considering that this body is frail like a jar, make your mind strong like a fortress and fight the great fight against MARA, all evil temptations. After victory guard well your conquests, and ever for ever watch.

41 For before long, how sad! this body will lifeless lie on the earth, cast aside like a useless log.

42 An enemy can hurt an enemy, and a man who hates can harm another man; but a man's own mind, if wrongly directed, can do him a far greater harm.

43 A father or a mother, or a relative, can indeed do good to a man; but his own right-directed mind can do to him a far greater good.

4

The Flowers of Life

44 Who shall conquer this world and the world of the gods, and also the world of Yama, of death and of pain? Who shall find the DHAMMAPADA, the clear Path of Perfection, even as a man who seeks flowers finds the most beautiful flower?

45 The wise student shall conquer this world, and the world

The Flowers of Life

of the gods, and also the world of Yama, of death and of pain. The wise student shall find the DHAMMAPADA, the clear Path of Perfection, even as a man who seeks flowers finds the most beautiful flower:

46 He who knows that this body is the foam of a wave, the shadow of a mirage, he breaks the sharp arrows of MARA, concealed in the flowers of sensuous passions and, unseen by the king of death, he goes on and follows his path.

47 But death carries away the man who gathers the flowers of sensuous passions, even as a torrent of rushing waters overflows a sleeping village, and then runs forward on its way.

48 And death, the end of all, makes an end of the man who, ever thirsty for desires, gathers the flowers of sensuous passions.

49 As the bee takes the essence of a flower and flies away without destroying its beauty and perfume, so let the sage wander in this life.

50 Think not of the faults of others, of what they have done or not done. Think rather of your own sins, of the things you have done or not done.

51 Just as a flower which seems beautiful and has colour but has no perfume, so are the fruitless words of the man who speaks them but does them not.

52 And just like a beautiful flower which has colour and also has perfume are the beautiful fruitful words of the man who speaks and does what he says.

53 As from a large heap of flowers many garlands and wreaths can be made, so by a mortal in this life there is much good work to be done.

54 The perfume of flowers goes not against the wind, not

even the perfume of sandalwood, of rose-bay, or of jasmine; but the perfume of virtue travels against the wind and reaches unto the ends of the world.

55 There is the perfume of sandalwood, of rose-bay, of the blue lotus and jasmine; but far above the perfume of those flowers the perfume of virtue is supreme.

56 Not very far goes the perfume of flowers, even that of rose-bay or of sandalwood; but the perfume of the good reaches heaven, and it is the perfume supreme amongst the gods.

57 The path of those who are rich in virtue, who are ever watchful, whose true light makes them free, cannot be crossed by MARA, by death.

58 Even as on a heap of rubbish thrown away by the side
59 of the road a lotus flower may grow and blossom with its pure perfume giving joy to the soul, in the same way among the blind multitudes shines pure the light of wisdom of the student who follows the Buddha, the ONE who is truly awake.

5

The Fool

60 How long is the night to the watchman; how long is the road to the weary; how long is the wandering of lives ending in death for the fool who cannot find the path!

61 If on the great journey of life a man cannot find one who is better or at least as good as himself, let him joyfully travel alone: a fool cannot help him on his journey.

The Fool

62 'These are my sons. This is my wealth.' In this way the fool troubles himself. He is not even the owner of himself: how much less of his sons and of his wealth!

63 If a fool can see his own folly, he in this at least is wise; but the fool who thinks he is wise, he indeed is the real fool.

64 If during the whole of his life a fool lives with a wise man, he never knows the path of wisdom as the spoon never knows the taste of the soup.

65 But if a man who watches and sees is only a moment with a wise man he soon knows the path of wisdom, as the tongue knows the taste of the soup.

66 A fool who thinks he is wise goes through life with himself as his enemy, and he ever does wrong deeds which in the end bear bitter fruit.

67 For that deed is not well done when being done one has to repent; and when one must reap with tears the bitter fruits of the wrong deed.

68 But the deed is indeed well done when being done one has not to repent; and when one can reap with joy the sweet fruits of the right deed.

69 The wrong action seems sweet to the fool until the reaction comes and brings pain, and the bitter fruits of wrong deeds have then to be eaten by the fool.

70 A fool may fast month after month eating his food with the sharp point of a blade of *kusa* grass, and his worth be not a sixteenth part of that of the wise man whose thoughts feed on truth.

71 A wrong action may not bring its reaction at once, even as fresh milk turns not sour at once: like a smouldering

fire concealed under ashes it consumes the wrongdoer, the fool.

72 And if ever to his own harm the fool increases in cleverness, this only destroys his own mind and his fate is worse than before.

73 For he will wish for reputation, for precedence among the monks, for authority in the monasteries and for veneration amongst the people.

74 'Let householders and hermits, both, think it was I who did that work; and let them ever ask me what they should do or not do.' These are the thoughts of the fool, puffed up with desire and pride.

75 But one is the path of earthly wealth, and another is the path of NIRVANA. Let the follower of Buddha think of this and, without striving for reputation, let him ever strive after freedom.

6

The Wise Man

76 Look upon the man who tells thee thy faults as if he told thee of a hidden treasure, the wise man who shows thee the dangers of life. Follow that man: he who follows him will see good and not evil.

77 Let him admonish and let him instruct, and let him restrain what is wrong. He will be loved by those who are good and hated by those who are not.

The Wise Man

78. Have not for friends those whose soul is ugly; go not with men who have an evil soul. Have for friends those whose soul is beautiful; go with men whose soul is good.

79. He who drinks of the waters of Truth, he rests in joy with mind serene. The wise find their delight in the DHAMMA, in the Truth revealed by the great.

80. Those who make channels for water control the waters; makers of arrows make the arrows straight; carpenters control their timber; and the wise control their own minds.

81. Even as a great rock is not shaken by the wind, the wise man is not shaken by praise or by blame.

82. Even as a lake that is pure and peaceful and deep, so becomes the soul of the wise man when he hears the words of DHAMMA.

83. Good men, at all times, surrender in truth all attachments. The holy spend not idle words on things of desire. When pleasure or pain comes to them, the wise feel above pleasure and pain.

84. He who for himself or others craves not for sons or power or wealth, who puts not his own success before the success of righteousness, he is virtuous, and righteous, and wise.

85. Few cross the river of time and are able to reach NIRVANA. Most of them run up and down only on this side of the river.

86. But those who when they know the law follow the path of the law, they shall reach the other shore and go beyond the realm of death.

87,88 Leaving behind the path of darkness and following the path of light, let the wise man leave his home life and go into a life of freedom. In solitude that few enjoy, let him find his joy supreme: free from possessions, free from desires, and free from whatever may darken his mind.

89 For he whose mind is well trained in the ways that lead to light, who surrenders the bondage of attachments and finds joy in his freedom from bondage, who free from the darkness of passions shines pure in a radiance of light, even in this mortal life he enjoys the immortal NIRVANA.

7

Infinite Freedom

90 The traveller has reached the end of the journey! In the freedom of the Infinite he is free from all sorrows, the fetters that bound him are thrown away, and the burning fever of life is no more.

91 Those who have high thoughts are ever striving: they are not happy to remain in the same place. Like swans that leave their lake and rise into the air, they leave their home for a higher home.

92 Who can trace the path of those who know the right food of life and, rejecting over-abundance, soar in the sky of liberation, the infinite Void without beginning? Their course is as hard to follow as that of the birds in the air.

Infinite Freedom

93 Who can trace the invisible path of the man who soars in the sky of liberation, the infinite Void without beginning, whose passions are peace, and over whom pleasures have no power? His path is as difficult to trace as that of the birds in the air.

94 The man who wisely controls his senses as a good driver controls his horses, and who is free from lower passions and pride, is admired even by the gods.

95 He is calm like the earth that endures; he is steady like a column that is firm; he is pure like a lake that is clear; he is free from *Samsara*, the ever-returning life-in-death.

96 In the light of his vision he has found his freedom: his thoughts are peace, his words are peace and his work is peace.

97 And he who is free from credulous beliefs since he has seen the eternal NIRVANA, who has thrown off the bondage of the lower life and, far beyond temptations, has surrendered all his desires, he is indeed great amongst men.

98 Wherever holy men dwell, that is indeed a place of joy – be it in the village, or in a forest, or in a valley or on the hills.

99 They make delightful the forests where other people could not dwell. Because they have not the burden of desires, they have that joy which others find not.

8

Better than a Thousand

100 Better than a thousand useless words is one single word that gives peace.
101 Better than a thousand useless verses is one single verse that gives peace.
102 Better than a hundred useless poems is one single poem that gives peace.
103 If a man should conquer in battle a thousand and a
104 thousand more, and another man should conquer him-
105 self, his would be the greater victory, because the greatest of victories is the victory over oneself; and neither the gods in heaven above nor the demons down below can turn into defeat the victory of such a man.
106 If month after month with a thousand offerings for a hundred years one should sacrifice; and another only for a moment paid reverence to a self-conquering man, this moment would have greater value than a hundred years of offerings.
107 If a man for a hundred years should worship the sacred fire in the forest; and if another only for a moment paid reverence to a self-conquering man, this reverence alone would be greater than a hundred years of worship.
108 Whatever a man for a year may offer in worship or in gifts to earn merit is not worth a fraction of the merit earned by one's reverence to a righteous man.

109 And whosoever honours in reverence those who are old in virtue and holiness, he indeed conquers four treasures: long life, and health, and power and joy.

110 Better than a hundred years lived in vice, without contemplation, is one single day of life lived in virtue and in deep contemplation.

111 Better than a hundred years lived in ignorance, without contemplation, is one single day of life lived in wisdom and in deep contemplation.

112 Better than a hundred years lived in idleness and in weakness is a single day of life lived with courage and powerful striving.

113 Better than a hundred years not considering how all things arise and pass away is one single day of life if one considers how all things arise and pass away.

114 Better than a hundred years not seeing one's own immortality is one single day of life if one sees one's own immortality.

115 Better than a hundred years not seeing the Path supreme is one single day of life if one sees the Path supreme.

9

Good and Evil

116 Make haste and do what is good; keep your mind away from evil. If a man is slow in doing good, his mind finds pleasure in evil.

117 If a man does something wrong, let him not do it again

and again. Let him not find pleasure in his sin. Painful is the accumulation of wrongdoings.

118 If a man does something good, let him do it again and again. Let him find joy in his good work. Joyful is the accumulation of good work.

119 A man may find pleasure in evil as long as his evil has not given fruit; but when the fruit of evil comes then that man finds evil indeed.

120 A man may find pain in doing good as long as his good has not given fruit; but when the fruit of good comes then that man finds good indeed.

121 Hold not a sin of little worth, thinking 'this is little to me'. The falling of drops of water will in time fill a water-jar. Even so the foolish man becomes full of evil, although he gather it little by little.

122 Hold not a deed of little worth, thinking 'this is little to me'. The falling of drops of water will in time fill a water-jar. Even so the wise man becomes full of good, although he gather it little by little.

123 Let a man avoid the dangers of evil even as a merchant carrying much wealth, but with a small escort, avoids the dangers of the road, or as a man who loves his life avoids the drinking of poison.

124 As a man who has no wound on his hand cannot be hurt by the poison he may carry in his hand, since poison hurts not where there is no wound, the man who has no evil cannot be hurt by evil.

125 The fool who does evil to a man who is good, to a man who is pure and free from sin, the evil returns to him like the dust thrown against the wind.

126 Some people are born on this earth; those who do evil are reborn in hell; the righteous go to heaven; but those who are pure reach NIRVANA.

127 Neither in the sky, nor deep in the ocean, nor in a mountain-cave, nor anywhere, can a man be free from the evil he has done.

128 Neither in the sky, nor deep in the ocean, nor in a mountain-cave, nor anywhere, can a man be free from the power of death.

10

Life

129 All beings tremble before danger, all fear death. When a man considers this, he does not kill or cause to kill.

130 All beings fear before danger, life is dear to all. When a man considers this, he does not kill or cause to kill.

131 He who for the sake of happiness hurts others who also want happiness, shall not hereafter find happiness.

132 He who for the sake of happiness does not hurt others who also want happiness, shall hereafter find happiness.

133 Never speak harsh words, for once spoken they may return to you. Angry words are painful and there may be blows for blows.

134 If you can be in silent quietness like a broken gong that is silent, you have reached the peace of NIRVANA and your anger is peace.

The Dhammapada

135 Just as a keeper of cows drives his cows into the fields, old age and death drive living beings far into the fields of death.

136 When a fool does evil work, he forgets that he is lighting a fire wherein he must burn one day.

137-140 He who hurts with his weapons those who are harmless and pure shall soon fall into one of these ten evils: fearful pain or infirmity; loss of limbs or terrible disease; or even madness, the loss of the mind; the king's persecution; a fearful indictment; the loss of possessions or the loss of relations; or fire from heaven that may burn his house. And when the evil-doer is no more, then he is reborn in hell.

141 Neither nakedness, nor entangled hair, nor uncleanliness, nor fasting, nor sleeping on the ground, nor covering the body with ashes, nor ever-squatting, can purify a man who is not pure from doubts and desires.

142 But although a man may wear fine clothing, if he lives peacefully; and is good, self-possessed, has faith and is pure; and if he does not hurt any living being, he is a holy Brahmin, a hermit of seclusion, a monk called a Bhikkhu.

143 Is there in this world a man so noble that he ever avoids all blame, even as a noble horse avoids the touch of the whip?

144 Have fire like a noble horse touched by the whip. By faith, by virtue and energy, by deep contemplation and vision, by wisdom and by right action, you shall overcome the sorrows of life.

145 Those who make channels for water control the waters; makers of arrows make the arrows straight; carpenters control their timber; and the holy control their soul.

11

Beyond Life

146 How can there be laughter, how can there be pleasure, when the whole world is burning? When you are in deep darkness, will you not ask for a lamp?

147 Consider this body! A painted puppet with jointed limbs, sometimes suffering and covered with ulcers, full of imaginings, never permanent, for ever changing.

148 This body is decaying! A nest of diseases, a heap of corruption, bound to destruction, to dissolution. All life ends in death.

149 Look at these grey-white dried bones, like dried empty gourds thrown away at the end of the summer. Who will feel joy in looking at them?

150 A house of bones is this body, bones covered with flesh and with blood. Pride and hypocrisy dwell in this house and also old age and death.

151 The glorious chariots of kings wear out, and the body wears out and grows old; but the virtue of the good never grows old, and thus they can teach the good to those who are good.

The Dhammapada

152 If a man tries not to learn he grows old just like an ox! His body indeed grows old but his wisdom does not grow.

153 I have gone round in vain the cycles of many lives ever
154 striving to find the builder of the house of life and death. How great is the sorrow of life that must die! But now I have seen thee, housebuilder: never more shalt thou build this house. The rafters of sins are broken, the ridge-pole of ignorance is destroyed. The fever of craving is past: for my mortal mind is gone to the joy of the immortal NIRVANA.

155 Those who in their youth did not live in self-harmony, and who did not gain the true treasures of life, are later like long-legged old herons standing sad by a lake without fish.

156 Those who in their youth did not live in self-harmony, and who did not gain the true treasures of life, are later like broken bows, ever deploring old things past and gone.

12

Self-Possession

157 If a man holds himself dear, let him guard himself well. Of the three watches of his time, let him at least watch over one.

158 Let him find first what is right and then he can teach it to others, avoiding thus useless pain.

Self-Possession

159 If he makes himself as good as he tells others to be, then he in truth can teach others. Difficult indeed is self-control.

160 Only a man himself can be the master of himself: who else from outside could be his master? When the Master and servant are one, then there is true help and self-possession.

161 Any wrong or evil a man does, is born in himself and is caused by himself; and this crushes the foolish man as a hard stone grinds the weaker stone.

162 And the evil that grows in a man is like the *malava* creeper which entangles the *sala* tree; and the man is brought down to that condition in which his own enemy would wish him to be.

163 It is easy to do what is wrong, to do what is bad for oneself; but very difficult to do what is right, to do what is good for oneself.

164 The fool who because of his views scorns the teachings of the holy, those whose soul is great and righteous, gathers fruits for his destruction, like the *kashta* reed whose fruits mean its death.

165 By oneself the evil is done, and it is oneself who suffers: by oneself the evil is not done, and by one's Self one becomes pure. The pure and the impure come from oneself: no man can purify another.

166 Let no man endanger his duty, the good of his soul, for the good of another, however great. When he has seen the good of his soul, let him follow it with earnestness.

13

Arise! Watch

167 Live not a low life; remember and forget not; follow not wrong ideas; sink not into the world.

168 Arise! Watch. Walk on the right path. He who follows the right path has joy in this world and in the world beyond.

169 Follow the right path: follow not the wrong path. He who follows the right path has joy in this world and in the world beyond.

170 When a man considers this world as a bubble of froth, and as the illusion of an appearance, then the king of death has no power over him.

171 Come and look at this world. It is like a royal painted chariot wherein fools sink. The wise are not imprisoned in the chariot.

172 He who in early days was unwise but later found wisdom, he sheds a light over the world like that of the moon when free from clouds.

173 He who overcomes the evil he has done with the good he afterwards does, he sheds a light over the world like that of the moon when free from clouds.

174 This world is indeed in darkness, and how few can see the light! Just as few birds can escape from a net, few souls can fly into the freedom of heaven.

175 Swans follow the path of the sun by the miracle of flying through the air. Men who are strong conquer evil and its armies; and then they arise far above the world.

176 A man whose words are lies, who transgresses the Great Law, and who scorns the higher world – there is no evil this man may not do.

177 Misers certainly do not go to the heaven of the gods, and fools do not praise liberality; but noble men find joy in generosity, and this gives them joy in higher worlds.

178 Better than power over all the earth, better than going to heaven and better than dominion over the worlds is the joy of the man who enters the river of life that leads to NIRVANA.

14

The Buddha

179 By what earthly path could you entice the Buddha who, enjoying all, can wander through the pathless ways of the Infinite? – the Buddha who is awake, whose victory cannot be turned into defeat, and whom no one can conquer?

180 By what earthly path could you entice the Buddha who, enjoying all, can wander through the pathless ways of the Infinite? – the Buddha who is awake, whom the net of poisonous desire cannot allure?

181 Even the gods long to be like the Buddhas who are awake and watch, who find peace in contemplation and who, calm and steady, find joy in renunciation.

182 It is a great event to be born a man; and his life is an ever-striving. It is not often he hears the doctrine of Truth; and a rare event is the arising of a Buddha.

183 Do not what is evil. Do what is good. Keep your mind pure. This is the teaching of Buddha.

184 Forbearance is the highest sacrifice. NIRVANA is the highest good. This say the Buddhas who are awake. If a man hurts another, he is not a hermit; if he offends another, he is not an ascetic.

185 Not to hurt by deeds or words, self-control as taught in the Rules, moderation in food, the solitude of one's room and one's bed, and the practice of the highest consciousness: this is teaching of the Buddhas who are awake.

186 Since a shower of golden coins could not satisfy craving

187 desires and the end of all pleasure is pain, how could a wise man find satisfaction even in the pleasures of the gods? When desires go, joy comes: the follower of Buddha finds this Truth.

188 Men in their fear fly for refuge to mountains or forests,

189 groves, sacred trees or shrines. But those are not a safe refuge, they are not the refuge that frees a man from sorrow.

190 He who goes for refuge to Buddha, to Truth and to those whom he taught, he goes indeed to a great refuge. Then he sees the four great truths:

191 Sorrow, the cause of sorrow, the end of sorrow, and the path of eight stages which leads to the end of sorrow.

192 That is the safe refuge, that is the refuge supreme. If a man goes to that refuge, he is free from sorrow.

193 A man of true vision is not easy to find, a Buddha who is awake is not born everywhere. Happy are the people where such a man is born.

194 Happy is the birth of a Buddha, happy is the teaching of DHAMMA, happy is the harmony of his followers, happy is the life of those who live in harmony.

195 Who could measure the excellence of the man who
196 pays reverence to those worthy of reverence, a Buddha or his disciples, who have left evil behind and have crossed the river of sorrow, who, free from all fear, are in the glory of NIRVANA?

15

Joy

197 O let us live in joy, in love amongst those who hate! Among men who hate, let us live in love.

198 O let us live in joy, in health amongst those who are ill! Among men who are ill, let us live in health.

199 O let us live in joy, in peace amongst those who struggle! Among men who struggle, let us live in peace.

200 O let us live in joy, although having nothing! In joy let us live like spirits of light!

201 Victory brings hate, because the defeated man is unhappy. He who surrenders victory and defeat, this man finds joy.

202 There is no fire like lust. There is no evil like hate. There is no pain like disharmony. There is no joy like NIRVANA.

203 The hunger of passions is the greatest disease. Disharmony is the greatest sorrow. When you know this well, then you know that NIRVANA is the greatest joy.

204 Health is the greatest possession. Contentment is the greatest treasure. Confidence is the greatest friend. NIRVANA is the greatest joy.

205 When a man knows the solitude of silence, and feels the joy of quietness, he is then free from fear and sin and he feels the joy of the DHAMMA.

206 It is a joy to see the noble and good, and to be with them makes one happy. If one were able never to see fools, then one could be for ever happy!

207 He who has to walk with fools has a long journey of sorrow, because to be with a fool is as painful as to be with an enemy; but the joy of being with the wise is like the joy of meeting a beloved kinsman.

208 If you find a man who is constant, awake to the inner light, learned, long-suffering, endowed with devotion, a noble man – follow this good and great man even as the moon follows the path of the stars.

16

Transient Pleasures

209 He who does what should not be done and fails to do what should be done, who forgets the true aim of life and sinks into transient pleasures – he will one day envy the man who lives in high contemplation.

210 Let a man be free from pleasure and let a man be free from pain; for not to have pleasure is sorrow and to have pain is also sorrow.

211 Be therefore not bound to pleasure for the loss of pleasure is pain. There are no fetters for the man who is beyond pleasure and pain.

212 From pleasure arises sorrow and from pleasure arises fear. If a man is free from pleasure, he is free from fear and sorrow.

213 From passion arises sorrow and from passion arises fear. If a man is free from passion, he is free from fear and sorrow.

214 From sensuousness arises sorrow and from sensuousness arises fear. If a man is free from sensuousness, he is free from fear and sorrow.

215 From lust arises sorrow and from lust arises fear. If a man is free from lust, he is free from fear and sorrow.

216 From craving arises sorrow and from craving arises fear. If a man is free from craving, he is free from fear and sorrow.

The Dhammapada

217 He who has virtue and vision, who follows DHAMMA, the Path of Perfection, whose words are truth, and does the work to be done – the world loves such a man.

218 And the man whose mind, filled with determination, is longing for the infinite NIRVANA, and who is free from sensuous pleasures, is called *uddham-soto*, 'he who goes upstream', for against the current of passions and worldly life he is bound for the joy of the Infinite.

219
220 Just as a man who has long been far away is welcomed with joy on his safe return by his relatives, well-wishers and friends; in the same way the good works of a man in his life welcome him in another life, with the joy of a friend meeting a friend on his return.

17

Forsake Anger

221 Forsake anger, give up pride. Sorrow cannot touch the man who is not in the bondage of anything, who owns nothing.

222 He who can control his rising anger as a coachman controls his carriage at full speed, this man I call a good driver: others merely hold the reins.

223 Overcome anger by peacefulness: overcome evil by good. Overcome the mean by generosity; and the man who lies by truth.

224 Speak the truth, yield not to anger, give what you can to him who asks: these three steps lead you to the gods.

Forsake Anger

225 The wise who hurt no living being, and who keep their body under self-control, they go to the immortal NIRVANA, where once gone they sorrow no more.

226 Those who are for ever watchful, who study themselves day and night, and who wholly strive for NIRVANA, all their passions pass away.

227 This is an old saying, Atula, it is not a saying of today: 'They blame the man who is silent, they blame the man who speaks too much, and they blame the man who speaks too little'. No man can escape blame in this world.

228 There never was, there never will be, nor is there now, a man whom men always blame, or a man whom they always praise.

229 But who would dare to blame the man whom the wise
230 praise day after day, whose life is pure and full of light, in whom there is virtue and wisdom, who is pure as a pure coin of gold of the Jambu river? Even the gods praise that man, even Brahma the Creator praises him.

231 Watch for anger of the body: let the body be self-controlled. Hurt not with the body, but use your body well.

232 Watch for anger of words: let your words be self-controlled. Hurt not with words, but use your words well.

233 Watch for anger of the mind: let your mind be self-controlled. Hurt not with the mind, but use your mind well.

234 There are men steady and wise whose body, words and mind are self-controlled. They are the men of supreme self-control.

18

Hasten and Strive

235 Yellow leaves hang on your tree of life. The messengers of death are waiting. You are going to travel far away. Have you any provision for the journey?

236 Make an island for yourself. Hasten and strive. Be wise. With the dust of impurities blown off, and free from sinful passions, you will come unto the glorious land of the great.

237 You are at the end of your life. You are going to meet Death. There is no resting-place on your way, and you have no provision for the journey.

238 Make therefore an island for yourself. Hasten and strive. Be wise. With the dust of impurities blown off, and free from sinful passions, you will be free from birth that must die, you will be free from old age that ends in death.

239 Let a wise man remove impurities from himself even as a silversmith removes impurities from the silver: one after one, little by little, again and again.

240 Even as rust on iron destroys in the end the iron, a man's own impure transgressions lead that man to the evil path.

241 Dull repetition is the rust of sacred verses; lack of repair is the rust of houses; want of healthy exercise is the rust of beauty; unwatchfulness is the rust of the watcher.

Hasten and Strive

242 Misconduct is sin in woman; meanness is sin in a benefactor; evil actions are indeed sins both in this world and in the next.

243 But the greatest of all sins is indeed the sin of ignorance. Throw this sin away, O man, and become pure from sin.

244 Life seems easy for those who shamelessly are bold and self-assertive, crafty and cunning, sensuously selfish, wanton and impure, arrogant and insulting, rotting with corruption.

245 But life seems difficult for those who peacefully strive for perfection, who free from self-seeking are not self-assertive, whose life is pure, who see the light.

246 He who destroys life, who utters lies, who takes what
247 is not given to him, who goes to the wife of another, who gets drunk with strong drinks – he digs up the very roots of his life.

248 Know this therefore, O man: that lack of self-control means wrongdoing. Watch that greediness and vice bring thee not unto long suffering.

249 People in this world give their gifts because of inner light or selfish pleasure. If a man's thoughts are disturbed by what others give or give not, how can he by day or night achieve supreme contemplation?

250 But he in whom the roots of jealousy have been uprooted and burnt away, then he both by day or by night can achieve supreme contemplation.

251 There is no fire like lust, and no chains like those of hate. There is no net like illusion, and no rushing torrent like desire.

252 It is easy to see the faults of others, but difficult to see one's own faults. One shows the faults of others like chaff winnowed in the wind, but one conceals one's own faults as a cunning gambler conceals his dice.

253 If a man sees the sins of others and for ever thinks of their faults, his own sins increase for ever and far off is he from the end of his faults.

254 There is no path in the sky and a monk must find the inner path. The world likes pleasures that are obstacles on the path; but the *Tatha-gatas*, the 'Thus-gone', have crossed the river of time and they have overcome the world.

255 There is no path in the sky and a monk must find the inner path. All things indeed pass away, but the Buddhas are for ever in Eternity.

19

Righteousness

256 A man is not on the path of righteousness if he settles
257 matters in a violent haste. A wise man calmly considers what is right and what is wrong, and faces different opinions with truth, non-violence and peace. This man is guarded by truth and is a guardian of truth. He is righteous and he is wise.

258 A man is not called wise because he talks and talks again; but if he is peaceful, loving and fearless then he is in truth called wise.

Righteousness

259 A man is not a follower of righteousness because he talks much learned talk; but although a man be not learned, if he forgets not the right path, if his work is rightly done, then he is a follower of righteousness.

260 A man is not old and venerable because grey hairs are on his head. If a man is old only in years then he is indeed old in vain.

261 But a man is a venerable 'elder' if he is in truth free from sin, and if in him there is truth and righteousness, non-violence, moderation and self-control.

262 Not by mere fine words and appearance can a man be
263 a man of honour, if envy, greed and deceit are in him. But he in whom these three sins are uprooted and who is wise and has love, he is in truth a man of honour.

264 Not by the tonsure, a shaven head, does a man become a *samana*, a monk. How can a man be a *samana* if he forgets his religious vows, if he speaks what is not true, if he still has desire and greed?

265 But he who turns into peace all evil, whether this be great or small, he in truth is a *samana*, because all his evil is peace.

266 He is not called a mendicant Bhikkhu because he leads a mendicant life. A man cannot be a true Bhikkhu unless he accepts the law of righteousness and rejects the law of the flesh.

267 But he who is above good and evil, who lives in chastity and goes through life in meditation, he in truth is called a Bhikkhu.

268 If a man is only silent because he is ignorant or a fool,
269 he is not a silent thinker, a MUNI who considers and

thinks. But as one who taking a pair of scales, puts in what is good and rejects what is bad, if a man considers the two worlds, then he is called a MUNI of silence, a man who considers and thinks.

270 A man is not a great man because he is a warrior and kills other men; but because he hurts not any living being he in truth is called a great man.

271 Not by mere morals or rituals, by much learning or high
272 concentration, or by a bed of solitude, can I reach that joy of freedom which is not reached by those of the world. Mendicant! Have not self-satisfaction, the victory has not yet been won.

20

The Path

273 The best of the paths is the path of eight. The best of truths, the four sayings. The best of states, freedom from passions. The best of men, the one who sees.

274 This is the path. There is no other that leads to vision. Go on this path, and you will confuse MARA, the devil of confusion.

275 Whoever goes on this path travels to the end of his sorrow. I showed this path to the world when I found the roots of sorrow.

276 It is you who must make the effort. The Great of the past only show the way. Those who think and follow the path become free from the bondage of MARA.

The Path

277 'All is transient.' When one sees this, he is above sorrow. This is the clear path.

278 'All is sorrow.' When one sees this, he is above sorrow. This is the clear path.

279 'All is unreal.' When one sees this, he is above sorrow. This is the clear path.

280 If a man when young and strong does not arise and strive when he should arise and strive, and thus sinks into laziness and lack of determination, he will never find the path of wisdom.

281 A man should control his words and mind and should not do any harm with his body. If these ways of action are pure he can make progress on the path of the wise.

282 Spiritual Yoga leads to light: lack of Yoga to darkness. Considering the two paths, let the wise man walk on the path that leads to light.

283 Cut down the forest of desires, not only a tree; for danger is in the forest. If you cut down the forest and its undergrowth, then, Bhikkhus, you will be free on the path of freedom.

284 As long as lustful desire, however small, of man for women is not controlled, so long the mind of man is not free, but is bound like a calf tied to a cow.

285 Pluck out your self-love as you would pull off a faded lotus in autumn. Strive on the path of peace, the path of NIRVANA shown by Buddha.

286 'Here shall I dwell in the season of rains, and here in winter and summer'; thus thinks the fool, but he does not think of death.

The Dhammapada

287 For death carries away the man whose mind is self-satisfied with his children and his flocks, even as a torrent carries away a sleeping village.

288 Neither father, sons nor one's relations can stop the King of Death. When he comes with all his power, a man's relations cannot save him.

289 A man who is virtuous and wise understands the meaning of this, and swiftly strives with all his might to clear a path to NIRVANA.

21

Wakefulness

290 If by forsaking a small pleasure one finds a great joy, he who is wise will look to the greater and leave what is less.

291 He who seeks happiness for himself by making others unhappy is bound in the chains of hate and from those he cannot be free.

292 By not doing what should be done, and by doing what should not be done, the sinful desires of proud and thoughtless men increase.

293 But those who are ever careful of their actions, who do not what should not be done, are those who are watchful and wise, and their sinful desires come to an end.

294 And a saint, a Brahmin, is pure from past sins; even if he had killed his father and mother, had murdered two noble kings, and had ravaged a whole kingdom and its people.

Wakefulness

295 A saint, a Brahmin, is pure from past sins; even if he had killed his father and mother, had murdered two holy kings, and had also murdered the best of men.

296 The followers of Buddha Gotama are awake and for ever watch; and ever by night and by day they remember Buddha, their Master.

297 The followers of Buddha Gotama are awake and for ever watch; and ever by night and by day they remember the Truth of the Law.

298 The followers of Buddha Gotama are awake and for ever watch; and ever by night and by day they remember the holy brotherhood.

299 The followers of Buddha Gotama are awake and for ever watch; and ever by night and by day they remember the mystery of the body.

300 The followers of Buddha Gotama are awake and for ever watch; and ever by night and by day they find joy in love for all beings.

301 The followers of Buddha Gotama are awake and for ever watch; and ever by night and by day they find joy in supreme contemplation.

302 It is painful to leave the world; it is painful to be in the world; and it is painful to be alone amongst the many. The long road of transmigration is a road of pain for the traveller: let him rest by the road and be free.

303 If a man has faith and has virtue, then he has true glory and treasure. Wherever that man may go, there he will be held in honour.

304 The good shine from far away, like the Himalaya mountains; but the wicked are in darkness, like arrows thrown in the night.

305 He who can be alone and rest alone and is never weary of his great work, he can live in joy, when master of himself, by the edge of the forest of desires.

22

In Darkness

306 He who says what is not goes down the path of hell; and he who says he has not done what he knows well he has done. Both in the end have to suffer, because both sinned against truth.

307 Many wear the yellow robe whose life is not pure, who have not self-control. Those evil men through their evil deeds are reborn in a hell of evil.

308 For it were better for an evil man to swallow a ball of red-hot iron rather than he should eat offerings of food given to him by good people.

309 Four things happen to the thoughtless man who takes another man's wife: he lowers himself, his pleasure is restless, he is blamed by others, he goes to hell.

310 Yes. The degradation of the soul, a frightened pleasure, the danger of the law, the path of hell. Considering these four, let not a man go after another man's wife.

311 Just as a hand of *kusa* grass if badly grasped will cut one's

In Darkness

hand, the life of a monk, if imperfectly followed, will only lead him to hell.

312 For when acts of devotion are carelessly performed, when sacred vows are broken, and when the holy life is not pure, no great fruit can come from such a life.

313 When a man has something to do, let him do it with all his might. A thoughtless pilgrim only raises dust on the road – the dust of dangerous desires.

314 Better to do nothing than to do what is wrong, for wrongdoing brings burning sorrow. Do therefore what is right, for good deeds never bring pain.

315 Like a border town that is well guarded both within and without, so let a man guard himself, and let not a moment pass by in carelessness. Those who carelessly allow their life to pass by, in the end have to suffer in hell.

316 Those who are ashamed when they should not be ashamed, and who are not ashamed when they should be, are men of very wrong views and they go the downward path.

317 Those who fear what they should not fear, and who do not fear what they should fear, are men of very wrong views and they go the downward path.

318 Those who think that right is wrong, and who think that wrong is right, they are the men of wrong views and they go the downward path.

319 But those who think that wrong is wrong, and who think that right is right, they are the men of right views and they go on the upward path.

23

Endurance

320 I will endure words that hurt in silent peace as the strong elephant endures in battle arrows sent by the bow, for many people lack self-control.

321 They take trained elephants to battle, and kings ride on royal trained elephants. The best of men are self-trained men, those who can endure abuse in peace.

322 Mules when trained are good, and so are noble horses of Sindh. Strong elephants when trained are good; but the best is the man who trains himself.

323 For it is not with those riding animals that a man will reach the land unknown. NIRVANA is reached by that man who wisely, heroically, trains himself.

324 The great elephant called Dhana-palaka is hard to control when in rut, and he will not eat his food when captive, for he remembers the elephant grove.

325 The man who is lazy and a glutton, who eats large meals and rolls in sleep, who is like a pig which is fed in the sty, this fool is reborn to a life of death.

326 In days gone by this mind of mine used to stray wherever selfish desire or lust or pleasure would lead it. To-day this mind does not stray and is under the harmony of control, even as a wild elephant is controlled by the trainer.

327 Find joy in watchfulness; guard well your mind. Uplift

Endurance

yourself from your lower self, even as an elephant draws himself out of a muddy swamp.

328 If on the journey of life a man can find a wise and intelligent friend who is good and self-controlled, let him go with that traveller; and in joy and recollection let them overcome the dangers of the journey.

329 But if on the journey of life a man cannot find a wise and intelligent friend who is good and self-controlled, let him then travel alone, like a king who has left his country, or like a great elephant alone in the forest.

330 For it is better to go alone on the path of life rather than to have a fool for a companion. With few wishes and few cares, and leaving all sins behind, let a man travel alone, like a great elephant alone in the forest.

331 It is sweet to have friends in need; and to share enjoyment is sweet. It is sweet to have done good before death; and to surrender all pain is sweet.

332 It is sweet in this world to be a mother; and to be a father is sweet. It is sweet in this world to be a monk; and to be a saintly Brahmin is sweet.

333 It is sweet to enjoy a lifelong virtue; and a pure firm faith is sweet. It is sweet to attain wisdom; and to be free from sin is sweet.

24

Cravings

334 If a man watches not for NIRVANA, his cravings grow like a creeper and he jumps from death to death like a monkey in the forest from one tree without fruit to another.

335 And when his cravings overcome him, his sorrows increase more and more, like the entangling creeper called *birana*.

336 But whoever in this world overcomes his selfish cravings, his sorrows fall away from him, like drops of water from a lotus flower.

337 Therefore in love I tell you, to you all who have come here: Cut off the bonds of desires, as the surface grass creeper *birana* is cut for its fragant root called *usira*. Be not like a reed by a stream which MARA, the devil of temptation, crushes again and again.

338 Just as a tree, though cut down, can grow again and again if its roots are undamaged and strong, in the same way if the roots of craving are not wholly uprooted sorrows will come again and again.

339 When the thirty-six streams of desire that run towards pleasures are strong, their powerful waves carry away that man without vision whose imaginings are lustful desires.

Cravings

340 Everywhere flow the streams. The creeper of craving grows everywhere. If you see the creeper grow, cut off its roots by the power of wisdom.

341 The sensuous pleasures of men flow everywhere. Bound for pleasures and seeking pleasures men suffer life and old age.

342 Men who are pursued by lust run around like a hunted hare. Held in fetters and in bonds they suffer and suffer again.

343 Men who are pursued by lust run round like a hunted hare. For a monk to conquer lust he must first conquer desires.

344 The man who free from desires finds joy in solitude, but when free he then returns to his life of old desires, people can say of that man: 'He was free and he ran back to his prison!'

345 The wise do not call a strong fetter that which is made of iron, of wood or of rope; much stronger is the fetter of passion for gold and for jewels, for sons or for wives.

346 This is indeed a strong fetter, say the wise. It seems soft but it drags a man down, and it is hard to undo. Therefore some men cut their fetters, renounce the life of the world and start to walk on the path, leaving pleasures behind.

347 Those who are slaves of desires run into the stream of desires, even as a spider runs into the web that it made. Therefore some men cut their fetters and start to walk on the path, leaving sorrows behind.

The Dhammapada

348 Leave the past behind; leave the future behind; leave the present behind. Thou art then ready to go to the other shore. Never more shalt thou return to a life that ends in death.

349 The man who is disturbed by wrong thoughts, whose selfish passions are strong and who only seeks sensuous pleasures, increases his craving desires and makes stronger the chains he forges for himself.

350 But he who enjoys peaceful thoughts, who considers the sorrows of pleasure, and who ever remembers the light of his life – he will see the end of his cravings, he will break the chains of death.

351 He has reached the end of his journey, he trembles not, his cravings are gone, he is free from sin, he has burnt the thorns of life: this is his last mortal body.

352 He is free from lust, he is free from greed, he knows the meaning of words, and the meaning of their combinations, he is a great man, a great man who sees the Light: this is his last mortal body.

353 I have conquered all; I know all, and my life is pure; I have left all, and I am free from craving. I myself found the way. Whom shall I call Teacher? Whom shall I teach?

354 The gift of Truth conquers all gifts. The taste of Truth conquers all sweetness. The Joy of Truth conquers all pleasures. The loss of desires conquers all sorrows.

355 Wealth destroys the fool who seeks not the Beyond. Because of greed for wealth the fool destroys himself as if he were his own enemy.

356 Weeds harm the fields, passions harm human nature: offerings given to those free from passions bring a great reward.
357 Weeds harm the fields, hate harms human nature: offerings given to those free from hate bring a great reward.
358 Weeds harm the fields, illusion harms human nature: offerings given to those free from illusion bring a great reward.
359 Weeds harm the fields, desire harms human nature: offerings given to those free from desire bring a great reward.

25

The Monk

360 Good is the control of the eye, and good is the control of the ear; good is the control of smell, and good is the control of taste.
361 Good is the control of the body, and good is the control of words; good is the control of the mind, and good is the control of our whole inner life. When a monk has achieved perfect self-control, he leaves all sorrows behind.
362 The man whose hands are controlled, whose feet are controlled, whose words are controlled, who is self-controlled in all things, who finds the inner joy, whose mind is self-possessed, who is one and has found perfect peace – this man I call a monk.

363 The monk whose words are controlled, peaceful and wise, who is humble, who throws light on the letter and the spirit of the sacred verses – sweet are his words.

364 Who abides in the truth of DHAMMA, whose joy is in the truth of DHAMMA, who ponders on DHAMMA, and remembers the truth of DHAMMA – this monk shall never fall from DHAMMA, from Truth.

365 Let him not despise the offerings given to him, and let him not be jealous of others, because the monk who feels envy cannot achieve deep contemplation.

366 However little a monk may receive, if he despises not what he receives, even the gods praise that monk, whose life is pure and full of endeavour.

367 For whom 'name and form' are not real, who never feels 'this is mine', and who sorrows not for things that are not, he in truth can be called a monk.

368 The monk who is full of love and who fully lives in the law of Buddha, he follows the path of NIRVANA, the path of the end of all sorrow, the path of infinite joy.

369 Empty the boat of your life, O man; when empty it will swiftly sail. When empty of passions and harmful desires you are bound for the land of NIRVANA.

370 Cut off the five – selfishness, doubt, wrong austerities and rites, lust, hate; throw off the five – desire to be born with a body, or without a body, self-will, restlessness, ignorance; but cherish five – faith, watchfulness, energy, contemplation, vision. He who has broken the five fetters – lust, hate, delusion, pride, false views – is one who has crossed to the other shore.

The Monk

371 Watch, Bhikkhu. Be in high contemplation, and think not of pleasure, so that you have not to think of pain, like those who in the fire of hell have to swallow a ball of red-hot iron.

372 He who has not wisdom has not contemplation, and he who has not contemplation has not wisdom; but he who has wisdom and contemplation, he is very near NIRVANA.

373 When with a mind in silent peace a monk enters his empty house, then he feels the unearthly joy of beholding the light of Truth.

374 And when he sees in a clear vision the coming and going of inner events, then he feels the infinite joy of those who see the immortal THAT; the NIRVANA immortal.

375 This is the beginning of the life of a wise monk; self-control of the senses, happiness, living under the moral law, and the association with good friends whose life is pure and who are ever striving.

376 Let him live in love. Let his work be well done. Then in a fulness of joy he will see the end of sorrow.

377 Even as the *vasika* jasmine lets its withered flowers fall, do you let fall from you, O monks, all ill passions and all ill-will.

378 The monk is said to be a Bhikkhu of peace when his body, words and mind are peaceful, when he is master of himself and when he has left behind the lower attractions of the world.

379 Arise! Rouse thyself by thy Self; train thyself by thy Self. Under the shelter of thy Self, and ever watchful, thou shalt live in supreme joy.

380 For thy Self is the master of thyself, and thy Self is thy refuge. Train therefore thyself well, even as a merchant trains a fine horse.

381 In a fulness of delight and of faith in the teaching of Buddha, the mendicant monk finds peace supreme and, beyond the transience of time, he will find the joy of Eternity, the joy supreme of NIRVANA.

382 When a mendicant monk, though young, follows with faith the path of Buddha, his light shines bright over the world, like the brightness of a moon free from clouds.

26

The Brahmin

383 Go beyond the stream, Brahmin, go with all your soul: leave desires behind. When you have crossed the stream of *Samsara*, you will reach the land of NIRVANA.

384 When beyond meditation and contemplation a Brahmin has reached the other shore, then he attains the supreme vision and all his fetters are broken.

385 He for whom there is neither this nor the further shore, nor both, who, beyond all fear, is free – him I call a Brahmin.

386 He who lives in contemplation, who is pure and is in peace, who has done what was to be done, who is free from passions, who has reached the Supreme end – him I call a Brahmin.

The Brahmin

387 By day the sun shines, and by night shines the moon. The warrior shines in his armour, and the Brahmin priest in his meditation. But the Buddha shines by day and by night – in the brightness of his glory shines the man who is awake.

388 Because he has put away evil, he is called a Brahmin; because he lives in peace, he is called a *Samana*; because he leaves all sins behind, he is called a *Pabbajita*, a pilgrim.

389 One should never hurt a Brahmin; and a Brahmin should never return evil for evil. Alas for the man who hurts a Brahmin! Alas for the Brahmin who returns evil for evil!

390 It is not a little good that a Brahmin gains if he holds back his mind from the pleasures of life. Every time the desire to hurt stops, every time a pain disappears.

391 He who hurts not with his thoughts, or words or deeds, who keeps these three under control – him I call a Brahmin.

392 He who learns the law of righteousness from one who teaches what Buddha taught, let him revere his teacher, as a Brahmin reveres the fire of sacrifice.

393 A man becomes not a Brahmin by long hair or family or birth. The man in whom there is truth and holiness, he is in joy and he is a Brahmin.

394 Of what use is your tangled hair, foolish man, of what use your antelope garment, if within you have tangled cravings, and without ascetic ornaments?

395 The man who is clothed in worn-out garments, thin, whose veins stand out, who in the forest is alone in contemplation – him I call a Brahmin.

The Dhammapada

396 I call not a man a Brahmin because he was born from a certain family or mother, for he may be proud, and he may be wealthy. The man who is free from possessions and free from desires – him I call a Brahmin.

397 He who has cut all fetters and whose mind trembles not, who in infinite freedom is free from all bonds – him I call a Brahmin.

398 Who has cut off the strap, the thong and the rope, with all their fastenings, who has raised the bar that closes the door, who is awake – him I call a Brahmin.

399 Who, though innocent, suffers insults, stripes and chains, whose weapons are endurance and soul-force – him I call a Brahmin.

400 Who is free from anger, faithful to his vows, virtuous, free from lusts, self-trained, whose mortal body is his last – him I call a Brahmin.

401 Who clings not to sensuous pleasures, even as water clings not to the leaf of the lotus, or a grain of mustard seed to the point of a needle – him I call a Brahmin.

402 He who even in this life knows the end of sorrow, who has laid down his burden and is free – him I call a Brahmin.

403 He whose vision is deep, who is wise, who knows the path and what is outside the path, who has attained the highest end – him I call a Brahmin.

404 Who keeps away from those who have a home and from those who have not a home, who wanders alone, and who has few desires – him I call a Brahmin.

405 Who hurts not any living being, whether feeble or strong, who neither kills nor causes to kill – him I call a Brahmin.

The Brahmin

406 Who is tolerant to the intolerant, peaceful to the violent, free from greed with the greedy – him I call a Brahmin.

407 He from whom lust and hate, and pride and insincerity fall down like a mustard seed from the point of a needle – him I call a Brahmin.

408 He who speaks words that are peaceful and useful and true, words that offend no one – him I call a Brahmin.

409 Who in this world does not take anything not given to him: be it long or short, large or small, good or bad – him I call a Brahmin.

410 He who has no craving desires, either for this world or for another world, who free from desires is in infinite freedom – him I call a Brahmin.

411 He who in his vision is free from doubts and, having all, longs for nothing, for he has reached the immortal NIRVANA – him I call a Brahmin.

412 He who in this world has gone beyond good and evil and both, who free from sorrows is free from passions and is pure – him I call a Brahmin.

413 He who like the moon is pure, bright, clear and serene; whose pleasure for things that pass away is gone – him I call a Brahmin.

414 He who has gone beyond the illusion of *Samsara*, the muddy road of transmigration so difficult to pass; who has crossed to the other shore and, free from doubts and temporal desires, has reached in his deep contemplation the joy of NIRVANA – him I call a Brahmin.

415 He who wanders without a home in this world, leaving behind the desires of the world, and the desires never return – him I call a Brahmin.

416 He who wanders without a home in this world, leaving behind the feverish thirst for the world, and the fever never returns – him I call a Brahmin.

417 He who is free from the bondage of men and also from the bondage of the gods: who is free from all things in creation – him I call a Brahmin.

418 He who is free from pleasure and pain, who is calm, and whose seeds of death-in-life are burnt, whose heroism has conquered all the inner worlds – him I call a Brahmin.

419 He who knows the going and returning of beings – the birth and rebirth of life – and in joy has arrived at the end of his journey, and now he is awake and can see – him I call a Brahmin.

420 He whose path is not known by men, nor by spirits or gods, who is pure from all imperfections, who is a saint, an Arahat – him I call a Brahmin.

421 He for whom things future or past or present are nothing, who has nothing and desires nothing – him I call a Brahmin.

422 He who is powerful, noble, who lives a life of inner heroism, the all-seer, the all-conqueror, the ever-pure, who has reached the end of the journey, who like Buddha is awake – him I call a Brahmin.

423 He who knows the river of his past lives and is free from life that ends in death, who knows the joys of heaven and the sorrows of hell, for he is a seer whose vision is pure, who in perfection is one with the Supreme Perfection – him I call a Brahmin.

1. BOCCACCIO · *Mrs Rosie and the Priest*
2. GERARD MANLEY HOPKINS · *As kingfishers catch fire*
3. *The Saga of Gunnlaug Serpent-tongue*
4. THOMAS DE QUINCEY · *On Murder Considered as One of the Fine Arts*
5. FRIEDRICH NIETZSCHE · *Aphorisms on Love and Hate*
6. JOHN RUSKIN · *Traffic*
7. PU SONGLING · *Wailing Ghosts*
8. JONATHAN SWIFT · *A Modest Proposal*
9. *Three Tang Dynasty Poets*
10. WALT WHITMAN · *On the Beach at Night Alone*
11. KENKŌ · *A Cup of Sake Beneath the Cherry Trees*
12. BALTASAR GRACIÁN · *How to Use Your Enemies*
13. JOHN KEATS · *The Eve of St Agnes*
14. THOMAS HARDY · *Woman much missed*
15. GUY DE MAUPASSANT · *Femme Fatale*
16. MARCO POLO · *Travels in the Land of Serpents and Pearls*
17. SUETONIUS · *Caligula*
18. APOLLONIUS OF RHODES · *Jason and Medea*
19. ROBERT LOUIS STEVENSON · *Olalla*
20. KARL MARX AND FRIEDRICH ENGELS · *The Communist Manifesto*
21. PETRONIUS · *Trimalchio's Feast*
22. JOHANN PETER HEBEL · *How a Ghastly Story Was Brought to Light by a Common or Garden Butcher's Dog*
23. HANS CHRISTIAN ANDERSEN · *The Tinder Box*
24. RUDYARD KIPLING · *The Gate of the Hundred Sorrows*
25. DANTE · *Circles of Hell*
26. HENRY MAYHEW · *Of Street Piemen*
27. HAFEZ · *The nightingales are drunk*
28. GEOFFREY CHAUCER · *The Wife of Bath*
29. MICHEL DE MONTAIGNE · *How We Weep and Laugh at the Same Thing*
30. THOMAS NASHE · *The Terrors of the Night*
31. EDGAR ALLAN POE · *The Tell-Tale Heart*
32. MARY KINGSLEY · *A Hippo Banquet*
33. JANE AUSTEN · *The Beautifull Cassandra*
34. ANTON CHEKHOV · *Gooseberries*
35. SAMUEL TAYLOR COLERIDGE · *Well, they are gone, and here must I remain*
36. JOHANN WOLFGANG VON GOETHE · *Sketchy, Doubtful, Incomplete Jottings*
37. CHARLES DICKENS · *The Great Winglebury Duel*
38. HERMAN MELVILLE · *The Maldive Shark*
39. ELIZABETH GASKELL · *The Old Nurse's Story*
40. NIKOLAY LESKOV · *The Steel Flea*

41. HONORÉ DE BALZAC · *The Atheist's Mass*
42. CHARLOTTE PERKINS GILMAN · *The Yellow Wall-Paper*
43. C.P. CAVAFY · *Remember, Body . . .*
44. FYODOR DOSTOEVSKY · *The Meek One*
45. GUSTAVE FLAUBERT · *A Simple Heart*
46. NIKOLAI GOGOL · *The Nose*
47. SAMUEL PEPYS · *The Great Fire of London*
48. EDITH WHARTON · *The Reckoning*
49. HENRY JAMES · *The Figure in the Carpet*
50. WILFRED OWEN · *Anthem For Doomed Youth*
51. WOLFGANG AMADEUS MOZART · *My Dearest Father*
52. PLATO · *Socrates' Defence*
53. CHRISTINA ROSSETTI · *Goblin Market*
54. *Sindbad the Sailor*
55. SOPHOCLES · *Antigone*
56. RYŪNOSUKE AKUTAGAWA · *The Life of a Stupid Man*
57. LEO TOLSTOY · *How Much Land Does A Man Need?*
58. GIORGIO VASARI · *Leonardo da Vinci*
59. OSCAR WILDE · *Lord Arthur Savile's Crime*
60. SHEN FU · *The Old Man of the Moon*
61. AESOP · *The Dolphins, the Whales and the Gudgeon*
62. MATSUO BASHŌ · *Lips too Chilled*
63. EMILY BRONTË · *The Night is Darkening Round Me*
64. JOSEPH CONRAD · *To-morrow*
65. RICHARD HAKLUYT · *The Voyage of Sir Francis Drake Around the Whole Globe*
66. KATE CHOPIN · *A Pair of Silk Stockings*
67. CHARLES DARWIN · *It was snowing butterflies*
68. BROTHERS GRIMM · *The Robber Bridegroom*
69. CATULLUS · *I Hate and I Love*
70. HOMER · *Circe and the Cyclops*
71. D. H. LAWRENCE · *Il Duro*
72. KATHERINE MANSFIELD · *Miss Brill*
73. OVID · *The Fall of Icarus*
74. SAPPHO · *Come Close*
75. IVAN TURGENEV · *Kasyan from the Beautiful Lands*
76. VIRGIL · *O Cruel Alexis*
77. H. G. WELLS · *A Slip under the Microscope*
78. HERODOTUS · *The Madness of Cambyses*
79. *Speaking of Siva*
80. *The Dhammapada*

'Can I bear
to leave these
blue hills?'

WANG WEI
Born c.699
Died c.761

LI PO
Born 701
Died 762

TU FU
Born 712
Died 770

WANG IN PENGUIN CLASSICS
Poems

LI AND TU IN PENGUIN CLASSICS
Poems

THREE TANG DYNASTY POETS

Translated by
G. W. Robinson and Arthur Cooper

PENGUIN BOOKS

PENGUIN CLASSICS

UK | USA | Canada | Ireland | Australia
India | New Zealand | South Africa

Penguin Books is part of the Penguin Random House group of companies
whose addresses can be found at global.penguinrandomhouse.com.

This selection published in Penguin Classics 2015
009

Wang Wei translations copyright © G. W. Robinson, 1973
Li Po and Tu Fu translations copyright © Arthur Cooper, 1973

The moral right of the translators has been asserted

Set in 9/12.4 pt Baskerville 10 Pro
Typeset by Jouve (UK), Milton Keynes

Printed and bound in Great Britain by Clays Ltd, Elcograf S.p.A.

A CIP catalogue record for this book is available from the British Library

ISBN: 978-0-141-39820-4

www.greenpenguin.co.uk

Penguin Random House is committed to a
sustainable future for our business, our readers
and our planet. This book is made from Forest
Stewardship Council® certified paper.

Contents

WANG WEI (WANG YOUCHENG)

Song of the Peach Tree Spring	3
Marching song	6
The Green Stream	7
The distant evening view when the weather has cleared	8
On leaving the Wang River retreat	9
A walk on a winter day	10
Passing the mountain cloister of the holy man, T'an-hsing, at Kanhua Temple	11
Return to Mount Sung	12
Seeing off Ch'en Tzu-fu to the east of the Yangtze	13
Song of the Kansu frontier	14
Good-bye to Li, Prefect of Tzŭchou	15
Watching a farewell	16

My Chungnan retreat 17

Taking the cool of the evening 18

LI PO (LI BAI)

Drinking with a Gentleman of Leisure
    in the Mountains 21

In the Mountains: a Reply to the Vulgar
    22

Marble Stairs Grievance 23

Letter to His Two Small Children
    staying in Eastern Lu at Wen Yang
    Village under Turtle Mountain 24

Remembering the Eastern Ranges 26

For his Wife 27

The Ballad of Ch'ang-Kan 28

The Ballad of Yü-Chang 31

Hard Is the Journey 32

Old Poem 33

TU FU (DU FU)

Lament by the Riverside 37

From The Journey North: The
    Homecoming 39

The Visitor 42

Nine Short Songs: Wandering Breezes: 1	43
Nine Short Songs: Wandering Breezes: 8	43
The Ballad of the Ancient Cypress	44
From a Height	46
Ballad on Seeing A Pupil of the Lady Kung-Sun Dance the Sword Mime	47
Night Thoughts Afloat	51
APPENDIX The Story of the Peach Blossom Spring by T'ao Ch'ien (Tao Yuan-ming) (365–427)	52

WANG WEI
(WANG YOUCHENG)

Song of the Peach Tree Spring

A fisherman sailed up a river
                        he loved spring in the hills

On both banks peach blossom
                        closed over the farther reaches

He sat and looked at the red trees
                        not knowing how far he was

And he neared the head of the green stream
                        seeing no one

A gap in the hills, a way through
                        twists and turns at first

Then hills gave on to a vastness
                        of level land all round

From far away all seemed
                        trees up to the clouds

He approached, and there were many houses
                        among flowers and bamboos

Foresters meeting would exchange
                        names from Han times

And the people had not altered
                        the Ch'in style of their clothes

They had all lived near
                        the head of Wuling River

And now cultivated their rice and gardens
                        out of the world

Bright moon and under the pines
                        outside their windows peace

Sun up and among the clouds
                        fowls and dogs call

Amazed to hear of the world's intruder
                        all vied to see him

And take him home and ask him
                        about his country and place

At first light in the alleys
                        they swept the flowers from their gates

At dusk fishermen and woodmen
                        came in on the stream

They had first come here
                        for refuge from the world

And then had become immortals
                        and never returned.

Who, clasped there in the hills,
                        would know of the world of men?

And whoever might gaze from the world
                        would make out only clouds and hills

The fisherman did not suspect
                              that paradise is hard to find

And his earthy spirit lived on
                              and he thought of his own
                              country

So he left that seclusion not reckoning
                              the barriers of mountain and
                              stream

To take leave at home and then return
                              for as long as it might please him.

He was sure of his way there
                              could never go wrong

How should he know that peaks and valleys
                              can so soon change?

When the time came he simply remembered
                              having gone deep into the hills

But how many green streams
                              lead into cloud-high woods –

When spring comes, everywhere
                              there are peach blossom streams

No one can tell which may be
                              the spring of paradise.

Marching song

The bugle is blown and rouses the marchers
With a great hubbub the marchers rise
The wailing notes set the horses neighing
As they struggle across the Golden River
The sun dropping down on the desert's rim
Martial sounds among smoke and dust
We will get the rope round that great king's neck
Then home to do homage to our Emperor.

The Green Stream

To get to the Yellow Flower River
I always follow the green water stream
Among the hills there must be a thousand twists
The distance there cannot be fifty miles
There is the murmur of water among rocks
And the quietness of colours deep in pines
Lightly lightly drifting water-chestnuts
Clearly clearly mirrored reeds and rushes
I have always been a lover of tranquillity
And when I see this clear stream so calm
I want to stay on some great rock
And fish for ever on and on.

The distant evening view when the weather has cleared

The sky has cleared and there is the vast plain
And so far as the eye can see no dust in the air
There is the outer gate facing the ford
And the village trees going down to the mouth of the stream
The white water shining beyond the fields
The blue peaks jutting behind the hills
This is no time for leisure on the land –
All hands at work in the fields to the south.

On leaving the Wang River retreat

At last I put my carriage in motion
Go sadly out from the ivied pines
Can I bear to leave these blue hills?
And the green stream – what of that?

A walk on a winter day

I walk out of the city by the eastern gate
And try to send my gaze a thousand miles
Blue hills crossed with green woods
Red sun round on the level plain
North of the Wei you get to Hantan
East of the Pass you go out to Han valley
This was where the Ch'in demesnes met
This was where the governors came to court
The cocks called in Hsienyang
And officers of state struggled for precedence
Ministers called on noblemen
Dukes assembled for official banquets
But Hsiang-ju became old and ill
And had to retire alone to Wuling.

Passing the mountain cloister of the holy man, T'an-hsing, at Kanhua Temple

In the evening he took his fine cane
And paused with his guests at the head of Tiger Stream
Urged us to listen for the sound in the mountains
Then went along by the water back to his house
    Profusion of lovely flowers in the wilds
    Vague sound of birds in the valley
When he sits down tonight the empty hills will be still
And the pine wind will suggest autumn.

Return to Mount Sung

The river ran clear between luxuriant banks
And my carriage jogged along on its way
And the water seemed to flow with a purpose
And in the evening the birds went back together –
Desolate town confronting an old ford
Setting sun filling the autumn hills
After a long journey, at the foot of Mount Sung
I have come home and shut my door.

Seeing off Ch'en Tzu-fu to the east of the Yangtze

Under the willows at the ford
               there are few travellers left

As the boatman steers away
               to the other curving shore

But my thoughts will follow you
               like the spring's returning colours

Returning from south of the Yangtze
               back to the north.

Song of the Kansu frontier

Two miles galloping all the way
Another one plying the whip –
A message arrives from headquarters
The Huns have surrounded Chouch'üan
The frontier passes are all flying snow
Beacons are out, no smoke.

Good-bye to Li, Prefect of Tzŭchou

In endless valleys trees reaching to the sky
In numberless hills the call of cuckoos
And in those hills half is all rain
Streaming off branches to multiply the springs –
The native women will bring in local cloth
The men will bring you actions about potato fields
Your revered predecessor reformed their ways
And will you be so bold as to repudiate him?

Watching a farewell

Green green the willowed road
The road where they are separating
A loved son off for far provinces
Old parents left at home

He must go or they could not live
But his going revives their grief
A charge to his brothers – gently
A word to the neighbours – softly
A last drink at the gates
And then he takes leave of his friends

Tears dried, he must catch up his companions
Swallowing grief, he sets his carriage in motion
At last the carriage passes out of sight
But still at times there's the dust thrown up from the road

I too, long ago, said good-bye to my family
And when I see this, my handkerchief is wet with tears.

My Chungnan retreat

Middle-aged, much drawn to the Way
Settled for my evening in the Chungnan foothills
Elation comes and off I go by myself
Where are the sights that I must know alone
I walk right on to the head of a stream
I sit and watch when clouds come up
Or I may meet an old woodman –
Talk, laughter, never a time to go home.

Taking the cool of the evening

Thousands of trunks of huge trees
Along the thread of a clear stream
Ahead the great estuary over which
Comes the far wind unobstructed
Rippling water wets white sands
Silver sturgeon swim in transparency
I lie down on a wet rock and let
Waves wash over my slight body
I rinse my mouth and wash my feet
Opposite there's an old man fishing.
How many fish come to the bait –
East of the lotus leaves – useless to think about it.

LI PO (LI BAI)

Drinking with a Gentleman of Leisure in the Mountains

We both have drunk their birth,
    the mountain flowers,
A toast, a toast, a toast,
    again another:

I am drunk, long to sleep;
    Sir, go a little –
Bring your lute (if you like)
    early tomorrow!

In the Mountains: A Reply to the Vulgar

    They ask me where's the sense
        on jasper mountains?
    I laugh and don't reply,
        in heart's own quiet:

    Peach petals float their streams
        away in secret
    To other skies and earths
        than those of mortals.

Marble Stairs Grievance

    On Marble Stairs
still grows the white dew
    That has all night
soaked her silk slippers,

    But she lets down
her crystal blind now
    And sees through glaze
the moon of autumn.

Letter to His Two Small Children Staying in Eastern Lu at Wen Yang Village under Turtle Mountain

Here in Wu Land mulberry leaves are green,
Silkworms in Wu have now had three sleeps:

My family, left in Eastern Lu,
Oh, to sow now Turtle-shaded fields,
Do the spring things I can never join,
Sailing Yangtze always on my own –

Let the South Wind blow you back my heart,
Fly and land it in the Tavern court
Where, to the East, there are sprays and leaves
Of one peach-tree, sweeping the blue mist;

This is the tree I myself put in
When I left you, nearly three years past;
A peach-tree now, level with the eaves,
And I sailing cannot yet turn home!

Pretty daughter, P'ing-yang is your name,
Breaking blossom, there beside my tree,
Breaking blossom, you cannot see me
And your tears flow like the running stream;

And little son, Po-ch'in you are called,
Your big sister's shoulder you must reach
When you come there underneath my peach,
Oh, to pat and pet you too, my child!

I dreamt like this till my wits went wild,
By such yearning daily burned within;
So tore some silk, wrote this distant pang
From me to you living at Wen Yang . . .

Remembering the East Ranges

1

Long since I turned
to my East Ranges:
 How many times
have their roses bloomed?

Have their white clouds
risen and vanished
 And their bright moon
set among strangers?

2

But I shall now
take Duke Hsieh's dancers:
 With a sad song
we shall leave the crowds

And call on him
in the East Ranges,
 Undo the gate,
sweep back the white clouds!

For His Wife

Three-sixty days with a muddled sot,
  That is Mistress Li Po's lot:
In what way different from the life
  Of the Grand Permanent's wife?

The Ballad of Ch'ang-Kan

(The Sailor's Wife)

1

I with my hair fringed on my forehead,
Breaking blossom, was romping outside:

And you rode up on your bamboo steed,
Round garden beds we juggled green plums;
Living alike in Ch'ang-kan village
We were both small, without doubts or guile . . .

When at fourteen I became your bride
I was bashful and could only hide
My face and frown against a dark wall:
A thousand calls, not once did I turn;

I was fifteen before I could smile,
Long to be one, like dust with ashes:
You'd ever stand by pillar faithful,
I'd never climb the Watcher's Mountain!

I am sixteen but you went away
Through Ch'ü-t'ang Gorge, passing Yen-yü Rock
And when in June it should not be passed,
Where the gibbons cried high above you.

Here by the door our farewell footprints,
They one by one are growing green moss,
The moss so thick I cannot sweep it,
And fallen leaves: autumn winds came soon!

September now: yellow butterflies
Flying in pairs in the west garden;
And what I feel hurts me in my heart,
Sadness to make a pretty face old . . .

Late or early coming from San-pa,
Before you come, write me a letter:
To welcome you, don't talk of distance,
I'll go as far as the Long Wind Sands!

2

I remember, in my maiden days
I did not know the world and its ways;
Until I wed a man of Ch'ang-kan:
Now, on the sands, I wait for the winds . . .

And when in June the south winds are fair,
I think: Pa-ling, it's soon you'll be there;
September now, and west winds risen,
I wish you'll leave the Yangtze Haven;

But, go or come, it's ever sorrow
For when we meet, you part tomorrow:
You'll make Hsiang-tan in how many days?
I dreamt I crossed the winds and the waves

Only last night, when the wind went mad
And tore down trees on the waterside
And waters raced where the dark wind ran
(Oh, where was then my travelling man?)

That we both rode dappled cloudy steeds
Eastward to bliss in Isles of Orchids:
A drake and duck among the green reeds,
Just as you've seen on a painted screen . . .

Pity me now, when I was fifteen
My face was pink as a peach's skin:
Why did I wed a travelling man?
Waters my grief . . . my grief in the wind!

The Ballad of Yü-Chang

A Tartar wind blows on Tai horses
Thronging northward through the Lu-yang Gap:

Wu cavalry like snowflakes seaward
Riding westward know of no return,
Where as they ford the Shang-liao shallows
A yellow cloud stares faceless on them;

An old mother parting from her son
Calls on Heaven in the wild grasses,
The white horses round flags and banners,
Sadly she keens and clasps him to her:

'"Poor white poplar in the autumn moon,
Soon it was felled on the Yü-chang Hills" –
You were ever a peaceful scholar,
You were not trained to kill and capture!'

'How can you weep for death in battle,
To free our Prince from stubborn bandits?
Given pure will, stones swallow feathers,
How can you speak of fearing dangers?

'Our towered ships look like flying whales
Where the squalls race on Fallen Star Lake:
This song you sing – if you sing loudly,
Three armies' hair will streak, too, with grey!'

Hard is the Journey

Gold vessels of fine wines,
    thousands a gallon,
Jade dishes of rare meats,
    costing more thousands,

I lay my chopsticks down,
    no more can banquet,
And draw my sword and stare
    wildly about me:

Ice bars my way to cross
    the Yellow River,
Snows from dark skies to climb
    the T'ai-hang Mountains!

At peace I drop a hook
    into a brooklet,
At once I'm in a boat
    but sailing sunward . . .

    (Hard is the Journey,
    Hard is the Journey,
    So many turnings,
    And now where am I?)

So when a breeze breaks waves,
    bringing fair weather,
I set a cloud for sails,
    cross the blue oceans!

Old Poem

Did Chuang Chou dream
he was the butterfly,
   Or the butterfly
that it was Chuang Chou?

In one body's
metamorphoses,
   All is present,
infinite virtue!

You surely know
Fairyland's oceans
   Were made again
a limpid brooklet,

Down at Green Gate
the melon gardener
   Once used to be
Marquis of Tung-ling?

Wealth and honour
were always like this:
   You strive and strive,
but what do you seek?

TU FU (DU FU)

Lament by the Riverside

The old man from Shao-ling,
   weeping inwardly,
Slips out by stealth in spring
   and walks by Serpentine,

And on its riverside
   sees the locked Palaces,
Young willows and new reeds
   all green for nobody;

Where Rainbow Banners once
   went through South Gardens,
Gardens and all therein
   with merry faces:

First Lady of the Land,
   Chao-yang's chatelaine,
Sits always by her Lord
   at board or carriage,

Carriage before which Maids
   with bows and arrows
Are mounted on white steeds
   with golden bridles;

They look up in the air
   and loose together,
What laughter when a pair
   of wings drop downward,

What bright eyes and white teeth,
 but now where is she?
The ghosts of those by blood
 defiled are homeless!

Where limpid River Wei's
 waters flow Eastward,
One goes, the other stays
 and has no tidings:

Though Pity, all our hours,
 weeping remembers,
These waters and these flowers
 remain as ever;

But now brown dusk and horse-
 men fill the City,
To gain the City's South
 I shall turn Northward!

From *The Journey North: the Homecoming*

Slowly, slowly we tramped country tracks,
With cottage smoke rarely on their winds:
Of those we met, many suffered wounds
Still oozing blood, and they moaned aloud!

I turned my head back to Feng-hsiang's camp,
Flags still flying in the fading light;
Climbing onward in the cold hills' folds,
Found here and there where cavalry once drank;

Till, far below, plains of Pin-chou sank,
Ching's swift torrent tearing them in two;
And 'Before us the wild tigers stood',
Had rent these rocks every time they roared:

Autumn daisies had begun to nod
Among crushed stones waggons once had passed;
To the great sky then my spirit soared,
That secret things still could give me joy!

Mountain berries, tiny, trifling gems
Growing tangled among scattered nuts,
Were some scarlet, sands of cinnabar,
And others black, as if lacquer-splashed:

By rain and dew all of them were washed
And, sweet or sour, equally were fruits;
They brought to mind Peach-tree River's springs,
And more I sighed for a life misspent!

Then I, downhill, spied Fu-chou far off
And rifts and rocks quickly disappeared
As I ran down to a river's edge,
My poor servant coming far behind;

There we heard owls hoot from mulberry
Saw fieldmice sit upright by their holes;
At deep of night crossed a battlefield,
The chill moonlight shining on white bones

Guarding the Pass once a million *men*,
But how many ever left this Pass?
True to orders half the men in Ch'in
Here had perished and were alien ghosts!

I had fallen, too, in Tartar dust
But can return with my hair like flour,
A year but past, to my simple home
And my own wife, in a hundred rags;

Who sees me, cried like the wind through trees
Weeps like the well sobbing underground
And then my son, pride of all my days,
With his face, too, whiter than the snows

Sees his father, turns his back to weep –
His sooty feet without socks or shoes;
Next by my couch two small daughters stand
In patched dresses scarcely to their knees

And the seawaves do not even meet
Where old bits of broidery are sewn;
Whilst the Serpent and the Purple Bird
On the short skirts both are upside-down

'Though your father is not yet himself,
Suffers sickness and must rest some days,
How could his script not contain some stuffs
To give you all, keep you from the cold?

'You'll find there, too, powder, eyebrow black
Wrapped in the quilts, rather neatly packed.'
My wife's thin face once again is fair,
Then the mad girls try to dress their hair:

Aping mother in her every act,
Morning make-up quickly smears their hands
Till in no time they have spread the rouge,
Fiercely painted great, enormous brows!

I am alive, with my children, home!
Seem to forget all that hunger, thirst:
These quick questions, as they tug my beard,
Who'd have the heart now to stop and scold?

Turning my mind to the Rebel Camp,
It's sweet to have all this nonsense, noise . . .

The Visitor

North and South of our hut
  spread the Spring waters,
And only flocks of gulls
  daily visit us;

For guests our path is yet
  unswept of petals,
To you our wattle gate
  the first time opens:

Dishes so far from town
  lack subtle flavours,
And wine is but the rough
  a poor home offers;

If you agree, I'll call
  my ancient neighbour
Across the fence, to come
  help us finish it!

Nine Short Songs: Wandering Breezes: 1

> The withies near my door
>   are slender, supple
> And like the waists of maids
>   of fifteen summers:
>
> Who said, when morning came,
>   'Nothing to mention'?
> A mad wind has been here
>   and broke the longest!

Nine Short Songs: Wandering Breezes: 8

> The catkins line the lanes,
>   making white carpets,
> And leaves on lotus streams
>   spread like green money:
>
> Pheasants root bamboo shoots,
>   nobody looking,
> While ducklings on the sands
>   sleep by their mothers.

The Ballad of the Ancient Cypress

In front of K'ung-ming Shrine
  stands an old cypress,
With branches like green bronze
  and roots like granite;

Its hoary bark, far round,
  glistens with raindrops,
And blueblack hues, high up,
  blend in with Heaven's:

Long ago Statesman, King
  kept Time's appointment,
But still this standing tree
  has men's devotion;

United with the mists
  of ghostly gorges,
Through which the moon brings cold
  from snowy mountains.

(I recall near my hut
  on Brocade River
Another Shrine is shared
  by King and Statesman

On civil, ancient plains
  with stately cypress:
The paint there now is dim,
  windows shutterless . . .)

Wide, wide though writhing roots
   maintain its station,
Far, far in lonely heights,
   many's the tempest

When its hold is the strength
   of Divine Wisdom
And straightness by the work
   of the Creator . . .

Yet if a crumbling Hall
   needed a rooftree,
Yoked herds would, turning heads,
   balk at this mountain:

By art still unexposed
   all have admired it;
But axe though not refused,
   who could transport it?

How can its bitter core
   deny ants lodging,
All the while scented boughs
   give Phoenix housing?

Oh, ambitious unknowns,
   sigh no more sadly:
Using timber as big
   was never easy!

From a Height

The winds cut, clouds are high,
    apes wail their sorrows,
The ait is fresh, sand white,
    birds fly in circles;

On all sides fallen leaves
    go rustling, rustling,
While ceaseless river waves
    come rippling, rippling:

Autumn's each faded mile
    seems like my journey
To mount, alone and ill,
    to this balcony;

Life's failures and regrets
    frosting my temples,
And wretched that I've had
    to give up drinking.

Ballad on Seeing a Pupil of the Lady Kung-Sun Dance the Sword Mime

On the 19th day of the Tenth Month of Year II of Ta-li (15 November 767), I saw the Lady Li, Twelfth, of Lin-ying dance the Mime of the Sword at the Residence of Lieutenant-Governor Yüan Ch'i of K'uei Chou Prefecture; and both the subtlety of her interpretation and her virtuosity on points so impressed me that I asked of her, who had been her Teacher? She replied: 'I was a Pupil of the great Lady Kung-sun!'

In Year V of K'ai-yüan (A.D. 717), when I was no more than a tiny boy, I remember being taken in Yü-yen City to see Kung-sun dance both this Mime and 'The Astrakhan Hat'.

For her combination of flowing rhythms with vigorous attack, Kung-sun had stood alone even in an outstanding epoch. No member at all of the *corps de ballet*, of any rank whatever, either of the Sweet Spring-time Garden or of the Pear Garden Schools, could interpret such dances as she could; throughout the reign of His Late Majesty, Saintly in Peace and Godlike in War! But where now is that jadelike face, where are those brocade costumes? And I whiteheaded! And her Pupil here, too, no longer young!

Having learned of this Lady's background, I came to realize that she had, in fact, been reproducing faithfully all the movements, all the little gestures, of her Teacher; and I was so stirred by that memory, that I decided to make a Ballad of the Mime of the Sword.

There was a time when the great calligrapher, Chang Hsü of Wu, famous for his wild running hand, had several opportunities of watching the Lady Kung-sun dance this Sword Mime (as it is danced in Turkestan); and he discovered, to his immense delight, that doing so had resulted in marked improvement in his own calligraphic art! From *that*, know the Lady Kung-sun!

> A Great Dancer there was,
>   the Lady Kung-sun,
> And her 'Mime of the Sword'
>   made the World marvel!
>
> Those, many as the hills,
>   who had watched breathless
> Thought sky and earth themselves
>   moved to her rhythms:
>
> As she flashed, the Nine Suns
>   fell to the Archer;
> She flew, was a Sky God
>   on saddled dragon;
>
> She came on, the pent storm
>   before it thunders;
> And she ceased, the cold light
>   off frozen rivers!

Her red lips and pearl sleeves
   are long since resting,
But a dancer revives
   of late their fragrance:

The Lady of Lin-ying
   in White King city
Did the piece with such grace
   and lively spirit

That I asked! Her reply
   gave the good reason
And we thought of those times
   with deepening sadness:

There had waited at Court
   eight thousand Ladies
(With Kung-sun, from the first,
   chief at the Sword Dance);

And fifty years had passed
   (a palm turned downward)
While the winds, bringing dust,
   darkened the Palace

And they scattered like mist
   those in Pear Garden,
On whose visages still
   its sun shines bleakly!

*

But now trees had clasped hands
   at Golden Granary
And grass played its sad tunes
   on Ch'ü-t'ang's Ramparts,

For the swift pipes had ceased
   playing to tortoiseshell;
The moon rose in the East,
   joy brought great sorrow:

An old man knows no more
   where he is going;
On these wild hills, footsore,
   he will not hurry!

Night Thoughts Afloat

    By bent grasses
in a gentle wind
    Under straight mast
I'm alone tonight,

    And the stars hang
above the broad plain
    But moon's afloat
in this Great River:

    Oh, where's my name
among the poets?
    Official rank?
'Retired for ill-health.'

    Drifting, drifting,
what am I more than
    A single gull
between sky and earth?

The Story of the Peach Blossom Spring by T'ao Ch'ien (T'ao Yüan-ming)

During the T'aiyüan period of the Ch'in dynasty there was a man of Wuling who lived by fishing. He went along a stream and forgot how far he had gone. Suddenly he found himself in a forest of peach blossom extending several hundred paces along both banks, unmixed with any other sort of tree. The fragrance was lovely, and fallen petals were everywhere. The fisherman was extremely surprised, and continued onwards in the hope of reaching the limit of this forest. The forest ended at the source of the stream. There he came on a hill, and in the hill a small opening, from which there seemed to come some light. So he abandoned his boat and went through the opening. The passage was at first so narrow that a man could only just pass, but after going some fifty paces or so, he found that it widened out into a broad and bright place. On the level ground there were dignified buildings, as well as good ricefields, fine pools, mulberry trees and bamboos. There were roads and lanes criss-crossing, and the sounds of fowls and dogs could be heard. People were coming and going, busy sowing seed, and the clothes of both the men and the women looked foreign. Both the grey-haired elders and the youngest children had an air of natural happiness.

They were much amazed at the sight of the fisherman, and asked him where he had come from, to which he replied fully. They then took him back to one of their houses, put wine before him, killed a fowl, and gave him a meal. When news of this man became known in the village, they all came along to find out about him. They said of themselves that their ancestors, escaping from the troubles of the Ch'in period, had brought away their wives and children and the other inhabitants of their locality to this isolated place, and that subsequently no one had left there. This had led to their being cut off from those outside. They asked what dynasty there was now, they themselves having no knowledge of the Han dynasty, not to mention those of Wei and Ch'in. The fisherman replied fully and precisely to their questions, and they were all dumbfounded. The others all came and invited the man to their houses, and all gave him food and drink. He stayed for several days before taking his leave and departing. The people had meanwhile told him that there was no object in divulging their existence to others.

When he emerged, he regained his boat and retraced his route, noting it at every turn. When he reached the prefecture, he went to the prefect and told his tale. The prefect thereupon dispatched someone to go with him and find the route he had noted, but they lost their way and could not find it again.

Liu Tzǔ-chi of Nanyang, a man of quality, heard the tale and was eager to go off to the place himself. But before anything had been achieved, he was taken ill and died, and since then no one has looked for the stream.

This story is the inspiration for Wang Wei's poem that opens this book.

1. BOCCACCIO · *Mrs Rosie and the Priest*
2. GERARD MANLEY HOPKINS · *As kingfishers catch fire*
3. *The Saga of Gunnlaug Serpent-tongue*
4. THOMAS DE QUINCEY · *On Murder Considered as One of the Fine Arts*
5. FRIEDRICH NIETZSCHE · *Aphorisms on Love and Hate*
6. JOHN RUSKIN · *Traffic*
7. PU SONGLING · *Wailing Ghosts*
8. JONATHAN SWIFT · *A Modest Proposal*
9. *Three Tang Dynasty Poets*
10. WALT WHITMAN · *On the Beach at Night Alone*
11. KENKŌ · *A Cup of Sake Beneath the Cherry Trees*
12. BALTASAR GRACIÁN · *How to Use Your Enemies*
13. JOHN KEATS · *The Eve of St Agnes*
14. THOMAS HARDY · *Woman much missed*
15. GUY DE MAUPASSANT · *Femme Fatale*
16. MARCO POLO · *Travels in the Land of Serpents and Pearls*
17. SUETONIUS · *Caligula*
18. APOLLONIUS OF RHODES · *Jason and Medea*
19. ROBERT LOUIS STEVENSON · *Olalla*
20. KARL MARX AND FRIEDRICH ENGELS · *The Communist Manifesto*
21. PETRONIUS · *Trimalchio's Feast*
22. JOHANN PETER HEBEL · *How a Ghastly Story Was Brought to Light by a Common or Garden Butcher's Dog*
23. HANS CHRISTIAN ANDERSEN · *The Tinder Box*
24. RUDYARD KIPLING · *The Gate of the Hundred Sorrows*
25. DANTE · *Circles of Hell*
26. HENRY MAYHEW · *Of Street Piemen*
27. HAFEZ · *The nightingales are drunk*
28. GEOFFREY CHAUCER · *The Wife of Bath*
29. MICHEL DE MONTAIGNE · *How We Weep and Laugh at the Same Thing*
30. THOMAS NASHE · *The Terrors of the Night*
31. EDGAR ALLAN POE · *The Tell-Tale Heart*
32. MARY KINGSLEY · *A Hippo Banquet*
33. JANE AUSTEN · *The Beautifull Cassandra*
34. ANTON CHEKHOV · *Gooseberries*
35. SAMUEL TAYLOR COLERIDGE · *Well, they are gone, and here must I remain*
36. JOHANN WOLFGANG VON GOETHE · *Sketchy, Doubtful, Incomplete Jottings*
37. CHARLES DICKENS · *The Great Winglebury Duel*
38. HERMAN MELVILLE · *The Maldive Shark*
39. ELIZABETH GASKELL · *The Old Nurse's Story*
40. NIKOLAY LESKOV · *The Steel Flea*

41. HONORÉ DE BALZAC · *The Atheist's Mass*
42. CHARLOTTE PERKINS GILMAN · *The Yellow Wall-Paper*
43. C.P. CAVAFY · *Remember, Body . . .*
44. FYODOR DOSTOEVSKY · *The Meek One*
45. GUSTAVE FLAUBERT · *A Simple Heart*
46. NIKOLAI GOGOL · *The Nose*
47. SAMUEL PEPYS · *The Great Fire of London*
48. EDITH WHARTON · *The Reckoning*
49. HENRY JAMES · *The Figure in the Carpet*
50. WILFRED OWEN · *Anthem For Doomed Youth*
51. WOLFGANG AMADEUS MOZART · *My Dearest Father*
52. PLATO · *Socrates' Defence*
53. CHRISTINA ROSSETTI · *Goblin Market*
54. *Sindbad the Sailor*
55. SOPHOCLES · *Antigone*
56. RYŪNOSUKE AKUTAGAWA · *The Life of a Stupid Man*
57. LEO TOLSTOY · *How Much Land Does A Man Need?*
58. GIORGIO VASARI · *Leonardo da Vinci*
59. OSCAR WILDE · *Lord Arthur Savile's Crime*
60. SHEN FU · *The Old Man of the Moon*
61. AESOP · *The Dolphins, the Whales and the Gudgeon*
62. MATSUO BASHŌ · *Lips too Chilled*
63. EMILY BRONTË · *The Night is Darkening Round Me*
64. JOSEPH CONRAD · *To-morrow*
65. RICHARD HAKLUYT · *The Voyage of Sir Francis Drake Around the Whole Globe*
66. KATE CHOPIN · *A Pair of Silk Stockings*
67. CHARLES DARWIN · *It was snowing butterflies*
68. BROTHERS GRIMM · *The Robber Bridegroom*
69. CATULLUS · *I Hate and I Love*
70. HOMER · *Circe and the Cyclops*
71. D. H. LAWRENCE · *Il Duro*
72. KATHERINE MANSFIELD · *Miss Brill*
73. OVID · *The Fall of Icarus*
74. SAPPHO · *Come Close*
75. IVAN TURGENEV · *Kasyan from the Beautiful Lands*
76. VIRGIL · *O Cruel Alexis*
77. H. G. WELLS · *A Slip under the Microscope*
78. HERODOTUS · *The Madness of Cambyses*
79. *Speaking of Siva*
80. *The Dhammapada*

'All nations,
colors,
barbarisms,
civilizations,
languages . . .'

WALT WHITMAN
Born 1819 West Hills, Long Island
Died 1892 Camden, New Jersey

Leaves of Grass published in many different editions,
with many additional poems, between 1855 and 1892.
This book makes a small selection.

WHITMAN IN PENGUIN CLASSICS
Leaves of Grass
The Complete Poems

WALT WHITMAN

On the Beach at Night Alone

PENGUIN BOOKS

PENGUIN CLASSICS

UK | USA | Canada | Ireland | Australia
India | New Zealand | South Africa

Penguin Books is part of the Penguin Random House group of companies
whose addresses can be found at global.penguinrandomhouse.com.

This selection published in Penguin Classics 2015
011

Set in 9/12.4 pt Baskerville 10 Pro
Typeset by Jouve (UK), Milton Keynes
Printed and bound in Great Britain by Clays Ltd, Elcograf S.p.A.

A CIP catalogue record for this book is available from the British Library

ISBN: 978–0–141–39822–8

www.greenpenguin.co.uk

Penguin Random House is committed to a
sustainable future for our business, our readers
and our planet. This book is made from Forest
Stewardship Council® certified paper.

Contents

Birds of Passage

Song of the Universal	1
Pioneers! O Pioneers!	5
To You	11
France, the 18th Year of These States	15
Myself and Mine	17
Year of Meteors (1859–60)	20
With Antecedents	22
A Broadway Pageant	25

Sea-Drift

Out of the Cradle Endlessly Rocking	31
As I Ebb'd with the Ocean of Life	40
Tears	45

To the Man-of-War Bird	46
Aboard at a Ship's Helm	47
On the Beach at Night	48
The World Below the Brine	50
On the Beach at Night Alone	51
Song for All Seas, All Ships	52
Patroling Barnegat	54
After the Sea-Ship	55

BIRDS OF PASSAGE

Song of the Universal

1

Come said the Muse,
Sing me a song no poet yet has chanted,
Sing me the universal.

In this broad earth of ours,
Amid the measureless grossness and the slag,
Enclosed and safe within its central heart,
Nestles the seed perfection.

By every life a share or more or less,
None born but it is born, conceal'd or unconceal'd the seed is waiting.

2

Lo! keen-eyed towering science,
As from tall peaks the modern overlooking,
Successive absolute fiats issuing.

Yet again, lo! the soul, above all science,
For it has history gather'd like husks around the globe,
For it the entire star-myriads roll through the sky.

In spiral routes by long detours,
(As a much-tacking ship upon the sea,)
For it the partial to the permanent flowing;
For it the real to the ideal tends.

For it the mystic evolution,
Not the right only justified, what we call evil also justified.

Forth from their masks, no matter what,
From the huge festering trunk, from craft and guile and tears,
Health to emerge and joy, joy universal.
Out of the bulk, the morbid and the shallow,
Out of the bad majority, the varied countless frauds of men and states,
Electric, antiseptic yet, cleaving, suffusing all,
Only the good is universal.

3

Over the mountain-growths disease and sorrow,
An uncaught bird is ever hovering, hovering,
High in the purer, happier air.

From imperfection's murkiest cloud,
Darts always forth one ray of perfect light,
One flash of heaven's glory.

Song of the Universal

To fashion's, custom's discord,
To the mad Babel-din, the deafening orgies,
Soothing each lull a strain is heard, just heard,
From some far shore the final chorus sounding.

O the blest eyes, the happy hearts,
That see, that know the guiding thread so fine,
Along the mighty labyrinth.

4

And thou America,
For the scheme's culmination, its thought and its reality,
For these (not for thyself) thou has arrived.

Thou too surroundest all,
Embracing carrying welcoming all, thou too by pathways
    broad and new,
To the ideal tendest.

The measur'd faiths of other lands, the grandeurs of the
    past,
Are not for thee, but grandeurs of thine own,
Deific faiths and amplitudes, absorbing,
    comprehending all,
All eligible to all.

All, all for immortality,
Love like the light silently wrapping all,
Nature's amelioration blessing all,
The blossoms, fruits of ages, orchards divine and certain,

Forms, objects, growths, humanities, to spirtual images
   ripening.

Give me O God to sing that thought,
Give me, give him or her I love this quenchless faith,
In Thy ensemble, whatever else withheld withhold not
   from us,
Belief in plan of Thee enclosed in Time and Space,
Health, peace, salvation universal.

Is it a dream?
Nay but the lack of it the dream,
And failing it life's lore and wealth a dream,
And all the world a dream.

Pioneers! O Pioneers!

    Come my tan-faced children,
Follow well in order, get your weapons ready,
Have you your pistols? have you your sharp-edged axes?
    Pioneers! O pioneers!

    For we cannot tarry here,
We must march my darlings, we must bear the brunt of
    danger,
We the youthful sinewy races, all the rest on us depend,
    Pioneers! O pioneers!

    O you youths, Western youths,
So impatient, full of action, full of manly pride and
    friendship,
Plain I see you Western youths, see you tramping with the
    foremost,
    Pioneers! O pioneers!

    Have the elder races halted?
Do they droop and end their lesson, wearied over there
    beyond the seas?
We take up the task eternal, and the burden and the lesson,
    Pioneers! O pioneers!

    All the past we leave behind,
We debouch upon a newer mightier world, varied world,
Fresh and strong the world we seize, world of labor and the
    march,
    Pioneers! O pioneers!

We detachments steady throwing,
Down the edges, through the passes, up the mountains
    steep,
Conquering, holding, daring, venturing as we go the
    unknown ways,
    Pioneers! O pioneers!

We primeval forests felling,
We the rivers stemming, vexing we and piercing deep the
    mines within,
We the surface broad surveying, we the virgin soil
    upheaving,
    Pioneers! O pioneers!

Colorado men are we,
From the peaks gigantic, from the giant sierras and the
    high plateaus,
From the mine and from the gully, from the hunting trail
    we come,
    Pioneers! O pioneers!

From Nebraska, from Arkansas,
Central inland race are we, from Missouri, with the
    continental blood intervein'd,
All the hands of comrades clasping, all the Southern, all
    the Northern,
    Pioneers! O pioneers!

Pioneers! O Pioneers!

    O resistless restless race!
O beloved race in all! O my breast aches with tender love
        for all!
O I mourn and yet exult, I am rapt with love for all,
        Pioneers! O pioneers!

    Raise the mighty mother mistress,
Waving high the delicate mistress, over all the starry
        mistress, (bend your heads all,)
Raise the fang'd and warlike mistress, stern, impassive,
        weapon'd mistress,
        Pioneers! O pioneers!

    See my children, resolute children,
By those swarms upon our rear we must never yield or falter,
Ages back in ghostly millions frowning there behind us
        urging,
        Pioneers! O pioneers!

    On and on the compact ranks,
With accessions ever waiting, with the places of the dead
        quickly fill'd,
Through the battle, through defeat, moving yet and never
        stopping,
        Pioneers! O pioneers!

    O to die advancing on!
Are there some of us to droop and die? has the hour come?
Then upon the march we fittest die, soon and sure the gap
        is fill'd,
        Pioneers! O pioneers!

All the pulses of the world,
Falling in they beat for us, with the Western movement beat,
Holding single or together, steady moving to the front, all for us,
    Pioneers! O pioneers!

Life's involv'd and varied pageants,
All the forms and shows, all the workmen at their work,
All the seamen and the landsmen, all the masters with their slaves,
    Pioneers! O pioneers!

All the hapless silent lovers,
All the prisoners in the prisons, all the righteous and the wicked,
All the joyous, all the sorrowing, all the living, all the dying,
    Pioneers! O pioneers!

I too with my soul and body,
We, a curious trio, picking, wandering on our way,
Through these shores amid the shadows, with the apparitions pressing,
    Pioneers! O pioneers!

Lo, the darting bowling orb!
Lo, the brother orbs around, all the clustering suns and planets,
All the dazzling days, all the mystic nights with dreams,
    Pioneers! O pioneers!

Pioneers! O Pioneers!

    These are of us, they are with us,
All for primal needed work, while the followers there in embryo wait behind,
We to-day's procession heading, we the route for travel clearing,
    Pioneers! O pioneers!

    O you daughters of the West!
O you young and elder daughters! O you mothers and you wives!
Never must you be divided, in our ranks you move united,
    Pioneers! O pioneers!

    Minstrels latent on the prairies!
(Shrouded bards of other lands, you may rest, you have done your work,)
Soon I hear you coming warbling, soon you rise and tramp amid us,
    Pioneers! O pioneers!

    Not for delectations sweet,
Not the cushion and the slipper, not the peaceful and the studious,
Not the riches safe and palling, not for us the tame enjoyment,
    Pioneers! O pioneers!

    Do the feasters gluttonous feast?
Do the corpulent sleepers sleep? have they lock'd and bolted doors?
Still be ours the diet hard, and the blanket on the ground,
    Pioneers! O pioneers!

Walt Whitman

    Has the night descended?
Was the road of late so toilsome? did we stop discouraged nodding on our way?
Yet a passing hour I yield you in your tracks to pause oblivious,
    Pioneers! O pioneers!

    Till with sound of trumpet,
Far, far off the daybreak call – hark! how loud and clear I hear it wind,
Swift! to the head of the army!–swift! spring to your places,
    Pioneers! O pioneers!

To You

Whoever you are, I fear you are walking the walks of
  dreams,
I fear these supposed realities are to melt from under your
  feet and hands,
Even now your features, joys, speech, house, trade,
  manners, troubles, follies, costume, crimes, dissipate
  away from you,
Your true soul and body appear before me,
They stand forth out of affairs, out of commerce, shops,
  work, farms, clothes, the house, buying, selling, eating,
  drinking, suffering, dying.

Whoever you are, now I place my hand upon you, that you
  be my poem,
I whisper with my lips close to your ear,
I have loved many women and men, but I love none better
  than you.

O I have been dilatory and dumb,
I should have made my way straight to you long ago,
I should have blabb'd nothing but you, I should have
  chanted nothing but you.

I will leave all and come and make the hymns of you,
None has understood you, but I understand you,
None has done justice to you, you have not done justice to
  yourself,

None but has found you imperfect, I only find no imperfection in you,
None but would subordinate you, I only am he who will never consent to subordinate you,
I only am he who places over you no master, owner, better, God, beyond what waits intrinsically in yourself.

Painters have painted their swarming groups and the centre-figure of all,
From the head of the centre-figure spreading a nimbus of gold-color'd light,
But I paint myriads of heads, but paint no head without its nimbus of gold-color'd light,
From my hand from the brain of every man and woman it streams, effulgently flowing forever.
O I could sing such grandeurs and glories about you!
You have not known what you are, you have slumber'd upon yourself all your life,
Your eyelids have been the same as closed most of the time,
What you have done returns already in mockeries,
(Your thrift, knowledge, prayers, if they do not return in mockeries, what is their return?)

The mockeries are not you,
Underneath them and within them I see you lurk,
I pursue you where none else has pursued you,
Silence, the desk, the flippant expression, the night, the accustom'd routine, if these conceal you from others or from yourself, they do not conceal you from me,

To You

The shaved face, the unsteady eye, the impure complexion,
   if these balk others they do not balk me,
The pert apparel, the deform'd attitude, drunkenness,
   greed, premature death, all these I part aside.

There is no endowment in man or woman that is not tallied
   in you,
There is no virtue, no beauty in man or woman, but as
   good is in you,
No pluck, no endurance in others, but as good is in you,
No pleasure waiting for others, but an equal pleasure waits
   for you.

As for me, I give nothing to any one except I give the like
   carefully to you,
I sing the songs of the glory of none, not God, sooner than
   I sing the songs of the glory of you.

Whoever you are! claim your own at any hazard!
These shows of the East and West are tame compared
   to you,
These immense meadows, these interminable rivers, you are
   immense and interminable as they,
These furies, elements, storms, motions of Nature, throes of
   apparent dissolution, you are he or she who is master or
   mistress over them,
Master or mistress in your own right over Nature, elements,
   pain, passion, dissolution.

Walt Whitman

The hopples fall from your ankles, you find an unfailing
    sufficiency,
Old or young, male or female, rude, low, rejected by the
    rest, whatever you are promulges itself,
Through birth, life, death, burial, the means are provided,
    nothing is scanted,
Through angers, losses, ambition, ignorance, ennui, what
    you are picks its way.

France, the 18th Year of These States

A great year and place.
A harsh discordant natal scream out-sounding, to touch the
 mother's heart closer than any yet.

I walk'd the shores of my Eastern sea,
Heard over the waves the little voice,
Saw the divine infant where she woke mournfully wailing,
 amid the roar of cannon, curses, shouts, crash of falling
 buildings,
Was not so sick from the blood in the gutters running, nor
 from the single corpses, nor those in heaps, nor those
 borne away in the tumbrils,
Was not so desperate at the battues of death – was not so
 shock'd at the repeated fusillades of the guns.

Pale, silent, stern, what could I say to that long-accrued
 retribution?
Could I wish humanity different?
Could I wish the people made of wood and stone?
Or that there be no justice in destiny or time?

O Liberty! O mate for me!
Here too the blaze, the grape-shot and the axe, in reserve,
 to fetch them out in case of need,
Here too, though long represt, can never be destroy'd,
Here too could rise at last murdering and ecstatic,
Here too demanding full arrears of vengeance.

Walt Whitman

Hence I sign this salute over the sea,
And I do not deny that terrible red birth and baptism,
But remember the little voice that I heard wailing, and wait with perfect trust, no matter how long,
And from to-day sad and cogent I maintain the bequeath'd cause, as for all lands,
And I send these words to Paris with my love,
And I guess some chansonniers there will understand them,
For I guess there is latent music yet in France, floods of it,
O I hear already the bustle of instruments, they will soon be drowning all that would interrupt them,
O I think the east wind brings a triumphal and free march,
It reaches hither, it swells me to joyful madness,
I will run transpose it in words, to justify it,
I will yet sing a song for you ma femme.

Myself and Mine

Myself and mine gymnastic ever,
To stand the cold or heat, to take good aim with a
 gun, to sail a boat, to manage horses, to beget
 superb children,
To speak readily and clearly, to feel at home among
 common people,
And to hold our own in terrible positions on land and sea.

Not for an embroiderer,
(There will always be plenty of embroiderers, I welcome
 them also,)
But for the fibre of things and for inherent men and
 women.

Not to chisel ornaments,
But to chisel with free stroke the heads and limbs of
 plenteous supreme Gods, that the States may realize
 them walking and talking.
Let me have my own way,
Let others promulge the laws, I will make no account of the
 laws,
Let others praise eminent men and hold up peace, I hold
 up agitation and conflict.
I praise no eminent man, I rebuke to his face the one that
 was thought most worthy.

(Who are you? and what are you secretly guilty of all your
   life?
Will you turn aside all your life? will you grub and chatter
   all your life?
And who are you, blabbing by rote, years, pages,
   languages, reminiscences,
Unwitting to-day that you do not know how to speak
   properly a single word?)

Let others finish specimens, I never finish specimens,
I start them by exhaustless laws as Nature does, fresh and
   modern continually.

I give nothing as duties,
What others give as duties I give as living impulses,
(Shall I give the heart's action as a duty?)

Let others dispose of questions, I dispose of nothing, I
   arouse unanswerable questions,
Who are they I see and touch, and what about them?
What about these likes of myself that draw me so close by
   tender directions and indirections?

I call to the world to distrust the accounts of my friends,
   but listen to my enemies, as I myself do,
I charge you forever reject those who would expound me,
   for I cannot expound myself,
I charge that there be no theory or school founded out
   of me,
I charge you to leave all free, as I have left all free.
After me, vista!
O I see life is not short, but immeasurably long,

Myself and Mine

I henceforth tread the world chaste, temperate, an early
   riser, a steady grower,
Every hour the semen of centuries, and still of centuries.

I must follow up these continual lessons of the air, water,
   earth,
I perceive I have no time to lose.

Year of Meteors (1859–60)

Year of meteors! brooding year!
I would bind in words retrospective some of your deeds and signs,
I would sing your contest for the 19th Presidentiad,
I would sing how an old man, tall, with white hair, mounted the scaffold in Virginia,
(I was at hand, silent I stood with teeth shut close, I watch'd,
I stood very near you old man when cool and indifferent, but trembling with age and your unheal'd wounds you mounted the scaffold;)
I would sing in my copious song your census returns of the States,
The tables of population and products, I would sing of your ships and their cargoes,
The proud black ships of Manhattan arriving, some fill'd with immigrants, some from the isthmus with cargoes of gold,
Songs thereof would I sing, to all that hitherward comes would I welcome give,
And you would I sing, fair stripling! welcome to you from me, young prince of England!
(Remember you surging Manhattan's crowds as you pass'd with your cortege of nobles?
There in the crowds stood I, and singled you out with attachment;)

Year of Meteors (1859–60)

Nor forget I to sing of the wonder, the ship as she swam up my bay,
Well-shaped and stately the Great Eastern swam up my bay, she was 600 feet long,
Her moving swiftly surrounded by myriads of small craft I forget not to sing;
Nor the comet that came unannounced out of the north flaring in heaven,
Nor the strange huge meteor-procession dazzling and clear shooting over our heads,
(A moment, a moment long it sail'd its balls of unearthly light over our heads,
Then departed, dropt in the night, and was gone;)
Of such, and fitful as they, I sing – with gleams from them would I gleam and patch these chants,
Your chants, O year all mottled with evil and good – year of forebodings!
Year of comets and meteors transient and strange – lo! even here one equally transient and strange!
As I flit through you hastily, soon to fall and be gone, what is this chant,
What am I myself but one of your meteors?

With Antecedents

1

With antecedents,
With my fathers and mothers and the accumulations of past ages,
With all which, had it not been, I would not now be here, as I am,
With Egypt, India, Phenicia, Greece and Rome,
With the Kelt, the Scandinavian, the Alb and the Saxon,
With antique maritime ventures, laws, artisanship, wars and journeys,
With the poet, the skald, the saga, the myth, and the oracle,
With the sale of slaves, with enthusiasts, with the troubadour, the crusader, and the monk,
With those old continents whence we have come to this new continent,
With the fading kingdoms and kings over there,
With the fading religions and priests,
With the small shores we look back to from our own large and present shores,
With countless years drawing themselves onward and arrived at these years,
You and me arrived – America arrived and making this year,
This year! sending itself ahead countless years to come.

With Antecedents

2

O but it is not the years – it is I, it is You,
We touch all laws and tally all antecedents,
We are the skald, the oracle, the monk and the knight, we easily include them and more,
We stand amid time beginningless and endless, we stand amid evil and good,
All swings around us, there is as much darkness as light,
The very sun swings itself and its system of planets around us,
Its sun, and its again, all swing around us.

As for me, (torn, stormy, amid these vehement days,)
I have the idea of all, and am all and believe in all,
I believe materialism is true and spiritualism is true, I reject no part.

(Have I forgotten any part? any thing in the past?
Come to me whoever and whatever, till I give you recognition.)

I respect Assyria, China, Teutonia, and the Hebrews,
I adopt each theory, myth, god, and demi-god,
I see that the old accounts, bibles, genealogies, are true, without exception,
I assert that all past days were what they must have been,
And that they could no-how have been better than they were,

And that to-day is what it must be, and that America is,
And that to-day and America could no-how be better than
    they are.

3

In the name of these States and in your and my name, the
    Past,
And in the name of these States and in your and my name,
    the Present time.

I know that the past was great and the future will be great,
And I know that both curiously conjoint in the present
    time,
(For the sake of him I typify, for the common average man's
    sake, your sake if you are he,)
And that where I am or you are this present day, there is the
    centre of all days, all races,
And there is the meaning to us of all that has ever come of
    races and days, or ever will come.

A Broadway Pageant

1

Over the Western sea hither from Niphon come,
Courteous, the swart-cheek'd two-sworded envoys,
Leaning back in their open barouches, bare-headed, impassive,
Ride to-day through Manhattan.

Libertad! I do not know whether others behold what I behold,
In the procession along with the nobles of Niphon, the errand-bearers,
Bringing up the rear, hovering above, around, or in the ranks marching,
But I will sing you a song of what I behold Libertad.
When million-footed Manhattan unpent descends to her pavements,
When the thunder-cracking guns arouse me with the proud roar I love,
When the round-mouth'd guns out of the smoke and smell I love spit their salutes,
When the fire-flashing guns have fully alerted me, and heaven-clouds canopy my city with a delicate thin haze,
When gorgeous the countless straight stems, the forests at the wharves, thicken with colors,
When every ship richly drest carries her flag at the peak,

When pennants trail and street-festoons hang from the windows,
When Broadway is entirely given up to foot-passengers and foot-standers, when the mass is densest,
When the façades of the houses are alive with people, when eyes gaze riveted tens of thousands at a time,
When the guests from the islands advance, when the pageant moves forward visible,
When the summons is made, when the answer that waited thousands of years answers,
I too arising, answering, descend to the pavements, merge with the crowd, and gaze with them.

2

Superb-faced Manhattan!
Comrade Americanos! to us, then at last the Orient comes.

To us, my city,
Where our tall-topt marble and iron beauties range on opposite sides, to walk in the space between,
To-day our Antipodes comes.

The Originatress comes,
The nest of languages, the bequeather of poems, the race of eld,
Florid with blood, pensive, rapt with musings, hot with passion,
Sultry with perfume, with ample and flowing garments,

With sunburnt visage, with intense soul and glittering eyes,
The race of Brahma comes.

See my cantabile! these and more are flashing to us from the procession,
As it moves changing, a kaleidoscope divine it moves changing before us.

For not the envoys nor the tann'd Japanee from his island only,
Lithe and silent the Hindoo appears, the Asiatic continent itself appears, the past, the dead,
The murky night-morning of wonder and fable inscrutable,
The envelop'd mysteries, the old and unknown hive-bees,
The north, the sweltering south, eastern Assyria, the Hebrews, the ancient of ancients,
Vast desolated cities, the gliding present, all of these and more are in the pageant-procession.

Geography, the world, is in it,
The Great Sea, the brood of islands, Polynesia, the coast beyond,
The coast you henceforth are facing – you Libertad! from your Western golden shores,
The countries there with their populations, the millions en-masse are curiously here,
The swarming market-places, the temples with idols ranged along the sides or at the end, bonze, brahmin, and llama,
Mandarin, farmer, merchant, mechanic, and fisherman,

The singing-girl and the dancing-girl, the ecstatic persons, the secluded emperors,
Confucious himself, the great poets and heroes, the warriors, the castes, all,
Trooping up, crowding from all directions, from the Altay mountains,
From Thibet, from the four winding and far-flowing rivers of China,
From the southern peninsulas and the demi-continental islands, from Malaysia,
These and whatever belongs to them palpable show forth to me, and are seiz'd by me,
And I am seiz'd by them, and friendlily held by them,
Till as here them all I chant, Libertad! for themselves and for you.

For I too raising my voice join the ranks of this pageant,
I am the chanter, I chant aloud over the pageant,
I chant the world on my Western sea,
I chant copious the islands beyond, thick as stars in the sky,
I chant the new empire grander than any before, as in a vision it comes to me,
I chant America the mistress, I chant a greater supremacy,
I chant projected a thousand blooming cities yet in time on those groups of sea-islands,
My sail-ships and steam-ships threading the archipelagoes,
My stars and stripes fluttering in the wind,
Commerce opening, the sleep of ages having done its work, races reborn, refresh'd,

A Broadway Pageant

Lives, works resumed – the object I know not – but the
  old, the Asiatic renew'd as it must be,
Commencing from this day surrounded by the world.

3

And you Libertad of the world!
You shall sit in the middle well-pois'd thousands and
  thousands of years,
As to-day from one side the nobles of Asia come to you,
As to-morrow from the other side the queen of England
  sends her eldest son to you.

The sign is reversing, the orb is enclosed,
The ring is circled, the journey is done,
The box-lid is but perceptibly open'd, nevertheless the
  perfume pours copiously out of the whole box.
Young Libertad! with the venerable Asia, the all-mother,
Be considerate with her now and ever hot Libertad, for you
  are all,
Bend your proud neck to the long-off mother now sending
  messages over the archipelagoes to you,
Bend your proud neck low for once, young Libertad.

Were the children straying westward so long? so wide the
  tramping?
Were the precedent dim ages debouching westward from
  Paradise so long?
Were the centuries steadily footing it that way, all the while
  unknown, for you, for reasons?

They are justified, they are accomplish'd, they shall now
 be turn'd the other way also, to travel toward you
 thence,
They shall now also march obediently eastward for your
 sake Libertad.

SEA-DRIFT

Out of the Cradle Endlessly Rocking

Out of the cradle endlessly rocking,
Out of the mocking-bird's throat, the musical shuttle,
Out of the Ninth-month midnight,
Over the sterile sands and the fields beyond, where the child leaving his bed wander'd alone, bareheaded, barefoot,
Down from the shower'd halo,
Up from the mystic play of shadows twining and twisting as if they were alive,
Out from the patches of briers and blackberries,
From the memories of the bird that chanted to me,
From your memories sad brother, from the fitful risings and fallings I heard,
From under that yellow half-moon late-risen and swollen as if with tears,
From those beginning notes of yearning and love there in the mist,
From the thousand responses of my heart never to cease,
From the myriad thence-arous'd words,
From the word stronger and more delicious than any,
From such as now they start the scene revisiting,
As a flock, twittering, rising, or overhead passing,

Walt Whitman

Borne hither, ere all eludes me, hurriedly,
A man, yet by these tears a little boy again,
Throwing myself on the sand, confronting the waves,
I, chanter of pains and joys, uniter of here and hereafter,
Taking all hints to use them, but swiftly leaping beyond them,
A reminiscence sing.

Once Paumanok,
When the lilac-scent was in the air and Fifth-month grass was growing,
Up this seashore in some briers,
Two feather'd guests from Alabama, two together,
And their nest, and four light-green eggs spotted with brown,
And every day the he-bird to and fro near at hand,
And every day the she-bird crouch'd on her nest, silent, with bright eyes,
And every day I, a curious boy, never too close, never disturbing them,
Cautiously peering, absorbing, translating.

Shine! shine! shine!
Pour down your warmth, great sun!
While we bask, we two together.

Two together!
Winds blow south, or winds blow north,
Day come white, or night come black,
Home, or rivers and mountains from home,
Singing all time, minding no time,
While we two keep together.

Out of the Cradle Endlessly Rocking

Till of a sudden,
May-be kill'd, unknown to her mate,
One forenoon the she-bird crouch'd not on the nest,
Nor return'd that afternoon, nor the next,
Nor ever appear'd again.

And thenceforward all summer in the sound of the sea,
And at night under the full of the moon in calmer
    weather,
Over the hoarse surging of the sea,
Or flitting from brier to brier by day,
I saw, I heard at intervals the remaining one, the he-bird,
The solitary guest from Alabama.

Blow! blow! blow!
Blow up sea-winds along Paumanok's shore;
I wait and I wait till you blow my mate to me.

Yes, when the stars glisten'd,
All night long on the prong of a moss-scallop'd stake,
Down almost amid the slapping waves,
Sat the lone singer wonderful causing tears.
He call'd on his mate,
He pour'd forth the meanings which I of all men know.

Yes my brother I know,
The rest might not, but I have treasur'd every note,
For more than once dimly down to the beach gliding,
Silent, avoiding the moonbeams, blending myself with the
    shadows,
Recalling now the obscure shapes, the echoes, the sounds
    and sights after their sorts,

Walt Whitman

The white arms out in the breakers tirelessly tossing,
I, with bare feet, a child, the wind wafting my hair,
Listen'd long and long.

Listen'd to keep, to sing, now translating the notes,
Following you my brother.

Soothe! soothe! soothe!
Close on its wave soothes the wave behind,
And again another behind embracing and lapping, every one
*   close,*
But my love soothes not me, not me.

Low hangs the moon, it rose late,
It is lagging – O I think it is heavy with love, with love.

O madly the sea pushes upon the land,
With love, with love.

O night! do I not see my love fluttering out among the
*   breakers?*
What is that little black thing I see there in the white?

Loud! loud! loud!
Loud I call to you, my love!
High and clear I shoot my voice over the waves,
Surely you must know who is here, is here,
You must know who I am, my love.
Low-hanging moon!
What is that dusky spot in your brown yellow?
O it is the shape, the shape of my mate!
O moon do not keep her from me any longer.

Land! land! O land!
Whichever way I turn, O I think you could give me my mate back again if you only would,
For I am almost sure I see her dimly whichever way I look.

O rising stars!
Perhaps the one I want so much will rise, will rise with some of you.

O throat! O trembling throat!
Sound clearer through the atmosphere!
Pierce the woods, the earth,
Somewhere listening to catch you must be the one I want.

Shake out carols!
Solitary here, the night's carols!
Carols of lonesome love! death's carols!
Carols under that lagging, yellow, waning moon!
O under that moon where she droops almost down into the sea!
O reckless despairing carols.

But soft! sink low!
Soft! let me just murmur,
And do you wait a moment you husky-nois'd sea,
For somewhere I believe I heard my mate responding to me,
So faint, I must be still, be still to listen,
But not altogether still, for then she might not come immediately to me.

Hither my love!
Here I am! here!
With this just-sustain'd note I announce myself to you,
This gentle call is for you my love, for you.
Do not be decoy'd elsewhere,
That is the whistle of the wind, it is not my voice,
That is the fluttering, the fluttering of the spray,
Those are the shadows of leaves.

O darkness! O in vain!
O I am very sick and sorrowful.

O brown halo in the sky near the moon, drooping upon the sea!
O troubled reflection in the sea!
O throat! O throbbing heart!
And I singing uselessly, uselessly all the night.

O past! O happy life! O songs of joy!
In the air, in the woods, over fields,
Loved! loved! loved! loved! loved!
But my mate no more, no more with me!
We two together no more.

The aria sinking,
All else continuing, the stars shining,
The winds blowing, the notes of the bird continuous echoing,
With angry moans the fierce old mother incessantly moaning,
On the sands of Paumanok's shore gray and rustling,
The yellow half-moon enlarged, sagging down, drooping, the face of the sea almost touching,

Out of the Cradle Endlessly Rocking

The boy ecstatic, with his bare feet the waves, with his hair
    the atmosphere dallying,
The love in the heart long pent, now loose, now at last
    tumultuously bursting,
The aria's meaning, the ears, the soul, swiftly depositing,
The strange tears down the cheeks coursing,
The colloquy there, the trio, each uttering,
The undertone, the savage old mother incessantly crying,
To the boy's soul's questions sullenly timing, some drown'd
    secret hissing,
To the outsetting bard.
Demon or bird! (said the boy's soul,)
Is it indeed toward your mate you sing? or is it really
    to me?
For I, that was a child, my tongue's use sleeping, now I
    have heard you,
Now in a moment I know what I am for, I awake,
And already a thousand singers, a thousand songs, clearer,
    louder and more sorrowful than yours,
A thousand warbling echoes have started to life within me,
    never to die.

O you singer solitary, singing by yourself, projecting me,
O solitary me listening, never more shall I cease
    perpetuating you,
Never more shall I escape, never more the reverberations,
Never more the cries of unsatisfied love be absent from me,
Never again leave me to be the peaceful child I was before
    what there in the night,
By the sea under the yellow and sagging moon,

Walt Whitman

The messenger there arous'd, the fire, the sweet hell within,
The unknown want, the destiny of me.

O give me the clew! (it lurks in the night here
    somewhere,)
O if I am to have so much, let me have more!

A word then, (for I will conquer it,)
The word final, superior to all,
Subtle, sent up – what is it? – I listen;
Are you whispering it, and have been all the time, you
    sea-waves?
Is that it from your liquid rims and wet sands?

Whereto answering, the sea,
Delaying not, hurrying not,
Whisper'd me through the night, and very plainly before
    daybreak,
Lisp'd to me the low and delicious word death,
And again death, death, death, death,
Hissing melodious, neither like the bird nor like my arous'd
    child's heart,
But edging near as privately for me rustling at my feet,
Creeping thence steadily up to my ears and laving me softly
    all over,
Death, death, death, death, death.

Which I do not forget,
But fuse the song of my dusky demon and brother,
That he sang to me in the moonlight on Paumanok's gray
    beach,
With the thousand responsive songs at random,

Out of the Cradle Endlessly Rocking

My own songs awaked from that hour,
And with them the key, the word up from the waves,
The word of the sweetest song and all songs,
That strong and delicious word which, creeping to my feet,
(Or like some old crone rocking the cradle, swathed in
    sweet garments, bending aside,)
The sea whisper'd me.

As I Ebb'd with the Ocean of Life

1

As I ebb'd with the ocean of life,
As I wended the shores I know,
As I walk'd where the ripples continually wash you Paumanok,
Where they rustle up hoarse and sibilant,
Where the fierce old mother endlessly cries for her castaways,
I musing late in the autumn day, gazing off southward,
Held by this electric self out of the pride of which I utter poems,
Was seiz'd by the spirit that trails in the lines underfoot,
The rim, the sediment that stands for all the water and all the land of the globe.

Fascinated, my eyes reverting from the south, dropt, to follow those slender windrows,
Chaff, straw, splinters of wood, weeds, and the sea-gluten,
Scum, scales from shining rocks, leaves of salt-lettuce, left by the tide,
Miles walking, the sound of breaking waves the other side of me,
Paumanok there and then as I thought the old thought of likenesses,
These you presented to me you fish-shaped island,

As I Ebb'd with the Ocean of Life

As I wended the shores I know,
As I walk'd with that electric self seeking types.

2

As I wend to the shores I know not,
As I list to the dirge, the voices of men and women wreck'd,
As I inhale the impalpable breezes that set in upon me,
As the ocean so mysterious rolls toward me closer and
　　closer,
I too but signify at the utmost a little wash'd-up drift,
A few sands and dead leaves to gather,
Gather, and merge myself as part of the sands and drift.

O baffled, balk'd, bent to the very earth,
Oppress'd with myself that I have dared to open my
　　mouth,
Aware now that amid all that blab whose echoes recoil
　　upon me I have not once had the least idea who or
　　what I am,
But that before all my arrogant poems the real Me stands
　　yet untouch'd, untold, altogether unreach'd,
Withdrawn far, mocking me with mock-congratulatory
　　signs and bows,
With peals of distant ironical laughter at every word I have
　　written,
Pointing in silence to these songs, and then to the sand
　　beneath.

I perceive I have not really understood any thing, not a
    single object, and that no man ever can,
Nature here in sight of the sea taking advantage of me to
    dart upon me and sting me,
Because I have dared to open my mouth to sing at all.

3

You oceans both, I close with you,
We murmur alike reproachfully rolling sands and drift,
    knowing not why,
These little shreds indeed standing for you and me and all.

You friable shore with trails of debris,
You fish-shaped island, I take what is underfoot,
What is yours is mine my father.

I too Paumanok,
I too have bubbled up, floated the measureless float, and
    been wash'd on your shores,
I too am but a trail of drift and debris,
I too leave little wrecks upon you, you fish-shaped island.

I throw myself upon your breast my father,
I cling to you so that you cannot unloose me,
I hold you so firm till you answer me something.

Kiss me my father,
Touch me with your lips as I touch those I love,
Breathe to me while I hold you close the secret of the
    murmuring I envy.

As I Ebb'd with the Ocean of Life

4

Ebb, ocean of life, (the flow will return,)
Cease not your moaning you fierce old mother,
Endlessly cry for your castaways, but fear not, deny
    not me,
Rustle not up so hoarse and angry against my feet as I
    touch you or gather from you.

I mean tenderly by you and all,
I gather for myself and for this phantom looking down
    where we lead, and following me and mine.

Me and mine, loose windrows, little corpses,
Froth, snowy white, and bubbles,
(See, from my dead lips the ooze exuding at last,
See, the prismatic colors glistening and rolling,)
Tufts of straw, sands, fragments,
Buoy'd hither from many moods, one contradicting
    another,
From the storm, the long calm, the darkness, the swell,
Musing, pondering, a breath, a briny tear, a dab of liquid
    or soil,
Up just as much out of fathomless workings fermented and
    thrown,
A limp blossom or two, torn, just as much over waves
    floating, drifted at random,
Just as much for us that sobbing dirge of Nature,
Just as much whence we come that blare of the
    cloud-trumpets,

Walt Whitman

We, capricious, brought hither we know not whence,
    spread out before you,
You up there walking or sitting,
Whoever you are, we too lie in drifts at your feet.

Tears

Tears! tears! tears!
In the night, in solitude, tears,
On the white shore dripping, dripping, suck'd in by the sand,
Tears, not a star shining, all dark and desolate,
Moist tears from the eyes of a muffled head;
O who is that ghost? that form in the dark, with tears?
What shapeless lump is that, bent, crouch'd there on the sand?
Streaming tears, sobbing tears, throes, choked with wild cries;
O storm, embodied, rising, careering with swift steps along the beach!
O wild and dismal night storm, with wind – O belching and desperate!
O shade so sedate and decorous by day, with calm countenance and regulated pace,
But away at night as you fly, none looking – O then the unloosen'd ocean,
Of tears! tears! tears!

To the Man-of-War Bird

Thou who hast slept all night upon the storm,
Waking renew'd on thy prodigious pinions,
(Burst the wild storm? above it thou ascended'st,
And rested on the sky, thy slave that cradled thee,)
Now a blue point, far, far, in heaven floating,
As to the light emerging here on deck I watch thee,
(Myself a speck, a point on the world's floating vast.)

Far, far at sea,
After the night's fierce drifts have strewn the shore with
    wrecks,
With re-appearing day as now so happy and serene,
The rosy and elastic dawn, the flashing sun,
The limpid spread of air cerulean,
Thou also re-appearest.
Thou born to match the gale, (thou art all wings,)
To cope with heaven and earth and sea and hurricane,
Thou ship of air that never furl'st thy sails,
Days, even weeks untired and onward, through spaces,
    realms gyrating,
At dusk that look'st on Senegal, at morn America,
That sport'st amid the lightning-flash and thunder-cloud,
In them, in thy experiences, had'st thou my soul,
What joys! what joys were thine!

Aboard at a Ship's Helm

Aboard at a ship's helm,
A young steersman steering with care.

Through fog on a sea-coast dolefully ringing,
An ocean-bell – O a warning bell, rock'd by the waves.

O you give good notice indeed, you bell by the sea-reefs ringing,
Ringing, ringing, to warn the ship from its wreck-place.

For as on the alert O steersman, you mind the loud admonition,
The bows turn, the freighted ship tacking speeds away under her gray sails,
The beautiful and noble ship with all her precious wealth speeds away gayly and safe.

But O the ship, the immortal ship! O ship aboard the ship!
Ship of the body, ship of the soul, voyaging, voyaging, voyaging.

On the Beach at Night

On the beach at night,
Stands a child with her father,
Watching the east, the autumn sky.

Up through the darkness,
While ravening clouds, the burial clouds, in black masses spreading,
Lower sullen and fast athwart and down the sky,
Amid a transparent clear belt of ether yet left in the east,
Ascends large and calm the lord-star Jupiter,
And nigh at hand, only a very little above,
Swim the delicate sisters the Pleiades.
From the beach the child holding the hand of her father,
Those burial-clouds that lower victorious soon to devour all,
Watching, silently weeps.

Weep not, child,
Weep not, my darling,
With these kisses let me remove your tears,
The ravening clouds shall not long be victorious,
They shall not long possess the sky, they devour the stars only in apparition,
Jupiter shall emerge, be patient, watch again another night, the Pleiades shall emerge,
They are immortal, all those stars both silvery and golden shall shine out again,

On the Beach at Night

The great stars and the little ones shall shine out again, they
    endure,
The vast immortal suns and the long-enduring pensive
    moons shall again shine.

Then dearest child mournest thou only for Jupiter?
Considerest thou alone the burial of the stars?

Something there is,
(With my lips soothing thee, adding I whisper,
I give thee the first suggestion, the problem and
    indirection,)
Something there is more immortal even than the stars,
(Many the burials, many the days and nights, passing
    away,)
Something that shall endure longer even than lustrous
    Jupiter,
Longer than sun or any revolving satellite,
Or the radiant sisters the Pleiades.

The World Below the Brine

The world below the brine,
Forests at the bottom of the sea, the branches and leaves,
Sea-lettuce, vast lichens, strange flowers and seeds, the thick tangle, openings, and pink turf,
Different colors, pale gray and green, purple, white, and gold, the play of light through the water,
Dumb swimmers there among the rocks, coral, gluten, grass, rushes, and the aliment of the swimmers,
Sluggish existences grazing there suspended, or slowly crawling close to the bottom,
The sperm-whale at the surface blowing air and spray, or disporting with his flukes,
The leaden-eyed shark, the walrus, the turtle, the hairy sea-leopard, and the sting-ray,
Passions there, wars, pursuits, tribes, sight in those ocean-depths, breathing that thick-breathing air, as so many do,
The change thence to the sight here, and to the subtle air breathed by beings like us who walk this sphere,
The change onward from ours to that of beings who walk other spheres.

On the Beach at Night Alone

On the beach at night alone,
As the old mother sways her to and fro singing her husky song,
As I watch the bright stars shining, I think a thought of the clef of the universes and of the future.

A vast similitude interlocks all,
All spheres, grown, ungrown, small, large, suns, moons, planets,
All distances of place however wide,
All distances of time, all inanimate forms,
All souls, all living bodies though they be ever so different, or in different worlds,
All gaseous, watery, vegetable, mineral processes, the fishes, the brutes,
All nations, colors, barbarisms, civilizations, languages,
All identities that have existed or may exist on this globe, or any globe,
All lives and deaths, all of the past, present, future,
This vast similitude spans them, and always has spann'd,
And shall forever span them and compactly hold and enclose them.

Song for All Seas, All Ships

1

To-day a rude brief recitative,
Of ships sailing the seas, each with its special flag or
 ship-signal,
Of unnamed heroes in the ships – of waves spreading and
 spreading far as the eye can reach,
Of dashing spray, and the winds piping and blowing,
And out of these a chant for the sailors of all nations,
Fitful, like a surge.

Of sea-captains young or old, and the mates, and of all
 intrepid sailors,
Of the few, very choice, taciturn, whom fate can never
 surprise nor death dismay,
Pick'd sparingly without noise by thee old ocean, chosen by
 thee,
Thou sea that pickest and cullest the race in time, and
 unitest nations,
Suckled by thee, old husky nurse, embodying thee,
Indomitable, untamed as thee.

(Ever the heroes on water or on land, by ones or twos
 appearing,
Ever the stock preserv'd and never lost, though rare,
 enough for seed preserv'd.)

2

Flaunt out O sea your separate flags of nations!
Flaunt out visible as ever the various ship-signals!
But do you reserve especially for yourself and for the soul
    of man one flag above all the rest,
A spiritual woven signal for all nations, emblem of man
    elate above death,
Token of all brave captains and all intrepid sailors and
    mates,
And all that went down doing their duty,
Reminiscent of them, twined from all intrepid captains
    young or old,
A pennant universal, subtly waving all time, o'er all brave
    sailors,
All seas, all ships.

Patroling Barnegat

Wild, wild the storm, and the sea high running,
Steady the roar of the gale, with incessant undertone muttering,
Shouts of demoniac laughter fitfully piercing and pealing,
Waves, air, midnight, their savagest trinity lashing,
Out in the shadows there milk-white combs careering,
On beachy slush and sand spirts of snow fierce slanting,
Where through the murk the easterly death-wind breasting,
Through cutting swirl and spray watchful and firm advancing,
(That in the distance! is that a wreck? is the red signal flaring?)
Slush and sand of the beach tireless till daylight wending,
Steadily, slowly, through hoarse roar never remitting,
Along the midnight edge by those milk-white combs careering,
A group of dim, weird forms, struggling, the night confronting,
That savage trinity warily watching.

After the Sea-Ship

After the sea-ship, after the whistling winds,
After the white-gray sails taut to their spars and ropes,
Below, a myriad myriad waves hastening, lifting up their necks,
Tending in ceaseless flow toward the track of the ship,
Waves of the ocean bubbling and gurgling, blithely prying,
Waves, undulating waves, liquid, uneven, emulous waves,
Toward that whirling current, laughing and buoyant, with curves,
Where the great vessel sailing and tacking displaces the surface,
Larger and smaller waves in the spread of the ocean yearnfully flowing,
The wake of the sea-ship after she passes, flashing and frolicsome under the sun,
A motley procession with many a fleck of foam and many fragments,
Following the stately and rapid ship, in the wake following.

1. BOCCACCIO · *Mrs Rosie and the Priest*
2. GERARD MANLEY HOPKINS · *As kingfishers catch fire*
3. *The Saga of Gunnlaug Serpent-tongue*
4. THOMAS DE QUINCEY · *On Murder Considered as One of the Fine Arts*
5. FRIEDRICH NIETZSCHE · *Aphorisms on Love and Hate*
6. JOHN RUSKIN · *Traffic*
7. PU SONGLING · *Wailing Ghosts*
8. JONATHAN SWIFT · *A Modest Proposal*
9. *Three Tang Dynasty Poets*
10. WALT WHITMAN · *On the Beach at Night Alone*
11. KENKŌ · *A Cup of Sake Beneath the Cherry Trees*
12. BALTASAR GRACIÁN · *How to Use Your Enemies*
13. JOHN KEATS · *The Eve of St Agnes*
14. THOMAS HARDY · *Woman much missed*
15. GUY DE MAUPASSANT · *Femme Fatale*
16. MARCO POLO · *Travels in the Land of Serpents and Pearls*
17. SUETONIUS · *Caligula*
18. APOLLONIUS OF RHODES · *Jason and Medea*
19. ROBERT LOUIS STEVENSON · *Olalla*
20. KARL MARX AND FRIEDRICH ENGELS · *The Communist Manifesto*
21. PETRONIUS · *Trimalchio's Feast*
22. JOHANN PETER HEBEL · *How a Ghastly Story Was Brought to Light by a Common or Garden Butcher's Dog*
23. HANS CHRISTIAN ANDERSEN · *The Tinder Box*
24. RUDYARD KIPLING · *The Gate of the Hundred Sorrows*
25. DANTE · *Circles of Hell*
26. HENRY MAYHEW · *Of Street Piemen*
27. HAFEZ · *The nightingales are drunk*
28. GEOFFREY CHAUCER · *The Wife of Bath*
29. MICHEL DE MONTAIGNE · *How We Weep and Laugh at the Same Thing*
30. THOMAS NASHE · *The Terrors of the Night*
31. EDGAR ALLAN POE · *The Tell-Tale Heart*
32. MARY KINGSLEY · *A Hippo Banquet*
33. JANE AUSTEN · *The Beautifull Cassandra*
34. ANTON CHEKHOV · *Gooseberries*
35. SAMUEL TAYLOR COLERIDGE · *Well, they are gone, and here must I remain*
36. JOHANN WOLFGANG VON GOETHE · *Sketchy, Doubtful, Incomplete Jottings*
37. CHARLES DICKENS · *The Great Winglebury Duel*
38. HERMAN MELVILLE · *The Maldive Shark*
39. ELIZABETH GASKELL · *The Old Nurse's Story*
40. NIKOLAY LESKOV · *The Steel Flea*

41. HONORÉ DE BALZAC · *The Atheist's Mass*
42. CHARLOTTE PERKINS GILMAN · *The Yellow Wall-Paper*
43. C.P. CAVAFY · *Remember, Body . . .*
44. FYODOR DOSTOEVSKY · *The Meek One*
45. GUSTAVE FLAUBERT · *A Simple Heart*
46. NIKOLAI GOGOL · *The Nose*
47. SAMUEL PEPYS · *The Great Fire of London*
48. EDITH WHARTON · *The Reckoning*
49. HENRY JAMES · *The Figure in the Carpet*
50. WILFRED OWEN · *Anthem For Doomed Youth*
51. WOLFGANG AMADEUS MOZART · *My Dearest Father*
52. PLATO · *Socrates' Defence*
53. CHRISTINA ROSSETTI · *Goblin Market*
54. *Sindbad the Sailor*
55. SOPHOCLES · *Antigone*
56. RYŪNOSUKE AKUTAGAWA · *The Life of a Stupid Man*
57. LEO TOLSTOY · *How Much Land Does A Man Need?*
58. GIORGIO VASARI · *Leonardo da Vinci*
59. OSCAR WILDE · *Lord Arthur Savile's Crime*
60. SHEN FU · *The Old Man of the Moon*
61. AESOP · *The Dolphins, the Whales and the Gudgeon*
62. MATSUO BASHŌ · *Lips too Chilled*
63. EMILY BRONTË · *The Night is Darkening Round Me*
64. JOSEPH CONRAD · *To-morrow*
65. RICHARD HAKLUYT · *The Voyage of Sir Francis Drake Around the Whole Globe*
66. KATE CHOPIN · *A Pair of Silk Stockings*
67. CHARLES DARWIN · *It was snowing butterflies*
68. BROTHERS GRIMM · *The Robber Bridegroom*
69. CATULLUS · *I Hate and I Love*
70. HOMER · *Circe and the Cyclops*
71. D. H. LAWRENCE · *Il Duro*
72. KATHERINE MANSFIELD · *Miss Brill*
73. OVID · *The Fall of Icarus*
74. SAPPHO · *Come Close*
75. IVAN TURGENEV · *Kasyan from the Beautiful Lands*
76. VIRGIL · *O Cruel Alexis*
77. H. G. WELLS · *A Slip under the Microscope*
78. HERODOTUS · *The Madness of Cambyses*
79. *Speaking of Siva*
80. *The Dhammapada*

'It is a most wonderful comfort to sit alone beneath a lamp, book spread before you, and commune with someone from the past whom you have never met.'

YOSHIDA KENKŌ
Born *c.* 1283, Japan
Died *c.* 1352, Japan

Selection taken from *Essays in Idleness* (*Tsurezuregusa*), which was probably written around 1329–31.

KENKŌ IN PENGUIN CLASSICS
Essays in Idleness and *Hōjōki*

YOSHIDA KENKŌ

A Cup of Sake Beneath the Cherry Trees

Translated by
Meredith McKinney

PENGUIN BOOKS

PENGUIN CLASSICS

UK | USA | Canada | Ireland | Australia
India | New Zealand | South Africa

Penguin Books is part of the Penguin Random House group of companies
whose addresses can be found at global.penguinrandomhouse.com.

This selection published in Penguin Classics 2015
013

Translation copyright © Meredith McKinney, 2013

The moral right of the translator has been asserted

Set in 9.5/13 pt Baskerville 10 Pro
Typeset by Jouve (UK), Milton Keynes
Printed and bound in Great Britain by Clays Ltd, Elcograf S.p.A.

A CIP catalogue record for this book is available from the British Library

ISBN: 978-0-141-39825-9

www.greenpenguin.co.uk

Penguin Random House is committed to a sustainable future for our business, our readers and our planet. This book is made from Forest Stewardship Council® certified paper.

What strange folly, to beguile the tedious hours like this all day before my ink stone, jotting down at random the idle thoughts that cross my mind . . .

*

To be born into this world of ours, it seems, brings with it so much to long for.

The rank of emperor is, of course, unspeakably exalted; even his remotest descendants fill one with awe, having sprung from no mere human seed.

Needless to say, the great ruler, and even the lesser nobles who are granted attendant guards to serve them, are also thoroughly magnificent. Their children and grandchildren too are still impressive, even if they have come down in the world. As for those of lesser degree, although they may make good according to their rank, and put on airs and consider themselves special, they are really quite pathetic.

No one could be less enviable than a monk. Sei

Shōnagon wrote that people treat them like unfeeling lumps of wood, and this is perfectly true. And there is nothing impressive about the way those with power will throw their weight around. As the holy man Sōga, I think, remarked, fame and fortune are an affliction for a monk, and violate the Buddha's teachings.

There is much to admire, though, in a dedicated recluse.

It is most important to present well, in both appearance and bearing. One never tires of spending time with someone whose speech is attractive and pleasing to the ear, and who does not talk overmuch. There is nothing worse than when someone you thought impressive reveals himself as lacking in sensibility. Status and personal appearance are things one is born with, after all, but surely the inner man can always be improved with effort. It is a great shame to see a fine upstanding fellow fall in with low and ugly types who easily run rings round him, and all for want of cultivation and learning.

A man should learn the orthodox literature, write poetry in Chinese as well as Japanese, and study music, and should ideally also be a model to others in his familiarity with ceremonial court customs and precedents. He should write a smooth, fair hand, carry the rhythm well when songs are sung at banquets, and when offered sake, make a show of declining it but nevertheless be able to drink.

*

No matter how splendid in every way, there is something dreadfully lacking in a man who does not pursue the art of love. He is, to coin the old phrase, like a beautiful wine cup that lacks a base.

The elegant thing is for a lover to wander aimlessly hither and yon, drenched with the frosts or dews of night, tormented by fears of his parents' reproaches and the censure of the world, the heart beset with uncertainties, yet for all that sleeping often alone, though always fitfully.

On the other hand, he shouldn't lose himself to love too thoroughly, or gain the reputation of being putty in women's hands.

*

If our life did not fade and vanish like the dews of Adashino's graves or the drifting smoke from Toribe's burning grounds, but lingered on for ever, how little the world would move us. It is the ephemeral nature of things that makes them wonderful.

Among all living creatures, it is man that lives longest. The brief dayfly dies before evening; summer's cicada knows neither spring nor autumn. What a glorious luxury it is to taste life to the full for even a single year. If you constantly regret life's passing, even a thousand long years will seem but the dream of a night.

Why cling to a life which cannot last for ever, only

to arrive at ugly old age? The longer you live, the greater your share of shame. It is most seemly to die before forty at the latest. Once past this age, people develop an urge to mix with others without the least shame at their own unsightliness; they spend their dwindling years fussing adoringly over their children and grandchildren, hoping to live long enough to see them make good in the world. Their greed for the things of this world grows ever deeper, till they lose all ability to be moved by life's pathos, and become really quite disgraceful.

*

Nothing so distracts the human heart as sexual desire. How foolish men's hearts are!

Aroma, for instance, is a mere transient thing, yet a whiff of delightful incense from a woman's robes will always excite a man, though he knows perfectly well that it is just a passing effect of robe-smoking.

The wizard priest of Kume is said to have lost his supernatural powers when he spied the white legs of a woman as she squatted washing clothes. I can quite believe it – after all, the beautiful, plump, glowing flesh of a woman's arm or leg is quite a different matter from some artificial allurement.

*

Beautiful hair on a woman will draw a man's gaze – but we can judge what manner of person she is and the nature of her sensibility even by simply hearing her speak from behind a screen. A mere unintended glimpse of a woman can distract a man's heart; and if a woman sleeps fitfully, and is prepared to endure impossible difficulties heedless of her own well-being, it is all because her mind is on love.

Yes indeed, the ways of love lie deep in us. Many are the allurements of our senses, yet we can distance ourselves from them all. But among them this one alone seems without exception to plague us all, young and old, wise and foolish.

So it is that we have those tales of how a woman's hair can snare and hold even an elephant, or how the rutting stag of autumn will always be drawn by the sound of a flute made from the wood of a woman's shoe.

We must discipline ourselves to be constantly prudent and vigilant lest we fall into this trap.

*

Though a home is of course merely a transient habitation, a place that is set up in beautiful taste to suit its owner is a delightful thing.

Even the moonlight is so much the more moving when it shines into a house where a refined person dwells in tranquil elegance. There is nothing fashionable or showy about the place, it is true, yet the grove of trees is redolent of age, the plants in the carefully untended garden carry a hint of delicate feelings, while the veranda and open-weave fence are tastefully done, and inside the house the casually disposed things have a tranquil, old-fashioned air. It is all most refined.

How ugly and depressing to see a house that has employed a bevy of craftsmen to work everything up to a fine finish, where all the household items set out for proud display are rare and precious foreign or Japanese objects, and where even the plants in the garden are clipped and contorted rather than left to grow as they will. How could anyone live for long in such a place? The merest glimpse will provoke the thought that all this could go up in smoke in an instant.

Yes, on the whole you can tell a great deal about the owner from his home.

The Later Tokudaiji Minister once had rope strung over the roof of the main house to stop the kites from roosting on it. 'What could be wrong with having kites on your roof? This shows what manner of man he is!' exclaimed the poet-monk Saigyō, and it is said he never called there again. I was reminded of this story when I noticed once that Prince Ayanokōji had laid rope over his Kosaka residence. Someone told me, however, that it was because he pitied the frogs in his pond when he observed how crows gathered on the roof to catch them. I was most impressed. Perhaps the Tokudaiji Minister too might have had some such reason for acting as he did?

A Cup of Sake Beneath the Cherry Trees

*

One day in the tenth month, I went to call on someone in a remote mountain village beyond Kurusuno.

Making my way along the mossy path, I came at length to the lonely hut where he lived. There was not a sound except for the soft drip of water from a bamboo pipe buried deep in fallen leaves. The vase on the altar shelf with its haphazard assortment of chrysanthemums and sprigs of autumn leaves bespoke someone's presence.

Moved, I said to myself, 'One could live like this' – but my mood was then somewhat spoiled by noticing at the far end of the garden a large mandarin tree, branches bowed with fruit, that was firmly protected by a stout fence. If only that tree weren't there! I thought.

*

What happiness to sit in intimate conversation with someone of like mind, warmed by candid discussion of the amusing and fleeting ways of this world . . . but such a friend is hard to find, and instead you sit there doing your best to fit in with whatever the other is saying, feeling deeply alone.

There is some pleasure to be had from agreeing with the other in general talk that interests you both, but it's better if he takes a slightly different position from yours. 'No, I can't agree with that,' you'll say to each other combatively, and you'll fall into arguing the matter out. This sort of lively discussion is a pleasant way to pass the idle hours, but in fact most people tend to grumble about things different from oneself, and though you can put up with the usual boring platitudes, such men are far indeed from the true friend after your own heart, and leave you feeling quite forlorn.

*

It is a most wonderful comfort to sit alone beneath a lamp, book spread before you, and commune with someone from the past whom you have never met.

As to books – those moving volumes of *Wenxuan*, the *Wenji* of Bai Juyi, the words of Laozi and *Zhuangzi*. There are many moving works from our own land, too, by scholars of former times.

*

It is an excellent thing to live modestly, shun luxury and wealth and not lust after fame and fortune. Rare has been the wise man who was rich.

In China once there was a man by the name of Xu You, who owned nothing and even drank directly from his cupped hands. Seeing this, someone gave him a 'singing gourd' to use as a cup; he hung it in a tree, but when he heard it singing in the wind one day he threw it away, annoyed by the noise it made, and went back to drinking his water from his hands. What a free, pure spirit!

Sun Chen had no bedclothes to sleep under in the winter months, only a bundle of straw which he slept in at night and put away again each morning.

The Chinese wrote these stories to hand down to later times because they found them so impressive. No one bothers to tell such tales in our country.

*

The changing seasons are moving in every way.

Everyone seems to feel that 'it is above all autumn that moves the heart to tears', and there is some truth in this, yet surely it is spring that stirs the heart more profoundly. Then, birdsong is full of the feel of spring, the plants beneath the hedges bud into leaf in the warm sunlight, the slowly deepening season brings soft mists, while the blossoms at last begin to open, only to meet with ceaseless winds and rain that send them flurrying restlessly to earth. Until the leaves appear on the boughs, the heart is endlessly perturbed.

The scented flowering orange is famously evocative, but it is above all plum blossom that has the power to carry you back to moments of cherished memory. The exquisite kerria, the hazy clusters of wisteria blossom – all these things linger in the heart.

Someone has said that at the time of the Buddha's birthday and the Kamo festival in the fourth month, when the trees are cool with luxuriant new leaf, one is particularly moved by the pathos of things and by a longing for others, and indeed it is true. And who could not be touched to melancholy in the fifth month, when the sweet flag iris leaves are laid on roofs, and the rice seedlings are planted out, and the water rail's knocking call is heard? The sixth month is also moving, with white evening-glory blooming over the walls of poor dwellings, and the smoke from smouldering smudge fires. The purifications of the sixth month are also delightful.

The festival of Tanabata is wonderfully elegant. Indeed so many things happen together in autumn – the nights grow slowly more chill, wild geese come crying over, and when the bush clover begins to yellow the early rice is harvested and hung to dry. The morning after a typhoon has blown through is also delightful.

Writing this, I realize that all this has already been spoken of long ago in *The Tale of Genji* and *The Pillow Book* – but that is no reason not to say it again. After all, things thought but left unsaid only fester inside you. So I let my brush run on like this for my own foolish solace; these pages deserve to be torn up and discarded, after all, and are not something others will ever see.

To continue – the sight of a bare wintry landscape is almost as lovely as autumn. It is delightful to see fallen autumn leaves scattered among the plants by the water's edge, or vapour rising from the garden stream on a morning white with frost. It is also especially moving to observe everyone bustling about at year's end, preparing for the new year. And then there is the forlornly touching sight of the waning moon around the twentieth day, hung in a clear, cold sky, although people consider it too dreary to look at. The Litany of Buddha Names and the Presentation of Tributes are thoroughly moving and magnificent, and in fact all the numerous court ceremonies and events at around this time, taking place as they do amidst the general end-of-year bustle, present an impressive sight. The way the Worship of the Four Directions follows so quickly upon the Great Demon Expulsion is wonderful too.

In the thick darkness of New Year's Eve, people light pine torches and rush about, so fast that their feet virtually skim the ground, making an extraordinary racket for some reason, and knocking on everyone's doors until late at night – but then at last around dawn all grows quiet, and you savour the touching moment of saying farewell to the old year. I was moved to find that in the East they still perform the ritual for dead souls on the night when the dead are said to return, although these days this has ceased to be done in the capital.

And so, watching the new year dawn in the sky, you are stirred by a sense of utter newness, although the sky looks no different from yesterday's. It is also touching to see the happy sight of new year pines gaily decorating the houses all along the main streets.

*

A certain recluse monk once remarked, 'I have relinquished all that ties me to the world, but the one thing that still haunts me is the beauty of the sky.' I can quite see why he would feel this.

*

How mutable the flower of the human heart, a fluttering blossom gone before the breeze's touch – so we recall the bygone years when the heart of another was our close companion, each dear word that stirred us then still unforgotten; and yet, it is the way of things that the beloved should move into worlds beyond our own, a parting far sadder than from the dead. Thus did Mozi grieve over a white thread that the dye would alter for ever, and at the crossroads Yang Zhu lamented the path's parting ways.

In Retired Emperor Horikawa's collection of one hundred poems, we read:

Where once I called on her	*mukashi mishi*
the garden fence is now in ruins –	*imo ga kakine wa*
flowering there I find	*arenikeri*
only wild violets, woven through	*tsubana majiri no*
with rank spring grasses.	*sumire nomi shite*

Such is the desolate scene that once must have met the poet's eye.

A Cup of Sake Beneath the Cherry Trees

*

Nothing is sadder than the aftermath of a death.

How trying it is to be jammed in together in some cramped and inconvenient mountain establishment for the forty-nine-day mourning period, performing the services for the dead. Never have the days passed faster. On the final day everyone is gruff and uncommunicative; each becomes engrossed in the importance of his own tidying and packing, then all go their separate ways. Once home again, the family will face all manner of fresh sorrows.

People go about warning each other of the various things that should be ritually avoided for the sake of the family. What a way to talk, at such a time! Really, what a wretched thing the human heart is!

Even with the passage of time the deceased is in no way forgotten, of course, but 'the dead grow more distant with each day', as the saying goes. And so, for all the memories, it seems our sorrow is no longer as acute as at death, for we begin to chatter idly and laugh again.

The corpse is buried on some deserted mountainside, we visit it only at the prescribed times, and soon moss has covered the grave marker, the grave is buried under fallen leaves, and only the howling evening winds and the moon at night come calling there.

It is all very well while there are those who remember and mourn the dead, but soon they too pass away; the descendants only know of him by hearsay, so they are hardly likely to grieve over his death. Finally, all ceremonies for him cease, no one any longer knows who he was or even his name, and only the grasses of each passing spring grow there to move the sensitive to pity; at length even the graveyard pine that sobbed in stormy winds is cut for firewood before its thousand years are up, the ancient mound is levelled by the plough, and the place becomes a field. The last trace of the grave itself has finally disappeared. It is sad to think of.

*

One morning after a beautiful fall of snow, I had reason to write a letter to an acquaintance, but I omitted to make any mention of the snow. I was delighted when she responded, 'Do you expect me to pay any attention to the words of someone so perverse that he fails to enquire how I find this snowy landscape? What deplorable insensitivity!'

The lady is no longer alive, so I treasure even this trifling memory.

*

Around the twentieth day of the ninth month, someone invited me along to view the moon with him. We wandered and gazed until first light. Along the way, my companion came upon a house he remembered. He had his name announced, and in he went. In the unkempt and dew-drenched garden, a hint of casual incense lingered in the air. It was all movingly redolent of a secluded life.

In due course my companion emerged, but the elegance of the scene led me to stay a little longer and watch from the shadows. Soon the double doors opened a fraction wider; it seemed the lady was gazing at the moon. It would have been very disappointing had she immediately bolted the doors as soon as the visit was over. She could not know that someone would still be watching. Such sensibility could only be the fruit of a habitual attitude of mind.

I heard that this lady died not long after.

*

It is foolish to be in thrall to fame and fortune, engaged in painful striving all your life with never a moment of peace and tranquillity.

Great wealth will drive you to neglect your own well-being in pursuit of it. It is asking for harm and tempting trouble. Though you leave behind at your death a mountain of gold high enough to prop up the North Star itself, it will only cause problems for those who come after you. Nor is there any point in all those pleasures that delight the eyes of fools. Big carriages, fat horses, glittering gold and jewels – any man of sensibility would view such things as gross stupidity. Toss your gold away in the mountains; hurl your jewels into the deep. Only a complete fool is led astray by avarice.

Everyone would like to leave their name unburied for posterity – but the high-born and exalted are not necessarily fine people, surely. A dull, stupid person can be born into a good house, attain high status thanks to opportunity and live in the height of luxury, while many wonderfully wise and saintly men choose to remain in lowly positions, and end their days without ever having met with good fortune. A fierce craving for high status and position is next in folly to the lust for fortune.

We long to leave a name for our exceptional wisdom and sensibility – but when you really think about it, desire for a good reputation is merely revelling in the praise of others. Neither those who praise us nor those who denigrate will remain in the world for long, and others who hear their opinions will be gone in short order as well. Just who should we feel ashamed before, then? Whose is the recognition we should crave? Fame in fact attracts abuse and slander. No, there is nothing to be gained from leaving a lasting name. The lust for fame is the third folly.

Let me now say a few words, however, to those who dedicate themselves to the search for knowledge and the desire for understanding. Knowledge leads to deception; talent and ability only serve to increase earthly desires. Knowledge acquired by listening to others or through study is not true knowledge. So what then should we call knowledge? Right and wrong are simply part of a single continuum. What should we call good? One who is truly wise has no knowledge or virtue, nor honour nor fame. Who then will know of him, and speak of him to others? This is not because he hides his virtue and pretends foolishness – he is beyond all distinctions such as wise and foolish, gain and loss.

I have been speaking of what it is to cling to one's delusions and seek after fame and fortune. All things of this phenomenal world are mere illusion. They are worth neither discussing nor desiring.

*

A certain novice monk in Inaba was rumoured to have a beautiful daughter, and many men came asking for her hand. But the girl ate nothing but chestnuts and never touched grains, so her father declared that she was too eccentric to be marriageable, and rejected them all.

*

When I went to see the horse racing at the Kamo Shrine on the fifth day of the fifth month, the view from our carriage was blocked by a throng of common folk. We all got down and moved towards the fence for a better view, but that area was particularly crowded and we couldn't make our way through.

We then noticed a priest who had climbed a chinaberry tree across the way to sit in its fork and watch from there. He was so sleepy as he clung there that he kept nodding off, and only just managed to start awake in time to save himself from falling each time. Those who saw him couldn't believe their eyes. 'What an extraordinary fool!' they all sneered. 'How can a man who's perched up there so precariously among the branches relax so much that he falls asleep?'

A thought suddenly occurred to me. 'Any of us may die from one instant to the next,' I said, 'and in fact we are far more foolish than this priest – here we are, contentedly watching the world go by, oblivious to death.'

'That's so true,' said those in front of me. 'It's really very stupid, isn't it,' and they turned around and invited me in and made room for me.

Anyone can have this sort of insight, but at that particular moment it came as a shock, which is no doubt why people were so struck by it. Humans are not mere insensate beings like trees or rocks, after all, and on occasion things can really strike home.

*

Those who feel the impulse to pursue the path of enlightenment should immediately take the step, and not defer it while they attend to all the other things on their mind.

A Cup of Sake Beneath the Cherry Trees

If you say to yourself, 'Let's just wait until after this is over,' or 'While I'm at it I'll just see to that,' or 'People will criticize me about such-and-such so I should make sure it's all dealt with and causes no problem later,' or 'There's been time enough so far, after all, and it won't take long just to await a little longer while I do this. Let's not rush into things,' one imperative thing after another will occur to detain you. There will be no end to it all, and the day of decision will never come.

In general, I find that reasonably sensitive and intelligent people will pass their whole life without taking the step they know they should. Would anyone with a fire close behind him choose to pause before fleeing? In a matter of life and death, one casts aside shame, abandons riches and runs. Does mortality wait on our choosing? Death comes upon us more swiftly than fire or flood. There is no escaping it. Who at that moment can refuse to part with all they love – aged parents, beloved children, lord and master, or the love of others?

*

The holy man of Shosha had accumulated such merit through recitations of *The Lotus Sutra* that he had attained purity of the Six Senses.

Once, on a journey, he entered the lodging where he was to stay the night and heard the bubbling of a pot of beans being boiled over a fire made from their husks.

'We're so closely related and yet you boil us so brutally!' they were crying, and the bean husks crackling in the flames seemed to him to reply, 'Do you imagine we're boiling you on purpose? It's excruciating for us to be burning like this, heaven knows, but we're powerless to stop. Enough of these recriminations!'

*

As soon as I hear someone's name, I feel I can picture their face, but when I actually meet them no one ever looks as I had been imagining all that time.

Also, I wonder if everyone, on hearing some old tale, imagines it as taking place in a certain part of some house he knows, and identifies the characters with people he sees in life, as I do.

And is it just I who sometimes feels a conviction that what someone is saying, or what you're seeing or thinking just then, has already happened before, though you cannot remember when?

*

Unpleasant things – a great many things cluttering up the area where someone is sitting. A lot of brushes lying on an ink stone. A crowd of Buddhist images in a private worship hall. A large collection of stones and plants in a garden. Too many children and grandchildren in a house.

Too much talk when meeting others. A long list of one's virtuous acts in a supplicatory prayer.

Things that are not unpleasant in large amounts are books on a book cart, and rubbish on a rubbish heap.

*

What kind of man will feel depressed at being idle? There is nothing finer than to be alone with nothing to distract you.

If you follow the ways of the world, your heart will be drawn to its sensual defilements and easily led astray; if you go among people, your words will be guided by others' responses rather than come from the heart. There is nothing firm or stable in a life spent between larking about together and quarrelling, exuberant one moment, aggrieved and resentful the next. You are forever pondering pros and cons, endlessly absorbed in questions of gain and loss. And on top of delusion comes drunkenness, and in that drunkenness you dream.

Scurrying and bustling, heedless and forgetful – such are all men. Even if you do not yet understand the True Way, you can achieve what could be termed temporary happiness at least by removing yourself from outside influences, taking no part in the affairs of the world, calming yourself and stilling the mind. As *The Great Cessation and Insight* says, we must 'break all ties with everyday life, human affairs, the arts and scholarship'.

*

I cannot bear the way people will make it their business to know all the details of some current rumour, even though it has nothing to do with them, and then proceed to pass the story on and do their best to learn more. Wandering monks up from some provincial backwater seem particularly adept at prying into tales about others as if it was their own concern, and spreading the word in such detail that you wonder how on earth they came to know so much.

*

Nor can I bear the way people will spread excited rumours about the latest marvels. A refined person will not learn of things until the rumours are old and stale.

If someone new comes visiting, the boorish and insensitive will always manage to make the visitor feel ignorant by exchanging cryptic remarks about something they all know among themselves, some story or name, chuckling and exchanging knowing glances.

*

When someone complained that it was a great shame the way fine silk covers are so soon damaged, Ton'a replied,

'It is only after the top and bottom edges of the silk have frayed, or when the mother-of-pearl has peeled off the roller, that a scroll is truly impressive' – an astonishingly fine remark, I felt. Similarly, an unmatched set of bound books can be considered unattractive, but Bishop Kōyū impressed me deeply by saying that only a boring man will always want things to match; real quality lies in irregularity – another excellent remark.

In all things, perfect regularity is tasteless. Something left not quite finished is very appealing, a gesture towards the future. Someone told me that even in the construction of the imperial palace, some part is always left uncompleted.

In the Buddhist scriptures and other works written by the great men of old there are also a number of missing sections.

*

The Dainagon Abbot employed a young acolyte by the name of Otozuru-maru, who came to be on intimate terms with one Yasura-dono and was constantly coming and going to visit him.

One day, seeing the lad return, the abbot asked where he had been. 'I've been to see Yasura-dono,' he replied.

'Is this Yasura-dono a layman, or a monk?' enquired the abbot.

Bringing his sleeves together in a polite bow, the acolyte replied, 'I really don't know, sir. I've never seen his head.'

I wonder why not – after all, he would have seen the rest of him.

*

The Yin-Yang masters do not concern themselves with those days of the calendar marked 'Red Tongue Days'. Nor did people of old treat the day as unpropitious. It seems someone more recently has declared it unlucky, and now everyone has begun to avoid it, believing that things undertaken on this day will miscarry. This idea – that whatever is said or done on this day will fail, that objects gained on the day will be lost and plans made will go awry – is ridiculous. If you count the number of failures that happen on an auspicious day, you will find there are just as many.

This is because, in this transient phenomenal world with its constant change, what appears to exist in fact does not. What is begun has no end. Aims go unfulfilled, yet desire is endless. The human heart changes ceaselessly. All things are passing illusion. What is there that remains unchanging? The folly of such beliefs springs from people's inability to understand this.

It is said that evil performed on an auspicious day is always ill-fated, while good performed on an inauspicious one will be blessed by good fortune. It is people who create good fortune and misfortune, not the calendar.

*

A man who was studying archery took two arrows in his hand and stood before the target.

'A beginner should not hold two arrows,' his teacher told him. 'You will be careless with the first, knowing you have a second. You must always be determined to hit the target with the single arrow you shoot, and have no thought beyond this.' With only two arrows, and standing before his master, would he really be inclined to be slapdash with one of them? Yet although he may not have been aware of his own carelessness, his teacher was. The same injunction surely applies in all matters.

A man engaged in Buddhist practice will tell himself at night that there is always the morning, or in the morning will anticipate the night, always intending to make more effort later. And if such are your days, how much less aware must you be of the passing moment's indolence. Why should it be so difficult to carry something out right now when you think of it, to seize the instant?

*

Someone told the following tale. A man sells an ox. The buyer says he will come in the morning to pay and take the beast. But during the night, the ox dies. 'The buyer thus gained, while the seller lost,' he concluded.

But a bystander remarked, 'The owner did indeed lose on the transaction, but he profited greatly in another way. Let me tell you why. Living creatures have no knowledge of the nearness of death. Such was the ox, and such too are we humans. As it happened, the ox died that night; as it happened, the owner lived on. One day's life is more precious than a fortune's worth of money, while an ox's worth weighs no more than a goose feather. One cannot say that a man who gains a fortune while losing a coin or two has made a loss.'

Everyone laughed at this. 'That reasoning doesn't only apply to the owner of the ox,' they scoffed.

The man went on. 'Well then, if people hate death they should love life. Should we not relish each day the joy of survival? Fools forget this – they go striving after other enjoyments, cease to appreciate the fortune they have and risk all to lay their hands on fresh wealth. Their desires are never sated. There is a deep contradiction in failing to enjoy life and yet fearing death when faced with it. It is because they have no fear of death that people fail to enjoy life – no, not that they don't fear it, but rather they forget its nearness. Of course, it must be said that the ultimate gain lies in transcending the relative world with its distinction between life and death.'

At this, everyone jeered more than ever.

A Cup of Sake Beneath the Cherry Trees

*

A lady who had reason to withdraw from the world for a time had retired to a lonely tumbledown house, where she was idling away the long days of her seclusion, when one dimly moonlit evening a certain man decided to call; but as he was creeping stealthily to her door, a dog set up a fierce barking. This brought one of the maidservants. 'Where do you hail from?' she enquired. The man promptly announced himself, and was shown in.

His heart was heavy as he took in his forlorn surroundings. How must she spend her time here? He stood hesitating on the veranda's rough wooden boards. 'This way,' came a wonderfully serene and youthful voice, so he slid open the door with some difficulty and entered.

The place was not so shabby after all, but was modest and refined. At the far end a lamp shone softly, revealing the beauty of the furnishings, and the scent of incense lit some time earlier imbued the place with an evocative and beguiling air.

He heard orders being given among the servants – 'Take care to lock the gate. It may rain. Put the carriage under the shelter of the gate roof' – and talk of where his retainers should spend the night. Then one added, in a soft murmur that nevertheless reached his ears because he was quite close, 'Tonight at least we can sleep easy.'

The two spoke together of all that had happened since

they last met, until the first cock crowed while it was yet night. On they talked earnestly, of matters past and to come, and now the cock's crow was loud and persistent. The day must by now have dawned, he thought, but this was not a place he must hasten to leave before light, so he lingered on a little, until sunlight whitened the cracks in the door. At last, with promises not to forget her, he departed.

Recalling the enchanting scene, he remembers how beautifully green the trees and garden plants glowed in that early summer daybreak, and even now, whenever he passes the house, he turns to gaze until the great camphor tree in the garden is lost to sight.

*

A man famed for his tree-climbing skills once directed another to climb a tall tree and cut branches. While the fellow was precariously balanced aloft, the tree-climber watched without a word, but when he was descending and had reached the height of the eaves the expert called to him, 'Careful how you go! Take care coming down!'

'Why do you say that? He's so far down now that he could leap to the ground from there,' I said.

'Just so,' replied the tree-climber. 'While he's up there among the treacherous branches I need not say a word – his fear is enough to guide him. It's in the easy places that mistakes will always occur.'

Lowly commoner though he was, his words echoed the warnings of the sages.

Apparently one of the laws of kickball also states that if you relax after achieving a difficult kick, this is the moment when the ball will always fall to the ground.

*

There are seven types of people one should not have as a friend.

The first is an exalted and high-ranking person. The second, somebody young. The third, anyone strong and in perfect health. The fourth, a man who loves drink. The fifth, a brave and daring warrior. The sixth, a liar. The seventh, an avaricious man.

The three to choose as friends are – one who gives gifts, a doctor and a wise man.

*

The domestic animals are the horse and the ox. It is a shame to tether the poor things and make them suffer, but it can't be helped, since they are indispensable to us. One should most certainly have a dog, as they are better than men at guarding the house. However, since all the houses around you will have dogs, you probably don't need to go out of your way to get one yourself.

All other creatures, be it bird or beast, are useless.

When you lock an animal that runs free into a cage or chain it up, when you snip the wings of a flying bird and confine it, the beast will ceaselessly pine for the wild and the bird for the clouds. Surely no one with a heart to imagine how unbearable he himself would find it could take pleasure in these creatures' torment. It would take the stony heart of a Jie or a Zhou to enjoy witnessing the suffering of a living creature.

Wang Huizhi loved birds. He watched them frolicking happily in the forest, and made them his companions in his rambles. He did not catch them and make them suffer. We should follow the words of the classic: 'Do not cultivate rare birds or strange beasts in your own land.'

*

Grand Counsellor Masafusa was a fine, scholarly man, and the retired emperor was planning to promote him to Commander of the Guards, when someone in close service informed His Majesty that he had just witnessed something dreadful.

'What was it?' His Majesty enquired.

'I watched through a gap in the fence as Count Masafusa cut off the leg of a live dog to feed to his hawk,' the man replied.

His Majesty was appalled. The thought of Masafusa revolted him, and he was not promoted after all.

It is extraordinary that such a man would own a hawk,

A Cup of Sake Beneath the Cherry Trees

and the story of the dog's leg is absolutely unfounded. The lie was most unfortunate, but how splendid of His Majesty to have reacted with such disgust when he heard the tale.

Overall, it must be said that those who kill or harm living creatures, or set them up to fight each other for their own pleasure, are no better than wild beasts themselves. If you pause and look carefully at the birds and animals, and even the little insects, you will see that they love their children, feel affection for their parents, live in couples, are jealous, angry, full of desire, self-protecting and fearful for their lives, and far more so than men, since they lack all intelligence. Surely one should pity them when they are killed or made to suffer? If you can look on any sentient being without compassion, you are less than human.

*

Yan Hui's firm belief was that he must avoid burdening others. One should not cause suffering and pain to others, nor undermine the will of the humble man.

Some will take pleasure in deceiving, frightening or mocking little children. Adults treat such tales lightly, knowing that they are quite unfounded, but those words will strike deep into the heart of a poor little child, and humiliate, terrify or appal it. It is heartless to enjoy tormenting children in this way.

The joys, angers, sorrows and pleasures of adults too are all based on illusion, but who among us is not attached to the seeming reality of this life?

It harms a man more to wound his heart than to hurt his body. Illness, too, often originates in the mind. Few illnesses come from without. There are times when medicine cannot produce the intended sweat, but shame or fear will always bring one on, which should prove to us that such things come from the mind. We find examples in the classics, after all – think of the man who was hoisted up the Ling Yun Tower to write its signboard, whose hair turned white from fear at the height.

*

Should we look at the spring blossoms only in full flower, or the moon only when cloudless and clear? To long for the moon with the rain before you, or to lie curtained in your room while the spring passes unseen, is yet more poignant and deeply moving. A branch of blossoms on the verge of opening, a garden strewn with fading petals, have more to please the eye. Could poems on the themes of 'Going to view the blossoms to find them already fallen' or 'Written when I was prevented from going to see the flowers' be deemed inferior to 'On seeing the blossoms'? It is natural human feeling to yearn over the falling blossoms and the setting moon – yet some, it seems, are so insensitive that they will declare that since this branch and that have already shed their flowers, there is nothing worth seeing any longer.

In all things, the beginning and end are the most engaging. Does the love of man and woman suggest only their embraces? No, the sorrow of lovers parted before they met, laments over promises betrayed, long lonely nights spent sleepless until dawn, pining thoughts for one in some far place, a woman left sighing over past love in her tumbledown abode – it is these, surely, that embody the romance of love.

Rather than gazing on a clear full moon that shines over a thousand leagues, it is infinitely more moving to see the moon near dawn and after long anticipation, tinged with most beautiful palest blue, a moon glimpsed among cedar branches deep in the mountains, its light now hidden again by the gathering clouds of an autumn shower. The moist glint of moonlight on the glossy leaves of the forest *shii* oak or the white oak pierces the heart, and makes you yearn for the distant capital and a friend of true sensibility to share the moment with you.

Are blossoms and the moon merely things to be gazed at with the eye? No, it brings more contentment and delight to stay inside the house in spring and, there in your bedroom, let your heart go out to the unseen moonlit night.

The man of quality never appears entranced by anything; he savours things with a casual air. Country bumpkins, however, take flamboyant pleasure in everything. They will wriggle their way in through the crowd and stand there endlessly gaping up at the blossoms, sit about under the trees drinking sake and indulging in linked verse-making together and, finally, oafishly break off great branches of blossom to carry away. They will dip their hands and feet into clear spring water, get down to stand in unsullied snow and leave their footprints everywhere, and in short throw themselves into everything with uninhibited glee.

I have observed such people behaving quite astonishingly when they came to see the Kamo festival. Declaring that the procession was horribly late so there was no point in hanging around on the viewing stand, a group retired to a house behind the stands and settled down to eat, drink and play *go* and *sugoroku*, leaving one of their number back on the stand to keep watch. 'It's coming by!' he shouted, whereupon they all leaped frantically to their feet and dashed back, elbowing each other out of the way as they scrambled up, nearly tumbling off in their eagerness to thrust aside the blinds for a better look, jostling for position and craning to miss nothing, and commenting volubly on everything they saw. Then, when that section of the procession had passed, off they went again, declaring they'd be back for the next one. They were clearly only there to see the spectacle.

The upper echelons from the capital, on the other hand, will sit there dozing without so much as a glance at the scene. Young gentlemen of lesser rank are constantly rising to wait on their superiors, while those seated in the back rows never rudely lean forward, and no one goes out of his way to watch as the procession passes.

On the day of the festival everything is elegantly strewn with the emblematic *aoi* leaves, and even before dawn the carriages quietly begin to arrive to secure a good viewing position, everyone intrigued about which carriage is whose, sometimes identifying them by an accompanying servant or ox-boy they recognize. It is endlessly fascinating to watch the carriages come and go, some charming, others more showy. By the time evening draws in, all those rows of carriages and the people who were crammed into the stands have disappeared, and hardly a soul is left. Once the chaos of departing carriages is over, the blinds and matting are taken down from the stands as you watch, and the place is left bare and forlorn, moving you to a poignant sense of the brevity of worldly things. It is this that is the real point of seeing the festival.

Among the people coming and going in front of the stands there are many you recognize, making you realize there are not really so many people in this world. Even if you were destined to die after all these others, clearly your own death cannot be far away. When a large vessel filled with water is pierced with a tiny hole, though each drop is small it will go on relentlessly leaking until soon the vessel is empty. The city is filled with people, but not a day would go by without someone dying. And is it only one or two a day? There are times when the corpses on the pyres of Toribe, Funaoka and elsewhere further afield are piled high, but no day passes without a funeral. And so the coffin sellers no sooner make one than it is sold. Be they young, be they strong, the time of death comes upon all unawares. It is an extraordinary miracle that we have escaped it until now. Can we ever, even briefly, have peace of mind in this world?

It is like the game of *mamakodate*, played with *sugoroku* pieces, in which no one knows which in the line of pieces will be removed next – when the count is made and a piece is taken, the rest seem to have escaped, but the count goes on and more are picked off in turn, so that no piece is finally spared. Soldiers going into battle, aware of the closeness of death, forget their home and their own safety. And it is sheer folly for a man who lives secluded from the world in his lowly hut, spending his days in idle delight in his garden, to pass off such matters as irrelevant to himself. Do you imagine that the enemy Impermanence will not come forcing its way into your peaceful mountain retreat? The recluse faces death as surely as the soldier setting forth to battle.

*

A sensible man will not die leaving valuables behind. A collection of vulgar objects looks bad, while good ones will suggest a futile attachment to worldly things. And it is even more unfortunate to leave behind a vast accumulation. There will be ugly fights over it after your death, with everyone determined to get things for himself. If you plan to leave something to a particular person, you should pass it on while you are still alive.

Some things are necessary for day-to-day living, but one should have nothing else.

*

Even people who seem to lack any finer feelings will sometimes say something impressive.

An alarming-looking ruffian from the eastern provinces once turned to the man beside him and asked if he had any children. 'Not one,' the man replied.

'Well then,' said the Easterner, 'you'll not know what true depth of feeling is. It frightens me to think of a man unacquainted with tenderness. It's having your own children that brings home to you the poignant beauty of life.'

This is indeed true. Without familial love, would such a man as this be able to feel compassion? Even a man who lacks all filial piety will discover how a parent feels when he himself has children.

It is wrong for a man who has taken the tonsure and cast all away to despise those he sees around him encumbered with worldly ties, who go crawling abjectly after this person and that and are full of craving. If you imagined yourself in his place, you would see how he might abase himself so far as to steal for the sake of his beloved parents or wife and children. Rather than seizing thieves and punishing their crimes, it would be better to make the world a place where people did not go hungry or cold. A man without stable means is a man whose heart is unstable. People steal from extremity. There will be no end to crime while the world is not governed well, and men suffer from cold and starvation. It is cruel to make people suffer and drive them to break the law, then treat the poor creatures as criminals.

As for how to improve people's lives, there can be no doubt that it would benefit those below if people in high positions were to cease their luxurious and wasteful ways and instead were kind and tender to the people, and encouraged agriculture. The true criminal must be defined as a man who commits a crime though he is as decently fed and clothed as others.

*

The imperial bodyguard Hada no Shigemi once said of one of the retired emperor's guard, the Shimotsuke Novice Shingan, 'He has the mark of one prone to falling from horses. He should take great care.' Shingan thought this very unlikely, but he did indeed fall from his horse and die. Everyone then decided that the words issuing from such an expert in his field were divinely prophetic.

So just what was this mark? people asked him. 'He

showed all the signs by having a very poor riding seat, and favouring horses that tend to buck,' replied the guard. 'Have I ever been wrong?'

*

It is not good to call on someone if you have no particular reason. Even if you go with some purpose, you should leave promptly once your business is accomplished. It is very annoying if a visit drags on.

There is so much talking when people get together. It is exhausting, disturbs the peace of mind and wastes time better spent on other things. There is nothing to be gained for either party. It is bad, too, to feel irritable as you talk. When you don't care for something, you should come right out and say so.

The exception to all this is when someone after your own heart, whom you feel inclined to talk with, is at a loose end and encourages you to stay a while longer for a peaceful chat. No doubt we all have Ruan Ji's 'welcoming green eyes' from time to time.

It is very nice when a friend simply drops in, has a quiet talk with you, and then leaves. It is also wonderfully pleasing to receive a letter that simply begins, 'I write because it's been some time since I sent news,' or some such.

*

A young man overflows with vigour, things stir his heart, and he is prone to passions. Like a flung ball, such a youth courts danger and physical harm. Riches are wasted in pursuit of magnificence, then all this is suddenly abandoned for the wretched robes of the monk; he is full of fervour and fight, suffers agonies of shame or bitterness, and his fancies are constantly shifting from day to day. He will devote himself to women and pursue infatuations, or take his example from those who have died with no thought to their own safety or longevity, behaving with such reckless daring that 'a long life lies ruined', or let himself be drawn wherever his heart urges, becoming the cause of talk for many years to come. It is indeed in youth that we make our mistakes.

In age, on the other hand, the spirit weakens, we become indifferent and apathetic, and nothing rouses us. The heart grows naturally calm, so that we no longer act in futile ways but instead tend to our bodies, live free of discontent and try to avoid troubling others. Age has more wisdom than youth, just as youth has more beauty than does age.

*

There are many incomprehensible things in this world.

I cannot understand why people will seize any occasion to immediately bring out the sake, delighting in forcing someone else to drink. The other will frown and grimace in painful protest, attempt to throw it away when no one's looking or do his best to escape, but this man will seize him, pin him down and make him swallow cup after cup. A genteel man will quickly be transformed into a madman and start acting the fool; a vigorous, healthy fellow will before your very eyes become shockingly afflicted and fall senseless to the floor. What a thing to do, on a day of celebration! Right into the next day his head hurts, he can't eat, and he lies there groaning with all memory of the previous day gone as if it were a former life. He neglects essential duties both public and private, with disastrous effects. It is both boorish and cruel to subject someone to this sort of misery. Surely a man who has had this bitter experience will be filled with regret and loathing. Anyone from a land that lacked this custom would be amazed and appalled to hear of its existence in another country.

It is depressing enough just to witness this happening to another. A man who had always seemed thoughtful and refined will burst into mindless laughter, prattle on and on, his lacquered court cap askew, the ties of his robes loosened and the skirts hauled up above his shins, and generally behave so obliviously that he seems a changed man. A woman will blatantly push her hair up away from her face, throw back her head and laugh quite shamelessly, and seize the hand of the person with the sake, while the more uncouth might grab one of the snacks and hold it to someone else's mouth or eat it herself – a quite disgraceful sight. People bellow at the top of their lungs, everyone sings and prances about, and an old monk is called in, who proceeds to bare his filthy black shoulder and writhe about so that you can hardly stand to watch, and you loathe just as much the others who sit there enjoying the spectacle.

Some will make you cringe by the way they sing their own praises, others will cry into their drink, while the lower orders abuse each other and get into quite shocking and appalling fights. Finally, after all manner of disgraceful and pitiful behaviour, the drunkard will seize things without permission, then end up hurting himself by rolling off the veranda or tumbling from his horse or carriage. If he's of a class that goes on foot he'll stagger away down the high road, doing unspeakable things against people's walls or gates as he goes. It is quite disgusting to see the old monk in his black robe stumbling off, steadying himself with his hand on the shoulder of the lad beside him and rambling on incomprehensibly.

If drinking like this profited us in this world or the next, what could one say? But in this world it leads to all manner of error, and causes both illness and loss of wealth. Wine has been called 'the greatest of medicines', but in fact all sickness springs from it. It is claimed that you forget your sorrows in drink, but from what I can see, men in their cups will in fact weep to recall their past unhappiness. As for the next world – having lost the wisdom you were born with, reduced all your good karma

A Cup of Sake Beneath the Cherry Trees

to ashes, built up a store of wickedness and broken all the Buddhist precepts, you are destined for hell. Remember, the Buddha teaches that those who lift the wine glass either to their own lips or to others' will spend five hundred lifetimes without hands.

Yet, loathsome though one finds it, there are situations when a cup of sake is hard to resist. On a moonlit night, a snowy morning, or beneath the flowering cherry trees, it increases all the pleasures of the moment to bring out the sake cups and settle down to talk serenely together over a drink. It is also a great comfort to have a drink together if an unexpected friend calls round when time is hanging heavy on your hands. And it is quite wonderful when sake and snacks are elegantly served from behind her curtains by some remote and exalted lady.

It is also quite delightful to sit across from a close friend in some cosy little nook in winter, roasting food over the coals and drinking lots of sake together. And delightful too on a journey to sit about on the grass together in some wayside hut or out in the wild, drinking and lamenting the lack of a suitable snack. And it's a fine thing when someone who really hates having sake pressed on them is forced to have just a little. You are thrilled when some grand person singles you out and offers to refill your cup, urging, 'Do have more. You've barely drunk.' And it is also very pleasing when someone you would like to get to know better is a drinker and becomes very pally with you in his cups.

All things considered, a drunkard is so entertaining he can be forgiven his sins. Think of the charming scene when a master throws open the door on his servant, who is sound asleep next morning after an exhausting night on the drink. The poor befuddled fellow rushes off, rubbing his bleary eyes, topknot exposed on his hatless head, only half dressed and clutching the rest of his trailing clothes, his hairy shins sticking out below his lifted skirts as he scampers into the distance – a typical drunk.

*

The one thing a man should not have is a wife.

One is impressed to hear that a certain man always lives alone, while someone who is reported to have married into this or that family, or to have taken a wife and be living together, will find himself quite looked down on. 'He must have married that nondescript girl because he thought she was something special,' people will say scornfully, or if she is a good woman they will think, 'He'll be so besotted that he treats her like his own personal buddha.' The impression is even more dreary when she runs the house well. It is depressing to watch her bear children and fuss over them, and things don't end with his death, for then you have the shameful sight of her growing old and decrepit as a nun.

No matter who the woman may be, you would grow to hate her if you lived with her and saw her day in day out, and the woman must become dissatisfied too. But if you lived separately and sometimes visited her, your feelings for each other would surely remain unchanged through the years. It keeps the relationship fresh to just drop in from time to time on impulse and spend the night.

*

What a shame it is to hear someone declare that things lose their beauty at night! All lustre, ornamentation and brilliance come into their own at night.

In daylight, one can keep things simple and dress sedately. But the best clothing for night is showy and dazzling formal wear. The same goes for people – a good-looking person will look still finer by lamplight, and it's charming to hear a careful voice speaking in darkness. Scents and music too are still lovelier at night.

It is a fine thing to see a man who calls on some great household looking his best late on an uneventful evening. Young people who pay attention to such things will always notice one's appearance no matter what the hour, so it is wise to dress well whatever the situation, whether formal or informal, and most especially at times when one is inclined to relax and unwind. Particularly delightful is when a fine gentleman has bothered to plaster down his hair though it is after dark, or when a lady slips from the room late at night to take up a mirror and see to her face before rejoining the company.

Yoshida Kenkō

*

When the now-deceased Tokudaiji Minister of the Right was Superintendent of Police, he was one day holding court at his central gate when the ox of one of the officers, Akikane, broke loose, got into the court room, scrambled up on to the Superintendent's seating platform and there settled down to chew its cud. This was deemed a disturbingly untoward event, and everyone present declared that the beast should be taken off for Yin-Yang divination to determine the meaning.

However, when the Superintendent's father the Minister heard of this, he declared, 'An ox has no understanding. It has its four legs which can take it anywhere. There is no reason to impound a skinny beast that happens to have brought some lowly official here.' He had the ox returned to its master, and changed the matting where the ox had lain. There were no ill consequences from the event.

It is sometimes said that if you see something sinister and choose to treat it as normal, you will thereby avert whatever it portended.

*

Nothing in this world can be trusted. Fools put all their faith in things, and so become angry and bitter.

The powerful should place no faith in their powerful

position. The strong are the first to go. The rich should never depend on their wealth. A fortune can easily disappear from one moment to the next. A scholar should never be complacent about his skills. Even Confucius did not meet with the reception he deserved. The virtuous should not rely on their virtue. Even the exemplary Yan Hui met with misfortune. Nor should those favoured by the emperor be smug. You may at any time find yourself instead faced with execution for some crime. Never rely on your servants to be loyal. They can rebel and flee. Never put your faith in others' goodwill. They will inevitably change their minds. Never depend on a promise made. People seldom keep their word.

If you rely neither on yourself nor on others, you will rejoice when things go well, and not be aggrieved when they don't. Maintain a clear space on either side, and nothing will obstruct you; keep open before and behind you, and you will be unimpeded. If you let yourself be hemmed in, you can be squeezed to breaking point. Without care and flexibility in your dealings with the world, you will find yourself in conflict and be damaged, while if you live calmly and serenely, not a hair on your head will come to harm.

Humans are the most miraculous and exalted of all things in heaven and earth. And heaven and earth are boundless. How, then, could we differ in essence? If our spirit is open and boundless, neither fear nor joy will obstruct it, and we will remain untroubled by the world.

*

There is a place in Tamba called Izumo, where the deity of the great Izumo Shrine has been installed in a magnificent shrine building. The area is ruled by a certain Shida, who one autumn invited a great many people, including the holy man Shōkai. 'Come and pray to Izumo,' he said, 'and let us feast on rice cakes.' He led them to the shrine, and every one of them prayed and was filled with faith.

The holy man was immensely moved by the sight of the guardian Chinese lion and Korean dog, which were placed back to back and facing backwards. 'How marvellous!' he exclaimed, close to tears. 'Such an unusual position to stand them in! There must be some deep reason behind it.' Then he turned to the others. 'How can you not have noticed this wonder?' he cried. 'I'm amazed at you.'

They were very struck. 'Yes indeed,' they all declared, 'they *are* different from elsewhere. We'll tell this to everyone back in the capital.'

The holy man now wished to learn more, so he called over an elderly and wise-looking shrine priest. 'There must be some interesting tale explaining the placement of these images,' he said. 'Do be so kind as to tell us.'

'Indeed there is,' replied the priest. 'Some naughty children did it. A disgraceful business,' and so saying he went over to the statues, set them to rights and walked off.

The holy man's tears of delight had been for nothing.

A Cup of Sake Beneath the Cherry Trees

*

He whose deep love spurs him to dare all and go to his beloved, though 'watchful eyes surround the stealthy lover' and 'guards are set to snare him in the dark', will leave them both replete with powerful memories of all the moments when they tasted life's poignancy to the full. It must feel very awkward and unromantic for the woman, however, if a man simply takes her as his wife with the full consent of the family and without further ado.

How dreary it is when a woman hard up in the world announces that she will 'answer the call of any current' so long as he is well-off, be it some unsuitable old priest or an uncouth Easterner, and a go-between sets about singing the praises of each to the other, with the result that she comes to someone's house as a bride without either knowing the other at all. What on earth would they say to each other when they first come face to face? On the other hand, a couple can find endless conversation in the memories of long hardships overcome, 'forging their way through the dense autumn woods' to be together at last.

It can generally be said that a great deal of dissatisfaction results from a marriage set up by a third party. If the wife is excellent and the man a lowly and ugly old fellow, he will despise her for allowing herself to be thrown away on the likes of himself, and feel ashamed in her presence – a deplorable situation.

If you can never linger beneath the clouded moon on

a plum-scented evening, nor find yourself recalling the dawns when you made your way home through the dew-soaked grasses by her gate after a night of love, you had best not aspire to be a lover at all.

*

The full moon's perfect roundness lasts barely a moment, and in no time is lost. Those with no eye for such things, it seems, fail to see how it changes in the course of a night.

An illness will grow graver as each moment passes, and death is already close at hand, yet while the sickness is still mild and you are not yet confronting death, you are lulled by your accustomed assumptions of a normal life in an unchanging world, and choose to wait until you have accomplished all you want in life before calmly turning your thoughts to salvation and a Buddhist practice, with the result that when you fall ill and confront death, none of your dreams has been fulfilled. Now, too late, you repent of your long years of negligence, and swear that if only you were to recover you would dedicate yourself unstintingly day and night to this thing and that – but for all your prayers your illness grows graver, until you lose your senses and die a raving death. It happens to so many of us. We must fully grasp this, here and now.

If you plan to turn your thoughts to the Buddhist Way after you have fulfilled all your desires, you will find that those desires are endless. What could be achieved, in this illusory life of ours? All desire is delusion. If desires arise within you, realize that they spring from your lost and deluded mind, and ignore them all. Relinquish all today and turn to the Buddhist path, and you will be freed of all obstruction, released from the need for action, and lasting peace will be yours body and soul.

*

The year I turned eight, I asked my father, 'What sort of thing is a buddha?'

'A buddha is what a human becomes,' he replied.

'How does a human become a buddha?' I asked.

'You become a buddha by following the Buddha's teaching,' he answered.

'So who taught the Buddha?' I asked.

'He became a buddha by following the teaching of previous buddhas,' he said.

'So what sort of buddha was the first one who began the teaching?' I asked.

My father laughed and replied, 'I suppose he just fell from the sky like rain or rose out of the earth like water.'

He used to enjoy recounting this story to others, adding, 'He had me cornered. I couldn't think what to reply.'

1. BOCCACCIO · *Mrs Rosie and the Priest*
2. GERARD MANLEY HOPKINS · *As kingfishers catch fire*
3. *The Saga of Gunnlaug Serpent-tongue*
4. THOMAS DE QUINCEY · *On Murder Considered as One of the Fine Arts*
5. FRIEDRICH NIETZSCHE · *Aphorisms on Love and Hate*
6. JOHN RUSKIN · *Traffic*
7. PU SONGLING · *Wailing Ghosts*
8. JONATHAN SWIFT · *A Modest Proposal*
9. *Three Tang Dynasty Poets*
10. WALT WHITMAN · *On the Beach at Night Alone*
11. KENKŌ · *A Cup of Sake Beneath the Cherry Trees*
12. BALTASAR GRACIÁN · *How to Use Your Enemies*
13. JOHN KEATS · *The Eve of St Agnes*
14. THOMAS HARDY · *Woman much missed*
15. GUY DE MAUPASSANT · *Femme Fatale*
16. MARCO POLO · *Travels in the Land of Serpents and Pearls*
17. SUETONIUS · *Caligula*
18. APOLLONIUS OF RHODES · *Jason and Medea*
19. ROBERT LOUIS STEVENSON · *Olalla*
20. KARL MARX AND FRIEDRICH ENGELS · *The Communist Manifesto*
21. PETRONIUS · *Trimalchio's Feast*
22. JOHANN PETER HEBEL · *How a Ghastly Story Was Brought to Light by a Common or Garden Butcher's Dog*
23. HANS CHRISTIAN ANDERSEN · *The Tinder Box*
24. RUDYARD KIPLING · *The Gate of the Hundred Sorrows*
25. DANTE · *Circles of Hell*
26. HENRY MAYHEW · *Of Street Piemen*
27. HAFEZ · *The nightingales are drunk*
28. GEOFFREY CHAUCER · *The Wife of Bath*
29. MICHEL DE MONTAIGNE · *How We Weep and Laugh at the Same Thing*
30. THOMAS NASHE · *The Terrors of the Night*
31. EDGAR ALLAN POE · *The Tell-Tale Heart*
32. MARY KINGSLEY · *A Hippo Banquet*
33. JANE AUSTEN · *The Beautifull Cassandra*
34. ANTON CHEKHOV · *Gooseberries*
35. SAMUEL TAYLOR COLERIDGE · *Well, they are gone, and here must I remain*
36. JOHANN WOLFGANG VON GOETHE · *Sketchy, Doubtful, Incomplete Jottings*
37. CHARLES DICKENS · *The Great Winglebury Duel*
38. HERMAN MELVILLE · *The Maldive Shark*
39. ELIZABETH GASKELL · *The Old Nurse's Story*
40. NIKOLAY LESKOV · *The Steel Flea*

41. HONORÉ DE BALZAC · *The Atheist's Mass*
42. CHARLOTTE PERKINS GILMAN · *The Yellow Wall-Paper*
43. C.P. CAVAFY · *Remember, Body . . .*
44. FYODOR DOSTOEVSKY · *The Meek One*
45. GUSTAVE FLAUBERT · *A Simple Heart*
46. NIKOLAI GOGOL · *The Nose*
47. SAMUEL PEPYS · *The Great Fire of London*
48. EDITH WHARTON · *The Reckoning*
49. HENRY JAMES · *The Figure in the Carpet*
50. WILFRED OWEN · *Anthem For Doomed Youth*
51. WOLFGANG AMADEUS MOZART · *My Dearest Father*
52. PLATO · *Socrates' Defence*
53. CHRISTINA ROSSETTI · *Goblin Market*
54. *Sindbad the Sailor*
55. SOPHOCLES · *Antigone*
56. RYŪNOSUKE AKUTAGAWA · *The Life of a Stupid Man*
57. LEO TOLSTOY · *How Much Land Does A Man Need?*
58. GIORGIO VASARI · *Leonardo da Vinci*
59. OSCAR WILDE · *Lord Arthur Savile's Crime*
60. SHEN FU · *The Old Man of the Moon*
61. AESOP · *The Dolphins, the Whales and the Gudgeon*
62. MATSUO BASHŌ · *Lips too Chilled*
63. EMILY BRONTË · *The Night is Darkening Round Me*
64. JOSEPH CONRAD · *To-morrow*
65. RICHARD HAKLUYT · *The Voyage of Sir Francis Drake Around the Whole Globe*
66. KATE CHOPIN · *A Pair of Silk Stockings*
67. CHARLES DARWIN · *It was snowing butterflies*
68. BROTHERS GRIMM · *The Robber Bridegroom*
69. CATULLUS · *I Hate and I Love*
70. HOMER · *Circe and the Cyclops*
71. D. H. LAWRENCE · *Il Duro*
72. KATHERINE MANSFIELD · *Miss Brill*
73. OVID · *The Fall of Icarus*
74. SAPPHO · *Come Close*
75. IVAN TURGENEV · *Kasyan from the Beautiful Lands*
76. VIRGIL · *O Cruel Alexis*
77. H. G. WELLS · *A Slip under the Microscope*
78. HERODOTUS · *The Madness of Cambyses*
79. *Speaking of Siva*
80. *The Dhammapada*

'Better mad
with the crowd
than sane
all alone . . .'

BALTASAR GRACIÁN
Born 1601, Aragon, Spain
Died 1658, Aragon, Spain

Selection taken from *The Pocket Oracle and Art of Prudence*,
first published in 1647.

GRACIÁN IN PENGUIN CLASSICS
The Pocket Oracle and Art of Prudence

BALTASAR GRACIÁN

How to Use Your Enemies

Translated by
Jeremy Robbins

PENGUIN BOOKS

PENGUIN CLASSICS

UK | USA | Canada | Ireland | Australia
India | New Zealand | South Africa

Penguin Books is part of the Penguin Random House group of companies
whose addresses can be found at global.penguinrandomhouse.com.

This selection published in Penguin Classics 2015
014

Translation copyright © Jeremy Robbins, 2011

The moral right of the translator has been asserted

Set in 9.5/13 pt Baskerville 10 Pro
Typeset by Jouve (UK), Milton Keynes
Printed and bound in Great Britain by Clays Ltd, Elcograf S.p.A.

A CIP catalogue record for this book is available from the British Library

ISBN: 978-0-141-39827-3

www.greenpenguin.co.uk

MIX
Paper from
responsible sources
FSC® C018179

Penguin Random House is committed to a
sustainable future for our business, our readers
and our planet. This book is made from Forest
Stewardship Council® certified paper.

In your affairs, create suspense. Admiration at their novelty means respect for your success. It's neither useful nor pleasurable to show all your cards. Not immediately revealing everything fuels anticipation, especially when a person's elevated position means expectations are greater. It bespeaks mystery in everything and, with this very secrecy, arouses awe. Even when explaining yourself, you should avoid complete frankness, just as you shouldn't open yourself up to everyone in all your dealings. Cautious silence is the refuge of good sense. A decision openly declared is never respected; instead, it opens the way to criticism, and if things turn out badly, you'll be unhappy twice over. Imitate divinity's way of doing things to keep people attentive and alert.

*

Knowledge and courage contribute in turn to greatness. Since they are immortal, they immortalize. You are as much as you know, and a wise person can do anything. A person without knowledge is a world in darkness. Judgement and strength, eyes and hands; without courage, wisdom is sterile.

*

Make people depend on you. An image is made sacred not by its creator but by its worshipper. The shrewd would rather people needed them than thanked them. To put your trust in vulgar gratitude is to devalue courteous hope, for whilst hope remembers, gratitude forgets. More can be gained from dependence than from courtesy; once thirst is quenched, people turn their backs on the fountain, and an orange once squeezed is tossed in the mud. When dependence ends, so does harmony, and with it esteem. Let experience's first lesson be to maintain and never satisfy dependence, keeping even royalty always in need of you. But you shouldn't go to the extreme of being so silent as to cause error, or make someone else's problems incurable for your own benefit.

*

The height of perfection. No one is born complete; perfect yourself and your activities day by day until you become a truly consummate being, your talents and your qualities all perfected. This will be evident in the excellence of your taste, the refinement of your intellect, the maturity of your judgement, the purity of your will. Some never manage to be complete; something is always missing. Others take a long time. The consummate man, wise in word and sensible in deed, is admitted into, and even sought out for, the singular company of the discreet.

*

Avoid outdoing your superior. All triumphs are despised, and triumphing over your superior is either stupid or fatal. Superiority has always been detested, especially by our superiors. Caution can usually hide ordinary advantages, just as it conceals beauty with a touch of carelessness. There will always be someone ready to admit others have better luck or temperaments, but no one, and especially not a sovereign, that someone has greater ingenuity. For this is the sovereign attribute and any crime against it is lese-majesty. Sovereigns, then, desire sovereignty over what matters most. Princes like to be helped, but not surpassed. Advice should be offered as if a reminder of what they've forgotten, not an insight that they've never had. The stars teach us such subtlety, for though they are children of the sun and shine brilliantly, they never compete with it in all its radiance.

*

Belie your national defects. Water acquires the good and bad qualities of the channels it passes through, people those of the country where they're born. Some owe more than others to their birthplace, for the heavens were more propitious to them there. No country, even the most civilized, is free from some national failing which neighbouring countries will always criticize, either for advantage or solace. It's a skilful triumph to correct, or at least to conceal, these national faults; you'll gain credit as unique among your countrymen, for what's least expected has always been more esteemed. There are also defects of lineage, status, occupation and age which, if they all appear in one person and are not carefully forestalled, will produce an unbearable monster.

*

Deal with people from whom you can learn. Let friendly interchange be a school of erudition, and conversation, civilized instruction. Make friends your teachers, joining learning's usefulness and conversation's pleasure. The intelligent combine two pleasures, enjoying the applause that greets what they say and the instruction received from what they hear. Usually, we are drawn to someone through our own interest, but here, that interest is ennobled. The circumspect frequent the company of eminent individuals whose houses are theatres of greatness rather than palaces of vanity. There are those renowned for their discretion whose example and behaviour are oracles in all matters of greatness and whose entourages are also courtly academies of good and gallant discretion.

*

Nature and art, material and craft. Beauty always needs a helping hand, and perfection is rough without the polish

How to Use Your Enemies

of artifice. It helps what is bad and perfects what is good. Nature usually lets us down when we need it most; let us then turn to art. Without it, our nature even at its best lacks refinement, and when culture is lacking, perfection remains incomplete. Everyone seems coarse without artifice, and everyone needs its polish in all areas to be perfect.

*

Reality and manner. Substance is insufficient, circumstance is also vital. A bad manner ruins everything, even justice and reason. A good manner makes up for everything: it gilds a 'no', sweetens truth, and beautifies old age itself. How something is done plays a key role in all affairs, and a good manner is a winning trick. Graceful conduct is the chief ornament of life; it gets you out of any tight situation.

*

Have intelligent support. The good fortune of the powerful: to be accompanied by outstanding minds that can save them from tight spots caused by their own ignorance and fight difficult battles for them. It shows exceptional greatness to make use of wise people, far better than the barbarous preference of Tigranes who wanted conquered kings as his servants. A new type of mastery over what's best in life: skilfully make those whom nature made superior your servants. There's much to know and life is short, and a life without knowledge is not a life. It's a singular skill effortlessly to learn much from many, gaining knowledge from all. Then you can speak in a meeting for many or, through your words, as many wise people as advised you will speak. You'll gain a reputation as an oracle through the sweat of others. Your learned helpers first select the subject, and then distil their knowledge and present it to you. If you can't have wisdom as your servant, at least be on intimate terms.

*

Vary your procedure. Not always the same way, so as to confound those observing you, especially if they are rivals. Don't always fulfil your declared intentions, for others will seize on your predictability, anticipating and frustrating your actions. It's easy to kill a bird that flies straight, but not one that twists and turns. But don't always do the opposite of what you say, for the trick will be understood the second time around. Malice is always lying in wait – great subtlety is needed to mislead it. Sharp players never move the piece their opponents are expecting, and especially not the one they want them to.

*

A person born in the right century. Truly outstanding people depend on their times. Not all were born at the time they deserved, and many, though they were, didn't manage to take advantage of it. Some were worthy of a better century, for every good doesn't triumph at all times. Everything has its time; even what's outstanding is subject to changing taste. But wisdom has the advantage of being eternal, and if this is not its century, many others will be.

*

Find everyone's weak spot. This is the art of moving people's wills. It consists more in skill than determination – a knowledge of how to get inside each person. Everyone's will has its own particular predilection, all different according to the variety of tastes. We all idolize something: for some, esteem; for others, self-interest; and for most, pleasure. The trick to influencing people lies in knowing what they idolize. Knowing each person's driving impulse is like having the key to their will. You should go direct to what most motivates a person, normally something base rather than anything noble, for there are more self-indulgent people than self-controlled ones in the world. You should first divine someone's character, then touch upon their fixation, and take control of their driving passion which, without fail, will defeat their free will.

*

Know the fortunate, to befriend them, and the unfortunate, to shun them. Misfortune is normally the crime of fools – and nothing is more contagious. You should never open the door to the smallest ill, for others, both many and greater, will come in after it and ambush you. The greatest trick is to know which cards to throw away: the lowest card that wins the current game is worth more than the highest that won an earlier one. If in doubt, a good move is to attach yourself to the wise and the prudent, for sooner or later they'll meet with good fortune.

*

Know how to leave things to one side, for if knowing how to refuse is one of life's great lessons, an even greater one is knowing how to say no to yourself, to important people, and in business. There are non-essential activities, moths of precious time, and it's worse to take an interest in irrelevant things than do nothing at all. To be circumspect, it's not enough to interfere; it's more important to make sure others don't interfere in your affairs. Don't so belong to others that you don't belong to yourself. Even friends should not be abused; you shouldn't want more from them than they're willing to concede. Any extreme is a vice, and especially in dealings with others. Sensible moderation is the best way to maintain goodwill and respect because ever-precious dignity won't be worn away. Be free in spirit, passionate about all that's fine, and never sin against your own good taste.

*

Know your key quality, your outstanding gift. Cultivate it, and improve the rest. Everyone could have been pre-eminent in something, if they had been aware of their best quality. Identify your key attribute and redouble its use. In some this is their judgement, in others courage. Most people misuse their capabilities, and so achieve superiority in nothing. What passion rushes to flatter, time is slow to disillusion us about.

*

Quit whilst fortune is smiling, as all good gamblers do. A graceful retreat is as important as a brave assault, safeguarding achievements once these are enough, and especially when they're more than enough. Always be suspicious of unbroken good fortune; far safer is fortune that's mixed, and for it to be bittersweet even whilst you are enjoying it. The more blessings there are rushing towards us, the greater the risk of them stumbling and bringing everything down. The intensity of fortune's favour sometimes compensates for the brevity of its duration. It quickly grows tired of carrying someone on its shoulders.

*

Be in people's good graces. It's a great thing to earn people's admiration, but more so their affection. This is partly a matter of luck, but mostly of effort; it begins with the first and is pursued with the second. Outstanding talent is not enough, although people imagine that it's easy to win affection once respect has been won. For benevolence, beneficence is required. Do endless good; good words, better deeds; love, in order to be loved. Courtesy is the greatest, most politic spell the great can cast. Reach for great deeds first, then for the pen; go from the sword to sheets of paper, for the favour of writers, which exists, is eternal.

*

Think with the few and speak with the many. To want to go against the current is as impossible for the wise as it is easy for the reckless. Only a Socrates could undertake this. Dissent is taken as an insult since it condemns another's judgement. Those offended multiply, either because of the point criticized or the person who'd endorsed it. Truth is for the few; deception is as common as it is vulgar. The wise cannot be identified by what they say in public, since they never speak there with their own voice but following common stupidity, however much their inner thoughts contradict this. The sensible flee being contradicted as much as contradicting: what they're quick to censure, they're slow to publicize. Thought is free; it cannot and should not be coerced. It retreats into the sanctuary of silence, and if it sometimes breaks this, it only does so among the select and the wise.

*

Caution – use it, but don't abuse it. Don't affect it, far less reveal it: all art should be concealed, for it's suspect, and especially the art of caution, which is odious. Deceit is widely used; suspicion should be everywhere but without revealing itself, for this would occasion distrust: it causes affront, provokes revenge, and arouses unimagined troubles. Reflective behaviour is of great advantage to our deeds: there is no greater proof of reason. An action's absolute perfection is secured by the mastery with which it is executed.

*

Never lose your composure. A prime aim of good sense: never lose your cool. This is proof of true character, of a perfect heart, because magnanimity is difficult to perturb. Passions are the humours of the mind and any imbalance in them unsettles good sense, and if this illness leads us to open our mouths, it will endanger our reputation. Be so in control of yourself that, whether things are going well or badly, nobody can accuse you of being perturbed and all can admire your superiority.

*

Know how to adapt yourself. You don't need to appear equally intelligent to all, nor should you employ more effort than is necessary. With knowledge and excellence, nothing should be squandered. A good falconer releases only as many birds as are needed for the chase. Don't continually flaunt your qualities or there'll be nothing left to admire. There must always be something novel with which to dazzle, for people who reveal something new each day keep interest alive and never allow the limits of their great abilities to be discovered.

*

Leave a good impression. In the house of Fortune, if you enter through pleasure's door, you'll leave through sorrow's, and vice versa. Pay attention to how things end, then, taking greater care to make a good exit than a widely applauded entrance. It's common for lucky people to have very favourable beginnings and truly tragic ends. The aim is not to have your entrance applauded by the rabble, for everyone's is greeted this way. What matters rather is the general feeling your exit arouses, for few are missed once gone. Good fortune rarely accompanies those on their way out; she is as polite to those who are arriving as she is rude to those who are leaving.

*

Make sure of a successful outcome. Some focus more on going about things the right way than on achieving their goal. But the discredit that comes with failure outweighs any credit gained by such diligence. Whoever wins need offer no explanations. Most people don't see the precise circumstances, only a good or bad outcome. Reputation is therefore never lost when goals are achieved. A successful conclusion makes everything golden, however mistaken the means. For it shows wisdom to go against received wisdom when there's no other way to achieve a happy outcome.

*

Know how to refuse. Not everything has to be granted, nor to everyone. This is as important as knowing how to grant something, and is a vital necessity for rulers. Your manner is important here: one person's 'no' is valued more than another's 'yes', because a gilded 'no' satisfies far more than a blunt 'yes'. Many are always ready to say 'no', turning everything sour. 'No' is always their first reaction, and although they subsequently grant everything, they are not held in esteem because of the taste left by the initial refusal. Things shouldn't be refused in one fell swoop; let disappointment sink in gradually. Nor should refusals be categoric, for dependants then give up all hope. Always let there be a few crumbs of hope to temper the bitterness of refusal. Let courtesy make up for the lack of favour, and fine words the lack of deeds. 'Yes' and 'no' are quick to say, and require much thought.

*

Know how to be evasive. This is the escape route of sensible people. With the charm of a witty phrase, they can normally extricate themselves from the most intricate labyrinth. They can avoid the most difficult confrontation with a smile: the courage of the greatest of the great captains was based on this. A polite tactic in refusing is to change the subject, and there's no greater act of caution than to conceal that you have understood.

*

Know how to be all things to all people. A discreet Proteus: with the learned, learned, and with the devout, devout. A great art to win everyone over, since similarity creates goodwill. Observe each person's temperament and tune yours to it. Whether with a serious or a jovial person, go with the current, undergoing a transformation that is politic – and essential for those in positions of dependency. Such vital subtlety requires great ability. It is less difficult for the universal man with his wide-ranging intellect and taste.

*

Take care when gathering information. We live mainly on information. We see very little for ourselves and live on others' testimony. Hearing is truth's last entry point, and a lie's first. Truth is normally seen and rarely heard. It rarely reaches us unadulterated, especially when it comes from far off. It is always tinged with the emotions through which it has passed. Passion tints everything it touches, making it odious or pleasing. It always tries to make an impression, so consider carefully a person offering praise, and even more so someone uttering abuse. The greatest attention is needed here to discover their intention by

How to Use Your Enemies

knowing beforehand where they're coming from. Let caution weigh up what's missing and what's false.

*

Dazzle anew. This is the privilege of the phoenix. Excellence normally grows old, and with it fame. Custom diminishes admiration, and mediocre novelty usually trumps aged pre-eminence. Valour, ingenuity, fortune, indeed everything, should be reborn. Dare to dazzle anew, rising repeatedly like the sun, shining in different fields, so that your absence in one area awakens desire and your novel appearance in another, applause.

*

Know how to use your enemies. You must know how to take hold of everything – not by the blade, which wounds, but by the hilt, which defends. This applies especially to envy. Enemies are of more use to the wise man than friends are to the fool. Ill will usually levels mountains of difficulty which goodwill would balk at tackling. The greatness of many has been fashioned thanks to malicious enemies. Flattery is more harmful than hatred, for the latter is an effective remedy for the flaws that the former conceals. Sensible people fashion a mirror from spite, more truthful than that of affection, and reduce or correct their defects, for great caution is needed when living on the frontier of envy and ill will.

Forestall malicious gossip. The mob is many-headed, with many malicious eyes and many slanderous tongues. Sometimes a rumour tarnishing the best reputation spreads through it, and if this results in your becoming a byword, it will destroy your name. The basis for this is normally some obvious defect, some ridiculous shortcomings, which are popular material for gossip. There are flaws secretly exposed by private envy to public malice, for there are malevolent tongues that destroy a great reputation more quickly with a joke than with open effrontery. It's very easy to gain a bad reputation, for badness is easy to believe and hard to erase. The sensible man should avoid such things and carefully forestall the insolence of the mob, for prevention is easier than cure.

*

Let your manner be lofty, endeavour to make it sublime. A great man's conduct should not be petty. You should never go into minute details, especially with unpleasant things, because although it's an advantage to notice everything casually, it isn't to want to inquire into every last thing. You should normally act with a noble generality, which is a form of gallantry. A large part of ruling is dissimulation; you should pass over most things that occur among your family, your friends and particularly your enemies. Triviality is annoying, and in a person's character, tedious. To keep coming back to a disagreement is a kind of mania. Normally, each person's behaviour follows their heart and their talents.

*

Understand yourself: your temperament, intellect, opinions, emotions. You can't be master of yourself if you don't first understand yourself. There are mirrors for the face, but none for the spirit: let discreet self-reflection be yours. And when you cease to care about your external image, focus on the inner one to correct and improve it. Know how strong your good sense and perspicacity are for any undertaking and evaluate your capacity for overcoming obstacles. Fathom your depths and weigh up your capacity for all things.

*

Unfathomable abilities. The circumspect man, if he wants to be venerated by everyone, should prevent the true depths of his knowledge or his courage being plumbed. He should allow himself to be known, but not fully understood. No one should establish the limits of his abilities, because of the danger of having their illusions shattered. He should never allow anyone to grasp everything about him. Greater veneration is created by conjecture and uncertainty over the extent of our ability than by firm evidence of this, however vast it might be.

*

On moral sense. It is the throne of reason, the foundation of prudence, and with it, success is easy. It's heaven's gift – the most wished for, because the greatest and the best. The most important piece of armour, so vital it's the only one whose absence is called a loss. Its lack is always noted first. All life's actions depend on its influence, and all seek its approval, for everything must be carried out with common sense. It consists of an innate propensity for all that most conforms to reason, and is always wedded to what's most right.

*

Conceal your wishes. Passions are breaches in the mind. The most practical kind of knowledge is dissimulation; whoever plays their hand openly runs the risk of losing. Let the reserve of the cautious compete against the scrutiny of the perceptive; against the sharp eyes of the lynx, the ink of the cuttlefish. Don't let your desires be known so that they won't be anticipated, either by opposition or flattery.

*

Half the world is laughing at the other half, and all are fools. Either everything is good or everything bad, depending on people's opinions. What one pursues, another flees.

How to Use Your Enemies

Whoever wants to make their own opinion the measure of all things is an insufferable fool. Perfection doesn't depend on one person's approval: tastes are as plentiful as faces, and as varied. There's not a single failing without its advocate. Nor should we lose heart if something doesn't please someone, for there'll always be someone else it does. But their applause shouldn't go to our heads, for others will condemn such praise. The measure of true satisfaction is the approval of reputable men who are experts in the relevant field. Life doesn't depend on any one opinion, any one custom, or any one century.

*

Understand what different jobs entail. They are all different and you need great knowledge and observation here. Some require courage, others subtlety. Those that depend on integrity are easier to handle, those on artifice, harder. With the right disposition, nothing else is needed for the former; but all the care and vigilance in the world are not enough for the latter. To govern people is a demanding job, and fools and madmen more so. Twice the wit is needed to deal with someone with none. A job that demands complete dedication, has fixed hours and is repetitive is intolerable; better is one which is free from boredom and which combines variety and importance, because change is refreshing. The best are those where dependency on others is minimal. The worst, one where you are held to account, both in this world and the next.

*

Don't be tedious. People with only one concern and only one subject are usually boring. Brevity flatters and opens more doors: it gains in courtesy what it loses in concision. What's good, if brief, is twice as good. Even bad things, if brief, are not so bad. Paring things down to their essence achieves more than verbosity. It's a commonplace that a tall person is rarely wise – not so much long-legged, as long-winded. There are those who, rather than embellish the world, are mere obstacles, worthless ornaments shunned by all. The discreet person should avoid being a hindrance, especially to the most powerful who are always very busy; worse to annoy one of them than the rest of the world. What's well said, is quickly said.

*

A short cut to being a true person: know how to rub shoulders with others. Interaction is very effective: custom and taste can be learnt, character and even ingenuity can rub off on you without your knowing. Let the impulsive get together with those who are restrained, and similarly other opposite temperaments. In this way, a proper balance will be effortlessly achieved. To know how to accommodate is a great skill. The alternation of opposites beautifies and sustains creation, and if it creates harmony in the natural world, even more so in the moral sphere. Make use of this politic advice when choosing friends and helpers, for from such communication between extremes, a discreet balance will be achieved.

*

Don't hang around to be a setting sun. The sensible person's maxim: abandon things before they abandon you. Know how to turn an ending into a triumph. Sometimes the sun itself, whilst still shining brilliantly, goes behind a cloud so nobody can see it setting, leaving people in suspense over whether it has or not. To avoid being slighted, avoid being seen to decline. Don't wait until everyone turns their back on you, burying you alive to regret but dead to esteem. Someone sharp retires a racehorse at the right time, not waiting until everyone laughs when it falls in mid-race. Let beauty astutely shatter her mirror when the time is right, not impatiently and too late when she sees her own illusions shattered in it.

*

Have friends. They are a second self. To a friend, another friend is always good and wise; between friends, everything turns out well. You are worth as much as others say you are, and to win their good words, win their hearts. Performing a service for another works like a charm, and the best way to win friends is to do people favours. The greatest and the best that we have depends on others.

You must live with either friends or enemies. You should make a new friend every day, if not a confidant, then at least a supporter, for if you have chosen well, some will later become confidants.

*

Win affection. Even the first and highest Cause, in its most important affairs, foresees this need and works towards it. Win someone's affection and their respect will follow. Some so trust merit that they underestimate diligence. But caution knows full well that without people's favour, merit alone is the longest route to take. Goodwill facilitates everything and makes good all deficiencies. It doesn't always take certain qualities – like courage, integrity, wisdom and even discretion – for granted, but will grant them. It never sees faults because it doesn't want to. It usually arises from some material connection, whether temperament, race, family, nationality or employment, or from a more sublime, intangible one, such as talent, duty, reputation or merit. The difficulty lies in gaining it, for it's easy to preserve. You can diligently acquire it and learn how to profit from it.

*

In good fortune prepare for bad. It's sensible to make provision for winter in the summer, and far easier. Favours are cheap then, and friends abundant. It's good to store things up against bad times, for adversity is costly and in

How to Use Your Enemies

need of everything. Have friends and grateful people set aside, for some day you will appreciate what you barely notice now. Villainy never has any friends, disowning them in prosperity, and in adversity being disowned.

*

Get used to the bad temperaments of those you deal with, like getting used to ugly faces. This is advisable in situations of dependency. There are horrible people you can neither live with nor live without. It's a necessary skill, therefore, to get used to them, as to ugliness, so you're not surprised each time their harshness manifests itself. At first they'll frighten you, but gradually your initial horror will disappear and caution will anticipate or tolerate the unpleasantness.

*

Live according to common practice. Even knowledge must keep in fashion; when it's not, you need to know how to appear ignorant. Reasoning and taste change with the times. You shouldn't reason and debate in an old-fashioned way and your taste should be up-to-the-minute. The preference of the majority sets the standard in all things. Follow it whilst it lasts, and move towards eminence. A sensible person must adapt the trappings of both body and soul to the fashion of the times, even if the past seems better. Only in matters of goodness does this rule of life not apply, for you should always practise virtue. Telling the truth and keeping your word are unknown today and seem like things from the past. Good men, though always loved, seem relics of better times, and so even if there happen to be any, they're not emulated because they're not in fashion. The misfortune of your century, that virtue is taken as unusual and malice as the norm! Let those with discretion live as they can, if not as they would prefer, and consider what fortune has given them to be better than what it has denied.

*

Be desired. Few win universal favour; if they win the favour of the wise, it's fortunate. Those on the way out are normally held in lukewarm esteem. There are ways to merit the prize of affection: eminence in your occupation and in your skills is a sure way, and an affable manner is effective. Make the eminent job depend on you so that people see that the job needed you, not you the job. Some confer honour on their position; others have honour conferred on them by it. It's no advantage to be thought good because your successor was bad, since this is not unqualified desire for you, but hatred for the other.

*

The fool is not someone who does something foolish, but someone who, once this is done, doesn't know how to hide it. Your emotions need to be concealed, and even more so your faults. Everyone errs, but with this difference: the shrewd dissimulate what they've done, while fools blab about what they're about to do. Reputation is more a matter of caution than of deeds; if you're not pure, be cautious. A great person's mistakes are observed more closely, like the eclipses of the largest planets. The only things that shouldn't be disclosed in a friendship are your faults; were it possible, these shouldn't even be disclosed to yourself. But another rule of life can be helpful here: know how to forget.

*

Reconsider things. Taking a second look at things provides security, especially when the solution isn't obvious. Take your time, whether to grant something or to improve your situation — new reasons to confirm and corroborate your personal judgement will appear. If it's a question of giving, then a gift is more valued because wisely given than quickly given; something long desired is always more appreciated. If you must refuse, then it allows time to think how, and for your refusal to taste less bitter, because more mature and considered. More often than not, once the initial desire for something has cooled, a refusal will not be felt as a rebuff. If someone asks for something quickly, delay granting it, which is a trick to deflect attention elsewhere.

*

Better mad with the crowd than sane all alone, say politicians. For if everyone is mad, you'll be different to none, and if good sense stands alone, it will be taken as madness. To go with the flow is so important. The greatest form of knowledge is, on occasion, not to know, or to affect not to know. You have to live with others, and most are ignorant. To live alone, you must be either very like God or a complete animal. But I would modify the aphorism and say: better sane with the majority than mad all alone. For some want to be unique in their fantastical illusions.

*

Have double of life's necessities. This is to double life. Don't depend on just one person, or limit yourself to a single resource, however excellent. Everything should be doubled, and especially the sources of advantage, favour and pleasure. The mutability of the moon pervades everything and sets a limit on all permanence, especially in areas that depend on our frail human will. Let your reserves help you against the fragility of life, and let a key rule of the art of living be to double the sources of your own benefit and comfort. Just as nature doubled the most important and exposed parts of the body, so human skill should double those things on which we depend.

*

The art of leaving things alone. Especially when the seas of public or personal life are stormiest. There are whirlwinds in the affairs of men, tempests of the will, and it makes good sense to retire and wait things out in a safe harbour.

How to Use Your Enemies

Remedies often make troubles worse. Let nature or morality take its course. The wise doctor needs to know when to prescribe something and when not, and often the art lies in not applying any remedy at all. Simply sitting back can be a way of calming the whirlwinds of the mob. Yielding to time now will lead to victory later. A spring's water is easily muddied; you will never make it clear by trying to, only by leaving it well alone. There is no better remedy for disorder than to let it run its course; it will then disappear on its own.

*

Know your unlucky days, for they exist. Nothing will work out right and, even though you change your game, your bad luck will remain. After a few moves you should recognize bad luck, and then withdraw, realizing whether it's your lucky day or not. Even understanding has its moments, for no one is knowledgeable on all occasions. It takes good fortune to reason successfully, just as to write a letter well. All perfection depends on the opportune moment. Even beauty is not always in fashion. Discretion contradicts itself, sometimes falling short, sometimes going too far. To work out well, everything depends on the right time. Just as on some days everything turns out badly, others it all goes well – and with less effort. It's as though everything has already been done; your ingenuity and character are perfectly aligned with your lucky star. Take advantage of such occasions and don't waste a single moment of them. But a judicious man given one obstacle shouldn't declare it a bad day, or a good one given the reverse, for the former might just be a setback, and the latter, luck.

*

Don't support the worse side out of stubbornness, simply because your opponent has already chosen the better one. The battle will be lost before it's begun and you'll inevitably have to surrender, scorned. You'll never come out best by supporting the worst. Your opponent showed astuteness in anticipating the better side, and you'd be stupid in then deciding to support the worse. Those obstinate in deeds are more stubborn than those obstinate in words, for actions carry more risk than words. The stupidity of stubborn people is seen in their not recognizing what's true or advantageous, preferring argument and contradiction. The circumspect are always on the side of reason, not passion, having got in first to support the best or, if not, having subsequently improved their position, for if their opponents are fools, their very stupidity will make them change course, switch sides, and thereby worsen their position. The only way to get your opponent to stop supporting what's best is to support it yourself, for their stupidity will then make them drop it, and their stubbornness will be their downfall.

*

Go in supporting the other person's interests so as to come out achieving your own. This is a strategy for achieving what you want. Even in matters concerning heaven, Christian teachers recommend such holy astuteness. It's an important kind of dissimulation, because the perceived benefit is just the bait to catch another's will. They'll think you are furthering their own aims, but this will be no more than a means of furthering your own. You should never enter into anything recklessly, especially when there's an undercurrent of danger. With people whose first word is usually 'no', it's also best to conceal your true intentions so that they won't focus on the difficulties of saying 'yes', especially when you sense their aversion to doing so. This piece of advice belongs with those about concealed intentions, for all involve extreme subtlety.

*

Don't expose your sore finger, or everything will knock against it. Don't complain about your sore points, for malice always attacks where our weaknesses hurt most. Getting annoyed will only serve to spur on someone else's enjoyment. The ill-intentioned are searching for a pretext to get your back up. Their dart-like insinuations aim to discover where you hurt, and they'll try a thousand different ways until they hit upon your most sensitive point. The circumspect pretend not to notice and never reveal their troubles, whether their own or their family's, for even fortune occasionally likes to hit where it hurts most, and it always cuts to the quick. You should therefore never reveal what causes you pain or pleasure, so that the former may quickly end and the latter long continue.

*

Don't be inaccessible. Nobody is so perfect that they don't sometimes need advice. Someone who refuses to listen is an incurable fool. The most independent person must still accept the need for friendly advice; even a monarch must be willing to be taught. There are individuals beyond all help because they are inaccessible and who come unstuck because nobody dares to stop them. The most self-sufficient person must leave a door open to friendship, from where all help will come. You need a friend of sufficient influence over you to be able to advise and admonish you freely. Your trust and high opinion of their loyalty and prudence should place them in this position of authority. Though such authority and respect shouldn't be handed to all and sundry, have in caution's innermost room a confidant, a faithful mirror, whose correction you value when disillusionment is necessary.

*

Know how to deflect trouble on to someone else. Having a shield against ill will is a great trick of rulers. To have someone else who can be criticized for mistakes and chastised by gossipmongers is a sign of superior skill, not lack of competence as malice thinks. Not everything can turn out well, nor can everyone be pleased. Have a fall guy, therefore, someone who, at the expense of their own ambition, can be a target for your misfortunes.

*

Think ahead: today for tomorrow, and even for many days after that. The greatest foresight is to have abundant time for it. For the far-sighted, nothing is unexpected; there are no tight spots for those who are prepared. Don't save your reason for when difficulties arise, use it well before that. Anticipate critical times with mature reflection. The pillow is a silent Sibyl and sleeping on things is better than lying awake under their weight. Some act first and think later, which is to search for excuses rather than consequences. Others think neither before nor after. The whole of life should be a process of deliberation to choose the right course. Reflection and foresight provide the means of living in anticipation.

*

Never be associated with someone who can cast you in a poor light, whether because they're better or worse than you. The more perfect they are, the higher their esteem. They will always play the lead role, and you a secondary one, and if you win any esteem, it will simply be their leftovers. The moon on its own stands out among the stars, but when the sun comes out, it either doesn't appear or it disappears. Never consort with someone who eclipses you, only with someone who enhances you. In this way Martial's discreet Fabulla was able to appear beautiful and to shine amidst the ugliness and slovenliness of her maids. Similarly, don't take the risk of keeping bad company, and don't honour others at the cost of your own reputation. To improve yourself, associate with the eminent; once perfected, with the mediocre.

*

Avoid stepping into great men's shoes. And if you do, be sure of your own superiority. To equal your predecessor you will need to be worth twice as much. Just as it's a good strategy to make sure your successor is such that people will miss you, so also to make sure your predecessor doesn't eclipse you. It's difficult to fill the void left by someone great because the past always seems better; even being their equal isn't enough, because they'll always have the advantage of having come first. To topple someone's greater reputation, then, you need qualities above and beyond theirs.

*

Choose your friends: they should become so after being examined by discretion, tested by fortune, and certified not simply by your will but your understanding. Although the most important thing in life, it's usually the one over which least care is taken: some are forced upon us, most are the result of pure chance. A person is defined by the friends they have, and the wise never make friends with fools. But liking someone's company need not suggest true intimacy – it can simply mean enjoying their humour rather than having any confidence in their actual abilities. Some friendships are like a marriage, others like an affair; the latter are for pleasure, the former for the abundant success they engender. Few are friends because of you yourself, many because of your good fortune. A friend's true understanding is worth more than the many good wishes of others. Make friends by choice, then, not by chance. A wise friend can prevent troubles, a foolish one can cause them. And don't wish friends too much good fortune, if you don't want to lose them.

*

Know how to use your friends. This requires its own art of discretion. Some are useful at a distance, others close to hand, and someone who is perhaps no good for conversation will be as a correspondent. Distance removes defects that are intolerable close up. You shouldn't simply seek enjoyment from friendship, but profit, for it should have the three qualities of goodness, though others argue it should have those of being – which is one, good and true – since a friend is all things. Few are capable of being good friends, and not knowing how to choose them makes their actual number even fewer. Knowing how to keep friends is harder than acquiring them. Look for friends who will last, and although they will be new at first, take satisfaction in knowing they will be old friends in time. The best are undoubtedly those most seasoned – although you may need to share a bushel of salt with them to reach this point. There's no desert like a life without friends: friendship multiplies blessings and divides troubles. It's the only remedy for bad fortune and is an oasis of comfort for the soul.

*

Talk circumspectly. With rivals, through caution; with everyone else, through decorum. There's always time to utter a word, but not to take it back. You should speak as wills are written, for the fewer the words, the fewer the disputes. Use occasions that don't matter to practise for those that do. Mystery has a hint of the divine about it. The loquacious are more easily conquered and convinced.

*

Know how to triumph over envy and malevolence. Showing contempt, even if prudent, achieves little; being polite is much better. Nothing is more worthy of applause than speaking well of someone who speaks ill of you, and no revenge more heroic than merit and talent conquering and tormenting envy. Each blessing is a further torture to ill will, and the glory of those envied is a personal hell to the envious. The greatest punishment is making your good fortune their poison. An envious person doesn't die straight off, but bit by bit every time the person envied receives applause, the enduring fame of one rivalling the punishment of the other, the former in everlasting glory, the latter everlasting torment. Fame's trumpet heralds one person's immortality and announces another's death – a sentence to hang by envy's anxious rope.

*

Never let compassion for the unfortunate earn you the disfavour of the fortunate. One person's misfortune is normally another's good fortune, for there can never be a lucky person without many unlucky ones. The unfortunate tend to attract the goodwill of people who want to compensate them for fortune's lack of favour with their own worthless favour. And it has sometimes been known for a person who was hated by everyone whilst they prospered to gain everyone's compassion in adversity; desire for revenge against the exalted turns to compassion for the fallen. But a shrewd person must pay close attention to fortune's shuffling of the cards. Some always side with the unfortunate, sidling up to them in their misfortune having previously shunned them when they enjoyed good fortune. This perhaps suggests innate nobility, but not an ounce of shrewdness.

*

Take more care not to fail once than to succeed a hundred times. Nobody looks at the sun when it's shining, everyone when it's eclipsed. The masses, ever critical, will not recount your successes, only your failures. The bad are better known through gossip than the good are through acclaim. Many people were never heard of until they went astray, and all our successes will never be enough to negate a single, tiny blemish. Let nobody be under any illusion: malevolence will point out every bad thing you do, but not a single good one.

*

Don't be brittle as glass in dealing with people. And especially with friends. Some people crack easily, revealing their fragility. They fill up with offence and fill others with annoyance. They reveal a nature so petty and sensitive that it tolerates nothing, in jest or in earnest. The slightest thing offends them, so insults are never necessary. Those who have dealings with them have to tread carefully, always attending to their sensibilities and adjusting to their temperaments, since the slightest snub annoys them. They are completely self-centred, slaves to their own pleasure, in pursuit of which they'll trample over everything, and idolaters of punctiliousness. Be instead like a lover, whose condition is akin to the diamond in its endurance and resistance.

*

Don't live in a hurry. To know how to parcel things out is to know how to enjoy them. With many people their happiness is all over with life still to spare. They waste happy moments, which they don't enjoy, and then want to go back later when they find themselves so far down the road. They are life's postilions, adding their own headlong rush to time's inexorable march. They want to devour in a day what could barely be digested in a lifetime. They anticipate every happiness, bolt down the years still to come, and since they're always in such a rush, quickly finish everything. Moderation is necessary even in our desire for knowledge so as not to know things badly. There are more days than joys to fill them. Take enjoyment slowly and tasks quickly. It's good when tasks are completed, but bad when happiness is over.

*

Never be ruled by what you think your enemy should do. Fools never do what a sensible person thinks they will, because they can't discern what's best. Neither will those with discretion, because they will want to hide their intentions which may have been discerned and even anticipated. The *pro* and the *contra* of every matter should be thought through and both sides analysed, anticipating the different courses things may take. Opinions vary: let impartiality be attentive not so much to what will happen as to what may.

*

Without lying, don't reveal every truth. Nothing requires more care than the truth, which is an opening up of the heart. It's as necessary to know how to reveal it as to conceal it. With a single lie, a reputation for integrity is lost: deceit is viewed as a fault, and a deceiver as false, which is worse. Not all truths can be spoken: some because they are important to me, others to someone else.

*

Don't hold opinions doggedly. Every fool is utterly convinced, and everyone utterly convinced is a fool, and the more mistaken their opinion, the greater their tenacity. Even when the evidence is clear, it's sensible to yield, for the correctness of your position will not go unnoticed, and your politeness will be recognized. More is lost with stubborn insistence than can be gained by winning; this is not to defend truth, but vulgarity. There are those who are completely stubborn, difficult to convince, incurably vehement; when caprice and conviction are found together, they are always indissolubly wed to folly. Your will must be tenacious, not your judgement. There are, however, exceptions when you mustn't lose and be doubly defeated, once in the argument, and again in its consequences.

*

Anything popular, do yourself; anything unpopular, use others to do it. With the one you garner affection, with the other you deflect hatred. The great are fortunate in their generosity, since for them, doing good is more pleasurable than receiving it. Rarely do you upset someone without upsetting yourself, either through compassion or remorse. Those at the top necessarily have to reward or punish. Let good things come directly, bad ones indirectly. Have something to deflect hatred and slander, the blows of the disgruntled. Common anger is normally like an angry dog which, not knowing the reason for its pain, attacks the instrument that inflicts it simply because this, though not the ultimate cause, is close at hand.

*

A truly peaceable person is a person with a long life. To live, let live. The peaceable not only live, but reign. You should see and hear, but remain silent. A day without an argument leads to a sleep-filled night. To live a lot and to enjoy life is to live twice: this is the fruit of peace. A person has everything who cares nothing about what matters little. There's no greater absurdity than taking everything seriously. Similarly, it's stupid to take things to heart that don't concern you, and not to take to heart those that are important.

*

Know your lucky star. There's nobody so hopeless that they don't have one, and if you are unfortunate, it's because you don't know which it is. Some are close to princes and the powerful without knowing how or why, except that their luck brought them this favour; all that remains is for their own hard work to help it along. Others find themselves smiled on by the wise. One person is more acceptable in one country than another, and better regarded in this city than that. People will have better luck in one job or position than in others for which they have equal or even identical qualities. Luck shuffles the cards as and when it wants. Let everyone know their lucky star as well as their abilities, for this is a matter of winning or losing. Know how to follow it and help it; never swap it or you will wander off course.

*

Know how to transplant yourself. There are people only valued when they move to other countries, especially in top positions. Countries are stepmothers to their eminent children; envy reigns there as over its own land, and the imperfections with which someone started are remembered more than the greatness they ended up achieving. A pin became valuable travelling from the old world to the new, and a piece of glass led to diamonds being scorned when it was transported. Anything foreign is valued, either because it comes from a distance or because it's only encountered perfect and complete. We have all seen individuals who were utterly scorned in their own backyards and who are now the toast of the world, held in high esteem by their countrymen because their deeds are followed from a distance, and by foreigners because they come from afar. A statue on an altar will never be venerated by someone who knew it as a tree trunk in a garden.

How to Use Your Enemies

*

Undertake what's easy as if it were hard, and what's hard as if it were easy. In the first case, so that confidence doesn't make you careless; in the second, so that lack of confidence doesn't make you discouraged. It takes nothing more for something not to be done than thinking that it is. Conversely, diligence removes impossibilities. Don't think over great undertakings, just seize them when they arise, so that consideration of their difficulty doesn't hold you back.

*

In heaven, everything is good; in hell, everything bad. In the world, since it lies between the two, you find both. We are placed between two extremes, and so participate in both. Good and bad luck alternate; not all is happy, nor all hostile. This world is a zero: on its own, it's worth nothing; joined to heaven, a great deal. Indifference to its variety constitutes good sense – the wise are never surprised. Our life is arranged like a play, everything will be sorted out in the end. Take care, then, to end it well.

*

Know how to contradict. This is provocation's great strategy, getting others to open up without opening up yourself. It's a unique form of coercion which makes hidden feelings fly out. Lukewarm belief is an emetic for secrets, a key to the most securely locked heart. It subtly probes both will and judgement. Scorn shrewdly expressed towards someone's veiled language is the way to hunt the deepest secrets, drawing these out until they trip off the tongue and are caught in the nets of artful deceit. When someone circumspect shows reserve, this makes someone cautious throw theirs away, revealing what they think in their otherwise inscrutable hearts. A feigned doubt is curiosity's subtlest picklock, enabling it to learn whatever it wants. Even where learning is concerned, contradiction is the pupil's strategy to make the teacher put all their effort into explaining and justifying the truth: a mild challenge leads to consummate instruction.

*

Neither love nor hate forever. Trust in today's friends as if tomorrow's worst enemies. Since this actually happens, anticipate it happening. You should never give arms to friendship's turncoats, since they'll wage a devastating war with them. With enemies, in contrast, always leave the door open for reconciliation, gallantry's door being the most effective. Sometimes an earlier act of revenge has subsequently caused torment, and pleasure in the harm done to our enemy, sorrow.

*

Don't be known for artifice, although you can't live without it now. Be prudent rather than astute. Everyone likes

How to Use Your Enemies

plain dealing, but not everyone practises it themselves. Don't let sincerity end up as extreme simplicity, nor shrewdness as astuteness. Be revered as wise rather than feared as calculating. Sincere people are loved, but deceived. The greatest artifice may be to conceal such artifice, for it's always viewed as deceit. Openness flourished in the age of gold; malice does in this age of iron. The reputation of someone who knows what they should do is an honourable one and inspires trust; that of someone full of artifice is false and provokes suspicion.

*

Know how to divide up your life wisely, not as things arise, but with foresight and discrimination. Life is arduous without any breaks, like a long journey without any inns. Learned variety makes it pleasant. Spend the first part of a fine life in communication with the dead. We are born to know and to know ourselves, and books reliably turn us into people. Spend the second part with the living: see and examine all that's good in the world. Not everything can be found in one country; the universal Father has shared out his gifts and sometimes endows the ugliest with the most. Let the third stage be spent entirely with yourself: the ultimate happiness, to philosophize.

*

Don't entrust your reputation to another without having their honour as security. Keeping silent should be to each other's advantage; speaking out to each other's detriment. Where honour is concerned, dealings must cut both ways, so that each looks after the other's reputation. You should never trust anyone; and if on occasion you have to, do so with such skill that you encourage caution even more than prudence. The risk should be equal and the matter mutual, so that someone who says they're your partner doesn't turn witness against you.

*

Know how to ask. There's nothing more difficult for some, or more easy for others. There are some who don't know how to refuse; with such people, no picklock is necessary. There are others whose first word on every occasion is 'no'; with these people, you need real skill. And with everyone, the right moment: catch them when they're in good spirits, when their bodies or their minds are satisfied. Unless the listener's careful attention detects the petitioner's subtlety, then happy days are the days when favours are granted, for inner happiness streams outwards. Don't go near when you see someone else has been refused, for any fear of saying 'no' will have vanished. There's no good time when people are down. Placing someone under an obligation beforehand is a good bill of exchange, unless you're dealing with someone base.

*

Grant something as a favour before it has to be given as a reward.
This is a skill of great politicians. Granting favours before they are merited is proof of an honourable person. A favour in advance is doubly excellent: the speed of the giver places the recipient under a greater obligation. A gift given afterwards is due payment; the same beforehand becomes an obligation. This is a subtle way of transforming obligations, for what was for the superior an obligation to reward becomes for the recipient an obligation to repay. This is the case with honourable people. With base individuals, a reward paid early is more of a bit than a spur.

*

Know how to appear the fool. The wisest sometimes play this card, and there are times when the greatest knowledge consists in appearing to lack knowledge. You mustn't be ignorant, just feign ignorance. With fools, being wise counts for little, and similarly with madmen, being sane: you need to talk to everyone in their own language. The person who feigns stupidity isn't a fool, just the person who suffers from it. Whilst real stupidity is just simple, feigned stupidity isn't, for genuine artifice is involved here. The only way to be well loved is to put on the skin of the most stupid of animals.

*

Take a joke, but don't make someone the butt of one. The first is a form of politeness; the second, of audacity. Whoever gets annoyed at some fun appears even more like a beast than they actually are. An excellent joke is enjoyable; to know how to take one is a mark of real character. Getting annoyed simply prompts others to poke fun again and again. Know how far to take a joke, and the safest thing is not to start one. The greatest truths have always arisen from jokes. Nothing demands greater care and skill: before making a joke, know just how far someone can take one.

*

Don't be completely dove-like. Let the craftiness of the snake alternate with the simplicity of the dove. There's nothing easier than deceiving a good person. The person who never lies is more ready to believe, and one who never deceives is more trusting. Being deceived is not always the result of stupidity, but sometimes of simple goodness. Two types of people often foresee danger: those who have learnt from experience, very much to their own cost, and the astute, very much to the cost of others. Let shrewdness be as versed in suspicion as astuteness is in intrigue, and don't try to be so good that you create opportunities for someone else to be bad. Be a combination of the dove and the serpent; not a monster, but a prodigy.

*

Don't offer an apology to someone who hasn't asked for one. And even if one is asked for, an over-the-top apology is like an admission of guilt. To apologize before it's necessary is to accuse yourself, and to be bled when healthy is to attract ill health and ill will. An excuse in advance awakens suspicion. Nor should a sensible person reveal their awareness of someone else's suspicions – this is to go looking for offence. They should try instead to refute these with the honesty of their actions.

*

Know how to do good: in small amounts, and often. An obligation should never be greater than someone's ability to fulfil it. Whoever gives a great deal is not giving but selling. Gratitude should not be placed in an impossible position; if it is, relations will be broken off. All it takes to lose many people is to place them under too much of an obligation: being unable to fulfil it, they'll back away, and since they are under it, they'll end up as enemies. The idol never wants to see before it the sculptor who created it, nor does someone under an obligation want to see their benefactor. The subtle art of giving: it should cost little, but be greatly desired, and hence greatly appreciated.

*

Never break off relations, because reputation is always damaged by this. Anyone makes a good enemy, not so a friend; few can do good, but almost everyone harm. The day the eagle broke with the beetle, its nest wasn't safe even in Jupiter's bosom. Hidden enemies, who wait for such opportunities, use a declared enemy to stoke the fires for them. Former friends make the worst enemies: they lay the blame for their misplaced esteem on your failings. Those looking on speak as they think and think as they wish, condemning both sides either for lacking foresight at the start of the friendship or for precipitousness at its end, and for lacking good sense in both instances. If a break is necessary, let it be forgivable, done with a cooling of favour, not a violent rage. The saying concerning a graceful retreat is relevant here.

*

You will never belong entirely to someone else nor they to you. Neither ties of blood, nor friendship, nor the most pressing obligation are sufficient for this, for there's a big difference between opening your heart and surrendering your will. Even the greatest intimacy has its limits, and the laws of courtesy are not offended by this. A friend always keeps some secret to himself and a son conceals something from his father. You conceal things from some people that you reveal to others, and vice versa, and by thus distinguishing between people, you end up revealing everything and withholding everything.

*

Know how to forget. This is more a matter of luck than skill. The things which should most be forgotten are the ones most remembered. Not only is memory base in failing when it's most needed, but stupid in turning up when it's best not to: it's meticulous with things that cause sorrow, and carefree with those that cause pleasure. Sometimes the remedy for misfortune consists in forgetting it – but we forget the remedy. It's therefore best to train our memory in good habits, because it can give us happiness or hell. The contented are an exception here, for in their state of innocence they enjoy their simple happiness.

*

Silken words, and a mild nature. Arrows pierce the body, but harsh words the soul. A pill can make your breath smell sweet, and to know how to sell air is one of life's subtlest skills. Most things are bought with words, and they're enough to achieve the impossible. All our dealings are in air, and the breath of a prince greatly inspires. So your mouth should always be full of sugar to sweeten your words so that they taste good even to your enemies. The only way to be loved is to be sweet-natured.

*

Know how to renew your character using nature and art. They say that our nature changes every seven years: let this improve and enhance your taste. After the first seven years we gain the use of reason; let there be a new perfection with each successive period. Observe this natural process to help it along, and expect others to improve as well. Thus many change their behaviour with their status or position, and sometimes this is not noticed until the full extent of such a change is apparent. At twenty, a person is a peacock; at thirty, a lion; at forty, a camel; at fifty, a snake; at sixty, a dog; at seventy, a monkey; and at eighty, nothing.

*

Show yourself off. It allows your qualities to shine. Each of these has its moment: seize it, for none can triumph every day. There are splendid individuals in whom the least accomplishment shines greatly and the greatest dazzles, provoking wonder. When display is joined to eminence, it's held to be prodigious. There are showy nations, and the Spanish surpass all in this. Light came first to enable all creation to shine. Display causes great satisfaction, makes good what's missing, and gives everything a second being, especially when grounded in reality. Heaven, which gives perfection, provides for its display, for one without the other would be unnatural. There's an art to all display; even what's truly excellent depends on circumstance and isn't always opportune. When the time isn't right, then display misfires. No quality should be less without affectation, and this always causes its downfall, since display is always close to vanity, and vanity to contempt. It should always be restrained so as not to end up being vulgar, and among the wise, excess has always been somewhat disparaged. It often consists in an eloquent silence, in a nonchalant show of perfection, for deft concealment is the most praiseworthy type of display, an apparent lack inciting profound curiosity. It's a great skill not to reveal perfection in its entirety straight off, but rather gradually to display it. Let one quality be a guarantee of a greater one, and applause for the first, an expectation of those to follow.

*

Don't meddle, and you won't be spurned. Respect yourself, if you want to be respected. Be sparing rather than lavish with your presence. Arrive when wanted, and you'll be well received; never come unless called, nor go unless sent. Someone who gets involved on their own initiative receives all the ill-will if they fail, and none of the thanks if they succeed. A meddler is the target of scorn, and since they brazenly interfere, they are discarded ignominiously.

*

Live as circumstances demand. Ruling, reasoning, everything must be opportune. Act when you can, for time and tide wait for no one. To live, don't follow generalizations, except where virtue is concerned, and don't insist on precise rules for desire, for you'll have to drink tomorrow the water you shunned today. There are some so outlandishly misguided that they expect all circumstances necessary for success to conform to their own whims, not the reverse. But the wise know that the lodestar of prudence is to behave as circumstances demand.

*

To combine esteem and affection is a real blessing. To maintain respect, don't be greatly loved. Love is more brazen than hate. Fondness and veneration don't sit well together. You should be neither greatly feared nor greatly loved. Love leads to familiarity, and when this makes its appearance, esteem departs. Be loved with appreciation rather than affection, for such love is a mark of great people.

*

Let your natural talents overcome the demands of the job, not the other way round. However great the position, a person must show that they are greater still. Real ability keeps on growing and dazzling with each new situation. Someone who lacks spirit will soon be overwhelmed and will be broken eventually by their duties and reputation. The great Augustus took pride in being a greater man than he was a prince. Nobility of spirit is beneficial here, and even sensible self-confidence.

*

Act as though always on view. The insightful man is the one who sees that others see or will see him. He knows that walls have ears, and that what's badly done is always bursting to come out. Even when alone, he acts as though seen by everyone, knowing that everything will eventually

How to Use Your Enemies

be known. He looks on those who will subsequently hear of his actions as witnesses to them already. The person who wanted everyone to see him wasn't daunted that others could see into his house from outside.

*

Leave people hungry: nectar should only ever brush the lips. Desire is the measure of esteem. Even with physical thirst, good taste's trick is to stimulate it, not quench it. What's good, if sparse is twice as good. The second time around, there's a sharp decline. A surfeit of pleasure is dangerous, for it occasions disdain even towards what's undisputedly excellent. The only rule in pleasing is to seize upon an appetite already whetted. If you must annoy it, do so through impatient desire rather than wearisome pleasure. Hard-won happiness is twice as enjoyable.

*

In a word, a saint, which says it once and for all. Virtue links all perfections and is the centre of all happiness. It makes a person prudent, circumspect, shrewd, sensible, wise, brave, restrained, upright, happy, praiseworthy, a true and comprehensive hero. Three S's make someone blessed: being saintly, sound and sage. Virtue is the sun of the little world of man and its hemisphere is a clear conscience. It is so fine, it gains the favour of both God and mankind. Nothing is worthy of love but virtue, nor of hate but vice. Virtue alone is real, everything else a mere jest. Ability and greatness must be measured by virtue, not by good fortune. It alone is self-sufficient. Whilst someone is alive, it makes them worthy of love; when dead, of being remembered.

1. BOCCACCIO · *Mrs Rosie and the Priest*
2. GERARD MANLEY HOPKINS · *As kingfishers catch fire*
3. *The Saga of Gunnlaug Serpent-tongue*
4. THOMAS DE QUINCEY · *On Murder Considered as One of the Fine Arts*
5. FRIEDRICH NIETZSCHE · *Aphorisms on Love and Hate*
6. JOHN RUSKIN · *Traffic*
7. PU SONGLING · *Wailing Ghosts*
8. JONATHAN SWIFT · *A Modest Proposal*
9. *Three Tang Dynasty Poets*
10. WALT WHITMAN · *On the Beach at Night Alone*
11. KENKŌ · *A Cup of Sake Beneath the Cherry Trees*
12. BALTASAR GRACIÁN · *How to Use Your Enemies*
13. JOHN KEATS · *The Eve of St Agnes*
14. THOMAS HARDY · *Woman much missed*
15. GUY DE MAUPASSANT · *Femme Fatale*
16. MARCO POLO · *Travels in the Land of Serpents and Pearls*
17. SUETONIUS · *Caligula*
18. APOLLONIUS OF RHODES · *Jason and Medea*
19. ROBERT LOUIS STEVENSON · *Olalla*
20. KARL MARX AND FRIEDRICH ENGELS · *The Communist Manifesto*
21. PETRONIUS · *Trimalchio's Feast*
22. JOHANN PETER HEBEL · *How a Ghastly Story Was Brought to Light by a Common or Garden Butcher's Dog*
23. HANS CHRISTIAN ANDERSEN · *The Tinder Box*
24. RUDYARD KIPLING · *The Gate of the Hundred Sorrows*
25. DANTE · *Circles of Hell*
26. HENRY MAYHEW · *Of Street Piemen*
27. HAFEZ · *The nightingales are drunk*
28. GEOFFREY CHAUCER · *The Wife of Bath*
29. MICHEL DE MONTAIGNE · *How We Weep and Laugh at the Same Thing*
30. THOMAS NASHE · *The Terrors of the Night*
31. EDGAR ALLAN POE · *The Tell-Tale Heart*
32. MARY KINGSLEY · *A Hippo Banquet*
33. JANE AUSTEN · *The Beautifull Cassandra*
34. ANTON CHEKHOV · *Gooseberries*
35. SAMUEL TAYLOR COLERIDGE · *Well, they are gone, and here must I remain*
36. JOHANN WOLFGANG VON GOETHE · *Sketchy, Doubtful, Incomplete Jottings*
37. CHARLES DICKENS · *The Great Winglebury Duel*
38. HERMAN MELVILLE · *The Maldive Shark*
39. ELIZABETH GASKELL · *The Old Nurse's Story*
40. NIKOLAY LESKOV · *The Steel Flea*

41. HONORÉ DE BALZAC · *The Atheist's Mass*
42. CHARLOTTE PERKINS GILMAN · *The Yellow Wall-Paper*
43. C.P. CAVAFY · *Remember, Body . . .*
44. FYODOR DOSTOEVSKY · *The Meek One*
45. GUSTAVE FLAUBERT · *A Simple Heart*
46. NIKOLAI GOGOL · *The Nose*
47. SAMUEL PEPYS · *The Great Fire of London*
48. EDITH WHARTON · *The Reckoning*
49. HENRY JAMES · *The Figure in the Carpet*
50. WILFRED OWEN · *Anthem For Doomed Youth*
51. WOLFGANG AMADEUS MOZART · *My Dearest Father*
52. PLATO · *Socrates' Defence*
53. CHRISTINA ROSSETTI · *Goblin Market*
54. *Sindbad the Sailor*
55. SOPHOCLES · *Antigone*
56. RYŪNOSUKE AKUTAGAWA · *The Life of a Stupid Man*
57. LEO TOLSTOY · *How Much Land Does A Man Need?*
58. GIORGIO VASARI · *Leonardo da Vinci*
59. OSCAR WILDE · *Lord Arthur Savile's Crime*
60. SHEN FU · *The Old Man of the Moon*
61. AESOP · *The Dolphins, the Whales and the Gudgeon*
62. MATSUO BASHŌ · *Lips too Chilled*
63. EMILY BRONTË · *The Night is Darkening Round Me*
64. JOSEPH CONRAD · *To-morrow*
65. RICHARD HAKLUYT · *The Voyage of Sir Francis Drake Around the Whole Globe*
66. KATE CHOPIN · *A Pair of Silk Stockings*
67. CHARLES DARWIN · *It was snowing butterflies*
68. BROTHERS GRIMM · *The Robber Bridegroom*
69. CATULLUS · *I Hate and I Love*
70. HOMER · *Circe and the Cyclops*
71. D. H. LAWRENCE · *Il Duro*
72. KATHERINE MANSFIELD · *Miss Brill*
73. OVID · *The Fall of Icarus*
74. SAPPHO · *Come Close*
75. IVAN TURGENEV · *Kasyan from the Beautiful Lands*
76. VIRGIL · *O Cruel Alexis*
77. H. G. WELLS · *A Slip under the Microscope*
78. HERODOTUS · *The Madness of Cambyses*
79. *Speaking of Siva*
80. *The Dhammapada*

'Hoodwinked with faery fancy...'

JOHN KEATS
Born 1795, London, England
Died 1821, Rome, Italy

Chosen from *Selected Poems*, edited by John Barnard and
published in Penguin Classics in 2007.

KEATS IN PENGUIN CLASSICS
The Complete Poems
Selected Poems
*So Bright and Delicate: Love Letters and Poems of
John Keats to Fanny Brawne*
Selected Letters

JOHN KEATS

The Eve of St Agnes

PENGUIN BOOKS

PENGUIN CLASSICS

UK | USA | Canada | Ireland | Australia
India | New Zealand | South Africa

Penguin Books is part of the Penguin Random House group of companies
whose addresses can be found at global.penguinrandomhouse.com.

This selection published in Penguin Classics 2015

010

Set in 9/12.4 pt Baskerville 10 Pro
Typeset by Jouve (UK), Milton Keynes
Printed and bound in Great Britain by Clays Ltd, Elcograf S.p.A.

A CIP catalogue record for this book is available from the British Library

ISBN: 978–0–141–39829–7

www.greenpenguin.co.uk

Penguin Random House is committed to a
sustainable future for our business, our readers
and our planet. This book is made from Forest
Stewardship Council® certified paper.

Contents

The Eve of St Agnes	1
La Belle Dame sans Merci. A Ballad	22
Lamia	26
Ode to Psyche	51
Ode on a Grecian Urn	54

The Eve of St Agnes

I

St Agnes' Eve – Ah, bitter chill it was!
The owl, for all his feathers, was a-cold;
The hare limped trembling through the frozen grass,
And silent was the flock in woolly fold:
Numb were the Beadsman's fingers, while he told
His rosary, and while his frosted breath,
Like pious incense from a censer old,
Seemed taking flight for heaven, without a death,
Past the sweet Virgin's picture, while his prayer he
    saith.

II

His prayer he saith, this patient, holy man;
Then takes his lamp, and riseth from his knees,
And back returneth, meagre, barefoot, wan,
Along the chapel aisle by slow degrees:
The sculptured dead, on each side, seem to freeze,
Emprisoned in black, purgatorial rails;
Knights, ladies, praying in dumb orat'ries,
He passeth by; and his weak spirit fails
To think how they may ache in icy hoods and mails.

III

Northward he turneth through a little door,
And scarce three steps, ere Music's golden tongue
Flattered to tears this agèd man and poor;
But no – already had his deathbell rung:
The joys of all his life were said and sung:
His was harsh penance on St Agnes' Eve.
Another way he went, and soon among
Rough ashes sat he for his soul's reprieve,
And all night kept awake, for sinners' sake to grieve.

IV

That ancient Beadsman heard the prelude soft;
And so it chanced, for many a door was wide,
From hurry to and fro. Soon, up aloft,
The silver, snarling trumpets 'gan to chide:
The level chambers, ready with their pride,
Were glowing to receive a thousand guests:
The carvèd angels, ever eager-eyed,
Stared, where upon their heads the cornice rests,
With hair blown back, and wings put cross-wise on their breasts.

The Eve of St Agnes

V

At length burst in the argent revelry,
With plume, tiara, and all rich array,
Numerous as shadows haunting faerily
The brain, new-stuffed, in youth, with triumphs gay
Of old romance. These let us wish away,
And turn, sole-thoughted, to one Lady there,
Whose heart had brooded, all that wintry day,
On love, and winged St Agnes' saintly care,
As she had heard old dames full many times declare.

VI

They told her how, upon St Agnes' Eve,
Young virgins might have visions of delight,
And soft adorings from their loves receive
Upon the honeyed middle of the night,
If ceremonies due they did aright;
As, supperless to bed they must retire,
And couch supine their beauties, lily white;
Nor look behind, nor sideways, but require
Of Heaven with upward eyes for all that they desire.

VII

Full of this whim was thoughtful Madeline:
The music, yearning like a God in pain,
She scarcely heard: her maiden eyes divine,
Fixed on the floor, saw many a sweeping train
Pass by – she heeded not at all: in vain
Came many a tip-toe, amorous cavalier,
And back retired – not cooled by high disdain,
But she saw not: her heart was otherwhere.
She sighed for Agnes' dreams, the sweetest of the year.

VIII

She danced along with vague, regardless eyes,
Anxious her lips, her breathing quick and short:
The hallowed hour was near at hand: she sighs
Amid the timbrels, and the thronged resort
Of whisperers in anger, or in sport;
'Mid looks of love, defiance, hate, and scorn,
Hoodwinked with faery fancy – all amort,
Save to St Agnes and her lambs unshorn,
And all the bliss to be before to-morrow morn.

The Eve of St Agnes

IX

So, purposing each moment to retire,
She lingered still. Meantime, across the moors,
Had come young Porphyro, with heart on fire
For Madeline. Beside the portal doors,
Buttressed from moonlight, stands he, and implores
All saints to give him sight of Madeline
But for one moment in the tedious hours,
That he might gaze and worship all unseen;
Perchance speak, kneel, touch, kiss – in sooth such
    things have been.

X

He ventures in – let no buzzed whisper tell,
All eyes be muffled, or a hundred swords
Will storm his heart, Love's fev'rous citadel:
For him, those chambers held barbarian hordes,
Hyena foemen, and hot-blooded lords,
Whose very dogs would execrations howl
Against his lineage: not one breast affords
Him any mercy, in that mansion foul,
Save one old beldame, weak in body and in soul.

XI

Ah, happy chance! the agèd creature came,
Shuffling along with ivory-headed wand,
To where he stood, hid from the torch's flame,
Behind a broad hall-pillar, far beyond
The sound of merriment and chorus bland:
He startled her; but soon she knew his face,
And grasped his fingers in her palsied hand,
Saying, 'Mercy, Porphyro! hie thee from this place:
They are all here to-night, the whole blood-thirsty race!

XII

'Get hence! get hence! there's dwarfish Hildebrand –
He had a fever late, and in the fit
He cursèd thee and thine, both house and land:
Then there's that old Lord Maurice, not a whit
More tame for his grey hairs – Alas me! flit!
Flit like a ghost away.' 'Ah, gossip dear,
We're safe enough; here in this arm-chair sit,
And tell me how –' 'Good Saints! not here, not here;
Follow me, child, or else these stones will be thy bier.'

XIII

He followed through a lowly archèd way,
Brushing the cobwebs with his lofty plume,
And as she muttered, 'Well-a – well-a-day!'
He found him in a little moonlight room,
Pale, latticed, chill, and silent as a tomb.
'Now tell me where is Madeline,' said he,
'O tell me, Angela, by the holy loom
Which none but secret sisterhood may see,
When they St Agnes' wool are weaving piously.'

XIV

'St Agnes? Ah! it is St Agnes' Eve –
Yet men will murder upon holy days:
Thou must hold water in a witch's sieve,
And be liege-lord of all the Elves and Fays,
To venture so: it fills me with amaze
To see thee, Porphyro! – St Agnes' Eve!
God's help! my lady fair the conjuror plays
This very night. Good angels her deceive!
But let me laugh a while, I've mickle time to grieve.'

XV

Feebly she laugheth in the languid moon,
While Porphyro upon her face doth look,
Like puzzled urchin on an agèd crone
Who keepeth closed a wondrous riddle-book,
As spectacled she sits in chimney nook.
But soon his eyes grew brilliant, when she told
His lady's purpose; and he scarce could brook
Tears, at the thought of those enchantments cold,
And Madeline asleep in lap of legends old.

XVI

Sudden a thought came like a full-blown rose,
Flushing his brow, and in his painèd heart
Made purple riot; then doth he propose
A stratagem, that makes the beldame start:
'A cruel man and impious thou art:
Sweet lady, let her pray, and sleep, and dream
Alone with her good angels, far apart
From wicked men like thee. Go, go! – I deem
Thou canst not surely be the same that thou didst seem.'

XVII

'I will not harm her, by all saints I swear,'
Quoth Porphyro: 'O may I ne'er find grace
When my weak voice shall whisper its last prayer,
If one of her soft ringlets I displace,
Or look with ruffian passion in her face:
Good Angela, believe me by these tears,
Or I will, even in a moment's space,
Awake, with horrid shout, my foeman's ears,
And beard them, though they be more fanged than wolves and bears.'

XVIII

'Ah! why wilt thou affright a feeble soul?
A poor, weak, palsy-stricken, churchyard thing,
Whose passing-bell may ere the midnight toll;
Whose prayers for thee, each morn and evening,
Were never missed.' – Thus plaining, doth she bring
A gentler speech from burning Porphyro,
So woeful, and of such deep sorrowing,
That Angela gives promise she will do
Whatever he shall wish, betide her weal or woe.

XIX

Which was, to lead him, in close secrecy,
Even to Madeline's chamber, and there hide
Him in a closet, of such privacy
That he might see her beauty unespied,
And win perhaps that night a peerless bride,
While legioned faeries paced the coverlet,
And pale enchantment held her sleepy-eyed.
Never on such a night have lovers met,
Since Merlin paid his Demon all the monstrous debt.

XX

'It shall be as thou wishest,' said the Dame:
'All cates and dainties shall be storèd there
Quickly on this feast-night; by the tambour frame
Her own lute thou wilt see. No time to spare,
For I am slow and feeble, and scarce dare
On such a catering trust my dizzy head.
Wait here, my child, with patience; kneel in prayer
The while. Ah! thou must needs the lady wed,
Or may I never leave my grave among the dead.'

XXI

So saying, she hobbled off with busy fear.
The lover's endless minutes slowly passed;
The dame returned, and whispered in his ear
To follow her; with agèd eyes aghast
From fright of dim espial. Safe at last,
Through many a dusky gallery, they gain
The maiden's chamber, silken, hushed, and chaste;
Where Porphyro took covert, pleased amain.
His poor guide hurried back with agues in her brain.

XXII

Her faltering hand upon the balustrade,
Old Angela was feeling for the stair,
When Madeline, St Agnes' charmèd maid,
Rose, like a missioned spirit, unaware:
With silver taper's light, and pious care,
She turned, and down the agèd gossip led
To a safe level matting. Now prepare,
Young Porphyro, for gazing on that bed –
She comes, she comes again, like ring-dove frayed and
    fled.

XXIII

Out went the taper as she hurried in;
Its little smoke, in pallid moonshine, died:
She closed the door, she panted, all akin
To spirits of the air, and visions wide –
No uttered syllable, or, woe betide!
But to her heart, her heart was voluble,
Paining with eloquence her balmy side;
As though a tongueless nightingale should swell
Her throat in vain, and die, heart-stiflèd, in her dell.

XXIV

A casement high and triple-arched there was,
All garlanded with carven imag'ries
Of fruits, and flowers, and bunches of knot-grass,
And diamonded with panes of quaint device,
Innumerable of stains and splendid dyes,
As are the tiger-moth's deep-damasked wings;
And in the midst, 'mong thousand heraldries,
And twilight saints, and dim emblazonings,
A shielded scutcheon blushed with blood of queens and
    kings.

The Eve of St Agnes

XXV

Full on this casement shone the wintry moon,
And threw warm gules on Madeline's fair breast,
As down she knelt for heaven's grace and boon;
Rose-bloom fell on her hands, together pressed,
And on her silver cross soft amethyst,
And on her hair a glory, like a saint:
She seemed a splendid angel, newly dressed,
Save wings, for Heaven – Porphyro grew faint;
She knelt, so pure a thing, so free from mortal taint.

XXVI

Anon his heart revives; her vespers done,
Of all its wreathèd pearls her hair she frees;
Unclasps her warmèd jewels one by one;
Loosens her fragrant bodice; by degrees
Her rich attire creeps rustling to her knees:
Half-hidden, like a mermaid in sea-weed,
Pensive awhile she dreams awake, and sees,
In fancy, fair St Agnes in her bed,
But dares not look behind, or all the charm is fled.

XXVII

Soon, trembling in her soft and chilly nest,
In sort of wakeful swoon, perplexed she lay,
Until the poppied warmth of sleep oppressed
Her soothèd limbs, and soul fatigued away –
Flown, like a thought, until the morrow-day;
Blissfully havened both from joy and pain;
Clasped like a missal where swart Paynims pray;
Blinded alike from sunshine and from rain,
As though a rose should shut, and be a bud again.

XXVIII

Stolen to this paradise, and so entranced,
Porphyro gazed upon her empty dress,
And listened to her breathing, if it chanced
To wake into a slumbrous tenderness;
Which when he heard, that minute did he bless,
And breathed himself: then from the closet crept,
Noiseless as fear in a wide wilderness,
And over the hushed carpet, silent, stepped,
And 'tween the curtains peeped, where, lo! – how fast
she slept.

XXIX

Then by the bed-side, where the faded moon
Made a dim, silver twilight, soft he set
A table, and, half anguished, threw thereon
A cloth of woven crimson, gold, and jet –
O for some drowsy Morphean amulet!
The boisterous, midnight, festive clarion,
The kettle-drum, and far-heard clarinet,
Affray his ears, though but in dying tone; –
The hall door shuts again, and all the noise is gone.

XXX

And still she slept an azure-lidded sleep,
In blanchèd linen, smooth, and lavendered,
While he from forth the closet brought a heap
Of candied apple, quince, and plum, and gourd,
With jellies soother than the creamy curd,
And lucent syrups, tinct with cinnamon;
Manna and dates, in argosy transferred
From Fez; and spicèd dainties, every one,
From silken Samarkand to cedared Lebanon.

XXXI

These delicates he heaped with glowing hand
On golden dishes and in baskets bright
Of wreathèd silver; sumptuous they stand
In the retirèd quiet of the night,
Filling the chilly room with perfume light.
'And now, my love, my seraph fair, awake!
Thou art my heaven, and I thine eremite:
Open thine eyes, for meek St Agnes' sake,
Or I shall drowse beside thee, so my soul doth ache.'

XXXII

Thus whispering, his warm, unnervèd arm
Sank in her pillow. Shaded was her dream
By the dusk curtains – 'twas a midnight charm
Impossible to melt as icèd stream:
The lustrous salvers in the moonlight gleam;
Broad golden fringe upon the carpet lies.
It seemed he never, never could redeem
From such a steadfast spell his lady's eyes;
So mused awhile, entoiled in woofèd fantasies.

XXXIII

Awakening up, he took her hollow lute,
Tumultuous, and, in chords that tenderest be,
He played an ancient ditty, long since mute,
In Provence called, 'La belle dame sans mercy',
Close to her ear touching the melody –
Wherewith disturbed, she uttered a soft moan:
He ceased – she panted quick – and suddenly
Her blue affrayèd eyes wide open shone.
Upon his knees he sank, pale as smooth-sculptured stone.

XXXIV

Her eyes were open, but she still beheld,
Now wide awake, the vision of her sleep –
There was a painful change, that nigh expelled
The blisses of her dream so pure and deep.
At which fair Madeline began to weep,
And moan forth witless words with many a sigh,
While still her gaze on Porphyro would keep;
Who knelt, with joinèd hands and piteous eye,
Fearing to move or speak, she looked so dreamingly.

XXXV

'Ah, Porphyro!' said she, 'but even now
Thy voice was at sweet tremble in mine ear,
Made tuneable with every sweetest vow,
And those sad eyes were spiritual and clear:
How changed thou art! How pallid, chill, and drear!
Give me that voice again, my Porphyro,
Those looks immortal, those complainings dear!
O leave me not in this eternal woe,
For if thou diest, my Love, I know not where to go.'

XXXVI

Beyond a mortal man impassioned far
At these voluptuous accents, he arose,
Ethereal, flushed, and like a throbbing star
Seen mid the sapphire heaven's deep repose;
Into her dream he melted, as the rose
Blendeth its odour with the violet –
Solution sweet. Meantime the frost-wind blows
Like Love's alarum pattering the sharp sleet
Against the window-panes; St Agnes' moon hath set.

XXXVII

'Tis dark: quick pattereth the flaw-blown sleet.
'This is no dream, my bride, my Madeline!'
'Tis dark: the icèd gusts still rave and beat.
'No dream, alas! alas! and woe is mine!
Porphyro will leave me here to fade and pine. –
Cruel! what traitor could thee hither bring?
I curse not, for my heart is lost in thine,
Though thou forsakest a deceivèd thing –
A dove forlorn and lost with sick unprunèd wing.'

XXXVIII

'My Madeline! sweet dreamer! lovely bride!
Say, may I be for aye thy vassal blessed?
Thy beauty's shield, heart-shaped and vermeil dyed?
Ah, silver shrine, here will I take my rest
After so many hours of toil and quest,
A famished pilgrim – saved by miracle.
Though I have found, I will not rob thy nest
Saving of thy sweet self; if thou think'st well
To trust, fair Madeline, to no rude infidel.

XXXIX

'Hark! 'tis an elfin-storm from faery land,
Of haggard seeming, but a boon indeed:
Arise – arise! the morning is at hand.
The bloated wassaillers will never heed –
Let us away, my love, with happy speed –
There are no ears to hear, or eyes to see, –
Drowned all in Rhenish and the sleepy mead;
Awake! arise! my love, and fearless be,
For o'er the southern moors I have a home for thee.'

XL

She hurried at his words, beset with fears,
For there were sleeping dragons all around,
At glaring watch, perhaps, with ready spears –
Down the wide stairs a darkling way they found.
In all the house was heard no human sound.
A chain-drooped lamp was flickering by each door;
The arras, rich with horseman, hawk, and hound,
Fluttered in the besieging wind's uproar;
And the long carpets rose along the gusty floor.

The Eve of St Agnes

XLI

They glide, like phantoms, into the wide hall;
Like phantoms, to the iron porch, they glide;
Where lay the Porter, in uneasy sprawl,
With a huge empty flaggon by his side:
The wakeful bloodhound rose, and shook his hide,
But his sagacious eye an inmate owns.
By one, and one, the bolts full easy slide –
The chains lie silent on the footworn stones –
The key turns, and the door upon its hinges groans.

XLII

And they are gone – ay, ages long ago
These lovers fled away into the storm.
That night the Baron dreamt of many a woe,
And all his warrior-guests, with shade and form
Of witch, and demon, and large coffin-worm,
Were long be-nightmared. Angela the old
Died palsy-twitched, with meagre face deform;
The Beadsman, after thousand aves told,
For aye unsought for slept among his ashes cold.

La Belle Dame sans Merci. A Ballad

I

O what can ail thee, knight-at-arms,
    Alone and palely loitering?
The sedge has withered from the lake,
    And no birds sing.

II

O what can ail thee, knight-at-arms,
    So haggard and so woe-begone?
The squirrel's granary is full,
    And the harvest's done.

III

I see a lily on thy brow,
    With anguish moist and fever-dew,
And on thy cheeks a fading rose
    Fast withereth too.

La Belle Dame sans Merci. A Ballad

IV

I met a lady in the meads,
    Full beautiful – a faery's child,
Her hair was long, her foot was light,
    And her eyes were wild.

V

I made a garland for her head,
    And bracelets too, and fragrant zone;
She looked at me as she did love,
    And made sweet moan.

VI

I set her on my pacing steed,
    And nothing else saw all day long,
For sidelong would she bend, and sing
    A faery's song.

VII

She found me roots of relish sweet,
    And honey wild, and manna-dew,
And sure in language strange she said –
    'I love thee true'.

VIII

She took me to her elfin grot,
    And there she wept and sighed full sore,
And there I shut her wild wild eyes
    With kisses four.

IX

And there she lullèd me asleep
    And there I dreamed – Ah! woe betide! –
The latest dream I ever dreamt
    On the cold hill side.

La Belle Dame sans Merci. A Ballad

X

I saw pale kings and princes too,
    Pale warriors, death-pale were they all;
They cried – 'La Belle Dame sans Merci
    Thee hath in thrall!'

XI

I saw their starved lips in the gloam,
    With horrid warning gapèd wide,
And I awoke and found me here,
    On the cold hill's side.

XII

And this is why I sojourn here
    Alone and palely loitering,
Though the sedge is withered from the lake,
    And no birds sing.

Lamia

PART I

Upon a time, before the faery broods
Drove Nymph and Satyr from the prosperous woods,
Before King Oberon's bright diadem,
Sceptre, and mantle, clasped with dewy gem,
Frighted away the Dryads and the Fauns
From rushes green, and brakes, and cowslipped lawns,
The ever-smitten Hermes empty left
His golden throne, bent warm on amorous theft:
From high Olympus had he stolen light,
On this side of Jove's clouds, to escape the sight
Of his great summoner, and made retreat
Into a forest on the shores of Crete.
For somewhere in that sacred island dwelt
A nymph, to whom all hoofèd Satyrs knelt,
At whose white feet the languid Tritons poured
Pearls, while on land they withered and adored.
Fast by the springs where she to bathe was wont,
And in those meads where sometime she might haunt,
Were strewn rich gifts, unknown to any Muse,
Though Fancy's casket were unlocked to choose.
Ah, what a world of love was at her feet!
So Hermes thought, and a celestial heat
Burnt from his wingèd heels to either ear,
That from a whiteness, as the lily clear,

Blushed into roses 'mid his golden hair,
Fallen in jealous curls about his shoulders bare.

   From vale to vale, from wood to wood, he flew,
Breathing upon the flowers his passion new,
And wound with many a river to its head
To find where this sweet nymph prepared her
     secret bed.
In vain; the sweet nymph might nowhere be found,
And so he rested, on the lonely ground,
Pensive, and full of painful jealousies
Of the Wood-Gods, and even the very trees.
There as he stood, he heard a mournful voice,
Such as, once heard, in gentle heart destroys
All pain but pity; thus the lone voice spake:
'When from this wreathèd tomb shall I awake!
When move in a sweet body fit for life,
And love, and pleasure, and the ruddy strife
Of hearts and lips! Ah, miserable me!'
The God, dove-footed, glided silently
Round bush and tree, soft-brushing, in his speed,
The taller grasses and full-flowering weed,
Until he found a palpitating snake,
Bright, and cirque-couchant in a dusky brake.

   She was a gordian shape of dazzling hue,
Vermilion-spotted, golden, green, and blue;
Striped like a zebra, freckled like a pard,
Eyed like a peacock, and all crimson barred;
And full of silver moons, that, as she breathed,
Dissolved, or brighter shone, or interwreathed

John Keats

Their lustres with the gloomier tapestries –
So rainbow-sided, touched with miseries,
She seemed, at once, some penanced lady elf,
Some demon's mistress, or the demon's self.
Upon her crest she wore a wannish fire
Sprinkled with stars, like Ariadne's tiar;
Her head was serpent, but ah, bitter-sweet!
She had a woman's mouth with all its pearls complete;
And for her eyes – what could such eyes do there
But weep, and weep, that they were born so fair,
As Proserpine still weeps for her Sicilian air?
Her throat was serpent, but the words she spake
Came, as through bubbling honey, for Love's sake,
And thus – while Hermes on his pinions lay,
Like a stooped falcon ere he takes his prey –

   'Fair Hermes, crowned with feathers, fluttering light,
I had a splendid dream of thee last night:
I saw thee sitting, on a throne of gold,
Among the Gods, upon Olympus old,
The only sad one; for thou didst not hear
The soft, lute-fingered Muses chanting clear,
Nor even Apollo when he sang alone,
Deaf to his throbbing throat's long, long melodious
    moan.
I dreamt I saw thee, robed in purple flakes,
Break amorous through the clouds, as morning breaks,
And, swiftly as a bright Phoebean dart,
Strike for the Cretan isle; and here thou art!
Too gentle Hermes, hast thou found the maid?'

Lamia

Whereat the star of Lethe not delayed
His rosy eloquence, and thus inquired:
'Thou smooth-lipped serpent, surely high inspired!
Thou beauteous wreath, with melancholy eyes,
Possess whatever bliss thou canst devise,
Telling me only where my nymph is fled –
Where she doth breathe!' 'Bright planet, thou hast said,'
Returned the snake, 'but seal with oaths, fair God!'
'I swear,' said Hermes, 'by my serpent rod,
And by thine eyes, and by thy starry crown!'
Light flew his earnest words, among the blossoms blown.
Then thus again the brilliance feminine:
'Too frail of heart! for this lost nymph of thine,
Free as the air, invisibly, she strays
About these thornless wilds; her pleasant days
She tastes unseen; unseen her nimble feet
Leave traces in the grass and flowers sweet;
From weary tendrils, and bowed branches green,
She plucks the fruit unseen, she bathes unseen;
And by my power is her beauty veiled
To keep it unaffronted, unassailed
By the love-glances of unlovely eyes
Of Satyrs, Fauns, and bleared Silenus' sighs.
Pale grew her immortality, for woe
Of all these lovers, and she grievèd so
I took compassion on her, bade her steep
Her hair in weïrd syrops, that would keep
Her loveliness invisible, yet free
To wander as she loves, in liberty.
Thou shalt behold her, Hermes, thou alone,

John Keats

If thou wilt, as thou swearest, grant my boon!'
Then, once again, the charmèd God began
An oath, and through the serpent's ears it ran
Warm, tremulous, devout, psalterian.
Ravished, she lifted her Circean head,
Blushed a live damask, and swift-lisping said,
'I was a woman, let me have once more
A woman's shape, and charming as before.
I love a youth of Corinth – O the bliss!
Give me my woman's form, and place me where he is.
Stoop, Hermes, let me breathe upon thy brow,
And thou shalt see thy sweet nymph even now.'
The God on half-shut feathers sank serene,
She breathed upon his eyes, and swift was seen
Of both the guarded nymph near-smiling on the green.
It was no dream; or say a dream it was,
Real are the dreams of Gods, and smoothly pass
Their pleasures in a long immortal dream.
One warm, flushed moment, hovering, it might seem
Dashed by the wood-nymph's beauty, so he burned;
Then, lighting on the printless verdure, turned
To the swooned serpent, and with languid arm,
Delicate, put to proof the lithe Caducean charm.
So done, upon the nymph his eyes he bent
Full of adoring tears and blandishment,
And towards her stepped: she, like a moon in wane,
Faded before him, cowered, nor could restrain
Her fearful sobs, self-folding like a flower
That faints into itself at evening hour:
But the God fostering her chillèd hand,

Lamia

She felt the warmth, her eyelids opened bland,
And, like new flowers at morning song of bees,
Bloomed, and gave up her honey to the lees.
Into the green-recessèd woods they flew;
Nor grew they pale, as mortal lovers do.

    Left to herself, the serpent now began
To change; her elfin blood in madness ran,
Her mouth foamed, and the grass, therewith besprent,
Withered at dew so sweet and virulent;
Her eyes in torture fixed, and anguish drear,
Hot, glazed, and wide, with lid-lashes all sear,
Flashed phosphor and sharp sparks, without one
        cooling tear.
The colours all inflamed throughout her train,
She writhed about, convulsed with scarlet pain:
A deep volcanian yellow took the place
Of all her milder-moonèd body's grace;
And, as the lava ravishes the mead,
Spoilt all her silver mail, and golden brede;
Made gloom of all her frecklings, streaks and bars,
Eclipsed her crescents, and licked up her stars.
So that, in moments few, she was undressed
Of all her sapphires, greens, and amethyst,
And rubious-argent; of all these bereft,
Nothing but pain and ugliness were left.
Still shone her crown; that vanished, also she
Melted and disappeared as suddenly;
And in the air, her new voice luting soft,
Cried, 'Lycius! gentle Lycius!' – Borne aloft

With the bright mists about the mountains hoar
These words dissolved: Crete's forests heard no more.

    Whither fled Lamia, now a lady bright,
A full-born beauty new and exquisite?
She fled into that valley they pass o'er
Who go to Corinth from Cenchreas' shore;
And rested at the foot of those wild hills,
The rugged founts of the Peræan rills,
And of that other ridge whose barren back
Stretches, with all its mist and cloudy rack,
South-westward to Cleone. There she stood
About a young bird's flutter from a wood,
Fair, on a sloping green of mossy tread,
By a clear pool, wherein she passionèd
To see herself escaped from so sore ills,
While her robes flaunted with the daffodils.

    Ah, happy Lycius! – for she was a maid
More beautiful than ever twisted braid,
Or sighed, or blushed, or on spring-flowered lea
Spread a green kirtle to the minstrelsy:
A virgin purest lipped, yet in the lore
Of love deep learnèd to the red heart's core;
Not one hour old, yet of sciential brain
To unperplex bliss from its neighbour pain,
Define their pettish limits, and estrange
Their points of contact, and swift counterchange;
Intrigue with the specious chaos, and dispart
Its most ambiguous atoms with sure art;
As though in Cupid's college she had spent

Lamia

Sweet days a lovely graduate, still unshent,
And kept his rosy terms in idle languishment.

   Why this fair creature chose so faerily
By the wayside to linger, we shall see;
But first 'tis fit to tell how she could muse
And dream, when in the serpent prison-house,
Of all she list, strange or magnificent:
How, ever, where she willed, her spirit went;
Whether to faint Elysium, or where
Down through tress-lifting waves the Nereids fair
Wind into Thetis' bower by many a pearly stair;
Or where God Bacchus drains his cups divine,
Stretched out, at ease, beneath a glutinous pine;
Or where in Pluto's gardens palatine
Mulciber's columns gleam in far piazzian line.
And sometimes into cities she would send
Her dream, with feast and rioting to blend;
And once, while among mortals dreaming thus,
She saw the young Corinthian Lycius
Charioting foremost in the envious race,
Like a young Jove with calm uneager face,
And fell into a swooning love of him.
Now on the moth-time of that evening dim
He would return that way, as well she knew,
To Corinth from the shore; for freshly blew
The eastern soft wind, and his galley now
Grated the quaystones with her brazen prow
In port Cenchreas, from Egina isle
Fresh anchored; whither he had been awhile

John Keats

To sacrifice to Jove, whose temple there
Waits with high marble doors for blood and incense rare.
Jove heard his vows, and bettered his desire;
For by some freakful chance he made retire
From his companions, and set forth to walk,
Perhaps grown wearied of their Corinth talk:
Over the solitary hills he fared,
Thoughtless at first, but ere eve's star appeared
His fantasy was lost, where reason fades,
In the calmed twilight of Platonic shades.
Lamia beheld him coming, near, more near –
Close to her passing, in indifference drear,
His silent sandals swept the mossy green;
So neighboured to him, and yet so unseen
She stood: he passed, shut up in mysteries,
His mind wrapped like his mantle, while her eyes
Followed his steps, and her neck regal white
Turned – syllabling thus, 'Ah, Lycius bright,
And will you leave me on the hills alone?
Lycius, look back! and be some pity shown.'
He did – not with cold wonder fearingly,
But Orpheus-like at an Eurydice –
For so delicious were the words she sung,
It seemed he had loved them a whole summer long.
And soon his eyes had drunk her beauty up,
Leaving no drop in the bewildering cup,
And still the cup was full – while he, afraid
Lest she should vanish ere his lip had paid
Due adoration, thus began to adore
(Her soft look growing coy, she saw his chain so sure):

Lamia

'Leave thee alone! Look back! Ah, Goddess, see
Whether my eyes can ever turn from thee!
For pity do not this sad heart belie –
Even as thou vanishest so I shall die.
Stay! though a Naiad of the rivers, stay!
To thy far wishes will thy streams obey.
Stay! though the greenest woods by thy domain,
Alone they can drink up the morning rain:
Though a descended Pleiad, will not one
Of thine harmonious sisters keep in tune
Thy spheres, and as thy silver proxy shine?
So sweetly to these ravished ears of mine
Came thy sweet greeting, that if thou shouldst fade
Thy memory will waste me to a shade –
For pity do not melt!' – 'If I should stay,'
Said Lamia, 'here, upon this floor of clay,
And pain my steps upon these flowers too rough,
What canst thou say or do of charm enough
To dull the nice remembrance of my home?
Thou canst not ask me with thee here to roam
Over these hills and vales, where no joy is –
Empty of immortality and bliss!
Thou art a scholar, Lycius, and must know
That finer spirits cannot breathe below
In human climes, and live. Alas! poor youth,
What taste of purer air hast thou to soothe
My essence? What serener palaces,
Where I may all my many senses please,
And by mysterious sleights a hundred thirsts appease?
It cannot be – Adieu!' So said, she rose

Tip-toe with white arms spread. He, sick to lose
The amorous promise of her lone complain,
Swooned, murmuring of love, and pale with pain.
The cruel lady, without any show
Of sorrow for her tender favourite's woe,
But rather, if her eyes could brighter be,
With brighter eyes and slow amenity,
Put her new lips to his, and gave afresh
The life she had so tangled in her mesh;
And as he from one trance was wakening
Into another, she began to sing,
Happy in beauty, life, and love, and every thing,
A song of love, too sweet for earthly lyres,
While, like held breath, the stars drew in their panting
    fires.
And then she whispered in such trembling tone,
As those who, safe together met alone
For the first time through many anguished days,
Use other speech than looks; bidding him raise
His drooping head, and clear his soul of doubt,
For that she was a woman, and without
Any more subtle fluid in her veins
Than throbbing blood, and that the self-same pains
Inhabited her frail-strung heart as his.
And next she wondered how his eyes could miss
Her face so long in Corinth, where, she said,
She dwelt but half retired, and there had led
Days happy as the gold coin could invent
Without the aid of love; yet in content
Till she saw him, as once she passed him by,

Lamia

Where 'gainst a column he leant thoughtfully
At Venus' temple porch, 'mid baskets heaped
Of amorous herbs and flowers, newly reaped
Late on that eve, as 'twas the night before
The Adonian feast; where of she saw no more,
But wept alone those days, for why should she adore?
Lycius from death awoke into amaze,
To see her still, and singing so sweet lays;
Then from amaze into delight he fell
To hear her whisper woman's lore so well;
And every word she spake enticed him on
To unperplexed delight and pleasure known.
Let the mad poets say whate'er they please
Of the sweets of Faeries, Peris, Goddesses,
There is not such a treat among them all,
Haunters of cavern, lake, and waterfall,
As a real woman, lineal indeed
From Pyrrha's pebbles or old Adam's seed.
Thus gentle Lamia judged, and judged aright,
That Lycius could not love in half a fright,
So threw the goddess off, and won his heart
More pleasantly by playing woman's part,
With no more awe than what her beauty gave,
That, while it smote, still guaranteed to save.
Lycius to all made eloquent reply,
Marrying to every word a twinborn sigh;
And last, pointing to Corinth, asked her sweet,
If 'twas was too far that night for her soft feet.
The way was short, for Lamia's eagerness

Made, by a spell, the triple league decrease
To a few paces; not at all surmised
By blinded Lycius, so in her comprised.
They passed the city gates, he knew not how,
So noiseless, and he never thought to know.

As men talk in a dream, so Corinth all,
Throughout her palaces imperial,
And all her populous streets and temples lewd,
Muttered, like tempest in the distance brewed,
To the wide-spreaded night above her towers.
Men, women, rich and poor, in the cool hours,
Shuffled their sandals o'er the pavement white,
Companioned or alone; while many a light
Flared, here and there, from wealthy festivals,
And threw their moving shadows on the walls,
Or found them clustered in the corniced shade
Of some arched temple door, or dusky colonnade.

Muffling his face, of greeting friends in fear,
Her fingers he pressed hard, as one came near
With curled grey beard, sharp eyes, and smooth bald crown,
Slow-stepped, and robed in philosophic gown:
Lycius shrank closer, as they met and passed,
Into his mantle, adding wings to haste,
While hurried Lamia trembled: 'Ah,' said he,
'Why do you shudder, love, so ruefully?
Why does your tender palm dissolve in dew?' –
'I'm wearied,' said fair Lamia, 'tell me who

Lamia

Is that old man? I cannot bring to mind
His features – Lycius! wherefore did you blind
Yourself from his quick eyes?' Lycius replied,
' 'Tis Apollonius sage, my trusty guide
And good instructor; but tonight he seems
The ghost of folly haunting my sweet dreams.'

   While yet he spake they had arrived before
A pillared porch, with lofty portal door,
Where hung a silver lamp, whose phosphor glow
Reflected in the slabbèd steps below,
Mild as a star in water; for so new,
And so unsullied was the marble hue,
So through the crystal polish, liquid fine,
Ran the dark veins, that none but feet divine
Could e'er have touched there. Sounds Aeolian
Breathed from the hinges, as the ample span
Of the wide doors disclosed a place unknown
Some time to any, but those two alone,
And a few Persian mutes, who that same year
Were seen about the markets: none knew where
They could inhabit; the most curious
Were foiled, who watched to trace them to their
     house.
And but the flitter-wingèd verse must tell,
For truth's sake, what woe afterwards befell,
'Twould humour many a heart to leave them thus,
Shut from the busy world, of more incredulous.

PART II

Love in a hut, with water and a crust,
Is – Love, forgive us! – cinder, ashes, dust;
Love in a palace is perhaps at last
More grievous torment than a hermit's fast.
That is a doubtful tale from faery land,
Hard for the non-elect to understand.
Had Lycius lived to hand his story down,
He might have given the moral a fresh frown,
Or clenched it quite: but too short was their bliss
To breed distrust and hate, that make the soft voice
    hiss.
Besides, there, nightly, with terrific glare,
Love, jealous grown of so complete a pair,
Hovered and buzzed his wings, with fearful roar,
Above the lintel of their chamber door,
And down the passage cast a glow upon the floor.

    For all this came a ruin: side by side
They were enthronèd, in the eventide,
Upon a couch, near to a curtaining
Whose airy texture, from a golden string,
Floated into the room, and let appear
Unveiled the summer heaven, blue and clear,
Betwixt two marble shafts. There they reposed,
Where use had made it sweet, with eyelids closed,
Saving a tithe which love still open kept,
That they might see each other while they almost slept;

Lamia

When from the slope side of a suburb hill,
Deafening the swallow's twitter, came a thrill
Of trumpets – Lycius started – the sounds fled,
But left a thought, a buzzing in his head.
For the first time, since first he harboured in
That purple-linèd palace of sweet sin,
His spirit passed beyond its golden bourne
Into the noisy world almost forsworn.
The lady, ever watchful, penetrant,
Saw this with pain, so arguing a want
Of something more, more than her empery
Of joys; and she began to moan and sigh
Because he mused beyond her, knowing well
That but a moment's thought is passion's passing-bell.
'Why do you sigh, fair creature?' whispered he:
'Why do you think?' returned she tenderly,
'You have deserted me – where am I now?
Not in your heart while care weighs on your brow:
No, no, you have dismissed me; and I go
From your breast houseless – ay, it must be so.'
He answered, bending to her open eyes,
Where he was mirrored small in paradise,
'My silver planet, both of eve and morn!
Why will you plead yourself so sad forlorn,
While I am striving how to fill my heart
With deeper crimson, and a double smart?
How to entangle, trammel up and snare
Your soul in mine, and labyrinth you there
Like the hid scent in an unbudded rose?
Ay, a sweet kiss – you see your mighty woes.

My thoughts! shall I unveil them? Listen then!
What mortal hath a prize, that other men
May be confounded and abashed withal,
But lets it sometimes pace abroad majestical,
And triumph, as in thee I should rejoice
Amid the hoarse alarm of Corinth's voice.
Let my foes choke, and my friends shout afar,
While through the throngèd streets your bridal car
Wheels round its dazzling spokes.' – The lady's cheek
Trembled; she nothing said, but, pale and meek,
Arose and knelt before him, wept a rain
Of sorrows at his words; at last with pain
Beseeching him, the while his hand she wrung,
To change his purpose. He thereat was stung,
Perverse, with stronger fancy to reclaim
Her wild and timid nature to his aim:
Besides, for all his love, in self-despite,
Against his better self, he took delight
Luxurious in her sorrows, soft and new.
His passion, cruel grown, took on a hue
Fierce and sanguineous as 'twas possible
In one whose brow had no dark veins to swell.
Fine was the mitigated fury, like
Apollo's presence when in act to strike
The serpent – Ha, the serpent! Certes, she
Was none. She burnt, she loved the tyranny,
And, all subdued, consented to the hour
When to the bridal he should lead his paramour.
Whispering in midnight silence, said the youth,
'Sure some sweet name thou hast, though, by my truth,

Lamia

I have not asked it, ever thinking thee
Not mortal, but of heavenly progeny,
As still I do. Hast any mortal name,
Fit appellation for this dazzling frame?
Or friends or kinsfolk on the citied earth,
To share our marriage feast and nuptial mirth?'
'I have no friends,' said Lamia, 'no, not one;
My presence in wide Corinth hardly known:
My parents' bones are in their dusty urns
Sepulchred, where no kindled incense burns,
Seeing all their luckless race are dead, save me,
And I neglect the holy rite for thee.
Even as you list invite your many guests;
But if, as now it seems, your vision rests
With any pleasure on me, do not bid
Old Apollonius – from him keep me hid.'
Lycius, perplexed at words so blind and blank,
Made close inquiry; from whose touch she shrank,
Feigning a sleep; and he to the dull shade
Of deep sleep in a moment was betrayed.

    It was the custom then to bring away
The bride from home at blushing shut of day,
Veiled, in a chariot, heralded along
By strewn flowers, torches, and a marriage song,
With other pageants: but this fair unknown
Had not a friend. So being left alone,
(Lycius was gone to summon all his kin)
And knowing surely she could never win
His foolish heart from its mad pompousness,

She set herself, high-thoughted, how to dress
The misery in fit magnificence.
She did so, but 'tis doubtful how and whence
Came, and who were her subtle servitors.
About the halls, and to and from the doors,
There was a noise of wings, till in short space
The glowing banquet-room shone with wide-archèd
    grace.
A haunting music, sole perhaps and lone
Supportress of the faery-roof, made moan
Throughout, as fearful the whole charm might fade.
Fresh carvèd cedar, mimicking a glade
Of palm and plantain, met from either side,
High in the midst, in honour of the bride;
Two palms and then two plantains, and so on,
From either side their stems branched one to one
All down the aislèd place; and beneath all
There ran a stream of lamps straight on from wall to wall.
So canopied, lay an untasted feast
Teeming with odours. Lamia, regal dressed,
Silently paced about, and as she went,
In pale contented sort of discontent,
Missioned her viewless servants to enrich
The fretted splendour of each nook and niche.
Between the tree-stems, marbled plain at first,
Came jasper panels; then anon, there burst
Forth creeping imagery of slighter trees,
And with the larger wove in small intricacies.
Approving all, she faded at self-will,

Lamia

And shut the chamber up, close, hushed and still,
Complete and ready for the revels rude,
When dreadful guests would come to spoil her
    solitude.

    The day appeared, and all the gossip rout.
O senseless Lycius! Madman! wherefore flout
The silent-blessing fate, warm cloistered hours,
And show to common eyes these secret bowers?
The herd approached; each guest, with busy brain,
Arriving at the portal, gazed amain,
And entered marvelling – for they knew the street,
Remembered it from childhood all complete
Without a gap, yet ne'er before had seen
That royal porch, that high-built fair demesne.
So in they hurried all, mazed, curious and keen –
Save one, who looked thereon with eye severe,
And with calm-planted steps walked in austere.
'Twas Apollonius: something too he laughed,
As though some knotty problem, that had daffed
His patient thought, had now begun to thaw,
And solve and melt – 'twas just as he foresaw.

    He met within the murmurous vestibule
His young disciple. ''Tis no common rule,
Lycius,' said he, 'for uninvited guest
To force himself upon you, and infest
With an unbidden presence the bright throng
Of younger friends; yet must I do this wrong,
And you forgive me.' Lycius blushed, and led

John Keats

> The old man through the inner doors broad-
>   spread;
> With reconciling words and courteous mien
> Turning into sweet milk the sophist's spleen.
>
>   Of wealthy lustre was the banquet-room,
> Filled with pervading brilliance and perfume:
> Before each lucid panel fuming stood
> A censer fed with myrrh and spicèd wood,
> Each by a sacred tripod held aloft,
> Whose slender feet wide-swerved upon the soft
> Wool-woofèd carpets; fifty wreaths of smoke
> From fifty censers their light voyage took
> To the high roof, still mimicked as they rose
> Along the mirrored walls by twin-clouds
>   odorous.
> Twelve spherèd tables, by silk seats ensphered,
> High as the level of a man's breast reared
> On libbard's paws, upheld the heavy gold
> Of cups and goblets, and the store thrice told
> Of Ceres' horn, and in huge vessels, wine
> Come from the gloomy tun with merry shine.
> Thus loaded with a feast the tables stood,
> Each shrining in the midst the image of a God.
>
>   When in an antechamber every guest
> Had felt the cold full sponge to pleasure pressed,
> By ministering slaves, upon his hands and feet,
> And fragrant oils with ceremony meet
> Poured on his hair, they all moved to the feast
> In white robes, and themselves in order placed

Around the silken couches, wondering
Whence all this mighty cost and blaze of wealth
    could spring.

   Soft went the music the soft air along,
While fluent Greek a vowelled undersong
Kept up among the guests, discoursing low
At first, for scarcely was the wine at flow;
But when the happy vintage touched their brains,
Louder they talk, and louder come the strains
Of powerful instruments. The gorgeous dyes,
The space, the splendour of the draperies,
The roof of awful richness, nectarous cheer,
Beautiful slaves, and Lamia's self, appear,
Now, when the wine has done its rosy deed,
And every soul from human trammels freed,
No more so strange; for merry wine, sweet wine,
Will make Elysian shades not too fair, too divine.

   Soon was God Bacchus at meridian height;
Flushed were their cheeks, and bright eyes double
    bright:
Garlands of every green, and every scent
From vales deflowered, or forest-trees branch-rent,
In baskets of bright osiered gold were brought
High as the handles heaped, to suit the thought
Of every guest – that each, as he did please,
Might fancy-fit his brows, silk-pillowed at his ease.

   What wreath for Lamia? What for Lycius?
What for the sage, old Apollonius?

John Keats

Upon her aching forehead be there hung
The leaves of willow and of adder's tongue;
And for the youth, quick, let us strip for him
The thyrsus, that his watching eyes may swim
Into forgetfulness; and, for the sage,
Let spear-grass and the spiteful thistle wage
War on his temples. Do not all charms fly
At the mere touch of cold philosophy?
There was an awful rainbow once in heaven:
We know her woof, her texture; she is given
In the dull catalogue of common things.
Philosophy will clip an Angel's wings,
Conquer all mysteries by rule and line,
Empty the haunted air, and gnomèd mine –
Unweave a rainbow, as it erewhile made
The tender-personed Lamia melt into a shade.

    By her glad Lycius sitting, in chief place,
Scarce saw in all the room another face,
Till, checking his love trance, a cup he took
Full brimmed, and opposite sent forth a look
'Cross the broad table, to beseech a glance
From his old teacher's wrinkled countenance,
And pledge him. The bald-head philosopher
Had fixed his eye, without a twinkle or stir
Full on the alarmèd beauty of the bride,
Brow-beating her fair form, and troubling her sweet pride.
Lycius then pressed her hand, with devout touch,
As pale it lay upon the rosy couch:
'Twas icy, and the cold ran through his veins;

Lamia

Then sudden it grew hot, and all the pains
Of an unnatural heat shot to his heart.
'Lamia, what means this? Wherefore dost thou start?
Know'st thou that man?' Poor Lamia answered not.
He gazed into her eyes, and not a jot
Owned they the lovelorn piteous appeal;
More, more he gazed; his human senses reel;
Some hungry spell that loveliness absorbs;
There was no recognition in those orbs.
'Lamia!' he cried – and no soft-toned reply.
The many heard, and the loud revelry
Grew hush; the stately music no more breathes;
The myrtle sickened in a thousand wreaths.
By faint degrees, voice, lute, and pleasure ceased;
A deadly silence step by step increased,
Until it seemed a horrid presence there,
And not a man but felt the terror in his hair.
'Lamia!' he shrieked; and nothing but the shriek
With its sad echo did the silence break.
'Begone, foul dream!' he cried, gazing again
In the bride's face, where now no azure vein
Wandered on fair-spaced temples; no soft bloom
Misted the cheek; no passion to illume
The deep-recessèd vision. All was blight;
Lamia, no longer fair, there sat a deadly white.
'Shut, shut those juggling eyes, thou ruthless man!
Turn them aside, wretch! or the righteous ban
Of all the Gods, whose dreadful images
Here represent their shadowy presences,
May pierce them on the sudden with the thorn

John Keats

Of painful blindness; leaving thee forlorn,
In trembling dotage to the feeblest fright
Of conscience, for their long offended might,
For all thine impious proud-heart sophistries,
Unlawful magic, and enticing lies.
Corinthians! look upon that grey-beard wretch!
Mark how, possessed, his lashless eyelids stretch
Around his demon eyes! Corinthians, see!
My sweet bride withers at their potency.'
'Fool!' said the sophist, in an undertone
Gruff with contempt; which a death-nighing moan
From Lycius answered, as heart-struck and lost,
He sank supine beside the aching ghost.
'Fool! Fool!' repeated he, while his eyes still
Relented not, nor moved: 'From every ill
Of life have I preserved thee to this day,
And shall I see thee made a serpent's prey?'
Then Lamia breathed death-breath; the sophist's eye,
Like a sharp spear, went through her utterly,
Keen, cruel, perceant, stinging: she, as well
As her weak hand could any meaning tell,
Motioned him to be silent; vainly so,
He looked and looked again a level – *No!*
'A Serpent!' echoed he; no sooner said,
Than with a frightful scream she vanishèd:
And Lycius' arms were empty of delight,
As were his limbs of life, from that same night.
On the high couch he lay! – his friends came round –
Supported him – no pulse, or breath they found,
And, in its marriage robe, the heavy body wound.

Ode to Psyche

O Goddess! hear these tuneless numbers, wrung
    By sweet enforcement and remembrance dear,
And pardon that thy secrets should be sung
    Even into thine own soft-conchèd ear:
Surely I dreamt to-day, or did I see
    The wingèd Psyche with awakened eyes?
I wandered in a forest thoughtlessly,
    And, on the sudden, fainting with surprise,
Saw two fair creatures, couchèd side by side
    In deepest grass, beneath the whispering roof
    Of leaves and tremblèd blossoms, where there ran
        A brooklet, scarce espied:
'Mid hushed, cool-rooted flowers, fragrant-eyed,
    Blue, silver-white, and budded Tyrian,
They lay calm-breathing on the bedded grass;
    Their arms embraced, and their pinions too:
    Their lips touched not, but had not bade adieu,
As if disjoined by soft-handed slumber,
And ready still past kisses to outnumber
    At tender eye-dawn of aurorean love:
        The wingèd boy I knew;
    But who wast thou, O happy, happy dove?
        His Psyche true!

O latest born and loveliest vision far
    Of all Olympus' faded hierarchy!
Fairer than Phoebe's sapphire-regioned star,

Or Vesper, amorous glow-worm of the sky;
Fairer than these, though temple thou hast none,
    Nor altar heaped with flowers;
Nor virgin-choir to make delicious moan
    Upon the midnight hours;
No voice, no lute, no pipe, no incense sweet
    From chain-swung censer teeming;
No shrine, no grove, no oracle, no heat
    Of pale-mouthed prophet dreaming.

O brightest! though too late for antique vows,
    Too, too late for the fond believing lyre,
When holy were the haunted forest boughs,
    Holy the air, the water, and the fire;
Yet even in these days so far retired
    From happy pieties, thy lucent fans,
    Fluttering among the faint Olympians,
I see, and sing, by my own eyes inspired.
So let me be thy choir, and make a moan
    Upon the midnight hours;
Thy voice, thy lute, thy pipe, thy incense sweet
    From swingèd censer teeming –
Thy shrine, thy grove, thy oracle, thy heat
    Of pale-mouthed prophet dreaming.

Yes, I will be thy priest, and build a fane
    In some untrodden region of my mind,
Where branchèd thoughts, new grown with pleasant pain,
    Instead of pines shall murmur in the wind:
Far, far around shall those dark-clustered trees

Ode to Psyche

 Fledge the wild-ridgèd mountains steep by steep;
And there by zephyrs, streams, and birds, and bees,
 The moss-lain Dryads shall be lulled to sleep;
And in the midst of this wide quietness
A rosy sanctuary will I dress
With the wreathed trellis of a working brain,
 With buds, and bells, and stars without a name,
With all the gardener Fancy e'er could feign,
 Who breeding flowers, will never breed the same:
And there shall be for thee all soft delight
 That shadowy thought can win,
A bright torch, and a casement ope at night,
 To let the warm Love in!

Ode on a Grecian Urn

I

Thou still unravished bride of quietness,
    Thou foster-child of silence and slow time,
Sylvan historian, who canst thus express
    A flowery tale more sweetly than our rhyme:
What leaf-fringed legend haunts about thy shape
    Of deities or mortals, or of both,
        In Tempe or the dales of Arcady?
    What men or gods are these? What maidens loth?
What mad pursuit? What struggle to escape?
        What pipes and timbrels? What wild ecstasy?

II

Heard melodies are sweet, but those unheard
    Are sweeter; therefore, ye soft pipes, play on;
Not to the sensual ear, but, more endeared,
    Pipe to the spirit ditties of no tone:
Fair youth, beneath the trees, thou canst not leave
    Thy song, nor ever can those trees be bare;
        Bold Lover, never, never canst thou kiss,
Though winning near the goal – yet, do not grieve:
    She cannot fade, though thou hast not thy bliss,
        For ever wilt thou love, and she be fair!

III

Ah, happy, happy boughs! that cannot shed
    Your leaves, nor ever bid the Spring adieu;
And, happy melodist, unwearièd,
    For ever piping songs for ever new;
More happy love! more happy, happy love!
    For ever warm and still to be enjoyed,
        For ever panting, and for ever young –
All breathing human passion far above,
    That leaves a heart high-sorrowful and cloyed,
        A burning forehead, and a parching tongue.

IV

Who are these coming to the sacrifice?
    To what green altar, O mysterious priest,
Lead'st thou that heifer lowing at the skies,
    And all her silken flanks with garlands dressed?
What little town by river or sea shore,
    Or mountain-built with peaceful citadel,
        Is emptied of this folk, this pious morn?
And, little town, thy streets for evermore
    Will silent be; and not a soul to tell
        Why thou art desolate, can e'er return.

V

O Attic shape! Fair attitude! with brede
    Of marble men and maidens overwrought,
With forest branches and the trodden weed;
    Thou, silent form, dost tease us out of thought
As doth eternity: Cold Pastoral!
    When old age shall this generation waste,
        Thou shalt remain, in midst of other woe
Than ours, a friend to man, to whom thou say'st,
    'Beauty is truth, truth beauty, – that is all
        Ye know on earth, and all ye need to know.'

1. BOCCACCIO · *Mrs Rosie and the Priest*
2. GERARD MANLEY HOPKINS · *As kingfishers catch fire*
3. *The Saga of Gunnlaug Serpent-tongue*
4. THOMAS DE QUINCEY · *On Murder Considered as One of the Fine Arts*
5. FRIEDRICH NIETZSCHE · *Aphorisms on Love and Hate*
6. JOHN RUSKIN · *Traffic*
7. PU SONGLING · *Wailing Ghosts*
8. JONATHAN SWIFT · *A Modest Proposal*
9. *Three Tang Dynasty Poets*
10. WALT WHITMAN · *On the Beach at Night Alone*
11. KENKŌ · *A Cup of Sake Beneath the Cherry Trees*
12. BALTASAR GRACIÁN · *How to Use Your Enemies*
13. JOHN KEATS · *The Eve of St Agnes*
14. THOMAS HARDY · *Woman much missed*
15. GUY DE MAUPASSANT · *Femme Fatale*
16. MARCO POLO · *Travels in the Land of Serpents and Pearls*
17. SUETONIUS · *Caligula*
18. APOLLONIUS OF RHODES · *Jason and Medea*
19. ROBERT LOUIS STEVENSON · *Olalla*
20. KARL MARX AND FRIEDRICH ENGELS · *The Communist Manifesto*
21. PETRONIUS · *Trimalchio's Feast*
22. JOHANN PETER HEBEL · *How a Ghastly Story Was Brought to Light by a Common or Garden Butcher's Dog*
23. HANS CHRISTIAN ANDERSEN · *The Tinder Box*
24. RUDYARD KIPLING · *The Gate of the Hundred Sorrows*
25. DANTE · *Circles of Hell*
26. HENRY MAYHEW · *Of Street Piemen*
27. HAFEZ · *The nightingales are drunk*
28. GEOFFREY CHAUCER · *The Wife of Bath*
29. MICHEL DE MONTAIGNE · *How We Weep and Laugh at the Same Thing*
30. THOMAS NASHE · *The Terrors of the Night*
31. EDGAR ALLAN POE · *The Tell-Tale Heart*
32. MARY KINGSLEY · *A Hippo Banquet*
33. JANE AUSTEN · *The Beautifull Cassandra*
34. ANTON CHEKHOV · *Gooseberries*
35. SAMUEL TAYLOR COLERIDGE · *Well, they are gone, and here must I remain*
36. JOHANN WOLFGANG VON GOETHE · *Sketchy, Doubtful, Incomplete Jottings*
37. CHARLES DICKENS · *The Great Winglebury Duel*
38. HERMAN MELVILLE · *The Maldive Shark*
39. ELIZABETH GASKELL · *The Old Nurse's Story*
40. NIKOLAY LESKOV · *The Steel Flea*

41. HONORÉ DE BALZAC · *The Atheist's Mass*
42. CHARLOTTE PERKINS GILMAN · *The Yellow Wall-Paper*
43. C.P. CAVAFY · *Remember, Body . . .*
44. FYODOR DOSTOEVSKY · *The Meek One*
45. GUSTAVE FLAUBERT · *A Simple Heart*
46. NIKOLAI GOGOL · *The Nose*
47. SAMUEL PEPYS · *The Great Fire of London*
48. EDITH WHARTON · *The Reckoning*
49. HENRY JAMES · *The Figure in the Carpet*
50. WILFRED OWEN · *Anthem For Doomed Youth*
51. WOLFGANG AMADEUS MOZART · *My Dearest Father*
52. PLATO · *Socrates' Defence*
53. CHRISTINA ROSSETTI · *Goblin Market*
54. *Sindbad the Sailor*
55. SOPHOCLES · *Antigone*
56. RYŪNOSUKE AKUTAGAWA · *The Life of a Stupid Man*
57. LEO TOLSTOY · *How Much Land Does A Man Need?*
58. GIORGIO VASARI · *Leonardo da Vinci*
59. OSCAR WILDE · *Lord Arthur Savile's Crime*
60. SHEN FU · *The Old Man of the Moon*
61. AESOP · *The Dolphins, the Whales and the Gudgeon*
62. MATSUO BASHŌ · *Lips too Chilled*
63. EMILY BRONTË · *The Night is Darkening Round Me*
64. JOSEPH CONRAD · *To-morrow*
65. RICHARD HAKLUYT · *The Voyage of Sir Francis Drake Around the Whole Globe*
66. KATE CHOPIN · *A Pair of Silk Stockings*
67. CHARLES DARWIN · *It was snowing butterflies*
68. BROTHERS GRIMM · *The Robber Bridegroom*
69. CATULLUS · *I Hate and I Love*
70. HOMER · *Circe and the Cyclops*
71. D. H. LAWRENCE · *Il Duro*
72. KATHERINE MANSFIELD · *Miss Brill*
73. OVID · *The Fall of Icarus*
74. SAPPHO · *Come Close*
75. IVAN TURGENEV · *Kasyan from the Beautiful Lands*
76. VIRGIL · *O Cruel Alexis*
77. H. G. WELLS · *A Slip under the Microscope*
78. HERODOTUS · *The Madness of Cambyses*
79. *Speaking of Siva*
80. *The Dhammapada*

'Woman much missed, how you call to me, call to me . . .'

THOMAS HARDY

Born 1840, Higher Bockhampton, near Dorchester, England
Died 1928, Dorchester, England

In 1870, Thomas Hardy went to Cornwall, where he met and fell in love with Emma Gifford, his first wife. Emma's death, on 27 November 1912, inspired some of the finest verse of Hardy's career, including the sequence 'Poems 1912–13'. This selection includes these poems, along with others relating to Hardy's courtship, marriage and widowed life.

HARDY IN PENGUIN CLASSICS

Selected Poems
A Laodicean
A Pair of Blue Eyes
Desperate Remedies
Far from the Madding Crowd
Jude the Obscure
Tess of the D'Urbervilles
The Hand of Ethelberta
The Mayor of Casterbridge
The Pursuit of the Well-beloved and *the well-beloved*
The Return of the Native
The Trumpet-Major
The Woodlanders
Two on a Tower
Under the Greenwood Tree
The Distracted Preacher and Other Tales
The Fiddler of the Reels and Other Stories
The Withered Arm and Other Stories

THOMAS HARDY

Woman much missed

PENGUIN BOOKS

PENGUIN CLASSICS

UK | USA | Canada | Ireland | Australia
India | New Zealand | South Africa

Penguin Books is part of the Penguin Random House group of companies whose addresses can be found at global.penguinrandomhouse.com.

This selection published in Penguin Classics 2015

010

Set in 9.5/13 pt Baskerville 10 Pro
Typeset by Jouve (UK), Milton Keynes

Printed and bound in Great Britain by Clays Ltd, Elcograf S.p.A.

A CIP catalogue record for this book is available from the British Library

ISBN: 978–0–141–39831–0

www.greenpenguin.co.uk

Penguin Random House is committed to a sustainable future for our business, our readers and our planet. This book is made from Forest Stewardship Council® certified paper.

Contents

'When I Set Out for Lyonnesse'	1
Shut Out That Moon	2

Poems of 1912–13

The Going	4
Your Last Drive	6
The Walk	8
Rain on a Grave	9
'I Found Her Out There'	11
Without Ceremony	13
Lament	14
The Haunter	16
The Voice	18
His Visitor	19
A Circular	20
A Dream or No	21

After a Journey	23
A Death-Day Recalled	25
Beeny Cliff	26
At Castle Boterel	28
Places	30
The Phantom Horsewoman	32
The Spell of the Rose	34
St Launce's Revisited	36
Where the Picnic Was	38
'We Sat at the Window'	40
At the Word 'Farewell'	41
Once at Swanage	43
The Musical Box	44
A Second Attempt	46
He Prefers Her Earthly	48
The Shadow on the Stone	49
'She Did Not Turn'	50
A Two-Years' Idyll	51
'If You Had Known'	53
The Marble Tablet	54
Days to Recollect	55

'When I Set Out for Lyonnesse'

1870

When I set out for Lyonnesse,
    A hundred miles away,
    The rime was on the spray,
And starlight lit my lonesomeness
When I set out for Lyonnesse
    A hundred miles away.

What would bechance at Lyonnesse
    While I should sojourn there
    No prophet durst declare,
Nor did the wisest wizard guess
What would bechance at Lyonnesse
    While I should sojourn there.

When I came back from Lyonnesse
    With magic in my eyes,
    All marked with mute surmise
My radiance rare and fathomless,
When I came back from Lyonnesse
    With magic in my eyes!

Shut Out That Moon

Close up the casement, draw the blind,
    Shut out that stealing moon,
She wears too much the guise she wore
    Before our lutes were strewn
With years-deep dust, and names we read
    On a white stone were hewn.

Step not forth on the dew-dashed lawn
    To view the Lady's Chair,
Immense Orion's glittering form,
    The Less and Greater Bear:
Stay in; to such sights we were drawn
    When faded ones were fair.

Brush not the bough for midnight scents
    That come forth lingeringly,
And wake the same sweet sentiments
    They breathed to you and me
When living seemed a laugh, and love
    All it was said to be.

Within the common lamp-lit room
    Prison my eyes and thought;
Let dingy details crudely loom,
    Mechanic speech be wrought:
Too fragrant was Life's early bloom,
    Too tart the fruit it brought!

POEMS OF 1912–13

Veteris vestigia flammae

The Going

Why did you give no hint that night
That quickly after the morrow's dawn,
And calmly, as if indifferent quite,
You would close your term here, up and be gone
      Where I could not follow
      With wing of swallow
To gain one glimpse of you ever anon!

      Never to bid good-bye,
        Or lip me the softest call,
Or utter a wish for a word, while I
Saw morning harden upon the wall,
      Unmoved, unknowing
      That your great going
Had place that moment, and altered all.

Why do you make me leave the house
And think for a breath it is you I see
At the end of the alley of bending boughs

Where so often at dusk you used to be;
        Till in darkening dankness
        The yawning blankness
Of the perspective sickens me!

        You were she who abode
        By those red-veined rocks far West,
You were the swan-necked one who rode
Along the beetling Beeny Crest,
        And, reining nigh me,
        Would muse and eye me,
While Life unrolled us its very best.

Why, then, latterly did we not speak,
Did we not think of those days long dead,
And ere your vanishing strive to seek
That time's renewal? We might have said,
        'In this bright spring weather
        We'll visit together
Those places that once we visited.'

        Well, well! All's past amend,
        Unchangeable. It must go.
I seem but a dead man held on end
To sink down soon . . . O you could not know
        That such swift fleeing
        No soul foreseeing –
Not even I – would undo me so!

Your Last Drive

Here by the moorway you returned,
And saw the borough lights ahead
That lit your face – all undiscerned
To be in a week the face of the dead,
And you told of the charm of that haloed view
That never again would beam on you.

And on your left you passed the spot
Where eight days later you were to lie,
And be spoken of as one who was not;
Beholding it with a heedless eye
As alien from you, though under its tree
You soon would halt everlastingly.

I drove not with you . . . Yet had I sat
At your side that eve I should not have seen
That the countenance I was glancing at
Had a last-time look in the flickering sheen,
Nor have read the writing upon your face,
'I go hence soon to my resting-place;

'You may miss me then. But I shall not know
How many times you visit me there,
Or what your thoughts are, or if you go
There never at all. And I shall not care.

Should you censure me I shall take no heed,
And even your praises no more shall need.'

True: never you'll know. And you will not mind.
But shall I then slight you because of such?
Dear ghost, in the past did you ever find
The thought 'What profit,' move me much?
Yet abides the fact, indeed, the same, –
You are past love, praise, indifference, blame.

The Walk

You did not walk with me
Of late to the hill-top tree
    By the gated ways,
    As in earlier days;
    You were weak and lame,
    So you never came,
And I went alone, and I did not mind,
Not thinking of you as left behind.

    I walked up there to-day
    Just in the former way;
        Surveyed around
        The familiar ground
        By myself again:
        What difference, then?
Only that underlying sense
Of the look of a room on returning thence.

Rain on a Grave

Clouds spout upon her
    Their waters amain
    In ruthless disdain, –
Her who but lately
    Had shivered with pain
As at touch of dishonour
If there had lit on her
So coldly, so straightly
    Such arrows of rain:

One who to shelter
    Her delicate head
Would quicken and quicken
    Each tentative tread
If drops chanced to pelt her
    That summertime spills
    In dust-paven rills
When thunder-clouds thicken
    And birds close their bills.

Would that I lay there
    And she were housed here!
Or better, together
Were folded away there
Exposed to one weather
We both, – who would stray there

When sunny the day there,
    Or evening was clear
    At the prime of the year.

Soon will be growing
    Green blades from her mound,
And daisies be showing
    Like stars on the ground,
Till she form part of them –
Ay – the sweet heart of them,
Loved beyond measure
With a child's pleasure
    All her life's round.

'I Found Her Out There'

I found her out there
On a slope few see,
That falls westwardly
To the salt-edged air,
Where the ocean breaks
On the purple strand,
And the hurricane shakes
The solid land.

I brought her here,
And have laid her to rest
In a noiseless nest
No sea beats near.
She will never be stirred
In her loamy cell
By the waves long heard
And loved so well.

So she does not sleep
By those haunted heights
The Atlantic smites
And the blind gales sweep,
Whence she often would gaze
At Dundagel's famed head,
While the dipping blaze
Dyed her face fire-red;

And would sigh at the tale
Of sunk Lyonnesse,
As a wind-tugged tress
Flapped her cheek like a flail;
Or listen at whiles
With a thought-bound brow
To the murmuring miles
She is far from now.

Yet her shade, maybe,
Will creep underground
Till it catch the sound
Of that western sea
As it swells and sobs
Where she once domiciled,
And joy in its throbs
With the heart of a child.

Without Ceremony

It was your way, my dear,
To vanish without a word
When callers, friends, or kin
Had left, and I hastened in
To rejoin you, as I inferred.

And when you'd a mind to career
Off anywhere – say to town –
You were all on a sudden gone
Before I had thought thereon,
Or noticed your trunks were down.

So, now that you disappear
For ever in that swift style,
Your meaning seems to me
Just as it used to be:
'Good-bye is not worth while!'

Lament

How she would have loved
A party to-day! –
Bright-hatted and gloved,
With table and tray
And chairs on the lawn
Her smiles would have shone
With welcomings . . . But
She is shut, she is shut
    From friendship's spell
    In the jailing shell
    Of her tiny cell.

Or she would have reigned
At a dinner to-night
With ardours unfeigned,
And a generous delight:
All in her abode
She'd have freely bestowed
On her guests . . . But alas,
She is shut under grass
    Where no cups flow,
    Powerless to know
    That it might be so.

And she would have sought
With a child's eager glance

The shy snowdrops brought
By the new year's advance,
And peered in the rime
Of Candlemas-time
For crocuses . . . chanced
It that she were not tranced
    From sights she loved best;
    Wholly possessed
    By an infinite rest!

And we are here staying
Amid these stale things,
Who care not for gaying,
And those junketings
That used so to joy her,
And never to cloy her
As us they cloy! . . . But
She is shut, she is shut
    From the cheer of them, dead
    To all done and said
    In her yew-arched bed.

The Haunter

He does not think that I haunt here nightly:
    How shall I let him know
That whither his fancy sets him wandering
    I, too, alertly go? –
Hover and hover a few feet from him
    Just as I used to do,
But cannot answer the words he lifts me –
    Only listen thereto!

When I could answer he did not say them:
    When I could let him know
How I would like to join in his journeys
    Seldom he wished to go.
Now that he goes and wants me with him
    More than he used to do,
Never he sees my faithful phantom
    Though he speaks thereto.

Yes, I companion him to places
    Only dreamers know,
Where the shy hares print long paces,
    Where the night rooks go;
Into old aisles where the past is all to him,
    Close as his shade can do,
Always lacking the power to call to him,
    Near as I reach thereto!

What a good haunter I am, O tell him!
    Quickly make him know
If he but sigh since my loss befell him
    Straight to his side I go.
Tell him a faithful one is doing
    All that love can do
Still that his path may be worth pursuing,
    And to bring peace thereto.

The Voice

Woman much missed, how you call to me, call to me,
Saying that now you are not as you were
When you had changed from the one who was all to me,
But as at first, when our day was fair.

Can it be you that I hear? Let me view you, then,
Standing as when I drew near to the town
Where you would wait for me: yes, as I knew you then,
Even to the original air-blue gown!

Or is it only the breeze, in its listlessness
Travelling across the wet mead to me here,
You being ever dissolved to wan wistlessness,
Heard no more again far or near?

    Thus I; faltering forward,
    Leaves around me falling,
Wind oozing thin through the thorn from norward,
    And the woman calling.

His Visitor

I come across from Mellstock while the moon wastes
                weaker
To behold where I lived with you for twenty years and
                more:
I shall go in the gray, at the passing of the mail-train,
And need no setting open of the long familiar door
                As before.

The change I notice in my once own quarters!
A formal-fashioned border where the daisies used to be,
The rooms new painted, and the pictures altered,
And other cups and saucers, and no cosy nook for tea
                As with me.

I discern the dim faces of the sleep-wrapt servants;
They are not those who tended me through feeble hours
                and strong,
But strangers quite, who never knew my rule here,
Who never saw me painting, never heard my softling song
                Float along.

So I don't want to linger in this re-decked dwelling,
I feel too uneasy at the contrasts I behold,
And I make again for Mellstock to return here never,
And rejoin the roomy silence, and the mute and manifold
                Souls of old.

A Circular

As 'legal representative'
I read a missive not my own,
On new designs the senders give
    For clothes, in tints as shown.

Here figure blouses, gowns for tea,
And presentation-trains of state,
Charming ball-dresses, millinery,
    Warranted up to date.

And this gay-pictured, spring-time shout
Of Fashion, hails what lady proud?
Her who before last year ebbed out
    Was costumed in a shroud.

A Dream or No

Why go to Saint-Juliot? What's Juliot to me?
    Some strange necromancy
    But charmed me to fancy
That much of my life claims the spot as its key.

Yes. I have had dreams of that place in the West,
    And a maiden abiding
    Thereat as in hiding;
Fair-eyed and white-shouldered, broad-browed and
        brown-tressed.

And of how, coastward bound on a night long ago,
    There lonely I found her,
    The sea-birds around her,
And other than nigh things uncaring to know.

So sweet her life there (in my thought has it seemed)
    That quickly she drew me
    To take her unto me,
And lodge her long years with me. Such have I
        dreamed.

But nought of that maid from Saint-Juliot I see;
    Can she ever have been here,
    And shed her life's sheen here,
The woman I thought a long housemate with me?

Does there even a place like Saint-Juliot exist?
    Or a Vallency Valley
    With stream and leafed alley,
Or Beeny, or Bos with its flounce flinging mist?

After a Journey

Hereto I come to view a voiceless ghost;
    Whither, O whither will its whim now draw me?
Up the cliff, down, till I'm lonely, lost,
    And the unseen waters' ejaculations awe me.
Where you will next be there's no knowing,
    Facing round about me everywhere,
        With your nut-coloured hair,
And gray eyes, and rose-flush coming and going.

Yes: I have re-entered your olden haunts at last;
    Through the years, through the dead scenes I have tracked you;
What have you now found to say of our past –
    Scanned across the dark space wherein I have lacked you?
Summer gave us sweets, but autumn wrought division?
    Things were not lastly as firstly well
        With us twain, you tell?
But all's closed now, despite Time's derision.

I see what you are doing: you are leading me on
    To the spots we knew when we haunted here together,
The waterfall, above which the mist-bow shone
    At the then fair hour in the then fair weather,

And the cave just under, with a voice still so hollow
    That it seems to call out to me from forty years ago,
        When you were all aglow,
And not the thin ghost that I now frailly follow!

Ignorant of what there is flitting here to see,
    The waked birds preen and the seals flop lazily,
Soon you will have, Dear, to vanish from me,
    For the stars close their shutters and the dawn
        whitens hazily.
Trust me, I mind not, though Life lours,
    The bringing me here; nay, bring me here again!
        I am just the same as when
Our days were a joy, and our paths through flowers.

PENTARGAN BAY

A Death-Day Recalled

Beeny did not quiver,
    Juliot grew not gray,
Thin Valency's river
    Held its wonted way.
Bos seemed not to utter
    Dimmest note of dirge,
Targan mouth a mutter
    To its creamy surge.

Yet though these, unheeding,
    Listless, passed the hour
Of her spirit's speeding,
    She had, in her flower,
Sought and loved the places –
    Much and often pined
For their lonely faces
    When in towns confined.

Why did not Valency
    In his purl deplore
One whose haunts were whence he
    Drew his limpid store?
Why did Bos not thunder,
    Targan apprehend
Body and Breath were sunder
    Of their former friend?

Beeny Cliff

(March 1870–March 1913)

I

O the opal and the sapphire of that wandering western sea,
And the woman riding high above with bright hair flapping free –
The woman whom I loved so, and who loyally loved me.

II

The pale mews plained below us, and the waves seemed far away
In a nether sky, engrossed in saying their ceaseless babbling say,
As we laughed light-heartedly aloft on that clear-sunned March day.

III

A little cloud then cloaked us, and there flew an irised rain,
And the Atlantic dyed its levels with a dull misfeatured stain,
And then the sun burst out again, and purples prinked the main.

IV

– Still in all its chasmal beauty bulks old Beeny to the
   sky,
And shall she and I not go there once again now March
   is nigh,
And the sweet things said in that March say anew there
   by and by?

V

What if still in chasmal beauty looms that wild weird
   western shore,
The woman now is – elsewhere – whom the ambling
   pony bore,
And nor knows nor cares for Beeny, and will laugh there
   nevermore.

At Castle Boterel

As I drive to the junction of lane and highway,
    And the drizzle bedrenches the waggonette,
I look behind at the fading byway,
    And see on its slope, now glistening wet,
        Distinctly yet

Myself and a girlish form benighted
    In dry March weather. We climb the road
Beside a chaise. We had just alighted
    To ease the sturdy pony's load
        When he sighed and slowed.

What we did as we climbed, and what we talked of
    Matters not much, nor to what it led, –
Something that life will not be balked of
    Without rude reason till hope is dead,
        And feeling fled.

It filled but a minute. But was there ever
    A time of such quality, since or before,
In that hill's story? To one mind never,
    Though it has been climbed, foot-swift, foot-sore,
        By thousands more.

Primaeval rocks form the road's steep border,
    And much have they faced there, first and last,
Of the transitory in Earth's long order;
    But what they record in colour and cast
        Is – that we two passed.

And to me, though Time's unflinching rigour,
    In mindless rote, has ruled from sight
The substance now, one phantom figure
    Remains on the slope, as when that night
        Saw us alight.

I look and see it there, shrinking, shrinking,
    I look back at it amid the rain
For the very last time; for my sand is sinking,
    And I shall traverse old love's domain
        Never again.

Places

Nobody says: Ah, that is the place
Where chanced, in the hollow of years ago,
What none of the Three Towns cared to know –
The birth of a little girl of grace –
The sweetest the house saw, first or last;
        Yet it was so
        On that day long past.

Nobody thinks: There, there she lay
In a room by the Hoe, like the bud of a flower,
And listened, just after the bedtime hour,
To the stammering chimes that used to play
The quaint Old Hundred-and-Thirteenth tune
        In Saint Andrew's tower
        Night, morn, and noon.

Nobody calls to mind that here
Upon Boterel Hill, where the waggoners skid,
With cheeks whose airy flush outbid
Fresh fruit in bloom, and free of fear,
She cantered down, as if she must fall
        (Though she never did),
        To the charm of all.

Nay: one there is to whom these things,
That nobody else's mind calls back,

Have a savour that scenes in being lack,
And a presence more than the actual brings;
To whom to-day is beneaped and stale,
        And its urgent clack
        But a vapid tale.

The Phantom Horsewoman

I

Queer are the ways of a man I know:
>He comes and stands
>In a careworn craze,
>And looks at the sands
>And the seaward haze
>With moveless hands
>And face and gaze,
>Then turns to go . . .
And what does he see when he gazes so?

II

They say he sees as an instant thing
>More clear than to-day,
>A sweet soft scene
>That once was in play
>By that briny green;
>Yes, notes alway
>Warm, real, and keen,
>What his back years bring –
A phantom of his own figuring.

III

Of this vision of his they might say more:
        Not only there
          Does he see this sight,
     But everywhere
      In his brain – day, night,
     As if on the air
      It were drawn rose bright –
    Yea, far from that shore
Does he carry this vision of heretofore:

IV

A ghost-girl-rider. And though, toil-tried,
       He withers daily,
      Time touches her not,
       But she still rides gaily
      In his rapt thought
       On that shagged and shaly
      Atlantic spot,
       And as when first eyed
Draws rein and sings to the swing of the tide.

The Spell of the Rose

'I mean to build a hall anon,
    And shape two turrets there,
    And a broad newelled stair,
And a cool well for crystal water;
    Yes; I will build a hall anon,
    Plant roses love shall feed upon,
    And apple-trees and pear.'

He set to build the manor-hall,
    And shaped the turrets there,
    And the broad newelled stair,
And the cool well for crystal water;
    He built for me that manor-hall,
    And planted many trees withal,
    But no rose anywhere.

And as he planted never a rose
    That bears the flower of love,
    Though other flowers throve
Some heart-bane moved our souls to sever
    Since he had planted never a rose;
    And misconceits raised horrid shows,
    And agonies came thereof.

'I'll mend these miseries,' then said I,
    And so, at dead of night,
    I went and, screened from sight,
That nought should keep our souls in severance,
    I set a rose-bush. 'This,' said I,
    'May end divisions dire and wry,
    And long-drawn days of blight.'

But I was called from earth – yea, called
    Before my rose-bush grew;
    And would that now I knew
What feels he of the tree I planted,
    And whether, after I was called
    To be a ghost, he, as of old,
    Gave me his heart anew!

Perhaps now blooms that queen of trees
    I set but saw not grow,
    And he, beside its glow –
Eyes couched of the mis-vision that blurred me –
    Ay, there beside that queen of trees
    He sees me as I was, though sees
    Too late to tell me so!

St Launce's Revisited

    Slip back, Time!
Yet again I am nearing
Castle and keep, uprearing
    Gray, as in my prime.

    At the inn
Smiling nigh, why is it
Not as on my visit
    When hope and I were twin?

    Groom and jade
Whom I found here, moulder;
Strange the tavern-holder,
    Strange the tap-maid.

    Here I hired
Horse and man for bearing
Me on my wayfaring
    To the door desired.

    Evening gloomed
As I journeyed forward
To the faces shoreward,
    Till their dwelling loomed.

    If again
Towards the Atlantic sea there
I should speed, they'd be there
    Surely now as then? . . .

    Why waste thought,
When I know them vanished
Under earth; yea, banished
    Ever into nought!

Where the Picnic Was

Where we made the fire
In the summer time
Of branch and briar
On the hill to the sea,
I slowly climb
Through winter mire,
And scan and trace
The forsaken place
Quite readily.

Now a cold wind blows,
And the grass is gray,
But the spot still shows
As a burnt circle – aye,
And stick-ends, charred,
Still strew the sward
Whereon I stand,
Last relic of the band
Who came that day!

Yes, I am here
Just as last year,
And the sea breathes brine
From its strange straight line
Up hither, the same
As when we four came.

– But two have wandered far
From this grassy rise
Into urban roar
Where no picnics are,
And one – has shut her eyes
For evermore.

'We Sat at the Window'

(Bournemouth, 1875)

We sat at the window looking out,
And the rain came down like silken strings
That Swithin's day. Each gutter and spout
Babbled unchecked in the busy way
      Of witless things:
Nothing to read, nothing to see
Seemed in that room for her and me
      On Swithin's day.

We were irked by the scene, by our own selves; yes,
For I did not know, nor did she infer
How much there was to read and guess
By her in me, and to see and crown
      By me in her.
Wasted were two souls in their prime,
And great was the waste, that July time
      When the rain came down.

At the Word 'Farewell'

She looked like a bird from a cloud
    On the clammy lawn,
Moving alone, bare-browed
    In the dim of dawn.
The candles alight in the room
    For my parting meal
Made all things withoutdoors loom
    Strange, ghostly, unreal.

The hour itself was a ghost,
    And it seemed to me then
As of chances the chance furthermost
    I should see her again.
I beheld not where all was so fleet
    That a Plan of the past
Which had ruled us from birthtime to meet
    Was in working at last:

No prelude did I there perceive
    To a drama at all,
Or foreshadow what fortune might weave
    From beginnings so small;
But I rose as if quicked by a spur
    I was bound to obey,
And stepped through the casement to her
    Still alone in the gray.

'I am leaving you . . . Farewell!' I said
    As I followed her on
By an alley bare boughs overspread;
    'I soon must be gone!'
Even then the scale might have been turned
    Against love by a feather,
– But crimson one cheek of hers burned
    When we came in together.

Once at Swanage

The spray sprang up across the cusps of the moon,
    And all its light loomed green
    As a witch-flame's weirdsome sheen
At the minute of an incantation scene;
And it greened our gaze – that night at demilune.

Roaring high and roaring low was the sea
    Behind the headland shores:
    It symboled the slamming of doors,
Or a regiment hurrying over hollow floors . . .
And there we two stood, hands clasped; I and she!

The Musical Box

      Lifelong to be
Seemed the fair colour of the time;
That there was standing shadowed near
A spirit who sang to the gentle chime
Of the self-struck notes, I did not hear,
          I did not see.

      Thus did it sing
To the mindless lyre that played indoors
As she came to listen for me without:
'O value what the nonce outpours –
This best of life – that shines about
          Your welcoming!'

      I had slowed along
After the torrid hours were done,
Though still the posts and walls and road
Flung back their sense of the hot-faced sun,
And had walked by Stourside Mill, where broad
          Stream-lilies throng.

   And I descried
The dusky house that stood apart,
And her, white-muslined, waiting there
In the porch with high-expectant heart,
While still the thin mechanic air
    Went on inside.

   At whiles would flit
Swart bats, whose wings, be-webbed and tanned,
Whirred like the wheels of ancient clocks:
She laughed a hailing as she scanned
Me in the gloom, the tuneful box
    Intoning it.

   Lifelong to be
I thought it. That there watched hard by
A spirit who sang to the indoor tune,
'O make the most of what is nigh!'
I did not hear in my dull soul-swoon –
    I did not see.

A Second Attempt

Thirty years after
I began again
An old-time passion:
And it seemed as fresh as when
The first day ventured on:
When mutely I would waft her
In Love's past fashion
Dreams much dwelt upon,
Dreams I wished she knew.

I went the course through,
From Love's fresh-found sensation –
Remembered still so well –
To worn words charged anew,
That left no more to tell:
Thence to hot hopes and fears,
And thence to consummation,
And thence to sober years,
Markless, and mellow-hued.

Firm the whole fabric stood,
Or seemed to stand, and sound
As it had stood before.
But nothing backward climbs,
And when I looked around

As at the former times,
There was Life – pale and hoar;
And slow it said to me,
'Twice-over cannot be!'

He Prefers Her Earthly

This after-sunset is a sight for seeing,
Cliff-heads of craggy cloud surrounding it.
   – And dwell you in that glory-show?
You may; for there are strange strange things in being,
     Stranger than I know.

Yet if that chasm of splendour claim your presence
Which glows between the ash cloud and the dun,
   How changed must be your mortal mould!
Changed to a firmament-riding earthless essence
     From what you were of old:

All too unlike the fond and fragile creature
Then known to me . . . Well, shall I say it plain?
   I would not have you thus and there,
But still would grieve on, missing you, still feature
     You as the one you were.

The Shadow on the Stone

    I went by the Druid stone
      That broods in the garden white and lone,
And I stopped and looked at the shifting shadows
      That at some moments fall thereon
      From the tree hard by with a rhythmic swing,
      And they shaped in my imagining
To the shade that a well-known head and shoulders
      Threw there when she was gardening.

    I thought her behind my back,
      Yea, her I long had learned to lack,
And I said: 'I am sure you are standing behind me,
      Though how do you get into this old track?'
      And there was no sound but the fall of a leaf
      As a sad response; and to keep down grief
I would not turn my head to discover
      That there was nothing in my belief.

    Yet I wanted to look and see
      That nobody stood at the back of me;
But I thought once more: 'Nay, I'll not unvision
      A shape which, somehow, there may be.'
      So I went on softly from the glade,
      And left her behind me throwing her shade,
As she were indeed an apparition –
      My head unturned lest my dream should fade.

'She Did Not Turn'

She did not turn,
But passed foot-faint with averted head
In her gown of green, by the bobbing fern,
Though I leaned over the gate that led
From where we waited with table spread;
   But she did not turn:
Why was she near there if love had fled?

   She did not turn,
Though the gate was whence I had often sped
In the mists of morning to meet her, and learn
Her heart, when its moving moods I read
As a book – she mine, as she sometimes said;
   But she did not turn,
And passed foot-faint with averted head.

A Two-Years' Idyll

Yes; such it was;
    Just those two seasons unsought,
Sweeping like summertide wind on our ways;
    Moving, as straws,
      Hearts quick as ours in those days;
Going like wind, too, and rated as nought
    Save as the prelude to plays
    Soon to come – larger, life-fraught:
      Yes; such it was.

'Nought' it was called,
    Even by ourselves – that which springs
Out of the years for all flesh, first or last,
    Commonplace, scrawled
      Dully on days that go past.
Yet, all the while, it upbore us like wings
    Even in hours overcast:
    Aye, though this best thing of things,
      'Nought' it was called!

What seems it now?
    Lost: such beginning was all;
Nothing came after: romance straight forsook
    Quickly somehow
    Life when we sped from our nook,

Primed for new scenes with designs smart and tall . . .
  – A preface without any book,
 A trumpet uplipped, but no call;
  That seems it now.

'If You Had Known'

    If you had known
When listening with her to the far-down moan
Of the white-selvaged and empurpled sea,
And rain came on that did not hinder talk,
Or damp your flashing facile gaiety
In turning home, despite the slow wet walk
By crooked ways, and over stiles of stone:
    If you had known

    You would lay roses,
Fifty years thence, on her monument, that discloses
Its graying shape upon the luxuriant green;
Fifty years thence to an hour, by chance led there,
What might have moved you? – yea, had you foreseen
That on the tomb of the selfsame one, gone where
The dawn of every day is as the close is,
    You would lay roses!

The Marble Tablet

There it stands, though alas, what a little of her
    Shows in its cold white look!
Not her glance, glide, or smile; not a tittle of her
    Voice like the purl of a brook;
      Not her thoughts, that you read like a book.

It may stand for her once in November
    When first she breathed, witless of all;
Or in heavy years she would remember
    When circumstance held her in thrall;
      Or at last, when she answered her call!

Nothing more. The still marble, date-graven,
    Gives all that it can, tersely lined;
That one has at length found the haven
    Which every one other will find;
      With silence on what shone behind.

Days to Recollect

    Do you recall
    That day in Fall
When we walked towards Saint Alban's Head,
Over thistledown that summer had shed,
    Or must I remind you?
Winged thistle-seeds which hitherto
Had lain as none were there, or few,
But rose at the brush of your petticoat-seam
(As ghosts might rise of the recent dead),
And sailed on the breeze in a nebulous stream
    Like a comet's tail behind you:
        You don't recall
        That day in Fall?

    Then do you remember
    That sad November
When you left me never to see me more,
And looked quite other than theretofore,
    As if it could not *be* you?
And lay by the window whence you had gazed
So many times when blamed or praised,
Morning or noon, through years and years,
Accepting the gifts that Fortune bore,

Sharing, enduring, joys, hopes, fears!
Well: I never more did see you. –
Say you remember
That sad November!

1. BOCCACCIO · *Mrs Rosie and the Priest*
2. GERARD MANLEY HOPKINS · *As kingfishers catch fire*
3. *The Saga of Gunnlaug Serpent-tongue*
4. THOMAS DE QUINCEY · *On Murder Considered as One of the Fine Arts*
5. FRIEDRICH NIETZSCHE · *Aphorisms on Love and Hate*
6. JOHN RUSKIN · *Traffic*
7. PU SONGLING · *Wailing Ghosts*
8. JONATHAN SWIFT · *A Modest Proposal*
9. *Three Tang Dynasty Poets*
10. WALT WHITMAN · *On the Beach at Night Alone*
11. KENKŌ · *A Cup of Sake Beneath the Cherry Trees*
12. BALTASAR GRACIÁN · *How to Use Your Enemies*
13. JOHN KEATS · *The Eve of St Agnes*
14. THOMAS HARDY · *Woman much missed*
15. GUY DE MAUPASSANT · *Femme Fatale*
16. MARCO POLO · *Travels in the Land of Serpents and Pearls*
17. SUETONIUS · *Caligula*
18. APOLLONIUS OF RHODES · *Jason and Medea*
19. ROBERT LOUIS STEVENSON · *Olalla*
20. KARL MARX AND FRIEDRICH ENGELS · *The Communist Manifesto*
21. PETRONIUS · *Trimalchio's Feast*
22. JOHANN PETER HEBEL · *How a Ghastly Story Was Brought to Light by a Common or Garden Butcher's Dog*
23. HANS CHRISTIAN ANDERSEN · *The Tinder Box*
24. RUDYARD KIPLING · *The Gate of the Hundred Sorrows*
25. DANTE · *Circles of Hell*
26. HENRY MAYHEW · *Of Street Piemen*
27. HAFEZ · *The nightingales are drunk*
28. GEOFFREY CHAUCER · *The Wife of Bath*
29. MICHEL DE MONTAIGNE · *How We Weep and Laugh at the Same Thing*
30. THOMAS NASHE · *The Terrors of the Night*
31. EDGAR ALLAN POE · *The Tell-Tale Heart*
32. MARY KINGSLEY · *A Hippo Banquet*
33. JANE AUSTEN · *The Beautifull Cassandra*
34. ANTON CHEKHOV · *Gooseberries*
35. SAMUEL TAYLOR COLERIDGE · *Well, they are gone, and here must I remain*
36. JOHANN WOLFGANG VON GOETHE · *Sketchy, Doubtful, Incomplete Jottings*
37. CHARLES DICKENS · *The Great Winglebury Duel*
38. HERMAN MELVILLE · *The Maldive Shark*
39. ELIZABETH GASKELL · *The Old Nurse's Story*
40. NIKOLAY LESKOV · *The Steel Flea*

41. HONORÉ DE BALZAC · *The Atheist's Mass*
42. CHARLOTTE PERKINS GILMAN · *The Yellow Wall-Paper*
43. C.P. CAVAFY · *Remember, Body . . .*
44. FYODOR DOSTOEVSKY · *The Meek One*
45. GUSTAVE FLAUBERT · *A Simple Heart*
46. NIKOLAI GOGOL · *The Nose*
47. SAMUEL PEPYS · *The Great Fire of London*
48. EDITH WHARTON · *The Reckoning*
49. HENRY JAMES · *The Figure in the Carpet*
50. WILFRED OWEN · *Anthem For Doomed Youth*
51. WOLFGANG AMADEUS MOZART · *My Dearest Father*
52. PLATO · *Socrates' Defence*
53. CHRISTINA ROSSETTI · *Goblin Market*
54. *Sindbad the Sailor*
55. SOPHOCLES · *Antigone*
56. RYŪNOSUKE AKUTAGAWA · *The Life of a Stupid Man*
57. LEO TOLSTOY · *How Much Land Does A Man Need?*
58. GIORGIO VASARI · *Leonardo da Vinci*
59. OSCAR WILDE · *Lord Arthur Savile's Crime*
60. SHEN FU · *The Old Man of the Moon*
61. AESOP · *The Dolphins, the Whales and the Gudgeon*
62. MATSUO BASHŌ · *Lips too Chilled*
63. EMILY BRONTË · *The Night is Darkening Round Me*
64. JOSEPH CONRAD · *To-morrow*
65. RICHARD HAKLUYT · *The Voyage of Sir Francis Drake Around the Whole Globe*
66. KATE CHOPIN · *A Pair of Silk Stockings*
67. CHARLES DARWIN · *It was snowing butterflies*
68. BROTHERS GRIMM · *The Robber Bridegroom*
69. CATULLUS · *I Hate and I Love*
70. HOMER · *Circe and the Cyclops*
71. D. H. LAWRENCE · *Il Duro*
72. KATHERINE MANSFIELD · *Miss Brill*
73. OVID · *The Fall of Icarus*
74. SAPPHO · *Come Close*
75. IVAN TURGENEV · *Kasyan from the Beautiful Lands*
76. VIRGIL · *O Cruel Alexis*
77. H. G. WELLS · *A Slip under the Microscope*
78. HERODOTUS · *The Madness of Cambyses*
79. *Speaking of Siva*
80. *The Dhammapada*

'They trailed in all their vulgar glory over the fresh green grass…'

GUY DE MAUPASSANT
Born 1850, Normandy, France
Died 1893, Paris, France

Selection from *A Parisian Affair and Other Stories*,
published in Penguin Classics 2004.

MAUPASSANT IN PENGUIN CLASSICS
A Parisian Affair and Other Stories
Bel-Ami
Pierre et Jean

GUY DE MAUPASSANT

Femme Fatale

Translated by
Siân Miles

PENGUIN BOOKS

PENGUIN CLASSICS

UK | USA | Canada | Ireland | Australia
India | New Zealand | South Africa

Penguin Books is part of the Penguin Random House group of companies
whose addresses can be found at global.penguinrandomhouse.com.

This selection published in Penguin Classics 2015

012

Translation copyright © Siân Miles, 2004

The moral right of the translator has been asserted

Set in 9/12.4 pt Baskerville 10 Pro
Typeset by Jouve (UK), Milton Keynes
Printed and bound in Great Britain by Clays Ltd, Elcograf S.p.A.

A CIP catalogue record for this book is available from the British Library

ISBN: 978-0-141-39833-4

www.greenpenguin.co.uk

Penguin Random House is committed to a
sustainable future for our business, our readers
and our planet. This book is made from Forest
Stewardship Council® certified paper.

Contents

Cockcrow	1
Femme Fatale	7
Hautot & Son	30
Laid to Rest	47

Cockcrow

Madame Berthe d'Avancelles had rejected the advances of her admirer Baron Joseph de Croissard to such an extent that he was now in despair. He had pursued her relentlessly throughout the winter in Paris, and now at his château at Carville in Normandy he was holding a series of hunting parties in her honour.

The husband, Monsieur d'Avancelles, turned a blind eye to all this. It was rumoured that they lived separate lives on account of a physical shortcoming of his which Madame could not overlook. He was a fat little man with short arms, short legs, a short neck, short nose, short everything in fact.

Madame d'Avancelles, in contrast, was a tall, chestnut-haired, determined-looking young woman. She laughed openly at old Pipe and Slippers as she called him to his face but looked with tender indulgence on her admirer, the titled Baron Joseph de Croissard, with his broad shoulders, his sturdy neck and his fair, drooping moustache.

Until now, however, she had granted him no favours despite the fact that he was spending a fortune on her, throwing a constant round of receptions, hunting parties, and all kinds of celebrations to which he invited the local aristocracy.

All day long the woods rang to the sound of hounds in full cry after a fox or a wild boar and every night a dazzling display of fireworks spiralled upwards to join the sparkling stars. A tracery of light from the drawing-room windows shone on the huge lawns where shadowy figures occasionally passed.

It was the russet season of autumn when leaves swirled over the gardens like flocks of birds. Wafting on the air came the tang of damp, bare earth, caught as the smell of a woman's naked flesh as her gown slips down to the floor after the ball.

On an evening during a reception held the previous spring, Madame d'Avancelles had replied to an imploring Monsieur de Croissard with the words: 'If I am to fall at all, my friend, it will certainly not be before the leaves do likewise. I've far too many things to do this summer to give it a thought.' He had remembered those daring words of hers spoken so provocatively and was now pressing his advantage. Each day he crept closer, gaining more and more of the bold beauty's heart until by this point her resistance seemed hardly more than symbolic.

Soon there was to be a great hunting party. The night before, Madame Berthe had said laughingly to the Baron: 'Tomorrow, Baron, if you manage to kill the beast I shall have something to give you.'

He was up at dawn reconnoitring where the wild boar was wallowing. He accompanied his whips, setting out the order of the hunt in such a way that he should return from the field in triumph. When the horns sounded for the meet, he appeared in a well-cut hunting costume of scarlet and gold. With his upright, broad-chested figure and flashing eyes he glowed with good health and manly vigour.

The hunt moved off. The boar was raised and ran, followed

by the baying hounds rushing through the undergrowth. The horses broke into a gallop, hurtling with their riders along the narrow forest paths while far behind the following carriages drove noiselessly over the softer verges.

Teasingly, Madame d'Avancelles kept the Baron at her side, slowing down to walking pace in an interminably long, straight avenue along which four rows of oaks arched vault-like towards each other. Trembling with both desire and frustration he listened with one ear to the young woman's light badinage, the other pricked for the hunting horns and the sound of the hounds growing fainter by the minute.

'So you love me no longer,' she was saying.

'How can you say such a thing?' he replied.

'You do seem to be more interested in the hunt than in me,' she went on. He groaned. 'You do remember your own orders don't you? To kill the beast myself.'

'Indeed I do,' she added with great seriousness. 'Before my very eyes.' At this he quivered impatiently in the saddle, spurred on his eager horse and finally lost his patience.

'For God's sake, Madame, not if we stay here a minute longer.'

'That is how it has to be nevertheless,' she cried laughingly. 'Otherwise, you're out of luck.'

Then she spoke to him gently, leaning her hand on his arm and, as if absentmindedly, stroking his horse's mane. They had turned right on to a narrow path overhung with trees when, suddenly swerving to avoid one of their low branches, she leaned against him so closely that he felt her hair tickling his neck. He threw his arms around her and pressing his thick moustache to her forehead planted upon it a passionate kiss.

At first she was motionless, stunned by his ardour, then with a start she turned her head and, either by chance or design, her own delicate lips met his beneath their blond cascade. Then, out of either embarrassment or regret for the incident she spurred her horse on the flank and galloped swiftly away. For a long while they rode straight on together, without so much as exchanging a glance.

The hunt in full cry was close and the thickets seemed to shake, when suddenly, covered in blood and shaking off the hounds that clung to him, the boar went rushing past through the bushes. The Baron gave a triumphant laugh, cried 'Let him who loves me follow me!' and disappeared, swallowed up by the forest. When Madame d'Avancelles reached an open glade a few minutes later he was just getting up, covered with mud, his jacket torn and his hands bloody, while the animal lay full length on the ground with the Baron's knife plunged up to the hilt in its shoulder.

The quarry was cut by torchlight on that mild and melancholy night. The moon gilded the red flames of the torches which filled the air with pine smoke. The dogs, yelping and snapping, devoured the stinking innards of the boar while the beaters and the gentlemen, standing in a circle around the spoil, blew their horns with all their might. The flourish of the hunting horns rose into the night air above the woods. Its echoes fell and were lost in the distant valleys beyond, alarming nervous stags, a barking fox and small grey rabbits at play on the edge of the glades. Terrified night birds fluttered above the crazed pack while the women, excited a little by the violence and vulnerability surrounding these events, leaned a little heavily on the men's arms and, without waiting for the hounds to finish, drifted off with their partners down the many forest paths. Feeling languid after all the exhausting emotion of the day Madame d'Avancelles said to the Baron: 'Would you care for a turn in the park, my friend?'

He gave no answer, but trembling and unsteady with desire pulled her to him. Instantly they kissed and as they walked very slowly under the almost leafless trees through which moonlight filtered, their love, their desire and their need for each other was so intense that they almost sank down at the foot of a tree.

The horns had fallen silent and the exhausted hounds were sleeping by now in their kennels.

'Let us go back,' the young woman said. They returned.

Just as they reached the château and were about to enter, she murmured in a faint voice: 'I'm so tired, my friend, I'm going straight to bed.' As he opened his arms for one last kiss she fled, with the parting words: 'No ... to sleep ... but ... let him who loves me follow me!'

An hour later when the whole sleeping château seemed dead to the world the Baron crept on tiptoe out of his room and scratched at the door of his friend. Receiving no reply he made to open it and found it unbolted.

She was leaning dreamily with her elbows on the window ledge. He threw himself at her knees which he showered with mad kisses through her nightdress. She said nothing, but ran her dainty fingers caressingly through the Baron's hair. Suddenly, as if coming to a momentous decision, she disengaged herself and whispered provocatively: 'Wait for me. I shall be back.' Her finger raised in shadow pointed to the far end of the room where loomed the vague white shape of her bed.

With wildly trembling hands he undressed quickly by feel and slipped between the cool sheets. He stretched out in bliss and almost forgot his friend as his weary body yielded to the linen's caress. Doubtless enjoying the strain on his patience, still she did not return. He closed his eyes in exquisitely pleasurable anticipation. His most cherished dream was about to come true. Little by little his limbs relaxed, as did his mind, where thoughts drifted, vague and indistinct. He succumbed at last to the power of great fatigue and finally fell asleep.

He slept the heavy, impenetrable sleep of the exhausted huntsman. He slept indeed till dawn. Then from a nearby tree through the still half-open window came the ringing cry of a cock. Startled awake, the Baron's eyes flew open. Finding himself, to his great surprise, in a strange bed and with a woman's body lying against his he remembered nothing and stammered as he struggled into consciousness: 'What? Where am I? What is it?'

At this, she, who had not slept a wink, looked at the puffy, red-eyed and dishevelled man at her side. She answered in the same dismissive tone she took with her husband. 'Nothing,' she said, 'it's a cock. Go back to sleep, Monsieur. It's nothing to do with you.'

Femme Fatale

The restaurant, Le Grillon, Mecca of the entire local boating community, was now slowly emptying. At the main entrance a large crowd of people were calling and shouting out to each other. With oars on their shoulders, strapping great fellows in white jerseys waved and gesticulated. Women in light spring frocks were stepping cautiously into the skiffs moored alongside and, having settled themselves in the stern of each, were smoothing out their dresses. The owner of the establishment, a tough-looking, red-bearded man of legendary strength, was helping the pretty young things aboard and with a practised hand was holding steady the gently bobbing craft.

The oarsmen then took their places, playing to the gallery and showing off broad chests and muscular arms in their sleeveless vests. The gallery in this case consisted of a crowd of suburbanites in their Sunday best, as well as a few workmen and some soldiers, all leaning on the parapet of the bridge and watching the scene below with keen interest. One by one the boats cast off from the landing stage. The oarsmen leaned forward and with a regular swing pulled back. At each stroke of the long, slightly curved blades the fast skiffs sped through the water making for La Grenouillère and growing progressively smaller till they disappeared beyond the railway bridge and into the distance.

Only one couple now remained. The slim, pale-faced young man, still a relatively beardless youth, had his arm around the waist of his girl, a skinny little grasshopper of a creature with brown hair. They stopped from time to time to gaze into each other's eyes.

The owner cried: 'Come on, Monsieur Paul, get a move on!'

The couple moved down closer. Of all the customers, Monsieur Paul, who paid regularly and in full, was the best liked and most respected. Many of the others ran up bills and frequently absconded without settling them. The son of a senator, he was also an excellent advertisement for the establishment. When some stranger asked, 'And who's that young chap over there with his eyes glued to the girl?' one of the regulars would murmur, in a mysterious, important sort of way, 'Oh, that's Paul Baron, you know, the son of the senator.' Then the stranger would inevitably have to comment, 'Poor young devil, he's got it bad.' The proprietress of Le Grillon, a good businesswoman and wise in the ways of the world, called the young man and his companion 'my two turtle doves' and looked with tender indulgence on the love affair which brought such glamour to her establishment.

The couple ambled slowly down to where a skiff called the *Madeleine* was ready. Before embarking, however, they stopped to kiss once more, much to the amusement of the audience gathered on the bridge. Finally, Monsieur Paul took up the oars and set off after the others also making for La Grenouillère.

When they arrived it was getting on for three and here too the vast floating café was swarming with people. It is in effect one huge raft with a tarpaulin roof supported by wooden columns. It is connected to the charming island of Croissy by two narrow footbridges, one of which runs right through to the centre of the café itself. The other connects at the far end with a tiny islet where a single tree grows and which is nicknamed the Pot-de-Fleurs. From there it connects with the land again via a bathing pool.

Monsieur Paul moored his boat alongside the café, climbed up to its balustrade then, holding his girl's two hands, guided her up also. They entered, found a place for two at the end of a table and sat down opposite each other.

Lining the towpath on the opposite side of the river was a long string of vehicles. Fiacres alternated with the flashy carriages of gay young men-about-town. The first were lumbering great hulks whose bodywork crushed the springs beneath and to which were harnessed broken-down old hacks with drooping necks. The other carriages were streamlined, with light suspension and fine, delicate wheels. These were drawn by horses with slender, straight, strong legs, heads held high and bits snowy with foam. Their solemn, liveried drivers, heads held stiffly inside huge collars, sat ramrod straight with their whips resting on their knees.

The river banks were crowded with people coming and going in different kinds of configurations: family parties, groups of friends, couples and individuals. They idly plucked at blades of grass, wandered down to the water's edge then climbed back up to the path. Having reached a certain spot they all congregated to wait for the ferryman whose heavy boat plied constantly back and forth, depositing passengers on the island.

The branch of the river, incidentally called the dead

branch, which this floating bar dominates, seemed asleep, so slowly did the current move there. Flotillas of gigs, skiffs, canoes, pedaloes and river craft of all kinds streamed over the still water, mingling and intersecting, meeting and parting, running foul of each other, stopping, and with a sudden jerk of their oarsmen's arms and a tensing of their muscles, taking off again, darting this way and that like shoals of red and yellow fish.

More were arriving all the time; some from Chatou upstream, some from Bougival, downstream. Gales of contagious laughter carried from one boat to another and the air was full of insults, complaints, protestations and howls. The men in the boats exposed their muscular, tanned bodies to the glare of the sun and, like exotic water-plants, the women's parasols of red, green and yellow silk blossomed in the sterns of their craft.

The July sun blazed in the middle of the sky and the atmosphere was gay and carefree, while in the windless air not a leaf stirred in the poplars and willows lining the banks of the river. In the distance ahead, the conspicuous bulk of Mont-Valérien loomed, rearing the ramparts of its fortifications in the glare of the sun. On the right, the gentle slopes of Louveciennes, following the curve of the river, formed a semi-circle within which could be glimpsed, through the dense and shady greenery of their spacious lawns, the white-painted walls of weekend retreats.

On the land adjoining La Grenouillère strollers were sauntering under the gigantic trees which help to make this part of the island one of the most delightful parks imaginable. Busty women with peroxided hair and nipped-in waists could be seen, made up to the nines with blood red lips and black-kohled eyes. Tightly laced into their garish dresses they trailed in all their vulgar glory over the fresh green grass. They were accompanied by men whose fashion-plate accessories, light gloves, patent-leather boots, canes as slender as threads and absurd monocles made them look like complete idiots.

The part of the island facing La Grenouillère is narrow and between it and the opposite bank where another ferry plies, bringing people over from Croissy, the current is very strong and very fast. Here it swirls and roars, raging like a torrent in a myriad of eddies and foam. A detachment of pontoon-builders wearing the uniform of artillerymen was camped on the bank and some of the soldiers, side by side on a long beam of wood, sat watching the river below.

A noisy, rambunctious crowd filled the floating restaurant. The wooden tables, sticky and awash with streams of spilt drink, were covered with half-empty glasses and surrounded by half-tipsy customers. The crowd sang and shouted and brawled. Red-faced, belligerent men, their hats tipped at the backs of their heads and their eyes glassy with booze, prowled like animals spoiling for a fight. The women, cadging free drinks in the meantime, were seeking their prey for the night. The space between the tables was filled with the usual clientèle – noisy young boating blades and their female companions in short flannel skirts.

One of the men was banging away at the piano using his feet as well as his hands. Four couples were dancing a quadrille and watching them was a group of elegantly dressed young men whose respectable appearance was ruined by the hideous incongruity of the setting.

The place reeked of vice and corruption and the dregs of Parisian society in all its rottenness gathered there: cheats, conmen and cheap hacks rubbed shoulders with under-age dandies, old roués and rogues, sleazy underworld types once notorious for things best forgotten mingled with other small-time crooks and speculators, dabblers in dubious ventures, frauds, pimps, and racketeers. Cheap sex, both male and female, was on offer in this tawdry meat-market of a place where petty rivalries were exploited, and quarrels picked over nothing in an atmosphere of fake gallantry where swords or pistols at dawn settled matters of highly questionable honour in the first place.

Every Sunday, out of sheer curiosity some of the people from the surrounding countryside would drop in. Every year would bring a fresh batch of young men, extremely young men at that, keen to make useful contacts. Casual cruisers would amble by and every so often a complete innocent would become embroiled.

La Grenouillère lived up to its name. There was a place for bathing between the tarpaulin-covered raft where drinks were served and the Pot-de-Fleurs. Women with the requisite curves came there to display their wares and their clients. Those less fortunate who required padding and corsetry to pass muster looked disdainfully on as their rivals cavorted and splashed about.

Awaiting their turn to plunge in and thronging around a small diving board were swimmers of every shape and size: some slim and straight as vine-poles, some round as pumpkins, some gnarled as olive-branches, some with bodies curved forward over pot-bellies, some whose vast stomachs threw the body backwards. Each was as ugly as the other as they leapt into the water and splashed the customers drinking at the café next door.

Despite the proximity of the river and the huge trees shading it, the place was suffocatingly hot. Mingling with the fumes of spilt drinks came the smell of flesh and the cheap perfume with which the skin of those trading in sex was drenched. Underlying all these smells was the slight but persistent aroma of talc, which wafted with varying intensity as if an unseen hand were waving some gigantic powder-puff over the entire scene.

All eyes were on the river where the comings and goings of the boats attracted everyone's attention. Girls sprawled in the stern opposite their strong-wristed menfolk looked with contempt at those still prowling about the island in search of a male to buy them dinner that night. Sometimes when a crew in full swing flashed past their friends ashore would shout and were joined by the crazy, yelling crowd inside the restaurant. At the bend of the river near Chatou boats were constantly coming into view. As they approached and grew more distinct, faces became recognizable and more shouts went up.

A boat with an awning and containing four women came slowly downstream towards them. The woman at the oars was small, lean and past her prime. She wore her hair pinned up inside an oilskin hat. Opposite her a big blonde dressed in a man's jacket was lying on her back at the bottom of the boat with a foot resting on the thwart on either side of the oarswoman. The blonde was smoking a cigarette and with each jerk of the oars her bosom and her belly quivered. At the very stern of the boat under the awning two beautiful, tall, slender girls, one blonde the other brunette, sat with their arms round each other's waists watching their two companions.

A shout went up from La Grenouillère: 'Aye-aye! Lesbos!' and suddenly a wild clamour broke out. In the terrifying scramble to see, glasses were knocked over and people started climbing on the tables. Everyone began to chant 'Lesbos! Lesbos! Lesbos!' The words merged into a vague howl before suddenly starting up again, rising into the air, filling the plain beyond, resounding in the dense foliage of the tall surrounding trees and echoing in the distance as if aimed at the sun itself.

During this ovation the oarswoman had calmly come to a halt. The big blonde lying at the bottom of the boat turned her head languorously and raised herself on her elbows. The two in the stern started laughing and waving to the crowd. At this there was even more of a hullabaloo and the place shook with the noise. The men raised their hats and the women waved their handkerchiefs. Every voice, deep and shrill alike, chanted in unison 'Lesbos!' This motley collection of undesirables seemed to be saluting a leader, as warships give a gun salute to their passing admiral. From the flotilla of boats also there was wild acclamation for the women's boat which now continued at its leisurely pace, to land a little further off.

Monsieur Paul's reaction was unlike that of the others. Pulling a key from his pocket he started using it as a whistle and blew hard. His girl, looking nervous now and even paler than before, pulled his arm to make him stop. This time when she looked into his eyes, it was with fury. But he was

Femme Fatale

beside himself with male jealousy and a deep, instinctive ungovernable rage. His lips trembling with indignation he stammered: 'Shouldn't be allowed! They should be drowned like puppies with stones round their necks!'

Madeleine suddenly lost her temper. Her shrill voice became piercing as she lashed out at him: 'Mind your own business, will you! They've got a perfect right to do whatever they want. They're not doing any harm to anyone. Why don't you just shut up and leave them alone . . .'

He cut her short. 'This a matter for the police! If it was up to me I'd have them locked up in Saint-Lazare!'

She gave a start. 'Oh you would, would you?'

'Certainly I would. And in the meantime I forbid you to have anything to do with them. I absolutely forbid it, do you understand?'

She shrugged her shoulders at this and said in a suddenly calm voice: 'Listen, dear, I shall do exactly as I please. If you don't like it you know what you can do. Get the hell out. Now. I'm not your wife, so shut up.'

He remained silent and they stood staring each other out, breathing rapidly, their mouths set.

At the other end of the café the women were now making their entrance. The two dressed as men led, one gaunt and weatherbeaten, ageing and very mannish. The other, more than amply filling the white flannel outfit with her large bottom and her huge thighs encased in the wide trousers, waddled forward like a fat, bow-legged goose. The two friends followed and the whole boating community surged forward to shake hands.

The four had rented a riverside cottage and lived together

there as two couples. Their vice was public, official and perfectly obvious to all. It was referred to quite naturally as something entirely normal. There were rumours about jealous scenes that took place there and about the various actresses and other famous women who frequented the little cottage near the water's edge. One neighbour, scandalized by the goings-on, alerted the police at one stage and an inspector accompanied by one of his men came to make enquiries. It was a delicate mission: there was nothing the women could be prosecuted for, least of all prostitution. The inspector was deeply puzzled and could not understand what these alleged misdemeanours could possibly be. He asked a whole lot of pointless questions, compiled a lengthy report and dismissed the charges out of hand. The joke spread as far as Saint-Germain.

Like queens they now walked slowly the entire length of La Grenouillère. They seemed happy to be in the limelight and delighted with the attention paid to them by all this riff-raff. Madeleine and her lover watched them, and as they approached the girl's face lit up.

When the leading couple reached their table Madeleine cried 'Pauline!' and the big girl, turning round, stopped, still arm in arm with her midshipwoman.

'Well good heavens! Madeleine! Darling! Come and join us for a bit. We must catch up!'

Paul tightened his grip on his girl's wrist but she said, 'You know what you can do, sweetheart, shove off.'

He kept quiet and let her be. Standing huddled together the women continued their animated conversation *sotto voce*. Pauline from time to time cast furtive glances at Paul and flashed him an evil, sardonic smile. Finally, unable to bear it a minute longer he suddenly stood up and trembling in every limb leapt towards her. He seized Madeleine by the shoulders and said: 'Come with me, do you hear? I said you were not to speak to these beastly women!'

Raising her voice, Pauline began to swear at him like a fishwife. People around started laughing. Others stood on tip-toe to get a better look. Under the hail of filthy abuse he was speechless. Feeling contaminated by it and fearing there might be worse to come he retreated, retraced his steps and went to lean on the balustrade overlooking the river, turning his back on the three triumphant women. He stayed there looking at the water and every so often brusquely wiping away the tears that sprang to his eyes.

The fact was that despite himself, without knowing why or how it had happened and very much against his better judgement, he had fallen hopelessly in love. He had fallen as if into some deep and muddy hole. By nature he was a delicate and sensitive soul. He had had ideals and dreamed of an exquisite and passionate affair. And now he had fallen for this little cricket of a creature. She was as stupid as every other woman and not even pretty to make up for it. Skinny and foul-tempered, she had taken possession of him entirely from tip to toe, body and soul. He had fallen under the omnipotent and mysterious spell of the female. He was overwhelmed by this colossal force of unknown origin, the demon in the flesh capable of hurling the most rational man in the world at the feet of a worthless harlot. There was no way he could explain its fatal and total power.

Behind his back now he could feel something evil brewing.

Their laughter pierced his heart. What should he do? He knew very well but had not the courage. He stared fixedly at the opposite bank where an angler was fishing, his line perfectly still. All of a sudden the man jerked out of the water a little silver fish which wriggled at the end of his line. Twisting and turning it this way and that he tried to extract his hook, but in vain. Losing patience he started pulling and, as he did so, tore out the entire bloody gullet of the fish with parts of its intestines attached. Paul shuddered, feeling himself equally torn apart. It seemed to him that the hook was like his own love and that if he were to tear it out he too would be gutted by a piece of curved wire hooked deep into his essential self at the end of a line held by Madeleine.

Feeling a hand on his shoulder he started and turned round. Madeleine was standing beside him. Neither spoke. She simply put her elbows on the balustrade beside him and leaned with him, staring out at the river. He tried to think of something to say but failed. He was incapable of analysing what was going on inside him. All he felt now was joy in the very nearness of her and a shameful cowardice on his own part. He wanted to forgive her, to let her do anything in the world she liked provided she never left him again.

After a while in a very gentle voice he asked, 'Would you like to leave now? We'll be better off in the boat.'

'All right my pet,' she said.

Awash with forgiveness and with tears still in his eyes he held her two hands tightly and helped her on board. Basking in the warmth of the afternoon they rowed upstream again past the willows and the grass-covered banks. When they reached Le Grillon once more it was not yet six, so, leaving

Femme Fatale

their skiff, they set off on foot towards Bezons across the meadows and past the high poplars bordering the banks.

The wide hayfields waiting to be harvested were full of flowers. The sinking sun cast a mantle of russet light over all and in the gentle warmth of the day's end the fragrance of the grass wafted in on them mingling with the damp smells of the river and filling the air with easy languor and an atmosphere of blessed well-being.

He felt soft and unresistant, in communion with the calm splendour of the evening and with the vague, mysterious thrill of life itself. He felt in tune with the all-embracing poetry of the moment in which plants and all that surrounded him revealed themselves to his senses at this lovely restful and reflective time of day. He was sensitive to it all but she appeared totally unaffected. They were walking side by side when suddenly, bored by the silence, she began to sing. In a squeaky, unmodulated voice she sang one of the catchy tunes of the day which jarred violently with the deeply serene mood of the evening. He looked at her and felt between them an unbridgeable abyss. She was swinging her parasol through the grass with her head down, looking at her feet as she sang, drawing out the notes and adding the odd little trill.

So behind the smooth little brow which he so much adored there was nothing! Absolutely nothing! Its sole concern at the moment was this caterwauling. The thoughts which from time to time passed through it were as vapid as the music. She had no understanding of him. They were as separate and distinct as if they had never met. His kisses had touched her lips only and nothing deeper within.

When, however, she raised her eyes to meet his and smiled,

he felt himself melt. Opening his arms out wide to her in a surge of renewed love he clasped her passionately to him. Since he was crushing her dress as he did so, she eventually broke free saying consolingly, 'Yes, yes, I love you, my pet, now that's enough.' In a mad rush of relief he grabbed her round the waist and started to run, dragging her with him. He kissed her on the cheeks, the temples and the neck, all the time dancing with joy. They threw themselves down at the edge of a thicket incandescent in the light of the setting sun. Even before catching their breath they came together. She could not understand the rapture he felt.

Walking back hand in hand they suddenly saw through the trees the river and on it the boat containing the four women. Big Pauline must have caught sight of them at the same time since she straightened up, blew kisses at Madeleine and shouted, 'See you tonight!'

'See you tonight!' shouted Madeleine in reply.

Paul felt his heart turn suddenly to ice. They returned for dinner and settling down in one of the arbours at the side of the water they began to eat in silence. When darkness fell, a candle enclosed in a globe was brought which shed a feeble, glimmering light on the two. All the time they could hear bursts of laughter coming from the large room on the first floor where the boat-trippers were. The couple were just about to order dessert when Paul, taking Madeleine's hand tenderly in his own, said: 'Darling, I feel so tired. Shall we make an early night of it?'

But she saw through his little ploy and shot him an enigmatic glance, one of those treacherous looks that so often

Femme Fatale

appear in women's eyes. She thought for a second, then said, 'You're perfectly welcome to go to bed if you like but I've promised to go to the dance at La Grenouillère.'

Attempting to mask his misery he gave her a pitiful smile and answered in a coaxing, wheedling tone: 'Be a darling. Let's both stay here. Please.'

She shook her head without saying a word. He tried again. 'Please, sweetheart . . .'

She cut him off. 'You know what I said. If you're not happy, you know where the door is. Nobody's stopping you. But I've promised, and I'm going.'

He put his two elbows on the table, sank his head into his hands and sat brooding. The trippers were coming down the stairs, yelling as usual before setting off for the dance at La Grenouillère. Madeleine said to Paul: 'Make up your mind. If you're not coming I'll ask one of these gentlemen to take me there.'

Paul rose. 'Come on then,' he muttered before they too set off. The night was dark and the sky full of stars. Around them the air was still hot and the atmosphere heavy with seething, unseen activity. The warm breeze caressed their faces, its hot breath stifling their own and making them gasp slightly. The skiffs set off, each with a Venetian lantern in the prow. It was too dark to see anything of the boats themselves except for the little patches of colour in the night bobbing and dancing like frenzied glow-worms. Voices sounded from the shadows on all sides as the young couple's skiff glided gently along. Sometimes when another overtook they would catch the flash of the oarsman's white-jerseyed back illuminated by his lantern. As they came round the bend of the river, La Grenouillère came into sight in the distance.

In gala mood, the place was decorated with bunting and with strings, clusters and garlands of fairy lights. On the surface of the Seine large barges moved slowly about, representing domes, pyramids and all kinds of monuments picked out in variously coloured lights. Illuminated festoons hung down as far as the water itself, and here and there an enormous red or blue lantern suspended from an invisible rod hung like a huge star in the sky.

All these illuminations shone on the café and floodlit the great trees on the bank whose trunks stood out pale grey and whose leaves were milky green against the deep, pitch black of the fields and of the sky. A band consisting of five local players blared shrill, syncopated music across the water and, hearing it, Madeleine began to sing along. She wanted to go in right away. Paul would have preferred to make a tour of the island first but had to give in. The clientèle had thinned out a little by this time, still consisting mostly of boatmen with the odd sprinkling of middle-class couples and a few young men flanked by girls. The director and organizer of the can-can strutted in his faded black suit and cast round the audience the world-weary, professional eye of a cheap music-hall master of ceremonies. Paul was relieved to see that Big Pauline and her chums were nowhere to be seen.

People were dancing. Couples faced each other and capered about madly, kicking their legs as high as their partners' noses. The women, who appeared to have double-jointed legs and hips, leapt about in a frou-frou of lifted skirts, flashing their knickers and kicking their legs up over their heads with amazing agility. They wriggled their bellies and shook their bosoms, spreading about them the powerful smell of female flesh in sweat. The males squatted like toads in front of them making faces and obscene gestures. They cavorted and turned cartwheels, posturing meanwhile in hideous parody, as one strapping maid and two waiters served the audience drinks.

Since the café-boat was covered by a roof only and had no side walls to separate it from the outdoors, the whole rumbustious dance was performed against the backdrop of the peaceful night and a firmament dusted with stars. Suddenly Mont-Valérien in the distance lit up as if a fire had started behind it. The glow deepened and spread, describing a wide, luminous circle of pale light. Then a ruby-coloured shape appeared, grew large, and glowed like red-hot metal. The circle widened further still and seemed to be emerging from the earth itself, as the moon, breaking free of the horizon, sailed gently upwards into space. As it rose, its crimson glow dimmed and turned to an increasingly light then bright yellow. As the planet climbed higher it grew smaller and smaller still in the distance.

Paul, lost in long contemplation of this sight, had become oblivious of his girl. When he turned round she had disappeared from view. He looked for her in vain. Having searched anxiously and systematically up and down the rows of tables he started asking people. No one had seen her. He then began to wander about wretchedly until one of the waiters said: 'If you're looking for Madame Madeleine, she went off a little while ago with Madame Pauline.'

Simultaneously, he caught sight of the midshipwoman and

the two beautiful girls sitting at the opposite end of the café, arms round each other's waists, watching him and whispering. Realizing what had happened, he ran off like a madman towards the island. Chasing first in the direction of Chatou, he stopped at the edge of the plain, turned and retraced his steps. He began to search the dense coppices, wandering about aimlessly and stopping every so often to listen. All he could hear around him was the short, metallic croak of frogs. Towards Bougival an unfamiliar bird sang a song which reached him faintly from a distance. Over the broad fields the moon shed a soft, filmy light. It filtered through the foliage, silvering the barks of the poplars and casting a shower of brilliant moonbeams on the shimmering tops of the tallest trees. Despite himself Paul was enchanted by the intoxicating loveliness of the night. It penetrated the terrible anguish he was feeling and stirred in his heart a fierce sense of irony. He longed with all his gentle and idealistic soul for a faithful woman to worship – someone in whose arms he could express all his love and tenderness as well as his passion.

Choked by racking sobs, he had to stop in his tracks. Having recovered a little he went on, only to feel a sudden stab in his heart. There, behind that bush . . . a pair of lovers! He ran forward and saw their silhouettes united in a seemingly endless kiss before they quickly ran off at his approach. He dared not call out, knowing full well that his own girl would not respond. He was desperately afraid now of coming upon them all of a sudden. The music of the quadrilles with its piercing solo cornets, the mock gaiety of the flute and the scraping of the fiddles pulled at his own heartstrings and deepened the pain he continued to feel.

Suddenly it occurred to him that she might have gone back in! Yes, that was it! She must have returned. He had lost all sense of proportion, he was stupid, he had been carried away by all the silly suspicions and fears that always haunted him. In one of those periods of strange calm which occur during periods of the blackest despair he turned and began to make for the café again.

He took in the whole room at a single glance. She was not there. He checked all the tables, and once again came face to face with the three women. He must have looked the picture of dejection for the three burst out laughing. Rushing out again, he ran back to the island. He threw himself into the coppices and stopped to listen once more. It was some time before he could hear anything save the roaring in his own ears. Finally, however, he thought he could hear some way ahead a shrill little laugh he knew only too well. Creeping forward he fell to his knees and crawled on, parting the branches cautiously as he went. His heart was beating so wildly in his chest that he could hardly breathe. Two voices were murmuring. He could not make out what they were saying. Then they fell silent again.

He had a sudden furious desire to run away, not to see, not to know and to keep on running to escape from the raging passion with which he was consumed. He would return to Chatou, catch a train and never come back. He would never see her again. Just as suddenly her face appeared in his mind's eye. He saw her as she was waking up next to him in their warm bed. He saw her snuggle up to him and throw her arms round his neck. Her hair was loose and a little tangled over her brow. Her eyes were still closed and her lips parted, waiting for the first kiss of the day. The thought of this morning's embrace filled him with unbearable regret and frantic desire.

They were talking again. He approached bent double. Then a cry rose from under the branches close to him. That cry! It was one of those he had come to know from their most tender, their most passionate love-making. He crept even closer, drawn irresistibly, blindly, despite himself . . . and then he saw them.

Oh! If only the other person had been a man! But this! He was transfixed by the loathsome sight before him. He remained there overwhelmed by shock. It was as though he had just stumbled upon the mutilated body of a loved one. It was a crime against nature, a monstrous and wicked desecration. Suddenly flashing into his mind's eye this time came the image of the little fish whose entrails he had earlier seen ripped out. Madeleine was moaning 'Pauline', exactly as she used to moan 'Paul' to him. Hearing it, he felt such pain that he turned and fled. He hurtled into one tree and ricocheted into another, fell over a root, picked himself up and ran again until suddenly he found himself at the edge of the river. The raging torrent made whirls and eddies on which the moonbeams now played. On the opposite side the bank loomed over the water like a cliff, leaving a wide band of black at its foot from which the sound of the swirling water rose in the darkness. Clearly visible on the other side were the weekend homes at Croissy.

Paul saw all this as if in a dream or as something remembered. He was no longer thinking. He understood nothing now. Everything including his own existence seemed vague, distant, forgotten and finished. There was the river. Did he know what he was doing? Did he want to die? He had lost his mind. Nevertheless he turned round to face the island where she was. Into the night in which the faint but persistent beat of the dance-band still throbbed back and forth, he shouted, 'Madeleine!'

His heart-rending call pierced the great silence of the sky and echoed, lost in the distance. Then with a furious animal-like leap he plunged into the river. The water splashed then closed over the spot setting up a series of ever-widening circles which rippled in the moonlight as far as the opposite bank. The two women had heard. Madeleine got up and said, 'That's Paul.' A suspicion arose suddenly in her mind. 'He's drowned himself,' she said and rushed towards the bank where Pauline caught up with her.

A heavy punt with two men in it was circling over and over around the same spot. One of the men rowed while the other was plunging a long pole into the water evidently looking for something. Pauline shouted: 'What's happened? What are you doing?'

A stranger's voice cried: 'A man's just drowned himself.'

With haggard faces the two women huddled together and watched the boat's manoeuvres. The music from La Grenouillère pounding in the distance provided a grim counterpoint to the movements of the solemn fishermen. The river, now containing a corpse in its depths, continued to swirl in the moonlight. The search was prolonged and

Madeleine, waiting in horrible suspense, shivered. Finally, after a good half-hour, one of the men announced: 'I've got him!'

Very gradually he pulled in the boathook. A large mass appeared at the surface of the water. The other boatman left his oars and between the two, each heaving with all his strength, they managed to haul the inert body and bring it tumbling into the boat. They soon reached the bank and found an open, flat space in the moonlight. As they landed, the women approached.

As soon as she saw him Madeleine recoiled in horror. In the light of the moon's rays he looked green already and his mouth, his eyes, his nose and his clothes were full of the river's slime. The stiff fingers of his clenched fist looked hideous. Black, liquid silt covered his entire body. The face looked swollen and from his hair now plastered down with ooze a stream of filthy water ran. The two men examined him.

'You know him?' asked one.

The other, the Croissy ferryman, hesitated.

'Seems to me I know the face . . .,' he said, 'but it's difficult to tell seeing him like this . . .'

Then suddenly: 'Oh! I know! It's Monsieur Paul!'

'Who's Monsieur Paul?' his friend asked.

The first went on: 'You know! Monsieur Paul Baron. Son of that senator. The kid who was so hooked on that girl, you remember?'

The other added philosophically: 'No more girls for him now, eh? Poor sod. And with all that money too!'

Madeleine, having collapsed on the ground, was sobbing.

Pauline approached the body and said, 'I suppose he really is dead . . . there's no chance he might . . . ?'

The men shrugged their shoulders.

'After that length of time no question.'

Then one of them asked: 'Was he staying at Le Grillon?'

'Yes,' said the other. 'We'd better take him back there. Handsome tip, mate.' Re-embarking they set off, moving slowly against the rapid current. Long after they had disappeared from the two women's sight the regular sound of their oars could still be heard.

Pauline took poor, weeping Madeleine in her arms, kissed and rocked her for a long time and then said: 'Now look. As long as you know it's not your fault. You can't stop men doing stupid things. It was his decision so it's just too bad, that's all.'

Then lifting her to her feet, she added, 'Come on darling! Come and sleep at the house. You can't go back to Le Grillon tonight.' She kissed her again. 'Come on, you'll feel better with us,' she said.

Madeleine got up, still sobbing, but less violently. She leaned her head on Pauline's shoulder. Seeming to find there a safer, warmer refuge and a closer, more intimate affection, she walked slowly away from the scene.

Hautot & Son

The house, half farm and half manor, was one of those combinations often found in the country of a property once vaguely seigneurial and now owned by farmers themselves rich in land. In front of it the dogs tied to the farmyard apple trees were barking and yelping as the keeper and some small boys arrived carrying gamebags.

It was the opening day of the season and in the vast kitchen which served as dining room Hautot senior, Hautot junior, Monsieur Bermont the tax-collector and Monsieur Mondaru the lawyer were having a drink and a bite to eat before setting off on the day's shoot. Hautot senior, very proud of his property, was telling his guests ahead of time what excellent game they would find on his land. He was a big-boned, ruddy-faced Norman, the powerfully built sort of man who can carry a whole barrel of apples on his shoulders. Somewhat authoritarian in manner, he was wealthy, respected and highly influential. He had sent his son César to school up to the fourth form so that he should have some education, then removed him lest he become so much of a gentleman that he no longer cared about his land.

César Hautot was nearly as tall as his father, but leaner. He was an easy-going, happy-go-lucky young man, a good son to his father whom he greatly admired and to whose every wish and opinion he was happy to defer.

Monsieur Bermont, the tax-collector, was a stout little man on whose red cheeks a maze of violet-coloured veins looked like a network of tortuous rivers and tributaries as might be seen on maps in an atlas. He asked, 'And hare? Will there be . . . hare?'

Hautot senior replied, 'As much as you like! Specially round Puysatier.'

'Where shall we start?' enquired the lawyer, a portly, well-fed man trussed up now in a new shooting jacket bought the previous week in Rouen.

'Down at the bottom, I think. We'll get the partridge out on the plain and then put them up from there.'

With this, Hautot senior rose. Following suit they all stood up and stamped their feet to bring warmth and suppleness to the leather of their newly-donned and tight-fitting boots. They collected the guns propped up in various corners of the room, examined the locks, then left the house. Outside, the dogs, still leashed, were now jumping up on their hind legs, yelping shrilly and pawing the air.

They set off towards the lower grounds and a small valley which was no more than a dip of poor-quality land left purposely uncultivated. It was criss-crossed with gullies and covered with fern – an excellent place for game. The guns spread out, with Hautot senior on the far right, Hautot junior on the far left and the two guests in the middle. The keeper and two gamebag carriers followed. Nervously fingering their triggers and with their hearts beating fast they stopped and stood waiting in solemn silence for the first shot of the season to ring out.

There it was! Hautot senior had fired. They saw one

partridge fall away from the headlong flight of birds and come down in a gully covered with thick brush. Highly excited, Hautot leapt up and ran off, tearing up everything in his way and finally disappearing into the undergrowth to pick up his quarry. Almost immediately a second shot rang out.

'The lucky devil!' cried old Bermont. 'He's picked off a hare while he's at it!'

They all waited, eyes fixed on the dense, impenetrable undergrowth. Cupping his hands round his mouth, the lawyer yelled: 'Have you got them?'

Since no answer came from Hautot senior, César, turning to the keeper, said: 'Go and give him a hand, Joseph, will you? We must spread out in line. We'll wait for you.'

Joseph, a great gnarled tree-trunk of a man, set off calmly down towards the gully. Like a fox he carefully reconnoitred the easiest way through the brush. Having found it and disappeared, he cried out suddenly: 'Come quick! Quick! There's been an accident!'

Each man tore through the bushes towards the scene. When they got there they saw Hautot lying on his side, unconscious, clasping his stomach from which long streams of blood were flowing inside his bullet-torn jacket and into the grass. His fallen partridge within reach, Hautot must have dropped the gun to pick it up and in so doing triggered a second shot which shattered his own entrails. They dragged him from the ditch and on removing some of his clothing found a terrible wound now spilling out his intestines. They ligatured him as best they could and carried him home where the doctor they had sent for was waiting, along with a priest.

When the doctor saw him he shook his head gravely, and turning to Hautot's son who was sobbing in a chair, said, 'My poor boy, I'm afraid it doesn't look at all good.'

But when a dressing had been applied, the injured man moved his fingers, opened his mouth, then a pair of haggard eyes, and cast a few anxious glances around him. He seemed to be searching his mind for something and then, when the whole sequence of events came flooding back, murmured: 'Christ almighty! I've had it now.'

The doctor took his hand.

'No! Certainly not! All you need is a few days' rest and you'll be absolutely fine.'

Hautot went on: 'No, I know the score. Shattered stomach. I've had it.'

Then suddenly: 'I want to talk to my son if I've got time.'

Young Hautot whimpered like a little boy: 'Papa! Papa! Oh, poor Papa!'

In a firmer tone his father said: 'Listen, stop crying. Doesn't help. I've got to talk to you. Come close, it'll only take a minute. Then I'll feel much better. You lot, can we have a minute or two if you don't mind?'

The others went out of the room, leaving father and son together. As soon as they were alone the father spoke: 'Listen, my boy, you're twenty-four, I can tell you everything now. Not that there's much to tell. Anyway you know when your mother died seven years ago I was . . . well I'm forty-five now. I was married at nineteen by the way, right?'

'Yes I know.'

'So when she died she left me a widower at thirty-seven.

Can you imagine? Chap like me. Can't be a permanent widower at thirty-seven, can you my boy?'

'No father, of course not.'

The father's face was pale and contorted with pain.

'God, I'm in agony here. Anyway, to continue. A chap can't live entirely on his own yet I couldn't remarry. I'd promised your mum. So . . . are you following?'

'Yes father.'

'So. I took up with this girl in Rouen. Rue de l'Éperlan, number 18, third floor, second door. You are taking all this in I hope? This girl, she's been so good to me, you know. I couldn't have wished for a sweeter little wife. Loving, devoted, you get the picture my boy?'

'Yes father.'

'Well, anyway, if I should pop off I reckon I owe her. A lot. Enough to set her up. You understand?'

'Yes, father.'

'When I say she's a good kid, I mean really good. If it hadn't been for you, and out of respect for your mother's memory, if it hadn't been for this house, and us having lived here, the three of us, I'd have brought her home here and married her, no question. Listen, listen, my boy. I could have made a will but I didn't. Didn't want to. Never put things down in writing. Not that sort of thing anyway. Upsets the family. Makes everything too complicated. Everybody at each other's throats. Who needs legal documents? Don't ever use them. That's how I've made my money, such as it is. Understand, my boy?'

'Yes, father.'

'Listen again, carefully. So I haven't made a will. Didn't

need to. Because I know you. You've got a good heart, you're not ... careful ... tight-fisted, you know what I mean? So I thought when the end came I'd just tell you how things stood and I'd ask you not to forget the girl: Caroline Donet, rue de l'Éperlan, number 18, third floor, second door, don't forget. Listen again. Go straight there when I've gone ... and make sure she's seen all right by me. You'll have plenty. You can do it. I'm leaving you enough. Listen. She won't be there most of the week, she works for Madame Moreau, rue Beauvoisine. But go on Thursday. That's when she expects me. That's my day, has been for six years now. Oh the poor girl! She's going to be so upset! I'm telling you all this because I know you, my boy. Not the sort of thing you tell everybody. Not the lawyer and not the curé. It happens, everybody knows that, but you don't discuss it. Not unless you have to. So, no strangers in on it. Just the family that's all. You understand?'

'Yes father.'

'Promise?'

'Yes father.'

'Swear?'

'Yes, father.'

'I beg of you, my boy, please. Please don't forget. You mustn't.'

'I won't father.'

'Go in person. You're in charge of everything.'

'Yes, father.'

'Then you'll see what she says. I can't talk any more. Swear to me.'

'Yes father.'

'That's good, my boy. Come and give me a kiss goodbye. I'm nearly finished. This is it. Tell them they can come in.'

Moaning, the younger Hautot kissed his father and, obedient as always, opened the door. The priest appeared wearing a white surplice and carrying the holy oils. But the dying man had closed his eyes and refused to open them again. He refused to reply and refused to give any sign that he knew what was going on.

He had talked enough and could not say another word. Besides, he felt relieved now. He could die in peace. What need was there for him to confess to this delegate of God since he had already confessed to his own son who really was family?

The last rites were administered, and he was given communion in the midst of his kneeling friends and servants with never a movement of his face to indicate that he was still alive. He died at around midnight after four hours of spasms indicative of appalling pain.

The season had opened on the Sunday and Hautot was buried the following Tuesday. Having returned from taking his father to the cemetery, César Hautot spent the rest of the day in tears. He hardly slept that night and was so miserable the next day that he wondered how he could carry on living. Nevertheless he spent the whole day thinking that, if his father's last wish was to be carried out, he should go to Rouen the following day and see this Caroline Donet at the rue de l'Éperlan, number 18, third floor, second door. He had repeated this like a mantra so many times so as not to forget it, that now he could think of little else. Both his mind and his ear were hypnotized by the phrase. Accordingly, the next morning around eight o'clock, having ordered Graindorge harnessed to the tilbury, he set off at a brisk pace behind the heavy Norman horse on the main road from Ainville to Rouen. He was wearing his black frock-coat, a tall silk topper and his trousers with the straps under the soles. In the circumstances he decided not to wear over his handsome suit the loose blue smock which, flapping in the wind, protected his better clothes against any dust or spots and which he normally shed as soon as he jumped down on arriving at his destination.

He got to Rouen just as ten o'clock was striking and went as usual to the Hôtel des Bons-Enfants, rue des Trois Mares. There he was embraced by the proprietor, the proprietor's wife and their five sons, all of whom had heard the sad news. After that he had to tell them exactly how the accident had happened and this set him off crying again. He turned down their offers of comfort, all the more insistent now that he was a man of substance, and even refused their invitation to dinner, which really offended them.

Having dusted off his hat, brushed down his frock-coat and given his boots a quick wipe, he set out to find the rue de l'Éperlan. He dared not ask for directions lest he be recognized and suspicions raised. Finally drawing a complete blank, he spotted a priest and counting on the professional discretion of a clergyman found out from him the way to the address. It was very close. In the next street on the right in fact.

He began to feel a little hesitant. Until this moment he had been blindly following his dead father's instructions.

Now he felt a confusing mixture of sorrow and shame as he thought of himself, a son, soon to be face to face with the woman who had been his father's mistress. All the old moral strictures lying buried in his unconscious under layer after layer of conventional, received wisdom handed down from generation to generation, everything he had learned from his catechism years and since about loose women and the instinctive mistrust men have of them even if they marry one – all these ignorant, peasant values clamoured inside him, held him back and brought a blush of shame to his cheeks.

Nevertheless, he thought, I promised my father. Mustn't let him down. The door marked 18 was ajar so he pushed it open and saw beyond it a dark stairway which he climbed as far as the third floor. There he saw first one door, then a second with a bell-pull which he now tugged. The tinkle which he heard echo into the room beyond made his heart sink. The door was opened and he found himself standing opposite a very well-dressed, fresh-faced brunette who was staring at him in astonishment.

He had no idea what to say and she, unaware of anything untoward and expecting his father any minute, did not invite him in. They looked at each other for a full thirty seconds, at the end of which she said: 'Can I help you, monsieur?'

He murmured, 'I'm Hautot, the son.'

She started, turned pale and stammered as if she had known him all her life: 'Oh! Monsieur César?'

'Yes.'

'What . . . what's . . . ?'

'I have a message for you from my father.'

She said, 'Oh my God!' and took a step backwards to let him in. He then saw a little boy playing with a cat on the floor in front of a stove where several dishes were cooking.

'Sit down,' she said.

He sat down.

'Well?' she asked.

He was struck dumb, his eyes on the table in the middle of the room laid for three including a child. He looked at the chair with its back to the fire, the plate, the napkin, the glasses, one bottle of red wine, already drunk from, and one unopened bottle of white. That must be his father's usual place with his back to the fire! He was still expected by her! That would have been his father's bread with all the crust removed because of his poor teeth. Raising his eyes, he saw hanging on the wall a large photograph of his father taken at the Paris Exhibition, the duplicate of one which hung over the bed in the master bedroom at Ainville.

The young woman went on: 'So? Monsieur César?'

He looked at her. She was pale with dread and her hands were trembling fearfully as she waited for him to speak. Eventually he gathered up enough courage to do so. 'Well Mam'zelle, I'm afraid Papa died on Sunday on the opening day of the shooting season.'

She was shocked literally rigid. After a few moments' silence she said in a barely audible voice, 'Oh no! He can't have!'

Then suddenly her eyes filled with tears. She raised her hands to cover her face and began to sob. The little boy, seeing his mother burst into tears and deducing that this stranger was the cause, hurled himself on César, grabbed him by the trouser-leg with one hand and started smacking him on the thigh as hard as he could with the other. César, frantic with grief himself, his own eyes still swollen with crying, was moved at the sight of this woman weeping for his father and the little boy defending the mother. He felt almost overwhelmed with emotion and, in order to keep from breaking down himself, started to speak: 'Yes,' he said, 'the tragedy occurred on Sunday morning at eight o'clock . . .'

He went on, assuming she was hearing it all and forgetting no detail, omitting not the smallest incident in a painstaking, plodding peasant way. The little boy continued to smack him and had now begun to kick him on the ankles. When Hautot junior came to the part where Hautot senior had talked about her, the young woman, hearing her own name, uncovered her face and asked: 'I'm sorry. Could you start again please? I wasn't taking it in . . . I really want to know what happened . . .'

He began again, using exactly the same words: 'The tragedy occurred on Sunday morning at eight o'clock . . .'

Again he told her everything, stopping every now and then to punctuate the story with little asides of his own. She listened attentively. With the sensitive perception of a woman, she seized every implication of each twist and turn of events, shuddering with horror and saying 'Oh my God' from time to time. The little boy, seeing his mother had calmed down, stopped hitting César and was now holding her hand, listening too as if he understood every word. When he came to the end Hautot junior said: 'And now what we must do is make sure his wishes are carried out. I'm in a comfortable position. He's left me property so . . . I wouldn't want you to feel in any need . . .'

She broke in abruptly: 'Oh, please, please, Monsieur César! Not today! My heart's breaking! Another time, another day, perhaps. But not today. And if I were to accept, I do want you to know it would not be for me, oh no, no, no, I swear I wouldn't want anything for myself but for the little one. We'll put any money in his name.'

César was aghast. Then the penny dropped. He stammered, 'You mean . . . he's his?'

'Oh yes,' she said.

Hautot junior looked at his half-brother with a mixture of emotions, all deeply painful. After a long silence, for she had begun to weep again, César was at a complete loss as to what to do. He said: 'Well then, Mam'zelle Donet, I'd better be going. When would you like us to meet and talk about arrangements?'

She cried out: 'Oh don't go! Please! Please don't leave me and Émile on our own. I'd die of grief. I've got nobody now except my little boy. Oh it's awful, Monsieur César, it's terrible! Please, please sit down! Talk to me some more. Tell me about what he used to do when he was away from here, when he was back home with you.'

And so César, obedient as always, sat down again. She drew her chair up close to his in front of the stove where the food was still cooking. She put Émile on her lap and asked César hundreds of little intimate questions about his father from which he could see or rather feel instinctively that this poor young woman had loved Hautot with all her heart.

The conversation naturally kept returning to the accident

and he told her all over again what had happened, in the same detail. When he said, 'The hole in his stomach was so big you could have put both hands in it', she gave a sort of cry and began sobbing yet again. This time César too broke down with her and started to weep. Softened by his own tears he leaned down towards Émile whose forehead was within reach and kissed it. His mother struggled to get her breath back.

'Poor little mite,' she said, 'he's fatherless now.'

'Me too,' said César.

At this, each stopped talking. Suddenly the young woman became the practical housewife who thinks of everything and everyone.

'I don't suppose you've eaten a thing all morning, have you, Monsieur César?'

'No, Mam'zelle.'

'Oh, you must be hungry! Will you have something to eat?'

'No thank you,' he said, 'I'm not hungry. Too upset.'

'Oh, but you've got to eat in spite of everything, you'll grant me that. Do stay a bit longer. I don't know what I'll do when you leave.'

After a few attempts at resistance, he sat down opposite her, and in the chair with its back to the fire he settled down to a dish of the tripe that had been sizzling in the oven, and to a glass of red wine. Several times he wiped the mouth of the little boy who had dribbled sauce all over his chin. As he rose to leave, he said: 'When would you like me to come back and talk business, Mam'zelle Donet?'

'If it's all the same to you, Monsieur César, next Thursday.

It'll save me taking time off. I've always got Thursday off anyway.'

'That's fine with me. Next Thursday.'

'You'll have lunch, won't you?'

'Oh, I don't know . . . really.'

'It's much easier to talk over a meal. Saves time too.'

'All right then. Let's say twelve o'clock.'

After giving little Émile another kiss and shaking Mademoiselle Donet's hand he left.

The week passed very slowly for César Hautot. He had never been on his own before and solitude seemed unbearable to him. Until then, he had shadowed his father all his life, following him into the fields, seeing that his orders were carried out, then, after a little while apart, he would see him again at dinner. In the evenings they would sit opposite each other smoking their pipes and talking about horses, cows and sheep. Their morning handshake was an expression of deep family attachment.

And now César was alone. He wandered about in the ploughed fields of autumn, all the time expecting to see the tall silhouette of his father waving to him from some field or other. To kill time he would drop in on neighbours, describe the accident to anyone who had not heard what had happened, and retell the story to those who had. Sometimes when he had run out of things that needed thinking about or doing he would sit down at the side of a cart track and wonder how much longer he could carry on.

He thought often of Mademoiselle Donet. He had liked her very much. He thought she was a very nice person indeed, a good, kind girl as his father had said. Yes, she was a lovely girl. A really lovely girl. He was determined to do her proud and to give her 2,000 francs in interest on capital to be settled on the child. He was rather pleased that he had to go and see her the following Thursday to sort things out with her. The thought of this brother, this new little fellow was a bit of a worry. It bothered him a little, yet at the same time it gave him a warm sort of feeling. There was a bit of kin for him there. The kid born on the other side of the blanket would never be called Hautot, but he was a bit of family with no pressure attached, a bit of his father after all.

When he found himself once more on the way to Rouen on Thursday morning, with these and similar thoughts in his head and the sound of Graindorge's rhythmical clip-clop, his heart was lighter and his mind calmer than at any time since the accident. As he entered Mademoiselle Donet's apartment he saw that everything was laid exactly as it had been the previous Thursday with one single exception – the crust of the bread at his place had not been removed.

He shook hands with the young woman, kissed Émile on both cheeks and sat down feeling both very much at home and extremely emotional. Mademoiselle Donet seemed slightly thinner and slightly paler. She must have cried her little heart out. This time she was a bit awkward in her manner towards him as if she had realized something she had been unable to absorb on that first occasion when she was still taking in the enormity of what had happened. She was extremely attentive to his needs and humble in her approach, as if trying to pay back in devotion and service towards him some of the generosity he was showing her. They took a long time over lunch and discussed the business which had brought him there. She did not want so much money. It was too much, far too much. She earned enough to keep herself; all she wanted was that Émile might have something to look forward to when he reached his majority. César, however, stuck to his guns and even added a present for herself as a token of mourning. As he finished his coffee, she asked, 'Do you smoke?'

'Yes, I've got my pipe here . . .,' he began.

He patted his pockets. Damnation. He had left it at home! He was just about to bemoan the fact when she produced one belonging to his father which she had kept tucked away in a cupboard. He took it from her and recognized it. Sniffing it and with emotion in his voice, declaring it to be one of the best, he filled and lit it. Then he put Émile on his knee and played ride-a-cock-horse with him while she cleared the table, stacking the dirty dishes in the sideboard to wash later after he had gone.

At about three, when he rose regretfully, he hated the idea of leaving.

'Well, Mamz'elle Donet,' he said, 'I'll wish you a very good afternoon. I'm delighted to have made your acquaintance like this.'

She remained standing in front of him, blushing and near to tears. As she looked at him she thought of his father.

'Are we not to see each other again then?' she asked.

He replied simply: 'We can, Mam'zelle, if that's what you'd like.'

'It most certainly is, Monsieur César. Shall we say next Thursday, if that's convenient for you?'

'Indeed it is, Mam'zelle Donet.'

'You'll come for lunch, of course?'

'Well, if you're offering I wouldn't say no.'

'Very well, Monsieur César. Thursday next it is, at twelve o'clock, like today.'

'Twelve o'clock on Thursday then, Mam'zelle Donet!'

Laid to Rest

Five friends had been dining together. They were all rich, middle-aged men of the world, two of them bachelors, three married men. These monthly meetings of theirs were some of the happiest evenings of their lives. They had all known each other since their youth, remained close friends, enjoyed one another's company and often stayed talking till two o'clock in the morning. The conversation was about anything and everything that might interest or amuse a Parisian and, as in most drawing rooms, it was a kind of verbal version of the news in the morning papers.

One of the most footloose and fancy-free among them was Joseph de Bardon, a bachelor who exploited to the full all the attractions Paris has to offer. Though not exactly decadent or debauched in his habits, he managed to satisfy all the natural curiosity of a fun-loving man in his late thirties. A man of the world in the best and widest sense of the word, he was witty rather than profound, knowledgeable rather than wise and possessed a quick rather than a deep understanding of human nature. His experiences and encounters provided him with a fund of anecdotes, some edifying, some frankly hilarious. He had a reputation in society as a bright fellow with a good sense of humour – everyone's favourite after-dinner speaker whose tales were always the ones most looked forward to. He never needed any urging to begin, as he did on this occasion.

Certain creatures at certain times and places look absolutely in their element, let's say a goldfish in its bowl, a nun in church, or what have you. Sitting there smoking a cigar, with his elbows on the table, a half-filled glass of liqueur brandy to hand and relaxing in a warm haze of coffee and tobacco, he looked like a man in his ideal milieu. Between a couple of puffs he spoke.

'The funniest thing happened to me not so long ago . . .'

A near-instantaneous chorus replied, 'Go on, do!'

And he was off.

'Thank you, I shall. You know I get around Paris a fair amount. As other people window-shop, I watch what's going on. I watch the world and his brother pass by, I watch what's going on around me. Well, some time towards the middle of last September, I left the house one afternoon with no clear idea of where I was going. You know how you always have a vague yen to go and see some pretty woman or other . . . you riffle through your little black book, you do a few mental comparisons, you weigh up the possible delights and you decide more or less on the spur of the moment. But when the sun's shining and it's warm outside you don't always want to be cooped up indoors. On this particular day, it was warm and sunny and I lit a cigar before starting to stroll along the outer boulevard. As I was sauntering along I decided to make for the cemetery in Montmartre and have a little wander about there. I like cemeteries, you know. They sadden and they soothe me and I find I need that from time to time. And of course some of one's chums are there, people nobody goes to see any more. I drop by every so often still.

Laid to Rest

And as it happens, an old flame of mine is buried in Montmatre Cemetery, a lovely little lady I was very keen on at one point in my life, very attached to. So although it's painful, I find it does me good. I mean all kinds of memories come flooding back while I'm there, letting my thoughts drift beside her grave. It's all over for her of course . . .

'The other reason I like cemeteries is because they're like cities in themselves, densely populated at that. Just think how many generations of Parisians are packed in there for ever; so many people stuck in their caves, their little holes just covered with a stone or marked with a cross, while the living take up so much room and make such a stupid racket.

'Then of course you've got all the monuments, some of them much more interesting than in a museum. Though I wouldn't put them in the same league, Cavaignac's grave reminded me so much of that masterpiece by Jean Goujon, the statue of Louis de Brézé in the underground chapel at Rouen cathedral. That's actually the root of all so-called modern, realist art, you know. That statue of the dead Louis de Brézé is more convincing, more terrible and more suggestive of inanimate flesh still convulsed in the death-agony than any of the tortured corpses you see sculpted these days on people's tombs.

'But in Montmartre Cemetery you can still admire the impressive monument to Baudin, the one to Gautier, and that to Murger, on which incidentally, only the other day I spotted one poor solitary wreath of helichrysums. I wonder who put that there. Perhaps the last of the *grisettes*, now a very old woman and possibly one of the local concierges. It's a pretty little statue by Millet, suffering badly from neglect and all the accumulated dirt of the years. Oh for the joys of youth, eh, Murger?

'Anyway there I was, stepping into Montmartre Cemetery, suddenly filled with sadness of a not entirely disagreeable kind, the sort that makes a healthy fellow think "Not the most cheerful of spots, but thank God I'm not stuck in here just yet." The feeling of autumn, the warm dampness of dead leaves in pale, weak sunshine heightened and romanticized the sense of solitude and finality surrounding this place of the dead.

'I wandered slowly along the streets of graves where neighbours no longer call, no longer sleep together and never hear the news. Then I started reading the epitaphs. I tell you gentlemen, they are absolutely killing. Not even Labiche or Meilhac can give me more of a laugh than the language of the headstone. When you read what the nearest and dearest have put on the marble slabs and crosses, pouring out their grief and their best wishes for the happiness of the departed in the next world, and their hopes – the liars! – for a speedy reunion, it's hilarious! Better than a Paul de Kock any day!

'But what I love most in that cemetery is the deserted, lonely part planted with all those tall yews and cypresses, the old district where those who died long ago now lie. Soon it will become the new part of town; the green trees nourished by human corpses will be felled to make room for the recently departed to be lined up in turn under their own little marble slabs.

'After I had wandered about long enough to refresh my mind, I realized I was now getting a little bored and that it was time to go to the last resting place of my old love and

Laid to Rest

pay her my ever-faithful respects. By the time I reached her graveside I was feeling quite upset. Poor darling, she was so sweet, so loving, so fair and rosy . . . and now . . . if this spot were ever opened up . . . Leaning on the iron railings I whispered to her a few sad words which I dare say she is unlikely to have heard. I was just about to leave when I saw a woman in deep mourning on her knees at the next graveside. She had lifted her crêpe veil and under it could be seen a pretty head of fair hair, a crown of bright dawn under the dark night of her head-dress. I lingered. In what was obviously deep distress she had buried her face in her hands and, stiff as a statue, was deep in meditation. Absorbed by her grief and telling the painful beads of memory behind closed and hidden eyes, she seemed herself dead to the world in her loss. Suddenly I saw that she was about to break down. I could tell from the slight movement her back made, like a willow stirring in the wind. She wept gently at first then more and more violently with her neck and shoulders shaking hard and rapidly. All of a sudden she uncovered her eyes. Full of tears they were lovely. She looked wildly about her as if waking from a nightmare. She saw me looking at her, seemed ashamed and buried her whole face once more in her hands. Then she burst into convulsive sobs and her head bent slowly down towards the marble slab. She rested her forehead on it and her veil, spreading about her, covered the white corners of her beloved sepulchre like a new mourning-cloth. I heard her moan before she collapsed with her cheek against the tombstone and lay there motionless and unconscious.

'I rushed over to her, slapped her hands and breathed on her eyelids while reading the simple epitaph beyond:

Guy de Maupassant

> HERE LIES LOUIS-THEODORE CARREL
> *Captain of Marines*
> *Killed by the enemy at Tonkin*
>
> PRAY FOR HIS SOUL

The date of death was some months earlier. I was moved to tears and redoubled my efforts to revive her. Finally they succeeded and she came to. I'm not bad-looking, not yet forty, remember, and at that moment I must have been looking extremely solicitous. At any rate, from her first glance I realized she would be both polite and grateful to me. I was not disappointed. Between further tears and sobs she told me about the officer who had been killed at Tonkin after they had been married for just one year. He had married her for love. She had been an orphan and possessed nothing but the smallest dowry.

'I comforted her, consoled her, lifted her up, then helped her to her feet.

"You can't stay here like this," I said, "come on . . ."

"I'm not sure I can manage to walk . . ."

"I'll help you, don't worry."

"Thank you, Monsieur, you're very kind. Did you have someone here yourself you wanted to mourn?"

"Yes, Madame."

"A lady?"

"Yes, Madame."

"Your wife?"

"A . . . friend."

"One can love a friend as much as a wife. Passion has its own laws."

Laid to Rest

"Indeed so, Madame."

'We walked away together, she leaning on me so heavily that I was almost carrying her along the paths of the cemetery. As we were leaving it, she said: "I think I'm going to faint."

"Would you like to go in and sit down somewhere? Let me get you something to . . ."

"Yes thank you, I would."

'I noticed a place nearby, one of those restaurants where the friends of the recently buried go when they have completed their grim duties. We went in and I made her drink a cup of hot tea which seemed to restore her strength somewhat. A faint smile came to her lips and she began to tell me a little about herself. How sad, how very sad it was to be all alone in the world, to be alone at home day and night, to have no one with whom to share love, trust and intimacy.

'It all seemed sincere and so genuine the way she told it. I felt my heart softening. She was very young, twenty at most. I flattered her a little and she responded gracefully. Then, as time was getting on, I offered to take her home by cab. She accepted. In the cab we were so close to each other, shoulder to shoulder, that we could feel the warmth of each other's bodies through our clothing – one of the most disturbing feelings in the world, as you know. When the cab drew up in front of her house she murmured: "I really don't think I can get up the stairs on my own. I live on the fourth floor. You've been so kind . . . could you possibly give me your arm again, please?"

'I said of course I could, and she went up slowly, breathing hard all the time. Then at her door she added: "Do come in for a few moments so that I can thank you."

'In I went, naturally.

'It was a modest, not to say poor little apartment furnished in simple but good taste. We sat side by side on a little sofa where she started talking again about how lonely she was. She rang for her maid to bring me something to drink. No one appeared. I was delighted about this and imagined that this maid must work mornings only, in other words, she only had a cleaner. She had taken off her hat. She really was quite a charmer. Her lovely, limpid eyes were fixed on me with such a clear, direct gaze that I suddenly felt an irresistible urge. I succumbed on the spot and clasped her in my arms. On her eyelids, which had instantly closed, I rained kiss after kiss after kiss. She struggled, pushing me away and repeating: "Please . . . please . . . please . . . have done!"

'What exactly did she mean? In the circumstances there were two ways of interpreting the words. To silence her I moved down from the eyes to the mouth and, putting my preferred interpretation on her request to please have done, complied with it. She put up little resistance and when later we looked at each other again after an insult to the memory of the captain killed at Tonkin she wore a languorous expression of tender resignation which dispelled any misgivings of my own.

'I showed my gratitude by being gallant and attentive, and after an hour or so's conversation asked: "Where do you normally dine?"

"At a little restaurant nearby."

"All on your own?"

"Yes, of course."

"Will you have dinner with me tonight?"

Laid to Rest

"Where did you have in mind?"

"Oh, a very good restaurant on the boulevard."

'She demurred for a while but I insisted and finally she gave in, reasoning that she would otherwise be terribly lonely again. Then she added, "I'd better change into something less severe," and disappeared into her bedroom. When she emerged she was in half-mourning and wearing a very simple but elegant grey dress in which she looked slender and charming. She obviously had markedly different outfits for the cemetery and for town.

'Dinner was very pleasant. She drank champagne, became very animated and excited, after which I went back to her apartment with her. This little liaison begun between the tombstones went on for some three weeks or so. But novelty, particularly with regard to women, eventually palls. I dropped her on the pretext of some unavoidable trip I had to make. I was very generous when we parted and she in turn very grateful. She made me promise, no, swear, to come back on my return and really seemed to care a little for me.

'I lost no time in forming other attachments, however, and about a month went by without my having felt any particular desire to resume my funereal fling. But nor did I forget her. The memory of her haunted me like some unsolved mystery, a psychological teaser, one of those nagging little puzzles you can't leave alone. One day, for some inexplicable reason, I wondered whether, if I went back to Montmartre Cemetery again, I might bump into her, and decided to return.

'I walked around for a long time but there was no one there apart from the usual sort of people who visit the place, mourners who have not yet severed all ties with their dead.

At the grave of the captain killed at Tonkin no one mourned over the marble slab, no flowers lay there, no wreaths. However, as I was walking through another district of the city of the departed I suddenly saw a couple, a man and a woman in deep mourning, coming towards me down a narrow avenue lined with crosses. To my amazement as they approached, I recognized the woman. It was she! Seeing me she blushed. As I brushed past her she gave me a tiny signal, the merest glance, but conveying in the clearest possible way both: "Don't show you know me," and "Come back and see me, darling."

'The man with her was about fifty, distinguished-looking and well-dressed, with the rosette of the *Légion d'honneur* in his lapel. He was supporting her just as I had done when we both left the cemetery that day.

'I went off, flabbergasted by what I had just seen and trying to imagine what tribe of creatures she belonged to, hunting as she obviously did on this sepulchral terrain. Was she a single prostitute who had struck on the brilliant idea of frequenting graveyards and picking up unhappy men still haunted by the loss of a wife or a mistress and troubled by the memory of past caresses? Was she unique? Or were there more like her? Was it a professional speciality to work the cemetery like the street? The loved ones of those laid to rest! Or was she alone in having conceived the psychologically sound idea of exploiting the feelings of amorous nostalgia awakened in these mournful venues?

'I was longing to know whose widow she had chosen to be that day.'

1. BOCCACCIO · *Mrs Rosie and the Priest*
2. GERARD MANLEY HOPKINS · *As kingfishers catch fire*
3. *The Saga of Gunnlaug Serpent-tongue*
4. THOMAS DE QUINCEY · *On Murder Considered as One of the Fine Arts*
5. FRIEDRICH NIETZSCHE · *Aphorisms on Love and Hate*
6. JOHN RUSKIN · *Traffic*
7. PU SONGLING · *Wailing Ghosts*
8. JONATHAN SWIFT · *A Modest Proposal*
9. *Three Tang Dynasty Poets*
10. WALT WHITMAN · *On the Beach at Night Alone*
11. KENKŌ · *A Cup of Sake Beneath the Cherry Trees*
12. BALTASAR GRACIÁN · *How to Use Your Enemies*
13. JOHN KEATS · *The Eve of St Agnes*
14. THOMAS HARDY · *Woman much missed*
15. GUY DE MAUPASSANT · *Femme Fatale*
16. MARCO POLO · *Travels in the Land of Serpents and Pearls*
17. SUETONIUS · *Caligula*
18. APOLLONIUS OF RHODES · *Jason and Medea*
19. ROBERT LOUIS STEVENSON · *Olalla*
20. KARL MARX AND FRIEDRICH ENGELS · *The Communist Manifesto*
21. PETRONIUS · *Trimalchio's Feast*
22. JOHANN PETER HEBEL · *How a Ghastly Story Was Brought to Light by a Common or Garden Butcher's Dog*
23. HANS CHRISTIAN ANDERSEN · *The Tinder Box*
24. RUDYARD KIPLING · *The Gate of the Hundred Sorrows*
25. DANTE · *Circles of Hell*
26. HENRY MAYHEW · *Of Street Piemen*
27. HAFEZ · *The nightingales are drunk*
28. GEOFFREY CHAUCER · *The Wife of Bath*
29. MICHEL DE MONTAIGNE · *How We Weep and Laugh at the Same Thing*
30. THOMAS NASHE · *The Terrors of the Night*
31. EDGAR ALLAN POE · *The Tell-Tale Heart*
32. MARY KINGSLEY · *A Hippo Banquet*
33. JANE AUSTEN · *The Beautifull Cassandra*
34. ANTON CHEKHOV · *Gooseberries*
35. SAMUEL TAYLOR COLERIDGE · *Well, they are gone, and here must I remain*
36. JOHANN WOLFGANG VON GOETHE · *Sketchy, Doubtful, Incomplete Jottings*
37. CHARLES DICKENS · *The Great Winglebury Duel*
38. HERMAN MELVILLE · *The Maldive Shark*
39. ELIZABETH GASKELL · *The Old Nurse's Story*
40. NIKOLAY LESKOV · *The Steel Flea*

41. HONORÉ DE BALZAC · *The Atheist's Mass*
42. CHARLOTTE PERKINS GILMAN · *The Yellow Wall-Paper*
43. C.P. CAVAFY · *Remember, Body . . .*
44. FYODOR DOSTOEVSKY · *The Meek One*
45. GUSTAVE FLAUBERT · *A Simple Heart*
46. NIKOLAI GOGOL · *The Nose*
47. SAMUEL PEPYS · *The Great Fire of London*
48. EDITH WHARTON · *The Reckoning*
49. HENRY JAMES · *The Figure in the Carpet*
50. WILFRED OWEN · *Anthem For Doomed Youth*
51. WOLFGANG AMADEUS MOZART · *My Dearest Father*
52. PLATO · *Socrates' Defence*
53. CHRISTINA ROSSETTI · *Goblin Market*
54. *Sindbad the Sailor*
55. SOPHOCLES · *Antigone*
56. RYŪNOSUKE AKUTAGAWA · *The Life of a Stupid Man*
57. LEO TOLSTOY · *How Much Land Does A Man Need?*
58. GIORGIO VASARI · *Leonardo da Vinci*
59. OSCAR WILDE · *Lord Arthur Savile's Crime*
60. SHEN FU · *The Old Man of the Moon*
61. AESOP · *The Dolphins, the Whales and the Gudgeon*
62. MATSUO BASHŌ · *Lips too Chilled*
63. EMILY BRONTË · *The Night is Darkening Round Me*
64. JOSEPH CONRAD · *To-morrow*
65. RICHARD HAKLUYT · *The Voyage of Sir Francis Drake Around the Whole Globe*
66. KATE CHOPIN · *A Pair of Silk Stockings*
67. CHARLES DARWIN · *It was snowing butterflies*
68. BROTHERS GRIMM · *The Robber Bridegroom*
69. CATULLUS · *I Hate and I Love*
70. HOMER · *Circe and the Cyclops*
71. D. H. LAWRENCE · *Il Duro*
72. KATHERINE MANSFIELD · *Miss Brill*
73. OVID · *The Fall of Icarus*
74. SAPPHO · *Come Close*
75. IVAN TURGENEV · *Kasyan from the Beautiful Lands*
76. VIRGIL · *O Cruel Alexis*
77. H. G. WELLS · *A Slip under the Microscope*
78. HERODOTUS · *The Madness of Cambyses*
79. *Speaking of Siva*
80. *The Dhammapada*

'You will hear it for yourselves, and it will surely fill you with wonder.'

MARCO POLO
Born 1254, Republic of Venice
Died 1324, Republic of Venice

Marco Polo left Venice in 1271 and spent twenty-four years in Asia, where he became an important agent for Kublai Khan and made many journeys through the Mongol Empire. On his way home in 1291, he accompanied a diplomatic mission that sailed on a fleet of junks via Sumatra, Sri Lanka and India to the Persian Gulf. He wrote his famous *Travels*, from which this selection is taken, while in prison in Genoa.

MARCO POLO IN PENGUIN CLASSICS
The Travels

MARCO POLO

*Travels in the Land of
Serpents and Pearls*

Translated by
Nigel Cliff

PENGUIN BOOKS

PENGUIN CLASSICS

UK | USA | Canada | Ireland | Australia
India | New Zealand | South Africa

Penguin Books is part of the Penguin Random House group of companies
whose addresses can be found at global.penguinrandomhouse.com.

This selection published in Penguin Classics 2015

011

Translation copyright © Nigel Cliff, 2015

The moral right of the translator has been asserted

Set in 10/14.5 pt Baskerville 10 Pro
Typeset by Jouve (UK), Milton Keynes
Printed in Great Britain by Clays Ltd, Elcograf S.p.A.

A CIP catalogue record for this book is available from the British Library

ISBN: 978-0-141-39835-8

www.greenpenguin.co.uk

Penguin Random House is committed to a sustainable future for our business, our readers and our planet. This book is made from Forest Stewardship Council® certified paper.

Travels in the Land of Serpents and Pearls

When the traveller leaves the island of Ceylon and sails westwards for about sixty miles he comes to the great province of Maabar, which is called Greater India. It is indeed the best of the Indies and forms part of the mainland. You should know that there are five kings in this province who are all brothers by birth; and we will tell you about each one in turn. You can also take my word for it that this province is the richest and most splendid in the whole world. And I will tell you why.

Now you should know that at this end of the province one of these brothers, Sundara Pandya Devar by name, is king. Fine pearls of great size and beauty are found in his kingdom; for the fact is that most of the world's pearls and precious stones are found in Maabar and Ceylon. And I will tell you how these pearls are found and gathered.

Marco Polo

Now you should know that in this sea there is a gulf between the island and the mainland; and across this entire gulf the water is no more than ten or twelve paces deep, while in some places it is no more than two paces deep. It is in this gulf that the pearls are gathered, and I will tell you how. A group of merchants will enter into partnership and form a company, and they will take a large ship specially fitted out for the purpose on which each will have his own room equipped and furnished for his use with a tub full of water and other necessities. There are many of these ships, for there are many merchants engaged in this type of fishing and they form numerous companies. The merchants who are associated together on one ship will also have several boats to tow the ship through the gulf. And they hire many men, giving them a fixed sum for the month of April and the first half of May, or as long as the fishing season lasts in this gulf.

These merchants take their big ships and small boats out into the gulf from the month of April till mid-May. They make for a place on the mainland called Bettala, this being where the greatest concentration of pearls is found. From here they head out to sea, sailing due south for sixty miles, and there they cast anchor. Then they go out in the little boats and begin to fish in the following manner. The men in the little boats, who have been hired by the merchants, jump overboard and dive into the water, some descending four or five paces or even twelve depending on the depth of the water in each spot. They stay underwater as long as they can. When they can hold out no longer they come to the surface and rest for a moment before once more diving to the bottom; and they continue in this way all day long. When they reach the seabed they find a type of shellfish called sea oysters, and they bring them to the surface in little net bags tied to their bodies. In these oysters are found pearls, both big and small and of every variety. The shells are split open and put into the tubs of water that are carried on the ships as mentioned, because the pearls are embedded in the flesh of the shellfish. As it soaks in water in these tubs, the flesh decomposes and rots until it resembles the white of an egg; it then floats to the surface while the clean pearls remain at the bottom.

This is how the pearls are gathered; and the quantities found are beyond all reckoning. For you should know that pearls from this gulf are exported throughout the world, because they are mostly round and lustrous. I can also tell you that the king of this kingdom receives a substantial duty on them, amounting to an enormous sum in revenue. The merchants pay the following duty on the pearls. First of all they pay a tenth to the king. Then they give some to the man who charms the fish so that they do not do harm to the divers who go underwater to find the pearls; they give him one in twenty. These men are called Brahmins and only charm the fish by day; at night they break the charm so the fish are free to do as they please. I can also tell you that these Brahmins are experts at charming every kind of creature, including all the birds and all the animals.

We have now told you how the pearls are found. And I give you my word that as soon as the middle of May comes round the fishing stops, because these shellfish – I mean the ones that produce pearls – are no longer found here. Yet it is true that about 300 miles away they are found from September to mid-October.

I can also tell you that in this whole province of

Maabar there is no need of tailors or needleworkers to cut or stitch clothes, because all the people go naked all year round. For I assure you that their weather is temperate at all seasons – which is to say it is never cold or hot – and so they always go naked, except for their private parts, which they cover with a scrap of cloth. The king goes round like the others, except for certain royal ornaments that I will describe to you. You may depend on it, then, that their king goes stark naked save that he covers his private parts with a beautiful cloth and wears round his neck a full collar so crammed with precious stones – rubies, sapphires, emeralds and other brilliant gems – that it is undoubtedly worth a fortune. He also has round his neck a thin silk cord that hangs down his chest to the length of a pace; and on this cord are strung very large, fine pearls and immensely valuable rubies, altogether 104 in number. I will tell you why there are 104 stones and pearls on this necklace. You may depend on it that he wears these 104 gems because every day, morning and evening, it falls to him to recite 104 prayers in honour of his idols, as ordained by their faith and customs and as practised by the kings who preceded him and who handed down the obligation to him. And this is the reason why the king wears these 104 gems round his neck. The prayer simply consists of the words '*Pauca, Pauca, Pacauca.*'

Let me further tell you that the king also wears, at three points on his arms, gold bracelets crammed with precious stones and pearls of great size and value. And let me add that this king likewise wears, in three places round his legs, gold bracelets crammed with opulent pearls and gems. I will tell you, too, that this king wears such beautiful pearls and other jewels on his toes that it is a marvellous sight to see. What else shall I tell you? You may take my word for it that this king wears so many gems and so many pearls that their value easily exceeds that of a substantial city; in fact there is no one who could reckon or estimate the great sum that these jewels worn by the king are worth. And no wonder he has as many jewels as I have said; for I assure you that all these precious stones and pearls are found in his kingdom.

Let me tell you something else. No one is allowed to take out of his kingdom any large and valuable gem, nor any pearl that weighs half a *saggio* or more. In fact several times a year the king issues a proclamation across his kingdom to the effect that all who possess fine pearls and precious stones must bring them to the court, and that in return he will give twice their value. It is the custom of the kingdom to pay double the value of all precious stones. So when merchants or other people have any of these precious stones and pearls, they readily take them to the court because they are well paid. And this is how this king comes to have so much wealth and so many precious stones.

Now I have told you about this. So next I will tell you about some other wonderful things.

I give you my word that this king has at least 500 wives or concubines. For I assure you that the moment he lays eyes on a beautiful woman or girl, he wants her for himself. On one occasion this led him into the shameful behaviour I will describe to you. Let me tell you that this king caught sight of a very beautiful woman who happened to be his brother's wife. And he took her from him and kept her for himself. His brother, who was a wise man, patiently bore his wrong and did not quarrel with him; and this was why. Despite his forbearance he was repeatedly on the brink of making war on him, but their mother would show them her breasts, saying, 'If you fight with each other I will cut off these breasts that suckled you.' And so the trouble was averted.

I will tell you yet another thing about this king that is truly to be marvelled at. I assure you that this king has large numbers of faithful followers who conduct themselves in the following way. The fact is that they declare themselves to be his followers in this world and the next. I will tell you more about this great wonder. These followers wait on the king at court; they go riding with him; they hold positions of great trust in his service. Wherever the king goes these barons accompany him, and they exercise high authority throughout the kingdom. And you should know that when the king dies and his body is burned in a great fire, then all these barons who were his faithful followers as I have told you above fling themselves into the fire and burn with the king in order to keep him company in the next world.

I will also tell you about a custom that prevails in this kingdom. The fact is that when a king dies leaving a great treasure, the sons who survive him would not touch it for anything in the world. For they say, 'I have the whole of my father's kingdom and all his subjects; surely I can find ways to profit from it as my father did.' Consequently the kings of this kingdom never touch their treasure but hand it down from one to another, each making his own fortune. And this is why this kingdom has such a titanic store of treasure.

Let me tell you next that this country does not breed horses. Consequently the entire annual revenue, or the greater part of it, is swallowed up by the purchase of horses; and I will tell you how this comes about. You may take my word for it that the merchants of Hormuz, Kish, Dhofar, Shihr and Aden – all provinces where chargers and other horses are plentiful – as I was saying, the merchants of these provinces buy up the best horses, load them on to ships and take them to this king and his four brothers, who are also kings. They sell each one for no less than 500 *saggi* of gold, which is worth more than 100 silver marks. And I assure you that this king buys no fewer than 2,000 of them every year and his brothers as many more. And by the end of the year not one of them has 100 left. They all die, because these people have no farriers and no idea how to care for them, so ill-treatment kills them off. And you can take it from me that the merchants who export these horses neither bring farriers with them nor allow any to come here, because they are only too glad for these kings' horses to die off in large numbers.

Let me move on to yet another custom of this kingdom, which I will describe to you. When a man has committed a crime that warrants the death sentence and the king has decreed his execution, the condemned man declares that he wishes to kill himself in honour and adoration of such-and-such an idol. The king replies that he approves of this. Then all the relatives and friends of the man who must kill himself take him and sit him in a chair and give him twelve swords or knives, and they carry him around the city proclaiming at every step, 'This brave man is going to kill himself out of devotion to such-and-such an idol.' They carry him like this round the whole city, and when they reach the place of execution the condemned man takes two of the knives and cries out loud, 'I kill myself for the love of such-and-such an idol!' Having uttered these words, at one stroke he thrusts the knives into his thighs. Then he thrusts two into his arms, two into his stomach, two into his chest and so on until he has stuck them all in his body, at every stroke calling out, 'I kill myself for the love of such-and-such an idol!' When all the knives are stuck in him, he takes a two-handled knife like those used for making hoops and holds it against the nape of his neck; then, jerking it violently forward, he severs his own neck, for the knife is razor sharp. And when he has killed himself his relatives burn his body amid great rejoicing.

I will go on to tell you about yet another custom of this kingdom. When a man is dead and his body is being burned, his wife flings herself on to the fire and lets herself burn with her husband out of love for him. The women who do this are highly praised by all. And believe me when I say that many women – though not all – do as I have told you.

I can also tell you that the people of this kingdom worship idols. Most worship the ox, because they say that an ox is a very good thing. None of them would eat beef for anything in the world, nor kill an ox on any account. I should tell you that there is a race of men among them called *gavi* who do eat beef, but even they would not dare kill an ox. Instead, when an ox dies of natural causes or gets killed by accident, these *gavi* whom I have mentioned eat it. And let me add that they daub their houses all over with ox dung.

I will move on to yet another custom of theirs, which I will describe to you. You should know that the king and the barons and all the other people sit on the earth. When asked why they did not seat themselves more honourably, they replied that it was honourable enough to sit on the ground since we are made of earth and to the earth we must return, from which it follows that no one can honour the earth too highly and no one should scorn it.

I can also tell you that these *gavi* – that is, that entire race of people who eat cattle when they die a natural death – are the same people whose ancestors killed Messer St Thomas the Apostle long ago. Let me tell you another thing, too: of all those of this tribe called *gavi*, none have been able to enter the place where the body of Messer St Thomas lies. For the fact is that ten men would not be able to cling on to one of these *gavi* in the presence of the holy body. I will go further: twenty or more men could not drag one of these *gavi* into the place where the body of

Messer St Thomas lies, because the place will not receive them by virtue of the holy body.

No grain grows in this kingdom with the sole exception of rice. And I will tell you an even stranger thing that is well worth relating. You should know that if a prize stallion mounts a prize mare, their offspring is a stunted colt with its feet askew that has no value and cannot be ridden.

I can also tell you that these people go into battle stark naked and armed only with a lance and shield. Far from being valiant or battle-hardened, they are mean-spirited cowards. They do not kill any animals or other living creatures; if they wish to eat the flesh of a sheep or any other beast or bird they have it slaughtered by Muslims or others who do not follow their faith or customs.

Let me tell you about another of their customs. All of them, men and women, bathe from head to toe in water twice a day – that is, morning and evening. They would neither eat nor drink without washing, and anyone who fails to wash himself twice a day is considered a heretic, much as we think of the Paterins. You should also know that in eating they use only the right hand; they never touch food with their left hand. Everything clean and pleasant they do and touch with the right hand, for the left hand is reserved for unpleasant and unclean necessities like wiping the nostrils, anus and suchlike. Another thing: they drink only from tankards, each from his own; for no one would drink from another's tankard. And when they drink they do not put the tankard to their lips but, holding it up high, pour the drink into their mouth. On no account would they touch the tankard with their lips or give it to a stranger to drink from. But if a stranger is thirsty and has not got his own tankard with him they pour the wine or other beverage into his palms and he drinks from them, making a cup of his own hands.

I can also tell you that harsh justice is administered in this kingdom to murderers, thieves and all other criminals. And as for debts, the following laws and procedures are observed among them. If a debtor who has been repeatedly asked by his creditor to pay a debt keeps on fobbing him off day after day with promises, and the creditor is able to get hold of him in such a way that he can draw a circle around him, the debtor cannot leave that circle until he has satisfied the creditor or given him a lawful and binding pledge that the debt will be discharged in full that very day. Otherwise, if the debtor ventured to leave the circle without paying the debt or pledging that the creditor would be paid the same day, he would incur the penalty of death for violating natural law and the justice established by the king. And Messer Marco saw this done in the case of the king himself. For it happened that the king was indebted to a certain foreign merchant for some goods he had had from him, and though the merchant had repeatedly petitioned him he kept on postponing the settlement date on the grounds of inconvenience. This delay was damaging him by blighting his business, so one day he made himself ready while the king was out riding and all at once drew a circle on the ground round him and his horse. When the king saw this, he reined in his horse and did not move from the spot until the merchant had been satisfied in full. When some bystanders saw this they exclaimed in astonishment, 'See how the king obeys the law!' And the king replied, 'Should I, who established this just law, break it because it goes against me? No, I more than anyone am obliged to observe it.'

Marco Polo

I can further tell you that most of these people abstain from drinking wine. A man who drinks wine is disqualified from acting as a witness or guarantor, as is one who sails the seas; for they say that a man who goes to sea must be a desperado, and so they reject him and discount his testimony. On the other hand, you should know that they do not regard any form of sexual indulgence as a sin.

The climate is amazingly hot, which explains why they go naked. There is no rain except in the months of June, July and August; and were it not for the rain that comes during those three months and freshens the air, the heat would be so oppressive that no one could endure it. But thanks to this rain the heat is moderated.

I can also tell you that among these people there are many experts in the field of physiognomy – that is, the study of men and women's characters and whether they are good or bad. They ascertain this merely by looking at the man or woman. They are also expert at divining the meaning of encounters with birds or beasts. They pay more attention to omens than any other people in the world, and they are better than any others at telling good omens from bad. For let me tell you that when a man sets out for some destination and happens along the way to hear someone sneeze, he immediately sits down on the road and will not budge. If the sneezer sneezes again, he gets up and continues on his way; but if he sneezes no more, he abandons his journey and turns back for home.

Likewise they say that for every day of the week there is one unlucky hour, which they call *choiach*. So, on Monday it is the hour after seven in the morning, on Tuesday after nine, on Wednesday the first hour after noon, and so on for each day throughout the year. They have recorded and defined all these things in their books. They tell the hour by measuring the length of a shadow in feet – that is, a man's shadow. So, on such-and-such a day, when a man's shadow reaches seven feet long in the opposite direction to the sun, then it will be the hour of *choiach*. And when this measurement changes, whether becoming longer or shorter (for as the sun rises the shadow shortens and as it sinks the shadow lengthens), then it is no longer *choiach*. On a different day it will be *choiach* when the shadow reaches twelve feet long; and when this measure passes, then *choiach* will likewise be over. They have set down all these things in writing. And you must know that during these hours they steer clear of trading or doing any kind of business. So two men may be in the middle of bargaining together when someone steps into the sunlight and measures the shadow; and if it is on the cusp of that day's hour, according to what is laid down for the day, he will at once say to them, 'It is *choiach*. Stop what you are doing.' And they will stop. Then he will take a second reading and finding that the hour is past will say to them, '*Choiach* is over. Carry on.' They have these calculations at their fingertips; for they say that if anyone strikes a bargain during these hours he will never profit by it but will find it turns out badly for him.

Again, their houses are infested with certain animals called tarantulas that run up the walls like lizards. These tarantulas have a poisonous bite and cause great pain if they bite a man. They make a sound as if they are saying '*Chis!*' and this is their cry. These tarantulas are taken as an omen in the following way: if some people are doing business in a house infested with these tarantulas and a tarantula utters its cry within their hearing, they check its position relative to each merchant, whether buyer or seller – in other words, whether it is to the left or right, in front or behind, or overhead – and according to the direction they know whether its significance is good or bad. If good, the bargain is struck; if bad, it is called off. Sometimes it augurs well for the seller and ill for the buyer, sometimes ill for the seller and well for the buyer, and sometimes well or ill for both; and they modify their actions accordingly. They have learned these things from experience.

I can also tell you that as soon as a child is born in this kingdom, whether boy or girl, the father or mother immediately has a written record made of his nativity – that is, the day, month, lunar cycle and hour of birth. They do this because they always act on the advice of astrologers and diviners who are well versed in enchantment and magic and geomancy. And some of them, as I have told you, also know astronomy.

Again, any man who has sons boots them out of the house the moment they turn thirteen and refuses to feed them at the family table. For he says that they are now old enough to feed themselves and trade at a profit as he himself did. And he gives each son twenty or twenty-four groats, or coins to that value, to bargain with and make a profit. The fathers do this so that the sons become practised and quick-witted in all their actions and accustomed to doing business. And this is exactly what happens; for the boys never stop running to and fro all day long, buying this and that and then selling it. When the pearl fishery is in full swing they run down to the port and buy five or six pearls from the fishermen, or as many as they can get. Then they take them to the dealers, who stay indoors for fear of the sun, and say, 'Do you want these? This is what they cost me, for real; let me have whatever profit you think fit.' And the dealers allow them some profit on top of the cost price. Then the boys run off again; or else they say to the dealers, 'Would you like me to go and buy something?' And in this way they become very able and very crafty traders. They still take groceries home for their mothers to cook and prepare for them, but this does not mean they eat anything at their father's expense.

You should also know that in this kingdom and throughout India the beasts and birds are different from ours – all except one bird, and that is the quail. This bird unmistakably resembles ours, but all the rest are very strange and different. I give you my word that they have bats – these are the birds that fly by night and have no quills or feathers – they have birds of this type as big as goshawks. There are goshawks as black as crows and much bigger than ours; they are good fliers and good hawkers. And let me add something else that is worth recounting. You should know that they feed their horses on cooked meat and rice and many other cooked foods.

Let me further tell you that they have many idols, both male and female, in their monasteries; and many girls are offered to these idols in the following manner. The fact is that their mother and father offer them to the idols of their choosing. Once they have been offered, then whenever the monks belonging to the monastery of the idol require the girls who have been offered to this idol to come to the monastery and entertain the idol, they go without delay; and, singing and dancing, they hold a high-spirited celebration. And there are great numbers of these girls forming huge troupes. Another thing: every month, several times a week, these girls bring food to the idols at the place where they were offered; and I will explain how they bring the food there and in what manner they say the idol has eaten. I can tell you that many of these girls whom I have mentioned prepare dishes of meat and other choice ingredients and take them to their idols in the monasteries. Then they spread a table before him with all the dishes they have brought and leave them there for some time. Meanwhile all these girls sing and dance non-stop and lay on the finest entertainment in the world. And when they have kept up this entertainment for as long as it would take a great baron to enjoy a leisurely meal, the girls say that the spirit of the idol has eaten the substance of the food. Then they gather it up and eat it all themselves with great relish and great gaiety. Afterwards they return to their homes. These girls carry on in this way until they get married. And there are plenty of girls like these throughout the kingdom, doing all the things I have told you about.

Why do they lay on these entertainments for the idols? Because the priests who serve the idols often declare, 'The god is angry with the goddess; they refuse to come together or speak to one another. So long as they are bad-tempered and angry and until they are reconciled and make their peace, all our affairs will be undone and will go from bad to worse because they will not bestow their blessing and favour.' And so the aforementioned girls go to the monastery in the way we have said, completely naked apart from covering their private parts, and sing before the god and goddess. The god stands by himself on an altar under a canopy, the goddess by herself on another altar under another canopy; the people say that he often takes his pleasure with her and they have intercourse together, but when they are angry they refrain from intercourse. This is when these girls come to placate them; and when they arrive they set about singing, dancing, leaping, tumbling and performing all sorts of diversions liable to cheer up the god and goddess and reconcile them. While they are performing they say, 'O Lord, why are you angry with the goddess and hard-hearted towards her? Is she not beautiful? Is she not delightful? May it please you therefore to be reconciled with her and take your pleasure with her, for she is unquestionably most delightful.' Then the girl who has spoken these words will lift her leg above her neck and perform a pirouette for the pleasure of the god and goddess. And when they have done enough coaxing they go home. In the morning the priest of the idols will announce as a great blessing that he has seen the god and goddess together and that harmony is restored between them. And then everyone rejoices and gives thanks.

So long as these girls remain virgins, their flesh is so firm that no one can grasp them or pinch them anywhere on their bodies. For a penny they will let a man try to pinch them as hard as he can. After they are married their flesh remains firm, but not as firm as before. Owing to this firmness their breasts do not hang down but stand pertly and conspicuously erect.

The men have very light cane beds fashioned in such a way that when they are in bed and want to go to sleep they can hoist themselves with ropes up to the ceiling and suspend themselves there. They do this in order to escape the aforementioned tarantulas, which have a nasty bite, as well as fleas and other vermin; and also to catch the breeze and combat the heat. Not all do this, though; only the nobles and heads of houses. The rest sleep in the streets. And we will tell you, apropos of the excellent justice kept by the king, that when a man is travelling by night (for on account of the lower temperatures they make their journeys by night rather than day) and wishes to sleep, he will, if he has a sack of pearls or other valuables, put the sack under his head and sleep where he is; and no one ever loses anything by theft or otherwise. And if he does lose something, he is reimbursed without delay – provided, that is, that he has slept on the road, because if he has slept away from the road he gets nothing. In fact he is presumed guilty. For the authorities say, 'Why would you have slept off the road unless you intended to rob others?' So he is punished and his loss is not made good.

We have now told you a great deal about the customs and manners and affairs of this kingdom. So we will leave it and move on to tell you about another kingdom, whose name is Motupalli.

Motupalli is a kingdom reached by travelling north from Maabar for about 1,000 miles. It belongs to a queen who is a woman of great wisdom. For let me tell you that it was a good forty years since the king her husband had died – a husband to whom she had been so deeply devoted that she declared God would never wish her to take another when he whom she had loved more than herself was dead. So for this reason she never sought to marry again. You may take my word for it that throughout her forty-year

Marco Polo

reign this queen has ruled her kingdom with great justice and great integrity, just as her husband did before her. And I assure you that she is more dearly loved by her subjects than any lady or lord has ever been.

The people are idolaters and pay tribute to no one. They live on rice, meat, milk, fish and fruit.

Diamonds are also produced in this kingdom, and we will tell you how. You should know that in this kingdom there are many mountains in which diamonds are found, as you will hear. For you should know that when it rains the water rushes down through these mountains, cascading wildly along vast ravines and caverns. And when the rain has stopped and the water has drained away the men head out into the ravines through which the water flowed in search of diamonds, which they find in plenty. In summer, when there is not a drop of water to be found here, they uncover plenty of them in the mountains themselves. The heat, though, is so intense as to be all but intolerable. And let me tell you that these mountains are so heavily infested with great fat serpents that men cannot go there without fearing for their lives. But all the same they make their way as best they can and find some very fine, large diamonds. I can also tell you that these serpents are highly venomous and vicious, so the men do not dare enter the caves where these vicious serpents live. And again I can tell you that the men extract the diamonds by other means. You should know that there are great, deep valleys whose rocky sides are so steep that no one can penetrate them. But I will tell you what the men do. They take some lumps of bloody meat and fling them down into the depths of the valleys; and the places where the meat is flung are littered with diamonds, which become embedded in the flesh. Now the fact is that many white eagles live among these mountains and prey on the serpents. And when these eagles see the meat lying at the bottom of the valleys, they swoop down, seize the lumps and carry them off. The men, meanwhile, have been carefully watching where the eagles go, and as soon as they see that one has alighted and is swallowing the meat they rush over as fast as they can. The eagles are so fearful of the men who have surprised them that they fly off and fail to take away the meat. And when the men reach the place where the meat is, they pick it up and find it studded with diamonds.

Marco Polo

The men also get hold of the diamonds in the following way. When the eagles eat the meat I have told you about, they also eat – or rather swallow – some of the diamonds. And at night, when they return to their nests, they pass the diamonds they have swallowed along with their faecal matter. Then the men arrive and collect the eagle's excrement, which also turns out to be rich in diamonds.

You have now heard three ways in which diamonds are gathered; there are many others besides. And you should know that diamonds are not found anywhere else in the world but in this kingdom alone. Here, though, they are both plentiful and of fine quality. And do not imagine that the best diamonds find their way to our Christian countries; on the contrary, they are taken to the Great Khan and the kings and barons of these various regions and realms. For they have the greatest treasures, and they buy all the costliest stones.

Now I have told you about the diamonds, so we will move on to other matters. You should know that this kingdom produces the best-quality buckrams – the finest, most beautiful and most valuable in the world. For I assure you that they resemble the linen fabrics of Rheims. There is not a king or queen in the world who would not gladly wear a fabric of such magnificence and beauty.

They have plenty of beasts, including the biggest sheep in the world. They are amply and richly endowed with all the means of life.

There is nothing else worth mentioning, so we will leave this kingdom and tell you about the burial place of Messer St Thomas the Apostle.

The body of Messer St Thomas the Apostle lies in a little town in the province of Maabar. There are few inhabitants, and merchants do not visit the place because it has no merchandise worth taking away and because it is in a very out-of-the-way spot. Yet the fact is that many Christians and many Muslims make pilgrimages to this place. For I can tell you that the Muslims of this country have great faith in him and declare that he was a Muslim; they say he was a great prophet and call him *avariun*, which means 'holy man'.

The Christians who guard the church have many trees that yield wine and bear coconuts. One of these nuts provides enough food and drink to make a meal for a man. They have first an outer husk covered, so to speak, with threads; these are used in all sorts of ways and serve many useful purposes. Inside this husk there is a type of food that provides a square meal for a man. It is really very tasty, as sweet as sugar and white as milk, and is formed in the shape of a cup like the surrounding husk. At the centre of this edible layer there is enough water to fill a flask. It is clear and cool and tastes delicious, and is drunk after eating the flesh. And so from one nut a man has his fill of both food and drink. For each of these trees the Christians pay one groat a month to one of the brothers who are kings in the province of Maabar.

You should also know that a marvel such as I will describe happens here. Now let me tell you that the Christians who come here on pilgrimage gather some of the earth from the place where the saint was killed and take it back to their own country. If anyone falls ill with a quartan or tertian ague or some such fever, they give him a potion made with a little of this earth; and no sooner has the sick man drunk it than he is cured. And every sick person who has drunk this earth has likewise been cured. Messer Marco took some of this earth with him to Venice and cured many people with it. And you should know that this earth is red.

Let me tell you, too, about a fine miracle that happened around the year 1288 from the incarnation of Christ. The fact is that a baron of this country had a vast quantity of the grain they call rice, and he filled up all the houses around the church with it. When the Christians who guard the church and the saint's body saw that this idolatrous baron was filling up the houses in this way and that the pilgrims would have nowhere to lodge, they were deeply distressed and earnestly begged him to desist. But he, being a cruel and haughty man, paid no heed to their prayers and filled up all these houses in accordance with his own wishes and contrary to the wishes of the Christians who guard the church. And when to the fury of the brethren this baron had filled up all the houses of St Thomas with his rice, the great miracle that I will tell you about took place. For you should know that the night after the baron had had these houses filled up, Messer St Thomas the Apostle appeared to him with a fork in his hand and held it to the baron's throat, calling him by name and saying to him, 'If you do not have my houses emptied immediately, you will die a terrible death.' As he said these words he pressed the fork hard against the throat of the baron, who was convinced he was in great pain and all but certain he was dying. And when Messer St Thomas had done this he went away. In the morning the baron arose early and had all the houses emptied. And he related everything that Messer St Thomas had done to him, which was held to be a great miracle. The Christians were filled with joy and gladness at it, and they repeatedly rendered great thanks and great honour to Messer St Thomas and profusely blessed his name. And I assure you that many other miracles happen here all year round which would undoubtedly be reckoned great marvels by anyone who heard of them – above all the healing of Christians who are lame or disabled.

Now that we have told you about this, we also want to tell you how St Thomas was killed according to the people of these parts. The fact is that Messer St Thomas was outside his hermitage in the woods, praying to the Lord his God. Around him were many peacocks, for you should know that in this country they are more common than anywhere else in the world. And while Messer St Thomas was at prayer an idolater of the lineage and race of the *gavi* let fly an arrow from his bow, intending to kill one of the peacocks that were gathered around the saint. He never even saw the saint; but instead of hitting the peacock as he thought, he had hit Messer St Thomas the Apostle in the middle of his right side. When he had received this blow he worshipped his creator with great gentleness; and I can tell you it was from this blow that he died. But it is a fact that before he came to this place where he died he made many converts in Nubia. As to the ways and means by which this came about, we will set it all out clearly for you in this book at the proper time and place.

Now we have told you about St Thomas, so we will move on to tell you about other things.

The fact is that when a child is born here they anoint him once a week with sesame oil, and this turns him a great deal darker than when he was born. For let me tell you that the blackest men here are held in highest regard and considered superior to those who are not so black. And I will tell you another thing, too. You may take my word for it that these people portray and paint all their gods and idols black and their devils white as snow. For they say that God and all the saints are black – speaking, of course, of their God and their saints – and that the devils are white. And so they portray and paint them in the way you have heard; and I can tell you that the statues they make of their idols are likewise all black.

You should also know that the men of this country have such faith in the ox and such belief in its sanctity that when they go to war they take with them some of the hair of the wild oxen I told you about before; those who are horsemen tie some of this ox hair to their horse's mane, while the foot soldiers fasten some of the ox hair to their shields or in some cases knot it on to their own hair. And they do this because they believe that this ox hair will help protect and save them from all kinds of danger. Everyone who joins the army follows suit. And you should know that for this reason the hair of the wild ox is worth a good deal here; for if a man has none he does not feel safe.

Since we have told you about this matter we will move on and tell you about a province of the Brahmins, as you will be able to hear.

Lar is a province that lies to the west of the place where St Thomas the Apostle is buried. All the

Brahmins in the world are sprung from this province, for this is where they originated. Let me tell you that these Brahmins are among the best and most trustworthy traders in the world; for they would not tell a lie for anything in the world or speak a word that was not true. You should know that if a foreign merchant who knows nothing of the manners and customs of these parts comes to this province to do business, he finds one of these Brahmins and entrusts him with his money and goods, asking him to conduct his business on his behalf lest he should be deceived through ignorance of the local customs. The Brahmin merchant promptly takes charge of the foreign merchant's goods and, when both selling and buying, deals with them as scrupulously and promotes the foreigner's interests at least as carefully as if he were acting for himself. In return for this service he asks for nothing, leaving any recompense to the foreigner's goodwill.

They do not eat meat or drink wine. They live very virtuous lives by their own lights. They do not have sex with any women except their wives. They would never take anything that belonged to someone else, or kill an animal, or do anything they believed might lead them to sin. I can also tell you that all Brahmins are known by an emblem they wear. For you should know that all the Brahmins in the world sling a cotton cord over one shoulder and tie it under the opposite arm, so that the cord crosses both the chest and back. And wherever they go they are known by this emblem. I can further tell you that they have a king who is mightily rich in treasure. This king is an enthusiastic purchaser of pearls and every other kind of precious stone. In fact he has struck a deal with all the merchants of his country that for all the pearls they bring him from the kingdom of Maabar known as Chola – which is the wealthiest and most sophisticated province in India and the source of the finest pearls – he will give them double the purchase price. So the Brahmins go to the kingdom of Maabar and buy up all the fine pearls they can find and take them to their king, declaring on their honour what they cost. And the king promptly has them paid double the cost price; not once have they received less than that. Thanks to this they have brought him enormous quantities of very fine, large pearls.

These Brahmins are idolaters who set more store by augury and the behaviour of beasts and birds than any other men in the world. So I will tell you a bit about what they do in this regard, beginning with a particular custom that is observed among them. The fact is that they have allotted a sign to every day of the week, as I will explain. If it happens that they are bargaining over some piece of merchandise, the prospective buyer stands up and examines his shadow in the sunlight, saying, 'What day is it today? Such-and-such a day.' Then he has his shadow measured. If it is the right length for that day, he makes the purchase; if it is not the length it should be, he absolutely does not make the purchase but rather waits till the shadow has reached the point laid down in their rule. Just as I have told you with respect to this day, so they have laid down the length the shadow ought to be on every day of the week; and until the shadow has reached the desired length they will not conduct any bargain or any other business. But when the shadow reaches the desired length for the day, they conclude all their bargains and business.

I will tell you something even more remarkable. Say they are in the middle of striking a bargain – whether indoors or out – and they see a tarantula approaching, these being very common here. If the purchaser sees it coming from a direction that seems auspicious to him, he will buy the goods without delay; but if the tarantula does not come from a direction he believes to be auspicious, he will call off the deal and abandon the purchase.

I can also tell you that if they are leaving their house when they hear someone sneeze and they decide it is not propitious, they will stop and go no further. And here is another thing. Say these Brahmins are going on their way when they see a swallow flying towards them, whether from ahead or from the left or right. If it appears according to their beliefs that the swallow comes from an auspicious direction, then they will go ahead; but if it appears to come from an inauspicious direction, then they will go no further but turn back.

These Brahmins live longer than any other people in the world; this is due to their sparse diet and strict abstinence. They have very healthy teeth thanks to a herb they chew with their meals, which is a great aid to digestion and very wholesome for the human body. And you should know that these Brahmins do not practise bloodletting, either from the veins or from any other part of the body.

Travels in the Land of Serpents and Pearls

Among them are some men living under a rule who are called *yogis*. They live even longer than the others, for they reach 150 to 200 years of age. Yet they remain so physically fit that they can still come and go wherever they want and perform all the necessary services for their monastery and idols, serving them just as well as if they were younger. This comes of the strict abstinence they practise by eating small portions of healthy food; for their customary diet consists chiefly of rice and milk. And I can further tell you that these *yogi* who live to the great age I have mentioned also ingest the following substance, which will surely strike you as an extraordinary thing. For I assure you that they take quicksilver and sulphur and mix them together to make a drink, which they then swallow. They say it prolongs life, and so they live all the longer. I can tell you that they take it twice a month. You should know, too, that these people start taking this drink from childhood in order to live longer. And certainly those who live to the age I have mentioned take this drink of sulphur and quicksilver.

There is also a religious order in this kingdom of Maabar of those called *yogi*. They carry abstinence to the extremes I will describe and lead a harsh and austere life. For you may take my word for it that they go stark naked and entirely unclothed, with their private parts and every other part of their bodies uncovered. They worship the ox, and most of them wear a miniature ox made of gilt copper or bronze in the middle of their foreheads; you understand that these are tied in place. I can also tell you that they burn ox dung and make a powder of it. Then they anoint various parts of their body with it, showing great reverence – at least as much as Christians do when using holy water. And if anyone salutes them in the street, they anoint his forehead with this powder as if it were the holiest of actions. They do not eat from bowls or trenchers; instead they take their food on the leaves of apples of paradise or other large leaves, but only when they are dried and no longer green. For they say that green leaves have souls and so it would be sinful. And let me tell you that they guard against acting towards any living creature in a way they believe will give rise to sin; for the fact is they would sooner die than do anything they deem sinful. When other men ask them why they go naked and are not ashamed to show their members, they reply, 'We go naked because we want nothing of this world; for we came into the world naked and unclothed. As for not being ashamed to show our members, the fact is that we do no sin with them and therefore have no more shame in them than you have when you show your hand or face or the other parts of your body that do not lead you into carnal sin; whereas you use your members to commit sin and lechery, and so you cover them up and are ashamed of them. But we are no more ashamed of showing them than we are of showing our fingers, because we do not sin with them.' This is the explanation they give to men who ask them why they are not ashamed to show their members. Again, I assure you they would never kill any creature or living thing on earth – be it a fly, flea, louse or any other kind of vermin – because they say they have souls. This, they say, is why they would never eat them; for if they did they would commit a sin. I can also tell you that they never eat anything green, be it herb or root, until it has been dried; for they say that green things have souls. When they wish to void their bowels, they go down to the beach or seashore and relieve themselves on the sand near the water's edge. When they are done they wash themselves thoroughly in the water, and when they are clean they take a little rod or twig and use it to flatten out their excrement, spreading it this way and that across the sand until no trace of it can be seen. When asked why they do this, they reply, 'Because it would breed worms, and when the sun dried out their source of nourishment, these worms that had been created would die for want of food; and since this substance emanates from our body (for we, too, cannot live without food) we would be committing a very grave sin by bringing about the death of so many souls that would have sprung from our substance. So we destroy this substance in such a way that worms cannot possibly be born from it only to die soon afterwards for want of food through our faults and failings.' And another thing: I can tell you that they sleep stark naked on the ground without a stitch to cover them or to lie on. It is quite astonishing that they do not die but rather live to the great age I mentioned above.

They are the most abstemious eaters, for they fast all year round and drink nothing but water.

I will tell you another thing about them, too. Among them are monks who live in monasteries to serve their idols. And when they are named to a new office or rank – for instance, if someone dies and his replacement needs to be chosen – they are put to the test in the following way. The girls who have been offered to the idols are brought in and made to touch the men who tend to the idols. They caress them in this place and that all over their bodies, embracing and kissing them and bringing them to the utmost pitch of earthly pleasure. If a man is fondled in this way by the girls I have told you about and his member does not in the least react but rather stays just as it was before the girls touched him, he passes muster and stays in the monastery. But if another man is fondled by the girls and his member reacts and grows erect, far from retaining him they drive him away at once, declaring that they cannot stand having a lecher among them. This is how cruel and false-hearted these idolaters are.

The reason they give for burning their dead is this. They say that if they did not burn the corpse it would breed worms, and after the worms had eaten the body from which they sprang they would have nothing left to eat and would perforce die. And they say that if the worms were to die the soul of the deceased would incur great sin. So this is the reason they give for burning their dead. And they say that worms have souls.

Now we have told you about the customs of these idolaters, so we will take our leave of them and tell you a delightful story that slipped our mind when we were dealing with the island of Ceylon. You will hear it for yourselves, and it will surely fill you with wonder.

Ceylon, as I told you earlier in this book, is a big island. Now the fact is that on this island there is a very high mountain, so precipitous and rocky that no one can climb it except in the way I will now tell you. For many iron chains are hung from the side of the mountain, so arranged that men can use them to climb to the summit. Now let me tell you this: it is said that on the top of this mountain is the monument of Adam, our first father. The Muslims say it is Adam's grave; the idolaters, though, say it is the monument of Sakyamuni Burkhan.

This Sakyamuni was the first man in whose name idols were made. For by their lights he was the best man who ever lived among them, and he was the first whom they revered as a saint and in whose name they made idols. He was the son of a great king who was both rich and powerful. And he – the son – was so pure of mind that he paid no heed to worldly affairs and did not wish to be king. When his father saw that he had no wish to be king and had no interest in worldly affairs, he was deeply troubled. So he made him a very generous offer: he said he would crown him king of the realm and that he could rule it at his pleasure. Moreover he was willing to resign the crown and issue no commands whatsoever, so that his son would be the sole ruler. His son replied that he wanted nothing. And when his father saw that nothing in the world would tempt him to accept the kingship, he was so deeply distressed that he came close to dying of grief. And no wonder; for he had no other son and no one else to whom he could leave his kingdom. So the king took the following course of action. He resolved to find a way to make his son willingly embrace worldly affairs and accept the crown and the kingdom. So he moved him into an exquisite palace and gave him 30,000 ravishing and captivating girls to serve him; not a single man was admitted but only these girls. And girls put him to bed and served him at table and kept him company all day long. They sang and danced for him and did everything they could to divert him, just as the king had commanded. Yet I can tell you that all these girls could not do enough to awaken any sexual appetites in the king's son; on the contrary, he lived more strictly and chastely than before and led a very virtuous life by their lights. I should also tell you that he was brought up so fastidiously that he had never left the palace nor seen a dead man or anyone who was not able-bodied, for his father had not let anyone old or infirm into his presence. Now it happened one day that this young man was riding along the road when he saw a dead body. He was quite horrified, as someone would be if they had never seen one before, and immediately asked his companions what it was. They told him it was a dead man. 'What,' said the king's son, 'do all men then die?' 'Indeed they do,' they replied. At this the young man fell silent and rode on deep in thought. He had not ridden far when he came across an ancient man who could not walk and had no teeth in his mouth, having lost them all through extreme old age. And when the king's son saw the old man he asked what he was and why he could not walk. His companions told him it was owing to old age that he could not walk and it was owing to old age that he had lost his teeth. And when the king's son had digested the truth about the dead man and the old man, he went back to his palace and resolved to remain no longer in this evil world but to set out in search of him who never dies and who had created him. And so he abandoned his palace and his father. He headed among vast, remote mountains and spent the rest of his days there, leading a life of virtue, chastity and great abstemiousness. If he had been a Christian he would undoubtedly be a great saint and dwell with our Lord Jesus Christ.

When this prince died, his body was brought to the king his father. And when the king saw that the son whom he loved more than himself was dead, there is no need to ask whether he was afflicted and grief-stricken. First he mourned deeply. Then he had an image made in his likeness, entirely of gold and precious stones, and had it honoured by all the people of the land and worshipped as a god. And they say that he died eighty-four times. For they say that the first time he died he became an ox, and the second time he died he became a horse. In this way they say he died eighty-four times, each time becoming a dog or another sort of animal until the eighty-fourth time, when they say he died and became a god. And the idolaters hold him to be the best and the greatest of their gods. You should know that this was the first idol the idolaters had, and all the idols derive from him. And this happened in the island of Ceylon in India.

Now you have heard how the idols originated. And I give you my word that the idolaters come here on pilgrimage from very distant parts, just as Christians make pilgrimages to the shrine of Messer St James. The idolaters say that the monument on this mountain is that of the king's son of whom you have heard, and that the teeth and the hair and the bowl that are kept here also belonged to this prince, whose name was Sakyamuni Burkhan, which means St Sakyamuni. But the Muslims, who also come here in great numbers on pilgrimage, say it is the monument of Adam, our first father, and that the teeth and hair and bowl also belonged to Adam. So now you have heard how the idolaters say he is the king's son who was their first idol and their first god, and how the Muslims say he is Adam, our first father. But God alone knows who he is and what he was. For we do not believe that Adam is in this place, since our Scripture of Holy Church says that he is in another part of the world.

Now it happened that the Great Khan heard that the monument of Adam was on this mountain, along with his teeth and his hair and the bowl from which he ate. He made up his mind that he must have the teeth and the bowl and the hair. So he sent a great embassy here in the year 1284 from the incarnation of Christ. What else shall I tell you? You may be quite certain that the Great Khan's messengers set out with a vast retinue and journeyed so far by land and sea that they came to the island of Ceylon. They went to the king and made such great efforts that they acquired two great big molar teeth as well as some of the hair and the bowl. The bowl was made of exquisite green porphyry. And when the Great Khan's messengers had these items I have mentioned in their possession, they set off and made their way back to their lord. When they were near the great city of Khanbaliq where the Great Khan was residing, they sent him word that they were coming and were bringing the things he had sent them for. At this the Great Khan ordered all the people, both the monks and the others, to go out and meet these relics, which they were given to understand belonged to Adam. But why make a long story of it? You may well believe that all the people of Khanbaliq went out to meet the relics; and the monks received them and brought them to the Great Khan, who accepted them with great joy and great ceremony and great reverence. And let me tell you that they found in their scriptures a passage declaring that the bowl possessed this property: that if food for one man were put inside, it would provide enough to feed five. And the Great Khan announced that he had put this to the proof and that it was quite true.

This is how the Great Khan came by these relics you have heard about; and undoubtedly the treasure it cost him to obtain them amounted to a substantial sum.

Now that we have told you this whole story in due order, with all the facts, we will move on and tell you about other things. And first of all we will tell you about the city of Kayal.

Kayal is a great and splendid city that belongs to Ashar, the eldest of the five royal brothers. And you may take my word for it that this is the port of call for all shipping coming from the west – that is, from Hormuz and Kish and Aden and all Arabia – laden with horses and other goods. The merchants use this city's port because it is conveniently situated and offers a good market for their wares, and also because merchants from many parts congregate here to buy merchandise and horses and other things. The king is very rich in treasure; he adorns his person with many valuable gems and goes about in great state. He governs his kingdom ably and maintains a high standard of justice, especially in the case of the merchants who come here from other parts – that is, the foreign merchants. He watches over their interests with great integrity. And the merchants, I assure you, are very glad to come here on account of this good king who looks after them so well. And it is certainly true that they make huge profits here and their business prospers.

I will also tell you that this king has at least 300 wives; for the more wives a man keeps here, the greater his honour is held to be. And I can tell you, too, that when a quarrel breaks out between these five kings (who are brothers-german born of the same father and mother) and they are determined to declare war on one another, then their mother, who is still alive, intervenes between them and refuses to let them fight. If, as often happens, her sons will not heed her prayers but are determined to defy her and fight, then their mother seizes a knife and cries, 'If you do not stop quarrelling and make peace with one another, I will kill myself here and now. And first of all I will cut from my bosom the breasts with which I gave you my milk.' And when the sons see how deeply their mother is grieved and how tenderly she pleads with them, and reflect that it is for their own good, they come to terms and make peace. This has happened time after time. Even so, I can tell you that after their mother's death an almighty quarrel will unavoidably break out among them and they will destroy one another.

You should also know that the people of this city, as of India as a whole, have the following custom: out of habit and for the pleasure it gives them, they almost constantly keep in their mouths a kind of leaf called *tambur*. They go round chewing this leaf and spitting out the resulting spittle. And this habit is especially prevalent among the nobles and magnates and kings. They have these leaves prepared with camphor and other spices and go about continually chewing them; lime is also added to the mix. And this keeps them very healthy. Moreover if anyone wishes to insult and taunt someone who has offended him, then when he meets him in the street he collects this mixture in his mouth and spits it in the other's face, saying, 'You are not worth this', referring to what he has spat out. The other, regarding this as a gross affront and insult, promptly complains to the king that so-and-so has slighted and abused him and asks the king's leave to avenge himself. To be precise, if the assailant has insulted him and his clan, he will ask leave to pit himself against the assailant and his clan against the assailant's clan until he has proved whether or not he is worth no more than that. But if it is a purely personal insult, he will ask leave to settle it man to man. Then the king grants leave to both parties. If it is to be a battle of the clans, each man gets ready for the fight with his own people; and the only armour they don and wear for protection is the skin their mothers gave them when they were born.

Marco Polo

When they are on the field and battle commences they strike, wound and kill one another, for their swords easily pierce their skin and they are all easy targets. The king will be present with a multitude of people to watch the proceedings; and when he sees that large numbers have been killed on both sides and that one side seems to have the upper hand and is overwhelming the other, he will take one end of the cloth he has wrapped round him and put it between his teeth, then hold out the other end at arm's length. At this the combatants will immediately stop fighting without striking another blow. And this is often how it turns out. If the combat is man to man they will both be naked, just as they are normally, and each will have a knife. They are very skilled at defending themselves with these knives, for they are adept at parrying a blow with them as well as attacking their opponent. This, then, is the procedure. As you have gathered, they are dark-skinned people. So one of them will draw a white circle wherever he chooses on the other's body, saying to him, 'Know that I will strike you in this circle and nowhere else; defend yourself as best you can.' And the other will do the same to him. Lucky for him who fares better, unlucky for him who fares worse; for whenever one of them strikes the other he feels it sharply enough.

[...]

Gujarat is also a large kingdom. The people are idolaters and have a king and their own language; they pay tribute to no one. The kingdom lies towards the west. And from here the Pole Star is still more clearly visible, for it appears at an altitude of at least six cubits. This kingdom is home to the most infamous pirates in the world. And I assure you that they perpetrate the enormity I will now describe. For you should know that when these wicked pirates capture merchants they make them drink tamarind mixed with seawater, which sends the merchants scurrying below to pass or vomit up the contents of their stomachs. The pirates then collect everything the merchants have produced and sift through it to see if it contains any pearls or other precious stones. For the pirates say that when the merchants are captured they swallow their pearls and other precious stones to keep them out of their captors' hands. And so these wicked pirates give the merchants this drink for the malicious purpose I have told you about.

They have huge quantities of pepper; they also have plenty of ginger and a great deal of indigo. They have plenty of cotton, too, for the trees that produce cotton grow here to a great height – as much as six paces after twenty years' growth. In truth when the trees reach this age they no longer produce cotton fit for spinning; instead it is used for wadding and quilting. And this is the rule with these trees: up to twelve years they produce fine cotton for spinning, but from twelve to twenty the cotton they produce is not as good as when they were young.

Immense quantities of skins are made into leather in this kingdom: that is, they tan the hides of goats, buffaloes, wild oxen, unicorns and many other beasts. I assure you they are tanned on such a scale that every year numerous ships load up with them and set sail for Arabia and many other parts; for this kingdom supplies many other kingdoms and provinces. I can also tell you that in this kingdom they make beautiful red leather mats embossed with birds and beasts and exquisitely embroidered with gold and silver thread. They are so beautiful that they are a marvel to behold. You should understand that these leather mats I am telling you about are used by the Muslims to sleep on; and how well you sleep on them! They also make cushions here, embroidered with gold and so beautiful that they are worth at least six silver marks. And some of the mats I have told you about are worth at least ten silver marks. What else shall I tell you? You may depend on it that in this kingdom they make the most finely crafted leather goods in the world, and the most expensive.

Now that we have given you all the facts about this kingdom in due order, we will go on our way . . .

1. BOCCACCIO · *Mrs Rosie and the Priest*
2. GERARD MANLEY HOPKINS · *As kingfishers catch fire*
3. *The Saga of Gunnlaug Serpent-tongue*
4. THOMAS DE QUINCEY · *On Murder Considered as One of the Fine Arts*
5. FRIEDRICH NIETZSCHE · *Aphorisms on Love and Hate*
6. JOHN RUSKIN · *Traffic*
7. PU SONGLING · *Wailing Ghosts*
8. JONATHAN SWIFT · *A Modest Proposal*
9. *Three Tang Dynasty Poets*
10. WALT WHITMAN · *On the Beach at Night Alone*
11. KENKŌ · *A Cup of Sake Beneath the Cherry Trees*
12. BALTASAR GRACIÁN · *How to Use Your Enemies*
13. JOHN KEATS · *The Eve of St Agnes*
14. THOMAS HARDY · *Woman much missed*
15. GUY DE MAUPASSANT · *Femme Fatale*
16. MARCO POLO · *Travels in the Land of Serpents and Pearls*
17. SUETONIUS · *Caligula*
18. APOLLONIUS OF RHODES · *Jason and Medea*
19. ROBERT LOUIS STEVENSON · *Olalla*
20. KARL MARX AND FRIEDRICH ENGELS · *The Communist Manifesto*
21. PETRONIUS · *Trimalchio's Feast*
22. JOHANN PETER HEBEL · *How a Ghastly Story Was Brought to Light by a Common or Garden Butcher's Dog*
23. HANS CHRISTIAN ANDERSEN · *The Tinder Box*
24. RUDYARD KIPLING · *The Gate of the Hundred Sorrows*
25. DANTE · *Circles of Hell*
26. HENRY MAYHEW · *Of Street Piemen*
27. HAFEZ · *The nightingales are drunk*
28. GEOFFREY CHAUCER · *The Wife of Bath*
29. MICHEL DE MONTAIGNE · *How We Weep and Laugh at the Same Thing*
30. THOMAS NASHE · *The Terrors of the Night*
31. EDGAR ALLAN POE · *The Tell-Tale Heart*
32. MARY KINGSLEY · *A Hippo Banquet*
33. JANE AUSTEN · *The Beautifull Cassandra*
34. ANTON CHEKHOV · *Gooseberries*
35. SAMUEL TAYLOR COLERIDGE · *Well, they are gone, and here must I remain*
36. JOHANN WOLFGANG VON GOETHE · *Sketchy, Doubtful, Incomplete Jottings*
37. CHARLES DICKENS · *The Great Winglebury Duel*
38. HERMAN MELVILLE · *The Maldive Shark*
39. ELIZABETH GASKELL · *The Old Nurse's Story*
40. NIKOLAY LESKOV · *The Steel Flea*

41. HONORÉ DE BALZAC · *The Atheist's Mass*
42. CHARLOTTE PERKINS GILMAN · *The Yellow Wall-Paper*
43. C.P. CAVAFY · *Remember, Body . . .*
44. FYODOR DOSTOEVSKY · *The Meek One*
45. GUSTAVE FLAUBERT · *A Simple Heart*
46. NIKOLAI GOGOL · *The Nose*
47. SAMUEL PEPYS · *The Great Fire of London*
48. EDITH WHARTON · *The Reckoning*
49. HENRY JAMES · *The Figure in the Carpet*
50. WILFRED OWEN · *Anthem For Doomed Youth*
51. WOLFGANG AMADEUS MOZART · *My Dearest Father*
52. PLATO · *Socrates' Defence*
53. CHRISTINA ROSSETTI · *Goblin Market*
54. *Sindbad the Sailor*
55. SOPHOCLES · *Antigone*
56. RYŪNOSUKE AKUTAGAWA · *The Life of a Stupid Man*
57. LEO TOLSTOY · *How Much Land Does A Man Need?*
58. GIORGIO VASARI · *Leonardo da Vinci*
59. OSCAR WILDE · *Lord Arthur Savile's Crime*
60. SHEN FU · *The Old Man of the Moon*
61. AESOP · *The Dolphins, the Whales and the Gudgeon*
62. MATSUO BASHŌ · *Lips too Chilled*
63. EMILY BRONTË · *The Night is Darkening Round Me*
64. JOSEPH CONRAD · *To-morrow*
65. RICHARD HAKLUYT · *The Voyage of Sir Francis Drake Around the Whole Globe*
66. KATE CHOPIN · *A Pair of Silk Stockings*
67. CHARLES DARWIN · *It was snowing butterflies*
68. BROTHERS GRIMM · *The Robber Bridegroom*
69. CATULLUS · *I Hate and I Love*
70. HOMER · *Circe and the Cyclops*
71. D. H. LAWRENCE · *Il Duro*
72. KATHERINE MANSFIELD · *Miss Brill*
73. OVID · *The Fall of Icarus*
74. SAPPHO · *Come Close*
75. IVAN TURGENEV · *Kasyan from the Beautiful Lands*
76. VIRGIL · *O Cruel Alexis*
77. H. G. WELLS · *A Slip under the Microscope*
78. HERODOTUS · *The Madness of Cambyses*
79. *Speaking of Siva*
80. *The Dhammapada*

'Because of his baldness and hairiness, he announced that it was a capital offence for anyone either to look down on him as he passed or to mention goats in any context.'

GAIUS SUETONIUS TRANQUILLUS
Born *c.* 70 CE
Died *c.* 130 CE

Taken from Robert Graves's translation of
The Twelve Caesars, first published in 1957.

SUETONIUS IN PENGUIN CLASSICS
The Twelve Caesars

SUETONIUS

Caligula

Translated by
Robert Graves

PENGUIN BOOKS

PENGUIN CLASSICS

UK | USA | Canada | Ireland | Australia
India | New Zealand | South Africa

Penguin Books is part of the Penguin Random House group of companies
whose addresses can be found at global.penguinrandomhouse.com.

This edition published in Penguin Classics 2015

011

Translation copyright © Robert Graves, 1957

The moral right of the translator has been asserted

Set in 10/14.5 pt Baskerville 10 Pro
Typeset by Jouve (UK), Milton Keynes
Printed and bound in Great Britain by Clays Ltd, Elcograf S.p.A.

A CIP catalogue record for this book is available from the British Library

ISBN: 978-0-141-39792-4

www.greenpenguin.co.uk

MIX
Paper from
responsible sources
FSC® C018179

Penguin Random House is committed to a
sustainable future for our business, our readers
and our planet. This book is made from Forest
Stewardship Council® certified paper.

Gaius Caligula

Germanicus, father of Gaius Caesar, was the son of Drusus and Antonia the younger, and was eventually adopted by Tiberius, his paternal uncle. He served as quaestor five years before he was legally eligible and became consul without holding any of the intermediary offices, and was then appointed to the command of the forces in Germany. When Augustus' death became known, the legions there were unanimously opposed to Tiberius' succession and would have acclaimed Germanicus emperor, but he showed a remarkable example of filial respect and personal integrity by diverting their attention from this project; he took the offensive in Germany, and won a triumph. As consul for the second time he was hurried to the east, where conditions were unsettled, before being able to take office. There he defeated the king of Armenia and reduced Cappadocia to provincial status, but he succumbed to a protracted illness at Antioch, being only thirty-four years old when he died. Because of the dark stains which covered his body and the foam on his lips, poison was suspected; significantly, they also found the heart intact among the ashes after cremation – a heart steeped in poison is supposedly proof against fire.

If we may accept the common verdict, Tiberius craftily arranged Germanicus' death with the advice and assistance of Gnaeus Piso. Piso had been appointed to govern Syria at about the same time, and there, deciding that he must make an enemy either of Germanicus or of Tiberius, took every opportunity to provoke Germanicus, even when on his sickbed, by the meanest acts and speeches – behaviour for which the Senate condemned him to death on his return to Rome, after he had narrowly escaped a popular lynching.

Germanicus is everywhere described as having been of outstanding physical and moral excellence. He was handsome, courageous, a past master of Greek and Latin oratory and learning, conspicuously kind-hearted, and gifted with the ability of winning universal respect and affection. Only his legs were somewhat undeveloped, but he strengthened them by assiduous exercise on horseback after meals. He often fought and killed an enemy in hand-to-hand combat, and did not cease to plead cases in the law courts even when he had gained a triumph. Some of his Greek comedies are extant, besides other literary works. At home or abroad he always behaved modestly, would dispense with lictors when visiting any free or allied town, and offered sacrifices at whatever tombs of famous men he came across. On deciding to bury under one mound all the scattered bones of Varus' fallen legionaries, he led the search party himself and took an active part in the collection. Towards his detractors Germanicus showed such tolerance and leniency, regardless of their identity or motives, that he would not even break with Piso (who was cancelling his orders and plaguing his subordinates) until he found that spells and potions were being used against him. And then he did no more than renounce his friendship in the traditional manner, and leave testamentary instructions for his family to take vengeance on Piso if anything should happen to himself.

Such virtuous conduct brought Germanicus rich

rewards. He was so deeply respected and loved by all his acquaintances that Augustus – I need hardly mention his other relatives – wondered for a long time whether to make him his successor, but at last ordered Tiberius to adopt him. Germanicus, the records show, had won such intense popular devotion that he was in danger of being mobbed to death whenever he arrived at a place or took his leave again. Indeed, when he came back from Germany after suppressing the native uprising, all the praetorian cohorts marched out in welcome, despite orders that only two were to do so, and the entire people of Rome – all ages and ranks and both sexes – flocked as far as the twentieth milestone to meet him.

But the most spectacular proof of the devotion in which Germanicus had been held appeared on the day of his death and immediately afterwards. The populace stoned temples and upset altars; heads of families threw their household gods into the street and abandoned their newly born children. Even the barbarians who were fighting us or one another are said to have made immediate peace as though a domestic tragedy had afflicted the whole world, some princes shaving their own beards and their wives' heads in token of profound grief. The King of Kings himself cancelled his hunting parties and banquets, which is a sign of public mourning in Parthia.

While Rome was still stunned by the first news of his illness and waiting for further bulletins, a rumour that he had recovered went the rounds one evening after dark and sent people rushing to the Capitol with torches and sacrificial victims; so eager were they to fulfil their vows that the temple gates were almost torn down. Tiberius was awakened by the joyful chant:

> All is well again at Rome,
> All is well again at home,
> Here's an end to all our pain:
> Germanicus is well again!

When the news of his death finally broke, neither edicts nor official expressions of sympathy could console the people; mourning continued throughout the festival days of December. The bitterness of their loss was aggravated by the horrors which followed, for everyone believed, and with good reason, that moral respect for Germanicus had alone kept Tiberius from displaying the cruelty of his wicked heart.

Suetonius

Germanicus married Agrippina, daughter of Marcus Agrippa and Julia, who bore him nine children. Two died in infancy, and a third, an extremely likeable boy, during early childhood. Livia dedicated a statue of him, dressed as Cupid, to Venus Capitolina; Augustus kept a replica in his bedroom, and used to kiss it fondly whenever he entered. The other children – three girls, Agrippina, Drusilla and Livilla, born in successive years, and three boys, Nero, Drusus and Gaius Caesar – survived their father; but Tiberius later brought charges against Nero and Drusus, whom he persuaded the Senate to execute as public enemies.

Gaius Caesar was born on 31 August, during the consulship shared by his father with Gaius Fonteius Capito. His birthplace is disputed. According to Gnaeus Lentulus Gaetulicus he was born at Tibur, but according to Pliny the Elder at the village of Ambitarvium in the territory of the Treveri, just above Confluens; Pliny supports his view by mentioning certain local altars inscribed 'In Honour of Agrippina's *Puerperium*'. A verse which went the rounds at his accession also suggests that he was born in the winter quarters of the legions:

> Born in a barracks,
>   Reared in the arts of war:
> A noble nativity
>   For a Roman emperor!

The public records, however, give his birthplace as Antium, and my researches convince me that this is correct. Pliny shows that Gaetulicus tried to flatter the proud young *princeps* by pretending that he came from Tibur, a city sacred to Hercules, and that he lied with greater confidence because Germanicus did have a son named Gaius Caesar born there the year before, whose sadly premature death I have already mentioned. Nevertheless, Pliny is himself mistaken, since Augustus' biographers agree that Germanicus' first visit to Gaul took place after he had been consul, by which time Gaius was already born. Moreover, the inscriptions on the altars do not prove Pliny's point, since Agrippina bore Germanicus two daughters in Gaul, and any confinement is a *puerperium*, regardless of the child's sex – girls were then still called *puerae* as often as *puellae*, and boys *puelli* as often as *pueri*. Finally, I have found a letter which Augustus wrote to his granddaughter Agrippina a few months before he died; the Gaius mentioned in it must have been this one, because no other child of that name was alive at the time. It reads, 'Yesterday, I made arrangements for Talarius and Asillius to bring your son Gaius to you on the eighteenth of May, if the gods will. I am also sending with him one of my slaves, a doctor who, as I have told Germanicus in a letter, need not be returned to me if he proves of use to you. Goodbye, my dear Agrippina! Keep well on the way back to your Germanicus.' Clearly, Gaius could not have been born in a country to which he was first taken from Rome at the age of nearly two. These details also weaken my confidence in that anonymous verse about his birth in a barracks. So we are, I think, reduced to accepting the only other authority, namely the public records, especially since Gaius preferred Antium to any other city and treated it as his native place; he even planned, they say, to transfer the seat of imperial government there when he wearied of Rome.

He won his cognomen Caligula from an army joke, because he grew up among the troops and wore the miniature uniform of a private soldier. An undeniable proof of the hold on their affections which this early

Caligula

experience of camp life gave him is that when they rioted at the news of Augustus' death and were ready for any madness, the mere sight of little Gaius calmed them down. As soon as they realized that he was being removed to a neighbouring city to protect him from their violence, they were overcome by contrition; some of them seized and stopped his carriage, pleading to be spared this disgrace.

Gaius also accompanied Germanicus to Syria. On his return he lived with his mother, and next, after she had been exiled, with his great-grandmother Livia Augusta, whose funeral oration he delivered from the Rostra though he had not yet come of age. He then lived with his grandmother Antonia until Tiberius summoned him to Capreae at the age of nineteen. He assumed the adult toga and shaved his first beard on one and the same day, but this was a most informal occasion compared with his brothers' coming-of-age celebrations. The courtiers tried every trick to force him into making complaints against Tiberius – always, however, without success. He not only failed to show any interest in the murder of his relatives, but affected an amazing indifference to his own ill treatment, behaving so obsequiously to his adoptive grandfather and to the entire household that someone said of him, very neatly, 'Never was there a better slave, or a worse master.'

Yet even in those days he could not control his natural brutality. He loved watching tortures and executions, and, disguised in a wig and a long robe, abandoned himself nightly to the pleasures of feasting and scandalous living. Tiberius was ready enough to indulge a passion which Gaius had for theatrical dancing and singing, on the ground that it might have a civilizing influence on him. With characteristic shrewdness, the old emperor had exactly gauged the young man's vicious inclinations, and would often remark that Gaius' advent portended his own death and the ruin of everyone else. 'I am nursing a viper in Rome's bosom,' he once said; 'I am educating a Phaethon for the whole world.'

Gaius shortly thereafter married Junia Claudilla, daughter of the distinguished senator Marcus Silanus. Then he was appointed augur in place of his brother Drusus, but transferred to the pontificate before his inauguration in compliment to his dutiful behaviour and exemplary life. This encouraged him in the hope of becoming Tiberius' successor, because Sejanus'

Caligula

downfall had reduced the court to a shadow of its former self; and when Junia died in childbirth he seduced Ennia, wife of Naevius Macro, the praetorian prefect, not only swearing to marry her if he became emperor, but putting the oath in writing. After Ennia helped him win Macro's support, he assailed Tiberius with poison, as some people think; he issued orders for his ring to be removed while he was still breathing, and when he would not let it go he had him smothered with a pillow. According to one account he throttled Tiberius with his own hands, and when a freedman cried out in protest at this wicked deed he crucified him at once. All this may be true; some writers report that Gaius later confessed to intended if not actual parricide. He would often boast, that is to say, of having carried a dagger into Tiberius' bedroom with the virtuous intention of avenging his mother and brothers; but, according to his own account, he found Tiberius asleep and, restrained by feelings of pity, threw down the dagger and went out. Tiberius, he said, was perfectly aware of what had happened, yet never dared question him or take any action in the matter.

Gaius' accession seemed to the Roman

people – one might almost say to the whole world – like the answer to their prayers. The memory of Germanicus and compassion for a family that had been practically wiped out by successive murders made most provincials and soldiers, many of whom had known him as a child, and the entire population of Rome as well, show extravagant joy that he was now emperor. When he escorted Tiberius' funeral procession from Misenum to Rome he was, of course, dressed in mourning, but a dense crowd greeted him ecstatically with altars, sacrifices and torches, and such endearments as 'star', 'chick', 'baby' and 'pet'.

On his arrival in the city the Senate (and a mob of people who had forced their way into the Senate House) immediately and unanimously conferred absolute power upon him. They set aside Tiberius' will, which made his other grandson, then still a child, joint heir with Gaius, and so splendid were the celebrations that 160,000 victims were publicly sacrificed during the next three months, or perhaps even a shorter period. A few days later he visited the prison islands off Campania, and vows were uttered for his safe return – at that time no opportunity of demonstrating a general concern for his welfare was ever disregarded. When he fell ill, anxious crowds besieged the Palatine all night. Some swore that they would fight as gladiators if the gods allowed him to recover; others even carried placards volunteering to die instead of him. To the great love in which he was held by his own people, foreigners added their own tribute of devotion. Artabanus, the king of the Parthians, who had always loathed and despised Tiberius, made unsolicited overtures of friendship to Gaius, attended a conference with the governor of Syria, and, before returning across the river Euphrates, paid homage to the Roman Eagles and standards and the statues of the Caesars.

Gaius strengthened his popularity by every possible means. He delivered a funeral speech in honour of Tiberius to a vast crowd, weeping profusely all the while, and gave him a magnificent burial. But as soon as this was over he sailed for Pandataria and the Pontian Islands to fetch back the remains of his mother and his brother Nero – and during rough weather too, in proof of devotion. He approached the ashes with the utmost reverence, and transferred them to the urns with his own hands. Equally dramatic was his gesture of raising a standard on the poop of the bireme which brought the urns to Ostia, and thence up the Tiber to Rome. He had arranged that the most distinguished *equites* available should carry them to the Mausoleum about noon, when the streets were at their busiest, and also appointed an annual day for commemorative rites, marked by chariot races in the Circus, at which Agrippina's image would be paraded in a covered carriage. He honoured his father's memory by renaming the month of September 'Germanicus', and sponsored a senatorial decree which awarded his grandmother Antonia, at a blow, all the honours won by Livia Augusta in her entire lifetime. As fellow consul he chose his uncle Claudius, who had hitherto been a mere *eques*, and adopted young Tiberius when he came of age, giving him the title of Youth Leader. He included the names of his sisters in the official oath which everyone had to take, which ran, 'I will not value my life or that of my children less highly than I do the safety of Gaius and his sisters,' and in the consular motions, as follows: 'Good fortune attend Gaius Caesar and his sisters!'

A similar bid for popularity was to recall all exiles and dismiss all criminal charges whatsoever that had been pending since the time of Tiberius. The batches

Caligula

of written evidence in his mother's and brothers' cases were brought to the Forum at his orders and burned, to set at rest the minds of such witnesses and informers as had testified against them, but first he swore before heaven that he had neither read nor abstracted a single document. He also refused to examine a report supposedly concerning his own safety, on the ground that nobody could have any reason to hate him, and swore that he would never listen to informers.

Gaius drove the spintrian perverts from the city, and could only with difficulty be restrained from drowning the lot. He gave permission for the works of Titus Labienus, Cremutius Cordus and Cassius Severus, which had been banned by order of the Senate, to be sought out and republished – making his desire known that posterity should be in full possession of all historical facts. In addition, he revived Augustus' practice, discontinued by Tiberius, of publishing an imperial budget, and invested the magistrates with full authority over court cases, not allowing litigants to come to him to appeal their decisions. He scrupulously scanned the list of *equites*, but, though publicly dismounting any who had behaved in a wicked or scandalous manner, was not unduly severe with those guilty of lesser misbehaviour – he merely omitted their names from the list which he read out. His creation of a fifth judicial division aided jurors to keep abreast of their work; his reviving of the electoral system was designed to restore voting rights to the people. He honoured every one of the bequests in Tiberius' will, though this had been set aside by the Senate, and in that of Julia Augusta, which Tiberius had suppressed; he abolished the Italian half-per-cent auction tax; and he paid compensation to a great many people whose houses had been damaged by fire. Any king whom he restored to the throne was awarded the taxes that had accumulated since his deposition – Antiochus of Commagene, for example, got a refund of 100 million sesterces. To show his interest in public morality, he awarded 800,000 sesterces to a freedwoman who, though put to extreme torture, had not revealed her patron's guilt. These acts won him many official honours, among them a golden shield, carried once a year to the Capitol by the colleges of priests marching in procession and followed by the Senate, while the children of the aristocracy chanted an anthem in praise of his virtues. By a senatorial decree, the day of his accession was called the Parilia, as though Rome had now been born again.

Gaius held four consulships: the earliest for two months, from the Kalends of July; the next for the whole month of January; the third for the first thirteen days of January; and the fourth for the first seven. Only the last two were in sequence. He assumed his third consulship at Lugdunum, without a colleague – not, as some people think, through arrogance or indifference, but because the news that his fellow consul-elect had died in Rome just before the Kalends of January had not reached him in time. He twice presented every member of the people with 300 sesterces, and twice invited all the senators and *equites*, with their wives and children, to an extravagant banquet. At the second of these banquets he gave every man a toga and every woman a purple scarf. In order to increase the public rejoicing in Rome for all time, he extended the Saturnalia with an additional day, which he called 'Youth Day'.

He held several gladiatorial contests, some in Statilius Taurus' amphitheatre and others in the Saepta, diversifying them with prize fights between the best boxers of Africa and Campania; he occasionally allowed magistrates or friends to preside at these instead of doing so himself. Again, he staged a great number of different theatrical shows in various buildings – sometimes at night, with the whole city illuminated – and would scatter vouchers among the audience entitling them to all sorts of gifts, over and above the basket of food which was everyone's due. At one banquet, noticing with what extraordinary gusto an *eques* seated opposite dug into the food, he sent him his own heaped plate as well, and rewarded a senator, who had been similarly enjoying himself, with a praetorship, though he was not yet qualified to hold this office. Many all-day games were celebrated in the Circus, and between races he introduced panther-baiting and the Troy Game. For certain special games, when all the charioteers were men of senatorial rank, he had the Circus decorated in red and green. Once, while he was inspecting the Circus equipment, from the Gelotian House which overlooks it, a group of people standing in the nearby balconies called out, 'What about a day's racing, Caesar?' So on the spur of the moment he gave immediate orders for games to be held.

Caligula

One of his spectacles was on such a fantastic scale that nothing like it had ever been seen before. He collected all available merchant ships and anchored them in two lines, close together, the whole way from Baiae to the mole at Puteoli, a distance of three miles and some 600 feet. Then he had the ships boarded over, with earth heaped on the planks, and made a kind of Via Appia along which he trotted back and forth for two consecutive days. On the first day he wore a civic crown, a sword, a shield and a cloth-of-gold cloak, and rode a gaily caparisoned charger. On the second he appeared in charioteer's costume driving a team of two famous horses, with a boy named Dareus, one of his Parthian hostages, triumphantly displayed in the car beside him; behind came a force of praetorians and a group of his friends mounted in Gallic chariots. Gaius is of course generally supposed to have built the bridge as an improvement on Xerxes' famous feat of bridging the much narrower Hellespont. Others believe that he planned this huge engineering feat to terrify the Germans and Britons, on whom he had his eye. But my grandfather used to tell me as a boy that, according to some courtiers in Gaius' confidence, the sole reason for the bridge was this: when Tiberius could not decide whom to appoint as his successor and inclined towards his grandson and namesake, Thrasyllus the astrologer had told him, 'As for Gaius, he has no more chance of becoming emperor than of riding a horse dry-shod across the Gulf of Baiae.'

Gaius gave several shows abroad – theatrical performances at Syracuse and mixed games at Lugdunum, where he also held a competition in Greek and Latin oratory. The losers, they say, had to present the winners with prizes and make speeches praising them, while those who failed miserably were forced to erase their entries with either sponges or their own tongues – at the threat of being thrashed and flung into the Rhône.

He completed certain projects neglected by Tiberius, namely the Temple of Augustus and Pompey's Theatre, and began the construction of an aqueduct in the Tibur district and an amphitheatre near the Saepta. (His successor Claudius finished the aqueduct, but work on the amphitheatre was abandoned.) Gaius rebuilt the ruinous walls and temples of Syracuse, and among his other projects were the restoration of Polycrates' palace at Samos, the completion of Didymaean Apollo's temple at Miletus, and the building of a city high up in the Alps. But he was most deeply interested in cutting a canal through the Isthmus of Corinth, and sent a *primipilaris* there to survey the site.

So much for Gaius the Emperor; the rest of this history must needs deal with Gaius the Monster.

He adopted a variety of titles, such as Pious, Son of the Camp, Father of the Army, Caesar Optimus Maximus. But when once, at the dinner table, some foreign kings who had come to pay homage were arguing which of them was the most nobly descended, he burst out, 'Nay, let there be one master, and one king!' And he nearly assumed a royal diadem then and there, transforming an ostensible principate into an actual kingdom. However, after his courtiers reminded him that he already outranked any king or local ruler, he insisted on being treated as a god – arranging for the most revered or artistically famous statues of the gods, including that of Jupiter at Olympia, to be brought from Greece and have their heads replaced by his own.

Next he extended his Palatine residence as far as the Forum, converted the shrine of Castor and Pollux into a vestibule, and would often stand between these divine brothers to be worshipped by all visitants, some of whom addressed him as 'Jupiter Latiaris'. He established a shrine to his own godhead, with priests, the costliest possible victims, and a life-sized golden image, which was dressed every day in clothes identical with those that he happened to be wearing. All the richest citizens tried to gain priesthoods here, either by influence or by bribery. Flamingos, peacocks, black grouse, guinea hens and pheasants were offered as sacrifices, each on a particular day. When the moon shone full and bright he always invited the moon goddess to his bed, and during the day he would indulge in whispered conversations with Jupiter Capitolinus, pressing his ear to the god's mouth and sometimes raising his voice in anger. Once he was overheard threatening the god, 'Either you throw me or I will throw you!' Finally he announced that Jupiter had persuaded him to share his home, and therefore connected the Palatine with the Capitol by throwing a bridge across the Temple of Divus Augustus; he next began building a new house inside the precincts of the Capitol itself, in order to live even nearer.

Caligula

Because of Agrippa's humble origin Gaius loathed being described as his grandson, and would fly into a rage if anyone mentioned him, in speech or song, as an ancestor of the Caesars. He nursed a fantasy that his mother had been born of an incestuous union between Augustus and Julia, and, not content with thus discrediting Augustus' name, cancelled the annual commemorations of his victories at Actium and Sicily, declaring that they had proved the ruin of the Roman people. He called his great-grandmother Livia Augusta a 'Ulysses in petticoats', and in a letter to the Senate he dared describe her as of low birth – 'her maternal grandfather Aufidius Lurco having been a mere town councillor from Fundi' – although the public records showed Lurco to have held high office at Rome. When his paternal grandmother Antonia begged him to grant her a private audience he insisted on taking Macro, the praetorian prefect, as his escort. Unkind treatment of this sort hurried her to the grave, though according to some he accelerated the process with poison; and when she died he showed so little respect that he sat in his dining room and watched the funeral pyre burn. He sent a military tribune to kill young Tiberius without warning, on the pretext that Tiberius had insulted him by taking an antidote against poison – his breath smelled of it – and he forced his father-in-law, Marcus Silanus, to cut his own throat with a razor, the charge being that he had not followed him when he put to sea in a storm, but had stayed on shore to seize power at Rome if anything happened to him. The truth was that Silanus, a notoriously bad sailor, could not face the voyage; and young Tiberius' breath smelled of medicine taken for a persistent cough which was gaining a hold on his lungs. Gaius preserved his uncle Claudius mainly as a butt for practical jokes.

It was his habit to commit incest with each of his three sisters in turn, and at large banquets, when his wife reclined above him, placed them all in turn below him. They say that he ravished his sister Drusilla before he came of age: their grandmother Antonia, at whose house they were both staying, caught them in bed together. Later, he took Drusilla from her husband, the former consul Lucius Cassius Longinus, quite unashamedly treating her as his wife; when he fell dangerously ill, he left her all his property, and the empire too. At her death he made it a capital offence to laugh, to bathe, or to dine with one's parents, wives or children while the period of public mourning lasted, and he was so crazed with grief that he suddenly rushed from Rome by night, drove through Campania, took ship to Sicily, and returned just as impetuously, without having shaved or cut his hair in the meantime. Afterwards, whenever he had to take an important oath, he swore by Drusilla's godhead, even at a public assembly or an army parade. He showed no such extreme love or respect for the two surviving sisters, and often, indeed, let his toy boys sleep with them; and at Aemilius Lepidus' trial he felt no compunction about denouncing them as adulteresses who were party to plots against him – openly producing letters in their handwriting (acquired by trickery and seduction) and dedicating to Mars Ultor the three swords with which, the accompanying placard alleged, they had meant to kill him.

It would be hard to say whether the way he got married, the way he dissolved his marriages or the way he behaved as a husband was the most disgraceful. He attended the wedding ceremony of Gaius Piso and Livia Orestilla, but had the bride carried off to his own home. After a few days, however, he sent her away, and two years later he banished her, suspecting that she had returned to Piso in the interval. According to one account, he told Piso, who was reclining opposite him at the wedding feast, 'Hands off my wife!' and took her home with him at once, and announced the next day that he had taken a wife in the style of Romulus and Augustus. Then he suddenly sent to the provinces for Lollia Paulina, wife of Gaius Memmius, the consular army commander, because somebody had remarked that her grandmother was once a famous beauty; but he soon discarded her, forbidding her ever again to sleep with another man. Caesonia was neither young nor beautiful and had three daughters by a former husband, besides being recklessly extravagant and utterly promiscuous, yet he loved her with a passionate faithfulness and often, when reviewing the troops, used to take her out riding in helmet, cloak and shield. For his friends he even paraded her naked, but he would not allow her the dignified title of wife until she had borne him a child, whereupon he announced the marriage and the birth simultaneously. He named the child Julia Drusilla, and carried her around the temples of all the goddesses in turn before finally entrusting her to the lap of Minerva, whom he called upon to supervise his daughter's growth and education. What he regarded as the surest proof of his paternity was her violent temper: while still an infant, she would try to scratch out her little playmates' eyes.

It seems hardly worthwhile to record how Gaius treated such relatives and friends as his cousin King Ptolemy (son of Juba and Mark Antony's daughter Selene) and even Macro and his wife Ennia, by whose help he had become emperor. Their very loyalty and nearness to him earned them cruel deaths. Nor was he any more respectful or considerate in his dealings with the Senate, but made some of the highest officials run for miles beside his chariot, dressed in their togas, or wait in short linen tunics at the head or foot of his dining couch. Often he would send for men whom he had secretly killed, as though they were still alive, and remark offhandedly a few days later that they must have committed suicide. When the consuls forgot to announce his birthday, he dismissed them and left the commonwealth for three days without its chief officers. One of his quaestors was charged with conspiracy; Gaius had his clothes stripped off and spread on the ground, to give the soldiers who flogged him a firmer foothold.

He behaved just as arrogantly and violently towards people of less exalted rank. A crowd bursting into the Circus in the middle of the night to secure free seats angered him so much that he had them driven away with clubs; more than a score of *equites*, as many married women, and numerous others were crushed to death in the ensuing panic. Gaius liked to stir up trouble in the theatre by scattering gift vouchers before the seats were occupied, thus tempting the common people to invade the rows reserved for *equites*. During gladiatorial shows he would have the canopies removed at the hottest time of the day and forbid anyone to leave; or cancel the regular programme and substitute worn-out wild beasts and feeble old fighters; or stage comic duels between respectable householders who happened to be physically disabled in some way or other. More than once he closed down the granaries and let the people go hungry.

The following instances will illustrate his cruelty. Having collected wild animals for one of his shows,

Caligula

he found butcher's meat too expensive and decided to feed them with criminals instead. He paid no attention to the charge sheets, but simply stood in the middle of a colonnade, glanced at the prisoners lined up before him, and gave the order 'Kill every man between that bald head and that other one over there.' Someone had sworn to fight in the arena if he recovered from his illness; Gaius forced him to fulfil this oath and watched his swordplay closely, not letting him go until he had won the match and begged abjectly to be released. Another fellow had pledged himself on the same occasion to commit suicide; Gaius, finding that he was still alive, ordered him to be dressed in wreaths and fillets and driven through Rome by the imperial slaves, who kept harping on his pledge and finally flung him over the rampart. Many men of decent family were branded at his command and sent down the mines, or put to work on the roads, or thrown to the wild beasts. Others were confined in narrow cages, where they had to crouch on all fours like animals, or were sawn in half – and not necessarily for major offences, but merely for criticizing his shows, failing to swear by his *genius*, and so forth.

Gaius made parents attend their sons' executions, and when one father excused himself on the ground of ill health he provided a litter for him. Having invited another father to dinner just after the son's execution, he overflowed with good fellowship in an attempt to make him laugh and joke. He watched the manager of his gladiatorial and wild-beast shows being flogged with chains for several days running, and had him killed only when the smell of suppurating brains became insupportable. A writer of Atellan farces was burned alive in the amphitheatre, because of a single line which had an amusing double entendre. One *eques*, on the point of being thrown to the wild beasts, shouted that he was innocent; Gaius brought him back, removed his tongue, and then ordered the sentence to be carried out.

Once he asked a returned exile how he had been spending his time. To flatter him the man answered, 'I prayed continuously to the gods for Tiberius' death and your accession, and my prayer was granted.' Gaius therefore concluded that the new batch of exiles must be praying for his own death, so he sent agents from island to island and had them all killed. Being anxious that one particular senator should be torn in pieces, he persuaded some of his colleagues to challenge him as a public enemy when he entered the Senate House, stab him with their pens, and then hand him over for lynching to the rest of the Senate; and he was not satisfied until the victim's limbs, organs and guts had been dragged through the streets and heaped up at his feet.

His savage crimes were matched by his brutal language. He claimed that no personal trait made him feel prouder than his 'inflexibility' – by which he must have meant 'brazen impudence'. As though mere deafness to his grandmother Antonia's good advice were not enough, he told her, 'Bear in mind that I can do anything I want to anyone I want!' Suspecting that young Tiberius had taken drugs as prophylactics to the poison he intended to administer, Gaius scoffed, 'Can there really be an antidote against Caesar?' And on banishing his sisters he remarked, 'I have swords as well as islands.' One man of praetorian status, taking a cure at Anticyra, made frequent requests for an extension of his sick leave; Gaius had his throat cut, suggesting that if hellebore had been of so little benefit over so long a period, he must need to be bled. When signing the execution list after the ten-day waiting period he used to say, 'I am clearing my accounts.' And one day, after sentencing a number of Gauls and Greeks to die in the same batch, he boasted of having 'subdued Gallograecia'.

The method of execution he preferred was to inflict numerous small wounds, avoiding the prisoner's vital organs, and his familiar order 'Make him feel that he is dying!' soon became proverbial. Once, when the wrong man had been killed, owing to a confusion of names, he announced that the victim had equally deserved death, and he often quoted the tragic line 'Let them hate me, so long as they fear me.' He would indiscriminately abuse the Senate as having been supporters of Sejanus or informers against his mother and brothers (at this point producing the papers which he was supposed to have burned), and exclaim that Tiberius' cruelty had been quite justified since, with so many accusers about, he was bound to believe their charges. The *equites* earned his constant displeasure for spending their time, or so he complained, at the plays or the games. On one occasion the people cheered the wrong team; he cried angrily, 'I wish all you Romans had only one neck!' When a shout arose in the amphitheatre for Tetrinius the bandit to come out and fight, he said that all those who called for him were Tetriniuses too. A group of net-and-trident gladiators, dressed in tunics, put up a very poor show against the five men-at-arms with whom they were matched; but when he sentenced them to death for cowardice, one of them seized a trident and killed each of his opponents in turn. Gaius then publicly expressed his horror at what he called 'this most bloody murder', and his disgust with those who had been able to stomach the sight.

He went about complaining how bad the times were, and particularly that there had been no public disasters like the Varus massacre under Augustus or the collapse of the amphitheatre at Fidenae under Tiberius. The prosperity of his own reign, he said, would lead to its being wholly forgotten, and he often prayed for a great military catastrophe or for famine, plague, fire or at least an earthquake.

Everything that Gaius said and did was marked with equal cruelty, even during his hours of rest and amusement and banquetry. He frequently had trials by torture held in his presence while he was eating or otherwise enjoying himself, and kept an expert headsman in readiness to decapitate the prisoners brought in from jail. When the bridge across the sea at Puteoli was being dedicated, he invited a number of spectators from the shore to inspect it and then abruptly tipped them into the water; some clung to the ships' rudders, but he had them dislodged with boathooks and oars and left to drown. At a public dinner in Rome he sent to his executioners a slave who had stolen a strip of silver from a couch; they were to lop off the man's hands, tie them around his neck so that they hung on his breast, and take him for a tour of the tables, displaying a placard in explanation of his punishment. On another occasion a gladiator against whom he was fencing with a wooden sword fell down deliberately, whereupon Gaius drew a real dagger, stabbed him to death, and ran about waving the palm branch of victory. Once, while serving at an altar in the role of sacrificial assistant, he swung his mallet as if at the victim, but instead felled his fellow assistant, whose duty it was to slit its throat. At one particularly extravagant banquet he burst into sudden peals of laughter. The consuls, who were reclining next to him, politely asked whether they might share the joke. 'What do you think?' he answered. 'It occurred to me that I have only to give one nod and both your throats will be cut on the spot!'

He played a prank on Apelles, the tragic actor, by striking a pose beside a statue of Jupiter and asking, 'Which of us two is the greater?' When Apelles hesitated momentarily, Gaius had him flogged, commenting on the musical quality even of his groans for mercy. He never kissed the neck of his wife or mistress without saying, 'And this beautiful throat will be cut whenever I please.' Sometimes he even threatened to torture Caesonia as a means of discovering why he was so devoted to her.

In his insolent pride and destructiveness he made malicious attacks on men of almost every epoch. Needing more room in the Capitol courtyard, Augustus had once shifted the statues of certain famous men to the Campus Martius; these Gaius dashed to the ground and shattered so completely that they could not possibly be restored, even though their bases were intact. After this no statue or bust of any living person could be set up without his permission. He toyed with the idea of suppressing Homer's poems – for surely, he would say, he might claim

Plato's privilege of banishing Homer from his republic. As for Virgil and Livy, Gaius came very near to having their works and busts removed from the libraries, claiming that Virgil had little knowledge and less skill and that Livy was a wordy and inaccurate historian. It seems also that he proposed to abolish the study of law; at any rate, he often swore by Hercules that no legal expert's advice would ever thwart his will.

Gaius deprived the noblest men at Rome of their ancient family emblems – Torquatus lost his golden torc, Cincinnatus his lock of hair, and Gnaeus Pompeius the famous cognomen Magnus. He invited King Ptolemy to visit Rome, welcomed him with appropriate honours, and then suddenly ordered his execution – as mentioned above – because at Ptolemy's entrance into the amphitheatre during a gladiatorial show the fine purple cloak which he wore had attracted universal admiration. Any good-looking man with a fine head of hair whom Gaius ran across had the back of his scalp brutally shaved. One Aesius Proculus, the son of a *primipilaris*, was so well built and handsome that people nicknamed him 'Colosseros'. Without warning, Gaius ordered Aesius to be dragged from his seat in the amphitheatre into the arena and matched first with a Thracian net fighter, then with a man-at-arms. Though Aesius won both combats, he was thereupon dressed in rags, led fettered through the streets to be jeered at by women, and finally strangled. In short, however low anyone's fortune or condition might be, Gaius always found some cause for envy. Thus he sent a stronger man to challenge the current King of the Grove, simply because he had held his priesthood for a number of years. A chariot fighter called Porius drew such tremendous applause for freeing his slave in celebration of a victory at the games that Gaius indignantly rushed from the amphitheatre. In so doing he tripped over the fringe of his robe and pitched down the steps, at the bottom of which he complained that the most powerful race in the world seemed to take greater notice of a gladiator's trifling gesture than of all their deified emperors, even the one still among them.

He had not the slightest regard for chastity, either his own or others', and is said to have had sexual relations, both active and passive, with Marcus Lepidus, Mnester the pantomime dancer, and various foreign hostages; moreover, a young man of consular family, Valerius Catullus, publicly announced that Gaius had been his passive sexual partner and had completely exhausted him with his demands. Besides incest with his sisters, and a notorious passion for the prostitute Pyrallis, Gaius made advances to almost every well-known married woman in Rome; after inviting a selection of them to dinner with their husbands, he would slowly and carefully examine each in turn while they passed his couch, as a purchaser might assess the value of a slave, and even stretch out his hand and lift up the chin of any woman who kept her eyes modestly cast down. Then, whenever he felt so inclined, he would send for whoever pleased him best and leave the banquet in her company. A little later he would return, showing obvious signs of what he had been about, and openly discuss his bedfellow in detail, dwelling on her good and bad physical points and criticizing her sexual performance. To some of these unfortunates he issued, and publicly registered, divorces in the name of their absent husbands.

No parallel can be found for Gaius' far-fetched extravagances. He invented new kinds of baths and the most unnatural dishes and drinks – bathing in hot and cold perfumes, drinking valuable pearls dissolved in vinegar, and providing his guests with golden bread and golden meat; he would remark that Caesar alone could not afford to be frugal. For several days in succession he scattered large sums of money from the roof of the Basilica Julia, and he built Liburnian galleys with ten banks of oars, jewelled poop decks, multicoloured sails, and huge baths, colonnades and banqueting halls aboard – not to mention growing vines and fruit trees of different varieties. In these vessels he used to take day-long cruises along the Campanian coast, reclining on his couch and listening to songs and choruses. Villas and country houses were run up for him regardless of expense. In fact Gaius seemed interested only in doing the apparently impossible, which led him to construct moles in deep, rough water far out to sea, drive tunnels through exceptionally hard rocks, raise flat ground to the height of mountains, and reduce mountains to the level of plains – and all at immense speed, because he punished delay with death. But why give details? Suffice it to record that in less than a year he squandered Tiberius' entire fortune of 2,700 million sesterces, and an enormous amount of other treasure besides.

When bankrupt and in need of funds, Gaius concentrated on wickedly ingenious methods of raising funds by false accusations, auctions, and taxes. He ruled that no man could inherit the Roman citizenship acquired by any ancestor more remote than his father, and when confronted with certificates of citizenship issued by Divus Julius or Divus Augustus he rejected them as obsolete. He also disallowed all property returns to which, for whatever reason, later additions had been appended. If a *primipilaris* had bequeathed nothing either to Tiberius or himself since the beginning of the former's reign, he would rescind the will on the ground of ingratitude, and he likewise voided the wills of all other persons who were said to have intended making him their heir when they died but had not done so. This caused widespread alarm, so that people would openly declare that he was one of their heirs, with strangers listing him among their friends and parents among their children; but if they continued to live after the declaration he considered himself tricked, and sent several of them presents of poisoned sweets. Gaius conducted these cases in person, first announcing the sum he meant to raise, and not stopping until he had raised it. The slightest delay nettled him; he once passed a single sentence on a batch of more than forty men charged with various offences, and then boasted to Caesonia, when she woke from her nap, that he had done very good business since she dozed off.

He would auction whatever properties were left over from a theatrical show, driving up the bidding to such heights that many of those present, forced to buy at fantastic prices, found themselves ruined and committed suicide by opening their veins. A famous occasion was when Aponius Saturninus fell asleep on a bench, and Gaius warned the auctioneer to keep an eye on the senator of praetorian rank who kept nodding his head. Before the bidding ended Aponius had unwittingly bought thirteen gladiators for a total of 9 million sesterces.

While in Gaul, Gaius did so well by selling the furniture, jewellery, slaves and even the freedmen of his condemned sisters at a ridiculous overvaluation that he decided to do the same with the furnishings of the old palace. So he sent to Rome, where his agents commandeered public conveyances and even draught animals from the bakeries to fetch the stuff north; this led to a bread shortage in Rome and to the loss of many lawsuits, because litigants who lived at a distance were unable to appear in court and meet their bail. He then used all kinds of tricks for disposing of the furniture: scolding the bidders for their avarice or for their shamelessness in being richer than he was, and pretending grief at this surrender of family property to commoners. Discovering that one wealthy provincial had paid his stewards 200,000 sesterces to be smuggled into a banquet, Caligula was delighted that the privilege of dining with him should be valued so highly, and when next day the same man turned up at the auction he made him pay 200,000 sesterces for some trifling object – but also sent him a personal invitation to dinner.

The publicans were ordered to raise new and unprecedented taxes, and found this so profitable that he detailed the tribunes and centurions of the praetorian guards to collect the money instead. No goods or services now avoided duty of some kind. He imposed a fixed tax on all foodstuffs sold in any quarter of the city, and a charge of 2½ per cent on the money involved in every lawsuit and legal transaction whatsoever, and also devised special penalties for anyone who settled out of court or abandoned a case. Porters had to hand over an eighth part of their day's earnings, and prostitutes their standard fee for a single act of intimacy, even if they had quitted their profession and were respectably married; pimps and ex-pimps also became liable to this public tax.

These new regulations having been announced by word of mouth only, many people failed to observe them through ignorance. At last he acceded to the urgent popular demand by posting the regulations up, but in an awkwardly cramped spot and written so small that no one could take a copy. He never missed a chance of making profits: setting aside a suite of rooms on the Palatine, he decorated them worthily, opened a brothel, stocked it with married women and freeborn boys, and then sent his pages around the squares and public places, inviting men of all ages to come and enjoy themselves. Those who appeared were lent money at interest, and clerks wrote down their names under the heading 'Contributors to Caesar's Revenue'.

Even when Gaius played at dice he would always

cheat and lie. Once he interrupted a game by giving up his seat to the man behind him and going out into the courtyard. A couple of rich *equites* passed; he immediately had them arrested and confiscated their property, and then resumed the game in high spirits, boasting that his luck had never been better.

His daughter's birth gave him an excuse for further complaints of poverty. 'In addition to the burden of sovereignty,' he said, 'I must now shoulder that of fatherhood' – and he promptly took up a collection for her education and dowry. He also announced that good-luck gifts would be welcomed on the Kalends of January, and then sat in the palace porch, grabbing the handfuls and capfuls of coins which a mixed crowd of all classes pressed on him. At last he developed a passion for the feel of money and, spilling heaps of gold pieces on an open space, would walk over them barefoot or else lie down and wallow.

Gaius had only a single taste of warfare, and even that was unpremeditated. At Mevania, where he went to visit the river Clitumnus and its sacred grove, he was reminded that he needed Batavian recruits for his bodyguard, and this suggested the idea of a

German expedition. He wasted no time in summoning legions and auxiliaries from all directions, levied troops with the utmost strictness, and collected military supplies on an unprecedented scale. Then he marched off with such rapidity that the praetorian cohorts could not keep up with him except by breaking tradition and tying their standards on the pack mules. Yet later he became so lazy and self-indulgent that he travelled in a litter borne by eight bearers, and whenever he approached a town he made the inhabitants sweep the roads and lay the dust with sprinklers.

After reaching the camp, Gaius showed how keen and severe a commander he intended to be by ignominiously dismissing any legate who was late in bringing along the auxiliaries he required. Then, when he reviewed the legions, he discharged several veteran *primipilares* on grounds of age and incapacity, though some had only a few more days of their service to run, and, calling the remainder a pack of greedy fellows, scaled down their retirement bonus to 6,000 sesterces each.

All that he accomplished in this expedition was to receive the surrender of Adminius, son of the British king Cynobellinus, who had been banished by his father and come over to the Romans with a few followers. Gaius nevertheless wrote an extravagant dispatch which might have persuaded any reader that the whole island had surrendered to him, and ordered the couriers to drive their chariots all the way to the Forum and the Senate House and to deliver his letter to the consuls in the Temple of Mars in the presence of the entire Senate.

Since the chance of military action appeared very remote, he soon ordered a few German prisoners to be taken across the Rhine and hidden among the trees. After lunch, scouts hurried in to tell him excitedly that the enemy were upon him. He at once galloped out at the head of his staff and part of the praetorian cavalry to halt in the nearest thicket, where they chopped branches from the trees and dressed them like trophies; then, riding back by torchlight, he taunted as cowards all who had failed to follow him and awarded his fellow heroes a novel fashion in crowns – he called it 'The Ranger's Crown' – ornamented with sun, moon and stars. On another day he took some German hostages from a school where they were being taught the rudiments of Latin and secretly ordered them on ahead of him. Later he left his dinner in a hurry and took his cavalry in pursuit of them, as though they had been fugitives. He was no less melodramatic about this foray: when he returned to the hall after catching the hostages and bringing them back in irons, and his officers reported that the army was marshalled, he made them recline at table, still in their corselets, and quoted Virgil's famous advice: 'Be steadfast, comrades, and preserve yourselves for happier occasions.' He also severely reprimanded the absent Senate and People for enjoying banquets and festivities and for hanging about the theatres or their luxurious country houses while their Caesar was exposed to all the hazards of war.

In the end, he drew up his army in battle array on the shore of the Ocean and moved the siege engines into position as though he intended to bring the campaign to a close. No one had the least notion what was in his mind, when suddenly he gave the order 'Gather seashells!' He referred to the shells as 'plunder from the sea, due to the Capitol and to the Palatine', and made the troops fill their helmets and the folds of their clothes with them; he commemorated this victory by the erection of a tall lighthouse, not unlike the one at Pharos, in which fires were to be kept going all night as a guide to ships. Then he promised every soldier a bounty of 100 denarii, and told them, 'Go rich, go happy!', as though he had surpassed every standard of generosity.

He now concentrated his attention on the imminent triumph. To supplement the few prisoners taken in frontier skirmishes and the deserters who had come over from the barbarians, he picked the tallest Gauls of the province – 'those worthy of a triumph', as he himself said – and some of their leaders as well, for his supposed train of captives. These had not only to grow their hair and dye it red, but also to learn Germanic speech and adopt Germanic names. The triremes used in the Ocean were carted to Rome, overland for most of the way. He sent a letter ahead instructing his agents to prepare a triumph more lavish than any hitherto known, but at the least possible expense, and added that everyone's property was at their disposal.

Before leaving Gaul he planned, in a sudden access of cruelty, to massacre the legionaries who, at news of Augustus' death, had mutinously besieged both his father Germanicus, their commander, and himself, still only a baby. His friends barely restrained him from carrying out this plan, and could not at all dissuade him from deciding on a decimation. And so he summoned the troops to assemble without any arms, even their swords, and surrounded them with armed horsemen. But when he noticed that a number of legionaries, scenting trouble, were slipping away to fetch their weapons, he hurriedly absconded and headed straight for Rome. There, to distract attention from his inglorious exploits, he vengefully threatened the Senate, who he said had cheated him of a well-earned triumph – though in point of fact he had expressly stated a few days before that they must do nothing to honour him, on pain of death.

So, when the distinguished senatorial delegates met him with an official plea for his immediate return, he shouted, 'I am coming, never fear, and this' – tapping the hilt of his sword – 'is coming too!' He proclaimed that he was returning only to those who would really welcome him, namely the *equites* and the people; so far as the senators were concerned, he would never again consider himself their fellow citizen or their *princeps*, and he even forbade any more of them to meet him. Having cancelled or at least postponed his triumph, he entered the city on his birthday and received an ovation. Within four months he was dead.

Gaius had dared commit fearful crimes and contemplated even worse ones, such as murdering the most distinguished of the senators and *equites* and then moving the seat of government first to Antium and afterwards to Alexandria. If at this point my readers become incredulous, let me record that two notebooks were found among his private papers entitled *Dagger* and *Sword*, each of them containing the names and particulars of men whom he had planned to kill. A huge chest filled with poisons also came to light. It is said that when Claudius later threw this into the sea, quantities of dead fish, cast up by the tide, littered the neighbouring beaches.

Gaius was tall, with a pallid complexion; he had a large body, but a thin neck and spindly legs; his eyes were sunken and his temples hollow, although his forehead was broad and forbidding. In contrast to his noticeably hairy body, the hair on his head was thin, and his crown was completely bald. Because of his baldness and hairiness, he announced that it was a capital offence for anyone either to look down on him as he passed or to mention goats in any context. He worked hard to make his naturally uncouth face even more repulsive by practising fearful grimaces in front of a mirror.

As to his health, Gaius was sick both physically and mentally. As a boy, he suffered from epilepsy, and, although his resistance to the disease gradually strengthened, there were times in his youth when he could hardly walk, stand, think or hold up his head, owing to sudden fits. He was well aware that he had mental trouble, and sometimes proposed taking a leave of absence from Rome to clear his brain; Caesonia is reputed to have given him an aphrodisiac which drove him mad. Insomnia was his worst torment. Three hours a night of fitful sleep were all that he ever got, and even then terrifying visions would haunt him – once, for instance, he dreamed that he had a conversation with the sea. He tired of lying awake the greater part of the night, and would alternately sit up in bed and wander through the long corridors, invoking the day which seemed as if it would never break.

I am convinced that this mental illness accounted for his two contradictory vices – overconfidence and extreme timorousness. Here was a man who despised the gods, yet shut his eyes and buried his head beneath the bedclothes at the most distant sound of thunder; and if the storm came closer he would jump out of bed and crawl underneath. In his travels through Sicily he poked fun at the miraculous stories associated with the various locales, yet on reaching Messana he suddenly fled in the middle of the night, terrified by the smoke and noise which came from the crater of Aetna. Despite his fearful threats against the barbarians, he showed so little courage after he had crossed the Rhine and gone riding in a chariot through a defile that when someone happened to remark 'What a panic there would be if the enemy unexpectedly appeared!' he leaped on a horse and galloped back to the bridges. These were crowded with army transport, but he had himself passed from hand to hand over the men's heads in his haste to regain the further bank. Even when safely home he was alarmed by reported revolts in Germany and decided to escape by sea. He fitted out a large fleet for this purpose, finding comfort only in the thought that, should the enemy be victorious and occupy the Alpine passes, as the Cimbri had done, or Rome, as

Caligula

the Senones had done, he would at least be able to hold his overseas provinces. This was probably what later gave his assassins the idea of quieting his vengeful German bodyguard with the story that rumours of a defeat had scared him into sudden suicide.

Gaius paid no attention to traditional or current fashions in his dress, but ignored masculine and even human conventions. Often he made public appearances in a cloak covered with embroidery and encrusted with precious stones, a long-sleeved tunic, and bracelets, and at other times in silk or even a woman's gown; and he came shod sometimes with slippers, sometimes with buskins, sometimes with military boots, sometimes with women's shoes. Occasionally he affected a golden beard and carried Jupiter's thunderbolt, Neptune's trident or Mercury's caduceus. He even dressed up as Venus, and long before his expedition he wore the uniform of a triumphant general, often embellished with the breastplate which he had stolen from the tomb of Alexander the Great.

Though no man of letters, Gaius took pains to study oratory, and showed remarkable eloquence and quickness of mind, especially when prosecuting.

Anger incited him to a flood of verbiage; he moved about excitedly while speaking, and his voice carried a great distance. At the start of every speech he would threaten to 'draw the sword which he had forged in his midnight study'; yet he so despised more elegant and melodious styles that he discounted Seneca, then at the height of his fame, as a 'mere textbook orator' and 'sand without lime'. He often published confutations of speakers who had successfully pleaded a case, or composed speeches for both the prosecution and the defence of important men who were on trial by the Senate – the verdict depending entirely on the caprice of his pen – and would invite the *equites* by proclamation to attend and listen.

Gaius practised many other arts – most enthusiastically too. He made appearances as a Thracian gladiator and a charioteer, as a singer and a dancer; he would fight with real weapons and drive chariots in the circuses that he had built in many places. Indeed, he was so proud of his singing and dancing that he could not resist the temptation of supporting the tragic actors at public performances, and would repeat their gestures by way of praise or criticism. On the very day of his death he seems to have ordered an all-night festival so that he could take advantage of the free-and-easy atmosphere to make his stage debut. He often danced even at night, and once, at the close of the second watch, summoned three senators of consular rank to the palace; arriving half-dead with fear, they were conducted to a stage upon which, amid a tremendous racket of flutes and castanets, Gaius suddenly burst, dressed in a shawl and an ankle-length tunic; he performed a song and dance, and disappeared as suddenly as he had entered. Yet with all these gifts he could not swim a stroke!

On those whom he loved he bestowed an almost insane passion. He would shower kisses on Mnester the pantomime dancer even in the theatre, and if anyone made the slightest noise during his performances Gaius had the offender dragged from his seat and beat him with his own hands. To an *eques* who created some disturbance while Mnester was on the stage, Gaius sent instructions by a centurion to sail from Ostia and convey a sealed message to King Ptolemy in Mauretania. The message read, 'Do nothing at all, either good or bad, to the bearer.'

He chose Thracian gladiators to officer his German bodyguard. Disliking the men-at-arms, he reduced their defensive armour; and when a gladiator of this sort, called Columbus, won a fight but was lightly wounded, Gaius treated him with a virulent poison which he afterwards called 'Columbinum' – at any rate that was how he described it in his catalogue of poisons. Gaius supported the Green faction with such ardour that he would often dine and spend the night in their stables, and on one occasion he gave the driver Eutychus presents worth 2 million sesterces. To prevent Incitatus, his favourite horse, from growing restive he always picketed the neighbourhood with troops on the day before the races, ordering them to enforce absolute silence. Incitatus owned a marble stable, an ivory stall, purple blankets and a jewelled collar, as well as a house, furniture and slaves – to provide suitable entertainment for guests whom Gaius invited in its name. It is said that he even planned to award Incitatus a consulship.

Such frantic and reckless behaviour roused murderous thoughts in certain minds. One or two plots for his assassination were discovered; others were still maturing when two tribunes of the praetorian guard put their heads together and succeeded in killing him, thanks to the cooperation of his most powerful freedmen and the praetorian prefects. Both these tribunes had been accused of being implicated in a previous plot and, although innocent, realized that Gaius hated and feared them. Once, in fact, he had subjected them to public shame and suspicion, taking them aside and announcing, as he waved a sword, that he would gladly kill himself if they thought him deserving of death. After this he accused them again and again, each to the other, and tried to make bad blood between them. At last they decided to kill him about noon at the conclusion of the Palatine Games, the principal part in this drama of blood being claimed by Cassius Chaerea. Gaius had persistently teased Cassius, who was no longer young, for his supposed effeminacy. Whenever he demanded the watchword, Gaius used to give him 'Priapus' or 'Venus'; and if he came to acknowledge a favour he always stuck out his middle finger for him to kiss, and wiggled it obscenely.

Many omens of Gaius' approaching death were reported. While the statue of Jupiter at Olympia was being dismantled before removal to Rome at his command, it burst into such a roar of laughter that the scaffolding collapsed and the workmen took to their heels, and a man named Cassius appeared immediately afterwards saying that Jupiter had ordered him in a dream to sacrifice a bull. The Capitol at Capua was struck by lightning on the Ides of March, which some interpreted as portending another death of the same sort that had previously occurred on that day. At Rome, the Palatine steward's lodge was likewise struck, and this seemed to mean that the master of the house stood in danger of attack by his own guards. On asking the astrologer Sulla for his horoscope, Gaius learned that he must expect to die very soon. The oracle of the goddesses of Fortune at Antium likewise warned him, 'Beware of Cassius!'; whereupon, forgetting Chaerea's nomen, he ordered the murder of Cassius Longinus, the consular governor of Asia. On the night before his assassination he dreamed that he was standing beside Jupiter's heavenly throne, when the god kicked him with the great toe of his right foot and sent him tumbling down to earth.

1. BOCCACCIO · *Mrs Rosie and the Priest*
2. GERARD MANLEY HOPKINS · *As kingfishers catch fire*
3. *The Saga of Gunnlaug Serpent-tongue*
4. THOMAS DE QUINCEY · *On Murder Considered as One of the Fine Arts*
5. FRIEDRICH NIETZSCHE · *Aphorisms on Love and Hate*
6. JOHN RUSKIN · *Traffic*
7. PU SONGLING · *Wailing Ghosts*
8. JONATHAN SWIFT · *A Modest Proposal*
9. *Three Tang Dynasty Poets*
10. WALT WHITMAN · *On the Beach at Night Alone*
11. KENKŌ · *A Cup of Sake Beneath the Cherry Trees*
12. BALTASAR GRACIÁN · *How to Use Your Enemies*
13. JOHN KEATS · *The Eve of St Agnes*
14. THOMAS HARDY · *Woman much missed*
15. GUY DE MAUPASSANT · *Femme Fatale*
16. MARCO POLO · *Travels in the Land of Serpents and Pearls*
17. SUETONIUS · *Caligula*
18. APOLLONIUS OF RHODES · *Jason and Medea*
19. ROBERT LOUIS STEVENSON · *Olalla*
20. KARL MARX AND FRIEDRICH ENGELS · *The Communist Manifesto*
21. PETRONIUS · *Trimalchio's Feast*
22. JOHANN PETER HEBEL · *How a Ghastly Story Was Brought to Light by a Common or Garden Butcher's Dog*
23. HANS CHRISTIAN ANDERSEN · *The Tinder Box*
24. RUDYARD KIPLING · *The Gate of the Hundred Sorrows*
25. DANTE · *Circles of Hell*
26. HENRY MAYHEW · *Of Street Piemen*
27. HAFEZ · *The nightingales are drunk*
28. GEOFFREY CHAUCER · *The Wife of Bath*
29. MICHEL DE MONTAIGNE · *How We Weep and Laugh at the Same Thing*
30. THOMAS NASHE · *The Terrors of the Night*
31. EDGAR ALLAN POE · *The Tell-Tale Heart*
32. MARY KINGSLEY · *A Hippo Banquet*
33. JANE AUSTEN · *The Beautifull Cassandra*
34. ANTON CHEKHOV · *Gooseberries*
35. SAMUEL TAYLOR COLERIDGE · *Well, they are gone, and here must I remain*
36. JOHANN WOLFGANG VON GOETHE · *Sketchy, Doubtful, Incomplete Jottings*
37. CHARLES DICKENS · *The Great Winglebury Duel*
38. HERMAN MELVILLE · *The Maldive Shark*
39. ELIZABETH GASKELL · *The Old Nurse's Story*
40. NIKOLAY LESKOV · *The Steel Flea*

41. HONORÉ DE BALZAC · *The Atheist's Mass*
42. CHARLOTTE PERKINS GILMAN · *The Yellow Wall-Paper*
43. C.P. CAVAFY · *Remember, Body...*
44. FYODOR DOSTOEVSKY · *The Meek One*
45. GUSTAVE FLAUBERT · *A Simple Heart*
46. NIKOLAI GOGOL · *The Nose*
47. SAMUEL PEPYS · *The Great Fire of London*
48. EDITH WHARTON · *The Reckoning*
49. HENRY JAMES · *The Figure in the Carpet*
50. WILFRED OWEN · *Anthem For Doomed Youth*
51. WOLFGANG AMADEUS MOZART · *My Dearest Father*
52. PLATO · *Socrates' Defence*
53. CHRISTINA ROSSETTI · *Goblin Market*
54. *Sindbad the Sailor*
55. SOPHOCLES · *Antigone*
56. RYŪNOSUKE AKUTAGAWA · *The Life of a Stupid Man*
57. LEO TOLSTOY · *How Much Land Does A Man Need?*
58. GIORGIO VASARI · *Leonardo da Vinci*
59. OSCAR WILDE · *Lord Arthur Savile's Crime*
60. SHEN FU · *The Old Man of the Moon*
61. AESOP · *The Dolphins, the Whales and the Gudgeon*
62. MATSUO BASHŌ · *Lips too Chilled*
63. EMILY BRONTË · *The Night is Darkening Round Me*
64. JOSEPH CONRAD · *To-morrow*
65. RICHARD HAKLUYT · *The Voyage of Sir Francis Drake Around the Whole Globe*
66. KATE CHOPIN · *A Pair of Silk Stockings*
67. CHARLES DARWIN · *It was snowing butterflies*
68. BROTHERS GRIMM · *The Robber Bridegroom*
69. CATULLUS · *I Hate and I Love*
70. HOMER · *Circe and the Cyclops*
71. D. H. LAWRENCE · *Il Duro*
72. KATHERINE MANSFIELD · *Miss Brill*
73. OVID · *The Fall of Icarus*
74. SAPPHO · *Come Close*
75. IVAN TURGENEV · *Kasyan from the Beautiful Lands*
76. VIRGIL · *O Cruel Alexis*
77. H. G. WELLS · *A Slip under the Microscope*
78. HERODOTUS · *The Madness of Cambyses*
79. *Speaking of Siva*
80. *The Dhammapada*

'The Argonauts were terrified at the sight. But Jason planting his feet apart stood to receive them, as a reef in the sea confronts the tossing billows in a gale.'

APOLLONIUS OF RHODES
Lived in the 3rd century BCE
Dates and location of birth and death unknown

Taken from E. V. Rieu's translation of *The Voyage of Argo*,
first published in 1959.

APOLLONIUS OF RHODES IN PENGUIN CLASSICS
The Voyage of Argo

APOLLONIUS OF RHODES

Jason and Medea

Translated by
E. V. Rieu

PENGUIN BOOKS

PENGUIN CLASSICS

UK | USA | Canada | Ireland | Australia
India | New Zealand | South Africa

Penguin Books is part of the Penguin Random House group of companies whose addresses can be found at global.penguinrandomhouse.com.

This selection published in Penguin Classics 2015

009

Translation copyright © E. V. Rieu, 1959, 1971

Set in 9.5/13 pt Baskerville 10 Pro
Typeset by Jouve (UK), Milton Keynes

A CIP catalogue record for this book is available from the British Library

ISBN: 978–0–141–39794–8

Printed and bound in Great Britain by Clays Ltd, Elcograf S.p.A.

www.greenpenguin.co.uk

Penguin Random House is committed to a sustainable future for our business, our readers and our planet. This book is made from Forest Stewardship Council® certified paper.

Come, Erato, come lovely Muse, stand by me and take up the tale. How did Medea's passion help Jason to bring back the fleece to Iolcus? You that share Aphrodite's powers must surely know; you that fill virgin hearts with love's inquietude and bear a name that speaks of love's delights.

We left the young lords lying there concealed among the rushes. But ambushed though they were, Here and Athene saw them and at once withdrew from Zeus and the rest of the immortal gods into a private room to talk the matter over.

Here began by sounding Athene. 'Daughter of Zeus,' she said, 'let me hear you first. What are we to do? Will you think of some ruse that might enable them to carry off Aeëtes' golden fleece to Hellas? Or should they speak him fair in the hope of winning his consent? I know the man is thoroughly intractable. But all the same, no method of approach should be neglected.'

'Here,' said Athene quickly, 'you have put to me the very questions I have been turning over in my mind. But

Apollonius of Rhodes

I must admit that, though I have racked my brains, I have failed so far to think of any scheme that might commend itself to the noble lords.'

For a while the two goddesses sat staring at the floor, each lost in her own perplexities. Here was the first to break the silence; an idea had struck her. 'Listen,' she said. 'We must have a word with Aphrodite. Let us go together and ask her to persuade her boy, if that is possible, to loose an arrow at Aeëtes' daughter, Medea of the many spells, and make her fall in love with Jason. I am sure that with her help he will succeed in bearing off the fleece to Hellas.'

This solution of their problem pleased Athene, who smilingly replied: 'Sprung as I am from Zeus, I have never felt the arrows of the Boy, and of love-charms I know nothing. However, if you yourself are satisfied with the idea, I will certainly go with you. But when we meet her you must be the one to speak.'

The two goddesses rose at once and made their way to the palace of Aphrodite, which her lame consort Hephaestus had built for her when he took her as his bride from the hands of Zeus. They entered the courtyard and paused below the veranda of the room where the goddess slept with her lord and master. Hephaestus himself had gone early to his forge and anvils in a vast cavern on a floating island, where he used to turn out all kinds of curious metalwork with the aid of fire and bellows; and Cypris, left at home alone, was sitting on an inlaid chair which faced the door. She had let her hair fall down on her white shoulders and was combing it with a golden comb before plaiting the long tresses. But when she saw the goddesses outside she stopped and called them in; and she rose to meet them and settled them in easy chairs before resuming her own seat. Then she bound up the uncombed locks with both hands, gave her visitors a smile, and spoke with mock humility:

'Ladies, you honour me! What brings you here after so long? We have seen little of you in the past. To what then do I owe a visit from the greatest goddesses of all?'

'This levity of yours,' said Here, 'is ill-timed. We two are facing a disaster. At this very moment the lord Jason and his friends are riding at anchor in the River Phasis. They have come to fetch the fleece, and since the time for action is at hand, we are gravely concerned for all of them, particularly Aeson's son. For him, I am prepared to fight with all my might and main, and I will save him, even if he sails to Hell to free Ixion from his brazen chains. For I will not have King Pelias boasting that he has escaped his evil doom, insolent Pelias, who left me out when he made offerings to the gods. Besides which I have been very fond of Jason ever since the time when I was putting human charity on trial and as he came home from the chase he met me at the mouth of the Anaurus. The river was in spate, for all the mountains and their high spurs were under snow and cataracts were roaring down their sides. I was disguised as an old woman and he took pity on me, lifted me up, and carried me across the flood on his shoulders. For that, I will never cease to honour him. But Pelias will not be brought to book for his outrageous conduct unless you yourself make it possible for Jason to return.'

Here had finished; but for a time words failed the Lady of Cyprus. The sight of Here begging her for favours struck her with awe; and her answer when it came was gracious. 'Queen of goddesses,' she said, 'regard me as the meanest creature in the world if I fail you in your need. Whatever I can say or do, whatever strength these feeble hands possess, is at your service. Moreover I expect no recompense.'

Here, choosing her words with care, replied: 'We are not asking you to use your hands: force is not needed. All we require of you is quietly to tell your boy to use his wizardry and make Aeëtes' daughter fall in love with Jason. With Medea on his side he should find it easy to carry off the golden fleece and make his way back to Iolcus. She is something of a witch herself.'

'But ladies,' said Cypris, speaking now to both of them, 'he is far more likely to obey you than me. There is no reverence in him, but faced by you he might display some spark of decent feeling. He certainly pays no attention to me: he defies me and always does the opposite of what I say. In fact I am so worn out by his naughtiness that I have half a mind to break his bow and wicked arrows in his very sight, remembering how he threatened me with them in one of his moods. He said, "If you don't keep your hands off me while I can still control my temper, you can blame yourself for the consequences."'

Here and Athene smiled at this and exchanged glances. But Aphrodite was hurt. She said: 'Other people find my troubles amusing. I really should not speak of them to all and sundry; it is enough for me to know them. However, as you have both set your hearts on it, I will try and coax my boy. He will not refuse.'

Here took Aphrodite's slender hand in hers and with a sweet smile replied: 'Very well, Cytherea. Play your part, just as you say; but quickly, please. And do not scold or argue with your child when he annoys you. He will improve by and by.'

With that she rose to go. Athene followed her, and the pair left for home. Cypris too set out, and after searching up and down Olympus for her boy, found him far away in the fruit-laden orchard of Zeus. With him was Ganymede, whose beauty had so captivated Zeus that he took him up to heaven to live with the immortals. The two lads, who had much in common, were playing with golden knuckle-bones. Eros, the greedy boy, was standing there with a whole handful of them clutched to his breast and a happy flush mantling his cheeks. Near by sat Ganymede, hunched up, silent and disconsolate, with only two left. He threw these for what they were worth in quick succession and was furious when Eros laughed. Of course he lost them both immediately – they joined the rest. So he went off in despair with empty hands and did not notice the goddess's approach.

Aphrodite came up to her boy, took his chin in her hand, and said: 'Why this triumphant smile, you rascal? I do believe you won the game unfairly by cheating a beginner. But listen now. Will you be good and do me a favour I am going to ask of you? Then I will give you one of Zeus's lovely toys, the one that his fond nurse Adresteia made for him in the Idaean cave when he was still a child and liked to play. It is a perfect ball; Hephaestus himself could not make you a better toy. It is made of golden hoops laced together all the way round with double stitching; but the seams are hidden by a winding, dark blue band. When you throw it up, it will leave a fiery trail behind it like a meteor in the sky. That is what I'll give you, if you let fly an arrow at Aeëtes' girl and make her fall in love with Jason. But you must act at once, or I may not be so generous.'

When he heard this, Eros was delighted. He threw down all his toys, flung his arms round his mother and hung on to her skirt with both hands, imploring her to let him have the ball at once. But she gently refused, and drawing him towards her, held him close and kissed his cheeks. Then with a smile she said, 'By your own dear head and mine, I swear I will not disappoint you. You shall have the gift when you have shot an arrow into Medea's heart.'

Eros gathered up his knuckle-bones, counted them all

carefully, and put them in the fold of his mother's shining robe. Fetching his quiver from where it leant against a tree, he slung it on his shoulder with a golden strap, picked up his crooked bow, and made his way through the luxuriant orchard of Zeus's palace. Then he passed through the celestial gates of Olympus, where a pathway for the gods leads down, and twin poles, earth's highest points, soar up in lofty pinnacles that catch the first rays of the risen sun. And as he swept on through the boundless air he saw an ever-changing scene beneath him, here the life-supporting land with its peopled cities and its sacred rivers, here mountain peaks, and here the all-encircling sea.

Meanwhile the Argonauts were sitting in conference on the benches of their ship where it lay hidden in the marshes of the river. Each man had taken his own seat, and Jason, who was speaking, was faced by row upon row of quiet listeners. 'My friends,' he said, 'I am going to tell you what action I myself should like to take, though its success depends on you. Sharing the danger as we do, we share the right of speech; and I warn the man who keeps his mouth shut when he ought to speak his mind that he will be the one to wreck our enterprise.

'I ask you all to stay quietly on board with your arms ready, while I go up to Aeëtes' palace with the sons of Phrixus and two other men. When I see him I intend to parley with him first and find out whether he means to treat us as friends and let us have the golden fleece, or dismiss us with contempt, relying on his own power. Warned thus, by the man himself, of any evil thoughts he may be entertaining, we will decide whether to face him in the field or find some way of getting what we want without recourse to arms. We ought not to use force to rob him of his own without so much as seeing what a few words may do; it would be much better to talk to him first and try to win him over. Speech, by smoothing the way, often succeeds where forceful measures might have failed. Remember too that Aeëtes welcomed the admirable Phrixus when he fled from a stepmother's treachery and a father who had planned to sacrifice him. Every man on earth, even the greatest rogue, fears Zeus the god of hospitality and keeps his laws.'

With one accord the young men approved the lord Jason's plan, and no one having risen to suggest another, he asked the sons of Phrixus, with Telamon and Augeias, to accompany him and himself took the Wand of Hermes in his hand. Leaving the ship they came to dry land beyond the reeds and water and passed on to the high ground of the plain which bears the name of Circe. Here osiers and willows stand in rows, with corpses dangling on ropes from their highest branches. To this day the Colchians would think it sacrilege to burn the bodies of their men. They never bury them or raise a mound above them, but wrap them in untanned oxhide and hang them up on trees at a distance from the town. Thus, since it is their custom to bury women, earth and air play equal parts in the disposal of their dead.

While Jason and his friends were on their way, Here had a kindly thought for them. She covered the whole town with mist so that they might reach Aeëtes' house unseen by any of the numerous Colchians. But as soon as they had come in from the country and reached the palace she dispersed the mist. At the entrance they paused for a moment to marvel at the king's courtyard with its wide gates, the rows of soaring columns round the palace walls, and high over all the marble cornice resting on triglyphs of bronze. They crossed the threshold of the court unchallenged. Near by, cultivated vines covered with greenery rose high in the air and underneath them four perennial springs gushed up. These were Hephaestus' work. One flowed with milk, and one with wine, the third with fragrant oil, while the fourth was a fountain of water which grew warm when the Pleiades set, but changed at their rising and bubbled up from the hollow rock as cold as ice. Such were the marvels that Hephaestus the great Engineer had contrived for the palace of Cytaean Aeëtes. He had also made him bulls with feet of bronze and bronze mouths from which the breath came out in flame, blazing and terrible. And he had forged a plough of indurated steel, all in one piece, as a thank-offering to Helios, who had taken him up in his chariot when he sank exhausted on the battlefield of Phlegra.

There was also an inner court, with many well-made folding doors leading to various rooms, and decorated galleries to right and left. Higher buildings stood at angles to this court on either side. In one of them, the highest, King Aeëtes lived with his queen; in another, his son Apsyrtus, whom a Caucasian nymph named Asterodeia had borne to him before he married Eidyia, the youngest daughter of Tethys and Ocean. 'Phaëthon' was the nickname that the young Colchians gave Apsyrtus because he outshone them all.

The other buildings housed the maidservants and Chalciope and Medea, the two daughters of Aeëtes. At the moment, Medea was going from room to room to find her sister. The goddess Here had kept her in the house, though as a rule she did not spend her time at home, but was busy all day in the temple of Hecate, of whom she was priestess. When she saw the men she gave a cry; Chalciope heard it, and her maids dropped their yarn and spindles on the floor and all ran out of doors.

When Chalciope saw her sons among the strangers, she lifted up her hands for joy. They greeted her in the same fashion and then in their happiness embraced her. But she had her moan to make. 'So after all,' she said, 'you were not allowed to roam so very far from your neglected mother: Fate turned you back. But how I have suffered! This mad desire of yours for Hellas! This blind obedience to your dying father's wishes! What misery, what heartache, they brought me! Why should you go to the city of

Jason and Medea

Orchomenus, whoever he may be, abandoning your widowed mother for the sake of your grandfather's estate?'

Last of all, Aeëtes with his queen, Eidyia, who had heard Chalciope speaking, came out of the house. And at once the whole courtyard was astir. A number of his men busied themselves over the carcass of a large bull; others chopped firewood; others heated water for the baths. Not one of them took a rest: they were working for the king.

Meanwhile Eros, passing through the clear air, had arrived unseen and bent on mischief, like a gadfly setting out to plague the grazing heifers, the fly that cowherds call the breese. In the porch, under the lintel of the door, he quickly strung his bow and from his quiver took a new arrow, fraught with pain. Still unobserved, he ran across the threshold glancing around him sharply. Then he crouched low at Jason's feet, fitted the notch to the middle of the string, and drawing the bow as far as his hands would stretch, shot at Medea. And her heart stood still.

With a happy laugh Eros sped out of the high-roofed hall on his way back, leaving his shaft deep in the girl's breast, hot as fire. Time and again she darted a bright glance at Jason. All else was forgotten. Her heart, brimful of this new agony, throbbed within her and overflowed with the sweetness of the pain.

A working woman, rising before dawn to spin and needing light in her cottage room, piles brushwood on a smouldering log, and the whole heap kindled by the little brand goes up in a mighty blaze. Such was the fire of Love, stealthy but all-consuming, that swept through Medea's heart. In the turmoil of her soul, her soft cheeks turned from rose to white and white to rose.

By now the servants had prepared a banquet for the newcomers, who gladly sat down to it after refreshing themselves in warm baths. When they had enjoyed the food and drink, Aeëtes put some questions to his grandsons:

'Sons of my daughter and of Phrixus, the most deserving guest I have ever entertained, how is it that you are back in Aea? Did some misadventure cut your journey short? You refused to listen when I told you what a long way you had to go. But I knew; for I myself was whirled along it in the chariot of my father Helios, when he took my sister Circe to the Western Land and we reached the coast of Tyrrhenia, where she still lives, far, far indeed from Colchis. But enough of that. Tell me plainly what befell you, who your companions are, and where you disembarked.'

To answer these questions, Argus stepped out in front of his brothers, being the eldest of the four. His heart misgave him for Jason and his mission; but he did his best to conciliate the king. 'My lord,' he said, 'that ship of ours soon fell to pieces in a storm. We hung on to one of her planks and were cast ashore on the Island of Ares in the pitch-dark night. But Providence looked after us: there was not a sign of the War-god's birds, who used to

Jason and Medea

haunt the desert isle. They were driven off by these men, who had landed on the previous day and been detained there by the will of Zeus in pity for ourselves – or was it only chance? In any case, they gave us plenty of food and clothing directly they heard the illustrious name of Phrixus, and your own, my lord, since it was your city they were bound for. As to their purpose, I will be frank with you. A certain king, wishing to banish and dispossess this man because he is the most powerful of the Aeolids, has sent him here on a desperate venture, maintaining that the House of Aeolus will not escape the inexorable wrath of Zeus, the heavy burden of their guilt, and vengeance for the sufferings of Phrixus, till the fleece returns to Hellas. The ship that brought him was built by Pallas Athene on altogether different lines from the Colchian craft, the rottenest of which, as luck would have it, fell to us. For *she* was smashed to pieces by the wind and waves, whereas the bolts of *Argo* hold her together in any gale that blows, and she runs as sweetly when the crew are tugging at the oars as she does before the wind. This ship he manned with the pick of all Achaea, and in her he has come to your city, touching at many ports and crossing formidable seas, in the hope that you will let him have the fleece. But it must be as you wish. He has not come here to force your hand. On the contrary, he is willing to repay you amply for the gift by reducing for you your bitter enemies, the Sauromatae, of whom I told him. But now you may wish to know the names and lineage of your visitors. Let me tell you. Here is the man to whom the others rallied from all parts of Hellas, Jason son of Aeson, Cretheus' son. He must be a kinsman of our own on the father's side, if he is a grandson of Cretheus, for Cretheus and Athamas were both sons of Aeolus, and our father Phrixus was a son of Athamas. Next, and in case you have heard that we have a son of Helios with us, behold the man, Augeias. And this is Telamon, son of the illustrious Aeacus, a son of Zeus himself. Much the same is true of all the rest of Jason's followers. They are all sons or grandsons of immortal gods.'

The king was filled with rage as he listened to Argus. And now, in a towering passion, he gave vent to his displeasure, the brunt of which fell on the sons of Chalciope, whom he held responsible for the presence of the rest. His eyes blazed with fury as he burst into speech:

'You scoundrels! Get out of my sight at once. Get out of my country, you and your knavish tricks, before you meet a Phrixus and a fleece you will not relish. It was no fleece that brought you and your confederates from Hellas, but a plot to seize my sceptre and my royal power. If you had not eaten at my table first, I would tear your tongues out and chop off your hands, both of them, and send you back with nothing but your feet, to teach you to think twice before starting on another expedition. As for all that about the blessed gods, it is nothing but a pack of lies.'

Telamon's gorge rose at this outburst from the angry

Jason and Medea

king, and he was on the point of flinging back defiance, to his own undoing, when he was checked by Jason, who forestalled him with a more politic reply.

'My lord,' he said, 'pray overlook our show of arms. We have not come to your city and palace with any such designs as you suspect. Nor have we predatory aims. Who of his own accord would brave so vast a sea to lay his hands on other people's goods? No; it was Destiny and the cruel orders of a brutal king that sent me here. Be generous to your suppliants, and I will make all Hellas ring with the glory of your name. And by way of more immediate recompense, we are prepared to take the field in your behalf against the Sauromatae or any other tribe you may wish to subdue.'

Jason's obsequious address had no effect. The king was plunged in sullen cogitation, wondering whether to leap up and kill them on the spot or to put their powers to the proof. He ended by deciding for a test and said to Jason:

'Sir, there is no need for me to hear you out. If you are really children of the gods or have other grounds for approaching me as equals in the course of your piratical adventure, I will let you have the golden fleece – that is, if you still want it when I have put you to the proof. For I am not like your overlord in Hellas, as you describe him; I am not inclined to be ungenerous to men of rank.

'I propose to test your courage and abilities by setting you a task which, though formidable, is not beyond the strength of my two hands. Grazing on the plain of Ares,

Apollonius of Rhodes

I have a pair of bronze-footed and fire-breathing bulls. These I yoke and drive over the hard fallow of the plain, quickly ploughing a four-acre field up to the ridge at either end. Then I sow the furrows, not with corn, but with the teeth of a monstrous serpent, which presently come up in the form of armed men, whom I cut down and kill with my spear as they rise up against me on all sides. It is morning when I yoke my team and by evening I have done my harvesting. That is what I do. If you, sir, can do as well, you may carry off the fleece to your king's palace on the very same day. If not, you shall not have it – do not deceive yourself. It would be wrong for a brave man to truckle to a coward.'

Jason listened to this with his eyes fixed on the floor; and when the king had finished, he sat there just as he was, without a word, resourceless in the face of his dilemma. For a long time he turned the matter over in his mind, unable boldly to accept a task so clearly fraught with peril. But at last he gave the king an answer which he thought would serve:

'Your Majesty, right is on your side and you leave me no escape whatever. Therefore I will take up your challenge, in spite of its preposterous terms, and though I may be courting death. Men serve no harsher mistress than Necessity, who drives me now and forced me to come here at another king's behest.'

He spoke in desperation and was little comforted by

Jason and Medea

Aeëtes' sinister reply: 'Go now and join your company: you have shown your relish for the task. But if you hesitate to yoke the bulls or shirk the deadly harvesting, I will take the matter up myself in a manner calculated to make others shrink from coming here and pestering their betters.'

He had made his meaning clear, and Jason rose from his chair. Augeias and Telamon followed him at once, and so did Argus, but without his brothers, whom he had warned by a nod to stay there for the time being. As the party went out of the hall, Jason's comeliness and charm singled him out from all the rest; and Medea, plucking her bright veil aside, turned wondering eyes upon him. Her heart smouldered with pain and as he passed from sight her soul crept out of her, as in a dream, and fluttered in his steps.

They left the palace with heavy hearts. Meanwhile Chalciope, to save herself from Aeëtes' wrath, had hastily withdrawn to her own room together with her sons. Medea too retired, a prey to all the inquietude that Love awakens. The whole scene was still before her eyes – how Jason looked, the clothes he wore, the things he said, the way he sat, and how he walked to the door. It seemed to her, as she reviewed these images, that there was nobody like Jason. His voice and the honey-sweet words that he had used still rang in her ears. But she feared for him. She was afraid that the bulls or Aeëtes with his own hands

Apollonius of Rhodes

might kill him; and she mourned him as one already dead. The pity of it overwhelmed her; a round tear ran down her cheek; and weeping quietly she voiced her woes:

'What is the meaning of this grief? Hero or villain (and why should I care which?) the man is going to his death. Well, let him go! And yet I wish he had been spared. Yes, sovran Lady Hecate, this is my prayer. Let him live to reach his home. But if he must be conquered by the bulls, may he first learn that I for one do not rejoice in his cruel fate.'

While Medea thus tormented herself, Jason was listening to some advice from Argus, who had waited to address him till the people and the town were left behind and the party were retracing their steps across the plain.

'My lord,' he said, 'I have a plan to suggest. You will not like it; but in a crisis no expedient should be left untried. You have heard me speak of a young woman who practises witchcraft under the tutelage of the goddess Hecate. If we could win her over, we might banish from our minds all fear of your defeat in the ordeal. I am only afraid that my mother may not support me in this scheme. Nevertheless, since we all stand to lose our lives together, I will go back and sound her.'

'My friend,' said Jason, responding to the good will shown by Argus, 'if you are satisfied, then I have no objections. Go back at once and seek your mother's aid, feeling your way with care. But oh, how bleak the prospect is, with our one hope of seeing home again in women's hands!'

Jason and Medea

Soon after this they reached the marsh. Their comrades, when they saw them coming up, greeted them with cheerful enquiries, which Jason answered in a gloomy vein. 'Friends,' he said, 'if I were to answer all your questions, we should never finish; but the cruel king has definitely set his face against us. He said he had a couple of bronze-footed and fire-breathing bulls grazing on the plain of Ares, and told me to plough a four-acre field with these. He will give me seed from a serpent's jaws which will produce a crop of earthborn men in panoplies of bronze. And I have got to kill them before the day is done. That is my task. I straightway undertook it, for I had no choice.'

The task, as Jason had described it, seemed so impossible to all of them that for a while they stood there without a sound or word, looking at one another in impotent despair. But at last Peleus took heart and spoke out to his fellow chieftains: 'The time has come. We must confer and settle what to do. Not that debate will help us much: I would rather trust to strength of arm. Jason, my lord, if you fancy the adventure and mean to yoke Aeëtes' bulls you will naturally keep your promise and prepare. But if you have the slightest fear that your nerve may fail you, do not force yourself. And you need not sit there looking round for someone else. I, for one, am willing. The worst that I shall suffer will be death.'

So said the son of Aeacus. Telamon too was stirred and eagerly leapt up; next Idas, full of lofty thoughts; then

Apollonius of Rhodes

Castor and Polydeuces; and with them one who was already numbered with the men of might though the down was scarcely showing on his cheeks, Meleager son of Oeneus, his heart uplifted by the courage that dares all. But the others made no move, leaving it to these; and Argus addressed the six devoted men:

'My friends, you certainly provide us with a last resource. But I have some hopes of timely help that may be coming from my mother. So I advise you, keen as you are, to do as you did earlier and wait here in the ship for a little while – it is always better to think twice before one throws away one's life for nothing. There is a girl living in Aeëtes' palace whom the goddess Hecate has taught to handle with extraordinary skill all the magic herbs that grow on dry land or in running water. With these she can put out a raging fire, she can stop rivers as they roar in spate, arrest a star, and check the movement of the sacred moon. We thought of her as we made our way down here from the palace. My mother, her own sister, might persuade her to be our ally in the hour of trial; and with your approval I am prepared to go back to Aeëtes' palace this very day and see what I can do. Who knows? Some friendly Power may come to my assistance.'

So said Argus. And the gods were kind: they sent them a sign. In her terror, a timid dove, hotly pursued by a great hawk, dropped straight down into Jason's lap, while the hawk fell impaled on the mascot at the stern. Mopsus at once made the omens clear to all:

Jason and Medea

'It is for you, my friends, that Heaven has designed this portent. We could construe it in no better way than by approaching the girl with every plea we can devise. And I do not think she will refuse, if Phineus was right when he told us that our safety lay in Aphrodite's care; for this gentle bird whose life was spared belongs to her. May all turn out as I foresee, reading the omens with my inward eye. And so, my friends, let us invoke Cytherea's aid and put ourselves at once in the hands of Argus.'

The young men applauded, remembering what Phineus had told them. But there was one dissentient voice, and that a loud one. Idas leapt up in a towering rage and shouted: 'For shame! Have we come here to trot along with women, calling on Aphrodite to support us, instead of the mighty god of battle? Do you look to doves and hawks to get you out of trouble? Well, please yourselves! Forget that you are fighters. Pay court to girls and turn their silly heads.'

This tirade from Idas was received by many of his comrades with muttered resentment, though no one took the floor to answer him back. He sat down in high dudgeon, and Jason rose immediately to give them his decision and his orders. 'We are all agreed,' he said. 'Argus sets out from the ship. And we ourselves will now make fast with hawsers from the river to the shore, where anyone can see us. We certainly ought not to hide here any longer as though we were afraid of fighting.'

With that, he despatched Argus on his way back to the

town; and the crew, taking their orders from Aeson's son, hauled the anchor-stones on board and rowed *Argo* close to dry land, a little way from the marsh.

At the same time Aeëtes, meaning to play the Minyae false and do them grievous injury, summoned the Colchians to assemble, not in his palace, but at another spot where meetings had been held before. He declared that as soon as the bulls had destroyed the man who had taken up his formidable challenge, he would strip a forest hill of brushwood and burn the ship with every man on board, to cure them once for all of the intolerable airs they gave themselves, these enterprising buccaneers. It was true that he had welcomed Phrixus to his palace, but whatever the man's plight, he certainly would not have done so, though he had never known a foreigner so gentle and so well-conducted, if Zeus himself had not sent Hermes speeding down from heaven to see that he met with a sympathetic host. Much less should pirates landing in his country be left unpunished, men whose sole concern it was to get their hands on other people's goods, to lie in ambush plotting a sudden stroke, to sally out, cry havoc, and raid the farmers' yards. Moreover, Phrixus' sons should make him suitable amends for coming back in league with a gang of ruffians to hurl him from the throne. The crazy fools! But it all chimed in with an ugly hint he had had long ago from his father Helios, warning him to beware of treasonable plots and evil machinations in his own family. So, to complete their chastisement, he would pack them off to Achaea, just as they and their father had wished; and that was surely far enough. As for his daughters, he had not the slightest fear of treachery from them. Nor from his son Apsyrtus; only Chalciope's sons were involved in the mischief. The angry king ended by informing his people of the drastic measures that he had in mind, and ordering them, with many threats, to watch the ship and the men themselves so that no one should escape his doom.

By now Argus had reached the palace and was urging his mother with every argument at his command to invoke Medea's aid. The same idea had already occurred to Chalciope herself; but she had hesitated. On the one hand, she was afraid of failure: Medea might be so appalled by thoughts of her father's wrath that all entreaties would fall upon deaf ears. On the other, she feared that if her sister yielded to her prayers the whole conspiracy would be laid bare.

Meanwhile the maiden lay on her bed, fast asleep, with all her cares forgotten. But not for long. Dreams assailed her, deceitful dreams, the nightmares of a soul in pain. She dreamt that the stranger had accepted the challenge, not in the hope of winning the ram's fleece – it was not that that had brought him to Aea – but in order that he might carry her off to his own home as his bride. Then it seemed that it was she who was standing up to the bulls; she found it easy to handle them. But when all was done, her parents backed out of the bargain, pointing out that it was Jason, not their daughter, whom they had dared to yoke the bulls. This led to an interminable dispute between her father and the Argonauts, which resulted in their leaving the decision to her – she could do as she pleased. And she, without a moment's thought, turned her back on her parents and chose the stranger. Her parents were cut to the quick; they screamed in their anger; and with their cries she woke.

She sat up, shivering with fright, and peered round the walls of her bedroom. Slowly and painfully she dragged herself back to reality. Then in self-pity she cried out and voiced the terror that her nightmare had engendered:

'These noblemen, their coming here, I fear it spells catastrophe. And how I tremble for their leader! He should pay court to some Achaean girl far away in his own country, leaving me content with spinsterhood and home. Ah no! Away with modesty! I will stand aside no longer; I will go to my sister. She is anxious for her sons and well might ask me for my help in the ordeal. And so my heartache would be eased.'

With that she rose, and in her gown, with nothing on her feet, went to her bedroom door and opened it. She was resolved to go to her sister and she crossed the threshold. But once outside she stayed for a long time where she was, inhibited by shame. Then she turned and went back into the room. Again she came out of it, and again she crept back, borne to and fro on hesitating feet.

Whenever she set out shame held her back; and all the time shame held her in the room shameless desire kept urging her to leave it. Three times she tried to go; three times she failed; and at the fourth attempt she threw herself face downward on the bed and writhed in pain.

Her plight was like that of a bride mourning in her bedroom for the young husband chosen for her by her brothers and parents, and lost by some stroke of Fate before the pair had enjoyed each other's love. Too shy and circumspect as yet to mingle freely with the maids and risk an unkind word or tactless jibe, she sits disconsolate in a corner of the room, looks at the empty bed and weeps in silence though her heart is bursting. Thus Medea wept.

But presently one of the servants, her own young maid, came to the room, and seeing her mistress lying there in tears, ran off to tell Chalciope, who was sitting with her sons considering how they might win Medea over. Chalciope did not make light of the girl's story, strange as it seemed. In great alarm she hurried through the house from her own to her sister's room, and there she found her lying in misery on the bed with both cheeks torn and her eyes red with weeping.

'My dear!' she cried. 'What is the meaning of these tears? What has made you so terribly unhappy? Have you suddenly been taken ill? Or has Father told you of some awful fate he has in mind for me and my sons? Oh, how

I wish I might never see this city and this home of ours again, and live at the world's end, where nobody has even heard of the Colchians!'

Medea blushed. She was eager to answer, but for a long while was checked by maiden modesty. Time and again the truth was on the tip of her tongue, only to be swallowed back. Time and again it tried to force a passage through her lovely lips, but no words came. At last, impelled by the bold hand of Love, she gave her sister a disingenuous reply: 'Chalciope, I am terrified for your sons. I am afraid that Father will destroy them out of hand, strangers and all. I had a little sleep just now and in a nightmare that is what I saw. God forfend such evil! May you never have to suffer so through them!'

Medea was trying to induce her sister to make the first move and appeal to her to save her sons. And indeed Chalciope was overwhelmed by horror at her disclosure. She said: 'My fears have been the same as yours. That is what brought me here. I hoped that you and I might put our heads together and find a way of rescuing my sons. But swear by Earth and Heaven that you will keep what I say to yourself and work in league with me. I implore you, by the happy gods, by your own head, and by your parents, not to stand by while they are mercilessly done to death. If you do so, may I die with my dear sons and haunt you afterwards from Hades like an avenging Fury.'

With that she burst into tears, sank down, and throwing her arms round her sister's knees buried her head in her

Jason and Medea

lap. Each of them wailed in pity for the other, and faint sounds of women weeping in distress were heard throughout the palace.

Medea was the first to speak. 'Sister,' she said, 'you left me speechless when you talked of curses and avenging Furies. How can I set your mind at rest? I only wish we could be sure of rescuing your sons. However, I will do as you ask and take the solemn oath of the Colchians, swearing by mighty Heaven and by Earth below, the Mother of the Gods, that provided your demands are not impossible I will help you as you wish, with all the power that in me lies.'

When Medea had taken the oath, Chalciope said: 'Well now, for the sake of my sons, could you not devise some stratagem, some cunning ruse that the stranger could rely on in his trial? He needs you just as much as they do. In fact he has sent Argus here to urge me to enlist your help. I left him in the palace when I came to you just now.'

At this, Medea's heart leapt up. Her lovely cheeks were crimsoned and her eyes grew dim with tears of joy. 'Chalciope,' she cried, 'I will do anything to please you and your sons, anything to make you happy. May I never see the light of dawn again and may you see me in the world no more, if I put anything before your safety and the lives of your sons, who are my brothers, my dear kinsmen, with whom I was brought up. And you, am I not as much your daughter as your sister, you that took me to your breast as you did them, when I was a baby, as I often heard my mother say? But go now and tell no one of my promise, so that my parents may not know how I propose to keep it. And at dawn I will go to Hecate's temple with magic medicine for the bulls.'

Thus assured, Chalciope withdrew from her sister's room and brought her sons the news of her success. But Medea, left alone, fell a prey once more to shame and horror at the way in which she planned to help a man in defiance of her father's wishes.

Night threw her shadow on the world. Sailors out at sea looked up at the circling Bear and the stars of Orion. Travellers and watchmen longed for sleep, and oblivion came at last to mothers mourning for their children's death. In the town, dogs ceased to bark and men to call to one another; silence reigned over the deepening dark. But gentle sleep did not visit Medea. In her yearning for Jason, fretful cares kept her awake. She feared the great strength of the bulls; she saw him face them in the field of Ares; she saw him meet an ignominious end. Her heart fluttered within her, restless as a patch of sunlight dancing up and down on a wall as the swirling water poured into a pail reflects it.

Tears of pity ran down her cheeks and her whole body was possessed by agony, a searing pain which shot along her nerves and deep into the nape of her neck, that vulnerable spot where the relentless archery of Love causes the keenest pangs. At one moment she thought she would give him the magic drug for the bulls; at the next she thought no, she would rather die herself; and then that she would do neither, but patiently endure her fate. In the end she sat down and debated with herself in miserable indecision:

'Evil on this side, evil on that; and must I choose between them? In either case my plight is desperate and there is no escape; this torture will go on. Oh how I wish that Artemis with her swift darts had put an end to me before I had seen that man, before Chalciope's sons had gone to Achaea! Some god, some Fury rather, must have brought them back with grief and tears for us. Let him be killed in the struggle, if it is indeed his fate to perish in the unploughed field. For how could I prepare the drug without my parents' knowledge? What story shall I tell them? What trickery will serve? How can I help him, and fail to be found out? Are he and I to meet alone? Indeed I am ill-starred, for even if he dies I have no hope of happiness; with Jason dead, I should taste real misery. Away with modesty, farewell to my good name! Saved from all harm by me, let him go where he pleases, and let me die. On the very day of his success I could hang myself from a rafter or take a deadly poison. Yet even so my death would never save me from their wicked tongues. My fate would be the talk of every city in the world; and here the Colchian women would bandy my name about and drag it in mud – the girl who fancied a foreigner enough to die for him, disgraced her parents and her home, went off her head for love. What infamy would not be mine? Ah, how I grieve now for the folly of my passion! Better to die here in my room this very night, passing from life unnoticed, unreproached, than to carry through this horrible, this despicable scheme.'

With that she went and fetched the box in which she kept her many drugs, healing or deadly, and putting it on her knees she wept. Tears ran unchecked in torrents down her cheeks and drenched her lap as she bemoaned her own sad destiny. She was determined now to take a poison from the box and swallow it; and in a moment she was fumbling with the fastening of the lid in her unhappy eagerness to reach the fatal drug. But suddenly she was overcome by the hateful thought of death, and for a long time she stayed her hand in silent horror. Visions of life and all its fascinating cares rose up before her. She thought of the pleasures that the living can enjoy. She thought of her happy playmates, as a young girl will. And now, setting its true value on all this, it seemed to her a sweeter thing to see the sun than it had ever been before. So, prompted by Here, she changed her mind and put the box away. Irresolute no longer, she waited eagerly for Dawn to come, so that she could meet the stranger face to face and give him the magic drug as she had promised. Time after time she opened her door to catch the first glimmer of day; and she rejoiced when early Dawn lit up the sky and people in the town began to stir.

Argus left the palace and returned to the ship. But he

told his brothers to wait before following him, in order to find out what Medea meant to do. She herself, as soon as she saw the first light of day, gathered up the golden locks that were floating round her shoulders in disorder, washed the stains from her cheeks and cleansed her skin with an ointment clear as nectar; then she put on a beautiful robe equipped with cunning brooches, and threw a silvery veil over her lovely head. And as she moved about, there in her own home, she walked oblivious of all evils imminent, and worse to come.

She had twelve maids, young as herself and all unmarried, who slept in the ante-chamber of her own sweet-scented room. She called them now and told them to yoke the mules to her carriage at once, as she wished to drive to the splendid Temple of Hecate; and while they were getting the carriage ready she took a magic ointment from her box. This salve was named after Prometheus. A man had only to smear it on his body, after propitiating the only-begotten Maiden with a midnight offering, to become invulnerable by sword or fire and for that day to surpass himself in strength and daring. It first appeared in a plant that sprang from the blood-like ichor of Prometheus in his torment, which the flesh-eating eagle had dropped on the spurs of Caucasus. The flowers, which grew on twin stalks a cubit high, were of the colour of Corycian saffron, while the root looked like flesh that has just been cut, and the juice like the dark sap of a mountain oak. To make the ointment, Medea, clothed in black, in the gloom of night, had drawn off this juice in a Caspian shell after bathing in seven perennial streams and calling seven times on Brimo, nurse of youth, Brimo, night-wanderer of the underworld, Queen of the dead. The dark earth shook and rumbled underneath the Titan root when it was cut, and Prometheus himself groaned in the anguish of his soul.

Such was the salve that Medea chose. Placing it in the fragrant girdle that she wore beneath her bosom, she left the house and got into her carriage, with two maids on either side. They gave her the reins, and taking the well-made whip in her right hand, she drove off through the town, while the rest of the maids tucked up their skirts above their white knees and ran behind along the broad highway, holding on to the wicker body of the carriage.

I see her there like Artemis, standing in her golden chariot after she has bathed in the gentle waters of Parthenius or the streams of Amnisus, and driving off with her fast-trotting deer over the hills and far away to some rich-scented sacrifice. Attendant nymphs have gathered at the source of Amnisus or flocked in from the glens and upland springs to follow her; and fawning beasts whimper in homage and tremble as she passes by. Thus Medea and her maids sped through the town, and on either side people made way for her, avoiding the princess's eye.

Leaving the city and its well-paved streets, she drove across the plain and drew up at the shrine. There she got quickly down from her smooth-running carriage and addressed her maids. 'My friends,' she said, 'I have done wrong. I forgot that we were told not to go among these foreigners who are wandering about the place. Everybody in the town is terrified, and in consequence none of the women who every day foregather here have come. But since we are here and it looks as though we shall be left in peace, we need not deny ourselves a little pleasure. Let us sing to our heart's content, and then, when we have gathered some of the lovely flowers in the meadow there, go back to town at the usual time. And if you will only fall in with a scheme of mine, you shall have something better than flowers to take home with you today. I will explain. Argus and Chalciope herself have persuaded me against my better judgement – but not a word to anyone of what I say; my father must not hear about it. They wish me to protect that stranger, the one who took up the challenge, in his mortal combat with the bulls and take some presents from him in return. I told them I thought well of the idea; and I have in fact invited him to come and see me here without his followers. But if he brings his gifts and hands them over, I mean to share them out among ourselves; and what we give him in return will be a deadlier drug than he expects. All I ask of you when he arrives is to leave me by myself.'

With this ingenious figment Medea satisfied her maids. Meanwhile Argus, when his brothers had told him she was going to the Temple of Hecate at dawn, drew Jason apart and conducted him across the plain. Mopsus son of Ampycus went with them, an excellent adviser for travellers setting out, and able to interpret any omen that a bird might offer on the way. As for Jason, by the grace of Here Queen of Heaven, no hero of the past, no son of Zeus himself, no offspring of the other gods, could have outshone him on that day, he was so good to look at, so delightful to talk to. Even his companions, as they glanced at him, were fascinated by his radiant charm. For Mopsus, it was a pleasurable journey: he had a shrewd idea how it would end.

Near the shrine and beside the path they followed, there stood a poplar, flaunting its myriad leaves. It was much frequented as a roost by garrulous crows, one of which flapped its wings as they were passing by, and cawing from the treetop expressed the sentiments of Here:

'Who is this inglorious seer who has not had the sense to realize, what even children know, that a girl does not permit herself to say a single word of love to a young man who brings an escort with him? Off with you, foolish prophet and incompetent diviner! You certainly are not inspired by Cypris or the gentle Loves.'

Mopsus listened to the bird's remarks with a smile at the reprimand from Heaven. Turning to Jason, he said: 'Proceed, my lord, to the temple, where you will find Medea and be graciously received, thanks to Aphrodite, who will be your ally in the hour of trial, as was foretold to us by Phineus son of Agenor. We two, Argus and I, will not go any nearer, but will wait here till you come back. You must go to her alone and attach her to yourself by your own persuasive eloquence.' This was sound advice and they both accepted it at once.

Meanwhile Medea, though she was singing and dancing with her maids, could think of one thing only. There was no melody, however gay, that did not quickly cease to please. Time and again she faltered and came to a halt. To keep her eyes fixed on her choir was more than she could do. She was for ever turning them aside to search the distant paths, and more than once she well-nigh fainted when she mistook the noise of the wind for the footfall of a passer-by.

But it was not so very long before the sight of Jason rewarded her impatient watch. Like Sirius rising from Ocean, brilliant and beautiful but full of menace for the flocks, he sprang into view, splendid to look at but fraught with trouble for the lovesick girl. Her heart stood still, a mist descended on her eyes, and a warm flush spread across her cheeks. She could neither move towards him nor retreat; her feet were rooted to the ground. And now her servants disappeared, and the pair of them stood face to face without a word or sound, like oaks or tall pines that stand in the mountains side by side in silence when the air is still, but when the wind has stirred them chatter without end. So these two, stirred by the breath of Love, were soon to pour out all their tale.

Jason, seeing how distraught Medea was, tried to put her at her ease. 'Lady,' he said, 'I am alone. Why are you so fearful of me? I am not a profligate as some men are, and never was, even in my own country. So you have no need to be on your guard, but may ask or tell me anything you wish. We have come together here as friends, in a consecrated spot which must not be profaned. Speak to me, question me, without reserve; and since you have already promised your sister to give me the talisman I need so much, pray do not put me off with pleasant speeches. I plead to you by Hecate herself, by your parents, and by Zeus. His hand protects all suppliants and strangers, and I that now address my prayers to you in my necessity am both a stranger and a suppliant. Without you and your sister I shall never succeed in my appalling task. Grant me your aid and in the days to come I will reward you duly, repaying you as best I can from the distant land where I shall sing your praises. My comrades too when they are back in Hellas will immortalize your name. So will their wives and mothers, whom I think of now as sitting by the sea, shedding tears in their anxiety for us – bitter tears, which you could wipe away. Remember Ariadne, young Ariadne, daughter of Minos and Pasiphae, who was a daughter of the Sun. She did not scruple to befriend Theseus and save him in his hour of trial; and then, when Minos had relented, she left her home and sailed away with him. She was the darling of the gods and she has her emblem in the sky: all night a ring of stars called Ariadne's Crown rolls on its way among the heavenly constellations. You too will be thanked by the gods if you save me and all my noble friends. Indeed your loveliness assures me of a kind and tender heart within.'

Jason's homage melted Medea. Turning her eyes aside she smiled divinely and then, uplifted by his praise, she looked him in the face. How to begin, she did not know; she longed so much to tell him everything at once. But with the charm, she did not hesitate; she drew it out from her sweet-scented girdle and he took it in his hands with joy. She revelled in his need of her and would have poured out all her soul to him as well, so captivating was the light of love that streamed from Jason's golden head and held her gleaming eyes. Her heart was warmed and melted like the dew on roses under the morning sun.

At one moment both of them were staring at the ground in deep embarrassment; at the next they were smiling and glancing at each other with the love-light in their eyes. But at last Medea forced herself to speak to him. 'Hear me now,' she said. 'These are my plans for you. When you have met my father and he has given you the deadly teeth from the serpent's jaws, wait for the moment of midnight and after bathing in an ever-running river, go out alone in sombre clothes and dig a round pit in the earth. There, kill a ewe and after heaping up a pyre over the pit, sacrifice it whole, with a libation of honey from the hive and prayers to Hecate, Perses' only Daughter. Then, when you have invoked the goddess duly, withdraw from the pyre. And do not be tempted to look behind you as you go,

Apollonius of Rhodes

either by footfalls or the baying of hounds, or you may ruin everything and never reach your friends alive.

'In the morning, melt this charm, strip, and using it like oil, anoint your body. It will endow you with tremendous strength and boundless confidence. You will feel yourself a match, not for mere men, but for the gods themselves. Sprinkle your spear and shield and sword with it as well; and neither the spear-points of the earth-born men nor the consuming flames that the savage bulls spew out will find you vulnerable. But you will not be immune for long – only for the day. Nevertheless, do not at any moment flinch from the encounter.

'And here is something else that will stand you in good stead. You have yoked the mighty bulls; you have ploughed the stubborn fallow (with those great hands and all that strength it will not take you long); you have sown the serpent's teeth in the dark earth; and now the giants are springing up along the furrows. Watch till you see a number of them rise from the soil, then, before they see you, throw a great boulder in among them; and they will fall on it like famished dogs and kill one another. That is your moment; plunge into the fray yourself.

'And so the task is done and you can carry off the fleece to Hellas – a long, long way from Aea, I believe. Go none the less, go where you will; go where the fancy takes you when you part from us.'

After this, Medea was silent for a while. She kept her eyes fixed on the ground, and the warm tears ran down

Jason and Medea

her lovely cheeks as she saw him sailing off over the high seas far away from her. Then she looked up at him and sorrowfully spoke again, taking his right hand in hers and no longer attempting to conceal her love. She said:

'But do remember, if you ever reach your home. Remember the name of Medea, and I for my part will remember you when you are far away. But now, pray tell me where you live. Where are you bound for when you sail across the sea from here? Will your journey take you near the wealthy city of Orchomenus or the Isle of Aea? Tell me too about that girl you mentioned, who won such fame for herself, the daughter of Pasiphae my father's sister.'

As he listened to this and noted her tears, unconscionable Love stole into the heart of Jason too. He replied: 'Of one thing I am sure. If I escape and live to reach Achaea; if Aeëtes does not set us a still more formidable task; never by night or day shall I forget you. But you asked about the country of my birth. If it pleases you to hear, I will describe it; indeed I should like nothing better. It is a land ringed by lofty mountains, rich in sheep and pasture, and the birthplace of Prometheus' son, the good Deucalion, who was the first man to found cities, build temples to the gods and rule mankind as king. Its neighbours call the land Haemonia, and in it stands Iolcus, my own town, and many others too where the very name of the Aeaean Island is unknown. Yet they do say that it was from these parts that the Aeolid Minyas migrated long ago to found Orchomenus, which borders on Cadmeian lands. But why do I trouble you with all this tiresome talk about my home and Minos' daughter, the far-famed Ariadne, that lovely lady with the glorious name who roused your curiosity? I can only hope that, as Minos came to terms with Theseus for her sake, your father will be reconciled with us.'

He had thought, by talking in this gentle way, to soothe Medea. But she was now obsessed by the gloomiest forebodings; embittered too. And she answered him with passion:

'No doubt in Hellas people think it right to honour their agreements. But Aeëtes is not the kind of man that Minos was, if what you say of him is true; and as for Ariadne, I cannot claim to be a match for her. So do not talk of friendliness to strangers. But oh, at least remember me when you are back in Iolcus; and I, despite my parents, will remember you. And may there come to me some whisper from afar, some bird to tell the tale, when you forget me. Or may the Storm-Winds snatch me up and carry me across the sea to Iolcus, to denounce you to your face and remind you that I saved your life. That is the moment I would choose to pay an unexpected visit to your house.'

As she spoke, tears of misery ran down her cheeks. But Jason said: 'Dear lady, you may spare the wandering Winds that task, and your tell-tale bird as well, for you are talking nonsense. If you come to us in Hellas you will be

Jason and Medea

honoured and revered by both the women and the men. Indeed they will treat you as a goddess, because it was through you that their sons came home alive, or their brothers, kinsmen, or beloved husbands were saved from hurt. And there shall be a bridal bed for you, which you and I will share. Nothing shall part us in our love till Death at his appointed hour removes us from the light of day.'

As she heard these words of his, her heart melted within her. And yet she shuddered as she thought of the disastrous step she was about to take. Poor girl! She was not going to refuse for long this offer of a home in Hellas. The goddess Here had arranged it all: Medea was to leave her native land for the sacred city of Iolcus, and there to bring his punishment to Pelias.

Her maids, who had been spying on them from afar, were now becoming restive, though they did not intervene. It was high time for the maiden to go home to her mother. But Medea had no thought of leaving yet; she was entranced both by his comeliness and his bewitching talk. At last however, Jason, who had kept his wits about him, said, 'Now we must part, or the sun will set before we know it. Besides, some passer-by might see us. But we will meet each other here again.'

By gentle steps they had advanced so far towards an understanding. And now they parted, he in a joyful mood to go back to his companions and the ship, she to rejoin her maids, who all ran up to meet her. But as they gathered round, she did not even notice them: her head was in the clouds. Without knowing what she did, she got into her carriage to drive the mules, taking the reins in one hand and the whip in the other. And off they trotted to the palace in the town.

She had no sooner arrived than Chalciope questioned her anxiously about her sons. But Medea had left her wits behind her. She neither heard a word her sister said nor showed the least desire to answer her inquiries. She sat down on a low stool at the foot of her bed, leant over and rested her cheek on her left hand, pondering with tears in her eyes on the infamous part she had played in a scene that she herself had staged.

Jason found his escort in the place where he had left them, and as they set out to rejoin the rest, he told them how he had fared. When the party reached the ship, he was received with open arms and in reply to the questions of his friends he told them of Medea's plans and showed them the powerful charm. Idas was the only member of the company who was not impressed. He sat aloof, nursing his resentment. The rest were overjoyed, and since the night permitted no immediate move, they settled down in peace and comfort. But at dawn they despatched two men to Aeetes to ask him for the seed, Telamon beloved of Ares, and Aethalides the famous son of Hermes. This pair set out on their errand, and they did not fail. When they reached the king, he handed them the deadly teeth that Jason was to sow.

Jason and Medea

The teeth were those of the Aonian serpent, the guardian of Ares' spring, which Cadmus killed in Ogygian Thebes. He had come there in his search for Europa, and there he settled, under the guidance of a heifer picked out for him by Apollo in an oracle. Athene, Lady of Trito, tore the teeth out of the serpent's jaws and divided them between Aeëtes and Cadmus, the slayer of the beast. Cadmus sowed them in the Aonian plain and founded an earthborn clan with all that had escaped the spear of Ares when he did his harvesting. Such were the teeth that Aeëtes let them take back to the ship. He gave them willingly, as he was satisfied that Jason, even if he yoked the bulls, would prove unable to finish off the task.

It was evening. Out in the west, beyond the farthest Ethiopian hills, the Sun was sinking under the darkening world; Night was harnessing her team; and the Argonauts were preparing their beds by the hawsers of the ship. But Jason waited for the bright constellation of the Bear to decline, and then, when all the air from heaven to earth was still, he set out like a stealthy thief across the solitary plain. During the day he had prepared himself, and so had everything he needed with him; Argus had fetched him some milk and a ewe from a farm; the rest he had taken from the ship itself. When he had found an unfrequented spot in a clear meadow under the open sky, he began by bathing his naked body reverently in the sacred river, and then put on a dark mantle which Hypsipyle of Lemnos had given him to remind him of their passionate embraces. Then he dug a pit a cubit deep, piled up billets, and laid the sheep on top of them after cutting its throat. He kindled the wood from underneath and poured mingled libations on the sacrifice, calling on Hecate Brimo to help him in the coming test. This done, he withdrew; and the dread goddess, hearing his words from the abyss, came up to accept the offering of Aeson's son. She was garlanded by fearsome snakes that coiled themselves round twigs of oak; the twinkle of a thousand torches lit the scene; and hounds of the underworld barked shrilly all around her. The whole meadow trembled under her feet, and the nymphs of marsh and river who haunt the fens by Amarantian Phasis cried out in fear. Jason was terrified; but even so, as he retreated, he did not once turn round. And so he found himself among his friends once more, and Dawn arrived, showing herself betimes above the snows of Caucasus.

At daybreak too, Aeëtes put on his breast the stiff cuirass which Ares had given him after slaying Mimas with his own hands in the field of Phlegra; and on his head he set his golden helmet with its four plates, bright as the Sun's round face when he rises fresh from Ocean Stream. And he took up his shield of many hides, and his unconquerable spear, a spear that none of the Argonauts could have withstood, now that they had deserted Heracles, who alone could have dealt with it in battle. Phaëthon was close at hand, holding his father's swift horses and well-built chariot in readiness. Aeëtes mounted, took the

Jason and Medea

reins in his hands, and drove out of the town along the broad highway to attend the contest, followed by hurrying crowds. Lord of the Colchians, he might have been Poseidon in his chariot driving to the Isthmian Games, to Taenarum, to the waters of Lerna, or through the grove of Onchestus, and on to Calaurea with his steeds, to the Haemonian Rock or the woods of Geraestus.

Meanwhile Jason, remembering Medea's instructions, melted the magic drug and sprinkled his shield with it and his sturdy spear and sword. His comrades watched him and put his weapons to the proof with all the force they had. But they could not bend the spear at all; even in their strong hands it proved itself unbreakable. Idas was furious with them. He hacked at the butt-end of the spear with his great sword, but the blade rebounded from it like a hammer from the anvil. And a great shout of joy went up; they felt that the battle was already won.

Next, Jason sprinkled his own body and was imbued with miraculous, indomitable might. As his hands increased in power, his very fingers twitched. Like a warhorse eager for battle, pawing the ground, neighing, pricking its ears and tossing up its head in pride, he exulted in the strength of his limbs. Time and again he leapt high in the air this way and that, brandishing his shield of bronze and ashen spear. The weapons flashed on the eye like intermittent lightning playing in a stormy sky from black clouds charged with rain.

After that there was no faltering; the Argonauts were

ready for the test. They took their places on the benches of the ship and rowed her swiftly upstream to the plain of Ares. This lay as far beyond the city as a chariot has to travel from start to turning-post when the kinsmen of a dead king are holding foot and chariot races in his honour. They found Aeëtes there and a full gathering of the Colchians. The tribesmen were stationed on the rocky spurs of Caucasus, and the king was wheeling around in his chariot on the river-bank.

Jason, as soon as his men had made the hawsers fast, leapt from the ship and entered the lists with spear and shield. He also took with him a shining bronze helmet full of sharp teeth, and his sword was slung from his shoulder. But his body was bare, so that he looked like Apollo of the golden sword as much as Ares god of war. Glancing round the field, he saw the bronze yoke for the bulls and beside it the plough of indurated steel, all in one piece. He went up to them, planted his heavy spear in the ground by its butt and laid the helmet down, leaning it against the spear. Then he went forward with his shield alone to examine the countless tracks that the bulls had made. And now, from somewhere in the bowels of the earth, from the smoky stronghold where they slept, the pair of bulls appeared, breathing flames of fire. The Argonauts were terrified at the sight. But Jason planting his feet apart stood to receive them, as a reef in the sea confronts the tossing billows in a gale. He held his shield

Jason and Medea

in front of him, and the two bulls, bellowing loudly, charged and butted it with their strong horns. But he was not shifted from his stance, not by so much as an inch. The bulls snorted and spurted from their mouths devouring flames, like a perforated crucible when the leather bellows of the smith, sometimes ceasing, sometimes blowing hard, have made a blaze and the fire leaps up from below with a terrific roar. The deadly heat assailed him on all sides with the force of lightning. But he was protected by Medea's magic. Seizing the right-hand bull by the tip of its horn, he dragged it with all his might towards the yoke, and then brought it down on its knees with a sudden kick on its bronze foot. The other charged, and was felled in the same way at a single blow; and Jason, who had cast his shield aside, stood with his feet apart, and though the flames at once enveloped him, held them both down on their fore-knees where they fell. Aeëtes marvelled at the man's strength.

Castor and Polydeuces picked up the yoke and gave it to Jason – they had been detailed for the task and were close at hand. Jason bound it tight on the bulls' necks, lifted the bronze pole between them and fastened it to the yoke by its pointed end, while the Twins backed out of the heat and returned to the ship. Then, taking his shield from the ground he slung it on his back, picked up the heavy helmet full of teeth and grasped his unconquerable spear, with which, like some ploughman using his Pelasgian goad, he pricked the bulls under their flanks and with a firm grip on its well-made handle guided the adamantine plough.

At first the bulls in their high fury spurted flames of fire. Their breath came out with a roar like that of the blustering wind that causes frightened mariners to take in sail. But presently, admonished by the spear, they went ahead, and the rough fallow cleft by their own and the great ploughman's might lay broken up behind them. The huge clods as they were torn away along the furrow groaned aloud; and Jason came behind, planting his feet down firmly on the field. As he ploughed he sowed the teeth, casting them far from himself with many a backward glance lest a deadly crop of earthborn men should catch him unawares. And the bulls, thrusting their bronze hoofs into the earth, toiled on till only a third of the passing day was left. Then, when weary labourers in other fields were hoping it would soon be time to free their oxen from the yoke, this indefatigable ploughman's work was done – the whole four-acre field was ploughed.

Jason freed his bulls from the plough and shooed them off. They fled across the plain; and he, seeing that no earthborn men had yet appeared in the furrows, seized the occasion to go back to the ship, where his comrades gathered round him with heartening words. He dipped his helmet in the flowing river and with its water quenched his thirst, then flexed his knees to keep them supple; and as fresh courage filled his heart, he lashed himself into a fury, like a wild boar when it whets its teeth to face the hunt and the foam drips to the ground from its savage mouth.

By now the earthborn men were shooting up like corn in all parts of the field. The deadly War-god's sacred plot bristled with stout shields, double-pointed spears, and glittering helmets. The splendour of it flashed through the air above and struck Olympus. Indeed this army springing from the earth shone out like the full congregation of the stars piercing the darkness of a murky night, when snow lies deep and the winds have chased the wintry clouds away. But Jason did not forget the counsel he had had from Medea of the many wiles. He picked up from the field a huge round boulder, a formidable quoit that Ares might have thrown, but four strong men together could not have budged from its place. Rushing forward with this in his hands he hurled it far away among the earthborn men, then crouched behind his shield, unseen and full of confidence. The Colchians gave a mighty shout like the roar of the sea beating on jagged rocks; and the king himself was astounded as he saw the great quoit hurtle through the air. But the earthborn men, like nimble hounds, leapt on one another and with loud yells began to slay. Beneath each other's spears they fell on their mother earth, as pines or oaks are blown down by a gale. And now, like a bright meteor that leaps from heaven and leaves a fiery trail behind it, portentous to all those who see it flash across the night, the son of Aeson hurled himself on them with his sword unsheathed and in promiscuous slaughter mowed them down, striking as he could, for many of them had but half emerged and showed their flanks and bellies only, some had their shoulders clear, some had just stood up, and others were afoot already and rushing into battle. So might some farmer threatened by a frontier war snatch up a newly sharpened sickle and, lest the enemy should reap his fields before him, hasten to cut down the unripe corn, not waiting for the season and the sun to ripen it. Thus Jason cut his crop of earthborn men. Blood filled the furrows as water fills the conduits of a spring. And still they fell, some on their faces biting the rough clods, some on their backs, and others on their hands and sides, looking like monsters from the sea. Many were struck before they could lift up their feet, and rested there with the death-dew on their brows, each trailing on the earth so much of him as had come up into the light of day. They lay like saplings in an orchard bowed to the ground when Zeus has sent torrential rain and snapped them at the root, wasting the gardeners' toil and bringing heartbreak to the owner of the plot, the man who planted them.

Such was the scene that King Aeëtes now surveyed, and such his bitterness. He went back to the city with his Colchians, pondering on the quickest way to bring the foreigners to book. And the sun sank and Jason's task was done.

1. BOCCACCIO · *Mrs Rosie and the Priest*
2. GERARD MANLEY HOPKINS · *As kingfishers catch fire*
3. *The Saga of Gunnlaug Serpent-tongue*
4. THOMAS DE QUINCEY · *On Murder Considered as One of the Fine Arts*
5. FRIEDRICH NIETZSCHE · *Aphorisms on Love and Hate*
6. JOHN RUSKIN · *Traffic*
7. PU SONGLING · *Wailing Ghosts*
8. JONATHAN SWIFT · *A Modest Proposal*
9. *Three Tang Dynasty Poets*
10. WALT WHITMAN · *On the Beach at Night Alone*
11. KENKŌ · *A Cup of Sake Beneath the Cherry Trees*
12. BALTASAR GRACIÁN · *How to Use Your Enemies*
13. JOHN KEATS · *The Eve of St Agnes*
14. THOMAS HARDY · *Woman much missed*
15. GUY DE MAUPASSANT · *Femme Fatale*
16. MARCO POLO · *Travels in the Land of Serpents and Pearls*
17. SUETONIUS · *Caligula*
18. APOLLONIUS OF RHODES · *Jason and Medea*
19. ROBERT LOUIS STEVENSON · *Olalla*
20. KARL MARX AND FRIEDRICH ENGELS · *The Communist Manifesto*
21. PETRONIUS · *Trimalchio's Feast*
22. JOHANN PETER HEBEL · *How a Ghastly Story Was Brought to Light by a Common or Garden Butcher's Dog*
23. HANS CHRISTIAN ANDERSEN · *The Tinder Box*
24. RUDYARD KIPLING · *The Gate of the Hundred Sorrows*
25. DANTE · *Circles of Hell*
26. HENRY MAYHEW · *Of Street Piemen*
27. HAFEZ · *The nightingales are drunk*
28. GEOFFREY CHAUCER · *The Wife of Bath*
29. MICHEL DE MONTAIGNE · *How We Weep and Laugh at the Same Thing*
30. THOMAS NASHE · *The Terrors of the Night*
31. EDGAR ALLAN POE · *The Tell-Tale Heart*
32. MARY KINGSLEY · *A Hippo Banquet*
33. JANE AUSTEN · *The Beautifull Cassandra*
34. ANTON CHEKHOV · *Gooseberries*
35. SAMUEL TAYLOR COLERIDGE · *Well, they are gone, and here must I remain*
36. JOHANN WOLFGANG VON GOETHE · *Sketchy, Doubtful, Incomplete Jottings*
37. CHARLES DICKENS · *The Great Winglebury Duel*
38. HERMAN MELVILLE · *The Maldive Shark*
39. ELIZABETH GASKELL · *The Old Nurse's Story*
40. NIKOLAY LESKOV · *The Steel Flea*

41. HONORÉ DE BALZAC · *The Atheist's Mass*
42. CHARLOTTE PERKINS GILMAN · *The Yellow Wall-Paper*
43. C.P. CAVAFY · *Remember, Body . . .*
44. FYODOR DOSTOEVSKY · *The Meek One*
45. GUSTAVE FLAUBERT · *A Simple Heart*
46. NIKOLAI GOGOL · *The Nose*
47. SAMUEL PEPYS · *The Great Fire of London*
48. EDITH WHARTON · *The Reckoning*
49. HENRY JAMES · *The Figure in the Carpet*
50. WILFRED OWEN · *Anthem For Doomed Youth*
51. WOLFGANG AMADEUS MOZART · *My Dearest Father*
52. PLATO · *Socrates' Defence*
53. CHRISTINA ROSSETTI · *Goblin Market*
54. *Sindbad the Sailor*
55. SOPHOCLES · *Antigone*
56. RYŪNOSUKE AKUTAGAWA · *The Life of a Stupid Man*
57. LEO TOLSTOY · *How Much Land Does A Man Need?*
58. GIORGIO VASARI · *Leonardo da Vinci*
59. OSCAR WILDE · *Lord Arthur Savile's Crime*
60. SHEN FU · *The Old Man of the Moon*
61. AESOP · *The Dolphins, the Whales and the Gudgeon*
62. MATSUO BASHŌ · *Lips too Chilled*
63. EMILY BRONTË · *The Night is Darkening Round Me*
64. JOSEPH CONRAD · *To-morrow*
65. RICHARD HAKLUYT · *The Voyage of Sir Francis Drake Around the Whole Globe*
66. KATE CHOPIN · *A Pair of Silk Stockings*
67. CHARLES DARWIN · *It was snowing butterflies*
68. BROTHERS GRIMM · *The Robber Bridegroom*
69. CATULLUS · *I Hate and I Love*
70. HOMER · *Circe and the Cyclops*
71. D. H. LAWRENCE · *Il Duro*
72. KATHERINE MANSFIELD · *Miss Brill*
73. OVID · *The Fall of Icarus*
74. SAPPHO · *Come Close*
75. IVAN TURGENEV · *Kasyan from the Beautiful Lands*
76. VIRGIL · *O Cruel Alexis*
77. H. G. WELLS · *A Slip under the Microscope*
78. HERODOTUS · *The Madness of Cambyses*
79. *Speaking of Siva*
80. *The Dhammapada*

'The proletarians have nothing to lose but their chains.'

KARL MARX
Born 1818, Trier, Prussia
Died 1883, London

FRIEDRICH ENGELS
Born 1820, Barmen, Prussia
Died 1895, London

Translation by Samuel Moore, first published 1888.

KARL MARX AND FRIEDRICH ENGELS
IN PENGUIN CLASSICS
The Communist Manifesto

KARL MARX IN PENGUIN CLASSICS
Capital
Dispatches for the New York Tribune
Early Writings
Grundrisse
The Portable Karl Marx
Revolution and War

KARL MARX and FRIEDRICH ENGELS

The Communist Manifesto

Translated by
Samuel Moore

PENGUIN BOOKS

PENGUIN CLASSICS

UK | USA | Canada | Ireland | Australia
India | New Zealand | South Africa

Penguin Books is part of the Penguin Random House group of companies
whose addresses can be found at global.penguinrandomhouse.com.

This edition published in Penguin Classics 2015

020

Set in 9.5/13 pt Baskerville 10 Pro
Typeset by Jouve (UK), Milton Keynes
Printed in Great Britain by Clays Ltd, Elcograf S.p.A

A CIP catalogue record for this book is available from the British Library

ISBN: 978-0-141-39798-6

www.greenpenguin.co.uk

Penguin Random House is committed to a
sustainable future for our business, our readers
and our planet. This book is made from Forest
Stewardship Council® certified paper.

Contents

THE MANIFESTO OF THE
COMMUNIST PARTY   1

1. Bourgeois and Proletarians   2
2. Proletarians and Communists   21
3. Socialist and Communist
   Literature   35
   I. *Reactionary Socialism*   35
       a) Feudal Socialism   35
       b) Petty-Bourgeois
          Socialism   37
       c) German, or 'True',
          Socialism   39
   II. *Conservative, or Bourgeois,
       Socialism*   44

III. *Critical-Utopian Socialism and Communism*   46

4. Position of the Communists in Relation to the Various Existing Opposition Parties   50

The Manifesto of the Communist Party

A spectre is haunting Europe – the spectre of Communism. All the Powers of old Europe have entered into a holy alliance to exorcize this spectre: Pope and Czar, Metternich and Guizot, French Radicals and German police spies.

Where is the party in opposition that has not been decried as Communistic by its opponents in power? Where the Opposition that has not hurled back the branding reproach of Communism, against the more advanced opposition parties, as well as against its reactionary adversaries?

Two things result from this fact:

I. Communism is already acknowledged by all European Powers to be itself a Power.

II. It is high time that Communists should openly, in the face of the whole world, publish their views, their aims, their tendencies, and meet this nursery tale of the Spectre of Communism with a Manifesto of the party itself.

To this end, Communists of various nationalities have assembled in London, and sketched the following Manifesto, to be published in the English, French, German, Italian, Flemish and Danish languages.

1. BOURGEOIS AND PROLETARIANS

The history of all hitherto existing society is the history of class struggles.

Freeman and slave, patrician and plebeian, lord and serf, guild-master and journeyman, in a word, oppressor and oppressed, stood in constant opposition to one another, carried on an uninterrupted, now hidden, now open fight, a fight that each time ended, either in a revolutionary reconstitution of society at large, or in the common ruin of the contending classes.

In the earlier epochs of history, we find almost everywhere a complicated arrangement of society into various orders, a manifold gradation of social rank. In ancient Rome we have patricians, knights, plebeians, slaves; in the Middle Ages, feudal lords, vassals, guild-masters, journeymen, apprentices, serfs; in almost all of these classes, again, subordinate gradations.

The modern bourgeois society that has sprouted from the ruins of feudal society has not done away with class antagonisms. It has but established new classes, new conditions of oppression, new forms of struggle in place of the old ones.

Bourgeois and Proletarians

Our epoch, the epoch of the bourgeoisie, possesses, however, this distinctive feature: it has simplified the class antagonisms. Society as a whole is more and more splitting up into two great hostile camps, into two great classes directly facing each other: Bourgeoisie and Proletariat.

From the serfs of the Middle Ages sprang the chartered burghers of the earliest towns. From these burgesses the first elements of the bourgeoisie were developed.

The discovery of America, the rounding of the Cape, opened up fresh ground for the rising bourgeoisie. The East-Indian and Chinese markets, the colonization of America, trade with the colonies, the increase in the means of exchange and in commodities generally, gave to commerce, to navigation, to industry, an impulse never before known, and thereby, to the revolutionary element in the tottering feudal society, a rapid development.

The feudal system of industry, under which industrial production was monopolized by closed guilds, now no longer sufficed for the growing wants of the new markets. The manufacturing system took its place. The guild-masters were pushed on one side by the manufacturing middle class; division of labour between the different corporate guilds vanished in the face of division of labour in each single workshop.

Meantime the markets kept ever growing, the demand ever rising. Even manufacture no longer sufficed.

Thereupon, steam and machinery revolutionized industrial production. The place of manufacture was taken by the giant, Modern Industry, the place of the industrial middle class, by industrial millionaires, the leaders of whole industrial armies, the modern bourgeois.

Modern industry has established the world market, for which the discovery of America paved the way. This market has given an immense development to commerce, to navigation, to communication by land. This development has, in its turn, reacted on the extension of industry; and in proportion as industry, commerce, navigation, railways extended, in the same proportion the bourgeoisie developed, increased its capital, and pushed into the background every class handed down from the Middle Ages.

We see, therefore, how the modern bourgeoisie is itself the product of a long course of development, of a series of revolutions in the modes of production and of exchange.

Each step in the development of the bourgeoisie was accompanied by a corresponding political advance of that class. An oppressed class under the sway of the feudal nobility, an armed and self-governing association in the medieval commune; here independent urban republic (as in Italy and Germany), there taxable 'third estate' of the monarchy (as in France), afterwards, in the period of manufacture proper, serving either the semi-feudal or the absolute monarchy as a counterpoise against the nobility, and, in fact, corner-stone of the great monarchies in general, the bourgeoisie has at last, since the establishment of Modern Industry and of the world market, conquered for itself, in the modern representative State, exclusive political sway. The executive of the modern State is but a committee for managing the common affairs of the whole bourgeoisie.

The bourgeoisie, historically, has played a most revolutionary part.

The bourgeoisie, wherever it has got the upper hand, has put an end to all feudal, patriarchal, idyllic relations. It has pitilessly torn asunder the motley feudal ties that bound man to his 'natural superiors', and has left remaining no other nexus between man and man than naked self-interest, than callous 'cash payment'. It has drowned the most heavenly ecstasies of religious fervour, of chivalrous enthusiasm, of philistine sentimentalism, in the icy water of egotistical calculation. It has resolved personal worth into exchange value, and in place of the numberless indefeasible chartered freedoms, has set up that single, unconscionable freedom – Free Trade. In one word, for exploitation, veiled by religious and political illusions, it has substituted naked, shameless, direct, brutal exploitation.

The bourgeoisie has stripped of its halo every occupation hitherto honoured and looked up to with reverent awe. It has converted the physician, the lawyer, the priest, the poet, the man of science, into its paid wage-labourers.

The bourgeoisie has torn away from the family its sentimental veil, and has reduced the family relation to a mere money relation.

The bourgeoisie has disclosed how it came to pass that the brutal display of vigour in the Middle Ages, which Reactionists so much admire, found its fitting complement in the most slothful indolence. It has been the first to show what man's activity can bring about. It has accomplished wonders far surpassing Egyptian pyramids, Roman aqueducts, and Gothic cathedrals; it has conducted expeditions that put in the shade all former Exoduses of nations and crusades.

The bourgeoisie cannot exist without constantly revolutionizing the instruments of production, and thereby the relations of production, and with them the whole relations of society. Conservation of the old modes of production in unaltered form, was, on the contrary, the first condition of existence for all earlier industrial classes. Constant revolutionizing of production, uninterrupted disturbance of all social conditions, everlasting uncertainty and agitation distinguish the bourgeois epoch from all earlier ones. All fixed, fast-frozen relations, with their train of ancient and venerable prejudices and opinions are swept away, all new-formed ones become antiquated before they can ossify. All that is solid melts into air, all that is holy is profaned, and man is at last compelled to face with sober senses, his real conditions of life, and his relations with his kind.

Bourgeois and Proletarians

The need of a constantly expanding market for its products chases the bourgeoisie over the whole surface of the globe. It must nestle everywhere, settle everywhere, establish connexions everywhere.

The bourgeoisie has through its exploitation of the world market given a cosmopolitan character to production and consumption in every country. To the great chagrin of Reactionists, it has drawn from under the feet of industry the national ground on which it stood. All old-established national industries have been destroyed or are daily being destroyed. They are dislodged by new industries, whose introduction becomes a life and death question for all civilized nations, by industries that no longer work up indigenous raw material, but raw material drawn from the remotest zones; industries whose products are consumed, not only at home, but in every quarter of the globe. In place of the old wants, satisfied by the productions of the country, we find new wants, requiring for their satisfaction the products of distant lands and climes. In place of the old local and national seclusion and self-sufficiency, we have intercourse in every direction, universal inter-dependence of nations. And as in material, so also in intellectual production. The intellectual creations of individual nations become common property. National one-sidedness and narrow-mindedness become more and more impossible, and from the numerous national and local literatures, there arises a world literature.

The bourgeoisie, by the rapid improvement of all instruments of production, by the immensely facilitated means of communication, draws all, even the most barbarian, nations into civilization. The cheap prices of its commodities are the heavy artillery with which it batters down all Chinese walls, with which it forces 'the barbarians'' intensely obstinate hatred of foreigners to capitulate. It compels all nations, on pain of extinction, to adopt the bourgeois mode of production; it compels them to introduce what it calls civilization into their midst, i.e., to become bourgeois themselves. In one word, it creates a world after its own image.

The bourgeoisie has subjected the country to the rule of the towns. It has created enormous cities, has greatly increased the urban population as compared with the rural, and has thus rescued a considerable part of the population from the idiocy of rural life. Just as it has made the country dependent on the towns, so it has made barbarian and semi-barbarian countries dependent on the civilized ones, nations of peasants on nations of bourgeois, the East on the West.

The bourgeoisie keeps more and more doing away with the scattered state of the population, of the means of production, and of property. It has agglomerated population, centralized means of production, and has concentrated property in a few hands. The necessary consequence of this was political centralization. Independent, or but loosely connected, provinces with separate interests, laws, governments and systems of taxation, became lumped together into one nation, with one government, one code of laws, one national class-interest, one frontier and one customs-tariff.

The bourgeoisie, during its rule of scarce one hundred years, has created more massive and more colossal productive forces than have all preceding generations together. Subjection of Nature's forces to man, machinery, application of chemistry to industry and agriculture, steam-navigation, railways, electric telegraphs, clearing of whole continents for cultivation, canalization of rivers, whole populations conjured out of the ground – what earlier century had even a presentiment that such productive forces slumbered in the lap of social labour?

We see then: the means of production and of exchange, on whose foundation the bourgeoisie built itself up, were generated in feudal society. At a certain stage in the development of these means of production and of exchange, the conditions under which feudal society produced and exchanged, the feudal organization of agriculture and manufacturing industry, in one word, the feudal relations of property became no longer compatible with the already developed productive forces; they became so many fetters. They had to be burst asunder; they were burst asunder.

Into their place stepped free competition, accompanied

by a social and political constitution adapted to it, and by the economical and political sway of the bourgeois class.

A similar movement is going on before our own eyes. Modern bourgeois society with its relations of production, of exchange and of property, a society that has conjured up such gigantic means of production and of exchange, is like the sorcerer, who is no longer able to control the powers of the nether world whom he has called up by his spells. For many a decade past the history of industry and commerce is but the history of the revolt of modern productive forces against modern conditions of production, against the property relations that are the conditions for the existence of the bourgeoisie and of its rule. It is enough to mention the commercial crises that by their periodical return put on its trial, each time more threateningly, the existence of the entire bourgeois society. In these crises a great part not only of the existing products, but also of the previously created productive forces, are periodically destroyed. In these crises there breaks out an epidemic that, in all earlier epochs, would have seemed an absurdity – the epidemic of overproduction. Society suddenly finds itself put back into a state of momentary barbarism; it appears as if a famine, a universal war of devastation had cut off the supply of every means of subsistence; industry and commerce seem to be destroyed; and why? Because there is too much civilization, too much means of subsistence, too much industry, too much commerce. The productive forces at the disposal of society no longer tend to further the development of the conditions of bourgeois property; on the contrary, they have become too powerful for these conditions, by which they are fettered, and so soon as they overcome these fetters, they bring disorder into the whole of bourgeois society, endanger the existence of bourgeois property. The conditions of bourgeois society are too narrow to comprise the wealth created by them. And how does the bourgeoisie get over these crises? On the one hand by enforced destruction of a mass of productive forces; on the other, by the conquest of new markets, and by the more thorough exploitation of the old ones. That is to say, by paving the way for more extensive and more destructive crises, and by diminishing the means whereby crises are prevented.

The weapons with which the bourgeoisie felled feudalism to the ground are now turned against the bourgeoisie itself.

But not only has the bourgeoisie forged the weapons that bring death to itself; it has also called into existence the men who are to wield those weapons – the modern working class – the proletarians.

In proportion as the bourgeoisie, i.e., capital, is developed, in the same proportion is the proletariat, the modern working class, developed – a class of labourers, who live only so long as they find work, and who find work only so long as their labour increases capital. These labourers, who must sell themselves piecemeal, are a commodity, like every other article of commerce, and are consequently exposed to all the vicissitudes of competition, to all the fluctuations of the market.

Owing to the extensive use of machinery and to division of labour, the work of the proletarians has lost all individual character, and, consequently, all charm for the workman. He becomes an appendage of the machine, and it is only the most simple, most monotonous, and most easily acquired knack, that is required of him. Hence, the cost of production of a workman is restricted, almost entirely, to the means of subsistence that he requires for his maintenance, and for the propagation of his race. But the price of a commodity, and therefore also of labour, is equal to its cost of production. In proportion, therefore, as the repulsiveness of the work increases, the wage decreases. Nay more, in proportion as the use of machinery and division of labour increases, in the same proportion the burden of toil also increases, whether by prolongation of the working hours, by increase of the work exacted in a given time or by increased speed of the machinery, etc.

Modern industry has converted the little workshop of the patriarchal master into the great factory of the industrial capitalist. Masses of labourers, crowded into the factory, are organized like soldiers. As privates of the industrial army they are placed under the command of a perfect hierarchy of officers and sergeants. Not only are

Bourgeois and Proletarians

they slaves of the bourgeois class, and of the bourgeois State; they are daily and hourly enslaved by the machine, by the overlooker, and, above all, by the individual bourgeois manufacturer himself. The more openly this despotism proclaims gain to be its end and aim, the more petty, the more hateful and the more embittering it is.

The less the skill and exertion of strength implied in manual labour, in other words, the more modern industry becomes developed, the more is the labour of men superseded by that of women. Differences of age and sex have no longer any distinctive social validity for the working class. All are instruments of labour, more or less expensive to use, according to their age and sex.

No sooner is the exploitation of the labourer by the manufacturer, so far, at an end, that he receives his wages in cash, than he is set upon by the other portions of the bourgeoisie, the landlord, the shopkeeper, the pawnbroker, etc.

The lower strata of the middle class – the small tradespeople, shopkeepers, and retired tradesmen generally, the handicraftsmen and peasants – all these sink gradually into the proletariat, partly because their diminutive capital does not suffice for the scale on which Modern Industry is carried on, and is swamped in the competition with the large capitalists, partly because their specialized skill is rendered worthless by new methods of production. Thus the proletariat is recruited from all classes of the population.

Karl Marx and Friedrich Engels

The proletariat goes through various stages of development. With its birth begins its struggle with the bourgeoisie. At first the contest is carried on by individual labourers, then by the work-people of a factory, then by the operatives of one trade, in one locality, against the individual bourgeois who directly exploits them. They direct their attacks not against the bourgeois conditions of production, but against the instruments of production themselves; they destroy imported wares that compete with their labour, they smash to pieces machinery, they set factories ablaze, they seek to restore by force the vanished status of the workman of the Middle Ages.

At this stage the labourers still form an incoherent mass scattered over the whole country, and broken up by their mutual competition. If anywhere they unite to form more compact bodies, this is not yet the consequence of their own active union, but of the union of the bourgeoisie, which class, in order to attain its own political ends, is compelled to set the whole proletariat in motion, and is moreover yet, for a time, able to do so. At this stage, therefore, the proletarians do not fight their enemies, but the enemies of their enemies, the remnants of absolute monarchy, the landowners, the non-industrial bourgeois, the petty bourgeoisie. Thus the whole historical movement is concentrated in the hands of the bourgeoisie; every victory so obtained is a victory for the bourgeoisie.

But with the development of industry the proletariat not only increases in number; it becomes concentrated

Bourgeois and Proletarians

in greater masses, its strength grows, and it feels that strength more. The various interests and conditions of life within the ranks of the proletariat are more and more equalized, in proportion as machinery obliterates all distinctions of labour, and nearly everywhere reduces wages to the same low level. The growing competition among the bourgeois, and the resulting commercial crises, make the wages of the workers ever more fluctuating. The unceasing improvement of machinery, ever more rapidly developing, makes their livelihood more and more precarious; the collisions between individual workmen and individual bourgeois take more and more the character of collisions between two classes. Thereupon the workers begin to form combinations (Trades Unions) against the bourgeois; they club together in order to keep up the rate of wages; they found permanent associations in order to make provision beforehand for these occasional revolts. Here and there the contest breaks out into riots.

Now and then the workers are victorious, but only for a time. The real fruit of their battles lies, not in the immediate result, but in the ever-expanding union of the workers. This union is helped on by the improved means of communication that are created by modern industry and that place the workers of different localities in contact with one another. It was just this contact that was needed to centralize the numerous local struggles, all of the same character, into one national struggle between classes. But every class struggle is a political struggle. And that union, to attain which the burghers of the Middle Ages, with their miserable highways, required centuries, the modern proletarians, thanks to railways, achieve in a few years.

This organization of the proletarians into a class, and consequently into a political party, is continually being upset again by the competition between the workers themselves. But it ever rises up again, stronger, firmer, mightier. It compels legislative recognition of particular interests of the workers, by taking advantage of the division among the bourgeoisie itself. Thus the Ten Hours bill in England was carried.

Altogether collisions between the classes of the old society further, in many ways, the course of development of the proletariat. The bourgeoisie finds itself involved in a constant battle. At first with the aristocracy; later on, with those portions of the bourgeoisie itself, whose interests have become antagonistic to the progress of industry; at all times, with the bourgeoisie of foreign countries. In all these battles it sees itself compelled to appeal to the proletariat, to ask for its help, and thus, to drag it into the political arena. The bourgeoisie itself, therefore, supplies the proletariat with its own elements of political and general education, in other words, it furnishes the proletariat with weapons for fighting the bourgeoisie.

Further, as we have already seen, entire sections of the ruling classes are, by the advance of industry, precipitated into the proletariat, or are at least threatened in their conditions of existence. These also supply the proletariat with fresh elements of enlightenment and progress.

Finally, in times when the class struggle nears the decisive hour, the process of dissolution going on within the ruling class, in fact within the whole range of old society, assumes such a violent, glaring character, that a small section of the ruling class cuts itself adrift, and joins the revolutionary class, the class that holds the future in its hands. Just as, therefore, at an earlier period, a section of the nobility went over to the bourgeoisie, so now a portion of the bourgeoisie goes over to the proletariat, and in particular, a portion of the bourgeois ideologists, who have raised themselves to the level of comprehending theoretically the historical movement as a whole.

Of all the classes that stand face to face with the bourgeoisie today, the proletariat alone is a really revolutionary class. The other classes decay and finally disappear in the face of modern industry; the proletariat is its special and essential product.

The lower middle class, the small manufacturer, the shop-keeper, the artisan, the peasant, all these fight against the bourgeoisie, to save from extinction their existence as fractions of the middle class. They are therefore not revolutionary, but conservative. Nay more, they are reactionary, for they try to roll back the wheel of history. If by chance they are revolutionary, they are so only in view of their impending transfer into the proletariat, they thus defend not their present, but their future interests, they desert their own standpoint to place themselves at that of the proletariat.

The 'dangerous class', the social scum, that passively rotting mass thrown off by the lowest layers of old society, may, here and there, be swept into the movement by a proletarian revolution; its conditions of life, however, prepare it far more for the part of a bribed tool of reactionary intrigue.

In the conditions of the proletariat, those of old society at large are already virtually swamped. The proletarian is without property; his relation to his wife and children has no longer anything in common with the bourgeois family relations; modern industrial labour, modern subjection to capital, the same in England as in France, in America as in Germany, has stripped him of every trace of national character. Law, morality, religion, are to him so many bourgeois prejudices, behind which lurk in ambush just as many bourgeois interests.

All the preceding classes that got the upper hand sought to fortify their already acquired status by subjecting society at large to their conditions of appropriation. The proletarians cannot become masters of the productive forces of society, except by abolishing their own previous mode of appropriation, and thereby also every other previous mode of appropriation. They have nothing of their own to secure and to fortify; their mission is to destroy all previous securities for, and insurances of, individual property.

Bourgeois and Proletarians

All previous historical movements were movements of minorities, or in the interest of minorities. The proletarian movement is the self-conscious, independent movement of the immense majority, in the interest of the immense majority. The proletariat, the lowest stratum of our present society, cannot stir, cannot raise itself up, without the whole superincumbent strata of official society being sprung into the air.

Though not in substance, yet in form, the struggle of the proletariat with the bourgeoisie is at first a national struggle. The proletariat of each country must, of course, first of all settle matters with its own bourgeoisie.

In depicting the most general phases of the development of the proletariat, we traced the more or less veiled civil war, raging within existing society, up to the point where that war breaks out into open revolution, and where the violent overthrow of the bourgeoisie lays the foundation for the sway of the proletariat.

Hitherto, every form of society has been based, as we have already seen, on the antagonism of oppressing and oppressed classes. But in order to oppress a class, certain conditions must be assured to it under which it can, at least, continue its slavish existence. The serf, in the period of serfdom, raised himself to membership in the commune, just as the petty bourgeois, under the yoke of feudal absolutism, managed to develop into a bourgeois. The modern labourer, on the contrary, instead of rising with the progress of industry, sinks deeper and deeper below the conditions of existence of his own class. He becomes a pauper, and pauperism develops more rapidly than population and wealth. And here it becomes evident, that the bourgeoisie is unfit any longer to be the ruling class in society, and to impose its conditions of existence upon society as an overriding law. It is unfit to rule because it is incompetent to assure an existence to its slave within his slavery, because it cannot help letting him sink into such a state, that it has to feed him, instead of being fed by him. Society can no longer live under this bourgeoisie, in other words, its existence is no longer compatible with society.

The essential condition for the existence, and for the sway of the bourgeois class, is the formation and augmentation of capital; the condition for capital is wage labour. Wage labour rests exclusively on competition between the labourers. The advance of industry, whose involuntary promoter is the bourgeoisie, replaces the isolation of the labourers, due to competition, by their revolutionary combination, due to association. The development of Modern Industry, therefore, cuts from under its feet the very foundation on which the bourgeoisie produces and appropriates products. What the bourgeoisie, therefore, produces, above all, is its own grave-diggers. Its fall and the victory of the proletariat are equally inevitable.

2. PROLETARIANS AND COMMUNISTS

In what relation do the Communists stand to the proletarians as a whole?

The Communists do not form a separate party opposed to other working-class parties.

They have no interests separate and apart from those of the proletariat as a whole.

They do not set up any sectarian principles of their own, by which to shape and mould the proletarian movement.

The Communists are distinguished from the other working-class parties by this only: 1. In the national struggles of the proletarians of the different countries, they point out and bring to the front the common interests of the entire proletariat, independently of all nationality. 2. In the various stages of development which the struggle of the working class against the bourgeoisie has to pass through, they always and everywhere represent the interests of the movement as a whole.

The Communists, therefore, are on the one hand, practically, the most advanced and resolute section of the working-class parties of every country, that section which pushes forward all others; on the other hand, theoretically, they have over the great mass of the proletariat the advantage of clearly understanding the line of march, the conditions, and the ultimate general results of the proletarian movement.

The immediate aim of the Communists is the same as that of all the other proletarian parties: formation of the proletariat into a class, overthrow of the bourgeois supremacy, conquest of political power by the proletariat.

The theoretical conclusions of the Communists are in no way based on ideas or principles that have been invented, or discovered, by this or that would-be universal reformer.

They merely express, in general terms, actual relations springing from an existing class struggle, from a historical movement going on under our very eyes. The abolition of existing property relations is not at all a distinctive feature of Communism.

All property relations in the past have continually been subject to historical change consequent upon the change in historical conditions.

The French Revolution, for example, abolished feudal property in favour of bourgeois property.

The distinguishing feature of Communism is not the abolition of property generally, but the abolition of bourgeois property. But modern bourgeois private property is the final and most complete expression of the system of producing and appropriating products, that is based on class antagonisms, on the exploitation of the many by the few.

Proletarians and Communists

In this sense, the theory of the Communists may be summed up in the single sentence: Abolition of private property.

We Communists have been reproached with the desire of abolishing the right of personally acquiring property as the fruit of a man's own labour, which property is alleged to be the ground work of all personal freedom, activity and independence.

Hard-won, self-acquired, self-earned property! Do you mean the property of the petty artisan and of the small peasant, a form of property that preceded the bourgeois form? There is no need to abolish that; the development of industry has to a great extent already destroyed it, and is still destroying it daily.

Or do you mean modern bourgeois private property?

But does wage labour create any property for the labourer? Not a bit. It creates capital, i.e., that kind of property which exploits wage labour, and which cannot increase except upon condition of begetting a new supply of wage labour for fresh exploitation. Property, in its present form, is based on the antagonism of capital and wage labour. Let us examine both sides of this antagonism.

To be a capitalist is to have not only a purely personal but a social *status* in production. Capital is a collective product, and only by the united action of many members, nay, in the last resort, only by the united action of all members of society, can it be set in motion.

Capital is, therefore, not a personal, it is a social power.

When, therefore, capital is converted into common property, into the property of all members of society, personal property is not thereby transformed into social property. It is only the social character of the property that is changed. It loses its class character.

Let us now take wage labour.

The average price of wage labour is the minimum wage, i.e., that quantum of the means of subsistence which is absolutely requisite to keep the labourer in bare existence as a labourer. What, therefore, the wage-labourer appropriates by means of his labour, merely suffices to prolong and reproduce a bare existence. We by no means intend to abolish this personal appropriation of the products of labour, an appropriation that is made for the maintenance and reproduction of human life, and that leaves no surplus wherewith to command the labour of others. All that we want to do away with is the miserable character of this appropriation, under which the labourer lives merely to increase capital, and is allowed to live only in so far as the interest of the ruling class requires it.

In bourgeois society, living labour is but a means to increase accumulated labour. In Communist society, accumulated labour is but a means to widen, to enrich, to promote the existence of the labourer.

In bourgeois society, therefore, the past dominates the present: in Communist society, the present dominates the past. In bourgeois society capital is independent and has individuality, while the living person is dependent and has no individuality.

And the abolition of this state of things is called by the bourgeois, abolition of individuality and freedom! And rightly so. The abolition of bourgeois individuality, bourgeois independence, and bourgeois freedom is undoubtedly aimed at.

By freedom is meant, under the present bourgeois conditions of production, free trade, free selling and buying.

But if selling and buying disappears, free selling and buying disappears also. This talk about free selling and buying, and all the other 'brave words' of our bourgeoisie about freedom in general, have a meaning, if any, only in contrast with restricted selling and buying, with the fettered traders of the Middle Ages, but have no meaning when opposed to the Communistic abolition of buying and selling, of the bourgeois conditions of production, and of the bourgeoisie itself.

You are horrified at our intending to do away with private property. But in your existing society, private property is already done away with for nine-tenths of the population; its existence for the few is solely due to its non-existence in the hands of those nine-tenths. You reproach us, therefore, with intending to do away with a form of property the necessary condition for whose existence is the non-existence of any property for the immense majority of society.

In one word, you reproach us with intending to do away with your property. Precisely so; that is just what we intend.

From the moment when labour can no longer be converted into capital, money, or rent, into a social power capable of being monopolized, i.e., from the moment when individual property can no longer be transformed into bourgeois property, into capital, from that moment, you say, individuality vanishes.

You must, therefore, confess that by 'individual' you mean no other person than the bourgeois, than the middle-class owner of property. This person must, indeed, be swept out of the way, and made impossible.

Communism deprives no man of the power to appropriate the products of society; all that it does is to deprive him of the power to subjugate the labour of others by means of such appropriation.

It has been objected that upon the abolition of private property all work will cease, and universal laziness will overtake us.

According to this, bourgeois society ought long ago to have gone to the dogs through sheer idleness; for those of its members who work, acquire nothing, and those who acquire anything, do not work. The whole of this objection is but another expression of the tautology: that there can no longer be any wage labour when there is no longer any capital.

Proletarians and Communists

All objections urged against the Communistic mode of producing and appropriating material products, have, in the same way, been urged against the Communistic modes of producing and appropriating intellectual products. Just as, to the bourgeois, the disappearance of class property is the disappearance of production itself, so the disappearance of class culture is to him identical with the disappearance of all culture.

That culture, the loss of which he laments, is, for the enormous majority, a mere training to act as a machine.

But don't wrangle with us so long as you apply, to our intended abolition of bourgeois property, the standard of your bourgeois notions of freedom, culture, law, &c. Your very ideas are but the outgrowth of the conditions of your bourgeois production and bourgeois property, just as your jurisprudence is but the will of your class made into a law for all, a will, whose essential character and direction are determined by the economical conditions of existence of your class.

The selfish misconception that induces you to transform into eternal laws of nature and of reason, the social forms springing from your present mode of production and form of property – historical relations that rise and disappear in the progress of production – this misconception you share with every ruling class that has preceded you. What you see clearly in the case of ancient property, what you admit in the case of feudal property, you are of course forbidden to admit in the case of your own bourgeois form of property.

Abolition of the family! Even the most radical flare up at this infamous proposal of the Communists.

On what foundation is the present family, the bourgeois family, based? On capital, on private gain. In its completely developed form this family exists only among the bourgeoisie. But this state of things finds its complement in the practical absence of the family among the proletarians, and in public prostitution. The bourgeois family will vanish as a matter of course when its complement vanishes, and both will vanish with the vanishing of capital.

Do you charge us with wanting to stop the exploitation of children by their parents? To this crime we plead guilty.

But, you will say, we destroy the most hallowed of relations, when we replace home education by social.

And your education! Is not that also social, and determined by the social conditions under which you educate, by the intervention, direct or indirect, of society, by means of schools, &c? The Communists have not invented the intervention of society in education; they do but seek to alter the character of that intervention, and to rescue education from the influence of the ruling class.

The bourgeois clap-trap about the family and education, about the hallowed co-relation of parent and child, becomes all the more disgusting, the more, by the action of Modern Industry, all family ties among the proletarians

Proletarians and Communists

are torn asunder, and their children transformed into simple articles of commerce and instruments of labour.

But you Communists would introduce community of women, screams the whole bourgeoisie in chorus.

The bourgeois sees in his wife a mere instrument of production. He hears that the instruments of production are to be exploited in common, and, naturally, can come to no other conclusion than that the lot of being common to all will likewise fall to the women.

He has not even a suspicion that the real point aimed at is to do away with the status of women as mere instruments of production.

For the rest, nothing is more ridiculous than the virtuous indignation of our bourgeois at the community of women which, they pretend, is to be openly and officially established by the Communists. The Communists have no need to introduce community of women; it has existed almost from time immemorial.

Our bourgeois, not content with having the wives and daughters of their proletarians at their disposal, not to speak of common prostitutes, take the greatest pleasure in seducing each other's wives.

Bourgeois marriage is in reality a system of wives in common and thus, at the most, what the Communists might possibly be reproached with, is that they desire to introduce, in substitution for a hypocritically concealed, an openly legalized community of women. For the rest, it is self-evident that the abolition of the present system of production must bring with it the abolition of the community of women springing from that system, i.e., of prostitution both public and private.

The Communists are further reproached with desiring to abolish countries and nationality.

The working men have no country. We cannot take from them what they have not got. Since the proletariat must first of all acquire political supremacy, must rise to be the leading class of the nation, must constitute itself *the* nation, it is, so far, itself national, though not in the bourgeois sense of the word.

National differences and antagonisms between peoples are daily more and more vanishing, owing to the development of the bourgeoisie, to freedom of commerce, to the world market, to uniformity in the mode of production and in the conditions of life corresponding thereto.

The supremacy of the proletariat will cause them to vanish still faster. United action, of the leading civilized countries at least, is one of the first conditions for the emancipation of the proletariat.

In proportion as the exploitation of one individual by another is put an end to, the exploitation of one nation by another will also be put an end to. In proportion as the antagonism between classes within the nation vanishes, the hostility of one nation to another will come to an end.

Proletarians and Communists

The charges against Communism made from a religious, a philosophical, and, generally, from an ideological standpoint, are not deserving of serious examination.

Does it require deep intuition to comprehend that man's ideas, views and conceptions, in one word, man's consciousness, changes with every change in the conditions of his material existence, in his social relations and in his social life?

What else does the history of ideas prove, than that intellectual production changes in character in proportion as material production is changed? The ruling ideas of each age have ever been the ideas of its ruling class.

When people speak of ideas that revolutionize society, they do but express the fact, that within the old society, the elements of a new one have been created, and that the dissolution of the old ideas keeps even pace with the dissolution of the old conditions of existence.

When the ancient world was in its last throes, the ancient religions were overcome by Christianity. When Christian ideas succumbed in the eighteenth century to rationalist ideas, feudal society fought its death battle with the then revolutionary bourgeoisie. The ideas of religious liberty and freedom of conscience, merely gave expression to the sway of free competition within the domain of knowledge.

'Undoubtedly,' it will be said, 'religious, moral, philosophical and juridical ideas have been modified in the course of historical development. But religion, morality, philosophy, political science, and law, constantly survived this change.

'There are, besides, eternal truths, such as Freedom, Justice, etc., that are common to all states of society. But Communism abolishes eternal truths, it abolishes all religion, and all morality, instead of constituting them on a new basis; it therefore acts in contradiction to all past historical experience.'

What does this accusation reduce itself to? The history of all past society has consisted in the development of class antagonisms, antagonisms that assumed different forms at different epochs.

But whatever form they may have taken, one fact is common to all past ages, viz., the exploitation of one part of society by the other. No wonder, then, that the social consciousness of past ages, despite all the multiplicity and variety it displays, moves within certain common forms, or general ideas, which cannot completely vanish except with the total disappearance of class antagonisms.

The Communist revolution is the most radical rupture with traditional property relations; no wonder that its development involves the most radical rupture with traditional ideas.

But let us have done with the bourgeois objections to Communism.

We have seen above, that the first step in the revolution by the working class, is to raise the proletariat to the position of ruling class, to win the battle of democracy.

Proletarians and Communists

The proletariat will use its political supremacy to wrest, by degrees, all capital from the bourgeoisie, to centralize all instruments of production in the hands of the State, i.e., of the proletariat organized as the ruling class; and to increase the total of productive forces as rapidly as possible.

Of course, in the beginning, this cannot be effected except by means of despotic inroads on the rights of property, and on the conditions of bourgeois production; by means of measures, therefore, which appear economically insufficient and untenable, but which, in the course of the movement, outstrip themselves, necessitate further inroads upon the old social order, and are unavoidable as a means of entirely revolutionizing the mode of production.

These measures will of course be different in different countries.

Nevertheless, in the most advanced countries, the following will be pretty generally applicable:

1. Abolition of property in land and application of all rents of land to public purposes.
2. A heavy progressive or graduated income tax.
3. Abolition of all right of inheritance.
4. Confiscation of the property of all emigrants and rebels.
5. Centralization of credit in the hands of the State, by means of a national bank with State capital and an exclusive monopoly.

6. Centralization of the means of communication and transport in the hands of the State.
7. Extension of factories and instruments of production owned by the State; the bringing into cultivation of wastelands, and the improvement of the soil generally in accordance with a common plan.
8. Equal liability of all to labour. Establishment of industrial armies, especially for agriculture.
9. Combination of agriculture with manufacturing industries; gradual abolition of the distinction between town and country, by a more equable distribution of the population over the country.
10. Free education for all children in public schools. Abolition of children's factory labour in its present form. Combination of education with industrial production, &c., &c.

When, in the course of development, class distinctions have disappeared, and all production has been concentrated in the hands of a vast association of the whole nation, the public power will lose its political character. Political power, properly so called, is merely the organized power of one class for oppressing another. If the proletariat during its contest with the bourgeoisie is compelled, by the force of circumstances, to organize itself as a class, if, by means of a revolution, it makes itself the ruling class, and, as such, sweeps away by force the old conditions of production, then it will, along with these conditions, have swept away the conditions for the existence of class antagonisms and of classes generally, and will thereby have abolished its own supremacy as a class.

In place of the old bourgeois society, with its classes and class antagonisms, we shall have an association, in which the free development of each is the condition for the free development of all.

3. SOCIALIST AND COMMUNIST LITERATURE

I. Reactionary Socialism

a. Feudal Socialism

Owing to their historical position, it became the vocation of the aristocracies of France and England to write pamphlets against modern bourgeois society. In the French revolution of July 1830, and in the English reform agitation, these aristocracies again succumbed to the hateful upstart. Thenceforth, a serious political contest was altogether out of question. A literary battle alone remained possible. But even in the domain of literature the old cries of the restoration period had become impossible.

In order to arouse sympathy, the aristocracy were obliged to lose sight, apparently, of their own interests, and to formulate their indictment against the bourgeoisie in the interest of the exploited working class alone. Thus the aristocracy took their revenge by singing lampoons on their new master, and whispering in his ears sinister prophecies of coming catastrophe.

In this way arose feudal Socialism: half lamentation, half lampoon: half echo of the past, half menace of the future; at times, by its bitter, witty and incisive criticism, striking the bourgeoisie to the very heart's core; but always ludicrous in its effect, through total incapacity to comprehend the march of modern history.

The aristocracy, in order to rally the people to them, waved the proletarian alms-bag in front for a banner. But the people, so often as it joined them, saw on their hindquarters the old feudal coats of arms, and deserted with loud and irreverent laughter.

One section of the French Legitimists and 'Young England' exhibited this spectacle.

In pointing out that their mode of exploitation was different to that of the bourgeoisie, the feudalists forget that they exploited under circumstances and conditions that were quite different, and that are now antiquated. In showing that, under their rule, the modern proletariat never existed, they forget that the modern bourgeoisie is the necessary offspring of their own form of society.

For the rest, so little do they conceal the reactionary character of their criticism that their chief accusation against the bourgeoisie amounts to this, that under the bourgeois *régime* a class is being developed, which is destined to cut up root and branch the old order of society.

What they upbraid the bourgeoisie with is not so much that it creates a proletariat, as that it creates a revolutionary proletariat.

In political practice, therefore, they join in all coercive measures against the working class; and in ordinary life, despite their high-falutin phrases, they stoop to pick up the golden apples dropped from the tree of industry, and to barter truth, love, honour for traffic in wool, beetroot-sugar, and potato spirits.

As the parson has ever gone hand in hand with the landlord, so has Clerical Socialism with Feudal Socialism.

Nothing is easier than to give Christian asceticism a Socialist tinge. Has not Christianity declaimed against private property, against marriage, against the State? Has it not preached in the place of these, charity and poverty, celibacy and mortification of the flesh, monastic life and Mother Church? Christian Socialism is but the holy water with which the priest consecrates the heart-burnings of the aristocrat.

b. Petty-Bourgeois Socialism

The feudal aristocracy was not the only class that was ruined by the bourgeoisie, not the only class whose conditions of existence pined and perished in the atmosphere of modern bourgeois society. The medieval burgesses and the small peasant proprietors were the precursors of the modern bourgeoisie. In those countries which are but little developed, industrially and commercially, these two classes still vegetate side by side with the rising bourgeoisie.

In countries where modern civilization has become fully developed, a new class of petty bourgeois has been formed, fluctuating between proletariat and bourgeoisie and ever renewing itself as a supplementary part of bourgeois society. The individual members of this class, however, are being constantly hurled down into the proletariat by the action of competition, and, as modern industry develops, they even see the moment approaching when they will completely disappear as an independent section of modern society, to be replaced, in manufacture, agriculture and commerce, by overlookers, bailiffs and shopmen.

In countries like France, where the peasants constitute far more than half of the population, it was natural that writers who sided with the proletariat against the bourgeoisie, should use, in their criticism of the bourgeois *régime*, the standard of the peasant and petty bourgeois, and from the standpoint of these intermediate classes should take up the cudgels for the working class. Thus arose petty-bourgeois Socialism. Sismondi was the head of this school, not only in France but also in England.

This school of Socialism dissected with great acuteness the contradictions in the conditions of modern production.

It laid bare the hypocritical apologies of economists. It proved, incontrovertibly, the disastrous effects of machinery and division of labour; the concentration of capital and land in a few hands; over-production and crises; it pointed out the inevitable ruin of the petty bourgeois and peasant, the misery of the proletariat, the anarchy in production, the crying inequalities in the distribution of wealth, the industrial war of extermination between nations, the dissolution of old moral bonds, of the old family relations, of the old nationalities.

In its positive aims, however, this form of Socialism aspires either to restoring the old means of production and of exchange, and with them the old property relations, and the old society, or to cramping the modern means of production and of exchange, within the framework of the old property relations that have been, and were bound to be, exploded by those means. In either case, it is both reactionary and Utopian.

Its last words are: corporate guilds for manufacture; patriarchal relations in agriculture.

Ultimately, when stubborn historical facts had dispersed all intoxicating effects of self-deception, this form of Socialism ended in a miserable fit of the blues.

c. German, or 'True', Socialism

The Socialist and Communist literature of France, a literature that originated under the pressure of a bourgeoisie in power, and that was the expression of the struggle against this power, was introduced into Germany at a time when the bourgeoisie, in that country, had just begun its contest with feudal absolutism.

German philosophers, would-be philosophers, and *beaux esprits*, eagerly seized on this literature, only forgetting, that when these writings immigrated from France into Germany, French social conditions had not immigrated along with them. In contact with German social conditions, this French literature lost all its immediate practical significance, and assumed a purely literary aspect. Thus, to the German philosophers of the Eighteenth Century, the demands of the first French Revolution were nothing more than the demands of 'Practical Reason' in general, and the utterance of the will of the revolutionary French bourgeoisie signified in their eyes the laws of pure Will, of Will as it was bound to be, of true human Will generally.

The work of the German *literati* consisted solely in bringing the new French ideas into harmony with their ancient philosophical conscience, or rather, in annexing the French ideas without deserting their own philosophic point of view.

This annexation took place in the same way in which a foreign language is appropriated, namely, by translation.

It is well known how the monks wrote silly lives of Catholic Saints *over* the manuscripts on which the

Socialist and Communist Literature

classical works of ancient heathendom had been written. The German *literati* reversed this process with the profane French literature. They wrote their philosophical nonsense beneath the French original. For instance, beneath the French criticism of the economic functions of money, they wrote 'Alienation of Humanity', and beneath the French criticism of the bourgeois State they wrote, 'Dethronement of the Category of the General', and so forth.

The introduction of these philosophical phrases at the back of the French historical criticisms they dubbed 'Philosophy of Action', 'True Socialism', 'German Science of Socialism', 'Philosophical Foundation of Socialism', and so on.

The French Socialist and Communist literature was thus completely emasculated. And, since it ceased in the hands of the German to express the struggle of one class with the other, he felt conscious of having overcome 'French onesidedness' and of representing, not true requirements, but the requirements of Truth; not the interests of the proletariat, but the interests of Human Nature, of Man in general, who belongs to no class, has no reality, who exists only in the misty realm of philosophical fantasy.

This German Socialism, which took its schoolboy task so seriously and solemnly, and extolled its poor stock-in-trade in such mountebank fashion, meanwhile gradually lost its pedantic innocence.

The fight of the German, and, especially of the Prussian bourgeoisie, against feudal aristocracy and absolute monarchy, in other words, the liberal movement, became more earnest.

By this, the long wished-for opportunity was offered to 'True' Socialism of confronting the political movement with the Socialist demands, of hurling the traditional anathemas against liberalism, against representative government, against bourgeois competition, bourgeois freedom of the press, bourgeois legislation, bourgeois liberty and equality, and of preaching to the masses that they had nothing to gain, and everything to lose, by this bourgeois movement. German Socialism forgot, in the nick of time, that the French criticism, whose silly echo it was, presupposed the existence of modern bourgeois society, with its corresponding economic conditions of existence, and the political constitution adapted thereto, the very things whose attainment was the object of the pending struggle in Germany.

To the absolute governments, with their following of parsons, professors, country squires and officials, it served as a welcome scarecrow against the threatening bourgeoisie.

It was a sweet finish after the bitter pills of floggings and bullets with which these same governments, just at that time, dosed the German working-class risings.

While this 'True' Socialism thus served the governments as a weapon for fighting the German bourgeoisie,

Socialist and Communist Literature

it, at the same time, directly represented a reactionary interest, the interest of the German Philistines. In Germany the *petty-bourgeois* class, a relic of the sixteenth century, and since then constantly cropping up again under various forms, is the real social basis of the existing state of things.

To preserve this class is to preserve the existing state of things in Germany. The industrial and political supremacy of the bourgeoisie threatens it with certain destruction; on the one hand, from the concentration of capital; on the other, from the rise of a revolutionary proletariat. 'True' Socialism appeared to kill these two birds with one stone. It spread like an epidemic.

The robe of speculative cobwebs, embroidered with flowers of rhetoric, steeped in the dew of sickly sentiment, this transcendental robe in which the German Socialists wrapped their sorry 'eternal truths', all skin and bone, served to wonderfully increase the sale of their goods amongst such a public.

And on its part, German Socialism recognized, more and more, its own calling as the bombastic representative of the petty-bourgeois Philistine.

It proclaimed the German nation to be the model nation, and the German petty Philistine to be the typical man. To every villainous meanness of this model man it gave a hidden, higher Socialistic interpretation, the exact contrary of its real character. It went to the extreme length of directly opposing the 'brutally destructive' tendency of Communism, and of proclaiming its supreme and impartial contempt of all class struggles. With very few exceptions, all the so-called Socialist and Communist publications that now (1847) circulate in Germany belong to the domain of this foul and enervating literature.

II. Conservative, or Bourgeois, Socialism

A part of the bourgeoisie is desirous of redressing social grievances, in order to secure the continued existence of bourgeois society.

To this section belong economists, philanthropists, humanitarians, improvers of the condition of the working class, organizers of charity, members of societies for the prevention of cruelty to animals, temperance fanatics, hole-and-corner reformers of every imaginable kind. This form of Socialism has, moreover, been worked out into complete systems.

We may cite Proudhon's *Philosophie de la Misère* as an example of this form.

The Socialistic bourgeois want all the advantages of modern social conditions without the struggles and dangers necessarily resulting therefrom. They desire the existing state of society minus its revolutionary and disintegrating elements. They wish for a bourgeoisie without a proletariat. The bourgeoisie naturally conceives the world in which it is supreme to be the best; and bourgeois

Socialism develops this comfortable conception into various more or less complete systems. In requiring the proletariat to carry out such a system, and thereby to march straightway into the social New Jerusalem, it but requires in reality, that the proletariat should remain within the bounds of existing society, but should cast away all its hateful ideas concerning the bourgeoisie.

A second and more practical, but less systematic, form of this Socialism sought to depreciate every revolutionary movement in the eyes of the working class, by showing that no mere political reform, but only a change in the material conditions of existence, in economical relations, could be of any advantage to them. By changes in the material conditions of existence, this form of Socialism, however, by no means understands abolition of the bourgeois relations of production, an abolition that can be effected only by a revolution, but administrative reforms, based on the continued existence of these relations; reforms, therefore, that in no respect affect the relations between capital and labour, but, at the best, lessen the cost, and simplify the administrative work, of bourgeois government.

Bourgeois Socialism attains adequate expression, when and only when, it becomes a mere figure of speech.

Free trade: for the benefit of the working class. Protective duties: for the benefit of the working class. Prison Reform: for the benefit of the working class. This is the last word and the only seriously meant word of bourgeois Socialism.

It is summed up in the phrase: the bourgeois is a bourgeois – for the benefit of the working class.

III. Critical-Utopian Socialism and Communism

We do not here refer to that literature which, in every great modern revolution, has always given voice to the demands of the proletariat, such as the writings of Babeuf and others.

The first direct attempts of the proletariat to attain its own ends, made in times of universal excitement, when feudal society was being overthrown, these attempts necessarily failed, owing to the then undeveloped state of the proletariat, as well as to the absence of the economic conditions for its emancipation, conditions that had yet to be produced, and could be produced by the impending bourgeois epoch alone. The revolutionary literature that accompanied these first movements of the proletariat had necessarily a reactionary character. It inculcated universal asceticism and social levelling in its crudest form.

The Socialist and Communist systems properly so called, those of Saint-Simon, Fourier, Owen and others, spring into existence in the early undeveloped period, described above, of the struggle between proletariat and bourgeoisie (see Section 1. Bourgeois and Proletarians).

The founders of these systems see, indeed, the class antagonisms, as well as the action of the decomposing elements in the prevailing form of society. But the proletariat, as yet in its infancy, offers to them the spectacle of a class without any historical initiative or any independent political movement.

Since the development of class antagonism keeps even pace with the development of industry, the economic situation, as they find it, does not as yet offer to them the material conditions for the emancipation of the proletariat. They therefore search after a new social science, after new social laws, that are to create these conditions.

Historical action is to yield to their personal inventive action, historically created conditions of emancipation to fantastic ones, and the gradual, spontaneous class organization of the proletariat to an organization of society specially contrived by these inventors. Future history resolves itself, in their eyes, into the propaganda and the practical carrying out of their social plans.

In the formation of their plans they are conscious of caring chiefly for the interests of the working class, as being the most suffering class. Only from the point of view of being the most suffering class does the proletariat exist for them.

The undeveloped state of the class struggle, as well as their own surroundings, causes Socialists of this kind to consider themselves far superior to all class antagonisms. They want to improve the condition of every member of society, even that of the most favoured. Hence, they habitually appeal to society at large, without distinction of class; nay, by preference, to the ruling class. For how can people, when once they understand their system, fail to see in it the best possible plan of the best possible state of society?

Hence, they reject all political, and especially all revolutionary, action; they wish to attain their ends by peaceful means, and endeavour, by small experiments, necessarily doomed to failure, and by the force of example, to pave the way for the new social Gospel.

Such fantastic pictures of future society, painted at a time when the proletariat is still in a very undeveloped state and has but a fantastic conception of its own position correspond with the first instinctive yearnings of that class for a general reconstruction of society.

But these Socialist and Communist publications contain also a critical element. They attack every principle of existing society. Hence they are full of the most valuable materials for the enlightenment of the working class. The practical measures proposed in them – such as the abolition of the distinction between town and country, of the family, of the carrying on of industries for the account of private individuals, and of the wage system, the proclamation of social harmony, the conversion of the functions of the State into a mere superintendence of production, all these proposals point solely to the disappearance of class antagonisms which were, at that time, only just cropping up, and which, in these publications, are recognized in their earliest indistinct and undefined forms only. These proposals, therefore, are of a purely Utopian character.

The significance of Critical-Utopian Socialism and

Socialist and Communist Literature

Communism bears an inverse relation to historical development. In proportion as the modern class struggle develops and takes definite shape, this fantastic standing apart from the contest, these fantastic attacks on it, lose all practical value and all theoretical justification. Therefore, although the originators of these systems were, in many respects, revolutionary, their disciples have, in every case, formed mere reactionary sects. They hold fast by the original views of their masters, in opposition to the progressive historical development of the proletariat. They, therefore, endeavour, and that consistently, to deaden the class struggle and to reconcile the class antagonisms. They still dream of experimental realization of their social Utopias, of founding isolated '*phalanstères*', of establishing 'Home Colonies', of setting up a 'Little Icaria' – duodecimo editions of the New Jerusalem – and to realize all these castles in the air, they are compelled to appeal to the feelings and purses of the bourgeois. By degrees they sink into the category of the reactionary conservative Socialists depicted above, differing from these only by more systematic pedantry, and by their fanatical and superstitious belief in the miraculous effects of their social science.

They, therefore, violently oppose all political action on the part of the working class; such action, according to them, can only result from blind unbelief in the new Gospel.

The Owenites in England and the Fourierists in France, respectively oppose the Chartists and the *Réformistes*.

4. POSITION OF THE COMMUNISTS IN RELATION TO THE VARIOUS EXISTING OPPOSITION PARTIES

Section 2 has made clear the relations of the Communists to the existing working-class parties, such as the Chartists in England and the Agrarian Reformers in America.

The Communists fight for the attainment of the immediate aims, for the enforcement of the momentary interests of the working class; but in the movement of present, they also represent and take care of the future of that movement. In France the Communists ally themselves with the Social-Democrats, against the conservative and radical bourgeoisie, reserving, however, the right to take up a critical position in regard to phrases and illusions traditionally handed down from the great Revolution.

In Switzerland they support the Radicals, without losing sight of the fact that this party consists of antagonistic elements, partly of Democratic Socialists, in the French sense, partly of radical bourgeois.

In Poland they support the party that insists on an agrarian revolution as the prime condition for national emancipation, that party which fomented the insurrection of Cracow in 1846.

Position of the Communists

In Germany they fight with the bourgeoisie whenever it acts in a revolutionary way, against the absolute monarchy, the feudal squirearchy, and the petty bourgeoisie.

But they never cease, for a single instant, to instil into the working class the clearest possible recognition of the hostile antagonism between bourgeoisie and proletariat, in order that the German workers may straightway use, as so many weapons against the bourgeoisie, the social and political conditions that the bourgeoisie must necessarily introduce along with its supremacy, and in order that, after the fall of the reactionary classes in Germany, the fight against the bourgeoisie itself may immediately begin.

The Communists turn their attention chiefly to Germany, because that country is on the eve of a bourgeois revolution that is bound to be carried out under more advanced conditions of European civilization, and with a much more developed proletariat, than that of England was in the seventeenth, and of France in the eighteenth century, and because the bourgeois revolution in Germany will be but the prelude to an immediately following proletarian revolution.

In short, the Communists everywhere support every revolutionary movement against the existing social and political order of things.

In all these movements they bring to the front, as the leading question in each, the property question, no matter what its degree of development at the time.

Finally, they labour everywhere for the union and agreement of the democratic parties of all countries.

The Communists disdain to conceal their views and aims. They openly declare that their ends can be attained only by the forcible overthrow of all existing social conditions. Let the ruling classes tremble at a Communistic revolution. The proletarians have nothing to lose but their chains. They have a world to win.

WORKING MEN OF ALL COUNTRIES, UNITE!

1. BOCCACCIO · *Mrs Rosie and the Priest*
2. GERARD MANLEY HOPKINS · *As kingfishers catch fire*
3. *The Saga of Gunnlaug Serpent-tongue*
4. THOMAS DE QUINCEY · *On Murder Considered as One of the Fine Arts*
5. FRIEDRICH NIETZSCHE · *Aphorisms on Love and Hate*
6. JOHN RUSKIN · *Traffic*
7. PU SONGLING · *Wailing Ghosts*
8. JONATHAN SWIFT · *A Modest Proposal*
9. *Three Tang Dynasty Poets*
10. WALT WHITMAN · *On the Beach at Night Alone*
11. KENKŌ · *A Cup of Sake Beneath the Cherry Trees*
12. BALTASAR GRACIÁN · *How to Use Your Enemies*
13. JOHN KEATS · *The Eve of St Agnes*
14. THOMAS HARDY · *Woman much missed*
15. GUY DE MAUPASSANT · *Femme Fatale*
16. MARCO POLO · *Travels in the Land of Serpents and Pearls*
17. SUETONIUS · *Caligula*
18. APOLLONIUS OF RHODES · *Jason and Medea*
19. ROBERT LOUIS STEVENSON · *Olalla*
20. KARL MARX AND FRIEDRICH ENGELS · *The Communist Manifesto*
21. PETRONIUS · *Trimalchio's Feast*
22. JOHANN PETER HEBEL · *How a Ghastly Story Was Brought to Light by a Common or Garden Butcher's Dog*
23. HANS CHRISTIAN ANDERSEN · *The Tinder Box*
24. RUDYARD KIPLING · *The Gate of the Hundred Sorrows*
25. DANTE · *Circles of Hell*
26. HENRY MAYHEW · *Of Street Piemen*
27. HAFEZ · *The nightingales are drunk*
28. GEOFFREY CHAUCER · *The Wife of Bath*
29. MICHEL DE MONTAIGNE · *How We Weep and Laugh at the Same Thing*
30. THOMAS NASHE · *The Terrors of the Night*
31. EDGAR ALLAN POE · *The Tell-Tale Heart*
32. MARY KINGSLEY · *A Hippo Banquet*
33. JANE AUSTEN · *The Beautifull Cassandra*
34. ANTON CHEKHOV · *Gooseberries*
35. SAMUEL TAYLOR COLERIDGE · *Well, they are gone, and here must I remain*
36. JOHANN WOLFGANG VON GOETHE · *Sketchy, Doubtful, Incomplete Jottings*
37. CHARLES DICKENS · *The Great Winglebury Duel*
38. HERMAN MELVILLE · *The Maldive Shark*
39. ELIZABETH GASKELL · *The Old Nurse's Story*
40. NIKOLAY LESKOV · *The Steel Flea*

41. HONORÉ DE BALZAC · *The Atheist's Mass*
42. CHARLOTTE PERKINS GILMAN · *The Yellow Wall-Paper*
43. C.P. CAVAFY · *Remember, Body . . .*
44. FYODOR DOSTOEVSKY · *The Meek One*
45. GUSTAVE FLAUBERT · *A Simple Heart*
46. NIKOLAI GOGOL · *The Nose*
47. SAMUEL PEPYS · *The Great Fire of London*
48. EDITH WHARTON · *The Reckoning*
49. HENRY JAMES · *The Figure in the Carpet*
50. WILFRED OWEN · *Anthem For Doomed Youth*
51. WOLFGANG AMADEUS MOZART · *My Dearest Father*
52. PLATO · *Socrates' Defence*
53. CHRISTINA ROSSETTI · *Goblin Market*
54. *Sindbad the Sailor*
55. SOPHOCLES · *Antigone*
56. RYŪNOSUKE AKUTAGAWA · *The Life of a Stupid Man*
57. LEO TOLSTOY · *How Much Land Does A Man Need?*
58. GIORGIO VASARI · *Leonardo da Vinci*
59. OSCAR WILDE · *Lord Arthur Savile's Crime*
60. SHEN FU · *The Old Man of the Moon*
61. AESOP · *The Dolphins, the Whales and the Gudgeon*
62. MATSUO BASHŌ · *Lips too Chilled*
63. EMILY BRONTË · *The Night is Darkening Round Me*
64. JOSEPH CONRAD · *To-morrow*
65. RICHARD HAKLUYT · *The Voyage of Sir Francis Drake Around the Whole Globe*
66. KATE CHOPIN · *A Pair of Silk Stockings*
67. CHARLES DARWIN · *It was snowing butterflies*
68. BROTHERS GRIMM · *The Robber Bridegroom*
69. CATULLUS · *I Hate and I Love*
70. HOMER · *Circe and the Cyclops*
71. D. H. LAWRENCE · *Il Duro*
72. KATHERINE MANSFIELD · *Miss Brill*
73. OVID · *The Fall of Icarus*
74. SAPPHO · *Come Close*
75. IVAN TURGENEV · *Kasyan from the Beautiful Lands*
76. VIRGIL · *O Cruel Alexis*
77. H. G. WELLS · *A Slip under the Microscope*
78. HERODOTUS · *The Madness of Cambyses*
79. *Speaking of Siva*
80. *The Dhammapada*

'Is it me you love, friend? or the race that made me?'

ROBERT LOUIS STEVENSON
Born 1850, Edinburgh, Scotland
Died 1894, Samoa

'Olalla' was first published in 1885.

STEVENSON IN PENGUIN CLASSICS
An Apology for Idlers
The Black Arrow
Dr Jekyll and Mr Hyde
In the South Seas
Kidnapped
The Master of Ballantrae
Treasure Island
Treasure Island and The Ebb-Tide
Selected Poems

ROBERT LOUIS STEVENSON

Olalla

PENGUIN BOOKS

PENGUIN CLASSICS

UK | USA | Canada | Ireland | Australia
India | New Zealand | South Africa

Penguin Books is part of the Penguin Random House group of companies
whose addresses can be found at global.penguinrandomhouse.com.

This edition published in Penguin Classics 2015
009

Set in 9/12.4 pt Baskerville 10 Pro
Typeset by Jouve (UK), Milton Keynes
Printed and bound in Great Britain by Clays Ltd, Elcograf S.p.A.

A CIP catalogue record for this book is available from the British Library

ISBN: 978-0-141-39796-2

www.greenpenguin.co.uk

Penguin Random House is committed to a
sustainable future for our business, our readers
and our planet. This book is made from Forest
Stewardship Council® certified paper.

'Now,' said the doctor, 'my part is done, and, I may say, with some vanity, well done. It remains only to get you out of this cold and poisonous city, and to give you two months of a pure air and an easy conscience. The last is your affair. To the first I think I can help you. It falls indeed rather oddly; it was but the other day the Padre came in from the country; and as he and I are old friends, although of contrary professions, he applied to me in a matter of distress among some of his parishioners. This was a family – but you are ignorant of Spain, and even the names of our grandees are hardly known to you; suffice it, then, that they were once great people, and are now fallen to the brink of destitution. Nothing now belongs to them but the residencia, and certain leagues of desert mountain, in the greater part of which not even a goat could support life. But the house is a fine old place, and stands at a great height among the hills, and most salubriously; and I had no sooner heard my friend's tale, than I remembered you. I told him I had a wounded officer, wounded in the good cause, who was now able to make a change; and I proposed that his friends should take you for a lodger. Instantly the Padre's face grew dark, as I had maliciously foreseen it would. It was out of the question, he said. Then let them starve, said I, for I have no sympathy with tatterdemalion pride. Thereupon we separated, not very content with one another; but yesterday, to my wonder, the Padre returned and made a submission: the difficulty, he said, he had found upon inquiry to be less than he had feared; or, in other words, these proud people had put their pride in their pocket. I closed with the offer; and, subject to your approval, I have taken rooms for you in the residencia. The air of these mountains will renew your blood; and the quiet in which you will there live is worth all the medicines in the world.'

'Doctor,' said I, 'you have been throughout my good angel, and your advice is a command. But tell me, if you please, something of the family with which I am to reside.'

'I am coming to that,' replied my friend; 'and, indeed, there is a difficulty in the way. These beggars are, as I have said, of very high descent and swollen with the most baseless vanity; they have lived for some generations in a growing isolation, drawing away, on either hand, from the rich who had now become too high for them, and from the poor, whom they still regarded as too low; and even today, when poverty forces them to unfasten their door to a guest, they cannot do so without a most ungracious stipulation. You are to remain, they say, a stranger; they will give you attendance, but they refuse from the first the idea of the smallest intimacy.'

I will not deny that I was piqued, and perhaps the feeling strengthened my desire to go, for I was confident that I could break down that barrier if I desired. 'There is nothing offensive in such a stipulation,' said I; 'and I even sympathize with the feeling that inspired it.'

'It is true they have never seen you,' returned the doctor

politely; 'and if they knew you were the handsomest and the most pleasant man that ever came from England (where I am told that handsome men are common, but pleasant ones not so much so), they would doubtless make you welcome with a better grace. But since you take the thing so well, it matters not. To me, indeed, it seems discourteous. But you will find yourself the gainer. The family will not much tempt you. A mother, a son, and a daughter; an old woman said to be half-witted, a country lout, and a country girl, who stands very high with her confessor, and is, therefore,' chuckled the physician, 'most likely plain; there is not much in that to attract the fancy of a dashing officer.'

'And yet you say they are high-born,' I objected.

'Well, as to that, I should distinguish,' returned the doctor. 'The mother is; not so the children. The mother was the last representative of a princely stock, degenerate both in parts and fortune. Her father was not only poor, he was mad: and the girl ran wild about the residencia till his death. Then, much of the fortune having died with him, and the family being quite extinct, the girl ran wilder than ever, until at last she married, Heaven knows whom, a muleteer some say, others a smuggler; while there are some who uphold there was no marriage at all, and that Felipe and Olalla are bastards. The union, such as it was, was tragically dissolved some years ago; but they live in such seclusion, and the country at that time was in so much disorder, that the precise manner of the man's end is known only to the priest – if even to him.'

'I begin to think I shall have strange experiences,' said I.

'I would not romance, if I were you,' replied the doctor;

'you will find, I fear, a very grovelling and commonplace reality. Felipe, for instance, I have seen. And what am I to say? He is very rustic, very cunning, very loutish, and, I should say, an innocent; the others are probably to match. No, no, Señor Commandante, you must seek congenial society among the great sights of our mountains; and in these at least, if you are at all a lover of the works of nature, I promise you will not be disappointed.'

The next day Felipe came for me in a rough country cart, drawn by a mule; and a little before the stroke of noon, after I had said farewell to the doctor, the innkeeper, and different good souls who had befriended me during my sickness, we set forth out of the city by the Eastern gate, and began to ascend into the Sierra. I had been so long a prisoner, since I was left behind for dying after the loss of the convoy, that the mere smell of the earth set me smiling. The country through which we went was wild and rocky, partially covered with rough woods, now of the cork-tree, and now of the great Spanish chestnut, and frequently intersected by the beds of mountain torrents. The sun shone, the wind rustled joyously; and we had advanced some miles, and the city had already shrunk into an inconsiderable knoll upon the plain behind us, before my attention began to be diverted to the companion of my drive. To the eye, he seemed but a diminutive, loutish, well-made country lad, such as the doctor had described, mighty quick and active, but devoid of any culture; and this first impression was with most observers final. What began to strike me was his familiar, chattering talk; so strangely inconsistent with the terms on which I was to be received; and partly from his imperfect enunciation, partly from the sprightly incoherence of the matter, so very difficult to follow clearly without an effort of the mind. It is true I had before talked with persons of a similar mental constitution; persons who seemed to live (as he did) by the senses, taken and possessed by the visual object of the moment and unable to discharge their minds of that impression. His seemed to me (as I sat, distantly giving ear) a kind of conversation proper to drivers, who pass much of their time in a great vacancy of the intellect and threading the sights of a familiar country. But this was not the case of Felipe; by his own account, he was a home-keeper; 'I wish I was there now,' he said; and then, spying a tree by the wayside, he broke off to tell me that he had once seen a crow among its branches.

'A crow?' I repeated, struck by the ineptitude of the remark, and thinking I had heard imperfectly.

But by this time he was already filled with a new idea; hearkening with a rapt intentness, his head on one side, his face puckered; and he struck me rudely, to make me hold my peace. Then he smiled and shook his head.

'What did you hear?' I asked.

'O, it is all right,' he said; and began encouraging his mule with cries that echoed unhumanly up the mountain walls.

I looked at him more closely. He was superlatively well-built, light, and lithe and strong; he was well-featured; his yellow eyes were very large, though, perhaps, not very expressive; take him altogether, he was a pleasant-looking lad, and I had no fault to find with him, beyond that he was of a dusky hue, and inclined to hairyness; two characteristics that I disliked. It was his mind that puzzled, and yet attracted me. The doctor's phrase – an innocent – came back to me; and I was wondering if that were, after all, the true description, when the road began to go down into the narrow and naked chasm of a torrent. The waters thundered tumultuously in the bottom; and the ravine was filled full of the sound, the thin spray, and the claps of wind, that accompanied their descent. The scene was certainly impressive; but the road was in that part very securely walled in; the mule went steadily forward; and I was astonished to perceive the paleness of terror in the face of my companion. The voice of that wild river was inconstant, now sinking lower as if in weariness, now doubling its hoarse tones; momentary freshets seemed to swell its volume, sweeping down the gorge, raving and booming against the barrier walls; and I observed it was at each of these accessions to the clamour, that my driver more particularly winced and blanched. Some thoughts of Scottish superstition and the river Kelpie passed across my mind; I wondered if perchance the like were prevalent in that part of Spain; and turning to Felipe, sought to draw him out.

'What is the matter?' I asked.

'O, I am afraid,' he replied.

'Of what are you afraid?' I returned. 'This seems one of the safest places on this very dangerous road.'

'It makes a noise,' he said, with a simplicity of awe that set my doubts at rest.

The lad was but a child in intellect; his mind was like his body, active and swift, but stunted in development; and I began from that time forth to regard him with a measure of pity, and to listen at first with indulgence, and at last even with pleasure, to his disjointed babble.

By about four in the afternoon we had crossed the summit of the mountain line, said farewell to the western sunshine, and began to go down upon the other side, skirting the edge of many ravines and moving through the shadow of dusky woods. There rose upon all sides the voice of falling water, not condensed and formidable as in the gorge of the river, but scattered and sounding gaily and musically from glen to glen. Here, too, the spirits of my driver mended, and he began to sing aloud in a falsetto voice, and with a singular bluntness of musical perception, never true either to melody or key, but wandering at will, and yet somehow with an effect that was natural and pleasing, like that of the song of birds. As the dusk increased, I fell more and more under the spell of this artless warbling, listening and waiting for some articulate air, and still disappointed; and when at last I asked him what it was he sang – 'O,' cried he, 'I am just singing!' Above all, I was taken with a trick he had of unweariedly repeating the same note at little intervals; it was not so monotonous as you would think, or, at least, not disagreeable; and it seemed to breathe a wonderful contentment with what is, such as we love to fancy in the attitude of trees, or the quiescence of a pool.

Night had fallen dark before we came out upon a plateau, and drew up a little after, before a certain lump of superior blackness which I could only conjecture to be the residencia. Here, my guide, getting down from the cart, hooted and whistled for a long time in vain; until at last an old peasant man came towards us from somewhere in the surrounding dark, carrying a candle in his hand. By the light of this I was able to perceive a great arched doorway of a Moorish character: it was closed by iron-studded gates, in one of the leaves of which Felipe opened a wicket. The peasant carried off the cart to some out-building; but my guide and I passed through the wicket, which was closed again behind us; and by the glimmer of the candle, passed through a court, up a stone stair, along a section of an open gallery, and up more stairs again, until we came at last to the door of a great and somewhat bare apartment. This room, which I understood was to be mine, was pierced by three windows, lined with some lustrous wood disposed in panels, and carpeted with the skins of many savage animals. A bright fire burned in the chimney, and shed abroad a changeful flicker; close up to the blaze there was drawn a table, laid for supper; and in the far end a bed stood ready. I was pleased by these preparations, and said so to Felipe; and he, with the same simplicity of disposition that I had already remarked in him, warmly re-echoed my praises. 'A fine room,' he said; 'a very fine room. And fire, too; fire is good; it melts out the pleasure in your bones. And the bed,' he continued, carrying over the candle in that direction – 'see what fine sheets – how soft, how smooth, smooth;' and he passed his hand again and again over their texture, and then laid down his head and rubbed his cheeks among them with a grossness of content that somehow offended me. I took the candle from his hand (for I feared he would set the bed on fire) and walked back to the supper-table, where, perceiving a measure of wine, I poured out a cup and called to him to come and drink of it.

Olalla

He started to his feet at once and ran to me with a strong expression of hope; but when he saw the wine, he visibly shuddered.

'Oh, no,' he said, 'not that; that is for you. I hate it.'

'Very well, Señor,' said I; 'then I will drink to your good health, and to the prosperity of your house and family. Speaking of which,' I added, after I had drunk, 'shall I not have the pleasure of laying my salutations in person at the feet of the Señora, your mother?'

But at these words all the childishness passed out of his face, and was succeeded by a look of indescribable cunning and secrecy. He backed away from me at the same time, as though I were an animal about to leap or some dangerous fellow with a weapon, and when he had got near the door, glowered at me suddenly with contracted pupils. 'No,' he said at last, and the next moment was gone noiselessly out of the room; and I heard his footing die away downstairs as light as rainfall, and silence closed over the house.

After I had supped I drew up the table nearer to the bed and began to prepare for rest; but in the new position of the light, I was struck by a picture on the wall. It represented a woman, still young. To judge by her costume and the mellow unity which reigned over the canvas, she had long been dead; to judge by the vivacity of the attitude, the eyes and the features, I might have been beholding in a mirror the image of life. Her figure was very slim and strong, and of a just proportion; red tresses lay like a crown over her brow; her eyes, of a very golden brown, held mine with a look; and her face, which was perfectly shaped, was yet marred by a cruel, sullen, and sensual expression. Something in both face and figure, something exquisitely intangible, like the echo of an echo, suggested the features and bearing of my guide; and I stood awhile, unpleasantly attracted and wondering at the oddity of the resemblance. The common, carnal stock of that race, which had been originally designed for such high dames as the one now looking on me from the canvas, had fallen to baser uses, wearing country clothes, sitting on the shaft and holding the reins of a mule cart, to bring home a lodger. Perhaps an actual link subsisted; perhaps some scruple of the delicate flesh that was once clothed upon with the satin and brocade of the dead lady, now winced at the rude contact of Felipe's frieze.

The first light of the morning shone full upon the portrait, and, as I lay awake, my eyes continued to dwell upon it with growing complacency; its beauty crept about my heart insidiously, silencing my scruples one after another; and while I knew that to love such a woman were to sign and seal one's own sentence of degeneration, I still knew that, if she were alive, I should love her. Day after day the double knowledge of her wickedness and of my weakness grew clearer. She came to be the heroine of many day-dreams, in which her eyes led on to, and sufficiently rewarded, crimes. She cast a dark shadow on my fancy; and when I was out in the free air of heaven, taking vigorous exercise and healthily renewing the current of my blood, it was often a glad thought to me that my enchantress was safe in the grave, her wand of beauty broken, her lips closed in silence, her philtre spilt. And yet I had a half-lingering terror that she might not be dead after all, but re-arisen in the body of some descendant.

Olalla

Felipe served my meals in my own apartment; and his resemblance to the portrait haunted me. At times it was not; at times, upon some change of attitude or flash of expression, it would leap out upon me like a ghost. It was above all in his ill tempers that the likeness triumphed. He certainly liked me; he was proud of my notice, which he sought to engage by many simple and childlike devices; he loved to sit close before my fire, talking his broken talk or singing his odd, endless, wordless songs, and sometimes drawing his hand over my clothes with an affectionate manner of caressing that never failed to cause in me an embarrassment of which I was ashamed. But for all that, he was capable of flashes of causeless anger and fits of sturdy sullenness. At a word of reproof, I have seen him upset the dish of which I was about to eat, and this not surreptitiously, but with defiance; and similarly at a hint of inquisition. I was not unnaturally curious, being in a strange place and surrounded by strange people; but at the shadow of a question, he shrank back, lowering and dangerous. Then it was that, for a fraction of a second, this rough lad might have been the brother of the lady in the frame. But these humours were swift to pass; and the resemblance died along with them.

In these first days I saw nothing of anyone but Felipe, unless the portrait is to be counted; and since the lad was plainly of weak mind, and had moments of passion, it may be wondered that I bore his dangerous neighbourhood with equanimity. As a matter of fact, it was for some time irksome; but it happened before long that I obtained over him so complete a mastery as set my disquietude at rest.

Robert Louis Stevenson

It fell in this way. He was by nature slothful, and much of a vagabond, and yet he kept by the house, and not only waited upon my wants, but laboured every day in the garden or small farm to the south of the residencia. Here he would be joined by the peasant whom I had seen on the night of my arrival, and who dwelt at the far end of the enclosure, about half a mile away, in a rude out-house; but it was plain to me that, of these two, it was Felipe who did most; and though I would sometimes see him throw down his spade and go to sleep among the very plants he had been digging, his constancy and energy were admirable in themselves, and still more so since I was well assured they were foreign to his disposition and the fruit of an ungrateful effort. But while I admired, I wondered what had called forth in a lad so shuttle-witted this enduring sense of duty. How was it sustained? I asked myself, and to what length did it prevail over his instincts? The priest was possibly his inspirer; but the priest came one day to the residencia. I saw him both come and go after an interval of close upon an hour, from a knoll where I was sketching, and all that time Felipe continued to labour undisturbed in the garden.

At last, in a very unworthy spirit, I determined to debauch the lad from his good resolutions, and, waylaying him at the gate, easily persuaded him to join me in a ramble. It was a fine day, and the woods to which I led him were green and pleasant and sweet-smelling and alive with the hum of insects. Here he discovered himself in a fresh character, mounting up to heights of gaiety that abashed me, and displaying an energy and grace of movement that delighted

Olalla

the eye. He leaped, he ran round me in mere glee; he would stop, and look and listen, and seem to drink in the world like a cordial; and then he would suddenly spring into a tree with one bound, and hang and gambol there like one at home. Little as he said to me, and that of not much import, I have rarely enjoyed more stirring company; the sight of his delight was a continual feast; the speed and accuracy of his movements pleased me to the heart; and I might have been so thoughtlessly unkind as to make a habit of these walks, had not chance prepared a very rude conclusion to my pleasure. By some swiftness or dexterity the lad captured a squirrel in a tree top. He was then some way ahead of me, but I saw him drop to the ground and crouch there, crying aloud for pleasure like a child. The sound stirred my sympathies, it was so fresh and innocent; but as I bettered my pace to draw near, the cry of the squirrel knocked upon my heart. I have heard and seen much of the cruelty of lads, and above all of peasants; but what I now beheld struck me into a passion of anger. I thrust the fellow aside, plucked the poor brute out of his hands, and with swift mercy killed it. Then I turned upon the torturer, spoke to him long out of the heat of my indignation, calling him names at which he seemed to wither; and at length, pointing towards the residencia, bade him begone and leave me, for I chose to walk with men, not with vermin. He fell upon his knees, and, the words coming to him with more clearness than usual, poured out a stream of the most touching supplications, begging me in mercy to forgive him, to forget what he had done, to look to the future. 'O, I try so hard,' he said. 'O, Commandante, bear with Felipe this once; he will never be a brute again!'

Thereupon, much more affected than I cared to show, I suffered myself to be persuaded, and at last shook hands with him and made it up. But the squirrel, by way of penance, I made him bury; speaking of the poor thing's beauty, telling him what pains it had suffered, and how base a thing was the abuse of strength. 'See, Felipe,' said I, 'you are strong indeed; but in my hands you are as helpless as that poor thing of the trees. Give me your hand in mine. You cannot remove it. Now suppose that I were cruel like you, and took a pleasure in pain. I only tighten my hold, and see how you suffer.' He screamed aloud, his face stricken ashy and dotted with needle points of sweat; and when I set him free, he fell to the earth and nursed his hand and moaned over it like a baby. But he took the lesson in good part; and whether from that, or from what I had said to him, or the higher notion he now had of my bodily strength, his original affection was changed into a dog-like, adoring fidelity.

Meanwhile I gained rapidly in health. The residencia stood on the crown of a stony plateau; on every side the mountains hemmed it about; only from the roof, where was a bartizan, there might be seen between two peaks, a small segment of plain, blue with extreme distance. The air in these altitudes moved freely and largely; great clouds congregated there, and were broken up by the wind and left in tatters on the hilltops; a hoarse, and yet faint rumbling of torrents rose from all round; and one could there study all the ruder and more ancient characters of nature in something of their pristine force. I delighted from the first in the vigorous scenery and changeful weather; nor less in the antique and

Olalla

dilapidated mansion where I dwelt. This was a large oblong, flanked at two opposite corners by bastion-like projections, one of which commanded the door, while both were loopholed for musketry. The lower storey was, besides, naked of windows, so that the building, if garrisoned, could not be carried without artillery. It enclosed an open court planted with pomegranate trees. From this a broad flight of marble stairs ascended to an open gallery, running all round and resting, towards the court, on slender pillars. Thence again, several enclosed stairs led to the upper storeys of the house, which were thus broken up into distinct divisions. The windows, both within and without, were closely shuttered; some of the stone-work in the upper parts had fallen; the roof, in one place, had been wrecked in one of the flurries of wind which were common in these mountains; and the whole house, in the strong, beating sunlight, and standing out above a grove of stunted cork-trees, thickly laden and discoloured with dust, looked like the sleeping palace of the legend. The court, in particular, seemed the very home of slumber. A hoarse cooing of doves haunted about the eaves; the winds were excluded, but when they blew outside, the mountain dust fell here as thick as rain, and veiled the red bloom of the pomegranates; shuttered windows and the closed doors of numerous cellars, and the vacant arches of the gallery, enclosed it; and all day long the sun made broken profiles on the four sides, and paraded the shadow of the pillars on the gallery floor. At the ground level there was, however, a certain pillared recess, which bore the marks of human habitation. Though it was open in front upon the court, it was yet provided with a chimney, where a wood fire would be always prettily blazing; and the tile floor was littered with the skins of animals.

It was in this place that I first saw my hostess. She had drawn one of the skins forward and sat in the sun, leaning against a pillar. It was her dress that struck me first of all, for it was rich and brightly coloured, and shone out in that dusty courtyard with something of the same relief as the flowers of the pomegranates. At a second look it was her beauty of person that took hold of me. As she sat back – watching me, I thought, though with invisible eyes – and wearing at the same time an expression of almost imbecile good-humour and contentment, she showed a perfectness of feature and a quiet nobility of attitude that were beyond a statue's. I took off my hat to her in passing, and her face puckered with suspicion as swiftly and lightly as a pool ruffles in the breeze; but she paid no heed to my courtesy. I went forth on my customary walk a trifle daunted, her idol-like impassivity haunting me; and when I returned, although she was still in much the same posture, I was half surprised to see that she had moved as far as the next pillar, following the sunshine. This time, however, she addressed me with some trivial salutation, civilly enough conceived, and uttered in the same deep-chested, and yet indistinct and lisping tones, that had already baffled the utmost niceness of my hearing from her son. I answered rather at a venture; for not only did I fail to take her meaning with precision, but the sudden disclosure of her eyes disturbed me. They were unusually large, the iris golden like Felipe's, but the pupil at that moment so distended that they seemed almost black; and what affected me was not so much their size as

Olalla

(what was perhaps its consequence) the singular insignificance of their regard. A look more blankly stupid I have never met. My eyes dropped before it even as I spoke, and I went on my way upstairs to my own room, at once baffled and embarrassed. Yet, when I came there and saw the face of the portrait, I was again reminded of the miracle of family descent. My hostess was, indeed, both older and fuller in person; her eyes were of a different colour; her face, besides, was not only free from the ill-significance that offended and attracted me in the painting; it was devoid of either good or bad – a moral blank expressing literally naught. And yet there was a likeness, not so much speaking as immanent, not so much in any particular feature as upon the whole. It should seem, I thought, as if when the master set his signature to that grave canvas, he had not only caught the image of one smiling and false-eyed woman, but stamped the essential quality of a race.

From that day forth, whether I came or went, I was sure to find the Señora seated in the sun against a pillar, or stretched on a rug before the fire; only at times she would shift her station to the top round of the stone staircase, where she lay with the same nonchalance right across my path. In all these days, I never knew her to display the least spark of energy beyond what she expended in brushing and re-brushing her copious copper-coloured hair, or in lisping out, in the rich and broken hoarseness of her voice, her customary idle salutations to myself. These, I think, were her two chief pleasures, beyond that of mere quiescence. She seemed always proud of her remarks, as though they had been witticisms: and, indeed, though they were empty enough, like the conversation of many respectable persons, and turned on a very narrow range of subjects, they were never meaningless or incoherent; nay, they had a certain beauty of their own, breathing, as they did, of her entire contentment. Now she would speak of the warmth, in which (like her son) she greatly delighted; now of the flowers of the pomegranate trees, and now of the white doves and long-winged swallows that fanned the air of the court. The birds excited her. As they raked the eaves in their swift flight, or skimmed sidelong past her with a rush of wind, she would sometimes stir, and sit a little up, and seem to awaken from her doze of satisfaction. But for the rest of her days she lay luxuriously folded on herself and sunk in sloth and pleasure. Her invincible content at first annoyed me, but I came gradually to find repose in the spectacle, until at last it grew to be my habit to sit down beside her four times in the day, both coming and going, and to talk with her sleepily, I scarce knew of what. I had come to like her dull, almost animal neighbourhood; her beauty and her stupidity soothed and amused me. I began to find a kind of transcendental good sense in her remarks, and her unfathomable good nature moved me to admiration and envy. The liking was returned; she enjoyed my presence half-unconsciously, as a man in deep meditation may enjoy the babbling of a brook. I can scarce say she brightened when I came, for satisfaction was written on her face eternally, as on some foolish statue's; but I was made conscious of her pleasure by some more intimate communication than the sight. And one day, as I sat within reach of her on the marble step, she suddenly shot forth one of her hands and patted mine. The thing was done, and she was back in her accustomed attitude, before my mind had received intelligence of the caress; and when I turned to look her in the face I could perceive no answerable sentiment. It was plain she attached no moment to the act, and I blamed myself for my own more uneasy consciousness.

The sight and (if I may so call it) the acquaintance of the mother confirmed the view I had already taken of the son. The family blood had been impoverished, perhaps by long inbreeding, which I knew to be a common error among the proud and the exclusive. No decline, indeed, was to be traced in the body, which had been handed down unimpaired in shapeliness and strength; and the faces of today were struck as sharply from the mint, as the face of two centuries ago that smiled upon me from the portrait. But the intelligence (that more precious heirloom) was degenerate; the treasure of ancestral memory ran low; and it had required the potent, plebeian crossing of a muleteer or mountain contrabandista to raise, what approached hebetude in the mother, into the active oddity of the son. Yet of the two, it was the mother I preferred. Of Felipe, vengeful and placable, full of starts and shyings, inconstant as a hare, I could even conceive as a creature possibly noxious. Of the mother I had no thoughts but those of kindness. And indeed, as spectators are apt ignorantly to take sides, I grew something of a partisan in the enmity which I perceived to smoulder between them. True, it seemed mostly on the mother's part. She would sometimes draw in her breath as he came near, and the pupils of her vacant eyes would contract as if with horror or fear. Her emotions, such as they were, were much upon the surface and readily shared; and this latent repulsion occupied my mind, and kept me wondering on what grounds it rested, and whether the son was certainly in fault.

I had been about ten days in the residencia, when there sprang up a high and harsh wind, carrying clouds of dust. It came out of malarious lowlands, and over several snowy sierras. The nerves of those on whom it blew were strung and jangled; their eyes smarted with the dust; their legs ached under the burden of their body; and the touch of one hand upon another grew to be odious. The wind, besides, came down the gullies of the hills and stormed about the house with a great, hollow buzzing and whistling that was wearisome to the ear and dismally depressing to the mind. It did not so much blow in gusts as with the steady sweep of a waterfall, so that there was no remission of discomfort while it blew. But higher upon the mountain, it was probably of a more variable strength, with accesses of fury; for there came down at times a far-off wailing, infinitely grievous to hear; and at times, on one of the high shelves or terraces, there would start up, and then disperse, a tower of dust, like the smoke of an explosion.

I no sooner awoke in bed than I was conscious of the nervous tension and depression of the weather, and the effect grew stronger as the day proceeded. It was in vain that I resisted; in vain that I set forth upon my customary morning's walk; the irrational, unchanging fury of the storm had soon beat down my strength and wrecked my temper; and I returned to the residencia, glowing with dry heat, and foul and gritty with dust. The court had a forlorn appearance; now and then a glimmer of sun fled over it; now and then

Olalla

the wind swooped down upon the pomegranates, and scattered the blossoms, and set the window shutters clapping on the wall. In the recess the Señora was pacing to and fro with a flushed countenance and bright eyes; I thought, too, she was speaking to herself, like one in anger. But when I addressed her with my customary salutation, she only replied by a sharp gesture and continued her walk. The weather had distempered even this impassive creature; and as I went on upstairs I was the less ashamed of my own discomposure.

All day the wind continued; and I sat in my room and made a feint of reading, or walked up and down, and listened to the riot overhead. Night fell, and I had not so much as a candle. I began to long for some society, and stole down to the court. It was now plunged in the blue of the first darkness; but the recess was redly lighted by the fire. The wood had been piled high, and was crowned by a shock of flames, which the draught of the chimney brandished to and fro. In this strong and shaken brightness the Señora continued pacing from wall to wall with disconnected gestures, clasping her hands, stretching forth her arms, throwing back her head as in appeal to heaven. In these disordered movements the beauty and grace of the woman showed more clearly; but there was a light in her eye that struck on me unpleasantly; and when I had looked on awhile in silence, and seemingly unobserved, I turned tail as I had come, and groped my way back again to my own chamber.

By the time Felipe brought my supper and lights, my nerve was utterly gone; and, had the lad been such as I was used to seeing him, I should have kept him (even by force had that been necessary) to take off the edge from my distasteful solitude. But on Felipe, also, the wind had exercised its influence. He had been feverish all day; now that the night had come he was fallen into a low and tremulous humour that reacted on my own. The sight of his scared face, his starts and pallors and sudden harkenings, unstrung me; and when he dropped and broke a dish, I fairly leaped out of my seat.

'I think we are all mad today,' said I, affecting to laugh.

'It is the black wind,' he replied dolefully. 'You feel as if you must do something, and you don't know what it is.'

I noted the aptness of the description; but, indeed, Felipe had sometimes a strange felicity in rendering into words the sensations of the body. 'And your mother, too,' said I; 'she seems to feel this weather much. Do you not fear she may be unwell?'

He stared at me a little, and then said, 'No,' almost defiantly; and the next moment, carrying his hand to his brow, cried out lamentably on the wind and the noise that made his head go round like a millwheel. 'Who can be well?' he cried; and, indeed, I could only echo his question, for I was disturbed enough myself.

I went to bed early, wearied with day-long restlessness; but the poisonous nature of the wind, and its ungodly and unintermittent uproar, would not suffer me to sleep. I lay there and tossed, my nerves and senses on the stretch. At times I would doze, dream horribly, and wake again; and these snatches of oblivion confused me as to time. But it must have been late on in the night, when I was suddenly startled by an outbreak of pitiable and hateful cries. I leaped from my bed, supposing I had dreamed; but the cries still continued to fill the house, cries of pain, I thought, but

Olalla

certainly of rage also, and so savage and discordant that they shocked the heart. It was no illusion; some living thing, some lunatic or some wild animal, was being foully tortured. The thought of Felipe and the squirrel flashed into my mind, and I ran to the door, but it had been locked from the outside; and I might shake it as I pleased, I was a fast prisoner. Still the cries continued. Now they would dwindle down into a moaning that seemed to be articulate, and at these times I made sure they must be human; and again they would break forth and fill the house with ravings worthy of hell. I stood at the door and gave ear to them, till at last they died away. Long after that, I still lingered and still continued to hear them mingle in fancy with the storming of the wind; and when at last I crept to my bed, it was with a deadly sickness and a blackness of horror on my heart.

It was little wonder if I slept no more. Why had I been locked in? What had passed? Who was the author of these indescribable and shocking cries? A human being? It was inconceivable. A beast? The cries were scarce quite bestial; and what animal, short of a lion or a tiger, could thus shake the solid walls of the residencia? And while I was thus turning over the elements of the mystery, it came into my mind that I had not yet set eyes upon the daughter of the house. What was more probable than that the daughter of the Señora, and the sister of Felipe, should be herself insane? Or, what more likely than that these ignorant and half-witted people should seek to manage an afflicted kinswoman by violence? Here was a solution; and yet when I called to mind the cries (which I never did without a shuddering chill) it seemed altogether insufficient: not even cruelty could wring such cries from madness. But of one thing I was sure: I could not live in a house where such a thing was half conceivable, and not probe the matter home and, if necessary, interfere.

The next day came, the wind had blown itself out, and there was nothing to remind me of the business of the night. Felipe came to my bedside with obvious cheerfulness; as I passed through the court, the Señora was sunning herself with her accustomed immobility; and when I issued from the gateway, I found the whole face of nature austerely smiling, the heavens of a cold blue, and sown with great cloud islands, and the mountainsides mapped forth into provinces of light and shadow. A short walk restored me to myself, and renewed within me the resolve to plumb this mystery; and when, from the vantage of my knoll, I had seen Felipe pass forth to his labours in the garden, I returned at once to the residencia to put my design in practice. The Señora appeared plunged in slumber; I stood awhile and marked her, but she did not stir; even if my design were indiscreet, I had little to fear from such a guardian; and turning away, I mounted to the gallery and began my exploration of the house.

All morning I went from one door to another, and entered spacious and faded chambers, some rudely shuttered, some receiving their full charge of daylight, all empty and unhomely. It was a rich house, on which Time had breathed his tarnish and dust had scattered disillusion. The spider swung there; the bloated tarantula scampered on the cornices; ants had their crowded highways on the floor of halls of audience; the big and foul fly, that lives on carrion and is often the messenger of death, had set up his nest in the rotten woodwork, and buzzed heavily about the rooms. Here

Olalla

and there a stool or two, a couch, a bed, or a great carved chair remained behind, like islets on the bare floors, to testify of man's bygone habitation; and everywhere the walls were set with the portraits of the dead. I could judge, by these decaying effigies, in the house of what a great and what a handsome race I was then wandering. Many of the men wore orders on their breasts and had the port of noble offices; the women were all richly attired; the canvases most of them by famous hands. But it was not so much these evidences of greatness that took hold upon my mind, even contrasted, as they were, with the present depopulation and decay of that great house. It was rather the parable of family life that I read in this succession of fair faces and shapely bodies. Never before had I so realized the miracle of the continued race, the creation and recreation, the weaving and changing and handing down of fleshly elements. That a child should be born of its mother, that it should grow and clothe itself (we know not how) with humanity, and put on inherited looks, and turn its head with the manner of one ascendant, and offer its hand with the gesture of another, are wonders dulled for us by repetition. But in the singular unity of look, in the common features and common bearing, of all these painted generations on the walls of the residencia, the miracle started out and looked me in the face. And an ancient mirror falling opportunely in my way, I stood and read my own features a long while, tracing out on either hand the filaments of descent and the bonds that knit me with my family.

At last, in the course of these investigations, I opened the door of a chamber that bore the marks of habitation. It was of large proportions and faced to the north, where the mountains were most wildly figured. The embers of a fire smouldered and smoked upon the hearth, to which a chair had been drawn close. And yet the aspect of the chamber was ascetic to the degree of sternness; the chair was uncushioned; the floor and walls were naked; and beyond the books which lay here and there in some confusion, there was no instrument of either work or pleasure. The sight of books in the house of such a family exceedingly amazed me; and I began with a great hurry, and in momentary fear of interruption, to go from one to another and hastily inspect their character. They were of all sorts, devotional, historical, and scientific, but mostly of a great age and in the Latin tongue. Some I could see to bear the marks of constant study; others had been torn across and tossed aside as if in petulance or disapproval. Lastly, as I cruised about that empty chamber, I espied some papers written upon with pencil on a table near the window. An unthinking curiosity led me to take one up. It bore a copy of verses, very roughly metred in the original Spanish, and which I may render somewhat thus –

> Pleasure approached with pain and shame,
> Grief with a wreath of lilies came.
> Pleasure showed the lovely sun;
> Jesu dear, how sweet it shone!
> Grief with her worn hand pointed on,
> > Jesu dear, to thee!

Shame and confusion at once fell on me; and, laying down the paper, I beat an immediate retreat from the apartment. Neither Felipe nor his mother could have read the book nor written these rough but feeling verses. It was plain I had

Olalla

stumbled with sacrilegious feet into the room of the daughter of the house. God knows, my own heart most sharply punished me for my indiscretion. The thought that I had thus secretly pushed my way into the confidence of a girl so strangely situated, and the fear that she might somehow come to hear of it, oppressed me like guilt. I blamed myself besides for my suspicions of the night before; wondered that I should ever have attributed those shocking cries to one of whom I now conceived as of a saint, spectral of mien, wasted with maceration, bound up in the practices of a mechanical devotion, and dwelling in a great isolation of soul with her incongruous relatives; and as I leaned on the balustrade of the gallery and looked down into the bright close of pomegranates and at the gaily dressed and somnolent woman, who just then stretched herself and delicately licked her lips as in the very sensuality of sloth, my mind swiftly compared the scene with the cold chamber looking northward on the mountains, where the daughter dwelt.

That same afternoon, as I sat upon my knoll, I saw the Padre enter the gates of the residencia. The revelation of the daughter's character had struck home to my fancy, and almost blotted out the horrors of the night before; but at sight of this worthy man the memory revived. I descended, then, from the knoll, and making a circuit among the woods, posted myself by the wayside to await his passage. As soon as he appeared I stepped forth and introduced myself as the lodger of the residencia. He had a very strong, honest countenance, on which it was easy to read the mingled emotions with which he regarded me, as a foreigner, a heretic, and yet one who had been wounded for the good cause. Of the family at the residencia he spoke with reserve, and yet with respect. I mentioned that I had not yet seen the daughter, whereupon he remarked that that was as it should be, and looked at me a little askance. Lastly, I plucked up courage to refer to the cries that had disturbed me in the night. He heard me out in silence, and then stopped and partly turned about, as though to mark beyond doubt that he was dismissing me.

'Do you take tobacco powder?' said he, offering his snuff-box; and then, when I had refused, 'I am an old man,' he added, 'and I may be allowed to remind you that you are a guest.'

'I have, then, your authority,' I returned, firmly enough, although I flushed at the implied reproof, 'to let things take their course, and not to interfere?'

He said 'yes,' and with a somewhat uneasy salute turned and left me where I was. But he had done two things: he had set my conscience at rest, and he had awakened my delicacy. I made a great effort, once more dismissed the recollections of the night, and fell once more to brooding on my saintly poetess. At the same time, I could not quite forget that I had been locked in, and that night when Felipe brought me my supper I attacked him warily on both points of interest.

'I never see your sister,' said I casually.

'Oh, no,' said he; 'she is a good, good girl,' and his mind instantly veered to something else.

'Your sister is pious, I suppose?' I asked in the next pause.

'Oh!' he cried, joining his hands with extreme fervour, 'a saint; it is she that keeps me up.'

Olalla

'You are very fortunate,' said I, 'for the most of us, I am afraid, and myself among the number, are better at going down.'

'Señor,' said Felipe earnestly, 'I would not say that. You should not tempt your angel. If one goes down, where is he to stop?'

'Why, Felipe,' said I, 'I had no guess you were a preacher, and I may say a good one; but I suppose that is your sister's doing?'

He nodded at me with round eyes.

'Well, then,' I continued, 'she has doubtless reproved you for your sin of cruelty?'

'Twelve times!' he cried; for this was the phrase by which the odd creature expressed the sense of frequency. 'And I told her you had done so – I remembered that,' he added proudly – 'and she was pleased.'

'Then, Felipe,' said I, 'what were those cries that I heard last night? for surely they were cries of some creature in suffering.'

'The wind,' returned Felipe, looking in the fire.

I took his hand in mine, at which, thinking it to be a caress, he smiled with a brightness of pleasure that came near disarming my resolve. But I trod the weakness down. 'The wind,' I repeated; 'and yet I think it was this hand,' holding it up, 'that had first locked me in.' The lad shook visibly, but answered never a word. 'Well,' said I, 'I am a stranger and a guest. It is not my part either to meddle or to judge in your affairs; in these you shall take your sister's counsel, which I cannot doubt to be excellent. But in so far as concerns my own I will be no man's prisoner, and

I demand that key.' Half an hour later my door was suddenly thrown open, and the key tossed ringing on the floor.

A day or two after I came in from a walk a little before the point of noon. The Señora was lying lapped in slumber on the threshold of the recess; the pigeons dozed below the eaves like snowdrifts; the house was under a deep spell of noontide quiet; and only a wandering and gentle wind from the mountain stole round the galleries, rustled among the pomegranates, and pleasantly stirred the shadows. Something in the stillness moved me to imitation, and I went very lightly across the court and up the marble staircase. My foot was on the topmost round, when a door opened, and I found myself face to face with Olalla. Surprise transfixed me; her loveliness struck to my heart; she glowed in the deep shadow of the gallery, a gem of colour; her eyes took hold upon mine and clung there, and bound us together like the joining of hands; and the moments we thus stood face to face, drinking each other in, were sacramental and the wedding of souls. I know not how long it was before I awoke out of a deep trance, and, hastily bowing, passed on into the upper stair. She did not move, but followed me with her great, thirsting eyes; and as I passed out of sight it seemed to me as if she paled and faded.

In my own room, I opened the window and looked out, and could not think what change had come upon that austere field of mountains that it should thus sing and shine under the lofty heaven. I had seen her – Olalla! And the stone crags answered, Olalla! and the dumb, unfathomable azure answered, Olalla! The pale saint of my dreams had vanished for ever; and in her place I beheld this maiden on

Olalla

whom God had lavished the richest colours and the most exuberant energies of life, whom he had made active as a deer, slender as a reed, and in whose great eyes he had lighted the torches of the soul. The thrill of her young life, strung like a wild animal's, had entered into me; the force of soul that had looked out from her eyes and conquered mine, mantled about my heart and sprang to my lips in singing. She passed through my veins: she was one with me.

I will not say that this enthusiasm declined; rather my soul held out in its ecstasy as in a strong castle, and was there besieged by cold and sorrowful considerations. I could not doubt but that I loved her at first sight, and already with a quivering ardour that was strange to my experience. What then was to follow? She was a child of an afflicted house, the Señora's daughter, the sister of Felipe; she bore it even in her beauty. She had the lightness and swiftness of the one, swift as an arrow, light as dew; like the other, she shone on the pale background of the world with the brilliancy of flowers. I could not call by the name of brother that half-witted lad, nor by the name of mother that immovable and lovely thing of flesh, whose silly eyes and perpetual simper now recurred to my mind like something hateful. And if I could not marry, what then? She was helplessly unprotected; her eyes, in that single and long glance which had been all our intercourse, had confessed a weakness equal to my own; but in my heart I knew her for the student of the cold northern chamber, and the writer of the sorrowful lines; and this was a knowledge to disarm a brute. To flee was more than I could find courage for; but I registered a vow of unsleeping circumspection.

As I turned from the window, my eyes alighted on the portrait. It had fallen dead, like a candle after sunrise; it followed me with eyes of paint. I knew it to be like, and marvelled at the tenacity of type in that declining race; but the likeness was swallowed up in difference. I remembered how it had seemed to me a thing unapproachable in the life, a creature rather of the painter's craft than of the modesty of nature, and I marvelled at the thought, and exulted in the image of Olalla. Beauty I had seen before, and not been charmed, and I had been often drawn to women, who were not beautiful except to me; but in Olalla all that I desired and had not dared to imagine was united.

I did not see her the next day, and my heart ached and my eyes longed for her, as men long for morning. But the day after, when I returned, about my usual hour, she was once more on the gallery, and our looks once more met and embraced. I would have spoken, I would have drawn near to her; but strongly as she plucked at my heart, drawing me like a magnet, something yet more imperious withheld me; and I could only bow and pass by; and she, leaving my salutation unanswered, only followed me with her noble eyes.

I had now her image by rote, and as I conned the traits in memory it seemed as if I read her very heart. She was dressed with something of her mother's coquetry, and love of positive colour. Her robe, which I knew she must have made with her own hands, clung about her with a cunning grace. After the fashion of that country, besides, her bodice stood open in the middle, in a long slit, and here, in spite of the poverty of the house, a gold coin, hanging by a ribbon, lay on her brown bosom. These were proofs, had any been needed, of her inborn delight in life and her own loveliness. On the other hand, in her eyes that hung upon mine, I could read depth beyond depth of passion and sadness, lights of poetry and hope, blacknesses of despair, and thoughts that were above the earth. It was a lovely body, but the inmate, the soul, was more than worthy of that lodging. Should I leave this incomparable flower to wither unseen on these rough mountains? Should I despise the great gift offered me in the eloquent silence of her eyes? Here was a soul immured; should I not burst its prison? All side considerations fell off from me; were she the child of Herod I swore I should make her mine; and that very evening I set myself, with a mingled sense of treachery and disgrace, to captivate the brother. Perhaps I read him with more favourable eyes, perhaps the thought of his sister always summoned up the better qualities of that imperfect soul; but he had never seemed to me so amiable, and his very likeness to Olalla, while it annoyed, yet softened me.

A third day passed in vain – an empty desert of hours. I would not lose a chance, and loitered all afternoon in the court where (to give myself a countenance) I spoke more than usual with the Señora. God knows it was with a most tender and sincere interest that I now studied her; and even as for Felipe, so now for the mother, I was conscious of a growing warmth of toleration. And yet I wondered. Even while I spoke with her, she would doze off into a little sleep, and presently awake again without embarrassment; and this composure staggered me. And again, as I marked her make infinitesimal changes in her posture, savouring and lingering on the bodily pleasure of the movement, I was driven to wonder at this depth of passive sensuality. She lived in her body; and her consciousness was all sunk into and disseminated through her members, where it luxuriously dwelt. Lastly, I could not grow accustomed to her eyes. Each time she turned on me these great beautiful and meaningless orbs, wide open to the day, but closed against human inquiry – each time I had occasion to observe the lively changes of her pupils which expanded and contracted in a breath – I know not what it was came over me, I can find no name for the mingled feeling of disappointment, annoyance, and distaste that jarred along my nerves. I tried her on a variety of subjects, equally in vain; and at last led the talk to her daughter. But even there she proved indifferent; said she was pretty, which (as with children) was her highest word of commendation, but was plainly incapable of any higher thought; and when I remarked that Olalla seemed silent, merely yawned in my face and replied that speech was of no great use when you had nothing to say. 'People speak much, very much,' she added, looking at me with expanded pupils; and then again yawned, and again showed me a mouth that was as dainty as a toy. This time I took the hint, and, leaving her to her repose, went up into my own chamber to sit by the open window, looking on the hills and not beholding them, sunk in lustrous and deep dreams, and hearkening in fancy to the note of a voice that I had never heard.

I awoke on the fifth morning with a brightness of anticipation that seemed to challenge fate. I was sure of myself, light of heart and foot, and resolved to put my love incontinently to the touch of knowledge. It should lie no longer under the bonds of silence, a dumb thing, living by the eye only, like the love of beasts; but should now put on the spirit, and enter upon the joys of the complete human intimacy. I thought of it with wild hopes, like a voyager to El Dorado; into that unknown and lovely country of her soul, I no longer trembled to adventure. Yet when I did indeed encounter her, the same force of passion descended on me and at once submerged my mind; speech seemed to drop away from me like a childish habit; and I but drew near to her as the giddy man draws near to the margin of a gulf. She drew back from me a little as I came; but her eyes did not waver from mine, and these lured me forward. At last, when I was already within reach of her, I stopped. Words were denied me; if I advanced I could but clasp her to my heart in silence; and all that was sane in me, all that was still unconquered, revolted against the thought of such an accost. So we stood for a second, all our life in our eyes, exchanging salvos of attraction and yet each resisting; and then, with a great effort of the will, and conscious at the same time of a sudden bitterness of disappointment, I turned and went away in the same silence.

What power lay upon me that I could not speak? And she, why was she also silent? Why did she draw away before me dumbly, with fascinated eyes? Was this love? or was it a mere brute attraction, mindless and inevitable, like that of the magnet for the steel? We had never spoken, we were wholly strangers; and yet an influence, strong as the grasp of a giant, swept us silently together. On my side, it filled me with impatience; and yet I was sure that she was worthy; I had seen her books, read her verses, and thus, in a sense, divined the soul of my mistress. But on her side, it struck me almost cold. Of me, she knew nothing but my bodily favour; she was drawn to me as stones fall to the earth; the laws that rule the earth conducted her, unconsenting, to my arms; and I drew back at the thought of such a bridal, and began to be jealous for myself. It was not thus that I desired to be loved. And then I began to fall into a great pity for the girl herself. I thought how sharp must be her mortification, that she, the student, the recluse, Felipe's saintly monitress, should have thus confessed an overweening weakness for a man with whom she had never exchanged a word. And at the coming of pity, all other thoughts were swallowed up; and I longed only to find and console and reassure her; to tell her how wholly her love was returned on my side, and how her choice, even if blindly made, was not unworthy.

The next day it was glorious weather; depth upon depth of blue over-canopied the mountains; the sun shone wide; and the wind in the trees and the many falling torrents in the mountains filled the air with delicate and haunting music. Yet I was prostrated with sadness. My heart wept for the sight of Olalla, as a child weeps for its mother. I sat down on a boulder on the verge of the low cliffs that bound the plateau to the north. Thence I looked down into the wooded valley of a stream, where no foot came. In the mood I was in, it was even touching to behold the place untenanted; it lacked Olalla; and I thought of the delight and glory of a life passed wholly with her in that strong air, and among these rugged and lovely surroundings, at first with a whimpering sentiment, and then again with such a fiery joy that I seemed to grow in strength and stature, like a Samson.

And then suddenly I was aware of Olalla drawing near.

Olalla

She appeared out of a grove of cork-trees, and came straight towards me; and I stood up and waited. She seemed in her walking a creature of such life and fire and lightness as amazed me; yet she came quietly and slowly. Her energy was in the slowness; but for inimitable strength, I felt she would have run, she would have flown to me. Still, as she approached, she kept her eyes lowered to the ground; and when she had drawn quite near, it was without one glance that she addressed me. At the first note of her voice I started. It was for this I had been waiting; this was the last test of my love. And lo, her enunciation was precise and clear, not lisping and incomplete like that of her family; and the voice, though deeper than usual with women, was still both youthful and womanly. She spoke in a rich chord; golden contralto strains mingled with hoarseness, as the red threads were mingled with the brown among her tresses. It was not only a voice that spoke to my heart directly; but it spoke to me of her. And yet her words immediately plunged me back upon despair.

'You will go away,' she said, 'today.'

Her example broke the bonds of my speech; I felt as lightened of a weight, or as if a spell had been dissolved. I know not in what words I answered; but, standing before her on the cliffs, I poured out the whole ardour of my love, telling her that I lived upon the thought of her, slept only to dream of her loveliness, and would gladly forswear my country, my language, and my friends, to live for ever by her side. And then, strongly commanding myself, I changed the note; I reassured, I comforted her; I told her I had divined in her a pious and heroic spirit, with which I was worthy to sympathize, and which I longed to share and lighten. 'Nature,' I told her, 'was the voice of God, which men disobey at peril; and if we were thus dumbly drawn together, ay, even as by a miracle of love, it must imply a divine fitness in our souls; we must be made,' I said – 'made for one another. We should be mad rebels,' I cried out – 'mad rebels against God, not to obey this instinct.'

She shook her head. 'You will go today,' she repeated, and then with a gesture, and in a sudden, sharp note – 'No, not today,' she cried, 'tomorrow!'

But at this sign of relenting, power came in upon me in a tide. I stretched out my arms and called upon her name; and she leaped to me and clung to me. The hills rocked about us, the earth quailed; a shock as of a blow went through me and left me blind and dizzy. And the next moment she had thrust me back, broken rudely from my arms, and fled with the speed of a deer among the cork-trees.

I stood and shouted to the mountains; I turned and went back towards the residencia, walking upon air. She sent me away, and yet I had but to call upon her name and she came to me. These were but the weaknesses of girls, from which even she, the strangest of her sex, was not exempted. Go? Not I, Olalla – O, not I, Olalla, my Olalla! A bird sang near by; and in that season, birds were rare. It bade me be of good cheer. And once more the whole countenance of nature, from the ponderous and stable mountains down to the lightest leaf and the smallest darting fly in the shadow of the groves, began to stir before me and to put on the lineaments of life and wear a face of awful joy. The sunshine struck upon the hills, strong as a hammer on the anvil, and the hills shook;

the earth, under that vigorous insolation, yielded up heady scents; the woods smouldered in the blaze. I felt the thrill of travail and delight run through the earth. Something elemental, something rude, violent, and savage, in the love that sang in my heart, was like a key to nature's secrets; and the very stones that rattled under my feet appeared alive and friendly. Olalla! Her touch had quickened, and renewed, and strung me up to the old pitch of concert with the rugged earth, to a swelling of the soul that men learn to forget in their polite assemblies. Love burned in me like rage; tenderness waxed fierce; I hated, I adored, I pitied, I revered her with ecstasy. She seemed the link that bound me in with dead things on the one hand, and with our pure and pitying God upon the other: a thing brutal and divine, and akin at once to the innocence and to the unbridled forces of the earth.

My head thus reeling, I came into the courtyard of the residencia, and the sight of the mother struck me like a revelation. She sat there, all sloth and contentment, blinking under the strong sunshine, branded with a passive enjoyment, a creature set quite apart, before whom my ardour fell away like a thing ashamed. I stopped a moment, and, commanding such shaken tones as I was able, said a word or two. She looked at me with her unfathomable kindness; her voice in reply sounded vaguely out of the realm of peace in which she slumbered, and there fell on my mind, for the first time, a sense of respect for one so uniformly innocent and happy, and I passed on in a kind of wonder at myself, that I should be so much disquieted.

On my table there lay a piece of the same yellow paper

Robert Louis Stevenson

I had seen in the north room; it was written on with pencil in the same hand, Olalla's hand, and I picked it up with a sudden sinking of alarm, and read, 'If you have any kindness for Olalla, if you have any chivalry for a creature sorely wrought, go from here today; in pity, in honour, for the sake of Him who died, I supplicate that you shall go.' I looked at this awhile in mere stupidity, then I began to awaken to a weariness and horror of life; the sunshine darkened outside on the bare hills, and I began to shake like a man in terror. The vacancy thus suddenly opened in my life unmanned me like a physical void. It was not my heart, it was not my happiness, it was life itself that was involved. I could not lose her. I said so, and stood repeating it. And then, like one in a dream, I moved to the window, put forth my hand to open the casement, and thrust it through the pane. The blood spurted from my wrist; and with an instantaneous quietude and command of myself, I pressed my thumb on the little leaping fountain, and reflected what to do. In that empty room there was nothing to my purpose; I felt, besides, that I required assistance. There shot into my mind a hope that Olalla herself might be my helper, and I turned and went down stairs, still keeping my thumb upon the wound.

There was no sign of either Olalla or Felipe, and I addressed myself to the recess, whither the Señora had not drawn quite back and sat dozing close before the fire, for no degree of heat appeared too much for her.

'Pardon me,' said I, 'if I disturb you, but I must apply to you for help.'

She looked up sleepily and asked me what it was, and with the very words I thought she drew in her breath with a widening of the nostrils and seemed to come suddenly and fully alive.

'I have cut myself,' I said, 'and rather badly. See!' And I held out my two hands from which the blood was oozing and dripping.

Her great eyes opened wide, the pupils shrank into points; a veil seemed to fall from her face, and leave it sharply expressive and yet inscrutable. And as I still stood, marvelling a little at her disturbance, she came swiftly up to me, and stooped and caught me by the hand; and the next moment my hand was at her mouth, and she had bitten me to the bone. The pang of the bite, the sudden spurting of blood, and the monstrous horror of the act, flashed through me all in one, and I beat her back; and she sprang at me again and again, with bestial cries, cries that I recognized, such cries as had awakened me on the night of the high wind. Her strength was like that of madness; mine was rapidly ebbing with the loss of blood; my mind besides was whirling with the abhorrent strangeness of the onslaught, and I was already forced against the wall, when Olalla ran betwixt us, and Felipe, following at a bound, pinned down his mother on the floor.

A trance-like weakness fell upon me; I saw, heard, and felt, but I was incapable of movement. I heard the struggle roll to and fro upon the floor, the yells of that catamount ringing up to Heaven as she strove to reach me. I felt Olalla clasp me in her arms, her hair falling on my face, and, with the strength of a man, raise and half drag, half carry me upstairs into my own room, where she cast me down upon the bed. Then I saw her hasten to the door and lock it, and stand an instant listening to the savage cries that shook the residencia. And then, swift and light as a thought, she was again beside me, binding up my hand, laying it in her bosom, moaning and mourning over it with dove-like sounds. They were not words that came to her, they were sounds more beautiful than speech, infinitely touching, infinitely tender; and yet as I lay there, a thought stung to my heart, a thought wounded me like a sword, a thought, like a worm in a flower, profaned the holiness of my love. Yes, they were beautiful sounds, and they were inspired by human tenderness; but was their beauty human?

All day I lay there. For a long time the cries of that nameless female thing, as she struggled with her half-witted whelp, resounded through the house, and pierced me with despairing sorrow and disgust. They were the death-cry of my love; my love was murdered; it was not only dead, but an offence to me; and yet, think as I pleased, feel as I must, it still swelled within me like a storm of sweetness, and my heart melted at her looks and touch. This horror that had sprung out, this doubt upon Olalla, this savage and bestial strain that ran not only through the whole behaviour of her family, but found a place in the very foundations and story of our love – though it appalled, though it shocked and sickened me, was yet not of power to break the knot of my infatuation.

When the cries had ceased, there came a scraping at the door, by which I knew Felipe was without; and Olalla went and spoke to him – I know not what. With that exception, she stayed close beside me, now kneeling by my bed and fervently praying, now sitting with her eyes upon mine. So then, for these six hours I drank in her beauty, and silently perused the story in her face. I saw the golden coin hover on her breasts; I saw her eyes darken and brighten, and still speak no language but that of an unfathomable kindness; I saw the faultless face, and, through the robe, the lines of the faultless body. Night came at last, and in the growing darkness of the chamber, the sight of her slowly melted; but even then the touch of her smooth hand lingered in mine and talked with me. To lie thus in deadly weakness and drink in the traits of the beloved, is to reawake to love from whatever shock of disillusion. I reasoned with myself; and I shut my eyes on horrors, and again I was very bold to accept the worst. What mattered it, if that imperious sentiment survived; if her eyes still beckoned and attached me; if now, even as before, every fibre of my dull body yearned and turned to her? Late on in the night some strength revived in me, and I spoke:

'Olalla,' I said, 'nothing matters; I ask nothing; I am content; I love you.'

She knelt down awhile and prayed, and I devoutly respected her devotions. The moon had begun to shine in upon one side of each of the three windows, and make a misty clearness in the room, by which I saw her indistinctly. When she re-arose she made the sign of the cross.

'It is for me to speak,' she said, 'and for you to listen. I know; you can but guess. I prayed, how I prayed for you to leave this place. I begged it of you, and I know you would have granted me even this; or if not, O let me think so!'

'I love you,' I said.

'And yet you have lived in the world,' she said; after a

pause, 'you are a man and wise; and I am but a child. Forgive me, if I seem to teach, who am as ignorant as the trees of the mountain; but those who learn much do but skim the face of knowledge; they seize the laws, they conceive the dignity of the design – the horror of the living fact fades from their memory. It is we who sit at home with evil who remember, I think, and are warned and pity. Go, rather, go now, and keep me in mind. So I shall have a life in the cherished places of your memory: a life as much my own, as that which I lead in this body.'

'I love you,' I said once more; and reaching out my weak hand, took hers, and carried it to my lips, and kissed it. Nor did she resist, but winced a little; and I could see her look upon me with a frown that was not unkindly, only sad and baffled. And then it seemed she made a call upon her resolution; plucked my hand towards her, herself at the same time leaning somewhat forward, and laid it on the beating of her heart. 'There,' she cried, 'you feel the very footfall of my life. It only moves for you; it is yours. But is it even mine? It is mine indeed to offer you, as I might take the coin from my neck, as I might break a live branch from a tree, and give it you. And yet not mine! I dwell, or I think I dwell (if I exist at all), somewhere apart, an impotent prisoner, and carried about and deafened by a mob that I disown. This capsule, such as throbs against the sides of animals, knows you at a touch for its master; ay, it loves you! But my soul, does my soul? I think not; I know not, fearing to ask. Yet when you spoke to me your words were of the soul; it is of the soul that you ask – it is only from the soul that you would take me.'

'Olalla,' I said, 'the soul and the body are one, and mostly so in love. What the body chooses, the soul loves; where the body clings, the soul cleaves; body for body, soul to soul, they come together at God's signal; and the lower part (if we can call aught low) is only the footstool and foundation of the highest.'

'Have you,' she said, 'seen the portraits in the house of my fathers? Have you looked at my mother or at Felipe? Have your eyes never rested on that picture that hangs by your bed? She who sat for it died ages ago; and she did evil in her life. But, look again: there is my hand to the least line, there are my eyes and my hair. What is mine, then, and what am I? If not a curve in this poor body of mine (which you love, and for the sake of which you dotingly dream that you love me) not a gesture that I can frame, not a tone of my voice, not any look from my eyes, no, not even now when I speak to him I love, but has belonged to others? Others, ages dead, have wooed other men with my eyes; other men have heard the pleading of the same voice that now sounds in your ears. The hands of the dead are in my bosom; they move me, they pluck me, they guide me; I am a puppet at their command; and I but reinform features and attributes that have long been laid aside from evil in the quiet of the grave. Is it me you love, friend? or the race that made me? The girl who does not know and cannot answer for the least portion of herself? or the stream of which she is a transitory eddy, the tree of which she is the passing fruit? The race exists; it is old, it is ever young, it carries its eternal destiny in its bosom; upon it, like waves upon the sea, individual succeeds to individual, mocked with a semblance of self-control, but they are nothing. We speak of the soul, but the soul is in the race.'

'You fret against the common law,' I said. 'You rebel against the voice of God, which he has made so winning to convince, so imperious to command. Hear it, and how it speaks between us! Your hand clings to mine, your heart leaps at my touch, the unknown elements of which we are compounded awake and run together at a look; the clay of the earth remembers its independent life and yearns to join us; we are drawn together as the stars are turned about in space, or as the tides ebb and flow, by things older and greater than we ourselves.'

'Alas!' she said, 'what can I say to you? My fathers, eight hundred years ago, ruled all this province: they were wise, great, cunning, and cruel; they were a picked race of the Spanish; their flags led in war; the king called them his cousin; the people, when the rope was slung for them or when they returned and found their hovels smoking, blasphemed their name. Presently a change began. Man has risen; if he has sprung from the brutes, he can descend again to the same level. The breath of weariness blew on their humanity and the cords relaxed; they began to go down; their minds fell on sleep, their passions awoke in gusts, heady and senseless like the wind in the gutters of the mountains; beauty was still handed down, but no longer the guiding wit nor the human heart; the seed passed on, it was wrapped in flesh, the flesh covered the bones, but they were the bones and the flesh of brutes, and their mind was as the mind of flies. I speak to you as I dare; but you have seen for yourself how the wheel has gone backward with my doomed race. I stand, as it were, upon a little rising ground in this desperate descent, and see both before and behind, both what we have lost and to what we are condemned to go farther downward. And shall I – I that dwell apart in the house of the dead, my body, loathing its ways – shall I repeat the spell? Shall I bind another spirit, reluctant as my own, into this bewitched and tempest-broken tenement that I now suffer in? Shall I hand down this cursed vessel of humanity, charge it with fresh life as with fresh poison, and dash it, like a fire, in the faces of posterity? But my vow has been given; the race shall cease from off the earth. At this hour my brother is making ready; his foot will soon be on the stair; and you will go with him and pass out of my sight for ever. Think of me sometimes as one to whom the lesson of life was very harshly told, but who heard it with courage; as one who loved you indeed, but who hated herself so deeply that her love was hateful to her; as one who sent you away and yet would have longed to keep you for ever; who had no dearer hope than to forget you, and no greater fear than to be forgotten.'

She had drawn towards the door as she spoke, her rich voice sounding softer and farther away; and with the last word she was gone, and I lay alone in the moonlit chamber. What I might have done had not I lain bound by my extreme weakness, I know not; but as it was there fell upon me a great and blank despair. It was not long before there shone in at the door the ruddy glimmer of a lantern, and Felipe coming, charged me without a word upon his shoulders, and carried me down to the great gate, where the cart was waiting. In the moonlight the hills stood out sharply, as if they were of cardboard; on the glimmering surface of the plateau, and from among the low trees which swung together and sparkled in the wind, the great black cube of the residencia stood out bulkily, its mass only broken by three dimly lighted windows in the northern front above the gate. They were Olalla's windows, and as the cart jolted onwards I kept my eyes fixed upon them till, where the road dipped into a valley, they were lost to my view for ever. Felipe walked in silence beside the shafts, but from time to time he would check the mule and seem to look back upon me; and at length drew quite near and laid his hand upon my head. There was such kindness in the touch, and such a simplicity, as of the brutes, that tears broke from me like the bursting of an artery.

'Felipe,' I said, 'take me where they will ask no questions.'

He said never a word, but he turned his mule about, end for end, retraced some part of the way we had gone, and, striking into another path, led me to the mountain village, which was, as we say in Scotland, the kirkton of that thinly peopled district. Some broken memories dwell in my mind of the day breaking over the plain, of the cart stopping, of arms that helped me down, of a bare room into which I was carried, and of a swoon that fell upon me like sleep.

The next day and the days following the old priest was often at my side with his snuff-box and prayer book, and after a while, when I began to pick up strength, he told me that I was now on a fair way to recovery, and must as soon as possible hurry my departure; whereupon, without naming any reason, he took snuff and looked at me sideways. I did not affect ignorance; I knew he must have seen Olalla. 'Sir,' said I, 'you know that I do not ask in wantonness. What of that family?'

He said they were very unfortunate; that it seemed a

declining race, and that they were very poor and had been much neglected.

'But she has not,' I said. 'Thanks, doubtless, to yourself, she is instructed and wise beyond the use of women.'

'Yes,' he said; 'the Señorita is well-informed. But the family has been neglected.'

'The mother?' I queried.

'Yes, the mother too,' said the Padre, taking snuff. 'But Felipe is a well-intentioned lad.'

'The mother is odd?' I asked.

'Very odd,' replied the priest.

'I think, sir, we beat about the bush,' said I. 'You must know more of my affairs than you allow. You must know my curiosity to be justified on many grounds. Will you not be frank with me?'

'My son,' said the old gentleman, 'I will be very frank with you on matters within my competence; on those of which I know nothing it does not require much discretion to be silent. I will not fence with you, I take your meaning perfectly; and what can I say, but that we are all in God's hands, and that His ways are not as our ways? I have even advised with my superiors in the church, but they, too, were dumb. It is a great mystery.'

'Is she mad?' I asked.

'I will answer you according to my belief. She is not,' returned the Padre, 'or she was not. When she was young – God help me, I fear I neglected that wild lamb – she was surely sane; and yet, although it did not run to such heights, the same strain was already notable; it had been so before her in her father, ay, and before him, and this inclined me, perhaps, to think too lightly of it. But these things go on growing, not only in the individual but in the race.'

'When she was young,' I began, and my voice failed me for a moment, and it was only with a great effort that I was able to add, 'was she like Olalla?'

'Now God forbid!' exclaimed the Padre. 'God forbid that any man should think so slightingly of my favourite penitent. No, no; the Señorita (but for her beauty, which I wish most honestly she had less of) has not a hair's resemblance to what her mother was at the same age. I could not bear to have you think so; though, Heaven knows, it were, perhaps, better that you should.'

At this, I raised myself in bed, and opened my heart to the old man; telling him of our love and of her decision, owning my own horrors, my own passing fancies, but telling him that these were at an end; and with something more than a purely formal submission, appealing to his judgement.

He heard me very patiently and without surprise; and when I had done, he sat for some time silent. Then he began: 'The church,' and instantly broke off again to apologize. 'I had forgotten, my child, that you were not a Christian,' said he. 'And indeed, upon a point so highly unusual, even the church can scarce be said to have decided. But would you have my opinion? The Señorita is, in a matter of this kind, the best judge; I would accept her judgement.'

On the back of that he went away, nor was he thenceforward so assiduous in his visits; indeed, even when I began to get about again, he plainly feared and deprecated my society, not as in distaste but much as a man might be disposed to flee from the riddling sphynx. The villagers, too,

Olalla

avoided me; they were unwilling to be my guides upon the mountain. I thought they looked at me askance, and I made sure that the more superstitious crossed themselves on my approach. At first I set this down to my heretical opinions; but it began at length to dawn upon me that if I was thus redoubted it was because I had stayed at the residencia. All men despise the savage notions of such peasantry; and yet I was conscious of a chill shadow that seemed to fall and dwell upon my love. It did not conquer, but I may not deny that it restrained my ardour.

Some miles westward of the village there was a gap in the sierra, from which the eye plunged direct upon the residencia; and thither it became my daily habit to repair. A wood crowned the summit; and just where the pathway issued from its fringes, it was overhung by a considerable shelf of rock, and that, in its turn, was surmounted by a crucifix of the size of life and more than usually painful in design. This was my perch; thence, day after day, I looked down upon the plateau, and the great old house, and could see Felipe, no bigger than a fly, going to and fro about the garden. Sometimes mists would draw across the view, and be broken up again by mountain winds; sometimes the plain slumbered below me in unbroken sunshine; it would sometimes be all blotted out by rain. This distant post, these interrupted sights of the place where my life had been so strangely changed, suited the indecision of my humour. I passed whole days there, debating with myself the various elements of our position; now leaning to the suggestions of love, now giving an ear to prudence, and in the end halting irresolute between the two.

Robert Louis Stevenson

One day, as I was sitting on my rock, there came by that way a somewhat gaunt peasant wrapped in a mantle. He was a stranger, and plainly did not know me even by repute; for, instead of keeping the other side, he drew near and sat down beside me, and we had soon fallen in talk. Among other things he told me he had been a muleteer, and in former years had much frequented these mountains; later on, he had followed the army with his mules, had realized a competence, and was now living retired with his family.

'Do you know that house?' I inquired, at last, pointing to the residencia, for I readily wearied of any talk that kept me from the thought of Olalla.

He looked at me darkly and crossed himself.

'Too well,' he said, 'it was there that one of my comrades sold himself to Satan; the Virgin shield us from temptations! He has paid the price; he is now burning in the reddest place in Hell!'

A fear came upon me; I could answer nothing; and presently the man resumed, as if to himself: 'Yes,' he said, 'O yes, I know it. I have passed its doors. There was snow upon the pass, the wind was driving it; sure enough there was death that night upon the mountains, but there was worse beside the hearth. I took him by the arm, Señor, and dragged him to the gate; I conjured him, by all he loved and respected, to go forth with me; I went on my knees before him in the snow; and I could see he was moved by my entreaty. And just then she came out on the gallery, and called him by his name; and he turned, and there was she standing with a lamp in her hand and smiling on him to come back. I cried out aloud to God, and threw my arms about him, but he put me by, and left me alone. He had made his choice; God help us. I would pray for him, but to what end? there are sins that not even the Pope can loose.'

'And your friend,' I asked, 'what became of him?'

'Nay, God knows,' said the muleteer. 'If all be true that we hear, his end was like his sin, a thing to raise the hair.'

'Do you mean that he was killed?' I asked.

'Sure enough, he was killed,' returned the man. 'But how? Ay, how? But these are things that it is sin to speak of.'

'The people of that house . . .' I began.

But he interrupted me with a savage outburst. 'The people?' he cried. 'What people? There are neither men nor women in that house of Satan's! What? Have you lived here so long, and never heard?' And here he put his mouth to my ear and whispered, as if even the fowls of the mountain might have overheard and been stricken with horror.

What he told me was not true, nor was it even original; being, indeed, but a new edition, vamped up again by village ignorance and superstition, of stories nearly as ancient as the race of man. It was rather the application that appalled me. In the old days, he said, the church would have burned out that nest of basilisks; but the arm of the church was now shortened; his friend Miguel had been unpunished by the hands of men, and left to the more awful judgment of an offended God. This was wrong; but it should be so no more. The Padre was sunk in age; he was even bewitched himself; but the eyes of his flock were now awake to their own danger; and some day – ay, and before long – the smoke of that house should go up to heaven.

He left me filled with horror and fear. Which way to turn

I knew not; whether first to warn the Padre, or to carry my ill-news direct to the threatened inhabitants of the residencia. Fate was to decide for me; for, while I was still hesitating, I beheld the veiled figure of a woman drawing near to me up the pathway. No veil could deceive my penetration; by every line and every movement I recognized Olalla; and keeping hidden behind a corner of the rock, I suffered her to gain the summit. Then I came forward. She knew me and paused, but did not speak; I, too, remained silent; and we continued for some time to gaze upon each other with a passionate sadness.

'I thought you had gone,' she said at length. 'It is all that you can do for me – to go. It is all I ever asked of you. And you still stay. But do you know, that every day heaps up the peril of death, not only on your head, but on ours? A report has gone about the mountain; it is thought you love me, and the people will not suffer it.'

I saw she was already informed of her danger, and I rejoiced at it. 'Olalla,' I said, 'I am ready to go this day, this very hour, but not alone.'

She stepped aside and knelt down before the crucifix to pray, and I stood by and looked now at her and now at the object of her adoration, now at the living figure of the penitent, and now at the ghastly, daubed countenance, the painted wounds, and the projected ribs of the image. The silence was only broken by the wailing of some large birds that circled sidelong, as if in surprise or alarm, about the summit of the hills. Presently Olalla rose again, turned towards me, raised her veil, and, still leaning with one hand on the shaft of the crucifix, looked upon me with a pale and sorrowful countenance.

'I have laid my hand upon the cross,' she said. 'The Padre says you are no Christian; but look up for a moment with my eyes, and behold the face of the Man of Sorrows. We are all such as He was – the inheritors of sin; we must all bear and expiate a past which was not ours; there is in all of us – ay, even in me – a sparkle of the divine. Like Him, we must endure for a little while, until morning returns bringing peace. Suffer me to pass on upon my way alone; it is thus that I shall be least lonely, counting for my friend Him who is the friend of all the distressed; it is thus that I shall be the most happy, having taken my farewell of earthly happiness, and willingly accepted sorrow for my portion.'

I looked at the face of the crucifix, and, though I was no friend to images, and despised that imitative and grimacing art of which it was a rude example, some sense of what the thing implied was carried home to my intelligence. The face looked down upon me with a painful and deadly contraction; but the rays of a glory encircled it, and reminded me that the sacrifice was voluntary. It stood there, crowning the rock, as it still stands on so many highway sides, vainly preaching to passers-by, an emblem of sad and noble truths: that pleasure is not an end, but an accident; that pain is the choice of the magnanimous; that it is best to suffer all things and do well. I turned and went down the mountain in silence; and when I looked back for the last time before the wood closed about my path, I saw Olalla still leaning on the crucifix.

1. BOCCACCIO · *Mrs Rosie and the Priest*
2. GERARD MANLEY HOPKINS · *As kingfishers catch fire*
3. *The Saga of Gunnlaug Serpent-tongue*
4. THOMAS DE QUINCEY · *On Murder Considered as One of the Fine Arts*
5. FRIEDRICH NIETZSCHE · *Aphorisms on Love and Hate*
6. JOHN RUSKIN · *Traffic*
7. PU SONGLING · *Wailing Ghosts*
8. JONATHAN SWIFT · *A Modest Proposal*
9. *Three Tang Dynasty Poets*
10. WALT WHITMAN · *On the Beach at Night Alone*
11. KENKŌ · *A Cup of Sake Beneath the Cherry Trees*
12. BALTASAR GRACIÁN · *How to Use Your Enemies*
13. JOHN KEATS · *The Eve of St Agnes*
14. THOMAS HARDY · *Woman much missed*
15. GUY DE MAUPASSANT · *Femme Fatale*
16. MARCO POLO · *Travels in the Land of Serpents and Pearls*
17. SUETONIUS · *Caligula*
18. APOLLONIUS OF RHODES · *Jason and Medea*
19. ROBERT LOUIS STEVENSON · *Olalla*
20. KARL MARX AND FRIEDRICH ENGELS · *The Communist Manifesto*
21. PETRONIUS · *Trimalchio's Feast*
22. JOHANN PETER HEBEL · *How a Ghastly Story Was Brought to Light by a Common or Garden Butcher's Dog*
23. HANS CHRISTIAN ANDERSEN · *The Tinder Box*
24. RUDYARD KIPLING · *The Gate of the Hundred Sorrows*
25. DANTE · *Circles of Hell*
26. HENRY MAYHEW · *Of Street Piemen*
27. HAFEZ · *The nightingales are drunk*
28. GEOFFREY CHAUCER · *The Wife of Bath*
29. MICHEL DE MONTAIGNE · *How We Weep and Laugh at the Same Thing*
30. THOMAS NASHE · *The Terrors of the Night*
31. EDGAR ALLAN POE · *The Tell-Tale Heart*
32. MARY KINGSLEY · *A Hippo Banquet*
33. JANE AUSTEN · *The Beautifull Cassandra*
34. ANTON CHEKHOV · *Gooseberries*
35. SAMUEL TAYLOR COLERIDGE · *Well, they are gone, and here must I remain*
36. JOHANN WOLFGANG VON GOETHE · *Sketchy, Doubtful, Incomplete Jottings*
37. CHARLES DICKENS · *The Great Winglebury Duel*
38. HERMAN MELVILLE · *The Maldive Shark*
39. ELIZABETH GASKELL · *The Old Nurse's Story*
40. NIKOLAY LESKOV · *The Steel Flea*

41. HONORÉ DE BALZAC · *The Atheist's Mass*
42. CHARLOTTE PERKINS GILMAN · *The Yellow Wall-Paper*
43. C.P. CAVAFY · *Remember, Body . . .*
44. FYODOR DOSTOEVSKY · *The Meek One*
45. GUSTAVE FLAUBERT · *A Simple Heart*
46. NIKOLAI GOGOL · *The Nose*
47. SAMUEL PEPYS · *The Great Fire of London*
48. EDITH WHARTON · *The Reckoning*
49. HENRY JAMES · *The Figure in the Carpet*
50. WILFRED OWEN · *Anthem For Doomed Youth*
51. WOLFGANG AMADEUS MOZART · *My Dearest Father*
52. PLATO · *Socrates' Defence*
53. CHRISTINA ROSSETTI · *Goblin Market*
54. *Sindbad the Sailor*
55. SOPHOCLES · *Antigone*
56. RYŪNOSUKE AKUTAGAWA · *The Life of a Stupid Man*
57. LEO TOLSTOY · *How Much Land Does A Man Need?*
58. GIORGIO VASARI · *Leonardo da Vinci*
59. OSCAR WILDE · *Lord Arthur Savile's Crime*
60. SHEN FU · *The Old Man of the Moon*
61. AESOP · *The Dolphins, the Whales and the Gudgeon*
62. MATSUO BASHŌ · *Lips too Chilled*
63. EMILY BRONTË · *The Night is Darkening Round Me*
64. JOSEPH CONRAD · *To-morrow*
65. RICHARD HAKLUYT · *The Voyage of Sir Francis Drake Around the Whole Globe*
66. KATE CHOPIN · *A Pair of Silk Stockings*
67. CHARLES DARWIN · *It was snowing butterflies*
68. BROTHERS GRIMM · *The Robber Bridegroom*
69. CATULLUS · *I Hate and I Love*
70. HOMER · *Circe and the Cyclops*
71. D. H. LAWRENCE · *Il Duro*
72. KATHERINE MANSFIELD · *Miss Brill*
73. OVID · *The Fall of Icarus*
74. SAPPHO · *Come Close*
75. IVAN TURGENEV · *Kasyan from the Beautiful Lands*
76. VIRGIL · *O Cruel Alexis*
77. H. G. WELLS · *A Slip under the Microscope*
78. HERODOTUS · *The Madness of Cambyses*
79. *Speaking of Siva*
80. *The Dhammapada*

'I blush to say what happened next.'

GAIUS PETRONIUS ARBITER
Lived in the Roman Empire in the first century CE
Died *c.* 66 CE

Taken from J. P. Sullivan's translation of *The Satyricon*,
first published in 1965.

PETRONIUS IN PENGUIN CLASSICS
The Satyricon

PETRONIUS

Trimalchio's Feast

Translated by
J. P. Sullivan

PENGUIN BOOKS

PENGUIN CLASSICS

UK | USA | Canada | Ireland | Australia
India | New Zealand | South Africa

Penguin Books is part of the Penguin Random House group of companies whose addresses can be found at global.penguinrandomhouse.com.

This selection published in Penguin Classics 2015
008

Translation copyright © J. P. Sullivan, 1965, 1969, 1974, 1977, 1986

The moral right of the translator has been asserted

Set in 9/12.4 pt Baskerville 10 Pro
Typeset by Jouve (UK), Milton Keynes

Printed and bound in Great Britain by Clays Ltd, Elcograf S.p.A.

A CIP catalogue record for this book is available from the British Library

ISBN: 978-0-141-39800-6

www.greenpenguin.co.uk

MIX
Paper from
responsible sources
FSC® C018179

Penguin Random House is committed to a sustainable future for our business, our readers and our planet. This book is made from Forest Stewardship Council® certified paper.

The next day but one finally arrived[, and that meant the prospect of a free dinner]. But we were so knocked about that we wanted to run rather than rest. We were mournfully discussing how to avoid the approaching storm, when one of Agamemnon's slaves broke in on our frantic debate.

'Here,' said he, 'don't you know who's your host today? It's Trimalchio – he's terribly elegant . . . He has a clock in the dining-room and a trumpeter all dressed up to tell him how much longer he's got to live.'

This made us forget all our troubles. We dressed carefully and told Giton, who was very kindly acting as our servant, to attend us at the baths.

We did not take our clothes off but began wandering around, or rather exchanging jokes while circulating among the little groups. Suddenly we saw a bald old man in a reddish shirt, playing ball with some long-haired boys. It was not so much the boys that made us watch, although they alone were worth the trouble, but the old gentleman himself. He was taking his exercise in slippers and throwing a green ball around. But he didn't pick it up if it touched the ground; instead there was a slave holding a bagful, and he supplied them to the players. We noticed other novelties. Two eunuchs stood around at different points: one of them carried a silver pissing bottle, the other counted the balls, not those flying from hand to hand according to the rules, but those that fell to the ground. We were still admiring these elegant arrangements when Menelaus hurried up to us.

'This is the man you'll be dining with,' he said. 'In fact, you are now watching the beginning of the dinner.'

No sooner had Menelaus spoken than Trimalchio snapped his fingers. At the signal the eunuch brought up the pissing bottle for him, while he went on playing. With the weight off his bladder, he demanded water for his hands, splashed a few drops on his fingers and wiped them on a boy's head.

It would take too long to pick out isolated incidents. Anyway, we entered the baths where we began sweating at once and we went immediately into the cold water. Trimalchio had been smothered in perfume and was already being rubbed down, not with linen towels, but with bath-robes of the finest wool. As this was going on, three masseurs sat drinking Falernian in front of him. Through quarrelling they spilled most of it and Trimalchio said they were drinking his health. Wrapped in thick scarlet felt he was put into a litter. Four couriers with lots of medals went in front, as well as a go-kart in which his favourite boy was riding – a wizened, bleary-eyed youngster, uglier than his master. As he was carried off, a musician with a tiny set of pipes took his place by Trimalchio's head and whispered a tune in his ear the whole way.

We followed on, choking with amazement by now, and arrived at the door with Agamemnon at our side. On the door-post a notice was fastened which read:

Trimalchio's Feast

ANY SLAVE LEAVING THE HOUSE WITHOUT
HIS MASTER'S PERMISSION WILL RECEIVE
ONE HUNDRED LASHES

Just at the entrance stood the hall-porter, dressed in a green uniform with a belt of cherry red. He was shelling peas into a silver basin. Over the doorway hung – of all things – a golden cage from which a spotted magpie greeted visitors.

As I was gaping at all this, I almost fell over backwards and broke a leg. There, on the left as one entered, not far from the porter's cubbyhole, was a huge dog with a chain round its neck. It was painted on the wall and over it, in big capitals, was written:

BEWARE OF THE DOG

My colleagues laughed at me, but when I got my breath back I went on to examine the whole wall. There was a mural of a slave market, price-tags and all. Then Trimalchio himself, holding a wand of Mercury and being led into Rome by Minerva. After this a picture of how he learned accounting and, finally, how he became a steward. The painstaking artist had drawn it all in great detail with descriptions underneath. Just where the colonnade ended Mercury hauled him up by the chin and rushed him to a high platform. Fortune with her horn of plenty and the three Fates spinning their golden threads were there in attendance.

I also noticed in the colonnade a company of runners practising with their trainer. In one corner was a large cabinet, which served as a shrine for some silver statues of the household deities with a marble figure of Venus and an impressive gold casket in which, they told me, the master's first beard was preserved.

I began asking the porter what were the pictures they had in the middle.

'The Iliad, the Odyssey,' he said, 'and the gladiatorial show given by Laenas.'

Time did not allow us to look at many things there... by now we had reached the dining-room, at the entrance to which sat a treasurer going over the accounts. There was one feature I particularly admired: on the door-posts were fixed rods and axes tapering off at their lowest point into something like the bronze beak of a ship. On it was the inscription:

> PRESENTED TO C. POMPEIUS TRIMALCHIO
> PRIEST OF THE AUGUSTAN COLLEGE
> BY HIS STEWARD CINNAMUS

Beneath this same inscription a fixture with twin lamps dangled from the ceiling and two notices, one on each door-post. One of them, if my memory is correct, had written on it:

> 30 AND 31 DECEMBER
> OUR GAIUS
> IS OUT TO DINNER

The other displayed representations of the moon's phases and the seven heavenly bodies. Lucky and unlucky days were marked with different coloured studs.

Trimalchio's Feast

Having had enough of these interesting things, we attempted to go in, but one of the slaves shouted: 'Right foot first!' Naturally we hesitated a moment in case one of us should cross the threshold the wrong way. But just as we were all stepping forward, a slave with his back bare flung himself at our feet and began pleading with us to get him off a flogging. He was in trouble for nothing very serious, he told us – the steward's clothes, hardly worth ten sesterces, had been stolen from him at the baths. Back went our feet, and we appealed to the steward, who was counting out gold pieces in the office, to let the man off.

He lifted his head haughtily: 'It is not so much the actual loss that annoys me,' he said, 'it's the wretch's carelessness. They were my dinner clothes he lost. A client had presented them to me on my birthday – genuine Tyrian purple, of course; however they had been laundered once. So what does it matter? He's all yours.'

We were very much obliged to him for this favour; and when we did enter the dining-room, that same slave whose cause we had pleaded ran up to us and, to our utter confusion, covered us with kisses and thanked us for our kindness.

'And what's more,' he said, 'you'll know right away who it is you have been so kind to. "The master's wine is the waiter's gift."'

Finally we took our places. Boys from Alexandria poured iced water over our hands. Others followed them and attended to our feet, removing any hangnails with great skill. But they were not quiet even during this troublesome operation: they sang away at their work. I wanted to find out if the whole staff were singers, so I asked for a drink. In a flash a boy was there, singing in a shrill voice while he attended to me – and anyone else who was asked for something did the same. It was more like a musical comedy than a respectable dinner party.

Some extremely elegant hors d'oeuvres were served at this point – by now everyone had taken his place with the exception of Trimalchio, for whom, strangely enough, the place at the top was reserved. The dishes for the first course included an ass of Corinthian bronze with two panniers, white olives on one side and black on the other. Over the ass were two pieces of plate, with Trimalchio's name and the weight of the silver inscribed on the rims. There were some small iron frames shaped like bridges supporting dormice sprinkled with honey and poppy seed. There were steaming hot sausages too, on a silver gridiron with damsons and pomegranate seeds underneath.

We were in the middle of these elegant dishes when Trimalchio himself was carried in to the sound of music and set down on a pile of tightly stuffed cushions. The sight of him drew an astonished laugh from the guests. His cropped head stuck out from a scarlet coat; his neck was well muffled up and he had put round it a napkin with a broad purple stripe and tassels dangling here and there. On the little finger of his left hand he wore a heavy gilt ring and a smaller one on the last joint of the next finger. This I thought was solid gold, but actually it was studded with little iron stars. And to show off even more of his jewellery, he had his right arm bare and set off by a gold armlet and an ivory circlet fastened with a gleaming metal plate.

Trimalchio's Feast

After picking his teeth with a silver toothpick, he began: 'My friends, I wasn't keen to come into the dining-room yet. But if I stayed away any more, I would have kept you back, so I've deprived myself of all my little pleasures for you. However, you'll allow me to finish my game.'

A boy was at his heels with a board of terebinth wood with glass squares, and I noticed the very last word in luxury – instead of white and black pieces he had gold and silver coins. While he was swearing away like a trooper over his game and we were still on the hors d'oeuvres, a tray was brought in with a basket on it. There sat a wooden hen, its wings spread round it the way hens are when they are broody. Two slaves hurried up and as the orchestra played a tune they began searching through the straw and dug out peahens' eggs, which they distributed to the guests.

Trimalchio turned to look at this little scene and said: 'My friends, I gave orders for that bird to sit on some peahens' eggs. I hope to goodness they are not starting to hatch. However, let's try them and see if they are still soft.'

We took up our spoons (weighing at least half a pound each) and cracked the eggs, which were made of rich pastry. To tell the truth, I nearly threw away my share, as the chicken seemed already formed. But I heard a guest who was an old hand say: 'There should be something good here.' So I searched the shell with my fingers and found the plumpest little figpecker, all covered with yolk and seasoned with pepper.

At this point Trimalchio became tired of his game and demanded that all the previous dishes be brought to him. He gave permission in a loud voice for any of us to have another glass of mead if we wanted it. Suddenly there was a crash from the orchestra and a troop of waiters – still singing – snatched away the hors d'oeuvres. However in the confusion one of the side-dishes happened to fall and a slave picked it up from the floor. Trimalchio noticed this, had the boy's ears boxed and told him to throw it down again. A cleaner came in with a broom and began to sweep up the silver plate along with the rest of the rubbish. Two long-haired Ethiopians followed him, carrying small skin bags like those used by the men who scatter the sand in the amphitheatre, and they poured wine over our hands – no one ever offered us water.

Our host was complimented on these elegant arrangements. 'Mars loves a fair fight,' he replied. 'That is why I gave orders for each guest to have his own table. At the same time these smelly slaves won't crowd so.'

Carefully sealed wine bottles were immediately brought, their necks labelled:

FALERNIAN
CONSUL OPIMIUS
ONE HUNDRED YEARS OLD

While we were examining the labels, Trimalchio clapped his hands and said with a sigh:

'Wine has a longer life than us poor folks. So let's wet our whistles. Wine is life. I'm giving you real Opimian. I didn't put out such good stuff yesterday, though the company was much better class.'

Trimalchio's Feast

Naturally we drank and missed no opportunity of admiring his elegant hospitality. In the middle of this a slave brought in a silver skeleton, put together in such a way that its joints and backbone could be pulled out and twisted in all directions. After he had flung it about on the table once or twice, its flexible joints falling into various postures, Trimalchio recited:

> 'O woe, woe, man is only a dot:
> Hell drags us off and that is the lot;
> So let us live a little space,
> At least while we can feed our face.'

After our applause the next course was brought in. Actually it was not as grand as we expected, but it was so novel that everyone stared. It was a deep circular tray with the twelve signs of the Zodiac arranged round the edge. Over each of them the chef had placed some appropriate dainty suggested by the subject. Over Aries the Ram, chickpeas; over Taurus the Bull, a beefsteak; over the Heavenly Twins, testicles and kidneys; over Cancer the Crab, a garland; over Leo the Lion, an African fig; over Virgo the Virgin, a young sow's udder; over Libra the Scales, a balance with a cheesecake in one pan and a pastry in the other; over Scorpio, a sea scorpion; over Sagittarius the Archer, a sea bream with eyespots; over Capricorn, a lobster; over Aquarius the Water-Carrier, a goose; over Pisces the Fishes, two mullets. In the centre was a piece of grassy turf bearing a honeycomb. A young Egyptian slave carried around bread in a silver oven . . . and in a sickening voice he mangled a song from the show *The Asafoetida Man*.

As we started rather reluctantly on this inferior fare, Trimalchio said:

'Let's eat, if you don't mind. This is the sauce of all order.' As he spoke, four dancers hurtled forward in time to the music and removed the upper part of the great dish, revealing underneath plump fowls, sows' udders, and a hare with wings fixed to his middle to look like Pegasus. We also noticed four figures of Marsyas with little skin bottles, which let a peppery fish-sauce go running over some fish, which seemed to be swimming in a little channel. We all joined in the servants' applause and amid some laughter we helped ourselves to these quite exquisite things.

Trimalchio was every bit as happy as we were with this sort of trick: 'Carve 'er!' he cried. Up came the man with the carving knife and, with his hands moving in time to the orchestra, he sliced up the victuals like a charioteer battling to the sound of organ music. And still Trimalchio went on saying insistently: 'Carve 'er, Carver!'

I suspected this repetition was connected with some witticism, and I went so far as to ask the man on my left what it meant. He had watched this sort of game quite often and said:

'You see the fellow doing the carving – he's called Carver. So whenever he says "Carver!" he's calling out his name and his orders.'

I couldn't face any more food. Instead I turned to this man to find out as much as I could. I began pestering him for gossip and information – who was the woman running round the place?

'Trimalchio's wife,' he told me, 'Fortunata is her name and

Trimalchio's Feast

she counts her money by the sackful. And before, before, what was she? You'll pardon me saying so, but you wouldn't of touched a bit of bread from her hand. Nowadays – and who knows how or why – she's in heaven, and she's absolutely everything to Trimalchio. In fact, if she tells him at high noon it's dark, he'll believe her. He doesn't know himself how much he's got, he's so loaded – but this bitch looks after everything; she's even in places you wouldn't think of. She's dry, sober and full of ideas – you see all that gold! – but she's got a rough tongue and she's a real magpie when she gets her feet up. If she likes you, she likes you – if she doesn't like you, she doesn't like you.

'The old boy himself now, he's got estates it'd take a kite to fly over – he's worth millions of millions. There's more silver plate lying in his porter's cubbyhole than any other man owns altogether. As for his servants – boy, oh boy! I honestly don't think there's one in ten knows his own master. In fact he could knock any of these smart boys into a cocked hat.

'And don't you think he buys anything, either. Everything is home-grown: wool, citrus, pepper. If you ask for hen's milk, you'll get it. In fact, there was a time when the wool he'd got wasn't good enough for him, so he brought some rams from Tarentum and banged them into his sheep. To get home-grown Attic honey, he ordered some bees from Athens – the Greek strain improved his own bees a bit at the same time.

'And here's something more – this last few days he wrote off for mushroom spores from India. Why, he hasn't a single mule that wasn't sired by a wild ass. You see all these cushions – every one of them has either purple or scarlet stuffing. There's happiness for you!

'But mind you, don't look down on the other freedmen here. They're dripping with the stuff. You see that man on the very bottom couch. At present he's got eight hundred thousand of his own. He started out with nothing. It's not long since he was humping wood on his own back. They say – I don't know myself, I've heard it – they say he stole a hobgoblin's cap and found its treasure. I don't begrudge anyone what god has given him. Besides, he can still feel his master's slap and wants to give himself a good time. For instance, the other day he put up a notice which said:

> GAIUS POMPEIUS DIOGENES
> IS MOVING TO HIS HOUSE AND
> WILL LET THE ROOM OVER
> HIS SHOP FROM 1 JULY

'Now that fellow in the freedman's place – look how well off he was once! I'm not blaming him – he had a million in his hands, but he slipped badly. I don't think he can call his hair his own. Yet I'd swear it wasn't his fault: there's not a better man alive. Some freedmen and crooks pocketed everything he had. One thing you can be sure of – you have partners and your pot never boils, and once things take a turn for the worse, friends get out from underneath. What a respectable business he had and look at him now! He was an undertaker. He used to eat like a king – boars roasted in their skins, elaborate pastry, braised game birds, as well as fish and hares. More wine was spilt under the table than another man keeps in his cellar. He wasn't a man, he was an absolute dream! When things were looking black, he didn't want his creditors to think he was bankrupt, so he put up notice of an auction like this:

GAIUS JULIUS PROCULUS
AUCTION OF SURPLUS STOCK'

Trimalchio interrupted these pleasant reminiscences. The dish had already been removed and the convivial guests had begun to concentrate on the drink and general conversation. Leaning on his elbow, Trimalchio said:

'Now you're supposed to be enjoying the wine. Fishes have to swim. I ask you, do you think I'm just content with that course you saw in the bottom of the dish? "Is this like the Ulysses you know?" Well then, we've got to display some culture at our dinner. My patron – God rest his bones! – wanted me to hold up my head in any company. There's nothing new to me, as that there dish proves. Look now, these here heavens, as there are twelve gods living in 'em, changes into that many shapes. First it becomes the Ram. So whoever is born under that sign has a lot of herds, a lot of wool, a hard head as well, a brassy front and a sharp horn. Most scholars are born under this sign, and most mutton-heads as well.'

We applauded the wit of our astrologer and he went on:

'Then the whole heavens turns into the little old Bull. So bullheaded folk are born then, and cow-herds and those who find their own feed. Under the Heavenly Twins on the other hand – pairs-in-hand, yokes of oxen, people with big ballocks and people who do it both ways. I was born under the Crab, so I have a lot of legs to stand on and a lot of property on land and sea, because the Crab takes both in his stride. And that's why I put nothing over him earlier, so as not to upset my horoscope. Under Leo are born greedy and bossy people. Under the Virgin, effeminates, runaways and candidates for the chain-gang. Under the Scales, butchers, perfume-sellers and anyone who weighs things up. Under Scorpio poisoners and murderers. Under Sagittarius are born cross-eyed people who look at the vegetables and take the bacon. Under Capricorn, people in trouble who sprout horns through their worries. Under the Water-Carrier, bartenders and jugheads. Under the Fishes, fish-fryers and people who spout in public.

'So the starry sky turns round like a millstone, always bringing some trouble, and men being born or dying.

'Now as for what you see in the middle, the piece of grass and on the grass the honeycomb, I don't do anything without a reason – it's Mother Earth in the middle, round like an egg, with all good things inside her like a honeycomb.'

'Oh, clever!' we all cried, raising our hands to the ceiling and swearing that Hipparchus and Aratus couldn't compete with *him*.

Then the servants came up and laid across the couches embroidered coverlets showing nets, hunters carrying broad spears, and all the paraphernalia of hunting. We were still wondering which way to look when a tremendous clamour arose outside the dining-room, and – surprise! – Spartan hounds began dashing everywhere, even round the table. Behind them came a great dish and on it lay a wild boar of

Trimalchio's Feast

the largest possible size, and, what is more, wearing a freedman's cap on its head. From its tusks dangled two baskets woven from palm leaves, one full of fresh Syrian dates, the other of dried Theban dates. Little piglets made of cake were all round as though at its dugs, suggesting it was a brood sow now being served. These were actually gifts to take home. Surprisingly the man who took his place to cut up the boar was not our old friend Carver but a huge bearded fellow, wearing leggings and a damask hunting coat. He pulled out a hunting knife and made a great stab at the boar's side and, as he struck, out flew a flock of thrushes. But there were fowlers all ready with their limed reeds, who caught them as soon as they began flying round the room.

Trimalchio gave orders for each guest to have his own bird, then added:

'And have a look at the delicious acorns our pig in the wood has been eating.'

Young slaves promptly went to the baskets and gave the guests their share of the two kinds of date.

As this was going on, I kept quiet, turning over a lot of ideas as to why the boar had come in with a freedman's cap on it. After working through all sorts of wild fancies, I ventured to put to my experienced neighbour the question I was racking my brains with. He of course replied:

'Even the man waiting on you could explain this obvious point – it's not puzzling at all, it's quite simple. The boar here was pressed into service for the last course yesterday, but the guests let it go. So today it returns to the feast as a freedman.'

I damned my own stupidity and asked no more questions in case I looked like someone who had never dined in decent company.

As we were talking, a handsome youth with a garland of vine-leaves and ivy round his head, pretending to be Bacchus the Reveller, then Bacchus the Deliverer and Bacchus the Inspirer, carried grapes round in a basket, all the time giving us a recital of his master's lyrics in a high-pitched voice. At the sound, Trimalchio called out, 'Dionysus, now be Bacchus the Liberat . . .'

The lad pulled the freedman's cap off the boar and stuck it on his head. Then Trimalchio commented:

'Now you won't deny my claim to be the liberated sort.' We applauded his joke and kissed the boy hard as he went round.

After this course Trimalchio got up and went to the toilet. Free of his domineering presence, we began to help ourselves to more drinks. Dama started off by calling for a cup of the grape.

'The day's nothin',' he said. 'It's night 'fore y'can turn around. So the best thing's get out of bed and go straight to dinner. Lovely cold weather we've had too. M'bath hardly thawed me out. Still, a hot drink's as good as an overcoat. I've been throwin' it back neat, and you can see I'm tight – the wine's gone to m'head.'

Seleucus took up the ball in the conversation:

'Me now,' he said, 'I don't have a bath every day. It's like getting rubbed with fuller's earth, havin' a bath. The water bites into you, and your heart begins to melt. But when I've knocked back a hot glass of wine and honey, "Go fuck yourself," I say to the cold weather. Mind you, I couldn't have a bath – I was at a funeral today. Poor old Chrysanthus has just given up the ghost – nice man he was! It was only the other day he stopped me in the street. I still seem to hear his voice. Dear, dear! We're just so many walking bags of wind. We're worse than flies – at least they have got some strength in them, but we're no more than empty bubbles.

'And yet he had been on an extremely strict diet? For five days he didn't take a drop of water or a crumb of bread into his mouth. But he's gone to join the majority. The doctors finished him – well, hard luck, more like. After all, a doctor is just to put your mind at rest. Still, he got a good send-off – he had a bier, and all beautifully draped. His mourners – several of his slaves were left their freedom – did him proud, even though his widow was a bit mean with her tears. And yet he had been extremely good to her! But women as a sex are real vultures. It's no good doing them a favour, you might as well throw it down a well. An old passion is just an ulcer.'

He was being a bore and Phileros said loudly:

'Let's think of the living. He's got what he deserved. He lived an honest life and he died an honest death. What has he got to complain about? He started out in life with just a penny and he was ready to pick up less than that from a muck-heap, even if he had to use his teeth. So whatever he put a finger to swelled up like a honeycomb. I honestly think he left a solid hundred thousand and he had the lot in hard cash. But I'll be honest about it, since I'm a bit of a cynic: he had a foul mouth and too much lip. He wasn't a man, he was just trouble.

'Now his brother was a brave lad, a real friend to his friends, always ready with a helping hand or a decent meal.

'Chrysanthus had bad luck at first, but the first vintage set him on his feet. He fixed his own price when he sold the wine. And what properly kept his head above water was a legacy he came in for, when he pocketed more than was left to him. And the blockhead, when he had a quarrel with his brother, cut him out of his will in favour of some sod we've never heard of. You're leaving a lot behind when you leave your own flesh and blood. But he kept listening to his slaves and they really fixed him. It's never right to believe all you're told, especially for a businessman. But it's true he enjoyed himself while he lived. You got it, you keep it. He was certainly Fortune's favourite – lead turned to gold in his hand. Mind you, it's easy when everything runs smoothly.

'And how old do you think he was? Seventy or more! But he was hard as a horn and carried his age well. His hair was black as a raven's wing. I knew the man for ages and ages and he was still an old lecher. I honestly don't think he left the dog alone. What's more, he liked little boys – he could turn his hand to anything. Well, I don't blame him – after all, he couldn't take anything else with him.'

This was Phileros, then Ganymedes said:

'You're all talking about things that don't concern heaven or earth. Meanwhile, no one gives a damn the way we're hit by the corn situation. Honest to god, I couldn't get hold of a mouthful of bread today. And look how there's still no rain. It's been absolute starvation for a whole year now. To hell with the food officers! They're in with the bakers – "You be nice to me and I'll be nice to you." So the little man suffers, while those grinders of the poor never stop celebrating. Oh, if only we still had the sort of men I found here when I first arrived from Asia. Like lions they were. That was the life! Come one, come all! If plain flour was inferior to the very finest, they'd thrash those bogeymen till they thought God Almighty was after them.

'I remember Safinius – he used to live by the old arch then; I was a boy at the time. He wasn't a man, he was all pepper. He used to scorch the ground wherever he went. But he was dead straight – don't let him down and he wouldn't let you down. You'd be ready to play *morra* with him in the dark. But on the city council, how he used to wade into some of them – no beating about the bush, straight from the shoulder! And when he was in court, his voice got louder and louder like a trumpet. He never sweated or spat – I think he'd been through the oven all right. And very affable he was when you met him, calling everyone by name just like one of us. Naturally at the time corn was dirt cheap. You could buy a penny loaf that two of you couldn't get through. Today – I've seen bigger bull's-eyes.

'Ah me! It's getting worse every day. This place is going down like a calf's tail. But why do we have a third-rate food officer who wouldn't lose a penny to save our lives? He sits at home laughing and rakes in more money a day than anyone else's whole fortune. I happen to know he's just made a thousand in gold. But if we had any balls at all, he wouldn't be feeling so pleased with himself. People today are lions at home and foxes outside.

'Take me. I've already sold the rags off my back for food and if this shortage continues I'll be selling my bit of a house. What's going to happen to this place if neither god nor man will help us? As I hope to go home tonight, I'm sure all this is heaven's doing.

'Nobody believes in heaven, see, nobody fasts, nobody gives a damn for the Almighty. No, people only bow their heads to count their money. In the old days high-class ladies used to climb up the hill barefoot, their hair loose and their hearts pure, and ask God for rain. And he'd send it down in bucketfuls right away – it was then or never – and everyone went home like drowned rats. Since we've given up religion the gods nowadays keep their feet wrapped up in wool. The fields just lie . . .'

'Please, please,' broke in Echion the rag-merchant, 'be a bit more cheerful. "First it's one thing, then another," as the yokel said when he lost his spotted pig. What we haven't got today, we'll have tomorrow. That's the way life goes. Believe me, you couldn't name a better country, if it had the people. As things are, I admit, it's having a hard time, but it isn't the only place. We mustn't be soft. The sky don't get no nearer wherever you are. If you were somewhere else, you'd be talking about the pigs walking round ready-roasted back here.

'And another thing, we'll be having a holiday with a three-day show that's the best ever – and not just a hack troupe of gladiators but freedmen for the most part. My old friend Titus has a big heart and a hot head. Maybe this, maybe that, but something at all events. I'm a close friend of his and he's no way wishy-washy. He'll give us cold steel, no quarter and the slaughterhouse right in the middle where all the stands can see it. And he's got the wherewithal – he was left thirty million when his poor father died. Even if he spent four hundred thousand, his pocket won't feel it and he'll go down in history. He's got some real desperadoes already, and a woman who fights in a chariot, and Glyco's steward who was caught having fun with his mistress. You'll see quite a quarrel in the crowd between jealous husbands and romantic lovers. But that half-pint Glyco threw his steward to the lions, which is just giving himself away. How is it the servant's fault when he's forced into it? It's that old piss-pot who really deserves to be tossed by a bull. But if you can't beat the ass you beat the saddle. But how did Glyco imagine that poisonous daughter of Hermogenes would ever turn out well? The old man could cut the claws off a flying kite, and a snake don't hatch old rope. Glyco – well, Glyco's got his. He's branded for as long as he lives and only the grave will get rid of it. But everyone pays for their sins.

'But I can almost smell the dinner Mammaea is going to give us – two denarii apiece for me and the family. If he really does it, he'll make off with all Norbanus's votes, I tell you he'll win at a canter. After all, what good has Norbanus done us? He put on some half-pint gladiators, so done in already that they'd have dropped if you blew at them. I've seen beast fighters give a better performance. As for the horsemen killed, he got them off a lamp – they ran round like cocks in a backyard. One was just a cart-horse, the other couldn't stand up, and the reserve was just one corpse instead of another – he was practically hamstrung. One boy did have a bit of spirit – he was in Thracian armour, and even he didn't show any initiative. In fact, they were all flogged afterwards, there were so many shouts of "Give 'em what for!" from the crowd. Pure cowards, that's all.

'"Well, I've put on a show for you," he says. "And I'm clapping you," says I. "Reckon it up – I'm giving more than I got. So we're quits."'

'Hey, Agamemnon! I suppose you're saying "What is that bore going on and on about?" It's because a good talker like you don't talk. You're a cut above us, and so you laugh at what us poor people say. We all know you're off your head with all that reading. But never mind! Will I get you some day to come down to my place in the country and have a look at our little cottage? We'll find something to eat – a chicken, some eggs. It'll be nice, even though the weather this year has ruined everything. Anyway, we'll find enough to fill our bellies.

'And by now my little lad is growing up to be a student of yours. He can divide by four already. If he stays well, you'll have him ready to do anything for you. In his spare time, he won't take his head out of his exercise book. He's clever and there's good stuff in him, even if he is crazy about birds. Only yesterday I killed his three goldfinches and told him a weasel ate them. But he's found some other silly hobbies, and he's having a fine time painting. Still, he's already well ahead with his Greek, and he's starting to take to his Latin, though his tutor is too pleased with himself and unreliable. He's well-educated but doesn't want to work. There is another one too, not so trained but he is conscientious – he teaches the boy more than he knows himself. In fact, he even makes a habit of coming around on holidays, and whatever you give him, he's happy.

'Anyway, I've just bought the boy some law books, as I want him to pick up some legal training for home use.

There's a living in that sort of thing. He's done enough dabbling in poetry and such like. If he objects, I've decided he'll learn a trade – barber, auctioneer, or at least a barrister – something he can't lose till he dies. Well, yesterday I gave it to him straight: "Believe me, my lad, any studying you do will be for your own good. You see Phileros the lawyer – if he hadn't studied, he'd be starving today. It's not so long since he was humping round stuff to sell on his back. Now he can even look Norbanus in the face. An education is an investment, and a proper profession never goes dead on you."'

This was the sort of chatter flying round when Trimalchio came in, dabbed his forehead and washed his hands in perfume. There was a very short pause, then he said:

'Excuse me, dear people, my inside has not been answering the call for several days now. The doctors are puzzled. But some pomegranate rind and resin in vinegar has done me good. But I hope now it will be back on its good behaviour. Otherwise my stomach rumbles like a bull. So if any of you wants to go out, there's no need for him to be embarrassed. None of us was born solid. I think there's nothing so tormenting as holding yourself in. This is the one thing even God Almighty can't object to. Yes, laugh, Fortunata, but you generally keep me up all night with this sort of thing.

'Anyway, I don't object to people doing what suits them even in the middle of dinner – and the doctors forbid you to hold yourself in. Even if it's a longer business, everything is there just outside – water, bowls, and all the other little comforts. Believe me, if the wind goes to your brain it starts flooding your whole body too. I've known a lot of people die from this because they wouldn't be honest with themselves.'

We thanked him for being so generous and considerate and promptly proceeded to bury our amusement in our glasses. Up to this point we'd not realized we were only half-way up the hill, as you might say.

The orchestra played, the tables were cleared, and then three white pigs were brought into the dining-room, all decked out in muzzles and bells. The first, the master of ceremonies announced, was two years old, the second three, and the third six. I was under the impression that some acrobats were on their way in and the pigs were going to do some tricks, the way they do in street shows. But Trimalchio dispelled this impression by asking:

'Which of these would you like for the next course? Any clodhopper can do you a barnyard cock or a stew and trifles like that, but my cooks are used to boiling whole calves.'

He immediately sent for the chef and without waiting for us to choose he told him to kill the oldest pig.

He then said to the man in a loud voice:

'Which division are you from?'

When he replied he was from number forty, Trimalchio asked:

'Were you bought or were you born here?'

'Neither,' said the chef, 'I was left to you in Pansa's will.'

'Well, then,' said Trimalchio, 'see you serve it up carefully – otherwise I'll have you thrown into the messengers' division.'

So the chef, duly reminded of his master's magnificence, went back to his kitchen, the next course leading the way.

Trimalchio looked round at us with a gentle smile: 'If you

Trimalchio's Feast

don't like the wine, I'll have it changed. It is up to you to do it justice. I don't buy it, thank heaven. In fact, whatever wine really tickles your palate this evening, it comes from an estate of mine which as yet I haven't seen. It's said to join my estates at Tarracina and Tarentum. What I'd like to do now is add Sicily to my little bit of land, so that when I want to go to Africa, I could sail there without leaving my own property.

'But tell me, Agamemnon, what was your debate about today? Even though I don't go in for the law, still I've picked up enough education for home consumption. And don't you think I turn my nose up at studying, because I have two libraries, one Greek, one Latin. So tell us, just as a favour, what was the topic of your debate?'

Agamemnon was just beginning, 'A poor man and a rich man were enemies . . .' when Trimalchio said: 'What's a poor man?' 'Oh, witty!' said Agamemnon, and then told us about some fictitious case or other. Like lightning Trimalchio said: 'If this happened, it's not a fictitious case – if it didn't happen, then it's nothing at all.'

We greeted this witticism and several more like it with the greatest enthusiasm.

'Tell me, my dear Agamemnon,' continued Trimalchio, 'do you remember the twelve labours of Hercules and the story of Ulysses – how the Cyclops tore out his eye with his thumb. I used to read about them in Homer, when I was a boy. In fact, I actually saw with my own eyes the Sybil at Cumae dangling in a bottle, and when the children asked her in Greek: "What do you want, Sybil?" she used to answer: "I want to die."'

He was still droning on when a server carrying the massive pig was put on the table. We started to express our amazement at this speed and swear that not even an ordinary rooster could be cooked so quickly, the more so as the pig seemed far larger than it had appeared before. Trimalchio looked closer and closer at it, and then shouted:

'What's this? Isn't this pig gutted? I'm damn certain it isn't. Call the chef in here, go on, call him!'

The downcast chef stood by the table and said he'd forgotten it.

'What, you forgot!' shouted Trimalchio. 'You'd think he'd only left out the pepper and cumin. Strip him!'

In a second the chef was stripped and standing miserably between two guards. But everyone began pleading for him:

'It does tend to happen,' they said, 'do let him off, please. If he does it any more, none of us will stand up for him again.'

Personally, given my tough and ruthless temperament, I couldn't contain myself. I leaned over and whispered in Agamemnon's ear:

'This has surely got to be the worst slave in the world. Could anyone forget to clean a pig? I damn well wouldn't let him off if he forgot to clean a fish.'

But not Trimalchio. His face relaxed into a smile.

'Well,' he said, 'since you have such a bad memory, gut it in front of us.'

The chef recovered his shirt, took up a knife and with a nervous hand cut open the pig's belly left and right. Suddenly, as the slits widened with the pressure, out poured sausages and blood-puddings.

The staff applauded this trick and gave a concerted cheer – 'Hurray for Gaius!' The chef of course was rewarded with a drink and a silver crown, and was also given a drinking cup on a tray of Corinthian bronze. Seeing Agamemnon staring hard at this cup, Trimalchio remarked:

'I'm the only person in the world with genuine Corinthian.'

I was expecting him with his usual conceit to claim that all his plate came from Corinth. But he was not as bad as that.

'Perhaps you're wondering,' he went on, 'how I'm the only one with genuine Corinthian dishes. The simple reason is that the manufacturer I buy from is named Corinth – but what can be Corinthian, if you don't have a Corinth to get it from?

'You mustn't take me for a fool: I know very well where Corinthian metalwork first came from. When Troy was captured that crafty snake Hannibal piled all the bronze, silver and gold statues into one heap and set them on fire, and they were all melted to a bronze alloy. The metalworkers took this solid mass and made plates, dishes, and statuettes out of it. That is how Corinthian plate was born, not really one thing or another, but everything in one. You won't mind my saying so, but I prefer glass – that's got no taste at all. If only it didn't break, I'd prefer it to gold, but it's cheap stuff the way it is.

'Mind you, there was a craftsman once who made a glass bowl that didn't break. So he got an audience with the Emperor, taking his present with him ... Then he made Caesar hand it back to him and dropped it on the floor. The Emperor couldn't have been more shaken. The man picked the bowl off the ground – it had been dinted like a bronze dish – took a hammer from his pocket and easily got the bowl as good as new. After this performance he thought he'd be in high heaven, especially when the Emperor said to him:

'"Is there anyone else who knows this process for making glass?"

'But now see what happens. When the man said no, the Emperor had his head cut off, the reason being that if it was made public, gold would have been as cheap as muck.

'Now I'm very keen on silver. I have some three-gallon bumpers more or less ... how Cassandra killed her sons, and the boys are lying there dead – very lifelike. I have a bowl my patron left to me with Daedalus shutting Niobe in the Trojan Horse. What's more, I have the fights of Hermeros and Petraites on some cups – all good and heavy. No, I wouldn't sell my know-how at any price.'

While he was talking, a young slave dropped a cup. Trimalchio looked in his direction.

'Get out and hang yourself,' he said, 'you're utterly useless.' Immediately the boy's lips trembled and he begged Trimalchio's pardon.

'What are you asking me for?' snapped his master, 'as though I was the trouble! I'm just asking you not to let yourself be such a useless fool.'

In the end however, as a favour to us, he let him off and the boy ran round the table to celebrate ... and shouted, 'Out with the water – in with the wine!'

We all showed our appreciation of his amusing wit – especially Agamemnon, who knew how to angle for further

Trimalchio's Feast

invitations. But our admiration went to Trimalchio's head. He drank with even greater cheerfulness and was very nearly drunk by now.

'Doesn't anyone want my dear Fortunata to dance?' he said. 'Honestly, no one dances the *Cordax* better.'

Then he stuck his hands up over his forehead and gave us a personal imitation of the actor Syrus, while all the staff sang in chorus:

'Madeia, Perimadeia.'

In fact, he would have taken the floor, if Fortunata had not whispered in his ear. She must have told him, I suppose, that such low fooling did not suit his dignity. But you never saw anyone so changeable – one minute he would be frightened of Fortunata and the next minute he would be back in character again.

What really interrupted his coarse insistence on dancing was his accountant, who sounded as though he was reading out a copy of the Gazette:

'26 July: Births on the estate at Cumae: male 30, female 40. Wheat threshed and stored: 500,000 pecks. Oxen broken in: 500.

'On the same date: the slave Mithridates crucified for insulting the guardian spirit of our dear Gaius.

'On the same date: Deposits to the strong-room (no further investment possible): 10,000,000 sesterces.

'On the same date: a fire broke out on the estate at Pompeii beginning at the house of Nasta the bailiff.'

'What!' said Trimalchio. 'When was an estate bought for me at Pompeii?'

'Last year,' said the accountant, 'so it hasn't yet come on the books.'

Trimalchio flared up:

'If any land is bought for me and I don't hear of it within six months, I refuse to have it entered on the books.'

The official edicts were read out and the wills of certain gamekeepers. In specific codicils they said they were leaving Trimalchio nothing. Then the names of some bailiffs; the divorce of a freed-woman, the wife of a watchman, on the grounds of adultery with a bath-attendant; the demotion of a hall-porter to a job at Baiae; the prosecution of a steward; and the result of an action between some bedroom attendants.

Finally the acrobats arrived. One was a silly idiot who stood there holding a ladder and made his boy climb up the rungs, give us a song and dance at the top, then jump through blazing hoops, and hold up a large wine-jar with his teeth.

Only Trimalchio was impressed by all this: art wasn't appreciated, he considered, but if there were two things in the world he really liked to watch, they were acrobats and horn-players. All the other shows were not worth a damn.

'As a matter of fact,' he said, 'once I even bought some comic-actors, but I preferred them putting on Atellan farces, and I told my conductor to keep his songs Latin.'

Just as he was saying this, the boy tumbled down on Trimalchio's couch. Everyone screamed, the guests as well as the servants – not because they were worried over such an awful person (they would happily have watched his neck being broken) but because it would have been a poor ending to the party if they had to offer their condolences for a comparative stranger. Trimalchio himself groaned heavily and leaned over his arm as though it were hurt. Doctors raced to the scene, but practically the first one there was Fortunata, hair flying and cup in hand, telling the world what a poor unfortunate thing she was. As for the boy who had fallen, he was already crawling round our feet, begging for mercy. I had a very uneasy feeling that his pleadings might be the prelude to some funny surprise ending, as I still remembered the chef who had forgotten to gut his pig. So I began looking round the dining-room for some machine to appear out of the wall, especially after a servant was beaten for using white instead of purple wool to bandage his master's bruised arm.

Nor were my suspicions far out, because instead of punishment, there came an official announcement from Trimalchio that the boy was free, so that no one could say that such a great figure had been injured by a slave.

We all applauded his action and started a desultory conversation about how uncertain life was.

'Well,' says Trimalchio, 'an occasion like this mustn't pass without a suitable record.' He immediately called for his notebook, and without much mental exertion he came out with:

> 'What comes next you never know,
> Lady Luck runs the show,
>   So pass the Falernian, lad.'

Petronius

This epigram brought the conversation round to poetry and for quite a time the first place among poets was given to Mopsus of Thrace until Trimalchio said:

'Tell me, professor, how would you compare Cicero and Publilius? I think Cicero was the better orator, but Publilius the better man. Now could there be anything finer than this:

> Down luxury's maw, Mars' walls now wilt.
> Your palate pens peacocks in plumage of gilt:
> These Babylon birds are plumped under lock
> With the guinea hen and the capon cock.
> That long-legged paragon, winged castanet,
> Summer's lingering lease and winter's regret –
> Even the stork, poor wandering guest,
> Is put in your pot and makes that his nest.
> Why are Indian pearls so dear in your sight?
> So your sluttish wife, draped in the diver's delight,
> May open her legs on her lover's divan?
> What use are green emeralds, glass ruin of man,
> Or carbuncles from Carthage with fire in their flint?
> Unless to let goodness gleam out in their glint.
> Is it right for a bride to be clad in a cloud
> Or wearing a wisp show off bare to the crowd?

'Well now, whose profession do we think is most difficult after literature? I think doctors and bankers. A doctor has to know what people have in their insides and what causes a fever – even though I do hate them terribly the way they put me on a diet of duck. A banker has to spot the brass under the silver. Well, among dumb animals the hardest worked are cattle and sheep. It's thanks to cattle we have

Trimalchio's Feast

bread to eat, and it's thanks to sheep and their wool that we're well dressed. It's a low trick the way we eat mutton and wear woollens. Bees, now, I think are heavenly creatures – they spew honey, though people suppose they get it from heaven. But at the same time they sting, because where there's sweet you'll find bitter there too.'

He was still putting the philosophers out of work when tickets were brought round in a cup and the boy whose job it was read out the presents. '*Rich man's prison* – a silver jug. *Pillow* – a piece of neck came up. *Old man's wit and a sour stick* – dry salt biscuits came up and an apple on a stick. *Lick and spit* got a whip and a knife. *Flies and a fly-trap* was raisins and Attic honey. *Dinner-clothes and city-suit* got a slice of meat and a notebook. *Head and foot* produced a hare and a slipper. *Lights and letters* got a lamprey and some peas.' We laughed for ages. There were hundreds of things like this but they've slipped my mind now.

Ascyltus, with his usual lack of restraint, found everything extremely funny, lifting up his hands and laughing till the tears came. Eventually one of Trimalchio's freedman friends flared up at him.

'You with the sheep's eyes,' he said, 'what's so funny? Isn't our host elegant enough for you? You're better off, I suppose, and used to a bigger dinner. Holy guardian here preserve me! If I was sitting by him, I'd stop his bleating! A fine pippin he is to be laughing at other people! Some fly-by-night from god knows where – not worth his own piss. In fact, if I pissed round him, he wouldn't know where to turn.

'By god, it takes a lot to make me boil, but if you're too

soft, worms like this only come to the top. Look at him laughing! What's he got to laugh at? Did his father pay cash for him? You're a Roman knight, are you? Well, my father was a king.

'"*Why are you only a freedman?*" did you say? Because I put myself into slavery. I wanted to be a Roman citizen, not a subject with taxes to pay. And today, I hope no one can laugh at the way I live. I'm a man among men, and I walk with my head up. I don't owe anybody a penny – there's never been a court-order out for me. No one's said "*Pay up*" to me in the street.

'I've bought a bit of land and some tiny pieces of plate. I've twenty bellies to feed, as well as a dog. I bought my old woman's freedom so nobody could wipe his dirty hands on *her* hair. Four thousand I paid for myself. I was elected to the Augustan College and it cost me nothing. I hope when I die I won't have to blush in my coffin.

'But you now, you're such a busybody you don't look behind you. You see a louse on somebody else, but not the fleas on your own back. You're the only one who finds us funny. Look at the professor now – he's an older man than you and we get along with him. But you're still wet from your mother's milk and not up to your ABC yet. Just a crackpot – you're like a piece of wash-leather in soak, softer but no better! You're grander than us – well, have two dinners and two suppers! I'd rather have my good name than any amount of money. When all's said and done, who's ever asked me for money twice? For forty years I slaved but nobody ever knew if I was a slave or a free man. I came to this colony when I was a lad with long hair – the town hall hadn't been built

Trimalchio's Feast

then. But I worked hard to please my master – there was a real gentleman, with more in his little finger-nail than there is in your whole body. And I had people in the house who tried to trip me up one way or another, but still – thanks be to his guardian spirit! – I kept my head above water. These are the prizes in life: being born free is as easy as all get-out. Now what are you gawping at, like a goat in a vetch-field?'

At this remark, Giton, who was waiting on me, could not suppress his laughter and let out a filthy guffaw, which did not pass unnoticed by Ascyltus' opponent. He turned his abuse on the boy.

'So!' he said. 'You're amused too, are you, you curly-headed onion? A merry Saturnalia to you! Is it December, I'd like to know? When did *you* pay your liberation tax? . . . Look, he doesn't know what to do, the gallow's bird, the crow's meat.

'God's curse on you, and your master too, for not keeping you under control! As sure as I get my bellyful, it's only because of Trimalchio that I don't take it out of you here and now. He's a freedman like myself. We're doing all right, but those good-for-nothings, well – . It's easy to see, like master, like man. I can hardly hold myself back, and I'm not naturally hot-headed – but once I start, I don't give a penny for my own mother.

'All right! I'll see you when we get outside, you rat, you excrescence. I'll knock your master into a cocked hat before I'm an inch taller or shorter. And I won't let you off either, by heaven, even if you scream down God Almighty. Your cheap curls and your no-good master won't be much use to you then – I'll see to that. I'll get my teeth into you all right. Either I'm much mistaken about myself or you won't be laughing at us behind your golden beard. Athena's curse on you and the man who first made you such a forward brat.

'I didn't learn no geometry or criticism and such silly rubbish, but I can read the letters on a notice board and I can do my percentages in metal, weights, and money. In fact, if you like, we'll have a bet. Come on, here's my cash. Now you'll see how your father wasted his money, even though you do know how to make a speech.

'Try this:

> Something we all have.
> Long I come, broad I come. What am I?

'I'll give you it: something we all have that runs and doesn't move from its place: something we all have that grows and gets smaller.

'You're running round in circles, you've had enough, like the mouse in the pisspot. So either keep quiet or keep out of the way of your betters – they don't even know you're alive – unless you think I care about your box-wood rings that you swiped from your girl-friend! Lord make me lucky! Let's go into town and borrow some money. You'll soon see they trust this iron one.

'Pah! a drownded fox makes a nice sight, I must say. As I hope to make my pile and die so famous that people swear by my dead body, I'll hound you to death. And he's a nice thing too, the one who taught you all these tricks – a muttonhead, not a master. We learned different. Our teacher used to say: "Are your things in order? Go straight home.

Trimalchio's Feast

No looking around. And be polite to your elders." Nowadays it's all an absolute muck-heap. They turn out nobody worth a penny. I'm like you see me and I thank god for the way I was learnt.'

Ascyltus began to answer this abuse, but Trimalchio, highly amused by his friend's fluency, said:

'No slanging matches! Let's all have a nice time. And you, Hermeros, leave the young fellow alone. His blood's a bit hot – you should know better. In things like this, the one who gives in always comes off best. Besides, when you were just a chicken, it was cock-a-doodle too, and you had no more brains yourself. So let's start enjoying ourselves again, that'll be better, and let's watch the recitations from Homer.'

In came the troupe immediately and banged their shields with their spears. Trimalchio sat up on his cushion and while the reciters spouted their Greek lines at one another in their usual impudent way, he read aloud in Latin in a sing-song voice. After a while, he got silence and asked:

'Do you know which scene they were acting? Diomede and Ganymede were the two brothers. Their sister was Helen. Agamemnon carried her off and offered a hind to Diana in her place. So now Homer is describing how the Trojans and Tarentines fought each other. Agamemnon, of course, won and married off his daughter Iphigenia to Achilles. This drove Ajax insane, and in a moment or two he'll explain how it ended.'

As Trimalchio said this, the reciters gave a loud shout, the servants made a lane, and a calf was brought in on a two-hundred pound plate: it was boiled whole and wearing a helmet. Following it came Ajax, slashing at the calf with a drawn sword like a madman. After rhythmically cutting and slicing, he collected the pieces on the point and shared them among the surprised guests.

But we were not given long to admire these elegant turns, for all of a sudden, the coffered ceiling began rumbling and the whole dining-room shook. I leapt to my feet in panic, as I was afraid some acrobat was coming down through the roof. The other guests also looked up to see what strange visitation this announced. Would you believe it – the panels opened and suddenly an enormous hoop was let down, with gold crowns and alabaster jars of toilet cream hanging from it. While we were being told to accept these as presents, I looked at the table . . . Already there was a tray of cakes in position, the centre of which was occupied by a Priapus made of pastry, holding the usual things in his very adequate lap – all kinds of apples and grapes.

Greedily enough, we stretched out our hands to this display, and in a flash a fresh series of jokes restored the general gaiety. Every single cake and every single apple needed only the slightest touch for a cloud of saffron to start pouring out and the irritating vapour to come right in our faces.

Naturally we thought the dish must have some religious significance to be smothered in such an odour of sanctity, so we raised ourselves to a sitting position and cried:

'God save Augustus, the Father of his People!'

All the same, even after this show of respect, some of the guests were snatching the apples – especially me, because I didn't think I was pushing a generous enough share into Giton's pocket.

Trimalchio's Feast

While all this was going on, three boys in brief white tunics came in. Two of them set down on the table the household deities, which had amulets round their necks; the other, carrying round a bowl of wine, kept shouting: 'God save all here!' . . .

Our host said that one of the gods was called Cobbler, the second Luck, and the third Lucre. There was also a golden image of Trimalchio himself, and as all the others were pressing their lips to it we felt too embarrassed not to do the same.

After we had all wished each other health and happiness, Trimalchio looked at Niceros and said:

'You used to be better company at a party. You're keeping very quiet nowadays: you don't say a word – I don't know why. Do me a favour to please me. Tell us about that adventure you had.'

Niceros was delighted by his friend's affable request and said:

'May I never make another penny if I'm not jumping for joy to see you in such form. Well, just for fun – though I'm worried about those schoolteachers there in case they laugh at me. That's up to them. I'll tell it all the same. Anyway, what do I care who laughs at me. It's better to be laughed at than laughed down.'

'When thus he spake,' he began this story:

'When I was still a slave, we were living down a narrow street – Gavilla owns the house now – and there as heaven would have it, I fell in love with the wife of Terentius the innkeeper.

'You all used to know Melissa from Tarentum, an absolute

peach to look at. But honest to god, it wasn't her body or just sex that made me care for her, it was more because she had such a nice nature. If I asked her for anything, it was never refused. If I had a penny or halfpenny, I gave it to her to look after and she never let me down.

'One day her husband died out at the villa. So I did my best by hook or by crook to get to her. After all, you know, a friend in need is a friend indeed.

'Luckily the master had gone off to Capua to look after some odds and ends. I seized my chance and I talked a guest of ours into walking with me as far as the fifth milestone. He was a soldier as it happened, and as brave as hell. About cock-crow we shag off, and the moon was shining like noontime. We get to where the tombs are and my chap starts making for the grave-stones, while I, singing away, keep going and start counting the stars. Then just as I looked back at my mate, he stripped off and laid all his clothes by the side of the road. My heart was in my mouth, I stood there like a corpse. Anyway, he pissed a ring round his clothes and suddenly turned into a wolf. Don't think I'm joking, I wouldn't tell a lie about this for a fortune. However, as I began to say, after he turned into a wolf, he started howling and rushed off into the woods.

'At first I didn't know where I was, then I went up to collect his clothes – but they'd turned to stone. If ever a man was dead with fright, it was me. But I pulled out my sword, and I fairly slaughtered the early morning shadows till I arrived at my girl's villa.

'I got into the house and I practically gasped my last, the sweat was pouring down my crotch, my eyes were blank and staring – I could hardly get over it. It came as a surprise to my poor Melissa to find I'd walked over so late.

'"If you'd come a bit earlier," she said, "at least you could've helped us. A wolf got into the grounds and tore into all the livestock – it was like a bloody shambles. But he didn't have the last laugh, even though he got away. Our slave here put a spear right through his neck."

'I couldn't close my eyes again after I heard this. But when it was broad daylight I rushed off home like the innkeeper after the robbery. And when I came to the spot where his clothes had turned to stone, I found nothing but blood-stains. However, when I got home, my soldier friend was lying in bed like a great ox with the doctor seeing to his neck. I realized he was a werewolf and afterwards I couldn't have taken a bite of bread in his company, not if you killed me for it. If some people think differently about this, that's up to them. But me – if I'm telling a lie may all your guardian spirits damn me!'

Everyone was struck with amazement.

'I wouldn't disbelieve a word,' said Trimalchio. 'Honestly, the way my hair stood on end – because I know Niceros doesn't go in for jokes. He's really reliable and never exaggerates.

'Now I'll tell you a horrible story myself. A real donkey on the roof! When I was still in long hair (you see, I led a very soft life from my boyhood) the master's pet slave died. He was a pearl, honest to god, a beautiful boy, and one of the best. Well, his poor mother was crying over him and the rest of us were deep in depression, when the witches suddenly started howling – you'd think it was a dog after a hare.

'At that time we had a Cappadocian chap, tall and a very brave old thing, quite the strong man – he could lift an angry ox. This fellow rushed outside with a drawn sword, first wrapping his left hand up very carefully, and he stabbed one of the women right through the middle, just about here – may no harm come to where I'm touching! We heard a groan but – naturally I'm not lying – we didn't see the things themselves. Our big fellow, however, once he was back inside, threw himself on his bed. His whole body was black and blue, as though he'd been whipped. The evil hand, you see, had been put on him.

'We closed the door and went back to what we had to do, but as the mother puts her arms round her son's body, she touches it and finds it's only a handful of straw. It had no heart, no inside, no anything. Of course the witches had already stolen the boy and put a straw baby in its place.

'I put it to you, you can't get away from it – there are such things as women with special powers and midnight hags that can turn everything upside down. But that great tall fellow of ours never got his colour back after what happened. In fact, not many days later, he went crazy and died.'

Equally thrilled and convinced, we kissed the table and asked the midnight hags to stay at home till we got back from dinner.

By this time, to tell the truth, there seemed to be more lights burning and the whole dining-room seemed different, when Trimalchio said:

'What about you, Plocamus, haven't you a story to entertain us with. You used to have a fine voice for giving recitations

Trimalchio's Feast

with a nice swing and putting songs over – ah me, the good old days are gone.'

'Well,' said Plocamus, 'my galloping days finished after I got gout. Besides, when I was really young I nearly got consumption through singing. How about my dancing? How about my recitations? How about my barber's shop act? When was there anybody so good apart from Apelles himself?'

Putting his hand to his mouth he let out some sort of obscene whistle which he afterwards insisted was Greek.

Trimalchio, after giving us his own imitation of a fanfare of trumpets, looked round for his little pet, whom he called Croesus. The boy, however, a bleary-eyed creature with absolutely filthy teeth, was busy wrapping a green cloth round a disgustingly fat black puppy. He put half a loaf on the couch and was cramming it down the animal's throat while it kept vomiting it back. This business reminded Trimalchio to send out for Scylax, 'protector of the house and the household'.

A hound of enormous size was immediately led in on a chain. A kick from the hall-porter reminded him to lie down and he stretched himself out in front of the table. Trimalchio threw him a piece of white bread, remarking:

'Nobody in the house is more devoted to me.'

The boy, however, annoyed by such a lavish tribute to Scylax, put his own little pup on the floor and encouraged her to hurry up and start a fight. Scylax, naturally following his canine instincts, filled the dining-room with a most unpleasant barking and almost tore Croesus' Pearl to pieces.

Nor was the trouble limited to the dog-fight. A lampstand was upset on the table as well and not only smashed all the glass but spilled hot oil over some of the guests.

Not wanting to seem disturbed by the damage, Trimalchio gave the boy a kiss and told him to climb on his back. The lad climbed on his mount without hesitation, and slapping his shoulder blades with the flat of his hand, shouted amid roars of laughter:

'Big mouth, big mouth, how many fingers have I got up?'

So Trimalchio was calmed down for a while and gave instructions for a huge bowl of drink to be mixed and served to all the servants, who were sitting by our feet. He added the condition:

'If anyone won't take it, pour it over his head. Day's the time for business, now's the time for fun.'

This display of kindness was followed by some savouries, the very recollection of which really and truly makes me sick. Instead of thrushes, a fat capon was brought round for each of us, as well as goose-eggs in pastry hoods. Trimalchio surpassed himself to make us eat them; he described them as boneless chickens. In the middle of all this, a lictor knocked at the double doors and a drunken guest entered wearing white, followed by a large crowd of people. I was terrified by this lordly apparition and thought it was the chief magistrate arriving. So I tried to rise and get my bare feet on the floor. Agamemnon laughed at this panic and said:

'Get hold of yourself, you silly fool. This is Habinnas – Augustan College and monumental mason.'

Relieved by this information I resumed my position and watched Habinnas' entry with huge admiration. Being

Trimalchio's Feast

already drunk, he had his hands on his wife's shoulders; loaded with several garlands, oil pouring down his forehead and into his eyes, he settled himself into the praetor's place of honour and immediately demanded some wine and hot water. Trimalchio, delighted by these high spirits, demanded a larger cup for himself and asked how he had enjoyed it all.

'The only thing we missed,' replied Habinnas, 'was yourself – the apple of my eye was here. Still, it was damn good. Scissa was giving a ninth-day dinner in honour of a poor slave of hers she'd freed on his death-bed. And I think she'll have a pretty penny to pay with the five per cent liberation tax, because they reckon he was worth fifty thousand. Still, it was pleasant enough, even if we did have to pour half our drinks over his wretched bones.'

'Well,' said Trimalchio, 'what did you have for dinner?'

'I'll tell you if I can – I've such a good memory that I often forget my own name. For the first course we had a pig crowned with sausages and served with blood-puddings and very nicely done giblets, and of course beetroot and pure wholemeal bread – which I prefer to white myself: it's very strengthening and I don't regret it when I do my business. The next course was cold tart and a concoction of first-class Spanish wine poured over hot honey. I didn't eat anything at all of the actual tart, but I got stuck into the honey. Scattered round were chickpeas, lupines, a choice of nuts and an apple apiece – though I took two. And look, I've got them tied up in a napkin, because if I don't take something in the way of a present to my little slave, I'll have a row on my hands.

'Oh yes, my good lady reminds me. We had a hunk of

bear-meat set before us, which Scintilla was foolish enough to try, and she practically spewed up her guts; but I ate more than a pound of it, as it tasted like real wild-boar. And I say if bears can eat us poor people, it's all the more reason why us poor people should eat bears.

'To finish up with, we had some cheese basted with new wine, snails all round, chitterlings, plates of liver, eggs in pastry hoods, turnips, mustard, and then, wait a minute, little tunny fish! There were pickled cumin seeds too, passed round in a bowl, and some people were that bad-mannered they took three handfuls. You see, we sent the ham away.

'But tell me something, Gaius, now I ask – why isn't Fortunata at the table?'

'You know her,' replied Trimalchio, 'unless she's put the silver away and shared out the leftovers among the slaves, she won't put a drop of water to her mouth.'

'All the same,' retorted Habinnas, 'unless she sits down, I'm shagging off.'

And he was starting to get up, when at a given signal all the servants shouted '*Fortunata*' four or more times. So in she came with her skirt tucked up under a yellow sash to show her cerise petticoat underneath, as well as her twisted anklets and gold-embroidered slippers. Wiping her hands on a handkerchief which she carried round her neck, she took her place on the couch where Habinnas' wife was reclining. She kissed her. 'Is it really you?' she said, clapping her hands together.

It soon got to the point where Fortunata took the bracelets from her great fat arms and showed them to the admiring Scintilla. In the end she even undid her anklets and her gold

Trimalchio's Feast

hair net, which she said was pure gold. Trimalchio noticed this and had it all brought to him and commented:

'A woman's chains, you see. This is the way us poor fools get robbed. She must have six and a half pounds on her. Still, I've got a bracelet myself, made up from one-tenth per cent to Mercury – and it weighs not an ounce less than ten pounds.'

Finally, for fear he looked like a liar, he even had some scales brought in and had them passed round to test the weight.

Scintilla was no better. From round her neck she took a little gold locket, which she called her 'lucky box'. From it she extracted two earrings and in her turn gave them to Fortunata to look at.

'A present from my good husband,' she said, 'and no one has a finer set.'

'Hey!' said Habinnas. 'You cleaned me out to buy you a glass bean. Honestly, if I had a daughter, I'd cut her little ears off. If there weren't any women, everything would be dirt cheap. As it is, we've got to drink cold water and piss it out hot.'

Meanwhile, the women giggled tipsily between themselves and kissed each other drunkenly, one crying up her merits as a housewife, the other crying about her husband's demerits and boy-friends. While they had their heads together like this, Habinnas rose stealthily and taking Fortunata's feet, flung them up over the couch.

'Oh, oh!' she shrieked, as her underskirt wandered up over her knees. So she settled herself in Scintilla's lap and hid her burning red face in her handkerchief.

Then came an interval, after which Trimalchio called for dessert. Slaves removed all the tables and brought in others. They scattered sawdust tinted with saffron and vermilion, and something I had never seen before – powdered mica. Trimalchio said at once:

'I could make you just settle for this. There's dessert for you! The first tables've deserted. However, if you people have anything nice, bring it on!'

Meanwhile a slave from Alexandria, who was taking round the hot water, started imitating a nightingale, only for Trimalchio to shout: 'Change your tune!'

More entertainment! A slave sitting by Habinnas' feet, prompted, I suppose, by his master, suddenly burst out in a sing-song voice:

'Meantime Aeneas was in mid-ocean with his fleet.'

No more cutting sound ever pierced my eardrums. Apart from his barbarous meandering up and down the scale, he mixed in Atellan verses, so that Virgil actually grated on me for the first time in my life. When he did finally stop through exhaustion, Habinnas said:

'He's never had any real training. I just had him taught by sending him along to peddlers on the street corner. He's no one to equal him if he wants to imitate mule-drivers or hawkers. He's terribly clever, really. He's a cobbler, a cook, a confectioner – a man that can turn his hand to anything. But he's got two faults; if he didn't have them, he'd be one in a million – he's circumcised and he snores. I don't mind him being cross-eyed – so is Venus. That's why he's never quiet and his eyes are hardly ever still. I got him for three hundred denarii.'

Scintilla interrupted him: 'Of course, you're not telling them all the tricks that wretch gets up to. He's a pimp – but I'll make sure he gets branded for it.'

Trimalchio laughed: 'I know a Cappadocian when I see one. He's not slow in looking after himself and, by heaven, I admire him for it. You can't take it with you.

'Now, Scintilla, don't be jealous. Believe me, we know all about you women too. As sure as I stand here, I used to bang the mistress so much that even the old boy suspected; so he sent me off to look after his farms. But I'd better save my breath to cool my porridge.'

As though he'd been complimented the wretched slave took out an earthenware lamp from his pocket and for more than half an hour gave imitations of trumpet-players, while Habinnas hummed an accompaniment, pressing down his lower lip with his hand. Finally coming right into the middle, he did a flute-player with some broken reeds, then he dressed up in a greatcoat and whip and did the Life of the Muleteer, till Habinnas called him over, kissed him, and gave him a drink:

'Better and better, Massa!' he said. 'I'll give you a pair of boots.'

There would have been no end to all these trials if an extra course had not arrived – pastry thrushes stuffed with raisins and nuts. After them came quinces with thorns stuck in them to look like sea urchins. All this would have been all right, but there was a far more horrible dish that made us prefer even dying of hunger. When it was put on the table, looking to us like a fat goose surrounded by fish and all sorts of game, Trimalchio said:

'Whatever you see here, friends, is made from one kind of stuff.'

I, of course, being very cautious by nature, spotted immediately what it was and glancing at Agamemnon, I said:

'I'll be surprised if it isn't all made of wax, or any rate mud. I've seen that sort of imitation food produced at the Saturnalia in Rome.'

I hadn't quite finished what I was saying when Trimalchio said:

'As sure as I hope to expand – my investments of course, not my waist-line – my chef made it all from pork. There couldn't be a more valuable man to have. Say the word and he'll produce a fish out of a sow's belly, a pigeon out of the lard, a turtle dove out of the ham, and fowl out of the knuckle. So he's been given a nice name I thought of myself – he's called Daedalus. And seeing he's a clever lad, I brought him some carvers of Styrian steel as a present from Rome.'

He immediately had them brought in and gazed at them with admiration. He even allowed us to test the point on our cheeks.

All of a sudden in came two slaves, apparently having had a quarrel at the well; at any rate they still had water jugs on their shoulders. But while Trimalchio was giving his decision about their respective cases, neither of them paid any attention to his verdict: instead they broke each other's jugs with their sticks. Staggered by their drunken insolence, we couldn't take our eyes away from the fight till we noticed

Trimalchio's Feast

oysters and scallops sliding out of the jugs, which a boy collected and carried round on a dish. The ingenious chef was equal to these elegant refinements – he brought in snails on a silver gridiron, singing all the time in a high grating voice.

I blush to say what happened next. Boys with their hair down their backs came round with perfumed cream in a silver bowl and rubbed it on our feet as we lay there, but first they wrapped our legs and ankles in wreaths of flowers. Some of the same stuff was dropped into the decanter and the lamp.

Fortunata was now wanting to dance, and Scintilla was doing more clapping than talking, when Trimalchio said:

'Philargyrus – even though you are such a terrible fan of the Greens – you have my permission to join us. And tell your dear Menophila to sit down as well.'

Need I say more? We were almost thrown out of our places, so completely did the household fill the dining-room. I even noticed that the chef, the one who had produced the goose out of pork, was actually given a place above me, and he was reeking of pickles and sauce. And he wasn't satisfied with just having a place, but he had to start straight off on an imitation of the tragedian Ephesus, and then challenge his master to bet against the Greens winning at the next races.

Trimalchio became expansive after this argument.

'My dear people,' he said, 'slaves are human beings too. They drink the same milk as anybody else, even though luck's been agin 'em. Still, if nothing happens to me, they'll have their taste of freedom soon. In fact, I'm setting them all free in my will. I'm giving Philargyrus a farm, what's more, and the woman he lives with. As for Cario, I'm leaving him a block of flats, his five per cent manumission tax, and a bed with all the trimmings. I'm making Fortunata my heir, and I want all my friends to look after her.

'The reason I'm telling everyone all this is so my household will love me now as much as if I was dead.'

Everyone began thanking his lordship for his kindness, when he became very serious and had a copy of his will brought in. Amid the sobs of his household he read out the whole thing from beginning to end.

Then looking at Habinnas, he said:

'What have you to say, my dear old friend? Are you building my monument the way I told you? I particularly want you to keep a place at the foot of my statue and put a picture of my pup there, as well as paintings of wreaths, scent-bottles, and all the contests of Petraites, and thanks to you I'll be able to live on after I'm dead. And another thing! See that it's a hundred feet facing the road and two hundred back into the field. I want all the various sorts of fruit round my ashes and lots and lots of vines. After all, it's a big mistake to have nice houses just for when you're alive and not worry about the one we have to live in for much longer. And that's why I want this written up before anything else:

THIS MONUMENT DOES NOT GO TO THE HEIR

'But I'll make sure in my will that I don't get done down once I'm dead. I'll put one of my freedmen in charge of my tomb to look after it and not let people run up and shit on

Trimalchio's Feast

my monument. I'd like you to put some ships there too, sailing under full canvas, and me sitting on a high platform in my robes of office, wearing five gold rings and pouring out a bagful of money for the people. You know I gave them all a dinner and two denarii apiece. Let's have in a banqueting hall as well, if you think it's a good idea, and show the whole town having a good time. Put up a statue of Fortunata on my right, holding a dove, and have her leading her little dog tied to her belt – and my little lad as well, and big wine-jars tightly sealed up so the wine won't spill. And perhaps you could carve me a broken one and a boy crying over it. A clock in the middle, so that anybody who looks at the time, like it or not, has got to read my name. As for the inscription now, take a good look and see if this seems suitable enough:

HERE SLEEPS

GAIUS POMPEIUS TRIMALCHIO

MAECENATIANUS

ELECTED TO THE AUGUSTAN COLLEGE IN HIS ABSENCE

HE COULD HAVE BEEN ON EVERY BOARD IN ROME

BUT HE REFUSED

GOD-FEARING BRAVE AND TRUE

A SELF-MADE MAN

HE LEFT AN ESTATE OF 30,000,000

AND HE NEVER HEARD A PHILOSOPHER

FAREWELL

AND YOU FARE WELL, TRIMALCHIO'

As he finished Trimalchio burst into tears. Fortunata was in tears, Habinnas was in tears, in the end the whole household filled the dining-room with their wailing, like people at a funeral. In fact, I'd even begun crying myself, when Trimalchio said:

'Well, since we know we've got to die, why don't we live a little. I want to see you enjoying yourselves. Let's jump into a bath – you won't be sorry, damn me! It's as hot as a furnace.'

'Hear! Hear!' said Habinnas. 'Turning one day into two – nothing I like better.' He got up in his bare feet and began to follow Trimalchio on his merry way.

I looked at Ascyltus. 'What do you think?' I said. 'Now me, if I see a bath, I'll die on the spot.'

'Let's say yes,' he suggested, 'and while they're going for their bath, we can slip out in the crowd.'

This seemed a good idea, so Giton led us through the portico till we reached the door, where the hound chained there greeted us with such a noise that Ascyltus actually fell into the fishpond. Not only that, as I was drunk too, when I tried to help the struggling Ascyltus I was dragged into the same watery trap. However, the hall-porter saved us and by his intervention pacified the dog and dragged us trembling to dry land. Giton had already bought off the beast in a most ingenious way. He had scattered whatever he had got from us at dinner in front of the barking hound, and distracted by the food, it had choked down its fury.

Nevertheless, when, shivering and wet, we asked the hall-porter to let us out through the front door, he said: 'You're wrong if you think you can leave through the door you came in. No guest has ever been let out through the same door. They come in one way and go out another.'

Trimalchio's Feast

What could we do after this piece of bad luck, shut up in this modern labyrinth and now beginning to regret that bath? We asked him to please show us the way to the bath-hall, and, throwing off our clothes, which Giton began drying at the door, we went in. There stood Trimalchio, and not even there could we get away from his filthy ostentation. He told us there was nothing better than a private bath, and that there had once been a bakery on that very spot. Then he sat down as though tired, and being tempted by the acoustics of the bath, with his drunken mouth gaping at the ceiling, he began murdering some songs by Menecrates – or so we were told by those who understood his words.

1. BOCCACCIO · *Mrs Rosie and the Priest*
2. GERARD MANLEY HOPKINS · *As kingfishers catch fire*
3. *The Saga of Gunnlaug Serpent-tongue*
4. THOMAS DE QUINCEY · *On Murder Considered as One of the Fine Arts*
5. FRIEDRICH NIETZSCHE · *Aphorisms on Love and Hate*
6. JOHN RUSKIN · *Traffic*
7. PU SONGLING · *Wailing Ghosts*
8. JONATHAN SWIFT · *A Modest Proposal*
9. *Three Tang Dynasty Poets*
10. WALT WHITMAN · *On the Beach at Night Alone*
11. KENKŌ · *A Cup of Sake Beneath the Cherry Trees*
12. BALTASAR GRACIÁN · *How to Use Your Enemies*
13. JOHN KEATS · *The Eve of St Agnes*
14. THOMAS HARDY · *Woman much missed*
15. GUY DE MAUPASSANT · *Femme Fatale*
16. MARCO POLO · *Travels in the Land of Serpents and Pearls*
17. SUETONIUS · *Caligula*
18. APOLLONIUS OF RHODES · *Jason and Medea*
19. ROBERT LOUIS STEVENSON · *Olalla*
20. KARL MARX AND FRIEDRICH ENGELS · *The Communist Manifesto*
21. PETRONIUS · *Trimalchio's Feast*
22. JOHANN PETER HEBEL · *How a Ghastly Story Was Brought to Light by a Common or Garden Butcher's Dog*
23. HANS CHRISTIAN ANDERSEN · *The Tinder Box*
24. RUDYARD KIPLING · *The Gate of the Hundred Sorrows*
25. DANTE · *Circles of Hell*
26. HENRY MAYHEW · *Of Street Piemen*
27. HAFEZ · *The nightingales are drunk*
28. GEOFFREY CHAUCER · *The Wife of Bath*
29. MICHEL DE MONTAIGNE · *How We Weep and Laugh at the Same Thing*
30. THOMAS NASHE · *The Terrors of the Night*
31. EDGAR ALLAN POE · *The Tell-Tale Heart*
32. MARY KINGSLEY · *A Hippo Banquet*
33. JANE AUSTEN · *The Beautifull Cassandra*
34. ANTON CHEKHOV · *Gooseberries*
35. SAMUEL TAYLOR COLERIDGE · *Well, they are gone, and here must I remain*
36. JOHANN WOLFGANG VON GOETHE · *Sketchy, Doubtful, Incomplete Jottings*
37. CHARLES DICKENS · *The Great Winglebury Duel*
38. HERMAN MELVILLE · *The Maldive Shark*
39. ELIZABETH GASKELL · *The Old Nurse's Story*
40. NIKOLAY LESKOV · *The Steel Flea*

41. HONORÉ DE BALZAC · *The Atheist's Mass*
42. CHARLOTTE PERKINS GILMAN · *The Yellow Wall-Paper*
43. C.P. CAVAFY · *Remember, Body . . .*
44. FYODOR DOSTOEVSKY · *The Meek One*
45. GUSTAVE FLAUBERT · *A Simple Heart*
46. NIKOLAI GOGOL · *The Nose*
47. SAMUEL PEPYS · *The Great Fire of London*
48. EDITH WHARTON · *The Reckoning*
49. HENRY JAMES · *The Figure in the Carpet*
50. WILFRED OWEN · *Anthem For Doomed Youth*
51. WOLFGANG AMADEUS MOZART · *My Dearest Father*
52. PLATO · *Socrates' Defence*
53. CHRISTINA ROSSETTI · *Goblin Market*
54. *Sindbad the Sailor*
55. SOPHOCLES · *Antigone*
56. RYŪNOSUKE AKUTAGAWA · *The Life of a Stupid Man*
57. LEO TOLSTOY · *How Much Land Does A Man Need?*
58. GIORGIO VASARI · *Leonardo da Vinci*
59. OSCAR WILDE · *Lord Arthur Savile's Crime*
60. SHEN FU · *The Old Man of the Moon*
61. AESOP · *The Dolphins, the Whales and the Gudgeon*
62. MATSUO BASHŌ · *Lips too Chilled*
63. EMILY BRONTË · *The Night is Darkening Round Me*
64. JOSEPH CONRAD · *To-morrow*
65. RICHARD HAKLUYT · *The Voyage of Sir Francis Drake Around the Whole Globe*
66. KATE CHOPIN · *A Pair of Silk Stockings*
67. CHARLES DARWIN · *It was snowing butterflies*
68. BROTHERS GRIMM · *The Robber Bridegroom*
69. CATULLUS · *I Hate and I Love*
70. HOMER · *Circe and the Cyclops*
71. D. H. LAWRENCE · *Il Duro*
72. KATHERINE MANSFIELD · *Miss Brill*
73. OVID · *The Fall of Icarus*
74. SAPPHO · *Come Close*
75. IVAN TURGENEV · *Kasyan from the Beautiful Lands*
76. VIRGIL · *O Cruel Alexis*
77. H. G. WELLS · *A Slip under the Microscope*
78. HERODOTUS · *The Madness of Cambyses*
79. *Speaking of Siva*
80. *The Dhammapada*

'The devil gave the woman a nudge: "Look at that belt full of money peeping out from under the butcher's shirt!"'

JOHANN PETER HEBEL
Born 1760, Basel, The Swiss Confederacy
Died 1826, Schwetzingen, Grand Duchy of Baden

The stories in this selection were mostly first published in
Johann Peter Hebel's *Schatzkästlein des rheinischen Hausfreundes*
in 1811 and are taken from *The Treasure Chest*, chosen and
translated by John Hibberd in 1994.

HEBEL IN PENGUIN CLASSICS
The Treasure Chest

JOHANN PETER HEBEL

How a Ghastly Story was Brought to Light by a Common or Garden Butcher's Dog

Translated by
John Hibberd and Nicholas Jacobs

PENGUIN BOOKS

PENGUIN CLASSICS

UK | USA | Canada | Ireland | Australia
India | New Zealand | South Africa

Penguin Books is part of the Penguin Random House group of companies
whose addresses can be found at global.penguinrandomhouse.com.

Original translation of *The Treasure Chest* first published in Great Britain by Libris 1994
Published in Penguin Books 1995
This selection published in Penguin Classics 2015
008

Translation copyright © John Hibberd, 1994
'The Safest Path' translation copyright © Nicholas Jacobs, 2015

The moral right of the translators has been asserted

Set in 9.5/13 pt Baskerville 10 Pro
Typeset by Jouve (UK), Milton Keynes
Printed and bound in Great Britain by Clays Ltd, Elcograf S.p.A.

A CIP catalogue record for this book is available from the British Library

ISBN: 978-0-141-39802-0

www.greenpenguin.co.uk

Penguin Random House is committed to a
sustainable future for our business, our readers
and our planet. This book is made from Forest
Stewardship Council® certified paper.

Contents

The Silver Spoon	1
The Cheap Meal	3
Dinner Outside	4
The Clever Judge	6
The Artful Hussar	7
The Dentist	9
A Short Stage	12
Strange Reckoning at the Inn	12
Unexpected Reunion	14
The Sly Pilgrim	17
The Commandant and the Light Infantry in Hersfeld	20
A Poor Reward	22
A Curious Ghost Story	23
One Word Leads to Another	28

A Bad Bargain	29
A Secret Beheading	32
The Fake Gem	34
How a Ghastly Story was Brought to Light by a Common or Garden Butcher's Dog	37
The Cunning Styrian	39
A Report from Turkey	41
The Lightest Death Sentence	42
A Stallholder Duped	43
Patience Rewarded	45
The Champion Swimmer	46
The Weather Man	50
The Safest Path	52

The Silver Spoon

An officer in Vienna was thinking, 'Just for once I'll dine at the Red Ox,' and into the Red Ox he went. There were regulars there and strangers, important and unimportant people, honest men and rascals such as you'll find anywhere. They were eating and drinking, some a great deal, others little. They talked and argued about this and that, about how it had rained rocks at Stannern in Moravia, for instance, or about Machin who fought the great wolf in France. When the meal was almost over one or two were drinking a small jug of Tokay to round things off, one man was making little balls from bread crumbs as if he were an apothecary making pills, another was fiddling with his knife or his fork or his silver spoon. It was then the officer happened to notice how a fellow in a green huntsman's coat was playing with a silver spoon when it suddenly disappeared up his sleeve and stayed there.

Someone else might have thought, 'It's no business of mine,' and said nothing, or have made a great fuss. The officer thought, 'I don't know who this green spoon-hunter is and what I might let myself in for,' and he kept as quiet as a mouse, until the landlord came to collect his money. But when the landlord came to collect his money the officer, too, picked up a silver spoon, and tucked it through two button holes in his coat, in one and out the other as soldiers sometimes do in war when they take their spoons with them, but no soup. As the officer was paying his bill the landlord was looking at his coat and thinking, 'That's a funny medal this gentleman's wearing! He must have distinguished himself battling with a bowl of crayfish soup to have got a silver spoon as a medal! Or could it just be one of mine?' But when the officer had paid the landlord he said, without a sign of a smile on his face, 'The spoon's included, I take it? The bill seems enough to cover it.' The landlord said, 'Nobody's tried that one on me before! If you don't have a spoon at home I'll give you a tin one, but you can't have one of my silver spoons!' Then the officer stood up, slapped the landlord on the shoulder and laughed. 'It was only a joke we were having,' he said, 'that gentleman over there in the green jacket and me! – My green friend, if you give back that spoon you have up your sleeve I'll give mine back too.' When the spoon-hunter saw that he had been caught in the act and that an honest eye had observed his dishonest hand, he thought, 'Better pretend it was a joke,' and gave back his spoon. So the landlord got his property back, and the spoon thief smiled too – but not for long. For when the other customers saw what had happened they set about him with curses and hounded him out of the Holy of Holies and the landlord sent the boots after him with a big stick. But he stood the worthy officer a bottle of Tokay to toast the health of all honest men.

Remember: You must not steal silver spoons!

Remember: Someone will always stand up for what is right.

The Cheap Meal

There is an old saying: The biter is sometimes bit. But the landlord at the Lion in a certain little town was bitten first. He received a well-dressed customer who curtly demanded a good bowl of broth, the best his money would buy. Then he ordered beef and vegetables too for his money. The landlord asked him, all politeness, if he wouldn't like a glass of wine with it. 'Indeed I would,' his guest replied, 'if I can have a good one for my money.' When he had finished, and he enjoyed it all, he took a worn six-kreuzer piece from his pocket and said, 'Here you are, landlord, there's my money!' The landlord said, 'What's this? You owe me a thaler!' The customer answered, 'I didn't ask for a meal for a thaler, but for my money. Here it is. It's all I have. If you gave me too much for it then that's your fault!' It wasn't really such a clever trick. It called only for cheek and a devil-may-care view of the consequences. But the best is yet to come.

'You're an utter villain,' said the landlord, 'and don't

deserve this. But you can have the meal for nothing and take this twenty-four kreuzer bit as well. Just keep quiet about it and go over to my neighbour who keeps the Bear and try the same trick on him!' He said this because he had had a quarrel with his neighbour and resented his success and each was keen to do the other down.

But the artful customer smiled as he took the money he was offered in his one hand and reached carefully for the door with the other, wished the innkeeper good afternoon, and said, 'I went to the Bear first, it was the landlord there who sent me over here!'

So really both of the innkeepers had been tricked; the cunning customer took advantage of their quarrel. Yet he might have also earned a further reward, grateful thanks from both of them, if they had learnt the right lesson from it and had made things up between them. For peace pays, whereas quarrels have to be paid for.

Dinner Outside

We often complain how difficult or impossible it is to get on with certain people. That may of course be true. But many such people are not bad but only strange, and if you got to know them well with all their ins and outs and learnt to deal with them properly, neither too wilfully nor too indulgently, then many of them might easily be brought to their senses. After all, one servant did manage

Dinner Outside

to do that with his master. Sometimes he could do nothing right by him and, as often happens in such situations, was blamed for many things that were not his fault. Thus one day his master came home in a very bad mood and sat down to dinner. The soup was too hot or too cold for him, or neither; no matter, he was in a bad mood! So he picked up the dish and threw it and its contents out of the open window into the yard below. So what do you think the servant did? He didn't hesitate, he threw the meat he was bringing to table down into the yard after the soup, then the bread, the wine, and finally the tablecloth and everything on it, all down into the yard too. 'What the devil do you think you're doing?' said his master angrily and rose threateningly to his feet. But the servant replied quietly and calmly, 'Pardon me if I misunderstood your wishes. I thought you wanted to eat outside today. The air's warm, the sky's blue, and look how lovely the apple blossom is and how happy the bees are sipping at the flowers!' Never again would the soup go out through the window! His master saw he was wrong, cheered up at the sight of the beautiful spring day, smiled to himself at his man's quick thinking, and in his heart he was grateful to him for teaching him a lesson.

Johann Peter Hebel

The Clever Judge

Not everything that happens in the East is so wrong. We are told the following event took place there. A rich man had been careless and lost a large sum of money sewn up in a cloth. He made his loss known, and in the usual way offered a reward for its return, in this case a hundred thalers. Soon a good honest man came to see him. 'I have found your money,' he said. 'This must be yours.' He had the open look of an upright fellow with a clear conscience, and that was good. The rich man looked happy too, but only at seeing his precious money again. As for his honesty, that we shall see! He counted the money and worked out quickly how he could cheat this man of the promised reward. 'My friend,' he said, 'there were in fact eight hundred thalers sewn up in this cloth. But I can find only seven hundred. So I take it you must have cut open a corner and taken your one hundred thalers' reward. You acted quite properly. I thank you!' That was not good. But we haven't got to the end yet. Honesty is the best policy, and wrongdoing never proves right. The honest man who had found the money and who was less concerned for his reward than for his blameless name protested that he had found the packet just as he handed it over, and had handed over exactly what he had found. In the end they appeared in court. Both of them stuck to their stories, one that eight hundred thalers were sewn up in the cloth, the other that he had left the packet just as he found it and had taken nothing from it. It was hard to know what to do. But the clever judge, who seemed from the outset to recognize the honesty of the one and the bad faith of the other, approached the problem as follows. He had both swear their statements on solemn oath, and then passed the following judgement: 'Since one of you lost eight hundred thalers and the other found a packet containing only seven hundred, the package found by that second party cannot be the one to which the first party has just claim. You, my honest friend, take back the money you found and put it into safe keeping until the person who lost only seven hundred thalers makes himself known. And you I can only advise to be patient until someone says he has found your eight hundred thalers.' That was his judgement, and that was final.

The Artful Hussar

A hussar in the last war knew that the farmer he met on the road had just sold his hay for a hundred guilders and was on his way home with the money. So he asked him for something to buy tobacco and brandy. Who knows, he might have been happy with a few coppers. But the farmer swore black and blue he had spent his last kreuzer in the nearby village and had nothing left. 'If we weren't

Johann Peter Hebel

so far from my quarters,' said the hussar, 'we could both be helped out of this difficulty; but you have nothing, and neither have I; so we'll just have to go to Saint Alphonsus! We'll share what he gives us like brothers.' This Saint Alphonsus stood carved from stone in an old, little frequented chapel in the fields. At first the farmer was not too keen to make the pilgrimage. But the hussar allowed no objection, and on the way he was so vigorous in his assurances that Saint Alphonsus had never let him down when in need that the farmer began to cherish hopes himself. So you think the hussar's comrade and accomplice was hiding in the deserted chapel, do you? Not a bit of it! No one was there, only the stone figure of Alphonsus, and they knelt before him, and the hussar appeared to be praying fervently. 'This is it!' he whispered to the farmer, 'the saint has just beckoned to me.' He got to his feet and went to put his ear to the lips of stone and came back delighted. 'He's given me a guilder, he says it's in my purse!' And indeed to the other's amazement the hussar took out a guilder, but one that he had had there all the time, and shared it like a brother as promised. That made sense to the farmer and he agreed that the hussar should try again. All went just as before. This time the hussar was even happier when he came back to the farmer. 'Now Saint Alphonsus has given us a hundred guilders all in one go! They're in your purse.' The farmer turned deadly white when he heard this and repeated his protests that he had no money at all. But the hussar persuaded him he must trust Saint Alphonsus and just take a look; Alphonsus had never deceived him! So whether he liked it or not he had to turn his pockets inside out and empty them. Then the hundred guilders appeared all right, and since he had taken half of the hussar's guilder it was no use pleading and imploring, he had to share his hundred.

That was all very artful and cunning, but that doesn't make it right, especially in a chapel.

The Dentist

Two loafers who had been roaming around the country together for some time because they were too lazy to work or had learnt no trade finally got into a tight corner because they had no money left, and they saw no quick way of getting any. Then they had this idea: they went begging at doors for bread which they intended to use, not to fill their stomachs, but to stage a trick. For they kneaded and rolled it into little balls and coated them with the dust from old, rotten worm-eaten wood so that they looked just like yellow pills from the chemist. Then for a couple of pence they bought some sheets of red paper at the bookbinder's (for a pretty colour often helps take people in). Next they cut up the paper and wrapped the pills in it, six or eight to a little packet. Then one of them went on ahead to a village where there was a fair and into the Red Lion where he hoped to find a good crowd. He ordered a glass of wine, but he didn't drink it but sat sadly in a corner holding his face in his hand, moaning under his breath and fidgeting and turning this way and that. The good farmers and townsfolk in the inn thought the poor fellow must have terrible toothache. Yet what could they do? They pitied him, they consoled him, saying it would soon go away, then went back to their drinks and their market-day affairs. Meanwhile the other idler came in. The two scoundrels pretended they had never seen each other in their lives before. They didn't look at each other until the one seemed to react to the other's moans in the corner. 'My friend,' he said, 'have you got toothache?' and he strode slowly over to him. 'I am Dr Schnauzius Rapunzius from Trafalgar,' he continued. Such resounding foreign names help take people in too, you know, like pretty colours. 'If you take my tooth pills,' he went on, 'I can easily get rid of the pain, one of them will do the trick, at most two.' 'Please God you're right!' said the other rogue. So now the fine doctor Rapunzius took one of the red packets from his pocket and prescribed one pill, to be placed on the tongue and bitten on firmly. The customers at the other tables now craned their necks and one by one they came over to observe the miracle cure. You can imagine what happened! But no, the first bite seemed to do the patient no good at all, he gave a terrible scream. The doctor was pleased! They had, he said, got the better of the pain, and

The Dentist

quickly he gave him the second pill to be taken likewise. Now suddenly the pain had all gone. The patient jumped for joy, wiped the sweat from his brow, though there was none there, and pretended to show his thanks by pressing more than a trifling sum into his saviour's hand. The trick was artfully done and had its desired effect. For all those present now wanted some of these excellent pills too. The doctor offered them at twenty-four kreuzers a packet, and they were all sold in a few minutes. Of course the two scoundrels now left separately one after the other, met up to laugh at the people's stupidity, and had a good time on their money.

The fools had paid dear for a few crumbs of bread! Even in times of famine you never got so little for twenty-four kreuzers. But the waste of money was not the worst part of it. For in time the pellets of breadcrumbs naturally became as hard as stone. So when a year later a poor dupe had toothache and confidently bit on a pill with the offending tooth, once and then again, just imagine the awful pain that he had got himself for twenty-four kreuzers instead of a cure!

From this we can learn how easy it is to be tricked if you believe what is told you by any vagrant whom you meet for the first time in your life, have never seen before and will never see again. Some of you who read this will perhaps be thinking: 'I was once silly like that too and brought suffering on myself!'

Remember: Those who can, earn their money elsewhere

and don't go around villages and fairs with holes in their stockings, or a white buckle on one shoe and a yellow one on the other.

A Short Stage

The postmaster told a Jew who drove up to his relay station with two horses, 'From here on you'll have to take three! It's a hard pull uphill and the surface is still soft. But that way you'll be there in three hours.' The Jew asked, 'When will I get there if I take four?' 'In two hours.' 'And if I take six?' 'In one hour.' 'I'll tell you what,' said the Jew after a while, 'Harness up eight. That way I shan't have to set off at all!'

Strange Reckoning at the Inn

Sometimes a cheeky trick comes off, sometimes it costs you your coat, often your skin as well. But in this case it was only coats. One day, you see, three merry students on their travels didn't have a brass farthing left between them, they had spent everything on a good time, but nevertheless they went into another inn intending to leave without sneaking out by the back door, and it suited them fine that they found only the landlord's nice young wife inside. They ate and drank merrily and talked very

Strange Reckoning at the Inn

learnedly about the world being many thousands of years old and how it would last as long again, and how each year, to the day and the hour, everything that happened came to pass as it had done on that day and at that hour six thousand years before. Eventually one of them turned to the landlady, who was sitting on one side by the window knitting and listening attentively, and said, 'That's how it is, ma'am, we've had to learn that from our learned tomes.' And one had the impudence to assert that he just about remembered their being there six thousand years ago, and he remembered the landlady's pretty friendly face very well indeed. They carried on talking for some time, and the more the landlady seemed to believe everything they said the more the young gadabouts tucked into the wine and the meat and a fistful of pretzels, and in the end their bill stood chalked up at five guilders and sixteen kreuzers. They had eaten and drunk their fill, and now they came out with the trick they had planned.

'Ma'am,' said one, 'this time we are short of money, for there are so many inns on the road. But since we know you're a clever woman we hope that as old friends we can have credit here, and if you agree, in six thousand years' time when we come again we'll pay our old bill together with the new one.' The sensible landlady was not upset by that, it was fine by her, she was delighted that the young gentlemen were well served. But before they had noticed her move she was standing in front of the door and was asking the gentlemen kindly just to settle now the bill of five guilders and sixteen kreuzers that they owed from six thousand years ago, since, as they said, everything that happened now was an exact repetition of what had taken place before. Unfortunately just at that moment the village mayor came in with a couple of sturdy men to enjoy a glass of wine together. That didn't suit our gay young dogs at all! For now the official verdict was pronounced and carried out: you had to give it to someone who had allowed credit for six thousand years! The gentlemen were therefore to pay their old debt immediately or leave their newish overcoats as a pledge. They were obliged to take the second option, and the landlady promised to return their coats in six thousand years' time when they came again with a bit more money.

This took place in 1805 on the 17th of April in the inn at Segringen.

Unexpected Reunion

At Falun in Sweden, a good fifty years ago, a young miner kissed his pretty young bride-to-be and said, 'On the feast of Saint Lucia the parson will bless our love and we shall be man and wife and start a home of our own.' 'And may peace and love dwell there with us,' said his lovely bride, and smiled sweetly, 'for you are everything to me, and without you I'd sooner be in the grave than anywhere

Unexpected Reunion

else.' When however, before the feast of Saint Lucia, the parson had called out their names in church for the second time: 'If any of you know cause, or just hindrance, why these two persons should not be joined together in holy Matrimony' – Death paid a call. For the next day when the young man passed her house in his black miner's suit (a miner is always dressed ready for his own funeral), he tapped at the window as usual and wished her good morning all right, but he did not wish her good evening. He did not return from the mine, and in vain that same morning she sewed a red border on a black neckerchief for him to wear on their wedding day, and when he did not come back she put it away, and she wept for him, and never forgot him.

In the meantime the city of Lisbon in Portugal was destroyed by an earthquake, the Seven Years War came and went, the Emperor Francis I died, the Jesuits were dissolved, Poland was partitioned, the Empress Maria Theresa died, and Struensee was executed, and America became independent, and the combined French and Spanish force failed to take Gibraltar. The Turks cooped up General Stein in the Veterane Cave in Hungary, and the Emperor Joseph died too. King Gustavus of Sweden conquered Russian Finland, the French Revolution came and the long war began, and the Emperor Leopold II too was buried. Napoleon defeated Prussia, the English bombarded Copenhagen, and the farmers sowed and reaped.

Johann Peter Hebel

The millers ground the corn, the blacksmiths wielded their hammers, and the miners dug for seams of metal in their workplace under the ground.

But in 1809, within a day or two of the feast of Saint John, when the miners at Falun were trying to open up a passage between two shafts, they dug out from the rubble and the vitriol water, a good three hundred yards below ground, the body of a young man soaked in ferrous vitriol but otherwise untouched by decay and unchanged, so that all his features and his age were still clearly recognizable, as if he had died only an hour before or had just nodded off at work. Yet when they brought him to the surface his father and mother and friends and acquaintances were all long since dead, and no one claimed to know the sleeping youth or to remember his misadventure, until the woman came who had once been promised to the miner who one day had gone below and had not returned. Grey and bent, she hobbled up on a crutch to where he lay and recognized her bridegroom; and, more in joyous rapture than in grief, she sank down over the beloved corpse, and it was some time before she had recovered from her fervent emotion. 'It is my betrothed,' she said at last, 'whom I have mourned these past fifty years, and now God grants that I see him once more before I die. A week before our wedding he went under ground and never came up again.' The hearts of all those there were moved to sadness and tears when they saw the former bride-to-be as an old woman whose beauty and strength had left her, and the groom still in the flower of his youth; and how the flame of young love was rekindled in her breast after fifty years, yet he did not open his mouth to smile, nor his eyes to recognize her; and how finally she, as the sole relative and the only person who had claim to him, had the miners carry him into her house until his grave was made ready for him in the churchyard.

The next day when the grave lay ready in the churchyard and the miners came to fetch him she opened a casket and put the black silk neckerchief with the red stripes on him, and then she went with him in her best Sunday dress, as if it were her wedding day, not the day of his burial. You see, as they lowered him into his grave in the churchyard she said, 'Sleep well for another day or a week or so longer in your cold wedding bed, and don't let time weigh heavy on you! I have only a few things left to do, and I shall join you soon, and soon the day will dawn.

'What the earth has given back once it will not withhold again at the final call', she said as she went away and looked back over her shoulder once more.

The Sly Pilgrim

A few years ago an idler roamed around the countryside pretending to be a pious pilgrim, saying he came from Paderborn and was making for the Holy Sepulchre in

Johann Peter Hebel

Jerusalem, and already at the Coach and Horses in Mülheim he was asking, 'How far is it to Jerusalem now?' They told him, 'Seven hundred hours. But you'll save a quarter of an hour if you take the path to Mauchen.' So he went by way of Mauchen to save himself a quarter of an hour on his long journey. That wasn't such a bad idea. You must not scorn a small gain or a bigger one won't come your way. You more often get a chance to save or make threepence than a florin. But eight threepennies make a florin, and if on a journey of seven hundred hours you can save a quarter of an hour every five hours, over the whole journey you will save – now, who can work that out? How many hours? But that wasn't how our supposed pilgrim saw it! Since he was only after an easy life and a good meal he didn't care which way he went. As the old saying goes, a beggar can never take the wrong turning, it's a poor village indeed where he can't collect more than the cost of the shoe leather he has worn out on the road, especially if he goes barefoot. Yet our pilgrim intended to get back as soon as he could to the main road where he'd find rich people's houses and good cooking. For this rascal wasn't content, as a true pilgrim should be, with common food given in compassion by a pious hand, he wanted nothing but nourishing pebble soup! You see, whenever he saw a nice inn by the road, for instance the Post House at Krozingen or the Basel Arms at Schliengen, he would go in and very humbly and hungrily ask for a nice soup made of pebbles and water, in God's name, he

The Sly Pilgrim

had no money. And when the innkeeper's wife took pity on him and said, 'Pious pilgrim, pebbles are not easy to digest!', he said, 'That's just it! Pebbles last longer than bread and it's a long way to Jerusalem. But if you were to give me a little glass of wine too, in God's name, it would help me digest them.' Now if she said, 'But good pilgrim, a soup like that won't give you any strength at all!' then he replied, 'Well, if you use broth instead of water then of course it would be more nourishing.' And when she brought him his broth and said, 'The bits at the bottom are still a bit hard, I'm afraid,' then he'd say, 'You're right, and the broth looks a little thin. Would you have a couple of spoonfuls of vegetables to add to it, or a scrap of meat, or maybe both?' If now the innkeeper's wife still felt sorry for him and put some meat and vegetables in the bowl, he said, 'God bless you! Now just hand me a piece of bread and I'll tuck into your soup!' Then he would push back the sleeves of his pilgrim's habit, sit down and set to work with relish, and when he had eaten the last crumb of bread, drained the wine, and finished the last morsel of meat and vegetables and the last drop of broth, he would wipe his mouth on the tablecloth or his sleeve, or perhaps he wouldn't bother, and he'd say, 'Missus, your soup has strengthened me as a good soup should, what a shame I can't find room for the nice pebbles now! But put them by, and when I come back I'll bring you a holy conch from the seashore at Ascalon or a Jericho rose.'

Johann Peter Hebel

The Commandant and the Light Infantry in Hersfeld

In the last campaign in Prussia and Russia when the French Army and a large part of the allied troops were in Poland and Prussia, a contingent of the Baden Light Infantry was in Hessen and stationed at Hersfeld. For the Emperor had taken that state at the beginning of the campaign and stationed troops there. The inhabitants who preferred the way things had been before defied the new order and there were several acts of lawlessness, particularly in the town of Hersfeld. In one incident a French officer was killed. The French Emperor was engaged face to face with great numbers of the enemy and couldn't allow hostilities behind his back or let a spark spread into a great fire. The unfortunate people of Hersfeld thus had cause to regret their rashness. For the Emperor ordered the town to be looted, set alight at each corner and burnt to the ground.

This town of Hersfeld has many factories and thus many rich inhabitants and fine buildings; and all of us with a heart can understand how its unfortunate people, those fathers and mothers with families, felt when they heard the dreadful news. The poor whose possessions could be carried off in one pair of arms were just as much affected as the rich whose goods couldn't all be loaded

The Commandant and the Light Infantry in Hersfeld

on a train of wagons. Great houses on the town square and small dwellings in the alleyways are all the same when burnt to the ground, just like rich and poor in the graveyard.

But the worst didn't happen. The French Commandant in Kassel and Hersfeld interceded and the punishment was reduced. Only four houses were to be burnt down, and that was lenient. But the plundering was to take place as ordered, and that was hard enough. The wretched townsfolk, hearing this latest decision, were so cowed and robbed of all presence of mind that the benevolent Commandant himself had to urge them, instead of weeping and pleading in vain, to remove their most precious possessions in the short time that was left. The dreadful hour arrived, the drums sounded over the wails of anguish. The soldiers hurried to their place of assembly through the crowds fleeing in despair. Then the stalwart Commandant of Hersfeld stood before the ranks of the infantry, and first he painted a vivid picture of the sad fate of the townspeople, then he said, 'Men, you now have permission to loot! Those who wish to take part, fall out!' Not one man moved. Not a single one! The order was repeated. Not one pair of boots stirred, and if the Commandant had intended the town to be plundered he would have had to do it himself. But no one was more pleased than he was that things turned out as they did, that is easy to tell. When the townsfolk learnt this, it was as if they woke from a bad dream. No one can describe their joy. They sent a delegation to the Commandant to thank him for his kindness and magnanimity, and offered him a handsome gift to mark their gratitude. Who knows what they might not have done! But the Commandant refused and said he wouldn't be paid for a good deed.

This happened in Hersfeld in the year 1807, and the town is still standing.

A Poor Reward

When in the last Prussian war the French came to Berlin where the King of Prussia resides, a great deal of the royal property as well as other people's was taken and carried off or sold. For war brings nothing, it only takes. Much was claimed as booty, however well it was hidden they found it, but not everything. A large store of royal building timber remained undiscovered and untouched for some time. But eventually a rascal among the king's own subjects thought, there's a fair penny to be made here, and with a smirk and a wink he went to tell the French commandant what a lovely stack of oak and pine logs was still at such and such a place, and it was worth a few thousand guilders. But the French commandant paid him badly for this betrayal and said, 'Just you leave those fine logs where they are! There's no call to deprive the enemy of his most basic needs. For when your king returns he will need timber for new gallows for trusty subjects like you!'

Your Family Friend can only applaud that, and he would make a present of a few logs from his own coppice if they were needed.

A Curious Ghost Story

Last autumn a gentleman was travelling through Schliengen, a nice little place. And as he was walking up the hill to spare the horses he told a man from Grenzach the following story of what had happened to him.

Six months earlier this gentleman was on his way to Denmark, and late one evening he arrived in a village with a fine mansion on a hill outside, and he wanted to stay the night. But the innkeeper said he had no room, there was a hanging the next day and three hangmen were staying with him. So the gentleman replied, 'Then I'll ask up there in the big house. The owner, the governor or whoever he is, will take me in and find a spare bed for me.' The innkeeper said, 'There are plenty of fine beds with silk hangings up there all ready made up, and I'm in charge of the keys. But I wouldn't advise you to go there! Three months ago the lord and the lady and the young master went away on a long journey, and since then the mansion house has been haunted by ghosts. The steward and the servants had to leave, and all the others who have been to the house never went back a second time.' Our stranger smiled. For he was a plucky man who

Johann Peter Hebel

wasn't afraid of ghosts, and he said, 'I'll risk it!' Despite all the innkeeper's objections he had to hand over the key, and after the traveller had put together what was needed to pay a visit on ghosts he went to the mansion with his servant who was travelling with him.

Once inside he didn't undress or get ready for bed, but waited to see what happened. He put two lights to burn on the table and a pair of loaded pistols next to them, and to pass away the time he picked up the Rhinelanders' Family Friend, bound in gold paper, which was hanging by a red silk ribbon under the mirror in its frame on the wall, and looked at the nice pictures. For a long time nothing happened. But when midnight stirred in the church tower and the clock struck twelve, and a rainstorm was passing over the house and large drops were beating against the window, there were three loud knocks on the door and a ghastly apparition with black squinting eyes, a nose half a yard long, gnashing teeth, a beard like a goat and hair all over its body came into the room and said in a horrible growl: 'I am the lord Mephistopheles. Welcome to my palace! Have you said your goodbyes to your wife and children?' The visitor felt a cold shiver run up from his big toes over his back and up under his nightcap, and his poor servant was in a worse state still. But when this Mephistopheles came towards him, scowling dreadfully and stepping high as if he was crossing a floor of flames, the unfortunate gentleman thought: in God's name, this is the test! And he stood up boldly and pointed

A Curious Ghost Story

his pistol at the monster and said, 'Halt, or I'll shoot!' Not every ghost can be stopped like that, for even if you pull the trigger it doesn't go off, or the bullet flies back and hits you instead of the target. But Mephistopheles raised his first finger in warning, turned slowly on his heels and strode away just as he had come. Now when our traveller saw that this devil had respect for gunpowder, he thought, 'There's no danger now!', picked up a light in his free hand and followed the ghost cautiously along the passage; and his servant who was standing behind him ran for all he was worth out of this blessed place and down to the village, thinking he'd sooner spend the night with the hangmen than with spooks.

But suddenly in the passage the ghost disappeared from under the eyes of its plucky pursuer just as if it had gone through the floor. And when the gentleman went on another few paces to see where it had gone, all at once there was no floor under his feet and he fell down through a hole towards a flaming fire, and he himself thought he was on the way to hell. But after dropping about ten feet he found himself lying unharmed on a heap of hay in a cellar. And six weird fellows were standing around the fire, that Mephistopheles with them. All sorts of strange implements were piled up around them, and two tables stood heaped with shining thalers, each one more lovely than the other.

Now the stranger knew what was going on. For this was a secret band of forgers, all with blood running in

Johann Peter Hebel

their veins. They had taken advantage of the owner's absence and set up their mint in his mansion, and some of them were probably servants of the house who knew their way about; and to make sure they were not disturbed and discovered they wailed like ghosts, and anyone who came to the house was so frightened he never came back to take a second look. Yet the plucky traveller now had cause to regret his lack of prudence in not listening to the innkeeper's warnings. For he was pushed through a narrow opening into a small dark room and could hear them deciding his fate: 'The best thing is to kill him!' said one. But another said, 'First we must question him, find out who he is and where he's from.' When they then learnt he was a man of consequence and on his way to Copenhagen to see the king they looked at each other wide-eyed. And when he was back in the dark storeroom they said, 'This is a bad business. For if he's missed and they find out from the innkeeper that he came here and didn't leave, the hussars will come overnight and fetch us out, and there's plenty of hemp in the fields this year, so hangmen's nooses come cheap.' So they told their prisoner they would let him go if he swore an oath not to betray them, threatening they would have him watched in Copenhagen. And he had to tell them on oath where he lived. He told them, 'Next to the Green Man, on the left in the big house with green shutters.' Then they poured him some Burgundy wine and he watched them coining their thalers until it was light.

A Curious Ghost Story

When the morning light shone down through the gratings, and they heard the sound of whips on the road and the cowherd blowing his horn, the traveller took leave of his night-time companions, thanked them for having him and went gaily back to the inn, quite forgetting that he had left his watch and pipe and the pistols behind in the mansion. The innkeeper said, 'Thank God you're back, I didn't get a wink of sleep! How did you get on?' But the traveller thought, an oath is an oath, and you mustn't take God's name in vain to save your life. So he said nothing, and as the bell was ringing and the wretched malefactor was being led out everyone ran off to watch. He said nothing in Copenhagen either, and almost forgot the incident himself.

A few weeks later, however, he received a parcel by the post, and in it were a pair of expensive new pistols inlaid with silver, a new gold watch set with diamonds, a Turkish pipe with a gold chain and a silk tobacco-pouch embroidered with gold, and in the pouch was a note. It said, 'We are sending you this to make up for the fright we gave you and to thank you for keeping quiet. It's all over now, and you can tell anyone you like.' So the traveller told the man from Grenzach, and it was that same gold watch that he took out at the top of the hill to check that the clock at Hertingen was striking noon on time, and later on in the Stork in Basel a French general offered him seventy-five new doubloons for it. But he wouldn't part with it.

Johann Peter Hebel

One Word Leads to Another

A rich man in Swabia sent his son to Paris to learn French and a few manners. After a year or more his father's farmhand came to see him. The son was greatly surprised and cried out joyfully, 'Hans, whatever are you doing here? How are things at home, what's the news?'

'Nothing much, Mr William, though your fine raven copped it two weeks ago, the one the gamekeeper gave you.'

'Oh, the poor bird,' replied Mr William. 'What happened to it?'

'Well, you see, he ate too much carrion when our fine horses died one after the other. I said he would.'

'What! My father's four fine greys are dead?' Mr William asked. 'How did that happen?'

'Well, you see, they were worked too hard hauling water when the house and the barns burned down, and it did no good.'

'Oh no!' exclaimed Mr William, horrified. 'Our house burnt down? When was that?'

'Well, you see, nobody thought of a fire when your father lay in his coffin. He was buried at night with torches. A small spark soon spreads.'

'That's terrible news!' exclaimed Mr William in his distress. 'My father dead? And how is my sister?'

'Well, you see, your late father died of grief when the young Miss had a child and no father for it. It's a boy.

'There's nothing much else to tell,' he added.

A Bad Bargain

In the great city of London and round about it there are an extraordinary number of silly fools who take a childish delight in other people's money or fob watches or precious rings and don't rest until they have them for themselves. Sometimes they get them by cunning and trickery, but more often by fearless assault, sometimes in broad daylight on the open road. Some of them do well, others don't. The London jailors and executioners can tell a few tales about that! One day, however, a strange thing happened to a certain rich and distinguished man. The King and many other great lords and their ladies were gathered on a lovely summer's day in a royal park where the winding paths led to a wood in the distance. Crowds of other people were there too, they didn't think their journey or their time wasted if they could see that their beloved King and his family were happy and well. There was food and drink, music and dancing. There were walks to be taken in pairs or alone along the inviting paths and between scented rose bushes. A man, well-dressed so that he appeared to be one of the company, took up his stand with a pistol under his coat by a tree at a secluded spot where the park bordered on the wood, waiting for someone to come his way. And someone did come, a gentleman with a ring sparkling on his finger, a tinkling watch chain, diamonds in his buckles, and a ribbon and a star on his breast. He was strolling in the cool shade and thinking of nothing in particular. And while he was thinking of nothing in particular the fellow behind the tree stepped out, bowed low, pulled his pistol from under his coat, pointed it at the gentleman's breast and asked him politely to keep quiet, no one need know about their conversation! You can't help feeling uneasy when a pistol is aimed at you, you can never be sure what's in it! The gentleman very sensibly thought: better your money than your life, better lose a ring than a finger! and he promised to keep quiet.

'Now, Your Honour,' said this fellow, 'would you part with your two gold watches for a good price? Our schoolmaster adjusts the clock every day, so we can never be sure of the right time, and you can't see the figures on the sundial.' The gentleman had no choice, he was obliged to sell his watches to the scoundrel for a few pence, hardly the price of a glass of wine. In this way the rascal bought his ring and his buckles and the decorations off his breast, one after another and each for a paltry sum, with the pistol in his left hand all the time. When at last the gentleman thought, now he'll let me go, thank God!, the rogue began again.

'Your Honour, since we do business so easily, why don't

A Bad Bargain

you buy some of my things from me?' The gentleman thought, I must grin and bear it, that's the expression, and said, 'Show me what you have!' The fellow took a collection of trinkets from his pocket, things he had bought at a tuppenny stall or filched from somewhere, and the gentleman had to buy them all from him, one after the other, none of them cheap. Eventually the rogue had nothing left but the pistol, but seeing that the gentleman still had a couple of lovely doubloons in his green silk purse he said, 'Sir, won't you buy this pistol of mine with what's left in your purse? It's made by the best gunmaker in London and it's worth two doubloons of anyone's money!' The gentleman was surprised. 'This robber's an idiot!' he thought, and bought the pistol. When he had bought it from the robber he turned the tables on him and said: 'Hands up, my fine friend, and do as I tell you, keep walking in front of me or I'll blow your brains out!' But the rogue darted off into the wood. 'Go ahead and shoot, Your Excellency,' he said, 'it's not loaded!' The gentleman pulled the trigger, and in fact it didn't go off. He pushed the ramrod into the barrel, there was no trace of powder. By now the thief was well away into the wood; and the distinguished Englishman walked back, red in the face at being frightened by an empty threat, and he had something to think about now.

Johann Peter Hebel

A Secret Beheading

Whether or not on that morning of 17 June that year the executioner at Landau said the Lord's Prayer with proper devotion and its 'Lead us not into temptation but deliver us from evil' – that I don't know. But a delivery came, a note posted from Nancy, and if he hadn't said his prayers, then it arrived on just the right day. The note said: 'Executioner at Landau, come to Nancy straight away and bring your big sword. You will be told what to do and paid well.' A coach was waiting outside. 'It's my job', thought the executioner and got into the coach. When he was still one hour this side of Nancy, it was evening already and the sun was setting among blood-red clouds, the driver drew up, saying, 'It will be fine again tomorrow', when suddenly three strong armed men were standing by the road, climbed in beside the executioner and promised that he wouldn't come to any harm, 'But you must let us blindfold you!' And when they had put the blindfold over his eyes they said, 'Driver, drive on!' The coachman drove on, and it seemed to the executioner that he was taken a good twelve hours further, and he had no way of telling where he was. He heard the midnight owls; he heard the cocks crow; he heard the morning bells. Then without warning the coach stopped again. They took him into a house and gave him something to drink and a nice roll and sausage too. When he was strengthened by food and drink they led him on inside the same building, through several doors and up stairs and down, and then they removed his blindfold and he saw he was in a large room. It was hung all around with black drapes, and wax candles burnt on the tables. In the middle sat a woman on a chair with her neck bared and a mask over her face, and she must have been gagged, for she couldn't speak, only sob. Round the walls stood a number of gentlemen dressed in black and with black crape over their faces so that the executioner could not have recognized them if he had met them again an hour later. And one of them handed him his sword and ordered him to cut off the head of the woman sitting on the chair. The poor executioner's blood ran cold and he said they must excuse him: his sword was dedicated to the service of justice and he could not defile it with murder. But one of the gentlemen by the wall pointed a pistol at him and said, 'Get on with it! Do as we tell you or you'll never set eyes on the church tower at Landau again!' The executioner thought of his wife and children at home. 'If I've no choice,' he said, 'and I must shed innocent blood, then on your head be it!' and with one blow he severed the poor woman's head from her body.

When it was done one of the men gave him a purse with two hundred doubloons. They put the blindfold over his eyes again and took him back to the coach he had come in. The men who had brought him there escorted him again. And when at last the coach drew up and they let him get out and remove the blindfold he was left standing where the three men had joined the coach, one hour this side of Nancy on the Landau road, and it was night. The coach sped off back.

That is what happened to the executioner at Landau, and Your Family Friend is not sorry that he can't say who that poor soul was who had to take such a bloody way to life everlasting. No, nobody found out who she was, what sin she had committed, and nobody knows where she is buried.

The Fake Gem

Outside the Butcher's Gate at Strassburg there is a pleasant garden where anyone can go and spend his money on decent pleasure, and there sat a well-dressed man drinking his wine like everyone else, and he had a ring with a precious stone on his finger and held it so it sparkled. So a Jew came up and said, 'Sir, you have a lovely gem in that ring on your finger, I wouldn't mind that myself! Doesn't it glitter like the Urim and Thummim in the breastplate of Aaron the priest?' The well-dressed stranger answered very curtly, 'The gem is a fake. If it weren't, it would be on someone else's finger, not mine!' The Jew asked to take a closer look at it. He turned it this way and that in his hand and bent his head to look at it

The Fake Gem

from every angle. 'He says this stone is a fake?' he thought, and offered the stranger two new doubloons for the ring. But the stranger said quite angrily, 'Why do you think I'm lying? I told you, it's a fake!' The Jew asked permission to show it to an expert, and someone sitting close by said, 'I'll vouch for the Israelite, he'll know what the jewel is worth!' The stranger said, 'I don't need to consult anyone, the stone's a fake.'

While this was happening Your Family Friend was sitting at another table in the same garden with good friends of his, happily spending money on decent pleasure, and one of the company was a goldsmith who knows all about gems. He fitted a soldier who lost his nose at the battle of Austerlitz with a silver one and painted it skin colour, and it was a good nose. The only thing he couldn't do was breathe the breath of life into it. The Jew came over to this goldsmith. 'Sir,' he said, 'would you say this is a fake stone? Can King Solomon have worn anything more splendid in his crown?' The goldsmith, who was also something of a stargazer, said, 'It shines like Aldebaran in the sky all right. I'll get you ninety doubloons for this ring. If you come by it cheaper the profit is yours.'

The Jew went back to the stranger. 'Fake or not, I'll give you six doubloons!' and he counted them out on the table, sparkling new from the mint. The stranger put the ring back on his finger and said, 'I have no intention of parting with it. If it's such a good fake that you think it's real that doesn't make it worth any less to me,' and he put his hand in his pocket so that the eager Israelite could no longer see the stone. 'Eight doubloons.' 'No.' 'Ten doubloons.' 'No.' 'Twelve – fourteen – fifteen doubloons.' 'Very well,' said the stranger at last, 'if you won't leave me in peace and insist on being deceived at all costs! But I tell you, in front of all these gentlemen here, the stone is a fake, and I'll not say it isn't. For I don't want any trouble. You can have the ring, it's yours.'

Now the Jew took the ring joyfully over to the goldsmith. 'I'll come for the money tomorrow.' But the goldsmith, who had never been taken in by anyone, opened his eyes wide in amazement. 'My friend, this isn't the ring you showed me two minutes ago! This stone is worth twenty kreuzers at most. This is the sort they make in the glass works at Sankt Blasien!' For actually the stranger had in his pocket a fake ring which looked as good as the one that had first sparkled on his finger, and while the Jew was bargaining with him and his hand was in his pocket, he pushed the genuine ring off his finger with his thumb and slipped his finger into the fake, and that was the one he had given the Jew. At once the dupe shot back to the stranger as if fired on a rocket: 'Oh, woe, woe unto me! I have been tricked, the stone is a fake!' But the stranger said coldly and calmly, 'I sold it to you for a fake. These gentlemen here are witnesses. It's yours now. Did I talk you into buying it or did you talk me into selling it?' All those present had to admit, 'Yes, he told you the stone was a fake when he said you could have it!' So the Jew had to keep the ring and no further fuss was made of the matter.

How a Ghastly Story was Brought to Light by a Common or Garden Butcher's Dog

Two butchers out in their district buying in animals came to a village and split up, one went left past the Swan, the other right, and they said, 'We'll meet up again in the Swan.' But they never did meet up again. For one of them went with a farmer into his cowshed. The farmer's wife went as well, though she was doing the washing in the kitchen, and their child decided to follow too. The devil gave the woman a nudge: 'Look at that belt full of money peeping out from under the butcher's shirt!' The woman gave her husband a wink, he gave her a nod, and they killed the poor butcher in the cowshed and hurriedly hid his body under some straw. The devil nudged the woman again: 'Look who's watching!' She looked round and saw the child. So, driven out of their minds by fear, they went back together into the house and locked the doors as if the enemy were near. Then the woman, whose heart was not just as black as sin but blacker and hotter than hell, said, 'Child, just look at you again! Come into the kitchen,' she said, 'I'll clean you up.' In the kitchen she

Johann Peter Hebel

pushed her child's head into the hot suds and scalded him to death. Now, she thought, there's no one to tell on us – but she didn't think of the murdered butcher's dog.

The murdered butcher's dog had run along a bit with the other butcher, and then, while the child was being boiled and then popped into the bread oven, the dog doubled back and picked up his master's scent, sniffed at the cowshed door, scratched at the door to the house, and knew that something was wrong. Off he ran at once, back into the village, looking for the other butcher. Soon he was whinging and whining and pulling at this butcher's coat, and the butcher, too, knew something was wrong. So he went with the dog back to the house, in no doubt that something dreadful had happened there. He beckoned over two men who were passing nearby. When the murderers heard the dog whining and the butcher shouting, they had nothing but the gallows before their eyes and the fear of hellfire in their hearts. The man tried to escape through the back window but his wife grabbed him by his coat and said, 'Stay here with me!' The man said, 'Come with me!' She answered, 'I can't, my legs won't move! Can't you see that ghastly figure outside the window, with its flaming eyes and fiery breath?' Meanwhile the door had been broken open. They soon found the two corpses. The criminals were taken and brought to court. Six weeks later they were put to death, their villainous corpses bound to the wheel, and even now the crows are still saying, 'That's tasty meat, that is!'

The Cunning Styrian

It was in Styria during the last war and some way off the main road, and a rich farmer was thinking: 'How can I keep my thalers and my dear little ducats safe in these evil times? I'm ever so fond of the Empress Maria Theresa, God bless her, and the Emperor Joseph, God bless him, and the Emperor Francis, God give him long life and health! And just when you think you have these dear sovereigns ever so safe and out of harm's way the enemy gets a whiff of them as soon as he sticks his nose into the village and takes them off prisoner to Lorraine or Champagne! It's enough to make a poor patriotic Austrian's heart bleed!' 'I've got it!' he said, 'I know what I'll do,' and in the dark moonless night he took his money out into the kitchen garden. 'The Seven Sisters will not betray me,' he said. Out in the garden he put the money straight down between the wallflowers and the sweet peas. Next to it he dug a hole in the path between the beds, threw all the soil on top of the coins and trampled on the beautiful flowers and the chard all around like someone treading down sauerkraut. The next Monday the Chasseurs were scouting all round the district, and on the Tuesday a patrol entered the village and went straight to the mill, and then with white elbows from the mill to our farmer. And an Alsatian brandished his sword and bawled

Johann Peter Hebel

at him, 'Out with your money, farmer, or say your last Our Father!' The farmer said they were welcome in God's name to take whatever they could find. He had nothing left, it had all gone yesterday and the day before that. 'You'll not find anything,' he said, 'you fine fellows!' When they found nothing except for a couple of coppers and a gilded threepenny piece with the image of the Empress Maria Theresa on it and a ring to hang it up by, the Alsatian said, 'Farmer, you've buried your money! Show us here and now where you buried your money or you'll leave for the hereafter without saying your last Our Father!' 'I can't show you it here and now,' said the farmer, 'I'm sorry, but you'll have to come with me out into the kitchen garden. I'll show you where it was hidden there and what happened. Our lords and masters, the enemy, were here before you, yesterday and the day before, and they found it and took the lot.' The Chasseurs saw how things looked in the garden, found everything just as the man said, and not one of them thought the money might be lying under the pile of earth, but each of them gazed into the empty hole and thought: 'If only I'd been here earlier!' 'And if only they hadn't ruined the wallflowers, and the chard as well!' said the farmer, and so he fooled them and all those who came after them, and so it was that he saved the whole family of archdukes, the Emperor Francis, the Emperor Joseph, the Empress Maria Theresa, and Leopold the First, the Most Blessed of All, and kept them safe in their own country.

A Report from Turkey

There is justice in Turkey. A merchant's man was overtaken on his journey by night and fatigue, tied his horse laden with precious goods to a tree not far from a guardhouse, lay down under the shelter of the tree and went to sleep. Early next day he was woken by the morning air and the quails calling. He had slept well, but his horse had gone.

So he rushed off to the governor of the province, Prince Carosman Oglu he was called and he was staying nearby, and complained that he had been robbed. The prince cut the hearing short: 'So close to the guardhouse! Why didn't you ride on another fifty yards, then you would have been safe! It's your own stupid fault!' But then the merchant's man said, 'O just prince, should I have feared to sleep in the open in a land where you rule?' That pleased the Prince Carosman, and it annoyed him too. 'Drink a little glass of Turkish brandy tonight,' he said to the merchant's man, 'and sleep under the same tree again.' The man did just as he was told. The next morning when he was woken by the morning air and the quails calling he had slept well again, for the horse was standing there tethered at his side together with all the precious goods, and in the tree hung a dead man, the thief, who never saw the sun rise again.

They do say there are trees enough in most parts, big ones and little ones.

The Lightest Death Sentence

People have said it's the guillotine. But it isn't, you know! A man who had done much for his country and was highly thought of by its ruler was sentenced to death for a crime he'd committed in a fit of passion. Petitions or prayers were no use. But since he was otherwise highly regarded by the ruler, he, the prince, let him choose how he would like to die: he was to die in whatever way he chose. So the chief secretary came to him in prison: 'The prince has determined to show you mercy. If you wish to be put to death on the wheel you shall be put on the wheel; if you wish to be hanged he will have you hanged – there are already two up on the gallows but everybody knows there's room for three at a time. If, however, you would rather take rat poison there is some at the chemist's. For whatever kind of death you choose the prince says it shall be yours. But, as you know, die you must!' The criminal replied, 'If I really must die, then death on the wheel can be bent to suit one's taste, and hanging can be turned to suit one's inclination if the wind lends a hand. But you haven't got the point! For my part I have always thought that death from old age is the easiest way, and since the prince leaves the choice to me I'll choose it and no other!'

And that was his final decision, he wouldn't be talked out of it. So they had to let him go free and live on until he died of old age. For the prince said, 'I gave my word and I'll not break it.'

This little story comes from our mother-in-law who doesn't like to let anyone die if she can possibly help it.

A Stallholder is Duped

A rouble is a silver coin in Russia, worth a bit less than two guilders, whereas an imperial is a gold coin and worth ten roubles. So you can get a rouble for an imperial, for instance if you lose nine roubles at cards, but you can't get an imperial for a rouble. Yet a cunning soldier in Moscow said, 'Want to bet? Tomorrow at the fair I'll get me an imperial for a rouble.' The next day long rows of stalls were set out at the fair, the people were already standing at all the booths, admiring or finding fault, making bids and haggling, the crowd was walking up and down and the boys were saying hello to the girls, when up came the soldier with a rouble in his hand. 'Whose is this rouble? Is it yours?' he asked all the stallkeepers in turn. One of them who wasn't doing much business looked on for some time and then thought: if that money's too hot for you to hold I can warm to it! 'Over here, musketeer, it's my rouble!' The soldier said, 'If you hadn't shouted I would never have found you in the crowd,' and he handed him the rouble. The trader turned it one way and the other and tested its ring; it was a good one all right, and he put it in his purse. 'Now give me back my imperial, please!' said the musketeer. The trader said, 'I don't have any imperial of yours, I owe you nothing. You can have this stupid rouble back if you're playing a trick on me!' But the musketeer said, 'Hand over my imperial, this is no joke, I'm serious and can easily fetch a constable!' One thing led to another, a polite word to a defiant one, defiance to insults, and a crowd gathered around the stall like bees round a honey pot. Then something was burrowing its way through the throng. 'What's going on here?' said the police sergeant who had pushed through the crowd with his men. 'I said, what's all this?' The stallkeeper couldn't say much, but the musketeer had a good story to tell.

Less than a quarter of an hour before, he said, he had bought this and that from this man for one rouble. But when it came to paying he could find only a double imperial, nothing smaller, one his godfather had given him when he was enlisted. So he gave him the imperial until he came back with a rouble. When he came back with the rouble he couldn't find the right stall, so he asked at all the booths, 'Who do I owe a rouble?' And this man said it was him, and it was too, and he took the rouble but pretended he didn't have his imperial. 'Now will you agree to give it back?' The police sergeant questioned those around and they said: Yes, the musketeer asked at all the stalls whose rouble it was and this man said it was his, and took it too, and tested it to see if it was genuine. When the police sergeant heard that, he settled the matter: 'You've got your rouble, so give this soldier his imperial or we'll close down your stall and nail it up with you inside and leave you to starve to death!' Thus the police officer, and the trader it was who had to give the musketeer an imperial for a rouble.

Remember: Other people's property can eat into your own just as fresh snow swallows up the old.

Patience Rewarded

One day a Frenchman rode up on to a bridge over a stream, and it was so narrow there was scarcely room for two horses at once. An Englishman was riding up from the other side, and when they met in the middle neither of them would give way. 'An Englishman does not make way for a Frenchman!' said the Englishman. 'Pardieu,' said the Frenchman, 'My horse has an English pedigree too! It's a pity I can't turn him round and let you have a good look at his backside in retreat! But you could at least let that English fellow you're riding step aside for this English mount of mine. In any case yours seems to be the junior; mine served under Louis XIV in the battle of Kieferholz, 1702!'

But the Englishman was not greatly impressed. 'I have

all the time in the world!' he said. 'This gives me a chance to read today's paper until you are pleased to make way.' So with the coolness the English are famed for he took a newspaper from his pocket and opened it up and sat on his horse on the bridge and read for an hour, and the sun didn't look as if it would shine on this pair of fools for ever, it was going down quickly towards the mountains. An hour later when he had finished reading and was about to fold up the newspaper again he looked at the Frenchman and said, 'Eh bien?' But the Frenchman had kept his head too and replied, 'Englishman, kindly lend me your paper a while, so that I can read it too until you are pleased to make way.' Now, when the Englishman saw that his adversary was a patient man, he said, 'Do you know what, Frenchman? Come on, I'll make way for you!' So the Englishman made way for the Frenchman.

The Champion Swimmer

Before the war and all its afflictions when you could still cross freely from France to England and drink a glass or two in Dover or buy material for a waistcoat, a large mail boat sailed from Calais across the straits to Dover and back again twice a week. For the sea between those two countries is only a few miles wide at that point, you see. But you had to get there before the boat left if you wanted to sail on it. A Frenchman from Gascony seemed not to

The Champion Swimmer

know that, for he came to Calais a quarter of an hour too late, just as they were shutting up the hens, and the sky was clouding over. 'Must I sit around here for a couple of days twiddling my thumbs? No,' he thought, 'I'd do better to pay a boatman a twelve-sous piece to go after the mail boat.' For a small craft can sail faster than the heavy mail boat, you understand, and will catch up with it. But when he was sitting in the open boat the boatman said, 'If I'd thought I'd have brought a tarpaulin!' For it began to rain, and how! Very soon it poured down from the night sky as if a sea up above was emptying itself into the sea below. But the Gascon thought, 'This is going to be fun!' 'Praise be,' said the boatman at last, 'I can see the mail boat.' And he pulled up alongside and the Gascon climbed aboard, and when he suddenly appeared through the narrow hatchway in the middle of the night and in the middle of the sea and joined the passengers on the ship they all wondered where he had sprung from, all on his own, so late and so wet. For on a ship like that it is like being in a cellar, you can't hear what is going on outside over the talk of the passengers, the sailors' shouts, the noise of the wind, the flapping sails and the crashing waves, and nobody had any idea it was raining. 'You look as if you've been keelhauled,' said one, 'pulled right under the ship from one side to the other, I mean.' 'Is that what you're thinking?' said the Gascon. 'Do you imagine you can go swimming and stay dry? If you can tell me how to do that I'll be glad to hear it, you see I'm

Johann Peter Hebel

the postman from Oléron and every Monday I swim over to the mainland with letters and messages, it's quicker that way. But now I have a message to take to England. With your permission I'll join you, since I was fortunate enough to meet up with you. Judging from the stars it can't be far to Dover now.' 'You're welcome, fellow countryman,' said one (though he wasn't a fellow Frenchman but an Englishman) and blew a cloud of tobacco smoke from his mouth. 'If you have swum this far across the sea from Calais you must be a class above the black swimmer in London!' 'I'm not afraid of competition,' said the Gascon. 'Will you take him on,' replied the Englishman, 'if I place a hundred louis d'or on you?' The Gascon said, 'You can bet I will!' It's the custom of rich Englishmen to bet with each other for large sums placed on men who excel at some physical activity. And so it was that this Englishman on the ship took the Gascon to London with him at his expense and had him eat and drink well so that he stayed fit and strong. 'My lord,' he said to a good friend of his in London, 'I have brought with me a swimmer I found at sea. I bet you a hundred guineas he can beat your Moor!' His friend said, 'You're on!'

The next day they both appeared with their swimmers at an agreed spot on the river Thames, and hundreds of curious people had gathered there and they laid their bets too, some on the Moor, some on the Gascon, one shilling, or six shillings, one, two, five, twenty guineas, and the

The Champion Swimmer

Moor didn't give the Gascon much of a chance. But when they had both undressed the Gascon tied a little box to his body with a leather strap without saying why, as if that were quite normal. The Moor said, 'What are you up to? Have you learnt that from the champion jumper who had to tie lead weights to his feet when he was set to catch a hare and was afraid he would jump right over it?' The Gascon opened his box and said, 'I've only got a bottle of wine in here, a couple of saveloys and a small loaf of bread! I was going to ask you where you have your eats. For I shall swim straight down the river Thames into the North Sea and down the Channel into the Atlantic and on to Cadiz, and I suggest we don't call in anywhere on the way, for I have to be back in Oléron by Monday, that's the 16th. But tomorrow morning in Cadiz at the White Horse I'll order a good dinner for you so it will be ready by the time you arrive.' You, good reader, will hardly be imagining that he could escape that way! But the Moor was scared stiff. 'I can't compete against that amphibian!' he told his master. 'You can please yourself what you do!' And he got dressed again.

So the bet was over, the Gascon was given a handsome reward by the Englishman who had brought him there and everyone scoffed at the Moor. For although they must have seen that the Frenchman was only shamming, they were all amused by his bravado and the unexpected outcome, and for a month after that he was treated in the inns and beerhouses by all those who had bet on him, and he admitted he had never been in the water in all his life.

The Weather Man

Just as a sieve-maker or a basket-weaver who lives in a small place cannot earn enough in his village or town to keep himself all year, but has to look for work and practise his craft in the countryside around, so our compasses-maker too does business away from home, and his trade is not in compasses but in knavish tricks that pay for a few drinks at the inn. Thus one day he appeared in Oberehingen and went straight to the mayor. 'Mr Mayor,' he said, 'could you do with different weather? I've seen how things are hereabouts. There's been too much rain on the bottom fields and the crops on the hill are behindhand.' The mayor thought that was easy to say but difficult to put right. 'Just so,' replied the compasses-maker, 'but that's my line of business! Didn't you know I'm the weather man from Bologna?' In Italy, he said, where the oranges and lemons grow, all the weather was made to order. 'You Germans are a bit behind in these matters.' The mayor was a good and trusting fellow and one of those who would like to get rich sooner rather than later. So he was attracted by the offer. But he also thought caution was called for! 'As a test run,' he said, 'make it a clear sky tomorrow with just a few fluffy white clouds, sunshine all day with some streaks of vapour glistening in the air. Let the first yellow butterflies come out round midday, and it can be a nice cool evening!' The compasses-maker replied, 'I can't commit myself just for one day, Mr Mayor! It wouldn't cover my costs. I can only take on the job by the year. But then you'll have problems finding room to store your crops and the new wine!' When the mayor wanted to know how much he would charge for the year he was careful and didn't ask for payment in advance, only a guilder a day and free drinks until the matter was properly in hand, that could take at least three days – 'But after that a pint from each gallon of wine over what you press in your best years, and a peck from every bushel of fruit.' 'That's risnible,' said the mayor. He stood in awe of the compasses-maker and was using refined language, and people in his part of the country think it's refined to say 'risnible' for reasonable. But when he took pen and paper from the cupboard and was drawing up a schedule for the weather month by month the compasses-maker came up with a further complication: 'You can't do that, Mr Mayor! You will have to consult the people. The weather is a community matter. You can't expect everyone to accept your choice of weather.' 'You're right!' said the mayor. 'You're a sensible man.'

You, good reader, will have taken the measure of our compasses-maker and will have foreseen that the people could not agree on the matter. At their first meeting no decision was reached, nor even at the seventh, at the eighth hard words were spoken, and in the end a level-headed lawyer concluded that the best thing to do, to preserve peace and avoid strife in the community, was to pay the weather man off and send him packing. So the mayor summoned the compasses-maker. 'Here are your nine guilders, you mischief-maker, now make sure you leave before there's blood shed in the village!' The compasses-maker didn't have to be told twice. He took the money, left owing for about twelve pints of wine at the inn, and the weather stayed as it was.

Now then, as always the compasses-maker has much to teach us! In this case how good it is that up till now the supreme ruler of the world has always governed the weather according to his will alone. Even we calendar-makers, luminaries and the other estates of the realm are scarcely consulted and need lose no sleep on that score.

The Safest Path

Now and then even someone drunk has the occasional notion or good idea, as a fellow did one day who didn't take his usual path home from town but walked straight into the stream running alongside it instead. There he met a good man ready to offer a hand to a fellow, even a drunk one, in trouble. 'My good friend,' said the man, 'haven't you noticed you're in the water? The footpath's

The Safest Path

over here.' He too, replied the drinker, generally found it best to use the path, but explained that this time he had had one too many. 'And that's just why I want to help you out of the stream,' said the good man. 'And that's just why I want to stay in it,' replied the drinker. 'Because if I walk in the stream and fall, I fall on to the path, but if I fell when walking on the path, I'd fall into the stream.' And that's what he said, tapping his forehead with his index finger, as if to show that he still knew a thing or two that might not have occurred to anyone else, despite being a bit the worse for wear.

1. BOCCACCIO · *Mrs Rosie and the Priest*
2. GERARD MANLEY HOPKINS · *As kingfishers catch fire*
3. *The Saga of Gunnlaug Serpent-tongue*
4. THOMAS DE QUINCEY · *On Murder Considered as One of the Fine Arts*
5. FRIEDRICH NIETZSCHE · *Aphorisms on Love and Hate*
6. JOHN RUSKIN · *Traffic*
7. PU SONGLING · *Wailing Ghosts*
8. JONATHAN SWIFT · *A Modest Proposal*
9. *Three Tang Dynasty Poets*
10. WALT WHITMAN · *On the Beach at Night Alone*
11. KENKŌ · *A Cup of Sake Beneath the Cherry Trees*
12. BALTASAR GRACIÁN · *How to Use Your Enemies*
13. JOHN KEATS · *The Eve of St Agnes*
14. THOMAS HARDY · *Woman much missed*
15. GUY DE MAUPASSANT · *Femme Fatale*
16. MARCO POLO · *Travels in the Land of Serpents and Pearls*
17. SUETONIUS · *Caligula*
18. APOLLONIUS OF RHODES · *Jason and Medea*
19. ROBERT LOUIS STEVENSON · *Olalla*
20. KARL MARX AND FRIEDRICH ENGELS · *The Communist Manifesto*
21. PETRONIUS · *Trimalchio's Feast*
22. JOHANN PETER HEBEL · *How a Ghastly Story Was Brought to Light by a Common or Garden Butcher's Dog*
23. HANS CHRISTIAN ANDERSEN · *The Tinder Box*
24. RUDYARD KIPLING · *The Gate of the Hundred Sorrows*
25. DANTE · *Circles of Hell*
26. HENRY MAYHEW · *Of Street Piemen*
27. HAFEZ · *The nightingales are drunk*
28. GEOFFREY CHAUCER · *The Wife of Bath*
29. MICHEL DE MONTAIGNE · *How We Weep and Laugh at the Same Thing*
30. THOMAS NASHE · *The Terrors of the Night*
31. EDGAR ALLAN POE · *The Tell-Tale Heart*
32. MARY KINGSLEY · *A Hippo Banquet*
33. JANE AUSTEN · *The Beautifull Cassandra*
34. ANTON CHEKHOV · *Gooseberries*
35. SAMUEL TAYLOR COLERIDGE · *Well, they are gone, and here must I remain*
36. JOHANN WOLFGANG VON GOETHE · *Sketchy, Doubtful, Incomplete Jottings*
37. CHARLES DICKENS · *The Great Winglebury Duel*
38. HERMAN MELVILLE · *The Maldive Shark*
39. ELIZABETH GASKELL · *The Old Nurse's Story*
40. NIKOLAY LESKOV · *The Steel Flea*

41. HONORÉ DE BALZAC · *The Atheist's Mass*
42. CHARLOTTE PERKINS GILMAN · *The Yellow Wall-Paper*
43. C.P. CAVAFY · *Remember, Body . . .*
44. FYODOR DOSTOEVSKY · *The Meek One*
45. GUSTAVE FLAUBERT · *A Simple Heart*
46. NIKOLAI GOGOL · *The Nose*
47. SAMUEL PEPYS · *The Great Fire of London*
48. EDITH WHARTON · *The Reckoning*
49. HENRY JAMES · *The Figure in the Carpet*
50. WILFRED OWEN · *Anthem For Doomed Youth*
51. WOLFGANG AMADEUS MOZART · *My Dearest Father*
52. PLATO · *Socrates' Defence*
53. CHRISTINA ROSSETTI · *Goblin Market*
54. *Sindbad the Sailor*
55. SOPHOCLES · *Antigone*
56. RYŪNOSUKE AKUTAGAWA · *The Life of a Stupid Man*
57. LEO TOLSTOY · *How Much Land Does A Man Need?*
58. GIORGIO VASARI · *Leonardo da Vinci*
59. OSCAR WILDE · *Lord Arthur Savile's Crime*
60. SHEN FU · *The Old Man of the Moon*
61. AESOP · *The Dolphins, the Whales and the Gudgeon*
62. MATSUO BASHŌ · *Lips too Chilled*
63. EMILY BRONTË · *The Night is Darkening Round Me*
64. JOSEPH CONRAD · *To-morrow*
65. RICHARD HAKLUYT · *The Voyage of Sir Francis Drake Around the Whole Globe*
66. KATE CHOPIN · *A Pair of Silk Stockings*
67. CHARLES DARWIN · *It was snowing butterflies*
68. BROTHERS GRIMM · *The Robber Bridegroom*
69. CATULLUS · *I Hate and I Love*
70. HOMER · *Circe and the Cyclops*
71. D. H. LAWRENCE · *Il Duro*
72. KATHERINE MANSFIELD · *Miss Brill*
73. OVID · *The Fall of Icarus*
74. SAPPHO · *Come Close*
75. IVAN TURGENEV · *Kasyan from the Beautiful Lands*
76. VIRGIL · *O Cruel Alexis*
77. H. G. WELLS · *A Slip under the Microscope*
78. HERODOTUS · *The Madness of Cambyses*
79. *Speaking of Siva*
80. *The Dhammapada*

'There sat the dog with eyes as big as mill wheels.'

HANS CHRISTIAN ANDERSEN
Born 1805, Odense, Denmark
Died 1875, Copenhagen

ANDERSEN IN PENGUIN CLASSICS
Fairy Tales

HANS CHRISTIAN ANDERSEN

The Tinderbox

Translated by
Tiina Nunnally

PENGUIN BOOKS

PENGUIN CLASSICS

UK | USA | Canada | Ireland | Australia
India | New Zealand | South Africa

Penguin Books is part of the Penguin Random House group of companies
whose addresses can be found at global.penguinrandomhouse.com.

This selection published in Penguin Classics 2015

011

Translation copyright © Tiina Nunnally, 2004

The moral right of the translator has been asserted.

Set in 9/12.4 pt Baskerville 10 Pro
Typeset by Jouve (UK), Milton Keynes
Printed and bound in Great Britain by Clays Ltd, Elcograf S.p.A.

A CIP catalogue record for this book is available from the British Library

ISBN: 978-0-141-39804-4

www.greenpenguin.co.uk

Penguin Random House is committed to a
sustainable future for our business, our readers
and our planet. This book is made from Forest
Stewardship Council® certified paper.

Contents

The Tinderbox	1
Little Claus and Big Claus	11
The Princess on the Pea	27
The Steadfast Tin Soldier	29
The Nightingale	35
The Red Shoes	48

The Tinderbox

A soldier came marching along the road: left, right! left, right! He had his knapsack on his back and a sword at his side, because he had been off to war, and now he was on his way home. Then he met an old witch on the road. She was so hideous, her lower lip hung all the way down to her breast. She said, 'Good evening, soldier. What a nice sword and big knapsack you have – you must be a real soldier! Now you shall have all the money you could ask for!'

'Well, thanks a lot, you old witch,' said the soldier.

'Do you see that big tree?' said the witch, pointing at a tree right next to them. 'It's completely hollow inside. Climb up to the top and you'll find a hole that you can slip into and slide all the way down inside the tree. I'll tie a rope around your waist so I can hoist you back up when you call me.'

'Why would I go inside that tree?' asked the soldier.

'To get the money!' said the witch. 'You see, when you reach the bottom of the tree, you'll be in a huge passageway that's very bright because it's lit by more than a hundred lamps. Then you'll see three doors, and you'll be able to open them because the keys are in the locks. If you go inside the first chamber you'll see a big chest in the middle of the room, and on top of it sits a dog. He has eyes as big as a pair of teacups, but never mind that. I'll give you my blue-checked apron that you can spread on the floor. Go right over and pick up the dog and set him on my apron. Then open the chest and take as many *skillings* as you like. They're all made of copper, but if you'd rather have silver, then go into the next room. In there is a dog with eyes as big as a pair of mill wheels, but never mind that. Set him on my apron and take the money. But if it's gold you want, you can have that too, and as much as you can carry, if you go into the third chamber. But the dog sitting on the money chest has two eyes that are each as big as the Round Tower. Now that's a real dog, believe me! But never you mind. Just set him on my apron and he won't harm you. Then take from the chest as much gold as you like.'

'Not bad,' said the soldier. 'But what do I have to give you in return, you old witch? Because I imagine there must be something you want.'

'No,' said the witch, 'I don't want a single *skilling*. All you have to bring me is an old tinderbox that my grandmother left behind when she was down there last.'

'Fine. Then let's have that rope around my waist,' said the soldier.

'Here it is,' said the witch. 'And here is my blue-checked apron.'

So the soldier climbed up the tree, tumbled down the hole, and then, just as the witch had said, he stood inside the huge passageway where hundreds of lamps were burning.

He opened the first door. Ooh! There sat the dog with eyes as big as teacups, staring at him.

'You're a handsome fellow!' said the soldier and set him

The Tinderbox

on the witch's apron. Then he took as many copper *skillings* as his pockets would hold, closed the chest, put the dog back, and went into the second room. Eeek! There sat the dog with eyes as big as mill wheels.

'You shouldn't look at me so hard,' said the soldier. 'You might hurt your eyes!' And then he set the dog on the witch's apron, but when he saw all the silver coins inside the chest he threw away the copper coins he was carrying and filled his pockets and his knapsack with nothing but silver. Next he went into the third chamber. Oh, how hideous! The dog in there really did have eyes as big as round towers, and they were spinning around in his head like wheels.

'Good evening,' said the soldier and doffed his cap, for he had never seen a dog like that before. But after he'd looked at him for a while, he thought to himself, 'All right, that's enough.' And he lifted him onto the floor and opened the chest. Good Lord, there was a lot of gold! Enough to buy all of Copenhagen and every single sugar-pig sold by the cake-wives, and all the tin soldiers, whips, and rocking horses in the whole world! Yes, there was certainly plenty of money! So the soldier threw away all the silver coins that filled his pockets and knapsack and took the gold instead. Yes, all his pockets, his knapsack, his cap, and his boots were so full that he could hardly walk. Now he had money! He put the dog back on the chest, slammed the door shut, and called up through the tree:

'Hoist me up now, you old witch!'

'Do you have the tinderbox?' asked the witch.

'Oh, that's right,' said the soldier. 'I forgot all about it.'

And he went over and picked it up. The witch hoisted him up and he once again stood on the road, with his pockets, boots, knapsack, and cap full of money.

'What do you want the tinderbox for?' asked the soldier.

'That's none of your business,' said the witch. 'You've got the money. Now just give me the tinderbox.'

'Pish posh!' said the soldier. 'Tell me right now what you want it for or I'll pull out my sword and chop off your head!'

'No,' said the witch.

So the soldier chopped off her head. There she lay! But he wrapped up all his money in her apron, slung it in a bundle over his shoulder, stuffed the tinderbox in his pocket, and headed straight for the city.

It was a lovely city, and he went inside the loveliest of inns and demanded the very best rooms and his favorite food, because now he had so much money that he was rich.

The servant who was supposed to polish his boots thought they were rather strange old boots for such a rich gentleman to be wearing, but he hadn't yet bought himself new ones. By the next day he had a good pair of boots and fine clothes to wear. The soldier was now a distinguished gentleman, and the people told him about all the splendid things to be found in their city, and about their king and what a charming princess his daughter was.

'Where might I catch a glimpse of her?' asked the soldier.

'It's impossible to catch a glimpse of her,' they all said. 'She lives in an enormous copper palace surrounded by dozens of walls and towers. No one but the king dares visit her,

The Tinderbox

because it was foretold that she would marry a simple soldier, and that certainly did not please the king.'

'She's someone I'd like to see,' thought the soldier, but that wasn't possible.

He was now leading a merry life, going to the theater, taking drives in the king's gardens, and giving away a great deal of money to the poor, which was a very nice gesture. No doubt he remembered from the old days how miserable it was not to have even a *skilling*. He was now rich and wore fine clothes, and had so many friends who all said that he was a pleasant fellow, a real gentleman, and that certainly pleased the soldier. But since he was spending money each day and not taking any in, he finally had no more than two *skillings* left and had to move out of the beautiful rooms where he had been living and into a tiny little garret room right under the roof. He had to brush his own boots and mend them with a darning needle, and none of his friends came to see him because there were too many stairs to climb.

It was a very dark evening, and he couldn't even afford to buy a candle, but then he remembered there was a little stump of one in the tinderbox he had taken from the hollow tree when the witch had helped him inside. He took out the tinderbox and the candle stump, but the minute he struck fire and sparks leaped from the flint, the door flew open and the dog that he had seen inside the tree, the one with eyes as big as two teacups, stood before him and said, 'What is my master's command?'

'What's this?' said the soldier. 'What an amusing

tinderbox, if I can wish for whatever I want! Bring me some money,' he said to the dog, and zip, he was gone; zip, he was back, holding a big sack of *skillings* in his mouth.

Now the soldier realized what a wonderful tinderbox it was. If he stuck it once, the dog who sat on the chest of copper coins came; if he struck it twice, the one with the silver coins came; and if he struck it three times, the one with the gold came. Now the soldier moved back downstairs to the beautiful rooms, dressed in fine clothing, and all his friends recognized him again, because they were so fond of him.

One day he thought, 'How odd that no one is allowed to see that princess. Everyone says she's supposed to be so lovely. But what good is it if she's always kept inside that enormous copper palace with all the towers? Couldn't I possibly have a look at her? Where's my tinderbox?' And then he struck fire and zip, the dog with eyes as big as teacups appeared.

'I know it's the middle of the night,' said the soldier, 'but I have such a great desire to see the princess, if only for a moment.'

The dog was out the door at once, and before the soldier knew it, he was back with the princess. She was sitting on the dog's back, asleep, and she was so lovely that anyone could see she was a real princess. The soldier couldn't resist, he had to kiss her, because he was a real soldier.

Then the dog ran back with the princess, but when morning came and the king and queen were pouring their tea, the princess said that she'd had a strange dream in the night about a dog and a soldier. She was riding on the dog's back, and the soldier had kissed her.

The Tinderbox

'That's certainly a fine story!' said the queen.

One of the old ladies-in-waiting was then ordered to keep watch at the bedside of the princess on the following night, to see if it was really a dream, or what else it might be.

The soldier was longing terribly to see the lovely princess once more, so the dog appeared in the night, picked her up, and ran as fast as he could, but the old lady-in-waiting put on her wading boots and ran just as swiftly right behind. When she saw them disappear inside a large building, she thought to herself: Now I know where it is. And with a piece of chalk she drew a big cross on the door. Then she returned home and went to bed, and the dog came back too, bringing the princess. But when he saw that a cross had been drawn on the door where the soldier lived, he took another piece of chalk and put a cross on all the doors in the whole city. That was a clever thing to do, because now the lady-in-waiting wouldn't be able to find the right door, since there were crosses on all of them.

Early the next morning the king and queen, the old lady-in-waiting, and all the officers went out to see where the princess had been.

'There it is!' said the king when he saw the first door with a cross on it.

'No, it's over there, my dear husband,' said the queen, who saw another door with a cross on it.

'But there's one there, and one there!' they all said. Wherever they looked, there was a cross on every door. Then they realized it was no use to go on searching.

But the queen was a very clever woman who was capable of more than just riding around in a coach. She took her

Hans Christian Andersen

big golden scissors, cut a large piece of silk into pieces, and then stitched together a charming little pouch, which she filled with fine grains of buckwheat. She tied it to the back of the princess, and when that was done, she cut a tiny hole in the pouch so the grains would sprinkle out wherever the princess went.

That night the dog appeared once again, put the princess on his back, and ran off with her to the soldier, who loved her so much and wanted dearly to be a prince so that he could make her his wife.

The dog didn't notice the grain sprinkling out all the way from the palace to the soldier's window, as he ran along the wall, carrying the princess. In the morning the king and queen could see quite well where their daughter had been, and they seized the soldier and threw him into jail.

And there he sat. Oh, how dark and dreary it was, and then they told him, 'Tomorrow you will hang.' That was not a pleasant thing to hear, and he had left his tinderbox behind at the inn. In the morning he could see through the iron bars on the little window that people were hurrying to the outskirts of the city to watch him hang. He heard the drums and saw the marching soldiers. Everyone was in a great rush, including a shoemaker's apprentice wearing a leather apron and slippers. He was moving along at such a gallop that one of his slippers flew off and struck the wall right where the soldier was sitting, peering out through the iron bars.

'Hey, shoemaker's apprentice! You don't have to be in such a rush,' said the soldier. 'Nothing's going to happen until I get there. But if you run over to the place where I was staying and bring me my tinderbox, I'll give you four *skillings*. But you have to be quick about it!' The shoemaker's apprentice wanted those four *skillings*, so he raced off to get the tinderbox, brought it to the soldier, and . . . well, let's hear what happened.

Outside the city a huge gallows had been built, and around it stood the soldiers and many hundreds of thousands of people. The king and queen sat on a lovely throne right across from the judge and the entire council.

The soldier was already standing on the ladder, but as they were about to put the rope around his neck, he said that before a sinner faced his punishment he was always allowed one harmless request. He dearly wanted to smoke a pipe of tobacco; it would be the last pipe he had in this world.

Now, that was not something the king could refuse, and so the soldier took out his tinderbox and struck fire, one, two, three! And there stood all three dogs: the one with eyes as big as teacups, the one with eyes like mill wheels, and the one with eyes as big as the Round Tower.

'Help me now, so I won't be hanged!' said the soldier, and then the dogs rushed at the judge and the entire council, seizing one by the leg and one by the nose, and flinging them high into the air so they fell back down and were crushed to bits.

'Not me!' said the king, but the biggest dog seized both him and the queen and tossed them after all the others. Then the soldiers were afraid, and all the people shouted, 'Little soldier, you shall be our king and wed the lovely princess!'

They put the soldier in the king's coach, and all three dogs danced before it, shouting, 'Hurrah!' The boys whistled through their fingers, and the soldiers presented arms. The princess came out of the copper palace and became queen, and that certainly pleased her! The wedding celebration lasted for a week, and the dogs sat at the table too, making big eyes.

Little Claus and Big Claus

There was a town where two men had the very same name. Both of them were named Claus, but one owned four horses while the other had only one. In order to tell them apart, people called the man with four horses Big Claus, and the man with only one horse Little Claus. Now we're going to hear what happened between those two, because this is a real story!

All week long Little Claus had to do the plowing for Big Claus, lending him his only horse. Then Big Claus would help him in return with all four of his horses, but only once a week, and that was on Sunday. Hee-ya! How Little Claus would crack his whip at all five horses. They might as well have belonged to him on that one day. The sun shone so wondrously, and all the bells in the tower rang, summoning people to church. Everyone was dressed in their best, walking with their hymnals under their arms, on their way to hear the pastor preach. And they looked at Little Claus, who was plowing with five horses, and he was so pleased that he cracked his whip again and shouted, 'Giddy-up, all my horses!'

'You shouldn't say that,' said Big Claus. 'Only one of those horses is yours.'

But when someone else passed by on his way to church,

Little Claus forgot that he wasn't supposed to say that and he shouted, 'Giddy-up, all my horses!'

'All right, now I really must ask you to stop that,' said Big Claus. 'Because if you say it one more time, I'm going to strike your horse on the forehead, and he'll drop dead on the spot, and that will be the end of him.'

'Well, I certainly won't say it again,' said Little Claus, but when people came past and nodded hello, he was so pleased and thought it looked so splendid that he had five horses plowing his field that he cracked his whip and shouted, 'Giddy-up, all my horses!'

'I'll giddy-up your horses!' said Big Claus, and he seized the tethering mallet and struck Little Claus's only horse on the forehead so that it fell to the ground, stone dead.

'Oh no, now I have no horse at all!' said Little Claus and began to cry. Later he flayed the horse and let the hide dry in the wind. Then he stuffed it in a sack that he hoisted onto his back and set off for town to sell his horsehide.

He had such a long way to go. He had to pass through a big, dark forest, and a terrible storm came up. He completely lost his way, and before he found the right road, dusk had fallen, and it was much too far to reach town or to go back home before night came.

Close to the road stood a large farm. The shutters on all the windows were closed, and yet there was a glimpse of light above. Surely they'll let me spend the night here, thought Little Claus, and he went over and knocked.

The farmer's wife opened the door, but when she heard what he wanted, she told him to keep on going. Her husband wasn't home, and she didn't take in strangers.

Little Claus and Big Claus

'Well, then I guess I'll have to sleep outside,' said Little Claus, and the farmer's wife shut the door in his face.

Nearby stood a big haystack, and between the haystack and house a little shed had been built with a flat, thatched roof.

'I can sleep up there,' said Little Claus when he saw the roof. 'That would make a lovely bed, and I'm sure the stork isn't going to fly down and bite me on the leg.' A real live stork was standing on the roof, where it had made a nest.

So Little Claus climbed up onto the shed, lay down, and turned onto his side to settle in properly. The wooden shutters on the windows of the house didn't quite meet at the top, which meant that he could peek into the room.

A great feast had been laid out with wine and a roast and such a lovely fish. The farmer's wife and the deacon were sitting at the table, all alone. She was pouring wine for him, and he began with the fish, because he was awfully fond of fish.

'If only I could have a bite too,' said Little Claus, craning his neck toward the window. Lord, what a lovely cake he could see in there. Oh yes, it was quite a feast.

Then he heard someone come riding along the road toward the house. It was the woman's husband, on his way home.

Now, it's true that he was a good man, but he had a strange affliction: He couldn't stand to see deacons. If he caught sight of a deacon, he would grow quite furious. That was also why the deacon had come to visit the woman when he knew that her husband wasn't home, and that's why the good woman had set out for him the best food she could offer. When they heard her husband coming, they were both terrified. The woman told the deacon to climb into a big empty chest that stood in the corner, which he did, because he knew full well that the poor man couldn't stand the sight of a deacon. The woman quickly hid all the wonderful food and wine inside her baking oven, because if her husband saw it, he was sure to ask what was going on.

'Oh no!' sighed Little Claus up on the shed when he saw all the food disappear.

'Is somebody up there?' asked the farmer, peering up at Little Claus. 'Why are you lying up there? Come on into the house!'

Then Little Claus told him how he had lost his way and asked if he might stay the night.

'Yes, of course,' said the farmer. 'But first we'll have a bite to eat.'

The woman welcomed them both, set dishes on a long table, and brought them a big bowl of porridge. The farmer was hungry and ate with gusto, but Little Claus couldn't help thinking about the wonderful roast, fish, and cake that he knew were hidden in the oven.

Under the table at his feet he had put the sack with the horsehide in it, because we know, after all, that this was what he had brought from home to sell in town. The porridge was not at all to his liking, and so he stepped on his sack, and the dry horsehide inside creaked quite loudly.

'Hush!' said Little Claus to his sack, but at the same instant he stepped on it again, and it creaked even louder than before.

'Tell me, what do you have in your bag?' asked the farmer.

Little Claus and Big Claus

'Oh, it's a troll,' said Little Claus. 'He says we shouldn't eat the porridge because he has conjured a whole oven full of roast and fish and cake.'

'Is that right?' said the farmer and quickly opened the oven. There he saw all the wonderful food that his wife had hidden, but he now thought the troll in the bag had conjured it up. His wife didn't dare say a word but set the food on the table at once, and so they ate the fish and the roast and the cake. Then Little Claus stepped on his sack again, making the hide creak.

'What's he saying now?' asked the farmer.

'He says,' said Little Claus, 'that he has also conjured up three bottles of wine for us, and they're standing over in the corner by the oven.' Then the woman had to bring out the wine she had hidden, and the farmer drank and grew quite merry. A troll like the one that Little Claus had in his bag was something that he would certainly like to own.

'Can he also conjure up the Devil?' asked the farmer. 'That's someone I'd really like to see, now that I'm feeling so merry.'

'Yes,' said Little Claus, 'my troll can do anything I ask. Isn't that right?' he said as he stepped on the bag, making it creak. 'Did you hear him say yes? But the Devil looks so horrid that you wouldn't want to look at him.'

'Oh, I'm not the least bit afraid. How bad do you think he could look?'

'Well, he's going to look exactly like a deacon.'

'Whoa!' said the farmer. 'That's ghastly, all right. I must tell you that I can't stand the sight of deacons. But that doesn't matter, because I'll know it's the Devil, so it won't bother me as much. I'm feeling brave now. But don't let him come too close.'

'Let me ask my troll,' said Little Claus, and he stepped on the bag, cupping his ear.

'What does he say?'

'He says that you can go over and open the chest that's standing in the corner, and you'll see the Devil moping inside, but you have to hold on to the lid so he doesn't get out.'

'Come and help me hold on to it,' said the farmer, and he went over to the chest where his wife had hidden the real deacon, who sat there completely terrified.

The farmer lifted the lid slightly and peeked inside. 'Whoa!' he yelled, jumping back. 'I saw him all right, and he looks just like our deacon! Oh, that was terrible!'

After that they had to have a drink, and then they kept on drinking until late into the night.

'You've got to sell me that troll,' said the farmer. 'Ask whatever price you like. Why, I'd even give you a whole bushelful of money!'

'No, I can't do that,' that Claus. 'Just think how much I'll gain from owning this troll.'

'Oh, but I'd certainly like to have it,' said the farmer, and he kept on begging.

'All right,' said Little Claus at last. 'Since you've been kind enough to give me shelter for the night, I can't refuse. You can have the troll for a bushel of money, but I want the bushel to be full to the brim.'

'And that's what you'll get,' said the farmer, 'but you have to take that chest over there with you. I refuse to have it in

Little Claus and Big Claus

the house for even an hour longer. There's no telling whether he's still inside.'

Little Claus gave the farmer the sack with the dried horse-hide and got in return a whole bushel of money, full to the brim. The farmer even presented him with a big wheelbarrow for carrying the money and the chest.

'Farewell!' said Little Claus, and then he set off with his money and the big chest in which the deacon was still sitting.

On the other side of the woods was a big, deep river. The water was running so fast that it was almost impossible to swim against the current. A big new bridge had been built across it. Little Claus stopped in the middle of the bridge and said very loudly so that the deacon inside the chest would hear him:

'Well, what do I need this stupid chest for? It's so heavy it feels like it's full of rocks. I'm getting awfully tired of carting it around, so I think I'll throw it in the river. If it floats home to me, that's fine, but if it doesn't, it won't matter at all.'

Then he grabbed one handle of the chest and lifted it slightly, as if he were going to shove it into the water.

'No, stop!' yelled the deacon inside the chest. 'Let me out!'

'Ooh!' said Little Claus, pretending to be scared. 'He's still inside! I've got to toss it in the river as quick as I can so he'll drown.'

'Oh no, oh no!' shouted the deacon. 'I'll give you a whole bushelful of money if you don't.'

'Well, that's a different story,' said Little Claus, and opened the chest. The deacon crawled out at once, shoved the empty chest into the water, and went off to his house, where he gave

Little Claus a whole bushelful of money. Little Claus already had one bushel from the farmer; now his whole wheelbarrow was full of money.

'Look at that, I certainly did get a good price for that horse,' he said to himself when he came back to his own house and dumped all the money in a big heap in the middle of the floor. 'Big Claus will be annoyed when he finds out how rich I've become from my only horse, but I'm not going to come right out and tell him about it.'

Then he sent a boy over to Big Claus to borrow a bushel measure.

'I wonder what he wants it for,' thought Big Claus, and smeared tar inside the bottom so that a little of whatever was being weighed would stick to it. And it did, because when he got the bushel measure back, there were three new silver eight-*skilling* coins stuck to it.

'What's this?' said Big Claus and ran right over to see Little Claus. 'Where did you get all this money?'

'Oh, I got it for my horsehide. I sold it last night.'

'That was certainly a good price!' said Big Claus, and he raced back home, picked up an ax, and struck every one of his four horses on the forehead. Then he skinned them and drove into town with the hides.

'Hides! Hides! Who wants to buy hides?' he shouted through the streets.

All the shoemakers and tanners came running and asked him how much he wanted for the hides.

'A bushel of money for each of them,' said Big Claus.

'Are you crazy?' they all said. 'Do you think we have bushels of money?'

Little Claus and Big Claus

'Hides, hides! Who wants to buy hides?' he shouted again, but to everyone who asked how much the hides cost, he replied, 'A bushel of money.'

'He's trying to make fools of us,' they all said. Then the shoemakers picked up their straps and the tanners their leather aprons, and they all started beating Big Claus.

'Hides, hides!' they jeered at him. 'Oh yes, we'll give you a hide that bleeds like a pig! Now get out of town!' they shouted, and Big Claus had to rush off as fast as he could. He had never been beaten so badly in his life.

'Well!' he said when he got home. 'Little Claus is going to pay for this. I'm going to murder him for this!'

But back at Little Claus's house his grandmother had just died. Now, it's true that she had been terribly ill-tempered and mean toward him, but even so he was quite sad. He took the dead woman and put her in his warm bed to see whether she might come back to life. There she would lie all night long while he slept in the corner, sitting on a chair; that was something he had done before.

As he was sitting there that night, the door opened and Big Claus came in with an ax. He knew where Little Claus's bed stood, and he went right over a struck the dead grandmother on the forehead, thinking that it was Little Claus.

'Take that!' he said. 'Now you won't make a fool of me anymore.' And then he went back home.

'What a mean and evil man,' said Little Claus. 'He wanted to murder me, but it's a good thing the old lady was already dead, or he would have taken her life.'

Then he dressed his old grandmother in her Sunday best, borrowed a horse from his neighbor, harnessed it to his wagon, and put his old grandmother on the back seat so that she wouldn't fall out when he started driving. Then they headed off through the woods. When the sun came up, they were outside a big inn, where Little Claus stopped and went inside to get a bite to eat.

The innkeeper was very, very rich, and he was also a good man, but hot-tempered, as if there were pepper and tobacco inside of him.

'Good morning,' he said to Little Claus. 'You've put on your fine clothes awfully early today.'

'Yes,' said Little Claus, 'I'm going to town with my old grandmother. She's sitting outside in the wagon, and I can't get her to come indoors. Would you mind taking her a glass of mead? But you'll have to speak up because she doesn't hear very well.'

'Why, certainly,' said the innkeeper. He poured a big glass of mead and took it outside to the dead grandmother, who was propped up in the wagon.

'Here's a glass of mead from your grandson,' said the innkeeper, but the dead woman didn't say a word, just sat there without moving.

'Didn't you hear me?' shouted the innkeeper as loud as he could. 'Here's a glass of mead from your grandson!'

Once again he shouted the same thing, and then one more time, when she didn't budge in the slightest, he got angry and tossed the glass of mead right in her face so it ran down her nose. And she toppled over backward into the wagon, because she had merely been propped up but wasn't tied down.

Little Claus and Big Claus

'What's this?' shouted Little Claus as he came running out the door and grabbed the innkeeper by the shirtfront. 'You've gone and killed my grandmother! Just look at that big hole in her forehead!'

'Oh, what bad luck!' cried the innkeeper, wringing his hands. 'It's all the fault of my bad temper. Dear Little Claus, I'll give you a whole bushelful of money and pay for your grandmother's burial as if she were my own, but don't say a word or they'll chop off my head, and that would be awful!'

So Little Claus got a whole bushelful of money, and the innkeeper buried the old grandmother as if she were his own.

As soon as Little Claus got back home with all the money, he at once sent his boy over to see Big Claus, to ask if he could borrow a bushel measure.

'What's this?' said Big Claus. 'I thought I killed him! I'm going to have to see this for myself.' And so he took the bushel measure over to Little Claus in person.

'Where on earth did you get all that money?' he asked, opening his eyes wide when he saw how much more Little Claus had accumulated.

'It was my grandmother, not me that you killed,' said Little Claus. 'But now I've sold her for a bushelful of money.'

'That was certainly a good price,' said Big Claus, and he rushed home, picked up an ax, and promptly killed his old grandmother. He put her in his wagon, drove into town to the apothecary's shop, and asked him whether he wanted to buy a dead body.

'Who is it, and where did you get it?' asked the apothecary.

'It's my grandmother,' said Big Claus. 'I've killed her for a bushelful of money.'

'Good Lord!' said the apothecary. 'You don't know what you're saying! Don't say things like that or you could lose your head.' And then he told him exactly what a dreadful, evil thing he had done, and what a bad person he was, and that he ought to be punished. Big Claus was so scared that he leaped straight from the apothecary's shop into his wagon, cracked his whip at the horses, and raced off home. The apothecary and everyone else thought he was mad, and so they let him go where he liked.

'You're going to pay for this!' said Big Claus when he was out on the road. 'Oh yes, you're going to pay for this, Little Claus!' As soon as he got home he took the biggest sack he could find and went over to Little Claus and said, 'You've made a fool of me again. First I killed my horses, and then my old grandmother. It's all your fault, but you're never going to trick me again.' And he grabbed Little Claus around the waist and stuffed him into the sack. Then he slung him over his back and shouted, 'Now I'm going to take you out and drown you!'

It was a long walk to reach the river, and Little Claus wasn't easy to carry. The road passed very close to the church, where the organ was playing and people were singing so beautifully inside. Then Big Claus put down the sack holding Little Claus right next to the church door, thinking that it might do him good to go inside and listen to a hymn first, before continuing on his way. Little Claus couldn't get out, and everyone else was in church, so Big Claus went inside.

Little Claus and Big Claus

'Oh me, oh my!' sighed Little Claus from inside the sack. He twisted and turned, but it was impossible for him to loosen the cord. At that moment an old, old cattle-driver with chalk-white hair and a big walking stick in his hand came by. He was driving a big herd of cows and bulls in front of him. They trampled over the sack that Claus was in, tumbling it onto its side.

'Oh my,' sighed Little Claus. 'I'm so young, but I'm already headed for Heaven.'

'And what a poor man am I,' said the cattle-driver. 'Here I am so old but it's not yet my time to go.'

'Open the sack!' shouted Little Claus. 'Climb in and take my place, and you'll end up in Heaven at once.'

'Oh, I'd like that very much,' said the cattle-driver, untying the sack. And Little Claus jumped right out.

'Could you take care of the cattle?' said the old man, and he climbed into the bag, which Little Claus tied up and then went on his way, taking along the cows and bulls.

A little while later Big Claus came out of the church and hoisted the sack onto his back, thinking that it certainly was a lot lighter, because the old cattle-driver was no more than half the weight of Little Claus. 'How easy it is to carry him now! Well, that's probably because I've been listening to a hymn.' Then he went over to the river, which was deep and wide, threw the sack with the old cattle-driver into the water, and shouted after him, thinking he was Little Claus, 'Take that! Now you won't be making a fool of me anymore!'

Then he headed home, but when he came to the crossroads, he met Little Claus walking along with all his cattle.

'What's this?' said Big Claus. 'Didn't I drown you?'

'Yes, you did,' said Little Claus. 'You threw me in the river less than half an hour ago.'

'But where did you get all these wonderful cattle?' asked Big Claus.

'They're sea cattle,' said Little Claus. 'Let me tell you the whole story. And by the way, thanks for drowning me, because now I'm back on my feet and let me tell you, I'm as rich as can be! I was so scared when I was inside that sack, and the wind whistled in my ears when you threw me off the bridge and into the cold water. I sank straight to the bottom, but I didn't hurt myself because the loveliest soft grass grows down there. That's where I landed, and the bag was opened at once. The loveliest maiden, wearing chalk-white clothing and with a green wreath on her wet hair, took my hand and said, "Is that you, Little Claus? Well, first let me give you these cattle. Five miles up the road there's another whole herd that I want you to have." Then I saw that the river was a great highway for the sea folk. Down on the bottom they were walking and driving all the way from the sea toward land, to the place where the river ends. It was so lovely with flowers and the freshest of grass, and fish swimming in the water; they flitted around my ears like the birds in the air. How handsome the people were and how many cattle there were, ambling along the ditches and fences.'

'But why did you come back to us so soon?' asked Big Claus. 'That's not what I would have done if it was so charming down there.'

'Well, you see,' said Little Claus, 'it was really very cunning of me. You heard me say that the mermaid told me that

Little Claus and Big Claus

five miles up the road – and by road she meant the river, of course, since she can't travel any other way – there was a whole herd of cattle waiting for me. I happen to know where the river starts to bend, first one way and then the other, making a whole detour. It's much shorter, if you can do it, to come up here on land and head straight across to the river. That way I saved almost two and a half miles and reached my sea cattle much quicker.'

'Oh, you certainly are a lucky man!' said Big Claus. 'Do you think I could get some sea cattle too, if I went down to the bottom of the river?'

'Oh yes, I imagine so,' said Little Claus. 'But I can't carry you in a sack to the river; you're much too heavy for me. But if you walk there yourself and then climb into the bag, I'd be more than happy to throw you in.'

'Thanks so much,' said Big Claus. 'But if I don't get any sea cattle when I get there, I'm going to give you a beating, believe you me!'

'Oh no! Don't be so mean!' And then they went down to the river. The cattle were so thirsty that when they saw the water, they ran as fast as they could down the slope to drink.

'Look how fast they're moving,' said Little Claus. 'They're longing to go back down to the bottom.'

'Yes, but help me first,' said Big Claus. 'Otherwise I'll give you a beating!' And then he climbed into the big sack that was lying across the back of one of the bulls. 'Put a rock inside, because otherwise I'm afraid I won't sink,' said Big Claus.

'Oh, I'm sure you will,' said Little Claus, but just the same, he put a big rock in the sack, tied the cord tight, and then gave it a shove. Plop! Big Claus landed in the river and promptly sank to the bottom.

'I'm afraid he's not going to find any cattle,' said Little Claus, and then he headed home with all he had.

The Princess on the Pea

Once upon a time there was a prince. He wanted a princess, but she had to be a real princess. So he traveled all over the world to find one, but wherever he went there was something wrong. There were plenty of princesses, but he wasn't quite sure if they were real princesses. There was always something that wasn't quite right. Then he went back home and was so sad because he dearly wanted to have a real princess.

One evening there was a terrible storm. Lightning flashed and thunder roared, the rain poured down, it was simply dreadful! Then there was a knock at the town gate, and the old king went to open it.

There was a princess standing outside. But good Lord how she looked because of the rain and terrible weather! Water was streaming from her hair and her clothes, running in the toes of her shoes and out of the heels. Then she said that she was a real princess.

'Well, we'll see about that,' thought the old queen, but she didn't say a word. She went into the bedroom, took off all the bedclothes, and placed a pea at the bottom of the bed. Then she took twenty mattresses and put them on top of the pea, and another twenty eiderdown quilts on top of the mattresses.

That's where the princess was to sleep that night.

The next morning they asked her how she had slept.

'Oh, dreadfully!' said the princess. 'I hardly closed my eyes all night. Lord knows what there was in my bed. I was lying on something hard, and I'm black and blue all over! It's simply dreadful!'

Then they could see that she was a real princess, since she had felt the pea through those twenty mattresses and those twenty eiderdown quilts. No one else could have such tender skin except for a real princess.

And so the prince took her as his wife, because now he knew that he had a real princess. And the pea was placed in the Royal Curiosity Cabinet, where it can still be seen today, as long as no one has taken it.

Now you see, that was a real story!

The Steadfast Tin Soldier

Once upon a time there were twenty-five tin soldiers. They were brothers, because they were all born from an old tin spoon. Rifles they held at their shoulders, and their faces looked straight ahead. Red and blue, and oh so lovely were their uniforms. When the lid was removed from the box in which they lay, the very first words they heard in the world were, 'Tin soldiers!' That's what a little boy cried, clapping his hands. They had been given to him because it was his birthday, and now he lined them up on the table. Each soldier looked exactly like the next, except for one who was slightly different. He had only one leg because he was the last to be cast, and there wasn't enough tin left. Yet he stood just as firmly on one leg as the others did on two, and he's the one who turned out to be remarkable.

On the table where they stood were many other toys, but the one that was most striking was a charming castle made of paper. Through the tiny windows you could see right into the halls. Outside stood small trees around a little mirror that was meant to look like a lake. Swans made of wax were swimming around on it, reflected in the mirror. The whole thing was so charming, and yet the most charming of all was a little maiden who stood in the open doorway to the castle. She had also been cut out of paper, but she was wearing a skirt of the sheerest tulle and a tiny narrow blue ribbon over her shoulder like a sash. In the middle sat a gleaming spangle as big as her face. The little maiden was stretching out both arms, because she was a dancer, and she was also lifting one leg so high in the air that the tin soldier couldn't see it at all, and he thought that she had only one leg, just like him.

'Now there's a wife for me!' he thought. 'But she looks rather refined, and she lives in a castle. I have only a box, and it has to hold twenty-five of us. That's no place for her! Still, I have to see about making her acquaintance.' And then he stretched out full-length behind a snuff box that stood on the table. From there he could get a good look at the elegant little lady, who continued to stand on one leg without losing her balance.

Later that evening all the other tin soldiers were put back in their box, and the people of the house went to bed. Then the toys began to play. They gave tea parties, fought battles, and danced. The tin soldiers rattled in their box because they wanted to play too, but they couldn't open the lid. The nutcracker turned somersaults, and the slate pencil scribbled all over the slate. There was such a commotion that the canary woke up and started chattering too, and in verse, of all things. The only two who didn't budge were the tin soldier and the little dancer. She held herself erect on her toes, with her arms held out. He was just as steadfast on one leg, and his eyes didn't leave her for a second.

Then the clock struck twelve, and *Bam!* the lid of the snuff box flew open, but there was no tobacco inside – no, there was a little black troll. What a wily trick that was.

'Tin soldier!' said the troll. 'Keep your eyes to yourself!'

But the tin soldier pretended not to hear him.

The Steadfast Tin Soldier

'Well, just wait till morning,' said the troll.

When morning came and the children got up, the tin soldier was moved over to the windowsill, and whether it was the troll or a gust of wind, all of a sudden the window flew open and the soldier plummeted headfirst from the fourth floor. What a terrifying speed, with his leg turned upward! He landed on his cap, with his bayonet stuck between the cobblestones.

The servant girl and the little boy went downstairs at once to look for him, but even though they nearly stepped on him, they couldn't see him. If the tin soldier had shouted 'Here I am!' they probably would have found him, but he didn't think it was proper to yell when he was in uniform.

Then it started to rain. One drop came down faster than the other; it turned into a regular downpour. When it was over, two street urchins came along.

'Hey, look!' said one of them. 'There's a tin soldier lying here. Let's send him out for a sail.'

And so they made a boat out of newspaper, set the tin soldier in the middle of it, and he sailed off down the gutter. The two boys ran alongside, clapping their hands. God save us, what waves there were in that gutter, and what a current! Well, it's true that there had just been a downpour. The paper boat pitched up and down, and at times it would spin so fast that the tin soldier swayed. But he remained steadfast, his expression unflinching, standing erect with his rifle at his shoulder.

All of a sudden the boat washed in under a plank that lay over the gutter. It grew just as dark as inside his box.

'I wonder where I'll end up now,' he thought. 'Yes, well,

this is all the troll's fault. Oh, if only the little maiden were sitting here in the boat, then I wouldn't care if it was twice as dark!'

At that moment a big water rat appeared. It lived under the gutter plank.

'Have you got a travel pass?' asked the rat. 'Let's see your travel pass!'

But the tin soldier didn't say a word, holding his rifle even tighter. The boat raced along, with the rat right behind. Oh, how it gnashed its teeth, shouting to sticks and pieces of straw:

'Stop him! Stop him! He didn't pay the toll! He didn't show his travel pass!'

But the current grew stronger and stronger. The tin soldier could already glimpse daylight up ahead where the plank ended, but he also heard a roaring sound that would scare even a brave man. Just imagine: Where the plank ended, the gutter plunged right into a huge canal. For him it would be just as dangerous as for us to sail over an enormous waterfall.

He was already so close that he couldn't stop. The boat rushed forward; the poor tin soldier held himself as upright as he could. No one was going to say that he so much as blinked an eye. The boat spun around three or four times and filled with water up to the rim. It was going to sink. The tin soldier was standing in water up to his neck, and the boat sank deeper and deeper, the paper began dissolving faster and faster. Then the water was over the soldier's head. That's when he thought about the charming little dancer, whom he would never see again. And in his ears the soldier heard:

The Steadfast Tin Soldier

'Flee, warrior, flee!
Death is after you!'

Then the paper fell apart, and the tin soldier plunged right through. But at that very instant he was swallowed by a big fish.

Oh, how dark it was inside! It was even worse than under the gutter plank, and it was much more cramped. But the tin soldier was steadfast and stretched out full-length with his rifle at his shoulder.

The fish thrashed about, making the most terrifying movements. Finally it grew quite still, and what looked like a bolt of lightning flashed through it. The light shone so bright, and someone cried loudly, 'Tin soldier!' The fish had been caught, brought to market, sold, and then ended up in a kitchen where the servant girl slit it open with a big knife. Putting two fingers around his waist, she plucked out the soldier and carried him into the parlor where everyone wanted to see the remarkable man who had traveled inside the belly of a fish. But the tin soldier was not the least bit proud of himself. They set him on the table and there . . . Oh, what strange things can happen in the world! The tin soldier was in the very same parlor where he had been before. He saw the very same children and the toys on the table and the lovely castle with the charming little dancer. She was still standing on one leg with the other lifted high in the air. She too was steadfast. The tin soldier was touched, he was just about to weep tears of tin, but that wouldn't be proper. He looked at her and she looked at him, but neither said a word.

At that moment one of the little boys picked up the soldier and tossed him right into the stove, giving no explanation at all. The troll in the box was most certainly to blame.

The tin soldier stood there, brightly lit, and felt a terrible heat, but whether it was from the actual fire or from love, he didn't know. The paint had worn right off him, but whether this had happened on his journey or from sorrow, no one could say. He looked at the little maiden, she looked at him, and he felt himself melting. But he still stood there, steadfast, with his rifle at his shoulder. Then a door opened, the wind seized hold of the dancer, and she flew like a sylph right into the stove to the tin soldier, burst into flame, and was gone. Then the tin soldier melted into a lump, and the next day, when the servant girl took out the ashes, she found him in the shape of a little tin heart. But all that was left of the dancer was the spangle, and that had been burned black as coal.

The Nightingale

In China, as you probably know, the Emperor is Chinese, and everyone around him is Chinese too. This story happened many years ago, but that's precisely why it's worth hearing, before it's forgotten. The Emperor's palace was the most magnificent in the world, made entirely of fine porcelain, so costly but so fragile, so delicate to the touch that you had to be extremely careful. In the garden you could see the most wondrous flowers. Tied to the most splendid of them were silver bells that jingled, and you couldn't walk past without noticing the flowers. Yes, everything was quite artful in the Emperor's garden, which stretched so far that even the gardener didn't know where it ended. If you kept on walking you would come to the loveliest forest with tall trees and deep lakes. The forest went right down to the sea, which was deep and blue. Great ships could sail right under the branches. And among the branches lived a nightingale who sang so blissfully that even the poor fisherman, who had many other things to tend to, would lie still and listen whenever he heard the nightingale as he pulled in his fishing nets at night. 'Dear Lord, how beautiful she sounds!' he said.

But then he had to go back to his work and forget about the bird. Yet the next night when she sang again and the fisherman appeared, he would say the same thing, 'Dear Lord, how beautiful she sounds!'

Travelers came from countries all over the world to admire the Emperor's city and the palace and the garden. But if they happened to hear the nightingale, they all said, 'That's the best thing of all!'

The travelers would talk about everything when they went back home, and the learned men wrote many books about the city, the palace, and the garden, but they didn't forget the nightingale; she was esteemed above all else. Those who could write poetry wrote the loveliest poems, every single one about the nightingale in the forest by the deep sea.

These books circulated around the world, and one day some of them even reached the Emperor. He sat on his golden chair, reading and reading, as he kept nodding his head, because it pleased him to hear the magnificent descriptions of the city, the palace, and the garden. 'Yet the nightingale is the best of all!' he read in the book.

'What's this?' said the Emperor. 'The nightingale? I know nothing about it! Is there such a bird in my empire, let alone in my own garden? I've never heard of her. To think I had to learn about her from a book!'

And then he called for his Lord Chamberlain, who was so refined that if anyone lower in rank dared speak to him or ask him about something, his only reply was 'P!' And that means nothing at all.

'Supposedly there is a truly extraordinary bird here called the nightingale,' said the Emperor. 'They say that she's the best thing in all my vast domain. Why hasn't anyone told me about her?'

'I've never heard her mentioned before,' said the Lord Chamberlain. 'She has never been presented at court.'

The Nightingale

'I want her to come here tonight and sing for me,' said the Emperor. 'The whole world knows what I have, but I do not.'

'I've never heard her mentioned before,' said the Lord Chamberlain. 'I'll search for her, I'll find her!'

But where was she to be found? The Lord Chamberlain ran up and down all the stairs, through the halls and corridors. Not a single person he met had ever heard mention of the nightingale. So the Lord Chamberlain ran back to the Emperor and said that she must be a fable concocted by those who write books. 'Your Imperial Majesty should not believe what people write. It's all fabrication and what's called black magic.'

'But the book I was reading was sent to me by the mighty Emperor of Japan,' said the Emperor, 'so it must be true. I want to hear the nightingale. She must be here tonight! I bestow on her my highest favor! And if she doesn't come, then all the members of the court will be punched in the stomach after they've eaten their supper.'

'*Xing-pei!*' said the Lord Chamberlain, and once again he ran up and down all the stairs, through all the halls and corridors. And half the court ran along with him, because they didn't want to be punched in the stomach. Everyone was asking about the remarkable nightingale that was known to the whole world but to no one at court.

Finally they came upon a poor little girl in the kitchen, and she said, 'Oh Lord, the nightingale! I know her well. Yes, how she can sing! Every evening I'm allowed to take home a few scraps from the table for my poor sick mother. She lives down near the shore, and when I walk back feeling tired, I take a rest in the forest, and then I hear the nightingale singing. It makes my eyes fill with tears. It's as if my mother were kissing me.'

'Little kitchen maid,' said the Lord Chamberlain, 'I shall arrange a permanent post for you in the kitchen and permission to watch the Emperor eat if you can lead us to the nightingale. She has been summoned here tonight.'

And so they all set off for the forest, to the place where the nightingale usually sang. Half the court went along. As they were walking, a cow began to moo.

'Oh!' said the royal squires. 'Now we've found her. What remarkable power for such a small creature! We're quite certain we've heard her before.'

'No, those are the cows mooing,' said the little kitchen maid. 'We're still quite far from the place.'

Now the frogs began croaking in the bog.

'Lovely!' said the Chinese Court Chaplain. 'Now I can hear her. It sounds just like little church bells.'

'No, those are the frogs,' said the little kitchen maid. 'But I think we'll hear her soon.'

Then the nightingale began to sing.

'There she is,' said the little girl. 'Listen! Listen! And there she sits!' And then she pointed at a little gray bird up in the branches.

'Is it possible?' said the Lord Chamberlain. 'That's not at all how I imagined her. How plain she looks! She must have lost her color from seeing so many refined people all around.'

'Little nightingale!' cried the little kitchen maid in a loud voice. 'Our Most Gracious Emperor would like so much for you to sing for him.'

The Nightingale

'With the greatest pleasure,' said the nightingale and sang so it was sheer delight.

'It sounds just like glass bells,' said the Lord Chamberlain. 'And look at her little throat – she's singing with all her might. It's strange that we've never heard this bird before. She will be a huge success at court.'

'Shall I sing some more for the Emperor?' asked the nightingale, who thought the Emperor was among them.

'My splendid little nightingale,' said the Lord Chamberlain, 'I have the great pleasure of summoning you to a royal celebration this evening, where you will enchant His Exalted Imperial Grace with your charming song.'

'My song sounds best out in nature,' said the nightingale, but she willingly went along with them when she heard that this was the Emperor's wish.

At the palace everything had been properly cleaned and polished. The walls and floors, which were made of porcelain, gleamed with thousands of golden lamps. The loveliest flowers, the ones with bells attached, had been placed in the corridors; there was a draft and a great commotion, making all the bells ring. You couldn't hear yourself think.

In the middle of the great hall, where the Emperor was seated, a golden perch had been placed, and that was where the nightingale was to sit. The entire court was present, and the little kitchen maid had been given permission to stand behind the door, since she now held the title of Real Kitchen Maid. Everyone was dressed in his very finest, and everyone was looking at the little gray bird, to whom the Emperor nodded.

And the nightingale sang so wondrously that tears filled the Emperor's eyes. Tears rolled down his cheeks, and then the nightingale sang even more beautifully; the song went straight to the heart. The Emperor was so happy that he said the nightingale must wear his golden slipper around her neck. But the nightingale thanked him and said that she had already received reward enough.

'I've seen tears in the Emperor's eyes. For me that is the richest treasure. An emperor's tears have a wondrous power. God knows, that is reward enough.' And then she sang again in her sweet, blessed voice.

'This is the most lovable coquetry we've ever known,' said the women all around, and then they put water in their mouths in order to cluck whenever anyone spoke to them. They thought they too could be nightingales. Even the lackeys and chambermaids announced that they were satisfied, and that is saying a great deal because they're the most difficult of all to please. Yes, the nightingale certainly was a success!

Now she would stay at court, and have her own cage, as well as the freedom to promenade twice a day and once at night. Twelve servants were sent along, each of them holding tight to a silk ribbon attached to her leg. There wasn't the least bit of pleasure in those excursions.

The whole city was talking about the extraordinary bird. If two people met, one of them would say to the other 'Night!' and the other would say 'Gale!' and then they would sigh, fully understanding each other. Why, eleven grocers' children were named after her, but not one of them could even carry a tune.

The Nightingale

One day a big package arrived for the Emperor. On the outside it said: 'Nightingale.'

'Here we have a new book about our famous bird,' said the Emperor. But it wasn't a book. A little work of art lay inside the box, a mechanical nightingale that was supposed to look like the live one, although it was completely encrusted with diamonds, rubies, and sapphires. As soon as they wound up the mechanical bird it sang one of the tunes that the real bird sang, and its tail moved up and down, glittering with silver and gold. Around its neck hung a little ribbon, and on it were the words: 'The Emperor of Japan's nightingale is paltry compared to the Emperor of China's.'

'It's lovely!' they all said, and the person who had brought the mechanical bird was at once given the title of Supreme Imperial Nightingale Bringer.

'Let's have them sing together. What a duet that will be!'

And then they had to sing together, but it was not a success, because the real nightingale sang in her own way, while the mechanical bird ran on cylinders. 'There's nothing wrong with that,' said the Music Master. 'It keeps perfect time and is obviously a follower of my own methods.' Then the mechanical bird had to sing alone. It brought just as much joy as the real bird, and on top of that it was much more charming in appearance. It glittered like bracelets and brooches.

Thirty-three times it sang the very same tune, and yet it never grew tired. Everyone could have listened to it all over again, but the Emperor felt that the live nightingale should also sing a little. But where was she? No one had noticed that she had flown out the open window, off to her green forests.

'Well, what sort of behavior is that?' said the Emperor. And all the members of court began scolding, saying that the nightingale was a most ungrateful creature. 'Yet we have the best bird of all,' they said, and then the mechanical bird had to sing some more, and that was the thirty-fourth time they heard the same tune. But they didn't yet know it by heart, because it was so complicated, and the Music Master lavished great praise on the bird. Yes, he assured them that it was better than the real nightingale, not only in terms of its attire and the scores of lovely diamonds, but also internally.

'For you see, ladies and gentlemen, and above all Your Imperial Highness! You can never count on what will come out of the real nightingale, but with the mechanical bird everything is certain. This is how it will sound, and no other way. You can explain it, you can open it up and demonstrate the human reasoning, how the cylinders are arranged, how they operate, and how one turns the other.'

'Those are my thoughts exactly,' they all said. And the Music Master was granted permission, on the following Sunday, to display the bird to the people. They too should hear it sing, said the Emperor. And they heard it and were as pleased as if they had drunk themselves giddy on tea; that was so typically Chinese. And everyone said 'Oh!' and held up in the air the finger that we call 'pot-licker' and then they nodded. But the poor fishermen who had heard the real nightingale said, 'It sounds nice enough, and it does look quite like it, but something is missing, we don't know what.'

The real nightingale was banished from the realm.

The mechanical bird had its place on a silk pillow close to

the Emperor's bed. All the gifts it had been given, gold and precious stones, were spread around it, and in title it had risen to Supreme Imperial Nightstand Singer. In rank it was number one on the left, because the Emperor considered the side of the heart to be the most noble, and even in an Emperor the heart is on the left. The Music Master wrote twenty-five volumes about the mechanical bird, books that were so learned and so lengthy, and written in the most difficult of Chinese words, that everyone said they had read and understood them, because otherwise they would have seemed stupid and then they would have been punched in the stomach.

A whole year passed in this fashion. The Emperor, the court, and all the other Chinese people knew by heart every little cluck of the mechanical bird's song, but that was precisely why they liked it above all else. They could sing it themselves, and they did. The street urchins sang 'Xi-xi-xi! Cluck-cluck-cluck!' And the Emperor sang it too. Oh yes, it was certainly lovely!

But one evening when the mechanical bird was singing its best and the Emperor was lying in bed and listening, it went 'Clunk!' inside. Something burst. 'Buzzzzzz!' all the gears spun around, and then the music stopped.

The Emperor sprang out of bed at once and called for his royal physician, but what good could he do? Then they summoned the watchmaker. After much discussion and a great deal of study, he managed to get the bird working fairly well, but he said that it would have to be played sparingly because the cylinder pegs were worn out. It would be impossible to replace them with new ones so that the music would play properly. That was a terrible shame! Only once a year did they dare let the mechanical bird sang, and even that was almost too often. But then the Music Master gave a little speech using big words and said that it was just as good as new, and so it was just as good as new.

Five years passed, and the whole land suffered a great sadness, because everyone was truly very fond of their Emperor. Now they said he was ill and about to die. A new emperor had already been chosen, and the people stood outside on the street and asked the Lord Chamberlain how things were going with their Emperor.

'P!' he said and shook his head.

Cold and pale, the Emperor lay in his big, magnificent bed. The entire court thought he was dead, and all of them had run off to greet the new Emperor. The valets had run outside to talk about it, and the palace maids were holding a big coffee party. All around in the halls and corridors cloth had been laid down so that no one's footsteps could be heard. That's why it was so quiet, so quiet. But the Emperor was not yet dead. Rigid and pale, he lay in the magnificent bed with the long velvet curtains and the heavy gold tassels. High above, a window stood open, and the moon was shining on the Emperor and the mechanical bird.

The poor Emperor could hardly breathe; it felt as if something were sitting on his chest. He opened his eyes and saw that it was Death sitting on his chest. He had put on the gold crown and was holding in one hand the Emperor's gold sword, and in the other his magnificent banner. All around in the folds of the great velvet bed curtains peculiar heads were sticking out, some of them quite horrid, others so

The Nightingale

blessedly gentle. They were all of the Emperor's good and bad deeds, looking at him, now that Death was sitting on his heart.

'Do you remember this?' one after the other whispered. 'Do you remember this?' And then they told him so many things that the sweat poured from his brow.

'I never knew that!' said the Emperor. 'Music, music, the great Chinese drum!' he shouted. 'So I won't have to listen to everything they're saying.'

But they kept on, and Death nodded, as the Chinese do, at everything that was said.

'Music, music!' screamed the Emperor. 'You blessed little golden bird! Sing now, sing! I've given you gold and precious things. I myself have hung my golden slipper around your neck. So sing now, sing!'

But the bird stood silent. There was no one to wind it up, and otherwise it couldn't sing. But Death kept on looking at the Emperor with his big, empty eye sockets, and it was so quiet, so horribly quiet.

At that moment, close to the window, the loveliest song was heard. It was the live little nightingale, who was sitting on a branch outside. She had heard about the Emperor's distress, and that's why she had come, to offer solace and hope. And as she sang, the figures grew more and more pale, the blood began to flow faster and faster through the Emperor's weak limbs, and Death himself listened and said, 'Keep singing, little nightingale! Keep singing!'

'Yes, if you give me the magnificent gold sword! Yes, if you give me the opulent banner! If you give me the Emperor's crown!'

Hans Christian Andersen

And Death returned each treasure for a song, and the nightingale still kept singing. She sang of the silent churchyard where the white roses grow, where the fragrant elder tree stands, and where the fresh grass is watered by the tears of the bereaved. Then Death had such a longing for his own garden that he floated out like a cold white fog, out the window.

'Thank you, thank you!' said the Emperor. 'You heavenly little bird, of course I recognize you! You're the one I chased from my realm. And yet you have sung the evil visions away from my bed and driven Death from my heart. How shall I reward you?'

'You have already rewarded me,' said the nightingale. 'I won tears from your eyes the first time I sang. I will never forget that about you. They are the jewels that make a singer's heart glad. But sleep now and grow strong and healthy. I will sing for you.'

And she sang. The Emperor fell into a sweet slumber, so gentle and refreshing was his sleep.

The sun was shining through the windows when he awoke, strong and healthy. None of his servants had yet returned, because they all thought he was dead. But the nightingale was still sitting there, singing.

'You must stay with me forever,' said the Emperor. 'You shall only sing when you want to, and I will smash the mechanical bird into a thousand pieces.'

'Don't do that,' said the nightingale. 'It has done the best it could. Keep it as you always have. I can't live in the palace, but let me come whenever I wish. Then in the evening I will sit on the branch by your window and sing for you, to make

The Nightingale

you both joyous and pensive. I will sing about those who are happy and those who suffer. I will sing about the evil and the good that is kept hidden from you. The little songbird flies far and wide, to the poor fisherman, to the farmer's rooftop, to everyone who is far from you and your court. I love your heart more than your crown, and yet the crown has a scent of something sacred about it. I will come, I will sing for you. But one thing you must promise me.'

'Anything!' said the Emperor, standing there in his imperial robes, which he had donned himself, and holding the sword that was heavy with gold pressed to his heart.

'One thing I ask of you. Tell no one that you have a little bird who tells you everything, and things will go even better.'

And then the nightingale flew off.

The servants came in to tend to their dead Emperor. Oh yes, there they stood. And the Emperor said, 'Good morning!'

The Red Shoes

There was a little girl who was so delicate and charming, but in the summer she always had to go barefoot because she was poor. In the winter she wore big wooden clogs that made her little ankles turn quite red, and that was awful.

In the middle of the village lived old Mother Shoemaker. She sat and sewed as best she could, using old strips of red cloth to make a little pair of shoes. Quite clumsy they were, but well-intended, and the little girl was to have them. The little girl's name was Karen.

On the very day that her mother was buried, Karen was given the red shoes, and she wore them for the first time. Now, it's true that they weren't the proper shoes for mourning, but she didn't have any others, and so she wore them on her bare feet, walking behind the humble coffin made of straw.

All at once a grand old carriage appeared, and inside sat a grand old woman. She looked at the little girl and felt sorry for her. Then she said to the pastor, 'Listen here, give me that little girl and I will be kind to her!'

Karen thought she said this because of her red shoes, but the old woman said they were awful, and they were burned, while Karen was dressed in nice, clean clothes. She had to learn to read and sew, and people said that she was charming, but the mirror said, 'You are much more than charming, you're lovely!'

The Red Shoes

Then the queen happened to travel through the land, and she brought along her little daughter, who was a princess. People came flocking to the palace, and Karen was there too. The little princess stood in a window for all to see dressed in fine white clothes. She wore neither a train nor a golden crown, but she had lovely, red kidskin shoes. Of course they were much prettier than the ones that Mother Shoemaker had sewn for little Karen. But nothing in the world could compare with red shoes!

Then Karen was old enough to be confirmed. She was given new clothes and she was also to have new shoes. The rich shoemaker in town measured her little foot. This was at home in his own parlor, where big glass cupboards stood filled with elegant shoes and shiny boots. Everything looked charming, but the old woman didn't see well, so it gave her no pleasure. In the midst of all the shoes stood a pair of red ones just like the ones the princess had worn. How beautiful they were! The shoemaker said they had been sewn for the child of a count, but they didn't fit properly.

'They must be made of the finest leather,' said the old woman. 'How they shine!'

'Yes, how they shine!' said Karen. And they fit, so they were bought. But the old woman didn't know that they were red, because she would never have allowed Karen to be confirmed wearing red shoes, and yet she did.

Everyone looked at her feet. When she walked up the church aisle toward the chancel doorway, she thought even the old paintings on the crypts, those portraits of pastors and their wives wearing stiff collars and long black gowns, had fixed their eyes on her red shoes. And that was all she could think of when the pastor placed his hand on her head and spoke of the holy baptism, of the pact with God, and the fact that she should now be a good Christian. The organ played so solemnly, the children sang so beautifully, and the old cantor sang too, but Karen thought only of her red shoes.

By that afternoon the old woman had heard from everyone that the shoes were red, and she said how dreadful that was. It wasn't the least bit proper. From that day on, whenever Karen went to church, she would always wear black shoes, even if they were old.

The following Sunday was her first communion, and Karen looked at the black shoes, she looked at the red ones – and then she looked at the red ones again and put them on.

It was lovely sunny weather. Karen and the old woman walked along the path through the grain fields where it was rather dusty.

At the church door stood an old soldier with a crutch and a long, odd-looking beard that was more red than white; in fact, it was red. He bowed all the way to the ground and asked the old woman whether he might wipe off her shoes. Karen stretched out her little foot too. 'Oh look, what lovely dancing shoes!' said the soldier. 'Stay on tight when you dance!' Then he slapped his hand on the soles.

The old woman gave the soldier a little *skilling* and then went with Karen into the church.

Everyone inside looked at Karen's red shoes; all the paintings looked at them too. And when Karen knelt before the altar and put the golden chalice to her lips, she thought only of the red shoes. They seemed to be swimming around in the

The Red Shoes

chalice before her, and she forgot to sing the hymn, she forgot to say the Lord's Prayer.

Then everyone left the church, and the old woman climbed into her carriage. As Karen lifted her foot to climb in after her, the old soldier who was standing close by said, 'Oh look, what lovely dancing shoes!' And Karen couldn't help herself, she had to take a few dance steps. As soon as she started, her feet kept on dancing. It was as if the shoes had taken control. She danced around the corner of the church, she couldn't stop herself. The coachman had to run after and grab her, and he lifted her into the carriage, but her feet kept on dancing and she kicked hard at the kind old woman. Finally they managed to take off the shoes, and her feet stopped moving.

At home the shoes were put in a cupboard, but Karen couldn't help looking at them.

Then the old woman fell ill, and they said she wouldn't live long. She needed someone to nurse and tend her, and who should do it but Karen? But over in town there was to be a great ball, and Karen was invited. She looked at the old woman, who didn't have long to live, after all. She looked at the red shoes, and she didn't think there was any sin in that. She put on the red shoes. Why shouldn't she? And then she went to the ball and began to dance.

But when she wanted to turn right, the shoes danced to the left, and when she wanted to move up the floor, the shoes danced down the floor, down the stairs, along the street, and out the town gate. Dance she did, and dance she must, right out into the dark forest.

Then she saw a light overhead among the trees, and she

thought it must be the moon, because it had a face, but it was the old soldier with the red beard. He sat there nodding and said, 'Oh look, what lovely dancing shoes!'

Then Karen was horrified and tried to take off the red shoes, but they wouldn't come off. She tore off her stockings, but the shoes had grown onto her feet; dance she did and dance she must, over field and meadow, in rain and in sunshine, night and day, but nighttime was the most terrible of all.

She danced into the open churchyard, but the dead weren't dancing. They had better things to do than dance. She wanted to sit down on the pauper's grave where bitter tansy grew, but for her there was no peace or rest. And when she danced toward the open church door, she saw an angel there in long white robes, with wings that reached from his shoulders to the ground. His face was stern and solemn, and in his hand he held a sword, gleaming and wide.

'Dance you shall!' he said. 'Dance in your red shoes until you turn pale and cold! Until your skin shrivels up like a mummy's! Dance from door to door. And wherever proud and vain children live, you will knock so they hear and fear you! Dance you shall, dance–!'

'Have mercy!' cried Karen. But she didn't hear what the angel replied, because her shoes carried her through the gate, out to the field, across the road, and along the path, and always she had to keep dancing.

Early one morning she danced past a door she knew quite well. Inside a hymn could be heard, and they carried out a coffin that was adorned with flowers. Then she knew that the

The Red Shoes

old woman was dead, and she felt as if she had now been forsaken by everyone and cursed by the angel of God.

Dance she did, and dance she must, dance into the dark night. Her shoes carried her over thickets and stumps, her feet were worn bloody. She danced across the heath to a lonely little house. She knew that this was where the executioner lived. She tapped her finger on the windowpane and said, 'Come out! Come out! I can't come inside, because I'm dancing!'

And the executioner said, 'Don't you know who I am? I chop off the heads of evil people, and I can feel my ax is trembling!'

'Don't chop off my head,' said Karen. 'Because then I won't be able to repent my sin. But chop off my feet with the red shoes!'

Then she confessed to her sin, and the executioner chopped off her feet with the red shoes. But the shoes kept dancing with the little feet across the fields and into the deep forest.

And he carved wooden feet and crutches for her, taught her a hymn that sinners always sing, and she kissed the hand that had wielded the ax and set out across the heath.

'Now I've suffered enough for those red shoes,' she said. 'Now I'm going to church so they can see me.' And she walked as fast as she could toward the church door, but when she got there, the red shoes were dancing in front of her. She was horrified and turned away.

All week long she was sad and wept many bitter tears, but when Sunday came, she said, 'All right! Now I've suffered and struggled enough! I should think that I'm just as good as many of those people sitting so proudly inside the church.' Then she set off quite boldly, but she got no farther than to the gate when she saw the red shoes dancing in front of her. She was horrified and turned away, repenting her sin with all her heart.

She went over to the parsonage and asked if she might be taken into service there. She would work hard and do everything she could. She had no wish for wages; all she asked for was a roof over her head and permission to stay with good people. The pastor's wife felt sorry for her and gave her a position. And she was hardworking and thoughtful. Quietly she would sit and listen when the pastor read aloud from the Bible in the evening. All the children were very fond of her, but whenever they spoke of adornments and finery and being as lovely as a queen, she would shake her head.

The next Sunday they all went to church and they asked if she would like to come along, but with tears in her eyes she looked sadly at her crutches. Then the others went to hear God's Word while she went alone into her tiny room. It was only big enough for a bed and a chair. There she sat with her hymnbook. As she began reading with a pious heart, the wind carried the tones of the organ from the church to her. She raised her tear-stained face and said, 'Oh, help me, God!'

Then the sun shone so bright, and right in front of her stood the angel of God in the white robes, the one she had seen that night at the church door. He was no longer holding a sharp sword but a lovely green bough that was covered with roses. He touched it to the ceiling, which raised up

The Red Shoes

high, and at the spot he had touched shone a golden star. He touched the walls and they moved outward. She saw the organ that was playing; she saw the old paintings of the pastors and their wives. The congregation was sitting in the carved pews and singing from their hymnals.

The church itself had come home to the poor girl in the tiny, cramped room, or perhaps she had gone to the church. She was sitting in a pew with the others from the parsonage. When they finished the hymn and looked up, they nodded and said, 'It was right for you to come, Karen.'

'It was God's mercy,' she said.

The organ soared, and the children's voices in the choir sounded gentle and lovely. The bright, warm sunshine streamed through the window, reaching the church pew where Karen sat. Her heart was so filled with sunlight, with peace and joy, that it burst. Her soul flew on the sunlight to God, and no one asked about the red shoes.

1. BOCCACCIO · *Mrs Rosie and the Priest*
2. GERARD MANLEY HOPKINS · *As kingfishers catch fire*
3. *The Saga of Gunnlaug Serpent-tongue*
4. THOMAS DE QUINCEY · *On Murder Considered as One of the Fine Arts*
5. FRIEDRICH NIETZSCHE · *Aphorisms on Love and Hate*
6. JOHN RUSKIN · *Traffic*
7. PU SONGLING · *Wailing Ghosts*
8. JONATHAN SWIFT · *A Modest Proposal*
9. *Three Tang Dynasty Poets*
10. WALT WHITMAN · *On the Beach at Night Alone*
11. KENKŌ · *A Cup of Sake Beneath the Cherry Trees*
12. BALTASAR GRACIÁN · *How to Use Your Enemies*
13. JOHN KEATS · *The Eve of St Agnes*
14. THOMAS HARDY · *Woman much missed*
15. GUY DE MAUPASSANT · *Femme Fatale*
16. MARCO POLO · *Travels in the Land of Serpents and Pearls*
17. SUETONIUS · *Caligula*
18. APOLLONIUS OF RHODES · *Jason and Medea*
19. ROBERT LOUIS STEVENSON · *Olalla*
20. KARL MARX AND FRIEDRICH ENGELS · *The Communist Manifesto*
21. PETRONIUS · *Trimalchio's Feast*
22. JOHANN PETER HEBEL · *How a Ghastly Story Was Brought to Light by a Common or Garden Butcher's Dog*
23. HANS CHRISTIAN ANDERSEN · *The Tinder Box*
24. RUDYARD KIPLING · *The Gate of the Hundred Sorrows*
25. DANTE · *Circles of Hell*
26. HENRY MAYHEW · *Of Street Piemen*
27. HAFEZ · *The nightingales are drunk*
28. GEOFFREY CHAUCER · *The Wife of Bath*
29. MICHEL DE MONTAIGNE · *How We Weep and Laugh at the Same Thing*
30. THOMAS NASHE · *The Terrors of the Night*
31. EDGAR ALLAN POE · *The Tell-Tale Heart*
32. MARY KINGSLEY · *A Hippo Banquet*
33. JANE AUSTEN · *The Beautifull Cassandra*
34. ANTON CHEKHOV · *Gooseberries*
35. SAMUEL TAYLOR COLERIDGE · *Well, they are gone, and here must I remain*
36. JOHANN WOLFGANG VON GOETHE · *Sketchy, Doubtful, Incomplete Jottings*
37. CHARLES DICKENS · *The Great Winglebury Duel*
38. HERMAN MELVILLE · *The Maldive Shark*
39. ELIZABETH GASKELL · *The Old Nurse's Story*
40. NIKOLAY LESKOV · *The Steel Flea*

41. HONORÉ DE BALZAC · *The Atheist's Mass*
42. CHARLOTTE PERKINS GILMAN · *The Yellow Wall-Paper*
43. C.P. CAVAFY · *Remember, Body...*
44. FYODOR DOSTOEVSKY · *The Meek One*
45. GUSTAVE FLAUBERT · *A Simple Heart*
46. NIKOLAI GOGOL · *The Nose*
47. SAMUEL PEPYS · *The Great Fire of London*
48. EDITH WHARTON · *The Reckoning*
49. HENRY JAMES · *The Figure in the Carpet*
50. WILFRED OWEN · *Anthem For Doomed Youth*
51. WOLFGANG AMADEUS MOZART · *My Dearest Father*
52. PLATO · *Socrates' Defence*
53. CHRISTINA ROSSETTI · *Goblin Market*
54. *Sindbad the Sailor*
55. SOPHOCLES · *Antigone*
56. RYŪNOSUKE AKUTAGAWA · *The Life of a Stupid Man*
57. LEO TOLSTOY · *How Much Land Does A Man Need?*
58. GIORGIO VASARI · *Leonardo da Vinci*
59. OSCAR WILDE · *Lord Arthur Savile's Crime*
60. SHEN FU · *The Old Man of the Moon*
61. AESOP · *The Dolphins, the Whales and the Gudgeon*
62. MATSUO BASHŌ · *Lips too Chilled*
63. EMILY BRONTË · *The Night is Darkening Round Me*
64. JOSEPH CONRAD · *To-morrow*
65. RICHARD HAKLUYT · *The Voyage of Sir Francis Drake Around the Whole Globe*
66. KATE CHOPIN · *A Pair of Silk Stockings*
67. CHARLES DARWIN · *It was snowing butterflies*
68. BROTHERS GRIMM · *The Robber Bridegroom*
69. CATULLUS · *I Hate and I Love*
70. HOMER · *Circe and the Cyclops*
71. D. H. LAWRENCE · *Il Duro*
72. KATHERINE MANSFIELD · *Miss Brill*
73. OVID · *The Fall of Icarus*
74. SAPPHO · *Come Close*
75. IVAN TURGENEV · *Kasyan from the Beautiful Lands*
76. VIRGIL · *O Cruel Alexis*
77. H. G. WELLS · *A Slip under the Microscope*
78. HERODOTUS · *The Madness of Cambyses*
79. *Speaking of Siva*
80. *The Dhammapada*

'Mind you, it was a *pukka*, respectable opium-house, and not one of those stifling, sweltering *chandoo-khanas* that you can find all over the City.'

RUDYARD KIPLING
Born 1865, Bombay
Died 1936, London

All stories taken from *Plain Tales from the Hills*,
first published in 1890

KIPLING IN PENGUIN CLASSICS
Captains Courageous
Just So Stories
Kim
Plain Tales from the Hills
Selected Poems
The Jungle Books
The Man Who Would Be King: Selected Stories

RUDYARD KIPLING

The Gate of the Hundred Sorrows

PENGUIN BOOKS

PENGUIN CLASSICS

UK | USA | Canada | Ireland | Australia
India | New Zealand | South Africa

Penguin Books is part of the Penguin Random House group of companies
whose addresses can be found at global.penguinrandomhouse.com.

This selection published in Penguin Classics 2015
011

Set in 9/12.4 pt Baskerville 10 Pro
Typeset by Jouve (UK), Milton Keynes
Printed and bound in Great Britain by Clays Ltd, Elcograf S.p.A.

A CIP catalogue record for this book is available from the British Library

ISBN: 978-0-141-39806-8

www.greenpenguin.co.uk

Penguin Random House is committed to a
sustainable future for our business, our readers
and our planet. This book is made from Forest
Stewardship Council® certified paper.

Contents

Thrown Away	1
False Dawn	12
In the House of Suddhoo	23
The Bisara of Pooree	33
The Gate of the Hundred Sorrows	40
The Story of Muhammad Din	48

Thrown Away

And some are sulky, while some will plunge.
  (*So ho! Steady! Stand still, you!*)
Some you must gentle, and some you must lunge.
  (*There! There! Who wants to kill you?*)
Some – there are losses in every trade –
Will break their hearts ere bitted and made,
Will fight like fiends as the rope cuts hard,
And die dumb-mad in the breaking-yard.

Toolungala Stockyard Chorus

To rear a boy under what parents call the 'sheltered life' system is, if the boy must go into the world and fend for himself, not wise. Unless he be one in a thousand he has certainly to pass through many unnecessary troubles; and may, possibly, come to extreme grief simply from ignorance of the proper proportions of things.

Let a puppy eat the soap in the bath-room or chew a newly-blacked boot. He chews and chuckles until, by and by, he finds out that blacking and Old Brown Windsor make him very sick. So he argues that soap and boots are not wholesome. Any old dog about the house will soon show him the unwisdom of biting big dogs' ears. Being young, he remembers, and goes abroad, at six months, a well-mannered little beast with a chastened appetite. If he had been kept away from boots, and soap, and big dogs till he came to the trinity full-grown and with developed teeth, consider how fearfully sick and thrashed he would be! Apply that notion to the 'sheltered life', and see how it works. It does not sound pretty, but it is the better of two evils.

There was a Boy once who had been brought up under the 'sheltered life' theory; and the theory killed him dead. He stayed with his people all his days, from the hour he was born till the hour he went into Sandhurst nearly at the top of the list. He was beautifully taught in all that wins marks by a private tutor, and carried the extra weight of 'never having given his parents an hour's anxiety in his life'. What he learnt at Sandhurst beyond the regular routine is of no great consequence. He looked about him, and he found soap and blacking, so to speak, very good. He ate a little, and came out of Sandhurst not so high as he went in. Then there was an interval and a scene with his people, who expected much from him. Next a year of living unspotted from the world in a third-rate depôt battalion where all the juniors were children and all the seniors old women; and lastly, he came out to India, where he was cut off from the support of his parents, and had no one to fall back on in time of trouble except himself.

Now India is a place beyond all others where one must not take things too seriously – the mid-day sun always excepted. Too much work and too much energy kill a man just as effectively as too much assorted vice or too much drink. Flirtation does not matter, because every one is being transferred, and either you or she leave the station and never return. Good work does not matter, because a man is judged by his worst output, and another man takes all the credit of his best as a rule. Bad work does not matter, because other men do worse, and incompetents hang on longer in India than anywhere else. Amusements do not matter, because you must repeat them as soon as you have accomplished them once, and most amusements only mean trying to win another person's money. Sickness does not matter, because it's all in the day's work, and if you die, another man takes over your place and your office in the eight hours between your death and burial. Nothing matters except Home-furlough and acting allowances, and these only because they are scarce. It is a slack country, where all men work with imperfect instruments, and the wisest thing is to escape as soon as ever you can to some place where amusement is amusement and a reputation worth the having.

But this Boy – the tale is as old as the Hills – came out, and took all things seriously. He was pretty and was petted. He took the pettings seriously, and fretted over women not worth saddling a pony to call upon. He found his new free life in India very good. It *does* look attractive in the beginning, from a subaltern's point of view – all ponies, partners, dancing, and so on. He tasted it as the puppy tastes the soap. Only he came late to the eating, with a grown set of teeth. He had no sense of balance – just like the puppy – and could not understand why he was not treated with the consideration he received under his father's roof. That hurt his feelings.

He quarrelled with other boys and, being sensitive to the marrow, remembered these quarrels, and they excited him.

He found whist, and gymkhanas, and things of that kind (meant to amuse one after office) good; but he took them seriously too, just as seriously as he took the 'head' that followed after drink. He lost his money over whist and gymkhanas because they were new to him.

He took his losses seriously, and wasted as much energy and interest over a two-goldmohur race for maiden *ekka*-ponies with their manes hogged, as if it had been the Derby. One-half of this came from inexperience – much as the puppy squabbles with the corner of the hearthrug – and the other half from the dizziness bred by stumbling out of his quiet life into the glare and excitement of a livelier one. No one told him about the soap and the blacking, because an average man takes it for granted that an average man is ordinarily careful in regard to them. It was pitiful to watch The Boy knocking himself to pieces, as an over-handled colt falls down and cuts himself when he gets away from his groom.

This unbridled licence in amusements not worth the trouble of breaking line for, much less rioting over, endured for six months – all through one cold weather – and then we thought that the heat and the knowledge of having lost his money and health and lamed his horses would sober The Boy down, and he would stand steady. In ninety-nine cases out of a hundred this would have happened. You can see the principle working in any Indian station. But this particular case fell through because The Boy was sensitive and took things seriously – as I may have said some seven times before. Of course, we could not tell how his excesses struck him personally. They were nothing very heartbreaking or above the average. He might be crippled for life financially, and want a little nursing. Still, the memory of his performances would wither away in one hot weather, and the bankers would help him to tide over the money-troubles. But he must have taken another view altogether, and have believed himself ruined beyond redemption. His Colonel talked to him severely when the cold weather ended. That made him more wretched than ever; and it was only an ordinary 'Colonel's wigging'!

What follows is a curious instance of the fashion in which we are all linked together and made responsible for one another. *The* thing that kicked the beam in The Boy's mind was a remark that a woman made when he was talking to her. There is no use in repeating it, for it was only a cruel little sentence, rapped out before thinking, that made him flush to the roots of his hair. He kept himself to himself for three days, and then put in for two days' leave to go shooting near a Canal Engineer's Rest House about thirty miles out. He got his leave, and that night at Mess was noisier and more offensive than ever. He said that he was 'going to shoot big game', and left at half-past ten o'clock in an *ekka*. Partridge – which was the only thing a man could get near the Rest House – is not big game; so every one laughed.

Next morning one of the Majors came in from short leave, and heard that The Boy had gone out to shoot 'big game'. The Major had taken an interest in The Boy, and had, more than once, tried to check him. The Major put up his eyebrows when he heard of the expedition, and went to The Boy's rooms, where he rummaged.

Presently he came out and found me leaving cards on the Mess. There was no one else in the ante-room.

He said, 'The Boy has gone out shooting. *Does* a man shoot partridge with a revolver and writing-case?'

I said, 'Nonsense, Major!' for I saw what was in his mind.

He said, 'Nonsense or no nonsense, I'm going to the Canal now – at once. I don't feel easy.'

Then he thought for a minute, and said, 'Can you lie?'

'You know best,' I answered. 'It's my profession.'

'Very well,' said the Major, 'you come out with me now – at once – in an *ekka* to the Canal to shoot black-buck. Go and put on *shikar*-kit – *quick* – and drive here with a gun.'

The Major was a masterful man, and I knew that he would not give orders for nothing. So I obeyed, and on return found the Major packed up in an *ekka* – gun-cases and food slung below – all ready for a shooting-trip.

He dismissed the driver and drove himself. We jogged along quietly while in the station; but, as soon as we got to the dusty road across the plains, he made that pony fly. A country-bred can do nearly anything at a pinch. We covered the thirty miles in under three hours, but the poor brute was nearly dead.

Once I said, 'What's the blazing hurry, Major?'

He said quietly, 'The Boy has been alone, by himself for – one, two, five, – fourteen hours now! I tell you, I don't feel easy.'

This uneasiness spread itself to me, and I helped to beat the pony.

When we came to the Canal Engineer's Rest House the Major called for The Boy's servant; but there was no answer. Then we went up to the house, calling for The Boy by name; but there was no answer.

'Oh, he's out shooting,' said I.

Just then I saw through one of the windows a little hurricane-lamp burning. This was at four in the afternoon. We both stopped dead in the veranda, holding our breath to catch every sound; and we heard, inside the room, the '*brr – brr – brr*' of a multitude of flies. The Major said nothing, but he took off his helmet and we entered very softly.

The Boy was dead on the bed in the centre of the bare, lime-washed room. He had shot his head nearly to pieces with his revolver. The gun-cases were still strapped, so was the bedding, and on the table lay The Boy's writing-case with photographs. He had gone away to die like a poisoned rat!

The Major said to himself softly, 'Poor Boy! Poor, *poor* devil!' Then he turned away from the bed and said, 'I want your help in this business.'

Knowing The Boy was dead by his own hand, I saw exactly what that help would be, so I passed over to the table, took a chair, lit a cheroot, and began to go through the writing-case; the Major looking over my shoulder and repeating to himself, 'We came too late! – Like a rat in a hole! – Poor, *poor* devil!'

The Boy must have spent half the night in writing to his people, to his Colonel, and to a girl at Home; and as soon as he had finished, must have shot himself, for he had been dead a long time when we came in.

I read all that he had written, and passed over each sheet to the Major as I finished it.

We saw from his accounts how very seriously he had taken everything. He wrote about 'disgrace which he was unable to bear' – 'indelible shame' – 'criminal folly' – 'wasted life', and so on; besides a lot of private things to his father and mother much too sacred to put into print. The letter to the girl at Home was the most pitiful of all, and I choked as I read it. The Major made no attempt to keep dry-eyed. I respected him for that. He read and rocked himself to and fro, and simply cried like a woman without caring to hide it. The letters were so dreary and hopeless and touching. We forgot all about The Boy's follies, and only thought of the poor Thing on the bed and the scrawled sheets in our hands. It was utterly impossible to let the letters go Home. They would have broken his father's heart and killed his mother after killing her belief in her son.

At last the Major dried his eyes openly, and said, 'Nice sort of thing to spring on an English family! What shall we do?'

I said, knowing what the Major had brought me out for, 'The Boy died of cholera. We were with him at the time. We can't commit ourselves to half-measures. Come along.'

Then began one of the most grimly comic scenes I have ever taken part in – the concoction of a big, written lie, bolstered with evidence to soothe The Boy's people at Home. I began the rough draft of the letter, the Major throwing in hints here and there while he gathered up all the stuff that The Boy had written and burnt it in the fireplace. It was a hot, still evening when we began, and the lamp burned very badly. In due course I made the draft to my satisfaction, setting forth how The Boy was the pattern of all virtues, beloved by his Regiment, with every promise of a great career before him, and so on; how we had helped him through the sickness – it was no time for little lies, you will understand – and how he had died without pain. I choked while I was putting down these things and thinking of the poor people who would read them. Then I laughed at the grotesqueness of the affair, and the laughter mixed itself up with the choke – and the Major said that we both wanted drinks.

I am afraid to say how much whisky we drank before the letter was finished. It had not the least effect on us. Then we took off The Boy's watch, locket, and ring.

Lastly, the Major said, 'We must send a lock of hair too. A woman values that.'

But there were reasons why we could not find a lock fit to send. The Boy was black-haired, and so was the Major, luckily. I cut off a piece of the Major's hair above the temple with a knife, and put it into the packet we were making. The laughing-fit and the chokes got hold of me again, and I had to stop. The Major was nearly as bad; and we both knew that the worst part of the work was to come.

We sealed up the packet, photographs, locket, seals, ring, letter, and lock of hair with The Boy's sealing-wax and The Boy's seal.

Then the Major said, 'For God's sake, let's get outside – away from the room – and think!'

We went outside, and walked on the banks of the Canal for an hour, eating and drinking what we had with us, until the moon rose. I know now exactly how a murderer feels. Finally, we forced ourselves back to the room with the lamp and the Other Thing in it, and began to take up the next piece of work. I am not going to write about this. It was too horrible. We burned the bedstead and dropped the ashes into the Canal; we took up the matting of the room and treated that in the same way. I went off to a village and borrowed two big hoes, – I did not want the villagers to help, – while the Major arranged – the other matters. It took us four hours' hard work to make the grave. As we worked, we argued out whether it was right to say as much as we remembered of the Burial of the Dead. We compromised things by saying the Lord's Prayer with a private unofficial prayer for the peace of the soul of The Boy. Then we filled in the grave and went into the veranda – not the house – to lie down to sleep. We were dead tired.

When we woke the Major said wearily, 'We can't go back till to-morrow. We must give him a decent time to die in. He died early *this* morning, remember. That seems more natural.' So the Major must have been lying awake all the time, thinking.

I said, 'Then why didn't we bring the body back to cantonments?'

The Major thought for a minute. 'Because the people bolted when they heard of the cholera. And the *ekka* has gone!'

That was strictly true. We had forgotten all about the *ekka*-pony, and he had gone home.

So we were left there alone, all that stifling day, in the Canal Rest House, testing and re-testing our story of The Boy's death to see if it was weak in any point. A native appeared in the afternoon, but we said that a Sahib was dead of cholera, and he ran away. As the dusk gathered, the Major told me all his fears about The Boy, and awful stories of suicide or nearly-carried-out suicide – tales that made one's hair crisp. He said that he himself had once gone into the same Valley of the Shadow as The Boy, when he was young and new to the country; so he understood how things fought together in The Boy's poor jumbled head. He also said that youngsters, in their repentant moments, consider their sins much more serious and ineffaceable than they really are. We talked together all through the evening and rehearsed the story of the death of The Boy. As soon as the moon was up, and The Boy, theoretically, just buried, we struck across country for the station. We walked from eight till six o'clock in the morning; but though we were dead tired, we did not forget to go to The Boy's rooms and put away his revolver with the proper amount of cartridges in the pouch. Also to set his writing-case on the table. We found the Colonel and reported the death, feeling more like murderers than ever. Then we went to bed and slept the clock round, for there was no more in us.

The tale had credence as long as was necessary; for every one forgot about The Boy before a fortnight was over. Many people, however, found time to say that the Major had behaved scandalously in not bringing in the body for a Regimental funeral. The saddest thing of all was the letter from The Boy's mother to the Major and me – with big inky blisters all over the sheet. She wrote the sweetest possible things about our great kindness, and the obligation she would be under to us as long as she lived.

All things considered, she was under an obligation, but not exactly as she meant.

False Dawn

> To-night, God knows what thing shall tide,
>   The Earth is racked and fain –
> Expectant, sleepless, open-eyed;
> And we, who from the Earth were made,
>   Thrill with our Mother's pain.
>
> In Durance

No man will ever know the exact truth of this story; though women may sometimes whisper it to one another after a dance, when they are putting up their hair for the night and comparing lists of victims. A man, of course, cannot assist at these functions. So the tale must be told from the outside – in the dark – all wrong.

Never praise a sister to a sister, in the hope of your compliments reaching the proper ears, and so preparing the way for you later on. Sisters are women first, and sisters afterwards; and you will find that you do yourself harm.

Saumarez knew this when he made up his mind to propose to the elder Miss Copleigh. Saumarez was a strange man, with few merits so far as men could see, though he was popular with women, and carried enough conceit to stock a Viceroy's Council and leave a little over for the Commander-in-Chief's Staff. He was a Civilian. Very many women took an interest

False Dawn

in Saumarez, perhaps because his manner to them was offensive. If you hit a pony over the nose at the outset of your acquaintance, he may not love you, but he will take a deep interest in your movements ever afterwards. The elder Miss Copleigh was nice, plump, winning, and pretty. The younger was not so pretty, and, from men disregarding the hint set forth above, her style was repellent and unattractive. Both girls had, practically, the same figure, and there was a strong likeness between them in look and voice; though no one could doubt for an instant which was the nicer of the two.

Saumarez made up his mind, as soon as they came into the station from Behar, to marry the elder one. At least, we all made sure that he would, which comes to the same thing. She was two-and-twenty, and he was thirty-three, with pay and allowances of nearly fourteen hundred rupees a month. So the match, as we arranged it, was in every way a good one. Saumarez was his name, and summary was his nature, as a man once said. Having drafted his Resolution, he formed a Select Committee of One to sit upon it, and resolved to take his time. In our unpleasant slang, the Copleigh girls 'hunted in couples'. That is to say, you could do nothing with one without the other. They were very loving sisters; but their mutual affection was sometimes inconvenient. Saumarez held the balance hair-true between them, and none but himself could have said to which side his heart inclined, though every one guessed. He rode with them a good deal and danced with them, but he never succeeded in detaching them from each other for any length of time.

Women said that the two girls kept together through deep

mistrust, each fearing that the other would steal a march on her. But that has nothing to do with a man. Saumarez was silent for good or bad, and as business-likely attentive as he could be, having due regard to his work and his polo. Beyond doubt both girls were fond of him.

As the hot weather drew nearer and Saumarez made no sign, women said that you could see their trouble in the eyes of the girls – that they were looking strained, anxious, and irritable. Men are quite blind in these matters unless they have more of the woman than the man in their composition; in which case it does not matter what they say or think. I maintain it was the hot April days that took the colour out of the Copleigh girls' cheeks. They should have been sent to the Hills early. No one – man or woman – feels an angel when the hot weather is approaching. The younger sister grew more cynical, not to say acid, in her ways; and the winningness of the elder wore thin. There was effort in it.

The station wherein all these things happened was, though not a little one, off the line of rail, and suffered through want of attention. There were no Gardens or bands or amusements worth speaking of, and it was nearly a day's journey to come into Lahore for a dance. People were grateful for small things to interest them.

About the beginning of May, and just before the final exodus of Hill-goers, when the weather was very hot and there were not more than twenty people in the station, Saumarez gave a moonlight riding-picnic at an old tomb, six miles away, near the bed of the river. It was a 'Noah's Ark' picnic; and there was to be the usual arrangement of quarter-mile intervals between each couple on account of

False Dawn

the dust. Six couples came altogether, including chaperons. Moonlight picnics are useful just at the very end of the season, before all the girls go away to the Hills. They lead to understandings, and should be encouraged by chaperons, especially those whose girls look sweetest in riding-habits. I knew a case once . . . But that is another story. That picnic was called the 'Great Pop Picnic', because every one knew Saumarez would propose then to the elder Miss Copleigh; and, besides his affair, there was another which might possibly come to happiness. The social atmosphere was heavily charged and wanted clearing.

We met at the parade-ground at ten. The night was fearfully hot. The horses sweated even at walking-pace, but anything was better than sitting still in our own dark houses. When we moved off under the full moon we were four couples, one triplet, and Me. Saumarez rode with the Copleigh girls, and I loitered at the tail of the procession wondering with whom Saumarez would ride home. Every one was happy and contented; but we all felt that things were going to happen. We rode slowly; and it was nearly midnight before we reached the old tomb, facing the ruined tank, in the decayed gardens where we were going to eat and drink. I was late in coming up; and, before I went into the garden, I saw that the horizon to the north carried a faint, dun-coloured feather. But no one would have thanked me for spoiling so well-managed an entertainment as this picnic – and a dust-storm, more or less, does no great harm.

We gathered by the tank. Some one had brought out a banjo – which is a most sentimental instrument – and three or four of us sang. You must not laugh at this. Our amusements in out-of-the-way stations are very few indeed. Then we talked in groups or together, lying under the trees, with the sun-baked roses dropping their petals on our feet, until supper was ready. It was a beautiful supper, as cold and as iced as you could wish; and we stayed long over it.

I had felt that the air was growing hotter and hotter; but nobody seemed to notice it until the moon went out and a burning hot wind began lashing the orange-trees with a sound like the noise of the sea. Before we knew where we were the dust-storm was on us, and everything was roaring, whirling darkness. The supper-table was blown bodily into the tank. We were afraid of staying anywhere near the old tomb for fear it might be blown down. So we felt our way to the orange-trees where the horses were picketed and waited for the storm to blow over. Then the little light that was left vanished, and you could not see your hand before your face. The air was heavy with dust and sand from the bed of the river, that filled boots and pockets, and drifted down necks, and coated eyebrows and moustaches. It was one of the worst dust-storms of the year. We were all huddled together close to the trembling horses, with the thunder chattering overhead, and the lightning spurting like water from a sluice, all ways at once. There was no danger, of course, unless the horses broke loose. I was standing with my head down wind and my hands over my mouth, hearing the trees thrashing each other. I could not see who was next me till the flashes came. Then I found that I was packed near Saumarez and the elder Miss Copleigh, with my own horse just in front of me. I recognized the elder Miss Copleigh, because she had a *pagri* round her helmet, and the younger

False Dawn

had not. All the electricity in the air had gone into my body, and I was quivering and tingling from head to foot – exactly as a corn shoots and tingles before rain. It was a grand storm. The wind seemed to be picking up the earth and pitching it to leeward in great heaps, and the heat beat up from the ground like the heat of the Day of Judgment.

The storm lulled slightly after the first half-hour, and I heard a despairing little voice close to my ear, saying to itself, quietly and softly, as if some lost soul were flying about with the wind, 'Oh, my God!' Then the younger Miss Copleigh stumbled into my arms, saying, 'Where is my horse? Get my horse. I want to go home. I want to go home. Take me home.'

I thought that the lightning and the black darkness had frightened her. So I said there was no danger, but she must wait till the storm blew over. She answered, 'It is not that! I want to go home! Oh, take me away from here!'

I said that she could not go till the light came; but I felt her brush past me and go away. It was too dark to see where. Then the whole sky was split open with one tremendous flash, as if the end of the world were coming, and all the women shrieked.

Almost directly after this I felt a man's hand on my shoulder, and heard Saumarez bellowing in my ear. Through the rattling of the trees and howling of the wind I did not catch his words at once, but at last I heard him say, 'I've proposed to the wrong one! What shall I do?' Saumarez had no occasion to make this confidence to me. I was never a friend of his, nor am I now; but I fancy neither of us were ourselves just then. He was shaking as he stood with excitement, and

I was feeling queer all over with the electricity. I could not think of anything to say except, 'More fool you for proposing in a dust-storm.' But I did not see how that would improve the mistake.

Then he shouted, 'Where's Edith – Edith Copleigh?' Edith was the younger sister. I answered out of my astonishment, 'What do you want with *her*?' For the next two minutes he and I were shouting at each other like maniacs, – he vowing that it was the younger sister he had meant to propose to all along, and I telling him, till my throat was hoarse, that he must have made a mistake! I cannot account for this except, again, by the fact that we were neither of us ourselves. Everything seemed to me like a bad dream – from the stamping of the horses in the darkness to Saumarez telling me the story of his loving Edith Copleigh from the first. He was still clawing my shoulder and begging me to tell him where Edith Copleigh was, when another lull came and brought light with it, and we saw the dust-cloud forming on the plain in front of us. So we knew the worst was over. The moon was low down, and there was just the glimmer of the false dawn that comes about an hour before the real one. But the light was very faint, and the dun cloud roared like a bull. I wondered where Edith Copleigh had gone; and as I was wondering I saw three things together: First, Maud Copleigh's face come smiling out of the darkness and move towards Saumarez who was standing by me. I heard the girl whisper, 'George,' and slide her arm through the arm that was not clawing my shoulder, and I saw that look on her face which only comes once or twice in a lifetime – when a woman is perfectly happy and the air is full of trumpets and

False Dawn

gorgeously-coloured fire, and the Earth turns into cloud because she loves and is loved. At the same time, I saw Saumarez's face as he heard Maud Copleigh's voice, and, fifty yards away from the clump of orange-trees, I saw a brown holland habit getting upon a horse.

It must have been my state of over-excitement that made me so ready to meddle with what did not concern me. Saumarez was moving off to the habit; but I pushed him back and said, 'Stop here and explain. I'll fetch her back!' And I ran out to get at my own horse. I had a perfectly unnecessary notion that everything must be done decently and in order, and that Saumarez's first care was to wipe the happy look out of Maud Copleigh's face. All the time I was linking up the curb-chain I wondered how he would do it.

I cantered after Edith Copleigh, thinking to bring her back slowly on some pretence or another. But she galloped away as soon as she saw me, and I was forced to ride after her in earnest. She called back over her shoulder, 'Go away! I'm going home. Oh, go away!' two or three times; but my business was to catch her first, and argue later. The ride fitted in with the rest of the evil dream. The ground was very rough, and now and again we rushed through the whirling, choking 'dust-devils' in the skirts of the flying storm. There was a burning hot wind blowing that brought up a stench of stale brick-kilns with it; and through the half-light and through the dust-devils, across that desolate plain, flickered the brown holland habit on the grey horse. She headed for the station at first. Then she wheeled round and set off for the river through beds of burnt-down jungle-grass, bad even to ride pig over. In cold blood I should never have dreamed of going over such a country at night, but it seemed quite right and natural with the lightning crackling overhead, and a reek like the smell of the Pit in my nostrils. I rode and shouted, and she bent forward and lashed her horse, and the aftermath of the dust-storm came up, and caught us both, and drove us down wind like pieces of paper.

I don't know how far we rode; but the drumming of the horse-hoofs and the roar of the wind and the race of the faint blood-red moon through the yellow mist seemed to have gone on for years and years, and I was literally drenched with sweat from my helmet to my gaiter when the grey stumbled, recovered himself, and pulled up dead lame. My brute was used up altogether. Edith Copleigh was bareheaded, plastered with dust, and crying bitterly. 'Why can't you let me alone?' she said. 'I only wanted to get away and go home. Oh, *please* let me go!'

'You have got to come back with me, Miss Copleigh. Saumarez has something to say to you.'

It was a foolish way of putting it; but I hardly knew Miss Copleigh, and, though I was playing Providence at the cost of my horse, I could not tell her in as many words what Saumarez had told me. I thought he could do that better himself. All her pretence about being tired and wanting to go home broke down, and she rocked herself to and fro in the saddle as she sobbed, and the hot wind blew her black hair to leeward. I am not going to repeat what she said, because she was utterly unstrung.

This was the cynical Miss Copleigh, and I, almost an utter stranger to her, was trying to tell her that Saumarez loved her, and she was to come back to hear him say so. I believe

False Dawn

I made myself understood, for she gathered the grey together and made him hobble somehow, and we set off for the tomb, while the storm went thundering down to Umballa and a few big drops of warm rain fell. I found out that she had been standing close to Saumarez when he proposed to her sister, and had wanted to go home to cry in peace, as an English girl should. She dabbed her eyes with her pocket-handkerchief as we went along, and babbled to me out of sheer lightness of heart and hysteria. That was perfectly unnatural; and yet it seemed all right at the time and in the place. All the world was only the two Copleigh girls, Saumarez, and I, ringed in with the lightning and the dark; and the guidance of this misguided world seemed to lie in my hands.

When we returned to the tomb in the deep, dead stillness that followed the storm, the dawn was just breaking and nobody had gone away. They were waiting for our return. Saumarez most of all. His face was white and drawn. As Miss Copleigh and I limped up, he came forward to meet us, and, when he helped her down from her saddle, he kissed her before all the picnic. It was like a scene in a theatre, and the likeness was heightened by all the dust-white, ghostly-looking men and women under the orange-trees clapping their hands – as if they were watching a play – at Saumarez's choice. I never knew anything so un-English in my life.

Lastly, Saumarez said we must all go home or the station would come out to look for us, and would I be good enough to ride home with Maud Copleigh? Nothing would give me greater pleasure, I said.

So we formed up, six couples in all, and went back two

by two; Saumarez walking at the side of Edith Copleigh, who was riding his horse. Maud Copleigh did not talk to me at any length.

The air was cleared; and, little by little, as the sun rose, I felt we were all dropping back again into ordinary men and women, and that the 'Great Pop Picnic' was a thing altogether a part and out of the world – never to happen again. It had gone with the dust-storm and the tingle in the hot air.

I felt tired and limp, and a good deal ashamed of myself, as I went in for a bath and some sleep.

There is a woman's version of this story, but it will never be written . . . unless Maud Copleigh cares to try.

In the House of Suddhoo

> A stone's throw out on either hand
> From that well-ordered road we tread,
>   And all the world is wild and strange:
> *Churel* and ghoul and *Djinn* and sprite
> Shall bear us company to-night,
> For we have reached the Oldest Land
>   Wherein the Powers of Darkness range.
>
>   *From the Dusk to the Dawn*

The house of Suddhoo, near the Taksali Gate, is two-storeyed, with four carved windows of old brown wood, and a flat roof. You may recognize it by five red hand-prints arranged like the Five of Diamonds on the whitewash between the upper windows. Bhagwan Dass the grocer and a man who says he gets his living by seal-cutting live in the lower storey with a troop of wives, servants, friends, and retainers. The two upper rooms used to be occupied by Janoo and Azizun, and a little black-and-tan terrier that was stolen from an Englishman's house and given to Janoo by a soldier. To-day, only Janoo lives in the upper rooms. Suddhoo sleeps on the roof generally, except when he sleeps in the street. He used to go to Peshawur in the cold weather to visit his son who sells curiosities near the Edwardes' Gate, and then he slept under a real mud roof. Suddhoo is a great friend of mine, because his cousin had a son who secured, thanks to my recommendation, the post of head-messenger to a big firm in the station. Suddhoo says that God will make me a Lieutenant-Governor one of these days. I daresay his prophecy will come true. He is very, very old, with white hair and no teeth worth showing, and he has outlived his wits – outlived nearly everything except his fondness for his son at Peshawur. Janoo and Azizun are Kashmiris, Ladies of the City, and theirs was an ancient and more or less honourable profession; but Azizun has since married a medical student from the North-West and has settled down to a most respectable life somewhere near Bareilly. Bhagwan Dass is an extortioner and an adulterator. He is very rich. The man who is supposed to get his living by seal-cutting pretends to be poor. This lets you know as much as is necessary of the four principal tenants in the house of Suddhoo. Then there is Me, of course; but I am only the chorus that comes in at the end to explain things. So I do not count.

Suddhoo was not clever. The man who pretended to cut seals was the cleverest of them all – Bhagwan Dass only knew how to lie – except Janoo. She was also beautiful, but that was her own affair.

Suddhoo's son at Peshawur was attacked by pleurisy, and old Suddhoo was troubled. The seal-cutter man heard of Suddhoo's anxiety and made capital out of it. He was abreast of the times. He got a friend in Peshawur to telegraph daily accounts of the son's health. And here the story begins.

Suddhoo's cousin's son told me, one evening, that Suddhoo wanted to see me; that he was too old and feeble

In the House of Suddhoo

to come personally, and that I should be conferring an everlasting honour on the House of Suddhoo if I went to him. I went; but I think, seeing how well off Suddhoo was then, that he might have sent something better than an *ekka*, which jolted fearfully, to haul out a future Lieutenant-Governor to the City on a muggy April evening. The *ekka* did not run quickly. It was full dark when we pulled up opposite the door of Ranjit Singh's Tomb near the main gate of the Fort. Here was Suddhoo, and he said that by reason of my condescension, it was absolutely certain that I should become a Lieutenant-Governor while my hair was yet black. Then we talked about the weather and the state of my health, and the wheat crops, for fifteen minutes, in the Huzuri Bagh, under the stars.

Suddhoo came to the point at last. He said that Janoo had told him that there was an order of the Sirkar against magic, because it was feared that magic might one day kill the Empress of India. I didn't know anything about the state of the law; but I fancied that something interesting was going to happen. I said that so far from magic being discouraged by the Government, it was highly commended. The greatest officials of the State practised it themselves. (If the Financial Statement isn't magic, I don't know what is.) Then, to encourage him further, I said that, if there was any *jadoo* afoot, I had not the least objection to giving it my countenance and sanction, and to seeing that it was clean *jadoo* – white magic, as distinguished from the unclean *jadoo* which kills folk. It took a long time before Suddhoo admitted that this was just what he had asked me to come for. Then he told me, in jerks and quavers, that the man who said he cut seals was a sorcerer of the cleanest kind; that every day he gave Suddhoo news of the sick son in Peshawur more quickly than the lightning could fly, and that this news was always corroborated by the letters. Further, that he had told Suddhoo how a great danger was threatening his son, which could be removed by clean *jadoo*; and, of course, heavy payment. I began to see exactly how the land lay, and told Suddhoo that I also understood a little *jadoo* in the Western line, and would go to his house to see that everything was done decently and in order. We set off together; and on the way Suddhoo told me that he had paid the seal-cutter between one hundred and two hundred rupees already; and the *jadoo* of that night would cost two hundred more. Which was cheap, he said, considering the greatness of his son's danger; but I do not think he meant it.

The lights were all cloaked in the front of the house when we arrived. I could hear awful noises from behind the seal-cutter's shop-front, as if some one were groaning his soul out. Suddhoo shook all over, and while we groped our way upstairs told me that the *jadoo* had begun. Janoo and Azizun met us at the stair-head, and told us that the *jadoo*-work was coming off in their rooms, because there was more space there. Janoo is a lady of a free-thinking turn of mind. She whispered that the *jadoo* was an invention to get money out of Suddhoo, and that the seal-cutter would go to a hot place when he died. Suddhoo was nearly crying with fear and old age. He kept walking up and down the room in the half-light, repeating his son's name over and over again, and asking Azizun if the seal-cutter ought not to make a reduction in the case of his own landlord. Janoo pulled me

In the House of Suddhoo

over to the shadow in the recess of the carved bow-windows. The boards were up, and the rooms were only lit by one tiny oil-lamp. There was no chance of my being seen if I stayed still.

Presently, the groans below ceased, and we heard steps on the staircase. That was the seal-cutter. He stopped outside the door as the terrier barked and Azizun fumbled at the chain, and he told Suddhoo to blow out the lamp. This left the place in jet darkness, except for the red glow from the two hookahs that belonged to Janoo and Azizun. The seal-cutter came in, and I heard Suddhoo throw himself down on the floor and groan. Azizun caught her breath, and Janoo backed on to one of the beds with a shudder. There was a clink of something metallic, and then shot up a pale blue-green flame near the ground. The light was just enough to show Azizun, pressed against one corner of the room with the terrier between her knees; Janoo, with her hands clasped, leaning forward as she sat on the bed; Suddhoo, face-down, quivering, and the seal-cutter.

I hope I may never see another man like that seal-cutter. He was stripped to the waist, with a wreath of white jasmine as thick as my wrist round his forehead, a salmon-coloured loin-cloth round his middle, and a steel bangle on each ankle. This was not awe-inspiring. It was the face of the man that turned me cold. It was blue-grey in the first place. In the second, the eyes were rolled back till you could see the whites of them; and, in the third, the face was the face of a demon – a ghoul – anything you please except of the sleek, oily old ruffian who sat in the daytime over his turning-lathe downstairs. He was lying on his stomach with his arms turned and crossed behind him, as if he had been thrown down pinioned. His head and neck were the only parts of him off the floor. They were nearly at right angles to the body, like the head of a cobra at spring. It was ghastly. In the centre of the room, on the bare earth floor, stood a big, deep, brass basin, with a pale blue-green light floating in the centre like a night-light. Round that basin the man on the floor wriggled himself three times. How he did it I do not know. I could see the muscles ripple along his spine and fall smooth again; but I could not see any other motion. The head seemed the only thing alive about him, except that slow curl and uncurl of the labouring back-muscles. Janoo from the bed was breathing seventy to the minute; Azizun held her hands before her eyes; and old Suddhoo, fingering at the dirt that had got into his white beard, was crying to himself. The horror of it was that the creeping, crawly thing made no sound – only crawled! And, remember, this lasted for ten minutes, while the terrier whined, and Azizun shuddered, and Janoo gasped, and Suddhoo cried!

I felt the hair lift at the back of my head, and my heart thump like a thermantidote-paddle. Luckily, the seal-cutter betrayed himself by his most impressive trick and made me calm again. After he had finished that unspeakable triple crawl, he stretched his head away from the floor as high as he could, and sent out a jet of fire from his nostrils. Now, I knew how fire-spouting is done – I can do it myself – so I felt at ease. The business was a fraud. If he had only kept to that crawl without trying to raise the effect, goodness knows what I might not have thought. Both the girls shrieked at the jet of fire, and the head dropped, chin down on the floor, with a thud; the whole body lying there like a corpse with its arms trussed. There was a pause of five full minutes after this, and the blue-green flame died down. Janoo stooped to settle one of her anklets, while Azizun turned her face to the wall and took the terrier in her arms. Suddhoo put out an arm mechanically to Janoo's hookah, and she slid it across the floor with her foot. Directly above the body and on the wall were a couple of flaming portraits, in stamped-paper frames, of the Queen and the Prince of Wales. They looked down on the performance, and, to my thinking, seemed to heighten the grotesqueness of it all.

Just when the silence was getting unendurable, the body turned over and rolled away from the basin to the side of the room, where it lay stomach-up. There was a faint 'plop' from the basin – exactly like the noise a fish makes when it takes a fly – and the green light in the centre revived.

I looked at the basin, and saw, bobbing in the water, the dried, shrivelled, black head of a native baby – open eyes, open mouth, and shaved scalp. It was worse, being so very sudden, than the crawling exhibition. We had no time to say anything before it began to speak.

Read Poe's account of the voice that came from the mesmerized dying man, and you will realize less than one-half of the horror of that head's voice.

There was an interval of a second or two between each word, and a sort of 'ring, ring, ring', in the note of the voice, like the timbre of a bell. It pealed slowly, as if talking to itself, for several minutes before I got rid of my cold sweat. Then the blessed solution struck me. I looked at the body lying near the doorway, and saw, just where the hollow of the throat joins on the shoulders, a muscle that had nothing to do with any man's regular breathing twitching away steadily. The whole thing was a careful reproduction of the Egyptian teraphim that one reads about sometimes; and the voice was as clever and as appalling a piece of ventriloquism as one could wish to hear. All this time the head was 'lip-lip-lapping' against the side of the basin, and speaking. It told Suddhoo, on his face again whining, of his son's illness and of the state of the illness up to the evening of that very night. I always shall respect the seal-cutter for keeping so faithfully to the time of the Peshawur telegrams. It went on to say that skilled doctors were night and day watching over the man's life; and that he would eventually recover if the fee to the potent sorcerer, whose servant was the head in the basin, were doubled.

Here the mistake from the artistic point of view came in. To ask for twice your stipulated fee in a voice that Lazarus might have used when he rose from the dead, is absurd. Janoo, who is really a woman of masculine intellect, saw this as quickly as I did. I heard her say, '*Asli nahin! Fareib!*' scornfully under her breath; and just as she said so, the light in the basin died out, the head stopped talking, and we heard the room door creak on its hinges. Then Janoo struck a match, lit the lamp, and we saw that the head, basin, and seal-cutter were gone. Suddhoo was wringing his hands, and explaining to anyone who cared to listen that, if his chances of eternal salvation depended on it, he could not raise another two hundred rupees. Azizun was nearly in hysterics in the corner; while Janoo sat down composedly on one of his beds to discuss the probabilities of the whole thing being a *bunao*, or 'make-up'.

I explained as much as I knew of the seal-cutter's way of

In the House of Suddhoo

jadoo; but her argument was much more simple. 'The magic that is always demanding gifts is no true magic,' said she. 'My mother told me that the only potent love-spells are those which are told you for love. This seal-cutter man is a liar and a devil. I dare not tell, do anything, or get anything done, because I am in debt to Bhagwan Dass the *bunnia* for two gold rings and a heavy anklet. I must get my food from his shop. The seal-cutter is the friend of Bhagwan Dass, and he would poison my food. A fool's *jadoo* has been going on for ten days, and has cost Suddhoo many rupees each night. The seal-cutter used black hens and lemons and charms before. He never showed us anything like this till to-night. Azizun is a fool, and will be a *purdah-nashin* soon. Suddhoo has lost his strength and lost his wits. See now! I had hoped to get from Suddhoo many rupees while he lived, and many more after his death; and behold, he is spending everything on that offspring of a devil and a she-ass, the seal-cutter!'

Here I said, 'But what induced Suddhoo to drag *me* into the business? Of course I can speak to the seal-cutter, and he shall refund. The whole thing is child's talk – shame – and senseless.'

'Suddhoo *is* an old child,' said Janoo. 'He has lived on the roofs these seventy years and is as senseless as a milch-goat. He brought you here to assure himself that he was not breaking any law of the Sirkar, whose salt he ate many years ago. He worships the dust off the feet of the seal-cutter, and that cow-devourer has forbidden him to go and see his son. What does Suddhoo know of your laws or the lightning-post? *I* have to watch his money going day by day to that lying beast below.'

Janoo stamped her foot on the floor and nearly cried with vexation; while Suddhoo was whimpering under a blanket in the corner, and Azizun was trying to guide the pipe-stem to his foolish old mouth.

Now, the case stands thus. Unthinkingly, I have laid myself open to the charge of aiding and abetting the seal-cutter in obtaining money under false pretences, which is forbidden by Section 420 of the Indian Penal Code. I am helpless in the matter for these reasons. I cannot inform the Police. What witnesses would support my statement? Janoo refuses flatly, and Azizun is a married woman somewhere near Bareilly – lost in this big India of ours. I dare not again take the law into my own hands, and speak to the seal-cutter; for certain am I that, not only would Suddhoo disbelieve me, but this step would end in the poisoning of Janoo, who is bound hand and foot by her debt to the *bunnia*. Suddhoo is an old dotard; and whenever we meet mumbles my idiotic joke that the Sirkar rather patronizes the Black Art than otherwise. His son is well now; but Suddhoo is completely under the influence of the seal-cutter, by whose advice he regulates the affairs of his life. Janoo watches daily the money that she hoped to wheedle out of Suddhoo taken by the seal-cutter and becomes daily more furious and sullen.

She will never tell, because she dare not; but, unless something happens to prevent her, I am afraid that the seal-cutter will die of cholera – the white arsenic kind – about the middle of May. And thus I shall be privy to a murder in the House of Suddhoo!

The Bisara of Pooree

> Little Blind Fish, thou art marvellous wise,
> Little Blind Fish, who put out thy eyes?
> Open thy ears while I whisper my wish –
> Bring me a lover, thou little Blind Fish.
>
> *The Charm of the Bisara*

Some natives say that it came from the other side of Kulu, where the eleven-inch Temple Sapphire is. Others that it was made at the Devil-Shrine of Ao-Chung in Tibet, was stolen by a Kafir, from him by a Gurkha, from him again by a Lahouli, from him by a *khitmutgar*, and by this latter sold to an Englishman, so all its virtue was lost; because, to work properly, the Bisara of Pooree must be stolen – with bloodshed if possible, but, at any rate, stolen.

These stories of the coming into India are all false. It was made at Pooree ages since – the manner of its making would fill a small book – was stolen by one of the Temple dancing-girls there, for her own purposes, and then passed on from hand to hand, steadily northward, till it reached Hanlé; always bearing the same name – the Bisara of Pooree. In shape it is a tiny square box of silver, studded outside with eight small balas-rubies. Inside the box, which opens with a spring, is a little eyeless fish, carved from some sort of dark, shiny nut and wrapped in a shred of faded gold cloth. That is the Bisara of Pooree, and it were better for a man to take a king-cobra in his hand than to touch the Bisara of Pooree.

All kinds of magic are out of date and done away with, except in India, where nothing changes in spite of the shiny, top-scum stuff that people call 'civilization'. Any man who know about the Bisara of Pooree will tell you what its powers are – always supposing that it has been honestly stolen. It is the only regularly working, trustworthy love-charm in the country, with one exception. (The other charm is in the hands of a trooper of the Nizam's Horse, at a place called Tuprani, due north of Hyderabad.) This can be depended upon for a fact. Some one else may explain it.

If the Bisara be not stolen, but given or bought or found, it turns against its owner in three years, and leads to ruin or death. This is another fact which you may explain when you have time. Meanwhile, you can laugh at it. At present the Bisara is safe on a hack-pony's neck, inside the blue bead-necklace that keeps off the Evil Eye. If the pony-driver ever finds it, and wears it, or gives it to his wife, I am sorry for him.

A very dirty Hill-coolie woman, with goitre, owned it at Theog in 1884. It came into Simla from the North before Churton's *khitmutgar* bought it, and sold it, for three times its silver-value, to Churton, who collected curiosities. The servant knew no more what he had bought than the master; but a man looking over Churton's collection of curiosities – Churton was an Assistant Commissioner, by the way – saw, and held his tongue. He was an Englishman, but

The Bisara of Pooree

knew how to believe. Which shows that he was different from most Englishmen. He knew that it was dangerous to have any share in the little box when working or dormant; for Love unsought is a terrible gift.

Pack – 'Grubby' Pack, as we used to call him – was, in every way, a nasty little man who must have crawled into the Army by mistake. He was three inches taller than his sword, but not half so strong. And the sword was a fifty-shilling, tailor-made one. Nobody liked him, and, I suppose, it was his wizenedness and worthlessness that made him fall so hopelessly in love with Miss Hollis, who was good and sweet, and five feet seven in her tennis-shoes. He was not content with falling in love quietly, but brought all the strength of his miserable little nature into the business. If he had not been so objectionable, one might have pitied him. He vapoured, and fretted, and fumed, and trotted up and down, and tried to make himself pleasing in Miss Hollis's big, quiet, grey eyes, and failed. It was one of the cases that you sometimes meet, even in our country, where we marry by Code, of a really blind attachment all on one side, without the faintest possibility of return. Miss Hollis looked on Pack as some sort of vermin running about the road. He had no prospects beyond Captain's pay, and no wits to help that out by one penny. In a large-sized man love like his would have been touching. In a good man it would have been grand. He being what he was, it was only a nuisance.

You will believe this much. What you will not believe is what follows: Churton, and The Man who Knew what the Bisara was, were lunching at the Simla Club together. Churton was complaining of life in general. His best mare had rolled out of stable down the cliff and had broken her back; his decisions were being reversed by the upper Courts more than an Assistant Commissioner of eight years' standing has a right to expect; he knew liver and fever, and for weeks past had felt out of sorts. Altogether, he was disgusted and disheartened.

Simla Club dining-room is built, as all the world knows, in two sections, with an arch-arrangement dividing them. Come in, turn to your own left, take the table under the window, and you cannot see any one who has come in, turned to the right, and taken a table on the right side of the arch. Curiously enough, every word that you say can be heard, not only by the other diner, but by the servants beyond the screen through which they bring dinner. This is worth knowing. An echoing-room is a trap to be forewarned against.

Half in fun, and half hoping to be believed, The Man who Knew told Churton the story of the Bisara of Pooree at rather greater length than I have told it to you in this place; winding up with a suggestion that Churton might as well throw the little box down the hill and see whether all his troubles would go with it. In ordinary ears, English ears, the tale was only an interesting bit of folklore. Churton laughed, said that he felt better for his tiffin, and went out. Pack had been tiffining by himself to the right of the arch, and had heard everything. He was nearly mad with his absurd infatuation for Miss Hollis, that all Simla had been laughing about.

It is a curious thing that, when a man hates or loves beyond reason, he is ready to go beyond reason to gratify

The Bisara of Pooree

his feelings; which he would not do for money or power merely. Depend upon it, Solomon would never have built altars to Ashtaroth and all those ladies with queer names, if there had not been trouble of some kind in his zenana, and nowhere else. But this is beside the story. The facts of the case are these: Pack called on Churton next day when Churton was out, left his card, and stole the Bisara of Pooree from its place under the clock on the mantelpiece! Stole it like the thief he was by nature! Three day later, all Simla was electrified by the news that Miss Hollis had accepted Pack – the shrivelled rat, Pack! Do you desire clearer evidence than this? The Bisara of Pooree had been stolen, and it worked as it had always done when won by foul means.

There are three or four times in a man's life when he is justified in meddling with other people's affairs to play Providence.

The Man who Knew felt that he was justified; but believing and acting on a belief are quite different things. The insolent satisfaction of Pack as he ambled by the side of Miss Hollis, and Churton's striking release from liver, as soon as the Bisara of Pooree had gone, decided The Man. He explained to Churton, and Churton laughed, because he was not brought up to believe that men on the Government House List steal – at least little things. But the miraculous acceptance by Miss Hollis of that tailor, Pack, decided him to take steps on suspicion. He vowed that he only wanted to find out where his ruby-studded silver box had vanished to. You cannot accuse a man on the Government House List of stealing; and if you rifle his room, you are a thief yourself. Churton, prompted by The Man who Knew, decided on burglary. If he found nothing in Pack's room . . . But it is not nice to think of what would have happened in that case.

Pack went to a dance at Benmore – Benmore was Benmore in those days, and not an office – and danced fifteen waltzes out of twenty-two with Miss Hollis. Churton and The Man took all the keys that they could lay hands on, and went to Pack's room in the hotel, certain that his servants would be away. Pack was a cheap soul. He had not purchased a decent cash-box to keep his papers in, but one of those native imitations that you buy for ten rupees. It opened to any sort of key, and there at the bottom, under Pack's Insurance Policy, lay the Bisara of Pooree!

Churton called Pack names, put the Bisara of Poore in his pocket, and went to the dance with The Man. At least, he came in time for supper, and saw the beginning of the end in Miss Hollis's eyes. She was hysterical after supper, and was taken away by her Mamma.

At the dance, with the abominable Bisara in his pocket, Churton twisted his foot on one of the steps leading down to the old Rink, and had to be sent home in a 'rickshaw, grumbling. He did not believe in the Bisara of Pooree any the more for this manifestation, but he sought out Pack and called him some ugly names; and 'thief' was the mildest of them. Pack took the names with the nervous smile of a little man who wants both soul and body to resent an insult, and went his way. There was no public scandal.

A week later Pack got his definite dismissal from Miss Hollis. There had been a mistake in the placing of her affections, she said. So he went away to Madras, where he can do no great harm even if he lives to be a Colonel.

Churton insisted upon The Man who Knew taking the Bisara of Pooree as a gift. The Man took it, went down to the Cart-Road at once, found a cart-pony with a blue bead-necklace, fastened the Bisara of Pooree inside the necklace with a piece of shoe-string and thanked Heaven that he was rid of a danger. Remember, in case you ever find it, that you must not destroy the Bisara of Pooree. I have not time to explain why just now, but the power lies in the little wooden fish. Mr Gubernatis or Max Müller could tell you more about it than I.

You will say that all this story is made up. Very well. If ever you come across a little, silver, ruby-studded box, seven-eighths of an inch long by three-quarters wide, with a dark-brown wooden fish, wrapped in gold cloth, inside it, keep it. Keep it for three years, and then you will discover for yourself whether my story is true or false.

Better still, steal it as Pack did, and you will be sorry that you had not killed yourself in the beginning.

The Gate of the Hundred Sorrows

If I can attain Heaven for a pice, why should you be envious?
Opium Smoker's Proverb

This is no work of mine. My friend, Gabral Misquitta, the half-caste, spoke it all, between moonset and morning, six weeks before he died; and I took it down from his mouth as he answered my questions. So: –

It lies between the Coppersmith's Gully and the pipe-stem sellers' quarter, within a hundred yards, too, as the crow flies, of the Mosque of Wazir Khan. I don't mind telling any one this much, but I defy him to find the Gate, however well he may think he knows the City. You might even go through the very gully it stands in a hundred times, and be none the wiser. We used to call the gully 'The Gully of the Black Smoke', but its native name is altogether different, of course. A loaded donkey couldn't pass between the walls; and, at one point, just before you reach the Gate, a bulged house-front makes people go along all sideways.

It isn't really a gate, though. It's a house. Old Fung-Tching had it first five years ago. He was a boot-maker in Calcutta. They say that he murdered his wife there when he was drunk. That was why he dropped bazar-rum and took to the Black Smoke instead. Later on, he came up north and opened the

The Gate of the Hundred Sorrows

Gate as a house where you could get your smoke in peace and quiet. Mind you, it was a *pukka*, respectable opium-house, and not one of those stifling, sweltering *chandoo-khanas* that you can find all over the City. No; the old man knew his business thoroughly, and he was most clean for a Chinaman. He was a one-eyed little chap, not much more than five feet high, and both his middle fingers were gone. All the same, he was the handiest man at rolling black pills I have ever seen. Never seemed to be touched by the Smoke, either; and what he took day and night, night and day, was a caution. I've been at it five years, and I can do my fair share of the Smoke with any one; but I was a child to Fung-Tching that way. All the same, the old man was keen on his money; very keen; and that's what I can't understand. I heard he saved a good deal before he died, but his nephew has got all that now; and the old man's gone back to China to be buried.

He kept the big upper room, where his best customers gathered, as neat as a new pin. In one corner used to stand Fung-Tching's Joss – almost as ugly as Fung-Tching – and there were always sticks burning under his nose; but you never smelt 'em when the pipes were going thick. Opposite the Joss was Fung-Tching's coffin. He had spent a good deal of his savings on that, and whenever a new man came to the Gate he was always introduced to it. It was lacquered black, with red and gold writings on it, and I've heard that Fung-Tching brought it out all the way from China. I don't know whether that's true or not, but I know that, if I came first in the evening, I used to spread my mat just at the foot of it. It was a quiet corner, you see, and a sort of breeze from the gully came in at the window now and then. Besides the mats, there was no other furniture in the room – only the coffin, and the old Joss all green and blue and purple with age and polish.

Fung-Tching never told us why he called the place 'The Gate of the Hundred Sorrows'. (He was the only Chinaman I know who used bad-sounding fancy names. Most of them are flowery. As you'll see in Calcutta.) We used to find that out for ourselves. Nothing grows on you so much, if you're white, as the Black Smoke. A yellow man is made different. Opium doesn't tell on him scarcely at all; but white and black suffer a good deal. Of course, there are some people that the Smoke doesn't touch any more than tobacco would at first. They just doze a bit, as one would fall asleep naturally, and next morning they are almost fit for work. Now, I was one of that sort when I began, but I've been at it for five years pretty steadily, and it's different now. There was an old aunt of mine, down Agra way, and she left me a little at her death. About sixty rupees a month secured. Sixty isn't much. I can recollect a time, seems hundreds and hundreds of years ago, that I was getting my three hundred a month, and pickings, when I was working on a big timber-contract in Calcutta.

I didn't stick to that work for long. The Black Smoke does not allow of much other business; and even though I am very little affected by it, as men go, I couldn't do a day's work now to save my life. After all, sixty rupees is what I want. When old Fung-Tching was alive he used to draw the money for me, give me about half of it to live on (I eat very little), and the rest he kept himself. I was free of the Gate at any time of the day and night, and could smoke and sleep there

The Gate of the Hundred Sorrows

when I liked; so I didn't care. I know the old man made a good thing out of it; but that's no matter. Nothing matters much to me; and besides, the money always came fresh and fresh each month.

There was ten of us met at the Gate when the place was first opened. Me, and two Babus from a Government Office somewhere in Anarkulli, but they got the sack and couldn't pay (no man who has to work in the daylight can do the Black Smoke for any length of time straight on); a Chinaman that was Fung-Tching's nephew; a bazar-woman that had got a lot of money somehow; an English loafer – MacSomebody, I think, but I have forgotten, – that smoked heaps, but never seemed to pay anything (they said he had saved Fung-Tching's life at some trial in Calcutta when he was barrister); another Eurasian, like myself, from Madras; a half-caste woman, and a couple of men who said they had come from the North. I think they must have been Persians or Afghans or something. There are not more than five of us living now, but we come regular. I don't know what happened to the Babus; but the bazar-woman, she died after six months of the Gate, and I think Fung-Tching took her bangles and nose-ring for himself. But I'm not certain. The Englishman, he drank as well as smoked, and he dropped off. One of the Persians got killed in a row at night by the big well near the mosque a long time ago, and the Police shut up the well, because they said it was full of foul air. They found him dead at the bottom of it. So, you see, there is only me, the Chinaman, the half-caste woman that we call the Memsahib (she used to live with Fung-Tching), the other Eurasian, and one of the Persians. The Memsahib looks very old now. I think she was

Rudyard Kipling

a young woman when the Gate was opened; but we are all old for the matter of that. Hundreds and hundreds of years old. It's very hard to keep count of time in the Gate, and, besides, time doesn't matter to me. I draw my sixty rupees fresh and fresh every month. A very, very long while ago, when I used to be getting three hundred and fifty rupees a month, and pickings, on a big timber-contract at Calcutta, I had a wife of sorts. But she's dead now. People said that I killed her by taking to the Black Smoke. Perhaps I did, but it's so long since that it doesn't matter. Sometimes, when I first came to the Gate, I used to feel sorry for it; but that's all over and done with long ago, and I draw my sixty rupees fresh and fresh every month, and am quite happy. Not *drunk* happy, you know, but always quiet and soothed and contented.

How did I take to it? It began at Calcutta. I used to try it in my own house, just to see what it was like. I never went very far, but I think my wife must have died then. Anyhow, I found myself here, and got to know Fung-Tching. I don't remember rightly how that came about; but he told me of the Gate and I used to go there, and, somehow, I have never got away from it since. Mind you, though, the Gate was a respectable place in Fung-Tching's time, where you could be comfortable, and not at all like the *chandoo-khanas* where the niggers go. No; it was clean, and quiet, and not crowded. Of course, there were others besides us ten and the man; but we always had a mat apiece, with a wadded woollen headpiece, all covered with black and red dragons and things, just like the coffin in the corner.

At the end of one's third pipe the dragons used to move

The Gate of the Hundred Sorrows

about and fight. I've watched 'em many and many a night through. I used to regulate my Smoke that way, and now it takes a dozen pipes to make 'em stir. Besides, they are all torn and dirty, like the mats, and old Fung-Tching is dead. He died a couple of years ago, and gave me the pipe I always use now – a silver one, with queer beasts crawling up and down the receiver-bottle below the cup. Before that, I think, I used a big bamboo stem with a copper cup, a very small one, and a green jade mouthpiece. It was a little thicker than a walking-stick stem, and smoked sweet, very sweet. The bamboo seemed to suck up the smoke. Silver doesn't, and I've got to clean it out now and then; that's a great deal of trouble, but I smoke it for the old man's sake. He must have made a good thing out of me, but he always gave me clean mats and pillows, and the best stuff you could get anywhere.

When he died, his nephew Tsin-ling took up the Gate, and he called it the 'Temple of the Three Possessions', but we old ones speak of it as the 'Hundred Sorrows', all the same. The nephew does things very shabbily, and I think the Memsahib must help him. She lives with him; same as she used to do with the old man. The two let in all sorts of low people, niggers and all, and the Black Smoke isn't as good as it used to be. I've found burnt bran in my pipe over and over again. The old man would have died if that had happened in his time. Besides, the room is never cleaned, and all the mats are torn and cut at the edges. The coffin is gone – gone to China again – with the old man and two ounces of Smoke inside it, in case he should want 'em on the way.

The Joss doesn't get so many sticks burnt under his nose

as he used to. That's a sign of ill-luck, as sure as death. He's all brown, too, and no one ever attends to him. That's the Memsahib's work, I know; because, when Tsin-ling tried to burn gilt paper before him, she said it was a waste of money, and, if he kept a stick burning very slowly, the Joss wouldn't know the difference. So now we've got the sticks mixed with a lot of glue, and they take half an hour longer to burn, and smell stinky. Let alone the smell of the room by itself. No business can get on if they try that sort of thing. The Joss doesn't like it. I can see that. Late at night, sometimes, he turns all sorts of queer colours – blue and green and red – just as he used to do when old Fung-Tching was alive; and he rolls his eyes and stamps his feet like a devil.

I don't know why I don't leave the place and smoke quietly in a little room of my own in the bazar. Most like, Tsin-ling would kill me if I went away – he draws my sixty rupees now – and besides, it's too much trouble, and I've grown to be very fond of the Gate. It's not much to look at. Not what it was in the old man's time, but I couldn't leave it. I've seen so many come in and out. And I've seen so many die here on the mats that I should be afraid of dying in the open now. I've seen some things that people would call strange enough; but nothing is strange when you're on the Black Smoke, except the Black Smoke. And if it was, it wouldn't matter.

Fung-Tching used to be very particular about his people, and never got in any one who'd give trouble by dying messy and such. But the nephew isn't half so careful. He tells everywhere that he keeps a 'first-chop' house. Never tries to get men in quietly, and make them comfortable like Fung-Tching did. That's why the Gate is getting a little bit more known than it used to be. Among the niggers of course. The nephew daren't get a white, or, for matter of that, a mixed skin into the place. He has to keep us three, of course – me and the Memsahib and the other Eurasian. We're fixtures. But he wouldn't give us credit for a pipeful – not for anything.

One of these days, I hope, I shall die in the Gate. The Persian and the Madras man are terribly shaky now. They've got a boy to light their pipes for them. I always do that myself. Most like, I shall see them carried out before me. I don't think I shall ever outlive the Memsahib or Tsin-ling. Women last longer than men at the Black Smoke, and Tsin-ling has a deal of the old man's blood in him, though he does smoke cheap stuff. The bazar-woman knew when she was going two days before her time; and she died on a clean mat with a nicely-wadded pillow, and the old man hung up her pipe just above the Joss. He was always fond of her, I fancy. But he took her bangles just the same.

I should like to die like the bazar-woman – on a clean, cool mat with a pipe of good stuff between my lips. When I feel I'm going, I shall ask Tsin-ling for them, and he can draw my sixty rupees a month, fresh and fresh, as long as he pleases. Then I shall lie back, quiet and comfortable, and watch the black and red dragons have their last big fight together; and then . . .

Well, it doesn't matter. Nothing matters much to me – only I wish Tsin-ling wouldn't put bran into the Black Smoke.

The Story of Muhammad Din

Who is the happy man? He that sees, in his own house at home, little children crowned with dust, leaping and falling and crying.

Munichandra, translated by Professor Peterson

The polo-ball was an old one, scarred, chipped, and dinted. It stood on the mantelpiece among the pipe-stems which Imam Din, *khitmutgar*, was cleaning for me.

'Does the Heaven-born want this ball?' said Imam Din deferentially.

The Heaven-born set no particular store by it; but of what use was a polo-ball to a *khitmutgar*?

'By Your Honour's favour, I have a little son. He has seen this ball, and desires it to play with. I do not want it for myself.'

No one would for an instant accuse portly old Imam Din of wanting to play with polo-balls. He carried out the battered thing into the veranda; and there followed a hurricane of joyful squeaks, a patter of small feet, and the *thud-thud-thud* of the ball rolling along the ground. Evidently the little son had been waiting outside the door to secure his treasure. But how had he managed to see that polo-ball?

The Story of Muhammad Din

Next day, coming back from office half an hour earlier than usual, I was aware of a small figure in the dining-room – a tiny, plump figure in a ridiculously inadequate shirt which came, perhaps, half-way down the tubby stomach. It wandered round the room, thumb in mouth, crooning to itself as it took stock of the pictures. Undoubtedly this was the 'little son'.

He had no business in my room, of course; but was so deeply absorbed in his discoveries that he never noticed me in the doorway. I stepped into the room and startled him nearly into a fit. He sat down on the ground with a gasp. His eyes opened, and his mouth followed suit. I knew what was coming, and fled, followed by a long, dry howl which reached the servants' quarters far more quickly than any command of mine had ever done. In ten seconds Imam Din was in the dining-room. Then despairing sobs arose, and I returned to find Imam Din admonishing the small sinner, who was using most of his shirt as a handkerchief.

'This boy,' said Imam Din judicially, 'is a *budmash* – a big *budmash*. He will, without doubt, go to the *jail-khana* for his behaviour.' Renewed yells from the penitent, and an elaborate apology to myself from Imam Din.

'Tell the baby,' said I, 'that the Sahib is not angry, and take him away.' Imam Din conveyed my forgiveness to the offender, who had now gathered all his shirt round his neck, stringwise, and the yell subsided into a sob. The two set off for the door. 'His name,' said Imam Din, as though the name were part of the crime, 'is Muhammad Din, and he is a *budmash*.' Freed from present danger, Muhammad Din turned

49

round in his father's arms, and said gravely, 'It is true that my name is Muhammad Din, Tahib, but I am not a *budmash*. I am a *man*!'

From that day dated my acquaintance with Muhammad Din. Never again did he come into my dining-room, but on the neutral ground of the garden we greeted each other with much state, though our conversation was confined to 'Talaam, Tahib' from his side, and 'Salaam, Muhammad Din' from mine. Daily on my return from office, the little white shirt and the fat little body used to rise from the shade of the creeper-covered trellis where they had been hid; and daily I checked my horse here, that my salutation might not be slurred over or given unseemly.

Muhammad Din never had any companions. He used to trot about the compound, in and out of the castor-oil bushes, on mysterious errands of his own. One day I stumbled upon some of his handiwork far down the grounds. He had half buried the polo-ball in dust, and stuck six shrivelled old marigold flowers in a circle round it. Outside that circle again was a rude square, traced out in bits of red brick alternating with fragments of broken china; the whole bounded by a little bank of dust. The water-man from the well-curb put in a plea for the small architect, saying that it was only the play of a baby and did not much disfigure my garden.

Heaven knows that I had no intention of touching the child's work then or later; but that evening, a stroll through the garden brought me unawares full on it; so that I trampled, before I knew, marigold-heads, dust-bank, and fragments of broken soap-dish into confusion past all hope of mending. Next morning, I came upon Muhammad Din

The Story of Muhammad Din

crying softly to himself over the ruin I had wrought. Some one had cruelly told him that the Sahib was very angry with him for spoiling the garden, and had scattered his rubbish, using bad language the while. Muhammad Din laboured for an hour at effacing every trace of the dusk-bank and pottery fragments, and it was with a tearful and apologetic face that he said, 'Talaam, Tahib,' when I came home from office. A hasty inquiry resulted in Imam Din informing Muhammad Din that, by my singular favour, he was permitted to disport himself as he pleased. Whereat the child took heart and fell to tracing the ground-plan of an edifice which was to eclipse the marigold-polo-ball creation.

For some months the chubby little eccentricity revolved in his humble orbit among the castor-oil bushes and in the dust; always fashioning magnificent palaces from stale flowers thrown away by the bearer, smooth water-worn pebbles, bits of broken glass, and feathers pulled, I fancy, from my fowls – always alone, and always crooning to himself.

A gaily-spotted sea-shell was dropped one day close to the last of his little buildings; and I looked that Muhammad Din should build something more than ordinarily splendid on the strength of it. Nor was I disappointed. He meditated for the better part of an hour, and his crooning rose to a jubilant song. Then he began tracing in the dust. It would certainly be a wondrous palace, this one, for it was two yards long and a yard broad in ground-plan. But the palace was never completed.

Next day there was no Muhammad Din at the head of the carriage-drive, and no 'Talaam, Tahib' to welcome my return. I had grown accustomed to the greeting, and its omission troubled me. Next day Imam Din told me that the child was suffering slightly from fever and needed quinine. He got the medicine, and an English Doctor.

'They have no stamina, these brats,' said the Doctor, as he left Imam Din's quarters.

A week later, though I would have given much to have avoided it, I met on the road to the Mussulman burying-ground Imam Din, accompanied by one other friend, carrying in his arms, wrapped in a white cloth, all that was left of little Muhammad Din.

1. BOCCACCIO · *Mrs Rosie and the Priest*
2. GERARD MANLEY HOPKINS · *As kingfishers catch fire*
3. *The Saga of Gunnlaug Serpent-tongue*
4. THOMAS DE QUINCEY · *On Murder Considered as One of the Fine Arts*
5. FRIEDRICH NIETZSCHE · *Aphorisms on Love and Hate*
6. JOHN RUSKIN · *Traffic*
7. PU SONGLING · *Wailing Ghosts*
8. JONATHAN SWIFT · *A Modest Proposal*
9. *Three Tang Dynasty Poets*
10. WALT WHITMAN · *On the Beach at Night Alone*
11. KENKŌ · *A Cup of Sake Beneath the Cherry Trees*
12. BALTASAR GRACIÁN · *How to Use Your Enemies*
13. JOHN KEATS · *The Eve of St Agnes*
14. THOMAS HARDY · *Woman much missed*
15. GUY DE MAUPASSANT · *Femme Fatale*
16. MARCO POLO · *Travels in the Land of Serpents and Pearls*
17. SUETONIUS · *Caligula*
18. APOLLONIUS OF RHODES · *Jason and Medea*
19. ROBERT LOUIS STEVENSON · *Olalla*
20. KARL MARX AND FRIEDRICH ENGELS · *The Communist Manifesto*
21. PETRONIUS · *Trimalchio's Feast*
22. JOHANN PETER HEBEL · *How a Ghastly Story Was Brought to Light by a Common or Garden Butcher's Dog*
23. HANS CHRISTIAN ANDERSEN · *The Tinder Box*
24. RUDYARD KIPLING · *The Gate of the Hundred Sorrows*
25. DANTE · *Circles of Hell*
26. HENRY MAYHEW · *Of Street Piemen*
27. HAFEZ · *The nightingales are drunk*
28. GEOFFREY CHAUCER · *The Wife of Bath*
29. MICHEL DE MONTAIGNE · *How We Weep and Laugh at the Same Thing*
30. THOMAS NASHE · *The Terrors of the Night*
31. EDGAR ALLAN POE · *The Tell-Tale Heart*
32. MARY KINGSLEY · *A Hippo Banquet*
33. JANE AUSTEN · *The Beautifull Cassandra*
34. ANTON CHEKHOV · *Gooseberries*
35. SAMUEL TAYLOR COLERIDGE · *Well, they are gone, and here must I remain*
36. JOHANN WOLFGANG VON GOETHE · *Sketchy, Doubtful, Incomplete Jottings*
37. CHARLES DICKENS · *The Great Winglebury Duel*
38. HERMAN MELVILLE · *The Maldive Shark*
39. ELIZABETH GASKELL · *The Old Nurse's Story*
40. NIKOLAY LESKOV · *The Steel Flea*

41. HONORÉ DE BALZAC · *The Atheist's Mass*
42. CHARLOTTE PERKINS GILMAN · *The Yellow Wall-Paper*
43. C.P. CAVAFY · *Remember, Body . . .*
44. FYODOR DOSTOEVSKY · *The Meek One*
45. GUSTAVE FLAUBERT · *A Simple Heart*
46. NIKOLAI GOGOL · *The Nose*
47. SAMUEL PEPYS · *The Great Fire of London*
48. EDITH WHARTON · *The Reckoning*
49. HENRY JAMES · *The Figure in the Carpet*
50. WILFRED OWEN · *Anthem For Doomed Youth*
51. WOLFGANG AMADEUS MOZART · *My Dearest Father*
52. PLATO · *Socrates' Defence*
53. CHRISTINA ROSSETTI · *Goblin Market*
54. *Sindbad the Sailor*
55. SOPHOCLES · *Antigone*
56. RYŪNOSUKE AKUTAGAWA · *The Life of a Stupid Man*
57. LEO TOLSTOY · *How Much Land Does A Man Need?*
58. GIORGIO VASARI · *Leonardo da Vinci*
59. OSCAR WILDE · *Lord Arthur Savile's Crime*
60. SHEN FU · *The Old Man of the Moon*
61. AESOP · *The Dolphins, the Whales and the Gudgeon*
62. MATSUO BASHŌ · *Lips too Chilled*
63. EMILY BRONTË · *The Night is Darkening Round Me*
64. JOSEPH CONRAD · *To-morrow*
65. RICHARD HAKLUYT · *The Voyage of Sir Francis Drake Around the Whole Globe*
66. KATE CHOPIN · *A Pair of Silk Stockings*
67. CHARLES DARWIN · *It was snowing butterflies*
68. BROTHERS GRIMM · *The Robber Bridegroom*
69. CATULLUS · *I Hate and I Love*
70. HOMER · *Circe and the Cyclops*
71. D. H. LAWRENCE · *Il Duro*
72. KATHERINE MANSFIELD · *Miss Brill*
73. OVID · *The Fall of Icarus*
74. SAPPHO · *Come Close*
75. IVAN TURGENEV · *Kasyan from the Beautiful Lands*
76. VIRGIL · *O Cruel Alexis*
77. H. G. WELLS · *A Slip under the Microscope*
78. HERODOTUS · *The Madness of Cambyses*
79. *Speaking of Siva*
80. *The Dhammapada*

'I truly thought I'd never make it back.'

DANTE ALIGHIERI
Born 1265, Florence, Italy
Died 1321, Ravenna, Italy

Dante wrote the *Divina Commedia* between 1308 and 1321.
This selection of cantos is taken from *Inferno* translated by
Robin Kirkpatrick, Penguin Classics, 2006.

DANTE IN PENGUIN CLASSICS
Inferno
Purgatorio
Paradiso
The Divine Comedy
Vita Nuova

DANTE ALIGHIERI

Circles of Hell

Translated by
Robin Kirkpatrick

PENGUIN BOOKS

PENGUIN CLASSICS

UK | USA | Canada | Ireland | Australia
India | New Zealand | South Africa

Penguin Books is part of the Penguin Random House group of companies
whose addresses can be found at global.penguinrandomhouse.com.

This selection published in Penguin Classics 2015

012

Translation copyright © Robin Kirkpatrick, 2006

The moral right of the translator has been asserted

Set in 9/12.4 pt Baskerville 10 Pro
Typeset by Jouve (UK), Milton Keynes
Printed and bound in Great Britain by Clays Ltd, Elcograf S.p.A.

A CIP catalogue record for this book is available from the British Library

ISBN: 978-0-141-98022-5

www.greenpenguin.co.uk

Penguin Random House is committed to a
sustainable future for our business, our readers
and our planet. This book is made from Forest
Stewardship Council® certified paper.

Contents

Canto III – Gates of Hell	1
Canto V – The lustful	6
Canto VI – The gluttonous	11
Canto VIII – The wrathful and the melancholic	15
Canto XIII – The violent against self	20
Canto XVII – Passage to the Eighth Circle	26
Canto XIX – Simonists	31
Canto XXIV – Thieves	36
Canto XXXIII – Traitors to nation and traitors to guests	42
Canto XXXIV – Traitors to benefactors	48

Canto III

GATES OF HELL

'Through me you go to the grief-wracked city.
Through me to everlasting pain you go.
Through me you go and pass among lost souls.
   Justice inspired my exalted Creator.
I am a creature of the Holiest Power,
of Wisdom in the Highest and of Primal Love.
   Nothing till I was made was made, only
eternal beings. And I endure eternally.
Surrender as you enter every hope you have.'
   These were the words that – written in dark tones –
I saw there, on the summit of a door.
I turned: 'Their meaning, sir, for me is hard.'
   And he in answering (as though he understood):
'You needs must here surrender all your doubts.
All taint of cowardice must here be dead.
   We now have come where, as I have said, you'll see
in suffering the souls of those who've lost
the good that intellect desires to win.'
   And then he placed his hand around my own,
he smiled, to give me some encouragement,
and set me on to enter secret things.
   Sighing, sobbing, moans and plaintive wailing
all echoed here through air where no star shone,
and I, as this began, began to weep.

Discordant tongues, harsh accents of horror,
tormented words, the twang of rage, strident
voices, the sound, as well, of smacking hands,

together these all stirred a storm that swirled
for ever in the darkened air where no time was,
as sand swept up in breathing spires of wind.

I turned, my head tight-bound in confusion,
to say to my master: 'What is it that I hear?
Who can these be, so overwhelmed by pain?'

'This baleful condition,' he said, 'is one
that grips those souls whose lives, contemptibly,
were void alike of honour and ill fame.

These all co-mingle with a noisome choir
of angels who – not rebels, yet not true
to God – existed for themselves alone.

To keep their beauty whole, the Heavens spurned them.
Nor would the depths of Hell receive them in,
lest truly wicked souls boast over them.'

And I: 'What can it be, so harsh, so heavy,
that draws such loud lamentings from these crowds?'
And he replied: 'My answer can be brief:

These have no hope that death will ever come.
And so degraded is the life they lead
all look with envy on all other fates.

The world allows no glory to their name.
Mercy and Justice alike despise them.
Let us not speak of them. Look, then pass on.'

I did look, intently. I saw a banner
running so rapidly, whirling forwards,
that nothing, it seemed, would ever grant a pause.

Canto III

Drawn by that banner was so long a trail
of men and women I should not have thought
that death could ever have unmade so many.

A few I recognized. And then I saw –
and knew beyond all doubt – the shadow of the one
who made, from cowardice, the great denial.

So I, at that instant, was wholly sure
this congregation was that worthless mob
loathsome alike to God and their own enemies.

These wretched souls were never truly live.
They now went naked and were sharply spurred
by wasps and hornets, thriving all around.

The insects streaked the face of each with blood.
Mixing with tears, the lines ran down; and then
were garnered at their feet by filthy worms.

And when I'd got myself to look beyond,
others, I saw, were ranged along the bank
of some great stream. 'Allow me, sir,' I said,

'to know who these might be. What drives them on,
and makes them all (as far, in this weak light,
as I discern) so eager for the crossing?'

'That will, of course, be clear to you,' he said,
'when once our footsteps are set firm upon
the melancholic shores of Acheron.'

At this – ashamed, my eyes cast humbly down,
fearing my words had weighed on him too hard –
I held my tongue until we reached the stream.

Look now! Towards us in a boat there came
an old man, yelling, hair all white and aged,
'Degenerates! Your fate is sealed! Cry woe!

Don't hope you'll ever see the skies again!
I'm here to lead you to the farther shore,
into eternal shadow, heat and chill.

And you there! You! Yes, you, the living soul!
Get right away from this gang! These are dead.'
But then, on seeing that I did not move:

'You will arrive by other paths and ports.
You'll start your journey from a different beach.
A lighter hull must carry you across.'

'Charon,' my leader, 'don't torment yourself.
For this is willed where all is possible
that is willed there. And so demand no more.'

The fleecy wattles of the ferry man –
who plied across the liverish swamp, eyeballs
encircled by two wheels of flame – fell mute.

But not the other souls. Naked and drained,
their complexions changed. Their teeth began
(hearing his raw command) to gnash and grind.

They raged, blaspheming God and their own kin,
the human race, the place and time, the seed
from which they'd sprung, the day that they'd been born.

And then they came together all as one,
wailing aloud along the evil margin
that waits for all who have no fear of God.

Charon the demon, with his hot-coal eyes,
glared what he meant to do. He swept all in.
He struck at any dawdler with his oar.

In autumn, leaves are lifted, one by one,
away until the branch looks down and sees
its tatters all arrayed upon the ground.

Canto III

    In that same way did Adam's evil seed
hurtle, in sequence, from the river rim,
as birds that answer to their handler's call.

    Then off they went, to cross the darkened flood.
And, long before they'd landed over there,
another flock assembled in their stead.

    Attentively, my master said: 'All those,
dear son, who perish in the wrath of God,
meet on this shore, wherever they were born.

    And they are eager to be shipped across.
Justice of God so spurs them all ahead
that fear in them becomes that sharp desire.

    But no good soul will ever leave from here.
And so when Charon thus complains of you,
you may well grasp the sense that sounds within.'

    His words now done, the desolate terrain
trembled with such great violence that the thought
soaks me once more in a terrified sweat.

    The tear-drenched earth gave out a gust of wind,
erupting in a flash of bright vermilion,
that overwhelmed all conscious sentiment.

    I fell like someone gripped by sudden sleep.

Canto V

THE LUSTFUL

And so from Circle One I now went down
deeper, to Circle Two, which bounds a lesser space
and therefore greater suffering. Its sting is misery.

Minos stands there – horribly there – and barking.
He, on the threshold, checks degrees of guilt,
then judges and dispatches with his twirling tail.

I mean that every ill-begotten creature,
when summoned here, confesses everything.
And he (his sense of sin is very fine)

perceives what place in Hell best suits each one,
and coils his tail around himself to tell
the numbered ring to which he'll send them down.

Before him, always, stands a crowd of souls.
By turns they go, each one, for sentencing.
Each pleads, attends – and then is tipped below.

'You there, arriving at this house of woe,'
so, when he saw me there, the judge spoke forth,
(to interrupt a while his formal role),

'watch as you enter – and in whom you trust.
Don't let yourself be fooled by this wide threshold.'
My leader's thrust: 'This yelling! Why persist?

Do not impede him on his destined way.
For this is willed where all is possible
that is willed there. And so demand no more.'

But now the tones of pain, continuing,

Canto V

demand I hear them out. And now I've come
where grief and weeping pierce me at the heart.

   And so I came where light is mute, a place
that moans as oceans do impelled by storms,
surging, embattled in conflicting squalls.

   The swirling wind of Hell will never rest.
It drags these spirits onwards in its force.
It chafes them – rolling, clashing – grievously.

   Then, once they reach the point from which they fell . . .
screams, keening cries, the agony of all,
and all blaspheming at the Holy Power.

   Caught in this torment, as I understood,
were those who – here condemned for carnal sin –
made reason bow to their instinctual bent.

   As starlings on the wing in winter chills
are borne along in wide and teeming flocks,
so on these breathing gusts the evil souls.

   This way and that and up and down they're borne.
Here is no hope of any comfort ever,
neither of respite nor of lesser pain.

   And now, as cranes go singing lamentations
and form themselves through air in long-drawn lines,
coming towards me, trailing all their sorrows,

   I saw new shadows lifted by this force.
'Who are these people, sir?' I said. 'Tell me
why black air scourges them so viciously.'

   'The first of those whose tale you wish to hear,'
he answered me without a moment's pause,
'governed as empress over diverse tongues.

   She was so wracked by lust and luxury,

licentiousness was legal under laws she made –
to lift the blame that she herself incurred.

   This is Semiramis. Of her one reads
that she, though heir to Ninus, was his bride.
Her lands were those where now the Sultan reigns.

   The other, lovelorn, slew herself and broke
her vow of faith to Sichaeus's ashes.
And next, so lascivious, Cleopatra.

   Helen. You see? Because of her, a wretched
waste of years went by. See! Great Achilles.
He fought with love until his final day.

   Paris you see, and Tristan there.' And more
than a thousand shadows he numbered, naming
them all, whom Love had led to leave our life.

   Hearing that man of learning herald thus
these chevaliers of old, and noble ladies,
pity oppressed me and I was all but lost.

   'How willingly,' I turned towards the poet,
'I'd speak to those two there who go conjoined
and look to be so light upon the wind.'

   And he to me: 'You'll see them clearer soon.
When they are closer, call to them. Invoke
the love that draws them on, and they will come.'

   The wind had swept them nearer to us now.
I moved to them in words: 'Soul-wearied creatures!
Come, if none forbids, to us and, breathless, speak.'

   As doves, when called by their desires, will come –
wings spreading high – to settle on their nest,
borne through the air by their own steady will,

   so these two left the flock where Dido is.

Canto V

They came, approaching through malignant air,
so strong for them had been my feeling cry.

'Our fellow being, gracious, kind and good!
You, on your journeying through this bruised air,
here visit two who tinged the world with blood.

Suppose the Sovereign of the Universe
were still our friend, we'd pray He grant you peace.
You pity so the ill perverting us.

Whatever you may please to hear or say,
we, as we hear, we, as we speak, assent,
so long – as now they do – these winds stay silent.

My native place is set along those shores
through which the river Po comes down, to be
at last at peace with all its tributaries.

Love, who so fast brings flame to generous hearts,
seized him with feeling for the lovely form,
now torn from me. The harm of how still rankles.

Love, who no loved one pardons love's requite,
seized me for him so strongly in delight
that, as you see, he does not leave me yet.

Love drew us onwards to consuming death.
Cain's ice awaits the one who quenched our lives.'
These words, borne on to us from them, were theirs.

And when I heard these spirits in distress,
I bowed my eyes and held them low, until,
at length, the poet said: 'What thoughts are these?'

I, answering in the end, began: 'Alas,
how many yearning thoughts, what great desire,
have led them through such sorrow to their fate?'

And turning to them now I came to say:

Dante Alighieri

'Francesca, how your suffering saddens me!
Sheer pity brings me to the point of tears.

But tell me this: the how of it – and why –
that Love, in sweetness of such sighing hours,
permitted you to know these doubtful pangs.'

To me she said: 'There is no sorrow greater
than, in times of misery, to hold at heart
the memory of happiness. (Your teacher knows.)

And yet, if you so deeply yearn to trace
the root from which the love we share first sprang,
then I shall say – and speak as though in tears.

One day we read together, for pure joy
how Lancelot was taken in Love's palm.
We were alone. We knew no suspicion.

Time after time, the words we read would lift
our eyes and drain all colour from our faces.
A single point, however, vanquished us.

For when at last we read the longed-for smile
of Guinevere – at last her lover kissed –
he, who from me will never now depart,

touched his kiss, trembling to my open mouth.
This book was *Galehault* – pander-penned, the pimp!
That day we read no further down those lines.'

And all the while, as one of them spoke on,
the other wept, and I, in such great pity,
fainted away as though I were to die.

And now I fell as bodies fall, for dead.

Canto VI

THE GLUTTONOUS

As now I came once more to conscious mind –
closed in those feelings for the kindred souls
that had, in sudden sadness, overcome me –

wherever I might turn I saw – wherever
I might move or send my gaze –
new forms of torment, new tormented souls.

I am in Circle Three. And rain falls there,
endlessly, chill, accursed and heavy,
its rate and composition never new.

Snow, massive hailstones, black, tainted water
pour down in sheets through tenebrae of air.
The earth absorbs it all and stinks, revoltingly.

Cerberus, weird and monstrously cruel,
barks from his triple throats in cur-like yowls
over the heads of those who lie there, drowned.

His eyes vermilion, beard a greasy black,
his belly broad, his fingers all sharp-nailed,
he mauls and skins, then hacks in four, these souls.

From all of them, rain wrings a wet-dog howl.
They squirm, as flank screens flank. They twist, they turn,
and then – these vile profanities – they turn again.

That reptile Cerberus now glimpsed us there.
He stretched his jaws; he showed us all his fangs.
And me? No member in my frame stayed still!

My leader, bending with his palms wide-spanned,

scooped dirt in each, and then – his fists both full –
hurled these as sops down all three ravening throats.

A hungry mongrel – yapping, thrusting out,
intent on nothing but the meal to come –
is silent only when its teeth sink in.

In that same way, with three repulsive muzzles,
the demon Cerberus. His thunderous growlings
stunned these souls. They wished themselves stone deaf.

Over such shadows, flat in that hard rain,
we travelled onwards still. Our tread now fell
on voided nothings only seeming men.

Across the whole terrain these shades were spread,
except that one, at seeing us pass by,
sat, on the sudden, upright and then cried:

'You there! Drawn onwards through this stretch of Hell,
tell me you know me. Say so, if so you can.
You! Made as man before myself unmade.'

And I replied: 'The awful pain you feel
perhaps has cancelled you from memory.
Till now, it seems, I've never even seen you.

Then tell me who you are, and why you dwell
in such a place? And why a pain like this?
Others may well be worse, none so disgusting.'

And he: 'That burgh of yours – that sack of bile
that brims by now to overflow – I lived
as hers throughout my own fine-weather years.

You knew me, like your city friends, as Hoggo.
So here I am, condemned for gullet sins,
lying, you see, squashed flat by battering rain.

I'm not alone in misery of soul.

Canto VI

These all lie subject to the self-same pain.
Their guilt is mine.' He spoke no further word.

   'Hoggo, your heavy labours,' I replied,
'weigh on me hard and prompt my heavy tears.
But tell me, if you can, where they'll all end,

   the citizens of that divided town?
Is there among them any honest man?
Why is that place assailed by so much strife?'

   His answer was: 'From each side, long harangues.
And then to blood. The Wildwood boys
will drive the others out. They'll do great harm.

   But then, within the span of three brief suns,
that side will fall and others rise and thrive,
spurred on by one who now just coasts between.

   For quite some time they'll hold their heads up high
and grind the others under heavy weights,
however much, for shame, these weep and writhe.

   Of this lot, two are honest yet not heard.
For pride and avarice and envy are
the three fierce sparks that set all hearts ablaze.'

   With this, his tear-drenched song now reached an end.
But I to him: 'I still want more instruction.
This gift I ask of you: please do say more.

   Tegghiaio, Farinata – men of rank –
Mosca, Arrigo, Rusticucci, too,
and others with their minds on noble deeds,

   tell me, so I may know them, where they are.
For I am gripped by great desire, to tell
if Heaven holds them sweet – or poisonous Hell.'

   And he: 'These dwell among the blackest souls,

loaded down deep by sins of differing types.
If you sink far enough, you'll see them all.

    But when you walk once more where life is sweet,
bring me, I beg, to others in remembrance.
No more I'll say, nor answer any more.'

    His forward gaze now twisted to a squint.
He stared at me a little, bent his head,
then fell face down and joined his fellow blind.

    My leader now addressed me: 'He'll not stir
until the trumpets of the angels sound,
at which his enemy, True Power, will come.

    Then each will see once more his own sad tomb,
and each, once more, assume its flesh and figure,
each hear the rumbling thunder roll for ever.'

    So on we fared across that filthy blend
of rain and shadow spirit, slow in step,
touching a little on the life to come.

    Concerning which, 'These torments, sir,' I said,
'when judgement has been finally proclaimed –
will these increase or simmer just the same?'

    'Return,' he said, 'to your first principles:
when anything (these state) becomes more perfect,
then all the more it feels both good and pain.

    Albeit these accursed men will not
achieve perfection full and true, they still,
beyond that Day, will come to sharper life.'

    So, circling on the curve around that path,
we talked of more than I shall here relate,
but reached the brow, from which the route descends,
    and found there Plutus, the tremendous foe.

Canto VIII

THE WRATHFUL AND THE
MELANCHOLIC

And so I say (continuing) that, long before
we reached the bottom of that lofty tower,
our eyes had travelled upwards to its summit,

   drawn by a pair of tiny flames, set there –
as now we saw – to signal to a third,
so far away the eye could hardly grasp it.

   I turned towards the ocean of all wisdom:
'What do they mean?' I said to him. 'What answer
follows from the farther fire? Who makes these signs?'

   And he: 'Across these waves of foaming mire,
you may already glimpse what they've been waiting for,
unless it still goes hidden by these marshy fumes.'

   No bow string ever shot through air an arrow
rapider than now, at speed, I saw come on
towards us there, a mean little vessel,

   within it – as pilot plying these waters –
a single galley man who strained the oar,
squealing: 'You fiend! You've got it coming now!'

   'Phlegyas, Phlegyas!' my master said.
'Your screams and shouts have, this time, little point.
We're yours – but only while we cross this marsh.'

   Like someone hearing that a massive hoax
has just, to his disgruntlement, been pulled on him,
so Phlegyas now stood, in pent-up rage.

Dante Alighieri

My lord stepped down, and, entering the boat,
he made me, in my turn, embark behind.
The hull seemed laden only when I did.

At once – my leader boarded, me as well –
the ancient prow put out. It sawed the waves
more deeply than it would with other crews.

So, rushing forwards on that lifeless slick,
there jerked up, fronting me, one brimming slime
who spoke: 'So who – you come too soon! – are you?'

And my riposte: 'I come, perhaps; I'll not remain.
But who might you be, brutishly befouled?'
His answer was: 'Just look at me. I'm one

who weeps.' And I to him: 'Weep on. In grief,
may you remain, you spirit of damnation!
I know who *you* are, filth as you may be.'

And then he stretched both hands towards our gunwales.
My teacher, though – alert – soon drove him back,
saying: 'Get down! Be off with all that dog pack!'

And then he ringed both arms around my neck.
He kissed my face, then said: 'You wrathful soul!
Blessed the one that held you in her womb.

That man, alive, flaunted his arrogance,
and nothing good adorns his memory.
So here his shadow is possessed with rage.

How many, in the world above, pose there
as kings but here will lie like pigs in muck,
leaving behind them horrible dispraise.'

'Sir,' I replied, 'this I should really like:
before we make our way beyond this lake,
to see him dabbled in the minestrone.'

Canto VIII

He gave me my answer: 'Before that shore
has come to view, you'll surely have your fill.
And rightly you rejoice in this desire.'

Then, moments on, I saw that sinner ripped
to vicious tatters by that mud-caked lot.
I praise God still, and still give thanks for that.

'Get him,' they howled. 'Let's get him – Silver Phil!'
That crazy Florentine! He bucked, he baulked.
Turning, the Guelf turned teeth upon himself.

We left him there. Of him, my story tells no more.
And yet my ears were pierced with cries of pain.
At which, I barred my eyes intently forwards.

'Dear son,' my teacher in his goodness said,
'we now approach the city known as Dis,
its teeming crowds and weighty citizens.'

'Already, sir,' I said, 'I clearly can
make out the minarets beyond this moat,
as bright and red, it seems, as if they sprang

from fire.' 'Eternal fire,' he answered me,
'burning within, projects, as you can see,
these glowing profiles from the depths of Hell.'

We now arrived within the deep-dug ditch –
the channel round that place disconsolate,
whose walls, it seemed to me, were formed of iron.

Not without, first, encircling it about,
we came to where the ferry man broke forth:
'Out you all get!' he yelled. 'The entry's here.'

I saw there, on that threshold – framed – more than
a thousand who had rained from Heaven. Spitting
in wrath. 'Who's that,' they hissed, 'who, yet undead,

    travels the kingdom of the truly dead?'
He gave a sign, my teacher in all wisdom,
saying he sought some secret word with them.

    At which they somewhat hid their fierce disdain.
'You come, but on your own!' they said. 'Let him,
so brazen entering our realm, walk by.

    He may retrace his foolish path alone –
or try it, if he can – while you'll stay here.
You've been his escort through this dark terrain.'

    Reader, imagine! I grew faint at heart,
to hear these cursed phrases ringing out.
I truly thought I'd never make it back.

    'My guide, my dearest master. Seven times –
or more by now – you've brought me safely through.
You've drawn me from the face of towering doom.

    Do not, I beg you, leave me here undone.
If we are now denied a clear way on,
then let us quickly trace our footsteps back.'

    My lord had led me onwards to that place –
and now he said: 'Do not be terrified.
No one can take from us our right to pass.

    Wait here a while. Refresh your weary soul.
Take strength. Be comforted. Feed on good hope.
I'll not desert you in this nether world.'

    So off he went. He there abandoned me,
my sweetest father. Plunged in 'perhapses',
I so remained, brain arguing 'yes' and 'no'.

    What he then said to them I could not tell.
Yet hardly had he taken up his stand
when all ran, jostling, to return inside.

Canto VIII

    They barred the door, these enemies of ours,
to meet his thrust. My lord remained shut out.
With heavy tread, he now came back to me.

    Eyes bent upon the ground, his forehead shaved
of all brave confidence, sighing, he said:
'Who dares deny me entrance to this house of grief?'

    To me he said: 'You see. I'm angry now.
Don't be dismayed. They'll fuss around in there.
They'll seek to keep us out. But I'll win through.

    This insolence of theirs is nothing new.
At some less secret gate they tried it once.
But that still stands without its lock, ajar.

    You've seen the door, dead words scribed on its beam.
And now already there descends the slope –
passing these circles, and without a guide –

    someone through whom the city will lie open.'

Canto XIII

THE VIOLENT AGAINST SELF

No, Nessus had not reached the other side
when we began to travel through a wood
that bore no sign of any path ahead.

No fresh green leaves but dismal in colour,
no boughs clean arc-ed but knotty and entwined,
no apples were there but thorns, poison-pricked.

No scrubby wilderness so bitter and dense
from Cécina as far as Corneto
offers a den to beasts that hate ploughed farmlands.

Their nest is there, those disgusting Harpies
who drove the Trojans from the Strophades,
with grim announcements of great harm to come.

Wings widespreading, human from neck to brow,
talons for feet, plumage around their paunches,
they sing from these uncanny trees their songs of woe.

Constant in kindness, my teacher now said:
'Before you venture further in, please know
that you now stand in Sub-ring Number Two,

and shall until you reach the Appalling Sands.
So look around. Take care. What you'll see here
would drain belief from any word I uttered.'

A wailing I heard, dragged out from every part,
and saw there no one who might make these sounds,
so that I stopped, bewildered, in my tracks.

Truly I think he truly thought that, truly,

Canto XIII

I might just have believed these voices rose
from persons hidden from us in the thorn maze.

Therefore: 'If you,' my teacher said, 'will wrench
away some sprig from any tree you choose,
that will lop short your feeling in such doubt.'

And so I reached my hand a little forwards.
I plucked a shoot (no more) from one great hawthorn.
At which its trunk screamed out: 'Why splinter me?'

Now darkened by a flow of blood, the tree
spoke out a second time: 'Why gash me so?
Is there no living pity in your heart?

Once we were men. We've now become dry sticks.
Your hand might well have proved more merciful
if we had been the hissing souls of snakes.'

Compare: a green brand, kindled at one end –
the other oozing sap – whistles and spits
as air finds vent, then rushes out as wind.

So now there ran, out of this fractured spigot,
both words and blood. At which I let the tip
drop down and stood like someone terror-struck.

'You injured soul!' my teacher (sane as ever)
now replied. 'If he had only earlier
believed what my own writings could have shown,

he'd not have stretched his hand so far towards you.
This, though, is all beyond belief. So I was forced
to urge a deed that presses on my own mind still.

But tell him now who once you were. He may,
in turn, as remedy, refresh your fame,
returning to the world above by leave.'

The trunk: 'Your words, sir, prove so sweet a bait,

I cannot here keep silence. Don't be irked
if I a while should settle on that lure and talk.

   I am the one who held in hand both keys
to Federigo's heart. I turned them there,
locking so smoothly and unlocking it

   that all men, almost, I stole from his secrets.
Faith I kept, so true in that proud office
I wasted sleep and lost my steady pulse.

   That harlot Scandal, then (her raddled eyes
she never drags from where the emperor dwells,
the vice of court life, mortal blight of all)

   enflamed the minds of everyone against me.
And they in flames enflamed the great Augustus.
So, happy honours turned to hapless grief.

   My mind – itself disdainful in its tastes –
believing it could flee disdain by dying,
made me unjust against myself so just.

   By all these weird, new-wooded roots, I swear
on oath before you: I did not break faith,
nor failed a lord so worthy of regard.

   Will you – should either head back to the world –
bring comfort to my memory, which lies
still lashed beneath the stroke of envious eyes?'

   Pausing a while, he said (my chosen poet),
'He's silent now, so waste no opportunity.
If there is more you wish to know, then say.'

   'You,' I replied, 'must speak once more and ask
what you believe will leave me satisfied.
I could not do it. Pity wrings my core.'

   And so he did once more begin: 'Suppose

Canto XIII

that freely, from a generous heart, someone
should do, imprisoned ghost, what your prayers seek,

tell us, if you should care to, this: how souls
are bound in these hard knots. And, if you can:
will anyone be ever loosed from limbs like these?'

At that (exhaling heavily) the trunk
converted wind to word and formed this speech:
'The answer you require is quick to give:

When any soul abandons savagely
its body, rending self by self away,
Minos consigns it to the seventh gulf.

Falling, it finds this copse. Yet no one place
is chosen as its plot. Where fortune slings it,
there (as spelt grains might) it germinates.

A sapling sprouts, grows ligneous, and then
the Harpies, grazing on its foliage,
fashion sharp pain and windows for that pain.

We (as shall all), come Judgement Day, shall seek
our cast-off spoil, yet not put on this vestment.
Keeping what we tore off would not be fair.

Our bodies we shall drag back here; and all
around this melancholy grove they'll swing,
each on the thorn of shades that wrought them harm.'

Attention trained entirely on that stock
(thinking, in truth, it might as yet say more),
we now were shocked by a sudden uproar,

as if (to make comparison) you'd heard some hog
and all the boar hunt baying round its stand –
a sound composed of beasts and thrashing twigs.

And look there, on the left-hand side, there came,

at speed, two fleeing, naked, scratched to bits,
who broke down every hurdle in that scrub.

    One was ahead: 'Quick, quick! Come, death! Come now!'
The other (seeming, to himself, too slow)
was yelling: 'Lano! Oh, your nimble heels
    weren't half so sharp at the Toppo rumble!'
And then (it may be his breath was failing),
he sank to form a clump beside a shrub.

    Behind these two, the wood was teeming, full
of black bitches, ravenous and rapid,
as greyhounds are when slipping from their leads.

    These set their teeth on that sad, hunkered form.
They tore him all to pieces, chunk by chunk.
And then they carried off those suffering limbs.

    My guide then took me gently by the hand,
and led me to the bush, which wept (in vain)
through all of its blood-stained lacerations,

    saying: 'O Jacopo da Santo Andrea!
What use was it to take me as your shield?
Am I to blame for your wild, wicked ways?'

    My teacher came and stood above that bush.
'So who were you,' he said, 'who, pierced to bits,
breathes painful utterance in jets of blood?'

    'You souls,' he said, 'you come – but just in time –
to see the massacre, in all its shame,
that rends away from me my fresh green fronds.

    Place all these leaves beneath this grieving stump.
I too was from that city, once, which chose
Saint John as patron over Mars – its first –
    whose arts, since spurned, have always brought us harm.

Canto XIII

And were there not, beneath the Arno bridge,
some traces visible of what he was,
   those citizens who built it all anew
on ashes that Attila left behind
would then have laboured with no end in view.
   Myself, I made a gallows of my house.'

Canto XVII

PASSAGE TO THE EIGHTH CIRCLE

'Behold! The beast who soars with needle tail
through mountains, shattering shields and city walls!
Behold! The beast that stinks out all the world!'

To me, my lord spoke thus, then beckoned up
the monster to approach the jutting prow
that marked the end of all our marble paths.

It came, that filthy image of deceit.
Its head and trunk it grounded on the shore.
It did not draw its tailpiece to the bank.

The face was that of any honest man,
the outer skin all generosity.
Its timber, though, was serpent through and through:

two clawing grabs, and hairy to the armpits,
its back and breast and ribcage all tattooed
with knot designs and spinning little whorls.

No Turk or Tartar has woven finer drapes,
more many-coloured in their pile or tuft.
Nor did Arachne thread such tapestries.

Compare: on foreshores, sometimes, dinghies stand
in water partly, partly on the shingle –
as likewise, in the land of drunken Germans,

beavers will do, advancing their attack.
So did this beast – the worst that there can be –
there on the rocky rim that locks the sand.

Out into emptiness it swung its tail,

Canto XVII

and twisted upwards its venomous fork.
The tip was armed like any scorpion's.

My leader said: 'We need to bend our path
a little further down, towards that vile
monstrosity that's lolling underneath.'

So down we went, towards the right-hand pap.
Ten paces, and we'd reached the very edge,
stepping well clear of flames and burning shoals.

And then, on getting to that spot, I saw,
a little further on along the sandbar,
a group just sitting near the gaping waste.

And here my teacher said: 'To carry back
experience of the ring that we're now in,
go over there and look at their behaviour.

But do not stay to talk at any length.
Till you return, I'll parley with this thing,
for him to grant us use of his great thews.'

So once again, along the outward brow
of Circle Seven I progressed alone
to where there sat these souls in misery.

The pain they felt erupted from their eyes.
All up and down and round about, their hands
sought remedies for burning air and ground.

Dogs in the heat of summer do the same,
stung by the bluebottle, gadfly and flea,
swatting at swarms with paw pads or with snout.

On some of these – these faces under showers
of grievous, never-ceasing rain – I set my eyes.
I recognized no single one, but noticed
round the neck of each a cash bag hung

27

(each with its own insignia and blaze),
on which their staring eyes appeared to graze.

  So I, too, gazing, passed among them all,
and saw, imprinted on a yellow purse,
a blue device, in face and pose a lion.

  Then, as my view went trundling further on,
I saw another, with a blood-red field –
the goose it bore was whiter, far, than butter.

  And then I heard (from one whose neat, white sack
was marked in azure with a pregnant sow):
'What are you after in this awful hole?

  Do go away! Yet you – as Vitaliano is –
are still alive. Then understand me, please:
he'll sit on my left flank, my one-time neighbour.

  I'm Paduan, among these Florentines,
and often they all thunder in my ears:
"Oh, let him come," they'll scream, "that sovereign knight,
  who'll bring the bag that bears three rampant goats."'
At which, in throes, he wrenched his mouth awry
and curled his tongue, like any ox, to lick his nose.

  And I, who feared that, if I lingered long,
I'd irritate the one who'd said 'Be brief',
now turned my back upon these worn-out souls.

  My leader, I discovered there, had jumped
already on that fearsome creature's rump.
'Come on,' he urged, 'be stalwart and courageous.

  From now on we'll descend by stairs like these.
Mount at the front so I can come between,
to see the tail won't bring you any harm.'

  Like someone shivering as the grip of 'flu

spreads over him, pale to the fingernails,
who trembles merely at the sight of shade . . .

    well, that was me, as these words carried over.
The threat of shame, however, when one's lord
is near, emboldens one to serve him well.

    I settled down between those gruesome shoulders.
I wished to say (my voice, though, would not come):
'Yes. Please! Be sure you hold me very firm.'

    He, who in many an earlier 'perhaps'
had aided me, as soon as I got on,
flinging his arms around me, hugged me tight,

    and said: 'Go on, then, Geryon. Cast out!
Wheel wide about to make a smooth descent.
Think of the strange new burden on your back.'

    Slowly astern, astern, as ferries leave
the quay where they had docked, so he moved out.
Then, only when he felt himself ride free,

    he turned the tail where breast had been before,
and – stretching long, as eels might do – set sail,
paddling the air towards him with his paws.

    No greater fear (so, truly, I believe)
was felt as Phaeton let the reins go loose,
and scorched the sky as still it is today,

    nor yet by ill-starred Icarus – his loins
unfeathering as the wax grew warm – to whom
his father screamed aloud: 'You're going wrong!'

    And then with fear I saw, on every side,
that I was now in air, and every sight
extinguished, save my view of that great beast.

    So swimming slowly, it goes on its way.

Dante Alighieri

It wheels. It descends. This I don't notice –
except an upward breeze now fans my face.
   By then I heard, beneath us to the right,
the roar of some appalling cataract.
And so I leant my head out, looking down.
   More timorous of falling still, I saw
that there were fires down there and heard shrill screams.
Trembling, I huddled back and locked my thighs.
   And then I saw, as I had not before,
the going-down – the spirals of great harm –
on every side now coming ever nearer.
   A falcon, having long been on the wing,
and seeing neither lure nor bird to prey on,
compels the falconer to sigh: 'You're coming in,'
   then sinks down wearily to where it left so fast.
A hundred turns – and then, far from its lord,
it lands, disdainful, spiteful in its scorn.
   So, too, did Geryon, to place us on the floor,
the very foot of that sheer, towering cliff.
And then, unburdened of our persons now,
   vanished at speed like barbed bolt from a bow.

Canto XIX

SIMONISTS

You! Magic Simon, and your sorry school!
Things that are God's own – things that, truly, are
the brides of goodness – lusting cruelly
    after gold and silver, you turn them all to whores.
The trumpet now (and rightly!) sounds for you.
There you all are, well set in Pocket Three.

    Onwards towards this yawning tomb, mounting
the ridge, by now we'd reached its summit –
the point that plumbs the middle of the ditch.

    O wisdom in the height, how great the art
that you display in Heaven, on earth and even
in that evil world! How justly you deal power!

    I saw how all the livid rock was drilled
with holes – along its flanks, across its floor –
all circular, and all of equal measure.

    To me they seemed, in radius, no more nor less
than fonts that, in my own beloved Saint John's,
allow the priest at baptisms a place to stand.

    (Not long ago, I shattered one of those.
Someone was drowning there. I got them out.
This, sealed and sworn, is nothing but the truth.)

    Out of the mouth of every single hole
there floated up a pair of sinner feet,
legs to the ham on show, the rest concealed.

    The soles of all these feet were set alight,

and each pair wriggled at the joint so hard
they'd easily have ripped a rope or lanyard.

As flames go flickering round some greasy thing
and hover just above its outer rind,
so these flames also, toe tip to heel end.

'Who, sir,' I said, 'is that one there? That one
who jerks in pain greater than his *confrères*,
sucked at by flames far more fiercely vermilion.'

'I'll lift you down,' he answered me, 'if you
insist. We'll take that bank the easier.
He'll talk to you himself about his twists.'

'Whatever pleases you,' I said, 'to me is good.
Lord, you remain: I'll not depart – you know –
from what you will. You read my silent thoughts.'

So on we went to the fourth embankment.
We turned around, descended on our left,
arriving at that pitted, straitened floor.

My teacher, kindly, did not set me down –
nor loose me from his hip hold – till we had reached
that fissure where (all tears) shanks shuddered.

'Whatever you might be there, upside down,
staked, you unhappy spirit, like a pole,
if you,' I said, 'are able, then speak out.'

So there I stood like any friar who shrives
the hired assassin – head down in the earth –
who calls him back to put off stifling death.

And he yelled out: 'Is that you standing there?
Are you there, on your feet still, Boniface?
The writings lied to me by quite some years.

Are you so sick of owning things already?

Canto XIX

Till now, you've hardly been afraid to cheat
our lovely woman, tearing her to shreds.'

  Well, I just stood there (you will know just how)
simply not getting what I'd heard come out,
feeling a fool, uncertain what to say.

  Then Virgil entered: 'Say this – and make speed:
"No, that's not me. I am not who you think."'
And so I answered as he'd said I should.

  At which – all feet – the spirit thrashed about,
then, sighing loudly in a tearful voice:
'So what is it you want of me?' he said.

  'If you're so keen to know who I might be,
and ran all down that slope to find me out,
you'd better know I wore the papal cope.

  A true Orsini, son of Ursa Bear,
I showed such greed in favouring her brats
that – up there well in pocket – I'm in pocket here.

  Below me, in great stacks beneath my head,
packed tight in every cranny of the rock,
are all my antecedents in the Simon line.

  Down there I'll sink, in that same way, when he
arrives whom I supposed that you might be,
and uttered, therefore, my abrupt inquiry.

  But I already – feet up on the grill, tossed
upside down – have passed more time
than Boniface will, stuck here with red hot toes.

  For after him from westwards there'll appear
that lawless shepherd, uglier in deed,
who then, for both of us, will form a lid.

  He shall be known as a "Jason-Once-Again".

33

Dante Alighieri

We read in Maccabees: "Priest Bribes a King."
This other will score well with one French prince.'

I may have been plain mad. I do not know.
But now, in measured verse, I sang these words:
'Tell me, I pray: what riches did Our Lord
  demand, as first instalment, from Saint Peter
before He placed the keys in his command?
He asked (be sure) no more than: "Come behind me."

  Nor did Saint Peter, or the rest of them,
receive from Matthias a gold or silver piece,
allotting him the place that Judas lost.

  So you stay put. You merit punishment.
But keep your eye on that ill-gotten coin
that made you bold with Charles the Angevin.

  And, were I not forbidden, as I am,
by reverence for those keys, supreme and holy,
that you hung on to in the happy life,

  I now would bring still weightier words to bear.
You and your greed bring misery to the world,
trampling the good and raising up the wicked.

  Saint John took heed of shepherds such as you.
He saw revealed that She-above-the-Waves,
whoring it up with Rulers of the earth,

  she who in truth was born with seven heads
and fed herself, in truth, from ten pure horns,
as long as she in virtue pleased her man.

  Silver and gold you have made your god. And what's
the odds – you and some idol-worshipper?
He prays to one, you to a gilded hundred.

  What harm you mothered, Emperor Constantine!

Canto XIX

Not your conversion but the dowry he –
that first rich Papa – thus obtained from you!'

    And all the time I chanted out these notes,
he, in his wrath or bitten by remorse,
flapped, with great force, the flat of both his feet.

    My leader, I believe, was very pleased.
In listening to these sounding words of truth,
he stood there satisfied, his lips compressed.

    So, too, he took me up in his embrace.
Then, bodily, he clasped me to his breast
and climbed again the path where he'd come down.

    Nor did he tire of holding me so tight.
He bore me to the summit of that arch
spanning the banks of Pockets Four and Five.

    And there he gently put his burden down,
gently on rocks so craggy and so steep
they might have seemed to goats too hard to cross.

    From there, another valley was disclosed.

Canto XXIV

THIEVES

In that still baby-boyish time of year,
when sunlight chills its curls beneath Aquarius,
when nights grow shorter equalling the day,
    and hoar frost writes fair copies on the ground
to mimic in design its snowy sister
(its pen, though, not chill-tempered to endure),
    the peasant in this season, when supplies
run short, rolls from his bed, looks out and sees
the fields are glistening white, so slaps his thigh,
    goes in, then grumbles up and down, as though
(poor sod) he couldn't find a thing to do,
till, out once more, he fills his wicker trug,
    with hope, at least. No time at all! The features
of the world transform. He grabs his goad.
Outdoors, he prods his lambs to open pasture.

    In some such way, I too was first dismayed
to see distress so written on my leader's brow.
But he, as quickly, plastered up the hurt.

    And so, arriving at the ruined bridge,
my leader turned that sour-sweet look on me
that first he'd shown me at the mountain foot.

    He spread his arms, then, having in his thought
surveyed the landslip, and (a man of sense)
assessed it well, he took me in his grip.

    Then, always with adjustments in his moves

Canto XXIV

(so that, it seemed, he foresaw everything),
in hauling me towards the pinnacle

   of one moraine, he'd see a spur beyond
and say: 'Next, take your hold on that niche there.
But test it first to see how well it bears.'

This was no route for someone warmly dressed.
Even for us – he, weightless, shoving me –
we hardly could progress from ledge to ledge.

   Had not the gradient been less severe
than that which faced it on the other side,
I'd have been beat. I cannot speak for him.

   But Rottenpockets slopes towards the flap
that opens on the lowest sump of all,
and so, in contour, every ditch is shaped

   with one rim proud, the other dipping down.
So, in the end, we came upon the point
where one last building block had sheared away.

   My lungs by now had so been milked of breath
that, come so far, I couldn't make it further.
I flopped, in fact, when we arrived, just there.

   'Now you must needs,' my teacher said, 'shake off
your wonted indolence. No fame is won
beneath the quilt or sunk in feather cushions.

   Whoever, fameless, wastes his life away,
leaves of himself no greater mark on earth
than smoke in air or froth upon the wave.

   So upwards! On! And vanquish laboured breath!
In any battle mind power will prevail,
unless the weight of body loads it down.

   There's yet a longer ladder you must scale.

Dante Alighieri

You can't just turn and leave all these behind.
You understand? Well, make my words avail.'

   So up I got, pretending to more puff
than, really, I could feel I'd got within.
'Let's go,' I answered, 'I'm all strength and dash.'

   Upwards we made our way, along the cliff –
poor, narrow-going where the rocks jut out,
far steeper than the slope had been before.

   Talking (to seem less feeble) on I went,
when, issuing from the ditch beyond, there came
a voice – though one unfit for human words.

   I made no sense of it. But now I neared
the arch that forms a span across that pocket.
The speaker seemed much moved by raging ire.

   Downwards I bent. But in such dark as that,
no eye alive could penetrate the depths.
But, 'Sir,' I said, 'make for the other edge,

   and let us then descend the pocket wall.
From here I hear but do not understand.
So, too, I see, yet focus not at all.'

   'I offer you,' he said to me, 'no answer
save "just do it". Noble demands, by right,
deserve the consequence of silent deeds.'

   So where the bridgehead meets Embankment Eight
we then went down, pursuing our descent,
so all that pocket was displayed to me.

   And there I came to see a dreadful brood
of writhing reptiles of such diverse kinds
the memory drains the very blood from me.

   Let Libya boast – for all her sand – no more!

Canto XXIV

Engender as she may chelydri, pharae,
chenchres and amphisbaenae, jaculi,
   never – and, yes, add Ethiopia, too,
with all, beyond the Red Sea, dry and waste –
has she displayed so many vicious pests.

   And through all this abundance, bitter and grim,
in panic naked humans ran – no holes
to hide in here or heliotropic charms.

   Behind their backs, the sinners' hands were bound
by snakes. These sent both tail and neck between
the buttocks, then formed the ends in knots up front.

   And near our point, at one of them (just look!)
a serpent headlong hurled itself and pierced
exactly at the knit of spine and nape.

   Then, faster than you scribble 'i' or 'o',
that shape caught fire, flash-flared and then (needs must)
descended in cascading showers of ash.

   There, lying in destruction on the ground,
the dead dust gathered of its own accord,
becoming instantly the self it was.

   Compare: the phoenix (as the sages say)
will come to its five-hundredth year, then die,
but then, on its own pyre, be born anew.

   Its lifelong food is neither grass nor grain,
but nurture drawn from weeping balm and incense.
Its shroud, at last, is fume of nard and myrrh.

   The sinner, first, drops down as someone might
when grappled down, not knowing how, by demons
(or else some other epileptic turn),
   who then, on rising, gazes all around,

Dante Alighieri

bewildered by the overwhelming ill
that came just now upon him, sighing, staring.
   So, too, this sinner, getting to his feet.
What power and might in God! How harsh it is!
How great the torrent of its vengeful blows!
   My leader then demanded who he was.
'I pelted down' – the sinner, in reply –
'to this wild gorge, right now, from Tuscany.
   Beast living suited me, not human life,
the mule that once I was. I'm Johnny Fucci,
animal. Pistoia is my proper hole.'
   I to my leader: 'Tell him, "Don't rush off!"
and make him say what guilt has thrust him down.
I've seen him. He's a man of blood and wrath.'
   The sinner, hearing this, made no pretence.
He fixed on me a concentrated eye,
and coloured up in brash embarrassment.
   'It pisses me right off,' he then declared,
'far more than being ripped away from life,
that you have got to see me in this misery.
   I can't say "no" to what you ask of me.
I'm stuck down here so deep 'cos it was me,
the thief who nicked the silver from the sanctuary.
   Then I just lied – to grass up someone else.
You won't, however, laugh at seeing this.
If ever you return from these dark dives,
   prick up your ears and hear my prophecy:
Pistoia first will slim and lose its Blacks.
Then Florence, too, renews its laws and ranks.
   Mars draws up fireballs from the Val di Magra,

wrapped all around in clouds and turbulence.
And these, in acrid, ever-driven storms,
   will battle high above the Picene acre.
A rapid bolt will rend the clouds apart,
and every single White be seared by wounds.
   I tell you this. I want it all to hurt.'

Canto XXXIII

TRAITORS TO NATION AND TRAITORS TO GUESTS

Jaws lifted now from that horrible dish,
the sinner – wiping clean each lip on hair that fringed
the mess he'd left the head in, at its rear –

began: 'You ask that I should tell anew
the pain that hopelessly, in thought alone,
before I voice it, presses at my heart.

Yet if I may, by speaking, sow the fruit
of hate to slur this traitor, caught between my teeth,
then words and tears, you'll see, will flow as one.

Who you might be, I do not know, nor how
you've come to be down here. But when you speak,
you seem (there's little doubt) a Florentine.

You need to see: I was Count Ugolino.
This is Ruggieri, the archbishop, there.
I'll tell you now why we two are so close.

That I, in consequence of his vile thoughts,
was captured – though I trusted in this man –
and after died, I do not need to say.

But this cannot have carried to your ears:
that is, how savagely I met my death.
You'll hear it now, and know if he has injured me.

One scant slit in the walls of Eaglehouse
(because of me, they call it now the Hunger Tower.
Be sure, though: others will be locked up there)

had shown me, in the shaft that pierces it,

Canto XXXIII

many new moons by now, when this bad dream
tore wide the veil of what my future was.

This thing here then appeared to me as Master
of the Hounds, who tracked the wolf – his cubs as well –
out on the hill where Lucca hides from Pisa.

In front, as leaders of the pack, he placed
the clans Gualandi, Sismond and Lanfranchi,
their bitches hunting eager, lean and smart.

The chase was brief. Father and sons, it seemed,
were wearying; and soon – or so it seemed –
I saw those sharp fangs raking down their flanks.

I woke before the day ahead had come,
and heard my sons (my little ones were there)
cry in their sleep and call out for some food.

How hard you are if, thinking what my heart
foretold, you do not feel the pain of it.
Whatever will you weep for, if not that?

By now they all had woken up. The time
was due when, as routine, our food was brought.
Yet each was doubtful, thinking of their dream.

Listening, I heard the door below locked shut,
then nailed in place against that dreadful tower.
I looked in their dear faces, spoke no word.

I did not weep. Inward, I turned to stone.
They wept. And then my boy Anselmo spoke:
"What are you staring at? Father, what's wrong?"

And so I held my tears in check and gave
no answer all that day, nor all the night
that followed on, until another sun came up.

A little light had forced a ray into

our prison, so full of pain. I now could see
on all four faces my own expression.

   Out of sheer grief, I gnawed on both my hands.
And they – who thought I did so from an urge
to eat – all, on the instant, rose and said:

   "Father, for us the pain would be far less
if you would chose to eat us. You, having dressed us
in this wretched flesh, ought now to strip it off."

   So I kept still, to not increase their miseries.
And that day and the day beyond, we all were mute.
Hard, cruel earth, why did you not gape wide?

   As then we reached the fourth of all those days,
Gaddo pitched forward, stretching at my feet.
"Help me," he said. "Why don't you help me, Dad!"

   And there he died. You see me here. So I saw them,
the three remaining, falling one by one
between the next days – five and six – then let

   myself, now blind, feel over them, calling
on each, now all were dead, for two days more.
Then hunger proved a greater power than grief.'

   His words were done. Now, eyes askew, he grabbed
once more that miserable skull – his teeth,
like any dog's teeth, strong against the bone.

   Pisa, you scandal of the lovely land
where 'yes' is uttered in the form of *sì,*
your neighbours may be slow to punish you,

   but let those reefs, Capraia and Gorgogna,
drift, as a barrage, to the Arno's mouth,
so that your people – every one – are drowned.

   So what if – as the rumour goes – the great Count

Canto XXXIII

Ugolino did cheat fortresses from you.
You had no right to crucify his children.

   Pisa, you are a newborn Thebes! Those boys
were young. That made them innocent. I've named
just two. I now name Uguiccione and Brigata.

   We now moved on, and came to where the ice
so roughly swaddled yet another brood.
And these – not hunched – bend back for all to view.

   They weep. Yet weeping does not let them weep.
Their anguish meets a blockage at the eye.
Turned in, this only makes their heartache more.

   Their tears first cluster into frozen buds,
and then – as though a crystal visor – fill
the socket of the eye beneath each brow.

   My own face now – a callus in the chill –
had ceased to be a throne to any kind
of sentiment. And yet, in spite of all,

   it seemed I felt a wind still stirring here.
'Who moves these currents, sir?' I now inquired.
'At depths like these, aren't vapours wholly spent?'

   He in reply: 'Come on, come on! You soon
will stand where your own probing eye shall see
what brings this drizzling exhalation on.'

   A case of icy-eye-scab now yelled out:
'You must be souls of such malignancy
you merit placement in the lowest hole.

   Prise off this rigid veil, to clear my eyes.
Let me awhile express the grief that swells
in my heart's womb before my tears next freeze.'

   I answered: 'Are you asking help from me?

Dante Alighieri

Tell me who you are. Then I'll free your gaze,
or travel – promise! – to the deepest ice.'

   'I,' he replied, 'am Brother Alberigo,
I of the Evil Orchard, Fruiterer.
Here I receive exquisite dates for figs.'

   'Oh,' I now said, 'so you're already dead?'
'Well, how my body fares above,' he said,
'still in the world, my knowledge is not sure.

   There is, in Ptolomea, this advantage,
that souls will frequently come falling down
before Fate Atropos has granted them discharge.

   I very willingly will tell you more,
but only scrape this tear glaze from my face.
The instant any soul commits, like me,

   some act of treachery, a demon takes
possession of that body-form and rules
its deeds until its time is done. Swirling,

   the soul runs downwards to this sink. And so
the body of that shade behind – a-twitter
all this winter through – still seems up there, perhaps.

   You're bound to know, arriving only now,
that this is Signor Branca ("Hookhand") d'Oria.
Years have gone by since he was ice-packed here.'

   'I think,' I said, 'that this must be a con.
For how can Branca d'Oria be dead?
He eats and drinks and sleeps and puts his clothes on.'

   'Recall that ditch,' he said, 'named Rotklorsville,
where, higher up, they brew adhesive pitch?
Well, long before Mike Zanche got to that,

   Hookhand was history. He, as proxy, left

46

Canto XXXIII

a devil in his skin (his kinsman's here as well,
the one who planned with him the double-cross).

    But please, now reach your hand to me down here.
Open my eyes for me.' I did not open them.
To be a swine in this case was pure courtesy.

    You Genovese, deviant, deranged
and stuffed with every sort of vicious canker!
Why have you not been wiped yet from the earth?

    Among the worst of all the Romagnuoli
I found there one of yours, whose works were such
his soul already bathes in Cocytus.

    His body, seemingly, lives on above.

Canto XXXIV

TRAITORS TO BENEFACTORS

'*Vexilla regis prodeunt inferni*,
marching towards us. Fix your eyes ahead,'
my teacher said, 'and see if you can see it.'

As though a windmill when a thick fog breathes –
or else when dark night grips our hemisphere –
seen from a distance, turning in the wind,

so there a great contraption had appeared.
And I now shrank, against the wind, behind
my guide. There were no glades to shelter in.

I was by now (I write this verse in fear)
where all the shades in ice were covered up,
transparent as are straws preserved in glass.

Some lay there flat, and some were vertical,
one with head raised, another soles aloft,
another like a bow, bent face to feet.

And then when we had got still further on,
where now my master chose to show to me
that creature who had once appeared so fair,

he drew away from me and made me stop,
saying: 'Now see! Great Dis! Now see the place
where you will need to put on all your strength.'

How weak I now became, how faded, dry –
reader, don't ask, I shall not write it down –
for anything I said would fall far short.

I neither died nor wholly stayed alive.

Canto XXXIV

Just think yourselves, if your minds are in flower,
what I became, bereft of life and death.

   The emperor of all these realms of gloom
stuck from the ice at mid-point on his breast.
And I am more a giant (to compare)
   than any giant measured to his arm.
So now you'll see how huge the whole must be,
when viewed in fit proportion to that limb.

   If, once, he was as lovely as now vile,
when first he raised his brow against his maker,
then truly grief must all proceed from him.

   How great a wonder it now seemed to me
to see three faces on a single head!
The forward face was brilliant vermilion.

   The other two attached themselves to that
along each shoulder on the central point,
and joined together at the crest of hair.

   The rightward face was whitish, dirty yellow.
The left in colour had the tint of those
beyond the source from which the Nile first swells.

   Behind each face there issued two great vanes,
all six proportioned to a fowl like this.
I never saw such size in ocean sails.

   Not feathered as a bird's wings are, bat-like
and leathery, each fanned away the air,
so three unchanging winds moved out from him,

   Cocytus being frozen hard by these.
He wept from all six eyes. And down each chin
both tears and bloody slobber slowly ran.

   In every mouth he mangled with his teeth

Dante Alighieri

(as flax combs do) a single sinning soul,
but brought this agony to three at once.

   Such biting, though, affects the soul in front
as nothing to the scratching he received.
His spine at times showed starkly, bare of skin.

   'That one up there, condemned to greater pain,
is Judas Iscariot,' my teacher said,
'his head inside, his feet out, wriggling hard.

   The other two, their heads hung down below,
are Brutus, dangling from the jet black snout
(look how he writhes there, uttering not a word!),

   the other Cassius with his burly look.
But night ascends once more. And now it's time
for us to quit this hole. We've seen it all.'

   As he desired, I clung around his neck.
With purpose, he selected time and place
and, when the wings had opened to the full,

   he took a handhold on the furry sides,
and then, from tuft to tuft, he travelled down
between the shaggy pelt and frozen crust.

   But then, arriving where the thigh bone turns
(the hips extended to their widest there),
my leader, with the utmost stress and strain,

   swivelled his head to where his shanks had been
and clutched the pelt like someone on a climb,
so now I thought: 'We're heading back to Hell.'

   'Take care,' my teacher said. 'By steps like these,'
breathless and panting, seemingly all-in,
'we need to take our leave of so much ill.'

   Then through a fissure in that rock he passed

Canto XXXIV

and set me down to perch there on its rim.
After, he stretched his careful stride towards me.

    Raising my eyes, I thought that I should see
Lucifer where I, just now, had left him,
but saw instead his legs held upwards there.

    If I was struggling then to understand,
let other dimwits think how they'd have failed
to see what point it was that I now passed.

    'Up on your feet!' my teacher ordered me.
'The way is long, the road is cruelly hard.
The sun is at the morning bell already.'

    This was no stroll, where now we had arrived,
through any palace but a natural cave.
The ground beneath was rough, the light was weak.

    'Before my roots are torn from this abyss,
sir,' I said, upright, 'to untangle me
from error, say a little more of this.

    Where is the ice? And why is that one there
fixed upside down? How is it that the sun
progressed so rapidly from evening on to day?'

    And he in answer: 'You suppose you're still
on that side of the centre where I gripped
that wormrot's coat that pierces all the world.

    While I was still descending, you were there.
But once I turned, you crossed, with me, the point
to which from every part all weight drags down.

    So you stand here beneath the hemisphere
that now is covered wholly with dry land,
under the highest point at which there died

    the one man sinless in his birth and life.

Dante Alighieri

Your feet are set upon a little sphere
that forms the other aspect of Giudecca.

    It's morning here. It's evening over there.
The thing that made a ladder of his hair
is still as fixed as he has always been.

    Falling from Heaven, when he reached this side,
the lands that then spread out to southern parts
in fear of him took on a veil of sea.

    These reached our hemisphere. Whatever now
is visible to us – in flight perhaps from him –
took refuge here and left an empty space.'

    There is a place (as distant from Beelzebub
as his own tomb extends in breadth)
known not by sight but rather by the sound

of waters falling in a rivulet
eroding, by the winding course it takes (which is
not very steep), an opening in that rock.

    So now we entered on that hidden path,
my lord and I, to move once more towards
a shining world. We did not care to rest.

    We climbed, he going first and I behind,
until through some small aperture I saw
the lovely things the skies above us bear.

    Now we came out, and once more saw the stars.

1. BOCCACCIO · *Mrs Rosie and the Priest*
2. GERARD MANLEY HOPKINS · *As kingfishers catch fire*
3. *The Saga of Gunnlaug Serpent-tongue*
4. THOMAS DE QUINCEY · *On Murder Considered as One of the Fine Arts*
5. FRIEDRICH NIETZSCHE · *Aphorisms on Love and Hate*
6. JOHN RUSKIN · *Traffic*
7. PU SONGLING · *Wailing Ghosts*
8. JONATHAN SWIFT · *A Modest Proposal*
9. *Three Tang Dynasty Poets*
10. WALT WHITMAN · *On the Beach at Night Alone*
11. KENKŌ · *A Cup of Sake Beneath the Cherry Trees*
12. BALTASAR GRACIÁN · *How to Use Your Enemies*
13. JOHN KEATS · *The Eve of St Agnes*
14. THOMAS HARDY · *Woman much missed*
15. GUY DE MAUPASSANT · *Femme Fatale*
16. MARCO POLO · *Travels in the Land of Serpents and Pearls*
17. SUETONIUS · *Caligula*
18. APOLLONIUS OF RHODES · *Jason and Medea*
19. ROBERT LOUIS STEVENSON · *Olalla*
20. KARL MARX AND FRIEDRICH ENGELS · *The Communist Manifesto*
21. PETRONIUS · *Trimalchio's Feast*
22. JOHANN PETER HEBEL · *How a Ghastly Story Was Brought to Light by a Common or Garden Butcher's Dog*
23. HANS CHRISTIAN ANDERSEN · *The Tinder Box*
24. RUDYARD KIPLING · *The Gate of the Hundred Sorrows*
25. DANTE · *Circles of Hell*
26. HENRY MAYHEW · *Of Street Piemen*
27. HAFEZ · *The nightingales are drunk*
28. GEOFFREY CHAUCER · *The Wife of Bath*
29. MICHEL DE MONTAIGNE · *How We Weep and Laugh at the Same Thing*
30. THOMAS NASHE · *The Terrors of the Night*
31. EDGAR ALLAN POE · *The Tell-Tale Heart*
32. MARY KINGSLEY · *A Hippo Banquet*
33. JANE AUSTEN · *The Beautifull Cassandra*
34. ANTON CHEKHOV · *Gooseberries*
35. SAMUEL TAYLOR COLERIDGE · *Well, they are gone, and here must I remain*
36. JOHANN WOLFGANG VON GOETHE · *Sketchy, Doubtful, Incomplete Jottings*
37. CHARLES DICKENS · *The Great Winglebury Duel*
38. HERMAN MELVILLE · *The Maldive Shark*
39. ELIZABETH GASKELL · *The Old Nurse's Story*
40. NIKOLAY LESKOV · *The Steel Flea*

41. HONORÉ DE BALZAC · *The Atheist's Mass*
42. CHARLOTTE PERKINS GILMAN · *The Yellow Wall-Paper*
43. C.P. CAVAFY · *Remember, Body . . .*
44. FYODOR DOSTOEVSKY · *The Meek One*
45. GUSTAVE FLAUBERT · *A Simple Heart*
46. NIKOLAI GOGOL · *The Nose*
47. SAMUEL PEPYS · *The Great Fire of London*
48. EDITH WHARTON · *The Reckoning*
49. HENRY JAMES · *The Figure in the Carpet*
50. WILFRED OWEN · *Anthem For Doomed Youth*
51. WOLFGANG AMADEUS MOZART · *My Dearest Father*
52. PLATO · *Socrates' Defence*
53. CHRISTINA ROSSETTI · *Goblin Market*
54. *Sindbad the Sailor*
55. SOPHOCLES · *Antigone*
56. RYŪNOSUKE AKUTAGAWA · *The Life of a Stupid Man*
57. LEO TOLSTOY · *How Much Land Does A Man Need?*
58. GIORGIO VASARI · *Leonardo da Vinci*
59. OSCAR WILDE · *Lord Arthur Savile's Crime*
60. SHEN FU · *The Old Man of the Moon*
61. AESOP · *The Dolphins, the Whales and the Gudgeon*
62. MATSUO BASHŌ · *Lips too Chilled*
63. EMILY BRONTË · *The Night is Darkening Round Me*
64. JOSEPH CONRAD · *To-morrow*
65. RICHARD HAKLUYT · *The Voyage of Sir Francis Drake Around the Whole Globe*
66. KATE CHOPIN · *A Pair of Silk Stockings*
67. CHARLES DARWIN · *It was snowing butterflies*
68. BROTHERS GRIMM · *The Robber Bridegroom*
69. CATULLUS · *I Hate and I Love*
70. HOMER · *Circe and the Cyclops*
71. D. H. LAWRENCE · *Il Duro*
72. KATHERINE MANSFIELD · *Miss Brill*
73. OVID · *The Fall of Icarus*
74. SAPPHO · *Come Close*
75. IVAN TURGENEV · *Kasyan from the Beautiful Lands*
76. VIRGIL · *O Cruel Alexis*
77. H. G. WELLS · *A Slip under the Microscope*
78. HERODOTUS · *The Madness of Cambyses*
79. *Speaking of Siva*
80. *The Dhammapada*

'. . . a good bit of spice to give the critlings a flavour, and plenty of treacle to make the mince-meat look rich.'

HENRY MAYHEW
Born 1812, London
Died 1887, London

MAYHEW IN PENGUIN CLASSICS
London Labour and the London Poor

HENRY MAYHEW

Of Street Piemen

Edited by
Christopher Gangadin

PENGUIN BOOKS

PENGUIN CLASSICS

UK | USA | Canada | Ireland | Australia
India | New Zealand | South Africa

Penguin Books is part of the Penguin Random House group of companies
whose addresses can be found at global.penguinrandomhouse.com.

This selection published in Penguin Classics 2015
009

Selection and notes copyright © Christopher Gangadin, 2015

Set in 9/12.4 pt Baskerville 10 Pro
Typeset by Jouve (UK), Milton Keynes
Printed and bound in Great Britain by Clays Ltd, Elcograf S.p.A.

A CIP catalogue record for this book is available from the British Library

ISBN: 978-0-141-98024-9

www.greenpenguin.co.uk

Penguin Random House is committed to a sustainable future for our business, our readers and our planet. This book is made from Forest Stewardship Council® certified paper.

Contents

Of Street Piemen	1
A Balloon Flight	6
The London Street Markets on a Saturday Night	12
Of the 'Penny Gaff'	17
The Port of London	23
Of Two Orphan Flower Girls	29
A Train to Clapham Common	35
Of the Street-Sellers of Live Birds	39
Of Sources	46

Of Street Piemen

The itinerant trade in pies is one of the most ancient of the street callings of London. The meat pies are made of beef or mutton; the fish pies of eels; the fruit of apples, currants, gooseberries, plums, damsons, cherries, raspberries, or rhubarb, according to the season – and occasionally of mince-meat. A few years ago the street pie-trade was very profitable, but it has been almost destroyed by the 'pie-shops,' and further, the few remaining street-dealers say 'the people now haven't the pennies to spare.' Summer fairs and races are the best places for the piemen. In London the best times are during any grand sight or holiday-making, such as a review in Hyde-park, the Lord Mayor's show, the opening of Parliament, Greenwich fair, &c. Nearly all the men of this class, whom I saw, were fond of speculating as to whether the Great Exposition would be 'any good' to them, or not.

The London piemen, who may number about forty in winter, and twice that number in summer, are seldom stationary. They go along with their pie-cans on their arms, crying, 'Pies all 'ot! Eel, beef, or mutton pies! Penny pies, all 'ot – all 'ot!' [. . .] The pies are kept hot by means of a charcoal fire beneath, and there is a partition in the body of the can to separate the hot and the cold pies. The 'can' has two tin drawers, one at the bottom, where the hot pies are kept, and above these are the cold pies. As fast as the hot dainties are sold, their place is supplied by the cold from the upper drawer.

A teetotal pieman in Billingsgate has a pony and 'shay cart.' His business is the most extensive in London. It is believed that he sells 20s. worth or 240 pies a day, but his brother tradesmen sell no such amount. 'I was out last night,' said one man to me, 'from four in the afternoon till half-past twelve. I went from Somers-town to the Horse Guards, and looked in at all the public-houses on my way, and I didn't take above 1s. 6d. I have been out sometimes from the beginning of the evening till long past midnight, and haven't taken more than 4d., and out of that I have to pay 1d. for charcoal.'

The pie-dealers usually make the pies themselves. The meat is bought in 'pieces,' of the same part as the sausage-makers purchase – the 'stickings' – at about 3d. the pound. 'People, when I go into houses,' said one man, 'often begin crying, "Mee-yow," or "Bow-wow-wow!" at me; but there's nothing of that kind now. Meat, you see, is so cheap.' About five-dozen pies are generally made at a time. These require a quarter of flour at 5d. or 6d.; 2 lbs. of suet at 6d.; 1½ lb. meat at 3d., amounting in all to about 2s. To this must be added 3d. for baking; 1d. for the cost of keeping hot, and 2d. for pepper, salt and eggs with which to season and wash them over. Hence the cost of the five dozen would be about 2s. 6d., and the profit of the same. The usual quantity of meat in each pie is about half an ounce. There are not more than 20 *hot*-piemen now in London. There are some who carry pies about on a tray slung before them; these are mostly

Of Street Piemen

boys, and, including them, the number amounts to about sixty all the year round, as I have stated.

The penny pie-shops, the street men say, have done their trade a great deal of harm. These shops have now got mostly all the custom, as they make the pies much larger for the money than those sold in the streets. The pies in Tottenham-court-road are very highly seasoned. 'I bought one there the other day, and it nearly took the skin off my mouth; it was full of pepper,' said a street-pieman, with considerable bitterness, to me. The reason why so large a quantity of pepper is put in is, because persons can't tell the flavour of the meat with it. Piemen generally are not very particular about the flavour of the meat they buy, as they can season it up into anything. In the summer, a street-pieman thinks he is doing a good business if the takes 5*s.* a day, and in the winter if he gets half that. On a Saturday night, however, he generally takes 5*s.* in the winter, and about 8*s.* in the summer. At Greenwich fair he will take about 14*s.* At a review in Hyde-park, if it is a good one, he will sell about 10*s.* worth. The generality of the customers are the boys of London. The women seldom, if ever, buy pies in the streets. At the public-houses a few pies are sold, and the pieman makes a practice of 'looking in' at all the taverns on his way. Here his customers are found principally in the tap-room. 'Here's all 'ot!' the pieman cries as he walks in; 'toss or Buy! Up and win 'em!' This is the only way that the pies can be got rid of. 'If it wasn't for tossing we shouldn't sell on.'

To 'toss the pieman' is a favourite pastime with costermongers' boys and all that class; some of whom aspire to the repute of being gourmands, and are critical on the quality of the comestible. If the pieman win the toss, he receives 1*d*. without giving a pie; if he lose, he hands it over for nothing. The pieman himself never 'tosses,' but always calls head or tail to his customer. At the week's end it comes to the same thing, they say, whether they toss or not, or rather whether they win or lose the toss: 'I've taken as much as 2*s*. 6*d*. at tossing, which I shouldn't have had if I had'nt done so. Very few people buy without tossing, and the boys in particular. Gentlemen "out on the spree" at the late public-houses will frequently toss when they don't want the pies, and when they win they will amuse themselves by throwing the pies at one another, or at me. Sometimes I have taken as much as half-a-crown, and the people of whom I had the money has never eaten a pie. The boys has the greatest love of gambling, and they seldom, if ever, buys without tossing.' One of the reasons why the street boys delight in tossing, is, that they can often obtain a pie by such means when they have only a halfpenny wherewith to gamble. If the lad wins he gets a penny pie for his halfpenny.

For street mince-meat pies the pieman usually makes 5lb. of mince-meat at a time, and for this he will put in 2 doz. of apples, 1lb. of sugar, 1lb. of currants, 2lb. of 'critlings' (critlings being the refuse left after boiling down the lard), a good bit of spice to give the critlings a flavour, and plenty of treacle to make the mince-meat look rich.

The 'gravy' that used to be given with the meat-pies was poured out of an oil-can, and consisted of a little salt and water browned. A hole was made with the little finger in the top of the meat pie, and the 'gravy' poured in until the crust rose. With this gravy a person in the line assured me that he

Of Street Piemen

has known pies four days old to go off very freely, and be pronounced excellent. The street-piemen are mostly bakers, who are unable to obtain employment at their trade. 'I myself,' said one, 'was a bread and biscuit baker. I have been at the pie business now about two years and a half, and I can't get a living at it. Last week my earnings were not more than 7*s*. all the week through, and I was out till three in the morning to get that.' The piemen seldom begin business till six o'clock, and some remain out all night. The best time for the sale of pies is generally from ten at night to one in the morning.

Calculating that there are only fifty street piemen plying their trade in London, the year through, and that their average earnings are 8*s*. a week, we find a street expenditure exceeding 3,000*l*., and a street consumption of pies amounting to three quarters of a million yearly.

To start in the penny-pie business of the streets requires *1l*. for a 'can', *2s*. *6d*. for a 'turn-halfpenny' board to gamble with, *12s*. for a gross of tin pie-dishes, *8d*. for an apron, and about *6s*. *6d*. for stock money – allowing 1*s*. for flour, 1*s*. *3d*. for meat, 2*d*. for apples, 4*d*. for eels, 2*s*. for pork flare or fat, 2*d*. for sugar, ½*d*. for cloves, 1*d*. for pepper and salt, 1*d*. for an egg to wash the pies over with, 6*d*. for baking, and 1*d*. for charcoal to keep the pies hot in the streets. Hence the capital required would be about 2*l*. in all.

A Balloon Flight

We had seen the Great Metropolis under almost every aspect. We had dived into the holes and corners hidden from the honest and well-to-do portion of the London community. We had visited Jacob's Island (the plague-spot of the British Capital) in the height of the cholera, when to inhale the very air of the place was to imbibe the breath of death. We had sought out the haunts of beggars and thieves, and passed hours communing with them as to their histories, habits, thoughts, and impulses. We had examined the World of London below the moral surface, as it were; and we had a craving, like the rest of mankind, to contemplate it from above; so, being offered a seat in the car of the Royal Nassau Balloon, we determined upon accompanying Mr Green into the clouds on his five hundredth ascent.

It was late in the evening (a fine autumn one) when the gun was fired that was the signal for the great gas-bag to be loosened from the ropes that held it down to the soil; and, immediately the buoyant machine bounded, like a big ball, into the air. Or, rather let us say, the earth seemed to sink suddenly down, as if the spot of ground to which it had been previously fastened had been constructed upon the same principle as the Adelphi stage, and admitted of being lowered at a moment's notice. Indeed, no sooner did the report of the gun clatter in the air, than the people, who had

A Balloon Flight

before been grouped about the car, appeared to fall from a level with the eye; and, instantaneously, there was seen a multitude of flat, upturned faces in the gardens below, with a dense *chevaux de frise* of arms extended above them, and some hundreds of outstretched hands fluttering farewell to us.

The moment after this, the balloon vaulted over the trees, and we saw the roadway outside the gardens stuck all over with mobs of little black Lilliputian people, while the hubbub of the voices below, and the cries of 'Ah *bal*-loon!' from the boys, rose to the ear like the sound of a distant school let loose to play.

Now began that peculiar panoramic effect which is the distinguishing feature of the first portion of a view from a balloon, and which arises from the utter absence of all sense of motion in the machine itself, and the consequent transference of the movement to the ground beneath. The earth, as the aeronautic vessel glided over it, seemed positively to consist of a continuous series of scenes which were being drawn along underneath us, as if it were some diorama laid flat upon the ground, and almost gave one the notion that the world was an endless landscape stretched upon rollers, which some invisible sprites below were busy revolving for our especial amusement.

Then, as we floated along, above the fields in a line with the Thames towards Richmond, and looked over the edge of the car in which we were standing (and which, by the bye, was like a big 'buck-basket,' reaching to one's breast), the sight was the most exquisite visual delight ever experienced. The houses directly underneath us looked like the tiny wooden things out of a child's box of toys, and the streets as if they were ruts in the ground; and we could hear the hum of the voices rising from every spot we passed over, faint as the buzzing of so many bees.

Far beneath, in the direction we were sailing, lay the suburban fields; and here the earth, with its tiny hills and plains and streams, assumed the appearance of the little coloured plaster models of countries. The roadways striping the land were like narrow brown ribbons, and the river, which we could see winding far away, resembled a long, gray, metallic-looking snake, creeping through the fields. The bridges over the Thames were positively like planks; and the tiny black barges, as they floated along the stream, seemed no bigger than summer insects on the water. The largest meadows were about the size of green-baize table covers; and across these we could just trace the line of the South-Western Railway, with the little whiff of white steam issuing from some passing engine, and no greater in volume than the jet of vapour from an ordinary tea-kettle.

Then, as the dusk of evening approached, and the gas-lights along the different lines of road started into light, one after another, the ground seemed to be covered with little illumination lamps, such as are hung on Christmas-trees, and reminding one of those that are occasionally placed, at intervals, along the grass at the edge of the gravel-walks in suburban tea-gardens; whilst the clusters of little lights at the spots where the hamlets were scattered over the scene, appeared like a knot of fire-flies in the air; and in the midst of these the eye could, here and there, distinguish the tiny crimson speck of some railway signal.

A Balloon Flight

In the opposite direction to that in which the wind was insensibly wafting the balloon, lay the leviathan Metropolis, with a dense canopy of smoke hanging over it, and reminding one of the fog of vapour that is often seen steaming up from the fields at early morning. It was impossible to tell where the monster city began or ended, for the buildings stretched not only to the horizon on either side, but far away into the distance, where, owing to the coming shades of evening and the dense fumes from the million chimneys, the town seemed to blend into the sky, so that there was no distinguishing earth from heaven. The multitude of roofs that extended back from the foreground was positively like a dingy red sea, heaving in bricken billows, and the seeming waves rising up one after the other till the eye grew wearied with following them. Here and there we could distinguish little bare green patches of parks, and occasionally make out the tiny circular enclosures of the principal squares, though, from the height, these appeared scarcely bigger than wafers. Further, the fog of smoke that over-shadowed the giant town was pierced with a thousand steeples and pin-like factory-chimneys.

That little building, no bigger than one of the small china houses that are used for burning pastilles in, is Buckingham Palace – with St James's Park, dwindled to the size of a card-table, stretched out before it. Yonder is Bethlehem Hospital, with its dome, now of about the same dimensions as a bell.

Then the little mites of men, crossing the bridges, seemed to have no more motion in them than the animalcules in cheese; while the streets appeared more like cracks in the soil than highways, and the tiny steamers on the river were only to be distinguished by the thin black thread of smoke trailing after them.

Indeed, it was a most wonderful sight to behold that vast bricken mass of churches and hospitals, banks and prisons, palaces and workhouses, docks and refuges for the destitute, parks and squares, and courts and alleys, which make up London – all blent into one immense black spot – to look down upon the whole as the birds of the air look down upon it, and see it dwindled into a mere rubbish heap – to contemplate from afar that strange conglomeration of vice, avarice, and low cunning, of noble aspirations and humble heroism, and to grasp it in the eye, in all its incongruous integrity, at one single glance – to take, as it were, an angel's view of that huge town where, perhaps, there is more virtue and more iniquity, more wealth and more want, brought together into one dense focus than in any other part of the earth – to hear the hubbub of the restless sea of life and emotion below, and hear it, like the ocean in a shell, whispering of the incessant stragglings and chafings of the distant tide – to swing in the air high above all the petty jealousies and heart-burnings, small ambitions and vain parade of 'polite' society, and feel, for once, tranquil as a babe in a cot, and that you are hardly of the earth earthy, as, Jacob-like, you mount the aerial ladder, and half lose sight of the 'great commercial world' beneath, where men are regarded as mere counters to play with, and where to do your neighbour as your neighbour would do you constitutes the first principle in the religion of trade – to feel yourself floating through the endless realms of space, and drinking in the pure thin air of

A Balloon Flight

the skies, as you go sailing along almost among the stars, free as 'the lark at heaven's gate,' and enjoying, for a brief half hour, at least, a foretaste of that Elysian destiny which is the ultimate hope of all.

Such is the scene we behold, and such the thoughts that stir the brain on contemplating London from the car of a balloon.

The London Street Markets on a Saturday Night

The street-sellers are to be seen in the greatest numbers at the London street markets on a Saturday night. Here, and in the shops immediately adjoining, the working-classes generally purchase their Sunday's dinner; and after pay-time on Saturday night, or early on Sunday morning, the crowd in the New-cut, and the Brill in particular, is almost impassable. Indeed, the scene in these parts has more of the character of a fair than a market. There are hundreds of stalls, and every stall has its one or two lights; either it is illuminated by the intense white light of the new self-generating gas-lamp, or else it is brightened up by the red smoky flame of the old-fashioned grease lamps. One man shows off his yellow haddock with a candle stuck in a bundle of firewood; his neighbour makes a candlestick of a huge turnip, and the tallow gutters over its sides; whilst the boy shouting 'Eight a penny, stunning pears!' has rolled his dip in a thick coat of brown paper, that flares away with the candle. Some stalls are crimson with the fire shining through the holes beneath the baked-chestnut stove; others have handsome octahedral lamps, while a few have a candle shining through a sieve; these, with the sparkling ground-glass globes of the tea-dealers' shops, and the butchers' gaslights streaming and fluttering in the wind, like flags of flame, pour forth such a

The London Street Markets on a Saturday Night

flood of light, that at a distance the atmosphere immediately above the spot is as lurid as if the pavement were on fire.

The pavement and the road are crowded with purchasers and street-sellers. The housewife in her thick shawl, with the market-basket on her arm, walks slowly on, stopping now to look at the stall of caps, and now to cheapen a bunch of greens. Little boys, holding three or four onions in their hand, creep between the people, wriggling their way through every interstice, and asking for custom in whining tones, as if seeking charity. Then the tumult of the thousand different cries of the eager dealers, all shouting at the top of their voices, at one and the same time, is almost bewildering. 'So-old again,' roars one. 'Chestnuts all 'ot, a penny a score,' bawls another. 'An 'aypenny a skin, blacking,' squeaks a boy. 'Buy, buy, buy, buy, buy – bu-u-uy!' cries the butcher. 'Half-quire of paper for a penny,' bellows the street stationer. 'An 'aypenny a lot ing-uns.' 'Twopence a pound grapes.' 'Three a penny Yarmouth bloaters.' 'Who'll buy a bonnet for fourpence?' 'Pick 'em out cheap here! Three pair for a halfpenny, bootlaces.' 'Now's your time! Beautiful whelks, a penny a lot.' 'Here's ha'p'orths,' shouts the perambulating confectioner. 'Come and look at 'em! Here's toasters!' bellows one with a Yarmouth bloater stuck on a toasting fork. 'Penny a lot, fine russets,' calls the apple woman: and so the Babel goes on.

One man stands with his red-edged mats hanging over his back and chest, like a herald's coat; and the girl with her basket of walnuts lifts her brown-stained fingers to her mouth, as she screams, 'Fine warnuts! Sixteen a penny, fine war-r-nuts.' A bootmaker, to 'ensure custom,' has illuminated his shop-front with a line of gas, and in its full glare stands a blind beggar, his eyes turned up so as to show only 'the whites,' and mumbling some begging rhymes, that are drowned in the shrill notes of the bamboo-flute-player next to him. The boy's sharp cry, the woman's cracked voice, the gruff, hoarse shout of the man, are all mingled together. Sometimes an Irishman is heard with his 'fine eating apples;' or else the jingling music of an unseen organ breaks out, as the trio of street singers rest between the verses.

Then the sights, as you elbow your way through the crowd, are equally multifarious. Here is a stall glittering with new tin saucepans; there another, bright with its blue and yellow crockery, and sparkling with white glass. Now you come to a row of old shoes arranged along the pavement; now to a stand of gaudy tea-trays; then to a shop with red handkerchiefs and blue checked shirts, fluttering backwards and forwards, and a counter built up outside on the kerb, beside which are boys beseeching custom. At the door of a tea-shop, with its hundred white globes of light, stands a man delivering bills, thanking the public for past favours, and 'defying competition.' Here, alongside the road, are some half-dozen headless tailors' dummies, dressed in Chesterfields and fustian jackets, each labelled, 'Look at the prices,' or 'Observe the quality.' After this a butcher's shop, crimson and white with meat piled up to the first-floor, in front of which the butcher himself, in his blue coat, walks up and down, sharpening his knife on the steel that hangs to his waist. A little further on stands the clean family, begging; the father with his head down as if in shame, and a box of lucifers held forth in his hand – the boys in newly-washed pinafores, and the

The London Street Markets on a Saturday Night

tidily got-up mother with a child at her breast. This stall is green and white with bunches of turnips – that red with apples, the next yellow with onions, and another purple with pickling cabbages. One minute you pass a man with an umbrella turned inside up and full of prints; the next, you hear one with a peep show of Mazeppa, and Paul Jones the pirate, describing the pictures to the boys looking in at the little round windows. Then is heard the sharp snap of the percussion-cap from the crowd of lads firing at the target for nuts; and the moment afterwards, you see either a black man half-clad in white, and shivering in the cold with tracts in his hand, or else you hear the sounds of music from 'Frazier's Circus,' on the other side of the road, and the man outside the door of the penny concert, beseeching you to 'Be in time – be in time!' as Mr Somebody is just about to sing his favourite song of the 'Knife Grinder.' Such, indeed, is the riot, the struggle, and the scramble for a living, that the confusion and uproar of the New-Cut on Saturday night have a bewildering and saddening effect upon the thoughtful mind.

Each salesman tries his utmost to sell his wares, tempting the passers-by with his bargains. The boy with his stock of herbs offers 'a double 'andful of fine parsley for a penny;' the man with the donkey-cart filled with turnips has three lads to shout for him to their utmost, with their 'Ho! ho! hi-i-i! What do you think of this here? A penny a bunch – hurrah for free trade! *Here's* your turnips!' Until it is seen and heard, we have no sense of the scramble that is going on throughout London for a living. The same scene takes place at the Brill – the same in Leather Lane – the same in

Tottenham-court-road – the same in Whitecross-street; go to whatever corner of the metropolis you please, either on a Saturday night or a Sunday morning, and there is the same shouting and the same struggling to get the penny profit out of the poor man's Sunday's dinner.

Since the above description was written the New-Cut has lost much of its noisy and brilliant glory. In consequence of a New Police regulation, 'stands' or 'pitches' have been forbidden, and each coster, on a market night, is now obliged, under pain of the lock-up house, to carry his tray, or keep moving with his barrow. The gay stalls have been replaced by deal boards, some sodden with wet fish, others stained purple with blackberries, or brown with walnut-peel; and the bright lamps are almost totally superseded by the dim, guttering candle. Even if the pole under the tray or 'shallow' is seen resting on the ground, the policeman on duty is obliged to interfere.

The mob of purchasers has diminished one-half; and instead of the road being filled with customers and trucks, the pavements and kerbstones are scarcely crowded.

Of the 'Penny Gaff'

In many of the thoroughfares of London there are shops which have been turned into a kind of temporary theatre (admission one penny), where dancing and singing take place every night. Rude pictures of the performers are arranged outside, to give the front a gaudy and attractive look, and at night-time coloured lamps and transparencies are displayed to draw an audience. These places are called by the costers 'Penny Gaffs;' and on a Monday night as many as six performances will take place, each one having its two hundred visitors . . .

The 'penny gaff' chosen was situated in a broad street near Smithfield; and for a great distance off, the jingling sound of music was heard, and the gas-light streamed out into the thick night air as from a dark lantern, glittering on the windows of the houses opposite, and lighting up the faces of the mob in the road, as on an illumination night. The front of a large shop had been entirely removed, and the entrance was decorated with paintings of the 'comic singers,' in their most 'humorous' attitudes. On a table against the wall was perched the band, playing what the costers call 'dancing tunes' with great effect, for the hole at the money-takers box was blocked up with hands tendering the penny. The crowd without was so numerous, that a policeman was in attendance to preserve order, and push the boys off the pavement – the music having the effect of drawing them insensibly towards the festooned green-baize curtain.

The shop itself had been turned into a waiting-room, and was crowded even to the top of the stairs leading to the gallery on the first floor. The ceiling of this 'lobby' was painted blue, and spotted with whitewash clouds, to represent the heavens; the boards of the trapdoor, and the laths that showed through the holes in the plaster, being all of the same colour. A notice was here posted, over the canvass door leading into the theatre, to the effect that 'Ladies and Gentlemen to the Front Places must pay Twopence.'

The visitors, with few exceptions, were all boys and girls, whose ages seemed to vary from eight to twenty years. Some of the girls – though their figures showed them to be mere children – were dressed in showy cotton-velvet polkas, and wore dowdy feathers in their crushed bonnets. They stood laughing and joking with the lads, in an unconcerned, impudent manner, that was almost appalling. Some of them, when tired of waiting, chose their partners, and commenced dancing grotesquely, to the admiration of the lookers-on, who expressed their approbation in obscene terms, that, far from disgusting the poor little women, were received as compliments, and acknowledged with smiles and coarse repartees. The boys clustered together, smoking their pipes, and laughing at each other's anecdotes, or else jingling halfpence in time with the tune, while they whistled an accompaniment to it. Presently one of the performers, with a gilt crown on his well-greased locks, descended from the staircase, his fleshings covered by a dingy dressing-gown, and mixed with the mob, shaking hands with old acquain-

Of the 'Penny Gaff'

tances. The 'comic singer,' too, made his appearance among the throng – the huge bow to his cravat, which nearly covered his waistcoat, and the red end to his nose, exciting neither merriment nor surprise.

To discover the kind of entertainment, a lad near me and my companion was asked 'if there was any flash dancing.' With a knowing wink the boy answered, 'Lots! Show their legs and all, prime!' and immediately the boy followed up his information by a request for a 'yennep' to get a 'tib of occabot.' After waiting in the lobby some considerable time, the performance inside was concluded, and the audience came pouring out through the canvass door. As they had to pass singly, I noticed them particularly. Above three-fourths of them were women and girls, the rest consisting chiefly of mere boys – for out of about two hundred persons I counted only eighteen men. Forward they came, bringing an overpowering stench with them, laughing and yelling as they pushed their way through the waiting-room. One woman carrying a sickly child with a bulging forehead, was reeling drunk, the saliva running down her mouth as she stared about her with a heavy fixed eye. Two boys were pushing her from side to side, while the poor infant slept, breathing heavily, as if stupefied, through the din. Lads jumping on girls' shoulders, and girls laughing hysterically from being tickled by the youths behind them, everyone shouting and jumping, presented a mad scene of frightful enjoyment.

When these had left, a rush for places by those in waiting began, that set at defiance the blows and strugglings of a lady in spangles who endeavoured to preserve order and take the checks. As time was a great object with the proprietor, the entertainment within began directly the first seat was taken, so that the lads without, rendered furious by the rattling of the piano within, made the canvas partition bulge in and out, with the struggling of those seeking admission, like a sail in a flagging wind.

To form the theatre, the first floor had been removed; the whitewashed beams however still stretched from wall to wall. The lower room had evidently been the warehouse, while the upper apartment had been the sitting-room, for the paper was still on the walls. A gallery, with a canvas front, had been hurriedly built up, and it was so fragile that the boards bent under the weight of those above. The bricks in the warehouse were smeared over with red paint, and had a few black curtains daubed upon them. The coster-youths require no very great scenic embellishment, and indeed the stage – which was about eight feet square – could admit of none. Two jets of gas, like those outside a butcher's shop, were placed on each side of the proscenium, and proved very handy for the gentlemen whose pipes required lighting. The band inside the 'theatre' could not compare with the band without. An old grand piano, whose canvas-covered top extended the entire length of the stage, sent forth its wiry notes under the be-ringed fingers of a 'professor Wilkinsini,' while another professional, with his head resting on his violin, played vigorously, as he stared unconcernedly at the noisy audience.

Singing and dancing formed the whole of the hour's performance, and, of the two, the singing was preferred. A young girl, of about fourteen years of age, danced with more energy than grace, and seemed to be well-known to the

Of the 'Penny Gaff'

spectators, who cheered her on by her Christian name. When the dance was concluded, the proprietor of the establishment threw down a penny from the gallery, in the hopes that others might be moved to similar acts of generosity; but no one followed up the offer, so the young lady hunted after the money and departed. The 'comic singer,' in a battered hat and the huge bow to his cravat, was received with deafening shouts. Several songs were named by the costers, but the 'funny gentleman' merely requested them 'to hold their jaws,' and putting on a 'knowing' look, sang a song, the whole point of which consisted in the mere utterance of some filthy word at the end of each stanza. Nothing, however, could have been more successful. The lads stamped their feet with delight; the girls screamed with enjoyment. Once or twice a young shrill laugh would anticipate the fun – as if the words were well known – or the boys would forestall the point by shouting it out before the proper time. When the song was ended the house was in a delirium of applause. The canvas front to the gallery was beaten with sticks, drum-like, and sent down showers of white powder on the heads in the pit. Another song followed, and the actor knowing on what his success depended, lost no opportunity of increasing his laurels. The most obscene thoughts, the most disgusting scenes were coolly described, making a poor child near me wipe away the tears that rolled down her eyes with the enjoyment of the poison. There were three or four of these songs sung during the course of the evening, each one being encored, and then changed. One written about 'Pine-apple rock,' was the grand treat of the night, and offered greater scope to the rhyming powers of the author than any of the others. In this, not a single chance had been missed; ingenuity had been exerted to its utmost lest an obscene thought should be passed by, and it was absolutely awful to behold the relish with which the young ones jumped to the hideous meaning of the verses.

There was one scene yet to come that was perfect in its wickedness. A ballet began between a man dressed up as a woman, and a country clown. The most disgusting attitudes were struck, the most immoral acts represented, without one dissenting voice. If there had been any feat of agility, any grimacing, or, in fact, anything with which the laughter of the uneducated classes is usually associated, the applause might have been accounted for; but here were two ruffians degrading themselves each time they stirred a limb, and forcing into the brains of the childish audience before them thoughts that must embitter a lifetime, and descend from father to child like some bodily infirmity.

The Port of London

Seen from the Custom House, this is indeed a characteristic sight; and some time since we were permitted, by the courtesy of the authorities, to witness the view from the 'long room' there.

The broad highway of the river – which at this part is near upon 300 yards in width – was almost blocked with the tiers of shipping; for there was merely a narrow pathway of grey, glittering water left open in the middle; and, on either side, the river was black with the dense mass of hulls collected alongside the quays; while the masts of the craft were as thick as the pine stems in their native forests.

The sun shone bright upon the water, and as its broken beams played upon the surface it sparkled and twinkled in the light, like a crumpled plate of golden foil; and down the 'silent highway,' barges, tide-borne, floated sideways, with their long slim oars projecting from their sides like the fins of a flying fish; whilst others went along, with their masts slanting down and their windlass clicking as men laboured to raise the 'warm-brown ' sail that they had lowered to pass under the bridge. Then came a raft of timber, towed by a small boat, and the boatman leaning far back in it as he tugged at the sculls; and presently a rapid river steamer flitted past, the deck crowded so densely with passengers that it reminded one of a cushion stuck all over with black pins;

and as it hurried past we caught a whiff, as it were, of music from the little band on board.

The large square blocks of warehouses on the opposite shore were almost hidden in the shadow which came slanting down far into the river, and covering, as with a thick veil of haze, the confused knot of sloops and schooners and 'bilanders' that lay there in the dusk, in front of the wharves. Over the tops of the warehouses we could see the trail of white steam, from the railway engines at the neighbouring terminus, darting from among the roofs as they hurried to and fro.

A little way down the river, stood a clump of Irish vessels, with the light peeping through the thicket, as it were, of their masts – some with their sails hanging all loose and limp, and others with them looped in rude festoons to the yards. Beside these lay barges stowed full of barrels of beer and sacks of flour; and a few yards farther on, a huge foreign steamer appeared, with short thick black funnel and blue paddle-boxes. Then came hoys laden with straw and coasting goods, and sunk so deep in the water that, as the steamers dashed by, the white spray was seen to beat against the dark tarpaulins that covered their heaped-up cargoes. Next to these the black, surly-looking colliers were noted, huddled in a dense mass together, with the bare backs of the coalwhippers flashing among the rigging as, in hoisting the 'Wallsend' from the hold, they leaped at intervals down upon the deck.

Behind, and through the tangled skeins of the rigging, the eye rested upon the old Suffranco wharves, with their peaked roofs and unwieldy cranes; and far at the back we caught sight of one solitary tree; whilst in the fog of the extreme distance the steeple of St Mary's, Rotherhithe, loomed over the mast-heads – grey, dim, and spectral-like.

Then, as we turned round and looked towards the bridge, we caught glimpses of barges and boats moving in the broad arcs of light showing through the arches; while above the bridge-parapet were seen just the tops of moving carts, and omnibuses, and high-loaded railway wagons, hurrying along in opposite directions.

Glancing thence to the bridge-wharves on the same side of the river as ourselves, we beheld bales of goods dangling in the air from the cranes that projected from the top of 'Nicholson's.' Here alongside the quay lay Spanish schooners and brigs, laden with fruits; and as we cast our eye below, we saw puppet-like figures of men with cases of oranges on their backs, bending beneath the load, on their way across the dumb-lighter to the wharf.

Next came Billingsgate, and here we could see the white bellies of the fish showing in the market beneath, and streams of men passing backwards and forwards to the river side, where lay a small crowd of Dutch eel boats, with their gutta-percha-like hulls, and unwieldy, green-tipped rudders. Immediately beneath us was the brown, gravelled walk of the Custom House quay, where trim children strolled with their nursemaids, and hatless and yellow-legged Blue-coat Boys, and there were youths fresh from school, who had come either to have a peep at the shipping, or to skip and play among the barges.

From the neighbouring stairs boats pushed off continually, while men standing in the stern wriggled themselves along by working a scull behind, after the fashion of a fish's tail.

Here, near the front of the quay, lay a tier of huge steamers with gilt sterns and mahogany wheels, and their bright brass binnacles shining as if on fire in the sun. At the foremast head of one of these the 'blue Peter' was flying as a summons to the hands on shore to come aboard, while the dense clouds of smoke that poured from the thick red funnel told that the boiler fires were ready lighted for starting.

Further on, might be seen the old 'Perseus,' the receiving-ship of the navy, with her topmasts down, her black sides towering high, like immense rampart-walls, out of the water, and her long white ventilating sacks hanging over the hatchways. Immediately beyond this, the eye could trace the Tower wharves, with their gravelled walks, and the high-capped and red-coated sentry pacing up and down them, and the square old grey lump of the Tower, with a turret at each of its four corners, peering over the water. In front of this lay another dense crowd of foreign vessels, and with huge lighters beside the wharf, while bales of hemp and crates of hardware swung from the cranes as they were lowered into the craft below.

In the distance, towered the huge massive warehouses of St Katherine's Dock, with their big signet letters on their sides, their many prison-like windows, and their cranes and doors to every floor. Beyond this, the view was barred out by the dense grove of masts that rose up from the water, thick as giant reeds beside the shore, and filmed over with the grey mist of vapour rising from the river so that their softened outlines melted gently into the dusk.

As we stood looking down upon the river, the hundred clocks of the hundred churches at our back, with the golden figures on their black dials shining in the sun, chimed the hour of noon, and in a hundred different tones; while solemnly above all boomed forth the deep metallic moan of St Paul's; and scarcely had the great bell ceased humming in the air, before there rose the sharp tinkling of eight bells from the decks of the multitude of sailing vessels and steamers packed below.

Indeed, there was an exquisite charm in the many different sounds that smote the ear from the busy Port of London. Now we could hear the ringing of the 'purlman's' bell, as, in his little boat, he flitted in and out among the several tiers of colliers to serve the grimy and half-naked coalwhippers with drink. Then would come the rattle of some heavy chain suddenly let go, and after this the chorus of many seamen heaving at the ropes; whilst high above all roared the hoarse voice of someone on the shore, bawling through his hands to a mate aboard the craft. Presently came the clicking of the capstan-palls, telling of the heaving of a neighbouring anchor; and mingling with all this might be heard the rumbling of the wagons and carts in the streets behind, and the panting and throbbing of the passing river steamers in front, together with the shrill scream of the railway whistle from the terminus on the opposite shore.

In fine, look or listen in whatever direction we might, the many sights and sounds that filled the eye and ear told each its different tale of busy trade, bold enterprise, and boundless capital. In the many bright-coloured flags that fluttered from the mastheads of the vessels crowding the port, we could read how all the corners of the earth had been ransacked each for its peculiar produce. The massive warehouses at the water-side looked really like the storehouses of the world's infinite products, and the tall mast-like factory chimneys behind us, with their black plumes of smoke streaming from them, told us how all around that port were hard at work fashioning the products into cunning fabrics.

Then, as we beheld the white clouds of steam from some passing railway engine puffed out once more from among the opposite roofs, and heard the clatter of the thousand vehicles in the streets hard by, and watched the dark tide of carts and wagons pouring over the bridge, and looked down the apparently endless vista of masts that crowded either side of the river – we could not help feeling how every power known to man was here used to bring and diffuse the riches of all parts of the world over our own, and indeed every other country.

Of Two Orphan Flower Girls

Of flower girls there are two classes. Some girls, and they are certainly the smaller class of the two, avail themselves of the sale of flowers in the streets for immoral purposes, or rather, they seek to eke out the small gains of their trade by such practices. They frequent the great thoroughfares, and offer their bouquets to gentlemen, whom on an evening they pursue for a hundred yards or two in such places as the Strand, mixing up a leer with their whine for custom or for charity. Their ages are from fourteen to nineteen or twenty, and sometimes they remain out offering their flowers – or dried lavender when no flowers are to be had – until late at night. They do not care, to make their appearance in the streets until towards evening, and though they solicit the custom of ladies, they rarely follow or importune them. Of this class I shall treat more fully under another head.

The other class of flower-girls is composed of the girls who, wholly or partially, depend upon the sale of flowers for their own support or as an assistance to their parents. Some of them are the children of street-sellers, some are orphans, and some are the daughters of mechanics who are out of employment, and who prefer any course rather than an application to the parish. These girls offer their flowers in the principal streets at the West End, and resort greatly to the suburbs; there are a few, also, in the business thoroughfares.

They walk up and down in front of the houses, offering their flowers to anyone looking out of the windows, or they stand at any likely place. They are generally very persevering, more especially the younger children, who will run along barefooted, with their 'Please, gentleman, do buy my flowers. Poor little girl!' – 'Please, kind lady, buy my violets. O, do! please! Poor little girl! Do buy a bunch, please, kind lady!'

The statement I give, 'of two orphan flower sellers' furnishes another proof, in addition to the many I have already given, of the heroic struggles of the poor, and of the truth of the saying 'What would the poor do without the poor?'

The better class of flower-girls reside in Lisson-grove, in the streets off Drury-lane, in St Giles's, and in other parts inhabited by the very poor. Some of them live in lodging-houses, the stench and squalor of which are in remarkable contrast to the beauty and fragrance of the flowers they sometimes have to carry thither with them unsold.

Of these girls the elder was fifteen and the younger eleven. Both were clad in old, but not torn, dark print frocks, hanging so closely, and yet so loosely, about them as to show the deficiency of underclothing; they wore old broken black chip bonnets. The older sister (or rather half-sister) had a pair of old worn-out shoes on her feet, the younger was barefoot, but trotted along, in a gait at once quick and feeble – as if the soles of her little feet were impervious, like horn, to the roughness of the road. The elder girl had a modest expression of countenance, with no pretensions to prettiness except in having tolerably good eyes. Her complexion was somewhat muddy, and her features somewhat pinched. The

Of Two Orphan Flower Girls

younger child had a round, chubby, and even rosy face, and quite a healthful look. [. . .]

They lived in one of the streets near Drury-lane. They were inmates of a house, not let out as a lodging house, in separate beds, but in rooms, and inhabited by street-sellers and street-labourers. The room they occupied was large, and one dim candle lighted it so insufficiently that it seemed to exaggerate the dimensions. The walls were bare and discoloured with damp. The furniture consisted of a crazy table and a few chairs, and in the centre of the room was an old four-post bedstead of the larger size. This bed was occupied nightly by the two sisters and their brother, a lad just turned thirteen. In a sort of recess in a corner of the room was the decency of an old curtain – or something equivalent, for I could hardly see in the dimness – and behind this was, I presume, the bed of the married couple. The three children paid 2*s.* a week for the room, the tenant an Irishman out of work paying 2*s.* 9*d.*, but the furniture was his, and his wife aided the children in their trifle of washing, mended their clothes, where such a thing was possible, and such like. The husband was absent at the time of my visit, but the wife seemed of a better stamp, judging by her appearance, and by her refraining from any direct, or even indirect, way of begging, as well as from the 'Glory be to Gods!' 'the heavens be your honour's bed!' or 'it's the thruth I'm telling of you sire,' that I so frequently meet with on similar visits.

The elder girl said, in an English accent, not at all garrulously, but merely in answer to my questions: 'I sell flowers, sir; we live almost on flowers when they are to be got. I sell, and so does my sister, all kinds, but it's very little use offering any that's not sweet. I think it's the sweetness as sells them. I sell primroses, when they're in, and violets, and wall-flowers, and stocks, and roses of different sorts, and pinks, and carnations, and mixed flowers, and lilies of the valley, and green lavender, and mignonette (but that I do very seldom), and violets again at this time of the year, for we get them both in spring and winter.' [They are forced in hot-houses for winter sale, I may remark.] 'The best sale of all is, I think, moss-roses, young moss-roses. We do best of all on them. Primroses are good, for people say: "Well, here's spring again to a certainty." Gentlemen are our best customers. I've heard that they buy flowers to give to the ladies. Ladies have sometimes said: "A penny, my poor girl, here's three-halfpence for the bunch." Or they've given me the price of two bunches for one; so have gentlemen. I never had a rude word said to me by a gentleman in my life. No, sir, neither lady nor gentleman ever gave me 6*d*. for a bunch of flowers. I never had a sixpence given to me in my life – never. I never go among boys, I know nobody but my brother. My father was a tradesman in Mitchelstown, in the County Cork. I don't know what sort of a tradesman he was. I never saw him. He was a tradesman I've been told. I was born in London. Mother was a chairwoman, and lived very well. None of us ever saw a father.' [It was evident that they were illegitimate children, but the landlady had never seen the mother, and could give me no information.] 'We don't know anything about our fathers. We were all "mother's children." Mother died seven years ago last Guy Faux day. I've got myself, and my brother and sister a bit of bread ever since, and never had any help but from the neighbours. I never troubled the parish. O, yes,

Of Two Orphan Flower Girls

sir, the neighbours is all poor people, very poor, some of them. We've lived with her' (indicating her landlady by a gesture) 'these two years, and off and on before that. I can't say how long.' 'Well, I don't know exactly,' said the landlady, 'but I've had them with me almost all the time, for four years, as near as I can recollect; perhaps more. I've moved three times, and they always followed me.' In answer to my inquiries the landlady assured me that these two poor girls, were never out of doors all the time she had known them after six at night. 'We've always good health. We can all read.' [Here the three somewhat insisted upon proving to me their proficiency in reading, and having produced a Roman Catholic book, the 'Garden of Heaven,' they read very well.] 'I put myself,' continued the girl, 'and I put my brother and sister to a Roman Catholic school – and to Ragged schools – but I could read before mother died. My brother can write, and I pray to God that he'll do well with it. I buy my flowers at Convent Garden; sometimes, but very seldom, at Farringdon. I pay 1*s.* for a dozen bunches, whatever flowers are in. Out of every two bunches I can make three, at 1*d.* a piece. Sometimes one or two over in the dozen, but not so often as I would like. We make the bunches up ourselves. We get the rush to tie them with for nothing. We put their own leaves round these violets (she produced a bunch). The paper for a dozen costs a penny; sometimes only a halfpenny. The two of us doesn't make less than 6*d.* a day, unless it's very ill luck. But religion teaches us that God will support us, and if we make less we say nothing. We do better on oranges in March or April, I think it is, than on flowers. Oranges keep better than flowers, you see, sir. We make 1*s.*

a day, and 9*d.* a day, on oranges, the two of us. I wish they was in all the year. I generally go St John's-wood way, and Hampstead and Highgate way with my flowers. I can get them nearly all the year, but oranges is better liked than flowers, I think. I always keep 1*s.* stock-money if I can. If it's bad weather, so bad that we can't sell flowers at all, and so if we've had to spend our stock-money for a bit of bread, *she* (the landlady) lends us 1*s.*, if she has one, or she borrows one of a neighbour, if she hasn't, or if the neighbours hasn't it, she borrows it at a dolly shop' [the illegal pawnshop]. 'There's 2*d.* a week to pay for 1*s.* at a dolly, and perhaps an old rug left for it; if it's very hard weather, the rug must be taken at night time, or we are starved with the cold. It sometimes has to be put into the dolly again next morning, and then there's 2*d.* to pay for it for the day. We've had a frock in for 6*d.*, and that's a penny a week, and the same for a day. We never pawned anything; we have nothing they would take in at the pawnshop. We live on bread and tea, and sometimes a fresh herring of a night. Sometimes we don't eat a bit all day when we're out; sometimes we take a bit of bread with us, or buy a bit. My sisters can't eat taturs; they sicken her. I don't know what emigrating means.' [I informed her and she continued]: 'No, sir, I wouldn't like to emigrate and leave brother and sister. If they went with me I don't think I should like it, not among strangers. I think our living costs us 2*s.* a week for the two of us; the rest goes in rent. That's all we make.'

The brother earned from 1*s.* 6*d.* to 2*s.* a week, with an occasional meal, as a costermonger's boy. Neither of them ever missed mass on a Sunday.

A Train to Clapham Common

The ascent of a mountain in the tropics, and gradual passage through the several atmospheric layers of different climates, reveals, as we rise above the plains, the mountain sides prismatically belted, as it were, with the rainbow hues of various zones of fruits and flowers – the same as if we had passed along rather than above the surface of the globe – from the brilliant and glowing tints of vegetable nature at the tropics, to the sombre shades of the hardier plants and trees peculiar to the colder regions, even till we ultimately reach, at the peak, the colourless desolation of the poles themselves. But this journeying upwards through the various botanical strata, as it were, of the earth is hardly more peculiar and marked than is the rapid transition now-a-days, while travelling on some London railway, from town to the country; for as we fly along the house-tops through the various suburban zones encircling the giant Metropolis, we can see the bricken city gradually melt away into the green fields, and the streets glide, like solid rivers, into the roads, and cabs and busses merge into wagons and ploughs, while factories give place to market-gardens, and parks and squares fade gradually into woods and corn-fields.

Perhaps this change, from civic to rustic scenery – this dissolving view, as it were, of the capital melting into the country, is nowhere better seen than in a half-hour's trip along the Southampton rail; for no sooner have we crossed the viaduct spanning the Westminster Road, and looked down upon the drivers at the back of the passing Hansoms, and the carters perched on the high box-seats of the railway-carriers' vans, as well as the passengers ranged along the roof of the Kennington omnibuses; and had a glimpse, moreover, at the bright-coloured rolls of carpets standing in the first-floor windows of the great linendrapery styled 'Lambeth House,' than we are whisked into the region of innumerable factories – the tall black chimneys piercing the air as thickly as the minarets of some Turkish city; and then, even with the eyes shut, the nose can tell, by the succession of chemical stenches assailing it, that we are being wafted through the several zones of Lambeth manufactures. Now we get a whiff of the gutta-percha works; then comes a faint gust from some floor-cloth shed; next we dash through an odoriferous belt of bone-boiling atmosphere; and after that through a film of fetor rank with the fumes from the glazing of the potteries; whereupon this is followed by bands of nauseous vapours from decomposing hides and horses' hoofs, resin and whiting works; and the next instant these give place to layer after layer of sickening exhalations from gas-factories, and soap-boiling establishments, and candle-companies; so that we are thus led by the nose along a chromatic scale, as it were, of the strong suburban stenches that encompass, in positive rings of nausea, the great cathedral dome of the Metropolis, like the phosphoric glory environing the head of some renowned Catholic saint.

Nor is the visional diorama that then glides past us less striking and characteristic than the nasal one. What a dense

A Train to Clapham Common

huddle and confused bricken crowd of houses and hovels does the city seem to be composed of; the very train itself appears to be ploughing its way through the walls of the houses, while each gable end that is turned towards the rail is used as a means to advertise the wares of some enterprising tradesman.

Now the cathedral-like dome of Bedlam flits before the eye, and now a huge announcement tells us that we are flying past the famed concert-tavern called Canterbury Hall. Then we catch just a glimpse of the green gardens and old ruby towers of Lambeth Palace; and no sooner has this whizzed by, and we have seen the river twinkle for a moment in the light, like a steel-plate flashing in the sun, than we are in the regions of the potteries, with their huge kilns, like enormous bricken skittles, and rows of yellow-looking pipes and pans ranged along the walls. The moment afterwards the gas-works, with their monster black iron drums, dart by the window of the carriage; and the next instant the old, gloomy, and desolate-looking Vauxhall Gardens, with its white rotunda, like a dingy twelfth-cake ornament, glides swiftly by. Then we have another momentary peep down into the road, and have hardly noted the monster railway taverns, and seen the small forest of factory chimneys here grouped about the bridge, with Price's gigantic candle-works hard by, than we are flying past the old Nine Elms station. No sooner has this flitted by than the scene is immediately shifted, and a small, muddy canal is beheld, skirted with willows; and then the tall metal syphon of the water-works, like a monster hair-pin stuck in the earth, shoots rapidly into sight; whereupon the view begins to open a bit, revealing

Henry Mayhew

Chelsea Hospital, with its green copper roof and red and white front, on the other side of the river; while the crowd of dwellings grows suddenly less dense, and the houses and factories dwindle into cottages with small patches of garden. Here, too, the London streets end, and the highroads, the lanes, and hedges make their appearance; while large, flat fields of the suburban market-garden rush by, each scored with line after line of plants. Nor is it many minutes more before these vast plains of cabbage and tracts of potatoes are succeeded by a glance of sloping lawns and pleasant-looking country villas, ranged alongside the raised roadway; immediately after which we are in the land of railway cuttings, with the line sunk in a trough of deep green shelving banks, instead of being buried, as it was only a few minutes before, among the sloping roofs and chimney-pots of the smoky London houses.

Another instant, and the train rattles through a little tunnel, and then is heard the sharp, shrill scream of the whistle; whereupon porters dart by the carriage windows, crying, 'Clapham Common! Clapham Common!' and the instant afterwards are landed at the little rustic station there.

Of the Street-Sellers of Live Birds

The bird-sellers in the streets are also the bird-catchers in the fields, plains, heaths and woods, which still surround the metropolis; and in compliance with established precedent it may be proper that I should give an account of the catching, before I proceed to any further statement of the procedure subsequent thereunto . . .

It is principally effected by means of nets. A bird-net is about twelve yards square; it is spread flat upon the ground, to which it is secured by four 'stars.' These are iron pins, which are inserted in the field, and hold the net, but so that the two 'wings' or 'flaps', which are indeed the sides of the net, are not confined by the stars. In the middle of the net is a cage with a fine wire roof, widely worked, containing the 'call-bird.' This bird is trained to sing loudly and cheerily, great care being bestowed upon its tuition, and its song attracts the wild birds. Sometimes a few stuffed birds are spread about the cage as if a flock were already assembling there. The bird-catcher lies flat and motionless on the ground, 20 or 30 yards distant from the edge of the net. As soon as he considers that a sufficiency of birds have congregated around his decoy, he rapidly draws towards him a line, called the 'pull-line' of which he has kept hold. This is so looped and run within the edges of the net, that on being smartly pulled, the two wings of the net collapse and fly together, the stars still keeping their hold, and the net encircles the cage of the call bird, and incloses in its folds all the wild birds allured round it. In fact it then resembles a great cage of network. The captives are secured in cages – the call-bird continuing to sing as if in mockery of their struggles – or in hampers proper for the purpose, which are carried on the man's back to London . . .

The bird-catcher's life has many, and to the constitution of some minds, irresistible charms. There is the excitement of 'sport' – not the headlong excitement of the chase, where the blood is stirred by motion and exercise – but still sport surpassing that of the angler, who plies his finest art to capture one fish at a time, while the bird-catcher despises an individual capture, but seeks to ensnare a flock at one twitch of the line. There is, moreover, the attraction of idleness, at least for intervals – perhaps the great charm of fishing – and basking in the lazy sunshine, to watch the progress of the snares. Birds, however, and more especially linnets, are caught in the winter, when it is not such quite holiday work. A bird-dealer (not a street dealer) told me that the greatest number of birds he had ever heard of as having been caught at one pull was nearly 200. My informant happened to be present on the occasion. 'Pulls' of 50, 100, and 150 are not very unfrequent when the young broods are all on the wing.

Of the bird-catchers, including all who reside in Woolwich, Greenwich, Hounslow, Isleworth, Barnet, Uxbridge, and places of similar distance, all working for the London market, there are about 200. The localities where these men 'catch', are the neighbourhoods of the places I have mentioned as their residences, and at Holloway, Hampstead,

Of the Street-Sellers of Live Birds

Highgate, Finchley, Battersea, Blackheath, Putney, Mortlake, Chiswick, Richmond, Hampton, Kingston, Eltham, Carshalton, Streatham, the Tootings, Woodford, Epping, Snaresbrook, Walthamstow, Tottenham, Edmonton – wherever, in fine, are open fields, plains or commons around the metropolis . . .

A young man, rather tall, and evidently active, but very thin, gave me the following account. His manners were quiet and his voice low. His dress could not so well be called mean as hard worn, with the unmistakable look of much of the attire of his class, that it was not made for the wearer; his surtout, for instance, which was fastened in front by two buttons, reached down to his ancles, and could have enclosed a bigger man. He resided in St Luke's, in which parish there are more bird-catchers living than in any other. A heavy old sofa, in the well of which was a bed, a table, two chairs, a fender, a small closet containing a few pots and tins, and some twenty empty bird-cages of different sizes hung against the walls. In a sort of wooden loft, which had originally been constructed, he believed, for the breeding of fancy-pigeons, and which was erected on the roof, were about a dozen or two of cages, some old and broken, and in them a few live goldfinches, which hopped about very merrily. They were all this year's birds, and my informant, who had 'a little connection of his own,' was rearing them in hopes they would turn out good specs, quite 'birds beyond the run of the streets.' The place and the cages, each bird having its own little cage, were very clean, but at the time of my visit the loft was exceedingly hot, as the day was one of the sultriest. Lest this heat should prove too great for the finches, the timbers on all sides were well wetted and re-wetted at intervals, for about an hour at noon, at which time only was the sun full on the loft.

'I shall soon have more birds, sir,' he said, 'but you see I only put aside here such as are the very best of the take; all cocks, of course. O, I've been in the trade all my life; I've had a turn at other things, certainly, but this life suits me best, I think, because I have my health best in it. My father – he's been dead a goodish bit – was a bird-catcher as well, and he used to take me out with him as soon as I was strong enough; when I was about ten I suppose. I don't remember my mother. Father was brought up to brick-making. I believe that most of the bird-catchers that have been trades, and that's not half, a quarter perhaps, were brick-makers, or something that way. Well, I don't know the reason. The brick-making was, in my father's young days, carried on more in the country, and the bird-catchers used to fall in with the brick-makers, and so perhaps that led to it. I've heard my father tell of an old soldier that had been discharged with a pension being the luckiest bird-catcher he knowed. The soldier was a bird-catcher before he first listed, and he listed drunk. I once – yes, sire, I dare say that's fifteen year back, for I was quite a lad – walked with my father and captain' [the pensioner's sobriquet] 'till they parted for work, and I remember very well I heard him tell how, when on march in Portingal – I think that's what he called it, but it's in foreign parts – he saw flocks of birds; he wished he could be after catching them, for he was well tired of sogering. I was sent to school twice or thrice, and can read a little and write a little; and I should like reading better if I could

Of the Street-Sellers of Live Birds

manage it better. I read a penny number, or "the police" in a newspaper, now and then, but very seldom. But on a fine day I hated being at school. I wanted to be at work, to make something at bird-catching. If a boy can make money, why shouldn't he? And if I'd had a net, or cage, and a mule of my own, then, I thought, I could make money.' [I may observe that the mule longed for by my informant was a 'cross' between two birds, and was wanted for the decoy. Some bird-catchers contend that a mule makes the best call-bird of any; others that the natural note of the linnet, for instance, was more alluring than the song of a mule between a linnet and a goldfinch. One birdman told me that the excellence of a mule was, that it had been bred and taught by its master, had never been at large, and was 'better to manage;' it was bolder, too, in a cage, and its notes were often loud and ringing, and might be heard to a considerable distance.]

'I couldn't stick school, sir,' my informant continued, 'and I don't know why, lest it be that one man's best suited for one business, and another for another. That may be seen every day. I was sent on trial to a shoemaker, and after that to a ropemaker, for father didn't seem to like my growing up and being a bird-catcher, like he was. But I never felt well, and knew I should never be any great hand at them trades, and so when my poor father went off rather sudden, I took to the catching at once and had all his traps. Perhaps, but I can't say to a niceness, that was eleven years back. Do I like the business, do you say, sir? Well, I'm forced to like it, for I've no other to live by.' [The reader will have remarked how this man attributed the course he pursued evidently from natural inclinations, to its being the best and most healthful means of subsistence in his power.] 'Last Monday, for my dealers like birds on a Monday or Tuesday best, and then they've the week before them, – I went to catch in the fields this side of Barnet, and started before two in the morning, when it was neither light nor dark. You must get to your place before daylight to be ready for the first flight, and have time to lay your net properly. When I'd done that, I lay down and smoked. No, smoke don't scare the birds; I think they're rather drawn to notice anything new, if all's quite quiet. Well, the first pull I had about 90 birds, nearly all linnets. There was, as well as I can remember, three hedge-sparrows among them, and two larks, and one or two other birds. Yes, there's always a terrible flutter and row when you make a catch, and often regular fights in the net. I then sorted my birds, and let the hens go, for I didn't want to be bothered with them. I might let such a thing as 35 hens go out of rather more than an 80 take, for I've always found, in catching young broods, that I've drawn more cocks than hens. How do I know the difference when the birds are so young? As easy as light from dark. You must lift up the wing, quite tender, and you'll find that a cock linnet has black, or nearly black, feathers on his shoulder, where the hens are a deal lighter. Then the cock has a broader and whiter stripe in the wing than the hen has. It's quite easy to distinguish, quite. A cock goldfinch is straighter and more larger in general than a hen, and has a broader white on his wing, as the cock linnet has; he's black round the beak and the eye too, and a hen's greenish thereabouts. There's some grey-pates (young birds) would deceive any one until he opens their wings. Well, I went on,

Of the Street-Sellers of Live Birds

sir, until about one o'clock, or a little after, as well as I could tell from the sun, and then came away with about 100 singing birds. I sold them in the lump to three shopkeepers at 2*s*. 2*d*. and 2*s*. 6*d*. the dozen. That was a good day, sir; a very lucky day. I got about 17*s*., the best I ever did but once, when I made 19*s*. in a day.

'Yes, it's hard work is mine, because there's such a long walking home when you've done catching. O, when you're at work it's not work but almost a pleasure. I've laid for hours though without a catch. I smoke to pass the time when I'm watching; sometimes I read a bit if I've had anything to take with me to read; then at other times I thinks. If you don't get a catch for hours, it's only like an angler without a nibble. O, I don't know what I think about; about nothing, perhaps. Yes, I've had a friend or two go out catching with me just for the amusement. They must lie about and wait as I do. We have a little talk of course: well, perhaps about sporting; no, not horse-racing, I care nothing for that, but it's hardly business taking any one with you. I supply the dealers and hawk as well. Perhaps I make 12*s*. a week the year through. Some weeks I've made between 3*l.s*. and 4*l.s*., and in winter, when there's rain every day, perhaps I haven't cleared a penny in a fortnight. That's the worst of it. But I make more than others because I have a connection and raise good birds.'

Of Sources

OF STREET PIEMEN

London Labour and the London Poor, Volume 1, 1851, pp. 197– [Penguin ed., pp. 94–7]

London Labour and the London Poor is the work Mayhew is remembered for today. It began as a series of letters commissioned by the *Morning Chronicle* exposing the working lives and conditions of the London poor. They formed part of a wider series on the condition of the working classes across England, with correspondents reporting from the industrial towns and rural areas too. The *Morning Chronicle* was an avowedly liberal national daily newspaper, the rival of the Tory *Times*. Starting in 1849, at first the weekly letters were anonymous, credited to the 'Metropolitan Correspondent', but as their fame grew, Mayhew's authorship became known. This came as a surprise to many. He had made his name as a satirical playwright and writer, and was one of the founders of *Punch* magazine in 1841, as well as a philosopher with a treatise on education and lectures under his belt, and was also known as something of a gifted amateur scientist. In his letters he developed his trademark method of letting the people speak for themselves, building up around their accounts a detailed picture of their communities and working lives, using a range of sources, from government statistics to their own housekeeping accounts, mixed in with first-hand accounts of his visits to the places they lived. After two years he fell out with the *Morning Chronicle*, accusing them of censoring his articles because they questioned the merits of free trade for the poor, and offended some lucrative advertisers. In December 1850 he launched his own weekly series, *London Labour and the London Poor*, using his own resources, taking some of the team he had built up at the *Morning Chronicle* with him. Here he continued his work, his main focus being on the street folk, with a parallel series soon launched on prostitution. Though recognized as a unique work, and said to be selling 18,000 copies a week at its height, its finances were shaky. On 16 March 1852 the printers gained a High Court injunction against Mayhew for non-payment of fees and *London Labour* was lost in Chancery for the next four years. Only one and a half volumes on the street folk and half of the volume on prostitution had been completed. Mayhew never finished them. In 1856 his publisher, David Bogue, a long-term friend and supporter, bought the copyright and work began on a relaunch, but Bogue died that same year and the project died with him. The copyright was sold on to Griffin and Bohn in 1861. They hired their own writers to complete the work, and reissued it September 1861, to become the four-volume edition it is known as today. It was out of print by the time of Mayhew's death in 1887, and lay forgotten for decades. It was only in the 1950s that new editions were brought out and Mayhew's work rediscovered.

Henry Mayhew

A BALLOON FLIGHT

The Great World of London, D. Bogue, 1856. Republished as *The Criminal Prisons of London*, Griffin and Co., 1862, pp. 8–10

This piece was first published in the *Illustrated London News* on 18 September 1852, not long after *London Labour and the London Poor* ended publication. It was republished as part of Mayhew's second series, *The Great World of London*, in 1856. Intended as an encyclopaedia of all aspects of London life and culture, an extension to his work in *London Labour* on the street folk, the series ran for under a year before collapsing through a combination of illness on Mayhew's part and the sudden death of his publisher, David Bogue. Only the introduction to the series, an overview of London, and the sections on the criminal prisons of London were ever completed. Bogue's executors tried to persuade Mayhew to continue the work, but he chose to walk away from it. Eventually, the copyright was brought by Griffin and Bohn from Bogue's executors, and the series, after some additional material commissioned by them from John Binney, was reissued in 1862 under the title of *The Criminal Prisons of London*, the name the work is known by today.

Of Sources

THE LONDON STREET MARKETS ON A SATURDAY NIGHT

London Labour and the London Poor, Volume 1, 1851, pp. 9–10 [Penguin ed., pp. 12–15]

Mayhew had a particular fascination for the London street markets. He saw them as the best places to observe people and how they lived their lives. They were where the poor went to do their late-night shopping. The New Cut market he describes here still exists behind Waterloo Station, albeit in reduced form. Of the other great street markets he visited, the Brill has been buried below King's Cross and Hungerford Market below Charing Cross, but Leather Lane and Whitecross markets still cling on today.

OF THE 'PENNY GAFF'

London Labour and the London Poor, Volume 1, 1851, pp. 36, 40–42 [Penguin ed., pp. 36–40]

As part of his exploration of the life of the costers, Mayhew visited their homes, pubs, theatres and dance halls (known as 'hops'). Here he visits a temporary theatre, thrown up in the streets around Smithfield. The ancient meat market was still a large open field where animals were driven through the streets of London to be sold and slaughtered. It was also the venue for a weekly donkey fair and races held by the costers. Mayhew relishes the atmosphere and the spectacle at the penny gaff. In a way he was at home here. He had started out in the 1830s in the theatre, and it was a life-long affair. He wrote *The Wandering Minstrel* in 1834, a short farce featuring a cockney love song, 'Villikins and his Dinah', and this remained a music hall favourite throughout the century. He was twenty-two, and perpetually hard up, so sold the copyright soon after for £25, losing out, as he later complained, on the £200 a year it had earned the owner since. He acted too, appearing in some of the amateur productions Charles Dickens staged. In the late 1830s he owned and managed the Queen's Theatre, off the Tottenham Court Road. In the late 1860s, he ran the theatre reviews for *The Times*. His last known venture on the stage was in the 1870s, when he co-wrote with his son, Athol, a comedy, *Mont Blanc*, which had a brief run at the Haymarket.

THE PORT OF LONDON

The Great World of London, D. Bogue, 1856. Republished as *The Criminal Prisons of London*, Griffin and Co., 1862, pp. 21–3

Mayhew stood on the balcony of Customs House to view the Port of London. To his right was London Bridge (still the medieval structure, though shorn of the houses that had adorned it), to his left the Tower of London, and across the river Southwark Cathedral and the Borough. Much of *London Labour* featured the lives of the people who earned a living here – the coal-whippers who unloaded the coal barges, the marine-store men, the dock workers, the sailors

Of Sources

and the prostitutes – and the streets, wharves, pubs and slums either side of the Thames that were drawn to serve this hub of world trade. When the wind was in an easterly direction, the ships were unable to dock, and thousands would be thrown out of work until it changed again. The Port of London was a microcosm of the world in the centre of the metropolis, with people and goods constantly coming and going from all regions of the world. Mayhew was a part of that movement. In 1827, aged fifteen, he boarded a ship at Blackwall Export Docks and sailed as a midshipman to Calcutta.

OF TWO ORPHAN FLOWER GIRLS

London Labour and the London Poor, Volume 1, 1851, pp. 134–6 [Penguin ed., pp. 61–4]

Mayhew interviewed his subjects at the offices of *London Labour*, in his home, in the streets, in pubs or, as here, in their own homes. His visits allowed him to provide a context for their stories, and record the minutiae of their day-to-day lives. Many of his subjects were children, finding one way or another to survive in the City, and to build a family life when parents were absent. The orphaned girls and their landlady expressed the dignity and kindness of the poor, as well as their strength and individuality, qualities Mayhew encountered again and again through the testimonies he collected. They were also part of the Irish diaspora, the 'Irish Cockneys' he described as a distinctive community of the poor in

London, whose numbers were swollen after 1848 by the Irish Potato Famine.

THE TRAIN TO CLAPHAM COMMON

The Great World of London, D. Bogue, 1856. Republished as *The Criminal Prisons of London*, Griffin and Co., 1862, pp. 487–9

This view of London was new to Mayhew's generation, as the railways had cut their way through the City within living memory. They epitomized relentless progress and transition. Mayhew had been caught up in the 'Railway Mania', the speculative frenzy that accompanied the burst of railway construction in the mid-1840s. He had been part-owner of the *Iron Times*, a daily newspaper devoted to railway news, share speculation and the ethos of change they carried with them. Thousands made fortunes in the boom, only to lose it all sharply in the crash. By 1846, with his wife heavily pregnant with their second child, the *Iron Times* folded. Mayhew was left bankrupt and his villa in Parsons Green, Fulham, was raided by bailiffs. Soon after, he left with his family for the Channel Islands and sanctuary from his creditors, remaining there for three years. The rail journey to Clapham Common was taken in 1856, to visit the Surrey House of Correction, Wandsworth, as part of his coverage of the criminal prisons of London for *The Great World of London*. For that series he visited the prisons at Pentonville, Millbank (on the site of the current Tate Britain), Brixton, Clerkenwell, the Woolwich Hulks (old battleships converted to floating prisons) and Tothill Fields in Westminster. He began each account with a description of the approach to the location, and the sights, sounds and smells of the immediate world outside the walls. The journey to Wandsworth Prison was his last. The series ended abruptly, midway through the description of the prison.

OF THE STREET-SELLERS OF LIVE BIRDS

London Labour and the London Poor, Volume 2, 1851, pp. 58–66

London, the 'Great Metropolis', was the largest city in the world and in a state of constant change. The poor made their living at the physical margins of this growth, in the brickfields, the leisure gardens, the fields, as much as in the streets, sweatshops, docks and factories. Some had lifestyles that Mayhew admired for their freedom. He never romanticized them, but expressed an affinity with them, as someone who lived on the margins too. The craft and knowledge of the street-bird seller straddled the rural and the urban, the one fast consuming the other, and the fields where he lay in wait for the flocks of birds would soon be lost beneath streets and houses.

1. BOCCACCIO · *Mrs Rosie and the Priest*
2. GERARD MANLEY HOPKINS · *As kingfishers catch fire*
3. *The Saga of Gunnlaug Serpent-tongue*
4. THOMAS DE QUINCEY · *On Murder Considered as One of the Fine Arts*
5. FRIEDRICH NIETZSCHE · *Aphorisms on Love and Hate*
6. JOHN RUSKIN · *Traffic*
7. PU SONGLING · *Wailing Ghosts*
8. JONATHAN SWIFT · *A Modest Proposal*
9. *Three Tang Dynasty Poets*
10. WALT WHITMAN · *On the Beach at Night Alone*
11. KENKŌ · *A Cup of Sake Beneath the Cherry Trees*
12. BALTASAR GRACIÁN · *How to Use Your Enemies*
13. JOHN KEATS · *The Eve of St Agnes*
14. THOMAS HARDY · *Woman much missed*
15. GUY DE MAUPASSANT · *Femme Fatale*
16. MARCO POLO · *Travels in the Land of Serpents and Pearls*
17. SUETONIUS · *Caligula*
18. APOLLONIUS OF RHODES · *Jason and Medea*
19. ROBERT LOUIS STEVENSON · *Olalla*
20. KARL MARX AND FRIEDRICH ENGELS · *The Communist Manifesto*
21. PETRONIUS · *Trimalchio's Feast*
22. JOHANN PETER HEBEL · *How a Ghastly Story Was Brought to Light by a Common or Garden Butcher's Dog*
23. HANS CHRISTIAN ANDERSEN · *The Tinder Box*
24. RUDYARD KIPLING · *The Gate of the Hundred Sorrows*
25. DANTE · *Circles of Hell*
26. HENRY MAYHEW · *Of Street Piemen*
27. HAFEZ · *The nightingales are drunk*
28. GEOFFREY CHAUCER · *The Wife of Bath*
29. MICHEL DE MONTAIGNE · *How We Weep and Laugh at the Same Thing*
30. THOMAS NASHE · *The Terrors of the Night*
31. EDGAR ALLAN POE · *The Tell-Tale Heart*
32. MARY KINGSLEY · *A Hippo Banquet*
33. JANE AUSTEN · *The Beautifull Cassandra*
34. ANTON CHEKHOV · *Gooseberries*
35. SAMUEL TAYLOR COLERIDGE · *Well, they are gone, and here must I remain*
36. JOHANN WOLFGANG VON GOETHE · *Sketchy, Doubtful, Incomplete Jottings*
37. CHARLES DICKENS · *The Great Winglebury Duel*
38. HERMAN MELVILLE · *The Maldive Shark*
39. ELIZABETH GASKELL · *The Old Nurse's Story*
40. NIKOLAY LESKOV · *The Steel Flea*

41. HONORÉ DE BALZAC · *The Atheist's Mass*
42. CHARLOTTE PERKINS GILMAN · *The Yellow Wall-Paper*
43. C.P. CAVAFY · *Remember, Body...*
44. FYODOR DOSTOEVSKY · *The Meek One*
45. GUSTAVE FLAUBERT · *A Simple Heart*
46. NIKOLAI GOGOL · *The Nose*
47. SAMUEL PEPYS · *The Great Fire of London*
48. EDITH WHARTON · *The Reckoning*
49. HENRY JAMES · *The Figure in the Carpet*
50. WILFRED OWEN · *Anthem For Doomed Youth*
51. WOLFGANG AMADEUS MOZART · *My Dearest Father*
52. PLATO · *Socrates' Defence*
53. CHRISTINA ROSSETTI · *Goblin Market*
54. *Sindbad the Sailor*
55. SOPHOCLES · *Antigone*
56. RYŪNOSUKE AKUTAGAWA · *The Life of a Stupid Man*
57. LEO TOLSTOY · *How Much Land Does A Man Need?*
58. GIORGIO VASARI · *Leonardo da Vinci*
59. OSCAR WILDE · *Lord Arthur Savile's Crime*
60. SHEN FU · *The Old Man of the Moon*
61. AESOP · *The Dolphins, the Whales and the Gudgeon*
62. MATSUO BASHŌ · *Lips too Chilled*
63. EMILY BRONTË · *The Night is Darkening Round Me*
64. JOSEPH CONRAD · *To-morrow*
65. RICHARD HAKLUYT · *The Voyage of Sir Francis Drake Around the Whole Globe*
66. KATE CHOPIN · *A Pair of Silk Stockings*
67. CHARLES DARWIN · *It was snowing butterflies*
68. BROTHERS GRIMM · *The Robber Bridegroom*
69. CATULLUS · *I Hate and I Love*
70. HOMER · *Circe and the Cyclops*
71. D. H. LAWRENCE · *Il Duro*
72. KATHERINE MANSFIELD · *Miss Brill*
73. OVID · *The Fall of Icarus*
74. SAPPHO · *Come Close*
75. IVAN TURGENEV · *Kasyan from the Beautiful Lands*
76. VIRGIL · *O Cruel Alexis*
77. H. G. WELLS · *A Slip under the Microscope*
78. HERODOTUS · *The Madness of Cambyses*
79. *Speaking of Siva*
80. *The Dhammapada*

'A glass of wine, a lover lovely as The moon...'

HAFEZ
Born *c.* 1317, Shiraz, Iran
Died 1390, Shiraz, Iran

All poems taken from *Faces of Love: Hafez and the Poets of Shiraz*, introduced and translated by Dick Davis.

HAFEZ IN PENGUIN CLASSICS
Faces of Love: Hafez and the Poets of Shiraz

HAFEZ

The nightingales are drunk

Translated by
Dick Davis

PENGUIN BOOKS

PENGUIN CLASSICS

UK | USA | Canada | Ireland | Australia
India | New Zealand | South Africa

Penguin Books is part of the Penguin Random House group of companies
whose addresses can be found at global.penguinrandomhouse.com.

First published by Mage Press 2012
This selection published in Penguin Classics 2015
011

Translation copyright © Mage Publishers, 2012
The moral right of the translator has been asserted

Set in 9.5/13 pt Baskerville 10 Pro
Typeset by Jouve (UK), Milton Keynes
Printed and bound in Great Britain by Clays Ltd, Elcograf S.p.A.

A CIP catalogue record for this book is available from the British Library

ISBN: 978–0–141–98026–3

www.greenpenguin.co.uk

Penguin Random House is committed to a
sustainable future for our business, our readers
and our planet. This book is made from Forest
Stewardship Council® certified paper.

Contents

A black mole graced his face	1
Ah, God forbid that I relinquish wine	2
Come, tell me what it is that I have gained	4
Dear friends	6
For years my heart inquired of me	8
Go mind your own business, preacher!	10
Good news! The days of grief and pain	12
I see no love in anyone	14
I've known the pains of love's frustration – ah, don't ask!	16
Last night I saw the angels	17
Life's garden flourishes	19

May I remember always	21
Mild breeze of morning	23
Moslems, time was I had a heart –	25
My body's dust is as a veil	27
My heart, good fortune is the only friend	29
Of all the roses in the world	31
The musky morning breeze	33
The nightgales are drunk	35
Though wine is pleasurable	37
To give up wine, and human beauty?	39
What does life give me in the end but sorrow?	41
What memories!	42
Where is the news we'll meet	44
Flirtatious games, and youth	46
With wine beside a gently flowing brook – this is best	48

A black mole graced his face; he stripped,
    and shone
Incomparable in splendor as the moon;
He was so slim his heart was visible,
As if clear water sluiced a granite stone.

Ah, god forbid that I relinquish wine
    When roses are in season;
How could I do this when I'm someone who
    Makes such a show of Reason?

Where's a musician, so that I can give
    The profit I once found
In self-control and knowledge for a flute's songs,
    And a lute's sweet sound?

The endless arguments within the schools –
    Whatever they might prove –
Sickened my heart; I'll give a little time
    To wine now, and to love.

Where is the shining messenger of dawn
    That I might now complain
To my good fortune's harbinger of this
    Long night of lonely pain?

But when did time keep faith with anyone?
    Bring wine, and I'll recall
The tales of kings, of Jamshid and Kavus,
    And how time took them all.

I'm not afraid of sins recorded in
    My name – I'll roll away

A hundred such accounts, by His benevolence
    And grace, on Judgment Day.

This lent soul, that the Friend once gave into
    Hafez's care, I'll place
Within His hands again, on that day when
    I see Him face to face.

Come, tell me what it is that I have gained
  From loving you,
Apart from losing all the faith I had
  And knowledge too?

Though longing for you scatters on the wind
  All my life's work,
Still, by the dust on your dear feet, I have
  Kept faith with you.

And even though I'm just a tiny mote
  In love's great kingdom,
I'm one now with the sun, before your face,
  In loving you.

Bring wine! In all my life I've never known
  A corner where
I could sit snugly, safely, and enjoy
  Contentment too.

And, if you're sensible, don't ply me with
  Advice; your words
Are wasted on me, and the reason is
  I'm drunk; it's true!

How can I not feel hopeless shame when I
 Am near my love?
What service could I offer him? What could
 I say or do?

Hafez is burned, but his bewitching love
 Has yet to say,
'Hafez, I wounded you, and here's the balm
 I send for you.'

Dear friends, that friend with whom we once
    Caroused at night –
His willing services to us
    And our delight . . . remember this.

And in your joy, when tinkling bells
    And harps are there,
Include within your songs the sound
    Of love's despair . . . remember this.

When wine bestows a smile upon
    Your server's face,
Keep in your songs, for lovers then,
    A special place . . . remember this.

So all that you have hoped for is
    Fulfilled at last?
All that we talked of long ago,
    Deep in the past . . . remember this.

When love is faithful, and it seems
    Nothing can hurt you,
Know that the world is faithless still
    And will desert you . . . remember this.

If Fortune's horse bolts under you,
    Then call to mind
Your riding whip, and see your friends
    Aren't left behind . . . remember this.

O you, who dwell in splendor now,
    Glorious and proud,
Pity Hafez, your threshold's where
    His face is bowed . . . remember this.

For years my heart inquired of me
   Where Jamshid's sacred cup might be,
And what was in its own possession
   It asked from strangers, constantly;
Begging the pearl that's slipped its shell
   From lost souls wandering by the sea.

Last night I took my troubles to
   The Magian sage whose keen eyes see
A hundred answers in the wine;
   Laughing, he showed the cup to me –
I asked him, 'When was this cup
   That shows the world's reality

Handed to you?' He said, 'The day
   Heaven's vault of lapis lazuli
Was raised, and marvelous things took place
   By Intellect's divine decree,
And Moses' miracles were made
   And Sameri's apostacy.'

He added then, 'That friend they hanged
   High on the looming gallows tree –
His sin was that he spoke of things
   Which should be pondered secretly;

The page of truth his heart enclosed
   Was annotated publicly.

But if the Holy Ghost once more
   Should lend his aid to us, we'd see
Others perform what Jesus did –
   Since in his heart-sick anguish he
Was unaware that God was there
   And called His name out ceaselessly.'

I asked him next, 'And beauties' curls
   That tumble down so sinuously,
What do they mean? Whence do they come?'
   'Hafez,' the sage replied to me,
'Their source is your distracted heart
   That asks these questions constantly.'

Go, mind your own business, preacher!
   what's all
   This hullabaloo?
My heart has left the road you travel, but
   What's that to you?

Until my lips are played on like a flute
   By his lips' beauty,
My ears can only hear as wind the world's
   Advice on duty –

God made him out of nothing, and within
   His being's state
There is a mystery no being's skill
   Can penetrate.

The beggar in your street disdains eight heavens
   For what he's given;
The captive in your chains is free of this world
   And of heaven;

And even though the drunkenness of love
   Has ruined me,
My being's built upon those ruins for
   Eternity.

My heart, don't whine so often that your friend's
   Unjust to you;
This is the fate he's given you, and this
   Is justice too.

Be off with you, Hafez! Enough of all
   These tales you tell;
I've heard these tales and fables many times;
   I know them well.

Good news! the days of grief and pain
        won't stay like this –
As others went, these won't remain
        or stay like this.

Though my belovèd thinks of me
        as dirt and dust,
My rival's status, and her trust,
        won't stay like this.

And though the doorman wields his sword
        against us all,
No rank remains immutable
        or stays like this.

When good or bad come, why give thanks,
        and why complain?
Since what is written won't remain
        or stay like this.

They say when Jamshid reigned, 'Bring wine'
        was his court's song,
'Since even Jamshid won't live long,
        or stay like this.'

And if you're wealthy help the poor,
        since, be assured,

The gold and silver that you hoard
>	won't stay like this!

O candle, prize the moth's love now
>	and hold it fast –
When dawn arrives it cannot last
>	or stay like this.

In words of gold they've written on
>	the emerald sky,
'Only compassion does not die
>	but stays like this.'

Do not despair of love, Hafez;
>	it can't be true
The heartlessness she's shown to you
>	will stay like this.

I see no love in anyone,
Where, then, have all the lovers gone?
And when did all our friendship end,
And what's become of every friend?

Life's water's muddied now, and where
Is Khezr to guide us from despair?
The rose has lost its coloring,
What's happened to the breeze of spring?

A hundred thousand flowers appear
But no birds sing for them to hear –
Thousands of nightingales are dumb:
Where are they now? Why don't they come?

For years no rubies have been found
In stony mines deep underground;
When will the sun shine forth again?
Where are the clouds brimful of rain?

Who thinks of drinking now? No one.
Where have the roistering drinkers gone?
This was a town of lovers once,
Of kindness and benevolence,

And when did kindness end? What brought
The sweetness of our town to naught?

The ball of generosity
Lies on the field for all to see –

No rider comes to strike it; where
Is everyone who should be there?
Silence, Hafez, since no one knows
The secret ways that heaven goes;

Who is it that you're asking how
The heavens are revolving now?

I've known the pains of love's frustration
   – ah, don't ask!
I've drained the dregs of separation – ah, don't ask!

I've been about the world and found at last
A lover worthy of my adoration – ah, don't ask!

So that my tears now lay the dust before
Her door in constant supplication – ah, don't ask!

Last night, with my own ears, I heard such words
Fall from her in our conversation – ah, don't ask!

You bite your lip at me? The lip I bite
Is all delicious delectation! – ah, don't ask!

Without you, in this beggarly poor hut,
I have endured such desolation – ah, don't ask!

Lost on love's road, like Hafez, I've attained
A stage . . . but stop this speculation – ah, don't ask!

Last night I saw the angels
   tapping at the wine-shop's door,
And kneading Adam's dust,
   and molding it as cups for wine;

And, where I sat beside the road,
   these messengers of heaven
Gave me their wine to drink,
   so that their drunkenness was mine.

The heavens could not bear
   the heavy trust they had been given,
And lots were cast, and crazed
   Hafez's name received the sign.

Forgive the seventy-two
   competing factions – all their tales
Mean that the Truth is what
   they haven't seen, and can't define!

But I am thankful that there's peace
   between Him now, and me;
In celebration of our pact
   the houris drink their wine –

And fire is not what gently smiles
   from candles' flames, it's what

Annihilates the flocking moths
   that flutter round His shrine.

No one has drawn aside the veil
   of Thought as Hafez has,
Or combed the curls of Speech
   as his sharp pen has, line by line.

Life's garden flourishes when your
    Bright countenance is here.
Come back! Without your face's bloom
    The spring has left the year.

If tears course down like raindrops now,
    It's no surprise, it's right –
My life's flashed by in longing for you
    As lightning splits the night.

Seize these few moments while we've still
    Time for our promised meeting,
Since no one knows what life will bring
    And life, my dear, is fleeting.

How long shall we enjoy our dawns'
    Sweet sleep, our morning wine?
Wake up, and think of this! Since life's
    Not yours for long, or mine.

She passed by yesterday, but gave
    Me not a glance, not one;
My wretched heart, you've witnessed nothing
    As life's passed by, and gone.

But those whose lives are centered on
    Your lovely mouth confess

No other thoughts than this, and think
    Nothing of Nothingness.

An ambush waits on every side
    Wherever we might tread,
And so life's rider rides slack-reined,
    Giving his horse its head.

I've lived my life without a life –
    Don't be surprised at this;
Who counts an absence as a life
    When life is what you miss?

Speak Hafez! On the world's page trace
    Your poems' narrative;
The words your pen writes will have life
    When you no longer live.

May I remember always when
  Your glance in secrecy met mine,
And in my face your love was like
  A visibly reflected sign.

May I remember always when
  Your chiding eyes were like my death
And your sweet lips restored my life
  Like Jesus's reviving breath.

May I remember always when
  We drank our wine as darkness died,
My friend and I, alone at dawn,
  Though God was there too, at our side.

May I remember always when
  Your face was pleasure's flame, and my
Poor fluttering heart was like a moth
  That's singed and is about to die.

May I remember always when
  The company that we were in
Was so polite, and when it seemed
  Only the wine would wink and grin!

May I remember always when
  Our goblet laughed with crimson wine –

What tales passed back and forth between
    Your ruby lips, my dear, and mine!

May I remember always when
    I was a canopy unfurled
That shaded you, and you were like
    The new moon riding through the world.

May I remember always when
    I sat and drank in wine-shops where
What I can't find in mosques today
    Accompanied the drinkers there.

May I remember always when
    The jewels of verse Hafez selected
Were set out properly by you,
    Arranged in order, and corrected.

Mild breeze of morning, gently tell
   That errant, elegant gazelle
She's made me wander far and wide
   About the hills and countryside.

My sugar-lipped, sweet girl – oh, may
   You live forever and a day! –
Where is your kindness? Come now, show it
   To your sweet-talking parrot-poet.

My rose, does vanity restrain you?
   Does beauty's arrogance detain you
From seeking out this nightingale
   Who wildly sings, to no avail?

With gentleness and kindness lies
   The surest way to win the wise,
Since birds that have become aware
   Of ropes and traps are hard to snare.

When you sit safely with your love,
   Sipping your wine, be mindful of
Those struggling lovers who still stray,
   Wind-tossed, upon their weary way.

I don't know why she isn't here,
   Why her tall presence won't appear,

Or why the full moon of her face,
   And her black eyes, avoid this place.

No fault can be imputed to
   Your beauty's excellence, or you,
Except that there is not a trace
   Of truth or kindness in your face.

When Hafez speaks, it's no surprise
   If Venus dances in the skies
And leads across the heavens' expanse
   Lord Jesus in the whirling dance.

Moslems, time was I had a heart –
        a good one too,
When problems came we'd talk, and I'd
        know what to do;

And if I tumbled in grief's whirlpool
        my heart was sure
To give me hope that soon enough
        I'd reach the shore –

A sympathetic, generous heart,
        a heart prepared
To help out any noble soul,
        a heart that cared.

This heart was lost to me within
        my lover's street;
God, what a place! – where I succumbed
        to sweet deceit.

There is no faultless art – we all
        fall short somehow,
But what poor beggar's more deprived
        than I am now?

Have pity on this wretched soul
        and sympathize

With one who once upon a time
>was strong and wise.

Since love has taught me how to talk,
>each little phrase
Of mine is cried up everywhere
>and showered with praise –

But don't call Hafez witty, wise,
>intelligent;
I've seen Hafez, I know him well;
>he's ignorant.

My body's dust is as a veil
   Spread out to hide
My soul – happy that moment when
   It's drawn aside!

To cage a songbird with so sweet
   A voice is wrong –
I'll fly to paradise's garden
   Where I belong.

But why I've come and whence I came
   Is all unclear –
Alas, to know so little of
   My being here!

How can I make my journey to
   My heavenly home
When I'm confined and cramped within
   This flesh and bone?

If my blood smells of longing, show no
   Astonishment –
Mine is the musk deer's pain as he
   Secretes his scent.

Don't think my golden shirt is like
   A candle's light –

The true flame burns beneath my shirt,
  Hidden from sight.

Come, and ensure Hafez's being
  Will disappear –
Since You exist, no one will hear
  Me say, 'I'm here.'

My heart, good fortune is the only friend
   Going along beside you that you need;
A breeze that's scented with Shiraz's gardens
   Is all the guard to guide you that you need.

Poor wretch, don't leave your lover's home again,
   Don't be in such a hurry to depart –
A corner of our Sufi meeting place,
   The journey in your heart . . . are all you need.

The claims of home, the promises you made
   An ancient friend – these are enough to say
When making your excuses to the travelers
   Who've been along life's way . . . they're all you need.

If grief should leap out from some corner of
   Your stubborn heart and ambush you, confide
Your troubles to our ancient Zoroastrian –
   His precincts will provide . . . you all you need.

Sit yourself down upon the wine-shop's bench
   And take a glass of wine – this is your share
Of all the wealth and glory of the world,
   And what you're given there . . . is all you need.

Let go, and make life easy for yourself,
   Don't strain and struggle, always wanting more;

A glass of wine, a lover lovely as
   The moon – you may be sure . . . they're all you need.

The heavens give the ignorant their head,
   Desire's the only bridle they acknowledge –
Your fault is that you're clever and accomplished,
   And this same sin of knowledge . . . is all you need.

And you require no other prayer, Hafez,
   Than that prayed in the middle of the night;
This and the morning lesson you repeat
   As dawn displays her light . . . are all you need.

Don't look for gifts from others; in both worlds –
   This world, the world that is to come – your king's
Kind bounty, and the Lord's approval, are
   The two essential things . . . they're all you need.

Of all the roses in the world
    A rosy face ... is quite enough for me;
Beneath this swaying cypress tree
    A shady place ... is quite enough for me.

May hypocrites find somewhere else
    To cant and prate –
Of all this weighty world, a full
    Wine-glass's weight ... is quite enough for me.

They hand out heaven for good deeds!
    The monastery
Where Magians live is better for
    A sot like me ... that's quite enough for me.

Sit by this stream and watch as life
    Flows swiftly on –
This emblem of the world that's all
    Too quickly gone ... is quite enough for me.

See how the world's bazaar pays cash,
    See the world's pain –
And if you're not content with this
    World's loss and gain ... they're quite enough for me.

My friend is here with me – what more
    Should I desire?

The riches of our talk are all
   That I require . . . they're quite enough for me.

Don't send me from your door, O God,
   To paradise –
For me, to wait here at Your street's
   End will suffice . . . that's quite enough for me.

Hafez, don't rail against your fate!
   Your nature flows,
As does your verse, like water as
   It comes and goes . . . that's quite enough for me.

The musky morning breeze
   Will gently blow again,
Once more the old world will
   Turn young and grow again;

White jasmine will take wine
   From glowing Judas trees,
Narcissi fondly glance
   At shy anemones;

Once more the banished, lovelorn
   Nightingale will bring
His passion to the rose
   And there sublimely sing;

And if I leave the mosque
   For wine, don't sneer at me –
Sermons are long, and time
   Moves on incessantly.

My heart, if you postpone
   Today's enjoyment, who
Will guarantee the cash
   Of happiness to you?

Drink before fasting, drink,
   Don't put your glass down yet –

Since Ramadan draws near
　　And pleasure's sun must set.

How sweet the roses are!
　　Enjoy them now, for they
As quickly as they bloomed
　　Will fall and fade away.

We're all friends here, my boy,
　　Sing love songs! Why should you
Sing yet again, 'As that
　　Has gone, so this must too'?

You are why Hafez lives –
　　But now, within your heart,
Prepare to say farewell,
　　Since he too must depart.

The nightingales are drunk, wine-red roses appear,
And, Sufis, all around us, happiness is here;

How firmly, like a rock, Repentance stood! Look how
A wine-glass taps it, and it lies in pieces now . . .

Bring wine! From the sequestered court where we're
    secluded,
Drunk or sober, king or soldier, none will be excluded;

This inn has two doors, and through one we have to go –
What does it matter if the doorway's high or low?

If there's no sorrow there can be no happiness,
And, when the world was made, men knew this, and
    said, 'Yes.'

Rejoice, don't fret at Being and Non-Being; say
That all perfection will be nothingness one day.

The horse that rode the wind, Asef in all his glory,
The language of the birds, are now an ancient story;

They've disappeared upon the wind, and Solomon,
The master of them all, has nothing now they've gone.

Don't rise on feathered wings, don't soar into the skies –
An arrow falls to earth, however far it flies;

How will your pen give thanks, Hafez, now men demand
Your verses everywhere, and pass them hand to hand?

Though wine is pleasurable, and though the
    breeze
  Seems soaked in roses, see your harp
Is silent when you drink – because the ears
  Of morals officers are sharp!

If you can find a wine jug and a friend,
  Drink sensibly, and with discretion,
Because the dreadful days we're living through
  Are rife with mischief, and oppression.

See that you hide your wine-cup in your sleeve;
  Your jug's lip sheds its wine, blood-red –
And, in the same way, these cruel times ensure
  Red blood is copiously shed.

We'd better wash away the wine stains from
  Our cloaks with tears of penitence –
Now is the season for sobriety,
  For days of pious abstinence.

The heavens have become a sieve that strains
  Upon us blood, and it is full
Of bloody scraps like royal Khosrow's crown,
  Together with King Kasra's skull.

Don't think that as the heavens turn they'll bring
  A trace of solace or relief;
Their hurtful curvature is through and through
  Made up of wretchedness and grief.

Pars knows the splendor of your verse, Hafez –
  It's made the towns of Eraq glad;
So now's the time to try it out elsewhere –
  Tabriz, perhaps, and then Baghdad.

To give up wine, and human beauty? And to give
  up love?
    No, I won't do it.
A hundred times I said I would; what was I thinking of?
    No, I won't do it.

To say that paradise, its houris, and its shade are more
To me than is the dusty street before my lover's door?
    No, I won't do it.

Sermons, and wise men's words, are signs, and that's
  how we should treat them;
I mouthed such metaphors before, but now – I won't
  repeat them;
    No, I won't do it.

I'll never understand myself, I'll never really know me,
Until I've joined the wine-shop's clientele, and that will
  show me;
    I have to do it.

The preacher told me, 'Give up wine' – contempt was
  in the saying;
'Sure,' I replied. Why should I listen to these
  donkeys braying?
    No, I won't do it.

The sheikh was angry when he told me, 'Give up love!' My brother,
There's no end to our arguing about it, so why bother?
    And I won't do it.

My abstinence is this: that when I wink and smile at beauty
It won't be from the pulpit in the mosque – I know my duty;
    No, I won't do it.

Hafez, good fortune's with the Magian sage, and I am sure
I'll never cease to kiss the dust that lies before his door;
    No, I won't do it.

What does life give me in the end but sorrow?
What do love's good and evil send but sorrow?
I've only seen one true companion – pain,
And I have known no faithful friend but sorrow.

What memories! I once lived on
    the street that you lived on,
And to my eyes how bright the dust
    before your doorway shone!

We were a lily and a rose:
    our talk was then so pure
That what was hidden in your heart
    and what I said were one!

And when our hearts discoursed
    with Wisdom's ancient words,
Love's commentary solved each crux
    within our lexicon.

I told my heart that I would never be
    without my friend;
But when our efforts fail, and hearts
    Are weak, what can be done?

Last night, for old times' sake, I saw
    the place where we once drank;
A cask was lying there, its lees
    like blood; mud was its bung.

How much I wandered, asking why
    the pain of parting came –

But Reason was a useless judge,
    and answers? He had none.

And though it's true the turquoise seal
    of Bu Es'haq shone brightly,
His splendid kingdom and his reign
    were all too quickly gone.

Hafez, you've seen a strutting partridge
    whose cry sounds like a laugh –
He's careless of the hawk's sharp claws
    by which he'll be undone.

Where is the news we'll meet, that from
    This life to greet you there   I may arise?
I am a bird from paradise,
    And from this world's cruel snare   I will arise.

Now by my love for you, I swear
    That if you summon me
To be your slave, from all existence
    And its sovereignty   I will arise.

O Lord, make rain fall from Your cloud
    Sent to us as a guide,
Send it before, like scattered dust
    That's wind-blown far and wide,   I will arise.

Sit by my dust with wine and music:
    From my imprisonment
Beneath the ground, within my grave,
    Dancing, drawn by your scent,   I will arise.

Rise now, my love, display your stature,
    Your sweetness, and I'll be,
Like Hafez, from the world itself
    And from my soul set free . . .   I will arise.

And though I'm old, if you'll embrace
   Me tightly in your arms all night,
Then from your side, as dawn appears,
   Young in the morning light,   I will arise.

Flirtatious games, and youth,
   And wine like rubies glowing;
Convivial company,
   And drink that's always flowing;

A sweet-mouthed boy to serve
   And sweet-voiced singers too,
An elegant, dear friend
   Who's seated next to you;

A kindly youngster whose
   Delightful purity
Would stir the Fount of Youth
   To angry jealousy –

A stealer of men's hearts
   Whose charm and loveliness
Would make the moon herself
   Turn pale and envious;

A meeting place as though
   Heaven's high courts surround us,
With paradise's roses
   Profusely growing round us;

Kind-hearted friends to drink with,
    Servants who act discreetly,
Companions who keep secrets,
    Whom we can trust completely;

With wine as red as roses,
    Astringent, light to sip,
Whose tale is garnets, rubies,
    Kissed in a lover's lip;

The server's glance to be
    A sword to plunder reason,
The lovers' curls like snares
    To trip hearts with their treason;

A wit like Hafez, all
    Sweet-talk and repartee,
A patron like Qavam,
    Whose generosity

Lights up the world . . . and may
    The man who turns away
From pleasures such as these
    Not know one happy day!

With wine beside a gently flowing brook – this is best;
Withdrawn from sorrow in some quiet nook – this is
    best;
Our life is like a flower's that blooms for ten short days,
Bright laughing lips, a friendly fresh-faced look – this is
    best.

1. BOCCACCIO · *Mrs Rosie and the Priest*
2. GERARD MANLEY HOPKINS · *As kingfishers catch fire*
3. *The Saga of Gunnlaug Serpent-tongue*
4. THOMAS DE QUINCEY · *On Murder Considered as One of the Fine Arts*
5. FRIEDRICH NIETZSCHE · *Aphorisms on Love and Hate*
6. JOHN RUSKIN · *Traffic*
7. PU SONGLING · *Wailing Ghosts*
8. JONATHAN SWIFT · *A Modest Proposal*
9. *Three Tang Dynasty Poets*
10. WALT WHITMAN · *On the Beach at Night Alone*
11. KENKŌ · *A Cup of Sake Beneath the Cherry Trees*
12. BALTASAR GRACIÁN · *How to Use Your Enemies*
13. JOHN KEATS · *The Eve of St Agnes*
14. THOMAS HARDY · *Woman much missed*
15. GUY DE MAUPASSANT · *Femme Fatale*
16. MARCO POLO · *Travels in the Land of Serpents and Pearls*
17. SUETONIUS · *Caligula*
18. APOLLONIUS OF RHODES · *Jason and Medea*
19. ROBERT LOUIS STEVENSON · *Olalla*
20. KARL MARX AND FRIEDRICH ENGELS · *The Communist Manifesto*
21. PETRONIUS · *Trimalchio's Feast*
22. JOHANN PETER HEBEL · *How a Ghastly Story Was Brought to Light by a Common or Garden Butcher's Dog*
23. HANS CHRISTIAN ANDERSEN · *The Tinder Box*
24. RUDYARD KIPLING · *The Gate of the Hundred Sorrows*
25. DANTE · *Circles of Hell*
26. HENRY MAYHEW · *Of Street Piemen*
27. HAFEZ · *The nightingales are drunk*
28. GEOFFREY CHAUCER · *The Wife of Bath*
29. MICHEL DE MONTAIGNE · *How We Weep and Laugh at the Same Thing*
30. THOMAS NASHE · *The Terrors of the Night*
31. EDGAR ALLAN POE · *The Tell-Tale Heart*
32. MARY KINGSLEY · *A Hippo Banquet*
33. JANE AUSTEN · *The Beautifull Cassandra*
34. ANTON CHEKHOV · *Gooseberries*
35. SAMUEL TAYLOR COLERIDGE · *Well, they are gone, and here must I remain*
36. JOHANN WOLFGANG VON GOETHE · *Sketchy, Doubtful, Incomplete Jottings*
37. CHARLES DICKENS · *The Great Winglebury Duel*
38. HERMAN MELVILLE · *The Maldive Shark*
39. ELIZABETH GASKELL · *The Old Nurse's Story*
40. NIKOLAY LESKOV · *The Steel Flea*

41. HONORÉ DE BALZAC · *The Atheist's Mass*
42. CHARLOTTE PERKINS GILMAN · *The Yellow Wall-Paper*
43. C.P. CAVAFY · *Remember, Body . . .*
44. FYODOR DOSTOEVSKY · *The Meek One*
45. GUSTAVE FLAUBERT · *A Simple Heart*
46. NIKOLAI GOGOL · *The Nose*
47. SAMUEL PEPYS · *The Great Fire of London*
48. EDITH WHARTON · *The Reckoning*
49. HENRY JAMES · *The Figure in the Carpet*
50. WILFRED OWEN · *Anthem For Doomed Youth*
51. WOLFGANG AMADEUS MOZART · *My Dearest Father*
52. PLATO · *Socrates' Defence*
53. CHRISTINA ROSSETTI · *Goblin Market*
54. *Sindbad the Sailor*
55. SOPHOCLES · *Antigone*
56. RYŪNOSUKE AKUTAGAWA · *The Life of a Stupid Man*
57. LEO TOLSTOY · *How Much Land Does A Man Need?*
58. GIORGIO VASARI · *Leonardo da Vinci*
59. OSCAR WILDE · *Lord Arthur Savile's Crime*
60. SHEN FU · *The Old Man of the Moon*
61. AESOP · *The Dolphins, the Whales and the Gudgeon*
62. MATSUO BASHŌ · *Lips too Chilled*
63. EMILY BRONTË · *The Night is Darkening Round Me*
64. JOSEPH CONRAD · *To-morrow*
65. RICHARD HAKLUYT · *The Voyage of Sir Francis Drake Around the Whole Globe*
66. KATE CHOPIN · *A Pair of Silk Stockings*
67. CHARLES DARWIN · *It was snowing butterflies*
68. BROTHERS GRIMM · *The Robber Bridegroom*
69. CATULLUS · *I Hate and I Love*
70. HOMER · *Circe and the Cyclops*
71. D. H. LAWRENCE · *Il Duro*
72. KATHERINE MANSFIELD · *Miss Brill*
73. OVID · *The Fall of Icarus*
74. SAPPHO · *Come Close*
75. IVAN TURGENEV · *Kasyan from the Beautiful Lands*
76. VIRGIL · *O Cruel Alexis*
77. H. G. WELLS · *A Slip under the Microscope*
78. HERODOTUS · *The Madness of Cambyses*
79. *Speaking of Siva*
80. *The Dhammapada*

'Those husbands that I had, Three of them were good and two were bad. The three that I call "good" were rich and old.'

GEOFFREY CHAUCER
Born *c.* 1343, London, England
Died *c.* 1400, England

Taken from Nevill Coghill's translation of *The Canterbury Tales*,
first published in 1951.

CHAUCER IN PENGUIN CLASSICS
The Canterbury Tales
Love Visions
Troilus and Criseyde

GEOFFREY CHAUCER

The Wife of Bath

Translated by
Nevill Coghill

PENGUIN BOOKS

PENGUIN CLASSICS

UK | USA | Canada | Ireland | Australia
India | New Zealand | South Africa

Penguin Books is part of the Penguin Random House group of companies whose addresses can be found at global.penguinrandomhouse.com.

This selection published in Penguin Classics 2015
008

Translation copyright © Nevill Coghill, 1958, 1960, 1975, 1977

Set in 9.5/13 pt Baskerville 10 Pro
Typeset by Jouve (UK), Milton Keynes
Printed and bound in Great Britain by Clays Ltd, Elcograf S.p.A.

A CIP catalogue record for this book is available from the British Library

ISBN: 978–0–141–39809–9

www.greenpenguin.co.uk

Penguin Random House is committed to a sustainable future for our business, our readers and our planet. This book is made from Forest Stewardship Council® certified paper.

Contents

The Wife of Bath's Prologue   1

The Wife of Bath's Tale   35

THE WIFE OF BATH'S PROLOGUE

'If there were no authority on earth
Except experience, mine, for what it's worth,
And that's enough for me, all goes to show
That marriage is a misery and a woe;
For let me say, if I may make so bold,
My lords, since when I was but twelve years old,
Thanks be to God Eternal evermore,
Five husbands have I had at the church door;
Yes, it's a fact that I have had so many,
All worthy in their way, as good as any.

  'Someone said recently for my persuasion
That as Christ only went on one occasion
To grace a wedding – in Cana of Galilee –
He taught me by example there to see
That it is wrong to marry more than once.
Consider, too, how sharply, for the nonce,
He spoke, rebuking the Samaritan
Beside the well, Christ Jesus, God and man.
"Thou has had five men husband unto thee
And he that even now thou hast," said He,
"Is not thy husband." Such the words that fell;
But what He meant thereby I cannot tell.
Why was her fifth – explain it if you can
No lawful spouse to the Samaritan?
How many might have had her, then, to wife?
I've never heard an answer all my life
To give the number final definition.

People may guess or frame a supposition;
But I can say for certain, it's no lie,
God bade us all to wax and multiply.
That kindly text I well can understand.
Is not my husband under God's command
To leave his father and mother and take me?
No word of what the number was to be,
Then why not marry two or even eight?
And why speak evil of the married state?

   'Take wise King Solomon of long ago;
We hear he had a thousand wives or so.
And would to God it were allowed to me
To be refreshed, aye, half so much as he!
He must have had a gift of God for wives,
No one to match him in a world of lives!
This noble king, one may as well admit,
On the first night threw many a merry fit
With each of them, he was so much alive.
Blessed be God that I have wedded five!
Welcome the sixth, whenever he appears.
I can't keep continent for years and years.
No sooner than one husband's dead and gone
Some other Christian man shall take me on,
For then, so says the Apostle, I am free
To wed, o' God's name, where it pleases me.
Wedding's no sin, so far as I can learn.
Better it is to marry than to burn.

   'What do I care if people choose to see

The Wife of Bath's Prologue

Scandal in Lamech for his bigamy?
I know that Abraham was a holy man
And Jacob too – I speak as best I can –
Yet each of them, we know, had several brides,
Like many another holy man besides.
Show me a time or text where God disparages
Or sets a prohibition upon marriages
Expressly, let me have it! Show it me!
And where did He command virginity?
I know as well as you do, never doubt it,
All the Apostle Paul has said about it;
He said that as for precepts he had none.
One may advise a woman to be one;
Advice is no commandment in my view.
He left it in our judgement what to do.

'Had God commanded maidenhood to all
Marriage would be condemned beyond recall,
And certainly if seed were never sown,
How ever could virginity be grown?
Paul did not dare pronounce, let matters rest,
His Master having given him no behest.
There's a prize offered for virginity;
Catch as catch can! Who's in for it? Let's see!

'It is not everyone who hears the call;
On whom God wills He lets His power fall.
The Apostle was a virgin, well I know;
Nevertheless, though all his writings show
He wished that everyone were such as he,

5

It's all mere counsel to virginity.
And as for being married, he lets me do it
Out of indulgence, so there's nothing to it
In marrying me, suppose my husband dead;
There's nothing bigamous in such a bed.
Though it were good a man should never touch
A woman (meaning here in bed and such)
And dangerous to assemble fire and tow
– What this allusion means you all must know –
He only says virginity is fresh,
More perfect than the frailty of the flesh
In married life – except when he and she
Prefer to live in married chastity.

'I grant it you. I'll never say a word
Decrying maidenhood although preferred
To frequent marriage; there are those who mean
To live in their virginity, as clean
In body as in soul, and never mate.
I'll make no boast about my own estate.
As in a noble household, we are told,
Not every dish and vessel's made of gold,
Some are of wood, yet earn their master's praise,
God calls His folk to Him in many ways.
To each of them God gave His proper gift,
Some this, some that, and left them to make shift.
Virginity is indeed a great perfection,
And married continence, for God's dilection,
But Christ, who of perfection is the well,

Bade not that everyone should go and sell
All that he had and give it to the poor
To follow in His footsteps, that is sure.
He spoke to those that would live perfectly,
And by your leave, my lords, that's not for me.
I will bestow the flower of life, the honey,
Upon the acts and fruit of matrimony.

  'Tell me to what conclusion or in aid
Of what were generative organs made?
And for what profit were those creatures wrought?
Trust me, they cannot have been made for naught.
Gloze as you will and plead the explanation
That they were only made for the purgation
Of urine, little things of no avail
Except to know a female from a male,
And nothing else. Did somebody say no?
Experience knows well it isn't so.
The learned may rebuke me, or be loth
To think it so, but they were made for both,
That is to say both use and pleasure in
Engendering, except in case of sin.
Why else the proverb written down and set
In books: "A man must yield his wife her debt"?
What means of paying her can he invent
Unless he use his silly instrument?
It follows they were fashioned at creation
Both to purge urine and for propagation.

  'But I'm not saying everyone is bound

Geoffrey Chaucer

Who has such harness as you heard me expound
To go and use it breeding; that would be
To show too little care for chastity.
Christ was a virgin, fashioned as a man,
And many of his saints since time began
Were ever perfect in their chastity.
I'll have no quarrel with virginity.
Let them be pure wheat loaves of maidenhead
And let us wives be known for barley-bread;
Yet Mark can tell that barley-bread sufficed
To freshen many at the hand of Christ.
In that estate to which God summoned me
I'll persevere; I'm not pernickety.
In wifehood I will use my instrument
As freely as my Maker me it sent.
If I turn difficult, God give me sorrow!
My husband, he shall have it eve and morrow
Whenever he likes to come and pay his debt,
I won't prevent him! I'll have a husband yet
Who shall be both my debtor and my slave
And bear his tribulation to the grave
Upon his flesh, as long as I'm his wife.
For mine shall be the power all his life
Over his proper body, and not he,
Thus the Apostle Paul has told it me,
And bade our husbands they should love us well;
There's a command on which I like to dwell . . .'

    The Pardoner started up, and thereupon

The Wife of Bath's Prologue

'Madam,' he said, 'by God and by St John,
That's noble preaching no one could surpass!
I was about to take a wife; alas!
Am I to buy it on my flesh so dear?
There'll be no marrying for me this year!'

   'You wait,' she said, 'my story's not begun.
You'll taste another brew before I've done;
You'll find it doesn't taste as good as ale;
And when I've finished telling you my tale
Of tribulation in the married life
In which I've been an expert as a wife,
That is to say, myself have been the whip.
So please yourself whether you want to sip
At that same cask of marriage I shall broach.
Be cautious before making the approach,
For I'll give instances, and more than ten.
And those who won't be warned by other men,
By other men shall suffer their correction,
So Ptolemy has said, in this connection.
You read his *Almagest*; you'll find it there.'

   'Madam, I put it to you as a prayer,'
The Pardoner said, 'go on as you began!
Tell us your tale, spare not for any man.
Instruct us younger men in your technique.'
'Gladly,' she said, 'if you will let me speak,
But still I hope the company won't reprove me
Though I should speak as fantasy may move me,
And please don't be offended at my views;

They're really only offered to amuse.

   'Now, gentlemen, I'll on and tell my tale
And as I hope to drink good wine and ale
I'll tell the truth. Those husbands that I had,
Three of them were good and two were bad.
The three that I call "good" were rich and old.
They could indeed with difficulty hold
The articles that bound them all to me;
(No doubt you understand my simile).
So help me God, I have to laugh outright
Remembering how I made them work at night!
And faith I set no store by it; no pleasure
It was to me. They'd given me their treasure,
And so I had no need of diligence
Winning their love, or showing reverence.
They loved me well enough, so, heavens above,
Why should I make a dainty of their love?

   'A knowing woman's work is never done
To get a lover if she hasn't one,
But as I had them eating from my hand
And as they'd yielded me their gold and land,
Why then take trouble to provide them pleasure
Unless to profit and amuse my leisure?
I set them so to work, I'm bound to say;
Many a night they sang, "Alack the day!"
Never for them the flitch of bacon though
That some have won in Essex at Dunmow!
I managed them so well by my technique

The Wife of Bath's Prologue

Each was delighted to go out and seek
And buy some pretty thing for me to wear,
Happy if I as much as spoke them fair.
God knows how spitefully I used to scold them.

'Listen, I'll tell you how I used to hold them,
You knowing women, who can understand,
First put them in the wrong, and out of hand.
No one can be so bold – I mean no man –
At lies and swearing as a woman can.
This is no news, as you'll have realized,
To knowing ones, but to the misadvised.
A knowing wife if she is worth her salt
Can always prove her husband is at fault,
And even though the fellow may have heard
Some story told him by a little bird
She knows enough to prove the bird is crazy
And get her maid to witness she's a daisy,
With full agreement, scarce solicited.
But listen. Here's the sort of thing I said:

'"Now, sir old dotard, what is that you say?
Why is my neighbour's wife so smart and gay?
She is respected everywhere she goes.
I sit at home and have no decent clothes.
Why haunt her house? What are you doing there?
Are you so amorous? Is she so fair?
What, whispering secrets to our maid? For shame,
Sir ancient lecher! Time you dropped that game.
And if I see my gossip or a friend

Geoffrey Chaucer

You scold me like a devil! There's no end
If I as much as stroll towards his house.
Then you come home as drunken as a mouse,
You mount your throne and preach, chapter and verse
– All nonsense – and you tell me it's a curse
To marry a poor woman – she's expensive;
Or if her family's wealthy and extensive
You say it's torture to endure her pride
And melancholy airs, and more beside.
And if she has a pretty face, old traitor,
You say she's game for any fornicator
And ask what likelihood will keep her straight
With all those men who lie about in wait.

'"You say that some desire us for our wealth,
Some for our shapeliness, our looks, our health,
Some for our singing, others for our dancing,
Some for our gentleness and dalliant glancing,
And some because our hands are soft and small;
By your account the devil gets us all.

'"You say what castle wall can be so strong
As to hold out against a siege for long?
And if her looks are foul you say that she
Is hot for every man that she can see,
Leaping upon them with a spaniel's airs
Until she finds a man to buy her wares.
Never was goose upon the lake so grey
But that she found a gander, so you say.
You say it's hard to keep a girl controlled

The Wife of Bath's Prologue

If she's the kind that no one wants to hold.
That's what you say as you stump off to bed,
You brute! You say no man of sense would wed,
That is, not if he wants to go to Heaven.
Wild thunderbolts and fire from the Seven
Planets descend and break your withered neck!

'"You say that buildings falling into wreck,
And smoke, and scolding women, are the three
Things that will drive a man from home. Dear me!
What ails the poor old man to grumble so?

'"We women hide our faults but let them show
Once we are safely married, so you say.
There's a fine proverb for a popinjay!

'"You say that oxen, asses, hounds and horses
Can be tried out on various ploys and courses;
And basins too, and dishes when you buy them,
Spoons, chairs and furnishings, a man can try them
As he can try a suit of clothes, no doubt,
But no one ever tries a woman out
Until he's married her; old dotard crow!
And then you say she lets her vices show.

'"You also say we count it for a crime
Unless you praise our beauty all the time,
Unless you're always poring on our faces
And call us pretty names in public places;
Or if you fail to treat me to a feast
Upon my birthday – presents at the least –
Or to respect my nurse and her grey hairs,

Or be polite to all my maids upstairs
And to my father's cronies and his spies.
That's what you say, old barrelful of lies!
   '"Then there's our young apprentice, handsome Johnny,
Because he has crisp hair that shines as bonny
As finest gold, and squires me up and down
You show your low suspicions in a frown.
I wouldn't have him, not if you died to-morrow!
   '"And tell me this, God punish you with sorrow,
Why do you hide the keys of coffer doors?
It's just as much my property as yours.
Do you want to make an idiot of your wife?
Now, by the Lord that gave me soul and life,
You shan't have both, you can't be such a noddy
As think to keep my goods and have my body!
One you must do without, whatever you say.
And do you need to spy on me all day?
I think you'd like to lock me in your coffer!
'Go where you please, dear wife,' you ought to offer,
'Amuse yourself! I shan't give ear to malice,
I know you for a virtuous wife, Dame Alice.'
We cannot love a husband who takes charge
Of where we go. We like to be at large.
   '"Above all other men may God confer
His blessing on that wise astrologer
Sir Ptolemy who, in his *Almagest*,
Has set this proverb down: 'Of men, the best

The Wife of Bath's Prologue

And wisest care not who may have in hand
The conduct of the world.' I understand
That means, 'If you've enough, you shouldn't care
How prosperously other people fare.'
Be sure, old dotard, if you call the bluff,
You'll get your evening rations right enough.
He's a mean fellow that lets no man handle
His lantern when it's just to light a candle
He has lost no light, he hasn't felt the strain;
And you have light enough, so why complain?

'"And when a woman tries a mild display
In dress or costly ornament, you say
It is a danger to her chastity,
And then, bad luck to you, start making free
With Bible tags in the Apostle's name;
'And in like manner, chastely and with shame,
You women should adorn yourselves,' said he,
'And not with braided hair or jewelry,
With pearl or golden ornament.' What next!
I'll pay as much attention to your text
And rubric in such things as would a gnat.

'"And once you said that I was like a cat,
For if you singe a cat it will not roam
And that's the way to keep a cat at home.
But when she feels her fur is sleek and gay
She can't be kept indoors for half a day
But off she takes herself as dusk is falling
To show her fur and go a-caterwauling.

Which means if I feel gay, as you suppose,
I shall run out to show my poor old clothes.

'"Silly old fool! You and your private spies!
Go on, beg Argus with his hundred eyes
To be my bodyguard, that's better still!
But yet he shan't, I say, against my will.
I'll pull him by the beard, believe you me!

'"And once you said that principally three
Misfortunes trouble earth, east, west and north,
And no man living could endure a fourth.
My dear sir shrew, Jesu cut short your life!
You preach away and say a hateful wife
Is reckoned to be one of these misfortunes.
Is there no other trouble that importunes
The world and that your parables could condemn?
Must an unhappy wife be one of them?

'"Then you compared a woman's love to Hell,
To barren land where water will not dwell,
And you compared it to a quenchless fire,
The more it burns the more is its desire
To burn up everything that burnt can be.
You say that just as worms destroy a tree
A wife destroys her husband and contrives,
As husbands know, the ruin of their lives."

'Such was the way, my lords, you understand
I kept my older husbands well in hand.
I told them they were drunk and their unfitness
To judge my conduct forced me to take witness

The Wife of Bath's Prologue

That they were lying. Johnny and my niece
Would back me up. O Lord, I wrecked their peace,
Innocent as they were, without remorse!
For I could bite and whinney like a horse
And launch complaints when things were all my fault;
I'd have been lost if I had called a halt.
First to the mill is first to grind your corn;
I attacked first and they were overborne,
Glad to apologize and even suing
Pardon for what they'd never thought of doing.

   'I'd tackle one for wenching, out of hand,
Although so ill the man could hardly stand,
Yet he felt flattered in his heart because
He thought it showed how fond of him I was.
I swore that all my walking out at night
Was just to keep his wenching well in sight.
That was a dodge that made me shake with mirth;
But all such wit is given us at birth.
Lies, tears and spinning are the things God gives
By nature to a woman, while she lives.
So there's one thing at least that I can boast,
That in the end I always ruled the roast;
Cunning or force was sure to make them stumble,
And always keeping up a steady grumble.

   'But bed-time above all was their misfortune;
That was the place to scold them and importune
And baulk their fun. I never would abide
In bed with them if hands began to slide

Geoffrey Chaucer

Till they had promised ransom, paid a fee:
And then I let them do their nicety.
And so I tell this tale to every man,
"It's all for sale and let him win who can."
No empty-handed man can lure a bird.
His pleasures were my profit; I concurred,
Even assumed fictitious appetite,
Though bacon never gave me much delight.
And that's the very fact that made me chide them.
And had the Pope been sitting there beside them
I wouldn't have spared them at their very table,
But paid them out as far as I was able.
I say, so help me God Omnipotent,
Were I to make my will and testament
I owe them nothing, paid them word for word
Putting my wits to use, and they preferred
To give it up and take it for the best
For otherwise they would have got no rest.
Though they might glower like a maddened beast
They got no satisfaction, not the least.

'I then would say, "My dear, just take a peep!
What a meek look on Willikin our sheep!
Come nearer, husband, let me kiss your cheek;
You should be just as patient, just as meek;
Sweeten your heart. Your conscience needs a probe.
You're fond of preaching patience out of Job,
And so be patient; practise what you preach,
And if you don't, my dear, we'll have to teach

The Wife of Bath's Prologue

You that it's nice to have a quiet life.
One of us must be master, man or wife,
And since a man's more reasonable, he
Should be the patient one, you must agree.

   '"What ails you, man, to grumble so and groan?
Just that you want my what-not all your own?
Why, take it all, man, take it, every bit!
St Peter, what a love you have for it!
For if I were to sell my *belle chose*,
I could go walking fresher than a rose;
But I will keep it for your private tooth.
By God, you are to blame, and that's the truth."

   'That's how my first three husbands were undone.
Now let me tell you of my last but one.

   'He was a reveller, was number four;
That is to say he kept a paramour.
Young, strong and stubborn, I was full of rage
And jolly as a magpie in a cage.
Play me the harp and I would dance and sing,
Believe me, like a nightingale in spring,
If I had had a draught of sweetened wine.

   'Metellius, that filthy lout – the swine
Who snatched a staff and took his woman's life
For drinking wine – if I had been his wife
He never would have daunted me from drink.
Whenever I take wine I have to think
Of Venus, for as cold engenders hail
A lecherous mouth begets a lecherous tail.

Geoffrey Chaucer

A woman in her cups has no defence,
As lechers know from long experience.

'But Christ! Whenever it comes back to me,
When I recall my youth and jollity,
It fairly warms the cockles of my heart!
This very day I feel a pleasure start,
Yes, I can feel it tickling at the root.
Lord, how it does me good! I've had my fruit,
I've had my world and time, I've had my fling!
But age that comes to poison everything
Has taken all my beauty and my pith.
Well, let it go, the devil go therewith!
The flour is gone, there is no more to say,
And I must sell the bran as best I may;
But still I mean to find my way to fun . . .
Now let me tell you of my last but one.

'I told you how it filled my heart with spite
To see another woman his delight,
By God and all His saints I made it good!
I carved him out a cross of the same wood,
Not with my body in a filthy way,
But certainly by seeming rather gay
To others, frying him in his own grease
Of jealousy and rage; he got no peace.
By God on earth I was his purgatory,
For which I hope his soul may be in glory.
God knows he sang a sorry tune, he flinched,
And bitterly enough, when the shoe pinched.

The Wife of Bath's Prologue

And God and he alone can say how grim,
How many were the ways I tortured him.

   'He died when I came back from Jordan Stream
And he lies buried under the rood-beam,
Albeit that his tomb can scarce supply us
With such a show as that of King Darius
– Apelles sculped it in a sumptuous taste –
Expensive funerals are just a waste.
Farewell to him, God give his spirit rest!
He's in his grave, he's nailed up in his chest.

   'Now of my fifth, last husband let me tell.
God never let his soul be sent to Hell!
And yet he was my worst, and many a blow
He struck me still can ache along my row
Of ribs, and will until my dying day.

   'But in our bed he was so fresh and gay,
So coaxing, so persuasive . . . Heaven knows
Whenever he wanted it – my *belle chose* –
Though he had beaten me in every bone
He still could wheedle me to love, I own.
I think I loved him best, I'll tell no lie.
He was disdainful in his love, that's why.
We women have a curious fantasy
In such affairs, or so it seems to me.
When something's difficult, or can't be had,
We crave and cry for it all day like mad.
Forbid a thing, we pine for it all night,
Press fast upon us and we take to flight;

Geoffrey Chaucer

We use disdain in offering our wares.
A throng of buyers sends prices up at fairs,
Cheap goods have little value, they suppose;
And that's a thing that every woman knows.

   'My fifth and last – God keep his soul in health!
The one I took for love and not for wealth,
Had been at Oxford not so long before
But had left school and gone to lodge next door,
Yes, it was to my godmother's he'd gone.
God bless her soul! *Her* name was Alison.
She knew my heart and more of what I thought
Than did the parish priest, and so she ought!
She was my confidante, I told her all.
For had my husband pissed against a wall
Or done some crime that would have cost his life,
To her and to another worthy wife
And to my niece, because I loved her well,
I'd have told everything there was to tell.
And so I often did, and Heaven knows
It used to set him blushing like a rose
For shame, and he would blame his lack of sense
In telling me secrets of such consequence.

   'And so one time it happened that in Lent,
As I so often did, I rose and went
To see her, ever wanting to be gay
And go a-strolling, March, April and May,
From house to house for chat and village malice.

   'Johnny (the boy from Oxford) and Dame Alice

The Wife of Bath's Prologue

And I myself, into the fields we went.
My husband was in London all that Lent;
All the more fun for me – I only mean
The fun of seeing people and being seen
By cocky lads; for how was I to know
Where or what graces Fortune might bestow?
And so I made a round of visitations,
Went to processions, festivals, orations,
Preachments and pilgrimages, watched the carriages
They use for plays and pageants, went to marriages,
And always wore my gayest scarlet dress.
  'These worms, these moths, these mites, I must confess,
Got little chance to eat it, by the way.
Why not? Because I wore it every day.
  'Now let me tell you all that came to pass.
We sauntered in the meadows through the grass
Toying and dallying to such extent,
Johnny and I, that I grew provident
And I suggested, were I ever free
And made a widow, he should marry me.
And certainly – I do not mean to boast –
I ever was more provident than most
In marriage matters and in other such.
I never think a mouse is up to much
That only has one hole in all the house;
If that should fail, well, it's good-bye the mouse.
  'I let him think I was as one enchanted

Geoffrey Chaucer

(That was a trick my godmother implanted)
And told him I had dreamt the night away
Thinking of him, and dreamt that as I lay
He tried to kill me. Blood had drenched the bed.
   '"But still it was a lucky dream," I said,
"For blood betokens gold as I recall."
It was a lie. I hadn't dreamt at all.
'Twas from my godmother I learnt my lore
In matters such as that, and many more.
   'Well, let me see . . . what had I to explain?
Aha! By God, I've got the thread again.

   'When my fourth husband lay upon his bier
I wept all day and looked as drear as drear,
As widows must, for it is quite in place,
And with a handkerchief I hid my face.
Now that I felt provided with a mate
I wept but little, I need hardly state.

   'To church they bore my husband on the morrow
With all the neighbours round him venting sorrow,
And one of them of course was handsome Johnny.
So help me God, I thought he looked so bonny
Behind the coffin! Heavens, what a pair
Of legs he had! Such feet, so clean and fair!
I gave my whole heart up, for him to hold.
He was, I think, some twenty winters old,
And I was forty then, to tell the truth.
But still, I always had a coltish tooth.
Yes, I'm gap-toothed; it suits me well I feel,

The Wife of Bath's Prologue

It is the print of Venus and her seal.
So help me God I was a lusty one,
Fair, young and well-to-do, and full of fun!
And truly, as my husbands said to me
I had the finest *quoniam* that might be.
For Venus sent me feeling from the stars
And my heart's boldness came to me from Mars.
Venus gave me desire and lecherousness
And Mars my hardihood, or so I guess,
Born under Taurus and with Mars therein.
Alas, alas, that ever love was sin!
I ever followed natural inclination
Under the power of my constellation
And was unable to deny, in truth,
My chamber of Venus to a likely youth.
The mark of Mars is still upon my face
And also in another privy place.
For as I may be saved by God above,
I never used discretion when in love
But ever followed on my appetite,
Whether the lad was short, long, black or white.
Little I cared, if he was fond of me,
How poor he was, or what his rank might be.

'What shall I say? Before the month was gone
This gay young student, my delightful John,
Had married me in solemn festival.
I handed him the money, lands and all
That ever had been given me before;

This I repented later, more and more.
None of my pleasures would he let me seek.
By God, he smote me once upon the cheek
Because I tore a page out of his book,
And that's the reason why I'm deaf. But look,
Stubborn I was, just like a lioness;
As to my tongue, a very wrangleress.
I went off gadding as I had before
From house to house, however much he swore.
Because of that he used to preach and scold,
Drag Roman history up from days of old,
How one Simplicius Gallus left his wife,
Deserting her completely all his life,
Only for poking out her head one day
Without a hat, upon the public way.

'Some other Roman – I forget his name –
Because his wife went to a summer's game
Without his knowledge, left her in the lurch.

'And he would take the Bible up and search
For proverbs in Ecclesiasticus,
Particularly one that has it thus:
"Suffer no wicked woman to gad about."
And then would come the saying (need you doubt?)
A man who seeks to build his house of sallows,
A man who spurs a blind horse over fallows,
Or lets his wife make pilgrimage to Hallows,
Is worthy to be hanged upon the gallows.
But all for naught. I didn't give a hen

The Wife of Bath's Prologue

For all his proverbs and his wise old men.
Nor would I take rebuke at any price;
I hate a man who points me out my vice,
And so, God knows, do many more than I.
That drove him raging mad, you may rely.
Nor more would I forbear him, I can promise.

'Now let me tell you truly by St Thomas
About that book and why I tore the page
And how he smote me deaf in very rage.

'He had a book, he kept it on his shelf,
And night and day he read it to himself
And laughed aloud, although it was quite serious.
He called it *Theophrastus and Valerius*.
There was another Roman, much the same,
A cardinal; St Jerome was his name.
He wrote a book against Jovinian,
Bound up together with Tertullian,
Chrysippus, Trotula and Heloise,
An abbess, lived near Paris. And with these
Were bound the parables of Solomon,
With Ovid's *Art of Love* another one.
All these were bound together in one book
And day and night he used to take a look
At what it said, when he had time and leisure
Or had no occupation but his pleasure,
Which was to read this book of wicked wives;
He knew more legends of them and their lives
Than there are good ones mentioned in the Bible.

For take my word for it, there is no libel
On women that the clergy will not paint,
Except when writing of a woman-saint,
But never good of other women, though.
Who called the lion savage? Do you know?
By God, if women had but written stories
Like those the clergy keep in oratories,
More had been written of man's wickedness
Than all the sons of Adam could redress.
Children of Mercury and we of Venus
Keep up the contrariety between us;
Mercury stands for wisdom, thrift and science,
Venus for revel, squandering and defiance.
Their several natures govern their direction;
One rises when the other's in dejection.
So Mercury is desolate when halted
In Pisces, just where Venus is exalted,
And Venus falls where Mercury is raised,
And women therefore never can be praised
By learned men, old scribes who cannot do
The works of Venus more than my old shoe.
These in their dotage sit them down to frowse
And say that women break their marriage-vows!

'Now to my purpose as I told you; look,
Here's how I got a beating for a book.
One evening Johnny, glowering with ire,
Sat with his book and read it by the fire.
And first he read of Eve whose wickedness

The Wife of Bath's Prologue

Brought all mankind to sorrow and distress,
Root-cause why Jesus Christ Himself was slain
And gave His blood to buy us back again.
Aye, there's the text where you expressly find
That woman brought the loss of all mankind.

'He read me then how Samson as he slept
Was shorn of all his hair by her he kept,
And by that treachery Samson lost his eyes.
And then he read me, if I tell no lies,
All about Hercules and Deianire;
She tricked him into setting himself on fire.

'He left out nothing of the miseries
Occasioned by his wives to Socrates.
Xantippe poured a piss-pot on his head.
The silly man sat still, as he were dead,
Wiping his head, but dared no more complain
Than say, "Ere thunder stops, down comes the rain."

'Next of Pasiphaë the Queen of Crete;
For wickedness he thought that story sweet;
Fie, say no more! It has a grisly sting,
Her horrible lust. How could she do the thing!

'And then he told of Clytemnestra's lechery
And how she made her husband die by treachery.
He read that story with a great devotion.

'He read me what occasioned the commotion
By which Amphiaraüs lost his life;
My husband had a legend about his wife
Eriphyle, who for a gaud in gold

Went to the Greeks in secret, and she told
Them where to find him, in what hiding-place.
At Thebes it was he met with sorry grace.

   'Of Livia and Lucilia then he read,
And both of course had killed their husbands dead,
The one for love, the other out of hate.
Livia prepared some poison for him late
One evening and she killed him out of spite,
Lucilia out of lecherous delight.
For she, in order he might only think
Of her, prepared an aphrodisiac drink;
He drank it and was dead before the morning.
Such is the fate of husbands; it's a warning.

   'And then he told how one Latumius
Lamented to his comrade Arrius
That in his orchard-plot there grew a tree
On which his wives had hanged themselves, all three,
Or so he said, out of some spite or other;
To which this Arrius replied, "Dear brother,
Give me a cutting from that blessed tree
And planted in my garden it shall be!"

   'Of wives of later date he also read,
How some had killed their husbands when in bed,
Then night-long with their lechers played the whore,
While the poor corpse lay fresh upon the floor.

   'One drove a nail into her husband's brain
While he was sleeping, and the man was slain;

The Wife of Bath's Prologue

Others put poison in their husbands' drink.
He spoke more harm of us than heart can think
And knew more proverbs too, for what they're worth,
Than there are blades of grass upon the earth.

'"Better," says he, "to share your habitation
With lion, dragon, or abomination
Than with a woman given to reproof.
Better," says he, "take refuge on the roof,
Than with an angry wife, down in the house;
They are so wicked and cantankerous
They hate the things their husbands like," he'd say.
"A woman always casts her shame away
When she casts off her smock, and that's in haste.
A pretty woman, if she isn't chaste,
Is like a golden ring in a sow's snout."

'Who could imagine, who could figure out
The torture in my heart? It reached the top
And when I saw that he would never stop
Reading this cursed book, all night no doubt,
I suddenly grabbed and tore three pages out
Where he was reading, at the very place,
And fisted such a buffet in his face
That backwards down into our fire he fell.

'Then like a maddened lion, with a yell
He started up and smote me on the head,
And down I fell upon the floor for dead.

'And when he saw how motionless I lay

Geoffrey Chaucer

He was aghast and would have fled away,
But in the end I started to come to.
"O have you murdered me, you robber, you,
To get my land?" I said. "Was that the game?
Before I'm dead I'll kiss you all the same."

'He came up close and kneeling gently down
He said, "My love, my dearest Alison,
So help me God, I never again will hit
You, love; and if I did, you asked for it.
Forgive me!" But for all he was so meek,
I up at once and smote him on the cheek
And said, "Take that to level up the score!
Now let me die, I can't speak any more."

'We had a mort of trouble and heavy weather
But in the end we made it up together.
He gave the bridle over to my hand,
Gave me the government of house and land,
Of tongue and fist, indeed of all he'd got.
I made him burn that book upon the spot.
And when I'd mastered him, and out of deadlock
Secured myself the sovereignty in wedlock,
And when he said, "My own and truest wife,
Do as you please for all the rest of life,
But guard your honour and my good estate,"
From that day forward there was no debate.
So help me God I was as kind to him
As any wife from Denmark to the rim
Of India, and as true. And he to me.

The Wife of Bath's Prologue

And I pray God that sits in majesty
To bless his soul and fill it with his glory.
Now, if you'll listen, I will tell my story.'

WORDS BETWEEN THE SUMMONER AND THE FRIAR

The Friar laughed when he had heard all this.
'Well, Ma'am,' he said, 'as God may send me bliss,
This is a long preamble to a tale!'
But when the Summoner heard the Friar rail,
'Just look!' he cried, 'by the two arms of God!
These meddling friars are always on the prod!
Don't we all know a friar and a fly
Go prod and buzz in every dish and pie!
What do you mean with your "preambulation"?
Amble yourself, trot, do a meditation!
You're spoiling all our fun with your commotion.'
The Friar smiled and said, 'Is that your motion?
I promise on my word before I go
To find occasion for a tale or so
About a summoner that will make us laugh.'
'Well, damn your eyes, and on my own behalf,'
The Summoner answered, 'mine be damned as well
If I can't think of several tales to tell
About the friars that will make you mourn
Before we get as far as Sittingbourne.

Have you no patience? Look, he's in a huff!'
   Our Host called out, 'Be quiet, that's enough!
Shut up, and let the woman tell her tale.
You must be drunk, you've taken too much ale.
Now, Ma'am, you go ahead and no demur.'
'All right,' she said, 'it's just as you prefer,
If I have licence from this worthy friar.'
'Nothing,' said he, 'that I should more desire.'

THE WIFE OF BATH'S TALE

When good King Arthur ruled in ancient days
(A king that every Briton loves to praise)
This was a land brim-full of fairy folk.
The Elf-Queen and her courtiers joined and broke
Their elfin dance on many a green mead,
Or so was the opinion once, I read,
Hundreds of years ago, in days of yore.
But no one now sees fairies any more.
For now the saintly charity and prayer
Of holy friars seem to have purged the air;
They search the countryside through field and stream
As thick as motes that speckle a sun-beam,
Blessing the halls, the chambers, kitchens, bowers,
Cities and boroughs, castles, courts and towers,
Thorpes, barns and stables, outhouses and dairies,
And that's the reason why there are no fairies.
Wherever there was wont to walk an elf
To-day there walks the holy friar himself
As evening falls or when the daylight springs,
Saying his mattins and his holy things,
Walking his limit round from town to town.
Women can now go safely up and down
By every bush or under every tree;
There is no other incubus but he,
So there is really no one else to hurt you
And he will do no more than take your virtue.

    Now it so happened, I began to say,

Geoffrey Chaucer

Long, long ago in good King Arthur's day,
There was a knight who was a lusty liver.
One day as he came riding from the river
He saw a maiden walking all forlorn
Ahead of him, alone as she was born.
And of that maiden, spite of all she said,
By very force he took her maidenhead.

   This act of violence made such a stir,
So much petitioning to the king for her,
That he condemned the knight to lose his head
By course of law. He was as good as dead
(It seems that then the statutes took that view)
But that the queen, and other ladies too,
Implored the king to exercise his grace
So ceaselessly, he gave the queen the case
And granted her his life, and she could choose
Whether to show him mercy or refuse.

   The queen returned him thanks with all her might,
And then she sent a summons to the knight
At her convenience, and expressed her will:
'You stand, for such is the position still,
In no way certain of your life,' said she,
'Yet you shall live if you can answer me:
What is the thing that women most desire?
Beware the axe and say as I require.

   'If you can't answer on the moment, though,
I will concede you this: you are to go

The Wife of Bath's Tale

A twelvemonth and a day to seek and learn
Sufficient answer, then you shall return.
I shall take gages from you to extort
Surrender of your body to the court.'

Sad was the knight and sorrowfully sighed,
But there! All other choices were denied,
And in the end he chose to go away
And to return after a year and day
Armed with such answer as there might be sent
To him by God. He took his leave and went.

He knocked at every house, searched every place,
Yes, anywhere that offered hope of grace.
What could it be that women wanted most?
But all the same he never touched a coast,
Country or town in which there seemed to be
Any two people willing to agree.

Some said that women wanted wealth and treasure,
'Honour,' said some, some 'Jollity and pleasure,'
Some 'Gorgeous clothes' and others 'Fun in bed,'
'To be oft widowed and remarried,' said
Others again, and some that what most mattered
Was that we should be cosseted and flattered.
That's very near the truth, it seems to me;
A man can win us best with flattery.
To dance attendance on us, make a fuss,
Ensnares us all, the best and worst of us.

Some say the things we most desire are these:
Freedom to do exactly as we please,

Geoffrey Chaucer

With no one to reprove our faults and lies,
Rather to have one call us good and wise.
Truly there's not a woman in ten score
Who has a fault, and someone rubs the sore,
But she will kick if what he says is true;
You try it out and you will find so too.
However vicious we may be within
We like to be thought wise and void of sin.
Others assert we women find it sweet
When we are thought dependable, discreet
And secret, firm of purpose and controlled,
Never betraying things that we are told.
But that's not worth the handle of a rake;
Women conceal a thing? For Heaven's sake!
Remember Midas? Will you hear the tale?

    Among some other little things, now stale,
Ovid relates that under his long hair
The unhappy Midas grew a splendid pair
Of ass's ears; as subtly as he might,
He kept his foul deformity from sight;
Save for his wife, there was not one that knew.
He loved her best, and trusted in her too.
He begged her not to tell a living creature
That he possessed so horrible a feature.
And she – she swore, were all the world to win,
She would not do such villainy and sin
As saddle her husband with so foul a name;
Besides to speak would be to share the shame.

The Wife of Bath's Tale

Nevertheless she thought she would have died
Keeping this secret bottled up inside;
It seemed to swell her heart and she, no doubt,
Thought it was on the point of bursting out.

    Fearing to speak of it to woman or man,
Down to a reedy marsh she quickly ran
And reached the sedge. Her heart was all on fire
And, as a bittern bumbles in the mire,
She whispered to the water, near the ground,
'Betray me not, O water, with thy sound!
To thee alone I tell it: it appears
My husband has a pair of ass's ears!
Ah! My heart's well again, the secret's out!
I could no longer keep it, not a doubt.'
And so you see, although we may hold fast
A little while, it must come out at last,
We can't keep secrets; as for Midas, well,
Read Ovid for his story; he will tell.

    This knight that I am telling you about
Perceived at last he never would find out
What it could be that women loved the best.
Faint was the soul within his sorrowful breast,
As home he went, he dared no longer stay;
His year was up and now it was the day.

    As he rode home in a dejected mood
Suddenly, at the margin of a wood,
He saw a dance upon the leafy floor
Of four and twenty ladies, nay, and more.

Geoffrey Chaucer

Eagerly he approached, in hope to learn
Some words of wisdom ere he should return;
But lo! Before he came to where they were,
Dancers and dance all vanished into air!
There wasn't a living creature to be seen
Save one old woman crouched upon the green.
A fouler-looking creature I suppose
Could scarcely be imagined. She arose
And said, 'Sir knight, there's no way on from here.
Tell me what you are looking for, my dear,
For peradventure that were best for you;
We old, old women know a thing or two.'

'Dear Mother,' said the knight, 'alack the day!
I am as good as dead if I can't say
What thing it is that women most desire;
If you could tell me I would pay your hire.'
'Give me your hand,' she said, 'and swear to do
Whatever I shall next require of you
– If so to do should lie within your might –
And you shall know the answer before night.'
'Upon my honour,' he answered, 'I agree.'
'Then,' said the crone, 'I dare to guarantee
Your life is safe; I shall make good my claim.
Upon my life the queen will say the same.
Show me the very proudest of them all
In costly coverchief or jewelled caul
That dare say no to what I have to teach.

The Wife of Bath's Tale

Let us go forward without further speech.'
And then she crooned her gospel in his ear
And told him to be glad and not to fear.

They came to court. This knight, in full array,
Stood forth and said, 'O Queen, I've kept my day
And kept my word and have my answer ready.'

There sat the noble matrons and the heady
Young girls, and widows too, that have the grace
Of wisdom, all assembled in that place,
And there the queen herself was throned to hear
And judge his answer. Then the knight drew near
And silence was commanded through the hall.

The queen gave order he should tell them all
What thing it was that women wanted most.
He stood not silent like a beast or post,
But gave his answer with the ringing word
Of a man's voice and the assembly heard:

'My liege and lady, in general,' said he,
'A woman wants the self-same sovereignty
Over her husband as over her lover,
And master him; he must not be above her.
That is your greatest wish, whether you kill
Or spare me; please yourself. I wait your will.'

In all the court not one that shook her head
Or contradicted what the knight had said;
Maid, wife and widow cried, 'He's saved his life!'

And on the word up started the old wife,

The one the knight saw sitting on the green,
And cried, 'Your mercy, sovereign lady queen!
Before the court disperses, do me right!
'Twas I who taught this answer to the knight,
For which he swore, and pledged his honour to it,
That the first thing I asked of him he'd do it,
So far as it should lie within his might.
Before this court I ask you then, sir knight,
To keep your word and take me for your wife;
For well you know that I have saved your life.
If this be false, deny it on your sword!'

'Alas!' he said, 'Old lady, by the Lord
I know indeed that such was my behest,
But for God's love think of a new request,
Take all my goods, but leave my body free.'
'A curse on us,' she said, 'if I agree!
I may be foul, I may be poor and old,
Yet will not choose to be, for all the gold
That's bedded in the earth or lies above,
Less than your wife, nay, than your very love!'

'My love?' said he. 'By heaven, my damnation!
Alas that any of my race and station
Should ever make so foul a misalliance!'
Yet in the end his pleading and defiance
All went for nothing, he was forced to wed.
He takes his ancient wife and goes to bed.

Now peradventure some may well suspect
A lack of care in me since I neglect

The Wife of Bath's Tale

To tell of the rejoicing and display
Made at the feast upon their wedding-day.
I have but a short answer to let fall;
I say there was no joy or feast at all,
Nothing but heaviness of heart and sorrow.
He married her in private on the morrow
And all day long stayed hidden like an owl,
It was such torture that his wife looked foul.

   Great was the anguish churning in his head
When he and she were piloted to bed;
He wallowed back and forth in desperate style.
His ancient wife lay smiling all the while;
At last she said, 'Bless us! Is this, my dear,
How knights and wives get on together here?
Are these the laws of good King Arthur's house?
Are knights of his all so contemptuous?
I am your own beloved and your wife,
And I am she, indeed, that saved your life;
And certainly I never did you wrong.
Then why, this first of nights, so sad a song?
You're carrying on as if you were half-witted.
Say, for God's love, what sin have I committed?
I'll put things right if you will tell me how.'

   'Put right?' he cried. 'That never can be now!
Nothing can ever be put right again!
You're old, and so abominably plain,
So poor to start with, so low-bred to follow;
It's little wonder if I twist and wallow!

God, that my heart would burst within my breast!'
   'Is that,' said she, 'the cause of your unrest?'
   'Yes, certainly,' he said, 'and can you wonder?'
   'I could set right what you suppose a blunder,
That's if I cared to, in a day or two,
If I were shown more courtesy by you.
Just now,' she said, 'you spoke of gentle birth,
Such as descends from ancient wealth and worth.
If that's the claim you make for gentlemen
Such arrogance is hardly worth a hen.
Whoever loves to work for virtuous ends,
Public and private, and who most intends
To do what deeds of gentleness he can,
Take him to be the greatest gentleman.
Christ wills we take our gentleness from Him,
Not from a wealth of ancestry long dim,
Though they bequeath their whole establishment
By which we claim to be of high descent.
Our fathers cannot make us a bequest
Of all those virtues that became them best
And earned for them the name of gentlemen,
But bade us follow them as best we can.

   'Thus the wise poet of the Florentines,
Dante by name, has written in these lines,
For such is the opinion Dante launches:
"Seldom arises by these slender branches
Prowess of men, for it is God, no less,

The Wife of Bath's Tale

Wills us to claim of Him our gentleness."
For of our parents nothing can we claim
Save temporal things, and these may hurt and maim.

  'But everyone knows this as well as I;
For if gentility were implanted by
The natural course of lineage down the line,
Public or private, could it cease to shine
In doing the fair work of gentle deed?
No vice or villainy could then bear seed.

  'Take fire and carry it to the darkest house
Between this kingdom and the Caucasus,
And shut the doors on it and leave it there,
It will burn on, and it will burn as fair
As if ten thousand men were there to see,
For fire will keep its nature and degree,
I can assure you, sir, until it dies.

  'But gentleness, as you will recognize,
Is not annexed in nature to possessions.
Men fail in living up to their professions;
But fire never ceases to be fire.
God knows you'll often find, if you enquire,
Some lording full of villainy and shame.
If you would be esteemed for the mere name
Of having been by birth a gentleman
And stemming from some virtuous, noble clan,
And do not live yourself by gentle deed

Or take your father's noble code and creed,
You are no gentleman, though duke or earl.
Vice and bad manners are what make a churl.

   'Gentility is only the renown
For bounty that your fathers handed down,
Quite foreign to your person, not your own;
Gentility must come from God alone.
That we are gentle comes to us by grace
And by no means is it bequeathed with place.

   'Reflect how noble (says Valerius)
Was Tullius surnamed Hostilius,
Who rose from poverty to nobleness.
And read Boethius, Seneca no less,
Thus they express themselves and are agreed:
"Gentle is he that does a gentle deed."
And therefore, my dear husband, I conclude
That even if my ancestors were rude,
Yet God on high – and so I hope He will –
Can grant me grace to live in virtue still,
A gentlewoman only when beginning
To live in virtue and to shrink from sinning.

   'As for my poverty which you reprove,
Almighty God Himself in whom we move,
Believe and have our being, chose a life
Of poverty, and every man or wife
Nay, every child can see our Heavenly King
Would never stoop to choose a shameful thing.
No shame in poverty if the heart is gay,

The Wife of Bath's Tale

As Seneca and all the learned say.
He who accepts his poverty unhurt
I'd say is rich although he lacked a shirt.
But truly poor are they who whine and fret
And covet what they cannot hope to get.
And he that, having nothing, covets not,
Is rich, though you may think he is a sot.

'True poverty can find a song to sing.
Juvenal says a pleasant little thing:
"The poor can dance and sing in the relief
Of having nothing that will tempt a thief."
Though it be hateful, poverty is good,
A great incentive to a livelihood,
And a great help to our capacity
For wisdom, if accepted patiently.
Poverty is, though wanting in estate,
A kind of wealth that none calumniate.
Poverty often, when the heart is lowly,
Brings one to God and teaches what is holy,
Gives knowledge of oneself and even lends
A glass by which to see one's truest friends.
And since it's no offence, let me be plain;
Do not rebuke my poverty again.

'Lastly you taxed me, sir, with being old.
Yet even if you never had been told
By ancient books, you gentlemen engage,
Yourselves in honour to respect old age.
To call an old man 'father' shows good breeding,

Geoffrey Chaucer

And this could be supported from my reading.
  'You say I'm old and fouler than a fen.
You need not fear to be a cuckold, then.
Filth and old age, I'm sure you will agree,
Are powerful wardens over chastity.
Nevertheless, well knowing your delights,
I shall fulfil your worldly appetites.
  'You have two choices; which one will you try?
To have me old and ugly till I die,
But still a loyal, true, and humble wife
That never will displease you all her life,
Or would you rather I were young and pretty
And chance your arm what happens in a city
Where friends will visit you because of me,
Yes, and in other places too, maybe.
Which would you have? The choice is all your own.'
  The knight thought long, and with a piteous groan
At last he said, with all the care in life,
'My lady and my love, my dearest wife,
I leave the matter to your wise decision.
You make the choice yourself, for the provision
Of what may be agreeable and rich
In honour to us both, I don't care which;
Whatever pleases you suffices me.'
  'And have I won the mastery?' said she,
'Since I'm to choose and rule as I think fit?'
'Certainly, wife,' he answered her, 'that's it.'
'Kiss me,' she cried. 'No quarrels! On my oath

The Wife of Bath's Tale

And word of honour, you shall find me both,
That is, both fair and faithful as a wife;
May I go howling mad and take my life
Unless I prove to be as good and true
As ever wife was since the world was new!
And if to-morrow when the sun's above
I seem less fair than any lady-love,
Than any queen or empress east or west,
Do with my life and death as you think best.
Cast up the curtain, husband. Look at me!'

And when indeed the knight had looked to see,
Lo, she was young and lovely, rich in charms.
In ecstasy he caught her in his arms,
His heart went bathing in a bath of blisses
And melted in a hundred thousand kisses,
And she responded in the fullest measure
With all that could delight or give him pleasure.

So they lived ever after to the end
In perfect bliss; and may Christ Jesus send
Us husbands meek and young and fresh in bed,
And grace to overbid them when we wed.
And – Jesu hear my prayer! – cut short the lives
Of those who won't be governed by their wives;
And all old, angry niggards of their pence,
God send them soon a very pestilence!

1. BOCCACCIO · *Mrs Rosie and the Priest*
2. GERARD MANLEY HOPKINS · *As kingfishers catch fire*
3. *The Saga of Gunnlaug Serpent-tongue*
4. THOMAS DE QUINCEY · *On Murder Considered as One of the Fine Arts*
5. FRIEDRICH NIETZSCHE · *Aphorisms on Love and Hate*
6. JOHN RUSKIN · *Traffic*
7. PU SONGLING · *Wailing Ghosts*
8. JONATHAN SWIFT · *A Modest Proposal*
9. *Three Tang Dynasty Poets*
10. WALT WHITMAN · *On the Beach at Night Alone*
11. KENKŌ · *A Cup of Sake Beneath the Cherry Trees*
12. BALTASAR GRACIÁN · *How to Use Your Enemies*
13. JOHN KEATS · *The Eve of St Agnes*
14. THOMAS HARDY · *Woman much missed*
15. GUY DE MAUPASSANT · *Femme Fatale*
16. MARCO POLO · *Travels in the Land of Serpents and Pearls*
17. SUETONIUS · *Caligula*
18. APOLLONIUS OF RHODES · *Jason and Medea*
19. ROBERT LOUIS STEVENSON · *Olalla*
20. KARL MARX AND FRIEDRICH ENGELS · *The Communist Manifesto*
21. PETRONIUS · *Trimalchio's Feast*
22. JOHANN PETER HEBEL · *How a Ghastly Story Was Brought to Light by a Common or Garden Butcher's Dog*
23. HANS CHRISTIAN ANDERSEN · *The Tinder Box*
24. RUDYARD KIPLING · *The Gate of the Hundred Sorrows*
25. DANTE · *Circles of Hell*
26. HENRY MAYHEW · *Of Street Piemen*
27. HAFEZ · *The nightingales are drunk*
28. GEOFFREY CHAUCER · *The Wife of Bath*
29. MICHEL DE MONTAIGNE · *How We Weep and Laugh at the Same Thing*
30. THOMAS NASHE · *The Terrors of the Night*
31. EDGAR ALLAN POE · *The Tell-Tale Heart*
32. MARY KINGSLEY · *A Hippo Banquet*
33. JANE AUSTEN · *The Beautifull Cassandra*
34. ANTON CHEKHOV · *Gooseberries*
35. SAMUEL TAYLOR COLERIDGE · *Well, they are gone, and here must I remain*
36. JOHANN WOLFGANG VON GOETHE · *Sketchy, Doubtful, Incomplete Jottings*
37. CHARLES DICKENS · *The Great Winglebury Duel*
38. HERMAN MELVILLE · *The Maldive Shark*
39. ELIZABETH GASKELL · *The Old Nurse's Story*
40. NIKOLAY LESKOV · *The Steel Flea*

41. HONORÉ DE BALZAC · *The Atheist's Mass*
42. CHARLOTTE PERKINS GILMAN · *The Yellow Wall-Paper*
43. C.P. CAVAFY · *Remember, Body . . .*
44. FYODOR DOSTOEVSKY · *The Meek One*
45. GUSTAVE FLAUBERT · *A Simple Heart*
46. NIKOLAI GOGOL · *The Nose*
47. SAMUEL PEPYS · *The Great Fire of London*
48. EDITH WHARTON · *The Reckoning*
49. HENRY JAMES · *The Figure in the Carpet*
50. WILFRED OWEN · *Anthem For Doomed Youth*
51. WOLFGANG AMADEUS MOZART · *My Dearest Father*
52. PLATO · *Socrates' Defence*
53. CHRISTINA ROSSETTI · *Goblin Market*
54. *Sindbad the Sailor*
55. SOPHOCLES · *Antigone*
56. RYŪNOSUKE AKUTAGAWA · *The Life of a Stupid Man*
57. LEO TOLSTOY · *How Much Land Does A Man Need?*
58. GIORGIO VASARI · *Leonardo da Vinci*
59. OSCAR WILDE · *Lord Arthur Savile's Crime*
60. SHEN FU · *The Old Man of the Moon*
61. AESOP · *The Dolphins, the Whales and the Gudgeon*
62. MATSUO BASHŌ · *Lips too Chilled*
63. EMILY BRONTË · *The Night is Darkening Round Me*
64. JOSEPH CONRAD · *To-morrow*
65. RICHARD HAKLUYT · *The Voyage of Sir Francis Drake Around the Whole Globe*
66. KATE CHOPIN · *A Pair of Silk Stockings*
67. CHARLES DARWIN · *It was snowing butterflies*
68. BROTHERS GRIMM · *The Robber Bridegroom*
69. CATULLUS · *I Hate and I Love*
70. HOMER · *Circe and the Cyclops*
71. D. H. LAWRENCE · *Il Duro*
72. KATHERINE MANSFIELD · *Miss Brill*
73. OVID · *The Fall of Icarus*
74. SAPPHO · *Come Close*
75. IVAN TURGENEV · *Kasyan from the Beautiful Lands*
76. VIRGIL · *O Cruel Alexis*
77. H. G. WELLS · *A Slip under the Microscope*
78. HERODOTUS · *The Madness of Cambyses*
79. *Speaking of Siva*
80. *The Dhammapada*

'No one characteristic clasps us purely and universally in its embrace.'

MICHEL DE MONTAIGNE
Born 1533, Aquitaine, France
Died 1592, Aquitaine, France

Montaigne wrote and revised his *Essays*
between 1570 and 1592.

MONTAIGNE IN PENGUIN CLASSICS
The Complete Essays
An Apology for Raymond Sebond
On Friendship
On Solitude
The Essays: A Selection

MICHEL DE MONTAIGNE

How We Weep and Laugh at the Same Thing

Translated by
M. A. Screech

PENGUIN BOOKS

PENGUIN CLASSICS

UK | USA | Canada | Ireland | Australia
India | New Zealand | South Africa

Penguin Books is part of the Penguin Random House group of companies
whose addresses can be found at global.penguinrandomhouse.com.

This edition published in Penguin Classics 2015

011

Translation and editorial material copyright © M. A. Screech, 1987, 1991, 2003

The moral right of the translator has been asserted

Set in 9.5/13 pt Baskerville 10 Pro
Typeset by Jouve (UK), Milton Keynes
Printed and bound in Great Britain by Clays Ltd, Elcograf S.p.A.

A CIP catalogue record for this book is available from the British Library

ISBN: 978-0-141-39722-1

www.greenpenguin.co.uk

Penguin Random House is committed to a
sustainable future for our business, our readers
and our planet. This book is made from Forest
Stewardship Council® certified paper.

Contents

How We Weep and Laugh at the Same Thing	1
On conscience	7
Fortune is often found in Reason's train	14
On punishing cowardice	19
On the vanity of words	22
To philosophize is to learn how to die	28

How We Weep and Laugh at the Same Thing

[An understanding of the complexity of conflicting emotions helps us to avoid trivial interpretations of great men and their grief.]

When we read in our history books that Antigonus was severely displeased with his son for having brought him the head of his enemy King Pyrrhus who had just been killed fighting against him and that he burst into copious tears when he saw it; and that Duke René of Lorraine also lamented the death of Duke Charles of Burgundy whom he had just defeated, and wore mourning at his funeral; and that at the battle of Auroy which the Count de Montfort won against Charles de Blois, his rival for the Duchy of Brittany, the victor showed great grief when he happened upon his enemy's corpse: we should not at once exclaim,

> *Et cosi aven che l'animo ciascuna*
> *Sua passion sotto et contrario manto*
> *Ricopre, con la vista hor' chiara hor bruna.*

[Thus does the mind cloak every passion with its opposite, our faces showing now joy, now sadness.]

When they presented Caesar with the head of Pompey our histories say that he turned his gaze away as from a spectacle both ugly and displeasing. There had been such a long understanding and fellowship between them in the management of affairs of State, they had shared the same fortunes and rendered each other so many mutual services as allies, that we should not believe that his behaviour was quite false and counterfeit – as this other poet thinks it was:

> *tutumque putavit*
> *Jam bonus esse socer; lachrimas non sponte cadentes*
> *Effudit, gemitusque expressit pectore læto.*

[And now he thought it was safe to play the good father-in-law; he poured out tears, but not spontaneous ones, and he forced out groans from his happy breast.]

For while it is true that most of our actions are but mask and cosmetic, and that it is sometimes true that

> *Hæredis fletus sub persona risus est;*

[Behind the mask, the tears of an heir are laughter;]

nevertheless we ought to consider when judging such events how our souls are often shaken by conflicting emotions. Even as there is said to be a variety of humours

How We Weep and Laugh at the Same Thing

assembled in our bodies, the dominant one being that which normally prevails according to our complexion, so too in our souls: although diverse emotions may shake them, there is one which must remain in possession of the field; nevertheless its victory is not so complete but that the weaker ones do not sometimes regain lost ground because of the pliancy and mutability of our soul and make a brief sally in their turn. That is why we can see that not only children, who artlessly follow Nature, often weep and laugh at the same thing, but that not one of us either can boast that, no matter how much he may want to set out on a journey, he still does not feel his heart a-tremble when he says goodbye to family and friends: even if he does not actually burst into tears at least he puts foot to stirrup with a sad and gloomy face. And however noble the passion which enflames the heart of a well-born bride, she still has to have her arms prised from her mother's neck before being given to her husband, no matter what that merry fellow may say:

> *Est ne novis nuptis odio venus, anne parentum*
> *Frustrantur falsis gaudia lachrimulis,*
> *Ubertim thalami quas intra limina fundunt?*
> *Non, ita me divi, vera gemunt, juverint.*

[Is Venus really hated by our brides, or do they mock their parents' joy with those false tears which they pour forth in abundance at their chamber-door? No. So help me, gods, their sobs are false ones.]

And so it is not odd to lament the death of a man whom we would by no means wish to be still alive.

When I rail at my manservant I do so sincerely with all my mind: my curses are real not feigned. But once I cease to fume, if he needs help from me I am glad to help him: I turn over the page. When I call him a dolt or a calf I have no intention of stitching such labels on to him for ever: nor do I believe I am contradicting myself when I later call him an honest fellow. No one characteristic clasps us purely and universally in its embrace. If only talking to oneself did not look mad, no day would go by without my being heard growling to myself, against myself, 'You silly shit!' Yet I do not intend that to be a definition of me.

If anyone should think when he sees me sometimes look bleakly at my wife and sometimes lovingly that either emotion is put on, then he is daft. When Nero took leave of his mother whom he was sending to be drowned, he nevertheless felt some emotion at his mother's departure and felt horror and pity.

The sun, they say, does not shed its light in one continuous flow but ceaselessly darts fresh rays so thickly at us, one after another, that we cannot perceive any gap between them:

> *Largus enim liquidi fons luminis, œtherius sol*
> *Inrigat assidue cœlum candore recenti,*
> *Suppeditatque novo confestim lumine lumen.*

How We Weep and Laugh at the Same Thing

[That generous source of liquid light, the aethereal sun, assiduously floods the heavens with new rays and ceaselessly sheds light upon new light.]

So, too, our soul darts its arrows separately but imperceptibly.

Artabanus happened to take his nephew Xerxes by surprise. He teased him about the sudden change which he saw come over his face. But Xerxes was in fact thinking about the huge size of his army as it was crossing the Hellespont for the expedition against Greece; he first felt a quiver of joy at seeing so many thousands of men devoted to his service and showed this by a happy and festive look on his face; then, all of a sudden his thoughts turned to all those lives which would wither in a hundred years at most: he knit his brow and was saddened to tears.

We have pursued revenge for an injury with a resolute will; we have felt a singular joy at our victory . . . and we weep: yet it is not for that that we weep. Nothing has changed; but our mind contemplates the matter in a different light and sees it from another aspect: for everything has many angles and many different sheens. Thoughts of kinship, old acquaintanceships and affections suddenly seize our minds and stir them each according to their worth: but the change is so sudden that it escapes us:

> *Nil adeo fieri celeri ratione videtur*
> *Quam si mens fieri proponit et inchoat ipsa.*

Michel de Montaigne

> *Ocius ergo animus quam res se perciet ulla,*
> *Ante oculos quarum in promptu natura videtur.*

[Nothing can be seen to match the rapidity of the thoughts which the mind produces and initiates. The mind is swifter than anything which the nature of our eyes allows them to see.]

That is why we deceive ourselves if we want to make this never-ending succession into one continuous whole. When Timoleon weeps for the murder which, with noble determination, he committed, he does not weep for the liberty he has restored to his country; he does not weep for the Tyrant: he weeps for his brother. He has done one part of his duty: let us allow him to do the other.

On conscience

[Conscience originally meant connivance. Conscience in the sense of our individual consciousness of right and wrong or of our own guilt or rectitude fascinated Montaigne. It became a vital concern of his during the Wars of Religion with their cruelties, their false accusations and their use of torture on prisoners. Such moral basis as there was for the 'question' (judicial torture) seems, curiously enough, to have been a respect for the power of conscience – of a man's inner sense of his guilt or innocence which would strengthen or weaken his power to withstand pain. A major source of Montaigne's ideas here is St Augustine and a passionate note by Juan Luis Vives in his edition of the City of God *designed to undermine confidence in torture.]*

During our civil wars I was travelling one day with my brother the Sieur de la Brousse when we met a gentleman of good appearance who was on the other side from us; I did not know anything about that since he feigned otherwise. The worst of these wars is that the cards are so mixed up, with your enemy indistinguishable from you by any clear indication of language or deportment, being brought up under the same laws, manners and climate, that it is not easy to avoid confusion and disorder. That made me fear that I myself would come upon our own troops in a place where I was not known, be obliged to state my name and wait for the worst. That did happen to me on another occasion: for, from just such a mishap, I lost men and horses. Among others, they killed one of my pages, pitifully: an Italian of good family whom I was carefully training; in him was extinguished a young life, beautiful and full of great promise.

But that man of mine was so madly afraid! I noticed that he nearly died every time we met any horsemen or passed through towns loyal to the King; I finally guessed that his alarm arose from his conscience. It seemed to that wretched man that you could read right into the very secret thoughts of his mind through his mask and the crosses on his greatcoat. So wondrous is the power of conscience! It makes us betray, accuse and fight against ourselves. In default of an outside testimony it leads us to witness against ourselves:

Occultum quatiens animo tortore flagellum.

[Lashing us with invisible whips, our soul torments us.]

The following story is on the lips of children: a Paeonian called Bessus was rebuked for having deliberately destroyed a nest of swallows, killing them all. He said he was right to do so: those little birds kept falsely accusing

On conscience

him of having murdered his father! Until then this act of parricide had been hidden and unknown; but the avenging Furies of his conscience made him who was to pay the penalty reveal the crime.

Hesiod corrects that saying of Plato's, that the punishment follows hard upon the sin. He says it is born at the same instant, with the sin itself; to expect punishment is to suffer it: to merit it is to expect it. Wickedness forges torments for itself,

> *Malum consilium consultori pessimum,*
>
> [Who counsels evil, suffers evil most,]

just as the wasp harms others when it stings but especially itself, for it loses sting and strength for ever:

> *Vitasque in vulnere ponunt.*
>
> [In that wound they lay down their lives.]

The Spanish blister-fly secretes an antidote to its poison, by some mutual antipathy within nature. So too, just when we take pleasure in vice, there is born in our conscience an opposite displeasure, which tortures us, sleeping and waking, with many painful thoughts.

> *Quippe ubi se multi, per somnia sæpe loquentes,*
> *Aut morbo delirantes, procraxe ferantur,*
> *Et celata diu in medium peccala dedisse.*

Michel de Montaigne

[Many indeed, often talking in their sleep or delirious in illness, have proclaimed, it is said, and betrayed long-hidden sins.]

Apollodorus dreamed that he saw himself being flayed by the Scythians then boiled in a pot while his heart kept muttering, 'I am the cause of all these ills.' No hiding-place awaits the wicked, said Epicurus, for they can never be certain of hiding there while their conscience gives them away.

> *Prima est hæc ultio, quod se*
> *Judice nemo nocens absolvitur.*

[This is the principal vengeance: no guilty man is absolved: he is his own judge.]

Conscience can fill us with fear, but she can also fill us with assurance and confidence. And I can say that I have walked more firmly through some dangers by reflecting on the secret knowledge I had of my own will and the innocence of my designs.

> *Conscia mens ut cuique sua est, ita concipit intra*
> *Pectora pro facto spemque metumque suo.*

[A mind conscious of what we have done conceives within our breast either hope or fear, according to our deeds.]

There are hundreds of examples: it will suffice to cite three of them about the same great man.

When Scipio was arraigned one day before the Roman

people on a grave indictment, instead of defending himself and flattering his judges he said: 'Your wishing to judge, on a capital charge, a man through whom you have authority to judge the Roman world, becomes you well!'

Another time his only reply to the accusations made against him by a Tribune of the People was not to plead his cause but to say: 'Come, fellow citizens! Let us go and give thanks to the gods for the victory they gave me over the Carthaginians on just such a day as this!' Then as he started to walk towards the temple all the assembled people could be seen following after him – even his prosecutor.

Again when Petilius, under the instigation of Cato, demanded that Scipio account for the monies that had passed through his hands in the province of Antioch, Scipio came to the Senate for this purpose, took his account-book from under his toga and declared that it contained the truth about his receipts and expenditure; but when he was told to produce it as evidence he refused to do so, saying that he had no wish to act so shamefully towards himself; in the presence of the Senate he tore it up with his own hands. I do not believe that a soul with seared scars could have counterfeited such assurance. He had, says Livy, a mind too great by nature, a mind too elevated by Fortune, even to know how to be a criminal or to condescend to the baseness of defending his innocence.

Torture is a dangerous innovation; it would appear that

it is an assay not of the truth but of a man's endurance. The man who can endure it hides the truth: so does he who cannot. For why should pain make me confess what is true rather than force me to say what is not true? And on the contrary if a man who has not done what he is accused of is able to support such torment, why should a man who has done it be unable to support it, when so beautiful a reward as life itself is offered him?

I think that this innovation is founded on the importance of the power of conscience. It would seem that in the case of the guilty man it would weaken him and assist the torture in making him confess his fault, whereas it strengthens the innocent man against the torture. But to speak the truth, it is a method full of danger and uncertainty. What would you *not* say, what would you *not* do, to avoid such grievous pain?

Etiam innocentes cogit mentiri dolor.

[Pain compels even the innocent to lie.]

This results in a man whom the judge has put to the torture lest he die innocent being condemned to die both innocent and tortured. Thousands upon thousands have falsely confessed to capital charges. Among them, after considering the details of the trial which Alexander made him face and the way he was tortured, I place Philotas.

All the same it is , so they say, the least bad method that human frailty has been able to discover. Very

On conscience

inhumanely, however, and very ineffectually in my opinion. Many peoples less barbarous in this respect than the Greeks and the Romans who call them the Barbarians reckon it horrifying and cruel to torture and smash a man of whose crime you are still in doubt. That ignorant doubt is yours: what has it to do with him? You are the unjust one, are you not? who do worse than kill a man so as not to kill him without due cause! You can prove that by seeing how frequently a man prefers to die for no reason at all rather than to pass through such a questioning which is more painful than the death-penalty itself and which by its harshness often anticipates that penalty by carrying it out.

I do not know where I heard this from, but it exactly represents the conscience of our own Justice: a village woman accused a soldier before his commanding general – a great man for justice – of having wrenched from her little children such sops as she had left to feed them with, the army having laid waste all the surrounding villages. As for proof, there was none. That general first summoned the woman to think carefully what she was saying, especially since she would be guilty of perjury if she were lying; she persisted, so he had the soldier's belly slit open in order to throw the light of truth on to the fact. The woman was found to be right. An investigatory condemnation!

Fortune is often found in Reason's train

[*The Roman censor was not too happy about Montaigne's writing about Fortune (as distinct from Providence) – strangely so, since fickle Fortune and Fortune's Wheel were centuries-old commonplaces. (The word* Fortune *itself occurs some 350 times in the* Essays*.)*]

The changeableness of Fortune's varied dance means that she must inevitably show us every kind of face. Has any of her actions ever been more expressly just than the following? The Duke of Valentinois decided to poison Adrian the Cardinal of Corneto, to whose home in the Vatican he and his father Pope Alexander VI were coming to dine; so he sent ahead a bottle of poisoned wine with instructions to the butler to look after it carefully. The Pope, chancing to arrive before his son, asked for a drink; that butler, who thought that the wine had been entrusted to him merely because of its quality, served it to him; then the Duke himself, arriving just in time for dinner and trusting that nobody would have touched his bottle, drank some too, so that the father died suddenly while the son, after being tormented by a long illness, was reserved for a worse and different fortune.

Sometimes it seems that Fortune is literally playing with us. The Seigneur d'Estrées (who was then ensign to Monseigneur de Vendôme) and the Seigneur de Licques (a lieutenant in the forces of the Duke of Aerschot) were both suitors of the sister of the Sieur de Fouquerolle – despite their being on opposite sides, as often happens with neighbours on the frontier. The Seigneur de Licques was successful. However, on his very wedding-day and, what is worse, before going to bed, the bridegroom desired to break a lance as a tribute to his new bride and went out skirmishing near St Omer; there, he was taken prisoner by the Seigneur d'Estrées who had proved the stronger. To exploit this advantage to the full, d'Estrées compelled the lady –

> *Conjugis ante coacta novi dimittere collum,*
> *Quam veniens una atque altera rursus hyems*
> *Noctibus in longis avidum saturasset amorem.*

[Forced to release her embrace of her young husband before the long nights of a couple of winters had sated her eager love] –

personally to beg him, of his courtesy, to surrender his prisoner to her. Which he did, the French nobility never refusing anything to the ladies . . .

Was the following not Fate apparently playing the artist? The Empire of Constantinople was founded by Constantine son of Helena: many centuries later it was ended by another Constantine son of Helena!

Sometimes it pleases Fortune to rival our Christian miracles. We hold that when King Clovis was besieging Angoulême, by God's favour the walls collapsed of themselves; Bouchet borrows from some other author an account of what happened when King Robert was laying siege to a certain city: he slipped off to Orleans to celebrate the festival of St Aignan; while he was saying his prayers, at a certain point in the Mass the walls of the besieged city collapsed without being attacked. But Fortune produced quite opposite results during our Milanese wars: for after Captain Renzo had mined a great stretch of the wall while besieging the town of Arona for us French it was blown right up in the air, only to fall straight back on to its foundations all in one piece so that the besieged were no worse off.

Sometimes Fortune dabbles in medicine. Jason Phereus was given up by his doctors because of a tumour on the breast; wishing to rid himself of it even by death, he threw himself recklessly into battle where the enemy was thickest; he was struck through the body at precisely the right spot, lancing his tumour and curing him.

Did Fortune not surpass Protogenes the painter in mastery of his art? He had completed a portrait of a tired and exhausted dog; he was pleased with everything else but could not paint its foaming slaver to his own satisfaction; irritated against his work, he grabbed a sponge and threw it at it, intending to blot everything out since the sponge was impregnated with a variety of paints: Fortune guided his throw right to the mouth of the dog and produced the effect which his art had been unable to attain.

Does she not sometimes direct our counsels and correct them? Queen Isabella of England had to cross over to her kingdom from Zealand with her army to come to the aid of her son against her husband; she would have been undone if she had landed at the port she had intended, for her enemies were awaiting her there; but Fortune drove her unwillingly to another place, where she landed in complete safety. And that Ancient who chucked a stone at a dog only to hit his stepmother and kill her could he not have rightly recited this verse:

Ταυτόματον ἡμῶν καλλίω βουλεύεται.

'Fortune has better counsel than we do.' Icetes had bribed two soldiers to murder Tomoleon during his stay in Adrana in Sicily. They chose a time when he was about to make some sacrifice or other; they mingled with the crowd; just as they were signalling to each other that the time was right for their deed, along comes a third soldier who landed a mighty sword-blow on the head of one of them and then ran away. His companion, believing he was discovered and undone, ran to the altar begging for sanctuary and promising to reveal all the truth. Just as he was giving an account of the conspiracy the third man was caught and was being dragged and manhandled through the crowd towards Timoleon and the more notable members of the congregation: he begged for mercy, saying that he had rightly killed his father's murderer, immediately proving by witnesses which good luck had conveniently provided that his father had indeed been murdered in the town of the Leontines by the very man against whom he had taken his revenge. He was granted ten Attic silver-pounds as a reward for his good luck in saving the life of the Father of the Sicilian People while avenging the death of his own father. Such fortune surpasses in rightness the right-rules of human wisdom.

To conclude. Does not the following reveal a most explicit granting of her favour as well as her goodness and singular piety? The two Ignatii, father and son, having been proscribed by the Roman Triumvirate, nobly decided that their duty was to take each other's life and so frustrate the cruelty of those tyrants. Sword in hand they fell on each other. Fortune guided their sword-points, made both blows equally mortal and honoured the beauty of such a loving affection by giving them just enough strength to withdraw their forearms from the wounds, blood-stained and still grasping their weapons, and to clasp each other, there as they lay, in such an embrace that the executioners cut off both their heads at once, allowing their bodies to remain nobly entwined together, wound against wound, lovingly soaking up each other's life-blood.

On punishing cowardice

[*Renaissance Jurisconsults such as Tiraquellus were concerned to temper the severity of the Law by examining motives and human limitations. Montaigne does so here in a matter of great concern to gentlemen in time of war.*]

I once heard a prince, a very great general, maintain that a soldier should not be condemned to death for cowardice: he was at table, being told about the trial of the Seigneur de Vervins who was sentenced to death for surrendering Boulogne.

In truth it is reasonable that we should make a great difference between defects due to our weakness and those due to our wickedness. In the latter we deliberately brace ourselves against reason's rules, which are imprinted on us by Nature; in the former it seems we can call Nature herself as a defence-witness for having left us so weak and imperfect. That is why a great many people believe that we can only be punished for deeds done against our conscience: on that rule is partly based the opinion of those who condemn the capital punishment of heretics and misbelievers as well as the opinion that a barrister or a judge cannot be arraigned if they fail in their duty merely from ignorance.

Where cowardice is concerned the usual way is, certainly, to punish it by disgrace and ignominy. It is said that this rule was first introduced by Charondas the lawgiver, and that before his time the laws of Greece condemned to death those who had fled from battle, whereas he ordered that they be made merely to sit for three days in the market-place dressed as women: he hoped he could still make use of them once he had restored their courage by this disgrace – '*Suffundere malis hominis sanguinem quam effundere.*' [Make the blood of a bad man blush not gush.]

It seems too that in ancient times the laws of Rome condemned deserters to death: Ammianus Marcellinus tells how the Emperor Julian condemned ten of his soldiers to be stripped of their rank and then suffer death, 'following,' he said, 'our Ancient laws'. Elsewhere however Julian for a similar fault condemned others to remain among the prisoners under the ensign in charge of the baggage. Even the harsh sentences decreed against those who had fled at Cannae and those who in that same war had followed Gnaeus Fulvius in his defeat did not extend to death.

Yet it is to be feared that disgrace, by making men desperate, may make them not merely estranged but hostile.

When our fathers were young the Seigneur de Franget,

On punishing cowardice

formerly a deputy-commander in the Company of My Lord Marshal de Châtillon, was sent by My Lord Marshal de Chabannes to replace the Seigneur Du Lude as Governor of Fuentarabia; he surrendered it to the Spaniards. He was sentenced to be stripped of his nobility, both he and his descendants being pronounced commoners, liable to taxation and unfit to bear arms. That severe sentence was executed at Lyons. Later all the noblemen who were at Guyse when the Count of Nassau entered it suffered a similar punishment; and subsequently others still.

Anyway, wherever there is a case of ignorance so crass and of cowardice so flagrant as to surpass any norm, that should be an adequate reason for accepting them as proof of wickedness and malice, to be punished as such.

On the vanity of words

[Montaigne, despite his own mastery of language, despised words and admired deeds or 'matter'. He showed this before he embarked on the Essays *in the dedicatory letter of his translation of Raymond Sebond's* Natural Theology, *addressed to his father. What Montaigne admired in ancient Sparta – and what he found lacking in his own day – was a genuine respect for action over rhetoric.]*

In former times there was a rhetorician who said his job was to make trivial things seem big and to be accepted as such. He is a cobbler who can make big shoes fit little feet. In Sparta they would have had him flogged for practising the art of lying and deception. And I am sure that Archidamus their king did not hear without amazement the answer given by Thucydides when he asked him whether he was better at wrestling than Pericles: 'That,' Thucydides replied, 'would be hard to prove: for after I have thrown him to the ground in the match he persuades the spectators that he did not have a fall and is declared the winner.' Those who hide women behind a mask of

On the vanity of words

make-up do less harm, since it is not much of a loss not to see them as they are by nature, whereas rhetoricians pride themselves on deceiving not our eyes but our judgement, bastardizing and corrupting things in their very essence. Countries such as Crete and Sparta which maintained themselves in a sound and regulated polity did not rate orators very highly.

Ariston wisely defined rhetoric as the art of persuading the people; Socrates and Plato, as the art of deceiving and flattering; and those who reject this generic description show it to be true by what they teach. The Mahometans will not allow their children to be taught it because of its uselessness. And the Athenians, despite the fact that the practice of it was esteemed in their city, realizing how pernicious it was, ordained that the main part of it which is to work on the emotions should be abolished, together with formal introductions and perorations.

It is a means invented for manipulating and stirring up the mob and a community fallen into lawlessness; it is a means which, like medicine, is used only when states are sick; in states such as Athens, Rhodes and Rome where the populace, or the ignorant, or all men, held all power and where everything was in perpetual turmoil, the orators flooded in. And in truth few great men in those countries managed to thrust themselves into positions of trust without the help of eloquent speech: Pompey, Caesar, Crassus, Lucullus, Lentulus and Metellus all made it their mainstay for scrambling up towards that grandiose authority which they finally achieved, helped more by rhetoric than by arms, contrary to what was thought right in better times. For Lucius Volumnius, making a public address in favour of the candidates Quintus Fabius and Publius Decius during the consular elections, declared, 'These are great men of action, born for war; they have consular minds, uncouth in verbal conflict. Subtle, eloquent, learned minds are good but for Praetors, administering justice in the City.'

Rhetoric flourished in Rome when their affairs were in their worst state and when they were shattered by the storms of civil war, just as a field left untamed bears the most flourishing weeds.

It would seem that polities which rely on a monarch have less use for it than the others: for that animal-stupidity and levity which are found in the masses, making them apt to be manipulated and swayed through the ears by those sweet harmonious sounds without succeeding in weighing the truth of anything by force of reason – such levity, I repeat, is not so readily found in one individual man; and it is easier to protect him by a good education and counsel from being impressed by that poison. No famous orator has ever been seen to come from Macedonia or from Persia.

What I have just said was prompted by my having talked with an Italian who served as chief steward to the late Cardinal Caraffa until his death. I got him to tell me

On the vanity of words

about his job. He harangued me on the art of feeding with a professional gravity and demeanour as though he were explaining some important point of Theology. He listed differences of appetite: the appetite you have when you are hungry, the one you have after the second and third courses; what means there are of simply satisfying it or of sometimes exciting it and stimulating it; how to govern the commonwealth of sauces, first in general then in particular, listing the qualities of every ingredient and its effects; the different green-stuffs in their season, the ones which must be served hot, the ones which must be served cold as well as the ways of decorating them and embellishing them to make them look even more appetizing. After all that he embarked upon how the service should be ordered, full of fine and weighty considerations:

> *nec minimo sane discrimine refert*
> *Quo gestu lepores, et quo gallina secetur!*

[For it is of no small importance to know how to carve a hare or a chicken!]

And all this was inflated with rich and magnificent words, the very ones we use to discuss the government of an empire. I was reminded of that man in the poem:

> *Hoc salsum est, hoc adustum est, hoc lautum est parum,*
> *Illud recte; iterum sic memento; sedulo*
> *Moneo quæ possum pro mea sapientia.*

Michel de Montaigne

> *Postremo, tanquam in speculum, in patinas, Demea,*
> *Inspicere jubeo, et moneo quid facto usus sit.*

['This is too salty; this has been burned; this needs to be properly washed; this is excellent – remember that next time.' I advise them carefully as far as my wisdom allows; finally I tell them, Demea, to polish the dishes until they can see their faces in them as in a mirror. I tell them the lot.]

Even the Greeks after all highly praised the order and arrangement which were observed in the banquet which Paulus Aemilius threw for them on his return from Macedonia; but I am not talking here of deeds but of words.

I cannot tell if others feel as I do, but when I hear our architects inflating their importance with big words such as pilasters, architraves, cornices, Corinthian style or Doric style, I cannot stop my thoughts from suddenly dwelling on the magic palaces of Apollidon: yet their deeds concern the wretched parts of my kitchen-door!

When you hear grammatical terms such as metonymy, metaphor and allegory do they not seem to refer to some rare, exotic tongue? Yet they are categories which apply to the chatter of your chambermaid.

It is a similar act of deception to use for our offices of state the same grandiloquent titles as the Romans did, even though they have no similarity of function and even less authority and power. Similar too – and a practice which will, in my judgement, bear witness one day to the singular ineptitude of our century – is our unworthily

On the vanity of words

employing for anybody we like those glorious cognomens with which Antiquity honoured one or two great men every few hundred years. By universal acclaim Plato bore the name *divine*, and nobody thought to dispute it with him: now the Italians, who rightly boast of having in general more lively minds and saner discourse than other peoples of their time, have made a gift of it to Aretino, in whom (apart from a style of writing stuffed and simmering over with pointed sayings, ingenious it is true but fantastical and far-fetched, and apart from his eloquence – such as it is) I can see nothing beyond the common run of authors of his century, so far is he from even approaching that 'divinity' of the Ancients.

And the title Great we now attach to kings who have nothing beyond routine greatness.

To philosophize is to learn how to die

[Montaigne comes to terms with his melancholy, now somewhat played down. He remains preoccupied with that fear of death – fear that is of the often excruciating act of dying – which in older times seems to have been widespread and acute. His treatment is rhetorical but not impersonal. Montaigne is on the way to discovering admirable qualities in common men and women.

Cicero says that philosophizing is nothing other than getting ready to die. That is because study and contemplation draw our souls somewhat outside ourselves, keeping them occupied away from the body, a state which both resembles death and which forms a kind of apprenticeship for it; or perhaps it is because all the wisdom and argument in the world eventually come down to one conclusion; which is to teach us not to be afraid of dying.

In truth, either reason is joking or her target must be our happiness; all the labour of reason must be to make us live well, and at our ease, as Holy Scripture says. All the opinions in the world reach the same point, that pleasure is our target even though they may get there by different means; otherwise we would throw them out immediately,

To philosophize is to learn how to die

for who would listen to anyone whose goal was to achieve for us pain and suffering?

In this case the disagreements between the schools of philosophy are a matter of words. '*Transcurramus solertissimas nugas.*' [Let us skip quickly through those most frivolous trivialities.] More stubbornness and prickliness are there than is appropriate for so dedicated a vocation, but then, no matter what role a man may assume, he always plays his own part within it.

Even in virtue our ultimate aim – no matter what they say – is pleasure. I enjoy bashing people's ears with that word which runs so strongly counter to their minds. When pleasure is taken to mean the most profound delight and an exceeding happiness it is a better companion to virtue than anything else; and rightly so. Such pleasure is no less seriously pleasurable for being more lively, taut, robust and virile. We ought to have given virtue the more favourable, noble and natural name of pleasure not (as we have done) a name derived from *vis* (vigour).

There is that lower voluptuous pleasure which can only be said to have a disputed claim to the name not a privileged right to it. I find it less pure of lets and hindrances than virtue. Apart from having a savour which is fleeting, fluid and perishable, it has its vigils, fasts and travails, its blood and its sweat; it also has its own peculiar sufferings, which are sharp in so many different ways and accompanied by a satiety of such weight that it amounts to repentance.

Since we reckon that obstacles serve as a spur to that pleasure and as seasoning to its sweetness (on the grounds that in Nature contraries are enhanced by their contraries) we are quite wrong to say when we turn to virtue that identical obstacles and difficulties overwhelm her, making her austere and inaccessible, whereas (much more appropriately than for voluptuous pleasure) they ennoble, sharpen and enhance that holy, perfect pleasure which virtue procures for us. A man is quite unworthy of an acquaintance with virtue who weighs her fruit against the price she exacts; he knows neither her graces nor her ways. Those who proceed to teach us that the questing after virtue is rugged and wearisome whereas it is delightful to possess her can only mean that she always lacks delight. (For what human means have ever brought anyone to the joy of possessing her?) Even the most perfect of men have been satisfied with aspiring to her – not possessing her but drawing near to her. The contention is wrong, seeing that in every pleasure known to Man the very pursuit of it is pleasurable: the undertaking savours of the quality of the object it has in view; it effectively constitutes a large proportion of it and is consubstantial with it. There is a happiness and blessedness radiating from virtue; they fill all that appertains to her and every approach to her, from the first way in to the very last barrier.

Now one of virtue's main gifts is a contempt for death, which is the means of furnishing our life with easy tranquillity, of giving us a pure and friendly taste for it; without it every other pleasure is snuffed out. That is why all rules meet and concur in this one clause. It is true that they all lead us by common accord to despise pain, poverty and the other misfortunes to which human lives are subject, but they do not do so with the same care. That is partly because such misfortunes are not inevitable. (Most of Mankind spend their lives without tasting poverty; some without even experiencing pain or sickness, like Xenophilus the musician, who lived in good health to a hundred and six.) It is also because, if the worse comes to worse, we can sheer off the bung of our misfortunes whenever we like: death can end them. But, as for death itself, that is inevitable.

> *Omnes eodem cogimur, omnium*
> *Versatur urna, serius ocius*
> *Sors exitura et nos in æter-*
> *Num exitium impositura cymbæ.*

[All of our lots are shaken about in the Urn, destined sooner or later to be cast forth, placing us in everlasting exile via Charon's boat.]

And so if death makes us afraid, that is a subject of continual torment which nothing can assuage. There is no place where death cannot find us – even if we constantly twist our heads about in all directions as in a suspect land: '*Quae quasi saxum Tantalo semper impendet.*' [It is like the rock for ever hanging over the head of Tantalus.] Our assizes often send prisoners to be executed at the scene of their crimes. On the way there, take them past fair mansions and ply them with good cheer as much as you like –

> . . . *non Siculæ dapes*
> *Dulcem elaborabunt saporem,*
> *Non avium cytharœque cantus*
> *Somnum reducent –*

[even Sicilian banquets produce no sweet savours; not even the music of birdsong nor of lyre can bring back sleep] –

do you think they can enjoy it or that having the final purpose of their journey ever before their eyes will not spoil their taste for such entertainment?

> *Audit iter, numeratque dies, spacioque viarum*
> *Metitur vitam, torquetur peste futura*

[He inquires about the way; he counts the days; the length of his life is the length of those roads. He is tortured by future anguish.]

The end of our course is death. It is the objective necessarily within our sights. If death frightens us how can we go one step forward without anguish? For ordinary people the remedy is not to think about it; but what

To philosophize is to learn how to die

brutish insensitivity can produce so gross a blindness? They lead the donkey by the tail:

> *Qui capite ipse suo instituit vestigia retro.*

[They walk forward with their heads turned backwards.]

No wonder that they often get caught in a trap. You can frighten such people simply by mentioning death (most of them cross themselves as when the Devil is named); and since it is mentioned in wills, never expect them to draw one up before the doctor has pronounced the death-sentence. And then, in the midst of pain and terror, God only knows what shape their good judgement kneads it into!

(That syllable 'death' struck Roman ears too roughly; the very word was thought to bring ill-luck, so they learned to soften and dilute it with periphrases. Instead of saying *He is dead* they said *He has ceased to live* or *He has lived*. They found consolation in living, even in a past tense! Whence our 'late' (*feu*) So-and-So: 'he was' So-and-So.)

Perhaps it is a case of, 'Repayment delayed means money in hand', as they say; I was born between eleven and noon on the last day of February, one thousand five hundred and thirty-three (as we date things nowadays, beginning the year in January); it is exactly a fortnight since I became thirty-nine: 'I ought to live at least as long again; meanwhile it would be mad to think of something so far off'. – Yes, but all leave life in the same circumstances, young and old alike. Everybody goes out as though he had just come in. Moreover, however decrepit a man may be, he thinks he still has another twenty years to go in the body, so long as he has Methuselah ahead of him. Silly fool, you! Where your life is concerned, who has decided the term? You are relying on doctors' tales; look at facts and experience instead. As things usually go, you have been living for some time now by favour extraordinary. You have already exceeded the usual term of life; to prove it, just count how many more of your acquaintances have died younger than you are compared with those who have reached your age. Just make a list of people who have ennobled their lives by fame: I wager that we shall find more who died before thirty-five than after. It is full of reason and piety to take as our example the manhood of Jesus Christ: his life ended at thirty-three. The same term applies to Alexander, the greatest man who was simply man.

Death can surprise us in so many ways:

> *Quid quisque vitet, nunquam homini satis*
> *Cautum est in horas.*

[No man knows what dangers he should avoid from one hour to another.]

Leaving aside fevers and pleurisies, who would ever have thought that a Duke of Brittany was to be crushed to death in a crowd, as one was during the state entry into Lyons of Pope Clement, who came from my part of the world! Have you not seen one of our kings killed at sport? And was not one of his ancestors killed by a bump from a pig? Aeschylus was warned against a falling house; he was always on the alert, but in vain: he was killed by the shell of a tortoise which slipped from the talons of an eagle in flight. Another choked to death on a pip from a grape; an Emperor died from a scratch when combing his hair; Aemilius Lepidus, from knocking his foot on his own doorstep; Aufidius from bumping into a door of his Council chamber. Those who died between a woman's thighs include Cornelius Gallus, a praetor; Tigillinus, a captain of the Roman Guard; Ludovico, the son of Guy di Gonzaga, the Marquis of Mantua; and – providing even worse examples – Speucippus the Platonic philosopher, and one of our Popes.

Then there was that wretched judge Bebius; he was just granting a week's extra time to a litigant when he died of a seizure: his own time had run out. Caius Julius, a doctor, was putting ointment on the eyes of a patient when death closed his. And if I may include a personal example, Captain Saint-Martin, my brother, died at the age of twenty-three while playing tennis; he was felled by a blow from a tennis-ball just above the right ear. There was no sign of bruising or of a wound. He did not even sit down or take a rest; yet five or six hours later he was dead from an apoplexy caused by that blow.

When there pass before our eyes examples such as these, so frequent and so ordinary, how can we ever rid ourselves of thoughts of death or stop imagining that death has us by the scruff of the neck at every moment?

You might say: 'But what does it matter how you do it, so long as you avoid pain?' I agree with that. If there were any way at all of sheltering from Death's blows – even by crawling under the skin of a calf – I am not the man to recoil from it. It is enough for me to spend my time contentedly. I deal myself the best hand I can, and then accept it. It can be as inglorious or as unexemplary as you please:

> *prœtulerim delirus inersque videri,*
> *Dum mea delectent mala me, vel denique fallant,*
> *Quam sapere et ringi.*

[I would rather be delirious or a dullard if my faults pleased me, or at least deceived me, rather than to be wise and snarling.]

But it is madness to think you can succeed that way. They come and they go and they trot and they dance: and never a word about death. All well and good. Yet when death does come – to them, their wives, their children, their friends – catching them unawares and unprepared, then what storms of passion overwhelm them, what cries, what fury, what despair! Have you ever seen anything brought so low, anything so changed, so confused?

We must start providing for it earlier. Even if such brutish indifference could find lodgings in the head of an intelligent man (which seems quite impossible to me) it sells its wares too dearly. If death were an enemy which could be avoided I would counsel borrowing the arms of cowardice. But it cannot be done. Death can catch you just as easily as a coward on the run or as an honourable man:

> *Nempe et fugacem persequitur virum,*
> *Nec parcit imbellis juventæ*
> *Poplitibus, timidoque tergo;*

[It hounds the man who runs away, and it does not spare the legs fearful backs of unwarlike youth;]

no tempered steel can protect your shoulders;

> *Ille licet ferro cautus se condat ære,*
> *Mors tamen inclusum protrahet inde caput;*

[No use a man hiding prudently behind iron or brass:
Death will know how to make him stick out his cowering head;]

we must learn to stand firm and to fight it.

To begin depriving death of its greatest advantage over us, let us adopt a way clean contrary to that common one; let us deprive death of its strangeness; let us frequent it, let us get used to it; let us have nothing more often in mind than death. At every instant let us evoke it in our imagination under all its aspects. Whenever a horse stumbles, a tile falls or a pin pricks however slightly, let us at once chew over this thought: 'Supposing that was death itself?' With that, let us brace ourselves and make an effort. In the midst of joy and feasting let our refrain be one which recalls our human condition. Let us never be carried away by pleasure so strongly that we fail to recall occasionally how many are the ways in which that joy of ours is subject to death or how many are the fashions in which death threatens to snatch it away. That is what the Egyptians did: in the midst of all their banquets and good cheer they would bring in a mummified corpse to serve as a warning to the guests:

> *Omnem crede diem tibi diluxisse supremum.*
> *Grata superveniet, quæ non sperabitur hora.*

[Believe that each day was the last to shine on you. If it comes, any unexpected hour will be welcome indeed.]

We do not know where death awaits us: so let us wait for it everywhere. To practise death is to practise freedom. A man who has learned how to die has unlearned how to be a slave. Knowing how to die gives us freedom from subjection and constraint. Life has no evil for him who has thoroughly understood that loss of life is not an evil. Paulus Aemilius was sent a messenger by that wretched King of Macedonia who was his prisoner, begging not to be led in his triumphant procession. He replied: 'Let him beg that favour from himself.'

To philosophize is to learn how to die

It is true that, in all things, if Nature does not lend a hand art and industry do not progress very far. I myself am not so much melancholic as an idle dreamer: from the outset there was no topic I ever concerned myself with more than with thoughts about death – even in the most licentious period of my life.

Jucundum cum aetas florida ver ageret.

[When my blossoming youth rejoiced in spring.]

Among the games and the courting many thought I was standing apart chewing over some jealousy or the uncertainty of my aspirations: meanwhile I was reflecting on someone or other who, on leaving festivities just like these, had been surprised by a burning fever and his end, with his head full of idleness, love and merriment – just like me; and the same could be dogging me now:

Jam fuerit, nec post unquam revocare licebit.

[The present will soon be the past, never to be recalled.]

Thoughts such as these did not furrow my brow any more than others did. At first it does seem impossible not to feel the sting of such ideas, but if you keep handling them and running through them you eventually tame them. No doubt about that. Otherwise I would, for my part, be in continual terror and frenzy: for no man ever had less confidence than I did that he would go on living;

and no man ever counted less on his life proving long. Up till now I have enjoyed robust good health almost uninterruptedly: yet that never extends my hopes for life any more than sickness shortens them. Every moment it seems to me that I am running away from myself. And I ceaselessly chant the refrain, 'Anything you can do another day can be done now.'

In truth risks and dangers do little or nothing to bring us nearer to death. If we think of all the millions of threats which remain hanging over us, apart from the one which happens to appear most menacing just now, we shall realize that death is equally near when we are vigorous or feverish, at sea or at home, in battle or in repose. *'Nemo altero fragilior est: nemo in crastinam sui certior.'* [No man is frailer than another: no man more certain of the morrow.]

If I have only one hour's work to do before I die, I am never sure I have time enough to finish it. The other day someone was going through my notebooks and found a declaration about something I wanted done after my death. I told him straight that, though I was hale and healthy and but a league away from my house, I had hastened to jot it down because I had not been absolutely certain of getting back home. Being a man who broods over his thoughts and stores them up inside him, I am always just about as ready as I can be: when death does suddenly appear, it will bear no new warning for me. As far as we possibly can we must always have our boots on,

To philosophize is to learn how to die

ready to go; above all we should take care to have no outstanding business with anyone else.

> *Quid brevi fortes jaculamur ævo*
> *Multa?*

[Why, in so brief a span do we find strength to make so many projects?]

We shall have enough to do then without adding to it.

One man complains less of death itself than of its cutting short the course of a fine victory; another, that he has to depart before marrying off his daughter or arranging the education of his children; one laments the company of his wife; another, of his son; as though they were the principal attributes of his being.

I am now ready to leave, thank God, whenever He pleases, regretting nothing except life itself – if its loss should happen to weigh heavy on me. I am untying all the knots. I have already half-said my adieus to everyone but myself. No man has ever prepared to leave the world more simply nor more fully than I have. No one has more completely let go of everything than I try to do.

> *Miser o miser, aiunt, omnia ademit*
> *Una dies infesta mihi tot præmia vitæ.*

['I am wretched, so wretched,' they say: 'One dreadful day has stripped me of all life's rewards.']

And the builder says:

Michel de Montaigne

> *Manent opera interrupta, minaeque*
> *Murorum ingentes.*

[My work remains unfinished; huge walls may fall down.]

We ought not to plan anything on so large a scale – at least, not if we are to get all worked up if we cannot see it through to the end.

We are born for action:

> *Cum moriar, medium solvare inter opus.*

[When I die, may I be in the midst of my work.]

I want us to be doing things, prolonging life's duties as much as we can; I want Death to find me planting my cabbages, neither worrying about it nor the unfinished gardening. I once saw a man die who, right to the last, kept lamenting that destiny had cut the thread of the history he was writing when he had only got up to our fifteenth or sixteenth king!

> *Illud in his rebus non addunt, nec tibi earum*
> *Jam desiderium rerum super insidet una!*

[They never add, that desire for such things does not linger on in your remains!]

We must throw off such humours; they are harmful and vulgar.

Our graveyards have been planted next to churches, says Lycurgus, so that women, children and lesser folk should grow accustomed to seeing a dead man without feeling terror, and so that this continual spectacle of bones, tombs and funerals should remind us of our human condition:

> *Quin etiam exhilarare viris convivia cæde*
> *Mos olim, et miscere epulis spectacula dira*
> *Certantum ferro, sæpe et super ipsa cadentum*
> *Pocula respersis non parco sanguine mensis;*

[It was once the custom, moreover, to enliven feasts with human slaughter and to entertain guests with the cruel sight of gladiators fighting: they often fell among the goblets, flooding the tables with their blood;]

so too, after their festivities the Egyptians used to display before their guests a huge portrait of death, held up by a man crying, 'Drink and be merry: once dead you will look like this'; similarly, I have adopted the practice of always having death not only in my mind but on my lips. There is nothing I inquire about more readily than how men have died: what did they say? How did they look? What expression did they have? There are no passages in the history books which I note more attentively. That I have a particular liking for such matters is shown by the examples with which I stuff my book. If I were a scribbler I would produce a compendium with commentaries of the various ways men have died. (Anyone who taught men how to die would teach them how to live.) Dicearchus did write a book with some such title, but for another and less useful purpose.

People will tell me that the reality of death so far exceeds the thought that when we actually get there all our fine fencing amounts to nothing. Let them say so: there is no doubt whatsoever that meditating on it beforehand confers great advantages. Anyway, is it nothing to get even that far without faltering or feverish agitation?

But there is more to it than that: Nature herself lends us a hand and gives us courage. If our death is violent and short we have no time to feel afraid: if it be otherwise, I have noticed that as an illness gets more and more hold on me I naturally slip into a kind of contempt for life. I find that a determination to die is harder to digest when I am in good health than when I am feverish, especially since I no longer hold so firmly to the pleasures of life once I begin to lose the use and enjoyment of them, and can look on death with a far less terrified gaze. That leads me to hope that the further I get from good health and the nearer I approach to death the more easily I will come to terms with exchanging one for the other. Just as I have in several other matters assayed the truth of Caesar's assertion that things often look bigger from afar than close to, I have also found that I was much more terrified of illness when I was well than when I felt ill. Being in a happy state, all pleasure and vigour, leads me to get the other state quite out of proportion, so that I mentally increase all its discomforts by half and imagine them heavier than they prove to be when I have to bear them.

I hope that the same will apply to me when I die. It is normal to experience change and decay: let us note how Nature robs us of our sense of loss and decline. What does an old man still retain of his youthful vigour and of his own past life?

> *Heu senibus vitae portio quanta manet.*

[Alas, what little of life's portion remains with the aged.]

When a soldier of Caesar's guard, broken and worn out, came up to him in the street and begged leave to kill himself, Caesar looked at his decrepit bearing and said with a smile: 'So you think you are still alive, then?'

If any of us were to be plunged into old age all of a sudden I do not think that the change would be bearable. But, almost imperceptibly, Nature leads us by the hand down a gentle slope; little by little, step by step, she engulfs us in that pitiful state and breaks us in, so that we feel no jolt when youth dies in us, although in essence and in truth that is a harsher death than the total extinction of a languishing life as old age dies. For it is not so grievous a leap from a wretched existence to non-existence as it is from a sweet existence in full bloom to one full of travail and pain.

When our bodies are bent and stooping low they have less strength for supporting burdens. So too for our souls:

we must therefore educate and train them for their encounter with that adversary, death; for the soul can find no rest while she remains afraid of him. But once she does find assurance she can boast that it is impossible for anxiety, anguish, fear or even the slightest dissatisfaction to dwell within her. And that almost surpasses our human condition.

> *Non vultus instantis tyranni*
> *Mente quatit solida, neque Auster*
> *Dux inquieti turbidus Adriæ,*
> *Nec fulminantis magna Jovis manus.*

[Nothing can shake such firmness: neither the threatening face of a tyrant, nor the South Wind (that tempestuous Master of the Stormy Adriatic) nor even the mighty hand of thundering Jove.]

She has made herself Mistress of her passions and her lusts, Mistress of destitution, shame, poverty and of all other injuries of Fortune. Let any of us who can gain such a superiority do so: for here is that true and sovereign freedom which enables us to cock a snook at force and injustice and to laugh at manacles and prisons:

> *in manicis, et*
> *Compedibus, sævo te sub custode tenebo.*
> *Ipse Deus simul atque volam, me solvet: opinor,*
> *Hoc sentit, moriar. Mors ultima linea rerum est.*

To philosophize is to learn how to die

['I will shackle your hands and feet and keep you under a cruel gaoler.' – 'God himself will set me free as soon as I ask him to.' (He means, I think, 'I will die': for death is the last line of all.)]

Our religion has never had a surer human foundation than contempt for life; rational argument (though not it alone) summons us to such contempt: for why should we fear to lose something which, once lost, cannot be regretted? And since we are threatened by so many kinds of death is it not worse to fear them all than to bear one? Death is inevitable: does it matter when it comes? When Socrates was told that the Thirty Tyrants had condemned him to death, he retorted, 'And nature, them!'

How absurd to anguish over our passing into freedom from all anguish. Just as our birth was the birth of all things for us, so our death will be the death of them all. That is why it is equally mad to weep because we shall not be alive a hundred years from now and to weep because we were not alive a hundred years ago. Death is the origin of another life. We wept like this and it cost us just as dear when we entered into this life, similarly stripping off our former veil as we did so. Nothing can be grievous which occurs but once; is it reasonable to fear for so long a time something which lasts so short a time? Living a long life or a short life are made all one by death: *long* and *short* do not apply to that which is no more. Aristotle says that there are tiny creatures on the river Hypanis whose life lasts one single day: those which die at eight in the morning die in youth; those which die at five in the evening die of senility. Which of us would not laugh if so momentary a span counted as happiness or unhappiness? Yet if we compare our own span against eternity or even against the span of mountains, rivers, stars, trees or, indeed, of some animals, then saying *shorter* or *longer* becomes equally ridiculous.

Nature drives us that way, too: 'Leave this world,' she says, 'just as you entered it. That same journey from death to life, which you once made without suffering or fear, make it again from life to death. Your death is a part of the order of the universe; it is a part of the life of the world:

> *inter se mortales mutua vivunt . . .*
> *Et quasi cursores vitaï lampada tradunt.*

[Mortal creatures live lives dependent on each other; like runners in a relay they pass on the torch of life.]

Shall I change, just for you, this beautiful interwoven structure! Death is one of the attributes you were created with; death is a part of you; you are running away from yourself; this *being* which you enjoy is equally divided between death and life. From the day you were born your path leads to death as well as life:

> *Prima, quae vitam dedit, hora, carpsit.*

[Our first hour gave us life and began to devour it.]

> *Nascentes morimur, finisque ab origine pendet.*

To philosophize is to learn how to die

[As we are born we die; the end of our life is attached to its beginning.]

All that you live, you have stolen from life; you live at her expense. Your life's continual task is to build your death. You are *in* death while you are *in* life: when you are no more *in* life you are after death. Or if you prefer it thus: after life you are dead, but during life you are dying: and death touches the dying more harshly than the dead, in more lively a fashion and more essentially.

'If you have profited from life, you have had your fill; go away satisfied:

> *Cur non ut plenus vitae conviva recedis?*

[Why not withdraw from life like a guest replete?]

But if you have never learned how to use life, if life is useless to you, what does it matter if you have lost it? What do you still want it for?

> *Cur amplius addere quæris*
> *Rursum quod pereat male, et ingratum occidat omne?*

[Why seek to add more, just to lose it again, wretchedly, without joy?]

Life itself is neither a good nor an evil: life is where good or evil find a place, depending on how you make it for them.

'If you have lived one day, you have seen everything.

Michel de Montaigne

One day equals all days. There is no other light, no other night. The Sun, Moon and Stars, disposed just as they are now, were enjoyed by your grandsires and will entertain your great-grandchildren:

> *Non alium videre patres: aliumve nepotes*
> *Aspicient.*

[Your fathers saw none other: none other shall your progeny discern.]

And at the worst estimate the division and variety of all the acts of my play are complete in one year. If you have observed the vicissitude of my four seasons you know they embrace the childhood, youth, manhood and old age of the World. Its play is done. It knows no other trick but to start all over again. Always it will be the same.

> *Versamur ibidem, atque insumus usque;*

[We turn in the same circle, for ever;]

> *Atque in se sua per vestigia volvitur annus.*

[And the year rolls on again through its own traces.]

I have not the slightest intention of creating new pastimes for you.

> *Nam tibi præterea quod machiner, inveniamque*
> *Quod placeat, nihil est, eadem sunt omnia semper.*

To philosophize is to learn how to die

[For there is nothing else I can make or discover to please you: all things are the same for ever.]

Make way for others as others did for you. The first part of equity is equality. Who can complain of being included when all are included?

'It is no good going on living: it will in no wise shorten the time you will stay dead. It is all for nothing: you will be just as long in that state which you fear as though you had died at the breast;

> *licet, quod vis, vivendo vincere secla,*
> *Mors æterna tamen nihilominus illa manebit.*

[Triumph over time and live as long as you please: death eternal will still be waiting for you.]

'And yet I shall arrange that you have no unhappiness:

> *In vera nescis nullum fore morte alium te,*
> *Qui possit vivus tibi te lugere peremptum,*
> *Stansque jacentem.*

[Do you not know that in real death there will be no second You, living to lament your death and standing by your corpse.]

"You" will not desire the life which now you so much lament.

> *Nec sibi enim quisquam tum se vitamque requirit . . .*
> *Nec desiderium nostri nos afficit ullum.*

[Then no one worries about his life or his self; . . . we feel no yearning for our own being.]

Death is less to be feared than nothing – if there be anything less than nothing:

> *multo mortem minus ad nos esse putandum*
> *Si minus esse potest quam quod nihil esse videmus.*

[We should think death to be less – if anything is 'less' than what we can see to be nothing at all.]

'Death does not concern you, dead or alive; alive, because you are: dead, because you are no more.

'No one dies before his time; the time you leave behind you is no more yours than the time which passed before you were born; and does not concern you either:

> *Respice enim quam nil ad nos ante acta vetustas*
> *Temporis æterní fuerit.*

[Look back and see that the aeons of eternity before we were born have been nothing to us.]

'Wherever your life ends, there all of it ends. The usefulness of living lies not in duration but in what you make of it. Some have lived long and lived little. See to it while you are still here. Whether you have lived enough depends not on a count of years but on your will.

'Do you think you will never arrive whither you are ceaselessly heading? Yet every road has its end. And, if it is a relief to have company, is not the whole world proceeding at the same pace as you are?

> *Omnia te vita perfuncta sequentur.*

> [All things will follow you when their life is done.]

Does not everything move with the same motion as you do? Is there anything which is not growing old with you? At this same instant that you die hundreds of men, of beasts and of other creatures are dying too.

> *Nam nox nulla diem, neque noctem aurora sequuta est,*
> *Qua non audierit mistos vagitibus ægris*
> *Ploratus, mortis comites et funeris atri.*

[No night has ever followed day, no dawn has ever followed night, without hearing, interspersed among the wails of infants, the cries of pain attending death and sombre funerals.]

'Why do you pull back when retreat is impossible? You have seen cases enough where men were lucky to die, avoiding great misfortunes by doing so: but have you ever seen anyone for whom death turned out badly? And it is very simple-minded of you to condemn something which you have never experienced either yourself or through another. Why do you complain of me or of Destiny? Do we do you wrong? Should you govern us or should we govern you? You may not have finished your stint but you have finished your life. A small man is no less whole than a tall one. Neither men nor their lives are measured by the yard. Chiron refused immortality when he was told of its characteristics by his father Saturn, the god of time and of duration.

'Truly imagine how much less bearable for Man, and how much more painful, would be a life which lasted for ever rather than the life which I have given you. If you did not have death you would curse me, for ever, for depriving you of it.

'Seeing what advantages death holds I have deliberately mixed a little anguish into it to stop you from embracing it too avidly or too injudiciously. To lodge you in that moderation which I require of you, neither fleeing from life nor yet fleeing from death, I have tempered them both between the bitter and the sweet.

'I taught Thales, the foremost of your Sages, that living and dying are things indifferent. So, when asked "why he did not go and die then," he very wisely replied: "Because it *is* indifferent."

'Water, Earth, Air and Fire and the other parts of this my edifice are no more instrumental to your life than to your death. Why are you afraid of your last day? It brings you no closer to your death than any other did. The last step does not make you tired: it shows that you are tired. All days lead to death: the last one gets there.'

Those are the good counsels of Nature, our Mother.

I have often wondered why the face of death, seen in ourselves or in other men, appears incomparably less terrifying to us in war than in our own homes – otherwise armies would consist of doctors and cry-babies – and why, since death is ever the same, there is always more steadfastness among village-folk and the lower orders than among all the rest. I truly believe that what frightens us more than death itself are those terrifying grimaces and preparations with which we surround it – a brand new way of life: mothers, wives and children weeping; visits from people stunned and beside themselves with grief; the presence of a crowd of servants, pale and tear-stained; a bedchamber without daylight; candles lighted; our bedside besieged by doctors and preachers; in short, all about us is horror and terror. We are under the ground, buried in our graves already! Children are frightened of their very friends when they see them masked. So are we. We must rip the masks off things as well as off people. Once we have done that we shall find underneath only that same death which a valet and a chambermaid got through recently, without being afraid. Blessed the death which leaves no time for preparing such gatherings of mourners.

1. BOCCACCIO · *Mrs Rosie and the Priest*
2. GERARD MANLEY HOPKINS · *As kingfishers catch fire*
3. *The Saga of Gunnlaug Serpent-tongue*
4. THOMAS DE QUINCEY · *On Murder Considered as One of the Fine Arts*
5. FRIEDRICH NIETZSCHE · *Aphorisms on Love and Hate*
6. JOHN RUSKIN · *Traffic*
7. PU SONGLING · *Wailing Ghosts*
8. JONATHAN SWIFT · *A Modest Proposal*
9. *Three Tang Dynasty Poets*
10. WALT WHITMAN · *On the Beach at Night Alone*
11. KENKŌ · *A Cup of Sake Beneath the Cherry Trees*
12. BALTASAR GRACIÁN · *How to Use Your Enemies*
13. JOHN KEATS · *The Eve of St Agnes*
14. THOMAS HARDY · *Woman much missed*
15. GUY DE MAUPASSANT · *Femme Fatale*
16. MARCO POLO · *Travels in the Land of Serpents and Pearls*
17. SUETONIUS · *Caligula*
18. APOLLONIUS OF RHODES · *Jason and Medea*
19. ROBERT LOUIS STEVENSON · *Olalla*
20. KARL MARX AND FRIEDRICH ENGELS · *The Communist Manifesto*
21. PETRONIUS · *Trimalchio's Feast*
22. JOHANN PETER HEBEL · *How a Ghastly Story Was Brought to Light by a Common or Garden Butcher's Dog*
23. HANS CHRISTIAN ANDERSEN · *The Tinder Box*
24. RUDYARD KIPLING · *The Gate of the Hundred Sorrows*
25. DANTE · *Circles of Hell*
26. HENRY MAYHEW · *Of Street Piemen*
27. HAFEZ · *The nightingales are drunk*
28. GEOFFREY CHAUCER · *The Wife of Bath*
29. MICHEL DE MONTAIGNE · *How We Weep and Laugh at the Same Thing*
30. THOMAS NASHE · *The Terrors of the Night*
31. EDGAR ALLAN POE · *The Tell-Tale Heart*
32. MARY KINGSLEY · *A Hippo Banquet*
33. JANE AUSTEN · *The Beautifull Cassandra*
34. ANTON CHEKHOV · *Gooseberries*
35. SAMUEL TAYLOR COLERIDGE · *Well, they are gone, and here must I remain*
36. JOHANN WOLFGANG VON GOETHE · *Sketchy, Doubtful, Incomplete Jottings*
37. CHARLES DICKENS · *The Great Winglebury Duel*
38. HERMAN MELVILLE · *The Maldive Shark*
39. ELIZABETH GASKELL · *The Old Nurse's Story*
40. NIKOLAY LESKOV · *The Steel Flea*

41. HONORÉ DE BALZAC · *The Atheist's Mass*
42. CHARLOTTE PERKINS GILMAN · *The Yellow Wall-Paper*
43. C.P. CAVAFY · *Remember, Body...*
44. FYODOR DOSTOEVSKY · *The Meek One*
45. GUSTAVE FLAUBERT · *A Simple Heart*
46. NIKOLAI GOGOL · *The Nose*
47. SAMUEL PEPYS · *The Great Fire of London*
48. EDITH WHARTON · *The Reckoning*
49. HENRY JAMES · *The Figure in the Carpet*
50. WILFRED OWEN · *Anthem For Doomed Youth*
51. WOLFGANG AMADEUS MOZART · *My Dearest Father*
52. PLATO · *Socrates' Defence*
53. CHRISTINA ROSSETTI · *Goblin Market*
54. *Sindbad the Sailor*
55. SOPHOCLES · *Antigone*
56. RYŪNOSUKE AKUTAGAWA · *The Life of a Stupid Man*
57. LEO TOLSTOY · *How Much Land Does A Man Need?*
58. GIORGIO VASARI · *Leonardo da Vinci*
59. OSCAR WILDE · *Lord Arthur Savile's Crime*
60. SHEN FU · *The Old Man of the Moon*
61. AESOP · *The Dolphins, the Whales and the Gudgeon*
62. MATSUO BASHŌ · *Lips too Chilled*
63. EMILY BRONTË · *The Night is Darkening Round Me*
64. JOSEPH CONRAD · *To-morrow*
65. RICHARD HAKLUYT · *The Voyage of Sir Francis Drake Around the Whole Globe*
66. KATE CHOPIN · *A Pair of Silk Stockings*
67. CHARLES DARWIN · *It was snowing butterflies*
68. BROTHERS GRIMM · *The Robber Bridegroom*
69. CATULLUS · *I Hate and I Love*
70. HOMER · *Circe and the Cyclops*
71. D. H. LAWRENCE · *Il Duro*
72. KATHERINE MANSFIELD · *Miss Brill*
73. OVID · *The Fall of Icarus*
74. SAPPHO · *Come Close*
75. IVAN TURGENEV · *Kasyan from the Beautiful Lands*
76. VIRGIL · *O Cruel Alexis*
77. H. G. WELLS · *A Slip under the Microscope*
78. HERODOTUS · *The Madness of Cambyses*
79. *Speaking of Siva*
80. *The Dhammapada*

'... dreaming of bears, or fire, or water ...'

THOMAS NASHE
Born 1567, Lowestoft, England
Died *c.* 1601

The Terrors of the Night first published 1594.

NASHE IN PENGUIN CLASSICS
The Unfortunate Traveller and Other Works

THOMAS NASHE

The Terrors of the Night, or
A Discourse of Apparitions

PENGUIN BOOKS

PENGUIN CLASSICS

UK | USA | Canada | Ireland | Australia
India | New Zealand | South Africa

Penguin Books is part of the Penguin Random House group of companies whose addresses can be found at global.penguinrandomhouse.com.

This edition published in Penguin Classics 2015
008

Set in 9.5/13 pt Baskerville 10 Pro
Typeset by Jouve (UK), Milton Keynes

Printed and bound in Great Britain by Clays Ltd, Elcograf S.p.A.

A CIP catalogue record for this book is available from the British Library

ISBN: 978–0–141–39724–5

www.greenpenguin.co.uk

Penguin Random House is committed to a sustainable future for our business, our readers and our planet. This book is made from Forest Stewardship Council® certified paper.

Glossary

bent on a head	rushing ahead
bill of parcels	catalogue
black saunt	discordant singing
bolings	bowlines
bonarobaes	courtesans
bosk	sketch
breaks with	confides in
buy wind	buy favours
cannot away with	cannot tolerate
chapmanable	saleable
chevala	'who goes there?' (*Qui va là?*)
cog	cheat (at a game)
colourable	deceitful
conceits	thoughts
conycatching	deceptive
countervailment	compensation
crepundio	empty talker
displin	disciplined
disposition	at his disposal
emayle	enamel
exornations	embellishments
extraught	derived

Glossary

foeculent	impure
gentilism	paganism
glick	jest
good big pop mouths	mouths suited to sharp yelling
incontinent	at once
a knot in a bulrush	trouble
linsey-wolsey	mixed up
lists	desires
make a coil	have a noisy conversation
make a shaft or bolt	make something definite
matachine	exotic sword dance
Molenax	Emeric Molyneux, a globe maker
Mounsier	Monsieur – the Duke of Anjou, who visited England in 1581 as a potential suitor of the Queen
pastance	food
Pater-Noster-while	the time it takes to say the Lord's Prayer
poses	catarrh
potestates	spiritual powers
Queen-Hive	Queenshithe
riding snarl	slip-knot
serena	evening rain (considered harmful)
sinkapace	lively dance
skirts and outshifts	suburbs
standish	ink-stand
surprised	captured
table	writing tablet

Glossary

Tittle est amen	conclusion
Tuns	Willem Tons, a painter
welt and gard	adorn and trim
worm in his tongue	a piece of cartilage thought then to be a parasite
yare	neat
y-clepped	called

The Terrors of the Night

OR

A DISCOURSE OF APPARITIONS

A little to beguile time idly discontented, and satisfy some of my solitary friends here in the country, I have hastily undertook to write of the weary fancies of the night, wherein if I weary none with my weak fancies, I will hereafter lean harder on my pen and fetch the pedigree of my praise from the utmost of pains.

As touching the terrors of the night, they are as many as our sins. The night is the devil's Black Book, wherein he recordeth all our transgressions. Even as, when a condemned man is put into a dark dungeon, secluded from all comfort of light or company, he doth nothing but despairfully call to mind his graceless former life, and the brutish outrages and misdemeanours that have thrown him into that desolate horror; so when night in her rusty dungeon hath imprisoned our eye-sight, and that we are shut separately in our chambers from resort, the devil keepeth his audit in our sin-guilty consciences, no sense but surrenders to our memory a true bill of parcels of his detestable impieties. The table of our heart is turned to an index of iniquities, and all our thoughts are nothing but texts to condemn us.

The rest we take in our beds is such another kind of rest as the weary traveller taketh in the cool soft grass in summer, who thinking there to lie at ease and refresh his tired limbs, layeth his fainting head unawares on a loathsome nest of snakes.

Well have the poets termed night the nurse of cares, the mother of despair, the daughter of hell.

Some divines have had this conceit, that God would have made all day and no night, if it had not been to put us in mind there is a hell as well as a heaven.

Such is the peace of the subjects as is the peace of the Prince under whom they are governed. As God is entitled the Father of Light, so is the devil surnamed the Prince of Darkness, which is the night. The only peace of mind that the devil hath is despair, wherefore we that live in his nightly kingdom of darkness must needs taste some disquiet.

The raven and the dove that were sent out of Noah's Ark to discover the world after the general deluge may well be an allegory of the day and the night. The day is our good angel, the dove, that returneth to our eyes with an olive branch of peace in his mouth, presenting quiet and security to our distracted souls and consciences; the night is that ill angel the raven, which never cometh back to bring any good tidings of tranquillity: a continual messenger he is of dole and misfortune. The greatest curse almost that in the scripture is threatened is that the ravens shall pick out their eyes in the valley of death. This cursed raven, the night, pecks out men's eyes in the valley of death. It hindreth them from looking to heaven for succour, where their Redeemer dwelleth; wherefore no doubt it is a time most fatal and unhallowed. This being proved, that the devil is a special predominant planet of the night, and that our creator for our punishment hath allotted it him as his peculiar signory and kingdom, from his inveterate envy I will amplify the ugly terrors of the night. The names importing his malice, which the scripture is plentiful of, I will here omit, lest some men should think I went about to conjure. Sufficeth us to have this heedful knowledge of him, that he is an ancient malcontent, and seeketh to make any one desperate like himself. Like a cunning fowler, to this end he spreadeth his nets of temptation in the dark, that men might not see to avoid them. As the poet saith:

Quae nimis apparent retia vitat avis.
(Too open nets even simple birds do shun)

Therefore in another place (which it cannot be but the devil hath read) he counseleth thus:

Noctem peccatis et fraudibus obiice nubem.
(By night-time sin, and cloak thy fraud with clouds)

When hath the devil commonly first appeared unto any man but in the night?

In the time of infidelity, when spirits were so familiar with men that they called them *Dii Penates*, their household Gods or their Lares, they never sacrificed unto them till sunsetting. The Robin Goodfellows, elves, fairies, hobgoblins of our latter age, which idolatrous former days and the fantastical world of Greece y-clepped fawns, satyrs, dryads, and hamadryads, did most of their merry pranks in the night. Then ground they malt, and had hempen shirts for their labours, danced in rounds in green meadows, pinched maids in their sleep that swept not their houses clean, and led poor travellers out of their way notoriously.

It is not to be gainsaid but the devil can transform himself into an angel of light, appear in the day as well as in the night, but not in this subtle world of Christianity so usual as before. If he do, it is when men's minds are extraordinarily thrown down with discontent, or inly terrified with some horrible concealed murder or other heinous crime close smothered in secret. In the day he may smoothly in some mild shape insinuate, but in the night he takes upon himself like a tyrant. There is no thief that is half so hardy in the day as in the night; no more is the devil. A general principle it is, he that doth ill hateth the light.

This Machiavellian trick hath he in him worth the noting, that those whom he dare not united or together encounter, disjoined and divided he will one by one assail in their sleep. And even as ruptures and cramps do then most torment a man when the body with any other disease is distempered, so the devil, when with any other sickness or malady the faculties of our reason are enfeebled and distempered, will be most busy to disturb us and torment us.

In the quiet silence of the night he will be sure to surprise us, when he unfallibly knows we shall be unarmed to resist, and that there will be full auditory granted him to undermine or persuade what he lists. All that ever he can scare us with are but Seleucus' airy castles, terrible bugbear brags, and nought else, which with the least thought of faith are quite evanished and put to flight. Neither in his own nature dare he come near us, but in the name of sin and as God's executioner. Those that catch birds imitate their voices; so will he imitate the voices of God's vengeance, to bring us like birds into the net of eternal damnation.

Children, fools, sick-men or madmen, he is most familiar with, for he still delights to work upon the advantage, and to them he boldly revealeth the whole astonishing treasury of his wonders.

It will be demanded why in the likeness of one's father or mother, or kinsfolks, he oftentimes presents himself unto us.

No other reason can be given of it but this, that in those shapes which he supposeth most familiar unto us, and that we are inclined to with a natural kind of love, we will sooner harken to him than otherwise.

Should he not disguise himself in such subtle forms of affection, we would fly from him as a serpent, and eschew him with that hatred he ought to be eschewed. If any ask why he is more conversant and busy in churchyards and places where men are buried than in any other places, it is to make us believe that the bodies and souls of the departed rest entirely in his possession and the peculiar power of death is resigned to his disposition. A rich man delights in nothing so much as to be uncessantly raking in his treasury, to be turning over his rusty gold every hour. The bones of the dead, the devil counts his chief treasury, and therefore is he continually raking amongst them; and the rather he doth it, that the living which hear it should be more unwilling to die, insomuch as after death their bones should take no rest.

It was said of Catiline, *Vultum gestavit in manibus*: with the turning of a hand he could turn and alter his countenance. Far more nimble and sudden is the devil in shifting his habit; his form he can change and cog as quick as thought.

What do we talk of one devil? There is not a room in any man's house but is pestered and close-packed with a camp-royal of devils. Chrisostom saith the air and earth are three parts inhabited with spirits. Hereunto the philosopher alluded when he said nature made no voidness in the whole universal; for no place (be it no bigger than a pockhole in a man's face) but is close thronged with them. Infinite millions of them will hang swarming about a worm-eaten nose.

Don Lucifer himself, their grand Capitano, asketh no better throne than a blear eye to set up his state in. Upon a hair they will sit like a nit, and overdredge a bald pate like a white scurf. The wrinkles in old witches' visages they eat out to entrench themselves in.

If in one man a whole legion of devils have been billetted, how many hundred thousand legions retain to a term in London? If I said but to a tavern, it were an infinite thing. In Westminster Hall a man can scarce breathe for them; for in every corner they hover as thick as motes in the sun.

The Druids that dwelt in the Isle of Man, which are famous for great conjurers, are reported to have been lousy with familiars. Had they but put their finger and their thumb into their neck, they could have plucked out a whole nest of them.

There be them that think every spark in a flame is a spirit, and that the worms which at sea eat through a ship are so also; which may very well be, for have not you seen one spark of fire burn a whole town and a man with a spark of lightning made blind or killed outright? It is impossible the guns should go off as they do, if there were not a spirit either in the fire or in the powder.

Now for worms: what makes a dog run mad but a worm in his tongue? And what should that worm be but a spirit? Is there any reason such small vermin as they are should devour such a vast thing as a ship, or have the teeth to gnaw through iron and wood? No, no, they are spirits, or else it were incredible.

Tullius Hostilius, who took upon him to conjure up Jove by Numa Pompilius' books, had no sense to quake and tremble at the wagging and shaking of every leaf but that he thought all leaves are full of worms, and those worms are wicked spirits.

If the bubbles in streams were well searched, I am persuaded they would be found to be little better. Hence it comes that mares, as Columella reporteth, looking their forms in the water run mad. A flea is but a little beast, yet if she were not possessed with a spirit, she could never leap and skip so as she doth. Froisard saith the Earl of Foix had a familiar that presented itself unto him in the likeness of two rushes fighting one with another. Not so much as Tewkesbury mustard but hath a spirit in it or else it would never bite so. Have we not read of a number of men that have ordinarily carried a familiar or a spirit in a ring instead of a spark of a diamond? Why, I tell ye we cannot break a crumb of bread so little as one of them will be if they list.

From this general discourse of spirits, let us digress and talk another while of their separate natures and properties.

The spirits of the fire which are the purest and perfectest are merry, pleasant, and well-inclined to wit, but nevertheless giddy and unconstant.

Those whom they possess they cause to excel in whatever they undertake. Or poets or boon companions they are, out of question.

Socrates' genius was one of this stamp, and the dove wherewith the Turks hold Mohamet their prophet to be inspired. What their names are and under whom they are governed *The Discovery of Witchcraft* hath amplified at large, wherefore I am exempted from that labour. But of the divinest quintessence of metals and of wines are many of these spirits extracted. It is almost impossible for any to be encumbered with ill spirits who is continually conversant in the excellent restorative distillations of wit and of alchemy. Those that ravenously englut themselves with gross meats and respect not the quality but the quantity of what they eat, have no affinity with these spirits of the fire.

A man that will entertain them must not pollute his body with any gross carnal copulation or inordinate beastly desires, but love pure beauty, pure virtue, and not have his affections linsey-wolsey, intermingled with lust and things worthy of liking.

As for example, if he love good poets he must not countenance ballad-makers; if he have learned physicians he must not favour horse-leeches and mountebanks. For a bad spirit and a good can never endure to dwell together.

Those spirits of the fire, however I term them comparatively good in respect of a number of bad, yet are they not simply well-inclined, for they be by nature ambitious, haughty, and proud; nor do they love virtue for itself any whit, but because they would overquell and outstrip others with the vain-glorious ostentation of it. A humour of monarchizing and nothing else it is, which makes them affect rare qualified studies. Many atheists are with these spirits inhabited.

To come to the spirits of the water, the earth and the air: they are dull phlegmatic drones, things that have much malice without any great might. Drunkards, misers and women they usually retain to. Water, you all know, breedeth a medley kind of liquor called beer; with these watery spirits they were possessed that first invented the art of brewing. A quagmire consisting of mud and sand sendeth forth the like puddly mixture.

All rheums, poses, sciaticas, dropsies and gouts are diseases of their phlegmatic engendering. Sea-faring men of what sort soever are chief entertainers of those spirits. Greedy vintners likewise give hospitality to a number of them; who, having read no more scripture than that miracle of Christ's turning water into wine in Canaan, think to do a far stranger miracle than ever he did, by turning wine into water.

Ale-houses and cooks' shady pavilions, by watery spirits are principally upholden.

The spirits of the earth are they which cry 'All bread and no drink', that love gold and a buttoned cap above heaven. The worth in nought they respect, but the weight; good wits they naturally hate, insomuch as the element of fire, their progenitor, is a waste-good and a consumer. If with their earth-ploughing snouts they can turn up a pearl out of a dunghill, it is all they desire. Witches have many of these spirits and kill kine with them. The giants and chieftains of those spirits are powerful sometimes to bring men to their ends, but not a jot of good can they do for their lives.

Soldiers with these terrestial spirits participate part of their essence; for nothing but iron and gold, which are earth's excrements, they delight in. Besides, in another kind they may be said to participate with them, insomuch as they confirm them in their fury and congeal their minds with a bloody resolution. Spirits of the earth they were that entered into the herd of swine in the gospel. There is no city merchant or country purchaser, but is haunted with a whole host of these spirits of the earth. The Indies is their metropolitan realm of abode.

As for the spirits of the air, which have no other visible bodies or form, but such as by the unconstant glimmering of our eyes is begotten, they are in truth all show and no substance, deluders of our imagination and naught else. Carpet knights, politic statesmen, women and children they most converse with. Carpet knights they inspire with a humour of setting big looks on it, being the basest cowards under heaven, covering an ape's heart with a lion's case, and making false alarums when they mean nothing but a may-game. Politic statesmen they privily incite to blear the world's eyes with clouds of commonwealth pretences, to broach any enmity or ambitious humour of their own under a title of their country's preservation; to make it fair or foul when they list, to procure popularity, or induce a preamble to some mighty piece of prowling, to stir up tempests round about, and replenish heaven with prodigies and wonders, the more to ratify their avaricious religion. Women they underhand instruct to pounce and bolster out their brawn-fallen deformities, to new parboil with painting their rake-lean withered visages, to set up flax shops on their foreheads when all their own hair is dead and rotten, to stick their gums round with comfits when they have not a tooth left in their heads to help them to chide withal.

Children they seduce with garish objects, and toyish babies, abusing them many years with slight vanities. So that you see all their whole influence is but thin overcast vapours, flying clouds dispersed with the least wind of wit or understanding.

None of these spirits of the air or the fire have so much predominance in the night as the spirits of the earth and the water; for they feeding on foggy-brained melancholy engender thereof many uncouth terrible monsters. Thus much observe by the way, that the grossest part of our blood is the melancholy humour, which in the spleen congealed whose office is to disperse it, with his thick steaming fenny vapours casteth a mist over the spirit and clean bemasketh the fantasy.

And even as slime and dirt in a standing puddle engender toads and frogs and many other unsightly creatures, so this slimy melancholy humour, still still thickening as it stands still, engendreth many misshapen objects in our imaginations. Sundry times we behold whole armies of men skirmishing in the air: dragons, wild beasts, bloody streamers, blazing comets, fiery streaks, with other apparitions innumberable. Whence have all these their conglomerate matter but from fuming meteors that arise from the earth? So from the fuming melancholy of our

The Terrors of the Night

spleen mounteth that hot matter into the higher region of the brain, whereof many fearful visions are framed. Our reason even like drunken fumes it displaceth and intoxicates, and yields up our intellective apprehension to be mocked and trodden under foot by every false object or counterfeit noise that comes near it. Herein specially consisteth our senses' defect and abuse, that those organical parts, which to the mind are ordained ambassadors, do not their message as they ought, but, by some misdiet or misgovernment being distempered, fail in their report and deliver up nothing but lies and fables.

Such is our brain oppressed with melancholy, as is a clock tied down with too heavy weights or plummets; which as it cannot choose but monstrously go a-square or not go at all, so must our brains of necessity be either monstrously distracted or utterly destroyed thereby.

Lightly this extremity of melancholy never cometh, but before some notable sickness; it faring with our brains as with bees, who, as they exceedingly toil and turmoil before a storm or change of weather, so do they beat and toil and are infinitely confused before sickness.

Of the effects of melancholy I need not dilate, or discourse how many encumbered with it have thought themselves birds and beasts, with feathers and horns and hides; others, that they have been turned into glass; others, that if they should make water they should drown all the world; others, that they can never bleed enough.

Physicians in their circuit every day meet with far more

ridiculous experience. Only it shall suffice a little by the way to handle one special effect of it, which is dreams.

A dream is nothing else but a bubbling scum or froth of the fancy, which the day hath left undigested; or an after-feast made of the fragments of idle imaginations.

How many sorts there be of them no man can rightly set down, since it scarce hath been heard there were ever two men that dreamed alike. Divers have written diversely of their causes, but the best reason among them all that I could ever pick out was this: that as an arrow which is shot out of a bow is sent forth many times with such force that it flieth far beyond the mark whereat it was aimed, so our thoughts, intensively fixed all the daytime upon a mark we are to hit, are now and then overdrawn with such force that they fly beyond the mark of the day into the confines of the night. There is no man put to any torment, but quaketh and trembleth a great while after the executioner hath withdrawn his hand from him. In the daytime we torment our thoughts and imaginations with sundry cares and devices; all the night-time they quake and tremble after the terror of their late suffering, and still continue thinking of the perplexities they have endured. To nothing more aptly can I compare the working of our brains after we have unyoked and gone to bed than to the glimmering and dazzling of a man's eyes when he comes newly out of the bright sun into the dark shadow.

Even as one's eyes glimmer and dazzle when they are withdrawn out of the light into darkness, so are our thoughts troubled and vexed when they are retired from labour to ease, and from skirmishing to surgery.

You must give a wounded man leave to groan while he is in dressing. Dreaming is no other than groaning, while sleep our surgeon hath us in cure.

He that dreams merrily is like a boy new breeched, who leaps and danceth for joy his pain is passed. But long that joy stays not with him, for presently after, his master, the day, seeing him so jocund and pleasant, comes and does as much for him again, whereby his hell is renewed.

No such figure as the first chaos whereout the world was extraught, as our dreams in the night. In them all states, all sexes, all places, are confounded and meet together.

Our cogitations run on heaps like men to part a fray where every one strikes his next fellow. From one place to another without consultation they leap, like rebels bent on a head. Soldiers just up and down they imitate at the sack of a city, which spare neither age nor beauty: the young, the old, trees, steeples and mountains, they confound in one gallimaufry.

Of those things which are most known to us, some of us that have moist brains make to ourselves images of memory. On those images of memory whereon we build in the day, comes some superfluous humour of ours, like a jackanapes, in the night, and erects a puppet stage or some such ridiculous idle childish invention.

A dream is nothing else but the echo of our conceits in the day.

Thomas Nashe

But otherwhile it falls out that one echo borrows of another; so our dreams, the echoes of the day, borrow of any noise we hear in the night.

As for example: if in the dead of the night there be any rumbling, knocking or disturbance near us, we straight dream of wars or of thunder. If a dog howl, we suppose we are transported into hell, where we hear the complaint of damned ghosts. If our heads lie double or uneasy, we imagine we uphold all heaven with our shoulders, like Atlas. If we be troubled with too many clothes, then we suppose the night mare rides us.

I knew one that was cramped, and he dreamed that he was torn in pieces with wild horses; and another, that having a black sant brought to his bedside at midnight, dreamt he was bidden to dinner at Ironmongers' Hall.

Any meat that in the daytime we eat against our stomachs, begetteth a dismal dream. Discontent also in dreams hath no little predominance; for even as from water that is troubled, the mud dispersingly ascendeth from the bottom to the top, so when our blood is chased, disquieted and troubled all the light imperfect humours of our body ascend like mud up aloft into the head.

The clearest spring a little touched is creased with a thousand circles; as those momentary circles for all the world, such are our dreams.

When all is said, melancholy is the mother of dreams, and of all terrors of the night whatsoever. Let it but affirm it hath seen a spirit, though it be but the moonshine on the wall, the best reason we have cannot infringe it.

Of this melancholy there be two sorts: one that, digested by our liver, swimmeth like oil above water and that is rightly termed women's melancholy, which lasteth but for an hour and is, as it were, but a copy of their countenance; the other sinketh down to the bottom like the lees of the wine, and that corrupteth all the blood and is the causer of lunacy. Well-moderated recreations are the medicine to both: surfeit or excessive study the causers of either.

There were gates in Rome out of which nothing was carried but dust and dung, and men to execution; so, many of the gates of our senses serve for nothing but to convey our excremental vapours and affrighting deadly dreams, that are worse than executioners unto us.

Ah, woe be to the solitary man that hath his sins continually about him, that hath no withdrawing place from the devil and his temptations.

Much I wonder how treason and murder dispense with the darkness of the night, how they can shrive themselves to it, and not rave and die. Methinks they should imagine that hell embraceth them round, when she overspreads them with her black pitchy mantle.

Dreams to none are so fearful, as to those whose accusing private guilt expects mischief every hour for their merit. Wonderful superstitious are such persons in observing every accident that befalls them; and that their superstition is as good as an hundred furies to torment them. Never in this world shall he enjoy one quiet day, that once hath given himself over to be her slave. His ears cannot glow, his nose itch, or his eyes smart, but his destiny stands upon her trial, and till she be acquitted or condemned he is miserable.

A cricket or a raven keep him forty times in more awe than God or the devil.

If he chance to kill a spider, he hath suppressed an enemy; if a spinner creep upon him, he shall have gold rain down from heaven. If his nose bleed, some of his kinsfolks is dead; if the salt fall right against him, all the stars cannot save him from some immediate misfortune.

The first witch was Proserpine, and she dwelt half in heaven and half in hell; half-witches are they that pretending any religion, meddle half with God and half with the devil. Meddling with the devil I call it, when ceremonies are observed which have no ground from divinity.

In another kind, witches may be said to meddle half with GOD and half with the Devil, because in their exorcisms, they use half scripture and half blasphemy.

The greatest and notablest heathen sorcerers that ever were, in all their hellish adjurations used the name of the one true and everliving God; but such a number of damned potestates they joined with him, that it might seem the stars had darkened the sun, or the moon was eclipsed by candlelight.

Of all countries under the sky, Persia was most addicted unto dreams. Darius, King of the Medes and Persians, before his fatal discomfiture, dreamt he saw an estrich with a winged crown overrunning the earth and devouring his jewel-coffer as if it had been an ordinary piece of iron. The jewel-coffer was by Alexander surprised, and afterward Homer's works in it carried before him, even as the mace or purse is customably carried before our Lord Chancellor.

Hannibal dreamed a little before his death that he was drowned in the poisonous Lake Asphaltites, when it was presently his hap within some days' distance, to seek his fate by the same means in a vault under the earth.

In India, the women very often conceive by devils in their sleep.

In Iceland, as I have read and heard, spirits in the likeness of one's father or mother after they are deceased do converse with them as naturally as if they were living.

Other spirits like rogues they have among them, destitute of all dwelling and habitation, and they chillingly complain if a constable ask them *Chevala* in the night, that they are going unto Mount Hecla to warm them.

That Mount Hecla a number conclude to be hell mouth; for near unto it are heard such yellings and groans as Ixion, Titius, Sisyphus and Tantalus blowing all in one trumpet of distress could never conjoined bellow forth.

Bondmen in Turkey or in Spain are not so ordinarily sold as witches sell familiars there. Far cheaper may you buy a wind amongst them than you can buy wind or fair words in the Court. Three knots in a thread, or an odd grandam's blessing in the corner of a napkin will carry you all the world over.

We when we frown knit our brows, but let a wizard there knit a noose or a riding snarl on his beard, and it is hail, storm and tempest a month after.

More might be spoken of the prodigies this country sends forth, if it were not too much erring from my scope. Whole islands they have of ice, on which they build and traffic as on the mainland.

Admirable, above the rest, are the incomprehensible wonders of the bottomless Lake Vether, over which no fowl flies but is frozen to death, nor any man passeth but he is senselessly benumbed like a statue of marble.

All the inhabitants round about it are deafened with the hideous roaring of his waters when the winter breaketh up, and the ice in his dissolving gives a terrible crack like to thunder, whenas out of the midst of it, as out of Mont-Gibell, a sulphureous stinking smoke issues, that wellnigh poisons the whole country.

A poison light on it, how come I to digress to such a dull, lenten, northern clime, where there is nothing but stock-fish, whetstones and cods' heads? Yet now I remember me: I have not lost my way so much as I thought, for my theme is the terrors of the night, and Iceland is one of the chief kingdoms of the night, they having scarce so much day there as will serve a child to ask his father blessing. Marry, with one commodity they are blest: they have

The Terrors of the Night

ale that they carry in their pockets like glue, and ever when they would drink, they set it on fire and melt it.

It is reported that the Pope long since gave them a dispensation to receive the sacrament in ale, insomuch as, for their uncessant frosts there, no wine but was turned to red emayle as soon as ever it came amongst them.

Farewell, frost: as much to say as 'Farewell, Iceland', for I have no more to say to thee.

I care not much if I dream yet a little more, and to say the troth, all this whole tractate is but a dream, for my wits are not half awaked in it; and yet no golden dream, but a leaden dream is it, for in a leaden standish I stand fishing all day, but have none of Saint Peter's luck to bring a fish to the hook that carries any silver in the mouth. And yet there be of them that carry silver in the mouth too, but none in the hand; that is to say, are very bountiful and honourable in their words, but (except it be to swear indeed) no other good deeds come from them.

Filthy Italianate compliment-mongers they are who would fain be counted the Court's *Gloriosos*, and the refined judges of wit when if their wardrobes and the withered bladders of their brains were well searched, they have nothing but a few moth-eaten cod-piece suits, made against the coming of Mounsier, in the one, and a few scraps of outlandish proverbs in the other, and these alone do buckler them from the name of beggars and idiots. Otherwhile perhaps they may keep a coil with the spirit of Tasso, and then they fold their arms like braggarts, writhe their necks *alla Neapolitano*, and turn up their eye-balls like men entranced.

Come, come, I am entranced from my text, I wote well, and talk idly in my sleep longer than I should. Those that will harken any more after dreams, I refer them to Artimidorus, Synesius, and Cardan, with many others which only I have heard by their names, but I thank God had never the plodding patience to read, for if they be no better than some of them I have perused, every weatherwise old wife might write better.

What sense is there that the yoke of an egg should signify gold, or dreaming of bears, or fire, or water, debate and anger, that everything must be interpreted backward as witches say their *Pater Noster*, good being the character of bad, and bad of good?

As well we may calculate from every accident in the day, and not go about any business in the morning till we have seen on which hand the crow sits.

'Oh Lord,' I have heard many a wise gentlewoman say, 'I am so merry and have laughed so heartily, that I am sure ere long to be crossed with some sad tidings or other' – all one as if men coming from a play should conclude, 'Well, we have seen a comedy today, and therefore there cannot choose but be a tragedy tomorrow.'

I do not deny but after extremity of mirth follow many sad accidents, but yet those sad accidents, in my opinion, we merely pluck on with the fear of coming mischief, and those means we in policy most use to prevent it soonest enwrap us in it; and that was Satan's trick in the old world of gentilism to bring to pass all his blind prophecies.

Could any men set down certain rules of expounding of dreams, and that their rules were general, holding in all as well as in some, I would begin a little to list to them; but commonly that which is portentive in a king is but a frivolous fancy in a beggar, and let him dream of angels, eagles, lions, griffons, dragons never so, all the augury under heaven will not allot him so much as a good alms.

Some will object unto me for the certainty of dreams, the dreams of Cyrus, Cambyses, Pompey, Caesar, Darius and Alexander. For those I answer that they were rather visions than dreams, extraordinarily sent from heaven to foreshow the translation of monarchies.

The Greek and Roman histories are full of them, and such a stir they keep with their augurers and soothsayers, how they foretold long before by dreams and beasts' and birds' entrails the loss of such a battle, the death of such a captain or emperor, when, false knaves, they were all as prophet Calchas, pernicious traitors to their country and them that put them in trust, and were many times hired by the adverse part to dishearten and discourage their masters by such conycatching riddles as might in truth be turned any way.

An easy matter was it for them to prognosticate treasons and conspiracies, in which they were underhand inlinked themselves; and however the world went, it was a good policy for them to save their heads by the shift, for if the treasons chanced afterwards to come to light, it would not be suspected they were practisers in them, insomuch as they revealed them; or if they should by their confederates be appealed as practisers, yet might they plead and pretend it was done but of spite and malice to supplant them for so bewraying and laying open their intents.

This trick they had with them besides, that never till the very instant that any treason was to be put in execution, and it was so near at hand that the Prince had no time to prevent it, would they speak one word of it, or offer to disclose it. Yea, and even then such unfit seasons for their colourable discovery would they pick forth, as they would be sure he should have no leisure to attend it.

But you will ask why at all as then, they should step forth to detect it. Marry, to clear themselves to his successors, that there might be no revenge prosecuted on their lives.

So did Spurina, the great astrologer; even as Caesar in the midst of all his business was going hastily to the Senate House, he popped a bill in his hand of Brutus' and Cassius' conspiracy, and all the names of those that were colleagued with them.

Well he might have thought that in such haste by the highway side, he would not stay to peruse any schedules, and well he knew and was ascertained that as soon as ever he came into the Capitol the bloody deed was to be accomplished.

Shall I impart unto you a rare secrecy how these great famous conjurors and cunning men ascend by degrees to

The Terrors of the Night

foretell secrets as they do? First and foremost they are men which have had some little sprinkling of grammar learning in their youth, or at least I will allow them to have been surgeons' or apothecaries' prentices; these, I say, having run through their thrift at the elbows, and riotously amongst harlots and make-shifts spent the annuity of halfpenny ale that was left them, fall a-beating their brains how to botch up an easy gainful trade, and set a new nap on an old occupation.

Hereupon presently they rake some dunghill for a few dirty boxes and plasters, and of toasted cheese and candles' ends temper up a few ointments and syrups; which having done, far north or into some such rude simple country they get them and set up.

Scarce one month have they stayed there, but what with their vaunting and prating, and speaking fustian instead of Greek, all the shires round about do ring with their fame; and then they begin to get them a library of three or four old rusty manuscript books, which they themselves nor any else can read, and furnish their shops with a thousand *quid pro quos*, that would choke any horse, besides some waste trinkets in their chambers hung up, which may make the world half in jealousy they can conjure.

They will evermore talk doubtfully, as if there were more in them than they meant to make public, or was appliable to every common man's capacity; when, God be their rightful judge, they utter all that they know and a great deal more.

To knit up their knaveries in short (which in sooth is the hangman's office and none's else), having picked up their crumbs thus prettily well in the country, they draw after a time a little nearer and nearer to London; and at length into London they filch themselves privily – but how? Not in the heart of the City will they presume at first dash to hang out their rat-banners, but in the skirts and outshifts steal out a sign over a cobbler's stall, like aqua vitae sellers, and stocking menders.

Many poor people they win to believe in them, who have not a barrelled herring or a piece of poor-john that looks ill on it, but they will bring the water that he was steeped in unto them in an urinal, and crave their judgement whether he be rotten, or merchant and chapmanable, or no. The bruit of their cunning thus travelling from ale-house to ale-house at length is transported in the great hilts of one or other country serving-man's sword to some good tavern or ordinary; where it is no sooner alive, but it is greedily snatched up by some dappert Monsieur Diego, who lives by telling of news, and false dice, and it may be hath a pretty insight into the cards also, together with a little skill in his Jacob's staff and his compasses, being able at all times to discover a new passage to Virginia.

This needy gallant, with the qualities aforesaid, straight trudgeth to some nobleman's to dinner, and there enlargeth the rumour of this new physician, comments upon every glass and vial that he hath, raleth on our Galenists, and calls them dull gardeners and hay-makers in a man's belly, compares them to dogs, who when they are sick eat grass, and says they are no better than pack or malt-horses, who, if a man should knock out their brains, will not go out of the beaten highway; whereas his horse-leach will leap over the hedge and ditch of a thousand Dioscorides and Hippocrates, and give a man twenty poisons in one, but he would restore him to perfect health. With this strange tale the nobleman inflamed desires to be acquainted with him; what does me he, but goes immediately and breaks with this mountebank, telling him if he will divide his gains with him, he will bring him in custom with such and such states, and he shall be countenanced in the Court as he would desire. The hungry druggier, ambitious after preferment, agrees to anything, and to Court he goes; where, being come to interview, he speaks nothing but broken English like a French doctor, pretending to have forgotten his natural tongue by travel, when he hath never been farther than either the Low Countries or Ireland, enforced thither to fly either for getting a maid with child, or marrying two wives. Sufficeth he set a good face on it, and will swear he can extract a better balsamum out of a chip than the balm of Judea; yea, all receipts and authors you can name he syllogizeth of, and makes a pish at, in comparison of them he hath seen and read; whose names if you ask, he claps you in the mouth with half-a-dozen spruce titles, never till he invented them heard of by any Christian. But this is most certain: if he be of any sect, he is a metal-brewing Paracelsian, having not passed one or two probatums for all diseases. Put case he be called to practise, he excuseth it by great cures he hath in hand; and will not encounter an infirmity but in the declining, that his credit may be more authentical, or else when by some secret intelligence he is throughly instructed of the whole process of his unrecoverable extremity, he comes gravely marching like a judge, and gives peremptory sentence of death; whereby he is accounted a prophet of deep prescience.

But how he comes to be the devil's secretary, all this long tale unrips not.

In secret be it spoken, he is not so great with the devil as you take it. It may be they are near akin, but yet you have many kindred that will do nothing for one another; no more will the devil for him, except it be to damn him.

This is the *Tittle est amen* of it: that when he waxeth stale, and all his pisspots are cracked and will no longer hold water, he sets up a conjuring school and undertakes to play the bawd to Lady Fortune.

Not a thief or a cut-purse, but a man that he keeps doth associate with, and is of their fraternity; only that his master when anything is stolen may tell who it is that hath it. In petty trifles having gotten some credit, great peers entertain him for one of their privy council, and if they have any dangerous enterprise in hand, they consult with him about success.

All malcontents intending any invasive violence against their Prince and country run headlong to his oracle.

Contrary factions enbosom unto him their inwardest complots, whilst he like a crafty jack-a-both-sides, as if he had a spirit still at his elbow, reciprocally embowelleth to the one what the other goes about, receiving no intelligence from any familiar, but their own mouths. I assure you most of our chief noted augurers and soothsayers in England at this day, by no other art but this gain their reputation.

They may very well pick men's purses, like the unskilfuller cozening kind of alchemists, with their artificial and ceremonial magic, but no effect shall they achieve thereby, though they would hang themselves. The reason is, the devil of late is grown a puritan and cannot away with any ceremonies; he sees all princes have left off their states, and he leaves off his state too and will not be invocated with such solemnity as he was wont.

Private and disguised, he passeth to and fro, and is in a thousand places in an hour.

Fair words cannot any longer beguile him, for not a cue of courtesy will he do any man, except it be upon a flat bill of sale, and so he chaffers with wizards and witches every hour.

Now the world is almost at an end, he hath left form and is all for matter; and like an embroiderer or a tailor, he maketh haste of work against a good time, which is the Day of Judgment. Therefore, you goodmen exorcisers, his old acquaintance, must pardon him, though (as heretofore) he stay not to dwell upon compliments.

In diebus illis [once upon a time] when Corineus and

Gogmagog were little boys, I will not gainsay but he was wont to jest and sport with country people, and play the Goodfellow amongst kitchen-wenches, sitting in an evening by the fireside making of possets, and come a-wooing to them in the likeness of a cooper, or a curmudgeonly purchaser; and sometimes he would dress himself like a barber, and wash and shave all those that lay in such a chamber. Otherwhile, like a stale cutter of Queen-hive, he would justle men in their own houses, pluck them out of bed by the heels, and dance in chains from one chamber to another. Now there is no goodness in him but miserableness and covetousness.

Sooner he will pare his nails cleanly than cause a man to dream of a pot of gold, or a money-bag that is hid in the eaves of a thatched house.

(Here is to be noted, that it is a blessed thing but to dream of gold, though a man never have it.)

Such a dream is not altogether ridiculous or impertinent, for it keeps flesh and blood from despair. All other are but as dust we raise by our steps, which awhile mounteth aloft and annoyeth our eye-sight, but presently disperseth and vanisheth.

Señor Satan, when he was a young stripling and had not yet gotten perfect audacity to set upon us in the daytime, was a sly politician in dreams; but those days are gone with him, and now that he is thoroughly steeled in his scutchery, he plays above-board boldly, and sweeps more stakes than ever he did before.

I have rid a false gallop these three or four pages. Now I care not if I breathe me and walk soberly and demurely half-a-dozen turns, like a grave citizen going about to take the air.

To make a shaft or a bolt of this drumbling subject of dreams, from whence I have been tossed off and on I know not how, this is my definitive verdict: that one may as well by the smoke that comes out of a kitchen guess what meat is there a-broach, as by paraphrasing on smoky dreams preominate of future events. Thus far notwithstanding I'll go with them: physicians by dreams may better discern the distemperature of their pale clients, than either by urine or ordure.

He that is inclining to a burning fever shall dream of frays, lightning and thunder, of skirmishing with the devil and a hundred such-like. He that is spiced with the gout or the dropsy frequently dreameth of fetters and manacles and being put on the bilbows, that his legs are turned to marble or adamant, and his feet, like the giants that scaled heaven, kept under with Mount Ossa and Pelion and erst-while that they are fast locked in quagmires. I have heard aged mumping beldams as they sat warming their knees over a coal scratch over the argument very curiously, and they would bid young folks beware on what day they pared their nails, tell what luck everyone should have by the day of the week he was born on; show how many years a man should live by the number of wrinkles on his forehead, and stand descanting not a little of the difference in fortune when they are turned upward and when they are bent downward; 'him that had a wart on his chin', they would confidently ascertain he should 'have no need of any of his kin'; marry, they would likewise distinguish between the standing of the wart on the right side and on the left. When I was a little child, I was a great auditor of theirs, and had all their witchcrafts at my fingers' ends, as perfect as good-morrow and good-even.

Of the signification of dreams, whole catalogues could I recite of theirs, which here there is no room for; but for a glance to this purpose this I remember they would very soberly affirm, that if one at supper eat birds, he should dream of flying; if fish, of swimming; if venison, of hunting, and so for the rest; as though those birds, fish, and venison being dead and digested did fly, swim and hold their chase in their brains; or the solution of our dreams should be nought else but to express what meats we ate over-night.

From the unequal and repugnant mixture of contrarious meats, I jump with them, many of our mystic cogitations procede; and even as fire maketh iron like itself, so the fiery inflammations of our liver or stomach transform our imaginations to their analogy and likeness.

No humour in general in our bodies overflowing or abounding, but the tips of our thoughts are dipped in his tincture. And as when a man is ready to drown, he takes hold of anything that is next him, so our fluttering thoughts, when we are drowned in deadly sleep, take hold and co-essence themselves with any overboiling humour which sourceth highest in our stomachs.

What heed then is there to be had of dreams that are no more but the confused giddy action of our brains, made drunk with the inundation of humours?

Just such-like impostures as is this art of exposition of dreams are the arts of physiognomy and palmistry, wherein who beareth most palm and praise is the palpablest fool and crepundio. Lives there any such slow, ice-brained, beef-witted gull, who by the rivelled bark or outward rind of a tree will take upon him to forespeak how long it shall stand, what mischances of worms, caterpillars, boughs breaking, frost bitings, cattle rubbing against, it shall have? As absurd is it, by the external branched seams or furrowed wrinkles in a man's face or hand, in particular or general to conjecture and foredoom of his fate.

According to every one's labour or exercise, the palm of his hand is written and plaited, and every day alters as he alters his employments or pastimes; wherefore well may we collect that he which hath a hand so brawned and interlined useth such-and-such toils or recreations; but for the mind or disposition, we can no more look into through it than we can into a looking glass through the wooden case thereof.

So also our faces, which sundry times with surfeits, grief, study or intemperance are most deformedly whelked and crumpled; there is no more to be gathered by their sharp embossed joiner's antique work or ragged overhangings or pitfalls but that they have been laid up in sloven's press, and with miscarriage and misgovernment are so fretted and galled.

My own experience is but small, yet thus much I can say by his warrantize that those fatal brands of physiognomy which condemn men for fools and for idiots, and on the other side for treacherous circumventers and false brothers, have in a hundred men I know been verified in the contrary.

So Socrates, the wisest man of Greece, was censured by a wrinkle-wizard for the lumpishest blockhead that ever went on two legs; whom though the philosopher in pity vouchsafed with a nice distinction of art and nature to raise and recover, when he was utterly confounded with a hiss and a laughter, yet sure his insolent simplicity might lawfully have sued out his patent of exemption, for he was a forlorn creature, both in discretion and wit-craft.

Will you have the sum of all: some subtle humourist, to feed fantastic heads with innovations and novelties, first invented this trifling childish glose upon dreams and physiognomy; wherein he strove only to boast himself of a pregnant probable conceit beyond philosophy or truth.

Let but any man who is most conversant in the superstition of dreams reckon me one that hath happened just, and I'll set down a hundred out of histories that have perished to foolery.

To come to late days. Lewis the xj. dreamt that he swam in blood on the top of the Alps, which one Father Robert,

The Terrors of the Night

a holy hermit of his time, interpreted to be present death in his next wars against Italy, though he lived and prospered in all his enterprises a long while after.

So Charles the Fifth, sailing to the siege of Tunis, dreamt that the City met him on the sea like an Argosy, and over-whelmed his whole navy; when by Cornelius Agrippa, the great conjurer, who went along with him, it was expounded to be the overthrow of that famous expedition. And thereupon Agrippa offered the Emperor, if it pleased him to blow up the City by art magic in the air before his eyes without any farther jeopardy of war or beseiging. The Emperor utterly refused it and said since it was God's wars against an infidel, he would never borrow aid of the devil.

Some have memorized that Agrippa seeing his counsel in that case rejected, and that the Emperor, notwithstanding his unfortunate presage, was prosperous and successful, within few days after died frantic and desperate.

Alphonso, King of Naples, in like case, before the rumour of the French King's coming into Italy, had a vision in the night presented unto him of Aeneas' ghost having Turnus in chase, and Juno Pronuba coming betwixt them, and parting them; whereby he guessed that by marriage their jarring kingdoms should be united. But far otherwise it fell out, for the French King came indeed and he was driven thereby into such a melancholy ecstasy that he thought the very fowls of the air would snatch his crown from him, and no bough or arbour that overshadowed him but enclosed him and took him prisoner, and that not so much but the stones of the street sought to justle him out of his throne.

These examples I allege, to prove there is no certainty in dreams, and that they are but according to our devisings and meditations in the daytime.

I confess the saints and martyrs of the Primitive Church had unfallible dreams fore-running their ends, as Policarpus and other; but those especially proceeded from heaven and not from any vaporous dreggy parts of our blood or our brains.

For this cause the Turks banish learning from amongst them, because it is every day setting men together by the ears, moving strange contentions and alterations, and making his professors faint-hearted and effeminate. Much more requisite were it that out of our civil Christian commonwealths we severely banish and exterminate those fabulous commentaries on toyish fantasies which fear-benumb and effeminate the hearts of the stoutest, cause a man without any ground to be jealous of his own friends and his kinsfolks, and withdraw him from the search and insight into more excellent things, to stand all his whole life sifting and winnowing dry rubbish chaff, whose best bottom quintescence proves in the end but sandy gravel and cockle.

Molestations and cares enough the ordinary course of our life tithes of his own accord unto us, though we seek not a knot in a bulrush, or stuff not our night-pillows with thistles to increase our disturbance.

In our sleep we are aghasted and terrified with the disordered skirmishing and conflicting of our sensitive faculties. Yet with this terror and aghastment cannot we rest ourselves satisfied, but we must pursue and hunt after a further fear in the recordation and too busy examining our pains over-passed.

Dreams in my mind if they have any premonstrances in them, the preparative fear of that they so premonstrate and denounce is far worse than the mischief itself by them denounced and premonstrated.

So there is no long sickness but is worse than death, for death is but a blow and away, whereas sickness is like a Chancery suit, which hangs two or three year ere it can come to a judgment.

Oh, a consumption is worse than a *Capias ad Ligatum*: to nothing can I compare it better than to a reprieve after a man is condemned, or to a boy with his hose about his heels, ready to be whipped, to whom his master stands preaching a long time all law and no gospel ere he proceed to execution. Or rather it is as a man should be roasted to death and melt away by little and little, whiles physicians like cooks stand stuffing him out with herbs and basting him with this oil and that syrup.

I am of the opinion that to be famished to death is far better, for his pain in seven or eight days is at an end, whereas he that is in a consumption continues languishing many years ere death have mercy on him.

The next plague and the nearest that I know in affinity

to a consumption is long depending hope frivolously defeated, than which there is no greater misery on earth, and so *per consequens* no men in earth more miserable than courtiers. It is a cowardly fear that is not resolute enough to despair. It is like a poor hunger-starved wretch at sea, who still in expectation of a good voyage endures more miseries than Job. He that writes this can tell, for he hath never had good voyage in his life but one, and that was to a fortunate blessed island near those pinacle rocks called the Needles. Oh, it is a purified continent, and a fertile plot fit to seat another paradise, where, or in no place, the image of the ancient hospitality is to be found.

While I live I will praise it and extol it for the true magnificence and continued honourable bounty that I saw there.

Far unworthy am I to spend the least breath of commendation in the extolling so delightful and pleasant a Tempe, or once to consecrate my ink with the excellent mention of the thrice-noble and illustrious chieftain under whom it is flourishingly governed.

That rare ornament of our country, learned Master Camden, whose desertful name is universally admired throughout Christendom, in the last re-polished edition of his *Britannia* hath most elaborate and exactly described the sovereign plenteous situation of that isle, as also the inestimable happiness it inherits, it being patronized and carefully protected by so heroical and courageous a commander.

Men that have never tasted that full spring of his liberality, wherewith, in my most forsaken extremities, right graciously he hath deigned to revive and refresh me, may rashly, at first sight, implead me of flattery and not esteem these my fervent terms as the necessary repayment of due debt, but words idly begotten with good looks, and in an over-joyed humour of vain hope slipped from me by chance; but therein they shall show themselves too uncivil injurious, both to my devoted observant duty and the condign dear purchased merit of his glory.

Too base a ground is this, whereon to embroider the rich story of his eternal renown; some longer-lived tractate I reserve for the full blaze of his virtues, which here only in the sparks I decipher. Many embers of encumbrances have I at this time, which forbid the bright flame of my zeal to mount aloft as it would. Perforce I must break from it, since other turbulent cares sit as now at the stern of my invention. Thus I conclude with this chance-medley parenthesis, that whatsoever minutes' intermission I have of calmed content, or least respite to call my wits together, principal and immediate proceedeth from him.

Through him my tender wainscot study door is delivered from much assault and battery. Through him I look into and am looked on in the world, from whence otherwise I were a wretched banished exile. Through him all my good, as by a conduit head, is conveyed unto me; and to him all my endeavours, like rivers, shall pay tribute as to the ocean.

Did Ovid entitle Carus, a nobleman of Rome, the only constant friend he had, in his ungrateful extrusion among the Getes, and writ to him thus:

Qui quod es id vere Care vocaris?

and in another elegy:

O mihi post nullos Care memorande sodales.*

Much more may I acknowledge all redundant prostrate vassalage to the royal descended family of the Careys, but for whom my spirit long ere this had expired, and my pen served as a poniard to gall my own heart.

Why do I use so much circumstance, and in a stream on which none but gnats and flies do swim sound Fame's trumpet like Triton to call a number of foolish skiffs and light cock-boats to parley?

Fear, if I be not deceived, was the last pertinent matter I had under my displing, from which I fear I have strayed beyond my limits; and yet fear hath no limits, for to hell and beyond hell it sinks down and penetrates.

But this was my position, that the fear of any expected evil is worse than the evil itself, which by divers comparisons I confirmed.

---

* 'After all my companions are gone, I will remember you, oh Carus.'

Now to visions and apparitions again, as fast as I can trudge.

The glasses of our sight, in the night, are like the prospective glasses one Hostius made in Rome, which represented the images of things far greater than they were. Each mote in the dark they make a monster, and every slight glimmering a giant.

A solitary man in his bed is like a poor bed-red lazar lying by the highway-side unto whose displayed wounds and sores a number of stinging flies do swarm for pastance and beverage. His naked wounds are his inward heart-griping woes, the wasps and flies his idle wandering thoughts; who to that secret smarting pain he hath already do add a further sting of impatience and new-lance his sleeping griefs and vexations.

Questionless, this is an unrefutable consequence, that the man who is mocked of his fortune, he that hath consumed his brains to compass prosperity and meets with no countervailment in her likeness, but hedge wine and lean mutton and peradventure some half-eyed good looks that can hardly be discerned from winking; this poor piteous perplexed miscreant either finally despairs, or like a lank frost-bitten plant loseth his vigour or spirit by little and little; any terror, the least illusion in the earth, is a Cacodaemon unto him. His soul hath left his body; for why, it is flying after these airy incorporate courtly promises, and glittering painted allurements, which when they vanish to nothing, it likewise vanisheth with them.

Excessive joy no less hath his defective and joyless operations, the spleen into water it melteth; so that except it be some momentary bubbles of mirth, nothing it yields but a cloying surfeit of repentance.

Divers instances have we of men whom too much sudden content and over-ravished delight hath brought untimely to their graves.

Four or five I have read of, whom the very extremity of laughter hath bereft of their lives; whereby I gather that even such another pernicious sweet, superfluous mirth is to the sense as a surfeit of honey to a man's stomach, than the which there is nothing more dangerous.

Be it as dangerous as it will, it cannot but be an easy kind of death. It is like one that is stung with an aspis, who in the midst of his pain falls delighted asleep, and in that suavity of slumber surrenders the ghost; whereas he whom grief undertakes to bring to his end, hath his heart gnawen in sunder by little and little with vultures, like Prometheus.

But this is nothing, you will object, to our journey's end of apparitions. Yes, altogether; for of the overswelling superabundance of joy and grief we frame to ourselves most of our melancholy dreams and visions.

There is an old philosophical common proverb, *Unusquisque fingit fortunam sibi*: everyone shapes his own fortune as he lists. More aptly may it be said: everyone shapes his own fears and fancies as he list.

In all points our brains are like the firmament, and

exhale in every respect the like gross mistempered vapours and meteors: of the more foeculent combustible airy matter whereof, affrighting forms and monstrous images innumerable are created, but of the slimy unwieldier drossy part, dull melancholy or drowsiness.

And as the firmament is still moving and working, so uncessant is the wheeling and rolling on of our brains, which every hour are tempering some new piece of prodigy or other, and turmoiling, mixing and changing the course of our thoughts.

I write not this for that I think there are no true apparitions or prodigies, but to show how easily we may be flouted if we take not great heed with our own antique suppositions. I will tell you a strange tale tending to this nature; whether of true melancholy or true apparition, I will not take upon me to determine.

It was my chance in February last to be in the country some threescore mile off from London, where a gentleman of good worship and credit falling sick, the very second day of his lying down he pretended to have miraculous waking visions, which before I enter to describe, thus much I will inform ye by the way, that at the reporting of them he was in perfect memory, nor had sickness yet so tyrannized over him to make his tongue grow idle. A wise, grave, sensible man he was ever reputed, and so approved himself in all his actions in his life-time. This which I deliver, with many preparative protestations, to a great man of this land he confidently avouched. Believe it or condemn it as you shall see cause, for I leave it to be censured indifferently.

The first day of his distemperature, he visibly saw, as he affirmed, all his chamber hung with silken nets and silver hooks, the devil, as it should seem, coming thither a-fishing. Whereupon, every *Pater-Noster*-while, he looked whether in the nets he should be entangled, or with the hooks ensnared. With the nets he feared to be strangled or smothered, and with the hooks to have his throat scratched out and his flesh rent and mangled. At length, he knew not how, they suddenly vanished and the whole chamber was cleared. Next a company of lusty sailors, every one a shirker or a swaggerer at the least, having made a brave voyage, came carousing and quaffing in large silver cans to his health. Fellows they were that had good big pop mouths to cry 'port, ahelm, Saint George', and knew as well as the best what belongs to haling of bolings yare and falling on the starboard buttock.

But to the issue of my tale. Their drunken proffers he utterly put by, and said he highly scorned and detested both them and their hellish disguisings; which notwithstanding, they tossed their cups to the skies, and reeled and staggered up and down the room like a ship shaking in the wind.

After all they danced lusty gallant and a drunken Danish lavalto or two, and so departed. For the third course, rushed in a number of stately devils, bringing in boisterous chests of massy treasure betwixt them. As brave they were as Turkish janissaries, having their apparel all powdered with gold and pearl, and their arms as it were bemailed with rich chains and bracelets, but faces far blacker than any ball of tobacco, great glaring eyes that had whole shelves of Kentish oysters in them, and terrible wide mouths, whereof not one of them but would well have made a case for Molenax' great globe of the world.

These lovely youths and full of favour, having stalked up and down the just measures of a sinkapace, opened one of the principal chests they brought, and out of it plucked a princely royal tent, whose empearled shining canopy they quickly advanced on high, and with all artificial magnificence adorned like a state; which performed, pompous Lucifer entered, imitating in goodly stature the huge picture of Laocoon at Rome, who sent unto him a gallant ambassador, signifying thus much, that if he would serve him, he should have all the rich treasure that he saw there, or any further wealth he would desire.

The gentleman returned this mild answer, that he knew not what he was, whether an angel or a wicked fiend, and if an angel, he was but his fellow servant, and no otherwise to be served or regarded; if a fiend, or a devil, he had nothing to do with him, for God had exalted and redeemed him above his desperate outcast condition, and a strong faith he had to defy and withstand all his juggling temptations. Having uttered these words, all the whole train of them invisibly avoided, and he never set eye on them after.

Then did there, for the third pageant, present themselves unto him an inveigling troop of naked virgins, thrice more amiable and beautiful than the bright vestals that brought in Augustus' Testament to the Senate after his decease; but no vestal-like ornament had they about them, for from top to toe bare despoiled they were, except some one or two of them that ware masks before their faces, and had transparent azured lawn veils before the chief jewel-houses of their honours.

Such goodly lustful bonarobaes they were, by his report, as if any sharp-eyed painter had been there to peruse them, he might have learned to exceed divine Michael Angelo in the true bosk of a naked, or curious Tuns in quick life, whom the great masters of that art do term the sprightly old man.

Their hair they ware loose unrolled about their shoulders, whose dangling amber trammels reaching down beneath their knees seemed to drop balm on their delicious bodies, and ever as they moved to and fro, with their light windy wavings, wantonly to correct their exquisite mistresses.

Their dainty feet in their tender birdlike trippings enamelled, as it were, the dusty ground; and their odoriferous breath more perfumed the air than ordnance would that is charged with amomum, musk, civet and ambergreece.

But to leave amplifications and proceed. Those sweet bewitching naked maids, having majestically paced about the chamber, to the end their natural unshelled shining mother pearl proportions might be more imprintingly apprehended, close to his bedside modestly blushing they approached, and made impudent proffer unto him of their lascivious embraces. He, obstinately bent to withstand these their sinful allurements, no less than the former, bad them go seek entertainment of hotter bloods, for he had not to satisfy them. A cold comfort was this to poor wenches no better clothed, yet they hearing what to trust to, very sorrowfully retired and shrunk away.

Lo, in the fourth act there sallied out a grave assembly of sober-attired matrons, much like the virgins of Mary Magdalen's order in Rome, which vow never to see man, or the chaste daughters of Saint Philip.

With no incontinent courtesy did they greet him, but told him if he thought good they would pray for him.

Thereupon, from the beginning to the ending he unfolded unto them how he had been mightily haunted with wicked illusions of late, but nevertheless, if he could be persuaded that they were angels or saints, their invocations could not hurt him; yea, he would add his desire to their requests to make their prayers more penetrably enforcing.

Without further parley, upon their knees they fell most devoutly and for half-an-hour never ceased extensively to intercessionate GOD for his speedy recovery.

Rising up again on the right hand of his bed, there appeared a clear light, and with that he might perceive a naked slender foot offering to steal betwixt the sheets in to him.

At which instant, entered a messenger from a knight of great honour thereabouts, who sent him a most precious extract quintessence to drink; which no sooner he tasted, but he thought he saw all the fore-named interluders at once hand-over-head leap, plunge and drown themselves in puddles and ditches hard by, and he felt perfect ease.

But long it lasted not with him, for within four hours after, having not fully settled his estate in order, he grew to trifling dotage, and raving died within two days following.

God is my witness, in all this relation I borrow no essential part from stretched-out invention, nor have I one jot abused my informations; only for the recreation of my readers, whom loath to tire with a coarse home-spun tale that should dull them worse than Holland cheese, here and there I welt and gard it with allusive exornations and comparisons; and yet methinks it comes off too gouty and lumbering.

Be it as it will, it is like to have no more allowance of English for me. If the world will give it any allowance of truth, so it is. For then I hope my excuse is already lawfully customed and authorized, since Truth is ever drawn and painted naked, and I have lent her but a leathern patched cloak at most to keep her from the cold; that is, that she come not off too lamely and coldly.

Upon the accidental occasion of this dream or

apparition (call or miscall it what you will, for it is yours as freely as any waste paper that ever you had in your lives) was this pamphlet (no bigger than an old preface) speedily botched up and compiled.

Are there any doubts which remain in your mind undigested, as touching this incredible narration I have unfolded? Well, doubt you not, but I am mild and tractable and will resolve you in what I may.

First, the house where this gentleman dwelt stood in a low marsh ground, almost as rotten a climate as the Low Countries, where their misty air is as thick as mould butter, and the dew lies like frothy barm on the ground. It was noted over and besides to have been an unlucky house to all his predecessors, situate in a quarter not altogether exempted from witches. The abrupt falling into his sickness was suspicious, proceeding from no apparent surfeit or misdiet. The outrageous tyranny of it in so short a time bred thrice more admiration and wonder, and his sudden death incontinent ensuing upon that his disclosed dream or vision, might seem some probable reason to confirm it, since none have such palpable dreams or visions but die presently after.

The like to this was Master Alington's vision in the beginning of Her Majesty's reign; than the which there is nothing more ordinarily bruited. Through Greek and Roman commonplaces to this purport I could run, if I were disposed to vaunt myself like a ridiculous pedant of deep reading in Fulgosius, Licosthenes and Valerius.

Go no further than the Court, and they will tell you of a mighty worthy man of this land, who riding in his coach from London to his house was all the way haunted with a couple of hogs, who followed him close, and do what his men could, they might not drive them from him. Wherefore at night he caused them to be shut up in a barn and commanded milk to be given them; the barn door was locked, and the key safely kept, yet were they gone by morning, and no man knew how.

A number of men there be yet living who have been haunted by their wives after their death about forswearing themselves and undoing their children of whom they promised to be careful fathers; whereof I can gather no reason but this, that women are born to torment a man both alive and dead.

I have heard of others likewise, that besides these night-terrors, have been, for whole months together, whithersoever they went or rid, pursued by weasels and rats, and oftentimes with squirrels and hares, that in the travelling of three hundred mile have still waited on their horse heels.

But those are only the exploits and stratagems of witches, which may well astonish a little at first sight, but if a man have the least heart or spirit to withstand one fierce blast of their bravadoes, he shall see them shrink faster than northern cloth, and outstrip time in dastardly flight.

Fie, fie, was ever poor fellow so far benighted in an old wive's tale of devils and urchins! Out upon it, I am weary of it, for it hath caused such a thick fulsome serena to descend on my brain that now my pen makes blots as broad as a furred stomacher, and my muse inspires me to put out my candle and go to bed; and yet I will not neither, till, after all these nights' revels I have solemnly bid you goodnight, as much to say as tell you how you shall have a good night, and sleep quietly without affrightment and annoyance.

First and foremost, drink moderately, and dice and drab not away your money prodigally and then foreswear yourselves to borrow more.

You that be poor men's children, know your own fathers; and though you can shift and cheat yourselves into good clothes here about town, yet bow your knees to their leathern bags and russet coats, that they may bless you from the ambition of Tyburn.

You that bear the name of soldiers and live basely swaggering in every ale-house, having no other exhibition but from harlots and strumpets, seek some new trade, and leave whoring and quarrelling, lest besides the nightly guilt of your own bankrout consciences, Bridewell or Newgate prove the end of your cavaliering.

You, whosoever or wheresoever you be, that live by spoiling and overreaching young gentlemen, and make but a sport to deride their simplicities to their undoing, to you the night at one time or other will prove terrible, except you forthwith think on restitution; or if you have not your night in this world, you will have it in hell.

You that are married and have wives of your own, and yet hold too near friendship with your neighbours', set up your rests that the night will be an ill neighbour to your rest and that you shall have as little peace of mind as the rest. Therefore was Troy burnt by night, because Paris by night prostituted Helena, and wrought such treason to Prince Menelaus.

You that are Machiavellian vain fools, and think it no wit or policy but to vow and protest what you never mean, that travel for nothing else but to learn the vices of other countries and disfigure the ill English faces that God hath given you with Tuscan glicks and apish tricks: the night is for you a black saunt or a matachine, except you presently turn and convert to the simplicity you were born to.

You that can cast a man into an Italian ague when you list, and imitate with your diet-drinks any disease or infirmity, the night likewise hath an infernal to act before ye.

Traitors that by night meet and consult how to walk in the day undiscovered, and think those words of Christ revealed and laid open: to you no less the night shall be as a night owl to vex and torment you.

And finally, on you judges and magistrates, if there be any amongst you that do wrest all the law into their own hands, by drawing and receiving every man's money into their hands, and making new golden laws of their own, which no prince nor parliament ever dreamed of; that look as just as Jehovah by day, enthroning grave zeal and religion on the elevated whites of their eyes, when by night corrupt gifts and rewards rush in at their gates in whole armies, like northern carriers coming to their inn; that instead of their books turn over their bribes, for the deciding of causes, adjudging him the best right that brings the richest present unto them. If any such there be, I say, as in our Commonwealth I know none, but have read of in other states, let them look to have a number of unwelcome clients of their own accusing thoughts and imaginations that will betray them in the night to every idle fear and illusion.

Therefore are the terrors of the night more than of the day, because the sins of the night surmount the sins of the day.

By night-time came the Deluge over the face of the whole earth; by night-time Judas betrayed Christ, Tarquin ravished Lucretia.

When any poet would describe a horrible tragical accident, to add the more probability and credence unto it, he dismally beginneth to tell how it was dark night when it was done and cheerful daylight had quite abandoned the firmament.

Hence it is, that sin generally throughout the scripture is called the works of darkness; for never is the devil so busy as then, and then he thinks he may as well undiscovered walk abroad, as homicides and outlaws.

Had we no more religion than we might derive from

heathen fables, methinks those doleful quiristers of the night, the scritch-owl, the nightingale, and croaking frogs, might overawe us from any insolent transgression at that time. The first for her lavish blabbing of forbidden secrets, being for ever ordained to be a blab of ill-news and misfortune, still is crying out in our ears that we are mortal and must die. The second puts us in mind of the end and punishment of lust and ravishment. And the third and last, that we are but slime and mud, such as those watery creatures are bred of; and therefore why should we delight to add more to our slime and corruption, by extraordinary surfeits and drunkenness?

But these are nothing neither in comparison. For he whom in the day heaven cannot exhale, the night will never help; she only pleading for her old grandmother hell as well as the day for heaven.

Thus I shut up my treatise abruptly: that he who in the day doth not good works enough to answer the objections of the night, will hardly answer at the Day of Judgment.

1. BOCCACCIO · *Mrs Rosie and the Priest*
2. GERARD MANLEY HOPKINS · *As kingfishers catch fire*
3. *The Saga of Gunnlaug Serpent-tongue*
4. THOMAS DE QUINCEY · *On Murder Considered as One of the Fine Arts*
5. FRIEDRICH NIETZSCHE · *Aphorisms on Love and Hate*
6. JOHN RUSKIN · *Traffic*
7. PU SONGLING · *Wailing Ghosts*
8. JONATHAN SWIFT · *A Modest Proposal*
9. *Three Tang Dynasty Poets*
10. WALT WHITMAN · *On the Beach at Night Alone*
11. KENKŌ · *A Cup of Sake Beneath the Cherry Trees*
12. BALTASAR GRACIÁN · *How to Use Your Enemies*
13. JOHN KEATS · *The Eve of St Agnes*
14. THOMAS HARDY · *Woman much missed*
15. GUY DE MAUPASSANT · *Femme Fatale*
16. MARCO POLO · *Travels in the Land of Serpents and Pearls*
17. SUETONIUS · *Caligula*
18. APOLLONIUS OF RHODES · *Jason and Medea*
19. ROBERT LOUIS STEVENSON · *Olalla*
20. KARL MARX AND FRIEDRICH ENGELS · *The Communist Manifesto*
21. PETRONIUS · *Trimalchio's Feast*
22. JOHANN PETER HEBEL · *How a Ghastly Story Was Brought to Light by a Common or Garden Butcher's Dog*
23. HANS CHRISTIAN ANDERSEN · *The Tinder Box*
24. RUDYARD KIPLING · *The Gate of the Hundred Sorrows*
25. DANTE · *Circles of Hell*
26. HENRY MAYHEW · *Of Street Piemen*
27. HAFEZ · *The nightingales are drunk*
28. GEOFFREY CHAUCER · *The Wife of Bath*
29. MICHEL DE MONTAIGNE · *How We Weep and Laugh at the Same Thing*
30. THOMAS NASHE · *The Terrors of the Night*
31. EDGAR ALLAN POE · *The Tell-Tale Heart*
32. MARY KINGSLEY · *A Hippo Banquet*
33. JANE AUSTEN · *The Beautifull Cassandra*
34. ANTON CHEKHOV · *Gooseberries*
35. SAMUEL TAYLOR COLERIDGE · *Well, they are gone, and here must I remain*
36. JOHANN WOLFGANG VON GOETHE · *Sketchy, Doubtful, Incomplete Jottings*
37. CHARLES DICKENS · *The Great Winglebury Duel*
38. HERMAN MELVILLE · *The Maldive Shark*
39. ELIZABETH GASKELL · *The Old Nurse's Story*
40. NIKOLAY LESKOV · *The Steel Flea*

41. HONORÉ DE BALZAC · *The Atheist's Mass*
42. CHARLOTTE PERKINS GILMAN · *The Yellow Wall-Paper*
43. C.P. CAVAFY · *Remember, Body . . .*
44. FYODOR DOSTOEVSKY · *The Meek One*
45. GUSTAVE FLAUBERT · *A Simple Heart*
46. NIKOLAI GOGOL · *The Nose*
47. SAMUEL PEPYS · *The Great Fire of London*
48. EDITH WHARTON · *The Reckoning*
49. HENRY JAMES · *The Figure in the Carpet*
50. WILFRED OWEN · *Anthem For Doomed Youth*
51. WOLFGANG AMADEUS MOZART · *My Dearest Father*
52. PLATO · *Socrates' Defence*
53. CHRISTINA ROSSETTI · *Goblin Market*
54. *Sindbad the Sailor*
55. SOPHOCLES · *Antigone*
56. RYŪNOSUKE AKUTAGAWA · *The Life of a Stupid Man*
57. LEO TOLSTOY · *How Much Land Does A Man Need?*
58. GIORGIO VASARI · *Leonardo da Vinci*
59. OSCAR WILDE · *Lord Arthur Savile's Crime*
60. SHEN FU · *The Old Man of the Moon*
61. AESOP · *The Dolphins, the Whales and the Gudgeon*
62. MATSUO BASHŌ · *Lips too Chilled*
63. EMILY BRONTË · *The Night is Darkening Round Me*
64. JOSEPH CONRAD · *To-morrow*
65. RICHARD HAKLUYT · *The Voyage of Sir Francis Drake Around the Whole Globe*
66. KATE CHOPIN · *A Pair of Silk Stockings*
67. CHARLES DARWIN · *It was snowing butterflies*
68. BROTHERS GRIMM · *The Robber Bridegroom*
69. CATULLUS · *I Hate and I Love*
70. HOMER · *Circe and the Cyclops*
71. D. H. LAWRENCE · *Il Duro*
72. KATHERINE MANSFIELD · *Miss Brill*
73. OVID · *The Fall of Icarus*
74. SAPPHO · *Come Close*
75. IVAN TURGENEV · *Kasyan from the Beautiful Lands*
76. VIRGIL · *O Cruel Alexis*
77. H. G. WELLS · *A Slip under the Microscope*
78. HERODOTUS · *The Madness of Cambyses*
79. *Speaking of Siva*
80. *The Dhammapada*

'Presently I heard a slight groan, and I knew it was a groan of mortal terror . . . the low stifled sound that arises from the bottom of the soul . . .'

EDGAR ALLAN POE
Born 1809, Boston, USA
Died 1849, Baltimore, USA

'The Fall of the House of Usher' was first published in 1839, 'The Tell-Tale Heart' in 1843, and 'The Cask of Amontillado' in 1846.

EDGAR ALLAN POE IN PENGUIN CLASSICS
The Complete Tales and Poems of Edgar Allan Poe
The Fall of the House of Usher and Other Writings
The Masque of the Red Death
The Murders in the Rue Morgue and Other Tales
The Narrative of Arthur Gordon Pym of Nantucket
The Pit and the Pendulum
The Portable Edgar Allan Poe
The Science Fiction of Edgar Allan Poe

EDGAR ALLAN POE

The Tell-Tale Heart

PENGUIN BOOKS

PENGUIN CLASSICS

UK | USA | Canada | Ireland | Australia
India | New Zealand | South Africa

Penguin Books is part of the Penguin Random House group of companies whose addresses can be found at global.penguinrandomhouse.com.

This selection published in Penguin Classics 2015

014

Set in 9.5/13 pt Baskerville 10 Pro
Typeset by Jouve (UK), Milton Keynes

Printed and bound in Great Britain by Clays Ltd, Elcograf S.p.A.

A CIP catalogue record for this book is available from the British Library

ISBN: 978-0-141-39726-9

www.greenpenguin.co.uk

MIX
Paper from
responsible sources
FSC® C018179

Penguin Random House is committed to a sustainable future for our business, our readers and our planet. This book is made from Forest Stewardship Council® certified paper.

Contents

The Tell-Tale Heart 1

The Fall of the House of
  Usher 9

The Cask of Amontillado 38

The Tell-Tale Heart

True! – nervous – very, very dreadfully nervous I had been and am; but why *will* you say that I am mad? The disease had sharpened my senses – not destroyed – not dulled them. Above all was the sense of hearing acute. I heard all things in the heaven and in the earth. I heard many things in hell. How, then, am I mad? Hearken! and observe how healthily – how calmly I can tell you the whole story.

It is impossible to say how first the idea entered my brain; but once conceived, it haunted me day and night. Object there was none. Passion there was none. I loved the old man. He had never wronged me. He had never given me insult. For his gold I had no desire. I think it was his eye! yes, it was this! He had the eye of a vulture – a pale blue eye, with a film over it. Whenever it fell upon me, my blood ran cold; and so by degrees – very gradually – I made up my mind to take the life of the old man, and thus rid myself of the eye forever.

Now this is the point. You fancy me mad. Madmen know nothing. But you should have seen *me*. You should have seen how wisely I proceeded – with what caution – with what foresight – with what dissimulation I went to work! I was never kinder to the old man than during the whole week before I killed him. And every night, about midnight, I turned the latch of his door and opened it – oh so gently! And then, when I had made an opening sufficient for my head, I put in a dark lantern, all closed, closed, so that no light shone out, and then I thrust in my head. Oh, you would have laughed to see how cunningly I thrust it in! I moved it slowly – very, very slowly, so that I might not disturb the old man's sleep. It took me an hour to place my whole head within the opening so far that I could see him as he lay upon his bed. Ha! – would a madman have been so wise as this? And then, when my head was well in the room, I undid the lantern cautiously – oh, so cautiously – cautiously (for the hinges creaked) – I undid it just so much that a single thin ray fell upon the vulture eye. And this I did for seven long nights – every night just at midnight – but I found the eye always closed; and so it was impossible to do the work; for it was not the old man who vexed me, but his Evil Eye. And every morning, when the day broke, I went boldly into the chamber, and spoke courageously to him, calling him by name in a hearty tone, and inquiring how he had passed the night. So you see he would have been a very profound old man, indeed, to suspect that every night, just at twelve, I looked in upon him while he slept.

Upon the eighth night I was more than usually cautious

in opening the door. A watch's minute hand moves more quickly than did mine. Never before that night, had I *felt* the extent of my own powers – of my sagacity. I could scarcely contain my feelings of triumph. To think that there I was, opening the door, little by little, and he not even to dream of my secret deeds or thoughts. I fairly chuckled at the idea; and perhaps he heard me; for he moved on the bed suddenly, as if startled. Now you may think that I drew back – but no. His room was as black as pitch with the thick darkness, (for the shutters were close fastened, through fear of robbers,) and so I knew that he could not see the opening of the door, and I kept pushing it on steadily, steadily.

I had my head in, and was about to open the lantern, when my thumb slipped upon the tin fastening, and the old man sprang up in bed, crying out – 'Who's there?'

I kept quite still and said nothing. For a whole hour I did not move a muscle, and in the meantime I did not hear him lie down. He was still sitting up in the bed listening; – just as I have done, night after night, hearkening to the death watches in the wall.

Presently I heard a slight groan, and I knew it was the groan of mortal terror. It was not a groan of pain or of grief – oh, no! – it was the low stifled sound that arises from the bottom of the soul when overcharged with awe. I knew the sound well. Many a night, just at midnight, when all the world slept, it has welled up from my own bosom, deepening, with its dreadful echo, the terrors that distracted me. I say I knew it well. I knew what the old man felt, and pitied him, although I chuckled at heart. I knew that he had been lying awake ever since the first slight noise, when he had turned in the bed. His fears had been ever since growing upon him. He had been trying to fancy them causeless, but could not. He had been saying to himself – 'It is nothing but the wind in the chimney – it is only a mouse crossing the floor,' or 'it is merely a cricket which has made a single chirp.' Yes, he had been trying to comfort himself with these suppositions: but he had found all in vain. *All in vain*; because Death, in approaching him had stalked with his black shadow before him, and enveloped the victim. And it was the mournful influence of the unperceived shadow that caused him to feel – although he neither saw nor heard – to *feel* the presence of my head within the room.

When I had waited a long time, very patiently, without hearing him lie down, I resolved to open a little – a very, very little crevice in the lantern. So I opened it – you cannot imagine how stealthily, stealthily – until, at length a simple dim ray, like the thread of the spider, shot from out the crevice and fell full upon the vulture eye.

It was open – wide, wide open – and I grew furious as I gazed upon it. I saw it with perfect distinctness – all a dull blue, with a hideous veil over it that chilled the very marrow in my bones; but I could see nothing else of the old man's face or person: for I had directed the ray as if by instinct, precisely upon the damned spot.

The Tell-Tale Heart

And have I not told you that what you mistake for madness is but over acuteness of the senses? – now, I say, there came to my ears a low, dull, quick sound, such as a watch makes when enveloped in cotton. I knew *that* sound well, too. It was the beating of the old man's heart. It increased my fury, as the beating of a drum stimulates the soldier into courage.

But even yet I refrained and kept still. I scarcely breathed. I held the lantern motionless. I tried how steadily I could maintain the ray upon the eye. Meantime the hellish tattoo of the heart increased. It grew quicker and quicker, and louder and louder every instant. The old man's terror *must* have been extreme! It grew louder, I say, louder every moment! – do you mark me well? I have told you that I am nervous: so I am. And now at the dead hour of the night, amid the dreadful silence of that old house, so strange a noise as this excited me to uncontrollable terror. Yet, for some minutes longer I refrained and stood still. But the beating grew louder, louder! I thought the heart must burst. And now a new anxiety seized me – the sound would be heard by a neighbour! The old man's hour had come! With a loud yell, I threw open the lantern and leaped into the room. He shrieked once – once only. In an instant I dragged him to the floor, and pulled the heavy bed over him. I then smiled gaily, to find the deed so far done. But, for many minutes, the heart beat on with a muffled sound. This, however, did not vex me; it would not be heard through the wall. At length it ceased. The old man was dead. I removed the bed and examined the corpse. Yes, he was stone, stone dead. I placed my hand upon the heart and held it there many minutes. There was no pulsation. He was stone dead. His eye would trouble me no more.

If still you think me mad, you will think so no longer when I describe the wise precautions I took for the concealment of the body. The night waned; and I worked hastily, but in silence. First of all I dismembered the corpse. I cut off the head and the arms and the legs.

I then took up three planks from the flooring of the chamber, and deposited all between the scantlings. I then replaced the boards so cleverly, so cunningly, that no human eye – not even *his* – could have detected any thing wrong. There was nothing to wash out – no stain of any kind – no blood-spot whatever. I had been too wary for that. A tub had caught all – ha! ha!

When I had made an end of these labours, it was four o'clock – still dark as midnight. As the bell sounded the hour, there came a knocking at the street door. I went down to open it with a light heart, – for what had I *now* to fear? There entered three men, who introduced themselves, with perfect suavity, as officers of the police. A shriek had been heard by a neighbour during the night; suspicion of foul play had been aroused; information had been lodged at the police office, and they (the officers) had been deputed to search the premises.

I smiled, – for *what* had I to fear? I bade the gentlemen

The Tell-Tale Heart

welcome. The shriek, I said, was my own in a dream. The old man, I mentioned, was absent in the country. I took my visitors all over the house. I bade them search – search *well*. I led them, at length, to *his* chamber. I showed them his treasures, secure, undisturbed. In the enthusiasm of my confidence, I brought chairs into the room, and desired them *here* to rest from their fatigues, while I myself, in the wild audacity of my perfect triumph, placed my own seat upon the very spot beneath which reposed the corpse of the victim.

The officers were satisfied. My *manner* had convinced them. I was singularly at ease. They sat, and while I answered cheerily, they chatted of familiar things. But, ere long, I felt myself getting pale and wished them gone. My head ached, and I fancied a ringing in my ears: but still they sat and still chatted. The ringing became more distinct: – it continued and became more distinct: I talked more freely to get rid of the feeling: but it continued and gained definiteness – until, at length, I found that the noise was *not* within my ears.

No doubt I now grew *very* pale; – but I talked more fluently, and with a heightened voice. Yet the sound increased – and what could I do? It was *a low, dull, quick sound – much such a sound as a watch makes when enveloped in cotton*. I gasped for breath – and yet the officers heard it not. I talked more quickly – more vehemently; but the noise steadily increased. I arose and argued about trifles, in a high key and with violent gesticulations; but the noise steadily increased. Why *would* they not be gone? I paced the floor to and fro with heavy strides, as if excited to fury by the observations of the men – but the noise steadily increased. Oh God! what *could* I do? I foamed – I raved – I swore! I swung the chair upon which I had been sitting, and grated it upon the boards, but the noise arose over all and continually increased. It grew louder – louder – *louder*! And still the men chatted pleasantly, and smiled. Was it possible they heard not? Almighty God! – no, no! They heard! – they suspected! – they *knew*! – they were making a mockery of my horror! – this I thought, and this I think. But anything was better than this agony! Anything was more tolerable than this derision! I could bear those hypocritical smiles no longer! I felt that I must scream or die! and now – again! – hark! louder! louder! louder! *louder*!

'Villains!' I shrieked, 'dissemble no more! I admit the deed! – tear up the planks! here, here! – it is the beating of his hideous heart!'

The Fall of the House of Usher

> Son coeur est un luth suspendu;
> Sitôt qu'on le touche il résonne.
>
> DE BÉRANGER

During the whole of a dull, dark, and soundless day in the autumn of the year, when the clouds hung oppressively low in the heavens, I had been passing alone, on horseback, through a singularly dreary tract of country; and at length found myself, as the shades of the evening drew on, within view of the melancholy House of Usher. I know not how it was – but, with the first glimpse of the building, a sense of insufferable gloom pervaded my spirit. I say insufferable; for the feeling was unrelieved by any of that half-pleasurable, because poetic, sentiment, with which the mind usually receives even the sternest natural images of the desolate or terrible. I looked upon the scene before me – upon the mere house, and the simple landscape features of the domain – upon the bleak walls – upon the vacant eye-like windows – upon a few rank sedges – and upon a few white trunks of decayed trees – with an utter depression of soul which I can compare to no earthly sensation more properly than to the afterdream of the reveller upon opium – the bitter lapse into everyday life – the hideous dropping off of the veil. There was an iciness, a sinking, a sickening of the heart – an unredeemed dreariness of thought which no goading of the imagination could torture into aught of the sublime. What was it – I paused to think – what was it that so unnerved me in the contemplation of the House of Usher? It was a mystery all insoluble; nor could I grapple with the shadowy fancies that crowded upon me as I pondered. I was forced to fall back upon the unsatisfactory conclusion, that while, beyond doubt, there *are* combinations of very simple natural objects which have the power of thus affecting us, still the analysis of this power lies among considerations beyond our depth. It was possible, I reflected, that a mere different arrangement of the particulars of the scene, of the details of the picture, would be sufficient to modify, or perhaps to annihilate its capacity for sorrowful impression; and, acting upon this idea, I reined my horse to the precipitous brink of a black and lurid tarn that lay in unruffled lustre by the dwelling, and gazed down – but with a shudder even more thrilling than before – upon the remodelled and inverted images of the gray sedge, and the ghastly tree-stems, and the vacant and eye-like windows.

Nevertheless, in this mansion of gloom I now proposed to myself a sojourn of some weeks. Its proprietor,

The Fall of the House of Usher

Roderick Usher, had been one of my boon companions in boyhood; but many years had elapsed since our last meeting. A letter, however, had lately reached me in a distant part of the country – a letter from him – which, in its wildly importunate nature, had admitted of no other than a personal reply. The MS. gave evidence of nervous agitation. The writer spoke of acute bodily illness – of a mental disorder which oppressed him – and of an earnest desire to see me, as his best, and indeed his only personal friend, with a view of attempting, by the cheerfulness of my society, some alleviation of his malady. It was the manner in which all this, and much more, was said – it was the apparent *heart* that went with his request – which allowed me no room for hesitation; and I accordingly obeyed forthwith what I still considered a very singular summons.

Although, as boys, we had been even intimate associates, yet I really knew little of my friend. His reserve had been always excessive and habitual. I was aware, however, that his very ancient family had been noted, time out of mind, for a peculiar sensibility of temperament, displaying itself, through long ages, in many works of exalted art, and manifested, of late, in repeated deeds of munificent yet unobtrusive charity, as well as in a passionate devotion to the intricacies, perhaps even more than to the orthodox and easily recognisable beauties, of musical science. I had learned, too, the very remarkable fact, that the stem of the Usher race, all time-honoured as it was, had put forth, at no period, any enduring branch; in other words, that the entire family lay in the direct line of descent, and had always, with very trifling and very temporary variation, so lain. It was this deficiency, I considered, while running over in thought the perfect keeping of the character of the premises with the accredited character of the people, and while speculating upon the possible influence which the one, in the long lapse of centuries, might have exercised upon the other – it was this deficiency, perhaps, of collateral issue, and the consequent undeviating transmission, from sire to son, of the patrimony with the name, which had, at length, so identified the two as to merge the original title of the estate in the quaint and equivocal appellation of the 'House of Usher' – an appellation which seemed to include, in the minds of the peasantry who used it, both the family and the family mansion.

I have said that the sole effect of my somewhat childish experiment – that of looking down within the tarn – had been to deepen the first singular impression. There can be no doubt that the consciousness of the rapid increase of my superstition – for why should I not so term it? – served mainly to accelerate the increase itself. Such, I have long known, is the paradoxical law of all sentiments having terror as a basis. And it might have been for this reason only, that, when I again uplifted my eyes to the house itself, from its image in the pool, there grew in my mind a strange fancy – a fancy so ridiculous, indeed, that I but mention it to show the vivid force of the sensations which oppressed me. I had so worked upon my imagination as really to believe that about the whole mansion and domain there hung an atmosphere peculiar to themselves and their immediate vicinity – an atmosphere which had no affinity with the air of heaven, but which had reeked up from the decayed trees, and the gray wall, and the silent tarn – a pestilent and mystic vapour, dull, sluggish, faintly discernible, and leaden-hued.

Shaking off from my spirit what *must* have been a dream, I scanned more narrowly the real aspect of the building. Its principal feature seemed to be that of an excessive antiquity. The discoloration of ages had been great. Minute fungi overspread the whole exterior, hanging in a fine tangled web-work from the eaves. Yet all this was apart from any extraordinary dilapidation. No portion of the masonry had fallen; and there appeared to be a wild inconsistency between its still perfect adaptation of parts, and the crumbling condition of the individual stones. In this there was much that reminded me of the specious totality of old wood-work which has rotted for long years in some neglected vault, with no disturbance from the breath of the external air. Beyond this indication of extensive decay, however, the fabric gave little token of instability. Perhaps the eye of a scrutinising observer might have discovered a barely perceptible fissure, which, extending from the roof of the building in front, made its way down the wall in a zigzag direction, until it became lost in the sullen waters of the tarn.

Noticing these things, I rode over a short causeway to the house. A servant in waiting took my horse and I entered the Gothic archway of the hall. A valet, of stealthy step, thence conducted me, in silence, through many dark and intricate passages in my progress to the *studio* of his master. Much that I encountered on the way contributed, I know not how, to heighten the vague sentiments of which I have already spoken. While the objects around me – while the carvings of the ceilings, the sombre tapestries of the walls, the ebon blackness of the floors, and the phantasmagoric armorial trophies which rattled as I strode, were but matters to which, or to such as which, I had been accustomed from my infancy – while I hesitated not to acknowledge how familiar was all this – I still wondered to find how unfamiliar were the fancies which ordinary images were stirring up. On one of the staircases, I met the physician of the family. His countenance, I thought, wore a mingled expression of low cunning and perplexity. He accosted me with trepidation and passed on. The valet now threw open a door and ushered me into the presence of his master.

The room in which I found myself was very large and lofty. The windows were long, narrow, and pointed, and at so vast a distance from the black oaken floor as to be altogether inaccessible from within. Feeble gleams of encrimsoned light made their way through the trellised panes, and served to render sufficiently distinct the more prominent objects around; the eye, however, struggled in vain to reach the remoter angles of the chamber, or the recesses of the vaulted and fretted ceiling. Dark draperies hung upon the walls. The general furniture was profuse, comfortless, antique, and tattered. Many books and musical instruments lay scattered about, but failed to give any vitality to the scene. I felt that I breathed an atmosphere of sorrow. An air of stern, deep, and irredeemable gloom hung over and pervaded all.

Upon my entrance, Usher arose from a sofa on which he had been lying at full length, and greeted me with a vivacious warmth which had much in it, I at first thought, of an overdone cordiality – of the constrained effort of the *ennuyé* man of the world. A glance, however, at his countenance, convinced me of his perfect sincerity. We sat down; and for some moments, while he spoke not, I gazed upon him with a feeling half of pity, half of awe. Surely, man had never before so terribly altered, in so brief a period, as had Roderick Usher! It was with difficulty that I could bring myself to admit the identity of the wan being before me with the companion of my early boyhood. Yet the character of his face had been at all times remarkable. A cadaverousness of complexion; an eye large, liquid, and luminous beyond comparison; lips somewhat thin and very pallid, but of a surpassingly beautiful curve; a nose of a delicate Hebrew model, but with a breadth of nostril unusual in similar formations; a finely moulded chin, speaking, in its want of prominence, of a want of moral energy; hair of a more than web-like softness and tenuity; these features, with an inordinate expansion above the regions of the temple, made up altogether a countenance not easily to be forgotten. And now in the mere exaggeration of the prevailing character of these features, and of the expression they were wont to convey, lay so much of change that I doubted to whom I spoke. The now ghastly pallor of the skin, and the now miraculous lustre of the eye, above all things startled and even awed me. The silken hair, too, had been suffered to grow all unheeded, and as, in its wild gossamer texture, it floated rather than fell about the face, I could not, even with effort, connect its Arabesque expression with any idea of simple humanity.

In the manner of my friend I was at once struck with an incoherence – an inconsistency; and I soon found this to arise from a series of feeble and futile struggles to overcome an habitual trepidancy – an excessive nervous agitation. For something of this nature I had indeed been prepared, no less by his letter, than by reminiscences of certain boyish traits, and by conclusions deduced from his peculiar physical conformation and temperament. His action was alternately vivacious and sullen. His voice varied rapidly from a tremulous indecision (when the animal spirits seemed utterly in abeyance) to that species of energetic concision – that abrupt, weighty, unhurried, and hollow-sounding enunciation – that leaden, self-balanced and perfectly modulated guttural utterance, which may be observed in the lost drunkard, or the irreclaimable eater of opium, during the periods of his most intense excitement.

It was thus that he spoke of the object of my visit, of his earnest desire to see me, and of the solace he expected me to afford him. He entered, at some length, into what he conceived to be the nature of his malady. It was, he said, a constitutional and a family evil, and one for which he despaired to find a remedy – a mere nervous affection, he immediately added, which would undoubtedly soon pass off. It displayed itself in a host of unnatural sensations. Some of these, as he detailed them, interested and bewildered me; although, perhaps, the terms, and the general manner of the narration had their weight. He suffered much from a morbid acuteness of the senses; the most insipid food was alone endurable; he could wear only garments of certain texture; the odours of all flowers were oppressive; his eyes were tortured by even a faint light; and there were but peculiar sounds, and these from stringed instruments, which did not inspire him with horror.

To an anomalous species of terror I found him a bounden slave. 'I shall perish,' said he, 'I *must* perish in this deplorable folly. Thus, thus, and not otherwise, shall I be lost. I dread the events of the future, not in themselves, but in their results. I shudder at the thought of any, even the most trivial, incident, which may operate upon this intolerable agitation of soul. I have, indeed, no abhorrence of danger, except in its absolute effect – in terror. In this unnerved – in this pitiable condition – I feel that the period will sooner or later arrive when I must abandon life and reason together, in some struggle with the grim phantasm, Fear.'

I learned, moreover, at intervals, and through broken and equivocal hints, another singular feature of his mental condition. He was enchained by certain superstitious impressions in regard to the dwelling which he tenanted, and whence, for many years, he had never ventured forth – in regard to an influence whose supposititious force was conveyed in terms too shadowy here to be re-stated – an influence which some peculiarities in the mere form and substance of his family mansion, had, by dint of long sufferance, he said, obtained over his spirit – an effect which the *physique* of the gray walls and turrets, and of the dim tarn into which they all looked down, had, at length, brought about upon the *morale* of his existence.

He admitted, however, although with hesitation, that much of the peculiar gloom which thus afflicted him could be traced to a more natural and far more palpable origin – to the severe and long-continued illness – indeed to the evidently approaching dissolution – of a tenderly beloved sister – his sole companion for long years – his last and only relative on earth. 'Her decease,' he said, with a bitterness which I can never forget, 'would leave him (him the hopeless and the frail) the last of the ancient race of the Ushers.' While he spoke, the lady Madeline (for so was she called) passed slowly through a remote portion of the apartment, and, without having noticed my presence, disappeared. I regarded her with an utter astonishment not unmingled with dread – and yet I found it impossible to account for such feelings. A sensation of stupor oppressed me, as my eyes followed her retreating steps. When a door, at length, closed upon her, my glance sought instinctively and eagerly the countenance of the brother – but he had buried his face in his hands, and I could only perceive that a far more than ordinary wanness had overspread the emaciated fingers through which trickled many passionate tears.

The disease of the lady Madeline had long baffled the skill of her physicians. A settled apathy, a gradual wasting away of the person, and frequent although transient affections of a partially cataleptical character, were the unusual diagnosis. Hitherto she had steadily borne up against the pressure of her malady, and had not betaken herself finally to bed; but, on the closing in of the evening of my arrival at the house, she succumbed (as her brother told me at night with inexpressible agitation) to the prostrating power of the destroyer; and I learned that the glimpse I had obtained of her person would thus probably be the last I should obtain – that the lady, at least while living, would be seen by me no more.

For several days ensuing, her name was unmentioned by either Usher or myself: and during this period I was busied in earnest endeavours to alleviate the melancholy of my friend. We painted and read together; or I listened, as if in a dream, to the wild improvisations of his speaking guitar. And thus, as a closer and still closer intimacy admitted me more unreservedly into the recesses of his spirit, the more bitterly did I perceive the futility of all attempt at cheering a mind from which darkness, as if an inherent positive quality, poured forth upon all objects of the moral and physical universe, in one unceasing radiation of gloom.

I shall ever bear about me a memory of the many solemn hours I thus spent alone with the master of the House of Usher. Yet I should fail in any attempt to convey an idea of the exact character of the studies, or of the occupations, in which he involved me, or led me the way. An excited and highly distempered ideality threw a sulphureous lustre over all. His long improvised dirges will ring forever in my ears. Among other things, I hold painfully in mind a certain singular perversion and amplification of the wild air of the last waltz of Von Weber. From the paintings over which his elaborate fancy brooded, and which grew, touch by touch, into vaguenesses at which I shuddered the more thrillingly, because I shuddered knowing not why; – from these paintings (vivid as their images now are before me) I would in vain endeavour to educe more than a small portion which should lie within the compass of merely written words. By the utter simplicity, by the nakedness of his designs, he arrested and overawed attention. If ever mortal painted an idea, that mortal was Roderick Usher. For me at least – in the circumstances then surrounding me – there arose out of the pure abstractions which the hypochondriac contrived to throw upon his canvas, an intensity of intolerable awe, no shadow of which felt I ever yet in the contemplation of the certainly glowing yet too concrete reveries of Fuseli.

One of the phantasmagoric conceptions of my friend, partaking not so rigidly of the spirit of abstraction, may be shadowed forth, although feebly, in words. A small picture presented the interior of an immensely long and rectangular vault or tunnel, with low walls, smooth, white, and without interruption or device. Certain accessory points of the design served well to convey the idea that this excavation lay at an exceeding depth below the surface of the earth. No outlet was observed in any portion of its vast extent, and no torch, or other artificial source of light was discernible; yet a flood of intense rays rolled throughout, and bathed the whole in a ghastly and inappropriate splendour.

I have just spoken of that morbid condition of the auditory nerve which rendered all music intolerable to the sufferer, with the exception of certain effects of stringed instruments. It was, perhaps, the narrow limits to which he thus confined himself upon the guitar, which gave birth, in great measure, to the fantastic character of his performances. But the fervid *facility* of his *impromptus* could not be so accounted for. They must have been, and were, in the notes, as well as in the words of his wild fantasias (for he not unfrequently accompanied himself with rhymed verbal improvisations), the result of that intense mental collectedness and concentration to which I have previously alluded as observable only in particular moments of the highest artificial excitement. The words of one of these rhapsodies I have easily remembered. I was, perhaps, the more forcibly impressed with it, as he gave it, because, in the under or mystic current of its meaning, I fancied that I perceived, and for the first time, a full consciousness on the part of Usher, of the tottering of his lofty reason upon her throne. The verses, which were entitled 'The Haunted Palace', ran very nearly, if not accurately, thus:

I

In the greenest of our valleys,
  By good angels tenanted,
Once a fair and stately palace –
  Radiant palace – reared its head.
In the monarch Thought's dominion –
  It stood there!
Never seraph spread a pinion
  Over fabric half so fair.

The Fall of the House of Usher

II

Banners yellow, glorious, golden,
    On its roof did float and flow;
(This – all this – was in the olden
    Time long ago)
And every gentle air that dallied,
    In that sweet day,
Along the ramparts plumed and pallid,
    A winged odour went away.

III

Wanderers in that happy valley
    Through two luminous windows saw
Spirits moving musically
    To a lute's well-tunèd law,
Round about a throne, where sitting
    (Porphyrogene!)
In state his glory well befitting,
    The ruler of the realm was seen.

IV

And all with pearl and ruby glowing
    Was the fair palace door,
Through which came flowing, flowing, flowing
    And sparkling evermore,

> A troop of Echoes whose sweet duty
>   Was but to sing,
> In voices of surpassing beauty,
>   The wit and wisdom of their king.
>
> V
>
> But evil things, in robes of sorrow,
>   Assailed the monarch's high estate;
> (Ah, let us mourn, for never morrow
>   Shall dawn upon him, desolate!)
> And, round about his home, the glory
>   That blushed and bloomed
> Is but a dim-remembered story
>   Of the old time entombed.
>
> VI
>
> And travellers now within that valley,
>   Through the red-litten windows, see
> Vast forms that move fantastically
>   To a discordant melody;
> While, like a rapid ghastly river,
>   Through the pale door,
> A hideous throng rush out forever,
>   And laugh – but smile no more.

I well remember that suggestions arising from this ballad, led us into a train of thought wherein there became

The Fall of the House of Usher

manifest an opinion of Usher's which I mention not so much on account of its novelty, (for other men have thought thus,) as on account of the pertinacity with which he maintained it. This opinion, in its general form, was that of the sentience of all vegetable things. But, in his disordered fancy, the idea had assumed a more daring character, and trespassed, under certain conditions, upon the kingdom of inorganization. I lack words to express the full extent, or the earnest *abandon* of his persuasion. The belief, however, was connected (as I have previously hinted) with the gray stones of the home of his forefathers. The conditions of the sentience had been here, he imagined, fulfilled in the method of collocation of these stones – in the order of their arrangement, as well as in that of the many *fungi* which overspread them, and of the decayed trees which stood around – above all, in the long undisturbed endurance of this arrangement, and in its reduplication in the still waters of the tarn. Its evidence – the evidence of the sentience – was to be seen, he said, (and I here started as he spoke,) in the gradual yet certain condensation of an atmosphere of their own about the waters and the walls. The result was discoverable, he added, in that silent, yet importunate and terrible influence which for centuries had moulded the destinies of his family, and which made *him* what I now saw him – what he was. Such opinions need no comment, and I will make none.

Our books – the books which, for years, had formed no small portion of the mental existence of the invalid – were, as might be supposed, in strict keeping with this character of phantasm. We pored together over such works as the Ververt et Chartreuse of Gresset; the Belphegor of Machiavelli; the Heaven and Hell of Swedenborg; the Subterranean Voyage of Nicholas Klimm by Holberg; the Chiromancy of Robert Flud, of Jean D'Indaginé, and of De la Chambre; the Journey into the Blue Distance of Tieck; and the City of the Sun of Campanella. One favourite volume was a small octavo edition of the *Directorium Inquisitorum*, by the Dominican Eymeric de Gironne; and there were passages in Pomponius Mela, about the old African Satyrs and Ægipans, over which Usher would sit dreaming for hours. His chief delight, however, was found in the perusal of an exceedingly rare and curious book in quarto Gothic – the manual of a forgotten church – the *Vigiliæ Mortuorum secundum Chorum Ecclesiæ Maguntinæ.*

I could not help thinking of the wild ritual of this work, and of its probable influence upon the hypochondriac, when, one evening, having informed me abruptly that the lady Madeline was no more, he stated his intention of preserving her corpse for a fortnight, (previously to its final interment,) in one of the numerous vaults within the main walls of the building. The worldly reason, however, assigned for this singular proceeding, was one which I did not feel at liberty to dispute. The brother had been led to his resolution (so he told me) by consideration of the unusual character of the malady of the deceased, of

The Fall of the House of Usher

certain obtrusive and eager inquiries on the part of her medical men, and of the remote and exposed situation of the burial-ground of the family. I will not deny that when I called to mind the sinister countenance of the person whom I met upon the staircase, on the day of my arrival at the house, I had no desire to oppose what I regarded as at best but a harmless, and by no means an unnatural, precaution.

At the request of Usher, I personally aided him in the arrangements for the temporary entombment. The body having been encoffined, we two alone bore it to its rest. The vault in which we placed it (and which had been so long unopened that our torches, half smothered in its oppressive atmosphere, gave us little opportunity for investigation) was small, damp, and entirely without means of admission for light; lying, at great depth, immediately beneath that portion of the building in which was my own sleeping apartment. It had been used, apparently, in remote feudal times, for the worst purposes of a donjon-keep, and, in later days, as a place of deposit for powder, or some other highly combustible substance, as a portion of its floor, and the whole interior of a long archway through which we reached it, were carefully sheathed with copper. The door, of massive iron, had been, also, similarly protected. Its immense weight caused an unusually sharp grating sound, as it moved upon its hinges.

Having deposited our mournful burden upon tressels within this region of horror, we partially turned aside the yet unscrewed lid of the coffin, and looked upon the face of the tenant. A striking similitude between the brother and sister now first arrested my attention; and Usher, divining, perhaps, my thoughts, murmured out some few words from which I learned that the deceased and himself had been twins, and that sympathies of a scarcely intelligible nature had always existed between them. Our glances, however, rested not long upon the dead – for we could not regard her unawed. The disease which had thus entombed the lady in the maturity of youth, had left, as usual in all maladies of a strictly cataleptical character, the mockery of a faint blush upon the bosom and the face, and that suspiciously lingering smile upon the lip which is so terrible in death. We replaced and screwed down the lid, and, having secured the door of iron, made our way, with toil, into the scarcely less gloomy apartments of the upper portion of the house.

And now, some days of bitter grief having elapsed, an observable change came over the features of the mental disorder of my friend. His ordinary manner had vanished. His ordinary occupations were neglected or forgotten. He roamed from chamber to chamber with hurried, unequal, and objectless step. The pallor of his countenance had assumed, if possible, a more ghastly hue – but the luminousness of his eye had utterly gone out. The once occasional huskiness of his tone was heard no more; and a tremulous quaver, as if of extreme terror, habitually characterized his utterance. There were times,

The Fall of the House of Usher

indeed, when I thought his unceasingly agitated mind was labouring with some oppressive secret, to divulge which he struggled for the necessary courage. At times, again, I was obliged to resolve all into the mere inexplicable vagaries of madness, for I beheld him gazing upon vacancy for long hours, in an attitude of the profoundest attention, as if listening to some imaginary sound. It was no wonder that his condition terrified – that it infected me. I felt creeping upon me, by slow yet certain degrees, the wild influences of his own fantastic yet impressive superstitions.

It was, especially, upon retiring to bed late in the night of the seventh or eighth day after the placing of the lady Madeline within the donjon, that I experienced the full power of such feelings. Sleep came not near my couch – while the hours waned and waned away. I struggled to reason off the nervousness which had dominion over me. I endeavoured to believe that much, if not all of what I felt, was due to the bewildering influence of the gloomy furniture of the room – of the dark and tattered draperies, which, tortured into motion by the breath of a rising tempest, swayed fitfully to and fro upon the walls, and rustled uneasily about the decorations of the bed. But my efforts were fruitless. An irrepressible tremour gradually pervaded my frame; and, at length, there sat upon my very heart an incubus of utterly causeless alarm. Shaking this off with a gasp and a struggle, I uplifted myself upon the pillows, and, peering earnestly within the intense darkness of the chamber, hearkened – I know not why, except that an instinctive spirit prompted me – to certain low and indefinite sounds which came, through the pauses of the storm, at long intervals, I knew not whence. Overpowered by an intense sentiment of horror, unaccountable yet unendurable, I threw on my clothes with haste (for I felt that I should sleep no more during the night), and endeavoured to arouse myself from the pitiable condition into which I had fallen, by pacing rapidly to and fro through the apartment.

I had taken but few turns in this manner, when a light step on an adjoining staircase arrested my attention. I presently recognised it as that of Usher. In an instant afterward he rapped, with a gentle touch, at my door, and entered, bearing a lamp. His countenance was, as usual, cadaverously wan – but, moreover, there was a species of mad hilarity in his eyes – an evidently restrained *hysteria* in his whole demeanour. His air appalled me – but anything was preferable to the solitude which I had so long endured, and I even welcomed his presence as a relief.

'And you have not seen it?' he said abruptly, after having stared about him for some moments in silence – 'you have not then seen it? – but, stay! you shall.' Thus speaking, and having carefully shaded his lamp, he hurried to one of the casements, and threw it freely open to the storm.

The impetuous fury of the entering gust nearly lifted us from our feet. It was, indeed, a tempestuous yet sternly beautiful night, and one wildly singular in its terror and

The Fall of the House of Usher

its beauty. A whirlwind had apparently collected its force in our vicinity; for there were frequent and violent alterations in the direction of the wind; and the exceeding density of the clouds (which hung so low as to press upon the turrets of the house) did not prevent our perceiving the life-like velocity with which they flew careering from all points against each other, without passing away into the distance. I say that even their exceeding density did not prevent our perceiving this – yet we had no glimpse of the moon or stars – nor was there any flashing forth of the lightning. But the under surfaces of the huge masses of agitated vapour, as well as all terrestrial objects immediately around us, were glowing in the unnatural light of a faintly luminous and distinctly visible gaseous exhalation which hung about and enshrouded the mansion.

'You must not – you shall not behold this!' said I, shudderingly, to Usher, as I led him, with a gentle violence, from the window to a seat. 'These appearances, which bewilder you, are merely electrical phenomena not uncommon – or it may be that they have their ghastly origin in the rank miasma of the tarn. Let us close this casement; – the air is chilling and dangerous to your frame. Here is one of your favourite romances. I will read, and you shall listen; – and so we will pass away this terrible night together.'

The antique volume which I had taken up was the 'Mad Trist' of Sir Launcelot Canning; but I had called it a favourite of Usher's more in sad jest than in earnest; for, in truth, there is little in its uncouth and unimaginative prolixity which could have had interest for the lofty and spiritual ideality of my friend. It was, however, the only book immediately at hand; and I indulged a vague hope that the excitement which now agitated the hypochondriac, might find relief (for the history of mental disorder is full of similar anomalies) even in the extremeness of the folly which I should read. Could I have judged, indeed, by the wild overstrained air of vivacity with which he hearkened, or apparently hearkened, to the words of the tale, I might well have congratulated myself upon the success of my design.

I had arrived at that well-known portion of the story where Ethelred, the hero of the Trist, having sought in vain for peaceable admission into the dwelling of the hermit, proceeds to make good an entrance by force. Here, it will be remembered, the words of the narrative run thus:

'And Ethelred, who was by nature of a doughty heart, and who was now mighty withal, on account of the powerfulness of the wine which he had drunken, waited no longer to hold parley with the hermit, who, in sooth, was of an obstinate and maliceful turn, but, feeling the rain upon his shoulders, and fearing the rising of the tempest, uplifted his mace outright, and, with blows, made quickly room in the plankings of the door for his gauntleted hand; and now pulling therewith sturdily, he so cracked, and ripped, and tore all asunder, that the noise of the dry and hollow-sounding wood alarumed and reverberated throughout the forest.'

The Fall of the House of Usher

At the termination of this sentence I started, and for a moment, paused; for it appeared to me (although I at once concluded that my excited fancy had deceived me) – it appeared to me that, from some very remote portion of the mansion, there came, indistinctly, to my ears, what might have been, in its exact similarity of character, the echo (but a stifled and dull one certainly) of the very cracking and ripping sound which Sir Launcelot had so particularly described. It was, beyond doubt, the coincidence alone which had arrested my attention; for, amid the rattling of the sashes of the casements, and the ordinary commingled noises of the still increasing storm, the sound, in itself, had nothing, surely, which should have interested or disturbed me. I continued the story:

'But the good champion Ethelred, now entering within the door, was sore enraged and amazed to perceive no signal of the maliceful hermit; but, in the stead thereof, a dragon of a scaly and prodigious demeanour, and of a fiery tongue, which sate in guard before a palace of gold, with a floor of silver; and upon the wall there hung a shield of shining brass with this legend enwritten –

> Who entereth herein, a conqueror hath bin;
> Who slayeth the dragon, the shield he shall win;

And Ethelred uplifted his mace, and struck upon the head of the dragon, which fell before him, and gave up his pesty breath, with a shriek so horrid and harsh, and withal so piercing, that Ethelred had fain to close his ears with his hands against the dreadful noise of it, the like whereof was never before heard.'

Here again I paused abruptly, and now with a feeling of wild amazement – for there could be no doubt whatever that, in this instance, I did actually hear (although from what direction it proceeded I found it impossible to say) a low and apparently distant, but harsh, protracted, and most unusual screaming or grating sound – the exact counterpart of what my fancy had already conjured up for the dragon's unnatural shriek as described by the romancer.

Oppressed, as I certainly was, upon the occurrence of the second and most extraordinary coincidence, by a thousand conflicting sensations, in which wonder and extreme terror were predominant, I still retained sufficient presence of mind to avoid exciting, by any observation, the sensitive nervousness of my companion. I was by no means certain that he had noticed the sounds in question; although, assuredly, a strange alteration had, during the last few minutes, taken place in his demeanour. From a position fronting my own, he had gradually brought round his chair, so as to sit with his face to the door of the chamber; and thus I could but partially perceive his features, although I saw that his lips trembled as if he were murmuring inaudibly. His head had dropped upon his breast – yet I knew that he was not asleep, from the wide and rigid opening of the eye as I caught a glance of it in profile. The motion of his body, too, was at variance with this idea – for he rocked from side to side with a gentle yet constant and uniform sway. Having rapidly taken notice of all this, I resumed the narrative of Sir Launcelot, which thus proceeded:

'And now, the champion, having escaped from the terrible fury of the dragon, bethinking himself of the brazen shield, and of the breaking up of the enchantment which was upon it, removed the carcass from out of the way before him, and approached valorously over the silver pavement of the castle to where the shield was upon the wall; which in sooth tarried not for his full coming, but fell down at his feet upon the silver floor, with a mighty great and terrible ringing sound.'

No sooner had these syllables passed my lips, than – as if a shield of brass had indeed, at the moment, fallen heavily upon a floor of silver – I became aware of a distinct, hollow, metallic, and clangorous, yet apparently muffled reverberation. Completely unnerved, I leaped to my feet; but the measured rocking movement of Usher was undisturbed. I rushed to the chair in which he sat. His eyes were bent fixedly before him, and throughout his whole countenance there reigned a stony rigidity. But, as I placed my hand upon his shoulder, there came a strong shudder over his whole person; a sickly smile quivered about his lips; and I saw that he spoke in a low, hurried, and gibbering murmur, as if unconscious of my presence. Bending closely over him, I at length drank in the hideous import of his words.

'Not hear it? – yes, I hear it, and *have* heard it. Long – long – long – many minutes, many hours, many days, have I heard it – yet I dared not – oh, pity me, miserable wretch that I am! – I dared not – I *dared* not speak! *We have put her living in the tomb!* Said I not that my senses were acute? I *now* tell you that I heard her first feeble movements in the hollow coffin. I heard them – many, many days ago – yet I dared not – I *dared not speak!* And now – to-night – Ethelred – ha! ha! – the breaking of the hermit's door, and the death-cry of the dragon, and the clangour of the shield! – say, rather, the rending of her coffin, and the grating of the iron hinges of her prison, and her struggles within the coppered archway of the vault! Oh whither shall I fly? Will she not be here anon? Is she not hurrying to upbraid me for my haste? Have I not heard her footstep on the stair? Do I not distinguish that heavy and horrible beating of her heart? MADMAN!' – here he sprang furiously to his feet, and shrieked out his syllables, as if in the effort he were giving up his soul – 'MADMAN! I TELL YOU THAT SHE NOW STANDS WITHOUT THE DOOR!'

As if in the superhuman energy of his utterance there had been found the potency of a spell – the huge antique panels to which the speaker pointed, threw slowly back, upon the instant, their ponderous and ebony jaws. It was the work of the rushing gust – but then without those doors there DID stand the lofty and enshrouded figure of the lady Madeline of Usher. There was blood upon her white robes, and the evidence of some bitter struggle upon every portion of her emaciated frame. For a moment she remained trembling and reeling to and fro upon the threshold, then, with a low moaning cry, fell heavily inward upon the person of her brother, and in her violent and now final death-agonies, bore him to the floor a corpse, and a victim to the terrors he had anticipated.

From that chamber, and from that mansion, I fled aghast. The storm was still abroad in all its wrath as I found myself crossing the old causeway. Suddenly there shot along the path a wild light, and I turned to see whence a gleam so unusual could have issued; for the vast house and its shadows were alone behind me. The radiance was that of the full, setting, and blood-red moon which now shone vividly through that once barely discernible fissure of which I have before spoken as extending from the roof of the building, in a zigzag direction, to the base. While I gazed, this fissure rapidly widened – there came a fierce breath of the whirlwind – the entire orb of the satellite burst at once upon my sight – my brain reeled as I saw the mighty walls rushing asunder – there was a long tumultuous shouting sound like the voice of a thousand waters – and the deep and dank tarn at my feet closed sullenly and silently over the fragments of the 'HOUSE OF USHER'.

The Cask of Amontillado

The thousand injuries of Fortunato I had borne as I best could, but when he ventured upon insult I vowed revenge. You, who so well know the nature of my soul, will not suppose, however, that I gave utterance to a threat. *At length* I would be avenged; this was a point definitely settled – but the very definitiveness with which it was resolved precluded the idea of risk. I must not only punish but punish with impunity. A wrong is unredressed when retribution overtakes its redresser. It is equally unredressed when the avenger fails to make himself felt as such to him who has done the wrong.

It must be understood that neither by word nor deed had I given Fortunato cause to doubt my good will. I continued, as was my wont, to smile in his face, and he did not perceive that my smile *now* was at the thought of his immolation.

He had a weak point – this Fortunato – although in other regards he was a man to be respected and even feared. He prided himself on his connoisseurship in wine.

The Cask of Amontillado

Few Italians have the true virtuoso spirit. For the most part their enthusiasm is adopted to suit the time and opportunity, to practise imposture upon the British and Austrian *millionaires*. In painting and gemmary, Fortunato, like his countrymen, was a quack, but in the matter of old wines he was sincere. In this respect I did not differ from him materially; – I was skilful in the Italian vintages myself, and bought largely whenever I could.

It was about dusk, one evening during the supreme madness of the carnival season, that I encountered my friend. He accosted me with excessive warmth, for he had been drinking much. The man wore motley. He had on a tight-fitting parti-striped dress, and his head was surmounted by the conical cap and bells. I was so pleased to see him that I thought I should never have done wringing his hand.

I said to him – 'My dear Fortunato, you are luckily met. How remarkably well you are looking today. But I have received a pipe of what passes for Amontillado, and I have my doubts.'

'How?' said he. 'Amontillado? A pipe? Impossible! And in the middle of the carnival!'

'I have my doubts,' I replied; 'and I was silly enough to pay the full Amontillado price without consulting you in the matter. You were not to be found, and I was fearful of losing a bargain.'

'Amontillado!'

'I have my doubts.'

'Amontillado!'

'And I must satisfy them.'

'Amontillado!'

'As you are engaged, I am on my way to Luchresi. If any one has a critical turn it is he. He will tell me –'

'Luchresi cannot tell Amontillado from Sherry.'

'And yet some fools will have it that his taste is a match for your own.'

'Come, let us go.'

'Whither?'

'To your vaults.'

'My friend, no; I will not impose upon your good nature. I perceive you have an engagement. Luchresi –'

'I have no engagement; – come.'

'My friend, no. It is not the engagement, but the severe cold with which I perceive you are afflicted. The vaults are insufferably damp. They are encrusted with nitre.'

'Let us go, nevertheless. The cold is merely nothing. Amontillado! You have been imposed upon. And as for Luchresi, he cannot distinguish Sherry from Amontillado.'

Thus speaking, Fortunato possessed himself of my arm; and putting on a mask of black silk and drawing a *roquelaire* closely about my person, I suffered him to hurry me to my palazzo.

There were no attendants at home; they had absconded to make merry in honour of the time. I had told them

The Cask of Amontillado

that I should not return until the morning, and had given them explicit orders not to stir from the house. These orders were sufficient, I well knew, to insure their immediate disappearance, one and all, as soon as my back was turned.

I took from their sconces two flambeaux, and giving one to Fortunato, bowed him through several suites of rooms to the archway that led into the vaults. I passed down a long and winding staircase, requesting him to be cautious as he followed. We came at length to the foot of the descent, and stood together upon the damp ground of the catacombs of the Montresors.

The gait of my friend was unsteady, and the bells upon his cap jingled as he strode.

'The pipe,' he said.

'It is farther on,' said I; 'but observe the white web-work which gleams from these cavern walls.'

He turned towards me, and looked into my eyes with two filmy orbs that distilled the rheum of intoxication.

'Nitre?' he asked, at length.

'Nitre,' I replied. 'How long have you had that cough?'

'Ugh! ugh! ugh! – ugh! ugh! ugh! – ugh! ugh! ugh! – ugh! ugh! ugh! – ugh! ugh! ugh!'

My poor friend found it impossible to reply for many minutes.

'It is nothing,' he said, at last.

'Come,' I said, with decision, 'we will go back; your health is precious. You are rich, respected, admired, beloved; you are happy, as once I was. You are a man to be missed. For me it is no matter. We will go back; you will be ill, and I cannot be responsible. Besides, there is Luchresi –'

'Enough,' he said; 'the cough is a mere nothing; it will not kill me. I shall not die of a cough.'

'True – true,' I replied; 'and, indeed, I had no intention of alarming you unnecessarily – but you should use all proper caution. A draught of this Medoc will defend us from the damps.'

Here I knocked off the neck of a bottle which I drew from a long row of its fellows that lay upon the mould.

'Drink,' I said, presenting him the wine.

He raised it to his lips with a leer. He paused and nodded to me familiarly, while his bells jingled.

'I drink,' he said, 'to the buried that repose around us.'

'And I to your long life.'

He again took my arm, and we proceeded.

'These vaults,' he said, 'are extensive.'

'The Montresors,' I replied, 'were a great and numerous family.'

'I forget your arms.'

'A huge human foot d'or, in a field azure; the foot crushes a serpent rampant whose fangs are imbedded in the heel.'

'And the motto?'

'*Nemo me impune lacessit.*'

'Good!' he said.

The wine sparkled in his eyes and the bells jingled. My

The Cask of Amontillado

own fancy grew warm with the Medoc. We had passed through long walls of piled skeletons, with casks and puncheons intermingling, into the inmost recesses of the catacombs. I paused again, and this time I made bold to seize Fortunato by an arm above the elbow.

'The nitre!' I said; 'see, it increases. It hangs like moss upon the vaults. We are below the river's bed. The drops of moisture trickle among the bones. Come, we will go back ere it is too late. Your cough –'

'It is nothing,' he said; 'let us go on. But first, another draught of the Medoc.'

I broke and reached him a flagon of De Grâve. He emptied it at a breath. His eyes flashed with a fierce light. He laughed and threw the bottle upwards with a gesticulation I did not understand.

I looked at him in surprise. He repeated the movement – a grotesque one.

'You do not comprehend?' he said.

'Not I,' I replied.

'Then you are not of the brotherhood.'

'How?'

'You are not of the masons.'

'Yes, yes,' I said; 'yes, yes.'

'You? Impossible! A mason?'

'A mason,' I replied.

'A sign,' he said, 'a sign.'

'It is this,' I answered, producing from beneath the folds of my *roquelaire* a trowel.

'You jest,' he exclaimed, recoiling a few paces. 'But let us proceed to the Amontillado.'

'Be it so,' I said, replacing the tool beneath the cloak and again offering him my arm. He leaned upon it heavily. We continued our route in search of the Amontillado. We passed through a range of low arches, descended, passed on, and descending again, arrived at a deep crypt, in which the foulness of the air caused our flambeaux rather to glow than flame.

At the most remote end of the crypt there appeared another less spacious. Its walls had been lined with human remains, piled to the vault overhead, in the fashion of the great catacombs of Paris. Three sides of this interior crypt were still ornamented in this manner. From the fourth side the bones had been thrown down, and lay promiscuously upon the earth, forming at one point a mound of some size. Within the wall thus exposed by the displacing of the bones, we perceived a still interior crypt or recess, in depth about four feet, in width three, in height six or seven. It seemed to have been constructed for no especial use within itself, but formed merely the interval between two of the colossal supports of the roof of the catacombs, and was backed by one of their circumscribing walls of solid granite.

It was in vain that Fortunato, uplifting his dull torch, endeavoured to pry into the depth of the recess. Its termination the feeble light did not enable us to see.

The Cask of Amontillado

'Proceed,' I said; 'herein is the Amontillado. As for Luchresi –'

'He is an ignoramus,' interrupted my friend, as he stepped unsteadily forward, while I followed immediately at his heels. In an instant he had reached the extremity of the niche, and finding his progress arrested by the rock, stood stupidly bewildered. A moment more and I had fettered him to the granite. In its surface were two iron staples, distant from each other about two feet, horizontally. From one of these depended a short chain, from the other a padlock. Throwing the links about his waist, it was but the work of a few seconds to secure it. He was too much astounded to resist. Withdrawing the key I stepped back from the recess.

'Pass your hand,' I said, 'over the wall; you cannot help feeling the nitre. Indeed, it is *very* damp. Once more let me *implore* you to return. No? Then I must positively leave you. But I must first render you all the little attentions in my power.'

'The Amontillado!' ejaculated my friend, not yet recovered from his astonishment.

'True,' I replied; 'the Amontillado.'

As I said these words I busied myself among the pile of bones of which I have before spoken. Throwing them aside, I soon uncovered a quantity of building stone and mortar. With these materials and with the aid of my trowel, I began vigorously to wall up the entrance of the niche.

Edgar Allan Poe

I had scarcely laid the first tier of the masonry when I discovered that the intoxication of Fortunato had in a great measure worn off. The earliest indication I had of this was a low moaning cry from the depth of the recess. It was *not* the cry of a drunken man. There was then a long and obstinate silence. I laid the second tier, and the third, and the fourth; and then I heard the furious vibrations of the chain. The noise lasted for several minutes, during which, that I might hearken to it with the more satisfaction, I ceased my labours and sat down upon the bones. When at last the clanking subsided, I resumed the trowel, and finished without interruption the fifth, the sixth, and the seventh tier. The wall was now nearly upon a level with my breast. I again paused, and holding the flambeaux over the mason-work, threw a few feeble rays upon the figure within.

A succession of loud and shrill screams, bursting suddenly from the throat of the chained form, seemed to thrust me violently back. For a brief moment I hesitated, I trembled. Unsheathing my rapier, I began to grope with it about the recess; but the thought of an instant reassured me. I placed my hand upon the solid fabric of the catacombs, and felt satisfied. I re-approached the wall; I replied to the yells of him who clamoured. I re-echoed, I aided, I surpassed them in volume and in strength. I did this, and the clamourer grew still.

It was now midnight, and my task was drawing to a

close. I had completed the eighth, the ninth and the tenth tier. I had finished a portion of the last and the eleventh; there remained but a single stone to be fitted and plastered in. I struggled with its weight; I placed it partially in its destined position. But now there came from out the niche a low laugh that erected the hairs upon my head. It was succeeded by a sad voice, which I had difficulty in recognizing as that of the noble Fortunato. The voice said –

'Ha! ha! ha! – he! he! he! – a very good joke, indeed – an excellent jest. We will have many a rich laugh about it at the palazzo – he! he! he! – over our wine – he! he! he!'

'The Amontillado!' I said.

'He! he! he! – he! he! he! – yes, the Amontillado. But is it not getting late? Will not they be awaiting us at the palazzo, the Lady Fortunato and the rest? Let us be gone.'

'Yes,' I said, 'let us be gone.'

'For the love of God, Montresor!'

'Yes,' I said, 'for the love of God!'

But to these words I hearkened in vain for a reply. I grew impatient. I called aloud –

'Fortunato!'

No answer. I called again –

'Fortunato!'

No answer still. I thrust a torch through the remaining aperture and let it fall within. There came forth in return only a jingling of the bells. My heart grew sick; it was the dampness of the catacombs that made it so. I hastened to make an end of my labour. I forced the last stone into its position; I plastered it up. Against the new masonry I re-erected the old rampart of bones. For the half of a century no mortal has disturbed them. *In pace requiescat!*

1. BOCCACCIO · *Mrs Rosie and the Priest*
2. GERARD MANLEY HOPKINS · *As kingfishers catch fire*
3. *The Saga of Gunnlaug Serpent-tongue*
4. THOMAS DE QUINCEY · *On Murder Considered as One of the Fine Arts*
5. FRIEDRICH NIETZSCHE · *Aphorisms on Love and Hate*
6. JOHN RUSKIN · *Traffic*
7. PU SONGLING · *Wailing Ghosts*
8. JONATHAN SWIFT · *A Modest Proposal*
9. *Three Tang Dynasty Poets*
10. WALT WHITMAN · *On the Beach at Night Alone*
11. KENKŌ · *A Cup of Sake Beneath the Cherry Trees*
12. BALTASAR GRACIÁN · *How to Use Your Enemies*
13. JOHN KEATS · *The Eve of St Agnes*
14. THOMAS HARDY · *Woman much missed*
15. GUY DE MAUPASSANT · *Femme Fatale*
16. MARCO POLO · *Travels in the Land of Serpents and Pearls*
17. SUETONIUS · *Caligula*
18. APOLLONIUS OF RHODES · *Jason and Medea*
19. ROBERT LOUIS STEVENSON · *Olalla*
20. KARL MARX AND FRIEDRICH ENGELS · *The Communist Manifesto*
21. PETRONIUS · *Trimalchio's Feast*
22. JOHANN PETER HEBEL · *How a Ghastly Story Was Brought to Light by a Common or Garden Butcher's Dog*
23. HANS CHRISTIAN ANDERSEN · *The Tinder Box*
24. RUDYARD KIPLING · *The Gate of the Hundred Sorrows*
25. DANTE · *Circles of Hell*
26. HENRY MAYHEW · *Of Street Piemen*
27. HAFEZ · *The nightingales are drunk*
28. GEOFFREY CHAUCER · *The Wife of Bath*
29. MICHEL DE MONTAIGNE · *How We Weep and Laugh at the Same Thing*
30. THOMAS NASHE · *The Terrors of the Night*
31. EDGAR ALLAN POE · *The Tell-Tale Heart*
32. MARY KINGSLEY · *A Hippo Banquet*
33. JANE AUSTEN · *The Beautifull Cassandra*
34. ANTON CHEKHOV · *Gooseberries*
35. SAMUEL TAYLOR COLERIDGE · *Well, they are gone, and here must I remain*
36. JOHANN WOLFGANG VON GOETHE · *Sketchy, Doubtful, Incomplete Jottings*
37. CHARLES DICKENS · *The Great Winglebury Duel*
38. HERMAN MELVILLE · *The Maldive Shark*
39. ELIZABETH GASKELL · *The Old Nurse's Story*
40. NIKOLAY LESKOV · *The Steel Flea*

41. HONORÉ DE BALZAC · *The Atheist's Mass*
42. CHARLOTTE PERKINS GILMAN · *The Yellow Wall-Paper*
43. C.P. CAVAFY · *Remember, Body . . .*
44. FYODOR DOSTOEVSKY · *The Meek One*
45. GUSTAVE FLAUBERT · *A Simple Heart*
46. NIKOLAI GOGOL · *The Nose*
47. SAMUEL PEPYS · *The Great Fire of London*
48. EDITH WHARTON · *The Reckoning*
49. HENRY JAMES · *The Figure in the Carpet*
50. WILFRED OWEN · *Anthem For Doomed Youth*
51. WOLFGANG AMADEUS MOZART · *My Dearest Father*
52. PLATO · *Socrates' Defence*
53. CHRISTINA ROSSETTI · *Goblin Market*
54. *Sindbad the Sailor*
55. SOPHOCLES · *Antigone*
56. RYŪNOSUKE AKUTAGAWA · *The Life of a Stupid Man*
57. LEO TOLSTOY · *How Much Land Does A Man Need?*
58. GIORGIO VASARI · *Leonardo da Vinci*
59. OSCAR WILDE · *Lord Arthur Savile's Crime*
60. SHEN FU · *The Old Man of the Moon*
61. AESOP · *The Dolphins, the Whales and the Gudgeon*
62. MATSUO BASHŌ · *Lips too Chilled*
63. EMILY BRONTË · *The Night is Darkening Round Me*
64. JOSEPH CONRAD · *To-morrow*
65. RICHARD HAKLUYT · *The Voyage of Sir Francis Drake Around the Whole Globe*
66. KATE CHOPIN · *A Pair of Silk Stockings*
67. CHARLES DARWIN · *It was snowing butterflies*
68. BROTHERS GRIMM · *The Robber Bridegroom*
69. CATULLUS · *I Hate and I Love*
70. HOMER · *Circe and the Cyclops*
71. D. H. LAWRENCE · *Il Duro*
72. KATHERINE MANSFIELD · *Miss Brill*
73. OVID · *The Fall of Icarus*
74. SAPPHO · *Come Close*
75. IVAN TURGENEV · *Kasyan from the Beautiful Lands*
76. VIRGIL · *O Cruel Alexis*
77. H. G. WELLS · *A Slip under the Microscope*
78. HERODOTUS · *The Madness of Cambyses*
79. *Speaking of Siva*
80. *The Dhammapada*

'While engaged on this hunt I felt the earth quiver under my feet, and heard a soft big soughing sound, and looking round saw I had dropped in on a hippo banquet'

MARY KINGSLEY
Born 1862, London, England
Died 1900, Simonstown, South Africa

Selection taken from *Travels in West Africa*,
first published in 1897.

KINGSLEY IN PENGUIN CLASSICS
Travels in West Africa

MARY KINGSLEY

A Hippo Banquet

PENGUIN BOOKS

PENGUIN CLASSICS

UK | USA | Canada | Ireland | Australia
India | New Zealand | South Africa

Penguin Books is part of the Penguin Random House group of companies
whose addresses can be found at global.penguinrandomhouse.com.

This selection published in Penguin Classics 2015

008

Set in 9/12.4 pt Baskerville 10 Pro
Typeset by Jouve (UK), Milton Keynes
Printed and bound in Great Britain by Clays Ltd, Elcograf S.p.A.

A CIP catalogue record for this book is available from the British Library

ISBN: 978-0-141-39728-3

www.greenpenguin.co.uk

Penguin Random House is committed to a sustainable future for our business, our readers and our planet. This book is made from Forest Stewardship Council® certified paper.

Contents

A Hippo Banquet	1
Five Gorillas	27
Elephant Hunt	43
Fight with a Leopard	48

A Hippo Banquet

Tuesday, July 23rd. – Am aroused by violent knocking at the door in the early gray dawn – so violent that two large centipedes and a scorpion drop on to the bed. They have evidently been tucked away among the folds of the bar all night. Well 'when ignorance is bliss 'tis folly to be wise,' particularly along here. I get up without delay, and find myself quite well. The cat has thrown a basin of water neatly over into my bag during her nocturnal hunts; and when my tea comes I am informed a man 'done die' in the night, which explains the firing of guns I heard. I inquire what he has died of, and am told 'He just truck luck, and then he die.' His widows are having their faces painted white by sympathetic lady friends, and are attired in their oldest, dirtiest clothes, and but very few of them; still, they seem to be taking things in a resigned spirit. These Ajumba seem pleasant folk. They play with their pretty brown children in a taking way. Last night I noticed some men and women playing a game new to me, which consisted in throwing a hoop at each other. The point was to get the hoop to fall over your adversary's head. It is a cheerful game. Quantities of the common house-fly about – and, during the early part of the morning, it rains in a gentle kind of way; but soon after we are afloat in our canoe it turns into a soft white mist.

We paddle still westwards down the broad quiet waters of

the O'Rembo Vongo. I notice great quantities of birds about here – great hornbills, vividly coloured kingfishers, and for the first time the great vulture I have often heard of, and the skin of which I will take home before I mention even its approximate spread of wing. There are also noble white cranes, and flocks of small black and white birds, new to me, with heavy razor-shaped bills, reminding one of the Devonian puffin. The hornbill is perhaps the most striking in appearance. It is the size of a small, or say a good-sized hen-turkey. Gray Shirt says the flocks, which are of eight or ten, always have the same quantity of cocks and hens, and that they live together 'white man fashion,' *i.e.*, each couple keeping together. They certainly do a great deal of courting, the cock filling out his wattles on his neck like a turkey, and spreading out his tail with great pomp and ceremony, but very awkwardly. To see hornbills on a bare sandbank is a solemn sight, but when they are dodging about in the hippo grass they sink ceremony, and roll and waddle, looking – my man said – for snakes and the little sand-fish, which are close in under the bank; and their killing way of dropping their jaws – I should say opening their bills – when they are alarmed is comic. I think this has something to do with their hearing, for I often saw two or three of them in a line on a long branch, standing, stretched up to their full height, their great eyes opened wide, and all with their great beaks open, evidently listening for something. Their cry is most peculiar and can only be mistaken for a native horn; and although there seems little variety in it to my ear, there must be more to theirs, for they will carry on long confabulations with each other across a river, and, I believe, sit up half the night and talk scandal.

There were plenty of plantain-eaters here, but, although their screech was as appalling as I have heard in Angola, they were not regarded, by the Ajumba at any rate, as being birds of evil omen, as they are in Angola. Still, by no means all the birds here only screech and squark. Several of them have very lovely notes. There is one who always gives a series of infinitely beautiful, soft, rich-toned whistles just before the first light of the dawn shows in the sky, and one at least who has a prolonged and very lovely song. This bird, I was told in Gaboon, is called *Telephonus erythropterus*. I expect an ornithologist would enjoy himself here, but I cannot – and will not – collect birds. I hate to have them killed any how, and particularly in the barbarous way in which these natives kill them.

The broad stretch of water looks like a long lake. In all directions sandbanks are showing their broad yellow backs, and there will be more showing soon, for it is not yet the height of the dry. We are perpetually grounding on those which by next month will be above water. These canoes are built, I believe, more with a view to taking sandbanks comfortably than anything else; but they are by no means yet sufficiently specialised for getting off them. Their flat bottoms enable them to glide on to the banks, and sit there, without either upsetting or cutting into the sand, as a canoe with a keel would; but the trouble comes in when you are getting off the steep edge of the bank, and the usual form it takes is upsetting. So far my Ajumba friends have only tried to meet this difficulty by tying the cargo in.

Mary Kingsley

I try to get up the geography of this region conscientiously. Fortunately I find Gray Shirt, Singlet, and Pagan can speak trade English; for my interpreter's knowledge of that language seems confined to 'Praps,' ''Tis better so,' and 'Lordy, Lordy, helpee me' – a valueless vocabulary. None of them, however, seem to recognise a single blessed name on the chart, which is saying nothing against the chart and its makers, who probably got their names up from M'pongwes and Igalwas instead of Ajumba, as I am trying to. Geographical research in this region is fraught with difficulty, I find, owing to different tribes calling one and the same place by different names; and I am sure the Royal Geographical Society ought to insert among their 'Hints' that every traveller in this region should carefully learn every separate native word, or set of words, signifying 'I don't know,' – four villages and two rivers I have come across out here solemnly set down with various forms of this statement, for their native name. Really I think the old Portuguese way of naming places after Saints, &c., was wiser in the long run, and it was certainly pleasanter to the ears. My Ajumba, however, know about my Ngambi and the Vinue all right and Elivã z' Ayzingo, so I must try and get cross bearings from these.

We have an addition to our crew this morning – a man who wants to go and get work at John Holt's sub-factory away on the Rembwé. He has been waiting a long while at Arevooma, unable to get across, I am told, 'because the road is now stopped between Ayzingo and the Rembwé by "those fearful Fans."' 'How are we going to get through that way?' says I, with natural feminine alarm. 'We are not, sir,' says Gray Shirt. This is what Lady MacDonald would term a

A Hippo Banquet

chatty little incident; and my hair begins to rise as I remember what I have been told about those Fans and the indications I have already seen of its being true when on the Upper Ogowé. Now here we are going to try to get through the heart of their country, far from a French station, and without the French flag. Why did I not obey Mr Hudson's orders not to go wandering about in a reckless way! Anyhow I am in for it, and Fortune favours the brave. The only question is: Do I individually come under this class? I go into details. It seems Pagan thinks he can depend on the friendship of two Fans he once met and did business with, and who now live on an island in Lake Ncovi – Ncovi is not down on my map and I have never heard of it before – anyhow thither we are bound now.

Each man has brought with him his best gun, loaded to the muzzle, and tied on to the baggage against which I am leaning – the muzzles sticking out each side of my head: the flint locks covered with cases, or sheaths, made of the black-haired skins of gorillas, leopard skin, and a beautiful bright bay skin, which I do not know, which they say is bush cow – but they call half a dozen things bush cow. These guns are not the 'gas-pipes' I have seen up north; but decent rifles which have had the rifling filed out and the locks replaced by flint locks and converted into muzzle loaders, and many of them have beautiful barrels. I find the Ajumba name for the beautiful shrub that has long bunches of red yellow and cream-coloured young leaves at the end of its branches is 'obãa.' I also learn that in their language ebony and a monkey have one name. The forest on either bank is very lovely. Some enormously high columns of green are formed by a sort of climbing plant having taken possession of lightning-struck trees, and in one place it really looks exactly as if some one had spread a great green coverlet over the forest, so as to keep it dry. No high land showing in any direction. Pagan tells me the extinguisher-shaped juju filled with medicine and made of iron is against drowning – the red juju is 'for keep foot in path.' Beautiful effect of a gleam of sunshine lighting up a red sandbank till it glows like the Nibelungen gold. Indeed the effects are Turneresque to-day owing to the mist, and the sun playing in and out among it.

The sandbanks now have their cliffs to the N. N. W. and N. W. At 9.30, the broad river in front of us is apparently closed by sandbanks which run out from the banks thus: – yellow S. bank bright-red yellow N. bank. Current running strong along south bank. This bank bears testimony of this also being the case in the wet season, for a fringe of torn-down trees hangs from it into the river. Pass Seke, a town on north bank, interchanging the usual observations regarding our destination. The river seems absolutely barred with sand again; but as we paddle down it, the obstructions resolve themselves into spits of sand from the north bank and the largest island in mid-stream, which also has a long tail, or train, of sandbank down river. Here we meet a picturesque series of canoes, fruit and trade laden, being poled up stream, one man with his pole over one side, the other with his pole over the other, making a St Andrew's cross as you meet them end on.

Most luxurious, charming, and pleasant trip this. The men are standing up swinging in rhythmic motion their long, rich red wood paddles in perfect time to their elaborate melancholy, minor key boat song. Nearly lost with all hands. Sandbank palaver – only when we were going over the end of it, slipped sideways over its edge. River deep, bottom sand and mud. This information may be interesting to the geologist, but I hope I shall not be converted by circumstances into a human sounding apparatus again to-day. Next time she strikes I shall get out and shove behind.

We are now skirting the real north bank, and not the bank of an island or islands as we have been for some time here-tofore. Lovely stream falls into this river over cascades. The water is now rough in a small way and the width of the river great, but it soon is crowded again with wooded islands. There are patches and wreaths of a lovely, vermilion-flowering bush rope decorating the forest, and now and again clumps of a plant that shows a yellow and crimson spike of bloom, very strikingly beautiful. We pass a long tunnel in the bush, quite dark as you look down it – evidently the path to some native town. The south bank is covered, where the falling waters have exposed it, with hippo grass. Terrible lot of mangrove flies about, although we are more than one hundred miles above the mangrove belt. River broad again – tending W. S. W., with a broad flattened island with attributive sandbanks in the middle. The fair way is along the south bank of the river. Gray Shirt tells me this river is called the O'Rembo Vongo, or small River, so as to distinguish it from the main stream of the Ogowé which goes down past the south side of Lembarene Island, as well I know after that canoe affair of mine. Ayzingo now bears due north – and native mahogany is called 'Okooma.' Pass village called Welli on north bank. It looks like some gipsy caravans stuck on poles. I expect that village has known what it means to be swamped by the rising river; it looks as if it had, very hastily in the middle of some night, taken to stilts, which I am sure, from their present rickety condition, will not last through the next wet season, and then some unfortunate spirit will get the blame of the collapse. I also learn that it is the natal spot of my friend Kabinda, the carpenter at Andande. Now if some of these good people I know would only go and distinguish themselves, I might write a sort of county family history of these parts; but they don't, and I fancy won't. For example, the entrance – or should I say the exit? – of a broadish little river is just away on the south bank. If you go up this river – it runs S. E. – you get to a good-sized lake; in this lake there is an island called Adole; then out of the other side of the lake there is another river which falls into the Ogowé main stream – but that is not the point of the story, which is that on that island of Adole, Ngouta, the interpreter, first saw the light. Why he ever did – there or anywhere – Heaven only knows! I know I shall never want to write his biography.

On the western bank end of that river going to Adole, there is an Igalwa town, notable for a large quantity of fine white ducks and a clump of Indian bamboo. My informants say, 'No white man ever live for this place,' so I suppose the ducks and bamboo have been imported by some black trader whose natal spot this is. The name of this village is Wande-regwoma. Stuck on sandbank – I flew out and shoved behind, leaving Ngouta to do the balancing performances in the stern. This O'Rembo Vongo divides up just below here, I am told, when we have re-embarked, into three streams. One goes into the main Ogowé opposite Ayshouka in Nkami country – Nkami country commences at Ayshouka and goes to the sea – one into the Ngumbi, and one into the Nunghi – all in the Ouroungou country. Ayzingo now lies N. E. according to Gray Shirt's arm. On our river there is here another broad low island with its gold-coloured banks shining out, seemingly barring the entire channel, but there is really a canoe channel along by both banks.

We turn at this point into a river on the north bank that runs north and south – the current is running very swift to the north. We run down into it, and then, it being more than time enough for chop, we push the canoe on to a sandbank in our new river, which I am told is the Karkola. I, after having had my tea, wander off. I find behind our high sandbank, which like all the other sandbanks above water now, is getting grown over with hippo grass – a fine light green grass, the beloved food of both hippo and manatee – a forest, and entering this I notice a succession of strange mounds or heaps, made up of branches, twigs, and leaves, and dead flowers. Many of these heaps are recent, while others have fallen into decay. Investigation shows they are burial places. Among the *débris* of an old one there are human bones, and out from one of the new ones comes a stench and a hurrying, exceedingly busy line of ants, demonstrating what is going on. I own I thought these mounds were some kind of bird's or animal's nest. They look entirely unhuman in this desolate reach of forest. Leaving these, I go down to the water edge of the sand, and find in it a quantity of pools of varying breadth and expanse, but each surrounded by a rim of dark red-brown deposit, which you can lift off the sand in a skin. On the top of the water is a film of exquisite iridescent colours like those on a soap bubble, only darker and brighter. In the river alongside the sand, there are thousands of those beautiful little fish with a black line each side of their tails. They are perfectly tame, and I feed them with crumbs in my hand. After making every effort to terrify the unknown object containing the food – gallant bulls, quite two inches long, sidling up and snapping at my fingers – they come and feed right in the palm, so that I could have caught them by the handful had I wished. There are also a lot of those weird, semi-transparent, yellow, spotted little sand-fish with cupshaped pectoral fins, which I see they use to enable them to make their astoundingly long leaps. These fish are of a more nervous and distrustful disposition, and hover round my hand but will not come into it. Indeed I do not believe the other cheeky little fellows would allow them to. They have grand butting matches among themselves, which wind up with a most comic tail fight, each combatant spinning round and going in for a spanking match with his adversary with his pretty little red-edged tail – the red rim round it and round his gill covers going claret-coloured with fury. I did not make out how you counted points in these fights – no one seemed a scale the worse.

The men, having had their rest and their pipes, shout for me, and off we go again. The Karkola soon widens to about 100 feet; it is evidently very deep here; the right bank (the east) is forested, the left, low and shrubbed, one patch looking as if it were being cleared for a plantation, but no village showing. A big rock shows up on the right bank, which is a

A Hippo Banquet

change from the clay and sand, and soon the whole character of the landscape changes. We come to a sharp turn in the river, from north and south to east and west – the current very swift. The river channel dodges round against a big bank of sword grass, and then widens out to the breadth of the Thames at Putney. I am told that a river runs out of it here to the west to Ouroungou country, and so I imagine this Karkola falls ultimately into the Nazareth. We skirt the eastern banks, which are covered with low grass with a scanty lot of trees along the top. High land shows in the distance to the S. S. W. and S. W., and then we suddenly turn up into a broad river or straith, shaping our course N. N. E. On the opposite bank, on a high dwarf cliff, is a Fan town. 'All Fan now,' says Singlet in anything but a gratified tone of voice.

It is a strange, wild, lonely bit of the world we are now in, apparently a lake or broad – full of sandbanks, some bare and some in the course of developing into permanent islands by the growth on them of that floating coarse grass, any joint of which being torn off either by the current, a passing canoe, or hippos, floats down and grows wherever it settles. Like most things that float in these parts, it usually settles on a sandbank, and then grows in much the same way as our couch grass grows on land in England, so as to form a network, which catches for its adopted sandbank all sorts of floating *débris*; so the sandbank comes up in the world. The waters of the wet season when they rise drown off the grass; but when they fall, up it comes again from the root, and so gradually the sandbank becomes an island and persuades real trees and shrubs to come and grow on it, and its future is then secured.

Mary Kingsley

We skirt alongside a great young island of this class; the sword grass some ten or fifteen feet high. It has not got any trees on it yet, but by next season or so it doubtless will have. The grass is stubbled down into paths by hippos, and just as I have realised who are the road-makers, they appear in person. One immense fellow, hearing us, stands up and shows himself about six feet from us in the grass, gazes calmly, and then yawns a yawn a yard wide and grunts his news to his companions, some of whom – there is evidently a large herd – get up and stroll towards us with all the flowing grace of Pantechnicon vans in motion. We put our helm paddles hard a starboard and leave that bank. These hippos always look to me as if they were the first or last creations in the animal world. At present I am undecided whether Nature tried 'her 'prentice hand' on them in her earliest youth, or whether, having got thoroughly tired of making the delicately beautiful antelopes, corallines, butterflies, and orchids, she just said: 'Goodness! I am quite worn out with this finicking work. Here, just put these other viscera into big bags – I can't bother any more.'

Our hasty trip across to the bank of the island on the other side being accomplished, we, in search of seclusion and in the hope that out of sight would mean out of mind to hippos, shot down a narrow channel between semi-island sandbanks, and those sandbanks, if you please, are covered with specimens – as fine a set of specimens as you could wish for – of the West African crocodile. These interesting animals are also having their siestas, lying sprawling in all directions on the sand, with their mouths wide open. One immense old lady has a family of lively young crocodiles running over

A Hippo Banquet

her, evidently playing like a lot of kittens. The heavy musky smell they give off is most repulsive, but we do not rise up and make a row about this, because we feel hopelessly in the wrong in intruding into these family scenes uninvited, and so apologetically pole ourselves along rapidly, not even singing. The pace the canoe goes down that channel would be a wonder to Henley Regatta. When out of ear-shot I ask Pagan whether there are many gorillas, elephants, or bush-cows round here. 'Plenty too much,' says he; and it occurs to me that the corn-fields are growing golden green away in England; and soon there rises up in my mental vision a picture that fascinated my youth in the *Fliegende Blätter* representing 'Friedrich Gerstaeker auf der Reise.' That gallant man is depicted tramping on a serpent, new to M. Boulenger, while he attempts to club, with the butt end of his gun, a most lively savage who, accompanied by a bison, is attacking him in front. A terrific and obviously enthusiastic crocodile is grabbing the tail of the explorer's coat, and the explorer says 'Hurrah! das gibt wieder einen prächtigen Artikel für *Die Allgemeine Zeitung.*' I do not know where in the world Gerstaeker was at the time, but I should fancy hereabouts. My vigorous and lively conscience also reminds me that the last words a most distinguished and valued scientific friend had said to me before I left home was, 'Always take measurements, Miss Kingsley, and always take them from the adult male.' I know I have neglected opportunities of carrying this commission out on both those banks, but I do not feel like going back. Besides, the men would not like it, and I have mislaid my yard measure.

The extent of water, dotted with sandbanks and islands in

all directions, here is great, and seems to be fringed uniformly by low swampy land, beyond which, to the north, rounded lumps of hills show blue. On one of the islands is a little white house which I am told was once occupied by a black trader for John Holt. It looks a desolate place for any man to live in, and the way the crocodiles and hippo must have come up on the garden ground in the evening time could not have enhanced its charms to the average cautious man. My men say, 'No man live for that place now.' The factory, I believe, has been, for some trade reason, abandoned. Behind it is a great clump of dark-coloured trees. The rest of the island is now covered with hippo grass looking like a beautifully kept lawn. We lie up for a short rest at another island, also a weird spot in its way, for it is covered with a grove of only one kind of tree, which has a twisted, contorted, gray-white trunk and dull, lifeless-looking, green, hard foliage.

I learn that these good people, to make topographical confusion worse confounded, call a river by one name when you are going up it, and by another when you are coming down; just as if you called the Thames the London when you were going up, and the Greenwich when you were coming down. The banks all round this lake or broad, seem all light-coloured sand and clay. We pass out of it into a channel. Current flowing north. As we are entering the channel between banks of grass-overgrown sand, a superb white crane is seen standing on the sand edge to the left. Gray Shirt attempts to get a shot at it, but it – alarmed at our unusual appearance – raises itself up with one of those graceful preliminary curtseys, and after one or two preliminary flaps

A Hippo Banquet

spreads its broad wings and sweeps away, with its long legs trailing behind it like a thing on a Japanese screen. Gray Shirt does not fire, but puts down his gun on the baggage again with its muzzle nestling against my left ear. A minute afterwards we strike a bank, and bang goes off the gun, deafening me, singeing my hair and the side of my face slightly. Fortunately the two men in front are at the moment in the recumbent position attributive to the shock of the canoe jarring against the cliff edge of a bank, or they would have had a miscellaneous collection of bits of broken iron pots and lumps of lead frisking among their vitals. It is a little difficult to make out how much credit Providence really deserves in this affair, but a good deal. Of course if It had taken the trouble to keep us off the bank, or to remind Gray Shirt to uncock his weapon, the thing would not have happened at all, but preliminary precaution is not Providence's peculiarity. Still, when the thing happened It certainly rose to it. I might have had the back of my head blown out, and the men might have been killed. I only hope this won't confirm Pagan permanently into superstition; for only a few minutes before, he had been showing me a big charm to keep him from being hurt by a gun. If he thinks about it, he will see there is nothing in the charm, because the other man who equally escaped was a charmless Christian.

The river into which we ran zig-zags about, and then takes a course S. S. E. It is studded with islands slightly higher than those we have passed, and thinly clad with forest. The place seems alive with birds; flocks of pelican and crane rise up before us out of the grass, and every now and then a crocodile slides off the bank into the water. Wonderfully like old logs they look, particularly when you see one letting himself roll and float down on the current. In spite of these interests I began to wonder where in this lonely land we were to sleep to-night. In front of us were miles of distant mountains, but in no direction the slightest sign of human habitation. Soon we passed out of our channel into a lovely, strangely melancholy, lonely-looking lake – Lake Ncovi, my friends tell me. It is exceedingly beautiful. The rich golden sunlight of the late afternoon soon followed by the short-lived, glorious flushes of colour of the sunset and the after-glow, play over the scene as we paddle across the lake to the N. N. E. – our canoe leaving a long trail of frosted silver behind her as she glides over the mirror-like water, and each stroke of the paddle sending down air with it to come up again in luminous silver bubbles – not as before in swirls of sand and mud. The lake shore is, in all directions, wreathed with nobly forested hills, indigo and purple in the dying daylight. On the N. N. E. and N. E. these come directly down into the lake; on N. W., N., S. W. and S. E. there is a band of well-forested ground, behind which they rise. In the north and north-eastern part of the lake several exceedingly beautiful wooded islands show, with gray rocky beaches and dwarf cliffs.

Sign of human habitation at first there was none; and in spite of its beauty, there was something which I was almost going to say was repulsive. The men evidently felt the same as I did. Had any one told me that the air that lay on the lake was poison, or that in among its forests lay some path to regions of utter death, I should have said – 'It looks like that'; but no one said anything, and we only looked round

A Hippo Banquet

uneasily, until the comfortable-souled Singlet made the unfortunate observation that he 'smelt blood.' We all called him an utter fool to relieve our minds, and made our way towards the second island. When we got near enough to it to see details, a large village showed among the trees on its summit, and a steep dwarf cliff, overgrown with trees and creeping plants came down to a small beach covered with large water-washed gray stones. There was evidently some kind of a row going on in that village, that took a lot of shouting too. We made straight for the beach, and drove our canoe among its outlying rocks, and then each of my men stowed his paddle quickly, slung on his ammunition bag, and picked up his ready loaded gun, sliding the skin sheath off the lock. Pagan got out on to the stones alongside the canoe just as the inhabitants became aware of our arrival, and, abandoning what I hope was a mass meeting to remonstrate with the local authorities on the insanitary state of the town, came – a brown mass of naked humanity – down the steep cliff path to attend to us, whom they evidently regarded as an imperial interest. Things did not look restful, nor these Fans personally pleasant. Every man among them – no women showed – was armed with a gun, and they loosened their shovel-shaped knives in their sheaths as they came, evidently regarding a fight quite as imminent as we did. They drew up about twenty paces from us in silence. Pagan and Gray Shirt, who had joined him, held out their unembarrassed hands, and shouted out the name of the Fan man they had said they were friendly with: 'Kiva-Kiva.' The Fans stood still and talked angrily among themselves for some minutes, and then, Silence said to me, 'It would be bad palaver if Kiva no live for this place,' in a tone that conveyed to me the idea he thought this unpleasant contingency almost a certainty. The Passenger exhibited unmistakable symptoms of wishing he had come by another boat. I got up from my seat in the bottom of the canoe and leisurely strolled ashore, saying to the line of angry faces 'M'boloani' in an unconcerned way, although I well knew it was etiquette for them to salute first. They grunted, but did not commit themselves further. A minute after they parted to allow a fine-looking, middle-aged man, naked save for a twist of dirty cloth round his loins and a bunch of leopard and wild cat tails hung from his shoulder by a strip of leopard skin, to come forward. Pagan went for him with a rush, as if he were going to clasp him to his ample bosom, but holding his hands just off from touching the Fan's shoulder in the usual way, while he said in Fan, 'Don't you know me, my beloved Kiva? Surely you have not forgotten your old friend?' Kiva grunted feelingly, and raised up his hands and held them just off touching Pagan, and we breathed again. Then Gray Shirt made a rush at the crowd and went through great demonstrations of affection with another gentleman whom he recognised as being a Fan friend of his own, and whom he had not expected to meet here. I looked round to see if there was not any Fan from the Upper Ogowé whom I knew to go for, but could not see one that I could on the strength of a previous acquaintance, and on their individual merits I did not feel inclined to do even this fashionable imitation embrace. Indeed I must say that never – even in a picture book – have I seen such a set of wild wicked-looking savages as those we faced this night, and with whom it was

A Hippo Banquet

touch-and-go for twenty of the longest minutes I have ever lived, whether we fought – for our lives, I was going to say, but it would not have been even for that, but merely for the price of them.

Peace having been proclaimed, conversation became general. Gray Shirt brought his friend up and introduced him to me, and we shook hands and smiled at each other in the conventional way. Pagan's friend, who was next introduced, was more alarming, for he held his hands for half a minute just above my elbows without quite touching me, but he meant well; and then we all disappeared into a brown mass of humanity and a fog of noise. You would have thought, from the violence and vehemence of the shouting and gesticulation, that we were going to be forthwith torn to shreds; but not a single hand really touched me, and as I, Pagan, and Gray Shirt went up to the town in the midst of the throng, the crowd opened in front and closed in behind, evidently half frightened at my appearance. The row when we reached the town redoubled in volume from the fact that the ladies, the children and the dogs joined in. Every child in the place as soon as it saw my white face let a howl out of it as if it had seen his Satanic Majesty, horns, hoofs, tail and all, and fled into the nearest hut, headlong, and I fear, from the continuance of the screams, had fits. The town was exceedingly filthy – the remains of the crocodile they had been eating the week before last, and piles of fish offal, and remains of an elephant hippo or manatee – I really can't say which, decomposition was too far advanced – united to form a most impressive stench. The bark huts are, as usual in a Fan town, in unbroken rows; but there are three or four streets here, not one only, as in most cases. The palaver house is in the innermost street, and there we went, and noticed that the village view was not in the direction in which we had come, but across towards the other side of the lake. I told the Ajumba to explain we wanted hospitality for the night, and wished to hire three carriers for to-morrow to go with us to the Rembwé.

For an hour and three-quarters by my watch I stood in the suffocating, smoky, hot atmosphere listening to, but only faintly understanding, the war of words and gesture that raged round us. At last the fact that we were to be received being settled, Gray Shirt's friend led us out of the guard house – the crowd flinching back as I came through it – to his own house on the right-hand side of the street of huts. It was a very different dwelling to Gray Shirt's residence at Arevooma. I was as high as its roof ridge and had to stoop low to get through the door-hole. Inside, the hut was fourteen or fifteen feet square, unlit by any window. The door-hole could be closed by pushing a broad piece of bark across it under two horizontally fixed bits of stick. The floor was sand like the street outside, but dirtier. On it in one place was a fire, whose smoke found its way out through the roof. In one corner of the room was a rough bench of wood, which from the few filthy cloths on it and a wood pillow I saw was the bed. There was no other furniture in the hut save some boxes, which I presume held my host's earthly possessions. From the bamboo roof hung a long stick with hooks on it, the hooks made by cutting off branching twigs. This was evidently the hanging wardrobe, and on it hung some few fetish charms, and a beautiful ornament of wild cat and leopard tails, tied on to a square piece of leopard skin, in the centre of which was a little mirror, and round the mirror were sewn dozens of common shirt buttons. In among the tails hung three little brass bells and a brass rattle; these bells and rattles are not only 'for dandy,' but serve to scare away snakes when the ornament is worn in the forest. A fine strip of silky-haired, young gorilla skin made the band to sling the ornament from the shoulder when worn. Gorillas seem well enough known round here. One old lady in the crowd outside, I saw, had a necklace made of sixteen gorilla canine teeth slung on a pineapple fibre string. Gray Shirt explained to me that this is the best house in the village, and my host the most renowned elephant hunter in the district.

We then returned to the canoe, whose occupants had been getting uneasy about the way affairs were going 'on top,' on account of the uproar they heard and the time we had been away. We got into the canoe and took her round the little promontory at the end of the island to the other beach, which is the main beach. By arriving at the beach when we did, we took our Fan friends in the rear, and they did not see us coming in the gloaming. This was all for the best it seems, as they said they should have fired on us before they had had time to see we were rank outsiders, on the apprehension that we were coming from one of the Fan towns we had passed, and with whom they were on bad terms regarding a lady who bolted there from her lawful lord, taking with her – cautious soul! – a quantity of rubber. The only white man who had been here before in the memory of man, was a French officer who paid Kiva six dollars to take him somewhere, I was told – but I could not find out when, or what happened to that Frenchman. It was a long time ago, Kiva said, but these folks have no definite way of expressing duration of time nor, do I believe, any great mental idea of it; although their ideas are, as usual with West Africans, far ahead of their language.

All the goods were brought up to my hut, and while Ngouta gets my tea we started talking the carrier palaver again. The Fans received my offer, starting at two dollars ahead of what M. Jacot said would be enough, with utter scorn, and every dramatic gesture of dissent; one man, pretending to catch Gray Shirt's words in his hands, flings them to the ground and stamps them under his feet. I affected an easy take-it-or-leave-it-manner, and looked on. A woman came out of the crowd to me, and held out a mass of slimy gray abomination on a bit of plantain leaf – smashed snail. I accepted it and gave her fish hooks. She was delighted and her companions excited, so she put them into her mouth for safe keeping. I hurriedly explained in my best Fan that I do not require any more snail; so another lady tried the effect of a pineapple. There might be no end to this, so I retired into trade and asked what she would sell it for. She did not want to sell it – she wanted to give it me; so I gave her fish hooks. Silence and Singlet interposed, saying the price for pineapples is one leaf of tobacco, but I explained I was not buying. Ngouta turned up with my tea, so I went inside, and had it on the bed. The door-hole was entirely filled with a mosaic of faces, but no one attempted to come in. All the time the carrier palaver went on without cessation, and I went out and offered to take Gray Shirt's and Pagan's place, knowing they must want their chop, but they refused relief,

A Hippo Banquet

and also said I must not raise the price; I was offering too big a price now, and if I once rise the Fan will only think I will keep on rising, and so make the palaver longer to talk. 'How long does a palaver usually take to talk round here?' I ask. 'The last one I talked,' says Pagan, 'took three weeks, and that was only a small price palaver.' 'Well,' say I, 'my price is for a start to-morrow – after then I have no price – after that I go away.' Another hour how ever sees the jam made, and to my surprise I find the three richest men in this town of M'fetta have personally taken up the contract – Kiva my host, Fika a fine young fellow, and Wiki, another noted elephant hunter. These three Fans, the four Ajumba and the Igalwa, Ngouta, I think will be enough. Moreover I fancy it safer not to have an overpowering percentage of Fans in the party, as I know we shall have considerable stretches of uninhabited forest to traverse; and the Ajumba say that the Fans will kill people, *i.e.*, the black traders who venture into their country, and cut them up into neat pieces, eat what they want at the time, and smoke the rest of the bodies for future use. Now I do not want to arrive at the Rembwé in a smoked condition, even should my fragments be neat, and I am going in a different direction to what I said I was when leaving Kangwe, and there are so many ways of accounting for death about here – leopard, canoe capsize, elephants, &c. – that even if I were traced – well, nothing could be done then, anyhow – so will only take three Fans. One must diminish dead certainties to the level of sporting chances along here, or one can never get on.

No one, either Ajumba or Fan, knew the exact course we were to take. The Ajumba had never been this way before – the way for black traders across being *viâ* Lake Ayzingo, the way Mr Goode of the American Mission once went, and the Fans said they only knew the way to a big Fan town called Efoua, where no white man or black trader had yet been. There is a path from there to the Rembwé they knew, because the Efoua people take their trade all to the Rembwé. They would, they said, come with me all the way if I would guarantee them safety if they 'found war' on the road. This I agreed to do, and arranged to pay off at Hatton and Cookson's sub-factory on the Rembwé, and they have 'Look my mouth and it be sweet, so palaver done set.' Every load then, by the light of the bush lights held by the women, we arranged. I had to unpack my bottles of fishes so as to equalise the weight of the loads. Every load is then made into a sort of cocoon with bush rope.

I was left in peace at about 11.30 P. M., and clearing off the clothes from the bench threw myself down and tried to get some sleep, for we were to start, the Fans said, before dawn. Sleep impossible – mosquitoes! lice!! – so at 12.40 I got up and slid aside my bark door. I found Pagan asleep under his mosquito bar outside, across the doorway, but managed to get past him without rousing him from his dreams of palaver which he was still talking aloud, and reconnoitred the town. The inhabitants seemed to have talked themselves quite out and were sleeping heavily. I went down then to our canoe and found it safe, high up among the Fan canoes on the stones, and then I slid a small Fan canoe off, and taking a paddle from a cluster stuck in the sand, paddled out on to the dark lake.

It was a wonderfully lovely quiet night with no light save

A Hippo Banquet

that from the stars. One immense planet shone pre-eminent in the purple sky, throwing a golden path down on to the still waters. Quantities of big fish sprung out of the water, their glistening silver-white scales flashing so that they look like slashing swords. Some bird was making a long, low boom-booming sound away on the forest shore. I paddled leisurely across the lake to the shore on the right, and seeing crawling on the ground some large glow-worms, drove the canoe on to the bank among some hippo grass, and got out to get them.

While engaged on this hunt I felt the earth quiver under my feet, and heard a soft big soughing sound, and looking round saw I had dropped in on a hippo banquet. I made out five of the immense brutes round me, so I softly returned to the canoe and shoved off, stealing along the bank, paddling under water, until I deemed it safe to run out across the lake for my island. I reached the other end of it to that on which the village is situated; and finding a miniature rocky bay with a soft patch of sand and no hippo grass, the incidents of the Fan hut suggested the advisability of a bath. Moreover, there was no china collection in that hut, and it would be a long time before I got another chance, so I go ashore again, and, carefully investigating the neighbourhood to make certain there was no human habitation near, I then indulged in a wash in peace. Drying one's self on one's cummerbund is not pure joy, but it can be done when you put your mind to it. While I was finishing my toilet I saw a strange thing happen. Down through the forest on the lake bank opposite came a violet ball the size of a small orange. When it reached the sand beach it hovered along it to and fro close to the ground. In a few minutes another ball of similarly coloured light came towards it from behind one of the islets, and the two waver to and fro over the beach, sometimes circling round each other. I made off towards them in the canoe, thinking – as I still do – they were some brand new kind of luminous insect. When I got on to their beach one of them went off into the bushes and the other away over the water. I followed in the canoe, for the water here is very deep, and, when I almost thought I had got it, it went down into the water and I could see it glowing as it sunk until it vanished in the depths. I made my way back hastily, fearing my absence with the canoe might give rise, if discovered, to trouble, and by 3.30 I was back in the hut safe, but not so comfortable as I had been on the lake. A little before five my men are stirring and I get my tea. I do not state my escapade to them, but ask what those lights were. 'Akom,' said the Fan, and pointing to the shore of the lake where I had been during the night they said, 'they came there, it was an "Aku"' – or devil bush. More than ever did I regret not having secured one of those sort of two phenomena. What a joy a real devil, appropriately put up in raw alcohol, would have been to my scientific friends!

Five Gorillas

I will not bore you with my diary in detail regarding our land journey, because the water-washed little volume attributive to this period is mainly full of reports of law cases, for reasons hereinafter to be stated; and at night, when passing through this bit of country, I was usually too tired to do anything more than make an entry such as: '5 S., 4 R. A., N. E. Ebony. T. I – 50, &c., &c.' – entries that require amplification to explain their significance, and I will proceed to explain.

Our first day's march was a very long one. Path in the ordinary acceptance of the term there was none. Hour after hour, mile after mile, we passed on, in the under-gloom of the great forest. The pace made by the Fans, who are infinitely the most rapid Africans I have ever come across, severely tired the Ajumba, who are canoe men, and who had been as fresh as paint, after their exceedingly long day's paddling from Arevooma to M'fetta. Ngouta, the Igalwa interpreter, felt pumped, and said as much, very early in the day. I regretted very much having brought him; for, from a mixture of nervous exhaustion arising from our M'fetta experiences, and a touch of chill he had almost entirely lost his voice, and I feared would fall sick. The Fans were evidently quite at home in the forest, and strode on over fallen trees and rocks with an easy, graceful stride. What saved us weaklings was the Fans' appetites; every two hours they sat down, and had a snack of a pound or so of meat and aguma apiece, followed by a pipe of tobacco. We used to come up with them at these halts. Ngouta and the Ajumba used to sit down; and rest with them, and I also, for a few minutes, for a rest and chat, and then I would go on alone, thus getting a good start. I got a good start, in the other meaning of the word, on the afternoon of the first day when descending into a ravine.

I saw in the bottom, wading and rolling in the mud, a herd of five elephants. I am certain that owing to some misapprehension among the Fates I was given a series of magnificent sporting chances, intended as a special treat for some favourite Nimrod of those three ladies, and I know exactly how I ought to have behaved. I should have felt my favourite rifle fly to my shoulder, and then, carefully sighting for the finest specimen, have fired. The noble beast should have stumbled forward, recovered itself, and shedding its life blood behind it have crashed away into the forest. I should then have tracked it, and either with one well-directed shot have given it its quietus, or have got charged by it, the elephant passing completely over my prostrate body; either termination is good form, but I never have these things happen, and never will. (In the present case I remembered, hastily, that your one chance when charged by several elephants is to dodge them round trees, working down wind all the time, until they lose smell and sight of you, then to lie quiet for a time, and go home.) It was evident from the utter unconcern of these monsters that I was down wind now, so I had only to attend to dodging, and I promptly dodged round a tree, thinking perhaps a dodge in time saves nine – and I lay down. Seeing

Five Gorillas

they still displayed no emotion on my account, and fascinated by the novelty of the scene, I crept forward from one tree to another, until I was close enough to have hit the nearest one with a stone, and spats of mud, which they sent flying with their stamping and wallowing came flap, flap among the bushes covering me.

One big fellow had a nice pair of 40 lb. or so tusks on him, singularly straight, and another had one big curved tusk and one broken one. If I were an elephant I think I would wear the tusks straight; they must be more effective weapons thus but there seems no fixed fashion among elephants here in this matter. Some of them lay right down like pigs in the deeper part of the swamp, some drew up trunkfuls of water and syringed themselves and each other, and every one of them indulged in a good rub against a tree. Presently when they had had enough of it they all strolled off up wind, a way elephants have; but why I do not know, because they know the difference, always carrying their trunk differently when they are going up wind to what they do when they are going down — arrested mental development, I suppose. They strolled through the bush in Indian file, now and then breaking off a branch, but leaving singularly little dead water for their tonnage and breadth of beam. One laid his trunk affectionately on the back of the one in front of him, which I believe to be the elephant equivalent to walking arm-in-arm. When they had gone I rose up, turned round to find the men, and trod on Kiva's back then and there, full and fair, and fell sideways down the steep hillside until I fetched up among some roots.

It seems Kiva had come on, after his meal; before the

others, and seeing the elephants, and being a born hunter, had crawled like me down to look at them. He had not expected to find me there, he said. I do not believe he gave a thought of any sort to me in the presence of these fascinating creatures, and so he got himself trodden on. I suggested to him we should pile the baggage, and go and have an elephant hunt. He shook his head reluctantly, saying 'Kor, kor,' like a depressed rook, and explained we were not strong enough; there were only three Fans – the Ajumba, and Ngouta did not count – and moreover that we had not brought sufficient ammunition owing to the baggage having to be carried, and the ammunition that we had must be saved for other game than elephant, for we might meet war before we met the Rembwé River.

We had by now joined the rest of the party, and were all soon squattering about on our own account in the elephant bath. It was shocking bad going – like a ploughed field exaggerated by a terrific nightmare. It pretty nearly pulled all the legs off me, and to this hour I cannot tell you if it is best to put your foot into a footmark – a young pond, I mean – about the size of the bottom of a Madeira work arm-chair, or whether you should poise yourself on the rim of the same, and stride forward to its other bank boldly and hopefully. The footmarks and the places where the elephants had been rolling were by now filled with water, and the mud underneath was in places hard and slippery. In spite of my determination to preserve an awesome and unmoved calm while among these dangerous savages, I had to give way and laugh explosively; to see the portly, powerful Pagan suddenly convert himself into a quadruped, while Gray Shirt

Five Gorillas

poised himself on one heel and waved his other leg in the air to advertise to the assembled nations that he was about to sit down, was irresistible. No one made such palaver about taking a seat as Gray Shirt; I did it repeatedly without any fuss to speak of. That lordly elephant-hunter, the Great Wiki, would, I fancy, have strode over safely and with dignity, but the man who was in front of him spun round on his own axis and flung his arms round the Fan, and they went to earth together; the heavy load on Wiki's back drove them into the mud like a pile-driver. However we got through in time, and after I had got up the other side of the ravine I saw the Fan let the Ajumba go on, and were busy searching themselves for something.

I followed the Ajumba, and before I joined them felt a fearful pricking irritation. Investigation of the affected part showed a tick of terrific size with its head embedded in the flesh; pursuing this interesting subject, I found three more and had awfully hard work to get them off and painful too for they give one not only a feeling of irritation at their holding-on place, but a streak of rheumatic-feeling pain up from it. On completing operations I went on and came upon the Ajumba in a state more approved of by Praxiteles than by the general public nowadays. They had found out about elephant ticks, so I went on and got an excellent start for the next stage.

By this time, shortly after noon on the first day, we had struck into a mountainous and rocky country, and also struck a track – a track you had to keep your eye on or you lost it in a minute, but still a guide as to direction.

The forest trees here were mainly ebony and great hard

wood trees, with no palms save my old enemy the climbing palm, *calamus*, as usual, going on its long excursions, up one tree and down another, bursting into a plume of fronds, and in the middle of each plume one long spike sticking straight up, which was an unopened frond, whenever it got a gleam of sunshine; running along the ground over anything it meets, rock or fallen timber, all alike, its long, dark-coloured, rope-like stem simply furred with thorns. Immense must be the length of some of these climbing palms. One tree I noticed that day that had hanging from its summit, a good one hundred and fifty feet above us, a long straight rope-like palm stem. Interested, I went to it, and tried to track it to root, and found it was only a loop that came down from another tree. I had no time to trace it further; for they go up a tree and travel along the surrounding tree-tops, take an occasional dip, and then up again.

The character of the whole forest was very interesting. Sometimes for hours we passed among thousands upon thousands of gray-white columns of uniform height (about 100–150 feet); at the top of these the boughs branched out and interlaced among each other, forming a canopy or ceiling, which dimmed the light even repetition of the equatorial sun to such an extent that no undergrowth could thrive in the gloom. The statement of the struggle for existence was published here in plain figures, but it was not, as in our climate, a struggle against climate mainly, but an internecine war from over population. Now and again we passed among vast stems of buttressed trees, sometimes enormous in girth; and from their far-away summits hung great bush-ropes, some as straight as plumb lines, others coiled round, and intertwined among each other, until one could fancy one was looking on some mighty battle between armies of gigantic serpents, that had been arrested at its height by some magic spell. All these bush-ropes were as bare of foliage as a ship's wire rigging, but a good many had thorns. I was very curious as to how they got up straight, and investigation showed me that many of them were carried up with a growing tree. The only true climbers were the *calamus* and the rubber vine (*Landolphia*), both of which employ hook tackle.

Some stretches of this forest were made up of thin, spindly stemmed trees of great height, and among these stretches I always noticed the ruins of some forest giant, whose death by lightning or by his superior height having given the demoniac tornado wind an extra grip on him, had allowed sunlight to penetrate the lower regions of the forest; and then evidently the seedlings and saplings, who had for years been living a half-starved life for light, shot up. They seemed to know that their one chance lay in getting with the greatest rapidity to the level of the top of the forest. No time to grow fat in the stem. No time to send out side branches, or any of those vanities. Up, up to the light level, and he among them who reached it first won in this game of life or death; for when he gets there he spreads out his crown of upper branches, and shuts off the life-giving sunshine from his competitors, who pale off and die, or remain dragging on an attenuated existence waiting for another chance, and waiting sometimes for centuries. There must be tens of thousands of seeds which perish before they get their chance; but the way the seeds of the hard wood African trees are packed, as it were, in cases specially made durable, is very wonderful.

Indeed the ways of Providence here are wonderful in their strange dual intention to preserve and to destroy; but on the whole, as Peer Gynt truly observes, '*Ein guter Wirth – nein das ist er nicht.*'

We saw this influence of light on a large scale as soon as we reached the open hills and mountains of the Sierra del Cristal, and had to pass over those fearful avalanche-like timber falls on their steep sides. The worst of these lay between Efoua and Egaja, where we struck a part of the range that was exposed to the south-east. These falls had evidently arisen from the tornados, which from time to time have hurled down the gigantic trees whose hold on the superficial soil over the sheets of hard bed rock was insufficient, in spite of all the anchors they had out in the shape of roots and buttresses, and all the rigging in the shape of bush ropes. Down they had come, crushing and dragging down with them those near them or bound to them by the great tough climbers.

Getting over these falls was perilous, not to say scratchy work. One or another member of our party always went through; and precious uncomfortable going it was I found, when I tried it in one above Egaja; ten or twelve feet of crashing creaking timber, and then flump on to a lot of rotten, wet *débris*, with more snakes and centipedes among it than you had any immediate use for, even though you were a collector; but there you had to stay, while Wiki, who was a most critical connoisseur, selected from the surrounding forest a bush-rope that he regarded as the correct remedy for the case, and then up you were hauled, through the sticks you had turned the wrong way on your down journey.

Five Gorillas

The Duke had a bad fall, going twenty feet or so before he found the rubbish heap; while Fika, who went through with a heavy load on his back, took us, on one occasion, half an hour to recover; and when we had just got him to the top, and able to cling on to the upper sticks, Wiki, who had been superintending operations, slipped backwards, and went through on his own account. The bush-rope we had been hauling on was too worn with the load to use again, and we just hauled Wiki out with the first one we could drag down and cut; and Wiki, when he came up, said we were reckless, and knew nothing of bush ropes, which shows how ungrateful an African can be. It makes the perspiration run down my nose whenever I think of it. The sun was out that day; we were neatly situated on the Equator, and the air was semi-solid, with the stinking exhalations from the swamps with which the mountain chain is fringed and intersected; and we were hot enough without these things, because of the violent exertion of getting these twelve to thirteen-stone gentlemen up among us again, and the fine varied exercise of getting over the fall on our own account.

When we got into the cool forest beyond it was delightful; particularly if it happened to be one of those lovely stretches of forest, gloomy down below, but giving hints that far away above us was a world of bloom and scent and beauty which we saw as much of as earth-worms in a flower-bed. Here and there the ground was strewn with great cast blossoms, thick, wax-like, glorious cups of orange and crimson and pure white, each one of which was in itself a handful, and which told us that some of the trees around us were showing a glory of colour to heaven alone. Sprinkled among them were bunches of pure stephanotis-like flowers, which said that the gaunt bush-ropes were rubber vines that had burst into flower when they had seen the sun. These flowers we came across in nearly every type of forest all the way, for rubber abounds here.

I will weary you no longer now with the different kinds of forest and only tell you I have let you off several. The natives have separate names for seven different kinds, and these might, I think, be easily run up to nine.

A certain sort of friendship soon arose between the Fans and me. We each recognised that we belonged to that same section of the human race with whom it is better to drink than to fight. We knew we would each have killed the other, if sufficient inducement were offered, and so we took a certain amount of care that the inducement should not arise. Gray Shirt and Pagan also, their trade friends, the Fans treated with an independent sort of courtesy; but Silence, Singlet, the Passenger, and above all Ngouta, they openly did not care a row of pins for, and I have small doubt that had it not been for us other three they would have killed and eaten these very amiable gentlemen with as much compunction as an English sportsman would kill as many rabbits. They on their part hated the Fan, and never lost an opportunity of telling me 'these Fan be bad man too much.' I must not forget to mention the other member of our party, a Fan gentleman with the manners of a duke and the habits of a dustbin. He came with us, quite uninvited by me, and never asked for any pay; I think he only wanted to see the fun, and drop in for a fight if there was one going on, and to pick up the pieces generally. He was evidently a man of some

Five Gorillas

importance, from the way the others treated him; and moreover he had a splendid gun, with a gorilla skin sheath for its lock, and ornamented all over its stock with brass nails. His costume consisted of a small piece of dirty rag round his loins; and whenever we were going through dense undergrowth, or wading a swamp, he wore that filament tucked up scandalously short. Whenever we were sitting down in the forest having one of our nondescript meals, he always sat next to me and appropriated the tin. Then he would fill his pipe, and turning to me with the easy grace of aristocracy, would say what may be translated as 'My dear Princess, could you favour me with a lucifer?'

I used to say, 'My dear Duke, charmed, I'm sure,' and give him one ready lit.

I dared not trust him with the box whole, having a personal conviction that he would have kept it. I asked him what he would do suppose I was not there with a box of lucifers; and he produced a bush-cow's horn with a neat wood lid tied on with tie, and from out of it he produced a flint and steel and demonstrated. Unfortunately all his grace's minor possessions, owing to the scantiness of his attire, were in one and the same pineapple-fibre bag which he wore slung across his shoulder; and these possessions, though not great, were as dangerous to the body as a million sterling is said to be to the soul, for they consisted largely of gunpowder and snuff, and their separate receptacles leaked and their contents, commingled, so that demonstration on fire-making methods among the Fan ended in an awful bang and blow-up in a small way, and the Professor and his pupil sneezed like fury for ten minutes, and a cruel world laughed till it nearly died, for twenty. Still that bag with all its failings was a wonder for its containing power.

The first day in the forest we came across a snake – a beauty with a new red-brown and yellow-patterned velvety skin, about three feet six inches long and as thick as a man's thigh. Ngouta met it, hanging from a bough, and shot backwards like a lobster, Ngouta having among his many weaknesses a rooted horror, of snakes. This snake the Ogowé natives all hold in great aversion. For the bite of other sorts of snakes they profess to have remedies, but for this they have none. If, however, a native is stung by one he usually conceals the fact that it was this particular kind, and tries to get any chance the native doctor's medicine may give. The Duke stepped forward and with one blow flattened its head against the tree with his gun butt, and then folded the snake up and got as much of it as possible into the bag, while the rest hung dangling out. Ngouta, not being able to keep ahead of the Duke, his Grace's pace being stiff, went to the extreme rear of the party, so that other people might be killed first if the snake returned to life, as he surmised it would. He fell into other dangers from this caution, but I cannot chronicle Ngouta's afflictions in full without running this book into an old-fashioned folio size. We had the snake for supper, that is to say the Fan and I; the others would not touch it, although a good snake, properly cooked, is one of the best meats one gets out here, far and away better than the African fowl.

The Fans also did their best to educate me in every way: they told me their names for things, while I told them mine, throwing in besides as 'a dash for top' a few colloquial phrases such as: 'Dear me, now,' 'Who'd have thought it,' 'Stuff, my dear sir,' and so on; and when I left them they had run each together as it were into one word, and a nice savage sound they had with them too, especially 'dearmenow,' so I must warn any philologist who visits the Fans, to beware of regarding any word beyond two syllables in length as being of native origin. I found several European words already slightly altered in use among them, such as 'Amuck' – a mug, 'Alas' – a glass, a tumbler. I do not know whether their 'Ami' – a person addressed, or spoken of – is French or not. It may come from 'Anwe' – M'pongwe for 'Ye,' 'You.' They use it as a rule in addressing a person after the phrase they always open up conversation with, 'Azuna' – Listen, or I am speaking.

They also showed me many things: how to light a fire from the pith of a certain tree, which was useful to me in after life, but they rather overdid this branch of instruction one way and another; for example, Wiki had, as above indicated, a mania for bush-ropes and a marvellous eye and knowledge of them; he would pick out from among the thousands surrounding us now one of such peculiar suppleness that you could wind it round anything, like a strip of cloth, and as strong withal as a hawser; or again another which has a certain stiffness, combined with a slight elastic spring, excellent for hauling, with the ease and accuracy of a lady who picks out the particular twisted strand of embroidery silk from a multi-coloured tangled ball. He would go into the bush after them while other people were resting, and particularly after the sort which, when split is bright yellow, and very supple and excellent to tie round loads.

On one occasion, between Egaja and Esoon, he came back from one of these quests and wanted me to come and see something, very quietly; I went, and we crept down into a rocky ravine, on the other side of which lay one of the outer most Egaja plantations. When we got to the edge of the cleared ground, we lay down, and wormed our way, with elaborate caution, among a patch of Koko; Wiki first, I following in his trail.

After about fifty yards of this, Wiki sank flat, and I saw before me some thirty yards off, busily employed in pulling down plantains, and other depredations, five gorillas: one old male, one young male, and three females. One of these had clinging to her a young fellow, with beautiful wavy black hair with just a kink in it. The big male was crouching on his haunches, with his long arms hanging down on either side, with the backs of his hands on the ground, the palms upwards. The elder lady was tearing to pieces and eating a pine-apple, while the others were at the plantains destroying more than they ate.

They kept up a sort of a whinnying, chattering noise, quite different from the sound I have heard gorillas give when enraged, or from the one you can hear them giving when they are what the natives call 'dancing' at night. I noticed that their reach of arm was immense, and that when they went from one tree to another, they squattered across the open ground in a most inelegant style, dragging their long arms with the knuckles downwards. I should think the big male and female were over six feet each. The others would be from four to five. I put out my hand and laid it on Wiki's gun to prevent him from firing, and he, thinking I was going to fire, gripped my wrist.

I watched the gorillas with great interest for a few seconds, until I heard Wiki make a peculiar small sound, and looking at him saw his face was working in an awful way as he clutched his throat with his hand violently.

Heavens! think I, this gentleman's going to have a fit; it's lost we are entirely this time. He rolled his head to and fro, and then buried his face into a heap of dried rubbish at the foot of a plantain stem, clasped his hands over it, and gave an explosive sneeze. The gorillas let go all, raised themselves up for a second, gave a quaint sound between a bark and a howl, and then the ladies and the young gentleman started home. The old male rose to his full height (it struck me at the time this was a matter of ten feet at least, but for scientific purposes allowance must be made for a lady's emotions) and looked straight towards us, or rather towards where that sound came from. Wiki went off into a paroxysm of falsetto sneezes the like of which I have never heard; nor evidently had the gorilla, who doubtless thinking, as one of his black co-relatives would have thought, that the phenomenon favoured Duppy, went off after his family with a celerity that was amazing the moment he touched the forest, and disappeared as they had, swinging himself along through it from bough to bough, in a way that convinced me that, given the necessity of getting about in tropical forests, man has made a mistake in getting his arms shortened. I have seen many wild animals in their native wilds, but never have I seen anything to equal gorillas going through bush; it is a graceful, powerful, superbly perfect hand-trapeze performance.*

---

*   I have no hesitation in saying that the gorilla is the most horrible wild animal I have seen. I have seen at close quarters specimens of the most important big game of Central Africa, and with the exception of snakes, I have run away from all of them; but although elephants, leopards and pythons give you a feeling of alarm, they do not give that feeling of horrible disgust that an old gorilla gives on account of its hideousness of appearance.

Elephant Hunt

I must now speak briefly on the most important article with which the Fan deals, namely ivory. His methods of collecting this are several, and many a wild story the handles of your table knives could tell you, if their ivory has passed through Fan hands. For ivory is everywhere an evil thing before which the quest for gold sinks into a parlour game; and when its charms seize such a tribe as the Fans, 'conclusions pass their careers.' A very common way of collecting a tooth is to kill the person who owns one. Therefore in order to prevent this catastrophe happening to you yourself, when you have one, it is held advisable, unless you are a powerful person in your own village, to bury or sink the said tooth and say nothing about it until the trader comes into your district or you get a chance of smuggling it quietly down to him. Some of these private ivories are kept for years and years before they reach the trader's hands. And quite a third of the ivory you see coming on board a vessel to go to Europe is dark from this keeping: some teeth a lovely brown like a well-coloured meerschaum, others quite black, and gnawed by that strange little creature – much heard of, and abused, yet little known in ivory ports – the ivory rat. This squirrel-like creature was first brought to Europe by Paul du Chaillu, and as far as I know no further specimen has been secured. I got two, but I am ashamed to say I lost them. Du Chaillu called it *Sciurus eborivorus*. Its main point, as may be imagined, is its teeth. The incisors in the upper jaw are long, and closely set together; those in the lower are still longer, and as they seem always to go in under the upper teeth, I wonder how the creature gets its mouth shut. The feet are hairless, and somewhat like those of a squirrel. The tail is long, and marked with transverse bars, and it is not carried over the back. Over the eyes, and on either side of the mouth, are very long stiff bristles. The mischief these little creatures play with buried ivory is immense, because, for some inscrutable reason, they seem to prefer the flavour of the points of the teeth, the most valuable part.

Ivory, however, that is obtained by murder is private ivory. The public ivory trade among the Fans is carried on in a way more in accordance with European ideas of a legitimate trade. The greater part of this ivory is obtained from dead elephants. There are in this region certain places where the elephants are said to go to die. A locality in one district pointed out to me as such a place, was a great swamp in the forest. A swamp that evidently was deep in the middle, for from out its dark waters no swamp plant, or tree grew, and evidently its shores sloped suddenly, for the band of swamp plants round its edge was narrow. It is just possible that during the rainy season when most of the surrounding country would be under water, elephants might stray into this natural trap and get drowned, and on the drying up of the waters be discovered, and the fact being known, be regularly sought for by the natives cognisant of this. I inquired carefully whether these places where the elephants came to die always had water in them, but they said no, and in one district spoke of a valley or round-shaped depression in among the mountains. But natives were naturally disinclined to take a stranger to these ivory mines, and a white person who has caught – as any one who has been in touch must catch – ivory fever, is naturally equally disinclined to give localities.

A certain percentage of ivory collected by the Fans is from live elephants, but I am bound to admit that their method of hunting elephants is disgracefully unsportsmanlike. A herd of elephants is discovered by rubber hunters or by depredations on plantations, and the whole village, men, women, children, babies and dogs turn out into the forest and stalk the monsters into a suitable ravine, taking care not to scare them. When they have gradually edged the elephants on into a suitable place, they fell trees and wreathe them very roughly together with bush rope, all round an immense enclosure, still taking care not to scare the elephants into a rush. This fence is quite inadequate to stop any elephant in itself, but it is made effective by being smeared with certain things, the smell whereof the elephants detest so much that when they wander up to it, they turn back disgusted. I need hardly remark that this preparation is made by the witch doctors and its constituents a secret of theirs, and I was only able to find out some of them. Then poisoned plantains are placed within the enclosure, and the elephants eat these and grow drowsier and drowsier; if the water supply within the enclosure is a pool it is poisoned, but if it is a running stream this cannot be done. During this time the crowd of men and women spend their days round the enclosure, ready to turn back any elephant who may attempt to break out, going to and fro to the village for their food. Their nights they spend in little bough shelters by the enclosure, watching more vigilantly than by day, as the elephants are more active at night, it being their usual feeding time. During the whole time the witch doctor is hard at work making incantations and charms, with a view to finding out the proper time to attack the elephants. In my opinion, his decision fundamentally depends on his knowledge of the state of poisoning the animals are in, but his version is that he gets his information from the forest spirits. When, however, he has settled the day, the best hunters steal into the enclosure and take up safe positions in trees, and the outer crowd set light to the ready-built fires, and make the greatest uproar possible, and fire upon the staggering, terrified elephants as they attempt to break out. The hunters in the trees fire down on them as they rush past, the fatal point at the back of the skull being well exposed to them.

When the animals are nearly exhausted, those men who do not possess guns dash into the enclosure, and the men who do, reload and join them, and the work is then completed. One elephant hunt I chanced upon at the final stage had taken two months' preparation, and although the plan sounds safe enough, there is really a good deal of danger left in it with all the drugging and ju-ju. There were eight elephants killed that day, but three burst through everything, sending energetic spectators flying, and squashing two men and a baby as flat as botanical specimens.

The subsequent proceedings were impressive. The whole of the people gorged themselves on the meat for days, and great chunks of it were smoked over the fires in all directions.

Elephant Hunt

A certain portion of the flesh of the hind leg was taken by the witch doctor for ju-ju, and was supposed to be put away by him, with certain suitable incantations in the recesses of the forest; his idea being apparently either to give rise to more elephants, or to induce the forest spirits to bring more elephants into the district. Meanwhile the carcases were going bad, rapidly bad, and the smell for a mile round was strong enough to have taken the paint off a door. Moreover there were flies, most of the flies in West Africa, I imagine, and – but I will say no more. I thought before this experience that I had touched bottom in smells when once I spent the outside of a week in a village, on the sand bank in front of which a portly hippopotamus, who had been shot up river, got stranded, and proceeded energetically to melt into its elemental gases; but that was a passing whiff to this.

Fight with a Leopard

I must say the African leopard is an audacious animal, although it is ungrateful of me to say a word against him, after the way he has let me off personally, and I will speak of his extreme beauty as compensation for my ingratitude. I really think, taken as a whole, he is the most lovely animal I have ever seen; only seeing him, in the one way you can gain a full idea of his beauty, namely in his native forest, is not an unmixed joy to a person, like myself, of a nervous disposition. I may remark that my nervousness regarding the big game of Africa is of a rather peculiar kind. I can confidently say I am not afraid of any wild animal – until I see it – and then – well I will yield to nobody in terror; fortunately as I say my terror is a special variety; fortunately because no one can manage their own terror. You can suppress alarm, excitement, fear, fright, and all those small-fry emotions, but the real terror is as dependent on the inner make of you as the colour of your eyes, or the shape of your nose; and when terror ascends its throne in my mind I become preternaturally artful, and intelligent to an extent utterly foreign to my true nature, and save, in the case of close quarters with bad big animals, a feeling of rage against some unknown person that such things as leopards, elephants, crocodiles, &c., should be allowed out loose in that disgracefully dangerous way, I do not think much about it

Fight with a Leopard

at the time. Whenever I have come across an awful animal in the forest and I know it has seen me I take Jerome's advice, and instead of relying on the power of the human eye rely upon that of the human leg, and effect a masterly retreat in the face of the enemy. If I know it has not seen me I sink in my tracks and keep an eye on it, hoping that it will go away soon. Thus I once came upon a leopard. I had got caught in a tornado in a dense forest. The massive, mighty trees were waving like a wheat-field in an autumn gale in England, and I dare say a field mouse in a wheat-field in a gale would have heard much the same uproar. The tornado shrieked like ten thousand vengeful demons. The great trees creaked and groaned and strained against it and their bush-rope cables groaned and smacked like whips, and ever and anon a thundering crash with snaps like pistol shots told that they and their mighty tree had strained and struggled in vain. The fierce rain came in a roar, tearing to shreds the leaves and blossoms and deluging everything. I was making bad weather of it, and climbing up over a lot of rocks out of a gully bottom where I had been half drowned in a stream, and on getting my head to the level of a block of rock I observed right in front of my eyes, broadside on, maybe a yard off, certainly not more, a big leopard. He was crouching on the ground, with his magnificent head thrown back and his eyes shut. His fore-paws were spread out in front of him and he lashed the ground with his tail, and I grieve to say, in face of that awful danger – I don't mean me, but the tornado – that depraved creature swore, softly, but repeatedly and profoundly. I did not get all these facts up in one glance, for no sooner did I see him than I ducked under the rocks, and remembered thankfully that leopards are said to have no power of smell. But I heard his observation on the weather, and the flip-flap of his tail on the ground. Every now and then I cautiously took a look at him with one eye round a rock-edge, and he remained in the same position. My feelings tell me he remained there twelve months, but my calmer judgment puts the time down at twenty minutes; and at last, on taking another cautious peep, I saw he was gone. At the time I wished I knew exactly where, but I do not care about that detail now, for I saw no more of him. He had moved off in one of those weird lulls which you get in a tornado, when for a few seconds the wild herd of hurrying winds seem to have lost themselves, and wander round crying and wailing like lost souls, until their common rage seizes them again and they rush back to their work of destruction. It was an immense pleasure to have seen the great creature like that. He was so evidently enraged and baffled by the uproar and dazzled by the floods of lightning that swept down into the deepest recesses of the forest, showing at one second every detail of twig, leaf, branch, and stone round you, and then leaving you in a sort of swirling dark until the next flash came; this, and the great conglomerate roar of the wind, rain and thunder, was enough to bewilder any living thing.

I have never hurt a leopard intentionally; I am habitually kind to animals, and besides I do not think it is ladylike to go shooting things with a gun. Twice, however, I have been in collision with them. On one occasion a big leopard had attacked a dog, who, with her family, was occupying a broken-down hut next to mine. The dog was a half-bred

Fight with a Leopard

boarhound, and a savage brute on her own account. I, being roused by the uproar, rushed out into the feeble moonlight, thinking she was having one of her habitual turns-up with other dogs, and I saw a whirling mass of animal matter within a yard of me. I fired two mushroom-shaped native stools in rapid succession into the brown of it, and the meeting broke up into a leopard and a dog. The leopard crouched, I think to spring on me. I can see its great, beautiful, lambent eyes still, and I seized an earthen water-cooler and flung it straight at them. It was a noble shot; it burst on the leopard's head like a shell and the leopard went for bush one time. Twenty minutes after people began to drop in cautiously and inquire if anything was the matter, and I civilly asked them to go and ask the leopard in the bush, but they firmly refused. We found the dog had got her shoulder slit open as if by a blow from a cutlass, and the leopard had evidently seized the dog by the scruff of her neck, but owing to the loose folds of skin no bones were broken and she got round all right after much ointment from me, which she paid me for with several bites. Do not mistake this for a sporting adventure. I no more thought it was a leopard than that it was a lotus when I joined the fight. My other leopard was also after a dog. Leopards always come after dogs, because once upon a time the leopard and the dog were great friends, and the leopard went out one day and left her whelps in charge of the dog, and the dog went out flirting, and a snake came and killed the whelps, so there is ill-feeling to this day between the two. For the benefit of sporting readers whose interest may have been excited by the mention of big game, I may remark that the largest leopard skin I ever measured myself was, tail included, 9 feet 7 inches. It was a dried skin, and every man who saw it said, 'It was the largest skin he had ever seen, except one that he had seen somewhere else.'

The largest crocodile I ever measured was 22 feet 3 inches, the largest gorilla 5 feet 7 inches. I am assured by the missionaries in Calabar, that there was a python brought into Creek Town in the Rev. Mr Goldie's time, that extended the whole length of the Creek Town mission-house verandah and to spare. This python must have been over 40 feet. I have not a shadow of doubt it was. Stay-at-home people will always discredit great measurements, but experienced bushmen do not, and after all, if it amuses the stay-at-homes to do so, by all means let them; they have dull lives of it and it don't hurt you, for you know how exceedingly difficult it is to preserve really big things to bring home, and how, half the time, they fall into the hands of people who would not bother their heads to preserve them in a rotting climate like West Africa.

1. BOCCACCIO · *Mrs Rosie and the Priest*
2. GERARD MANLEY HOPKINS · *As kingfishers catch fire*
3. *The Saga of Gunnlaug Serpent-tongue*
4. THOMAS DE QUINCEY · *On Murder Considered as One of the Fine Arts*
5. FRIEDRICH NIETZSCHE · *Aphorisms on Love and Hate*
6. JOHN RUSKIN · *Traffic*
7. PU SONGLING · *Wailing Ghosts*
8. JONATHAN SWIFT · *A Modest Proposal*
9. *Three Tang Dynasty Poets*
10. WALT WHITMAN · *On the Beach at Night Alone*
11. KENKŌ · *A Cup of Sake Beneath the Cherry Trees*
12. BALTASAR GRACIÁN · *How to Use Your Enemies*
13. JOHN KEATS · *The Eve of St Agnes*
14. THOMAS HARDY · *Woman much missed*
15. GUY DE MAUPASSANT · *Femme Fatale*
16. MARCO POLO · *Travels in the Land of Serpents and Pearls*
17. SUETONIUS · *Caligula*
18. APOLLONIUS OF RHODES · *Jason and Medea*
19. ROBERT LOUIS STEVENSON · *Olalla*
20. KARL MARX AND FRIEDRICH ENGELS · *The Communist Manifesto*
21. PETRONIUS · *Trimalchio's Feast*
22. JOHANN PETER HEBEL · *How a Ghastly Story Was Brought to Light by a Common or Garden Butcher's Dog*
23. HANS CHRISTIAN ANDERSEN · *The Tinder Box*
24. RUDYARD KIPLING · *The Gate of the Hundred Sorrows*
25. DANTE · *Circles of Hell*
26. HENRY MAYHEW · *Of Street Piemen*
27. HAFEZ · *The nightingales are drunk*
28. GEOFFREY CHAUCER · *The Wife of Bath*
29. MICHEL DE MONTAIGNE · *How We Weep and Laugh at the Same Thing*
30. THOMAS NASHE · *The Terrors of the Night*
31. EDGAR ALLAN POE · *The Tell-Tale Heart*
32. MARY KINGSLEY · *A Hippo Banquet*
33. JANE AUSTEN · *The Beautifull Cassandra*
34. ANTON CHEKHOV · *Gooseberries*
35. SAMUEL TAYLOR COLERIDGE · *Well, they are gone, and here must I remain*
36. JOHANN WOLFGANG VON GOETHE · *Sketchy, Doubtful, Incomplete Jottings*
37. CHARLES DICKENS · *The Great Winglebury Duel*
38. HERMAN MELVILLE · *The Maldive Shark*
39. ELIZABETH GASKELL · *The Old Nurse's Story*
40. NIKOLAY LESKOV · *The Steel Flea*

41. HONORÉ DE BALZAC · *The Atheist's Mass*
42. CHARLOTTE PERKINS GILMAN · *The Yellow Wall-Paper*
43. C.P. CAVAFY · *Remember, Body . . .*
44. FYODOR DOSTOEVSKY · *The Meek One*
45. GUSTAVE FLAUBERT · *A Simple Heart*
46. NIKOLAI GOGOL · *The Nose*
47. SAMUEL PEPYS · *The Great Fire of London*
48. EDITH WHARTON · *The Reckoning*
49. HENRY JAMES · *The Figure in the Carpet*
50. WILFRED OWEN · *Anthem For Doomed Youth*
51. WOLFGANG AMADEUS MOZART · *My Dearest Father*
52. PLATO · *Socrates' Defence*
53. CHRISTINA ROSSETTI · *Goblin Market*
54. *Sindbad the Sailor*
55. SOPHOCLES · *Antigone*
56. RYŪNOSUKE AKUTAGAWA · *The Life of a Stupid Man*
57. LEO TOLSTOY · *How Much Land Does A Man Need?*
58. GIORGIO VASARI · *Leonardo da Vinci*
59. OSCAR WILDE · *Lord Arthur Savile's Crime*
60. SHEN FU · *The Old Man of the Moon*
61. AESOP · *The Dolphins, the Whales and the Gudgeon*
62. MATSUO BASHŌ · *Lips too Chilled*
63. EMILY BRONTË · *The Night is Darkening Round Me*
64. JOSEPH CONRAD · *To-morrow*
65. RICHARD HAKLUYT · *The Voyage of Sir Francis Drake Around the Whole Globe*
66. KATE CHOPIN · *A Pair of Silk Stockings*
67. CHARLES DARWIN · *It was snowing butterflies*
68. BROTHERS GRIMM · *The Robber Bridegroom*
69. CATULLUS · *I Hate and I Love*
70. HOMER · *Circe and the Cyclops*
71. D. H. LAWRENCE · *Il Duro*
72. KATHERINE MANSFIELD · *Miss Brill*
73. OVID · *The Fall of Icarus*
74. SAPPHO · *Come Close*
75. IVAN TURGENEV · *Kasyan from the Beautiful Lands*
76. VIRGIL · *O Cruel Alexis*
77. H. G. WELLS · *A Slip under the Microscope*
78. HERODOTUS · *The Madness of Cambyses*
79. *Speaking of Siva*
80. *The Dhammapada*

'She has many rare and charming qualities, but Sobriety is not one of them . . .'

JANE AUSTEN
Born 1775, Hampshire, England
Died 1817, Hampshire, England

Selected from *Love and Freindship and Other Youthful Writings*,
edited by Christine Alexander.

AUSTEN IN PENGUIN CLASSICS
Love and Freindship and Other Youthful Writings
Northanger Abbey
Sense and Sensibility
Pride and Prejudice
Mansfield Park
Emma
Persuasion
Lady Susan / The Watsons / Sanditon

JANE AUSTEN

The Beautifull Cassandra

PENGUIN BOOKS

PENGUIN CLASSICS

UK | USA | Canada | Ireland | Australia
India | New Zealand | South Africa

Penguin Books is part of the Penguin Random House group of companies whose addresses can be found at global.penguinrandomhouse.com.

This selection published in Penguin Classics 2015

013

Set in 9.5/13 pt Baskerville 10 Pro
Typeset by Jouve (UK), Milton Keynes

Printed and bound in Great Britain by Clays Ltd, Elcograf S.p.A.

A CIP catalogue record for this book is available from the British Library

ISBN: 978–0–141–39707–8

www.greenpenguin.co.uk

Penguin Random House is committed to a sustainable future for our business, our readers and our planet. This book is made from Forest Stewardship Council® certified paper.

Contents

Jack and Alice	1
Henry and Eliza	24
The beautifull Cassandra	33
From A young Lady in distress'd Circumstances to her freind	37
From a Young Lady very much in love to her Freind	43
A Letter from a Young Lady, whose feelings being too Strong for her Judgement led her into the commission of Errors which her Heart disapproved	54

Jack and Alice

a novel

Is respectfully inscribed to Francis William Austen Esqr Midshipman on board his Majesty's Ship the Perseverance
by his obedient humble
Servant The Author

CHAPTER THE FIRST

Mr Johnson was once upon a time about 53; in a twelvemonth afterwards he was 54, which so much delighted him that he was determined to celebrate his next Birth day by giving a Masquerade to his Children and Freinds. Accordingly on the Day he attained his 55th year tickets were dispatched to all his Neighbours to that purpose. His acquaintance indeed in that part of the World were not very numerous as they consisted only of Lady Williams, M^r and Mrs Jones, Charles Adams and the 3 Miss Simpsons, who composed the neighbourhood of Pammydiddle and formed the Masquerade.

Before I proceed to give an account of the Evening, it

will be proper to describe to my reader, the persons and Characters of the party introduced to his acquaintance.

M^r and Mrs Jones were both rather tall and very passionate, but were in other respects, good tempered, wellbehaved People. Charles Adams was an amiable, accomplished and bewitching young Man; of so dazzling a Beauty that none but Eagles could look him in the Face.

Miss Simpson was pleasing in her person, in her Manners and in her Disposition; an unbounded ambition was her only fault. Her second sister Sukey was Envious, Spitefull and Malicious. Her person was short, fat and disagreable. Cecilia (the youngest) was perfectly handsome but too affected to be pleasing.

In Lady Williams every virtue met. She was a widow with a handsome Jointure and the remains of a very handsome face. Tho' Benevolent and Candid, she was Generous and sincere; Tho' Pious and Good, she was Religious and amiable, and Tho' Elegant and Agreable, she was Polished and Entertaining.

The Johnsons were a family of Love, and though a little addicted to the Bottle and the Dice, had many good Qualities.

Such was the party assembled in the elegant Drawing Room of Johnson Court, amongst which the pleasing figure of a Sultana was the most remarkable of the female Masks. Of the Males a Mask representing the Sun, was the most universally admired. The Beams that darted from his Eyes were like those of that glorious Luminary

The Beautifull Cassandra

tho' infinitely superior. So strong were they that no one dared venture within half a mile of them; he had therefore the best part of the Room to himself, its size not amounting to more than 3 quarters of a mile in length and half a one in breadth. The Gentleman at last finding the feirceness of his beams to be very inconvenient to the concourse by obliging them to croud together in one corner of the room, half shut his eyes by which means, the Company discovered him to be Charles Adams in his plain green Coat, without any mask at all.

When their astonishment was a little subsided their attention was attracted by 2 Dominos who advanced in a horrible Passion; they were both very tall, but seemed in other respects to have many good qualities. 'These,' said the witty Charles, 'these are M^r and Mrs Jones,' and so indeed they were.

No one could imagine who was the Sultana! Till at length on her addressing a beautifull Flora who was reclining in a studied attitude on a couch, with 'Oh Cecilia, I wish I was really what I pretend to be', she was discovered by the never failing genius of Charles Adams, to be the elegant but ambitious Caroline Simpson, and the person to whom she addressed herself, he rightly imagined to be her lovely but affected sister Cecilia.

The Company now advanced to a Gaming Table where sat 3 Dominos (each with a bottle in their hand) deeply engaged; but a female in the character of Virtue fled with hasty footsteps from the shocking scene, whilst a little fat woman representing Envy, sate alternately on the foreheads of the 3 Gamesters. Charles Adams was still as bright as ever; he soon discovered the party at play to be the 3 Johnsons, Envy to be Sukey Simpson and Virtue to be Lady Williams.

The Masks were then all removed and the Company retired to another room, to partake of an elegant and well managed Entertainment, after which the Bottle being pretty briskly pushed about by the 3 Johnsons, the whole party not excepting even Virtue were carried home, Dead Drunk.

CHAPTER THE SECOND

For three months did the Masquerade afford ample subject for conversation to the inhabitants of Pammydiddle; but no character at it was so fully expatiated on as Charles Adams. The singularity of his appearance, the beams which darted from his eyes, the brightness of his Wit, and the whole <u>tout ensemble</u> of his person had subdued the hearts of so many of the young Ladies, that of the six present at the Masquerade but five had returned uncaptivated. Alice Johnson was the unhappy sixth whose heart had not been able to withstand the power of his Charms. But as it may appear strange to my Readers, that so much worth and Excellence as he possessed should have conquered only hers, it will be necessary to inform them that the Miss Simpsons were defended from his Power by Ambition, Envy, and Selfadmiration.

Every wish of Caroline was centered in a titled Husband; whilst in Sukey such superior excellence could only raise her Envy not her Love, and Cecilia was too tenderly attached to herself to be pleased with any one besides. As for Lady Williams and Mrs Jones, the former of them was too sensible, to fall in love with one so much her Junior and the latter, tho' very tall and very passionate was too fond of her Husband to think of such a thing.

Yet in spite of every endeavour on the part of Miss Johnson to discover any attachment to her in him; the cold and indifferent heart of Charles Adams still to all appearance, preserved its native freedom; polite to all but partial to none, he still remained the lovely, the lively, but insensible Charles Adams.

One evening, Alice finding herself somewhat heated by wine (no very uncommon case) determined to seek a releif for her disordered Head and Love-sick Heart in the Conversation of the intelligent Lady Williams.

She found her Ladyship at home as was in general the Case, for she was not fond of going out, and like the great Sir Charles Grandison scorned to deny herself when at Home, as she looked on that fashionable method of shutting out disagreable Visitors, as little less than downright Bigamy.

In spite of the wine she had been drinking, poor Alice was uncommonly out of spirits; she could think of nothing but Charles Adams, she could talk of nothing but him, and in short spoke so openly that Lady Williams soon discovered the unreturned affection she bore him, which excited her Pity and Compassion so strongly that she addressed her in the following Manner.

'I perceive but too plainly my dear Miss Johnson, that your Heart has not been able to withstand the fascinating Charms of this Young Man and I pity you sincerely. Is it a first Love?'

'It is.'

'I am still more greived to hear <u>that</u>; I am myself a sad example of the Miseries, in general attendant on a first Love and I am determined for the future to avoid the like Misfortune. I wish it may not be too late for you to do the same; if it is not endeavour my dear Girl to secure yourself from so great a Danger. A second attachment is seldom attended with any serious consequences; against <u>that</u> therefore I have nothing to say. Preserve yourself from a first Love and you need not fear a second.'

'You mentioned Madam something of your having yourself been a sufferer by the misfortune you are so good as to wish me to avoid. Will you favour me with your Life and Adventures?'

'Willingly my Love.'

CHAPTER THE THIRD

'My Father was a gentleman of considerable Fortune in Berkshire; myself and a few more his only Children. I was but six years old when I had the misfortune of losing my Mother and being at that time young and Tender, my father instead of sending me to School, procured an able handed Governess to superintend my Education at Home. My Brothers were placed at Schools suitable to their Ages and my Sisters being all younger than myself, remained still under the Care of their Nurse.

'Miss Dickins was an excellent Governess. She instructed me in the Paths of Virtue; under her tuition I daily became more amiable, and might perhaps by this time have nearly attained perfection, had not my worthy Preceptoress been torn from my arms, e'er I had attained my seventeenth year. I never shall forget her last words. "My dear Kitty" she said. "Good night t'ye." I never saw her afterwards,' continued Lady Williams wiping her eyes, 'She eloped with the Butler the same night.

'I was invited the following year by a distant relation of my Father's to spend the Winter with her in town. Mrs Watkins was a Lady of Fashion, Family and fortune; she was in general esteemed a pretty Woman, but I never thought her very handsome, for my part. She had too high a forehead, Her eyes were too small and she had too much colour.'

'How can <u>that</u> be?' interrupted Miss Johnson reddening with anger; 'Do you think that any one can have too much colour?'

'Indeed I do, and I'll tell you why I do my dear Alice; when a person has too great a degree of red in their Complexion, it gives their face in my opinion, too red a look.'

'But can a face my Lady have too red a look?'

'Certainly my dear Miss Johnson and I'll [tell] you why. When a face has too red a look it does not appear to so much advantage as it would were it paler.'

'Pray Ma'am proceed in your story.'

'Well, as I said before, I was invited by this Lady to spend some weeks with her in town. Many Gentlemen thought her Handsome but in my opinion, Her forehead was too high, her eyes too small and she had too much colour.'

'In that Madam as I said before your Ladyship must have been mistaken. Mrs Watkins could not have too much colour since no one can have too much.'

'Excuse me my Love if I do not agree with you in that particular. Let me explain myself clearly; my idea of the case is this. When a Woman has too great a proportion of red in her Cheeks, she must have too much colour.'

'But Madam I deny that it is possible for any one to have too great a proportion of red in their Cheeks.'

'What my Love not if they have too much colour?'

Miss Johnson was now out of all patience, the more so perhaps as Lady Williams still remained so inflexibly cool.

It must be remembered however that her Ladyship had in one respect by far the advantage of Alice; I mean in not being drunk, for heated with wine and raised by Passion, she could have little command of her Temper.

The Dispute at length grew so hot on the part of Alice that 'From Words she almost came to Blows' When Mr Johnson luckily entered and with some difficulty forced her away from Lady Williams, Mrs Watkins and her red cheeks.

CHAPTER THE FOURTH

My Readers may perhaps imagine that after such a fracas, no intimacy could longer subsist between the Johnsons and Lady Williams, but in that they are mistaken for her Ladyship was too sensible to be angry at a conduct which she could not help perceiving to be the natural consequence of inebriety and Alice had too sincere a respect for Lady Williams and too great a relish for her Claret, not to make every concession in her power.

A few days after their reconciliation Lady Williams called on Miss Johnson to propose a walk in a Citron Grove which led from her Ladyship's pigstye to Charles Adams's Horsepond. Alice was too sensible of Lady Williams's kindness in proposing such a walk and too much pleased with the prospect of seeing at the end of it, a Horsepond of Charles's, not to accept it with visible delight. They had not proceeded far before she was roused from the reflection of the happiness she was going to enjoy, by Lady Williams's thus addressing her.

'I have as yet forborn my dear Alice to continue the narrative of my Life from an unwillingness of recalling to your Memory a scene which (since it reflects on you rather disgrace than credit) had better be forgot than remembered.'

Alice had already begun to colour up and was beginning to speak, when her Ladyship perceiving her displeasure, continued thus.

'I am afraid my dear Girl that I have offended you by what I have just said; I assure you I do not mean to distress you by a retrospection of what cannot now be helped; considering all things I do not think you so much to blame as many People do; for when a person is in Liquor, there is no answering for what they may do.'

'Madam, this is not to be borne; I insist—'

'My dear Girl don't vex yourself about the matter; I assure you I have entirely forgiven every thing respecting it; indeed I was not angry at the time, because as I saw all along, you were nearly dead drunk. I knew you could not help saying the strange things you did. But I see I distress you; so I will change the subject and desire it may never again be mentioned; remember it is all forgot – I will now pursue my story; but I must insist upon not giving you any description of Mrs Watkins; it would only be reviving old stories and as you never saw her, it can

The Beautifull Cassandra

be nothing to you, if her forehead <u>was</u> too high, her eyes <u>were</u> too small, or if she <u>had</u> too much colour.'

'Again! Lady Williams: this is too much—'

So provoked was poor Alice at this renewal of the old story, that I know not what might have been the consequence of it, had not their attention been engaged by another object. A lovely young Woman lying apparently in great pain beneath a Citron-tree, was an object too interesting not to attract their notice. Forgetting their own dispute they both with simpathizing Tenderness advanced towards her and accosted her in these terms.

'You seem fair Nymph to be labouring under some misfortune which we shall be happy to releive if you will inform us what it is. Will you favour us with your Life and adventures?'

'Willingly Ladies, if you will be so kind as to be seated.' They took their places and she thus began.

CHAPTER THE FIFTH

'I am a native of North Wales and my Father is one of the most capital Taylors in it. Having a numerous family, he was easily prevailed on by a sister of my Mother's who is a widow in good circumstances and keeps an alehouse in the next Village to ours, to let her take me and breed me up at her own expence. Accordingly I have lived with her for the last 8 years of my Life, during which time she provided me with some of the first rate Masters, who taught me all the accomplishments requisite for one of my sex and rank. Under their instructions I learned Dancing, Music, Drawing and various Languages, by which means I became more accomplished than any other Taylor's Daughter in Wales. Never was there a happier Creature than I was, till within the last half year – but I should have told you before that the principal Estate in our Neighbourhood belongs to Charles Adams, the owner of the brick House, you see yonder.'

'Charles Adams!' exclaimed the astonished Alice; 'are you acquainted with Charles Adams?'

'To my sorrow madam I am. He came about half a year ago to receive the rents of the Estate I have just mentioned. At that time I first saw him; as you seem ma'am acquainted with him, I need not describe to you how charming he is. I could not resist his attractions;—'

'Ah! who can,' said Alice with a deep sigh.

'My Aunt being in terms of the greatest intimacy with his cook, determined, at my request, to try whether she could discover, by means of her freind if there were any chance of his returning my affection. For this purpose she went one evening to drink tea with Mrs Susan, who in the course of Conversation mentioned the goodness of her Place and the Goodness of her Master; upon which my Aunt began pumping her with so much dexterity that in a short time Susan owned, that she did not think her Master would ever marry, "for (said she) he has often and

The Beautifull Cassandra

often declared to me that his wife, whoever she might be, must possess, Youth, Beauty, Birth, Wit, Merit, and Money. I have many a time (she continued) endeavoured to reason him out of his resolution and to convince him of the improbability of his ever meeting with such a Lady; but my arguments have had no effect and he continues as firm in his determination as ever." You may imagine Ladies my distress on hearing this; for I was fearfull that tho' possessed of Youth, Beauty, Wit and Merit, and tho' the probable Heiress of my Aunts House and business, he might think me deficient in Rank, and in being so, unworthy of his hand.

'However I was determined to make a bold push and therefore wrote him a very kind letter, offering him with great tenderness my hand and heart. To this I received an angry and peremptory refusal, but thinking it might be rather the effect of his modesty than any thing else, I pressed him again on the subject. But he never answered any more of my Letters and very soon afterwards left the Country. As soon as I heard of his departure I wrote to him here, informing him that I should shortly do myself the honour of waiting on him at Pammydiddle, to which I received no answer; therefore choosing to take, Silence for Consent, I left Wales, unknown to my Aunt, and arrived here after a tedious Journey this Morning. On enquiring for his House I was directed thro' this Wood, to the one you there see. With a heart elated by the expected happiness of beholding him I entered it and had proceeded thus far in my progress thro' it, when I found myself suddenly seized by the leg and on examining the cause of it, found that I was caught in one of the steel traps so common in gentlemen's grounds.'

'Ah,' cried Lady Williams, 'how fortunate we are to meet with you; since we might otherwise perhaps have shared the like misfortune—'

'It is indeed happy for you Ladies, that I should have been a short time before you. I screamed as you may easily imagine till the woods resounded again and till one of the inhuman Wretch's servants came to my assistance and released me from my dreadfull prison, but not before one of my legs was entirely broken.'

CHAPTER THE SIXTH

At this melancholy recital the fair eyes of Lady Williams, were suffused in tears and Alice could not help exclaiming,

'Oh! cruel Charles to wound the hearts and legs of all the fair.'

Lady Williams now interposed and observed that the young Lady's leg ought to be set without farther delay. After examining the fracture therefore, she immediately began and performed the operation with great skill which was the more wonderfull on account of her having never performed such a one before. Lucy, then arose from the ground and finding that she could walk with the greatest

The Beautifull Cassandra

ease, accompanied them to Lady Williams's House at her Ladyship's particular request.

The perfect form, the beautifull face, and elegant manners of Lucy so won on the affections of Alice that when they parted, which was not till after Supper, she assured her that except her Father, Brother, Uncles, Aunts, Cousins and other relations, Lady Williams, Charles Adams and a few dozen more of particular freinds, she loved her better than almost any other person in the world.

Such a flattering assurance of her regard would justly have given much pleasure to the object of it, had she not plainly perceived that the amiable Alice had partaken too freely of Lady Williams's claret.

Her Ladyship (whose discernment was great) read in the intelligent countenance of Lucy her thoughts on the subject and as soon as Miss Johnson had taken her leave, thus addressed her.

'When you are more intimately acquainted with my Alice you will not be surprised, Lucy, to see the dear Creature drink a little too much; for such things happen every day. She has many rare and charming qualities, but Sobriety is not one of them. The whole Family are indeed a sad drunken set. I am sorry to say too that I never knew three such thorough Gamesters as they are, more particularly Alice. But she is a charming girl. I fancy not one of the sweetest tempers in the world; to be sure I have seen her in such passions! However she is a sweet young Woman. I am sure you'll like her. I scarcely know any one so amiable. – Oh! that you could but have seen her the other Evening! How she raved! and on such a trifle too! She is indeed a most pleasing Girl! I shall always love her!'

'She appears by your ladyship's account to have many good qualities', replied Lucy. 'Oh! a thousand,' answered Lady Williams; 'tho' I am very partial to her, and perhaps am blinded by my affection, to her real defects.'

CHAPTER THE SEVENTH

The next morning brought the three Miss Simpsons to wait on Lady Williams, who received them with the utmost politeness and introduced to their acquaintance Lucy, with whom the eldest was so much pleased that at parting she declared her sole <u>ambition</u> was to have her accompany them the next morning to Bath, whither they were going for some weeks.

'Lucy,' said Lady Williams, 'is quite at her own disposal and if she chooses to accept so kind an invitation, I hope she will not hesitate, from any motives of delicacy on my account. I know not indeed how I shall ever be able to part with her. She never was at Bath and I should think that it would be a most agreable Jaunt to her. Speak my Love,' continued she, turning to Lucy, 'what say you to accompanying these Ladies? I shall be miserable without you – t'will be a most pleasant tour to you – I hope you'll

The Beautifull Cassandra

go; if you do I am sure t'will be the Death of me – pray be persuaded'—

Lucy begged leave to decline the honour of accompanying them, with many expressions of gratitude for the extream politeness of Miss Simpson in inviting her.

Miss Simpson appeared much disappointed by her refusal. Lady Williams insisted on her going – declared that she would never forgive her if she did not, and that she should never survive it if she did, and inshort used such persuasive arguments that it was at length resolved she was to go. The Miss Simpsons called for her at ten o'clock the next morning and Lady Williams had soon the satisfaction of receiving from her young freind, the pleasing intelligence of their safe arrival in Bath.

It may now be proper to return to the Hero of this Novel, the brother of Alice, of whom I beleive I have scarcely ever had occasion to speak; which may perhaps be partly oweing to his unfortunate propensity to Liquor, which so compleatly deprived him of the use of those faculties Nature had endowed him with, that he never did anything worth mentioning. His Death happened a short time after Lucy's departure and was the natural Consequence of this pernicious practice. By his decease, his sister became the sole inheritress of a very large fortune, which as it gave her fresh Hopes of rendering herself acceptable as a wife to Charles Adams could not fail of being most pleasing to her – and as the effect was Joyfull the Cause could scarcely be lamented.

Jane Austen

Finding the violence of her attachment to him daily augment, she at length disclosed it to her Father and desired him to propose a union between them to Charles. Her father consented and set out one morning to open the affair to the young Man. M.r Johnson being a man of few words his part was soon performed and the answer he received was as follows—

'Sir, I may perhaps be expected to appear pleased at and gratefull for the offer you have made me: but let me tell you that I consider it as an affront. I look upon myself to be Sir a perfect Beauty – where would you see a finer figure or a more charming face. Then, sir I imagine my Manners and Address to be of the most polished kind; there is a certain elegance a peculiar sweetness in them that I never saw equalled and cannot describe—. Partiality aside, I am certainly more accomplished in every Language, every Science, every Art and every thing than any other person in Europe. My temper is even, my virtues innumerable, my self unparalelled. Since such Sir is my character, what do you mean by wishing me to marry your Daughter? Let me give you a short sketch of yourself and of her. I look upon you Sir to be a very good sort of Man in the main; a drunken old Dog to be sure, but that's nothing to me. Your daughter sir, is neither sufficiently beautifull, sufficiently amiable, sufficiently witty, nor sufficiently rich for me—. I expect nothing more in my wife than my wife will find in me – Perfection. These sir, are

The Beautifull Cassandra

my sentiments and I honour myself for having such. One freind I have and glory in having but one—. She is at present preparing my Dinner, but if you choose to see her, she shall come and she will inform you that these have ever been my sentiments.'

Mr Johnson was satisfied; and expressing himself to be much obliged to Mr Adams for the characters he had favoured him with of himself and his Daughter, took his leave.

The unfortunate Alice on receiving from her father the sad account of the ill success his visit had been attended with, could scarcely support the disappointment – She flew to her Bottle and it was soon forgot.

CHAPTER THE EIGHTH

While these affairs were transacting at Pammydiddle, Lucy was conquering every Heart at Bath. A fortnight's residence there had nearly effaced from her remembrance the captivating form of Charles – The recollection of what her Heart had formerly suffered by his charms and her Leg by his trap, enabled her to forget him with tolerable Ease, which was what she determined to do; and for that purpose dedicated five minutes in every day to the employment of driving him from her remembrance.

Her second Letter to Lady Williams contained the

pleasing intelligence of her having accomplished her undertaking to her entire satisfaction; she mentioned in it also an offer of marriage she had received from the Duke of —— an elderly Man of noble fortune whose ill health was the chief inducement of his Journey to Bath. 'I am distressed (she continued) to know whether I mean to accept him or not. There are a thousand advantages to be derived from a marriage with the Duke, for besides those more inferior ones of Rank and Fortune it will procure me a home, which of all other things is what I most desire. Your Ladyship's kind wish of my always remaining with you, is noble and generous but I cannot think of becoming so great a burden on one I so much love and esteem. That One should receive obligations only from those we despise, is a sentiment instilled into my mind by my worthy Aunt, in my early years, and cannot in my opinion be too strictly adhered to. The excellent woman of whom I now speak, is I hear too much incensed by my imprudent departure from Wales, to receive me again—. I most earnestly wish to leave the Ladies I am now with. Miss Simpson is indeed (setting aside ambition) very amiable, but her 2^d Sister the envious and malvolent Sukey is too disagreable to live with. – I have reason to think that the admiration I have met with in the circles of the great at this Place, has raised her Hatred and Envy; for often has she threatened, and sometimes endeavoured to cut my throat. – Your Ladyship will therefore allow that I am not wrong in wishing to leave Bath, and in wishing

The Beautifull Cassandra

to have a home to receive me, when I do. I shall expect with impatience your advice concerning the Duke and am your most obliged

etc etc – Lucy.'

Lady Williams sent her, her opinion on the subject in the following Manner.

'Why do you hesitate my dearest Lucy, a moment with respect to the Duke? I have enquired into his Character and find him to be an unprincipled, illiterate Man. Never shall my Lucy be united to such a one! He has a princely fortune, which is every day encreasing. How nobly will you spend it!, what credit will you give him in the eyes of all! How much will he be respected on his Wife's account! But why my dearest Lucy, why will you not at once decide this affair by returning to me and never leaving me again? Altho' I admire your noble sentiments with respect to obligations, yet, let me beg that they may not prevent your making me happy. It will to be sure be a great expence to me, to have you always with me – I shall not be able to support it – but what is that in comparison with the happiness I shall enjoy in your society?—'twill ruin me I know–you will not therefore surely, withstand these arguments, or refuse to return to yours most affectionately–etc etc.

C. Williams'

CHAPTER THE NINTH

What might have been the effect of her Ladyship's advice, had it ever been received by Lucy, is uncertain, as it reached Bath a few Hours after she had breathed her last. She fell a sacrifice to the Envy and Malice of Sukey who jealous of her superior charms took her by poison from an admiring World at the age of seventeen.

Thus fell the amiable and lovely Lucy whose Life had been marked by no crime, and stained by no blemish but her imprudent departure from her Aunts, and whose death was sincerely lamented by every one who knew her. Among the most afflicted of her freinds were Lady Williams, Miss Johnson and the Duke; the 2 last of whom had a most sincere regard for her, more particularly Alice, who had spent a whole evening in her company and had never thought of her since. His Grace's affliction may likewise be easily accounted for, since he lost one for whom he had experienced during the last ten days, a tender affection and sincere regard. He mourned her loss with unshaken constancy for the next fortnight at the end of which time, he gratified the ambition of Caroline Simpson by raising her to the rank of a Dutchess. Thus was she at length rendered compleatly happy in the gratification of her favourite passion. Her sister the perfidious Sukey, was likewise shortly after exalted in a manner she truly deserved, and by her actions appeared to have

The Beautifull Cassandra

always desired. Her barbarous Murder was discovered and in spite of every interceding freind she was speedily raised to the Gallows—. The beautifull but affected Cecilia was too sensible of her own superior charms, not to imagine that if Caroline could engage a Duke, she might without censure aspire to the affections of some Prince – and knowing that those of her native Country were cheifly engaged, she left England and I have since heard is at present the favourite Sultana of the great Mogul—.

In the mean time the inhabitants of Pammydiddle were in a state of the greatest astonishment and Wonder, a report being circulated of the intended marriage of Charles Adams. The Lady's name was still a secret. M^r and Mrs Jones imagined it to be, Miss Johnson; but <u>she</u> knew better; all <u>her</u> fears were centered in his Cook, when to the astonishment of every one, he was publicly united to Lady Williams—

Finis

Henry and Eliza

a novel

Is humbly dedicated to Miss Cooper by her obedient
Humble Servant
The Author

As Sir George and Lady Harcourt were superintending the Labours of their Haymakers, rewarding the industry of some by smiles of approbation, and punishing the idleness of others, by a cudgel, they perceived lying closely concealed beneath the thick foliage of a Haycock, a beautifull little Girl not more than 3 months old.

Touched with the enchanting Graces of her face and delighted with the infantine tho' sprightly answers she returned to their many questions, they resolved to take her home and, having no Children of their own, to educate her with care and cost.

Being good People themselves, their first and principal care was to incite in her a Love of Virtue and a Hatred of Vice, in which they so well succeeded (Eliza having a natural turn that way herself) that when she grew up, she was the delight of all who knew her.

The Beautifull Cassandra

Beloved by Lady Harcourt, adored by Sir George and admired by all the World, she lived in a continued course of uninterrupted Happiness, till she had attained her eighteenth year, when happening one day to be detected in stealing a banknote of 50£, she was turned out of doors by her inhuman Benefactors. Such a transition to one who did not possess so noble and exalted a mind as Eliza, would have been Death, but she, happy in the conscious knowledge of her own Excellence, amused herself, as she sate beneath a tree with making and singing the following Lines.

SONG.

Though misfortunes my footsteps may ever attend
   I hope I shall never have need of a Freind
as an innocent Heart I will ever preserve
   and will never from Virtue's dear boundaries swerve.

Having amused herself some hours, with this song and her own pleasing reflections, she arose and took the road to M. a small market town of which place her most intimate freind kept the red Lion.

To this freind she immediately went, to whom having recounted her late misfortune, she communicated her wish of getting into some family in the capacity of Humble Companion.

Mʳˢ Wilson, who was the most amiable creature on earth, was no sooner acquainted with her Desire, than she sate down in the Bar and wrote the following Letter to the Dutchess of F., the woman whom of all others, she most Esteemed.

'TO THE DUTCHESS OF F.'

Receive into your Family, at my request a young woman of unexceptionable Character, who is so good as to choose your Society in preference to going to Service. Hasten, and take her from the arms of your

Sarah Wilson.

The Dutchess, whose freindship for Mʳˢ Wilson would have carried her any lengths, was overjoyed at such an opportunity of obliging her and accordingly sate out immediately on the receipt of her letter for the red Lion, which she reached the same Evening. The Dutchess of F. was about 45 and a half; Her passions were strong, her freindships firm and her Enmities, unconquerable. She was a widow and had only one Daughter who was on the point of marriage with a young Man of considerable fortune.

The Dutchess no sooner beheld our Heroine than throwing her arms around her neck, she declared herself so much pleased with her, that she was resolved they never

The Beautifull Cassandra

more should part. Eliza was delighted with such a protestation of freindship, and after taking a most affecting leave of her dear Mrs Wilson, accompanied her grace the next morning to her seat in Surry.

With every expression of regard did the Dutchess introduce her to Lady Harriet, who was so much pleased with her appearance that she besought her, to consider her as her Sister, which Eliza with the greatest Condescension promised to do.

Mr Cecil, the Lover of Lady Harriet, being often with the family was often with Eliza. A mutual Love took place and Cecil having declared his first, prevailed on Eliza to consent to a private union, which was easy to be effected, as the Dutchess's chaplain being very much in love with Eliza himself, would they were certain do anything to oblige her.

The Dutchess and Lady Harriet being engaged one evening to an assembly, they took the opportunity of their absence and were united by the enamoured Chaplain.

When the Ladies returned, their amazement was great at finding instead of Eliza the following Note.

'Madam
   We are married and gone.

                              Henry and Eliza Cecil.'

Her Grace as soon as she had read the letter, which sufficiently explained the whole affair, flew into the most violent passion and after having spent an agreable half hour, in calling them by all the shocking Names her rage could suggest to her, sent out after them 300 armed Men, with orders not to return without their Bodies, dead or alive; intending that if they should be brought to her in the latter condition to have them put to Death in some torture-like manner, after a few years Confinement.

In the mean time Cecil and Eliza continued their flight to the Continent, which they judged to be more secure than their native Land, from the dreadfull effects of the Dutchess's vengeance, which they had so much reason to apprehend.

In France they remained 3 years, during which time they became the parents of two Boys, and at the end of it Eliza became a widow without any thing to support either her or her Children. They had lived since their Marriage at the rate of 12,000£ a year, of which Mr Cecil's estate being rather less than the twentieth part, they had been able to save but a trifle, having lived to the utmost extent of their Income.

Eliza, being perfectly conscious of the derangement in their affairs, immediately on her Husband's death set sail for England, in a man of War of 55 Guns, which they had built in their more prosperous Days. But no sooner had she stepped on Shore at Dover, with a Child in each hand, than she was seized by the officers of the Dutchess, and conducted by them to a snug little Newgate

The Beautifull Cassandra

of their Lady's which she had erected for the reception of her own private Prisoners.

No sooner had Eliza entered her Dungeon than the first thought which occurred to her, was how to get out of it again.

She went to the Door; but it was locked. She looked at the Window; but it was barred with iron; disappointed in both her expectations, she dispaired of effecting her Escape, when she fortunately perceived in a Corner of her Cell, a small saw and Ladder of ropes. With the saw she instantly went to work and in a few weeks had displaced every Bar but one to which she fastened the Ladder.

A difficulty then occurred which for some time, she knew not how to obviate. Her Children were too small to get down the Ladder by themselves, nor would it be possible for her to take them in her arms, when she did. At last she determined to fling down all her Cloathes, of which she had a large Quantity, and then having given them strict Charge not to hurt themselves, threw her Children after them. She herself with ease discended by the Ladder, at the bottom of which she had the pleasure of finding Her little boys in perfect Health and fast asleep.

Her wardrobe she now saw a fatal necessity of selling, both for the preservation of her Children and herself. With tears in her eyes, she parted with these last reliques of her former Glory, and with the money she got for them, bought others more usefull, some playthings for her Boys and a gold Watch for herself.

But scarcely was she provided with the above-mentioned necessaries, than she began to find herself rather hungry, and had reason to think, by their biting off two of her fingers, that her Children were much in the same situation.

To remedy these unavoidable misfortunes, she determined to return to her old freinds, Sir George and Lady Harcourt, whose generosity she had so often experienced and hoped to experience as often again.

She had about 40 miles to travel before she could reach their hospitable Mansion, of which having walked 30 without stopping, she found herself at the Entrance of a Town, where often in happier times, she had accompanied Sir George and Lady Harcourt to regale themselves with a cold collation at one of the Inns.

The reflections that her adventures since the last time she had partaken of these happy <u>Junketings</u>, afforded her, occupied her mind, for some time, as she sate on the steps at the door of a Gentleman's house. As soon as these reflections were ended, she arose and determined to take her station at the very inn, she remembered with so much delight, from the Company of which, as they went in and out, she hoped to receive some Charitable Gratuity.

She had but just taken her post at the Innyard before a Carriage drove out of it, and on turning the Corner at which she was stationed, stopped to give the Postilion an opportunity of admiring the beauty of the prospect. Eliza

The Beautifull Cassandra

then advanced to the carriage and was going to request their Charity, when on fixing her Eyes on the Lady, within it, she exclaimed,

'Lady Harcourt!'

To which the lady replied,

'Eliza!'

'Yes Madam it is the wretched Eliza herself.'

Sir George, who was also in the Carriage, but too much amazed to speek, was proceeding to demand an explanation from Eliza of the Situation she was then in, when Lady Harcourt in transports of Joy, exclaimed.

'Sir George, Sir George, she is not only Eliza our adopted Daughter, but our real Child.'

'Our real Child! What Lady Harcourt, do you mean? You know you never even was with child. Explain yourself, I beseech you.'

'You must remember Sir George that when you sailed for America, you left me breeding.'

'I do, I do, go on dear Polly.'

'Four months after you were gone, I was delivered of this Girl, but dreading your just resentment at her not proving the Boy you wished, I took her to a Haycock and laid her down. A few weeks afterwards, you returned, and fortunately for me, made no enquiries on the subject. Satisfied within myself of the wellfare of my Child, I soon forgot I had one, insomuch that when, we shortly after found her in the very Haycock, I had placed her, I had no more idea of her being my own, than you had, and

31

nothing I will venture to say would have recalled the circumstance to my remembrance, but my thus accidentally hearing her voice, which now strikes me as being the very counterpart of my own Child's.'

'The rational and convincing Account you have given of the whole affair,' said Sir George, 'leaves no doubt of her being our Daughter and as such I freely forgive the robbery she was guilty of.'

A mutual Reconciliation then took place, and Eliza, ascending the Carriage with her two Children returned to that home from which she had been absent nearly four years.

No sooner was she reinstated in her accustomed power at Harcourt Hall, than she raised an Army, with which she entirely demolished the Dutchess's Newgate, snug as it was, and by that act, gained the Blessings of thousands, and the Applause of her own Heart.

Finis

The beautifull Cassandra

*a novel in twelve Chapters dedicated
by permission to Miss Austen.*

DEDICATION.

Madam

    You are a Phoenix. Your taste is refined, your Sentiments are noble, and your Virtues innumerable. Your Person is lovely, your Figure, elegant, and your Form, magestic. Your Manners are polished, your Conversation is rational and your appearance singular. If therefore the following Tale will afford one moment's amusement to you, every wish will be gratified of

your most obedient
humble Servant
The Author

CHAPTER THE FIRST

Cassandra was the Daughter and the only Daughter of a celebrated Millener in Bond Street. Her father was of noble Birth, being the near relation of the Dutchess of ——'s Butler.

CHAPTER THE 2^D

When Cassandra had attained her 16th year, she was lovely and amiable and chancing to fall in love with an elegant Bonnet, her Mother had just compleated bespoke by the Countess of —— she placed it on her gentle Head and walked from her Mother's shop to make her Fortune.

CHAPTER THE 3^D

The first person she met, was the Viscount of —— a young Man, no less celebrated for his Accomplishments and Virtues, than for his Elegance and Beauty. She curtseyed and walked on.

CHAPTER THE 4TH

She then proceeded to a Pastry-cooks where she devoured six ices, refused to pay for them, knocked down the Pastry Cook and walked away.

CHAPTER THE 5ᵀᴴ

She next ascended a Hackney Coach and ordered it to Hampstead, where she was no sooner arrived than she ordered the Coachman to turn round and drive her back again.

CHAPTER THE 6ᵀᴴ

Being returned to the same spot of the same Street she had sate out from, the Coachman demanded his Pay.

CHAPTER THE 7ᵀᴴ

She searched her pockets over again and again; but every search was unsuccessfull. No money could she find. The man grew peremptory. She placed her bonnet on his head and ran away.

CHAPTER THE 8ᵀᴴ

Thro' many a street she then proceeded and met in none the least Adventure till on turning a Corner of Bloomsbury Square, she met Maria.

CHAPTER THE 9^(TH)

Cassandra started and Maria seemed surprised; they trembled, blushed, turned pale and passed each other in a mutual silence.

CHAPTER THE 10^(TH)

Cassandra was next accosted by her freind the Widow, who squeezing out her little Head thro' her less window, asked her how she did? Cassandra curtseyed and went on.

CHAPTER THE 11^(TH)

A quarter of a mile brought her to her paternal roof in Bond Street from which she had now been absent nearly 7 hours.

CHAPTER THE 12^(TH)

She entered it and was pressed to her Mother's bosom by that worthy woman. Cassandra smiled and whispered to herself 'This is a day well spent.'

Finis

Letter the third

*From A young Lady in distress'd
Circumstances to her freind*

A few days ago I was at a private Ball given by Mr Ashburnham. As my Mother never goes out she entrusted me to the care of Lady Greville who did me the honour of calling for me in her way and of allowing me to sit forwards, which is a favour about which I am very indifferent especially as I know it is considered as confering a great obligation on me. 'So Miss Maria' (said her Ladyship as she saw me advancing to the door of the Carriage) 'you seem very smart to night – <u>My</u> poor Girls will appear quite to disadvantage by <u>you</u> – I only hope your Mother may not have distressed herself to set <u>you</u> off. Have you got a new Gown on?'

'Yes Ma'am,' replied I with as much indifference as I could assume.

'Aye, and a fine one too I think—' (feeling it, as by her permission I seated myself by her) 'I dare say it is all very smart – But I must own, for you know I always speak my mind, that I think it was quite a needless peice of expence – Why could not you have worn your old striped one? It is not my way to find fault with people because they are poor, for I always think that they are more to be despised and pitied than blamed for it, especially if they cannot help it, but at the same time I must say that in my opinion your old striped Gown would have been quite fine enough for its Wearer – for to tell you the truth (I always speak my mind) I am very much afraid that one half of the people in the room will not know whether you have a Gown on or not – But I suppose you intend to make your fortune tonight—: Well, the sooner the better; and I wish you success.'

'Indeed, Ma'am, I have no such intention—'

'Who ever heard a Young Lady own that she was a Fortune-hunter?' Miss Greville laughed, but I am sure Ellen felt for me.

'Was your Mother gone to bed before you left her?' said her Ladyship—

'Dear Ma'am,' said Ellen, 'it is but nine o'clock.'

'True, Ellen, but Candles cost money, and Mrs Williams is too wise to be extravagant.'

'She was just sitting down to supper, Ma'am—'

'And what had she got for Supper?' 'I did not observe.' 'Bread and Cheese I suppose.' 'I should never wish for a better supper,' said Ellen. 'You have never any reason' replied her Mother, 'as a better is always provided for you.' Miss Greville laughed excessively, as she constantly does at her Mother's wit.

Such is the humiliating Situation in which I am forced to appear while riding in her Ladyship's Coach – I dare

The Beautifull Cassandra

not be impertinent, as my Mother is always admonishing me to be humble and patient if I wish to make my way in the world. She insists on my accepting every invitation of Lady Greville, or you may be certain that I would never enter either her House, or her Coach, with the disagreable certainty I always have of being abused for my Poverty while I am in them. – When we arrived at Ashburnham, it was nearly ten o'clock, which was an hour and a half later than we were desired to be there; but Lady Greville is too fashionable (or fancies herself to be so) to be punctual. The Dancing however was not begun as they waited for Miss Greville. I had not been long in the room before I was engaged to dance by Mr Bernard, but just as we were going to stand up, he recollected that his Servant had got his white Gloves, and immediately ran out to fetch them. In the mean time the Dancing began and Lady Greville in passing to another room went exactly before me – She saw me and instantly stopping, said to me though there were several people close to us;

'Hey day, Miss Maria! What cannot you get a partner? Poor Young Lady! I am afraid your new Gown was put on for nothing. But do not despair; perhaps you may get a hop before the Evening is over.' So saying, she passed on without hearing my repeated assurance of being engaged, and leaving me very provoked at being so exposed before every one – Mr Bernard however soon returned and by coming to me the moment he entered the room, and leading me to the Dancers, my Character I hope was cleared from the imputation Lady Greville had thrown on it, in the eyes of all the old Ladies who had heard her speech. I soon forgot all my vexations in the pleasure of dancing and of having the most agreable partner in the room. As he is moreover heir to a very large Estate I could see that Lady Greville did not look very well pleased when she found who had been his Choice – She was determined to mortify me, and accordingly when we were sitting down between the dances, she came to me with <u>more</u> than her usual insulting importance attended by Miss Mason and said loud enough to be heard by half the people in the room, 'Pray, Miss Maria, in what way of business was your Grandfather? for Miss Mason and I cannot agree whether he was a Grocer or a Bookbinder.' I saw that she wanted to mortify me, and was resolved if I possibly could to prevent her seeing that her scheme succeeded. 'Neither Madam; he was a Wine Merchant.' 'Aye, I knew he was in some such low way – He broke did not he?' 'I beleive not Ma'am.' 'Did not he abscond?' 'I never heard that he did.' 'At least he died insolvent?' 'I was never told so before.' 'Why, was not your <u>Father</u> as poor as a Rat?' 'I fancy not.' 'Was not he in the King's Bench once?' 'I never saw him there.' <u>She</u> gave me <u>such</u> a look, and turned away in a great passion; while I was half delighted with myself for my impertinence, and half afraid of being thought too saucy. As Lady Greville was extremely angry with me, she took no

The Beautifull Cassandra

further notice of me all the Evening, and indeed had I been in favour I should have been equally neglected, as she was got into a party of great folks and she never speaks to me when she can to any one else. Miss Greville was with her Mother's party at Supper, but Ellen preferred staying with the Bernards and me. We had a very pleasant Dance and as Lady G —— slept all the way home, I had a very comfortable ride.

The next day while we were at dinner Lady Greville's Coach stopped at the door, for that is the time of day she generally contrives it should. She sent in a message by the Servant to say that 'she should not get out but that Miss Maria must come to the Coach-door, as she wanted to speak to her, and that she must make haste and come immediately—' 'What an impertinent Message Mama!' said I—'Go Maria—' replied She – Accordingly I went and was obliged to stand there at her Ladyship's pleasure though the Wind was extremely high and very cold.

'Why I think, Miss Maria, you are not quite so smart as you were last night – But I did not come to examine your dress, but to tell you that you may dine with us the day after tomorrow – Not tomorrow, remember, do not come tomorrow, for we expect Lord and Lady Clermont and Sir Thomas Stanley's family – There will be no occasion for your being very fine for I shan't send the Carriage – If it rains you may take an umbrella—' I could hardly help laughing at hearing her give me leave to keep myself dry – 'And pray remember to be in time, for

Jane Austen

I shan't wait – I hate my Victuals over-done – But you need not come <u>before</u> the time – How does your Mother do? She is at dinner is not she?' 'Yes, Ma'am, we were in the middle of dinner when your Ladyship came.' 'I am afraid you find it very cold, Maria,' said Ellen. 'Yes, it is an horrible East wind'—said her Mother—'I assure you I can hardly bear the window down – But you are used to be blown about the wind, Miss Maria, and that is what has made your Complexion so ruddy and coarse. You young Ladies who cannot often ride in a Carriage never mind what weather you trudge in, or how the wind shews your legs. I would not have <u>my</u> Girls stand out of doors as you do in such a day as this. But some sort of people have no feelings either of cold or Delicacy – Well, remember that we shall expect you on Thursday at 5 o'clock – You must tell your Maid to come for you at night – There will be no Moon – and you will have an horrid walk home – My Compliments to your Mother – I am afraid your dinner will be cold – Drive on—' And away she went, leaving me in a great passion with her as she always does.

Maria Williams

From a Young Lady very much in love to her Freind

My Uncle gets more stingy, my Aunt more particular, and I more in love every day. What shall we all be at the rate by the end of the year! I had this morning the happiness of receiving the following Letter from my dear Musgrove.

Sackville St: Jan^{ry} 7th

It is a month to day since I beheld my lovely Henrietta, and the sacred anniversary must and shall be kept in a manner becoming the day – by writing to her. Never shall I forget the moment when her Beauties first broke on my sight – No time as you well know can erase it from my Memory. It was at Lady Scudamore's. Happy Lady Scudamore to live within a mile of the divine Henrietta! When the lovely Creature first entered the room, Oh! what were my sensations? The sight of you was like the sight of a wonderful fine Thing. I started – I gazed at her with Admiration – She appeared every moment more Charming, and the unfortunate Musgrove became a Captive to your Charms before I had time to look about me.

Yes Madam, I had the happiness of adoring you, an unhappiness for which I cannot be too grateful. 'What,' said he to himself, 'is Musgrove allowed to die for Henrietta? Enviable Mortal! and may he pine for her who is the object of universal Admiration, who is adored by a Colonel, and toasted by a Baronet!—' Adorable Henrietta how beautiful you are! I declare you are quite divine! You are more than Mortal. You are an Angel. You are Venus herself. Inshort, Madam, you are the prettiest Girl I ever saw in my Life – and her Beauty is encreased in her Musgrove's Eyes, by permitting him to love her and allowing me to hope. And Ah! Angelic Miss Henrietta, Heaven is my Witness how ardently I do hope for the death of your villanous Uncle and his Abandoned Wife, Since my fair one will not consent to be mine till their decease has placed her in affluence above what my fortune can procure—. Though it is an improvable Estate—. Cruel Henrietta to persist in such a resolution! I am at present with my Sister where I mean to continue till my own house which tho' an excellent one is at present somewhat out of repair, is ready to receive me. Amiable princess of my Heart farewell – Of that Heart which trembles while it signs itself your most ardent Admirer

and devoted humble Servt
T. Musgrove

There is a pattern for a Love-letter Matilda! Did you ever read such a masterpeice of Writing? Such Sense,

The Beautifull Cassandra

Such Sentiment, Such purity of Thought, Such flow of Language and such unfeigned Love in one Sheet? No, never I can answer for it, since a Musgrove is not to be met with by every Girl. Oh! how I long to be with him! I intend to send him the following in answer to his Letter tomorrow.

My dearest Musgrove—. Words can not express how happy your Letter made me; I thought I should have cried for Joy, for I love you better than any body in the World. I think you the most amiable, and the handsomest Man in England, and so to be sure you are. I never read so sweet a Letter in my Life. Do write me another just like it, and tell me you are in love with me in every other line. I quite die to see you. How shall we manage to see one another? for we are so much in love that we cannot live asunder. Oh! my dear Musgrove you cannot think how impatiently I wait for the death of my Uncle and Aunt – If they will not die soon, I beleive I shall run mad, for I get more in love with you every day of my Life. How happy your Sister is to enjoy the pleasure of your Company in her house, and how happy every body in London must be because you are there. I hope you will be so kind as to write to me again soon, for I never read such sweet Letters as yours. I am, my dearest Musgrove, most truly and faithfully yours for ever and ever

Henrietta Halton

I hope he will like my answer; it is as good a one as I can write, though nothing to his; Indeed I had always heard what a dab he was at a Love-letter. I saw him you know for the first time at Lady Scudamore's – And when I saw her Ladyship afterwards she asked me how I liked her Cousin Musgrove?

'Why upon my word' said I, 'I think he is a very handsome young Man.'

'I am glad you think so,' replied she, 'for he is distractedly in love with you.'

'Law! Lady Scudamore,' said I, 'how can you talk so ridiculously?'

'Nay, 'tis very true,' answered She, 'I assure you, for he was in love with you from the first moment he beheld you.'

'I wish it may be true,' said I, 'for that is the only kind of love I would give a farthing for – There is some Sense in being in love at first sight.'

'Well, I give you Joy of your conquest,' replied Lady Scudamore, 'and I beleive it to have been a very complete one; I am sure it is not a contemptible one, for my Cousin is a charming young fellow, has seen a great deal of the World, and writes the best Love-letters I ever read.'

This made me very happy, and I was excessively pleased with my conquest. However I thought it was proper to give myself a few Airs – So I said to her—

'This is all very pretty, Lady Scudamore, but you know that we young Ladies who are Heiresses must not throw ourselves away upon Men who have no fortune at all.'

'My dear Miss Halton,' said She, 'I am as much convinced of that as you can be, and I do assure you that I should be the last person to encourage your marrying any one who had not some pretensions to expect a fortune with you. Mr Musgrove is so far from being poor that he has an estate of Several hundreds an year which is capable of great Improvement, and an excellent House, though at present it is not quite in repair.'

'If that is the case,' replied I, 'I have nothing more to say against him, and if as you say he is an informed young Man and can write good Love-letters, I am sure I have no reason to find fault with him for admiring me, tho' perhaps I may not marry him for all that, Lady Scudamore.'

'You are certainly under no obligation to marry him,' answered her Ladyship, 'except that which love himself will dictate to you, for if I am not greatly mistaken you are at this very moment unknown to yourself, cherishing a most tender affection for him.'

'Law, Lady Scudamore,' replied I blushing, 'how can you think of such a thing?'

'Because every look, every word betrays it,' answered She; 'Come, my dear Henrietta, consider me as a freind, and be sincere with me – Do not you prefer Mr Musgrove to any man of your acquaintance?'

'Pray do not ask me such questions, Lady Scudamore,' said I turning away my head, 'for it is not fit for me to answer them.'

'Nay my Love,' replied she, 'now you confirm my suspicions. But why, Henrietta, should you be ashamed to own a well-placed Love, or why refuse to confide in me?'

'I am not ashamed to own it;' said I taking Courage. 'I do not refuse to confide in you or blush to say that I do love your cousin Mr Musgrove, that I am sincerely attached to him, for it is no disgrace to love a handsome Man. If he were plain indeed I might have had reason to be ashamed of a passion which must have been mean since the Object would have been unworthy. But with such a figure and face, and such beautiful hair as your Cousin has, why should I blush to own that such Superior Merit has made an impression on me.'

'My sweet Girl' (said Lady Scudamore embracing me with great Affection) 'what a delicate way of thinking you have in these Matters, and what a quick discernment for one of your years! Oh! how I honour you for such Noble Sentiments!'

'Do you, Ma'am?' said I; 'You are vastly obliging. But pray, Lady Scudamore, did your Cousin himself tell you of his Affection for me? I shall like him the better if he did, for what is a Lover without a Confidante?'

'Oh! my Love' replied She, 'you were born for each other. Every word you say more deeply convinces me that your Minds are actuated by the invisible power of simpathy, for your opinions and Sentiments so exactly coincide. Nay, the colour of your Hair is not very different. Yes, my dear Girl, the poor despairing Musgrove did reveal to me the story of his Love—. Nor was I surprised at it – I know not how it was, but I had a kind of presentiment that he <u>would</u> be in love with you.'

'Well, but how did he break it to you?'

'It was not till after supper. We were sitting round the fire together talking on indifferent subjects, though to say the truth the Conversation was cheifly on my side, for he was thoughtful and silent, when on a sudden he interrupted me in the midst of something I was saying, by exclaiming in a most Theatrical tone—

"Yes I'm in love I feel it now

And Henrietta Halton has undone me—"'

'Oh! What a sweet Way' replied I, 'of declaring his Passion! To make such a couple of charming Lines about me! What a pity it is that they are not in rhime!'

'I am very glad you like it,' answered She; 'To be sure there was a great deal of Taste in it. "And are you in love with her, Cousin?" said I. "I am very sorry for it, for unexceptionable as you are in every respect, with a pretty Estate capable of Great improvements, and an excellent House tho' somewhat out of repair, Yet who can hope to aspire with success to the adorable Henrietta who has had an offer from a Colonel and been toasted by a Baronet—"'

'<u>That</u> I have—' cried I. Lady Scudamore continued. '"Ah, dear Cousin," replied he, "I am so well convinced of the little Chance I can have of winning her who is adored by thousands, that I need no assurances of yours to make me more thoroughly so. Yet surely neither you or the fair

Henrietta herself will deny me the exquisite Gratification of dieing for her, of falling a victim of her Charms. And when I am dead" – continued he—'

'Oh Lady Scudamore,' said I wiping my eyes, 'that such a sweet Creature should talk of dieing!'

'It is an affecting Circumstance indeed,' replied Lady Scudamore. '"When I am dead," said he, "Let me be carried and lain at her feet, and perhaps she may not disdain to drop a pitying tear on my poor remains."'

'Dear Lady Scudamore' interrupted I, 'say no more on this affecting Subject. I cannot bear it.'

'Oh! how I admire the sweet Sensibility of your Soul, and as I would not for Worlds wound it too deeply, I will be silent.'

'Pray go on' said I. She did so.

'"And then," added he, "Ah! Cousin, imagine what my transports will be when I feel the dear precious drops trickle o'er my face! Who would not die to taste such extacy! And when I am interred, may the divine Henrietta bless some happier Youth with her affection, May he be as tenderly attached to her as the hapless Musgrove and while <u>he</u> crumbles to dust, May they live an example of Felicity in the Conjugal state!"'

'Did you ever hear any thing so pathetic? What a charming wish, to be lain at my feet when he was dead! Oh! what an exalted mind he must have to be capable of such a wish!' Lady Scudamore went on.

'"Ah! my dear Cousin," replied I to him, "Such noble

The Beautifull Cassandra

behaviour as this, must melt the heart of any Woman however obdurate it may naturally be; and could the divine Henrietta but hear your generous wishes for her happiness, all gentle as is her Mind, I have not a doubt but that she would pity your affection and endeavour to return it." "Oh! Cousin," answered he, "do not endeavour to raise my hopes by such flattering Assurances. No, I cannot hope to please this angel of a Woman, and the only thing which remains for me to do, is to die." "True Love is ever desponding," replied I, "but I, my dear Tom, will give you even greater hopes of conquering this fair one's heart, than I have yet given you, by assuring you that I watched her with the strictest attention during the whole day, and could plainly discover that she cherishes in her bosom though unknown to herself, a most tender affection for you."'

'Dear Lady Scudamore,' cried I, 'This is more than I ever knew!'

'Did not I say that it was unknown to yourself? "I did not," continued I to him, "encourage you by saying this at first, that Surprise might render the pleasure Still Greater." "No, Cousin," replied he in a languid voice, "nothing will convince me that I can have touched the heart of Henrietta Halton, and if you are deceived yourself, do not attempt deceiving me." Inshort my Love it was the work of some hours for me to persuade the poor despairing Youth that you had really a preference for him; but when at last he could no longer deny the force of my arguments, or discredit what I told him, his transports, his Raptures, his Extacies are beyond my power to describe.'

'Oh! the dear Creature,' cried I, 'how passionately he loves me! But, dear Lady Scudamore, did you tell him that I was totally dependant on my Uncle and Aunt?'

'Yes, I told him every thing.'

'And what did he say?'

'He exclaimed with virulence against Uncles and Aunts; Accused the Laws of England for allowing them to possess their Estates when wanted by their Nephews or Neices, and wished <u>he</u> were in the House of Commons, that he might reform the Legislature, and rectify all its abuses.'

'Oh! the sweet Man! What a spirit he has!' said I.

'He could not flatter himself, he added, that the adorable Henrietta would condescend for his Sake to resign those Luxuries and that Splendor to which She had been used, and accept only in exchange the Comforts and Elegancies which his limited Income could afford her, even supposing that his house were in Readiness to receive her. I told him that it could not be expected that she would; it would be doing her an injustice to suppose her capable of giving up the power she now possesses and so nobly uses of doing such extensive Good to the poorer part of her fellow Creatures, merely for the gratification of you and herself.'

'To be sure,' said I, 'I <u>am</u> very Charitable every now and then. And what did Mr Musgrove say to this?'

'He replied that he was under a melancholy Necessity of owning the truth of what I said, and therefore if he should be the happy Creature destined to be the Husband of the Beautiful Henrietta he must bring himself to wait, however impatiently, for the fortunate day, when she might be freed from the power of worthless Relations and able to bestow herself on him.'

What a noble Creature he is! Oh! Matilda what a fortunate one <u>I am</u>, who am to be his Wife! My Aunt is calling to me to come and make the pies. So adeiu my dear freind,

        and beleive me yours etc. – H. Halton

Finis

*A Letter from a Young Lady, whose feelings
being too Strong for her Judgement led her
into the commission of Errors which
her Heart disapproved*

Many have been the cares and vicissitudes of my past life, my beloved Ellinor, and the only consolation I feel for their bitterness is that on a close examination of my conduct, I am convinced that I have strictly deserved them. I murdered my father at a very early period of my Life, I have since murdered my Mother, and I am now going to murder my Sister. I have changed my religion so often that at present I have not an idea of any left. I have been a perjured witness in every public tryal for these last twelve Years, and I have forged my own Will. In short there is scarcely a crime that I have not committed – But I am now going to reform. Colonel Martin of the Horse guards has paid his Addresses to me, and we are to be married in a few days. As there is something singular in our Courtship, I will give you an account of it. Colonel Martin is the second son of the late Sir John Martin who died immensely rich, but bequeathing only one hundred thousand pound apiece to his three younger Children, left the bulk of his fortune, about eight Million to the present Sir Thomas. Upon his small pittance the Colonel lived tolerably contented for nearly four months when he took it into his head to determine on getting the whole of his eldest Brother's Estate. A new will was forged and the Colonel produced it in Court – but nobody would swear to it's being the right Will except himself, and he had sworn so much that Nobody beleived him. At that moment I happened to be passing by the door of the Court, and was beckoned in by the Judge who told the Colonel that I was a Lady ready to witness anything for the cause of Justice, and advised him to apply to me. In short the Affair was soon adjusted. The Colonel and I swore to its' being the right will, and Sir Thomas has been obliged to resign all his illgotten Wealth. The Colonel in gratitude waited on me the next day with an offer of his hand—. I am now going to murder my Sister.

                        Yours Ever,

                                Anna Parker

1. BOCCACCIO · *Mrs Rosie and the Priest*
2. GERARD MANLEY HOPKINS · *As kingfishers catch fire*
3. *The Saga of Gunnlaug Serpent-tongue*
4. THOMAS DE QUINCEY · *On Murder Considered as One of the Fine Arts*
5. FRIEDRICH NIETZSCHE · *Aphorisms on Love and Hate*
6. JOHN RUSKIN · *Traffic*
7. PU SONGLING · *Wailing Ghosts*
8. JONATHAN SWIFT · *A Modest Proposal*
9. *Three Tang Dynasty Poets*
10. WALT WHITMAN · *On the Beach at Night Alone*
11. KENKŌ · *A Cup of Sake Beneath the Cherry Trees*
12. BALTASAR GRACIÁN · *How to Use Your Enemies*
13. JOHN KEATS · *The Eve of St Agnes*
14. THOMAS HARDY · *Woman much missed*
15. GUY DE MAUPASSANT · *Femme Fatale*
16. MARCO POLO · *Travels in the Land of Serpents and Pearls*
17. SUETONIUS · *Caligula*
18. APOLLONIUS OF RHODES · *Jason and Medea*
19. ROBERT LOUIS STEVENSON · *Olalla*
20. KARL MARX AND FRIEDRICH ENGELS · *The Communist Manifesto*
21. PETRONIUS · *Trimalchio's Feast*
22. JOHANN PETER HEBEL · *How a Ghastly Story Was Brought to Light by a Common or Garden Butcher's Dog*
23. HANS CHRISTIAN ANDERSEN · *The Tinder Box*
24. RUDYARD KIPLING · *The Gate of the Hundred Sorrows*
25. DANTE · *Circles of Hell*
26. HENRY MAYHEW · *Of Street Piemen*
27. HAFEZ · *The nightingales are drunk*
28. GEOFFREY CHAUCER · *The Wife of Bath*
29. MICHEL DE MONTAIGNE · *How We Weep and Laugh at the Same Thing*
30. THOMAS NASHE · *The Terrors of the Night*
31. EDGAR ALLAN POE · *The Tell-Tale Heart*
32. MARY KINGSLEY · *A Hippo Banquet*
33. JANE AUSTEN · *The Beautifull Cassandra*
34. ANTON CHEKHOV · *Gooseberries*
35. SAMUEL TAYLOR COLERIDGE · *Well, they are gone, and here must I remain*
36. JOHANN WOLFGANG VON GOETHE · *Sketchy, Doubtful, Incomplete Jottings*
37. CHARLES DICKENS · *The Great Winglebury Duel*
38. HERMAN MELVILLE · *The Maldive Shark*
39. ELIZABETH GASKELL · *The Old Nurse's Story*
40. NIKOLAY LESKOV · *The Steel Flea*

41. HONORÉ DE BALZAC · *The Atheist's Mass*
42. CHARLOTTE PERKINS GILMAN · *The Yellow Wall-Paper*
43. C.P. CAVAFY · *Remember, Body . . .*
44. FYODOR DOSTOEVSKY · *The Meek One*
45. GUSTAVE FLAUBERT · *A Simple Heart*
46. NIKOLAI GOGOL · *The Nose*
47. SAMUEL PEPYS · *The Great Fire of London*
48. EDITH WHARTON · *The Reckoning*
49. HENRY JAMES · *The Figure in the Carpet*
50. WILFRED OWEN · *Anthem For Doomed Youth*
51. WOLFGANG AMADEUS MOZART · *My Dearest Father*
52. PLATO · *Socrates' Defence*
53. CHRISTINA ROSSETTI · *Goblin Market*
54. *Sindbad the Sailor*
55. SOPHOCLES · *Antigone*
56. RYŪNOSUKE AKUTAGAWA · *The Life of a Stupid Man*
57. LEO TOLSTOY · *How Much Land Does A Man Need?*
58. GIORGIO VASARI · *Leonardo da Vinci*
59. OSCAR WILDE · *Lord Arthur Savile's Crime*
60. SHEN FU · *The Old Man of the Moon*
61. AESOP · *The Dolphins, the Whales and the Gudgeon*
62. MATSUO BASHŌ · *Lips too Chilled*
63. EMILY BRONTË · *The Night is Darkening Round Me*
64. JOSEPH CONRAD · *To-morrow*
65. RICHARD HAKLUYT · *The Voyage of Sir Francis Drake Around the Whole Globe*
66. KATE CHOPIN · *A Pair of Silk Stockings*
67. CHARLES DARWIN · *It was snowing butterflies*
68. BROTHERS GRIMM · *The Robber Bridegroom*
69. CATULLUS · *I Hate and I Love*
70. HOMER · *Circe and the Cyclops*
71. D. H. LAWRENCE · *Il Duro*
72. KATHERINE MANSFIELD · *Miss Brill*
73. OVID · *The Fall of Icarus*
74. SAPPHO · *Come Close*
75. IVAN TURGENEV · *Kasyan from the Beautiful Lands*
76. VIRGIL · *O Cruel Alexis*
77. H. G. WELLS · *A Slip under the Microscope*
78. HERODOTUS · *The Madness of Cambyses*
79. *Speaking of Siva*
80. *The Dhammapada*

""Oh, good God," he kept saying with great relish. "Good God . . .""

ANTON CHEKHOV
Born 1860, Taganrog, Russia
Died 1904, Badenweiler, Germany

'The Kiss' was first published in 1887; 'The Two Volodyas' in 1893; and 'Gooseberries' in 1898. This selection has been taken from the three volumes of Chekhov's short stories available in Penguin Classics.

CHEKHOV IN PENGUIN CLASSICS
The Steppe and Other Stories, 1887–1891
Ward No. 6 and Other Stories, 1892–1895
The Lady with the Little Dog and Other Stories, 1896–1904
The Shooting Party
Plays
A Life in Letters

ANTON CHEKHOV

Gooseberries

Translated by
Ronald Wilks

PENGUIN BOOKS

PENGUIN CLASSICS

UK | USA | Canada | Ireland | Australia
India | New Zealand | South Africa

Penguin Books is part of the Penguin Random House group of companies
whose addresses can be found at global.penguinrandomhouse.com.

This selection published in Penguin Classics 2015

012

'The Kiss' and 'Gooseberries', translation copyright © Ronald Wilks, 1982
'The Two Volodyas', translation copyright © Ronald Wilks, 1984

The moral right of the translator has been asserted

Set in 9/12.4 pt Baskerville 10 Pro
Typeset by Jouve (UK), Milton Keynes
Printed and bound in Great Britain by Clays Ltd, Elcograf S.p.A.

A CIP catalogue record for this book is available from the British Library

ISBN: 978-0-141-39709-2

www.greenpenguin.co.uk

Penguin Random House is committed to a sustainable future for our business, our readers and our planet. This book is made from Forest Stewardship Council® certified paper.

Contents

The Kiss	1
The Two Volodyas	26
Gooseberries	42

The Kiss

On 20 May, at eight o'clock in the evening, all six batteries of a reserve artillery brigade, on their way back to headquarters, stopped for the night at the village of Mestechki. At the height of all the confusion – some officers were busy with the guns, while others had assembled in the main square by the churchyard fence to receive their billetings – someone in civilian dress rode up from behind the church on a strange horse: it was small and dun-coloured with a fine neck and short tail, and seemed to move sideways instead of straight ahead, making small dancing movements with its legs as if they were being whipped. When the rider came up to the officers he doffed his hat and said, 'Our squire, His Excellency, Lieutenant-General von Rabbeck, invites you for tea and would like you to come now . . .'

The horse performed a bow and a little dance, and retreated with the same sideways motion. The rider raised his hat again and quickly disappeared behind the church on his peculiar horse.

'To hell with it!' some of the officers grumbled as they rode off to their quarters. 'We want to sleep and up pops this von Rabbeck with his tea! We know what *that* means all right!'

Every officer in the six batteries vividly remembered the previous year when they were on manoeuvres with officers from a Cossack regiment and had received a similar invitation from a landowning count, who was a retired officer. This hospitable and genial count had plied them with food and drink, would not hear of them returning to their billets and made them stay the night. That was all very well, of course, and they could not have hoped for better. But the trouble was that this retired officer was overjoyed beyond measure at having young men as his guests and he regaled them with stories from his glorious past until dawn, led them on a tour of the house, showed them his valuable paintings, old engravings and rare guns, and read out signed letters from eminent personages; and all this time the tired and weary officers listened, looked, pined for bed, and continuously yawned in their sleeves. When their host finally let them go, it was too late for bed.

Now, was this von Rabbeck one of the same breed? Whether he was or not, there was nothing they could do about it. The officers put clean uniforms on, smartened themselves up and went off en masse to look for the squire's house. On the square by the church they were told that they could either take the lower path leading down to the river behind the church, and then go along the bank to the garden, or they could ride direct from the church along the higher road which would bring them to the count's barns about a quarter of a mile from the village. The officers decided on the higher route.

'Who is this von Rabbeck?' they argued as they rode along. 'Is he the one who commanded a cavalry division at Plevna?'

'No, that wasn't von Rabbeck, just Rabbe, and without the "von".'

'It's marvellous weather, anyway!'

The road divided when they reached the first barn: one fork led straight on and disappeared in the darkness of the evening, while the other turned towards the squire's house on the right. The officers took the right fork and began to lower their voices . . . Stone barns with red tiled roofs stood on both sides of the road and they had the heavy, forbidding look of some provincial barracks. Ahead of them were the lighted windows of the manor-house.

'That's a good sign, gentlemen!' one of the officers said. 'Our setter's going on in front. That means he scents game!'

Lieutenant Lobytko, a tall, strongly built officer, who was riding ahead of the others, who had no moustache (although he was over twenty-five there wasn't a trace of hair on his face), and who was renowned in the brigade for his keen senses and ability to sniff a woman out from miles away, turned round and said, 'Yes, there must be women here, my instinct tells me.'

The officers were met at the front door by von Rabbeck himself – a fine-looking man of about sixty, wearing civilian clothes. He said how very pleased and happy he was to see the officers as he shook hands, but begged them most sincerely, in the name of God, to excuse him for not inviting them to stay the night, as two sisters with their children, his brothers and some neighbours had turned up, and he didn't have one spare room.

The general shook everyone's hand, apologized and smiled, but they could tell from his face that he wasn't nearly as pleased to have guests as last year's count and he had only asked them as it was the done thing. And, as they climbed the softly carpeted stairs and listened, the officers sensed that they had been invited only because it would have caused embarrassment if they had *not* been invited. At the sight of footmen dashing around lighting the lamps in the hall and upstairs, they felt they had introduced a note of uneasiness and anxiety into the house. And how could any host be pleased at having nineteen strange officers descend on a house where two sisters, children, brothers and neighbours had already arrived, most probably to celebrate some family anniversary. They were met in the ballroom upstairs by a tall, stately old lady with black eyebrows and a long face – the living image of Empress Eugénie. She gave them a majestic, welcoming smile and said how glad and happy she was to have them as guests and apologized for the fact that she and her husband weren't able to invite the officers to stay overnight on this occasion. Her beautiful, majestic smile, which momentarily disappeared every time she turned away from her guests, revealed that in her day she had seen many officers, that she had no time for them now, and that she had invited them and was apologizing only because her upbringing and social position demanded it.

The officers entered the large dining-room where about ten gentlemen and ladies, old and young, were sitting along one side of the table having tea. Behind their chairs, enveloped in a thin haze of cigar smoke, was a group of men with a rather lean, young, red-whiskered man in the middle, rolling his 'r's as he spoke out loud in English. Behind them, through a door, was a bright room with light blue furniture.

'Gentlemen, there's so many of you, it's impossible to

introduce *everyone*!' the general was saying in a loud voice, trying to sound cheerful. 'So don't stand on ceremony, introduce yourselves!'

Some officers wore very serious, even solemn expressions; others forced a smile, and all of them felt awkward as they bowed rather indifferently and sat down to tea.

Staff-Captain Ryabovich, a short, stooping officer, with spectacles and lynx-like side whiskers, was more embarrassed than anyone else. While his fellow-officers were trying to look serious or force a smile, his face, lynx-like whiskers and spectacles seemed to be saying, 'I'm the shyest, most modest and most insignificant officer in the whole brigade!' When he first entered the dining-room and sat down to tea, he found it impossible to concentrate on any one face or object. All those faces, dresses, cut-glass decanters, steaming glasses, moulded cornices, merged into one composite sensation, making Ryabovich feel ill at ease, and he longed to bury his head somewhere. Like a lecturer at his first appearance in public, he could see everything in front of him well enough, but at the same time he could make little sense of it (physicians call this condition, when someone sees without understanding, 'psychic blindness'). But after a little while Ryabovich began to feel more at home, recovered his normal vision and began to take stock of his surroundings. Since he was a timid and unsociable person, he was struck above all by what he himself had never possessed – the extraordinary boldness of these unfamiliar people. Von Rabbeck, two elderly ladies, a young girl in a lilac dress, and the young man with red whiskers – Rabbeck's youngest son – had sat themselves very cunningly among the officers, as though it had all been rehearsed. Straight away they had launched into a heated argument, which the guests could not help joining. The girl in lilac very excitedly insisted that the artillery had a much easier time than either the cavalry or the infantry, while Rabbeck and the elderly ladies argued the contrary. A rapid conversational crossfire ensued. Ryabovich glanced at the lilac girl who was arguing so passionately about something that was so foreign to her, so utterly boring, and he could see artificial smiles flickering over her face.

Von Rabbeck and family skilfully drew the officers into the argument, at the same time watching their wine glasses with eagle eyes to check whether they were filled, that they had enough sugar, and one officer who wasn't eating biscuits or drinking any brandy worried them. The more Ryabovich looked and listened, the more he began to like this insincere but wonderfully disciplined family.

After tea the officers went into the ballroom. Lieutenant Lobytko's instinct had not failed him: the room was full of girls and young married women. Already this 'setter' lieutenant had positioned himself next to a young blonde in a black dress, bending over dashingly as though leaning on some invisible sabre, smiling and flirting with his shoulders. Most probably he was telling her some intriguing nonsense as the blonde glanced superciliously at his well-fed face and said, 'Really?'

If that 'setter' had had any brains, that cool 'Really?' should have told him that he would never be called 'to heel'.

The grand piano suddenly thundered out. The sounds of a sad waltz drifted through the wide-open windows and everyone remembered that outside it was spring, an evening in May, and they smelt the fragrance of the young leaves of the poplars, of roses and lilac. Ryabovich, feeling the effects of the brandy and the music, squinted at a window, smiled and watched the movements of the women. Now it seemed that the fragrance of the roses, the poplars and lilac wasn't coming from the garden but from the ladies' faces and dresses.

Rabbeck's son had invited a skinny girl to dance and waltzed twice round the room with her. Lobytko glided over the parquet floor as he flew up to the girl in lilac and whirled her round the room. They all began to dance . . . Ryabovich stood by the door with guests who were not dancing and watched. Not once in his life had he danced, not once had he put his arm round an attractive young woman's waist. He would usually be absolutely delighted when, with everyone looking on, a man took a young girl he hadn't met before by the waist and offered his shoulders for her to rest her hands on, but he could never imagine himself in that situation. There had been times when he envied his fellow-officers' daring and dashing ways and it made him very depressed. The realization that he was shy, round-shouldered, quite undistinguished, that he had a long waist, lynx-like side whiskers, hurt him deeply. But over the years this realization had become something of a habit and as he watched his friends dance or talk out loud he no longer envied them but was filled with sadness.

When the quadrille began, young von Rabbeck went over to the officers who were not dancing and invited two of them to a game of billiards. They accepted and left the great hall with him. As he had nothing else to do, and feeling he would like to take at least some part in what was going on, Ryabovich trudged off after them. First they went into the drawing-room, then down a narrow corridor with a glass ceiling, then into a room where three sleepy footmen leapt up from a sofa the moment they entered. Finally, after passing through a whole series of rooms, young Rabbeck and company reached a small billiard-room and the game began.

Ryabovich, who never played any games except cards, stood by the table and indifferently watched the players, cue in hand, walking up and down in their unbuttoned tunics, making puns and shouting things he could not understand. The players ignored him, only turning round to say, 'I beg your pardon', when one of them happened accidentally to nudge him with an elbow or prod him with a cue. Even before the first game was over, he was bored and began to feel he was not wanted, that he was in the way ... He felt drawn back to the ballroom and walked away.

As he walked back he had a little adventure. Halfway, he realized he was lost – he knew very well he had to go by those three sleepy footmen, but already he had passed through five or six rooms and those footmen seemed to have vanished into thin air. He realized his mistake, retraced his steps a little and turned to the right, only to find himself in a small, dimly lit room he had not seen on the way to the billiard-room. He stood still for a minute or so, opened the first door he came to with determination and entered a completely dark room. Ahead of him he could see light coming through a crack in the door and beyond was the muffled sound of a sad mazurka. The windows here had been left open as they had in the ballroom and he could smell poplars, lilac and roses . . .

Ryabovich stopped, undecided what to do . . . Just then he was astonished to hear hurried footsteps, the rustle of a dress and a female voice whispering breathlessly, 'At last!' Two soft, sweet-smelling arms (undoubtedly a woman's) encircled his neck, a burning cheek pressed against his and at the same time there was the sound of a kiss. But immediately after the kiss the woman gave a faint cry and shrank backwards in disgust – that was how it seemed to Ryabovich.

He was on the point of crying out too and he rushed towards the bright chink in the door.

His heart pounded away when he was back in the hall and his hands trembled so obviously that he hastily hid them behind his back. At first he was tormented by shame and he feared everyone there knew he had just been embraced and kissed, and this made him hesitate and look around anxiously. But when he had convinced himself that everyone was dancing and gossiping just as peacefully as before, he gave himself up to a totally new kind of sensation, one he had never experienced before in all his life. Something strange was happening to him . . . his neck, which just a few moments ago had been embraced by sweet-smelling hands, seemed anointed with oil. And on his left cheek, just by his moustache, there was a faint, pleasant, cold, tingling sensation, the kind you get from peppermint drops and the more he rubbed the spot the stronger the tingling became. From head to heels he was overcome by a strange, new feeling which grew stronger every minute. He wanted to dance, speak to everyone, run out into the garden, laugh out loud. He completely forgot his stoop, his insignificant appearance, his lynx-like whiskers and 'vague appearance' (once he happened to hear some ladies saying this about him). When Rabbeck's wife went by he gave her such a broad, warm smile that she stopped and gave him a very searching look.

'I love this house so much!' he said, adjusting his spectacles.

The general's wife smiled and told him that the house still belonged to her father. Then she asked if his parents were still alive, how long he had been in the army, why he was so thin, and so on... When Ryabovich had replied, she moved on, leaving him smiling even more warmly and he began to think he was surrounded by the most wonderful people...

Mechanically, Ryabovich ate and drank everything he was offered at the dinner table, deaf to everything as he tried to find an explanation for what had just happened. It was a mysterious, romantic incident, but it wasn't difficult to explain. No doubt some girl or young married woman had a rendezvous with someone in that dark room, had waited for a long time, and then mistook Ryabovich for her hero in her nervous excitement. This was the most likely explanation, all the more so as Ryabovich had hesitated in the middle of the room, which made it look as though he were expecting someone...

'But who *is* she?' he thought as he surveyed the ladies' faces. 'She must be young, as old ladies don't have rendezvous. And intelligent – I could tell from the rustle of her dress, her smell, her voice.'

He stared at the girl in lilac and found her very attractive.

The Kiss

She had beautiful shoulders and arms, a clever face and a fine voice. As he gazed at her, Ryabovich wanted *her*, no one else, to be that mysterious stranger . . . But she gave a rather artificial laugh and wrinkled her long nose, which made her look old. Then he turned to the blonde in black. She was younger, simpler and less affected, with charming temples and she sipped daintily from her wine glass. Now Ryabovich wanted her to be the stranger. But he soon discovered that she had a featureless face and he turned to her neighbour . . . 'It's hard to say,' he wondered dreamily. 'If I could just take the lilac girl's shoulders and arms away, add the blonde's temples, then take those eyes away from the girl on Lobytko's left, *then*.' He merged them all into one, so that he had an image of the girl who had kissed him, the image he desired so much, but which he just could not find among the guests around the table.

After dinner the officers, well-fed and slightly tipsy by now, began to make their farewells and expressed their thanks. Once again the hosts apologized for not having them stay the night.

'Delighted, gentlemen, absolutely delighted,' the general was saying and this time he meant it – probably because people are usually more sincere and better-humoured saying goodbye to guests than welcoming them.

'Delighted! Glad to see you back any time, so don't stand on ceremony. Which way are you going? The higher road? No, go through the garden, it's quicker.'

The officers went into the garden, where it seemed very dark and quiet after the bright lights and the noise. They did not say a word all the way to the gate. They were half-drunk, cheerful and contented, but the darkness and the silence made them pause for thought. Probably they were thinking the same as Ryabovich: would they ever see the day when they would own a large house, have a family, a garden, when *they* too would be able to entertain people (however much of a pretence this might be), feed them well, make them drunk and happy?

As they went through the garden gate they all started talking at once and, for no apparent reason, laughed out loud. Now they were descending the path that led down to the river and then ran along the water's edge, weaving its way around the bushes, the little pools of water and the willows which overhung the river. The bank and the path were barely visible, and the far side was plunged in darkness. Here and there were reflections of the stars in the water, quivering and breaking up into little patches – the only sign that the river was flowing fast. All was quiet. Sleepy sandpipers called plaintively from the far bank and on the near side a nightingale in a bush poured out its song, ignoring the passing officers.

The men paused by the bush, touched it, but still the nightingale sang.

'That's a bird for you!' approving voices murmured. 'Here we are, right next to him and he doesn't take a blind bit of notice! What a rascal!'

The path finally turned upwards and came out on to the high road by the church fence. The officers were exhausted from walking up the hill and sat down for a smoke. On the far bank they could make out a dim red light and they tried to pass the time by guessing whether it was a camp fire, a light in a window, or something else . . . Ryabovich looked at it and imagined that the light was winking at him and smiling, as though it knew all about that kiss.

When he reached his quarters Ryabovich quickly undressed and lay on his bed. In the same hut were Lobytko and Lieutenant Merzlyakov, a gentle, rather quiet young man, who was considered well-educated in his own little circle. He was always reading the *European Herald* when he had the chance and took it with him everywhere. Lobytko undressed, paced up and down for a long time, with the expression of a dissatisfied man, and sent the batman for some beer.

Merzlyakov lay down, placed a candle near his pillow and immersed himself in the *European Herald*.

'Who *is* she?' Ryabovich wondered as he glanced at the grimy ceiling. His neck still felt as if it had been anointed with oil and he had that tingling sensation around his mouth – just like peppermint drops. He had fleeting visions of the lilac girl's shoulders and arms, the temples and truthful eyes of the blonde in black, waists, dresses, brooches. He tried to fix these visions firmly in his mind, but they kept dancing about, dissolving, flickering. When these visions vanished completely against that darkened background everyone has when he closes his eyes, he began to hear hurried steps, rustling dresses, the sound of a kiss and he was gripped by an inexplicable, overwhelming feeling of joy. Just as he was abandoning himself to it, he heard the batman come back and report that there wasn't any beer. Lobytko became terribly agitated and started pacing up and down again.

'Didn't I tell you he's an idiot?' he said, stopping first in front of Ryabovich, then Merzlyakov. 'A man must really be a blockhead and idiot to come back without any beer! The man's a rogue, eh?'

'Of course, you won't find any beer in this place,' Merzlyakov said without taking his eyes off the *European Herald*.

'Oh, do you really think so?' Lobytko persisted. 'Good God, put me on the moon and I'll find you beer and women right away! Yes, I'll go now and find some . . . Call me a scoundrel if I don't succeed!'

He slowly dressed and pulled on his high boots. Then he finished his cigarette in silence and left.

'Rabbeck, Grabbeck, Labbeck,' he muttered, pausing in the hall. 'I don't feel like going on my own, dammit! Fancy a little walk, Ryabovich?'

There was no reply, so he came back, slowly undressed and got into bed. Merzlyakov sighed, put the *European Herald* away and snuffed the candle.

'Hm,' Lobytko murmured as he puffed his cigarette in the dark.

Ryabovich pulled the blankets over his head, curled himself into a ball and tried to merge the visions fleeting through his mind into one fixed image. But he failed completely. Soon he fell asleep and his last waking thought was of someone caressing him and making him happy, of something absurd and unusual, but nonetheless exceptionally fine and joyful, that had entered his life. And his dreams centred around this one thought.

When he woke up, the sensation of oil on his cheek and the minty tingling near his lips had vanished, but the joy of yesterday still filled his heart. Delighted, he watched the window frames, gilded now by the rising sun, and listened intently to the street noises. Outside, just by the window, he could hear loud voices – Lebedetsky, Ryabovich's battery commander, who had just caught up with the brigade, was shouting at his sergeant – simply because he had lost the habit of talking softly.

'Is there anything else?' he roared.

'When they were shoeing yesterday, sir, someone drove a nail into Pigeon's hoof. The medical orderly put clay and vinegar on it and they're keeping the horse reined, away from the others. And artificer Artemyev got drunk yesterday and the lieutenant had him tied to the fore-carriage of an auxiliary field-gun.'

And the sergeant had more to report. Karpov had forgotten the new cords for the trumpets and the stakes for the tents, and the officers had spent the previous evening as guests of General von Rabbeck. During the conversation, Lebedetsky's head and red beard appeared at the window. He blinked his short-sighted eyes at the sleepy officers and bade them good morning.

'Everything all right?' he asked.

'One of the shaft-horses damaged its withers – it was the new collar,' Lobytko answered, yawning.

The commander sighed, pondered for a moment and said in a loud voice, 'I'm still wondering whether to pay Aleksandra a visit, I really ought to go and see how she is. Well, goodbye for now, I'll catch you up by evening.'

A quarter of an hour later the brigade moved off. As it passed the general's barns, Ryabovich looked to the right where the house was. The blinds were drawn in all the windows. Clearly, everyone was still asleep. And the girl who had kissed Ryabovich the day before was sleeping too. He tried to imagine her as she slept and he had a clear and distinct picture of the wide-open windows, the little green branches peeping into her bedroom, the morning freshness, the smell of poplars, lilac and roses, her bed and the chair with that dress which had rustled the day before lying over it, tiny slippers, a watch on the table. But the actual features of that face, that sweet, dreamy smile, exactly what was most characteristic of her, slipped through his imagination like mercury through the fingers. When he had ridden about a quarter of a mile, he looked back. The yellow church, the house, the river and garden were flooded in sunlight and the river, with its bright green banks and its waters reflecting the light blue sky and glinting silver here and there, looked very beautiful. Ryabovich took a last look at Mestechki and he felt so sad, as if he were saying farewell to what was very near and dear to him.

But there were only long-familiar, boring scenes ahead of him. On both sides of the road there were fields of young rye and buckwheat, where crows were hopping about. Ahead, all he could see was dust and the backs of soldiers' heads; and behind, the same dust, the same faces. The brigade was led by a vanguard of four soldiers bearing sabres and behind them rode the military choristers, followed by trumpeters. Every now and then, like torchbearers in a funeral cortège, the vanguard and singers ignored the regulation distance and pushed on far ahead. Ryabovich rode alongside the first field-gun of the fifth battery and he could see the other four in front. These long, ponderous processions formed by brigades on the move can strike civilians as very peculiar, an unintelligible muddle, and non-military people just cannot fathom why a single field-gun has to be escorted by so many soldiers, why it has to be drawn by so many horses all tangled up in such strange harness, as if it really was such a terrible, heavy object. But Ryabovich understood everything perfectly well and for that reason he found it all extremely boring. He had long known why a hefty bombardier always rides with the officer at the head of every battery and why he is called an outrider. Immediately behind this bombardier came the riders on the first, then the middle-section trace-horses. Ryabovich knew that the horses to the left were saddle-horses, while those on the right were auxiliary – all this was very boring. The horsemen were followed by two shaft-horses, one ridden by a horseman with yesterday's dust still on his back and who had a clumsy-looking, very comical piece of wood fixed to his right leg. Ryabovich knew what it was for and did not find it funny. All the riders waved their whips mechanically and shouted now and again. As for the field-gun, it was an ugly thing. Sacks of oats covered with tarpaulin lay on the fore-carriage and the gun itself was hung with kettles, kitbags and little sacks: it resembled a small harmless animal which had been surrounded, for some reason, by men and horses. On the side sheltered from the wind a team of six strode along, swinging their arms. This gun was followed by more bombardiers, riders, shaft-horses and another field-gun – just as ugly and uninspiring as the first – lumbering along in the rear. After the second gun came a third, then a fourth with an officer riding alongside (there are six batteries to a brigade and four guns to a battery). The whole procession stretched about a quarter of a mile and ended with the baggage wagons, where a most likeable creature plodded thoughtfully along, his long-eared head drooping: this was Magar the donkey, brought from Turkey by a certain battery commander.

Ryabovich looked apathetically at all those necks and faces in front and behind. At any other time he would have dozed off, but now he was immersed in new, pleasant thoughts. When the brigade had first set off, he had tried to convince himself that the incident of the kiss was only some unimportant, mysterious adventure and that essentially it was trivial and too ridiculous for serious thought. But very quickly he waved logic aside and gave himself up to his dreams. First he pictured himself in von Rabbeck's drawing-room, sitting next to a girl who resembled both the girl in lilac and the blonde in black. Then he closed his eyes and imagined himself with another, completely strange girl, with very indeterminate features: in his thoughts he spoke to her, caressed her and leaned his head on her shoulder. Then he thought of war and separation, reunion, dinner with his wife and children . . .

'Brakes on!' rang out the command every time they went downhill. He shouted the command too, and feared that his own shouts would shatter his daydreams and bring him back to reality.

As they passed some estate, Ryabovich peeped over the fence into the garden. There he saw a long avenue, straight as a ruler, strewn with yellow sand and lined with young birches. With the eagerness of a man who has surrendered himself to daydreaming, he imagined tiny female feet walking over the yellow sand. And, quite unexpectedly, he had a clear mental picture of the girl who had kissed him, the girl he had visualized the previous evening during dinner. This image had planted itself in his mind and would not leave him.

At midday someone shouted from a wagon in the rear, 'Attention, eyes left! Officers!'

The brigadier drove up in an open carriage drawn by two white horses. He ordered it to stop near the second battery and shouted something no one understood. Several officers galloped over to him, Ryabovich among them.

'Well, what's the news?' asked the brigadier, blinking his red eyes. 'Anyone ill?'

When they had replied, the brigadier, a small skinny man, chewed for a moment, pondered and then turned to one of the officers: 'One of your drivers, on the third gun, has taken his knee-guard off and the devil's hung it on the fore-carriage. Reprimand him!'

He looked up at Ryabovich and continued: 'It strikes me your harness breeches are too long.'

After a few more tiresome comments, the brigadier glanced at Lobytko and grinned. 'You look down in the dumps today, Lieutenant Lobytko. Pining for Madame Lopukhov, eh? Gentlemen, he's pining for Madame Lopukhov!'

Madame Lopukhov was a very plump, tall lady, well past forty. The brigadier, who had a passion for large women, no matter what age, suspected his officers nurtured similar passions. They smiled politely. Then the brigadier, delighted with himself for having made a very amusing, cutting remark, roared with laughter, tapped his driver on the back and saluted. The carriage drove off.

'All the things I'm dreaming about now and which seem impossible, out of this world, are in fact very ordinary,' Ryabovich thought as he watched the clouds of dust rising in the wake of the brigadier's carriage. 'It's all so very ordinary, everyone experiences it . . . The brigadier, for example. He was in love once, now he's married, with children. Captain Vachter is married and loved, despite having an extremely ugly red neck and no waistline. Salmanov is coarse and too much of a Tartar, but *he* had an affair that finished in marriage. I'm the same as everyone else . . . sooner or later I'll have to go through what they did . . .'

And he was delighted and encouraged by the thought that he was just an ordinary man, leading an ordinary life. Now he was bold enough to picture *her* and his happiness as much as he liked and he gave full rein to his imagination.

In the evening, when the brigade had reached its destination and the officers were resting in their tents, Ryabovich, Merzlyakov and Lobytko gathered round a trunk and had supper. Merzlyakov took his time, holding his *European Herald* on his knees and reading it as he slowly munched his food.

Lobytko could not stop talking and kept filling his glass with beer, while Ryabovich, whose head was rather hazy from dreaming all day long, said nothing as he drank. Three glasses made him tipsy and weak and he felt an irrepressible longing to share his new feelings with his friends.

'A strange thing happened to me at the Rabbecks,' he

said, trying to sound cool and sarcastic. 'I went to the billiard-room, you know . . .'

He began to tell them, in great detail, all about the kiss, but after a minute fell silent. In that one minute he had told them everything and he was astonished when he considered how little time was needed to tell his story: he had imagined it would take until morning. After he heard the story, Lobytko – who was a great liar and therefore a great sceptic – looked at him in disbelief and grinned. Merzlyakov twitched his eyebrows and kept his eyes glued to the *European Herald* as he calmly remarked, 'Damned if I know what to make of it! Throwing herself round a stranger's neck without saying a word first . . . She must have been a mental case . . .'

'Yes, some kind of neurotic,' Ryabovich agreed.

'Something similar happened to me once,' Lobytko said, assuming a frightened look. 'Last year I was travelling to Kovno . . . second class. The compartment was chock-full and it was impossible to sleep. So I tipped the guard fifty copeks . . . he took my luggage and got me a berth in a sleeper. I lay down and covered myself with a blanket. It was dark, you understand. Suddenly someone was touching my shoulder and breathing into my face. So I moved my arm and felt an elbow. I opened my eyes and – can you imagine! – it was a woman. Black eyes, lips as red as the best salmon, nostrils breathing passion, breasts like buffers! . . .'

'Just a minute,' Merzlyakov calmly interrupted. 'I don't dispute what you said about her breasts, but how could you see her lips if it was dark?'

Lobytko tried to wriggle out by poking fun at Merzlyakov's

obtuseness and this jarred on Ryabovich. He went away from the trunk, lay down and vowed never again to tell his secrets.

Camp life fell back into its normal routine. The days flashed by, each exactly the same as the other. All this time Ryabovich felt, thought and behaved like someone in love. When his batman brought him cold water in the mornings, he poured it over his head and each time he remembered that there was something beautiful and loving in his life.

In the evenings, when his fellow-officers talked about love and women, he would listen very attentively, sitting very close to them and assuming the habitual expression of a soldier hearing stories about battles he himself fought in. On those evenings when senior officers, led by 'setter' Lobytko, carried out 'sorties' on the local village, in true Don Juan style, Ryabovich went along with them and invariably returned feeling sad, deeply guilty and imploring *her* forgiveness. In his spare time, or on nights when he couldn't sleep, when he wanted to recall his childhood days, his parents, everything that was near and dear to him, he would always find himself thinking of Mestechki instead, of that strange horse, of von Rabbeck and his wife, who looked like the Empress Eugénie, of that dark room with the bright chink in the door.

On 31 August he left camp – not with his own brigade, however, but with two batteries. All the way he daydreamed and became very excited, as though he were going home. He wanted passionately to see that strange horse again, the church, those artificial Rabbecks, the dark room. Some inner voice, which so often deceives those in love, whispered that he was *bound* to see her again. And he was tormented by such questions as: how could he arrange a meeting, what would she say, had she forgotten the kiss? If the worst came to the worst, he would at least have the pleasure of walking through that dark room and remembering . . .

Towards evening, that familiar church and the white barns appeared on the horizon. His heart began to pound. He did not listen to what the officer riding next to him was saying, he was oblivious of everything and looked eagerly at the river gleaming in the distance, at the loft above which pigeons were circling in the light of the setting sun.

As he rode up to the church and heard the quartermaster speaking, he expected a messenger on horseback to appear from behind the fence any minute and invite the officers to tea . . . but the quartermaster read the billeting list out, the officers dismounted and strolled off into the village – and no messenger came.

'The people in the village will tell Rabbeck we're here and he'll send for us,' Ryabovich thought as he went into his hut. He just could not understand why a fellow-officer was lighting a candle, why the batmen were hurriedly heating the samovars.

He was gripped by an acute feeling of anxiety. He lay down, then got up and looked out of the window to see if the messenger was coming. But there was no one. He lay down again but got up again after half an hour, unable to control his anxiety, went out into the street and strode off towards the church.

The square near the fence was dark and deserted. Some soldiers were standing in a row at the top of the slope, saying nothing. They jumped when they saw Ryabovich and saluted. He acknowledged the salute and went down the familiar path.

The entire sky over the far bank was flooded with crimson; the moon was rising. Two peasant women were talking loudly and picking cabbage leaves as they walked along the edge of a kitchen garden. Beyond the gardens were some dark huts. On the near bank everything was much the same as in May: the path, the bushes, the willows overhanging the river . . . only there was no bold nightingale singing, no fragrant poplars or young grass. Ryabovich reached the garden and peered over the gate. It was dark and quiet and all he could see were the white trunks of the nearest birches and here and there little patches of avenue – everything else had merged into one black mass. Ryabovich looked hard, listened eagerly, and after standing and waiting for about a quarter of an hour, without hearing a sound or seeing a single light, he trudged wearily away . . .

He went down to the river, where he could see the general's bathing-hut and towels hanging over the rail on the little bridge. He went on to the bridge, stood for a moment and aimlessly fingered the towels. They felt cold and rough. He looked down at the water . . . the current was swift and purled, barely audibly, against the piles of the hut. The red moon was reflected in the water near the left bank; tiny waves rippled through the reflection, pulling it apart and breaking it up into little patches, as if trying to bear it away.

'How stupid, how very stupid!' Ryabovich thought as he looked at the fast-flowing water. Now, when he hoped for nothing, that adventure of the kiss, his impatience, his vague longings and disillusionment appeared in a new light. He

The Kiss

didn't think it at all strange that he hadn't waited for the general's messenger or that he would never see the girl who had kissed him by mistake. On the contrary, he would have thought it strange if he *had* seen her . . .

The water raced past and he did not know where or why; it had flowed just as swiftly in May, when it grew from a little stream into a large river, flowed into the sea, evaporated and turned into rain. Perhaps this was the same water flowing past. To what purpose?

And the whole world, the whole of life, struck Ryabovich as a meaningless, futile joke. As he turned his eyes from the water to the sky, he remembered how fate had accidentally caressed him – in the guise of an unknown woman. He recalled the dreams and visions of that summer and his life seemed terribly empty, miserable, colourless . . . When he returned to his hut, none of the officers was there.

The batman reported that they had all gone to 'General Fontryabkin's' – he'd sent a messenger on horseback with the invitation. There was a brief flicker of joy in his heart, but he snuffed it out at once, lay on his bed and in defiance of fate – as though he wanted to bring its wrath down on his own head – he did not go to the general's.

The Two Volodyas

'Let me go, *I* want to drive. I'm going to sit next to the driver,' Sophia Lvovna shouted. 'Driver, wait. I'm coming up on to the box to sit next to you.'

She stood on the sledge while her husband Vladimir Nikitych and her childhood friend Vladimir Mikhaylych held her by the arm in case she fell. Away sped the troika.

'I said you shouldn't have given her brandy,' Vladimir Nikitych whispered irritably to his companion. 'You're a fine one!'

From past experience the Colonel knew that when women like his wife Sophia Lvovna had been in riotous, rather inebriated high spirits he could normally expect fits of hysterical laughter and tears to follow. He was afraid that once they got home he would have to run around with the cold compresses and medicine instead of being able to go to bed.

'Whoa!' Sophia Lvovna shouted. 'I want to drive.'

She was really very gay and in an exultant mood. For two months after her wedding she had been tormented by the thought that she had married Colonel Yagich for his money or, as they say, *par dépit*. That same evening, in the out-of-town restaurant, she finally became convinced that she loved him passionately. In spite of his fifty-four years, he was so trim, sprightly and athletic, and he told puns and joined in the gypsy girls' songs with such charm. It is true that nowadays old men are a thousand times more interesting than young ones, as though age and youth had changed places. The Colonel was two years older than her father, but was that important if, to be quite honest, he was infinitely stronger, more energetic and livelier than she was, even though she was only twenty-three?

'Oh, my darling!' she thought. 'My wonderful man!'

In the restaurant she had come to the conclusion too that not a spark remained of her old feelings. To her childhood friend Vladimir Mikhaylych, whom only yesterday she had loved to distraction, she now felt completely indifferent. The whole evening he had struck her as a lifeless, sleepy, boring nobody and the habitual coolness with which he avoided paying restaurant bills exasperated her so much this time that she very nearly told him, 'You should have stayed at home if you're so poor.' The Colonel footed the bill.

Perhaps it was the trees, telegraph poles and snowdrifts all flashing past that aroused the most varied thoughts. She reflected that the meal had cost one hundred and twenty roubles – with a hundred for the gypsies – and that the next day, if she so wished, she could throw a thousand roubles away, whereas two months ago, before the wedding, she did not have three roubles to call her own and she had to turn to her father for every little thing. How her life had changed!

Her thoughts were in a muddle and she remembered how, when she was about ten, Colonel Yagich, her husband now, had made advances to her aunt and how everyone in the house had said that he had ruined her. In fact, her aunt often came down to dinner with tear-stained eyes and was always going away somewhere; people said the poor woman was suffering terribly. In those days he was very handsome and had extraordinary success with women; the whole town knew him and he was said to visit his admirers every day, like a doctor doing his rounds. Even now, despite his grey hair, wrinkles and spectacles, his thin face looked handsome, especially in profile.

Sophia Lvovna's father was an army doctor and had once served in Yagich's regiment. Volodya senior's father had also been an army doctor and had once served in the same regiment as her own father and Yagich. Despite some highly involved and frantic amorous adventures Volodya junior had been an excellent student. He graduated with honours from university, had decided to specialize in foreign literature and was said to be writing his thesis. He lived in the barracks with his doctor father and he had no money of his own, although he was now thirty. When they were children, Sophia Lvovna and he had lived in different flats, but in the same building, and he often came to play with her; together they had dancing and French lessons. But when he grew up into a well-built, exceedingly good-looking young man, she began to be shy of him. Then she fell madly in love with him and was still in love until shortly before she married Yagich. He too had extraordinary success with women, from the age of fourteen almost, and the ladies who deceived their husbands with him exonerated themselves by saying Volodya was 'so little'. Not long before, he was said to be living in digs close to the university and every time you knocked, his footsteps could be heard on the other side of the door and then the whispered apology: '*Pardon, je ne suis pas seul.*' Yagich was delighted with him, gave him his blessing for the future as Derzhavin had blessed Pushkin, and was evidently very fond of him. For hours on end they would silently play billiards or piquet, and if Yagich went off somewhere in a troika, he would take Volodya with him; only Yagich shared the secret of his thesis. In earlier days, when the Colonel was younger, they were often rivals, but were never jealous of one another. When they were in company, which they frequented together, Yagich was called 'Big Volodya' and his friend 'Little Volodya'.

Besides Big Volodya and Little Volodya, and Sophia Lvovna, there was someone else in the sledge, Margarita Aleksandrovna – or Rita as everyone called her – Mrs Yagich's cousin. She was a spinster, in her thirties, very pale, with black eyebrows, pince-nez, who chain-smoked even when it was freezing; there was always ash on her lap and chest. She spoke through her nose and drawled; she was cold and unemotional, could drink any quantity of liqueur or brandy without getting drunk and told stories abounding in *doubles entendres* in a dull, tasteless way. At home she read the learned reviews all day long, scattering ash all over them; or she would eat crystallized apples.

'Sophia, don't play the fool,' she drawled; 'it's really so stupid.'

When the town gates came into view the troika slowed down; they caught glimpses of people and houses, and Sophia quietened down, snuggled against her husband and gave herself up to her thoughts. And now gloomy thoughts began to mingle with her happy, carefree fantasies. The man opposite knew that she had loved him (so she thought), and of course he believed the reports that she had married the

Colonel *par dépit*. Not once had she confessed her love and she did not want him to know. She had concealed her feelings, but his expression clearly showed that he understood her perfectly, and so her pride suffered. But most humiliating of all about her situation was the fact that Little Volodya had suddenly started paying attention to her after her marriage, which had never happened before. He would sit with her for hours on end, in silence, or telling her some nonsense; and now in the sledge he was gently touching her leg or squeezing her hand, without saying a word. Evidently, all he wanted was for her to get married. No less obviously, he did not think much of her and she interested him only in a certain way, as an immoral, disreputable woman. And this mingling of triumphant love for her husband and injured pride was the reason for her behaving so irresponsibly, prompting her to sit on the box and shout and whistle . . .

Just as they were passing the convent the great twenty-ton bell started clanging away. Rita crossed herself.

'Our Olga is in that convent,' Sophia Lvovna said, crossing herself and shuddering.

'Why did she become a nun?' the Colonel asked.

'*Par dépit*,' Rita answered angrily, obviously hinting at Sophia Lvovna's marriage to Yagich. 'This *par dépit* is all the rage now. It's a challenge to the whole of society. She was a proper good-time girl, a terrible flirt, all she liked was dances and dancing partners. And then suddenly we have all this! She took us all by surprise!'

'That's not true,' Little Volodya said, lowering the collar of his fur coat and revealing his handsome face. 'This wasn't a case of *par dépit*, but something really terrible. Her brother

Dmitry was sentenced to hard labour in Siberia and no one knows where he is now. The mother died of grief.' He raised his collar again. 'And Olga did the right thing,' he added dully. 'Living as a ward, and with a treasure like our Sophia Lvovna, what's more – that's enough food for thought!'

Sophia Lvovna noted the contempt in his voice and wanted to say something very nasty in reply, but she said nothing. Once more euphoria gripped her. She stood up and shouted tearfully, 'I want to go to morning service. Driver, turn back! I want to see Olga!'

They turned back. The convent bell had a dull peal and Sophia Lvovna felt there was something in it reminding her of Olga and her life. Bells rang out from other churches. When the driver had brought the troika to a halt, Sophia leapt from the sledge and rushed unescorted to the gates.

'Please don't be long!' her husband shouted. 'It's late.'

She went through the dark gates, then along the path leading to the main church; the light snow crunched under her feet and the tolling of the bells sounded right over her head now and seemed to penetrate her whole being. First she came to the church door, the three steps down, then the porch, with paintings of the saints on both sides; there was a smell of juniper and incense. Then came another door, which a dark figure opened, bowing very low ... In the church the service had not yet begun. One of the nuns was in front of the icon-screen lighting candles in their holders, another was lighting a chandelier. Here and there, close to the columns and side-chapels, were motionless, black figures. 'They'll be standing in exactly the same places till morning,' Sophia Lvovna thought and the whole place struck her as dark, cold, depressing – more depressing than a graveyard. Feeling bored, she glanced at the motionless, frozen figures and suddenly her heart sank. Somehow she recognized one of the nuns – short, with thin shoulders and a black shawl on her head – as Olga, although when she had entered the convent she had been plump and taller, she thought. Deeply disturbed for some reason, Sophia Lvovna hesitantly walked over to the lay sister, looked over her shoulder into her face and saw it *was* Olga.

'Olga!' she said, clasping her hands and too excited to say anything else. 'Olga!'

The nun recognized her immediately, raised her eyebrows in astonishment and her pale, freshly washed face (even, it seemed, her white kerchief visible under her shawl) glowed with joy.

'God has performed a miracle,' she said and also clasped her thin, pale little hands.

Sophia Lvovna firmly embraced her and kissed her, frightened as she did so that her breath might smell of drink.

'We were just passing and we thought of you,' she said breathlessly, as though she had just completed a fast walk. 'Heavens, how pale you are! I'm . . . I'm very pleased to see you. Well, how are you? Bored?' Sophia Lvovna looked round at the other nuns and now she lowered her voice: 'So much has happened . . . you know I married Volodya Yagich. You must remember him . . . I'm very happy.'

'Well, thank the Lord for that! And is your father well?'

'Yes, he often remembers you. But you must come and see us during the holidays, Olga. Will you do that?'

The Two Volodyas

'Yes, I'll come,' Olga said smiling. 'I'll come the day after tomorrow.'

Without even knowing why, Sophia burst into tears and cried in silence for a whole minute. Then she dried her eyes and said, 'Rita will be very sorry she didn't see you. She's with us too. And Little Volodya. They're at the gate. How pleased they would be to see you! Come out and see them, the service hasn't started yet.'

'All right,' Olga agreed. She crossed herself three times and walked out with Sophia Lvovna.

'So, you said you're happy, Sophia,' she said after they were past the gates.

'Very.'

'Well, thank God.'

When Big Volodya and Little Volodya saw the nun they got off the sledge and greeted her respectfully. They were visibly moved by her pale face and her nun's black habit, and they were both pleased that she remembered them and had come to greet them. Sophia Lvovna wrapped her in a rug and covered her with one flap of her fur coat to protect her from the cold. Her recent tears had lightened and cleansed her soul and she was glad that the noisy, riotous and essentially immoral night had unexpectedly come to such a pure and quiet conclusion. Then to keep Olga by her side longer, she suggested, 'Let's take her for a ride! Olga, get in. Just a little one.'

The men expected the nun to refuse – religious people don't go around in troikas – but to their amazement she agreed and got in. When the troika hurtled off towards the town gates, no one said a word; their only concern was to make her warm and comfortable. Each one of them thought about the difference in her from before. Her face was impassive, somewhat expressionless, cold, pale, transparent, as though water flowed in her veins instead of blood. Two or three years ago she had been buxom and rosy-cheeked, had talked about eligible bachelors and laughed loud at the least thing.

The troika turned round at the town gates. Ten minutes later they were back at the convent and Olga climbed out. The bells were ringing a series of chimes.

'God be with you,' Olga said, giving a low, nun-like bow.

'So you will come then, Olga?'

'Of course I will.'

She quickly left and soon disappeared through the dark gateway. After the troika had moved on everyone somehow felt very sad. No one said a word. Sophia Lvovna felt weak all over and her heart sank. Making a nun get into a sledge and go for a ride with that drunken crowd struck her now as stupid, tactless and almost sacrilegious. The desire for self-deception vanished with her tipsiness and now she clearly realized that she did not and could not love her husband, it was all nothing but silly nonsense. She had married for money because, as her ex-schoolgirl friends put it, he was 'madly rich', because she was terrified of becoming an old maid, like Rita, because her doctor father got on her nerves and because she wanted to annoy Little Volodya. Had she guessed when she was contemplating marriage that it would turn out to be so nasty, painful and ugly, she would never have agreed to it, not for anything in the world. But the damage was done now, she had to accept things.

The Two Volodyas

They arrived home. As she lay in her warm, soft bed and covered herself with a blanket, Sophia Lvovna recalled the dark porch, the smell of incense, the figures by the columns, and she was distressed at the thought that these figures would still be standing there, quite motionless, all the time she was sleeping. Early morning service would be interminably long, and after that there would be the hours, then Mass, then more prayers . . .

'But surely God exists? He certainly exists and I must certainly die. Therefore, sooner or later, I must think of my soul, eternal life, like Olga does. Olga is saved now, she has solved all her problems for herself . . . But what if there is *no* God? Then her life has been wasted. But how has it been wasted? Why?'

A minute later another thought entered her head. 'God exists, death will certainly come. I should be thinking of my soul. If Olga could see her death this very minute she would not be afraid. She's ready. But the most important thing is, she's solved the riddle of existence for herself. God exists . . . yes. But isn't there another way out apart from becoming a nun? *That* means renouncing life, destroying it . . .' Sophia Lvovna became rather scared and hid her head under the pillow. 'I mustn't think about it,' she whispered, 'I mustn't.'

Yagich was walking up and down in the next room, his spurs softly jingling; he was deep in thought. Sophia Lvovna thought that this man was near and dear to her only in one thing – he was called Volodya too. She sat on her bed and tenderly called, 'Volodya!'

'What do you want?' her husband replied.

'Nothing.'

She lay down again. There were bells tolling – from that same convent, perhaps – and once again she recalled the porch and the dark figures. Thoughts of God and inescapable death wandered through her mind; she pulled the blanket over her head to drown the sound of the bells. She expected, before old age and death came, that her life would drag on for such a terribly long time, and from one day to the next she would have to cope with the nearness of someone she did not love, and who had come into the room just at that moment and was getting into bed; and she would have to suppress that hopeless love for another – someone who was so young, so charming and apparently so unusual. She looked at her husband and wanted to say good night, but she suddenly burst into tears instead. She felt annoyed with herself.

'Well, we're off again,' Yagich said.

She did calm down, but not until later, towards ten in the morning. She had stopped crying and shaking all over; she developed a severe headache, however. Yagich was hurrying, getting ready for late Mass and in the next room he was grumbling at the batman helping him dress. He came into the bedroom once, his spurs softly jingling, took something, and when he came in a second time he was wearing epaulettes and decorations; he limped slightly from rheumatism. He gave Sophia Lvovna the impression he was a beast of prey, prowling and looking round.

Then she heard him on the telephone. 'Please put me through to the Vasilyevsky Barracks,' he said. A minute later he went on, 'Is that Vasilyevsky Barracks? Please ask Dr Salimovich to come to the phone.' Then, a minute later, 'Who am I speaking to? Volodya? Fine. My dear chap, please ask your father to come over right away, my wife is terribly off colour after what happened yesterday. What's that? He's out? Hm . . . thanks . . . Yes, I'd be much obliged. *Merci*.'

Yagich came into the bedroom for the third time, bent over his wife, made the sign of the cross over her, let her kiss his hand (women who loved him would kiss his hand, he was used to this), and said he would be back for dinner. And he left.

Towards noon the maid announced Little Volodya. Swaying from weariness and her headache, Sophia Lvovna quickly put on her stunning new lilac, fur-trimmed negligee and hurriedly tidied her hair. In her heart she felt inexpressibly tender and trembled for joy – and for fear he might leave. She wanted just one look at him.

Little Volodya was paying her a visit in formal dress – tailcoat and white tie. When Sophia Lvovna came into the drawing-room he kissed her hand, said how deeply sorry he was to see her so unwell. When they had sat down he praised her negligee.

'Seeing Olga last night has upset me,' she said. 'At first it was painful for me, but now I envy her. She is like an immovable rock, it's impossible to budge her. But was there really no other way out for her, Volodya? Can burying oneself alive really solve life's problems? You'd call that death, not life, wouldn't you?' At the mention of Olga, Little Volodya's face showed deep emotion. 'Now look, Volodya, you're a clever man,' Sophia Lvovna said. 'Teach me to be like her. Of course, I'm a non-believer and I couldn't become a nun. But couldn't I do something that would be just as good? I find life hard enough.' After a brief silence she continued, 'Teach me . . . tell me something that will convince me. Just one word.'

'One word? Okay. Ta-ra-ra-boomdeay.'

'Volodya, why do you despise me?' she asked excitedly. 'You speak to me in some special – if you'll forgive the expression – fancy language that one doesn't use with friends and respectable women. You're a successful scholar, you love your studies, but why do you never tell me about them? Why? Aren't I good enough?'

Little Volodya frowned irritably and said, 'Why this sudden passion for scholarship? Perhaps you want us to have a constitution? Or perhaps sturgeon with horseradish?'

'Oh, have it your way then. I'm a mediocre, worthless, unprincipled, stupid woman . . . I've made thousands, thousands of mistakes. I'm not right in the head, a loose woman, and for that I deserve contempt. But you're ten years older than me, Volodya, aren't you? And my husband is thirty years older. You watched me grow up and if you'd wanted to, you could have made me anything you wanted, an angel even. But you . . .' (here her voice shook) 'treat me dreadfully. Yagich was an old man when he married me, and you . . .'

'Well, enough of that. Enough,' Volodya said, drawing closer to her and kissing both her hands. 'We'll leave the Schopenhauers to philosophize and argue about anything they like, but now we're going to kiss these sweet little hands.'

'You despise me and if only you knew the suffering it causes me,' she said hesitantly, knowing beforehand that he

The Two Volodyas

would not believe her. 'If you only knew how I want to improve myself, to start a new life! It fills me with joy just thinking about it,' she murmured and actually shed a few joyous tears. 'To be a good, honest, decent person, not to lie, to have a purpose in life.'

'Stop it please! You don't have to put on an act for me, I don't like it,' Volodya said, looking peevish. 'Heavens, you'd think we were at the theatre! Let's behave like normal human beings!'

To prevent him from leaving in a temper she began to make excuses, forced herself to smile – to please him – mentioned Olga again and that she wanted to solve the riddle of her existence, to become a real human being.

'Ta-ra-ra-boomdeay,' he chanted softly. 'Ta-ra-ra-boomdeay!'

And then quite suddenly he clasped her waist. Barely conscious of what she was doing she put her hands on his shoulders and for a whole minute looked rapturously at his clever, sarcastic face, his forehead, eyes, handsome beard...

'You've known for a long time that I love you,' she confessed with an agonized blush and she felt that even her lips had twisted in a paroxysm of shame. 'I love you. So why do you torment me?'

She closed her eyes and kissed him firmly on the lips. For a long time – a whole minute perhaps – she just could not bring herself to end this kiss, although she knew very well that she was behaving badly, that he might tell her off, or that a servant might come in...

Half an hour later, when he had got what he wanted, he sat in the dining-room eating a snack while she knelt before him, staring hungrily into his face. He told her she was like a small dog waiting for someone to toss it a piece of ham. Then he sat her on one knee, rocked her like a child and sang, 'Ta-ra-ra-boomdeay . . . Ta-ra-ra-boomdeay!'

When he was about to leave she asked him passionately, 'When? Later on? Where?' And she held out both hands to his mouth, as if wanting to catch his reply in them.

'It's not really convenient today,' he said after a moment's thought. 'Perhaps tomorrow, though.'

And they parted. Before lunch Sophia Lvovna went off to the convent to see Olga, but was told that she was reading the Psalter for someone who had died. From the convent she went to her father's and drove aimlessly up and down the main streets and side-streets until evening. While she was riding, for some reason she kept remembering that aunt with the tear-stained eyes, who was fretting her life away.

That night they all went riding on troikas again and heard the gypsies in that out-of-town restaurant. And when they were once again passing the convent Sophia Lvovna thought of Olga and became terrified at the thought that there was no escape for girls and women in her circle, except perpetual troika-rides or entering a convent to mortify the flesh . . .

The following day she had a lovers' rendezvous once again. She went for solitary cab-rides around town and thought of her aunt.

A week later Little Volodya dropped her. Then life reverted to normal and was just as boring, dreary – and sometimes just as excruciating as it had ever been. The Colonel and Little Volodya had long billiards and piquet sessions, Rita told her tasteless anecdotes in the same lifeless fashion,

Sophia Lvovna kept driving in cabs and asking her husband to take her for troika-rides.

Almost every day she called at the convent, boring Olga with her complaints of intolerable suffering; she cried and felt that she had brought something impure, pathetic and shabby into the cell. Olga, however, as if repeating a well-learnt lesson parrot-fashion, told her that there was nothing to worry about, that it would all pass and that God would forgive her.

Gooseberries

The sky had been overcast with rain clouds since early morning. The weather was mild, and not hot and oppressive as it can be on dull grey days when storm clouds lie over the fields for ages and you wait for rain which never comes. Ivan Ivanych, the vet, and Burkin, a teacher at the high school, were tired of walking and thought they would never come to the end of the fields. They could just make out the windmills at the village of Mironositskoye in the far distance – a range of hills stretched away to the right and disappeared far beyond it. They both knew that the river was there, with meadows, green willows and farmsteads, and that if they climbed one of the hills they would see yet another vast expanse of fields, telegraph wires and a train resembling a caterpillar in the distance. In fine weather they could see even as far as the town. And now, in calm weather, when the whole of nature had become gentle and dreamy, Ivan Ivanych and Burkin were filled with love for those open spaces and they both thought what a vast and beautiful country it was.

'Last time we were in Elder Prokofy's barn, you were going to tell me a story,' Burkin said.

'Yes, I wanted to tell you about my brother.'

Ivan Ivanych heaved a long sigh and lit his pipe before beginning his narrative; but at that moment down came the rain. Five minutes later it was simply teeming. Ivan Ivanych and Burkin were in two minds as to what they should do. The dogs were already soaked through and stood with their tails drooping, looking at them affectionately.

'We must take shelter,' Burkin said. 'Let's go to Alyokhin's, it's not very far.'

'All right, let's go there.'

They changed direction and went across mown fields, walking straight on at first, and then bearing right until they came out on the high road. Before long, poplars, a garden, then the red roofs of barns came into view. The river glinted, and then they caught sight of a wide stretch of water and a white bathing-hut. This was Sofino, where Alyokhin lived.

The mill was turning and drowned the noise of the rain. The wall of the dam shook. Wet horses with downcast heads were standing by some carts and peasants went around with sacks on their heads. Everything was damp, muddy and bleak, and the water had a cold, malevolent look. Ivan Ivanych and Burkin felt wet, dirty and terribly uncomfortable. Their feet were weighed down by mud and when they crossed the dam and walked up to the barns near the manor house they did not say a word and seemed to be angry with each other.

A winnowing fan was droning away in one of the barns and dust poured out of the open door. On the threshold stood the master himself, Alyokhin, a man of about forty, tall, stout, with long hair, and he looked more like a professor or an artist than a landowner. He wore a white shirt that hadn't been washed for a very long time, and it was tied round with a piece of rope as a belt. Instead of trousers he was wearing underpants; mud and straw clung to his boots. His nose and eyes were black with dust. He immediately recognized Ivan Ivanych and Burkin, and was clearly delighted to see them.

'Please come into the house, gentlemen,' he said, smiling, 'I'll be with you in a jiffy.'

It was a large house, with two storeys. Alyokhin lived on the ground floor in the two rooms with vaulted ceilings and small windows where his estate managers used to live. They were simply furnished and smelled of rye bread, cheap vodka and harness. He seldom used the main rooms upstairs, reserving them for guests. Ivan Ivanych and Burkin were welcomed by the maid, who was such a beautiful young woman that they both stopped and stared at each other.

'You can't imagine how glad I am to see you, gentlemen,' Alyokhin said as he followed them into the hall. 'A real surprise!' Then he turned to the maid and said, 'Pelageya, bring some dry clothes for the gentlemen. I suppose I'd better change too. But I must have a wash first, or you'll think I haven't had one since spring. Would you like to come to the bathing-hut while they get things ready in the house?'

The beautiful Pelageya, who had such a dainty look and gentle face, brought soap and towels, and Alyokhin went off with his guests to the bathing-hut.

'Yes, it's ages since I had a good wash,' he said as he undressed. 'As you can see, it's a nice hut. My father built it, but I never find time these days for a swim.'

He sat on one of the steps and smothered his long hair and neck with soap; the water turned brown.

'Yes, I must confess . . .' Ivan Ivanych muttered, with a meaningful look at his head.

'Haven't had a wash for ages,' Alyokhin repeated in his embarrassment and soaped himself again; the water turned a dark inky blue.

Ivan Ivanych came out of the cabin, dived in with a loud splash and swam in the rain, making broad sweeps with his arms and sending out waves with white lilies bobbing about on them. He swam right out to the middle of the reach and dived. A moment later he popped up somewhere else and swam on, continually trying to dive right to the bottom.

'Oh, good God,' he kept saying with great relish. 'Good God . . .'

He reached the mill, said a few words to the peasants, then he turned and floated on his back in the middle with his face under the rain. Burkin and Alyokhin were already dressed and ready to leave, but he kept on swimming and diving.

'Oh, dear God,' he said. 'Oh, God!'

'Now that's enough,' Burkin shouted.

They went back to the house. Only when the lamp in the large upstairs drawing-room was alight and Burkin and Ivan Ivanych, wearing silk dressing-gowns and warm slippers, were sitting in armchairs and Alyokhin, washed and combed now and with a new frock-coat on, was walking up and down, obviously savouring the warmth, cleanliness, dry clothes and light shoes, while his beautiful Pelageya glided silently over the carpet and gently smiled as she served tea and jam on a tray – only then did Ivan Ivanych begin his story. It seemed that Burkin and Alyokhin were not the only ones who were listening, but also the ladies (young and old) and the officers, who were looking down calmly and solemnly from their gilt frames on the walls.

'There are two of us brothers,' he began, 'myself – Ivan Ivanych – and Nikolay Ivanych, who's two years younger. I studied to be a vet, while Nikolay worked in the district tax office from the time he was nineteen. Chimsha-Gimalaysky, our father, had served as a private, but when he was promoted to officer we became hereditary gentlemen and owners of a small estate. After he died, this estate was sequestrated to pay off his debts, but despite this we spent our boyhood in the country free to do what we wanted. Just like any other village children, we stayed out in the fields and woods for days and nights, minded horses, stripped bark, went fishing, and so on . . . As you know very well, anyone who has ever caught a ruff or watched migrating thrushes swarming over his native village on cool clear autumn days can never live in a town afterwards and he'll always hanker after the free and open life until his dying day. My brother was miserable in the tax office. The years passed, but there he stayed, always at the same old desk, copying out the same old documents and obsessed with this longing for the country. And gradually this longing took the form of a definite wish, a dream of buying a nice little estate somewhere in the country, beside a river or a lake.

'He was a kind, gentle man and I was very fond of him, but I could never feel any sympathy for him in this longing to lock himself away in a country house for the rest of his life. They say a man needs only six feet of earth, but surely they must mean a corpse – not a *man*! These days they seem to think that it's very good if our educated classes want to go back to the land and set their hearts on a country estate. But in reality these estates are only that same six feet all over again. To leave the town and all its noise and hubbub, to go and shut yourself away on your little estate – that's no life! It's selfishness, laziness, a peculiar brand of monasticism that achieves nothing. A man needs more than six feet of earth and a little place in the country, he needs the whole wide world, the whole of nature, where there's room for him to display his potential, all the manifold attributes of his free spirit.

'As he sat there in his office, my brother Nikolay dreamt of soup made from his own home-grown cabbages, soup that would fill the whole house with a delicious smell; eating meals on the green grass; sleeping in the sun; sitting on a bench outside the main gates for hours on end and looking at the fields and woods. Booklets on agriculture and words of wisdom from calendars were his joy, his favourite spiritual nourishment. He liked newspapers as well, but he only read property adverts – for so many acres of arable land and meadows, with "house, river, garden, mill, and ponds fed by running springs". And he had visions of garden paths, flowers, fruit, nesting-boxes for starlings, ponds teeming with carp – you know the kind of thing. These visions varied according to the adverts he happened to see, but for some reason, in every single one, there *had* to be gooseberry bushes. "Life in the country has its comforts," he used to say. "You can sit drinking tea on your balcony, while your ducks are swimming in the pond . . . it all smells so good and um . . . there's your gooseberries growing away!"

'He drew up a plan for his estate and it turned out exactly

the same every time: (a) manor house; (b) servants' quarters; (c) kitchen garden; (d) gooseberry bushes. He lived a frugal life, economizing on food and drink, dressing any-old-how – just like a beggar – and putting every penny he saved straight into the bank. He was terribly mean. It was really painful to look at him, so I used to send him a little money on special occasions. But he would put that in the bank too. Once a man has his mind firmly made up there's nothing you can do about it.

'Years passed and he was transferred to another province. He was now in his forties, still reading newspaper adverts and still saving up. Then I heard that he'd got married. So that he could buy a country estate with gooseberry bushes, he married an ugly old widow, for whom he felt nothing and only because she had a little money tucked away. He made her life miserable too, half-starved her and banked her money into his own account. She'd been married to a postmaster and was used to pies and fruit liqueurs, but with her second husband she didn't even have enough black bread. This kind of life made her wither away, and within three years she'd gone to join her maker. Of course, my brother didn't think that *he* was to blame – not for one minute! Like vodka, money can make a man do the most peculiar things. There was once a merchant living in our town who was on his deathbed. Just before he died, he asked for some honey, stirred it up with all his money and winning lottery tickets, and swallowed the lot to stop anyone else from laying their hands on it. And another time, when I was inspecting cattle at some railway station, a dealer fell under a train and had his leg cut off. We took him to the local casualty department.

The blood simply gushed out, a terrible sight, but all he did was ask for his leg back and was only bothered about the twenty roubles he had tucked away in the boot. Scared he might lose them, I dare say!'

'But that's neither here nor there,' Burkin said.

'When his wife died,' Ivan continued, after a pause for thought, 'my brother started looking for an estate. Of course, you can look around for five years and still make the wrong choice and you finish up with something you never even dreamt of. So brother Nikolay bought about three hundred acres, with manor house, servants' quarters and a park, on a mortgage through an estate agent. But there wasn't any orchard, gooseberries or duck pond. There *was* a river, but the water was always the colour of coffee because of the brickworks on one side of the estate and a bone-ash factory on the other. But my dear Nikolay didn't seem to care. He ordered twenty gooseberry bushes, planted them out and settled down to a landowner's life.

'Last year I visited him, as I wanted to see what was going on. In his letter my brother had called his estate "Chumbaroklov Patch" or "Gimalaysky's". One afternoon I turned up at "Gimalaysky's". It was a hot day. Everywhere there were ditches, fences, hedges, rows of small fir trees and there seemed no way into the yard or anywhere to leave my horse. I went up to the house, only to be welcomed by a fat ginger dog that looked rather like a pig. It wanted to bark, but it was too lazy. Then a barefooted, plump cook – she resembled a pig as well – came out of the kitchen and told me the master was having his after-lunch nap. So I went to my brother's room and there he was sitting up in bed with a blanket over his knees. He'd aged, put on weight and looked very flabby. His cheeks, nose and lips stuck out and I thought any moment he was going to grunt into his blanket, like a pig.

'We embraced and wept for joy, and at the sad thought that once we were young and now both of us were grey, and that our lives were nearly over. He got dressed and led me on a tour of the estate.

'"Well, how's it going?" I asked.

'"All right, thank God. It's a good life."

'No longer was he the poor, timid little clerk of before, but a real squire, a *gentleman*. He felt quite at home, being used to country life by then and he was enjoying himself. He ate a great deal, took proper baths, and he was putting on weight. Already he was suing the district council and both factories, and he got very peeved when the villagers didn't call him "sir". He paid great attention to his spiritual well-being (as a gentleman should) and he couldn't dispense charity nice and quietly, but had to make a great show of it. And what did it all add up to? He doled out bicarbonate of soda or castor oil to his villagers – regardless of what they were suffering from – and on his name-day held a thanksgiving service in the village, supplying vodka in plenty, as he thought this was the right thing to do. Oh, those horrid pints of vodka! Nowadays your fat squire drags his villagers off to court for letting their cattle stray on his land and the very next day (if it's a high holiday) stands them all a few pints of vodka. They'll drink it, shout hurray and fall at his feet in a drunken stupor. Better standards of living, plenty to eat, idleness – all this makes us Russians terribly smug. Back in his office, Nikolay had been too scared even to voice any opinions of his own, but now he was expounding the eternal verities in true ministerial style: "Education is essential, but premature as far as the common people are concerned" or "Corporal punishment, generally speaking, is harmful, but in certain cases it can be useful and irreplaceable". And he'd say, "I know the working classes and how to handle them. They *like* me, I only have to lift my little finger and they'll do *anything* for me."

'And he said all this, mark you, with a clever, good-natured smile. Time after time he'd say "we *gentlemen*" or "speaking as *one of the gentry*". He'd evidently forgotten that our grandfather had been a peasant and our father a common soldier. Even our absolutely ridiculous surname, Chimsha-Gimalaysky, was melodious, distinguished and highly agreeable to his ears now.

'But it's myself I'm concerned with, not him. I'd like to tell you about the change that came over me during the few hours I spent on his estate. Later, when we were having tea, his cook brought us a plateful of gooseberries. They weren't shop gooseberries, but home-grown, the first fruits of the bushes he'd planted. Nikolay laughed and stared at them for a whole minute, with tears in his eyes. He was too deeply moved for words. Then he popped one in his mouth, looked at me like an enraptured child that has finally been given a long-awaited toy and said, "Absolutely delicious!" He ate some greedily and kept repeating, "So tasty, you *must* try one!"

'They were hard and sour, but as Pushkin says: "Uplifting illusion is dearer to us than a host of truths." This was a happy man whose cherished dreams had clearly come true, who had achieved his life's purpose, had got what he wanted and was happy with his lot – and himself. My thoughts about human happiness, for some peculiar reason, had always been tinged with a certain sadness. But now, seeing this happy man, I was overwhelmed by a feeling of despondency that was close to utter despair. I felt particularly low that night. They made up a bed for me in the room next to my brother's. He was wide awake and I could hear him getting up, going over to the plate and helping himself to one gooseberry at a time. And I thought how many satisfied, happy people really do exist in this world! And what a powerful force they are! Just take a look at this life of ours and you will see the arrogance and idleness of the strong, the ignorance and bestiality of the weak. Everywhere there's unspeakable poverty, overcrowding, degeneracy, drunkenness, hypocrisy and stupid lies . . . And yet peace and quiet reign in every house and street. Out of fifty thousand people you won't find one who is prepared to shout out loud and make a strong protest. We see people buying food in the market, eating during the day, sleeping at night-time, talking nonsense, marrying, growing old and then contentedly carting their dead off to the cemetery. But we don't hear or see those who suffer: the real tragedies of life are enacted somewhere behind the scenes. Everything is calm and peaceful and the only protest comes from statistics – and they can't talk. Figures show that so many went mad, so many bottles of vodka were emptied, so many children died from malnutrition. And clearly this kind of system is what people need. It's obvious that the happy man feels contented only because the unhappy ones bear their burden without saying a word: if it weren't for their silence, happiness would be quite impossible. It's a kind of mass hypnosis. Someone ought to stand with a hammer at the door of every happy contented man, continually banging on it to remind him that there are unhappy people around and that however happy *he* may be at the time, sooner or later life will show him its claws and disaster will overtake him in the form of illness, poverty, bereavement and there will be no one to hear or see him. But there isn't anyone holding a hammer, so our happy man goes his own sweet way and is only gently ruffled by life's trivial cares, as an aspen is ruffled by the breeze. All's well as far as *he's* concerned.

'That night I realized that I too was happy and contented,' Ivan Ivanych went on, getting to his feet. 'I too had lectured people over dinner – or out hunting – on how to live, on what to believe, on how to handle the common people. And I too had told them that knowledge is a shining lamp, that education is essential, and that plain reading and writing is good enough for the masses, for the moment. Freedom is a blessing, I told them, and we need it like the air we breathe, but we must wait for it patiently.'

Ivan Ivanych turned to Burkin and said angrily, 'Yes, that's what I used to say and now I'd like to know *what* is it we're waiting for? I'm asking you, *what*? What is it we're trying to prove? I'm told that nothing can be achieved in five minutes, that it takes time for any kind of idea to be realized; it's a gradual process. But who says so? And what is there to prove he's right? You refer to the natural order of things, to the law of cause and effect. But *is* there any law or order in a state of affairs where a lively, thinking person like myself should have to stand by a ditch and wait until it's choked with weeds, or silted up, when I could quite easily, perhaps, leap across it or bridge it? I ask you again, what are we waiting for? Until we have no more strength to live, although we long to and *need* to go on living?

'I left my brother early next morning and ever since then I've found town life unbearable. I'm depressed by peace and quiet, I'm scared of peering through windows, nothing makes me more dejected than the sight of a happy family sitting round the table drinking tea. But I'm old now, no longer fit for the fray, I'm even incapable of hating. I only feel sick at heart, irritable and exasperated. At night my head seems to be on fire with so many thoughts crowding in and I can't get any sleep . . . Oh, if only I were young again!'

Ivan Ivanych paced the room excitedly, repeating, 'If only I were young again!'

Suddenly he went up to Alyokhin and squeezed one hand, then the other. 'Pavel Konstantinych,' he pleaded, 'don't go to sleep or be lulled into complacency! While you're still young, strong and healthy, never stop doing good! Happiness doesn't exist, we don't need any such thing. If life has *any* meaning or purpose, you won't find it in happiness, but in something more rational, in something greater. Doing good!'

Ivan Ivanych said all this with a pitiful, imploring smile, as though pleading for himself.

Afterwards all three of them sat in armchairs in different parts of the room and said nothing. Ivan Ivanych's story satisfied neither Burkin nor Alyokhin. It was boring listening

Gooseberries

to that story about some poor devil of a clerk who ate gooseberries, while those generals and ladies, who seemed to have come to life in the gathering gloom, peered out of their gilt frames. For some reason they would have preferred discussing and hearing about refined people, about ladies. The fact that they were all sitting in a drawing-room where everything – the draped chandeliers, the armchairs, the carpets underfoot – indicated that those same people who were now looking out of their frames had once walked around, sat down and drunk their tea there ... and with beautiful Pelageya moving about here without a sound – all this was better than any story.

Alyokhin was dying to get to bed. That morning he had been up and about very early (before three) working on the farm, and he could hardly keep his eyes open. However, he was frightened he might miss some interesting story if he left now, so he stayed. He didn't even try to fathom if everything that Ivan Ivanych had just been saying was clever, or even true: he was only too glad that his guests did not discuss oats or hay or tar, but things that had nothing to do with his way of life, and he wanted them to continue ...

'But it's time we got some sleep,' Burkin said, standing up. 'May I wish you all a very good night!'

Alyokhin bade them good night and went down to his room, while his guests stayed upstairs. They had been given the large room with two old, elaborately carved beds and an ivory crucifix in one corner. These wide, cool beds had been made by the beautiful Pelageya and the linen had a pleasant fresh smell.

Ivan Ivanych undressed without a word and got into bed.

Then he muttered, 'Lord have mercy on us sinners!' and pulled the blankets over his head. His pipe, which was lying on a table, smelt strongly of stale tobacco and Burkin was so puzzled as to where the terrible smell was coming from that it was a long time before he fell asleep.

All night long the rain beat against the windows.

1. BOCCACCIO · *Mrs Rosie and the Priest*
2. GERARD MANLEY HOPKINS · *As kingfishers catch fire*
3. *The Saga of Gunnlaug Serpent-tongue*
4. THOMAS DE QUINCEY · *On Murder Considered as One of the Fine Arts*
5. FRIEDRICH NIETZSCHE · *Aphorisms on Love and Hate*
6. JOHN RUSKIN · *Traffic*
7. PU SONGLING · *Wailing Ghosts*
8. JONATHAN SWIFT · *A Modest Proposal*
9. *Three Tang Dynasty Poets*
10. WALT WHITMAN · *On the Beach at Night Alone*
11. KENKŌ · *A Cup of Sake Beneath the Cherry Trees*
12. BALTASAR GRACIÁN · *How to Use Your Enemies*
13. JOHN KEATS · *The Eve of St Agnes*
14. THOMAS HARDY · *Woman much missed*
15. GUY DE MAUPASSANT · *Femme Fatale*
16. MARCO POLO · *Travels in the Land of Serpents and Pearls*
17. SUETONIUS · *Caligula*
18. APOLLONIUS OF RHODES · *Jason and Medea*
19. ROBERT LOUIS STEVENSON · *Olalla*
20. KARL MARX AND FRIEDRICH ENGELS · *The Communist Manifesto*
21. PETRONIUS · *Trimalchio's Feast*
22. JOHANN PETER HEBEL · *How a Ghastly Story Was Brought to Light by a Common or Garden Butcher's Dog*
23. HANS CHRISTIAN ANDERSEN · *The Tinder Box*
24. RUDYARD KIPLING · *The Gate of the Hundred Sorrows*
25. DANTE · *Circles of Hell*
26. HENRY MAYHEW · *Of Street Piemen*
27. HAFEZ · *The nightingales are drunk*
28. GEOFFREY CHAUCER · *The Wife of Bath*
29. MICHEL DE MONTAIGNE · *How We Weep and Laugh at the Same Thing*
30. THOMAS NASHE · *The Terrors of the Night*
31. EDGAR ALLAN POE · *The Tell-Tale Heart*
32. MARY KINGSLEY · *A Hippo Banquet*
33. JANE AUSTEN · *The Beautifull Cassandra*
34. ANTON CHEKHOV · *Gooseberries*
35. SAMUEL TAYLOR COLERIDGE · *Well, they are gone, and here must I remain*
36. JOHANN WOLFGANG VON GOETHE · *Sketchy, Doubtful, Incomplete Jottings*
37. CHARLES DICKENS · *The Great Winglebury Duel*
38. HERMAN MELVILLE · *The Maldive Shark*
39. ELIZABETH GASKELL · *The Old Nurse's Story*
40. NIKOLAY LESKOV · *The Steel Flea*

41. HONORÉ DE BALZAC · *The Atheist's Mass*
42. CHARLOTTE PERKINS GILMAN · *The Yellow Wall-Paper*
43. C.P. CAVAFY · *Remember, Body . . .*
44. FYODOR DOSTOEVSKY · *The Meek One*
45. GUSTAVE FLAUBERT · *A Simple Heart*
46. NIKOLAI GOGOL · *The Nose*
47. SAMUEL PEPYS · *The Great Fire of London*
48. EDITH WHARTON · *The Reckoning*
49. HENRY JAMES · *The Figure in the Carpet*
50. WILFRED OWEN · *Anthem For Doomed Youth*
51. WOLFGANG AMADEUS MOZART · *My Dearest Father*
52. PLATO · *Socrates' Defence*
53. CHRISTINA ROSSETTI · *Goblin Market*
54. *Sindbad the Sailor*
55. SOPHOCLES · *Antigone*
56. RYŪNOSUKE AKUTAGAWA · *The Life of a Stupid Man*
57. LEO TOLSTOY · *How Much Land Does A Man Need?*
58. GIORGIO VASARI · *Leonardo da Vinci*
59. OSCAR WILDE · *Lord Arthur Savile's Crime*
60. SHEN FU · *The Old Man of the Moon*
61. AESOP · *The Dolphins, the Whales and the Gudgeon*
62. MATSUO BASHŌ · *Lips too Chilled*
63. EMILY BRONTË · *The Night is Darkening Round Me*
64. JOSEPH CONRAD · *To-morrow*
65. RICHARD HAKLUYT · *The Voyage of Sir Francis Drake Around the Whole Globe*
66. KATE CHOPIN · *A Pair of Silk Stockings*
67. CHARLES DARWIN · *It was snowing butterflies*
68. BROTHERS GRIMM · *The Robber Bridegroom*
69. CATULLUS · *I Hate and I Love*
70. HOMER · *Circe and the Cyclops*
71. D. H. LAWRENCE · *Il Duro*
72. KATHERINE MANSFIELD · *Miss Brill*
73. OVID · *The Fall of Icarus*
74. SAPPHO · *Come Close*
75. IVAN TURGENEV · *Kasyan from the Beautiful Lands*
76. VIRGIL · *O Cruel Alexis*
77. H. G. WELLS · *A Slip under the Microscope*
78. HERODOTUS · *The Madness of Cambyses*
79. *Speaking of Siva*
80. *The Dhammapada*

'Ye Ice-falls! ye that from the mountain's brow Adown enormous ravines slope amain –...'

SAMUEL TAYLOR COLERIDGE
Born 1772, Ottery St Mary, England
Died 1834, Highgate, England

These poems were written roughly between 1795 and 1818, although there are some uncertainties and they are published here in approximate date order.

COLERIDGE IN PENGUIN CLASSICS
Selected Poetry
The Penguin Book of Romantic Poetry

SAMUEL TAYLOR COLERIDGE

*Well, they are gone,
and here must I remain*

PENGUIN BOOKS

PENGUIN CLASSICS

UK | USA | Canada | Ireland | Australia
India | New Zealand | South Africa

Penguin Books is part of the Penguin Random House group of companies whose addresses can be found at global.penguinrandomhouse.com.

This selection published in Penguin Classics 2015
008

Set in 9/12.4 pt Baskerville 10 Pro
Typeset by Jouve (UK), Milton Keynes

Printed and bound in Great Britain by Clays Ltd, Elcograf S.p.A.

A CIP catalogue record for this book is available from the British Library

ISBN: 978-0-141-39711-5

www.greenpenguin.co.uk

Penguin Random House is committed to a sustainable future for our business, our readers and our planet. This book is made from Forest Stewardship Council® certified paper.

Contents

1. Lines Composed while Climbing the Left Ascent of Brockley Coomb, Somersetshire, May 1795 — 1
2. The Eolian Harp — 2
3. This Lime-Tree Bower My Prison — 5
4. Frost at Midnight — 8
5. Fears in Solitude — 11
6. The Nightingale — 20
7. Love — 24
8. Lines Written in the Album at Elbingerode, in the Hartz Forest — 28
9. Hymn before Sun-Rise, in the Vale of Chamouni — 30
10. Lady, to Death we're Doom'd . . . — 34

Contents

11. The Blossoming of the
    Solitary Date-Tree   35

12. O Sara! Never Rashly
    Let Me Go   40

13. You Mould My Hopes   41

14. The Tropic Tree   42

15. The Yellow Hammer   43

16. The Pang More Sharp
    Than All   44

17. Limbo   47

18. The Pains of Sleep   49

19. The Knight's Tomb   51

20. Fancy in Nubibus   52

Lines Composed while Climbing the Left Ascent of Brockley Coomb, Somersetshire, May 1795

With many a pause and oft reverted eye
I climb the Coomb's ascent: sweet songsters near
Warble in shade their wild-wood melody:
Far off the unvarying Cuckoo soothes my ear.
Up scour the startling stragglers of the flock
That on green plots o'er precipices browze:
From the deep fissures of the naked rock
The Yew-tree bursts! Beneath its dark green boughs
(Mid which the May-thorn blends its blossoms white)
Where broad smooth stones jut out in mossy seats,
I rest: – and now have gain'd the topmost site.
Ah! what a luxury of landscape meets
My gaze! Proud towers, and Cots more dear to me,
Elm-shadow'd Fields, and prospect-bounding Sea!
Deep sighs my lonely heart: I drop the tear:
Enchanting spot! O were my Sara here!

The Eolian Harp

COMPOSED AT CLEVEDON, SOMERSETSHIRE

My pensive Sara! thy soft cheek reclined
Thus on mine arm, most soothing sweet it is
To sit beside our Cot, our Cot o'ergrown
With white-flower'd Jasmin, and the broad-leav'd Myrtle,
(Meet emblems they of Innocence and Love!)
And watch the clouds, that late were rich with light,
Slow saddening round, and mark the star of eve
Serenely brilliant (such should Wisdom be)
Shine opposite! How exquisite the scents
Snatch'd from yon bean-field! and the world *so* hush'd!
The stilly murmur of the distant Sea
Tells us of silence.

                      And that simplest Lute,
Placed length-ways in the clasping casement, hark!
How by the desultory breeze caress'd,
Like some coy maid half yielding to her lover,
It pours such sweet upbraiding, as must needs
Tempt to repeat the wrong! And now, its strings
Boldlier swept, the long sequacious notes
Over delicious surges sink and rise,
Such a soft floating witchery of sound
As twilight Elfins make, when they at eve
Voyage on gentle gales from Fairy-Land,
Where Melodies round honey-dropping flowers,

The Eolian Harp

Footless and wild, like birds of Paradise,
Nor pause, nor perch, hovering on untam'd wing!
O! the one Life within us and abroad,
Which meets all motion and becomes its soul,
A light in sound, a sound-like power in light,
Rhythm in all thought, and joyance every where –
Methinks, it should have been impossible
Not to love all things in a world so fill'd;
Where the breeze warbles, and the mute still air
Is Music slumbering on her instrument.

    And thus, my Love! as on the midway slope
Of yonder hill I stretch my limbs at noon,
Whilst through my half-clos'd eye-lids I behold
The sunbeams dance, like diamonds, on the main,
And tranquil muse upon tranquillity;
Full many a thought uncall'd and undetain'd,
And many idle flitting phantasies,
Traverse my indolent and passive brain,
As wild and various as the random gales
That swell and flutter on this subject Lute!

    And what if all of animated nature
Be but organic Harps diversely fram'd,
That tremble into thought, as o'er them sweeps
Plastic and vast, one intellectual breeze,
At once the Soul of each, and God of all?

    But thy more serious eye a mild reproof
Darts, O belovéd Woman! nor such thoughts
Dim and unhallow'd dost thou not reject,

And biddest me walk humbly with my God.
Meek Daughter in the family of Christ!
Well hast thou said and holily disprais'd
These shapings of the unregenerate mind;
Bubbles that glitter as they rise and break
On vain Philosophy's aye-babbling spring.
For never guiltless may I speak of him,
The Incomprehensible! save when with awe
I praise him, and with Faith that inly *feels*;
Who with his saving mercies healéd me,
A sinful and most miserable man,
Wilder'd and dark, and gave me to possess
Peace, and this Cot, and thee, heart-honour'd Maid!

This Lime-Tree Bower My Prison

In the June of 1797 some long-expected friends paid a visit to the author's cottage; and on the morning of their arrival, he met with an accident, which disabled him from walking during the whole time of their stay. One evening, when they had left him for a few hours, he composed the following lines in the garden-bower.

> Well, they are gone, and here must I remain,
> This lime-tree bower my prison! I have lost
> Beauties and feelings, such as would have been
> Most sweet to my remembrance even when age
> Had dimm'd mine eyes to blindness! They, meanwhile,
> Friends, whom I never more may meet again,
> On springy heath, along the hill-top edge,
> Wander in gladness, and wind down, perchance,
> To that still roaring dell, of which I told;
> The roaring dell, o'erwooded, narrow, deep,
> And only speckled by the mid-day sun;
> Where its slim trunk the ash from rock to rock
> Flings arching like a bridge; – that branchless ash,
> Unsunn'd and damp, whose few poor yellow leaves,
> Ne'er tremble in the gale, yet tremble still,
> Fann'd by the water-fall! and there my friends
> Behold the dark green file of long lank weeds,
> That all at once (a most fantastic sight!)
> Still nod and drip beneath the dripping edge
> Of the blue clay-stone.

Samuel Taylor Coleridge

                        Now, my friends emerge
Beneath the wide wide Heaven – and view again
The many-steepled tract magnificent
Of hilly fields and meadows, and the sea,
With some fair bark, perhaps, whose sails light up
The slip of smooth clear blue betwixt two Isles
Of purple shadow! Yes! they wander on
In gladness all; but thou, methinks, most glad,
My gentle-hearted Charles! for thou hast pined
And hunger'd after Nature, many a year,
In the great City pent, winning thy way
With sad yet patient soul, through evil and pain
And strange calamity! Ah! slowly sink
Behind the western ridge, thou glorious Sun!
Shine in the slant beams of the sinking orb,
Ye purple heath-flowers! richlier burn, ye clouds!
Live in the yellow light, ye distant groves!
And kindle, thou blue Ocean! So my friend
Struck with deep joy may stand, as I have stood,
Silent with swimming sense; yea, gazing round
On the wide landscape, gaze till all doth seem
Less gross than bodily; and of such hues
As veil the Almighty Spirit, when yet he makes
Spirits perceive his presence.

                        A delight
Comes sudden on my heart, and I am glad
As I myself were there! Nor in this bower,
This little lime-tree bower, have I not mark'd
Much that has sooth'd me. Pale beneath the blaze

This Lime-Tree Bower My Prison

Hung the transparent foliage; and I watch'd
Some broad and sunny leaf, and lov'd to see
The shadow of the leaf and stem above
Dappling its sunshine! And that walnut-tree
Was richly ting'd, and a deep radiance lay
Full on the ancient ivy, which usurps
Those fronting elms, and now, with blackest mass
Makes their dark branches gleam a lighter hue
Through the late twilight: and though now the bat
Wheels silent by, and not a swallow twitters,
Yet still the solitary humble-bee
Sings in the bean-flower! Henceforth I shall know
That Nature ne'er deserts the wise and pure;
No plot so narrow, be but Nature there,
No waste so vacant, but may well employ
Each faculty of sense, and keep the heart
Awake to Love and Beauty! and sometimes
'Tis well to be bereft of promis'd good,
That we may lift the soul, and contemplate
With lively joy the joys we cannot share.
My gentle-hearted Charles! when the last rook
Beat its straight path along the dusky air
Homewards, I blest it! deeming its black wing
(Now a dim speck, now vanishing in light)
Had cross'd the mighty Orb's dilated glory,
While thou stood'st gazing; or, when all was still,
Flew creeking o'er thy head, and had a charm
For thee, my gentle-hearted Charles, to whom
No sound is dissonant which tells of Life.

Frost at Midnight

The Frost performs its secret ministry,
Unhelped by any wind. The owlet's cry
Came loud – and hark, again! loud as before.
The inmates of my cottage, all at rest,
Have left me to that solitude, which suits
Abstruser musings: save that at my side
My cradled infant slumbers peacefully.
'Tis calm indeed! so calm, that it disturbs
And vexes meditation with its strange
And extreme silentness. Sea, hill, and wood,
This populous village! Sea, and hill, and wood,
With all the numberless goings-on of life,
Inaudible as dreams! the thin blue flame
Lies on my low-burnt fire, and quivers not;
Only that film, which fluttered on the grate,
Still flutters there, the sole unquiet thing.
Methinks, its motion in this hush of nature
Gives it dim sympathies with me who live,
Making it a companionable form,
Whose puny flaps and freaks the idling Spirit
By its own moods interprets, every where
Echo or mirror seeking of itself,
And makes a toy of Thought.

                      But O! how oft,
How oft, at school, with most believing mind,
Presageful, have I gazed upon the bars,

Frost at Midnight

To watch that fluttering *stranger*! and as oft
With unclosed lids, already had I dreamt
Of my sweet birth-place, and the old church-tower,
Whose bells, the poor man's only music, rang
From morn to evening, all the hot Fair-day,
So sweetly, that they stirred and haunted me
With a wild pleasure, falling on mine ear
Most like articulate sounds of things to come!
So gazed I, till the soothing things, I dreamt,
Lulled me to sleep, and sleep prolonged my dreams!
And so I brooded all the following morn,
Awed by the stern preceptor's face, mine eye
Fixed with mock study on my swimming book:
Save if the door half opened, and I snatched
A hasty glance, and still my heart leaped up,
For still I hoped to see the *stranger's* face,
Townsman, or aunt, or sister more beloved,
My play-mate when we both were clothed alike!

   Dear Babe, that sleepest cradled by my side,
Whose gentle breathings, heard in this deep calm,
Fill up the interspersèd vacancies
And momentary pauses of the thought!
My babe so beautiful! it thrills my heart
With tender gladness, thus to look at thee,
And think that thou shalt learn far other lore,
And in far other scenes! For I was reared
In the great city, pent 'mid cloisters dim,
And saw nought lovely but the sky and stars.
But *thou*, my babe! shalt wander like a breeze

Samuel Taylor Coleridge

By lakes and sandy shores, beneath the crags
Of ancient mountain, and beneath the clouds,
Which image in their bulk both lakes and shores
And mountain crags: so shalt thou see and hear
The lovely shapes and sounds intelligible
Of that eternal language, which thy God
Utters, who from eternity doth teach
Himself in all, and all things in himself.
Great universal Teacher! he shall mould
Thy spirit, and by giving make it ask.

    Therefore all seasons shall be sweet to thee,
Whether the summer clothe the general earth
With greenness, or the redbreast sit and sing
Betwixt the tufts of snow on the bare branch
Of mossy apple-tree, while the nigh thatch
Smokes in the sun-thaw; whether the eave-drops fall
Heard only in the trances of the blast,
Or if the secret ministry of frost
Shall hang them up in silent icicles,
Quietly shining to the quiet Moon.

Fears in Solitude

WRITTEN IN APRIL 1798,
DURING THE ALARM OF AN INVASION

A green and silent spot, amid the hills,
A small and silent dell! O'er stiller place
No singing sky-lark ever poised himself.
The hills are heathy, save that swelling slope,
Which hath a gay and gorgeous covering on,
All golden with the never-bloomless furze,
Which now blooms most profusely: but the dell,
Bathed by the mist, is fresh and delicate
As vernal corn-field, or the unripe flax,
When, through its half-transparent stalks, at eve,
The level sunshine glimmers with green light.
Oh! 'tis a quiet spirit-healing nook!
Which all, methinks, would love; but chiefly he,
The humble man, who, in his youthful years,
Knew just so much of folly, as had made
His early manhood more securely wise!
Here he might lie on fern or withered heath,
While from the singing lark (that sings unseen
The minstrelsy that solitude loves best),
And from the sun, and from the breezy air,
Sweet influences trembled o'er his frame;
And he, with many feelings, many thoughts,
Made up a meditative joy, and found
Religious meanings in the forms of Nature!

Samuel Taylor Coleridge

And so, his senses gradually wrapt
In a half sleep, he dreams of better worlds,
And dreaming hears thee still, O singing lark,
That singest like an angel in the clouds!

   My God! it is a melancholy thing
For such a man, who would full fain preserve
His soul in calmness, yet perforce must feel
For all his human brethren – O my God!
It weighs upon the heart, that he must think
What uproar and what strife may now be stirring
This way or that way o'er these silent hills –
Invasion, and the thunder and the shout,
And all the crash of onset; fear and rage,
And undetermined conflict – even now,
Even now, perchance, and in his native isle:
Carnage and groans beneath this blessed sun!
We have offended, Oh! my countrymen!
We have offended very grievously,
And been most tyrannous. From east to west
A groan of accusation pierces Heaven!
The wretched plead against us; multitudes
Countless and vehement, the sons of God,
Our brethren! Like a cloud that travels on,
Steamed up from Cairo's swamps of pestilence,
Even so, my countrymen! have we gone forth
And borne to distant tribes slavery and pangs,
And, deadlier far, our vices, whose deep taint
With slow perdition murders the whole man,
His body and his soul! Meanwhile, at home,

Fears in Solitude

All individual dignity and power
Engulfed in Courts, Committees, Institutions,
Associations and Societies,
A vain, speech-mouthing, speech-reporting Guild,
One Benefit-Club for mutual flattery,
We have drunk up, demure as at a grace,
Pollutions from the brimming cup of wealth;
Contemptuous of all honourable rule,
Yet bartering freedom and the poor man's life
For gold, as at a market! The sweet words
Of Christian promise, words that even yet
Might stem destruction, were they wisely preached,
Are muttered o'er by men, whose tones proclaim
How flat and wearisome they feel their trade:
Rank scoffers some, but most too indolent
To deem them falsehoods or to know their truth.
Oh! blasphemous! the Book of Life is made
A superstitious instrument, on which
We gabble o'er the oaths we mean to break;
For all must swear – all and in every place,
College and wharf, council and justice-court;
All, all must swear, the briber and the bribed,
Merchant and lawyer, senator and priest,
The rich, the poor, the old man and the young;
All, all make up one scheme of perjury,
That faith doth reel; the very name of God
Sounds like a juggler's charm; and, bold with joy,
Forth from his dark and lonely hiding-place,
(Portentous sight!) the owlet Atheism,
Sailing on obscene wings athwart the noon,

Drops his blue-fringéd lids, and holds them close,
And hooting at the glorious sun in Heaven,
Cries out, 'Where is it?'

                        Thankless too for peace,
(Peace long preserved by fleets and perilous seas)
Secure from actual warfare, we have loved
To swell the war-whoop, passionate for war!
Alas! for ages ignorant of all
Its ghastlier workings, (famine or blue plague,
Battle, or siege, or flight through wintry snows,)
We, this whole people, have been clamorous
For war and bloodshed; animating sports,
The which we pay for as a thing to talk of,
Spectators and not combatants! No guess
Anticipative of a wrong unfelt,
No speculation on contingency,
However dim and vague, too vague and dim
To yield a justifying cause; and forth,
(Stuffed out with big preamble, holy names,
And adjurations of the God in Heaven,)
We send our mandates for the certain death
Of thousands and ten thousands! Boys and girls,
And women, that would groan to see a child
Pull off an insect's leg, all read of war,
The best amusement for our morning meal!
The poor wretch, who has learnt his only prayers
From curses, who knows scarcely words enough
To ask a blessing from his Heavenly Father,
Becomes a fluent phraseman, absolute

Fears in Solitude

And technical in victories and defeats,
And all our dainty terms for fratricide;
Terms which we trundle smoothly o'er our tongues
Like mere abstractions, empty sounds to which
We join no feeling and attach no form!
As if the soldier died without a wound;
As if the fibres of this godlike frame
Were gored without a pang; as if the wretch,
Who fell in battle, doing bloody deeds,
Passed off to Heaven, translated and not killed;
As though he had no wife to pine for him,
No God to judge him! Therefore, evil days
Are coming on us, O my countrymen!
And what if all-avenging Providence,
Strong and retributive, should make us know
The meaning of our words, force us to feel
The desolation and the agony
Of our fierce doings?

      Spare us yet awhile,
Father and God! O! spare us yet awhile!
Oh! let not English women drag their flight
Fainting beneath the burthen of their babes,
Of the sweet infants, that but yesterday
Laughed at the breast! Sons, brothers, husbands, all
Who ever gazed with fondness on the forms
Which grew up with you round the same fire-side,
And all who ever heard the sabbath-bells
Without the infidel's scorn, make yourselves pure!
Stand forth! be men! repel an impious foe,

Samuel Taylor Coleridge

   Impious and false, a light yet cruel race,
Who laugh away all virtue, mingling mirth
With deeds of murder; and still promising
Freedom, themselves too sensual to be free,
Poison life's amities, and cheat the heart
Of faith and quiet hope, and all that soothes,
And all that lifts the spirit! Stand we forth;
Render them back upon the insulted ocean,
And let them toss as idly on its waves
As the vile sea-weed, which some mountain-blast
Swept from our shores! And oh! may we return
Not with a drunken triumph, but with fear,
Repenting of the wrongs with which we stung
So fierce a foe to frenzy!

                     I have told,
O Britons! O my brethren! I have told
Most bitter truth, but without bitterness.
Nor deem my zeal or factious or mistimed;
For never can true courage dwell with them,
Who, playing tricks with conscience, dare not look
At their own vices. We have been too long
Dupes of a deep delusion! Some, belike,
Groaning with restless enmity, expect
All change from change of constituted power;
As if a Government had been a robe,
On which our vice and wretchedness were tagged
Like fancy-points and fringes, with the robe
Pulled off at pleasure. Fondly these attach
A radical causation to a few

Fears in Solitude

Poor drudges of chastising Providence,
Who borrow all their hues and qualities
From our own folly and rank wickedness,
Which gave them birth and nursed them. Others, meanwhile,
Dote with a mad idolatry; and all
Who will not fall before their images,
And yield them worship, they are enemies
Even of their country!

                    Such have I been deemed. –
But, O dear Britain! O my Mother Isle!
Needs must thou prove a name most dear and holy
To me, a son, a brother, and a friend,
A husband, and a father! who revere
All bonds of natural love, and find them all
Within the limits of thy rocky shores.
O native Britain! O my Mother Isle!
How shouldst thou prove aught else but dear and holy
To me, who from thy lakes and mountain-hills,
Thy clouds, thy quiet dales, thy rocks and seas,
Have drunk in all my intellectual life,
All sweet sensations, all ennobling thoughts,
All adoration of the God in nature,
All lovely and all honourable things,
Whatever makes this mortal spirit feel
The joy and greatness of its future being?
There lives nor form nor feeling in my soul
Unborrowed from my country! O divine
And beauteous island! thou hast been my sole

Samuel Taylor Coleridge

And most magnificent temple, in the which
I walk with awe, and sing my stately songs,
Loving the God that made me! –

                      May my fears,
My filial fears, be vain! and may the vaunts
And menace of the vengeful enemy
Pass like the gust, that roared and died away
In the distant tree: which heard, and only heard
In this low dell, bowed not the delicate grass.

    But now the gentle dew-fall sends abroad
The fruit-like perfume of the golden furze:
The light has left the summit of the hill,
Though still a sunny gleam lies beautiful,
Aslant the ivied beacon. Now farewell,
Farewell, awhile, O soft and silent spot!
On the green sheep-track, up the heathy hill,
Homeward I wind my way; and lo! recalled
From bodings that have well-nigh wearied me,
I find myself upon the brow, and pause
Startled! And after lonely sojourning
In such a quiet and surrounded nook,
This burst of prospect, here the shadowy main,
Dim-tinted, there the mighty majesty
Of that huge amphitheatre of rich
And elmy fields, seems like society –
Conversing with the mind, and giving it
A livelier impulse and a dance of thought!
And now, beloved Stowey! I behold
Thy church-tower, and, methinks, the four huge elms

Clustering, which mark the mansion of my friend;
And close behind them, hidden from my view,
Is my own lowly cottage, where my babe
And my babe's mother dwell in peace! With light
And quickened footsteps thitherward I tend,
Remembering thee, O green and silent dell!
And grateful, that by nature's quietness
And solitary musings, all my heart
Is softened, and made worthy to indulge
Love, and the thoughts that yearn for human kind.

The Nightingale

No cloud, no relique of the sunken day
Distinguishes the West, no long thin slip
Of sullen light, no obscure trembling hues.
Come, we will rest on this old mossy bridge!
You see the glimmer of the stream beneath,
But hear no murmuring: it flows silently,
O'er its soft bed of verdure. All is still,
A balmy night! and though the stars be dim,
Yet let us think upon the vernal showers
That gladden the green earth, and we shall find
A pleasure in the dimness of the stars.
And hark! the Nightingale begins its song,
'Most musical, most melancholy' bird!
A melancholy bird? Oh! idle thought!
In Nature there is nothing melancholy.
But some night-wandering man whose heart was pierced
With the remembrance of a grievous wrong,
Or slow distemper, or neglected love,
(And so, poor wretch! filled all things with himself,
And made all gentle sounds tell back the tale
Of his own sorrow) he, and such as he,
First named these notes a melancholy strain.
And many a poet echoes the conceit;
Poet who hath been building up the rhyme
When he had better far have stretched his limbs
Beside a brook in mossy forest-dell,
By sun or moon-light, to the influxes

The Nightingale

Of shapes and sounds and shifting elements
Surrendering his whole spirit, of his song
And of his fame forgetful! so his fame
Should share in Nature's immortality,
A venerable thing! and so his song
Should make all Nature lovelier, and itself
Be loved like Nature! But 'twill not be so;
And youths and maidens most poetical,
Who lose the deepening twilights of the spring
In ball-rooms and hot theatres, they still
Full of meek sympathy must heave their sighs
O'er Philomela's pity-pleading strains.

My Friend, and thou, our Sister! we have learnt
A different lore: we may not thus profane
Nature's sweet voices, always full of love
And joyance! 'Tis the merry Nightingale
That crowds, and hurries, and precipitates
With fast thick warble his delicious notes,
As he were fearful that an April night
Would be too short for him to utter forth
His love-chant, and disburthen his full soul
Of all its music!

               And I know a grove
Of large extent, hard by a castle huge,
Which the great lord inhabits not; and so
This grove is wild with tangling underwood,
And the trim walks are broken up, and grass,
Thin grass and king-cups grow within the paths.
But never elsewhere in one place I knew

Samuel Taylor Coleridge

So many nightingales; and far and near,
In wood and thicket, over the wide grove,
They answer and provoke each other's song,
With skirmish and capricious passagings,
And murmurs musical and swift jug jug,
And one low piping sound more sweet than all –
Stirring the air with such a harmony,
That should you close your eyes, you might almost
Forget it was not day! On moonlight bushes,
Whose dewy leaflets are but half-disclosed,
You may perchance behold them on the twigs,
Their bright, bright eyes, their eyes both bright and full,
Glistening, while many a glow-worm in the shade
Lights up her love-torch.

                A most gentle Maid,
Who dwelleth in her hospitable home
Hard by the castle, and at latest eve
(Even like a Lady vowed and dedicate
To something more than Nature in the grove)
Glides through the pathways; she knows all their notes,
That gentle Maid! and oft, a moment's space,
What time the moon was lost behind a cloud,
Hath heard a pause of silence; till the moon
Emerging, hath awakened earth and sky
With one sensation, and those wakeful birds
Have all burst forth in choral minstrelsy,
As if some sudden gale had swept at once
A hundred airy harps! And she hath watched
Many a nightingale perch giddily

The Nightingale

On blossomy twig still swinging from the breeze,
And to that motion tune his wanton song
Like tipsy Joy that reels with tossing head.

Farewell, O Warbler! till to-morrow eve,
And you, my friends! farewell, a short farewell!
We have been loitering long and pleasantly,
And now for our dear homes. – That strain again!
Full fain it would delay me! My dear babe,
Who, capable of no articulate sound,
Mars all things with his imitative lisp,
How he would place his hand beside his ear,
His little hand, the small forefinger up,
And bid us listen! And I deem it wise
To make him Nature's play-mate. He knows well
The evening-star; and once, when he awoke
In most distressful mood (some inward pain
Had made up that strange thing, an infant's dream –)
I hurried with him to our orchard-plot,
And he beheld the moon, and, hushed at once,
Suspends his sobs, and laughs most silently,
While his fair eyes, that swam with undropped tears,
Did glitter in the yellow moon-beam! Well! –
It is a father's tale: But if that Heaven
Should give me life, his childhood shall grow up
Familiar with these songs, that with the night
He may associate joy. – Once more, farewell,
Sweet Nightingale! once more, my friends! farewell.

Love

All thoughts, all passions, all delights,
Whatever stirs this mortal frame,
All are but ministers of Love,
    And feed his sacred flame.

Oft in my waking dreams do I
Live o'er again that happy hour,
When midway on the mount I lay,
    Beside the ruined tower.

The moonshine, stealing o'er the scene
Had blended with the lights of eve;
And she was there, my hope, my joy,
    My own dear Genevieve!

She leant against the armèd man,
The statue of the armèd knight;
She stood and listened to my lay,
    Amid the lingering light.

Few sorrows hath she of her own,
My hope! my joy! my Genevieve!
She loves me best, whene'er I sing
    The songs that make her grieve.

I played a soft and doleful air,
I sang an old and moving story –
An old rude song, that suited well
    That ruin wild and hoary.

Love

She listened with a flitting blush,
With downcast eyes and modest grace;
For well she knew, I could not choose
    But gaze upon her face.

I told her of the Knight that wore
Upon his shield a burning brand;
And that for ten long years he wooed
    The Lady of the Land.

I told her how he pined: and ah!
The deep, the low, the pleading tone
With which I sang another's love,
    Interpreted my own.

She listened with a flitting blush,
With downcast eyes, and modest grace;
And she forgave me, that I gazed
    Too fondly on her face!

But when I told the cruel scorn
That crazed that bold and lovely Knight,
And that he crossed the mountain-woods,
    Nor rested day nor night;

That sometimes from the savage den,
And sometimes from the darksome shade,
And sometimes starting up at once
    In green and sunny glade, –

There came and looked him in the face
An angel beautiful and bright;
And that he knew it was a Fiend,
    This miserable Knight!

And that unknowing what he did,
He leaped amid a murderous band,
And saved from outrage worse than death
    The Lady of the Land!

And how she wept, and clasped his knees;
And how she tended him in vain –
And ever strove to expiate
    The scorn that crazed his brain; –

And that she nursed him in a cave;
And how his madness went away,
When on the yellow forest-leaves
    A dying man he lay; –

His dying words – but when I reached
That tenderest strain of all the ditty,
My faultering voice and pausing harp
    Disturbed her soul with pity!

All impulses of soul and sense
Had thrilled my guileless Genevieve;
The music and the doleful tale,
    The rich and balmy eve;

Love

And hopes, and fears that kindle hope,
An undistinguishable throng,
And gentle wishes long subdued,
    Subdued and cherished long!

She wept with pity and delight,
She blushed with love, and virgin-shame;
And like the murmur of a dream,
    I heard her breathe my name.

Her bosom heaved – she stepped aside,
As conscious of my look she stepped –
Then suddenly, with timorous eye
    She fled to me and wept.

She half enclosed me with her arms,
She pressed me with a meek embrace;
And bending back her head, looked up,
    And gazed upon my face.

'Twas partly love, and partly fear,
And partly 'twas a bashful art,
That I might rather feel, than see,
    The swelling of her heart.

I calmed her fears, and she was calm,
And told her love with virgin pride;
And so I won my Genevieve,
    My bright and beauteous Bride.

Lines Written in the Album at Elbingerode, in the Hartz Forest

I stood on Brocken's sovran height, and saw
Woods crowding upon woods, hills over hills,
A surging scene, and only limited
By the blue distance. Heavily my way
Downward I dragged through fir groves evermore,
Where bright green moss heaves in sepulchral forms
Speckled with sunshine; and, but seldom heard,
The sweet bird's song became a hollow sound;
And the breeze, murmuring indivisibly,
Preserved its solemn murmur most distinct
From many a note of many a waterfall,
And the brook's chatter; 'mid whose islet-stones
The dingy kidling with its tinkling bell
Leaped frolicsome, or old romantic goat
Sat, his white beard slow waving. I moved on
In low and languid mood: for I had found
That outward forms, the loftiest, still receive
Their finer influence from the Life within; –
Fair cyphers else: fair, but of import vague
Or unconcerning, where the heart not finds
History or prophecy of friend, or child,
Or gentle maid, our first and early love,
Or father, or the venerable name
Of our adoréd country! O thou Queen,
Thou delegated Deity of Earth,

Lines Written in the Album at Elbingerode, in the Hartz Forest

O dear, dear England! how my longing eye
Turned westward, shaping in the steady clouds
Thy sands and high white cliffs!

                          My native Land!
Filled with the thought of thee this heart was proud,
Yea, mine eye swam with tears: that all the view
From sovran Brocken, woods and woody hills,
Floated away, like a departing dream,
Feeble and dim! Stranger, these impulses
Blame thou not lightly; nor will I profane,
With hasty judgment or injurious doubt,
That man's sublimer spirit, who can feel
That God is everywhere! the God who framed
Mankind to be one mighty family,
Himself our Father, and the World our Home.

Hymn before Sun-Rise, in the Vale of Chamouni

Besides the Rivers, Arve and Arveiron, which have their sources in the foot of Mont Blanc, five conspicuous torrents rush down its sides; and within a few paces of the Glaciers, the Gentiana Major grows in immense numbers, with its 'flowers of loveliest blue.'

Hast thou a charm to stay the morning-star
In his steep course? So long he seems to pause
On thy bald awful head, O sovran BLANC,
The Arve and Arveiron at thy base
Rave ceaselessly; but thou, most awful Form!
Risest from forth thy silent sea of pines,
How silently! Around thee and above
Deep is the air and dark, substantial, black,
An ebon mass: methinks thou piercest it,
As with a wedge! But when I look again,
It is thine own calm home, thy crystal shrine,
Thy habitation from eternity!
O dread and silent Mount! I gazed upon thee,
Till thou, still present to the bodily sense,
Didst vanish from my thought: entranced in prayer
I worshipped the Invisible alone.

    Yet, like some sweet beguiling melody,
So sweet, we know not we are listening to it,
Thou, the meanwhile, wast blending with my Thought,
Yea, with my Life and Life's own secret joy:

Hymn before Sun-Rise, in the Vale of Chamouni

Till the dilating Soul, enrapt, transfused,
Into the mighty vision passing – there
As in her natural form, swelled vast to Heaven!

    Awake, my soul! not only passive praise
Thou owest! not alone these swelling tears,
Mute thanks and secret ecstasy! Awake,
Voice of sweet song! Awake, my heart, awake!
Green vales and icy cliffs, all join my Hymn.

    Thou first and chief, sole sovereign of the Vale!
O struggling with the darkness all the night,
And visited all night by troops of stars,
Or when they climb the sky or when they sink:
Companion of the morning-star at dawn,
Thyself Earth's rosy star, and of the dawn
Co-herald: wake, O wake, and utter praise!
Who sank thy sunless pillars deep in Earth?
Who filled thy countenance with rosy light?
Who made thee parent of perpetual streams?

    And you, ye five wild torrents fiercely glad!
Who called you forth from night and utter death,
From dark and icy caverns called you forth,
Down those precipitous, black, jaggéd rocks,
For ever shattered and the same for ever?
Who gave you your invulnerable life,
Your strength, your speed, your fury, and your joy,
Unceasing thunder and eternal foam?
And who commanded (and the silence came),
Here let the billows stiffen, and have rest?

Samuel Taylor Coleridge

Ye Ice-falls! ye that from the mountain's brow
Adown enormous ravines slope amain –
Torrents, methinks, that heard a mighty voice,
And stopped at once amid their maddest plunge!
Motionless torrents! silent cataracts!
Who made you glorious as the Gates of Heaven
Beneath the keen full moon? Who bade the sun
Clothe you with rainbows? Who, with living flowers
Of loveliest blue, spread garlands at your feet? –
God! let the torrents, like a shout of nations,
Answer! and let the ice-plains echo, God!
God! sing ye meadow-streams with gladsome voice!
Ye pine-groves, with your soft and soul-like sounds!
And they too have a voice, yon piles of snow,
And in their perilous fall shall thunder, God!

Ye living flowers that skirt the eternal frost!
Ye wild goats sporting round the eagle's nest!
Ye eagles, play-mates of the mountain-storm!
Ye lightnings, the dread arrows of the clouds!
Ye signs and wonders of the element!
Utter forth God, and fill the hills with praise!

Thou too, hoar Mount! with thy sky-pointing peaks,
Oft from whose feet the avalanche, unheard,
Shoots downward, glittering through the pure serene
Into the depth of clouds, that veil thy breast –
Thou too again, stupendous Mountain! thou
That as I raise my head, awhile bowed low
In adoration, upward from thy base
Slow travelling with dim eyes suffused with tears,

Hymn before Sun-Rise, in the Vale of Chamouni

Solemnly seemest, like a vapoury cloud,
To rise before me – Rise, O ever rise,
Rise like a cloud of incense from the Earth!
Thou kingly Spirit throned among the hills,
Thou dread ambassador from Earth to Heaven,
Great Hierarch! tell thou the silent sky,
And tell the stars, and tell yon rising sun
Earth, with her thousand voices, praises GOD.

Lady, to Death we're Doom'd...

TRANSLATED FROM MARINO

Lady, to Death we're doom'd, our crime the same!
Thou, that in me thou kindled'st such fierce heat;
I, that my heart did of a Sun so sweet
The rays concentre to so hot a flame.
I, fascinated by an Adder's eye –
Deaf as an Adder thou to all my pain;
Thou obstinate in Scorn, in Passion I –
I lov'd too much, too much didst thou disdain.
Hear then our doom in Hell as just as stern,
Our sentence equal as our crimes conspire –
Who living bask'd at Beauty's earthly fire,
In living flames eternal these must burn –
Hell for us both fit places too supplies –
In my heart *thou* wilt burn, I *roast* before thine eyes.

The Blossoming of the Solitary Date-Tree

A LAMENT

I seem to have an indistinct recollection of having read either in one of the ponderous tomes of George of Venice, or in some other compilation from the uninspired Hebrew writers, an apologue or Rabbinical tradition to the following purpose:

> While our first parents stood before their offended Maker, and the last words of the sentence were yet sounding in Adam's ear, the guileful false serpent, a counterfeit and a usurper from the beginning, presumptuously took on himself the character of advocate or mediator, and pretending to intercede for Adam, exclaimed: 'Nay, Lord, in thy justice, not so! for the man was the least in fault. Rather let the Woman return at once to the dust, and let Adam remain in this thy Paradise.' And the word of the Most High answered Satan: *'The tender mercies of the wicked are cruel.* Treacherous Fiend! if with guilt like thine, it had been possible for thee to have the heart of a Man, and to feel the yearning of a human soul for its counterpart, the sentence, which thou now counsellest, should have been inflicted on thyself.'

The title of the following poem was suggested by a fact mentioned by Linnaeus, of a date-tree in a nobleman's garden which year after year had put forth a full show of blossoms, but never produced fruit, till a branch from another date-tree had been conveyed from a distance of some hundred leagues. The first leaf of the MS from which the poem has been transcribed, and which contained the two or three introductory stanzas, is wanting: and the author has in vain taxed his memory to repair the loss. But a rude draught of the poem contains the substance of the stanzas, and the reader is requested to receive it as the substitute. It is not impossible, that some congenial spirit, whose years do not exceed those of the Author at the time the poem was written, may find a pleasure in restoring the Lament to its original integrity by a reduction of the thoughts to the requisite metre.

S.T.C.

I

Beneath the blaze of a tropical sun the mountain peaks are the Thrones of Frost, through the absence of objects to reflect the rays. 'What no one with us shares, seems scarce our own.' The presence of a ONE,

> The best belov'd, who loveth me the best,

is for the heart, what the supporting air from within is for the hollow globe with its suspended car. Deprive it of this, and all without, that would have buoyed it aloft even to the seat of the gods, becomes a burthen and crushes it into flatness.

2

The finer the sense for the beautiful and the lovely, and the fairer and lovelier the object presented to the sense; the more exquisite the individual's capacity of joy, and the more ample his means and opportunities of enjoyment, the more heavily will he feel the ache of solitariness, the more unsubstantial becomes the feast spread around him. What matters it, whether in fact the viands and the ministering graces are shadowy or real, to him who has not hand to grasp nor arms to embrace them?

3

Imagination; honourable aims;
Free commune with the choir that cannot die;
Science and song; delight in little things,
The buoyant child surviving in the man;
Fields, forests, ancient mountains, ocean, sky,
With all their voices – O dare I accuse
My earthly lot as guilty of my spleen,
Or call my destiny niggard! O no! no!
It is her largeness, and her overflow,
Which being incomplete, disquieteth me so!

Samuel Taylor Coleridge

4

For never touch of gladness stirs my heart,
But tim'rously beginning to rejoice
Like a blind Arab, that from sleep doth start
In lonesome tent, I listen for thy voice.
Belovéd! 'tis not thine; thou art not there!
Then melts the bubble into idle air,
And wishing without hope I restlessly despair.

5

The mother with anticipated glee
Smiles o'er the child, that, standing by her chair
And flatt'ning its round cheek upon her knee,
Looks up, and doth its rosy lips prepare
To mock the coming sounds. At that sweet sight
She hears her own voice with a new delight;
And if the babe perchance should lisp the notes aright,

6

Then is she tenfold gladder than before!
But should disease or chance the darling take,
What then avail those songs, which sweet of yore

The Blossoming of the Solitary Date-Tree

Were only sweet for their sweet echo's sake?
Dear maid! no prattler at a mother's knee
Was e'er so dearly prized as I prize thee:
Why was I made for Love and Love denied to me?

O Sara! Never Rashly Let Me Go

O Sara! never rashly let me go
Beyond the precincts of this holy Place,
Where streams as pure as in Elysium flow
And flowrets view reflected Grace:
What though in vain the melted Metals glow,
We die, and dying own a more than mortal Love.

You Mould My Hopes

You mould my Hopes you fashion me within:
And to the leading love-throb in the heart,
Through all my being, through my pulses beat;
You lie in all my many thoughts like Light,
Like the fair light of Dawn, or summer Eve,
On rippling stream, or cloud-reflecting lake;
And looking to the Heaven that bends above you,
How oft! I bless the lot that made me love you.

The Tropic Tree

As some vast Tropic tree, itself a wood,
That crests its head with clouds, beneath the flood
Feeds its deep roots, and with the bulging flank
Of its wide base controls the fronting bank –
(By the slant current's pressure scoop'd away
The fronting bank becomes a foam-piled bay)
High in the Fork the uncouth Idol knits
His channel'd brow; low murmurs stir by fits
And dark below the horrid Faquir sits –
An Horror from its broad Head's branching wreath
Broods o'er the rude Idolatry beneath –

The Yellow Hammer

The spruce and limber yellow-hammer
In the dawn of spring and sultry summer,
In hedge or tree the hours beguiling
With notes as of one who brass is filing.

The Pang More Sharp Than All

AN ALLEGORY

I

He too has flitted from his secret nest,
Hope's last and dearest child without a name! –
Has flitted from me, like the warmthless flame,
That makes false promise of a place of rest
To the tired Pilgrim's still believing mind; –
Or like some Elfin Knight in kingly court,
Who having won all guerdons in his sport,
Glides out of view, and whither none can find!

II

Yes! he hath flitted from me – with what aim,
Or why, I know not! 'Twas a home of bliss,
And he was innocent, as the pretty shame
Of babe, that tempts and shuns the menaced kiss,
From its twy-cluster'd hiding place of snow!
Pure as the babe, I ween, and all aglow
As the dear hopes, that swell the mother's breast –
Her eyes down gazing o'er her claspéd charge; –
Yet gay as that twice happy father's kiss,
That well might glance aside, yet never miss,
Where the sweet mark emboss'd so sweet a targe –
Twice wretched he who hath been doubly blest!

The Pang More Sharp Than All

III

Like a loose blossom on a gusty night
He flitted from me – and has left behind
(As if to them his faith he ne'er did plight)
Of either sex and answerable mind
Two playmates, twin-births of his foster-dame: –
The one a steady lad (Esteem he hight)
And Kindness is the gentler sister's name.
Dim likeness now, though fair she be and good,
Of that bright Boy who hath us all forsook; –
But in his full-eyed aspect when she stood,
And while her face reflected every look,
And in reflection kindled – she became
So like Him, that almost she seem'd the same!

IV

Ah! he is gone, and yet will not depart! –
Is with me still, yet I from him exiled!
For still there lives within my secret heart
The magic image of the magic Child,
Which there he made up-grow by his strong art,
As in that crystal orb – wise Merlin's feat, –
The wondrous 'World of Glass,' wherein inisled
All long'd-for things their beings did repeat; –
And there he left it, like a Sylph beguiled,
To live and yearn and languish incomplete!

V

Can wit of man a heavier grief reveal?
Can sharper pang from hate or scorn arise? –
Yes! one more sharp there is that deeper lies,
Which fond Esteem but mocks when he would heal.
Yet neither scorn nor hate did it devise,
But sad compassion and atoning zeal!
One pang more blighting-keen than hope betray'd!
And this it is my woeful hap to feel,
When, at her Brother's hest, the twin-born Maid
With face averted and unsteady eyes,
Her truant playmate's faded robe puts on;
And inly shrinking from her own disguise
Enacts the faery Boy that's lost and gone.
O worse than all! O pang all pangs above
Is Kindness counterfeiting absent Love!

Limbo

'Tis a strange place, this Limbo! – not a Place,
Yet name it so; – where Time and weary Space
Fettered from flight, with night-mare sense of fleeing,
Strive for their last crepuscular half-being, –
Lank Space, and scytheless Time with branny hands
Barren and soundless as the measuring sands,
Not mark'd by flit of Shades, – unmeaning they
As moonlight on the dial of the day!

But that is lovely – looks like human Time, –
An Old Man with a steady look sublime,
That stops his earthly task to watch the skies;
But he is blind – a statue hath such eyes; –
Yet having moonward turn'd his face by chance,
Gazes the orb with moon-like countenance,
With scant white hairs, with foretop bald and high,
He gazes still, – his eyeless face all eye; –
As 'twere an organ full of silent sight,
His whole face seemeth to rejoice in light! –
Lip touching lip, all moveless, bust and limb –
He seems to gaze at that which seems to gaze on him!

    No such sweet sights doth Limbo den immure,
Wall'd round, and made a spirit-jail secure,
By the mere horror of blank Naught-at-all,
Whose circumambience doth these ghosts enthrall.

Samuel Taylor Coleridge

    A lurid thought is growthless, dull Privation,
    Yet that is but a Purgatory curse;
    Hell knows a fear far worse,
    A fear – a future state; –'tis positive Negation!

The Pains of Sleep

Ere on my bed my limbs I lay,
It hath not been my use to pray
With moving lips or bended knees;
But silently, by slow degrees,
My spirit I to Love compose,
In humble trust mine eye-lids close,
With reverential resignation,
No wish conceived, no thought exprest,
Only a sense of supplication;
A sense o'er all my soul imprest
That I am weak, yet not unblest,
Since in me, round me, every where
Eternal Strength and Wisdom are.

But yester-night I prayed aloud
In anguish and in agony,
Up-starting from the fiendish crowd
Of shapes and thoughts that tortured me:
A lurid light, a trampling throng,
Sense of intolerable wrong,
And whom I scorned, those only strong!
Thirst of revenge, the powerless will
Still baffled, and yet burning still!
Desire with loathing strangely mixed
On wild or hateful objects fixed.
Fantastic passions! maddening brawl!
And shame and terror over all!

Samuel Taylor Coleridge

>Deeds to be hid which were not hid,
>Which all confused I could not know
>Whether I suffered, or I did:
>For all seemed guilt, remorse or woe,
>My own or others still the same
>Life-stifling fear, soul-stifling shame.
>So two nights passed: the night's dismay
>Saddened and stunned the coming day.
>Sleep, the wide blessing, seemed to me
>Distemper's worst calamity.
>The third night, when my own loud scream
>Had waked me from the fiendish dream,
>O'ercome with sufferings strange and wild,
>I wept as I had been a child;
>And having thus by tears subdued
>My anguish to a milder mood,
>Such punishments, I said, were due
>To natures deepliest stained with sin, –
>For aye entempesting anew
>The unfathomable hell within,
>The horror of their deeds to view,
>To know and loathe, yet wish and do!
>Such griefs with such men well agree,
>But wherefore, wherefore fall on me?
>To be beloved is all I need,
>And whom I love, I love indeed.

The Knight's Tomb

Where is the grave of Sir Arthur O'Kellyn?
Where may the grave of that good man be? –
By the side of a spring, on the breast of Helvellyn,
Under the twigs of a young birch tree!
The oak that in summer was sweet to hear,
And rustled its leaves in the fall of the year,
And whistled and roared in the winter alone,
Is gone, – and the birch in its stead is grown. –
The Knight's bones are dust,
And his good sword rust; –
His soul is with the saints, I trust.

Fancy in Nubibus

OR THE POET IN THE CLOUDS

O! It is pleasant, with a heart at ease,
    Just after sunset, or by moonlight skies,
To make the shifting clouds be what you please,
    Or let the easily persuaded eyes
Own each quaint likeness issuing from the mould
    Of a friend's fancy; or with head bent low
And cheek aslant see rivers flow of gold
    'Twixt crimson banks; and then, a traveller, go
From mount to mount through Cloudland, gorgeous land!
    Or list'ning to the tide, with closéd sight,
Be that blind bard, who on the Chian strand
    By those deep sounds possessed with inward light,
Beheld the Iliad and the Odyssee
    Rise to the swelling of the voiceful sea.

1. BOCCACCIO · *Mrs Rosie and the Priest*
2. GERARD MANLEY HOPKINS · *As kingfishers catch fire*
3. *The Saga of Gunnlaug Serpent-tongue*
4. THOMAS DE QUINCEY · *On Murder Considered as One of the Fine Arts*
5. FRIEDRICH NIETZSCHE · *Aphorisms on Love and Hate*
6. JOHN RUSKIN · *Traffic*
7. PU SONGLING · *Wailing Ghosts*
8. JONATHAN SWIFT · *A Modest Proposal*
9. *Three Tang Dynasty Poets*
10. WALT WHITMAN · *On the Beach at Night Alone*
11. KENKŌ · *A Cup of Sake Beneath the Cherry Trees*
12. BALTASAR GRACIÁN · *How to Use Your Enemies*
13. JOHN KEATS · *The Eve of St Agnes*
14. THOMAS HARDY · *Woman much missed*
15. GUY DE MAUPASSANT · *Femme Fatale*
16. MARCO POLO · *Travels in the Land of Serpents and Pearls*
17. SUETONIUS · *Caligula*
18. APOLLONIUS OF RHODES · *Jason and Medea*
19. ROBERT LOUIS STEVENSON · *Olalla*
20. KARL MARX AND FRIEDRICH ENGELS · *The Communist Manifesto*
21. PETRONIUS · *Trimalchio's Feast*
22. JOHANN PETER HEBEL · *How a Ghastly Story Was Brought to Light by a Common or Garden Butcher's Dog*
23. HANS CHRISTIAN ANDERSEN · *The Tinder Box*
24. RUDYARD KIPLING · *The Gate of the Hundred Sorrows*
25. DANTE · *Circles of Hell*
26. HENRY MAYHEW · *Of Street Piemen*
27. HAFEZ · *The nightingales are drunk*
28. GEOFFREY CHAUCER · *The Wife of Bath*
29. MICHEL DE MONTAIGNE · *How We Weep and Laugh at the Same Thing*
30. THOMAS NASHE · *The Terrors of the Night*
31. EDGAR ALLAN POE · *The Tell-Tale Heart*
32. MARY KINGSLEY · *A Hippo Banquet*
33. JANE AUSTEN · *The Beautifull Cassandra*
34. ANTON CHEKHOV · *Gooseberries*
35. SAMUEL TAYLOR COLERIDGE · *Well, they are gone, and here must I remain*
36. JOHANN WOLFGANG VON GOETHE · *Sketchy, Doubtful, Incomplete Jottings*
37. CHARLES DICKENS · *The Great Winglebury Duel*
38. HERMAN MELVILLE · *The Maldive Shark*
39. ELIZABETH GASKELL · *The Old Nurse's Story*
40. NIKOLAY LESKOV · *The Steel Flea*

41. HONORÉ DE BALZAC · *The Atheist's Mass*
42. CHARLOTTE PERKINS GILMAN · *The Yellow Wall-Paper*
43. C.P. CAVAFY · *Remember, Body . . .*
44. FYODOR DOSTOEVSKY · *The Meek One*
45. GUSTAVE FLAUBERT · *A Simple Heart*
46. NIKOLAI GOGOL · *The Nose*
47. SAMUEL PEPYS · *The Great Fire of London*
48. EDITH WHARTON · *The Reckoning*
49. HENRY JAMES · *The Figure in the Carpet*
50. WILFRED OWEN · *Anthem For Doomed Youth*
51. WOLFGANG AMADEUS MOZART · *My Dearest Father*
52. PLATO · *Socrates' Defence*
53. CHRISTINA ROSSETTI · *Goblin Market*
54. *Sindbad the Sailor*
55. SOPHOCLES · *Antigone*
56. RYŪNOSUKE AKUTAGAWA · *The Life of a Stupid Man*
57. LEO TOLSTOY · *How Much Land Does A Man Need?*
58. GIORGIO VASARI · *Leonardo da Vinci*
59. OSCAR WILDE · *Lord Arthur Savile's Crime*
60. SHEN FU · *The Old Man of the Moon*
61. AESOP · *The Dolphins, the Whales and the Gudgeon*
62. MATSUO BASHŌ · *Lips too Chilled*
63. EMILY BRONTË · *The Night is Darkening Round Me*
64. JOSEPH CONRAD · *To-morrow*
65. RICHARD HAKLUYT · *The Voyage of Sir Francis Drake Around the Whole Globe*
66. KATE CHOPIN · *A Pair of Silk Stockings*
67. CHARLES DARWIN · *It was snowing butterflies*
68. BROTHERS GRIMM · *The Robber Bridegroom*
69. CATULLUS · *I Hate and I Love*
70. HOMER · *Circe and the Cyclops*
71. D. H. LAWRENCE · *Il Duro*
72. KATHERINE MANSFIELD · *Miss Brill*
73. OVID · *The Fall of Icarus*
74. SAPPHO · *Come Close*
75. IVAN TURGENEV · *Kasyan from the Beautiful Lands*
76. VIRGIL · *O Cruel Alexis*
77. H. G. WELLS · *A Slip under the Microscope*
78. HERODOTUS · *The Madness of Cambyses*
79. *Speaking of Siva*
80. *The Dhammapada*

'I can promise to be candid, not, however, to be impartial.'

JOHANN WOLFGANG VON GOETHE
Born 1749, Frankfurt, Germany
Died 1832, Weimar, Germany

This selection is taken from *Maxims and Reflections*,
translated by Elisabeth Stopp,
Penguin Classics, 1998.

GOETHE IN PENGUIN CLASSICS
Faust, Part I
Faust, Part II
Maxims and Reflections
Elective Affinities
The Sorrows of Young Werther
Selected Poetry
Italian Journey 1786–1788

JOHANN WOLFGANG VON GOETHE

Sketchy, Doubtful, Incomplete Jottings

Translated by
Elisabeth Stopp

PENGUIN BOOKS

PENGUIN CLASSICS

UK | USA | Canada | Ireland | Australia
India | New Zealand | South Africa

Penguin Books is part of the Penguin Random House group of companies whose addresses can be found at global.penguinrandomhouse.com.

This selection published in Penguin Classics 2015

011

Translation copyright © the Estate of Elisabeth Stopp, 1998

Set in 10/14.5 pt Baskerville 10 Pro
Typeset by Jouve (UK), Milton Keynes

Printed and bound in Great Britain by Clays Ltd, Elcograf S.p.A.

A CIP catalogue record for this book is available from the British Library

ISBN: 978-0-141-39713-9

www.greenpenguin.co.uk

Penguin Random House is committed to a sustainable future for our business, our readers and our planet. This book is made from Forest Stewardship Council® certified paper.

It is much easier to recognize error than to find truth; the former lies on the surface, this is quite manageable; the latter resides in depth, and this quest is not everyone's business.

*

We all live on the past and perish by the past.

*

When we are called to learn something great, we at once take refuge in our native poverty and yet have still learnt something.

*

Johann Wolfgang von Goethe

The Germans are indifferent about staying together, yet they do want to be on their own. Each person, never mind who he may be, has his own way of being alone and is unwilling to be deprived of this.

*

The empirical-moral world consists largely of bad will and envy.

*

Superstition is the poetry of life; so it does the poet no harm to be superstitious.

*

Trust is a curious matter. Listen only to one person: he may be wrong or deceiving himself; listen to many: they are in the same case, and as a rule you don't really discover the truth.

*

Sketchy, Doubtful, Incomplete Jottings

One should not wish anyone disagreeable conditions of life; but for him who is involved in them by chance, they are touchstones of character and of the most decisive value to man.

*

A limited, honest man often sees right through the knavery of the sharpest tricksters.

*

One who feels no love must learn to flatter, otherwise he won't make out.

*

You can neither protect nor defend yourself against criticism; you have to act in defiance of it and this is gradually accepted.

*

Johann Wolfgang von Goethe

The crowd cannot do without efficient people and always finds efficiency burdensome.

*

Anyone who tells on my faults is my master, even if it happens to be my servant.

*

Memoirs from above downwards, or from below upwards: they are always bound to meet.

*

If you demand duties from people and will not concede them rights, you have to pay them well.

*

When a landscape is described as romantic, this means that there is a tranquil sense of the sublime in the form of the past, or, what amounts to the same, of solitude, remoteness, seclusion.

*

The splendid liturgical song '*Veni Creator Spiritus*' is in actual fact a call addressed to genius; and this is also why it appeals powerfully to people who are spirited and strong.

*

Beauty is a manifestation of secret natural laws which without this appearance would have remained eternally hidden from us.

*

I can promise to be candid, not, however, to be impartial.

*

Ingratitude is always a kind of weakness. I have never known competent people to be ungrateful.

*

We are all so blinkered that we always imagine we are right; and so we can imagine an extraordinary spirit, a person who not only makes a mistake but even enjoys being wrong.

*

Completely moderate action to achieve what is good and right is very rare; what we usually see is pedantry seeking to retard, impertinence seeking to precipitate.

*

Word and image are correlatives which are always in quest of one another as metaphors and comparisons show us clearly enough. Thus, from of old, what is inwardly said or sung for the ear is at the same time intended for the eye. And so in ages which seem to us childlike, we see in codes of law and salvational doctrine, in bible and in primer, a continual balance of word and image. If they put into words what did not go into images, or formed an image of what could not be put into words, that was quite proper; but people often went wrong about this and used the spoken word instead of the pictorial image, which was the origin of those doubly wicked symbolically mystical monsters.

*

Anyone who devotes himself to the sciences suffers, firstly through retardations and then through preoccupations. To begin with, people are reluctant to admit the value of what we are providing; later on they act as though they already knew what we might be able to provide.

*

A collection of anecdotes and maxims is the greatest treasure for a man of the world – as long as he knows how to weave the former into apposite points of the course of conversation, and to recall the latter on fitting occasions.

*

People say, 'Artist, study nature!' But it is no small matter to develop what is noble out of what is common, beauty out of what lacks form.

*

Where concern is lost, memory fares likewise.

*

The world is a bell that is cracked: it clatters, but does not ring out clearly.

*

One must put up kindly with the pressing overtures of young dilettantes: with age they become the truest votaries of art and of the master.

*

When people really deteriorate, their only contribution is malicious joy in the misfortune of others.

*

Intelligent people are always the best encyclopaedia.

*

There are people who never make mistakes because they never have sensible projects.

*

Knowing my attitude to myself and to the world outside me is what I call truth. And so everyone can have his own truth and yet it remains the self-same truth.

*

What is particular is eternally defeated by what is general; the general has eternally to fit in with the particular.

*

Johann Wolfgang von Goethe

No one can control what is really creative, and everybody just has to let it go its own way.

*

Anyone to whom nature begins to unveil its open mystery feels an irresistible yearning for nature's noblest interpreter, for art.

*

Time is itself an element.

*

Man never understands how anthropomorphic he is.

*

A difference which gives reason nothing to register is not a difference.

*

Sketchy, Doubtful, Incomplete Jottings

In phanerogamy there is still so much of what is cryptogamic that centuries will not suffice to unriddle it.

*

Exchanging one consonant for another might perhaps be due to some organ deficiency, transforming a vowel into a diphthong the result of conceited pathos.

*

If one had to study all laws, one would have no time at all to transgress them.

*

One can't live for everyone, more especially not for those with whom one wouldn't care to live.

*

A call to posterity originates in the clear vital feeling that there is such a thing as permanence and that even if this is not immediately acknowledged it will, in the end, win the recognition of a minority and finally of a majority.

*

Mysteries do not as yet amount to miracles.

*

I convertiti stanno freschi appresso di me. [The converted are puzzled by me.]

*

Reckless, passionate favouritism of problematic men of talent was a failing of my younger years of which I could never completely rid myself.

*

I would like to be honest with you without us parting company; but this isn't possible. You are acting wrongly and trying to sit between two stools, not getting any followers and losing your friends. What's to come of this!

*

No matter whether you're of high rank or low, you can't avoid paying the price of your common humanity.

*

Writers of a liberal persuasion are now on to a good game; they have the whole public at their feet.

*

When I hear talk about liberal ideas, I'm always amazed how people like to delude themselves with the sound of empty words: an idea is not allowed to be liberal! Let it be forceful, doughty, self-enclosed, so as to fulfil its God-given mission of being productive. Still less is a concept allowed to be liberal; for its commission is completely different.

*

But where we have to look for liberality is in people's attitudes and these are their feelings come to life.

*

Attitudes, however, are seldom liberal because an attitude springs directly from the person, his immediate context and his needs.

*

We'll leave it at that; by this yardstick we should measure what we hear day after day!

*

It's always only our eyes, the way we imagine things; nature quite alone knows what it wills, what it intended.

>'Give me where I stand!'
>Archimedes.

> 'Take where you stand!'
> Nose.
> Declare where you stand!
> G.

It is general causal relationships which the observer will explore, and he will attribute similar phenomena to a general cause; rarely will he think of the immediate cause.

*

No intelligent man experiences a minor stupidity.

*

In every work of art, great or small, and down to the smallest detail, everything depends on the initial conception.

*

There is no such thing as poetry without tropes as poetry is a single trope writ large.

Johann Wolfgang von Goethe

*

A kindly old examiner whispers into a schoolboy's ear: '*Etiam nihil didicisti*' [you haven't learnt anything as yet] and gives him a pass-mark.

*

Excellence is unfathomable; tackle it in what way you will.

*

Aemilium Paulum – virum in tantum landandum, in quantum intelligi virtus potest. [Aemilius Paulus – a man to be praised as highly as virtue can be understood.]

*

I was intent on pursuing what is general until such time as I came to comprehend the achievement of outstanding people in what is particular.

*

Sketchy, Doubtful, Incomplete Jottings

You really only know when you know little; doubt grows with knowledge.

*

It's really a person's mistakes that make him endearing.

*

Bonus vir semper tiro. [A good man is always a beginner.]

*

There are people who love and seek out those like themselves, and, then again, those who love and pursue their opposites.

*

Anyone who had always allowed himself to take so poor a view of the world as our adversaries make out would have turned into a rotten subject.

Johann Wolfgang von Goethe

*

Envy and hatred limit the observer's view to the surface even if this is also associated with acumen; if this, however, goes hand in hand with kindliness and love, the observer can see right through the world and mankind; indeed, he can hope to reach the Allhighest.

*

An English critic credits me with 'panoramic ability', for which I must tender my most cordial thanks.

*

A certain measure of poetical talent is desirable for every German as the right way to cloak his condition, of whatever kind it may be, with a certain degree of worth and charm.

*

Sketchy, Doubtful, Incomplete Jottings

The subject-matter is visible to everyone, content is only discovered by him who has something to contribute, and form is a mystery to most.

*

People's inclinations favour what is vitally alive. And youth again forms itself by youth.

*

We may get to know the world however we choose, it will always keep a day and a night aspect.

*

Error is continually repeated in action, and that is why we must not tire of repeating in words what is true.

*

Just as in Rome, besides the Romans, there was also a people of statues, so, too, apart from this real world, there is also an illusory world, mightier almost, where the majority live.

*

People are like the Red Sea: the staff has hardly kept them apart, immediately afterwards they flow together again.

*

The historian's duty: to distinguish truth from falsehood, certainty from uncertainty, doubtful matters from those which are to be rejected.

*

Only someone to whom the present is important writes a chronicle.

*

Thoughts recur, convictions perpetuate themselves; circumstances pass by irretrievably.

Sketchy, Doubtful, Incomplete Jottings

*

Among all peoples, the Greeks have dreamt life's dream most beautifully.

*

Translators are to be regarded as busy matchmakers who exalt the great loveliness of a half-veiled beauty: they kindle an irresistible longing for the original.

*

We like to rate Antiquity higher than ourselves, but not posterity. It's only a father who doesn't envy a son's talent.

*

It's not at all hard to subordinate yourself; but when you are set on a declining course, in the descendant, how hard it is to admit that what is, in fact, below you is above you!

Johann Wolfgang von Goethe

*

Our whole achievement is to give up our existence in order to exist.

*

All we devise and do is exhausting; happy the man who doesn't get weary.

*

'Hope is the second soul of those who are unfortunate.'

*

'*L'amour est un vrai recommenceur.*' [Love is truly a new beginning.]

*

There is, too, in man a desire to serve; hence French chivalry is a form of service, '*servage*'.

*

'In the theatre visual and aural entertainment greatly limit reflection.'

*

Experience can be extended into infinity; in not quite the same sense theory can be purified and perfected. To the former the universe is open in all directions; the latter remains locked within the confines of human capacity. This is why all modes of conceptual thinking are bound to reappear, and that is why, strangely enough, a theory of limited value can regain favour in spite of wider experience.

*

It is always the same world which lies open to our view, is always contemplated or surmised, and it is always the same people who live in truth or wrong-headedly, more comfortably in the latter way than in the former.

Johann Wolfgang von Goethe

*

Truth is contrary to our nature, not so error, and this for a very simple reason: truth demands that we should recognize ourselves as limited, error flatters us that, in one way or another, we are unlimited.

*

It is now nearly twenty years since all Germans 'transcend'. Once they notice this, they are bound to realize how odd they are.

*

It is natural enough that people should imagine they can still do what they were once able to do; that others imagine themselves capable of doing what they never could do is perhaps strange but not infrequent.

*

At all times only individuals have had an effect on scientific knowledge, not the epoch. It was the epoch that did Socrates to death by poison, the epoch that burnt Huss: epochs have always remained true to type.

*

This is true symbolism, where the particular represents the general, not as dream and shadow, but as a live and immediate revelation of the unfathomable.

*

As soon as the ideal makes a demand on the real, it in the end consumes it and also itself. Thus credit (paper money) consumes silver and its own self.

*

Mastery is often seen as egoism.

*

As soon as good works and their merit cease, sentimentality immediately takes over in the case of Protestants.

Johann Wolfgang von Goethe

*

If you can seek out good advice, it's as though you yourself have the capacity for action.

*

There's nothing clever that hasn't been thought of before – you've just got to try to think it all over again.

*

How can we learn self-knowledge? Never by taking thought but rather by action. Try to do your duty and you'll soon discover what you're like.

*

But what is your duty? The demands of the day.

*

The reasonable world is to be seen as a great individual not subject to mortality and forever bringing about what is needed, in this way even mastering chance events.

*

The longer I live, the more depressing I find the spectacle of a man, whose optimal function is to be a lord over nature so as to free himself and his fellow men from tyrannical necessity, doing the exact opposite of what he really wants to do, and all because of some preconceived false notion; and in the end, because the structure of the project as a whole has been ruined, he just muddles on miserably with odd details.

*

Man of ability and action, be worthy of, and expect:

grace	–from those who are great
favour	–from the powerful
a helping hand	–from those who are active and good
affection	–from the crowd
love	–from an individual

Johann Wolfgang von Goethe

*

When a dilettante has done what lies within his capacity to complete a work, he usually makes the excuse that of course it's as yet unfinished. Clearly, it never can be finished because it was never properly started. The master of his art, by means of a few strokes, produces a finished work; fully worked out or not, it is already completed. The cleverest kind of dilettante gropes about in uncertainties and, as the work proceeds, the dubiousness of the initial structure becomes more and more apparent. Right at the end the faulty nature of the work, impossible to correct, shows up clearly and so, of course, the work can never be finished.

*

For true art there is no such thing as preparatory schooling, but there are certainly preparations; the best, however, is when the least pupil takes a share in the master's work. Colour-grinders have turned into very good artists.

*

Sketchy, Doubtful, Incomplete Jottings

Copycat work, casually stimulating people's natural activity in imitating an important artist who achieves with ease what is difficult, is quite a different matter.

*

We are quite convinced that it is essential for the artist to make studies from nature; we won't however deny that it often grieves us to perceive the misuse of such praiseworthy endeavours.

*

We are convinced that the young artist should rarely, if at all, set out to do studies from nature without at the same time considering how he might round off every sheet and make a whole of it, transforming this unit into a pleasing picture set within a frame, and offer it courteously to the amateur and the expert.

*

Johann Wolfgang von Goethe

Much that is beautiful stands as an isolated entity in the world, but the spirit has to discover connections and thus to create works of art. The flower unfolds its full beauty only through the insect that clings to it, through the dewdrop that makes it glisten, through the calix from out of which it may be drawing its last sustenance. No bush, no tree whose charm may not be enhanced by a neighbouring rock or brook, by a simple prospect in the distance. And so it is with human figures and so with animals of every kind.

*

The advantages accruing to a young artist in this way are indeed manifold. He learns to think out the best way of fitting together related things and, when he thus composes intelligently, he will, in the end, assuredly not lack what is termed invention, the capacity to develop a manifold whole out of single units.

*

And, as well as conforming to the tenets of art pedagogy, he gains the great advantage, by no means to

Sketchy, Doubtful, Incomplete Jottings

be despised, of learning to create saleable pictures that are a pleasure and delight to the art lover.

*

A work of this kind need not be complete down to the last detail; if it is well envisaged, thought out and finished, it is often more appealing to the art lover than a larger, more fully completed picture.

*

Let every young artist take a look at the studies in his sketch book and portfolio and consider how many of these sheets he might have been able to make enjoyable and desirable in this way.

*

We are not talking about the higher regions of art which might of course also be discussed; this is no more than a warning to recall the artist from a devious path and point the way to higher regions.

*

Let the artist put this to a practical test, if only for half a year, and not make use of either charcoal or brush unless he has the firm intention of actually structuring a picture out of the natural object or scene confronting him. If he has inborn talent, what we intended by our comments will soon be revealed.

*

Tell me with whom you consort and I will tell you who you are; if I know how you spend your time, then I know what might become of you.

*

Every individual must think in his own personal way; for on his way he always finds a truth or a kind of truth which helps him get through life. But he mustn't let himself go, he has got to keep a check on himself; purely naked instinct is unseemly.

*

Sketchy, Doubtful, Incomplete Jottings

Absolute activity, of whatever kind, ultimately leads to bankruptcy.

*

In the works of man as in those of nature, what most deserves notice is his intention.

*

People are at a loss with regard to themselves and one another because they use means as ends, and then, because of sheer busyness, nothing whatever happens or perhaps, even worse, something which is disagreeable.

*

What we think out, what we undertake, should have achieved such perfect clarity and beauty that anything the world could do to it could only spoil it; this would leave us with the advantage of only having to adjust what has been misplaced and refashion what has been destroyed.

Johann Wolfgang von Goethe

*

Whole, half- and quarter-errors are most difficult and wearisome to put right, to sort out.

*

Truth need not always take corporeal form; enough for it to be around in spiritual form, bringing about harmony as it floats on the breeze as a spiritual presence like the solemn-friendly sound of bells.

*

When I ask young German artists, even those who have spent some time in Italy, why they use such crudely bright colours, especially in their landscapes, and seem to shun anything like harmony, they are apt to answer boldly and cheerfully that this is precisely how they see nature.

*

Sketchy, Doubtful, Incomplete Jottings

Kant has drawn our attention to the fact that there is such a thing as a Critique of Reason, and that this, the highest faculty possessed by man, has cause to keep watch over itself. Let everyone judge for himself what great advantages the voice of Kant has brought him. I, for my part, would similarly like to urge that a Critique of the Senses should be worked out, if art, especially German art, is in any way to recover and to proceed and progress at a pleasing and lively pace.

*

Man, born to be a creature of reason, nevertheless needs much education, whether this comes gradually by way of careful parents and tutors, by peaceful example or by stern experience. Similarly, there is such a thing as a born potential artist, but no one is born perfect. He may have an inborn clarity of vision, a happy eye for shape, proportion, movement: but without becoming aware of this lack, he may be without a natural instinct for composition in its higher aspects, for correct tonal proportion, for light, shade and colouring.

Johann Wolfgang von Goethe

*

Now if he is not inclined to learn from more highly skilled contemporary or earlier artists what he himself lacks in order to be a true artist, he will lag behind his own potential because of a wrong-headed idea that he is safeguarding his own originality; for we own not just what we are born with, but also what we can acquire, and this is what we are.

*

General notions and great conceit are always potential creators of shocking misfortune.

*

'You don't play the flute just by blowing – you've got to move your fingers.'

*

Botanists have a plant-category which they call 'Incompletae'; similarly one can say that there are incomplete and uncompleted people. These are the ones whose longings and strivings are out of proportion with what they actually do and what they achieve.

*

The least gifted man can be complete if he keeps within the limits of his capacities and skills, but real excellence is obscured, cancelled out and destroyed if there is not that absolutely essential sense of proportion. This disastrous lack is bound to crop up frequently in our own day; for who can possibly keep up with the demands of an exorbitant present, and that at maximum speed?

*

Only those people who are both clever and active, who are clear about their own capacities and can use them with moderation and common sense, will really get on in the world as it is.

*

Johann Wolfgang von Goethe

A great failing: to see yourself as more than you are and to value yourself at less than your true worth.

*

From time to time I meet a young man whom I wouldn't wish different or improved in any way; but what worries me is that some of these people seem to me just the kind who let themselves drift along with the current of the stream of time, and this is where I keep wanting to point out that man is put at the helm of his own fragile craft precisely so that he may not follow the whim of the waves, the determination of his own insight.

*

But how is a young man independently to reach the insight that what everyone else pursues, approves and furthers may be reprehensible and damaging? Why shouldn't he let himself and his own natural disposition go the same way?

*

Sketchy, Doubtful, Incomplete Jottings

The greatest evil of our time – which lets nothing come to fruition – is, I think, that one moment consumes the next, wastes the day within that same day and so is always living from hand to mouth without achieving anything of substance. Don't we already have news-sheets for every point of the day! A clever man might well be able to slip in one or two more. In this way everything that anyone does, is working at or writing, indeed plans to write, is dragged out into the open. No one is allowed to be happy or miserable except as a pastime for the rest of the world, and so news rushes from house to house, from town to town, from one country to another, and, in the end, from one continent to the next, and all on the principle of speed and velocity.

*

As little as steam engines can be quelled, so little is this possible in the behavioural realm: the lively pace of trade, the rapid rush of paper-money, the inflated increase of debts made in order to pay off other debts, these are the monstrous elements to which a young man is now exposed. How good for him if nature has endowed him with a moderate and calm attitude so that he makes no disproportionate claims on the world nor yet allows it to determine his course!

*

But the spirit of the day threatens him in every sphere and nothing is more important than to make him realize early enough the direction in which his will should steer.

*

As one grows older, the most innocent talk and action grow in significance, and to those I see around me for any length of time I always try to point out the shades of difference between sincerity, frankness and indiscretion, and that there is really no difference between them, but just an intangible transition from the most harmless comment to the most damaging, and that this subtle transition has to be observed or indeed felt.

*

Sketchy, Doubtful, Incomplete Jottings

In this matter we have to use tact, else we run the risk of losing people's favour without being in the least aware of this and precisely in the way we came by it. This we probably come to understand in the course of life, but only after we have paid a high price for our experience, and from this we cannot, alas, spare those who come after us.

*

The relationship of the arts and the sciences to life is very varied according to the way their temporal stages are related to the nature of their epoch and a thousand other chance contingencies; which is why it isn't easy to make sense of all this.

Poetry is most effective at the start of any set of circumstances, irrespective of whether these are quite crude, half-cultured, or when a culture is in the process of change as it begins to become aware of a foreign culture; in such cases one can claim the effect of the new is definitely to be felt.

Johann Wolfgang von Goethe

*

Music at its best hardly needs to be new; indeed, the older it is, the more familiar to us, the more effective it can be.

*

The dignity of art perhaps appears most eminent in music because it has no material of a kind for which detailed accounting might be needed. It is all form and content and it heightens and ennobles all it expresses.

*

Music is either sacred or profane. What is sacred accords completely with its nobility, and this is where music most immediately influences life; such influence remains unchanged at all times and in every epoch. Profane music should be altogether cheerful.

*

Sketchy, Doubtful, Incomplete Jottings

Music of a kind that mixes the sacred with the profane is godless and shoddy music which goes in for expressing feeble, wretched, deplorable feelings, and is just insipid. For it is not serious enough to be sacred and it lacks the chief quality of the opposite kind: cheerfulness.

*

The numinous nature of church music, the cheerfulness and playfulness of folk melodies are the two pivots of true music. At these two focal points music always and inevitably leads either towards reverence or else to dance. Any mixture of the two is confusing, dilution is boring, and if music consorts with didactic or descriptive poems and texts of that kind, the result is coldness.

*

Plastic art is really only effective at its highest level; it is true that the middle zone can perhaps impress us for more reasons than one, but all middle-range art of this kind is more confusing than gladdening.

Sculpture therefore has to discover subject-matter of interest and this is to be found in the portraits of people of some significance. But here, too, it has to reach a high degree of excellence if it is to be at the same time true and dignified.

*

Painting is the slackest and most easy-going of all the arts. The slackest because, on account of the material and subject-matter, we condone and enjoy much that is no more than skilled craftsmanship and can hardly be called art. In part it is also because a good technical performance, even though it may be dull, can be admired by the cultured as well as the uneducated, and need only remotely resemble art in order to be highly acceptable. True colours, surfaces and a true relationship of visible objects – all this is in itself pleasing; and, since the eye is in any case used to seeing everything, it does not find misshapen or mistaken form as objectionable as a jarring note is for the listening ear. We tolerate the worst portrayal because we are used to seeing even worse originals. So the painter need only be remotely artistic so as to find a bigger public than a musician of equal merit; the minor painter can at least always operate on his own, whereas the minor musician has to associate with others in order to achieve some sort of resonance by means of a combined musical effort.

*

The question 'Are we to compare or not to compare when considering works of art' is one we would like to answer as follows: the trained connoisseur should make comparisons, for he has a general idea, a preconceived notion of what could be and should be achieved; the amateur, still involved in the process of being educated, can make the best progress if he does not compare but judges each achievement on its individual merit: this gradually forms an instinct and idea for the general situation. Comparison by the unknowing is really only a lazy and conceited way of avoiding judgement.

*

Johann Wolfgang von Goethe

To find and to appreciate goodness everywhere is the sign of a love of truth.

*

The sign of a historical feeling for humanity is that, at the same time as we appreciate the merits and attainments of the present, we also take into account the merits of the past.

*

The best we get from history is that it rouses our enthusiasm.

*

Idiosyncrasy calls forth idiosyncrasy.

*

One has to remember that there are quite a lot of people who would like to say something significant without being productive, and then the most peculiar things see the light of day.

*

People who think deeply and seriously are on bad terms with the public.

*

If I'm to listen to someone else's opinion, it must be put in a positive way; I have enough problematic speculations in my own head.

*

Superstition is innate in the human make-up, and when you think you have completely ousted it, it takes refuge in the strangest nooks and crannies and then suddenly emerges when one thinks one is tolerably safe.

*

We would know much more about things if we weren't intent on discerning them too precisely. For, surely, an object can only be comprehensible to us when viewed at an angle of forty-five degrees.

*

Microscopes and telescopes really only serve to confuse the unaided human senses.

*

I hold my peace about many things; for I don't like to confuse people and am quite content if they are happy while I am cross.

*

Everything that liberates our mind without at the same time imparting self-control is pernicious.

*

Sketchy, Doubtful, Incomplete Jottings

The 'what' of a work of art interests people more than the 'how'; they can grasp the subject-matter in detail but not the method as a whole. That is why they pick out individual passages, in which, if you observe closely, the total effect is not actually lost but remains unconscious to all.

*

And the question, too, 'Where has the poet got it from?' gets no further than the 'what'; it helps no one to understand the 'how'.

*

Imagination is only ordered and structured by poetry. There is nothing more awful than imagination devoid of taste.

*

Mannerism is an ideology gone wrong, a subjective ideology; that's why, as a rule, it isn't without wit.

Johann Wolfgang von Goethe

*

The philologist is dependent on the congruence of what has been handed down in written form. There is a basic manuscript and this has real gaps, errors of transcription which lead to a break in the meaning and to other difficulties common to manuscript tradition. Then a second copy is found, a third one; collating these leads to growing perception of what makes sense and meaning in the transmitted material. Indeed, the philologist goes further and requires that it should increasingly reveal and structure its inner meaning and the congruence of its subject-matter without dependence on philological aides. This calls for a special degree of sensitive judgement, a special absorption in an author long dead and a certain amount of inventive power; one cannot, therefore, take it amiss if the philologist allows himself to make a judgement in matters of taste even if this doesn't always succeed.

*

The poet is dependent on representation, the climax of which is reached when it vies with reality, that is, when the descriptions are so full of living power that everyone can see them as being actually present. At the summit of its excellence poetry appears as something completely external; the more it withdraws into the inner realm, the more it is on its way towards sinking. The kind of poetry which concentrates on the inner realm without giving it outward substance or without allowing the outward to be perceived through the inward – both are the last steps from which poetry steps down into ordinary life.

*

Oratory is dependent on all the advantages of poetry, on all its rights. It takes possession of these and misuses them in order to get hold of certain outer momentary advantages, whether moral or immoral, in civic life.

*

Literature is the fragment of fragments; only the least amount of what has happened and has been spoken was written down, the least of what has been recorded in writing has survived.

*

Although Lord Byron's talent is wild and uncomfortable in its structure, hardly anyone can compare with him in natural truth and grandeur.

*

The really important value of folksong, so called, is that its themes are taken directly from nature. But the educated poet too might well avail himself of this advantage if only he knew how to set about it.

*

But the advantage inherent in folksong is that natural people, as distinct from the educated, are on better terms with what is laconic.

*

Sketchy, Doubtful, Incomplete Jottings

Shakespeare is dangerous reading for talents in the process of formation: he forces them to reproduce him, and they imagine they are producing themselves.

*

Nobody can make judgements about history except those who have experienced history as a part of their own development. This applies to whole nations. The Germans have only been able to judge literature since the point they themselves have had literature.

*

One is really only alive when one enjoys the good will of others.

*

Piety is not an end but a means to attain by the greatest peace of mind the highest degree of culture.

*

This is why we may say that those who parade piety as a purpose and an aim mostly turn into hypocrites.

*

'When one is old one has to do more than when one was young.'

*

A duty absolved still feels like an unpaid debt, because one can never quite live up to one's expectations.

*

Human failings are only descried by an unloving person; that is why, in order to realize them, one has to become unloving oneself, but not more than is strictly to the purpose.

*

It is our greatest good fortune to have our failings corrected and our faults adjusted.

Sketchy, Doubtful, Incomplete Jottings

*

Three things are not recognized except in the due course of time:
> a hero in wartime,
> a wise man in a rage,
> a friend in need.

*

Three classes of fools:
> men because of pride,
> girls by love,
> women by jealousy.

*

The following are mad:
> he who tries to teach simpletons,
> contradicts the wise,
> is moved by empty speeches,
> believes whores,
> entrusts secrets to the garrulous.

Johann Wolfgang von Goethe

*

Man can only live together with his own kind and not with them either; for in the long run he cannot bear the thought that anyone is like him.

*

The most mediocre novel is still better than mediocre readers, indeed the worst novel still participates in some way in the excellence of the genre as a whole.

*

Actors win hearts and don't give away their own; they cheat, but do it with charm.

*

The Germans know how to correct, but not how to give supportive help.

*

Whichever way you look at nature, it is the source of what is infinite.

*

You have to have actually found a thing if you want to know where it is situated.

*

He who acts as though he's glad, and is glad about what he has done, is happy.

1. BOCCACCIO · *Mrs Rosie and the Priest*
2. GERARD MANLEY HOPKINS · *As kingfishers catch fire*
3. *The Saga of Gunnlaug Serpent-tongue*
4. THOMAS DE QUINCEY · *On Murder Considered as One of the Fine Arts*
5. FRIEDRICH NIETZSCHE · *Aphorisms on Love and Hate*
6. JOHN RUSKIN · *Traffic*
7. PU SONGLING · *Wailing Ghosts*
8. JONATHAN SWIFT · *A Modest Proposal*
9. *Three Tang Dynasty Poets*
10. WALT WHITMAN · *On the Beach at Night Alone*
11. KENKŌ · *A Cup of Sake Beneath the Cherry Trees*
12. BALTASAR GRACIÁN · *How to Use Your Enemies*
13. JOHN KEATS · *The Eve of St Agnes*
14. THOMAS HARDY · *Woman much missed*
15. GUY DE MAUPASSANT · *Femme Fatale*
16. MARCO POLO · *Travels in the Land of Serpents and Pearls*
17. SUETONIUS · *Caligula*
18. APOLLONIUS OF RHODES · *Jason and Medea*
19. ROBERT LOUIS STEVENSON · *Olalla*
20. KARL MARX AND FRIEDRICH ENGELS · *The Communist Manifesto*
21. PETRONIUS · *Trimalchio's Feast*
22. JOHANN PETER HEBEL · *How a Ghastly Story Was Brought to Light by a Common or Garden Butcher's Dog*
23. HANS CHRISTIAN ANDERSEN · *The Tinder Box*
24. RUDYARD KIPLING · *The Gate of the Hundred Sorrows*
25. DANTE · *Circles of Hell*
26. HENRY MAYHEW · *Of Street Piemen*
27. HAFEZ · *The nightingales are drunk*
28. GEOFFREY CHAUCER · *The Wife of Bath*
29. MICHEL DE MONTAIGNE · *How We Weep and Laugh at the Same Thing*
30. THOMAS NASHE · *The Terrors of the Night*
31. EDGAR ALLAN POE · *The Tell-Tale Heart*
32. MARY KINGSLEY · *A Hippo Banquet*
33. JANE AUSTEN · *The Beautifull Cassandra*
34. ANTON CHEKHOV · *Gooseberries*
35. SAMUEL TAYLOR COLERIDGE · *Well, they are gone, and here must I remain*
36. JOHANN WOLFGANG VON GOETHE · *Sketchy, Doubtful, Incomplete Jottings*
37. CHARLES DICKENS · *The Great Winglebury Duel*
38. HERMAN MELVILLE · *The Maldive Shark*
39. ELIZABETH GASKELL · *The Old Nurse's Story*
40. NIKOLAY LESKOV · *The Steel Flea*

41. HONORÉ DE BALZAC · *The Atheist's Mass*
42. CHARLOTTE PERKINS GILMAN · *The Yellow Wall-Paper*
43. C.P. CAVAFY · *Remember, Body...*
44. FYODOR DOSTOEVSKY · *The Meek One*
45. GUSTAVE FLAUBERT · *A Simple Heart*
46. NIKOLAI GOGOL · *The Nose*
47. SAMUEL PEPYS · *The Great Fire of London*
48. EDITH WHARTON · *The Reckoning*
49. HENRY JAMES · *The Figure in the Carpet*
50. WILFRED OWEN · *Anthem For Doomed Youth*
51. WOLFGANG AMADEUS MOZART · *My Dearest Father*
52. PLATO · *Socrates' Defence*
53. CHRISTINA ROSSETTI · *Goblin Market*
54. *Sindbad the Sailor*
55. SOPHOCLES · *Antigone*
56. RYŪNOSUKE AKUTAGAWA · *The Life of a Stupid Man*
57. LEO TOLSTOY · *How Much Land Does A Man Need?*
58. GIORGIO VASARI · *Leonardo da Vinci*
59. OSCAR WILDE · *Lord Arthur Savile's Crime*
60. SHEN FU · *The Old Man of the Moon*
61. AESOP · *The Dolphins, the Whales and the Gudgeon*
62. MATSUO BASHŌ · *Lips too Chilled*
63. EMILY BRONTË · *The Night is Darkening Round Me*
64. JOSEPH CONRAD · *To-morrow*
65. RICHARD HAKLUYT · *The Voyage of Sir Francis Drake Around the Whole Globe*
66. KATE CHOPIN · *A Pair of Silk Stockings*
67. CHARLES DARWIN · *It was snowing butterflies*
68. BROTHERS GRIMM · *The Robber Bridegroom*
69. CATULLUS · *I Hate and I Love*
70. HOMER · *Circe and the Cyclops*
71. D. H. LAWRENCE · *Il Duro*
72. KATHERINE MANSFIELD · *Miss Brill*
73. OVID · *The Fall of Icarus*
74. SAPPHO · *Come Close*
75. IVAN TURGENEV · *Kasyan from the Beautiful Lands*
76. VIRGIL · *O Cruel Alexis*
77. H. G. WELLS · *A Slip under the Microscope*
78. HERODOTUS · *The Madness of Cambyses*
79. *Speaking of Siva*
80. *The Dhammapada*

'Desperate-minded villain!'

CHARLES DICKENS
Born 1812, Landport, England
Died 1870, Higham, England

Both stories taken from *Sketches by Boz*,
first published in 1839.

DICKENS IN PENGUIN CLASSICS
A Christmas Carol and Other Christmas Writings
A Tale of Two Cities
American Notes
Barnaby Rudge
Bleak House
David Copperfield
Dombey and Son
Great Expectations
Hard Times
Little Dorrit
Martin Chuzzlewit
Nicholas Nickleby
Oliver Twist
Our Mutual Friend
Pictures From Italy
Selected Journalism 1850–1870
Selected Short Fiction
Sketches by Boz
The Mystery of Edwin Drood
The Old Curiosity Shop
The Pickwick Papers

CHARLES DICKENS

The Great Winglebury Duel

PENGUIN BOOKS

PENGUIN CLASSICS

UK | USA | Canada | Ireland | Australia
India | New Zealand | South Africa

Penguin Books is part of the Penguin Random House group of companies whose addresses can be found at global.penguinrandomhouse.com.

This selection published in Penguin Classics 2015
010

Set in 9/12.4 pt Baskerville 10 Pro
Typeset by Jouve (UK), Milton Keynes
Printed and bound in Great Britain by Clays Ltd, Elcograf S.p.A.

A CIP catalogue record for this book is available from the British Library

ISBN: 978-0-141-39715-3

www.greenpenguin.co.uk

Penguin Random House is committed to a sustainable future for our business, our readers and our planet. This book is made from Forest Stewardship Council® certified paper.

Contents

The Great Winglebury Duel   1
The Steam Excursion   26

The Great Winglebury Duel

The little town of Great Winglebury is exactly forty-two miles and three-quarters from Hyde Park corner. It has a long, straggling, quiet High-street, with a great black and white clock at a small red Town-hall, half-way up – a market-place – a cage – an assembly-room – a church – a bridge – a chapel – a theatre – a library – an inn – a pump – and a Post-office. Tradition tells of a 'Little Winglebury' down some cross-road about two miles off; and as a square mass of dirty paper, supposed to have been originally intended for a letter, with certain tremulous characters inscribed thereon, in which a lively imagination might trace a remote resemblance to the word 'Little,' was once stuck up to be owned in the sunny window of the Great Winglebury Post-office, from which it only disappeared when it fell to pieces with dust and extreme old age, there would appear to be some foundation for the legend. Common belief is inclined to bestow the name upon a little hole at the end of a muddy lane about a couple of miles long, colonized by one wheelwright, four paupers, and a beer-shop; but even this authority, slight as it is, must be regarded with extreme suspicion, inasmuch as the inhabitants of the hole aforesaid concur in opining that it never had any name at all, from the earliest ages down to the present day.

The Winglebury Arms in the centre of the High-street,

opposite the small building with the big clock, is the principal inn of Great Winglebury – the commercial inn, posting-house, and excise-office; the 'Blue' house at every election, and the Judges' house at every assizes. It is the head-quarters of the Gentlemen's Whist Club of Winglebury Blues (so called in opposition to the Gentlemen's Whist Club of Winglebury Buffs, held at the other house, a little further down); and whenever a juggler, or wax-work man, or concert-giver, takes Great Winglebury in his circuit, it is immediately placarded all over the town that Mr So-and-so, 'trusting to that liberal support which the inhabitants of Great Winglebury have long been so liberal in bestowing, has at a great expense engaged the elegant and commodious assembly-rooms, attached to the Winglebury Arms.' The house is a large one, with a red brick and stone front; a pretty spacious hall ornamented with evergreen plants, terminates in a perspective view of the bar, and a glass case, in which are displayed a choice variety of delicacies ready for dressing, to catch the eye of a new-comer the moment he enters, and excite his appetite to the highest possible pitch. Opposite doors lead to the 'coffee' and 'commercial' rooms; and a great wide, rambling staircase, – three stairs and a landing – four stairs and another landing – one step and another landing – half a dozen stairs and another landing – and so on – conducts to galleries of bedrooms, and labyrinths of sitting-rooms, denominated 'private,' where you may enjoy yourself as privately as you can in any place where some bewildered being or other walks into your room every five minutes by mistake, and then walks out

The Great Winglebury Duel

again, to open all the doors along the gallery till he finds his own.

Such is the Winglebury Arms at this day, and such was the Winglebury Arms some time since – no matter when – two or three minutes before the arrival of the London stage. Four horses with cloths on – change for a coach – were standing quietly at the corner of the yard, surrounded by a listless group of post-boys in shiny hats and smock-frocks, engaged in discussing the merits of the cattle; half a dozen ragged boys were standing a little apart, listening with evident interest to the conversation of these worthies; and a few loungers were collected round the horse-trough, awaiting the arrival of the coach.

The day was hot and sunny, the town in the zenith of its dulness, and with the exception of these few idlers, not a living creature was to be seen. Suddenly the loud notes of a key-bugle broke the monotonous stillness of the street; in came the coach, rattling over the uneven paving with a noise startling enough to stop even the large-faced clock itself. Down got the outsides, up went the windows in all directions; out came the waiters, up started the ostlers, and the loungers, and the post-boys, and the ragged boys, as if they were electrified – unstrapping, and unchaining, and unbuckling, and dragging willing horses out, and forcing reluctant horses in, and making a most exhilarating bustle. 'Lady inside, here,' said the guard. 'Please to alight, ma'am,' said the waiter. 'Private sitting-room?' interrogated the lady. – 'Certainly, ma'am,' responded the chambermaid. 'Nothing but these 'ere trunks, ma'am?' inquired the guard. 'Nothing more,' replied the lady. Up got the outsides again, and the guard, and the coachman; off came the cloths, with a jerk – 'All right' was the cry; and away they went. The loungers lingered a minute or two in the road, watching the coach till it turned the corner, and then loitered away one by one. The street was clear again, and the town, by contrast, quieter than ever.

'Lady in number twenty-five,' screamed the landlady. – 'Thomas!'

'Yes, ma'am.'

'Letter just been left for the gentleman in number nineteen. – Boots at the Lion left it. – No answer.'

'Letter for you, sir,' said Thomas, depositing the letter on number nineteen's table.

'For me?' said number nineteen, turning from the window, out of which he had been surveying the scene we have just described.

'Yes, sir, – (waiters always speak in hints, and never utter complete sentences) – yes, sir, – Boots at the Lion, sir – Bar, sir – Missis said number nineteen, sir – Alexander Trott, Esq., sir? – Your card at the bar, sir, I think, sir?'

'My name *is* Trott,' replied number nineteen, breaking the seal. 'You may go, waiter.' The waiter pulled down the window-blind, and then pulled it up again – for a regular waiter must do something before he leaves the room – adjusted the glasses on the sideboard, brushed a place which was *not* dusty, rubbed his hands very hard, walked stealthily to the door, and evaporated.

There was evidently something in the contents of the letter of a nature, if not wholly unexpected, certainly extremely disagreeable. Mr Alexander Trott laid it down and took it

The Great Winglebury Duel

up again, and walked about the room on particular squares of the carpet, and even attempted, though very unsuccessfully, to whistle an air. It wouldn't do. He threw himself into a chair and read the following epistle aloud:

'Blue Lion and Stomach-warmer,
Great Winglebury.

'Wednesday Morning.

'Sir,

'Immediately on discovering your intentions, I left our counting-house, and followed you. I know the purport of your journey; – that journey shall never be completed.

'I have no friend here just now, on whose secrecy I can rely. This shall be no obstacle to my revenge. Neither shall Emily Brown be exposed to the mercenary solicitations of a scoundrel, odious in her eyes, and contemptible in every body else's: nor will I tamely submit to the clandestine attacks of a base umbrella-maker.

'Sir, – from Great Winglebury Church, a footpath leads through four meadows to a retired spot known to the townspeople as Stiffun's Acre (Mr Trott shuddered). I shall be waiting there alone, at twenty minutes before six o'clock to-morrow morning. Should I be disappointed of seeing you there, I will do myself the pleasure of calling with a horsewhip.

'Horace Hunter.

'PS. There is a gunsmith's in the High-street; and they won't sell gunpowder after dark – you understand me.

'PPS. You had better not order your breakfast in the morning till you have seen me. It may be an unnecessary expense.'

'Desperate-minded villain! I knew how it would be!' ejaculated the terrified Trott. 'I always told father, that once start me on this expedition, and Hunter would pursue me like the wandering Jew. It's bad enough as it is, to marry with the old people's commands, and without the girl's consent: but what will Emily think of me, if I go down there, breathless with running away from this infernal salamander? What *shall* I do? What *can* I do? If I go back to the city I'm disgraced for ever – lose the girl, and what's more lose the money too. Even if I did go on to the Brown's by the coach, Hunter would be after me in a post-chaise; and if I go to this place, this Stiffun's Acre, (another shudder) I'm as good as dead. I've seen him hit the man at the Pall-mall shooting gallery, in the second button-hole of the waistcoat five times out of every six, and when he didn't hit him there, he hit him in the head.' And with this consolatory reminiscence, Mr Alexander Trott again ejaculated, 'What shall I do?'

Long and weary were his reflections as, burying his face in his hands, he sat ruminating on the best course to be pursued. His mental direction-post pointed to London. He thought of 'the governor's' anger, and the loss of the fortune which the paternal Brown had promised the paternal Trott his daughter should contribute to the coffers of his son. Then the words 'To Brown's' were legibly inscribed on the said direction-post, but Horace Hunter's denunciation rung in his ears: – last of all it bore, in red letters, the words, 'To Stiffun's Acre;' and then Mr Alexander Trott decided on adopting a plan which he presently matured.

First and foremost he despatched the under-boots to the Blue Lion and Stomach-warmer, with a gentlemanly note to

The Great Winglebury Duel

Mr Horace Hunter, intimating that he thirsted for his destruction and would do himself the pleasure of slaughtering him next morning without fail. He then wrote another letter, and requested the attendance of the other boots – for they kept a pair. A modest knock at the room-door was heard – 'Come in,' said Mr Trott. A man thrust in a red head with one eye in it, and being again desired to 'come in,' brought in the body and legs to which the head belonged and a fur cap which belonged to the head.

'You are the upper-boots, I think?' inquired Mr Trott.

'Yes, I am the upper-boots,' replied a voice from inside a velveteen case with mother-of-pearl buttons – 'that is, I'm the boots as b'longs to the house; the other man's my man, as goes errands and does odd jobs – top-boots and half-boots I calls us.'

'You're from London?' inquired Mr Trott.

'Driv a cab once,' was the laconic reply.

'Why don't you drive it now?' asked Mr Trott.

'Cos I over-driv the cab, and driv over a 'ooman,' replied the top-boots, with brevity.

'Do you know the mayor's house?' inquired Trott.

'Rather,' replied the boots, significantly, as if he had some good reason to remember it.

'Do you think you could manage to leave a letter there?' interrogated Trott.

'Shouldn't wonder,' responded boots.

'But this letter,' said Trott, holding a deformed note with a paralytic direction in one hand, and five shillings in the other – 'this letter is anonymous.'

'A – what?' interrupted the boots.

'Anonymous – he's not to know who it comes from.'

'Oh! I see,' responded the rig'lar, with a knowing wink, but without evincing the slightest disinclination to undertake the charge – 'I see – bit o' sving, eh?' and his one eye wandered round the room as if in quest of a dark lantern and phosphorous-box. 'But I say,' he continued, recalling the eye from its search, and bringing it to bear on Mr Trott – 'I say, he's a lawyer, our mayor, and insured in the County. If you've a spite agen him, you'd better not burn his house down – blessed if I don't think it would be the greatest favour you could do him.' And he chuckled inwardly.

If Mr Alexander Trott had been in any other situation, his first act would have been to kick the man down stairs by deputy; or, in other words, to ring the bell, and desire the landlord to take his boots off. He contented himself, however, with doubling the fee and explaining that the letter merely related to a breach of the peace. The top-boots retired, solemnly pledged to secrecy; and Mr Alexander Trott sat down to a fried sole, maintenon cutlet, Madeira, and sundries, with much greater composure than he had experienced since the receipt of Horace Hunter's letter of defiance.

The lady who alighted from the London coach had no sooner been installed in number twenty-five, and made some alteration in her travelling-dress, than she endited a note to Joseph Overton, esquire, solicitor, and mayor of Great Winglebury, requesting his immediate attendance on private business of paramount importance – a summons which that worthy functionary lost no time in obeying; for after sundry openings of his eyes, divers ejaculations of 'Bless me!' and

The Great Winglebury Duel

other manifestations of surprise, he took his broad-brimmed hat from its accustomed peg in his little front office, and walked briskly down the High-street to the Winglebury Arms; through the hall and up the staircase of which establishment he was ushered by the landlady, and a crowd of officious waiters, to the door of number twenty-five.

'Show the gentleman in,' said the stranger lady, in reply to the foremost waiter's announcement. The gentleman was shown in accordingly.

The lady rose from the sofa; the mayor advanced a step from the door, and there they both paused for a minute or two, looking at one another as if by mutual consent. The mayor saw before him a buxom richly-dressed female of about forty; and the lady looked upon a sleek man about ten years older, in drab shorts and continuations, black coat, neckcloth, and gloves.

'Miss Julia Manners!' exclaimed the mayor at length, 'you astonish me.'

'That's very unfair of you, Overton,' replied Miss Julia, 'for I have known you long enough not to be surprised at any thing you do, and you might extend equal courtesy to me.'

'But to run away – actually run away – with a young man!' remonstrated the mayor.

'You would not have me actually run away with an old one I presume?' was the cool rejoinder.

'And then to ask me – me – of all people in the world – a man of my age and appearance – mayor of the town – to promote such a scheme!' pettishly ejaculated Joseph Overton; throwing himself into an arm-chair, and producing Miss

Julia's letter from his pocket, as if to corroborate the assertion that he had been asked.

'Now, Overton,' replied the lady, impatiently, 'I want your assistance in this matter, and I must have it. In the lifetime of that poor old dear, Mr Cornberry, who – who –'

'Who was to have married you, and didn't because he died first; and who left you his property unencumbered with the addition of himself,' suggested the mayor, in a sarcastic tone.

'Well,' replied Miss Julia, reddening slightly, 'in the lifetime of the poor old dear, the property had the incumbrance of your management; and all I will say of that is, that I only wonder *it* didn't die of consumption instead of its master. You helped yourself then: – help me now.'

Mr Joseph Overton was a man of the world, and an attorney; and as certain indistinct recollections of an odd thousand pounds or two, appropriated by mistake, passed across his mind, he hemmed deprecatingly, smiled blandly, remained silent for a few seconds; and finally inquired, 'What do you wish me to do?'

'I'll tell you,' replied Miss Julia – 'I'll tell you in three words. Dear Lord Peter –'

'That's the young man, I suppose –' interrupted the mayor.

'That's the young nobleman,' replied the lady, with a great stress on the last word. 'Dear Lord Peter is considerably afraid of the resentment of his family; and we have therefore thought it better to make the match a stolen one. He left town to avoid suspicion, on a visit to his friend, the Honourable Augustus Flair, whose seat, as you know, is about thirty miles from this, accompanied only by his favourite tiger. We arranged that I should come here alone in the

The Great Winglebury Duel

London coach; and that he, leaving his tiger and cab behind him, should come on, and arrive here as soon as possible this afternoon.'

'Very well,' observed Joseph Overton, 'and then he can order the chaise, and you can go on to Gretna Green together, without requiring the presence or interference of a third party, can't you?'

'No,' replied Miss Julia. 'We have every reason to believe – dear Lord Peter not being considered very prudent or sagacious by his friends, and they having discovered his attachment to me – that immediately on his absence being observed, pursuit will be made in this direction: to elude which, and to prevent our being traced, I wish it to be understood in this house, that dear Lord Peter is slightly deranged, though perfectly harmless; and that I am, unknown to him, waiting his arrival to convey him in a post-chaise to a private asylum – at Berwick, say. If I don't show myself much, I dare say I can manage to pass for his mother.'

The thought occurred to the mayor's mind that the lady might show herself a good deal without fear of detection; seeing that she was about double the age of her intended husband. He said nothing, however, and the lady proceeded –

'With the whole of this arrangement, dear Lord Peter is acquainted: and all I want you to do is, to make the delusion more complete by giving it the sanction of your influence in this place, and assigning this as a reason to the people of the house for my taking the young gentleman away. As it would not be consistent with the story that I should see him until after he has entered the chaise, I also wish you to communicate with him, and inform him that it is all going on well.'

'Has he arrived?' inquired Overton.

'I don't know,' replied the lady.

'Then how am I to know?' inquired the mayor. 'Of course he will not give his own name at the bar.'

'I begged him, immediately on his arrival, to write you a note,' replied Miss Manners; 'and to prevent the possibility of our project being discovered through its means, I desired him to write anonymously, and in mysterious terms to acquaint you with the number of his room.'

'God bless me!' exclaimed the mayor, rising from his seat, and searching his pockets – 'most extraordinary circumstance – he *has* arrived – mysterious note left at my house in a most mysterious manner, just before yours – didn't know what to make of it before, and certainly shouldn't have attended to it. – Oh! here it is.' And Joseph Overton pulled out of an inner coat-pocket the identical letter penned by Alexander Trott. 'Is this his lordship's hand?'

'Oh yes,' replied Julia; 'good, punctual creature! I have not seen it more than once or twice, but I know he writes very badly and very large. These dear, wild young noblemen, you know, Overton –'

'Ay, ay, I see,' replied the mayor. – 'Horses and dogs, play and wine – grooms, actresses, and cigars, – the stable, the green-room, the brothel, and the tavern; and the legislative assembly at last.'

'Here's what he says,' pursued the mayor; '"Sir, – A young gentleman in number nineteen at the Winglebury Arms, is bent on committing a rash act to-morrow morning at an early hour. (That's good – he means marrying.) If you have

The Great Winglebury Duel

any regard for the peace of this town, or the preservation of one – it may be two – human lives" – What the deuce does he mean by that?'

'That he's so anxious for the ceremony, he will expire if it's put off, and that I may possibly do the same,' replied the lady with great complacency.

'Oh! I see – not much fear of that; – well – "two human lives, you will cause him to be removed to-night. – (He wants to start at once.) Fear not to do this on your responsibility: for to-morrow, the absolute necessity of the proceeding will be but too aparent. Remember: number nineteen. The name is Trott. No delay; for life and death depend upon your promptitude." – Passionate language, certainly. – Shall I see him?'

'Do,' replied Miss Julia; 'and entreat him to act his part well. I am half afraid of him. Tell him to be cautious.'

'I will,' said the mayor.

'Settle all the arrangements.'

'I will,' said the mayor again.

'And say I think the chaise had better be ordered for one o'clock.'

'Very well,' cried the mayor once more; and ruminating on the absurdity of the situation in which fate and old acquaintance had placed him, he desired a waiter to herald his approach to the temporary representative of number nineteen.

The announcement – 'Gentleman to speak with you, sir,' induced Mr Trott to pause half-way in the glass of port, the contents of which he was in the act of imbibing at the moment; to rise from his chair, and retreat a few paces towards the window, as if to secure a retreat in the event of the visitor assuming the form and appearance of Horace Hunter. One glance at Joseph Overton, however, quieted his apprehensions. He courteously motioned the stranger to a seat. The waiter after a little jingling with the decanter and glasses, consented to leave the room; and Joseph Overton placing the broad-brimmed hat on the chair next him, and bending his body gently forward, opened the business by saying in a very low and cautious tone,

'My lord –'

'Eh?' said Mr Alexander Trott in a very loud key, with the vacant and mystified stare of a chilly somnambulist.

'Hush – hush!' said the cautious attorney: 'to be sure – quite right – no titles here – my name is Overton, sir.'

'Overton!'

'Yes: the mayor of this place – you sent me a letter with anonymous information, this afternoon.'

'I, sir?' exclaimed Trott with ill-dissembled surprise; for, coward as he was, he would willingly have repudiated the authorship of the letter in question. 'I, sir?'

'Yes, you, sir; did you not?' responded Overton, annoyed with what he supposed to be an extreme degree of unnecessary suspicion. 'Either this letter is yours, or it is not. If it be, we can converse securely upon the subject at once. If it be not, of course I have no more to say.'

'Stay, stay,' said Trott, 'it *is* mine; I *did* write it. What could I do, sir? I had no friend here.'

'To be sure – to be sure,' said the mayor, encouragingly, 'you could not have managed it better. Well, sir; it will be necessary for you to leave here to-night in a post-chaise and

The Great Winglebury Duel

four. And the harder the boys drive the better. You are not safe from pursuit here.'

'Bless me!' exclaimed Trott, in an agony of apprehension, 'can such things happen in a country like this? Such unrelenting and cold-blooded hostility!' He wiped off the concentrated essence of cowardice that was oozing fast down his forehead, and looked aghast at Joseph Overton.

'It certainly is a very hard case,' replied the mayor with a smile, 'that, in a free country, people can't marry whom they like without being hunted down as if they were criminals. However, in the present instance the lady is willing, you know, and that's the main point, after all.'

'Lady willing!' repeated Trott, mechanically – 'How do you know the lady's willing?'

'Come, that's a good one,' said the mayor, benevolently tapping Mr Trott on the arm with his broad-brimmed hat, 'I have known her, well, for a long time, and if any body could entertain the remotest doubt on the subject, I assure you I have none, nor need you.'

'Dear me!' said Mr Trott, ruminating – 'Dear me! – this is very extraordinary!'

'Well, Lord Peter,' said the mayor, rising.

'Lord Peter?' repeated Mr Trott.

'Oh – ah, I forgot; well, Mr Trott, then – Trott – very good, ha! ha! – Well, sir, the chaise shall be ready at half-past twelve.'

'And what is to become of me till then?' inquired Mr Trott, anxiously. 'Wouldn't it save appearances if I were placed under some restraint?'

'Ah!' replied Overton, 'very good thought – capital idea indeed. I'll send somebody up directly. And if you make a little resistance when we put you in the chaise it wouldn't be amiss – look as if you didn't want to be taken away, you know.'

'To be sure,' said Trott – 'to be sure.'

'Well, my lord,' said Overton, in a low tone, 'till then, I wish your lordship a good evening.'

'Lord – lordship!' ejaculated Trott again, falling back a step or two, and gazing in unutterable wonder on the countenance of the mayor.

'Ha-ha! I see, my lord – practising the madman? – very good indeed – very vacant look – capital, my lord, capital – good evening, Mr Trott – ha! ha! ha!'

'That mayor's decidedly drunk,' soliloquised Mr Trott, throwing himself back in his chair, in an attitude of reflection.

'He is a much cleverer fellow than I thought him, that young nobleman – he carries it off uncommonly well,' thought Overton, as he wended his way to the bar, there to complete his arrangements. This was soon done: every word of the story was implicitly believed, and the one-eyed boots was immediately instructed to repair to number nineteen, to act as custodian of the person of the supposed lunatic until half-past twelve o'clock. In pursuance of this direction, that somewhat eccentric gentleman armed himself with a walking-stick of gigantic dimensions, and repaired with his usual equanimity of manner to Mr Trott's apartment, which he entered without any ceremony, and mounted guard in, by quietly depositing himself upon a chair near the door,

The Great Winglebury Duel

where he proceeded to beguile the time by whistling a popular air with great apparent satisfaction.

'What do you want here, you scoundrel?' exclaimed Mr Alexander Trott, with a proper appearance of indignation at his detention.

The boots beat time with his head, as he looked gently round at Mr Trott with a smile of pity, and whistled an *adagio* movement.

'Do you attend in this room by Mr Overton's desire?' inquired Trott, rather astonished at the man's demeanour.

'Keep yourself to yourself, young feller,' calmly responded the boots, 'and don't say nothin' to nobody.' And he whistled again.

'Now mind,' ejaculated Mr Trott, anxious to keep up the farce of wishing with great earnestness to fight a duel if they'd let him, – 'I protest against being kept here. I deny that I have any intention of fighting with any body. But as it's useless contending with superior numbers, I shall sit quietly down.'

'You'd better,' observed the placid boots, shaking the large stick expressively.

'Under protest, however,' added Alexander Trott, seating himself, with indignation in his face but great content in his heart. 'Under protest.'

'Oh, certainly!' responded the boots; 'any thing you please. If you're happy, I'm transported; only don't talk too much – it'll make you worse.'

'Make me worse!' exclaimed Trott, in unfeigned astonishment: 'the man's drunk!'

The Great Winglebury Duel

'You'd better be quiet, young feller,' remarked the boots, going through a most threatening piece of pantomime with the stick.

'Or mad!' said Mr Trott, rather alarmed. 'Leave the room, sir, and tell them to send somebody else.'

'Won't do!' replied the boots.

'Leave the room!' shouted Trott, ringing the bell violently; for he began to be alarmed on a new score.

'Leave that 'ere bell alone, you wretched loo-nattic!' said the boots, suddenly forcing the unfortunate Trott back into his chair, and brandishing the stick aloft. 'Be quiet, you mis'rable object, and don't let every body know there's a madman in the house.'

'He *is* a madman! He *is* a madman!' exclaimed the terrified Mr Trott, gazing on the one eye of the red-headed boots with a look of abject horror.

'Madman!' replied the boots – 'dam'me, I think he *is* a madman with a vengeance! Listen to me, you unfort'nate. Ah! would you? – [a slight tap on the head with the large stick, as Mr Trott made another move towards the bell-handle] I caught you there! did I?'

'Spare my life!' exclaimed Trott, raising his hands imploringly.

'I don't want your life,' replied the boots, disdainfully, 'though I think it 'ud be a charity if somebody took it.'

'No, no, it wouldn't,' interrupted poor Mr Trott, hurriedly; 'no, no, it wouldn't! I – I –'d rather keep it!'

'O werry well,' said the boots; 'that's a mere matter of taste – ev'ry one to his liking. Hows'ever, all I've got to say is this here: You sit quietly down in that chair, and I'll sit hoppersite you here, and if you keep quiet and don't stir, I won't damage you; but if you move hand or foot till half-past twelve o'clock, I shall alter the expression of your countenance so completely, that the next time you look in the glass you'll ask vether you're gone out of town, and ven you're likely to come back again. So sit down.'

'I will – I will,' responded the victim of mistakes; and down sat Mr Trott and down sat the boots too, exactly opposite him, with the stick ready for immediate action in case of emergency.

Long and dreary were the hours that followed. The bell of Great Winglebury church had just struck ten, and two hours and a half would probably elapse before succour arrived. For half an hour the noise occasioned by shutting up the shops in the street beneath betokened something like life in the town, and rendered Mr Trott's situation a little less insupportable; but when even these ceased, and nothing was heard beyond the occasional rattling of a post-chaise as it drove up the yard to change horses, and then drove away again, or the clattering of horses' hoofs in the stables behind, it became almost unbearable. The boots occasionally moved an inch or two, to knock superfluous bits of wax off the candles, which were burning low, but instantaneously resumed his former position; and as he remembered to have heard somewhere or other that the human eye had an unfailing effect in controlling mad people, he kept his solitary organ of vision constantly fixed on Mr Alexander Trott. That unfortunate individual stared at his companion in his turn, until his features grew more and more indistinct – his hair gradually less red – and the room more misty and obscure.

The Great Winglebury Duel

Mr Alexander Trott fell into a sound sleep, from which he was awakened by a rumbling in the street, and a cry of – 'Chaise-and-four for number twenty-five!' A bustle on the stairs succeeded; the room-door was hastily thrown open; and Mr Joseph Overton entered, followed by four stout waiters, and Mrs Williamson, the stout landlady of the Winglebury Arms.

'Mr Overton!' exclaimed Mr Alexander Trott, jumping up in a frenzy of passionate excitement – 'Look at this man, sir; consider the situation in which I have been placed for three hours past – the person you sent to guard me, sir, was a madman – a madman – a raging, ravaging, furious madman.'

'Bravo!' whispered Overton.

'Poor dear!' said the compassionate Mrs Williamson, 'mad people always thinks other people's mad.'

'Poor dear!' ejaculated Mr Alexander Trott, 'What the devil do you mean by poor dear! are you the landlady of this house?'

'Yes, yes,' replied the stout old lady, 'don't exert yourself, there's a dear – consider your health, now; do.'

'Exert myself!' shouted Mr Alexander Trott, 'it's a mercy, ma'am, that I have any breath to exert myself with, I might have been assassinated three hours ago by that one-eyed monster with the oakum head. How dare you have a madman, ma'am – how dare you have a madman, to assault and terrify the visiters to your house?'

'I'll never have another,' said Mrs Williamson, casting a look of reproach at the mayor.

'Capital – capital,' whispered Overton again, as he enveloped Mr Alexander Trott in a thick travelling-cloak.

'Capital, sir!' exclaimed Trott, aloud, 'it's horrible. The very recollection makes me shudder. I'd rather fight four duels in three hours if I survived the first three, than I'd sit for that time face to face with a madman.'

'Keep it up, as you go down stairs,' whispered Overton, 'your bill is paid, and your portmanteau in the chaise.' And then he added aloud, 'Now, waiters, the gentleman's ready.'

At this signal the waiters crowded round Mr Alexander Trott. One took one arm, another the other, a third walked before with a candle, the fourth behind with another candle; the boots and Mrs Williamson brought up the rear, and down stairs they went, Mr Alexander Trott expressing alternately at the very top of his voice either his feigned reluctance to go, or his unfeigned indignation at being shut up with a madman.

Mr Overton was waiting at the chaise-door, the boys were ready mounted, and a few ostlers and stable nondescripts were standing round to witness the departure of 'the mad gentleman.' Mr Alexander Trott's foot was on the step, when he observed (which the dim light had prevented his doing before) a human figure seated in the chaise, closely muffled up in a cloak like his own.

'Who's that?' he inquired of Overton, in a whisper.

'Hush, hush,' replied the mayor; 'the other party of course.'

'The other party!' exclaimed Trott, with an effort to retreat.

'Yes, yes; you'll soon find that out, before you go far, I should think – but make a noise, you'll excite suspicion if you whisper to me so much.'

'I won't go in this chaise,' shouted Mr Alexander Trott, all

The Great Winglebury Duel

his original fears recurring with tenfold violence. 'I shall be assassinated – I shall be –'

'Bravo, bravo,' whispered Overton. 'I'll push you in.'

'But I won't go,' exclaimed Mr Trott. 'Help here, help! they're carrying me away against my will. This is a plot to murder me.'

'Poor dear!' said Mrs Williamson again.

'Now, boys, put 'em along,' cried the mayor, pushing Trott in and slamming the door. 'Off with you as quick as you can, and stop for nothing till you come to the next stage – all right.'

'Horses are paid, Tom,' screamed Mrs Williamson; and away went the chaise at the rate of fourteen miles an hour, with Mr Alexander Trott and Miss Julia Manners carefully shut up in the inside.

Mr Alexander Trott remained coiled up in one corner of the chaise, and his mysterious companion in the other, for the first two or three miles; Mr Trott edging more and more into his corner as he felt his companion gradually edging more and more from hers; and vainly endeavouring in the darkness to catch a glimpse of the furious face of the supposed Horace Hunter.

'We may speak now,' said his fellow traveller, at length; 'the post-boys can neither see nor hear us.'

'That's not Hunter's voice!' – thought Alexander, astonished.

'Dear Lord Peter!' said Miss Julia, most winningly: putting her arm on Mr Trott's shoulder – 'Dear Lord Peter. Not a word?'

Charles Dickens

'Why, it's a woman!' exclaimed Mr Trott in a low tone of excessive wonder.

'Ah – whose voice is that?' said Julia – ''tis not Lord Peter's.'

'No, – it's mine,' replied Mr Trott.

'Yours!' ejaculated Miss Julia Manners, 'a strange man! Gracious Heaven – how came you here?'

'Whoever you are, you might have known that I came against my will, ma'am,' replied Alexander, 'For I made noise enough when I got in.'

'Do you come from Lord Peter?' inquired Miss Manners.

'Damn Lord Peter,' replied Trott pettishly – 'I don't know any Lord Peter – I never heard of him before to-night, when I've been Lord Peter'd by one and Lord Peter'd by another, till I verily believe I'm mad, or dreaming –'

'Whither are we going?' inquired the lady tragically.

'How should *I* know, ma'am?' replied Trott with singular coolness; for the events of the evening had completely hardened him.

'Stop! stop!' cried the lady, letting down the front glasses of the chaise.

'Stay, my dear ma'am!' said Mr Trott, pulling the glasses up again with one hand, and gently squeezing Miss Julia's waist with the other. 'There is some mistake here; give me till the end of this stage to explain my share of it. We must go so far; you cannot be set down here alone, at this hour of the night.'

The lady consented; the mistake was mutually explained. Mr Trott was a young man, had highly promising whiskers,

The Great Winglebury Duel

an undeniable tailor, and an insinuating address – he wanted nothing but valour, and who wants that with three thousand a-year? The lady had this, and more; she wanted a young husband, and the only course open to Mr Trott to retrieve his disgrace was a rich wife. So, they came to the conclusion that it would be a pity to have all this trouble and expense for nothing, and that as they were so far on the road already, they had better go to Gretna Green, and marry each other, and they did so. And the very next preceding entry in the Blacksmith's book was an entry of the marriage of Emily Brown with Horace Hunter. Mr Hunter took his wife home, and begged pardon, and *was* pardoned; and Mr Trott took *his* wife home, begged pardon too, and was pardoned also. And Lord Peter, who had been detained beyond his time by drinking champagne and riding a steeple-chase, went back to the Honourable Augustus Flair's, and drank more champagne, and rode another steeple-chase, and was thrown and killed. And Horace Hunter took great credit to himself for practising on the cowardice of Alexander Trott; and all these circumstances were discovered in time, and carefully noted down; and if ever you stop a week at the Winglebury Arms, they'll give you just this account of The Great Winglebury Duel.

The Steam Excursion

Mr Percy Noakes was a law-student, inhabiting a set of chambers on the fourth floor, in one of those houses in Gray's-inn-square which command an extensive view of the gardens, and their usual adjuncts – flaunting nursery-maids, and town-made children, with parenthetical legs. Mr Percy Noakes was what is generally termed – 'a devilish good fellow.' He had a large circle of acquaintance, and seldom dined at his own expense. He used to talk politics to papas, flatter the vanity of mammas, do the amiable to their daughters, make pleasure engagements with their sons, and romp with the younger branches. Like those paragons of perfection, advertising footmen out of place, he was always 'willing to make himself generally useful.' If any old lady, whose son was in India, gave a ball, Mr Percy Noakes was master of the ceremonies; if any young lady made a stolen match, Mr Percy Noakes gave her away; if a juvenile wife presented her husband with a blooming cherub, Mr Percy Noakes was either godfather, or deputy-godfather; and if any member of a friend's family died, Mr Percy Noakes was invariably to be seen in the second mourning coach, with a white handkerchief to his eyes, sobbing – to use his own appropriate and expressive description – 'like winkin!'

It may readily be imagined that these numerous avocations were rather calculated to interfere with Mr Percy

Noakes's professional studies. Mr Percy Noakes was perfectly aware of the fact, and he had, therefore, after mature reflection, made up his mind not to study at all – a laudable determination, to which he adhered in the most praiseworthy manner. His sitting-room presented a strange chaos of dress-gloves, boxing-gloves, caricatures, albums, invitation-cards, foils, cricket-bats, card-board drawings, paste, gum, and fifty other extraordinary articles heaped together in the strangest confusion. He was always making something for somebody, or planning some party of pleasure, which was his great *forte*. He invariably spoke with astonishing rapidity; was smart, spoffish, and eight-and-twenty.

'Splendid idea, 'pon my life!' soliloquized Mr Percy Noakes, over his morning's coffee, as his mind reverted to a suggestion which had been thrown out the previous night, by a lady at whose house he had spent the evening. 'Glorious idea! – Mrs Stubbs,' cried the student, raising his voice.

'Yes, sir,' replied a dirty old woman with an inflamed countenance, emerging from the bedroom, with a barrel of dirt and cinders. – This was the laundress. 'Did you call, sir?'

'Oh! Mrs Stubbs, I'm going out: if that tailor should call again, you'd better say – you'd better say, I'm out of town, and shan't be back for a fortnight; and if that bootmaker should come, tell him I've lost his address, or I'd have sent him that little amount. Mind he writes it down; and if Mr Hardy should call – you know Mr Hardy?'

'The funny gentleman, sir?'

'Ah! the funny gentleman. If Mr Hardy should call, say I've gone to Mrs Taunton's about that water-party.'

'Yes, sir.'

'And if any fellow calls, and says he's come about a steamer, tell him to be here at five o'clock this afternoon, Mrs Stubbs.'

'Very well, sir.'

Mr Percy Noakes brushed his hat, whisked the crumbs off his inexplicables with a silk handkerchief, gave the ends of his hair a persuasive roll round his forefinger, and sallied forth for Mrs Taunton's domicile in Great Marlborough-street, where she and her daughters occupied the upper part of a house. She was a good-looking widow of fifty, with the form of a giantess and the mind of a child. The pursuit of pleasure, and some means of killing time, appeared the sole end of her existence. She doted on her daughters, who were as frivolous as herself.

A general exclamation of satisfaction hailed the arrival of Mr Percy Noakes, who went through the ordinary salutations and threw himself into an easy chair near the ladies' work-table, with all the ease of a regularly established friend of the family. Mrs Taunton was busily engaged in planting immense bright bows on every part of a smart cap on which it was possible to stick one; Miss Emily Taunton was making a watch-guard; and Miss Sophia was at the piano, practising a new song – poetry by the young officer, or the police officer, or the custom-house officer, or some equally interesting amateur.

'You good creature!' said Mrs Taunton, addressing the gallant Percy. 'You really are a good soul! You've come about the water-party, I know.'

'I should rather suspect I had,' replied Mr Noakes, triumphantly. 'Now come here, girls, and I'll tell you all about it.' Miss Emily and Miss Sophia advanced to the table, with that

The Steam Excursion

ballet sort of step which some young ladies seem to think so fascinating – something between a skip and a canter.

'Now,' continued Mr Percy Noakes, 'it seems to me that the best way will be to have a committee of ten, to make all the arrangements, and manage the whole set-out. Then I propose that the expenses shall be paid by these ten fellows jointly.'

'Excellent, indeed!' said Mrs Taunton, who highly approved of this part of the arrangements.

'Then my plan is, that each of these ten fellows shall have the power of asking five people. There must be a meeting of the committee at my chambers, to make all the arrangements, and these people shall be then named; every member of the committee shall have the power of black-balling any one who is proposed, and one black ball shall exclude that person. This will ensure our having a pleasant party, you know.'

'What a manager you are!' interrupted Mrs Taunton again.

'Charming!' said the lovely Emily.

'I never did!' ejaculated Sophia.

'Yes, I think it'll do,' replied Mr Percy Noakes, who was now quite in his element. 'I think it'll do. Then you know we shall go down to the Nore and back, and have a regular capital cold dinner laid out in the cabin before we start, so that every thing may be ready without any confusion; and we shall have the lunch laid out on deck in those little tea-garden-looking concerns by the paddle-boxes – I don't know what you call 'em. Then we shall hire a steamer expressly for our party, and a band, and have the deck chalked, and we shall be able to dance quadrilles all day: and then whoever we know that's musical, you know, why they'll make themselves useful and agreeable; and – and – upon the whole, I really hope we shall have a glorious day, you know.'

The announcement of these arrangements was received with the utmost enthusiasm. Mrs Taunton, Emily, and Sophia, were loud in their praises.

'Well, but tell me, Percy,' said Mrs Taunton, 'who are the ten gentlemen to be?'

'Oh! I know plenty of fellows who'll be delighted with the scheme,' replied Mr Percy Noakes; 'of course, we shall have —'

'Mr Hardy,' interrupted the servant, announcing a visiter. Miss Sophia and Miss Emily hastily assumed the most interesting attitudes that could be adopted on so short a notice.

'How are you?' said a stout gentleman of about forty, pausing at the door in the attitude of an awkward harlequin. This was Mr Hardy, whom we have before described, on the authority of Mrs Stubbs, as 'the funny gentleman.' He was an Astley-Cooperish Joe Miller – a practical joker, immensely popular with married ladies, and a general favourite with young men. He was always engaged in some pleasure excursion or other, and delighted in getting somebody into a scrape on such occasions. He could sing comic songs, imitate hackney-coachmen and fowls, play airs on his chin, and execute concertos on the Jews'-harp. He always eat and drank most immoderately, and was the bosom friend of Mr Percy Noakes. He had a red face, a somewhat husky voice, and a tremendously loud laugh.

'How are you?' said this worthy, laughing, as if it were the finest joke in the world to make a morning call, and shaking hands with the ladies with as much vehemence as if their arms were so many pump-handles.

'You're just the very man I wanted,' said Mr Percy Noakes,

who proceeded to explain the cause of his being in requisition.

'Ha! ha! ha!' shouted Hardy, after hearing the statement, and receiving a detailed account of the proposed excursion. 'Oh, capital! glorious! What a day it will be! what fun! – But, I say, when are you going to begin making the arrangements?'

'No time like the present – at once, if you please.'

'Oh, charming!' cried the ladies. 'Pray, do.'

Writing materials were laid before Mr Percy Noakes, and the names of the different members of the committee were agreed on, after as much discussion between him and Mr Hardy as if at least the fate of nations had depended on their appointment. It was then agreed that a meeting should take place at Mr Percy Noakes's chambers on the ensuing Wednesday evening at eight o'clock, and the visiters departed.

Wednesday evening arrived, eight o'clock came, and eight members of the committee were punctual in their attendance. Mr Loggins, the solicitor, of Boswell-court, sent an excuse, and Mr Samuel Briggs, the ditto of Furnival's Inn, sent his brother, much to his (the brother's) satisfaction, and greatly to the discomfiture of Mr Percy Noakes. Between the Briggses and the Tauntons there existed a degree of implacable hatred, quite unprecedented. The animosity between the Montagues and Capulets was nothing to that which prevailed between these two illustrious houses. Mrs Briggs was a widow, with three daughters and two sons; Mr Samuel, the eldest, was an attorney, and Mr Alexander, the youngest, was under articles to his brother. They resided in Portland-street, Oxford-street, and moved in the same orbit as the

Tauntons – hence their mutual dislike. If the Miss Briggs appeared in smart bonnets, the Miss Tauntons eclipsed them with smarter. If Mrs Taunton appeared in a cap of all the hues of the rainbow, Mrs Briggs forthwith mounted a toque, with all the patterns of a kaleidescope. If Miss Sophia Taunton learnt a new song, two of the Miss Briggses came out with a new duet. The Tauntons had once gained a temporary triumph with the assistance of a harp, but the Briggses brought three guitars into the field, and effectually routed the enemy. There was no end to the rivalry between them.

Now, as Mr Samuel Briggs was a mere machine, a sort of self-acting legal walking-stick; and as the party was known to have originated, however remotely, with Mrs Taunton, the female branches of the Briggs family had arranged that Mr Alexander should attend instead of his brother; and as the said Mr Alexander was deservedly celebrated for possessing all the pertinacity of a bankruptcy-court attorney, combined with the obstinacy of that pleasing animal which browses upon the thistle – he required but little tuition. He was especially enjoined to make himself as disagreeable as possible; and, above all, to black-ball the Tauntons at every hazard.

The proceedings of the evening were opened by Mr Percy Noakes. After successfully urging upon the gentlemen present the propriety of their mixing some brandy-and-water, he briefly stated the object of the meeting, and concluded by observing that the first step must be the selection of a chairman, necessarily possessing some arbitrary – he trusted not unconstitutional – powers, to whom the personal direction of the whole of the arrangements (subject to the approval of the committee) should be confided. A pale young gentleman

The Steam Excursion

in a green stock and spectacles of the same, a member of the honourable society of the Inner Temple, immediately rose for the purpose of proposing Mr Percy Noakes. He had known him long, and this he would say, that a more honourable, a more excellent, or a better-hearted fellow, never existed – (hear, hear!) The young gentleman, who was a member of a debating society, took this opportunity of entering into an examination of the state of the English law, from the days of William the Conqueror down to the present period: he briefly adverted to the code established by the ancient Druids; slightly glanced at the principles laid down by the Athenian lawgivers; and concluded with a most glowing eulogium on pic-nics and constitutional rights.

Mr Alexander Briggs opposed the motion. He had the highest esteem for Mr Percy Noakes as an individual, but he did consider that he ought not to be intrusted with these immense powers – (oh, oh!) – He believed that in the proposed capacity Mr Percy Noakes would not act fairly, impartially, or honourably; but he begged it to be distinctly understood, that he said this without the slightest personal disrespect. Mr Hardy defended his honourable friend, in a voice rendered partially unintelligible by emotion and brandy-and-water. The proposition was put to the vote, and there appearing to be only one dissentient voice, Mr Percy Noakes was declared duly elected, and took the chair accordingly.

The business of the meeting now proceeded with great rapidity. The chairman delivered in his estimate of the probable expense of the excursion, and every one present subscribed his proportion thereof. The question was put that 'The Endeavour' be hired for the occasion; Mr Alexander Briggs moved as an amendment, that the word 'Fly' be substituted for the word 'Endeavour;' but after some debate consented to withdraw his opposition. The important ceremony of balloting then commenced. A tea-caddy was placed on a table in a dark corner of the apartment, and every one was provided with two backgammon men; one black and one white.

The chairman with great solemnity then read the following list of the guests whom he proposed to introduce: – Mrs Taunton and two daughters, Mr Wizzle, Mr Simson. The names were respectively balloted for, and Mrs Taunton and her daughters were declared to be black-balled. Mr Percy Noakes and Mr Hardy exchanged glances.

'Is your list prepared, Mr Briggs?' inquired the chairman.

'It is,' replied Alexander, delivering in the following: – 'Mrs Briggs and three daughters, Mr Samuel Briggs.' The previous ceremony was repeated, and Mrs Briggs and three daughters were declared to be black-balled. Mr Alexander Briggs looked rather foolish, and the remainder of the company appeared somewhat overawed by the mysterious nature of the proceedings.

The balloting proceeded; but one little circumstance which Mr Percy Noakes had not originally foreseen, prevented the system working quite as well as he had anticipated – every body was black-balled. Mr Alexander Briggs, by way of retaliation, exercised his power of exclusion in every instance, and the result was, that after three hours had been consumed in incessant balloting, the names of only three gentlemen were found to have been agreed to. In this dilemma what was to be done? either the whole plan must fall to the ground, or a compromise must be effected. The latter alternative was preferable; and Mr

The Steam Excursion

Percy Noakes therefore proposed that the form of balloting should be dispensed with, and that every gentleman should merely be required to state whom he intended to bring. The proposal was readily acceded to; the Tauntons and the Briggses were reinstated, and the party was formed.

The next Wednesday was fixed for the eventful day, and it was unanimously resolved that every member of the committee should wear a piece of blue sarsenet ribbon round his left arm. It appeared from the statement of Mr Percy Noakes, that the boat belonged to the General Steam Navigation Company, and was then lying off the Custom-house; and as he proposed that the dinner and wines should be provided by an eminent city purveyor, it was arranged that Mr Percy Noakes should be on board by seven o'clock to superintend the arrangements, and that the remaining members of the committee, together with the company generally, should be expected to join her by nine o'clock. More brandy-and-water was despatched; several speeches were made by the different law students present; thanks were voted to the chairman, and the meeting separated.

The weather had been beautiful up to this period, and beautiful it continued to be. Sunday passed over, and Mr Percy Noakes became unusually fidgety – rushing constantly to and from the Steam Packet Wharf, to the astonishment of the clerks, and the great emolument of the Holborn cabmen. Tuesday arrived, and the anxiety of Mr Percy Noakes knew no bounds: he was every instant running to the window to look out for clouds; and Mr Hardy astonished the whole square by practising a new comic song for the occasion, in the chairman's chambers.

Charles Dickens

Uneasy were the slumbers of Mr Percy Noakes that night: he tossed and tumbled about, and had confused dreams of steamers starting off, and gigantic clocks with the hands pointing to a quarter past nine, and the ugly face of Mr Alexander Briggs looking over the boat's side, and grinning as if in derision of his fruitless attempts to move. He made a violent effort to get on board, and awoke. The bright sun was shining cheerfully into the bedroom, and Mr Percy Noakes started up for his watch, in the dreadful expectation of finding his worst dreams realized.

It was just five o'clock. He calculated the time – he should be a good half-hour dressing himself; and as it was a lovely morning, and the tide would be then running down, he would walk leisurely to Strand-lane, and have a boat to the Custom-house.

He dressed himself, took a hasty apology for a breakfast, and sallied forth. The streets looked as lonely and deserted as if they had been crowded overnight for the last time. Here and there an early apprentice, with quenched-looking sleepy eyes, was taking down the shutters of a shop; and a policeman or milkwoman might occasionally be seen pacing slowly along; the servants had not yet begun to clean the doors, or light the fires, and London looked the picture of desolation. At the corner of a bye-street, near Temple-bar, was stationed a 'street breakfast.' The coffee was boiling over a charcoal fire, and large slices of bread and butter were piled one upon the other, like deals in a timber-yard. The company were seated on a form, which, with a view both to security and comfort, was placed against a neighbouring wall. Two young men, whose uproarious mirth and disordered dress bespoke the conviviality of the preceding

The Steam Excursion

evening, were treating three 'ladies' and an Irish labourer. A little sweep was standing at a short distance, casting a longing eye at the tempting delicacies; and a policeman was watching the group from the opposite side of the street. The wan looks, and gaudy finery of the wretched thinly-clad females, contrasted as strangely with the gay sun-light, as did their forced merriment with the boisterous hilarity of the two young men, who now and then varied their amusements by 'bonneting' the proprietor of this itinerant coffee-house.

Mr Percy Noakes walked briskly by, and when he turned down Strand-lane, and caught a glimpse of the glistening water, he thought he had never felt so important or so happy in his life.

'Boat, sir!' cried one of the three watermen who were mopping out their boats, and all whistling different tunes. 'Boat, sir!'

'No,' replied Mr Percy Noakes, rather sharply; for the inquiry was not made in a manner at all suitable to his dignity.

'Would you prefer a wessel, sir?' inquired another, to the infinite delight of the 'Jack-in-the-water.'

Mr Percy Noakes replied with a look of the most supreme contempt.

'Did you want to be put on board a steamer, sir?' inquired an old fireman-waterman, very confidentially. He was dressed in a faded red suit, just the colour of the cover of a very old Court-guide.

'Yes, make haste – the Endeavour – off the Custom-house.'

'Endeavour!' cried the man who had convulsed the 'Jack' before. 'Vy, I see the Endeavour go up half an hour ago.'

'So did I,' said another; 'and I should think she'd gone down by this time, for she's a precious sight too full of ladies and gen'lmen.'

Mr Percy Noakes affected to disregard these representations, and stepped into the boat, which the old man, by dint of scrambling, and shoving, and grating, had brought up to the causeway. 'Shove her off,' cried Mr Percy Noakes, and away the boat glided down the river, Mr Percy Noakes seated on the recently mopped seat, and the watermen at the stairs offering to bet him any reasonable sum that he'd never reach the 'Custum-us.'

'Here she is, by Jove!' said the delighted Percy, as they ran alongside the Endeavour.

'Hold hard!' cried the steward over the side, and Mr Percy Noakes jumped on board.

'Hope you'll find every thing as you wished, sir. She looks uncommon well this morning.'

'She does, indeed,' replied the manager, in a state of ecstasy which it is impossible to describe. The deck was scrubbed, and the seats were scrubbed, and there was a bench for the band, and a place for dancing, and a pile of camp-stools, and an awning; and then Mr Percy Noakes bustled down below, and there were the pastrycook's men, and the steward's wife laying out the dinner on two tables the whole length of the cabin; and then Mr Percy Noakes took off his coat, and rushed backwards and forwards, doing nothing, but quite convinced he was assisting every body; and the steward's wife laughed till she cried, and Mr Percy Noakes panted with the violence of his exertions. And then the bell at London-bridge wharf rang, and a Margate boat was just starting, and a Gravesend boat was just starting,

The Steam Excursion

and people shouted, and porters ran down the steps with luggage that would crush any men but porters; and sloping boards, with bits of wood nailed on them, were placed between the outside boat and the inside boat, and the passengers ran along them, and looked like so many fowls coming out of an area; and then the bell ceased, and the boards were taken away, and the boats started; and the whole scene was one of the most delightful bustle and confusion that can be imagined.

The time wore on; half-past eight o'clock arrived; the pastry-cook's men went ashore; the dinner was completely laid out, and Mr Percy Noakes locked the principal cabin, and put the key into his pocket, in order that it might be suddenly disclosed in all its magnificence to the eyes of the astonished company. The band came on board, and so did the wine.

Ten minutes to nine, and the committee embarked in a body. There was Mr Hardy in a blue jacket and waistcoat, white trousers, silk stockings, and pumps; habited in full aquatic costume, with a straw hat on his head, and an immense telescope under his arm; and there was the young gentleman with the green spectacles, in nankeen inexplicables, with a ditto waistcoat and bright buttons, like the pictures of Paul – not the saint, but he of Virginia notoriety. The remainder of the committee, dressed in white hats, light jackets, waistcoats, and trousers, looked something between waiters and West India planters.

Nine o'clock struck, and the company arrived in shoals. Mr Samuel Briggs, Mrs Briggs, and the Misses Briggs made their appearance in a smart private wherry. The three guitars, in their respective dark green cases, were carefully stowed away in the bottom of the boat, accompanied by two immense portfolios of music, which it would take at least a week's incessant playing to get through. The Tauntons arrived at the same moment with more music, and a lion – a gentleman with a bass voice and an incipient red moustache. The colours of the Taunton party were pink; those of the Briggses a light blue. The Tauntons had artificial flowers in their bonnets; here the Briggses gained a decided advantage – they wore feathers.

'How d'ye do, dear?' said the Misses Briggs to the Misses Taunton. (The word 'dear' among girls is frequently synonymous with 'wretch.')

'Quite well, thank you, dear,' replied the Misses Taunton to the Misses Briggs; and then there was such a kissing, and congratulating, and shaking of hands, as would induce one to suppose that the two families were the best friends in the world, instead of each wishing the other overboard, as they most sincerely did.

Mr Percy Noakes received the visiters, and bowed to the strange gentleman, as if he should like to know who he was. This was just what Mrs Taunton wanted. Here was an opportunity to astonish the Briggses.

'Oh! I beg your pardon,' said the general of the Taunton party, with a careless air. – 'Captain Helves – Mr Percy Noakes – Mrs Briggs – Captain Helves.'

Mr Percy Noakes bowed very low; the gallant captain did the same with all due ferocity, and the Briggses were clearly overcome.

'Our friend, Mr Wizzle, being unfortunately prevented from coming,' resumed Mrs Taunton, 'I did myself the pleasure of bringing the captain, whose musical talents I knew would be a great acquisition.'

'In the name of the committee I have to thank you for

doing so, and to offer you a most sincere welcome, sir,' replied Percy. (Here the scraping was renewed.) 'But pray be seated – won't you walk aft? Captain, will you conduct Miss Taunton? – Miss Briggs, will you allow me?'

'Where could they have picked up that military man?' inquired Mrs Briggs of Miss Kate Briggs, as they followed the little party.

'I can't imagine,' replied Miss Kate, bursting with vexation; for the very fierce air with which the gallant captain regarded the company, had impressed her with a high sense of his importance.

Boat after boat came alongside, and guest after guest arrived. The invites had been excellently arranged, Mr Percy Noakes having considered it as important that the number of young men should exactly tally with that of the young ladies, as that the quantity of knives on board should be in precise proportion to the forks.

'Now, is every one on board?' inquired Mr Percy Noakes. The committee (who, with their bits of blue ribbon, looked as if they were all going to be bled) bustled about to ascertain the fact, and reported that they might safely start.

'Go on,' cried the master of the boat from the top of one of the paddle-boxes.

'Go on,' echoed the boy, who was stationed over the hatchway to pass the directions down to the engineer; and away went the vessel with that agreeable noise which is peculiar to steamers, and which is composed of a pleasant mixture of creaking, gushing, clanging, and snorting.

'Hoi–oi–oi–oi–oi–oi–o–i–i–i!' shouted half-a-dozen voices from a boat about a quarter of a mile astern.

'Ease her!' cried the captain: 'do these people belong to us, sir?'

'Noakes,' exclaimed Hardy, who had been looking at every object, far and near, through the large telescope, 'it's the Fleetwoods and the Wakefields – and two children with them, by Jove!'

'What a shame to bring children!' said every body; 'how very inconsiderate!'

'I say, it would be a good joke to pretend not to see 'em, wouldn't it?' suggested Hardy, to the immense delight of the company generally. A council of war was hastily held, and it was resolved that the new comers should be taken on board, on Mr Hardy's solemnly pledging himself to tease the children during the whole of the day.

'Stop her!' cried the captain.

'Stop her!' repeated the boy; whizz went the steam, and all the young ladies, as in duty bound, screamed in concert. They were only appeased by the assurance of the martial Helves, that the escape of steam consequent on stopping a vessel was seldom attended with any great loss of human life.

Two men ran to the side, and after a good deal of shouting, and swearing, and angling for the wherry with a boat-hook, Mr Fleetwood, and Mrs Fleetwood, and Master Fleetwood, and Mr Wakefield, and Mrs Wakefield, and Miss Wakefield, were safely deposited on the deck. The girl was about six years old, the boy about four; the former was dressed in a white frock with a pink sash and a dog's-eared-looking little spencer, a straw bonnet and green veil, six inches by three and a half: the latter was attired for the occasion in a nankeen frock, between the bottom of which and the top of his plaid socks a

The Steam Excursion

considerable portion of two small mottled legs was discernible. He had a light blue cap with a gold band and tassel on his head, and a damp piece of gingerbread in his hand, with which he had slightly embossed his dear little countenance.

The boat once more started off; the band played 'Off she goes;' the major part of the company conversed cheerfully in groups, and the old gentlemen walked up and down the deck in pairs, as perseveringly and gravely as if they were doing a match against time for an immense stake. They ran briskly down the Pool; the gentlemen pointed out the Docks, the Thames Police-office, and other elegant public edifices; and the young ladies exhibited a proper display of horror and bashfulness at the appearance of the coal-whippers and ballast-heavers. Mr Hardy told stories to the married ladies, at which they laughed very much in their pocket-handkerchiefs, and hit him on the knuckles with their fans, declaring him to be 'a naughty man – a shocking creature' – and so forth; and Captain Helves gave slight descriptions of battles and duels, with a most bloodthirsty air, which made him the admiration of the women, and the envy of the men. Quadrilling commenced; Captain Helves danced one set with Miss Emily Taunton, and another set with Miss Sophia Taunton. Mrs Taunton was in ecstasies. The victory appeared to be complete; but, alas! the inconstancy of man! Having performed this necessary duty, he attached himself solely to Miss Julia Briggs, with whom he danced no less than three sets consecutively, and from whose side he evinced no intention of stirring for the remainder of the day.

Mr Hardy having played one or two very brilliant fantasias on the Jews'-harp, and having frequently repeated the exquisitely amusing joke of slily chalking a large cross on the back of some member of the committee, Mr Percy Noakes expressed his hope that some of their musical friends would oblige the company by a display of their abilities.

'Perhaps,' he said in a very insinuating manner, 'Captain Helves will oblige us.' Mrs Taunton's countenance lighted up, for the captain only sang duets, and couldn't sing them with any body but one of her daughters.

'Really,' said that warlike individual, 'I should be very happy, but –'

'Oh! pray do,' cried all the young ladies.

'Miss Sophia, have you any objection to join in a duet?'

'Oh! not the slightest,' returned the young lady, in a tone which clearly showed she had the greatest possible objection.

'Shall I accompany you, dear?' inquired one of the Miss Briggses, with the bland intention of spoiling the effect.

'Very much obliged to you, Miss Briggs,' sharply retorted Mrs Taunton, who saw through the manœuvre; 'my daughters always sing without accompaniments.'

'And without voices,' tittered Mrs Briggs, in a low tone.

'Perhaps,' said Mrs Taunton, reddening, for she guessed the tenor of the observation, though she had not heard it clearly – 'Perhaps it would be as well for some people, if their voices were not quite so audible as they are to other people.'

'And perhaps, if gentlemen, who are kidnapped to pay attention to some persons' daughters, had not sufficient discernment to pay attention to other persons' daughters,' returned Mrs Briggs, 'some persons would not be so ready to display that ill-temper, which, thank God, distinguishes them from other persons.'

'Persons!' ejaculated Mrs Taunton.

The Steam Excursion

'Yes; persons, ma'am,' replied Mrs Briggs.

'Insolence!'

'Creature!'

'Hush! hush!' interrupted Mr Percy Noakes, who was one of the very few by whom this dialogue had been overheard. 'Hush! – pray silence for the duet.'

After a great deal of preparatory crowing and humming, the captain began the following duet from the opera of 'Paul and Virginia,' in that grunting tone in which a man gets down, Heaven knows where, without the remotest chance of ever getting up again. This, in private circles, is frequently designated 'a bass voice.'

>   'See (sung the captain) from o–ce–an ri–sing
>   Bright flames the or–b of d–ay.
>   From yon gro–ve, the varied so–ngs —'

Here the singer was interrupted by varied cries of the most dreadful description, proceeding from some grove in the immediate vicinity of the starboard paddle-box.

'My child!' screamed Mrs Fleetwood. 'My child! it is his voice – I know it.'

Mr Fleetwood, accompanied by several gentlemen, here rushed to the quarter from whence the noise proceeded, and an exclamation of horror burst from the company; the general impression being, that the little innocent had either got his head in the water, or his legs in the machinery.

'What is the matter?' shouted the agonized father, as he returned with the child in his arms.

'Oh! oh! oh!' screamed the small sufferer again.

'What is the matter, dear?' inquired the father once more – hastily stripping off the nankeen frock, for the purpose of ascertaining whether the child had one bone which was not smashed to pieces.

'Oh! oh! – I'm so frightened.'

'What at, dear? – what at?' said the mother, soothing the sweet infant.

'Oh! he's been making such dreadful faces at me,' cried the boy, relapsing into convulsions at the bare recollection.

'He! – who?' cried every body, crowding round him.

'Oh! – him,' replied the child, pointing at Hardy, who affected to be the most concerned of the whole group.

The real state of the case at once flashed upon the minds of all present, with the exception of the Fleetwoods and the Wakefields. The facetious Hardy, in fulfilment of his promise, had watched the child to a remote part of the vessel, and, suddenly appearing before him with the most awful contortions of visage, had produced his paroxysm of terror. Of course, he now observed that it was hardly necessary for him to deny the accusation; and the unfortunate little victim was accordingly led below, after receiving sundry thumps on the head from both his parents, for having the wickedness to tell a story.

This little interruption having been adjusted, the captain resumed and Miss Emily chimed in, in due course. The duet was loudly applauded, and, certainly, the perfect independence of the parties deserved great commendation. Miss Emily sung her part without the slightest reference to the captain, and the captain sang so loud that he had not the slightest idea of what was being done by his partner. After

The Steam Excursion

having gone through the last few eighteen or nineteen bars by himself, therefore, he acknowledged the plaudits of the circle with that air of self-denial which men always assume when they think they have done something to astonish the company, though they don't exactly know what.

'Now,' said Mr Percy Noakes, who had just ascended from the fore-cabin, where he had been busily engaged in decanting the wine, 'if the Misses Briggs will oblige us with something before dinner, I am sure we shall be very much delighted.'

One of those hums of admiration followed the suggestion, which one frequently hears in society, when nobody has the most distant notion of what he is expressing his approval of. The three Misses Briggs looked modestly at their mamma, and the mamma looked approvingly at her daughters, and Mrs Taunton looked scornfully at all of them. The Misses Briggs asked for their guitars, and several gentlemen seriously damaged the cases in their anxiety to present them. Then there was a very interesting production of three little keys for the aforesaid cases, and a melodramatic expression of horror at finding a string broken; and a vast deal of screwing and tightening, and winding and tuning, during which Mrs Briggs expatiated to those near her on the immense difficulty of playing a guitar, and hinted at the wondrous proficiency of her daughters in that mystic art. Mrs Taunton whispered to a neighbour that it was 'quite sickening!' and the Misses Taunton tried to look as if they knew how to play, but disdained to do so.

At length the Misses Briggs began in real earnest. It was a new Spanish composition, for three voices and three guitars. The effect was electrical. All eyes were turned upon the captain, who was reported to have once passed through Spain with his regiment, and who, of course, must be well acquainted with the national music. He was in raptures. This was sufficient; the trio was encored – the applause was universal, and never had the Tauntons suffered such a complete defeat.

'Bravo! bravo!' ejaculated the captain; – 'Bravo!'

'Pretty! isn't it, sir?' inquired Mr Samuel Briggs, with the air of a self-satisfied showman. By the by, these were the first words he had been heard to utter since he left Boswell-court the evening before.

'De–lightful!' returned the captain, with a flourish, and a military cough; – 'de–lightful!'

'Sweet instrument!' said an old gentleman with a bald head, who had been trying all the morning to look through a telescope, inside the glass of which Mr Hardy had fixed a large black wafer.

'Did you ever hear a Portuguese tambarine?' inquired that jocular individual.

'Did *you* ever hear a tom-tom, sir?' sternly inquired the captain, who lost no opportunity of showing off his travels, real or pretended.

'A what?' asked Hardy, rather taken aback.

'A tom-tom.'

'Never!'

'Nor a gum-gum?'

'Never!'

'What *is* a gum-gum?' eagerly inquired several young ladies.

'When I was in the East Indies,' replied the captain, (here was a discovery – he had been in the East Indies!) – 'when I was in the East Indies, I was once stopping a few thousand miles up the country, on a visit at the house of a very particular friend of mine, Ram Chowdar Doss Azuph Al Bowlar – a devilish pleasant fellow. As we were enjoying our hookahs one evening in the cool verandah in front of his villa, we were rather surprised by the sudden appearance of thirty-four of his Kit-ma-gars (for he had rather a large establishment there), accompanied by an equal number of Consumars, approaching the house with a threatening aspect, and beating a tom-tom. The Ram started up —'

'The who?' inquired the bald gentleman, intensely interested.

'The Ram – Ram Chowdar –'

'Oh!' said the old gentleman, 'I beg your pardon; it really didn't occur to me; pray go on.'

'– Started up and drew a pistol. "Helves," said he, "my boy," – he always called me, my boy – "Helves," said he, "do you hear that tom-tom?" – "I do," said I. His countenance, which before was pale, assumed a most frightful appearance; his whole visage was distorted, and his frame shaken by violent emotions. "Do you see that gum-gum?" said he. "No," said I, staring about me. "You don't?" said he. "No, I'll be damned if I do", said I; "and what's more, I don't know what a gum-gum is," said I. I really thought the man would have dropped. He drew me aside, and, with an expression of agony I shall never forget, said in a low whisper —'

'Dinner's on the table, ladies,' interrupted the steward's wife.

'Will you allow me?' said the captain, immediately suiting the action to the word, and escorting Miss Julia Briggs to the cabin, with as much ease as if he had finished the story.

'What an extraordinary circumstance!' ejaculated the same old gentleman, preserving his listening attitude.

'What a traveller!' said the young ladies.

'What a singular name!' exclaimed the gentlemen, rather confused by the coolness of the whole affair.

'I wish he had finished the story,' said an old lady. 'I wonder what a gum-gum really is?'

'By Jove!' exclaimed Hardy, who until now had been lost in utter amazement, 'I don't know what it may be in India, but in England I think a gum-gum has very much the same meaning as a humbug.'

'How illiberal! how envious!' said every body, as they made for the cabin, fully impressed with a belief in the captain's amazing adventures. Helves was the sole lion for the remainder of the day – impudence and the marvellous are sure passports to any society.

The party had by this time reached their destination, and put about on their return home. The wind, which had been with them the whole day, was now directly in their teeth; the weather had become gradually more and more overcast; and the sky, water, and shore, were all of that dull, heavy, uniform lead-colour, which house-painters daub in the first instance over a street-door which is gradually approaching a state of convalescence. It had been 'spitting' with rain for the last half-hour, and now began to pour in good earnest. The wind was freshening very fast, and the waterman at the wheel had unequivocally expressed his opinion that there would shortly be a squall. A slight motion on the part of the vessel now and then, seemed to suggest the possibility of its pitching to a very uncomfortable extent in the event of its blowing harder; and every timber began to creak as if the boat were an overladen clothes-basket. Sea-sickness, however, is like a belief in ghosts – every one entertains some misgivings on the subject, but few will acknowledge them. The majority of the company, therefore, endeavoured to look peculiarly happy, feeling all the while especially miserable.

'Don't it rain?' inquired the old gentleman before noticed, when, by dint of squeezing and jamming, they were all seated at table.

'I think it does – a little,' replied Mr Percy Noakes, who could hardly hear himself speak, in consequence of the pattering on the deck.

'Don't it blow?' inquired some one else.

'No – I don't think it does,' responded Hardy, sincerely wishing that he could persuade himself it did not, for he sat near the door, and was almost blown off his seat.

'It'll soon clear up,' said Mr Percy Noakes, in a cheerful tone.

'Oh, certainly!' ejaculated the committee generally.

'No doubt of it,' said the remainder of the company, whose attention was now pretty well engrossed by the serious business of eating, carving, taking wine, and so forth.

The throbbing motion of the engine was but too perceptible. There was a large, substantial cold boiled leg of mutton at the bottom of the table, shaking like blanc-mange; a hearty sirloin of beef looked as if it had been suddenly seized with the palsy; and some tongues, which were placed on dishes rather too large for them, were going through the most surprising evolutions, darting from side to side, and from end to end, like a fly in an inverted wine-glass. Then the sweets shook and trembled till it was quite impossible to help them, and people gave up the attempt in despair; and the pigeon-pies looked as if the birds, whose legs were stuck outside, were trying to get them in. The table vibrated and started like a feverish pulse, and the very legs were slightly convulsed – every thing was shaking and jarring. The beams in the roof of the cabin seemed as if they were put there for the sole purpose of giving people headaches, and several elderly gentlemen became ill-tempered in consequence. As fast as the steward put the fire-irons up, they *would* fall down again; and the more the ladies and gentlemen tried to sit comfortably on their seats, the more the seats seemed to slide away from the ladies and gentlemen. Several ominous demands were made for small glasses of brandy; the countenances of the company gradually underwent the most extraordinary changes; and one gentleman was observed suddenly to rush from table without the slightest ostensible reason, and dart up the steps with incredible swiftness, thereby greatly damaging both himself and the steward, who happened to be coming down at the same moment.

The cloth was removed; the dessert was laid on the table, and the glasses were filled. The motion of the boat increased; several members of the party began to feel rather vague and misty, and looked as if they had only just got up. The young gentleman with the spectacles, who had been in a fluctuating state for some time – one moment bright, and another dismal, like a revolving light on the sea-coast – rashly announced his wish to propose a toast. After several ineffectual attempts to preserve his perpendicular, the young gentleman, having managed to hook himself to the centre leg of the table with his left hand, proceeded as follows:

'Ladies and gentlemen. – A gentleman is among us – I may say a stranger – (here some painful thought seemed to

The Steam Excursion

strike the orator; he paused, and looked extremely odd) whose talents, whose travels, whose cheerfulness –'

'I beg your pardon, Edkins,' hastily interrupted Mr Percy Noakes. – 'Hardy, what's the matter?'

'Nothing,' replied the 'funny gentleman', who had just life enough left to utter two consecutive syllables.

'Will you have some brandy?'

'No,' replied Hardy, in a tone of great indignation, and looking about as comfortable as Temple-bar in a Scotch mist; 'what should I want brandy for?'

'Will you go on deck?'

'No, I will not.' This was said with a most determined air, and in a voice which might have been taken for an imitation of any thing; it was quite as much like a guinea-pig as a bassoon.

'I beg your pardon, Edkins,' said the courteous Percy; 'I thought our friend was ill. Pray go on.'

A pause.

'Pray go on.'

'Mr Edkins *is* gone,' cried somebody.

'I beg your pardon, sir,' said the steward, running up to Mr Percy Noakes, 'I beg your pardon, sir, but the gentleman as just went on deck – him with the green spectacles – is uncommon bad, to be sure; and the young man as played the wiolin says, that unless he has some brandy he can't answer for the consequences. He says he has a wife and two children, whose werry subsistence depends on his breaking a wessel, and that he expects to do so every moment. The flageolet's been very ill, but he's better, only he's in such a dreadful prusperation.'

All disguise was now useless; the company staggered on deck, the gentlemen tried to see nothing but the clouds, and

The Steam Excursion

the ladies, muffled up in such shawls and cloaks as they had brought with them, lay about on the seats and under the seats, in the most wretched condition. Never was such a blowing, and raining, and pitching, and tossing, endured by any pleasure party before. Several remonstrances were sent down below on the subject of Master Fleetwood, but they were totally unheeded in consequence of the indisposition of his natural protectors. That interesting child screamed at the very top of his voice, until he had no voice left to scream with, and then Miss Wakefield began, and screamed for the remainder of the passage.

Mr Hardy was observed some hours afterwards in an attitude which induced his friends to suppose that he was busily engaged in contemplating the beauties of the deep; they only regretted that his taste for the picturesque should lead him to remain so long in a position, very injurious at all times, but especially so to an individual labouring under a tendency of blood to the head.

The party arrived off the Custom-house at about two o'clock on the Thursday morning – dispirited and worn out. The Tauntons were too ill to quarrel with the Briggses, and the Briggses were too wretched to annoy the Tauntons. One of the guitar-cases was lost on its passage to a hackney-coach, and Mrs Briggs has not scrupled to state that the Tauntons bribed a porter to throw it down an area. Mr Alexander Briggs opposes vote by ballot – he says from personal experience of its inefficacy; and Mr Samuel Briggs, whenever he is asked to express his sentiments on the point, says that he has no opinion on that or any other subject.

Mr Edkins – the young gentleman in the green

spectacles – makes a speech on every occasion on which a speech can possibly be made, the eloquence of which can only be equalled by its length. In the event of his not being previously appointed to a judgeship, it is most probable that he will practise as a barrister in the New Central Criminal Court.

Captain Helves continued his attention to Miss Julia Briggs, whom he might possibly have espoused, if it had not unfortunately happened that Mr Samuel arrested him in the way of business, pursuant to instructions received from Messrs Scroggins and Payne, whose town debts the gallant captain had condescended to collect, but whose accounts, with the indiscretion so peculiar to military minds, he had omitted to keep with that dull accuracy which custom has rendered necessary. Mrs Taunton complains that she has been much deceived in him. He introduced himself to the family on board a Gravesend steam-packet, and certainly, therefore, ought to have proved respectable.

Mr Percy Noakes is as light-hearted and careless as ever. We have described him as a general favourite in his private circle, and trust he may find a kindly-disposed friend or two in public.

1. BOCCACCIO · *Mrs Rosie and the Priest*
2. GERARD MANLEY HOPKINS · *As kingfishers catch fire*
3. *The Saga of Gunnlaug Serpent-tongue*
4. THOMAS DE QUINCEY · *On Murder Considered as One of the Fine Arts*
5. FRIEDRICH NIETZSCHE · *Aphorisms on Love and Hate*
6. JOHN RUSKIN · *Traffic*
7. PU SONGLING · *Wailing Ghosts*
8. JONATHAN SWIFT · *A Modest Proposal*
9. *Three Tang Dynasty Poets*
10. WALT WHITMAN · *On the Beach at Night Alone*
11. KENKŌ · *A Cup of Sake Beneath the Cherry Trees*
12. BALTASAR GRACIÁN · *How to Use Your Enemies*
13. JOHN KEATS · *The Eve of St Agnes*
14. THOMAS HARDY · *Woman much missed*
15. GUY DE MAUPASSANT · *Femme Fatale*
16. MARCO POLO · *Travels in the Land of Serpents and Pearls*
17. SUETONIUS · *Caligula*
18. APOLLONIUS OF RHODES · *Jason and Medea*
19. ROBERT LOUIS STEVENSON · *Olalla*
20. KARL MARX AND FRIEDRICH ENGELS · *The Communist Manifesto*
21. PETRONIUS · *Trimalchio's Feast*
22. JOHANN PETER HEBEL · *How a Ghastly Story Was Brought to Light by a Common or Garden Butcher's Dog*
23. HANS CHRISTIAN ANDERSEN · *The Tinder Box*
24. RUDYARD KIPLING · *The Gate of the Hundred Sorrows*
25. DANTE · *Circles of Hell*
26. HENRY MAYHEW · *Of Street Piemen*
27. HAFEZ · *The nightingales are drunk*
28. GEOFFREY CHAUCER · *The Wife of Bath*
29. MICHEL DE MONTAIGNE · *How We Weep and Laugh at the Same Thing*
30. THOMAS NASHE · *The Terrors of the Night*
31. EDGAR ALLAN POE · *The Tell-Tale Heart*
32. MARY KINGSLEY · *A Hippo Banquet*
33. JANE AUSTEN · *The Beautifull Cassandra*
34. ANTON CHEKHOV · *Gooseberries*
35. SAMUEL TAYLOR COLERIDGE · *Well, they are gone, and here must I remain*
36. JOHANN WOLFGANG VON GOETHE · *Sketchy, Doubtful, Incomplete Jottings*
37. CHARLES DICKENS · *The Great Winglebury Duel*
38. HERMAN MELVILLE · *The Maldive Shark*
39. ELIZABETH GASKELL · *The Old Nurse's Story*
40. NIKOLAY LESKOV · *The Steel Flea*

41. HONORÉ DE BALZAC · *The Atheist's Mass*
42. CHARLOTTE PERKINS GILMAN · *The Yellow Wall-Paper*
43. C.P. CAVAFY · *Remember, Body . . .*
44. FYODOR DOSTOEVSKY · *The Meek One*
45. GUSTAVE FLAUBERT · *A Simple Heart*
46. NIKOLAI GOGOL · *The Nose*
47. SAMUEL PEPYS · *The Great Fire of London*
48. EDITH WHARTON · *The Reckoning*
49. HENRY JAMES · *The Figure in the Carpet*
50. WILFRED OWEN · *Anthem For Doomed Youth*
51. WOLFGANG AMADEUS MOZART · *My Dearest Father*
52. PLATO · *Socrates' Defence*
53. CHRISTINA ROSSETTI · *Goblin Market*
54. *Sindbad the Sailor*
55. SOPHOCLES · *Antigone*
56. RYŪNOSUKE AKUTAGAWA · *The Life of a Stupid Man*
57. LEO TOLSTOY · *How Much Land Does A Man Need?*
58. GIORGIO VASARI · *Leonardo da Vinci*
59. OSCAR WILDE · *Lord Arthur Savile's Crime*
60. SHEN FU · *The Old Man of the Moon*
61. AESOP · *The Dolphins, the Whales and the Gudgeon*
62. MATSUO BASHŌ · *Lips too Chilled*
63. EMILY BRONTË · *The Night is Darkening Round Me*
64. JOSEPH CONRAD · *To-morrow*
65. RICHARD HAKLUYT · *The Voyage of Sir Francis Drake Around the Whole Globe*
66. KATE CHOPIN · *A Pair of Silk Stockings*
67. CHARLES DARWIN · *It was snowing butterflies*
68. BROTHERS GRIMM · *The Robber Bridegroom*
69. CATULLUS · *I Hate and I Love*
70. HOMER · *Circe and the Cyclops*
71. D. H. LAWRENCE · *Il Duro*
72. KATHERINE MANSFIELD · *Miss Brill*
73. OVID · *The Fall of Icarus*
74. SAPPHO · *Come Close*
75. IVAN TURGENEV · *Kasyan from the Beautiful Lands*
76. VIRGIL · *O Cruel Alexis*
77. H. G. WELLS · *A Slip under the Microscope*
78. HERODOTUS · *The Madness of Cambyses*
79. *Speaking of Siva*
80. *The Dhammapada*

'No voice, no low, no howl is heard; the chief sound of life here is a hiss.'

HERMAN MELVILLE
Born 1819, New York City
Died 1891, New York City

The three poems first published 1888 in *John Marr and Other Sailors*. *The Encantadas or Enchanted Isles* first published in 1854. 'Sketch Eighth' and 'Sketch Ninth' have been omitted.

MELVILLE IN PENGUIN CLASSICS
Billy Budd and Other Stories
Israel Potter
Moby-Dick
Omoo
Pierre
Redburn
The Confidence-Man

HERMAN MELVILLE

The Maldive Shark

PENGUIN BOOKS

PENGUIN CLASSICS

UK | USA | Canada | Ireland | Australia
India | New Zealand | South Africa

Penguin Books is part of the Penguin Random House group of companies
whose addresses can be found at global.penguinrandomhouse.com.

This selection published in Penguin Classics 2015

008

Set in 9.5/12.5 pt Baskerville 10 Pro
Typeset by Jouve (UK), Milton Keynes
Printed and bound in Great Britain by Clays Ltd, Elcograf S.p.A.

A CIP catalogue record for this book is available from the British Library

ISBN: 978-0-141-39717-7

www.greenpenguin.co.uk

Penguin Random House is committed to a
sustainable future for our business, our readers
and our planet. This book is made from Forest
Stewardship Council® certified paper.

Contents

The Maldive Shark   1

The Berg (A Dream)   2

The Enviable Isles *(from 'Rammon')*   4

from *The Encantadas or Enchanted Isles*

Sketch First: The Isles at Large   5

Sketch Second: Two Sides to a Tortoise   13

Sketch Third: Rock Rodondo   19

Sketch Fourth: A Pisgah View from the Rock   26

Sketch Fifth: The Frigate, and Ship Flyaway   36

Sketch Sixth: Barrington Isle and the Buccaneers   39

Sketch Seventh: Charles's Isle
and the Dog-King   44

Sketch Tenth: Runaways,
Castaways, Solitaries,
Grave-Stones, etc.   51

The Maldive Shark

About the Shark, phlegmatical one,
Pale sot of the Maldive sea,
The sleek little pilot-fish, azure and slim,
How alert in attendance be.
From his saw-pit of mouth, from his charnel of maw
They have nothing of harm to dread,
But liquidly glide on his ghastly flank
Or before his Gorgonian head;
Or lurk in the port of serrated teeth
In white triple tiers of glittering gates,
And there find a haven when peril's abroad,
An asylum in jaws of the Fates!
They are friends; and friendly they guide him to prey,
Yet never partake of the treat –
Eyes and brains to the dotard lethargic and dull,
Pale ravener of horrible meat.

The Berg
(A Dream)

I saw a ship of martial build
(Her standards set, her brave apparel on)
Directed as by madness mere
Against a stolid iceberg steer,
Nor budge it, though the infatuate ship went down.
The impact made huge ice-cubes fall
Sullen, in tons that crashed the deck;
But that one avalanche was all –
No other movement save the foundering wreck.

Along the spurs of ridges pale,
Not any slenderest shaft and frail,
A prism over glass-green gorges lone,
Topple; nor lace of traceries fine,
Nor pendant drops in grot or mine
Were jarred, when the stunned ship went down.
Nor sole the gulls in cloud that wheeled
Circling one snow-flanked peak afar,
But nearer fowl the floes that skimmed
And crystal beaches, felt no jar.
No thrill transmitted stirred the lock
Of jack-straw needle-ice at base;
Towers undermined by waves – the block

The Berg (A Dream)

Atilt impending – kept their place.
Seals, dozing sleek on sliddery ledges
Slipt never, when by loftier edges
Through very inertia overthrown,
The impetuous ship in bafflement went down.

Hard Berg (methought), so cold, so vast,
With mortal damps self-overcast;
Exhaling still thy dankish breath –
Adrift dissolving, bound for death;
Though lumpish thou, a lumbering one –
A lumbering lubbard loitering slow,
Impingers rue thee and go down,
Sounding thy precipice below,
Nor stir the slimy slug that sprawls
Along thy dense stolidity of walls.

The Enviable Isles
(From 'Rammon')

Through storms you reach them and from storms are free.
    Afar descried, the foremost drear in hue,
But, nearer, green; and, on the marge, the sea
    Makes thunder low and mist of rainbowed dew.

But, inland, where the sleep that folds the hills
A dreamier sleep, the trance of God, instills –
    On uplands hazed, in wandering airs aswoon,
Slow-swaying palms salute love's cypress tree
    Adown in vale where pebbly runlets croon
A song to lull all sorrow and all glee.

Sweet-fern and moss in many a glade are here,
    Where, strown in flocks, what cheek-flushed myriads lie
Dimpling in dream – unconscious slumberers mere,
    While billows endless round the beaches die.

THE ENCANTADAS OR ENCHANTED ISLES

Sketch First

THE ISLES AT LARGE

— *'That may not be, said then the* Ferryman
Least we unweeting hap to be fordonne:
For those same Islands, seeming now and then,
Are not firme lande, nor any certein wonne,
But straggling plots, which to and fro do ronne
In the wide waters: therefore are they hight
The wandring Islands. *Therefore doe them shonne;*
For they have oft drawne many a wandring wight
Into most deadly daunger and distressed plight;
For whosoever once hath fastened
His foot thereon, may never it recure,
But wandreth ever more uncertain and unsure.'

'Darke, dolefull, drearie, like a greedie grave,
That still for carrion carcases doth crave:
On top whereof aye dwelt the ghastly Owle,
Shrieking his balefull note, which ever drave
Farre from that haunt all other chearefull fowle;
And all about it wandring ghostes did waile and howle.'

Take five-and-twenty heaps of cinders dumped here and there in an outside city lot; imagine some of them magnified into mountains, and the vacant lot the sea; and you will have a fit idea of the general aspect of the Encantadas, or Enchanted Isles. A group rather of extinct volcanoes than of isles; looking much as the world at large might, after a penal conflagration.

It is to be doubted whether any spot of earth can, in desolateness, furnish a parallel to this group. Abandoned cemeteries of long ago, old cities by piecemeal tumbling to their ruin, these are melancholy enough; but, like all else which has but once been associated with humanity, they still awaken in us some thoughts of sympathy, however sad. Hence, even the Dead Sea, along with whatever other emotions it may at times inspire, does not fail to touch in the pilgrim some of his less unpleasurable feelings.

And as for solitariness; the great forests of the north, the expanses of unnavigated waters, the Greenland ice-fields, are the profoundest of solitudes to a human observer; still the magic of their changeable tides and seasons mitigates their terror; because, though unvisited by men, those forests are visited by the May; the remotest seas reflect familiar stars even as Lake Erie does; and, in the clear air of a fine Polar day, the irradiated, azure ice shows beautifully as malachite.

But the special curse, as one may call it, of the Encantadas, that which exalts them in desolation above Idumea and the Pole, is, that to them change never comes; neither the change of seasons nor of sorrows. Cut by the Equator,

Sketch First

they know not autumn, and they know not spring; while already reduced to the lees of fire, ruin itself can work little more upon them. The showers refresh the deserts; but in these isles, rain never falls. Like split Syrian gourds left withering in the sun, they are cracked by an everlasting drought beneath a torrid sky. 'Have mercy upon me,' the wailing spirit of the Encantadas seems to cry, 'and send Lazarus that he may dip the tip of his finger in water and cool my tongue, for I am tormented in this flame.'

Another feature in these isles is their emphatic uninhabitableness. It is deemed a fit type of all-forsaken overthrow, that the jackal should den in the wastes of weedy Babylon; but the Encantadas refuse to harbor even the outcasts of the beasts. Man and wolf alike disown them. Little but reptile life is here found: tortoises, lizards, immense spiders, snakes, and that strangest anomaly of outlandish nature, the *aguano*. No voice, no low, no howl is heard; the chief sound of life here is a hiss.

On most of the isles where vegetation is found at all, it is more ungrateful than the blankness of Aracama. Tangled thickets of wiry bushes, without fruit and without a name, springing up among deep fissures of calcined rock, and treacherously masking them; or a parched growth of distorted cactus trees.

In many places the coast is rock-bound, or, more properly, clinker-bound; tumbled masses of blackish or greenish stuff like the dross of an iron-furnace, forming dark clefts and caves here and there, into which a ceaseless sea pours a fury of foam; overhanging them with a swirl of gray, haggard mist, amidst which sail screaming flights of unearthly birds heightening the dismal din. However calm the sea without, there is no rest for these swells and those rocks; they lash and are lashed, even when the outer ocean is most at peace with itself. On the oppressive, clouded days, such as are peculiar to this part of the watery Equator, the dark, vitrified masses, many of which raise themselves among white whirlpools and breakers in detached and perilous places off the shore, present a most Plutonian sight. In no world but a fallen one could such lands exist.

Those parts of the strand free from the marks of fire, stretch away in wide level beaches of multitudinous dead shells, with here and there decayed bits of sugar-cane, bamboos, and cocoanuts, washed upon this other and darker world from the charming palm isles to the westward and southward; all the way from Paradise to Tartarus; while mixed with the relics of distant beauty you will sometimes see fragments of charred wood and mouldering ribs of wrecks. Neither will any one be surprised at meeting these last, after observing the conflicting currents which eddy throughout nearly all the wide channels of the entire group. The capriciousness of the tides of air sympathizes with those of the sea. Nowhere is the wind so light, baffling, and every way unreliable, and so given to perplexing calms, as at the Encantadas. Nigh a month has been spent by a ship going from one isle to another, though but ninety miles between; for owing to the force of the current, the boats employed to tow barely

Sketch First

suffice to keep the craft from sweeping upon the cliffs, but do nothing towards accelerating her voyage. Sometimes it is impossible for a vessel from afar to fetch up with the group itself, unless large allowances for prospective lee-way have been made ere its coming in sight. And yet, at other times, there is a mysterious indraft, which irresistibly draws a passing vessel among the isles, though not bound to them.

True, at one period, as to some extent at the present day, large fleets of whalemen cruised for spermaceti upon what some seamen call the Enchanted Ground. But this, as in due place will be described, was off the great outer isle of Albemarle, away from the intricacies of the smaller isles, where there is plenty of sea-room; and hence, to that vicinity, the above remarks do not altogether apply; though even there the current runs at times with singular force, shifting, too, with as singular a caprice.

Indeed, there are seasons when currents quite unaccountable prevail for a great distance round about the total group, and are so strong and irregular as to change a vessel's course against the helm, though sailing at the rate of four or five miles the hour. The difference in the reckonings of navigators, produced by these causes, along with the light and variable winds, long nourished a persuasion, that there existed two distinct clusters of isles in the parallel of the Encantadas, about a hundred leagues apart. Such was the idea of their earlier visitors, the Buccaneers; and as late as 1750, the charts of that part of the Pacific accorded with the strange delusion. And this apparent fleetingness and unreality of the locality of the isles was most probably one reason for the Spaniards calling them the Encantada, or Enchanted Group.

But not uninfluenced by their character, as they now confessedly exist, the modern voyager will be inclined to fancy that the bestowal of this name might have in part originated in that air of spell-bound desertness which so significantly invests the isles. Nothing can better suggest the aspect of once living things malignly crumbled from ruddiness into ashes. Apples of Sodom, after touching, seem these isles.

However wavering their place may seem by reason of the currents, they themselves, at least to one upon the shore, appear invariably the same: fixed, cast, glued into the very body of cadaverous death.

Nor would the appellation, enchanted, seem misapplied in still another sense. For concerning the peculiar reptile inhabitant of these wilds – whose presence gives the group its second Spanish name, Gallipagos – concerning the tortoises found here, most mariners have long cherished a superstition, not more frightful than grotesque. They earnestly believe that all wicked sea-officers, more especially commodores and captains, are at death (and, in some cases, before death) transformed into tortoises; thenceforth dwelling upon these hot aridities, sole solitary lords of Asphaltum.

Doubtless, so quaintly dolorous a thought was originally inspired by the woe-begone landscape itself; but more particularly, perhaps, by the tortoises. For, apart from

Sketch First

their strictly physical features, there is something strangely self-condemned in the appearance of these creatures. Lasting sorrow and penal hopelessness are in no animal form so suppliantly expressed as in theirs; while the thought of their wonderful longevity does not fail to enhance the impression.

Nor even at the risk of meriting the charge of absurdly believing in enchantments, can I restrain the admission that sometimes, even now, when leaving the crowded city to wander out July and August among the Adirondack Mountains, far from the influences of towns and proportionally nigh to the mysterious ones of nature; when at such times I sit me down in the mossy head of some deep-wooded gorge, surrounded by prostrate trunks of blasted pines and recall, as in a dream, my other and far-distant rovings in the baked heart of the charmed isles: and remember the sudden glimpses of dusky shells, and long languid necks protruded from the leafless thickets; and again have beheld the vitreous inland rocks worn down and grooved into deep ruts by ages and ages of the slow draggings of tortoises in quest of pools of scanty water; I can hardly resist the feeling that in my time I have indeed slept upon evilly enchanted ground.

Nay, such is the vividness of my memory, or the magic of my fancy, that I know not whether I am not the occasional victim of optical delusion concerning the Gallipagos. For, often in scenes of social merriment, and especially at revels held by candle-light in old-fashioned mansions, so that shadows are thrown into the further recesses of an angular and spacious room, making them put on a look of haunted undergrowth of lonely woods, I have drawn the attention of my comrades by my fixed gaze and sudden change of air, as I have seemed to see, slowly emerging from those imagined solitudes, and heavily crawling along the floor, the ghost of a gigantic tortoise, with 'Memento * * * * *' burning in live letters upon his back.

Sketch Second

TWO SIDES TO A TORTOISE

'Most ugly shapes, and horrible aspects,
Such as Dame Nature selfe mote feare to see,
Or shame, that ever should so fowle defects
From her most cunning hand escaped bee;
All dreadfull pourtraicts of deformitee.
Ne wonder, if these do a man appall;
For all that here at home we dreadfull hold,
Be but as bugs to fearen babes withall,
Compared to the creatures in these isles' entrall.

Feare nought, (then said the Palmer well aviz'd;)
For these same Monsters are not there in deed,
But are into these fearfull shapes disguiz'd.

And lifting up his vertuous staffe on bye,
Then all that dreadfull Armie fast gan flye
Into great Tethys *bosome, where they hidden lye.'*

In view of the description given, may one be gay upon the Encantadas? Yes: that is, find one the gayety, and he will be gay. And indeed, sackcloth and ashes as they are, the isles are not perhaps unmitigated gloom. For while no spectator can deny their claims to a most solemn and superstitious consideration, no more than my firmest resolutions can decline to behold the spectre-tortoise when emerging from its shadowy recess; yet even the tortoise, dark and melancholy as it is upon the back, still possesses a bright side; its calipee or breast-plate being sometimes of a faint yellowish or golden tinge. Moreover, every one knows that tortoises as well as turtles are of such a make, that if you but put them on their backs you thereby expose their bright sides without the possibility of their recovering themselves, and turning into view the other. But after you have done this, and because you have done this, you should not swear that the tortoise has no dark side. Enjoy the bright, keep it turned up perpetually if you can, but be honest, and don't deny the black. Neither should he, who cannot turn the tortoise from its natural position so as to hide the darker and expose his livelier aspect, like a great October pumpkin in the sun, for that cause declare the creature to be one total inky blot. The tortoise is both black and bright. But let us to particulars.

Some months before my first stepping ashore upon the group, my ship was cruising in its close vicinity. One noon we found ourselves off the South Head of Albemarle, and not very far from the land. Partly by way of freak, and partly by way of spying out so strange a country, a boat's crew was sent ashore, with orders to see all they could, and besides, bring back whatever tortoises they could conveniently transport.

Sketch Second

It was after sunset, when the adventurers returned. I looked down over the ship's high side as if looking down over the curb of a well, and dimly saw the damp boat deep in the sea with some unwonted weight. Ropes were dropt over, and presently three huge antediluvian-looking tortoises, after much straining, were landed on deck. They seemed hardly of the seed of earth. We had been broad upon the waters for five long months, a period amply sufficient to make all things of the land wear a fabulous hue to the dreamy mind. Had three Spanish custom-house officers boarded us then, it is not unlikely that I should have curiously stared at them, felt of them, and stroked them much as savages serve civilized guests. But instead of three custom-house officers, behold these really wondrous tortoises – none of your schoolboy mud-turtles – but black as widower's weeds, heavy as chests of plate, with vast shells medallioned and orbed like shields, and dented and blistered like shields that have breasted a battle, shaggy, too, here and there, with dark green moss, and slimy with the spray of the sea. These mystic creatures, suddenly translated by night from unutterable solitudes to our peopled deck, affected me in a manner not easy to unfold. They seemed newly crawled forth from beneath the foundations of the world. Yea, they seemed the identical tortoises whereon the Hindoo plants this total sphere. With a lantern I inspected them more closely. Such worshipful venerableness of aspect! Such furry greenness mantling the rude peelings and healing the fissures of their shattered shells. I no more saw three tortoises. They expanded – became transfigured. I seemed to see three Roman Coliseums in magnificent decay.

Ye oldest inhabitants of this, or any other isle, said I, pray, give me the freedom of your three-walled towns.

The great feeling inspired by these creatures was that of age: – dateless, indefinite endurance. And in fact that any other creature can live and breathe as long as the tortoise of the Encantadas, I will not readily believe. Not to hint of their known capacity of sustaining life, while going without food for an entire year, consider that impregnable armor of their living mail. What other bodily being possesses such a citadel wherein to resist the assaults of Time?

As, lantern in hand, I scraped among the moss and beheld the ancient scars of bruises received in many a sullen fall among the marly mountains of the isle – scars strangely widened, swollen, half obliterate, and yet distorted like those sometimes found in the bark of very hoary trees, I seemed an antiquary of a geologist, studying the bird-tracks and ciphers upon the exhumed slates trod by incredible creatures whose very ghosts are now defunct.

As I lay in my hammock that night, overhead I heard the slow weary draggings of the three ponderous strangers along the encumbered deck. Their stupidity or their resolution was so great, that they never went aside for any impediment. One ceased his movements altogether just before the mid-watch. At sunrise I found him butted like a battering-ram against the immovable foot of the

Sketch Second

foremast, and still striving, tooth and nail, to force the impossible passage. That these tortoises are the victims of a penal, or malignant, or perhaps a downright diabolical enchanter, seems in nothing more likely than in that strange infatuation of hopeless toil which so often possesses them. I have known them in their journeyings ram themselves heroically against rocks, and long abide there, nudging, wriggling, wedging, in order to displace them, and so hold on their inflexible path. Their crowning curse is their drudging impulse to straightforwardness in a belittered world.

Meeting with no such hinderance as their companion did, the other tortoises merely fell foul of small stumbling-blocks – buckets, blocks, and coils of rigging – and at times in the act of crawling over them would slip with an astounding rattle to the deck. Listening to these draggings and concussions, I thought me of the haunt from which they came; an isle full of metallic ravines and gulches, sunk bottomlessly into the hearts of splintered mountains, and covered for many miles with inextricable thickets. I then pictured these three straightforward monsters, century after century, writhing through the shades, grim as blacksmiths; crawling so slowly and ponderously, that not only did toad-stools and all fungus things grow beneath their feet, but a sooty moss sprouted upon their backs. With them I lost myself in volcanic mazes; brushed away endless boughs of rotting thickets; till finally in a dream I found myself sitting crosslegged upon the foremost, a Brahmin similarly mounted upon either side, forming a tripod of foreheads which upheld the universal cope.

Such was the wild nightmare begot by my first impression of the Encantadas tortoise. But next evening, strange to say, I sat down with my shipmates, and made a merry repast from tortoise steaks and tortoise stews; and supper over, out knife, and helped convert the three mighty concave shells into three fanciful soup-tureens, and polished the three flat yellowish calipees into three gorgeous salvers.

Sketch Third

ROCK RODONDO

'*For they this hight* The Rocke of *vile* Reproch,
A daungerous and dreadfull place,
To which nor fish nor fowle did once approch,
But yelling Meawes, with Seagulles hoarse and bace,
And Cormoyrants, with birds of ravenous race,
Which still sate waiting on that dreadfull clift.'

'*With that the rolling sea resounding soft,*
In his big base them fitly answered,
And on the rocke the waves breaking aloft,
A solemne Meane unto them measured.'

'*Then he the boateman bad row easily,*
And let him heare some part of that rare melody.'

'*Suddeinly an innumerable flight*
Of harmefull fowles about them fluttering, cride,
And with their wicked wings them oft did smight,
And sore annoyed, groping in that griesly night.'

'*Even all the nation of unfortunate*
And fatall birds about them flocked were.'

Herman Melville

To go up into a high stone tower is not only a very fine thing in itself, but the very best mode of gaining a comprehensive view of the region round about. It is all the better if this tower stand solitary and alone, like that mysterious Newport one, or else be sole survivor of some perished castle.

Now, with reference to the Enchanted Isles, we are fortunately supplied with just such a noble point of observation in a remarkable rock, from its peculiar figure called of old by the Spaniards, Rock Rodondo, or Round Rock. Some two hundred and fifty feet high, rising straight from the sea ten miles from land, with the whole mountainous group to the south and east, Rock Rodondo occupies, on a large scale, very much the position which the famous Campanile or detached Bell Tower of St Mark does with respect to the tangled group of hoary edifices around it.

Ere ascending, however, to gaze abroad upon the Encantadas, this sea-tower itself claims attention. It is visible at the distance of thirty miles; and, fully participating in that enchantment which pervades the group, when first seen afar invariably is mistaken for a sail. Four leagues away, of a golden, hazy noon, it seems some Spanish Admiral's ship, stacked up with glittering canvas. Sail ho! Sail ho! Sail ho! from all three masts. But coming nigh, the enchanted frigate is transformed apace into a craggy keep.

My first visit to the spot was made in the gray of the morning. With a view of fishing, we had lowered three

Sketch Third

boats, and pulling some two miles from our vessel, found ourselves just before dawn of day close under the moon-shadow of Rodondo. Its aspect was heightened, and yet softened, by the strange double twilight of the hour. The great full moon burnt in the low west like a half-spent beacon, casting a soft mellow tinge upon the sea like that cast by a waning fire of embers upon a midnight hearth; while along the entire east the invisible sun sent pallid intimations of his coming. The wind was light; the waves languid; the stars twinkled with a faint effulgence; all nature seemed supine with the long night watch, and half-suspended in jaded expectation of the sun. This was the critical hour to catch Rodondo in his perfect mood. The twilight was just enough to reveal every striking point, without tearing away the dim investiture of wonder.

From a broken stair-like base, washed, as the steps of a water-palace, by the waves, the tower rose in entablatures of strata to a shaven summit. These uniform layers, which compose the mass, form its most peculiar feature. For at their lines of junction they project flatly into encircling shelves, from top to bottom, rising one above another in graduated series. And as the eaves of any old barn or abbey are alive with swallows, so were all these rocky ledges with unnumbered sea-fowl. Eaves upon eaves, and nests upon nests. Here and there were long bird-lime streaks of a ghostly white staining the tower from sea to air, readily accounting for its sail-like look afar. All would have been bewitchingly quiescent, were it not for the demoniac din created by the birds. Not only were the eaves rustling with them, but they flew densely overhead, spreading themselves into a winged and continually shifting canopy. The tower is the resort of aquatic birds for hundreds of leagues around. To the north, to the east, to the west, stretches nothing but eternal ocean; so that the man-of-war hawk coming from the coasts of North America, Polynesia, or Peru, makes his first land at Rodondo. And yet though Rodondo be terra-firma, no land-bird ever lighted on it. Fancy a red-robin or a canary there! What a falling into the hands of the Philistines, when the poor warbler should be surrounded by such locust-flights of strong bandit birds, with long bills cruel as daggers.

I know not where one can better study the Natural History of strange sea-fowl than at Rodondo. It is the aviary of Ocean. Birds light here which never touched mast or tree; hermit-birds, which ever fly alone; cloud-birds, familiar with unpierced zones of air.

Let us first glance low down to the lowermost shelf of all, which is the widest, too, and but a little space from high-water mark. What outlandish beings are these? Erect as men, but hardly as symmetrical, they stand all round the rock like sculptured caryatides, supporting the next range of eaves above. Their bodies are grotesquely misshapen; their bills short; their feet seemingly legless; while the members at their sides are neither fin, wing, nor arm. And truly neither fish, flesh, nor fowl is the penguin; as an edible, pertaining neither to Carnival nor Lent; without exception the most ambiguous and least lovely

Sketch Third

creature yet discovered by man. Though dabbling in all three elements, and indeed possessing some rudimental claims to all, the penguin is at home in none. On land it stumps; afloat it sculls; in the air it flops. As if ashamed of her failure, Nature keeps this ungainly child hidden away at the ends of the earth, in the Straits of Magellan, and on the abased sea-story of Rodondo.

But look, what are yon woebegone regiments drawn up on the next shelf above? what rank and file of large strange fowl? what sea Friars of Orders Gray? Pelicans. Their elongated bills, and heavy leathern pouches suspended thereto, give them the most lugubrious expression. A pensive race, they stand for hours together without motion. Their dull, ashy plumage imparts an aspect as if they had been powdered over with cinders. A penitential bird, indeed, fitly haunting the shores of the clinkered Encantadas, whereon tormented Job himself might have well sat down and scraped himself with potsherds.

Higher up now we mark the gony, or gray albatross, anomalously so called, an unsightly, unpoetic bird, unlike its storied kinsman, which is the snow-white ghost of the haunted Capes of Hope and Horn.

As we still ascend from shelf to shelf, we find the tenants of the tower serially disposed in order of their magnitude: – gannets, black and speckled haglets, jays, sea-hens, sperm-whale-birds, gulls of all varieties: – thrones, princedoms, powers, dominating one above another in senatorial array; while, sprinkled over all, like an ever-repeated fly in a great piece of broidery, the stormy petrel or Mother Cary's chicken sounds his continual challenge and alarm. That this mysterious humming-bird of ocean – which, had it but brilliancy of hue, might, from its evanescent liveliness, be almost called its butterfly, yet whose chirrup under the stern is ominous to mariners as to the peasant the death-tick sounding from behind the chimney jamb – should have its special haunt at the Encantadas, contributes, in the seaman's mind, not a little to their dreary spell.

As day advances the dissonant din augments. With ear-splitting cries the wild birds celebrate their matins. Each moment, flights push from the tower, and join the aerial choir hovering overhead, while their places below are supplied by darting myriads. But down through all this discord of commotion, I hear clear, silver, bugle-like notes unbrokenly falling, like oblique lines of swift-slanting rain in a cascading shower. I gaze far up, and behold a snow-white angelic thing, with one long, lance-like feather thrust out behind. It is the bright, inspiriting chanticleer of ocean, the beauteous bird, from its bestirring whistle of musical invocation, fitly styled the 'Boatswain's Mate.'

The winged, life-clouding Rodondo had its full counterpart in the finny hosts which peopled the waters at its base. Below the water-line, the rock seemed one honeycomb of grottoes, affording labyrinthine lurking-places for swarms of fairy fish. All were strange; many exceedingly beautiful; and would have well graced the costliest glass globes in which gold-fish are kept for a show.

Sketch Third

Nothing was more striking than the complete novelty of many individuals of this multitude. Here hues were seen as yet unpainted, and figures which are unengraved.

To show the multitude, avidity, and nameless fearlessness and tameness of these fish, let me say, that often, marking through clear spaces of water – temporarily made so by the concentric dartings of the fish above the surface – certain larger and less unwary wights, which swam slow and deep; our anglers would cautiously essay to drop their lines down to these last. But in vain; there was no passing the uppermost zone. No sooner did the hook touch the sea, than a hundred infatuates contended for the honor of capture. Poor fish of Rodondo! in your victimized confidence, you are of the number of those who inconsiderately trust, while they do not understand, human nature.

But the dawn is now fairly day. Band after band, the sea-fowl sail away to forage the deep for their food. The tower is left solitary, save the fish-caves at its base. Its bird-lime gleams in the golden rays like the whitewash of a tall light-house, or the lofty sails of a cruiser. This moment, doubtless, while we know it to be a dead desert rock, other voyagers are taking oaths it is a glad populous ship.

But ropes now, and let us ascend. Yet soft, this is not so easy.

Sketch Fourth

A PISGAH VIEW FROM THE ROCK

'That done, he leads him to the highest Mount,
From whence, far off he unto him did shew . . .'

If you seek to ascend Rock Rodondo, take the following prescription. Go three voyages round the world as a main-royal-man of the tallest frigate that floats; then serve a year or two apprenticeship to the guides who conduct strangers up the Peak of Teneriffe; and as many more respectively to a rope-dancer, an Indian juggler, and a chamois. This done, come and be rewarded by the view from our tower. How we get there, we alone know. If we sought to tell others, what the wiser were they? Suffice it, that here at the summit you and I stand. Does any balloonist, does the outlooking man in the moon, take a broader view of space? Much thus, one fancies, looks the universe from Milton's celestial battlements. A boundless watery Kentucky. Here Daniel Boone would have dwelt content.

Never heed for the present yonder Burnt District of the Enchanted Isles. Look edgeways, as it were, past them, to the South. You see nothing; but permit me to point

Sketch Fourth

out the direction, if not the place, of certain interesting objects in the vast sea, which, kissing this tower's base, we behold unscrolling itself towards the Antarctic Pole.

We stand now ten miles from the Equator. Yonder, to the East, some six hundred miles, lies the continent; this Rock being just about on the parallel of Quito.

Observe another thing here. We are at one of three uninhabited clusters, which, at pretty nearly uniform distances from the main, sentinel, at long intervals from each other, the entire coast of South America. In a peculiar manner, also, they terminate the South American character of country. Of the unnumbered Polynesian chains to the westward, not one partakes of the qualities of the Encantadas or Gallipagos, the isles of St Felix and St Ambrose, the isles Juan Fernandez and Massafuero. Of the first, it needs not here to speak. The second lie a little above the Southern Tropic; lofty, inhospitable, and uninhabitable rocks, one of which, presenting two round hummocks connected by a low reef, exactly resembles a huge double-headed shot. The last lie in the latitude of 33°; high, wild and cloven. Juan Fernandez is sufficiently famous without further description. Massafuero is a Spanish name, expressive of the fact, that the isle so called lies *more without*, that is further off the main than its neighbor Juan. This isle Massafuero has a very imposing aspect at a distance of eight or ten miles. Approached in one direction, in cloudy weather, its great overhanging height and rugged contour, and more especially a peculiar slope of its broad summits, give it much the air of a vast iceberg drifting in tremendous poise. Its sides are split with dark cavernous recesses, as an old cathedral with its gloomy lateral chapels. Drawing nigh one of these gorges from sea, after a long voyage, and beholding some tatterdemalion outlaw, staff in hand, descending its steep rocks toward you, conveys a very queer emotion to a lover of the picturesque.

On fishing parties from ships, at various times, I have chanced to visit each of these groups. The impression they give to the stranger pulling close up in his boat under their grim cliffs is, that surely he must be their first discoverer, such, for the most part, is the unimpaired ... silence and solitude. And here, by the way, the mode in which these isles were really first lighted upon by Europeans is not unworthy of mention, especially as what is about to be said, likewise applies to the original discovery of our Encantadas.

Prior to the year 1563, the voyages made by Spanish ships from Peru to Chili, were full of difficulty. Along this coast, the winds from the South most generally prevail; and it had been an invariable custom to keep close in with the land, from a superstitious conceit on the part of the Spaniards, that were they to lose sight of it, the eternal trade-wind would waft them into unending waters, from whence would be no return. Here, involved among tortuous capes and headlands, shoals and reefs, beating, too, against a continual head wind, often light, and sometimes for days and weeks sunk into utter calm, the provincial vessels, in many cases, suffered the extremest hardships,

Sketch Fourth

in passages, which at the present day seem to have been incredibly protracted. There is on record in some collections of nautical disasters, an account of one of these ships, which, starting on a voyage whose duration was estimated at ten days, spent four months at sea, and indeed never again entered harbor, for in the end she was cast away. Singular to tell, this craft never encountered a gale, but was the vexed sport of malicious calms and currents. Thrice, out of provisions, she put back to an intermediate port, and started afresh, but only yet again to return. Frequent fogs enveloped her; so that no observation could be had of her place, and once, when all hands were joyously anticipating sight of their destination, lo! the vapors lifted and disclosed the mountains from which they had taken their first departure. In the like deceptive vapors she at last struck upon a reef, whence ensued a long series of calamities too sad to detail.

It was the famous pilot, Juan Fernandez, immortalized by the island named after him, who put an end to these coasting tribulations, by boldly venturing the experiment – as De Gama did before him with respect to Europe – of standing broad out from land. Here he found the winds favorable for getting to the South, and by running westward till beyond the influences of the trades, he regained the coast without difficulty; making the passage which, though in a high degree circuitous, proved far more expeditious than the nominally direct one. Now it was upon these new tracks, and about the year 1670, or thereabouts, that the Enchanted Isles, and the rest of the sentinel groups, as they may be called, were discovered. Though I know of no account as to whether any of them were found inhabited or no, it may be reasonably concluded that they have been immemorial solitudes. But let us return to Rodondo.

Southwest from our tower lies all Polynesia, hundreds of leagues away; but straight West, on the precise line of his parallel, no land rises till your keel is beached upon the Kingsmills, a nice little sail of, say 5000 miles.

Having thus by such distant references – with Rodondo the only possible ones – settled our relative place on the sea, let us consider objects not quite so remote. Behold the grim and charred Enchanted Isles. This nearest crater-shaped headland is part of Albemarle, the largest of the group, being some sixty miles or more long, and fifteen broad. Did you ever lay eye on the real genuine Equator? Have you ever, in the largest sense, toed the Line? Well, that identical crater-shaped headland there, all yellow lava, is cut by the Equator exactly as a knife cuts straight through the centre of a pumpkin pie. If you could only see so far, just to one side of that same headland, across yon low dikey ground, you would catch sight of the isle of Narborough, the loftiest land of the cluster; no soil whatever; one seamed clinker from top to bottom; abounding in black caves like smithies; its metallic shore ringing under foot like plates of iron; its central volcanoes standing grouped like a gigantic chimney-stack.

Narborough and Albemarle are neighbors after a quite

Sketch Fourth

curious fashion. A familiar diagram will illustrate this strange neighborhood:

Cut a channel at the above letter joint, and the middle transverse limb is Narborough, and all the rest is Albemarle. Volcanic Narborough lies in the black jaws of Albemarle like a wolf's red tongue in his open mouth.

If now you desire the population of Albemarle, I will give you, in round numbers, the statistics, according to the most reliable estimates made upon the spot:

Men,	none
Ant-eaters,	unknown
Man-haters,	unknown
Lizards,	500,000
Snakes,	500,000
Spiders,	10,000,000
Salamanders,	unknown
Devils,	do.
Making a clean total of	11,000,000

exclusive of an incomputable host of fiends, ant-eaters, man-haters, and salamanders.

Albemarle opens his mouth towards the setting sun. His distended jaws form a great bay, which Narborough, his tongue, divides into halves, one whereof is called Weather Bay, the other Lee Bay; while the volcanic promontories, terminating his coasts, are styled South Head and North Head. I note this, because these bays are famous in the annals of the Sperm Whale Fishery. The whales come here at certain seasons to calve. When ships first cruised hereabouts, I am told, they used to blockade the entrance of Lee Bay, when their boats going round by Weather Bay, passed through Narborough channel, and so had the Leviathans very neatly in a pen.

The day after we took fish at the base of this Round Tower, we had a fine wind, and shooting round the north headland, suddenly descried a fleet of full thirty sail, all beating to windward like a squadron in line. A brave sight as ever man saw. A most harmonious concord of rushing keels. Their thirty kelsons hummed like thirty harp-strings, and looked as straight whilst they left their parallel traces on the sea. But there proved too many hunters for the game. The fleet broke up, and went their separate ways out of sight, leaving my own ship and two trim gentlemen of London. These last, finding no luck either, likewise vanished; and Lee Bay, with all its appurtenances, and without a rival, devolved to us.

The way of cruising here is this. You keep hovering about the entrance of the bay, in one beat and out the next. But at times – not always, as in other parts of the group – a racehorse of a current sweeps right across its mouth. So, with all sails set, you carefully ply your tacks. How often, standing at the foremast head at sunrise, with our patient prow pointed in between these isles, did I gaze upon that land, not of cakes, but of clinkers, not of streams of sparkling water, but arrested torrents of tormented lava.

As the ship runs in from the open sea, Narborough

Sketch Fourth

presents its side in one dark craggy mass, soaring up some five or six thousand feet, at which point it hoods itself in heavy clouds, whose lowest level fold is as clearly defined against the rocks as the snow-line against the Andes. There is dire mischief going on in that upper dark. There toil the demons of fire, who, at intervals, irradiate the nights with a strange spectral illumination for miles and miles around, but unaccompanied by any further demonstration; or else, suddenly announce themselves by terrific concussions, and the full drama of a volcanic eruption. The blacker that cloud by day, the more may you look for light by night. Often whalemen have found themselves cruising nigh that burning mountain when all aglow with a ball-room blaze. Or, rather, glass-works, you may call this same vitreous isle of Narborough, with its tall chimney-stacks.

Where we still stand, here on Rodondo, we cannot see all the other isles, but it is a good place from which to point out where they lie. Yonder, though, to the E.N.E., I mark a distant dusky ridge. It is Abington Isle, one of the most northerly of the group; so solitary, remote, and blank, it looks like No-Man's Land seen off our northern shore. I doubt whether two human beings ever touched upon that spot. So far as yon Abington Isle is concerned, Adam and his billions of posterity remain uncreated.

Ranging south of Abington, and quite out of sight behind the long spine of Albemarle, lies James's Isle, so called by the early Buccaneers after the luckless Stuart, Duke of York. Observe here, by the way, that, excepting the isles particularized in comparatively recent times, and which mostly received the names of famous Admirals, the Encantadas were first christened by the Spaniards; but these Spanish names were generally effaced on English charts by the subsequent christenings of the Buccaneers, who, in the middle of the seventeenth century, called them after English noblemen and kings. Of these loyal freebooters and the things which associate their name with the Encantadas, we shall hear anon. Nay, for one little item, immediately; for between James's Isle and Albemarle, lies a fantastic islet, strangely known as 'Cowley's Enchanted Isle.' But, as all the group is deemed enchanted, the reason must be given for the spell within a spell involved by this particular designation. The name was bestowed by that excellent Buccaneer himself, on his first visit here. Speaking in his published voyages of this spot, he says – 'My fancy led me to call it Cowley's Enchanted Island, for we having had a sight of it upon several points of the compass, it appeared always in as many different forms; sometimes like a ruined fortification; upon another point like a great city, etc.' No wonder though, that among the Encantadas all sorts of ocular deceptions and mirages should be met.

That Cowley linked his name with this self-transforming and bemocking isle, suggests the possibility that it conveyed to him some meditative image of himself. At least, as is not impossible, if he were any relative of the mildly-thoughtful and self-upbraiding poet Cowley, who lived about his time, the conceit might seem not unwarranted; for that sort of thing evinced in the naming of this isle runs in the blood, and may be seen in pirates as in poets.

Still south of James's Isle lie Jervis Isle, Duncan Isle, Crossman's Isle, Brattle Isle, Wood's Isle, Chatham Isle, and various lesser isles, for the most part an archipelago of aridities, without inhabitant, history, or hope of either in all time to come. But not far from these are rather notable isles – Barrington, Charles's, Norfolk, and Hood's. Succeeding chapters will reveal some ground for their notability.

Sketch Fifth

THE FRIGATE, AND SHIP FLYAWAY

'Looking far foorth into the Ocean wide,
A goodly ship with banners bravely dight,
And flag in her top-gallant I espide,
Through the maine sea making her merry flight.'

Ere quitting Rodondo, it must not be omitted that here, in 1813, the U.S. frigate *Essex*, Captain David Porter, came near leaving her bones. Lying becalmed one morning with a strong current setting her rapidly towards the rock, a strange sail was descried, which – not out of keeping with alleged enchantments of the neighborhood – seemed to be staggering under a violent wind, while the frigate lay lifeless as if spell-bound. But a light air springing up, all sail was made by the frigate in chase of the enemy, as supposed – he being deemed an English whale-ship – but the rapidity of the current was so great, that soon all sight was lost of him; and, at meridian, the *Essex*, spite of her drags, was driven so close under the foam-lashed cliffs of Rodondo that, for a time, all hands gave her up. A smart breeze, however, at last helped her off, though the escape was so critical as to seem almost miraculous.

Sketch Fifth

Thus saved from destruction herself, she now made use of that salvation to destroy the other vessel, if possible. Renewing the chase in the direction in which the stranger had disappeared, sight was caught of him the following morning. Upon being descried he hoisted American colors and stood away from the *Essex*. A calm ensued; when, still confident that the stranger was an Englishman, Porter dispatched a cutter, not to board the enemy, but drive back his boats engaged in towing him. The cutter succeeded. Cutters were subsequently sent to capture him; the stranger now showing English colors in place of American. But, when the frigate's boats were within a short distance of their hoped-for prize, another sudden breeze sprang up; the stranger, under all sail, bore off to the westward, and, ere night, was hull down ahead of the *Essex*, which, all this time, lay perfectly becalmed.

This enigmatic craft – American in the morning, and English in the evening – her sails full of wind in a calm – was never again beheld. An enchanted ship no doubt. So, at least, the sailors swore.

This cruise of the *Essex* in the Pacific during the war of 1812, is, perhaps, the strangest and most stirring to be found in the history of the American navy. She captured the furthest wandering vessels; visited the remotest seas and isles; long hovered in the charmed vicinity of the enchanted group; and, finally, valiantly gave up the ghost fighting two English frigates in the harbor of Valparaiso. Mention is made of her here for the same reason that the Buccaneers will likewise receive record; because, like them, by long cruising among the isles, tortoise-hunting upon their shores, and generally exploring them; for these and other reasons, the *Essex* is peculiarly associated with the Encantadas.

Here be it said that you have but three eye-witness authorities worth mentioning touching the Enchanted Isles: – Cowley, the Buccaneer (1684); Colnet, the whaling-ground explorer (1798); Porter, the post captain (1813). Other than these you have but barren, bootless allusions from some few passing voyagers or compilers.

Sketch Sixth

BARRINGTON ISLE AND THE BUCCANEERS

> *'Let us all servile base subiection scorne;*
> *And as we bee sonnes of the earth so wide,*
> *Let us our fathers heritage divide,*
> *And chalenge to our selves our portions dew*
> *Of all the patrimonie, which a few*
> *Now hold in hugger mugger in their hand.'*

> *'Lords of the world, and so will wander free*
> *Where so us listeth, uncontrol'd of anie.'*

> *'How bravely now we live, how jocund, how near the first inheritance, without fear, how free from little troubles!'*

Near two centuries ago Barrington Isle was the resort of that famous wing of the West Indian Buccaneers, which, upon their repulse from the Cuban waters, crossing the Isthmus of Darien, ravaged the Pacific side of the Spanish colonies, and, with the regularity and timing of a modern mail, waylaid the royal treasure-ships plying between Manilla and Acapulco. After the toils of piratic war, here they came to say their prayers, enjoy their free-and-easies, count their crackers from the cask, their doubloons from the keg, and measure their silks of Asia with long Toledos for their yard-sticks.

As a secure retreat, an undiscoverable hiding-place, no spot in those days could have been better fitted. In the centre of a vast and silent sea, but very little traversed – surrounded by islands, whose inhospitable aspect might well drive away the chance navigator – and yet within a few days' sail of the opulent countries which they made their prey – the unmolested Buccaneers found here that tranquillity which they fiercely denied to every civilized harbor in that part of the world. Here, after stress of weather, or a temporary drubbing at the hands of their vindictive foes, or in swift flight with golden booty, those old marauders came, and lay snugly out of all harm's reach. But not only was the place a harbor of safety, and a bower of ease, but for utility in other things it was most admirable.

Barrington Isle is, in many respects, singularly adapted to careening, refitting, refreshing, and other seamen's purposes. Not only has it good water, and good anchorage, well sheltered from all winds by the high land of Albemarle, but it is the least unproductive isle of the group. Tortoises good for food, trees good for fuel, and long grass good for bedding, abound here, and there are pretty natural walks, and several landscapes to be seen. Indeed, though in its locality belonging to the Enchanted group, Barrington Isle is so unlike most of its neighbors, that it would hardly seem of kin to them.

Sketch Sixth

'I once landed on its western side,' says a sentimental voyager long ago, 'where it faces the black buttress of Albemarle. I walked beneath groves of trees – not very lofty, and not palm trees, or orange trees, or peach trees, to be sure – but, for all that, after long sea-faring, very beautiful to walk under, even though they supplied no fruit. And here, in calm spaces at the heads of glades, and on the shaded tops of slopes commanding the most quiet scenery – what do you think I saw? Seats which might have served Brahmins and presidents of peace societies. Fine old ruins of what had once been symmetric lounges of stone and turf, they bore every mark both of artificialness and age, and were, undoubtedly, made by the Buccaneers. One had been a long sofa, with back and arms, just such a sofa as the poet Gray might have loved to throw himself upon, his Crébillon in hand.

'Though they sometimes tarried here for months at a time, and used the spot for a storing-place for spare spars, sails, and casks; yet it is highly improbable that the Buccaneers ever erected dwelling-houses upon the isle. They never were here except their ships remained, and they would most likely have slept on board. I mention this, because I cannot avoid the thought, that it is hard to impute the construction of these romantic seats to any other motive than one of pure peacefulness and kindly fellowship with nature. That the Buccaneers perpetrated the greatest outrages is very true – that some of them were mere cut-throats is not to be denied; but we know that here and there among their host was a Dampier, a Wafer, and a Cowley, and likewise other men, whose worst reproach was their desperate fortunes – whom persecution, or adversity, or secret and unavengeable wrongs, had driven from Christian society to seek the melancholy solitude or the guilty adventures of the sea. At any rate, long as those ruins of seats on Barrington remain, the most singular monuments are furnished to the fact, that all of the Buccaneers were not unmitigated monsters.

'But during my ramble on the isle I was not long in discovering other tokens, of things quite in accordance with those wild traits, popularly, and no doubt truly enough, imputed to the freebooters at large. Had I picked up old sails and rusty hoops I would only have thought of the ship's carpenter and cooper. But I found old cutlasses and daggers reduced to mere threads of rust, which, doubtless, had stuck between Spanish ribs ere now. These were signs of the murderer and robber; the reveler likewise had left his trace. Mixed with shells, fragments of broken jars were lying here and there, high up upon the beach. They were precisely like the jars now used upon the Spanish coast for the wine and Pisco spirits of that country.

'With a rusty dagger-fragment in one hand, and a bit of a wine-jar in another, I sat me down on the ruinous green sofa I have spoken of, and bethought me long and deeply of these same Buccaneers. Could it be possible, that they robbed and murdered one day, reveled the next, and rested themselves by turning meditative philosophers, rural poets, and seat-builders on the third? Not very improbable, after all. For consider the vacillations of a man. Still, strange as it may seem, I must also abide by the more charitable thought; namely, that among these adventurers were some gentlemanly, companionable souls, capable of genuine tranquillity and virtue.'

Sketch Seventh

CHARLES'S ISLE AND THE DOG-KING

'Loe with outragious cry
A thousand villeins round about him swarmd
Out of the rockes and caves adjoining nye,
Vile caytive wretches, ragged, rude, deformd,
All threatning death, all in straunge manner armd,
Some with unweldy clubs, some with long speares,
Some rusty knives, some staves in fire warmd.'

'We will not be of anie occupation,
Let such vile vassals, borne to base vocation
Drudge in the world, and for their living droyle
Which have no wit to live withouten toyle.'

Southwest of Barrington lies Charles's Isle. And hereby hangs a history which I gathered long ago from a shipmate learned in all the lore of outlandish life.

During the successful revolt of the Spanish provinces from Old Spain, there fought on behalf of Peru a certain Creole adventurer from Cuba, who, by his bravery and good fortune, at length advanced himself to high rank in the patriot army. The war being ended, Peru found itself

Sketch Seventh

like many valorous gentlemen, free and independent enough, but with few shot in the locker. In other words, Peru had not wherewithal to pay off its troops. But the Creole – I forget his name – volunteered to take his pay in lands. So they told him he might have his pick of the Enchanted Isles, which were then, as they still remain, the nominal appanage of Peru. The soldier straightaway embarks thither, explores the group, returns to Callao, and says he will take a deed of Charles's Isle. Moreover, this deed must stipulate that henceforth Charles's Isle is not only the sole property of the Creole, but is for ever free of Peru, even as Peru of Spain. To be short, this adventurer procures himself to be made in effect Supreme Lord of the Island, one of the princes of the powers of the earth.*

He now sends forth a proclamation inviting subjects to his as yet unpopulated kingdom. Some eighty souls, men and women, respond; and being provided by their leader with necessaries, and tools of various sorts, together with a few cattle and goats, take ship for the promised land; the last arrival on board, prior to sailing, being the Creole himself, accompanied, strange to say, by a disciplined cavalry company of large grim dogs. These, it was observed on the

---

* The American Spaniards have long been in the habit of making presents of islands to deserving individuals. The pilot Juan Fernandez procured a deed of the isle named after him, and for some years resided there before Selkirk came. It is supposed, however, that he eventually contracted the blues upon his princely property, for after a time he returned to the main, and as report goes, became a very garrulous barber in the city of Lima.

passage, refusing to consort with the emigrants, remained aristocratically grouped around their master on the elevated quarter-deck, casting disdainful glances forward upon the inferior rabble there; much as, from the ramparts, the soldiers of a garrison, thrown into a conquered town, eye the inglorious citizen-mob over which they are set to watch.

Now Charles's Isle not only resembles Barrington Isle in being much more inhabitable than other parts of the group, but it is double the size of Barrington, say forty or fifty miles in circuit.

Safely debarked at last, the company, under direction of their lord and patron, forthwith proceeded to build their capital city. They make considerable advance in the way of walls of clinkers, and lava floors, nicely sanded with cinders. On the least barren hills they pasture their cattle, while the goats, adventurers by nature, explore the far inland solitudes for a scanty livelihood of lofty herbage. Meantime, abundance of fish and tortoises supply their other wants.

The disorders incident to settling all primitive regions, in the present case were heightened by the peculiarly untoward character of many of the pilgrims. His Majesty was forced at last to proclaim martial law, and actually hunted and shot with his own hand several of his rebellious subjects, who, with most questionable intentions, had clandestinely encamped in the interior, whence they stole by night, to prowl barefooted on tiptoe round the precincts of the lava-palace. It is to be remarked, however, that prior to such stern proceedings, the more reliable

Sketch Seventh

men had been judiciously picked out for an infantry body-guard, subordinate to the cavalry body-guard of dogs. But the stage of politics in this unhappy nation may be somewhat imagined, from the circumstances that all who were not of the body-guard were downright plotters and malignant traitors. At length the death penalty was tacitly abolished, owing to the timely thought, that were strict sportsman's justice to be dispensed among such subjects, ere long the Nimrod King would have little or no remaining game to shoot. The human part of the life-guard was now disbanded, and set to work cultivating the soil, and raising potatoes; the regular army now solely consisting of the dog-regiment. These, as I have heard, were of a singularly ferocious character, though by severe training rendered docile to their master. Armed to the teeth, the Creole now goes in state, surrounded by his canine janizaries, whose terrific bayings prove quite as serviceable as bayonets in keeping down the surgings of revolt.

But the census of the isle, sadly lessened by the dispensation of justice, and not materially recruited by matrimony, began to fill his mind with sad mistrust. Some way the population must be increased. Now, from its possessing a little water, and its comparative pleasantness of aspect, Charles's Isle at this period was occasionally visited by foreign whalers. These His Majesty had always levied upon for port charges, thereby contributing to his revenue. But now he had additional designs. By insidious arts he, from time to time, cajoles certain sailors to desert their ships, and enlist beneath his banner. Soon as missed, their captains crave permission to go and hunt them up. Whereupon His Majesty first hides them very carefully away, and then freely permits the search. In consequence, the delinquents are never found, and the ships retire without them.

Thus, by a two-edged policy of this crafty monarch, foreign nations were crippled in the number of their subjects, and his own were greatly multiplied. He particularly petted these renegado strangers. But alas for the deep-laid schemes of ambitious princes, and alas for the vanity of glory. As the foreign-born Pretorians, unwisely introduced into the Roman state, and still more unwisely made favorites of the Emperors, at last insulted and overturned the throne, even so these lawless mariners, with all the rest of the body-guard and all the populace, broke out into a terrible mutiny, and defied their master. He marched against them with all his dogs. A deadly battle ensued upon the beach. It raged for three hours, the dogs fighting with determined valor, and the sailors reckless of everything but victory. Three men and thirteen dogs were left dead upon the field, many on both sides were wounded, and the king was forced to fly with the remainder of his canine regiment. The enemy pursued, stoning the dogs with their master into the wilderness of the interior. Discontinuing the pursuit, the victors returned to the village on the shore, stove the spirit casks, and proclaimed a Republic. The dead men were interred with the honors of war, and the dead dogs ignominiously thrown into the sea. At last, forced by stress of suffering, the fugitive Creole came down from the hills and offered to treat for

Sketch Seventh

peace. But the rebels refused it on any other terms than his unconditional banishment. Accordingly, the next ship that arrived carried away the ex-king to Peru.

The history of the king of Charles's Island furnishes another illustration of the difficulty of colonizing barren islands with unprincipled pilgrims.

Doubtless for a long time the exiled monarch, pensively ruralizing in Peru, which afforded him a safe asylum in his calamity, watched every arrival from the Encantadas, to hear news of the failure of the Republic, the consequent penitence of the rebels, and his own recall to royalty. Doubtless he deemed the Republic but a miserable experiment which would soon explode. But no, the insurgents had confederated themselves into a democracy neither Grecian, Roman, nor American. Nay, it was no democracy at all, but a permanent *Riotocracy*, which gloried in having no law but lawlessness. Great inducements being offered to deserters, their ranks were swelled by accessions of scamps from every ship which touched their shores. Charles's Island was proclaimed the asylum of the oppressed of all navies. Each runaway tar was hailed as a martyr in the cause of freedom, and became immediately installed a ragged citizen of this universal nation. In vain the captains of absconding seamen strove to regain them. Their new compatriots were ready to give any number of ornamental eyes in their behalf. They had few cannon, but their fists were not to be trifled with. So at last it came to pass that no vessels acquainted with the character of that country durst touch there, however sorely in want of refreshment. It became Anathema – a sea Alsatia – the unassailed lurking-place of all sorts of desperadoes, who in the name of liberty did just what they pleased. They continually fluctuated in their numbers. Sailors, deserting ships at other islands, or in boats at sea anywhere in that vicinity, steered for Charles's Isle, as to their sure home of refuge; while, sated with the life of the isle, numbers from time to time crossed the water to the neighboring ones, and there presenting themselves to strange captains as shipwrecked seamen, often succeeded in getting on board vessels bound to the Spanish coast, and having a compassionate purse made up for them on landing there.

One warm night during my first visit to the group, our ship was floating along in languid stillness, when some one on the forecastle shouted 'Light ho!' We looked and saw a beacon burning on some obscure land off the beam. Our third mate was not intimate with this part of the world. Going to the captain he said, 'Sir, shall I put off in a boat? These must be shipwrecked men.'

The captain laughed rather grimly, as, shaking his fist towards the beacon, he rapped out an oath, and said – 'No, no, you precious rascals, you don't juggle one of my boats ashore this blessed night. You do well, you thieves – you do benevolently to hoist a light yonder as on a dangerous shoal. It tempts no wise man to pull off and see what's the matter, but bids him steer small and keep off shore – that is Charles's Island; brace up, Mr Mate, and keep the light astern.'

Sketch Tenth

RUNAWAYS, CASTAWAYS, SOLITARIES,
GRAVE-STONES, ETC.

'And all about old stockes and stubs of trees,
Whereon nor fruit, nor leafe was ever seene,
Did hang upon the ragged knotty knees,
On which had many wretches hanged beene.'

Some relics of the hut of Oberlus partially remain to this day at the head of the clinkered valley. Nor does the stranger, wandering among other of the Enchanted Isles, fail to stumble upon still other solitary abodes, long abandoned to the tortoise and the lizard. Probably few parts of earth have, in modern times, sheltered so many solitaries. The reason is, that these isles are situated in a distant sea, and the vessels which occasionally visit them are mostly all whalers, or ships bound on dreary and protracted voyages, exempting them in a good degree from both the oversight and the memory of human law. Such is the character of some commanders and some seamen, that under these untoward circumstances, it is quite impossible but that scenes of unpleasantness and discord should occur between them. A sullen hatred of the tyrannic ship will seize the sailor, and he gladly exchanges it for isles, which, though blighted as by a continual sirocco and burning breeze, still offer him, in their labyrinthine interior, a retreat beyond the possibility of capture. To flee the ship in any Peruvian or Chilian port, even the smallest and most rustical, is not unattended with great risk of apprehension, not to speak of jaguars. A reward of five pesos sends fifty dastardly Spaniards into the wood, who, with long knives, scour them day and night in eager hopes of securing their prey. Neither is it, in general, much easier to escape pursuit at the isles of Polynesia. Those of them which have felt a civilizing influence present the same difficulty to the runaway with the Peruvian ports, the advanced natives being quite as mercenary and keen of knife and scent as the retrograde Spaniards; while, owing to the bad odor in which all Europeans lie, in the minds of aboriginal savages who have chanced to hear aught of them, to desert the ship among primitive Polynesians, is, in most cases, a hope not unforlorn. Hence the Enchanted Isles become the voluntary tarrying places of all sorts of refugees; some of whom too sadly experience the fact, that flight from tyranny does not of itself insure a safe asylum, far less a happy home.

Moreover, it has not seldom happened that hermits have been made upon the isles by the accidents incident to tortoise-hunting. The interior of most of them is tangled and difficult of passage beyond description; the air is sultry and stifling; an intolerable thirst is provoked, for

Sketch Tenth

which no running stream offers its kind relief. In a few hours, under an equatorial sun, reduced by these causes to entire exhaustion, woe betide the straggler at the Enchanted Isles! Their extent is such as to forbid an adequate search, unless weeks are devoted to it. The impatient ship waits a day or two; when, the missing man remaining undiscovered, up goes a stake on the beach, with a letter of regret, and a keg of crackers and another of water tied to it, and away sails the craft.

Nor have there been wanting instances where the inhumanity of some captains has led them to wreak a secure revenge upon seamen who have given their caprice or pride some singular offense. Thrust ashore upon the scorching marl, such mariners are abandoned to perish outright, unless by solitary labors they succeed in discovering some precious dribblets of moisture oozing from a rock or stagnant in a mountain pool.

I was well acquainted with a man, who, lost upon the Isle of Narborough, was brought to such extremes by thirst, that at last he only saved his life by taking that of another being. A large hair-seal came upon the beach. He rushed upon it, stabbed it in the neck, and then throwing himself upon the panting body quaffed at the living wound; the palpitations of the creature's dying heart injected life into the drinker.

Another seaman, thrust ashore in a boat upon an isle at which no ship ever touched, owing to its peculiar sterility and the shoals about it, and from which all other parts of the group were hidden – this man, feeling that it was sure death to remain there, and that nothing worse than death menaced him in quitting it, killed two seals, and inflating their skins, made a float, upon which he transported himself to Charles's Island, and joined the republic there.

But men, not endowed with courage equal to such desperate attempts, find their only resource in forthwith seeking some watering-place, however precarious or scanty; building a hut; catching tortoises and birds; and in all respects preparing for a hermit life, till tide or time, or a passing ship arrives to float them off.

At the foot of precipices on many of the isles, small rude basins in the rocks are found, partly filled with rotted rubbish or vegetable decay, or overgrown with thickets, and sometimes a little moist; which, upon examination, reveal plain tokens of artificial instruments employed in hollowing them out, by some poor castaway or still more miserable runaway. These basins are made in places where it was supposed some scanty drops of dew might exude into them from the upper crevices.

The relics of hermitages and stone basins are not the only signs of vanishing humanity to be found upon the isles. And, curious to say, that spot which of all others in settled communities is most animated, at the Enchanted Isles presents the most dreary of aspects. And though it may seem very strange to talk of post-offices in this barren region, yet post-offices are occasionally to be found there. They consist of a stake and a bottle. The letters being not only sealed, but corked. They are generally deposited by

Sketch Tenth

captains of Nantucketers for the benefit of passing fishermen, and contain statements as to what luck they had in whaling or tortoise-hunting. Frequently, however, long months and months, whole years glide by and no applicant appears. The stake rots and falls, presenting no very exhilarating object.

If now it be added that grave-stones, or rather grave-boards, are also discovered upon some of the isles, the picture will be complete.

Upon the beach of James's Isle, for many years, was to be seen a rude finger-post, pointing inland. And, perhaps, taking it for some signal of possible hospitality in this otherwise desolate spot – some good hermit living there with his maple dish – the stranger would follow on in the path thus indicated, till at last he would come out in a noiseless nook, and find his only welcome, a dead man – his sole greeting the inscription over a grave. Here, in 1813, fell, in a daybreak duel, a lieutenant of the U.S. frigate *Essex*, aged twenty-one: attaining his majority in death.

It is but fit that, like those old monastic institutions of Europe, whose inmates go not out of their own walls to be inurned, but are entombed there where they die, the Encantadas, too, should bury their own dead, even as the great general monastery of earth does hers.

It is known that burial in the ocean is a pure necessity of sea-faring life, and that it is only done when land is far astern, and not clearly visible from the bow. Hence, to vessels cruising in the vicinity of the Enchanted Isles, they afford a convenient Potter's Field. The interment over, some good-natured forecastle poet and artist seizes his paintbrush, and inscribes a doggerel epitaph. When, after a long lapse of time, other good-natured seamen chance to come upon the spot, they usually make a table of the mound, and quaff a friendly can to the poor soul's repose.

As a specimen of these epitaphs, take the following, found in a bleak gorge of Chatham Isle: –

> *'Oh, Brother Jack, as you pass by,*
> *As you are now, so once was I.*
> *Just so game, and just so gay,*
> *But now, alack, they've stopped my pay.*
> *No more I peep out of my blinkers,*
> *Here I be – tucked in with clinkers!'*

1. BOCCACCIO · *Mrs Rosie and the Priest*
2. GERARD MANLEY HOPKINS · *As kingfishers catch fire*
3. *The Saga of Gunnlaug Serpent-tongue*
4. THOMAS DE QUINCEY · *On Murder Considered as One of the Fine Arts*
5. FRIEDRICH NIETZSCHE · *Aphorisms on Love and Hate*
6. JOHN RUSKIN · *Traffic*
7. PU SONGLING · *Wailing Ghosts*
8. JONATHAN SWIFT · *A Modest Proposal*
9. *Three Tang Dynasty Poets*
10. WALT WHITMAN · *On the Beach at Night Alone*
11. KENKŌ · *A Cup of Sake Beneath the Cherry Trees*
12. BALTASAR GRACIÁN · *How to Use Your Enemies*
13. JOHN KEATS · *The Eve of St Agnes*
14. THOMAS HARDY · *Woman much missed*
15. GUY DE MAUPASSANT · *Femme Fatale*
16. MARCO POLO · *Travels in the Land of Serpents and Pearls*
17. SUETONIUS · *Caligula*
18. APOLLONIUS OF RHODES · *Jason and Medea*
19. ROBERT LOUIS STEVENSON · *Olalla*
20. KARL MARX AND FRIEDRICH ENGELS · *The Communist Manifesto*
21. PETRONIUS · *Trimalchio's Feast*
22. JOHANN PETER HEBEL · *How a Ghastly Story Was Brought to Light by a Common or Garden Butcher's Dog*
23. HANS CHRISTIAN ANDERSEN · *The Tinder Box*
24. RUDYARD KIPLING · *The Gate of the Hundred Sorrows*
25. DANTE · *Circles of Hell*
26. HENRY MAYHEW · *Of Street Piemen*
27. HAFEZ · *The nightingales are drunk*
28. GEOFFREY CHAUCER · *The Wife of Bath*
29. MICHEL DE MONTAIGNE · *How We Weep and Laugh at the Same Thing*
30. THOMAS NASHE · *The Terrors of the Night*
31. EDGAR ALLAN POE · *The Tell-Tale Heart*
32. MARY KINGSLEY · *A Hippo Banquet*
33. JANE AUSTEN · *The Beautifull Cassandra*
34. ANTON CHEKHOV · *Gooseberries*
35. SAMUEL TAYLOR COLERIDGE · *Well, they are gone, and here must I remain*
36. JOHANN WOLFGANG VON GOETHE · *Sketchy, Doubtful, Incomplete Jottings*
37. CHARLES DICKENS · *The Great Winglebury Duel*
38. HERMAN MELVILLE · *The Maldive Shark*
39. ELIZABETH GASKELL · *The Old Nurse's Story*
40. NIKOLAY LESKOV · *The Steel Flea*

41. HONORÉ DE BALZAC · *The Atheist's Mass*
42. CHARLOTTE PERKINS GILMAN · *The Yellow Wall-Paper*
43. C.P. CAVAFY · *Remember, Body . . .*
44. FYODOR DOSTOEVSKY · *The Meek One*
45. GUSTAVE FLAUBERT · *A Simple Heart*
46. NIKOLAI GOGOL · *The Nose*
47. SAMUEL PEPYS · *The Great Fire of London*
48. EDITH WHARTON · *The Reckoning*
49. HENRY JAMES · *The Figure in the Carpet*
50. WILFRED OWEN · *Anthem For Doomed Youth*
51. WOLFGANG AMADEUS MOZART · *My Dearest Father*
52. PLATO · *Socrates' Defence*
53. CHRISTINA ROSSETTI · *Goblin Market*
54. *Sindbad the Sailor*
55. SOPHOCLES · *Antigone*
56. RYŪNOSUKE AKUTAGAWA · *The Life of a Stupid Man*
57. LEO TOLSTOY · *How Much Land Does A Man Need?*
58. GIORGIO VASARI · *Leonardo da Vinci*
59. OSCAR WILDE · *Lord Arthur Savile's Crime*
60. SHEN FU · *The Old Man of the Moon*
61. AESOP · *The Dolphins, the Whales and the Gudgeon*
62. MATSUO BASHŌ · *Lips too Chilled*
63. EMILY BRONTË · *The Night is Darkening Round Me*
64. JOSEPH CONRAD · *To-morrow*
65. RICHARD HAKLUYT · *The Voyage of Sir Francis Drake Around the Whole Globe*
66. KATE CHOPIN · *A Pair of Silk Stockings*
67. CHARLES DARWIN · *It was snowing butterflies*
68. BROTHERS GRIMM · *The Robber Bridegroom*
69. CATULLUS · *I Hate and I Love*
70. HOMER · *Circe and the Cyclops*
71. D. H. LAWRENCE · *Il Duro*
72. KATHERINE MANSFIELD · *Miss Brill*
73. OVID · *The Fall of Icarus*
74. SAPPHO · *Come Close*
75. IVAN TURGENEV · *Kasyan from the Beautiful Lands*
76. VIRGIL · *O Cruel Alexis*
77. H. G. WELLS · *A Slip under the Microscope*
78. HERODOTUS · *The Madness of Cambyses*
79. *Speaking of Siva*
80. *The Dhammapada*

'Even in the stillness of that dead-cold weather, I had heard no sound of little battering hands upon the window-glass...'

ELIZABETH GASKELL
Born 1810, London
Died 1865, Hampshire, England

'The Old Nurse's Story' first appeared in a Christmas edition of Charles Dickens' magazine, *Household Words*, in 1852. 'Curious, if True' was one of the earliest stories published by William Thackeray's *Cornhill Magazine*, in 1860.

GASKELL IN PENGUIN CLASSICS
Cranford
Cranford and *Cousin Phillis*
Gothic Tales
Mary Barton
North and South
Ruth
Sylvia's Lovers
The Life of Charlotte Brontë
Wives and Daughters

ELIZABETH GASKELL

The Old Nurse's Story

PENGUIN BOOKS

PENGUIN CLASSICS

UK | USA | Canada | Ireland | Australia
India | New Zealand | South Africa

Penguin Books is part of the Penguin Random House group of companies whose addresses can be found at global.penguinrandomhouse.com.

This selection published in Penguin Classics 2015

009

Set in 9/12.4 pt Baskerville 10 Pro
Typeset by Jouve (UK), Milton Keynes
Printed and bound in Great Britain by Clays Ltd, Elcograf S.p.A.

A CIP catalogue record for this book is available from the British Library

ISBN: 978-0-141-39737-5

www.greenpenguin.co.uk

Penguin Random House is committed to a sustainable future for our business, our readers and our planet. This book is made from Forest Stewardship Council® certified paper.

Contents

The Old Nurse's Story   1

Curious, if True   31

The Old Nurse's Story

You know, my dears, that your mother was an orphan, and an only child; and I daresay you have heard that your grandfather was a clergyman up in Westmoreland, where I come from. I was just a girl in the village school, when, one day, your grandmother came in to ask the mistress if there was any scholar there who would do for a nurse-maid; and mighty proud I was, I can tell ye, when the mistress called me up, and spoke to my being a good girl at my needle, and a steady, honest girl, and one whose parents were very respectable, though they might be poor. I thought I should like nothing better than to serve the pretty young lady, who was blushing as deep as I was, as she spoke of the coming baby, and what I should have to do with it. However, I see you don't care so much for this part of my story, as for what you think is to come, so I'll tell you at once. I was engaged and settled at the parsonage before Miss Rosamond (that was the baby, who is now your mother) was born. To be sure, I had little enough to do with her when she came, for she was never out of her mother's arms, and slept by her all night long; and proud enough was I sometimes when missis trusted her to me. There never was such a baby before or since, though you've all of you been fine enough in your turns; but for sweet, winning ways, you've none of you come up to your mother. She took after her mother, who was a real lady born; a Miss Furnivall, a grand-daughter of Lord Furnivall's, in Northumberland. I believe she had neither brother nor sister, and had been brought up in my lord's family till she had married your grandfather, who was just a curate, son to a shopkeeper in Carlisle – but a clever, fine gentleman as ever was – and one who was a right-down hard worker in his parish, which was very wide, and scattered all abroad over the Westmoreland Fells. When your mother, little Miss Rosamond, was about four or five years old, both her parents died in a fortnight – one after the other. Ah! that was a sad time. My pretty young mistress and me was looking for another baby, when my master came home from one of his long rides, wet and tired, and took the fever he died of; and then she never held up her head again, but just lived to see her dead baby, and have it laid on her breast, before she sighed away her life. My mistress had asked me, on her death-bed, never to leave Miss Rosamond; but if she had never spoken a word, I would have gone with the little child to the end of the world.

The next thing, and before we had well stilled our sobs, the executors and guardians came to settle the affairs. They were my poor young mistress's own cousin, Lord Furnivall, and Mr Esthwaite, my master's brother, a shopkeeper in Manchester; not so well to do then as he was afterwards, and with a large family rising about him. Well! I don't know if it were their settling, or because of a letter my mistress wrote on her death-bed to her cousin, my lord; but somehow it was settled that Miss Rosamond and me were to go to Furnivall Manor House, in Northumberland, and my lord spoke as if it had been her mother's wish that she should live with his

The Old Nurse's Story

family, and as if he had no objections, for that one or two more or less could make no difference in so grand a household. So, though that was not the way in which I should have wished the coming of my bright and pretty pet to have been looked at – who was like a sunbeam in any family, be it never so grand – I was well pleased that all the folks in the Dale should stare and admire, when they heard I was going to be young lady's-maid at my Lord Furnivall's at Furnivall Manor.

But I made a mistake in thinking we were to go and live where my lord did. It turned out that the family had left Furnivall Manor House fifty years or more. I could not hear that my poor young mistress had ever been there, though she had been brought up in the family; and I was sorry for that, for I should have liked Miss Rosamond's youth to have passed where her mother's had been.

My lord's gentleman, from whom I asked as many questions as I durst, said that the Manor House was at the foot of the Cumberland Fells, and a very grand place; that an old Miss Furnivall, a great-aunt of my lord's, lived there, with only a few servants; but that it was a very healthy place, and my lord had thought that it would suit Miss Rosamond very well for a few years, and that her being there might perhaps amuse his old aunt.

I was bidden by my lord to have Miss Rosamond's things ready by a certain day. He was a stern, proud man, as they say all the Lords Furnivall were; and he never spoke a word more than was necessary. Folk did say he had loved my young mistress; but that, because she knew that his father would object, she would never listen to him, and married

Mr Esthwaite; but I don't know. He never married, at any rate. But he never took much notice of Miss Rosamond; which I thought he might have done if he had cared for her dead mother. He sent his gentleman with us to the Manor House, telling him to join him at Newcastle that same evening; so there was no great length of time for him to make us known to all the strangers before he, too, shook us off; and we were left, two lonely young things (I was not eighteen) in the great old Manor House. It seems like yesterday that we drove there. We had left our own dear parsonage very early, and we had both cried as if our hearts would break, though we were travelling in my lord's carriage, which I thought so much of once. And now it was long past noon on a September day, and we stopped to change horses for the last time at a little smoky town, all full of colliers and miners. Miss Rosamond had fallen asleep, but Mr Henry told me to waken her, that she might see the park and the Manor House as we drove up. I thought it rather a pity; but I did what he bade me, for fear he should complain of me to my lord. We had left all signs of a town, or even a village, and were then inside the gates of a large wild park – not like the parks here in the south, but with rocks, and the noise of running water, and gnarled thorn-trees, and old oaks, all white and peeled with age.

The road went up about two miles, and then we saw a great and stately house, with many trees close around it, so close that in some places their branches dragged against the walls when the wind blew; and some hung broken down; for no one seemed to take much charge of the place; – to lop the wood, or to keep the moss-covered carriage-way in order.

The Old Nurse's Story

Only in front of the house all was clear. The great oval drive was without a weed; and neither tree nor creeper was allowed to grow over the long, many-windowed front; at both sides of which a wing projected, which were each the ends of other side fronts; for the house, although it was so desolate, was even grander than I expected. Behind it rose the Fells, which seemed unenclosed and bare enough; and on the left hand of the house, as you stood facing it, was a little, old-fashioned flower-garden, as I found out afterwards. A door opened out upon it from the west front; it had been scooped out of the thick, dark wood for some old Lady Furnivall; but the branches of the great forest-trees had grown and overshadowed it again, and there were very few flowers that would live there at that time.

When we drove up to the great front entrance, and went into the hall, I thought we should be lost – it was so large, and vast, and grand. There was a chandelier all of bronze, hung down from the middle of the ceiling; and I had never seen one before, and looked at it all in amaze. Then, at one end of the hall, was a great fire-place, as large as the sides of the houses in my country, with massy andirons and dogs to hold the wood; and by it were heavy, old-fashioned sofas. At the opposite end of the hall, to the left as you went in – on the western side – was an organ built into the wall, and so large that it filled up the best part of that end. Beyond it, on the same side, was a door; and opposite, on each side of the fire-place, were also doors leading to the east front; but those I never went through as long as I stayed in the house, so I can't tell you what lay beyond.

The afternoon was closing in, and the hall, which had no

fire lighted in it, looked dark and gloomy, but we did not stay there a moment. The old servant, who had opened the door for us, bowed to Mr Henry, and took us in through the door at the further side of the great organ, and led us through several smaller halls and passages into the west drawing-room, where he said that Miss Furnivall was sitting. Poor little Miss Rosamond held very tight to me, as if she were scared and lost in that great place; and as for myself, I was not much better. The west drawing-room was very cheerful-looking, with a warm fire in it, and plenty of good, comfortable furniture about. Miss Furnivall was an old lady not far from eighty, I should think, but I do not know. She was thin and tall, and had a face as full of fine wrinkles as if they had been drawn all over it with a needle's point. Her eyes were very watchful to make up, I suppose, for her being so deaf as to be obliged to use a trumpet. Sitting with her, working at the same great piece of tapestry, was Mrs Stark, her maid and companion, and almost as old as she was. She had lived with Miss Furnivall ever since they both were young, and now she seemed more like a friend than a servant; she looked so cold, and grey, and stony, as if she had never loved or cared for any one; and I don't suppose she did care for any one, except her mistress; and, owing to the great deafness of the latter, Mrs Stark treated her very much as if she were a child. Mr Henry gave some message from my lord, and then he bowed good-by to us all, – taking no notice of my sweet little Miss Rosamond's out-stretched hand – and left us standing there, being looked at by two old ladies through their spectacles.

I was right glad when they rung for the old footman who

The Old Nurse's Story

had shown us in at first, and told him to take us to our rooms. So we went out of that great drawing-room, and into another sitting-room, and out of that, and then up a great flight of stairs, and along a broad gallery – which was something like a library, having books all down one side, and windows and writing-tables all down the other – till we came to our rooms, which I was not sorry to hear were just over the kitchens; for I began to think I should be lost in that wilderness of a house. There was an old nursery, that had been used for all the little lords and ladies long ago, with a pleasant fire burning in the grate, and the kettle boiling on the hob, and tea-things spread out on the table; and out of that room was the night-nursery, with a little crib for Miss Rosamond close to my bed. And old James called up Dorothy, his wife, to bid us welcome; and both he and she were so hospitable and kind, that by-and-by Miss Rosamond and me felt quite at home; and by the time tea was over, she was sitting on Dorothy's knee, and chattering away as fast as her little tongue could go. I soon found out that Dorothy was from Westmoreland, and that bound her and me together, as it were; and I would never wish to meet with kinder people than were old James and his wife. James had lived pretty nearly all his life in my lord's family, and thought there was no one so grand as they. He even looked down a little on his wife; because, till he had married her, she had never lived in any but a farmer's household. But he was very fond of her, as well he might be. They had one servant under them, to do all the rough work. Agnes they called her; and she and me, and James and Dorothy, with Miss Furnivall and Mrs Stark, made up the family; always remembering my sweet little Miss Rosamond! I used to wonder what they had done before she came, they thought so much of her now. Kitchen and drawing-room, it was all the same. The hard, sad Miss Furnivall, and the cold Mrs Stark, looked pleased when she came fluttering in like a bird, playing and pranking hither and thither, with a continual murmur, and pretty prattle of gladness. I am sure, they were sorry many a time when she flitted away into the kitchen, though they were too proud to ask her to stay with them, and were a little surprised at her taste; though to be sure, as Mrs Stark said, it was not to be wondered at, remembering what stock her father had come of. The great, old rambling house was a famous place for little Miss Rosamond. She made expeditions all over it, with me at her heels; all, except the east wing, which was never opened, and whither we never thought of going. But in the western and northern part was many a pleasant room; full of things that were curiosities to us, though they might not have been to people who had seen more. The windows were darkened by the sweeping boughs of the trees, and the ivy which had overgrown them: but, in the green gloom, we could manage to see old China jars and carved ivory boxes, and great heavy books, and, above all, the old pictures!

Once, I remember, my darling would have Dorothy go with us to tell us who they all were; for they were all portraits of some of my lord's family, though Dorothy could not tell us the names of every one. We had gone through most of the rooms, when we came to the old state drawing-room over the hall, and there was a picture of Miss Furnivall; or, as she was called in those days, Miss Grace, for she was the younger sister. Such a beauty she must have been! but with such a set, proud look, and such scorn looking out of her handsome eyes, with her eyebrows just a little raised, as if she wondered how any one could have the impertinence to look at her, and her lip curled at us, as we stood there gazing. She had a dress on, the like of which I had never seen before, but it was all the fashion when she was young: a hat of some soft white stuff like beaver, pulled a little over her brows, and a beautiful plume of feathers sweeping round it on one side; and her gown of blue satin was open in front to a quilted white stomacher.

'Well, to be sure!' said I, when I had gazed my fill. 'Flesh is grass, they do say; but who would have thought that Miss Furnivall had been such an out-and-out beauty, to see her now?'

'Yes,' said Dorothy. 'Folks change sadly. But if what my master's father used to say was true, Miss Furnivall, the elder sister, was handsomer than Miss Grace. Her picture is here somewhere; but, if I show it you, you must never let on, even to James, that you have seen it. Can the little lady hold her tongue, think you?' asked she.

I was not so sure, for she was such a little sweet, bold, open-spoken child, so I set her to hide herself; and then I helped Dorothy to turn a great picture, that leaned with its face towards the wall, and was not hung up as the others were. To be sure, it beat Miss Grace for beauty; and, I think, for scornful pride, too, though in that matter it might be hard to choose. I could have looked at it an hour, but Dorothy seemed half frightened at having shown it to me, and hurried it back again, and bade me run and find Miss Rosamond, for that there were some ugly places about the house, where she should like ill for the child to go. I was a brave, high-spirited girl, and thought little of what the old woman said, for I liked hide-and-seek as well as any child in the parish; so off I ran to find my little one.

As winter drew on, and the days grew shorter, I was sometimes almost certain that I heard a noise as if some one was playing on the great organ in the hall. I did not hear it every evening; but, certainly, I did very often, usually when I was sitting with Miss Rosamond, after I had put her to bed, and keeping quite still and silent in the bedroom. Then I used to hear it booming and swelling away in the distance. The first night, when I went down to my supper, I asked Dorothy who had been playing music, and James said very shortly that I was a gowk to take the wind soughing among the trees for music: but I saw Dorothy look at him very fearfully, and Agnes, the kitchen-maid, said something beneath her breath, and went quite white. I saw they did not like my question, so I held my peace till I was with Dorothy alone, when I knew I could get a good deal out of her. So, the next day, I watched my time, and I coaxed and asked her who it was that played the organ; for I knew that it was the organ and not the wind well enough, for all I had kept silence before James. But Dorothy had had her lesson, I'll warrant, and never a word could I get from her. So then I tried Agnes, though I had always held my head rather above her, as I was evened to James and Dorothy, and she was little better than their servant. So she said I must never, never tell; and if I ever told, I was never to say *she* had told me; but it was a very strange noise, and she had heard it many a time, but most of all on winter nights, and before storms; and folks did say it was the old lord playing on the great organ in the hall, just as he used to do when he was alive; but who the old lord was, or why he played, and why he played on stormy winter evenings in particular, she either could not or would not tell me. Well! I told you I had a brave heart; and I thought it was rather pleasant to have that grand music rolling about the house, let who would be the player; for now it rose above the great gusts of wind, and wailed and triumphed just like a living creature, and then it fell to a softness most complete, only it was always music, and tunes, so it was nonsense to call it the wind. I thought at first, that it might be Miss Furnivall who played, unknown to Agnes; but, one day when I was in the hall by myself, I opened the organ and peeped all about it and around it, as I had done to the organ in Crosthwaite Church once before, and I saw it was all broken and destroyed inside, though it looked so brave and fine; and then, though it was noonday, my flesh began to creep a little, and I shut it up, and run away pretty quickly to my own bright nursery; and I did not like hearing the music for some time after that, any more than James and Dorothy did. All this time Miss Rosamond was making herself more and more beloved. The old ladies liked her to dine with them at their early dinner. James stood behind Miss Furnivall's chair, and I behind Miss Rosamond's all in state; and after dinner, she would play about in a corner of the great drawing-room as still as any mouse, while Miss Furnivall slept, and I had my dinner in the kitchen. But she was glad enough to come to me in the nursery afterwards; for, as she said, Miss Furnivall was so sad, and Mrs Stark so dull; but she and I were merry enough; and, by-and-by, I got not to care for that weird rolling music, which did one no harm, if we did not know where it came from.

That winter was very cold. In the middle of October the frosts began, and lasted many, many weeks. I remember one day, at dinner, Miss Furnivall lifted up her sad, heavy eyes, and said to Mrs Stark, 'I am afraid we shall have a terrible winter,' in a strange kind of meaning way. But Mrs Stark pretended not to hear, and talked very loud of something else. My little lady and I did not care for the frost; not we! As long as it was dry, we climbed up the steep brows behind the house, and went up on the Fells, which were bleak and bare enough, and there we ran races in the fresh, sharp air; and once we came down by a new path, that took us past the two old gnarled holly-trees, which grew about halfway down by the east side of the house. But the days grew shorter and shorter, and the old lord, if it was he, played away, more and more stormily and sadly, on the great organ. One Sunday afternoon – it must have been towards the end of November – I asked Dorothy to take charge of little Missey when she came out of the drawing-room, after Miss Furnivall had had her nap; for it was too cold to take her with me to church, and yet I wanted to go. And Dorothy was glad enough to promise, and was so fond of the child, that all seemed well; and Agnes and I set off very briskly, though the sky hung heavy and black over the white earth; as if the night had never fully gone away, and the air, though still, was very biting and keen.

'We shall have a fall of snow,' said Agnes to me. And sure enough, even while we were in church, it came down thick,

The Old Nurse's Story

in great large flakes – so thick, it almost darkened the windows. It had stopped snowing before we came out, but it lay soft, thick and deep beneath our feet, as we tramped home. Before we got to the hall, the moon rose, and I think it was lighter then – what with the moon, and what with the white dazzling snow – than it had been when we went to church, between two and three o'clock. I have not told you that Miss Furnivall and Mrs Stark never went to church; they used to read the prayers together, in their quiet, gloomy way; they seemed to feel the Sunday very long without their tapestry-work to be busy at. So when I went to Dorothy in the kitchen, to fetch Miss Rosamond and take her upstairs with me, I did not much wonder when the old woman told me that the ladies had kept the child with them, and that she had never come to the kitchen, as I had bidden her, when she was tired of behaving pretty in the drawing-room. So I took off my things and went to find her, and bring her to her supper in the nursery. But when I went into the best drawing-room, there sat the two old ladies, very still and quiet, dropping out a word now and then, but looking as if nothing so bright and merry as Miss Rosamond had ever been near them. Still I thought she might be hiding from me; it was one of her pretty ways, – and that she had persuaded them to look as if they knew nothing about her; so I went softly peeping under this sofa, and behind that chair, making believe I was sadly frightened at not finding her.

'What's the matter, Hester?' said Mrs Stark, sharply. I don't know if Miss Furnivall had seen me, for, as I told you, she was very deaf, and she sat quite still, idly staring into the fire, with her hopeless face. 'I'm only looking for my little Rosy Posy,' replied I, still thinking that the child was there, and near me, though I could not see her.

'Miss Rosamond is not here,' said Mrs Stark. 'She went away, more than an hour ago, to find Dorothy.' And she, too, turned and went on looking into the fire.

My heart sank at this, and I began to wish I had never left my darling. I went back to Dorothy and told her. James was gone out for the day, but she, and me, and Agnes took lights, and went up into the nursery first; and then we roamed over the great, large house, calling and entreating Miss Rosamond to come out of her hiding-place, and not frighten us to death in that way. But there was no answer; no sound.

'Oh!' said I, at last, 'can she have got into the east wing and hidden there?'

But Dorothy said it was not possible, for that she herself had never been in there; that the doors were always locked, and my lord's steward had the keys, she believed; at any rate, neither she nor James had ever seen them: so I said I would go back, and see if, after all, she was not hidden in the drawing-room, unknown to the old ladies; and if I found her there, I said, I would whip her well for the fright she had given me; but I never meant to do it. Well, I went back to the west drawing-room, and I told Mrs Stark we could not find her anywhere, and asked for leave to look all about the furniture there, for I thought now that she might have fallen asleep in some warm, hidden corner; but no! we looked – Miss Furnivall got up and looked, trembling all over – and she was nowhere there; then we set off again, every one in the house, and looked in all the places we had searched

The Old Nurse's Story

before, but we could not find her. Miss Furnivall shivered and shook so much, that Mrs Stark took her back into the warm drawing-room; but not before they had made me promise to bring her to them when she was found. Well-a-day! I began to think she never would be found, when I bethought me to look out into the great front court, all covered with snow. I was upstairs when I looked out; but, it was such clear moonlight, I could see, quite plain, two little footprints, which might be traced from the hall-door and round the corner of the east wing. I don't know how I got down, but I tugged open the great stiff hall-door, and, throwing the skirt of my gown over my head for a cloak, I ran out. I turned the east corner, and there a black shadow fell on the snow; but when I came again into the moonlight, there were the little footmarks going up – up to the Fells. It was bitter cold; so cold, that the air almost took the skin off my face as I ran; but I ran on, crying to think how my poor little darling must be perished and frightened. I was within sight of the holly-trees, when I saw a shepherd coming down the hill, bearing something in his arms wrapped in his maud. He shouted to me, and asked me if I had lost a bairn; and, when I could not speak for crying, he bore towards me, and I saw my wee bairnie lying still, and white, and stiff in his arms, as if she had been dead. He told me he had been up the Fells to gather in his sheep, before the deep cold of night came on, and that under the holly-trees (black marks on the hill-side, where no other bush was for miles around) he had found my little lady – my lamb – my queen – my darling – stiff and cold, in the terrible sleep which is frost-begotten. Oh! the joy and the tears of having her in my arms once again! for I would not let him carry her; but took her, maud and all, into my own arms, and held her near my own warm neck and heart, and felt the life stealing slowly back again into her little gentle limbs. But she was still insensible when we reached the hall, and I had no breath for speech. We went in by the kitchen-door.

'Bring the warming-pan,' said I; and I carried her upstairs, and began undressing her by the nursery fire, which Agnes had kept up. I called my little lammie all the sweet and playful names I could think of, – even while my eyes were blinded by my tears; and at last, oh! at length she opened her large blue eyes. Then I put her into her warm bed, and sent Dorothy down to tell Miss Furnivall that all was well; and I made up my mind to sit by my darling's bedside the live-long night. She fell away into a soft sleep as soon as her pretty head had touched the pillow, and I watched by her till morning light; when she wakened up bright and clear – or so I thought at first – and, my dears, so I think now.

She said, that she had fancied that she should like to go to Dorothy, for that both the old ladies were asleep, and it was very dull in the drawing-room; and that, as she was going through the west lobby, she saw the snow through the high window falling – falling – soft and steady; but she wanted to see it lying pretty and white on the ground; so she made her way into the great hall; and then, going to the window, she saw it bright and soft upon the drive; but while she stood there, she saw a little girl, not so old as she was, 'but so pretty,' said my darling, 'and this little girl beckoned to me to come out; and oh, she was so pretty and so sweet, I could not choose but go.' And then this other little girl had

The Old Nurse's Story

taken her by the hand, and side by side the two had gone round the east corner.

'Now you are a naughty little girl, and telling stories,' said I. 'What would your good mamma, that is in heaven, and never told a story in her life, say to her little Rosamond if she heard her – and I daresay she does – telling stories!'

'Indeed, Hester,' sobbed out my child, 'I'm telling you true. Indeed I am.'

'Don't tell me!' said I, very stern. 'I tracked you by your foot-marks through the snow; there were only yours to be seen: and if you had had a little girl to go hand-in-hand with you up the hill, don't you think the footprints would have gone along with yours?'

'I can't help it, dear, dear Hester,' said she, crying, 'if they did not; I never looked at her feet, but she held my hand fast and tight in her little one, and it was very, very cold. She took me up the Fell-path, up to the holly-trees; and there I saw a lady weeping and crying; but when she saw me, she hushed her weeping, and smiled very proud and grand, and took me on her knee, and began to lull me to sleep; and that's all, Hester – but that is true; and my dear mamma knows it is,' said she, crying. So I thought the child was in a fever, and pretended to believe her, as she went over her story – over and over again, and always the same. At last Dorothy knocked at the door with Miss Rosamond's breakfast; and she told me the old ladies were down in the eating parlour, and that they wanted to speak to me. They had both been into the night-nursery the evening before, but it was after Miss Rosamond was asleep; so they had only looked at her – not asked me any questions.

'I shall catch it,' thought I to myself, as I went along the north gallery. 'And yet,' I thought, taking courage, 'it was in their charge I left her; and it's they that's to blame for letting her steal away unknown and unwatched.' So I went in boldly, and told my story. I told it all to Miss Furnivall, shouting it close to her ear; but when I came to the mention of the other little girl out in the snow, coaxing and tempting her out, and wiling her up to the grand and beautiful lady by the holly-tree, she threw her arms up – her old and withered arms – and cried aloud, 'Oh! Heaven forgive! Have mercy!'

Mrs Stark took hold of her; roughly enough, I thought; but she was past Mrs Stark's management, and spoke to me, in a kind of wild warning and authority.

'Hester! keep her from that child! It will lure her to her death! That evil child! Tell her it is a wicked, naughty child.' Then, Mrs Stark hurried me out of the room; where, indeed, I was glad enough to go; but Miss Furnivall kept shrieking out, 'Oh, have mercy! Wilt Thou never forgive! It is many a long year ago – '

I was very uneasy in my mind after that. I durst never leave Miss Rosamond, night or day, for fear lest she might slip off again, after some fancy or other; and all the more, because I thought I could make out that Miss Furnivall was crazy, from their odd ways about her; and I was afraid lest something of the same kind (which might be in the family, you know) hung over my darling. And the great frost never ceased all this time; and, whenever it was a more stormy night than usual, between the gusts, and through the wind, we heard the old lord playing on the great organ. But, old

The Old Nurse's Story

lord, or not, wherever Miss Rosamond went, there I followed; for my love for her, pretty, helpless orphan, was stronger than my fear for the grand and terrible sound. Besides, it rested with me to keep her cheerful and merry, as beseemed her age. So we played together, and wandered together, here and there, and everywhere; for I never dared to lose sight of her again in that large and rambling house. And so it happened that one afternoon, not long before Christmas-day, we were playing together on the billiard-table in the great hall (not that we knew the right way of playing, but she liked to roll the smooth ivory balls with her pretty hands, and I liked to do whatever she did); and, by-and-by, without our noticing it, it grew dusk indoors, though it was still light in the open air, and I was thinking of taking her back into the nursery, when, all of a sudden, she cried out –

'Look, Hester! look! there is my poor little girl out in the snow!'

I turned towards the long narrow windows, and there, sure enough, I saw a little girl, less than my Miss Rosamond – dressed all unfit to be out-of-doors such a bitter night – crying, and beating against the window-panes, as if she wanted to be let in. She seemed to sob and wail, till Miss Rosamond could bear it no longer, and was flying to the door to open it, when, all of a sudden, and close upon us, the great organ pealed out so loud and thundering, it fairly made me tremble; and all the more, when I remembered me that, even in the stillness of that dead-cold weather, I had heard no sound of little battering hands upon the window-glass, although the phantom child had seemed to put forth all its force; and, although I had seen it wail and cry, no faintest touch of sound had fallen upon my ears. Whether I remembered all this at the very moment, I do not know; the great organ sound had so stunned me into terror; but this I know, I caught up Miss Rosamond before she got the hall-door opened, and clutched her, and carried her away, kicking and screaming, into the large, bright kitchen, where Dorothy and Agnes were busy with their mince-pies.

'What is the matter with my sweet one?' cried Dorothy, as I bore in Miss Rosamond, who was sobbing as if her heart would break.

'She won't let me open the door for my little girl to come in; and she'll die if she is out on the Fells all night. Cruel, naughty Hester,' she said, slapping me; but she might have struck harder, for I had seen a look of ghastly terror on Dorothy's face, which made my very blood run cold.

'Shut the back-kitchen door fast, and bolt it well,' said she to Agnes. She said no more; she gave me raisins and almonds to quiet Miss Rosamond; but she sobbed about the little girl in the snow, and would not touch any of the good things. I was thankful when she cried herself to sleep in bed. Then I stole down to the kitchen, and told Dorothy I had made up my mind. I would carry my darling back to my father's house in Applethwaite; where, if we lived humbly, we lived at peace. I said I had been frightened enough with the old lord's organ-playing; but now that I had seen for myself this little moaning child, all decked out as no child in the neighbourhood could be, beating and battering to get in, yet always without any sound or noise – with the dark wound on its right shoulder; and that Miss Rosamond had known it again for the phantom that had nearly lured her to her

The Old Nurse's Story

death (which Dorothy knew was true); I would stand it no longer.

I saw Dorothy change colour once or twice. When I had done, she told me she did not think I could take Miss Rosamond with me, for that she was my lord's ward, and I had no right over her; and she asked me would I leave the child that I was so fond of just for sounds and sights that could do me no harm; and that they had all had to get used to in their turns? I was all in a hot, trembling passion; and I said it was very well for her to talk, that knew what these sights and noises betokened, and that had, perhaps, had something to do with the spectre child while it was alive. And I taunted her so, that she told me all she knew at last; and then I wished I had never been told, for it only made me more afraid than ever.

She said she had heard the tale from old neighbours that were alive when she was first married; when folks used to come to the hall sometimes, before it had got such a bad name on the countryside: it might not be true, or it might, what she had been told.

The old lord was Miss Furnivall's father — Miss Grace, as Dorothy called her, for Miss Maude was the elder, and Miss Furnivall by rights. The old lord was eaten up with pride. Such a proud man was never seen or heard of; and his daughters were like him. No one was good enough to wed them, although they had choice enough; for they were the great beauties of their day, as I had seen by their portraits, where they hung in the state drawing-room. But, as the old saying is, 'Pride will have a fall'; and these two haughty beauties fell in love with the same man, and he no better than a foreign musician, whom their father had down from London to play music with him at the Manor House. For, above all things, next to his pride, the old lord loved music. He could play on nearly every instrument that ever was heard of; and it was a strange thing it did not soften him; but he was a fierce dour old man, and had broken his poor wife's heart with his cruelty, they said. He was mad after music, and would pay any money for it. So he got this foreigner to come; who made such beautiful music, that they said the very birds on the trees stopped their singing to listen. And, by degrees, this foreign gentleman got such a hold over the old lord, that nothing would serve him but that he must come every year; and it was he that had the great organ brought from Holland, and built up in the hall, where it stood now. He taught the old lord to play on it; but many and many a time, when Lord Furnivall was thinking of nothing but his fine organ, and his finer music, the dark foreigner was walking abroad in the woods with one of the young ladies; now Miss Maude, and then Miss Grace.

Miss Maude won the day and carried off the prize, such as it was; and he and she were married, all unknown to any one; and, before he made his next yearly visit, she had been confined of a little girl at a farm-house on the Moors, while her father and Miss Grace thought she was away at Doncaster Races. But though she was a wife and a mother, she was not a bit softened, but as haughty and as passionate as ever; and perhaps more so, for she was jealous of Miss Grace, to whom her foreign husband paid a deal of court – by way of blinding her – as he told his wife. But Miss Grace triumphed over Miss Maude, and Miss Maude grew fiercer and fiercer,

The Old Nurse's Story

both with her husband and with her sister; and the former – who could easily shake off what was disagreeable, and hide himself in foreign countries – went away a month before his usual time that summer, and half-threatened that he would never come back again. Meanwhile, the little girl was left at the farm-house, and her mother used to have her horse saddled and gallop wildly over the hills to see her once every week, at the very least; for where she loved she loved, and where she hated she hated. And the old lord went on playing – playing on his organ; and the servants thought the sweet music he made had soothed down his awful temper, of which (Dorothy said) some terrible tales could be told. He grew infirm too, and had to walk with a crutch; and his son – that was the present Lord Furnivall's father – was with the army in America, and the other son at sea; so Miss Maude had it pretty much her own way, and she and Miss Grace grew colder and bitterer to each other every day; till at last they hardly ever spoke, except when the old lord was by. The foreign musician came again the next summer, but it was for the last time; for they led him such a life with their jealousy and their passions, that he grew weary, and went away, and never was heard of again. And Miss Maude, who had always meant to have her marriage acknowledged when her father should be dead, was left now a deserted wife, whom nobody knew to have been married, with a child that she dared not own, although she loved it to distraction; living with a father whom she feared, and a sister whom she hated. When the next summer passed over, and the dark foreigner never came, both Miss Maude and Miss Grace grew gloomy and sad; they had a haggard look about them, though they looked handsome as ever. But, by-and-by, Miss Maude brightened; for her father grew more and more infirm, and more than ever carried away by his music; and she and Miss Grace lived almost entirely apart, having separate rooms, the one on the west side, Miss Maude on the east – those very rooms which were now shut up. So she thought she might have her little girl with her, and no one need ever know except those who dared not speak about it, and were bound to believe that it was, as she said, a cottager's child she had taken a fancy to. All this, Dorothy said, was pretty well known; but what came afterwards no one knew, except Miss Grace, and Mrs Stark, who was even then her maid, and much more of a friend to her than ever her sister had been. But the servants supposed, from words that were dropped, that Miss Maude had triumphed over Miss Grace, and told her that all the time the dark foreigner had been mocking her with pretended love – he was her own husband. The colour left Miss Grace's cheek and lips that very day for ever, and she was heard to say many a time that sooner or later she would have her revenge; and Mrs Stark was for ever spying about the east rooms.

One fearful night, just after the New Year had come in, when the snow was lying thick and deep, and the flakes were still falling – fast enough to blind any one who might be about and abroad – there was a great and violent noise heard, and the old lord's voice above all, cursing and swearing awfully, and the cries of a little child, and the proud defiance of a fierce woman, and the sound of a blow, and a dead stillness, and moans and wailings dying away on the hill-side! Then the old lord summoned all his servants, and told them, with terrible oaths, and words more terrible, that his daughter had disgraced herself, and that he had turned her out of doors – her, and her child – and that if ever they gave her help, or food, or shelter, he prayed that they might never enter heaven. And, all the while, Miss Grace stood by him, white and still as any stone; and, when he had ended, she heaved a great sigh, as much as to say her work was done, and her end was accomplished. But the old lord never touched his organ again, and died within the year; and no wonder! for, on the morrow of that wild and fearful night, the shepherds, coming down the Fell side, found Miss Maude sitting, all crazy and smiling, under the holly-trees, nursing a dead child, with a terrible mark on its right shoulder. 'But that was not what killed it,' said Dorothy: 'it was the frost and the cold. Every wild creature was in its hole, and every beast in its fold, while the child and its mother were turned out to wander on the Fells! And now you know all! and I wonder if you are less frightened now?'

I was more frightened than ever; but I said I was not. I wished Miss Rosamond and myself well out of that dreadful house for ever; but I would not leave her, and I dared not take her away. But oh, how I watched her, and guarded her! We bolted the doors, and shut the window-shutters fast, an hour or more before dark, rather than leave them open five minutes too late. But my little lady still heard the weird child crying and mourning; and not all we could do or say, could keep her from wanting to go to her, and let her in from the cruel wind and the snow. All this time I kept away from Miss Furnivall and Mrs Stark, as much as ever I could; for I feared them – I knew no good could be about them, with their grey, hard faces, and their dreamy eyes, looking back into the ghastly years that were gone. But, even in my fear, I had a kind of pity for Miss Furnivall, at least. Those gone down to the pit can hardly have a more hopeless look than that which was ever on her face. At last I even got so sorry for her – who never said a word but what was quite forced from her – that I prayed for her; and I taught Miss Rosamond to pray for one who had done a deadly sin; but often when she came to those words, she would listen, and start up from her knees, and say, 'I hear my little girl plaining and crying very sad – oh, let her in, or she will die!'

One night – just after New Year's Day had come at last, and the long winter had taken a turn, as I hoped – I heard the west drawing-room bell ring three times, which was the signal for me. I would not leave Miss Rosamond alone, for all she was asleep – for the old lord had been playing wilder than ever – and I feared lest my darling should waken to hear the spectre child; see her I knew she could not. I had fastened the windows too well for that. So I took her out of her bed, and wrapped her up in such outer clothes as were most handy, and carried her down to the drawing-room, where the old ladies sat at their tapestry work as usual. They looked up when I came in, and Mrs Stark asked, quite astounded, 'Why did I bring Miss Rosamond there, out of her warm bed?' I had begun to whisper, 'Because I was afraid of her being tempted out while I was away, by the wild child in the snow,' when she stopped me short (with a glance at Miss Furnivall), and said Miss Furnivall wanted me to undo some work she had done wrong, and which neither of

The Old Nurse's Story

them could see to unpick. So I laid my pretty dear on the sofa, and sat down on a stool by them, and hardened my heart against them, as I heard the wind rising and howling.

Miss Rosamond slept on sound, for all the wind blew so; and Miss Furnivall said never a word, nor looked round when the gusts shook the windows. All at once she started up to her full height, and put up one hand, as if to bid us listen.

'I hear voices!' said she. 'I hear terrible screams – I hear my father's voice!'

Just at that moment my darling wakened with a sudden start: 'My little girl is crying, oh, how she is crying!' and she tried to get up and go to her, but she got her feet entangled in the blanket, and I caught her up; for my flesh had begun to creep at these noises, which they heard while we could catch no sound. In a minute or two the noises came, and gathered fast, and filled our ears; we, too, heard voices and screams, and no longer heard the winter's wind that raged abroad. Mrs Stark looked at me, and I at her, but we dared not speak. Suddenly Miss Furnivall went towards the door, out into the ante-room, through the west lobby, and opened the door into the great hall. Mrs Stark followed, and I durst not be left, though my heart almost stopped beating for fear. I wrapped my darling tight in my arms, and went out with them. In the hall the screams were louder than ever; they seemed to come from the east wing – nearer and nearer – close on the other side of the locked-up doors – close behind them. Then I noticed that the great bronze chandelier seemed all alight, though the hall was dim, and that a fire was blazing in the vast hearth-place, though it gave no heat; and I shuddered up with terror, and folded my darling closer to me. But as I did so, the east door shook, and she, suddenly struggling to get free from me, cried, 'Hester! I must go! My little girl is there! I hear her; she is coming! Hester, I must go!'

I held her tight with all my strength; with a set will, I held her. If I had died, my hands would have grasped her still, I was so resolved in my mind. Miss Furnivall stood listening, and paid no regard to my darling, who had got down to the ground, and whom I, upon my knees now, was holding with both my arms clasped round her neck; she still striving and crying to get free.

All at once, the east door gave way with a thundering crash, as if torn open in a violent passion, and there came into that broad and mysterious light, the figure of a tall old man, with grey hair and gleaming eyes. He drove before him, with many a relentless gesture of abhorrence, a stern and beautiful woman, with a little child clinging to her dress.

'Oh, Hester! Hester!' cried Miss Rosamond; 'it's the lady! the lady below the holly-trees; and my little girl is with her. Hester! Hester! let me go to her; they are drawing me to them. I feel them – I feel them. I must go!'

Again she was almost convulsed by her efforts to get away; but I held her tighter and tighter, till I feared I should do her a hurt; but rather that than let her go towards those terrible phantoms. They passed along towards the great hall-door, where the winds howled and ravened for their

The Old Nurse's Story

prey; but before they reached that, the lady turned; and I could see that she defied the old man with a fierce and proud defiance; but then she quailed – and then she threw up her arms wildly and piteously to save her child – her little child – from a blow from his uplifted crutch.

And Miss Rosamond was torn as by a power stronger than mine, and writhed in my arms, and sobbed (for by this time the poor darling was growing faint).

'They want me to go with them on to the Fells – they are drawing me to them. Oh, my little girl! I would come, but cruel, wicked Hester holds me very tight.' But when she saw the uplifted crutch, she swooned away, and I thanked God for it. Just at this moment – when the tall old man, his hair streaming as in the blast of a furnace, was going to strike the little shrinking child – Miss Furnivall, the old woman by my side, cried out, 'Oh, father! father! spare the little innocent child!' But just then I saw – we all saw – another phantom shape itself, and grow clear out of the blue and misty light that filled the hall; we had not seen her till now, for it was another lady who stood by the old man, with a look of relentless hate and triumphant scorn. That figure was very beautiful to look upon, with a soft, white hat drawn down over the proud brows, and a red and curling lip. It was dressed in an open robe of blue satin. I had seen that figure before. It was the likeness of Miss Furnivall in her youth; and the terrible phantoms moved on, regardless of old Miss Furnivall's wild entreaty, – and the uplifted crutch fell on the right shoulder of the little child, and the younger sister looked on, stony, and deadly serene. But at that moment, the dim lights, and the fire that gave no heat, went out of themselves, and Miss Furnivall lay at our feet stricken down by the palsy – death-stricken.

Yes! she was carried to her bed that night never to rise again. She lay with her face to the wall, muttering low, but muttering always: 'Alas! alas! what is done in youth can never be undone in age! What is done in youth can never be undone in age!'

Curious, if True

(EXTRACT FROM A LETTER FROM
RICHARD WHITTINGHAM, ESQ.)

You were formerly so much amused at my pride in my descent from that sister of Calvin's, who married a Whittingham, Dean of Durham, that I doubt if you will be able to enter into the regard for my distinguished relation that has led me to France, in order to examine registers and archives, which, I thought, might enable me to discover collateral descendants of the great reformer, with whom I might call cousins. I shall not tell you of my troubles and adventures in this research; you are not worthy to hear of them; but something so curious befell me one evening last August, that if I had not been perfectly certain I was wide awake, I might have taken it for a dream.

For the purpose I have named, it was necessary that I should make Tours my head-quarters for a time. I had traced descendants of the Calvin family out of Normandy into the centre of France; but I found it was necessary to have a kind of permission from the bishop of the diocese before I could see certain family papers, which had fallen into the possession of the Church; and, as I had several English friends at Tours, I awaited the answer to my request to Monseigneur de ——, at that town. I was ready to accept any invitation;

but I received very few; and was sometimes a little at a loss what to do with my evenings. The *table d'hôte* was at five o'clock; I did not wish to go to the expense of a private sitting-room, disliked the dinnery atmosphere of the *salle à manger*, could not play either at pool or billiards, and the aspect of my fellow guests was unprepossessing enough to make me unwilling to enter into any *tête-à-tête* gamblings with them. So I usually rose from table early, and tried to make the most of the remaining light of the August evenings in walking briskly off to explore the surrounding country; the middle of the day was too hot for this purpose, and better employed in lounging on a bench in the Boulevards, lazily listening to the distant band and noticing with equal laziness the faces and figures of the women who passed by.

One Thursday evening, the 18th of August it was, I think, I had gone further than usual in my walk, and I found that it was later than I had imagined when I paused to turn back. I fancied I could make a round; I had enough notion of the direction in which I was, to see that by turning up a narrow straight lane to my left I should shorten my way back to Tours. And so I believe I should have done, could I have found an outlet at the right place, but field-paths are almost unknown in that part of France, and my lane, stiff and straight as any street, and marked into terribly vanishing perspective by the regular row of poplars on each side, seemed interminable. Of course night came on, and I was in darkness. In England I might have had a chance of seeing a light in some cottage only a field or two off, and asking my way from the inhabitants; but here I could see no such welcome sight; indeed, I believe French peasants go to bed with the summer daylight, so if there were any habitations in the neighbourhood I never saw them. At last – I believe I must have walked two hours in the darkness, – I saw the dusky outline of a wood on one side of the weariful lane, and, impatiently careless of all forest laws and penalties for trespassers, I made my way to it, thinking that if the worst came to the worst, I could find some covert – some shelter where I could lie down and rest, until the morning light gave me a chance of finding my way back to Tours. But the plantation, on the outskirts of what appeared to me a dense wood, was of young trees, too closely planted to be more than slender stems growing up to a good height, with scanty foliage on their summits. On I went towards the thicker forest, and once there I slackened my pace, and began to look about me for a good lair. I was as dainty as Lochiel's grandchild, who made his grandsire indignant at the luxury of his pillow of snow; this brake was too full of brambles, that felt damp with dew; there was no hurry, since I had given up all hope of passing the night between four walls; and I went leisurely groping about, and trusting that there were no wolves to be poked up out of their summer drowsiness by my stick, when all at once I saw a château before me, not a quarter of a mile off, at the end of what seemed to be an ancient avenue (now overgrown and irregular), which I happened to be crossing, when I looked to my right, and saw the welcome sight. Large, stately and dark was its outline against the dusky night-sky; there were pepper-boxes and tourelles and what-not fantastically going up into the dim starlight. And more to the purpose still, though I could not see the details of the building that I was now facing, it was plain enough that there were lights in many windows, as if some great entertainment was going on.

'They are hospitable people, at any rate,' thought I. 'Perhaps they will give me a bed. I don't suppose French propriétaires have traps and horses quite as plentiful as English gentlemen; but they are evidently having a large party, and some of their guests may be from Tours, and will give me a cast back to the Lion d'Or. I am not proud, and I am dog-tired. I am not above hanging on behind, if need be.'

So, putting a little briskness and spirit into my walk, I went up to the door, which was standing open, most hospitably, and showing a large lighted hall, all hung round with spoils of the chase, armour, &c., the details of which I had not time to notice, for the instant I stood on the threshold a huge porter appeared, in a strange, old-fashioned dress, a kind of livery which well befitted the general appearance of the house. He asked me, in French (so curiously pronounced that I thought I had hit upon a new kind of *patois*), my name, and whence I came. I thought he would not be much the wiser, still it was but civil to give it before I made my request for assistance; so, in reply, I said –

'My name is Whittingham – Richard Whittingham, an English gentleman, staying at – .' To my infinite surprise, a light of pleased intelligence came over the giant's face; he made me a low bow, and said (still in the same curious dialect) that I was welcome, that I was long expected.

'Long expected!' What could the fellow mean? Had I stumbled on a nest of relations by John Calvin's side, who had heard of my genealogical inquiries, and were gratified and interested by them? But I was too much pleased to be

Curious, if True

under shelter for the night to think it necessary to account for my agreeable reception before I enjoyed it. Just as he was opening the great heavy *battants* of the door that led from the hall to the interior, he turned round and said, –

'Apparently Monsieur le Géanquilleur is not come with you.'

'No! I am all alone; I have lost my way,' – and I was going on with my explanation, when he, as if quite indifferent to it, led the way up a great stone staircase, as wide as many rooms, and having on each landing-place massive iron wickets, in a heavy framework; these the porter unlocked with the solemn slowness of age. Indeed, a strange, mysterious awe of the centuries that had passed away since this château was built, came over me as I waited for the turning of the ponderous keys in the ancient locks. I could almost have fancied that I heard a mighty rushing murmur (like the ceaseless sound of a distant sea, ebbing and flowing for ever and for ever), coming forth from the great vacant galleries that opened out on each side of the broad staircase, and were to be dimly perceived in the darkness above us. It was as if the voices of generations of men yet echoed and eddied in the silent air. It was strange, too, that my friend the porter going before me, ponderously infirm, with his feeble old hands striving in vain to keep the tall *flambeau* he held steadily before him, – strange, I say, that he was the only domestic I saw in the vast halls and passages, or met with on the grand staircase. At length we stood before the gilded doors that led into the saloon where the family – or it might be the company, so great was the buzz of voices – was assembled. I would have remonstrated when I found he was going to introduce me, dusty and travel-smeared, in a morning costume that was not even my best, into this grand *salon*, with nobody knew how many ladies and gentlemen assembled; but the obstinate old man was evidently bent upon taking me straight to his master, and paid no heed to my words.

The doors flew open, and I was ushered into a saloon curiously full of pale light, which did not culminate on any spot, nor proceed from any centre, nor flicker with any motion of the air, but filled every nook and corner, making all things deliciously distinct; different from our light of gas or candle, as is the difference between a clear southern atmosphere and that of our misty England.

At the first moment, my arrival excited no attention, the apartment was so full of people, all intent on their own conversation. But my friend the porter went up to a handsome lady of middle age, richly attired in that antique manner which fashion has brought round again of late years, and, waiting first in an attitude of deep respect till her attention fell upon him, told her my name and something about me, as far as I could guess from the gestures of the one and the sudden glance of the eye of the other.

She immediately came towards me with the most friendly actions of greeting, even before she had advanced near enough to speak. Then, – and was it not strange? – her words and accent were that of the commonest peasant of the country. Yet she herself looked high-bred, and would have been dignified had she been a shade less restless, had her countenance worn a little less lively and inquisitive expression. I had been poking a good deal about the old parts of Tours,

Curious, if True

and had had to understand the dialect of the people who dwelt in the Marché au Vendredi and similar places, or I really should not have understood my handsome hostess, as she offered to present me to her husband, a henpecked, gentlemanly man, who was more quaintly attired than she in the very extreme of that style of dress. I thought to myself that in France, as in England, it is the provincials who carry fashion to such an excess as to become ridiculous.

However, he spoke (still in the *patois*) of his pleasure in making my acquaintance, and led me to a strange uneasy easy-chair, much of a piece with the rest of the furniture, which might have taken its place without any anachronism by the side of that in the Hôtel Cluny. Then again began the clatter of French voices, which my arrival had for an instant interrupted, and I had leisure to look about me. Opposite to me sat a very sweet-looking lady, who must have been a great beauty in her youth, I should think, and would be charming in old age, from the sweetness of her countenance. She was, however, extremely fat, and on seeing her feet laid up before her on a cushion, I at once perceived that they were so swollen as to render her incapable of walking, which probably brought on her excessive *embonpoint*. Her hands were plump and small, but rather coarse-grained in texture, not quite so clean as they might have been, and altogether not so aristocratic-looking as the charming face. Her dress was of superb black velvet, ermine-trimmed, with diamonds thrown all abroad over it.

Not far from her stood the least little man I had ever seen; of such admirable proportions no one could call him a dwarf, because with that word we usually associate something of deformity; but yet with an elfin look of shrewd, hard, worldly wisdom in his face that marred the impression which his delicate regular little features would otherwise have conveyed. Indeed, I do not think he was quite of equal rank with the rest of the company, for his dress was inappropriate to the occasion (and he apparently was an invited, while I was an involuntary guest); and one or two of his gestures and actions were more like the tricks of an uneducated rustic than anything else. To explain what I mean: his boots had evidently seen much service, and had been re-topped, re-heeled, re-soled to the extent of cobbler's powers. Why should he have come in them if they were not his best – his only pair? And what can be more ungenteel than poverty? Then again he had an uneasy trick of putting his hand up to his throat, as if he expected to find something the matter with it; and he had the awkward habit – which I do not think he could have copied from Dr Johnson, because most probably he had never heard of him – of trying always to retrace his steps on the exact boards on which he had trodden to arrive at any particular part of the room. Besides, to settle the question, I once heard him addressed as Monsieur Poucet, without any aristocratic 'de' for a prefix; and nearly every one else in the room was a marquis, at any rate.

I say, 'nearly every one'; for some strange people had the *entrée*; unless, indeed, they were, like me, benighted. One of the guests I should have taken for a servant, but for the extraordinary influence he seemed to have over the man I took for his master, and who never did anything without, apparently, being urged thereto by this follower. The master, magnificently dressed, but ill at ease in his clothes, as if they

Curious, if True

had been made for some one else, was a weak-looking, handsome man, continually sauntering about, and I almost guessed an object of suspicion to some of the gentlemen present, which, perhaps, drove him on the companionship of his follower, who was dressed something in the style of an ambassador's *chasseur*; yet it was not a *chasseur*'s dress after all; it was something more thoroughly old-world; boots half way up his ridiculously small legs, which clattered as he walked along, as if they were too large for his little feet; and a great quantity of grey fur, as trimming to coat, court-mantle, boots, cap – everything. You know the way in which certain countenances remind you perpetually of some animal, be it bird or beast! Well, this *chasseur* (as I will call him for want of a better name) was exceedingly like the great Tom-cat that you have seen so often in my chambers, and laughed at almost as often for his uncanny gravity of demeanour. Grey whiskers has my Tom – grey whiskers had the chasseur: grey hair overshadows the upper lip of my Tom – grey mustachios hid that of the chasseur. The pupils of Tom's eyes dilate and contract as I had thought cats' pupils only could do, until I saw those of the *chasseur*. To be sure, canny as Tom is, the *chasseur* had the advantage in the more intelligent expression. He seemed to have obtained most complete sway over his master or patron, whose looks he watched, and whose steps he followed, with a kind of distrustful interest that puzzled me greatly.

There were several other groups in the more distant part of the saloon, all of the stately old school, all grand and noble, I conjectured from their bearing. They seemed perfectly well acquainted with each other, as if they were in the habit of meeting. But I was interrupted in my observations by the tiny little gentleman on the opposite side of the room coming across to take a place beside me. It is no difficult matter to a Frenchman to slide into conversation, and so gracefully did my pigmy friend keep up the character of the nation, that we were almost confidential before ten minutes had elapsed.

Now I was quite aware that the welcome which all had extended to me, from the porter up to the vivacious lady and meek lord of the castle, was intended for some other person. But it required either a degree of moral courage, of which I cannot boast, or the self-reliance and conversational powers of a bolder and cleverer man than I, to undeceive people who had fallen into so fortunate a mistake for me. Yet the little man by my side insinuated himself so much into my confidence, that I had half a mind to tell him of my exact situation, and to turn him into a friend and an ally.

'Madame is perceptibly growing older,' said he, in the midst of my perplexity, glancing at our hostess.

'Madame is still a very fine woman,' replied I.

'Now, is it not strange,' continued he, lowering his voice, 'how women almost invariably praise the absent, or departed, as if they were angels of light, while as for the present, or the living' – here he shrugged up his little shoulders, and made an expressive pause. 'Would you believe it! Madame is always praising her late husband to monsieur's face; till, in fact, we guests are quite perplexed how to look: for, you know, the late M. de Retz's character was quite notorious, – everybody has heard of him.' All the world of Touraine, thought I, but I made an assenting noise.

Curious, if True

At this instant, monsieur our host came up to me, and with a civil look of tender interest (such as some people put on when they inquire after your mother, about whom they do not care one straw), asked if I had heard lately how my cat was? 'How my cat was!' What could the man mean? My cat! Could he mean the tailless Tom, born in the Isle of Man, and now supposed to be keeping guard against the incursions of rats and mice into my chambers in London? Tom is, as you know, on pretty good terms with some of my friends, using their legs for rubbing-posts without scruple, and highly esteemed by them for his gravity of demeanour, and wise manner of winking his eyes. But could his fame have reached across the Channel? However, an answer must be returned to the inquiry, as monsieur's face was bent down to mine with a look of polite anxiety; so I, in my turn, assumed an expression of gratitude, and assured him that, to the best of my belief, my cat was in remarkably good health.

'And the climate agrees with her?'

'Perfectly,' said I, in a maze of wonder at this deep solicitude in a tailless cat who had lost one foot and half an ear in some cruel trap. My host smiled a sweet smile, and, addressing a few words to my little neighbour, passed on.

'How wearisome those aristocrats are!' quoth my neighbour, with a slight sneer. 'Monsieur's conversation rarely extends to more than two sentences to any one. By that time his faculties are exhausted, and he needs the refreshment of silence. You and I, monsieur, are, at any rate, indebted to our own wits for our rise in the world!'

Here again I was bewildered! As you know, I am rather

proud of my descent from families which, if not noble themselves, are allied to nobility, – and as to my 'rise in the world' – if I had risen, it would have been rather for balloon-like qualities than for mother-wit, to being unencumbered with heavy ballast either in my head or my pockets. However, it was my cue to agree: so I smiled again.

'For my part,' said he, 'if a man does not stick at trifles, if he knows how to judiciously add to, or withhold facts, and is not sentimental in his parade of humanity, he is sure to do well; sure to affix a *de* or *von* to his name, and end his days in comfort. There is an example of what I am saying' – and he glanced furtively at the weak-looking master of the sharp, intelligent servant, whom I have called the *chasseur*.

'Monsieur le Marquis would never have been anything but a miller's son, if it had not been for the talents of his servant. Of course you know his antecedents?'

I was going to make some remarks on the changes in the order of the peerage since the days of Louis XVI – going, in fact, to be very sensible and historical – when there was a slight commotion among the people at the other end of the room. Lacqueys in quaint liveries must have come in from behind the tapestry, I suppose (for I never saw them enter, though I sat right opposite to the doors), and were handing about the slight beverages and slighter viands which are considered sufficient refreshments, but which looked rather meagre to my hungry appetite. These footmen were standing solemnly opposite to a lady, – beautiful, splendid as the dawn, but – sound asleep in a magnificent settee. A gentleman who showed so much irritation at her ill-timed slumbers, that I think he must have been her husband, was

Curious, if True

trying to awaken her with actions not far removed from shakings. All in vain; she was quite unconscious of his annoyance, or the smiles of the company, or the automatic solemnity of the waiting footman, or the perplexed anxiety of monsieur and madame.

My little friend sat down with a sneer, as if his curiosity was quenched in contempt.

'Moralists would make an infinity of wise remarks on that scene,' said he. 'In the first place, note the ridiculous position into which their superstitious reverence for rank and title puts all these people. Because monsieur is a reigning prince over some minute principality, the exact situation of which no one has as yet discovered, no one must venture to take their glass of *eau sucré* till Madame la Princesse awakens; and, judging from past experience, those poor lacqueys may have to stand for a century before that happens. Next – always speaking as a moralist, you will observe – note how difficult it is to break off bad habits acquired in youth!'

Just then the prince succeeded, by what means I did not see, in awaking the beautiful sleeper. But at first she did not remember where she was, and looking up at her husband with loving eyes, she smiled and said:

'Is it you, my prince?'

But he was too conscious of the suppressed amusement of the spectators and his own consequent annoyance, to be reciprocally tender, and turned away with some little French expression, best rendered into English by 'Pooh, pooh, my dear!'

After I had had a glass of delicious wine of some unknown quality, my courage was in rather better plight than before, and I told my cynical little neighbour – whom I must say I was beginning to dislike – that I had lost my way in the wood, and had arrived at the château quite by mistake.

He seemed mightily amused at my story; said that the same thing had happened to himself more than once; and told me that I had better luck than he had on one of these occasions, when, from his account, he must have been in considerable danger of his life. He ended his story by making me admire his boots, which he said he still wore, patched though they were, and all their excellent quality lost by patching, because they were of such a first-rate make for long pedestrian excursions. 'Though, indeed,' he wound up by saying, 'the new fashion of railroads would seem to supersede the necessity for this description of boots.'

When I consulted him as to whether I ought to make myself known to my host and hostess as a benighted traveller, instead of the guest whom they had taken me for, he exclaimed, 'By no means! I hate such squeamish morality.' And he seemed much offended by my innocent question, as if it seemed by implication to condemn something in himself. He was offended and silent; and just at this moment I caught the sweet, attractive eyes of the lady opposite – that lady whom I named at first as being no longer in the bloom of youth, but as being somewhat infirm about the feet, which were supported on a raised cushion before her. Her looks seemed to say, 'Come here, and let us have some conversation together'; and, with a bow of silent excuse to my little companion, I went across to the lame old lady. She acknowledged my coming with the prettiest gesture of thanks possible; and, half apologetically, said, 'It is a little dull to be unable to move about on such evenings as this; but it is a just punishment to me for my early vanities. My poor feet, that were by nature so small, are now taking their revenge for my cruelty in forcing them into such little slippers ... Besides, monsieur,' with a pleasant smile, 'I thought it was possible you might be weary of the malicious sayings of your little neighbour. He has not borne the best character in his youth, and such men are sure to be cynical in their old age.'

'Who is he?' asked I, with English abruptness.

'His name is Poucet, and his father was, I believe, a wood-cutter, or charcoal burner, or something of the sort. They do tell sad stories of connivance at murder, ingratitude and obtaining money on false pretences – but you will think me as bad as he if I go on with my slanders. Rather let us admire the lovely lady coming up towards us, with the roses in her hand – I never see her without roses, they are so closely connected with her past history, as you are doubtless aware. Ah, beauty!' said my companion to the lady drawing near to us, 'it is like you to come to me, now that I can no longer go to you.' Then turning to me, and gracefully drawing me into the conversation, she said, 'You must know that, although we never met until we were both married, we have been almost like sisters ever since. There have been so many points of resemblance in our circumstances, and I think I may say in our characters. We had each two elder sisters – mine were but half-sisters, though – who were not so kind to us as they might have been.'

'But have been sorry for it since,' put in the other lady.

'Since we have married princes,' continued the same lady, with an arch smile that had nothing of unkindness in it, 'for we both have married far above our original stations in life; we are both unpunctual in our habits, and, in consequence of this failing of ours, we have both had to suffer mortification and pain.'

'And both are charming,' said a whisper close behind me. 'My lord the marquis, say it – say, "And both are charming."'

'And both are charming,' was spoken aloud by another voice. I turned, and saw the wily cat-like *chasseur*, prompting his master to make civil speeches.

The ladies bowed with that kind of haughty acknowledgment which shows that compliments from such a source are distasteful. But our trio of conversation was broken up, and I was sorry for it. The marquis looked as if he had been stirred up to make that one speech, and hoped that he would not be expected to say more; while behind him stood the *chasseur*, half impertinent and half servile in his ways and attitudes. The ladies, who were real ladies, seemed to be sorry for the awkwardness of the marquis, and addressed some trifling questions to him, adapting themselves to the subjects on which he could have no trouble in answering. The *chasseur*, meanwhile, was talking to himself in a growling tone of voice. I had fallen a little into the background at this interruption in a conversation which promised to be so pleasant, and I could not help hearing his words.

'Really, De Carabas grows more stupid every day. I have a great mind to throw off his boots, and leave him to his fate. I was intended for a court, and to a court I will go, and make my own fortune as I have made his. The emperor will appreciate my talents.'

And such are the habits of the French, or such his forgetfulness of good manners in his anger, that he spat right and left on the parquetted floor.

Just then a very ugly, very pleasant-looking man, came towards the two ladies to whom I had lately been speaking, leading up to them a delicate, fair woman, dressed all in the softest white, as if she were *vouée au blanc*. I do not think there was a bit of colour about her. I thought I heard her making, as she came along, a little noise of pleasure, not exactly like the singing of a tea-kettle, nor yet like the cooing of a dove, but reminding me of each sound.

'Madame de Mioumiou was anxious to see you,' said he, addressing the lady with the roses, 'so I have brought her across to give you a pleasure!' What an honest, good face! but oh! how ugly! And yet I liked his ugliness better than most persons' beauty. There was a look of pathetic acknowledgment of his ugliness, and a deprecation of your too hasty judgment, in his countenance that was positively winning. The soft, white lady kept glancing at my neighbour the *chasseur*, as if they had had some former acquaintance, which puzzled me very much, as they were of such different rank. However, their nerves were evidently strung to the same tune, for at a sound behind the tapestry, which was more like the scuttering of rats and mice than anything else, both Madame de Mioumiou and the chasseur started with the most eager look of anxiety on their countenances, and by their restless movements – madame's panting, and the fiery dilation of his eyes – one might see that commonplace sounds affected them both in a manner very different to the rest of the company. The ugly husband of the lovely lady with the roses now addressed himself to me.

'We are much disappointed,' he said, 'in finding that monsieur is not accompanied by his countryman – *le grand* Jean d'Angleterre; I cannot pronounce his name rightly' – and he looked at me to help him out.

'*Le grand* Jean d'Angleterre!' now who was *le grand* Jean d'Angleterre? John Bull? John Russell? John Bright?

'Jean – Jean' – continued the gentleman, seeing my embarrassment. 'Ah, these terrible English names – "Jean de Géanquilleur"!'

I was as wise as ever. And yet the name struck me as familiar, but slightly disguised. I repeated it to myself. It was mighty like John the Giant-killer, only his friends always call that worthy 'Jack'. I said the name aloud.

'Ah, that is it!' said he. 'But why has he not accompanied you to our little reunion to-night?'

I had been rather puzzled once or twice before, but this serious question added considerably to my perplexity. Jack the Giant-killer had once, it is true, been rather an intimate friend of mine, as far as (printer's) ink and paper can keep up a friendship, but I had not heard his name mentioned for years; and for aught I knew he lay enchanted with King Arthur's knights, who lie entranced until the blast of the trumpets of four mighty kings shall call them to help at England's need. But the question had been asked in serious earnest by that gentleman, whom I more wished to think well of me than I did any other person in the room. So I answered respectfully that it was long since I had heard

Curious, if True

anything of my countryman; but that I was sure it would have given him as much pleasure as it was doing myself to have been present at such an agreeable gathering of friends. He bowed, and then the lame lady took up the word.

'To-night is the night when, of all the year, this great old forest surrounding the castle is said to be haunted by the phantom of a little peasant girl who once lived hereabouts; the tradition is that she was devoured by a wolf. In former days I have seen her on this night out of yonder window at the end of the gallery. Will you, *ma belle*, take monsieur to see the view outside by the moonlight (you may possibly see the phantom-child); and leave me to a little *tête-à-tête* with your husband?'

With a gentle movement the lady with the roses complied with the other's request, and we went to a great window, looking down on the forest, in which I had lost my way. The tops of the far-spreading and leafy trees lay motionless beneath us in that pale, wan light, which shows objects almost as distinct in form, though not in colour, as by day. We looked down on the countless avenues, which seemed to converge from all quarters to the great old castle; and suddenly across one, quite near to us, there passed the figure of a little girl, with the '*capuchon*' on, that takes the place of a peasant girl's bonnet in France. She had a basket on one arm, and by her, on the side to which her head was turned, there went a wolf. I could almost have said it was licking her hand, as if in penitent love, if either penitence or love had ever been a quality of wolves, – but though not of living, perhaps it may be of phantom wolves.

'There, we have seen her!' exclaimed my beautiful

companion. 'Though so long dead, her simple story of household goodness and trustful simplicity still lingers in the hearts of all who have ever heard of her; and the country-people about here say that seeing that phantom-child on this anniversary brings good luck for the year. Let us hope that we shall share in the traditionary good fortune. Ah! here is Madame de Retz – she retains the name of her first husband, you know, as he was of higher rank than the present.' We were joined by our hostess.

'If monsieur is fond of the beauties of nature and art,' said she, perceiving that I had been looking at the view from the great window, 'he will perhaps take pleasure in seeing the picture.' Here she sighed, with a little affectation of grief. 'You know the picture I allude to,' addressing my companion, who bowed assent, and smiled a little maliciously, as I followed the lead of madame.

I went after her to the other end of the saloon, noting by the way with what keen curiosity she caught up what was passing either in word or action on each side of her. When we stood opposite to the end wall, I perceived a full-length picture of a handsome, peculiar-looking man, with – in spite of his good looks – a very fierce and scowling expression. My hostess clasped her hands together as her arms hung down in front, and sighed once more. Then, half in soliloquy, she said –

'He was the love of my youth; his stern yet manly character first touched this heart of mine. When – when shall I cease to deplore his loss!'

Not being acquainted with her enough to answer this question (if, indeed, it were not sufficiently answered by the

Curious, if True

fact of her second marriage), I felt awkward; and, by way of saying something, I remarked, –

'The countenance strikes me as resembling something I have seen before – in an engraving from an historical picture, I think; only, it is there the principal figure in a group: he is holding a lady by her hair, and threatening her with his scimitar, while two cavaliers are rushing up the stairs, apparently only just in time to save her life.'

'Alas, alas!' said she, 'you too accurately describe a miserable passage in my life, which has often been represented in a false light. The best of husbands' – here she sobbed, and became slightly inarticulate with her grief – 'will sometimes be displeased. I was young and curious, he was justly angry with my disobedience – my brothers were too hasty – the consequence is, I became a widow!'

After due respect for her tears, I ventured to suggest some commonplace consolation. She turned round sharply: –

'No, monsieur: my only comfort is that I have never forgiven the brothers who interfered so cruelly, in such an uncalled-for manner, between my dear husband and myself. To quote my friend Monsieur Sganarelle – "*Ce sont petites choses qui sont de temps en temps nécessaires dans l'amitié; et cinq ou six coups d'épée entre gens qui s'aiment ne font que ragaillardir l'affection.*"* You observe the colouring is not quite what it should be?'

'In this light the beard is of rather a peculiar tint,' said I.

---

* 'There are little things which are necessary from time to time in friendship; and five or six blow with a sword between people who love each other can only revive their affection.'

'Yes: the painter did not do it justice. It was most lovely, and gave him such a distinguished air, quite different from the common herd. Stay, I will show you the exact colour, if you will come near this *flambeau*!' And going near the light, she took off a bracelet of hair, with a magnificent clasp of pearls. It was peculiar, certainly. I did not know what to say. 'His precious lovely beard!' said she. 'And the pearls go so well with the delicate blue!'

Her husband, who had come up to us, and waited till her eye fell upon him before venturing to speak, now said, 'It is strange Monsieur Ogre is not yet arrived!'

'Not at all strange,' said she, tartly. 'He was always very stupid, and constantly falls into mistakes, in which he comes worse off; and it is very well he does, for he is a credulous and cowardly fellow. Not at all strange! If you will' – turning to her husband, so that I hardly heard her words, until I caught – 'Then everybody would have their rights, and we should have no more trouble. Is it not, monsieur?' addressing me.

'If I were in England, I should imagine madame was speaking of the reform bill, or the millennium, but I am in ignorance.'

And just as I spoke, the great folding-doors were thrown open wide, and every one started to their feet to greet a little old lady, leaning on a thin black wand – and –

'Madame la Féemarraine,'* was announced by a chorus of sweet shrill voices.

---

*   Madame Fairy Godmother.

And in a moment I was lying in the grass close by a hollow oak-tree, with the slanting glory of the dawning day shining full in my face, and thousands of little birds and delicate insects piping and warbling out their welcome to the ruddy splendour.

1. BOCCACCIO · *Mrs Rosie and the Priest*
2. GERARD MANLEY HOPKINS · *As kingfishers catch fire*
3. *The Saga of Gunnlaug Serpent-tongue*
4. THOMAS DE QUINCEY · *On Murder Considered as One of the Fine Arts*
5. FRIEDRICH NIETZSCHE · *Aphorisms on Love and Hate*
6. JOHN RUSKIN · *Traffic*
7. PU SONGLING · *Wailing Ghosts*
8. JONATHAN SWIFT · *A Modest Proposal*
9. *Three Tang Dynasty Poets*
10. WALT WHITMAN · *On the Beach at Night Alone*
11. KENKŌ · *A Cup of Sake Beneath the Cherry Trees*
12. BALTASAR GRACIÁN · *How to Use Your Enemies*
13. JOHN KEATS · *The Eve of St Agnes*
14. THOMAS HARDY · *Woman much missed*
15. GUY DE MAUPASSANT · *Femme Fatale*
16. MARCO POLO · *Travels in the Land of Serpents and Pearls*
17. SUETONIUS · *Caligula*
18. APOLLONIUS OF RHODES · *Jason and Medea*
19. ROBERT LOUIS STEVENSON · *Olalla*
20. KARL MARX AND FRIEDRICH ENGELS · *The Communist Manifesto*
21. PETRONIUS · *Trimalchio's Feast*
22. JOHANN PETER HEBEL · *How a Ghastly Story Was Brought to Light by a Common or Garden Butcher's Dog*
23. HANS CHRISTIAN ANDERSEN · *The Tinder Box*
24. RUDYARD KIPLING · *The Gate of the Hundred Sorrows*
25. DANTE · *Circles of Hell*
26. HENRY MAYHEW · *Of Street Piemen*
27. HAFEZ · *The nightingales are drunk*
28. GEOFFREY CHAUCER · *The Wife of Bath*
29. MICHEL DE MONTAIGNE · *How We Weep and Laugh at the Same Thing*
30. THOMAS NASHE · *The Terrors of the Night*
31. EDGAR ALLAN POE · *The Tell-Tale Heart*
32. MARY KINGSLEY · *A Hippo Banquet*
33. JANE AUSTEN · *The Beautifull Cassandra*
34. ANTON CHEKHOV · *Gooseberries*
35. SAMUEL TAYLOR COLERIDGE · *Well, they are gone, and here must I remain*
36. JOHANN WOLFGANG VON GOETHE · *Sketchy, Doubtful, Incomplete Jottings*
37. CHARLES DICKENS · *The Great Winglebury Duel*
38. HERMAN MELVILLE · *The Maldive Shark*
39. ELIZABETH GASKELL · *The Old Nurse's Story*
40. NIKOLAY LESKOV · *The Steel Flea*

41. HONORÉ DE BALZAC · *The Atheist's Mass*
42. CHARLOTTE PERKINS GILMAN · *The Yellow Wall-Paper*
43. C.P. CAVAFY · *Remember, Body . . .*
44. FYODOR DOSTOYEVSKY · *The Meek One*
45. GUSTAVE FLAUBERT · *A Simple Heart*
46. NIKOLAI GOGOL · *The Nose*
47. SAMUEL PEPYS · *The Great Fire of London*
48. EDITH WHARTON · *The Reckoning*
49. HENRY JAMES · *The Figure in the Carpet*
50. WILFRED OWEN · *Anthem For Doomed Youth*
51. WOLFGANG AMADEUS MOZART · *My Dearest Father*
52. PLATO · *Socrates' Defence*
53. CHRISTINA ROSSETTI · *Goblin Market*
54. *Sindbad the Sailor*
55. SOPHOCLES · *Antigone*
56. RYŪNOSUKE AKUTAGAWA · *The Life of a Stupid Man*
57. LEO TOLSTOY · *How Much Land Does A Man Need?*
58. GIORGIO VASARI · *Leonardo da Vinci*
59. OSCAR WILDE · *Lord Arthur Savile's Crime*
60. SHEN FU · *The Old Man of the Moon*
61. AESOP · *The Dolphins, the Whales and the Gudgeon*
62. MATSUO BASHŌ · *Lips too Chilled*
63. EMILY BRONTË · *The Night is Darkening Round Me*
64. JOSEPH CONRAD · *To-morrow*
65. RICHARD HAKLUYT · *The Voyage of Sir Francis Drake Around the Whole Globe*
66. KATE CHOPIN · *A Pair of Silk Stockings*
67. CHARLES DARWIN · *It was snowing butterflies*
68. BROTHERS GRIMM · *The Robber Bridegroom*
69. CATULLUS · *I Hate and I Love*
70. HOMER · *Circe and the Cyclops*
71. D. H. LAWRENCE · *Il Duro*
72. KATHERINE MANSFIELD · *Miss Brill*
73. OVID · *The Fall of Icarus*
74. SAPPHO · *Come Close*
75. IVAN TURGENEV · *Kasyan from the Beautiful Lands*
76. VIRGIL · *O Cruel Alexis*
77. H. G. WELLS · *A Slip under the Microscope*
78. HERODOTUS · *The Madness of Cambyses*
79. *Speaking of Siva*
80. *The Dhammapada*

'He gave orders that they were not to get any hot glum pudding in flames, for fear the spirits in their innards might catch fire . . .'

NIKOLAY SEMYONOVICH LESKOV
Born 1831, Oryol, Russia
Died 1895, Saint Petersburg, Russia

'The Steel Flea' was first published in Russian in 1881.

LESKOV IN PENGUIN CLASSICS
Russian Short Stories from Pushkin to Buida
Lady Macbeth of Mtsensk and Other Stories

NIKOLAY LESKOV

The Steel Flea

Translated by
William Edgerton

PENGUIN BOOKS

PENGUIN CLASSICS

UK | USA | Canada | Ireland | Australia
India | New Zealand | South Africa

Penguin Books is part of the Penguin Random House group of companies whose addresses can be found at global.penguinrandomhouse.com.

This edition published in Penguin Classics 2015

010

Translation copyright © The Estate of William Edgerton, 1969, 2015

The moral right of the translator has been asserted

Set in 9.5/13 pt Baskerville 10 Pro
Typeset by Jouve (UK), Milton Keynes

Printed and bound in Great Britain by Clays Ltd, Elcograf S.p.A.

A CIP catalogue record for this book is available from the British Library

ISBN: 978-0-141-39739-9

www.greenpenguin.co.uk

Penguin Random House is committed to a sustainable future for our business, our readers and our planet. This book is made from Forest Stewardship Council® certified paper.

The Steel Flea

(The Tale of the Cross-Eyed, Left-Handed Gunsmith from Tula and the Steel Flea)

1

When Emperor Aleksandr the First had finished the Council of Vienna he decided he would like to take a trip around Europe and look at the marvels in the different countries. He travelled through all the nations, and everywhere his friendliness always helped him get into the most intimidating conversations with all kinds of people, and everybody would amaze him with one thing or another and try to win him over to their side. But along with him was the Don Cossack Platov, who didn't like all this persuasion; he hankered to get back to his farm, and he kept trying to talk the Emperor into going home. And if Platov noticed the Emperor getting really interested in something foreign, then just as soon as all the guides stopped talking for a minute, Platov would pop up and say this, that and the other, telling them ours at home was just as good, and one way or another he would get their minds onto something else.

The Englishmen knew this, and they thought up all kinds of shifty tricks for the Emperor's visit, so as to get him in their power with their outlandishness and get his mind off the Russians, and in a lot of cases they managed it, especially at their big meetings, where Platov couldn't say everything completely in French. But then he was not very much interested in that, since he was a married man and looked on all French conversations as trifles not worthy of serious imagination. And when the Englishmen started inviting the Emperor into all their store houses, gun works and soapy-rope factories, so as to show how much better they were than us in everything and then brag about it, Platov said to himself, 'Well, this has gone far enough. I've put up with it so far, but I can't take any more. Maybe I'll succeed and maybe I'll fail, but at least I won't go back on my own people.'

And he had no sooner said this to himself than the Emperor told him, 'Tomorrow you and I are going to look at their military museum. There they've got such natures of perfection that just as soon as you've seen them you'll agree that we Russians with our significance don't mean a thing.'

Platov said nothing in reply to the Emperor, but just stuck his humpbacked nose down into his shaggy felt overcoat and went to his room. He told his orderly to get a bottle of Caucasian grape vodka out of their travelling supplies. He gulped down a big glassful, said his prayers before the folding travelling icon, covered himself with his overcoat and started snoring such a time that none of the Englishmen in the whole house could get any sleep.

He thought, 'Wait until the morning light; it's always wiser than the night.'

2

The next day the Emperor and Platov went to the museums. The Emperor took none of his other Russians with him, because the carriage they gave him was only a two-sitter.

They came to a great big building, with an entrance beyond description, corridors beyond measure, and one room after another, until at last they came into the biggest hall of all, with tremendulous estuaries, and right in the middle, under a canoply, stood the Apollo Velvet Ear.

The Emperor glanced around sideways at Platov to see what he was looking at and whether he was very much amazed; but Platov was walking along with his eyes looking down at the ground as if he didn't see anything, and he was only winding his moustaches into rings.

The Englishmen started at once to show off all sorts of marvels and explain how everything in them was fitted together with everything else for military circumstances. There were nautical whether-meters, gamblehair coats for the infantry and waterproof rein coats for the cavalry. The Emperor was glad to see all this, and he thought everything looked very good; but Platov held his impatience and said it all didn't mean a thing for him.

The Emperor said, 'How is that possible? How can you be so unfeeling? Doesn't anything at all impress you here?'

And Platov replied, 'Just one thing impresses me here: my Don River boys fought without all this and drove out old Bony Part.'

The Emperor said, 'That's just prejudunce.'

Platov answered, 'I don't know what to call it, but I ain't allowed to argue so I'll keep quiet.'

The Englishmen, seeing this exchange between the Emperor, at once took him up to the statue of Apollo Velvet Ear itself and took a Mortimer rifle out of one hand and a pistol out of the other.

'Here's the kind of production we've got,' they said, and they handed him the rifle.

The Emperor looked calmly at the Mortimer rifle, because he had some like it at home in his Summer Palace, and then they handed him the pistol and said, 'This is a pistol of unknown and inimitable workmanship. Our admiral snatched it off the belt of a robber chieftain at Candelabria.'

The Emperor fastened his eyes on the pistol and couldn't get enough of looking at it.

He oh-ed and ah-ed something awful.

'Oh! Oh! Oh!' he says. 'What do you know about that! How is it possible to do such fine work!' And he turned to Platov and said to him in Russian: 'Now if only I had just one craftsman like that in Russia I would be a very happy man; I'd be so proud I would make a nobleman of him on the spot.'

At these words Platov stuck his right hand into his big wide trousers and pulled out a gunsmith's screwdriver. The Englishmen said, 'This won't come open,' but Platov, paying no attention to them, started tinkering with the gunlock. He turned it once, he turned it twice – and the gun opened up. Platov showed the Emperor the trigger, and right there in the crook was a Russian inscription: *Ivan Moskvin in Tula Town.*

The Englishmen were amazed and nudged each other: 'Uh-oh!' they said. 'We slipped up that time.'

But the Emperor said sadly to Platov, 'Why did you have to embarrass them so much? Let's go.'

They got into their two-sitter again and started off, and the Emperor went to a ball that evening, but Platov downed a still bigger glass of grape vodka and slept the sound sleep of the Cossacks.

He had been glad to put the Englishmen to rout and attract contention to the Tula gunsmith, but he had been put out as well: why did the Emperor have to feel sorry for the Englishmen in a case like this?

'Why did the Emperor feel bad about it?' thought Platov. 'I can't figure it out at all.' And in this consideration he got up twice, crossed himself, and drank vodka until at last he forced himself into a sound sleep.

At that same time the Englishmen were not asleep either, because their heads were spinning, too. While the Emperor was having a good time at the ball, they cooked up such a new marvel for him that they completely knocked the imagination out of Platov.

3

The next day, when Platov reported to the Emperor to say good morning, he told Platov, 'Have the two-sitter carriage hitched up, and let's go to look at some more museums.'

Platov even made bold to ask the Emperor whether they hadn't looked at enough outlandish products, and wouldn't it be better to get ready to go back to Russia, but the Emperor said, 'No, I wish to see still other novelties here; they have boasted to me about how they make sugar of the very highest quality.'

They started off.

The Englishmen showed everything to the Emperor – just how many different highest qualities they had – and

Platov looked and looked, and then suddenly he said, 'But won't you show us your factories where you make Molvo sugar?'

The Englishmen didn't know what 'Molvo' was. They whispered back and forth to each other, winked back and forth to each other, and repeated to each other, 'Molvo, Molvo,' but they couldn't understand what kind of sugar that was that we made in our country, and they had to admit that they had all kinds of sugar – but no 'Molvo'.

Platov said, 'Well, then, you haven't got anything to brag about. Come to our country and we'll fill you full of tea with genuwine Molvo sugar from Bobrinsky's factory.'

But the Emperor tugged him by the sleeve and said quietly: 'Now, please don't go and spoil my politics.'

Then the Englishmen invited the Emperor to their very latest museum, where they had brought together mineral stones and nymphusorias from all over the world, beginning with the most enormous Egyptian hobble lists and coming down to the hide-bound flea, which you can't see with your eyes but can only feel when he bites you between your hide and your body.

The Emperor set out.

They looked at the hobble lists and all kinds of stuffed animals, and then came out and Platov thought to himself, 'There now, thank the Lord, everything is turning out all right: the Emperor hasn't marvelled at anything.'

But as soon as they got to the very last room, there were workmen standing around in everyday jackets and aprons holding a tray that had nothing on it.

Then the Emperor really did marvel because they offered him an empty tray.

'What does this mean?' he asked, and the English craftsmen replied, 'This is our humble offering to your Highness.'

'But what *is* it?'

'Well,' they said, 'does your Highness kindly see this little speck?'

The Emperor took a look and saw that there really was the tiniest little speck lying on the tray.

The workmen said, 'Be so kind as to spit on your finger and pick it up and put it on your hand.'

'What good is that speck to me?'

'That,' they answered, 'is not a speck but a nymphusoria.'

'Is it alive?'

'No, sir,' they answered, 'it's not alive. We made it in the shape of a flea out of pure English steel, and inside it is a motor and a spring. Be so kind as to wind it up with the key: then it will do a little *dansez*.'

The Emperor got curious and asked, 'But where is the key?'

The Englishmen replied, 'Here is the key, right in front of your eyes.'

'Then why can't I see it?' asked the Emperor.

The Steel Flea

'Because,' they said, 'you have to blow it up in a nitroscope.'

A nitroscope was brought in, and the Emperor saw that a little key really was lying on the tray beside the flea.

'Be so kind as to take it in your hand,' they said. 'There's a hole in its belly for the key, and the key will take seven turns. Then it will start its *dansez*.'

The Emperor could barely pick up the key and barely hold it in his fingers. He took hold of the flea with his other hand and hadn't hardly stuck the key in before he felt the whiskers move, and then the legs started working, and at last it suddenly jumped up and in one bound did a straight *dansez* and two fairiations to one side and then to the other, and danced like that through a whole cod drill in three fairiations.

The Emperor gave orders on the spot to give a million to the Englishmen in any kind of money they wanted — either in silver five-kopek coins, if they wished, or else in small bills.

The Englishmen asked for it in silver, because they couldn't make heads or tails out of paper money, and then right off they pulled another one of their shifty tricks: they handed over the flea as a gift, but they hadn't brought any case for it. Without a case you couldn't keep either the flea or the key, because they would get lost and thrown out with the trash. But they had made a case out of a diamond in the shape of a nut, with a hole dug out of the middle for the flea. They didn't make a gift of this, because they said the case was government property, and they are very strict over there about government property, even for the Emperor – you can't give it away.

Platov was about to get hot under the collar, and he said, 'What's the idea of all this swindle! They gave us a gift and they got a million for it, and still that isn't enough! The case,' he says, 'always goes with such things as these.'

But the Emperor said, 'Leave off, please, this isn't your affair – don't go and spoil my politics. They have their own customs.' And he asked, 'How much does that nut cost that the flea fits into?'

The Englishmen reckoned that would be five thousand more.

Emperor Aleksandr said, 'Pay them,' and put the flea in that nut himself, and the key along with it, and so as not to lose the nut he put it into his gold snuffbox, and he ordered the snuffbox put into his little travelling casket, which was all covered with the mother of pearl and fishbones. The Emperor dismissed the English workmen with honour and said to them, 'You are the finest workmen in the whole world, and my men can't do anything compared to you.'

They were very pleased with this, and Platov could say nothing against the words of his Emperor. Only he took the nitroscope and slipped it in his pocket without saying anything, because 'it goes with it,' he says, 'and you've taken a lot of money from us already.'

The Steel Flea

The Emperor knew nothing about that till he got to Russia. They left right away, because military affairs had filled the Emperor with melancholy and he wanted to go to spiritual confession before Father Fedot in Taganrog. On the way he and Platov had a mighty unpleasant conversation, because they had entirely different ideas in their heads: the Emperor thought nobody could come up to the Englishmen in art, and Platov begged to report that our people could make anything once they got a good look at it, only they didn't have any useful training. And he pointed out to the Emperor that the English workmen have completely different rules of life, science and production for everything, and every man among them has all the absolute circumstances before him, and for that reason he has a completely different meaning.

The Emperor would not listen very long to that, and when Platov saw this he didn't insist. So they rode along in silence, only Platov would get out at every station and in his aggravation he would drink up a big glass of vodka, eat a little salt mutton, light up his enormous pipe, which was big enough to hold a whole pound of Zhukov tobacco, and then take his seat and sit without saying a word beside the Tsar in the carriage. The Emperor would look off in one direction, and Platov would stick his chibouk out the other window and smoke into the wind. This was how they rode all the way to Petersburg, and when the Emperor went on to see Father Fedot he didn't take Platov at all.

'You,' he said, 'are intemperate in spiritual conversation, and you smoke so much that my head is full of soot from your pipe.'

Platov felt insulted and he lay down at home on his bed of ire, and just kept on lying there, smoking his Zhukov tobacco without intercession.

4

The marvellous flea of blue English steel remained in Aleksandr the First's little fishbone casket until he died in Taganrog, after turning it over to Father Fedot to pass on to the Empress when she calmed down. Empress Elizabeth Alexeyevna looked at the flea's fairiations and smiled, but she didn't take an interest in it.

'My affairs now,' she said, 'are widow's affairs, and no amusements can win my attention,' and when she got back to Petersburg she handed over this wonder with all her other valuables as an inheritance for the new emperor.

In the beginning Tsar Nicholas the First also paid no attention to the flea, because there was trouble at the time he got up on the throne, but after that one day he started looking through the little casket that had come down to him from his brother, and he took out the snuffbox, and out of the snuffbox he took the diamond nut, and in it he found the steel flea, which had not been wound up in

The Steel Flea

a long time and for that reason was not moving, but lay there quietly like it was numb.

The Emperor looked at it in amazement.

'What can this trifle be, and to what purpose did my brother preserve it in this way?'

The courtiers wanted to throw it out, but the Emperor said, 'No, this must mean something.'

They called a druggist from the pharmacy effacing the Anichkin Bridge, who weighed poisons in the very finest scales. They showed it to him, and he took the flea and put it on his tongue and said, 'I feel something cold, like strong metal.' And then he mashed it a little with his teeth and announced, 'Say what you please, but this is not a genuine flea but a nymphusoria, and it is made of metal, and the work is not ours – not Russian.'

The Emperor ordered that inquiries should be made at once about where it had come from and what it signified.

They plunged into an examination of the records and the lists, but nothing was written in the records. They began asking this one and that, but nobody knew anything. By good luck, though, Platov the Don Cossack was still alive and even still lying on his bed of ire and smoking his pipe. As soon as he heard about all that disturbance at the Court, he rose up from his bed, threw down his pipe and reported to the Emperor with all his decorations. The Emperor said, 'What need have you of me, courageous old man?'

And Platov answered, 'I need nothing for myself, Your Majesty, since I eat and drink all I want and I'm satisfied with everything. But,' he says, 'I have come to report about that nymphusoria they found. This is the way it was,' he says, 'this is how it happened right before my eyes in England, and right here beside it is the key, and I've got their own nitroscope, that you can use to blow it up and look at it, and with this key you can wind up the nymphusoria through its belly, and it will hop around in any space you want and do fairiations to each side.'

They wound it up, it began to jump, and Platov said, 'You're right, Your Majesty,' he says, 'that the work is mighty fine and interesting, only it's not right for us to marvel at it with nothing but the rapture of our feelings. It ought to be submitted for Russian inspection at Tula or Sesterbek (at that time Sestroretsk was still called Sesterbek), to see whether our craftsmen can't outdo it, so that the Englishmen won't keep lording it over us Russians.'

Emperor Nicholas had great confidence in his Russian men and didn't like to yield to any foreigner, and so he answered Platov, 'You speak well, courageous old man, and I charge you with the task of proving this matter. With all my cares I do not need this little box. You take it with you, and lie no more on your bed of ire, but go to the silent Don, and strike up intimidating conversations there with my Don people about their life and devotion and what is pleasing to them. And when you go through

Tula, show this nymphusoria to my Tula craftsmen, that they may ponder over it. Tell them from me that my brother marvelled at this thing, and he praised above all others the foreigners who made this nymphusoria, but I place my hope in my own people, that they are surpassed by no one. They will heed my word and will do something.'

5

Platov took the steel flea, and when he went through Tula toward the Don, he showed it to the Tula gunsmiths and passed the Emperor's words on to them and then asked, 'Now what can we do about it, Orthodox brethren?'

The gunsmiths replied, 'Worthy old man we feel the gracious word of the Emperor, and we never can forget it, because he puts his hope in his own people, but what we can do about it in this here case we can't say in just one minute, because the English nation ain't stupid either; they're even sort of cunning, and their art is full of horse sense. We mustn't go out after them till we've pondered about it and got God's blessing. Now, if you have confidence in us like the Emperor, then journey hence to your home upon the silent Don, and leave us this here little flea just like it is, in its case and in the golden snuffbox of the Tsar. Make yourself merry along the Don and heal the wounds you have suffered for our fatherland, and when you return through Tula, tarry and send for us: by that time, God willing, it may be that we'll have something thunk up.'

Platov was not completely satisfied because the Tula workmen demanded so much time and didn't talk very clearly about just what they hoped to make. He asked them this way and that, and using his Don Cossack cunning he talked with them in every sort of way, but the Tula men were no less cunning than he was, because they already had thought up such a plan that they couldn't really hope even Platov would believe them, and they wanted to carry out their bold idea right away and then hand it over.

They said, 'Even we ourselves don't know yet what we'll do, but we'll only rest our faith in God and trust that the Tsar's word won't be put to shame through our doings.'

Platov kept twisting and turning this way and that, and so did the men from Tula.

Platov wriggled and wriggled till he saw that he couldn't outwriggle a Tula man, and then he handed over the snuffbox with the nymphusoria and said, 'Well, there's nothing to do. Let it be your way,' he says. 'I know you – what kind you are. Still, there's nothing to do – I believe you. Only take care and don't try to swap diamonds on me, and don't spoil the fine English workmanship, and don't fool around very long, because I travel fast. Two weeks won't go by before I return again from the silent

Don to Petersburg. At that time see to it that I have something to show the Emperor.'

The gunsmiths reassured him completely, 'We ain't going to harm the fine workmanship,' they said, 'and we won't change diamonds on you, and two weeks are enough time for us, and by the time you come back you will have *something* worthy to be shown to his Imperial Splendour.'

But exactly *what* it was they just wouldn't say.

6

Platov departed from Tula; and three of the gunsmiths, the most skilful of them all – one of them a cross-eyed left-handed man with a birthmark on his cheek and bald spots on his temples where the hair had been pulled out when he was an apprentice – these three bade farewell to their fellow workmen and their families, and without saying anything to anybody they took their bags, put what food they needed into them, and disappeared from town.

The only thing anybody noticed was that they didn't go out through the Moscow gate, but through the one on the other side, in the direction of Kiev, and people thought they had gone to Kiev to bow down before the saints resting there in peace or to take counsel with some of the holy men still alive there, who were always available in abundance in Kiev.

But this was only close to the truth and not the truth itself. Neither time nor distance allowed the Tula craftsmen in three weeks to walk to Kiev and then on top of that to make something that would put the English nation to shame. They might have done better to go and pray in Moscow, which was only 'twice fifty miles away', and a good many holy saints rest in peace there too. In the other direction too it was 'twice fifty miles' to Oryol and then another good three hundred from Oryol to Kiev. You won't get over that much ground in a hurry, and even when you've done it you won't get rested in a hurry: for a long time your feet will feel as numb as glass and your hands will tremble.

Some people even thought the craftsmen had bragged a little too much to Platov and then after they thought it over had got scared and run away for good, taking along the Tsar's gold snuffbox, and the diamond, and the English steel flea in its case that had brought them all the trouble.

However, this supposition too was completely unfounded, and was unworthy of the clever men on whom the hope of the nation now rested.

7

The inhabitants of Tula, who are intelligent people and knowledgeable about metal work, are also well known as the finest experts in religion. Their fame in this connection has spread all over their native land and has even reached Mount Athos: they are not only masters at singing their fancy trills; they also know how to paint the picture *Evening Bells*, and if any of them dedicate themselves to greater service and enter monastic life, they become famous as the best managers of monastery household affairs, and they make the most capable collectors of alms. On holy Mount Athos everybody knows that the Tula inhabitants are a most remunerative people, and if it wasn't for them, most likely the dark corners of Russia would not see very many holy relics from the distant East, and Mount Athos would be deprived of many useful contributions from Russian generosity and piety. Today the 'Tula men of Mount Athos' carry holy relics all over our native land and skilfully collect contributions even where there is nothing to collect. The Tula man is full of churchly piety and is highly practical in this matter, and so the three master craftsmen who took it on themselves to uphold Platov, and with him all Russia, made no mistake when they headed south instead of towards Moscow. They didn't go to Kiev at all but to Mtsensk, to the district town of Oryol Province in which there stands the ancient 'stone-graven' icon of Saint Nicholas, which was brought here in the most ancient times along the river Zusha on a large cross, likewise made of stone. This icon is 'awesome and most terrible' in appearance. The sainted archbishop of Myra in Lycia is represented on it full-length, clothed all over in silver-gilt clothing, swarthy of face and holding a temple in one hand and the sword of 'Military Conquest' in the other. It was just this 'Conquest' that held the meaning of the whole thing: Saint Nicholas in general and 'Nicholas of Mtsensk' in particular was the patron saint of commerce and warfare, and so the Tula gunsmiths went to make their bows to him. They held their prayer service right in front of the icon, and then in front of the stone cross, and finally, returning home by night and saying nothing to anybody, they set about their work in awful secrecy. All three of them got together in Lefty's house; they locked the doors, boarded up the windows, lighted a lamp before the icon of Saint Nicholas and started to work.

One day, two days, three days they sat without going out anywhere, all of them tapping away with their hammers. They were making something, but what it was they were making nobody knew.

Everyone was curious, but nobody could find out a thing, because the workmen said nothing and never stuck their noses outside. All sorts of people would go up to the little house and knock on the door with all sorts of excuses, to ask for fire or borrow some salt, but the three experts would not open up for any kind of request. Even how they got food nobody knew. People tried to scare them, and pretended that the house next door was on fire to see whether they wouldn't run out in fright and give away the secret of what they were making, but nothing could take in those shrewd workmen. Lefty stuck his head out only once and shouted, 'Go ahead and burn up; we ain't got time,' and then he drew in his plucked head, banged the shutters tight and got to work again. Through the tiny cracks people could only see the glitter of a light and hear the ringing blows of tiny hammers tapping on anvils.

In a word, the whole thing was handled in such awful secrecy that there was no way to find out anything about it, and it lasted right up to the return of the Cossack Platov from the silent Don on his way to the Emperor, and during all that time the craftsmen saw nobody and said nothing.

8

Platov travelled in great haste and ceremony: he himself sat in the carriage, and on the coach-boxes two Cossack scurriers holding whips sat on each side of the driver and poured it on him unmercifully so as to make him hurry. If either one of the Cossacks dozed off, Platov would give him a kick from inside the carriage, and they would tear along even more wildly. These measures worked so well that there was no holding back the horses at a single station anywhere; they would always gallop on a hundred paces past the halting-place. Then the Cossack would work on the driver once more in the opposite direction, and they would go back to the entrance.

That was the way they rolled into Tula: there too at first they flew a hundred paces beyond the Moscow gate, and then the Cossack worked on the driver with his whip in the opposite direction, and at the entrance they started hitching up fresh horses. Platov didn't get out of the carriage, but only told his scurrier to go as fast as possible and get the craftsmen he had left the flea with.

One scurrier dashed off to get them to come as fast as possible and bring him the work that was to put the Englishmen to shame, and that scurrier had run only a short distance when Platov sent first one and then another after him so as to speed things up.

He sent off all his scurriers and then began dispatching ordinary people from the curious crowd, and in impatience he even stuck his own legs out of the carriage and was about to start running impatiently himself, and he gritted his teeth because they were all so slow in coming into sight.

In those days everything had to be done just right and very fast, so as not to lose a minute that might be useful to Russia.

9

At that very moment the Tula craftsmen who were making the marvellous thing had finished their work. The scurriers ran up to them puffing and blowing, and the ordinary people from the curious crowd – well, they didn't even get there at all, because their legs, being out of practice, scattered and fell all along the way, and then in terror, for fear they might catch sight of Platov, they lit out for home and hid wherever they could.

As soon as the scurriers ran up, they gave a shout, and when they saw that nobody opened up, they jerked at the bolts on the shutters, but the bolts were so strong they wouldn't give at all; they pulled at the doors, but the doors were fastened from the inside with heavy oak bars. Then the scurriers picked up a beam from the street and stuck it under the eave of the roof the way firemen do, and in one blow they prized the whole roof off the hut. But as soon as they got the roof off, they themselves keeled over, because the workmen with their unceaseless labour in their crowded little shanty had expired so much that a man who wasn't used to it, coming right in when the wind was dead, instinkly choked.

The messengers cried out, 'What are you doing, you so-and-so's, you swine? What do you mean by knocking us over with that expiration? Or ain't you got any fear of God left in you?'

And they answered, 'Just a minute, we're driving in the last nail, and as soon as we hammer it down we'll bring out our work.'

The messengers said, 'He'll eat us alive before then and won't even leave our souls for the funeral.'

But the craftsmen answered, 'He won't have time to

gobble you up, because we drove the last nail in while you were standing there talking. Run and tell him we're bringing it right now.'

The scurriers dashed off, but their hearts weren't in it, because they thought the craftsmen might fool them, and for that reason they ran and ran, but kept looking back. But the craftsmen were coming along behind them, and they had hurried so fast they hadn't even got dressed quite the way they ought for a meeting with an important person, and while they ran they were still fastening the hooks of their kaftans. Two of them had nothing in their hands, but the third one, Lefty, had the Tsar's jewel casket wrapped in a green cloth cover with the English steel flea inside.

10

The scurriers ran up to Platov and said, 'Here they are in person!'

Platov barked at the craftsmen, 'Is it ready?'

'It's all ready,' they answered.

'Give it here.'

They handed it over.

The carriage was already hitched up, and the driver and postillion were in their places. The Cossacks at once took their seats beside the driver and raised their whips over his head and held them brandished there.

The Steel Flea

Platov snatched off the green cover, opened the little casket, took the gold snuffbox out of its padding and the diamond nut out of the snuffbox. He saw the English flea lying there just the way it had before, and apart from it nothing else was there.

Platov said, 'What's the meaning of this? Where is your work that you wanted to console the Emperor with?'

The gunsmiths answered, 'Our work is right there.'

Platov asked, 'What kind of work?'

The gunsmiths answered, 'What's the use of explaining? Everything is right there in front of your eyes. Just take a look at it.'

Platov squared his shoulders and shouted, 'Where's the key to the flea?'

'Why, it's right here,' they answered. 'Where the flea is, there the key is – in the same nut.'

Platov tried to take hold of the key, but his fingers were too stubby. He grabbed and grabbed but couldn't catch either the flea or the key to its bellyworks, and suddenly he burst out and started swearing with colourful Cossack words.

He shouted, 'You scoundrels, you've done nothing at all, and on top of it you've probably ruined the whole thing! I'll take off your heads!'

But the Tula men answered him, 'There ain't no use insulting us. From you, as the Emperor's messenger, we've got to put up with all insults, but just because you wouldn't trust us and thought we were the kind that would even cheat the Emperor hisself, we ain't going to tell you the secret of our work now; just be so kind as to take it to the Emperor, and he'll see what sort of men he's got in us, and whether we've done anything to make him ashamed of us.'

Platov shouted, 'You're lying, you scoundrels, and I won't let you get away from me like that. One of you will go with me to Petersburg, and there I'll get out of him what kind of scullduggery you've been up to.'

And with this he reached out, grabbed the cross-eyed Lefty by the collar with his stubby fingers, so that all the hooks flew off his kazakin shirt, and pitched him into the carriage at his feet.

'Lie there like a puddle,' he said, 'till we get to Petersburg. You'll answer to me for all of them. And you,' he said to the scurriers, 'get a move on! Look sharp now, and see to it that I'm in Petersburg at the Emperor's the day after tomorrow!'

The craftsmen stuck their necks out for their comrade and asked how he could be taken away from them like that without his grasp port. Then he would have no way to get back! But instead of answering them Platov just showed them his fist – a frightful one, all knotty and hacked apart and somehow grown back together again – and waving it in front of them he said, 'There's a grasp port for you!'

And he said to his Cossacks, 'Let's go, boys!'

His Cossacks, drivers and steeds all started working at

The Steel Flea

once and they whisked Lefty away without his grasp port, and two days later, just as Platov had ordered, they rolled up to the Emperor's palace, arriving at such a properly furious gallop that they drove right past the columns.

Platov stood up, hooked on his decorations and went in to the Emperor, telling his Cossack scurriers to keep watch at the entrance over cross-eyed Lefty.

11

Platov was afraid to report to the Emperor in person, because it was awful how noticeable and memorable Tsar Nicholas was – he never forgot anything. Platov knew he was bound to ask him about the flea. And even though he was afraid of no enemy on earth, right here he got cold feet: he carried the little casket into the palace and very quietly laid it down in the hall behind the stove. With the box hidden he presented himself to the Emperor in his office and quickly began reporting on the intimidating conversations he'd had with the Cossacks on the silent Don. He figured he would try to keep the Emperor busy with this. Then if the Emperor remembered and started talking about the flea, he would have to hand it over and answer, but if the Emperor didn't say anything about it, he could just keep quiet. He would tell the Emperor's servant to hide the little casket and lock up Lefty in a fortress cell so as to keep him handy in case he might be needed.

But Emperor Nicholas forgot about nothing, and Platov had barely finished about the intimidating conversations when he asked at once, 'And how about it – how did my Tula craftsmen justify themselves against the English nymphusoria?'

Platov answered the way the matter looked to him.

'Your Majesty,' he says, 'the nymphusoria is still lying in that same space, and I have brought it back, but the Tula craftsmen couldn't make anything more marvellous.'

The Emperor replied, 'You are a courageous old man, but what you report to me cannot be so.'

Platov tried to convince him and told him how the whole thing had happened, and when he got to the part where the Tula workmen asked him to show the flea to the Emperor, Tsar Nicholas slapped him on the back and said, 'Give it here. I know my men won't let me down. Something has been done here that is past all understanding.'

12

They brought the little casket out from behind the stove, they took the cloth cover off, they opened the gold snuffbox and the diamond nut – and there the flea was, lying just the way it had before.

The Emperor took a look and said, 'What a misfortune!' But his faith in his Russian craftsmen didn't slacken, and he sent for his favourite daughter Aleksandra and commanded her, 'You have slender fingers: hasten, take that little key and wind up the bellyworks of that nymphusoria.'

The princess began to wind it up, and the flea at once started wiggling its whiskers, but it didn't move its feet. Aleksandra pulled on the whole works, but still the nymphusoria wouldn't do a single *dansez* or fairiation, the way it used to.

Platov turned green all over and shouted, 'Oh those rascally dogs! Now I understand why they wouldn't tell me anything. It's lucky I brought one of their blockheads along with me.'

With these words he ran out to the entrance, grabbed Lefty by the hair, and began to swing him back and forth so hard that tufts of it started flying. When Platov had stopped beating him, Lefty straightened himself out and said, 'That's the way all my hair got pulled out while I was an apprentice. I don't know what need there is now to go through all that again.'

'That's because I'd counted on you and vouched for you,' said Platov, 'and then you went and spoiled that rarity.'

Lefty answered, 'We're mighty glad you vouched for us, and as for spoiling – we didn't spoil nothing. Just blow it up in your strongest nitroscope and take a look.'

Platov ran back to tell them about the nitroscope, but

to Lefty he only warned, 'I'll give you this-that-and-the-other even yet.'

He ordered the scurriers to twist Lefty's arms even harder behind his back, and he himself went up the steps, puffing and blowing and repeating the prayer, 'Blessed Tsar's Most Blessed Mother, immaculate and pure,' and so on, as needed. And the courtiers who were standing on the steps all turned their backs on him. They thought, 'Platov is done for now, and he'll soon be chased out of the palace,' because they couldn't stand him on account of his bravery.

13

As soon as Platov reported Lefty's words to the Emperor, he said full of joy, 'I know my Russian men will not let me down.' And he ordered the nitroscope to be brought forward on a pillow.

The nitroscope was brought forward that very minute, and the Emperor took the flea and laid it under the glass, first on its belly, then on its side and then on its back. In a word, it was turned in every direction, but nothing could be seen. Still the Emperor didn't lose faith. He only said, 'Bring hither at once that gunsmith who is waiting below.'

Platov reported, 'They'd have to dress him up. He's still

The Steel Flea

got the clothes on he was caught in, and now he's in bad shape.'

But the Emperor replied, 'Never mind; bring him in just as he is.'

Platov said, 'Come in here, now, you so-and-so, and answer to the Emperor before his eyes.'

Lefty replied, 'Why, sure, I'll go like this and I'll answer.'

He went like he was: in ragged boots, with one trouser-leg tucked in and the other dangling, with an old jacket that wouldn't fasten because the hooks were lost, and with the collar that was torn; but it didn't matter – he wasn't embarrassed.

'What of it?' he thought. 'If the Emperor wants to see me, I've got to go, and if I ain't got a grasp port, it ain't my fault, and I'll tell him how it happened.'

As soon as Lefty came in and bowed, the Emperor said to him, 'What does this mean, my good man? We have looked this way and that and have blown it up in the nitroscope and we still can't find anything remarkable.'

Lefty answered, 'Did Your Majesty be so kind as to look at it the right way?'

The nobles motioned to him to tell him that was not the way to talk, but he didn't understand how to talk courtier language – with flattery or cunning – and he kept on talking simply.

The Emperor said to them, 'Stop making things complicated for him; let him answer as he knows how.'

And then he explained to Lefty, 'This is the way we laid it,' he says. And he put the flea under the nitroscope. 'Look at it yourself,' he says. 'You can't see a thing.'

Lefty answered, 'You can't see nothing that way, Your Majesty, because our work is a lot too secret for that size.'

The Emperor asked, 'Then how *do* we manage it?'

'You have to put just one of its feet in detail under the whole nitroscope, and look one at a time at each foot it walks on.'

'Goodness Gracious,' said the Emperor. 'That's powerfully small.'

'But what else can you do,' answered Lefty, 'if that's the only way you can get a look at our work? Then you can see the whole amazement.'

They laid it down the way Lefty said and as soon as the Emperor looked in the upper glass, he beamed all over. He grabbed Lefty just the way he was – dirty, dusty, unwashed – and put his arms around him and kissed him on the cheek, and then he turned to all the courtiers and said, 'You see, I knew better than everybody that my Russians would not let me down. Just look: why, the rascals have taken the English flea and nailed flea-shoes on its feet!'

14

They all came up to look: all the flea's feet really were shod with genuine flea-shoes, and Lefty reported that this was not the only marvel.

'If you had a better nitroscope,' he said, 'one that would blow it up five million times, then you could be so kind as to see that a craftsman's name was put on each shoe, so as to show which Russian gunsmith made that shoe.'

'Is your name there too?' asked the Emperor.

'No, sir,' answered Lefty. 'Mine is the only one that ain't.'

'Why isn't it?'

'Because I did smaller work than these flea-shoes,' he said. 'I made the nails the shoes were fastened on with, and they are too small for any nitroscope to blow them up.'

The Emperor asked, 'But where is your nitroscope, which you used to produce this marvel?'

Lefty answered, 'We are poor people – too poor to own a nitroscope, so we just sharpened our eyes.'

Seeing that Lefty's business had turned out well, the other courtiers began to kiss him and Platov gave him a hundred roubles and said, 'Forgive me, brother, for dragging you around by the hair.'

Lefty answered, 'God will forgive you – it ain't the first time that kind of snow has fallen on my head.'

He would say no more – and he didn't even have time to say more, because the Emperor ordered the iron-shod nymphusoria to be packed up and sent back at once to England, as a sort of gift, to make them understand that it wasn't any marvel to us. And the Emperor ordered the flea to be carried by a special courier who was learned in all languages, and ordered the left-handed smith to go with him so that he himself could show their work to the Englishmen and show them what kind of craftsmen we have in Tula.

Platov made the sign of the Cross over him.

'Blessings be upon you,' he said. 'I'll send you some of my own grape vodka for the journey. Don't drink too little and don't drink too much – drink middlesome.'

And so he did – he sent it.

Count Nestlebroad gave orders to wash Lefty in the Tula Public Baths, cut his hair in a barber shop, and deck him out in the full-dress coat of a singer in the royal choir, so that he would look like he had some kind of paid government rank.

As soon as they had worked him over this way, they filled him with tea and Platov's grape vodka, drew up his belt as tight as possible so that his guts wouldn't shake, and sent him off to London. That is when foreign sights started happening to Lefty.

15

The courier travelled powerfully fast with Lefty, so that they didn't stop to rest anywhere between Petersburg and London, but only drew their belts another notch tighter at every station, so that their guts wouldn't get mixed up with their lungs; but since Lefty on Platov's orders was allotted as much government vodka as he wanted after he had been presented to the Emperor, he kept up his strength on this alone, without eating anything, and he sang Russian songs all the way through Europe – only adding a refrain of foreign words,

> *Aye loolee*
> *Say tray Joe Lee.*

As soon as the courier got him to London, he reported to the proper authorities and handed over the box, and then put Lefty down in a hotel room; but there he soon began to get restless, and besides, he was hungry. He knocked on the door and pointed to his mouth when the servant came, and the servant took him right off to the feeding room.

Here Lefty sat down at a table and waited. He didn't know how to ask for anything in English. But then he figured it out, again he just tapped on the table with his finger and pointed to his mouth; the Englishmen guessed what he meant and served him, only they didn't always bring what he wanted. But he wouldn't take anything that didn't suit him. They brought him their kind of hot glum pudding in flames. He said, 'I don't see how anybody can eat that,' and he wouldn't take a bite. They exchanged it for him and brought him something else to eat. He wouldn't drink their vodka, either, because it was green – like they had flavoured it with sulphuric acid. He picked out the plainest stuff they had, and waited in the cool with his canteen for the courier.

And the people the courier had handed the nymphusoria over to looked at it that very minute through their strongest nitroscope and sent a description right off to a calumnist on the *Daily Telegraft*, so that he could tell everybody about it the very next day.

'And as for that craftsman,' they said, 'we want to see him at once.' The courier took them to the hotel room and from there to the feeding room, where our Lefty had begun to glow very decently, and said, 'There he is.'

The Englishmen slapped Lefty on the back right away and took him by the hands just like their own equal. 'Comrade,' they said, 'comrade, you're a good craftsman. We'll talk to you afterwards when there is time, but now we want to drink to your prosperity.'

They ordered a lot of wine and gave Lefty the first glass, but out of politeness he wouldn't be the first to drink. He thought, 'Maybe you're so aggravated you want to poison me.'

The Steel Flea

'No,' he said, 'that's not the way to do it. Even with a Polish thirst, you have to let the host drink first. You yourselves drink on ahead.'

The Englishmen tasted all their wines in front of him and then started filling his glass. He stood up, crossed himself with his left hand, and drank to the health of them all.

They noticed that he had crossed himself with his left hand, and they asked the courier, 'What is he – a Lutheranian or a Protesterian?'

The courier answered, 'He's not either a Lutheranian or a Protesterian; he belongs to the Russian faith.'

'But why does he cross himself with his left hand?'

The courier replied, 'He's a left-handed man, and he does everything with his left hand.'

The Englishmen marvelled even more and started pumping both Lefty and the courier full of wine, and kept on this way for three whole days, and then they said, 'Now that's enough.' They symphonied some water out of a bottle with impressed air, and when they were refreshed all over they started asking Lefty all about where had he studied, and what had he studied, and how far had he gone in arithmetic.

Lefty answered, 'Our learning is simple – according to the Psalter and the *Dream-Book*. We don't know no arithmetic at all.'

The Englishmen looked at each other and said, 'That's amazing.'

And Lefty answered, 'It's that way all over in our country.'

'But what sort of book is that in Russia,' they asked, 'that dream-book?'

'That book,' he said, 'refers to if King David didn't reveal some fortune-telling clearly in the Psalter, then you can get some extra fortunes out of the *Dream-Book*.'

They said, 'That's too bad. It would be better if you at least knew the four rules of addition; that would be a lot more utilifying to you than your whole *Dream-Book*. Then you would be able to understand that every machine has its balance of forces. As it is, even though you are mighty skilful with your hands, you didn't realize that such a little machine as the one in the nymphusoria was calculated for the most accurate exactness, and it can't carry the flea-shoes. That's why the nymphusoria won't jump or dance any *dansez*.'

Lefty agreed, 'About that there ain't no argument,' he said. 'We didn't get very far in book-learning, but only faithfully serve our fatherland.'

And the Englishmen said to him, 'Stay here with us; we'll give you a big education and you'll turn out to be a superbluous craftsman.'

But Lefty wouldn't agree. 'I've got my parents at home,' he said.

The Englishmen offered to send his parents money, but Lefty wouldn't take it.

'We are devoted to our country,' he said, 'and my

daddy's an old man and my mother's an old woman, and they're used to going to church in their own parish, and it would be mighty lonely here for me all by myself, because I'm still a bachelor by calling.'

'You'll get used to it,' they said. 'You'll accept our laws, and we'll get you married.'

'That can never be,' answered Lefty.

'Why not?'

'Because,' he answered, 'our Russian faith is the rightest one, and the way our forefathers believed is just the way their dissentants have to believe.'

'You don't know our faith,' said the Englishmen. 'We've got the same Christian law and hold to the same Gospel.'

'It's true,' said Lefty, 'that everybody's got the same Gospel, but our books are thicker than yours, and our faith is fuller.'

'How can you judge that way?'

'We've got all the evident proofs of it,' he answered.

'What kind?'

'Why, we've got God-wondering icons and prism-working relics, and you ain't got nothing – except for Sunday you ain't even got any special holidays. And the second reason is that even if I was married in the law to an English girl it would be confusing to live with her.'

'How's that?' they asked. 'Don't turn up your nose at our girls – they too dress neatly and they're good housekeepers.'

But Lefty said, 'I don't know them.'

The Englishmen replied, 'That's no problem – you'll get to know them. We'll fix up a roundy-view for you.'

Lefty started blushing. 'What's the use of stringing the girls along for no reason?' he said, and he wouldn't budge. 'That's something for fine gentlemen. It wouldn't suit us. And if they found out about it at home, in Tula, they'd make fun of me something awful.'

The Englishmen got curious, 'Then suppose we did it without a roundy-view,' they said. 'How do you manage in your country so as to make a favourable choice?'

Lefty explained our way to them. 'In our country,' he said, 'when a man wants to reveal a circumstantial intention in regard to a girl, he sends over a conversational woman, and when she has made a preposition, they politely go to the house together and look the girl over without concealment, and in front of all the relationships.'

They understood, but they answered that they had no conversational women and followed no such custom, and Lefty said, 'That's all the better, because if you go in for that kind of thing you have to do it with a circumstantial intention, and since I don't feel none towards a foreign nation, what's the use of stringing the girls along?'

The Englishmen were pleased with him for these opinions too, and so they started off again in their friendly way, slapping him on the back and the knees, and they asked: 'Just out of curiosity,' they said, 'we'd like to know

The Steel Flea

what signs of defects you've noticed in our girls, and why you keep away from them?'

At this Lefty answered them frankly, 'I don't mean to run them down; I just don't like the way their dresses sort of swish back and forth, so that you can't make out just what they've got on and what it's for. There'll be one thing here, and below something else will be pinned on, and on their arms they'll have some kind of socks. In them velveteen coats of theirs they look just like capuchin monkeys.'

The Englishmen laughed and said, 'Why does that get in your way?'

'It don't get in my way,' answered Lefty, 'only I'm scared I'd be ashamed to look and wait until she got untangled from all that stuff.'

'But do you really think your fashions are better?' they asked.

'Our fashions in Tula,' he replied, 'are simple: every girl is dressed in her own lace. Our lace is worn even by fine ladies.'

Then they showed him off to their own ladies, and there they served him tea and asked him, 'What are you frowning for?'

He answered that 'We ain't used to drinking it so sweet.'

Then they served it to him in the Russian way, with a lump of sugar to suck.

This didn't seem to be as good to them, but Lefty said, 'To our taste this way it's tastier.'

The Englishmen couldn't find any bait at all that could make him take to their life. They could only talk him into staying with them for a short while as their guest, and said they would take him to all sorts of factories and show him all their arts.

And after that, they said, they would put him on their own ship and 'deliver him safe and sound in Petersburg.'

He agreed to that.

16

The Englishmen took charge of Lefty and sent the Russian courier back to Russia. Even though the courier had government rank and was learned in various languages, they weren't interested in him, but they *were* interested in Lefty, and they set out to take Lefty around and show him everything. He looked at all their production: he really liked their metallic mills and their soapy-rope factories, and the way they managed things – especially the way they took care of their workers. Every one of their workmen was always well fed, none was dressed in rags, each one had on a capable everyday jacket and wore thick hard-nail boots with iron caps, so that he wouldn't stump his toes anywhere on anything. Along with his work he got teaching instead of beatings, and he worked with comprehension. In front of each one, hung up right in full view, was a stultification table, and within arm's reach was a racing slate. Whatever any craftsman did, he would look up at the tables, and then check it with comprehension, and then write one thing down on the slate, race another thing, and put it together accurately: whatever was written down in the figures really came out that way. And when a holiday came, they would all get together in couples, each one would take a walking stick in his hand, and they would go for a walk in a proper way, all proud and polite.

Lefty got a good look at all their life and all their work, but above all else he paid attention to something that surprised the Englishmen a lot. He wasn't interested so much in how they made new rifles as in how they took care of the old ones. He would walk around everything and praise it and say, 'We can do that too.'

But whenever he came to an old rifle, he would stick his finger in the barrel, rub it around inside, and sigh, 'That is way yonder better than ours.'

The Englishmen couldn't figure out what Lefty noticed. He asked them, 'Might I know whether or not our generals have ever looked at this?'

They answered, 'Those who have been here must have taken a look.'

'But when they were here,' he asked, 'did they have gloves on or not?'

'Yours are full-dress generals,' they said. 'Gloves come with them, so they must have had them on here.'

Lefty said nothing. But suddenly he began to feel an uneasy homesickness. He pined away and pined away and said to the Englishmen, 'I thank you kindly for your entertainment, and I like everything in your country, and I've seen everything I needed to see – and now I'd like to go home in a hurry.'

They couldn't hold him back any longer. There was no way to let him go by land because he didn't know all languages, and it was a bad time to go by sea because it was the fall of the year and stormy, but he insisted, 'Let me go.'

'We've looked at the whether-meter,' they said. 'A storm is coming; you could drown; after all, this is not like your Gulf of Finland – this is the real Militerranean Sea.'

'It's all the same where a man dies,' he answered. 'It's all God's will alone, and I want to get back home in a hurry; because if I don't, I might get a kind of craziness in the head.'

They couldn't hold him back by force. They fed him till he creaked, they rewarded him with money, they gave him an alarmed gold watch as a souvenir, and for the cold weather at sea on the late fall voyage they gave him a woollen overcoat with a windy hurricane hat for his head. They dressed him warmly and took him down to the ship that was sailing for Russia. There they gave Lefty the very best cabin, like a real nobleman, but he felt ashamed and didn't like to sit shut up with the other gentlemen, and

The Steel Flea

he would go up on deck and sit down under the tar poling and ask, 'Where is our Russia?'

The Englishman he asked would point or nod off in that direction, and then Lefty would turn his head that way and impatiently look for his native land.

When they sailed out of the bay into the Militerranean Sea, his longing for Russia became so strong that there was no way to calm him down. The rolling and pitching was awful, but Lefty still wouldn't go down to his cabin; he sat under the tar poling, pulled his hurricane hat down over his eyes and kept looking towards his homeland.

Often the Englishmen would come up and invite him to a warm spot down below, and he even began to lie his way out so that they would stop bothering him. 'No,' he would answer. 'I feel better out here; if I went inside with all this rolling and pitching the sea wretch would get me.'

And so the whole time he would never go below until he had to for special reasons, and because of this the thirst mate took a liking to him. This thirst mate, to the misfortune of our Lefty, knew how to talk Russian, and he couldn't get over marvelling that a Russian landlubber could hold out like that through all the rough weather.

'Good lad, Russ!' he said. 'Let's take a drink!'

Lefty took a drink.

And the thirst mate said, 'Another one!'

So Lefty took another one, and they drank themselves tight. The thirst mate asked him, 'What kind of secret is it you're taking to Russia from our country?'

Lefty answered, 'That's my business.'

'Well, if that's the way it is,' answered the thirst mate, 'then let me make an English bet with you.'

Lefty asked, 'What kind?'

'That we'll never drink alone and will always drink the same – one just as much as the other – and whoever drinks the other one down will win.'

Lefty thought, 'Dark skies, bellies rise; the boredom's strong and the way is long. We still can't see the homeland beyond the waves – it will be merrier after all to make the bet.'

'All right,' he said. 'It's a bet.'

'Only let it be honest.'

'As far as that goes,' he said, 'you ain't got no worry.'

They agreed and shook hands on it.

17

Their bet began in the Militerranean Sea, and they drank all the way to the Riga Dunamunde, but they ran neck and neck, and neither one fell behind the other, and they kept so strictly even with each other that when one of them looked down into the sea and saw a devil climbing up out of the water, the very same thing immediately appeared to the other one. Only, the thirst mate saw a red-headed devil, and Lefty claimed it was dark, like a blackamoor.

The Steel Flea

Lefty said, 'Cross yourself and turn away; that's a devil from the deep.'

But the Englishman argued that it was only a 'deep-sea driver'. 'If you want me to,' he said, 'I'll pitch you overboard. Don't be afraid – he'll bring you right back to me.'

And Lefty answered, 'If that's true, then pitch me over.'

The thirst mate picked him up by the shoulders and carried him to the rail.

The sailors saw this and stopped them and reported it to the captain. He ordered them both to be locked up below and kept on rations of rum and wine and cold food, so that they could both eat and drink and stick to their bet, but he gave orders that they were not to get any hot glum pudding in flames, for fear the spirits in their innards might catch fire.

So they travelled locked up all the way to Petersburg, and neither one of them won the bet. There they were spread out in separate sleighs, and the Englishman was sent to the embassy on the English quay and Lefty to the police station.

From this point their destinies became very different.

18

When the Englishman was brought to the Ambassador's house, they at once called in a doctor and a druggist for him. The doctor ordered him put into a warm bath on

Nikolay Leskov

the spot, and the druggist right away rolled up a gutta-percha pill and personally stuck it in his mouth, and then both of them together took and laid him on a feather bed and covered him over with a fur coat and left him to sweat; and to keep anyone from disturbing him the order was sent out through the whole embassy to let nobody sneeze. The doctor and the druggist waited till the thirst mate went to sleep, and then they made another gutta-percha pill for him, laid it on a little table at the head of his bed and went off.

But at the police station they threw Lefty on the floor and started questioning him, 'Who was he, and where was he from, and did he have a grasp port or any other kind of document?'

But he was so weak from his illness and the drinking and the rolling and pitching that he didn't answer a word, but only groaned.

Then they searched him right away, relieved him of his colourful clothes and his alarmed watch and fleeced him of his money; and the police officer gave orders that the first passing sleigh-driver should take him free to the hospital.

The policeman took Lefty out to put him into a sleigh, but for a long time he couldn't catch a single one, because sleigh-drivers avoid policemen. Lefty was lying all this time on the cold depravement. Then the policeman caught a sleigh-driver, only one without a warm fur lap-robe, because in cases like that they hide the fur lap-robe by sitting on it, in order to make policemen's feet freeze faster. So they carried Lefty in an open sleigh, and whenever they transferred him from one sleigh to another they would keep dropping him, and when they picked him up they would pull his ears to make him come to. They got him to one hospital, but there they wouldn't accept him without a grasp port; they took him to another, and they wouldn't accept him there either; and then to a third, and a fourth. All night long they kept dragging him through all the little winding alleys and transferring him over and over, until he was half dead. Then one doctor's assistant told the policeman to take him to the Obukhvin Public Hospital, where everybody of unknown social class was taken in to die.

There they gave orders to write out a receipt and deposit Lefty on the floor in the corridor till they could inspect him.

And at that very same time the next day the English thirst mate got up, swallowed the second gutta-percha pill down to his innards, ate a light breakfast of chicken and rice, took a drink of impressed air, and said, 'Where is my Russian buddy? I'm going to look for him.'

19

He got dressed and off he ran.

In some amazing way the thirst mate found Lefty very quickly; only, they hadn't yet put him on a bed. He was still lying in the hall on the floor, and he complained to the Englishman. 'I've just got to have two words with the Emperor,' he said.

The Englishman ran off to Count Kleinmichel and ripped and roared, 'Really, now, this is the limit!' he said. 'Though only a sheep-skin coat it be, in its wearer a human soul we see.'

For this statement the Englishman was turned out at once, so that he shouldn't dare mention the human soul again. After that somebody said to him, 'You'd do better to go around to Platov the Cossack; he's got simple feelings.'

The Englishman got hold of Platov, who by this time was lying again on his bed. Platov listened to his story and remembered Lefty.

'Why, of course, brother,' he said. 'I know him very well. I've even dragged him around by the hair. Only, I don't know how I can help him in this kind of trouble, because I've served out my time and got a full apple plexy – now they don't pay attention to me any more. But you just run over to the Commandant Skobelev; he's in full force, and he's also had experience in this line – he'll do something.'

The thirst mate went to Skobelev and told all about what sort of illness Lefty had and how it had happened. Skobelev said, 'I understand that illness; only, the Germans don't know how to treat it; here you have to have some kind of doctor from the spiritual profession, because they have grown up with these cases and they can help; I'll send over the Russian doctor Martyn-Solsky right away.'

But when Martyn-Solsky got there, Lefty was already dying, because he had cracked open the back of his head when they dropped him on the cold depravement; and he was able to say only one thing clearly, 'Tell the Emperor that the English don't clean their rifles with brick dust, and we must stop it too, or else God save us from a war, because they won't be any good for shooting.'

And with this loyalty, Lefty crossed himself and kicked the bucket.

Martyn-Solsky went out at once and reported this to Count Chernyshov, so that he could tell the Emperor, but Count Chernyshov shouted at him, 'Look here now,' he said, 'your job is laxatives and purgatives. Don't stick your nose into other people's business: in Russia we've got generals for that.'

So nothing was said to the Emperor, and the cleaning went on in the same old way right up to the Crimean War. At that time when they started loading their rifles, the bullets just rattled around in them, because the barrels had been cleaned out with brick dust.

Then Martyn-Solsky reminded Count Chernyshov about Lefty, and Count Chernyshov said, 'Go to the devil, you public enema, and don't stick your nose into other people's business or I'll deny I ever heard about that from you, and then you yourself will catch it.'

Martyn-Solsky thought, 'And he really will deny it.' So he kept quiet.

But if only they had reported Lefty's words in time to the Emperor, the war against the enemy in Crimea would have taken an entirely different turn.

Now all this is 'affairs of long-gone days' and 'traditions of yore' even though this yore is not very old. But there is no need to be hasty about forgetting these traditions, despite the incredible nature of the legend and the epic character of its principal hero. Lefty's real name, like the names of many of the greatest geniuses, has been lost to posterity forever; but he is interesting as the embodiment of a myth in the popular imagination, and his adventures can serve to remind us of an epoch whose general spirit has been portrayed here clearly and accurately.

It goes without saying that Tula no longer has such master craftsmen as the legendary Lefty: machines have evened up the inequalities in gifts and talents, and genius no longer strains itself in a struggle against diligence and exactness. Even though they encourage the raising of salaries, machines do not encourage artistic daring, which sometimes went so far beyond ordinary bounds as to inspire the folk imagination to create unbelievable legends like this one.

The workmen, of course, can appreciate the advantages they have gained through practical applications of mechanical science, but they still recall those olden times with pride and affection. These memories are their epic – an epic that has a genuinely 'human soul'.

1. BOCCACCIO · *Mrs Rosie and the Priest*
2. GERARD MANLEY HOPKINS · *As kingfishers catch fire*
3. *The Saga of Gunnlaug Serpent-tongue*
4. THOMAS DE QUINCEY · *On Murder Considered as One of the Fine Arts*
5. FRIEDRICH NIETZSCHE · *Aphorisms on Love and Hate*
6. JOHN RUSKIN · *Traffic*
7. PU SONGLING · *Wailing Ghosts*
8. JONATHAN SWIFT · *A Modest Proposal*
9. *Three Tang Dynasty Poets*
10. WALT WHITMAN · *On the Beach at Night Alone*
11. KENKŌ · *A Cup of Sake Beneath the Cherry Trees*
12. BALTASAR GRACIÁN · *How to Use Your Enemies*
13. JOHN KEATS · *The Eve of St Agnes*
14. THOMAS HARDY · *Woman much missed*
15. GUY DE MAUPASSANT · *Femme Fatale*
16. MARCO POLO · *Travels in the Land of Serpents and Pearls*
17. SUETONIUS · *Caligula*
18. APOLLONIUS OF RHODES · *Jason and Medea*
19. ROBERT LOUIS STEVENSON · *Olalla*
20. KARL MARX AND FRIEDRICH ENGELS · *The Communist Manifesto*
21. PETRONIUS · *Trimalchio's Feast*
22. JOHANN PETER HEBEL · *How a Ghastly Story Was Brought to Light by a Common or Garden Butcher's Dog*
23. HANS CHRISTIAN ANDERSEN · *The Tinder Box*
24. RUDYARD KIPLING · *The Gate of the Hundred Sorrows*
25. DANTE · *Circles of Hell*
26. HENRY MAYHEW · *Of Street Piemen*
27. HAFEZ · *The nightingales are drunk*
28. GEOFFREY CHAUCER · *The Wife of Bath*
29. MICHEL DE MONTAIGNE · *How We Weep and Laugh at the Same Thing*
30. THOMAS NASHE · *The Terrors of the Night*
31. EDGAR ALLAN POE · *The Tell-Tale Heart*
32. MARY KINGSLEY · *A Hippo Banquet*
33. JANE AUSTEN · *The Beautifull Cassandra*
34. ANTON CHEKHOV · *Gooseberries*
35. SAMUEL TAYLOR COLERIDGE · *Well, they are gone, and here must I remain*
36. JOHANN WOLFGANG VON GOETHE · *Sketchy, Doubtful, Incomplete Jottings*
37. CHARLES DICKENS · *The Great Winglebury Duel*
38. HERMAN MELVILLE · *The Maldive Shark*
39. ELIZABETH GASKELL · *The Old Nurse's Story*
40. NIKOLAY LESKOV · *The Steel Flea*

41. HONORÉ DE BALZAC · *The Atheist's Mass*
42. CHARLOTTE PERKINS GILMAN · *The Yellow Wall-Paper*
43. C.P. CAVAFY · *Remember, Body . . .*
44. FYODOR DOSTOEVSKY · *The Meek One*
45. GUSTAVE FLAUBERT · *A Simple Heart*
46. NIKOLAI GOGOL · *The Nose*
47. SAMUEL PEPYS · *The Great Fire of London*
48. EDITH WHARTON · *The Reckoning*
49. HENRY JAMES · *The Figure in the Carpet*
50. WILFRED OWEN · *Anthem For Doomed Youth*
51. WOLFGANG AMADEUS MOZART · *My Dearest Father*
52. PLATO · *Socrates' Defence*
53. CHRISTINA ROSSETTI · *Goblin Market*
54. *Sindbad the Sailor*
55. SOPHOCLES · *Antigone*
56. RYŪNOSUKE AKUTAGAWA · *The Life of a Stupid Man*
57. LEO TOLSTOY · *How Much Land Does A Man Need?*
58. GIORGIO VASARI · *Leonardo da Vinci*
59. OSCAR WILDE · *Lord Arthur Savile's Crime*
60. SHEN FU · *The Old Man of the Moon*
61. AESOP · *The Dolphins, the Whales and the Gudgeon*
62. MATSUO BASHŌ · *Lips too Chilled*
63. EMILY BRONTË · *The Night is Darkening Round Me*
64. JOSEPH CONRAD · *To-morrow*
65. RICHARD HAKLUYT · *The Voyage of Sir Francis Drake Around the Whole Globe*
66. KATE CHOPIN · *A Pair of Silk Stockings*
67. CHARLES DARWIN · *It was snowing butterflies*
68. BROTHERS GRIMM · *The Robber Bridegroom*
69. CATULLUS · *I Hate and I Love*
70. HOMER · *Circe and the Cyclops*
71. D. H. LAWRENCE · *Il Duro*
72. KATHERINE MANSFIELD · *Miss Brill*
73. OVID · *The Fall of Icarus*
74. SAPPHO · *Come Close*
75. IVAN TURGENEV · *Kasyan from the Beautiful Lands*
76. VIRGIL · *O Cruel Alexis*
77. H. G. WELLS · *A Slip under the Microscope*
78. HERODOTUS · *The Madness of Cambyses*
79. *Speaking of Siva*
80. *The Dhammapada*

'This is as much
a mystery as
the Immaculate
Conception,
which of itself
must make
a doctor an
unbeliever.'

HONORÉ DE BALZAC
Born 1799, Tours, France
Died 1850, Paris

'The Atheist's Mass' and 'The Conscript' were first published
in their original French in 1836 and 1831 respectively.
They are taken from *Selected Short Stories*.

BALZAC IN PENGUIN CLASSICS
Old Man Goriot
Cousin Bette
History of the Thirteen
Selected Short Stories
Cousin Pons
A Harlot High and Low
Eugénie Grandet
The Wild Ass's Skin
The Black Sheep
Lost Illusions

HONORÉ DE BALZAC

The Atheist's Mass

Translated by
Sylvia Raphael

PENGUIN BOOKS

PENGUIN CLASSICS

UK | USA | Canada | Ireland | Australia
India | New Zealand | South Africa

Penguin Books is part of the Penguin Random House group of companies
whose addresses can be found at global.penguinrandomhouse.com.

This edition published in Penguin Classics 2015

011

Translation copyright © Sylvia Raphael, 1977

The moral right of the translator has been asserted

Set in 9.5/13 pt Baskerville 10 Pro
Typeset by Jouve (UK), Milton Keynes
Printed and bound in Great Britain by Clays Ltd, Elcograf S.p.A.

A CIP catalogue record for this book is available from the British Library

ISBN: 978-0-141-39742-9

www.greenpenguin.co.uk

Penguin Random House is committed to a sustainable future for our business, our readers and our planet. This book is made from Forest Stewardship Council® certified paper.

Contents

The Atheist's Mass   1

The Conscript   27

The Atheist's Mass

A doctor to whom science owes a fine physiological theory and who, while still young, achieved a place amongst the celebrities of the Paris school of medicine (that centre of enlightenment to which all the doctors of Europe pay homage), Doctor Bianchon, practised surgery for a long time before devoting himself to medicine. His early studies were directed by one of the greatest of French surgeons, by the celebrated Desplein who passed through the world of science like a meteor. Even his enemies admit that he took with him to the grave a method that could not be handed on to others. Like all men of genius he had no heirs; he carried his skill within him and he carried it away with him. A surgeon's fame is like an actor's. It exists only so long as he is alive and his talent can no longer be appreciated once he has gone. Actors and surgeons, great singers too, and virtuoso musicians who by their playing increase tenfold the power of music, are all heroes of the moment. Desplein's life is a proof of the resemblance between the destinies of these transitory geniuses. His name which was so famous yesterday is almost forgotten today. It will remain only in his own field without going beyond it. But extraordinary conditions are surely necessary for the name of a scholar to pass from the domain of Science into the general history of humanity. Did Desplein have that width of knowledge which makes a man the mouthpiece or the representative of an age? Desplein possessed a god-like glance; he understood the patient and his disease by means of a natural or acquired intuition which allowed him to appreciate the diagnosis appropriate to the individual, to decide the precise moment, the hour, the minute at which he should operate, taking into account atmospheric conditions and temperamental peculiarities. To be able to collaborate with Nature in this way, had he then studied the endless combination of beings and elemental substances contained in the atmosphere or provided by the earth for man, who absorbs them and uses them for a particular purpose? Did he use that power of deduction and analogy to which Cuvier owes his genius? However that may be, this man understood the secrets of the flesh; he understood its past as well as its future, by studying the present. But did he contain all science in his person as did Hippocrates, Galen, Aristotle? Did he lead a whole school towards new worlds? No. If it is impossible to refuse to this constant observer of human chemistry the ancient science of Magism, that is to say, the knowledge of the elements in fusion, of the causes of life, of life before life, of what it will be, judging from its antecedents before it exists, all this unfortunately was personal to him. In his life he was isolated by egoism, and today that

The Atheist's Mass

egoism is the death of his fame. Over his tomb there is no statue proclaiming to the future, in ringing tones, the mysteries which Genius seeks out at its own expense. But perhaps Desplein's talent was in keeping with his beliefs, and consequently mortal. For him the terrestrial atmosphere was like a generative bag; he saw the earth as if it were an egg in its shell, and unable to know whether the egg or the hen came first, he denied both the fowl and the egg. He believed neither in the animal anterior to man nor in the spirit beyond him. Desplein was not in doubt, he affirmed his opinion. He was like many other scholars in his frank, unmixed atheism. They are the best people in the world but incorrigible atheists, atheists such as religious people don't believe exist. It was hardly possible for such a man to hold a different opinion, for from his youth he was used to dissecting the living being *par excellence*, before, during and after life, and to examining all its functions without finding the unique soul that is indispensable to religious theories. Desplein recognized a cerebral centre, a nervous centre and a circulatory centre, of which the first two do duty for each other so well that at the end of his life he was convinced that the sense of hearing was not absolutely necessary to hear, nor the sense of sight absolutely necessary to see, and that the solar plexus could replace them without anyone noticing it. He thus found two souls in man and this fact confirmed his atheism, although it still tells us nothing about God. He died, they say, impenitent to the last, as unfortunately do many fine geniuses. May God forgive them!

This really great man's life exhibited many pettinesses, to use the expression of his enemies who in their jealousy wanted to diminish his fame, but it would be more appropriate to call them apparent contradictions. Envious or stupid people who do not know the reasons which explain the activities of superior minds immediately take advantage of a few superficial contradictions to make accusations on which they obtain a momentary judgement. If, later on, the plans which have been attacked are crowned with success, when the preparations are correlated with the results, some of the calumnies which were made beforehand remain. Thus, in our own time, Napoleon was condemned by our contemporaries when he spread out the wings of his eagle over England: but we needed the events of 1822 to explain 1804 and the flat-bottomed boats at Boulogne.*

Since Desplein's fame and scientific knowledge were unassailable, his enemies attacked his strange disposition and his character, while in fact he was simply what the English call eccentric. At times he dressed magnificently

---

* In 1804 Napoleon planned to invade England, using a fleet of flat-bottomed boats based on Boulogne. But he was unable to gain command of the sea, and abandoned this plan in favour of the land conquest of Europe. In 1822 the French Government wanted to intervene in the civil conflict in Spain, in spite of the vigorous protest of Great Britain. Balzac's point is, however, unclear.

The Atheist's Mass

like the tragedian Crébillon, at times he seemed unusually indifferent to clothes. Sometimes he was to be seen in a carriage, sometimes on foot. He was now sharp-tempered, now kind, apparently hard and stingy, yet capable of offering his fortune to his exiled rulers who honoured him by accepting it for a few days. No man has inspired more contradictory judgements. Although, to obtain the Order of Saint Michael (which doctors are not supposed to solicit), he was capable of dropping a Book of Hours from his pocket at Court, you can be sure that inwardly he laughed at the whole thing. He had a profound contempt for mankind, having studied them from above and from below, having surprised them without pretence, as they performed the most solemn as well as the pettiest acts of life. A great man's gifts often hang together. If one of these giants has more talent than wit, his wit is still greater than that of a man of whom one says simply, 'He is witty.' All genius presupposes moral insight. This insight may be applied to some speciality, but he who sees the flower must see the sun. The doctor who heard a diplomat whose life he had saved ask, 'How is the Emperor?', and who replied, 'The courtier is coming back to life, the man will follow!' was not only a surgeon or a physician, he was also extremely witty. Thus the close and patient observer of humanity will justify Desplein's exorbitant pretensions and will realize, as he himself realized, that he was capable of being as great a minister as he was a surgeon.

Honoré de Balzac

Among the riddles which Desplein's life reveals to his contemporaries we have chosen one of the most interesting, because the solution will be found at the end of this tale and will answer some of the foolish accusations which have been made against him.

Of all the pupils whom Desplein had at his hospital, Horace Bianchon was one of those to whom he became most warmly attached. Before doing his internship at the Hôtel Dieu,* Horace Bianchon was a medical student, living in a miserable boarding-house in the Latin Quarter, known by the name of La Maison Vauquer.† There this poor young man experienced that desperate poverty which is a kind of melting-pot whence great talents emerge pure and incorruptible, just as diamonds can be subjected to any kind of shock without breaking. In the violence of their unleashed passions, they acquire the most unshakeable honesty, and by dint of the constant labour with which they have contained their balked appetites, they become used to the struggles which are the lot of genius. Horace was an upright young man, incapable of double-dealing in affairs of honour, going straight to the point without fuss, as capable of pawning his coat for his friends as of giving them his time and his night's rest.

---

* L'Hôtel-Dieu was one of the oldest and most important hospitals in Paris.

† Life in La Maison Vauquer is depicted in Balzac's novel *Le Père Goriot*.

In short, Horace was one of those friends who are not worried about what they receive in exchange for what they give, certain as they are to receive in their turn more than they will give. Most of his friends had for him that inner respect which is inspired by unostentatious goodness, and several of them were afraid of his strictures. But Horace exercised these virtues without being prudish. He was neither a puritan nor a preacher; he swore quite readily when giving advice, and enjoyed a good meal in gay company when opportunity offered. He was good company, no more squeamish than a soldier, bluff and open, not like a sailor – for the sailor of today is a wily diplomatist – but like a fine young man who has nothing to hide in his life; he walked with his head high and his heart light. In a word, Horace was the Pylades of more than one Orestes, creditors being today the most real shape assumed by the ancient Furies. He wore his poverty with that gaiety which is perhaps one of the greatest elements of courage, and like all those who have nothing, he contracted few debts. Sober as a camel, brisk as a stag, he was unwavering both in his principles and in his behaviour. The happiness of Bianchon's life began on the day when the famous surgeon obtained evidence of the good qualities and failings which, the one as much as the other, made Doctor Horace Bianchon doubly precious to his friends. When a clinical chief adopts a young man, that young man has, as they say, his foot in the stirrup. Desplein always took Bianchon with him to act as his assistant in well-to-do homes, where some reward would nearly always find its way into the student's purse, and where little by little the mysteries of Parisian life were revealed to the young provincial. Desplein also kept him in his surgery during consultations and gave him work to do there. Sometimes he would send him to accompany a rich patient to a spa. In short, he was making a practice for him. The result of all this was that after a time the lord of surgery had a devoted slave. These two men, the one at the height of his fame and leader of his profession, enjoying an immense fortune and an immense reputation, the other, a modest Omega, having neither fortune nor fame, became intimate friends. The great Desplein told his assistant everything. He knew if a certain lady had sat down on a chair beside the master, or on the famous surgery couch where Desplein slept. Bianchon knew the mysteries of that temperament, both lion-like and bull-like, which in the end expanded and abnormally developed the great man's chest and caused his death from enlargement of the heart. The student studied the eccentricities of Desplein's very busy life, the plans made by his sordid avarice, the hopes of the politician concealed behind the scientist; he foresaw the disappointments in store for the only feeling hidden in that heart which was hardened rather than hard.

One day Bianchon told Desplein that a poor water-carrier from the Saint-Jacques quarter had a horrible illness caused by fatigue and poverty; this poor Auvergnat

The Atheist's Mass

had eaten only potatoes during the severe winter of 1821. Desplein left all his patients. At the risk of working his horse to death, he rode as fast as he could, followed by Bianchon, to the poor man's house and himself had him carried to the nursing-home founded by the famous Dubois in the Faubourg Saint-Denis. Desplein attended the man, and when he had cured him, gave him the money to buy a horse and a water-cart. This Auvergnat was remarkable for one original characteristic. One of his friends fell ill; he took him straight away to Desplein and said to his benefactor, 'I would not have allowed him to go to another doctor.' Surly as he was, Desplein grasped the water-carrier's hand and said, 'Bring them all to me.' And he had the peasant from the Cantal admitted to the Hôtel Dieu, where he took the greatest care of him. Bianchon had already noticed several times that his chief had a predilection for Auvergnats, and especially for water-carriers. But as Desplein had a kind of pride in his treatments at the Hôtel Dieu, his pupil didn't see anything very strange in that.

One day, as Bianchon was crossing the Place Saint-Sulpice, he noticed his master going into the church about nine o'clock in the morning. Desplein, who at that period of his life never moved a step except by carriage, was on foot and slipping in by the door of the Rue du Petit-Lion, as if he had been going into a house of doubtful reputation. Bianchon's curiosity was naturally aroused, since he knew his master's opinions and that he was a 'devyl' of a Cabanist* (devyl with a y, which in Rabelais seems to suggest a superiority in devilry). Slipping into Saint-Sulpice, he was not a little astonished to see the great Desplein, that atheist without pity for the angels, who cannot be subjected to the surgeon's knife, who cannot have sinus or gastric trouble, that dauntless scoffer, kneeling humbly, and where? ... in the chapel of the Virgin, where he listened to a Mass, paid for the cost of the service, gave alms for the poor, all as solemnly as if he had been performing an operation.

'He certainly didn't come to clear up questions about the Virgin birth,' said Bianchon in boundless astonishment. 'If I had seen him holding one of the tassels of the canopy on Corpus Christi day, I would have taken it as a joke; but at this hour, alone, with no one to see him, that certainly gives one food for thought!'

Bianchon did not want to look as if he was spying on the chief surgeon of the Hôtel Dieu and he went away. By chance Desplein invited him to dinner that very day, not at home but at a restaurant.

Between the fruit and the cheese, Bianchon managed skilfully to bring the conversation round to the subject of the Mass, calling it a masquerade and a farce.

'A farce,' said Desplein, 'which has cost Christendom

---

* Cabanis was the author of the *Traité du physique et du moral de l'homme*, an influential atheistic and materialistic work.

The Atheist's Mass

more blood than all Napoleon's battles and all Broussais' leeches! The Mass is a papal invention which goes no further back than the sixth century and which is based on *Hoc est corpus*. What torrents of blood had to be spilt to establish Corpus Christi day! By the institution of this Feast the court of Rome intended to proclaim its victory in the matter of the Real Presence, a schism which troubled the Church for three centuries. The wars of the Counts of Toulouse and the Albigensians are the tail-end of this affair. The Vaudois and the Albigensians* refused to recognize this innovation.'

In short Desplein enjoyed himself, giving free rein to his atheistic wit, and pouring out a flood of Voltairean jokes, or, to be more precise, a horrible parody of the *Citateur*.†

'Well,' Bianchon said to himself, 'where is the pious man I saw this morning?'

He said nothing; he had doubts whether he really had seen his chief at Saint-Sulpice. Desplein would not have bothered to lie to Bianchon. They both knew each other too well; they had already exchanged ideas on subjects which were just as serious, and they had discussed systems *de natura rerum*, probing or dissecting them with the knives and the scalpel of incredulity. Three months went

---

* The Vaudois and the Albigensians were twelfth-century heretical sects in the south of France.

† *Le Citateur* was an anti-clerical pamphlet by Pigault-Lebrun.

by. Bianchon did not follow up the incident, although it remained stamped on his memory. One day in the course of that year, one of the doctors at the Hôtel Dieu took Desplein by the arm, in Bianchon's presence, as if to ask him a question.

'What were you going to do at Saint-Sulpice, my dear chief?' he asked.

'I went to see a priest who had a diseased knee. Madame la Duchesse d'Angoulême did me the honour of recommending me,' said Desplein.

The doctor was satisfied with this excuse, but not so Bianchon.

'Oh! So he goes to see bad knees in church! He was going to hear Mass,' the student said to himself.

Bianchon determined to keep a watch on Desplein. He recalled the day and the time on which he had surprised him going in to Saint-Sulpice and he determined to go there the following year on the same day and at the same time, to find out if he would surprise him there again. If that happened, the regularity of his worship would justify a scientific investigation, for in such a man there should not be a direct contradiction between thought and deed. The following year, on the day and at the hour in question, Bianchon, who was by this time no longer Desplein's assistant, saw the surgeon's carriage stop at the corner of the Rue de Tournon and the Rue du Petit-Lion. From there his friend crept stealthily along by the walls of Saint-Sulpice where he again heard Mass at the altar of the Virgin. It was certainly Desplein, the chief surgeon, the atheist *in petto*, the pious man on occasion. The plot became more involved. The famous scientist's persistence complicated everything. When Desplein had left the church, Bianchon went up to the sacristan who came to minister to the chapel, and asked him if the gentleman was a regular attendant.

'I have been here for twenty years,' said the sacristan, 'and for all that time Monsieur Desplein has been coming four times a year to hear this Mass; it was he who founded it.'

'*He* founded it!' said Bianchon as he walked away. 'This is as much a mystery as the Immaculate Conception, which of itself must make a doctor an unbeliever.'

Although Dr Bianchon was a friend of Desplein's, some time went by before he was in a position to speak to him about this strange circumstance of his life. If they met at a consultation or in society, it was difficult to find that moment of confidence and solitude when, with feet up on the fire-dogs and heads leaning against the backs of their chairs, two men tell each other their secrets. Finally, seven years later, after the 1830 Revolution, when the people stormed the Archbishopric, when, inspired by Republican sentiments, they destroyed the golden crosses which appeared, like flashes of lightning, in this vast sea of houses, when Disbelief and Violence swaggered together through the streets, Bianchon surprised Desplein going into Saint-Sulpice. The doctor followed him in and took a place near him without his friend making the least sign or showing the least surprise. Both of them heard the foundation Mass.

'Will you tell me, my friend,' Bianchon said to Desplein when they were outside the church, 'the reason for this display of piety? I have already caught you three times going to Mass, you! You must tell me the reason for this mysterious activity, and explain to me the flagrant discrepancy between your opinions and your behaviour. You don't believe in God, yet you go to Mass! My dear chief, you must answer me.'

'I am like many pious men, men who appear to be profoundly religious but are quite as atheistic as we are, you and I.'

And he let forth a torrent of epigrams about political personalities of whom the best known provides us in this century with a new edition of Molière's Tartuffe.

'That's not what I am talking about,' said Bianchon. 'I want to know the reason for what you have just been doing here. Why did you found this Mass?'

'Well, my dear friend,' said Desplein, 'since I am on the brink of the grave, there is no reason why I shouldn't speak to you about the beginning of my life.'

At this moment Bianchon and the great man happened to be in the Rue des Quatre-Vents, one of the most horrible streets in Paris. Desplein pointed to the sixth storey of one of those houses which are shaped like an obelisk and have a medium-sized door opening on to a passage.

The Atheist's Mass

At the end of the passage is a spiral staircase lit by apertures called *jours de souffrance*. The house was a greenish colour; on the ground floor lived a furniture dealer; a different kind of poverty seemed to lodge on each floor. Raising his arm with an emphatic gesture, Desplein said to Bianchon, 'I lived up there for two years.'

'I know the place; d'Arthez lived there and I came here almost every day in my youth. At that time we called it the "jar of great men"! Well, what of it?'

'The Mass that I have just heard is linked to events which took place at the time when I lived in the attic where, so you tell me, d'Arthez lived. It is the one where a line of washing is dangling at the window above a pot of flowers. I had such a difficult time to start with, my dear Bianchon, that I can dispute the palm of the sufferings of Paris with anyone. I have put up with everything, hunger, thirst, lack of money, lack of clothes, of footwear, of linen, everything that is hardest about poverty. I have blown on my numbed fingers in that "jar of great men" which I should like to visit again with you. I worked during one winter, when I could see my own head steaming and a cloud of my own breath rising like horses' breath on a frosty day. I don't know what enables a man to stand up to such a life. I was alone, without help, without a farthing either to buy books or to pay the expenses of my medical education. I had no friends and my irritable, sensitive, restless temperament did me no good. No one could see that my bad temper was caused by the difficulties and the work of a man who, from his position at the bottom of the social ladder, was striving to reach the top. But I can tell *you*, you to whom I don't need to pretend, that I had that basis of good feeling and keen sensitivity which will always be the prerogative of men who, after having been stuck for a long time in the slough of poverty, are strong enough to climb to any kind of summit. I could get nothing from my family or my home beyond the inadequate allowance they made me. In short, at this period of my life, all I had to eat in the mornings was a roll which the baker in the Rue du Petit-Lion sold me more cheaply because it was yesterday's, or the day before yesterday's. I crumbled it up into some milk and so my morning meal cost me only two sous. I dined only every other day at a boarding-house where dinner cost sixteen sous. In this way I spent only nine sous a day. You know as well as I do the care I had to take of my clothes and my footwear. I don't think, later on in life, we are as much distressed by a colleague's disloyalty as you and I were when we saw the mocking grin of a shoe that was becoming unsewn, or heard the armhole of a frock-coat split. I drank only water; I had the greatest respect for cafés. Zoppi's seemed to me like a promised land which the Luculli of the Latin Quarter alone had the right to patronize. Sometimes I wondered whether I would ever be able to have a cup of white coffee there, or play a game of dominoes. In short, I transferred to my work the fury which poverty inspired in me. I tried to master scientific

The Atheist's Mass

knowledge so that I should have an immense personal worth deserving of the place I would reach when I emerged from my obscurity. I consumed more oil than bread; the light which lit up those stubborn vigils cost me more than my food. The struggle was long, hard and unrelieved. I aroused no feelings of friendship in those around me. To make friends, you must mix with young people, have a few sous so that you can go and have a drink with them, go with them everywhere where students go. I had nothing. And no one in Paris realizes that "nothing" is "nothing". When there was any question of revealing my poverty I experienced that nervous contraction of the throat which makes our patients think that a ball is rising up from the gullet into the larynx. Later on I met people who, born rich and never having lacked for anything, don't know the problem of this rule of three: "A young man is to crime as a hundred sous piece is to X." These gilded fools say to me, "Why did you get into debt? Why did you take on such crushing obligations?" They remind me of the princess who, knowing that the people were dying of hunger, asked, "Why don't they buy cake?" I should very much like to see one of those rich people, who complains that I charge too much for operating on him, alone in Paris, without a penny, without a friend, without credit and forced to work with his two hands to live. What would he do? Where would he satisfy his hunger? Bianchon, if at times you have seen me bitter and hard, it was because I was superimposing my early sufferings on the lack of feeling, the selfishness, of which I had thousands of examples in high places; or I was thinking of the obstacles which hatred, envy, jealousy, and calumny have placed between me and success. In Paris, when certain people see you ready to put your foot in the stirrup, some of them pull you back by the coat-tail, others loosen the buckle of the saddle-girth so that you'll fall and break your head; this one takes the shoes of your horse, that one steals your whip. The least treacherous is the one you see coming up to shoot you at point-blank range. You have enough talent, my dear fellow, soon to be acquainted with the horrible, unending battle which mediocrity wages against superiority. If one evening you lose twenty-five louis, the next day you will be accused of being a gambler and your best friends will say that the day before you lost twenty-five thousand francs. If you have a headache, you will be called a lunatic. If you have one outburst of temper, they will say you are a social misfit. If, in order to resist this army of pygmies, you muster your superior forces, your best friends will cry out that you want to eat up everything, that you claim to have the right to dominate and lord it over others. In short, your good qualities will become failings, your failings will become vices, and your virtues will be crimes. If you have saved a man, they'll say you have killed him; if your patient is in circulation again, they will affirm that you have sacrificed the future to the present; if he is not dead, he will die. Hesitate, and you will be lost! Invent anything

The Atheist's Mass

at all, claim your just due, you will be regarded as a sly character, difficult to deal with, who is standing in the way of the young men. So, my dear fellow, if I don't believe in God, I believe still less in man. You recognize in me a Desplein very different from the Desplein everyone speaks ill of, don't you? But let's not rummage in this muck heap. Well, I used to live in this house; I was busy working to pass my first examination and I hadn't a sou. I had reached one of those extreme situations where, you know, a man says to himself, "I shall join the army." I had one last hope. I was expecting from home a trunk full of linen, a present from old aunts of the kind who, knowing nothing of Paris, think of your shirts and imagine that with thirty francs a month their nephew lives on caviar. The trunk arrived while I was at the school; the carriage cost forty francs. The porter, a German cobbler who lived in a garret, had paid the money and was keeping the trunk. I went for a walk in the Rue des Fossés-Saint-Germain-des-Prés and in the Rue de l'Ecole-de-Médecine, but I could not think up a plan which would deliver my trunk to me without my having to pay the forty francs; naturally I would have paid them after I had sold the linen. My stupidity made me realize that I was gifted for nothing but surgery. My dear fellow, sensitive souls whose gifts are deployed in a lofty sphere are lacking in that spirit of intrigue which is so resourceful in contriving schemes. *Their* genius lies in chance; they don't seek for things, they come on them by chance. Well, I returned at nightfall at the same time that my neighbour, a water-carrier named Bourgeat, a man from Saint-Flour, was going home. We knew each other in the way two tenants do who have rooms on the same landing, and who hear each other sleeping, coughing, and dressing, till in the end they get used to one another. My neighbour informed me that the landlord, to whom I owed three quarters' rent, had turned me out; I would have to clear out the next day. He himself had been given notice because of his calling. I spent the most unhappy night of my life. Where would I find a carrier to remove my poor household affairs and my books? How would I be able to pay the carrier and the porter? Where was I to go? I kept on asking myself these unanswerable questions through my tears, like a madman repeating a refrain. I fell asleep. Poverty has in its favour an exquisite sleep filled with beautiful dreams. The next morning, just as I was eating my bowlful of crumbled bread and milk, Bourgeat came in and said in his bad French, "*Monchieur l'étudiant*, I'm a poor man, a foundling from the Chain-Flour hospital. I've no father or mother and I'm not rich enough to get married. You haven't many relations either, or much in the way of hard cash. Now listen. I've got a hand-cart downstairs which I've hired for two *chous* an hour. It'll take all our things. If you're willing, we'll look for digs together since we're turned out of here. After all, this place isn't an earthly paradise."

'"I know that alright, Bourgeat, my good fellow," I

The Atheist's Mass

replied. "But I'm in rather a jam. Downstairs I have a trunk containing linen worth a hundred crowns. With that I could pay the landlord and what I owe the porter, but I haven't got a hundred sous."

'"That doesn't matter, I've got some cash," Bourgeat replied cheerfully, showing me a filthy old leather purse. "Keep your linen."

'Bourgeat paid my three quarters' rent and his own and settled with the porter. Then he put our furniture and my linen on to his cart and dragged it through the streets, stopping in front of every house which had a "to let" sign hanging out. My job was to go up and see if the place to let would suit us. At midday we were still wandering about the Latin Quarter without having found anything. The price was a great difficulty. Bourgeat suggested that we should have lunch at a wine-shop; we left our cart at the door. Towards evening, I discovered in the Cour de Rohan, Passage du Commerce, two rooms, separated by the stair in the attic at the top of a house. The rent was sixty francs a year each. We were housed at last, my humble friend and I. We had dinner together. Bourgeat, who earned about fifty sous a day, had about a hundred crowns. He was soon going to be able to realize his ambition and buy a water-cart and a horse. When he learned about my situation (for he dragged my secrets out of me with a deep cunning and a good nature the memory of which still touches my heart), he gave up for some time his whole life's ambition. Bourgeat had been a street-merchant for twenty-two years; he sacrificed his hundred crowns to my future.'

Desplein gripped Bianchon's arm with emotion.

'He gave me the money I needed for my exams. My friend, that man realized that I had a mission, that the needs of my intelligence were more important than his own. He took care of me; he called me his child and lent me the money I needed to buy books. Sometimes he would come in very quietly to watch me working. Last but not least, he took care, as a mother might have done, to see that instead of the bad and insufficient food which I had been forced to put up with, I had a healthy and plentiful diet. Bourgeat, who was a man of about forty, had the face of a medieval burgess, a dome-like forehead and a head that a painter might have used as a model for Lycurgus. The poor man's heart was filled with affections which had no outlet. The only creature that had ever loved him was a poodle which had died a short time before. He talked to me continually about it and asked me if I thought that the Church would be willing to say Masses for the repose of its soul. His dog was, so he said, a true Christian and it had gone to church with him for twelve years, without ever barking there. It had listened to the organ without opening its mouth and squatted beside him with a look that made him think it was praying with him. This man transferred all his affections to me; he accepted me as a lonely and unhappy creature. He became for me the most attentive of mothers, the most

The Atheist's Mass

tactful of benefactors, in short, the ideal of that virtue which delights in its own work. Whenever I met him in the street, he would glance at me with an understanding look filled with remarkable nobility; then he would pretend to walk as if he was carrying nothing. He seemed happy to see me in good health and well-dressed. In short, it was the devotion of a man of the people, the love of a working-girl transferred to a higher sphere. Bourgeat did my errands; he woke me up at night at the hours I asked him to. He cleaned my lamp and polished our landing. He was as good a servant as he was a father, and tidy as an English girl. He did the housework. Like Philopoemen he used to saw up our wood, doing everything with simplicity and dignity, for he seemed to realize that his objective added nobility to everything he did. When I left this good man to do my residence at the Hôtel Dieu, he felt an indescribable grief at the thought that he could no longer live with me. But he consoled himself with the prospect of saving up the money needed for the expenses of my thesis, and made me promise to come and see him on my days off. Bourgeat was proud of me; he loved me both for my sake and for his own. If you look up my thesis you will see that it was dedicated to him. During the last year of my internship, I had earned enough money to pay back everything I owed to this admirable Auvergnat, by buying him a horse and a water-cart. He was furious when he knew that I had been depriving myself of my money, and nevertheless he was delighted to see his wishes realized. He both laughed and scolded me. He looked at his cart and his horse, wiping a tear from his eyes as he said, "That's bad! Oh, what a splendid cart! You shouldn't have done it. The horse is as strong as an Auvergnat." I have never seen anything more moving than this scene. Bourgeat absolutely insisted on buying me that case of instruments mounted in silver which you have seen in my study, and which is for me the most valuable thing I have there. Although he was thrilled by my first successes, he never let slip the least word or gesture which implied, "That man's success is due to me." And yet, without him, poverty would have killed me. The poor man had dug his own grave to help me. He had eaten nothing but bread rubbed with garlic, so that I could have coffee to help me work at night. He fell ill. As you can imagine, I spent the nights at his bedside. I pulled him through the first time, but he had a relapse two years later, and in spite of the most constant care, in spite of the greatest efforts of medical science, his end had come. No king was ever as well cared for as he was. Yes, Bianchon, to snatch that life from death I made supreme efforts. I wanted to make him live long enough for me to show him the results of his work and realize all his hopes for me; I wanted to satisfy the only gratitude which has ever filled my heart and put out a fire which still burns me today.'

After a pause, Desplein, visibly moved, resumed his tale. 'Bourgeat, my second father, died in my arms leaving me everything he possessed in a will which he had had

The Atheist's Mass

made by a public letter-writer and dated the year when we went to live in the Cour de Rohan. This man had the simple faith of a charcoal-burner. He loved the Blessed Virgin as he would have loved his wife. Although he was an ardent Catholic, he had never said a word to me about my lack of religion. When his life was in danger, he begged me to do everything possible to enable him to have the help of the Church. I had Mass said for him every day. Often, during the night, he would express fears for his future; he was afraid that he had not lived a sufficiently holy life. Poor man! He worked from morning to night. To whom then would Paradise belong – if there is a Paradise? He received the last rites like the saint he was and his death was worthy of his life. I was the only person to attend his funeral. When I had buried my only benefactor, I tried to think of a way of paying my debt to him. I realized that he had neither family nor friends, wife nor children. But he was a believer, he had a religious conviction. Had I any right to dispute it? He had spoken to me shyly about Masses said for the repose of the dead. He didn't want to impose this duty upon me, thinking that it would be like asking payment for his services. As soon as I could establish an endowment fund, I gave Saint-Sulpice the necessary amount to have four Masses said there a year. As the only thing I can give to Bourgeat is the satisfaction of his religious wishes, the day when this Mass is said at the beginning of each season, I say with the good faith of a doubter, "Oh God, if there is a sphere where, after their death, you place all those who have been perfect, think of good Bourgeat. And if there is anything for him to suffer, give me his sufferings so that he may enter more quickly into what is called Paradise." That, my dear fellow, is the most that a man with my opinions can allow himself. God must be a decent chap; he couldn't hold it against me. I swear to you, I would give my fortune to be a believer like Bourgeat.'

Bianchon, who looked after Desplein in his last illness, dares not affirm nowadays that the distinguished surgeon died an atheist. Believers will like to think that the humble Auvergnat will have opened the gate of heaven for him as, earlier, he had opened for him the gate of that earthly temple on whose doorway is written *Aux grands hommes la patrie reconnaissante.**

---

*   These words (meaning 'To our great men from their grateful country') are inscribed above the doorway of the Panthéon in Paris where many of the great men of France are buried.

The Conscript

Sometimes they saw that, by a phenomenon of vision or movement, he could abolish space in its two aspects of Time and Distance, one of these being intellectual and the other physical.

Histoire Intellectuelle de Louis Lambert.

One evening in the month of November 1793, the most important people in Carentan were gathered together in the drawing-room of Madame de Dey, who received company every day. Certain circumstances, which would not have attracted attention in a large town but which were bound to arouse curiosity in a small one, gave an unwonted interest to this everyday gathering. Two days earlier, Madame de Dey had closed her doors to visitors, and she had not received any the previous day either, pretending that she was unwell. In normal times these two events would have had the same effect in Carentan as the closing of the theatres has in Paris. On such days existence is, in a way, incomplete. But in 1793 Madame de Dey's behaviour could have the most disastrous consequences. At that time if an aristocrat risked the least step, he was nearly always involved in a matter of life and death. To understand properly the eager curiosity and the narrow-minded cunning which, during that evening, were expressed on the faces of all these Norman worthies, but above all to appreciate the secret worries of Madame de Dey, the part she played at Carentan must be explained. As the critical position in which she was placed at that time was, no doubt, that of many people during the Revolution, the sympathies of more than one reader will give an emotional background to this narrative.

Madame de Dey, the widow of a lieutenant-general, a chevalier of several orders, had left the Court at the beginning of the emigration. As she owned a considerable amount of property in the Carentan region, she had taken refuge there, hoping that the influence of the Terror would be little felt in those parts. This calculation, founded on an accurate knowledge of the region, was correct. The Revolution wrought little havoc in Lower Normandy. Although, in the past, when Madame de Dey visited her property in Normandy, she associated only with the noble families of the district, she now made a policy of opening her doors to the principal townspeople and to the new authorities, trying to make them proud of having won her over, without arousing either their hatred or their jealousy. She was charming and kind, and gifted with that indescribable gentleness which enabled her to please without having to lower herself or ask favours. She had succeeded in winning general esteem thanks to her perfect tact which enabled her to keep wisely to a narrow path, satisfying the demands of that mixed society without humiliating the touchy *amour propre* of the parvenus, or upsetting the sensibilities of her old friends.

She was about thirty-eight years old, and she still retained, not the fresh, rounded good looks which distinguish the girls of Lower Normandy, but a slender, as it were aristocratic, type of beauty. Her features were neat and delicate; her figure was graceful and slender. When she spoke, her pale face seemed to light up and come to life. Her large black eyes were full of friendliness, but their calm, religious expression seemed to show that the mainspring of her existence was no longer within herself. In the prime of her youth she had been married to a jealous old soldier, and her false position at a flirtatious court no doubt helped to spread a veil of serious melancholy over a face which must once have shone with the charms and vivacity of love. Since, at an age when a woman still feels rather than reflects, she had always had to repress her instinctive feminine feelings and emotions, passion had remained unawakened in the depths of her heart. And so her principal attraction stemmed from this inner youthfulness which was, at times, revealed in her face and which gave her thoughts an expression of innocent desire. Her appearance commanded respect, but in her bearing and in her voice there was always the expectancy of an unknown future as with a young girl. Soon after meeting her the least susceptible of men would find himself in love with her and yet retain a kind of respectful fear of her, inspired by her courteous, dignified manner. Her soul, naturally great but strengthened by cruel struggles, seemed far removed from ordinary humanity, and men recognized their inferiority. This soul needed a dominating passion. Madame de Dey's affections were thus concentrated in one single feeling, that of maternity. The happiness and the satisfactions of which she had been deprived as a wife, she found instead in the intense love she had for her son. She loved him not only with the pure and profound devotion of a mother, but with the coquetry of a mistress and the jealousy of a wife. She was unhappy when he was away, and, anxious during his absence, she could never see enough of him and lived only through and for him. To make the reader appreciate the strength of this feeling, it will suffice to add that this son was not only Madame de Dey's only child, but also her last surviving relative, the one being on whom she could fasten the fears, the hopes and the joys of her life. The late Comte de Dey was the last of his family and she was the sole heiress of hers. Material motives and interests thus combined with the noblest needs of the soul to intensify in the countess's heart a feeling which is already so strong in women. It was only by taking the greatest of care that she had managed to bring up her son and this had made him even more dear to her. Twenty times the doctors told her she would lose him, but confident in her own hopes and instincts, she had the inexpressible joy of seeing him safely overcome the perils of childhood, and of marvelling at the improvement in his health, in spite of the doctors' verdict.

Due to her constant care, this son had grown up and developed into such a charming young man that at the age of twenty he was regarded as one of the most accomplished young courtiers at Versailles. Above all, thanks to a good fortune which does not crown the efforts of every mother, she was adored by her son; they understood each other in fraternal sympathy. If they had not already been linked by the ties of nature, they would instinctively have felt for each other that mutual friendship which one meets so rarely in life. At the age of eighteen the young count had been appointed a sub-lieutenant of dragoons and in obedience to the code of honour of the period he had followed the princes when they emigrated.

Madame de Dey, noble, rich and the mother of an *émigré*, thus could not conceal from herself the dangers of her cruel situation. As her only wish was to preserve her large fortune for her son, she had denied herself the happiness of going with him, and when she read the strict laws under which the Republic was confiscating every day the property of *émigrés* at Carentan, she congratulated herself on this act of courage. Was she not watching over her son's wealth at the risk of her life? Then, when she heard of the terrible executions decreed by the Convention, she slept peacefully in the knowledge that her only treasure was in safety, far from the danger of the scaffold. She was happy in the belief that she had done what was best to save both her son and her fortune. To this private thought she made the concessions demanded by those unhappy times, without compromising her feminine dignity or her aristocratic convictions, but hiding her sorrows with a cold secrecy. She had understood the difficulties which awaited her at Carentan. To come there and occupy the first place, wasn't that a way of defying the scaffold every day? But, supported by the courage of a mother, she knew how to win the affection of the poor by relieving all kinds of distress without distinction, and made herself indispensable to the rich by ministering to their pleasures. She entertained at her house the *procureur** of the commune, the mayor, the president of the district, the public prosecutor and even the judges of the revolutionary tribunal. The first four of these were unmarried and so they courted her, hoping to marry her either by making her afraid of the harm they could do her or by offering her their protection. The public prosecutor, who had been *procureur* at Caen and used to look after the countess's business interests, tried to make her love him, by behaving with devotion and generosity – a dangerous form of cunning! He was the most formidable of all the suitors. As she had formerly been a client of his, he was the only

---

* An official elected to represent the central government on local courts and administration.

one who had an intimate knowledge of the state of her considerable fortune. His passion was reinforced by all the desires of avarice and supported by an immense power, the power of life and death throughout the district. This man, who was still young, behaved with such an appearance of magnanimity that Madame de Dey had not yet been able to form an opinion of him. But, despising the danger which lay in vying in cunning with Normans, she made use of the inventive craftiness with which Nature has endowed women to play off these rivals against each other. By gaining time, she hoped to survive safe and sound to the end of the revolutionary troubles. At that period, the royalists who had stayed in France deluded themselves each day that the next day would see the end of the Revolution, and this conviction caused the ruin of many of them.

In spite of these difficulties, the countess had very skilfully maintained her independence until the day on which, with unaccountable imprudence, she took it into her head to close her door. The interest she aroused was so deep and genuine that the people who had come to her house that evening became extremely anxious when they learned that it was impossible for her to receive them. Then, with that frank curiosity which is engrained in provincial manners, they made inquiries about the misfortune, the sorrow, or the illness which Madame de Dey must be suffering from. An old servant named Brigitte answered these questions saying that her mistress had shut herself up in her room and wouldn't see anyone, not even the members of her own household. The almost cloister-like existence led by the inhabitants of a small town forms in them the habit of analysing and explaining the actions of others. This habit is naturally so invincible that after pitying Madame de Dey, and without knowing whether she was really happy or sad, everyone began to look for the causes of her sudden retreat.

'If she were ill,' said the first inquirer, 'she would have sent for the doctor. But the doctor spent the whole day at my house playing chess. He said to me jokingly that nowadays there is only one illness . . . and that unfortunately it is incurable.'

This jest was made with caution. Men and women, old men and girls then began to range over the vast field of conjectures. Each one thought he spied a secret, and this secret filled all their imaginations. The next day their suspicions had grown nastier. As life is lived in public in a small town, the women were the first to find out that Brigitte had bought more provisions than usual at the market. This fact could not be denied. Brigitte had been seen first thing in the morning in the market-square and – strange to relate – she had bought the only hare available. The whole town knew that Madame de Dey did not like game. The hare became a starting point for endless conjectures. As they took their daily walk, the old men noticed in the countess's house a kind of concentrated activity which was revealed by the very precautions taken by the servants to conceal it. The valet was beating a carpet in the garden. The previous day no one would have paid any attention to it, but this carpet became a piece of evidence in support of the fanciful tales which everyone was inventing. Each person had his own. The second day, when they heard that Madame de Dey said she was unwell, the leading inhabitants of Carentan gathered together in the evening at the mayor's brother's house. He was a retired merchant, married, honourable, generally respected, and the countess had a high regard for him. That evening all the suitors for the hand of the rich widow had a more or less probable tale to tell, and each one of them considered how to turn to his own profit the secret event which forced her to place herself in this compromising position. The public prosecutor imagined a whole drama in which Madame de Dey's son would be brought to her house at night. The mayor thought that a non-juring priest had arrived from La Vendée and sought asylum with her.* But the purchase of a hare on a Friday couldn't be explained by this story. The president of the district was convinced that she was hiding a chouan† or a Vendéen leader who was being hotly pursued. Others thought it was a noble who had escaped from the Paris

---

* The priests often helped the inhabitants of La Vendée in the west of France in their risings against the Revolution.
† The chouans were royalist insurgents from Western France who engaged in guerrilla warfare against the Revolution.

prisons. In short, everyone suspected the countess of being guilty of one of those acts of generosity which the laws of that period called a crime and which could lead to the scaffold. The public prosecutor, however, whispered that they must be silent and try to save the unfortunate woman from the abyss towards which she was hastening.

'If you make this affair known,' he added, 'I shall be obliged to intervene, to search her house, and then! . . .' He said no more but everyone understood what he meant.

The countess's real friends were so alarmed for her that, on the morning of the third day, the *procureur-syndic** of the commune got his wife to write her a note urging her to receive company that evening as usual. Bolder still, the retired merchant called at Madame de Dey's house during the morning. Very conscious of the service which he wanted to render her, he insisted on being allowed in to see her, and was amazed when he caught sight of her in the garden, busy cutting the last flowers from her borders to fill her vases.

'She must have given refuge to her lover,' the old man said to himself, as he was overcome with pity for this charming woman. The strange expression of the countess's face confirmed his suspicions. The merchant was deeply moved by this devotion which is so natural to

* See note 1 above.

women, but which men always find touching because they are all flattered by the sacrifices which a woman makes for a man; he told the countess about the rumours which were all over the town, and of the danger in which she was placed. 'For,' he said in conclusion, 'though some of our officials may be willing to forgive you for acting heroically to save a priest, nobody will pity you if they find out you are sacrificing yourself for the sake of a love affair.'

At these words, Madame de Dey looked at the old man with a distraught and crazy expression which made him shudder, despite his age.

'Come with me,' she said taking him by the hand and leading him into her room where, having first made sure that they were alone, she took a dirty crumpled letter from the bodice of her dress. 'Read that,' she cried pronouncing the words with great effort.

She collapsed into her chair, as if she were overcome. While the old merchant was looking for his glasses and cleaning them, she looked up at him, examined him for the first time with interest and said gently in a faltering voice, 'I can trust you.'

'Have I not come to share in your crime?' replied the worthy man simply.

She gave a start. For the first time in this little town, her soul felt sympathy with another's. The merchant understood at once both the dejection and the joy of the countess. Her son had taken part in the Granville expedition;* his letter to his mother was written from the depths of his prison, giving her one sad, yet joyful hope. He had no doubts about his means of escape, and he mentioned three days in the course of which he would come to her house, in disguise. The fatal letter contained heart-rending farewells in case he would not be at Carentan by the evening of the third day, and he begged his mother to give a fairly large sum of money to the messenger who, braving countless dangers, had undertaken to bring her this letter. The paper shook in the old man's hands.

'And this is the third day,' cried Madame de Dey as she got up quickly, took back the letter, and paced up and down the room.

'You have acted rashly,' said the merchant. 'Why did you have food bought in?'

'But he might arrive, dying with hunger, exhausted, and . . .' She said no more.

'I can count on my brother,' continued the old man, 'I will go and bring him over to your side.'

In this situation the merchant deployed again all the subtlety which he had formerly used in business and gave the countess prudent and wise advice. After they had

---

* Granville is a small town, south-west of Carentan, on the other side of the Cotentin peninsula. In 1793 the Vendéens tried unsuccessfully to capture it for the royalists.

The Conscript

agreed on what they both should say and do, the old man, on cleverly invented pretexts, went to the principal houses in Carentan. There he announced that he had just seen Madame de Dey, who would receive company that evening, although she was not very well. As he was a good match for the cunning Norman minds who, in every family, cross-examined him about the nature of the countess's illness, he managed to deceive nearly everybody who was interested in this mysterious affair. His first visit worked wonders. He told a gouty old lady that Madame de Dey had nearly died from an attack of stomach gout. The famous Doctor Tronchin had on a former, similar occasion advised her to lay on her chest the skin of a hare, which had been flayed alive, and to stay absolutely immobile in bed. The countess who, two days ago, had been in mortal danger, was now, after having punctiliously obeyed Tronchin's extraordinary instructions, well enough to receive visitors that evening. This tale had an enormous success, and the Carentan doctor, a secret royalist, added to the effect by the seriousness with which he discussed the remedy. Nevertheless, suspicions had taken root too strongly in the minds of some obstinate people, or of some doubters, to be entirely dissipated. So, that evening, Madame de Dey's visitors came eagerly, in good time, some to observe her face carefully, others out of friendship, most of them amazed at her recovery. They found the countess by the large fireplace in her drawing-room, which was almost as small as the other drawing-rooms in Carentan, for to avoid offending the narrow-minded ideas of her guests, she had denied herself the luxuries she had been used to and so had made no changes in her house. The floor of the reception room was not even polished. She left dingy old hangings on the walls, kept the local furniture, burnt tallow candles and followed the fashions of the place. She adopted provincial life, without shrinking from its most uncomfortable meannesses or its most disagreeable privations. But, as she knew that her guests would forgive her any lavishness conducive to their comfort, she left nothing undone which would minister to their personal pleasures. And so she always provided excellent dinners. She went as far as to feign meanness in order to please these calculating minds and she skilfully admitted to certain concessions to luxury, in order to give in gracefully. And so, about seven o'clock that evening, the best of Carentan's poor society was at Madame de Dey's house and formed a large circle around the hearth. The mistress of the house, supported in her trouble by the old merchant's sympathetic glances, endured with remarkable courage her guests' detailed questioning and their frivolous and stupid arguments. But at every knock on the door, and whenever there was a sound of footsteps in the street, she hid her violent emotion by raising questions of importance to the prosperity of the district. She started off lively discussions about the quality of the ciders and was so well supported by her confidant that the company almost forgot to spy

The Conscript

on her, since the expression of her face was so natural and her self-possession so imperturbable. Nevertheless the public prosecutor and one of the judges of the revolutionary tribunal said little, watching carefully the least changes in her expression and, in spite of the noise, listening to every sound in the house. Every now and then they asked the countess awkward questions but she answered them with admirable presence of mind. A mother has so much courage! When Madame de Dey had arranged the card-players, and settled everyone at the tables to play boston or reversis or whist, she still lingered in quite a carefree manner to chat with some young people. She was playing her part like a consummate actress. She got someone to ask for lotto, pretended to be the only person who knew where the set was, and left the room.

'I feel stifled, my dear Brigitte,' she exclaimed as she wiped the tears springing from her eyes which shone with fever, grief and impatience. 'He is not coming,' she continued, as she went upstairs and looked round the bedroom. 'Here, I can breathe and live. Yet in a few more moments he will be here! For he is alive, of that I am sure. My heart tells me so. Don't you hear anything, Brigitte? Oh! I would give the rest of my life to know whether he is in prison or walking across the countryside. I wish I could stop thinking.'

She looked round the room again to see if everything was in order. A good fire was burning brightly in the grate, the shutters were tightly closed, the polished furniture was gleaming, the way the bed had been made showed that the countess had discussed the smallest details with Brigitte. Her hopes could be discerned in the fastidious care which had obviously been lavished on this room; in the scent of the flowers she had placed there could be sensed the gracious sweetness and the most chaste caresses of love. Only a mother could have anticipated a soldier's wants and made preparations which satisfied them so completely. A superb meal, choice wines, slippers, clean linen, in short everything that a weary traveller could need or desire was brought together so that he should lack for nothing, so that the delights of home should show him a mother's love.

'Brigitte,' cried the countess in a heart-rending voice as she went to place a chair at the table. It was as if she wanted to make her prayers come true, as if she wanted to add strength to her illusions.

'Ah, Madame, he will come. He is not far away – I am sure that he is alive and on his way. I put a key in the Bible and I kept it on my fingers while Cottin read the Gospel of St John . . . and, Madame, the key didn't turn.'

'Is that a reliable sign?' asked the countess.

'Oh, yes! Madame, it's well known. I would stake my soul he's still alive. God cannot be wrong.'

'I would love to see him, in spite of the danger he will be in when he gets here.'

'Poor Monsieur Auguste,' cried Brigitte, 'he must be on the way, on foot.'

The Conscript

'And there's the church clock striking eight,' exclaimed the countess in terror.

She was afraid that she had stayed longer than she should have done in this room where, as everything bore witness to her son's life, she could believe that he was still alive. She went downstairs but before going into the drawing-room, she paused for a moment under the pillars of the staircase, listening to hear if any sound disturbed the silent echoes of the town. She smiled at Brigitte's husband, who kept guard like a sentinel and seemed dazed with the effort of straining to hear the sounds of the night from the village square. She saw her son in everything and everywhere. She soon went back into the room, putting on an air of gaiety, and began to play lotto with some little girls. But every now and then she complained of not feeling well and sat down in her armchair by the fireplace.

That is how people and things were in Madame de Dey's house while on the road from Paris to Cherbourg a young man wearing a brown *carmagnole*, the obligatory dress of the period, was making his way to Carentan. When the conscription of August 1793 first came into force, there was little or no discipline. The needs of the moment were such that the Republic could not equip its soldiers immediately, and it was not uncommon to see the roads full of conscripts still wearing their civilian clothes. These young men reached their halting places ahead of their battalions, or lagged behind, for their progress depended on their ability to endure the fatigues of a long march. The traveller in question was some way ahead of a column of conscripts which was going to Cherbourg and which the mayor of Carentan was expecting from hour to hour, intending to billet the men on the inhabitants. The young man was marching with a heavy tread, but he was still walking steadily and his bearing suggested that he had long been familiar with the hardships of military life. Although the meadow-land around Carentan was lit up by the moon, he had noticed big white clouds threatening a snowfall over the countryside. The fear of being caught in a storm probably made him walk faster, for he was going at a pace ill-suited to his fatigue. On his back he had an almost empty rucksack, and in his hand was a boxwood stick cut from one of the high, thick hedges which this shrub forms around most of the estates of Lower Normandy. A moment after the solitary traveller had caught sight of the towers of Carentan silhouetted in the eerie moonlight, he entered the town. His step aroused the echoes of the silent, deserted streets and he had to ask a weaver who was still at work the way to the mayor's house. This official did not live far away and the conscript soon found himself in the shelter of the porch of the mayor's house. He applied for a billeting order and sat down on a stone seat to wait. But he had to appear before the mayor who had sent for him and he was subjected to a scrupulous cross-examination. The soldier was a young man of good appearance who seemed to belong to a good family. His demeanour indicated that he was of noble birth and his face expressed that intelligence which comes from a good education.

'What's your name?' asked the mayor looking at him knowingly.

'Julien Jussien,' replied the conscript.

'And where do you come from?' asked the official with an incredulous smile.

'From Paris.'

'Your comrades must be some distance away,' continued the Norman half jokingly.

'I am three miles ahead of the battalion.'

'Some special feeling attracts you to Carentan, no doubt, *citoyen réquisitionnaire*,'* said the mayor shrewdly.

'It is all right,' he added, as with a gesture he imposed silence on the young man who was about to speak. 'We know where to send you. There you are,' he added giving him his billeting order. 'Off you go, *citoyen Jussien*.'

There was a tinge of irony in the official's tone as he pronounced these last two words and handed out a billet order giving the address of Madame de Dey's house. The young man read the address with an air of curiosity.

'He knows quite well that he hasn't far to go. And once

---

* *Citoyen* was a form of address during the Revolution replacing *monsieur*. A decree passed by the National Convention in 1793 called for military service all men between eighteen and twenty-five. The conscripts were known as *réquisitionnaires*.

he's outside he'll soon be across the square,' exclaimed the mayor talking to himself as the young man went out. He's got some nerve! May God guide him! He has an answer to everything. Yes, but if anyone but me had asked to see his papers, he would have been lost.'

At this moment, the Carentan clocks had just struck half past nine. The torches were being lit in Madame de Dey's ante-chamber; the servants were helping their masters and mistresses to put on their clogs, their overcoats or their capes; the card-players had settled their accounts and they were all leaving together, according to the established custom in all little towns.

'It looks as if the prosecutor wants to stay,' said a lady, who noticed that this important personage was missing when, having exhausted all the formulae of leave-taking, they separated in the square to go to their respective homes.

In fact that terrible magistrate was alone with the countess who was waiting, trembling, till he chose to go.

After a long and rather frightening silence, he said at last, 'I am here to see that the laws of the Republic are obeyed . . .'

Madame de Dey shuddered.

'Have you nothing to reveal to me?' he asked.

'Nothing,' she replied, amazed.

'Ah, Madame,' cried the prosecutor sitting down beside her and changing his tone, 'at this moment, one word could send you or me to the scaffold. I have observed your

The Conscript

character, your feelings, your ways too closely to share the mistake into which you managed to lead your guests this evening. I have no doubt at all that you are expecting your son.'

The countess made a gesture of denial, but she had grown pale and the muscles of her face had contracted under the necessity of assuming a false air of calmness.

'Well, receive him,' continued the magistrate of the Revolution, 'but don't let him stay under your roof after seven o'clock in the morning. At daybreak, tomorrow, I shall come to your house armed with a denunciation which I shall have drawn up . . .'

She looked at him with a dazed expression which would have melted the heart of a tiger.

He went on gently, 'I shall demonstrate the falsity of the denunciation by a minute search, and by the nature of my report you will be protected from all further suspicion. I shall speak of your patriotic gifts, of your civic devotion, and we shall all be saved.'

Madame de Dey was afraid of a trap. She stood there motionless but her face was burning and her tongue was frozen. The sound of the door-knocker rang through the house.

'Ah,' cried the terrified mother, falling on her knees. 'Save him, save him!'

'Yes, let us save him!' replied the public prosecutor, looking at her passionately, 'even at the cost of *our* lives.'

'I am lost,' she cried as the prosecutor politely helped her to rise.

'Ah! Madame,' he replied with a fine oratorical gesture, 'I want to owe you to nothing . . . but yourself.'

'Madame, he's –,' cried Brigitte thinking her mistress was alone.

At the sight of the public prosecutor, the old servant who had been flushed with joy, became pale and motionless.

'Who is it, Brigitte?' asked the magistrate gently, with a knowing expression.

'A conscript sent by the mayor to be put up here,' replied the servant showing the billet order.

'That's right,' said the prosecutor after reading the order. 'A battalion is due in the town tonight.' And he went out.

At that moment the countess needed so much to believe in the sincerity of her former lawyer that she could not entertain the slightest doubt of it. Quickly she went upstairs, though she scarcely had the strength to stand. Then she opened her bedroom door, saw her son, and fell half-dead into his arms. 'Oh, my child, my child,' she cried sobbing and covering him with wild kisses.

'Madame,' said the stranger.

'Oh! It's someone else,' she cried. She recoiled in horror and stood in front of the conscript, gazing at him with a haggard look.

The Conscript

'Oh, good God, what a strong resemblance!' said Brigitte.

There was silence for a moment and even the stranger shuddered at the sight of Madame de Dey.

She leaned for support on Brigitte's husband and felt the full extent of her grief; this first blow had almost killed her. 'Monsieur,' she said, 'I cannot bear to see you any longer; I hope you won't mind if my servants take my place and look after you.'

She went down to her own room half carried by Brigitte and her old manservant.

'What, Madame!' cried the housekeeper as she helped her mistress to sit down. 'Is that man going to sleep in Monsieur Auguste's bed, put on Monsieur Auguste's slippers and eat the *pâté* that I made for Monsieur Auguste? If I were to be sent to the guillotine, I . . .'

'Brigitte,' cried Madame de Dey.

Brigitte said no more.

'Be quiet, you chatterbox,' said her husband in a low voice. 'You'll be the death of Madame.'

At this moment, the conscript made a noise in his room as he sat down to table.

'I can't stay here,' exclaimed Madame de Dey. 'I shall go into the conservatory. From there I shall be able to hear better what's going on outside during the night.'

She was still wavering between the fear of having lost her son and the hope of seeing him come back. The silence of the night was horrible. When the conscript battalion came into town and each man had to seek out his lodgings, it was a terrible time for the countess. Her hopes were dashed at every footstep, at every sound; then soon the awful stillness of Nature returned. Towards morning, the countess had to go back to her own room. Brigitte, who was watching her mistress's movements, did not see her come out; she went into the room and there found the countess dead.

'She must have heard the conscript finishing dressing and walking about in Monsieur Auguste's room singing their damned *Marseillaise*, as if he were in a stable,' cried Brigitte. 'That will have killed her!'

The countess's death was caused by a more important feeling and, very likely, by a terrible vision. At the exact moment when Madame de Dey was dying in Carentan, her son was being shot in Le Morbihan. We can add this tragic fact to all the observations that have been made of sympathies which override the laws of space. Some learned recluses, in their curiosity, have collected this evidence in documents which will one day serve as a foundation for a new science – a science that has hitherto failed to produce its man of genius.

1. BOCCACCIO · *Mrs Rosie and the Priest*
2. GERARD MANLEY HOPKINS · *As kingfishers catch fire*
3. *The Saga of Gunnlaug Serpent-tongue*
4. THOMAS DE QUINCEY · *On Murder Considered as One of the Fine Arts*
5. FRIEDRICH NIETZSCHE · *Aphorisms on Love and Hate*
6. JOHN RUSKIN · *Traffic*
7. PU SONGLING · *Wailing Ghosts*
8. JONATHAN SWIFT · *A Modest Proposal*
9. *Three Tang Dynasty Poets*
10. WALT WHITMAN · *On the Beach at Night Alone*
11. KENKŌ · *A Cup of Sake Beneath the Cherry Trees*
12. BALTASAR GRACIÁN · *How to Use Your Enemies*
13. JOHN KEATS · *The Eve of St Agnes*
14. THOMAS HARDY · *Woman much missed*
15. GUY DE MAUPASSANT · *Femme Fatale*
16. MARCO POLO · *Travels in the Land of Serpents and Pearls*
17. SUETONIUS · *Caligula*
18. APOLLONIUS OF RHODES · *Jason and Medea*
19. ROBERT LOUIS STEVENSON · *Olalla*
20. KARL MARX AND FRIEDRICH ENGELS · *The Communist Manifesto*
21. PETRONIUS · *Trimalchio's Feast*
22. JOHANN PETER HEBEL · *How a Ghastly Story Was Brought to Light by a Common or Garden Butcher's Dog*
23. HANS CHRISTIAN ANDERSEN · *The Tinder Box*
24. RUDYARD KIPLING · *The Gate of the Hundred Sorrows*
25. DANTE · *Circles of Hell*
26. HENRY MAYHEW · *Of Street Piemen*
27. HAFEZ · *The nightingales are drunk*
28. GEOFFREY CHAUCER · *The Wife of Bath*
29. MICHEL DE MONTAIGNE · *How We Weep and Laugh at the Same Thing*
30. THOMAS NASHE · *The Terrors of the Night*
31. EDGAR ALLAN POE · *The Tell-Tale Heart*
32. MARY KINGSLEY · *A Hippo Banquet*
33. JANE AUSTEN · *The Beautifull Cassandra*
34. ANTON CHEKHOV · *Gooseberries*
35. SAMUEL TAYLOR COLERIDGE · *Well, they are gone, and here must I remain*
36. JOHANN WOLFGANG VON GOETHE · *Sketchy, Doubtful, Incomplete Jottings*
37. CHARLES DICKENS · *The Great Winglebury Duel*
38. HERMAN MELVILLE · *The Maldive Shark*
39. ELIZABETH GASKELL · *The Old Nurse's Story*
40. NIKOLAY LESKOV · *The Steel Flea*

41. HONORÉ DE BALZAC · *The Atheist's Mass*
42. CHARLOTTE PERKINS GILMAN · *The Yellow Wall-Paper*
43. C.P. CAVAFY · *Remember, Body . . .*
44. FYODOR DOSTOEVSKY · *The Meek One*
45. GUSTAVE FLAUBERT · *A Simple Heart*
46. NIKOLAI GOGOL · *The Nose*
47. SAMUEL PEPYS · *The Great Fire of London*
48. EDITH WHARTON · *The Reckoning*
49. HENRY JAMES · *The Figure in the Carpet*
50. WILFRED OWEN · *Anthem For Doomed Youth*
51. WOLFGANG AMADEUS MOZART · *My Dearest Father*
52. PLATO · *Socrates' Defence*
53. CHRISTINA ROSSETTI · *Goblin Market*
54. *Sindbad the Sailor*
55. SOPHOCLES · *Antigone*
56. RYŪNOSUKE AKUTAGAWA · *The Life of a Stupid Man*
57. LEO TOLSTOY · *How Much Land Does A Man Need?*
58. GIORGIO VASARI · *Leonardo da Vinci*
59. OSCAR WILDE · *Lord Arthur Savile's Crime*
60. SHEN FU · *The Old Man of the Moon*
61. AESOP · *The Dolphins, the Whales and the Gudgeon*
62. MATSUO BASHŌ · *Lips too Chilled*
63. EMILY BRONTË · *The Night is Darkening Round Me*
64. JOSEPH CONRAD · *To-morrow*
65. RICHARD HAKLUYT · *The Voyage of Sir Francis Drake Around the Whole Globe*
66. KATE CHOPIN · *A Pair of Silk Stockings*
67. CHARLES DARWIN · *It was snowing butterflies*
68. BROTHERS GRIMM · *The Robber Bridegroom*
69. CATULLUS · *I Hate and I Love*
70. HOMER · *Circe and the Cyclops*
71. D. H. LAWRENCE · *Il Duro*
72. KATHERINE MANSFIELD · *Miss Brill*
73. OVID · *The Fall of Icarus*
74. SAPPHO · *Come Close*
75. IVAN TURGENEV · *Kasyan from the Beautiful Lands*
76. VIRGIL · *O Cruel Alexis*
77. H. G. WELLS · *A Slip under the Microscope*
78. HERODOTUS · *The Madness of Cambyses*
79. *Speaking of Siva*
80. *The Dhammapada*

'The color is hideous enough, and unreliable enough, and infuriating enough, but the pattern is torturing . . .'

CHARLOTTE PERKINS GILMAN
Born 1860, New England, USA
Died 1935, California, USA

'The Yellow Wall-Paper' was first published in 1892; 'The Rocking-Chair' in 1893; and 'Old Water' in 1911.

GILMAN IN PENGUIN CLASSICS
The Yellow Wall-Paper, Herland and Selected Writings

CHARLOTTE PERKINS GILMAN

The Yellow Wall-Paper

PENGUIN BOOKS

PENGUIN CLASSICS

UK | USA | Canada | Ireland | Australia
India | New Zealand | South Africa

Penguin Books is part of the Penguin Random House group of companies
whose addresses can be found at global.penguinrandomhouse.com.

This selection published in Penguin Classics 2015

012

Set in 9.5/13 pt Baskerville 10 Pro
Typeset by Jouve (UK), Milton Keynes
Printed in Great Britain by Clays Ltd, Elcograf S.p.A.

A CIP catalogue record for this book is available from the British Library

ISBN: 978–0–141–39741–2

www.greenpenguin.co.uk

Penguin Random House is committed to a
sustainable future for our business, our readers
and our planet. This book is made from Forest
Stewardship Council® certified paper.

Contents

The Yellow Wall-Paper   1

The Rocking-Chair   27

Old Water   43

The Yellow Wall-Paper

It is very seldom that mere ordinary people like John and myself secure ancestral halls for the summer.

A colonial mansion, a hereditary estate, I would say a haunted house, and reach the height of romantic felicity – but that would be asking too much of fate!

Still I will proudly declare that there is something queer about it.

Else, why should it be let so cheaply? And why have stood so long untenanted?

John laughs at me, of course, but one expects that in marriage.

John is practical in the extreme. He has no patience with faith, an intense horror of superstition, and he scoffs openly at any talk of things not to be felt and seen and put down in figures.

John is a physician, and *perhaps* – (I would not say it to a living soul, of course, but this is dead paper and a great relief to my mind –) *perhaps* that is one reason I do not get well faster.

You see he does not believe I am sick!

And what can one do?

If a physician of high standing, and one's own husband,

assures friends and relatives that there is really nothing the matter with one but temporary nervous depression – a slight hysterical tendency – what is one to do?

My brother is also a physician, and also of high standing, and he says the same thing.

So I take phosphates or phosphites – whichever it is, and tonics, and journeys, and air, and exercise, and am absolutely forbidden to 'work' until I am well again.

Personally, I disagree with their ideas.

Personally, I believe that congenial work, with excitement and change, would do me good.

But what is one to do?

I did write for a while in spite of them; but it *does* exhaust me a good deal – having to be so sly about it, or else meet with heavy opposition.

I sometimes fancy that in my condition if I had less opposition and more society and stimulus – but John says the very worst thing I can do is to think about my condition, and I confess it always makes me feel bad.

So I will let it alone and talk about the house.

The most beautiful place! It is quite alone, standing well back from the road, quite three miles from the village. It makes me think of English places that you read about, for there are hedges and walls and gates that lock, and lots of separate little houses for the gardeners and people.

There is a *delicious* garden! I never saw such a garden – large and shady, full of box-bordered paths, and lined with long grape-covered arbors with seats under them.

There were greenhouses, too, but they are all broken now.

There was some legal trouble, I believe, something about the heirs and co-heirs; anyhow, the place has been empty for years.

That spoils my ghostliness, I am afraid, but I don't care – there is something strange about the house – I can feel it.

I even said so to John one moonlight evening, but he said what I felt was a *draught*, and shut the window.

I get unreasonably angry with John sometimes. I'm sure I never used to be so sensitive. I think it is due to this nervous condition.

But John says if I feel so, I shall neglect proper self-control; so I take pains to control myself – before him, at least, and that makes me very tired.

I don't like our room a bit. I wanted one downstairs that opened on the piazza and had roses all over the window, and such pretty old-fashioned chintz hangings! but John would not hear of it.

He said there was only one window and not room for two beds, and no near room for him if he took another.

He is very careful and loving, and hardly lets me stir without special direction.

I have a schedule prescription for each hour in the day; he takes all care from me, and so I feel basely ungrateful not to value it more.

He said we came here solely on my account, that I was

to have perfect rest and all the air I could get. 'Your exercise depends on your strength, my dear,' said he, 'and your food somewhat on your appetite; but air you can absorb all the time.' So we took the nursery at the top of the house.

It is a big, airy room, the whole floor nearly, with windows that look all ways, and air and sunshine galore. It was nursery first and then playroom and gymnasium, I should judge; for the windows are barred for little children, and there are rings and things in the walls.

The paint and paper look as if a boys' school had used it. It is stripped off – the paper – in great patches all around the head of my bed, about as far as I can reach, and in a great place on the other side of the room low down. I never saw a worse paper in my life.

One of those sprawling flamboyant patterns committing every artistic sin.

It is dull enough to confuse the eye in following, pronounced enough to constantly irritate and provoke study, and when you follow the lame uncertain curves for a little distance they suddenly commit suicide – plunge off at outrageous angles, destroy themselves in unheard of contradictions.

The color is repellant, almost revolting; a smouldering unclean yellow, strangely faded by the slow-turning sunlight.

It is a dull yet lurid orange in some places, a sickly sulphur tint in others.

No wonder the children hated it! I should hate it myself if I had to live in this room long.

There comes John, and I must put this away, – he hates to have me write a word.

We have been here two weeks, and I haven't felt like writing before, since that first day.

I am sitting by the window now, up in this atrocious nursery, and there is nothing to hinder my writing as much as I please, save lack of strength.

John is away all day, and even some nights when his cases are serious.

I am glad my case is not serious!

But these nervous troubles are dreadfully depressing.

John does not know how much I really suffer. He knows there is no *reason* to suffer, and that satisfies him.

Of course it is only nervousness. It does weigh on me so not to do my duty in any way!

I meant to be such a help to John, such a real rest and comfort, and here I am a comparative burden already!

Nobody would believe what an effort it is to do what little I am able, – to dress and entertain, and order things.

It is fortunate Mary is so good with the baby. Such a dear baby!

And yet I *cannot* be with him, it makes me so nervous.

I suppose John never was nervous in his life. He laughs at me so about this wall-paper!

At first he meant to repaper the room, but afterwards he said that I was letting it get the better of me, and that nothing was worse for a nervous patient than to give way to such fancies.

He said that after the wall-paper was changed it would be the heavy bedstead, and then the barred windows, and then that gate at the head of the stairs, and so on.

'You know the place is doing you good,' he said, 'and really, dear, I don't care to renovate the house just for a three months' rental.'

'Then do let us go downstairs,' I said, 'there are such pretty rooms there.'

Then he took me in his arms and called me a blessed little goose, and said he would go down to the cellar, if I wished, and have it whitewashed into the bargain.

But he is right enough about the beds and windows and things.

It is an airy and comfortable room as any one need wish, and, of course, I would not be so silly as to make him uncomfortable just for a whim.

I'm really getting quite fond of the big room, all but that horrid paper.

Out of one window I can see the garden, those mysterious deep-shaded arbors, the riotous old-fashioned flowers, and bushes and gnarly trees.

Out of another I get a lovely view of the bay and a little private wharf belonging to the estate. There is a beautiful shaded lane that runs down there from the house. I always fancy I see people walking in these numerous paths and arbors, but John has cautioned me not to give way to fancy in the least. He says that with my imaginative power and habit of story-making, a nervous weakness like mine is sure to lead to all manner of excited fancies, and that I ought to use my will and good sense to check the tendency. So I try.

I think sometimes that if I were only well enough to write a little it would relieve the press of ideas and rest me.

But I find I get pretty tired when I try.

It is so discouraging not to have any advice and companionship about my work. When I get really well, John says we will ask Cousin Henry and Julia down for a long visit; but he says he would as soon put fireworks in my pillow-case as to let me have those stimulating people about now.

I wish I could get well faster.

But I must not think about that. This paper looks to me as if it *knew* what a vicious influence it had!

There is a recurrent spot where the pattern lolls like a broken neck and two bulbous eyes stare at you upside down.

I get positively angry with the impertinence of it and the everlastingness. Up and down and sideways they crawl, and those absurd, unblinking eyes are everywhere. There is one place where two breadths didn't match, and the eyes go all up and down the line, one a little higher than the other.

I never saw so much expression in an inanimate thing before, and we all know how much expression they have! I used to lie awake as a child and get more entertainment and terror out of blank walls and plain furniture than most children could find in a toy-store.

I remember what a kindly wink the knobs of our big, old bureau used to have, and there was one chair that always seemed like a strong friend.

I used to feel that if any of the other things looked too fierce I could always hop into that chair and be safe.

The furniture in this room is no worse than inharmonious, however, for we had to bring it all from downstairs. I suppose when this was used as a playroom they had to take the nursery things out, and no wonder! I never saw such ravages as the children have made here.

The wall-paper, as I said before, is torn off in spots, and it sticketh closer than a brother – they must have had perseverance as well as hatred.

Then the floor is scratched and gouged and splintered, the plaster itself is dug out here and there, and this great heavy bed which is all we found in the room, looks as if it had been through the wars.

But I don't mind it a bit – only the paper.

There comes John's sister. Such a dear girl as she is, and so careful of me! I must not let her find me writing.

She is a perfect and enthusiastic housekeeper, and hopes for no better profession. I verily believe she thinks it is the writing which made me sick!

But I can write when she is out, and see her a long way off from these windows.

There is one that commands the road, a lovely shaded winding road, and one that just looks off over the country. A lovely country, too, full of great elms and velvet meadows.

This wallpaper has a kind of subpattern in a different shade, a particularly irritating one, for you can only see it in certain lights, and not clearly then.

But in the places where it isn't faded and where the sun is just so – I can see a strange, provoking, formless sort of figure, that seems to skulk about behind that silly and conspicuous front design.

There's sister on the stairs!

Well, the Fourth of July is over! The people are all gone and I am tired out. John thought it might do me good to see a little company, so we just had mother and Nellie and the children down for a week.

Of course I didn't do a thing. Jennie sees to everything now.

But it tired me all the same.

John says if I don't pick up faster he shall send me to Weir Mitchell in the fall.

But I don't want to go there at all. I had a friend who was in his hands once, and she says he is just like John and my brother, only more so!

Besides, it is such an undertaking to go so far.

I don't feel as if it was worth while to turn my hand over for anything, and I'm getting dreadfully fretful and querulous.

I cry at nothing, and cry most of the time.

Of course I don't when John is here, or anybody else, but when I am alone.

And I am alone a good deal just now. John is kept in town very often by serious cases, and Jennie is good and lets me alone when I want her to.

So I walk a little in the garden or down that lovely lane, sit on the porch under the roses, and lie down up here a good deal.

I'm getting really fond of the room in spite of the wall-paper. Perhaps *because* of the wall-paper.

It dwells in my mind so!

I lie here on this great immovable bed – it is nailed down, I believe – and follow that pattern about by the hour. It is as good as gymnastics, I assure you. I start, we'll say, at the bottom, down in the corner over there where it has not been touched, and I determine for the thousandth time that I *will* follow that pointless pattern to some sort of a conclusion.

I know a little of the principle of design, and I know this thing was not arranged on any laws of radiation, or alternation, or repetition, or symmetry, or anything else that I ever heard of.

It is repeated, of course, by the breadths, but not otherwise.

Looked at in one way each breadth stands alone, the bloated curves and flourishes – a kind of 'debased Romanesque' with *delirium tremens* – go waddling up and down in isolated columns of fatuity.

But, on the other hand, they connect diagonally, and the sprawling outlines run off in great slanting waves of optic horror, like a lot of wallowing seaweeds in full chase.

The whole thing goes horizontally, too, at least it seems so, and I exhaust myself in trying to distinguish the order of its going in that direction.

They have used a horizontal breadth for a frieze, and that adds wonderfully to the confusion.

There is one end of the room where it is almost intact, and there, when the crosslights fade and the low sun shines directly upon it, I can almost fancy radiation after all, – the interminable grotesques seem to form around a common centre and rush off in headlong plunges of equal distraction.

It makes me tired to follow it. I will take a nap I guess.

I don't know why I should write this.

I don't want to.

I don't feel able.

And I know John would think it absurd. But I *must* say what I feel and think in some way – it is such a relief!

But the effort is getting to be greater than the relief.

Half the time now I am awfully lazy, and lie down ever so much.

John says I mustn't lose my strength, and has me take cod liver oil and lots of tonics and things, to say nothing of ale and wine and rare meat.

Dear John! He loves me very dearly, and hates to have me sick. I tried to have a real earnest reasonable talk with him the other day, and tell him how I wish he would let me go and make a visit to Cousin Henry and Julia.

But he said I wasn't able to go, nor able to stand it after I got there; and I did not make out a very good case for myself, for I was crying before I had finished.

It is getting to be a great effort for me to think straight. Just this nervous weakness I suppose.

And dear John gathered me up in his arms, and just carried me upstairs and laid me on the bed, and sat by me and read to me till it tired my head.

He said I was his darling and his comfort and all he had, and that I must take care of myself for his sake, and keep well.

He says no one but myself can help me out of it, that I must use my will and self-control and not let any silly fancies run away with me.

There's one comfort, the baby is well and happy, and does not have to occupy this nursery with the horrid wallpaper.

If we had not used it, that blessed child would have!

The Yellow Wall-Paper

What a fortunate escape! Why, I wouldn't have a child of mine, an impressionable little thing, live in such a room for worlds.

I never thought of it before, but it is lucky that John kept me here after all, I can stand it so much easier than a baby, you see.

Of course I never mention it to them any more – I am too wise, – but I keep watch of it all the same.

There are things in that paper that nobody knows but me, or ever will.

Behind that outside pattern the dim shapes get clearer every day.

It is always the same shape, only very numerous.

And it is like a woman stooping down and creeping about behind that pattern. I don't like it a bit. I wonder – I begin to think – I wish John would take me away from here!

It is so hard to talk with John about my case, because he is so wise, and because he loves me so.

But I tried it last night.

It was moonlight. The moon shines in all around just as the sun does.

I hate to see it sometimes, it creeps so slowly, and always comes in by one window or another.

John was asleep and I hated to waken him, so I kept still and watched the moonlight on that undulating wall-paper till I felt creepy.

The faint figure behind seemed to shake the pattern, just as if she wanted to get out.

I got up softly and went to feel and see if the paper *did* move, and when I came back John was awake.

'What is it, little girl?' he said. 'Don't go walking about like that – you'll get cold.'

I thought it was a good time to talk, so I told him that I really was not gaining here, and that I wished he would take me away.

'Why, darling!' said he, 'our lease will be up in three weeks, and I can't see how to leave before.

'The repairs are not done at home, and I cannot possibly leave town just now. Of course if you were in any danger, I could and would, but you really are better, dear, whether you can see it or not. I am a doctor, dear, and I know. You are gaining flesh and color, your appetite is better, I feel really much easier about you.'

'I don't weigh a bit more,' said I, 'nor as much; and my appetite may be better in the evening when you are here, but it is worse in the morning when you are away!'

'Bless her little heart!' said he with a big hug, 'she shall be as sick as she pleases! But now let's improve the shining hours by going to sleep, and talk about it in the morning!'

'And you won't go away?' I asked gloomily.

'Why, how can I, dear? It is only three weeks more and then we will take a nice little trip of a few days while

Jennie is getting the house ready. Really, dear, you are better!'

'Better in body perhaps –' I began, and stopped short, for he sat up straight and looked at me with such a stern, reproachful look that I could not say another word.

'My darling,' said he, 'I beg of you, for my sake and for our child's sake, as well as for your own, that you will never for one instant let that idea enter your mind! There is nothing so dangerous, so fascinating, to a temperament like yours. It is a false and foolish fancy. Can you not trust me as a physician when I tell you so?'

So of course I said no more on that score, and we went to sleep before long. He thought I was asleep first, but I wasn't, and lay there for hours trying to decide whether that front pattern and the back pattern really did move together or separately.

On a pattern like this, by daylight, there is a lack of sequence, a defiance of law, that is a constant irritant to a normal mind.

The color is hideous enough, and unreliable enough, and infuriating enough, but the pattern is torturing.

You think you have mastered it, but just as you get well underway in following, it turns a back-somersault and there you are. It slaps you in the face, knocks you down, and tramples upon you. It is like a bad dream.

The outside pattern is a florid arabesque, reminding

one of a fungus. If you can imagine a toadstool in joints, an interminable string of toadstools, budding and sprouting in endless convolutions – why, that is something like it.

That is, sometimes!

There is one marked peculiarity about this paper, a thing nobody seems to notice but myself, and that is that it changes as the light changes.

When the sun shoots in through the east window – I always watch for that first long, straight ray – it changes so quickly that I never can quite believe it.

That is why I watch it always.

By moonlight – the moon shines in all night when there is a moon – I wouldn't know it was the same paper.

At night in any kind of light, in twilight, candlelight, lamplight, and worst of all by moonlight, it becomes bars! The outside pattern I mean, and the woman behind it is as plain as can be.

I didn't realize for a long time what the thing was that showed behind, that dim sub-pattern, but now I am quite sure it is a woman.

By daylight she is subdued, quiet. I fancy it is the pattern that keeps her so still. It is so puzzling. It keeps me quiet by the hour.

I lie down ever so much now. John says it is good for me, and to sleep all I can.

Indeed he started the habit by making me lie down for an hour after each meal.

It is a very bad habit I am convinced, for you see I don't sleep.

And that cultivates deceit, for I don't tell them I'm awake – O no!

The fact is I am getting a little afraid of John.

He seems very queer sometimes, and even Jennie has an inexplicable look.

It strikes me occasionally, just as a scientific hypothesis, – that perhaps it is the paper!

I have watched John when he did not know I was looking, and come into the room suddenly on the most innocent excuses, and I've caught him several times *looking at the paper!* And Jennie too. I caught Jennie with her hand on it once.

She didn't know I was in the room, and when I asked her in a quiet, a very quiet voice, with the most restrained manner possible, what she was doing with the paper – she turned around as if she had been caught stealing, and looked quite angry – asked me why I should frighten her so!

Then she said that the paper stained everything it touched, that she had found yellow smooches on all my clothes and John's, and she wished we would be more careful!

Did not that sound innocent? But I know she was studying that pattern, and I am determined that nobody shall find it out but myself!

*

Life is very much more exciting now than it used to be. You see I have something more to expect, to look forward to, to watch. I really do eat better, and am more quiet than I was.

John is so pleased to see me improve! He laughed a little the other day, and said I seemed to be flourishing in spite of my wall-paper.

I turned it off with a laugh. I had no intention of telling him it was *because* of the wall-paper – he would make fun of me. He might even want to take me away.

I don't want to leave now until I have found it out. There is a week more, and I think that will be enough.

I'm feeling ever so much better! I don't sleep much at night, for it is so interesting to watch developments; but I sleep a good deal in the daytime.

In the daytime it is tiresome and perplexing.

There are always new shoots on the fungus, and new shades of yellow all over it. I cannot keep count of them, though I have tried conscientiously.

It is the strangest yellow, that wall-paper! It makes me think of all the yellow things I ever saw – not beautiful ones like buttercups, but old foul, bad yellow things.

But there is something else about that paper – the smell! I noticed it the moment we came into the room, but with so much air and sun it was not bad. Now we have had a week of fog and rain, and whether the windows are open or not, the smell is here.

The Yellow Wall-Paper

It creeps all over the house.

I find it hovering in the dining-room, skulking in the parlor, hiding in the hall, lying in wait for me on the stairs.

It gets into my hair.

Even when I go to ride, if I turn my head suddenly and surprise it – there is that smell!

Such a peculiar odor, too! I have spent hours in trying to analyze it, to find what it smelled like.

It is not bad – at first, and very gentle, but quite the subtlest, most enduring odor I ever met.

In this damp weather it is awful, I wake up in the night and find it hanging over me.

It used to disturb me at first. I thought seriously of burning the house – to reach the smell.

But now I am used to it. The only thing I can think of that it is like is the *color* of the paper! A yellow smell.

There is a very funny mark on this wall, low down, near the mopboard. A streak that runs round the room. It goes behind every piece of furniture, except the bed, a long, straight, even *smooch*, as if it had been rubbed over and over.

I wonder how it was done and who did it, and what they did it for. Round and round and round – round and round and round – it makes me dizzy!

I really have discovered something at last.

Through watching so much at night, when it changes so, I have finally found out.

The front pattern *does* move – and no wonder! The woman behind shakes it!

Sometimes I think there are a great many women behind, and sometimes only one, and she crawls around fast, and her crawling shakes it all over.

Then in the very bright spots she keeps still, and in the very shady spots she just takes hold of the bars and shakes them hard.

And she is all the time trying to climb through. But nobody could climb through that pattern – it strangles so; I think that is why it has so many heads.

They get through, and then the pattern strangles them off and turns them upside down, and makes their eyes white!

If those heads were covered or taken off it would not be half so bad.

I think that woman gets out in the daytime!

And I'll tell you why – privately – I've seen her!

I can see her out of every one of my windows!

It is the same woman, I know, for she is always creeping, and most women do not creep by daylight.

I see her in that long shaded lane, creeping up and down. I see her in those dark grape arbors, creeping all around the garden.

I see her on that long road under the trees, creeping along, and when a carriage comes she hides under the blackberry vines.

I don't blame her a bit. It must be very humiliating to be caught creeping by daylight!

I always lock the door when I creep by daylight. I can't do it at night, for I know John would suspect something at once.

And John is so queer now, that I don't want to irritate him. I wish he would take another room! Besides, I don't want anybody to get that woman out at night but myself.

I often wonder if I could see her out of all the windows at once.

But, turn as fast as I can, I can only see out of one at one time.

And though I always see her, she *may* be able to creep faster than I can turn!

I have watched her sometimes away off in the open country, creeping as fast as a cloud shadow in a high wind.

If only that top pattern could be gotten off from the under one! I mean to try it, little by little.

I have found out another funny thing, but I shan't tell it this time! It does not do to trust people too much.

There are only two more days to get this paper off, and I believe John is beginning to notice. I don't like the look in his eyes.

And I heard him ask Jennie a lot of professional questions about me. She had a very good report to give.

She said I slept a good deal in the daytime.

John knows I don't sleep very well at night, for all I'm so quiet!

He asked me all sorts of questions, too, and pretended to be very loving and kind.

As if I couldn't see through him!

Still, I don't wonder he acts so, sleeping under this paper for three months.

It only interests me, but I feel sure John and Jennie are secretly affected by it.

Hurrah! This is the last day, but it is enough. John is to stay in town over night, and won't be out until this evening.

Jennie wanted to sleep with me – the sly thing! but I told her I should undoubtedly rest better for a night all alone.

That was clever, for really I wasn't alone a bit! As soon as it was moonlight and that poor thing began to crawl and shake the pattern, I got up and ran to help her.

I pulled and she shook, I shook and she pulled, and before morning we had peeled off yards of that paper.

A strip about as high as my head and half around the room.

And then when the sun came and that awful pattern began to laugh at me, I declared I would finish it to-day!

We go away to-morrow, and they are moving all my furniture down again to leave things as they were before.

Jennie looked at the wall in amazement, but I told her merrily that I did it out of pure spite at the vicious thing.

She laughed and said she wouldn't mind doing it herself, but I must not get tired.

How she betrayed herself that time!

But I am here, and no person touches this paper but me, – not *alive!*

She tried to get me out of the room – it was too patent! But I said it was so quiet and empty and clean now that I believed I would lie down again and sleep all I could; and not to wake me even for dinner – I would call when I woke.

So now she is gone, and the servants are gone, and the things are gone, and there is nothing left but that great bedstead nailed down, with the canvas mattress we found on it.

We shall sleep downstairs to-night, and take the boat home tomorrow.

I quite enjoy the room, now it is bare again.

How those children did tear about here!

This bedstead is fairly gnawed!

But I must get to work.

I have locked the door and thrown the key down into the front path.

I don't want to go out, and I don't want to have anybody come in, till John comes.

I want to astonish him.

I've got a rope up here that even Jennie did not find. If that woman does get out, and tries to get away, I can tie her!

But I forgot I could not reach far without anything to stand on!

This bed will *not* move!

I tried to lift and push it until I was lame, and then I got so angry I bit off a little piece at one corner – but it hurt my teeth.

Then I peeled off all the paper I could reach standing on the floor. It sticks horribly and the pattern just enjoys it! All those strangled heads and bulbous eyes and waddling fungus growths just shriek with derision!

I am getting angry enough to do something desperate. To jump out of the window would be admirable exercise, but the bars are too strong even to try.

Besides I wouldn't do it. Of course not. I know well enough that a step like that is improper and might be misconstrued.

I don't like to *look* out of the windows even – there are so many of those creeping women, and they creep so fast.

I wonder if they all come out of that wall-paper as I did?

But I am securely fastened now by my well-hidden rope – you don't get *me* out in the road there!

I suppose I shall have to get back behind the pattern when it comes night, and that is hard!

The Yellow Wall-Paper

It is so pleasant to be out in this great room and creep around as I please!

I don't want to go outside. I won't, even if Jennie asks me to.

For outside you have to creep on the ground, and everything is green instead of yellow.

But here I can creep smoothly on the floor, and my shoulder just fits in that long smooch around the wall, so I cannot lose my way.

Why there's John at the door!

It is no use, young man, you can't open it!

How he does call and pound!

Now he's crying for an axe.

It would be a shame to break down that beautiful door!

'John dear!' said I in the gentlest voice, 'the key is down by the front steps, under a plantain leaf!'

That silenced him for a few moments.

Then he said – very quietly indeed, 'Open the door, my darling!'

'I can't,' said I. 'The key is down by the front door under a plantain leaf!'

And then I said it again, several times, very gently and slowly, and said it so often that he had to go and see, and he got it of course, and came in. He stopped short by the door.

'What is the matter?' he cried. 'For God's sake, what are you doing!'

I kept on creeping just the same, but I looked at him over my shoulder.

'I've got out at last,' said I, 'in spite of you and Jane! And I've pulled off most of the paper, so you can't put me back!'

Now why should that man have fainted? But he did, and right across my path by the wall, so that I had to creep over him every time!

The Rocking-Chair

A waving spot of sunshine, a signal light that caught the eye at once in a waste of commonplace houses, and all the dreary dimness of a narrow city street.

Across some low roof that made a gap in the wall of masonry, shot a level, brilliant beam of the just-setting sun, touching the golden head of a girl in an open window.

She sat in a high-backed rocking-chair with brass mountings that glittered as it swung, rocking slowly back and forth, never lifting her head, but fairly lighting up the street with the glory of her sunlit hair.

We two stopped and stared, and, so staring, caught sight of a small sign in a lower window – 'Furnished Lodgings.' With a common impulse we crossed the street and knocked at the dingy front door.

Slow, even footsteps approached from within, and a soft girlish laugh ceased suddenly as the door opened, showing us an old woman, with a dull, expressionless face and faded eyes.

Yes, she had rooms to let. Yes, we could see them. No, there was no service. No, there were no meals. So murmuring monotonously, she led the way up-stairs. It was an ordinary house enough, on a poor sort of street, a house in no way remarkable or unlike its fellows.

She showed us two rooms, connected, neither better nor worse than most of their class, rooms without a striking feature about them, unless it was the great brass-bound chair we found still rocking gently by the window.

But the gold-haired girl was nowhere to be seen.

I fancied I heard the light rustle of girlish robes in the inner chamber – a breath of that low laugh – but the door leading to this apartment was locked, and when I asked the woman if we could see the other rooms she said she had no other rooms to let.

A few words aside with Hal, and we decided to take these two, and move in at once. There was no reason we should not. We were looking for lodgings when that swinging sunbeam caught our eyes, and the accommodations were fully as good as we could pay for. So we closed our bargain on the spot, returned to our deserted boarding-house for a few belongings, and were settled anew that night.

Hal and I were young newspaper men, 'penny-a-liners,' part of that struggling crowd of aspirants who are to literature what squires and pages were to knighthood in olden days. We were winning our spurs. So far it was slow work, unpleasant and ill-paid – so was squireship and pagehood, I am sure; menial service and laborious polishing of armor; long running afoot while the master rode. But the squire could at least honor his lord and

The Rocking-Chair

leader, while we, alas! had small honor for those above us in our profession, with but too good reason. We, of course, should do far nobler things when these same spurs were won!

Now it may have been mere literary instinct – the grasping at 'material' of the pot-boiling writers of the day, and it may have been another kind of instinct – the unacknowledged attraction of the fair unknown; but, whatever the reason, the place had drawn us both, and here we were.

Unbroken friendship begun in babyhood held us two together, all the more closely because Hal was a merry, prosaic, clear-headed fellow, and I sensitive and romantic.

The fearless frankness of family life we shared, but held the right to unapproachable reserves, and so kept love unstrained.

We examined our new quarters with interest. The front room, Hal's, was rather big and bare. The back room, mine, rather small and bare.

He preferred that room, I am convinced, because of the window and the chair. I preferred the other, because of the locked door. We neither of us mentioned these prejudices.

'Are you sure you would not rather have this room?' asked Hal, conscious, perhaps, of an ulterior motive in his choice.

'No, indeed,' said I, with a similar reservation; 'you

only have the street and I have a real "view" from my window. The only thing I begrudge you is the chair!'

'You may come and rock therein at any hour of the day or night,' said he magnanimously. 'It is tremendously comfortable, for all its black looks.'

It was a comfortable chair, a very comfortable chair, and we both used it a great deal. A very high-backed chair, curving a little forward at the top, with heavy square corners. These corners, the ends of the rockers, the great sharp knobs that tipped the arms, and every other point and angle were mounted in brass.

'Might be used for a battering-ram!' said Hal.

He sat smoking in it, rocking slowly and complacently by the window, while I lounged on the foot of the bed, and watched a pale young moon sink slowly over the western housetops.

It went out of sight at last, and the room grew darker and darker till I could only see Hal's handsome head and the curving chair-back move slowly to and fro against the dim sky.

'What brought us here so suddenly, Maurice?' he asked, out of the dark.

'Three reasons,' I answered. 'Our need of lodgings, the suitability of these, and a beautiful head.'

'Correct,' said he. 'Anything else?'

'Nothing you would admit the existence of, my sternly logical friend. But I am conscious of a certain compul-

The Rocking-Chair

sion, or at least attraction, in the case, which does not seem wholly accounted for, even by golden hair.'

'For once I will agree with you,' said Hal. 'I feel the same way myself, and I am not impressionable.'

We were silent for a little. I may have closed my eyes, – it may have been longer than I thought, but it did not seem another moment when something brushed softly against my arm, and Hal in his great chair was rocking beside me.

'Excuse me,' said he, seeing me start. 'This chair evidently "walks," I've seen 'em before.'

So had I, on carpets, but there was no carpet here, and I thought I was awake.

He pulled the heavy thing back to the window again, and we went to bed.

Our door was open, and we could talk back and forth, but presently I dropped off and slept heavily until morning. But I must have dreamed most vividly, for he accused me of rocking in his chair half the night, said he could see my outline clearly against the starlight.

'No,' said I, 'you dreamed it. You've got that rocking-chair on the brain.'

'Dream it is, then,' he answered cheerily. 'Better a nightmare than a contradiction; a vampire than a quarrel! Come on, let's go to breakfast!'

We wondered greatly as the days went by that we saw nothing of our golden-haired charmer. But we wondered in silence, and neither mentioned it to the other.

Sometimes I heard her light movements in the room next mine, or the soft laugh somewhere in the house; but the mother's slow, even steps were more frequent, and even she was not often visible.

All either of us saw of the girl, to my knowledge, was from the street, for she still availed herself of our chair by the window. This we disapproved of, on principle, the more so as we left the doors locked, and her presence proved the possession of another key. No; there was the door in my room! But I did not mention the idea. Under the circumstances, however, we made no complaint, and used to rush stealthily and swiftly up-stairs, hoping to surprise her. But we never succeeded. Only the chair was often found still rocking, and sometimes I fancied a faint sweet odor lingering about, an odor strangely saddening and suggestive. But one day when I thought Hal was there I rushed in unceremoniously and caught her. It was but a glimpse – a swift, light, noiseless sweep – she vanished into my own room. Following her with apologies for such a sudden entrance, I was too late. The envious door was locked again.

Our landlady's fair daughter was evidently shy enough when brought to bay, but strangely willing to take liberties in our absence.

Still, I had seen her, and for that sight would have forgiven much. Hers was a strange beauty, infinitely attractive yet infinitely perplexing. I marveled in secret, and longed with painful eagerness for another meeting;

The Rocking-Chair

but I said nothing to Hal of my surprising her – it did not seem fair to the girl! She might have some good reason for going there; perhaps I could meet her again.

So I took to coming home early, on one excuse or another, and inventing all manner of errands to get to the room when Hal was not in.

But it was not until after numberless surprises on that point, finding him there when I supposed him downtown, and noticing something a little forced in his needless explanations, that I began to wonder if he might not be on the same quest.

Soon I was sure of it. I reached the corner of the street one evening just at sunset, and – yes, there was the rhythmic swing of that bright head in the dark frame of the open window. There also was Hal in the street below. She looked out, she smiled. He let himself in and went up-stairs.

I quickened my pace. I was in time to see the movement stop, the fair head turn, and Hal standing beyond her in the shadow.

I passed the door, passed the street, walked an hour – two hours – got a late supper somewhere, and came back about bedtime with a sharp and bitter feeling in my heart that I strove in vain to reason down. Why he had not as good a right to meet her as I it were hard to say, and yet I was strangely angry with him.

When I returned the lamplight shone behind the white curtain, and the shadow of the great chair stood motionless against it. Another shadow crossed – Hal – smoking. I went up.

He greeted me effusively and asked why I was so late. Where I got supper. Was unnaturally cheerful. There was a sudden dreadful sense of concealment between us. But he told nothing and I asked nothing, and we went silently to bed.

I blamed him for saying no word about our fair mystery, and yet I had said none concerning my own meeting. I racked my brain with questions as to how much he had really seen of her; if she had talked to him; what she had told him; how long she had stayed.

I tossed all night and Hal was sleepless too, for I heard him rocking for hours, by the window, by the bed, close to my door. I never knew a rocking-chair to 'walk' as that one did.

Towards morning the steady creak and swing was too much for my nerves or temper.

'For goodness' sake, Hal, do stop that and go to bed!'

'What?' came a sleepy voice.

'Don't fool!' said I, 'I haven't slept a wink to-night for your everlasting rocking. Now do leave off and go to bed.'

'Go to bed! I've been in bed all night and I wish you had! Can't you use the chair without blaming me for it?'

And all the time I *heard* him rock, rock, rock, over by the hall door!

I rose stealthily and entered the room, meaning to surprise the ill-timed joker and convict him in the act.

The Rocking-Chair

Both rooms were full of the dim phosphorescence of reflected moonlight; I knew them even in the dark; and yet I stumbled just inside the door, and fell heavily.

Hal was out of bed in a moment and had struck a light.

'Are you hurt, my dear boy?'

I was hurt, and solely by his fault, for the chair was not where I supposed, but close to my bedroom door, where he must have left it to leap into bed when he heard me coming. So it was in no amiable humor that I refused his offers of assistance and limped back to my own sleepless pillow. I had struck my ankle on one of those brass-tipped rockers, and it pained me severely. I never saw a chair so made to hurt as that one. It was so large and heavy and ill-balanced, and every joint and corner so shod with brass. Hal and I had punished ourselves enough on it before, especially in the dark when we forgot where the thing was standing, but never so severely as this. It was not like Hal to play such tricks, and both heart and ankle ached as I crept into bed again to toss and doze and dream and fitfully start till morning.

Hal was kindness itself, but he would insist that he had been asleep and I rocking all night, till I grew actually angry with him.

'That's carrying a joke too far,' I said at last. 'I don't mind a joke, even when it hurts, but there are limits.'

'Yes, there are!' said he, significantly, and we dropped the subject.

Several days passed. Hal had repeated meetings with

the gold-haired damsel; this I saw from the street; but save for these bitter glimpses I waited vainly.

It was hard to bear, harder almost than the growing estrangement between Hal and me, and that cut deeply. I think that at last either one of us would have been glad to go away by himself, but neither was willing to leave the other to the room, the chair, the beautiful unknown.

Coming home one morning unexpectedly, I found the dull-faced landlady arranging the rooms, and quite laid myself out to make an impression upon her, to no purpose.

'That is a fine old chair you have there,' said I, as she stood mechanically polishing the brass corners with her apron.

She looked at the darkly glittering thing with almost a flash of pride.

'Yes,' said she, 'a fine chair!'

'Is it old?' I pursued.

'Very old,' she answered briefly.

'But I thought rocking-chairs were a modern American invention?' said I.

She looked at me apathetically.

'It is Spanish,' she said, 'Spanish oak, Spanish leather, Spanish brass, Spanish —.' I did not catch the last word, and she left the room without another.

It was a strange ill-balanced thing, that chair, though so easy and comfortable to sit in. The rockers were long and sharp behind, always lying in wait for the unwary,

The Rocking-Chair

but cut short in front: and the back was so high and so heavy on top, that what with its weight and the shortness of the front rockers, it tipped forward with an ease and a violence equally astonishing.

This I knew from experience, as it had plunged over upon me during some of our frequent encounters. Hal also was a sufferer, but in spite of our manifold bruises, neither of us would have had the chair removed, for did not she sit in it, evening after evening, and rock there in the golden light of the setting sun.

So, evening after evening, we two fled from our work as early as possible, and hurried home alone, by separate ways, to the dingy street and the glorified window.

I could not endure forever. When Hal came home first, I, lingering in the street below, could see through our window that lovely head and his in close proximity. When I came first, it was to catch perhaps a quick glance from above – a bewildering smile – no more. She was always gone when I reached the room, and the inner door of my chamber irrevocably locked.

At times I even caught the click of the latch, heard the flutter of loose robes on the other side; and sometimes this daily disappointment, this constant agony of hope deferred, would bring me to my knees by that door begging her to open to me, crying to her in every term of passionate endearment and persuasion that tortured heart of man could think to use.

Hal had neither word nor look for me now, save those

of studied politeness and cold indifference, and how could I behave otherwise to him, so proven to my face a liar?

I saw him from the street one night, in the broad level sunlight, sitting in that chair, with the beautiful head on his shoulder. It was more than I could bear. If he had won, and won so utterly, I would ask but to speak to her once, and say farewell to both forever. So I heavily climbed the stairs, knocked loudly, and entered at Hal's 'Come in!' only to find him sitting there alone, smoking – yes, smoking in the chair which but a moment since had held her too!

He had but just lit the cigar, a paltry device to blind my eyes.

'Look here, Hal,' said I, 'I can't stand this any longer. May I ask you one thing? Let me see her once, just once, that I may say good-bye, and then neither of you need see me again!'

Hal rose to his feet and looked me straight in the eye. Then he threw that whole cigar out of the window, and walked to within two feet of me.

'Are you crazy,' he said. '*I* ask her! *I!* I have never had speech of her in my life! And *you* –' He stopped and turned away.

'And I what?' I would have it out now whatever came.

'And you have seen her day after day – talked with her – I need not repeat all that my eyes have seen!'

'You need not, indeed,' said I. 'It would tax even your

The Rocking-Chair

invention. I have never seen her in this room but once, and then but for a fleeting glimpse – no word. From the street I have seen her often – with you!'

He turned very white and walked from me to the window, then turned again.

'I have never seen her in this room for even such a moment as you own to. From the street I have seen her often – *with you!*'

We looked at each other.

'Do you mean to say,' I inquired slowly, 'that I did not see you just now sitting in that chair, by that window, with her in your arms?'

'Stop!' he cried, throwing out his hand with a fierce gesture. It struck sharply on the corner of the chair-back. He wiped the blood mechanically from the three-cornered cut, looking fixedly at me.

'I saw you,' said I.

'You did not!' said he.

I turned slowly on my heel and went into my room. I could not bear to tell that man, my more than brother, that he lied.

I sat down on my bed with my head on my hands, and presently I heard Hal's door open and shut, his step on the stair, the front door slam behind him. He had gone, I knew not where, and if he went to his death and a word of mine would have stopped him, I would not have said it. I do not know how long I sat there, in the company of hopeless love and jealousy and hate.

Suddenly, out of the silence of the empty room, came the steady swing and creak of the great chair. Perhaps – it must be! I sprang to my feet and noiselessly opened the door. There she sat by the window, looking out, and – yes – she threw a kiss to some one below. Ah, how beautiful she was! How beautiful! I made a step toward her. I held out my hands, I uttered I know not what – when all at once came Hal's quick step upon the stairs.

She heard it, too, and, giving me one look, one subtle, mysterious, triumphant look, slipped past me and into my room just as Hal burst in. He saw her go. He came straight to me and I thought he would have struck me down where I stood.

'Out of my way,' he cried. 'I will speak to her. Is it not enough to see?' – he motioned toward the window with his wounded hand – 'Let me pass!'

'She is not there,' I answered. 'She has gone through into the other room.'

A light laugh sounded close by us, a faint, soft, silver laugh, almost at my elbow.

He flung me from his path, threw open the door, and entered. The room was empty.

'Where have you hidden her?' he demanded. I coldly pointed to the other door.

'So her room opens into yours, does it?' he muttered with a bitter smile. 'No wonder you preferred the "view"! Perhaps I can open it too?' And he laid his hand upon the latch.

The Rocking-Chair

I smiled then, for bitter experience had taught me that it was always locked, locked to all my prayers and entreaties. Let him kneel there as I had! But it opened under his hand! I sprang to his side, and we looked into – a closet, two by four, as bare and shallow as an empty coffin!

He turned to me, as white with rage as I was with terror. I was not thinking of him.

'What have you done with her?' he cried. And then contemptuously – 'That I should stop to question a liar!'

I paid no heed to him, but walked back into the other room, where the great chair rocked by the window.

He followed me, furious with disappointment, and laid his hand upon the swaying back, his strong fingers closing on it till the nails were white.

'Will you leave this place?' said he.

'No,' said I.

'I will live no longer with a liar and a traitor,' said he.

'Then you will have to kill yourself,' said I.

With a muttered oath he sprang upon me, but caught his foot in the long rocker, and fell heavily.

So wild a wave of hate rose in my heart that I could have trampled upon him where he lay – killed him like a dog – but with a mighty effort I turned from him and left the room.

When I returned it was broad day. Early and still, not sunrise yet, but full of hard, clear light on roof and wall and roadway. I stopped on the lower floor to find the landlady and announce my immediate departure. Door after door I knocked at, tried and opened; room after room I entered and searched thoroughly; in all that house, from cellar to garret, was no furnished room but ours, no sign of human occupancy. Dust, dust, and cobwebs everywhere. Nothing else.

With a strange sinking of the heart I came back to our own door.

Surely I heard the landlady's slow, even step inside, and that soft, low laugh. I rushed in.

The room was empty of all life; both rooms utterly empty.

Yes, of all life; for, with the love of a lifetime surging in my heart, I sprang to where Hal lay beneath the window, and found him dead.

Dead, and most horribly dead. Three heavy marks – blows – three deep, three-cornered gashes – I started to my feet – even the chair had gone!

Again the whispered laugh. Out of that house of terror I fled desperately.

From the street I cast one shuddering glance at the fateful window.

The risen sun was gilding all the housetops, and its level rays, striking the high panes on the building opposite, shone back in a calm glory on the great chair by the window, the sweet face, down-dropped eyes, and swaying golden head.

Old Water

The lake lay glassy in level golden light. Where the long shadows of the wooded bank spread across it was dark, fathomless. Where the little cliff rose on the eastern shore its bright reflection went down endlessly.

Slowly across the open gold came a still canoe, sent swiftly and smoothly on by well-accustomed arms.

'How strong! How splendid! Ah! she is like a Valkyr!' said the poet; and Mrs Osgood looked up at the dark bulk with appreciative eyes.

'You don't know how it delights me to have you speak like that!' she said softly. 'I feel those things myself, but have not the gift of words. And Ellen is so practical.'

'She could not be your daughter and not have a poetic soul,' he answered, smiling gravely.

'I'm sure I hope so. But I have never felt sure! When she was little I read to her from the poets, always; but she did not care for them – unless it was what she called "story poetry." And as soon as she had any choice of her own she took to science.'

'The poetry is there,' he said, his eyes on the smooth brown arms, now more near. 'That poise! That motion!

It is the very soul of poetry – and the body! Her body is a poem!'

Mrs Osgood watched the accurate landing, the strong pull that brought the canoe over the roller and up into the little boathouse. 'Ellen is so practical!' she murmured. 'She will not even admit her own beauty.'

'She is unawakened,' breathed the poet – 'Unawakened!' And his big eyes glimmered as with a stir of hope.

'It's very brave of her, too,' the mother went on. 'She does not really love the water, and just makes herself go out on it. I think in her heart she's afraid – but will not admit it. O Ellen! Come here dear. This is Mr Pendexter – the Poet.'

Ellen gave her cool brown hand; a little wet even, as she had casually washed them at the water's edge; but he pressed it warmly, and uttered his admiration of her skill with the canoe.

'O that's nothing,' said the girl. 'Canoeing's dead easy.'

'Will you teach it to me?' he asked. 'I will be a most docile pupil.'

She looked up and down his large frame with a somewhat questioning eye. It was big enough surely, and those great limbs must mean strength; but he lacked something of the balance and assured quickness which speaks of training.

'Can't you paddle?' she said.

'Forgive my ignorance – but I have never been in one of those graceful slim crafts. I shall be so glad to try.'

Old Water

'Mr Pendexter has been more in Europe than America,' her mother put in hastily, 'and you must not imagine, my dear, that all men care for these things. I'm sure that if you are interested, my daughter will be very glad to teach you, Mr Pendexter.'

'Certainly,' said Ellen. 'I'll teach him in two tries. Want to start tomorrow morning? I'm usually out pretty early.'

'I shall be delighted,' he said. 'We will greet Aurora together.'

'The Dawn, dear,' suggested her mother with an apologetic smile.

'O yes,' the girl agreed. 'I recognize Aurora, mama. Is dinner ready?'

'It will be when you are dressed,' said her mother. 'Put on your blue frock, dear – the light one.'

'All right,' said Ellen, and ran lightly up the path.

'Beautiful! Beautiful!' he murmured, his eyes following her flying figure. 'Ah, madam! What it must be to you to have such a daughter! To see your own youth – but a moment passed – repeated before your eyes!' And he bent an admiring glance on the outlines of his hostess.

Mrs Osgood appeared at dinner in a somewhat classic gown, her fine hair banded with barbaric gold; and looked with satisfaction at her daughter, who shone like a juvenile Juno in her misty blue. Ellen had her mother's beauty and her father's strength. Her frame was large, her muscles had power under their flowing grace of line. She carried herself like a queen, but wore the cheerful unconscious air of a healthy schoolgirl, which she was.

Her appetite was so hearty that her mother almost feared it would pain the poet, but she soon observed that he too showed full appreciation of her chef's creations. Ellen too observed him, noting with frank disapproval that he ate freely of sweets and creams, and seemed to enjoy the coffee and liqueurs exceedingly.

'Ellen never takes coffee,' Mrs Osgood explained, as they sat in the luxurious drawing room, 'she has some notion about training I believe.'

'Mother! I am training!' the girl protested. 'Not officially – there's no race on; but I like to keep in good condition. I'm stroke at college, Mr Pindexter.'

'*Pen*dexter, dear,' her mother whispered.

The big man took his second demitasse, and sat near the girl.

'I can't tell you how much I admire it,' he said, leaning forward. 'You are like Nausicaa – like Atalanta – like the women of my dreams!'

She was not displeased with his open admiration – even athletic girls are not above enjoying praise – but she took it awkwardly.

'I don't believe in dreams,' she said.

'No,' he agreed, 'No – one must not. And yet – have you never had a dream that haunts you – a dream that comes again?'

Old Water

'I've had bad dreams,' she admitted, 'horrid ones; but not the same dream twice.'

'What do you dream of when your dreams are terrible?'

'Beasts,' she answered promptly. 'Big beasts that jump at me! And I run and run – ugh!'

Mrs Osgood sipped her coffee and watched them. There was no young poet more promising than this. He represented all that her own girlhood had longed for – all that the highly prosperous mill-owner she married had utterly failed to give. If her daughter could have what she had missed!

'They say those dreams come from our remote past,' she suggested. 'Do you believe that, Mr Pendexter?'

'Yes,' he agreed, 'from our racial infancy. From those long buried years of fear and pain.'

'And when we have that queer feeling of *having been there before* – isn't that the same thing?'

'We do not know,' said he. 'Some say it is from a moment's delay in action of one-half of the brain. I cannot tell. To me it is more mysterious, more interesting, to think that when one has that wonderful sudden sense of previous acquaintance it means vague memories of a former life.' And he looked at Ellen as if she had figured largely in his previous existence. 'Have you ever had that feeling, Miss Osgood?'

The girl laughed rather shamefacedly. 'I've had it about one thing,' she said. 'That's why I'm afraid of water.'

'Afraid of water! You! A water goddess!'

'O, I don't encourage it, of course. But it's the only thing I ever was nervous about. I've had it from childhood – that horrid feeling!'

She shivered a little, and asked if he wouldn't like some music.

'Ah! You make music too?'

She laughed gaily. 'Only with the pianola – or the other machine. Shall I start it?'

'A moment,' he said. 'In a moment. But tell me, will you not, of this dream of something terrible? I am so deeply interested.'

'Why, it isn't much,' she said. 'I don't dream it, really – it comes when I'm awake. Only two or three times – once when I was about ten or eleven, and twice since. It's water – black, still, smooth water – way down below me. And I can't get away from it. I want to – and then something grabs me – ugh!'

She got up decidedly and went to the music stand. 'If that's a relic of my past I must have been prematurely cut off by an enraged ape! Anyhow, I don't like water – unless it's wild ocean. What shall I play?'

He meant to rise next morning with the daylight, but failed to awaken; and when he did look out he saw the canoe shooting lightly home in time for breakfast.

She laughed at him for his laziness, but promised a lesson later, and was pleased to find that he could play

Old Water

tennis. He looked well in his white flannels, in fact his appearance was more admirable than his playing, and the girl beat him till he grew almost angry.

Mrs Osgood watched delightedly on occasions where watching was agreeable, and on other occasions she took herself off with various excuses, and left them much together.

He expressed to her privately a question as to whether he was not too heavy for the canoe, but she reassured him.

'O, no, indeed, Mr Pendexter; it's a specially wide canoe, and has air chambers in it – it can't sink.' Her father had made it for her. 'He's a heavy man himself, and loves canoeing.'

So the stalwart poet was directed to step softly into the middle, and given the bow paddle.

It grieved him much that he could not see his fair instructress, and he proposed that they change places.

'No, indeed!' she said. 'Trust you with the other paddle? – Not yet!'

Could he not at least face her, he suggested. At which she laughed wickedly, and told him he'd better learn to paddle forward before he tried to do it backward.

'If you want to look at me you might get another canoe and try to follow,' she added, smiling; whereat he declared her would obey orders absolutely.

He sat all across the little rattan bow seat, and rolled up his sleeves as she did. She gave him the paddle, showed him how to hold it, and grinned silently as his mighty strokes swung them to right or left, for all her vigorous steering.

'Not so hard!' she said. 'You are stronger than I, and your stroke is so far out you swing me around.'

With a little patience he mastered the art sufficiently to wield a fairly serviceable bow paddle, but she would not trust him with the stern; and not all the beauties of the quiet lake consoled him for losing sight of her. Still, he reflected, she could see him. Perhaps that was why she kept him there in front! – and he sat straighter at the thought.

She did rather enjoy the well proportioned bulk of him, but she had small respect for his lack of dexterity, and felt a real dislike for the heavy fell of black hair on his arms and hands.

He tired of canoeing. One cannot direct speaking glances over one's shoulder, nor tender words; not with good effect, that is. At tennis he found her so steadily victor that he tired of that too. Golf she did not care for; horses he was unfamiliar with; and when she ran the car her hands and eyes and whole attention were on the machine. So he begged for walking.

'You must having charming walks in these woods,' he said. 'I own inferiority in many ways – but I can walk!'

'All right,' she cheerily agreed, and tramped about the country with him, brisk and tireless.

Her mother watched breathlessly. She wholly admired

Old Water

this ox-eyed man with the velvet voice, the mouth so red under his soft mustache. She thought his poetry noble and musical beyond measure. Ellen thought it was 'no mortal use.'

'What on earth does he want to make over those old legends for, anyway!' she said, when her mother tried to win her to some appreciation. 'Isn't there enough to write about today without going back to people who never existed anyhow – nothing but characters out of other people's stories?'

'They are parts of the world's poetic material, my dear; folk-lore, race-myths. They are among our universal images.'

'Well, I don't like poetry about universal images, that's all. It's like mummies – sort of warmed over and dressed up!'

'I am so sorry!' said her mother, with some irritation. 'Here we are honored with a visit from one of our very greatest poets – perhaps the greatest; and my own child hasn't sense enough to appreciate his beautiful work. You are so like your father!'

'Well, I can't help it,' said Ellen. 'I don't like those foolish old stories about people who never did anything useful, and hadn't an idea in their heads except being in love and killing somebody! They had no sense, and no courage, and no decency!'

Her mother tried to win her to some admission of merit in his other work.

'It's no use, mama! You may have your poet, and get all the esthetic satisfaction you can out of it. And I'll be polite to him, of course. But I don't like his stuff.'

'Not his "Lyrics of the Day," dear? And "The Woods"?'

'No, mumsy, not even those. I don't believe he ever saw a sunrise – unless he got up on purpose and set himself before it like a camera! And woods! Why he don't know one tree from another!'

Her mother almost despaired of her; but the poet was not discouraged.

'Ah! Mrs Osgood! Since you honor me with your confidence I can but thank you and try my fate. It is so beautiful, this budding soul – not opened yet! So close – so almost hard! But when its rosy petals do unfold –'

He did not, however, give his confidence to Mrs Osgood beyond this gentle poetic outside view of a sort of floricultural intent. He told her nothing of the storm of passion which was growing within him; a passion of such seething intensity as would have alarmed that gentle soul exceedingly and make her doubt, perhaps, the wisdom of her selection.

She remained in a state of eager but restrained emotion; saying little to Ellen lest she alarm her, but hoping that the girl would find happiness with this great soul.

The great soul, meanwhile, pursued his way, using every art he knew – and his experience was not narrow – to reach the heart of the brown and ruddy nymph beside him.

She was ignorant and young. Too whole-souled in her

Old Water

indifference to really appreciate the stress he labored under; much less to sympathize. On the contrary she took a mischievous delight in teasing him, doing harm without knowing it, like a playful child. She teased him about his tennis playing, about his paddling, about his driving; allowed that perhaps he might play golf well, but she didn't care for golf herself – it was too slow; mocked even his walking expeditions.

'He don't want to walk!' she said gaily to her mother one night at dinner. 'He just wants to go somewhere and arrange himself gracefully under a tree and read to me about Eloise, or Araminta or somebody; all slim and white and wavy and golden-haired; and how they killed themselves for love!'

She laughed frankly at him, and he laughed with her; but his heart was hot and dark within him. The longer he pursued and failed the fiercer was his desire for her. Already he had loved longer than was usual to him. Never before had his overwhelming advances been so lightly parried and set aside.

'Will you take a walk with me this evening after dinner?' he proposed. 'There is a most heavenly moon – and I cannot see to read to you. It must be strangely lovely – the moonlight – on your lake, is it not, Mrs Osgood?'

'It is indeed,' she warmly agreed, looking disapprovingly on the girl, who was still giggling softly at the memory of golden-haired Araminta. 'Take him on the cliff walk, Ellen, and do try to be more appreciative of beauty!'

'Yes, mama,' said Ellen, 'I'll be good.'

She was so good upon the moonlit walk; so gentle and sympathetic, and so honestly tried to find some point of agreement, that his feelings were too much for his judgment, and he seized her hand and kissed it. She pushed him away, too astonished for words.

'Why, Mr Pendexter! What are you thinking of!'

Then he poured out his heart to her. He told her how he loved her – madly, passionately, irresistably. He begged her to listen to him.

'Ah! You young Diana! You do not know how I suffer! You are so young, so cold! So heavenly beautiful! Do not be cruel! Listen to me! Say you will be my wife! Give me one kiss! Just one!'

She was young, and cold, and ignorantly cruel. She laughed at him, laughed mercilessly, and turned away.

He followed her, the blood pounding in his veins, his voice shaken with the intensity of his emotions. He caught her hand and drew her toward him again. She broke from him with a little cry, and ran. He followed, hotly, madly; rushed upon her, caught her, held her fast.

'You shall love me! You shall!' he cried. His hands were hot and trembling, but he held her close and turned her face to his.

'I will not!' she cried, struggling. 'Let me go! I hate you, I tell you. I hate you! You are – disgusting!' She pushed as far from him as he could.

They had reached the top of the little cliff opposite the

Old Water

house. Huge dark pines hung over them, their wide boughs swaying softly.

The water lay below in the shadow, smooth and oil-black.

The girl looked down at it, and a sudden shudder shook her tense frame. She gave a low moan and hid her face in her hands.

'Ah!' he cried. 'It is your fate! Our fate! We have lived through this before! We will die together if we cannot live together!'

He caught her to him, kissed her madly, passionately, and together they went down into the black water.

'It's pretty lucky I could swim,' said Ellen, as she hurried home. 'And he couldn't. The poor man! O, the poor man! He must have been crazy!'

1. BOCCACCIO · *Mrs Rosie and the Priest*
2. GERARD MANLEY HOPKINS · *As kingfishers catch fire*
3. *The Saga of Gunnlaug Serpent-tongue*
4. THOMAS DE QUINCEY · *On Murder Considered as One of the Fine Arts*
5. FRIEDRICH NIETZSCHE · *Aphorisms on Love and Hate*
6. JOHN RUSKIN · *Traffic*
7. PU SONGLING · *Wailing Ghosts*
8. JONATHAN SWIFT · *A Modest Proposal*
9. *Three Tang Dynasty Poets*
10. WALT WHITMAN · *On the Beach at Night Alone*
11. KENKŌ · *A Cup of Sake Beneath the Cherry Trees*
12. BALTASAR GRACIÁN · *How to Use Your Enemies*
13. JOHN KEATS · *The Eve of St Agnes*
14. THOMAS HARDY · *Woman much missed*
15. GUY DE MAUPASSANT · *Femme Fatale*
16. MARCO POLO · *Travels in the Land of Serpents and Pearls*
17. SUETONIUS · *Caligula*
18. APOLLONIUS OF RHODES · *Jason and Medea*
19. ROBERT LOUIS STEVENSON · *Olalla*
20. KARL MARX AND FRIEDRICH ENGELS · *The Communist Manifesto*
21. PETRONIUS · *Trimalchio's Feast*
22. JOHANN PETER HEBEL · *How a Ghastly Story Was Brought to Light by a Common or Garden Butcher's Dog*
23. HANS CHRISTIAN ANDERSEN · *The Tinder Box*
24. RUDYARD KIPLING · *The Gate of the Hundred Sorrows*
25. DANTE · *Circles of Hell*
26. HENRY MAYHEW · *Of Street Piemen*
27. HAFEZ · *The nightingales are drunk*
28. GEOFFREY CHAUCER · *The Wife of Bath*
29. MICHEL DE MONTAIGNE · *How We Weep and Laugh at the Same Thing*
30. THOMAS NASHE · *The Terrors of the Night*
31. EDGAR ALLAN POE · *The Tell-Tale Heart*
32. MARY KINGSLEY · *A Hippo Banquet*
33. JANE AUSTEN · *The Beautifull Cassandra*
34. ANTON CHEKHOV · *Gooseberries*
35. SAMUEL TAYLOR COLERIDGE · *Well, they are gone, and here must I remain*
36. JOHANN WOLFGANG VON GOETHE · *Sketchy, Doubtful, Incomplete Jottings*
37. CHARLES DICKENS · *The Great Winglebury Duel*
38. HERMAN MELVILLE · *The Maldive Shark*
39. ELIZABETH GASKELL · *The Old Nurse's Story*
40. NIKOLAY LESKOV · *The Steel Flea*

41. HONORÉ DE BALZAC · *The Atheist's Mass*
42. CHARLOTTE PERKINS GILMAN · *The Yellow Wall-Paper*
43. C.P. CAVAFY · *Remember, Body . . .*
44. FYODOR DOSTOEVSKY · *The Meek One*
45. GUSTAVE FLAUBERT · *A Simple Heart*
46. NIKOLAI GOGOL · *The Nose*
47. SAMUEL PEPYS · *The Great Fire of London*
48. EDITH WHARTON · *The Reckoning*
49. HENRY JAMES · *The Figure in the Carpet*
50. WILFRED OWEN · *Anthem For Doomed Youth*
51. WOLFGANG AMADEUS MOZART · *My Dearest Father*
52. PLATO · *Socrates' Defence*
53. CHRISTINA ROSSETTI · *Goblin Market*
54. *Sindbad the Sailor*
55. SOPHOCLES · *Antigone*
56. RYŪNOSUKE AKUTAGAWA · *The Life of a Stupid Man*
57. LEO TOLSTOY · *How Much Land Does A Man Need?*
58. GIORGIO VASARI · *Leonardo da Vinci*
59. OSCAR WILDE · *Lord Arthur Savile's Crime*
60. SHEN FU · *The Old Man of the Moon*
61. AESOP · *The Dolphins, the Whales and the Gudgeon*
62. MATSUO BASHŌ · *Lips too Chilled*
63. EMILY BRONTË · *The Night is Darkening Round Me*
64. JOSEPH CONRAD · *To-morrow*
65. RICHARD HAKLUYT · *The Voyage of Sir Francis Drake Around the Whole Globe*
66. KATE CHOPIN · *A Pair of Silk Stockings*
67. CHARLES DARWIN · *It was snowing butterflies*
68. BROTHERS GRIMM · *The Robber Bridegroom*
69. CATULLUS · *I Hate and I Love*
70. HOMER · *Circe and the Cyclops*
71. D. H. LAWRENCE · *Il Duro*
72. KATHERINE MANSFIELD · *Miss Brill*
73. OVID · *The Fall of Icarus*
74. SAPPHO · *Come Close*
75. IVAN TURGENEV · *Kasyan from the Beautiful Lands*
76. VIRGIL · *O Cruel Alexis*
77. H. G. WELLS · *A Slip under the Microscope*
78. HERODOTUS · *The Madness of Cambyses*
79. *Speaking of Siva*
80. *The Dhammapada*

'All those excessive, useless regrets . . .'

C. P. CAVAFY
Born 1863, Alexandria, Egypt
Died 1933, Alexandria, Egypt

This selection of poetry covers a thirty-six-year period in Cavafy's life, 1897–1933. Originally written in Greek, this selection is taken from *The Selected Poems of Cavafy*, translated by Avi Sharon, Penguin Classics, 2008.

CAVAFY IN PENGUIN CLASSICS
The Selected Poems of Cavafy

C. P. CAVAFY

Remember, Body . . .

Translated by
Avi Sharon

PENGUIN BOOKS

PENGUIN CLASSICS

UK | USA | Canada | Ireland | Australia
India | New Zealand | South Africa

Penguin Books is part of the Penguin Random House group of companies whose addresses can be found at global.penguinrandomhouse.com.

This selection published in Penguin Classics 2015

009

Translation copyright © Avi Sharon, 2008

The moral right of the translator has been asserted

Set in 9/12.4 pt Baskerville 10 Pro
Typeset by Jouve (UK), Milton Keynes
Printed and bound in Great Britain by Clays Ltd, Elcograf S.p.A.

A CIP catalogue record for this book is available from the British Library

ISBN: 978-0-141-39746-7

www.greenpenguin.co.uk

Penguin Random House is committed to a sustainable future for our business, our readers and our planet. This book is made from Forest Stewardship Council® certified paper.

Contents

Desires	1
Candles	2
Dangerous Things	3
Very Seldom	4
Painted Things	5
Morning Sea	6
The Café Entrance	7
One Night	8
Return	9
Far Away	10
He Vows	11
I Left	12
Chandelier	13
Since Nine O'Clock	14
Insight	15
When They Come Alive	16
Pleasure	17

I Have Gazed So Much	18
In The Street	19
The Tobacconist's Window	20
The Passage	21
In the Evening	22
Grey	23
Beside the House	24
The Next Table	25
Remember, Body . . .	26
Days of 1903	27
The Afternoon Sun	28
To Live	29
On the Ship	30
That They May Come	31
Their Beginning	32
In an Old Book	33
In Despair	34
Before Time Could Change Them	35
He Came to Read	36
In the Twenty-fifth Year of His Life	37
The Dreary Village	38
In the Bars	39

Days of 1896	40
Two Young Men, Twenty-three to Twenty-four Years Old	41
Days of 1901	43
Days of 1908	44
A Young Writer – in His Twenty-fourth Year	46
Picture of a Young Man of Twenty-three, Painted by His Friend of the Same Age, an Amateur	47
Days of 1909, 1910 and 1911	48
Lovely Flowers, White Ones, That Matched So Well	49
In the Same Space	51
The Mirror in the Entrance Hall	52
He Asked About the Quality	53

Desires

Like the beautiful bodies of those who died young,
tearfully interred in a grand mausoleum
with roses by their heads and jasmine at their feet –
so seem those desires that have passed
without fulfilment; without a single night
of pleasure, or one of its radiant mornings.

Candles

The days of the future stand before us
like a line of burning candles –
golden candles, warm with life.

Behind them stand the days of our past,
a pitiful row of candles extinguished,
the nearest still sending up their smoke:
cold and melted, withered sticks.

I don't want to look; their image makes me sad,
it saddens me to recall their kindling.
I look ahead at the ones still burning.

I don't want to turn and see, with horror,
how quickly the line of shadow lengthens,
how quickly the number of snuffed candles grows.

Dangerous Things

Myrtias, a Syrian studying in Alexandria
during the reigns of Constans and Constantius,
half pagan and half Christian convert:
'Fortified with contemplation and long study,
I will not fear my passions, like a coward;
I will give my body entirely to pleasure,
to dreamed-of joys, the most brazen
erotic desires, the most depraved passions in my blood,
all without fear. For when I so wish it –
and I *will* so wish it, fortified as I'll be
with contemplation and long study –
at those critical moments I will find again
my ascetic spirit, as pure as it was before.'

Very Seldom

An old man, stooped and spent,
crippled by the years and by excess,
walks slowly across the alley.
But as he enters his house
to hide his wretched state and his old age,
he muses on that share of youth he still claims.

Young boys today recite his verses.
His fancies pass across their waking eyes.
Their healthy, sensuous minds,
their muscular, smooth limbs,
are stirred by his vision of beauty.

Painted Things

I love my work and take pains with it. But today
I find the slow pace of composition discouraging.
The weather has got into me. It just gets darker
and darker. Non-stop wind and rain.
I'd rather watch than write.
I'm looking at this painting now:
it shows a handsome boy lying near a spring,
out of breath from running.
Such a beautiful boy! And such a divine noon
which has taken him and induced him to sleep!
I sit and gaze like this for a long time.
Immersed again in art, I recover from the labour of
    creating it.

Morning Sea

Let me stop right here. Let me, too, have a look at nature:
the morning sea and the cloudless sky,
both a luminous blue, the yellow shore, all of it
beautiful, and in such magnificent light.

Let me stop right here. Let me pretend this is actually
what I'm seeing (I really did see it, when I first stopped)
and not, here too, more of those fantasies of mine,
more of those memories, those voluptuous illusions.

The Café Entrance

Something they said beside me
turned my attention towards the café entrance.
There I saw a beautiful body
that Eros must have fashioned with his boundless skill,
designing with delight the symmetrical limbs,
moulding the tall, sculpted frame,
tenderly drawing the face,
and bestowing, with a touch of his hand,
a feeling on the brow, in the eyes and on the lips.

One Night

The room was shabby and miserable,
tucked above a suspect tavern.
A window opened on to the alley,
narrow and unclean. From the tavern beneath
came the voices of workmen
playing cards and carousing.

There, in that humble, commonplace bed,
I possessed the body of love; I possessed
those sensual, rose-red lips of intoxication –
red lips so intoxicating that even now,
as I write these lines, after so many years
all alone in this house, I am drunk with it again.

Return

Return often and take me,
beloved sensation, return and take me –
when the body's memory awakens,
and old longings pulse again in my blood,
when lips and skin remember,
and hands could almost touch again.

Return often and take me at night,
when lips and skin remember.

Far Away

I would like to speak of this memory . . .
But it has grown dim . . . as if no trace of it remains –
for it lies far off in the first years of my youth.

Skin as if made of jasmine . . .
an August evening – was it August? –
I barely recall the eyes now: they were blue, I think.
Ah yes . . . blue, a sapphire blue.

He Vows

Every now and then   he vows to live a better life.
But when night comes   with her own counsels,
with her promises   and her compromises,
when night   comes with her power
over the body   that seeks and yearns,
he returns, lost,   to the same fatal pleasures.

I Left

I allowed no restraint. I gave in completely and left.
I ran toward pleasures that were half real
and half spun by my own mind.
I ran in the radiant night
and drank down strong wines, the kind
that champions of pleasure drink.

Chandelier

In a small, empty room, nothing
but four walls covered in green fabric,
an elegant chandelier glows, ablaze with light;
and in each of the chandelier's flames
burns an erotic fever, an erotic urge.

The fire raging in the chandelier
fills the tiny room, which shines
with a radiance that is in no way familiar.
And from its heat comes a kind of pleasure
not suited for timid bodies.

Since Nine O'Clock

Half past twelve. The time has passed quickly
since I first lit the lamp at nine o'clock,
and sat down here. I've sat without reading,
without speaking. With whom could I speak,
all alone in this house?

Since nine o'clock when I lit the lamp
a ghostly image of my adolescent body
came to me, reminding me
of closed and scented chambers,
and past pleasures – what brazen pleasures!
It brought before my eyes
streets now unrecognizable,
bars once filled with movement, now closed,
cafés and theatres that once existed.

The vision of my body in its youth
brought sorrowful memories also:
the grieving of my family, separations,
the feelings I had for my own kin, feelings
for the dead, whom I little acknowledged.

Half past twelve; how the time has passed.
Half past twelve; how the years have passed.

Insight

The years of my youth, my sensual adolescence –
how clearly I see their meaning now.

All those excessive, useless regrets . . .

I didn't see the meaning then.

For in the dissolute life of my youth
the plans for my poetry were taking shape;
the boundaries of my art were being drawn.

That's why my regrets were never firm,
and my determination to refrain, to change my ways,
lasted two weeks at most.

When They Come Alive

Try to preserve them, poet,
your visions of love,
however few may stay for you.
Cast them, half hidden, into your verse.
Try to hold on to them, poet,
when they come alive in your mind
at night or in the brightness of noon.

Pleasure

The joy and balm of my life is the memory of those hours
when I found and held pleasure just as I had wished it.
The joy and balm of my life is that I was able to avoid
any sensual gratification that seemed routine.

I Have Gazed So Much

I have gazed so much on beauty
that my eyes overflow with it.

The body's curves. Red lips. Voluptuous limbs.
Hair as if taken from a Greek statue,
always lovely, even if uncombed,
tumbling lightly over the snowy brow:
the Dramatis Personae of love that my poetry
demanded . . . in the nights of my youth,
encountered, secretly, in those nights . . .

In the Street

His face, appealing, a little wan;
his languid eyes a chestnut colour;
twenty-five years old but seeming twenty,
with an artist's sense for clothing –
the colour of the tie, the collar's shape –
aimlessly wandering the street
as if still dazed from the illicit passion,
the quite illicit passion he has just enjoyed.

The Tobacconist's Window

Near the brightly lit window
of a tobacconist's shop, they stood amid a crowd of people.
By chance their gazes met
and hesitantly they half expressed
the illicit longing of their flesh.
Later, after several anxious steps along the pavement –
they smiled and gently nodded.

Then the closed carriage . . .
the sensuous mingling of their bodies;
the hands, the lips coming together.

The Passage

Those things he only timidly imagined as a schoolboy
stand open now, revealed before him.
He goes to parties, stays out all night,
gets swept off his feet. And this is perfectly fitting (for our
    art, that is)
as his blood, young and hot,
is pleasure's prize. Lawless, erotic ecstasy
overcomes his body. And his young limbs
give in. In this way a simple youth
becomes worthy of our regard, and briefly he too
crosses over to the Exalted World of Poetry –
this appealing boy with his blood young and hot.

In the Evening

It would not have lasted long in any case.
Years of experience taught me that. And yet,
it was rather hasty, the way Fate ended it.
The good times were brief.
But how powerful the fragrances;
how wonderful the bed we lay in;
what pleasure we gave our bodies!

An echo from those days of pleasure,
an echo from those days came near,
an ember from our youth's fire;
I took one of his letters
and read it over and over until the light faded.

Melancholic, I stepped out on to the balcony –
I stepped out to change my mood by seeing at least
a little of this city that I love,
a little movement in the streets and in the shops.

Grey

Gazing upon a half-grey opal
I suddenly recalled two beautiful grey eyes
I'd once seen. It must have been twenty years ago . . .

We were lovers for a month.
Then he left; to Smyrna I think,
looking for work, and we never saw each other again.

Their beauty must have dimmed by now – if he's even
    alive – those grey eyes;
that beautiful face has surely gone to ruin.

Memory, keep those eyes just as they were.
And memory, whatever you can salvage of that passion of
    mine,
whatever you can, bring back to me tonight.

Beside the House

Yesterday, strolling in a remote neighbourhood,
I passed beside the house
I had entered when I was just a boy.
It was there that Eros first seized my limbs
with his delicious force.

And yesterday,
as I crossed that same old street, suddenly,
through the enchantment that Eros gives,
it was all made beautiful again . . . the shops, the
    pavements, the stones,
the walls and terraces and windows;
nothing unseemly remained.

And while I stood there, gazing up at the door,
while I stood loitering beside the house,
my entire being exuded
a sensual feeling confined within.

The Next Table

He can't be more than twenty-two.
And yet I'm certain it was at least that many years ago
that I enjoyed the very same body.

This isn't some erotic fantasy.
I've only just come into the casino
and there hasn't been time enough to drink.
I tell you, that's the very same body I once enjoyed.

And if I can't recall precisely where – that means nothing.

Now that he's sitting there at the next table,
I recognize each of his movements – and beneath his
     clothes
I see those beloved, naked limbs again.

Remember, Body . . .

Body, remember not only how deeply you were loved,
not only the many beds where you lay,
but also those desires that flashed
openly in their eyes
or trembled in the voice – and were thwarted
by some chance impediment.
Now that all of them are locked away in the past,
it almost seems as if you surrendered
to even those pre-empted desires – how they flashed,
    remember,
in the eyes of those who looked at you, how they trembled
in the voice for you, remember, body.

Days of 1903

I never found them again – so quickly lost,
the poetic eyes, the pallid face,
seen on the street at nightfall.

I never found them again – possessed entirely by chance,
then given up so easily,
and now so agonizingly longed for.
The poetic eyes, the pallid face,
those lips I never found again.

The Afternoon Sun

This room, how well I know it.
Now they're renting it and the one next door
as commercial space. The whole house is now
offices for brokers, salesmen, entire firms.

Ah, this room, how familiar it is!

Here, near the door, stood the sofa,
a Turkish carpet just before it;
nearby was a shelf with two yellow vases;
on the right – no, facing it – was an armoire with a mirror.
The desk where he wrote stood in the middle,
along with three large, wicker chairs.
Beside the window lay the bed
where we made love so many times.

All of these poor old furnishings must still exist
    somewhere.

Beside the window lay the bed;
the afternoon sunlight reached only half way across it . . .

That afternoon, at four o'clock, we parted,
just for a week . . . alas,
that week became forever.

To Live

It must have been one o'clock in the morning,
or one-thirty.

In a corner of the tavern;
behind the wooden partition.
Except for us, the space entirely empty.
An oil lamp was barely glowing.
The waiter on the night shift lay dozing at the door.

No one could have seen us. Regardless,
we'd reached such a state already,
we were past all thought of caution.

Our clothes half undone now – the few we had on,
with divine July burning.

Gratification of the flesh
between half-opened clothes,
the quick baring of the flesh – the ideal image of it
has travelled across twenty-six years, and now has come
to live in these verses.

On the Ship

It certainly bears some resemblance, this small portrait, done in pencil.

Hastily drawn right there on the ship's deck
one magical afternoon,
the Ionian Sea all around us.

It bears a resemblance. But I remember him as even more
    handsome,
more sensual, almost painfully so,
which casts his features in a more vivid light.
He seems even more handsome to me
now that my soul calls him back, out of Time.

Out of Time. All of these things are so very old –
the sketch, the ship, that afternoon.

That They May Come

One candle will suffice.   The gentle light it gives
suits the ambience better,   makes the room more alluring
for the Shades of Love,   whenever they may come.

One candle will suffice.   The room tonight
should have very faint light.   For deep in reverie
and suggestiveness –   in the softest light –
I will conjure my visions,   lost in feeling,
so the shades may come,   the Shades of Love.

Their Beginning

The fulfilling of their lawless pleasures
now complete, they rise from the bed
and hurriedly dress without speaking.
They emerge separately, furtively from the house,
and as they walk somewhat uneasily down the street,
it appears they suspect something about them betrays
the sort of bed they fell upon just a moment ago.

But what great profit to the artist's life:
tomorrow, the day after, or years later, he'll write
the powerful lines that had their beginning here.

In an Old Book

In an antique book – about a hundred years old –
I found a watercolour sandwiched amid the pages,
totally forgotten, with no signature.
You could see it was the work of a skilful artist;
it bore the title: 'Representation of Love'.

But it should have been 'love of the most extreme
    voluptuaries'.

For it was clear when you looked at the work
(the intent of the artist was easily grasped)
that the boy in this painting was not intended
for those who love in any healthy way,
who remain within the bounds of what is normally permitted –
his deep, chestnut eyes, the exquisite beauty
of his face, his idealized lips that bring
such pleasure to the beloved's body;
those ideal limbs fashioned for the sort of activity
the current morality would call shameless.

In Despair

He's lost him for good,   and now on the lips
of each new lover   he seeks the lips
of the one he lost;   in every embrace
with each new lover   he tries to believe
that he's giving himself   to the same young man.

He's lost him for good,   as if he'd never existed.
The boy wished – so he said –   he wished to be freed
from the stigma and reproach   of that unhealthy pleasure;
from the stigma and reproach   of that shameful pleasure.
It wasn't too late – he said –   for him to break free.

He's lost him for good,   as if he'd never existed.
Through imagination,   and self-delusion,
he seeks those lips   on the lips of others;
he's trying to feel   that lost love again.

Before Time Could Change Them

They wept horribly   at the separation.
Neither had wished it;   it was circumstance,
the need to earn a living,   where one or the other was obliged
to go far away –   New York or Canada.
Yet at that point their love   was no longer what it had been.
Their old attraction   had diminished by degrees;
their old attraction   had diminished a good deal.
But neither desired   to be split apart.
It was circumstance, surely.   Or perhaps Destiny itself
was working now as an artist,   separating them at the point
when their passion subsided,   before time could change them;
and each to the other   would remain always as he was:
a handsome young man   of twenty-four.

He Came to Read

He came to read; two or three books
are lying open: history and poetry.
But after just ten minutes of reading
he lets them drop. There on the sofa
he falls asleep. He truly is devoted to reading –
but he is twenty-three years old, and very handsome.
And just this afternoon, Eros surged
within his perfect limbs and on his lips.
Into his beautiful flesh came the heat of passion,
and there was no foolish embarrassment
about the form that pleasure took . . .

In the Twenty-fifth Year of His Life

He goes nightly to the saloon
where they'd met the month before.
He made inquiries, but they could tell him nothing.
From what little they'd said, he knew he'd met up
with an entirely unknown subject:
one of the many suspicious, shadowy
young forms who frequented that spot.
Yet he goes to the tavern every night
and sits there watching the entrance,
doggedly watching the entrance.
Perhaps he'll come. Perhaps tonight he'll come.

For three weeks he repeats the ritual.
His mind grows sick with lust.
Kisses linger on his lips.
Every inch of his flesh is racked by longing.
He feels that body's touch all over.
He longs to embrace him again.

He tries, of course, not to betray his emotions.
But sometimes he is almost beyond caring.
Besides, he is well aware of the risk;
he's made up his mind. It's not improbable that this life he
    leads
will expose him to some ruinous scandal.

The Dreary Village

In the dreary village where he works –
an assistant in one of the commercial establishments,
and quite young – he waits
for two or three months to pass,
for two or three months when business might slow
and he could leave for the city, to plunge straight
into the hurly-burly and amusement there;
in the dreary village where he waits –
he fell into bed tonight in a fit of passion,
all of his youth burning with carnal desire,
all of his beautiful youth in its beautiful intensity.
And in his sleep, pleasure came upon him; in his sleep
he sees and holds those limbs, the flesh he desired . . .

In the Bars

I'm wallowing in the bars   and brothels of Beirut.
I had no desire   to stay in Alexandria.
Tamides has left me   for the Eparch's son,
for a villa on the Nile,   and a mansion in town.
To stay in Alexandria   wouldn't do for me.
I'm wallowing in the bars   and brothels of Beirut.
In base debauchery   I lead a dirty, sordid life.
My one consolation,   like long-lasting beauty,
like a scent that has stayed   lingering on my skin,
is that for two years I had   that most exquisite youth,
Tamides, as my own,   as my very own,
and not for a house   or a villa on the Nile.

Days of 1896

He is utterly disgraced.   An erotic proclivity,
quite forbidden   and widely condemned
(yet congenital nonetheless),   was the cause:
for public opinion   was terribly prudish.
Bit by bit he was deprived   of the little income he had;
then came a loss in status,   and the respect he once
                                commanded.
He was nearing thirty   but had never gone a year
in full employment,   or at least a job he could talk about.
At times he earned   some semblance of a livelihood
by brokering meetings   considered shameful.
He ended up one of those who,   if you were seen with him
often enough, you could be   terribly compromised.

But no, that will not do;   this picture isn't right.
The memory of his beauty   deserves better than this.
There is another point of view,   and seen from that angle
he is quite appealing;   a simple and true
child of Eros who,   without hesitation,
placed far above his honour   and reputation,
the pure pleasure   that his pure flesh could give.

Above his own reputation?   But public opinion,
which was so terribly prudish,   so often got it wrong.

Two Young Men, Twenty-three to Twenty-four Years Old

He'd been sitting at the café since half past ten,
expecting him to appear at any moment.
Midnight came and went, and he still waited.
Soon it would be one thirty; the café
was almost completely empty.
He grew tired of reading the newspapers mechanically.
Of his original three shillings
only one remained: while waiting there
he'd spent the rest on coffee and brandy.
He'd smoked all his cigarettes.
The waiting had exhausted him. Alone
all those hours, insidious thoughts began to rankle
about the wayward life he led.

But when he saw his friend arrive – at once
the fatigue, the boredom, and the dark thoughts all
    vanished.

His friend brought unexpected good news:
he'd won sixty pounds playing cards.

Their handsome faces, their buoyant youth,
the sensuous love they both shared
were refreshed, had come alive and were fortified
by those sixty pounds won at cards.

C. P. Cavafy

Now full of joy and strength, sensuousness and beauty,
they departed – not to the homes of their respectable families
(where, after all, they were no longer welcome):
but to a place known only to them, a special
establishment of vice, where they requested
a room with a bed, expensive cocktails, and started to drink again.
When the drinks ran dry
and it was nearing four in the morning,
they gave themselves, happy at last, to love.

Days of 1901

This is what was so exceptional about him:
that despite all his profligacy
and his vast experience of love,
despite the fact that his comportment
matched his years perfectly,
there were moments – extremely rare
of course – when he gave the impression
that his flesh had almost never been touched.

The beauty of his twenty-nine years,
a beauty so well tested by pleasure,
could at times make one believe
he was a mere adolescent who – a bit awkwardly –
surrenders his chaste body to love for the very first time.

Days of 1908

That year he found himself out of work,
and so he made a living playing cards
or backgammon, and from whatever he could borrow.

He'd been offered work at a small stationer's
for three pounds a month.
Without a second thought he turned it down.
It wouldn't do. That was no salary for him,
a young man of twenty-five,
with a decent education.

He made – or failed to make – two or three shillings a day.
What else could a youth expect to win at cards
or backgammon in the sort of working-class cafés he
    frequented,
no matter how skilfully he played, or how stupid his
    opponents?
As for the loans, that was even worse.
On rare occasions he got a crown. More often, half.
Sometimes just a shilling.

When he was able to escape the grim, nightly ritual
for a week, or sometimes longer,
he would go and freshen up at the baths, with a morning
    swim.

His clothes were in terrible disrepair.
He wore the same suit all the time,
a faded cinnamon-coloured suit.

Days of 1908

Ah, days of summer, nineteen hundred and eight,
your vision of him, for beauty's sake,
omitted that faded cinnamon-coloured suit.

Instead, your vision preserved him
just as he was taking it off, casting away
that unworthy clothing, and the mended underwear,
and he stood completely naked, flawless in his beauty; a
    miracle.
His hair uncombed, tossed back,
his limbs lightly tanned
from those naked mornings at the baths and on the beach.

A Young Writer – in His Twenty-fourth Year

Now, brain, work as hard as you can.
A one-sided passion is wearing him thin.
He's in a state of nervous anxiety.
He kisses that adored face every day,
his hands all over those exquisite limbs.
He never loved before with so intense
a passion, but the happy fulfilment of Eros
is wanting; missing is the satisfaction that comes
when there are two who long with the same intensity.

(But these two are not equally given to their illicit passion.
    It possessed only him in full.)

So he is worn down, his nerves completely frayed.
He's jobless too, which makes matters worse.
He borrows a few pounds here and there,
and with difficulty (sometimes he almost has to beg)
he just about gets by.
He kisses those lips he adores; and upon
that exquisite body – which he now knows
merely tolerates him – he takes his pleasure.
Then he drinks and smokes; drinks and smokes,
and loiters in the coffee shops all day,
tediously lugging his heart-ache for that beauty.
Now, brain, work as hard as you can.

Picture of a Young Man of Twenty-three, Painted by His Friend of the Same Age, an Amateur

He completed the portrait   yesterday afternoon.
Now he scans it carefully: the subject is shown
in a grey jacket, dark grey,   unbuttoned, with no vest
and no tie underneath.   The shirt is pink
and left just open enough   to allow a glance
at his fine-looking chest   and his elegant neck.
The brow, on his right,   is almost completely obscured
by a curl of his hair,   that rich, thick hair
(done in the style   he wore that year).
Throughout the portrait   you see the extreme sensuousness
with which he endowed it,   when he painted the eyes,
when he drew the lips . . .   the mouth, those lips,
created for the fulfilment   of a particular pleasure.

Days of 1909, 1910 and 1911

The son of a put-upon, dirt-poor sailor
(from some island in the Aegean),
he worked as a blacksmith's apprentice. He had rags
for clothes, his pitiful working boots were in tatters,
his hands filthy with rust and oil.

In the evening, when the shop closed,
if there were something he especially wanted,
a necktie with a rather high price-tag,
a necktie to wear on Sundays,
or if he caught a glimpse of a nice blue shirt
in the shop window and hankered after it,
he'd sell his body for a shilling or two.

I wonder if Alexandria, in all its glory, in all the long history
of its ancient days, had ever seen a youth more exquisite,
more perfect than this boy – who went utterly to waste.
For, of course, no statue or portrait
was ever made. Stuck there in that grimy blacksmith's shop,
worn down by the wrack and strain of work,
and by the working man's rough pleasures, the boy went quickly to ruin.

Lovely Flowers, White Ones,
That Matched So Well

He entered the café   they used to frequent together.
It was here that his friend   three months ago had said:
'We haven't a farthing between us.   We're utterly broke.
There's nothing left   but loitering in cheap taverns.
I'm telling you straight,   I can't afford to be with you.
Someone else, you know,   is interested in me now.'
This other had promised him   two suits and a few
silk handkerchiefs.   To get him to come back
he searched everywhere   and found twenty pounds.
For twenty pounds,   his friend returned;
but beyond that, surely,   he returned for their friendship,
for the love they shared,   the deep feeling between them.
The other one had lied,   he was a nasty piece of work;
he'd only placed one suit   on order for him, and that
only grudgingly,   after a thousand requests.

But now he no longer   has any desire for the suit,
he has no desire   for silk handkerchiefs,
or twenty pounds,   or even twenty pence.

They buried him on Sunday,   at ten in the morning.
They buried him on Sunday,   a week ago now.

And on the cheap coffin   he laid some flowers,
lovely flowers, white ones,   that matched so well
his youthful beauty,   his twenty-two years.

When he went in the evening to the same café
they used to frequent together – he happened to find work;

he still had to earn a living – that dark café
they used to frequent together was like a knife in his heart.

In the Same Space

This setting of houses and cafés, the neighbourhood
where I gaze and where I stroll, for years and years.

I have fashioned you in joy and in sorrow,
through so many happenings, out of so many things.

You've been wholly transformed into feeling, for me.

The Mirror in the Entrance Hall

In the entrance hall of the elegant home
stood a large mirror, very old,
acquired at least eighty years ago.

A handsome youth, a tailor's apprentice
(on Sundays an amateur athlete),
was standing with a package. He handed it
to someone at the door who took it inside;
then he waited for the receipt. The tailor's apprentice
remained alone and waited.
He approached the mirror, gazed at his reflection
and straightened his tie. Five minutes later
they came with the receipt. He took it and left.

But the old mirror that during all the many years
of its existence had looked upon
thousands of objects and faces,
the old mirror was happy now,
filled with the satisfaction that it had received,
if only for a few minutes, beauty in all its perfection.

He Asked About the Quality

From the office where he'd been taken on
to fill a position that was trivial and poorly paid
(eight pounds a month, including bonus) –
he emerged as soon as he'd finished the dreary tasks
that kept him bent over his desk all afternoon.
At seven he came out and began to stroll
slowly down the street. He was handsome
in an interesting way, with the look of a man
who had reached the peak of his sensual potential.
He'd turned twenty-nine a month before.

He dawdled along the street, then down
the shabby alleys that led to his apartment.

As he passed a little shop that sold cheap
imitation goods for workmen,
inside he saw a face, a physique
that urged him on, and in he walked,
inquiring about some coloured handkerchiefs.

He asked about the quality of the handkerchiefs
and what they cost; his voice
breaking, almost stifled by desire.
The answers came back in the same tone,
distracted, the low timbre
suggesting veiled consent.

They went on talking about the merchandise –
but their sole aim was for their hands to touch

over the handkerchiefs, for their faces,
their lips, as if by chance, to brush against each other:
for some momentary contact of the flesh.

Swiftly and in secret, so that the shop owner,
seated at the back, would never notice.

1. BOCCACCIO · *Mrs Rosie and the Priest*
2. GERARD MANLEY HOPKINS · *As kingfishers catch fire*
3. *The Saga of Gunnlaug Serpent-tongue*
4. THOMAS DE QUINCEY · *On Murder Considered as One of the Fine Arts*
5. FRIEDRICH NIETZSCHE · *Aphorisms on Love and Hate*
6. JOHN RUSKIN · *Traffic*
7. PU SONGLING · *Wailing Ghosts*
8. JONATHAN SWIFT · *A Modest Proposal*
9. *Three Tang Dynasty Poets*
10. WALT WHITMAN · *On the Beach at Night Alone*
11. KENKŌ · *A Cup of Sake Beneath the Cherry Trees*
12. BALTASAR GRACIÁN · *How to Use Your Enemies*
13. JOHN KEATS · *The Eve of St Agnes*
14. THOMAS HARDY · *Woman much missed*
15. GUY DE MAUPASSANT · *Femme Fatale*
16. MARCO POLO · *Travels in the Land of Serpents and Pearls*
17. SUETONIUS · *Caligula*
18. APOLLONIUS OF RHODES · *Jason and Medea*
19. ROBERT LOUIS STEVENSON · *Olalla*
20. KARL MARX AND FRIEDRICH ENGELS · *The Communist Manifesto*
21. PETRONIUS · *Trimalchio's Feast*
22. JOHANN PETER HEBEL · *How a Ghastly Story Was Brought to Light by a Common or Garden Butcher's Dog*
23. HANS CHRISTIAN ANDERSEN · *The Tinder Box*
24. RUDYARD KIPLING · *The Gate of the Hundred Sorrows*
25. DANTE · *Circles of Hell*
26. HENRY MAYHEW · *Of Street Piemen*
27. HAFEZ · *The nightingales are drunk*
28. GEOFFREY CHAUCER · *The Wife of Bath*
29. MICHEL DE MONTAIGNE · *How We Weep and Laugh at the Same Thing*
30. THOMAS NASHE · *The Terrors of the Night*
31. EDGAR ALLAN POE · *The Tell-Tale Heart*
32. MARY KINGSLEY · *A Hippo Banquet*
33. JANE AUSTEN · *The Beautifull Cassandra*
34. ANTON CHEKHOV · *Gooseberries*
35. SAMUEL TAYLOR COLERIDGE · *Well, they are gone, and here must I remain*
36. JOHANN WOLFGANG VON GOETHE · *Sketchy, Doubtful, Incomplete Jottings*
37. CHARLES DICKENS · *The Great Winglebury Duel*
38. HERMAN MELVILLE · *The Maldive Shark*
39. ELIZABETH GASKELL · *The Old Nurse's Story*
40. NIKOLAY LESKOV · *The Steel Flea*

41. HONORÉ DE BALZAC · *The Atheist's Mass*
42. CHARLOTTE PERKINS GILMAN · *The Yellow Wall-Paper*
43. C.P. CAVAFY · *Remember, Body . . .*
44. FYODOR DOSTOEVSKY · *The Meek One*
45. GUSTAVE FLAUBERT · *A Simple Heart*
46. NIKOLAI GOGOL · *The Nose*
47. SAMUEL PEPYS · *The Great Fire of London*
48. EDITH WHARTON · *The Reckoning*
49. HENRY JAMES · *The Figure in the Carpet*
50. WILFRED OWEN · *Anthem For Doomed Youth*
51. WOLFGANG AMADEUS MOZART · *My Dearest Father*
52. PLATO · *Socrates' Defence*
53. CHRISTINA ROSSETTI · *Goblin Market*
54. *Sindbad the Sailor*
55. SOPHOCLES · *Antigone*
56. RYŪNOSUKE AKUTAGAWA · *The Life of a Stupid Man*
57. LEO TOLSTOY · *How Much Land Does A Man Need?*
58. GIORGIO VASARI · *Leonardo da Vinci*
59. OSCAR WILDE · *Lord Arthur Savile's Crime*
60. SHEN FU · *The Old Man of the Moon*
61. AESOP · *The Dolphins, the Whales and the Gudgeon*
62. MATSUO BASHŌ · *Lips too Chilled*
63. EMILY BRONTË · *The Night is Darkening Round Me*
64. JOSEPH CONRAD · *To-morrow*
65. RICHARD HAKLUYT · *The Voyage of Sir Francis Drake Around the Whole Globe*
66. KATE CHOPIN · *A Pair of Silk Stockings*
67. CHARLES DARWIN · *It was snowing butterflies*
68. BROTHERS GRIMM · *The Robber Bridegroom*
69. CATULLUS · *I Hate and I Love*
70. HOMER · *Circe and the Cyclops*
71. D. H. LAWRENCE · *Il Duro*
72. KATHERINE MANSFIELD · *Miss Brill*
73. OVID · *The Fall of Icarus*
74. SAPPHO · *Come Close*
75. IVAN TURGENEV · *Kasyan from the Beautiful Lands*
76. VIRGIL · *O Cruel Alexis*
77. H. G. WELLS · *A Slip under the Microscope*
78. HERODOTUS · *The Madness of Cambyses*
79. *Speaking of Siva*
80. *The Dhammapada*

'I could see that she was still terribly afraid, but I didn't soften anything; instead, seeing that she was afraid I deliberately intensified it.'

FYODOR DOSTOYEVSKY
Born 1821, Moscow, Russia
Died 1881, Saint Petersburg, Russia

The story was first published in its original Russian as 'Krotkaya' in 1876 and is taken from the *The Gambler and Other Stories*.

DOSTOYEVSKY IN PENGUIN CLASSICS

Crime and Punishment
The Idiot
The Double
The Gambler and Other Stories
The Grand Inquisitor
Notes from the Underground
Netochka Nezvanova
The House of the Dead
The Brothers Karamazov
The Village of Stepanchikovo
Russian Short Stories from Pushkin to Buida
Demons
Poor Folk and Other Stories

FYODOR DOSTOYEVSKY

The Meek One

A Fantastic Story

Translated by
Ronald Meyer

PENGUIN BOOKS

PENGUIN CLASSICS

UK | USA | Canada | Ireland | Australia
India | New Zealand | South Africa

Penguin Books is part of the Penguin Random House group of companies
whose addresses can be found at global.penguinrandomhouse.com.

This edition published in Penguin Classics 2015

012

Translation copyright © Ronald Mayer, 2010

The moral right of the translator has been asserted

Set in 9/12.4 pt Baskerville 10 Pro
Typeset by Jouve (UK), Milton Keynes
Printed and bound in Great Britain by Clays Ltd, Elcograf S.p.A.

A CIP catalogue record for this book is available from the British Library

ISBN: 978–0–141–39748–1

www.greenpenguin.co.uk

Penguin Random House is committed to a
sustainable future for our business, our readers
and our planet. This book is made from Forest
Stewardship Council® certified paper.

Chapter 1

I. WHO I WAS AND WHO SHE WAS

... Now as long as she's here – everything is still all right: I'm constantly going over and looking at her; but tomorrow they'll take her away and – how will I ever stay behind all on my own? Now she's on the table in the sitting room, on two card tables that were put together, and the coffin will come tomorrow, a white one, with white *gros de Naples*, however, that's not it . . . I keep pacing and want to make sense of it for myself. Now it's six hours that I've been trying to make sense of it and I still can't collect my thoughts to a T. The fact of the matter is that I keep pacing, pacing, pacing . . . Here's how it was. I'll simply tell it in order. (Order!) Gentlemen, I'm far from being a literary man, as you'll see, well, so be it, but I'll tell it as I myself understand it. That's the horror of it for me, that I understand everything!

If you want to know, that is, if we take it from the very beginning, then quite simply she used to come to me to pawn things in order to pay for advertising in the *Voice*, saying, well, that there's a governess, willing to travel and give lessons in the home and so forth and so on. That was in the very beginning and of course I didn't single her out from the others: she came like all the others and so forth. But afterwards I began to single her out. She was so thin, fair, a bit taller than average; with me she was always awkward, as if she were embarrassed (I think that she was exactly the same with all strangers, and, it goes without saying, I was no different than anyone else, that is, if taken not as a pawnbroker but as a man). As soon as she received her money she would immediately turn around and leave. And all in silence. Others argue, beg, haggle to be given more; but not this one, whatever she was given . . . It seems to me that I keep getting muddled . . . Yes; first of all, I was struck by her things: silver gilt earrings, a worthless little locket – things worth twenty kopecks. She herself knew that they were worth all of ten kopecks, but I could see from her face that for her they were objects of great value – and indeed, as I learned later, this was all that she had left from her papa and mama. Only once did I permit myself to smile at her things. That is, you see, I never permit myself that, I maintain a gentlemanly tone with the public: a few words said respectfully and sternly. 'Sternly, sternly and sternly.' But she suddenly permitted herself to bring the remnants (quite literally, that is) of an old rabbit-skin jacket – and I couldn't resist and suddenly said something to her in the way of a witticism, as it were. Goodness gracious, how she flared up! Her eyes were blue, large, thoughtful, but how they blazed! But she didn't let drop a single word, she picked up her 'remnants' and left. That was the first time that I noticed her *particularly* and thought something of that sort about her, that is, precisely something of that particular sort. Yes; I recall yet another impression, that is, if you wish, the main impression, the synthesis of everything: namely, that she was terribly young, so young, as if she were fourteen years old. Whereas she was then three months shy of sixteen. However, that wasn't what I wanted to say, that wasn't the synthesis at all. She came again the next day. I later learned that she had been to Dobronravov and Mozer with that jacket, but they don't take anything except gold and didn't even bother to talk to her. I, on the other hand, had once taken a cameo from her (a worthless little thing) – and when I gave it some thought later on I was surprised: I also don't buy anything except gold and silver and yet I had taken a cameo. That was my second thought about her then, I remember that.

This time, that is, after going to Mozer, she brought an amber cigar holder – a so-so little piece, for the connoisseur, but something of no worth to us, because we deal only in gold. Since she had come after yesterday's *rebellion*, I greeted her sternly. Sternness for me means dryness. However, as I was giving her the two roubles, I couldn't resist and said with some irritation, as it were: 'I'm doing this only *for you*, Mozer wouldn't take a thing like this from you.' I particularly emphasized the words 'for you', and precisely with a *certain insinuation*. I was angry. Once again she flared up, upon hearing that 'for you', but she held her tongue, didn't throw down the money, took it – that's what poverty is! But how she flared up! I understood that I had wounded her. But when she had gone, I suddenly asked myself: So is this triumph over her really worth two roubles? Hee-hee-hee! I remember that I asked precisely that very question twice: 'Is it worth it? Is it worth it?' And, laughing, I answered this question to myself in the affirmative. Then I really cheered up. But this wasn't a nasty feeling: I had a plan, a purpose; I wanted to test her, because suddenly I began to have some thoughts about her. That was my third *particular* thought about her.

Fyodor Dostoyevsky

... Well, it was from that time that it all started. It goes without saying, I immediately tried to find out all her circumstances indirectly and waited for her arrival with particular impatience. You see, I had a feeling that she would come soon. When she came, I launched into an amiable conversation with unusual politeness. You see, I wasn't badly brought up and have manners. Hmm. That was when I guessed that she was kind and meek. The kind and meek don't resist for long, and although they are by no means very open, they don't at all know how to avoid a conversation: they answer grudgingly, but they answer and the longer it goes on, the more they answer; but if this is what you want, you can't let yourself get tired. It goes without saying that she didn't explain anything to me then. It was later that I learned about the *Voice* and about everything else. She was then mustering every last bit she had to advertise – at first, it goes without saying, presumptuously: 'Governess, willing to travel, send terms by post'; but later: 'Willing to do anything, tutor, be a companion, housekeeping, care for the sick, can sew' and so forth and so on. The usual! It goes without saying that all this was added to the advertisement at different stages, and towards the end, when despair had set it, there was even 'without salary, for board'. No, she didn't find a position! I made up my mind then to test her for the last time: I suddenly picked up today's *Voice* and showed her an advertisement: 'Young female, orphan, seeks position as governess of small children, preferably with an elderly widower. Willing to do light housework.'

'There, you see, this was published this morning and by

The Meek One

evening she's sure to have found a job. That's the way to advertise!'

Again she flared up, again her eyes blazed; she turned around and immediately walked out. I was very pleased. However, by then I was already sure of everything and had no fears: nobody would take her cigar holders. Besides, she had already run out of cigar holders. And so it was, two days later she comes, such a pale, agitated little thing – I understood that something had happened at home, and indeed something had happened. I'll explain straight away what happened, but now I merely wish to recall how I suddenly did something chic and rose in her eyes. A plan suddenly occurred to me. The fact of the matter is that she brought this icon (she had steeled herself to bring it) ... Oh, listen! Listen! This is where it began, but I keep getting muddled ... The fact of the matter is that I now want to recall everything, every trifle, every little detail. I still want to collect my thoughts to a T and – I can't, and now there are these little details, these little details ...

An icon of the Mother of God. The Mother of God with Child, a family heirloom, an antique, with a silver gilt frame – worth – well, worth about six roubles. I see that the icon is dear to her, and she's pawning the whole icon, without removing the mounting. I tell her that it would be better if she removed the mounting and took the icon with her, because after all it's an icon.

'Surely you're not forbidden?'

'No, it's not that it's forbidden, but just that, perhaps, you yourself ...'

'Well, remove it.'

'You know what, I won't remove it, but I'll put it over there in the icon case,' I said, after giving it some thought, 'with the other icons, under the lamp.' (I've always had the lamp burning ever since I opened my shop.) 'And I'll give you ten roubles – it's as simple as that.'

'I don't need ten, give me five; I'll redeem it without fail.'

'But don't you want ten? The icon is worth it,' I added, after observing that her little eyes had flashed once again. She held her tongue. I brought her five roubles.

'Don't despise anybody – I've been in tight squeezes myself, and even a bit worse, and if you now see me in such an occupation . . . well, you see, after all that I've endured . . .'

'You're taking revenge on society? Is that it?' she suddenly interrupted me with a rather sarcastic gibe, in which, however, there was a good deal of innocence (that is, of a general sort, because she certainly did not single me out from the others then, so it was said almost inoffensively). 'Aha!' I thought, 'so that's what you're like, your character is showing itself, you belong to the new movement.'

'You see,' I immediately observed, half-jokingly, half-mysteriously. 'I – I am part of that part of the whole that desires to do evil, but creates good . . .'

She looked at me quickly and with great curiosity, in which, however, there was a great deal of childishness:

'Wait a moment . . . What's that saying? Where's it from? I've heard it somewhere . . .'

'Don't rack your brains: Mephistopheles recommends himself to Faust in those words. Have you read *Faust*?'

'No . . . not carefully.'

'That is, you haven't read it at all. You should read it. However, once again I see a sardonic grin on your lips. Please, don't suppose that I have so little taste that I wished to paint over my role as a pawnbroker by recommending myself to you as Mephistopheles. Once a pawnbroker, always a pawnbroker. We know that, miss.'

'You're such a strange person . . . I didn't in the least want to say anything of the kind . . .'

She wanted to say: I didn't expect that you were an educated man, but she didn't say it, though I knew that she had thought it; I had pleased her terribly much.

'You see,' I observed, 'one can do good in any walk of life. Of course, I'm not speaking of myself; let's suppose that I do nothing but bad things . . .'

'Of course, one can do good in any position,' she said, looking at me with a quick and penetrating glance. 'Precisely in any position,' she added suddenly.

Oh, I remember, I remember all those moments! And I also want to add that when these young people, these dear young people, want to say something intelligent and penetrating, then their faces suddenly show you all too sincerely and naively: 'Here I am, I'm telling you something intelligent and penetrating.' And it's not at all from vanity, as is the case with the likes of us, but you see that she herself sets great store on all this terribly, and she believes, and respects and thinks that you, too, respect all this just as she does. Oh, sincerity! That's what they win you over with! And it was so charming in her!

I remember, I have forgotten nothing! When she left, I made up my mind at once. That same day I made my final enquiries and learned absolutely everything else there was to know about her present particulars; all the particulars of her past I already knew from Lukerya, who was then their servant and whom I had bribed several days earlier. These circumstances were so horrible that I don't understand how it had been possible for her to laugh, as she had that day, and be curious about Mephistopheles' words, when she herself was faced with such horrors. But – youth! That's precisely what I thought about her then with pride and joy, because, you see, there was also magnanimity about it, as if she were to say: the great works of Goethe shine even on the brink of ruin. Youth is always magnanimous, if only ever so slightly and ever so distortedly. That is, I'm speaking of her, you see, her alone. And the main thing, I then looked upon her as *mine* and did not doubt my power. You know, that's a most voluptuous thought, when you no longer have any doubt.

But what's wrong with me? If I keep going on like this, then when will I collect everything to a T? Quickly, quickly – this isn't the point at all, oh God!

II. A MARRIAGE PROPOSAL

The 'particulars' I learned about her I can set forth in a few words: her father and mother had died a long time ago, three years previously, and she had been left with her disreputable aunts. That is, it's saying too little to call them disreputable. One aunt was a widow with a large family, six children, each one smaller than the next; the other was a spinster, old and

The Meek One

nasty. Both of them were nasty. Her father had been a government official, but only a clerk, and a non-hereditary nobleman – in a word: everything played into my hands. I appeared as if from some higher world: after all, I was a retired staff captain of a brilliant regiment, a nobleman by birth, independent and so on, and as far as the pawnshop went, the aunts could only look at it with respect. She had been slaving for her aunts for three years, but nevertheless she had passed an examination somewhere – she had managed to pass it, snatched a free minute to pass it, despite relentless work day in and day out – and that meant something about aspirations for the noble and the sublime on her part. After all, why did I want to get married? But who cares about me, we'll save that for later ... As if that were the point! She taught her aunt's children, she sewed their underclothes, and towards the end she washed not only these underclothes, but she, with her bad chest, also washed the floors. To put it bluntly, they even beat her, reproaching her for every crumb. It ended with them intending to sell her. Ugh! I'll omit the dirty details. Later she told me everything in detail. A neighbour, a fat shopkeeper, had been observing all this for a whole year, and he wasn't just an ordinary shopkeeper, but the owner of two grocery stores. He had already beat two wives to death and was looking for a third, and had cast his eye on her: 'She's a quiet one,' he thought, 'she grew up in poverty and I'm marrying for the sake of my orphans.' Indeed, he did have orphans. He began to seek her hand, started negotiations with the aunts, and on top of that – he's fifty years old; she's horrified. And that's when she started coming to me to get money for advertisements in the *Voice*.

In the end, she began asking the aunts to give her just the littlest bit of time to think it over. They gave her that little bit, but only one, they didn't give her another; they badgered her: 'We don't know where we'll get our next meal, even without an extra mouth to feed.' I already knew all this, and on that same day, after her visit in the morning, I made up my mind. That evening the merchant came, he had brought from the shop a pound of candies worth fifty kopecks; she's sitting with him, and I summon Lukerya from the kitchen and tell her to go to her and whisper that I'm standing by the gate and wish to tell her something most urgently. I remained pleased with myself. And in general I was terribly pleased with myself that entire day.

Right there at the gate, already dumbfounded that I had summoned her, I explained to her, in Lukerya's presence, that I would consider myself happy and honoured . . . Secondly, she was not surprised by my manner or by the fact that this was taking place by the gate: 'I am a straightforward man,' I said, 'and have studied the circumstances of the matter.' And I wasn't lying that I'm straightforward. Well, to hell with it. I spoke not only decently, that is, by showing myself to be a person of good breeding, but originally as well, and that's the main thing. What, is it a sin to acknowledge this? I want to judge myself and am doing so. I must speak both *pro* and *contra*, and I am doing so. I recalled it with delight afterwards, even though it was stupid: I announced straight out then, without any embarrassment, that, in the first place, I wasn't particularly talented, not particularly intelligent, and perhaps not even particularly kind, that I was a rather cheap egoist (I remember this expression, I had composed

The Meek One

it on my way there and remained pleased with it) and that – very, very likely – there was much that was unpleasant about me in other respects as well. All this was said with a particular kind of pride – we know how these sorts of things are said. Of course, I had sufficient good taste, after nobly declaring my deficiencies, not to launch into a declaration of my virtues: 'But to make up for this, I have this, that and the other.' I could see that she was still terribly afraid, but I didn't soften anything; instead, seeing that she was afraid I deliberately intensified it: I said straight out that she wouldn't go hungry, but as for fancy clothes, the theatre and balls – there would be none of that, though perhaps later, when I had achieved my goal. I was definitely carried away by this stern tone. I added, and as casually as possible, that if I had taken up such an occupation, that is, keeping this pawnshop, it was for one purpose only – that is, there was a certain circumstance, so to speak . . . But you see I had a right to speak like that: I really did have such a purpose and such a circumstance. Wait a moment, gentlemen, all my life I have been the first to hate this pawnbroking business, but in essence, you see, even though it's ridiculous to talk to oneself in mysterious phrases, I was 'taking revenge on society', you see, I really, really, really was! Therefore, her joke about the fact that I was 'taking revenge' was unfair. That is, you see, if I had said to her straight out in so many words: 'Yes, I'm taking revenge on society', and she had burst out laughing, the way she did that morning, it would indeed have come out ridiculous. But with an indirect hint and by dropping a mysterious phrase it turned out that it was possible to engage her imagination. Moreover, I wasn't afraid of anything then: you see, I knew that in any event the fat shopkeeper was more repulsive than I and that I, standing by the gate, was her liberator. I understood that, you see. Oh, man understands baseness particularly well! But was it baseness? How is one to judge a man in a case like this? Didn't I love her already even then?

Wait a moment: it goes without saying that I didn't say a word to her about doing a good deed: on the contrary, oh, on the contrary: 'It is *I*,' I said, 'who am being done the favour, and not *you*.' So that I even expressed this in words, I couldn't help myself, and perhaps it came out stupidly, because I noticed a fleeting grin on her face. But on the whole I had definitely won. Wait a moment, if I'm going to recall all this filth, then I'll recall this final bit of swinishness: I was standing there and this is what was going through my head: You're tall, fit, educated and – and finally, to speak without any boasting, you're not bad looking. That's what was running through my head. It goes without saying, she said 'yes' there and then by the gate. But . . . but I should add: she thought it over for a long time, right there and then by the gate, before she said 'yes'. She was so deep in thought, so deep in thought that I was on the verge of asking, 'Well, what is it going to be?' – and I couldn't even help myself from asking with a certain sense of chic: 'Well, what is it going to be, Miss?' – adding the 'Miss' for good measure.

'Wait, I'm thinking.'

And her little face was so serious, so serious – that even then I might have read it! But instead I was offended: 'Is she really,' I thought to myself, 'choosing between me and the merchant?' Oh, I still didn't understand then! I still didn't understand anything, anything then! I didn't understand until today! I remember Lukerya ran after me when I was already walking away, stopped me in the street and said, catching her breath: 'God will reward you, sir, for taking our dear young lady – only don't say anything about it to her, she's proud.'

Well now, proud! I like them proud, I said to myself. The proud ones are particularly nice, when . . . well, when you no longer harbour any doubts about your power over them. Eh? Oh, base, awkward man! Oh, how pleased I was! Do you know, while she was standing there by the gate deep in thought about whether to say 'yes' to me, and I was surprised, do you know, that she might even have been thinking: 'If it's to be misfortune either way, isn't it better to choose the worst straight away, that is, the fat shopkeeper; let him get drunk, the sooner the better, and beat me to death!' Eh? What do you think, could that have been what she was thinking?

And even now I don't understand, even now I don't understand anything! I just now said that she might have been thinking that she should choose the worse of the two misfortunes, that is, the merchant. But who was worse for her then – the merchant or I? The merchant or the pawnbroker who quotes Goethe? That's still a question! What question? You don't understand even that: the answer is lying on the table, and you say 'what question'! But to hell with me! I'm not the point here at all . . . And at the same time, what do I care now – whether I'm the point or not? That's something I'm utterly incapable of deciding. I'd better go to bed. I have a headache . . .

III. THE NOBLEST OF MEN, BUT I DON'T BELIEVE IT MYSELF

I didn't fall asleep. And how could I with that pulse hammering away in my head. I want to absorb all this, all this filth. Oh, the filth! Oh, the filth I dragged her out of then! She should have realized that, you know, she should have appreciated my deed! I was pleased, too, by various thoughts, for example, that I was forty-one years old and that she was only sixteen. That fascinated me, this sense of inequality, it was very sweet, very sweet.

I, for example, wanted to have the wedding *à l'anglaise*, that is, just the two of us, perhaps with two witnesses, one of whom would be Lukerya, and then at once to the train, for example, if only to Moscow (it so happened that I had business there), to a hotel for a fortnight or so. She was against it, she wouldn't have it and I was forced to visit her aunts and pay my respects to them as the relatives from whom I was taking her. I gave in, and the aunts were rendered their due. I even made a present of a hundred roubles each to those creatures and promised more, of course, without saying a word to her, so as not to distress her with the baseness of the situation. The aunts at once became as soft as silk. There was an argument about the trousseau as well: she didn't have anything, almost literally, but she didn't want anything either. However, I managed to convince her that it wasn't possible to have absolutely nothing, and so I arranged for the trousseau myself, because who else would do anything for her? Well, but to hell with me! Various ideas of

The Meek One

mine, however, I nevertheless did manage to convey to her then, so that she would at least know. Perhaps I was even too hasty. The main thing is that from the very beginning, however much she tried to hold out, she would throw herself at me with her love; she would meet me when I came home in the evening with rapture, she would tell me in her prattle (the charming prattle of innocence!) all about her childhood, youth, about her parental home, about her father and mother. But I immediately threw cold water on all these ecstasies right then and there. That was the whole point of my idea. I answered her raptures with silence, gracious, of course . . . but she nevertheless quickly saw that we were different and that I was – a riddle. And the main thing is that I had set my sights on this riddle! You see, it was in order to pose this riddle perhaps that I committed all this foolishness! First of all, sternness – it was with sternness that I took her into my house. In a word, even though I was quite pleased with things as they were, I began to create a complete system. Oh, it took shape on its own, without any effort. And it couldn't have been otherwise, I had to create this system on account of one incontrovertible circumstance – really, what is this? I'm slandering myself! The system was genuine. No, listen, if you're going to judge a person, then you should judge him knowing the case . . . Listen.

How should I begin this, because it's very difficult. When you begin justifying yourself – that's when it gets difficult. You see: young people despise money, for example – I hammered away about money; I pressed home about money. And I hammered away so that she began to fall silent more and more. She would open her big eyes, listen, look and fall silent. You see: young people are magnanimous, that is, the good ones are magnanimous and impetuous, but they have little tolerance, as soon as something's not quite right – you get their contempt. But I wanted breadth, I wanted to instil breadth right into her heart, to instil it into her heart's vista, isn't that so? I'll take a trivial example: How could I explain, for example, my pawnshop to a person like that? It goes without saying that I didn't bring it up directly, or it would have looked like I was asking her forgiveness for the pawnshop; instead I acted, so to speak, with pride – I spoke almost silently. And I'm a master of speaking silently – all my life I've spoken silently and I've lived through entire tragedies in silence. Oh, and I too have been unhappy! I was cast aside by everyone, cast aside and forgotten, and no one, no one knows it! And suddenly this sixteen-year-old girl got hold of details about me afterwards from vile people and thought that she knew everything, but meanwhile the secret remained only in this man's breast! I went on being silent, and I was particularly, particularly silent with her until just yesterday – why was I silent? Because I'm a proud man. I wanted her to find out on her own, without me, but not from stories told by scoundrels, but that she should *guess herself* about this man and comprehend him! When I received her into my house, I wanted her complete respect. I wanted her to stand before me beseechingly, on account of my suffering – and I was worthy of that. Oh, I've always been proud, I've always wanted all or nothing! And that's precisely why I'm not for half-measures in happiness, but wanted everything – and that's precisely why I was forced

The Meek One

to act as I did then, as if to say: 'Figure it out for yourself and appreciate me!' Because, you must agree, if I had begun by explaining and prompting, being evasive and asking for respect – then, you see, it would have been as if I were asking for charity ... However ... However, why am I talking about this!

Stupid, stupid, stupid, stupid! I straight away and ruthlessly (and I want to emphasize that it was ruthlessly) explained to her then, in a few words, that the magnanimity of young people was lovely, but not worth a brass button. Why not? Because it comes cheap, they get it without having lived; it's all, so to speak, the 'first impressions of existence', but let's see you do some work! Cheap magnanimity is always easy, and even to give your life – even that's easy, because that's just a matter of the blood boiling and an over-abundance of energy, one passionately longs for beauty! No, take an act of magnanimity that is difficult, quiet, muted, without splendour, where you're slandered, where there's much sacrifice and not a drop of glory – where you, a shining man, are brought forward before everyone as a scoundrel, when you are the most honest man in the world – come on, try your hand at that sort of deed, no, sir, you'll give it up! While I – all I've done my whole life is to shoulder that sort of deed. In the beginning she would argue – and how! But then she began to fall silent, completely and totally, she would just open her eyes terribly wide as she listened, such big, big eyes, and so attentive. And ... and besides that I suddenly saw a smile, a mistrustful, silent, bad smile. It was with that smile that I brought her into my house. And it's also true that she had nowhere else to go ...

Fyodor Dostoyevsky

IV. PLANS AND MORE PLANS

Which of us was the first to begin then?

Neither. It began on its own from the very first. I have said that I had brought her into my house with sternness; however, I softened it from the very first. When she was still my fiancée it had been explained to her that she would assist in taking in the pledges and paying out the money, and she didn't say anything then (note that). And what's more, she even took to the business with zeal. Well, of course, the apartment, the furniture – everything remained the same as before. The apartment has two rooms: one is a large room in which the shop is partitioned off from the rest, and the other one is also a large room in which we have our sitting room and bedroom. My furniture isn't much; even her aunts had better. My icon-stand with the lamp is in the room with the shop; in the other room I have my bookcase with some books and a trunk to which I have the keys; and there's a bed, tables, chairs. When she was still my fiancée I told her that one rouble a day and no more was allotted for our board, that is, food, for me, her and Lukerya, whom I had enticed away: 'I need 30,000 in three years,' I told her, 'otherwise I won't be able to save up enough money.' She didn't stand in the way, but I myself added to our board by thirty kopecks. It was the same thing with the theatre. When she was still my fiancée I told her that there wouldn't be any theatre; however, I decided that we should go to the theatre once a month, and decently at that, in the orchestra. We went

The Meek One

together, three times, and saw *In Pursuit of Happiness* and *Songbirds*, I think. (Oh, to hell with it, to hell with it!) We went in silence and returned in silence. Why, why did we from the very beginning choose to be silent? After all, there weren't any quarrels in the beginning, but there was silence then, too. As I recall, she somehow kept looking at me then on the sly; when I noticed that I increased my silence. True, I was the one who insisted upon silence, and not she. On her part there were outbursts once or twice, when she would rush to embrace me; but since these outbursts were unhealthy and hysterical, and what I required was steadfast happiness, together with her respect, I received them coldly. And I was right to do so: each time the outburst was followed the next day by a quarrel.

That is, there weren't any quarrels, but there was silence and – and on her part a more and more insolent look. 'Rebellion and independence' – that's what it was, only she didn't know how. Yes, that meek face was becoming more and more insolent. Can you believe it? I was becoming repulsive to her – I came to understand that. And there could be no doubt about these outbursts that came over her. For example, after leaving behind such filth and beggary, after scrubbing floors, how could she suddenly begin to grumble about our poverty! You see, gentlemen: it wasn't poverty, it was economy, and where necessary there was some luxury, when it came to linens and cleanliness, for example. I had always dreamed before that cleanliness in a husband attracts a wife. However, it wasn't poverty, but my supposed miserly economy that bothered her: 'He has goals, he's showing his firm character.' She suddenly declined to go to the theatre. And there was more and more of that sardonic grin . . . While I intensified my silence, I intensified my silence.

Surely there was no need to justify my actions? The main thing here was the pawnshop. Come now, sirs: I knew that a woman, especially one who was sixteen years old, couldn't help but submit completely to a man. Women have no originality, that's – that's an axiom, even now it's an axiom for me! Never mind what's lying there in the front room: truth is truth, and even Mill himself can't do anything about it! But a loving woman, oh, a loving woman idolizes even the vices, even the villainy of her beloved being. He would not seek such justifications for his villainy as she will find for him. That's magnanimous but not original. It is this lack of originality alone that has been the undoing of women. And what, I repeat, what are you pointing to there on the table? Is there really anything original about what's there on the table? Oh-h-h!

Listen: I was certain of her love then. You see, she would throw herself on my neck then. That meant she loved me, or rather – she wished to love me. Yes, that's what it was: she wished to love, she sought to love. But the main thing, you see, is that there weren't any villainies for which she needed to find justifications. You say a 'pawnbroker' and that's what everyone says. But what if I am a pawnbroker? That means there are reasons, if the most magnanimous of men became a pawnbroker. You see, gentlemen, there are ideas . . . that is, you see, when some ideas are said out loud, put into words, they come out terribly stupid. They come out so that you're ashamed of them yourself. But why? For no reason at all. Because we're all good-for-nothings and can't bear the truth, or I don't know why else. I said just now 'the most magnanimous of men'. That's ridiculous, you see, and yet that's how it was. You see, it's the truth, that is, it's the most truthful truth of all! Yes, I *had the right* then to want to provide for myself and open this shop: 'You, that is, you people, have spurned me, you have driven me away with your contemptuous silence. You have answered my outbursts of passion with an insult that I will feel for the rest of my life. Consequently, I now am within my rights to protect myself from you with a wall, to amass those 30,000 roubles and end my days somewhere in the Crimea, on the southern shore, amidst mountains and vineyards, on my own estate purchased with that 30,000, and the main thing, far away from you all, but without malice towards you, with an ideal in my soul, with my beloved woman at my heart, with a family if God should send one, and – helping out the neighbouring peasants.' It goes without saying that it's good that I'm telling this to myself now, but what could have been more stupid than if I had described all this out loud to her then? That was the reason behind my proud silence, and that was the reason we sat in silence. Because what would she have understood? Just sixteen years old, so very young – what could she have understood of my justifications, of my suffering? I was dealing with straightforwardness, ignorance of life, cheap, youthful convictions, the blindness of 'beautiful hearts', and the main thing, the pawnshop and – *basta*! (But was I a scoundrel in the pawnshop, didn't she see how I conducted myself and did I charge more than I should?) Oh, how terrible is truth on this earth! This charming one, this meek one, this heaven – she was a tyrant, the unbearable tyrant of my soul and my tormentor! I'd be slandering myself, you see, if I didn't say that! You think I didn't love her? Who can say that I didn't love her? You see: there was irony here, the malicious irony of fate and nature! We are accursed, the life of people in general is accursed! (And mine in particular!) I understand now, you see, that I made some mistake here! Something didn't come out the way it was supposed to. Everything was clear, my plan was as clear as the sky: 'Severe, proud, requires no moral consolation, suffers in silence.' That's how it was, I wasn't lying, I wasn't lying! 'She'll see for herself later on that there was magnanimity here, but she just wasn't able to see it now – and when she does fathom it some day, she'll appreciate it ten times more and will fall down in the dust with her hands folded in supplication.' That was the plan. But I forgot something here or failed to take it into account. I wasn't able to do something here. But enough, enough. And of whom can I ask forgiveness now? What's done is done. Take courage, man, and be proud! It's not you who are to blame! . . .

Now then, I'll tell the truth, I won't be afraid to stand face to face with the truth: *she* is to blame, *she* is to blame! . . .

V. THE MEEK ONE REBELS

The quarrels began when she suddenly took it into her head to pay out money as she saw fit, to appraise things for more than they were worth, and a couple of times she even thought

The Meek One

fit to enter into an argument with me on the subject. I didn't agree. But then this captain's widow turned up.

An old lady, the widow of a captain, came with a locket – a present from her late husband, well, you know, a keepsake. I gave thirty roubles. She started to whine plaintively, begging me to keep the thing for her; it goes without saying that we keep it. Well, in a word, suddenly she comes five days later to exchange it for a bracelet that's not worth even eight roubles; it goes without saying that I refused. She must have guessed then something from my wife's eyes, but in any case she came when I wasn't there, and my wife exchanged the locket.

When I learned about it that very same day, I began by speaking meekly, but firmly and reasonably. She was sitting on the bed, looking at the floor, tapping the rug with the toe of her right shoe (her gesture); an unpleasant smile played on her lips. Then without raising my voice at all I announced calmly that the money was *mine*, that I had the right to look at life with *my own* eyes and that when I invited her into my house I had not concealed anything from her.

She suddenly jumped up, suddenly began trembling all over and – what do you think – she suddenly began stamping her feet at me; this was a wild animal, this was a fit, this was a wild animal having a fit. I froze in astonishment: I had never expected such an outburst. But I didn't become flustered, I didn't even move a muscle, and once again in the same calm voice I declared plainly that from that time forward I refused to let her take part in my affairs. She laughed in my face and walked out of the apartment.

The fact of the matter is that she had no right to leave the apartment. Nowhere without me, that was the agreement we made when she was still my fiancée. She returned towards evening; I didn't say a word.

The next day, too, she went out in the morning, and it was the same thing the following day. I locked up the shop and set off to see her aunts. I had broken off relations with them from the day of the wedding – I hadn't invited them to visit me, we didn't visit them. Now it turned out that she wasn't with them. They heard me out with curiosity and laughed in my face. 'Serves you right,' they said. But I had expected their laughter. I then and there bribed the younger aunt, the spinster, with a hundred roubles, and gave her twenty-five in advance. Two days later she comes to me: 'An officer,' she says, 'a Lieutenant Yefimovich, a former comrade of yours from the regiment, is mixed up in this.' I was quite astonished. This Yefimovich had done me more harm than anyone else in the regiment, and a month ago he stopped by my shop a couple of times, and being the shameless fellow that he is, under the pretence of pawning something, I remember, he began laughing with my wife. I went up to him then and told him that, considering our relations, he should not presume to visit me; but no idea of anything like that crossed my mind, I simply thought that he was an insolent fellow. But now suddenly her auntie informs me that she had made an appointment to see him and that this whole affair is being handled by a certain former acquaintance of the aunts, Yuliya Samsonovna, a widow, and a colonel's widow at that – 'It's her that your spouse goes to visit now,' she says.

I'll cut this story short. This business cost me almost 300 roubles, but in two days it was arranged that I would stand in the adjoining room, behind closed doors, and listen to my wife's first *rendezvous* alone with Yefimovich. Meanwhile, the previous evening a brief but for me very significant scene between myself and my wife took place.

She returned towards evening, sat down on the bed, looked at me mockingly and thumped the rug with her foot. Suddenly, as I was looking at her, the idea flew into my head then that all this past month, or, rather, for the past two weeks, she had not been herself at all – one could even say that she had been exactly the opposite: a wild, aggressive being had made its appearance; I can't say shameless, but disorderly and looking for trouble. Asking for trouble. Meekness, however, held her back. When a girl like that starts creating an uproar, even if she does cross the line, it's nevertheless plain to see that she's only hurting herself, that she's egging herself on and that she will be the first who is unable to cope with her feelings of modesty and shame. That's why girls like that sometimes go too far, so that you don't believe your own eyes when you witness it. A soul accustomed to debauchery, on the contrary, always softens it, making it more vile, but in a guise of decorum and decency that claims to be superior to you.

'And is it true that you were driven out of your regiment, because you were too cowardly to fight a duel?' she asked suddenly, out of the blue, and her eyes flashed.

'It's true; the officers rendered the verdict that I was to be asked to leave the regiment, although I had in any case already tendered my resignation.'

'You were driven out as a coward?'

'Yes, they judged me a coward. But I refused to duel not

because I was a coward, but because I didn't wish to submit to their tyrannical verdict and issue a challenge to a duel when I did not consider myself to be insulted. You should know,' I couldn't restrain myself here, 'that flying in the face of such tyranny through my actions and accepting all the consequences took far more courage than any duel would have done.'

I couldn't contain myself, with this phrase I launched into self-justifications, as it were, and that was all she needed, a fresh instance of my humiliation. She burst out in malicious laughter.

'And is it true that for the next three years you wandered the streets of Petersburg like a tramp, and begged for kopecks, and slept under billiard tables?'

'I even spent some nights in the Vyazemsky House on Haymarket Square. Yes, it's true; in my life after leaving the regiment there was much shame and degradation, but not moral degradation, because I was the first to loathe my actions even then. It was merely the degradation of my will and mind, and it was brought about only by the desperation of my situation. But this passed . . .'

'Oh, now you're an important person – a financier!'

That is, a hint at my pawnshop. But I had already managed to hold myself in check. I saw that she thirsted for explanations that would be humiliating for me and – I didn't give them. Fortunately, a client rang the bell just then and I went to see him in the front room. Afterwards, an hour later, when she had suddenly dressed to go out, she stopped in front of me and said:

The Meek One

'You didn't tell me anything about this before the wedding, however.'

I didn't answer, and she left.

And so, the next day I stood in this room behind the door and listened to my fate being decided, and in my pocket there was a revolver. She was dressed up, sitting at the table, and Yefimovich was putting on airs. And what do you know: it turned out (I say this to my credit), it turned out exactly as I had foreseen and supposed, though without realizing that I had foreseen and supposed this. I don't know whether I'm expressing myself clearly.

This is what happened. I listened for a whole hour and for that hour I witnessed a duel between the most noble and lofty woman and a worldly, depraved, dim-witted creature with a grovelling soul. And how, I thought to myself in amazement, how does this naive, this meek, this reserved girl know all this? The cleverest author of a high-society comedy could not have created this scene of ridicule, the most naive laughter and the holy contempt of virtue for vice. And such brilliance in her words and little turns of speech; what wit in her quick replies, what truth in her censure! And at the same time what almost girlish ingenuousness. She laughed in his face at his declarations of love, at his gestures, at his proposals. Coming straight to the matter with a crude assault and not foreseeing any opposition, all of a sudden he had the wind taken out of his sails. At first I might have thought that it was simply coquetry on her part – the 'coquetry of a clever though depraved creature in order to show herself more lavishly'. But no, the truth shone through like the sun and it was impossible to have any doubts. It was only out of hatred for me, affected and impetuous though it was, that she, inexperienced as she was, could have decided to undertake this meeting, but as soon as it had become reality – her eyes were opened at once. Here was a creature who was simply flailing about so as to insult me no matter what, but once she had decided on such filth she couldn't bear the disorder. And could she, blameless and pure, with ideals, have been attracted to Yefimovich or any of those other high-society brutes? On the contrary, he aroused only laughter. The whole truth rose up from her soul, and indignation called forth sarcasm from her heart. I repeat, towards the end this fool was utterly dazed and sat scowling, barely responding, so that I even began to fear that he would venture to insult her out of mean-spirited revenge. And I repeat once again: to my credit I heard this scene out almost without astonishment. It was as though I had encountered something familiar. It was as though I had gone in order to encounter it. I had gone, believing nothing, no accusation, although I did put a revolver in my pocket – that's the truth! And could I have really imagined her otherwise? Wasn't that why I loved her, wasn't that why I cherished her, wasn't that why I had married her? Oh, of course, I was all too convinced that she hated me then, but I was also convinced of her purity. I brought the scene swiftly to a close by opening the door. Yefimovich jumped to his feet, I took her by the hand and invited her to leave with me. Yefimovich found his bearings and suddenly burst out in resounding peals of laughter.

'Oh, I have no objections to sacred conjugal rights, take

her away, take her away! And you know,' he shouted after me, 'even though a respectable person can't fight you, yet out of respect for your lady, I am at your service . . . If you, however, want to risk it . . .'

'Do you hear that!' I stopped her for a second on the threshold.

Then not a word all the way home. I led her by the hand, and she didn't resist. On the contrary, she was utterly dumbfounded, but only until we got home. On our arrival, she sat down on a chair and fastened her gaze on me. She was extraordinarily pale; though her lips had at once formed a mocking smile, she was already regarding me with a solemn and severe challenge, and, I believe, she was seriously convinced those first few moments that I was going to kill her with the revolver. But I took the revolver out of my pocket in silence and laid it on the table. She looked at me and at the revolver. (Note: she was already familiar with this revolver. I had acquired it and kept it loaded ever since opening the shop. When I was getting ready to open the shop I had decided not to keep hulking dogs or a burly lackey like Mozer did, for example. The cook opens the door for my visitors. But people who engage in my trade cannot deprive themselves of self-defence, just in case, and I kept a loaded revolver. During those first days when she had come to live in my house she showed a lot of interest in this revolver, she asked a lot of questions, and I even explained the mechanism and how it worked; moreover, I persuaded her once to shoot at a target. Note all that.) Paying no notice of her frightened look, I lay down on the bed half-undressed. I was very tired; it was already almost eleven o'clock. She went on sitting in the same place, without moving, for almost another hour, then she put out the candle and lay down, also dressed, on the sofa by the wall. It was the first time that she didn't come to bed with me – note that as well . . .

VI. A TERRIBLE MEMORY

Now, this terrible memory . . .

I woke up in the morning, between seven and eight, I think, and it was already almost completely light in the room. I woke up all at once fully conscious and suddenly opened my eyes. She was standing by the table, holding the revolver. She didn't see that I was awake and watching. And suddenly I saw that she had started to move towards me, holding the revolver. I quickly shut my eyes and pretended to be fast asleep.

She came up to the bed and stood over me. I heard everything; although a dead silence had fallen, I heard even that silence. Then there came a convulsive movement – and I suddenly, uncontrollably, opened my eyes against my will. She was looking me right in the eyes, and the revolver was already by my temple. Our eyes met. But we looked at each other for no more than a moment. I forced myself to shut my eyes again and at the same moment I resolved with every fibre of my being that I would not stir or open my eyes, no matter what awaited me.

In fact, it does happen sometimes that a person who is sound asleep suddenly opens his eyes, even raises his head for a second and looks about the room, then, a moment later, he lays his head on the pillow again and falls asleep without remembering a thing. When, after meeting her gaze and feeling the revolver at my temple, I suddenly shut my eyes again and didn't stir, like someone sound asleep, she certainly could have supposed that I indeed was asleep and that I hadn't seen anything, particularly since it was altogether incredible that having seen what I saw I would shut my eyes again at *such* a moment.

Yes, incredible. But she still might have guessed the truth – that was what suddenly flashed through my mind, at that very same moment. Oh, what a whirlwind of thoughts, sensations raced through my mind in less than a moment; long live the electricity of human thought! In that case (I felt), if she had guessed the truth and knew that I wasn't sleeping, then I had already crushed her with my readiness to accept death and her hand might now falter. Her former resolve might be shattered by this new extraordinary impression. They say that people standing on a height are drawn downwards, as it were, of their own accord, to the abyss. I think that a lot of suicides and murders have been committed merely because the revolver was already in hand. There's an abyss here as well, there's a forty-five-degree slope down which you can't help but slide and something relentlessly challenges you to pull the trigger. But the awareness that I had seen everything, that I knew everything and that I was awaiting my death from her in silence – might hold her back from that slope.

The silence continued, and suddenly I felt on my temple, at my hairline, the cold touch of iron. You will ask: did I firmly hope that I would be saved? I will answer you as if

I were before God himself: I had no hope whatsoever, except perhaps one chance in a hundred. Why, then, did I accept death? But I will ask: What need would I have of life after the revolver was raised against me by the being whom I adored? Moreover, I knew with all the force of my being that a struggle was going on between us at that very moment, a terrible duel for life and death, a duel of that same coward of yesterday, driven out by his comrades. I knew it, and she knew it, if only she had guessed the truth that I wasn't sleeping.

Perhaps it wasn't like that, perhaps I didn't think that then, but still it must have been like that, even without thought, because all I've done since is think about it every hour of my life.

But you'll ask me the question again: why didn't I save her then from this treachery? Oh, I have asked myself that question a thousand times since – each time when, with a shiver down my spine, I recalled that second. But my soul then was plunged in dark despair: I was lost, I myself was lost, so whom could I have saved? And how do you know whether I still wanted to save somebody then? How can you know what I might have been feeling then?

My consciousness, however, was seething; the seconds passed, there was dead silence; she was still standing over me – and then suddenly I shuddered with hope! I quickly opened my eyes. She was no longer in the room. I got up from the bed: I had defeated her – and she was forever defeated!

I went out to the samovar. We always had the samovar brought to the outer room and she was always the one to pour the tea. I sat down at the table in silence and took a glass of tea from her. About five minutes later I glanced at her. She was terribly pale, even paler than yesterday, and she was looking at me. And suddenly – and suddenly, seeing that I was looking at her, she gave a pale smile with her pale lips, a timid question in her eyes. 'That means that she still has doubts and is asking herself: does he know or not, did he see or didn't he?' I indifferently turned my eyes away. After tea I locked up the shop, went to the market and bought an iron bed and a screen. When I returned home, I had the bed installed in the front room with the screen around it. This bed was for her, but I didn't say a word to her. Even without words she understood from this bed alone that I 'had seen everything and knew everything' and that there was no longer any doubt about this. I left the revolver on the table for the night as always. At night she silently got into her new bed: the marriage was dissolved, 'she had been defeated but not forgiven'. During the night she became delirious, and by morning she had a fever. She was confined to bed for six weeks.

Chapter 2

I. A DREAM OF PRIDE

Lukerya just announced that she won't stay with me and that she'll leave as soon as the mistress is buried. I prayed on my knees for five minutes, and I had wanted to pray for an hour, but I keep thinking, and thinking, and they're all such aching thoughts and my head aches – what's the use of praying – it's nothing but a sin! It's also strange that I don't want to sleep: in great, in such great sorrow, after the first violent outbursts, one always wants to sleep. They say that people who are condemned to death sleep extremely soundly on their last night. As they should, it's only natural, otherwise they wouldn't have the strength to endure it . . . I lay down on the sofa, but I didn't fall asleep . . .

. . . For the six weeks of her illness we took care of her day and night – Lukerya and I and a trained nurse from the hospital, whom I had hired. I didn't begrudge the money, and even wanted to spend money on her. I called in Dr Schroeder and paid him ten roubles a visit. When she regained consciousness, I started to show myself less often. But why am I describing this? When she was completely on her feet again, she sat quietly and silently in my room at a special table, which I had also bought for her at the time . . . Yes, it's true, we were perfectly silent; that is, we began to talk later on, but only about the usual things. Of course, I deliberately refrained from becoming expansive, but I could see very well that she also was happy not to say a word more than was necessary. This seemed perfectly natural on her part: 'She is too shaken and too defeated,' I thought, 'and of course she needs time to forget and get used to things.' And so it was that we were silent, but every minute I was secretly preparing myself for the future. I thought that she was doing the same as well, and it was terribly entertaining for me to guess: Exactly what is she thinking about now?

I'll say one more thing: Oh, of course, nobody knows what

The Meek One

I endured as I grieved over her during her illness. But I kept my grief to myself and kept the grieving in my heart even from Lukerya. I couldn't imagine, I couldn't even suppose that she would die without learning everything. When she was out of danger and her health started to return, I remember this, I quickly calmed down and very much so. What's more, I decided *to postpone our future* for as long as possible, and for the present to leave everything as it was now. Yes, then something happened to me that was strange and peculiar, I don't know what else to call it: I had triumphed and this thought alone proved to be quite sufficient for me. And that's how the whole winter passed. Oh, I was pleased as I had never been before, and that for the whole winter.

You see: in my life there had been one terrible external circumstance, which until then, that is, until the catastrophe with my wife, weighed heavily on me every day and every hour, namely, the loss of my reputation and leaving the regiment. To put it in a nutshell: this had been a tyrannical injustice against me. True, my comrades disliked me on account of my difficult and, perhaps, ridiculous character, although it often happens that what you find sublime, what you hold dear and esteem, for some reason at the same time makes a group of your comrades laugh. Oh, I was never liked, even in school. I've never been liked anywhere. Even Lukerya cannot like me. The incident in the regiment, though a consequence of this dislike for me, without a doubt bore an accidental character. I mention this because there's nothing more exasperating and intolerable than to be ruined by an incident that might or might not have happened, by an unfortunate chain of circumstances that might have passed over, like a cloud. It's humiliating for an educated man. The incident was as follows.

During the intermission at the theatre I went to the bar. Hussar A—v came in suddenly and began talking loudly with two of his fellow hussars in the presence of all the officers and public gathered there about how Bezumtsev, the captain of our regiment, had just caused a scandal in the corridor 'and he seems to be drunk'. The conversation moved on to other things; besides, there had been a mistake, because Captain Bezumtsev wasn't drunk, and there hadn't really been a scandal. The hussars began talking about something else, and that was the end of it, but the next day the story made its way to our regiment, and at once they began saying how I was the only person at the bar from our regiment and that when Hussar A—v spoke insolently of Captain Bezumtsev I had not gone over to A—v and put a stop to it by reprimanding him. But why on earth should I have done that? If he had it in for Bezumtsev, then it was their personal affair, and why should I get involved? Meanwhile, the officers began to take the position that the affair was not personal but concerned the regiment, and that since I was the only officer of our regiment present, I had proved by my conduct to all the officers at the bar as well as the public that there might be officers in our regiment who were not overly scrupulous concerning their honour and the regiment's. I could not agree with this verdict. I was given to understand that I might still set everything right even now, belatedly, if I should wish to demand a formal explanation from A—v. I did not wish to do so and since I was annoyed, I refused with

The Meek One

pride. I then at once resigned my commission – and that's the whole story. I left proud, but with my spirit crushed. My mind and will both foundered. It was just then that my sister's husband squandered our little fortune and my portion of it, a tiny portion, so I was left on the street without a kopeck. I could have found employment in a private business, but I didn't: after wearing my splendid regimental uniform I couldn't go work on some railroad. And so – if it's shame, let it be shame, if it's disgrace, let it be disgrace, if it's degradation, let it be degradation, and the worse, the better – that's what I chose. There followed three years of gloomy memories, even of the Vyazemsky House. A year and a half ago a rich old lady, my godmother, died in Moscow and among other bequests unexpectedly left me 3,000 in her will. I gave it some thought and then decided my fate. I settled on the pawnshop, with no apologies to anyone: money, then a corner and – a new life far away from my former memories – that was the plan. Nevertheless, my gloomy past and the reputation of my honour, forever ruined, tormented me every hour, every minute. But then I married. By chance or not – I don't know. But when I brought her into my house, I thought that I was bringing a friend, I greatly needed a friend. But I saw clearly that my friend had to be prepared, given the finishing touches, and even defeated. And could I have explained anything straight off like that to this sixteen-year-old girl with her prejudices? For example, how could I, without the accidental assistance of the terrible catastrophe with the revolver, have convinced her that I wasn't a coward and that I had been unjustly accused by the regiment of being a coward? But the catastrophe arrived just at the right moment. Having stood up to the revolver, I had avenged all of my gloomy past. And even though nobody knew about it, *she* knew about it, and that was everything for me, because she was everything to me, all my hopes for the future in my dreams! She was the only person whom I was preparing for myself, and I didn't need another – and now she knew everything; at least she knew that she had unjustly hurried to join my enemies. This thought delighted me. In her eyes I could no longer be a scoundrel, but merely a peculiar person, and even this thought, after everything that had happened, did not at all displease me: peculiarity is not a vice; on the contrary, it sometimes attracts the feminine character. In a word, I deliberately postponed the finale: what had taken place was more than sufficient, for the time being, for my peace of mind and contained more than enough pictures and material for my dreams. That's the nasty thing about this – I'm a dreamer: I had enough material; as for her, I thought that *she would wait*.

And so the whole winter passed in some sort of expectation of something. I liked to steal looks at her, when she happened to be sitting at her little table. She would be busy with her needlework, with the linen, and in the evenings she would sometimes read books which she would take from my bookcase. The choice of books in the bookcase should also have spoken in my favour. She hardly ever went out. Every day after dinner, before dusk, I would take her for a walk and we would go for our constitutional, but not completely in silence, as before. I precisely tried to make it look as though we weren't being silent and were speaking harmoniously, but as I've

The Meek One

already said we both avoided getting carried away talking. I was doing this on purpose, while she, I thought, needed to be 'given time'. Of course, it's strange that it did not once occur to me until almost the very end of the winter that though I liked to look at her on the sly, I never once caught her looking at me that whole winter! I thought that it was timidity on her part. Moreover, she had an air about her of such timid meekness, such weakness after her illness. No, better to bide one's time and – 'and she will suddenly come to you on her own . . .'

That thought delighted me irresistibly. I will add one thing: sometimes it was as if I had deliberately inflamed myself and really brought my heart and mind to the point that I would feel that I had been wronged by her. And so it continued for some time. But my hatred could never ripen and take root in my soul. And I even felt that it was only some sort of game. And even then, although I had dissolved our marriage by buying the bed and screen, never, never could I see her as a criminal. And not because I judged her crime lightly, but because it made sense to forgive her completely, from the very first day, even before I bought the bed. In a word, this was a strange move on my part, for I am morally stern. On the contrary, in my eyes she was so defeated, so humiliated, so crushed that I sometimes felt tormenting pity for her, even though at the same time I sometimes definitely found the idea of her humiliation pleasing. The idea of our inequality pleased me . . .

That winter it so happened that I deliberately performed several good deeds. I forgave two debts, I gave money to one poor woman without any pledge. And I didn't tell my wife about this, and I hadn't done this so that she would find out; but the woman came to thank me herself, she was practically on her knees. And that was how it became known; it seemed to me that she was truly pleased to find out about the woman.

But spring was approaching, it was already the middle of April, the storm windows had been taken down, and the sun began to light up our silent rooms with its bright pencils of light. But scales hung before my eyes and blinded my reason. Fateful, terrible scales! How did it come about that they suddenly fell from my eyes and that I suddenly could see clearly and understand everything! Was it chance, was it that the appointed day had come, was it a ray of sunshine that had kindled the thought and conjecture in my benumbed mind? No, it wasn't a matter of a thought but rather a nerve began to play up, a nerve that had grown numb began to quiver and came to life and illuminated my entire benumbed soul and my demonic pride. It was as if I had suddenly jumped up from my seat then. And it happened suddenly and unexpectedly. It happened towards evening, at about five o'clock, after dinner . . .

II. THE SCALES SUDDENLY FALL

A couple of words first. A month earlier I had noticed a strange pensiveness in her, not just silence, but pensiveness. I had also noticed this suddenly. She was sitting at her work at the time, her head bent over her sewing, and she didn't see that I was looking at her. And suddenly I was struck by how delicate and thin she had become, that her face was pale, her lips were drained of colour – all this as a whole, taken together with her pensiveness, shocked me all at once in the extreme. I had already heard earlier a little dry cough, particularly at night. I got up at once and set off to ask Schroeder to pay us a visit, without saying anything to her.

Schroeder came the following day. She was very surprised and looked first at Schroeder and then at me.

'But I'm fine,' she said with an uncertain smile.

Schroeder didn't examine her very thoroughly (these medical men sometimes are condescendingly offhand), and merely told me in the other room that it was the remnants of her illness and that come spring it wouldn't be a bad idea to take a trip somewhere to the sea or if that were not possible, then simply to find a place in the country. In a word, he didn't say anything other than that there was some weakness or something of the sort. When Schroeder had gone, she suddenly said to me again, looking at me terribly seriously:

'I'm really, really fine.'

But after saying this, she then and there suddenly flushed, apparently from shame. Apparently, it was shame. Oh, now I understand: She was ashamed that I was still *her husband*, that I was taking care of her as if I were still her real husband. But I didn't understand then and ascribed her blush to humility. (The scales!)

And then, a month later, between five and six o'clock, in April, on a bright sunny day I was sitting in the shop and doing the accounts. Suddenly I heard her in our room, at her table, over her work, singing ever so softly . . . This new development made a tremendous impression on me, and to this day I don't understand it. Until then I had almost never heard her sing, except perhaps in the very first days when I brought her into my house and we could still have some fun, target shooting with the revolver. Then her voice was still rather strong, ringing, though a bit off-key, but terribly pleasant and healthy. But now her little song sounded so feeble – oh, not that it was doleful (it was some romance), but it was as if there was something cracked, broken, in her voice, as if the little voice couldn't cope, as if the song itself were ailing. She was singing under her breath, and suddenly, after rising, the voice broke – such a poor little voice, it broke so pitifully; she cleared her throat and started singing again, ever so softly, you could barely hear her . . .

My agitation may be laughable, but no one will ever understand why I had become so agitated! No, I didn't feel sorry for her yet; it was still something altogether different. At the beginning, for the first moments at least, I suddenly felt bewilderment and terrible surprise, terrible and strange, painful and almost vindictive: 'She is singing and in my presence! *Has she forgotten about me, is that it?*'

Completely shaken, I stayed where I was, then I suddenly rose, took my hat and left, without thinking it through, as it were. At least I didn't know why or where I was going. Lukerya started helping me on with my coat.

'She sings?' I said to Lukerya unintentionally. She didn't understand and looked at me, still not understanding; but I really had been incomprehensible.

'Is this the first time that she's been singing?'

The Meek One

'No, she sometimes sings when you're not here,' Lukerya replied.

I remember everything. I walked down the stairs, went out into the street and set off for nowhere in particular. I walked as far as the corner and began to stare off into the distance. People passed by me, jostled me, but I didn't feel it. I hailed a cab and told him to take me to the Police Bridge, I don't know why. But then I suddenly changed my mind and gave him a twenty-kopeck piece.

'That's for your trouble,' I said, laughing senselessly, but some sort of rapture had suddenly begun to fill my heart.

I turned around and went home, quickening my step. The cracked, poor, broken little note suddenly rang out in my heart again. It took my breath away. The scales were falling, falling from my eyes! If she'd started singing in my presence, then she had forgotten about me – that's what was clear and terrible. My heart sensed this. But rapture shone in my soul and overcame my fear.

Oh, the irony of fate! You see, there had been nothing else and there could not have been anything else in my soul all winter except this very rapture, but where had I myself been all winter long? Had I been there with my soul? I ran up the stairs in a great hurry, I don't know whether I walked in timidly or not. I remember only that the entire floor seemed to be rippling and it was as if I were floating down a river. I walked into the room, she was sitting in the same place, sewing, with her head bent, but no longer singing. She threw me a fleeting and incurious glance, but it wasn't even a glance, merely the usual, indifferent gesture one makes when somebody enters a room.

I walked straight up to her and sat down on a chair right beside her, like a madman. She gave me a quick look, as though she were frightened: I took her by the hand and I don't remember what I said to her, that is, what I wanted to say, because I couldn't even speak properly. My voice kept breaking and wouldn't obey me. And I didn't know what to say, I just kept gasping for breath.

'Let's talk . . . you know . . . say something!' I suddenly babbled something stupid – oh, but was I capable of making sense? She flinched again and recoiled, badly frightened, looking at my face, but suddenly – *stern surprise* appeared in her eyes. Yes, surprise, and *stern*. She was looking at me wide-eyed. This sternness, this stern surprise came crashing down on me all at once: 'So you still want love? Love?' that surprise seemed to ask suddenly, although she was silent as well. But I could read it all, all of it. My whole being was shaken and I simply fell to the ground at her feet. Yes, I collapsed at her feet. She quickly jumped up, but I restrained her by taking hold of both her hands with extraordinary force.

And I fully understood my despair, oh, I understood! But would you believe it, rapture was seething in my heart so irrepressibly that I thought I would die. I kissed her feet in ecstasy and happiness. Yes, in happiness, immeasurable and infinite, yet understanding nonetheless all my hopeless despair! I wept, said something, but couldn't speak. Her fright and surprise suddenly gave way to some anxious thought, some extreme question, and she looked at me strangely, wildly even – she wanted to understand something quickly, and she smiled. She was terribly ashamed that I was kissing her feet, and she kept moving back, but I would at once kiss the spot on the floor where she had been standing. She saw this and suddenly began to laugh from shame (you know how people laugh from shame). Hysterics weren't far off, I saw that, her hands quivered – I didn't give it a thought and kept muttering that I loved her, that I wouldn't get up, '... let me kiss your dress ... I'll worship you like this for as long as you live ...' I don't know, I don't remember – and suddenly she burst out into sobs and started trembling; a terrible fit of hysteria had set in. I had frightened her.

I carried her over to the bed. When the fit had passed, she sat up on the bed and with a terribly distraught look, seized me by the hands and pleaded with me to calm myself: 'Enough, don't torment yourself, calm yourself!' and she began to weep again. I didn't leave her side all that evening. I kept telling her that I'd take her to Boulogne to bathe in the sea, now, right away, in two weeks, that she had such a cracked little voice, I had heard it earlier that day, that I would close the pawnshop, sell it to Dobronravov, that everything would begin afresh, and the main thing, to Boulogne, to Boulogne! She listened and was still afraid. She was more and more afraid. But that wasn't the main thing for me, but rather that I more and more irrepressibly wanted to lie down again at her feet, and once again, to kiss, to kiss the ground on which her feet stood, and to idolize her and – 'I'll ask nothing more of you, nothing,' I kept repeating every minute. 'Don't answer me anything, don't take any notice of me at all, and only let me look at you from the corner, turn me into your thing, into your little dog ...' She wept.

'*But I thought that you were going to leave me like that,*' suddenly burst forth from her involuntarily, so involuntarily that perhaps she didn't notice at all how she had said it, and yet – oh, it was the most important, her most fateful word and the most comprehensible for me that evening, and it was as if it had slashed my heart like a knife. It explained everything to me, everything, but as long as she was there beside me, before my eyes, I went on hoping irrepressibly and was terribly happy. Oh, I wore her out terribly that evening and I understood that, but I kept thinking that I would change everything at once. Finally, towards nightfall, she broke down completely; I persuaded her to go to sleep, and she immediately fell sound asleep. I expected delirium, and there was delirium, but it was very mild. I got up during the night every few minutes, and would quietly go in my slippers to look at her. I wrung my hands over her, as I looked at this sick being lying on that pathetic little cot, the iron bedstead that I had bought for her then for three roubles. I got down on my knees but I didn't dare kiss her feet while she was sleeping (against her wishes!). I would start praying to God, and then jump up again. Lukerya watched me closely and kept coming out of the kitchen. I went to her and told her to go to bed and that tomorrow 'something quite different' would begin.

And I believed that blindly, madly, terribly. Oh, I was surging with rapture, rapture. I couldn't wait for tomorrow. The main thing, I didn't believe in any misfortune, despite the symptoms. My powers of understanding had not yet fully returned, even though the scales had fallen, and for a long, long time would not return – oh, not until today, not until this very day! And how, how could my understanding have returned then: you see, she was still alive then, you see, she was right there before me, and I before her. 'She'll wake up tomorrow, and I'll tell her all this, and she'll see it all.' That was my reasoning then, clear and simple, hence the rapture! The main thing was this trip to Boulogne. For some reason I thought that Boulogne was everything, that there was something final about Boulogne. 'To Boulogne, to Boulogne! . . .' I waited for morning in a state of madness.

III. I UNDERSTAND ALL TOO WELL

But this was only a few days ago, you see, five days, only five days ago, just last Tuesday! No, no, if only there had been a little more time, if only she had waited just a little bit longer and – and I would have dispelled the darkness! And hadn't she calmed down? The very next day she listened to me with a smile even, despite her confusion. The main thing was that during all this time, all five days, she was either confused or ashamed . . . She was also afraid, very afraid. I don't dispute it, I won't deny it, like some madman: there was fear, but then how could she not be afraid? You see, we'd been strangers to each other for so long, we had grown so far apart from one another, and suddenly all this . . . But I didn't pay attention to her fear – something new was shining! . . . Yes, it's undoubtedly true that I'd made a mistake. And perhaps even many mistakes. And as soon as we woke up the next day, when it was still morning (this was on Wednesday), I suddenly made a mistake right away: I suddenly made her my friend. I was in a hurry, much too much of a hurry, but a confession was necessary, essential – and much more than a confession! I didn't even conceal that which I had concealed from myself all my life. I told her straight out that I had done nothing all winter long but be certain of her love. I explained to her that the pawnshop had been merely the degradation of my will and mind, my personal idea of self-flagellation and self-exaltation. I explained to her that I had indeed turned coward that time at the bar, and that it was owing to my character, my touchiness: I was struck by the surroundings, I was struck by the bar; I was struck by how I would end up looking in all this and wouldn't it end up looking stupid? I didn't turn coward on account of the duel, but because it would end up looking stupid . . . And then later I didn't want to admit it, and tormented everyone, and tormented her for it as well, and then I married her so that I could torment her on account of it. In general, for the most part I spoke as though I were in a fever. She herself took me by the hands and begged me to stop: 'You're exaggerating . . . you're tormenting yourself', and the tears would begin again, and again there'd almost be a fit of hysteria. She kept pleading with me not to say or remember any of this.

I paid little or no attention to her pleas: spring, Boulogne! There was the sun, there was our new sun, that was all I talked about! I locked up the shop, handed over the business to Dobronravov. I suddenly suggested to her that we give away everything to the poor, except for the initial 3,000 I had received from my godmother, which we would use to travel to Boulogne, and then we'd come back and begin our new working life. And so it was decided, because she didn't say anything . . . she merely smiled. And I believe she smiled more out of a sense of delicacy, so as not to upset me. Of course, I saw that I was a burden to her, don't think that I was so stupid or such an egoist that I didn't see that. I saw everything, everything, right down to the last detail, I saw and knew better than anyone else; my despair was there for all to see!

I told her everything about myself and about her. And about Lukerya. I told her that I had wept . . . Oh, I'd change the subject, you see, I was also trying not to remind her of certain things at all. And, you see, she even livened up once or twice, you see, I remember, I remember! Why do you say that I looked and saw nothing? And if only *this* had not happened, everything would have been resurrected. You see, it was she who told me the day before yesterday, when the conversation turned to reading and what she had read that winter – you see, it was she who told me and laughed, when she recalled that scene between Gil Blas and the Archbishop of Granada. And what a childish laugh, sweet, just like when she was still my fiancée (an instant! an instant!); I was so happy! I was terribly struck, however, by the archbishop: you see, that meant she had found enough peace of mind and happiness to laugh at that masterpiece while she sat there that winter. That means that she had already begun to find herself wholly at peace, that she had already begun to be wholly persuaded that I would leave her *like that*. 'I thought that you were going to leave me *like that*' – that's what she had said then on Tuesday! Oh, the thought of a ten-year-old girl! And you see, she believed, believed that everything would in fact remain *like that*: she at her table, I at mine, and that's how it would be for both of us until we were sixty. And suddenly – here I come forward, her husband, and her husband needs love! Oh, the incomprehensibility, oh, my blindness!

It was also a mistake to look at her with rapture; I should have exercised restraint, because the rapture frightened her. But you see, I did exercise restraint, I didn't kiss her feet anymore. Not once did I make a show of the fact . . . well, that I was her husband – oh, and it didn't even cross my mind, I only worshipped her! But you see, I couldn't be completely silent, I couldn't say nothing at all, you see! I suddenly told her that I enjoyed her conversation and that I considered her incomparably, incomparably more educated and developed than I. Embarrassed, she blushed bright red and said that I was exaggerating. At this point, unable to contain myself, I foolishly told her what rapture I'd felt when I stood behind the door and listened to her duel, a duel of innocence with that beast, and how I had taken pleasure in her intelligence, her sparkling wit, combined with such childlike simple-heartedness. She seemed to shudder all over, murmured again that I was exaggerating, but suddenly her whole face darkened, she covered it with her hands and burst into sobs . . . Here I was unable to hold myself back: I again fell down before her, I again started to kiss her feet and again it ended in a fit, just as it had on Tuesday. That was yesterday evening, but the next morning . . .

Next morning?! Madman, but that morning was today, just now, only just now!

Listen and consider carefully: you see, when we met just

The Meek One

now (this was after yesterday's attack), she even struck me with her calmness, that's how it was! While all night long I had been trembling with fear over what had happened yesterday. But suddenly she comes up to me, stands before me and with her arms folded (just now, just now!), began by telling me that she's a criminal, that she knows this, that the crime has tormented her all winter long, and is tormenting her now ... that she values my magnanimity all too much ... 'I'll be your true wife, I'll respect you ...' Here I jumped up and embraced her like a madman! I kissed her, I kissed her face, her lips, like a husband, for the first time after a long separation. But why did I go out just now, for only two hours ... our foreign passports ... Oh, God! If only I had returned five minutes earlier, just five minutes! ... And now there's this crowd at our gate, these eyes fixed on me ... Oh, Lord!

Lukerya says (oh, I won't let Lukerya go now for anything, she knows everything, she was here all winter, she'll tell me everything), she says that after I left the house and only some twenty minutes before my return – she suddenly went into our room to see the mistress to ask her something, I don't remember what, and she saw that her icon (the same icon of the Mother of God) had been taken down and was on the table before her, and that her mistress seemed to have been praying before it. 'What's wrong, mistress?' 'Nothing, Lukerya, you may go ... Wait, Lukerya,' she walked up to her and kissed her. 'Are you happy, mistress?' I ask. 'Yes, Lukerya.' 'The master should have come to ask your forgiveness long ago ... Thank God, you've made up.' 'All right, Lukerya,' she says, 'leave me, Lukerya.' And she smiled, but so strangely. So strangely that ten minutes later Lukerya suddenly went back to look in on her: 'She was standing by the wall, right by the window, she had placed her hand on the wall, and laid her head on her hand, she was standing like that and thinking. And she was so lost in thought standing there that she didn't hear me standing there and watching her from the other room. I saw that she was smiling, as it were, standing, thinking and smiling. I looked at her, turned around ever so quietly and walked out, thinking to myself, only suddenly I hear the window being opened. I at once went to say that "it's fresh, mistress, you'll catch cold" – and suddenly I see that she's climbed up on to the window and is already standing there upright, in the open window, with her back towards me and holding the icon. My heart just sank then and I cried out: "Mistress, mistress!" She heard, made a move as if to turn around towards me, but didn't, instead she took a step, clutched the icon to her breast – and threw herself out the window!'

I only remember that when I entered the gates she was still warm. The main thing is that they're all looking at me. At first they were shouting, but then they suddenly fell silent and they all make way for me and . . . and she's lying there with the icon. I remember, though darkly, that I walked over in silence and looked for a long time, and they all gathered round and are saying something to me. Lukerya was there, but I didn't see her. She says that she spoke with me. I remember only that tradesman: he kept shouting at me 'only a handful of blood came out of her mouth, a handful, a handful!' and pointing to the blood on a stone. I think I touched the blood with my finger, smeared some on my finger, looked at my finger (I remember that), and he kept saying to me: 'A handful, a handful!'

'And what do you mean "a handful"?' I wailed, they say, with all my might, I raised my arms and threw myself at him . . .

Oh, it's absurd, absurd! Incomprehensibility! Improbability! Impossibility!

IV. ONLY FIVE MINUTES TOO LATE

But is it really? Is it really probable? Can one really say that it was possible? Why, for what reason did this woman die?

Oh, believe me, I understand; but why she died is still a question. She was frightened of my love, she asked herself seriously whether she should accept it or not, and she couldn't bear the question and it was better to die. I know, I know, there's no use in racking my brains over it: she had made too many promises, got frightened that she couldn't keep them – that's clear. There are a number of circumstances here that are quite terrible.

Because why did she die? The question persists, all the same. The question hammers, hammers away in my brain. I would even have left her *like that* if she had wished to be left *like that*. She didn't believe it, that's what! No, no, I'm lying, that's not it at all. It was simply because with me it had to be honest: to love meant to love completely, and not like she would have loved the merchant. And since she was too chaste, too pure to agree to a love like a merchant needs, she didn't want to deceive me. She didn't want to deceive me with half a love or a quarter of a love under the guise of love. She was much too honest, that's what it is, gentlemen! I wanted to cultivate breadth of heart then, do you remember? A strange thought.

I'm terribly curious: did she respect me? I don't know. Did she despise me or not? I don't think she did. It's terribly strange: why didn't it occur to me all winter long that she despised me? I was utterly convinced of the contrary right until the moment when she looked at me then with *stern surprise*. Precisely, *stern*. It was then that I understood at once that she despised me. I understood irrevocably and forever! Ah, let her, let her despise me, for her whole life even, but let her live, live! Just now she was still walking, talking. I don't at all understand how she could throw herself out the window! And how could I have supposed that even five minutes earlier? I summoned Lukerya. I won't let Lukerya go now for anything, not for anything!

Oh, we could still have come to an understanding. It's just that we had grown so terribly unused to each other during the winter, but couldn't we have become accustomed to one another again? Why, why couldn't we have come together and begun a new life again? I'm magnanimous, and so is she – that's the point of connection! Just a few words more, two days, no more, and she would have understood everything.

The main thing, it's a pity that it all comes down to chance – simple, barbaric inertia, chance. That's the pity of it! All of five minutes, I was only five minutes late! If I had arrived five minutes earlier – the moment would have passed by, like a cloud, and it would never have occurred to her

The Meek One

again. And it would have ended by her understanding everything. But now the rooms stand empty again and I'm alone once again. There's the pendulum ticking, it doesn't care, it doesn't feel sorry for anyone. There's no one – that's the awful thing!

I pace, I keep pacing. I know, I know, don't try to put words in my mouth: you think it's ridiculous that I complain about chance and the five minutes? But it's obvious, you see. Consider one thing: she didn't even leave a note saying, 'Don't blame anyone for my death', like everyone does. Could she really not have considered that even Lukerya might get into trouble? They might say, 'You were alone with her, so you must have pushed her.' In any event, she would have been dragged away, innocent though she was, if four people in the courtyard hadn't seen from the windows of the wing and the courtyard how she stood there holding the icon and hurled herself down. But, you see, that's chance as well that people were standing and saw it. No, this was all a moment, just one inexplicable moment. Suddenness and fantasy! So what if she was praying before the icon? That doesn't mean that this was before death. The entire moment lasted, perhaps, all of some ten minutes, the entire decision – precisely when she was standing by the wall, with her head resting on her arm, and smiling. The thought flew into her head, her head started spinning and – and she couldn't withstand it.

It was a clear misunderstanding, say what you will. She could still have lived with me. But what if it was anaemia? Simply on account of anaemia, the exhaustion of vital energy? She had grown tired during the winter, that's what it was . . .

Fyodor Dostoyevsky

I was late!!!

How very thin she is in the coffin, how sharp her little nose has become! Her eyelashes lie like arrows. And she fell, you see – without smashing or breaking anything! Just this one 'handful of blood'. A dessertspoon, that is. Internal concussion. A strange thought: What if it were possible not to bury her? Because if they take her away, then ... Oh, no, it's almost impossible that she'll be taken away! Oh, of course, I know that she must be taken away, I'm not a madman and I'm not the least bit delirious; on the contrary, my mind has never been so lucid – but how can it be that again there'll be no one in the house, again the two rooms, and again I'm alone with the pledges. Delirium, delirium, that's where the delirium lies! I tormented her – that's what it was!

What are your laws to me now? What do I need with your customs, your ways, your life, your government, your faith? Let your judges judge me, let them take me to court, to your public court, and I will say that I acknowledge nothing. The judge will shout: 'Silence, officer!' And I will cry out to him: 'What power do you now possess that I should obey you? Why has dark inertia shattered that which was dearest of all? What need have I now of your laws? I part company with you.' Oh, it's all the same to me!

Blind, she's blind! Dead, she doesn't hear! You don't know with what paradise I would have surrounded you. The paradise was in my soul; I would have planted it all round you! Well, you wouldn't have loved me – so be it, what of it? Everything would have been *like that*, everything would have stayed *like that*. You would have talked to me only as a friend – and we would have rejoiced and laughed with joy, as we looked into each other's eyes. That's how we would have lived. And if you had fallen in love with somebody else – well, so be it, so be it! You would have walked with him and laughed, while I looked on from the other side of the street . . . Oh, let it be anything, anything, if only she would open her eyes just once! For one moment, just one! If she would look at me as she did just now, when she stood before me and swore to be my faithful wife! Oh, she would have understood it all in one glance!

Inertia! Oh, nature! People are alone on this earth – that's the problem! 'Is there a man alive on the field?' the Russian *bogatyr* cries out. And I cry out as well, though I am not a *bogatyr*, and no one answers. They say that the sun gives life to the universe. The sun will rise and – look at it, isn't it dead? Everything is dead, the dead are everywhere. There are only people, and all around them is silence – that's the earth. 'People, love one another' – who said that? Whose commandment is that? The pendulum ticks insensibly, disgustingly. It's two o'clock in the morning. Her little shoes are by the bed, as if they were waiting for her . . . No, seriously, when they take her away tomorrow, what will become of me?

1876

1. BOCCACCIO · *Mrs Rosie and the Priest*
2. GERARD MANLEY HOPKINS · *As kingfishers catch fire*
3. *The Saga of Gunnlaug Serpent-tongue*
4. THOMAS DE QUINCEY · *On Murder Considered as One of the Fine Arts*
5. FRIEDRICH NIETZSCHE · *Aphorisms on Love and Hate*
6. JOHN RUSKIN · *Traffic*
7. PU SONGLING · *Wailing Ghosts*
8. JONATHAN SWIFT · *A Modest Proposal*
9. *Three Tang Dynasty Poets*
10. WALT WHITMAN · *On the Beach at Night Alone*
11. KENKŌ · *A Cup of Sake Beneath the Cherry Trees*
12. BALTASAR GRACIÁN · *How to Use Your Enemies*
13. JOHN KEATS · *The Eve of St Agnes*
14. THOMAS HARDY · *Woman much missed*
15. GUY DE MAUPASSANT · *Femme Fatale*
16. MARCO POLO · *Travels in the Land of Serpents and Pearls*
17. SUETONIUS · *Caligula*
18. APOLLONIUS OF RHODES · *Jason and Medea*
19. ROBERT LOUIS STEVENSON · *Olalla*
20. KARL MARX AND FRIEDRICH ENGELS · *The Communist Manifesto*
21. PETRONIUS · *Trimalchio's Feast*
22. JOHANN PETER HEBEL · *How a Ghastly Story Was Brought to Light by a Common or Garden Butcher's Dog*
23. HANS CHRISTIAN ANDERSEN · *The Tinder Box*
24. RUDYARD KIPLING · *The Gate of the Hundred Sorrows*
25. DANTE · *Circles of Hell*
26. HENRY MAYHEW · *Of Street Piemen*
27. HAFEZ · *The nightingales are drunk*
28. GEOFFREY CHAUCER · *The Wife of Bath*
29. MICHEL DE MONTAIGNE · *How We Weep and Laugh at the Same Thing*
30. THOMAS NASHE · *The Terrors of the Night*
31. EDGAR ALLAN POE · *The Tell-Tale Heart*
32. MARY KINGSLEY · *A Hippo Banquet*
33. JANE AUSTEN · *The Beautifull Cassandra*
34. ANTON CHEKHOV · *Gooseberries*
35. SAMUEL TAYLOR COLERIDGE · *Well, they are gone, and here must I remain*
36. JOHANN WOLFGANG VON GOETHE · *Sketchy, Doubtful, Incomplete Jottings*
37. CHARLES DICKENS · *The Great Winglebury Duel*
38. HERMAN MELVILLE · *The Maldive Shark*
39. ELIZABETH GASKELL · *The Old Nurse's Story*
40. NIKOLAY LESKOV · *The Steel Flea*

41. HONORÉ DE BALZAC · *The Atheist's Mass*
42. CHARLOTTE PERKINS GILMAN · *The Yellow Wall-Paper*
43. C.P. CAVAFY · *Remember, Body . . .*
44. FYODOR DOSTOEVSKY · *The Meek One*
45. GUSTAVE FLAUBERT · *A Simple Heart*
46. NIKOLAI GOGOL · *The Nose*
47. SAMUEL PEPYS · *The Great Fire of London*
48. EDITH WHARTON · *The Reckoning*
49. HENRY JAMES · *The Figure in the Carpet*
50. WILFRED OWEN · *Anthem For Doomed Youth*
51. WOLFGANG AMADEUS MOZART · *My Dearest Father*
52. PLATO · *Socrates' Defence*
53. CHRISTINA ROSSETTI · *Goblin Market*
54. *Sindbad the Sailor*
55. SOPHOCLES · *Antigone*
56. RYŪNOSUKE AKUTAGAWA · *The Life of a Stupid Man*
57. LEO TOLSTOY · *How Much Land Does A Man Need?*
58. GIORGIO VASARI · *Leonardo da Vinci*
59. OSCAR WILDE · *Lord Arthur Savile's Crime*
60. SHEN FU · *The Old Man of the Moon*
61. AESOP · *The Dolphins, the Whales and the Gudgeon*
62. MATSUO BASHŌ · *Lips too Chilled*
63. EMILY BRONTË · *The Night is Darkening Round Me*
64. JOSEPH CONRAD · *To-morrow*
65. RICHARD HAKLUYT · *The Voyage of Sir Francis Drake Around the Whole Globe*
66. KATE CHOPIN · *A Pair of Silk Stockings*
67. CHARLES DARWIN · *It was snowing butterflies*
68. BROTHERS GRIMM · *The Robber Bridegroom*
69. CATULLUS · *I Hate and I Love*
70. HOMER · *Circe and the Cyclops*
71. D. H. LAWRENCE · *Il Duro*
72. KATHERINE MANSFIELD · *Miss Brill*
73. OVID · *The Fall of Icarus*
74. SAPPHO · *Come Close*
75. IVAN TURGENEV · *Kasyan from the Beautiful Lands*
76. VIRGIL · *O Cruel Alexis*
77. H. G. WELLS · *A Slip under the Microscope*
78. HERODOTUS · *The Madness of Cambyses*
79. *Speaking of Siva*
80. *The Dhammapada*

'She decided she would teach him to speak and he was very soon able to say, "Pretty boy!", "Your servant, sir!" and "Hail Mary!"'

GUSTAVE FLAUBERT
Born 1821, Rouen, France
Died 1880, Croisset, France

This story was first published in its original French
in Gustave Flaubert's *Trois Contes* in 1877,
translated as *Three Tales*.

FLAUBERT IN PENGUIN CLASSICS
Madame Bovary
Sentimental Education
Three Tales
Salammbo

GUSTAVE FLAUBERT

A Simple Heart

Translated by
Roger Whitehouse

PENGUIN BOOKS

PENGUIN CLASSICS

UK | USA | Canada | Ireland | Australia
India | New Zealand | South Africa

Penguin Books is part of the Penguin Random House group of companies
whose addresses can be found at global.penguinrandomhouse.com.

This edition published in Penguin Classics 2015

012

Translation copyright © Roger Whitehouse, 2005

The moral right of the translator has been asserted

Set in 9.5/13 pt Baskerville 10 Pro
Typeset by Jouve (UK), Milton Keynes

Printed and bound in Great Britain by Clays Ltd, Elcograf S.p.A.

A CIP catalogue record for this book is available from the British Library

ISBN: 978-0-141-39750-4

www.greenpenguin.co.uk

Penguin Random House is committed to a
sustainable future for our business, our readers
and our planet. This book is made from Forest
Stewardship Council® certified paper.

A Simple Heart

1

For half a century, Madame Aubain's housemaid Félicité was the envy of all the good ladies of Pont-l'Evêque.

For just one hundred francs a year, she did all the cooking and the housework, she saw to the darning, the washing and the ironing, she could bridle a horse, keep the chickens well fed and churn the butter. What is more she remained faithful to her mistress, who, it must be said, was not the easiest of people to get on with.

Madame Aubain had married a handsome but impecunious young man, who had died at the beginning of 1809, leaving her with two very young children and substantial debts. Upon his death, she sold her properties, with the exception of the two farms at Toucques and Geffosses, which between them provided her with an income of no more than five thousand francs in rent, and she moved out of her house in Saint-Melaine to live in another which was less costly to maintain, which had belonged to her family and which was situated behind the market.

This house had a slate roof and stood between an alley

and a narrow street leading down to the river. Inside, the floors were at different levels, making it very easy to trip up. A narrow hallway separated the kitchen from the living room in which Madame Aubain remained all day long, sitting in a wicker armchair close to the casement window. Against the wainscoting, which was painted white, there stood a row of eight mahogany chairs. A barometer hung on the wall above an old piano, piled high with a pyramid-shaped assortment of packets and cardboard boxes. Two easy chairs upholstered in tapestry stood on either side of a Louis-Quinze-style mantelpiece in yellow marble. The clock, in the middle, was designed to look like a Temple of Vesta, and the whole room smelt musty, due to the fact that the floor level was lower than the garden.

On the first floor, there was 'Madame's' bedroom, a very large room, decorated with pale, flowery wallpaper and containing a picture of 'Monsieur' dressed up in the fanciful attire that was fashionable at the time. This room led directly to a smaller bedroom which housed two children's beds, each with the mattress removed. Next came the parlour, which was always kept locked and was full of furniture draped in dust-sheets. Finally, there was a corridor leading to a study; books and papers lay stacked on the shelves of a bookcase which ran around three walls of the room and surrounded a large writing-desk in dark wood. The two end panels of this bookcase were covered in line drawings, landscapes in gouache and etchings by

Audran, a reminder of better days and of more expensive tastes that were now a thing of the past. On the second floor was Félicité's bedroom, lit by a dormer window which looked out over the fields.

Félicité always rose at first light to make sure she was in time for mass, and then worked without a break until the evening. As soon as dinner was finished, the crockery cleared away and the door firmly bolted, she would cover the log fire with ashes and go to sleep in front of the fireplace, holding her rosary in her hand. No one could have been more persistent when it came to haggling over prices and, as for cleanliness, the spotless state of her saucepans was the despair of all the other serving maids in Pont-l'Evêque. She wasted nothing and ate slowly, gathering every crumb of her loaf from the table with her fingers, a twelve-pound loaf baked especially for her and which lasted her twenty days.

In all weathers she wore a printed kerchief fastened behind with a pin, a bonnet which completely covered her hair, grey stockings, a red skirt and over her jacket a bibbed apron like those worn by hospital nurses.

Her face was thin and her voice was shrill. At twenty-five, people took her to be as old as forty. After her fiftieth birthday, it became impossible to say what age she was at all. She hardly ever spoke, and her upright stance and deliberate movements gave her the appearance of a woman made out of wood, driven as if by clockwork.

2

Like other girls, she had once fallen in love.

Her father, a stonemason by trade, had been killed falling from some scaffolding. Following this, her mother died and her sisters went their separate ways. A farmer took her in and, even though she was still a very young girl, he would send her out into the fields to look after the cows. She was dressed in mere rags, she shivered with cold and would lie flat on her stomach to drink water from ponds. She was regularly beaten for no reason at all and was eventually turned out of the house for having stolen thirty sous, a theft of which she was quite innocent. She was taken on at another farm, where she looked after the poultry and, because she was well liked by her employers, her friends were jealous of her.

One evening in August (she was eighteen at the time), she was taken to the village fête at Colleville. She was instantly overcome, bewildered by the boisterous sounds of the fiddle music, the lamps in the trees, the array of brightly coloured clothes, the gold crosses and the lace, all those people moving as one in time to the tune. She was standing on her own, shyly, when a young man, fairly well off to judge by his appearance and who had been leaning against the shaft of a farm wagon smoking his pipe, approached her and asked her to dance. He bought her a glass of cider, a cup of coffee, a cake and a silk scarf

A Simple Heart

and, imagining that she understood his motive, offered to accompany her back home. As they were walking along the edge of a field of oats, he thrust her to the ground. She was terrified and began to scream. He ran off.

One evening a little later, she was walking along the road leading to Beaumont and was trying to get past a large hay wagon as it lumbered slowly along. As she was edging her way round the wheels, she recognized Théodore.

He looked at her quite unabashed and said she should forgive his behaviour of the other night; he 'had just had too much to drink'.

She did not know how to answer him and wanted to run away.

He immediately began to talk about the harvest and various important people in the district and told her that his father had left Colleville and bought a farm at Les Ecots, which meant that they were now neighbours. 'Oh, are we!' she said. He said that his parents wanted him to settle down but that he was in no rush and preferred to wait until the right woman came along before he married. She lowered her eyes. He then asked her if she was thinking of marrying. She smiled and said that he was wrong to tease her. 'But I am not teasing you, I swear,' he said, and slipped his left arm around her waist. She walked on with his arm still around her. They were now walking more slowly. There was a gentle breeze, the stars were shining, the huge wagon-load of hay swayed from side to side in front of them and dust rose from the feet of the four horses as they plodded along. Then, without any word of command, the horses turned off to the right. He kissed her once more and she vanished into the darkness.

The following week, Théodore persuaded her to go out with him on several other occasions.

They would meet in a corner of some farmyard, behind a wall or beneath a solitary tree. Félicité was not naive like other young girls of her age; working with the farm animals had taught her a great deal. However, her natural discretion and an intuitive sense of honour prevented her from giving in to Théodore's demands. Théodore found this resistance so frustrating that, in order to satisfy his passion (or maybe out of sheer simple-mindedness), he proposed to her. She was not sure whether to believe him or not, but he insisted that he was serious.

He then announced something rather disturbing: a year ago his parents had paid for someone else to do his military service but he might still be called up at any time. The prospect of serving in the army terrified him. Félicité took this cowardice as a sign of his affection for her and it made her love him all the more. She would slip out of the house at night to meet Théodore, who assailed her with his fears and entreaties.

Eventually, he declared that he would go to the Préfecture himself and find out what the situation was. He would come back and tell Félicité the following Sunday, between eleven o'clock and midnight.

A Simple Heart

At the appointed time, Félicité ran to meet her lover.

But instead of Théodore, it was one of his friends who stood waiting to meet her.

He informed her that she would never see Théodore again. In order to make sure he could not be called up, he had married a wealthy old lady from Toucques, by the name of Madame Lehoussais.

Félicité's distress was unbounded. She threw herself to the ground, weeping and wailing; she implored God to come to her aid and lay moaning, all alone in the fields, until daylight. Then she made her way back to the farm and announced that she had decided to leave. At the end of the month, having received her wages, she wrapped her few belongings in a shawl and left for Pont-l'Evêque.

Outside the inn she spoke to a woman wearing a widow's hood who, as it happened, was looking for a cook. The young girl knew precious little about cooking but she seemed so willing and so ready to oblige that Madame Aubain eventually said: 'Very well, you may work for me.'

A quarter of an hour later, Félicité was installed in her house.

At first she lived in a constant state of trepidation as a result of 'the sort of house it was' and the memory of 'Monsieur' which seemed to hover over everything! Paul and Virginie, one aged seven and the other barely four, seemed made of some precious material; she liked to give them piggyback rides and was mortified when Madame Aubain instructed her not to keep kissing them. Even so, she was happy. Her new surroundings were very pleasant and her earlier unhappiness quickly faded.

Every Thursday, a group of Madame Aubain's friends came to play Boston. Félicité would set out the cards and the foot-warmers in readiness. The guests always arrived punctually at eight and left as the clock struck eleven.

On Monday mornings, the secondhand dealer who had a shop at the end of the lane would spread his various bits and pieces of ironmongery out on the pavement. The town would be filled with the buzz of voices, with the sounds of horses neighing, lambs bleating, pigs grunting and carts rattling through the streets. At about midday, just when the market was at its busiest, an old peasant would present himself on Madame Aubain's front doorstep – a tall man with a hooked nose and with his hat perched on the back of his head. This was Robelin, the farmer from Geffosses. He would be followed shortly afterwards by Liébard, the farmer from Toucques, short, fat and red in the face, wearing a grey jacket and leather gaiters complete with spurs.

They would both come bearing chickens or cheeses which they hoped they might persuade their landlady to buy. But Félicité was more than a match for their banter and they always respected her for this.

Madame Aubain also received sporadic visits from the Marquis de Grémanville, an uncle of hers who had squandered his money in loose living and who now lived at Falaise on the last bit of property he could still call his own. He would always turn up at lunch time with a

A Simple Heart

loathsome little poodle which left its muddy paw marks all over the furniture. Despite his efforts to behave like a gentleman, raising his hat every time he mentioned his 'late father', habit would soon get the better of him and he would pour himself glass after glass and start telling bawdy jokes. Félicité would politely show him to the door. 'I think you have had enough for today, Monsieur de Grémanville! Do come and see us again soon!' And she would close the door behind him.

But she was always delighted to welcome Monsieur Bourais, a retired solicitor. His white cravat and bald head, the flounces on his shirt-front and the generous cut of his brown frock-coat, the special way he had of bending his arm when taking snuff, indeed everything about his person prompted in Félicité the sort of agitation we always feel when in the presence of some great man.

He looked after the management of 'Madame's' properties and would shut himself away with her for hours on end in 'Monsieur's' study. He lived in constant fear for his own reputation, had an inordinate respect for the judiciary and claimed to know some Latin.

Thinking that it would help the children to derive some enjoyment from their studies, he bought them an illustrated geography book. It depicted scenes from different parts of the world, cannibals wearing feathered head-dresses, a monkey abducting a young girl, a group of Bedouins in the desert, a whale being harpooned, and so on.

Paul carefully explained all these pictures to Félicité.

In fact, this was the only time anyone ever taught her how to read a book.

The children received their lessons from Guyot, a rather pitiful character who worked at the Town Hall, who was noted for his fine handwriting and who used to sharpen his penknife on the sole of his shoe.

Whenever the weather was fine, the whole family would get up early and spend the day at the farm at Geffosses.

The farmyard there was on a slope, with the farmhouse in the middle. One could just see the sea, a little streak of grey in the distance.

Félicité would take a few slices of cold meat from her basket and they would eat in a room adjoining the dairy. This room was all that now remained of a country house which had fallen into ruin. The paper hung in strips from the wall and fluttered in the draught. Madame Aubain sat with her head bowed, absorbed in her memories, the children hardly daring to speak. 'Off you go and play,' she would say. And off they went.

Paul would climb up into the barn, catch birds, play ducks and drakes on the pond or bang the great farm barrels with a stick to make them boom like drums.

Virginie would go and feed the rabbits or run off across the fields gathering cornflowers, showing her dainty embroidered knickers as she ran.

One evening in autumn, they were coming back through the fields.

A Simple Heart

The moon, which was in its first quarter, lit up part of the sky, and a mist drifted like a scarf over the windings of the river Toucques. A group of cattle, lying in the middle of a field, lazily watched them go by. When they came to the third field, a few of them got to their feet and stood in a circle in front of them. 'There's nothing to be frightened of!' said Félicité and, humming a wistful little tune as she approached, she went up to the nearest of the animals and patted it on the back. It turned away and the others did the same. But no sooner had they got through the next field when they heard a terrifying bellowing. It was a bull that had been hidden by the mist. It began to come towards the two women. Madame Aubain wanted to run. 'No, no, we must not move too quickly!' said Félicité. They walked more quickly, even so, and could hear the bull's loud breathing getting nearer behind them and the pounding of its hoofs on the grass. They knew it was now galloping towards them! Félicité turned round to face it, grabbed clods of earth from the ground and flung them into the bull's face. It lowered its muzzle, shook its horns and began to shudder and bellow with rage. Madame Aubain had now reached the edge of the field with the two children and was frantically trying to find a way of getting over the hedge. Félicité was still steadily retreating before the bull, throwing lumps of turf into its eyes and calling out, 'Hurry up! Hurry up!'

Madame Aubain got down into the ditch, pushing first Virginie and then Paul in front of her. She fell several times as she tried to climb the bank and at last, by dint of sheer determination, she succeeded.

The bull had driven Félicité up against a gate and was blowing slaver into her face. A second later and it would have gored her. In the nick of time she managed to squeeze herself between two bars in the gate. The huge animal was taken completely by surprise and stopped in its tracks.

People in Pont-l'Evêque talked about this adventure for years afterwards. But Félicité never boasted about it and hardly seemed to realize that she had done anything heroic.

Virginie commanded all her attention. The frightening experience with the bull had affected her nerves and Monsieur Poupart, the doctor, recommended sea bathing at Trouville.

In those days, very few people visited the resort. Madame Aubain made enquiries, sought the advice of Bourais and made preparations as if for a long journey.

The day before they left, the luggage was sent off in Liébard's farm wagon. The next day he returned with two horses. One of them had a woman's saddle with a velvet backrest and the other had a cloak rolled up across its back as a makeshift seat. Madame Aubain sat on this behind Liébard. Félicité looked after Virginie on the other horse and Paul rode separately on Monsieur Lechaptois's donkey, which had been lent on the clear understanding that they took great care of it.

The road was so bad that the five-mile journey took them two hours. The horses sank up to their pasterns in the mud and lurched forward in order to pull themselves free. They lost their footing in the ruts and sometimes had to jump. At certain points on the road, Liébard's mare would suddenly stop dead. Liébard would wait patiently for her to move forward again. As they rode on, he would tell them stories about the people who lived along the way, always adding a few personal comments of his own for good measure. In the town centre of Toucques, for instance, as they were passing alongside a house with nasturtiums growing around the windows, he said, with a shrug of his shoulders, 'There's a Madame Lehoussais lives there and, rather than take a young man . . .' Félicité did not hear the rest, for the horses had broken into a trot and the donkey had run on ahead. They turned down a track, a gate swung open, two young farmhands appeared and they all dismounted beside the manure-heap right outside the front door of the farmhouse.

Old Madame Liébard greeted her mistress with effusive expressions of delight. For lunch she served a sirloin of beef, along with tripe, black pudding, a fricassee of chicken, sparkling cider, a fruit tart and plums in brandy, all accompanied by a stream of compliments to Madame who seemed 'in much better health', to Mademoiselle who had grown up into such 'a fine looking young woman', to Monsieur Paul who was such a 'strapping' young man, not forgetting their dear departed grandparents whom the Liébards had known personally, having been in service to the family for several generations. The farm, like the Liébards themselves, had an old-world feel to it. The beams in the ceiling were pitted with woodworm, the walls blackened with smoke, the window panes grey with dust. There was an oak dresser, cluttered with all manner of implements – jugs, plates, pewter bowls, wolf-traps, shears for the sheep and a huge syringe which particularly amused the children. In the three yards outside, there was not a single tree which did not have mushrooms growing at its foot or clumps of mistletoe in its branches. Several had been blown down by the wind but had begun to grow again where the trunk had been split and all of them were bent beneath the weight of apples. The thatched roofs looked like brown velvet of unequal thickness and weathered the fiercest winds. But the shed for the carts was falling down. Madame Aubain said that she would arrange to have it repaired and asked for the horses to be reharnessed.

It took them another half-hour to reach Trouville. The little caravan had to dismount when they came to the Ecores, a cliff which jutted out over the boats below. Three minutes later they had arrived at the end of the quay and turned into the courtyard of the Golden Lamb, an inn run by old Madame David.

Virginie very quickly began to recover her strength as a result of the change of air and of bathing in the sea. She did not have a bathing costume and so she went into the water wearing a chemise. Afterwards, her maid would help her to get dressed in a customs officer's hut that was also used by the bathers.

A Simple Heart

In the afternoon, they would take the donkey and walk out beyond the Roches-Noires, towards Hennequeville. At first the path wound up between gently rolling meadows like the lawn in a park and then came to a plateau where there were grazing pastures and ploughed fields. The path was lined by holly bushes which grew amongst the tangles of brambles, and here and there the branches of a large dead tree traced their zigzag patterns against the blue of the sky.

There was one particular field in which they usually stopped to rest themselves, looking down towards Deauville to their left, Le Havre to their right and, in front of them, the open sea. It lay shimmering in the sunshine, as smooth as the surface of a mirror and so calm that they could barely hear the murmur of the waves. Sparrows twittered from somewhere nearby and the great dome of the sky lay spread out above them. Madame Aubain would sit with her needlework, Virginie would sit beside her, plaiting rushes, Félicité gathered bunches of wild lavender and Paul, utterly bored, would always be itching to move on.

At other times they would take the ferry across the Toucques and go looking for shells. At low tide, sea urchins, ormers and jellyfish were left behind on the sand. The children would chase after flecks of foam blown about by the breeze. The waves broke lazily on the sand from one end of the beach to the other. The beach stretched as far as the eye could see but was bounded on the landward side by sand dunes which separated it from the Marais, a broad meadow in the shape of a racecourse. As they walked back through it towards Trouville, which lay at the foot of the hill, the town appeared to grow bigger at every step they took and, with its motley assortment of houses, it seemed to blossom like a flower garden in colourful disarray.

When it was too hot, they kept to their room. The dazzling brightness outside cast bars of light through the slats in the window blinds. There was not a sound to be heard in the village. Not a soul ventured out into the streets. The prevailing quiet made everything seem all the more peaceful. From far away came the sound of the caulkers' hammers beating against the hull of a boat and the smell of tar was wafted to them on the listless breeze.

The most exciting event of the day was when the fishing boats came in. Once past the entrance buoys, they would begin to tack from side to side. Their main sails would be lowered to half-mast and, with their foresail swollen like a great balloon, they would come gliding through the splashing waves right into the middle of the harbour and suddenly drop anchor. The boat would then be brought alongside the quay. The sailors would hoist their fish ashore, still live and quivering. A line of carts was ready waiting and women in cotton bonnets rushed forward to take the baskets and to kiss their menfolk.

One day one of these women came up to Félicité. A moment or two later, Félicité was back in the room at the inn, beside herself with excitement. She had found one

A Simple Heart

of her lost sisters, and into the room walked Nastasie Barette, now Leroux, with a baby at her breast, another child holding her right hand and, on her left, a little ship's boy with his hands on his hips and his beret over one ear.

After a quarter of an hour, Madame Aubain asked her to leave.

But after that there was no getting away from them. They would wait just outside the kitchen or follow them when they went for walks. The husband always kept well out of sight.

Félicité became very attached to them. She bought them a blanket, some shirts and a cooking stove. They were obviously out to take advantage of her. Madame Aubain was annoyed that Félicité was not more firm with them. She also took objection to the familiar way in which the nephew spoke to Paul. So, because Virginie had developed a cough and the weather had taken a turn for the worse, she returned to Pont-l'Evêque.

Monsieur Bourais offered his advice on choosing a good school for Paul. The one at Caen was generally considered to be the best. So Paul was sent away to Caen. He said his goodbyes bravely, really quite pleased that he was going to live somewhere where he would have some friends of his own.

Madame Aubain resigned herself to her son going away, knowing that he must have a good education. Virginie quickly got used to being on her own, but Félicité found the house very quiet without him. Soon, however, she had something else to occupy her mind. From Christmas onwards she had to take Virginie to catechism every day.

3

Genuflecting as she went in through the door, Félicité walked up the aisle beneath the high ceiling of the nave, opened the door of Madame Aubain's pew, sat herself down and looked all around her.

The children were seated in the choir stalls, the boys on the right and the girls on the left. The priest stood in front of them beside the lectern. One of the stained-glass windows in the apse showed the Holy Spirit looking down on the Virgin Mary. In another, the Virgin knelt before the infant Jesus and behind the tabernacle there was a carving in wood representing Saint Michael slaying the dragon.

The priest began with a summary of the Holy Scriptures. Félicité's mind was filled with images of Paradise, the Flood, the Tower of Babel, cities consumed by flames, peoples dying and idols cast down. This dazzling recital of events instilled in her a wholesome respect for the Almighty and a profound fear of his wrath. She wept at the story of Christ's Passion. Why had they crucified a man who was so kind to children, fed the hungry, gave sight to the blind, and who had chosen, out of his own

A Simple Heart

gentle nature, to be born amongst the poor on the rough straw of a stable? Seed-time and harvest, the fruits of the vine, all those familiar things mentioned in the gospels had their place in her life too. They now seemed sanctified by contact with God. Félicité loved lambs all the more because of her love for the Lamb of God, and doves now reminded her of the Holy Spirit.

She found it difficult to imagine what the Holy Spirit actually looked like because he was not only a bird but sometimes a fire and sometimes a breath. Perhaps it was the light of the Holy Spirit that she would see at night-time, flickering at the edge of the marshes, or his breath which drove the clouds across the sky, or his voice which made the church bells ring so beautifully. She sat rapt in adoration of these wonders, delighting in the coolness of the stone walls and the peacefulness of the church.

Of church dogma she understood not a word and did not even attempt to understand it. As the curé stood explaining it all to the children and the children repeated what they had learnt, Félicité would drop off to sleep, to be woken suddenly by the clatter of wooden shoes on the stone floor as the children left the church. And so Félicité came to learn her catechism by dint of hearing the children recite it, for her own religious education had been neglected when she was young. From then on, she copied the religious observances of Virginie, fasting when she fasted and going to confession whenever she did. For the feast of Corpus Christi, Félicité and Virginie made an altar of repose together.

For days beforehand, Félicité fretted over the preparations for Virginie's first communion. She worried about her shoes, her rosary, her missal and her gloves. Her hands trembled as she helped Madame Aubain to dress her.

All through the mass she was on tenterhooks. One half of the choir stalls was hidden from her sight by Monsieur Bourais, but straight in front of her she could see the flock of young girls all wearing white crowns over their lowered veils and looking like a field of snow. Even from a distance, she could recognize her beloved little Virginie by the delicate line of her neck and her attitude of reverent contemplation. The bell tinkled. They all bowed their heads and knelt in silence. Then, with a mighty flourish from the organ, the choir and congregation sang the *Agnus Dei*. After the boys had processed forwards, the girls stood up. With their hands joined in prayer, they moved slowly towards the candle-lit altar, knelt at the altar-step, received the Host one by one and returned in the same order to their place in the choir stalls. When it came to Virginie's turn, Félicité leant further forwards so that she could see her and, with that singular imagination that is born of true love, she felt she was herself Virginie, assuming her expression, wearing her dress and with her heart beating inside her breast. As Virginie opened her mouth, Félicité closed her eyes and almost fainted.

The next morning, bright and early, Félicité went to the sacristy and asked to be given communion. She

A Simple Heart

received it with due reverence but did not experience the same rapture.

Madame Aubain wanted the best possible education for her daughter and, because Guyot was unable to teach her either English or music, she resolved to send her to the Ursuline convent school in Honfleur.

Virginie had no objection to this plan but Félicité was most unhappy and felt that Madame was being too strict. However, she came to accept that it was not really for her to decide and that her mistress probably knew best.

Then one day, an old carriage drew up outside the door. Out of it got a nun who had come to collect Mademoiselle. Félicité loaded the luggage up on to the rack, issued some parting instructions to the driver and put six pots of jam, a dozen pears and a bunch of violets in the boot.

Just as they were about to leave, Virginie burst into tears. She clung to her mother, who kissed her on the forehead and kept telling her: 'Come, come, we must be brave!' The step was pulled up and the carriage drove away.

When it had gone, Madame Aubain broke down and that evening all her friends, Monsieur and Madame Lormeau, Madame Lechaptois, the two Rochefeuille sisters, Monsieur de Houppeville and Bourais, came round to comfort her.

At first, the loss of her daughter left her feeling very sad. But she received letters from her on three days each week and on the other days she wrote back to her, walked in her garden, read a little and so managed to occupy her time.

Every morning, out of habit, Félicité would go into Virginie's bedroom and gaze at the walls. She missed being able to comb her hair for her, tie her bootlaces and tuck her up in bed; she missed seeing her sweet little face always beside her and holding her hand when they went out for walks. For want of something to do, she tried to take up lace work. But she was too clumsy with her fingers and she kept breaking the threads. She could not put her mind to anything and was losing sleep. She was, in her own words, 'all empty inside'.

In order to provide herself with 'a bit of company', she asked Madame Aubain if her nephew Victor might be allowed to visit her.

He would always arrive on Sundays, just after mass, rosy-cheeked, his shirt unbuttoned and bringing with him the smells of the countryside through which he had travelled. She straight away laid the table for him. They would eat lunch sitting opposite each other, Félicité taking care to eat as little as possible so as to save on expense and giving Victor so much to eat that he ended up falling asleep. As the first bell for vespers began to ring, she would wake him up, give his trousers a good brush, tie his tie, and make her way to church, leaning on his arm like a proud mother.

His parents always told him to make sure he brought something back with him, a bag of sugar, a piece of soap, a little brandy or even money. He brought with him any

A Simple Heart

of his clothes that needed mending and Félicité always did the work willingly, glad of any opportunity of encouraging him to visit her again.

In August, Victor went to join his father on his sea trips along the coast.

It was the beginning of the school holidays and it was some consolation to Félicité to have the children back at home. But Paul had become rather temperamental and Virginie was now too grown-up to be treated as a little child, which created a sense of awkwardness and distance between them.

Victor's travels took him to Morlaix, to Dunkirk and to Brighton and after each trip he brought back a present for Félicité. The first was a little box made out of shells, the second a coffee cup and the third a big gingerbread man. He was growing into a handsome young man, with a fine figure, the first signs of a moustache, a frank and open expression and a little leather cap which he wore perched on the back of his head like a sea pilot. He would entertain Félicité by telling her stories laced with all sorts of nautical jargon.

One Monday, 14 July 1819 (it was a date that Félicité was never to forget), Victor announced that he had been signed on to the crew of an ocean-going ship and that in two days' time he would be taking the night ferry from Honfleur to join his schooner, which was due shortly to set sail from Le Havre. He might be away for two years.

The prospect of such a long separation left Félicité

feeling very saddened. In order to say one final farewell to him, on the Wednesday evening, after Madame had finished her dinner, she put on her clogs and ran the ten miles from Pont-l'Evêque to Honfleur.

When she came to the Calvary, instead of turning left, she turned right, got lost in the shipyards and had to retrace her steps. She asked directions from some passers-by, who told her she would have to hurry. She walked all the way round the harbour, which was full of boats, getting caught up in the moorings as she went. Suddenly the ground seemed to fall away beneath her, beams of light criss-crossed before her eyes and she thought she must be losing her senses when she saw some horses in the sky overhead.

On the quayside, more horses were neighing, frightened by the sea. They were being hoisted into the air by a derrick and then lowered into a boat which was already crammed with passengers trying to squeeze their way between barrels of cider, baskets of cheese and sacks of grain. Hens were cackling and the captain was swearing. One of the deck-hands, apparently oblivious to everything around him, stood leaning against the cat-head. Félicité had not recognized him and was calling out 'Victor!' again and again. He looked up and she rushed forward, but just at that moment the gangway was suddenly pulled ashore.

The boat moved out of the harbour, hauled along by a group of women who sang in chorus as they went about their work. Its ribs creaked and heavy waves lashed its

A Simple Heart

bows. The sail swung round and hid everyone from view. The surface of the sea shone like silver in the moonlight and on it the ship appeared as a black spot, growing paler as it moved away. Eventually it was swallowed up in the distance and vanished from sight.

Returning home, Félicité passed by the Calvary and was taken by a sudden desire to commend to God's mercy all that she held dear. She stood there praying for a long time, with tears running down her cheeks and her eyes fixed on the clouds above. The town was fast asleep; the only people about were the customs men. Water could be heard gushing through the holes in the lock-gate like a running torrent. A clock struck two.

The convent would not be open to visitors before daybreak and Félicité knew that, if she arrived back late, Madame was sure to be annoyed. So, although she would have loved just one small kiss from Virginie, she set off back home. The maids at the inn were just waking up as she walked into Pont-l'Evêque.

So poor little Victor was to spend months on end being tossed around on the waves! His previous trips at sea had not bothered her. England and Brittany were places one came back from. But America, the colonies and the Antilles were lost in some unknown region on the other side of the world.

From the day he left, Félicité could not stop thinking about her nephew. When it was hot and sunny, she worried that he might be thirsty and when there was a storm, she feared he might be struck by lightning. As she listened to the wind howling in the chimney and blowing slates off the roof, she pictured him buffered by the same storm, clinging to the top of a broken mast and being flung backwards into a sheet of foam. At other times, prompted by her recollection of the pictures in the geography book, she imagined him being eaten by savages, captured by monkeys in a forest or dying on some deserted beach. But she never spoke about these worries to anyone.

Madame Aubain had worries of her own about her daughter.

The sisters at the convent said that she was an affectionate child, but over-sensitive. The slightest emotion unsettled her and she had to give up playing the piano.

Her mother insisted that she wrote home regularly. One morning, when the postman had failed to appear, she could scarcely contain her impatience and kept pacing backwards and forwards in her room between her armchair and the window. This really was extraordinary! No news for four days!

Thinking that her own situation might serve as some comfort to her mistress, Félicité ventured:

'But Madame, I haven't received any news for six months!'

'News from whom?'

'Why, news from my nephew,' Félicité gently replied.

'Oh, your nephew!' And with a shrug of her shoulders, Madame Aubain began pacing about the room again, as

A Simple Heart

if to say, 'I hadn't given him a thought! And in any case, he's no concern of mine! A mere ship's boy, a scrounger; he's not worth bothering about! But someone like my daughter . . . Really!'

Although Félicité had been fed such rough treatment since she was a child, she felt very offended by Madame Aubain. But she soon got over it.

After all, it was to be expected that Madame should get upset about her own daughter.

For Félicité, the two children were of equal importance; they were bound together by her love for them and it seemed right that they should share the same fate.

Félicité learnt from the chemist that Victor's ship had arrived in Havana. He had read the announcement in a newspaper.

Because of its association with cigars, Félicité imagined Havana to be a place in which the only thing people did was to smoke and she pictured Victor walking amongst crowds of Negroes in a cloud of tobacco smoke. Was it possible to return from Havana by land, 'if need be'? How far was it from Pont-l'Evêque? In order to find out, she went to consult Monsieur Bourais.

He reached for his atlas and launched into a disquisition on lines of longitude. Félicité was utterly bewildered. Bourais sat in front of her, beaming smugly to himself, like the know-all he was. Eventually, he picked up his pencil and pointed to an almost invisible black dot in one of the little indentations in the contour of an oval-shaped patch on the map. 'Here it is,' he said. Félicité peered closely at the map. The network of coloured lines was a strain on her eyes, but it told her nothing. Bourais asked her what was puzzling her and she asked him if he would show her the house in which Victor was living. Bourais raised his arms in the air, sneezed and roared with laughter, delighted to come across someone so simple-minded. Félicité, whose understanding was so limited that she probably even expected to see a picture of her nephew, could not understand what he found so funny.

It was a fortnight after this, at his usual time on market day, that Liébard came into the kitchen and handed Félicité a letter which he had received from her brother-in-law. As neither of them could read, Félicité showed the letter to her mistress.

Madame Aubain, who was counting the stitches on a piece of knitting, put her work to one side, opened the letter, gave a sudden start and then, lowering her voice and looking very serious, she said, 'They are sending you . . . bad news. Your nephew . . .'

Victor was dead. That was all the letter said.

Félicité sank down on to a chair and leant her head against the wall. Her eyelids closed and suddenly flushed pink. She remained there, her head bowed, her hands hanging limply at her side, staring in front of her and repeating over and over again, 'The poor boy! The poor boy!'

Liébard stood looking at her and sighing. Madame Aubain was shaking slightly.

A Simple Heart

She suggested that Félicité might go and see her sister at Trouville.

Félicité gave a wave of her hand to indicate that it was not necessary.

There was a silence. Old Liébard thought it best to leave.

When he had gone, Félicité said, 'It doesn't matter a bit, not to them it doesn't.'

She lowered her head again and sat there, now and then toying distractedly with the knitting needles that lay on the work-table.

A group of women passed by in the yard, wheeling a barrow-load of dripping linen.

Félicité caught sight of them through the window and suddenly remembered that she had washing to do herself. She had passed the lye through it the day before and today it needed rinsing. She got up and left the room.

Her washing board and her tub were on the bank of the Toucques. She flung her pile of chemises on to the ground beside the river, rolled up her sleeves and seized her battledore. The drubbing could be heard in all the neighbouring gardens. The fields lay deserted and the wind rippled the surface of the river. On the river-bed, long strands of weed drifted with the current, like the hair of corpses floating downstream in the water. Félicité managed to restrain her grief and was very brave until the evening, but when she was alone in her room she gave in to it, lying prone on her mattress with her face buried in the pillow and pressing her fists to her temples.

Much later, she came to learn the circumstances of Victor's death from the captain of his ship. He had caught yellow fever and had been bled too much in the hospital. Four separate doctors had given him the same treatment and he had died immediately. The chief doctor's comment was, 'Good, that's one more to add to the list!'

Victor had always been treated cruelly by his parents and Félicité preferred not to see them again. They did not get in touch with Félicité either; perhaps they had simply forgotten about her or perhaps poverty had hardened their hearts.

Virginie was now growing weaker.

Difficulty in breathing, a persistent cough, a constant high temperature and pale blotches on her cheeks all pointed to some underlying disorder. Monsieur Poupart had advised a holiday in Provence. Madame Aubain decided to follow his advice and would have brought Virginie back home immediately, had it not been for the weather at Pont-l'Evêque.

She had a standing arrangement with a job-master, who drove her to the convent every Tuesday. In the convent garden there was a terrace overlooking the Seine where Virginie would walk up and down over the fallen vine leaves, leaning on her mother's arm. She would look out at the sails in the distance and the whole sweep of the estuary from the chateau at Tancarville to the lighthouses at Le Havre. Sometimes the sun would suddenly break through the clouds and make her blink. Afterwards, they would rest under the arbour. Her mother had procured a little flask of the choicest Malaga wine, from which Virginie would take just two tiny sips, laughing at the thought of making herself tipsy.

She began to recover her strength. Autumn gradually slipped by. Félicité did all she could to reassure Madame Aubain. But one evening, on her way back from an errand in the town, she noticed Monsieur Poupart's gig standing at the front door. Monsieur Poupart himself was in the entrance hall and Madame Aubain was fastening her bonnet.

'Bring me my foot-warmer, my purse and my gloves! Hurry!'

Virginie had pneumonia and Madame feared she was beyond recovery.

'I'm sure it's not that bad,' said the doctor, and the two of them climbed into his carriage, with the snowflakes falling in great flurries around them. Night was drawing on and it was bitterly cold.

Félicité dashed into the church to light a candle and then began to run after Monsieur Poupart's gig. It was a full hour before she caught up with it. She jumped up behind it and clung to the fringe. Suddenly a thought occurred to her. 'The gate to the courtyard was not locked! What if thieves should break in!' She jumped back down on to the road.

The next day, at the very first sign of daylight, she went to the doctor's house. The doctor had returned but had already left again to visit patients in the country. She waited at the inn, thinking that someone or other might arrive with a letter. Eventually, in the half-light of morning, she boarded the Lisieux stagecoach.

The convent was situated at the foot of a steep narrow street. When she was about half-way down the street, she began to make out strange sounds coming from the convent; it was the tolling of a death bell. 'It must be for someone else', she thought, and gave the door-knocker a loud rap.

After some considerable time, she heard the shuffle of footsteps, the door was inched open and a nun appeared.

The good sister solemnly announced that 'she had just passed away'. At precisely the same moment, the bell of Saint-Léonard's began to toll even more strongly.

Félicité went up to the second floor.

She stood in the doorway of the bedroom and could see Virginie laid out on her back, her hands clasped together, her mouth open and her head tilted backwards. Above her head and inclined towards her was a black crucifix; her face was whiter than the drapes which hung stiffly around her. Madame Aubain lay hugging the foot of the bed and sobbing wildly. The Mother Superior stood beside her on the right. On the chest of drawers, three candlesticks gave out little circles of red light; outside, the fog whitened the window panes. Some nuns came and led Madame Aubain away.

Félicité did not leave Virginie's bedside for two whole

nights. She sat there, repeating the same prayers over and over again; she would get up to sprinkle holy water on the sheets, then come back to her chair and continue to gaze fixedly at the dead girl. At the end of her first night's vigil, she noticed that her face was beginning to turn yellow, her lips were turning blue, her nose had grown thinner and her eyes had become sunken. More than once she kissed her eyes and would not have been in the least surprised if Virginie had opened them again; to minds like hers, the supernatural appears perfectly ordinary. She laid her out, wrapped her in her shroud, put her in her coffin, placed a wreath upon her and spread out her hair. Her hair was fair and amazingly long for a girl of her age. Félicité cut off a large lock of it and slipped half of it into her bosom, resolving that it would never be separated from her.

The body was brought back to Pont-l'Evêque, according to Madame Aubain's instructions. Madame Aubain followed the hearse in a closed carriage.

After the funeral mass, it took another three-quarters of an hour to get to the cemetery. Paul led the procession, sobbing. Monsieur Bourais walked behind him, followed in turn by various dignitaries from Pont-l'Evêque, the women, all wearing black veils, and lastly Félicité. Félicité could not help thinking of her nephew and, having been unable to offer him these last honours, she now felt an added grief, as if he were being buried along with Virginie.

Madame Aubain's despair knew no bounds.

At first she rebelled against God, thinking it was unjust

that He should take her daughter from her when she had never done any wrong and when there was nothing for her to feel guilty about. But perhaps there was. She should have taken her to the South. Other doctors would have cured her. She blamed herself, wished she could follow her daughter to the grave and called out in anguish in the middle of her dreams. One dream in particular tormented her. Her husband, dressed like a sailor, had returned from a long voyage and, choking back his tears, told her that he had received an order to take Virginie away. They then both racked their brains to think of a hiding place for her.

On one occasion she came in from the garden distraught. Just a moment before (and she pointed to the spot), the father and daughter had appeared in front of her, one after the other. They were not doing anything; they were just staring at her.

For several months she remained in her room, totally listless. Félicité gently admonished her, telling her that she should look after herself for the sake of her son and her late husband and in memory of 'her'.

'Her?' said Madame Aubain as though waking from sleep. 'Oh yes, of course. You haven't forgotten her, have you!' This was a reference to the cemetery, which Madame Aubain had been expressly forbidden to visit.

Félicité went there every day.

On the stroke of four, she would walk past the row of houses, climb the hill, open the gate and approach

A Simple Heart

Virginie's grave. There was a little column of pink marble standing on a stone base, with a small garden surrounded by chains. The separate beds could hardly be seen beneath the covering of flowers. Félicité would water the leaves, place fresh sand on the garden and get down on her hands and knees to make sure the ground was properly weeded. When Madame Aubain was eventually able to come to see the grave, she found it a source of comfort, a kind of consolation for her loss.

The years passed, one very much like another, marked only by the annual recurrence of the church festivals: Easter, the Assumption, All Saints' Day. It was only little incidents in their daily lives that, in later years, enabled them to recall a particular date. Thus in 1825 two glaziers whitewashed the entrance hall; in 1827 a part of the roof fell into the courtyard and nearly killed a passer-by. In the summer of 1828 it was Madame's turn to distribute consecrated bread to the parishioners. This was also about the same time that Bourais mysteriously left the town. One by one, all their old acquaintances went away: Guyot, Liébard, Madame Lechaptois, Robelin and old Uncle Gremanville, who had been paralysed for many years.

One night, the driver of the mail-coach arrived in Pont-l'Évêque with news of the July Revolution. A few days later, a new subprefect was appointed: the Baron de Larsonnière, who had previously been a consul in America. He arrived in Pont-l'Évêque accompanied not only by his wife but also by his sister-in-law and three young girls, all of them already quite grown up. They were often to be seen on their lawn, dressed in long, flowing smocks. They also had a Negro servant and a parrot. They called on Madame Aubain to pay their respects and she made a point of doing likewise. As soon as she spotted them approaching in the distance, Félicité would come running in to tell Madame Aubain that they were on their way. But there was only one thing that could really awaken her interest and that was her son's letters.

Paul seemed unable to settle down to a career and spent much of his time in the tavern. Madame Aubain would pay off his debts, but he immediately ran up new ones. She would sit at her knitting by the window and heave sighs that Félicité could hear even in the kitchen, where she was working at her spinning wheel.

The two women would often take a stroll together alongside the trellised wall of the garden. They still talked constantly about Virginie, wondering whether she would have liked such and such a thing or trying to imagine what she would have said on such and such an occasion.

All her belongings were still in a cupboard in the children's bedroom. Madame Aubain had avoided looking inside it as much as possible. Then, one summer day, she resigned herself. Moths came flying from the cupboard.

Virginie's frocks hung in a row beneath a shelf upon which there were three dolls, some hoops, a set of doll's furniture and her own hand-basin. The two women took out all the petticoats, stockings and handkerchiefs and

A Simple Heart

spread them out on the two beds before folding them again. This sorry collection of objects lay there, caught in a beam of sunlight which brought out all the stains and the creases that had been made by the movements of Virginie's body. The air was warm, the sky was blue, a blackbird sang outside and the world seemed to be utterly at peace. They found a little chestnut-coloured hat made of long-piled plush, but it had been completely destroyed by the moths. Félicité asked if she might have it as a keepsake. The two women looked at each other and their eyes filled with tears. Madame Aubain opened her arms and Félicité threw herself into them. Mistress and servant embraced each other, uniting their grief in a kiss which made them equal.

It was the first time that this had ever happened, Madame Aubain being, by nature, very reserved. Félicité could not have been more grateful if she had been offered a priceless gift and from then on she doted on her mistress with dog-like fidelity and the reverence that might be accorded to a saint.

As time went by, Félicité's natural kind-heartedness increased.

One day she heard the sound of drums from a regiment marching along the street and she stood at the door with a jug of cider, handing out drinks to the soldiers. She helped to nurse cholera victims and to look after the refugees from Poland. One of the Poles even said he would like to marry her, but they had a serious argument when she came back one morning from the angelus to find him ensconced in her kitchen, calmly helping himself to a salad which she had prepared for lunch.

After the Poles had left, she turned her attention to an old man by the name of Colmiche, who was rumoured to have committed terrible atrocities in '93. He now lived down by the river in a ruined pigsty. The boys in the town used to spy on him through the cracks in the wall and throw stones at him as he lay coughing and choking on his straw bed. He had long, straggling hair, his eyelids were inflamed and on one arm there was a swelling bigger than his head. Félicité provided him with linen and did what she could to keep his hovel clean; she even hoped she might be able to install him in the outhouse, where he would not disturb Madame. When the tumour burst, she changed his dressing every single day. Sometimes she would bring him a small piece of cake or help him outside on to a bundle of straw, where he could lie in the sun. The poor old wretch would splutter and shake and thank her in a barely audible whisper, saying he could not bear to lose her and stretching out his hands the minute he saw her preparing to leave him. He died and Félicité had a mass said for the repose of his soul.

On the same day, she received the most wonderful surprise. Just as she was serving dinner, Madame de Larsonnière's Negro servant arrived, carrying the parrot in its cage, along with its perch, chain and padlock. There was a note from the Baroness, informing Madame Aubain that her husband had been promoted to a Préfecture and that they were leaving Pont-l'Evêque that very evening. She asked Madame Aubain if she would be kind enough to accept the parrot as a memento of their friendship and as a token of her respect.

The parrot had been a source of wonder to Félicité for a long time, for it came from America, a word which always reminded her of Victor. She had already questioned the servant about it and, on one occasion, had even said that 'Madame would be delighted to look after it!'

The Negro had mentioned this to his mistress and, because she could not take it away with her, she readily seized this opportunity of getting it off her hands.

4

The parrot was called Loulou. His body was green, the tips of his wings were pink, the top of his head was blue and his breast was gold-coloured.

Unfortunately, he had the tiresome habit of chewing his perch and he kept plucking out his feathers, scattering his droppings everywhere and splashing the water from his bath all over his cage. He thoroughly irritated Madame Aubain and so she gave him to Félicité to look after.

She decided she would teach him to speak and he was very soon able to say, 'Pretty boy!', 'Your servant, sir!' and 'Hail Mary!' She put him near the front door and a number of visitors were surprised that he would not answer to the name 'Polly', which is what all parrots are supposed to be called. Some people said he looked more like a turkey or called him a blockhead. Félicité found their jibes very hurtful. There was a curious stubborn streak in Loulou which never ceased to amaze Félicité; he would refuse to talk the minute anyone looked at him!

Even so, there was no doubt that he appreciated company. On Sundays, when the Rochefeuille sisters, Monsieur de Houppeville and some of Madame Aubain's new friends – the apothecary Onfroy, Monsieur Varin and Captain Mathieu – came round to play cards, Loulou would beat on the window panes with his wings and make such a furious commotion that no one could hear themselves speak.

He obviously found Bourais's face a source of great amusement. He only had to see it and he would break into fits of uncontrollable laughter. His squawks could be heard echoing round the yard. The neighbours would come to their windows and start laughing too. To avoid being seen by the parrot, Bourais would slink past the house along the side of the wall, hiding his face behind his hat. He would go down to the river and come into the house by way of the back garden. The looks he gave the bird were not of the tender variety.

The butcher's boy had once flipped Loulou on the ear for trying to help himself to something from his basket and, since then, Loulou always tried to give him a peck through his shirt. Fabu threatened to wring his neck,

A Simple Heart

although he was not cruel by nature, despite what the tattoos on his arms and his long side whiskers might have led one to believe. In fact, he was rather fond of the parrot and, just for the fun of it, he had even tried to teach him a few swear words. Félicité was alarmed at the thought of his acquiring such bad habits and moved him into the kitchen. His chain was removed and he was allowed to wander all over the house.

When he came down the stairs, he would position the curved part of his beak on the step in front of him and then raise first his right foot, followed by his left. Félicité was always worried that these weird acrobatics would make the parrot giddy. He fell ill and could not talk or eat due to an ulcer under his tongue, such as chickens sometimes have. Félicité cured him herself, extracting the lump in his mouth with her fingernails. One day, Monsieur Paul was silly enough to blow cigar smoke up his nose. On another occasion, when Madame Lormeau was teasing him with the end of her parasol, he bit off the metal ferrule with his beak. Then there was the time he got lost.

Félicité had put him out on the grass to get some fresh air. She went indoors for a minute and, when she came back, the parrot had disappeared. She searched for him in the bushes, by the river and even on the rooftops, oblivious to her mistress's shouts of 'Do be careful! You must be mad!' She then hunted through every single garden in Pont-l'Evêque and stopped all the people in the street, asking, 'You don't happen to have seen my parrot by any chance?' Those who did not already know the parrot were given a full description. Suddenly, she thought she saw something green flying about behind the mills at the bottom of the hill. But when she got to the top of the hill, there was nothing to be seen. A pedlar told her he had definitely seen the bird only a short while ago in old Madame Simon's shop at Saint-Melaine. Félicité ran all the way there, but nobody knew what she was talking about. In the end she came back home, utterly exhausted, her shoes torn to shreds and feeling sick at heart. She sat down on the middle of the garden bench, next to Madame, and she was telling her everything that she had done when she suddenly felt something drop gently on to her shoulder. It was Loulou! What on earth had he been up to? Perhaps he had just gone for a little walk around the town!

It took Félicité quite a while to recover from this shock. If the truth were known, she never really recovered from it completely.

She caught tonsillitis, as a result of getting thoroughly chilled, and shortly afterwards developed pains in her ears. Within three years she was completely deaf and spoke in a very loud voice, even in church. Even though her sins could have been proclaimed in every corner of the diocese without bringing any discredit to her or causing offence to others, the curé decided that it would now be best to hear her confession in the sacristy.

Imaginary buzzing noises in her head added to her troubles. Her mistress would often say, 'Goodness me!

You're just being silly!' Félicité would answer, 'Yes, Madame,' still looking around her to see where the noises were coming from.

She became enclosed in an ever-diminishing world of her own; gone for ever was the pealing of church bells and the lowing of cattle in the fields. Every living thing passed by her in ghostly silence. Only one sound now reached her ears, and that was the voice of her parrot.

Almost as if he were deliberately trying to entertain her, he would imitate the clicking of the turnspit, the shrill cry of the fishmonger or the sound of sawing from the joiner's shop on the other side of the street. Whenever the front door bell rang, he would imitate Madame Aubain: 'Félicité! The door, the door!'

They would hold conversations with each other, the parrot endlessly repeating the three stock phrases from his repertory and Félicité replying with words that made very little sense but which all came straight from the heart. In her isolation, Loulou was almost a son to her; she simply doted on him. He used to climb up her fingers, peck at her lips and hang on to her shawl. Sometimes she would put her face close to his and shake her head in the way a nurse does to a baby, with the wings of her bonnet and the bird's wings all fluttering together.

When storm clouds gathered and thunder rumbled, the bird would squawk loudly, no doubt remembering the sudden cloud-bursts of his native forests. The sound of falling rain would send him into a frenzy. He would fly madly about the house, shooting up to the ceiling, knocking everything over and finally escaping through the window into the garden to splash around in the puddles. But he would soon come back, perch on one of the fire-dogs, jump up and down to dry his feathers and then proudly display his tail or his beak.

One morning in the terrible winter of 1837, when she had put him near the fireplace because of the cold, she found him dead in his cage, hanging head downwards with his claws caught in the metal bars. He had probably died of a stroke, but the thought crossed Félicité's mind that he might have been poisoned with parsley and, although there was no definite proof, her suspicions fell on Fabu.

She wept so much that her mistress eventually said, 'Well, why don't you have him stuffed?'

Félicité went to consult the chemist, who had always been kind to the parrot.

He wrote to Le Havre and a man by the name of Fellacher agreed to do the job. But, knowing that the mail-coach sometimes mislaid parcels, Félicité decided that she would take the parrot as far as Honfleur herself.

The road ran between endless lines of apple trees, bare and leafless. Ice lay in the ditches. Dogs barked as she walked past the farms. With her hands tucked under her mantlet and her basket on her arm, Félicité walked briskly along the middle of the road in her little black clogs.

She followed the road through the forest, passed Le Haut-Chêne and eventually reached Saint-Gatien.

A Simple Heart

On the road behind her, in a cloud of dust and gathering speed on its way down the hill, a mail-coach at full gallop came rushing towards her like a whirlwind. The coachman, seeing that this woman was making no attempt to get out of the way, stood up and looked out over the roof of the carriage and both he and his postilion shouted at her for all their worth. The four horses, which he was vainly trying to rein in, galloped faster and faster towards her and the leading pair struck her as they went by. With a sharp tug on the reins, the coachman forced them to swerve on to the side of the road. In his rage, he raised his arm and lashed out at her with his long whip as the coach lurched past. The blow struck Félicité full across her face and the upper part of her body, and with such force that she fell flat on her back.

The first thing she did when she regained consciousness was to open her basket. Fortunately, Loulou had come to no harm. She felt a burning sensation on her right cheek. She put her hand to her face and saw that her hand was red. She was bleeding.

She sat down on a pile of stones and dabbed her face with her handkerchief. Then she ate a crust of bread which she had brought with her in case she needed it and tried to take her mind off her wound by looking at the parrot.

As she came to the top of the hill at Ecquemauville, she saw the lights of Honfleur twinkling in the night like clusters of stars and, beyond them, the sea, stretching dimly into the distance. She was suddenly overcome with a fit of giddiness and her wretched childhood, the disappointment of her first love affair, the departure of her nephew and the death of Virginie all came flooding back to her like the waves of an incoming tide, welling up inside her and taking her breath away.

She insisted on speaking personally to the captain of the ship and, although she did not tell him what was in her parcel, she asked him to look after it carefully.

Fellacher kept the parrot for a long time. He kept promising that it would arrive the following week. After six months, he announced that a box had been dispatched, but that was the last they heard of it. Félicité began to fear that Loulou would never come back. 'He has been stolen, I know it!' she thought to herself.

But at last he arrived. And quite magnificent he looked too, perched on a branch which was screwed on to a mahogany plinth, with one foot held raised, his head cocked to one side and holding in his beak a nut which the taxidermist, in order to add a little touch of grandeur, had gilded.

Félicité installed him in her room.

This room, which few were allowed into, was filled with a mixture of religious knick-knacks and other miscellaneous bits and pieces and resembled something between a chapel and a bazaar.

A large wardrobe made it awkward to open the door fully. Opposite the window that looked out on to the garden was a smaller circular window which looked out on to

A Simple Heart

the courtyard. There was a plain, unsprung bed and beside it a table with a water jug, two combs and a small cake of blue soap on a chipped plate. Fixed to the walls were rosaries, medals, several pictures of the Virgin and a holy-water stoop made out of a coconut shell. On the chest of drawers, which was draped with a cloth like an altar, was the shell box that Victor had given her, a watering can and a ball, some handwriting books, the illustrated geography book and a pair of little ankle boots. Hanging by its two ribbons from the nail which supported the mirror was the little plush hat! These keepsakes meant so much to Félicité. She had even kept one of Monsieur's frock-coats. If there was anything that Madame Aubain wanted to get rid of, she would find a place for it in her room, like the artificial flowers beside her chest of drawers and the portrait of the Comte d'Artois in the window recess.

Loulou was placed on a little shelf made especially for the purpose and fixed to a chimney breast which protruded into the room. Every morning, as she woke, she would catch sight of him in the early morning light and would recall the days gone by, trivial incidents, right down to the tiniest detail, remembered not in sadness but in perfect tranquillity.

Being unable to hold a conversation with anyone, she lived her life as if in a sleepwalker's trance. The only thing that seemed capable of bringing her back to life was the Corpus Christi procession, when she would visit all the neighbours, collecting candlesticks and mats to decorate the altar of repose that was always set up outside in the street.

When she went to church, she would sit gazing at the picture of the Holy Spirit and it struck her that it looked rather like her parrot. The resemblance was even more striking in an Epinal colour print depicting Our Lord's baptism. The dove had wings of crimson and a body of emerald-green and it looked for all the world like Loulou. Félicité bought the picture and hung it in place of the portrait of the Comte d'Artois, so that she could see them both together at the same time. In her mind, the one became associated with the other, the parrot becoming sanctified by connection with the Holy Spirit and the Holy Spirit in turn acquiring added life and meaning. Surely it could not have been a dove that God had chosen to speak through, since doves cannot talk. It must have been one of Loulou's ancestors. Félicité would say her prayers with her eyes turned towards the picture but every now and then she would turn her head slightly to look at the parrot.

She thought of entering the sisterhood of the Ladies of the Virgin but Madame Aubain persuaded her not to.

There now occurred an event of considerable importance – Paul's wedding.

Having worked first as a lawyer's clerk, Paul had subsequently tried his hand at business, worked for the Customs and for the Inland Revenue and had even considered joining the Department of Forests and Waterways. Now, at the age of thirty-six, as if by divine inspiration,

A Simple Heart

he had suddenly discovered his vocation – the Registry Office! Indeed, he had displayed such a talent for the job that one of the inspectors had offered him his daughter's hand in marriage and had promised to use his influence to advance his career.

By now, Paul took his responsibilities seriously and he brought his intended to see his mother.

Not a thing at Pont-l'Evêque met with her approval. She expected to be treated like royalty and she hurt Félicité's feelings badly. Madame Aubain was relieved to see her go.

The following week, they learned of the death of Monsieur Bourais in an inn somewhere in Lower Brittany. Rumour had it that he had committed suicide. This turned out to be true and questions were raised about his honesty. Madame Aubain went through her accounts and the catalogue of his misdeeds soon became apparent: embezzlement of arrears of rent, undeclared sales of wood, forged receipts, and so forth. It was also discovered that he was the father of an illegitimate child and that he was having 'an illicit relationship with someone from Dozulé'.

This sordid business was a source of great distress to Madame Aubain. In March 1853, she began to feel pains in her chest. A grey coating covered her tongue. She was treated with leeches but this failed to improve her breathing. On the ninth evening of her illness, she died, aged just seventy-two.

People took her to be younger than this because of her dark hair, which she had always worn in bandeaux round her pale, pockmarked face. She had very few friends to lament her death; there was a certain haughtiness about her that had always kept people at a distance.

Félicité wept for her in a way that servants rarely weep for their masters. That Madame should die before her disturbed her whole way of thinking; it seemed to go against the natural order of things; it was something unacceptable and unreal.

Ten days later, just as soon as they could get there from Besançon, the heirs arrived on the scene. Madame Aubain's daughter-in-law went through all the drawers, chose a few pieces of furniture for herself and sold what was left. Then they all went back to the Registry Office.

Madame's armchair, her little table, her foot-warmer and the eight chairs had all gone! On the walls, yellow patches marked the places where pictures had once hung. They had taken away the children's beds, along with their mattresses, and the cupboard had been cleared of all Virginie's things. Félicité went from room to room, heartbroken.

The following day, a notice appeared on the front door. The apothecary shouted into Félicité's ear that the house was for sale.

Félicité's head began to swim and she had to sit down.

What most upset her was the thought of having to move out of her own room; it was the perfect place for poor Loulou. In her anguish she would gaze at him and beg the Holy Spirit to come to her aid. She developed the idolatrous habit of kneeling in front of the parrot to say her prayers. Sometimes the sun would catch the parrot's glass eye as it came through the little window, causing an emanation of radiant light that sent her into ecstasies.

Félicité had been left a pension of three hundred and eighty francs by her mistress. The garden provided her with vegetables. As for clothes, she had sufficient to last her her lifetime and she saved on lighting by going to bed as soon as it began to get dark.

She hardly ever went out, because she disliked walking past the secondhand dealer's shop, where some of the old furniture was on display. Ever since her fit of giddiness, she had been dragging one leg and, as she was now growing frail, old Madame Simon, whose grocery business had recently collapsed, used to come round every morning to chop her firewood and draw her water.

Her eyes grew weaker. The shutters were no longer opened. Many years passed. Nobody came to rent the house and nobody came to buy it.

Félicité never asked for any repairs to be done, because she was frightened she might be evicted. The laths in the roof rotted and for one whole winter her bolster was permanently wet from the rain. Shortly after Easter, she coughed blood.

Madame Simon called for a doctor. Félicité wanted to know what was wrong with her. But by now she was too deaf to hear what was said and she only managed to catch one word: 'pneumonia'. It was a word she knew and she quietly answered, 'Ah! Like Madame', finding it quite natural that she should follow in her mistress's footsteps.

The time for preparing the altars of repose was drawing near.

The first of them was always placed at the foot of the hill, the second outside the post office and the third about half-way up the street. The exact position of this last altar was a matter of some rivalry, but the women of the parish eventually agreed that it should be placed in Madame Aubain's courtyard.

Félicité's breathing was getting worse and she was becoming more feverish. She fretted at not being able to do anything for the altar. If only there were at least something that she could put on it! And then she thought of the parrot. The neighbours objected, saying that it was not really suitable. But the curé gave his permission and this made Félicité so happy that she asked him to accept Loulou, the one treasure she possessed, as a gift from her when she died.

From Tuesday to Saturday, the eve of Corpus Christi, her coughing increased. By the evening, her face looked drawn, her lips were sticking to her gums and she began vomiting. The following morning, at first light, feeling very low, she sent for a priest. Three good women stood round her as she was given extreme unction. She then announced that she needed to speak to Fabu.

Fabu arrived dressed in his Sunday best and feeling very ill at ease in such sombre surroundings.

'Please forgive me,' she said, summoning all her

strength to extend her arm towards him, 'I thought it was you who had killed him.'

What was all this nonsense? How could she suspect someone like him of having committed a murder! Fabu was most indignant and was on the point of losing his temper.

'Her mind is wandering,' they said. 'Surely you can see that.'

From time to time Félicité seemed to be speaking to phantoms. The women went away. Madame Simon ate her lunch.

A little later she went to fetch Loulou and held him close to Félicité. 'Come on,' she said. 'Say goodbye to him.'

Although Loulou was not a corpse, he was being eaten away by maggots. One of his wings was broken and the stuffing was coming out of his stomach. But Félicité was now blind. She kissed him on his forehead and held him against her cheek. Madame Simon took him from her and went to replace him on the altar.

5

The smells of summer drifted in from the meadows. The air was filled with the buzzing of flies. The sun glinted on the surface of the river and warmed the slates of the roof. Madame Simon had come back into the room and was gently nodding off to sleep.

Gustave Flaubert

She was awoken by the sound of bells; they were coming out of vespers. Félicité grew suddenly calmer. She thought of the procession and saw everything as clearly as if she were there.

All the schoolchildren, the choristers and the firemen were walking along the pavements. In the middle of the street, at the head of the procession, came the church officer with his halberd, the beadle carrying the great cross, the schoolmaster in charge of the boys and the nun keeping a motherly eye on the girls. Three of the prettiest, looking like curly headed angels, were throwing rose petals in the air. They were followed by the deacon conducting the band with arms outstretched and two censer-bearers turning round at every step to face the Holy Sacrament, which was carried by Monsieur le Curé, clad in his magnificent chasuble and protected by a canopy of bright red velvet held aloft by four churchwardens. A great throng of people followed on behind as the procession made its way between the white sheets which draped the walls of the houses and eventually arrived at the bottom of the hill.

Félicité's forehead was bathed in a cold sweat. Madame Simon sponged it with a cloth, telling herself that one day she would go the same way.

The noise of the crowd gradually increased, at one point becoming very loud and then fading away.

A sudden burst of gunfire rattled the window panes. The postilions were saluting the monstrance. Félicité rolled her eyes and, trying to raise her voice above a whisper, she asked, 'Is he all right?' She was still worrying about the parrot.

Félicité was now entering her final moments. Her breath came in short raucous gasps, making her sides heave. Beads of froth gathered in the corners of her mouth and her whole body began to shake.

From the street outside came the blaring of ophicleides, the high-pitched voices of the children and the deeper voices of the men. There were moments when all was quiet and all that could be heard was the tread of feet, cushioned by the scattered petals and sounding like a flock of sheep crossing a field.

The group of clergy entered the courtyard. Madame Simon climbed up on to a chair to look out of the little window and was able to see the altar directly below.

It was hung with green garlands and covered with a flounce in English point lace. Standing in the centre was a little square frame containing some relics and at each end there was an orange tree. Along the length of the altar there was a row of silver candlesticks and china vases containing a vivid display of sunflowers, lilies, peonies, foxgloves and bunches of hydrangea. A cascade of bright colours fell from the top of the altar down to the carpet spread out on the cobblestones beneath it. In amongst the flowers could be seen a number of other treasured ornaments: a silver-gilt sugar-bowl decorated with a ring of violets, a set of pendants cut from Alençon gemstones glittering on a little carpet of moss, two Chinese screens with painted landscapes. Loulou lay hidden beneath some roses and all that could be seen of him was the spot of blue on the top of his head, like a disc of lapis lazuli.

The churchwardens, the choristers and the children took up their places around three sides of the courtyard. The priest slowly walked up the steps and placed his great shining orb on the lace altar cloth. Everyone fell to their knees. There was a deep silence in which all that could be heard was the sound of the censers sliding on their chains as they were swung backwards and forwards.

A blue haze of incense floated up into Félicité's room. She opened her nostrils wide to breathe it in, savouring it with mystical fervour. Her eyes closed and a smile played on her lips. One by one her heartbeats became slower, growing successively weaker and fainter like a fountain running dry, an echo fading away. With her dying breath she imagined she saw a huge parrot hovering above her head as the heavens parted to receive her.

1. BOCCACCIO · *Mrs Rosie and the Priest*
2. GERARD MANLEY HOPKINS · *As kingfishers catch fire*
3. *The Saga of Gunnlaug Serpent-tongue*
4. THOMAS DE QUINCEY · *On Murder Considered as One of the Fine Arts*
5. FRIEDRICH NIETZSCHE · *Aphorisms on Love and Hate*
6. JOHN RUSKIN · *Traffic*
7. PU SONGLING · *Wailing Ghosts*
8. JONATHAN SWIFT · *A Modest Proposal*
9. *Three Tang Dynasty Poets*
10. WALT WHITMAN · *On the Beach at Night Alone*
11. KENKŌ · *A Cup of Sake Beneath the Cherry Trees*
12. BALTASAR GRACIÁN · *How to Use Your Enemies*
13. JOHN KEATS · *The Eve of St Agnes*
14. THOMAS HARDY · *Woman much missed*
15. GUY DE MAUPASSANT · *Femme Fatale*
16. MARCO POLO · *Travels in the Land of Serpents and Pearls*
17. SUETONIUS · *Caligula*
18. APOLLONIUS OF RHODES · *Jason and Medea*
19. ROBERT LOUIS STEVENSON · *Olalla*
20. KARL MARX AND FRIEDRICH ENGELS · *The Communist Manifesto*
21. PETRONIUS · *Trimalchio's Feast*
22. JOHANN PETER HEBEL · *How a Ghastly Story Was Brought to Light by a Common or Garden Butcher's Dog*
23. HANS CHRISTIAN ANDERSEN · *The Tinder Box*
24. RUDYARD KIPLING · *The Gate of the Hundred Sorrows*
25. DANTE · *Circles of Hell*
26. HENRY MAYHEW · *Of Street Piemen*
27. HAFEZ · *The nightingales are drunk*
28. GEOFFREY CHAUCER · *The Wife of Bath*
29. MICHEL DE MONTAIGNE · *How We Weep and Laugh at the Same Thing*
30. THOMAS NASHE · *The Terrors of the Night*
31. EDGAR ALLAN POE · *The Tell-Tale Heart*
32. MARY KINGSLEY · *A Hippo Banquet*
33. JANE AUSTEN · *The Beautifull Cassandra*
34. ANTON CHEKHOV · *Gooseberries*
35. SAMUEL TAYLOR COLERIDGE · *Well, they are gone, and here must I remain*
36. JOHANN WOLFGANG VON GOETHE · *Sketchy, Doubtful, Incomplete Jottings*
37. CHARLES DICKENS · *The Great Winglebury Duel*
38. HERMAN MELVILLE · *The Maldive Shark*
39. ELIZABETH GASKELL · *The Old Nurse's Story*
40. NIKOLAY LESKOV · *The Steel Flea*

41. HONORÉ DE BALZAC · *The Atheist's Mass*
42. CHARLOTTE PERKINS GILMAN · *The Yellow Wall-Paper*
43. C.P. CAVAFY · *Remember, Body . . .*
44. FYODOR DOSTOEVSKY · *The Meek One*
45. GUSTAVE FLAUBERT · *A Simple Heart*
46. NIKOLAI GOGOL · *The Nose*
47. SAMUEL PEPYS · *The Great Fire of London*
48. EDITH WHARTON · *The Reckoning*
49. HENRY JAMES · *The Figure in the Carpet*
50. WILFRED OWEN · *Anthem For Doomed Youth*
51. WOLFGANG AMADEUS MOZART · *My Dearest Father*
52. PLATO · *Socrates' Defence*
53. CHRISTINA ROSSETTI · *Goblin Market*
54. *Sindbad the Sailor*
55. SOPHOCLES · *Antigone*
56. RYŪNOSUKE AKUTAGAWA · *The Life of a Stupid Man*
57. LEO TOLSTOY · *How Much Land Does A Man Need?*
58. GIORGIO VASARI · *Leonardo da Vinci*
59. OSCAR WILDE · *Lord Arthur Savile's Crime*
60. SHEN FU · *The Old Man of the Moon*
61. AESOP · *The Dolphins, the Whales and the Gudgeon*
62. MATSUO BASHŌ · *Lips too Chilled*
63. EMILY BRONTË · *The Night is Darkening Round Me*
64. JOSEPH CONRAD · *To-morrow*
65. RICHARD HAKLUYT · *The Voyage of Sir Francis Drake Around the Whole Globe*
66. KATE CHOPIN · *A Pair of Silk Stockings*
67. CHARLES DARWIN · *It was snowing butterflies*
68. BROTHERS GRIMM · *The Robber Bridegroom*
69. CATULLUS · *I Hate and I Love*
70. HOMER · *Circe and the Cyclops*
71. D. H. LAWRENCE · *Il Duro*
72. KATHERINE MANSFIELD · *Miss Brill*
73. OVID · *The Fall of Icarus*
74. SAPPHO · *Come Close*
75. IVAN TURGENEV · *Kasyan from the Beautiful Lands*
76. VIRGIL · *O Cruel Alexis*
77. H. G. WELLS · *A Slip under the Microscope*
78. HERODOTUS · *The Madness of Cambyses*
79. *Speaking of Siva*
80. *The Dhammapada*

'Strangely enough, I mistook it for a gentleman at first. Fortunately I had my spectacles with me so I could see it was really a nose.'

NIKOLAI GOGOL
Born 1809, Poltava, Russian Empire
Died 1852, Moscow, Russian Empire

'The Nose' and 'The Carriage' were published separately in their original Russian in 1836. They are taken from *Diary of a Madman, The Government Inspector & Selected Stories*.

GOGOL IN PENGUIN CLASSICS
Dead Souls
Diary of a Madman, The Government Inspector & Selected Stories
The Night before Christmas

NIKOLAI GOGOL

The Nose

Translated by
Ronald Wilks

PENGUIN BOOKS

PENGUIN CLASSICS

UK | USA | Canada | Ireland | Australia
India | New Zealand | South Africa

Penguin Books is part of the Penguin Random House group of companies
whose addresses can be found at global.penguinrandomhouse.com.

This edition published in Penguin Classics 2015

012

Translation copyright © Ronald Wilks, 1972, revised 2005

The moral right of the translator has been asserted

Set in 9/12.4 pt Baskerville 10 Pro
Typeset by Jouve (UK), Milton Keynes
Printed and bound in Great Britain by Clays Ltd, Elcograf S.p.A.

A CIP catalogue record for this book is available from the British Library

ISBN: 978–0–141–39752–8

www.greenpenguin.co.uk

Penguin Random House is committed to a
sustainable future for our business, our readers
and our planet. This book is made from Forest
Stewardship Council® certified paper.

Contents

The Nose   1
The Carriage   37

The Nose

1

An extraordinarily strange event took place in St Petersburg on 25 March. Ivan Yakovlevich, a barber who lived on Voznesensky Prospekt (his surname has been lost and all that his shop sign shows is a gentleman with a lathered cheek and the inscription 'We also let blood'), woke up rather early one morning and smelt hot bread. Raising himself slightly on his bed he saw his wife, who was a quite respectable lady and a great coffee-drinker, taking some freshly baked rolls out of the oven.

'I don't want any coffee today, Praskovya Osipovna,' said Ivan Yakovlevich, 'I'll make do with a hot roll and onion instead.' (Here I must explain that Ivan Yakovlevich would really have liked to have had some coffee as well, but knew it was quite out of the question to expect both coffee *and* rolls, since Praskovya Osipovna did not take very kindly to these whims of his.) 'Let the old fool have his bread, I don't mind,' she thought. 'That means extra coffee for me!' And she threw a roll on to the table.

Ivan pulled his frock-coat over his nightshirt for decency's sake, sat down at the table, poured out some salt, peeled two onions, took a knife and with a determined expression on his face started cutting one of the rolls.

When he had sliced the roll in two, he peered into the middle and was amazed to see something white there. Ivan carefully picked at it with his knife, and felt it with his finger. 'Quite thick,' he said to himself. 'What on earth can it be?'

He poked two fingers in and pulled out – a nose!

Ivan Yakovlevich let his arms drop to his sides and began rubbing his eyes and feeling around in the roll again. Yes, it was a nose all right, no mistake about that. And, what's more, it seemed a very familiar nose. His face filled with horror. But this horror was nothing compared with his wife's indignation.

'You beast, whose nose is *that* you've cut off?' she cried furiously. 'You scoundrel! You drunkard! I'll report it to the police myself, I will. You thief! Come to think of it, I've heard three customers say that when they come in for a shave you start tweaking their noses about so much it's a wonder they stay on at all!'

But Ivan felt more dead than alive. He knew that the nose belonged to none other than Collegiate Assessor Kovalyov, whom he shaved on Wednesdays and Sundays.

'Wait a minute, Praskovya! I'll wrap it up in a piece of cloth and put it over there in the corner. Let's leave it there for a bit, then I'll try and get rid of it.'

'I don't want to know! Do you think I'm going to let a sawn-off nose lie around in *my* room ... you fathead! All you can do is strop that blasted razor of yours and let everything else go to pot. Layabout! Night-bird! And you expect me to cover up for you with the police! You filthy pig! Blockhead! Get that nose out of here, out! Do what you like with it, but I don't want that thing hanging around here a minute

The Nose

longer!' Ivan Yakovlevich was absolutely stunned. He thought and thought, but just didn't know what to make of it.

'I'm damned if I know what's happened!' he said at last, scratching the back of his ear. 'I can't say for certain if I came home drunk or not last night. All I know is, it's crazy. After all, bread is something you bake, but a nose is quite different. Can't make head or tail of it! . . .'

Ivan Yakovlevich lapsed into silence. The thought that the police might search the place, find the nose and afterwards bring a charge against him, very nearly sent him out of his mind. Already he could see that scarlet collar beautifully embroidered with silver, that sword . . . and he began shaking all over. Finally he put on his undergarments and boots, pulled on all that nonsense and with Praskovya Osipovna's vigorous invective ringing in his ears, wrapped the nose up in a piece of cloth and went out into the street.

All he wanted was to stuff it away somewhere, either hiding it between two curb-stones by someone's front door or else 'accidentally' dropping it and slinking off down a side-street. But as luck would have it, he kept bumping into friends, who would insist on asking: 'Where are *you* off to?' or 'It's a bit early for shaving customers, isn't it?' with the result that he didn't have a chance to get rid of it. Once he *did* manage to drop it, but a policeman pointed with his halberd and said: 'Pick that up! Can't you see you dropped something!' And Ivan Yakovlevich had to pick it up and hide it in his pocket. Despair gripped him, especially as the streets were getting more and more crowded now as the shops and stalls began to open.

He decided to make his way to St Isaac's Bridge and see if he could throw the nose into the River Neva without anyone seeing him. But here I am rather at fault for not having told you before something about Ivan Yakovlevich, who in many ways was a man worthy of respect.

Ivan Yakovlevich, like any honest Russian working man, was a terrible drunkard. And although he spent all day shaving other people's beards, his own was perpetually unshaven. His frock-coat (Ivan Yakovlevich never wore a dress-coat) could best be described as piebald: that is to say, it was black, but with brownish-yellow and grey spots all over it. His collar was very shiny, and three loosely hanging threads showed that some buttons had once been there. Ivan Yakovlevich was a great cynic, and whenever Kovalyov the collegiate assessor said 'Your hands always stink!' while he was being shaved, Ivan Yakovlevich would say: 'But why *should* they stink?' The collegiate assessor used to reply: 'Don't ask me, my dear chap. All I know is, they *stink*.' Ivan Yakovlevich would answer by taking a pinch of snuff and then, by way of retaliation, lather all over Kovalyov's cheeks, under his nose, behind the ears and beneath his beard – in short, wherever he felt like covering him with soap.

By now this respectable citizen of ours had already reached St Isaac's Bridge. First of all he had a good look round. Then he leant over the rails, trying to pretend he was looking under the bridge to see if there were many fish there, and furtively threw the packet into the water. He felt as if a couple of hundredweight had been lifted all at once from his shoulders and he even managed to produce a smile.

Instead of going off to shave civil servants' chins, he

headed for a shop bearing the sign 'Hot Meals and Tea' for a glass of punch. Suddenly he saw a policeman at one end of the bridge, looking very impressive with broad whiskers, a three-cornered hat and a sword. He went cold all over as the policeman beckoned to him and said: 'Come here, my friend!'

Recognizing the uniform, Ivan Yakovlevich took his cap off before he had taken half a dozen steps, tripped up to him and greeted him with: 'Good morning, Your Honour!'

'No, no, my dear chap, none of your "Honour". Just tell me what you were up to on the bridge?'

'Honest, officer, I was on my way to shave a customer and stopped to see how fast the current was.'

'You're lying. You really can't expect me to believe that! You'd better come clean at once!'

'I'll give Your Honour a free shave twice, even three times a week, honest I will,' answered Ivan Yakovlevich.

'No, no, my friend, that won't do. Three barbers look after me already, and it's an *honour* for them to shave me. Will you please tell me what you were up to?'

Ivan Yakovlevich turned pale ... But at this point everything became so completely enveloped in mist it is really impossible to say what happened afterwards.

2

Collegiate Assessor Kovalyov woke up rather early and made a 'brrr' noise with his lips. He always did this when he woke up, though, if you asked him why, he could not give any good reason. Kovalyov stretched himself and asked for the small mirror that stood on the table to be brought over to him. He wanted to have a look at a pimple that had made its appearance on his nose the previous evening, but to his extreme astonishment found that instead of a nose there was nothing but an absolutely flat surface! In a terrible panic Kovalyov asked for some water and rubbed his eyes with a towel. No mistake about it: his nose had gone. He began pinching himself to make sure he was not sleeping, but to all intents and purposes he was wide awake. Collegiate Assessor Kovalyov sprang out of bed and shook himself: still no nose! He asked for his clothes and off he dashed straight to the Head of Police.

In the meantime, however, a few words should be said about Kovalyov, so that the reader may see what kind of collegiate assessor this man was. You really cannot compare those collegiate assessors who acquire office through academic qualifications with the variety appointed in the Caucasus. The two species are quite distinct. Collegiate assessors with diplomas from learned bodies . . . But Russia is such an amazing country, that if you pass any remark about *one* collegiate assessor, every assessor from Riga to Kamchatka will take it personally. And the same goes for all people holding titles and government ranks. Kovalyov belonged to the Caucasian variety.

He had been a collegiate assessor for only two years and therefore could not forget it for a single minute. To make himself sound more important and to give more weight and nobility to his status he never called himself collegiate assessor, but 'Major'. If he met a woman in the street selling shirt

The Nose

fronts he would say: 'Listen dear, come and see me at home. My flat's in Sadovaya Street. All you have to do is ask if Major Kovalyov lives there and anyone will show you the way.' If he happened to meet a pretty girl he would whisper some secret instructions and then say: 'Just ask for Major Kovalyov, my dear.' Therefore, throughout this story, we will call this collegiate assessor 'Major'.

Major Kovalyov was in the habit of taking a daily stroll along Nevsky Prospekt. His shirt collar was always immaculately clean and well-starched. His whiskers were the kind you usually find among provincial surveyors, architects and regimental surgeons, as well as those who have some sort of connection with the police, with anyone in fact who has full rosy cheeks and plays a good hand at whist. These were the kind of whiskers that usually reach from the middle of the face right across to the nostrils. Major Kovalyov always carried plenty of seals with him – seals bearing coats of arms or engraved with the words: 'Wednesday, Thursday, Monday', and so on. Major Kovalyov had come to St Petersburg with the express purpose of finding a position in keeping with his rank. If he was successful, he would get a vice-governorship, but failing that, a job as an administrative clerk in some important government department would have to do. Major Kovalyov was not averse to marriage, as long as his bride happened to be worth 200,000 roubles. And now the reader can judge for himself this major's state of mind when, instead of a fairly presentable and reasonably sized nose, all he saw was an absolutely preposterous smooth flat space. As if this were not bad enough, there was not a cab in sight, and he had to walk home, keeping himself huddled up in his cloak and with a handkerchief over his face to make people think he was bleeding. 'But perhaps I dreamt it! How could I be so stupid as to go and lose my nose?' With these thoughts he dropped into a coffee-house to take a look at himself in a mirror. Fortunately the shop was empty, except for some waiters sweeping up and tidying the chairs. A few of them, rather bleary-eyed, were carrying trays laden with hot pies. Yesterday's newspapers, covered in coffee stains, lay scattered on the tables and chairs. 'Well, thank God there's no one about,' he said. 'Now I can have a look.' He approached the mirror rather gingerly and peered into it. 'Damn it! What kind of trick is this?' he cried, spitting on the floor. 'If only there were *something* to take its place, but there's nothing!'

He bit his lips in annoyance, left the coffee-house and decided not to smile or look at anyone, which was not like him at all. Suddenly he stood rooted to the spot near the front door of some house and witnessed a most incredible spectacle. A carriage drew up at the entrance porch. The doors flew open and out jumped a uniformed, stooping gentleman who dashed up the steps. The feeling of horror and amazement that gripped Kovalyov when he recognized his own nose defies description! After this extraordinary sight everything went topsy-turvy. He could hardly keep to his feet, but decided at all costs to wait until the nose returned to the carriage, although he was shaking all over and felt quite feverish.

About two minutes later a nose really did come out. It was wearing a gold-braided uniform with a high stand-up collar and chamois trousers, and had a sword at its side. From the plumes on its hat one could tell that it held the exalted rank of state counsellor. And it was abundantly clear that the nose was going to visit someone. It looked right, then left, shouted to the coachman 'Let's go!', climbed in and drove off.

Poor Kovalyov nearly went out of his mind. He did not know what to make of it. How, in fact, could a nose, which only yesterday was in the middle of his face, and which could not possibly walk around or drive in a carriage, suddenly turn up in a uniform! He ran after the carriage which fortunately did not travel very far and came to a halt outside Kazan Cathedral. Kovalyov rushed into the cathedral square, elbowed his way through a crowd of beggarwomen who always used to make him laugh because of the way they covered their faces, leaving only slits for the eyes, and made his way in. Only a few people were at prayer, all of them standing by the entrance. Kovalyov felt so distraught that he was in no condition for praying, and his eyes searched every nook and cranny for the nose in uniform. At length he spotted it standing by one of the walls to the side. The nose's face was completely hidden by the high collar and it was praying with an expression of profound piety.

'What's the best way of approaching it?' thought Kovalyov. 'Judging by its uniform, its hat, and its whole appearance, it must be a state counsellor. But I'm damned if I know how to go about it!'

He tried to attract its attention by coughing, but the nose did not interrupt its devotions for one second and continued to perform low bows.

'My dear sir,' Kovalyov said, summoning up his courage, 'my dear sir . . .'

'What do you want?' replied the nose, turning round.

'I don't know how best to put it, sir, but it strikes me as very peculiar . . . Don't you know where you belong? And where do I find you? In church, of all places! I'm sure you'll agree that . . .'

'Please forgive me, but would you mind telling me what you're talking about? . . . Explain yourself.'

'How can I make myself clear?' Kovalyov wondered. Nerving himself once more he said: 'Of course, I am, as it happens, a major. You will agree that it's not done for someone in my position to walk around minus a nose. It's all right for some old woman selling peeled oranges on the Voskresensky Bridge to sit there without one. But as I'm hoping to be promoted soon . . . Besides, as I'm acquainted with several highly placed ladies: Madame Chekhtaryev, for example, a state counsellor's wife and others . . . you can judge for yourself . . . I really don't know what to say, my dear sir . . .' (He shrugged his shoulders as he said this.) 'If one considers this from the point of view of duty and honour . . . then you yourself will understand.'

'I don't understand a thing,' the nose replied. 'Please make yourself clear.'

'My dear sir,' continued Kovalyov in a smug voice, 'I really don't know what you mean by that. It's plain enough for anyone to see . . . Unless you want . . . Don't you realize you are *my own nose!*'

The nose looked at the major and frowned a little.

'My dear fellow, you are mistaken. I am a person in my own right. Furthermore, I don't see that we can have any-

The Nose

thing in common. Judging from your uniform buttons, I should say you're from another government department.'

With these words the nose turned away and continued its prayers.

Kovalyov was so confused he did not know what to do or think. At that moment he heard the pleasant rustle of a woman's dress, and an elderly lady, bedecked with lace, came by, accompanied by a slim girl wearing a white dress, which showed her shapely figure to very good advantage, and a pale yellow hat as light as pastry. A tall footman, with enormous whiskers and what seemed to be a dozen collars, stationed himself behind them and opened his snuff-box. Kovalyov went closer, pulled the linen collar of his shirt front up high, straightened the seals hanging on his gold watch chain and, smiling all over his face, turned his attention to the slim girl, who bent over to pray like a spring flower and kept lifting her little white hand with its almost transparent fingers to her forehead.

The smile on Kovalyov's face grew even more expansive when he saw, beneath her hat, a little rounded chin of dazzling white, and cheeks flushed with the colour of the first rose of spring.

But suddenly he jumped backwards as though he had been burnt: he remembered that instead of a nose he had absolutely nothing, and tears streamed from his eyes. He swung round to tell the nose in uniform straight out that it was only masquerading as a state counsellor, that it was an impostor and a scoundrel, and really nothing else than his own private property, *his* nose . . . But the nose had already gone: it had managed to slip off unseen, probably to pay somebody a visit.

This reduced Kovalyov to utter despair. He went out, and stood for a minute or so under the colonnade, carefully looking around him in the hope of spotting the nose. He remembered quite distinctly that it was wearing a plumed hat and a gold-embroidered uniform. But he had not noticed what its greatcoat was like, or the colour of its carriage, or its horses, or even if there was a liveried footman at the back. What's more, there were so many carriages careering to and fro, so fast, that it was practically impossible to recognize any of them, and even if he could, there was no way of making them stop.

It was a beautiful sunny day. Nevsky Prospekt was packed. From the Police Headquarters right down to the Anichkov Bridge a whole floral cascade of ladies flowed along the pavements. Not far off he could see that court counsellor whom he referred to as lieutenant-colonel, especially if there happened to be other people around. And over there was Yarygin, a head clerk in the Senate, and a very close friend of his who always lost at whist when he played in a party of eight. Another major, a collegiate assessor, of the Caucasian variety, waved to him to come over and have a chat.

'Blast and damn!' said Kovalyov, hailing a droshky. 'Driver, take me straight to the Chief of Police.'

He climbed into the droshky and shouted: 'Drive like the devil!'

'Is the Police Commissioner in?' he said as soon as he entered the hall.

'No, he's not, sir,' said the porter. 'He left only a few minutes ago.'

'This really *is* my day.'

'Yes,' added the porter, 'you've only just missed him. A minute ago you'd have caught him.'

Kovalyov, his handkerchief still pressed to his face, climbed into the droshky again and cried out in a despairing voice: 'Let's go!'

'Where?' asked the driver.

'Straight on!'

'Straight on? But it's a dead end here – you can only go right or left.'

This last question made Kovalyov stop and think. In his position the best thing to do was to go first to the City Security Office, not because it was directly connected with the police, but because things got done there much quicker than in any other government department. There was no sense in going for satisfaction direct to the head of the department where the nose claimed to work since anyone could see from the answers he had got before that the nose considered nothing holy and was just as capable now of lying as it had done before, claiming never to have set eyes on him.

So just as Kovalyov was about to tell the driver to go straight to the Security Office, it again struck him that the scoundrel and impostor who had behaved so shamelessly at their first encounter could quite easily take advantage of the delay and slip out of the city, in which event all his efforts to find it would be futile and might even drag on for another month, God forbid. Finally inspiration came from above.

He decided to go straight to the newspaper offices and publish an advertisement, giving such a detailed description of the nose that anyone who happened to meet it would at once turn it over to Kovalyov, or at least tell him where he could find it. Deciding this was the best course of action, he ordered the driver to go straight to the newspaper offices and throughout the whole journey never once stopped pummelling the driver in the back with his fist and shouting: 'Faster, damn you, faster!'

'But sir . . .' the driver retorted as he shook his head and flicked his reins at his horse, which had a coat as long as a spaniel's. Finally the droshky came to a halt and the breathless Kovalyov tore into a small waiting-room where a grey-haired bespectacled clerk in an old frock-coat was sitting at a table with his pen between his teeth, counting out copper coins.

'Who sees to advertisements here?' Kovalyov shouted. 'Ah, good morning.'

'Good morning,' replied the grey-haired clerk, raising his eyes for one second, then looking down again at the little piles of money spread out on the table.

'I want to publish an advertisement.'

'Just one moment, if you don't mind,' the clerk answered, as he wrote down a figure with one hand and moved two beads on his abacus with the other.

A footman who, judging by his gold-braided livery and generally very smart appearance, obviously worked in some noble house, was standing by the table holding a piece of paper and, considering it the right thing to display a certain degree of bonhomie, started rattling away:

The Nose

'Believe me, sir, that nasty little dog just isn't worth eighty copecks. I mean, I wouldn't even give eight for it. But the Countess adores it, just dotes on it she does, and she'll give anyone who finds it a reward of a hundred roubles! If we're going to be honest with one another, I'll tell you quite openly, there's no accounting for taste. I can understand a fancier paying anything up to five hundred, even a thousand for a deerhound or a poodle, as long as it's a good dog.'

The worthy clerk listened to him solemnly while he carried on totting up the words in the advertisement. The room was crowded with old women, salesmen and house-porters, all holding advertisements. In one of these a coachman of 'sober disposition' was seeking employment; in another a carriage, hardly used, and brought from Paris in 1814, was up for sale; in another a nineteen-year-old servant girl, with laundry experience, and prepared to do *other* work, was looking for a job. Other advertisements offered a droshky for sale – in good condition apart from one missing spring; a 'young' and spirited dapple-grey colt seventeen years old; radish and turnip seeds only just arrived from London; a country house, with every modern convenience, including stabling for two horses and enough land for planting an excellent birch or fir forest. And one invited prospective buyers of old boot soles to attend certain auction rooms between the hours of eight and three daily. The room into which all these people were crammed was small and extremely stuffy. But Collegiate Assessor Kovalyov could not smell anything as he had covered his face with a handkerchief – and he could not have smelt anything anyway, as his nose had disappeared God knows where.

'My dear sir, if I may request your . . . it's really most urgent,' he said, beginning to lose patience.

'Just a minute, if you *don't* mind! Two roubles forty-three copecks. Nearly ready. One rouble sixty-four copecks,' the grey-haired clerk muttered as he shoved pieces of paper at the old ladies and servants standing around. Finally he turned to Kovalyov and said: 'What do you want?'

'I want . . .' Kovalyov began. 'Something very fishy's been going on, whether it's some nasty practical joke or a plain case of fraud I can't say as yet. All I want you to do is to offer a substantial reward for the first person to find the blackguard . . .'

'May I inquire as to your name, sir?'

'Why do you need that? I can't tell you. Too many people know me – Mrs Chekhtaryev, for example, who's married to a state counsellor, Mrs Palageya Podtochin, a staff officer's wife . . . they'd find out who it was at once, God forbid! Just put "Collegiate Assessor", or even better, "Gentleman holding the rank of major".'

'And the missing person was a household serf of yours?'

'Household serf? The crime wouldn't be half as serious! It's my *nose* that's disappeared God knows where.'

'Hm, strange name. And did this Mr Nose steal much?'

'*My* nose, I'm trying to say. You don't understand! It's my own nose that's disappeared. It's a diabolical practical joke someone's played on me.'

'How did it disappear? I don't follow.'

'I can't tell you how. But please understand, my nose is driving at this very moment all over town, calling itself a state counsellor. That's why I'm asking you to print this advertisement announcing the first person who catches it should return the nose to its rightful owner as soon as possible. Imagine what it's like being without such a conspicuous part of your anatomy! If it were just a small toe, then I could put my shoe on and no one would be any the wiser. On Thursdays I go to Mrs Chekhtaryev's (she's married to a state counsellor) and Mrs Podtochin, who has a staff officer for a husband – and a very pretty little daughter as well. Also, they're all very close friends of mine, so just imagine what it would be like . . . In *my* state I can't possibly visit any of them.'

The clerk's tightly pressed lips showed he was deep in thought. 'I can't print an advertisement like that in our paper,' he said after a long silence.

'What? Why not?'

'I'll tell you. A paper can get a bad name. If everyone started announcing his nose had run away, I don't know how it would all end. And enough false reports and rumours get past editorial already . . .'

'But why does it strike you as so absurd? *I* certainly don't think so.'

'That's what *you* think. But only last week there was a similar case. A clerk came here with an advertisement, just like you. It cost him two roubles seventy-three copecks, and all he wanted to advertise was a runaway black poodle. And what do you think he was up to really? In the end we had a libel case on our hands: the poodle was meant as a satire on a government cashier – I can't remember what ministry he came from.'

'But I want to publish an advertisement about my nose, not a poodle, and that's as near myself as dammit!'

'No, I can't accept that kind of advertisement.'

'But I've lost my *nose*!'

'Then you'd better see a doctor about it. I've heard there's a certain kind of specialist who can fix you up with any kind of nose you like. Anyway, you seem the cheery sort, and I can see you like to have your little joke.'

'By all that's holy, I swear I'm telling you the truth. If you really want me to, I'll *show* you what I mean.'

'I shouldn't bother if I were you,' the clerk continued, taking a pinch of snuff. 'However, if it's *really* no trouble,' he added, leaning forward out of curiosity, 'then I shouldn't mind having a quick look.'

The collegiate assessor removed his handkerchief.

'Well, how very peculiar! It's quite flat, just like a freshly cooked pancake. Incredibly flat.'

'So much for your objections! Now you've seen it with your own eyes and you can't possibly refuse. I will be particularly grateful for this little favour, and I'm delighted that this incident has afforded me the pleasure of making your acquaintance.'

The major, evidently, had decided that a little toadying might do the trick.

'Of course, it's no problem *printing* the advertisement,' the clerk said. 'But I can't see what you can stand to gain by it. If you like, why not give it to someone with a flair for journalism, then he can write it up as a very rare freak of nature and have it published as an article in the *Northern Bee* (here he took another pinch of snuff) so that young people might benefit from it (here he wiped his nose). Or else, as something of interest to the general public.'

The Nose

The collegiate assessor's hopes were completely dashed. He looked down at the bottom of the page at the theatre guide. The name of a rather pretty actress almost brought a smile to his face, and he reached down to his pocket to see if he had a five-rouble note, since in his opinion staff officers should sit only in the stalls. But then he remembered his nose, and knew he could not possibly think of going to the theatre.

Apparently even the clerk was touched by Kovalyov's terrible predicament and thought it would not hurt to cheer him up with a few words of sympathy.

'I deeply regret that such a strange thing has happened to you. Would you care for a pinch of snuff? It's very good for headaches – and puts fresh heart into you. It's even good for piles.'

With these words he offered Kovalyov his snuff-box, deftly flipping back the lid which bore a portrait of some lady in a hat.

This unintentionally thoughtless action made Kovalyov lose patience altogether.

'I don't understand how you can joke at a time like this,' he said angrily. 'Are you so blind you can't see that I've nothing to smell with? To hell with your snuff! I can't bear to look at it, and anyway you might at least offer me some real French rappee, not that filthy Berezinsky brand.'

After this declaration he strode furiously out of the newspaper office and went off to the local Inspector of Police (a fanatical lover of sugar whose hall and dining room were crammed full of sugar cubes presented by merchants who wanted to keep well in with him). At that moment the cook was removing the Inspector's regulation jackboots. His sword and all his military trappings were hanging peacefully in the corner and his three-year-old son was already fingering his awesome tricorn. And he himself, after a warrior's life of martial exploits, was now preparing to savour the pleasures of peace. Kovalyov arrived just when he was having a good stretch, grunting, and saying, 'Now for a nice two hours' nap.' Our collegiate assessor had clearly chosen a very bad time for his visit.

The Inspector was a great patron of the arts and industry, but most of all he loved government banknotes. 'There's nothing finer than banknotes,' he used to say. 'They don't need feeding, take up very little room and slip nicely into the pocket. And they don't break if you drop them.'

The Inspector gave Kovalyov a rather cold welcome and said that after dinner wasn't at all the time to start investigations, that Nature herself had decreed a rest after meals (from this our collegiate assessor concluded the Inspector was well versed in the wisdom of antiquity), that *respectable* men do not get their noses ripped off, and that there were no end of majors knocking around who were not too fussy about their underwear and who were in the habit of visiting the most disreputable places.

These few home truths stung Kovalyov to the quick. Here I must point out that Kovalyov was an extremely sensitive man. He did not so much mind people making personal remarks about him, but it was a different matter when aspersions were cast on his rank or social standing.

As far as he was concerned they could say what they liked

The Nose

about subalterns on the stage, but staff officers should be exempt from attack.

The reception given him by the Inspector startled him so much that he shook his head, threw out his arms and said in a dignified voice, 'To be frank, after these remarks of yours, which I find very offensive, I have nothing more to say . . .' and walked out. He arrived home hardly able to feel his feet beneath him. It was already getting dark. After his fruitless inquiries his flat seemed extremely dismal and depressing. As he entered the hall he saw his footman Ivan lying on a soiled leather couch spitting at the ceiling, managing to hit the same spot with a fair degree of success. The nonchalance of the man infuriated him and Kovalyov hit him across the forehead with his hat and said: 'You fat pig! Haven't you anything better to do!'

Ivan promptly jumped up and rushed to take off Kovalyov's coat. Tired and depressed, the major went to his room, threw himself into an armchair and after a few sighs said:

'My God, my God! What have I done to deserve this? If I'd lost an arm or a leg it wouldn't be so bad. Even without any *ears* things wouldn't be very pleasant, but it wouldn't be the end of the world. A man without a nose, though, is God knows what, neither fish nor fowl. Just something to be thrown out of the window. If my nose had been lopped off during the war, or in a duel, at least I might have had some say in the matter. But to lose it for no reason at all and with nothing to show for it, not even a copeck! No, it's absolutely impossible . . . It can't have gone just like that! Never! Must have been a dream, or perhaps I drank some of that vodka

I use for rubbing down my beard after shaving instead of water: that idiot Ivan couldn't have put it away and I must have picked it up by mistake.'

To convince himself that he was not in fact drunk the major pinched himself so hard that he cried out in pain, which really did convince him he was awake and in full possession of his senses. He stealthily crept over to the mirror and screwed up his eyes in the hope that his nose would reappear in its proper place, but at once he jumped back, exclaiming:

'That ridiculous blank space again!'

It was absolutely incomprehensible. If a button, or a silver spoon, or his watch, or something of that sort had been missing, that would have been understandable. But for his *nose* to disappear from his own flat ... Major Kovalyov weighed up all the evidence and decided that the most likely explanation of all was that Mrs Podtochin, the staff officer's wife, who wanted to marry off her daughter to him, was to blame, and no one else. In fact he liked chasing after her, but never came to proposing. And when the staff officer's wife told him straight out that she was offering him her daughter's hand, he politely withdrew, excusing himself on the grounds that he was still a young man, and that he wanted to devote another five years to the service, by which time he would be just forty-two. So, to get her revenge, the staff officer's wife must have decided to ruin him and for that purpose had hired some old witches – it was quite inconceivable that his nose had been cut off – no one had visited him in his flat, his barber Ivan Yakovlevich had shaved him only last Wednesday, and the rest of that day and the whole of Thursday his nose had been intact. All this he remembered quite clearly. Moreover, he would have been in pain and the wound could not have healed as flat as a pancake in such a short time. He began planning what to do: either he would sue the staff officer's wife for damages, or he would go and see her personally and accuse her point blank.

But he was distracted from these thoughts by the sight of some chinks of light in the door, which meant Ivan had lit a candle in the hall. Soon afterwards Ivan appeared in person, holding the candle in front of him, so that it brightened up the whole room. Kovalyov's first reaction was to seize his handkerchief and cover up the bare place where only yesterday his nose had been, to stop that stupid man gaping at his master's weird appearance. No sooner had Ivan gone back to his cubby-hole than a strange voice was heard in the hall:

'Does Collegiate Assessor Kovalyov live here?'

'Please come in. The major's home,' said Kovalyov, springing to his feet and opening the door.

A smart-looking police officer, with plump cheeks and whiskers that were neither too light nor too dark – the same police officer who had stood on St Isaac's Bridge at the beginning of our story – made his entrance.

'Are you the gentleman who has lost his nose?'

'Yes, that's me.'

'It's been found.'

'What did you say?' cried Major Kovalyov. He could hardly speak for joy. He looked wide-eyed at the police officer, the candle-light flickering on his fat cheeks and thick lips.

'How did you find it?'

'Very strange. We intercepted it just as it was boarding the stagecoach bound for Riga. Its passport was made out in the name of some civil servant. Strangely enough, I mistook it for a gentleman at first. Fortunately I had my spectacles with me so I could see it was really a nose. I'm very short-sighted, and if you happen to stand just in front of me, I can only make out your face, but not your nose, or beard, or anything else in fact. My mother-in-law (that's to say, on my *wife's* side) suffers from the same complaint.'

Kovalyov was beside himself.

'Where is it? I'll go right away to claim it.'

'Don't excite yourself, sir. I knew how much you wanted it back, so I've brought it with me. Very strange, but the main culprit in this little affair seems to be that swindler of a barber from Voznesensky Street: he's down at the station now. I've had my eyes on him a long time now on suspicion of drunkenness and larceny, and only the day before yesterday he was found stealing a dozen buttons from a shop. You'll find your nose just as it was when you lost it.'

And the police officer dipped into his pocket and pulled out the nose wrapped up in a piece of paper.

'That's it!' cried Kovalyov, 'no mistake! You *must* stay and have a cup of tea with me.'

'That would give me great pleasure, but I just couldn't. From here I have to go direct to the House of Correction . . . The price of food has rocketed . . . My mother-in-law (on my *wife's* side) is living with me, and all the children as well; the eldest boy seems very promising, very bright, but we haven't the money to send him to school . . .'

Kovalyov guessed what he was after and took a note from

the table and pressed it into the officer's hands. The police officer bowed very low and went out into the street, and almost simultaneously Kovalyov could hear him telling some stupid peasant who had driven his cart up on the pavement what he thought of him.

When the police officer had gone, our collegiate assessor felt rather bemused and only after a few minutes did he come to his senses at all, so intense and unexpected was the joy he felt. He carefully took the nose in his cupped hands and once more subjected it to close scrutiny.

'Yes, that's it, that's it!' Major Kovalyov said, 'and there's the pimple that came up yesterday on the left-hand side.' The major almost laughed with joy.

But nothing is lasting in this world. Even joy begins to fade after only one minute. Two minutes later, and it is weaker still, until finally it is swallowed up in our everyday, prosaic state of mind, just as a ripple made by a pebble gradually merges with the smooth surface of the water. After some thought Kovalyov concluded that all was not right: yes – the nose had been found but there still remained the problem of putting it back in place.

'What if it doesn't stick?'

And this question which he now asked himself made the major turn pale.

With a feeling of inexpressible horror he rushed to the table, and pulled the mirror nearer, as he was afraid that he might stick the nose on crooked. His hands trembled. With great care and caution he pushed it into place. But oh! the nose just would not stick. He warmed it a little by pressing it to his mouth and breathing on it, and then pressed it again to the smooth space between his cheeks. But try as he might the nose would not stay on.

'Come on now – stay on, you fool!' he said. But the nose seemed to be made of wood and fell on to the table with a strange cork-like sound. The major's face quivered convulsively. 'Perhaps I can graft it,' he said apprehensively. But no matter how many times he tried to put it back, all his efforts were futile.

He called Ivan and told him to fetch the doctor, who happened to live in the same block, in the best flat, on the first floor.

This doctor was a handsome man with fine whiskers as black as pitch, and a fresh-looking, healthy wife. Every morning he used to eat apples and was terribly meticulous about keeping his mouth clean, spending at least three quarters of an hour rinsing it out every day and using five different varieties of toothbrush to polish his teeth. He came right away. When he had asked the major if he had had this trouble for very long the doctor lifted Major Kovalyov's head by the chin and prodded him with his thumb in the spot once occupied by his nose – so sharply that the major hit the wall very hard with the back of his head. The doctor told him not to worry and made him stand a little way from the wall and lean his head first to the right. Pinching the place where his nose had been the doctor said 'Hm!' Then he ordered him to move his head to the left and produced another 'Hm!' Finally he prodded him again, making Kovalyov's head twitch like a horse having its teeth inspected.

After this examination the doctor shook his head and said:

'It's no good. It's best to stay as you are, otherwise you'll only make it worse. Of course, it's possible to have it stuck on, and I could do this for you quite easily. But I assure you it would look terrible.'

'That's *marvellous*, that is! How can I carry on without a nose?' said Kovalyov. 'Things can't get any worse! The devil knows what's going on! How can I go around looking like a freak? I mix with nice people. I'm expected at two soirées today. I know nearly all the best people – Mrs Chekhtaryev, a state counsellor's wife, Mrs Podtochin, a staff officer's wife . . . after the way *she's* behaved I won't have any more to do with *her*, except when I get the police on her trail.' Kovalyov went on pleading: 'Please do me this one favour – isn't there *any* way? Even if you only get it to hold on, it wouldn't be so bad, and if there were any risk of it falling off, I could keep it there with my hand. I don't dance, which is a help, because any violent movement might make it drop off. And you may rest assured I wouldn't be slow in showing my appreciation – as far as my pocket will allow of course . . .'

The doctor then said in a voice which could not be called loud, or even soft, but persuasive and arresting: 'I never practise my art from purely mercenary motives. That is contrary to my code of conduct and all professional ethics. True, I make a charge for private visits, but only so as not to offend patients by refusing to take their money. Of course, I could put your nose back if I wanted to. But I give you my word of honour, if you know what's good for you, it would be far worse if I tried. Let nature take its course. Wash the area as much as you can with cold water and believe me you'll feel just as good as when you had a nose. Now, as far as the nose is concerned, put it in a jar of alcohol; better still, soak it in two tablespoonsful of sour vodka and warmed-up vinegar, and you'll get good money for it. I'll take it myself if you don't want it.'

'No! I wouldn't sell it for anything,' Kovalyov cried desperately. 'I'd rather lose it again.'

'Then I'm sorry,' replied the doctor, bowing himself out. 'I wanted to help you . . . at least I've tried hard enough.'

With these words the doctor made a very dignified exit. Kovalyov did not even look at his face, and felt so dazed that all he could make out were the doctor's snowy-white cuffs sticking out from the sleeves of his black dress-coat.

The very next day he decided – before going to the police – to write to the staff officer's wife to ask her to put back in its proper place what belonged to him, without further ado. The letter read as follows:

Dear Mrs Alexandra Grigoryevna,

I cannot understand this strange behaviour on your part. You can be sure, though, that it won't get you anywhere and you certainly won't force me to marry your daughter. Moreover, you can rest assured that, regarding my nose, I am familiar with the whole history of this affair from the very beginning, and I also know that you, and no one else, are the prime instigator. Its sudden detachment from its rightful place, its subsequent flight, its masquerading as a civil servant and then its reappearance in its natural state, are nothing else than the result of black magic carried out by yourself or by those practising the same very honourable art. I consider it my duty to warn you that if

The Nose

the above-mentioned nose is not back in its proper place by today, then I shall be compelled to ask for the law's protection.

I remain, dear Madam,

               Your very faithful servant,

                      Platon Kovalyov.

Dear Mr Kovalyov!

I was simply staggered by your letter. To be honest, I never expected anything of this kind from you, particularly those remarks which are quite uncalled-for. I would have you know I have never received that civil servant mentioned by you in my house, whether disguised or not. True, Philip Ivanovich Potanchikov used to call. Although he wanted to ask for my daughter's hand, and despite the fact that he was a very sober, respectable and learned gentleman, I never gave him any cause for hope. And then you go on to mention your nose. If by this you mean to say I wanted to make you look foolish, that is, to put you off with a formal refusal, then all I can say is that I am very surprised that you can talk like this, as you know well enough my feelings on the matter are quite different. And if you care to make an official proposal to my daughter, I will gladly give my consent, for this has always been my dearest wish, and in this hope I am always at your disposal.

               Yours sincerely,

                      Alexandra Podtochin.

'No,' said Kovalyov when he had read the letter. 'She's not to blame. Impossible! A guilty person could never write a letter like that.' The collegiate assessor knew what he was talking about in this case as he had been sent to the Caucasus several times to carry out legal inquiries. 'How on earth did this happen then? It's impossible to make head or tail of it!' he said, letting his arms drop to his side.

Meanwhile rumours about the strange occurrence had spread throughout the capital, not, need we say, without a few embellishments. At the time everyone seemed very preoccupied with the supernatural: only a short time before, some experiments in magnetism had been all the rage. Besides, the story of the dancing chairs in Konyushenny Street was still fresh in people's minds, so no one was particularly surprised to hear about Collegiate Assessor Kovalyov's nose taking a regular stroll along Nevsky Prospekt at exactly three o'clock every afternoon. Every day crowds of inquisitive people flocked there. Someone said they had seen the nose in Junker's Store and this produced such a crush outside that the police had to be called.

One fairly respectable-looking, bewhiskered entrepreneur, who sold stale cakes outside the theatre, knocked together some handsome, solid-looking wooden benches, and hired them out at eighty copecks a time for the curious to stand on.

One retired colonel left home especially early one morning and after a great struggle managed to barge his way through to the front. But to his great annoyance, instead of a nose in the shop window, all he could see was an ordinary woollen jersey and a lithograph showing a girl adjusting her stocking while a dandy with a small beard and cutaway waistcoat peered out at her from behind a tree – a picture which had hung there in that identical spot for more than ten years. He left feeling very cross and was heard to say: 'Misleading the public with such ridiculous and far-fetched stories shouldn't be allowed.'

Afterwards it was rumoured that Major Kovalyov's nose was no longer to be seen strolling along Nevsky Prospekt but was in the habit of walking in Tavrichesky Park and that it had been doing this for some time. When Khozrev-Mirza lived there, he was astonished at this freak of nature. Some of the students from the College of Surgeons went to have a look. One well-known, very respectable lady wrote specially to the head park-keeper, asking him to show her children this very rare phenomenon and, if possible, give them an instructive and edifying commentary at the same time.

These events came as a blessing to those socialites (indispensable for any successful party) who loved amusing the ladies and whose stock of stories was completely exhausted at the time.

A few respectable and high-minded citizens were very upset. One indignant gentleman said that he was at a loss to understand how such absurd cock-and-bull stories could gain currency in the present enlightened century, and that the complete indifference shown by the authorities was past comprehension. Clearly this gentleman was the type who likes to make the government responsible for everything, even their daily quarrels with their wives. And afterwards ... but there again the whole incident becomes enveloped in mist and what happened later remains a complete mystery.

3

This world is full of the most outrageous nonsense. Sometimes things happen which you would hardly think possible: that very same nose, which had paraded itself as a state counsellor and created such an uproar in the city, suddenly turned up, as if nothing had happened, in its rightful place, that is, between Major Kovalyov's two cheeks. This was on 7 April. He woke up and happened to glance at the mirror – there was his nose! He grabbed it with his hand to make sure – but there was no doubt this time. 'Aha!' cried Kovalyov, and if Ivan hadn't come in at that very moment, he would have joyfully danced a trepak round the room in his bare feet.

He ordered some soap and water to be brought right away, and as he washed himself looked into the mirror again: the nose was there. He had another look as he dried himself – yes, the nose was still there!

'Look, Ivan, I think I've got a pimple on my nose.'

Kovalyov thought: 'God, supposing he replies: "Not only is there no pimple, but no nose either!"' But Ivan answered: 'Your nose is quite all right, sir, I can't see any pimple.'

'Thank God for that,' the major said to himself and clicked his fingers.

At this moment Ivan Yakovlevich the barber poked his head round the corner, but timidly this time, like a cat which had just been beaten for stealing fat.

'Before you start, are your hands clean?' Kovalyov shouted from the other side of the room.

'Perfectly clean.'

'You're lying.'

'On my life, sir, they're clean!'

'Well, they'd better be!'

Kovalyov sat down. Ivan Yakovlevich covered him with a towel and in a twinkling, with the help of his shaving brush, had transformed his whole beard and part of his cheeks into the kind of cream served up at merchants' birthday parties.

'Well, I'll be damned,' Ivan Yakovlevich muttered to himself, staring at the nose. He bent Kovalyov's head to one side and looked at him from a different angle. 'That's *it* all right! You'd never credit it . . .' he continued and contemplated the nose for a long time. Finally, ever so gently, with a delicacy that the reader can best imagine, he lifted two fingers to hold the nose by its tip. This was how Ivan Yakovlevich normally shaved his customers.

'Come on now, and mind what you're doing!' shouted Kovalyov. Ivan Yakovlevich let his arms fall to his side and stood there more frightened and embarrassed than he had ever been in his life. At last he started tickling Kovalyov carefully under the chin with his razor. And although with only his olfactory organ to hold on to without any other means of support made shaving very awkward, by planting his rough, wrinkled thumb on his cheek and lower gum (in this way gaining some sort of leverage) he finally succeeded in overcoming all obstacles.

When everything was ready, Kovalyov rushed to get dressed and took a cab straight to the café. He had hardly got inside before he shouted, 'Waiter, a cup of chocolate,' and went straight up to the mirror. Yes, his nose was there!

Gaily he turned round, screwed up his eyes and looked superciliously at two soldiers, one of whom had a nose no bigger than a *waistcoat* button. Then he went off to the ministerial department where he was petitioning for a vice-governorship. (Failing this he was going to try for an administrative post.) As he crossed the entrance hall he had another look in the mirror: his nose was still there!

Then he went to see another collegiate assessor (or major), a great wag whose sly digs Kovalyov used to counter by saying: 'I'm used to your quips by now, you old niggler!'

On the way he thought: 'If the major doesn't split his sides when he sees me, that's a sure sign everything is in its proper place.' But the collegiate assessor did not pass any remarks. 'That's all right then, dammit!' thought Kovalyov. In the street he met Mrs Podtochin, the staff officer's wife, who was with her daughter, and they replied to his bow with delighted exclamations: clearly, he had suffered no lasting injury. He had a long chat with them, made a point of taking out his snuff-box, and stood there for ages ostentatiously stuffing both nostrils as he murmured to himself: 'That'll teach you, you old hens! And I'm not going to marry your daughter, simply *par amour*, as they say! If you *don't* mind!'

And from that time onwards Major Kovalyov was able to stroll along Nevsky Prospekt, visit the theatre, in fact go everywhere as though absolutely nothing had happened. And, as though absolutely nothing *had* happened, his nose stayed in the middle of his face and showed no signs of absenting itself. After that he was in perpetual high spirits, always smiling, chasing all the pretty girls, and on one occasion even stopping at a small shop in the Gostiny Dvor to buy ribbon for some medal, no one knows why, as he did not belong to any order of knighthood.

And all this took place in the northern capital of our vast empire! Only now, after much reflection, can we see that there is a great deal that is very far-fetched in this story. Apart from the fact that it's *highly* unlikely for a nose to disappear in such a fantastic way and then reappear in various parts of the town dressed as a state counsellor, it is hard to believe that Kovalyov was so ignorant as to think newspapers would accept advertisements about noses. I'm not saying I consider such an advertisement too expensive and a waste of money: that's nonsense, and what's more, I don't think I'm a mercenary person. But it's all very nasty, not quite the thing at all, and it makes me feel very awkward! And, come to think of it, how *did* the nose manage to turn up in a loaf of bread, and how *did* Ivan Yakovlevich . . .? No, I don't understand it, not one bit! But the strangest, most incredible thing of all is that authors should write about such things. That, I confess, is beyond my comprehension. It's just . . . no, no, I don't understand it at all! Firstly, it's no use to the country whatsoever; secondly – but even then it's no use either . . . I simply don't know *what* one can make of it . . . However, when all is said and done, one can concede this point or the other and perhaps you can even find . . . well then you won't find much that *isn't* on the absurd side *somewhere*, will you?

And yet, if you stop to think for a moment, there's a grain of truth in it. Whatever you may say, these things do happen in this world – rarely, I admit, but they do happen.

The Carriage

The little town of B— brightened up considerably when the *** cavalry regiment set up quarters there. Before then life had been terribly dull. If you happened to be passing through and took one look at those squat little adobe houses peering out into the street with an incredibly sour expression – well, words cannot describe the oppressive feeling that came over you! It was as if you had lost at cards or blurted out something silly and inappropriate: in short, really depressing. The plaster on the houses has peeled off with the rain and walls that once were white have turned piebald and blotchy. Most of the roofs are thatched with reeds, as is usual in our southern towns. To improve the general aspect of the place, the mayor had long ago ordered the little gardens to be cut down. Rarely do you meet anyone in the street – perhaps a cockerel might venture across the road that becomes as soft as pillows when the least drop of rain turns the inch-deep dust into mud. And then the streets of the little town of B— are filled with those portly beasts called 'Frenchies' by the mayor. Thrusting their proud snouts into the air out of their 'baths', they emit such deafening grunts that the traveller can only whip on his horses as hard as he can. However, you would be hard put to find any travellers at all in the town of B—; only very rarely some squire owning eleven serfs and clad in his nankeen frock-coat clatters along the road in a contraption that is a cross between a brichka and a cart, peeping out from piles of flour sacks and lashing his bay mare with her following foal. Even the market-place has a rather forlorn look. The tailor's house has been built very stupidly, with one corner to the street, so that it does not face it squarely. Opposite, some brick edifice with two windows has been under construction for the past fifteen years. Further on, and standing by itself, is a stylish wooden fence, painted grey to match the mud and erected by the major as a model for other projects in his younger days, before he acquired the habit of taking a nap immediately after dinner and drinking – as a nightcap – some peculiar decoction distilled from dried gooseberries. Elsewhere there were only plain wattle fences.

In the middle of the square are the tiniest stalls, where you are sure to see a bundle of bread-rings, a market-woman in a red kerchief, thirty-six pounds of soap, a few pounds of bitter almonds, grapeshot for the huntsman, a roll of demi-cotton and two shop boys playing pitch and toss all day in front of them. But the moment the cavalry regiment was stationed in the little town of B— everything changed. The streets were filled with life and colour – in fact, they were completely transformed. Those squat little houses would often witness a sprightly, well-turned-out officer passing by in his plumed hat, on his way to chat about promotion, or the best tobacco with a friend – and occasionally to play cards for what might justifiably be called the 'regimental' droshky since, without ever leaving the regiment, it went the rounds of all the officers: one day the major would be bowling along in it, the next it would turn up in the lieutenant's

The Carriage

stables and a week later – lo and behold! – the major's batman would be greasing its axles again.

The wooden fence between the houses was always festooned with soldiers' forage caps hanging in the sun; a grey overcoat was invariably draped over a gate somewhere. In the side-streets one would see soldiers with moustaches that bristled like boot brushes. These moustaches were everywhere in view. If the women of the town gathered at the market with their jugs, a moustache was always to be glimpsed behind their shoulders. By the town scaffold one could always see a mustachioed soldier reprimanding some country bumpkin who would only grunt and goggle by way of reply. The officers revitalized local society, which until then had consisted only of the judge, who shared lodgings with a deacon's widow, and the mayor, who, being a very sensible man, was apt to spend all day sleeping from lunch to dinner, from dinner to lunch. Social life expanded and became more interesting when the brigadier general was transferred to the town. Local squires whose existence no one would have suspected before took to visiting the town more frequently, calling on the officers – sometimes for a game of whist, of which they had a very hazy notion, so lumbered were their heads with crops, hares and instructions from their wives. I regret that I cannot remember what actually inspired the brigadier general to give a sumptuous dinner. The scale of the preparations for this grand event was vast: the clatter of chefs' knives could be heard almost as far as the town gates; the entire market was commandeered for this dinner, so that the judge and his deaconess had to subsist on buckwheat cakes and fish jelly. The small courtyard at the general's quarters was packed with droshkies and other carriages. The company was male, consisting of officers and sundry local landowners. Most eminent among the latter was one Pifagor Pifagorovich Chertokutsky, one of the foremost aristocrats in B— province, who made his voice heard above all others at the elections, turning up in a very fancy carriage. Once he had served in a cavalry regiment and had been one of its most notable and prominent officers. At least, he was seen at numerous balls and gatherings wherever his regiment happened to be stationed: the young ladies of Tambov and Simbirsk provinces can vouch for that. He might equally have acquired fame in other provinces had he not been obliged to resign his commission as a result of one of those incidents commonly called 'an unpleasant business'. Whether he had slapped someone's face in the old days, or whether someone had slapped his, I cannot say for certain. Whatever the facts, he had to resign. However, his authority was not diminished one bit. He gallivanted around in a military-style, high-waisted tail-coat, wore spurs on his boots and sported a moustache under his nose, for without one the local gentry might think that he had served in the infantry, which he sometimes contemptuously referred to as 'infantillery' and sometimes as 'infantery'. He visited all the crowded fairs, where the very heart of Russia, consisting of mammas, daughters and fat squires, would flock to amuse themselves, in their brichkas, tarantasses and such preposterous carriages as you would never even see in your dreams. He had a pronounced talent for sniffing out a cavalry regiment's quarters, leaping with the utmost aplomb from his light carriage or droshky, and in no time at all he would

The Carriage

make the officers' acquaintance. At the last election he had given a splendid dinner for the gentry, at which he announced that if only he were elected marshal he would not fail to 'set them up'. By and large, he lorded it like a real gentleman, as they say in the provinces, married a pretty girl with a dowry of two hundred serfs and several thousand in cash. These funds were immediately lavished on a team of six truly excellent horses, gilt locks for the doors, a tame monkey for the house and a French butler. The young lady's two hundred serfs, together with two hundred of his own, were mortgaged for some business transaction. In brief, he was an exemplary landowner, a real paragon. Apart from him, there were several other landowners at the general's dinner, but there is nothing much to say about them. The remaining guests were officers from the same regiment, and two staff officers: a colonel and a rather corpulent major. The general himself was rather stout and stocky, but, in the words of his officers, a good commander. He spoke in a rather thick, portentous bass.

The dinner was magnificent: the profusion of sturgeon, beluga sterlet, bustards, quails and partridges amply testified that the chef had gone without food and sleep for the past two days, and that four soldiers, knife in hand, had toiled all night to help him prepare fricassees and gêlées. The multitude of bottles – tall slender ones of Lafitte, short-necked ones of madeira, the fine summer's day, the wide-open windows, the plates of ice, the officers with their last waistcoat button undone, the crumpled shirt-fronts of the owners of exceedingly capacious tail-coats, the conversational crossfire drowned by the general's voice and lubricated with champagne – all made for perfect harmony.

After dinner the guests rose with an agreeable heaviness in their stomachs. When they had lit their long- and short-stemmed pipes, they stepped out on to the porch with cups of coffee in their hands. The general's, the colonel's and even the major's uniforms were completely unbuttoned, so that their pure silk, rather aristocratic braces were visible. But the other officers, duly observing regimental etiquette, kept their tunics fastened – except for the last three buttons.

'Now you can have a look at her,' the general was saying. 'Here, my dear fellow,' he muttered, turning to his adjutant – a rather smart young man of pleasant appearance – 'tell them to bring the bay mare. Then you can see for yourselves!'

At this the general took a pull on his pipe and released a plume of smoke. 'She's not properly groomed yet, there's no decent stabling in this wretched little town. But she's a very presentable ... *puff* ... *puff* ... horse!'

'And has Your Excellency ... *puff* ... *puff* ... had her long?' asked Chertokutsky.

'Well ... *puff* ... *puff* ... *pu* ... *ff* ... well, not so long. It's only two years since I had her from stud.'

'And did Your Excellency take her broken in, or did you have her broken in here?'

'*Puff* ... *puff* ... *pu* ... *pu* ... *u* ... *u* ... *ff* ... here' – and at this the general vanished completely in smoke.

Meanwhile a soldier sprang out from the stables, the clatter of hooves was heard and finally another soldier appeared, wearing white overalls and with enormous black moustaches, leading by the bridle a trembling, terrified mare which suddenly reared and almost lifted the soldier – moustaches and all – into the air.

The Carriage

'Now, now, Agrafena Ivanovna,' the soldier said, bringing her up to the porch steps.

Agrafena Ivanovna was the mare's name. As spirited and as wild as a southern beauty, she nervously stamped her hooves on the wooden steps and then suddenly stopped.

Putting down his pipe, the general began surveying her with evident satisfaction. The colonel came down from the steps and took Agrafena Ivanovna by the muzzle. The major patted Agrafena Ivanovna on the leg, while the others clicked their tongues in approval. Then Chertokutsky went down and followed the mare; the soldier holding the bridle and standing to attention stared the guests right in the eyes, as if he intended jumping right into them.

'Very fine, very fine!' exclaimed Chertokutsky. 'Excellent points. If I may ask Your Excellency, how does she go?'

'She has a good stride only – damn and blast! – that idiot of a vet gave her some sort of pills and for the past two days she's done nothing but sneeze.'

'She's a fine horse – very fine! And does Your Excellency have the right kind of carriage?'

'Carriage? But she's a saddle-horse.'

'I know. But what I really meant is – does Your Excellency have the right kind of carriage for your other horses?'

'Well, I don't have much in the way of carriages. I must confess that for some time I've been wanting an up-to-date calash. I've written to my brother in St Petersburg about it, but I've no idea if he's going to send me one or not.'

'In my opinion, Your Excellency . . . observed the colonel, 'you can't beat a Viennese calash.'

'There you are right . . . *puff* . . . *puff* . . . *puff*.'

'I have an exceptional calash, of real Viennese make, Your Excellency!'

'Which one? The one you came in?'

'Oh no, that's purely for riding around in, for short trips. But as for the other, why, it's truly amazing – as light as a feather! And when you sit in it – if I may put it like this – it's as if your nurse were rocking you in the cradle.'

'You mean it's comfortable?'

'Very, very comfortable! The cushions, springs – all top-notch!'

'Well, that's nice!'

'And so roomy! Oh yes, I've never seen one like it, Your Excellency. When I was in the army I used to get ten bottles of rum and twenty pounds of tobacco into the boxes, not to mention six uniforms, underlinen and two pipes as long as tapeworms, if I may put it like that, Your Excellency. And you could stow a whole ox in the pockets!'

'That's good!'

'It cost four thousand, Your Excellency.'

'At that price it *should* be good. And did you buy it yourself?'

'No, Your Excellency. I acquired it by chance. It was bought by a friend of mine – a fine chap and childhood pal, a man with whom you would have got along perfectly. We used to share everything. I won it off him at cards. Now, would you do me the honour, Your Excellency, of coming to have dinner with me tomorrow? You could inspect the calash at the same time.'

'I really don't know what to say – it's a bit awkward, you

know, coming on my own. Would you allow me to bring my fellow officers along?'

'The officers will be most welcome too! . . . Gentlemen, I should consider it an honour to have the pleasure of entertaining you in my home!'

The colonel, major and the other officers thanked him with polite bows.

'In my opinion, Your Excellency, if one buys something it should be good and if it's no good there's no point in buying it. When you do me the honour of visiting me tomorrow I'll show you a few improvements I've introduced on my estate.'

The general glanced at him and blew more smoke out of his mouth. Chertokutsky was really delighted that he had invited the gentlemen officers. Mentally he was already ordering the pâtés and sauces as he cheerfully looked at them. For their part, the look in their eyes and their little gestures in the way of half-bows showed that they were twice as well disposed towards him as before.

Chertokutsky now became more free and easy and there was a languid note in his voice, as though it were simply weighed down with pleasure.

'There you will meet the lady of the house, Your Excellency.'

'That will be most pleasant,' replied the general, stroking his moustache.

After this Chertokutsky could not wait to return home and ensure that the preparations for receiving his dinner guests next day were made in good time. He was about to pick up his hat, but for some strange reason he stayed on a little longer.

Meanwhile card-tables had already been set up in the room. Soon the whole company was divided into foursomes for whist and sat down in different parts of the general's rooms. Candles were brought. Chertokutsky was a long time making up his mind whether or not to sit down to whist. But since the officers were pressing him, he considered that it might be terribly bad form to refuse and so he took a seat. As if by magic there suddenly appeared before him a glass of punch which he immediately downed, without thinking. After two rubbers there again appeared a glass of punch at Chertokutsky's elbow and he downed that too, again without thinking, declaring beforehand: 'It's really time I went home, gentlemen.' But again he sat down, to a second game. Meanwhile private conversations were struck up in various parts of the room. The whist players were rather quiet, but the others who were not playing sat to one side on sofas, engaged in conversation of their own. In one corner the staff captain who was reclining with a cushion thrust under one side, his pipe between his teeth, was regaling a group of fascinated listeners with a fairly spicy and flowing account of his amorous adventures. One extraordinarily fat squire with short hands rather like overgrown potatoes was listening with an unusually cloying expression as he made sporadic attempts to extract his snuff-box from his back pocket. In another corner a rather heated argument about squadron drill had broken out and Chertokutsky, who had about that time twice played a jack instead of a queen, suddenly interrupted the conversation that did not concern him

The Carriage

at all, calling out from his corner: 'In which year? Which regiment?', oblivious of the fact that his questions were quite malapropos. Finally, a few minutes before supper, the whist came to an end, although the games continued verbally and everyone's head was bursting with whist. Chertokutsky clearly remembered that he had won a great deal, but he did not pick up his winnings. After getting up from the table he stood there for a long time, like a man who finds he has no handkerchief in his pocket. Meanwhile supper was served. It goes without saying there was no shortage of wine and that Chertokutsky felt almost compelled to refill his glass from time to time, as there were bottles to left and right of him.

An interminable conversation dragged on at table, but it was conducted rather oddly. One squire who had served in the 1812 campaign told of a battle that had certainly never taken place and then, for some mysterious reason, removed the stopper from a decanter and stuck it in the pudding. In brief, by the time the party started to break up it was already three in the morning and the coachmen had to carry several of the guests in their arms as if they were parcels from some shopping expedition. Despite his aristocratic pretensions, Chertokutsky bowed so low and with such a broad sweep of the head as he climbed into his carriage that he later found he had brought home with him two thistles in his moustache.

At home everyone was fast asleep. The coachman had difficulty finding a footman, who conducted his master across the drawing-room and handed him over to a chambermaid, whom Chertokutsky somehow managed to follow to the bedroom, and he lay down beside his pretty young wife, who was sleeping in the most enchanting posture in her snow-white nightdress. The jolt made by him falling on the bed woke her. Stretching, raising her eyelashes and blinking three times in quick succession, she opened her eyes with a half-angry smile, but when she realized that her husband had no intention of showing her any kind of endearment, turned over on her other side in pique. Resting her fresh cheek on her hand she fell asleep soon after him.

When the young mistress of the house awoke beside her snoring spouse it was at an hour that country folk would not consider early. Mindful that he had returned after three o'clock in the morning, she did not have the heart to wake him and so, donning her bedroom slippers that her husband had specially ordered from St Petersburg, her white nightdress draped around her like a flowing stream, she went to her dressing-room, washed herself in water as fresh as herself and went over to her dressing-table. After a couple of glances in the mirror she saw that she was looking really quite pretty that morning. This apparently insignificant circumstance led her to sit in front of her mirror exactly two hours longer than usual. Finally she dressed herself very charmingly and went out into the garden for some fresh air. As if by design, the weather was glorious, as only a summer's day in the south of Russia can be. The noonday sun beat down fiercely, but it was cool walking down the shady paths with their overarching foliage; the flowers were three times as fragrant in the warmth of the sun. The pretty young wife forgot that it was already twelve o'clock and that her husband was still

The Carriage

asleep. The post-prandial snores of the two coachmen and the postilion, who were fast asleep in the stable behind the garden, already reached her ears, but she continued to sit in the shady avenue from which the totally deserted high road was clearly visible. Suddenly a cloud of dust in the distance caught her attention.

Straining her eyes, she soon made out several carriages, headed by an open two-seated trap, in which were sitting the general, his thick epaulettes glinting in the sun, with the colonel at his side. This was followed by a four-seated carriage with the major and the general's adjutant, with two other officers sitting opposite. This carriage was followed by the regimental droshky, familiar to all and which was then in the stout major's possession. The droshky was followed by a *bonvoyage* in which four officers were seated, with a fifth squeezed in. After the *bonvoyage* three officers on their fine dappled bays came into view.

'Surely they're not coming here?' wondered the mistress of the house. 'Oh, my god! They *are*! They've turned at the bridge!'

She shrieked, wrung her hands and dashed right across the flowerbeds and shrubbery to the bedroom, where her husband was sleeping like a log.

'Get up! Hurry now! Get up!!' she cried, tugging at his arm.

'Ehhhh?' Chertokutsky said, stretching, without opening his eyes.

'Get up, poppet! Do you hear? We've visitors!'

'Visitors? *What* visitors?' – and having said this he

moaned plaintively, like a calf nuzzling its mother's udder. 'Mmmmmm . . .' he mumbled, 'give me your little neck, sweetie, I want to kiss it.'

'Darling! for heaven's sake get up! At once! It's the general and the officers. Oh – you've thistle in your moustache!'

'The general? So, he's on his way already? Why on earth didn't anyone wake me up? Now, about dinner . . . has everything been properly prepared?'

'What dinner?'

'But didn't I give instructions for dinner . . .?'

'Give instructions? You came home at four o'clock in the morning and however hard I tried I couldn't get one word out of you . . . I didn't wake you, poppet . . . because I felt sorry for you . . . you needed your sleep.'

She spoke these last words in a particularly languid and pleading voice.

His eyes goggling, Chertokutsky lay on his bed for a minute as if struck by a thunderbolt. Finally he leapt out of bed with only his nightshirt on, forgetting that this was highly improper.

'God! I'm such an ass!' he exclaimed, slapping his forehead. 'Yes, I did invite them for dinner. So, what are we going to do? Are they far off?'

'No, they're not! They'll be here any minute.'

'Darling, you go, and hide . . . Hey, who's there? Oh, it's you, you wretched girl! Now come here, you silly thing . . . what are you afraid of? Now, the officers will be here any minute, so you must tell them the master's not at home . . .

The Carriage

tell them he won't be here at all . . . that he went away early this morning. Do you hear? And tell all the other servants. Now, hurry up!'

With these words he grabbed his dressing-gown and ran to hide in the carriage-shed, assuming he would be perfectly safe there. But as he stood in a corner he realized that even there someone might spot him.

'Now, this is better!' flashed through his mind and in no time at all he had pulled down the steps of the carriage standing right by him, jumped in and slammed the door after him. For greater security he covered himself with the leather apron and travelling rug and lay there absolutely still, huddled in his dressing-gown.

Meanwhile the carriages had driven up to the front steps. The general alighted and gave himself a little shake; the colonel followed, smoothing the plumes of his hat. Then out of the droshky jumped the stout major, his sabre under his arm. Then the slim subalterns sprang down from the *bonvoyage*, with the ensign who had been squeezed in with them. Lastly the officers who had been elegantly prancing about on horseback dismounted.

'The Master's not at home,' announced a footman as he came out on to the front steps.

'Not at home! I suppose he'll be back for dinner then.'

'Oh no, sir. Master's gone out for the day. He won't be back until around this time tomorrow.'

'Well I'll be damned!' said the general. 'What the hell's going on here!?'

'I must admit, it's all rather odd!' laughed the colonel.

'And how! What's he playing at?' continued the general, visibly put out. 'Hell and damnation! If he can't receive people why did he invite them in the first place?'

'I do agree, Your Excellency. I too cannot understand how anyone can behave so badly,' observed a young officer.

'*What!!?*' shouted the general, who was in the habit of using the interrogative particle whenever he addressed a junior officer.

'I was saying, Your Excellency ... how could anyone behave like that?'

'Quite so ... well, if something unexpected had happened he could at least have told us. Otherwise he shouldn't have invited us.'

'No, Your Excellency, there's nothing we can do about it ... Let's go back,' said the colonel.

'Yes, of course, that's all we can do ... but we might take a look at that carriage of his without him. I'm sure he wouldn't have gone away in it. Hey ... you! Come here, old chap!'

'What can I do for Yer Excellency?'

'Are you the stable-boy?'

'That I am, Yer Excellency.'

'Well, show us the new calash your master bought recently.'

'If you'd please come into the carriage-shed, sir.'

The general went with his officers into the shed.

'Shall I move it out a bit, sir, it's rather dark in here.'

'Yes ... enough ... that's enough ... that's fine!'

The general walked around the calash with his officers and carefully inspected the wheels and springs.

'Well, it's nothing special,' remarked the general. 'It's nothing out of the ordinary.'

The Carriage

'Yes, nothing much at all,' agreed the colonel. 'Can't say anything good about it.'

'It seems to me, Your Excellency, that it can't possibly be worth four thousand,' commented one of the young officers.

'*What!!?*'

'Your Excellency, I said that I don't think it's worth four thousand.'

'Four thousand – my eye! It's not even worth two thousand – sheer junk!'

'Well, perhaps there's something special about the inside. Please unbutton the apron, my dear chap.'

And right before the officers' eyes there was Chertokutsky, sitting in his dressing-gown and curled up in the most bizarre fashion.

'Aha! So here you are!' exclaimed the astonished general.

And with these words the general immediately slammed the door, pulled the apron back over Chertokutsky and rode off with his officers.

1. BOCCACCIO · *Mrs Rosie and the Priest*
2. GERARD MANLEY HOPKINS · *As kingfishers catch fire*
3. *The Saga of Gunnlaug Serpent-tongue*
4. THOMAS DE QUINCEY · *On Murder Considered as One of the Fine Arts*
5. FRIEDRICH NIETZSCHE · *Aphorisms on Love and Hate*
6. JOHN RUSKIN · *Traffic*
7. PU SONGLING · *Wailing Ghosts*
8. JONATHAN SWIFT · *A Modest Proposal*
9. *Three Tang Dynasty Poets*
10. WALT WHITMAN · *On the Beach at Night Alone*
11. KENKŌ · *A Cup of Sake Beneath the Cherry Trees*
12. BALTASAR GRACIÁN · *How to Use Your Enemies*
13. JOHN KEATS · *The Eve of St Agnes*
14. THOMAS HARDY · *Woman much missed*
15. GUY DE MAUPASSANT · *Femme Fatale*
16. MARCO POLO · *Travels in the Land of Serpents and Pearls*
17. SUETONIUS · *Caligula*
18. APOLLONIUS OF RHODES · *Jason and Medea*
19. ROBERT LOUIS STEVENSON · *Olalla*
20. KARL MARX AND FRIEDRICH ENGELS · *The Communist Manifesto*
21. PETRONIUS · *Trimalchio's Feast*
22. JOHANN PETER HEBEL · *How a Ghastly Story Was Brought to Light by a Common or Garden Butcher's Dog*
23. HANS CHRISTIAN ANDERSEN · *The Tinder Box*
24. RUDYARD KIPLING · *The Gate of the Hundred Sorrows*
25. DANTE · *Circles of Hell*
26. HENRY MAYHEW · *Of Street Piemen*
27. HAFEZ · *The nightingales are drunk*
28. GEOFFREY CHAUCER · *The Wife of Bath*
29. MICHEL DE MONTAIGNE · *How We Weep and Laugh at the Same Thing*
30. THOMAS NASHE · *The Terrors of the Night*
31. EDGAR ALLAN POE · *The Tell-Tale Heart*
32. MARY KINGSLEY · *A Hippo Banquet*
33. JANE AUSTEN · *The Beautifull Cassandra*
34. ANTON CHEKHOV · *Gooseberries*
35. SAMUEL TAYLOR COLERIDGE · *Well, they are gone, and here must I remain*
36. JOHANN WOLFGANG VON GOETHE · *Sketchy, Doubtful, Incomplete Jottings*
37. CHARLES DICKENS · *The Great Winglebury Duel*
38. HERMAN MELVILLE · *The Maldive Shark*
39. ELIZABETH GASKELL · *The Old Nurse's Story*
40. NIKOLAY LESKOV · *The Steel Flea*

41. HONORÉ DE BALZAC · *The Atheist's Mass*
42. CHARLOTTE PERKINS GILMAN · *The Yellow Wall-Paper*
43. C.P. CAVAFY · *Remember, Body . . .*
44. FYODOR DOSTOEVSKY · *The Meek One*
45. GUSTAVE FLAUBERT · *A Simple Heart*
46. NIKOLAI GOGOL · *The Nose*
47. SAMUEL PEPYS · *The Great Fire of London*
48. EDITH WHARTON · *The Reckoning*
49. HENRY JAMES · *The Figure in the Carpet*
50. WILFRED OWEN · *Anthem For Doomed Youth*
51. WOLFGANG AMADEUS MOZART · *My Dearest Father*
52. PLATO · *Socrates' Defence*
53. CHRISTINA ROSSETTI · *Goblin Market*
54. *Sindbad the Sailor*
55. SOPHOCLES · *Antigone*
56. RYŪNOSUKE AKUTAGAWA · *The Life of a Stupid Man*
57. LEO TOLSTOY · *How Much Land Does A Man Need?*
58. GIORGIO VASARI · *Leonardo da Vinci*
59. OSCAR WILDE · *Lord Arthur Savile's Crime*
60. SHEN FU · *The Old Man of the Moon*
61. AESOP · *The Dolphins, the Whales and the Gudgeon*
62. MATSUO BASHŌ · *Lips too Chilled*
63. EMILY BRONTË · *The Night is Darkening Round Me*
64. JOSEPH CONRAD · *To-morrow*
65. RICHARD HAKLUYT · *The Voyage of Sir Francis Drake Around the Whole Globe*
66. KATE CHOPIN · *A Pair of Silk Stockings*
67. CHARLES DARWIN · *It was snowing butterflies*
68. BROTHERS GRIMM · *The Robber Bridegroom*
69. CATULLUS · *I Hate and I Love*
70. HOMER · *Circe and the Cyclops*
71. D. H. LAWRENCE · *Il Duro*
72. KATHERINE MANSFIELD · *Miss Brill*
73. OVID · *The Fall of Icarus*
74. SAPPHO · *Come Close*
75. IVAN TURGENEV · *Kasyan from the Beautiful Lands*
76. VIRGIL · *O Cruel Alexis*
77. H. G. WELLS · *A Slip under the Microscope*
78. HERODOTUS · *The Madness of Cambyses*
79. *Speaking of Siva*
80. *The Dhammapada*

'With one's face in the wind you were almost burned with a shower of Firedrops . . .'

SAMUEL PEPYS
Born 1633, London
Died 1703, Clapham

PEPYS IN PENGUIN CLASSICS
The Diary of Samuel Pepys

SAMUEL PEPYS

The Great Fire of London

PENGUIN BOOKS

PENGUIN CLASSICS

UK | USA | Canada | Ireland | Australia
India | New Zealand | South Africa

Penguin Books is part of the Penguin Random House group of companies
whose addresses can be found at global.penguinrandomhouse.com.

This selection published in Penguin Classics 2015

010

Copyright © The Masters, Fellows and Scholars of Magdalene College, Cambridge,
Robert Latham and the Executors of William Matthews, 1985

Set in 9.5/13 pt Baskerville 10 Pro
Typeset by Jouve (UK), Milton Keynes
Printed and bound in Great Britain by Clays Ltd, Elcograf S.p.A.

A CIP catalogue record for this book is available from the British Library

ISBN: 978–0–141–39754–2

www.greenpenguin.co.uk

Penguin Random House is committed to a
sustainable future for our business, our readers
and our planet. This book is made from Forest
Stewardship Council® certified paper.

Contents

MAY 1ST–JUNE 30TH 1665   1

SEPTEMBER 2ND–15TH 1666   29

During this period Pepys is Clerk of the Acts to the Navy Board and concerned with the ultimately abortive English colony of 'Tanger' (Tangier), part of Catherine of Braganza's dowry (together with Bombay) when she married the now reigning monarch Charles II. Pepys is also engaged more broadly with the management of the Royal Navy which is fighting what proved to be the unsuccessful Second Anglo-Dutch War. Much of the first extract is concerned both with the spread of the Plague and with the prosecution of the war. The news of the English victory off Lowestoft is described, with the fleet commanded by Charles II's younger brother the Duke of York (later James II). The second extract describes the Great Fire of London. Throughout the text Pepys refers to personal friends and family, scientific colleagues and naval colleagues. The Duke of Albemarle (the former George Monck) is Captain-General. The Earl of Sandwich ('My Lord') is Pepys' patron. 'Mr Evelings' is the diarist John Evelyn.

May 1665

1. Up, and to Mr Povy's, and by his bedside talked a good while. Thence to the Duke of Albemarle, where I sorry to find myself to come a little late. And so home, and at noon, going to the Change, met my Lord Brunkerd, Sir Robert Murry, Deane Wilkins, and Mr Hooke, going by coach to Coll. Blunt's to dinner. So they stopped and took me with them. Landed at the Tower wharf and thence by water to Greenwich, and there coaches met us and to his house, a very stately seat for situation and brave plantations; and among others, a Vineyard. No extraordinary dinner, nor any other entertainment good – but only, after dinner to the tryall of some experiments about making of coaches easy. And several we tried, but one did prove mighty easy (not here for me to describe, but the whole body of that coach lies upon one long spring) and we all, one after another, rid in it; and it is very fine and likely to take. These experiments were the intent of their coming, and pretty they are. Thence back by coach to Greenwich and in his pleasure-boat to Deptford; and there stopped, and in to Mr Evelings, which is a most

beautiful place, but it being dark and late, I stayed not; but Dean Wilkins and Mr Hooke and I walked to Redriffe, and noble discourse all day long did please me. And it being late, did take them to my house to drink, and did give them some sweetmeats – and thence sent them with a lanthorn home – two worthy persons as are in England, I think, or the world. So to my Lady Batten, where my wife is tonight; and so after some merry talk, home to bed.

3. Up betimes, and walked to Sir Ph. Warwickes, where a long time with him in his chamber alone, talking of Sir G. Carteret's business and the abuses he puts on the nation by his bad payments – to both our vexations; but no hope of remedy for aught I see. So to the Change and thence home to dinner; and so out to Gresham College and saw a cat killed with the Duke of Florence's poison. And saw it proved that the oyle of Tobacco, drawn by one of the Society, doth the same effect, and is judged to be the same thing with the poison, both in colour and smell and effect. (I saw also an abortive child, preserved fresh in spirit of salt). Thence parted, and to Whitehall to the council chamber about an order touching the Navy (our being impowered to commit seamen or maisters that do not, being hired or pressed, fallow their work), but they could give us none. So, a little vexed at that, because I put in the memorial to the Duke of Albemarle alone,

May 1665

under my own hand – home; and after some time at the office, home to bed.

5. Up betimes, and by water to Westminster, there to speak the first time with Sir Robt. Long, to give him my privy seal and my Lord Treasurers order for Tanger Tallys. He received me kindly enough. Thence home by water; and presently down to Woolwige and back to Blackewall, and there viewed the Breach, in order to a mast-Docke; and so to Deptford to the Globe, where my Lord Brunkard, Sir J. Mennes, Sir W. Batten, and Comissioner Pett were at dinner, having been at the Breach also – but they find it will be of too great charge to make use of it. After dinner to Mr Evelings; he being abroad, we walked in his garden, and a lovely noble ground he hath endeed. And among other rarities, a hive of Bees; so, as being hived in glass, you may see the Bees making their honey and Combs mighty pleasantly. Thence home, and I by and by to Mr Povy's to see him, who is yet in his chamber, not well. And thence by his advice to one Lovetts, a Varnisher, to see his manner of new varnish, but found not him at home; but his wife a very beautiful woman, who showed me much variety of admirable work; and is in order to my having of some papers fitted with lines, for my use for Tables and the like. I know not whether I was more pleased with the thing, or that I was showed it by her. But resolved I am to have some made.

So home to my office late, and then to supper and to bed. My wife tells me that she hears that my poor aunt James hath had her breast cut off here in town – her breast having long been out of order. This day, after I had suffered my own hayre to grow long, in order to wearing it, I find the convenience of Perrywiggs is so great, that I have cut off all short again, and will keep to periwigs.

7. *Lords day*. Up, and to church with my wife. Home and dined. After dinner came Mr Andrews, and spent the afternoon with me about our Tanger business of the victuals and then parted. And after sermon comes Mr Hill and a gentleman, a friend of his, one Mr Scott, that sings well also; and then comes Mr Andrews, and we all sung and supped; and then to sing again, and passed the Sunday very pleasantly and soberly; and so I to my office a little, and then home to prayers and to bed. Yesterday begun my wife to learn to Limb of one Browne, which Mr Hill helps her to. And by her beginning, upon some eyes, I think she will [do] very fine things – and I shall take great delight in it.

9. Up betimes, and to my business at the office, where all the morning. At noon comes Mrs The[oph]. Turner and dines with us. And my wife's painting-maister stayed and dined, and I take great pleasure in thinking that my wife will really come to something in that business. Here

May 1665

dined also Luellin. So after dinner to the office and there very busy till almost midnight, and so home to supper and to bed. This day we have news of eight ships being taken by some of ours, going into the Texell, their two men of war that convoyed [them] running in. They came from about Ireland, round to the North.

10. Up betimes, and abroad to the Cockepitt, where the Duke[1] did give Sir W. Batten and me an account of the late taking of eight ships and of his[2] intent to come back to the Gunfleete with the fleet presently – which creates us much work and haste therein, against the fleet comes. So to Mr Povy; and after discourse with him, home and thence to the Guard in Southworke, there to get some soldiers, by the Duke's order, to go keep press-men on board our ships. So to the Change and did much business; and then home to dinner and there find my poor mother come out of the country today, in good health; and I am glad to see her, but my business, which I am sorry for, keeps me from paying the respect I ought to her at her first coming – she being grown very weak in her judgment, and doting again in her discourse, through age and some trouble in her family. Left her and my wife to go abroad to buy something, and then I to my office.

1. Albemarle.
2. The Duke of York's.

Samuel Pepys

In the evening, by appointment to Sir W. Warren and Mr Dering at a tavern hard by, with intent to do some good upon their agreement in a great bargain of plank. So home to my office again, and then to supper and to bed, my mother being in bed already.

12. By water to the Exchequer, and there up and down through all the offices to strike my tallies for 17500*l* – which methinks is so great a testimony of the goodness of God to me; that I, from a mean clerk there, should come to strike tallies myself for that sum, and in the authority that I do now, is a very stupendous mercy to me. I shall have them struck tomorrow. But to see how every little fellow looks after his fees, and to get what he can for everything, is a strange consideration – the King's Fees, that he must pay himself for this 17500*l*, coming to above 100*l*. Thence, called my wife at Unthankes, to the New Exchange and elsewhere to buy a lace band for me, but we did not buy. But I find it so necessary to have some handsome clothes, that I cannot but lay out some money there-upon.

13. Up, and all day in some little grutchings of pain, as I use to have – from Winde – arising, I think, from my fasting so long and want of exercise – and I think, going so hot in clothes, the weather being hot and I in the same clothes I wore all winter. To the Change after office, and received my Wach from the watchmaker; and a very fine

May 1665

[one] it is – given me by Briggs the Scrivener. But Lord, to see how much of my old folly and childishnesse hangs upon me still, that I cannot forbear carrying my watch in my hand in the coach all this afternoon, and seeing what a-clock it is 100 times. And am apt to think with myself: how could I be so long without one – though I remember since, I had one and found it a trouble, and resolved to carry one no more about me while I lived.

14. *Lords day*. Up, and with my wife to church, it being Whitsunday. My wife very fine in a new yellow birds-eye Hood, as the fashion is now. We had a most sorry sermon. So home to dinner, my mother having her new suit brought home, which makes her very fine. After dinner my wife and she and Mercer to Tho. Pepys's wife's christening of his first child. And I took a coach and to Wanstead, the house where Sir H. Mildmay did [live] and now Sir Rob. Brookes lives, having bought it of the Duke of Yorke, it being forfeited to him. A fine seat, but an old-fashion house and being not full of people, looks desolately. Thence to Walthamstow, where Sir W. Batten by and by came home, I walking up and down the house and garden with my Lady, very pleasant. Then to supper, very merry; and then back by coach by dark night – I, all the afternoon in the coach, reading the treasonous book of the Court of King James, printed a great while ago and worth reading, though ill intended. As soon as came

home, upon a letter from Duke of Albemarle, I took boat, at about 12 at night, and down the River in a galley, my boy and I, down to the Hope, and so up again, sleeping and waking with great pleasure; my business, to call upon every one of our victualling ships to set them a-going.

15. And so home; and after dinner, to the King's playhouse all alone, and saw *Loves Maistresse*. Some pretty things and good variety in it, but no or little fancy in it. Thence to the Duke of Albemarle to give him account of my day's works – where he showed me letters from Sir G. Downing, of four days' date, that the Duch are come out and joyned – well-manned and resolved to board our best ships; and fight for certain they will. Thence to the Swan at Herberts, and there the company of Sarah a little while; and so away and called at the Harp and Ball, where the maid, Mary, is very formosa; but Lord, to see in what readiness I am, upon the expiring of my vowes this day, to begin to run into all my pleasures and neglect of business. Thence home; and being sleepy, to bed.

22. Up, and down to the ships, which now are hindered from going to the fleet (to our great sorrow and shame) with the provisions, the wind being against them. So to the Duke of Albemarle – and thence down by water to Deptford, it being Trinity Monday and so the day of choosing the Master of Trinity house for the next year – where, to my great content, I find that contrary to the

May 1665

practice and design of Sir W. Batten to break the rule and custom of the Company in choosing their Masters by succession, he would have brought in Sir W. Rider or Sir W. Pen over the head of Hurleston (who is a knave too besides, I believe): the Younger Brothers did all oppose it against the Elder, and with great heat did carry it for Hurleston – which I know will vex him to the heart. Thence, the election being over, to church; where an idle sermon from that conceited fellow Dr Britton, saving that his advice to unity and laying aside all envy and enmity among them was very apposite. Thence walked to Redriffe, and so to the Trinity house; and a great dinner, as is usual. And so to my office, where busy all the afternoon till late; and then home to bed – being much troubled in mind for several things. First, for the condition of the fleet for lack of provisions. The blame this office lies under, and the shame that they deserve to have brought upon them for the ships not being gone out of the River. And then for my business of Tanger, which is not settled; and lastly, for fear that I am not observed to have attended the office business of late as much as I ought to do, though there hath been nothing but my attendance on Tanger that hath occasioned my absence, and that of late not much.

24. Up by 4 a-clock in the morning; and with W. Hewer there till 12 without intermission, putting some papers in order. Thence to the coffee-house with Creed, where I

have not been a great while – where all the news is of the Dutch being gone out – and of the plague growing upon us in this town and of remedies against it; some saying one thing, some another.

28. *Lords day*. Went to chapel and heard a little Musique and there met with Creed, and with him a little while walking and to Wilkinsons for me to drink, being troubled with Winde; and at noon to Sir Ph. Warwicke's to dinner, where abundance of company came in unexpectedly. And here I saw one pretty piece of household stuff; as the company encreaseth, to put a larger leaf upon an Ovall table. After dinner much good discourse with Sir Phillip, who I find, I think, a most pious good man, and a professor of a philosiphicall manner of life and principles like Epictetus, whom he cites in many things. Thence to my Lady Sandwiches, where to my shame I had not been a great while before. Here, upon my telling her a story of my Lord of Rochester's running away on Friday night last with Mrs Mallet, the great beauty and fortune of the [West], who had supped at Whitehall with Mrs Stewart and was going home to her lodgings with her grandfather, my Lord Haly, by coach, and was at Charing cross seized on by both horse- and foot-men and forcibly taken from him, and put into a coach with six horses and two women provided to receive her, and carried away. Upon immediate pursuit, my Lord of Rochester (for whom the King had spoke to the lady often, but with

no success) was taken at Uxbridge; but the lady is not yet heard of, and the King mighty angry and the Lord sent to the Tower. Hereupon, my Lady did confess to me, as a great secret, her being concerned in this story – for if this match breaks between my Lord Rochester and her, then, by the consent of all her friends, my Lord Hinchingbrooke stands fair, and is invited for her. She is worth, and will be at her mother's death (who keeps but a little from her), 2500*l* per annum. Pray God give a good success to it. But my poor Lady, who is afeared of the sickness and resolved to be gone into the country, is forced to stay in town a day or two or three about it, to see the event of it. Thence home, and to see my Lady Pen – where my wife and I were shown a fine rarity: of fishes kept in a glass of water, that will live so for ever; and finely marked they are, being foreign. So to supper at home and to bed.

29. Lay long in bed, being in some little pain of the wind, Collique. Then up and to the Duke of Albemarle, and so to the Swan and there drank at Herberts; and so by coach home, it being kept a great holiday through the City, for the birth and restoration of the King. To my office, where I stood by and saw Symson the Joyner do several things, little Jobbs, to the rendering of my closet handsome and the setting up of some neat plats that Burston hath for my money made me. And so home to dinner; and then, with my wife, mother, and Mercer in one boat, and I in another, down to Woolwich, I walking

from Greenwich, the others going to and fro upon the water till my coming back, having done but little business. So home and to supper, and weary to bed. We have everywhere taken some prizes. Our merchants have good luck to come home safe: Colliers from the North, and some Streights-men just now – and our Hambrough ships, of whom we were so much afeared, are safe in Hambrough. Our Fleete resolved to sail out again from Harwich in a day or two.

June 1665

1. Up, and to the office, where sat all the morning. At noon to the Change and there did some business and home to dinner, whither Creed comes. And after dinner I put on my new silk Camelott Sute, the best that ever I wore in my life, the suit costing me above 24*l*. In this I went with him to Goldsmiths hall to the burial of Sir Tho. Viner; which hall, and Haberdashers also, was so full of people, that we were fain for ease and coolness to go forth to Paternoster row to choose a silk to make me a plain ordinary suit. That done, we walked to Cornehill, and there at Mr Cades stood in the Balcon and saw all the funerals, which was with the Bluecoat boys and old men – all the Aldermen, and Lord Mayor, &c., and the number of the company very great – the greatest I ever did see for a Taverne. Hither came up to us Dr Allen – and then Mr Povy and Mr Fox. The show being over, and my discourse with Mr Povy – I took coach and to Westminster hall, where I took the fairest flower and by coach to Tothill fields for the ayre, till it was dark. I light, and in with the fairest flower to eat a cake, and there did do as

much as was safe with my flower, and that was enough on my part. Broke up, and away without any notice; and after delivering the rose where it should be, I to the Temple and light; and came to the middle door and there took another coach, and so home – to write letters; but very few, God knows, being (by my pleasure) made to forget everything that is. The coachman that carried [us] cannot know me again, nor the people at the house where we were. Home to bed, certain news being come that our fleet is in sight of the Dutch ships.

2. Met an express from Sir W. Batten at Harwich, that the fleet is all sailed from Solebay, having spied the Dutch Fleete at sea – and that if the Calmes hinder not, they must needs be now engaged with them.

3. All this day, by all people upon the River and almost everywhere else hereabout, were heard the Guns, our two fleets for certain being engaged; which was confirmed by letters from Harwich, but nothing perticular; and all our hearts full of concernment for the Duke, and I perticularly for my Lord Sandwich and Mr Coventry after his Royal Highness.

7. This day, much against my Will, I did in Drury lane see two or three houses marked with a red cross upon the doors, and 'Lord have mercy upon us' writ there – which was a sad sight to me, being the first of that kind that to

my remembrance I ever saw. It put me into an ill conception of myself and my smell, so that I was forced to buy some roll tobacco to smell to and chaw – which took away the apprehension.

8. About 5 a-clock my wife came home, it having lightened all night hard, and one great shower of rain. She came and lay upon the bed. I up, and to the office, where all the morning. I alone at home to dinner, my wife, mother, and Mercer dining at W. Joyces, I giving her a caution to go round by the Half Moone to his house, because of the plague. I to my Lord Treasurer's, by appointment of Sir Tho. Ingram's, to meet the goldsmiths – where I met with the great news, at last newly come, brought by Bab May from the Duke of Yorke, that we have totally routed the Dutch. That the Duke himself, the Prince, my Lord Sandwich, and Mr Coventry are all well. Which did put me into such a joy, that I forgot almost all other thoughts. The sum of the news is:

Victory over the Dutch. June. 3. 1665.

This day they engaged – the Dutch neglecting greatly the opportunity of the wind they had of us – by which they lost the benefit of their fireships. The Earl of Falmouth, Muskery, and Mr Rd. Boyle killed on board the Dukes ship, the *Royall Charles*, with one shot. Their blood and brains flying in the Duke's face – and the head of Mr Boyle striking down the Duke, as some say. Earle of

Marlbrough, Portland, Rere-[A]dm. Sansum (to Prince Rupert) killed, and Capt. Kirby and Ableson. Sir Jo. Lawson wounded on the knee – hath had some bones taken out, and is likely to be well again. Upon receiving the hurt, he sent to the Duke for another to command the *Royall Oake*. The Duke sent Jordan out of the *St George*, who did brave things in her. Capt. Jer. Smith of the *Mary* was second to the Duke, and stepped between him and Capt. Seaton of the *Urania* (76 guns and 400 men), who had sworn to board the Duke. Killed him, 200 men, and took the ship. Himself losing 99 men, and never an officer saved but himself and Lieutenant. His maister endeed is saved, with his leg cut off. Adm. Opdam blown up. Trump killed, and said by Holmes. All the rest of their Admiralls, as they say, but Everson (whom they dare not trust for his affection to the prince of Orange) are killed. We have taken and sunk, as is believed, about 24 of their best ships. Killed and taken near 8 or 10000 men; and lost, we think, not above 700. A great victory, never known in the world. They are all fled; some 43 got into the Texell and others elsewhere, and we in pursuit of the rest.

Thence, with my heart full of Joy, home, and to my office a little; then to my Lady Pen's, where they are all joyed and not a little puffed up at the good success of their father; and good service endeed is said to have been done by him. Had a great bonefire at the gate; and I with my Lady Pens people and others to Mrs Turner's great

June 1665

room, and then down into the street. I did give the boys 4s. among them – and mighty merry; so home to bed – with my heart at great rest and quiet, saving that the consideration of the victory is too great for me presently to comprehend.

10. Lay long in bed; and then up and at the office all the morning. At noon dined at home, and then to the office, busy all the afternoon. In the evening home to supper, and there to my great trouble hear that the plague is come into the City (though it hath these three or four weeks since its beginning been wholly out of the City); but where should it begin but in my good friend and neighbour's, Dr Burnett in Fanchurch street – which in both points troubles me mightily.

11. *Lords day*. Up, and expected long a new suit; but coming not, dressed myself in my late new black silk camelot suit; and when full ready, comes my new one of Colour'd Farrinden, which my wife puts me out of love with; which vexes [me], but I think it is only my not being used to wear Colours, which makes it look a little unusual upon me. To my chamber, and there spent the morning reading. At noon by invitation comes my two cousin Joyces and their wifes – my aunt James, and he-cousin Harman – his wife being ill. I had a good dinner for them, and as merry as I could be in such company. They being gone, I out of doors a little to show forsooth my new suit,

and back again; and in going, saw poor Dr Burnets door shut. But he hath, I hear, gained great goodwill among his neighbours; for he discovered it himself first, and caused himself to be shut up of his own accord – which was very handsome. In the evening comes Mr Andrews and his wife and Mr Hill, and stayed and played and sung and supped – most excellent pretty company; so pleasant, ingenious, and harmless, I cannot desire better. They gone, we to bed – my mind in great present ease.

13. Up, and to the office, where all the morning doing business. At noon with Sir G. Carteret to my Lord Mayors to dinner, where much company in a little room – and though a good, yet no extraordinary Table. His name, Sir John Lawrence – whose father, a very ordinary old man, sat there at table – but it seems a very rich man. [Ald. Sir Richard Browne] did here openly tell in boasting, how he had, only upon suspicion of disturbances (if there had been any bad news from sea), clapped up several persons that he was afeared of. And that he had several times done the like and would do, and take no bail where he saw it unsafe for the King.

14. I met with Mr Cowling, who observed to me how he finds everybody silent in the praise of my Lord of Sandwich, to set up the Duke and the Prince. But that the Duke did, both to the King and my Lord Chancellor, write abundantly of my Lord's courage and service. And

June 1665

I this day met with a letter of Capt. Ferrers, where he tells us my Lord was with his ship in all the heat of the day, and did most worthily. Met with Creed, and he and I to Westminster and there saw my Lord Marlborough brought to be buried – several Lords of the Council carrying him, and with the Heralds in some state. Thence, vexed in my mind to think that I do so little in my Tanger business, and so home, and after supper to bed.

15. Up, and put on my new stuff suit with close knees, which becomes me most nobly as my wife says. At the office all day. At noon put on my first laced band, all lace, and to Kate Joyce's to dinner; where my mother, wife, and abundance of their friends, and good usage. Thence wife and Mercer and I to the Old Exchange and there bought two lace bands more, one of my Semstresse, whom my wife concurs with me to be a pretty woman. So down to Deptford and Woolwich, my boy and I. At Woolwich discoursed with Mr Shelden about my bringing my wife down for a month or two to his house; which he approves of, and I think will be very convenient. So late back and to the office, wrote letters, and so home to supper and to bed. This day the Newsbook (upon Mr Moores showing Lestrange Capt. Ferrers letter) did do my Lord Sandwich great right as to the late victory. The Duke of Yorke not yet come to town.

The town grows very sickly, and people to be afeared of it – there dying this last week of the plague 112, from

Samuel Pepys

43 the week before – whereof, one in Fanchurch street and one in Broadstreete by the Treasurer's office.

16. Up, and to the office, where I set hard to business – but was informed that the Duke of Yorke is come, and hath appointed us to attend him this afternoon. So after dinner and doing some business at the office, I to Whitehall, where the Court is full of the Duke and his Courtiers, returned from sea – all fat and lusty, and ruddy by being in the sun. I kissed his hands, and we waited all the afternoon. By and by saw Mr Coventry, which rejoiced my very heart. Anon he and I from all the rest of the company walked into the matted gallery – where after many expressions of love, we fell to talk of business. Among other things, how my Lord Sandwich, both in his counsels and personal service, hath done most honorably and serviceably. Sir J. Lawson is come to Greenwich, but his wound in his knee yet very bad. Jonas Poole in the *Vantguard* did basely, so as to be, or will be, turned out of his ship. Capt. Holmes, expecting upon Sansums death to be made Rere-admirall to the Prince (but Harman is put in), hath delivered up to the Duke his commission, which the Duke took and tore. He, it seems, had bid the Prince, who first told him of Holmes's intention, that he should dissuade him from it, for that he was resolved to take it if he offered it. Yet Holmes would do it, like a rash, proud coxcomb – but he is rich, and hath it seems sought an occasion of leaving the service. Several of our Captains have done ill.

June 1665

The great Shipps are the ships do the business, they quite deadening the enemy – they run away upon sight of the *Prince*. It is strange, to see how people do already slight Sir Wm. Berkely, my Lord Fitzharding's brother, who three months since was the delight of the Court. Capt. Smith of the *Mary*, the Duke talks mightily of, and some great thing will be done for him. Strange, to hear how the Dutch do relate, as the Duke says, that they are the conquerors – and bonefires are made in Dunkirke in their behalf – though a clearer victory can never be expected. Mr Coventry thinks they cannot have lost less then 6000 men; and we not dead above 200, and wounded about 400; in all, about 600. Thence home, and to my office till past 12 and then home to supper and to bed – my wife and mother not being yet come home from W. Hewres chamber, who treats my mother tonight. Capt. Grove, the Duke told us this day, hath done the basest thing at Lastoffe, in hearing of the guns and could not (as others) be got out, but stayed there – for which he will be tried; and is reckoned a prating coxcombe, and of no courage.

17. It stroke me very deep this afternoon, going with a Hackny-coach from my Lord Treasurer's down Holborne – the coachman I found to drive easily and easily; at last stood still, and came down hardly able to stand; and told me that he was suddenly stroke very sick and almost blind, he could not see. So I light and went into another

coach, with a sad heart for the poor man and trouble for myself, lest he should have been stroke with the plague – being at that end of the town that I took him up. But God have mercy upon us all. Sir Jo. Lawson, I hear, is worse then yesterday – the King went to see him today, most kindly. It seems his wound is not very bad, but he hath a fever – a thrush and a Hickup, all three together; which are, it seems, very bad symptoms.

20. *Thanksgiving day for Victory over the Dutch*. Up, and to the office, where very busy alone all the morning till church time; and there heard a mean sorry sermon of Mr Mills. Then to the Dolphin Taverne, where all we officers of the Navy met with the Comissioners of the Ordnance by agreement and dined – where good Musique, at my direction. Our club came to 34s. a man – nine of us. Thence after dinner I to Whitehall with Sir W. Berkely in his coach. And so I walked to Herberts and there spent a little time avec la mosa, sin hazer algo con ella que kiss and tocar ses mamelles, que me haza hazer la cosa a mi mismo con gran plaisir. Thence by water to Foxhall, and there walked an hour alone, observing the several humours of the citizens that were there this holiday, pulling of cherries and God knows what. And so home to my office, where late, my wife not being come home with my mother, who have been this day all abroad upon the water, my mother being to go out of town speedily. So I home and to supper and to bed. This day I

June 1665

informed myself that there died four or five at Westminster of the plague, in one alley in several houses upon Sunday last – Bell Alley, over against the Palace gate. Yet people do think that the number will be fewer in the town then it was the last week.

24. *Midsummer Day*. Up very betimes, by 6, and at Dr Clerkes at Westminster by 7 of the clock, having overnight by a note acquainted him with my intention of coming. And there I, in the best manner I could, broke my errand about a match between Sir G. Carterets eldest son and my Lord Sandwiches eldest daughter – which he (as I knew he would) took with great content; and we both agreed that my Lord and he, being both men relating to the sea – under a kind aspect of His Majesty – already good friends, and both virtuous and good families, their allyance might be of good use to us. And he did undertake to find out Sir George this morning, and put the business in execution. So being both well pleased with the proposition, I saw his neece there and made her sing me two or three songs, very prettily; and so home to the office – where to my great trouble, I found Mr Coventry and the board met before I came. I excused my late coming, by having been upon the River about office business. So to business all the morning. [After dinner] to Dr Clerke, and there find that he hath broke the business to Sir G. Carteret and that he takes the thing mighty well. Thence I to Sir G. Carteret at his Chamber, and in the

best manner I could, and most obligingly, moved that business; he received it with great respect and content and thanks to me, and promised that he would do what he could possibly for his son, to render him fit for my Lord's daughter. And showed great kindness to me, and sense of my kindness to him herein. Sir Wm. Pen told me this day that Mr Coventry is to be sworn a Privy Counsellor – at which my soul is glad. So home and to my letters by the post, and so home – to supper and bed.

25. *Lords day*. Up, and several people about business came to me by appointment, relating to the office; thence I to my closet about my Tanger papers. At noon dined. And then I abroad by water, it raining hard, thinking to have gone down to Woolwich; but I did not, but back through bridge to Whitehall – where after I had again visited Sir G. Carteret and received his (and now his Lady's) full content in my proposal, I went to my Lord Sandwich; and having told him how Sir G. Carteret received it, he did direct me to return to Sir G. Carteret and give him thanks for his kind reception of this offer, and that he would the next day be willing to enter discourse with him about that business. Which message I did presently do, and so left the business, with great joy to both sides. My Lord, I perceive, entends to give 5000*l* with her, and expects about 800*l* per annum joynture. So by water home and to supper and bed, being weary with

long walking at Court. But had a psalm or two with my boy and Mercer before bed, which pleased me mightily.

26. The plague encreases mightily – I this day seeing a house, at a bittmakers over against St Clements church in the open street, shut up; which is a sad sight.

29. Up, and by water to Whitehall, where the Court full of waggons and people ready to go out of town. The Mortality bill is come to 267 – which is about 90 more then the last; and of these, but 4 in the City – which is a great blessing to us. So home, calling at Somersett house, where all are packing up too; the Queene-mother setting out for France this day to drink Bourbon waters this year, she being in a consumption – and entends not to come till winter come twelvemonths. To the office, where busy a while, putting some things in my office in order, and then to letters till night. About 10 a-clock home – the days being sensibly shorter: before, I have once kept a summer's day by shutting up office by daylight, but my life hath been still as it was in winter almost. But I will for a month try what I can do by daylight. So home to supper and to bed.

30. Thus this book of two years ends. Myself and family in good health, consisting of myself and wife – Mercer, her woman – Mary, Alice and Su, our maids; and Tom,

my boy. In a sickly time, of the plague growing on. Having upon my hands the troublesome care of the Treasury of Tanger, with great sums drawn upon me and nothing to pay them with. Also, the business of the office great. Consideration of removing my wife to Woolwich. She lately busy in learning to paint, with great pleasure and successe. All other things well; especially a new interest I am making, by a match in hand between the eldest son of Sir G. Carteret and my Lady Jemimah Mountagu. The Duke of York gone down to the fleet; but, all suppose, not with intent to stay there – as it is not fit, all men conceive, he should.[1]

---

1. sc. as heir presumptive to the King.

September 1666

2. *Lords day*. Some of our maids sitting up late last night to get things ready against our feast today, Jane called us up, about 3 in the morning, to tell us of a great fire they saw in the City. So I rose, and slipped on my nightgown and went to her window, and thought it to be on the back side of Markelane at the furthest; but being unused to such fires as fallowed, I thought it far enough off, and so went to bed again and to sleep. About 7 rose again to dress myself, and there looked out at the window and saw the fire not so much as it was, and further off. So to my closet to set things to rights after yesterday's cleaning. By and by Jane comes and tells me that she hears that above 300 houses have been burned down tonight by the fire we saw, and that it was now burning down all Fishstreet by London Bridge. So I made myself ready presently, and walked to the Tower and there got up upon one of the high places, Sir J. Robinsons little son going up with me; and there I did see the houses at that end of the bridge all on fire, and an infinite great fire on this and the other side the end of the bridge – which, among other people,

did trouble me for poor little Michell and our Sarah on the Bridge. So down, with my heart full of trouble, to the Lieutenant of the Tower, who tells me that it begun this morning in the King's bakers house in Pudding lane, and that it hath burned down St Magnes Church and most part of Fishstreete already. So I down to the waterside and there got a boat and through the bridge, and there saw a lamentable fire. Poor Michells house, as far as the Old Swan, already burned that way and the fire running further, that in a very little time it got as far as the Stillyard while I was there. Everybody endeavouring to remove their goods, and flinging into the River or bringing them into lighters that lay off. Poor people staying in their houses as long as till the very fire touched them, and then running into boats or clambering from one pair of stair by the waterside to another. And among other things, the poor pigeons I perceive were loath to leave their houses, but hovered about the windows and balconies till they were some of them burned, their wings, and fell down.

Having stayed, and in an hour's time seen the fire rage every way, and nobody to my sight endeavouring to quench it, but to remove their goods and leave all to the fire; and having seen it get as far as the Steeleyard, and the wind mighty high and driving it into the city, and everything, after so long a drougth, proving combustible, even the very stones of churches, and among other things, the poor steeple by which pretty Mrs [Horsley] lives, and

September 1666

whereof my old schoolfellow Elborough is parson, taken fire in the very top and there burned till it fall down – I to Whitehall with a gentleman with me who desired to go off from the Tower to see the fire in my boat – to Whitehall, and there up to the King's closet in the chapel, where people came about me and I did give them an account dismayed them all; and word was carried in to the King, so I was called for and did tell the King and Duke of York what I saw, and that unless his Majesty did command houses to be pulled down, nothing could stop the fire. They seemed much troubled, and the King commanded me to go to my Lord Mayor from him and command him to spare no houses but to pull down before the fire every way. The Duke of York bid me tell him that if he would have any more soldiers, he shall; and so did my Lord Arlington afterward, as a great secret. Here meeting with Capt. Cocke, I in his coach, which he lent me, and Creed with me, to Pauls; and there walked along Watling street as well as I could, every creature coming away loaden with goods to save – and here and there sick people carried away in beds. Extraordinary good goods carried in carts and on backs. At last met my Lord Mayor in Canning Streete, like a man spent, with a handkercher about his neck. To the King's message, he cried like a fainting woman, 'Lord, what can I do? I am spent! People will not obey me. I have been pull[ing] down houses. But the fire overtakes us faster then we can do it.' That he needed no more soldiers; and that for himself, he must go and refresh himself, having been up all night. So he left me, and I him, and walked home – seeing people all almost distracted and no manner of means used to quench the fire. The houses too, so very thick thereabouts, and full of matter for burning, as pitch and tar, in Thames street – and warehouses of oyle and wines and Brandy and other things. Here I saw Mr Isaccke Houblon, that handsome man – prettily dressed and dirty at his door at Dowgate, receiving some of his brothers things whose houses were on fire; and as he says, have been removed twice already, and he doubts (as it soon proved) that they must be in a little time removed from his house also – which was a sad consideration. And to see the churches all filling with goods, by people who themselfs should have been quietly there at this time. By this time it was about 12 a-clock, and so home and there find my guests, which was Mr Wood and his wife, Barbary Shelden, and also Mr Moone – she mighty fine, and her husband, for aught I see, a likely man. But Mr Moones design and mine, which was to look over my closet and please him with the sight thereof, which he hath long desired, was wholly disappointed, for we were in great trouble and disturbance at this fire, not knowing what to think of it. However, we had an extraordinary good dinner, and as merry as at this time we could be. While at dinner, Mrs Batelier came to enquire after Mr Woolfe and Stanes (who it seems are related to them), whose houses in

Fishstreet are all burned, and they in a sad condition. She would not stay in the fright.

As soon as dined, I and Moone away and walked through the City, the streets full of nothing but people and horses and carts loaden with goods, ready to run over one another, and removing goods from one burned house to another – they now removing out of Canning street (which received goods in the morning) into Lumbard Streete and further; and among others, I now saw my little goldsmith Stokes receiving some friend's goods, whose house itself was burned the day after. We parted at Pauls, he home and I to Pauls Wharf, where I had appointed a boat to attend me; and took in Mr Carcasse and his brother, whom I met in the street, and carried them below and above bridge, to and again, to see the fire, which was now got further, both below and above, and no likelihood of stopping it. Met with the King and Duke of York in their Barge, and with them to Queen Hith and there called Sir Rd. Browne to them. Their order was only to pull down houses apace, and so below bridge at the waterside; but little was or could be done, the fire coming upon them so fast. Good hopes there was of stopping it at the Three Cranes above, and at Buttolphs Wharf below bridge, if care be used; but the wind carries it into the City, so as we know not by the waterside what it doth there. River full of lighter[s] and boats taking in goods, and good goods swimming in the water; and only,

Samuel Pepys

I observed that hardly one lighter or boat in three that had goods of a house in, but there was a pair of virginalls in it. Having seen as much as I could now, I away to Whitehall by appointment, and there walked to St James's Park, and there met my wife and Creed and Wood and his wife and walked to my boat, and there upon the water again, and to the fire up and down, it still increasing and the wind great. So near the fire as we could for smoke; and all over the Thames, with one's face in the wind you were almost burned with a shower of Firedrops – this is very true – so as houses were burned by these drops and flakes of fire, three or four, nay five or six houses, one from another. When we could endure no more upon the water, we to a little alehouse on the Bankside over against the Three Cranes, and there stayed till it was dark almost and saw the fire grow; and as it grow darker, appeared more and more, and in Corners and upon steeples and between churches and houses, as far as we could see up the hill of the City, in a most horrid malicious bloody flame, not like the fine flame of an ordinary fire. Barbary and her husband away before us. We stayed till, it being darkish, we saw the fire as only one entire arch of fire from this to the other side of the bridge, and in a bow up the hill, for an arch of above a mile long. It made me weep to see it. The churches, houses, and all on fire and flaming at once, and a horrid noise the flames made, and the cracking of houses at their ruine.

So home with a sad heart, and there find everybody

discoursing and lamenting the fire; and poor Tom Hater came with some few of his goods saved out of his house, which is burned upon Fish street hill. I invited him to lie at my house, and did receive his goods: but was deceived in his lying there, the noise coming every moment of the growth of the Fire, so as we were forced to begin to pack up our own goods and prepare for their removal. And did by Mooneshine (it being brave, dry, and moonshine and warm weather) carry much of my goods into the garden, and Mr Hater and I did remove my money and Iron chests into my cellar – as thinking that the safest place. And got my bags of gold into my office ready to carry away, and my chief papers of accounts also there, and my tallies into a box by themselfs. So great was our fear, as Sir W. Batten had carts come out of the country to fetch away his goods this night. We did put Mr Hater, poor man, to bed a little; but he got but very little rest, so much noise being in my house, taking down of goods.

3. About 4 a-clock in the morning, my Lady Batten sent me a cart to carry away all my money and plate and best things to Sir W. Riders at Bednall greene; which I did, riding myself in my nightgown in the Cart; and Lord, to see how the streets and the highways are crowded with people, running and riding and getting of carts at any rate to fetch away thing[s]. I find Sir W. Rider tired with being called up all night and receiving things from several friends. His house full of goods – and much of Sir W.

Samuel Pepys

Batten and Sir W. Penn's. I am eased at my heart to have my treasure so well secured. Then home with much ado to find a way. Nor any sleep all this night to me nor my poor wife. But then, and all this day, she and I and all my people labouring to get away the rest of our things, and did get Mr Tooker to get me a lighter to take them in, and we did carry them (myself some) over Tower hill, which was by this time full of people's goods, bringing their goods thither. And down to the lighter, which lay at the next quay above the Tower dock. And there was my neighbour's wife, Mrs [Buckworth], with her pretty child and some few of her things, which I did willingly give way to be saved with mine. But there was no passing with anything through the postern, the crowd was so great. The Duke of York came this day by the office and spoke to us, and did ride with his guard up and down the City to keep all quiet (he being now General, and having the care of all). This day, Mercer being not at home, but against her mistress order gone to her mother's, and my wife going thither to speak with W. Hewer, met her there and was angry; and her mother saying that she was not a prentice girl, to ask leave every time she goes abroad, my wife with good reason was angry, and when she came home, bid her be gone again. And so she went away, which troubled me; but yet less then it would, because of the condition we are in fear of coming into in a little time, of being less able to keep one in her quality. At night, lay down a little upon a quilt of W. Hewer in the office (all my own things being packed up or gone); and after me, my poor wife did the like – we having fed upon the remains of yesterday's dinner, having no fire nor dishes, nor any opportunity of dressing anything.

4. Up by break of day to get away the remainder of my things, which I did by a lighter at the Iron gate; and my hands so few, that it was the afternoon before we could get them all away. Sir W. Penn and I to Tower street, and there met the fire Burning three or four doors beyond Mr Howells; whose goods, poor man (his trayes and dishes, Shovells &c., were flung all along Tower street in the kennels, and people working therewith from one end to the other), the fire coming on in that narrow street, on both sides, with infinite fury. Sir W. Batten, not knowing how to remove his wind, did dig a pit in the garden and laid it in there; and I took the opportunity of laying all the papers of my office that I could not otherwise dispose of. And in the evening Sir W. Penn and I did dig another and put our wine in it, and I my parmazan cheese as well as my wine and some other things. The Duke of York was at the office this day at Sir W. Penn's, but I happened not to be within. This afternoon, sitting melancholy with Sir W. Penn in our garden and thinking of the certain burning of this office without extraordinary means, I did propose for the sending up of all our workmen from Woolwich and Deptford yards (none whereof yet appeared), and to write to Sir W. Coventry to have the

Samuel Pepys

Duke of York's permission to pull down houses rather then lose this office, which would much hinder the King's business. So Sir W. Penn he went down this night, in order to the sending them up tomorrow morning; and I wrote to Sir W. Coventry about the business, but received no answer.

This night Mrs Turner (who, poor woman, was removing her goods all this day – good goods, into the garden, and knew not how to dispose of them) – and her husband supped with my wife and I at night in the office, upon a shoulder of mutton from the cook's, without any napkin or anything, in a sad manner but were merry. Only, now and then walking into the garden and saw how horridly the sky looks, all on a fire in the night, was enough to put us out of our wits; and endeed it was extremely dreadfull – for it looks just as if it was at us, and the whole heaven on fire. I after supper walked in the dark down to Tower street, and there saw it all on fire at the Trinity house on that side and the Dolphin tavern on this side, which was very near us – and the fire with extraordinary vehemence. Now begins the practice of blowing up of houses in Tower street, those next the Tower, which at first did frighten people more then anything; but it stop[ped] the fire where it was done – it bringing down the houses to the ground in the same places they stood, and then it was easy to quench what little fire was in it, though it kindled nothing almost. W. Hewer this day went to see how his mother did, and comes late home, but telling us how he hath been forced to remove her to Islington, her house in Pye Corner being burned. So that it is got so far that way and all the Old Bayly, and was running down to Fleet street. And Pauls is burned, and all Cheapside. I wrote to my father this night; but the post-house being burned, the letter could not go.

5. I lay down in the office again upon W. Hewer's quilt, being mighty weary and sore in my feet with going till I was hardly able to stand. About 2 in the morning my wife calls me up and tells of new Cryes of 'Fyre!' – it being come to Barkeing Church, which is the bottom of our lane. I up; and finding it so, resolved presently to take her away; and did, and took my gold (which was about 23 50*l*), W. Hewer, and Jane down by Poundy's boat to Woolwich. But Lord, what a sad sight it was by moonlight to see the whole City almost on fire – that you might see it plain at Woolwich, as if you were by it. There when I came, I find the gates shut, but no guard kept at all; which troubled me, because of discourses now begun that there is plot in it and that the French had done it. I got the gates open, and to Mr Shelden's, where I locked up my gold and charged my wife and W. Hewer never to leave the room without one of them in it night nor day. So back again, by the way seeing my goods well in the lighters at Deptford and watched well by people. Home, and whereas I expected to have seen our house on fire, it being now about 7 a-clock, it was not. But to the Fyre, and there

find greater hopes then I expected; for my confidence of finding our office on fire was such, that I durst not ask anybody how it was with us, till I came and saw it not burned. But going to the fire, I find, by the blowing up of houses and the great help given by the workmen out of the King's yards, sent up by Sir W. Penn, there is a good stop given to it, as well at Marke lane end as ours – it having only burned the Dyall of Barkeing Church, and part of the porch, and was there quenched. I up to the top of Barkeing steeple, and there saw the saddest sight of desolation that I ever saw. Everywhere great fires. Oyle cellars and brimstone and other things burning. I became afeared to stay there long; and therefore down again as fast as I could, the fire being spread as far as I could see it, and to Sir W. Penn's and there eat a piece of cold meat, having eaten nothing since Sunday but the remains of Sunday's dinner.

Here I met with Mr Young and Whistler; and having removed all my things, and received good hopes that the fire at our end is stopped, they and I walked into the town and find Fanchurch street, Gracious street, and Lumbard street all in dust. The Exchange a sad sight, nothing standing there of all the statues or pillars but Sir Tho. Gresham's picture in the corner. Walked into Moorefields (our feet ready to burn, walking through the town among the hot coles) and find that full of people, and poor wretches carrying their goods there, and everybody keeping his goods together by themselfs (and a great blessing

September 1666

it is to them that it is fair weather for them to keep abroad night and day); drank there, and paid twopence for a plain penny loaf. Thence homeward, having passed through Cheapside and Newgate market, all burned – and seen Anthony Joyces house in fire. And took up (which I keep by me) a piece of glass of Mercer's chapel in the street, where much more was, so melted and buckled with the heat of the fire, like parchment. I also did see a poor Catt taken out of a hole in the chimney joyning to the wall of the Exchange, with the hair all burned off the body and yet alive. So home at night, and find there good hopes of saving our office – but great endeavours of watching all night and having men ready; and so we lodged them in the office, and had drink and bread and cheese for them. And I lay down and slept a good night about midnight – though when I rose, I hear that there had been a great alarme of French and Duch being risen – which proved nothing. But it is a strange thing to see how long this time did look since Sunday, having been alway full of variety of actions, and little sleep, that it looked like a week or more. And I had forgot almost the day of the week.

6. Up about 5 a-clock, and there met Mr Gawden at the gate of the office (I entending to go out, as I used every now and then to do, to see how the fire is) to call our men to Bishoppsgate, where no fire had yet been near, and there is now one broke out – which did give great grounds

Samuel Pepys

to people, and to me too, to think that there is some kind of plott in this (on which many by this time have been taken, and it hath been dangerous for any stranger to walk in the streets); but I went with the men and we did put it out in a little time, so that that was well again. It was pretty to see how hard the women did work in the cannells sweeping of water; but then they would scold for drink and be as drunk as devils. I saw good Butts of sugar broke open in the street, and people go and take handfuls out and put into beer and drink it. And now all being pretty well, I took boat and over to Southwarke, and took boat on the other side the bridge and so to Westminster, thinking to Shift myself, being all in dirt from top to bottom. But could not there find any place to buy a Shirt or pair of gloves, Westminster hall being full of people's goods – those in Westminster having removed all their goods, and the Exchequer money put into vessels to carry to Nonsuch. But to the Swan, and there was trimmed. And then to Whitehall, but saw nobody, and so home. A sad sight to see how the River looks – no houses nor church near it to the Temple – where it stopped. At home did go with Sir W. Batten and our neighbour Knightly (who, with one more, was the only man of any fashion left in all the neighbourhood hereabouts, they all removing their goods and leaving their houses to the mercy of the fire) to Sir R. Ford's, and there dined, in an earthen platter a fried breast of mutton, a great many of us. But very merry; and endeed as good

September 1666

a meal, though as ugly a one, as ever I had in my life. Thence down to Deptford, and there with great satisfaction landed all my goods at Sir G. Carteret's, safe, and nothing missed I could see, or hurt. This being done to my great content, I home; and to Sir W. Batten's and there with Sir R. Ford, Mr Knightly, and one Withers, a professed lying rogue, supped well; and mighty merry and our fears over. From them to the office and there slept, with the office full of labourers, who talked and slept and walked all night long there. But strange it was to see Cloathworkers hall on fire these three days and nights in one body of Flame – it being the cellar, full of Oyle.

7. Up by 5 a-clock and, blessed be God, find all well, and by water to Paul's wharfe. Walked thence and saw all the town burned, and a miserable sight of Pauls church, with all the roofs fallen and the body of the Quire fallen into St Fayths – Paul's school also – Ludgate – Fleet street – my father's house, and the church, and a good part of the Temple the like. So to Creeds lodging near the New Exchange, and there find him laid down upon a bed – the house all unfurnished, there being fears of the fire's coming to them. There borrowed a shirt of him – and washed. To Sir W. Coventry at St James's, who lay without Curtains, having removed all his goods – as the King at Whitehall and everybody had done and was doing. He hopes we shall have no public distractions upon this fire, which is what everybody fears – because of the talk of

Samuel Pepys

the French having a hand in it. And it is a proper time for discontents – but all men's minds are full of care to protect themselfs and save their goods. The Militia is in armes everywhere. Our fleetes, he tells me, have been in sight of one another, and most unhappily by Fowle weather were parted, to our great loss, as in reason they do conclude – the Duch being come out only to make a show and please their people; but in very bad condition as to stores, victuals, and men. They are at Bullen, and our fleet come to St Ellens. We have got nothing, but have lost one ship, but he knows not what.

Thence to the Swan and there drank; and so home and find all well. My Lord Brouncker at Sir W. Batten's, and tells us the Generall is sent for up to come to advise with the King about business at this juncture, and to keep all quiet – which is great honour to him, but I am sure is but a piece of dissimulation. So home and did give order for my house to be made clean; and then down to Woolwich and there find all well. Dined, and Mrs Markeham came to see my wife. So I up again, and calling at Deptford for some things of W. Hewer, he being with me; and then home and spent the evening with Sir R. Ford, Mr Knightly, and Sir W. Penn at Sir W. Batten's. This day our Merchants first met at Gresham College, which by proclamation is to be their Exchange. Strange to hear what is bid for houses all up and down here – a friend of Sir W. Riders having 150*l* for what he used to let for 40*l* per annum. Much dispute where the Custome house shall be; thereby the growth of the City again to be foreseen. My Lord Treasurer, they say, and others, would have it at the other end of the town. I home late to Sir W. Penn, who did give me a bed – but without curtains or hangings, all being down. So here I went the first time into a naked bed, only my drawers on – and did sleep pretty well; but still, both sleeping and waking, had a fear of fire in my heart, that I took little rest. People do all the world over cry out of the simplicity of my Lord Mayor in general, and more perticularly in this business of the fire, laying it all upon him. A proclamation is come out for markets to be kept at Leadenhall and Mile end greene and several other places about the town, and Tower hill, and all churches to be set open to receive poor people.

8. Up, and with Sir W. Batten and Sir W. Penn by water to Whitehall, and they to St James's. I stopped with Sir G. Carteret, to desire him to go with us and to enquire after money. But the first he cannot do, and the other as little, or says, 'When can we get any, or what shall we do for it?' He, it seems, is imployed in the correspondence between the City and the King every day, in settling of things. I find him full of trouble to think how things will go. I left him, and to St James's, where we met first at Sir W. Coventry's chamber and there did what business we can without any books. Our discourse, as everything else, was confused. The fleet is at Portsmouth, there staying a wind to carry them to the Downes or toward Bullen,

Samuel Pepys

where they say the Duch fleete is gone and stays. We concluded upon private meetings for a while, not having any money to satisfy any people that may come to us. I bought two eeles upon the Thames, cost me 6*s*. Thence with Sir W. Batten to the Cockpit, whither the Duke of Albemarle is come. It seems the King holds him so necessary at this time, that he hath sent for him and will keep him here. Endeed, his interest in the City, being acquainted, and his care in keeping things quiet, is reckoned that wherein he will be very serviceable. We to him. He is courted in appearance by everybody. He very kind to us. I perceive he lays by all business of the fleet at present and minds the City, and is now hastening to Gresham College to discourse with the Aldermen. Sir W. Batten and I home (where met by my Brother John, come to town to see how things are with us). And then presently he with me to Gresham College – where infinite of people; partly through novelty to see the new place, and partly to find out and hear what is become one man of another. I met with many people undone, and more that have extraordinary great losses. People speaking their thoughts variously about the beginning of the fire and the rebuilding of the City. Then to Sir W. Batten and took my brother with me, and there dined with a great company of neighbours, and much good discourse; among others, of the low spirits of some rich men in the City, in sparing any encouragement to the poor people that wrought for the saving their houses. Among others, Ald. Starling, a very rich man, without children, the fire at next door to him in our Lane – after our men had saved his house, did give 2*s*. 6*d*. among 30 of them, and did quarrel with some that would remove the rubbish out of the way of the fire, saying that they came to steal. Sir. W. Coventry told me of another this morning in Holborne, which he showed the King – that when it was offered to stop the fire near his house for such a reward, that came but to 2*s*. 6*d*. a man among the neighbours, he would give but 18*d*. Thence to Bednall green by coach, my brother with me, and saw all well there and fetched away my Journall-book to enter for five days past. To the office, and late writing letters; and then to Sir W. Penn, my brother lying with me, and Sir W. Penn gone down to rest himself at Woolwich. But I was much frighted, and kept awake in my bed, by some noise I heard a great while below-stairs and the boys not coming up to me when I knocked. It was by their discovery of people stealing of some neighbours' wine that lay in vessels in the street. So to sleep. And all well all night.

9. *Sunday*. Up, and was trimmed, and sent my brother to Woolwich to my wife to dine with her. I to church, where our parson made a melancholy but good sermon – and many, and most, in the church cried, especially the women. The church mighty full, but few of fashion, and most strangers. I walked to Bednall green; and there dined well, but a bad venison pasty, at Sir W. Rider's.

Good people they are, and good discourse. And his daughter Middleton, a fine woman and discreet. Thence home, and to church again, and there preached Deane Harding; but methinks a bad poor sermon, though proper for the time – nor eloquent, in saying at this time that the City is reduced from a large Folio to a Decimo tertio. So to my office, there to write down my journall and take leave of my brother, whom I sent back this afternoon, though rainy – which it hath not done a good while before. But I had no room nor convenience for him here till my house is fitted; but I was very kind to him, and do take very well of him his journey. I did give him 40s. for his pocket; and so he being gone, and it presently rayning, I was troubled for him, though it is good for the Fyre. Anon to Sir W. Penn to bed, and made my boy Tom to read me asleep.

13. Up, and down to Tower wharfe; and there with Balty and labourers from Deptford did get my goods housed well at home. So down to Deptford again to fetch the rest, and there eat a bit of dinner at the Globe, with the maister of the *Bezan* with me, while the labourers went to dinner. Here I hear that this poor town doth bury still of the plague seven or eight in a day. So to Sir G. Carteret's to work; and there did, to my great content, ship off into the *Bezan* all the rest of my goods, saving my pictures and fine things, that I will bring home in wherrys when my house is fit to receive them. And so home and unloaden

them by carts and hands before night, to my exceeding satisfaction; and so after supper to bed in my house, the first time I have lain there; and lay with my wife in my old closet upon the ground, and Balty and his wife in the best chamber, upon the ground also.

14. Up, and to work, having Carpenters come to help in setting up bedsteads and hangings; and at that trade my people and I all the morning, till pressed by public business to leave them, against my will, in the afternoon; and yet I was troubled in being at home, to see all my goods lie up and down the house in a bad condition, and strange workmen going to and fro might take what they would almost. All the afternoon busy; and Sir W. Coventry came to me, and found me, as God would have it, in my office, and people about me setting my papers to rights; and there discoursed about getting an account ready against the Parliament, and thereby did create me infinite of business, and to be done on a sudden, which troubled me; but however, he being gone, I about it late to good purpose; and so home, having this day also got my wine out of the ground again and set it in my cellar; but with great pain to keep the port[er]s that carried it in from observing the money-chests there. So to bed as last night; only, my wife and I upon a bedstead with curtains in that which was Mercer's chamber, and Balty and his wife (who are here and do us good service) where we lay last night.

Samuel Pepys

15. All morning at the office, Harman being come, to my great satisfaction, to put up my beds and hangings; so I am at rest, and fallowed my business all day. Dined with Sir W. Batten. Mighty busy about this account, and while my people were busy, myself wrote near 30 letters and orders with my own hand. At it till 11 at night; and it is strange to see how clear my head was, being eased of all the matter of all those letters; whereas one would think that I should have been dozed – I never did observe so much of myself in my life. In the evening there comes to me Capt. Cocke, and walked a good while in the garden; he says he hath computed that the rents of houses lost this fire in the City comes to 600000*l* per annum. That this will make the Parliament more quiet then otherwise they would have been and give the King a more ready supply. That the supply must be by excise, as it is in holland. That the Parliament will see it necessary to carry on the war. That the late storm hindered our beating the Duch fleet, who were gone out only to satisfy the people, having no business to do but to avoid us. That the French, as late in the year as it is, are coming. That the Duch are really in bad condition, but that this unhappiness of ours doth give them heart. That, certainly, never so great a loss as this was borne so well by citizens in the world as this; he believing that not one merchant upon the Change will break upon it. That he doth not apprehend there will be any disturbances in estate upon it, for that all men are busy in looking after their own business, to save

September 1666

themselfs. He gone, I to finish my letters; and home to bed and find, to my infinite joy, many rooms clean, and myself and wife lie in our own chamber again. But much terrified in the nights nowadays with dreams of fire and falling down of houses.

1. BOCCACCIO · *Mrs Rosie and the Priest*
2. GERARD MANLEY HOPKINS · *As kingfishers catch fire*
3. *The Saga of Gunnlaug Serpent-tongue*
4. THOMAS DE QUINCEY · *On Murder Considered as One of the Fine Arts*
5. FRIEDRICH NIETZSCHE · *Aphorisms on Love and Hate*
6. JOHN RUSKIN · *Traffic*
7. PU SONGLING · *Wailing Ghosts*
8. JONATHAN SWIFT · *A Modest Proposal*
9. *Three Tang Dynasty Poets*
10. WALT WHITMAN · *On the Beach at Night Alone*
11. KENKŌ · *A Cup of Sake Beneath the Cherry Trees*
12. BALTASAR GRACIÁN · *How to Use Your Enemies*
13. JOHN KEATS · *The Eve of St Agnes*
14. THOMAS HARDY · *Woman much missed*
15. GUY DE MAUPASSANT · *Femme Fatale*
16. MARCO POLO · *Travels in the Land of Serpents and Pearls*
17. SUETONIUS · *Caligula*
18. APOLLONIUS OF RHODES · *Jason and Medea*
19. ROBERT LOUIS STEVENSON · *Olalla*
20. KARL MARX AND FRIEDRICH ENGELS · *The Communist Manifesto*
21. PETRONIUS · *Trimalchio's Feast*
22. JOHANN PETER HEBEL · *How a Ghastly Story Was Brought to Light by a Common or Garden Butcher's Dog*
23. HANS CHRISTIAN ANDERSEN · *The Tinder Box*
24. RUDYARD KIPLING · *The Gate of the Hundred Sorrows*
25. DANTE · *Circles of Hell*
26. HENRY MAYHEW · *Of Street Piemen*
27. HAFEZ · *The nightingales are drunk*
28. GEOFFREY CHAUCER · *The Wife of Bath*
29. MICHEL DE MONTAIGNE · *How We Weep and Laugh at the Same Thing*
30. THOMAS NASHE · *The Terrors of the Night*
31. EDGAR ALLAN POE · *The Tell-Tale Heart*
32. MARY KINGSLEY · *A Hippo Banquet*
33. JANE AUSTEN · *The Beautifull Cassandra*
34. ANTON CHEKHOV · *Gooseberries*
35. SAMUEL TAYLOR COLERIDGE · *Well, they are gone, and here must I remain*
36. JOHANN WOLFGANG VON GOETHE · *Sketchy, Doubtful, Incomplete Jottings*
37. CHARLES DICKENS · *The Great Winglebury Duel*
38. HERMAN MELVILLE · *The Maldive Shark*
39. ELIZABETH GASKELL · *The Old Nurse's Story*
40. NIKOLAY LESKOV · *The Steel Flea*

41. HONORÉ DE BALZAC · *The Atheist's Mass*
42. CHARLOTTE PERKINS GILMAN · *The Yellow Wall-Paper*
43. C.P. CAVAFY · *Remember, Body . . .*
44. FYODOR DOSTOYEVSKY · *The Meek One*
45. GUSTAVE FLAUBERT · *A Simple Heart*
46. NIKOLAI GOGOL · *The Nose*
47. SAMUEL PEPYS · *The Great Fire of London*
48. EDITH WHARTON · *The Reckoning*
49. HENRY JAMES · *The Figure in the Carpet*
50. WILFRED OWEN · *Anthem For Doomed Youth*
51. WOLFGANG AMADEUS MOZART · *My Dearest Father*
52. PLATO · *Socrates' Defence*
53. CHRISTINA ROSSETTI · *Goblin Market*
54. *Sindbad the Sailor*
55. SOPHOCLES · *Antigone*
56. RYŪNOSUKE AKUTAGAWA · *The Life of a Stupid Man*
57. LEO TOLSTOY · *How Much Land Does A Man Need?*
58. GIORGIO VASARI · *Leonardo da Vinci*
59. OSCAR WILDE · *Lord Arthur Savile's Crime*
60. SHEN FU · *The Old Man of the Moon*
61. AESOP · *The Dolphins, the Whales and the Gudgeon*
62. MATSUO BASHŌ · *Lips too Chilled*
63. EMILY BRONTË · *The Night is Darkening Round Me*
64. JOSEPH CONRAD · *To-morrow*
65. RICHARD HAKLUYT · *The Voyage of Sir Francis Drake Around the Whole Globe*
66. KATE CHOPIN · *A Pair of Silk Stockings*
67. CHARLES DARWIN · *It was snowing butterflies*
68. BROTHERS GRIMM · *The Robber Bridegroom*
69. CATULLUS · *I Hate and I Love*
70. HOMER · *Circe and the Cyclops*
71. D. H. LAWRENCE · *Il Duro*
72. KATHERINE MANSFIELD · *Miss Brill*
73. OVID · *The Fall of Icarus*
74. SAPPHO · *Come Close*
75. IVAN TURGENEV · *Kasyan from the Beautiful Lands*
76. VIRGIL · *O Cruel Alexis*
77. H. G. WELLS · *A Slip under the Microscope*
78. HERODOTUS · *The Madness of Cambyses*
79. *Speaking of Siva*
80. *The Dhammapada*

'If marriage was the slow life-long acquittal of a debt contracted in ignorance, then marriage was a crime against human nature.'

EDITH WHARTON
Born 1862, New York City, USA
Died 1937, Saint-Brice-sous-Forêt, France

'Mrs Manstey's View', Edith Wharton's first published story, appeared in 1891. 'The Reckoning' was published in 1902.

WHARTON IN PENGUIN CLASSICS
Ethan Frome
The Age of Innocence
The Custom of the Country
The House of Mirth
Three Novels of New York

EDITH WHARTON

The Reckoning

PENGUIN BOOKS

PENGUIN CLASSICS

UK | USA | Canada | Ireland | Australia
India | New Zealand | South Africa

Penguin Books is part of the Penguin Random House group of companies
whose addresses can be found at global.penguinrandomhouse.com.

This selection published in Penguin Classics 2015
009

Set in 9.5/13 pt Baskerville 10 Pro
Typeset by Jouve (UK), Milton Keynes
Printed and bound in Great Britain by Clays Ltd, Elcograf S.p.A.

A CIP catalogue record for this book is available from the British Library

ISBN: 978-0-141-39756-6

www.greenpenguin.co.uk

Penguin Random House is committed to a sustainable future for our business, our readers and our planet. This book is made from Forest Stewardship Council® certified paper.

Contents

Mrs Manstey's View   1
The Reckoning   17

Mrs Manstey's View

The view from Mrs Manstey's window was not a striking one, but to her at least it was full of interest and beauty. Mrs Manstey occupied the back room on the third floor of a New York boarding-house, in a street where the ash-barrels lingered late on the sidewalk and the gaps in the pavement would have staggered a Quintus Curtius. She was the widow of a clerk in a large wholesale house, and his death had left her alone, for her only daughter had married in California, and could not afford the long journey to New York to see her mother. Mrs Manstey, perhaps, might have joined her daughter in the West, but they had now been so many years apart that they had ceased to feel any need of each other's society, and their intercourse had long been limited to the exchange of a few perfunctory letters, written with indifference by the daughter, and with difficulty by Mrs Manstey, whose right hand was growing stiff with gout. Even had she felt a stronger desire for her daughter's companionship, Mrs Manstey's increasing infirmity, which caused her to dread the three flights of stairs between her room and the street, would have given her pause on the eve of undertaking so long a journey; and without perhaps formulating these reasons she had long since accepted as a matter of course her solitary life in New York.

She was, indeed, not quite lonely, for a few friends still toiled up now and then to her room; but their visits grew rare as the years went by. Mrs Manstey had never been a sociable woman, and during her husband's lifetime his companionship had been all-sufficient to her. For many years she had cherished a desire to live in the country, to have a hen-house and a garden; but this longing had faded with age, leaving only in the breast of the uncommunicative old woman a vague tenderness for plants and animals. It was, perhaps, this tenderness which made her cling so fervently to her view from her window, a view in which the most optimistic eye would at first have failed to discover anything admirable.

Mrs Manstey, from her coign of vantage (a slightly projecting bow-window where she nursed an ivy and a succession of unwholesome-looking bulbs), looked out first upon the yard of her own dwelling, of which, however, she could get but a restricted glimpse. Still, her gaze took in the topmost boughs of the ailanthus below her window, and she knew how early each year the clump of dicentra strung its bending stalk with hearts of pink.

But of greater interest were the yards beyond. Being for the most part attached to boarding-houses they were in a state of chronic untidiness and fluttering, on certain days of the week, with miscellaneous garments and frayed table-cloths. In spite of this Mrs Manstey found much to admire in the long vista which she commanded. Some of the yards were, indeed, but stony wastes, with grass in the cracks of the pavement and no shade in spring save that afforded by the intermittent leafage of the clothes-lines. These yards Mrs Manstey disapproved of, but the others, the green ones, she loved. She had grown used to their disorder; the broken barrels, the empty bottles and paths unswept no longer annoyed her; hers was the happy faculty of dwelling on the pleasanter side of the prospect before her.

In the very next enclosure did not a magnolia open its hard white flowers against the watery blue of April? And was there not, a little way down the line, a fence foamed over every May by lilac waves of wistaria? Farther still, a horse-chestnut lifted its candelabra of buff and pink blossoms above broad fans of foliage; while in the opposite yard June was sweet with the breath of a neglected syringa, which persisted in growing in spite of the countless obstacles opposed to its welfare.

But if nature occupied the front rank in Mrs Manstey's view, there was much of a more personal character to interest her in the aspect of the houses and their inmates. She deeply disapproved of the mustard-colored curtains which had lately been hung in the doctor's window opposite; but she glowed with pleasure when the house farther down had its old bricks washed with a coat of paint. The occupants of the houses did not often show themselves at the back windows, but the servants were always in sight. Noisy slatterns, Mrs Manstey pronounced the greater number; she knew their ways and hated them. But to the quiet cook in the newly painted house, whose mistress bullied her, and who secretly fed the stray cats at nightfall, Mrs Manstey's warmest sympathies were given. On one occasion her feelings were racked by the neglect of a house-maid, who for two days forgot to feed the parrot committed to her care. On the third day, Mrs Manstey, in spite of her gouty hand, had just penned a letter, beginning: 'Madam, it is now three days since your parrot has been fed,' when the forgetful maid appeared at the window with a cup of seed in her hand.

But in Mrs Manstey's more meditative moods it was the narrowing perspective of far-off yards which pleased her best. She loved, at twilight, when the distant brown-stone spire seemed melting in the fluid yellow of the west, to lose herself in vague memories of a trip to Europe, made years ago, and now reduced in her mind's eye to a pale phantasmagoria of indistinct steeples and dreamy skies. Perhaps at heart Mrs Manstey was an artist; at all events she was sensible of many changes of color unnoticed by the average eye, and dear to her as the green of early spring was the black lattice of branches against a cold sulphur sky at the close of a snowy day. She enjoyed, also, the sunny thaws of March, when patches of earth showed through the snow, like ink-spots spreading on a sheet of white blotting-paper; and, better still, the haze of boughs, leafless but swollen, which replaced the clear-cut tracery of winter. She even watched with a certain interest the trail of smoke from a far-off factory chimney, and missed a detail in the landscape when the factory was closed and the smoke disappeared.

Mrs Manstey, in the long hours which she spent at her window, was not idle. She read a little, and knitted numberless stockings; but the view surrounded and shaped her life as the sea does a lonely island. When her rare callers came it was difficult for her to detach herself from the contemplation of the opposite window-washing, or the scrutiny of certain green points in a neighboring flower-bed which might, or might not, turn into hyacinths, while she feigned an interest in her visitor's anecdotes about some unknown grandchild. Mrs Manstey's real friends were the denizens of the yards, the hyacinths, the magnolia, the green parrot, the maid who fed the cats, the doctor who studied late behind his mustard-colored curtains; and the confidant of her tenderer musings was the church-spire floating in the sunset.

One April day, as she sat in her usual place, with knitting cast aside and eyes fixed on the blue sky mottled with round clouds, a knock at the door announced the entrance of her landlady. Mrs Manstey did not care for her landlady, but she submitted to her visits with ladylike resignation. To-day, however, it seemed harder than usual to turn from the blue sky and the blossoming magnolia to Mrs Sampson's unsuggestive face, and Mrs Manstey was conscious of a distinct effort as she did so.

'The magnolia is out earlier than usual this year, Mrs Sampson,' she remarked, yielding to a rare impulse, for she seldom alluded to the absorbing interest of her life. In the first place it was a topic not likely to appeal to her visitors and, besides, she lacked the power of expression and could not have given utterance to her feelings had she wished to.

'The what, Mrs Manstey?' inquired the landlady, glancing about the room as if to find there the explanation of Mrs Manstey's statement.

'The magnolia in the next yard – in Mrs Black's yard,' Mrs Manstey repeated.

'Is it, indeed? I didn't know there was a magnolia there,' said Mrs Sampson, carelessly. Mrs Manstey looked at her; she did not know that there was a magnolia in the next yard!

'By the way,' Mrs Sampson continued, 'speaking of Mrs Black reminds me that the work on the extension is to begin next week.'

'The what?' it was Mrs Manstey's turn to ask.

'The extension,' said Mrs Sampson, nodding her head in the direction of the ignored magnolia. 'You knew, of course, that Mrs Black was going to build an extension to her house? Yes, ma'am. I hear it is to run right back to the end of the yard. How she can afford to build an extension in these hard times I don't see; but she always was crazy about building. She used to keep a boarding-house in Seventeenth Street, and she nearly ruined herself then by sticking out bow-windows and what not; I should have thought that would have cured her of building, but I guess it's a disease, like drink. Anyhow, the work is to begin on Monday.'

Mrs Manstey had grown pale. She always spoke slowly, so the landlady did not heed the long pause which followed. At last Mrs Manstey said: 'Do you know how high the extension will be?'

'That's the most absurd part of it. The extension is to be built right up to the roof of the main building; now, did you ever?'

Mrs Manstey paused again. 'Won't it be a great annoyance to you, Mrs Sampson?' she asked.

'I should say it would. But there's no help for it; if people have got a mind to build extensions there's no law to prevent 'em, that I'm aware of.' Mrs Manstey, knowing this, was silent. 'There is no help for it,' Mrs Sampson repeated, 'but if I *am* a church member, I wouldn't be so sorry if it ruined Eliza Black. Well, good-day, Mrs Manstey; I'm glad to find you so comfortable.'

So comfortable – so comfortable! Left to herself the old woman turned once more to the window. How lovely the view was that day! The blue sky with its round clouds shed a brightness over everything; the ailanthus had put on a tinge of yellow-green, the hyacinths were budding, the magnolia flowers looked more than ever like rosettes carved in alabaster. Soon the wistaria would bloom, then the horse-chestnut; but not for her. Between her eyes and them a barrier of brick and mortar would swiftly rise; presently even the spire would disappear, and all her radiant world be blotted out. Mrs Manstey sent away untouched the dinner-tray brought to her that evening. She lingered in the window until the windy sunset died in bat-colored dusk; then, going to bed, she lay sleepless all night.

Early the next day she was up and at the window. It was raining, but even through the slanting gray gauze the scene had its charm – and then the rain was so good for the trees. She had noticed the day before that the ailanthus was growing dusty.

'Of course I might move,' said Mrs Manstey aloud, and turning from the window she looked about her room. She might move, of course; so might she be flayed alive; but she was not likely to survive either operation. The room, though far less important to her happiness than the view, was as much a part of her existence. She had lived in it seventeen years. She knew every stain on the wall-paper, every rent in the carpet; the light fell in a certain way on her engravings, her books had grown shabby on their shelves, her bulbs and ivy were used to their window and knew which way to lean to the sun. 'We are all too old to move,' she said.

That afternoon it cleared. Wet and radiant the blue

reappeared through torn rags of cloud; the ailanthus sparkled; the earth in the flower-borders looked rich and warm. It was Thursday, and on Monday the building of the extension was to begin.

On Sunday afternoon a card was brought to Mrs Black, as she was engaged in gathering up the fragments of the boarders' dinner in the basement. The card, black-edged, bore Mrs Manstey's name.

'One of Mrs Sampson's boarders; wants to move, I suppose. Well, I can give her a room next year in the extension. Dinah,' said Mrs Black, 'tell the lady I'll be upstairs in a minute.'

Mrs Black found Mrs Manstey standing in the long parlor garnished with statuettes and antimacassars; in that house she could not sit down.

Stooping hurriedly to open the register, which let out a cloud of dust, Mrs Black advanced to her visitor.

'I'm happy to meet you, Mrs Manstey; take a seat, please,' the landlady remarked in her prosperous voice, the voice of a woman who can afford to build extensions. There was no help for it; Mrs Manstey sat down.

'Is there anything I can do for you, ma'am?' Mrs Black continued. 'My house is full at present, but I am going to build an extension, and – '

'It is about the extension that I wish to speak,' said Mrs Manstey, suddenly. 'I am a poor woman, Mrs Black, and I have never been a happy one. I shall have to talk about myself first to – to make you understand.'

Mrs Black, astonished but imperturbable, bowed at this parenthesis.

'I never had what I wanted,' Mrs Manstey continued. 'It was always one disappointment after another. For years I wanted to live in the country. I dreamed and dreamed about it; but we never could manage it. There was no sunny window in our house, and so all my plants died. My daughter married years ago and went away – besides, she never cared for the same things. Then my husband died and I was left alone. That was seventeen years ago. I went to live at Mrs Sampson's, and I have been there ever since. I have grown a little infirm, as you see, and I don't get out often; only on fine days, if I am feeling very well. So you can understand my sitting a great deal in my window – the back window on the third floor – '

'Well, Mrs Manstey,' said Mrs Black, liberally, 'I could give you a back room, I dare say; one of the new rooms in the ex – '

'But I don't want to move; I can't move,' said Mrs Manstey, almost with a scream. 'And I came to tell you that if you build that extension I shall have no view from my window – no view! Do you understand?'

Mrs Black thought herself face to face with a lunatic, and she had always heard that lunatics must be humored.

'Dear me, dear me,' she remarked, pushing her chair back a little way, 'that is too bad, isn't it? Why, I never thought of that. To be sure, the extension *will* interfere with your view, Mrs Manstey.'

Mrs Mansfey's View

'You do understand?' Mrs Manstey gasped.

'Of course I do. And I'm real sorry about it, too. But there, don't you worry, Mrs Manstey. I guess we can fix that all right.'

Mrs Manstey rose from her seat, and Mrs Black slipped toward the door.

'What do you mean by fixing it? Do you mean that I can induce you to change your mind about the extension? Oh, Mrs Black, listen to me. I have two thousand dollars in the bank and I could manage, I know I could manage, to give you a thousand if – ' Mrs Manstey paused; the tears were rolling down her cheeks.

'There, there, Mrs Manstey, don't you worry,' repeated Mrs Black, soothingly. 'I am sure we can settle it. I am sorry that I can't stay and talk about it any longer, but this is such a busy time of day, with supper to get – '

Her hand was on the door-knob, but with sudden vigor Mrs Manstey seized her wrist.

'You are not giving me a definite answer. Do you mean to say that you accept my proposition?'

'Why, I'll think it over, Mrs Manstey, certainly I will. I wouldn't annoy you for the world – '

'But the work is to begin to-morrow, I am told,' Mrs Manstey persisted.

Mrs Black hesitated. 'It shan't begin, I promise you that; I'll send word to the builder this very night.' Mrs Manstey tightened her hold.

'You are not deceiving me, are you?' she said.

'No – no,' stammered Mrs Black. 'How can you think such a thing of me, Mrs Manstey?'

Slowly Mrs Manstey's clutch relaxed, and she passed through the open door. 'One thousand dollars,' she repeated, pausing in the hall; then she let herself out of the house and hobbled down the steps, supporting herself on the cast-iron railing.

'My goodness,' exclaimed Mrs Black, shutting and bolting the hall-door, 'I never knew the old woman was crazy! And she looks so quiet and ladylike, too.'

Mrs Manstey slept well that night, but early the next morning she was awakened by a sound of hammering. She got to her window with what haste she might and, looking out, saw that Mrs Black's yard was full of workmen. Some were carrying loads of brick from the kitchen to the yard, others beginning to demolish the old-fashioned wooden balcony which adorned each story of Mrs Black's house. Mrs Manstey saw that she had been deceived. At first she thought of confiding her trouble to Mrs Sampson, but a settled discouragement soon took possession of her and she went back to bed, not caring to see what was going on.

Toward afternoon, however, feeling that she must know the worst, she rose and dressed herself. It was a laborious task, for her hands were stiffer than usual, and the hooks and buttons seemed to evade her.

When she seated herself in the window, she saw that the workmen had removed the upper part of the balcony,

Mrs Manstey's View

and that the bricks had multiplied since morning. One of the men, a coarse fellow with a bloated face, picked a magnolia blossom and, after smelling it, threw it to the ground; the next man, carrying a load of bricks, trod on the flower in passing.

'Look out, Jim,' called one of the men to another who was smoking a pipe, 'if you throw matches around near those barrels of paper you'll have the old tinder-box burning down before you know it.' And Mrs Manstey, leaning forward, perceived that there were several barrels of paper and rubbish under the wooden balcony.

At length the work ceased and twilight fell. The sunset was perfect and a roseate light, transfiguring the distant spire, lingered late in the west. When it grew dark Mrs Manstey drew down the shades and proceeded, in her usual methodical manner, to light her lamp. She always filled and lit it with her own hands, keeping a kettle of kerosene on a zinc-covered shelf in a closet. As the lamp-light filled the room it assumed its usual peaceful aspect. The books and pictures and plants seemed, like their mistress, to settle themselves down for another quiet evening, and Mrs Manstey, as was her wont, drew up her armchair to the table and began to knit.

That night she could not sleep. The weather had changed and a wild wind was abroad, blotting the stars with close-driven clouds. Mrs Manstey rose once or twice and looked out of the window; but of the view nothing was discernible save a tardy light or two in the opposite windows. These lights at last went out, and Mrs Manstey, who had watched for their extinction, began to dress herself. She was in evident haste, for she merely flung a thin dressing-gown over her night-dress and wrapped her head in a scarf; then she opened her closet and cautiously took out the kettle of kerosene. Having slipped a bundle of wooden matches into her pocket she proceeded, with increasing precautions, to unlock her door, and a few moments later she was feeling her way down the dark staircase, led by a glimmer of gas from the lower hall. At length she reached the bottom of the stairs and began the more difficult descent into the utter darkness of the basement. Here, however, she could move more freely, as there was less danger of being overheard; and without much delay she contrived to unlock the iron door leading into the yard. A gust of cold wind smote her as she stepped out and groped shiveringly under the clothes-lines.

That morning at three o'clock an alarm of fire brought the engines to Mrs Black's door, and also brought Mrs Sampson's startled boarders to their windows. The wooden balcony at the back of Mrs Black's house was ablaze, and among those who watched the progress of the flames was Mrs Manstey, leaning in her thin dressing-gown from the open window.

The fire, however, was soon put out, and the frightened occupants of the house, who had fled in scant attire, reassembled at dawn to find that little mischief had been done beyond the cracking of window panes and smoking of

Mrs Mansey's View

ceilings. In fact, the chief sufferer by the fire was Mrs Manstey, who was found in the morning gasping with pneumonia, a not unnatural result, as everyone remarked, of her having hung out of an open window at her age in a dressing-gown. It was easy to see that she was very ill, but no one had guessed how grave the doctor's verdict would be, and the faces gathered that evening about Mrs Sampson's table were awe-struck and disturbed. Not that any of the boarders knew Mrs Manstey well; she 'kept to herself,' as they said, and seemed to fancy herself too good for them; but then it is always disagreeable to have anyone dying in the house and, as one lady observed to another: 'It might just as well have been you or me, my dear.'

But it was only Mrs Manstey; and she was dying, as she had lived, lonely if not alone. The doctor had sent a trained nurse, and Mrs Sampson, with muffled step, came in from time to time; but both, to Mrs Manstey, seemed remote and unsubstantial as the figures in a dream. All day she said nothing; but when she was asked for her daughter's address she shook her head. At times the nurse noticed that she seemed to be listening attentively for some sound which did not come; then again she dozed.

The next morning at daylight she was very low. The nurse called Mrs Sampson and as the two bent over the old woman they saw her lips move.

'Lift me up – out of bed,' she whispered.

They raised her in their arms, and with her stiff hand she pointed to the window.

'Oh, the window – she wants to sit in the window. She used to sit there all day,' Mrs Sampson explained. 'It can do her no harm, I suppose?'

'Nothing matters now,' said the nurse.

They carried Mrs Manstey to the window and placed her in her chair. The dawn was abroad, a jubilant spring dawn; the spire had already caught a golden ray, though the magnolia and horse-chestnut still slumbered in shadow. In Mrs Black's yard all was quiet. The charred timbers of the balcony lay where they had fallen. It was evident that since the fire the builders had not returned to their work. The magnolia had unfolded a few more sculptural flowers; the view was undisturbed.

It was hard for Mrs Manstey to breathe; each moment it grew more difficult. She tried to make them open the window, but they would not understand. If she could have tasted the air, sweet with the penetrating ailanthus savor, it would have eased her; but the view at least was there – the spire was golden now, the heavens had warmed from pearl to blue, day was alight from east to west, even the magnolia had caught the sun.

Mrs Manstey's head fell back and smiling she died.

That day the building of the extension was resumed.

The Reckoning

'The marriage law of the new dispensation will be: *Thou shalt not be unfaithful – to thyself.*'

A discreet murmur of approval filled the studio, and through the haze of cigarette smoke Mrs Clement Westall, as her husband descended from his improvised platform, saw him merged in a congratulatory group of ladies. Westall's informal talks on 'The New Ethics' had drawn about him an eager following of the mentally unemployed – those who, as he had once phrased it, liked to have their brain-food cut up for them. The talks had begun by accident. Westall's ideas were known to be 'advanced,' but hitherto their advance had not been in the direction of publicity. He had been, in his wife's opinion, almost pusillanimously careful not to let his personal views endanger his professional standing. Of late, however, he had shown a puzzling tendency to dogmatize, to throw down the gauntlet, to flaunt his private code in the face of society; and the relation of the sexes being a topic always sure of an audience, a few admiring friends had persuaded him to give his after-dinner opinions a larger circulation by summing them up in a series of talks at the Van Sideren studio.

The Herbert Van Siderens were a couple who subsisted, socially, on the fact that they had a studio. Van Sideren's pictures were chiefly valuable as accessories to the *mise en scène* which differentiated his wife's 'afternoons' from the blighting functions held in long New York drawing-rooms, and permitted her to offer their friends whiskey-and-soda instead of tea. Mrs Van Sideren, for her part, was skilled in making the most of the kind of atmosphere which a lay-figure and an easel create; and if at times she found the illusion hard to maintain, and lost courage to the extent of almost wishing that Herbert could paint, she promptly overcame such moments of weakness by calling in some fresh talent, some extraneous re-enforcement of the 'artistic' impression. It was in quest of such aid that she had seized on Westall, coaxing him, somewhat to his wife's surprise, into a flattered participation in her fraud. It was vaguely felt, in the Van Sideren circle, that all the audacities were artistic, and that a teacher who pronounced marriage immoral was somehow as distinguished as a painter who depicted purple grass and a green sky. The Van Sideren set were tired of the conventional color-scheme in art and conduct.

Julia Westall had long had her own views on the immorality of marriage; she might indeed have claimed her husband as a disciple. In the early days of their union she had secretly resented his disinclination to proclaim himself a follower of the new creed; had been inclined to tax him with moral cowardice, with a failure to live up to the convictions for which their marriage was supposed to stand. That was in the first burst of propagandism, when, womanlike, she wanted to turn her disobedience into a law. Now she felt differently. She could hardly account for the change, yet being a woman who never allowed her impulses to remain unaccounted for, she tried to do so by saying that she did not care to have the articles of her faith misinterpreted by the vulgar. In this connection, she was beginning to think that almost every one was vulgar; certainly there were few to whom she would have cared to entrust the defense of so esoteric a doctrine. And it was precisely at this point that Westall, discarding his unspoken principles, had chosen to descend from the heights of privacy, and stand hawking his convictions at the street-corner!

It was Una Van Sideren who, on this occasion, unconsciously focused upon herself Mrs Westall's wandering resentment. In the first place, the girl had no business to be there. It was 'horrid' – Mrs Westall found herself slipping back into the old feminine vocabulary – simply 'horrid' to think of a young girl's being allowed to listen to such talk. The fact that Una smoked cigarettes and sipped an occasional cocktail did not in the least tarnish a certain radiant innocency which made her appear the victim, rather than the accomplice, of her parents' vulgarities. Julia Westall felt in a hot helpless way that something ought to be done – that some one ought to speak to the girl's mother. And just then Una glided up.

'Oh, Mrs Westall, how beautiful it was!' Una fixed her with large limpid eyes. 'You believe it all, I suppose?' she asked with seraphic gravity.

'All – what, my dear child?'

The girl shone on her. 'About the higher life – the freer expansion of the individual – the law of fidelity to one's self,' she glibly recited.

Mrs Westall, to her own wonder, blushed a deep and burning blush.

'My dear Una,' she said, 'you don't in the least understand what it's all about!'

Miss Van Sideren stared, with a slowly answering blush. 'Don't *you*, then?' she murmured.

Mrs Westall laughed. 'Not always – or altogether! But I should like some tea, please.'

Una led her to the corner where innocent beverages were dispensed. As Julia received her cup she scrutinized the girl more carefully. It was not such a girlish face, after all – definite lines were forming under the rosy haze of youth. She reflected that Una must be six-and-twenty, and wondered why she had not married. A nice stock of ideas she would have as her dower! If *they* were to be a part of the modern girl's trousseau –

Mrs Westall caught herself up with a start. It was as though some one else had been speaking – a stranger who had borrowed her own voice: she felt herself the dupe of some fantastic mental ventriloquism. Concluding suddenly that the room was stifling and Una's tea too sweet, she set down her cup and looked about for Westall: to meet his eyes had long been her refuge from every uncertainty. She met them now, but only, as she felt, in transit; they included her parenthetically in a larger flight. She followed the flight, and it carried her to a corner to which Una had withdrawn – one of the palmy nooks to which Mrs Van Sideren attributed the success of her Saturdays. Westall, a moment later, had overtaken his look, and found a place at the girl's side. She bent forward, speaking eagerly; he leaned back, listening, with the depreciatory smile which acted as a filter to flattery, enabling him to swallow the strongest doses without apparent grossness of appetite. Julia winced at her own definition of the smile.

On the way home, in the deserted winter dusk, Westall surprised his wife by a sudden boyish pressure of her arm. 'Did I open their eyes a bit? Did I tell them what you wanted me to?' he asked gaily.

Almost unconsciously, she let her arm slip from his. 'What *I* wanted – ?'

'Why, haven't you – all this time?' She caught the honest wonder of his tone. 'I somehow fancied you'd rather blamed me for not talking more openly – before – . You almost made me feel, at times, that I was sacrificing principles to expediency.'

She paused a moment over her reply; then she asked quietly: 'What made you decide not to – any longer?'

She felt again the vibration of a faint surprise. 'Why – the wish to please you!' he answered, almost too simply.

'I wish you would not go on, then,' she said abruptly.

He stopped in his quick walk, and she felt his stare through the darkness.

'Not go on – ?'

'Call a hansom, please. I'm tired,' broke from her with a sudden rush of physical weariness.

Instantly his solicitude enveloped her. The room had been infernally hot – and then that confounded cigarette smoke – he had noticed once or twice that she looked pale – she mustn't come to another Saturday. She felt herself yielding, as she always did, to the warm influence of his concern for her, the feminine in her leaning on the man in him with a conscious intensity of abandonment.

He put her in the hansom, and her hand stole into his in the darkness. A tear or two rose, and she let them fall. It was so delicious to cry over imaginary troubles!

That evening, after dinner, he surprised her by reverting to the subject of his talk. He combined a man's dislike of uncomfortable questions with an almost feminine skill in eluding them; and she knew that if he returned to the subject he must have some special reason for doing so.

'You seem not to have cared for what I said this afternoon. Did I put the case badly?'

'No – you put it very well.'

The Reckoning

'Then what did you mean by saying that you would rather not have me go on with it?'

She glanced at him nervously, her ignorance of his intention deepening her sense of helplessness.

'I don't think I care to hear such things discussed in public.'

'I don't understand you,' he exclaimed. Again the feeling that his surprise was genuine gave an air of obliquity to her own attitude. She was not sure that she understood herself.

'Won't you explain?' he said with a tinge of impatience.

Her eyes wandered about the familiar drawing-room which had been the scene of so many of their evening confidences. The shaded lamps, the quiet-colored walls hung with mezzotints, the pale spring flowers scattered here and there in Venice glasses and bowls of old Sèvres, recalled, she hardly knew why, the apartment in which the evenings of her first marriage had been passed – a wilderness of rosewood and upholstery, with a picture of a Roman peasant above the mantelpiece, and a Greek slave in 'statuary marble' between the folding-doors of the back drawing-room. It was a room with which she had never been able to establish any closer relation than that between a traveler and a railway station; and now, as she looked about at the surroundings which stood for her deepest affinities – the room for which she had left that other room – she was startled by the same sense of strangeness and unfamiliarity. The prints, the flowers, the subdued tones of the old porcelains, seemed to typify a superficial refinement which had no relation to the deeper significances of life.

Suddenly she heard her husband repeating his question.

'I don't know that I can explain,' she faltered.

He drew his armchair forward so that he faced her across the hearth. The light of a reading-lamp fell on his finely drawn face, which had a kind of surface-sensitiveness akin to the surface-refinement of its setting.

'Is it that you no longer believe in our ideas?' he asked.

'In our ideas – ?'

'The ideas I am trying to teach. The ideas you and I are supposed to stand for.' He paused a moment. 'The ideas on which our marriage was founded.'

The blood rushed to her face. He had his reasons, then – she was sure now that he had his reasons! In the ten years of their marriage, how often had either of them stopped to consider the ideas on which it was founded? How often does a man dig about the basement of his house to examine its foundation? The foundation is there, of course – the house rests on it – but one lives above-stairs and not in the cellar. It was she, indeed, who in the beginning had insisted on reviewing the situation now and then, on recapitulating the reasons which justified her course, on proclaiming, from time to time, her adherence to the religion of personal independence; but she had long ceased to feel the want of any such ideal standards, and had accepted her marriage as frankly and naturally as though it had been based on the primitive needs of the heart, and required no special sanction to explain or justify it.

'Of course I still believe in our ideas!' she exclaimed.

'Then I repeat that I don't understand. It was a part of your theory that the greatest possible publicity should be given to our view of marriage. Have you changed your mind in that respect?'

She hesitated. 'It depends on circumstances – on the public one is addressing. The set of people that the Van Siderens get about them don't care for the truth or falseness of a doctrine. They are attracted simply by its novelty.'

'And yet it was in just such a set of people that you and I met, and learned the truth from each other.'

'That was different.'

'In what way?'

'I was not a young girl, to begin with. It is perfectly unfitting that young girls should be present at – at such times – should hear such things discussed – '

'I thought you considered it one of the deepest social wrongs that such things never *are* discussed before young girls; but that is beside the point, for I don't remember seeing any young girl in my audience to-day – '

'Except Una Van Sideren!'

He turned slightly and pushed back the lamp at his elbow.

'Oh, Miss Van Sideren – naturally – '

'Why naturally?'

'The daughter of the house – would you have had her sent out with her governess?'

'If I had a daughter I should not allow such things to go on in my house!'

Westall, stroking his mustache, leaned back with a faint smile. 'I fancy Miss Van Sideren is quite capable of taking care of herself.'

'No girl knows how to take care of herself – till it's too late.'

'And yet you would deliberately deny her the surest means of self-defense?'

'What do you call the surest means of self-defense?'

'Some preliminary knowledge of human nature in its relation to the marriage tie.'

She made an impatient gesture. 'How should you like to marry that kind of a girl?'

'Immensely – if she were my kind of girl in other respects.'

She took up the argument at another point.

'You are quite mistaken if you think such talk does not affect young girls. Una was in a state of the most absurd exaltation – ' She broke off, wondering why she had spoken.

Westall reopened a magazine which he had laid aside at the beginning of their discussion. 'What you tell me is immensely flattering to my oratorical talent – but I fear you overrate its effect. I can assure you that Miss Van Sideren doesn't have to have her thinking done for her. She's quite capable of doing it herself.'

'You seem very familiar with her mental processes!' flashed unguardedly from his wife.

He looked up quietly from the pages he was cutting.

'I should like to be,' he answered. 'She interests me.'

II

If there be a distinction in being misunderstood, it was one denied to Julia Westall when she left her first husband. Every one was ready to excuse and even to defend her. The world she adorned agreed that John Arment was 'impossible,' and hostesses gave a sigh of relief at the thought that it would no longer be necessary to ask him to dine.

There had been no scandal connected with the divorce: neither side had accused the other of the offense euphemistically described as 'statutory.' The Arments had indeed been obliged to transfer their allegiance to a State which recognized desertion as a cause for divorce, and construed the term so liberally that the seeds of desertion were shown to exist in every union. Even Mrs Arment's second marriage did not make traditional morality stir in its sleep. It was known that she had not met her second husband till after she had parted from the first, and she had, moreover, replaced a rich man by a poor one. Though Clement Westall was acknowledged to be a rising lawyer, it was generally felt that his fortunes would not rise as rapidly as his reputation. The Westalls would probably always have to live quietly and go out to dinner in cabs. Could there be better evidence of Mrs Arment's complete disinterestedness?

If the reasoning by which her friends justified her course was somewhat cruder and less complex than her own elucidation of the matter, both explanations led to the same conclusion: John Arment was impossible. The only difference was that, to his wife, his impossibility was something deeper than a social disqualification. She had once said, in ironical defense of her marriage, that it had at least preserved her from the necessity of sitting next to him at dinner; but she had not then realized at what cost the immunity was purchased. John Arment was impossible; but the sting of his impossibility lay in the fact that he made it impossible for those about him to be other than himself. By an unconscious process of elimination he had excluded from the world everything of which he did not feel a personal need: had become, as it were, a climate in which only his own requirements survived. This might seem to imply a deliberate selfishness; but there was nothing deliberate about Arment. He was as instinctive as an animal or a child. It was this childish element in his nature which sometimes for a moment unsettled his wife's estimate of him. Was it possible that he was simply undeveloped, that he had delayed, somewhat longer than is usual, the laborious process of growing up? He had the kind of sporadic shrewdness which causes it to be said of a dull man that he is 'no fool'; and it was this quality that his wife found most trying. Even to the naturalist it is annoying to have his deductions disturbed by some unforeseen aberrancy of form or function; and how much more so to the wife whose estimate of herself is inevitably bound up with her judgment of her husband!

Arment's shrewdness did not, indeed, imply any latent intellectual power; it suggested, rather, potentialities of feeling, of suffering, perhaps, in a blind rudimentary way, on which Julia's sensibilities naturally declined to linger. She so fully understood her own reasons for leaving him that she disliked to think they were not as comprehensible to her husband. She was haunted, in her analytic moments, by the look of perplexity, too inarticulate for words, with which he had acquiesced in her explanations.

These moments were rare with her, however. Her marriage had been too concrete a misery to be surveyed philosophically. If she had been unhappy for complex reasons, the unhappiness was as real as though it had been uncomplicated. Soul is more bruisable than flesh, and Julia was wounded in every fiber of her spirit. Her husband's personality seemed to be closing gradually in on her, obscuring the sky and cutting off the air, till she felt herself shut up among the decaying bodies of her starved hopes. A sense of having been decoyed by some world-old conspiracy into this bondage of body and soul filled her with despair. If marriage was the slow life-long acquittal of a debt contracted in ignorance, then marriage was a crime against human nature. She, for one, would have no share in maintaining the pretense of which she had been a victim: the pretense that a man and a woman, forced into the narrowest of personal relations, must remain there till the end, though they may have outgrown the span of each other's natures as the mature tree outgrows the iron brace about the sapling.

It was in the first heat of her moral indignation that she had met Clement Westall. She had seen at once that he was 'interested,' and had fought off the discovery, dreading any influence that should draw her back into the bondage of conventional relations. To ward off the peril she had, with an almost crude precipitancy, revealed her opinions to him. To her surprise, she found that he shared them. She was attracted by the frankness of a suitor who, while pressing his suit, admitted that he did not believe in marriage. Her worst audacities did not seem to surprise him: he had thought out all that she had felt, and they had reached the same conclusion. People grew at varying rates, and the yoke that was an easy fit for the one might soon become galling to the other. That was what divorce was for: the readjustment of personal relations. As soon as their necessarily transitive nature was recognized they would gain in dignity as well as in harmony. There would

The Reckoning

be no farther need of the ignoble concessions and connivances, the perpetual sacrifice of personal delicacy and moral pride, by means of which imperfect marriages were now held together. Each partner to the contract would be on his mettle, forced to live up to the highest standard of self-development, on pain of losing the other's respect and affection. The low nature could no longer drag the higher down, but must struggle to rise, or remain alone on its inferior level. The only necessary condition to a harmonious marriage was a frank recognition of this truth, and a solemn agreement between the contracting parties to keep faith with themselves, and not to live together for a moment after complete accord had ceased to exist between them. The new adultery was unfaithfulness to self.

It was, as Westall had just reminded her, on this understanding that they had married. The ceremony was an unimportant concession to social prejudice: now that the door of divorce stood open, no marriage need be an imprisonment, and the contract therefore no longer involved any diminution of self-respect. The nature of their attachment placed them so far beyond the reach of such contingencies that it was easy to discuss them with an open mind; and Julia's sense of security made her dwell with a tender insistence on Westall's promise to claim his release when he should cease to love her. The exchange of these vows seemed to make them, in a sense, champions of the new law, pioneers in the forbidden realm of individual freedom: they felt that they had somehow achieved beatitude without martyrdom.

This, as Julia now reviewed the past, she perceived to have been her theoretical attitude toward marriage. It was unconsciously, insidiously, that her ten years of happiness with Westall had developed another conception of the tie; a reversion, rather, to the old instinct of passionate dependency and possessorship that now made her blood revolt at the mere hint of change. Change? Renewal? Was that what they had called it, in their foolish jargon? Destruction, extermination rather – this rending of a myriad fibers interwoven with another's being! Another? But he was not other! He and she were one, one in the mystic sense which alone gave marriage its significance. The new law was not for them, but for the disunited creatures forced into a mockery of union. The gospel she had felt called on to proclaim had no bearing on her own case . . . She sent for the doctor and told him she was sure she needed a nerve tonic.

She took the nerve tonic diligently, but it failed to act as a sedative to her fears. She did not know what she feared; but that made her anxiety the more pervasive. Her husband had not reverted to the subject of his Saturday talks. He was unusually kind and considerate, with a softening of his quick manner, a touch of shyness in his consideration, that sickened her with new fears. She told herself that it was because she looked badly – because he knew about the doctor and the nerve tonic – that he showed this deference to her wishes, this eagerness to screen her from moral drafts; but the explanation simply cleared the way for fresh inferences.

The week passed slowly, vacantly, like a prolonged Sunday. On Saturday the morning post brought a note from Mrs Van Sideren. Would dear Julia ask Mr Westall to come half an hour earlier than usual, as there was to be some music after his 'talk'? Westall was just leaving for his office when his wife read the note. She opened the drawing-room door and called him back to deliver the message.

He glanced at the note and tossed it aside. 'What a bore! I shall have to cut my game of racquets. Well, I suppose it can't be helped. Will you write and say it's all right?'

Julia hesitated a moment, her hand stiffening on the chair-back against which she leaned.

'You mean to go on with these talks?' she asked.

'I – why not?' he returned; and this time it struck her that his surprise was not quite unfeigned. The perception helped her to find words.

'You said you had started them with the idea of pleasing me – '

'Well?'

'I told you last week that they didn't please me.'

'Last week? – Oh – ' He seemed to make an effort of memory. 'I thought you were nervous then; you sent for the doctor the next day.'

'It was not the doctor I needed; it was your assurance – '

'My assurance?'

Suddenly she felt the floor fail under her. She sank into the chair with a choking throat, her words, her reasons slipping away from her like straws down a whirling flood.

'Clement,' she cried, 'isn't it enough for you to know that I hate it?'

He turned to close the door behind them; then he walked toward her and sat down. 'What is it that you hate?' he asked gently.

She had made a desperate effort to rally her routed argument.

'I can't bear to have you speak as if – as if – our marriage – were like the other kind – the wrong kind. When I heard you there, the other afternoon, before all those inquisitive gossiping people, proclaiming that husbands and wives had a right to leave each other whenever they were tired – or had seen some one else – '

Westall sat motionless, his eyes fixed on a pattern of the carpet.

'You *have* ceased to take this view, then?' he said as she broke off. 'You no longer believe that husbands and wives *are* justified in separating – under such conditions?'

'Under such conditions?' she stammered. 'Yes – I still believe that – but how can we judge for others? What can we know of the circumstances – ?'

He interrupted her. 'I thought it was a fundamental article of our creed that the special circumstances produced by marriage were not to interfere with the full assertion of individual liberty.' He paused a moment. 'I thought that was your reason for leaving Arment.'

She flushed to the forehead. It was not like him to give a personal turn to the argument.

'It was my reason,' she said simply.

'Well, then – why do you refuse to recognize its validity now?'

'I don't – I don't – I only say that one can't judge for others.'

He made an impatient movement. 'This is mere hair-splitting. What you mean is that, the doctrine having served your purpose when you needed it, you now repudiate it.'

'Well,' she exclaimed, flushing again, 'what if I do? What does it matter to us?'

Westall rose from his chair. He was excessively pale, and stood before his wife with something of the formality of a stranger.

'It matters to me,' he said in a low voice, 'because I do *not* repudiate it.'

'Well – ?'

'And because I had intended to invoke it as – '

He paused and drew his breath deeply. She sat silent, almost deafened by her heart-beats.

' – as a complete justification of the course I am about to take.'

Julia remained motionless. 'What course is that?' she asked.

He cleared his throat. 'I mean to claim the fulfillment of your promise.'

For an instant the room wavered and darkened; then she recovered a torturing acuteness of vision. Every detail of her surroundings pressed upon her: the tick of the clock, the slant of sunlight on the wall, the hardness of the chair-arms that she grasped, were a separate wound to each sense.

'My promise – ' she faltered.

'Your part of our mutual agreement to set each other free if one or the other should wish to be released.'

She was silent again. He waited a moment, shifting his position nervously; then he said, with a touch of irritability: 'You acknowledge the agreement?'

The question went through her like a shock. She lifted her head to it proudly. 'I acknowledge the agreement,' she said.

'And – you don't mean to repudiate it?'

A log on the hearth fell forward, and mechanically he advanced and pushed it back.

'No,' she answered slowly, 'I don't mean to repudiate it.'

There was a pause. He remained near the hearth, his elbow resting on the mantelshelf. Close to his hand stood a little cup of jade that he had given her on one of their wedding anniversaries. She wondered vaguely if he noticed it.

'You intend to leave me, then?' she said at length.

His gesture seemed to deprecate the crudeness of the allusion.

'To marry some one else?'

Again his eye and hand protested. She rose and stood before him.

'Why should you be afraid to tell me? Is it Una Van Sideren?'

He was silent.

'I wish you good luck,' she said.

III

She looked up, finding herself alone. She did not remember when or how he had left the room, or how long afterward she had sat there. The fire still smoldered on the hearth, but the slant of sunlight had left the wall.

Her first conscious thought was that she had not broken her word, that she had fulfilled the very letter of their bargain. There had been no crying out, no vain appeal to the past, no attempt at temporizing or evasion. She had marched straight up to the guns.

Now that it was over, she sickened to find herself alive. She looked about her, trying to recover her hold on reality. Her identity seemed to be slipping from her, as it disappears in a physical swoon. 'This is my room – this is my house,' she heard herself saying. Her room?

Her house? She could almost hear the walls laugh back at her.

She stood up, weariness in every bone. The silence of the room frightened her. She remembered, now, having heard the front door close a long time ago: the sound suddenly re-echoed through her brain. Her husband must have left the house, then – her *husband?* She no longer knew in what terms to think: the simplest phrases had a poisoned edge. She sank back into her chair, overcome by a strange weakness. The clock struck ten – it was only ten o'clock! Suddenly she remembered that she had not ordered dinner . . . or were they dining out that evening? *Dinner – dining out* – the old meaningless phraseology pursued her! She must try to think of herself as she would think of some one else, a some one dissociated from all the familiar routine of the past, whose wants and habits must gradually be learned, as one might spy out the ways of a strange animal . . .

The clock struck another hour – eleven. She stood up again and walked to the door: she thought she would go upstairs to her room. *Her* room? Again the word derided her. She opened the door, crossed the narrow hall, and walked up the stairs. As she passed, she noticed Westall's sticks and umbrellas: a pair of his gloves lay on the hall table. The same stair-carpet mounted between the same walls; the same old French print, in its narrow black frame, faced her on the landing. This visual continuity was intolerable. Within, a gaping chasm; without, the

The Reckoning

same untroubled and familiar surface. She must get away from it before she could attempt to think. But, once in her room, she sat down on the lounge, a stupor creeping over her . . .

Gradually her vision cleared. A great deal had happened in the interval – a wild marching and countermarching of emotions, arguments, ideas – a fury of insurgent impulses that fell back spent upon themselves. She had tried, at first, to rally, to organize these chaotic forces. There must be help somewhere, if only she could master the inner tumult. Life could not be broken off short like this, for a whim, a fancy; the law itself would side with her, would defend her. The law? What claim had she upon it? She was the prisoner of her own choice: she had been her own legislator, and she was the predestined victim of the code she had devised. But this was grotesque, intolerable – a mad mistake, for which she could not be held accountable! The law she had despised was still there, might still be invoked . . . invoked, but to what end? Could she ask it to chain Westall to her side? *She* had been allowed to go free when she claimed her freedom – should she show less magnanimity than she had exacted? Magnanimity? The word lashed her with its irony – one does not strike an attitude when one is fighting for life! She would threaten, grovel, cajole . . . she would yield anything to keep her hold on happiness. Ah, but the difficulty lay deeper! The law could not help her – her own apostasy could not help her. She was the victim of the theories she renounced. It was as though some giant machine of her own making had caught her up in its wheels and was grinding her to atoms ...

It was afternoon when she found herself out-of-doors. She walked with an aimless haste, fearing to meet familiar faces. The day was radiant, metallic: one of those searching American days so calculated to reveal the shortcomings of our street-cleaning and the excesses of our architecture. The streets looked bare and hideous; everything stared and glittered. She called a passing hansom, and gave Mrs Van Sideren's address. She did not know what had led up to the act; but she found herself suddenly resolved to speak, to cry out a warning. It was too late to save herself – but the girl might still be told. The hansom rattled up Fifth Avenue; she sat with her eyes fixed, avoiding recognition. At the Van Siderens' door she sprang out and rang the bell. Action had cleared her brain, and she felt calm and self-possessed. She knew now exactly what she meant to say.

The ladies were both out ... the parlor-maid stood waiting for a card. Julia, with a vague murmur, turned away from the door and lingered a moment on the sidewalk. Then she remembered that she had not paid the cab-driver. She drew a dollar from her purse and handed it to him. He touched his hat and drove off, leaving her alone in the long empty street. She wandered away westward, toward strange thoroughfares, where she was not likely to meet acquaintances. The feeling of aimlessness

The Reckoning

had returned. Once she found herself in the afternoon torrent of Broadway, swept past tawdry shops and flaming theatrical posters, with a succession of meaningless faces gliding by in the opposite direction . . .

A feeling of faintness reminded her that she had not eaten since morning. She turned into a side-street of shabby houses, with rows of ash-barrels behind bent area-railings. In a basement window she saw the sign *Ladies' Restaurant*: a pie and a dish of doughnuts lay against the dusty pane like petrified food in an ethnological museum. She entered, and a young woman with a weak mouth and a brazen eye cleared a table for her near the window. The table was covered with a red and white cotton cloth and adorned with a bunch of celery in a thick tumbler and a salt-cellar full of grayish lumpy salt. Julia ordered tea, and sat a long time waiting for it. She was glad to be away from the noise and confusion of the streets. The low-ceilinged room was empty, and two or three waitresses with thin pert faces lounged in the background staring at her and whispering together. At last the tea was brought in a discolored metal teapot. Julia poured a cup and drank it hastily. It was black and bitter, but it flowed through her veins like an elixir. She was almost dizzy with exhilaration. Oh, how tired, how unutterably tired she had been!

She drank a second cup, blacker and bitterer, and now her mind was once more working clearly. She felt as vigorous, as decisive, as when she had stood on the Van

Siderens' door-step – but the wish to return there had subsided. She saw now the futility of such an attempt – the humiliation to which it might have exposed her . . . The pity of it was that she did not know what to do next. The short winter day was fading, and she realized that she could not remain much longer in the restaurant without attracting notice. She paid for her tea and went out into the street. The lamps were alight, and here and there a basement shop cast an oblong of gas-light across the fissured pavement. In the dusk there was something sinister about the aspect of the street, and she hastened back toward Fifth Avenue. She was not used to being out alone at that hour.

At the corner of Fifth Avenue she paused and stood watching the stream of carriages. At last a policeman caught sight of her and signed to her that he would take her across. She had not meant to cross the street, but she obeyed automatically, and presently found herself on the farther corner. There she paused again for a moment; but she fancied the policeman was watching her, and this sent her hastening down the nearest side-street . . . After that she walked a long time, vaguely . . . Night had fallen, and now and then, through the windows of a passing carriage, she caught the expanse of an evening waistcoat or the shimmer of an opera cloak . . .

Suddenly she found herself in a familiar street. She stood still a moment, breathing quickly. She had turned the corner without noticing whither it led; but now, a few yards ahead of her, she saw the house in which she had once lived – her first husband's house. The blinds were drawn, and only a faint translucence marked the windows and the transom above the door. As she stood there she heard a step behind her, and a man walked by in the direction of the house. He walked slowly, with a heavy middle-aged gait, his head sunk a little between the shoulders, the red crease of his neck visible above the fur collar of his overcoat. He crossed the street, went up the steps of the house, drew forth a latch-key, and let himself in . . .

There was no one else in sight. Julia leaned for a long time against the area-rail at the corner, her eyes fixed on the front of the house. The feeling of physical weariness had returned, but the strong tea still throbbed in her veins and lit her brain with an unnatural clearness. Presently she heard another step draw near, and moving quickly away, she too crossed the street and mounted the steps of the house. The impulse which had carried her there prolonged itself in a quick pressure of the electric bell – then she felt suddenly weak and tremulous, and grasped the balustrade for support. The door opened and a young footman with a fresh inexperienced face stood on the threshold. Julia knew in an instant that he would admit her.

'I saw Mr Arment going in just now,' she said. 'Will you ask him to see me for a moment?'

The footman hesitated. 'I think Mr Arment has gone up to dress for dinner, madam.'

Julia advanced into the hall. 'I am sure he will see me – I will not detain him long,' she said. She spoke quietly, authoritatively, in the tone which a good servant does not mistake. The footman had his hand on the drawing-room door.

'I will tell him, madam. What name, please?'

Julia trembled: she had not thought of that. 'Merely say a lady,' she returned carelessly.

The footman wavered and she fancied herself lost; but at that instant the door opened from within and John Arment stepped into the hall. He drew back sharply as he saw her, his florid face turning sallow with the shock; then the blood poured back to it, swelling the veins on his temples and reddening the lobes of his thick ears.

It was long since Julia had seen him, and she was startled at the change in his appearance. He had thickened, coarsened, settled down into the enclosing flesh. But she noted this insensibly: her one conscious thought was that, now she was face to face with him, she must not let him escape till he had heard her. Every pulse in her body throbbed with the urgency of her message.

She went up to him as he drew back. 'I must speak to you,' she said.

Arment hesitated, red and stammering. Julia glanced at the footman, and her look acted as a warning. The instinctive shrinking from a 'scene' predominated over every other impulse, and Arment said slowly: 'Will you come this way?'

The Reckoning

He followed her into the drawing-room and closed the door. Julia, as she advanced, was vaguely aware that the room at least was unchanged: time had not mitigated its horrors. The contadina still lurched from the chimney-breast, and the Greek slave obstructed the threshold of the inner room. The place was alive with memories: they started out from every fold of the yellow satin curtains and glided between the angles of the rosewood furniture. But while some subordinate agency was carrying these impressions to her brain, her whole conscious effort was centered in the act of dominating Arment's will. The fear that he would refuse to hear her mounted like fever to her brain. She felt her purpose melt before it, words and arguments running into each other in the heat of her longing. For a moment her voice failed her, and she imagined herself thrust out before she could speak; but as she was struggling for a word Arment pushed a chair forward, and said quietly: 'You are not well.'

The sound of his voice steadied her. It was neither kind nor unkind – a voice that suspended judgment, rather, awaiting unforeseen developments. She supported herself against the back of the chair and drew a deep breath.

'Shall I send for something?' he continued, with a cold embarrassed politeness.

Julia raised an entreating hand. 'No – no – thank you. I am quite well.'

He paused midway toward the bell, and turned on her. 'Then may I ask – ?'

'Yes,' she interrupted him. 'I came here because I wanted to see you. There is something I must tell you.'

Arment continued to scrutinize her. 'I am surprised at that,' he said. 'I should have supposed that any communication you may wish to make could have been made through our lawyers.'

'Our lawyers!' She burst into a little laugh. 'I don't think they could help me – this time.'

Arment's face took on a barricaded look. 'If there is any question of help – of course – '

It struck her, whimsically, that she had seen that look when some shabby devil called with a subscription-book. Perhaps he thought she wanted him to put his name down for so much in sympathy – or even in money ... The thought made her laugh again. She saw his look change slowly to perplexity. All his facial changes were slow, and she remembered, suddenly, how it had once diverted her to shift that lumbering scenery with a word. For the first time it struck her that she had been cruel. 'There *is* a question of help,' she said in a softer key; 'you can help me; but only by listening ... I want to tell you something ... '

Arment's resistance was not yielding. 'Would it not be easier to – write?' he suggested.

She shook her head. 'There is no time to write ... and it won't take long.' She raised her head and their eyes met. 'My husband has left me,' she said.

'Westall – ?' he stammered, reddening again.

'Yes. This morning. Just as I left you. Because he was tired of me.'

The words, uttered scarcely above a whisper, seemed to dilate to the limit of the room. Arment looked toward the door; then his embarrassed glance returned to Julia.

'I am very sorry,' he said awkwardly.

'Thank you,' she murmured.

'But I don't see – '

'No – but you will – in a moment. Won't you listen to me? Please!' Instinctively she had shifted her position, putting herself between him and the door. 'It happened this morning,' she went on in short breathless phrases. 'I never suspected anything – I thought we were – perfectly happy ... Suddenly he told me he was tired of me ... there is a girl he likes better ... He has gone to her ... ' As she spoke, the lurking anguish rose upon her, possessing her once more to the exclusion of every other emotion. Her eyes ached, her throat swelled with it, and two painful tears ran down her face.

Arment's constraint was increasing visibly. 'This – this is very unfortunate,' he began. 'But I should say the law – '

'The law?' she echoed ironically. 'When he asks for his freedom?'

'You are not obliged to give it.'

'You were not obliged to give me mine – but you did.'

He made a protesting gesture.

'You saw that the law couldn't help you – didn't you?'

she went on. 'That is what I see now. The law represents material rights – it can't go beyond. If we don't recognize an inner law . . . the obligation that love creates . . . being loved as well as loving . . . there is nothing to prevent our spreading ruin unhindered . . . is there?' She raised her head plaintively, with the look of a bewildered child. 'That is what I see now . . . what I wanted to tell you. He leaves me because he's tired . . . but *I* was not tired; and I don't understand why he is. That's the dreadful part of it – the not understanding: I hadn't realized what it meant. But I've been thinking of it all day, and things have come back to me – things I hadn't noticed . . . when you and I . . . ' She moved closer to him, and fixed her eyes on his with the gaze which tries to reach beyond words. 'I see now that *you* didn't understand – did you?'

Their eyes met in a sudden shock of comprehension: a veil seemed to be lifted between them. Arment's lip trembled.

'No,' he said, 'I didn't understand.'

She gave a little cry, almost of triumph. 'I knew it! I knew it! You wondered – you tried to tell me – but no words came . . . You saw your life falling in ruins . . . the world slipping from you . . . and you couldn't speak or move!'

She sank down on the chair against which she had been leaning. 'Now I know – now I know,' she repeated.

'I am very sorry for you,' she heard Arment stammer.

She looked up quickly. 'That's not what I came for. I

don't want you to be sorry. I came to ask you to forgive me . . . for not understanding that *you* didn't understand . . . That's all I wanted to say.' She rose with a vague sense that the end had come, and put out a groping hand toward the door.

Arment stood motionless. She turned to him with a faint smile.

'You forgive me?'

'There is nothing to forgive – '

'Then you will shake hands for good-bye?' She felt his hand in hers: it was nerveless, reluctant.

'Good-bye,' she repeated. 'I understand now.'

She opened the door and passed out into the hall. As she did so, Arment took an impulsive step forward; but just then the footman, who was evidently alive to his obligations, advanced from the background to let her out. She heard Arment fall back. The footman threw open the door, and she found herself outside in the darkness.

1. BOCCACCIO · *Mrs Rosie and the Priest*
2. GERARD MANLEY HOPKINS · *As kingfishers catch fire*
3. *The Saga of Gunnlaug Serpent-tongue*
4. THOMAS DE QUINCEY · *On Murder Considered as One of the Fine Arts*
5. FRIEDRICH NIETZSCHE · *Aphorisms on Love and Hate*
6. JOHN RUSKIN · *Traffic*
7. PU SONGLING · *Wailing Ghosts*
8. JONATHAN SWIFT · *A Modest Proposal*
9. *Three Tang Dynasty Poets*
10. WALT WHITMAN · *On the Beach at Night Alone*
11. KENKŌ · *A Cup of Sake Beneath the Cherry Trees*
12. BALTASAR GRACIÁN · *How to Use Your Enemies*
13. JOHN KEATS · *The Eve of St Agnes*
14. THOMAS HARDY · *Woman much missed*
15. GUY DE MAUPASSANT · *Femme Fatale*
16. MARCO POLO · *Travels in the Land of Serpents and Pearls*
17. SUETONIUS · *Caligula*
18. APOLLONIUS OF RHODES · *Jason and Medea*
19. ROBERT LOUIS STEVENSON · *Olalla*
20. KARL MARX AND FRIEDRICH ENGELS · *The Communist Manifesto*
21. PETRONIUS · *Trimalchio's Feast*
22. JOHANN PETER HEBEL · *How a Ghastly Story Was Brought to Light by a Common or Garden Butcher's Dog*
23. HANS CHRISTIAN ANDERSEN · *The Tinder Box*
24. RUDYARD KIPLING · *The Gate of the Hundred Sorrows*
25. DANTE · *Circles of Hell*
26. HENRY MAYHEW · *Of Street Piemen*
27. HAFEZ · *The nightingales are drunk*
28. GEOFFREY CHAUCER · *The Wife of Bath*
29. MICHEL DE MONTAIGNE · *How We Weep and Laugh at the Same Thing*
30. THOMAS NASHE · *The Terrors of the Night*
31. EDGAR ALLAN POE · *The Tell-Tale Heart*
32. MARY KINGSLEY · *A Hippo Banquet*
33. JANE AUSTEN · *The Beautifull Cassandra*
34. ANTON CHEKHOV · *Gooseberries*
35. SAMUEL TAYLOR COLERIDGE · *Well, they are gone, and here must I remain*
36. JOHANN WOLFGANG VON GOETHE · *Sketchy, Doubtful, Incomplete Jottings*
37. CHARLES DICKENS · *The Great Winglebury Duel*
38. HERMAN MELVILLE · *The Maldive Shark*
39. ELIZABETH GASKELL · *The Old Nurse's Story*
40. NIKOLAY LESKOV · *The Steel Flea*

41. HONORÉ DE BALZAC · *The Atheist's Mass*
42. CHARLOTTE PERKINS GILMAN · *The Yellow Wall-Paper*
43. C.P. CAVAFY · *Remember, Body...*
44. FYODOR DOSTOEVSKY · *The Meek One*
45. GUSTAVE FLAUBERT · *A Simple Heart*
46. NIKOLAI GOGOL · *The Nose*
47. SAMUEL PEPYS · *The Great Fire of London*
48. EDITH WHARTON · *The Reckoning*
49. HENRY JAMES · *The Figure in the Carpet*
50. WILFRED OWEN · *Anthem For Doomed Youth*
51. WOLFGANG AMADEUS MOZART · *My Dearest Father*
52. PLATO · *Socrates' Defence*
53. CHRISTINA ROSSETTI · *Goblin Market*
54. *Sindbad the Sailor*
55. SOPHOCLES · *Antigone*
56. RYŪNOSUKE AKUTAGAWA · *The Life of a Stupid Man*
57. LEO TOLSTOY · *How Much Land Does A Man Need?*
58. GIORGIO VASARI · *Leonardo da Vinci*
59. OSCAR WILDE · *Lord Arthur Savile's Crime*
60. SHEN FU · *The Old Man of the Moon*
61. AESOP · *The Dolphins, the Whales and the Gudgeon*
62. MATSUO BASHŌ · *Lips too Chilled*
63. EMILY BRONTË · *The Night is Darkening Round Me*
64. JOSEPH CONRAD · *To-morrow*
65. RICHARD HAKLUYT · *The Voyage of Sir Francis Drake Around the Whole Globe*
66. KATE CHOPIN · *A Pair of Silk Stockings*
67. CHARLES DARWIN · *It was snowing butterflies*
68. BROTHERS GRIMM · *The Robber Bridegroom*
69. CATULLUS · *I Hate and I Love*
70. HOMER · *Circe and the Cyclops*
71. D. H. LAWRENCE · *Il Duro*
72. KATHERINE MANSFIELD · *Miss Brill*
73. OVID · *The Fall of Icarus*
74. SAPPHO · *Come Close*
75. IVAN TURGENEV · *Kasyan from the Beautiful Lands*
76. VIRGIL · *O Cruel Alexis*
77. H. G. WELLS · *A Slip under the Microscope*
78. HERODOTUS · *The Madness of Cambyses*
79. *Speaking of Siva*
80. *The Dhammapada*

'Did she know
and if she knew
would she speak?'

HENRY JAMES
Born 1843, New York, USA
Died 1916, London

'The Figure in the Carpet' first published in 1896.

JAMES IN PENGUIN CLASSICS
The Portrait of a Lady
The Europeans
What Maisie Knew
The Awkward Age
The Figure in the Carpet and Other Stories
The Turn of the Screw
The Aspern Papers and Other Tales
The Wings of the Dove
Washington Square
The Tragic Muse
Daisy Miller
The Ambassadors
The Golden Bowl
Selected Tales
Roderick Hudson
The Princess Casamassima
The American

HENRY JAMES

The Figure in the Carpet

PENGUIN BOOKS

PENGUIN CLASSICS

UK | USA | Canada | Ireland | Australia
India | New Zealand | South Africa

Penguin Books is part of the Penguin Random House group of companies whose addresses can be found at global.penguinrandomhouse.com.

This edition published in Penguin Classics 2015
010

Set in 9.5/13 pt Baskerville 10 Pro
Typeset by Jouve (UK), Milton Keynes
Printed and bound in Great Britain by Clays Ltd, Elcograf S.p.A.

A CIP catalogue record for this book is available from the British Library

ISBN: 978-0-141-39758-0

www.greenpenguin.co.uk

Penguin Random House is committed to a sustainable future for our business, our readers and our planet. This book is made from Forest Stewardship Council® certified paper.

The Figure in the Carpet

I

I had done a few things and earned a few pence – I had perhaps even had time to begin to think I was finer than was perceived by the patronising; but when I take the little measure of my course (a fidgety habit, for it's none of the longest yet) I count my real start from the evening George Corvick, breathless and worried, came in to ask me a service. He had done more things than I, and earned more pence, though there were chances for cleverness I thought he sometimes missed. I could only however that evening declare to him that he never missed one for kindness. There was almost rapture in hearing it proposed to me to prepare for *The Middle*, the organ of our lucubrations, so called from the position in the week of its day of appearance, an article for which he had made himself responsible, and of which, tied up with a stout string, he laid on my table the subject. I pounced upon my opportunity – that is on the first volume of it – and paid scant attention to my friend's explanation of his appeal. What explanation could be more to the point than my obvious fitness for the task? I had written on Hugh Vereker, but never a word in *The*

Middle, where my dealings were mainly with the ladies and the minor poets. This was his new novel, an advance copy, and whatever much or little it should do for his reputation I was clear on the spot as to what it should do for mine. Moreover if I always read him as soon as I could get hold of him I had a particular reason for wishing to read him now: I had accepted an invitation to Bridges for the following Sunday, and it had been mentioned in Lady Jane's note that Mr Vereker was to be there. I was young enough for a flutter at meeting a man of his renown, and innocent enough to believe the occasion would demand the display of an acquaintance with his 'last'.

Corvick, who had promised a review of it, had not even had time to read it; he had gone to pieces in consequence of news requiring – as on precipitate reflection he judged – that he should catch the night-mail to Paris. He had had a telegram from Gwendolen Erme in answer to his letter offering to fly to her aid. I knew already about Gwendolen Erme; I had never seen her, but I had my ideas, which were mainly to the effect that Corvick would marry her if her mother would only die. That lady seemed now in a fair way to oblige him; after some dreadful mistake about a climate or a 'cure' she had suddenly collapsed on the return from abroad. Her daughter, unsupported and alarmed, desiring to make a rush for home but hesitating at the risk, had accepted our friend's assistance, and it was my secret belief that at sight of him Mrs Erme would pull round. His own belief was scarcely to be called secret, it discernibly at any rate differed from mine. He had showed me Gwendolen's photograph with the remark that she wasn't pretty but was awfully interesting; she had published at the age of nineteen a novel in three volumes, 'Deep Down', about which, in *The Middle*, he had been really splendid. He appreciated my present eagerness and undertook that the periodical in question should do no less; then at the last, with his hand on the door, he said to me: 'Of course you'll be all right, you know.' Seeing I was a trifle vague he added: 'I mean you won't be silly.'

'Silly – about Vereker! Why what do I ever find him but awfully clever?'

'Well, what's that but silly? What on earth does "awfully clever" mean? For God's sake try to get *at* him. Don't let him suffer by our arrangement. Speak of him, you know, if you can, as *I* should have spoken of him.'

I wondered an instant. 'You mean as far and away the biggest of the lot – that sort of thing?'

Corvick almost groaned. 'Oh you know, I don't put them back to back that way; it's the infancy of art! But he gives me a pleasure so rare; the sense of' – he mused a little – 'something or other.'

I wondered again. 'The sense, pray, of what?'

'My dear man, that's just what I want *you* to say!'

Even before he had banged the door I had begun, book in hand, to prepare myself to say it. I sat up with Vereker half the night; Corvick couldn't have done more than that. He was awfully clever – I stuck to that, but he wasn't a bit the biggest of the lot. I didn't allude to the lot, however; I flattered myself that I emerged on this occasion from the infancy of art. 'It's all right,' they declared vividly at the office; and when the number appeared I felt there was a basis on which I could meet the great man. It gave me confidence for a day or two – then that confidence dropped. I had fancied him reading it with relish, but if Corvick wasn't satisfied how could Vereker himself be? I reflected indeed that the heat of the admirer was sometimes grosser even than the appetite of the scribe. Corvick at all events wrote me from Paris a little ill-humouredly. Mrs Erme was pulling round, and I hadn't at all said what Vereker gave him the sense of.

II

The effect of my visit to Bridges was to turn me out for more profundity. Hugh Vereker, as I saw him there, was of a contact so void of angles that I blushed for the poverty of imagination involved in my small precautions. If he was in spirits it wasn't because he had read my review; in fact on the Sunday morning I felt sure he hadn't read it, though *The Middle* had been out three days and bloomed, I assured myself, in the stiff garden of periodicals which gave one of the ormolu tables the air of a stand at a station. The impression he made on me personally was such that I wished him to read it, and I corrected to this end with a surreptitious hand what might be wanting in the careless conspicuity of the sheet. I'm afraid I even watched the result of my manoeuvre, but up to luncheon I watched in vain.

When afterwards, in the course of our gregarious walk, I found myself for half an hour, not perhaps without another manoeuvre, at the great man's side, the result of his affability was a still livelier desire that he shouldn't remain in ignorance of the peculiar justice I had done him. It wasn't that he seemed to thirst for justice; on the contrary I hadn't yet caught in his talk the faintest grunt of a grudge – a note for which my young experience had already given me an ear. Of late he had had more recognition, and it was pleasant, as we used to say in *The Middle*, to see how it drew him out. He wasn't of course popular, but I judged one of the sources of his good humour to be precisely that his success was independent of that. He had none the less become in a manner the fashion; the critics at least had put on a spurt and caught up with him. We had found out at last how clever he was, and he had had to make the best of the loss of his mystery. I was strongly tempted, as I walked beside him, to let him know how much of that unveiling was my act; and there was a moment when I probably should have done so had not one of the ladies of our party, snatching a place at his other elbow, just then appealed to him in a spirit comparatively selfish. It was very discouraging: I almost felt the liberty had been taken with myself.

I had had on my tongue's end, for my own part, a phrase or two about the right word at the right time, but later on

I was glad not to have spoken, for when on our return we clustered at tea I perceived Lady Jane, who had not been out with us, brandishing *The Middle* with her longest arm. She had taken it up at her leisure; she was delighted with what she had found, and I saw that, as a mistake in a man may often be a felicity in a woman, she would practically do for me what I hadn't been able to do for myself. 'Some sweet little truths that needed to be spoken,' I heard her declare, thrusting the paper at rather a bewildered couple by the fireplace. She grabbed it away from them again on the reappearance of Hugh Vereker, who after our walk had been upstairs to change something. 'I know you don't in general look at this kind of thing, but it's an occasion really for doing so. You *haven't* seen it? Then you must. The man has actually got *at* you, at what *I* always feel, you know.' Lady Jane threw into her eyes a look evidently intended to give an idea of what she always felt; but she added that she couldn't have expressed it. The man in the paper expressed it in a striking manner. 'Just see there, and there, where I've dashed it, how he brings it out.' She had literally marked for him the brightest patches of my prose, and if I was a little amused Vereker himself may well have been. He showed how much he was when before us all Lady Jane wanted to read something aloud. I liked at any rate the way he defeated her purpose by jerking the paper affectionately out of her clutch. He'd take it upstairs with him and look at it on going to dress. He did this half an hour later – I saw it in his hand when he repaired to his room. That was the moment at which, thinking to give her pleasure, I mentioned to Lady Jane that I was the author of the review. I did give her pleasure, I judged, but perhaps not quite so much as I had expected. If the author was 'only me' the thing didn't seem quite so remarkable. Hadn't I had the effect rather of diminishing the lustre of the article than of adding to my own? Her ladyship was subject to the most extraordinary drops. It didn't matter; the only effect I cared about was the one it would have on Vereker up there by his bedroom fire.

At dinner I watched for the signs of this impression, tried to fancy some happier light in his eyes; but to my disappointment Lady Jane gave me no chance to make sure. I had hoped she'd call triumphantly down the table, publicly demand if she hadn't been right. The party was large – there were people from outside as well, but I had never seen a table long enough to deprive Lady Jane of a triumph. I was just reflecting in truth that this interminable board would deprive *me* of one when the guest next me, dear woman – she was Miss Poyle, the vicar's sister, a robust unmodulated person – had the happy inspiration and the unusual courage to address herself across it to Vereker, who was opposite, but not directly, so that when he replied they were both leaning forward. She enquired, artless body, what he thought of Lady Jane's 'panegyric', which she had read – not connecting it however with her right-hand neighbour; and while I strained my ear for his reply I heard him, to my stupefaction, call back gaily, his mouth full of bread: 'Oh it's all right – the usual twaddle!'

I had caught Vereker's glance as he spoke, but Miss Poyle's surprise was a fortunate cover for my own. 'You mean he doesn't do you justice?' said the excellent woman.

Vereker laughed out, and I was happy to be able to do the same. 'It's a charming article,' he tossed us.

Miss Poyle thrust her chin half across the cloth. 'Oh you're so deep!' she drove home.

'As deep as the ocean! All I pretend is that the author doesn't see –' But a dish was at this point passed over his shoulder, and we had to wait while he helped himself.

'Doesn't see what?' my neighbour continued.

'Doesn't see anything.'

'Dear me – how very stupid!'

'Not a bit,' Vereker laughed again. 'Nobody does.'

The lady on his further side appealed to him and Miss Poyle sank back to myself. 'Nobody sees anything!' she cheerfully announced; to which I replied that I had often thought so too, but had somehow taken the thought for a proof on my own part of a tremendous eye. I didn't tell her the article was mine; and I observed that Lady Jane, occupied at the end of the table, had not caught Vereker's words.

I rather avoided him after dinner, for I confess he struck me as cruelly conceited, and the revelation was a pain. 'The usual twaddle' – my acute little study! That one's admiration should have had a reserve or two could gall him to that point? I had thought him placid, and he was placid enough; such a surface was the hard polished glass that encased the bauble of his vanity. I was really ruffled, and the only comfort was that if nobody saw anything George Corvick was quite as much out of it as I. This comfort however was not sufficient, after the ladies had dispersed, to carry me in the proper manner – I mean in a spotted jacket and humming an air – into the smoking-room. I took my way in some dejection to bed; but in the passage I encountered Mr Vereker, who had been up once more to change, coming out of his room. *He* was humming an air and had on a spotted jacket, and as soon as he saw me his gaiety gave a start.

'My dear young man,' he exclaimed, 'I'm so glad to lay hands on you! I'm afraid I most unwittingly wounded you by those words of mine at dinner to Miss Poyle. I learned but half an hour ago from Lady Jane that you're the author of the little notice in *The Middle*.'

I protested that no bones were broken; but he moved with me to my own door, his hand, on my shoulder, kindly feeling for a fracture; and on hearing that I had come up to bed he asked leave to cross my threshold and just tell me in three words what his qualification of my remarks had represented. It was plain he really feared I was hurt, and the sense of his solicitude suddenly made all the difference to me. My cheap review fluttered off into space, and the best things I had said in it became flat enough beside the brilliancy of his being there. I can see him there still, on my rug, in the firelight and his spotted jacket, his fine clear face all bright with the desire to be tender to my youth. I don't know what he had at first meant to say, but I think the sight of my relief touched him, excited him, brought up words to his lips from far within. It was so these words presently conveyed to me something that, as I afterwards knew, he had never uttered to anyone. I've always done justice to the generous impulse that made him speak; it was simply compunction for a snub unconsciously administered to a man of letters in a position inferior to his own, a man of letters moreover in the very act of praising him. To make the thing right he talked to me exactly as an equal and on the ground of what we both loved best. The hour, the place, the unexpectedness deepened the impression: he couldn't have done anything more intensely effective.

III

'I don't quite know how to explain it to you,' he said, 'but it was the very fact that your notice of my book had a spice of intelligence, it was just your exceptional sharpness, that produced the feeling – a very old story with me, I beg you to believe – under the momentary influence of which I used in speaking to that good lady the words you so naturally resent. I don't read the things in the newspapers unless they're thrust upon me as that one was – it's always one's best friend who does it! But I used to read them sometimes – ten years ago. I dare say they were in general rather stupider then; at any rate it always struck me they missed my little point with a perfection exactly as admirable when they patted me on the back as when they kicked me in the shins. Whenever since I've happened to have a glimpse of them they were still blazing away – still missing it, I mean, deliciously. *You* miss it, my dear fellow, with inimitable assurance; the fact of your being awfully clever and your article's being awfully nice doesn't make a hair's breadth of difference. It's quite with you rising young men,' Vereker laughed, 'that I feel most what a failure I am!'

I listened with keen interest; it grew keener as he talked. '*You* a failure – heavens! What then may your "little point" happen to be?'

'Have I got to *tell* you, after all these years and labours?' There was something in the friendly reproach of this – jocosely exaggerated – that made me, as an ardent young seeker for truth, blush to the roots of my hair. I'm as much in the dark as ever, though I've grown used in a sense to my obtuseness; at that moment, however, Vereker's happy accent made me appear to myself, and probably to him, a rare dunce. I was on the point of exclaiming 'Ah yes, don't tell me: for my honour, for that of the craft, don't!' when he went on in a manner that showed he had read my thoughts and had his own idea of the probability of our some day redeeming ourselves. 'By my little point I mean – what shall I call it? – the particular thing I've written my books most *for*. Isn't there for every writer a particular thing of that sort, the thing that most makes him apply himself, the thing without the effort to achieve which he wouldn't write at all, the very passion of his passion, the part of the business in which, for him, the flame of art burns most intensely? Well, it's *that*!'

I considered a moment – that is I followed at a respectful distance, rather gasping. I was fascinated – easily, you'll say; but I wasn't going after all to be put off my guard. 'Your description's certainly beautiful, but it doesn't make what you describe very distinct.'

'I promise you it would be distinct if it should dawn on you at all.' I saw that the charm of our topic overflowed for my companion into an emotion as lively as my own. 'At any rate,' he went on, 'I can speak for myself: there's an idea in my work without which I wouldn't have given a straw for the whole job. It's the finest fullest intention of the lot, and the application of it has been, I think, a triumph of patience, of ingenuity. I ought to leave that to somebody else to say; but that nobody does say it is precisely what we're talking about. It stretches, this little trick of mine, from book to book, and every thing else, comparatively, plays over the surface of it. The order, the form, the texture of my books will perhaps some day constitute for the initiated a complete representation of it. So it's naturally the thing for the critic to look for. It strikes me,' my visitor added, smiling, 'even as the thing for the critic to find.'

This seemed a responsibility indeed. 'You call it a little trick?'

'That's only my little modesty. It's really an exquisite scheme.'

'And you hold that you've carried the scheme out?'

'The way I've carried it out is the thing in life I think a bit well of myself for.'

I had a pause. 'Don't you think you ought – just a trifle – to assist the critic?'

'Assist him? What else have I done with every stroke of my pen? I've shouted my intention in his great blank face!' At this, laughing out again, Vereker laid his hand on my shoulder to show the allusion wasn't to my personal appearance.

'But you talk about the initiated. There must therefore, you see, *be* initiation.'

'What else in heaven's name is criticism supposed to be?' I'm afraid I coloured at this too; but I took refuge in repeating that his account of his silver lining was poor in something or other that a plain man knows things by. 'That's only because you've never had a glimpse of it,' he returned. 'If you had had one the element in question would soon have become practically all you'd see. To me it's exactly as palpable as the marble of this chimney. Besides, the critic just *isn't* a plain man: if he were, pray, what would he be doing in his neighbour's garden? You're anything but a plain man yourself, and the very *raison d'être* of you all is that you're little demons of subtlety. If my great affair's a secret, that's only because it's a secret in spite of itself – the amazing event has made it one. I not only never took the smallest precaution to keep it so, but never dreamed of any such accident. If I had I shouldn't in advance have had the heart to go on. As it was, I only became aware little by little, and meanwhile I had done my work.'

'And now you quite like it?' I risked.

'My work?'

'Your secret. It's the same thing.'

'Your guessing that,' Vereker replied, 'is a proof that you're as clever as I say!' I was encouraged by this to remark that he would clearly be pained to part with it, and he confessed that it was indeed with him now the great amusement of life. 'I live almost to see if it will ever be detected.' He looked at me for a jesting challenge; something far within his eyes seemed to peep out. 'But I needn't worry – it won't!'

'You fire me as I've never been fired,' I declared; 'you make me determined to do or die.' Then I asked: 'Is it a kind of esoteric message?'

His countenance fell at this – he put out his hand as if to bid me good night. 'Ah my dear fellow, it can't be described in cheap journalese!'

I knew of course he'd be awfully fastidious, but our talk had made me feel how much his nerves were exposed. I was unsatisfied – I kept hold of his hand. 'I won't make use of the expression then,' I said, 'in the article which I shall eventually announce my discovery, though I dare say I shall have hard work to do without it. But meanwhile, just

The Figure in the Carpet

to hasten that difficult birth, can't you give a fellow a clue?' I felt much more at my ease.

'My whole lucid effort gives him the clue – every page and line and letter. The thing's as concrete there as a bird in a cage, a bait on a hook, a piece of cheese in a mouse-trap. It's stuck into every volume as your foot is stuck into your shoe. It governs every line, it chooses every word, it dots every i, it places every comma.'

I scratched my head. 'Is it something in the style or something in the thought? An element of form or an element of feeling?'

He indulgently shook my hand again, and I felt my questions to be crude and my distinctions pitiful. 'Good night, my dear boy – don't bother about it. After all, you do like a fellow.'

'And a little intelligence might spoil it?' I still detained him.

He hesitated. 'Well, you've got a heart in your body. Is that an element of form or an element of feeling? What I contend that nobody has ever mentioned in my work is the organ of life.'

'I see – it's some idea *about* life, some sort of philosophy. Unless it be,' I added with the eagerness of a thought perhaps still happier, 'some kind of game you're up to with your style, something you're after in the language. Perhaps it's a preference for the letter P!' I ventured profanely to break out. 'Papa, potatoes, prunes – that sort of thing?' He was suitably indulgent: he only said I hadn't got the right letter. But his amusement was over; I could see he was bored. There was nevertheless something else I had absolutely to learn. 'Should you be able, pen in hand, to state it clearly yourself – to name it, phrase it, formulate, it?'

'Oh,' he almost passionately sighed, 'if I were only, pen in hand, one of *you* chaps!'

'That would be a great chance for you of course. But why should you despise us chaps for not doing what you can't do yourself?'

'Can't do?' He opened his eyes. 'Haven't I done it in twenty volumes? I do it in my way,' he continued. 'Go *you* and don't do it in yours.'

'Ours is so devilish difficult,' I weakly observed.

'So's mine! We each choose our own. There's no compulsion. You won't come down and smoke?'

'No. I want to think this thing out.'

'You'll tell me then in the morning that you've laid me bare?'

'I'll see what I can do; I'll sleep on it. But just one word more,' I added. We had left the room – I walked again with him a few steps along the passage. 'This extraordinary "general intention," as you call it – for that's the most vivid description I can induce you to make of it – is then, generally, a sort of buried treasure?'

His face lighted. 'Yes, call it that, though it's perhaps not for me to do so.'

'Nonsense!' I laughed. 'You know you're hugely proud of it.'

'Well, I didn't propose to tell you so; but it *is* the joy of my soul!'

'You mean it's a beauty so rare, so great?'

He waited a little again. 'The loveliest thing in the world!' We had stopped, and on these words he left me; but at the end of the corridor, while I looked after him rather yearningly, he turned and caught sight of my puzzled face. It made him earnestly, indeed I thought quite anxiously, shake his head and wave his finger. 'Give it up – give it up!'

This wasn't a challenge – it was fatherly advice. If I had had one of his books at hand I'd have repeated my recent act of faith – I'd have spent half the night with him. At three o'clock in the morning, not sleeping, remembering moreover how indispensable he was to Lady Jane, I stole down to the library with a candle. There wasn't, so far as I could discover, a line of his writing in the house.

IV

Returning to town I feverishly collected them all; I picked out each in its order and held it up to the light. This gave me a maddening month, in the course of which several things took place. One of these, the last, I may as well immediately mention, was that I acted on Vereker's advice: I renounced my ridiculous attempt. I could really make nothing of the business; it proved a dead loss. After all I had always, as he had himself noted, liked him; and what now occurred was simply that my new intelligence and vain preoccupation damaged my liking. I not only failed to run a general intention to earth, I found myself missing the subordinate intentions I had formerly enjoyed. His books didn't even remain the charming things they had been for me; the exasperation of my search put me out of conceit of them. Instead of being a pleasure the more they became a resource the less; for from the moment I was unable to follow up the author's hint I of course felt it a point of honour not to make use professionally of my knowledge of them. I *had* no knowledge – nobody had any. It was humiliating, but I could bear it – they only annoyed me now. At last they even bored me, and I accounted for my confusion – perversely, I allow – by the idea that Vereker had made a fool of me. The buried treasure was a bad joke, the general intention a monstrous *pose*.

The great point of it all is, however, that I told George Corvick what had befallen me and that my information had an immense effect on him. He had at last come back, but so, unfortunately, had Mrs Erme, and there was as yet, I could see, no question of his nuptials. He was immensely stirred up by the anecdote I had brought from Bridges; it fell in so completely with the sense he had had from the first that there was more in Vereker than met the eye. When I remarked that the eye seemed what the printed page had been expressly invented to meet he immediately accused me of being spiteful because I had been foiled.

The Figure in the Carpet

Our commerce had always that pleasant latitude. The thing Vereker had mentioned to me was exactly the thing he, Corvick, had wanted me to speak of in my review. On my suggesting at last that with the assistance I had now given him he would doubtless be prepared to speak of it himself he admitted freely that before doing this there was more he must understand. What he would have said, had he reviewed the new book, was that there was evidently in the writer's inmost art something to *be* understood. I hadn't so much as hinted at that: no wonder the writer hadn't been flattered! I asked Corvick what he really considered he meant by his own supersubtlety, and, unmistakably kindled, he replied: 'It isn't for the vulgar – it isn't for the vulgar!' He had hold of the tail of something: he would pull hard, pull it right out. He pumped me dry on Vereker's strange confidence and, pronouncing me the luckiest of mortals, mentioned half a dozen questions he wished to goodness I had had the gumption to put. Yet on the other hand he didn't want to be told too much – it would spoil the fun of seeing what would come. The failure of *my* fun was at the moment of our meeting not complete, but I saw it ahead, and Corvick saw that I saw it. I, on my side, saw likewise that one of the first things he would do would be to rush off with my story to Gwendolen.

On the very day after my talk with him I was surprised by the receipt of a note from Hugh Vereker, to whom our encounter at Bridges had been recalled, as he mentioned, by his falling, in a magazine, on some article to which my signature was attached. 'I read it with great pleasure,' he wrote, 'and remembered under its influence our lively conversation by your bedroom fire. The consequence of this has been that I begin to measure the temerity of my having saddled you with a knowledge that you may find something of a burden. Now that the fit's over I can't imagine how I came to be moved so much beyond my wont. I had never before mentioned, no matter in what state of expansion, the fact of my little secret, and I shall never speak of the mystery again. I was accidentally so much more explicit with you than it had ever entered into my game to be, that I find this game – I mean the pleasure of playing it – suffers considerably. In short, if you can understand it, I've rather spoiled my sport. I really don't want to give anybody what I believe you clever young men call the tip. That's of course a selfish solicitude, and I name it to you for what it may be worth to you. If you're disposed to humour me don't repeat my revelation. Think me demented – it's your right; but don't tell anybody why.'

The sequel to this communication was that as early on the morrow as I dared I drove straight to Mr Vereker's door. He occupied in those years one of the honest old houses in Kensington Square. He received me immediately, and as soon as I came in I saw I hadn't lost my power to minister to his mirth. He laughed out at sight of my face, which doubtless expressed my perturbation. I had been indiscreet – my compunction was great. 'I *have* told somebody,' I panted, 'and I'm sure that person will by this time have told somebody else! It's a woman, into the bargain.'

'The person you've told?'

'No, the other person. I'm quite sure he must have told her.'

'For all the good it will do her – or do *me*! A woman will never find out.'

'No, but she'll talk all over the place: she'll do just what you don't want.'

Vereker thought a moment, but wasn't so disconcerted as I had feared: he felt that if the harm was done it only served him right. 'It doesn't matter – don't worry.'

'I'll do my best, I promise you, that your talk with me shall go no further.'

'Very good; do what you can.'

'In the meantime,' I pursued, 'George Corvick's possession of the tip may, on his part, really lead to something.'

'That will be a brave day.'

I told him about Corvick's cleverness, his admiration, the intensity of his interest in my anecdote; and without making too much of the divergence of our respective estimates mentioned that my friend was already of opinion that he saw much further into a certain affair than most people. He was quite as fired as I had been at Bridges. He was moreover in love with the young lady: perhaps the two together would puzzle something out.

Vereker seemed struck with this. 'Do you mean they're to be married?'

21

'I dare say that's what it will come to.'

'That may help them,' he conceded, 'but we must give them time!'

I spoke of my own renewed assault and confessed my difficulties; whereupon he repeated his former advice: 'Give it up, give it up!' He evidently didn't think me intellectually equipped for the adventure. I stayed half an hour, and he was most good-natured, but I couldn't help pronouncing him a man of unstable moods. He had been free with me in a mood, he had repented in a mood, and now in a mood he had turned indifferent. This general levity helped me to believe that, so far as the subject of the tip went, there wasn't much in it. I contrived however to make him answer a few more questions about it, though he did so with visible impatience. For himself, beyond doubt, the thing we were all so blank about was vividly there. It was something, I guessed, in the primal plan; something like a complex figure in a Persian carpet. He highly approved of this image when I used it, and he used another himself. 'It's the very string,' he said, 'that my pearls are strung on!' The reason of his note to me had been that he really didn't want to give us a grain of succour – our density was a thing too perfect in its way to touch. He had formed the habit of depending on it, and if the spell was to break it must break by some force of its own. He comes back to me from that last occasion – for I was never to speak to him again – as a man with some safe preserve for sport. I wondered as I walked away where he had got *his* tip.

V

When I spoke to George Corvick of the caution I had received he made me feel that any doubt of his delicacy would be almost an insult. He had instantly told Gwendolen, but Gwendolen's ardent response was in itself a pledge of discretion. The question would now absorb them and would offer them a pastime too precious to be shared with the crowd. They appeared to have caught instinctively at Vereker's high idea of enjoyment. Their intellectual pride, however, was not such as to make them indifferent to any further light I might throw on the affair they had in hand. They were indeed of the 'artistic temperament', and I was freshly struck with my colleague's power to excite himself over a question of art. He'd call it letters, he'd call it life, but it was all one thing. In what he said I now seemed to understand that he spoke equally for Gwendolen, to whom, as soon as Mrs Erme was sufficiently better to allow her a little leisure, he made a point of introducing me. I remember our going together one Sunday in August to a huddled house in Chelsea, and my renewed envy of Corvick's possession of a friend who had some light to mingle with his own. He could say things to her that I could never say to him. She had indeed no sense of humour and, with her pretty way of holding her head on one side, was one of those persons whom you want, as the phrase is, to shake, but who have learnt Hungarian by themselves. She conversed perhaps in Hungarian with Corvick; she had remarkably little English for his friend. Corvick afterwards told me that I had chilled her by my apparent indisposition to oblige them with the detail of what Vereker had said to me. I allowed that I felt I had given thought enough to that indication: hadn't I even made up my mind that it was vain and would lead nowhere? The importance they attached to it was irritating and quite envenomed my doubts.

That statement looks unamiable, and what probably happened was that I felt humiliated at seeing other persons deeply beguiled by an experiment that had brought me only chagrin. I was out in the cold while, by the evening fire, under the lamp, they followed the chase for which I myself had sounded the horn. They did as I had done, only more deliberately and sociably – they went over their author from the beginning. There was no hurry, Corvick said – the future was before them and the fascination could only grow; they would take him page by page, as they would take one of the classics, inhale him in slow draughts and let him sink all the way in. They would scarce have got so wound up, I think, if they hadn't been in love: poor Vereker's inner meaning gave them endless occasion to put and to keep their young heads together. None the less it represented the kind of problem for which Corvick had a special aptitude, drew out the particular pointed patience of which, had he lived, he would have given more striking and, it is to be hoped, more fruitful examples. He at least was, in Vereker's words, a little demon of subtlety. We had

The Figure in the Carpet

begun by disputing, but I soon saw that without my stirring a finger his infatuation would have its bad hours. He would bound off on false scents as I had done – he would clap his hands over new lights and see them blown out by the wind of the turned page. He was like nothing, I told him, but the maniacs who embrace some bedlamitical theory of the cryptic character of Shakespeare. To this he replied that if we had had Shakespeare's own word for his being cryptic he would at once have accepted it. The case there was altogether different – we had nothing but the word of Mr Snooks. I returned that I was stupefied to see him attach such importance even to the word of Mr Vereker. He wanted thereupon to know if I treated Mr Vereker's word as a lie. I wasn't perhaps prepared, in my unhappy rebound, to go so far as that, but I insisted that till the contrary was proved I should view it as too fond an imagination. I didn't, I confess, say – I didn't at that time quite know – all I felt. Deep down, as Miss Erme would have said, I was uneasy, I was expectant. At the core of my disconcerted state – for my wonted curiosity lived in its ashes – was the sharpness of a sense that Corvick would at last probably come out somewhere. He made, in defence of his credulity, a great point of the fact that from of old, in his study of this genius, he had caught whiffs and hints of he didn't know what, faint wandering notes of a hidden music. That was just the rarity, that was the charm: it fitted so perfectly into what I reported.

If I returned on several occasions to the little house in

Chelsea I dare say it was as much for news of Vereker as for news of Miss Erme's ailing parent. The hours spent there by Corvick were present to my fancy as those of a chessplayer bent with a silent scowl, all the lamplit winter, over his board and his moves. As my imagination filled it out the picture held me fast. On the other side of the table was a ghostlier form, the faint figure of an antagonist good-humouredly but a little wearily secure – an antagonist who leaned back in his chair with his hands in his pockets and a smile on his fine clear face. Close to Corvick, behind him, was a girl who had begun to strike me as pale and wasted and even, on more familiar view, as rather handsome, and who rested on his shoulder and hung on his moves. He would take up a chessman and hold it poised a while over one of the little squares, and then would put it back in its place with a long sigh of disappointment. The young lady, at this, would slightly but uneasily shift her position and look across, very hard, very long, very strangely, at their dim participant. I had asked them at an early stage of the business if it mightn't contribute to their success to have some closer communication with him. The special circumstances would surely be held to have given me a right to introduce them. Corvick immediately replied that he had no wish to approach the altar before he had prepared the sacrifice. He quite agreed with our friend both as to the delight and as to the honour of the chase – he would bring down the animal with his own rifle. When I asked him if Miss Erme were as keen a shot he said after thinking: 'No, I'm ashamed to say she wants to set a trap. She'd give anything to see him; she says she requires another tip. She's really quite morbid about it. But she must play fair – she *shan't* see him!' he emphatically added. I wondered if they hadn't even quarrelled a little on the subject – a suspicion not corrected by the way he more than once exclaimed to me: 'She's quite incredibly literary, you know – quite fantastically!' I remember his saying of her that she felt in italics and thought in capitals. 'Oh when I've run him to earth,' he also said, 'then, you know, I shall knock at his door. Rather – I beg you to believe. I'll have it from his own lips: "Right you are, my boy; you've done it this time!" He shall crown me victor – with the critical laurel.'

Meanwhile he really avoided the chances London life might have given him of meeting the distinguished novelist; a danger, however, that disappeared with Vereker's leaving England for an indefinite absence, as the newspapers announced – going to the south for motives connected with the health of his wife, which had long kept her in retirement. A year – more than a year – had elapsed since the incident at Bridges, but I had had no further sight of him. I think I was at bottom rather ashamed – I hated to remind him that, though I had irremediably missed his point, a reputation for acuteness was rapidly overtaking me. This scruple led me a dance; kept me out of Lady Jane's house, made me even decline, when in spite of my bad manners she was a second time so good as to make me a sign, an invitation to her beautiful seat. I once became aware of her under Vereker's escort at a concert, and was sure I was seen by them, but I slipped out without being caught. I felt, as on that occasion I splashed along in the rain, that I couldn't have done anything else; and yet I remember saying to myself that it was hard, was even cruel. Not only had I lost the books, but I had lost the man himself: they and their author had been alike spoiled for me. I knew too which was the loss I most regretted. I had taken to the man still more than I had ever taken to the books.

VI

Six months after our friend had left England George Corvick, who made his living by his pen, contracted for a piece of work which imposed on him an absence of some length and a journey of some difficulty, and his undertaking of which was much of a surprise to me. His brother-in-law had become editor of a great provincial paper, and the great provincial paper, in a fine flight of fancy, had conceived the idea of sending a 'special commissioner' to India. Special commissioners had begun, in the 'metropolitan press,' to be the fashion, and the journal in question must have felt it had passed too long for a mere country cousin. Corvick had no hand, I knew, for the big brush of the correspondent, but that was his brother-in-law's affair, and the fact that a particular task was not in his line was apt to be with himself exactly a reason for accepting it. He was prepared to out-Herod the metropolitan press; he took solemn precautions against priggishness, he exquisitely outraged taste. Nobody ever knew it – that offended principle was all his own. In addition to his expenses he was to be conveniently paid, and I found myself able to help him, for the usual fat book, to a plausible arrangement with the usual fat publisher. I naturally inferred that his obvious desire to make a little money was not unconnected with the prospect of a union with Gwendolen Erme. I was aware that her mother's opposition was largely addressed to his want of means and of lucrative abilities, but it so happened that, on my saying the last time I saw him something that bore on the question of his separation from our young lady, he brought out with an emphasis that startled me: 'Ah I'm not a bit engaged to her, you know!'

'Not overtly,' I answered, 'because her mother doesn't like you. But I've always taken for granted a private understanding.'

'Well, there *was* one. But there isn't now.' That was all he said save something about Mrs Erme's having got on her feet again in the most extraordinary way – a remark pointing, as I supposed, the moral that private understandings were of little use when the doctor didn't share them. What I took the liberty of more closely inferring was that the girl might in some way have estranged him.

Well, if he had taken the turn of jealousy for instance it could scarcely be jealousy of me. In that case – over and above the absurdity of it – he wouldn't have gone away just to leave us together. For some time before his going we had indulged in no allusion to the buried treasure, and from his silence, which my reserve simply emulated, I had drawn a sharp conclusion. His courage had dropped, his ardour had gone the way of mine – this appearance at least he left me to scan. More than that he couldn't do; he couldn't face the triumph with which I might have greeted an explicit admission. He needn't have been afraid, poor dear, for I had by this time lost all need to triumph. In fact I considered I showed magnanimity in not reproaching him with his collapse, for the sense of his having thrown up the game made me feel more than ever how much I at last depended on him. If Corvick had broken down I should never know; no one would be of any use if *he* wasn't. It wasn't a bit true I had ceased to care for knowledge; little by little my curiosity not only had begun to ache again, but had become the familiar torment of my days and my nights. There are doubtless people to whom torments of such an order appear hardly more natural than the contortions of disease; but I don't after all know why I should in this connection so much as mention them. For the few persons, at any rate, abnormal or not, with whom my anecdote is concerned, literature was a game of skill, and skill meant courage, and courage meant honour, and honour meant passion, meant life. The stake on the table was of a special substance and our roulette the revolving mind, but we sat round the green board as intently as the grim gamblers at Monte Carlo. Gwendolen Erme, for that matter, with her white face and her fixed eyes, was of the very type of the lean ladies one had met in the temples of chance. I recognised in Corvick's absence that she made this analogy vivid. It was extravagant, I admit, the way she lived for the art of the pen. Her passion visibly preyed on her, and in her presence I felt almost tepid. I got hold of 'Deep Down' again: it was a desert in which she had lost herself, but in which too she had dug a wonderful hole in the sand – a cavity out of which Corvick had still more remarkably pulled her.

Early in March I had a telegram from her, in consequence of which I repaired immediately to Chelsea, where the first thing she said to me was 'He has got it, he has got it!'

She was moved, as I could see, to such depths that she must mean the great thing. 'Vereker's idea?'

'His general intention. George has cabled from Bombay.'

She had the missive open there; it was emphatic though concise. 'Eureka. Immense.' That was all – he had saved the cost of the signature. I shared her emotion, but I was disappointed. 'He doesn't say what it is.'

'How could he – in a telegram? He'll write it.'

'But how does he know?'

'Know it's the real thing? Oh I'm sure that when you see it you do know. *Vera incessu patuit dea!*'

'It's you, Miss Erme, who are a "dear" for bringing me such news!' – I went all lengths in my high spirits. 'But fancy finding our goddess in the temple of Vishnu! How strange of George to have been able to go into the thing again in the midst of such different and such powerful solicitations!'

'He hasn't gone into it, I know; it's the thing itself, let severely alone for six months, that has simply sprung out at him like a tigress out of the jungle. He didn't take a book with him – on purpose; indeed he wouldn't have needed to – he knows every page, as I do, by heart. They all worked in him together, and some day somewhere, when he wasn't thinking, they fell, in all their superb intricacy, into the one right combination. The figure in the carpet came out. That's the way he knew it would come and the real reason – you didn't in the least understand, but I suppose I may tell you now – why he went and why I consented to his going. We knew the change would do it – that the difference of thought, of scene, would give the needed touch, the magic shake. We had perfectly, we had admirably calculated. The elements were all in his mind, and in the *secousse* of a new and intense experience they just struck light.' She positively struck light herself – she was literally, facially luminous. I stammered something about unconscious cerebration, and she continued: 'He'll come right home – this will bring him.'

'To see Vereker, you mean?'

'To see Vereker – and to see *me*. Think what he'll have to tell me!'

I hesitated. 'About India?'

'About fiddlesticks! About Vereker – about the figure in the carpet.'

'But, as you say, we shall surely have that in a letter.'

She thought like one inspired, and I remembered how Corvick had told me long before that her face was interesting. 'Perhaps it can't be got into a letter if it's "immense".'

'Perhaps not if it's immense bosh. If he has hold of something that can't be got into a letter he hasn't hold of *the* thing. Vereker's own statement to me was exactly that the "figure" *would* fit into a letter.'

'Well, I cabled to George an hour ago – two words,' said Gwendolen.

'Is it indiscreet of me to ask what they were?'

She hung fire, but at last brought them out. '"Angel, write."'

'Good!' I cried. 'I'll make it sure – I'll send him the same.'

VII

My words however were not absolutely the same – I put something instead of 'angel'; and in the sequel my epithet seemed the more apt, for when eventually we heard from our traveller it was merely, it was thoroughly to be tantalised. He was magnificent in his triumph, he described his discovery as stupendous; but his ecstasy only obscured it – there were to be no particulars till he should have submitted his conception to the supreme authority. He had thrown up his commission, he had thrown up his book, he had thrown up everything but the instant need to hurry to Rapallo, on the Genoese shore, where Vereker was making a stay. I wrote him a letter which was to await him at Aden – I besought him to relieve my suspense. That he had found my letter was indicated by a telegram which, reaching me after weary days and in the absence of any answer to my laconic dispatch to him at Bombay, was evidently intended as a reply to both communications. Those few words were in familiar French, the French of the day, which Corvick often made use of to show he wasn't a prig. It had for some persons the opposite effect, but his message may fairly be paraphrased. 'Have patience; I want to see, as it breaks on you, the face you'll make!' 'Tellement envie de voir ta tête!' – that was what I had to sit down with. I can certainly not be said to have sat down, for I seem to remember myself at this time as rattling constantly between the little house in Chelsea and my own. Our impatience, Gwendolen's and mine, was equal, but I kept hoping her light would be greater. We all spent during this episode, for people of our means, a great deal of money in telegrams and cabs, and I counted on the receipt of news from Rapallo immediately after the junction of the discoverer with the discovered. The interval seemed an age, but late one day I heard a hansom precipitated to my door with the crash engendered by a hint of liberality. I lived with my heart in my mouth and accordingly bounded to the window – a movement which gave me a view of a young lady erect on the footboard of the vehicle and eagerly looking up at my house. At sight of me she flourished a paper with a movement that brought me straight down, the movement with which, in melodramas, handkerchiefs and reprieves are flourished at the foot of the scaffold.

'Just seen Vereker – not a note wrong. Pressed me to bosom – keeps me a month.' So much I read on her paper while the cabby dropped a grin from his perch. In my excitement I paid him profusely and in hers she suffered it; then as he drove away we started to walk about and talk. We had talked, heavens knows, enough before, but this was a wondrous lift. We pictured the whole scene at Rapallo, where he would have written, mentioning my name, for permission to call; that is *I* pictured it, having more material than my companion, whom I felt hang on my lips as we stopped on purpose before shop-windows we didn't look into. About one thing we were clear: if he was staying on for fuller communication we should at least have a letter from him that would help us through the dregs of delay. We understood his staying on, and yet each of us saw, I think, that the other hated it. The letter we were clear about arrived; it was for Gwendolen, and I called on her in time to save her the trouble of bringing it to me. She didn't read it out, as was natural enough; but she repeated to me what it chiefly embodied. This consisted of the remarkable statement that he'd tell her after they were married exactly what she wanted to know.

'Only *then*, when I'm his wife – not before,' she explained. "It's tantamount to saying – isn't it? – that I must marry him straight off!' She smiled at me while I flushed with disappointment, a vision of fresh delay that made me at first unconscious of my surprise. It seemed more than a hint that on me as well he would impose some tiresome condition. Suddenly, while she reported several more things from his letter, I remembered what he had told me before going away. He had found Mr Vereker deliriously interesting and his own possession of the secret a real intoxication. The buried treasure was all gold and gems. Now that it was there it seemed to grow and grow before him; it would have been, through all time and taking all tongues, one of the most wonderful flowers of literary art. Nothing, in especial, once you were face to face with it, could show for more consummately *done*. When once it came out it came out, was there with a splendour that made you ashamed; and there hadn't been, save in the bottomless vulgarity of the age, with every one tasteless and tainted, every sense stopped, the smallest reason why it should have been overlooked. It was great, yet so simple, was simple, yet so great, and the final knowledge of it was an experience quite apart. He intimated that the charm of such an experience, the desire to drain it, in its freshness, to the last drop, was what kept him there close to the source. Gwendolen, frankly radiant as she tossed me these fragments, showed the elation of a prospect more assured than my own. That brought me back to the question of her marriage, prompted me to ask if what she meant by what she had just surprised me with was that she was under an engagement.

'Of course I am!' she answered. 'Didn't you know it?' She seemed astonished, but I was still more so, for Corvick had told me the exact contrary. I didn't mention this, however; I only reminded her how little I had been on that score in her confidence, or even in Corvick's and that moreover I wasn't in ignorance of her mother's interdict. At bottom I was troubled by the disparity of the two accounts; but after a little I felt Corvick's to be the one I least doubted. This simply reduced me to asking myself if the girl had on the spot improvised an engagement – vamped up an old one or dashed off a new – in order to arrive at the satisfaction she desired. She must have had resources of which I was destitute, but she made her case slightly more intelligible by returning presently: 'What the state of things has been is that we felt of course bound to do nothing in mamma's lifetime.'

'But now you think you'll just dispense with mamma's consent?'

'Ah it mayn't come to that!' I wondered what it might come to, and she went on: 'Poor dear, she may swallow the dose. In fact, you know,' she added with a laugh, 'she really *must*!' – a proposition of which, on behalf of every one concerned, I fully acknowledged the force.

VIII

Nothing more vexatious had ever happened to me than to become aware before Corvick's arrival in England that I shouldn't be there to put him through. I found myself abruptly called to Germany by the alarming illness of my younger brother, who, against my advice, had gone to Munich to study, at the feet indeed of a great master, the art of portraiture in oils. The near relative who made him an allowance had threatened to withdraw it if he should, under specious pretexts, turn for superior truth to Paris – Paris being somehow, for a Cheltenham aunt, the school of evil, the abyss. I deplored this prejudice at the time, and the deep injury of it was now visible – first in the fact that it hadn't saved the poor boy, who was clever, frail and foolish, from congestion of the lungs, and second in the greater break with London to which the event condemned me. I'm afraid that what was uppermost in my mind during several anxious weeks was the sense that if we had only been in Paris I might have run over to see Corvick. This was actually out of the question from every point of view: my brother, whose recovery gave us both plenty to do, was ill for three months, during which I never left him and at the end of which we had to face the absolute prohibition of a return to England. The consideration of climate imposed itself, and he was in no state to meet it alone. I took him to Meran and there spent the summer with him, trying to show him by example how to get back to work and nursing a rage of another sort that I tried *not* to show him.

The whole business proved the first of a series of phenomena so strangely interlaced that, taken all together – which was how I had to take them – they form as good an illustration as I can recall of the manner in which, for the good of his soul doubtless, fate sometimes deals with a man's avidity. These incidents certainly had larger bearings than the comparatively meagre consequence we are here concerned with – though I feel that consequence also a thing to speak of with some respect. It's mainly in such a light, I confess, at any rate, that the ugly fruit of my exile is at this hour present to me. Even at first indeed the spirit in which my avidity, as I have called it, made me regard that term owed no element of ease to the fact that before coming back from Rapallo George Corvick addressed me in a way I objected to. His letter had none of the sedative action I must today profess myself sure he had wished to give it, and the march of occurrences was not so ordered as to make up for what it lacked. He had begun on the spot, for one of the quarterlies, a great last word on Vereker's writings, and this exhaustive study, the only one that would have counted, have existed, was to turn on the new light, to utter – oh so quietly! – the unimagined truth. It was in other words to trace the figure in the carpet through every convolution, to reproduce it in every tint. The result, according to my friend, would be the greatest literary portrait ever painted, and what he asked of me was just to be so good as not to trouble him with questions till he should hang up his masterpiece before me. He did me the honour to declare that, putting aside the great sitter himself, all aloft in his indifference, I was individually the connoisseur he was most working for. I was therefore to be a good boy and not try to peep under the curtain before the show was ready: I should enjoy it all the more if I sat very still.

I did my best to sit very still, but I couldn't help giving a jump on seeing in *The Times,* after I had been a week or two in Munich and before, as I knew, Corvick had reached London, the announcement of the sudden death of poor Mrs Erme. I instantly, by letter, appealed to Gwendolen for particulars, and she wrote me that her mother had yielded to long-threatened failure of the heart. She didn't say, but I took the liberty of reading into her words, that from the point of view of her marriage and also of her eagerness, which was quite a match for mine, this was a solution more prompt than could have been expected and more radical than waiting for the old lady to swallow the dose. I candidly admit indeed that at the time – for I heard from her repeatedly – I read some singular things into Gwendolen's words and some still more extraordinary ones into her silences. Pen in hand, this way, I live the time over, and it brings back the oddest sense of my

The Figure in the Carpet

having been, both for months and in spite of myself, a kind of coerced spectator. All my life had taken refuge in my eyes, which the procession of events appeared to have committed itself to keep astare. There were days when I thought of writing to Hugh Vereker and simply throwing myself on his charity. But I felt more deeply that I hadn't fallen quite so low – besides which, quite properly, he would send me about my business. Mrs Erme's death brought Corvick straight home, and within the month he was united 'very quietly' – as quietly, I seemed to make out, as he meant in his article to bring out his *trouvaille* – to the young lady he had loved and quitted. I use this last term, I may parenthetically say, because I subsequently grew sure that at the time he went to India, at the time of his great news from Bombay, there had been no positive pledge between them whatever. There had been none at the moment she was affirming to me the very opposite. On the other hand he had certainly become engaged the day he returned. The happy pair went down to Torquay for their honeymoon, and there, in a reckless hour, it occurred to poor Corvick to take his young bride for a drive. He had no command of that business: this had been brought home to me of old in a little tour we had once made together in a dog-cart. In a dog-cart he perched his companion for a rattle over Devonshire hills, on one of the likeliest of which he brought his horse, who, it was true, had bolted, down with such violence that the occupants of the cart were hurled forward and that he fell horribly on his head. He was killed on the spot; Gwendolen escaped unhurt.

I pass rapidly over the question of this unmitigated tragedy, of what the loss of my best friend meant for me, and I complete my little history of my patience and my pain by the frank statement of my having, in a postscript to my very first letter to her after the receipt of the hideous news, asked Mrs Corvick whether her husband mightn't at least have finished the great article on Vereker. Her answer was as prompt as my question: the article, which had been barely begun, was a mere heartbreaking scrap. She explained that our friend, abroad, had just settled down to it when interrupted by her mother's death, and that then, on his return, he had been kept from work by the engrossments into which that calamity was to plunge them. The opening pages were all that existed; they were striking, they were promising, but they didn't unveil the idol. That great intellectual feat was obviously to have formed his climax. She said nothing more, nothing to enlighten me as to the state of her own knowledge – the knowledge for the acquisition of which I had fancied her prodigiously acting. This was above all what I wanted to know: had *she* seen the idol unveiled? Had there been a private ceremony for a palpitating audience of one? For what else but that ceremony had the nuptials taken place? I didn't like as yet to press her, though when I thought of what had passed between us on the subject in Corvick's absence her reticence surprised me. It was therefore not till much later, from Meran, that I risked another appeal, risked it in some trepidation, for she continued to tell me nothing. 'Did you hear in those few days of your blighted bliss,' I wrote, 'what we desired so to hear?' I said 'we' as a little hint; and she showed me she could take a little hint. 'I heard everything,' she replied, 'and I mean to keep it to myself!'

IX

It was impossible not to be moved with the strongest sympathy for her, and on my return to England I showed her every kindness in my power. Her mother's death had made her means sufficient, and she had gone to live in a more convenient quarter. But her loss had been great and her visitation cruel; it never would have occurred to me moreover to suppose she could come to feel the possession of a technical tip, of a piece of literary experience, a counterpoise to her grief. Strange to say, none the less, I couldn't help believing after I had seen her a few times that I caught a glimpse of some such oddity. I hasten to add that there had been other things I couldn't help believing, or at least imagining; and as I never felt I was really clear about these, so, as to the point I here touch on, I give her memory the benefit of the doubt. Stricken and solitary, highly accomplished and now, in her deep mourning, her maturer grace and her uncomplaining sorrow, incontestably handsome, she presented herself as leading a life of singular dignity and beauty. I had at first found a way to persuade myself that I should soon get the better of the reserve formulated, the week after the catastrophe, in her reply to an appeal as to which I was not unconscious that it might strike her as mistimed. Certainly that reserve was something of a shock to me – certainly it puzzled me the more I thought of it and even though I tried to explain it (with moments of success) by an imputation of exalted sentiments, of superstitious scruples, of a refinement of loyalty. Certainly it added at the same time hugely to the price of Vereker's secret, precious as this mystery already appeared. I may as well confess abjectly that Mrs Corvick's unexpected attitude was the final tap on the nail that was to fix fast my luckless idea, convert it into the obsession of which I'm for ever conscious.

But this only helped me the more to be artful, to be adroit, to allow time to elapse before renewing my suit. There were plenty of speculations for the interval, and one of them was deeply absorbing. Corvick had kept his information from his young friend till after the removal of the last barrier to their intimacy – then only had he let the cat out of the bag. Was it Gwendolen's idea, taking a hint from him, to liberate this animal only on the basis of the renewal of such a relation? Was the figure in the carpet traceable or describable only for husbands and wives – for lovers supremely united? It came back to me in a mystifying manner that in Kensington Square, when I mentioned that Corvick would have told the girl he loved, some word had dropped from Vereker that gave colour to this possibility. There might be little in it, but there was enough to make me wonder if I should have to marry Mrs Corvick to get what I wanted. Was I prepared to offer her this price for the blessing of her knowledge? Ah that way madness lay! – so I at least said to myself in bewildered hours. I could see meanwhile the torch she refused to pass on flame away in her chamber of memory – pour through her eyes a light that shone in her lonely house. At the end of six months I was fully sure of what this warm presence made up to her for. We had talked again and again of the man who had brought us together – of his talent, his character, his personal charm, his certain career, his dreadful doom, and even of his clear purpose in that great study which was to have been a supreme literary portrait, a kind of critical Vandyke or Velasquez. She had conveyed to me in abundance that she was tongue-tied by her perversity, by her piety, that she would never break the silence it had not been given to the 'right person,' as she said, to break. The hour however finally arrived. One evening when I had been sitting with her longer than usual I laid my hand firmly on her arm. 'Now at last what *is* it?'

She had been expecting me and was ready. She gave a long slow soundless headshake, merciful only in being inarticulate. This mercy didn't prevent its hurling at me the largest finest coldest 'Never!' I had yet, in the course of a life that had known denials, had to take full in the face. I took it and was aware that with the hard blow the tears had come into my eyes. So for a while we sat and looked at each other; after which I slowly rose. I was wondering if some day she would accept me; but this was not what I brought out. I said as I smoothed down my hat: 'I know what to think then. It's nothing!'

A remote disdainful pity for me gathered in her dim smile; then she spoke in a voice that I hear at this hour. 'It's my *life*!' As I stood at the door she added: 'You've insulted him!'

'Do you mean Vereker?'

'I mean the Dead!'

I recognised when I reached the street the justice of her charge. Yes, it was her life – I recognised that too; but her life none the less made room with the lapse of time for another interest. A year and a half after Corvick's death she published in a single volume her second novel, 'Overmastered,' which I pounced on in the hope of finding in it some tell-tale echo or some peeping face. All I found was a much better book than her younger performance, showing I thought the better company she had kept. As a tissue tolerably intricate it was a carpet with a figure of its own; but the figure was not the figure I was looking for. On sending a review of it to *The Middle* I was surprised to learn from the office that a notice was already in type. When the paper came out I had no hesitation in attributing this article, which I thought rather vulgarly overdone, to Drayton Deane, who in the old days had been something of a friend of Corvick's, yet had only within a few weeks made the acquaintance of his widow. I had had an early copy of the book, but Deane had evidently had an earlier. He lacked all the same the light hand with which Corvick had gilded the gingerbread – he laid on the tinsel in splotches.

X

Six months later appeared 'The Right of Way', the last chance, though we didn't know it, that we were to have to redeem ourselves. Written wholly during Vereker's sojourn abroad, the book had been heralded, in a hundred paragraphs, by the usual ineptitudes. I carried it, as early a copy as any, I this time flattered myself, straightway to Mrs Corvick. This was the only use I had for it; I left the inevitable tribute of *The Middle* to some more ingenious mind and some less irritated temper. 'But I already have it,' Gwendolen said. 'Drayton Deane was so good as to bring it to me yesterday, and I've just finished it.'

'Yesterday? How did he get it so soon?'

'He gets everything so soon! He's to review it in *The Middle*.'

'He – Drayton Deane – review Vereker?' I couldn't believe my ears.

'Why not? One fine ignorance is as good as another.'

I winced but I presently said: 'You ought to review him yourself!'

'I don't "review,"' she laughed. 'I'm reviewed!'

Just then the door was thrown open. 'Ah yes, here's your reviewer!' Drayton Deane was there with his long legs and his tall forehead: he had come to see what she thought of 'The Right of Way,' and to bring news that was singularly relevant. The evening papers were just out with a telegram on the author of that work, who, in Rome, had been ill for some days with an attack of malarial fever. It had at first not been thought grave, but had taken, in consequence of complications, a turn that might give rise to anxiety. Anxiety had indeed at the latest hour begun to be felt.

I was struck in the presence of these tidings with the fundamental detachment that Mrs Corvick's overt concern quite failed to hide: it gave me the measure of her consummate independence. That independence rested on her knowledge, the knowledge which nothing now could destroy and which nothing could make different. The figure in the carpet might take on another twist or two, but the sentence had virtually been written. The writer might go down to his grave: she was the person in the world to whom – as if she had been his favoured heir – his continued existence was least of a need. This reminded me how I had observed at a particular moment – after Corvick's death – the drop of her desire to see him face to face. She had got what she wanted without that. I had been sure that if she hadn't got it she wouldn't have been restrained from the endeavour to sound him personally by those superior reflections, more conceivable on a man's part than on a woman's, which in my case had served as

The Figure in the Carpet

a deterrent. It wasn't however, I hasten to add, that my case, in spite of this invidious comparison, wasn't ambiguous enough. At the thought that Vereker was perhaps at that moment dying there rolled over me a wave of anguish – a poignant sense of how inconsistently I still depended on him. A delicacy that it was my one compensation to suffer to rule me had left the Alps and the Apennines between us, but the sense of the waning occasion suggested that I might in my despair at last have gone to him. Of course I should really have done nothing of the sort. I remained five minutes, while my companions talked of the new book, and when Drayton Deane appealed to me for my opinion of it I made answer, getting up, that I detested Hugh Vereker and simply couldn't read him. I departed with the moral certainty that as the door closed behind me Deane would brand me for awfully superficial. His hostess wouldn't contradict *that* at least.

I continue to trace with a briefer touch our intensely odd successions. Three weeks after this came Vereker's death, and before the year was out the death of his wife. That poor lady I had never seen, but I had had a futile theory that, should she survive him long enough to be decorously accessible, I might approach her with the feeble flicker of my plea. Did she know and if she knew would she speak? It was much to be presumed that for more reasons than one she would have nothing to say; but when she passed out of all reach I felt renouncement indeed my appointed lot. I was shut up in my obsession for ever – my gaolers had gone off with the key. I find myself quite as vague as a captive in a dungeon about the time that further elapsed before Mrs Corvick became the wife of Drayton Deane. I had foreseen, through my bars, this end of the business, though there was no indecent haste and our friendship had rather fallen off. They were both so 'awfully intellectual' that it struck people as a suitable match, but I had measured better than any one the wealth of understanding the bride would contribute to the union. Never, for a marriage in literary circles – so the newspapers described the alliance – had a lady been so bravely dowered. I began with due promptness to look for the fruit of the affair – that fruit, I mean, of which the premonitory symptoms would be peculiarly visible in the husband. Taking for granted the splendour of the other party's nuptial gift, I expected to see him make a show commensurate with his increase of means. I knew what his means had been – his article on 'The Right of Way' had distinctly given one the figure. As he was now exactly in the position in which still more exactly I was not I watched from month to month, in the likely periodicals, for the heavy message poor Corvick had been unable to deliver and the responsibility of which would have fallen on his successor. The widow and wife would have broken by the rekindled hearth the silence that only a widow and wife might break, and Deane would be as aflame with the knowledge as Corvick in his own hour, as Gwendolen in hers, had been. Well, he was aflame doubtless, but the fire was apparently not to become a public blaze. I scanned the periodicals in vain: Drayton Deane filled them with exuberant pages, but he withheld the page I most feverishly sought. He wrote on a thousand subjects, but never on the subject of Vereker. His special line was to tell truths that other people either 'funked,' as he said, or overlooked, but he never told the only truth that seemed to me in these days to signify. I met the couple in those literary circles referred to in the papers: I have sufficiently intimated that it was only in such circles we were all constructed to revolve. Gwendolen was more than ever committed to them by the publication of her third novel, and I myself definitely classed by holding the opinion that this work was inferior to its immediate predecessor. Was it worse because she had been keeping worse company? If her secret was, as she had told me, her life – a fact discernible in her increasing bloom, an air of conscious privilege that, cleverly corrected by pretty charities, gave distinction to her appearance – it had yet not a direct influence on her work. That only made one – everything only made one – yearn the more for it; only rounded it off with a mystery finer and subtler.

XI

It was therefore from her husband I could never remove my eyes: I beset him in a manner that might have made him uneasy. I went even so far as to engage him in conversation. *Didn't* he know, hadn't he come into it as a matter of course? – that question hummed in my brain. Of course he knew; otherwise he wouldn't return my stare so queerly. His wife had told him what I wanted and he was amiably amused at my impotence. He didn't laugh – he wasn't a laugher: his system was to present to my irritation, so that I should crudely expose myself, a conversational blank as vast as his big bare brow. It always happened that I turned away with a settled conviction from these unpeopled expanses, which seemed to complete each other geographically and to symbolise together Drayton Deane's want of voice, want of form. He simply hadn't the art to use what he knew, he literally was incompetent to take up the duty where Corvick had left it. I went still further – it was the only glimpse of happiness I had. I made up my mind that the duty didn't appeal to him. He wasn't interested, he didn't care. Yes, it quite comforted me to believe him too stupid to have joy of the thing I lacked. He was as stupid after as he had been before, and that deepened for me the golden glory in which the mystery was wrapped. I had of course none the less to recollect that his wife might have imposed her conditions and exactions. I had above all to remind myself that with Vereker's death the major incentive dropped. He was still there to be honoured by what might be done – he was no longer there to give it his sanction. Who alas but he had the authority?

Two children were born to the pair, but the second cost

the mother her life. After this stroke I seemed to see another ghost of a chance. I jumped at it in thought, but I waited a certain time for manners, and at last my opportunity arrived in a remunerative way. His wife had been dead a year when I met Drayton Deane in the smoking-room of a small club of which we both were members, but where for months – perhaps because I rarely entered it – I hadn't seen him. The room was empty and the occasion propitious. I deliberately offered him, to have done with the matter for ever, that advantage for which I felt he had long been looking.

'As an older acquaintance of your late wife's than even you were,' I began, 'you must let me say to you something I have on my mind. I shall be glad to make any terms with you that you see fit to name for the information she must have had from George Corvick – the information, you know, that had come to *him*, poor chap, in one of the happiest hours of his life, straight from Hugh Vereker.'

He looked at me like a dim phrenological bust. 'The information –?'

'Vereker's secret, my dear man – the general intention of his books: the string the pearls were strung on, the buried treasure, the figure in the carpet.'

He began to flush – the numbers on his bumps to come out. 'Vereker's books had a general intention?'

I started in my turn. 'You don't mean to say you don't know it?' I thought for a moment he was playing with me. 'Mrs Deane knew it; she had it, as I say, straight from

Corvick, who had, after infinite search and to Vereker's own delight, found the very mouth of the cave. Where *is* the mouth? He told after their marriage – and told alone – the person who, when the circumstances were reproduced, must have told *you*. Have I been wrong in taking for granted that she admitted you, as one of the highest privileges of the relation in which you stood to her, to the knowledge of which she was after Corvick's death the sole depositary? All *I* know is that that knowledge is infinitely precious, and what I want you to understand is that if you'll in your turn admit me to it you'll do me a kindness for which I shall be lastingly grateful.'

He had turned at last very red; I dare say he had begun by thinking I had lost my wits. Little by little he followed me; on my own side I stared with a livelier surprise. Then he spoke. 'I don't know what you're talking about.'

He wasn't acting – it was the absurd truth. 'She *didn't* tell you –?'

'Nothing about Hugh Vereker.'

I was stupefied; the room went round. It had been too good even for that! 'Upon your honour?'

'Upon my honour. What the devil's the matter with you?' he growled.

'I'm astounded – I'm disappointed. I wanted to get it out of you.'

'It isn't *in* me!' he awkwardly laughed. 'And even if it were –'

The Figure in the Carpet

'If it were you'd let me have it – oh yes, in common humanity. But I believe you. I see – I see!' I went on, conscious, with the full turn of the wheel, of my great delusion, my false view of the poor man's attitude. What I saw, though I couldn't say it, was that his wife hadn't thought him worth enlightening. This struck me as strange for a woman who had thought him worth marrying. At last I explained it by the reflection that she couldn't possibly have married him for his understanding. She had married him for something else.

He was to some extent enlightened now, but he was even more astonished, more disconcerted: he took a moment to compare my story with his quickened memories. The result of his meditation was his presently saying with a good deal of rather feeble form: 'This is the first I hear of what you allude to. I think you must be mistaken as to Mrs Drayton Deane's having had any unmentioned, and still less any unmentionable, knowledge of Hugh Vereker. She'd certainly have wished it – should it have borne on his literary character – to be used.'

'It *was* used. She used it herself. She told me with her own lips that she "lived" on it.'

I had no sooner spoken than I repented of my words; he grew so pale that I felt as if I had struck him. 'Ah "lived" –!' he murmured, turning short away from me.

My compunction was real; I laid my hand on his shoulder. 'I beg you to forgive me – I've made a mistake. You *don't* know what I thought you knew. You could, if I had been right, have rendered me a service; and I had my reasons for assuming that you'd be in a position to meet me.'

'Your reasons?' he echoed. 'What were your reasons?'

I looked at him well; I hesitated; I considered. 'Come and sit down with me here and I'll tell you.' I drew him to a sofa, I lighted another cigar and, beginning with the anecdote of Vereker's one descent from the clouds, I recited to him the extraordinary chain of accidents that had, in spite of the original gleam, kept me till that hour in the dark. I told him in a word just what I've written out here. He listened with deepening attention, and I became aware, to my surprise, by his ejaculations, by his questions, that he would have been after all not unworthy to be trusted by his wife. So abrupt an experience of her want of trust had now a disturbing effect on him; but I saw the immediate shock throb away little by little and then gather again into waves of wonder and curiosity – waves that promised, I could perfectly judge, to break in the end with the fury of my own highest tides. I may say that today as victims of unappeased desire there isn't a pin to choose between us. The poor man's state is almost my consolation, there are really moments when I feel it to be quite my revenge.

1. BOCCACCIO · *Mrs Rosie and the Priest*
2. GERARD MANLEY HOPKINS · *As kingfishers catch fire*
3. *The Saga of Gunnlaug Serpent-tongue*
4. THOMAS DE QUINCEY · *On Murder Considered as One of the Fine Arts*
5. FRIEDRICH NIETZSCHE · *Aphorisms on Love and Hate*
6. JOHN RUSKIN · *Traffic*
7. PU SONGLING · *Wailing Ghosts*
8. JONATHAN SWIFT · *A Modest Proposal*
9. *Three Tang Dynasty Poets*
10. WALT WHITMAN · *On the Beach at Night Alone*
11. KENKŌ · *A Cup of Sake Beneath the Cherry Trees*
12. BALTASAR GRACIÁN · *How to Use Your Enemies*
13. JOHN KEATS · *The Eve of St Agnes*
14. THOMAS HARDY · *Woman much missed*
15. GUY DE MAUPASSANT · *Femme Fatale*
16. MARCO POLO · *Travels in the Land of Serpents and Pearls*
17. SUETONIUS · *Caligula*
18. APOLLONIUS OF RHODES · *Jason and Medea*
19. ROBERT LOUIS STEVENSON · *Olalla*
20. KARL MARX AND FRIEDRICH ENGELS · *The Communist Manifesto*
21. PETRONIUS · *Trimalchio's Feast*
22. JOHANN PETER HEBEL · *How a Ghastly Story Was Brought to Light by a Common or Garden Butcher's Dog*
23. HANS CHRISTIAN ANDERSEN · *The Tinder Box*
24. RUDYARD KIPLING · *The Gate of the Hundred Sorrows*
25. DANTE · *Circles of Hell*
26. HENRY MAYHEW · *Of Street Piemen*
27. HAFEZ · *The nightingales are drunk*
28. GEOFFREY CHAUCER · *The Wife of Bath*
29. MICHEL DE MONTAIGNE · *How We Weep and Laugh at the Same Thing*
30. THOMAS NASHE · *The Terrors of the Night*
31. EDGAR ALLAN POE · *The Tell-Tale Heart*
32. MARY KINGSLEY · *A Hippo Banquet*
33. JANE AUSTEN · *The Beautifull Cassandra*
34. ANTON CHEKHOV · *Gooseberries*
35. SAMUEL TAYLOR COLERIDGE · *Well, they are gone, and here must I remain*
36. JOHANN WOLFGANG VON GOETHE · *Sketchy, Doubtful, Incomplete Jottings*
37. CHARLES DICKENS · *The Great Winglebury Duel*
38. HERMAN MELVILLE · *The Maldive Shark*
39. ELIZABETH GASKELL · *The Old Nurse's Story*
40. NIKOLAY LESKOV · *The Steel Flea*

41. HONORÉ DE BALZAC · *The Atheist's Mass*
42. CHARLOTTE PERKINS GILMAN · *The Yellow Wall-Paper*
43. C.P. CAVAFY · *Remember, Body . . .*
44. FYODOR DOSTOEVSKY · *The Meek One*
45. GUSTAVE FLAUBERT · *A Simple Heart*
46. NIKOLAI GOGOL · *The Nose*
47. SAMUEL PEPYS · *The Great Fire of London*
48. EDITH WHARTON · *The Reckoning*
49. HENRY JAMES · *The Figure in the Carpet*
50. WILFRED OWEN · *Anthem For Doomed Youth*
51. WOLFGANG AMADEUS MOZART · *My Dearest Father*
52. PLATO · *Socrates' Defence*
53. CHRISTINA ROSSETTI · *Goblin Market*
54. *Sindbad the Sailor*
55. SOPHOCLES · *Antigone*
56. RYŪNOSUKE AKUTAGAWA · *The Life of a Stupid Man*
57. LEO TOLSTOY · *How Much Land Does A Man Need?*
58. GIORGIO VASARI · *Leonardo da Vinci*
59. OSCAR WILDE · *Lord Arthur Savile's Crime*
60. SHEN FU · *The Old Man of the Moon*
61. AESOP · *The Dolphins, the Whales and the Gudgeon*
62. MATSUO BASHŌ · *Lips too Chilled*
63. EMILY BRONTË · *The Night is Darkening Round Me*
64. JOSEPH CONRAD · *To-morrow*
65. RICHARD HAKLUYT · *The Voyage of Sir Francis Drake Around the Whole Globe*
66. KATE CHOPIN · *A Pair of Silk Stockings*
67. CHARLES DARWIN · *It was snowing butterflies*
68. BROTHERS GRIMM · *The Robber Bridegroom*
69. CATULLUS · *I Hate and I Love*
70. HOMER · *Circe and the Cyclops*
71. D. H. LAWRENCE · *Il Duro*
72. KATHERINE MANSFIELD · *Miss Brill*
73. OVID · *The Fall of Icarus*
74. SAPPHO · *Come Close*
75. IVAN TURGENEV · *Kasyan from the Beautiful Lands*
76. VIRGIL · *O Cruel Alexis*
77. H. G. WELLS · *A Slip under the Microscope*
78. HERODOTUS · *The Madness of Cambyses*
79. *Speaking of Siva*
80. *The Dhammapada*

'Tonight he noticed how the women's eyes Passed from him to the strong men that were whole.'

WILFRED OWEN
Born 1893, Oswestry, England
Died 1918, Sambre–Oise Canal, France

This selection of poems is taken from *Three Poets of the First World War: Ivor Gurney, Isaac Rosenberg, Wilfred Owen*, Penguin Classics, 2011.

OWEN IN PENGUIN CLASSICS
Three Poets of the First World War: Ivor Gurney, Isaac Rosenberg, Wilfred Owen

WILFRED OWEN

Anthem for Doomed Youth

PENGUIN BOOKS

PENGUIN CLASSICS

UK | USA | Canada | Ireland | Australia
India | New Zealand | South Africa

Penguin Books is part of the Penguin Random House group of companies
whose addresses can be found at global.penguinrandomhouse.com.

This selection published in Penguin Classics 2015
011

'The Last Laugh' and 'The Letter' copyright © the Executors of
Harold Owen's Estate, 1963, 1983

Set in 9/12.4 pt Baskerville 10 Pro
Typeset by Jouve (UK), Milton Keynes
Printed and bound in Great Britain by Clays Ltd, Elcograf S.p.A.

A CIP catalogue record for this book is available from the British Library

ISBN: 978-0-141-39760-3

www.greenpenguin.co.uk

Penguin Random House is committed to a
sustainable future for our business, our readers
and our planet. This book is made from Forest
Stewardship Council® certified paper.

Contents

1. 1914 — 1
2. Dulce et Decorum Est — 2
3. Arms and the Boy — 4
4. Inspection — 5
5. From My Diary, July 1914 — 6
6. Apologia pro Poemate Meo — 8
7. S.I.W. — 10
8. The Last Laugh — 13
9. The Send-Off — 14
10. Exposure — 15
11. Smile, Smile, Smile — 17
12. The Letter — 18
13. Anthem for Doomed Youth — 19
14. With an Identity Disc — 20
15. Le Christianisme — 21
16. 'Cramped in that funnelled hole' — 22

17.	Hospital Barge	23
18.	At a Calvary near the Ancre	24
19.	Conscious	25
20.	Futility	26
21.	Disabled	27
22.	Miners	29
23.	Insensibility	31
24.	Strange Meeting	34
25.	Asleep	36
26.	The Show	37
27.	Mental Cases	39
28.	The Chances	41
29.	The Parable of the Old Man and the Young	42
30.	The End	43
31.	A Terre	44
32.	The Kind Ghosts	47
33.	The Sentry	48
34.	Spring Offensive	50
35.	Greater Love	52
36.	The Next War	54

1914

War broke: and now the Winter of the world
With perishing great darkness closes in.
The foul tornado, centred at Berlin,
Is over all the width of Europe whirled,

Rending the sails of progress. Rent or furled
Are all Art's ensigns. Verse wails. Now begin
Famines of thought and feeling. Love's wine's thin.
The grain of human Autumn rots, down-hurled.

For after Spring had bloomed in early Greece,
And Summer blazed her glory out with Rome,
An Autumn softly fell, a harvest home,
A slow grand age, and rich with all increase.
But now, for us, wild Winter, and the need
Of sowings for new Spring, and blood for seed.

Dulce et Decorum Est

Bent double, like old beggars under sacks,
Knock-kneed, coughing like hags, we cursed through sludge,
Till on the haunting flares we turned our backs
And towards our distant rest began to trudge.
Men marched asleep. Many had lost their boots
But limped on, blood-shod. All went lame; all blind;
Drunk with fatigue; deaf even to the hoots
Of tired, outstripped Five-nines that dropped behind.

Gas! GAS! Quick, boys! – An ecstasy of fumbling,
Fitting the clumsy helmets just in time;
But someone still was yelling out and stumbling,
And flound'ring like a man in fire or lime . . .
Dim, through the misty panes and thick green light,
As under a green sea, I saw him drowning.

In all my dreams, before my helpless sight,
He plunges at me, guttering, choking, drowning.

If in some smothering dreams you too could pace
Behind the wagon that we flung him in,
And watch the white eyes writhing in his face,
His hanging face, like a devil's sick of sin;
If you could hear, at every jolt, the blood
Come gargling from the froth-corrupted lungs,
Obscene as cancer, bitter as the cud

Of vile, incurable sores on innocent tongues, –
My friend, you would not tell with such high zest
To children ardent for some desperate glory,
The old Lie: Dulce et decorum est
Pro patria mori.

Arms and the Boy

Let the boy try along this bayonet-blade
How cold steel is, and keen with hunger of blood;
Blue with all malice, like a madman's flash;
And thinly drawn with famishing for flesh.

Lend him to stroke these blind, blunt bullet-leads,
Which long to nuzzle in the hearts of lads,
Or give him cartridges whose fine zinc teeth
Are sharp with sharpness of grief and death.

For his teeth seem for laughing round an apple.
There lurk no claws behind his fingers supple;
And God will grow no talons at his heels,
Nor antlers through the thickness of his curls.

Inspection

'You! What d'you mean by this?' I rapped.
'You dare come on parade like this?'
'Please, sir, it's –' ''Old yer mouth,' the sergeant snapped.
'I takes 'is name, sir?' – 'Please, and then dismiss.'

Some days 'confined to camp' he got,
For being 'dirty on parade'.
He told me, afterwards, the damnèd spot
Was blood, his own. 'Well, blood is dirt,' I said.

'Blood's dirt,' he laughed, looking away,
Far off to where his wound had bled
And almost merged for ever into clay.
'The world is washing out its stains,' he said.
'It doesn't like our cheeks so red:
Young blood's its great objection.
But when we're duly white-washed, being dead,
The race will bear Field Marshal God's inspection.'

From My Diary, July 1914

Leaves
   Murmuring by myriads in the shimmering trees.
Lives
   Wakening with wonder in the Pyrenees.
Birds
   Cheerily chirping in the early day.
Bards
   Singing of summer, scything through the hay.
Bees
   Shaking the heavy dews from bloom and frond.
Boys
   Bursting the surface of the ebony pond.
Flashes
   Of swimmers carving through the sparkling cold.
Fleshes
   Gleaming with wetness to the morning gold.
A mead
   Bordered about with warbling waterbrooks.
A maid
   Laughing the love-laugh with me; proud of looks.
The heat
   Throbbing between the upland and the peak.
Her heart
   Quivering with passion to my pressèd cheek.
Braiding
   Of floating flames across the mountain brow.

Brooding
  Of stillness; and a sighing of the bough.
Stirs
  Of leaflets in the gloom; soft petal-showers;
Stars
  Expanding with the starr'd nocturnal flowers.

Apologia pro Poemate Meo

I, too, saw God through mud, –
    The mud that cracked on cheeks when wretches smiled.
    War brought more glory to their eyes than blood,
    And gave their laughs more glee than shakes a child.

Merry it was to laugh there –
    Where death becomes absurd and life absurder.
    For power was on us as we slashed bones bare
    Not to feel sickness or remorse of murder.

I, too, have dropped off Fear –
    Behind the barrage, dead as my platoon,
    And sailed my spirit surging light and clear
    Past the entanglement where hopes lay strewn;

And witnessed exultation –
    Faces that used to curse me, scowl for scowl,
    Shine and lift up with passion of oblation,
    Seraphic for an hour; though they were foul.

I have made fellowships –
    Untold of happy lovers in old song.
    For love is not the binding of fair lips
    With the soft silk of eyes that look and long,

By Joy, whose ribbon slips, –
    But wound with war's hard wire whose stakes are strong;
    Bound with the bandage of the arm that drips;
    Knit in the webbing of the rifle-thong.

I have perceived much beauty
   In the hoarse oaths that kept our courage straight;
   Heard music in the silentness of duty;
   Found peace where shell-storms spouted reddest spate.

Nevertheless, except you share
   With them in hell the sorrowful dark of hell,
   Whose world is but the trembling of a flare
   And heaven but as the highway for a shell,

You shall not hear their mirth:
   You shall not come to think them well content
   By any jest of mine. These men are worth
   Your tears. You are not worth their merriment.

S.I.W.

> I will to the King,
> And offer him consolation in his trouble,
> For that man there has set his teeth to die,
> And being one that hates obedience,
> Discipline, and orderliness of life,
> I cannot mourn him.
>
> W. B. YEATS

I. THE PROLOGUE

Patting goodbye, doubtless they told the lad
He'd always show the Hun a brave man's face;
Father would sooner him dead than in disgrace, –
Was proud to see him going, aye, and glad.
Perhaps his mother whimpered how she'd fret
Until he got a nice safe wound to nurse.
Sisters would wish girls too could shoot, charge, curse . . .
Brothers – would send his favourite cigarette.
Each week, month after month, they wrote the same,
Thinking him sheltered in some Y. M. Hut,
Because he said so, writing on his butt
Where once an hour a bullet missed its aim.
And misses teased the hunger of his brain.
His eyes grew old with wincing, and his hand
Reckless with ague. Courage leaked, as sand

From the best sandbags after years of rain.
But never leave, wound, fever, trench-foot, shock,
Untrapped the wretch. And death seemed still withheld
For torture of lying machinally shelled,
At the pleasure of this world's Powers who'd run amok.
He'd seen men shoot their hands, on night patrol.
Their people never knew. Yet they were vile.
'Death sooner than dishonour, that's the style!'
So Father said.

II. THE ACTION

                One dawn, our wire patrol
Carried him. This time, Death had not missed.
We could do nothing but wipe his bleeding cough.
Could it be accident? – Rifles go off . . .
Not sniped? No. (Later they found the English ball.)

III. THE POEM

It was the reasoned crisis of his soul
Against more days of inescapable thrall,
Against infrangibly wired and blind trench wall
Curtained with fire, roofed in with creeping fire,
Slow grazing fire, that would not burn him whole
But kept him for death's promises and scoff,
And life's half-promising, and both their riling.

IV. THE EPILOGUE

With him they buried the muzzle his teeth had kissed,
And truthfully wrote the mother, 'Tim died smiling.'

The Last Laugh

'Oh! Jesus Christ! I'm hit,' he said; and died.
Whether he vainly cursed or prayed indeed,
   The Bullets chirped – In vain, vain, vain!
   Machine-guns chuckled – Tut-tut! Tut-tut!
   And the Big Gun guffawed.

Another sighed – 'O Mother, – Mother, – Dad!'
Then smiled at nothing, childlike, being dead.
   And the lofty Shrapnel-cloud
   Leisurely gestured, – Fool!
   And the splinters spat, and tittered.

'My Love!' One moaned. Love-languid seemed his mood,
Till slowly lowered, his whole face kissed the mud.
   And the Bayonet's long teeth grinned;
   Rabbles of Shells hooted and groaned;
   And the Gas hissed.

The Send-Off

Down the close darkening lanes they sang their way
To the siding-shed,
And lined the train with faces grimly gay.

Their breasts were stuck all white with wreath and spray
As men's are, dead.

Dull porters watched them, and a casual tramp
Stood staring hard,
Sorry to miss them from the upland camp.

Then, unmoved, signals nodded, and a lamp
Winked to the guard.

So secretly, like wrongs hushed-up, they went.
They were not ours:
We never heard to which front these were sent;

Nor there if they yet mock what women meant
Who gave them flowers.

Shall they return to beating of great bells
In wild train-loads?
A few, a few, too few for drums and yells,

May creep back, silent, to village wells,
Up half-known roads.

Exposure

Our brains ache, in the merciless iced east winds that knive
  us . . .
Wearied we keep awake because the night is silent . . .
Low, drooping flares confuse our memory of the salient . . .
Worried by silence, sentries whisper, curious, nervous,
  But nothing happens.

Watching, we hear the mad gusts tugging on the wire,
Like twitching agonies of men among its brambles.
Northward, incessantly, the flickering gunnery rumbles,
Far off, like a dull rumour of some other war.
  What are we doing here?

The poignant misery of dawn begins to grow . . .
We only know war lasts, rain soaks, and clouds sag stormy.
Dawn massing in the east her melancholy army
Attacks once more in ranks on shivering ranks of grey,
  But nothing happens.

Sudden successive flights of bullets streak the silence.
Less deathly than the air that shudders black with snow,
With sidelong flowing flakes that flock, pause, and renew;
We watch them wandering up and down the wind's
    nonchalance,
  But nothing happens.

Pale flakes with fingering stealth come feeling for our faces –
We cringe in holes, back on forgotten dreams, and stare,
  snow-dazed,

Deep into grassier ditches. So we drowse, sun-dozed,
Littered with blossoms trickling where the blackbird fusses.
 – Is it that we are dying?

Slowly our ghosts drag home: glimpsing the sunk fires, glozed
With crusted dark-red jewels; crickets jingle there;
For hours the innocent mice rejoice: the house is theirs;
Shutters and doors, all closed: on us the doors are closed, –
 We turn back to our dying.

Since we believe not otherwise can kind fires burn;
Nor ever suns smile true on child, or field, or fruit.
For God's invincible spring our love is made afraid;
Therefore, not loath we lie out here; therefore were born,
 For love of God seems dying.

Tonight, this frost will fasten on this mud and us,
Shrivelling many hands, puckering foreheads crisp.
The burying-party, picks and shovels in shaking grasp,
Pause over half-known faces. All their eyes are ice,
 But nothing happens.

Smile, Smile, Smile

Head to limp head, the sunk-eyed wounded scanned
Yesterday's *Mail;* the casualties (typed small)
And (large) Vast Booty from our Latest Haul.
Also, they read of Cheap Homes, not yet planned,
'For', said the paper, 'when this war is done
The men's first instincts will be making homes.
Meanwhile their foremost need is aerodromes,
It being certain war has but begun.
Peace would do wrong to our undying dead, –
The sons we offered might regret they died
If we got nothing lasting in their stead.
We must be solidly indemnified.
Though all be worthy Victory which all bought,
We rulers sitting in this ancient spot
Would wrong our very selves if we forgot
The greatest glory will be theirs who fought,
Who kept this nation in integrity.'
Nation? – The half-limbed readers did not chafe
But smiled at one another curiously
Like secret men who know their secret safe.
(This is the thing they know and never speak,
That England one by one had fled to France,
Not many elsewhere now, save under France.)
Pictures of these broad smiles appear each week,
And people in whose voice real feeling rings
Say: How they smile! They're happy now, poor things.

The Letter

With B.E.F. June 10. Dear Wife,
(Oh blast this pencil. 'Ere, Bill, lend's a knife.)
I'm in the pink at present, dear.
I think the war will end this year.
We don't see much of them square-'eaded 'Uns.
We're out of harm's way, not bad fed.
I'm longing for a taste of your old buns.
(Say, Jimmie, spare's a bite of bread.)
There don't seem much to say just now.
(Yer what? Then don't, yer ruddy cow!
And give us back me cigarette!)
I'll soon be 'ome. You mustn't fret.
My feet's improvin', as I told you of.
We're out in rest now. Never fear.
(VRACH! By crumbs, but that was near.)
Mother might spare you half a sov.
Kiss Neil and Bert. When me and you –
(Eh? What the 'ell! Stand to? Stand to!
Jim, give's a hand with pack on, lad.
Guh! Christ! I'm hit. Take 'old. Aye, bad.
No, damn your iodine. Jim? 'Ere!
Write my old girl, Jim, there's a dear.)

Anthem for Doomed Youth

What passing-bells for these who die as cattle?
   – Only the monstrous anger of the guns.
   Only the stuttering rifles' rapid rattle
Can patter out their hasty orisons.
No mockeries now for them; no prayers nor bells;
   Nor any voice of mourning save the choirs, –
The shrill, demented choirs of wailing shells;
   And bugles calling for them from sad shires.

What candles may be held to speed them all?
   Not in the hands of boys but in their eyes
Shall shine the holy glimmers of goodbyes.
   The pallor of girls' brows shall be their pall;
Their flowers the tenderness of patient minds,
And each slow dusk a drawing-down of blinds.

With an Identity Disc

If ever I had dreamed of my dead name
High in the heart of London, unsurpassed
By Time for ever, and the Fugitive, Fame,
There taking a long sanctuary at last,

I better that; and recollect with shame
How once I longed to hide it from life's heats
Under those holy cypresses, the same
That keep in shade the quiet place of Keats.

Now, rather, thank I God there is no risk
Of gravers scoring it with florid screed,
But let my death be memoried on this disc.
Wear it, sweet friend. Inscribe no date nor deed.
But let thy heart-beat kiss it night and day,
Until the name grow vague and wear away.

Le Christianisme

So the church Christ was hit and buried
   Under its rubbish and its rubble.
In cellars, packed-up saints lie serried,
   Well out of hearing of our trouble.

One Virgin still immaculate
   Smiles on for war to flatter her.
She's halo'd with an old tin hat,
   But a piece of hell will batter her.

'Cramped in that funnelled hole'

Cramped in that funnelled hole, they watched the dawn
Open jagged rim around; a yawn
Of death's jaws, which had all but swallowed them
Stuck in the bottom of his throat of phlegm.

They were in one of many mouths of Hell
Not seen of seem in visions; only felt
As teeth of traps; when bones and the dead are smelt
Under the mud where long ago they fell
Mixed with the sour sharp odour of the shell.

Hospital Barge

Budging the sluggard ripples of the Somme,
A barge round old Cérisy slowly slewed.
Softly her engines down the current screwed,
And chuckled softly with contented hum,
Till fairy tinklings struck their croonings dumb.
The waters rumpling at the stern subdued;
The lock-gate took her bulging amplitude;
Gently from out the gurgling lock she swum.

One reading by that calm bank shaded eyes
To watch her lessening westward quietly.
Then, as she neared the bend, her funnel screamed.
And that long lamentation made him wise
How unto Avalon, in agony,
Kings passed in the dark barge which Merlin dreamed.

At a Calvary near the Ancre

One ever hangs where shelled roads part.
   In this war He too lost a limb,
But His disciples hide apart;
   And now the Soldiers bear with Him.

Near Golgotha strolls many a priest,
   And in their faces there is pride
That they were flesh-marked by the Beast
   By whom the gentle Christ's denied.

The scribes on all the people shove
   And bawl allegiance to the state,
But they who love the greater love
   Lay down their life; they do not hate.

Conscious

His fingers wake, and flutter; up the bed.
His eyes come open with a pull of will,
Helped by the yellow mayflowers by his head.
The blind-cord drawls across the window-sill . . .
What a smooth floor the ward has! What a rug!
Who is that talking somewhere out of sight?
Three flies are creeping round the shiny jug . . .
'Nurse! Doctor!' – 'Yes, all right, all right.'

But sudden evening blurs and fogs the air.
There seems no time to want a drink of water.
Nurse looks so far away. And here and there
Music and roses burst through crimson slaughter.
He can't remember where he saw blue sky . . .
The trench is narrower. Cold, he's cold; yet hot –
And there's no light to see the voices by . . .
There is no time to ask . . . he knows not what.

Futility

Move him into the sun –
Gently its touch awoke him once,
At home, whispering of fields half-sown.
Always it woke him, even in France,
Until this morning and this snow.
If anything might rouse him now
The kind old sun will know.

Think how it wakes the seeds –
Woke once the clays of a cold star.
Are limbs, so dear achieved, are sides
Full-nerved, still warm, too hard to stir?
Was it for this the clay grew tall?
– O what made fatuous sunbeams toil
To break earth's sleep at all?

Disabled

He sat in a wheeled chair, waiting for dark,
And shivered in his ghastly suit of grey,
Legless, sewn short at elbow. Through the park
Voices of boys rang saddening like a hymn,
Voices of play and pleasure after day,
Till gathering sleep had mothered them from him.

* * *

About this time Town used to swing so gay
When glow-lamps budded in the light blue trees,
And girls glanced lovelier as the air grew dim, –
In the old times, before he threw away his knees.
Now he will never feel again how slim
Girls' waists are, or how warm their subtle hands.
All of them touch him like some queer disease.

* * *

There was an artist silly for his face,
For it was younger than his youth, last year.
Now, he is old; his back will never brace;
He's lost his colour very far from here,
Poured it down shell-holes till the veins ran dry,
And half his lifetime lapsed in the hot race
And leap of purple spurted from his thigh.

* * *

One time he liked a blood-smear down his leg,
After the matches, carried shoulder-high.
It was after football, when he'd drunk a peg,
He thought he'd better join. – He wonders why.
Someone had said he'd look a god in kilts,
That's why; and maybe, too, to please his Meg,
Aye, that was it, to please the giddy jilts
He asked to join. He didn't have to beg;
Smiling they wrote his lie: aged nineteen years.
Germans he scarcely thought of; all their guilt,
And Austria's, did not move him. And no fears
Of Fear came yet. He thought of jewelled hilts
For daggers in plaid socks; of smart salutes;
And care of arms; and leave; and pay arrears;
Esprit de corps; and hints for young recruits.
And soon, he was drafted out with drums and cheers.

* * *

Some cheered him home, but not as crowds cheer Goal.
Only a solemn man who brought him fruits
Thanked him; and then enquired about his soul.

* * *

Now, he will spend a few sick years in institutes,
And do what things the rules consider wise,
And take whatever pity they may dole.
Tonight he noticed how the women's eyes
Passed from him to the strong men that were whole.
How cold and late it is! Why don't they come
And put him into bed? Why don't they come?

Miners

There was a whispering in my hearth,
  A sigh of the coal,
Grown wistful of a former earth
  It might recall.

I listened for a tale of leaves
  And smothered ferns,
Frond-forests, and the low sly lives
  Before the fauns.

My fire might show steam-phantoms simmer
  From Time's old cauldron,
Before the birds made nests in summer,
  Or men had children.

But the coals were murmuring of their mine,
  And moans down there
Of boys that slept wry sleep, and men
  Writhing for air.

And I saw white bones in the cinder-shard,
  Bones without number.
Many the muscled bodies charred,
  And few remember.

I thought of all that worked dark pits
  Of war, and died
Digging the rock where Death reputes
  Peace lies indeed.

Comforted years will sit soft-chaired,
  In rooms of amber;
The years will stretch their hands, well-cheered
  By our life's ember;

The centuries will burn rich loads
  With which we groaned,
Whose warmth shall lull their dreaming lids,
  While songs are crooned;
But they will not dream of us poor lads,
  Left in the ground.

Insensibility

1

Happy are men who yet before they are killed
Can let their veins run cold.
Whom no compassion fleers
Or makes their feet
Sore on the alleys cobbled with their brothers.
The front line withers.
But they are troops who fade, not flowers,
For poets' tearful fooling:
Men, gaps for filling:
Losses, who might have fought
Longer; but no one bothers.

2

And some cease feeling
Even themselves or for themselves.
Dullness best solves
The tease and doubt of shelling,
And Chance's strange arithmetic
Comes simpler than the reckoning of their shilling.
They keep no check on armies' decimation.

3

Happy are these who lose imagination:
They have enough to carry with ammunition.
Their spirit drags no pack.
Their old wounds, save with cold, can not more ache.
Having seen all things red,
Their eyes are rid
Of the hurt of the colour of blood for ever.
And terror's first constriction over,
Their hearts remain small-drawn.
Their senses in some scorching cautery of battle
Now long since ironed,
Can laugh among the dying, unconcerned.

4

Happy the soldier home, with not a notion
How somewhere, every dawn, some men attack,
And many sighs are drained.
Happy the lad whose mind was never trained:
His days are worth forgetting more than not.
He sings along the march
Which we march taciturn, because of dusk,
The long, forlorn, relentless trend
From larger day to huger night.

5

We wise, who with a thought besmirch
Blood over all our soul,
How should we see our task
But through his blunt and lashless eyes?
Alive, he is not vital overmuch;
Dying, not mortal overmuch;
Nor sad, nor proud,
Nor curious at all.
He cannot tell
Old men's placidity from his.

6

But cursed are dullards whom no cannon stuns,
That they should be as stones.
Wretched are they, and mean
With paucity that never was simplicity.
By choice they made themselves immune
To pity and whatever moans in man
Before the last sea and the hapless stars;
Whatever mourns when many leave these shores;
Whatever shares
The eternal reciprocity of tears.

Strange Meeting

It seemed that out of battle I escaped
Down some profound dull tunnel, long since scooped
Through granites which titanic wars had groined.

Yet also there encumbered sleepers groaned,
Too fast in thought or death to be bestirred.
Then, as I probed them, one sprang up, and stared
With piteous recognition in fixed eyes,
Lifting distressful hands, as if to bless.
And by his smile, I knew that sullen hall, –
By his dead smile I knew we stood in Hell.

With a thousand pains that vision's face was grained;
Yet no blood reached there from the upper ground,
And no guns thumped, or down the flues made moan.
'Strange friend,' I said, 'here is no cause to mourn.'
'None,' said that other, 'save the undone years,
The hopelessness. Whatever hope is yours,
Was my life also; I went hunting wild
After the wildest beauty in the world,
Which lies not calm in eyes, or braided hair,
But mocks the steady running of the hour,
And if it grieves, grieves richlier than here.
For by my glee might many men have laughed,
And of my weeping something had been left,
Which must die now. I mean the truth untold,
The pity of war, the pity war distilled.
Now men will go content with what we spoiled,

Or, discontent, boil bloody, and be spilled.
They will be swift with swiftness of the tigress.
None will break ranks, though nations trek from progress.
Courage was mine, and I had mystery,
Wisdom was mine, and I had mastery:
To miss the march of this retreating world
Into vain citadels that are not walled.
Then, when much blood had clogged their chariot-wheels,
I would go up and wash them from sweet wells,
Even with truths that lie too deep for taint.
I would have poured my spirit without stint
But not through wounds; not on the cess of war.
Foreheads of men have bled where no wounds were.

'I am the enemy you killed, my friend.
I knew you in this dark: for so you frowned
Yesterday through me as you jabbed and killed.
I parried; but my hands were loath and cold.
Let us sleep now . . .'

Asleep

Under his helmet, up against his pack,
After so many days of work and waking,
Sleep took him by the brow and laid him back.

There, in the happy no-time of his sleeping,
Death took him by the heart. There heaved a quaking
Of the aborted life within him leaping,
Then chest and sleepy arms once more fell slack.

And soon the slow, stray blood came creeping
From the intruding lead, like ants on track.

Whether his deeper sleep lie shaded by the shaking
Of great wings, and the thoughts that hung the stars,
High-pillowed on calm pillows of God's making,
Above these clouds, these rains, these sleets of lead,
And these winds' scimitars,

– Or whether yet his thin and sodden head
Confuses more and more with the low mould,
His hair being one with the grey grass
Of finished fields, and wire-scrags rusty-old,
Who knows? Who hopes? Who troubles? Let it pass!
He sleeps. He sleeps less tremulous, less cold,
Than we who wake, and waking say Alas!

The Show

> We have fallen in the dreams the ever-living
> Breathe on the tarnished mirror of the world,
> And then smooth out with ivory hands and sigh.
>
> W. B. YEATS

My soul looked down from a vague height, with Death,
As unremembering how I rose or why,
And saw a sad land, weak with sweats of dearth,
Grey, cratered like the moon with hollow woe,
And pitted with great pocks and scabs of plagues.

Across its beard, that horror of harsh wire,
There moved thin caterpillars, slowly uncoiled.
It seemed they pushed themselves to be as plugs
Of ditches, where they writhed and shrivelled, killed.

By them had slimy paths been trailed and scraped
Round myriad warts that might be little hills.

From gloom's last dregs these long-strung creatures crept,
And vanished out of dawn down hidden holes.

(And smell came up from those foul openings
As out of mouths, or deep wounds deepening.)

On dithering feet upgathered, more and more,
Brown strings, towards strings of grey, with bristling spines,
All migrants from green fields, intent on mire.

Those that were grey, of more abundant spawns,
Ramped on the rest and ate them and were eaten.

I saw their bitten backs curve, loop, and straighten.
I watched those agonies curl, lift and flatten.

Whereat, in terror what that sight might mean,
I reeled and shivered earthward like a feather.

And Death fell with me, like a deepening moan.
And He, picking a manner of worm, which half had hid
Its bruises in the earth, but crawled no further,
Showed me its feet, the feet of many men,
And the fresh-severed head of it, my head.

Mental Cases

Who are these? Why sit they here in twilight?
Wherefore rock they, purgatorial shadows,
Drooping tongues from jaws that slob their relish,
Baring teeth that leer like skulls' teeth wicked?
Stroke on stroke of pain, – but what slow panic,
Gouged these chasms round their fretted sockets?
Ever from their hair and through their hands' palms
Misery swelters. Surely we have perished
Sleeping, and walk hell; but who these hellish?

– These are men whose minds the Dead have ravished.
Memory fingers in their hair of murders,
Multitudinous murders they once witnessed.
Wading sloughs of flesh these helpless wander,
Treading blood from lungs that had loved laughter.
Always they must see these things and hear them,
Batter of guns and shatter of flying muscles,
Carnage incomparable, and human squander
Rucked too thick for these men's extrication.

Therefore still their eyeballs shrink tormented
Back into their brains, because on their sense
Sunlight seems a blood-smear; night comes blood-black;
Dawn breaks open like a wound that bleeds afresh.
– Thus their heads wear this hilarious, hideous,
Awful falseness of set-smiling corpses.

– Thus their hands are plucking at each other;
Picking at the rope-knouts of their scourging;
Snatching after us who smote them, brother,
Pawing us who dealt them war and madness.

The Chances

I 'mind as how the night before that show
Us five got talkin'; we was in the know.
'Ah well,' says Jimmy, and he's seen some scrappin',
'There ain't no more than five things as can happen, –
You get knocked out; else wounded, bad or cushy;
Scuppered; or nowt except you're feelin' mushy.'
One of us got the knock-out, blown to chops;
One lad was hurt, like, losin' both his props;
And one – to use the word of hypocrites –
Had the misfortune to be took by Fritz.
Now me, I wasn't scratched, praise God Almighty,
Though next time please I'll thank Him for a blighty.
But poor old Jim, he's livin' and he's not;
He reckoned he'd five chances, and he had:
He's wounded, killed, and pris'ner, all the lot,
The flamin' lot all rolled in one. Jim's mad.

The Parable of the Old Man and the Young

So Abram rose, and clave the wood, and went,
And took the fire with him, and a knife.
And as they sojourned both of them together,
Isaac the first-born spake and said, My Father,
Behold the preparations, fire and iron,
But where the lamb, for this burnt-offering?
Then Abram bound the youth with belts and straps,
And builded parapets and trenches there,
And stretchèd forth the knife to slay his son.
When lo! an Angel called him out of heaven,
Saying, Lay not thy hand upon the lad,
Neither do anything to him, thy son.
Behold! Caught in a thicket by its horns,
A Ram. Offer the Ram of Pride instead.

But the old man would not so, but slew his son,
And half the seed of Europe, one by one.

The End

After the blast of lightning from the east,
   The flourish of loud clouds, the Chariot Throne;
After the drums of time have rolled and ceased,
   And by the bronze west long retreat is blown,
Shall Life renew these bodies? Of a truth,
   All death will he annul, all tears assuage?
Or fill these void veins full again with youth,
   And wash, with an immortal water, age?

When I do ask white Age, he saith not so:
   'My head hangs weighed with snow.'
And when I hearken to the Earth, she saith:
   'My fiery heart shrinks, aching. It is death.
Mine ancient scars shall not be glorified,
Nor my titanic tears, the seas, be dried.'

A Terre
(being the philosophy of many soldiers)

Sit on the bed. I'm blind, and three parts shell.
Be careful; can't shake hands now; never shall.
Both arms have mutinied against me, – brutes.
My fingers fidget like ten idle brats.

I tried to peg out soldierly, – no use!
One dies of war like any old disease.
This bandage feels like pennies on my eyes.
I have my medals? – Discs to make eyes close.
My glorious ribbons? – Ripped from my own back
In scarlet shreds. (That's for your poetry book.)

A short life and a merry one, my buck!
We used to say we'd hate to live dead-old, –
Yet now . . . I'd willingly be puffy, bald,
And patriotic. Buffers catch from boys
At least the jokes hurled at them. I suppose
Little I'd ever teach a son, but hitting,
Shooting, war, hunting, all the arts of hurting.
Well, that's what I learnt, – that, and making money.

Your fifty years ahead seem none too many?
Tell me how long I've got? God! For one year
To help myself to nothing more than air!
One Spring! Is one too good to spare, too long?
Spring wind would work its own way to my lung,
And grow me legs as quick as lilac-shoots.

My servant's lamed, but listen how he shouts!
When I'm lugged out, he'll still be good for that.
Here in this mummy-case, you know, I've thought
How well I might have swept his floors for ever.
I'd ask no nights off when the bustle's over,
Enjoying so the dirt. Who's prejudiced
Against a grimed hand when his own's quite dust,
Less live than specks that in the sun-shafts turn,
Less warm than dust that mixes with arms' tan?
I'd love to be a sweep, now, black as Town,
Yes, or a muckman. Must I be his load?

O Life, Life, let me breathe, – a dug-out rat!
Not worse than ours the lives rats lead –
Nosing along at night down some safe rut,
They find a shell-proof home before they rot.
Dead men may envy living mites in cheese,
Or good germs even. Microbes have their joys,
And subdivide, and never come to death.
Certainly flowers have the easiest time on earth.
'I shall be one with nature, herb, and stone,'
Shelley would tell me. Shelley would be stunned:
The dullest Tommy hugs that fancy now.
'Pushing up daisies' is their creed, you know.

To grain, then, go my fat, to buds my sap,
For all the usefulness there is in soap.
D'you think the Boche will ever stew man-soup?
Some day, no doubt, if . . .

                    Friend, be very sure

I shall be better off with plants that share
More peaceably the meadow and the shower.
Soft rains will touch me, – as they could touch once,
And nothing but the sun shall make me ware.
Your guns may crash around me. I'll not hear;
Or, if I wince, I shall not know I wince.

Don't take my soul's poor comfort for your jest.
Soldiers may grow a soul when turned to fronds,
But here the thing's best left at home with friends.

My soul's a little grief, grappling your chest,
To climb your throat on sobs; easily chased
On other sighs and wiped by fresher winds.

Carry my crying spirit till it's weaned
To do without what blood remained these wounds.

The Kind Ghosts

She sleeps on soft, last breaths; but no ghost looms
Out of the stillness of her palace wall,
Her wall of boys on boys and dooms on dooms.

She dreams of golden gardens and sweet glooms,
Not marvelling why her roses never fall
Nor what red mouths were torn to make their blooms.

The shades keep down which well might roam her hall.
Quiet their blood lies in her crimson rooms
And she is not afraid of their footfall.

They move not from her tapestries, their pall,
Nor pace her terraces, their hecatombs,
Lest aught she be disturbed, or grieved at all.

The Sentry

We'd found an old Boche dug-out, and he knew,
And gave us hell; for shell on frantic shell
Lit full on top, but never quite burst through.
Rain, guttering down in waterfalls of slime,
Kept slush waist-high and rising hour by hour,
And choked the steps too thick with clay to climb.
What murk of air remained stank old, and sour
With fumes from whizz-bangs, and the smell of men
Who'd lived there years, and left their curse in the den,
If not their corpses . . .
                    There we herded from the blast
Of whizz-bangs; but one found our door at last, –
Buffeting eyes and breath, snuffing the candles,
And thud! flump! thud! down the steep steps came
    thumping
And sploshing in the flood, deluging muck,
The sentry's body; then his rifle, handles
Of old Boche bombs, and mud in ruck on ruck.
We dredged it up, for dead, until he whined,
'O sir – my eyes, – I'm blind, – I'm blind, – I'm blind.'
Coaxing, I held a flame against his lids
And said if he could see the least blurred light
He was not blind; in time they'd get all right.
'I can't,' he sobbed. Eyeballs, huge-bulged like squids',
Watch my dreams still, – yet I forgot him there
In posting Next for duty, and sending a scout

To beg a stretcher somewhere, and flound' ring about
To other posts under the shrieking air.

Those other wretches, how they bled and spewed,
And one who would have drowned himself for good, –
I try not to remember these things now.
Let Dread hark back for one word only: how,
Half-listening to that sentry's moans and jumps,
And the wild chattering of his shivered teeth,
Renewed most horribly whenever crumps
Pummelled the roof and slogged the air beneath, –
Through the dense din, I say, we heard him shout
'I see your lights!' – But ours had long gone out.

Spring Offensive

Halted against the shade of a last hill
They fed, and eased of pack-loads, were at ease;
And leaning on the nearest chest or knees
Carelessly slept.
               But many there stood still
To face the stark blank sky beyond the ridge,
Knowing their feet had come to the end of the world.
Marvelling they stood, and watched the long grass swirled
By the May breeze, murmurous with wasp and midge;
And though the summer oozed into their veins
Like an injected drug for their bodies' pains,
Sharp on their souls hung the imminent ridge of grass,
Fearfully flashed the sky's mysterious glass.

Hour after hour they ponder the warm field
And the far valley behind, where buttercups
Had blessed with gold their slow boots coming up;
When even the little brambles would not yield
But clutched and clung to them like sorrowing arms.
They breathe like trees unstirred.

Till like a cold gust thrills the little word
At which each body and its soul begird
And tighten them for battle. No alarms
Of bugles, no high flags, no clamorous haste, –
Only a lift and flare of eyes that faced
The sun, like a friend with whom their love is done.

O larger shone that smile against the sun, –
Mightier than his whose bounty these have spurned.

So, soon they topped the hill, and raced together
Over an open stretch of herb and heather
Exposed. And instantly the whole sky burned
With fury against them; earth set sudden cups
In thousands for their blood; and the green slope
Chasmed and deepened sheer to infinite space.

Of them who running on that last high place
Breasted the surf of bullets, or went up
On the hot blast and fury of hell's upsurge,
Or plunged and fell away past this world's verge,
Some say God caught them even before they fell.

But what say such as from existence' brink
Ventured but drave too swift to sink,
The few who rushed in the body to enter hell,
And there out-fiending all its fiends and flames
With superhuman inhumanities,
Long-famous slowly, immemorial shames –
And crawling slowly back, have by degrees
Regained cool peaceful air in wonder –
Why speak not they of comrades that went under?

Greater Love

Red lips are not so red
   As the stained stones kissed by the English dead.
Kindness of wooed and wooer
Seems shame to their love pure.
O Love, your eyes lose lure
   When I behold eyes blinded in my stead!

Your slender attitude
   Trembles not exquisite like limbs knife-skewed,
Rolling and rolling there
Where God seems not to care;
Till the fierce love they bear
   Cramps them in death's extreme decrepitude.

Your voice sings not so soft, –
   Though even as wind murmuring through raftered loft, –
Your dear voice is not dear,
Gentle, and evening clear,
As theirs whom none now hear,
   Now earth has stopped their piteous mouths that coughed.

Heart, you were never hot
    Nor large, nor full like hearts made great with shot;
And though your hand be pale,
Paler are all which trail
Your cross through flame and hail:
    Weep, you may weep, for you may touch them not.

The Next War

War's a joke for me and you,
While we know such dreams are true.

SIEGFRIED SASSOON

Out there, we walked quite friendly up to Death, –
    Sat down and ate beside him, cool and bland, –
    Pardoned his spilling mess-tins in our hand.
We've sniffed the green thick odour of his breath, –

Our eyes wept, but our courage didn't writhe.
    He's spat at us with bullets, and he's coughed
    Shrapnel. We chorused if he sang aloft,
We whistled while he shaved us with his scythe.

Oh, Death was never enemy of ours!
    We laughed at him, we leagued with him, old chum.
No soldier's paid to kick against His powers.
    We laughed, – knowing that better men would come,
And greater wars: when every fighter brags
He fights on Death, for lives; not men, for flags.

1. BOCCACCIO · *Mrs Rosie and the Priest*
2. GERARD MANLEY HOPKINS · *As kingfishers catch fire*
3. *The Saga of Gunnlaug Serpent-tongue*
4. THOMAS DE QUINCEY · *On Murder Considered as One of the Fine Arts*
5. FRIEDRICH NIETZSCHE · *Aphorisms on Love and Hate*
6. JOHN RUSKIN · *Traffic*
7. PU SONGLING · *Wailing Ghosts*
8. JONATHAN SWIFT · *A Modest Proposal*
9. *Three Tang Dynasty Poets*
10. WALT WHITMAN · *On the Beach at Night Alone*
11. KENKŌ · *A Cup of Sake Beneath the Cherry Trees*
12. BALTASAR GRACIÁN · *How to Use Your Enemies*
13. JOHN KEATS · *The Eve of St Agnes*
14. THOMAS HARDY · *Woman much missed*
15. GUY DE MAUPASSANT · *Femme Fatale*
16. MARCO POLO · *Travels in the Land of Serpents and Pearls*
17. SUETONIUS · *Caligula*
18. APOLLONIUS OF RHODES · *Jason and Medea*
19. ROBERT LOUIS STEVENSON · *Olalla*
20. KARL MARX AND FRIEDRICH ENGELS · *The Communist Manifesto*
21. PETRONIUS · *Trimalchio's Feast*
22. JOHANN PETER HEBEL · *How a Ghastly Story Was Brought to Light by a Common or Garden Butcher's Dog*
23. HANS CHRISTIAN ANDERSEN · *The Tinder Box*
24. RUDYARD KIPLING · *The Gate of the Hundred Sorrows*
25. DANTE · *Circles of Hell*
26. HENRY MAYHEW · *Of Street Piemen*
27. HAFEZ · *The nightingales are drunk*
28. GEOFFREY CHAUCER · *The Wife of Bath*
29. MICHEL DE MONTAIGNE · *How We Weep and Laugh at the Same Thing*
30. THOMAS NASHE · *The Terrors of the Night*
31. EDGAR ALLAN POE · *The Tell-Tale Heart*
32. MARY KINGSLEY · *A Hippo Banquet*
33. JANE AUSTEN · *The Beautifull Cassandra*
34. ANTON CHEKHOV · *Gooseberries*
35. SAMUEL TAYLOR COLERIDGE · *Well, they are gone, and here must I remain*
36. JOHANN WOLFGANG VON GOETHE · *Sketchy, Doubtful, Incomplete Jottings*
37. CHARLES DICKENS · *The Great Winglebury Duel*
38. HERMAN MELVILLE · *The Maldive Shark*
39. ELIZABETH GASKELL · *The Old Nurse's Story*
40. NIKOLAY LESKOV · *The Steel Flea*

41. HONORÉ DE BALZAC · *The Atheist's Mass*
42. CHARLOTTE PERKINS GILMAN · *The Yellow Wall-Paper*
43. C.P. CAVAFY · *Remember, Body . . .*
44. FYODOR DOSTOEVSKY · *The Meek One*
45. GUSTAVE FLAUBERT · *A Simple Heart*
46. NIKOLAI GOGOL · *The Nose*
47. SAMUEL PEPYS · *The Great Fire of London*
48. EDITH WHARTON · *The Reckoning*
49. HENRY JAMES · *The Figure in the Carpet*
50. WILFRED OWEN · *Anthem For Doomed Youth*
51. WOLFGANG AMADEUS MOZART · *My Dearest Father*
52. PLATO · *Socrates' Defence*
53. CHRISTINA ROSSETTI · *Goblin Market*
54. *Sindbad the Sailor*
55. SOPHOCLES · *Antigone*
56. RYŪNOSUKE AKUTAGAWA · *The Life of a Stupid Man*
57. LEO TOLSTOY · *How Much Land Does A Man Need?*
58. GIORGIO VASARI · *Leonardo da Vinci*
59. OSCAR WILDE · *Lord Arthur Savile's Crime*
60. SHEN FU · *The Old Man of the Moon*
61. AESOP · *The Dolphins, the Whales and the Gudgeon*
62. MATSUO BASHŌ · *Lips too Chilled*
63. EMILY BRONTË · *The Night is Darkening Round Me*
64. JOSEPH CONRAD · *To-morrow*
65. RICHARD HAKLUYT · *The Voyage of Sir Francis Drake Around the Whole Globe*
66. KATE CHOPIN · *A Pair of Silk Stockings*
67. CHARLES DARWIN · *It was snowing butterflies*
68. BROTHERS GRIMM · *The Robber Bridegroom*
69. CATULLUS · *I Hate and I Love*
70. HOMER · *Circe and the Cyclops*
71. D. H. LAWRENCE · *Il Duro*
72. KATHERINE MANSFIELD · *Miss Brill*
73. OVID · *The Fall of Icarus*
74. SAPPHO · *Come Close*
75. IVAN TURGENEV · *Kasyan from the Beautiful Lands*
76. VIRGIL · *O Cruel Alexis*
77. H. G. WELLS · *A Slip under the Microscope*
78. HERODOTUS · *The Madness of Cambyses*
79. *Speaking of Siva*
80. *The Dhammapada*

'They wanted me to give a concert; I wanted them to beg me. And so they did. I gave a concert.'

WOLFGANG AMADEUS MOZART
Born 1756, Salzburg
Died 1791, Vienna

This selection of letters between Mozart and his father was written between October 1777 and July 1778.

MOZART IN PENGUIN CLASSICS
Mozart: A Life in Letters

WOLFGANG AMADEUS MOZART

My Dearest Father

Translated by
Stewart Spencer

PENGUIN BOOKS

PENGUIN CLASSICS

UK | USA | Canada | Ireland | Australia
India | New Zealand | South Africa

Penguin Books is part of the Penguin Random House group of companies whose addresses can be found at global.penguinrandomhouse.com.

This selection published in Penguin Classics 2015

012

Translation copyright © Stewart Spencer, 2006

The moral right of the translator has been asserted.

Set in 9.5/13 pt Baskerville 10 Pro
Typeset by Jouve (UK), Milton Keynes
Printed and bound in Great Britain by Clays Ltd, Elcograf S.p.A.

A CIP catalogue record for this book is available from the British Library

ISBN: 978-0-141-39762-7

www.greenpenguin.co.uk

Penguin Random House is committed to a sustainable future for our business, our readers and our planet. This book is made from Forest Stewardship Council® certified paper.

Mozart to his father,
17 October 1777, Augsburg

Mon très cher Père,

I must start with Stein's pianofortes. Before I saw any of Stein's work, I'd always preferred Späth's pianos; but now I prefer Stein's, as they damp so much better than the Regensburg instruments. If I strike hard, it doesn't matter whether I keep my finger down or raise it, the sound ceases the moment I produce it. However I attack the keys, the tone is always even. It doesn't produce a clattering sound, it doesn't get louder or softer or fail to sound at all; in a word, it's always even. It's true, he won't part with a pianoforte like this for under 300 florins, but the effort and labour that he expends on it can't be paid for. A particular feature of his instruments is their escape action. Not one maker in a hundred bothers with this. But without escape action it's impossible for a pianoforte not to produce a clattering sound or to go on sounding after the note has been struck; when you strike the keys, his hammers fall back again the moment they hit the strings, whether you hold down the keys or release them. He told me that only when he's finished making a piano like this does he sit down and try out all the passagework, runs and leaps, and, using a shave, works away at the instrument until it can do everything. For he works only to serve the music, not just for his own profit, otherwise he'd be finished at once.

He often says that if he weren't such a great music lover and didn't have some slight skill on the instrument, he'd long since have run out of patience with his work; but he loves an instrument that never lets the player down and that will last. His pianos will really last. He guarantees that the sounding board won't break or crack. Once he's finished making a sounding board for a piano he puts it outside, exposing it to the air, rain, snow, heat of the sun and all the devils in order for it to crack, and then he inserts wedges, which he glues in, so that it's very strong and firm. He's perfectly happy for it to crack as he's then assured that nothing more can happen to it. Indeed, he often cuts into it himself and then glues it back together again and makes it really strong. He has completed three such pianofortes. Not until today did I play on one of them again. Today – the 17th – we had lunch with young Herr Gasser, a young and handsome widower who's lost his young and beautiful wife. They'd been married for only 2 years. He's a most excellent and polite young man. We were splendidly entertained. Also there was a colleague of Abbé Henri, Bullinger and Wieshofer, an ex-Jesuit who's now Kapellmeister at the cathedral here. He knows Herr *Schachtner* very well, he was his

My Dearest Father

choirmaster in Ingolstadt. He's called Pater Gerbl. I'm to give his best wishes to Herr Schachtner. After lunch Herr Gasser and I went to Herr *Stein's*, where we were accompanied by one of his sisters-in-law as well as Mama and our cousin. At 4 o'clock we were joined by the Kapellmeister and Herr Schmidbaur, the organist at St Ulrich's, a fine old gentleman who's very well-spoken; and I then sight-read a sonata by Beecke that was quite hard and *miserable al solito*; I can't begin to tell you how the Kapellmeister and organist crossed themselves. Both here and in Munich I've played my 6 sonatas many times from memory. I played the fifth one in G at the aristocrats' concert in the Bauernstube. The last one, in D, sounds amazing on *Stein's* pianoforte. The device that you depress with your knee is also better made on his instrument than on others. I scarcely need to touch it and it works; and as soon as you remove your knee even a little, you no longer hear the slightest reverberation. Tomorrow I may get round to his organs – – I mean, *to write about them*; I'm saving up his little daughter till the end. When I told Herr *Stein* that I'd like to play on his organ as the organ was my passion, he was very surprised and said: What, a man like you, so great a keyboard player wants to play on an instrument that has no douceur, no expression, no piano or forte but always sounds the same? – – None of that matters. In my eyes and ears the organ is the king of instruments. Well, as you like. We went off together. I could already tell from what he

3

said that he didn't think I'd do much on his organ and that – for example – I'd play in a way more suited to a piano. He told me that Schubart had asked to be shown his organ, and I was afraid – he said – as Schubart had told everyone, and the church was quite full; for I thought he'd be all spirit, fire and speed, none of which works on the organ; but as soon as he started I changed my mind. I said only this: What do you think, Herr Stein? Do you think I'll run all over the organ? – – Oh, you, that's quite different. We reached the choir. I began to improvise, by which point he was already laughing, and then a fugue. I can well believe – he said – that you enjoy playing the organ if you play like that – – at first the pedal was a little strange as it wasn't divided. It began with C, then D, E in the same row. But with us D and E are above, as E flat and F sharp are here. But I soon got used to it. I also played on the old organ at St Ulrich's. The steps up to it are a nightmare. I asked if someone could play on it for me as I wanted to go down and listen. From up there the organ is totally ineffectual. But I could make nothing of it, as the young choirmaster, a priest, played only scales, so it was impossible to form any impression. And when he tried to play some chords, he produced only discords as it was out of tune. After that we had to go to a coffee-room as my mother and cousin and Herr Stein were with us. A certain Pater Aemilian, an arrogant ass and a simpleton of his profession, was in an especially hearty mood. He kept wanting to joke with my cousin, but she

My Dearest Father

just made fun of him – – finally, when he was drunk (which didn't take long), he started to talk about music. He sang a canon and I said I'd never in my whole life heard a finer one. I said I'm sorry, I can't join in as I've no natural gift for intoning. That doesn't matter, he said. He started. I was the third voice, but I made up some very different words, for example, O you prick, lick my arse. *Sotto voce* to my cousin. We laughed about it for half an hour. He said to me: if only we could have spent longer together. I'd like to discuss the art of composition with you. Then the discussion would soon be over, I said. *Get lost*. To be continued.

W. A. Mozart

Leopold Mozart to his son,
23 October 1777, Salzburg

Mon très cher Fils,
I must congratulate you on your name day! But what can I wish you today that I don't always wish you? – – I wish you the grace of God, that it may accompany you everywhere and never abandon you, as indeed it will never do if you strive to fulfil the obligations of a true Catholic Christian.

You know me. – I'm no pedant, I'm not holier than thou, and I'm certainly no hypocrite: but you surely won't refuse a request from your father? – It is this: that you should be concerned for your soul's welfare and not cause your father any anxiety in his hour of death, so that at that difficult time he won't have to reproach himself for neglecting your soul's salvation. Farewell! Be happy! Lead a sensible life! Honour and esteem your mother, who has much toil in her old age, love me as I love you. Your truly solicitous father

Leop. Mozart

Leopold Mozart to his son,
24 November 1777, Salzburg

Mon très cher Fils,

I really don't know what to say, I was so stunned by your last letter of the 16th. In it you announced with a display of the *greatest nonchalance* that Herr *Schmalz* – presumably the father, brother or relation of Herr Schmalz of the leather factory in Munich or possibly even Herr Schmalz himself – had apologized for the fact that he had no instructions to give you any money. I can well believe that; and he was right: you should have asked Herr Herzog or the firm of Nocker & Schiedl to provide you with a little extra credit, *as I used to do*: for they had no orders from Hagenauer's house to extend this credit elsewhere, and no businessman exceeds his literal orders: but it would have been done if you'd asked them. But this incident was described in such matter-of-fact and indifferent terms as though I'd whole chests full of money and should have been terribly annoyed that you'd not been paid at once. I won't waste time with a long-winded account of our circumstances, you know them yourself, as does Mama, and in my letter *of the 20th* I listed the main items, although I forgot a sizeable *sum* that we owe to Hagenauer *for goods* but with whom we're not *writing up a single farthing more on credit*. But what amazed me most of all on receiving your letter was that you suddenly came out with this story without telling me about it in your previous letter, in which you simply said that money would have been more useful and appropriate for your journey than a trinket, as you knew even then that you were low on funds. If Herr Schmalz had been willing, I would have been lumbered with instructions for payment *without having received the slightest advance notice* and at a time *when I suspected nothing*. That's a pretty state of affairs indeed! – I leave you to think it over, in the light of my present circumstances. You wrote to me from Augsb. that you'd lost only 27 florins. – According to my own calculations, you must still have 170 florins even if you'd lost 30 florins. Even if that stupid trip to Mannheim via Wallerstein cost you 70 florins, you should still be left with 100 florins. Even if it cost you more, *can you really not have enough left* to be able to make the journey to Mainz? You'd then be near Frankfurt and if absolutely necessary would be able to draw a little with your second letter of credit from Herr Bolongaro in Frankfurt. Then you'd only have to ask some businessman in Mainz who's in contact with Herr Bolongaro; he would have undertaken to send the letter of credit to Herr Bolong. and to draw what you require.

Wouldn't this have been more sensible than to settle

My Dearest Father

down in Mannheim and squander your money to no avail, as this money would presumably have enabled you to make the journey, which would have cost perhaps 15 or 16 florins. It's only $1\frac{1}{4}$ stages to *Worms*, 2 to Oppenheim and 1 to Mainz, so only $3\frac{3}{4}$ in all. And even if you'd had little or no money on your arrival, we have acquaintances there who would help you, and no gentleman need be ashamed if he hasn't a farthing in his pocket but can produce a letter of credit: this can happen to the wealthiest and most distinguished people, indeed it's a maxim when travelling that, if possible, you should carry only as much money as you need. I'm still in the dark and if I speak of *Mainz* it's pure supposition as you haven't done me the honour in any of your letters of telling me where you are intending to go, only at the very last moment did you write to me from Augsb. and say you were going to Wallerstein; and Herr Stein wrote to say that you left for Wallerstein and Mannheim at half past 7 on Sunday. But such things should be announced some time in advance, as I can sometimes make useful preparations and send reminders, just as I was at pains to do by writing to Herr Otto and Herr Pfeil in Frankfurt. – – Of course, your journey is no concern of mine! Isn't that so? – – You could, of course, have taken a very different route from Mannheim: namely, Würzburg and from there to the Margrave of Darmstadt, then Frankfurt and Mainz. But how can I guess what you're thinking or make suggestions as I'm never consulted and didn't know how things stood in Mannheim, indeed to judge by your letter in which you had an opportunity to speak so familiarly with the elector I was bound to assume that you had very different plans and were intending to stay there for some time; all of which – whatever your opinions, inclinations, aims etc. may be – you should have reported honestly and in good time as it takes *12 days* to receive and reply to a letter even if all goes smoothly. But you didn't bother to consider this either as in your last letter of the 16th you wrote that *I could continue to write to you in Mannheim*, although it would be 12 days at the quickest before you received this letter, in other words, not until the 28th, by which time Herr Herzog will long since have replied and you will have left. But I did not receive your letter until Friday the 21st, as a present on our *wedding day*, and was unable therefore to reply until the 24th; you'll have read this letter – God knows where – on 1 or 2 December. Neither of you must think that I don't know how many incidental expenses are incurred on a journey and how money vanishes into thin air, especially when one's overgenerous or too kind. My dear wife prided herself on getting up early, on not lingering and on doing everything quickly and economically. *16 days in Munich*, *14 days in Augsburg* and now, according to your letter of *16 Nov.*, *17 days in Mannheim*, which, including the time spent waiting for a reply from Augsb., will turn out to be 3 weeks. That's sorcery indeed; you've been away 8 weeks, in other words, 2 months, and you're already in Mannheim? – – That's

My Dearest Father

incredibly quick! When we travelled to England, we spent *9 days* in Munich, called on the *elector* and Duke *Clemens*, and had to wait for our present. – We were *15 days* in Augsb., but we gave *3 concerts* there, namely, on 28 and 30 June and 4 July. – We left Salzburg on *9 June* and did not arrive in Munich until the 12th as new wheels had to be made in Wasserburg, yet in spite of this we were in Schwetzingen by *13 July*, although we broke our journey in Ulm, Ludwigsburg and Bruchsal. So you see that your long and unnecessary stay has ruined everything, the most beautiful autumn in living memory has come and gone, and so far you've regarded your journey as no more than a pleasure trip and spent the time enjoying yourselves: now the bad weather, shorter days and cold are here, with more of the same to come, while your prospects and goals are now correspondingly expensive and distant.

You can't spend the whole winter travelling; and if you plan to stay anywhere, it should be in a large town with lots of people where there are hopes and opportunities of earning some money: and where is such a place to be found in the whole of this region? – Apart from Paris: – – but life in Paris requires a completely different attitude to life, a different way of thinking, you have to be attentive and every day think of ways of earning money and exercise extreme politeness in order to ingratiate yourself with people of standing: I'll write more on this in my next letter, in which I shall also set out my ideas on a quite different route that may be worth taking and which, I believe, will get you to Paris more quickly, namely, from *Koblenz* to *Trier, Luxembourg, Sedan*, where Herr *Ziegenhagen*, who visited us with Herr Wahler, has a textile factory. Perhaps he'll be there now. Then Rethel, *Rheims*, Soissons and Paris. Note that from Paris to Rethel there are 22 French post stages. From Rethel it's only a stone's throw to Sedan – Luxembourg, too, isn't far, and Trier is close to Luxembourg. Luxembourg is an imposing fortress and there'll be lots of officers there. *Rheims* and *Soissons* are large towns. In all these places it will be relatively easy to earn some money in order to recover your travelling expenses as virtuosos rarely visit such places. By contrast, it's 34 post stages from Brussels to Paris, and these cost us *20 louis d'or* for 6 horses, without our receiving a farthing in return. And between Koblenz and Brussels there's nothing that can be done, except perhaps with the elector of Cologne. Perhaps? – And what about Brussels? – – – – –

Meanwhile, whichever route you take, make sure that you obtain some letters of recommendation to take with you to Paris, it doesn't matter who writes them – businessmen, courtiers etc. etc. And is there no French ambassador or resident in Mainz or Koblenz? I don't think there is. You haven't got any letters of recommendation, whereas I had a lot; they're vital in providing you with both patronage and contacts. A journey like this is no joke, you've no experience of this sort of thing, you need to have other, more important thoughts on your mind than foolish games, you have to try to anticipate a hundred different things, otherwise you'll suddenly find yourself in the shit without any money, – – and where you've no money you'll have no friends either, even if you give a hundred lessons for nothing, and even if you write sonatas and spend every night fooling around from 10 till 12 instead of devoting yourself to more important matters. Then try asking for credit! – That'll wipe the smile off your face. I'm not blaming you for a moment for placing the Cannabichs under an obligation to you by your acts of kindness, that was well done: but you should have devoted a few of your otherwise idle hours each evening to your father, who is so concerned about you, and sent him not simply a mishmash tossed off in a hurry but a proper, confidential and detailed account of the expenses incurred on your journey, of the money you still have left, of the journey you plan to take in future and of your intentions in Mannheim etc. etc. In short, you should have sought my advice; I hope you'll be sensible enough to see this, for who has to shoulder this whole burden if not your poor old father? As I've already said, I didn't receive your letter until the 21st and was unable to reply until today. Yesterday, the 23rd, I confessed my sins at Holy Trinity and with tears in my eyes commended you both to the protection of Almighty God. In the afternoon we had target practice. The prize was offered by Cajetan Antretter and I won. *Herr Bullinger*, who sends his best wishes, was also somewhat taken aback by your letter and it struck me that, in the present serious situation, he didn't appreciate your joke about a public debt. At half past 5 I then went to see Herr Hagenauer to ask him *that if Messrs Nocker & Schiedl had not informed him by post that they had transferred some money to you, he might care to write to Augsb. by today's post*. I returned to the shop this morning and spoke to Herr Joseph. I discovered that although they'd received letters from *Nocker & Schiedl*, there'd been no word about you. He promised to write today. I've now done all I can and hope that in the meantime you'll have received some money, *Nocker* & Schiedl won't send me a report until they know how much you've been given. NB: It's always better when drawing money to accept not *florins* but the local currency, e.g., 6, 7 etc. *louis d'or*, *carolins* or whatever. I've now told you what was weighing on my mind, it is God's own truth. You'll have to learn for yourself that it is no joke to undertake a journey like this and to have to live on random income: above all you must pray most earnestly to God for good health, be on your guard against wicked people, earn money by every means that is known and available to you, and then spend it with the greatest care. I prefer to give too little to someone who is travelling with me and whom I may never see again and risk being called a skinflint, rather than have him laugh at me behind my back for giving him too much. I've no more paper, and I'm tired, especially my eyes.

Nannerl and I wish you the best of health and with all

My Dearest Father

our hearts kiss you a million times. I am your old husband and father but NB not your son

Mozart

I hope you'll have received my letter of the 20th in which I told you to write to *Monsieur Grimm* in Paris, also what you should write to the Prince of Chiemsee in Munich. By the next post I'll send you a list of all the stages to Paris and my opinion etc., also a list of all our former acquaintances in Paris. *Addio.*

Mozart to his father,
29 November 1777, Mannheim

Mon très cher Père,
I received your letter of the 24th this morning and see from it that you're unable to reconcile yourself to fate, be it good or bad, when it takes us by surprise; until now, and as things stand, the four of us have never been happy or unhappy, and for that I thank God. You reproach us both for many things, without our deserving it. We are not incurring any expenses that are not necessary; and what is necessary when travelling you know as well as we do, if not better. That we stayed so long in Munich was the fault of no one but *myself*; and if I'd been alone, I'd certainly have stayed in Munich. Why did we spend 2 weeks in Augsburg? – – I'm tempted to think that you didn't receive my letters from Augsburg. – – I wanted to give a concert – I was let down; meanwhile a whole week went by. I was absolutely determined to leave. They wouldn't let me. They wanted me to give a concert; I wanted them to beg me. And so they did. I gave a concert. There are your 2 weeks. Why did we go straight to Mannheim? – – I answered this question in my last letter. Why

My Dearest Father

are we still here? – – Yes – – can you really think that I'd remain somewhere for no reason? – – But I could have told my father – – all right, you shall know the reason and indeed the whole course of events. But God knows that I had no wish to speak about it because I was unable to go into detail – any more than I can today – and I know you well enough to appreciate that a *vague* account would have caused you worry and distress, something I've always tried to avoid; but if you ascribe the cause to my negligence, thoughtlessness and indolence, I can only thank you for your high opinion of me and sincerely regret that you don't know your own son.

I'm not thoughtless but am prepared for anything and as a result can wait patiently for whatever the future holds in store, and I'll be able to endure it—as long as my honour and the good name of Mozart don't suffer in consequence. Well, if it must be so, then let it be so. But I must ask you at the outset not to rejoice or grieve prematurely; for whatever happens, all is well as long as we remain healthy; for happiness consists – – simply in our imagination. Last Tuesday week, the 18th, the day before St Elisabeth's Day, I saw Count Savioli in the morning and asked him if there was any chance that the elector would keep me here this winter? – – I wanted to teach the young princes. He said yes, I'll suggest it to the elector; and if it's up to me, it will certainly happen. That afternoon I saw Cannabich and as it was at his suggestion that I'd been to see the count, he asked me at once if I'd been

Wolfgang Amadeus Mozart

there. – I told him all that had happened, he said to me I'd very much like you to spend the winter here with us, but I'd like it even more if you had a proper, permanent appointment. I said that there was nothing I'd like more than to be always near them but that I really didn't know how it would be possible for me to stay permanently. You've already got two Kapellmeisters, so I don't know what I could do, as I wouldn't like to be under *Vogler*! Nor shall you, he said. None of the members of the orchestra here is under the Kapellmeister or even under the intendant. The elector could make you his chamber composer. Wait, I'll speak to the count about it. There was a big concert on Thursday. When the count saw me, he apologized for not having said anything, but the galas were still going on; but as soon as the galas were over, namely, on Monday, he would certainly speak to the elector. I left it for 3 days, and as I'd heard nothing, I went to see him in order to make enquiries. He said: My dear Monsieur Mozart (this was Friday, namely, yesterday), there was a hunt today so I've been unable to *ask* the elector; but by this time tomorrow I shall certainly be able to give you an answer: I begged him not to forget. To tell the truth, I was rather angry when I left him and decided to take the young count my six easiest variations on Fischer's minuet – which I'd already had copied out here for this very purpose – in order to have an opportunity to speak to the elector in person. When I arrived, you can't imagine how pleased the governess was to see

My Dearest Father

me. I received a most courteous welcome. When I took out the variations and said that they were for the count, she said Oh, that's good of you; but have you also got something for the countess? – – Not yet, I said, but if I were to stay here long enough to write something, I'll – – By the way, she said, I'm glad that you'll be staying here all winter. Me? – – I didn't know that! – – That surprises me. It's curious. The elector himself told me so recently. By the way, he said, Mozart is staying here this winter. Well, if he did indeed say that, then he's the one person who *can* say it, for without the elector I certainly can't remain here. I told her the whole story. We agreed that I'd return the next day – namely, *today* – after 4 o'clock and bring something for the countess. You'll speak to the elector – before I arrive – and he'll still be with you when I get there. I went back there today, but he didn't come. But I'll go again tomorrow. I've written a rondeau for the countess. Don't I have reason enough to remain here and await the outcome? – – Should I leave now that the greatest step has been taken? – – I now have a chance to speak to the elector himself. I think I shall probably remain here all winter as the elector is fond of me, he thinks highly of me and knows what I can do. I hope to be able to give you some good news in my next letter. I beg you once again not to rejoice or worry too soon and to confide this story in no one except Herr Bullinger and my sister. I'm sending my sister the allegro and andante from the sonata for Mlle Cannabich. The rondeau will follow shortly. It would have been too much to send them all together. You'll have to make do with the original; you can have it copied more easily at 6 kreuzers a page than I can at 24 kreuzers. Don't you find that expensive? – – Adieu. I kiss your hands 100,000 times and embrace my sister with all my heart. I am your obedient son

Wolfgang Amadé Mozart

You'll probably already have heard a little of the sonata, as it's sung, banged out, fiddled and whistled at least 3 times a day at Cannabich's. – Only *sotto voce*, of course.

[*Maria Anna Mozart's postscript*]
My dear husband, I kiss you and Nannerl many 1000 times and ask you to give our best wishes to all our acquaintances, I'll write more next time, but it's turned midnight, *addio*, I remain your faithful wife

Maria Anna Mozart

Leopold Mozart to his wife and son, 4 December 1777, Salzburg

My Dear Wife and Dear Son,

I've no objection to your having to wait for what you told me about in your last letter, and there's nothing more that can be said about all that has happened on your journey and that has turned out differently from what I'd expected and worked out to our disadvantage and even caused us obvious harm, as it is all over and done with and can no longer be changed. – But the fact that you, my son, write *that all speculation is superfluous and of no avail as we cannot know what is to happen* – this is indeed ill considered and was undoubtedly written unthinkingly. No sensible person – I shall not say no Christian – will deny that *everything will and must happen according to God's will*. But does it follow from this that we should act blindly, live carefree lives, make no provisions for the future and simply wait for things to befall us of their own accord? – Does God himself and, indeed, do all rational people not demand that in all our actions we consider their consequences and outcome, at least as far as our human powers of reason enable us to, and that we make every effort to see as far ahead as we can? – – If this is necessary in all our actions, how much more so is it in the present circumstances, on a journey? Or have you not already suffered the consequences of this? – – Is it enough for you to have taken the step *with the elector in order to remain there throughout the winter*? – – Should you not – shouldn't you long ago have thought of a plan that can be implemented if things don't work out: and shouldn't you have told me about it long ago and learnt my views on it? – – And now you write – what? If we were after all to leave here we'll go straight to Weilburg to the Princess of Nassau-Weilburg – for whom you wrote the sonatas in Holland – etc. – There we'll stay as long as *the officers' table* is to our liking – what sort of a tale is that? Like everything else you wrote, this is the language of a *desperate man* who is trying to console both himself and me. – – But there's still a *hope* that you'll receive 6 louis d'or, and that will make everything all right. – But my question to you now is whether you're certain that the princess is there: she won't be there without good reason as her husband is based in The Hague on account of his military office. Shouldn't you have told me about this long ago? – Another question: wouldn't you do better to go to Mainz – and from there to Weilburg via Frankfurt? After all, if you go from Mannheim to Weilburg, you'll cross the Frankfurt road: and as you're not staying in Weilburg for ever, the Mainz road will take you back through Frankfurt. If you first go to Mainz and then to Weilburg, you'll have only a short distance from Weilburg to Koblenz, which will presumably take you via *Nassau*. Or do you intend to avoid Mainz, where we've so many good friends and where we earned *200 florins from 3 concerts*, even without playing for the elector, who was ill. Tell me, my dear son, are these useless speculations? – – Your dear good Mama told me she'd keep a careful note of your expenses. Good! I've never asked for a detailed account and never thought of demanding one: but when you arrived in Augsburg you should have written to say: We paid such and such at Albert's in Munich, and such and such was spent on travelling expenses, so that we still have *such and such* a sum. From Augsb. you wrote to say that after taking account of the concert receipts you were about 20 florins out of pocket. In your 2nd letter from Mannheim you should at least have said that the journey cost us such and such an amount and we're *now* left with – –, so that I could have made arrangements in good time – – was my arrangement to send you a letter of credit in Augsburg a useless speculation? – – Do you really think that Herr Herzog – *who's a good old friend of mine* – would have provided you with money in response to all your letters from Mannheim if you'd not already given him a letter of credit? – – Certainly not! The most that he would have done would have been to make enquiries with me first. – – Why did I have to discover that you needed money only when you were in trouble? *You wanted to wait to see what the elector gave you.* Isn't that so? Perhaps in order to spare me the worry – – but it would have caused me less worry if I'd been told everything honestly and in good time, as I know better than either of you how one must be prepared for all eventualities on such a journey in order not to be placed in some terrible predicament at the very moment when one least expects it. – At such times all your *friends* disappear! *One must be cheerful; one must enjoy oneself!* But one must also find time *to give serious thought to these matters*, and this must be your main concern when travelling and when not a single day should be allowed to pass to your disadvantage – – the days slip past – days which are in any case very short at present and which all cost money at an inn. Merciful heavens! You ask me not to speculate now that *I'm 450 florins in debt entirely thanks to you two*. – And you think that you may be able to put me in a good mood by telling me a hundred foolish jokes. I'm pleased that you're in good spirits: but instead of the good wishes set out in the form of the alphabet, I'd have felt happier if you'd told me the reasons for, and the circumstances of, your journey to *Weilburg* and what you planned to do afterwards and, most of all, if you'd listened to my opinion; and this could have been done before a post day, as you can't only just have hit on the idea, nor can you know independently that the princess is there, unless someone had already suggested the idea to you. In a word, it is no idle speculation when one has something in mind and formulates 2 or 3 plans and makes all the necessary arrangements in advance so that if one plan doesn't work out, one can easily turn to another. Anyone who acts otherwise is an unintelligent or thoughtless person who, especially *in today's world*, will always be left behind, no matter how clever he is, and who will even be unhappy as he will always be duped by flatterers, false friends and those who envy him. My son, to find *one man in a 1000* who is your true friend for reasons other than self-interest *is one of the greatest wonders of this world*. Examine all who call themselves your friends or who make a show of friendship and you'll find the reason why this is so. If they're not motivated by self-interest on their own account, then they'll be acting in the interests of some other friend whom they need; or they are your friends so that by singling you out they can annoy some third party. If nothing comes of *Mannheim*, you still have your plan to go to *Mainz, Frankfurt, Weilburg, Koblenz* etc.; one should always look for places as close to each other as possible so that, if you can, the journeys should be kept short and you can soon get to a place where you'll find a source of income. If this letter doesn't reach you in *Mannheim* and you're already in *Weilburg*, I can't help you. But if you're still in Mannheim and have to leave, then Mama will see from the map that your best plan is to go to *Mainz* first, otherwise you'll either have to forgo Mainz or retrace your steps a little. In Weilburg you need to bear in mind that you'll not find a *Catholic church* there as everyone is *Lutheran* or *Calvinist*. So I'd prefer you *not to spend too long* there.

And who told you that you'd have to go through the forest of Spessart to get from *Würzburg to Mannheim* as the *Spessart* is near *Aschaffenburg*, between *Fulda and Frankfurt*? – – This is no doubt some other trick that Herr Beecke has played on you. *Aschaffenburg* and *Würzburg* are 10 miles apart. – It may be that one drives past the forest on the right-hand side for some hours as one approaches Mannheim. But there's nothing near Würzburg, whether you've been there or not.

NB: I've another observation to make about any journey that you may choose to make from *Weilburg* to *Koblenz*, namely, that the road is across country and will be safer than the one from *Mainz* to *Koblenz*, which is too near the Rhine. I now want to know all your other plans, *I'd never have suspected that my own dear wife wouldn't have given me the occasional accurate account of your travelling expense, as I've twice asked about Albert's bill and should also have been told about the bill from the landlord of the Lamb* etc. etc. But I'm not allowed to know about all your expenses. *And so I must ask Mama to write me a confidential letter on this point – I don't want a wordy explanation but would just like to see from the landlord's bill how people have been treating you and where all the money has gone.* We must now give serious thought to the ways and means of getting you out of the present situation, of travelling as economically as possible and of making sensible arrangements, but at all events you must let me know at once what may be to our detriment or advantage. *On no account* must you *sell* the chaise.

My Dearest Father

May God keep both you and me well. Nannerl and I kiss you many 100,000,000 times. I am your own husband and father

Mzt

Count Czernin has asked me to give you his best wishes. There was a rumour not only that the archbishop will be sending Haydn to Italy but that he had already wanted to send him to Bozen with Triendl. But Herr Triendl excused himself. I beg you, my dear Wolfg., consider everything and don't always write about things when they're already over and done with. Otherwise we'll all be unhappy.

Leopold Mozart to his son,
5 February 1778, Salzburg

My Dear Son,

In all probability this will be the last letter that you can be certain of receiving from me in Mannheim, and so it is addressed to you alone. How hard it is for me to accept that you're moving even further away from me is something you may perhaps be able to imagine, but you cannot feel as acutely as I do the weight that lies on my mind. If you take the trouble to recall what I did with you two children during your tender youth, you'll not accuse me of timidity but, like everyone else, will concede that I am a man and have always had the courage to risk everything. But I did everything with the greatest caution and consideration that were humanly possible: – one can't prevent accidents, for God alone can foretell the future. Until now, of course, we've been neither happy nor unhappy, but, thanks be to God, we've trodden a middle course. We've tried everything to make you happy and, through you, to make ourselves happier and at least to place your destiny on a firmer footing; but fate was against us. As you know, our last step has left me in very deep waters,

My Dearest Father

and you also know that I'm now around 700 florins *in debt* and don't know how I shall *support myself, your mother and your sister* on my *monthly income*, for as long as I live I cannot *hope to receive another farthing* from *the prince*. So it must be clear as day to you that the future fate of your old parents and of your sister, who undoubtedly loves you with all her heart, lies solely in your hands. Ever since you were born and, indeed, before that – in other words, ever since I was married – there is no doubt that I've had a difficult time *providing a livelihood* for a wife and 7 children, 2 servants and Mama's mother, all on a fixed monthly income of only a little more than 20 florins, and to *pay for* accouchements, deaths and illnesses, expenses which, if you think them over, will convince you not only that I have never spent a farthing on the least pleasure for myself, but that, without God's special mercy, I'd never have managed to *keep out of debt* in spite of all my hopes and bitter efforts: yet this is *the first time I've been in debt*. I gave up every hour of my life to you 2 in the hope of ensuring not only that in due course you'd both be able to count on being able to provide for yourselves but that I too would be able to enjoy a peaceful old age and be accountable to God for my children's education, with no more cares but being able to live solely for my soul's salvation and calmly awaiting my end. But God has willed and ordained that I must once again take on the *undoubtedly wearisome task* of giving lessons and of doing so, moreover, in a town where these strenuous efforts are so badly paid that it is not possible every month *to earn enough to support oneself and one's family.* Yet one must be glad and talk oneself hoarse in order to *earn* at least *something.* Not only do I not distrust you, my dear Wolfgang, no, not in the very least, but I place all my trust and hope in your filial love: all depends on your good sense, which you certainly have – if only you will listen to it – and on fortunate circumstances. This latter cannot be coerced; but you will always consult your good sense – at least I hope so and beg of you to do so.

You're now entering a completely different world: and you mustn't think that it is simply prejudice that makes me see Paris as such a dangerous place, *au contraire* – from my own experience I've no reason at all to regard Paris as so very dangerous. But my situation then could not be more different from yours now. We stayed with an ambassador, and on the second occasion in a self-contained apartment; I was a man of mature years and you were children; I avoided all contact with others and in particular *preferred not to become over-familiar with people of our own profession*; remember that I did the same in Italy. I made the acquaintance and sought out the friendship only of people of a higher social class – and among these only mature people, not young lads, not even if they were of the foremost rank. I never invited anyone to visit me regularly in my rooms in order to be able to maintain my freedom, and I always considered it more sensible to visit others at my convenience. If I don't like a person or if I'm working or have business to attend to, I can then stay away. – Conversely, if people come to me and behave badly, I don't know how to get rid of them, and even a person who is otherwise not unwelcome may prevent me from getting on with some important work. You're a young man of 22; and so you don't have that earnestness of old age that could deter a young lad of whatever social class, be he an adventurer, joker or fraud and be he young or old, from seeking out your acquaintance and friendship and drawing you into his company and then gradually into his plans. One is drawn imperceptibly into this and cannot then escape. I shan't even mention women, for here one needs the greatest restraint and reason, as nature herself is our enemy, and the man who does not apply his whole reason and show the necessary restraint will later do so in vain in his attempt to escape from the labyrinth, *a misfortune that mostly ends only in death*. You yourself may perhaps already have learnt from your limited experience how blindly we may often be taken in by jests, flatteries and jokes that initially seem unimportant but at which reason, when she awakes later on, is ashamed; I don't want to reproach you. I know that you love me not just as your father but also as your staunchest and surest friend; and that you know and realize that our happiness and misfortune and, indeed, my very life – whether I live to a ripe old age or die suddenly – are in your hands as much as God's. If I know you, I can hope for nothing but contentment, and this alone must console me during your absence, when I am deprived of a father's delight in hearing, seeing and embracing you. Live like a good Catholic, live and fear God, pray most fervently to Him in reverence and trust, and lead so Christian a life that, even if I am never to see you again, the hour of my death may be free from care. With all my heart I give you a father's blessing and remain until death your faithful father and surest friend

Leopold Mozart

Here are our Paris acquaintances, all of whom will be delighted to see you. [. . .]

[*Leopold's postscript to his wife on the envelope*]
My Dear Wife,

As you'll receive this letter on the 11th or 12th and as I doubt whether a further letter will reach Wolfg. in Mannheim, I'll take my leave of him with this enclosure! I'm writing this with tears in my eyes. Nannerl kisses her dear brother Wolfg. a million times. She would have added a note to my letter and said goodbye, but the letter was already full and in any case I didn't let her read it. We ask Wolfg. *to take care of his health and to stick to the diet that he got used to at home*; otherwise he'll have *to be bled* as soon as he arrives in Paris, *everything spicy* is bad for him. I

My Dearest Father

expect he'll take with him the big *Latin prayer book* that contains *all the psalms* for the full office of Our Lady. If he wants to have the *German* text of the office of Our Lady in Mannheim in order to have it in German too, he'll have to try to obtain the very smallest format as the Latin psalms are difficult to understand. It would be better if he also had them in German. Learned contrapuntal settings of the psalms are also performed at the Concert Spirituel; it's possible to gain a great reputation in this way. Perhaps he could also have his *Misericordias* performed there. The opera singers aren't coming but have gone instead to Straubing to entertain the Austrian officers. The prince has again forced the magistrature to hold 9 balls, the first one was yesterday and was attended by 30 persons; it lasted till half past one, but not a soul had arrived by half past 9 and it wasn't till 10 that they started dancing; 1 capon and 6 mugs of wine were consumed. I hope you received the 2 sonatas for 4 hands, the Fischer variations and the rondo, which were all parcelled up in the same letter. – – The late Herr Adlgasser hasn't found a decent bellows blower in the afterlife; the cathedral's old bellows blower, the 80-year-old Thomas, has followed him into the next world. The main news is that Mme Barisani has become incredibly jealous of her old and respectable husband as he and Checco have on a handful of occasions been to perform at the home of handsome Herr Freysauff, who has a relatively pretty but witless wife. There was an incredible fuss. Farewell. We kiss you millions of times

Mzt

Everyone sends their best wishes, especially Herr Bullinger and the wife of the sergeant of the bodyguards, Herr *Clessin*, Waberl Mölk etc.

Mozart to his father, 3 July 1778, Paris

Monsieur
mon très cher Père!

I have some very disagreeable and sad news for you, which is also the reason why I have been unable until now to reply to your last letter of the 11th. –

My dear mother is very ill – she was bled, as usual, and very necessary it was, too; she felt very well afterwards – but a few days later she complained of shivering and feverishness – she had diarrhoea and a headache – at first we just used our home remedies, antispasmodic powder, we'd like to have used the black one too, but we didn't have any and couldn't get any here, it's not known here even under the name of *Pulvis epilepticus*. – But when things started to get worse – she could hardly speak and lost her hearing so we had to shout – Baron *Grimm* sent his doctor – she's very weak and is still feverish and delirious – I'm told to be hopeful, but I'm not – for long days and nights I've been hovering between fear and hope – but I've resigned myself to God's will – and I hope that you and my dear sister will do the same; what other means is there to remain calm? – or, rather, calmer, as we can't be entirely calm; – come what may, I feel comforted – because I know that God, who orders everything for the best, however contrary it may seem to us, wills it so; for I believe – and I won't be persuaded otherwise – that no doctor, no individual, no misfortune and no accident can give a man his life or take it away, God alone can do that – these are only the instruments that He generally uses, although not always – after all, we can see people fainting, collapsing and dying – once our time comes, all remedies are useless, they hasten death rather than prevent it – we saw this in the case of our late friend Herr Heffner! – I'm not saying by this that my mother will and must die and that all hope is lost – she may yet be hale and hearty again, but only if God so wills it – after praying to my God with all my strength for health and life for my dear mother, I like to think this and derive comfort from such thoughts, as I then feel heartened, calmer and consoled – and you'll easily imagine that I need this! – Now for something different; let's banish these sad thoughts. Let us hope, but not too much; let us put our trust in God and console ourselves with the thought that all is well if it accords with the will of the Almighty as He knows best what is most advantageous and beneficial to our temporal and eternal happiness and salvation –

I've had to write a symphony to open the Concert Spirituel. It was performed to general acclaim on Corpus

Christi; I also hear that there was a report on it in the *Courrier de l'Europe*. – Without exception, people liked it. I was very afraid at the rehearsal as I've never in all my life heard anything worse; you can't imagine how twice in succession they bungled and scraped their way through it. – I was really very afraid – I'd have liked to rehearse it again, but there are always so many things to rehearse and so there was no more time; and so I had to go to bed with a fearful heart and in a discontented and angry frame of mind. The next day I decided not to go to the concert at all; but in the evening the weather was fine and so I decided to go, determined that if it went as badly as it had done during the rehearsal, I'd go into the orchestra, take the fiddle from the hands of the first violin, Herr Lahoussaye, and conduct myself. I prayed to *God* that it would go well because everything is to His greater glory and honour; and behold, the symphony started, Raaff was standing next to me, and in the middle of the opening allegro there was a passage that I knew very well people were bound to like, the whole audience was carried away by it – and there was loud applause – but as I knew when I wrote it what effect it would produce, I introduced it again at the end – now people wanted to have it encored. They liked the andante, too, but especially the final allegro – I'd heard that all the final allegros and opening ones too begin here with all the instruments playing together and generally in unison, and so I began mine with 2 violins only, playing piano for 8 whole bars, followed at once by a forte – the audience, as I expected, went 'shush' at the piano – then came the forte – and as soon as they heard it, they started to clap – I was so happy that as soon as the symphony was over I went to the Palais Royal – had a large ice – said the rosary, as I'd promised – and went home – just as I'm always happiest at home and always will be – or with some good, true, honest German who, if he's single, lives on his own as a good Christian or, if married, loves his wife and brings up his children well –

You probably already know that that godless arch-rogue Voltaire has died like a dog, like a beast – that's his reward! – As you say, we owe Tresel her wages for 5 quarters – you'll have realized long ago that I don't like it here – there are many reasons for this, but as I'm here, it would serve no useful purpose to go into them. It's not my fault and never will be, I'll do my very best – well, God will make all things right! – I've something in mind for which I pray to God every day – if it's His divine will, it will happen, if not, then I'm also content – at least I'll have done my part – when all is sorted out and if things work out as I want, you too must do your part or the whole business will be incomplete – I trust in your kindness to do so – but for the present you mustn't waste time thinking about it, the only favour I wanted to beg of you now is not to ask me to reveal my thoughts until it's time to do so.

As for the opera, it's now like this. It's very difficult to find a good libretto. The old ones are the best but they're not suited to the modern style, and the new ones are all useless; poetry was the one thing of which the French could be proud but this is now getting worse by the day – and yet poetry is the one thing that must be good here as they don't understand music – there are now 2 aria-based operas that I could write, one *en deux actes*, the other *en trois*. The one *en deux* is *Alexandre et Roxane* – but the poet who's writing it is still out of town – the one *en trois* is a translation of *Demofoonte* by Metastasio, combined with choruses and dances and in general arranged for the French theatre. Of this I've not yet been able to see anything –

Let me know if you've got Schroeter's concertos in Salzburg. And Hüllmandel's sonatas. – I was thinking of buying them and sending them to you. Both sets of pieces are very fine – I never thought of going to Versailles – I asked Baron Grimm and some other good friends for their advice – they all thought like me.

It's not much money, you have to spend 6 months languishing in a place where you can't earn anything else and your talent lies buried. Anyone in the king's service is forgotten in Paris. And then, to be an organist! – I'd like a decent appointment, but only as a Kapellmeister, and well paid.

Farewell for now – take care of your health, put your trust in God – it's there that you must find consolation; my dear mother is in the hands of the Almighty – if He returns her to us, as I hope, we shall thank Him for this mercy, but if it is His will to take her to Him, our fears and cares and despair will be of no avail – let us rather resign ourselves steadfastly to His divine will, fully convinced that it will be for our own good, for He does nothing without good cause – farewell, dearest Papa, keep well for my sake; I kiss your hands 1000 times and embrace my sister with all my heart. I am your most obedient son

Wolfgang Amadè Mozart

Mozart to his father, 9 July 1778, Paris

Monsieur
mon très cher Père!

I hope that you are prepared to hear with fortitude a piece of news that could not be sadder or more painful – my last letter of the 3rd will have placed you in the position of knowing that the news, when it came, would not be good – that same day, the 3rd, at 10.21 in the evening, my mother passed away peacefully; – when I wrote to you, she was already enjoying the delights of heaven – by then it was all over – I wrote to you during the night – I hope that you and my dear sister will forgive me this slight but very necessary deception – concluding from my own grief and sadness what yours must be, I couldn't possibly bring myself to spring such a terrible piece of news on you – but I hope that you're both now ready to hear the worst and that, after giving way to natural and only too justified grief and tears, you will eventually resign yourselves to God's will and worship His inscrutable, unfathomable and all-wise providence – you'll easily be able to imagine what I have had to bear – what courage and fortitude I needed to endure it all calmly as things grew progressively worse – and yet God in His goodness granted me this mercy – I have suffered enough anguish and wept enough tears – but what use was it all? – and so I had to console myself; you, my dear father and sister, must do the same! – Weep, weep your fill – but ultimately you must take comfort, – remember that Almighty God willed it so – and what can we do against Him? – We should rather pray and thank Him that it all turned out for the best – for she died a very happy death; – in these sad circumstances, I consoled myself with three things, namely, my entire trust and submission in God's will – then the fact that I was present at so easy and beautiful a death, as I imagined how happy she had become in a single moment – how much happier she is now than we are – so much so that at that moment I wanted to take the same journey as she had just done – in turn this wish and desire gave rise to my third source of consolation, namely, that she is not lost to us for ever – we shall see her again – we shall be happier and more contented to be with her than we have been in this world; we do not know when our time may come – but this is no cause for anxiety – when God wills it, then I too shall will it – well, God's most hallowed will has been done – let us therefore say a devout prayer for her soul and proceed to other matters, there is a time for everything – I'm writing this at the home of Madame d'Épinay and Monsieur Grimm, where I'm now lodging, a pretty little room with a very pleasant view and, so far as my state allows, I'm

My Dearest Father

happy here – it will help me to regain my contentment to hear that my dear father and sister have accepted God's will with composure and fortitude and that they trust in Him with all their hearts in the firm conviction that He orders all things for the best – dearest father! Look after yourself! – Dearest sister – look after yourself – you've not yet enjoyed your brother's kind heart as he's not yet been able to demonstrate it – dearest father and sister – look after your health – remember that you have a son and a brother who is doing everything in his power to make you happy – knowing full well that one day you'll not refuse to grant him his desire and his happiness – which certainly does him honour – and that you'll do everything possible to make him happy – Oh, then we'll live together as peacefully, honourably and contentedly as is possible in this world – and finally, when God wills it, we shall meet again there – for this we are destined and created –

Your last letter of 29 June has arrived safely and I'm pleased to learn that you are both well, all praise and thanks be to God, I couldn't help laughing at your account of Haydn's drunkenness, – if I'd been there, I'd certainly have whispered in his ear: *Adlgasser*. But it's a disgrace that such an able man should be rendered incapable of performing his duties and have only himself to blame for it – in a post that's in God's honour – when the archbishop and the whole court are there – and the whole church is full of people – it's appalling – this is also one of the main reasons why I detest Salzburg – the coarse, ill-mannered and dissolute court musicians – no honest man of good breeding could live with them; – instead of taking an interest in them, he should be ashamed of them! – also – and this is probably the reason – the musicians aren't very popular with us and are simply not respected – if only the orchestra were organized as it is in Mannheim! – the discipline that obtains in that orchestra! – the authority that Cannabich wields – there everything is taken seriously; Cannabich, who's the best music director I've ever seen, is loved and feared by his subordinates. – He's also respected by the whole town, as are his troops – but they certainly behave very differently – they're well-mannered, dress well, don't frequent taverns and don't get drunk – but this can never be the case with you, unless, that is, the prince trusts you or me and gives us full authority, *at least as far as the orchestra is concerned* – otherwise it's no good; in *Salzburg* everyone – or rather no one – bothers about the orchestra – if I were to take it on, I'd have to have a completely free hand – the chief steward should have nothing to say to me on orchestral matters and, indeed, on anything bound up with the orchestra. A courtier can't stand in for a Kapellmeister, though a Kapellmeister could no doubt stand in for a courtier – by the way, the elector is now back in Mannheim – Madame Cannabich and her husband are in correspondence with me. I'm afraid that the orchestra will be much reduced in size, which would

My Dearest Father

be an eternal shame, but if this doesn't happen, I may still remain hopeful – you know that there's nothing I want more than a good position, good in character and good in terms of the money – it doesn't matter where it is – as long as it's in a Catholic area. – You acted in a masterly way, just like Ulysses, throughout the whole affair with Count Starhemberg – only continue as before and don't allow yourself to be taken in – and in particular you should be on your guard if conversation turns to that arrogant goose – I know her, and you can be assured that she has sugar and honey on her lips but pepper in her head and heart – it's entirely natural that the whole business is still open to discussion and that many points must be conceded before I could make up my mind and that even if everything were all right I'd still prefer to be anywhere else but Salzburg – but I don't need to worry, as it's unlikely that everything will be granted to me as I'm asking for so much –. But it's not impossible – I'd not hesitate for a moment if everything were properly organized – if only to have the pleasure of being with you – but if the Salzburgers want me, they must satisfy me and all my wishes – otherwise they'll certainly not get me. – So the abbot of Baumberg has died the usual abbot's death! – I didn't know that the abbot of the Holy Cross had died too – I'm very sorry – he was a good, honest, decent man; so you didn't think that Dean Zöschinger would be made abbot? – Upon my honour, I never imagined it otherwise; I really don't know who else it could have been! – Of course, he's a good abbot for the orchestra! – So the *young lady's* daily walk with her faithful lackey bore fruit after all! – They were certainly busy and haven't been idle – the devil makes work for idle hands: – so the amateur theatricals have finally started up? – But how long will they last? – I don't suppose Countess Lodron will be wanting any more concerts like the last one – Czernin is a young whippersnapper and Brunetti a foul-mouthed oaf.

My friend Raaff is leaving tomorrow; but he's going via Brussels to Aix-la-Chapelle and Spa – and from there to Mannheim; he'll let me know as soon as he gets there, for we intend to stay in touch – he sends you and my sister his good wishes, even though he doesn't know you. You say in your letter that you've heard no more about my composition pupil for a long time – that's true, but what shall I tell you about her? – She's not the sort of person who will ever become a composer – all my efforts are in vain – in the first place, she's thoroughly stupid and also thoroughly lazy – I told you about the opera in my last letter – as for Noverre's ballet, all I've ever said is that he may write a new one – he needed just half a ballet and so I wrote the music for it – in other words, 6 numbers are by others and consist entirely of dreadful old French airs, whereas I've written the symphony and contredanses, making 12 pieces in all – the ballet has already been given 4 times to great acclaim – but I'm now absolutely determined not to write anything else unless

My Dearest Father

I know in advance what I'm going to get for it – I did this just as a favour for Noverre. – Monsieur Wendling left on the last day of May – if I wanted to see Baron Bagge, I'd have to have very good eyes as he's not here but in London – is it possible that I've not already told you this? – You'll see that in future I'll answer all your letters accurately – it's said that Baron Bagge will be returning soon, which I should like very much – for many reasons – but especially because there's always an opportunity at his house to hold proper rehearsals – Kapellmeister Bach will also be here soon – I think he'll be writing an opera – the French are asses and will always remain so, they can do nothing themselves – they have to rely on foreigners. I spoke to Piccinni at the Concert Spirituel – he's very polite to me and I to him – whenever we happen to meet – otherwise I've not made any new acquaintances – either with him or with other composers – I know what I'm doing – and so do they – and that's enough: – I've already told you that my symphony was a great success at the Concert Spirituel. – If I'm asked to write an opera, it'll no doubt be a source of considerable annoyance, but I don't mind too much as I'm used to it – if only the confounded French language weren't such a dastardly enemy of music! – It's pitiful – German is divine in comparison. – And then there are the singers – – they simply don't deserve the name as they don't sing but scream and howl at the tops of their voices, a nasal, throaty sound – I'll have to write a French oratorio for the Concert Spirituel next Lent – the director Legros is amazingly taken with me; I should add that although I used to see him every day, I've not seen him since Easter, I was so annoyed that he'd not performed my sinfonia concertante; I often visited his house in order to see Monsieur Raaff and each time had to pass his rooms – on each occasion the servants and maids saw me and on each occasion I asked them to give him my best wishes. – I think it's a shame that he didn't perform it, people would have liked it – but he no longer has any opportunity to do so. Where could he find 4 such people for it? One day, when I was planning to visit Raaff, he wasn't at home but I was assured that he'd soon be back. And so I waited – Monsieur Legros came into the room – it's a miracle that I've finally had the pleasure of seeing you again – yes, I've got so much to do – are you staying for lunch? – I'm sorry, but I've a prior engagement. – Monsieur Mozart, we must spend more time together; – it'll be a pleasure. – Long silence – finally: by the way, won't you write a grand symphony for me for Corpus Christi? – Why not? – But can I rely on it? – Oh yes, as long as I can rely on its being performed – and that it doesn't suffer the same fate as the sinfonia concertante – then the dance began – he apologized as best he could – but there wasn't much he could say – in a word, the symphony was universally liked – and Legros is so pleased that he says it's his best symphony – only the andante hasn't had the good fortune to win his approval – he says it contains too many modulations and

My Dearest Father

that it's too long – but this is because the audience forgot to clap as loudly and make as much noise as they did for the first and final movements – but the andante won the greatest approval *from me* and from all the connoisseurs and music lovers and most other listeners – it's exactly the opposite of what Legros says – it's entirely natural – and short. – But in order to satisfy him – and, as he claims, several others – I've written another one – each is fitting in its own way – for each has a different character – but I like the last one even more – when I have a moment, I'll send you the symphony, together with the violin tutor, some keyboard pieces and Vogler's *Tonwissenschaft und Tonsezkunst* – and I shall then want to know what you think about them – the symphony will be performed for the second time – with the new andante – on 15 August – the Feast of the Assumption – the symphony is in re and the andante in sol – you're not supposed to say D or G here. – Well, Legros is now right behind me. – It's time to start thinking about ending this letter – if you write to me, I think it would be better if you were to do so *chez Monsieur Le Baron de Grimm, Chaussée d'Antin près le Boulevard* – Monsieur Grimm will be writing to you himself very shortly. He and Madame d'Épinay both ask to be remembered to you and send you their heartfelt condolences – but they hope that you will be able to remain composed in the face of a matter that can't be changed – take comfort – and pray fervently, this is the only expedient that is left to us – I was going to ask you to have Holy Masses said at Maria Plain and Loreto – I've also done so here. As for the letter of recommendation for Herr Beer, I don't think it'll be necessary to send it to me – I still haven't met him; I know only that he's a good clarinettist but a dissolute companion – I don't like associating with such people – it does one no credit; and I've no wish to give him a letter of recommendation – I'd be truly ashamed to do so – even if he could do something for me! – But he's by no means respected – many people haven't even heard of him – Of the 2 Stamitzes, only the younger one is here – the older (the real composer *à la* Hafeneder) is in London – they're 2 wretched scribblers – and gamblers – drunkards – and whoremongers – not the kind of people for me – the one who's here has scarcely a decent coat to his back – by the way, if things don't work out with Brunetti, I'd very much like to recommend a good friend of mine to the archbishop as first violin, a decent, honest, upstanding man – a stolid individual; – I'd put him at around 40 – a widower – he's called Rothfischer – he's concert master to the princess of Nassau-Weilburg at Kirchheimbolanden – between ourselves, he's dissatisfied as the prince doesn't like him – or rather he doesn't like *his music* – he's commended himself to me and it would give me real pleasure to help him – he's the best of men. – Adieu. I kiss your hands 100,000 times and embrace my sister with all my heart. I am your most obedient son

                                           Wolfgang Amadè Mozart

Leopold Mozart to his wife and son, 13 July 1778, Salzburg

My Dear Wife and Son,

In order not to miss your name day, my dear wife, I'm writing to you today, even though the letter will no doubt arrive a few days early. I wish you a million joys in being able to celebrate it once more and ask Almighty God to keep you well on this day and for many years to come and allow you to live as contented a life as is possible in this inconstant world theatre. I'm absolutely convinced that for you to be truly happy you need your husband and daughter. God in His unfathomable decree and most holy providence will do what is best for us. Would you have thought a year ago that you'd be spending your next name day in Paris? – – However incredible this would have seemed to many people then, although not to ourselves, it is possible that with God's help we may be reunited even before we expect it: for my one concern is that I am separated from you and *living so far away, so very far away from you*; otherwise we're well, God be praised! We both kiss you and Wolfgang a million times and beg you above all to take great care of your health. – *The theatre of war has finally opened!* In Paris you'll already know that on the 5th of this month the king of Prussia entered Bohemia from Glatz and that he's passed through Nachod and penetrated as far as Königgrätz. War was bound to break out as neither power could withdraw its armies without losing face. For several weeks Austria, with its marches and countermarches, has provided the king with occasional opportunities to make an incursion and launch an attack: but the king didn't think it advisable to undertake such an attack; now the emperor has established a very powerful *false arsenal* at Nachod, and this persuaded the king to attack. But the arsenal was a *feint* and contained only a semblance of the real thing. They had to take this risk, whatever the outcome, as Austria was neither able nor willing to be the aggressor, while the Croats were merely an advance guard (the only position in which they can really be used) and could barely be restrained any longer, as these people always hope to win booty, which is why they're so keen to go to war. The Saxon troops have formed an alliance with Prussia, and it's presumably true that they've joined forces with Prince Heinrich and will no doubt attack *Eger* and the *Upper* Palatinate. More news will no doubt arrive with the next post: this came with the Austrian post on the 11th. This war will be one of the bloodiest, the king wants to die a glorious death, and the emperor wants to start his army life on an equally glorious note.

I wrote the foregoing yesterday, the 12th. This morning, the

13th, shortly before 10 o'clock, I received your distressing letter of 3 July. You can well imagine how we are both feeling. We wept so much that we could scarcely read your letter. – And your sister! – Great God in your mercy! May your most hallowed will be done! My dear son! For all that I am resigned as far as possible to God's will, you'll none the less find it entirely human and natural that I'm almost unable to write for weeping. What am I to conclude from all this –? Only that even as I write these lines, she is presumably already dead – or that she has recovered, for you wrote on the 3rd and today is already the 13th. You say that after being bled she felt well, but that a few days later she complained of shivering and feverishness. The last letter from the two of you was dated 12 June, and in it she wrote – *I was bled yesterday*: so that was the 11th – and why was it done on a Saturday – a fast day? – – I expect she ate some meat. She waited too long to be bled. Knowing her very well, I remember that she likes to put things off, especially in a foreign place, where she'd first have to enquire after a surgeon. Well, so the matter stands – it can't be helped any longer – I have complete confidence in your filial love and know that you have taken all possible care of your mother, who is undoubtedly *good*, and that if God restores her to us, you will always continue to do so – your *good* mother, who always saw you as *the apple of her eye* and whose love for you was exceptional, who was exceedingly proud of you and who – I know this better than you – lived for you alone.

But if all our hopes are in vain! Could we really have lost her! – Good God! *You need friends, honest friends!* Otherwise you'll lose everything, what with the funeral expenses etc. My God! There are many expenses about which you know nothing and where strangers are cheated – taken for a ride – tricked – put to unnecessary expense and exploited if they don't have honest friends: you can have no conception of this. If this misfortune has befallen you, ask Baron Grimm if you can store your mother's effects at his house, so that you don't have to keep an eye on so many things: or lock everything up, because if you're often away for whole days at a time, people could break into your room and rob you. God grant that all my precautions are unnecessary: but you will recognize your father in this. My dear wife! My dear son! – as she fell ill a few days after being bled, she must have been ill since 16 or 17 June. But you waited too long – she thought she'd get better through bed rest – by dieting – by her own devices, I know how it is, one hopes for the best and puts things off: but, my dear Wolfgang, diarrhoea when one has a fever requires a doctor to know if the fever should be reduced or allowed to run its course as medicines designed to reduce the temperature cause an increase in diarrhoea: and if the diarrhoea is stopped at the wrong time, the *materia peccans* leads to gangrene. – God! We are in your hands.

Congratulations on the success of your symphony at the Concert Spirituel. I can imagine how anxious you

My Dearest Father

must have been. – Your determination to rush out into the orchestra if things hadn't gone well was presumably just a wild idea. God forbid! You must put this and all such notions out of your head; they're ill considered, such a step would cost you your life, which no man in his right senses risks for a symphony. – Such an affront – and a public affront to boot – would inevitably be avenged by the sword not just by a *Frenchman* but by all who value their honour. An Italian would say nothing but would lie in wait at a street corner and shoot you dead. – From Munich I've received reliable reports that Count Seeau has been confirmed as intendant of music for Munich and Mannheim; that a list of all the orchestral players has been sent to Mannheim; that the two orchestras will be combined and the worst players weeded out; Herr *Wotschitka* and the other *valets de chambre* have been pensioned off on a pension of 400 florins, *which surprises me*; Dr *Sänfftel* had the effrontery to demand 3000 florins for his treatment, whereupon he was stripped of his title and salary; finally, it is hoped in Munich that the elector and his wife, the electress, will be back in Munich with their entire court by 10 August. – I began this letter with my congratulations, – and Nannerl was planning to end it with her own. But, as you can imagine, she's incapable of writing a single word, now that she has to write – each letter that she's supposed to write down brings a flood of tears to her eyes. You, her dear brother, must take her place, if – as we hope and desire – you can still do so.

Wolfgang Amadeus Mozart

But no! You can no longer do so – she has passed away – you are trying too hard to console me, no one is as eager as that unless driven to it quite naturally by the loss of all human hope or by the event itself. I'm now going to have some lunch, though I don't suppose I'll have much of an appetite.

I'm writing this at half past 3 in the afternoon. I now know that my dear wife is in heaven. I'm writing this with tears in my eyes but in total submission to God's will! Yesterday was the annual celebration of the dedication of the Holy Trinity, so our usual target practice was postponed till today. I was unable to cancel it at such a late hour and didn't want to either, in spite of your sad letter. We ate little, but Nannerl, who had cried a lot before lunch, was violently sick and had a terrible headache, so she went to lie down on her bed. Herr Bullinger and the rest of them found us in this deeply distressing situation. Without saying a word, I gave him your letter to read, and he acted his part very well and asked me what I thought of it. I told him that I was firmly convinced that my dear wife was already dead: he said that he was indeed inclined to suspect as much himself; and he then comforted me and as a true friend told me all that I had *already* told *myself*. I made an effort to cheer up and to remain so, while submitting to God's most holy will, we finished our target practice and everyone left, feeling very saddened, Herr Bullinger remained with me and, without appearing to do so, asked me if I thought that there was

My Dearest Father

any hope in the condition that had been described to us. I replied that I thought that not only was she now dead but that she was already dead on the day you wrote your letter; that I had submitted to the will of God and had to remember *that I still had 2 children who I hoped would continue to love me inasmuch as I lived only for them*; that I was so firmly convinced that she was dead that I'd even written to you, reminding you to take care of her succession etc. To this he said, *yes, she's dead*. At that moment the scales fell from my eyes, scales that had been put in place by this sudden and unexpected turn of events, preventing me from seeing what had happened, for otherwise I'd have quickly suspected that you'd secretly written the truth to Herr Bullinger as soon as I'd read your letter. But your letter had really stunned me – at first I was too dumbfounded to be able to think properly. Even now I still don't know what to write! You don't need to worry about me; I shall play the man. But just think of your mother's tender love for you and you'll realize how much she cared for you – just as when you reach maturity you'll love me more and more after my death – if you love me – *as I do not doubt* – you should take care of your health, – *my life depends on yours*, as does the future support of your sister, who honestly loves you with all her heart. It is unbelievably difficult when death severs a good and happy marriage, but you have to experience that for yourself to know it. – *Write and tell me all the details*; perhaps she wasn't bled enough? – – The only thing that's certain is that she trusted too much in herself and called in the doctor too late; meanwhile the inflammation of her intestines gained the upper hand. *Take good care of your health!* Don't make us all unhappy! Nannerl doesn't yet know about Bullinger's letter, but I've already prepared her to believe that her dear mother is dead. – Write to me soon – tell me everything – when she was buried – and where. – – Good God! To think that I'll have to go to Paris in search of my dear wife's grave! – We kiss you both with all our heart. I must close as the post is leaving. Your honest and utterly distraught father

Mozart

Make sure that none of your things are lost.

1. BOCCACCIO · *Mrs Rosie and the Priest*
2. GERARD MANLEY HOPKINS · *As kingfishers catch fire*
3. *The Saga of Gunnlaug Serpent-tongue*
4. THOMAS DE QUINCEY · *On Murder Considered as One of the Fine Arts*
5. FRIEDRICH NIETZSCHE · *Aphorisms on Love and Hate*
6. JOHN RUSKIN · *Traffic*
7. PU SONGLING · *Wailing Ghosts*
8. JONATHAN SWIFT · *A Modest Proposal*
9. *Three Tang Dynasty Poets*
10. WALT WHITMAN · *On the Beach at Night Alone*
11. KENKŌ · *A Cup of Sake Beneath the Cherry Trees*
12. BALTASAR GRACIÁN · *How to Use Your Enemies*
13. JOHN KEATS · *The Eve of St Agnes*
14. THOMAS HARDY · *Woman much missed*
15. GUY DE MAUPASSANT · *Femme Fatale*
16. MARCO POLO · *Travels in the Land of Serpents and Pearls*
17. SUETONIUS · *Caligula*
18. APOLLONIUS OF RHODES · *Jason and Medea*
19. ROBERT LOUIS STEVENSON · *Olalla*
20. KARL MARX AND FRIEDRICH ENGELS · *The Communist Manifesto*
21. PETRONIUS · *Trimalchio's Feast*
22. JOHANN PETER HEBEL · *How a Ghastly Story Was Brought to Light by a Common or Garden Butcher's Dog*
23. HANS CHRISTIAN ANDERSEN · *The Tinder Box*
24. RUDYARD KIPLING · *The Gate of the Hundred Sorrows*
25. DANTE · *Circles of Hell*
26. HENRY MAYHEW · *Of Street Piemen*
27. HAFEZ · *The nightingales are drunk*
28. GEOFFREY CHAUCER · *The Wife of Bath*
29. MICHEL DE MONTAIGNE · *How We Weep and Laugh at the Same Thing*
30. THOMAS NASHE · *The Terrors of the Night*
31. EDGAR ALLAN POE · *The Tell-Tale Heart*
32. MARY KINGSLEY · *A Hippo Banquet*
33. JANE AUSTEN · *The Beautifull Cassandra*
34. ANTON CHEKHOV · *Gooseberries*
35. SAMUEL TAYLOR COLERIDGE · *Well, they are gone, and here must I remain*
36. JOHANN WOLFGANG VON GOETHE · *Sketchy, Doubtful, Incomplete Jottings*
37. CHARLES DICKENS · *The Great Winglebury Duel*
38. HERMAN MELVILLE · *The Maldive Shark*
39. ELIZABETH GASKELL · *The Old Nurse's Story*
40. NIKOLAY LESKOV · *The Steel Flea*

41. HONORÉ DE BALZAC · *The Atheist's Mass*
42. CHARLOTTE PERKINS GILMAN · *The Yellow Wall-Paper*
43. C.P. CAVAFY · *Remember, Body . . .*
44. FYODOR DOSTOEVSKY · *The Meek One*
45. GUSTAVE FLAUBERT · *A Simple Heart*
46. NIKOLAI GOGOL · *The Nose*
47. SAMUEL PEPYS · *The Great Fire of London*
48. EDITH WHARTON · *The Reckoning*
49. HENRY JAMES · *The Figure in the Carpet*
50. WILFRED OWEN · *Anthem For Doomed Youth*
51. WOLFGANG AMADEUS MOZART · *My Dearest Father*
52. PLATO · *Socrates' Defence*
53. CHRISTINA ROSSETTI · *Goblin Market*
54. *Sindbad the Sailor*
55. SOPHOCLES · *Antigone*
56. RYŪNOSUKE AKUTAGAWA · *The Life of a Stupid Man*
57. LEO TOLSTOY · *How Much Land Does A Man Need?*
58. GIORGIO VASARI · *Leonardo da Vinci*
59. OSCAR WILDE · *Lord Arthur Savile's Crime*
60. SHEN FU · *The Old Man of the Moon*
61. AESOP · *The Dolphins, the Whales and the Gudgeon*
62. MATSUO BASHŌ · *Lips too Chilled*
63. EMILY BRONTË · *The Night is Darkening Round Me*
64. JOSEPH CONRAD · *To-morrow*
65. RICHARD HAKLUYT · *The Voyage of Sir Francis Drake Around the Whole Globe*
66. KATE CHOPIN · *A Pair of Silk Stockings*
67. CHARLES DARWIN · *It was snowing butterflies*
68. BROTHERS GRIMM · *The Robber Bridegroom*
69. CATULLUS · *I Hate and I Love*
70. HOMER · *Circe and the Cyclops*
71. D. H. LAWRENCE · *Il Duro*
72. KATHERINE MANSFIELD · *Miss Brill*
73. OVID · *The Fall of Icarus*
74. SAPPHO · *Come Close*
75. IVAN TURGENEV · *Kasyan from the Beautiful Lands*
76. VIRGIL · *O Cruel Alexis*
77. H. G. WELLS · *A Slip under the Microscope*
78. HERODOTUS · *The Madness of Cambyses*
79. *Speaking of Siva*
80. *The Dhammapada*

'. . . I'll stop doing it as soon as I understand what I'm doing.'

PLATO

Born *c.* 424 BC, Athens, Greece
Died *c.* 347 BC, Athens, Greece

The account was written following Socrates' trial in 399 BC
and is taken from *The Last Days of Socrates*.

PLATO IN PENGUIN CLASSICS

Republic
The Last Days of Socrates
The Laws
Phaedrus
Protagoras and Meno
Timaeus and Critias
Theaetetus
Early Socratic Dialogues
The Symposium
Gorgias

PLATO

Socrates' Defence

Translated by
Christopher Rowe

PENGUIN BOOKS

PENGUIN CLASSICS

UK | USA | Canada | Ireland | Australia
India | New Zealand | South Africa

Penguin Books is part of the Penguin Random House group of companies whose addresses can be found at global.penguinrandomhouse.com.

This edition published in Penguin Classics 2015

014

Translation and editorial material copyright © Christopher Rowe, 2010

The moral right of the translator has been asserted

Set in 10/14.5 pt Baskerville 10 Pro
Typeset by Jouve (UK), Milton Keynes

Printed and bound in Great Britain by Clays Ltd, Elcograf S.p.A.

A CIP catalogue record for this book is available from the British Library

ISBN: 978-0-141-39764-1

www.greenpenguin.co.uk

Penguin Random House is committed to a sustainable future for our business, our readers and our planet. This book is made from Forest Stewardship Council® certified paper.

Socrates' Defence

SOCRATES

I don't know what effect my accusers have had on you, men of Athens, but I can tell you they almost made even me forget where I was, so convincingly did they speak. But when it comes to the truth, they've said virtually nothing. The most astounding of the many lies they told came when they claimed that you needed to take care not to be deceived by me, because of my artfulness as a speaker. Their lack of concern that their claim will immediately be proved false, as I display my total lack of artfulness as a speaker, seemed to me more shameful than anything else – unless, of course, 'artful speaker' is what these people call someone who tells the truth; because if that's what they have in mind, I'll admit to being an orator, and one in a different league from them. In any case, I repeat, they've said either little or nothing that's true, whereas you'll hear from me the whole truth. What you won't hear from me at all, I swear to you by Zeus, men of Athens, is language like theirs, full of fine words and phrases and arranged in due order. What you will hear will be in the words that come to me at the time, and as they come to me, since I'm confident that what I say is just. Let none of you expect any more. It wouldn't be fitting in any case for someone of my age, Athenians, to come before you and fiddle with words like an adolescent boy. But if there is one thing I ask of you, men of Athens, it's that if you hear me talking, in my defence, in the same language I habitually use in the marketplace around the bankers' stalls (where many of you have heard me) and elsewhere, you shouldn't be astonished or protest at it. This is the way it is: this is the first time, in my seventy years, that I've come before a law-court, and so the way people talk here is simply alien to me. So just as, if I were actually an alien, you'd obviously be sympathetic to me if I spoke in the same kind of Greek and the same style that I'd been brought up to speak, so I ask you here and now (and it's a just request, at least as I see it) to disregard the manner of my delivery – perhaps it won't stand comparison, perhaps it will – and to consider just this, and give your minds to this alone:

whether or not what I say is just. For that is what makes for excellence in a juryman, just as what makes an excellent orator is telling the truth.

Well, then, the right thing for me to do first, men of Athens, is to defend myself against the first false accusations made against me, and my first accusers, leaving till after that the accusations and accusers that have come along later. The fact is that it's nothing new for you Athenians to hear accusations against me; plenty of people have made them for plenty of years now, without saying anything that's true. Those accusers are the ones I fear more than Anytus and his lot, frightening though these latter ones are; more frightening, Athenians, are the ones who've been filling the ears of most of you since you were children and trying to convince you of something that's not the slightest bit truer than the rest: that there's a Socrates around who's an expert – one who dabbles in theories about the heavenly bodies, who's already searched out everything beneath the earth and who makes the weaker argument the stronger. It's the people spreading accusations like these, men of Athens, that are genuinely frightening. Why? Because their audience thinks that people who conduct research into these things don't even believe in the gods. There are also a large number of these accusers, and they've been making their accusations for a long time; what's more they were already talking to you at an age when you would have most readily believed them, being children, some of you, or adolescents, and they were prosecuting a case that went by default because there was no one there to defend it. But what is most unreasonable of all is that even their names aren't available to be listed, unless, that is, one or another of them happens to be a comic writer. The ones who have slandered me out of malice and convinced you of their slanders, and the ones who, having been convinced themselves, have gone on to convince others – all these accusers are the most difficult to deal with, because it isn't even possible to have them appear in court, or to cross-examine a single one of them; I must simply shadow-box my defence against them, as it were, and mount my cross-examination with no one there to answer me. So I ask you to accept that, as I say, my accusers are twofold: apart from the ones who have spoken out recently, there are these other, more long-standing accusers I'm talking of, and I ask you to join me in supposing that I must defend myself first against the latter sort – for you yourselves heard them making their accusations earlier, and you were exposed to them much more than to these later accusers.

So, then: defend myself I must, men of Athens, and attempt to remove from your minds, in this short time allotted to me, the slander that you have been exposed to for so long. Well, that's what I would like to achieve, if it's in any way the better outcome whether for you or for me. I would like to have some sort of success in my defence. But I think it's going to be hard, and I'm well aware what kind of task it is. Never mind; let it go as it pleases the god, and meanwhile the law must be obeyed and a defence made.

Let's start, then, from the beginning, by asking what the accusation is that lies at the root of all the slander on which I suppose Meletus must be relying in taking out the present indictment against me. Well, then: what did the slanderers actually say when they slandered me? I should read it out, as if it were the prosecutors' affidavit: 'Socrates is guilty of busying himself with research into what's beneath the earth and in the heavens and making the weaker argument the stronger and teaching the same things to others.' That's the sort of thing that's in my pretend affidavit: you saw it for

Plato

yourselves in Aristophanes' comedy – a 'Socrates' being whirled around above the stage, claiming he's 'walking on air' and uttering a whole lot of other nonsense about things of which, speaking for myself, I have no inkling whatsoever. Nor do I say this out of disrespect for such knowledge, if there's someone around with expertise in such matters (please let me not have to defend myself against another suit brought by Meletus!); the simple fact is, men of Athens, that I have nothing to do with these things. As witnesses, I offer you yourselves, or most of you: I ask those of you who've ever heard me in conversation (and there are plenty of you who have) to tell the others, if any one of you has ever yet heard me making the smallest mention of such things, and then you'll be in a position to see that the same also holds good for all the other things that people in general say about me.

In fact not only is none of these things true, but also, if you've heard from any source that I undertake to teach people and charge money for it – that's not true either, though I think it would be a fine thing if someone did turn out to be able to teach people, like Gorgias of Leontini, or Prodicus of Ceos, or Hippias of Elis. Each of these individuals, Athenians, is able to go into

Socrates' Defence

one city after another and persuade her young men, who have the option of spending time with whichever of their own fellow citizens they wish for no charge at all, to get together with *them* instead and not only pay good money for it but be grateful to them as well. Indeed I've learned there's another expert, a Parian, who's here in Athens at the moment. As it happened, I recently went up to someone who's paid out more money to sophists than everyone else put together, Callias son of Hipponicus, and I asked him – he has two sons – 'Callias, if your two sons had been born colts or calves, we could find someone to hire to take charge of them and make them fine and good, equipped with the appropriate excellence; and this person would be an expert in horse-training or farming. But as it is, since the two of them are human beings, whom do you have in mind to put in charge of them? Who is expert in this sort of excellence – the human, citizen sort? I imagine, seeing that you've acquired sons, that you've looked into the question. Is there anyone like this,' I said, 'or not?' 'Yes, absolutely,' he said. I asked 'Who is it? Where does he come from? And how much does he charge for his teaching?' 'It's Evenus, Socrates,' he said; 'he's from Paros, and he charges five minas.' My reaction was to call Evenus a fortunate man if he genuinely possessed this expertise, and teaches it at so low a price. I'd certainly be preening myself and putting on all sorts of airs if I had this knowledge. But the fact is that I don't, men of Athens.

One of you will probably then interject 'But Socrates, what is it about you? Where have these slanders against you come from? So much gossip and talk can't have come about because you were up to nothing more extraordinary than anyone else; you must be doing something different from what ordinary people do. So tell us what it is, so that we don't get things wrong about you in the way others do.' Now *this* seems to me a legitimate thing to say, and I will try to show you just what it is that has brought about the false reputation that I have. So hear me out. Probably some of you will think I'm not being serious; but I can assure you that what I'm going to say will be the whole truth. I have earned my reputation, men of Athens, for no reason other than that I possess a certain sort of wisdom. What sort of wisdom could this be? Probably a wisdom of a human sort. It's likely enough that I really am wise in this way; whereas those others I mentioned just now will be wise with a sort of wisdom

Socrates' Defence

that's beyond the human – or if that's not so, I don't know what to say, because *I* certainly don't have their wisdom, and anyone who says I do is lying and deliberately misrepresenting me.

Now please don't protest, men of Athens, even if I may seem to you to be boasting a bit. What I say won't be coming from me; it comes from a source you'll find impeccable. As to my ... well, as to whether it actually *is* wisdom, and what sort of wisdom it is, as witness I mean to offer you: the god at Delphi. How so? I imagine you know Chaerephon. He was not only a friend of mine from my youth, but a friend of the people, who shared your recent exile and returned from exile with you. You also know what kind of person Chaerephon was, and how single-minded he was about anything he undertook. This time he actually went to Delphi and had the face to ask the oracle (once again, Athenians, I ask you not to protest) – he actually asked whether anyone was wiser than I was, and the Pythia duly replied that there was no one wiser. Chaerephon's brother here will testify to all this, since the man himself is dead.

Consider why I'm telling you this: to explain to you the source of the slander against me. When I heard what the Pythia had said, I thought to myself 'What can the god be saying? It's a riddle: what can it mean? I've no knowledge of my being wise in any respect, great or small, so what is he saying when he claims that I'm the wisest? He certainly can't be *lying*; that's out of the question for him.' For a long time I was at a loss as to what the god was saying, but then, with great reluctance, I turned to inquiring into his response. I went about it like this: I approached one of those individuals people suppose to be wise, on the basis that here if anywhere I could challenge the oracle's response by pointing out someone it had missed – 'This person here is wiser than me, and you said I was wiser than him!' Well, I examined this person – I've no need to mention his name, but the person with whom I had the sort of experience I'm about to describe, when I examined him, was one of the political experts; and as I conversed with him, I formed the conclusion that, while this person seemed wise to lots of other people, and especially to himself, in reality he wasn't; upon which I made a concerted attempt to demonstrate to him that he only thought he was wise, but really wasn't. Well, that made him hate me, as it did a lot of those who were present; but

Socrates' Defence

I reasoned to myself, as I left him, like this – 'I am actually wiser than this person; likely enough neither of us knows anything of importance, but he *thinks* he knows something when he doesn't, whereas just as I don't know anything, so I don't think I do, either. So I appear to be wiser, at least than him, in just this one small respect: that when I don't know things, I don't think that I do either.' After that I went on to someone else, supposedly wiser than him, and reached exactly the same conclusion; at that point I became an object of hate both for him and for many others.

Well, after that I went on to another person, and another; distressed and fearful though I was as I perceived their hatred for me, I thought I must make my business with the god the first priority. So, as I searched for the meaning of the oracle, there was nothing for it but to approach everyone with a reputation for knowing something. And by the Dog, men of Athens, because I'm bound to tell you the truth, I swear to you that it turned out something like this: that those with the greatest reputations seemed to me, as I continued my divinely instigated search, practically the most deficient, while others who were supposedly inferior seemed better endowed when it came to good sense.

I should give you a picture of these wanderings of mine – these labours, as it were, that I undertook in order to leave the oracle's response unrefuted. After the political experts I went on to the poets – tragic, dithyrambic and the rest – on the basis that it was here I'd catch myself red-handed, as actually more ignorant than them. So, picking out those of their poetic compositions they seemed to me to have spent most effort on, I would ask them what they were trying to say, with a view to learning a thing or two from them as well. Well, Athenians, I blush to tell you the truth, but it has to be told: practically speaking, almost everyone present would have better things to say than they did about their own compositions. So I quickly came to the same conclusion about the poets as I had about the others, that it wasn't through wisdom that they did what they did, but rather through some sort of natural talent, or because they were inspired like the seers and the soothsayers, who make many fine utterances but have no knowledge about the things they're saying. That, I thought, was clearly the case with the poets too; and I noticed that they thought their poetry-making also made them the wisest of men about everything else too, which they weren't. So I left the poets thinking

Socrates' Defence

that I'd outdone them in the same respect that I'd outdone the political experts. Finally, I went on to the craftsmen. I knew that I myself had practically no knowledge, whereas I knew that I'd find them knowing lots of fine things. Nor was I mistaken about that. They did know things I didn't, and in that respect they were wiser than me. But, men of Athens, the good craftsmen too seemed to me to suffer from the same failing as the poets: because they were accomplished in practising their skill, each one of them claimed to be wisest about other things too, the most important ones at that – and this error of theirs seemed to me to obscure the wisdom they did possess. The outcome was that I asked myself, in defence of the oracle, whether I'd prefer to be as I am, and not be either in the least bit wise with their wisdom or ignorant with their ignorance, or to have both their wisdom and their ignorance together. And the answer I gave myself, and the oracle, was that I was better off as I was.

The result of my inquiry, then, men of Athens, has been that I have become an object of hatred for many people, and hatred of a particularly intractable and intolerable kind, which has brought about numerous slanders against me and given me that reputation of being *wise*; for on every occasion the onlookers suppose that if I refute someone else I must myself be an expert in whatever the discussion is about. But the truth most likely is, Athenians, that it's the god who's really wise, and that in this utterance of the oracle he's simply saying that human wisdom is worth very little, or nothing at all. And in mentioning this 'Socrates', he appears to be using my name just to treat me as an illustration – as if he were to say 'The wisest among you, humans, is the one who like Socrates has recognized that in truth he's worth nothing when it comes to wisdom.' That's why I, for my part, still go around even now on this search of mine, instigated by the god, so that if I think anyone, whether fellow citizen or foreigner, might be wise, I'll sniff him out; and whenever I conclude that he isn't wise, I come to the aid of the god by demonstrating that he isn't. It's because of this preoccupation of mine that I've not had the leisure to make any contribution worth speaking of either to the city's affairs or to my own; instead I find myself in extreme poverty, because of my service to the god.

In addition to all of this the young ones follow me around, since they have all the leisure in the world – that is, the wealthiest of them, and they do it of their own accord, because they love hearing those fellows being put to the test; often they copy me amongst themselves, and then they go on to try out their technique by examining others, and I imagine that as a result they find a great superfluity of people who think they know something but actually know little or nothing. So the next thing is that their victims get angry with me instead of with themselves, and talk about some quite abominable Socrates who corrupts the young; and when anyone asks them what they have against him, and what he teaches that has this effect, they have nothing to say and simply don't know; but so as to avoid seeming to be at a loss they produce the slogans that are ready to hand for use against all philosophers: 'things up in the heavens and below the earth', 'not believing in the gods', 'making the weaker argument the stronger'. They wouldn't want to admit the truth, which is that they're shown up by their questioners as pretending to know when they actually know nothing. So because of what I take to be their desire to get ahead, their vigour, and their sheer numbers, and because they talk so earnestly and convincingly about me, they've managed to fill your ears from way back with an equally vigorous slander. On the back of all of this, Meletus has now joined in the attack on me, along with Anytus and Lycon: Meletus out of irritation on behalf of the poets, Anytus on behalf of the craftsmen and the political experts, and Lycon on behalf of the orators. So, as I was saying at the beginning, I'd be astonished if I turned out to be able to remove all this slander from your minds in so short a time, when you have been exposed to it for so long. What I'm telling you, men of Athens, is the truth, and I address you without concealing anything, significant or not, and without dissimulation. But that's the reason, I'm pretty sure, that I'm so hated; and that in itself is proof that I'm right, and that the slanders against me and their causes are as I have described them. No matter whether you look into the matter now or later, that's what you'll find.

Let this, then, be a sufficient defence before you in relation to the charges made against me by my first accusers; next I shall try to defend myself against Meletus – good, patriotic Meletus, as he represents himself – and the other later accusers.

Let's do as we did before, then; let's read their affidavit, as if it belonged to a different set of accusers. It's something like this; it says that Socrates is guilty

Socrates' Defence

of corrupting the young and not believing in the gods the city believes in, but in other new divinities. So the charge is like that. Let's examine each aspect of this charge, one by one.

The man says I'm guilty of corrupting the young. But I say, men of Athens, that it's Meletus who's the guilty party, for treating serious matters as a joke – taking people to court as if it were a light matter, and pretending a serious concern for things that never meant anything to him up till now. I'll try to demonstrate to you that this is so.

[*There follows a period of cross-examination.*]

Here, Meletus, and tell me this: am I right in saying it's your first priority that the younger among us should be in the best possible condition?

'It is.'

So come on, tell these people: who is it that makes them better? Plainly you must know, since it means so much to you. At any rate you've found the person who's corrupting them, as you claim, namely me, and you're bringing him before these jurymen here and charging him; so who's the one to make them better? Come on, say who it is; reveal to them who it is. – Do you see, Meletus? You say nothing, because you've nothing *to* say. But doesn't that seem to you to be shameful, and already sufficient proof of exactly what I'm saying, that it's not a meaningful subject to you? Fine. So tell me, my good man, who makes our young ones better people?

'It's the laws.'

That wasn't what I was asking, my fine fellow; I was asking you what *person* makes them better – someone who knows these very things, the laws, above anything else.

'These people here, Socrates, the members of the jury.'

What are you saying, Meletus? These people are able to teach the young, make them better?

'Certainly.'

All of them? Or just some of them, and not others?

'All of them.'

A happy answer, by Hera; you're saying there's a great superfluity of people to help them. What about the spectators over there – do they make the young better as well, or not?

'They do too.'

What about the members of the Council?

'The Councillors too.'

Socrates' Defence

Surely, then, Meletus, those who sit in the Assembly, the Assemblymen – *they* don't corrupt the younger ones? All of these make them better too?

'They do too.'

In that case, Meletus, it seems that every single Athenian makes them into fine and upstanding people except for me; I alone corrupt them. Is that what you're saying?

'That's what I'm saying, most emphatically.'

What great misfortune you've condemned me to! Answer me this: does it seem to you to be like this with horses too? That it's all mankind that improves them, and just one person who corrupts them? Or is the situation quite the opposite of this, that there's one person or a very small number of people who can improve them, namely the horse-experts, whereas most people, if they even have anything to do with horses, or use them, actually make them worse? Isn't that how it is, Meletus, whether with horses or with any other sort of animal? Yes indeed it is, whether you and Anytus deny it or accept it; because if there's one person and only one who corrupts our young men, while everyone else benefits them, it would be a great piece of good fortune in their case. But the fact is,

Meletus, that your behaviour is sufficient demonstration of your total lack of concern for the young up till now; you clearly show your own negligence, and the fact that the things you're bringing me to court for aren't a meaningful subject for you at all.

And answer for me this further question, for heaven's sake, Meletus: is it better to live among fellow citizens who are good or those who are vicious? Sir, answer the question – it's not a difficult one. Don't vicious people do some sort of damage to those closest to them, in whatever context, whereas good people correspondingly do them some sort of good?

'Yes, absolutely.'

Well, is there anyone who prefers to be damaged rather than benefited by the people he has to deal with? Answer, my good man, since the law says you must. Is there anyone who wishes to be damaged?

'Certainly not.'

Come on, then: are you bringing me before the court for corrupting the young and making them more vicious intentionally or unintentionally?

'Intentionally.'

What's this, Meletus? Are you so much wiser than me, even though you're so young and I'm so old, that

Socrates' Defence

you've noticed that the bad always do some damage to those who are nearest to them and the good benefit them, whereas *I* have reached such a pitch of ignorance that I'm actually unaware of the fact that if I make anyone among the people I associate with into a depraved person, I shall very likely be the recipient of some damage from him? You're telling me I'm intentionally doing something *that* bad? You don't convince me that I am, and I don't think you'll convince anyone else in the world, either. Either I don't corrupt people, or, if I do, I corrupt them unintentionally, so that whichever way you take it your charge is false. And if I do corrupt people unintentionally, then the law is that for such offences a person shouldn't be brought to court; instead he should be taken off for private instruction and a private telling off, since evidently, if I'm acting unintentionally, I'll stop doing it as soon as I understand what I'm doing. But you shied away from getting together with me to give me my lesson; you refused that option and preferred to bring me to court, when the law says prosecution is for those needing punishment, not lecturing.

So there it is, men of Athens: what I was claiming, that Meletus has never yet concerned himself in the slightest degree with these things, is by now clear enough. But all the same tell us *how* you say I corrupt the younger among us, Meletus. Or is it, clearly, to go by the indictment as you've framed it, by teaching them not to believe in the gods the city believes in but to treat new and different things as 'divine'? Isn't that what you say I teach and so corrupt them?

'Yes, absolutely, that's what I say, emphatically.'

Well then, Meletus, by those very gods we're talking about, make things even clearer than you have so far, both to me and to the jurymen here. I'm unable to establish whether you're saying I teach the young to believe that there are gods of some sort (in which case I believe there are gods myself, so that I'm not a total atheist; I'm innocent on that score), just different ones, not the ones the city believes in – I'm unclear whether *that*'s what you're charging me with, believing in different gods, or whether your charge is unqualified on both counts: that I don't myself believe in gods at all, and that this is what I teach others.

'This is what I'm saying, that you're a total non-believer in the gods.'

Meletus, my dear man, why on earth are you saying

Socrates' Defence

that? Don't I suppose the sun, even, or the moon to be gods, then, like the rest of mankind?

'I swear to Zeus he doesn't, men of the jury, because he says the sun is a rock and the moon is made of earth.'

Do you suppose you're prosecuting Anaxagoras, my dear Meletus? Are you so contemptuous of these people here, and think them so illiterate as not to know that these assertions are bursting out of Anaxagoras' books? Are the young really supposed to be learning things from me that sometimes they'd be able to pick up from the orchestra for a drachma at the very most? Wouldn't they laugh at Socrates if he should ever pretend they were his and not Anaxagoras', especially when they're so strange? By Zeus, is that really how you think of me? You think I don't believe in any god at all?

'None at all, by Zeus; none whatsoever.'

You're not credible, Meletus, and in this instance I don't think you even believe yourself. Men of Athens, this person here seems to me totally insolent and unscrupulous; that's all that lies behind this indictment of his – a kind of youthful insolence and lack of scruple. He's like someone who's putting together a riddle, to see if I'll get the point: 'Will Socrates, who's so wise, see that I'm making a joke of contradicting myself, or will I bamboozle him and the rest of those listening?' For in fact he does appear to me to be contradicting himself in the indictment: it's as if he were saying, 'Socrates is guilty of not believing in gods, but believing in gods.' Someone who says that is merely playing about and not serious.

So let me explain to you, Athenians, why I take him to be saying this. You, Meletus, answer my questions; meanwhile I ask you, the jury, to remember the request I made to you at the beginning of my defence, not to protest if I express myself in my habitual style.

Is there anyone on earth, Meletus, who believes in the existence of human things, but not in the existence of humans? I demand that the man answer, Athenians, instead of making one protest after another. Is there anyone who doesn't believe in horses, but does believe in horsey things? Or doesn't believe pipers exist, but does believe in piperish things? There's no such person, Meletus, best of men; if you won't give the answer, I'll say it for you, and for these people here. At least answer the next question: is there anyone who believes in the existence of divine things, but not in the existence of divinities?

Socrates' Defence

'There's no one.'

How good of you to answer – even if you could barely get the words out, and because the jury here forced you to. Well then: you say that I both believe and teach that there are divine things, whether these are new ones or old ones – for the moment I don't mind; at any rate, on your account I do believe in divine things, and you've sworn to precisely that in your indictment of me. But if I believe in divine things, then surely there's no way I can avoid believing in divinities? Isn't that so? It is; since you don't reply, I'll put you down as agreeing with me. And divinities – don't we suppose these either actually to be gods, or at any rate children of gods? Do you agree or not?

'Yes, absolutely.'

Fine: so if in fact I believe in divinities, as you yourself claim I do, then if divinities are some sort of gods, that'll be the riddle I'm saying you're putting together, as your way of making a joke, that while I don't believe in gods, then again I do believe in gods, given that I believe in divinities; if on the other hand these divinities are only the children of gods, whether bastards of some sort, or born from nymphs, or whoever it is they're said to be from, who on earth would believe in children of gods and not in gods? It would be just as strange as if someone were to believe in the offspring of mares and donkeys, namely mules, but didn't believe there were mares or donkeys. When you composed your indictment like this, Meletus, it *must* have been to see if we'd get the joke – or else it was because you were at a loss as to what true crime you could charge me with. If you're seriously proposing to convince anyone with even a bit of intelligence *both* that someone who believes in divine things must also believe in things to do with gods *and* that this same person won't believe in divinities, or gods, or heroes – well, there's no way you can possibly convince anyone at all.

[*The cross-examination of Meletus ends.*]

So there you are, men of Athens. To show that I'm not guilty according to the terms of Meletus' indictment doesn't seem to me to require much from me; just the little I've offered is enough. But believe you me, there's no mistake about my earlier claim. I've earned myself a lot of hatred, and from a lot of people, and this is what will convict me, if that's how it turns out: not Meletus, and not Anytus either, but the malicious slander of people in general. That's taken down

Socrates' Defence

many others before me, good men too, and I imagine it'll take more; there's no danger it will end with me.

Well, probably someone will say to me, 'Then aren't you ashamed of yourself, Socrates, for going in for the kind of activity that puts you in the danger you're in now, of being put to death?' To this person I'll retort, and justly, 'You're wrong, my man, if you think a person who's of any use at all should take danger into account, weighing up his chances of living or dying, instead of making it the sole consideration, whenever he acts, whether his actions are just or unjust, and whether they're what a good man would do or a bad one. By your reasoning all those demi-gods who died at Troy would be poor creatures; not least the son of Thetis, who was so contemptuous of danger when he compared it with incurring disgrace that when his mother, a goddess, addressed him, eager as he was to kill Hector – with words that were I imagine something like this: "Son, if you take revenge for the killing of your friend Patroclus, and kill Hector, you'll prepare your own death; for straightway," the poet says, "after Hector's is your death prepared" – when he heard this, he looked down on death and danger and, having much greater fear of living a coward and not avenging those he loved, the poet has him saying, "Then straightway let me die, with the guilty punished; or here shall I lie, an object of mirth beside the beaked ships, a dead weight upon earth." Surely you don't think *he* cared about death and danger?'

That's how it is, men of Athens, in truth: wherever a person makes his stand, either because that's where he thinks it best for him to be or under orders from a superior, that, it seems to me, is where he must stay and face danger, taking nothing into account, even death, before avoiding what is shameful. I myself would have been behaving in a shocking fashion, men of Athens, if I stood firm, like everyone else, and risked death when the commanders you chose to command me gave me the order to do so, whether at Potidaea or Amphipolis or Delium, but then, when the god gave me my orders, as I thought and supposed he had, to live a life of philosophy, examining myself and others, at *that* point I conceived a fear either of death or of whatever else it might be and abandoned my post. It would indeed be a shocking thing to do, and would truly give someone just cause for taking me to court for not believing in the gods; after all, there I'd be, disobeying the oracle, fearing death and thinking I was wise

Socrates' Defence

when I wasn't. For I tell you, Athenians, the fear of death is simply this, thinking yourself wise when you are not; it's thinking you know what you don't know. Death may even be the greatest of all good things for a human being – no one knows, yet people fear it as if they knew for sure that it's the greatest of bad things. And how is this kind of ignorance not reprehensible – thinking one knows what one doesn't? As for me, Athenians, it's just in this one respect that I probably am superior to the majority of mankind; if there's any way in which I'd claim to be wiser than the next man, it would be because, not possessing enough knowledge about the things in Hades, I actually think I don't know; whereas I do know that to be guilty of disobeying someone better than me, whether god or man, is bad and shameful. So, faced as I am with bad things that I know to be bad, I'll never turn tail for fear of things that, for all I know, may even be good. So now imagine you're prepared to let me go, and refuse to listen to Anytus, who said that either I shouldn't have been brought to court in the first place or, since I have been brought here, it was not an option not to apply the death penalty – because, he said, if I get off, your sons will all set about doing what Socrates teaches and all be totally corrupted: imagine that you said to me, in response to this, 'Socrates, for the moment we're not going to listen to Anytus, and we're prepared to let you go, but on this one condition, that you stop spending your time in this search of yours, and you stop doing philosophy. But if you're caught doing this in the future, we'll put you to death.' Well, my point was that, if you let me go on these conditions, I'd say to you, 'I have the greatest respect and love for you, men of Athens, but I shall obey the god rather than you, and so long as I breathe and so long as I am able I shall never stop doing philosophy, exhorting you all the while and declaring myself to whichever of you I meet – saying the sort of things that it's my habit to say: "Best of men, I ask you this: when you're an Athenian, and so belong to the greatest city, the one with the highest reputation for wisdom and strength, aren't you ashamed of caring about acquiring the greatest possible amount of money, together with reputation and honours, while not caring about, even sparing a thought for, wisdom and truth, and making your soul as good as possible?" And every time one of you disputes the matter with me and claims that he *does* care, I won't let him get away with it and walk away. Instead I'll question and examine and

Socrates' Defence

challenge him, and if he doesn't seem to me to have acquired excellence, but claims that he has, I'll rebuke him for making things that are most valuable his lowest priority and giving higher priority to things of lesser worth. That's what I'll do for any one of you I meet, whether young or old, foreigner or citizen – though I put my fellow citizens first, insofar as you are more akin to me. This is what the god tells me to do, make no mistake about it, and I don't think you've ever yet benefited more from anything than you have from my service to the god. What I *do*, as I move around among you, is just this: I try to persuade you, whether younger or older, to give less priority, and devote less zeal, to the care of your bodies or of your money than to the care of your soul and trying to make it as good as it can be. What I say to you is: "It's not from money that excellence comes, but from excellence money and the other things, all of them, come to be good for human beings, whether in private or in public life." So if it's by saying *this* that I corrupt the young, it will be this that is damaging them; and if anyone claims that I say something other than this, they're talking nonsense. So, men of Athens,' I'd say to you, 'that's what you need to take into account when you make your decision either to do what Anytus says or not – either let me go or don't, knowing that I would behave no differently even if that meant I'd be put to death many times over.'

Don't protest, men of Athens, but keep to the terms of my request to you, to hear me out and not protest at anything I say, because I think you'll benefit if you do listen. In any case I'm now going to say more things that probably will have you shouting out at me; just don't do it. What you should know is that if I'm the sort of person I say I am, your killing me will do me less damage than it does you; for neither will Meletus damage me, nor Anytus – nor could he, since I think it's not permitted for a better man to be damaged by a worse one. He'll have me killed, no doubt, or sent into exile, or stripped of my citizenship, and probably – I imagine he isn't alone in this – he thinks of these as great evils; but that's not how I think of them. I think it a much worse thing to be doing what he's now doing, trying to have a man put to death without just cause. So as a matter of fact, men of Athens, far from defending myself, as one might suppose, what I'm doing now is actually defending *you*, so that you don't make a mistake with the god's gift to you by casting your votes against me. Because if you do put me to death, you

Socrates' Defence

won't easily find anyone else quite like me, attached by the god to the city, if it's not too comic an image, as if to a horse – a big and noble horse, but one that's rather sleepy because of its size, all the time needing to be woken up by some sort of gadfly: this is the kind of role the god gave me when he attached me to the city, and the result is that there's never a moment when I'm not waking you up and cajoling and rebuking you, each one of you, the whole day long, settling on you wherever you may be. Another one like me, Athenians, as I say, it won't be easy for you to find, and if you take my advice you'll spare me; but probably you'll be irritated at me, and like people who are woken up as they're nodding off you'll hit out at me, taking Anytus' advice instead of mine, and take the easy course of putting me to death, after which you'll spend the rest of your lives asleep, unless in his care for you the god should send someone else to stop you. That I really am the sort of person to have been given by the god to the city you might infer from something about me that doesn't look quite human: that I've totally neglected my own affairs, and put up with the neglect of what belongs to me for so many years now, while always acting in your interest, approaching each of you privately as if I were a father or elder brother and trying to persuade you to care for excellence. That would be a reasonable way for me to behave, if I made something out of it, and got paid for my exhortations, but as it is you can see for yourselves that, while my accusers show no sense of shame in anything else they say about me, in this one respect they weren't able to brazen it out and provide a single witness to say that I ever either received or asked for payment. I offer my poverty as witness that I'm telling the truth; that should be enough.

Now it will probably seem strange that I go about as I do, busying myself with giving advice in private but not venturing to advise the city in public, when you're gathered together in the Assembly. The cause of this is something that you yourselves have often heard me talking about, all over the place, that some god or 'divinity' intervenes with me – something Meletus caricatured in his indictment. It's something that started in my boyhood, a sort of voice that comes to me and, when it comes, always discourages me from doing what I'm about to do, never encourages me. It's this that opposes my playing the statesman, and it's a fine thing that it does, it seems to me, for

Socrates' Defence

you can be quite sure, men of Athens, that if I'd set about a political career all those years ago, I'd long ago have come to a sticky end and would have been of no use either to you or to myself. Don't be annoyed with me for telling the truth: there isn't anyone in the world who'll survive if he genuinely opposes you or any other popular majority and tries to prevent widespread injustice and lawlessness from occurring in the city. Anyone who's really fighting for justice must live as a private citizen and not as a public figure if he's going to survive even a short time.

What I'll offer you as evidence for all this is not just words but the hard facts that you set such store by. You've heard the details of my history, which show you that fear of death will not make me give in to anything or anyone if it means going against what's just; I'll even die not giving in. What I'm going to mention to you is vulgar, the sort of thing that's typically talked about in court cases, but all the same it's true. I've never in my life held any office in the city, men of Athens, except that I did serve as a member of the Council; and it happened that my tribe, Antiochis, held the presidency when you approved the proposal to put the ten generals who failed to pick up the dead from the sea-battle on trial together – contrary to the law, as all of you decided later on. At the time, I alone among those presiding opposed your doing anything contrary to the laws and voted against; and when the orators were ready to move against me and have me taken away, with your loud support, I thought I should rather take my chances on the side of law and justice than be on your side, out of a fear of imprisonment or death, when you were approving things that were not just. This was during the time when the city was still ruled by the democracy; when the oligarchy was instituted, the Thirty had their go at me, sending for me and four others to come to the Roundhouse, and ordering us to bring Leon of Salamis from Salamis for execution; lots of other people found this sort of thing happening to them all the time, as the oligarchs gave out orders so as to spread responsibility for what was going on as widely as possible. Then it was that I showed not by mere talk but by my actions that the amount I care about dying – if it's not too boorish to say so – is zero, and that all my care is devoted to doing nothing unjust, or impious. The fact is that that regime, for all its power, did not terrify me into doing something that was unjust. Instead, when we left the

Socrates' Defence

Roundhouse, the other four went off to Salamis and brought Leon in, but I went off home. I would probably have been executed for this if the regime hadn't been brought to an end shortly afterwards. You'll find plenty of witnesses for all of this.

So do you think I would have survived for so many years if I had taken a public role and performed it – as any good man should – as the ally of everything just, and making this, as it must be, the highest priority? Not by a long way, men of Athens; and no one else in the world would survive for long like that, either. But if I have ever performed any action in any public context, you'll find me exactly as I've described, and in private the same: someone who has never yet agreed to anything contrary to justice with anyone at all, and certainly not with any of those they slanderously call my pupils. I have never, ever, been anybody's teacher; if anyone, young or old, wants to listen to me as I talk and do what I do, I've never begrudged it to anyone, nor do I talk to people if I get money for it but otherwise not. Instead, I offer myself to rich and poor alike, for them to ask their questions and, if anyone wishes, to listen to whatever I have to say and answer *my* questions. Whether any one of these people turns out well or not, it wouldn't be fair for me to be held responsible for things that I never to this day promised anyone he'd learn from me, and have never taught, and if anyone says he ever learned or heard from me something in private of a sort that all the rest didn't hear as well, then you can be certain that he's not telling the truth.

Why is it, then, that some people enjoy spending large amounts of time with me? You have heard my explanation, men of Athens – and it's no less than the truth of the matter: that they enjoy witnessing the examination of people who think they're wise when they're not; and it has its delights. But what I do, as I say, I do because the god has assigned it to me, whether he communicates through oracular responses, or dreams, or any other means gods use to assign whatever task it may be to human beings.

And what I say, men of Athens, is both true and easily checked. Just think. If I'm currently corrupting some of the young, and I have corrupted others, then surely – let's suppose that some of them are now old enough to realize that I advised them badly in their youth: surely now is the time they should be stepping up and pressing charges by way of getting their own

Socrates' Defence

back? Or, if they were reluctant to do it themselves, shouldn't some of their relatives be stepping in, whether fathers, brothers, or whichever? If their kinsmen were the victims of some malfeasance on my part, shouldn't they now be mindful of it and pay me back? There are more than enough of them here: I can see them with my own eyes – first of all there's Crito, my coeval and fellow demesman, who's the father of Critobulus here; next there's Lysanias of Sphettus, father of Aeschines, and also Antiphon of Cephissus, Epigenes' father, both there with their sons; and then there are others whose brothers have spent their time with me, Nicostratus son of Theozotides, brother of Theodotus – admittedly, Theodotus is dead, so he couldn't have asked Nicostratus to act for him; Paralius too, son of Demodocus, whose brother was Theages; and there's Adimantus, son of Ariston, whose brother is Plato there, and Aiantodorus, whose brother is Apollodorus – also here. I can identify lots of others as well, one of whom Meletus should surely have offered you as a witness, preferably during his own speech; or if he forgot to do it then, let him do it now (I'll make him that concession), and let him say whether he has something like that up his sleeve. In fact you'll find it's quite the opposite. You'll find them all ready to help me, the corrupter, the one that's doing damage, or so Meletus and Anytus claim, to members of their family. It might perhaps be reasonable for those who've been corrupted to come to my aid themselves; but those who weren't corrupted, and are more grown up now, the relatives of those others – what reason do they have for coming to my aid except the one that's correct and just, that they know Meletus is lying and I'm telling the truth?

So there you are, Athenians; that's pretty much all I have to say in my defence, apart from some other things probably of the same sort. Perhaps one of you will take offence when he remembers how *he* behaved, if even when fighting a case less serious than the one I'm fighting he resorted to begging and supplicating the jury, in floods of tears, bringing his little children into court so that everyone should feel as sorry as anything for him, other relatives too, and lots of friends; and here I am, apparently proposing to do none of these things even when faced – so people will suppose – with the last and worst of all dangers. Perhaps these thoughts will cause one or another of you to harden his view of me; he'll get angry with me on these very grounds, and cast his vote accordingly. If any one of you is in this position – I don't think he should be, but in any case, if he is – I think it would be a decent response to him to say, 'Actually, best of men, even I have *relatives*, I imagine; this is that saying of Homer's – I'm not born "from oak or from rock", but from human beings, so that I do have relatives, and, yes, sons too, men of Athens, three of them, one by now a lad but the other two still small; all the same I will not bring any one of them into court and beg you to acquit me.' So *why* won't I do any of these things? Not out of wilfulness, men of Athens, nor out of disrespect for you; whether I face death with confidence or not is a different issue, but so far as appearances are concerned, doing any of the things in question would seem to me not to reflect well on me, or you, or the city as a whole, given my age and the name that I have – whether it's true or it's false, it's the established view that 'Socrates' is in some respect superior to the common run of mankind. Well, if those among you who are thought to excel in wisdom, or courage, or any other kind of excellence are going to behave like that, it'd be shameful; I've seen people doing it, when they're on trial – people who are thought to be of some worth, but then go on to do surprising things because they think something awful will be happening to them if they die, as if they'll be immortal providing *you* don't kill them off. People like that seem to me to hang a badge of shame on the city, so that a visitor might even suppose that those outstandingly excellent Athenians whom their fellow citizens choose over themselves for public offices and other kinds of honour are no better than women. Behaviour like that, men of Athens, is not only something you shouldn't indulge in yourselves, if you've any worth whatever in people's eyes, but if I indulge in it, you shouldn't let me; you should give a clear indication that you'll much sooner vote against someone who makes the city a laughing-stock by bringing on these pitiful exhibitions than against the man who keeps his peace.

But quite apart from the question of appearances, Athenians, it also doesn't seem to me just to *beg* a member of the jury, or to get off by begging. The just thing is to inform and convince. A juryman doesn't sit for the purpose of giving out justice as a favour, but to decide where justice lies; and he's sworn an oath that he won't dispense favours as he sees fit, but will make his decision according to the laws. Neither, then, should I try to get you into the habit of breaking your oath, nor should you acquire the habit, because then neither I nor you would be behaving piously. So, men of Athens, please don't expect me to behave towards you in ways that I don't think either honourable, or just, or pious, particularly and especially – Zeus! – when it's on a charge of impiety that I'm in the process of defending myself against Meletus here. Plainly, if I were to persuade you by begging, browbeating you when you're under oath, I'd turn out to be teaching *you* that the gods don't exist, and I'd literally be making it part of my defence to accuse myself of not believing in them. But that's not the case at all; I do believe in the gods, men of Athens, as none of my accusers does, and I leave it in your hands and in the god's to reach whatever decision about me is going to be best both for me and for you.

[*Socrates speaks again after the voting.*]

There are many reasons, men of Athens, why I'm not upset about what has occurred, and at your having voted against me, but the main reason is that it was not unexpected. In fact I'm much more surprised at the numbers of votes on the two sides. I didn't think the margin would be so small; I thought it would be a big one. As it is, it seems that if a mere thirty votes had gone the other way, I would have been acquitted. So far as Meletus' contribution is concerned, I think I actually do stand acquitted, even now, and not only that, it's obvious to anyone that if Anytus hadn't come forward to accuse me, and Lycon, Meletus would have been fined a thousand drachmas for not getting the required fifth of the votes.

In any case, the man proposes the penalty of death. Fine: what alternative penalty shall I put to you, men of Athens? Or is it clear – the one I deserve? What, then? What do I deserve to have done to me, or what fine do I deserve to pay, for the crime of not spending my life keeping to myself? What I have done is to turn my back on the things most people care about – money-making, managing a household, generalships, popular speech-making and all the other aspects of communal life in the city, whether public offices or private clubs and factions – because I concluded that I was truly too fair-minded a person to go in for this sort of thing and stay alive. So I didn't take that turning, because I knew that that way I would be no use at all either to you or to myself. Instead I headed along

Socrates' Defence

a different route, one that would lead, as I claim, to my doing you, privately, the greatest of good turns, as I try to persuade each one of you both to stop caring for your possessions before caring for yourself and making yourself as good and wise as possible, and to stop caring for the city's possessions before caring for the city itself – and to apply the same rule in the same way in caring for everything else. What, then, do I deserve to have happen to me, if that's the kind of person I am? Something good, I submit, men of Athens, if I'm to set my penalty in accordance with what I truly deserve, and not only that, the sort of good thing that would fit my case. So what does fit the case of a poor man who's your benefactor and needs free time to exhort you all? There's nothing that fits better, men of Athens, than to have such a person fed at public expense in the Prytaneum; much better him than one of you who's won a horse-race at Olympia, or won with a pair or a team of four, because someone like that makes you seem happy, whereas because of me you *are* happy, and what's more he doesn't need feeding and I do. So if I'm to make a just assessment of the penalty I deserve, this is it – free food in the Prytaneum.

Probably when I say this too I'll seem to you to be

Plato

talking in the same wilful sort of way as when I talked about the practice of making pitiful appeals. But it isn't like that, men of Athens; rather it's like this – I'm convinced that I wrong no one in the world, intentionally, but I don't convince you of it, because the time we've had for conversation between us is too short. In fact, in my opinion, if the law were the same here as everywhere else, and you had to spend not just one but several days judging capital cases, you would have been convinced; as it is, the slanders against me are too great to be undone in so short a time. In any case, given my conviction that I do no wrong to anyone, I'm hardly likely to go on to wrong myself by saying on my own account I deserve something bad and myself proposing that kind of penalty. Why would I do that? Out of fear? Fear of having done to me what Meletus proposes, when I say I don't know whether it's a good thing or a bad thing? Instead, then, am I to choose one of the things I know very well to be bad, proposing that as my penalty? Imprisonment, perhaps? Why, I ask you, should I live in prison, as the slave of whichever collection of people happened to make up the Eleven, year after year? A fine, then, and imprisonment until I pay it? It's the same answer I

Socrates' Defence

gave just now – I don't have any money to pay with. So what about my proposing exile – since probably you'd accept that? I'd have to be possessed with a great passion for life, men of Athens, to make me so poor at adding up that I couldn't do a simple calculation: when it was even beyond you, my fellow citizens, to put up with my discourses and arguments, how likely would it be that others would easily manage it? They were just too much for you, too hateful, so now you're setting out to be permanently rid of them; why should *others* put up with them? Of course I can work it out, men of Athens. A fine life it would be if I did leave Athens, a person of my age, moving on to one city after another and living the life of a fugitive. Because that's what it would be; I'm sure that wherever I go the young will listen to me talk as they do here. If I drive them away, they'll be the ones who'll persuade their elders to drive me out; and if I don't, their fathers and other relatives will drive me out on their account anyway.

Someone will probably say, 'But, Socrates, can't you live in exile without talking, just keeping your peace? Surely you can do that?' To convince some of you about this is the most difficult thing of all. If I say 'That would be to disobey the god; how *can* I keep my peace, then?', you'll not believe me because you'll think I'm dissembling; if on the other hand I say that it actually is the greatest good for a human being to get into discussion, every day, about goodness and the other subjects you hear me talking and examining myself and others about, and that for a human being a life without examination is actually not worth living – if I say that, you'll be even less convinced. But that's how I say it is, Athenians; it's just not easy to convince you.

At the same time, I'm not used to thinking I deserve anything bad at all. In fact if I'd had any money available, I'd propose a fine of whatever amount I'd be in a position to pay, since it wouldn't have done me any damage to pay it. But actually I don't have money – unless of course you're willing to set the penalty at what I *could* pay. I imagine I'd probably be able to find a mina of silver for you. So that's what I propose.

[*A message is passed from the audience.*]

One moment – Plato here, men of Athens, along with Crito and Critobulus and Apollodorus – they're telling me to propose thirty minae, with them as guarantors; so that's the amount I propose, and as

Socrates' Defence

guarantors of the money these people will be creditworthy enough.

[*The sentence of death is approved; Socrates addresses the court for the final time.*]

You'll not have bought a lot of time at this price, men of Athens: getting the name – from anyone who wants to abuse the city – for being the ones who killed off 'Socrates, a wise man'. (People who want to find fault with Athens will of course say that I'm wise even if I'm not.) At any rate if you'd waited a little time, you'd have had the same outcome without doing anything. You can see my age for yourselves, how far on I am in life, how near to death. I say this not to all of you, just to those of you who've voted to put me to death. And I've got something else to say to these people. You probably imagine, Athenians, that I stand condemned because I lacked the sorts of arguments with which I could have persuaded you, given always that I supposed I should do and say everything to escape the penalty. Far from it. If I've been condemned for the lack of something, it's not a lack of arguments but a lack of effrontery and shamelessness and the willingness to address you in the sorts of ways that it'd please you most to hear – wailing and lamenting and doing and saying plenty of other things unworthy of me, as I claim, even if they're the sorts of things you're used to hearing from everyone else. I didn't think then that I should do anything unworthy of a free man, despite the danger I face, nor do I now regret having made my defence as I did. I'd far rather make that defence and die than demean myself and live. No one, whether it's in court or in war, whether it's myself or anyone else, should try to escape death by any means he can devise. In battles the opportunity is often there to avoid death by throwing away one's arms or turning to supplicate one's pursuers, and there are other devices for avoiding death in every sort of danger, if only one has the face to do and say anything no matter what. But I hazard, Athenians, that the difficult thing is not to avoid death; more difficult is avoiding viciousness, because viciousness is a faster runner than death. So now, because I'm so slow and old, I've been caught by the slower runner, but because they're so quick and clever my accusers have been caught by the quicker one; and if I'm going to leave the court condemned by you to death, *they* will leave it convicted by truth

Socrates' Defence

of depravity and injustice. They accept their penalty as I do mine. I suppose it's probably how it had to be, and I think it's a fair result.

The next thing I want to do is to make a prophecy to you, the ones who voted against me; I'm now at that moment when human beings are most prone to turn prophet, when they're about to die. I tell you, you Athenians who have become my killers, that just as soon as I'm dead you'll meet with a punishment that – Zeus knows – will be much harsher than the one you've meted out to me by putting me to death. You've acted as you have now because you think it'll let you off being challenged for an account of your life; in fact, I tell you, you'll find the case quite the opposite. There'll be more, not fewer, people challenging you – people that I was holding back, without your noticing it, and they'll be all the harsher because they're younger, and you'll be crosser than you are now. If you think killing people will stop anyone reproaching you for not living correctly, you're not thinking straight. Being let off like that is not only quite impossible, it's the opposite of fine; the finest and easiest kind of letting off is when, instead of trying to cut other people down to size, each of you takes the measures needed to make yourself as good as you can be. So that's the prophecy I leave behind for those who voted to condemn me.

As for those of you who voted for me, I'll be happy to talk to you about this thing that's happened to me, just while the court authorities are busy and before I go off to the place where I'm to go and die. [*Some of the jury are making to leave.*] Do stay, Athenians, just for those few moments, because there's nothing to stop us having a good talk to each other while we can. You're my friends, and I do want to show you what this thing that's now happened to me actually signifies. Men of the jury (because 'jurymen' is the correct name to give you), I've something striking to report to you. In all my time before now that accustomed prophetic ability of mine, the one I get from my 'divinity', was always with me, intervening again and again and opposing me in quite small matters, if ever I were to be going to act incorrectly in some respect. And now things have turned out for me as you yourselves observe, in a way that might be thought, and people actually think, the worst that can happen to anyone; but the god's sign failed to oppose either my leaving my house at dawn, or my coming up here to the court, or my saying anything I was going to say at any point in my speech. And yet on other occasions when I've been talking it has held me back all over the place in mid-speech; now, in relation to this whole business it has nowhere opposed my doing or saying anything. What do I suppose to be the reason for this? I'll tell you: it's because this thing that's happened has very likely been good for me. There's no way that those of us who think dying is a bad thing can be right; and I've had a powerful indication of that – there's no way that my accustomed sign wouldn't have opposed me if I wasn't going to do something good.

Let us look at things in the following way too, to see how great a hope there is that it's a good thing. Death is one or the other of two things: either the dead are nothing, as it were, and have no perception of anything, or else, as some people say, death is really a kind of change, a relocation of the soul from its residence here to another place. Now if the dead perceive nothing, but are as it were asleep, as when a sleeper sees nothing even in dreams, death would be a striking gain; for I imagine that if anyone had to pick out the night in which he'd slept so soundly as not even to see a dream and compare not just all other nights but the days of his life with that night – if he had to say, after thinking about it, how many days and nights in his life he'd lived through better and more pleasantly than *this* night, I imagine that not just any private individual but the Great King himself would find these days and nights easy to count by comparison with those other, dreamless ones; so that if death is something like that, I myself count it a gain, since from that perspective there'll be no difference between a single night and the whole of time. If on the other hand death is a kind of change of residence from here to another place, and what we're told is true, that all who have died are there, what greater good could there be, men of the jury? For if any new arrival in Hades, who has got away from those who call themselves judges here, will find himself before the true judges who are said to sit in judgement there, Minos, Rhadamanthus, Aeacus and Triptolemus, and those other demi-gods who became just in their own life, would that be a poor destination to move to? And what would any of you give to get together with Orpheus, or Musaeus, or Hesiod, or Homer? I'd happily die, myself, many times over if that's truly what awaits us, because I for one would pass the time wonderfully, when I met

Socrates' Defence

Palamedes, or Ajax son of Telamon, or any such figure from the past, dead because of an unjust judgement – I'd be able to compare my experiences with theirs, and I think it'd be delightful enough; but the greatest thing is that I'd be able to spend my time examining people there and sniffing them out as I do people here, to see which of them is wise and which merely thinks he is but really isn't. What would one give, men of the jury, to examine the man who led that great army against Troy, or Odysseus, or Sisyphus, or – well, one could list countless others, women as well as men with whom it'd give immeasurable happiness to talk, to be with them and to examine them. People there certainly don't put one to death for it, I imagine; they're happier than people here in every respect, and especially because for the rest of time they are deathless, if indeed what we are told is true.

But you too, men of the jury, should be of good hope when you think of death, keeping the truth of this one thing in mind: that there is nothing bad that can happen to a good man whether in life or after he has died, nor are his affairs neglected by the gods. This business of mine now hasn't come about by accident; no, it's clear to me that it was *better* for me to die now and to be rid of life's ordinary business altogether. That's the reason why that sign of mine at no point turned me back, and why I'm not at all angry with those who voted against me, or with my accusers. All the same, that wasn't what was in their minds when they were voting against me and making their accusations. They did it thinking they were damaging me, and that's what they deserve to be blamed for. This much I ask of them: if my sons seem to you, when they reach puberty, to be caring about money or anything else before excellence, punish them, Athenians, by making them suffer in the very same way I used to make you suffer, and if they think they're something when they're not, reproach them as I have reproached you for not caring about the things they should and thinking they're something when they're not worth anything. If you do that, then I shall have had my just deserts from you, both for myself and for my sons.

But now it is time for us to leave: for me, to go to my death, and for you to go on living. Whether it's you or I who are going to a better thing is clear to no one but the god.

1. BOCCACCIO · *Mrs Rosie and the Priest*
2. GERARD MANLEY HOPKINS · *As kingfishers catch fire*
3. *The Saga of Gunnlaug Serpent-tongue*
4. THOMAS DE QUINCEY · *On Murder Considered as One of the Fine Arts*
5. FRIEDRICH NIETZSCHE · *Aphorisms on Love and Hate*
6. JOHN RUSKIN · *Traffic*
7. PU SONGLING · *Wailing Ghosts*
8. JONATHAN SWIFT · *A Modest Proposal*
9. *Three Tang Dynasty Poets*
10. WALT WHITMAN · *On the Beach at Night Alone*
11. KENKŌ · *A Cup of Sake Beneath the Cherry Trees*
12. BALTASAR GRACIÁN · *How to Use Your Enemies*
13. JOHN KEATS · *The Eve of St Agnes*
14. THOMAS HARDY · *Woman much missed*
15. GUY DE MAUPASSANT · *Femme Fatale*
16. MARCO POLO · *Travels in the Land of Serpents and Pearls*
17. SUETONIUS · *Caligula*
18. APOLLONIUS OF RHODES · *Jason and Medea*
19. ROBERT LOUIS STEVENSON · *Olalla*
20. KARL MARX AND FRIEDRICH ENGELS · *The Communist Manifesto*
21. PETRONIUS · *Trimalchio's Feast*
22. JOHANN PETER HEBEL · *How a Ghastly Story Was Brought to Light by a Common or Garden Butcher's Dog*
23. HANS CHRISTIAN ANDERSEN · *The Tinder Box*
24. RUDYARD KIPLING · *The Gate of the Hundred Sorrows*
25. DANTE · *Circles of Hell*
26. HENRY MAYHEW · *Of Street Piemen*
27. HAFEZ · *The nightingales are drunk*
28. GEOFFREY CHAUCER · *The Wife of Bath*
29. MICHEL DE MONTAIGNE · *How We Weep and Laugh at the Same Thing*
30. THOMAS NASHE · *The Terrors of the Night*
31. EDGAR ALLAN POE · *The Tell-Tale Heart*
32. MARY KINGSLEY · *A Hippo Banquet*
33. JANE AUSTEN · *The Beautifull Cassandra*
34. ANTON CHEKHOV · *Gooseberries*
35. SAMUEL TAYLOR COLERIDGE · *Well, they are gone, and here must I remain*
36. JOHANN WOLFGANG VON GOETHE · *Sketchy, Doubtful, Incomplete Jottings*
37. CHARLES DICKENS · *The Great Winglebury Duel*
38. HERMAN MELVILLE · *The Maldive Shark*
39. ELIZABETH GASKELL · *The Old Nurse's Story*
40. NIKOLAY LESKOV · *The Steel Flea*

41. HONORÉ DE BALZAC · *The Atheist's Mass*
42. CHARLOTTE PERKINS GILMAN · *The Yellow Wall-Paper*
43. C.P. CAVAFY · *Remember, Body . . .*
44. FYODOR DOSTOEVSKY · *The Meek One*
45. GUSTAVE FLAUBERT · *A Simple Heart*
46. NIKOLAI GOGOL · *The Nose*
47. SAMUEL PEPYS · *The Great Fire of London*
48. EDITH WHARTON · *The Reckoning*
49. HENRY JAMES · *The Figure in the Carpet*
50. WILFRED OWEN · *Anthem For Doomed Youth*
51. WOLFGANG AMADEUS MOZART · *My Dearest Father*
52. PLATO · *Socrates' Defence*
53. CHRISTINA ROSSETTI · *Goblin Market*
54. *Sindbad the Sailor*
55. SOPHOCLES · *Antigone*
56. RYŪNOSUKE AKUTAGAWA · *The Life of a Stupid Man*
57. LEO TOLSTOY · *How Much Land Does A Man Need?*
58. GIORGIO VASARI · *Leonardo da Vinci*
59. OSCAR WILDE · *Lord Arthur Savile's Crime*
60. SHEN FU · *The Old Man of the Moon*
61. AESOP · *The Dolphins, the Whales and the Gudgeon*
62. MATSUO BASHŌ · *Lips too Chilled*
63. EMILY BRONTË · *The Night is Darkening Round Me*
64. JOSEPH CONRAD · *To-morrow*
65. RICHARD HAKLUYT · *The Voyage of Sir Francis Drake Around the Whole Globe*
66. KATE CHOPIN · *A Pair of Silk Stockings*
67. CHARLES DARWIN · *It was snowing butterflies*
68. BROTHERS GRIMM · *The Robber Bridegroom*
69. CATULLUS · *I Hate and I Love*
70. HOMER · *Circe and the Cyclops*
71. D. H. LAWRENCE · *Il Duro*
72. KATHERINE MANSFIELD · *Miss Brill*
73. OVID · *The Fall of Icarus*
74. SAPPHO · *Come Close*
75. IVAN TURGENEV · *Kasyan from the Beautiful Lands*
76. VIRGIL · *O Cruel Alexis*
77. H. G. WELLS · *A Slip under the Microscope*
78. HERODOTUS · *The Madness of Cambyses*
79. *Speaking of Siva*
80. *The Dhammapada*

'She kissed and kissed her with a hungry mouth.'

CHRISTINA ROSSETTI
Born 1830, London
Died 1894, London

ROSSETTI IN PENGUIN CLASSICS
The Complete Poems
The Penguin Book of Victorian Verse
The Pre-Raphaelites

CHRISTINA ROSSETTI

Goblin Market

PENGUIN BOOKS

PENGUIN CLASSICS

UK | USA | Canada | Ireland | Australia
India | New Zealand | South Africa

Penguin Books is part of the Penguin Random House group of companies
whose addresses can be found at global.penguinrandomhouse.com.

This selection published in Penguin Classics 2015
010

Set in 9/12.4 pt Baskerville 10 Pro
Typeset by Jouve (UK), Milton Keynes
Printed and bound in Great Britain by Clays Ltd, Elcograf S.p.A.

A CIP catalogue record for this book is available from the British Library

ISBN: 978-0-141-39766-5

www.greenpenguin.co.uk

Penguin Random House is committed to a
sustainable future for our business, our readers
and our planet. This book is made from Forest
Stewardship Council® certified paper.

Contents

Goblin Market	1
Dream Land	21
Song ['When I am dead, my dearest']	23
An End	24
A Pause of Thought	25
Sweet Death	26
A Birthday	27
Babylon the Great	28
On Keats	29
In an Artist's Studio	30
The Queen of Hearts	31
A Christmas Carol	33
An Old-World Thicket	35
Spring Quiet	42
Up-Hill	43
Song ['Two doves upon the selfsame branch']	44

A Dirge	45
A Frog's Fate	46
My Dream	48
Nursery Rhymes from *Sing-Song*	50

Goblin Market

Morning and evening
Maids heard the goblins cry:
'Come buy our orchard fruits,
Come buy, come buy:
Apples and quinces,
Lemons and oranges,
Plump unpecked cherries,
Melons and raspberries,
Bloom-down-cheeked peaches,
Swart-headed mulberries,
Wild free-born cranberries,
Crab-apples, dewberries,
Pine-apples, blackberries,
Apricots, strawberries; –
All ripe together
In summer weather, –
Morns that pass by,
Fair eves that fly;
Come buy, come buy:
Our grapes fresh from the vine,
Pomegranates full and fine.
Dates and sharp bullaces,
Rare pears and greengages,
Damsons and bilberries,
Taste them and try:
Currants and gooseberries,
Bright-fire-like barberries,

Figs to fill your mouth,
Citrons from the South,
Sweet to tongue and sound to eye;
Come buy, come buy.'

    Evening by evening
Among the brookside rushes,
Laura bowed her head to hear,
Lizzie veiled her blushes:
Crouching close together
In the cooling weather,
With clasping arms and cautioning lips,
With tingling cheeks and finger tips.
'Lie close,' Laura said,
Pricking up her golden head:
'We must not look at goblin men,
We must not buy their fruits:
Who knows upon what soil they fed
Their hungry thirsty roots?'
'Come buy,' call the goblins
Hobbling down the glen.
'Oh,' cried Lizzie, 'Laura, Laura,
You should not peep at goblin men.'
Lizzie covered up her eyes,
Covered close lest they should look;
Laura reared her glossy head,
And whispered like the restless brook:
'Look, Lizzie, look, Lizzie,
Down the glen tramp little men.

Goblin Market

One hauls a basket,
One bears a plate,
One lugs a golden dish
Of many pounds weight.
How fair the vine must grow
Whose grapes are so luscious;
How warm the wind must blow
Through those fruit bushes.'
'No,' said Lizzie: 'No, no, no;
Their offers should not charm us,
Their evil gifts would harm us.'
She thrust a dimpled finger
In each ear, shut eyes and ran:
Curious Laura chose to linger
Wondering at each merchant man.
One had a cat's face,
One whisked a tail,
One tramped at a rat's pace,
One crawled like a snail,
One like a wombat prowled obtuse and furry,
One like a ratel tumbled hurry skurry.
She heard a voice like voice of doves
Cooing all together:
They sounded kind and full of loves
In the pleasant weather.

    Laura stretched her gleaming neck
Like a rush-imbedded swan,
Like a lily from the beck,

Like a moonlit poplar branch,
Like a vessel at the launch
When its last restraint is gone.

Backwards up the mossy glen
Turned and trooped the goblin men,
With their shrill repeated cry,
'Come buy, come buy.'
When they reached where Laura was
They stood stock still upon the moss,
Leering at each other,
Brother with queer brother;
Signalling each other,
Brother with sly brother.
One set his basket down,
One reared his plate;
One began to weave a crown
Of tendrils, leaves and rough nuts brown
(Men sell not such in any town);
One heaved the golden weight
Of dish and fruit to offer her:
'Come buy, come buy,' was still their cry.
Laura stared but did not stir,
Longed but had no money:
The whisk-tailed merchant bade her taste
In tones as smooth as honey,
The cat-faced purr'd,
The rat-paced spoke a word
Of welcome, and the snail-paced even was heard;

One parrot-voiced and jolly
Cried 'Pretty Goblin' still for 'Pretty Polly;' –
One whistled like a bird.

    But sweet-tooth Laura spoke in haste:
'Good folk, I have no coin;
To take were to purloin:
I have no copper in my purse,
I have no silver either,
And all my gold is on the furze
That shakes in windy weather
Above the rusty heather.'
'You have much gold upon your head,'
They answered all together:
'Buy from us with a golden curl.'
She clipped a precious golden lock,
She dropped a tear more rare than pearl,
Then sucked their fruit globes fair or red:
Sweeter than honey from the rock,
Stronger than man-rejoicing wine,
Clearer than water flowed that juice;
She never tasted such before,
How should it cloy with length of use?
She sucked and sucked and sucked the more
Fruits which that unknown orchard bore;
She sucked until her lips were sore;
Then flung the emptied rinds away
But gathered up one kernel-stone,
And knew not was it night or day
As she turned home alone.

Christina Rossetti

    Lizzie met her at the gate
Full of wise upbraidings:
'Dear, you should not stay so late,
Twilight is not good for maidens;
Should not loiter in the glen
In the haunts of goblin men.
Do you not remember Jeanie,
How she met them in the moonlight,
Took their gifts both choice and many,
Ate their fruits and wore their flowers
Plucked from bowers
Where summer ripens at all hours?
But ever in the noonlight
She pined and pined away;
Sought them by night and day,
Found them no more but dwindled and grew grey;
Then fell with the first snow,
While to this day no grass will grow
Where she lies low:
I planted daisies there a year ago
That never blow.
You should not loiter so.'
'Nay, hush,' said Laura:
'Nay, hush, my sister:
I ate and ate my fill,
Yet my mouth waters still;
To-morrow night I will
Buy more:' and kissed her:
'Have done with sorrow;
I'll bring you plums to-morrow

Goblin Market

Fresh on their mother twigs,
Cherries worth getting;
You cannot think what figs
My teeth have met in,
What melons icy-cold
Piled on a dish of gold
Too huge for me to hold,
What peaches with a velvet nap,
Pellucid grapes without one seed:
Odorous indeed must be the mead
Whereon they grow, and pure the wave they drink
With lilies at the brink,
And sugar-sweet their sap.'

    Golden head by golden head,
Like two pigeons in one nest
Folded in each other's wings,
They lay down in their curtained bed:
Like two blossoms on one stem,
Like two flakes of new-fall'n snow,
Like two wands of ivory
Tipped with gold for awful kings.
Moon and stars gazed in at them,
Wind sang to them lullaby,
Lumbering owls forbore to fly,
Not a bat flapped to and fro
Round their rest:
Cheek to cheek and breast to breast
Locked together in one nest.

Christina Rossetti

    Early in the morning
When the first cock crowed his warning,
Neat like bees, as sweet and busy,
Laura rose with Lizzie:
Fetched in honey, milked the cows,
Aired and set to rights the house,
Kneaded cakes of whitest wheat,
Cakes for dainty mouths to eat,
Next churned butter, whipped up cream,
Fed their poultry, sat and sewed;
Talked as modest maidens should:
Lizzie with an open heart,
Laura in an absent dream,
One content, one sick in part;
One warbling for the mere bright day's delight,
One longing for the night.

    At length slow evening came:
They went with pitchers to the reedy brook;
Lizzie most placid in her look,
Laura most like a leaping flame.
They drew the gurgling water from its deep;
Lizzie plucked purple and rich golden flags,
Then turning homewards said: 'The sunset flushes
Those furthest loftiest crags;
Come, Laura, not another maiden lags,
No wilful squirrel wags,
The beasts and birds are fast asleep.'

But Laura loitered still among the rushes
And said the bank was steep.

    And said the hour was early still,
The dew not fall'n, the wind not chill:
Listening ever, but not catching
The customary cry,
'Come buy, come buy,'
With its iterated jingle
Of sugar-baited words:
Not for all her watching
Once discerning even one goblin
Racing, whisking, tumbling, hobbling;
Let alone the herds
That used to tramp along the glen,
In groups or single,
Of brisk fruit-merchant men.

    Till Lizzie urged, 'O Laura, come;
I hear the fruit-call but I dare not look:
You should not loiter longer at this brook
Come with me home.
The stars rise, the moon bends her arc,
Each glowworm winks her spark,
Let us get home before the night grows dark:
For clouds may gather
Though this is summer weather,
Put out the lights and drench us through;
Then if we lost our way what should we do?'

Laura turned cold as stone
To find her sister heard that cry alone,
That goblin cry,
'Come buy our fruits, come buy.'
Must she then buy no more such dainty fruits?
Must she no more that succous pasture find,
Gone deaf and blind?
Her tree of life drooped from the root:
She said not one word in her heart's sore ache;
But peering thro' the dimness, nought discerning,
Trudged home, her pitcher dripping all the way;
So crept to bed, and lay
Silent till Lizzie slept;
Then sat up in a passionate yearning,
And gnashed her teeth for baulked desire, and wept
As if her heart would break.

Day after day, night after night,
Laura kept watch in vain
In sullen silence of exceeding pain.
She never caught again the goblin cry:
'Come buy, come buy;' –
She never spied the goblin men
Hawking their fruits along the glen:
But when the noon waxed bright
Her hair grew thin and grey;
She dwindled, as the fair full moon doth turn
To swift decay and burn
Her fire away.

One day remembering her kernel-stone
She set it by a wall that faced the south;
Dewed it with tears, hoped for a root,
Watched for a waxing shoot,
But there came none;
It never saw the sun,
It never felt the trickling moisture run:
While with sunk eyes and faded mouth
She dreamed of melons, as a traveller sees
False waves in desert drouth
With shade of leaf-crowned trees,
And burns the thirstier in the sandful breeze.

She no more swept the house,
Tended the fowls or cows,
Fetched honey, kneaded cakes of wheat,
Brought water from the brook:
But sat down listless in the chimney-nook
And would not eat.

Tender Lizzie could not bear
To watch her sister's cankerous care
Yet not to share.
She night and morning
Caught the goblins' cry:
'Come buy our orchard fruits,
Come buy, come buy:' –
Beside the brook, along the glen,
She heard the tramp of goblin men,
The voice and stir

Christina Rossetti

Poor Laura could not hear;
Longed to buy fruit to comfort her,
But feared to pay too dear.
She thought of Jeanie in her grave,
Who should have been a bride;
But who for joys brides hope to have
Fell sick and died
In her gay prime,
In earliest Winter time,
With the first glazing rime,
With the first snow-fall of crisp Winter time.

   Till Laura dwindling
Seemed knocking at Death's door:
Then Lizzie weighed no more
Better and worse;
But put a silver penny in her purse,
Kissed Laura, crossed the heath with clumps of furze
At twilight, halted by the brook:
And for the first time in her life
Began to listen and look.

   Laughed every goblin
When they spied her peeping:
Came towards her hobbling,
Flying, running, leaping,
Puffing and blowing,
Chuckling, clapping, crowing,
Clucking and gobbling,
Mopping and mowing,
Full of airs and graces,

Pulling wry faces,
Demure grimaces,
Cat-like and rat-like,
Ratel- and wombat-like,
Snail-paced in a hurry,
Parrot-voiced and whistler,
Helter skelter, hurry skurry,
Chattering like magpies,
Fluttering like pigeons,
Gliding like fishes, –
Hugged her and kissed her,
Squeezed and caressed her:
Stretched up their dishes,
Panniers, and plates:
'Look at our apples
Russet and dun,
Bob at our cherries,
Bite at our peaches,
Citrons and dates,
Grapes for the asking,
Pears red with basking
Out in the sun,
Plums on their twigs;
Pluck them and suck them.
Pomegranates, figs.' –

   'Good folk,' said Lizzie,
Mindful of Jeanie:
'Give me much and many;' –
Held out her apron,

Tossed them her penny.
'Nay, take a seat with us,
Honour and eat with us,'
They answered grinning:
'Our feast is but beginning.
Night yet is early,
Warm and dew-pearly,
Wakeful and starry:
Such fruits as these
No man can carry;
Half their bloom would fly,
Half their dew would dry,
Half their flavour would pass by.
Sit down and feast with us,
Be welcome guest with us,
Cheer you and rest with us.' –
'Thank you,' said Lizzie: 'But one waits
At home alone for me:
So without further parleying,
If you will not sell me any
Of your fruits though much and many,
Give me back my silver penny
I tossed you for a fee.' –
They began to scratch their pates,
No longer wagging, purring,
But visibly demurring,
Grunting and snarling.
One called her proud,
Cross-grained, uncivil;
Their tones waxed loud,

Their looks were evil.
Lashing their tails
They trod and hustled her,
Elbowed and jostled her,
Clawed with their nails,
Barking, mewing, hissing, mocking,
Tore her gown and soiled her stocking,
Twitched her hair out by the roots,
Stamped upon her tender feet,
Held her hands and squeezed their fruits
Against her mouth to make her eat.

    White and golden Lizzie stood,
Like a lily in a flood, –
Like a rock of blue-veined stone
Lashed by tides obstreperously, –
Like a beacon left alone
In a hoary roaring sea,
Sending up a golden fire, –
Like a fruit-crowned orange-tree
White with blossoms honey-sweet
Sore beset by wasp and bee, –
Like a royal virgin town
Topped with gilded dome and spire
Close beleaguered by a fleet
Mad to tug her standard down.

    One may lead a horse to water,
Twenty cannot make him drink.
Though the goblins cuffed and caught her,
Coaxed and fought her,

Bullied and besought her,
Scratched her, pinched her black as ink,
Kicked and knocked her,
Mauled and mocked her,
Lizzie uttered not a word;
Would not open lip from lip
Lest they should cram a mouthful in:
But laughed in heart to feel the drip
Of juice that syrupped all her face,
And lodged in dimples of her chin,
And streaked her neck which quaked like curd.
At last the evil people
Worn out by her resistance
Flung back her penny, kicked their fruit
Along whichever road they took,
Not leaving root or stone or shoot;
Some writhed into the ground,
Some dived into the brook
With ring and ripple,
Some scudded on the gale without a sound,
Some vanished in the distance.

    In a smart, ache, tingle,
Lizzie went her way;
Knew not was it night or day;
Sprang up the bank, tore thro' the furze,
Threaded copse and dingle,
And heard her penny jingle
Bouncing in her purse, –
Its bounce was music to her ear.

Goblin Market

She ran and ran
As if she feared some goblin man
Dogged her with gibe or curse
Or something worse:
But not one goblin skurried after,
Nor was she pricked by fear;
The kind heart made her windy-paced
That urged her home quite out of breath with haste
And inward laughter.

   She cried 'Laura,' up the garden,
'Did you miss me?
Come and kiss me.
Never mind my bruises,
Hug me, kiss me, suck my juices
Squeezed from goblin fruits for you,
Goblin pulp and goblin dew.
Eat me, drink me, love me;
Laura, make much of me:
For your sake I have braved the glen
And had to do with goblin merchant men.'

   Laura started from her chair,
Flung her arms up in the air,
Clutched her hair:
'Lizzie, Lizzie, have you tasted
For my sake the fruit forbidden?
Must your light like mine be hidden,
Your young life like mine be wasted,
Undone in mine undoing
And ruined in my ruin,

Thirsty, cankered, goblin-ridden?' –
She clung about her sister,
Kissed and kissed and kissed her:
Tears once again
Refreshed her shrunken eyes,
Dropping like rain
After long sultry drouth;
Shaking with aguish fear, and pain,
She kissed and kissed her with a hungry mouth.

    Her lips began to scorch,
That juice was wormwood to her tongue,
She loathed the feast:
Writhing as one possessed she leaped and sung,
Rent all her robe, and wrung
Her hands in lamentable haste,
And beat her breast.
Her locks streamed like the torch
Borne by a racer at full speed,
Or like the mane of horses in their flight,
Or like an eagle when she stems the light
Straight toward the sun,
Or like a caged thing freed,
Or like a flying flag when armies run.

    Swift fire spread through her veins, knocked at her
      heart,
Met the fire smouldering there
And overbore its lesser flame;
She gorged on bitterness without a name:
Ah! fool, to choose such part

Of soul-consuming care!
Sense failed in the mortal strife:
Like the watch-tower of a town
Which an earthquake shatters down,
Like a lightning-stricken mast,
Like a wind-uprooted tree
Spun about,
Like a foam-topped waterspout
Cast down headlong in the sea,
She fell at last;
Pleasure past and anguish past,
Is it death or is it life?

    Life out of death.
That night long Lizzie watched by her,
Counted her pulse's flagging stir,
Felt for her breath,
Held water to her lips, and cooled her face
With tears and fanning leaves:
But when the first birds chirped about their eaves,
And early reapers plodded to the place
Of golden sheaves,
And dew-wet grass
Bowed in the morning winds so brisk to pass,
And new buds with new day
Opened of cup-like lilies on the stream,
Laura awoke as from a dream,
Laughed in the innocent old way,
Hugged Lizzie but not twice or thrice;
Her gleaming locks showed not one thread of grey,

Her breath was sweet as May
And light danced in her eyes.

    Days, weeks, months, years,
Afterwards, when both were wives
With children of their own;
Their mother-hearts beset with fears,
Their lives bound up in tender lives;
Laura would call the little ones
And tell them of her early prime,
Those pleasant days long gone
Of not-returning time:
Would talk about the haunted glen,
The wicked, quaint fruit-merchant men,
Their fruits like honey to the throat
But poison in the blood;
(Men sell not such in any town:)
Would tell them how her sister stood
In deadly peril to do her good,
And win the fiery antidote:
Then joining hands to little hands
Would bid them cling together,
'For there is no friend like a sister
In calm or stormy weather;
To cheer one on the tedious way,
To fetch one if one goes astray,
To lift one if one totters down,
To strengthen whilst one stands.'

Dream Land

Where sunless rivers weep
Their waves into the deep,
She sleeps a charmèd sleep:
    Awake her not.
Led by a single star,
She came from very far
To seek where shadows are
    Her pleasant lot.

She left the rosy morn,
She left the fields of corn,
For twilight cold and lorn
    And water springs.
Through sleep, as through a veil,
She sees the sky look pale,
And hears the nightingale
    That sadly sings.

Rest, rest, a perfect rest
Shed over brow and breast;
Her face is toward the west,
    The purple land.
She cannot see the grain
Ripening on hill and plain;
She cannot feel the rain
    Upon her hand.

Christina Rossetti

    Rest, rest, for evermore
    Upon a mossy shore;
    Rest, rest at the heart's core
        Till time shall cease:
    Sleep that no pain shall wake,
    Night that no morn shall break
    Till joy shall overtake
        Her perfect peace.

Song

When I am dead, my dearest,
  Sing no sad songs for me;
Plant thou no roses at my head,
  Nor shady cypress tree:
Be the green grass above me
  With showers and dewdrops wet:
And if thou wilt, remember,
  And if thou wilt, forget.

I shall not see the shadows,
  I shall not feel the rain;
I shall not hear the nightingale
  Sing on as if in pain:
And dreaming through the twilight
  That doth not rise nor set,
Haply I may remember,
  And haply may forget.

An End

Love, strong as Death, is dead
Come, let us make his bed
Among the dying flowers:
A green turf at his head;
And a stone at his feet,
Whereon we may sit
In the quiet evening hours.

He was born in the Spring,
And died before the harvesting:
On the last warm summer day
He left us; he would not stay
For Autumn twilight cold and grey.
Sit we by his grave, and sing
He is gone away.

To few chords and sad and low
Sing we so:
Be our eyes fixed on the grass
Shadow-veiled as the years pass,
While we think of all that was
In the long ago.

A Pause of Thought

I looked for that which is not, nor can be,
    And hope deferred made my heart sick in truth:
    But years must pass before a hope of youth
        Is resigned utterly.

I watched and waited with a steadfast will:
    And though the object seemed to flee away
    That I so longed for, ever day by day
        I watched and waited still.

Sometimes I said: This thing shall be no more;
    My expectation wearies and shall cease;
    I will resign it now and be at peace:
        Yet never gave it o'er.

Sometimes I said: It is an empty name
    I long for; to a name why should I give
    The peace of all the days I have to live? –
        Yet gave it all the same.

Alas, thou foolish one! alike unfit
    For healthy joy and salutary pain:
    Thou knowest the chase useless, and again
        Turnest to follow it.

Sweet Death

The sweetest blossoms die.
    And so it was that, going day by day
    Unto the Church to praise and pray,
And crossing the green churchyard thoughtfully,
    I saw how on the graves the flowers
    Shed their fresh leaves in showers,
And how their perfume rose up to the sky
    Before it passed away.

The youngest blossoms die.
    They die and fall and nourish the rich earth
    From which they lately had their birth;
Sweet life, but sweeter death that passeth by
    And is as though it had not been: –
    All colours turn to green;
The bright hues vanish and the odours fly,
    The grass hath lasting worth.

And youth and beauty die.
    So be it, O my God, Thou God of truth:
    Better than beauty and than youth
Are Saints and Angels, a glad company;
    And Thou, O Lord, our Rest and Ease,
    Art better far than these.
Why should we shrink from our full harvest? why
    Prefer to glean with Ruth?

A Birthday

My heart is like a singing bird
    Whose nest is in a watered shoot;
My heart is like an appletree
    Whose boughs are bent with thickset fruit;
My heart is like a rainbow shell
    That paddles in a halcyon sea;
My heart is gladder than all these
    Because my love is come to me.

Raise me a dais of silk and down;
    Hang it with vair and purple dyes;
Carve it in doves, and pomegranates,
    And peacocks with a hundred eyes;
Work it in gold and silver grapes,
    In leaves, and silver fleurs-de-lys;
Because the birthday of my life
    Is come, my love is come to me.

Babylon the Great

Foul is she and ill-favoured, set askew:
    Gaze not upon her till thou dream her fair,
    Lest she should mesh thee in her wanton hair,
Adept in arts grown old yet ever new.
Her heart lusts not for love, but thro' and thro'
    For blood, as spotted panther lusts in lair;
    No wine is in her cup, but filth is there
Unutterable, with plagues hid out of view.
Gaze not upon her; for her dancing whirl
    Turns giddy the fixed gazer presently:
    Gaze not upon her, lest thou be as she
        When at the far end of her long desire
Her scarlet vest and gold and gem and pearl
    And she amid her pomp are set on fire.

On Keats

A garden in a garden: a green spot
    Where all is green: most fitting slumber-place
    For the strong man grown weary of a race
Soon over. Unto him a goodly lot
Hath fallen in fertile ground; there thorns are not,
    But his own daisies; silence, full of grace,
    Surely hath shed a quiet on his face;
His earth is but sweet leaves that fall and rot.
What was his record of himself, ere he
    Went from us? 'Here lies one whose name was writ
    In water.' While the chilly shadows flit
    Of sweet St Agnes' Eve, while basil springs –
    His name, in every humble heart that sings,
Shall be a fountain of love, verily.

In an Artist's Studio

One face looks out from all his canvases,
    One selfsame figure sits or walks or leans:
    We found her hidden just behind those screens,
That mirror gave back all her loveliness.
A queen in opal or in ruby dress,
    A nameless girl in freshest summer-greens,
    A saint, an angel – every canvas means
The same one meaning, neither more nor less.
He feeds upon her face by day and night,
    And she with true kind eyes looks back on him,
Fair as the moon and joyful as the light:
    Not wan with waiting, not with sorrow dim;
Not as she is, but was when hope shone bright;
    Not as she is, but as she fills his dream.

The Queen of Hearts

How comes it, Flora, that, whenever we
Play cards together, you invariably,
    However the pack parts,
    Still hold the Queen of Hearts?

I've scanned you with a scrutinizing gaze,
Resolved to fathom these your secret ways:
    But, sift them as I will,
    Your ways are secret still.

I cut and shuffle; shuffle, cut, again;
But all my cutting, shuffling, proves in vain:
    Vain hope, vain forethought too;
    That Queen still falls to you.

I dropped her once, prepense; but, ere the deal
Was dealt, your instinct seemed her loss to feel:
    'There should be one card more,'
    You said, and searched the floor.

I cheated once; I made a private notch
In Heart-Queen's back, and kept a lynx-eyed watch;
    Yet such another back
    Deceived me in the pack;

The Queen of Clubs assumed by arts unknown
An imitative dint that seemed my own;
    This notch, not of my doing,
    Misled me to my ruin.

Christina Rossetti

> It baffles me to puzzle out the clue,
> Which must be skill, or craft, or luck in you:
> > Unless, indeed, it be
> > Natural affinity.

A Christmas Carol

In the bleak mid-winter
    Frosty wind made moan,
Earth stood hard as iron,
    Water like a stone;
Snow had fallen, snow on snow,
    Snow on snow,
In the bleak mid-winter
    Long ago.

Our God, Heaven cannot hold Him
    Nor earth sustain;
Heaven and earth shall flee away
    When He comes to reign:
In the bleak mid-winter
    A stable-place sufficed
The Lord God Almighty
    Jesus Christ.

Enough for Him, whom cherubim
    Worship night and day,
A breastful of milk
    And a mangerful of hay;
Enough for Him, whom angels,
    Fall down before,
The ox and ass and camel
    Which adore.

Christina Rossetti

Angels and archangels
    May have gathered there,
Cherubim and seraphim
    Throng'd the air,
But only His mother
    In her maiden bliss
Worshipped the Beloved
    With a kiss.

What can I give Him,
    Poor as I am?
If I were a shepherd
    I would bring a lamb,
If I were a Wise Man
    I would do my part, –
Yet what I can I give Him,
    Give my heart.

An Old-World Thicket

'Una selva oscura.'

– Dante

Awake or sleeping (for I know not which)
    I was or was not mazed within a wood
      Where every mother-bird brought up her brood
        Safe in some leafy niche
Of oak or ash, of cypress or of beech,

Of silvery aspen trembling delicately,
    Of plane or warmer-tinted sycomore,
    Of elm that dies in secret from the core,
      Of ivy weak and free,
Of pines, of all green lofty things that be.

Such birds they seemed as challenged each desire;
    Like spots of azure heaven upon the wing,
    Like downy emeralds that alight and sing,
      Like actual coals on fire,
Like anything they seemed, and everything.

Such mirth they made, such warblings and such chat
    With tongue of music in a well-tuned beak,
    They seemed to speak more wisdom than we speak,
      To make our music flat
And all our subtlest reasonings wild or weak.

Christina Rossetti

Their meat was nought but flowers like butterflies,
    With berries coral-coloured or like gold;
      Their drink was only dew, which blossoms hold
        Deep where the honey lies;
Their wings and tails were lit by sparkling eyes.

The shade wherein they revelled was a shade
    That danced and twinkled to the unseen sun;
      Branches and leaves cast shadows one by one,
        And all their shadows swayed
In breaths of air that rustled and that played.

A sound of waters neither rose nor sank,
    And spread a sense of freshness through the air;
      It seemed not here or there, but everywhere,
        As if the whole earth drank,
Root fathom-deep and strawberry on its bank.

But I who saw such things as I have said
    Was overdone with utter weariness;
      And walked in care, as one whom fears oppress
        Because above his head
Death hangs, or damage, or the dearth of bread.

Each sore defeat of my defeated life
    Faced and outfaced me in that bitter hour;
      And turned to yearning palsy all my power,
        And all my peace to strife,
Self stabbing self with keen lack-pity knife.

Sweetness of beauty moved me to despair,
    Stung me to anger by its mere content,

An Old-World Thicket

Made me all lonely on that way I went,
    Piled care upon my care,
Brimmed full my cup, and stripped me empty and bare:

For all that was but showed what all was not,
    But gave clear proof of what might never be;
    Making more destitute my poverty,
        And yet more blank my lot,
And me much sadder by its jubilee.

Therefore I sat me down: for wherefore walk?
    And closed mine eyes: for wherefore see or hear?
    Alas, I had no shutter to mine ear,
        And could not shun the talk
Of all rejoicing creatures far or near.

Without my will I hearkened and I heard
    (Asleep or waking, for I know not which),
    Till note by note the music changed its pitch;
        Bird ceased to answer bird,
And every wind sighed softly if it stirred.

The drip of widening waters seemed to weep,
    All fountains sobbed and gurgled as they sprang,
    Somewhere a cataract cried out in its leap
        Sheer down a headlong steep;
High over all cloud-thunders gave a clang.

Such universal sound of lamentation
    I heard and felt, fain not to feel or hear;
    Nought else there seemed but anguish far and near;
        Nought else but all creation
Moaning and groaning wrung by pain or fear,

Shuddering in the misery of its doom:
    My heart then rose a rebel against light,
        Scouring all earth and heaven and depth and height,
            Ingathering wrath and gloom,
Ingathering wrath to wrath and night to night.

Ah me, the bitterness of such revolt,
    All impotent, all hateful, and all hate,
        That kicks and breaks itself against the bolt
            Of an imprisoning fate,
And vainly shakes, and cannot shake the gate.

Agony to agony, deep called to deep,
    Out of the deep I called of my desire;
        My strength was weakness and my heart was fire;
            Mine eyes that would not weep
Or sleep, scaled height and depth, and could not sleep;

The eyes, I mean, of my rebellious soul,
    For still my bodily eyes were closed and dark:
        A random thing I seemed without a mark,
            Racing without a goal,
Adrift upon life's sea without an ark.

More leaden than the actual self of lead
    Outer and inner darkness weighed on me.
        The tide of anger ebbed. Then fierce and free
            Surged full above my head
The moaning tide of helpless misery.

An Old-World Thicket

Why should I breathe, whose breath was but a sigh?
    Why should I live, who drew such painful breath?
    Oh weary work, the unanswerable why! –
        Yet I, why should I die,
Who had no hope in life, no hope in death?

Grasses and mosses and the fallen leaf
    Make peaceful bed for an indefinite term;
    But underneath the grass there gnaws a worm –
        Haply, there gnaws a grief –
Both, haply always; not, as now, so brief.

The pleasure I remember, it is past;
    The pain I feel, is passing passing by;
    Thus all the world is passing, and thus I:
        All things that cannot last
Have grown familiar, and are born to die.

And being familiar, have so long been borne
    That habit trains us not to break but bend:
    Mourning grows natural to us who mourn
        In foresight of an end,
But that which ends not who shall brave or mend?

Surely the ripe fruits tremble on their bough,
    They cling and linger trembling till they drop:
    I, trembling, cling to dying life; for how
        Face the perpetual Now?
Birthless and deathless, void of start or stop,

Christina Rossetti

Void of repentance, void of hope and fear,
    Of possibility, alternative,
      Of all that ever made us bear to live
        From night to morning here,
Of promise even which has no gift to give.

The wood, and every creature of the wood,
    Seemed mourning with me in an undertone;
      Soft scattered chirpings and a windy moan,
        Trees rustling where they stood
And shivered, showed compassion for my mood.

Rage to despair; and now despair had turned
    Back to self-pity and mere weariness,
      With yearnings like a smouldering fire that burned,
        And might grow more or less,
And might die out or wax to white excess.

Without, within me, music seemed to be;
    Something not music, yet most musical,
      Silence and sound in heavenly harmony;
        At length a pattering fall
Of feet, a bell, and bleatings, broke through all.

Then I looked up. The wood lay in a glow
    From golden sunset and from ruddy sky;
      The sun had stooped to earth though once so high;
        Had stooped to earth, in slow
Warm dying loveliness brought near and low.

Each water drop made answer to the light,
    Lit up a spark and showed the sun his face;

An Old-World Thicket

Soft purple shadows paved the grassy space
    And crept from height to height,
From height to loftier height crept up apace.

While opposite the sun a gazing moon
    Put on his glory for her coronet,
    Kindling her luminous coldness to its noon,
        As his great splendour set;
One only star made up her train as yet.

Each twig was tipped with gold, each leaf was edged
    And veined with gold from the gold-flooded west;
    Each mother-bird, and mate-bird, and unfledged
        Nestling, and curious nest,
    Displayed a gilded moss or beak or breast.

And filing peacefully between the trees,
    Having the moon behind them, and the sun
    Full in their meek mild faces, walked at ease
        A homeward flock, at peace
With one another and with every one.

A patriarchal ram with tinkling bell
    Led all his kin; sometimes one browsing sheep
    Hung back a moment, or one lamb would leap
        And frolic in a dell;
Yet still they kept together, journeying well,

And bleating, one or other, many or few,
    Journeying together toward the sunlit west;
    Mild face by face, and woolly breast by breast,
        Patient, sun-brightened too,
Still journeying toward the sunset and their rest.

Spring Quiet

Gone were but the Winter,
    Come were but the Spring,
I would go to a covert
    Where the birds sing;

Where in the whitethorn
    Singeth a thrush,
And a robin sings
    In the holly-bush.

Full of fresh scents
    Are the budding boughs
Arching high over
    A cool green house:

Full of sweet scents,
    And whispering air
Which sayeth softly:
    'We spread no snare;

'Here dwell in safety,
    Here dwell alone,
With a clear stream
    And a mossy stone.

'Here the sun shineth
    Most shadily;
Here is heard an echo
    Of the far sea,
      Though far off it be.'

Up-Hill

Does the road wind up-hill all the way?
    Yes, to the very end.
Will the day's journey take the whole long day?
    From morn to night, my friend.

But is there for the night a resting-place?
    A roof for when the slow dark hours begin.
May not the darkness hide it from my face?
    You cannot miss that inn.

Shall I meet other wayfarers at night?
    Those who have gone before.
Then must I knock, or call when just in sight?
    They will not keep you standing at that door.

Shall I find comfort, travel-sore and weak?
    Of labour you shall find the sum.
Will there be beds for me and all who seek?
    Yea, beds for all who come.

Song

Two doves upon the selfsame branch,
    Two lilies on a single stem,
Two butterflies upon one flower: –
    Oh happy they who look on them!

Who look upon them hand in hand
    Flushed in the rosy summer light;
Who look upon them hand in hand,
    And never give a thought to night.

A Dirge

Why were you born when the snow was falling?
You should have come to the cuckoo's calling,
Or when grapes are green in the cluster,
Or at least when lithe swallows muster
    For their far off flying
    From summer dying.

Why did you die when the lambs were cropping?
You should have died at the apples' dropping,
When the grasshopper comes to trouble,
And the wheat-fields are sodden stubble,
    And all winds go sighing
    For sweet things dying.

A Frog's Fate

Contemptuous of his home beyond
The village and the village pond,
A large-souled Frog who spurned each byeway
Hopped along the imperial highway.

Nor grunting pig nor barking dog
Could disconcert so great a Frog.
The morning dew was lingering yet,
His sides to cool, his tongue to wet:
The night-dew when the night should come
A travelled Frog would send him home.

Not so, alas! The wayside grass
Sees him no more: not so, alas!
A broad-wheeled waggon unawares
Ran him down, his joys, his cares.
From dying choke one feeble croak

The Frog's perpetual silence broke: –
'Ye buoyant Frogs, ye great and small,
Even I am mortal after all!
My road to fame turns out a wry way:
I perish on the hideous highway;
Oh for my old familiar byeway!'

The choking Frog sobbed and was gone;
The Waggoner strode whistling on.
Unconscious of the carnage done,
Whistling that Waggoner strode on –

A Frog's Fate

Whistling (it may have happened so)
'A froggy would a-wooing go.'
A hypothetic frog trolled he
Obtuse to a reality.

O rich and poor, O great and small,
Such oversights beset us all:
The mangled Frog abides incog,
The uninteresting actual frog:
The hypothetic frog alone
Is the one frog we dwell upon.

My Dream

Hear now a curious dream I dreamed last night,
Each word whereof is weighed and sifted truth.

    I stood beside Euphrates while it swelled
Like overflowing Jordan in its youth:
It waxed and coloured sensibly to sight;
Till out of myriad pregnant waves there welled
Young crocodiles, a gaunt blunt-featured crew,
Fresh-hatched perhaps and daubed with birthday dew.
The rest if I should tell, I fear my friend
My closest friend would deem the facts untrue;
And therefore it were wisely left untold;
Yet if you will, why hear it to the end.

    Each crocodile was girt with massive gold
And polished stones that with their wearers grew:
But one there was who waxed beyond the rest,
Wore kinglier girdle and a kingly crown,
Whilst crowns and orbs and sceptres starred his breast.
All gleamed compact and green with scale on scale,
But special burnishment adorned his mail
And special terror weighed upon his frown;
His punier brethren quaked before his tail,
Broad as a rafter, potent as a flail.
So he grew lord and master of his kin:
But who shall tell the tale of all their woes?
An execrable appetite arose,
He battened on them, crunched, and sucked them in.

My Dream

He knew no law, he feared no binding law,
But ground them with inexorable jaw:
The luscious fat distilled upon his chin,
Exuded from his nostrils and his eyes,
While still like hungry death he fed his maw;
Till every minor crocodile being dead
And buried too, himself gorged to the full,
He slept with breath oppressed and unstrung claw.
Oh marvel passing strange which next I saw:
In sleep he dwindled to the common size,
And all the empire faded from his coat.
Then from far off a wingèd vessel came,
Swift as a swallow, subtle as a flame:
I know not what it bore of freight or host,
But white it was as an avenging ghost.
It levelled strong Euphrates in its course;
Supreme yet weightless as an idle mote
It seemed to tame the waters without force
Till not a murmur swelled or billow beat:
Lo, as the purple shadow swept the sands,
The prudent crocodile rose on his feet
And shed appropriate tears and wrung his hands.

What can it mean? you ask. I answer not
For meaning, but myself must echo, What?
And tell it as I saw it on the spot.

Nursery Rhymes from Sing-Song

My baby has a father and a mother,
    Rich little baby!
Fatherless, motherless, I know another
    Forlorn as may be:
    Poor little baby!

Our little baby fell asleep,
    And may not wake again
For days and days, and weeks and weeks;
    But then he'll wake again,
And come with his own pretty look,
    And kiss Mamma again.

    Baby cry—
    Oh fie!—
At the physic in the cup:
    Gulp it twice
    And gulp it thrice,
Baby gulp it up.

Eight o'clock;
The postman's knock!
Five letters for Papa;
    One for Lou,
    And none for you,
And three for dear Mamma.

Nursery Rhymes from Sing-Song

Bread and milk for breakfast,
    And woollen frocks to wear,
And a crumb for robin redbreast
    On the cold days of the year.

There's snow on the fields,
    And cold in the cottage,
While I sit in the chimney nook
    Supping hot pottage.

My clothes are soft and warm,
    Fold upon fold,
But I'm so sorry for the poor
    Out in the cold.

Dead in the cold, a song-singing thrush,
Dead at the foot of a snowberry bush,—
Weave him a coffin of rush,
Dig him a grave where the soft mosses grow,
Raise him a tombstone of snow.

I dug and dug amongst the snow,
And thought the flowers would never grow;
I dug and dug amongst the sand,
And still no green thing came to hand.

Melt, O snow! the warm winds blow
To thaw the flowers and melt the snow;
But all the winds from every land
Will rear no blossom from the sand.

Christina Rossetti

A city plum is not a plum;
A dumb-bell is no bell, though dumb;
A party rat is not a rat;
A sailor's cat is not a cat;
A soldier's frog is not a frog;
A captain's log is not a log.

Your brother has a falcon,
    Your sister has a flower;
But what is left for mannikin,
    Born within an hour?

I'll nurse you on my knee, my knee,
    My own little son;
I'll rock you, rock you, in my arms,
    My least little one.

Hear what the mournful linnets say:
    'We built our nest compact and warm,
But cruel boys came round our way
    And took our summerhouse by storm.

'They crushed the eggs so neatly laid;
    So now we sit with drooping wing,
And watch the ruin they have made,
    Too late to build, too sad to sing.'

A baby's cradle with no baby in it,
    A baby's grave where autumn leaves drop sere;
The sweet soul gathered home to Paradise,
    The body waiting here.

Nursery Rhymes from Sing-Song

Hope is like a harebell trembling from its birth,
Love is like a rose the joy of all the earth;
Faith is like a lily lifted high and white,
Love is like a lovely rose the world's delight;
Harebells and sweet lilies show a thornless growth,
But the rose with all its thorns excels them both.

O wind, why do you never rest,
    Wandering, whistling to and fro,
Bringing rain out of the west,
    From the dim north bringing snow?

A linnet in a gilded cage,—
    A linnet on a bough,—
In frosty winter one might doubt
    Which bird is luckier now.

But let the trees burst out in leaf,
    And nests be on the bough,
Which linnet is the luckier bird,
    Oh who could doubt it now?

Wrens and robins in the hedge,
    Wrens and robins here and there;
Building, perching, pecking, fluttering,
      Everywhere!

My baby has a mottled fist,
    My baby has a neck in creases;
My baby kisses and is kissed,
    For he's the very thing for kisses.

Christina Rossetti

Why did baby die,
Making Father sigh,
Mother cry?

Flowers, that bloom to die,
Make no reply
Of 'why?'
But bow and die.

If all were rain and never sun,
    No bow could span the hill;
If all were sun and never rain,
    There'd be no rainbow still.

O wind, where have you been,
    That you blow so sweet?
Among the violets
    Which blossom at your feet.

The honeysuckle waits
    For Summer and for heat.
But violets in the chilly Spring
    Make the turf so sweet.

Heartsease in my garden bed,
    With sweetwilliam white and red,
Honeysuckle on my wall:—
    Heartsease blossoms in my heart
When sweet William comes to call,
    But it withers when we part,
And the honey-trumpets fall.

Nursery Rhymes from Sing-Song

If I were a Queen,
    What would I do?
I'd make you King,
    And I'd wait on you.

If I were a King,
    What would I do?
I'd make you Queen,
    For I'd marry you.

1. BOCCACCIO · *Mrs Rosie and the Priest*
2. GERARD MANLEY HOPKINS · *As kingfishers catch fire*
3. *The Saga of Gunnlaug Serpent-tongue*
4. THOMAS DE QUINCEY · *On Murder Considered as One of the Fine Arts*
5. FRIEDRICH NIETZSCHE · *Aphorisms on Love and Hate*
6. JOHN RUSKIN · *Traffic*
7. PU SONGLING · *Wailing Ghosts*
8. JONATHAN SWIFT · *A Modest Proposal*
9. *Three Tang Dynasty Poets*
10. WALT WHITMAN · *On the Beach at Night Alone*
11. KENKŌ · *A Cup of Sake Beneath the Cherry Trees*
12. BALTASAR GRACIÁN · *How to Use Your Enemies*
13. JOHN KEATS · *The Eve of St Agnes*
14. THOMAS HARDY · *Woman much missed*
15. GUY DE MAUPASSANT · *Femme Fatale*
16. MARCO POLO · *Travels in the Land of Serpents and Pearls*
17. SUETONIUS · *Caligula*
18. APOLLONIUS OF RHODES · *Jason and Medea*
19. ROBERT LOUIS STEVENSON · *Olalla*
20. KARL MARX AND FRIEDRICH ENGELS · *The Communist Manifesto*
21. PETRONIUS · *Trimalchio's Feast*
22. JOHANN PETER HEBEL · *How a Ghastly Story Was Brought to Light by a Common or Garden Butcher's Dog*
23. HANS CHRISTIAN ANDERSEN · *The Tinder Box*
24. RUDYARD KIPLING · *The Gate of the Hundred Sorrows*
25. DANTE · *Circles of Hell*
26. HENRY MAYHEW · *Of Street Piemen*
27. HAFEZ · *The nightingales are drunk*
28. GEOFFREY CHAUCER · *The Wife of Bath*
29. MICHEL DE MONTAIGNE · *How We Weep and Laugh at the Same Thing*
30. THOMAS NASHE · *The Terrors of the Night*
31. EDGAR ALLAN POE · *The Tell-Tale Heart*
32. MARY KINGSLEY · *A Hippo Banquet*
33. JANE AUSTEN · *The Beautifull Cassandra*
34. ANTON CHEKHOV · *Gooseberries*
35. SAMUEL TAYLOR COLERIDGE · *Well, they are gone, and here must I remain*
36. JOHANN WOLFGANG VON GOETHE · *Sketchy, Doubtful, Incomplete Jottings*
37. CHARLES DICKENS · *The Great Winglebury Duel*
38. HERMAN MELVILLE · *The Maldive Shark*
39. ELIZABETH GASKELL · *The Old Nurse's Story*
40. NIKOLAY LESKOV · *The Steel Flea*

41. HONORÉ DE BALZAC · *The Atheist's Mass*
42. CHARLOTTE PERKINS GILMAN · *The Yellow Wall-Paper*
43. C.P. CAVAFY · *Remember, Body . . .*
44. FYODOR DOSTOEVSKY · *The Meek One*
45. GUSTAVE FLAUBERT · *A Simple Heart*
46. NIKOLAI GOGOL · *The Nose*
47. SAMUEL PEPYS · *The Great Fire of London*
48. EDITH WHARTON · *The Reckoning*
49. HENRY JAMES · *The Figure in the Carpet*
50. WILFRED OWEN · *Anthem For Doomed Youth*
51. WOLFGANG AMADEUS MOZART · *My Dearest Father*
52. PLATO · *Socrates' Defence*
53. CHRISTINA ROSSETTI · *Goblin Market*
54. *Sindbad the Sailor*
55. SOPHOCLES · *Antigone*
56. RYŪNOSUKE AKUTAGAWA · *The Life of a Stupid Man*
57. LEO TOLSTOY · *How Much Land Does A Man Need?*
58. GIORGIO VASARI · *Leonardo da Vinci*
59. OSCAR WILDE · *Lord Arthur Savile's Crime*
60. SHEN FU · *The Old Man of the Moon*
61. AESOP · *The Dolphins, the Whales and the Gudgeon*
62. MATSUO BASHŌ · *Lips too Chilled*
63. EMILY BRONTË · *The Night is Darkening Round Me*
64. JOSEPH CONRAD · *To-morrow*
65. RICHARD HAKLUYT · *The Voyage of Sir Francis Drake Around the Whole Globe*
66. KATE CHOPIN · *A Pair of Silk Stockings*
67. CHARLES DARWIN · *It was snowing butterflies*
68. BROTHERS GRIMM · *The Robber Bridegroom*
69. CATULLUS · *I Hate and I Love*
70. HOMER · *Circe and the Cyclops*
71. D. H. LAWRENCE · *Il Duro*
72. KATHERINE MANSFIELD · *Miss Brill*
73. OVID · *The Fall of Icarus*
74. SAPPHO · *Come Close*
75. IVAN TURGENEV · *Kasyan from the Beautiful Lands*
76. VIRGIL · *O Cruel Alexis*
77. H. G. WELLS · *A Slip under the Microscope*
78. HERODOTUS · *The Madness of Cambyses*
79. *Speaking of Siva*
80. *The Dhammapada*

'The valley was full of snakes and serpents as big as palm trees, so huge that they could have swallowed any elephant that met them…'

This selection of stories is taken from the collection of seven stories entitled *Sindbad the Sailor* from *Tales from 1,001 Nights*, Penguin Classics, 2010. *Tales from 1,001 Nights* is an abridged version of the three volumes published by Penguin Classics 2008.

ARABIAN NIGHTS IN PENGUIN CLASSICS
The Arabian Nights: Tales of 1,001 Nights (Volume I)
The Arabian Nights: Tales of 1,001 Nights (Volume II)
The Arabian Nights: Tales of 1,001 Nights (Volume III)
Tales from 1,001 Nights
Three Tales from the Arabian Nights

ANONYMOUS

Sindbad the Sailor

Translated by
Malcolm C. Lyons

PENGUIN BOOKS

PENGUIN CLASSICS

UK | USA | Canada | Ireland | Australia
India | New Zealand | South Africa

Penguin Books is part of the Penguin Random House group of companies
whose addresses can be found at global.penguinrandomhouse.com.

This selection published in Penguin Classics 2015
009

Translation copyright © Malcolm C. Lyons, 2008

The moral right of the translator has been asserted

Set in 10/14.5 pt Baskerville 10 Pro
Typeset by Jouve (UK), Milton Keynes
Printed and bound in Great Britain by Clays Ltd, Elcograf S.p.A.

A CIP catalogue record for this book is available from the British Library

ISBN: 978–0–141–39768–9

www.greenpenguin.co.uk

Penguin Random House is committed to a
sustainable future for our business, our readers
and our planet. This book is made from Forest
Stewardship Council® certified paper.

Contents

Sindbad the Sailor — 1
  1. The Valley of Diamonds — 6
  2. The Black Giant — 19
  3. The Cannibal King — 37

Sindbad the Sailor

In the time of the caliph Harun al-Rashid, the Commander of the Faithful, there was in the city of Baghdad a man called Sindbad the porter, a poor fellow who earned his living by carrying goods on his head. On one particularly hot day he was tired, sweating and feeling the heat with a heavy load, when he passed by the door of a merchant's house. The ground in front of it had been swept and sprinkled with water and a temperate breeze was blowing. As there was a wide bench at the side of the house, he set down his bundle in order to rest there and to sniff the breeze.

From the door came a refreshing breath of air and a pleasant scent which attracted him, and as he sat he heard coming from within the house the sound of stringed instruments and lutes, together with singing and clearly chanted songs. In addition, he could hear birds twittering and praising God Almighty in all their varied tongues – turtledoves, nightingales, thrushes, bulbuls, ringdoves and curlews. He wondered at this and, filled as he was with pleasure, he moved forward and discovered within the grounds of the house a vast orchard in which he could see pages, black slaves, eunuchs, retainers and so forth, such as are only to be found in the palaces of kings and sultans. When he smelt the scent of all kinds of appetizing foods, together with fine wines, he looked up to heaven and said: 'Praise be to You, my Lord, Creator and Provider, Who sustains those whom You wish beyond all reckoning. I ask You to forgive all my sins, and I repent of my faults to You. My Lord, none can oppose Your judgement or power, or question Your acts, for You are omnipotent, praise be to You. You make one man rich and another poor, as You choose; You exalt some and humble others in accordance with Your will and there is no other god but You. How great You are! How strong is Your power and how excellent is Your governance! You show favour to those of Your servants whom You choose, for here is the owner of this house living in the greatest prosperity, enjoying pleasant scents, delicious food and all kinds of splendid wines. You have decreed what You wish with regard to your servants in accordance with Your power. Some are worn out and others live at ease; some are fortunate while others, like me, live laborious and humble lives.'

He then recited these lines:

> How many an unfortunate, who has no rest,
> Comes later to enjoy the pleasant shade.
> But as for me, my drudgery grows worse,
> And so, remarkably, my burdens now increase.
> Others are fortunate, living without hardship,
> And never once enduring what I must endure.
> They live in comfort all their days,
> With ease and honour, food and drink.
> All are created from a drop of sperm;
> I'm like the next man and he is like me,
> But oh how different are the lives we lead!
> How different is wine from vinegar.
> I do not say this as a calumny;
> God is All-Wise and His decrees are just.

When Sindbad the porter had finished these lines, he was about to pick up his load and carry it off when a splendidly dressed young boy, well proportioned and with a handsome face, came through the door, took his hand and said: 'Come and have a word with my master, for he invites you in.' Sindbad wanted to

Sindbad the Sailor

refuse, but finding that impossible, he left his load with the gatekeeper in the entrance hall and entered. He found an elegant house with an atmosphere of friendliness and dignity, and there he saw a large room filled with men of rank and importance. It was decked out with all kinds of flowers and scented herbs; there were fruits both dried and fresh, together with expensive foods of all kinds as well as wines of rare vintages; and there were musical instruments played by beautiful slave girls of various races. Everyone was seated in his appointed place and at their head was a large and venerable man whose facial hair was touched with grey. He was handsome and well shaped, with an imposing air of dignity, grandeur and pride. Sindbad the porter was taken aback, saying to himself: 'By God, this is one of the regions of Paradise, or perhaps the palace of a king or a sultan.' Then, remembering his manners, he greeted the company, invoking blessings on them and kissing the ground before them.

He stood there with his head bowed in an attitude of humility until the master of the house gave him permission to sit and placed him on a chair near his own, welcoming him and talking to him in a friendly way before offering him some of the splendid, delicious and expensive foods that were there. The porter, after invoking the Name of God, ate his fill and then exclaimed: 'Praise be to God in all things!' before washing his hands and thanking the company. The master of the house, after again welcoming him and wishing him good fortune, asked his name and his profession. 'My name is Sindbad the porter,' his guest replied, 'and in return for a fee I carry people's goods on my head.' The master smiled and said: 'You must know, porter, that your name is the same as mine, and I am Sindbad the sailor. I would like you to let me hear the verses which you were reciting as you stood at the door.' Sindbad the porter was embarrassed and said: 'For the sake of God, don't hold this against me, for toil and hardship together with a lack of means teach a man bad manners and stupidity.' 'Don't be ashamed,' said his host. 'You have become a brother to me, so repeat the verses that I admired when I heard you recite them at the door.' Sindbad the porter did this, moving Sindbad the sailor to delighted appreciation, after which THIS SECOND SINDBAD SAID:

The Valley of Diamonds

I was enjoying a life of the greatest pleasure and happiness until one day I got the idea of travelling to foreign parts, as I wanted to trade, to look at other countries and islands and to earn my living. After I had thought this over, I took out a large sum of money and bought trade goods and other things that would be useful on a voyage. I packed these up and when I went down to the coast I found a fine new ship with a good set of sails, fully manned and well equipped. A number of other merchants were there and they and I loaded our goods on board. We put to sea that day and had a pleasant voyage, moving from one sea and one island to another, and wherever we anchored we were met by the local traders and dignitaries as well as by buyers and sellers, with whom we bought, sold and bartered our goods.

Things went on like this until fate brought us to a

The Valley of Diamonds

pleasant island, full of trees with ripe fruits, scented flowers, singing birds and limpid streams, but without any houses or inhabitants. The captain anchored there and the merchants, together with the crew, disembarked to enjoy its trees and its birds, giving praise to the One Omnipotent God, and wondering at His great power. I had gone with this landing party and I sat down by a spring of clear water among the trees. I had some food with me and I sat there eating what God had provided for me; there was a pleasant breeze; I had no worries and, as I felt drowsy, I stretched out at my ease, enjoying the breeze and the delightful scents, until I fell fast asleep. When I woke up, there was no one to be found there, human or *jinn*. The ship had sailed off leaving me, as not a single one on board, merchants or crew, had remembered me. I turned right and left, and when I failed to find anyone at all, I fell into so deep a depression that my gall bladder almost exploded through the force of my cares, sorrow and distress. I had no possessions, no food and no drink; I was alone, and in my distress I despaired of life. I said to myself: 'The pitcher does not always remain unbroken. I escaped the first time by meeting someone who took me with him from the island to an inhabited part, but this time how very,

Sindbad the Sailor

very unlikely it is that I shall meet anyone to bring me to civilization!'

I started to weep and wail, blaming myself in my grief for what I had done, for the voyage on which I had embarked, and for the hardships I had inflicted on myself after I had been sitting at home in my own land at my ease, enjoying myself and taking pleasure in eating well, drinking good wine and wearing fine clothes, in no need of more money or goods. I regretted having left Baghdad to go to sea after what I had had to endure on my first voyage, which had brought me close to death. I recited the formula: 'We belong to God and to Him do we return,' and I was close to losing my reason. Then I got up and began to wander around, not being able to sit still in any one place. I climbed a high tree and from the top of it I started to look right and left, but all I could see was sky, water, trees, birds, islands and sand. Then, when I stared more closely, I caught sight of something white and huge on the island. I climbed down from my tree and set out to walk towards it. On I went until, when I reached it, I found it to be a white dome, very tall and with a large circumference. I went nearer and walked around it but I could find no door and the dome itself was so smoothly polished that I had

The Valley of Diamonds

neither the strength nor the agility to climb it. I marked my starting point and made a circuit of it to measure its circumference, which came to fifty full paces, and then I started to think of some way to get inside it.

It was coming on towards evening. I could no longer see the sun, and the sky had grown dark; I thought that the sun must have been hidden by a cloud, but since it was summer I found this surprising and I raised my head to look again. There, flying in the sky, I caught sight of an enormous bird with a huge body and broad wings. It was this that had covered the face of the sun, screening its rays from the island. I was even more amazed, but I remembered an old travellers' tale of a giant bird called the *rukh* that lived on an island and fed its chicks on elephants, and I became sure that my 'dome' was simply a *rukh*'s egg. While I was wondering at what Almighty God had created, the parent bird flew down and settled on the egg, covering it with its wings and stretching its legs behind it on the ground. It fell asleep – glory be to God, Who does not sleep – and I got up and undid my turban, which I folded and twisted until it was like a rope. I tied this tightly round my waist and attached myself as firmly as

I could to the bird's legs in the hope that it might take me to a civilized region, which would be better for me than staying on the island.

I spent the night awake, fearful that if I slept, the bird might fly off before I realized what was happening. When daylight came, it rose from the egg and with a loud cry it carried me up into the sky, soaring higher and higher until I thought that it must have reached the empyrean. It then began its descent and brought me back to earth, settling on a high peak. As soon as it had landed I quickly cut myself free from its legs, as I was afraid of it, although it hadn't noticed that I was there. I was trembling as I undid my turban, freeing it from the bird's legs, and I then walked off, while, for its part, the bird took something in its talons from the surface of the ground and then flew back up into the sky. When I looked to see what it had taken, I discovered that this was a huge snake with an enormous body. I watched in wonder as it left with its prey, and I then walked on further, to find myself on a high ridge under which there was a broad and deep valley, flanked by a vast and unscalable mountain that towered so high into the sky that its summit was invisible. I blamed myself for what I had done and wished that I had stayed on the island,

The Valley of Diamonds

saying to myself: 'That was better than this barren place, as there were various kinds of fruits to eat and streams from which to drink, whereas here there are no trees, fruits or streams.' I recited the formula: 'There is no power and no might except with God, the Exalted, the Almighty,' adding: 'Every time I escape from one disaster, I fall into another that is even worse.'

I got up and, plucking up my courage, walked down into the valley, where I discovered that its soil was composed of diamonds, the hard and compact stone that is used for boring holes in metals, gems, porcelain and onyx. Neither iron nor rock has any effect on it; no part of it can be cut off and the only way in which it can be broken is by the use of lead. The valley was full of snakes and serpents as big as palm trees, so huge that they could have swallowed any elephant that met them, but these only came out at night and hid away by day for fear of *rukhs* and eagles, lest they be carried away and torn in bits, although I don't know why that should be. I stayed there filled with regret at what I had done, saying to myself: 'By God, you have hastened your own death.' As evening drew on, I walked around looking for a place where I could spend the night, and I was so

Sindbad the Sailor

afraid of the snakes that in my concern for my safety I forgot about eating and drinking. Nearby I spotted a cave and when I approached it, I found that its entrance was narrow. I went into it and then pushed a large stone that I found nearby in order to block it behind me. 'I'm safe in here,' I told myself, 'and when day breaks I shall go out and see what fate brings me.'

At that point I looked inside my cave only to see a huge snake asleep over its eggs at the far end. All the hairs rose on my body and, raising my head, I entrusted myself to fate. I spent a wakeful night, and when dawn broke I removed the stone that I had used to block the entrance and came out, staggering like a drunken man through the effects of sleeplessness, hunger and fear. Then, as I was walking, suddenly, to my astonishment, a large carcass fell in front of me, although there was no one in sight. I thought of a travellers' tale that I had heard long ago of the dangers of the diamond mountains and of how the only way the diamond traders can reach these is to take and kill a sheep, which they skin and cut up. They then throw it down from the mountain into the valley and, as it is fresh when it falls, some of the stones there stick to it. The traders leave it until midday, at which point eagles and vultures swoop down

The Valley of Diamonds

on it and carry it up to the mountain in their talons. Then the traders come and scare them away from the flesh by shouting at them, after which they go up and remove the stones that are sticking to it. The flesh is left for the birds and beasts and the stones are taken back home by the traders. This is the only way in which they can get hold of the diamonds.

I looked at the carcass and remembered the story. So I went up to it and cleared away a large number of diamonds which I put in my purse and among my clothes, while I stored others in my pockets, my belt, my turban and elsewhere among my belongings. While I was doing this, another large carcass fell down and, lying on my back, I set it on my breast and tied myself to it with my turban, holding on to it and lifting it up from the ground. At that point an eagle came down and carried it off into the air in its talons, with me fastened to it. The eagle flew up to the mountain top where it deposited the carcass, and it was about to tear at it when there came a loud shout from behind it, together with the noise of sticks striking against rocks. The eagle took fright and flew off, and, having freed myself from the carcass, I stood there beside it, with my clothes all smeared with blood. At that point the trader who had shouted at the eagle came up, but when he saw me standing there he trembled and was too afraid of me to speak. He went to the carcass and turned it over, giving a great cry of disappointment and reciting the formula: 'There is no might and no power except with God. We take refuge with God from Satan, the accursed.' In his regret he struck the palms of his hands together, exclaiming: 'Alas, alas, what is this?'

I went up to him, and when he asked me who I was and why I had come there, I told him: 'Don't be afraid. I am a mortal man, of good stock, a former merchant. My story is very remarkable indeed, and there is a strange tale attached to my arrival at this mountain and this valley. There is no need for you to be frightened, for I have enough to make you happy – a large number of diamonds, of which I will give what will satisfy you, and each of my stones is better than anything else that you can get. So don't be unhappy or alarmed.'

The man thanked me, calling down blessings on me, and as we talked the other traders, each of whom had thrown down a carcass, heard the sound of our voices and came up to us. They congratulated me on my escape and, when they had taken me away with them, I told them my whole story, explaining the perils that I had endured on my voyage as well as the reason why I had got to the valley. After that, I presented many of the diamonds that I had with me to the man who had thrown down the carcass that I had used, and in his delight he renewed his blessings. The others exclaimed: 'By God, fate has granted you a second life, for you are the first man ever to come here and escape from the valley. God be praised that you are safe.'

I passed the night with them in a spot that was both pleasant and safe, delighted that I had escaped unhurt from the valley of the snakes and had got back to inhabited parts. At dawn we got up, and as we moved across the great mountain we could see huge numbers of snakes in the valley, but we kept on our way until we reached an orchard on a large and beautiful island, where there were camphor trees, each one of which could provide shade for a hundred people. Whoever wants to get some camphor must use a long tool to bore a hole at the top of the tree and then collect what comes out. The liquid camphor flows down and then solidifies like gum, as this is the sap of the tree, and when it dries up, it can be used for firewood. On the island is a type of wild beast known as the rhinoceros, which grazes there just as cows and buffaloes do in our own parts. It is a huge beast with a body larger than that of a camel, a herbivore with a single horn some ten cubits long in the centre of its head containing what looks like the image of a man. There is also a species of cattle there. According to seafarers and travellers who have visited the mountain and its districts there, this rhinoceros can carry a large elephant on its horn and go on pasturing in the island and on the shore without paying any attention to it. The elephant, impaled on its horn, will then die, and in the heat of the sun grease from its corpse will trickle on to the head of the rhinoceros. When this gets into its eyes, it will go blind, and as it then lies down by the coast, a *rukh* will swoop on it and carry it off in its talons in order to feed its chicks both with the beast itself and with what is on its horn. On the island I saw many buffaloes of a type unlike any that we have at home.

I exchanged a number of the stones that I had brought with me in my pocket from the diamond valley with the traders in return for a cash payment and some of the goods that they had brought with them, which they carried for me. I travelled on in their company, inspecting different lands and God's creations, from one valley and one city to another, buying and selling as we went, until we arrived at Basra. We stayed there for a few days and then I returned to Baghdad.

When Sindbad reached Baghdad, the City of Peace, he went to his own district and entered his house. He had with him a large number of diamonds, as well as cash and a splendid display of all kinds of goods. After he had met his family and his relatives, he dispensed alms and gave gifts to every one of his relations and companions. He began to enjoy good food and wine, to dress in fine clothes and to frequent the company of his friends. He forgot all his past sufferings, and he continued to enjoy a pleasant, relaxed and contented life, with entertainments of all sorts. All those who had heard of his return would come and ask him about his voyage and about the lands that he had visited. He would tell them of his experiences and amaze them by recounting the difficulties with which he had to contend, after which they would congratulate him on his safe return.

When he had told all this to Sindbad the landsman, those present were filled with astonishment. They all dined with him that evening and he gave orders that the second Sindbad be given a hundred *mithqals* of gold. Sindbad the landsman took these and went on his way, marvelling at what his host had endured, and, filled with gratitude, when he reached his own house, he called down blessings on him.

The next morning, when it was light, he got up and, having performed the morning prayer, he went back to the house of Sindbad the sailor as he had been told to do. On his arrival he said good morning to his host, who welcomed him, and the two sat together until the rest of the company arrived. When they had eaten and drunk and were pleasantly and cheerfully relaxed, SINDBAD THE SAILOR SAID:

The Black Giant

Listen with attention to this tale of mine, my brothers, for it is more wonderful than what I told you before, and it is God Whose knowledge and decree regulate the unknown. When I got back from my voyage I was happy, relaxed and glad to be safe, and, as I told you yesterday, I had made a large amount of money, since God had replaced for me all that I had lost. So I stayed in Baghdad for a time, enjoying my good fortune with happiness and contentment, but then I began to feel an urge to travel again and to see the world, as well as to make a profit by trading, for as the proverb says: 'The soul instructs us to do evil.' After thinking the matter over, I bought a large quantity of goods suitable for a trading voyage, packed them up and took them from Baghdad to Basra. I went to the shore, where I saw a large ship on which were many virtuous merchants and passengers, as well as a pious crew of devout and godly sailors. I embarked with them and we set sail with the blessing of Almighty God and His beneficent aid, confident of success and safety.

On we sailed from sea to sea, island to island and city to city, enjoying the sights that we saw, and happy with our trading, until one day, when we were in the middle of a boisterous sea with buffeting waves, the captain, who was keeping a lookout from the gunwale, gave a great cry, slapped his face, plucked at his beard and tore his clothes. He ordered the sails to be furled and the anchors dropped. 'What is it, captain?' we asked him, and he told us to pray for safety, explaining: 'The wind got the better of us, forcing us out to sea, and ill fortune has driven us to the mountain of the hairy ones, an ape-like folk. No one who has come there has ever escaped, and I feel in my heart that we shall all die.' Before he had finished speaking we were surrounded on all sides by apes who were like a flock of locusts, approaching our ship and spreading out on the shore. We were afraid to kill any of them or to strike them and drive them off, as we thought that if we did, they would be certain to kill us because of their numbers, since 'numbers defeat courage', as the proverb has it. We could only wait in fear lest they plunder our stores and our goods.

These apes are the ugliest of creatures, with hair like black felt and a horrifying appearance; no one can understand anything they say and they have an aversion to men. They have yellow eyes and black faces and are small, each being four spans in height. They climbed on to the anchor cables and gnawed through them with their teeth before proceeding to cut all the other ropes throughout the ship. As we could not keep head to wind, the ship came to rest by the mountain of the ape men and grounded there. The apes seized all the merchants and the others, bringing them to shore, after which they took the ship and everything in it, carrying off their spoils and going on their way. We were left on the island, unable to see the ship and without any idea where they had taken it.

We stayed there eating fruits and herbs and drinking from the streams until we caught sight of some form of habitation in the centre of the island. We walked towards this and found that it was a strongly built castle with high walls and an ebony gate whose twin leaves were standing open. We went through the gate and discovered a wide space like an extensive

Sindbad the Sailor

courtyard around which were a number of lofty doors, while at the top of it was a large and high stone bench. Cooking pots hung there on stoves surrounded by great quantities of bones, but there was nobody to be seen. We were astonished by all this and we sat down there for a while, after which we fell asleep and stayed sleeping from the forenoon until sunset. It was then that the earth shook beneath us, there was a thunderous sound, and from the top of the castle down came an enormous creature shaped like a man, black, tall as a lofty palm tree, with eyes like sparks of fire. He had tusks like those of a boar, a huge mouth like the top of a well, lips like those of a camel, which hung down over his chest, ears like large boats resting on his shoulders, and fingernails like the claws of a lion. When we saw what he looked like, we were so terrified that we almost lost our senses and were half-dead from fear and terror.

When he had reached the ground, he sat for a short while on the bench before getting up and coming over to us. He singled me out from among the other traders who were with me, grasping my hand and lifting me from the ground. Then he felt me and turned me over, but in his hands I was no more than a small mouthful, and when he had examined me as a butcher examines a sheep for slaughter, he found that I had been weakened by my sufferings and emaciated by the discomforts of the voyage, which had left me skinny. So he let go of me and picked another of my companions in my place. After turning him over and feeling him as he had felt me, he let him go too and he kept on doing this with us, one after the other, until he came to the captain, a powerful man, stout and thickset with broad shoulders. He was pleased with what he had found and, after laying hold of the man as a butcher holds his victim, he threw him down on the ground and set his foot on his neck, which he broke. Then he took a long spit, which he thrust up from the captain's backside to the crown of his head, after which the creature lit a large fire and over this he placed the spit on which the captain was skewered. He turned this round and round over the coals until, when the flesh was cooked, he took it off the fire, put it down in front of him and dismembered it, as a man dismembers a chicken. He started to tear the flesh with his fingernails and then to eat it. When he had finished it all, he gnawed the bones, leaving none of them untouched, before throwing away what was left of them at the side of the castle. He then sat for a while before stretching himself out on the bench and falling asleep, snorting like a sheep or a beast with its throat cut. He slept until morning and then got up and went off about his business.

When we were sure that he had gone we began to talk to one another, weeping over our plight and exclaiming: 'Would that we had been drowned or eaten by the ape men, for this would have been better than being roasted over the coals! That is a terrible death, but God's will be done, for there is no might and no power except with Him, the Exalted, the Omnipotent. We shall die miserably without anyone knowing about us, as there is no way left to us to escape from this place.' Then we went off into the island to look for a hiding place or a means of escape, as we didn't mind dying provided we were not roasted over the fire. But we found nowhere to hide and when evening came we were so afraid that we went back to the castle.

We had only been sitting there for a short while before the ground beneath us began to shake again and the black giant came up to us. He started turning us over and inspecting us one by one as he had done the first time, until he found one to his liking. He

The Black Giant

seized this man and treated him as he had treated the captain the day before, roasting and eating him. He then went to sleep on the bench and slept the night through, snorting like a slaughtered beast. When day broke he got up and went away, leaving us, as he had done before. We gathered together to talk, telling one another: 'By God, it would be better to throw ourselves into the sea and drown rather than be roasted, for that is an abominable death.' At that point one of our number said: 'Listen to me. We must find some way of killing the giant so as to free ourselves from the distress that he has caused us, and also to free our fellow Muslims from his hostility and tyranny.' I said: 'Brothers, listen. If we have to kill him, we must move some of these timbers and this wood and make ourselves a species of ship. If we then think of a way of killing him, we can embark on it and put out to sea, going wherever God wills, or else we could stay here until a ship sails by on which we might take passage. If we fail to kill him, we can come down and put out to sea, for even if we drown we would still escape being slaughtered and roasted over the fire. If we escape, we escape, and if we drown, we die as martyrs.' 'This is sound advice,' they all agreed, and we then set to work moving timbers

Sindbad the Sailor

out of the castle and building a boat which we moored by the shore, loading it with some provisions. Afterwards we went back to the castle.

When evening came, the earth shook and the black giant arrived like a ravening dog. He turned us over and felt us one by one before picking out one of us, whom he treated as he had done the others. Having eaten him he fell asleep on the bench, with thunderous snorts. We got up and took two iron spits from those that were standing there. We put them in the fierce fire until they were red hot, like burning coals, and then, gripping them firmly, we carried them to the sleeping, snoring giant, placed them on his eyes and then bore down on them with our combined strength as firmly as we could. The spits entered his eyes and blinded him, at which he terrified us by uttering a great cry. He sprang up from the bench and began to hunt for us as we fled right and left. In his blinded state he could not see us, but we were still terrified of him, thinking that our last hour had come and despairing of escape. He felt his way to the door and went out bellowing, leaving us quaking with fear as the earth shook beneath our feet because of the violence of his cries. We followed him out as he went off in search of us, but then he came back

The Black Giant

with two others, larger and more ferocious-looking than himself. When we saw him and his even more hideous companions, we panicked, and as they caught sight of us and hurried towards us, we boarded our boat, cast off its moorings and drove it out to sea. Each of the giants had a huge rock in his hands, which they threw at us, killing most of us and leaving only me and two others.

The boat took us to another island and there we walked until nightfall, when, in our wretched state, we fell asleep for a little while, but when we woke, it was only to see that a huge snake with an enormous body and a wide belly had coiled around us. It made for one of us and swallowed his body as far as the shoulders, after which it gulped down the rest of him and we could hear his ribs cracking in its belly. Then it went off, leaving us astonished, filled with grief for our companion and fearful for our own safety. We exclaimed: 'By God, it is amazing that each death should be more hideous than the one before! We were glad to have got away from the black giant but our joy has been short-lived, and there is no might and no power except with God. By God, we managed to escape from the giant and from death by drowning, but how are we to escape from this sinister monster?'

Sindbad the Sailor

We walked around the island until evening, eating its fruits and drinking from its streams, until we discovered a huge and lofty tree which we climbed in order to sleep there. I was up on the top-most branch, and when night fell the snake came through the darkness and, having looked right and left, it made for our tree and swarmed up until it had reached my companion. It swallowed his body as far as the shoulders, and then coiled round the tree with him until I heard his bones cracking in its belly, after which it swallowed the rest of him before my eyes. It then slid down the tree and went away. I stayed on my branch for the rest of the night and when daylight came, I climbed down again, half-dead with fear and terror. I thought of throwing myself into the sea to find rest from the troubles of the world, but I could not bring myself to commit suicide, as life is dear. So I fastened a broad wooden beam across my feet with two other similar beams on my right and my left sides, another over my stomach, and a very large one laterally over my head, to match the one beneath my feet. I was in the middle of these beams, which encased me on all sides, and after I had fastened them securely, I threw myself, with all of them, on to the ground. I lay between them as though I was in a cupboard, and

The Black Giant

when night fell and the snake arrived as usual, it saw me and made for me but could not swallow me up as I was protected on all sides by the beams and, although it circled round, it could find no way to reach me. I watched it, nearly dead with fear, as it went off and then came back, constantly trying to get to me in order to swallow me, but the beams that I had fastened all around me prevented it. This continued from sunset until dawn, and when the sun rose the snake went off, frustrated and angry, and I then stretched out my hand and freed myself from the beams, still half-dead because of the terror that it had inflicted on me.

After I had got up, I walked to the end of the island, and when I looked out from the shore, there far out at sea was a ship. I took a large branch and waved it in its direction, calling out to the sailors. They saw me and told each other: 'We must look to see what this is, as it might be a man.' When they had sailed near enough to hear my shouts, they came in and brought me on board. They asked for my story, and I told them everything that had happened to me from beginning to end, and they were amazed at the hardships I had endured. They gave me some of their own clothes to hide my nakedness and then brought me

Sindbad the Sailor

some food, allowing me to eat my fill, as well as providing me with cold, fresh water. This revived and refreshed me, and such was my relief that it was as though God had brought me back from the dead. I praised and thanked Him for His abundant grace, and although I had been sure that I was doomed, I regained my composure to such an extent that it seemed as if all my perils had been a dream.

My rescuers sailed on with a fair wind granted by Almighty God until we came in sight of an island called al-Salahita, where the captain dropped anchor. Everyone disembarked, merchants and passengers alike, unloading their wares in order to trade. The master of the ship then turned to me and said: 'Listen to me. You are a poor stranger who has gone through a terrifying ordeal, as you have told us, and so I want to do something for you that may help you get back to your own land and cause you to bless me for the rest of your life.' When I had thanked him for this he went on to say: 'We lost one of our passengers, and we don't know whether he is alive or dead, as we have heard no news of him. I propose to hand over his goods to you so that you may sell them here in return for payment that we shall give you for your trouble. Anything left over we shall keep until we get back to

The Black Giant

Baghdad, where we can make enquiries about his family, and we shall then hand over the rest of the goods to them, as well as the price of what has been sold. Are you prepared to take charge of these things, land them on the island and trade with them?' 'To hear is to obey, sir,' I said, adding my blessings and thanks for his generous conduct. So he ordered the porters and members of the crew to unload the goods on the shore and then to hand them over to me. The ship's clerk asked him whose goods these were so that he could enter the name of the merchant who owned them. 'Write on them the name of Sindbad the sailor,' the master told him, 'the man who came out with us but was lost on an island. We never heard of him again, and I want this stranger to sell them and give us what they fetch in return for a fee for his trouble in selling them. Whatever is unsold we can take back to Baghdad, and if we find Sindbad, we can give it back to him, but if not, we can hand it over to his family in the city.' 'Well said!' exclaimed the clerk. 'That is a good plan.'

When I heard the master say that the bales were to be entered under my name, I told myself: 'By God, I am Sindbad the sailor, who was one of those lost on the island,' but I waited in patience until the

Sindbad the Sailor

merchants had left the ship and were all there together talking about trade. It was then that I went up to the master and said: 'Sir, do you know anything about the owner of these bales that you have entrusted to me to sell for him?' 'I know nothing about his circumstances,' the master replied, 'only that he was a Baghdadi called Sindbad the sailor. We anchored off an island, where a large number of our people were lost in the sea, including Sindbad, and until this day we have heard nothing more about him.' At that I gave a great cry and said: 'Master, may God keep you safe. Know that I am Sindbad the sailor and that I was not drowned. When you anchored there, I landed with the other merchants and passengers and went off to a corner of the island, taking some food with me. I so enjoyed sitting there that I became drowsy and fell into the soundest of sleeps, and when I woke up I found the ship gone and no one else there with me. So these are my belongings and my goods. All the merchants who fetch diamonds saw me when I was on the diamond mountain and they will confirm that I am, in fact, Sindbad. For I told them the story of what had happened to me on your ship and how you forgot about me and left me lying asleep on the island and what happened to me after I woke up and found no one there.'

When the merchants and the passengers heard what I had to say, they gathered around me, some believing me and some convinced that I was lying. While things were still undecided, one of the merchants who heard me mention the diamond valley got up and came to me. He asked the company to listen to him and said: 'I told you of the most remarkable thing that I saw on my travels, which happened when my companions and I were throwing down carcasses into the diamond valley. I threw mine down as usual and when it was brought up by an eagle there was a man attached to it. You didn't believe me and thought that I was lying.' 'Yes,' said the others, 'you certainly told us this and we didn't believe you.' 'Here is the man who was clinging to it,' said the merchant. 'He presented me with valuable diamonds whose like is nowhere to be found, giving me more than I had ever got from a carcass, and he then stayed with me until we reached Basra, after which he went off to his own city. My companions and I said goodbye to him and went back to our own lands. This is the man. He told us that his name was Sindbad the sailor and that his ship had gone off leaving him on the island. He has come here as proof to you that I was telling the truth. All these goods are his; he told us about them when we met and what he has said has been shown to be true.'

When the master heard this he came up to me and looked carefully at me for some time. Then he asked: 'What mark is on your goods?' I told him what it was and then I mentioned some dealings that we had had together on our voyage from Basra. He was then convinced that I really was Sindbad and embraced me, saluting me and congratulating me on my safe return. 'By God, sir,' he said, 'yours is a remarkable story and a strange affair. Praise be to God, Who has reunited us and returned your goods and possessions to you.' After that I used my expertise to dispose of my goods, making a great profit on the trip. I was delighted by this, congratulating myself on my safety and on the return of my possessions.

We continued to trade among the islands until we came to Sind, where we bought and sold, and in the sea there I came across innumerable wonders. Among them was a fish that looked like a cow and another resembling a donkey, together with a bird that came out of a mollusc shell, laying its eggs and rearing its

The Black Giant

chicks on the surface of the sea and never coming out on to dry land at all. On we sailed, with the permission of Almighty God, enjoying a fair wind and a pleasant voyage until we got back to Basra. I stayed there for a few days before going to Baghdad, where I went to my own district and entered my house, greeting my family as well as my friends and companions. Feeling joyful at my safe return to my country, my family, my city and my properties, I distributed alms, made gifts, clothed widows and orphans and gathered together my companions and friends. I went on like this, eating, drinking and enjoying myself with good food, good wine and friends, having made a vast profit from my voyage and having forgotten all that had happened to me and the hardships and terrors that I had endured.

Sindbad the sailor then gave orders that Sindbad the porter should be given his usual hundred *mithqals* of gold and that tables should be laid with food. The whole company ate with him, still filled with amazement at the tale of their host's experiences, and then after supper they went on their ways. As for Sindbad the porter, he took his gold and went off astonished by what he had heard. He spent the night at home

Sindbad the Sailor

and the next morning, when it was light, he got up, performed the morning prayer and walked to the house of Sindbad the sailor, greeting him as he went in. His host welcomed him with gladness and delight, making him sit with him until the rest of his companions arrived. Food was produced and they ate, drank and enjoyed themselves, until SINDBAD BEGAN TO SPEAK:

The Cannibal King

Know, my brothers, that when I got back to Baghdad and met my companions, my family and my friends I enjoyed a life of the greatest happiness, contentment and relaxation, forgetting everything in my well-being, and drowning in pleasure and delight in the company of my friends and companions. It was while my life was at its most pleasant that I felt a pernicious urge to travel to foreign parts, to associate with different races and to trade and make a profit. Having thought this over, I bought more valuable goods, suitable for a voyage, than I had ever taken before, packing them into bales. When I had gone down from Baghdad to Basra I loaded them on a ship, taking with me a number of the leading Basran merchants. We put out, with the blessing of Almighty God, on to the turbulent and boisterous sea and for a number of nights and days we had a good voyage, passing

Sindbad the Sailor

from island to island and sea to sea until one day we met a contrary wind. The master used the anchors to bring us to a halt in mid-ocean lest we founder there, but while we were addressing our supplications to Almighty God a violent gale blew up, which tore our sails to shreds, plunging all on board into the sea, together with all their bales, goods and belongings.

I was with the others in the sea. I swam for half a day, but I had given up all hope when Almighty God sent me part of one of the ship's timbers on to which I climbed, together with some of the other merchants. We huddled together as we rode on it, paddling with our legs, and being helped by the waves and the wind. This went on for a day and a night, but in the forenoon of the second day the wind rose and the sea became stormy, with powerful waves. The current then cast us up on an island, half-dead through lack of sleep, fatigue and cold, hunger, thirst and fear. Later, when we walked around the place, we found many plants, some of which we ate to allay our hunger and sustain us, and we spent the night by the shore. The next day, when it was light, we got up and continued to explore the various parts of the island. In the distance we caught sight of a building and kept on walking towards it until we stood at its

The Cannibal King

door. While we were there, out came a crowd of naked men, who took hold of us without a word and brought us to their king. We sat down at his command and food was brought which we did not recognize and whose like we had never seen in our lives. I could not bring myself to take it and so I ate nothing, unlike my companions, and this abstemiousness on my part was thanks to the grace of Almighty God as it was this that has allowed me to live until now.

When my companions tasted the food, their wits went wandering; they fell on it like madmen and were no longer the same men. The king's servants then fetched them coconut oil, some of which was poured out as drink and some of which was smeared over them. When my companions drank the oil their eyes swivelled in their heads and they started to eat the food in an unnatural way. I felt sorry for them, but I did not know what to do about it and I was filled with great uneasiness, fearing for my own life at the hands of the naked men. For when I looked at them closely I could see that they were Magians and that the king of their city was a *ghul*. They would bring him everyone who came to their country or whom they saw or met in their valley or its roads. The newcomer would then be given that food and anointed with that oil;

Sindbad the Sailor

his belly would swell so that he could eat more and more; he would lose his mind and his powers of thought until he became like an imbecile. The Magians would continue to stuff him with food and coconut oil drink until, when he was fat enough, they would cut his throat and feed him to the king. They themselves would eat human flesh unroasted and raw.

When I saw this I was filled with distress both for myself and for my comrades, who, in their bewildered state, did not realize what was being done to them. They were put in the charge of a man who would herd them around the island like cattle; as for me, fear and hunger made me weak and sickly, and my flesh clung to my bones. The Magians, seeing my condition, left me alone and forgot about me. Not one of them remembered me or thought about me, and so one day I contrived to move from the place where they were, and walked away, leaving it far behind me. I then saw a herdsman sitting on a high promontory, and when I looked more closely I could see that he was the man who had been given the job of pasturing not only my companions but many others as well, who were in the same state. When he saw me he realized that I was still in possession of my wits and was not suffering from what had affected the others. So

The Cannibal King

he gestured to me from far off, indicating that I should turn back and then take the road to the right, which would lead to the main highway. I followed his instructions and went back, and when I saw a road on my right I followed it, at times running in terror and then walking more slowly until I was rested. I went on like this until I was out of sight of the man who had shown me the way and I could no longer see him nor could he see me.

The sun then set and as darkness fell I sat down to rest, intending to go to sleep, but I was too afraid, too hungry and too tired to sleep that night. At midnight I got up and walked further into the island, carrying on until daybreak, when the sun rose over the hilltops and the valleys. I was exhausted, hungry and thirsty and so I started to eat grass and some of the island plants, going on until I had satisfied my hunger and was satiated. Then I got up and walked on, and I continued like this for the whole of the day and the night, eating plants whenever I was hungry. This went on for seven days and seven nights until, on the morning of the eighth day, I caught sight of something in the distance and set off towards it. I got to my destination after sunset and looked carefully at it from far off, as my heart was still fluttering because of my earlier sufferings, but it turned out to be a group of men gathering peppercorns. They saw me as I approached and quickly came and surrounded me on all sides, asking me who I was and where I had come from. I told them that I was a poor unfortunate and then went on to give them my whole story, explaining my perils, hardships and sufferings.

'By God,' they exclaimed, 'this is an amazing story, but how did you escape from the blacks and get away from them on the island? There are vast numbers of them and as they are cannibals no one can pass them in safety.' So I told them what had happened to me and how they had taken my companions by feeding them on some food which I did not eat. They were astonished by my experiences and, after congratulating me on my safety, they made me sit with them until they had finished their work, after which they brought me some tasty food, which I ate because I was starving. I stayed with them for some time and then they took me with them on a ship, which brought me to the island where they lived. There they presented me to their king, whom I greeted and who welcomed me courteously and asked me about myself. I told him of my circumstances and of all my experiences from the day that I left Baghdad until I came to him. He and those with him were filled

The Cannibal King

with astonishment at this tale. He told me to sit by him and he then ordered food to be brought, from which I ate my fill. Then I washed my hands and thanked, praised and extolled Almighty God for His grace.

When I left the king's court I looked around the city, which was a thriving place, populous and wealthy, well stocked with provisions and full of markets and trade goods, as well as with both buyers and sellers. I was pleased and happy to have got there, and I made friends with the people, and their king, who treated me with more honour and respect than he showed to his own leading citizens. I observed that all of them, high and low alike, rode good horses but without saddles. I was surprised at that and I asked the king why it was, pointing out that a saddle made things more comfortable for the rider and allowed him to exert more force. 'What is a saddle?' he asked, adding: 'I have never seen one or ridden on one in my life.' 'Would you allow me to make you one so that you could ride on it and see its advantages?' I asked, and when he told me to carry on, I asked him to provide me with some wood. He ordered everything I needed to be fetched, after which I looked for a clever carpenter and sat teaching him how saddles should be made. Then I got wool, carded it and made it into felt, after which I covered the saddle in leather and polished it before attaching bands and fastening the girth. Next I fetched a smith and explained to him how to make stirrups. When he had made a large pair, I filed them down and then covered them with tin, giving them fringes of silk. I fetched one of the best of the king's horses, a stallion, which I then saddled and bridled, and when I had attached the stirrups I brought him to the king. What I had done took the fancy of the king, who was filled with admiration, and, having thanked me, he mounted the horse and was delighted by the saddle. In return for my work he gave me a huge reward, and when his vizier saw what I had made, he asked for another saddle like it. I made him one and after that all the principal officers of state and the state officials began to ask me to make them saddles. I taught the carpenter how to produce them and showed the smith how to make stirrups, after which we started to manufacture them and to sell them to great men and the employers of labour. This brought me a great deal of money and I became a man of importance in the city, commanding ever greater affection and enjoying high status both with the king and with his court, and also with the leading citizens and state officials.

The Cannibal King

One day, while I was sitting with the king enjoying my dignity to the full, he said to me: 'You have become a respected and honoured companion of ours; you are one of us and we cannot bear to be parted from you or that you should leave our city. I have something to ask of you, and I want you to obey me and not to reject my request.' 'What is it that you want of me, your majesty?' I asked, adding: 'I cannot refuse you, because you have treated me with such kindness, favour and generosity, and I thank God that I have become one of your servants.' The king said: 'I want you to take a wife here, a beautiful, graceful and witty lady, as wealthy as she is lovely, so that you may become one of our citizens and I can lodge you with me in my palace. Do not disobey me or reject my proposal.' When I heard what he said, I was too embarrassed to speak and stayed silent. Then, when he asked why I did not answer, I said: 'My master, king of the age, your commands must be obeyed.' He sent at once for the *qadi* and the notaries, and he married me on the spot to a noble lady of high birth and great wealth, who combined beauty and grace with her distinguished ancestry, and who was the owner of houses, properties and estates.

After the king had married me to the great lady,

Sindbad the Sailor

he presented me with a fine, large detached house, providing me with eunuchs and retainers and assigning me pay and allowances. I lived a life of ease, happy and relaxed, forgetting all the toils, difficulties and hardships that I had experienced. I told myself that when I went back to my own country, I would take my wife with me, but there is no avoiding fate and no one knows what will happen to him. My wife and I were deeply in love; we lived in harmony, enjoying a life of pleasure and plenty over a period of time. Almighty God then widowed a neighbour of mine, and, as he was a friend of mine, I went to his house to offer my condolences on his loss. I found him in the worst of states, full of care and sick at heart. I tried to console him by saying: 'Don't grieve for your wife. Almighty God will see that you are well recompensed by providing you with another, more beautiful one, and, if it is His will, you will live a long life.' He wept bitterly and said: 'My friend, how can I marry another wife and how can God compensate me with a better one when I have only one day left to live?' 'Come back to your senses, brother,' I told him, 'and don't forecast your own death, for you are sound and healthy.' 'My friend,' he said, 'I swear by your life that tomorrow you will lose me and never see me

The Cannibal King

again.' 'How can that be?' I asked him, and he told me: 'Today my wife will be buried and I shall be buried with her in the same grave. It is the custom here that, when a wife dies, her husband is buried alive with her, while if the husband dies it is the wife who suffers this fate, so that neither partner may enjoy life after the death of the other.' 'By God,' I exclaimed, 'what a dreadful custom! This is unbearable!'

While we were talking, a group comprising the bulk of the citizens of the town arrived and started to pay condolences to my friend on the loss of his wife and on his own fate. They began to lay out the corpse in their usual way, fetching a coffin in which they carried it, accompanied by the husband. They took it out of the city to a place on the side of a mountain overlooking the sea. When they got there, they lifted up a huge stone, under which could be seen a rocky cleft like the shaft of a well.

They threw the woman's body down this, into what I could see was a great underground pit. Then they brought my friend, tied a rope round his waist and lowered him into the pit, providing him with a large jug of fresh water and seven loaves by way of provisions. When he had been lowered down, he freed himself from the rope, which they pulled up before

Sindbad the Sailor

putting the stone back in its place and going away, leaving my friend with his wife in the pit.

I said to myself: 'By God, this death is even more frightful than the previous one,' and I went to the king and asked him how it was that in his country they buried the living with the dead. He said: 'This is our custom here. When the husband dies we bury his wife with him, and when the wife dies we bury her husband alive so that they may not be parted either in life or in death. This is a tradition handed down from our ancestors.' I asked him: 'O king of the age, in the case of a foreigner like me, if his wife dies here, would you treat him as you treated my friend?' 'Yes,' he replied, 'we would bury him with her just as you have seen.'

When I heard this, I was so concerned and distressed for myself that my gall bladder almost split and in my dismay I began to fear that my wife might die before me and that I would be buried alive with her. Then I tried to console myself, telling myself that it might be I who died first, for no one knows who will be first and who second. I tried to amuse myself in various ways, but within a short time my wife fell ill and a few days later she was dead. Most of the townsfolk came to pay their condolences to me and her family, and among those who came in accordance

The Cannibal King

with their custom was the king. They fetched professionals who washed her corpse and dressed her in the most splendid of her clothes together with the best of her jewellery, necklaces and precious gems before placing her in her coffin. They then carried her off to the mountain, removed the stone from the mouth of the pit and threw her into it. My friends and my wife's family came up to take a last farewell of me. I was calling out: 'I'm a foreigner! I don't have to put up with your customs,' but they did not listen or pay any attention to me. Instead they seized me and used force to tie me up, attaching the seven loaves and the jug of fresh water that their custom required, before lowering me into the pit, which turned out to be a vast cavern under the mountain. 'Loose yourself from the rope!' they shouted, but I wasn't willing to do that and so they threw the rest of it down on top of me before replacing the huge stone that covered the entrance and going away.

In the pit I came across very many corpses together with a foul stink of putrefaction and I blamed myself for my own actions, telling myself that I deserved everything that had happened to me. While I was there I could not distinguish night from day and I began by putting myself on short rations, not eating until I was half-dead with hunger and drinking only when I was violently thirsty, because I was afraid of exhausting my food and my water. I recited the formula: 'There is no might and no power except with God, the Exalted, the Omnipotent,' adding: 'Why did I have the misfortune to marry in this city? Every time I say to myself that I have escaped from one disaster, I fall into another that is worse. By God, this is a terrible death. I wish that I had been drowned at sea or had died on the mountains, for that would have been better than this miserable end.'

I went on like this, blaming myself, sleeping on the bones of the dead and calling on Almighty God to aid me. I longed for death, but, in spite of my plight, death would not come and this continued until I was consumed by hunger and parched by thirst. I sat down and felt for my bread, after which I ate a little and drank a little before getting up and walking round the cavern. This was wide with some empty hollows, but the surface was covered with bodies as well as old dry bones. I made a place for myself at the side of it, far away from the recent corpses, and there I slept. I now had very little food left and I would only take one mouthful and one sip of water each day or at even longer intervals for fear of using

The Cannibal King

up both food and water before my death. Things went on like this until one day, as I was sitting thinking about what I would do when my provisions were exhausted, the stone was suddenly moved and light shone down on me. While I was wondering what was happening, I saw people standing at the head of the shaft. They lowered a dead man and a live woman, who was weeping and screaming, and with her they sent down a large quantity of food and water. I watched her but she didn't see me, and when the stone had been replaced and the people had gone, I stood up with the shin bone of a dead man in my hand and, going up to her, I struck her on the middle of her head. She fell unconscious on the ground and I struck her a second and a third time, so killing her. I took her bread and what else she had, for I noticed she had with her a large quantity of ornaments, robes, necklaces, jewels and precious stones. When I had removed her food and water, I sat down to sleep in my place by the side of the cavern. Later I began to eat as little of the food as was needed to keep me alive lest it be used up too soon, leaving me to die of hunger and thirst.

I stayed down there for some time, killing all those who were buried alive with the dead and taking their food and water in order to survive. Then, one day, I

Sindbad the Sailor

woke from sleep to hear something making a noise at the side of the cavern. I asked myself what it could be, and so I got up and went towards whatever it was, carrying with me a dead man's shin bone. When the thing that was making the noise heard me, it fled away and I could see that it was an animal. I followed it to the upper part of the cave and there coming through a little hole I could see a ray of light like a star, appearing and then disappearing. At the sight of this, I made my way towards it, and the nearer I got, the broader the beam of light became, leaving me certain that there was an opening in the cave leading to the outer world. 'There must be some reason for this,' I said to myself. 'Either it is another opening, like the one through which I was lowered, or it is crack leading out of here.' I thought the matter over for a while and then went towards the light. Here I discovered that there was a tunnel dug by wild beasts from the surface of the mountain to allow them to get in, eat their fill of the corpses and then get out again. On seeing this I calmed down, regained my composure and relaxed, being certain that, after my brush with death, I would manage to stay alive.

Like a man in a dream, I struggled through the tunnel to find myself overlooking the sea coast on a

The Cannibal King

high and impassable mountain promontory that cut off the island and its city from the seas that met there. In my delight, I gave praise and thanks to God, and then, taking heart, I went back through the tunnel to the cave and removed all the food and water that I had saved. I took some clothes from the dead to put on in place of my own, and I also collected a quantity of what they were wearing in the way of necklaces, gems, strings of pearls and jewellery of silver and gold, studded with precious stones of all kinds, together with other rare items. I fastened the clothes of the dead to my own and went through the tunnel to stand by the seashore. Every day I would go back down to inspect the cave, and whenever there was a burial I would kill the survivor, whether it was a man or a woman, and take the food and the water. Then I would go out of the tunnel and sit by the shore, waiting for Almighty God to send me relief in the form of a passing ship. I started to remove all the jewellery that I could see from the cave, tying it up in dead men's clothes.

Things went on like this for some time until one day, while I was sitting by the shore, I saw a passing ship out at sea in the middle of the waves. I took something white from the clothes of the dead, fastened it to a stick and ran along with it, parallel to the shore, waving it

Sindbad the Sailor

towards the ship, until the crew turned and caught sight of me as I stood on a high point. They put in towards me until they could hear my voice, and then they sent me a boat manned by some of their crew. As they came close they said: 'Who are you and why are you sitting there? How did you get to this mountain? Never in our lives have we seen anyone who managed to reach it.' I told them: 'I'm a merchant whose ship was sunk. I got on a plank together with my belongings, and by God's aid I was able to come up on shore here, bringing them with me, but only after I had exerted myself and used all my skill in a hard struggle.'

The sailors took me with them in the boat, carrying what I had fetched from the cave tied up in clothes and shrouds. They brought me to the ship, together with all of these things, and took me to the master, who asked: 'Man, how did you get here? This is a huge mountain with a great city on the other side of it, but although I have spent my life sailing this sea and passing by it, I have never seen anything on it except beasts and birds.' 'I'm a merchant,' I told him, 'but the large ship on which I was sailing broke up and sank. All these goods of mine, and the clothes that you see, were plunged into the water, but I managed to load them on to a large beam from the ship

The Cannibal King

and fate helped me to come to shore by this mountain, after which I waited for someone to pass by and take me off.' I said nothing about what had happened to me in the city or in the cave, for fear that someone on board might be from the city. Then I took a quantity of my goods to the master of the ship and said: 'Sir, it is thanks to you that I have escaped from this mountain, so please take these things in return for the kindness you have shown me.' The master did not accept, insisting: 'We take no gifts from anyone, and if we see a shipwrecked man on the coast or on an island we take him with us and give him food and water. If he is naked we clothe him, and when we reach a safe haven we give him a present from what we have with us as an act of generosity for the sake of Almighty God.' On hearing that, I prayed God to grant him a long life.

We then sailed on from island to island and from sea to sea. I was hopeful that I would escape my difficulties, but although I was full of joy that I had been saved, whenever I thought of how I had sat in the cave with my wife I would almost go out of my mind. Through the power of God we came safely to Basra, where I landed and spent a few days before going on to Baghdad. There I went to my own district

Sindbad the Sailor

and, when I had entered my house, I met my family and friends and asked them how they were. They were delighted by my safe return and congratulated me. I then stored all the goods that I had with me in my warehouses and distributed alms and gifts, providing clothes for the widows and orphans. I was filled with joy and delight and renewed old ties with friends and companions, enjoying amusements and entertainments.

These, then, were the most remarkable things that happened to me on my fourth voyage, but, my brother, dine with me this evening, take your usual present of gold, come back tomorrow and I shall tell you of my experiences on my fifth voyage, as these were stranger and more wonderful than anything that happened before.

Sindbad the sailor then ordered that Sindbad the porter be given a hundred *mithqals* of gold. Tables were set and the company dined, before dispersing in a state of astonishment, as each story was more surprising than the last. Sindbad the porter went home and spent the night filled with happiness and contentedness as well as with amazement.

1. BOCCACCIO · *Mrs Rosie and the Priest*
2. GERARD MANLEY HOPKINS · *As kingfishers catch fire*
3. *The Saga of Gunnlaug Serpent-tongue*
4. THOMAS DE QUINCEY · *On Murder Considered as One of the Fine Arts*
5. FRIEDRICH NIETZSCHE · *Aphorisms on Love and Hate*
6. JOHN RUSKIN · *Traffic*
7. PU SONGLING · *Wailing Ghosts*
8. JONATHAN SWIFT · *A Modest Proposal*
9. *Three Tang Dynasty Poets*
10. WALT WHITMAN · *On the Beach at Night Alone*
11. KENKŌ · *A Cup of Sake Beneath the Cherry Trees*
12. BALTASAR GRACIÁN · *How to Use Your Enemies*
13. JOHN KEATS · *The Eve of St Agnes*
14. THOMAS HARDY · *Woman much missed*
15. GUY DE MAUPASSANT · *Femme Fatale*
16. MARCO POLO · *Travels in the Land of Serpents and Pearls*
17. SUETONIUS · *Caligula*
18. APOLLONIUS OF RHODES · *Jason and Medea*
19. ROBERT LOUIS STEVENSON · *Olalla*
20. KARL MARX AND FRIEDRICH ENGELS · *The Communist Manifesto*
21. PETRONIUS · *Trimalchio's Feast*
22. JOHANN PETER HEBEL · *How a Ghastly Story Was Brought to Light by a Common or Garden Butcher's Dog*
23. HANS CHRISTIAN ANDERSEN · *The Tinder Box*
24. RUDYARD KIPLING · *The Gate of the Hundred Sorrows*
25. DANTE · *Circles of Hell*
26. HENRY MAYHEW · *Of Street Piemen*
27. HAFEZ · *The nightingales are drunk*
28. GEOFFREY CHAUCER · *The Wife of Bath*
29. MICHEL DE MONTAIGNE · *How We Weep and Laugh at the Same Thing*
30. THOMAS NASHE · *The Terrors of the Night*
31. EDGAR ALLAN POE · *The Tell-Tale Heart*
32. MARY KINGSLEY · *A Hippo Banquet*
33. JANE AUSTEN · *The Beautifull Cassandra*
34. ANTON CHEKHOV · *Gooseberries*
35. SAMUEL TAYLOR COLERIDGE · *Well, they are gone, and here must I remain*
36. JOHANN WOLFGANG VON GOETHE · *Sketchy, Doubtful, Incomplete Jottings*
37. CHARLES DICKENS · *The Great Winglebury Duel*
38. HERMAN MELVILLE · *The Maldive Shark*
39. ELIZABETH GASKELL · *The Old Nurse's Story*
40. NIKOLAY LESKOV · *The Steel Flea*

41. HONORÉ DE BALZAC · *The Atheist's Mass*
42. CHARLOTTE PERKINS GILMAN · *The Yellow Wall-Paper*
43. C.P. CAVAFY · *Remember, Body . . .*
44. FYODOR DOSTOEVSKY · *The Meek One*
45. GUSTAVE FLAUBERT · *A Simple Heart*
46. NIKOLAI GOGOL · *The Nose*
47. SAMUEL PEPYS · *The Great Fire of London*
48. EDITH WHARTON · *The Reckoning*
49. HENRY JAMES · *The Figure in the Carpet*
50. WILFRED OWEN · *Anthem For Doomed Youth*
51. WOLFGANG AMADEUS MOZART · *My Dearest Father*
52. PLATO · *Socrates' Defence*
53. CHRISTINA ROSSETTI · *Goblin Market*
54. *Sindbad the Sailor*
55. SOPHOCLES · *Antigone*
56. RYŪNOSUKE AKUTAGAWA · *The Life of a Stupid Man*
57. LEO TOLSTOY · *How Much Land Does A Man Need?*
58. GIORGIO VASARI · *Leonardo da Vinci*
59. OSCAR WILDE · *Lord Arthur Savile's Crime*
60. SHEN FU · *The Old Man of the Moon*
61. AESOP · *The Dolphins, the Whales and the Gudgeon*
62. MATSUO BASHŌ · *Lips too Chilled*
63. EMILY BRONTË · *The Night is Darkening Round Me*
64. JOSEPH CONRAD · *To-morrow*
65. RICHARD HAKLUYT · *The Voyage of Sir Francis Drake Around the Whole Globe*
66. KATE CHOPIN · *A Pair of Silk Stockings*
67. CHARLES DARWIN · *It was snowing butterflies*
68. BROTHERS GRIMM · *The Robber Bridegroom*
69. CATULLUS · *I Hate and I Love*
70. HOMER · *Circe and the Cyclops*
71. D. H. LAWRENCE · *Il Duro*
72. KATHERINE MANSFIELD · *Miss Brill*
73. OVID · *The Fall of Icarus*
74. SAPPHO · *Come Close*
75. IVAN TURGENEV · *Kasyan from the Beautiful Lands*
76. VIRGIL · *O Cruel Alexis*
77. H. G. WELLS · *A Slip under the Microscope*
78. HERODOTUS · *The Madness of Cambyses*
79. *Speaking of Siva*
80. *The Dhammapada*

'It's a dreadful thing to yield . . . but resist now? Lay my pride bare to the blows of ruin? That's dreadful too.'

SOPHOCLES
Born 496 BC, Colonus, Greece
Died *c.* 406 BC, Athens, Greece

The play was written in its original Greek in or before
441 BC and is taken from *The Three Theban Plays*,
translated by Robert Fagles.

SOPHOCLES IN PENGUIN CLASSICS
The Three Theban Plays
Electra and Other Plays

SOPHOCLES

Antigone

Translated by
Robert Fagles

PENGUIN BOOKS

PENGUIN CLASSICS

UK | USA | Canada | Ireland | Australia
India | New Zealand | South Africa

Penguin Books is part of the Penguin Random House group of companies
whose addresses can be found at global.penguinrandomhouse.com.

This edition published in Penguin Classics 2015

012

Translation copyright © Robert Fagles, 1982, 1984

The moral right of the translator has been asserted

Set in 7.25/10 pt Baskerville 10 Pro
Typeset by Jouve (UK), Milton Keynes
Printed and bound in Great Britain by Clays Ltd, Elcograf S.p.A.

A CIP catalogue record for this book is available from the British Library

ISBN: 978-0-141-39770-2

www.greenpenguin.co.uk

Penguin Random House is committed to a sustainable future for our business, our readers and our planet. This book is made from Forest Stewardship Council® certified paper.

Characters

ANTIGONE
daughter of Oedipus and Jocasta

ISMENE
sister of Antigone

A CHORUS
of old Theban citizens and their **LEADER**

CREON
king of Thebes, uncle of Antigone and Ismene

A SENTRY

HAEMON
son of Creon and Eurydice

TIRESIAS
a blind prophet

A MESSENGER

EURYDICE
wife of Creon

Guards, attendants, and a boy

TIME AND SCENE: *The royal house of Thebes. It is still night, and the invading armies of Argos have just been driven from the city. Fighting on opposite sides, the sons of Oedipus, Eteocles and Polynices, have killed each other in combat. Their uncle,* CREON, *is now king of Thebes.*

Enter ANTIGONE, *slipping through the central doors of the palace. She motions to her sister,* ISMENE, *who follows her cautiously toward an altar at the center of the stage.*

ANTIGONE:
My own flesh and blood – dear sister, dear Ismene,
how many griefs our father Oedipus handed down!
Do you know one, I ask you, one grief
that Zeus will not perfect for the two of us
while we still live and breathe? There's nothing,
no pain – our lives are pain – no private shame,
no public disgrace, nothing I haven't seen
in your griefs and mine. And now this:
an emergency decree, they say, the Commander
has just now declared for all of Thebes.
What, haven't you heard? Don't you see?
The doom reserved for enemies
marches on the ones we love the most.

ISMENE:
Not I, I haven't heard a word, Antigone.
Nothing of loved ones,
no joy or pain has come my way, not since
the two of us were robbed of our two brothers,
both gone in a day, a double blow –
not since the armies of Argos vanished,
just this very night. I know nothing more,
whether our luck's improved or ruin's still to come.

Sophocles

ANTIGONE:
I thought so. That's why I brought you out here,
past the gates, so you could hear in private.

ISMENE:
What's the matter? Trouble, clearly . . .
you sound so dark, so grim.

ANTIGONE:
Why not? Our own brothers' burial!
Hasn't Creon graced one with all the rites,
disgraced the other? Eteocles, they say,
has been given full military honors,
rightly so – Creon has laid him in the earth
and he goes with glory down among the dead.
But the body of Polynices, who died miserably –
why, a city-wide proclamation, rumor has it,
forbids anyone to bury him, even mourn him.
He's to be left unwept, unburied, a lovely treasure
for birds that scan the field and feast to their heart's content.

Such, I hear, is the martial law our good Creon
lays down for you and me – yes, me, I tell you –
and he's coming here to alert the uninformed
in no uncertain terms,
and he won't treat the matter lightly. Whoever
disobeys in the least will die, his doom is sealed:
stoning to death inside the city walls!

There you have it. You'll soon show what you are,
worth your breeding, Ismene, or a coward –
for all your royal blood.

ISMENE:
My poor sister, if things have come to this,
who am I to make or mend them, tell me,
what good am I to you?

ANTIGONE: Decide.
Will you share the labor, share the work?

ISMENE:
What work, what's the risk? What do you mean?

ANTIGONE: *Raising her hands.*
Will you lift up his body with these bare hands
and lower it with me?

ISMENE: What? You'd bury him –
when a law forbids the city?

ANTIGONE: Yes!
He is my brother and – deny it as you will –
your brother too.
No one will ever convict me for a traitor.

ISMENE:
So desperate, and Creon has expressly –

ANTIGONE: No,
he has no right to keep me from my own.

ISMENE:
Oh my sister, think –
think how our own father died, hated,
his reputation in ruins, driven on
by the crimes he brought to light himself
to gouge out his eyes with his own hands –
then mother . . . his mother and wife, both in one,
mutilating her life in the twisted noose –
and last, our two brothers dead in a single day,
both shedding their own blood, poor suffering boys,
battling out their common destiny hand-to-hand.

Now look at the two of us, left so alone . . .
think what a death we'll die, the worst of all
if we violate the laws and override
the fixed decree of the throne, its power –

we must be sensible. Remember we are women,
we're not born to contend with men. Then too,
we're underlings, ruled by much stronger hands,
so we must submit in this, and things still worse.

I, for one, I'll beg the dead to forgive me –
I'm forced, I have no choice – I must obey
the ones who stand in power. Why rush to extremes?
It's madness, madness.

ANTIGONE: I won't insist,
no, even if you should have a change of heart,
I'd never welcome you in the labor, not with me.
So, do as you like, whatever suits you best –
I will bury him myself.
And even if I die in the act, that death will be a glory.
I will lie with the one I love and loved by him –
an outrage sacred to the gods! I have longer
to please the dead than please the living here:
in the kingdom down below I'll lie forever.
Do as you like, dishonor the laws
the gods hold in honor.

ISMENE: I'd do them no dishonor . . .
but defy the city? I have no strength for that.

ANTIGONE:
You have your excuses. I am on my way,
I will raise a mound for him, for my dear brother.

ISMENE:
Oh Antigone, you're so rash – I'm so afraid for you!

ANTIGONE:
Don't fear for me. Set your own life in order.

ISMENE:
Then don't, at least, blurt this out to anyone.
Keep it a secret. I'll join you in that, I promise.

ANTIGONE:
Dear god, shout it from the rooftops. I'll hate you
all the more for silence – tell the world!

ISMENE:
So fiery – and it ought to chill your heart.

ANTIGONE:
I know I please where I must please the most.

ISMENE:
Yes, if you can, but you're in love with impossibility.

ANTIGONE:
Very well then, once my strength gives out
I will be done at last.

ISMENE: You're wrong from the start,
you're off on a hopeless quest.

ANTIGONE:
If you say so, you will make me hate you,
and the hatred of the dead, by all rights,
will haunt you night and day.
But leave me to my own absurdity, leave me
to suffer this – dreadful thing. I will suffer
nothing as great as death without glory.

Exit to the side.

ISMENE:
Then go if you must, but rest assured,
wild, irrational as you are, my sister,
you are truly dear to the ones who love you.

Withdrawing to the palace.

Enter a CHORUS, *the old citizens
of Thebes, chanting as the sun begins
to rise.*

Sophocles

CHORUS:

Glory! – great beam of the sun, brightest of all
that ever rose on the seven gates of Thebes,
   you burn through night at last!
       Great eye of the golden day,
mounting the Dirce's banks you throw him back –
the enemy out of Argos, the white shield, the man of bronze –
he's flying headlong now
       the bridle of fate stampeding him with pain!

   And he had driven against our borders,
   launched by the warring claims of Polynices –
   like an eagle screaming, winging havoc
   over the land, wings of armor
   shielded white as snow,
   a huge army massing,
   crested helmets bristling for assault.

He hovered above our roofs, his vast maw gaping
closing down around our seven gates,
   his spears thirsting for the kill
       but now he's gone, look,
before he could glut his jaws with Theban blood
or the god of fire put our crown of towers to the torch.
He grappled the Dragon none can master – Thebes –
       the clang of our arms like thunder at his back!

   Zeus hates with a vengeance all bravado,
   the mighty boasts of men. He watched them
   coming on in a rising flood, the pride
   of their golden armor ringing shrill –
   and brandishing his lightning
   blasted the fighter just at the goal,
   rushing to shout his triumph from our walls.

Down from the heights he crashed, pounding down on the earth!
And a moment ago, blazing torch in hand –
       mad for attack, ecstatic

he breathed his rage, the storm
   of his fury hurling at our heads!
But now his high hopes have laid him low
and down the enemy ranks the iron god of war
      deals his rewards, his stunning blows – Ares
      rapture of battle, our right arm in the crisis.

   Seven captains marshaled at seven gates
   seven against their equals, gave
   their brazen trophies up to Zeus,
   god of the breaking rout of battle,
   all but two: those blood brothers,
   one father, one mother – matched in rage,
   spears matched for the twin conquest –
   clashed and won the common prize of death.

But now for Victory! Glorious in the morning,
joy in her eyes to meet our joy
   she is winging down to Thebes,
our fleets of chariots wheeling in her wake –
   Now let us win oblivion from the wars,
thronging the temples of the gods
in singing, dancing choirs through the night!
      Lord Dionysus, god of the dance
      that shakes the land of Thebes, now lead the way!

Enter CREON *from the palace,*
attended by his guard.

   But look, the king of the realm is coming,
   Creon, the new man for the new day,
   whatever the gods are sending now . . .
   what new plan will he launch?
   Why this, this special session?
   Why this sudden call to the old men
   summoned at one command?

Sophocles

CREON: My countrymen,
the ship of state is safe. The gods who rocked her,
after a long, merciless pounding in the storm,
have righted her once more.
                            Out of the whole city
I have called you here alone. Well I know,
first, your undeviating respect
for the throne and royal power of King Laius.
Next, while Oedipus steered the land of Thebes,
and even after he died, your loyalty was unshakable,
you still stood by their children. Now then,
since the two sons are dead – two blows of fate
in the same day, cut down by each other's hands,
both killers, both brothers stained with blood –
as I am next in kin to the dead,
I now possess the throne and all its powers.

Of course you cannot know a man completely,
his character, his principles, sense of judgment,
not till he's shown his colors, ruling the people,
making laws. Experience, there's the test.
As I see it, whoever assumes the task,
the awesome task of setting the city's course,
and refuses to adopt the soundest policies
but fearing someone, keeps his lips locked tight,
he's utterly worthless. So I rate him now,
I always have. And whoever places a friend
above the good of his own country, he is nothing:
I have no use for him. Zeus my witness,
Zeus who sees all things, always –

I could never stand by silent, watching destruction
march against our city, putting safety to rout,
nor could I ever make that man a friend of mine
who menaces our country. Remember this:
our country *is* our safety.
Only while she voyages true on course

can we establish friendships, truer than blood itself.
Such are my standards. They make our city great.

Closely akin to them I have proclaimed,
just now, the following decree to our people
concerning the two sons of Oedipus.
Eteocles, who died fighting for Thebes,
excelling all in arms: he shall be buried,
crowned with a hero's honors, the cups we pour
to soak the earth and reach the famous dead.

But as for his blood brother, Polynices,
who returned from exile, home to his father-city
and the gods of his race, consumed with one desire –
to burn them roof to roots – who thirsted to drink
his kinsmen's blood and sell the rest to slavery:
that man – a proclamation has forbidden the city
to dignify him with burial, mourn him at all.
No, he must be left unburied, his corpse
carrion for the birds and dogs to tear,
an obscenity for the citizens to behold!

These are my principles. Never at my hands
will the traitor be honored above the patriot.
But whoever proves his loyalty to the state –
I'll prize that man in death as well as life.

LEADER:
If this is your pleasure, Creon, treating
our city's enemy and our friend this way . . .
The power is yours, I suppose, to enforce it
with the laws, both for the dead and all of us,
the living.

CREON: Follow my orders closely then,
be on your guard.

LEADER: We are too old.
Lay that burden on younger shoulders.

Sophocles

CREON: No, no,
I don't mean the body – I've posted guards already.

LEADER:
What commands for us then? What other service?

CREON:
See that you never side with those who break my orders.

LEADER:
Never. Only a fool could be in love with death.

CREON:
Death is the price – you're right. But all too often
the mere hope of money has ruined many men.

A SENTRY *enters from the side.*

SENTRY: My lord,
I can't say I'm winded from running, or set out
with any spring in my legs either – no sir,
I was lost in thought, and it made me stop, often,
dead in my tracks, wheeling, turning back,
and all the time a voice inside me muttering,
'Idiot, why? You're going straight to your death.'
Then muttering, 'Stopped again, poor fool?
If somebody gets the news to Creon first,
what's to save your neck?'
 And so,
mulling it over, on I trudged, dragging my feet,
you can make a short road take forever . . .
but at last, look, common sense won out,
I'm here, and I'm all yours,
and even though I come empty-handed
I'll tell my story just the same, because
I've come with a good grip on one hope,
what will come will come, whatever fate –

Antigone

CREON:
Come to the point!
What's wrong – why so afraid?

SENTRY:
First, myself, I've got to tell you,
I didn't do it, didn't see who did –
Be fair, don't take it out on me.

CREON:
You're playing it safe, soldier,
barricading yourself from any trouble.
It's obvious, you've something strange to tell.

SENTRY:
Dangerous too, and danger makes you delay
for all you're worth.

CREON:
Out with it – then dismiss!

SENTRY:
All right, here it comes. The body –
someone's just buried it, then run off . . .
sprinkled some dry dust on the flesh,
given it proper rites.

CREON: What?
What man alive would dare –

SENTRY: I've no idea, I swear it.
There was no mark of a spade, no pickaxe there,
no earth turned up, the ground packed hard and dry,
unbroken, no tracks, no wheelruts, nothing,
the workman left no trace. Just at sunup
the first watch of the day points it out –
it was a wonder! We were stunned . . .
a terrific burden too, for all of us, listen:
you can't see the corpse, not that it's buried,

really, just a light cover of road-dust on it,
as if someone meant to lay the dead to rest
and keep from getting cursed.
Not a sign in sight that dogs or wild beasts
had worried the body, even torn the skin.

But what came next! Rough talk flew thick and fast,
guard grilling guard – we'd have come to blows
at last, nothing to stop it; each man for himself
and each the culprit, no one caught red-handed,
all of us pleading ignorance, dodging the charges,
ready to take up red-hot iron in our fists,
go through fire, swear oaths to the gods –
'I didn't do it, I had no hand in it either,
not in the plotting, not the work itself!'

Finally, after all this wrangling came to nothing,
one man spoke out and made us stare at the ground,
hanging our heads in fear. No way to counter him,
no way to take his advice and come through
safe and sound. Here's what he said:
'Look, we've got to report the facts to Creon,
we can't keep this hidden.' Well, that won out,
and the lot fell to me, condemned me,
unlucky as ever, I got the prize. So here I am,
against my will and yours too, well I know –
no one wants the man who brings bad news.

LEADER: My king,
ever since he began I've been debating in my mind,
could this possibly be the work of the gods?

CREON: Stop –
before you make me choke with anger – the gods!
You, you're senile, must you be insane?
You say – why it's intolerable – say the gods
could have the slightest concern for that corpse?
Tell me, was it for meritorious service
they proceeded to bury him, prized him so? The hero

who came to burn their temples ringed with pillars,
their golden treasures – scorch their hallowed earth
and fling their laws to the winds.
Exactly when did you last see the gods
celebrating traitors? Inconceivable!

No, from the first there were certain citizens
who could hardly stand the spirit of my regime,
grumbling against me in the dark, heads together,
tossing wildly, never keeping their necks beneath
the yoke, loyally submitting to their king.
These are the instigators, I'm convinced –
they've perverted my own guard, bribed them
to do their work.
                    Money! Nothing worse
in our lives, so current, rampant, so corrupting.
Money – you demolish cities, root men from their homes,
you train and twist good minds and set them on
to the most atrocious schemes. No limit,
you make them adept at every kind of outrage,
every godless crime – money!
                              Everyone –
the whole crew bribed to commit this crime,
they've made one thing sure at least:
sooner or later they will pay the price.

Wheeling on the SENTRY.

                              You –
I swear to Zeus as I still believe in Zeus,
if you don't find the man who buried that corpse,
the very man, and produce him before my eyes,
simple death won't be enough for you,
not till we string you up alive
and wring the immorality out of you.
Then you can steal the rest of your days,
better informed about where to make a killing.
You'll have learned, at last, it doesn't pay

to itch for rewards from every hand that beckons.
Filthy profits wreck most men, you'll see –
they'll never save your life.

SENTRY: Please,
may I say a word or two, or just turn and go?

CREON:
Can't you tell? Everything you say offends me.

SENTRY:
Where does it hurt you, in the ears or in the heart?

CREON:
And who are you to pinpoint my displeasure?

SENTRY:
The culprit grates on your feelings,
I just annoy your ears.

CREON: Still talking?
You talk too much! A born nuisance –

SENTRY: Maybe so,
but I never did this thing, so help me!

CREON: Yes you did –
what's more, you squandered your life for silver!

SENTRY:
Oh it's terrible when the one who does the judging
judges things all wrong.

CREON: Well now,
you just be clever about your judgments –
if you fail to produce the criminals for me,
you'll swear your dirty money brought you pain.

*Turning sharply, reentering
the palace.*

SENTRY:
I hope he's found. Best thing by far.
But caught or not, that's in the lap of fortune:
I'll never come back, you've seen the last of me.
I'm saved, even now, and I never thought,
I never hoped –
dear gods, I owe you all my thanks!

Rushing out.

CHORUS: Numberless wonders
terrible wonders walk the world but none the match for man –
that great wonder crossing the heaving gray sea,
                driven on by the blasts of winter
on through breakers crashing left and right,
   holds his steady course
and the oldest of the gods he wears away –
the Earth, the immortal, the inexhaustible –
as his plows go back and forth, year in, year out
   with the breed of stallions turning up the furrows.

And the blithe, lightheaded race of birds he snares,
the tribes of savage beasts, the life that swarms the depths –
                with one fling of his nets
woven and coiled tight, he takes them all,
   man the skilled, the brilliant!
He conquers all, taming with his techniques
the prey that roams the cliffs and wild lairs,
training the stallion, clamping the yoke across
   his shaggy neck, and the tireless mountain bull.

And speech and thought, quick as the wind
and the mood and mind for law that rules the city –
   all these he has taught himself
and shelter from the arrows of the frost
when there's rough lodging under the cold clear sky
and the shafts of lashing rain –
       ready, resourceful man!
            Never without resources

never an impasse as he marches on the future –
only Death, from Death alone he will find no rescue
but from desperate plagues he has plotted his escapes.

Man the master, ingenious past all measure
past all dreams, the skills within his grasp –
   he forges on, now to destruction
now again to greatness. When he weaves in
the laws of the land, and the justice of the gods
that binds his oaths together
        he and his city rise high –
            but the city casts out
that man who weds himself to inhumanity
thanks to reckless daring. Never share my hearth
never think my thoughts, whoever does such things.

Enter ANTIGONE *from the side,*
accompanied by the SENTRY.

Here is a dark sign from the gods –
what to make of this? I know her,
how can I deny it? That young girl's Antigone!
Wretched, child of a wretched father,
Oedipus. Look, is it possible?
They bring you in like a prisoner –
why? did you break the king's laws?
Did they take you in some act of mad defiance?

SENTRY:
She's the one, she did it single-handed –
we caught her burying the body. Where's Creon?

Enter CREON *from the palace.*

LEADER:
Back again, just in time when you need him.

CREON:
In time for what? What is it?

Antigone

SENTRY: My king,
there's nothing you can swear you'll never do –
second thoughts make liars of us all.
I could have sworn I wouldn't hurry back
(what with your threats, the buffeting I just took),
but a stroke of luck beyond our wildest hopes,
what a joy, there's nothing like it. So,
back I've come, breaking my oath, who cares?
I'm bringing in our prisoner – this young girl –
we took her giving the dead the last rites.
But no casting lots this time; this is *my* luck,
my prize, no one else's.
                    Now, my lord,
here she is. Take her, question her,
cross-examine her to your heart's content.
But set me free, it's only right –
I'm rid of this dreadful business once for all.

CREON:
Prisoner! Her? You took her – where, doing what?

SENTRY:
Burying the man. That's the whole story.

CREON: What?
You mean what you say, you're telling me the truth?

SENTRY:
She's the one. With my own eyes I saw her
bury the body, just what you've forbidden.
There. Is that plain and clear?

CREON:
What did you see? Did you catch her in the act?

SENTRY:
Here's what happened. We went back to our post,
those threats of yours breathing down our necks –
we brushed the corpse clean of the dust that covered it,
stripped it bare . . . it was slimy, going soft,

Sophocles

and we took to high ground, backs to the wind
so the stink of him couldn't hit us;
jostling, baiting each other to keep awake,
shouting back and forth – no napping on the job,
not this time. And so the hours dragged by
until the sun stood dead above our heads,
a huge white ball in the noon sky, beating,
blazing down, and then it happened –
suddenly, a whirlwind!
Twisting a great dust-storm up from the earth,
a black plague of the heavens, filling the plain,
ripping the leaves off every tree in sight,
choking the air and sky. We squinted hard
and took our whipping from the gods.

And after the storm passed – it seemed endless –
there, we saw the girl!
And she cried out a sharp, piercing cry,
like a bird come back to an empty nest,
peering into its bed, and all the babies gone . . .
Just so, when she sees the corpse bare
she bursts into a long, shattering wail
and calls down withering curses on the heads
of all who did the work. And she scoops up dry dust,
handfuls, quickly, and lifting a fine bronze urn,
lifting it high and pouring, she crowns the dead
with three full libations.

                       Soon as we saw
we rushed her, closed on the kill like hunters,
and she, she didn't flinch. We interrogated her,
charging her with offenses past and present –
she stood up to it all, denied nothing. I tell you,
it made me ache and laugh in the same breath.
It's pure joy to escape the worst yourself,
it hurts a man to bring down his friends.
But all that, I'm afraid, means less to me
than my own skin. That's the way I'm made.

Antigone

CREON: *Wheeling on* ANTIGONE.

You,
with your eyes fixed on the ground – speak up.
Do you deny you did this, yes or no?

ANTIGONE:
I did it. I don't deny a thing.

CREON: *To the* SENTRY.
You, get out, wherever you please –
you're clear of a very heavy charge.

He leaves; CREON *turns back to*
ANTIGONE.

You, tell me briefly, no long speeches –
were you aware a decree had forbidden this?

ANTIGONE:
Well aware. How could I avoid it? It was public.

CREON:
And still you had the gall to break this law?

ANTIGONE:
Of course I did. It wasn't Zeus, not in the least,
who made this proclamation – not to me.
Nor did that Justice, dwelling with the gods
beneath the earth, ordain such laws for men.
Nor did I think your edict had such force
that you, a mere mortal, could override the gods,
the great unwritten, unshakable traditions.
They are alive, not just today or yesterday:
they live forever, from the first of time,
and no one knows when they first saw the light.

These laws – I was not about to break them,
not out of fear of some man's wounded pride,
and face the retribution of the gods.
Die I must, I've known it all my life –

how could I keep from knowing? – even without
your death-sentence ringing in my ears.
And if I am to die before my time
I consider that a gain. Who on earth,
alive in the midst of so much grief as I,
could fail to find his death a rich reward?
So for me, at least, to meet this doom of yours
is precious little pain. But if I had allowed
my own mother's son to rot, an unburied corpse –
that would have been an agony! This is nothing.
And if my present actions strike you as foolish,
let's just say I've been accused of folly
by a fool.

LEADER: Like father like daughter,
passionate, wild . . .
she hasn't learned to bend before adversity.

CREON:
No? Believe me, the stiffest stubborn wills
fall the hardest; the toughest iron,
tempered strong in the white-hot fire,
you'll see it crack and shatter first of all.
And I've known spirited horses you can break
with a light bit – proud, rebellious horses.
There's no room for pride, not in a slave,
not with the lord and master standing by.

This girl was an old hand at insolence
when she overrode the edicts we made public.
But once she had done it – the insolence,
twice over – to glory in it, laughing,
mocking us to our face with what she'd done.
I am not the man, not now: she is the man
if this victory goes to her and she goes free.

Never! Sister's child or closer in blood
than all my family clustered at my altar
worshiping Guardian Zeus – she'll never escape,

Antigone

she and her blood sister, the most barbaric death.
Yes, I accuse her sister of an equal part
in scheming this, this burial.

To his attendants.

Bring her here!
I just saw her inside, hysterical, gone to pieces.
It never fails: the mind convicts itself
in advance, when scoundrels are up to no good,
plotting in the dark. Oh but I hate it more
when a traitor, caught red-handed,
tries to glorify his crimes.

ANTIGONE:
Creon, what more do you want
than my arrest and execution?

CREON:
Nothing. Then I have it all.

ANTIGONE:
Then why delay? Your moralizing repels me,
every word you say – pray god it always will.
So naturally all I say repels you too.
Enough.
Give me glory! What greater glory could I win
than to give my own brother decent burial?
These citizens here would all agree,

To the CHORUS.

they would praise me too
if their lips weren't locked in fear.

Pointing to CREON.

Lucky tyrants – the perquisites of power!
Ruthless power to do and say whatever pleases *them*.

CREON:
You alone, of all the people in Thebes,
see things that way.

Sophocles

ANTIGONE: They see it just that way
but defer to you and keep their tongues in leash.

CREON:
And you, aren't you ashamed to differ so from them?
So disloyal!

ANTIGONE: Not ashamed for a moment,
not to honor my brother, my own flesh and blood.

CREON:
Wasn't Eteocles a brother too – cut down, facing him?

ANTIGONE:
Brother, yes, by the same mother, the same father.

CREON:
Then how can you render his enemy such honors,
such impieties in his eyes?

ANTIGONE:
He will never testify to that,
Eteocles dead and buried.

CREON: He will –
if you honor the traitor just as much as him.

ANTIGONE:
But it was his brother, not some slave that died –

CREON:
Ravaging our country! –
but Eteocles died fighting in our behalf.

ANTIGONE:
No matter – Death longs for the same rites for all.

CREON:
Never the same for the patriot and the traitor.

ANTIGONE:
Who, Creon, who on earth can say the ones below
don't find this pure and uncorrupt?

CREON:
Never. Once an enemy, never a friend,
not even after death.

ANTIGONE:
I was born to join in love, not hate –
that is my nature.

CREON: Go down below and love,
if love you must – love the dead! While I'm alive,
no woman is going to lord it over me.

Enter ISMENE *from the palace, under guard.*

CHORUS: Look,

Ismene's coming, weeping a sister's tears,
loving sister, under a cloud . . .
her face is flushed, her cheeks streaming.
Sorrow puts her lovely radiance in the dark.

CREON: You –
in my own house, you viper, slinking undetected,
sucking my life-blood! I never knew
I was breeding twin disasters, the two of you
rising up against my throne. Come, tell me,
will you confess your part in the crime or not?
Answer me. Swear to me.

ISMENE: I did it, yes –
if only she consents – I share the guilt,
the consequences too.

ANTIGONE: No,
Justice will never suffer that – not you,
you were unwilling. I never brought you in.

Sophocles

ISMENE:
But now you face such dangers . . . I'm not ashamed
to sail through trouble with you,
make your troubles mine.

ANTIGONE: Who did the work?
Let the dead and the god of death bear witness!
I have no love for a friend who loves in words alone.

ISMENE:
Oh no, my sister, don't reject me, please,
let me die beside you, consecrating
the dead together.

ANTIGONE: Never share my dying,
don't lay claim to what you never touched.
My death will be enough.

ISMENE:
What do I care for life, cut off from you?

ANTIGONE:
Ask Creon. Your concern is all for him.

ISMENE:
Why abuse me so? It doesn't help you now.

ANTIGONE: You're right –
if I mock you, I get no pleasure from it,
only pain.

ISMENE: Tell me, dear one,
what can I do to help you, even now?

ANTIGONE:
Save yourself. I don't grudge you your survival.

ISMENE:
Oh no, no, denied my portion in your death?

ANTIGONE:
You chose to live, I chose to die.

Antigone

ISMENE: Not, at least,
without every kind of caution I could voice.

ANTIGONE:
Your wisdom appealed to one world – mine, another.

ISMENE:
But look, we're both guilty, both condemned to death.

ANTIGONE:
Courage! Live your life. I gave myself to death,
long ago, so I might serve the dead.

CREON:
They're both mad, I tell you, the two of them.
One's just shown it, the other's been that way
since she was born.

ISMENE: True, my king,
the sense we were born with cannot last forever . . .
commit cruelty on a person long enough
and the mind begins to go.

CREON: Yours did,
when you chose to commit your crimes with her.

ISMENE:
How can I live alone, without her?

CREON: Her?
Don't even mention her – she no longer exists.

ISMENE:
What? You'd kill your own son's bride?

CREON: Absolutely:
there are other fields for him to plow.

ISMENE: Perhaps,
but never as true, as close a bond as theirs.

CREON:
A worthless woman for my son? It repels me.

ISMENE:
Dearest Haemon, your father wrongs you so!

CREON:
Enough, enough – you and your talk of marriage!

ISMENE:
Creon – you're really going to rob your son of Antigone?

CREON:
Death will do it for me – break their marriage off.

LEADER:
So, it's settled then? Antigone must die?

CREON:
Settled, yes – we both know that.

To the guards.

Stop wasting time. Take them in.
From now on they'll act like women.
Tie them up, no more running loose;
even the bravest will cut and run,
once they see Death coming for their lives.

The guards escort ANTIGONE *and* ISMENE *into the palace.* CREON *remains while the old citizens form their* CHORUS.

CHORUS:
Blest, they are the truly blest who all their lives
have never tasted devastation. For others, once
the gods have rocked a house to its foundations
　the ruin will never cease, cresting on and on
from one generation on throughout the race –
like a great mounting tide
driven on by savage northern gales,
　　surging over the dead black depths
roiling up from the bottom dark heaves of sand

Antigone

and the headlands, taking the storm's onslaught full-force,
roar, and the low moaning
                      echoes on and on
                                    and now
as in ancient times I see the sorrows of the house,
the living heirs of the old ancestral kings,
piling on the sorrows of the dead
  and one generation cannot free the next –
some god will bring them crashing down,
the race finds no release.
And now the light, the hope
    springing up from the late last root
in the house of Oedipus, that hope's cut down in turn
by the long, bloody knife swung by the gods of death
by a senseless word
                    by fury at the heart.
                                  Zeus,
yours is the power, Zeus, what man on earth
can override it, who can hold it back?
Power that neither Sleep, the all-ensnaring
  no, nor the tireless months of heaven
can ever overmaster – young through all time,
mighty lord of power, you hold fast
  the dazzling crystal mansions of Olympus.
And throughout the future, late and soon
as through the past, your law prevails:
no towering form of greatness
    enters into the lives of mortals
                          free and clear of ruin.
                                      True,
our dreams, our high hopes voyaging far and wide
bring sheer delight to many, to many others
  delusion, blithe, mindless lusts
and the fraud steals on one slowly . . . unaware
till he trips and puts his foot into the fire.
  He was a wise old man who coined
the famous saying: 'Sooner or later

foul is fair, fair is foul
to the man the gods will ruin' –
   He goes his way for a moment only
                     free of blinding ruin.

Enter HAEMON *from the palace.*

   Here's Haemon now, the last of all your sons.
   Does he come in tears for his bride,
   his doomed bride, Antigone –
   bitter at being cheated of their marriage?

CREON:
We'll soon know, better than seers could tell us.

Turning to HAEMON.

Son, you've heard the final verdict on your bride?
Are you coming now, raving against your father?
Or do you love me, no matter what I do?

HAEMON:
Father, I'm your *son* . . . you in your wisdom
set my bearings for me – I obey you.
No marriage could ever mean more to me than you,
whatever good direction you may offer.

CREON: Fine, Haemon.
That's how you ought to feel within your heart,
subordinate to your father's will in every way.
That's what a man prays for: to produce good sons –
a household full of them, dutiful and attentive,
so they can pay his enemy back with interest
and match the respect their father shows his friend.
But the man who rears a brood of useless children,
what has he brought into the world, I ask you?
Nothing but trouble for himself, and mockery
from his enemies laughing in his face.
                        Oh Haemon,
never lose your sense of judgment over a woman.

Antigone

The warmth, the rush of pleasure, it all goes cold
in your arms, I warn you . . . a worthless woman
in your house, a misery in your bed.
What wound cuts deeper than a loved one
turned against you? Spit her out,
like a mortal enemy – let the girl go.
Let her find a husband down among the dead.
Imagine it: I caught her in naked rebellion,
the traitor, the only one in the whole city.
I'm not about to prove myself a liar,
not to my people, no, I'm going to kill her!
That's right – so let her cry for mercy, sing her hymns
to Zeus who defends all bonds of kindred blood.
Why, if I bring up my own kin to be rebels,
think what I'd suffer from the world at large.
Show me the man who rules his household well:
I'll show you someone fit to rule the state.
That good man, my son,
I have every confidence he and he alone
can give commands and take them too. Staunch
in the storm of spears he'll stand his ground,
a loyal, unflinching comrade at your side.

But whoever steps out of line, violates the laws
or presumes to hand out orders to his superiors,
he'll win no praise from me. But that man
the city places in authority, his orders
must be obeyed, large and small,
right and wrong.
         Anarchy –
show me a greater crime in all the earth!
She, she destroys cities, rips up houses,
breaks the ranks of spearmen into headlong rout.
But the ones who last it out, the great mass of them
owe their lives to discipline. Therefore
we must defend the men who live by law,
never let some woman triumph over us.
Better to fall from power, if fall we must,

at the hands of a man – never be rated
inferior to a woman, never.

LEADER: To us,
unless old age has robbed us of our wits,
you seem to say what you have to say with sense.

HAEMON:
Father, only the gods endow a man with reason,
the finest of all their gifts, a treasure.
Far be it from me – I haven't the skill,
and certainly no desire, to tell you when,
if ever, you make a slip in speech . . . though
someone else might have a good suggestion.

Of course it's not for you,
in the normal run of things, to watch
whatever men say or do, or find to criticize.
The man in the street, you know, dreads your glance,
he'd never say anything displeasing to your face.
But it's for me to catch the murmurs in the dark,
the way the city mourns for this young girl.
'No woman,' they say, 'ever deserved death less,
and such a brutal death for such a glorious action.
She, with her own dear brother lying in his blood –
she couldn't bear to leave him dead, unburied,
food for the wild dogs or wheeling vultures.
Death? She deserves a glowing crown of gold!'
So they say, and the rumor spreads in secret,
darkly . . .
            I rejoice in your success, father –
nothing more precious to me in the world.
What medal of honor brighter to his children
than a father's growing glory? Or a child's
to his proud father? Now don't, please,
be quite so single-minded, self-involved,
or assume the world is wrong and you are right.
Whoever thinks that he alone possesses intelligence,

the gift of eloquence, he and no one else,
and character too . . . such men, I tell you,
spread them open – you will find them empty.

                              No,
it's no disgrace for a man, even a wise man,
to learn many things and not to be too rigid.
You've seen trees by a raging winter torrent,
how many sway with the flood and salvage every twig,
but not the stubborn – they're ripped out, roots and all.
Bend or break. The same when a man is sailing:
haul your sheets too taut, never give an inch,
you'll capsize, and go the rest of the voyage
keel up and the rowing-benches under.

Oh give way. Relax your anger – change!
I'm young, I know, but let me offer this:
it would be best by far, I admit,
if a man were born infallible, right by nature.
If not – and things don't often go that way,
it's best to learn from those with good advice.

LEADER:
You'd do well, my lord, if he's speaking to the point,
to learn from him,

                      Turning to HAEMON.

                and you, my boy, from him.
You both are talking sense.

CREON: So,
men our age, we're to be lectured, are we? –
schooled by a boy his age?

HAEMON:
Only in what is right. But if I seem young,
look less to my years and more to what I do.

CREON:
Do? Is admiring rebels an achievement?

Sophocles

HAEMON:
I'd never suggest that you admire treason.

CREON: Oh? –
isn't that just the sickness that's attacked her?

HAEMON:
The whole city of Thebes denies it, to a man.

CREON:
And is Thebes about to tell me how to rule?

HAEMON:
Now, you see? Who's talking like a child?

CREON:
Am I to rule this land for others – or myself?

HAEMON:
It's no city at all, owned by one man alone.

CREON:
What? The city *is* the king's – that's the law!

HAEMON:
What a splendid king you'd make of a desert island –
you and you alone.

CREON: *To the* CHORUS.
This boy, I do believe,
is fighting on her side, the woman's side.

HAEMON:
If you are a woman, yes –
my concern is all for you.

CREON:
Why, you degenerate – bandying accusations,
threatening me with justice, your own father!

HAEMON:
I see my father offending justice – wrong.

Antigone

CREON: Wrong?
To protect my royal rights?

HAEMON: Protect your rights?
When you trample down the honors of the gods?

CREON:
You, you soul of corruption, rotten through –
woman's accomplice!

HAEMON: That may be,
but you will never find me accomplice to a criminal.

CREON:
That's what *she* is,
and every word you say is a blatant appeal for her –

HAEMON:
And you, and me, and the gods beneath the earth.

CREON:
You will never marry her, not while she's alive.

HAEMON:
Then she will die . . . but her death will kill another.

CREON:
What, brazen threats? You go too far!

HAEMON: What threat?
Combating your empty, mindless judgments with a word?

CREON:
You'll suffer for your sermons, you and your empty wisdom!

HAEMON:
If you weren't my father, I'd say you were insane.

CREON:
Don't flatter me with Father – you woman's slave!

HAEMON:
You really expect to fling abuse at me

and not receive the same?

CREON: Is that so!
Now, by heaven, I promise you, you'll pay –
taunting, insulting me! Bring her out,
that hateful – she'll die now, here,
in front of his eyes, beside her groom!

HAEMON:
No, no, she will never die beside me –
don't delude yourself. And you will never
see me, never set eyes on my face again.
Rage your heart out, rage with friends
who can stand the sight of you.

Rushing out.

LEADER:
Gone, my king, in a burst of anger.
A temper young as his . . . hurt him once,
he may do something violent.

CREON: Let him do –
dream up something desperate, past all human limit!
Good riddance. Rest assured,
he'll never save those two young girls from death.

LEADER:
Both of them, you really intend to kill them both?

CREON:
No, not her, the one whose hands are clean –
you're quite right.

LEADER: But Antigone –
what sort of death do you have in mind for her?

CREON:
I will take her down some wild, desolate path
never trod by men, and wall her up alive
in a rocky vault, and set out short rations,
just the measure piety demands

to keep the entire city free of defilement.
There let her pray to the one god she worships:
Death – who knows? – may just reprieve her from death.
Or she may learn at last, better late than never,
what a waste of breath it is to worship Death.

Exit to the palace.

CHORUS:
Love, never conquered in battle
Love the plunderer laying waste the rich!
Love standing the night-watch
                guarding a girl's soft cheek,
you range the seas, the shepherds' steadings off in the wilds –
not even the deathless gods can flee your onset,
nothing human born for a day –
whoever feels your grip is driven mad.
                            Love! –
you wrench the minds of the righteous into outrage,
swerve them to their ruin – you have ignited this,
this kindred strife, father and son at war
                        and Love alone the victor –
warm glance of the bride triumphant, burning with desire!
Throned in power, side-by-side with the mighty laws!
Irresistible Aphrodite, never conquered –
Love, you mock us for your sport.

*ANTIGONE is brought from the
palace under guard.*

But now, even I would rebel against the king,
I would break all bounds when I see this –
I fill with tears, I cannot hold them back,
not any more . . . I see Antigone make her way
to the bridal vault where all are laid to rest.

ANTIGONE:
Look at me, men of my fatherland,
  setting out on the last road

Sophocles

looking into the last light of day
the last I will ever see . . .
the god of death who puts us all to bed
takes me down to the banks of Acheron alive –
   denied my part in the wedding-songs,
no wedding-song in the dusk has crowned my marriage –
I go to wed the lord of the dark waters.

CHORUS:
>   Not crowned with glory or with a dirge,
>   you leave for the deep pit of the dead.
>   No withering illness laid you low,
>   no strokes of the sword – a law to yourself,
>   alone, no mortal like you, ever, you go down
>   to the halls of Death alive and breathing.

ANTIGONE:
But think of Niobe – well I know her story –
   think what a living death she died,
Tantalus' daughter, stranger queen from the east:
there on the mountain heights, growing stone
binding as ivy, slowly walled her round
and the rains will never cease, the legends say
the snows will never leave her . . .
   wasting away, under her brows the tears
showering down her breasting ridge and slopes –
a rocky death like hers puts me to sleep.

CHORUS:
>   But she was a god, born of gods,
>   and we are only mortals born to die.
>   And yet, of course, it's a great thing
>   for a dying girl to hear, even to hear
>   she shares a destiny equal to the gods,
>   during life and later, once she's dead.

ANTIGONE: O you mock me!
Why, in the name of all my fathers' gods
why can't you wait till I am gone –

Antigone

    must you abuse me to my face?
O my city, all your fine rich sons!
And you, you springs of the Dirce,
holy grove of Thebes where the chariots gather,
    you at least, you'll bear me witness, look,
unmourned by friends and forced by such crude laws
I go to my rockbound prison, strange new tomb –
    always a stranger, O dear god,
    I have no home on earth and none below,
      not with the living, not with the breathless dead.

CHORUS:
    You went too far, the last limits of daring –
    smashing against the high throne of Justice!
      Your life's in ruins, child – I wonder . . .
    do you pay for your father's terrible ordeal?

ANTIGONE:
There – at last you've touched it, the worst pain
the worst anguish! Raking up the grief for father
    three times over, for all the doom
that's struck us down, the brilliant house of Laius.
O mother, your marriage-bed
the coiling horrors, the coupling there –
    you with your own son, my father – doomstruck mother!
Such, such were my parents, and I their wretched child.
I go to them now, cursed, unwed, to share their home –
    I am a stranger! O dear brother, doomed
    in your marriage – your marriage murders mine,
    your dying drags me down to death alive!

                      Enter Creon.

CHORUS:
    Reverence asks some reverence in return –
    but attacks on power never go unchecked,
      not by the man who holds the reins of power.
    Your own blind will, your passion has destroyed you.

Sophocles

ANTIGONE:
>   No one to weep for me, my friends,
>   no wedding-song – they take me away
>   in all my pain . . . the road lies open, waiting.
>   Never again, the law forbids me to see
>   the sacred eye of day. I am agony!
>   No tears for the destiny that's mine,
>   no loved one mourns my death.

CREON: Can't you see?
>   If a man could wail his own dirge *before* he dies,
>   he'd never finish.

To the guards.

>   Take her away, quickly!
>   Wall her up in the tomb, you have your orders.
>   Abandon her there, alone, and let her choose –
>   death or a buried life with a good roof for shelter.
>   As for myself, my hands are clean. This young girl –
>   dead or alive, she will be stripped of her rights,
>   her stranger's rights, here in the world above.

ANTIGONE:
>   O tomb, my bridal-bed – my house, my prison
>   cut in the hollow rock, my everlasting watch!
>   I'll soon be there, soon embrace my own,
>   the great growing family of our dead
>   Persephone has received among her ghosts.
>
>   I,
>   the last of them all, the most reviled by far,
>   go down before my destined time's run out.
>   But still I go, cherishing one good hope:
>   my arrival may be dear to father,
>   dear to you, my mother,
>   dear to you, my loving brother, Eteocles –
>   When you died I washed you with my hands,
>   I dressed you all, I poured the sacred cups
>   across your tombs. But now, Polynices,

because I laid your body out as well,
this, this is my reward. Nevertheless
I honored you – the decent will admit it –
well and wisely too.

                Never, I tell you,
if I had been the mother of children
or if my husband died, exposed and rotting –
I'd never have taken this ordeal upon myself,
never defied our people's will. What law,
you ask, do I satisfy with what I say?
A husband dead, there might have been another.
A child by another too, if I had lost the first.
But mother and father both lost in the halls of Death,
no brother could ever spring to light again.
For this law alone I held you first in honor.
For this, Creon, the king, judges me a criminal
guilty of dreadful outrage, my dear brother!
And now he leads me off, a captive in his hands,
with no part in the bridal-song, the bridal-bed,
denied all joy of marriage, raising children –
deserted so by loved ones, struck by fate,
I descend alive to the caverns of the dead.

What law of the mighty gods have I transgressed?
Why look to the heavens any more, tormented as I am?
Whom to call, what comrades now? Just think,
my reverence only brands me for irreverence!
Very well: if this is the pleasure of the gods,
once I suffer I will know that I was wrong.
But if these men are wrong, let them suffer
nothing worse than they mete out to me –
these masters of injustice!

LEADER:
Still the same rough winds, the wild passion
raging through the girl.

CREON: *To the guards.*
Take her away.
You're wasting time – you'll pay for it too.

ANTIGONE:
Oh god, the voice of death. It's come, it's here.

CREON:
True. Not a word of hope – your doom is sealed.

ANTIGONE:
    Land of Thebes, city of all my fathers –
    O you gods, the first gods of the race!
    They drag me away, now, no more delay.
    Look on me, you noble sons of Thebes –
    the last of a great line of kings,
    I alone, see what I suffer now
    at the hands of what breed of men –
    all for reverence, my reverence for the gods!

She leaves under guard: the CHORUS *gathers.*

CHORUS:
    Danaë, Danaë –
even she endured a fate like yours,
  in all her lovely strength she traded
the light of day for the bolted brazen vault –
buried within her tomb, her bridal-chamber,
wed to the yoke and broken.
    But she was of glorious birth
              my child, my child
and treasured the seed of Zeus within her womb,
the cloudburst streaming gold!
    The power of fate is a wonder,
    dark, terrible wonder –
    neither wealth nor armies
    towered walls nor ships
    black hulls lashed by the salt
    can save us from that force.

Antigone

The yoke tamed him too
   young Lycurgus flaming in anger
king of Edonia, all for his mad taunts
Dionysus clamped him down, encased
in the chain-mail of rock
   and there his rage
          his terrible flowering rage burst –
sobbing, dying away . . . at last that madman
came to know his god –
    the power he mocked, the power
    he taunted in all his frenzy
    trying to stamp out
    the women strong with the god –
    the torch, the raving sacred cries –
    enraging the Muses who adore the flute.
And far north where the Black Rocks
   cut the sea in half
and murderous straits
split the coast of Thrace
 a forbidding city stands
where once, hard by the walls
the savage Ares thrilled to watch
a king's new queen, a Fury rearing in rage
  against his two royal sons –
   her bloody hands, her dagger-shuttle
stabbing out their eyes – cursed, blinding wounds –
their eyes blind sockets screaming for revenge!

They wailed in agony, cries echoing cries
   the princes doomed at birth . . .
and their mother doomed to chains,
walled up in a tomb of stone –
 but she traced her own birth back
to a proud Athenian line and the high gods
and off in caverns half the world away,
born of the wild North Wind
  she sprang on her father's gales,

Sophocles

racing stallions up the leaping cliffs –
child of the heavens. But even on her the Fates
the gray everlasting Fates rode hard
my child, my child.

> *Enter* TIRESIAS, *the blind prophet,
> led by a boy.*

TIRESIAS: Lords of Thebes,
I and the boy have come together,
hand in hand. Two see with the eyes of one . . .
so the blind must go, with a guide to lead the way.

CREON:
What is it, old Tiresias? What news now?

TIRESIAS:
I will teach you. And you obey the seer.

CREON: I will,
I've never wavered from your advice before.

TIRESIAS:
And so you kept the city straight on course.

CREON:
I owe you a great deal, I swear to that.

TIRESIAS:
Then reflect, my son: you are poised,
once more, on the razor-edge of fate.

CREON:
What is it? I shudder to hear you.

TIRESIAS: You will learn
when you listen to the warnings of my craft.
As I sat on the ancient seat of augury,
in the sanctuary where every bird I know
will hover at my hands – suddenly I heard it,
a strange voice in the wingbeats, unintelligible,

barbaric, a mad scream! Talons flashing, ripping,
they were killing each other – that much I knew –
the murderous fury whirring in those wings
made that much clear!
                         I was afraid,
I turned quickly, tested the burnt-sacrifice,
ignited the altar at all points – but no fire,
the god in the fire never blazed.
Not from those offerings . . . over the embers
slid a heavy ooze from the long thighbones,
smoking, sputtering out, and the bladder
puffed and burst – spraying gall into the air –
and the fat wrapping the bones slithered off
and left them glistening white. No fire!
The rites failed that might have blazed the future
with a sign. So I learned from the boy here:
he is my guide, as I am guide to others.
                                    And it is you –
your high resolve that sets this plague on Thebes.
The public altars and sacred hearths are fouled,
one and all, by the birds and dogs with carrion
torn from the corpse, the doomstruck son of Oedipus!
And so the gods are deaf to our prayers, they spurn
the offerings in our hands, the flame of holy flesh.
No birds cry out an omen clear and true –
they're gorged with the murdered victim's blood and fat.
Take these things to heart, my son, I warn you.
All men make mistakes, it is only human.
But once the wrong is done, a man
can turn his back on folly, misfortune too,
if he tries to make amends, however low he's fallen,
and stops his bullnecked ways. Stubbornness
brands you for stupidity – pride is a crime.
No, yield to the dead!
Never stab the fighter when he's down.
Where's the glory, killing the dead twice over?

Sophocles

I mean you well. I give you sound advice.
It's best to learn from a good adviser
when he speaks for your own good:
it's pure gain.

CREON: Old man – all of you! So,
you shoot your arrows at my head like archers at the target –
I even have *him* loosed on me, this fortune-teller.
Oh his ilk has tried to sell me short
and ship me off for years. Well,
drive your bargains, traffic – much as you like –
in the gold of India, silver-gold of Sardis.
You'll never bury that body in the grave,
not even if Zeus's eagles rip the corpse
and wing their rotten pickings off to the throne of god!
Never, not even in fear of such defilement
will I tolerate his burial, that traitor.
Well I know, we can't defile the gods –
no mortal has the power.
                          No,
reverend old Tiresias, all men fall,
it's only human, but the wisest fall obscenely
when they glorify obscene advice with rhetoric –
all for their own gain.

TIRESIAS:
Oh god, is there a man alive
who knows, who actually believes . . .

CREON: What now?
What earth-shattering truth are you about to utter?

TIRESIAS:
. . . just how much a sense of judgment, wisdom
is the greatest gift we have?

CREON: Just as much, I'd say,
as a twisted mind is the worst affliction known.

TIRESIAS:
You are the one who's sick, Creon, sick to death.

CREON:
I am in no mood to trade insults with a seer.

TIRESIAS:
You have already, calling my prophecies a lie.

CREON: Why not?
You and the whole breed of seers are mad for money!

TIRESIAS:
And the whole race of tyrants lusts for filthy gain.

CREON:
This slander of yours –
are you aware you're speaking to the king?

TIRESIAS:
Well aware. Who helped you save the city?

CREON: You –
you have your skills, old seer, but you lust for injustice!

TIRESIAS:
You will drive me to utter the dreadful secret in my heart.

CREON:
Spit it out! Just don't speak it out for profit.

TIRESIAS:
Profit? No, not a bit of profit, not for you.

CREON:
Know full well, you'll never buy off my resolve.

TIRESIAS:
Then know this too, learn this by heart!
The chariot of the sun will not race through
so many circuits more, before you have surrendered
one born of your own loins, your own flesh and blood,
a corpse for corpses given in return, since you have thrust

to the world below a child sprung for the world above,
ruthlessly lodged a living soul within the grave –
then you've robbed the gods below the earth,
keeping a dead body here in the bright air,
unburied, unsung, unhallowed by the rites.

You, you have no business with the dead,
nor do the gods above – this is violence
you have forced upon the heavens.
And so the avengers, the dark destroyers late
but true to the mark, now lie in wait for you,
the Furies sent by the gods and the god of death
to strike you down with the pains that you perfected!

There. Reflect on that, tell me I've been bribed.
The day comes soon, no long test of time, not now,
when the mourning cries for men and women break
throughout your halls. Great hatred rises against you –
cities in tumult, all whose mutilated sons
the dogs have graced with burial, or the wild beasts
or a wheeling crow that wings the ungodly stench of carrion
back to each city, each warrior's hearth and home.

These arrows for your heart! Since you've raked me
I loose them like an archer in my anger,
arrows deadly true. You'll never escape
their burning, searing force.

> *Motioning to his escort.*

Come, boy, take me home.
So he can vent his rage on younger men,
and learn to keep a gentler tongue in his head
and better sense than what he carries now.

> *Exit to the side.*

LEADER:
The old man's gone, my king –
terrible prophecies. Well I know,

since the hair on this old head went gray,
he's never lied to Thebes.

CREON:
I know it myself – I'm shaken, torn.
It's a dreadful thing to yield . . . but resist now?
Lay my pride bare to the blows of ruin?
That's dreadful too.

LEADER: But good advice,
Creon, take it now, you must.

CREON:
What should I do? Tell me . . . I'll obey.

LEADER:
Go! Free the girl from the rocky vault
and raise a mound for the body you exposed.

CREON:
That's your advice? You think I should give in?

LEADER:
Yes, my king, quickly. Disasters sent by the gods
cut short our follies in a flash.

CREON: Oh it's hard,
giving up the heart's desire . . . but I will do it –
no more fighting a losing battle with necessity.

LEADER:
Do it now, go, don't leave it to others.

CREON:
Now – I'm on my way! Come, each of you,
take up axes, make for the high ground,
over there, quickly! I and my better judgment
have come round to this – I shackled her,
I'll set her free myself. I am afraid . . .
it's best to keep the established laws
to the very day we die.

Sophocles

> *Rushing out, followed by his entourage. The* CHORUS *clusters around the altar.*

CHORUS:
God of a hundred names!

                Great Dionysus –
     Son and glory of Semele! Pride of Thebes –
Child of Zeus whose thunder rocks the clouds –
Lord of the famous lands of evening –
King of the Mysteries!

                    King of Eleusis, Demeter's plain
her breasting hills that welcome in the world –
Great Dionysus!

             Bacchus, living in Thebes
the mother-city of all your frenzied women –

                            Bacchus
   living along the Ismenus' rippling waters
standing over the field sown with the Dragon's teeth!

You – we have seen you through the flaring smoky fires,
  your torches blazing over the twin peaks
where nymphs of the hallowed cave climb onward
                    fired with you, your sacred rage –
we have seen you at Castalia's running spring
and down from the heights of Nysa crowned with ivy
the greening shore rioting vines and grapes
   down you come in your storm of wild women
           ecstatic, mystic cries –

                        Dionysus –
down to watch and ward the roads of Thebes!
First of all cities, Thebes you honor first
you and your mother, bride of the lighting –
come, Dionysus! now your people lie
in the iron grip of plague,
come in your racing, healing stride
               down Parnassus' slopes
or across the moaning straits.

Antigone

                    Lord of the dancing –
dance, dance the constellations breathing fire!
Great master of the voices of the night!
Child of Zeus, God's offspring, come, come forth!
Lord, king, dance with your nymphs, swirling, raving
arm-in-arm in frenzy through the night
  they dance you, Iacchus –
                    Dance, Dionysus
giver of all good things!

Enter a MESSENGER *from the side.*

MESSENGER: Neighbors,
friends of the house of Cadmus and the kings,
there's not a thing in this mortal life of ours
I'd praise or blame as settled once for all.
Fortune lifts and Fortune fells the lucky
and unlucky every day. No prophet on earth
can tell a man his fate. Take Creon:
there was a man to rouse your envy once,
as I see it. He saved the realm from enemies,
taking power, he alone, the lord of the fatherland,
he set us true on course – he flourished like a tree
with the noble line of sons he bred and reared . . .
and now it's lost, all gone.
                    Believe me,
when a man has squandered his true joys,
he's good as dead, I tell you, a living corpse.
Pile up riches in your house, as much as you like –
live like a king with a huge show of pomp,
but if real delight is missing from the lot,
I wouldn't give you a wisp of smoke for it,
not compared with joy.

LEADER: What now?
What new grief do you bring the house of kings?

MESSENGER:
Dead, dead – and the living are guilty of their death!

Sophocles

LEADER:
Who's the murderer? Who is dead? Tell us.

MESSENGER:
Haemon's gone, his blood spilled by the very hand –

LEADER:
His father's or his own?

MESSENGER: His own . . .
raging mad with his father for the death –

LEADER: Oh great seer,
you saw it all, you brought your word to birth!

MESSENGER:
Those are the facts. Deal with them as you will.

As he turns to go, EURYDICE *enters from the palace.*

LEADER:
Look, Eurydice. Poor woman, Creon's wife,
so close at hand. By chance perhaps,
unless she's heard the news about her son.

EURYDICE: My countrymen,
all of you – I caught the sound of your words
as I was leaving to do my part,
to appeal to queen Athena with my prayers.
I was just loosing the bolts, opening the doors,
when a voice filled with sorrow, family sorrow,
struck my ears, and I fell back, terrified,
into the women's arms – everything went black.
Tell me the news, again, whatever it is . . .
sorrow and I are hardly strangers.
I can bear the worst.

MESSENGER: I – dear lady,
I'll speak as an eye-witness. I was there.
And I won't pass over one word of the truth.
Why should I try to soothe you with a story,

Antigone

only to prove a liar in a moment?
Truth is always best.
                    So,
I escorted your lord, I guided him
to the edge of the plain where the body lay,
Polynices, torn by the dogs and still unmourned.
And saying a prayer to Hecate of the Crossroads,
Pluto too, to hold their anger and be kind,
we washed the dead in a bath of holy water
and plucking some fresh branches, gathering . . .
what was left of him, we burned them all together
and raised a high mound of native earth, and then
we turned and made for that rocky vault of hers,
the hollow, empty bed of the bride of Death.
And far off, one of us heard a voice,
a long wail rising, echoing
out of that unhallowed wedding-chamber,
he ran to alert the master and Creon pressed on,
closer – the strange, inscrutable cry came sharper,
throbbing around him now, and he let loose
a cry of his own, enough to wrench the heart,
'Oh god, am I the prophet now? going down
the darkest road I've ever gone? My son –
it's *his* dear voice, he greets me! Go, men,
closer, quickly! Go through the gap,
the rocks are dragged back –
right to the tomb's very mouth – and look,
see if it's Haemon's voice I think I hear,
or the gods have robbed me of my senses.'

The king was shattered. We took his orders,
went and searched, and there in the deepest,
dark recesses of the tomb we found her . . .
hanged by the neck in a fine linen noose,
strangled in her veils – and the boy,
his arms flung around her waist,
clinging to her, wailing for his bride,

dead and down below, for his father's crimes
and the bed of his marriage blighted by misfortune.
When Creon saw him, he gave a deep sob,
he ran in, shouting, crying out to him,
'Oh my child – what have you done? what seized you,
what insanity? what disaster drove you mad?
Come out, my son! I beg you on my knees!'
But the boy gave him a wild burning glance,
spat in his face, not a word in reply,
he drew his sword – his father rushed out,
running as Haemon lunged and missed! –
and then, doomed, desperate with himself,
suddenly leaning his full weight on the blade,
he buried it in his body, halfway to the hilt,
And still in his senses, pouring his arms around her,
he embraced the girl and breathing hard,
released a quick rush of blood,
bright red on her cheek glistening white.
And there he lies, body enfolding body . . .
he has won his bride at last, poor boy,
not here but in the houses of the dead.

Creon shows the world that of all the ills
afflicting men the worst is lack of judgment.

> EURYDICE *turns and re-enters the palace.*

LEADER:
What do you make of that? The lady's gone,
without a word, good or bad.

MESSENGER: I'm alarmed too
but here's my hope – faced with her son's death
she finds it unbecoming to mourn in public.
Inside, under her roof, she'll set her women
to the task and wail the sorrow of the house.
She's too discreet. She won't do something rash.

Antigone

LEADER:
I'm not so sure. To me, at least,
a long heavy silence promises danger,
just as much as a lot of empty outcries.

MESSENGER:
We'll see if she's holding something back,
hiding some passion in her heart.
I'm going in. You may be right – who knows?
Even too much silence has its dangers.

Exit to the palace. Enter CREON
*from the side, escorted by attendants
carrying* HAEMON's *body on a bier.*

LEADER:
    The king himself! Coming toward us,
    look, holding the boy's head in his hands.
    Clear, damning proof, if it's right to say so –
    proof of his own madness, no one else's,
        no, his own blind wrongs.

CREON: Ohhh,
so senseless, so insane . . . my crimes,
my stubborn, deadly –
Look at us, the killer, the killed,
father and son, the same blood – the misery!
My plans, my mad fanatic heart,
my son, cut off so young!
Ai, dead, lost to the world,
not through your stupidity, no, my own.

LEADER: Too late,
too late, you see what justice means.

CREON: Oh I've learned
    through blood and tears! Then, it was then,
    when the god came down and struck me – a great weight
    shattering, driving me down that wild savage path,

ruining, trampling down my joy. Oh the agony,
the heartbreaking agonies of our lives.

Enter the MESSENGER *from the palace.*

MESSENGER: Master,
what a hoard of grief you have, and you'll have more.
The grief that lies to hand you've brought yourself –

Pointing to HAEMON's *body.*

the rest, in the house, you'll see it all too soon.

CREON:
What now? What's worse than this?

MESSENGER: The queen is dead.
The mother of this dead boy . . . mother to the end –
poor thing, her wounds are fresh.

CREON: No, no,
harbor of Death, so choked, so hard to cleanse! –
why me? why are you killing me?
Herald of pain, more words, more grief?
I died once, you kill me again and again!
What's the report, boy . . . some news for me?
My wife dead? O dear god!
Slaughter heaped on slaughter?

The doors open; the body of EURYDICE *is brought out on her bier.*

MESSENGER: See for yourself:
now they bring her body from the palace.

CREON: Oh no,
another, a second loss to break the heart.
What next, what fate still waits for me?
I just held my son in my arms and now,
look, a new corpse rising before my eyes –
wretched, helpless mother – O my son!

MESSENGER:
She stabbed herself at the altar,
then her eyes went dark, after she'd raised
a cry for the noble fate of Megareus, the hero
killed in the first assault, then for Haemon,
then with her dying breath she called down
torments on your head – you killed her sons.

CREON: Oh the dread,
　I shudder with dread! Why not kill me too? –
　run me through with a good sharp sword?
　Oh god, the misery, anguish –
　I, I'm churning with it, going under.

MESSENGER:
Yes, and the dead, the woman lying there,
piles the guilt of all their deaths on you.

CREON:
How did she end her life, what bloody stroke?

MESSENGER:
She drove home to the heart with her own hand,
once she learned her son was dead . . . that agony.

CREON:
　And the guilt is all mine –
　can never be fixed on another man,
　no escape for me. I killed you,
　I, god help me, I admit it all!

To his attendants.

　Take me away, quickly, out of sight.
　I don't even exist – I'm no one. Nothing.

LEADER:
Good advice, if there's any good in suffering.
Quickest is best when troubles block the way.

Sophocles

CREON: *Kneeling in prayer.*
> Come, let it come! – that best of fates for me
> that brings the final day, best fate of all.
> Oh quickly, now –
> so I never have to see another sunrise.

LEADER:
That will come when it comes;
we must deal with all that lies before us.
The future rests with the ones who tend the future.

CREON:
> That prayer – I poured my heart into that prayer!

LEADER:
No more prayers now. For mortal men
there is no escape from the doom we must endure.

CREON:
> Take me away, I beg you, out of sight.
> A rash, indiscriminate fool!
> I murdered you, my son, against my will –
> you too, my wife . . .
>   Wailing wreck of a man,
> whom to look to? where to lean for support?

Desperately turning from HAEMON
to EURYDICE *on their biers.*

> Whatever I touch goes wrong – once more
> a crushing fate's come down upon my head!

The MESSENGER *and attendants lead*
CREON *into the palace.*

CHORUS:
> Wisdom is by far the greatest part of joy,
> and reverence toward the gods must be safeguarded.
> The mighty words of the proud are paid in full
> with mighty blows of fate, and at long last
> those blows will teach us wisdom.

The old citizens exit to the side.

1. BOCCACCIO · *Mrs Rosie and the Priest*
2. GERARD MANLEY HOPKINS · *As kingfishers catch fire*
3. *The Saga of Gunnlaug Serpent-tongue*
4. THOMAS DE QUINCEY · *On Murder Considered as One of the Fine Arts*
5. FRIEDRICH NIETZSCHE · *Aphorisms on Love and Hate*
6. JOHN RUSKIN · *Traffic*
7. PU SONGLING · *Wailing Ghosts*
8. JONATHAN SWIFT · *A Modest Proposal*
9. *Three Tang Dynasty Poets*
10. WALT WHITMAN · *On the Beach at Night Alone*
11. KENKŌ · *A Cup of Sake Beneath the Cherry Trees*
12. BALTASAR GRACIÁN · *How to Use Your Enemies*
13. JOHN KEATS · *The Eve of St Agnes*
14. THOMAS HARDY · *Woman much missed*
15. GUY DE MAUPASSANT · *Femme Fatale*
16. MARCO POLO · *Travels in the Land of Serpents and Pearls*
17. SUETONIUS · *Caligula*
18. APOLLONIUS OF RHODES · *Jason and Medea*
19. ROBERT LOUIS STEVENSON · *Olalla*
20. KARL MARX AND FRIEDRICH ENGELS · *The Communist Manifesto*
21. PETRONIUS · *Trimalchio's Feast*
22. JOHANN PETER HEBEL · *How a Ghastly Story Was Brought to Light by a Common or Garden Butcher's Dog*
23. HANS CHRISTIAN ANDERSEN · *The Tinder Box*
24. RUDYARD KIPLING · *The Gate of the Hundred Sorrows*
25. DANTE · *Circles of Hell*
26. HENRY MAYHEW · *Of Street Piemen*
27. HAFEZ · *The nightingales are drunk*
28. GEOFFREY CHAUCER · *The Wife of Bath*
29. MICHEL DE MONTAIGNE · *How We Weep and Laugh at the Same Thing*
30. THOMAS NASHE · *The Terrors of the Night*
31. EDGAR ALLAN POE · *The Tell-Tale Heart*
32. MARY KINGSLEY · *A Hippo Banquet*
33. JANE AUSTEN · *The Beautifull Cassandra*
34. ANTON CHEKHOV · *Gooseberries*
35. SAMUEL TAYLOR COLERIDGE · *Well, they are gone, and here must I remain*
36. JOHANN WOLFGANG VON GOETHE · *Sketchy, Doubtful, Incomplete Jottings*
37. CHARLES DICKENS · *The Great Winglebury Duel*
38. HERMAN MELVILLE · *The Maldive Shark*
39. ELIZABETH GASKELL · *The Old Nurse's Story*
40. NIKOLAY LESKOV · *The Steel Flea*

41. HONORÉ DE BALZAC · *The Atheist's Mass*
42. CHARLOTTE PERKINS GILMAN · *The Yellow Wall-Paper*
43. C.P. CAVAFY · *Remember, Body . . .*
44. FYODOR DOSTOEVSKY · *The Meek One*
45. GUSTAVE FLAUBERT · *A Simple Heart*
46. NIKOLAI GOGOL · *The Nose*
47. SAMUEL PEPYS · *The Great Fire of London*
48. EDITH WHARTON · *The Reckoning*
49. HENRY JAMES · *The Figure in the Carpet*
50. WILFRED OWEN · *Anthem For Doomed Youth*
51. WOLFGANG AMADEUS MOZART · *My Dearest Father*
52. PLATO · *Socrates' Defence*
53. CHRISTINA ROSSETTI · *Goblin Market*
54. *Sindbad the Sailor*
55. SOPHOCLES · *Antigone*
56. RYŪNOSUKE AKUTAGAWA · *The Life of a Stupid Man*
57. LEO TOLSTOY · *How Much Land Does A Man Need?*
58. GIORGIO VASARI · *Leonardo da Vinci*
59. OSCAR WILDE · *Lord Arthur Savile's Crime*
60. SHEN FU · *The Old Man of the Moon*
61. AESOP · *The Dolphins, the Whales and the Gudgeon*
62. MATSUO BASHŌ · *Lips too Chilled*
63. EMILY BRONTË · *The Night is Darkening Round Me*
64. JOSEPH CONRAD · *To-morrow*
65. RICHARD HAKLUYT · *The Voyage of Sir Francis Drake Around the Whole Globe*
66. KATE CHOPIN · *A Pair of Silk Stockings*
67. CHARLES DARWIN · *It was snowing butterflies*
68. BROTHERS GRIMM · *The Robber Bridegroom*
69. CATULLUS · *I Hate and I Love*
70. HOMER · *Circe and the Cyclops*
71. D. H. LAWRENCE · *Il Duro*
72. KATHERINE MANSFIELD · *Miss Brill*
73. OVID · *The Fall of Icarus*
74. SAPPHO · *Come Close*
75. IVAN TURGENEV · *Kasyan from the Beautiful Lands*
76. VIRGIL · *O Cruel Alexis*
77. H. G. WELLS · *A Slip under the Microscope*
78. HERODOTUS · *The Madness of Cambyses*
79. *Speaking of Siva*
80. *The Dhammapada*

'Ah, what is the life of a human being – a drop of dew, a flash of lightning? This is so sad, so sad.'

RYŪNOSUKE AKUTAGAWA
Born 1892, Tokyo
Died 1927, Tokyo

This selection is taken from Jay Rubin's translation of *Rashōmon and Seventeen Other Stories*, first published in 2006.

RYŪNOSUKE AKUTAGAWA IN PENGUIN CLASSICS
Rashōmon and Seventeen Other Stories

RYŪNOSUKE AKUTAGAWA

The Life of a Stupid Man

Translated by
Jay Rubin

PENGUIN BOOKS

PENGUIN CLASSICS

UK | USA | Canada | Ireland | Australia
India | New Zealand | South Africa

Penguin Books is part of the Penguin Random House group of companies
whose addresses can be found at global.penguinrandomhouse.com.

This selection published in Penguin Classics 2015
013

Translation copyright © Jay Rubin, 2006

The moral right of the translator has been asserted

Set in 9.5/13 pt Baskerville 10 Pro
Typeset by Jouve (UK), Milton Keynes
Printed in Great Britain by Clays Ltd, Elcograf S.p.A.

A CIP catalogue record for this book is available from the British Library

ISBN: 978–0–141–39772–6

www.greenpenguin.co.uk

Penguin Random House is committed to a
sustainable future for our business, our readers
and our planet. This book is made from Forest
Stewardship Council® certified paper.

Contents

In a Bamboo Grove   1
Death Register   16
The Life of a Stupid Man   26

In a Bamboo Grove

THE TESTIMONY OF A WOODCUTTER
UNDER QUESTIONING BY THE MAGISTRATE

That is true, Your Honor. I am the one who found the body. I went out as usual this morning to cut cedar in the hills behind my place. The body was in a bamboo grove on the other side of the mountain. Its exact location? A few hundred yards off the Yamashina post road. A deserted place where a few scrub cedar trees are mixed in with the bamboo.

The man was lying on his back in his pale blue robe with the sleeves tied up and one of those fancy Kyoto-style black hats with the sharp creases. He had only one stab wound, but it was right in the middle of his chest; the bamboo leaves around the body were soaked with dark red blood. No, the bleeding had stopped. The wound looked dry, and I remember it had a big horsefly sucking on it so hard the thing didn't even notice my footsteps.

Did I see a sword or anything? No, Sir, not a thing. Just a length of rope by the cedar tree next to the body.

And – oh yes, there was a comb there, too. Just the rope and the comb is all. But the weeds and the bamboo leaves on the ground were pretty trampled down: he must have put up a tremendous fight before they killed him. How's that, Sir – a horse? No, a horse could never have gotten into that place. It's all bamboo thicket between there and the road.

THE TESTIMONY OF A TRAVELING PRIEST UNDER QUESTIONING BY THE MAGISTRATE

I'm sure I passed the man yesterday, Your Honor. Yesterday at – about noon, I'd say. Near Checkpoint Hill on the way to Yamashina. He was walking toward the checkpoint with a woman on horseback. She wore a stiff, round straw hat with a long veil hanging down around the brim; I couldn't see her face, just her robe. I think it had a kind of dark-red outer layer with a blue-green lining. The horse was a dappled gray with a tinge of red, and I'm fairly sure it had a clipped mane. Was it a big horse? I'd say it was a few inches taller than most, but I'm a priest after all. I don't know much about horses. The man? No, Sir, he had a good-sized sword, and he was equipped with a bow and arrows. I can still see that black-lacquered quiver of his: he must have had twenty arrows in it, maybe more. I would never have dreamt that a thing like this could happen to such a man. Ah, what is the life of a human

In a Bamboo Grove

being – a drop of dew, a flash of lightning? This is so sad, so sad. What can I say?

THE TESTIMONY OF A POLICEMAN UNDER QUESTIONING BY THE MAGISTRATE

The man I captured, Your Honor? I am certain he is the famous bandit, Tajōmaru. True, when I caught him he had fallen off his horse, and he was moaning and groaning on the stone bridge at Awataguchi. The time, Sir? It was last night at the first watch. He was wearing the same dark blue robe and carrying the same long sword he used the time I almost captured him before. You can see he also has a bow and arrows now. Oh, is that so, Sir? The dead man, too? That settles it, then: I'm sure this Tajōmaru fellow is the murderer. A leather-wrapped bow, a quiver in black lacquer, seventeen hawk-feather arrows – they must have belonged to the victim. And yes, as you say, Sir, the horse is a dappled gray with a touch of red, and it has a clipped mane. It's only a dumb animal, but it gave that bandit just what he deserved, throwing him like that. It was a short way beyond the bridge, trailing its reins on the ground and eating plume grass by the road.

Of all the bandits prowling around Kyoto, this Tajōmaru is known as a fellow who likes the women. Last fall, people at Toribe Temple found a pair of worshippers murdered – a woman and a child – on the hill behind the statue of Binzuru. Everybody said Tajōmaru must have done it. If it turns out he killed the man, there's no telling what he might have done to the woman who was on the horse. I don't mean to meddle, Sir, but I do think you ought to question him about that.

THE TESTIMONY OF AN OLD WOMAN UNDER QUESTIONING BY THE MAGISTRATE

Yes, Your Honor, my daughter was married to the dead man. He is not from the capital, though. He was a samurai serving in the Wakasa provincial office. His name was Kanazawa no Takehiro, and he was twenty-six years old. No, Sir, he was a very kind man. I can't believe anyone would have hated him enough to do this.

My daughter, Sir? Her name is Masago, and she is nineteen years old. She's as bold as any man, but the only man she has ever known is Takehiro. Her complexion is a little on the dark side, and she has a mole by the outside corner of her left eye, but her face is a tiny, perfect oval.

Takehiro left for Wakasa yesterday with my daughter, but what turn of fate could have led to this? There's nothing I can do for my son-in-law anymore, but what could have happened to my daughter? I'm worried sick about her. Oh please, Sir, do everything you can to find her, leave no stone unturned: I have lived a long time, but I have never wanted anything so badly in my life. Oh how I hate that bandit – that, that Tajōmaru! Not only my son-in-law, but my daughter . . . (Here the old woman broke down and was unable to go on speaking.)

*   *   *   *   *

TAJŌMARU'S CONFESSION

Sure, I killed the man. But I didn't kill the woman. So, where did she go? I don't know any better than you do. Now, wait just a minute – you can torture me all you want, but I can't tell you what I don't know. And besides, now that you've got me, I'm not going to hide anything. I'm no coward.

I met that couple yesterday, a little after noon. The second I saw them, a puff of wind lifted her veil and I caught a peek at her. Just a peek: that's maybe why she looked so perfect to me – an absolute bodhisattva of a woman. I made up my mind right then to take her even if I had to kill the man.

Oh come on, killing a man is not as big a thing as people like you seem to think. If you're going to take somebody's woman, a man has to die. When *I* kill a man, I do it with my sword, but people like you don't use swords. You gentlemen kill with your power, with your money, and sometimes just with your words: you tell people you're doing them a favor. True, no blood flows, the man is still alive, but you've killed him all the same. I don't know whose sin is greater – yours or mine. (A sarcastic smile.)

Of course, if you can take the woman without killing the man, all the better. Which is exactly what I was hoping to do yesterday. It would have been impossible on the Yamashina post road, of course, so I thought of a way to lure them into the hills.

It was easy. I fell in with them on the road and made up a story. I told them I had found an old burial mound in the hills, and when I opened it it was full of swords and mirrors and things. I said I had buried the stuff in a bamboo grove on the other side of the mountain to keep anyone from finding out about it, and I'd sell it cheap to the right buyer. He started getting interested soon enough. It's scary what greed can do to people, don't you think? In less than an hour, I was leading that couple and their horse up a mountain trail.

When we reached the grove, I told them the treasure was buried in there and they should come inside with me and look at it. The man was so hungry for the stuff by then, he couldn't refuse, but the woman said she'd wait there on the horse. I figured that would happen – the woods are so thick. They fell right into my trap. We left the woman alone and went into the grove.

It was all bamboo at first. Fifty yards or so inside, there was a sort of open clump of cedars – the perfect place for

In a Bamboo Grove

what I was going to do. I pushed through the thicket and made up some nonsense about how the treasure was buried under one of them. When he heard that, the man charged toward some scrawny cedars visible up ahead. The bamboo thinned out, and the trees were standing there in a row. As soon as we got to them, I grabbed him and pinned him down. I could see he was a strong man – he carried a sword – but I took him by surprise, and he couldn't do a thing. I had him tied to the base of a tree in no time. Where did I get the rope? Well, I'm a thief, you know – I might have to scale a wall at any time – so I've always got a piece of rope in my belt. I stuffed his mouth full of bamboo leaves to keep him quiet. That's all there was to it.

Once I finished with the man, I went and told the woman that her husband had suddenly been taken ill and she should come and have a look at him. This was another bull's-eye, of course. She took off her hat and let me lead her by the hand into the grove. As soon as she saw the man tied to the tree, though, she whipped a dagger out of her breast. I never saw a woman with such fire! If I'd been off my guard, she'd have stuck that thing in my gut. And the way she kept coming, she would have done me some damage eventually no matter how much I dodged. Still, I *am* Tajōmaru. One way or another, I managed to knock the knife out of her hand without drawing my sword. Even the most spirited woman is going to be helpless if she hasn't got a weapon. And so I was able to make the woman mine without taking her husband's life.

Yes, you heard me: without taking her husband's life. I wasn't planning to kill him on top of everything else. The woman was on the ground, crying, and I was getting ready to run out of the grove and leave her there when all of a sudden she grabbed my arm like some kind of crazy person. And then I heard what she was shouting between sobs. She could hardly catch her breath: 'Either you die or my husband dies. It has to be one of you. It's worse than death for me to have two men see my shame. I want to stay with the one left alive, whether it's you or him.' That gave me a wild desire to kill her husband. (Sullen excitement.)

When I say this, you probably think I'm crueler than you are. But that's because you didn't see the look on her face – and especially, you never saw the way her eyes were burning at that moment. When those eyes met mine, I knew I wanted to make her my wife. Let the thunder god kill me, I'd make her my wife – that was the only thought in my head. And no, not just from lust. I know that's what you gentlemen are thinking. If lust was all I felt for her, I'd already taken care of that. I could've just kicked her down and gotten out of there. And the man wouldn't have stained my sword with his blood. But the moment my eyes locked onto hers in that dark grove, I knew I couldn't leave there until I had killed him.

In a Bamboo Grove

Still, I didn't want to kill him in a cowardly way. I untied him and challenged him to a sword fight. (That piece of rope they found was the one I threw aside then.) The man looked furious as he drew his big sword, and without a word he sprang at me in a rage. I don't have to tell you the outcome of the fight. My sword pierced his breast on the twenty-third thrust. Not till the twenty-third: I want you to keep that in mind. I still admire him for that. He's the only man who ever lasted even twenty thrusts with me. (Cheerful grin.)

As he went down, I lowered my bloody sword and turned toward the woman. But she was gone! I looked for her among the cedars, but the bamboo leaves on the ground showed no sign she'd ever been there. I cocked my ear for any sound of her, but all I could hear was the man's death rattle.

Maybe she had run through the underbrush to call for help when the sword fight started. The thought made me fear for my life. I grabbed the man's sword and his bow and arrows and headed straight for the mountain road. The woman's horse was still there, just chewing on grass. Anything else I could tell you after that would be a waste of breath. I got rid of his sword before coming to Kyoto, though.

So that's my confession. I always knew my head would end up hanging in the tree outside the prison some day, so let me have the ultimate punishment. (Defiant attitude.)

Ryūnosuke Akutagawa

PENITENT CONFESSION OF A WOMAN IN THE KIYOMIZU TEMPLE

After the man in the dark blue robe had his way with me, he looked at my husband, all tied up, and taunted him with laughter. How humiliated my husband must have felt! He squirmed and twisted in the ropes that covered his body, but the knots ate all the deeper into his flesh. Stumbling, I ran to his side. No – I *tried* to run to him, but instantly the man kicked me down. And that was when it happened: that was when I saw the indescribable glint in my husband's eyes. Truly, it was indescribable. It makes me shudder to recall it even now. My husband was unable to speak a word, and yet, in that moment, his eyes conveyed his whole heart to me. What I saw shining there was neither anger nor sorrow. It was the cold flash of contempt – contempt for *me*. This struck me more painfully than the bandit's kick. I let out a cry and collapsed on the spot.

When I regained consciousness, the man in blue was gone. The only one there in the grove was my husband, still tied to the cedar tree. I just barely managed to raise myself on the carpet of dead bamboo leaves, and look into my husband's face. His eyes were exactly as they had been before, with that same cold look of contempt and hatred. How can I describe the emotion that filled my heart then? Shame . . . sorrow . . . anger . . . I staggered over to him.

'Oh, my husband! Now that this has happened, I

In a Bamboo Grove

cannot go on living with you. I am prepared to die here and now. But you – yes, I want you to die as well. You witnessed my shame. I cannot leave you behind with that knowledge.'

I struggled to say everything I needed to say, but my husband simply went on staring at me in disgust. I felt as if my breast would burst open at any moment, but holding my feelings in check, I began to search the bamboo thicket for his sword. The bandit must have taken it – I couldn't find it anywhere – and my husband's bow and arrows were gone as well. But then I had the good luck to find the dagger at my feet. I brandished it before my husband and spoke to him once again.

'This is the end, then. Please be so good as to allow me to take your life. I will quickly follow you in death.'

When he heard this, my husband finally began moving his lips. Of course his mouth was stuffed with bamboo leaves, so he couldn't make a sound, but I knew immediately what he was saying. With total contempt for me, he said only, 'Do it.' Drifting somewhere between dream and reality, I thrust the dagger through the chest of his pale blue robe.

Then I lost consciousness again. When I was able to look around me at last, my husband, still tied to the tree, was no longer breathing. Across his ashen face shone a streak of light from the setting sun, filtered through the bamboo and cedar. Gulping back my tears, I untied him and cast the rope aside. And then – and then what happened to me? I no longer have the strength to tell it. That I failed to kill myself is obvious. I tried to stab myself in the throat. I threw myself in a pond at the foot of the mountain. Nothing worked. I am still here, by no means proud of my inability to die. (Forlorn smile.) Perhaps even Kanzeon, bodhisattva of compassion, has turned away from me for being so weak. But now – now that I have killed my husband, now that I have been violated by a bandit – what am I to do? Tell me, what am I to ... (Sudden violent sobbing.)

THE TESTIMONY OF THE DEAD MAN'S SPIRIT TOLD THROUGH A MEDIUM

After the bandit had his way with my wife, he sat there on the ground, trying to comfort her. I could say nothing, of course, and I was bound to the cedar tree. But I kept trying to signal her with my eyes: *Don't believe anything he tells you. He's lying, no matter what he says*. I tried to convey my meaning to her, but she just went on cringing there on the fallen bamboo leaves, staring at her knees. And, you know, I could see she was listening to him. I writhed with jealousy, but the bandit kept his smooth talk going from one point to the next. 'Now that your flesh has been sullied, things will never be the same with your husband. Don't stay with him – come and be my wife! It's because

In a Bamboo Grove

I love you so much that I was so wild with you.' The bandit had the gall to speak to her like that!

When my wife raised her face in response to him, she seemed almost spellbound. I had never seen her look so beautiful as she did at that moment. And what do you think this beautiful wife of mine said to the bandit, in my presence — in the presence of her husband bound hand and foot? My spirit may be wandering now between one life and the next, but every time I recall her answer, I burn with indignation. 'All right,' she told him, 'take me anywhere you like.' (Long silence.)

And that was not her only crime against me. If that were all she did, I would not be suffering so here in the darkness. With him leading her by the hand, she was stepping out of the bamboo grove as if in a dream, when suddenly the color drained from her face and she pointed back to me. 'Kill him!' she screamed. 'Kill him! I can't be with you as long as he is alive!' Again and again she screamed, as if she had lost her mind, 'Kill him!' Even now her words like a windstorm threaten to blow me headlong into the darkest depths. Have such hateful words ever come from the mouth of a human being before? Have such damnable words ever reached the ears of a human being before? Have such — (An explosion of derisive laughter.) Even the bandit went pale when he heard her. She clung to his arm and screamed again, 'Kill him!' The bandit stared at her, saying neither that he would kill me nor that he would not. The next thing I knew, however, he sent my wife sprawling on the bamboo leaves with a single kick. (Another explosion of derisive laughter.) The bandit calmly folded his arms and turned to look at me.

'What do you want me to do with her?' he asked. 'Kill her or let her go? Just nod to answer. Kill her?' For this if for nothing else, I am ready to forgive the bandit his crimes. (Second long silence.)

When I hesitated with my answer, my wife let out a scream and darted into the depths of the bamboo thicket. He sprang after her, but I don't think he even managed to lay a hand on her sleeve. I watched the spectacle as if it were some kind of vision.

After my wife ran off, the bandit picked up my sword and bow and arrows, and he cut my ropes at one place. 'Now it's my turn to run,' I remember hearing him mutter as he disappeared from the thicket. Then the whole area was quiet. No – I could hear someone weeping. While I was untying myself, I listened to the sound, until I realized – I realized that I was the one crying. (Another long silence.)

I finally raised myself, exhausted, from the foot of the tree. Lying there before me was the dagger that my wife had dropped. I picked it up and shoved it into my chest. Some kind of bloody mass rose to my mouth, but I felt no pain at all. My chest grew cold, and then everything sank into stillness. What perfect silence! In the skies

In a Bamboo Grove

above that grove on the hidden side of the mountain, not a single bird came to sing. The lonely glow of the sun lingered among the high branches of cedar and bamboo. The sun – but gradually, even that began to fade, and with it the cedars and bamboo. I lay there wrapped in a deep silence.

Then stealthy footsteps came up to me. I tried to see who it was, but the darkness had closed in all around me. Someone – that someone gently pulled the dagger from my chest with an invisible hand. Again a rush of blood filled my mouth, but then I sank once and for all into the darkness between lives.

Death Register

1

My mother was a madwoman. I never did feel close to her, as a son should feel toward his mother. Hair held in place by a comb, she would sit alone all day puffing on a long, skinny pipe in the house of my birth family in Tokyo's Shiba Ward. She had a tiny face on a tiny body, and that face of hers, for some reason, was always ashen and lifeless. Once, reading *The Story of the Western Wing*, I came upon the phrase 'smell of earth, taste of mud', and thought immediately of my mother – of her emaciated face in profile.

And so I never had the experience of a mother's care. I do seem to recall that one time, when my adoptive mother made a point of taking me upstairs to see her, she suddenly conked me on the head with her pipe. In general, though, she was a quiet lunatic. I or my elder sister would sometimes press her to paint a picture for us, and she would do it on a sheet of paper folded in four. And not just with black ink, either. She would apply my sister's watercolors to blossoming

Death Register

plants or the costumes of children on an outing. The people in her pictures, though, always had fox faces.

My mother died in the autumn of my eleventh year, not so much from illness, I think, as from simply wasting away. I have a fairly clear memory of the events surrounding her death.

A telegram must have arrived to alert us. Late on a windless night, I climbed into a rickshaw with my adoptive mother and sped across the city from Honjo to Shiba. Otherwise in my life I have never used a scarf, but I do recall that on that particular night I had a thin silk handkerchief wrapped around my neck. I also recall that it had some kind of Chinese landscape motif, and that it smelled strongly of Iris Bouquet.

My mother lay on a futon in the eight-mat parlor directly beneath her upstairs room. I knelt beside her, wailing, with my four-year-older sister. I felt especially miserable when I heard someone behind me say, 'The end is near.' My mother had been lying there as good as dead, but suddenly she opened her eyes and spoke. Sad as everyone felt, we couldn't help giggling.

I stayed up by my mother through the following night as well, but that night, for some reason, my tears simply wouldn't flow. Ashamed to be so unfeeling while right next to me my sister wept almost constantly, I struggled to pretend. Yet I also believed that as long as I was unable to cry, my mother would not die.

On the evening of the third day, though, she did die, with very little suffering. A few times before it happened, she would seem to regain consciousness, look us all in the face, and release an endless stream of tears, but as usual she said not a thing.

Even after her body had been placed in the coffin, I couldn't keep from breaking down time and again. The old woman we called our 'Ōji Auntie', a distant relative, would say, 'I'm so impressed with you!' My only thought was that here was a person who let herself be impressed by very strange things.

The day of my mother's funeral, my sister climbed into a rickshaw holding the memorial tablet, and I followed her inside, holding the censer. I dozed off now and then, waking with a start each time the censer was about to drop from my hand. Still, we seemed never to reach Yanaka. Always I would wake to find the long funeral procession still winding its way through the streets of Tokyo in the autumn sunlight.

The anniversary of my mother's death is 28 November. The priest gave her the posthumous name of Kimyōin Myōjō Nisshin Daishi. I can remember neither the anniversary of my birth father's death two decades later nor his posthumous name. Memorizing such things had probably been a matter of pride for me at the age of eleven.

Death Register

2

I have just the one elder sister. Not very healthy, she is nevertheless the mother of two children. She is not, of course, one of those I want to include in this 'Death Register.' Rather, it is the sister who died suddenly just before I was born. Among us three siblings, she was said to be the smartest.

She was certainly the first – which is why they named her 'Hatsuko' (First Daughter). Even now a small framed portrait of 'Little Hatsu' adorns the Buddhist altar in my house. There is nothing at all sickly-looking about her. Her cheeks, with their little dimples, are as round as ripe apricots.

Little Hatsu was by far the one who received the greatest outpouring of love from my parents. They made a point of sending her all the way from Shiba Shinsenza to attend the kindergarten of a Mrs Summers – I think it was – in Tsukiji. On weekends, though, she would stay with my mother's family, the Akutagawas, in Honjo. On these outings of hers, Little Hatsu would probably wear Western dresses, which still, in the Meiji twenties, would have seemed very modish. When I was in elementary school, I remember, I used to get remnants of her clothes to put on my rubber doll. Without exception, all the cloth patches were imported calico scattered with tiny printed flowers or musical instruments.

Ryūnosuke Akutagawa

One Sunday afternoon in early spring, when Little Hatsu was strolling through the garden (wearing a Western dress, as I imagine her), she called out to our aunt Fuki in the parlor, 'Auntie, what's the name of this tree?'

'Which one?'

'This one, with the buds.'

In the garden of my mother's family, a single low *boke** trailed its branches over the old well. Little Hatsu, in pigtails, was probably looking up at its thorny branches with big round eyes.

'It has the same name as you,' my aunt said, but before she could explain her joke, Hatsu made up one of her own:

'Then it must be a "dummy" tree.'

My aunt always tells this story whenever the conversation turns to Little Hatsu. Indeed, it's the only story left to tell about her. Probably not too many days later, Little Hatsu was in her coffin. I don't remember the posthumous name engraved on her tiny memorial tablet. I do have a strangely clear memory of her death date, though: 5 April.

For some unknown reason, I feel close to this sister I never knew. If 'Little Hatsu' were still living, she would

---

* *boke*: The name of the tree, known as a Japanese quince (*Pyrus japonica*) in English, is a homonym for 'dimwit'. Before the aunt can joke with her that both she and the tree are '*boke*', Hatsu cleverly makes up her own remarkably similar word play using '*baka*' (dummy).

be over forty now. And maybe, at that age, she would look like my mother as I recall her upstairs in the Shiba house, blankly puffing away on her pipe. I often feel as if there is a fortyish woman somewhere – a phantom not exactly my mother nor this dead sister – watching over my life. Could this be the effect of nerves wracked by coffee and tobacco? Or might it be the work of some supernatural power giving occasional glimpses of itself to the real world?

3

Because my mother lost her mind, I was adopted into the family of her elder brother shortly after I was born, and so my real father was another parent for whom I had little feeling. He owned a dairy and seems to have been a small-scale success. That father was the person who taught me all about the newly imported fruits and drinks of the day: *banana*, *ice cream*, *pineapple*, *rum* – and probably much more. I remember once drinking rum in the shade of an oak tree outside the pasture, which was then located in Shinjuku. Rum was an amber-colored drink with little alcohol.

When I was very young, my father would try to entice me back from my adoptive family by plying me with these rare treats. I remember how he once openly tempted me into running away while feeding me ice cream in the Uoei restaurant in Ōmori. At times like this he could be a smooth talker and exude real charm. Unfortunately for him, though, his enticements never worked. This was because I loved my adoptive family too much – and especially my mother's elder sister, Aunt Fuki.

My father had a short temper and was always fighting with people. When I was in the third year of middle school, I beat him at sumo wrestling by tripping him backwards using a special judo move of mine. He got up and came right after me saying 'One more go.' I threw him easily again. He came charging at me for a third time, again saying 'One more go,' but now I could see he was angry. My other aunt (Aunt Fuyu, my mother's younger sister – by then my father's second wife) was watching all this, and she winked at me a few times behind my father's back. After grappling with him for a little while, I purposely fell over backwards. I'm sure if I hadn't lost to him, I would have ended up another victim of my father's temper.

When I was twenty-eight and still teaching, I received a telegram saying 'Father hospitalized,' and I rushed from Kamakura to Tokyo. He was in the Tokyo Hospital with influenza. I spent the next three days there with my Aunts Fuyu and Fuki, sleeping in a corner of the room. I was beginning to feel bored when a call came for me from an Irish reporter friend inviting me out for a meal at a Tsukiji tea house. Using his upcoming departure for America as

Death Register

an excuse, I left for Tsukiji even though my father was on the verge of death.

We had a delightful Japanese dinner in the company of four or five geisha. I think the meal ended around ten o'clock. Leaving the reporter, I was headed down the steep, narrow stairway when, from behind, I heard a soft feminine voice calling me 'Ah-san' in that playful geisha way. I stopped in mid-descent and turned to look up toward the top of the stairs. There, one of the geisha was looking down, her eyes fixed on mine. Wordlessly, I continued down the stairs and stepped into the cab waiting at the front door. The car moved off immediately, but instead of my father what came to mind was the fresh face of that geisha in her Western hairstyle – and in particular her eyes.

Back at the hospital, I found my father eagerly awaiting my return. He sent everyone else outside the two-panel folding screen by the bed, and, gripping and caressing my hand, he began to talk about long-ago matters that I had never known – things from the time when he married my mother. They were inconsequential things – how he and she had gone to shop for a storage chest, or how they had eaten home-delivered sushi – but before I knew it my eyelids were growing hot inside, and down my father's wasted cheeks, too, tears were flowing.

My father died the next morning without a great deal of suffering. His mind seemed to grow confused before he died, and he would say things like 'Here comes a warship! Look at all the flags it has flying! Three cheers, everybody!' I don't remember his funeral at all. What I do remember is that when we transported his body from the hospital to his home, a great big spring moon was shining down on the hearse.

4

In mid-March of this year, when it was still cold enough for us to carry pocket warmers, my wife and I visited the cemetery for the first time in a long while – a very long while. Still, however, there was no change at all in either the small grave itself (of course) nor in the red pine stretching its branches above it.

The bones of all three people I have included in this 'Death Register' lie buried in the same corner of the cemetery in Yanaka – indeed, beneath the same gravestone. I recalled the time my mother's coffin was gently lowered into the grave. They must have done the same with Little Hatsu. In my father's case, though, I remember the gold teeth mixed in with the tiny white shards of bone at the crematorium.

I don't much like visiting the cemetery, and I would prefer to forget about my parents and sister if I could. On that particular day, though, perhaps because I was physically debilitated, I found myself staring at the blackened gravestone in the early spring afternoon sunlight and wondering which of the three had been the most fortunate.

> A shimmering of heat –
> Outside the grave
> Alone I dwell.

Never before had I sensed these feelings of Jōsō's pressing in upon me with the force they truly had for me that day.

The Life of a Stupid Man

To my friend, Kume Masao:

I leave it to you to decide when and where to publish this manuscript – or whether to publish it at all.

You know most of the people who appear here, but if you do publish this, I don't want you adding an index identifying them.

I am living now in the unhappiest happiness imaginable. Yet, strangely, I have no regrets. I just feel sorry for anyone unfortunate enough to have had a bad husband, a bad son, a bad father like me. So goodbye, then. I have not tried – *consciously*, at least – to vindicate myself here.

Finally, I entrust this manuscript to you because I believe you probably know me better than anyone else. I may wear the skin of an urbane sophisticate, but in this manuscript I invite you to strip it off and laugh at my stupidity.

Akutagawa Ryūnosuke
20 June 1927

The Life of a Stupid Man

1. THE ERA

He was upstairs in a bookstore. Twenty years old at the time, he had climbed a ladder set against a bookcase and was searching for the newly-arrived Western books: Maupassant, Baudelaire, Strindberg, Ibsen, Shaw, Tolstoy . . .

The sun threatened to set before long, but he went on reading book spines with undiminished intensity. Lined up before him was not so much an array of books as the *fin de siècle* itself. Nietzsche, Verlaine, the Goncourt brothers, Dostoevsky, Hauptmann, Flaubert . . .

He took stock of their names as he struggled with the impending gloom. The books began to sink into the somber shadows. Finally his stamina gave out and he made ready to climb down. At that very moment, directly overhead, a single bare light bulb came on. Standing on his perch on top of the ladder, he looked down at the clerks and customers moving among the books. They were strangely small – and shabby.

Life is not worth a single line of Baudelaire.

He stood on the ladder, watching them below . . .

2. MOTHER

All the lunatics had been dressed in the same gray clothing, which seemed to give the large room an even more depressing look. One of them sat at an organ, playing a hymn over and over with great intensity. Another was dancing – or, rather, leaping about – in the very center of the room.

He stood watching this spectacle with a doctor of notably healthy complexion. Ten years earlier, his mother had been in no way different from these lunatics. In no way. And in fact in their smell he caught a whiff of his own mother's smell.

'Shall we go, then?'

The doctor led him down a corridor to another room. In a corner there were several brains soaking in large jars of alcohol. On one of the brains he noticed something faintly white, almost like a dollop of egg white. As he stood there chatting with the doctor, he thought again of his mother.

'The man who had this brain here was an engineer for the XX lighting company. He always thought of himself as a big shiny black dynamo.'

To avoid the doctor's eyes, he kept looking out the window. There was nothing out there but a brick wall topped with embedded broken bottles. It did, though, have thin growths of moss in dull white patches.

The Life of a Stupid Man

3. THE HOUSE

He was living in the upstairs room of a house in the suburbs. The second story tilted oddly because the ground was unstable.

In this room, his aunt would often quarrel with him, though not without occasional interventions from his adoptive parents. Still, he loved this aunt more than anyone. She never married, and by the time he was twenty, she was an old woman close to sixty.

He often wondered, in that suburban second story, if people who loved each other had to cause each other pain. Even as the thought crossed his mind, he was aware of the floor's eerie tilt.

4. TOKYO

A thick layer of cloud hung above the Sumida River. From the window of the little steamer, he watched the Mukōjima bank drawing closer. To his eyes, the blossoming cherry trees there looked as dreary as rags in a row. But almost before he knew it, in those trees – those cherry trees that had lined the bank of Mukōjima since the Edo Period – he was beginning to discover himself.

5. EGO

He and an elder colleague sat at a café table puffing on cigarettes. He said very little, but he paid close attention to his companion's every word.

'I spent half the day riding around in an automobile.'

'Was there something you needed to do?'

Cheek resting on his hand, the elder colleague replied with complete abandon, 'No, I just felt like riding around.'

The words released him into a world of which he knew nothing – a world of 'ego' close to the gods. He felt a kind of pain but, at the same time, a kind of joy.

The café was extremely small. Beneath a framed picture of the god Pan, however, a rubber tree in a red pot thrust its thick leaves out and down.

6. ILLNESS

In a steady ocean breeze, he spread out the large English dictionary and let his fingertip find words for him.

Talaria: A winged sandal.

Tale: A story.

Talipot: A coconut palm native to the East Indies. Trunk from 50 to 100 feet in height, leaves used for umbrellas, fans, hats, etc. Blooms once in 70 years . . .

His imagination painted a vivid picture of this bloom.

He then experienced an unfamiliar scratchy feeling in his throat, and before he knew it he had dropped a glob of phlegm on the dictionary. Phlegm? But it was not phlegm. He thought of the shortness of life and once again imagined the coconut blossom – the blossom of the coconut palm soaring on high far across the ocean.

7. PICTURE

It happened for him suddenly – quite suddenly. He was standing outside a bookstore, looking at a Van Gogh volume, when he suddenly understood what a 'picture' was. True, the Van Gogh was just a book of reproductions, but even in the photographs of those paintings, he sensed the vivid presence of nature.

This passion for pictures gave him a whole new way of looking at the world. He began to pay constant attention to the curve of a branch or the swell of a woman's cheek.

One rainy autumn evening, he was walking beneath an iron railroad bridge in the suburbs. Below the bank on the far side of the bridge stood a horse cart. As he passed it, he sensed that someone had come this way before. Someone? There was no need for him to wonder who that 'someone' might have been. In his twenty-three-year-old heart, a Dutchman with a cut ear and a long pipe in his mouth was fixing his gaze on this dreary landscape.

8. SPARKS: FLOWERS OF FIRE

Soaked by the rain, he trod along the asphalt. It was a heavy downpour. In the enveloping spray, he caught the smell of his rubberized coat.

Just then he saw the overhead trolley line giving off purple sparks and was strangely moved. His jacket pocket concealed the manuscript of the piece he was planning to publish in their little magazine. Walking through the rain, he looked back and up once again at the trolley line.

The cable was still sending sharp sparks into the air. He could think of nothing in life that he especially desired, but those purple sparks – those wildly-blooming flowers of fire – he would trade his life for the chance to hold them in his hands.

9. CADAVERS

A tag on a wire dangled from the big toe of each cadaver. The tags were inscribed with names, ages, and such. His friend bent over one corpse, peeling back the skin of its face with a deftly wielded scalpel. An expanse of beautiful yellow fat lay beneath the skin.

He studied the cadaver. He needed to do this to finish writing a story – a piece set against a Heian Period background – but he hated the stink of the corpses, which was like the smell of rotting apricots. Meanwhile, with wrinkled brow, his friend went on working his scalpel.

'You know, we're running out of cadavers these days,' his friend said.

His reply was ready: 'If *I* needed a corpse, I'd kill someone without the slightest malice.' Of course the reply stayed where it was – inside his heart.

10. THE MASTER

He was reading the Master's book beneath a great oak tree. Not a leaf stirred on the oak in the autumn sunlight. Far off in the sky, a scale with glass pans hung in perfect balance. He imagined such a vision as he read the Master's book . . .

11. DAWN

Night gradually gave way to dawn. He found himself on a street corner surveying a vast market. The swarming people and vehicles in the market were increasingly bathed in rose light.

He lit a cigarette and ambled into the market. Just then a lean black dog started barking at him, but he was not afraid. Indeed, he even loved this dog.

In the very center of the marketplace, a sycamore spread

its branches in all directions. He stood at the foot of the tree and looked up through the branches at the sky. A single star shone directly above him.

It was his twenty-fifth year – the third month after he first met the Master.

12. NAVAL PORT

Gloom filled the interior of the miniature submarine. Crouching down amid all the machinery, he peered into a small scope. What he saw there was a view of the bright naval port.

'You should be able to see the *Kongō*, too,' the naval officer explained to him.

As he was looking at the small warship through the square eyepiece, the thought of parsley popped into his mind for no reason – faintly aromatic parsley on top of a thirty-yen serving of beefsteak.

13. THE MASTER'S DEATH

In the wind after the rain, he walked down the platform of the new station. The sky was still dark. Across from the platform three or four railway laborers were swinging picks and singing loudly. The wind tore at the men's song and at his own emotions.

He left his cigarette unlit and felt a pain close to joy. 'Master near death,' read the telegram he had thrust into his coat pocket.

Just then the 6 a.m. Tokyo-bound train began to snake its way toward the station, rounding a pine-covered hill in the distance and trailing a wisp of smoke.

14. MARRIAGE

The day after he married her, he delivered a scolding to his wife: 'No sooner do you arrive here than you start wasting our money.' But the scolding was less from him than from his aunt, who had ordered him to deliver it. His wife apologized to him, of course, and to the aunt as well – with the potted jonquils she had bought for him in the room.

15. HE AND SHE

They led a peaceful life, surrounded by the garden's broad green *bashō* leaves.

It helped that their house was located in a town by the shore a full hour's train ride from Tokyo.

16. PILLOW

Pillowing his head on his rose-scented skepticism, he read a book by Anatole France. That even such a pillow might hold a god half-horse, he remained unaware.

17. BUTTERFLY

A butterfly fluttered its wings in a wind thick with the smell of seaweed. His dry lips felt the touch of the butterfly for the briefest instant, yet the wisp of wing dust still shone on his lips years later.

18. MOON

He happened to pass her on the stairway of a certain hotel. Her face seemed to be bathed in moonglow even now, in daylight. As he watched her walk on (they had never met), he felt a loneliness he had not known before.

19. MAN-MADE WINGS

He moved on from Anatole France to the eighteenth-century philosophers, though not to Rousseau. Perhaps this was

The Life of a Stupid Man

because one side of him – the side easily moved by passion – was too close to Rousseau. Instead, he approached the author of *Candide*, who was closer to another side of him – the cool and richly intellectual side.

At twenty-nine, life no longer held any brightness for him, but Voltaire supplied him with man-made wings.

Spreading these man-made wings, he soared with ease into the sky. The higher he flew, the farther below him sank the joys and sorrows of a life bathed in the light of intellect. Dropping ironies and smiles upon the shabby towns below, he climbed through the open sky, straight for the sun – as if he had forgotten about that ancient Greek who plunged to his death in the ocean when his man-made wings were singed by the sun.

20. SHACKLES

He and his wife came to live with his adoptive parents when he went to work for a newspaper. He saw his contract, written on a single sheet of yellow paper, as a great source of strength. Later, however, he came to realize that the contract saddled *him* with all the obligations and the company with none.

21. CRAZY GIRL

Two rickshaws sped down a deserted country road beneath overcast skies. From the sea breeze it was clear that the road was headed toward the ocean. Puzzled that he felt not the slightest excitement about this rendezvous, he sat in the second rickshaw thinking about what had drawn him here. It was certainly not love. And if it was not love, then . . . but to avoid the conclusion, he had to tell himself, *At least we are in this as equals.*

The person riding in the front rickshaw was a crazy girl. And she was not alone in her madness: her younger sister had killed herself out of jealousy.

There's nothing I can do about this anymore.

He now felt a kind of loathing for this crazy girl – this woman who was all powerful animal instinct.

The two rickshaws soon passed a cemetery where the smell of the shore was strong. Several blackened, pagoda-shaped gravestones stood within the fence, which was woven of brushwood and decorated with oyster shells. He caught a glimpse of the ocean gleaming beyond the gravestones and suddenly – inexplicably – he felt contempt for the woman's husband for having failed to capture her heart.

The Life of a Stupid Man

22. A PAINTER

It was just a magazine illustration, but the ink drawing of a rooster showed a remarkable individuality. He asked a friend to tell him about the painter.

A week later, the painter himself came to pay him a visit. This was one of the most remarkable events in his entire life. He discovered in this painter a poetry of which no one else was aware. In addition, he discovered in himself a soul of which he himself had been unaware.

One chilly autumn evening, he was reminded of the painter by a stalk of corn: the way it stood there armed in its rough coat of leaves, exposing its delicate roots atop the mounded earth like so many nerves, it was also a portrait of his own most vulnerable self. The discovery only served to increase his melancholy.

It's too late now. But when the time comes . . .

23. THE WOMAN

From where he stood, the plaza was beginning to darken. He walked into the open space feeling slightly feverish. The electric lights in the windows of several large office buildings flashed against the clear, faintly silvery sky.

He halted at the curb and decided to wait for the woman there. Five minutes later she came walking toward him looking somewhat haggard. 'I'm exhausted,' she said with a smile when she caught sight of him. They walked through the fading light of the plaza side-by-side. This was their first time together. He felt ready to abandon anything and everything to be with her.

In the automobile she stared at him and asked, 'You're not going to regret this?'

'Not at all,' he answered with conviction.

She pressed her hand on his and said, 'I know *I* won't have any regrets.'

Again, as she said this, her face seemed to be bathed in moonlight.

24. THE BIRTH

He stood by the sliding screen, looking down at the midwife in her white surgical gown washing the baby. Whenever soap got in its eyes, the baby would wrinkle up its sad little face and let out a loud wail. It looked like a baby rat, and its odor stirred him to these irrepressible thoughts –

Why did this one have to be born – to come into the world like all the others, this world so full of suffering? Why did this one have to bear the destiny of having a father like me?

This was the first son his wife bore him.

25. STRINDBERG

He stood in the doorway, watching some grimy Chinese men playing Mahjongg in the moonlight where figs bloomed. Back in his room, he started reading *The Confessions of a Fool* beneath a squat lamp. He had barely read two pages when he caught himself with a sour smile. So – the lies that Strindberg wrote to his lover, the Countess, were hardly different from his own.

26. ANTIQUITY

He was nearly overwhelmed by peeling Buddhas, heavenly beings, horses and lotus blossoms. Looking up at them, he forgot everything – even his good fortune at having escaped the clutches of the crazy girl.

27. SPARTAN DISCIPLINE

He was walking down a back street with a friend when a hooded rickshaw came charging in their direction. He was surprised to recognize the passenger as the woman he had been with the night before. Her face seemed to be bathed in moonglow even now, in the daylight. With his friend present, they could not exchange even ordinary greetings.

'Pretty woman,' his friend said.

Eyes on the spring hills at the end of the street, he answered without the slightest hesitation:

'Yes, very.'

28. MURDER

The country road stank of cow manure in the sun. Mopping his sweat, he struggled up the steep hill. The ripened wheat on either side of the road gave off a pleasant scent.

'Kill him, kill him . . .'

Before he knew it, he was muttering this aloud to himself over and over. Kill whom? It was obvious to him. He recalled the cringing fellow with close-cropped hair.

Just then, the domed roof of a Catholic church appeared beyond the yellow wheat.

29. FORM

It was a cast-iron saké bottle. With its finely incised lines, it had managed at some point to teach him the beauty of 'form'.

30. RAIN

In the big bed he talked with her about many things. Beyond the bedroom window it was raining. The blossoms of the crinum tree had begun to rot in the rain, it seemed. Her face, as always, looked as if it were in moonlight, yet talking with her was not entirely free of boredom. He lay on his stomach, had himself a quiet smoke, and realized he had now been with her for seven years.

Do I still love this woman? he asked himself. He was in the habit of observing himself so closely that the answer came as a surprise to him: *I do.*

31. THE GREAT EARTHQUAKE

The odor was something close to overripe apricots. Catching a hint of it as he walked through the charred ruins, he found himself thinking such thoughts as these: *The smell of corpses rotting in the sun is not as bad as I would have expected.* When he stood before a pond where bodies were piled upon bodies, however, he discovered that the old Chinese expression, 'burning the nose', was no mere sensory exaggeration of grief and horror. What especially moved him was the corpse of a child of twelve or thirteen. He felt something like envy as he looked at it, recalling such expressions as 'Those whom the gods love die young.' Both his sister and his half-brother had lost their houses to fire. His sister's husband, though, was on a suspended sentence for perjury.

Too bad we didn't all die.

Standing in the charred ruins, he could hardly keep from feeling this way.

32. FIGHT

He had a quarrel with his half-brother that ended in a physical brawl. True, he was a constant source of pressure for this younger brother, who in turn cost him a good deal of freedom. Relatives were always telling the young man, 'be like your brother', but for him, this was like being bound hand and foot. Locked in each other's grip, they fell near the edge of the veranda. He still remembers the one crape myrtle bush in the garden by the veranda – its load of brilliant red blossoms beneath a sky about to drop its rainy burden.

33. HERO

From the window of Voltaire's house, he found himself looking up toward a high mountain. There was nothing to be seen on the glacier-topped mountain, not even a vulture. There was, however, a short Russian man doggedly climbing the trail.

The Life of a Stupid Man

After night fell, beneath the bright lamp in Voltaire's house, he wrote this didactic poem (still picturing that Russian man climbing the mountain).

> You who more than anyone obeyed the Ten
>   Commandments
> Are you who more than anyone broke the Ten
>   Commandments.
>
> You who more than anyone loved the masses
> Are you who more than anyone despised the masses.
>
> You who more than anyone burned with ideals
> Are you who more than anyone knew reality.
>
> You are what our Eastern world has bred –
> An electric locomotive that smells of flowering
>   grasses.

34. COLOR

At thirty he found himself loving a piece of vacant land. It contained only some moss and scattered bits of brick and tile. To his eyes, however, it was exactly like a Cezanne landscape.

He suddenly recalled his passions of seven or eight years earlier. And when he did so, he realized that seven or eight years earlier he had known nothing about color.

35. COMIC PUPPET

He wanted to live life so intensely that he could die at any moment without regrets. But still, out of deference to his adoptive parents and his aunt, he kept himself in check. This created both light and dark sides to his life. Seeing a comic puppet in a Western tailor's shop made him wonder how close he himself was to such a figure. His self beyond consciousness, however – his 'second self' – had long since put such feelings into a story.

36. TEDIUM

He was walking through a field of plume grass with a university student. 'You fellows still have a strong will to live, I suppose?'

'Yes, of course, but you, too . . .'

'Not any more,' he said. He was telling the truth. At some point he had lost interest in life. 'I *do* have the will to create, though.'

'But surely the will to create is a form of the will to live . . . ?'

To this he did not reply. Above the field's red plumes rose the sharp outline of an active volcano. He viewed the peak with something close to envy, though he had no idea why this was so . . .

37. 'WOMAN OF HOKURIKU'

He met a woman he could grapple with intellectually. He barely extricated himself from the crisis by writing a number of lyric poems, some under the title 'Woman of Hokuriku'. These conveyed a sense of heartbreak as when one knocks away a brilliant coating of snow frozen onto a tree trunk.

> Hat of sedge dancing in the wind:
> How could it fail to drop into the road?
> What need I fear for my name?
> For your name alone do I fear.

38. PUNISHMENT

They were on the balcony of a hotel surrounded by trees in bud. He was drawing pictures to amuse a little boy – the only son of the crazy girl, with whom he had broken off relations seven years earlier.

The crazy girl lit a cigarette and watched them play. With an oppressive feeling, he went on drawing trains and airplanes. Fortunately, the boy was not his, but it still pained him greatly when the child called him 'uncle'.

After the boy wandered off, the crazy girl, still smoking her cigarette, said suggestively:

'Don't you think he looks like you?'
'Not at all. Besides –'
'But you do know about "prenatal influence", I'm sure.'

He looked away from her in silence, but in his heart he wanted to strangle her.

39. MIRRORS

He was in the corner of a café, chatting with a friend. The friend was eating a baked apple and talking about the recent cold weather when he himself began to sense a certain contradiction in the conversation.

'Hey, wait a minute – you're still a bachelor, right?'
'Not exactly: I'm getting married next month.'

That silenced him. The mirrors set in the café walls reflected him in endless numbers. Coldly. Menacingly.

40. DIALOGUE

Why do you attack the present social system?
  Because I see the evils that capitalism has engendered.
  Evils? I thought you recognized no difference between good and evil. How do you make a living, then?

He engaged thus in dialogue with an angel – an angel in an impeccable top hat.

41. ILLNESS

He suffered an onslaught of insomnia. His physical strength began to fade as well. The doctors gave him various diagnoses – gastric hyperacidity, gastric atony, dry pleurisy, neurasthenia, chronic conjunctivitis, brain fatigue . . .

But he knew well enough what was wrong with him: he was ashamed of himself and afraid of *them* – afraid of the society he so despised.

One afternoon when snow clouds hung over the city, he was in the corner of a café, smoking a cigar and listening to music from the gramophone on the other side of the room. He found the music permeating his emotions in a strange new way. When it ended, he walked over to the gramophone to read the label on the record.

'Magic Flute – Mozart.'

All at once it became clear to him: Mozart too had broken the Ten Commandments and suffered. Probably not the way *he* had, but . . .

He bowed his head and returned to his table in silence.

42. THE LAUGHTER OF THE GODS

At thirty-five, he was walking through a pinewood with the spring sun beating down on it. He was recalling, too, the words he had written a few years earlier: 'It is unfortunate for the gods that, unlike us, they cannot commit suicide.'

43. NIGHT

Night closed in again. The rough sea sent up spray in the fading light. Beneath these skies, he married his wife anew. This brought them joy, but there was suffering as well. With them, their three sons watched the lightning over the open sea. His wife, holding one of the boys in her arms, seemed to be fighting back tears.

'See the boat over there?' he asked her.

'Yes . . .'

'That boat with the mast cracked in two . . .'

44. DEATH

Taking advantage of his sleeping alone, he tried to hang himself with a sash tied over the window lattice. When he slipped his head into the sash, however, he suddenly became afraid of death. Not that he feared the suffering he would have to experience at the moment of dying. He decided to try it again, using his pocket watch to see how long it would take. This time, everything began to cloud over after a short interval of pain. He was sure that once he got past that, he would enter death. Checking the hands of his watch, he discovered that the pain lasted one minute and twenty-some seconds. It was pitch dark outside the lattices, but the wild clucking of chickens echoed in the darkness.

45. DIVAN

Divan was giving him new inner power. This was an 'Oriental Goethe' he had not known before. He saw the author standing with quiet confidence on the Other Shore, far beyond good and evil, and he felt an envy close to despair. In his eyes, the poet Goethe was even greater than the poet Christ. For in the heart of the poet Goethe, there bloomed not only the roses of the Acropolis and Golgotha but the rose of Arabia as well. If only he had the least ability to follow in this poet's footsteps!

Once he had finished reading *Divan* and recovered somewhat from its terrifying emotional impact, he could only despise himself for having been born such a eunuch in life!

46. LIES

He felt the suicide of his sister's husband as a terrible blow. Now he was responsible for his sister's family as well. To him at least, his future looked as gloomy as the end of the day. He felt something like a sneer for his own spiritual bankruptcy (he was aware of all of his faults and weak points, every single one of them), but he went on reading one book after another. Even Rousseau's *Confessions*, though, was full of the most heroic lies. And when it came to Tōson's *New Life*, he felt he had never met such a cunning hypocrite as that novel's protagonist. The one who truly moved him, though, was François Villon. He found in that poet's many works the 'beautiful male'.

Sometimes in his dreams the image would come to him of Villon waiting to be hanged. Like Villon, he had several times nearly fallen to the ultimate depths of life, but neither his situation nor his physical energy would permit him to keep this up. He grew gradually weaker, like the tree Swift saw so long ago, withering from the top down.

47. PLAYING WITH FIRE

She had a radiant face, like the morning sun on a thin sheet of ice. He was fond of her, but he did not love her, nor had he ever laid a finger on her.

'I've heard you want to die,' she said.

'Yes – or rather, it's not so much that I want to die as that I'm tired of living.'

This dialogue led to a vow to die together.

'It would be a Platonic suicide, I suppose,' she said.

'A Platonic double suicide.'

He was amazed at his own sangfroid.

48. DEATH

He did not die with her, but he took a certain satisfaction in his never having touched her. She often spoke with him as though their dialogue had never happened. She did once give him a bottle of cyanide with the remark, 'As long as we have this, it will give us both strength.'

And it did indeed give him strength. Sitting in a rattan chair, observing the new growth of a *shii* tree, he often thought of the peace that death would give him.

49. STUFFED SWAN

With the last of his strength, he tried to write his autobiography, but it did not come together as easily as he had hoped. This was because of his remaining pride and skepticism, and a calculation of what was in his own best interest. He couldn't help despising these qualities in himself; but neither could he help feeling that 'Everyone is the same under the skin.' He tended to think that Goethe's title 'Poetry and Truth' could serve for anyone's autobiography, but he knew that not everyone is moved by literature. His own works were unlikely to appeal to people who were not like him and had not lived a life like his – this was another feeling that worked upon him. And so he decided to write his own brief 'Poetry and Truth'.

Once he had finished writing 'The Life of a Stupid Man', he happened to see a stuffed swan in a secondhand shop. It stood with its head held high, but its wings were yellowed and moth-eaten. As he thought about his life, he felt both tears and mockery welling up inside him. All that lay before him was madness or suicide. He walked down the darkening street alone, determined now to wait for the destiny that would come to annihilate him.

50. CAPTIVE

One of his friends went mad. He had always felt close to this man because he understood far more deeply than anyone else the loneliness that lurked beneath his jaunty mask. He visited him a few times after the madness struck.

'You and I are both possessed by a demon,' the friend whispered, 'the demon of the *fin de siècle*.'

Two or three days later, he heard, the man ate roses on the way to a hot-spring resort. When the friend was hospitalized, he recalled once sending him a terra cotta piece. It was a bust of the author of *The Inspector General*, one of the friend's favorite writers. Thinking how Gogol, too, had gone mad, he could not help feeling that there was a force governing all of them.

Just as he reached the point of utter exhaustion, he happened to read Raymond Radiguet's dying words, 'God's soldiers are coming to get me,' and sensed once again the laughter of the gods. He tried to fight against his own superstitions and sentimentalism, but he was physically incapable of putting up any kind of struggle. The 'demon of the *fin de siècle*' was preying on him without a doubt. He envied medieval men's ability to find strength in God. But for him, believing in God – in God's love – was an impossibility, though even Cocteau had done it!

51. DEFEAT

The hand with the pen began to tremble, and before long he was even drooling. The only time his head ever cleared was after a sleep induced by eight-tenths of a gram of Veronal, and even then it never lasted more than thirty minutes or an hour. He barely made it through each day in the gloom, leaning as it were upon a chipped and narrow sword.

1. BOCCACCIO · *Mrs Rosie and the Priest*
2. GERARD MANLEY HOPKINS · *As kingfishers catch fire*
3. *The Saga of Gunnlaug Serpent-tongue*
4. THOMAS DE QUINCEY · *On Murder Considered as One of the Fine Arts*
5. FRIEDRICH NIETZSCHE · *Aphorisms on Love and Hate*
6. JOHN RUSKIN · *Traffic*
7. PU SONGLING · *Wailing Ghosts*
8. JONATHAN SWIFT · *A Modest Proposal*
9. *Three Tang Dynasty Poets*
10. WALT WHITMAN · *On the Beach at Night Alone*
11. KENKŌ · *A Cup of Sake Beneath the Cherry Trees*
12. BALTASAR GRACIÁN · *How to Use Your Enemies*
13. JOHN KEATS · *The Eve of St Agnes*
14. THOMAS HARDY · *Woman much missed*
15. GUY DE MAUPASSANT · *Femme Fatale*
16. MARCO POLO · *Travels in the Land of Serpents and Pearls*
17. SUETONIUS · *Caligula*
18. APOLLONIUS OF RHODES · *Jason and Medea*
19. ROBERT LOUIS STEVENSON · *Olalla*
20. KARL MARX AND FRIEDRICH ENGELS · *The Communist Manifesto*
21. PETRONIUS · *Trimalchio's Feast*
22. JOHANN PETER HEBEL · *How a Ghastly Story Was Brought to Light by a Common or Garden Butcher's Dog*
23. HANS CHRISTIAN ANDERSEN · *The Tinder Box*
24. RUDYARD KIPLING · *The Gate of the Hundred Sorrows*
25. DANTE · *Circles of Hell*
26. HENRY MAYHEW · *Of Street Piemen*
27. HAFEZ · *The nightingales are drunk*
28. GEOFFREY CHAUCER · *The Wife of Bath*
29. MICHEL DE MONTAIGNE · *How We Weep and Laugh at the Same Thing*
30. THOMAS NASHE · *The Terrors of the Night*
31. EDGAR ALLAN POE · *The Tell-Tale Heart*
32. MARY KINGSLEY · *A Hippo Banquet*
33. JANE AUSTEN · *The Beautifull Cassandra*
34. ANTON CHEKHOV · *Gooseberries*
35. SAMUEL TAYLOR COLERIDGE · *Well, they are gone, and here must I remain*
36. JOHANN WOLFGANG VON GOETHE · *Sketchy, Doubtful, Incomplete Jottings*
37. CHARLES DICKENS · *The Great Winglebury Duel*
38. HERMAN MELVILLE · *The Maldive Shark*
39. ELIZABETH GASKELL · *The Old Nurse's Story*
40. NIKOLAY LESKOV · *The Steel Flea*

41. HONORÉ DE BALZAC · *The Atheist's Mass*
42. CHARLOTTE PERKINS GILMAN · *The Yellow Wall-Paper*
43. C.P. CAVAFY · *Remember, Body . . .*
44. FYODOR DOSTOYEVSKY · *The Meek One*
45. GUSTAVE FLAUBERT · *A Simple Heart*
46. NIKOLAI GOGOL · *The Nose*
47. SAMUEL PEPYS · *The Great Fire of London*
48. EDITH WHARTON · *The Reckoning*
49. HENRY JAMES · *The Figure in the Carpet*
50. WILFRED OWEN · *Anthem For Doomed Youth*
51. WOLFGANG AMADEUS MOZART · *My Dearest Father*
52. PLATO · *Socrates' Defence*
53. CHRISTINA ROSSETTI · *Goblin Market*
54. *Sindbad the Sailor*
55. SOPHOCLES · *Antigone*
56. RYŪNOSUKE AKUTAGAWA · *The Life of a Stupid Man*
57. LEO TOLSTOY · *How Much Land Does A Man Need?*
58. GIORGIO VASARI · *Leonardo da Vinci*
59. OSCAR WILDE · *Lord Arthur Savile's Crime*
60. SHEN FU · *The Old Man of the Moon*
61. AESOP · *The Dolphins, the Whales and the Gudgeon*
62. MATSUO BASHŌ · *Lips too Chilled*
63. EMILY BRONTË · *The Night is Darkening Round Me*
64. JOSEPH CONRAD · *To-morrow*
65. RICHARD HAKLUYT · *The Voyage of Sir Francis Drake Around the Whole Globe*
66. KATE CHOPIN · *A Pair of Silk Stockings*
67. CHARLES DARWIN · *It was snowing butterflies*
68. BROTHERS GRIMM · *The Robber Bridegroom*
69. CATULLUS · *I Hate and I Love*
70. HOMER · *Circe and the Cyclops*
71. D. H. LAWRENCE · *Il Duro*
72. KATHERINE MANSFIELD · *Miss Brill*
73. OVID · *The Fall of Icarus*
74. SAPPHO · *Come Close*
75. IVAN TURGENEV · *Kasyan from the Beautiful Lands*
76. VIRGIL · *O Cruel Alexis*
77. H. G. WELLS · *A Slip under the Microscope*
78. HERODOTUS · *The Madness of Cambyses*
79. *Speaking of Siva*
80. *The Dhammapada*

'If I stopped now, after coming all this way – well, they'd call me an idiot!'

LEO TOLSTOY

Born 1828, Yasnaya Polyana, Russian Empire
Died 1910, Astapovo, Russian Empire

'How Much Land Does A Man Need?' and 'What Men Live By',
published in their original Russian in 1836 and 1835 respectively.
They are taken from *How Much Land Does a Man Need? and
Other Stories*.

TOLSTOY IN PENGUIN CLASSICS

Anna Karenina
War and Peace
Childhood, Boyhood, Youth
The Cossacks and Other Stories
The Kreutzer Sonata and Other Stories
What is Art?
Resurrection
The Death of Ivan Ilyich and Other Stories
Master and Man and Other Stories
How Much Land Does a Man Need? and Other Stories
A Confession and Other Religious Writings
Last Steps: The Late Writings of Leo Tolstoy

LEO TOLSTOY

How Much Land Does A Man Need?

Translated by
Ronald Wilks

PENGUIN BOOKS

PENGUIN CLASSICS

UK | USA | Canada | Ireland | Australia
India | New Zealand | South Africa

Penguin Books is part of the Penguin Random House group of companies
whose addresses can be found at global.penguinrandomhouse.com.

This edition published in Penguin Classics 2015

017

Translation copyright © Ronald Wilks, 1993

The moral right of the translator has been asserted

Set in 9/12.4 pt Baskerville 10 Pro
Typeset by Jouve (UK), Milton Keynes

Printed and bound in Great Britain by Clays Ltd, Elcograf S.p.A.

A CIP catalogue record for this book is available from the British Library

ISBN: 978-0-141-39774-0

www.greenpenguin.co.uk

Penguin Random House is committed to a sustainable future for our business, our readers and our planet. This book is made from Forest Stewardship Council® certified paper.

Contents

How Much Land Does A
  Man Need?   1
What Men Live By   22

How Much Land Does A Man Need?

1

An elder sister came from the town to visit her younger sister in the country. This elder sister was married to a merchant and the younger to a peasant in the village. The two sisters sat down for a talk over a cup of tea and the elder started boasting about the superiority of town life, with all its comforts, the fine clothes her children wore, the exquisite food and drink, the skating, parties and visits to the theatre.

The younger sister resented this and in turn scoffed at the life of a merchant's wife and sang the praises of her own life as a peasant.

'I wouldn't care to change my life for yours,' she said. 'I admit mine is dull, but at least we have no worries. You live in grander style, but you must do a great deal of business or you'll be ruined. You know the proverb, "Loss is Gain's elder brother." One day you are rich and the next you might find yourself out in the street. Here in the country we don't have those ups and downs. A peasant's life may be poor, but it's long. Although we may never be rich, we'll always have enough to eat.'

Then the elder sister said her piece.

'Enough to eat indeed with nothing but those filthy pigs and calves! What do you know about nice clothes and good manners! However hard your good husband slaves away you'll spend your lives in the muck and that's where you'll die. And the same goes for your children.'

'Well, what of it?' the younger sister retorted. 'That's how it is here. But at least we know where we are. We don't have to crawl to anyone and we're afraid of no one. But you in the town are surrounded by temptations. All may be well one day, the next the Devil comes along and tempts your husband with cards, women and drink. And then you're ruined. It does happen, doesn't it?'

Pakhom, the younger sister's husband, was lying over the stove listening to the women's chatter.

'It's true what you say,' he said. 'Take me. Ever since I was a youngster I've been too busy tilling the soil to let that kind of nonsense enter my head. My only grievance is that I don't have enough land. Give me enough of that and I'd fear no one — not even the Devil himself!'

The sisters finished their tea, talked a little longer about dresses, cleared away the tea things and went to bed.

But the Devil had been sitting behind the stove and had heard everything. He was delighted that a peasant's wife had led her husband to boast that if he had enough land he would fear no one, not even the Devil. 'Good!' he thought. 'I'll have a little game with you. I shall see that you have plenty of land and that way I'll get you in my clutches!'

2

Not far from the village lived a lady with a small estate of about three hundred acres. She had always been on good terms with the peasants and had never ill-treated them. But then she had taken on an old soldier to manage her estate and he proceeded to harass the peasants by constantly imposing fines. No matter how careful Pakhom was, one of his horses might stray into the lady's oats, or a cow might sometimes wander into her garden, or some calves might venture out on to her meadows. Every time this happened he would have to pay a fine.

Pakhom would pay up and then he would go and swear at his family and beat them. All that summer Pakhom had to put up with a great deal from that manager, so he welcomed winter when it came and his cattle had to be kept in the shed: although he begrudged the fodder, at least he wouldn't have to worry about them straying.

That winter word got round that the lady wanted to sell some of her land and that the innkeeper on the highway was trying to agree on a price with her. The peasants took this news very badly. 'If that innkeeper gets his hands on that land he'll start slapping even more fines on us than that manager. But we can't survive without it, we all depend on it for our living.'

So a few peasants, in the name of the village commune, begged the lady not to sell any of her land to the innkeeper and to let them buy it, offering her a better price. The lady agreed. Then the members of the commune thought of buying the whole estate. They met once, they met twice, but no progress was made: the Devil had set them at loggerheads and there was nothing they could agree upon. In the end they decided to buy the land in separate lots, each according to what he could afford. The lady agreed to this as well.

One day Pakhom learned that one of his neighbours was buying about fifty acres and that the lady had taken half payment in cash, allowing the man one year to pay the balance. This made Pakhom very envious. 'They'll buy up all the land,' he thought, 'and I'll be left with nothing.' So he conferred with his wife.

'Everyone's buying land,' he said. 'We must get hold of twenty acres, or thereabouts. If we don't we won't be able to live, what with that manager bleeding us white with fines.'

So they racked their brains as to how they could buy some of the land. They had a hundred roubles saved up, so that by selling a foal and half their bees, by sending one of their sons out to work for someone who paid wages in advance and borrowing from a brother-in-law, they managed to scrape together half the money.

Then Pakhom took the money, chose about thirty acres of partly wooded land and went off to the lady to see if he could strike a deal. He managed to get the thirty acres, they shook hands on it and Pakhom paid a deposit. Then they went into town and signed the deeds, Pakhom paying half cash down and pledging to settle the balance within two years.

And so Pakhom now had land. He borrowed money for seeds and sowed the newly bought land; the harvest was excellent. Within a year he had repaid both the lady and his brother-in-law. Now he was a landowner, in the full sense of the word: he ploughed and sowed his own fields, reaped his own hay, cut his own timber and could pasture his cattle on his own land. Whenever he rode out to plough the land which was now his for ever, or to inspect his young corn and meadows, he was filled with joy. He felt that the grass that grew and the flowers that bloomed were different from any other grass and flowers. Before, when he had ridden over that land, it had seemed the same as any other. But now it was something quite special.

3

So Pakhom lived a landowner's life and he was happy. And in fact all would have been well had other peasants not trespassed on his cornfields and meadows. He spoke to them very politely, but they took no notice. Herdsmen let their cows stray on to his meadows, then horses wandered into his corn on their way home from night pasture. Again and again Pakhom drove them out without taking further action, but in the end he lost patience and complained to the District Court. He knew very well that the peasants weren't doing it deliberately but because they were short of land. But still he thought, 'I can't let this go on. Before long they'll have destroyed all I have. I must teach them a lesson.'

So he taught them a lesson in court, then another, making several of them pay fines. Pakhom's neighbours resented this and once again began to let their cattle stray on his land, this time on purpose. One night someone managed to get into Pakhom's wood and felled about ten young lime-trees for their bark. Next day, when Pakhom was riding through his wood, he suddenly noticed something white on the ground. He went nearer and saw tree-trunks lying all around, stripped of their bark, with the stumps lying nearby. 'If he'd only just cut one or two down, but that devil's left me with one tree standing and cleared the rest.' Pakhom seethed with anger. 'Oh, if I knew who did it I'd show him a thing or two!' For a long time he racked his brains and finally concluded, 'It must be Semyon, it can't be anyone else.' So off he went to search Semyon's place, but he found nothing and all the two men did was swear at each other. Pakhom was more convinced than ever that it was Semyon's work and he lodged a complaint. The magistrates sat for ages debating the case and finally acquitted Semyon for lack of evidence. This incensed Pakhom even more and he had a stormy session with the village elder and the magistrates.

'You are hand in glove with thieves,' he protested. 'If you were honest men you wouldn't let a thief like him off the hook.'

As a result Pakhom fell out with the magistrates as well as his neighbours, who threatened to burn his cottage down.

And so, although Pakhom had plenty of leg-room now, he felt that the commune was hemming him in.

Around that time rumours were in the air that many peasants were leaving to settle in new parts of the country. Pakhom thought, '*I* don't really need to go away, what with all that land of mine. But if some of the villagers were to go there'd be more room for others. I could buy their land and make my estate bigger. Life would be easier then, but as things are, it's still too cramped here for my liking.'

One day a peasant who was passing through stopped at Pakhom's cottage. They let him stay the night and gave him food. Pakhom asked where he was from and the man replied that he had come from the south, from the other side of the Volga, where he had been working. Then he told how people from his own village had settled there, joined the commune and had been allotted twenty-five acres each. 'The land is so fertile,' he said, 'that rye grows as high as a horse and it's so thick you can make a whole sheaf from only five handfuls! One peasant arrived with a copeck and only his bare hands to work with and now he has six horses and two cows.'

Pakhom was terribly excited by this news. 'Why should I have to scrape a living cooped up here,' he thought, 'when I could be leading a good life somewhere else? I could sell the land and cottage and with the money I'd be able to build myself a house there and start a whole new farm. But here there's no room to breathe and I get nothing but aggravation. I must go and find out what it's like for myself.'

When summer came he was ready and he set off. He went down the Volga to Samara by steamboat, then walked the remaining three hundred miles to the new settlement, which was just as the visitor had described. All the men had plenty of space, each having been allotted twenty-five acres without charge and welcomed into the commune. Anyone who had the money could also buy as much of the finest freehold land as he wanted, at three roubles an acre – there was no limit!

Towards autumn, after finding out all he needed to know, Pakhom went home and started selling up. He sold the land at a profit, his home and all his cattle, resigned from the commune and waited until the spring, when he left with his family for the new settlement.

4

When he arrived with his family Pakhom managed to get himself on the register of a large village commune, having duly moistened the elders' throats. All was signed and sealed and Pakhom was granted a hundred acres (twenty for each member of his family, in different fields), besides the use of the communal pasture. Then he put up some buildings and stocked his farm with cattle. The allotted land alone was three times as much as at home and it was perfect for growing corn. He was ten times better off here, for he had plenty of arable land and pasturage, and he was able to keep as many cattle as he wanted.

At first, while he was busy building and stocking up, everything seemed wonderful. But no sooner had he settled down to his new life than he began to feel cramped even here. During the first year he had sowed wheat on the allotted land and the crop had been excellent. But when he wanted to sow more wheat he found he needed more land: the other land he had been allotted was not suitable for wheat. In the south wheat is sown only on grass or on fallow land. They sow it for one or two years and then leave it fallow until the land is overgrown with feather-grass again. This type of land was in great demand and there wasn't enough to go round, so that people quarrelled over it. The richer ones sowed their own, whilst the poorer ones had to mortgage theirs to merchants to pay their taxes. Pakhom wanted to sow more wheat, so the following year he rented some fields from a dealer for one year. He sowed a great deal of wheat and had a good crop. But the fields were a long way from the village and the wheat had to be carted more than ten miles. Then Pakhom noticed that some peasant farmers with large homesteads in the neighbourhood were becoming very wealthy. 'What if I bought some freehold land and built myself a homestead like theirs?' he wondered. 'Then everything would be within easy reach.' And he tried to think how he could buy some.

Pakhom farmed the same way for three years, renting land and sowing wheat. They were good years, the crops were good and he was able to save some money. But Pakhom grew tired of having to rent land, year after year, of having to waste his time scrambling after it. Whenever good land came up for sale the peasants would immediately fall over themselves to buy it and it would all be gone before he could do anything: he was never quick enough and so he had no land for sowing his wheat. So in the third year he went halves with a merchant in buying a plot of pasture land outright from some peasants. They had already ploughed it when someone sued the peasants over it and as a result all their work was wasted. 'If it had been *my* land,' Pakhom thought, 'I wouldn't have been under an obligation to anyone and I wouldn't have got into that mess.'

So Pakhom tried to discover where to buy some freehold land. He came across a peasant who, having purchased some thirteen hundred acres, had then gone bankrupt and was selling the land off very cheaply. Pakhom bargained with him. After much haggling they finally agreed upon fifteen hundred roubles, half cash down, half to be paid at a later date. The deal was all but signed and sealed when a passing merchant called at Pakhom's to have his horses fed. They drank tea together and got into conversation. The merchant said that he was on his way back from the far-off land of the Bashkirs, where he had bought some thirteen thousand acres for a mere thousand roubles. When Pakhom questioned him further the merchant told him, 'All I had to do was give the old men there a few presents – a hundred roubles' worth of silk robes and carpets, a chest of tea, and vodka for anyone who wanted it. I managed to get the land for twenty copecks an acre.' He showed Pakhom the title deeds. 'The land is near a river and it's all beautiful grassy steppe.'

Pakhom continued to ply him with questions.

'There's so much land that you couldn't walk round it all in a year. It all belongs to the Bashkirs. Yes, the people there are as stupid as sheep and you can get land off them for practically nothing.'

'Well,' Pakhom thought, 'why should I pay a thousand roubles for thirteen hundred acres and saddle myself with debt? To think what I could buy with the same money down there!'

5

Pakhom asked him how to get there and as soon as he had said goodbye to the merchant he prepared to leave. He left his wife behind and set off, taking a workman with him. First they stopped off in town and bought a chest of tea, vodka and other presents, just as the old merchant had advised. Then they travelled for miles and miles until, on the seventh day, they reached the Bashkir settlement. Everything was as the merchant had described: the people lived on the steppe, near a river, in tents of thick felt. They neither ploughed the soil nor ate bread, and their cattle and horses wandered in herds over the steppe. The foals were tethered behind the tents and the mares brought over to them twice a day. These mares were milked and from the milk kumiss was made. The women also made cheese from the kumiss and all the men seemed concerned with was drinking kumiss and tea, eating mutton and playing their pipes. All of them were cheerful and well-fed, and they spent the whole summer idling about. The Bashkirs were very ignorant, knew no Russian, but were kindly people.

The moment they spotted Pakhom, the Bashkirs streamed out of their tents and surrounded their visitor. An interpreter was found and Pakhom told him that he had come about some land. The Bashkirs were delighted and took Pakhom off to one of the finest tents, where they made him sit on some rugs piled with cushions, while they formed a circle and offered him tea and kumiss. Then they slaughtered a sheep and fed him with mutton. Pakhom fetched the presents from his cart, handed them round and shared the tea out. The Bashkirs were delighted. For a while they talked away amongst themselves and then told the interpreter to translate.

'They want me to tell you,' the interpreter said, 'that they've taken a great liking to you and that it's our custom to do all we can to please a guest and repay him for his gifts. You have given us presents, so please tell us if there is anything of ours that you would like so we can show our gratitude.'

'What I like most of all here,' Pakhom replied, 'is your land. Back home there isn't enough to go round and, what's more, the soil is exhausted. But here you have plenty and it looks very good. I've never seen soil like it.'

The interpreter translated and then the Bashkirs went into a lengthy conference. Although Pakhom did not understand, he could see how cheerful they were, laughing and shouting. Then they all became quiet, glanced at Pakhom and the interpreter continued, 'I'm to tell you that they would be only too pleased to let you have as much land as you like in return for your kindness. All you have to do is point it out and it will be yours.'

Then they conferred again and started arguing about something. Pakhom asked what it was and the interpreter told him, 'Some of them are saying they should first consult the elder about the land. They can't do anything without his permission, but some of the others say it's not necessary.'

6

While the Bashkirs were arguing, a man in a fox-fur cap suddenly came into the tent, whereupon they all became quiet and stood up.

'It's the elder,' the interpreter explained.

Pakhom immediately fetched his best robe and presented it with five pounds of tea to the elder, who accepted the gifts and then sat in the place of honour. The Bashkirs immediately started telling him something. After listening for a while the elder motioned with his head for them to be quiet and then spoke to Pakhom in Russian.

'Well now,' he said. 'It's all right. Choose whatever land you like, there's plenty of it.'

'How can I just go and take whatever I like?' Pakhom wondered. 'I must have it all signed and sealed somehow. Now they tell me it's mine, but who knows, they might change their minds?' So he told them, 'Thank you for your kind words. Yes, you do have a great deal of land, but I need only a little. However, I would like to be sure which will be mine, so couldn't it be measured and made over to me by some sort of contract? Our lives are in God's hands and although you good people are willing to give me the land now, it's possible your children might want it back again.'

'What you say is true,' said the elder. 'We can have a contract drawn up.'

Pakhom said, 'I've heard that you made some land over to a merchant not long ago, together with the title deeds. I would like you to do the same with me.'

The elder understood. 'That's no problem,' he said. 'We have a clerk here and we can ride into town and have the documents properly witnessed and signed.'

'But what about the price?' Pakhom asked.

'We have a set price – a thousand roubles a day.'

Pakhom did not understand.

'What kind of rate is that – a *day*? How many acres would that be?'

'We don't reckon your way. We sell by the day. However

much you can walk round in one day will be yours. And the price is a thousand roubles a day.'

Pakhom was amazed. 'Well, a man can walk round a lot of land in one day,' he said.

The elder burst out laughing. 'Well, all of it will be yours,' he replied. 'But there's one condition: if you don't return to your starting-point the same day, your money will be forfeited.'

'But how can I mark where I've been?'

'We'll all go to whatever place you select and wait until you've completed your circuit. You must take a spade, dig a hole at every turning and leave the turf piled up. Afterwards, we will go from hole to hole with a plough. You may make as large a circuit as you like, only you must be back at your starting-point by sunset. All the land you can walk round will be yours.'

Pakhom was absolutely delighted. An early start was decided on and after talking for a while they drank kumiss, ate some mutton and then had tea. This went on until nightfall. Then the Bashkirs made up a feather-bed for Pakhom and left. They promised to be ready to ride out to the chosen spot before sunrise.

7

Pakhom lay down on the feather-bed, but the thought of all that land kept him awake. 'Tomorrow,' he thought, 'I shall mark out a really large stretch. In one day I can easily walk thirty-five miles. The days are long now – just think how much land I'll have from walking that distance! I'll sell the poorer bits, or let it to the peasants. I'll take the best for myself and farm it. I'll have two ox-ploughs and hire a couple of labourers to work them. Yes, I'll cultivate about a hundred and fifty acres and let the cattle graze the rest.'

Pakhom did not sleep a wink that night and dozed off only just before dawn. The moment he fell asleep he had a dream: he seemed to be lying in the same tent and could hear someone roaring with laughter outside. Wondering who was laughing like that he got up, went out and saw that same Bashkir elder sitting there, holding his sides and rolling about in fits of laughter. He went closer and asked, 'What are you laughing at?' And then he saw that it wasn't the elder at all, but the merchant who had called on him a few days before and told him about the land. And just as Pakhom asked him, 'Have you been here long?' the merchant turned into the peasant who had come up from the Volga and visited him at home. And then Pakhom saw that it wasn't the peasant, but the Devil himself, with horns and hoofs, sitting there laughing his head off, while before him lay a barefoot man wearing only shirt and trousers. When Pakhom took a closer look he saw that the man was dead and that it was himself. Pakhom woke up in a cold sweat. 'The things one dreams about!' he thought. Then he looked round and saw that it was getting light at the open door – dawn was breaking. 'I must go and wake them,' he thought, 'it's time to start.' So Pakhom got up, roused the workman, who was sleeping in the cart, ordered him to harness the horse and went off to wake the Bashkirs. 'It's time to go out on the steppe and measure the land,' he said. The Bashkirs got up, assembled, and then the elder came and joined them. They drank some more kumiss and offered Pakhom tea, but he was impatient to be off. 'If we're going,' he said, 'let's go. It's time.'

8

So the Bashkirs got ready and left, some on horses, others in carts. Pakhom went to his little cart with him. They came out on to the open steppe just as the sun was rising. They climbed a small hill (called a 'shikhan' in Bashkir). Then the Bashkirs got out of their carts, dismounted from their horses and gathered in one place. The elder went over to Pakhom and pointed.

'Look,' he said, 'that's all ours, as far as the eye can see. Choose any part you like.'

Pakhom's eyes lit up, for the land was all virgin soil, flat as the palm of one's hand, black as poppy-seed, with different kinds of grass growing breast-high in the hollows.

The elder took off his fox-fur cap and put it on the ground.

'Let this be the marker: this is the starting point to which you must return. All the land you can walk round will be yours.'

Pakhom took out his money, placed it on the cap, took off his outer coat, so that he was wearing only a sleeveless undercoat, tightened his belt below the waist and stuffed a small bag of bread inside his shirt. Then he tied a flask of water to the belt, pulled up his boots, took the spade from his workman and was ready to leave. He could not decide which direction to take at first as the land was so good everywhere. Then he decided, 'It's all good land, so I'll walk towards the sunrise.' He turned to the east, stretching himself as he waited for the sun to appear above the horizon. 'There's no point in wasting time,' he thought. 'And it's easier walking while it's still cool.' The moment the sun's rays came flooding over the horizon Pakhom put the spade on one shoulder and walked out on to the steppe.

Pakhom walked neither quickly nor slowly. When he had gone about three quarters of a mile he stopped, dug a hole and piled the pieces of turf high on top of each other so that they were easily visible. The stiffness had now gone from his legs and he lengthened his stride. A little further on he stopped again and dug another hole.

When Pakhom looked back he could see quite clearly the small hill tyres of the cart-wheels. Pakhom guessed that he had covered about three miles. He was beginning to feel warmer, so he tool off his undercoat, flung it over his shoulder and walked another three miles. It was hot, and a look at the sun reminded him it was time for breakfast.

'Well, that's the first stretch completed!' he thought. 'But there are four to a day and it's too early to start turning. I must take these boots off, though.'

So he sat down, took off his boots, stuck them behind his belt and moved on. The going was easy now and he thought. 'I'll do another three miles and then turn left. The land's so beautiful here, it would be a pity to miss out on any of it. The further I go, the better the land gets.' So for a while he carried straight on and when he looked back the hill was barely visible and the people on it looked like black ants; he could just glimpse something that glinted in the sun.

'Well,' thought Pakhom, 'I've walked enough in this direction, I should be turning now. Besides, I'm stewing in this heat and terribly thirsty.' So he stopped, dug a large hole, piled up the turf, untied his flask, drank and then turned sharp left. On and on he walked – the grass was higher here and it was very hot.

Pakhom began to feel tired. He glanced at the sun and saw that it was noon. 'Well,' he thought, 'I must have a little rest.' So he stopped, sat down and had some bread and water. He did not stretch out, though, thinking, 'Once I lie down I'll fall asleep.' After a few minutes he carried on. At first it was easy – the food had given him strength. But by now it was extremely hot and he began to feel sleepy. Still, he kept going and thought of the proverb, 'A moment's pain can be a lifetime's gain.'

He had walked a long way in the same direction and was just about to turn left when he spotted a lush hollow and decided it would be a pity to lose it. 'What a good place for growing flax!' he thought. So he carried straight on until he had walked right round the low-lying meadows, dug a hole the other side, and then he turned the second corner. Pakhom looked back at the hill: it was shimmering in the heat and through the haze it was difficult to see all the people there – they were at least ten miles away. 'Well,' thought Pakhom, 'I've made those sides too long, this one has to be shorter.' So he started the third side, quickening his step. He looked at the sun and saw that it was already half way to the horizon, but he had completed only about one mile of the third side. The starting-point was still ten miles away. 'No,' he thought, 'although it will make the land a bit lopsided I must take the shortest way back. It's no good trying to grab too much, I've quite enough already!'

Pakhom hastily dug another hole and headed straight for the hill.

9

On the way back Pakhom found the going tough. The heat had exhausted him, his bare feet were cut and bruised and his legs were giving way. He wanted to rest, but this was out of the question – he would never get back by sunset. The sun waits for no man and was sinking lower and lower. 'Oh,' he wondered, 'have I blundered, trying to take too much? What if I'm not back in time?' He looked towards the hill, then at the sun. The hill was far off, the sun was close to the horizon.

But Pakhom struggled on. Although it was very hard, he walked faster and faster. On and on he went – but there was still a long way to go. He started running and threw away his coat, boots, flask, cap, keeping only the spade which he used for leaning on. 'Oh dear,' he thought, 'I've been too greedy. Now I've ruined it. I'll never get back by sunset.' His fear made him only more breathless. On he ran, his shirt soaking and his trousers clinging to him: his throat was parched. His lungs were working like a blacksmith's bellows, his heart beat like a hammer and his legs did not seem to be his – he felt that they were breaking ... Pakhom was terrified and thought, 'All this strain will be the death of me.'

Although he feared death, he could not stop. 'If I stopped now, after coming all this way – well, they'd call me an idiot!' So on he ran until he was close enough to hear the Bashkirs yelling and cheering him on. Their shouts spurred him on all the more, so he summoned his last ounce of strength and kept running. But by now the sun was almost touching the horizon: veiled in mist, it was large and blood-red. It was about to set, but although it did not have very far to sink it was no distance to the starting-point either. Pakhom could see the people on the hill now, waving their arms and urging him on. He could see the fox-fur cap on the ground with the money on it; he could see the elder sitting there with his arms pressed to his sides. And Pakhom remembered his dream. 'I've plenty of land now, but will God let me live to enjoy it? No, I'm finished . . . I'll never make it.'

Pakhom looked at the sun – it had reached the earth now: half of its great disc had dipped below the horizon. With all the strength he had left Pakhom lurched forwards with his full weight, hardly able to move his legs quickly enough to stop himself falling. He reached the hill – and everything suddenly became dark. He looked round and saw that the sun had set. Pakhom groaned. 'All that effort has been in vain,' he thought. He wanted to stop, when he heard the Bashkirs still cheering him on and he realized that from where he was at the bottom of the hill the sun had apparently set, but not for those on top. Pakhom took a deep breath and rushed up the hill which was still bathed in sunlight. When he reached the top he saw his cap with the elder sitting by it, holding his sides and laughing his head off. Then he remembered the dream and he groaned. His legs gave way, he fell forward and managed to reach the cap with his hands.

'Oh, well done!' exclaimed the elder. 'That's a lot of land you've earned yourself!'

Pakhom's workman ran up and tried to lift his master, but the blood flowed from his mouth. Pakhom was dead.

The Bashkirs clicked their tongues sympathetically.

Pakhom's workman picked up the spade, dug a grave for his master – six feet from head to heel, which was exactly the right length – and buried him.

What Men Live By

We know that we have passed from death unto life, because we love the brethren. He that loveth not his brother abideth in death. (I John iii, 14)

But whoso hath this world's good, and seeth his brother have need, and shutteth up his bowels of compassion from him, how dwelleth the love of God in him? (I John iii, 17)

My little children, let us not love in word, neither in tongue: but in deed and in truth. (I John iii, 18)

... for love is of God; and every one that loveth is born of God, and knoweth God. (I John iv, 7)

He that loveth not knoweth not God; for God is love. (I John iv, 8)

No man hath seen God at any time. If we love one another, God dwelleth in us ... (I John iv, 12)

God is love; and he that dwelleth in love dwelleth in God, and God in him. (I John iv, 16)

If a man say, I love God, and hateth his brother, he is a liar: for he that loveth not his brother whom he hath seen, how can he love God whom he hath not seen? (I John iv, 20)

Leo Tolstoy

1

Once there was a shoemaker who had neither house nor land of his own and who lived in a peasant's cottage with his wife and children, supporting them by what work he could get. Bread was expensive but his work was cheap and the little he earned was spent on food for his family. He and his wife had only one winter coat between them and even that was in a sorry state. For the past two years he had been saving to buy sheepskins for a new one.

By autumn he had scraped together a small sum: there was the three-rouble note that his wife kept in a little wooden box, as well as the five roubles and twenty copecks that some of the villagers owed him.

One morning he decided to go to the village to buy the skins. He put his wife's wadded twill jacket over his shirt and over that his own cloth coat. After breakfast he put the three-rouble note in his pocket, cut himself a walking-stick and set off.

'With the five roubles that one of them owes me,' he thought, 'plus the three I already have, I should have enough to buy the sheepskins.'

When he reached the village he stopped at a cottage, but the owner was out. His wife did not have the money, but she promised to send her husband over with it by the end of the week. So he called on another peasant who swore he was short of cash and that all he could manage was twenty copecks that were owing for some boot repairs. And then, when the shoemaker tried to buy the skins on credit, the dealer would not trust him.

'Bring me the money first,' he said. 'Then you can pick whatever skins you like. We all know how hard it is to collect what's owing to us!'

And so the shoemaker did no business that day, apart from twenty copecks for the repairs and a pair of felt boots that needed soling.

All this depressed the shoemaker and after spending the twenty copecks on vodka he set off for home without any skins. Earlier that morning he had felt a sharp nip in the air, but after a few vodkas he warmed up – even though he had no proper winter coat. As he walked down the road, striking frozen clods of earth with his stick in one hand and swinging the felt boots in the other, he started talking to himself.

'I feel quite warm without a coat,' he said. 'I've only had a drop, yet I can feel it rushing through every vein in my body. I don't need any sheepskins! I'm going home, with all my troubles behind me. That's the sort of man I am! Why should I worry? I can survive without a new coat – I won't need one for ages. Only, the wife won't be too happy. But it's really rotten when you do a job and the customer tries to string you along and doesn't pay up. You just wait – if you don't bring me the money I'll have the shirt off your back, I swear it! It's a bit much, what with a measly twenty copecks at a time. What can I do with twenty copecks? Spend it on drink, that's all. You say you're hard up. Well, what about me? You've a house, cattle, everything, but all I have is on my back. You grow your own corn, while I have to go out and buy mine. Whatever happens I must spend three roubles a week on bread alone. By the time I get home there won't be any left and I'll have to fork out another rouble and a half. So, you'd better pay up!'

The shoemaker kept rambling on like this until he drew near the wayside chapel at the bend in the road where something whitish just behind it caught his eye. But by now it was growing dark and although he strained his eyes he could not make out what it was. 'There wasn't any stone there before,' he thought. 'Perhaps it's a cow? No, it doesn't look like one at all. From the head it looks like a man and it's all white. But what would a man be doing there?'

He went a few steps closer and could now make it out quite clearly. How amazing! It *was* a man sitting there, but he could not see if he were dead or alive, and he was naked and quite motionless, his back propped against the chapel wall. The shoemaker was terrified and thought, 'A man's been murdered, stripped naked and dumped. If I go any nearer I might get mixed up in all sorts of troubles.'

And so the shoemaker went on his way. He walked behind the chapel to avoid having to look at him again. After a short distance he turned round and saw that the man was no longer leaning against the wall, but was moving, as if trying to see who he was. The shoemaker felt even more frightened and thought, 'Shall I go back or simply carry on? If I go back something terrible might happen. Who knows what kind of man he might be? I bet he's up to no good. Besides, he might suddenly jump to his feet and start choking the life out of me – and there'd be nothing I could do about it. And if he doesn't throttle me I might get lumbered with looking after him. But how can I help a naked man? I couldn't let him have the last shirt off my back. Please God, help me!'

And the shoemaker quickened his stride. He had almost left the chapel behind when his conscience began to prick him. He stopped in the middle of the road.

'How could you do such a thing, Semyon?' he reproached himself. 'That man might be dying miserably and you're such a coward you'd leave him there to die. Or have you become so rich all of a sudden that you're scared stiff he might steal all your money? You should be ashamed, Semyon!'

And he turned round again and went right up to the man.

2

After a close look Semyon could see that he was young and healthy. There were no bruises on his body: he was just chilled to the bone and terrified. There he sat, leaning forward without looking at Semyon and apparently too weak to raise his eyes. When Semyon was right next to him he suddenly seemed to wake as if from a trance. He turned his head, opened his eyes and looked straight at Semyon. That one look was enough to allay all Semyon's fears. He threw down the felt boots, undid his belt, laid it over the boots and took off his cloth coat.

'There's no time for talking,' he said. 'Put that on – and be quick about it!'

Then Semyon took the man under the arms and tried to lift him, but he got to his feet without any help. And then

Semyon saw that his body was slender and clean, that his legs and arms bore no trace of any wounds; his face was mild and gentle. Semyon threw his coat over his shoulders, but the man could not find the sleeves, so Semyon guided his arms into them, pulled on the coat, wrapped it around him and fastened it with his belt.

Then Semyon took off his tattered cap, intending to put it on the naked man's head, but he felt the cold on his own head and thought, 'I'm completely bald, while he's got long, curly hair.' And he put it back on again. 'It would be better to give him the boots,' he thought.

So he made the man sit down again and put the felt boots on his feet, after which he said, 'There you are, my friend. Stretch your legs a bit and warm yourself. Don't worry, it will all be sorted out later. Now, can you walk?'

The man stood up, looked tenderly at Semyon, but was unable to say one word.

'Why don't you say something? Come on, we can't spend all winter here, we must be on our way. Here, you can lean on my stick if you feel weak. Right, come on!'

And the man started walking – and he walked effortlessly, without lagging behind.

As they went down the road Semyon asked, 'Where are you from?'

'Not from these parts.'

'I thought so – I know everyone round here. But how did you come to be there, by the chapel?'

'I cannot tell you that.'

'Did some men attack you?'

'No, no one harmed me. It was God who punished me.'

'Well, we are all in His hands. All the same, you must have somewhere to go. Where are you heading?'

'Nowhere in particular.'

Semyon was amazed. The man did not strike him as a ruffian, he was so softly spoken, yet he revealed nothing about himself. 'Anything can happen in this world,' Semyon reflected and he told the man, 'All right, come home with me, even if it is a bit out of your way.'

As Semyon walked down the road the stranger did not lag behind for one moment, but kept abreast. The wind got up and the cold air crept under Semyon's shirt. The drink was beginning to wear off and he felt chilled to the marrow.

Sniffling as he went, he wrapped his wife's jacket tighter around himself and thought, 'So much for sheepskins! I go off to buy some and all I do is come home without even the old coat on my back, and with a naked stranger into the bargain! Matryona won't be too pleased about that!' And the thought of his wife depressed him. But the moment he looked at the stranger he remembered the look he had given him at the chapel and his heart filled with joy.

3

Semyon's wife had finished her chores early that day. She had chopped the wood, fetched water, fed the children, had a bite to eat herself and had then sat for a long time wondering when she should bake the bread – that same day or the next. There was still one thick slice left.

'If Semyon has his dinner in the village,' she thought, 'then he won't want much for supper and there'll be enough bread for tomorrow.'

She turned the slice over, 'I shan't do any baking today,' she decided, 'there's only enough flour for one loaf. But we can make this last till Friday.'

So Matryona put the bread away and sat down at the table to patch her husband's shirt. As she worked she thought of him buying the sheepskins for the new winter coat.

'I hope the dealer won't swindle him. He's so simple, that husband of mine. He'd never cheat a soul himself and even a little child could trick him. Eight roubles is a lot of money, enough to buy very good sheepskins. Not the best quality tanned ones perhaps, but still good enough for a nice coat. Last winter was so hard without a proper one! I couldn't even go down to the river, couldn't go anywhere. And when he left this morning he took all the warm clothes we have, leaving me with nothing to wear. Now, he didn't leave all that early. All the same, it's time he was back. I hope my old man hasn't gone drinking!'

These thoughts had just crossed Matryona's mind when the front steps creaked and someone came in. Matryona stuck her needle into the shirt and went out into the hall. There she saw two men – Semyon and someone in felt boots and without a cap.

Matryona immediately smelt the vodka on her husband's breath. 'So, I was right, he's been on the drink,' she thought. And when she saw him standing there, empty-handed and with a guilty grin on his face, wearing nothing but the jacket she had lent him, her heart sank. 'He's gone and spent all that money drinking with some good-for-nothing. What's more, he's got the nerve to bring him home.'

Matryona ushered them in and followed them into the living-room. Now she could see that the stranger was a thin young man and that he was wearing her husband's coat. She could see no shirt under it and he had no cap. Once inside he stood quite still and kept looking down. Matryona concluded that he was a bad lot, as he seemed so nervous.

Frowning, she went over to the stove and waited to see what they would do next.

Semyon took off his cap and sat down on the bench as if he had done no wrong.

'Come on, Matryona, let's have some supper!' he said.

Matryona muttered something to herself and stayed quite still by the stove. She kept looking first at one, then the other, shaking her head. Semyon realized that his wife was annoyed, but there was nothing he could do about it. Pretending not to notice, he took the stranger by the arm.

'Sit down,' he said. 'Let's have something to eat.'

The stranger sat on the bench.

'Well, don't you have anything?'

Matryona lost her temper. 'Yes, I do, but not for you. It seems you've drunk your brains away. You went out to buy some sheepskins and back you come without even the coat you left in. What's more, you bring some half-naked tramp back with you. I don't have any supper for a pair of drunkards like you!'

'Now that's enough of your stupid tongue-wagging, Matryona! You might at least ask who he is.'

'And you can tell me what you did with the money.'

Semyon felt in his pocket, took out the three-rouble note and unfolded it.

'Here it is. Trifonov wouldn't give me any money, but he promised to pay up in a day or so.'

Matryona grew even more furious: in addition to not buying the sheepskins, her husband had lent their only coat to some naked stranger. What's more, he'd brought him back home.

She snatched the note from the table and went off to hide it somewhere.

'I've no supper for you,' she told them. 'You can't expect me to feed every naked drunkard.'

'And you mind your tongue, Matryona. First hear what he has to say . . .'

'What sense will I get from a drunken fool like him? I was right in not wanting to marry an old soak like you! You sold all Mother's linen for drink. And then, instead of buying sheepskins you spend the money on drink.'

Semyon tried hard to make his wife understand that all he had spent on drink was a mere twenty copecks and to explain where he had found the stranger. But she would not let him get a word in edgeways, rattling away nineteen to the dozen and even reminding him of things that had happened ten years ago. On and on she went, until finally she dashed over to Semyon and grabbed his sleeve.

'Give me my jacket back, it's the only one I have and you took it to wear yourself. Give it back, you flea-bitten dog. May you die of a fit!'

Semyon began taking the jacket off and turned a sleeve

inside-out, but his wife tugged so hard that it came apart at the seams. Then she seized it, threw it over her head and made for the door. But then she stopped. Her heart seemed to melt and she felt that she wanted to banish all those spiteful feelings and to find out who that man really was.

4

As she stood there, quite still, Matryona said, 'If he were an honest man he wouldn't be going around without a shirt to his back. And if you'd been doing what you were supposed to you'd have told me where you picked up this fine young fellow!'

'All right, I'll tell you. I was on my way home when I saw this man sitting by the chapel, naked and frozen. Now, it's not the kind of weather to go about naked! God must have led me to him, or he'd have perished. What could I do? Who knows what may have happened to him? So, I made him stand up, clothed him and brought him back here. Please don't be angry, Matryona, it's sinful. Don't forget that we must all die one day.'

Matryona was about to give him a piece of her mind again, but then she looked at the stranger and became silent. There he sat, motionless, on the edge of the bench, his hands folded on his knees, his head drooping on his breast. His eyes were closed and he wrinkled his face as if something were choking him. Matryona still said nothing, but Semyon asked, 'Matryona, is there no love of God within you?'

At these words Matryona glanced at the stranger and her heart suddenly filled with pity. She came back from the door, went over to the stove, took out the supper, placed a cup on the table, poured out some kvass, brought out the last slice of bread and set out a knife and some spoons. Please eat,' she said.

Semyon nudged the stranger and told him, 'Come and sit at the table.'

Semyon divided the bread into small pieces and they started eating. Matryona sat at one corner of the table, her head on her hand, gazing at the stranger. And she was filled with pity and her heart went out to him. Suddenly, his face brightened, the wrinkles disappeared and he looked up at Matryona and smiled.

After supper Matryona cleared the table and began questioning him.

'Where are you from?'

'Not from these parts.'

'How did you come to be by the wayside?'

'I cannot tell you.'

'Who stole your clothes?'

'God punished me.'

'And you were lying there, all naked?'

'Yes, naked and freezing. And then Semyon saw me and took pity on me. He took off his coat, put it over me and insisted I came home with him. You have given me food and drink and shown compassion. God will reward you!'

Matryona got up, took from the window-sill the old shirt of Semyon's she had been patching and handed it to the stranger. Then she found him some trousers.

'Here, I see you've no shirt, so put this on and lie down where you like – up on the sleeping-bench or over the stove.'

The stranger took off the coat, put on the shirt and trousers and lay on the sleeping-bench. Matryona blew out the candle, took the coat and joined her husband over the stove.

Matryona drew the skirts of the coat over herself and lay down. But she did not fall asleep, for she could not get that stranger out of her mind.

When she remembered that he had eaten their last slice of bread and that they would have none for tomorrow, and that she had given him the shirt and trousers, she became terribly dejected. But then, when she recalled his smile her heart leapt up. For a long time she lay awake and she noticed that Semyon was awake too, as he kept pulling the coat up.

'Semyon!'

'What is it?'

'You two have eaten the last slice of bread and I haven't prepared any more. I don't know what we're going to do tomorrow. Perhaps I can borrow some from our neighbour Malanya.'

'Yes, we'll get by, we won't starve.'

Matryona lay silently for a while and then she said, 'He seems to be a good man, only he doesn't tell us anything about himself.'

'I suppose he can't.'

'Semyon!'

'What?'

'We're always giving, but why does nobody ever give *us* anything?'

Semyon didn't know what to reply. All he said was, 'Let's

talk about that another time,' after which he turned over and went to sleep.

5

Next morning, when Semyon woke up, the children were still asleep and his wife had gone over to the neighbour's to borrow some bread. Only the stranger was sitting on the bench, wearing the old trousers and shirt and looking up. His face was brighter than the evening before. Semyon said, 'Well, my friend. The belly needs food and the body clothes. We all have to earn a living, so what sort of work can you do?'

'I can't do anything.'

Semyon was amazed and replied, 'If a man has the will he can learn anything.'

'Yes, men work for their living, so I'll work too.'

'What's your name?'

'Mikhail.'

'Well, Mikhail, if you don't want to tell us about yourself that's your affair. But we have to earn our living. If you do as I tell you I'll see you have enough to eat.'

'God bless you! I'll learn how to work, just tell me what to do.'

Semyon took a piece of yarn, wound it round his fingers and twisted it.

'It's not hard, just watch . . .'

Mikhail watched and right away he caught the knack, winding the yarn and twisting it just like Semyon.

Then Semyon showed him how to wax it and Mikhail understood at once. Then he showed him how to draw it through and how to stitch. Again Mikhail immediately understood.

Whatever Semyon showed him he mastered right away and within three days was working as if he had been making shoes all his life. He would work without any let-up and ate very little. Only when one job was finished would he stop for a moment and silently look up. He never went out, only spoke when he really had to, and he never joked or laughed.

And in fact the only time they had seen him smile was on that very first evening, when Matryona had given him supper.

6

The days passed, weeks passed, and a year ran its course. Mikhail was still living with Semyon and working for him. The word got round that Semyon's new workman could make boots better and stronger than anyone else. People from all over the district came to Semyon for new boots and he prospered.

One winter's day Semyon and Mikhail were sitting at their work when a three-horse carriage on sleigh runners drove up to the cottage, its bells gaily ringing. When they looked out of the window they saw it had stopped right outside. A boy jumped down from the box and opened the carriage door. A gentleman in a fur coat stepped out, walked up to the front door and climbed the steps. Matryona rushed to fling open the door.

As he came in, the gentleman had to lower his head and then straighten up. But still his head almost touched the ceiling and he filled a whole corner of the room.

Semyon stood up and marvelled at the gentleman: he had never seen anyone like him. Semyon himself was lean, Mikhail was skinny, while Matryona was as thin as a rake. But this visitor seemed like someone from another world: with his full red face and his bull's neck he seemed to be made of cast iron.

He puffed, took off his fur coat, sat on the bench and asked, 'Who is the master bootmaker here?'

Semyon stepped forward and said, 'I am, Your Honour.'

Then the gentleman shouted to his boy, 'Hey, Fedka, bring the leather!'

The boy ran in with a parcel, which the gentleman took and placed on the table.

'Untie it,' he said. The boy untied it.

Then the gentleman pointed at the leather and told Semyon, 'Now, listen to me, bootmaker. Do you see that leather?'

'Yes, I do, Your Honour.'

'Do you know what kind it is?'

Semyon felt it and said, 'It's very good quality.'

'I should say it's good quality! You fool, I bet you've never set eyes on leather like that. It's German and I paid twenty roubles for it.'

Semyon quailed and said, 'Now where would *I* see leather like that?'

'Yes, where indeed! Could you make me a pair of boots out of it?'

'It's possible, Your Honour.'

'I'll give you possible!' the gentleman shouted. 'Now, see you don't forget for whom you're making them and the quality of the leather you'll be using. I want a pair of boots that will last me a year without losing their shape or coming apart at the stitches. If you can do the job, take the leather and cut it up. But if you can't, you'd better tell me here and now. I'm warning you: if the boots split or lose their shape before the year's out I'll have you clapped in prison. But if they keep their shape and don't split for a year I'll pay you ten roubles.'

Semyon was quite afraid and did not know what to reply. He glanced at Mikhail, nudged him with his elbow and whispered, 'Well, shall I take it on?'

Mikhail nodded as if to say, 'Yes, take it on.'

So Semyon followed Mikhail's advice and undertook to make a pair of boots that would not lose their shape or split for a whole year.

Then the gentleman called the boy over to take off his left boot for him and stretched out his leg.

'Take my measurements!'

Semyon sewed together a strip of paper about seventeen inches long, smoothed it out, knelt down, wiped his hands thoroughly on his apron so as not to dirty the gentleman's sock and started measuring. He took the sole and instep measurements. But when he tried to measure the calf he found that the strip of paper was not long enough – the gentleman's calf was as thick as a log.

'Mind you don't make them too tight in the leg,' he said.

Semyon sewed another piece to the strip of paper, while the gentleman sat wriggling his toes in his sock and surveying the people in the room. And then he noticed Mikhail.

'Who's that over there?' he asked.

'He's my master craftsman, he'll be making the boots.'

'Now you watch out,' the gentleman said, 'remember they have to last a whole year.'

When Semyon turned towards Mikhail he saw that he was not even looking at the gentleman, but staring into the corner, as if someone was standing behind him. Mikhail kept staring until suddenly he smiled and his whole face lit up.

'What are you grinning at, idiot?' the gentleman asked. 'You'd better see to it that the boots are ready on time!'

'They'll be ready whenever you want them,' Mikhail replied.

'Good.'

The gentleman put on his boots again, then his fur coat, which he wrapped tightly around him, and went to the door. But he forgot to lower his head and banged it against the lintel. He cursed and rubbed it. Then he climbed into the carriage and drove off.

As soon as he had gone Semyon remarked, 'He's as tough as nails! You couldn't kill him with a mallet. Why, he nearly knocked the lintel out and still he hardly felt a thing!'

'You'd expect him to be strong with the kind of life he leads,' Matryona said. 'Death itself couldn't touch that iron girder!'

7

'Well, we've taken on the work now,' Semyon told Mikhail, 'and I only hope it doesn't land us in trouble. The leather's very expensive and the gentleman's short-tempered, so we'd better not slip up. Your eyes are sharper than mine and your hands are more skilled, so take the measure and start cutting the leather. I'll sew the vamps later.'

Mikhail obediently took the leather, spread it on the table, folded it in two, took a knife and started cutting.

Matryona went over to watch Mikhail working and was amazed to see what he was doing. Naturally she knew all about boot-making and could see that instead of cutting the leather into the normal shape for boots Mikhail was cutting it into round pieces.

Matryona felt she should point it out, but then she thought, 'Maybe I don't understand how a *gentleman's* boots should be made. Maybe Mikhail knows best, so I won't interfere.'

When he had finished cutting Mikhail took some thread and started sewing the pieces together – not with two ends, as he should have done for boots, but with one end, as if for slippers.

Although Matryona was astonished by this as well, she did not interfere and Mikhail carried on sewing until midday.

When Semyon got up and saw that Mikhail had made a pair of slippers from the gentleman's leather he groaned.

'I don't understand,' he thought, 'how Mikhail, who's

been with me for a whole year without making one mistake, should now go and make such a dreadful mess of things. The gentleman ordered welted high boots and he's made slippers without soles and ruined the leather. How can I face the gentleman now? I can't replace leather of that quality.'

And he told Mikhail, 'What on earth have you done, my friend? You've ruined me! The gentleman ordered high boots and just look what you've made!'

And he was just about to give Mikhail a stern lecture when someone knocked hard on the front door with the iron ring. They looked out of the window and saw that someone had ridden up and was tethering his horse. When the door was opened in came the same young boy who had accompanied the gentleman.

'Good afternoon to you!'

'Good afternoon. What can we do for you?'

'The mistress sent me about those boots.'

'What about them?'

'Just this: the master won't be needing them. He's dead.'

'What did you say?'

'He died in the carriage even before we got home. When we reached the house the others came to help him out, but there he lay, slumped like a sack of potatoes. He was already stiff, stone-dead, and we had a real struggle getting him out. So the mistress told me to come back here. "Tell that shoemaker," she said, "that the gentleman who called and ordered some boots and left the leather won't be needing them and that instead he must make a pair of soft corpse-slippers as soon as he can." She told me to wait until they're ready. So here I am.'

What Men Live By

Mikhail collected the offcuts from the table and rolled them up. Then he took the soft slippers he had already made, slapped them together, wiped them with his apron and handed them to the boy, who took them.

'Goodbye, masters! Good luck to you!' he said as he left.

8

Another year passed, then another, until Mikhail was in his sixth year with Semyon. He lived just as before, never going out, speaking only when he had to. And all that time he smiled only twice – when the old woman had first given him supper and then when the rich gentleman called. Semyon thought the world of his workman and no longer inquired where he was from. His only fear was that Mikhail might leave him.

One day they were all at home and Matryona was putting iron pots into the oven, while the children were scampering along the benches and looking out of the windows. Semyon was stitching at one window, while Mikhail was heeling a boot at the other.

One of the little boys ran along the bench to Mikhail, leant on his shoulder and looked through the window.

'Look, Uncle Mikhail! There's a lady with two little girls. I think she's coming here. One of the girls is limping.'

When the boy said this, Mikhail put down his work, turned to the window and looked out into the street.

Semyon was amazed: Mikhail had never looked out into the street before, but now he was glued to the window and staring at something. Semyon, too, looked out and saw that a well-dressed woman with two little girls in fur coats and thick woollen shawls were in fact coming towards the cottage. The girls were so alike it would have been impossible to tell them apart were it not that one had a crippled left leg and walked with a limp.

The woman climbed the steps, fumbled for the latch and opened the door. She let the little girls in first and then followed them.

'Good day, everyone!' she said.

'Welcome! What can we do for you?'

The woman sat at the table while the girls, feeling shy with all those people in the room, snuggled against her knees.

'I'd like some leather shoes for the girls, for the spring,' she said.

'That's no problem. Although we've never made such small ones before we can do them – either welted or lined with linen. This is Mikhail, my master shoemaker.'

Semyon turned to Mikhail and saw that he had stopped working and was sitting there with his eyes fixed on the little girls.

Semyon was quite surprised. True, the girls were very pretty – plump, with black eyes and rosy little cheeks – and wore fine fur coats and shawls. Still, he could not understand why Mikhail should be staring like that, as if he knew them.

Semyon kept wondering and then started discussing the price with the woman. This was finally agreed and Semyon took his measure. The woman lifted the lame girl on to one knee and said, 'Measure her twice and make one shoe for her lame foot and three for the sound one: they take exactly the same size, because they're twins.'

Semyon took the measurements and inquired about the little lame girl.

'What happened? Such a pretty little girl. Was she born like that?'

'No, she was crushed by her mother.'

Just then Matryona joined in. She was wondering who the woman was and whose children they were.

'You're their mother, aren't you?'

'No, dear woman, I'm not their mother, nor am I a relative. They were complete strangers and I adopted them.'

'They're not your own and yet you seem so fond of them!'

'How can I help being fond of them? I breast-fed them both. I did have a child of my own once, but it pleased God to take him. I didn't love him as much as these little girls, though.'

'So whose are they?'

9

And the woman proceeded to tell them the whole story.

'It all started about six years ago, when these little girls lost their father and mother the same week – the father was buried on the Tuesday and the mother died on the Friday. So, for three days they had no father and on the fourth they lost their mother. At that time my husband and I were farm-workers and our yard was right next door. The father was a lone wolf and worked as a woodcutter. One day when they were cutting down some trees they let one fall right on him and it crushed his insides. They had hardly got him back to the village when his soul went up to heaven and the same week his widow gave birth to twins – these little girls. She was a poor woman, all on her own, with no other women, young or old, to help her. Alone she gave birth and alone she died.

'The next morning I went to see how she was, but the poor thing was already stiff and cold. When she died she'd rolled over on to this little girl and twisted her leg out of shape. Then the villagers came, washed the body and laid it out. Then they made a coffin and buried her. Good folk they were. So the two little girls were left alone in the world, and who was going to look after them? I happened to be the only woman in that village who'd had a baby at the time and I'd been breast-feeding my first-born for about eight weeks. So I took care of the girls for the time being. The men thought hard about what to do with the orphans and in the end they told me, "You'd better look after them for now, Marya, until we manage to sort something out." So I breast-fed the girl who hadn't been harmed, but not the one who'd been crippled, as I didn't expect her to live. And then I thought to myself, "Why should that little angel be left to fade away?" I took pity on her too and started feeding her, so that in the end I was feeding all three of them – my own first-born and these two, at my own breasts! I was young, strong and well-nourished and God gave me so much milk that it filled my breasts to overflowing. Sometimes I'd feed two at a time, with the third waiting, and when one had had its fill, I'd put the third to my breast. But it was God's will that I should nurse these little girls and bury my own child before he was two years old. And God never gave me another one. But after that I became quite well off. My second husband's working for a corn merchant and we live at the mill. He earns good money and we live well. But as we've no children of our own I'd be terribly lonely without these two little girls. How can I help loving them? They are the apple of my eye!'

The woman pressed the lame girl to her with one hand and wiped the tears from her cheeks with the other.

Matryona sighed. 'There's a lot of truth in the saying "You can live without mother or father, but you can't live without God."'

They chatted together for a while and then the woman got up to leave. Semyon and his wife saw them out and then they looked at Mikhail: he was sitting there, his arms folded on his knees, and he was looking up and smiling.

10

Semyon went over to Mikhail and asked, 'What is it?'

Mikhail rose from the bench, put down his work, took off his apron, bowed to Semyon and Matryona and said, 'Please forgive me, you good people. God has forgiven me, so please forgive me too.'

And the shoemaker and his wife saw a light shining from Mikhail. And Semyon stood up, bowed in turn and said, 'I can see you are no ordinary mortal and I cannot detain you any longer or question you. But please tell me one thing: why were you so miserable when I first found you and brought you home? And why, when my wife gave you supper, did you smile and from that time onwards brighten up?

And why, when that rich gentleman ordered those boots, did you smile again and become even more cheerful? And why, when that woman brought those little girls here just now, did you smile a third time and become the very picture of joy? Please tell me, Mikhail. What is that light coming from you and why did you smile three times?'

'The light is radiating from me,' Mikhail replied, 'because I had been punished, but now God has forgiven me. And I smiled three times because I was commanded to discover three truths and I have discovered them. I discovered the first truth when your wife took pity on me – that is why I smiled for the first time. The second truth I discovered when that rich gentleman ordered the boots – and then I smiled again. And just now, when I saw those two little girls, I discovered the last of the three truths – and I smiled for the third time.'

'Tell me, Mikhail,' Semyon asked, 'why did God punish you and what are those three truths, so that I too may know them?'

Mikhail replied, 'God punished me because I disobeyed Him. I was an angel of the Lord and I disobeyed Him. Yes, I was an angel in heaven and the Lord sent me down to earth to take a woman's soul. I flew down and saw the woman lying there. She was sick, all alone and had just given birth to twins, two little girls. There they were, crawling around their mother, but she was unable to put them to her breasts. When she saw me she understood that God had sent me to take her soul. She burst into tears and said, "Angel of the Lord! My husband has just been buried, killed by a falling tree. I have no sister, no aunt, no grandmother – no one to bring up my little orphans. So please don't take my soul, let me suckle my babies, bring them up and set them on their feet. Children cannot live without father or mother!" And I did what she asked, pressed one little girl to her breast, put the other in her arms and ascended to heaven. I flew to God and told Him, "I could not bring myself to take the soul of a woman who had just borne twins. The father was killed by a falling tree and the mother had just given birth and begged me not to take her soul. 'Let me suckle my children, bring them up and set them on their feet. Children cannot live without a father or mother,' she pleaded. So I did not take that woman's soul." And then God said, "If you go down to earth and take that woman's soul you will discover three truths: you will learn *what dwells in man, what is not given to man* and *what men live by*. When you have learnt these truths you shall return to heaven." So I flew down to earth again and took the mother's soul. The babies dropped from her breasts and her body rolled over on to one of them, crushing its leg. Then I rose above the village, wishing to return her soul to God, but I was seized by a strong wind and my wings drooped and fell off. And so the soul alone returned to God and I fell to earth, by the roadside.'

11

And now Semyon and Matryona realized whom they had been clothing and feeding and had taken in to live with them. And they both wept for joy and fear. And the angel said, 'I was alone and naked in that field. Never before had

I known the needs of man, never had I known cold or hunger. But now I was an ordinary mortal, cold and hungry and not knowing what to do. And then I saw a chapel in the field, built for the glory of God. So I went to it to seek shelter. But it was locked and I could not enter. So I sat down behind it to shelter from the wind. Evening came and I was famished, freezing and in pain. Suddenly I heard a man coming down the road. He was carrying a pair of boots and talking to himself. For the first time since I became a man I saw the mortal face of man. It terrified me and I turned away. And I could hear this man wondering how to protect his body from the winter cold and feed his wife and children. And I thought, "I am perishing with cold and hunger, but here is someone whose only thought is how to find a warm coat for himself and his wife, and food for his family. I cannot expect any help from him." When the man saw me he frowned, looking even more terrifying, and he passed me by. I was desperate. But suddenly I heard him coming back. As I looked he no longer seemed the same man. Before, his face had borne the stamp of death, but now he had suddenly become alive again and in that face I could see God. He came up to me, clothed me and took me to his home. When we arrived a woman came out to meet us and she spoke. This woman was even more terrifying than the man. Her breath seemed to come from the grave and I was almost choked by that deathly stench. She wished to cast me out into the cold and I knew that if she did that she would die. Then suddenly her husband told her to think of God and at once she was transformed. When she had given us supper I returned the look she gave me and saw that death no longer dwelt in her, but life. And in her too I could see God.

'And I recalled God's first lesson: *thou shalt learn what dwelleth in man*. And now I knew that it is Love that dwells in man. I was overjoyed that God had begun to reveal what He had promised to reveal, and I smiled for the first time. But I did not know the whole truth yet. I did not yet know what is not given to man and what men live by.

'And so I came to live with you and one year passed. One day a rich gentleman came to order a pair of boots that would last a year without splitting or losing their shape. When I looked at him I suddenly saw my comrade, the Angel of Death, standing behind him. No one but I could see that angel. And I knew that he would take the gentleman's soul before sunset. And I thought, "Here is a man who wants to provide for himself for a year from now but does not know that by evening he will be dead.' And so I remembered God's second lesson: *thou shalt learn what is not given to man*.

'What dwells in man I already knew. Now I knew that which is not given to man: it is not given to him to know his bodily needs. And I smiled for the second time. I rejoiced that I had seen my fellow angel and that God had revealed His second truth.

'But still I did not know everything. I did not understand what it is that men live by. And so I lived on, waiting for God to reveal this last truth to me. In my sixth year that woman came here with the two little girls. I recognized the girls and learnt how they had stayed alive. After this discovery I thought, "The mother pleaded with me for her children's sake and I believed what she said, thinking that children cannot live without father or mother. But the other woman had nursed them and brought them up." And when I saw how much love this woman had for the children and how she wept over them I saw the living God in her and understood *what men live by*. And I realized that God had revealed His last lesson and had forgiven me. So I smiled for the third time.'

12

And the angel's body was bared and it was robed in light, so that the eye could not look upon it. And the angel's voice grew louder, as though it came not from him, but from heaven itself. And the angel said, 'I have learned that men live not by selfishness, but by love.

'It was not given to the mother to know what her children needed for their lives. Nor was it given to the rich man to know what his true needs were. Nor is it given to any man to know, before the sun has set, whether he will need boots for his living body or slippers for his corpse. When I became a mortal I survived not by thinking of myself, but through the love that dwelt in a passer-by and his wife, and the compassion and love they showed me. The two orphans' lives were preserved, not by what others may have intended for them, but by the love that dwelt in the heart of a woman, a complete stranger, and by the love and compassion she showed them. Indeed, all men live not by what they may intend for their own well-being, but by the love that dwells in others.

'Previously I had known that God gave life to men and desired that they should live. But then I came to know something else.

'I came to understand that God does not wish men to live apart and that is why He does not reveal to each man what he needs for himself *alone*. On the contrary, He wishes men to live in peace and harmony with each other and for this reason He has revealed to each and every one of them what *all* men need, as well as themselves.

'And I understood that men only think that they live by caring only about themselves: in reality they live by love alone. He who dwells in love dwells in God, and God in him, for God is love.'

And the angel sang the Lord's praises and the hut shook with the sound of his voice. And the roof parted and a pillar of fire rose from earth to heaven. Semyon and his wife and children prostrated themselves; the angel's wings unfurled and he soared into the sky.

When Semyon came to his senses the hut was just as it had always been and there was no one there but him and his family.

1. BOCCACCIO · *Mrs Rosie and the Priest*
2. GERARD MANLEY HOPKINS · *As kingfishers catch fire*
3. *The Saga of Gunnlaug Serpent-tongue*
4. THOMAS DE QUINCEY · *On Murder Considered as One of the Fine Arts*
5. FRIEDRICH NIETZSCHE · *Aphorisms on Love and Hate*
6. JOHN RUSKIN · *Traffic*
7. PU SONGLING · *Wailing Ghosts*
8. JONATHAN SWIFT · *A Modest Proposal*
9. *Three Tang Dynasty Poets*
10. WALT WHITMAN · *On the Beach at Night Alone*
11. KENKŌ · *A Cup of Sake Beneath the Cherry Trees*
12. BALTASAR GRACIÁN · *How to Use Your Enemies*
13. JOHN KEATS · *The Eve of St Agnes*
14. THOMAS HARDY · *Woman much missed*
15. GUY DE MAUPASSANT · *Femme Fatale*
16. MARCO POLO · *Travels in the Land of Serpents and Pearls*
17. SUETONIUS · *Caligula*
18. APOLLONIUS OF RHODES · *Jason and Medea*
19. ROBERT LOUIS STEVENSON · *Olalla*
20. KARL MARX AND FRIEDRICH ENGELS · *The Communist Manifesto*
21. PETRONIUS · *Trimalchio's Feast*
22. JOHANN PETER HEBEL · *How a Ghastly Story Was Brought to Light by a Common or Garden Butcher's Dog*
23. HANS CHRISTIAN ANDERSEN · *The Tinder Box*
24. RUDYARD KIPLING · *The Gate of the Hundred Sorrows*
25. DANTE · *Circles of Hell*
26. HENRY MAYHEW · *Of Street Piemen*
27. HAFEZ · *The nightingales are drunk*
28. GEOFFREY CHAUCER · *The Wife of Bath*
29. MICHEL DE MONTAIGNE · *How We Weep and Laugh at the Same Thing*
30. THOMAS NASHE · *The Terrors of the Night*
31. EDGAR ALLAN POE · *The Tell-Tale Heart*
32. MARY KINGSLEY · *A Hippo Banquet*
33. JANE AUSTEN · *The Beautifull Cassandra*
34. ANTON CHEKHOV · *Gooseberries*
35. SAMUEL TAYLOR COLERIDGE · *Well, they are gone, and here must I remain*
36. JOHANN WOLFGANG VON GOETHE · *Sketchy, Doubtful, Incomplete Jottings*
37. CHARLES DICKENS · *The Great Winglebury Duel*
38. HERMAN MELVILLE · *The Maldive Shark*
39. ELIZABETH GASKELL · *The Old Nurse's Story*
40. NIKOLAY LESKOV · *The Steel Flea*

41. HONORÉ DE BALZAC · *The Atheist's Mass*
42. CHARLOTTE PERKINS GILMAN · *The Yellow Wall-Paper*
43. C.P. CAVAFY · *Remember, Body...*
44. FYODOR DOSTOEVSKY · *The Meek One*
45. GUSTAVE FLAUBERT · *A Simple Heart*
46. NIKOLAI GOGOL · *The Nose*
47. SAMUEL PEPYS · *The Great Fire of London*
48. EDITH WHARTON · *The Reckoning*
49. HENRY JAMES · *The Figure in the Carpet*
50. WILFRED OWEN · *Anthem For Doomed Youth*
51. WOLFGANG AMADEUS MOZART · *My Dearest Father*
52. PLATO · *Socrates' Defence*
53. CHRISTINA ROSSETTI · *Goblin Market*
54. *Sindbad the Sailor*
55. SOPHOCLES · *Antigone*
56. RYŪNOSUKE AKUTAGAWA · *The Life of a Stupid Man*
57. LEO TOLSTOY · *How Much Land Does A Man Need?*
58. GIORGIO VASARI · *Leonardo da Vinci*
59. OSCAR WILDE · *Lord Arthur Savile's Crime*
60. SHEN FU · *The Old Man of the Moon*
61. AESOP · *The Dolphins, the Whales and the Gudgeon*
62. MATSUO BASHŌ · *Lips too Chilled*
63. EMILY BRONTË · *The Night is Darkening Round Me*
64. JOSEPH CONRAD · *To-morrow*
65. RICHARD HAKLUYT · *The Voyage of Sir Francis Drake Around the Whole Globe*
66. KATE CHOPIN · *A Pair of Silk Stockings*
67. CHARLES DARWIN · *It was snowing butterflies*
68. BROTHERS GRIMM · *The Robber Bridegroom*
69. CATULLUS · *I Hate and I Love*
70. HOMER · *Circe and the Cyclops*
71. D. H. LAWRENCE · *Il Duro*
72. KATHERINE MANSFIELD · *Miss Brill*
73. OVID · *The Fall of Icarus*
74. SAPPHO · *Come Close*
75. IVAN TURGENEV · *Kasyan from the Beautiful Lands*
76. VIRGIL · *O Cruel Alexis*
77. H. G. WELLS · *A Slip under the Microscope*
78. HERODOTUS · *The Madness of Cambyses*
79. *Speaking of Siva*
80. *The Dhammapada*

'. . . in this painting of Leonardo's there was a smile so pleasing that it seemed divine rather than human . . .'

GIORGIO VASARI
Born 1511, Arezzo, Italy
Died 1574, Florence, Italy

This selection of biographies published in its original Italian in 1550. They are taken from *Lives of the Artists (Volume I)*, Penguin Classics, 1987.

VASARI IN PENGUIN CLASSICS
Lives of the Artists (Volume I)
Lives of the Artists (Volume II)

GIORGIO VASARI

Leonardo da Vinci

Translated by
George Bull

PENGUIN BOOKS

PENGUIN CLASSICS

UK | USA | Canada | Ireland | Australia
India | New Zealand | South Africa

Penguin Books is part of the Penguin Random House group of companies whose addresses can be found at global.penguinrandomhouse.com.

This selection published in Penguin Classics 2015

011

Translation copyright © George Bull, 1965

The moral right of the translator has been asserted

Set in 9.5/13 pt Baskerville 10 Pro
Typeset by Jouve (UK), Milton Keynes
Printed and bound in Great Britain by Clays Ltd, Elcograf S.p.A.

A CIP catalogue record for this book is available from the British Library

ISBN: 978-0-141-39776-4

www.greenpenguin.co.uk

MIX
Paper from responsible sources
FSC® C018179

Penguin Random House is committed to a sustainable future for our business, our readers and our planet. This book is made from Forest Stewardship Council® certified paper.

Contents

Life of Leonardo da Vinci   1
Life of Fra Filippo Lippi   26
Life of Sandro Botticelli   40

Life of Leonardo da Vinci

FLORENTINE PAINTER AND
SCULPTOR, 1452−1519

In the normal course of events many men and women are born with various remarkable qualities and talents; but occasionally, in a way that transcends nature, a single person is marvellously endowed by heaven with beauty, grace, and talent in such abundance that he leaves other men far behind, all his actions seem inspired, and indeed everything he does clearly comes from God rather than from human art.

Everyone acknowledged that this was true of Leonardo da Vinci, an artist of outstanding physical beauty who displayed infinite grace in everything he did and who cultivated his genius so brilliantly that all problems he studied he solved with ease. He possessed great strength and dexterity; he was a man of regal spirit and tremendous breadth of mind; and his name became so famous that not only was he esteemed during his lifetime but his reputation endured and became even greater after his death.

This marvellous and divinely inspired Leonardo was

the son of Piero da Vinci. He would have been very proficient at his early lessons if he had not been so volatile and unstable; for he was always setting himself to learn many things only to abandon them almost immediately. Thus he began to learn arithmetic, and after a few months he had made so much progress that he used to baffle his master with the questions and problems that he raised. For a little while he attended to music, and then he very soon resolved to learn to play the lyre, for he was naturally of an elevated and refined disposition; and with this instrument he accompanied his own charming improvised singing. All the same, for all his other enterprises Leonardo never ceased drawing and working in relief, pursuits which best suited his temperament.

Realizing this, and considering the quality of his son's intelligence, Piero one day took some of Leonardo's drawings along to Andrea del Verrocchio (who was a close friend of his) and earnestly begged him to say whether it would be profitable for the boy to study design. Andrea was amazed to see what extraordinary beginnings Leonardo had made and he urged Piero to make him study the subject. So Piero arranged for Leonardo to enter Andrea's workshop. The boy was delighted with this decision, and he began to practise not only one branch of the arts but all the branches in which design plays a part. He was marvellously gifted, and he proved himself to be a first-class geometrician in his work as a sculptor and architect. In his youth Leonardo made in clay several heads of women, with smiling faces, of which plaster casts are still being made, as well as some children's heads executed as if by a mature artist. He also did many architectural drawings both of ground plans and of other elevations, and, while still young, he was the first to propose reducing the Arno to a navigable canal between Pisa and Florence. He made designs for mills, fulling machines, and engines that could be driven by water-power; and as he intended to be a painter by profession he carefully studied drawing from life. Sometimes he made clay models, draping the figures with rags dipped in plaster, and then drawing them painstakingly on fine Rheims cloth or prepared linen. These drawings were done in black and white with the point of the brush, and the results were marvellous, as one can see from the examples I have in my book of drawings. Besides this, Leonardo did beautiful and detailed drawings on paper which are unrivalled for the perfection of their finish. (I have an example of these in a superb head in coloured silverpoint.) Altogether, his genius was so wonderfully inspired by the grace of God, his powers of expression were so powerfully fed by a willing memory and intellect, and his writing conveyed his ideas so precisely, that his arguments and reasonings confounded the most formidable critics. In addition, he used to make models and plans showing how to excavate and tunnel through mountains without difficulty, so as to pass from one level to another; and he demonstrated how to lift and draw great weights by means of levers, hoists, and winches, and ways of cleansing harbours and using pumps to suck up water from great depths. His brain was always busy on such devices, and one can find drawings of his ideas and experiments scattered among our craftsmen today; I myself have seen many of them. He also spent a great deal of time in making a pattern of a series of knots, so arranged that the connecting thread can be traced from one end to the other and the complete design fills a round space. There exists a splendid engraving of one of these fine and intricate designs, with these words in the centre: *Leonardus Vinci Academia*.

Among his models and plans there was one which Leonardo would often put before the citizens who were then governing Florence – many of them men of great discernment – showing how he proposed to raise and place steps under the church of San Giovanni without damaging the fabric. His arguments were so cogent that they would allow themselves to be convinced, although when they all went their several ways each of them would realize the impossibility of what Leonardo suggested.

Leonardo's disposition was so lovable that he commanded everyone's affection. He owned, one might say, nothing and he worked very little, yet he always kept servants as well as horses. These gave him great pleasure as indeed did all the animal creation which he treated with wonderful love and patience. For example, often when he was walking past the places where birds were sold he would pay the price asked, take them from their cages, and let them fly off into the air, giving them back their lost freedom. In return he was so favoured by nature that to whatever he turned his mind or thoughts the results were always inspired and perfect; and his lively and delightful works were incomparably graceful and realistic.

Clearly, it was because of his profound knowledge of painting that Leonardo started so many things without finishing them; for he was convinced that his hands, for all their skill, could never perfectly express the subtle and wonderful ideas of his imagination. Among his many interests was included the study of nature; he investigated the properties of plants and then observed the motion of the heavens, the path of the moon, and the course of the sun.

I mentioned earlier that when he was still young Leonardo entered the workshop of Andrea del Verrocchio. Now at that time Verrocchio was working on a panel picture showing the Baptism of Christ by St John, for which Leonardo painted an angel who was holding some garments; and despite his youth, he executed it in such a manner that his angel was far better than the figures painted by Andrea. This was the reason why Andrea would never touch colours again, he was so ashamed that a boy understood their use better than he did. Leonardo was then commissioned to make a cartoon (for a tapestry to be woven of gold and silk in Flanders and sent to the king of Portugal) showing the sin of Adam and Eve in the Garden of Paradise. For this he drew with the brush in chiaroscuro, with the lights in lead-white, a luxuriant meadow full of different kinds of animals; and it can truthfully be said that for diligence and faithfulness to nature nothing could be more inspired or perfect. There is a fig tree, for example, with its leaves foreshortened and its branches drawn from various aspects, depicted with such loving care that the brain reels at the thought that a man could have such patience. And there is a palm tree, the radiating crown of which is drawn with such marvellous skill that no one without Leonardo's understanding and patience could have done it. The work was not carried any farther and so today the cartoon is still in Florence, in the blessed house of the Magnificent Ottaviano de' Medici to whom it was presented not long ago by Leonardo's uncle.

The story goes that once when Piero da Vinci was at his house in the country one of the peasants on his farm, who had made himself a buckler out of a fig tree that he had cut down, asked him as a favour to have it painted for him in Florence. Piero was very happy to do this, since the man was very adept at snaring birds and fishing and Piero himself very often made use of him in these pursuits. He took the buckler to Florence, and without saying a word about whom it belonged to he asked Leonardo to paint something on it. Some days later Leonardo examined the buckler, and, finding that it was warped, badly made, and clumsy, he straightened it in the fire and then gave it to a turner who, from the rough and clumsy thing that it was, made it smooth and even. Then having given it a coat of gesso and prepared it in his own way Leonardo started to think what he could paint on it so as to terrify anyone who saw it and produce the same effect as the head of Medusa. To do what he wanted Leonardo carried into a room of his own, which no one ever entered except himself, a number of green and other kinds of lizards, crickets, serpents, butterflies, locusts, bats, and various strange creatures of this nature; from all these he took and assembled different parts to create a fearsome and horrible monster which emitted a poisonous breath and turned the air to fire. He depicted the creature emerging from the dark cleft of a rock, belching forth venom from its open throat, fire from its eyes and smoke from its nostrils in so macabre a fashion that the effect was altogether monstrous and horrible. Leonardo took so long over the work that the stench of the dead animals in his room became unbearable, although he himself failed to notice because of his great love of painting. By the time he had finished the painting both the peasant and his father had stopped inquiring after it; but all the same he told his father that he could send for the buckler when convenient, since his work on it was completed. So one morning Piero went along to the room in order to get the buckler, knocked at the door, and was told by Leonardo to wait for a moment. Leonardo went back into the room, put the buckler on an easel in the light, and shaded the window; then he asked Piero to come in and see it. When his eyes fell on it Piero was completely taken by surprise and gave a sudden start, not realizing that he was looking at the buckler and that the form he saw was, in fact, painted on it. As he backed away, Leonardo checked him and said:

'This work certainly serves its purpose. It has produced the right reaction, so now you can take it away.'

Piero thought the painting was indescribably marvellous and he was loud in praise of Leonardo's ingenuity. And then on the quiet he bought from a pedlar another buckler, decorated with a heart pierced by a dart, and he gave this to the peasant, who remained grateful to him for the rest of his days. Later on Piero secretly sold Leonardo's buckler to some merchants in Florence for a hundred ducats; and not long afterwards it came into the hands of the duke of Milan, who paid those merchants three hundred ducats for it.

Leonardo then painted a Madonna, a very fine work which came into the possession of Pope Clement VII; one of the details in this picture was a vase of water containing some flowers, painted with wonderful realism, which had on them dewdrops that looked more convincing than the real thing.

For his very close friend Antonio Segni, Leonardo drew on a sheet of paper a Neptune executed with such fine draughtsmanship and diligence that it was utterly convincing. In this picture could be seen the restless ocean and Neptune's chariot drawn by sea-horses, and the sprites, the sea-monsters, and the winds, along with some very beautiful heads of sea-gods. This was presented by Antonio's son Fabio to Giovanni Gaddi, with this epigram:

> *Pinxit Virgilius Neptunum, pinxit Homerus,*
> *Dum maris undisoni per vada flectit equos.*
> *Mente quidem vates illum conspexit uterque,*
> *Vincius ast oculis; jureque vincit eos.**

Leonardo then took it in mind to do a painting in oils showing the head of Medusa attired with a coil of serpents, the strangest and most extravagant invention imaginable. But this was a work that needed time, and so as with most of the things he did it was never finished. Today it is kept among the fine works of art in the palace of Duke Cosimo, along with the head of an angel raising one arm, which is foreshortened as it comes forward from the shoulder to the elbow, and lifting a hand to its breast with the other.

One of the remarkable aspects of Leonardo's talent was the extremes he went to, in his anxiety to achieve solidity of modelling, in the use of inky shadows. Thus to get the

---

* Virgil and Homer both have shown us Neptune guide
  His steeds amid the billows of the roaring main.
  These poets, though, have seen him but with mental gaze,
  Vinci with vision real; and 'tis truth to hail
  Vinci as victor.

darkest possible grounds Leonardo selected blacks that made deeper shadows and were indeed blacker than any other, endeavouring to make his lights all the brighter by contrast. However, he eventually succeeded so well that his paintings were wholly devoid of light and the subjects looked as if they were being seen by night rather than clearly defined by daylight. All this came from his striving to obtain ever more relief and to bring his art to absolute perfection. I must mention another habit of Leonardo's: he was always fascinated when he saw a man of striking appearance, with a strange head of hair or beard; and anyone who attracted him he would follow about all day long and end up seeing so clearly in his mind's eye that when he got home he could draw him as if he were standing there in the flesh. There are many drawings of both male and female heads which he did in this way, and I have several examples of them in the book of drawings mentioned so often before, such as the sketch of Amerigo Vespucci, which shows the head of a very handsome old man drawn in charcoal, or of Scaramuccia, the leader of the gipsies, which Giambullari subsequently left to Donato Valdambrini of Arezzo, canon of San Lorenzo.

Leonardo also started work on a panel picture showing the Adoration of the Magi and containing a number of beautiful details, especially the heads; this painting, however, which was in the house of Amerigo Benci, opposite the Loggia de' Peruzzi, like so many of his works remained unfinished.

Life of Leonardo da Vinci

Meanwhile in Milan, following the death of Duke Gian Galeazzo, Ludovico Sforza took over the state (in the year 1494) and did Leonardo the honour of inviting him to visit Milan so that he could hear him play the lyre, an instrument of which the new duke was very fond. Leonardo took with him a lyre that he had made himself, mostly of silver, in the shape of a horse's head (a very strange and novel design) so that the sound should be more sonorous and resonant. Leonardo's performance was therefore superior to that of all the other musicians who had come to Ludovico's court. Leonardo was also the most talented improviser in verse of his time. Moreover, he was a sparkling conversationalist, and after they had spoken together the duke developed almost boundless love and admiration for his talents. He begged Leonardo to paint for him an altarpiece containing a Nativity, which he then sent to the emperor.

Leonardo also executed in Milan, for the Dominicans of Santa Maria delle Grazie, a marvellous and beautiful painting of the Last Supper. Having depicted the heads of the apostles full of splendour and majesty, he deliberately left the head of Christ unfinished, convinced he would fail to give it the divine spirituality it demands. This all but finished work has ever since been held in the greatest veneration by the Milanese and others. In it Leonardo brilliantly succeeded in envisaging and reproducing the tormented anxiety of the apostles to know who had betrayed their master; so in their faces one can read the emotions of love, dismay, and anger, or rather sorrow, at their failure to grasp the meaning of Christ. And this excites no less admiration than the contrasted spectacle of the obstinacy, hatred, and treachery in the face of Judas or, indeed, than the incredible diligence with which every detail of the work was executed. The texture of the very cloth on the table is counterfeited so cunningly that the linen itself could not look more realistic.

It is said that the prior used to keep pressing Leonardo, in the most importunate way, to hurry up and finish the work, because he was puzzled by Leonardo's habit of sometimes spending half a day at a time contemplating what he had done so far; if the prior had had his way, Leonardo would have toiled like one of the labourers hoeing in the garden and never put his brush down for a moment. Not satisfied with this, the prior then complained to the duke, making such a fuss that the duke was constrained to send for Leonardo and, very tactfully, question him about the painting, although he showed perfectly well that he was only doing so because of the prior's insistence. Leonardo, knowing he was dealing with a prince of acute and discerning intelligence, was willing (as he never had been with the prior) to explain his mind at length; and so he talked to the duke for a long time about the art of painting. He explained that men of genius sometimes accomplish most when they work the least; for, he added, they are thinking out inventions and forming in their minds the perfect ideas which they

Life of Leonardo da Vinci

subsequently express and reproduce with their hands. Leonardo then said that he still had two heads to paint: the head of Christ was one, and for this he was unwilling to look for any human model, nor did he dare suppose that his imagination could conceive the beauty and divine grace that properly belonged to the incarnate Deity. Then, he said, he had yet to do the head of Judas, and this troubled him since he did not think he could imagine the features that would form the countenance of a man who, despite all the blessings he had been given, could so cruelly steel his will to betray his own master and the creator of the world. However, added Leonardo, he would try to find a model for Judas, and if he did not succeed in doing so, why then he was not without the head of that tactless and importunate prior. The duke roared with laughter at this and said that Leonardo had every reason in the world for saying so. The unfortunate prior retired in confusion to worry the labourers working in his garden, and he left off worrying Leonardo, who skilfully finished the head of Judas and made it seem the very embodiment of treachery and inhumanity. The head of Christ remained, as was said, unfinished.

This noble painting was so finely composed and executed that the King of France subsequently wanted to remove it to his kingdom. He tried all he could to find architects to make cross-stays of wood and iron with which the painting could be protected and brought safely to France, without any regard for expense, so great was his desire to have it. But as the painting was done on a wall his majesty failed to have his way and it remained in the possession of the Milanese. While he was working on the Last Supper, in the same refectory where there is a painting of the Passion done in the old manner, on the end wall, Leonardo portrayed Ludovico himself with his eldest son, Massimiliano; and on the other side, with the Duchess Beatrice, his other son Francesco, both of whom later became dukes of Milan; and all these figures are beautifully painted.

While he was engaged on this work Leonardo proposed to the duke that he should make a huge equestrian statue in bronze as a memorial to his father; then he started and carried the work forward on such a scale that it was impossible to finish it. There have even been some to say (men's opinions are so various and, often enough, so envious and spiteful) that Leonardo had no intention of finishing it when he started. This was because it was so large that it proved an insoluble problem to cast it in one piece; and one can realize why, the outcome being what it was, many came to the conclusion they did, seeing that so many of his works remained unfinished. The truth, however, is surely that Leonardo's profound and discerning mind was so ambitious that this was itself an impediment; and the reason he failed was because he endeavoured to add excellence to excellence and perfection to perfection. As our Petrarch has said, the desire outran the performance. In fact, those who saw the great clay model that Leonardo made considered that they had never seen a finer or more magnificent piece of work. It was preserved until the French came to Milan under King Louis and smashed it to pieces. Also lost is a little wax model which was held to be perfect, together with a reference book which Leonardo composed on the anatomy of horses. Leonardo then applied himself, even more assiduously, to the study of human anatomy, in which he collaborated with that excellent philosopher Marc Antonio della Torre, who was then lecturing at Pavia and who wrote on the subject. Della Torre, I have heard, was one of the first to illustrate the problems of medicine by the teachings of Galen and to throw true light on anatomy, which up to then had been obscured by the shadows of ignorance. In this he was wonderfully served by the intelligence, work, and hand of Leonardo, who composed a book annotated in pen and ink in which he did meticulous drawings in red chalk of bodies he had dissected himself. He showed all the bone structure, adding in order all the nerves and covering them with the muscles: the first attached to the skeleton, the second that hold it firm and the third that move it. In the various sections he wrote his observations in puzzling characters (written in reverse with the left hand) which cannot be deciphered by anyone who does not know the trick of reading them in a mirror.

Many of Leonardo's manuscripts on human anatomy are in the possession of Francesco Melzi, a Milanese gentleman who was a handsome boy when Leonardo was alive and who was greatly loved by him. Francesco cherishes and preserves these papers as relics of Leonardo, together with the portrait of that artist of such happy memory. Reading Leonardo's writings one is astonished at the brilliant way in which this inspired artist discussed so thoroughly art and anatomy (the muscles, nerves, and veins) and indeed every kind of subject. There are also some of his papers in the possession of a Milanese painter (again written in reverse with the left hand) which discuss painting and methods of drawing and colouring. Not long ago this man came to Florence to see me with the object of having the work printed, and later he went to Rome to put this into effect; but I do not know what happened then.

Anyhow, to return to Leonardo's works: when during his lifetime the king of France came to Milan, Leonardo was asked to devise some unusual entertainment, and so he constructed a lion which after walking a few steps opened its breast to reveal a cluster of lilies. It was in Milan that Leonardo took for his servant a Milanese called Salai, a very attractive youth of unusual grace and looks, with very beautiful hair which he wore curled in ringlets and which delighted his master. Leonardo taught Salai a great deal about painting, and some of the works in Milan which are attributed to him were retouched by Leonardo.

Then Leonardo went back to Florence where he found

that the Servite friars had commissioned Filippino to paint the altarpiece for the high altar of the Annunziata. Leonardo remarked that he would gladly have undertaken the work himself, and when he heard this, like the good-hearted person he was, Filippino decided to withdraw. Then the friars, to secure Leonardo's services, took him into their house and met all his expenses and those of his household. He kept them waiting a long time without even starting anything, and then finally he did a cartoon showing Our Lady with St Anne and the Infant Christ. This work not only won the astonished admiration of all the artists but when finished for two days it attracted to the room where it was exhibited a crowd of men and women, young and old, who flocked there, as if they were attending a great festival, to gaze in amazement at the marvels he had created. For in the face of Our Lady are seen all the simplicity and loveliness and grace that can be conferred on the mother of Christ, since Leonardo wanted to show the humility and the modesty appropriate to an image of the Virgin who is overflowing with joy at seeing the beauty of her Son. She is holding him tenderly on her lap, and she lets her pure gaze fall on St John, who is depicted as a little boy playing with a lamb; and this is not without a smile from St Anne, who is supremely joyful as she contemplates the divinity of her earthly progeny. These ideas were truly worthy of Leonardo's intellect and genius. As I shall describe, this cartoon was subsequently taken to France.

Giorgio Vasari

Leonardo also did a portrait of Ginevra, the wife of Amerigo Benci, a very beautiful painting. He abandoned the work he was doing for the friars and they went back to Filippino, who, however, died before he could finish it.

For Francesco del Giocondo Leonardo undertook to execute the portrait of his wife, Mona Lisa. He worked on this painting for four years, and then left it still unfinished; and today it is in the possession of King Francis of France, at Fontainebleau. If one wanted to see how faithfully art can imitate nature, one could readily perceive it from this head; for here Leonardo subtly reproduced every living detail. The eyes had their natural lustre and moistness, and around them were the lashes and all those rosy and pearly tints that demand the greatest delicacy of execution. The eyebrows were completely natural, growing thickly in one place and lightly in another and following the pores of the skin. The nose was finely painted, with rosy and delicate nostrils as in life. The mouth, joined to the flesh-tints of the face by the red of the lips, appeared to be living flesh rather than paint. On looking closely at the pit of her throat one could swear that the pulses were beating. Altogether this picture was painted in a manner to make the most confident artist – no matter who – despair and lose heart. Leonardo also made use of this device: while he was painting Mona Lisa, who was a very beautiful woman, he employed singers and musicians or jesters to keep her full of merriment and so chase away the melancholy that painters usually give

Life of Leonardo da Vinci

to portraits. As a result, in this painting of Leonardo's there was a smile so pleasing that it seemed divine rather than human; and those who saw it were amazed to find that it was as alive as the original.

The great achievements of this inspired artist so increased his prestige that everyone who loved art, or rather every single person in Florence, was anxious for him to leave the city some memorial; and it was being proposed everywhere that Leonardo should be commissioned to do some great and notable work which would enable the state to be honoured and adorned by his discerning talent, grace, and judgement. As it happened the great hall of the council was being constructed under the architectural direction of Giuliano Sangallo, Simone Pollaiuolo (known as Cronaca), Michelangelo Buonarroti, and Baccio d'Agnolo, as I shall relate at greater length in the right place. It was finished in a hurry, and after the head of the government and the chief citizens had conferred together, it was publicly announced that a splendid painting would be commissioned from Leonardo. And then he was asked by Piero Soderini, the Gonfalonier of Justice, to do a decorative painting for the council hall. As a start, therefore, Leonardo began work in the Hall of the Pope, in Santa Maria Novella, on a cartoon illustrating an incident in the life of Niccolò Piccinino, a commander of Duke Filippo of Milan. He showed a group of horsemen fighting for a standard, in a drawing which was regarded as very fine and successful because of the wonderful ideas he expressed in his interpretation of the battle. In the drawing, rage, fury, and vindictiveness are displayed both by the men and by the horses, two of which with their forelegs interlocked are battling with their teeth no less fiercely than their riders are struggling for the standard, the staff of which has been grasped by a soldier who, as he turns and spurs his horse to flight, is trying by the strength of his shoulders to wrest it by force from the hands of four others. Two of them are struggling for it with one hand and attempting with the other to cut the staff with their raised swords; and an old soldier in a red cap roars out as he grips the staff with one hand and with the other raises a scimitar and aims a furious blow to cut off both the hands of those who are gnashing their teeth and ferociously defending their standard. Besides this, on the ground between the legs of the horses there are two figures, foreshortened, shown fighting together; the one on the ground has over him a soldier who has raised his arm as high as possible to plunge his dagger with greater force into the throat of his enemy, who struggles frantically with his arms and legs to escape death.

It is impossible to convey the fine draughtsmanship with which Leonardo depicted the soldiers' costumes, with their distinctive variations, or the helmet-crests and the other ornaments, not to speak of the incredible mastery that he displayed in the forms and lineaments of the horses which, with their bold spirit and muscles and shapely beauty, Leonardo portrayed better than any other artist. It is said that to draw the cartoon Leonardo constructed an ingenious scaffolding that he could raise or lower by drawing it together or extending it. He also conceived the wish to paint the picture in oils, but to do this he mixed such a thick composition for laying on the wall that, as he continued his painting in the hall, it started to run and spoil what had been done. So shortly afterwards he abandoned the work.

Leonardo was very proud and instinctively generous. According to one story, he once went along to the bank to draw his usual monthly salary from Piero Soderini and the cashier wanted to give him a few packets of pennies which he refused to take, saying that he was no 'penny painter'. As the painting had not been finished, he was accused of cheating Piero Soderini and there were murmurings against him. So Leonardo went round his friends and got the money together to repay Soderini; but Piero would not accept it.

Leonardo went to Rome with Duke Giuliano de' Medici on the election of Pope Leo who was a great student of natural philosophy, and especially of alchemy. And in Rome he experimented with a paste made out of a certain kind of wax and made some light and billowy figures in the form of animals which he inflated with his mouth as he walked along and which flew above the ground until all the air escaped. To the back of a very odd-looking lizard that was found by the gardener of the Belvedere he attached with a mixture of quicksilver some wings, made from the scales stripped from other lizards, which quivered as it walked along. Then, after he had given it eyes, horns, and a beard he tamed the creature, and keeping it in a box he used to show it to his friends and frighten the life out of them. Again, Leonardo used to get the intestines of a bullock scraped completely free of their fat, cleaned and made so fine that they could be compressed into the palm of one hand; then he would fix one end of them to a pair of bellows lying in another room, and when they were inflated they filled the room in which they were and forced anyone standing there into a corner. Thus he could expand this translucent and airy stuff to fill a large space after occupying only a little, and he compared it to genius. He perpetrated hundreds of follies of this kind, and he also experimented with mirrors and made the most outlandish experiments to discover oils for painting and varnish for preserving the finished works.

At that time for Baldassare Turini of Pescia, who was Pope Leo's datary, Leonardo executed with extraordinary diligence and skill a small picture of the Madonna and Child. But either because of the mistakes made by whoever primed the panel with gesso, or because of his own capricious way of mixing any number of grounds and colours, it is now spoilt. In another small picture he did the portrait of a little boy which is wonderfully beautiful and graceful. And both of these pictures are now in the possession of Giulio Turini at Pescia.

Once, when he was commissioned a work by the Pope, Leonardo is said to have started at once to distil oils and various plants in order to prepare the varnish; and the Pope is supposed to have exclaimed: 'Oh dear, this man will never do anything. Here he is thinking about finishing the work before he even starts it!'

Leonardo and Michelangelo strongly disliked each other, and so Michelangelo left Florence because of their rivalry (with permission from Duke Giuliano) after he had been summoned by the Pope to discuss the completion of the façade of San Lorenzo; and when he heard this Leonardo also left Florence and went to France. The king had obtained several of his works and was very devoted to him, and he asked Leonardo to paint the cartoon of St Anne. But, characteristically, Leonardo for a long time put him off with mere words.

Finally, in his old age Leonardo lay sick for several months, and feeling that he was near to death he earnestly resolved to learn about the doctrines of the Catholic faith and of the good and holy Christian religion. Then, lamenting bitterly, he confessed and repented, and, although he could not stand up, supported by his friends and servants he received the Blessed Sacrament from his bed. He was joined by the king, who often used to pay him affectionate visits, and having respectfully raised himself in his bed he told the king about his illness and what had caused it, and he protested that he had offended God and mankind by not working at his art as he should have done. Then he was seized by a paroxysm, the forerunner of death, and, to show him favour and to soothe his pain, the king held his head. Conscious of the great honour being done to him, the inspired Leonardo breathed his last in the arms of the king; he was then seventy-five years old.

All who had known Leonardo were grieved beyond words by their loss, for no one had ever shed such lustre on the art of painting.

In appearance he was striking and handsome, and his magnificent presence brought comfort to the most troubled soul; he was so persuasive that he could bend other people to his own will. He was physically so strong that he could withstand any violence; with his right hand he would bend the iron ring of a doorbell or a horseshoe as if they were lead. He was so generous that he sheltered and fed all his friends, rich or poor, provided they were of some talent or worth. By his every action Leonardo adorned and honoured the meanest and humblest dwelling-place. Through his birth, therefore, Florence received a very great gift, and through his death it sustained an incalculable loss. In painting he brought to the technique of colouring in oils a way of darkening the shadows which has enabled modern painters to give great vigour and relief to their figures. He showed his powers as a sculptor in the three bronze figures over the north door of San Giovanni which were executed by Giovanfrancesco Rustici, under Leonardo's direction, and which

Life of Leonardo da Vinci

as far as design and finish are concerned are the finest casts yet seen in modern times.

Because of Leonardo we have a deeper knowledge of human anatomy and the anatomy of the horse. And because of his many wonderful gifts (although he accomplished far more in words than in deeds) his name and fame will never be extinguished. This was written in praise of Leonardo by Giovan Battista Strozzi:

> *Vince costui pur solo*
> *Tutti altri, e vince Fidia e vince Apelle,*
> *E tutto lor vittoriosi stuolo.**

One of Leonardo's pupils was Giovanni Antonio Boltraffio of Milan, a very skilful and discerning artist who in 1500 in the church of the Misericordia, outside Bologna, painted in oils a carefully finished picture of the Madonna and Child, St John the Baptist, and a nude St Sebastian, with a portrait of the donor kneeling in prayer. On this very beautiful panel he signed his name, adding that he was a pupil of Leonardo. He did other works at Milan and elsewhere, but it is enough to have described the best of them.

Another of Leonardo's pupils was Marco Uggioni, who in Santa Maria della Pace painted the Assumption of the Virgin and the Marriage of Cana in Galilee.

---

* Da Vinci vanquished alone all others, he vanquished Phidias and Apelles, and all their victorious followers.

Life of Fra Filippo Lippi

FLORENTINE PAINTER, *c*. 1406–69

Fra Filippo di Tommaso Lippi, a Carmelite, was born in Florence, in a street called Ardiglione, below the Canto alla Cucilia and behind the Carmelite Convent. The death of his father left him, at the age of two, a sad and solitary orphan, since his mother had died not long after he was born. He was put under the care of his aunt, Mona Lapaccia, Tommaso's sister, but she found it a struggle to bring him up and, when she could no longer manage, sent him, at the age of eight, to be a friar in the Carmelite Convent. At the convent he showed himself dexterous and ingenious in any work he had to do with his hands, but equally dull and incapable of learning when it came to his books; so he never spent any time studying his letters, which he regarded with great distaste. The boy (who was called by his secular name, Filippo) was placed with the other novices in the charge of the master teaching grammar to see what he could learn; but instead of studying he spent all his time scrawling pictures on his own books and those of others, and so eventually the prior decided to give him every chance and opportunity of learning to paint.

Life of Fra Filippo Lippi

At that time the chapel of the Carmine had been freshly painted by Masaccio and its great beauty attracted Fra Filippo so much that he used to go every day in his spare time and practise in company with many other young artists who were always drawing there. He showed himself so superior to the rest in skill and knowledge that it was held for certain that one day he would do marvellous things; indeed, it was a miracle how many fine works he did produce before his maturity, while he was still in his salad days. Before very long he did a painting in *terra verde* in the cloister, near to Masaccio's *Consecration*, of a pope approving the Rule of the Carmelites, and he executed various frescoes on walls in many parts of the church, notably a St John the Baptist with some scenes from his life. His work improved every day and he came to understand Masaccio's style so well that his own pictures resembled those of Masaccio, and it was often said that Masaccio's soul had entered into his body. On a pilaster in the church, near the organ, he did a painting of St Marziale which bore comparison with Masaccio's work and which made his reputation. Then, in response to the praises he heard from all sides, at the age of seventeen he boldly threw off his friar's habit.

Now one day he happened to be enjoying himself with some of his friends in a little boat on the sea off the March of Ancona when they were all seized by the Moorish galleys that were scouring those parts, taken captive to Barbary, and put in chains. He stayed in this wretched condition for eighteen months. But one day when the opportunity presented itself he took it into his head to do a portrait of his master, with whom he was very familiar, and using a piece of dead coal from the fire he drew him on a white wall, full length in his Moorish costume. The other slaves reported this to his master, and since neither drawing nor painting were known in those parts everyone was astounded by what he had accomplished and he was, as a result, freed from the chains in which he had been kept so long. It was a glorious thing for the art of painting that it caused someone with the lawful authority to condemn and punish to do the opposite, giving his slave affection and liberty in the place of torture and death.

So, after he had done some painting in colour for his master, Fra Filippo was brought safely to Naples where for King Alfonso, then duke of Calabria, he painted a panel in tempera for the castle chapel, where the guardroom is now. He then determined to return to Florence, where he stayed for several months, executing a very beautiful altarpiece for the nuns of Sant' Ambrogio. This won him the affection of Cosimo de' Medici who became a close friend of his.

Fra Filippo also did a panel picture for the chapter-house of Santa Croce and another, which was placed in the chapel in the house of the Medici, showing the Nativity of Christ. As well as this, for the wife of Cosimo de' Medici he painted a panel picture of the Nativity of Christ

Life of Fra Filippo Lippi

with St John the Baptist, which was to be placed in the hermitage of Camaldoli in one of the hermits' cells dedicated to St John the Baptist which she had had built as an act of devotion. And he painted some little scenes that Cosimo sent as a gift to Pope Eugene IV, the Venetian. This work won Fra Filippo the favour of the Pope himself.

It is said that Fra Filippo was so lustful that he would give anything to enjoy a woman he wanted if he thought he could have his way; and if he couldn't buy what he wanted, then he would cool his passion by painting her portrait and reasoning with himself. His lust was so violent that when it took hold of him he could never concentrate on his work. And because of this, one time or other when he was doing something for Cosimo de' Medici in Cosimo's house, Cosimo had him locked in so that he wouldn't wander away and waste time. After he had been confined for a few days, Fra Filippo's amorous or rather his animal desires drove him one night to seize a pair of scissors, make a rope from his bed-sheets and escape through a window to pursue his own pleasures for days on end. When Cosimo discovered that he was gone, he searched for him and eventually got him back to work. And after that he always allowed him to come and go as he liked, having regretted the way he had shut him up before and realizing how dangerous it was for such a madman to be confined. Cosimo determined for the future to keep a hold on him by affection and kindness and, being served all the more readily, he used to say that artists of genius were to be treated with respect, not used as hacks.

For the church of Santa Maria Primerana, on the piazza at Fiesole, Fra Filippo did a panel picture of the Annunciation of Our Lady, finished with wonderful care, in which the figure of the angel is so beautiful that one can hardly doubt it has come from heaven. He did two panel pictures for the Murate, the convent of the enclosed Order of nuns: one for the high altar, showing the Annunciation, and the other over another altar in the same church containing scenes from the lives of SS. Benedict and Bernard. And in the palace of the Signoria he executed a panel picture of the Annunciation which is over one of the doors, and a painting of St Bernard which is over another. For the sacristy of Santo Spirito at Florence he did a panel picture showing Our Lady surrounded by angels and with saints on either side. This is an outstanding work which our leading artists have always held in reverence.

In the chapel of the wardens in San Lorenzo Fra Filippo painted a panel picture again showing the Annunciation, as well as another for the Della Stufa Chapel which was left unfinished. In Santi Apostoli at Florence, for one of the chapels, he painted a panel with various figures, grouped round Our Lady, and in Arezzo he was commissioned by Carlo Marsuppini to paint for the monks of Monte Oliveto the altarpiece for the chapel of St Bernard,

Life of Fra Filippo Lippi

showing the Coronation of Our Lady with a number of saints. When he painted this picture (which is still so fresh that it looks as if it has only just been finished) Fra Filippo was told by Carlo to pay special attention to the rendering of the hands, as his work had been adversely criticized in this respect. So from then onwards Filippo always covered the hands he painted with draperies or else used some other technique to escape censure. In this particular work he did a portrait of Carlo Marsuppini from life. Meanwhile, for the nuns of the Annalena at Florence he painted a panel picture showing Christ in the Manger; and there are also some paintings of his in Padua. To Cardinal Barbo at Rome he sent two small scenes with tiny figures which were skilfully executed and very carefully finished: it may be said here, in fact, that his paintings were always done with astonishing grace and finely composed and finished, and, consequently, he has always won the most lavish praise and respect from our artists, both living and dead. So long as his innumerable works are left undamaged by the ravages of time, their qualities will always command the highest respect.

In Prato near Florence, where he had some relations, Fra Filippo stayed for many months doing a great deal of work in various parts of the district in company with Fra Diamante of the Carmelite convent at Prato, who had been his companion when they were novices together. Subsequently, he was asked by the nuns to paint the altarpiece for the high altar of Santa Margherita, and it was when he was working at this that he one day caught sight of the daughter of Francesco Buti of Florence, who was living there as a novice or ward. Fra Filippo made advances to the girl, who was called Lucrezia and who was very beautiful and graceful, and he succeeded in persuading the nuns to let him use her as a model for the figure of Our Lady in his painting. This opportunity left him even more infatuated, and by various ways and means he managed to steal her from the nuns, taking her away on the very day that she was going to see the exposition of the Girdle of Our Lady, one of the great relics of Prato. This episode disgraced the nuns, and Francesco, the girl's father, never smiled again. He did all he could to get her back, but either from fear or some other reason she would never leave Fra Filippo; and by him she had a son, Filippo, who became, like his father, a famous and accomplished painter.

There are two of Fra Filippo's panel pictures in San Domenico of Prato; and a Madonna in the gallery of the church of San Francesco. It proved possible to move this painting from its original position to where it is now without damaging it by cutting away the wall and giving the section a wooden framework. There is also a little panel by Fra Filippo, over a well in the courtyard of the alms-house of Francesco di Marco, which contains the portrait of Francesco, who was the creator and founder of that pious foundation. And in the parish church at Prato there is a small panel of his, over the side door as

Life of Fra Filippo Lippi

one ascends the steps, showing the death of St Bernard, by the touch of whose bier many cripples are being restored to health. In this painting are a number of friars lamenting their dead master; and it is marvellous to see how skilfully and truthfully Fra Filippo has expressed grief and sadness in the attitudes of their heads. The draperies in this picture, namely, the friars' robes, are shown with a number of very beautiful folds, and their excellent design, colouring, and composition deserve every praise, as do the grace and proportion with which Fra Filippo delicately executed the whole work.

To have some memorial of him, the wardens of the parish church commissioned Fra Filippo to paint the chapel of the high altar; and he fully demonstrated his capabilities in the excellence and artistry of the work as a whole and, in particular, in its marvellous draperies and heads. In these frescoes Fra Filippo made his figures larger than life, thus showing the way to modern artists to achieve the grandeur of the style of our own day. They contain also various figures dressed in clothes which were not contemporary, and by this departure Fra Filippo prompted the artists of that time to abandon the kind of simplicity which, far from reflecting the style of the ancient world, was simply old-fashioned. The work includes scenes from the life of St Stephen, the patron saint of the church, covering the right-hand wall, namely, the Disputation, the Stoning, and the Death of the first martyr. Fra Filippo showed such zeal and fervour in

Giorgio Vasari

St Stephen's face as he disputes with the Jews that it is difficult to imagine let alone to describe; and this is to say nothing of the contempt and hatred, and the anger at being vanquished, expressed in the faces and the various attitudes of those Jews. He depicted even more convincingly the fury and brutality of St Stephen's executioners, who are seizing stones of all sizes, with a fearsome grinding of teeth and with cruel and outrageous gestures. Yet St Stephen stands serene before this terrible onslaught, his face lifted towards heaven, praying with great charity and fervour to the Eternal Father for the very men who are murdering him. These concepts are all extremely fine, and they show other painters how important it is to be able to express new ideas and to convey the emotions. Fra Filippo was so expert in this respect that one cannot look at the grief-stricken attitudes of those burying St Stephen and the sad and afflicted expressions of some of the mourners without being deeply moved.

On the other side of the chapel he painted scenes from the life of John the Baptist: the Nativity, the Preaching in the Wilderness, the Baptism, the Feast of Herod, and the Beheading. The light of divine inspiration shines from the face of the preacher and the various gestures of the crowd express the joy and sorrow of the men and women held and absorbed by the ministrations of St John. Beauty and goodness are apparent in the Baptism scene; and in the picture of Herod's banquet we see depicted all the sumptuousness of this occasion, along with the skill of

Herodias, the stupor of the guests and the horrified consternation caused when the head is offered on a charger. About the table Fra Filippo painted a great many figures, in very expressive poses, with beautifully executed draperies and expressions. Among them he included a portrait of himself, drawn with a mirror, clothed in the black habit of a priest; and in the scene showing the mourning for St Stephen he showed his pupil, Fra Diamante. (This work was certainly his best for the reasons I have already given and also because in it he made the figures somewhat larger than life; and this prompted those who came after him to paint with more grandeur. Fra Filippo was so highly regarded for his good qualities and his virtuosity that the many blameworthy circumstances in his life were passed over in silence.) He also portrayed in the work I have been discussing Cosimo de' Medici's natural son, Carlo, at that time the provost of the church, which received many benefactions from him and his family.

After he had finished these frescoes, Fra Filippo, in 1463, painted a panel in tempera for the church of San Jacopo at Pistoia, containing a very beautiful Annunciation, with a lively portrait of Jacopo Bellucci, who commissioned the work. In the house of Pulidoro Bracciolini there is a picture by Fra Filippo of the Birth of Our Lady; and for the hall of the Tribunal of the Eight at Florence he painted in tempera a Madonna and Child on a lunette. There is a very beautiful Madonna from his hand in the house of Lodovico Capponi; and in the possession of Bernardo Vecchietti, a Florentine gentleman of outstanding accomplishment and merit, is a beautiful little picture of his, showing St Augustine at his studies. Finer still is the St Jerome in Penitence, a picture of the same size which is in Duke Cosimo's wardrobe.

All Fra Filippo's work was outstanding, but in his smaller paintings he excelled even himself, producing pictures of incomparable grace and beauty, as we can see in all the predellas he did for his panels. His stature as a painter was such that none of his contemporaries and few modern painters have surpassed him. Michelangelo himself has always sung his praises and in many particulars has even imitated him. One of the paintings Fra Filippo did was for the church of San Domenico Vecchio at Perugia, a panel (subsequently placed on the high altar) containing a Madonna, St Peter, St Paul, St Louis, and St Anthony Abbot. And Alessandro degli Alessandri, a knight of that time and a friend of Fra Filippo's, commissioned from him, for the church of his villa at Vincigliata on the hillside of Fiesole, a panel depicting St Lawrence and other saints, among whom he painted Alessandro and two sons of his.

Fra Filippo liked to have cheerful people as his friends and himself lived a very merry life. He taught the art of painting to Fra Diamante, who executed many pictures for the Carmine at Prato and by imitating his master's

Life of Fra Filippo Lippi

style very closely achieved the highest perfection. Among those who studied with Fra Filippo in their youth were Sandro Botticelli, Pesellino, and Jacopo del Sellaio of Florence, who painted two panel pictures for San Frediano and one for the Carmine, in tempera. There were countless other artists to whom he affectionately taught the art of painting. He lived honourably from his work and he spent extravagantly on his love affairs, which he pursued all his life until the day he died.

Through the mediation of Cosimo de' Medici, Fra Filippo was asked by the commune of Spoleto to decorate the chapel in their principal church, dedicated to Our Lady. Working with Fra Diamante he made excellent progress, but he died before he could finish: they say that in one of those sublime love affairs he was always having the relations of the woman concerned had him poisoned. At any rate, Fra Filippo ended this life at the age of fifty-seven in the year 1438.

In his will he left his son Filippo, who was then ten years old, to the care of Fra Diamante, who brought the boy back to Florence and taught him the art of painting. On his return to Florence Fra Diamante took with him three hundred ducats that were owing from the commune, giving some of them to the boy and using the rest to buy things for himself. Filippo was placed with Sandro Botticelli, who was then regarded as a first-rate artist; and Fra Filippo himself was buried in a tomb of red-and-white marble erected by the people of Spoleto in the church he had painted.

Fra Filippo's death deeply grieved his many friends, especially Cosimo de' Medici and Pope Eugene. When he was alive the Pope wanted to give him a dispensation so that he could make Lucrezia, Francesco Buti's daughter, his legitimate wife; but as he wanted to stay free and give full rein to his desires Fra Filippo refused the offer. During the lifetime of Sixtus IV, Lorenzo de' Medici, who had been made an ambassador of Florence, went to Spoleto to ask the citizens for permission to remove Fra Filippo's body to Santa Maria del Fiore at Florence; but they told him that Spoleto lacked any great marks of distinction and especially the adornment of eminent men; and so they asked him as a favour to allow them to keep Filippo's body to honour Spoleto, adding that Florence had countless famous citizens, almost a superfluity, and so it could do without this one. So Lorenzo failed to get what he wanted. However, subsequently he determined to pay him the greatest honour he could, and he sent his son, Filippino, to Rome to decorate a chapel in his father's memory for the cardinal of Naples. On his way through Spoleto, Filippino was commissioned by Lorenzo to construct a marble tomb under the organ over the sacristy; and on this he spent a hundred gold ducats which were paid by Nofri Tornabuoni, director of the Medici Bank. He obtained from Angelo Politian the following epigram, which was carved on the tomb in antique letters:

Life of Fra Filippo Lippi

Conditus hic ego sum picturae fama Philippus,
  Nulli ignota meae est gratia mira manus.
Artifices potuit digitis animare colores,
  Sperataque animos fallere voce diu.
Ipsa meis stupuit natura expressa figuris,
  Meque suis fassa est artibus esse parem.
Marmoreo tumolo Medices Laurentius hic me
  *Condidit, ante humili pulvere tectus eram.**

Fra Filippo was a first-rate draughtsman, as can be seen in our book of drawings by the most famous painters, notably in some sheets containing his design for the picture of Santo Spirito and others showing the chapel of Prato.

---

* Here in this place do I, Filippo, rest
  Enshrin'd in token of my art's renown.
  All know the wondrous beauty of my skill;
  My touch gave life to lifeless paint, and long
  Deceiv'd the mind to think the forms would speak.
  Nature herself, as I reveal'd her, own'd
  In wonderment that I could match her arts.
  Beneath the lowly soil was I interr'd
  Ere this; but now Lorenzo Medici
  Hath laid me here within this marble tomb.

Life of Sandro Botticelli

FLORENTINE PAINTER, *c*. 1445–1510

In the time of the elder Lorenzo de' Medici, Lorenzo the Magnificent, truly a golden age for men of talent, there flourished an artist called Alessandro (which we shorten to Sandro), whose second name, for reasons we shall see later, was Botticelli. He was the son of a Florentine, Mariano Filipepi, who brought him up very conscientiously and had him instructed in all those things usually taught to young children before they are apprenticed. However, although he easily mastered all that he wanted to, the boy refused to settle down or be satisfied with reading, writing, and arithmetic; and finally, exasperated by his son's restless mind, his father apprenticed him as a goldsmith to a close companion of his own called Botticelli, who was a very competent craftsman. Now at that time there was a very close connexion – almost a constant intercourse – between the goldsmiths and the painters, and so Sandro, who was a very agile-minded young man and who had already become absorbed by the arts of design, became entranced by painting and determined to devote himself

Life of Sandro Botticelli

to it. He told his father about his ambition, and Mariano, seeing the way his mind was inclined, took him to Fra Filippo of the Carmine, a great painter of that time, and, as Sandro himself wished, placed him with Fra Filippo to study painting.

Botticelli threw all his energies into his work, following and imitating his master so well that Fra Filippo grew very fond of him and taught him to such good effect that very soon his skill was greater than anyone would have anticipated. While still a young man Botticelli painted in the Mercanzia of Florence, among the pictures of virtues executed by Antonio and Piero Pollaiuolo, a figure representing Fortitude. In Santo Spirito in Florence, for the Bardi Chapel, he did a panel picture, very carefully painted and beautifully finished, with some olive trees and palms depicted with loving care. He also painted a panel picture for the Convertite Convent and another for the nuns of Santa Barnaba. In the church of Ognissanti, in the gallery by the door leading to the choir, he painted for the Vespucci family a fresco of St Augustine, over which he took very great pains in an attempt to surpass all his contemporaries but especially Domenico Ghirlandaio, who had painted a St Jerome on the other side. This work was very favourably received, for Botticelli succeeded in expressing in the head of the saint that air of profound meditation and subtle perception characteristic of men of wisdom who ponder continuously on difficult and elevated matters. As I said in my *Life* of Ghirlandaio, this year (1564) this painting of Botticelli's was removed safe and sound from its original position.

Because of the credit and reputation he acquired through his St Augustine, Botticelli was commissioned by the Guild of Porta Santa Maria to do a panel picture for San Marco showing the Coronation of Our Lady surrounded by a choir of angels, which he designed and executed very competently. He also carried out many works in the house of the Medici for Lorenzo the Magnificent, notably a life-size Pallas on a shield wreathed with fiery branches, and a St Sebastian. And in Santa Maria Maggiore at Florence, beside the chapel of the Panciatichi, there is a very beautiful Pietà with little figures.

For various houses in Florence Botticelli painted a number of round pictures, including many female nudes, of which there are still two extant at Castello, Duke Cosimo's villa, one showing the Birth of Venus, with her Cupids, being wafted to land by the winds and zephyrs, and the other Venus as a symbol of spring, being adorned with flowers by the Graces; all this work was executed with exquisite grace. In the Via de' Servi around a room in Giovanni Vespucci's house (which now belongs to Piero Salviati) Botticelli painted several pictures showing many beautiful and very vivacious figures, which were enclosed in walnut panelling and ornamentation. In the house of the Pucci he illustrated – with various little figures in four paintings of considerable charm and beauty – Boccaccio's story about Nastagio degli Onesto, and he also did a circular picture of the Epiphany. For a chapel belonging to the monks of Cestello he did a panel picture of the Annunciation. Then for San Piero Maggiore, by the side door, he did a panel for Matteo Palmieri, with a vast number of figures, showing the Assumption of Our Lady and the circles of heaven, the patriarchs, prophets and apostles, the evangelists, martyrs, confessors, doctors, virgins, and the hierarchy of angels, all taken from a drawing given to him by Matteo, a very learned and talented man. Botticelli painted this work with exquisite care and assurance, introducing the portraits of Matteo and his wife kneeling at the foot. Although the painting is so great that it should have silenced envy, it provoked some malevolent critics to allege, not being able to fault it on any other score, that both Matteo and Sandro had fallen into the sin of heresy. Whether this was so or not I am not the one to say; it is enough for me that the figures which Sandro painted in this picture are admirable for the care lavished on them, and the manner in which he has shown the circles of the heavens, introducing foreshortenings and intervals between his variously composed groups of angels and other figures, and executing the whole work with a fine sense of design.

At that time Sandro was commissioned to paint a small panel, with figures a foot and a half in length, which was placed in Santa Maria Novella between two doors in the principal façade on the left as one goes in by the centre door. The subject is the Adoration of the Magi, and the picture is remarkable for the emotion shown by the elderly man as he kisses the foot of Our Lord with wonderful tenderness and conveys his sense of relief at having come to the end of his long journey. This figure, the first of the kings, is a portrait of the elder Cosimo de' Medici, and it is the most convincing and natural of all the surviving portraits. The second king (a portrait of Giuliano de' Medici, the father of Pope Clement VII) is shown doing reverence with utterly absorbed devotion as he offers his gift to the Child. The third, also on his knees, is shown gratefully adoring the Child whom he acknowledges as the true Messiah; and this is Cosimo's son, Giovanni. The beauty of the heads that Sandro painted in this picture defies description: they are shown in various poses, some full-face, some in profile, some in three-quarters, some looking down, with a great variety of expressions and attitudes in the figures of young and old, and with all those imaginative details that demonstrate the artist's complete mastery of his craft. For Botticelli clearly distinguished the retinues belonging to each of the three kings, producing in the completed work a marvellous painting which today amazes every artist by its colouring, its design, and its composition.

His Adoration of the Magi made Botticelli so famous, both in Florence and elsewhere, that Pope Sixtus IV, having finished the building of the chapel for his palace at

Life of Sandro Botticelli

Rome and wanting to have it painted, decided that he should be put in charge of the work. So Botticelli himself painted the following scenes for the chapel: Christ tempted by the devil; Moses slaying the Egyptian and accepting drink from the daughters of Jethro the Midianite; fire falling from heaven on the sacrifice of the sons of Aaron; and several portraits of canonized Popes in the niches above. Having won even greater fame and reputation among the many competitors who worked with him, artists from Florence and elsewhere, Botticelli was generously paid by the Pope; but living in his usual haphazard fashion he spent and squandered all he earned during his stay in Rome. Then, when he had finished and unveiled the work he had been commissioned, he immediately returned to Florence where, being a man of inquiring mind, he completed and printed a commentary on a part of Dante, illustrating the *Inferno*. He wasted a great deal of time on this, neglecting his work and thoroughly disrupting his life. He also printed many of his other drawings, but the results were inferior because the plates were badly engraved; the best was the Triumph of the Faith of Fra Girolamo Savonarola of Ferrara. Botticelli was a follower of Savonarola's, and this was why he gave up painting and then fell into considerable distress as he had no other source of income. None the less, he remained an obstinate member of the sect, becoming one of the *piagnoni*, the snivellers, as they were called then, and abandoning his work; so finally, as an old man, he found himself so poor that if Lorenzo de' Medici (for whom he had among other things done some work at the little hospital at Volterra) and then his friends and other worthy men who loved him for his talent had not come to his assistance, he would have almost died of hunger.

One of Sandro's paintings, a very highly regarded work to be found in San Francesco outside the Porta a San Miniato, is a Madonna in a circular picture with some angels, all lifesize.

He was a very good-humoured man and much given to playing jokes on his pupils and friends. For example, the story goes that one of his pupils, called Biagio, painted a circular picture exactly like the one of Botticelli's mentioned above, and that Sandro sold it for him to one of the citizens for six gold florins; then he found Biagio and told him:

'I've finally sold this picture of yours. So now you must hang it up high this evening so that it looks better, and then tomorrow morning go along and find the man who bought it so that you can show it to him properly displayed in a good light, and then he'll give you your money.'

'Oh, you've done marvellously,' said Biagio, who then went along to the shop, hung his picture at a good height, and left. In the meantime, Sandro and another of his pupils, Jacopo, had made several paper hats (like the ones the citizens wore) which they stuck with white wax over the heads of the eight angels that surrounded the

Madonna in his picture. Then, when the morning came, Biagio arrived with the citizen who had bought the painting (and who had been let into the joke). They went into the shop, where Biagio looked up and saw his Madonna seated not in the midst of angels but in the middle of the councillors of Florence, all wearing their paper hats! He was just about to roar out in anger and make excuses when he noticed that the man he was with had said nothing at all, and was in fact starting to praise the picture . . . so Biagio kept quiet himself. And at length he went home with him and was given his six florins, as the price agreed by Botticelli. Then he went back to the shop, a moment or two after Sandro and Jacopo had removed those paper hats, and he found that the angels he had painted were angels after all and was so stupefied that he was at a loss for words. Eventually he turned to Sandro and said:

'Sir, I don't know if I'm dreaming or if this is reality, but when I was here earlier those angels were wearing red hats, and now they're not. What's the meaning of it?'

'You've taken leave of your senses,' said Sandro. 'All that money has gone to your head. If what you say were true, do you think he'd have bought your picture?'

'That's so,' said Biagio, 'He didn't say a word. But all the same it struck me as very strange.'

Then all the other apprentices flocked round him and convinced him that he had had some kind of giddy spell.

Another time, a cloth-weaver moved into the house next to Sandro's and set up no less than eight looms which when they were working not only deafened poor Sandro with the noise of the treadles and the movement of the frames but also shook his whole house, the walls of which were no stronger than they should be. What with one thing and the other, he couldn't work or even stay in the house. Several times he begged his neighbour to do something about the nuisance, but the weaver retorted that in his own home he could and would do just what he liked. Finally, Sandro grew very angry, and on top of his roof, which was higher than his neighbour's and not all that substantial, he balanced an enormous stone (big enough to fill a wagon) which threatened to fall at the least movement of the wall and wreck the man's roof, ceilings, floors, and looms. Terrified at the prospect the cloth-weaver ran to Sandro only to be told, in his own words, that in his own house Botticelli could and would do just what he wanted to. So there being nothing else for it the man was obliged to come to reasonable terms and make himself a good neighbour.

According to another anecdote, for a joke Sandro once denounced one of his friends to the vicar as a heretic. The man appeared and demanded to know who had accused him and of what. When he was told that his accuser was Sandro, who had alleged that he believed with the Epicureans that the soul dies with the body, he demanded to see him before the judge. And when Sandro appeared on the scene, he said:

'Certainly that is what I believe as far as this man is

Life of Sandro Botticelli

concerned, seeing that he's a brute. But apart from that, isn't it he who is the heretic, since although he scarcely knows how to read and write he did a commentary on Dante and took his name in vain?'

It is also said of Sandro that he was extraordinarily fond of any serious student of painting, and that he earned a great deal of money but wasted it all through carelessness and lack of management. Anyhow, after he had grown old and useless, unable to stand upright and moving about with the help of crutches, he died, ill and decrepit, at the age of seventy-eight, and he was buried in Ognissanti in Florence.

In Duke Cosimo's wardrobe there are two very beautiful female heads in profile by Botticelli, one of which is said to be the mistress of Lorenzo's brother, Giuliano de' Medici, and the other, Madonna Lucrezia de' Tornabuoni, Lorenzo's wife. In the same place there is a Bacchus of Sandro's, a very graceful figure shown raising a cask with both hands and putting it to its lips. In the Duomo at Pisa, in the chapel of the Impagliata, he started an Assumption with a choir of angels, but it displeased him and he left it unfinished. In San Francesco at Montevarchi he did the panel for the high altar, and he also did two angels for the parish church at Empoli, on the same side as Rossellino's St Sebastian.

Botticelli was one of the first to find out how to make standards and other draperies by plaiting the material so that the colours show on both sides without running.

That was how he made the baldachin of Orsanmichele, full of Madonnas, all different and all beautiful. It is clear that this method of treating the cloth preserves the work better than the use of acids, which eat the material away, even though because of its relative cheapness the latter is nowadays the more usual technique.

Sandro was an uncommonly good draughtsman and, in consequence, for some time after his death artists used to search out his drawings, and I have some of them in my book which show great skill and judgement. In the scenes he did he made a lavish use of figures, as can be seen in the decorative work he designed for the frieze of the processional cross of the friars of Santa Maria Novella.

Altogether, Sandra Botticelli's pictures merited the highest praise; he threw himself into his work with diligence and enthusiasm, as can be seen in the Adoration of the Magi in Santa Maria Novella, which I described earlier and which is a marvellous painting. Also very fine is the small circular picture by Sandro that can be seen in the prior's room in the Angeli at Florence, the figures being tiny but very graceful and beautifully composed. A Florentine gentleman, Fabio Segni, has in his possession a painting of the same size as the panel picture of the Magi; the subject is Apelles' Calumny. He himself gave this unimaginably beautiful painting to his close friend, Antonio Segni, and underneath it can be read these lines by Fabio:

Life of Sandro Botticelli

Iudicio quemquam ne falso laedere tentent
Terrarum reges, parva tabella monet.
Huic similem Aegypti regi donavit Apelles;
Rex fuit et dignus munere, munus eo.*

---

* This little picture warns the rulers of the earth
To shun the tyranny of judgement false.
Apelles gave its like to Egypt's king; that king
Was worthy of the gift, and it of him.

1. BOCCACCIO · *Mrs Rosie and the Priest*
2. GERARD MANLEY HOPKINS · *As kingfishers catch fire*
3. *The Saga of Gunnlaug Serpent-tongue*
4. THOMAS DE QUINCEY · *On Murder Considered as One of the Fine Arts*
5. FRIEDRICH NIETZSCHE · *Aphorisms on Love and Hate*
6. JOHN RUSKIN · *Traffic*
7. PU SONGLING · *Wailing Ghosts*
8. JONATHAN SWIFT · *A Modest Proposal*
9. *Three Tang Dynasty Poets*
10. WALT WHITMAN · *On the Beach at Night Alone*
11. KENKŌ · *A Cup of Sake Beneath the Cherry Trees*
12. BALTASAR GRACIÁN · *How to Use Your Enemies*
13. JOHN KEATS · *The Eve of St Agnes*
14. THOMAS HARDY · *Woman much missed*
15. GUY DE MAUPASSANT · *Femme Fatale*
16. MARCO POLO · *Travels in the Land of Serpents and Pearls*
17. SUETONIUS · *Caligula*
18. APOLLONIUS OF RHODES · *Jason and Medea*
19. ROBERT LOUIS STEVENSON · *Olalla*
20. KARL MARX AND FRIEDRICH ENGELS · *The Communist Manifesto*
21. PETRONIUS · *Trimalchio's Feast*
22. JOHANN PETER HEBEL · *How a Ghastly Story Was Brought to Light by a Common or Garden Butcher's Dog*
23. HANS CHRISTIAN ANDERSEN · *The Tinder Box*
24. RUDYARD KIPLING · *The Gate of the Hundred Sorrows*
25. DANTE · *Circles of Hell*
26. HENRY MAYHEW · *Of Street Piemen*
27. HAFEZ · *The nightingales are drunk*
28. GEOFFREY CHAUCER · *The Wife of Bath*
29. MICHEL DE MONTAIGNE · *How We Weep and Laugh at the Same Thing*
30. THOMAS NASHE · *The Terrors of the Night*
31. EDGAR ALLAN POE · *The Tell-Tale Heart*
32. MARY KINGSLEY · *A Hippo Banquet*
33. JANE AUSTEN · *The Beautifull Cassandra*
34. ANTON CHEKHOV · *Gooseberries*
35. SAMUEL TAYLOR COLERIDGE · *Well, they are gone, and here must I remain*
36. JOHANN WOLFGANG VON GOETHE · *Sketchy, Doubtful, Incomplete Jottings*
37. CHARLES DICKENS · *The Great Winglebury Duel*
38. HERMAN MELVILLE · *The Maldive Shark*
39. ELIZABETH GASKELL · *The Old Nurse's Story*
40. NIKOLAY LESKOV · *The Steel Flea*

41. HONORÉ DE BALZAC · *The Atheist's Mass*
42. CHARLOTTE PERKINS GILMAN · *The Yellow Wall-Paper*
43. C.P. CAVAFY · *Remember, Body . . .*
44. FYODOR DOSTOEVSKY · *The Meek One*
45. GUSTAVE FLAUBERT · *A Simple Heart*
46. NIKOLAI GOGOL · *The Nose*
47. SAMUEL PEPYS · *The Great Fire of London*
48. EDITH WHARTON · *The Reckoning*
49. HENRY JAMES · *The Figure in the Carpet*
50. WILFRED OWEN · *Anthem For Doomed Youth*
51. WOLFGANG AMADEUS MOZART · *My Dearest Father*
52. PLATO · *Socrates' Defence*
53. CHRISTINA ROSSETTI · *Goblin Market*
54. *Sindbad the Sailor*
55. SOPHOCLES · *Antigone*
56. RYŪNOSUKE AKUTAGAWA · *The Life of a Stupid Man*
57. LEO TOLSTOY · *How Much Land Does A Man Need?*
58. GIORGIO VASARI · *Leonardo da Vinci*
59. OSCAR WILDE · *Lord Arthur Savile's Crime*
60. SHEN FU · *The Old Man of the Moon*
61. AESOP · *The Dolphins, the Whales and the Gudgeon*
62. MATSUO BASHŌ · *Lips too Chilled*
63. EMILY BRONTË · *The Night is Darkening Round Me*
64. JOSEPH CONRAD · *To-morrow*
65. RICHARD HAKLUYT · *The Voyage of Sir Francis Drake Around the Whole Globe*
66. KATE CHOPIN · *A Pair of Silk Stockings*
67. CHARLES DARWIN · *It was snowing butterflies*
68. BROTHERS GRIMM · *The Robber Bridegroom*
69. CATULLUS · *I Hate and I Love*
70. HOMER · *Circe and the Cyclops*
71. D. H. LAWRENCE · *Il Duro*
72. KATHERINE MANSFIELD · *Miss Brill*
73. OVID · *The Fall of Icarus*
74. SAPPHO · *Come Close*
75. IVAN TURGENEV · *Kasyan from the Beautiful Lands*
76. VIRGIL · *O Cruel Alexis*
77. H. G. WELLS · *A Slip under the Microscope*
78. HERODOTUS · *The Madness of Cambyses*
79. *Speaking of Siva*
80. *The Dhammapada*

'He was not blind to the fact that murder, like the religions of the Pagan world, requires a victim as well as a priest.'

OSCAR WILDE
Born 1854, Dublin, Ireland
Died 1900, Paris, France

This story was first published in *Lord Arthur Savile's Crime and Other Stories* in 1891.

WILDE IN PENGUIN CLASSICS
De Profundis and Other Prison Writings
The Complete Short Fiction
The Importance of Being Earnest and Other Plays
The Picture of Dorian Gray
The Soul of Man Under Socialism and Selected Critical Prose

OSCAR WILDE

Lord Arthur Savile's Crime

PENGUIN BOOKS

PENGUIN CLASSICS

UK | USA | Canada | Ireland | Australia
India | New Zealand | South Africa

Penguin Books is part of the Penguin Random House group of companies whose addresses can be found at global.penguinrandomhouse.com.

This edition published in Penguin Classics 2015
013

Set in 9.5/13 pt Baskerville 10 Pro
Typeset by Jouve (UK), Milton Keynes
Printed and bound in Great Britain by Clays Ltd, Elcograf S.p.A.

A CIP catalogue record for this book is available from the British Library

ISBN: 978–0–141–39778–8

www.greenpenguin.co.uk

Penguin Random House is committed to a sustainable future for our business, our readers and our planet. This book is made from Forest Stewardship Council® certified paper.

Lord Arthur Savile's Crime

A STUDY OF DUTY

I

It was Lady Windermere's last reception before Easter, and Bentinck House was even more crowded than usual. Six Cabinet Ministers had come on from the Speaker's Levée in their stars and ribands, all the pretty women wore their smartest dresses, and at the end of the picture-gallery stood the Princess Sophia of Carlsrühe, a heavy Tartar-looking lady, with tiny black eyes and wonderful emeralds, talking bad French at the top of her voice, and laughing immoderately at everything that was said to her. It was certainly a wonderful medley of people. Gorgeous peeresses chatted affably to violent Radicals, popular preachers brushed coat-tails with eminent sceptics, a perfect bevy of bishops kept following a stout prima-donna from room to room, on the staircase stood several Royal Academicians, disguised as artists, and it was said that at one time the supper-room was absolutely crammed with geniuses. In fact, it was one of Lady

Windermere's best nights, and the Princess stayed till nearly half-past eleven.

As soon as she had gone, Lady Windermere returned to the picture-gallery, where a celebrated political economist was solemnly explaining the scientific theory of music to an indignant virtuoso from Hungary, and began to talk to the Duchess of Paisley. She looked wonderfully beautiful with her grand ivory throat, her large blue forget-me-not eyes, and her heavy coils of golden hair. *Or pur* they were – not that pale straw colour that nowadays usurps the gracious name of gold, but such gold as is woven into sunbeams or hidden in strange amber; and they gave to her face something of the frame of a saint, with not a little of the fascination of a sinner. She was a curious psychological study. Early in life she had discovered the important truth that nothing looks so like innocence as an indiscretion; and by a series of reckless escapades, half of them quite harmless, she had acquired all the privileges of a personality. She had more than once changed her husband; indeed, Debrett credits her with three marriages; but as she had never changed her lover, the world had long ago ceased to talk scandal about her. She was now forty years of age, childless, and with that inordinate passion for pleasure which is the secret of remaining young.

Suddenly she looked eagerly round the room, and said, in her clear contralto voice, 'Where is my cheiromantist?'

Lord Arthur Savile's Crime

'Your what, Gladys?' exclaimed the Duchess, giving an involuntary start.

'My cheiromantist, Duchess; I can't live without him at present.'

'Dear Gladys! you are always so original,' murmured the Duchess, trying to remember what a cheiromantist really was, and hoping it was not the same as a cheiropodist.

'He comes to see my hand twice a week regularly,' continued Lady Windermere, 'and is most interesting about it.'

'Good heavens!' said the Duchess to herself, 'he is a sort of cheiropodist after all. How very dreadful. I hope he is a foreigner at any rate. It wouldn't be quite so bad then.'

'I must certainly introduce him to you.'

'Introduce him!' cried the Duchess; 'you don't mean to say he is here?' and she began looking about for a small tortoise-shell fan and a very tattered lace shawl, so as to be ready to go at a moment's notice.

'Of course he is here, I would not dream of giving a party without him. He tells me I have a pure psychic hand, and that if my thumb had been the least little bit shorter, I should have been a confirmed pessimist, and gone into a convent.'

'Oh, I see!' said the Duchess, feeling very much relieved; 'he tells fortunes, I suppose?'

'And misfortunes, too,' answered Lady Windermere, 'any amount of them. Next year, for instance, I am in great danger, both by land and sea, so I am going to live in a balloon, and draw up my dinner in a basket every evening. It is all written down on my little finger, or on the palm of my hand, I forget which.'

'But surely that is tempting Providence, Gladys.'

'My dear Duchess, surely Providence can resist temptation by this time. I think every one should have their hands told once a month, so as to know what not to do. Of course, one does it all the same, but it is so pleasant to be warned. Now, if some one doesn't go and fetch Mr Podgers at once, I shall have to go myself.'

'Let me go, Lady Windermere,' said a tall handsome young man, who was standing by, listening to the conversation with an amused smile.

'Thanks so much, Lord Arthur; but I am afraid you wouldn't recognise him.'

'If he is as wonderful as you say, Lady Windermere, I couldn't well miss him. Tell me what he is like, and I'll bring him to you at once.'

'Well, he is not a bit like a cheiromantist. I mean he is not mysterious, or esoteric, or romantic-looking. He is a little, stout man, with a funny, bald head, and great gold-rimmed spectacles; something between a family doctor and a country attorney. I'm really very sorry, but it is not my fault. People are so annoying. All my pianists look exactly like poets, and all my poets look exactly like pianists; and I remember last season asking a most dreadful conspirator to dinner, a man who had blown up ever so many people, and always wore a coat of mail, and carried a dagger up his shirt-sleeve; and do you know that when he came he looked just like a nice old clergyman, and cracked jokes all the evening? Of course, he was very amusing, and all that, but I was awfully disappointed; and when I asked him about the coat of mail, he only laughed, and said it was far too cold to wear in England. Ah, here is Mr Podgers! Now, Mr Podgers, I want you to tell the Duchess of Paisley's hand. Duchess, you must take your glove off. No, not the left hand, the other.'

'Dear Gladys, I really don't think it is quite right,' said the Duchess, feebly unbuttoning a rather soiled kid glove.

'Nothing interesting ever is,' said Lady Windermere: '*on a fait le monde ainsi*. But I must introduce you. Duchess, this is Mr Podgers, my pet cheiromantist. Mr Podgers, this is the Duchess of Paisley, and if you say that she has a larger mountain of the moon than I have, I will never believe in you again.'

'I am sure, Gladys, there is nothing of the kind in my hand,' said the Duchess gravely.

'Your Grace is quite right,' said Mr Podgers, glancing at the little fat hand with its short square fingers, 'the mountain of the moon is not developed. The line of life, however, is excellent. Kindly bend the wrist. Thank you. Three distinct lines on the *rascette*! You will live to a great age, Duchess, and be extremely happy. Ambition – very moderate, line of intellect not exaggerated, line of heart –'

'Now, do be indiscreet, Mr Podgers,' cried Lady Windermere.

'Nothing would give me greater pleasure,' said Mr Podgers, bowing, 'if the Duchess ever had been, but I am sorry to say that I see great permanence of affection, combined with a strong sense of duty.'

'Pray go on, Mr Podgers,' said the Duchess, looking quite pleased.

'Economy is not the least of your Grace's virtues,' continued Mr Podgers, and Lady Windermere went off into fits of laughter.

'Economy is a very good thing,' remarked the Duchess complacently; 'when I married Paisley he had eleven castles, and not a single house fit to live in.'

'And now he has twelve houses, and not a single castle,' cried Lady Windermere.

'Well, my dear,' said the Duchess, 'I like –'

'Comfort,' said Mr Podgers, 'and modern improvements, and hot water laid on in every bedroom. Your Grace is quite right. Comfort is the only thing our civilisation can give us.'

'You have told the Duchess's character admirably, Mr Podgers, and now you must tell Lady Flora's;' and in answer to a nod from the smiling hostess, a tall girl, with sandy Scotch hair, and high shoulder-blades, stepped awkwardly from behind the sofa, and held out a long, bony hand with spatulate fingers.

'Ah, a pianist! I see,' said Mr Podgers, 'an excellent pianist, but perhaps hardly a musician. Very reserved, very honest, and with a great love of animals.'

'Quite true!' exclaimed the Duchess, turning to Lady Windermere, 'absolutely true! Flora keeps two dozen collie dogs at Macloskie, and would turn our town house into a menagerie if her father would let her.'

'Well, that is just what I do with my house every Thursday evening,' cried Lady Windermere, laughing, 'only I like lions better than collie dogs.'

'Your one mistake, Lady Windermere,' said Mr Podgers, with a pompous bow.

'If a woman can't make her mistakes charming, she is only a female,' was the answer. 'But you must read some more hands for us. Come, Sir Thomas, show Mr Podgers yours;' and a genial-looking old gentleman, in a white waistcoat, came forward, and held out a thick rugged hand, with a very long third finger.

'An adventurous nature; four long voyages in the past, and one to come. Been shipwrecked three times. No, only twice, but in danger of a shipwreck your next journey. A strong Conservative, very punctual, and with a passion for collecting curiosities. Had a severe illness between the ages of sixteen and eighteen. Was left a fortune when about thirty. Great aversion to cats and Radicals.'

'Extraordinary!' exclaimed Sir Thomas; 'you must really tell my wife's hand, too.'

'Your second wife's,' said Mr Podgers quietly, still keeping Sir Thomas's hand in his. 'Your second wife's. I shall be charmed;' but Lady Marvel, a melancholy-looking woman, with brown hair and sentimental eyelashes, entirely declined to have her past or her future exposed; and nothing that Lady Windermere could do would induce Monsieur de Koloff, the Russian Ambassador, even to take his gloves off. In fact, many people seemed afraid to face the odd little man with his stereotyped smile, his gold spectacles, and his bright, beady eyes; and when he told poor Lady Fermor, right out before every one, that she did not care a bit for music, but was extremely fond of musicians, it was generally felt that cheiromancy was a most dangerous science, and one that ought not to be encouraged, except in a *tête-à-tête*.

Lord Arthur Savile, however, who did not know anything about Lady Fermor's unfortunate story, and who had been watching Mr Podgers with a great deal of interest, was filled with an immense curiosity to have his own hand read, and feeling somewhat shy about putting himself forward, crossed over the room to where Lady Windermere was sitting, and, with a charming blush, asked her if she thought Mr Podgers would mind.

'Of course, he won't mind,' said Lady Windermere, 'that is what he is here for. All my lions, Lord Arthur, are performing lions, and jump through hoops whenever I

Lord Arthur Savile's Crime

ask them. But I must warn you beforehand that I shall tell Sybil everything. She is coming to lunch with me to-morrow, to talk about bonnets, and if Mr Podgers finds out that you have a bad temper, or a tendency to gout, or a wife living in Bayswater, I shall certainly let her know all about it.'

Lord Arthur smiled, and shook his head. 'I am not afraid,' he answered. 'Sybil knows me as well as I know her.'

'Ah! I am a little sorry to hear you say that. The proper basis for marriage is a mutual misunderstanding. No, I am not at all cynical, I have merely got experience, which, however, is very much the same thing. Mr Podgers, Lord Arthur Savile is dying to have his hand read. Don't tell him that he is engaged to one of the most beautiful girls in London, because that appeared in the *Morning Post* a month ago.

'Dear Lady Windermere,' cried the Marchioness of Jedburgh, 'do let Mr Podgers stay here a little longer. He has just told me I should go on the stage, and I am so interested.'

'If he has told you that, Lady Jedburgh, I shall certainly take him away. Come over at once, Mr Podgers, and read Lord Arthur's hand.'

'Well,' said Lady Jedburgh, making a little *moue* as she rose from the sofa, 'if I am not to be allowed to go on the stage, I must be allowed to be part of the audience at any rate.'

'Of course; we are all going to be part of the audience,' said Lady Windermere; 'and now, Mr Podgers, be sure and tell us something nice. Lord Arthur is one of my special favourites.'

But when Mr Podgers saw Lord Arthur's hand he grew curiously pale, and said nothing. A shudder seemed to pass through him, and his great bushy eyebrows twitched convulsively, in an odd, irritating way they had when he was puzzled. Then some huge beads of perspiration broke out on his yellow forehead, like a poisonous dew, and his fat fingers grew cold and clammy.

Lord Arthur did not fail to notice these strange signs of agitation, and, for the first time in his life, he himself felt fear. His impulse was to rush from the room, but he restrained himself. It was better to know the worst, whatever it was, than to be left in this hideous uncertainty.

'I am waiting, Mr Podgers,' he said.

'We are all waiting,' cried Lady Windermere, in her quick, impatient manner, but the cheiromantist made no reply.

'I believe Arthur is going on the stage,' said Lady Jedburgh, 'and that, after your scolding, Mr Podgers is afraid to tell him so.'

Suddenly Mr Podgers dropped Lord Arthur's right hand, and seized hold of his left, bending down so low to examine it that the gold rims of his spectacles seemed almost to touch the palm. For a moment his face became a white mask of horror, but he soon recovered his *sang-froid*, and looking up at Lady Windermere, said with a forced smile, 'It is the hand of a charming young man.'

'Of course it is!' answered Lady Windermere, 'but will he be a charming husband? That is what I want to know.'

'All charming young men are,' said Mr Podgers.

'I don't think a husband should be too fascinating,' murmured Lady Jedburgh pensively, 'it is so dangerous.'

'My dear child, they never are too fascinating,' cried Lady Windermere. 'But what I want are details. Details are the only things that interest. What is going to happen to Lord Arthur?'

'Well, within the next few months Lord Arthur will go on a voyage –'

'Oh yes, his honeymoon, of course!'

'And lose a relative.'

'Not his sister, I hope?' said Lady Jedburgh, in a piteous tone of voice.

'Certainly not his sister,' answered Mr Podgers, with a deprecating wave of the hand, 'a distant relative merely.'

'Well, I am dreadfully disappointed,' said Lady Windermere. 'I have absolutely nothing to tell Sybil to-morrow. No one cares about distant relatives nowadays. They went out of fashion years ago. However, I suppose she had better have a black silk by her; it always does for church, you know. And now let us go to supper. They are sure to have eaten everything up, but we may find some hot soup.

François used to make excellent soup once, but he is so agitated about politics at present, that I never feel quite certain about him. I do wish General Boulanger would keep quiet. Duchess, I am sure you are tired?'

'Not at all, dear Gladys,' answered the Duchess, waddling towards the door. 'I have enjoyed myself immensely, and the cheiropodist, I mean the cheiromantist, is most interesting. Flora, where can my tortoise-shell fan be? Oh, thank you, Sir Thomas, so much. And my lace shawl, Flora? Oh, thank you, Sir Thomas, very kind, I'm sure;' and the worthy creature finally managed to get downstairs without dropping her scent-bottle more than twice.

All this time Lord Arthur Savile had remained standing by the fireplace, with the same feeling of dread over him, the same sickening sense of coming evil. He smiled sadly at his sister, as she swept past him on Lord Plymdale's arm, looking lovely in her pink brocade and pearls, and he hardly heard Lady Windermere when she called to him to follow her. He thought of Sybil Merton, and the idea that anything could come between them made his eyes dim with tears.

Looking at him, one would have said that Nemesis had stolen the shield of Pallas, and shown him the Gorgon's head. He seemed turned to stone, and his face was like marble in its melancholy. He had lived the delicate and luxurious life of a young man of birth and fortune, a life exquisite in its freedom from sordid care, its beautiful boyish insouciance; and now for the first time he became

Lord Arthur Savile's Crime

conscious of the terrible mystery of Destiny, of the awful meaning of Doom.

How mad and monstrous it all seemed! Could it be that written on his hand, in characters that he could not read himself, but that another could decipher, was some fearful secret of sin, some blood-red sign of crime? Was there no escape possible? Were we no better than chessmen, moved by an unseen power, vessels the potter fashions at his fancy, for honour or for shame? His reason revolted against it, and yet he felt that some tragedy was hanging over him, and that he had been suddenly called upon to bear an intolerable burden. Actors are so fortunate. They can choose whether they will appear in tragedy or in comedy, whether they will suffer or make merry, laugh or shed tears. But in real life it is different. Most men and women are forced to perform parts for which they have no qualifications. Our Guildensterns play Hamlet for us, and our Hamlets have to jest like Prince Hal. The world is a stage, but the play is badly cast.

Suddenly Mr Podgers entered the room. When he saw Lord Arthur he started, and his coarse, fat face became a sort of greenish-yellow colour. The two men's eyes met, and for a moment there was silence.

'The Duchess has left one of her gloves here, Lord Arthur, and has asked me to bring it to her,' said Mr Podgers finally. 'Ah, I see it on the sofa! Good evening.'

'Mr Podgers, I must insist on your giving me a straightforward answer to a question I am going to put to you.'

'Another time, Lord Arthur, but the Duchess is anxious. I am afraid I must go.'

'You shall not go. The Duchess is in no hurry.'

'Ladies should not be kept waiting, Lord Arthur,' said Mr Podgers, with his sickly smile. 'The fair sex is apt to be impatient.'

Lord Arthur's finely-chiselled lips curled in petulant disdain. The poor Duchess seemed to him of very little importance at that moment. He walked across the room to where Mr Podgers was standing, and held his hand out.

'Tell me what you saw there,' he said. 'Tell me the truth. I must know it. I am not a child.'

Mr Podgers's eyes blinked behind his gold-rimmed spectacles, and he moved uneasily from one foot to the other, while his fingers played nervously with a flash watch-chain.

'What makes you think that I saw anything in your hand, Lord Arthur, more than I told you?'

'I know you did, and I insist on your telling me what it was. I will pay you. I will give you a cheque for a hundred pounds.'

The green eyes flashed for a moment, and then became dull again.

'Guineas?' said Mr Podgers at last, in a low voice.

'Certainly. I will send you a cheque to-morrow. What is your club?'

'I have no club. That is to say, not just at present. My address is –, but allow me to give you my card;' and producing a bit of gilt-edged pasteboard from his waistcoat pocket, Mr Podgers handed it, with a low bow, to Lord Arthur, who read on it,

> MR SEPTIMUS R. PODGERS
> *Professional Cheiromantist*
> 103a West Moon Street

'My hours are from ten to four,' murmured Mr Podgers mechanically, 'and I make a reduction for families.'

'Be quick,' cried Lord Arthur, looking very pale, and holding his hand out.

Mr Podgers glanced nervously round, and drew the heavy *portière* across the door.

'It will take a little time, Lord Arthur, you had better sit down.'

'Be quick, sir,' cried Lord Arthur again, stamping his foot angrily on the polished floor.

Mr Podgers smiled, drew from his breast-pocket a small magnifying glass, and wiped it carefully with his handkerchief.

'I am quite ready,' he said.

II

Ten minutes later, with face blanched by terror, and eyes wild with grief, Lord Arthur Savile rushed from Bentinck House, crushing his way through the crowd of fur-coated footmen that stood round the large striped awning, and seeming not to see or hear anything. The night was bitter cold, and the gas-lamps round the square flared and flickered in the keen wind; but his hands were hot with fever, and his forehead burned like fire. On and on he went, almost with the gait of a drunken man. A policeman looked curiously at him as he passed, and a beggar, who slouched from an archway to ask for alms, grew frightened, seeing misery greater than his own. Once he stopped under a lamp, and looked at his hands. He thought he could detect the stain of blood already upon them, and a faint cry broke from his trembling lips.

Murder! that is what the cheiromantist had seen there. Murder! The very night seemed to know it, and the desolate wind to howl it in his ear. The dark corners of the streets were full of it. It grinned at him from the roofs of the houses.

First he came to the Park, whose sombre woodland seemed to fascinate him. He leaned wearily up against the railings, cooling his brow against the wet metal, and listening to the tremulous silence of the trees. 'Murder! murder!' he kept repeating, as though iteration could dim the horror of the word. The sound of his own voice made him shudder, yet he almost hoped that Echo might hear him, and wake the slumbering city from its dreams. He felt a mad desire to stop the casual passer-by, and tell him everything.

Then he wandered across Oxford Street into narrow, shameful alleys. Two women with painted faces mocked at him as he went by. From a dark courtyard came a sound of oaths and blows, followed by shrill screams, and, huddled upon a damp doorstep, he saw the crook-backed forms of poverty and eld. A strange pity came over him. Were these children of sin and misery predestined to their end, as he to his? Were they, like him, merely the puppets of a monstrous show?

And yet it was not the mystery, but the comedy of suffering that struck him; its absolute uselessness, its grotesque want of meaning. How incoherent everything seemed! How lacking in all harmony! He was amazed at the discord between the shallow optimism of the day, and the real facts of existence. He was still very young.

After a time he found himself in front of Marylebone Church. The silent roadway looked like a long riband of polished silver, flecked here and there by the dark arabesques of waving shadows. Far into the distance curved the line of flickering gas-lamps, and outside a little walled-in house stood a solitary hansom, the driver asleep inside. He walked hastily in the direction of Portland Place, now and then looking round, as though he feared that he was being followed. At the corner of Rich Street stood two men, reading a small bill upon a hoarding. An odd feeling of curiosity stirred him, and he crossed over. As he came near, the word 'Murder,' printed in black letters, met his eye. He started, and a deep flush came into his cheek. It was an advertisement offering a reward for any information leading to the arrest of a man of medium height, between thirty and forty years of age, wearing a billy-cock hat, a black coat, and check trousers, and with a scar upon his right cheek. He read it over and over again, and wondered if the wretched man would be caught, and how he had been scarred. Perhaps, some day, his own name might be placarded on the walls of London. Some day, perhaps, a price would be set on his head also.

The thought made him sick with horror. He turned on his heel, and hurried on into the night.

Where he went he hardly knew. He had a dim memory of wandering through a labyrinth of sordid houses, of being lost in a giant web of sombre streets, and it was bright dawn when he found himself at last in Piccadilly Circus. As he strolled home towards Belgrave Square, he met the great waggons on their way to Covent Garden. The white-smocked carters, with their pleasant sunburnt faces and coarse curly hair, strode sturdily on, cracking their whips, and calling out now and then to each other; on the back of a huge grey horse, the leader of a jangling team, sat a chubby boy, with a bunch of primroses in his battered hat, keeping tight hold of the mane with his little hands, and laughing; and the great piles of vegetables looked like masses of jade against the morning sky, like masses of green jade against the pink petals of some marvellous rose. Lord Arthur felt curiously affected, he could not tell why. There was something in the dawn's delicate loveliness that seemed to him inexpressibly pathetic, and he thought of all the days that break in beauty, and that set in storm. These rustics, too, with their rough, good-humoured voices, and their nonchalant ways, what a strange London they saw! A London free from the sin of night and the smoke of day, a pallid, ghost-like city, a desolate town of tombs! He wondered what they thought of it, and whether they knew anything of its splendour and its shame, of its fierce, fiery-coloured joys, and its horrible hunger, of all it makes and mars from morn to eve. Probably it was to them merely a mart where they brought their fruits to sell, and where they tarried for a few hours at most, leaving the streets still silent, the houses still asleep. It gave him pleasure to watch them as they went by. Rude as they were, with their heavy, hob-nailed shoes, and their awkward gait, they brought a little of Arcady with them. He felt that they had lived with Nature, and that she had taught them peace. He envied them all that they did not know.

By the time he had reached Belgrave Square the sky was a faint blue, and the birds were beginning to twitter in the gardens.

III

When Lord Arthur woke it was twelve o'clock, and the mid-day sun was streaming through the ivory-silk curtains of his room. He got up and looked out of the window. A dim haze of heat was hanging over the great city, and the roofs of the houses were like dull silver. In the flickering green of the square below some children were flitting about like white butterflies, and the pavement was crowded with people on their way to the Park. Never had life seemed lovelier to him, never had the things of evil seemed more remote.

Then his valet brought him a cup of chocolate on a tray. After he had drunk it, he drew aside a heavy *portière* of peach-coloured plush, and passed into the bathroom. The light stole softly from above, through thin slabs of transparent onyx, and the water in the marble tank glimmered like a moonstone. He plunged hastily in, till the cool ripples touched throat and hair, and then dipped his head right under, as though he would have wiped away the stain of some shameful memory. When he stepped out he felt almost at peace. The exquisite physical conditions of the moment had dominated him, as indeed often happens in the case of very finely-wrought natures, for the senses, like fire, can purify as well as destroy.

After breakfast, he flung himself down on a divan, and lit a cigarette. On the mantel-shelf, framed in dainty old

Lord Arthur Savile's Crime

brocade, stood a large photograph of Sybil Merton, as he had seen her first at Lady Noel's ball. The small, exquisitely-shaped head drooped slightly to one side, as though the thin, reed-like throat could hardly bear the burden of so much beauty; the lips were slightly parted, and seemed made for sweet music; and all the tender purity of girlhood looked out in wonder from the dreaming eyes. With her soft, clinging dress of *crêpe-de-chine*, and her large leaf-shaped fan, she looked like one of those delicate little figures men find in the olive-woods near Tanagra; and there was a touch of Greek grace in her pose and attitude. Yet she was not *petite*. Yet she was simply perfectly proportioned – a rare thing in an age when so many women are either over life-size or insignificant.

Now as Lord Arthur looked at her, he was filled with the terrible pity that is born of love. He felt that to marry her, with the doom of murder hanging over his head, would be a betrayal like that of Judas, a sin worse than any the Borgia had ever dreamed of. What happiness could there be for them, when at any moment he might be called upon to carry out the awful prophecy written in his hand? What manner of life would be theirs while Fate still held this fearful fortune in the scales? The marriage must be postponed, at all costs. Of this he was quite resolved. Ardently though he loved the girl, and the mere touch of her fingers, when they sat together, made each nerve of his body thrill with exquisite joy, he recognised none the less clearly where his duty lay, and was fully conscious of the fact that he had no right to marry until he had committed the murder. This done, he could stand before the altar with Sybil Merton, and give his life into her hands without terror of wrongdoing. This done, he could take her to his arms, knowing that she would never have to blush for him, never have to hang her head in shame. But done it must be first; and the sooner the better for both.

Many men in his position would have preferred the primrose path of dalliance to the steep heights of duty; but Lord Arthur was too conscientious to set pleasure above principle. There was more than mere passion in his love; and Sybil was to him a symbol of all that is good and noble. For a moment he had a natural repugnance against what he was asked to do, but it soon passed away. His heart told him that it was not a sin, but a sacrifice; his reason reminded him that there was no other course open. He had to choose between living for himself and living for others, and terrible though the task laid upon him undoubtedly was, yet he knew that he must not suffer selfishness to triumph over love. Sooner or later we are all called upon to decide on the same issue – of us all, the same question is asked. To Lord Arthur it came early in life – before his nature had been spoiled by the calculating cynicism of middle-age, or his heart corroded by the shallow, fashionable egotism of our day, and he felt no hesitation about doing his duty. Fortunately also, for him, he was no mere dreamer, or idle dilettante. Had he been so, he would have hesitated, like Hamlet, and let irresolution mar his purpose. But he was essentially practical. Life to him meant action, rather than thought. He had that rarest of all things, common sense.

The wild, turbid feelings of the previous night had by this time completely passed away, and it was almost with a sense of shame that he looked back upon his mad wanderings from street to street, his fierce emotional agony. The very sincerity of his sufferings made them seem unreal to him now. He wondered how he could have been so foolish as to rant and rave about the inevitable. The only question that seemed to trouble him was, whom to make away with; for he was not blind to the fact that murder, like the religions of the Pagan world, requires a victim as well as a priest. Not being a genius, he had no enemies, and indeed he felt that this was not the time for the gratification of any personal pique or dislike, the mission in which he was engaged being one of great and grave solemnity. He accordingly made out a list of his friends and relatives on a sheet of notepaper, and after careful consideration, decided in favour of Lady Clementina Beauchamp, a dear old lady who lived in Curzon Street, and was his own second cousin by his mother's side. He had always been very fond of Lady Clem, as every one called her, and as he was very wealthy himself, having come into all Lord Rugby's property when he came of age, there was no possibility of his deriving any vulgar monetary advantage by her death. In fact, the more he thought over the matter, the more she seemed to him to be just the right person, and, feeling that any delay would be unfair to Sybil, he determined to make his arrangements at once.

The first thing to be done was, of course, to settle with the cheiromantist; so he sat down at a small Sheraton writing-table that stood near the window, drew a cheque for £105, payable to the order of Mr Septimus Podgers, and, enclosing it in an envelope, told his valet to take it to West Moon Street. He then telephoned to the stables for his hansom, and dressed to go out. As he was leaving the room, he looked back at Sybil Merton's photograph, and swore that, come what may, he would never let her know what he was doing for her sake, but would keep the secret of his self-sacrifice hidden always in his heart.

On his way to the Buckingham, he stopped at a florist's, and sent Sybil a beautiful basket of narcissi, with lovely white petals and staring pheasants' eyes, and on arriving at the club, went straight to the library, rang the bell, and ordered the waiter to bring him a lemon-and-soda, and a book on Toxicology. He had fully decided that poison was the best means to adopt in this troublesome business. Anything like personal violence was extremely distasteful to him, and besides, he was very anxious not to murder Lady Clementina in any way that might attract public attention, as he hated the idea of being lionised at Lady Windermere's, or seeing his name figuring in the paragraphs of vulgar society-newspapers. He had also to think

Lord Arthur Savile's Crime

of Sybil's father and mother, who were rather old-fashioned people, and might possibly object to the marriage if there was anything like a scandal, though he felt certain that if he told them the whole facts of the case they would be the very first to appreciate the motives that had actuated him. He had every reason, then, to decide in favour of poison. It was safe, sure, and quiet, and did away with any necessity for painful scenes, to which, like most Englishmen, he had a rooted objection.

Of the science of poisons, however, he knew absolutely nothing, and as the waiter seemed quite unable to find anything in the library but Ruff's *Guide* and Bailey's *Magazine*, he examined the book-shelves himself, and finally came across a handsomely-bound edition of the *Pharmacopoeia*, and a copy of Erskine's *Toxicology*, edited by Sir Mathew Reid, the President of the Royal College of Physicians, and one of the oldest members of the Buckingham, having been elected in mistake for somebody else; a *contretemps* that so enraged the Committee, that when the real man came up they black-balled him unanimously. Lord Arthur was a good deal puzzled at the technical terms used in both books, and had begun to regret that he had not paid more attention to his classics at Oxford, when in the second volume of Erskine, he found a very interesting and complete account of the properties of aconitine, written in fairly clear English. It seemed to him to be exactly the poison he wanted. It was swift – indeed, almost immediate, in its effect – perfectly painless, and when taken in the form of a gelatine capsule, the mode recommended by Sir Mathew, not by any means unpalatable. He accordingly made a note, upon his shirt-cuff, of the amount necessary for a fatal dose, put the books back in their places, and strolled up St James's Street, to Pestle and Humbey's, the great chemists. Mr Pestle, who always attended personally on the aristocracy, was a good deal surprised at the order, and in a very deferential manner murmured something about a medical certificate being necessary. However, as soon as Lord Arthur explained to him that it was for a large Norwegian mastiff that he was obliged to get rid of, as it showed signs of incipient rabies, and had already bitten the coachman twice in the calf of the leg, he expressed himself as being perfectly satisfied, complimented Lord Arthur on his wonderful knowledge of Toxicology, and had the prescription made up immediately.

Lord Arthur put the capsule into a pretty little silver *bonbonnière* that he saw in a shop-window in Bond Street, threw away Pestle and Humbey's ugly pill-box, and drove off at once to Lady Clementina's.

'Well, *monsieur le mauvais sujet*,' cried the old lady, as he entered the room, 'why haven't you been to see me all this time?'

'My dear Lady Clem, I never have a moment to myself,' said Lord Arthur, smiling.

'I suppose you mean that you go about all day long with Miss Sybil Merton, buying *chiffons* and talking nonsense? I cannot understand why people make such a fuss about being married. In my day we never dreamed of billing and cooing in public, or in private for that matter.'

'I assure you I have not seen Sybil for twenty-four hours, Lady Clem. As far as I can make out, she belongs entirely to her milliners.'

'Of course; that is the only reason you come to see an ugly old woman like myself. I wonder you men don't take warning. *On a fait des folies pour moi*, and here I am, a poor, rheumatic creature, with a false front and a bad temper. Why, if it were not for dear Lady Jansen, who sends me all the worst French novels she can find, I don't think I could get through the day. Doctors are no use at all, except to get fees out of one. They can't even cure my heartburn.'

'I have brought you a cure for that, Lady Clem,' said Lord Arthur gravely. 'It is a wonderful thing, invented by an American.'

'I don't think I like American inventions, Arthur. I am quite sure I don't. I read some American novels lately, and they were quite nonsensical.'

'Oh, but there is no nonsense at all about this, Lady Clem! I assure you it is a perfect cure. You must promise to try it;' and Lord Arthur brought the little box out of his pocket, and handed it to her.

'Well, the box is charming, Arthur. Is it really a present? That is very sweet of you. And is this the wonderful medicine? It looks like a *bonbon*. I'll take it at once.'

'Good heavens! Lady Clem,' cried Lord Arthur, catching hold of her hand, 'you mustn't do anything of the kind. It is a homoeopathic medicine, and if you take it without having heartburn, it might do you no end of harm. Wait till you have an attack, and take it then. You will be astonished at the result.'

'I should like to take it now,' said Lady Clementina, holding up to the light the little transparent capsule, with its floating bubble of liquid aconitine. 'I am sure it is delicious. The fact is that, though I hate doctors, I love medicines. However, I'll keep it till my next attack.'

'And when will that be?' asked Lord Arthur eagerly. 'Will it be soon?'

'I hope not for a week. I had a very bad time yesterday morning with it. But one never knows.'

'You are sure to have one before the end of the month then, Lady Clem?'

'I am afraid so. But how sympathetic you are to-day, Arthur! Really, Sybil has done you a great deal of good. And now you must run away, for I am dining with some very dull people, who won't talk scandal, and I know that if I don't get my sleep now I shall never be able to keep awake during dinner. Good-bye, Arthur, give my love to Sybil, and thank you so much for the American medicine.'

'You won't forget to take it, Lady Clem, will you?' said Lord Arthur, rising from his seat.

'Of course I won't, you silly boy. I think it is most kind

Lord Arthur Savile's Crime

of you to think of me, and I shall write and tell you if I want any more.'

Lord Arthur left the house in high spirits, and with a feeling of immense relief.

That night he had an interview with Sybil Merton. He told her how he had been suddenly placed in a position of terrible difficulty, from which neither honour nor duty would allow him to recede. He told her that the marriage must be put off for the present, as until he had got rid of his fearful entanglements, he was not a free man. He implored her to trust him, and not to have any doubts about the future. Everything would come right, but patience was necessary.

The scene took place in the conservatory of Mr Merton's house, in Park Lane, where Lord Arthur had dined as usual. Sybil had never seemed more happy, and for a moment Lord Arthur had been tempted to play the coward's part, to write to Lady Clementina for the pill, and to let the marriage go on as if there was no such person as Mr Podgers in the world. His better nature, however, soon asserted itself, and even when Sybil flung herself weeping into his arms, he did not falter. The beauty that stirred his senses had touched his conscience also. He felt that to wreck so fair a life for the sake of a few months' pleasure would be a wrong thing to do.

He stayed with Sybil till nearly midnight, comforting her and being comforted in turn, and early the next morning he left for Venice, after writing a manly, firm letter to

Mr Merton about the necessary postponement of the marriage.

IV

In Venice he met his brother, Lord Surbiton, who happened to have come over from Corfu in his yacht. The two young men spent a delightful fortnight together. In the morning they rode on the Lido, or glided up and down the green canals in their long black gondola; in the afternoon they usually entertained visitors on the yacht; and in the evening they dined at Florian's, and smoked innumerable cigarettes on the Piazza. Yet somehow Lord Arthur was not happy. Every day he studied the obituary column in the *Times*, expecting to see a notice of Lady Clementina's death, but every day he was disappointed. He began to be afraid that some accident had happened to her, and often regretted that he had prevented her taking the aconitine when she had been so anxious to try its effect. Sybil's letters, too, though full of love, and trust, and tenderness, were often very sad in their tone, and sometimes he used to think that he was parted from her for ever.

After a fortnight Lord Surbiton got bored with Venice, and determined to run down the coast to Ravenna, as he heard that there was some capital cock-shooting in the Pinetum. Lord Arthur, at first, refused absolutely to come, but Surbiton, of whom he was extremely fond, finally persuaded him that if he stayed at Danielli's by himself he would be moped to death, and on the morning of the 15th they started, with a strong nor'-east wind blowing, and a rather sloppy sea. The sport was excellent, and the free, open-air life brought the colour back to Lord Arthur's cheeks, but about the 22nd he became anxious about Lady Clementina, and, in spite of Surbiton's remonstrances, came back to Venice by train.

As he stepped out of his gondola on to the hotel steps, the proprietor came forward to meet him with a sheaf of telegrams. Lord Arthur snatched them out of his hand, and tore them open. Everything had been successful. Lady Clementina had died quite suddenly on the night of the 17th!

His first thought was for Sybil, and he sent her off a telegram announcing his immediate return to London. He then ordered his valet to pack his things for the night mail, sent his gondoliers about five times their proper fare, and ran up to his sitting-room with a light step and a buoyant heart. There he found three letters waiting for him. One was from Sybil herself, full of sympathy and condolence. The others were from his mother, and from Lady Clementina's solicitor. It seemed that the old lady had dined with the Duchess that very night, had delighted every one by her wit and *esprit*, but had gone home somewhat early, complaining of heartburn. In the morning she was found dead in her bed, having apparently suffered no pain. Sir Mathew Reid had been sent for at once, but, of course, there was nothing to be done, and she was to be buried on the 22nd at Beauchamp Chalcote. A few days before she died she had made her will, and left Lord Arthur her little house in Curzon Street, and all her furniture, personal effects, and pictures, with the exception of her collection of miniatures, which was to go to her sister, Lady Margaret Rufford, and her amethyst necklace, which Sybil Merton was to have. The property was not of much value; but Mr Mansfield the solicitor was extremely anxious for Lord Arthur to return at once, if possible, as there were a great many bills to be paid, and Lady Clementina had never kept any regular accounts.

Lord Arthur was very much touched by Lady Clementina's kind remembrance of him, and felt that Mr Podgers had a great deal to answer for. His love of Sybil, however, dominated every other emotion, and the consciousness that he had done his duty gave him peace and comfort. When he arrived at Charing Cross, he felt perfectly happy.

The Mertons received him very kindly, Sybil made him promise that he would never again allow anything to come between them, and the marriage was fixed for the 7th June. Life seemed to him once more bright and beautiful, and all his old gladness came back to him again.

One day, however, as he was going over the house in Curzon Street, in company with Lady Clementina's solicitor and Sybil herself, burning packages of faded letters, and turning out drawers of odd rubbish, the young girl suddenly gave a little cry of delight.

'What have you found, Sybil?' said Lord Arthur, looking up from his work, and smiling.

'This lovely little silver *bonbonnière*, Arthur. Isn't it quaint and Dutch? Do give it to me! I know amethysts won't become me till I am over eighty.'

It was the box that had held the aconitine.

Lord Arthur started, and a faint blush came into his cheek. He had almost entirely forgotten what he had done, and it seemed to him a curious coincidence that Sybil, for whose sake he had gone through all that terrible anxiety, should have been the first to remind him of it.

'Of course you can have it, Sybil. I gave it to poor Lady Clem myself.'

'Oh! thank you, Arthur; and may I have the *bonbon* too? I had no notion that Lady Clementina liked sweets. I thought she was far too intellectual.'

Lord Arthur grew deadly pale, and a horrible idea crossed his mind.

'*Bonbon*, Sybil? What do you mean?' he said, in a slow, hoarse voice.

'There is one in it, that is all. It looks quite old and dusty, and I have not the slightest intention of eating it. What is the matter, Arthur? How white you look!'

Lord Arthur rushed across the room, and seized the

box. Inside it was the amber-coloured capsule, with its poison-bubble. Lady Clementina had died a natural death after all!

The shock of the discovery was almost too much for him. He flung the capsule into the fire, and sank on the sofa with a cry of despair.

V

Mr Merton was a good deal distressed at the second postponement of the marriage, and Lady Julia, who had already ordered her dress for the wedding, did all in her power to make Sybil break off the match. Dearly, however, as Sybil loved her mother, she had given her whole life into Lord Arthur's hands, and nothing that Lady Julia could say could make her waver in her faith. As for Lord Arthur himself, it took him days to get over his terrible disappointment, and for a time his nerves were completely unstrung. His excellent common sense, however, soon asserted itself, and his sound, practical mind did not leave him long in doubt about what to do. Poison having proved a complete failure, dynamite, or some other form of explosive, was obviously the proper thing to try.

He accordingly looked again over the list of his friends and relatives, and, after careful consideration, determined to blow up his uncle, the Dean of Chichester. The Dean, who was a man of great culture and learning, was extremely fond of clocks, and had a wonderful collection of timepieces, ranging from the fifteenth century to the present day, and it seemed to Lord Arthur that this hobby of the good Dean's offered him an excellent opportunity for carrying out his scheme. Where to procure an explosive machine was, of course, quite another matter. The London Directory gave him no information on the point, and he felt that there was very little use in going to Scotland Yard about it, as they never seemed to know anything about the movements of the dynamite faction till after an explosion had taken place, and not much even then.

Suddenly he thought of his friend Rouvaloff, a young Russian of very revolutionary tendencies, whom he had met at Lady Windermere's in the winter. Count Rouvaloff was supposed to be writing a life of Peter the Great, and to have come over to England for the purpose of studying the documents relating to that Tsar's residence in this country as a ship carpenter; but it was generally suspected that he was a Nihilist agent, and there was no doubt that the Russian Embassy did not look with any favour upon his presence in London. Lord Arthur felt that he was just the man for his purpose, and drove down one morning to his lodgings in Bloomsbury, to ask his advice and assistance.

'So you are taking up politics seriously?' said Count Rouvaloff, when Lord Arthur had told him the object of his mission; but Lord Arthur, who hated swagger of any kind, felt bound to admit to him that he had not the slightest interest in social questions, and simply wanted the explosive machine for a purely family matter, in which no one was concerned but himself.

Count Rouvaloff looked at him for some moments in amazement, and then seeing that he was quite serious, wrote an address on a piece of paper, initialled it, and handed it to him across the table.

'Scotland Yard would give a good deal to know this address, my dear fellow.'

'They shan't have it,' cried Lord Arthur, laughing; and after shaking the young Russian warmly by the hand he ran downstairs, examined the paper, and told the coachman to drive to Soho Square.

There he dismissed him, and strolled down Greek Street, till he came to a place called Bayle's Court. He passed under the archway, and found himself in a curious cul-de-sac, that was apparently occupied by a French Laundry, as a perfect network of clothes-lines was stretched across from house to house, and there was a flutter of white linen in the morning air. He walked right to the end, and knocked at a little green house. After some delay, during which every window in the court became a blurred mass of peering faces, the door was opened by a rather rough-looking foreigner, who asked him in very bad English what his business was. Lord Arthur handed him the paper Count Rouvaloff had given him. When the man saw it he bowed, and invited Lord Arthur into a very shabby front parlour on the ground-floor, and in a few

Lord Arthur Savile's Crime

moments Herr Winckelkopf, as he was called in England, bustled into the room, with a very wine-stained napkin round his neck, and a fork in his left hand.

'Count Rouvaloff has given me an introduction to you,' said Lord Arthur, bowing, 'and I am anxious to have a short interview with you on a matter of business. My name is Smith, Mr Robert Smith, and I want you to supply me with an explosive clock.'

'Charmed to meet you, Lord Arthur,' said the genial little German, laughing. 'Don't look so alarmed, it is my duty to know everybody, and I remember seeing you one evening at Lady Windermere's. I hope her ladyship is quite well. Do you mind sitting with me while I finish my breakfast? There is an excellent *pâté*, and my friends are kind enough to say that my Rhine wine is better than any they get at the German Embassy,' and before Lord Arthur had got over his surprise at being recognised, he found himself seated in the back-room, sipping the most delicious Marcobrünner out of a pale yellow hock-glass marked with the Imperial monogram, and chatting in the friendliest manner possible to the famous conspirator.

'Explosive clocks,' said Herr Winckelkopf, 'are not very good things for foreign exportation, as, even if they succeed in passing the Custom House, the train service is so irregular, that they usually go off before they have reached their proper destination. If, however, you want one for home use, I can supply you with an excellent article, and guarantee that you will be satisfied with the result. May

I ask for whom it is intended? If it is for the police, or for any one connected with Scotland Yard, I'm afraid I cannot do anything for you. The English detectives are really our best friends, and I have always found that by relying on their stupidity, we can do exactly what we like. I could not spare one of them.'

'I assure you,' said Lord Arthur, 'that it has nothing to do with the police at all. In fact, the clock is intended for the Dean of Chichester.'

'Dear me! I had no idea that you felt so strongly about religion, Lord Arthur. Few young men do nowadays.'

'I am afraid you overrate me, Herr Winckelkopf,' said Lord Arthur, blushing. 'The fact is, I really know nothing about theology.'

'It is a purely private matter then?'

'Purely private.'

Herr Winckelkopf shrugged his shoulders, and left the room, returning in a few minutes with a round cake of dynamite about the size of a penny, and a pretty little French clock, surmounted by an ormolu figure of Liberty trampling on the hydra of Despotism.

Lord Arthur's face brightened up when he saw it. 'That is just what I want,' he cried, 'and now tell me how it goes off.'

'Ah! there is my secret,' answered Herr Winckelkopf, contemplating his invention with a justifiable look of pride; 'let me know when you wish it to explode, and I will set the machine to the moment.'

Lord Arthur Savile's Crime

'Well, to-day is Tuesday, and if you could send it off at once –'

'That is impossible; I have a great deal of important work on hand for some friends of mine in Moscow. Still, I might send it off to-morrow.'

'Oh, it will be quite time enough!' said Lord Arthur politely, 'if it is delivered to-morrow night or Thursday morning. For the moment of the explosion, say Friday at noon exactly. The Dean is always at home at that hour.'

'Friday, at noon,' repeated Herr Winckelkopf, and he made a note to that effect in a large ledger that was lying on a bureau near the fireplace.

'And now,' said Lord Arthur, rising from his seat, 'pray let me know how much I am in your debt.'

'It is such a small matter, Lord Arthur, that I do not care to make any charge. The dynamite comes to seven and sixpence, the clock will be three pounds ten, and the carriage about five shillings. I am only too pleased to oblige any friend of Count Rouvaloff's.'

'But your trouble, Herr Winckelkopf?'

'Oh, that is nothing! It is a pleasure to me. I do not work for money; I live entirely for my art.'

Lord Arthur laid down £4:2:6 on the table, thanked the little German for his kindness, and, having succeeded in declining an invitation to meet some Anarchists at a meat-tea on the following Saturday, left the house and went off to the Park.

For the next two days he was in a state of the greatest

excitement, and on Friday at twelve o'clock he drove down to the Buckingham to wait for news. All the afternoon the stolid hall-porter kept posting up telegrams from various parts of the country giving the results of horse-races, the verdicts in divorce suits, the state of the weather, and the like, while the tape ticked out wearisome details about an all-night sitting in the House of Commons, and a small panic on the Stock Exchange. At four o'clock the evening papers came in, and Lord Arthur disappeared into the library with the *Pall Mall*, the *St James's*, the *Globe*, and the *Echo*, to the immense indignation of Colonel Goodchild, who wanted to read the reports of a speech he had delivered that morning at the Mansion House, on the subject of South African Missions, and the advisability of having black Bishops in every province, and for some reason or other had a strong prejudice against the *Evening News*. None of the papers, however, contained even the slightest allusion to Chichester, and Lord Arthur felt that the attempt must have failed. It was a terrible blow to him, and for a time he was quite unnerved. Herr Winckelkopf, whom he went to see the next day, was full of elaborate apologies, and offered to supply him with another clock free of charge, or with a case of nitro-glycerine bombs at cost price. But he had lost all faith in explosives, and Herr Winckelkopf himself acknowledged that everything is so adulterated nowadays, that even dynamite can hardly be got in a pure condition. The little German, however, while admitting that something must have gone wrong with the machinery, was not without hope that the clock might still go off, and instanced the case of a barometer that he had once sent to the military Governor at Odessa, which, though timed to explode in ten days, had not done so for something like three months. It was quite true that when it did go off, it merely succeeded in blowing a housemaid to atoms, the Governor having gone out of town six weeks before, but at least it showed that dynamite, as a destructive force, was, when under the control of machinery, a powerful, though a somewhat unpunctual agent. Lord Arthur was a little consoled by this reflection, but even here he was destined to disappointment, for two days afterwards, as he was going upstairs, the Duchess called him into her boudoir, and showed him a letter she had just received from the Deanery.

'Jane writes charming letters,' said the Duchess; 'you must really read her last. It is quite as good as the novels Mudie sends us.'

Lord Arthur seized the letter from her hand. It ran as follows: –

'The Deanery, Chichester,
'27th May.

'My Dearest Aunt,

'Thank you so much for the flannel for the Dorcas Society, and also for the gingham. I quite agree with you that it is nonsense their wanting to wear pretty things, but everybody is so Radical and irreligious nowadays, that it is difficult to make them see that they should not try and dress like the upper classes. I am sure I don't know what we are coming to. As papa has often said in his sermons, we live in an age of unbelief.

'We have had great fun over a clock that an unknown admirer sent papa last Thursday. It arrived in a wooden box from London, carriage paid; and papa feels it must have been sent by some one who had read his remarkable sermon, "Is Licence Liberty?" for on the top of the clock was a figure of a woman, with what papa said was the cap of Liberty on her head. I didn't think it very becoming myself, but papa said it was historical, so I suppose it is all right. Parker unpacked it, and papa put it on the mantelpiece in the library, and we were all sitting there on Friday morning, when just as the clock struck twelve, we heard a whirring noise, a little puff of smoke came from the pedestal of the figure, and the goddess of Liberty fell off, and broke her nose on the fender! Maria was quite alarmed, but it looked so ridiculous, that James and I went off into fits of laughter, and even papa was amused. When we examined it, we found it was a sort of alarum clock, and that, if you set it to a particular hour, and put some gunpowder and a cap under a little hammer, it went off whenever you wanted. Papa said it must not remain in the library, as it made a noise, so Reggie carried it away to the schoolroom, and does nothing but have small explosions all day long. Do you think Arthur would like one for a wedding present? I suppose they are quite fashionable in London. Papa says they should do a great deal of good, as they show that Liberty can't last, but must fall down. Papa says Liberty was invented at the time of the French Revolution. How awful it seems!

'I have now to go to the Dorcas, where I will read them your most instructive letter. How true, dear aunt, your idea is, that in their rank of life they should wear what is unbecoming. I must say it is absurd, their anxiety about dress, when there are so many more important things in this world, and in the next. I am so glad your flowered poplin turned out so well, and that your lace was not torn. I am wearing my yellow satin, that you so kindly gave me, at the Bishop's on Wednesday, and think it will look all right. Would you have bows or not? Jennings says that every one wears bows now, and that the underskirt should be frilled. Reggie has just had another explosion, and papa has ordered the clock to be sent to the stables. I don't think papa likes it so much as he did at first, though he is very flattered at being sent such a pretty and ingenious toy. It shows that people read his sermons, and profit by them.

'Papa sends his love, in which James, and Reggie, and Maria all unite, and, hoping that Uncle Cecil's gout is better, believe me, dear aunt, ever your affectionate niece,

'Jane Percy

'P. S. – Do tell me about the bows. Jennings insists they are the fashion.'

Lord Arthur looked so serious and unhappy over the letter, that the Duchess went into fits of laughter.

'My dear Arthur,' she cried, 'I shall never show you a young lady's letter again! But what shall I say about the clock? I think it is a capital invention, and I should like to have one myself.'

'I don't think much of them,' said Lord Arthur, with a sad smile, and, after kissing his mother, he left the room.

When he got upstairs, he flung himself on a sofa, and his eyes filled with tears. He had done his best to commit this murder, but on both occasions he had failed, and through no fault of his own. He had tried to do his duty, but it seemed as if Destiny herself had turned traitor. He was oppressed with the sense of the barrenness of good intentions, of the futility of trying to be fine. Perhaps, it would be better to break off the marriage altogether. Sybil would suffer, it is true, but suffering could not really mar a nature so noble as hers. As for himself, what did it matter? There is always some war in which a man can die, some cause to which a man can give his life, and as life had no pleasure for him, so death had no terror. Let Destiny work out his doom. He would not stir to help her.

At half-past seven he dressed, and went down to the club. Surbiton was there with a party of young men, and he was obliged to dine with them. Their trivial conversation and idle jests did not interest him, and as soon as coffee was brought he left them, inventing some engagement in order to get away. As he was going out of the club, the hall porter handed him a letter. It was from Herr Winckelkopf, asking him to call down the next evening, and look at an explosive umbrella, that went off as soon as it was opened. It was the very latest invention, and had just arrived from Geneva. He tore the letter up into fragments. He had made up his mind not to try any more experiments. Then he wandered down to the Thames Embankment, and sat for hours by the river. The moon peered through a mane of tawny clouds, as if it were a lion's eye, and innumerable stars spangled the hollow vault, like gold dust powdered on a purple dome. Now and then a barge swung out into the turbid stream, and floated away with the tide, and the railway signals changed from green to scarlet as the trains ran shrieking across the bridge. After some time, twelve o'clock boomed from the tall tower at Westminster, and at each stroke of the sonorous bell the night seemed to tremble. Then the railway lights went out, one solitary lamp left gleaming like a large ruby on a giant mast, and the roar of the city became fainter.

At two o'clock he got up, and strolled towards Blackfriars. How unreal everything looked! How like a strange dream! The houses on the other side of the river seemed built out of darkness. One would have said that silver and shadow had fashioned the world anew. The huge dome of St Paul's loomed like a bubble through the dusky air.

As he approached Cleopatra's Needle he saw a man

leaning over the parapet, and as he came nearer the man looked up, the gas-light falling full upon his face.

It was Mr Podgers, the cheiromantist! No one could mistake the fat, flabby face, the gold-rimmed spectacles, the sickly feeble smile, the sensual mouth.

Lord Arthur stopped. A brilliant idea flashed across him, and he stole softly up behind. In a moment he had seized Mr Podgers by the legs, and flung him into the Thames. There was a coarse oath, a heavy splash, and all was still. Lord Arthur looked anxiously over, but could see nothing of the cheiromantist but a tall hat, pirouetting in an eddy of moonlit water. After a time it also sank, and no trace of Mr Podgers was visible. Once he thought that he caught sight of the bulky misshapen figure striking out for the staircase by the bridge, and a horrible feeling of failure came over him, but it turned out to be merely a reflection, and when the moon shone out from behind a cloud it passed away. At last he seemed to have realised the decree of destiny. He heaved a deep sigh of relief, and Sybil's name came to his lips.

'Have you dropped anything, sir?' said a voice behind him suddenly.

He turned round, and saw a policeman with a bull's-eye lantern.

'Nothing of importance, sergeant,' he answered, smiling, and hailing a passing hansom, he jumped in, and told the man to drive to Belgrave Square.

For the next few days he alternated between hope and

fear. There were moments when he almost expected Mr Podgers to walk into the room, and yet at other times he felt that Fate could not be so unjust to him. Twice he went to the cheiromantist's address in West Moon Street, but he could not bring himself to ring the bell. He longed for certainty, and was afraid of it.

Finally it came. He was sitting in the smoking-room of the club having tea, and listening rather wearily to Surbiton's account of the last comic song at the Gaiety, when the waiter came in with the evening papers. He took up the *St James's*, and was listlessly turning over its pages, when this strange heading caught his eye:

SUICIDE OF A CHEIROMANTIST.

He turned pale with excitement, and began to read. The paragraph ran as follows: –

Yesterday morning, at seven o'clock, the body of Mr Septimus R. Podgers, the eminent cheiromantist, was washed on shore at Greenwich, just in front of the Ship Hotel. The unfortunate gentleman had been missing for some days, and considerable anxiety for his safety had been felt in cheiromantic circles. It is supposed that he committed suicide under the influence of a temporary mental derangement, caused by overwork, and a verdict to that effect was returned this afternoon by the coroner's jury. Mr Podgers had just completed an elaborate treatise on the subject of the Human Hand, that will shortly be published, when it will no doubt attract much attention. The deceased was sixty-five years of age, and does not seem to have left any relations.

Lord Arthur rushed out of the club with the paper still in his hand, to the immense amazement of the hall-porter, who tried in vain to stop him, and drove at once to Park Lane. Sybil saw him from the window, and something told her that he was the bearer of good news. She ran down to meet him, and, when she saw his face, she knew that all was well.

'My dear Sybil,' cried Lord Arthur, 'let us be married tomorrow!'

'You foolish boy! Why the cake is not even ordered!' said Sybil, laughing through her tears.

VI

When the wedding took place, some three weeks later, St Peter's was crowded with a perfect mob of smart people. The service was read in a most impressive manner by the Dean of Chichester, and everybody agreed that they had never seen a handsomer couple than the bride and bridegroom. They were more than handsome, however – they were happy. Never for a single moment did Lord Arthur regret all that he had suffered for Sybil's sake, while she, on her side, gave him the best things a woman can give to any man – worship, tenderness, and love. For them romance was not killed by reality. They always felt young.

Some years afterwards, when two beautiful children had been born to them, Lady Windermere came down on a visit to Alton Priory, a lovely old place, that had been the Duke's wedding present to his son; and one afternoon as she was sitting with Lady Arthur under a lime-tree in the garden, watching the little boy and girl as they played up and down the rose-walk, like fitful sunbeams, she suddenly took her hostess's hand in hers, and said, 'Are you happy, Sybil?'

'Dear Lady Windermere, of course I am happy. Aren't you?'

'I have no time to be happy, Sybil. I always like the last person who is introduced to me; but, as a rule, as soon as I know people I get tired of them.'

'Don't your lions satisfy you, Lady Windermere?'

'Oh dear, no! lions are only good for one season. As soon as their manes are cut, they are the dullest creatures going. Besides, they behave very badly, if you are really nice to them. Do you remember that horrid Mr Podgers? He was a dreadful impostor. Of course, I didn't mind that at all, and even when he wanted to borrow money I forgave him, but I could not stand his making love to me. He has really made me hate cheiromancy. I go in for telepathy now. It is much more amusing.'

'You mustn't say anything against cheiromancy here,

Lady Windermere; it is the only subject that Arthur does not like people to chaff about. I assure you he is quite serious over it.'

'You don't mean to say that he believes in it, Sybil?'

'Ask him, Lady Windermere, here he is;' and Lord Arthur came up the garden with a large bunch of yellow roses in his hand, and his two children dancing round him.

'Lord Arthur?'

'Yes, Lady Windermere.'

'You don't mean to say that you believe in cheiromancy?'

'Of course I do,' said the young man, smiling.

'But why?'

'Because I owe to it all the happiness of my life,' he murmured, throwing himself into a wicker chair.

'My dear Lord Arthur, what do you owe to it?'

'Sybil,' he answered, handing his wife the roses, and looking into her violet eyes.

'What nonsense!' cried Lady Windermere. 'I never heard such nonsense in all my life.'

1. BOCCACCIO · *Mrs Rosie and the Priest*
2. GERARD MANLEY HOPKINS · *As kingfishers catch fire*
3. *The Saga of Gunnlaug Serpent-tongue*
4. THOMAS DE QUINCEY · *On Murder Considered as One of the Fine Arts*
5. FRIEDRICH NIETZSCHE · *Aphorisms on Love and Hate*
6. JOHN RUSKIN · *Traffic*
7. PU SONGLING · *Wailing Ghosts*
8. JONATHAN SWIFT · *A Modest Proposal*
9. *Three Tang Dynasty Poets*
10. WALT WHITMAN · *On the Beach at Night Alone*
11. KENKŌ · *A Cup of Sake Beneath the Cherry Trees*
12. BALTASAR GRACIÁN · *How to Use Your Enemies*
13. JOHN KEATS · *The Eve of St Agnes*
14. THOMAS HARDY · *Woman much missed*
15. GUY DE MAUPASSANT · *Femme Fatale*
16. MARCO POLO · *Travels in the Land of Serpents and Pearls*
17. SUETONIUS · *Caligula*
18. APOLLONIUS OF RHODES · *Jason and Medea*
19. ROBERT LOUIS STEVENSON · *Olalla*
20. KARL MARX AND FRIEDRICH ENGELS · *The Communist Manifesto*
21. PETRONIUS · *Trimalchio's Feast*
22. JOHANN PETER HEBEL · *How a Ghastly Story Was Brought to Light by a Common or Garden Butcher's Dog*
23. HANS CHRISTIAN ANDERSEN · *The Tinder Box*
24. RUDYARD KIPLING · *The Gate of the Hundred Sorrows*
25. DANTE · *Circles of Hell*
26. HENRY MAYHEW · *Of Street Piemen*
27. HAFEZ · *The nightingales are drunk*
28. GEOFFREY CHAUCER · *The Wife of Bath*
29. MICHEL DE MONTAIGNE · *How We Weep and Laugh at the Same Thing*
30. THOMAS NASHE · *The Terrors of the Night*
31. EDGAR ALLAN POE · *The Tell-Tale Heart*
32. MARY KINGSLEY · *A Hippo Banquet*
33. JANE AUSTEN · *The Beautifull Cassandra*
34. ANTON CHEKHOV · *Gooseberries*
35. SAMUEL TAYLOR COLERIDGE · *Well, they are gone, and here must I remain*
36. JOHANN WOLFGANG VON GOETHE · *Sketchy, Doubtful, Incomplete Jottings*
37. CHARLES DICKENS · *The Great Winglebury Duel*
38. HERMAN MELVILLE · *The Maldive Shark*
39. ELIZABETH GASKELL · *The Old Nurse's Story*
40. NIKOLAY LESKOV · *The Steel Flea*

41. HONORÉ DE BALZAC · *The Atheist's Mass*
42. CHARLOTTE PERKINS GILMAN · *The Yellow Wall-Paper*
43. C.P. CAVAFY · *Remember, Body...*
44. FYODOR DOSTOEVSKY · *The Meek One*
45. GUSTAVE FLAUBERT · *A Simple Heart*
46. NIKOLAI GOGOL · *The Nose*
47. SAMUEL PEPYS · *The Great Fire of London*
48. EDITH WHARTON · *The Reckoning*
49. HENRY JAMES · *The Figure in the Carpet*
50. WILFRED OWEN · *Anthem For Doomed Youth*
51. WOLFGANG AMADEUS MOZART · *My Dearest Father*
52. PLATO · *Socrates' Defence*
53. CHRISTINA ROSSETTI · *Goblin Market*
54. *Sindbad the Sailor*
55. SOPHOCLES · *Antigone*
56. RYŪNOSUKE AKUTAGAWA · *The Life of a Stupid Man*
57. LEO TOLSTOY · *How Much Land Does A Man Need?*
58. GIORGIO VASARI · *Leonardo da Vinci*
59. OSCAR WILDE · *Lord Arthur Savile's Crime*
60. SHEN FU · *The Old Man of the Moon*
61. AESOP · *The Dolphins, the Whales and the Gudgeon*
62. MATSUO BASHŌ · *Lips too Chilled*
63. EMILY BRONTË · *The Night is Darkening Round Me*
64. JOSEPH CONRAD · *To-morrow*
65. RICHARD HAKLUYT · *The Voyage of Sir Francis Drake Around the Whole Globe*
66. KATE CHOPIN · *A Pair of Silk Stockings*
67. CHARLES DARWIN · *It was snowing butterflies*
68. BROTHERS GRIMM · *The Robber Bridegroom*
69. CATULLUS · *I Hate and I Love*
70. HOMER · *Circe and the Cyclops*
71. D. H. LAWRENCE · *Il Duro*
72. KATHERINE MANSFIELD · *Miss Brill*
73. OVID · *The Fall of Icarus*
74. SAPPHO · *Come Close*
75. IVAN TURGENEV · *Kasyan from the Beautiful Lands*
76. VIRGIL · *O Cruel Alexis*
77. H. G. WELLS · *A Slip under the Microscope*
78. HERODOTUS · *The Madness of Cambyses*
79. *Speaking of Siva*
80. *The Dhammapada*

'Our passion was so great. Will the Old Man understand and help us once again?'

SHEN FU
Born 1763, Jiangsu province, China

Selection taken from *Six Records of a Floating Life*, written in 1809 and discovered in the 1870s.

SHEN FU IN PENGUIN CLASSICS
Six Records of a Floating Life

SHEN FU

The Old Man of the Moon

Translated by
Leonard Pratt and Chiang Su-hui

PENGUIN BOOKS

PENGUIN CLASSICS

UK | USA | Canada | Ireland | Australia
India | New Zealand | South Africa

Penguin Books is part of the Penguin Random House group of companies
whose addresses can be found at global.penguinrandomhouse.com.

This selection published in Penguin Classics 2015
011

Translation copyright © Leonard Pratt, 1983

The moral right of the translator has been asserted

Set in 9.5/13 pt Baskerville 10 Pro
Typeset by Jouve (UK), Milton Keynes

Printed and bound in Great Britain by Clays Ltd, Elcograf S.p.A.
A CIP catalogue record for this book is available from the British Library

ISBN: 978-0-141-39780-1

www.greenpenguin.co.uk

Penguin Random House is committed to a
sustainable future for our business, our readers
and our planet. This book is made from Forest
Stewardship Council® certified paper.

I was born in the winter of the 27th year of the reign of the Emperor Chien Lung, on the second and twentieth day of the eleventh month. Heaven blessed me, and life then could not have been more full. It was a time of great peace and plenty, and my family was an official one that lived next to the Pavilion of the Waves in Soochow. As the poet Su Tung-po wrote, 'All things are like spring dreams, passing with no trace.' If I did not make a record of that time, I should be ungrateful for the blessings of heaven.

The very first of the three hundred chapters of the *Book of Odes* concerns husbands and wives, so I too will write of other matters in their turn. Unfortunately I never completed my studies, so my writing is not very skilful. But here my purpose is merely to record true feelings and actual events. Criticism of my writing will be like the shining of a bright light into a dirty mirror.

When I was young I was engaged to Chin Sha-yu, but she died when she was eight years old. Eventually I married Chen Yün, the daughter of my uncle, Mr Chen Hsin-yü. Her literary name was Shu-chen.

Even while small, she was very clever. While she was learning to talk she was taught the poem *The Mandolin Song* and could repeat it almost immediately.

Yün's father died when she was four years old, leaving her mother, whose family name was Chin, and her younger brother, Ko-chang. At first they had virtually nothing, but as Yün grew older she became very adept at needlework, and the labour of her ten fingers came to provide for all three of them. Thanks to her work, they were always able to afford to pay the tuition for her brother's teachers.

One day Yün found a copy of *The Mandolin Song* in her brother's book-box and, remembering her lessons as a child, was able to pick out the characters one by one. That is how she began learning to read. In her spare moments she gradually learned how to write poetry, one line of which was, 'We grow thin in the shadows of autumn, but chrysanthemums grow fat with the dew.'

When I was thirteen, my mother took me along on a visit to her relatives. That was the first time I met my cousin Yün, and we two children got on well together. I had a chance to see her poems that day, and though I sighed at her brilliance I privately feared she was too sensitive to be completely happy in life. Still, I could not forget her, and I remember saying to my mother, 'If you are going to choose a wife for me, I will marry no other than Yün.'

Mother also loved her gentleness, so she was quick to

arrange our engagement, sealing the match by giving Yün a gold ring from her own finger. This was in the 39th year of the reign of the Emperor Chien Lung, on the 16th day of the seventh month.

That winter mother took me to their home once again, for the marriage of Yün's cousin. Yün and I were born in the same year, but because she was ten months older than I, I had always called her 'elder sister', while she called me 'younger brother'. We continued to call one another by these names even after we were engaged.

At her cousin's wedding the room was full of beautifully dressed people. Yün alone wore a plain dress; only her shoes were new. I noticed they were skilfully embroidered, and when she told me she had done them herself I began to appreciate that her cleverness lay not only in her writing.

Yün had delicate shoulders and a stately neck, and her figure was slim. Her brows arched over beautiful, lively eyes. Her only blemish was two slightly protruding front teeth, the sign of a lack of good fortune. But her manner was altogether charming, and she captivated all who saw her.

I asked to see more of her poems that day, and found some had only one line, others three or four, and most were unfinished. I asked her why.

'I have done them without a teacher,' she replied, laughing. 'I hope you, my best friend, can be my teacher now and help me finish them.' Then as a joke I wrote on her book, 'The Embroidered Bag of Beautiful Verses'. I did not then realize that the origin of her early death already lay in that book.

That night after the wedding I escorted my relatives out of the city, and it was midnight by the time I returned. I was terribly hungry and asked for something to eat. A servant brought me some dried plums, but they were too sweet for me. So Yün secretly took me to her room, where she had hidden some warm rice porridge and some small dishes of food. I delightedly picked up my chopsticks, but suddenly heard Yün's cousin Yu-heng call, 'Yün, come quickly!'

Yün hurriedly shut the door and called back, 'I'm very tired. I was just going to sleep.' But Yu-heng pushed open the door and came in anyway.

He saw me just about to begin eating the rice porridge, and chuckled, looking out of the corner of his eye at Yün. 'When I asked you for some rice porridge just now, you said there wasn't any more! But I see you were just hiding it in here and saving it for your "husband"!'

Yün was terribly embarrassed, and ran out. The whole household broke into laughter. I was also embarrassed and angry, roused my servant, and left early.

Every time I returned after that, Yün would hide. I knew she was afraid that everyone would laugh at her.

On the night of the 22nd day of the first month in the 44th year of the reign of the Emperor Chien Lung I saw by the light of our wedding candles that Yün's figure was as slim as before. When her veil was lifted we smiled at each other. After we had shared the ceremonial cup of wine and sat down together for the wedding banquet, I secretly took her small hand under the table. It was warm and it was soft, and my heart beat uncontrollably.

I asked her to begin eating, but it turned out to be a day on which she did not eat meat, a Buddhist practice which she had followed for several years. I thought to myself that she had begun this practice at the very time I had begun to break out with acne, and I asked her, 'Since my skin is now clear and healthy, couldn't you give up this custom?' Her eyes smiled amusement, and her head nodded agreement.

That same night of the 22nd there was a wedding-eve party for my elder sister. She was to be married on the 24th, but the 23rd was a day of national mourning on which all entertaining was forbidden and the holding of the wedding-eve party would have been impossible. Yün attended the dinner, but I spent the time in our bedroom drinking with my sister's maid of honour. We played a drinking game which I lost frequently, and I wound up getting very drunk and falling asleep. By the time I woke up the next morning, Yün was already putting on her make-up.

During the day a constant stream of relatives and friends came to congratulate Yün and me on our marriage. In the evening there were some musical performances in honour of the wedding, after the lamps had been lit.

At midnight I escorted my sister to her new husband's home, and it was almost three in the morning when I returned. The candles had burned low and the house was silent. I stole quietly into our room to find my wife's servant dozing beside the bed and Yün herself with her make-up off but not yet asleep. A candle burned brightly beside her; she was bent intently over a book, but I could not tell what it was that she was reading with such concentration. I went up to her, rubbed her shoulder, and said, 'You've been so busy these past few days, why are you reading so late?'

Yün turned and stood up. 'I was just thinking of going to sleep, but I opened the bookcase and found this book, *The Romance of the Western Chamber*. Once I had started reading it, I forgot how tired I was. I had often heard it spoken of, but this was the first time I had had a chance to read it. The author really is as talented as people say, but I do think his tale is too explicitly told.'

I laughed and said, 'Only a talented writer could be so explicit.'

Yün's servant then urged us to go to sleep, but we told her she should go to sleep first, and to shut the door to our room. We sat up making jokes, like two close friends meeting after a long separation. I playfully felt her breast and found her heart was beating as fast as mine. I pulled her to me and whispered in her ear, 'Why is your heart beating so fast?' She answered with a bewitching smile that made me feel a love so endless it shook my soul. I held her close as I parted the curtains and led her into bed. We never noticed what time the sun rose in the morning.

As a new bride, Yün was very quiet. She never got angry, and when anyone spoke to her she always replied with a smile. She was respectful to her elders and amiable to everyone else. Everything she did was orderly, and was done properly. Each morning when she saw the first rays of the sun touch the top of the window, she would dress quickly and hurry out of bed, as if someone were calling her. I once laughed at her about it; 'This is not like that time with the rice porridge! Why are you still afraid of someone laughing at you?'

'True,' she answered, 'my hiding the rice porridge for you that time has become a joke. But I'm not worried about people laughing at me now. I am afraid your parents will think I'm lazy.'

While I would have liked it if she could have slept more, I had to agree that she was right. So every morning I got up early with her, and from that time on we were inseparable, like a man and his shadow. Words could not describe our love.

We were so happy that our first month together passed in the twinkling of an eye. At that time my father, the Honourable Chia-fu, was working as a private secretary in the prefectural government office at Kuichi. He sent for me, having enrolled me as a student of Mr Chao Sheng-chai at Wulin. Mr Chao taught me patiently and well; the fact that I can write at all today is due to his efforts.

I had, however, originally planned to continue my studies with my father after my marriage, so I was disappointed when I received his letter. I feared Yün would weep when she heard of it, but she showed no emotion, encouraged me to go, and helped me pack my bag. The night before I left she was slightly subdued, but that was all. When it was time for me to go, though, she whispered to me, 'There will be no one there to look after you. Please take good care of yourself.'

My boat cast off just as the peach and the plum flowers were in magnificent bloom. I felt like a bird that had lost its flock. My world was shaken. After I arrived at the offices where my father worked, he immediately began preparations to go east across the river.

Our separation of three months seemed as if it were ten years long. Yün wrote to me frequently, but her letters asked about me twice as often as they told me anything about herself. Most of what she wrote was merely to encourage me in my studies, and the rest was just polite chatter. I really was a little angry with her. Every time the wind would rustle the bamboo trees in the yard, or the moon would shine through the leaves of the banana tree outside my window, I would look out and miss her so terribly that dreams of her took possession of my soul.

My teacher understood how I felt, and wrote to tell my

The Old Man of the Moon

father about it. He then assigned me ten compositions and sent me home for a while to write them. I felt like a prisoner who has been pardoned.

Once I was on the boat each quarter of an hour seemed to pass as slowly as a year. After I got home and paid my respects to my mother, I went into our room and Yün rose to greet me. She held my hands without saying a word. Our souls became smoke and mist. I thought I heard something, but it was as if my body had ceased to exist.

It was then the sixth month, and steamy hot in our room. Fortunately we lived just west of the Pavilion of the Waves' Lotus Lovers' Hall, where it was cooler. By a bridge and overlooking a stream there was a small hall called My Desire, because, as desired, one could 'wash my hat strings in it when it is clean, and wash my feet in it when it is dirty'. Almost under the eaves of the hall there was an old tree that cast a shadow across the windows so deep that it turned one's face green. Strollers were always walking along the opposite bank of the stream. This was where my father, the Honourable Chia-fu, used to entertain guests privately, and I obtained my mother's permission to take Yün there to escape the summer's heat. Because it was so hot, Yün had given up her embroidery. She spent all day with me as I studied, and we talked of ancient times, analysed the moon, and discussed the flowers. Yün could not take much drink, and would accept at the most three cups of wine when I forced her to. I taught her a literary game, in which the loser has to drink a cup. We were certain two people had never been happier than we were.

One day Yün asked me, 'Of all the ancient literary masters, who do you think is the best?'

'*The Annals of the Warring States* and *Chuang Tsu* are known for their liveliness,' I replied. 'Kuang Heng and Liu Hsiang are known for their elegance. Shih Chien and Pan Ku are known for their breadth. Change Li is known for his extensive knowledge, and Liu Chou for his vigorous style. Lu Ling is known for his originality, and Su Hsün and his two sons for their essays. There are also the policy debates of Chia and Tung, the poetic styles of Yü and Hsü, and the Imperial memorials of Lu Chih. I could never give a complete list of all the talented writers there have been. Besides, which one you like depends upon which one you feel in sympathy with.'

'It takes great knowledge and a heroic spirit to appreciate ancient literature,' said Yün. 'I fear a woman's learning is not enough to master it. The only way we have of understanding it is through poetry, and I understand but a bit of that.'

'During the Tang Dynasty all candidates had to pass an examination in poetry before they could become officials,' I remarked. 'Clearly the best were Li Pai and Tu Fu. Which of them do you like best?'

Yün said her opinion was that 'Tu Fu's poetry is very pure and carefully tempered, while Li Pai's is ethereal and

The Old Man of the Moon

open. Personally, I would rather have Li Pai's liveliness than Tu Fu's strictness.'

'But Tu Fu was the more successful, and most scholars prefer him. Why do you alone like Li Pai?'

'Tu Fu is alone,' Yün replied, 'in the detail of his verse and the vividness of his expression. But Li Pai's poetry flows like a flower tossed into a stream. It's enchanting. I would not say Li Pai is a better poet than Tu Fu, but only that he appeals to me more.'

I smiled and said, 'I never thought you were such an admirer of Li Pai's.'

Yün smiled back. 'Apart from him, there is only my first teacher, Mr Pai Lo-tien. I have always had a feeling in my heart for him that has never changed.'

'Why do you say that?' I asked.

'Didn't he write *The Mandolin Song?*'

I laughed. 'Isn't that strange! You are an admirer of Li Pai's, and Pai Lo-tien was your first tutor. And as it happens, the literary name of your husband is San-pai. What is this affinity you have for the character *pai*?'

Yün laughed and said, 'Since I do have an affinity for the character *pai*, I'm afraid that in the future my writing will be full of *pai* characters.' (Our Kiangsu accent pronounces the character *pieh* as *pai*.) We both shook with laughter.

'Since you know poetry,' I said, 'you must know the good and bad points of the form called *fu*.'

'I know it's descended from the ancient Chu Tzu

poetry,' Yün replied, 'but I have only studied it a little and it's hard to understand. Of the *fu* poets of the Han and Chin Dynasties, who had the best meter and the most refined language, I think Hsiang-ju was the best.'

I jokingly said, 'So perhaps Wen-chün did not fall in love with Hsiang-ju because of the way he played the lute after all, but because of his poetry?' The conversation ended with us both laughing loudly.

I am by nature candid and unconstrained, but Yün was scrupulous and meticulously polite. When I would occasionally put a cape over her shoulders or help her adjust her sleeves, she would invariably say, 'I beg your pardon.' If I gave her a handkerchief or a fan, she would always stand to take it. At first I did not like her acting like this, and once I said to her, 'Do you think that by being so polite you can make me do as you like? For it is said that "Deceit hides behind too much courtesy".'

Yün blushed. 'Why should respect and good manners be called deceit?'

'True respect comes from the heart, not from empty words,' I said.

'There is no one closer to us than our parents,' Yün said, arguing with me now. 'But how could we merely respect them in our hearts while being rude in our treatment of them?'

'But I was only joking,' I protested.

'Most arguments people have begin with a joke,' Yün

said. 'Don't ever argue with me for the fun of it again – it makes me so angry I could die!'

I pulled her close to me, patted her back, and comforted her. Her anger passed and she began to smile. From then on, the polite phrases 'How dare I?' and 'I beg your pardon' became mere expressions to us. We lived together with the greatest mutual respect for three and twenty years, and as the years passed we grew ever closer.

Whenever we would meet one another in a darkened room or a narrow hallway of the house, we would hold hands and ask, 'Where are you going?' We felt furtive, as if we were afraid others would see us. In fact, at first we even avoided being seen walking or sitting together, though after a while we thought nothing of it. If Yün were sitting and talking with someone and saw me come in, she would stand up and move over to me and I would sit down beside her. Neither of us thought about this and it seemed quite natural; and though at first we felt embarrassed about it, we gradually grew accustomed to doing it. The strangest thing to me then was how old couples seemed to treat one another like enemies. I did not understand why. Yet people said, 'Otherwise, how could they grow old together?' Could this be true? I wondered.

On the evening of the 7th day of the seventh month that year, Yün lit candles and set out fruit on the altar by the Pavilion of My Desire, and we worshipped Tien Sun together. I had had two matching seals engraved with the inscription, 'May we remain husband and wife in all our lives to come'; on mine the characters were raised and on hers they were incised. We used them to sign the letters we wrote one another. That night the moonlight was very lovely, and as it was reflected in the stream it turned the ripples of the water as white as silk. We sat together near the water wearing light robes and fanned ourselves gently as we looked up at the clouds flying across the sky and changing into ten thousand shapes.

Yün said, 'The world is so vast, but still everyone looks up at the same moon. I wonder if there is another couple in the world as much in love as we are.'

'Naturally there are people everywhere who like to enjoy the night air and gaze at the moon,' I said, 'and there are more than a few women who enjoy discussing the sunset. But when a man and wife look at it together, I don't think it is the sunset they will wind up talking about.' The candles soon burned out, and the moon set. We took the fruit inside and went to bed.

The 15th day of the seventh month, when the moon is full, is the day called the Ghost Festival. Yün had prepared some small dishes, and we had planned to invite the moon to drink with us. But when night came, clouds suddenly darkened the sky.

Yün grew melancholy and said, 'If I am to grow old together with you, the moon must come out.'

I also felt depressed. On the opposite bank I could see will-o'-the-wisps winking on and off like ten thousand fireflies, as their light threaded through the high grass and willow trees that grew on the small island in the stream. To get ourselves into a better mood Yün and I began composing a poem out loud, with me offering the first couplet, her the second, and so on. After the first two couplets we gradually became less and less restrained and more and more excited, until we were saying anything that came into our heads. Yün was soon laughing so hard that she cried, and had to lean up against me, unable to speak a word. The heavy scent of jasmine in her hair assailed my nostrils, so to stop her laughing I patted her on the back and changed the subject, saying, 'I thought women of ancient times put jasmine flowers in their hair because they resembled pearls. I never realized that the jasmine is so attractive when mixed with the scent of women's make-up, much more attractive than the lime.'

Yün stopped laughing. 'Lime is the gentleman of perfumes,' she said, 'and you notice its scent unconsciously. But the jasmine is a commoner that has to rely on a woman's make-up for its effect. It's suggestive, like a wicked smile.'

'So why are you avoiding the gentleman and taking up with the commoner?'

'I'm only making fun of gentlemen who love commoners,' she replied.

Just as we were speaking, the water clock showed midnight. The wind gradually began to sweep the clouds away, and the full moon finally came out. We were delighted, and drank some wine leaning against the windowsill. But before we had finished three cups we heard a loud noise from under the bridge, as if someone had fallen into the water. We leaned out of the window and looked around carefully. The surface of the stream was as bright as a mirror, but we saw not a thing. We only heard the sound of a duck running quickly along the river bank. I knew that the ghosts of people who had drowned often appeared by the river near the Pavilion of the Waves, but I was worried that Yün would be afraid and so I did not dare tell her.

'Yi!' she said, none the less frightened for my silence. 'Where did that sound come from?'

We could not keep ourselves from trembling. I closed the window and we took the wine into the bedroom. The flame in the lamp was as small as a bean, and the curtains around the bed cast shadows that writhed like snakes. We were still frightened. I turned up the lamp and we got into bed, but Yün was already suffering hot and cold attacks from the shock. I caught the same fever, and we were ill for twenty days. It is true what people say, that happiness carried to an extreme turns into sadness. The events of that day were another omen that we were not to grow old together.

By the time of the Mid-Autumn Festival I had just started to feel better, though I was still a little weak. Yün had by this time been my wife for half a year without once going next door to the Pavilion of the Waves, so one evening I sent an old servant there to tell the gate-keeper not to let in any other visitors. Just as night was falling, Yün, my little sister, and I walked there. Two servants helped me along and another led the way. We crossed the stone bridge, went in at the gate, and took a small winding path along the eastern side of the gardens. There were rocks piled up into small artificial mountains, and trees with luxuriant light green leaves. The pavilion itself stood on top of a small hill. Steps led up to the summit, from where you could see all around for several miles. The smoke of cooking fires rose up from every direction into the brilliant twilight. On the opposite bank was a place called Chinshan Woods, where high officials would hold formal banquets; at that time the Chengyi Academy had not yet been established there. We had taken along a blanket which we spread out in the middle of the pavilion, and we all sat around in a circle on it, while the gate-keeper made tea and brought it up to us. A full moon soon rose above the trees, and we gradually felt a breeze beginning to tug at our sleeves. The moon shone on the stream below, and quickly drove away our cares.

'This is such fun!' said Yün. 'Wouldn't it be wonderful if we had a small skiff to row around in the stream down there?'

The time had come to light the lanterns, so, still thinking of the shock we had received on the night of the Ghost Festival, we left the pavilion and went home, holding hands all the way. It is a Soochow custom that on the night of the Mid-Autumn Festival women, regardless of whether they come from a well-off family or not, all come out in groups to stroll. This is called the 'moonlight walk'. But although the Pavilion of the Waves was elegant and peaceful, no one had come there that night.

My father, the Honourable Chia-fu, liked to adopt sons, so I had twenty-six brothers with surnames different from mine. My mother too had adopted nine daughters; Miss Wang, the second of them, and Miss Yü, the sixth, got on best with Yün. Miss Wang was a simple girl who enjoyed drinking, while Miss Yü was open and loved to talk. Every time they got together they would exile me so that the three of them could sleep in the same bed. This was Miss Yü's idea.

'After you are married,' I once joked with her, 'I will invite your husband over and make him stay at least ten days.'

'I'll come along too,' she replied, 'and sleep with your wife. Won't that be fun?' Yün and Miss Wang said nothing, but only smiled.

At the time of my younger brother Chi-tang's marriage, we moved to Granary Lane, near the Drinking Horses Bridge. Although the new house was big, it was not as elegant as the one near the Pavilion of the Waves. For my mother's birthday that year we had an opera troupe come to perform, and Yün at first thought it was quite wonderful. My father had never been superstitious, however, so he had no compunctions about asking for the performance of *The Sad Parting*. The actors were excellent and, watching it, we were very moved.

But while the performance was still going on, I saw Yün suddenly get up from behind the screen where the women were seated and go to our room. After a long while she had still not returned, so I went in to look for her, Miss Yü and Miss Wang following me. We found Yün sitting alone beside the dressing table with her head in her hands.

'Are you unhappy about something?' I asked her.

'Seeing an opera is supposed to be entertaining,' Yün said. 'But today's is heartbreaking.'

Both Miss Yü and Miss Wang were laughing at her, but I told them they had to understand what a very emotional person she was. Still, Miss Yü asked her, 'Are you going to sit here by yourself all day?'

'When there's something I like, I'll go back and watch it,' Yün replied. Miss Wang went out as soon as she'd heard this, and asked my mother to tell them to perform things like *Tse Liang* and *Hou So*. After some urging Yün came out to watch, and soon began to cheer up.

My father's cousin, the Honourable Su-tsun, died young leaving no descendants, so my father named me to inherit from him. His grave was on ancestral ground at Hsikuatang on the Mountain of Prosperity and Longevity, and every spring I had to take Yün there to sweep the grave and perform the rites. Second sister Wang had heard of a beautiful place on the mountain called the Ko Garden, and so she once asked to go along with us.

That day Yün saw some stones on the mountainside that were streaked with beautiful colours. 'If we put some in a bowl to make a little mountain,' she said, 'they would look even better than white stones from Hsüanchou.'

I told Yün I feared it would be hard to find enough stones to do that, but Miss Wang volunteered to collect them. She immediately went to the grave-keeper and borrowed a hempen bag, and then began collecting the stones, walking along as slowly and as deliberately as a crane. She would pick up each one, and if I said 'good' she would keep it; if I said 'no', she would throw it away.

Before long she was perspiring heavily and, dragging her bag, she came back to us and said, 'I don't have the strength to pick up any more.'

'I've heard that if you want to collect fruit in the mountains,' said Yün as she selected the stones she wanted, 'you have to get a monkey to do it for you. Now I know that that's true!'

Miss Wang rubbed her hands together furiously, as if she were going to tickle Yün in revenge for her joke. I stood between them to stop her, and scolded Yün. 'Miss Wang has been working while you've been relaxing, and still you talk like that. No wonder she's angry.'

On the way back we strolled through the Ko Garden, where the fresh, light green leaves and the delicate red flowers seemed to be competing over which was the most beautiful. Miss Wang always had been a foolish girl, and as soon as she saw the flowers she thought she had to pick some. Yün scolded her. 'You have no vase to put them in, and you're not going to put them in your hair either. Why are you picking so many?'

'They feel no pain,' Miss Wang said, 'so what's the harm?'

I laughed and told her, 'You are going to marry a pock-marked, hairy fellow. That will be the flowers' revenge.'

Miss Wang looked at me angrily, threw the flowers on the ground, and kicked them into a pond with her tiny foot. 'How can you make fun of me like this?' she said. But Yün joked with her, and her anger passed.

When we were first married Yün was very quiet, and enjoyed listening to me discuss things. But I drew her out, as a man will use a blade of grass to encourage a cricket to chirp, and she gradually became able to express herself, as the following conversation proves.

Every day Yün would mix her rice with tea. She liked to eat a spicy, salty kind of beancurd that Soochow people call 'stinking beancurd'. She also liked pickled cucumber. These last two were things I had hated all my life, so one day I said to her, 'Dogs have no stomach, and eat dung because they do not realize how bad it smells. A beetle rolls in its dung so it can become a cicada, because it wants to fly as high as it can. Which are you, a dog or a beetle?'

'That kind of beancurd is cheap,' Yün said, 'and it tastes good with either rice porridge or plain rice. I've eaten it since I was a child. As I am now living in your home I'm like the beetle that has become a cicada, and the reason I still like to eat the beancurd is that I have not forgotten my former life. As for pickled cucumber, the first time I had it was here in your home.'

'In other words, my house is a doghouse?' I said, continuing to joke with her.

Yün was embarrassed and quickly explained. 'There is dung in every house. The only question is whether one eats it. I don't like garlic, but I still eat it because you like it. I would never ask you to eat stinking beancurd; but as for pickled cucumber, if you would only hold your nose and eat some you would realize how good it is. It's like the old stories about the girl named Wu-yen, who was ugly but virtuous.'

'Now are you trying to get me to behave like a dog?'

'I've been acting like a dog for a long time,' Yün said. 'Why don't you try it?' Upon which she picked up a piece of pickled cucumber with her chopsticks and forced it into my mouth. I held my nose and chewed, and it did seem quite good. I took my hand away and continued chewing, and to my surprise found it did have rather a special taste. From then on, I too began to enjoy eating it.

Yün also ate salted beancurd by pouring sesame seed oil and a little sugar over it, and that was wonderful. She would sometimes eat the beancurd by mixing it with a paste of pickled cucumber; this she called 'double-delicious sauce', and it was very good.

One day I said to her, 'At first I did not like any of these things, but now I have come to like all of them very much. I cannot understand why.'

'If you like something,' said Yün, 'you don't care if it's ugly.'

My younger brother Chi-tang's wife is the granddaughter of Wang Hsü-chou. As the time for their marriage approached, she discovered she did not have enough pearl flowers. Yün took out her own pearls that she had been given when we were married, and gave them to my mother for her to give to my brother's fiancée. The servants thought it was a pity that she should give up her own jewellery.

'Women are entirely *yin* in nature,' Yün told them, 'and pearls are the essence of *yin*. If you wear them in your hair, they completely overcome the spirit of *yang*. So why should I value them?'

On the other hand, she prized shabby old books and tattered paintings. She would take the partial remnants of old books, separate them all into sections by topic, and then have them rebound. These she called her 'Fragments of Literature'. When she found some calligraphy or a painting that had been ruined, she felt she had to search for a piece of old paper on which to remount it. If there were portions missing, she would ask me to restore them. These she named the 'Collection of Discarded Delights'.

Yün would work on these projects the whole day without becoming tired, whenever she could take time off from her sewing and cooking. If, in an old trunk or a shabby book, she came across a piece of paper with something on it, she acted as if she had found something very special. Every time our neighbour, old lady Fung, got hold of some scraps of old books, she would sell them to Yün.

Yün's habits and tastes were the same as mine. She understood what my eyes said, and the language of my brows. She did everything according to my expression, and everything she did was as I wished it.

Once I said to her, 'It's a pity that you are a woman and have to remain hidden away at home. If only you could become a man we could visit famous mountains and search out magnificent ruins. We could travel the whole world together. Wouldn't that be wonderful?'

'What is so difficult about that?' Yün replied. 'After my hair begins to turn white, although we could not go so far as to visit the Five Sacred Mountains, we could still visit places nearer by. We could probably go together to Hufu and Lingyen, and south to the West Lake and north to Ping Mountain.'

'By the time your hair begins to turn white, I'm afraid you will find it hard to walk,' I told her.

'Then if we can't do it in this life, I hope we will do it in the next.'

'In our next life I hope you will be born a man,' I said. 'I will be a woman, and we can be together again.'

The Old Man of the Moon

'That would be lovely,' said Yün, 'especially if we could still remember this life.'

I laughed. 'We still haven't finished talking about that business with the rice porridge when we were young. If in the next life we can still remember this one, we will have so much to talk about on our wedding night that we will never get to sleep!'

'People say that marriages are arranged by the "Old Man of the Moon",' said Yün. 'He has already pulled us together in this life, and in the next we will have to depend on him too. Why don't we have a picture of him painted so we can worship him?'

At that time the famous portraitist Chi Liu-ti, whose literary name was Chun, was living in Tiaohsi, and we asked him to paint the picture for us. He portrayed the old man carrying his red silk cord in one hand, while with the other he grasped his walking stick with the *Book of Marriages* tied to the top of it. Though his hair was white, his face was that of a child, and he was striding through mist and fog. This was the best painting that Mr Chi ever did. My friend Shih Cho-tang wrote a complimentary inscription at the top of the painting, and I hung it in our room. On the 1st and the 15th days of each month, Yün and I would light incense and worship in front of it. Later, because of the many things that happened to our family, the painting was somehow lost and I have no idea in whose home it hangs now. 'Our next life is not known, while this life closes.' Our passion was so great. Will the Old Man understand and help us once again?

After we moved to Granary Lane, I called our upstairs bedroom the Pavilion of My Guest's Fragrance, after Yün's name and the idea that husbands and wives should treat each other like guests. The new house had only a small garden and high walls, and there was nothing much that we liked about it. At the back there was a row of small rooms off the library, but when their windows were open there was nothing to see but the overgrown Lu Family Garden, which was a desolate sight. It was from this time that Yün began to miss the scenery of the Pavilion of the Waves.

There was then an old woman who lived east of the Chinmu Bridge and north of Keng Lane. Her cottage was surrounded by a vegetable garden, and had a rattan gate. Outside the gate there was a pond about one *mou* in size that reflected the interwoven images of the flowers and the shadows of the trees. The place was the site of the ruins of the palace that Chang Shih-cheng had built at the end of the Yüan Dynasty. Immediately to the west of her house there was a pile of broken bricks as big as a small hill, and if you climbed to the top you could see for a long way, a large area with few people and great wild beauty. The old woman once spoke of the place to Yün, who wanted very much to go and see it. 'Since we left the Pavilion of the Waves,' she told me, 'I dream about it night and day. As we cannot go back there, the only thing

The Old Man of the Moon

I can think of now is trying to find a substitute for it. What about this old woman's house?'

'In the worst heat of the early autumn,' I said, 'I think every morning of having a cool place to pass the long days. If you're interested, I'll have a look first and see whether the house is habitable. If it is, we could take our bedding and stay there for a month. What would you think of that?'

'I'm afraid your parents will disapprove,' Yün said.

I told her I would ask their permission myself, and the next day I went to look over the house. It had only two rooms, one in front and one at the back, each divided by a partition. The windows were paper and the bed of bamboo, and the place had altogether a subtle charm about it. When the old woman heard what we wanted, she was very happy to rent the bedroom to us. I pasted white paper up on the walls, and soon it looked like a different place entirely. I then respectfully informed my mother, and took Yün to live there.

Our only neighbours were an old couple who raised vegetables for a living. Learning we had come to escape the summer's heat, they came to call on us, bringing gifts of fish from the pond and vegetables from the garden. I tried to pay for them, but they would not take anything, so Yün made them some shoes, which we finally prevailed on them to accept.

It was then the beginning of the seventh month, with dark shadows among the green trees. There was a breeze across the water, and the songs of cicadas were everywhere. The old couple also made us a fishing pole, and I took Yün fishing in the deep shadows of the willow trees.

When the sun was going down, we would climb to the top of the small hill and admire the twilight. We used to make up impromptu poems there, one line of which was, 'Beast-like clouds eat the setting sun, the bow-like moon shoots falling stars.' After a while, when the moonlight fell directly into the pond and the sound of insects came from all around, we would move the bed out beside the fence. The old woman would come to tell us when the wine was warm and the food was hot. We would drink in the moonlight until we were a little tipsy, and then eat. After having a wash, we would fan ourselves with banana leaves, and sit or lie down and listen to our old neighbours telling stories of sin and retribution. At three strokes of the night watch we would go in to sleep feeling cool and refreshed. It was almost like not living in the city at all.

We had asked the old couple to buy chrysanthemums and plant them all the way around the fence, and when the flowers bloomed in the ninth month I decided to stay there with Yün for ten more days. About then my mother came to visit us, and seemed quite happy with what she saw. We ate crabs beside the flowers, and thoroughly enjoyed the day.

'One day we should build a cottage here and buy ten

mou of land to make a garden around it,' said Yün happily. 'We could have servants plant melons and vegetables that would be enough to live on. What with your painting and my embroidery, it would give us enough to have a little to drink while we wrote poetry. We could live quite happily wearing cotton clothes and eating nothing but vegetables and rice. We would never have to leave here.' I deeply wished we could do so. The cottage is still there, but now I have lost my most intimate friend. It is enough to make one sigh deeply.

About half a *li* from my house, on Vinegar Warehouse Lane, was the Tungting Temple, which we usually called the Narcissus Temple. Inside there were winding covered paths and a small park with pavilions. Every year on the god's birthday the members of each family association would gather in their corner of the temple, hang up a special glass lantern, and erect a throne below it. Beside the throne they would set out vases filled with flowers, in a competition to see whose decorations were most beautiful. During the day operas were performed, and at night candles of different lengths were set out among the vases and the flowers. This was called the 'lighting of the flowers'. The colours of the flowers, the shadows of the lamps, and the fragrant smoke floating up from the incense urns, made it all seem like a night banquet at the palace of the Dragon King himself. The heads of the family associations would play the flute and sing, or brew fine tea and chat with one another. Townspeople gathered like ants to watch this spectacle, and a fence had to be put up under the eaves of the temple to keep them out.

One year some friends of mine invited me to go and help to arrange their flowers, so I had a chance to see the festival myself. I went home and told Yün how beautiful it was.

'What a shame that I cannot go just because I am not a man,' said Yün.

'If you wore one of my hats and some of my clothes, you could look like a man.'

Yün thereupon braided her hair into a plait and made up her eyebrows. She put on my hat, and though her hair showed a little around her ears it was easy to conceal. When she put on my robe we found it was an inch and a half too long, but she took it up around the waist and put on a riding jacket over it.

'What about my feet?' Yün asked.

'In the street they sell "butterfly shoes",' I said, 'in all sizes. They're easy to buy, and afterwards you can wear them around the house. Wouldn't they do?'

Yün was delighted, and when she had put on my clothes after dinner she practised for a long time, putting her hands into her sleeves and taking large steps like a man.

But suddenly she changed her mind. 'I am not going! It would be awful if someone found out. If your parents knew, they would never allow us to go.'

I still encouraged her to go, however. 'Everyone at the temple knows me. Even if they find out, they will only take it as a joke. Mother is at ninth sister's house, so if we come and go secretly no one will ever know.'

Yün looked at herself in the mirror and laughed endlessly. I pulled her along, and we left quietly. We walked all around inside the temple, with no one realizing she was a woman. If someone asked who she was, I would tell them she was my cousin. They would only fold their hands and bow to her.

At the last place we came to, young women and girls were sitting behind the throne that had been erected there. They were the family of a Mr Yang, one of the organizers of the festival. Without thinking, Yün walked over and began to chat with them as a woman quite naturally might, and as she bent over to do so she inadvertently laid her hand on the shoulder of one of the young ladies.

One of the maids angrily jumped up and shouted, 'What kind of a rogue are you, to behave like that!' I went over to try to explain, but Yün, seeing how embarrassing the situation could become, quickly took off her hat and kicked up her foot, saying, 'See, I am a woman too!'

At first they all stared at Yün in surprise, but then their anger turned to laughter. We stayed to have some tea and refreshments with them, and then called sedan chairs and went home.

* * *

In the seventh month of the Chiayen year of the reign of the Emperor Chien Lung I returned from Yüehtung with my friend Hsü Hsiu-feng, who was my cousin's husband. He brought a new concubine back with him, raving about her beauty to everyone, and one day he invited Yün to go and see her. Afterwards Yün said to Hsiu-feng, 'She certainly is beautiful, but she is not the least bit charming.'

'If your husband were to take a concubine,' Hsiu-feng asked, 'would she have to be charming as well as beautiful?'

'Naturally,' said Yün.

From then on, Yün was obsessed with the idea of finding me a concubine, even though we had nowhere near enough money for such an ambition.

There was a courtesan from Chekiang named Wen Leng-hsiang then living in Soochow. She was something of a poet, and had written four stanzas on the theme of willow catkins that had taken the city by storm, many talented writers composing couplets in response to her originals. My friend from Wuchiang, Chang Hsien-han, had long admired Leng-hsiang, and asked us to help him write some verses to accompany hers. Yün thought little of her and so declined, but I longed to write, and thus composed some verses to her rhyme. One couplet that Yün liked very much was, 'They arouse my springtime wistfulness, and ensnare her wandering fancy.'

A year later, on the 5th day of the eighth month, mother was planning to take Yün on a visit to Tiger Hill, when my friend Hsien-han suddenly arrived at our house. 'I am going to Tiger Hill too,' he said, 'and today I came

The Old Man of the Moon

especially to invite you to go with me and admire some flowers along the way.'

I then asked mother to go on ahead, and said I would meet her at Pantang near Tiger Hill. Hsien-han took me to Leng-hsiang's home, where I discovered that she was already middle-aged.

However, she had a daughter named Han-yüan, who, though not yet fully mature, was as beautiful as a piece of jade. Her eyes were as lovely as the surface of an autumn pond, and while they entertained us it became obvious that her literary knowledge was extensive. She had a younger sister named Wen-yüan who was still quite small.

At first I had no wild ideas and wanted only to have a cup of wine and chat with them. I well knew that a poor scholar like myself could not afford this sort of thing, and once inside I began to feel quite nervous. While I did not show my unease in my conversation, I did quietly say to Hsien-han 'I'm only a poor fellow. How can you invite these girls to entertain me?'

Hsien-han laughed. 'It's not that way at all. A friend of mine had invited me to come and be entertained by Han-yüan today, but then he was called away by an important visitor. He asked me to be the host and invite someone else. Don't worry about it.'

At that, I began to relax. Later, when our boat reached Pantang, I told Han-yüan to go aboard my mother's boat and pay her respects. That was when Yün met Han-yüan and, as happy as old friends at a reunion, they soon set off hand in hand to climb the hill in search of all the scenic spots it offered. Yün especially liked the height and vista of Thousand Clouds, and they sat there enjoying the view for some time. When we returned to Yehfangpin, we moored the boats side by side and drank long and happily.

As the boats were being unmoored, Yün asked me if Han-yüan could return aboard hers, while I went back with Hsien-han. To this, I agreed. When we returned to the Tuting Bridge we went back aboard our own boats and took leave of one another. By the time we arrived home it was already the third night watch.

'Today I have met someone who is both beautiful and charming,' said Yün. 'I have just invited Han-yüan to come and see me tomorrow, so I can try to arrange things for you.'

'But we're not a rich family,' I said, worried. 'We cannot afford to keep someone like that. How could people as poor as ourselves dare think of such a thing? And we are so happily married, why should we look for someone else?'

'But I love her too,' Yün said, laughing. 'You just let me take care of everything.'

The next day at noon, Han-yüan actually came. Yün entertained her warmly, and during the meal we played a game – the winner would read a poem, while the loser had to drink a cup of wine. By the end of the meal still not a word had been said about our obtaining Han-yüan.

The Old Man of the Moon

As soon as she left, Yün said to me, 'I have just made a secret agreement with her. She will come here on the 18th, and we will pledge ourselves as sisters. You will have to prepare animals for the sacrifice.'

Then, laughing and pointing to the jade bracelet on her arm, she said, 'If you see this bracelet on Han-yüan's arm then, it will mean she has agreed to our proposal. I have just told her my idea, but I am still not very sure what she thinks about it all.'

I only listened to what she said, making no reply.

It rained very hard on the 18th, but Han-yüan came all the same. She and Yün went into another room and were alone there for some time. They were holding hands when they emerged, and Han-yüan looked at me shyly. She was wearing the jade bracelet!

We had intended, after the incense was burned and they had become sisters, that we should carry on drinking. As it turned out, however, Han-yüan had promised to go on a trip to Stone Lake, so she left as soon as the ceremony was over.

'She has agreed,' Yün told me happily. 'Now, how will you reward your go-between?' I asked her the details of the arrangement.

'Just now I spoke to her privately because I was afraid she might have another attachment. When she said she did not, I asked her, "Do you know why we have invited you here today, little sister?"

'"The respect of an honourable lady like yourself makes

me feel like a small weed leaning up against a great tree," she replied, "but my mother has high hopes for me, and I'm afraid I cannot agree without consulting her. I do hope, though, that you and I can think of a way to work things out."

'When I took off the bracelet and put it on her arm I said to her, "The jade of this bracelet is hard and represents the constancy of our pledge; and like our pledge, the circle of the bracelet has no end. Wear it as the first token of our understanding." To which she replied, "The power to unite us rests entirely with you." So it seems as if we have already won over Han-yüan. The difficult part will be convincing her mother, but I will think of a plan for that.'

I laughed, and asked her, 'Are you trying to imitate Li-weng's *Pitying the Fragrant Companion*?'

'Yes,' she replied.

From that time on there was not a day that Yün did not talk about Han-yüan. But later Han-yüan was taken off by a powerful man, and all the plans came to nothing. In fact, it was because of this that Yün died.

* * *

Yün had had the blood sickness ever since her younger brother Ko-chang had run away from home and her mother had missed him so much that she died of grief. Yün was so distraught she had fallen ill herself. From the time she met Han-yüan, she passed no blood for over a

The Old Man of the Moon

year, and I was delighted that Yün had found such a good cure in her friend, when Han-yüan was snatched away by an influential man who paid a thousand golds for her and also promised to take care of her mother. 'The beauty belongs to Sha-shih-li!' I had learned of all this but had not dared to say anything to Yün, so she did not find out about it until one day when she went to see Han-yüan. She returned weeping, and said, 'I had not thought Han's feelings could be so shallow!'

'Your own feelings are too deep,' I said. 'How can that sort of person be said to have feelings? Someone who is used to beautiful clothes and delicate foods could never grow accustomed to thorn hairpins and plain cloth dresses. It's better that we should be unsuccessful now than to have her regret things later.'

I comforted her repeatedly, but having been so wounded Yün still suffered great discharges of blood. She was bedridden and did not respond to any treatment. She suffered relapses, and became so thin you could see her bones. After a few years the money we owed increased daily, and so did the gossip about us. And because she had pledged sisterhood with a sing-song girl, my parents' scorn for Yün deepened daily. I became the mediator between my parents and my wife. It was no way to live!

Yün had given birth to a girl named Ching-chün, who by then was fourteen years old. She could read and write well and was also very capable, so fortunately we could rely on her help in pawning hairpins and clothes. Our son was named Feng-sen; at this time he was twelve years old and was studying reading with a teacher. I was then without employment for several years, so I had opened up a shop in our home, selling books and paintings. But I did not make enough in three days to pay the expenses of one. I was weary and beset by hardships, and we often had no money. In the deepest winter I had no furs, but there was nothing to do but to be strong and bear the cold. Ching-chün, too, shivered in an unlined dress, though she bravely denied being cold. On account of this, Yün swore she would never spend the money to see a doctor or buy medicine.

Once during a period when Yün was able to get out of bed, it happened that my friend Chou Chun-hsi had just returned from Prince Fu's secretariat and wanted to hire someone to embroider the Heart Sutra for him. Yün thought that by embroidering a sutra she might bring us some luck to ease our difficulties, as well as getting a good price for her work, so despite her illness she agreed to do it. As it turned out Chun-hsi was only on a quick visit and could not wait long, needing the job completed in ten days. Yün was still weak, and the sudden work made her waist hurt and gave her dizzy spells. Who would have thought her fate was so bad that even the Buddha would not show her mercy! After she had embroidered the sutra, her illness worsened. First she would call for water, then she would want soup. The family began to grow weary of her.

The Old Man of the Moon

There was a Westerner who had rented the house to the left of my painting shop. He made his living by lending out money at interest, and I had come to know him when he asked me to do paintings for him. A friend of mine had once borrowed fifty golds from him, asking me to be the guarantor. I would have been embarrassed to refuse and so agreed to it, but then he ended up by running off with the loan. The Westerner had only me to ask for repayment, and often came to demand his money. At first I gave him paintings in lieu of payment, but gradually I came to have nothing left to give him. At the end of the year while my father was at home, he came again to demand repayment, and made a commotion at the gate.

When my father heard the noise he called for me and scolded me angrily, saying, 'We are a house of robes and caps. How could we owe money to someone like this!'

Just as I was about to explain, a messenger arrived. He had been sent by a woman who had been a sworn sister of Yün's as a child, who had married a man named Hua from Hsishan, and who had heard of her illness and wanted to inquire after her.

My father, however, mistakenly thought he was a messenger from Han-yüan and so became even angrier, saying, 'Your wife does not behave as a woman should, swearing sisterhood with a sing-song girl. Nor do you think to learn from your elders, running around with riff-raff. I cannot bear to send you to the execution ground, but I will give you only three days. Make plans to leave home, and make them quickly. If you take longer, you will lose your head for your disobedience!'

When Yün heard this she wept, and said, 'It is all my fault that father is so angry. Yet if I committed suicide and you left home, you could not bear it; and if I stayed here while you left, you could not stand it. Go secretly and tell the messenger from the Huas to come here. I will force myself to get out of bed and talk to him.'

I told Ching-chün to help her out of the bedroom, and fetched the messenger from the Huas. 'Did your mistress send you here specially,' Yün asked, 'or did you come because you just happened to be passing this way?'

The messenger replied, 'My mistress had heard of madam's illness some time ago, and originally wanted to come personally to visit you. But because she had never entered your gate before, she did not dare to come herself. As I was leaving she told me to say that if madam does not mind a plain and rustic life, she could come and build up her strength in the countryside, according to the pledge they made to one another under the lamplight when they were young.' This last referred to a pledge Yün and she had made once when they were embroidering together, to help one another if they were ever ill.

So Yün told him to go home quickly and ask his mistress to send a boat for us secretly two days later.

After he left, Yün said to me, 'Sister Hua is closer to me than my own flesh and blood. If you don't mind moving to her home, we can go there together. I'm afraid we won't be able to take the children with us, though, and we certainly cannot leave them here to trouble our parents. We will have to make arrangements for them in the next two days.'

At that time my cousin Wang Chin-chen had a son named Yün-shih and wanted to have Ching-chün for his daughter-in-law. 'I hear young Wang is timid and without much ability,' said Yün, 'and that while he will be able to keep up what the Wangs own, they do not own much to keep up. On the other hand, they are a respectable family and have only the one son. I think we should allow the marriage.'

I met with Chin-chen and said, 'My father and you have the friendship of Weiyang. If you want Ching-chün for your daughter-in-law I do not think he will refuse you. But she must be brought up a little longer before she is ready for marriage, and in the circumstances we will not be able to do that. After my wife and I have gone to Hsishan, how would you feel about going to my parents and asking for her first to be your child daughter-in-law?' He happily agreed to my suggestion.

I also made arrangements for our son Feng-sen, asking my friend Hsia Yi-shan to introduce him to someone from whom he could learn the business of trading. This was no sooner done than the Huas' boat arrived. It was then the 25th day of the twelfth month of 1800.

Yün said to me, 'Since we are leaving alone, I am afraid that not only will the neighbours laugh at us, but also that the Westerner will not let us go as we still cannot repay his loan. We must go quietly tomorrow morning at the fifth night watch.'

'But you are ill,' I protested. 'Can you stand the morning cold?'

'Life and death are governed by fate,' Yün replied. 'Do not worry about me.'

I secretly informed my father of what we were going to do, and he agreed to it. That night I first carried a little baggage down to the boat on a shoulder pole, and then told Feng-sen to go to sleep. Ching-chün was crying at her mother's side.

These were Yün's parting instructions to our daughter: 'Your mother has had a bitter fate and emotions that run too deep; therefore we have had these many problems. Fortunately your father has been kind to me, and there is nothing to worry about in our leaving. In two or three years we will be able to arrange for us all to be reunited. Go to your new home, behave as a proper woman in everything you do, and do not be like your mother. Your father-in-law and mother-in-law will be happy to have you, and will surely treat you well. You can take with you all the cases, boxes, and anything else we have left behind. Your little brother is still young, so we have not told him what we are doing. When we are about to leave, we will tell him that I am going to see a doctor and will be back in a few days; after we have left, explain everything to him, and let grandfather take care of him.'

At our side was the old woman who had once rented us her house so that we could escape the summer's heat. She wanted to go with us to the countryside, and since she could not she stood beside us wiping away her tears. Just before the striking of the fifth night watch we all ate some warm rice porridge.

Yün laughed bravely. 'Once it was rice porridge that brought us together,' she said, 'and now it is rice porridge that sends us away. If someone wrote a play about it, he could call it *The Romance of the Rice Porridge*.'

Feng-sen heard her talking and woke up, saying sleepily, 'What are you doing, mother?'

'I am going out to see a doctor,' Yün replied.

'Why so early?'

'Because it is far away. You and elder sister should stay home and be good. Do not make grandmother angry. I am going with your father and will be back in a few days.'

As the cock crowed three times, Yün, with tears in her eyes and her arm around the old woman, was just opening the back door to go out when Feng-sen cried loudly, 'Yi! My mother is not coming back!'

Ching-chün feared he would awaken others, so she quickly covered his mouth with her hand and comforted him. By this time Yün and I felt as if we were being torn apart, but there was nothing more we could say. We could only tell him not to cry.

After Ching-chün shut the door, Yün was able to walk only about a dozen steps from our lane before she was too tired to go any farther. We continued with me carrying Yün on my back and the old woman holding up the lantern. We had nearly reached the boat when we were almost arrested by a night patrolman, but fortunately the servant woman told him that Yün was her daughter who was ill and that I was her son-in-law. When the boatmen (who all worked for the Hua family) heard us talking, they came to meet us and helped us down to the boat. After we cast off Yün finally burst out crying, and wept bitterly. After this separation, mother and son never saw each other again.

Hua was named Ta-cheng, and he lived facing the mountains at Tungkaoshan in Wuhsi. He farmed the land himself, and was very simple and sincere. His wife – Yün's sworn sister – was from the Hsia family. It was early in the afternoon of that day before we arrived at their house. Madam Hua had been waiting for us by the gate, and when we arrived she led her two small daughters to the boat to greet us. Everyone was very happy to see us. Yün was helped ashore and we were treated very hospitably. After a while the neighbours' wives burst into the room along with their children, and stood around Yün looking her over. Some asked her questions, some offered her condolences, while others whispered to one another, all filling the house with the sound of their chatter.

Yün told Madam Hua, 'Today I feel just like the fisherman who wandered into Peach Blossom Spring!'

'Please don't laugh at our country folk,' replied

The Old Man of the Moon

Mrs Hua. 'That which they seldom see they consider most wonderful.'

Thus we settled down to pass the New Year. Only two score days after we arrived, by the Festival of the First Moon, Yün was starting to be able to get up and around. That night as we watched the dragon lanterns on the threshing floor, her spirits began to revive. I then began to feel at peace myself, and decided to talk our situation over with her. 'We have no future living here,' I said, 'but we are too short of money to go anywhere else. What do you think we should do?'

'I have been thinking about this too,' said Yün. 'Your elder sister's husband Fan Hui-lai is now chief accountant at the Chingchiang Salt Office. Ten years ago when he wanted to borrow ten golds from you we did not have the money and I pawned my hairpins to get it. Do you remember?'

'I had forgotten!'

'I hear Chingchiang is not far away. Why don't you go and see if he can help us?'

I did as she suggested. At the time it was very warm, and I felt the heat even dressed only in a woollen gown and a worsted short jacket. This was the 16th day of the first month of 1801. That night I spent at an inn at Hsishan, where I rented bedding.

The next morning I took a boat for Chiangyin, but the winds were against us and there was a continuous drizzle. By the time we reached the river mouth at Chiangyin the spring cold was cutting me to the bone. I bought some wine to ward off the cold, but that exhausted my purse. All night I tried to decide whether I should sell my undergarments to get money for the ferry.

By the 19th the north wind was stronger and the snow was deeper everywhere. I could not hold back bitter tears. Alone, I worked out lodging and ferry expenses, and did not dare to buy any more to drink. I was trembling in soul and body when an old man suddenly entered the inn, wearing straw sandals and a felt hat and carrying a yellow bag on his back. He looked at me as if he knew me.

'Aren't you Tsao from Taichou?' I asked.

'I am,' he replied, 'and if it were not for you I would be lying dead in a ditch by now! My little girl is well, and she often sings your praises. What a surprise to meet you today! What are you hanging about here for?'

Now when I was working in the government offices at Taichou there was this same Tsao, a poor man with a beautiful daughter who had already been betrothed. But then a man of some influence had loaned him money in a plan to obtain his daughter, and it had all led to legal proceedings. I had helped protect them and send his daughter back to her betrothed. In his gratitude, Tsao had volunteered as a servant at the *yamen* and kowtowed to me, and so I had come to know him. I told him how I had been going to see my brother-in-law and had run into the snowstorm.

'I am heading that way myself,' Tsao said. 'If the

The Old Man of the Moon

weather clears tomorrow I will take you there.' Then he took out money to buy wine, and was most courteous to me.

On the 20th, as soon as the monastery's morning bells began to ring, I heard the ferryman's shouts by the river mouth. I got up in a hurry and called to Tsao to come along. 'Don't be in such a rush,' he said. 'We should eat our fill before boarding the boat.'

Then he paid for my room and my meals, and took me off to buy something for breakfast. I had been delayed for days, and was anxious to get across on the ferry, so I did not feel like eating, but I forced down two sesame cakes. As we boarded the boat, the river wind cut through our garments like an arrow, and soon I was trembling in all four limbs.

'I hear a Chiangyin man has hung himself in Chingchiang,' said Tsao, 'and that his wife has chartered this boat to go there. We have to wait for her before we can cross.' I had to wait until noon before we cast off, still hungry and fighting the cold. By the time we reached Chingchiang the smoke from evening cooking fires was rising on all sides.

'There are two *yamen* at Chingchiang,' said Tsao. 'Is the man you are visiting at the one inside the wall or the one outside the wall?'

Staggering along behind him, I confessed I did not know. 'Then we might just as well stop here for the night,' Tsao said, 'and go to look for him tomorrow.'

My shoes and stockings were filthy with mud and wet through, so at the inn that night I asked to dry them by the fire. I gulped down a meal and fell into an exhausted sleep, however, so that by the time I awoke the next day my stockings were half burned.

That morning Tsao once again paid for my room and board. We arrived at the *yamen* inside the wall to find that Hui-lai had not yet got up, but on hearing that I had arrived he threw on some clothes and came out. Seeing the state I was in, he was very upset; 'What calamity has brought you here?' he asked.

'Just a moment,' I said. 'First, have you got two golds you can loan me to repay the man who brought me here?'

Hui-lai gave me two barbarian cakes and I offered them to Tsao. He was determined to refuse them, but finally accepted one and left. I then told Hui-lai everything that had happened, and why I had come.

'You and I are relatives by marriage,' he said, 'and even if there were no old debt I should do everything I could for you. But unfortunately our sea-going salt boats have just been taken by pirates. We are now trying to straighten out the accounts, and I have no means of finding the money. The best I could do would be to give you twenty coins of barbarian silver to repay the debt. Would that be all right?'

I had not had any extravagant hopes to begin with, so I accepted. I stayed on two more days, but when the sky cleared and the weather turned warmer I made plans to go back, returning to the Huas on the 25th.

The Old Man of the Moon

Yün asked whether I had run into the snow, and I told her about my ordeal. 'When it snowed I thought you had already reached Chingchiang,' she said sadly, 'but you were still held up at the river mouth. You were lucky to run into old Tsao. It's true that heaven watches over the good.'

Several days later we received a letter from Ching-chün telling us that Yi-shan had already found Feng-sen a job in a shop. Chin-chen had asked permission of my father and on the 24th day of the first month had taken Ching-chün to his home. Our children's affairs seemed well in order, but we were still sad at being parted from them.

By the beginning of the second month the sun was warmer and the wind less strong, and with the money I had got at Chingchiang I made some simple preparations to visit my old friend Hu Ken-tang at the Hanchiang Salt Bureau. There was a tax office there, where I succeeded in obtaining a position as secretary, after which body and soul were a little more settled.

In the eighth month of the next year, 1802, I received a letter from Yün saying, 'My illness is now completely cured. I don't think it is a good idea for me to live and board indefinitely at a home where I have neither relatives nor friends. I would like to join you at Hanchiang, and see the glory of Ping Mountain.'

After receiving this letter I rented a house of two spans facing the river outside the Hsienchun Gate at

Hanchiang, and went myself to the Huas to fetch Yün. Madam Hua presented us with a child servant called Ah Shuang, to help with housework and meals, and we agreed that one day we should all be neighbours. By this time it was already the tenth month, and bitterly cold on Ping Mountain, so Yün and I decided not to go there until spring.

With Yün recovered we were happy again, and full of hope that we could reunite our family. But before the month was out the tax bureau suddenly cut its staff by fifteen persons, and as I was only the friend of a friend, I was dismissed. At first Yün still managed to come up with a hundred plans for us, putting on a brave front to comfort me. Never did she in the least find fault, though by the second month of spring, 1803, she began to suffer great discharges of blood once again. I wanted to return to Chingchiang and beg my brother-in-law for more help, but, as Yün put it, 'It's better to ask for help from a friend than from a relative.'

'That's true,' I replied, 'but all our friends are now out of work as well. While they may be concerned about us, they could not help us if they wanted to.'

'Then fortunately the weather at least has turned warm,' said Yün, 'so you won't have to worry about the road being blocked by snow. Please go quickly, come back as soon as you can, and don't worry about my being ill. If anything were to happen to you, my sins would be even heavier.'

The Old Man of the Moon

Our income was irregular, but so that Yün would not worry I pretended to her that I was hiring a mule. In fact I walked, with some cakes in my bag and eating as I went. I headed south-east for about eighty or ninety *li*, twice taking a ferry across a forked river, and finally coming to a district where I could see no villages in any direction. I walked on until it grew late, but still saw only endless stretches of yellow sand and bright, twinkling stars. Finally I came to an earth god shrine, about five feet tall and surrounded by a low wall. A pair of cypress trees was planted beside it.

I kowtowed to the god and said a prayer. 'My name is Shen and I am from Soochow. I am going to visit relatives, but have lost my way. Let me borrow your temple for a night's rest. Blessed spirit, protect me.'

I then moved aside the small stone incense pot and squeezed myself into the shrine. It was big enough for only half my body, so I turned my wind cap around to cover my face and lay half inside the shrine with my knees sticking out. I shut my eyes and listened quietly, but the only sound was the whistling of the wind. With my feet tired and my spirits weak, I collapsed into sleep.

When I awoke it was already light in the east, and suddenly I heard the sound of walking and talking outside the wall. I rushed out to see who it was, and it turned out to be some local people passing by on their way to market. I asked the way to Chingchiang, and one of them told me, 'Go south ten *li* and you will come to the county seat at Taihsing City. Go straight through the town and then head east for another ten *li*, when you will come to an earthen mound. Pass eight of these mounds and you will come to Chingchiang. All these places are along the main road.'

I went back inside the shrine to return the incense pot to its original position, then kowtowed my thanks to the god and left. After passing through Taihsing I was able to take a wheelbarrow, and arrived at Chingchiang about four o'clock in the afternoon. I sent my calling card in to my brother-in-law's office, but only after a long while did the gate-keeper come out and tell me, 'His Honour Mr Fan has gone to Changchou on business.'

From the way he spoke, this sounded like an excuse. 'When will he be back?' I asked.

'I don't know.'

'Then I will wait for him,' I said, 'even if I have to wait a year.'

The gate-keeper saw that I meant what I said, and quietly asked me, 'Is His Honour Mr Fan's mother-in-law really your mother?'

'If she were not, I would not be waiting for Mr Fan to come back!'

'Then you just wait for him,' the gate-keeper said. After three days I was told Hui-lai had returned, and was given twenty-five golds. I hired a mule and hurried home.

I returned to find Yün moaning and weeping, looking as if something awful had happened. As soon as she saw me she burst out, 'Did you know that yesterday noon Ah Shuang stole all our things and ran away? I have asked people to search everywhere, but they still have not found him. Losing our things is a small matter, but what of our relationship with our friends? As we were leaving, his mother told me over and over again to take good care of him. I'm terribly worried he's running back home and will have to cross the Great River. And what will we do if his parents have hidden him to blackmail us? How can I face my sworn sister again?'

'Please calm down,' I said. 'You've been worrying about it too much. You can only blackmail someone who has money; with you and me, it's all our four shoulders can do to support our two mouths. Besides, in the half year the boy has been with us, we have given him clothing and shared our food with him. Our neighbours all know we have never once beaten him or scolded him. What's really happened is that the wretched child has ignored his conscience and taken advantage of our problems to run away with our belongings. Your sworn sister at the Huas' gave us a thief. How can you say you cannot face her? It is she who should not be able to face you. What we should do now is report this case to the magistrate, so as to avoid any questions being raised about it in the future.'

After Yün heard me speak, her mind seemed somewhat eased, but from then on she began frequently to talk in her sleep, calling out, 'Ah Shuang has run away!' or 'How could Han-yüan turn her back on me?' Her illness worsened daily.

Finally I was about to call a doctor to treat her, but she stopped me. 'My illness began because of my terribly deep grief over my brother's running away and my mother's death,' said Yün. 'It continued because of my affections, and now it has returned because of my indignation. I have always worried too much about things, and while I have tried my best to be a good daughter-in-law, I have failed.

'These are the reasons why I have come down with dizziness and palpitations of the heart. The disease has already entered my vitals, and there is nothing a doctor can do about it. Please do not spend money on something that cannot help.

'I have been happy as your wife these twenty-three years. You have loved me and sympathized with me in everything, and never rejected me despite my faults. Having had for my husband an intimate friend like you, I have no regrets over this life. I have had warm cotton clothes, enough to eat, and a pleasant home. I have strolled among streams and rocks, at places like the Pavilion of the Waves and the Villa of Serenity. In the midst of life, I have been just like an Immortal. But a true Immortal must go through many incarnations before reaching enlightenment. Who could dare hope to become an Immortal in only one lifetime? In our eagerness for immortality, we have only incurred the wrath of the Creator, and

The Old Man of the Moon

brought on our troubles with our passion. Because you have loved me too much, I have had a short life!'

Later she sobbed and spoke again. 'Even someone who lives a hundred years must still die one day. I am only sorry at having to leave you so suddenly and for so long, halfway through our journey. I will not be able to serve you for all your life, or to see Feng-sen's wedding with my own eyes.' When she finished, she wept great tears.

I forced myself to be strong and comforted her saying, 'You have been ill for eight years, and it has seemed critical many times. Why do you suddenly say such heartbreaking things now?'

'I have been dreaming every night that my parents have sent a boat to fetch me,' said Yün. 'When I shut my eyes it feels as if I'm floating, as if I were walking in the mist. Is my spirit leaving me, while only my body remains?'

'That is only because you are upset,' I said. 'If you will relax, drink some medicine, and take care of yourself, you will get better.'

Yün only sobbed again and said, 'If I thought I had the slightest thread of life left in me I would never dare alarm you by talking to you like this. But the road to the next world is near, and if I do not speak to you now there will never be a day when I can.

'It is all because of me that you have lost the affection of your parents and drifted apart from them. Do not worry, for after I die you will be able to regain their hearts. Your parents' springs and autumns are many, and when I die you should return to them quickly. If you cannot take my bones home, it does not matter if you leave my coffin here for a while until you can come for it. I also want you to find someone who is attractive and capable, to serve our parents and bring up my children. If you will do this for me, I can die in peace.'

When she had said this a great sad moan forced itself from her, as if she was in an agony of heartbreak.

'If you part from me half way I would never want to take another wife,' I said. 'You know the saying, "One who has seen the ocean cannot desire a stream, and compared with Wu Mountain there are no clouds anywhere."'

Yün then took my hand and it seemed there was something else she wanted to say, but she could only brokenly repeat the two words 'next life'. Suddenly she fell silent and began to pant, her eyes staring into the distance. I called her name a thousand times, but she could not speak. Two streams of agonized tears flowed from her eyes in torrents, until finally her panting grew shallow and her tears dried up. Her spirit vanished in the mist and she began her long journey. This was on the 30th day of the third month in the 7th year of the reign of the Emperor Chia Ching. When it happened there was a solitary lamp burning in the room. I looked up but saw nothing, there was nothing for my two hands to hold, and my heart felt as if it would shatter. How can there be anything greater than my everlasting grief?

My friend Hu Ken-tang loaned me ten golds, and by

selling every single thing remaining in the house I put together enough money to give my beloved a proper burial.

Alas! Yün came to this world a woman, but she had the feelings and abilities of a man. After she entered the gate of my home in marriage, I had to rush about daily to earn our clothing and food, there was never enough, but she never once complained. When I was living at home, all we had for entertainment was talk about literature. What a pity that she should have died in poverty and after long illness. And whose fault was it that she did? It was my fault, what else can I say? I would advise all the husbands and wives in the world not to hate one another, certainly, but also not to love too deeply. As it is said, 'An affectionate couple cannot grow old together.' My example should serve as a warning to others.

1. BOCCACCIO · *Mrs Rosie and the Priest*
2. GERARD MANLEY HOPKINS · *As kingfishers catch fire*
3. *The Saga of Gunnlaug Serpent-tongue*
4. THOMAS DE QUINCEY · *On Murder Considered as One of the Fine Arts*
5. FRIEDRICH NIETZSCHE · *Aphorisms on Love and Hate*
6. JOHN RUSKIN · *Traffic*
7. PU SONGLING · *Wailing Ghosts*
8. JONATHAN SWIFT · *A Modest Proposal*
9. *Three Tang Dynasty Poets*
10. WALT WHITMAN · *On the Beach at Night Alone*
11. KENKŌ · *A Cup of Sake Beneath the Cherry Trees*
12. BALTASAR GRACIÁN · *How to Use Your Enemies*
13. JOHN KEATS · *The Eve of St Agnes*
14. THOMAS HARDY · *Woman much missed*
15. GUY DE MAUPASSANT · *Femme Fatale*
16. MARCO POLO · *Travels in the Land of Serpents and Pearls*
17. SUETONIUS · *Caligula*
18. APOLLONIUS OF RHODES · *Jason and Medea*
19. ROBERT LOUIS STEVENSON · *Olalla*
20. KARL MARX AND FRIEDRICH ENGELS · *The Communist Manifesto*
21. PETRONIUS · *Trimalchio's Feast*
22. JOHANN PETER HEBEL · *How a Ghastly Story Was Brought to Light by a Common or Garden Butcher's Dog*
23. HANS CHRISTIAN ANDERSEN · *The Tinder Box*
24. RUDYARD KIPLING · *The Gate of the Hundred Sorrows*
25. DANTE · *Circles of Hell*
26. HENRY MAYHEW · *Of Street Piemen*
27. HAFEZ · *The nightingales are drunk*
28. GEOFFREY CHAUCER · *The Wife of Bath*
29. MICHEL DE MONTAIGNE · *How We Weep and Laugh at the Same Thing*
30. THOMAS NASHE · *The Terrors of the Night*
31. EDGAR ALLAN POE · *The Tell-Tale Heart*
32. MARY KINGSLEY · *A Hippo Banquet*
33. JANE AUSTEN · *The Beautifull Cassandra*
34. ANTON CHEKHOV · *Gooseberries*
35. SAMUEL TAYLOR COLERIDGE · *Well, they are gone, and here must I remain*
36. JOHANN WOLFGANG VON GOETHE · *Sketchy, Doubtful, Incomplete Jottings*
37. CHARLES DICKENS · *The Great Winglebury Duel*
38. HERMAN MELVILLE · *The Maldive Shark*
39. ELIZABETH GASKELL · *The Old Nurse's Story*
40. NIKOLAY LESKOV · *The Steel Flea*

41. HONORÉ DE BALZAC · *The Atheist's Mass*
42. CHARLOTTE PERKINS GILMAN · *The Yellow Wall-Paper*
43. C.P. CAVAFY · *Remember, Body...*
44. FYODOR DOSTOEVSKY · *The Meek One*
45. GUSTAVE FLAUBERT · *A Simple Heart*
46. NIKOLAI GOGOL · *The Nose*
47. SAMUEL PEPYS · *The Great Fire of London*
48. EDITH WHARTON · *The Reckoning*
49. HENRY JAMES · *The Figure in the Carpet*
50. WILFRED OWEN · *Anthem For Doomed Youth*
51. WOLFGANG AMADEUS MOZART · *My Dearest Father*
52. PLATO · *Socrates' Defence*
53. CHRISTINA ROSSETTI · *Goblin Market*
54. *Sindbad the Sailor*
55. SOPHOCLES · *Antigone*
56. RYŪNOSUKE AKUTAGAWA · *The Life of a Stupid Man*
57. LEO TOLSTOY · *How Much Land Does A Man Need?*
58. GIORGIO VASARI · *Leonardo da Vinci*
59. OSCAR WILDE · *Lord Arthur Savile's Crime*
60. SHEN FU · *The Old Man of the Moon*
61. AESOP · *The Dolphins, the Whales and the Gudgeon*
62. MATSUO BASHŌ · *Lips too Chilled*
63. EMILY BRONTË · *The Night is Darkening Round Me*
64. JOSEPH CONRAD · *To-morrow*
65. RICHARD HAKLUYT · *The Voyage of Sir Francis Drake Around the Whole Globe*
66. KATE CHOPIN · *A Pair of Silk Stockings*
67. CHARLES DARWIN · *It was snowing butterflies*
68. BROTHERS GRIMM · *The Robber Bridegroom*
69. CATULLUS · *I Hate and I Love*
70. HOMER · *Circe and the Cyclops*
71. D. H. LAWRENCE · *Il Duro*
72. KATHERINE MANSFIELD · *Miss Brill*
73. OVID · *The Fall of Icarus*
74. SAPPHO · *Come Close*
75. IVAN TURGENEV · *Kasyan from the Beautiful Lands*
76. VIRGIL · *O Cruel Alexis*
77. H. G. WELLS · *A Slip under the Microscope*
78. HERODOTUS · *The Madness of Cambyses*
79. *Speaking of Siva*
80. *The Dhammapada*

'An ass, clothed in the skin of a lion . . .'

AESOP

Generally believed to have lived in the 6th century BC.

AESOP IN PENGUIN CLASSICS
The Complete Fables

AESOP

The Dolphins, the Whales and the Gudgeon

Translated by
Robert *and* Olivia Temple

PENGUIN BOOKS

PENGUIN CLASSICS

UK | USA | Canada | Ireland | Australia
India | New Zealand | South Africa

Penguin Books is part of the Penguin Random House group of companies whose addresses can be found at global.penguinrandomhouse.com.

This selection published in Penguin Classics 2015
010

Translation copyright © Robert and Olivia Temple, 1998

Set in 9/11.9 pt Baskerville 10 Pro
Typeset by Jouve (UK), Milton Keynes
Printed and bound in Great Britain by Clays Ltd, Elcograf S.p.A.

A CIP catalogue record for this book is available from the British Library

ISBN: 978-0-141-39843-3

www.greenpenguin.co.uk

Penguin Random House is committed to a sustainable future for our business, our readers and our planet. This book is made from Forest Stewardship Council® certified paper.

The Eagle, the Jackdaw and the Shepherd

An eagle, dropping suddenly from a high rock, carried off a lamb. A jackdaw saw this, was smitten by a sense of rivalry and determined to do the same. So, with a great deal of noise, he pounced upon a ram. But his claws merely got caught in the thick ringlets of the ram's fleece, and no matter how frantically he flapped his wings, he was unable to get free and take flight.

Finally the shepherd bestirred himself, hurried up to the jackdaw and got hold of him. He clipped the end of his wings and, when evening fell, he carried him back for his children. The children wanted to know what sort of bird this was. So the shepherd replied:

'As far as I can see, it's a jackdaw, but it would like us to think it's an eagle!'

Just so, to compete with the powerful is not only not worth the effort and labour lost, but also brings mockery and calamity upon us.

The Cat and the Cock

A cat who had caught a cock wanted to give a plausible reason for devouring it. So she accused it of annoying people by crowing at night and disturbing their sleep.

The cock defended himself by saying that he did it to be helpful. For, if he woke people up, it was to summon them to their accustomed work.

Then the cat produced another grievance and accused the cock of insulting Nature by his relationship with his mother and sisters.

The cock replied that in this also he was serving his master's interests, since it was thanks to this that the chickens laid lots of eggs.

'Ah well!' cried the cat, 'I'm not going to go without food just because you can produce a lot of justifications!' And she ate the cock.

This fable shows that someone with a wicked nature who is determined to do wrong, when he cannot do so in the guise of a good man, does his evil deeds openly.

The Goat and the Donkey

A man kept a goat and a donkey. The goat became jealous of the donkey, because it was so well fed. So she said to him:

'What with turning the millstone and all the burdens you carry, your life is just a torment without end.'

She advised him to pretend to have epilepsy and to fall into a hole in order to get some rest. The donkey followed her advice, fell down and was badly bruised all over. His master went to get the vet and asked him for a remedy for these injuries. The vet prescribed an infusion of goat's lung; this remedy would surely restore him to health. As a result, the man sacrificed the goat to cure the donkey.

Whosoever schemes against others owes his own misfortune to himself.

The Two Cocks and the Eagle

Two cockerels were fighting over some hens. One triumphed and saw the other off. The defeated one then withdrew into a thicket where he hid himself. The victor fluttered up into the air and sat atop a high wall, where he began to crow with a loud voice.

Straight away an eagle fell upon him and carried him off. And, from then on, the cockerel hidden in the shadows possessed all the hens at his leisure.

This fable shows that the Lord resisteth the proud but giveth grace unto the humble.

The Fisherman and the Large and Small Fish

A fisherman drew in his net from the sea. He could catch big fish, which he spread out in the sun, but the small fish slipped through the mesh, escaping into the sea.

People of a mediocre fortune escape danger easily, but one rarely sees a man of great note escape when there is a disaster.

The Fox and the Woodcutter

A fox who was fleeing ahead of some hunters saw a woodcutter and pleaded with him to find a hiding-place. The woodcutter promised to hide him in his hut, and did so. Some moments later the huntsmen arrived and asked the woodcutter if he had seen a fox in the vicinity. He replied in words that he had not seen one go past, but by signalling with his hands he indicated where the fox was hidden. The huntsmen, however, took no notice of his gestures and simply took him at his word.

After they had gone, the fox emerged from the hut without saying anything. When the woodcutter reproached him for showing no gratitude for having saved him, the fox replied:

'I would thank you if your gestures and your conduct had agreed with your words.'

One could apply this fable to men who make protestations of virtue but who actually behave like rascals.

The Fox and the Billy-goat

A fox, having fallen into a well, was faced with the prospect of being stuck there. But then a billy-goat came along to that same well because he was thirsty and saw the fox. He asked him if the water was good.

The fox decided to put a brave face on it and gave a tremendous speech about how wonderful the water was down there, so very excellent. So the billy-goat climbed down the well, thinking only of his thirst. When he had had a good drink, he asked the fox what he thought was the best way to get back up again.

The fox said:

'Well, I have a very good way to do that. Of course, it will mean our working together. If you just push your front feet up against the wall and hold your horns up in the air as high as you can, I will climb up on to them, get out, and then I can pull you up behind me.'

The billy-goat willingly consented to this idea, and the fox briskly clambered up the legs, the shoulders, and finally the horns of his companion. He found himself at the mouth of the well, pulled himself out, and immediately scampered off. The billy-goat shouted after him, reproaching him for breaking their agreement of mutual assistance. The fox came back to the top of the well and shouted down to the billy-goat:

'Ha! If you had as many brains as you have hairs on your

chin, you wouldn't have got down there in the first place without thinking of how you were going to get out again.'

It is thus that sensible men should not undertake any action without having first examined the end result.

The Man Bitten by an Ant, and Hermes

One day, a sailing ship sank to the bottom of the sea with all its passengers. A man who was a witness of the shipwreck claimed that the decrees of the gods were unjust, for to lose a single impious person they had also made the innocent perish.

There were a great many ants on the spot where he was standing. As he was saying this, it happened that one of them bit him. In order to kill it, he crushed them all.

Then Hermes appeared to him, and struck him with his wand [*rhabdos*], saying:

'And now do you not admit that the gods judge men in the same way you judge the ants?'

Don't blaspheme against the gods. When misfortune befalls you, examine your own faults.

The Cheat

A poor man, being very ill and getting worse, promised the gods to sacrifice to them one hundred oxen if they saved him from death. The gods, wishing to put him to the test, restored him to health very quickly. Soon he was up and out of bed.

But, as he didn't really have any oxen, he modelled one hundred of them out of tallow and burned them on an altar, saying:

'Receive my votive offering, oh gods!'

But the gods, wanting to trick him in their turn, sent him a dream saying that if he would go to the seashore it would result in one thousand Athenian drachmas for him. Unable to contain his joy, he ran to the beach, where he came across some pirates who took him away and sold him into slavery. And they did indeed obtain one thousand Athenian drachmas for him.

This fable is well applied to a liar.

The Man and the Lion Travelling Together

A man and a lion were travelling along together one day when they began to argue about which of them was the stronger. Just then they passed a stone statue representing a man strangling a lion.

'There, you see, we are stronger than you,' said the man, pointing it out to the lion.

But the lion smiled and replied:

'If lions could make statues, you would see plenty of men under the paws of lions.'

Many people boast of how brave and fearless they are, but when put to the test are exposed as frauds.

The Bear and the Fox

A bear once boasted to a fox that he had a great love for mankind, since he made it a point never to eat a corpse.

The fox replied:

'I wish to heaven you would mangle the dead rather than the living!'

This fable unmasks the covetous who live in hypocrisy and vainglory.

The Frogs Who Demanded a King

The frogs, annoyed with the anarchy in which they lived, sent a deputation to Zeus to ask him to give them a king. Zeus, seeing that they were but very simple creatures, threw a piece of wood into their marsh. The frogs were so alarmed by the sudden noise that they plunged into the depths of the bog. But when the piece of wood did not move, they clambered out again. They developed such a contempt for this new king that they jumped on his back and crouched there.

The frogs were deeply ashamed at having such a king, so they sent a second deputation to Zeus asking him to change their monarch. For the first was too passive and did nothing.

Zeus now became impatient with them and sent down a water-serpent [*hydra*] which seized them and ate them all up.

This fable teaches us that it is better to be ruled by passive, worthless men who bear no spitefulness than by productive but wicked ones.

The Ox-driver and Herakles

An ox-driver was bringing a wagon towards a town. The wagon fell down into a deep ravine. But instead of doing anything to get it out, the ox-driver stood without doing a thing, and merely invoked Herakles among all the gods whom he particularly honoured. Herakles appeared to him and said:

'Put your hand to the wheels, goad the oxen, and do not invoke the gods without making some effort yourself. Otherwise you will invoke them in vain.'

The House-ferret and Aphrodite

A house-ferret, having fallen in love with a handsome young man, begged Aphrodite, goddess of love, to change her into a human girl. The goddess took pity on this passion and changed her into a gracious young girl. The young man, when he saw her, fell in love with her and led her to his home. As they rested in the nuptial chamber [*thalamos*], Aphrodite, wanting to see if in changing body the house-ferret had also changed in character, released a mouse in the middle of the room. The house-ferret, forgetting her present condition, leapt up from the bed and chased the mouse in order to eat it. Then the indignant goddess changed her back to her former state.

Bad people who change their appearance do not change their character.

The House-ferret and the File

A house-ferret slipped into a blacksmith's workshop and began to lick the file that she found there. Now it happened that using her tongue thus, the blood flowed from it. But she was delighted, imagining that she had extracted something from the iron. And in the end she lost her tongue.

This fable is aimed at people who pick arguments with others, thereby doing harm to themselves.

The Ploughman and the Frozen Snake

One winter, a ploughman found a snake stiff with cold. He took pity on it, picked it up and put it under his shirt. When the snake had warmed up again against the man's chest, it reverted to its nature, struck out and killed its benefactor. When he realized that he was dying, the man bemoaned:
 'I well deserve it, for taking pity on a wicked wretch.'

This fable shows that perversity of nature does not change under the influence of kindness.

The Wife and Her Drunken Husband

There was a woman whose husband was a drunkard. To get the better of him and his vice she devised a plan. She waited for the moment when her husband was so drunk that he was like a corpse, then she heaved him up over her shoulders, carried him to the cemetery and dumped him there. When she thought he had slept it off, she went back to the cemetery and knocked on the door of the vault.

'Who's that at the door?' the drunkard called out.

'It's me, who comes to bring food for the dead,' replied his wife mournfully.

'Don't bring me anything to eat, my good man. Bring me more to drink. You distress me by talking about food and not drink.'

The wife, beating her breast, cried out:

'Alas! How miserable I am! My plan has had no effect on you, husband! For not only are you not sober but you have become even worse. Your weakness has now become second nature to you.'

This fable shows that you shouldn't become habituated to a loose way of life, for there comes a time when habit forces itself upon you, whether you like it or not.

The Woman and the Hen

A widow had a hen which laid an egg every day. She imagined that if she gave the hen more barley it would lay twice a day. So she increased the hen's ration accordingly. But the hen became fat and wasn't even capable of laying one egg a day.

This fable shows that if, through greed, you look for more than you have, you lose even that which you do possess.

The Dolphins, the Whales and the Gudgeon

Some dolphins and some whales were engaged in battle. As the fight went on and became desperate, a gudgeon poked his head above the surface of the water and tried to reconcile them. But one of the dolphins retorted:

'It is less humiliating for us to fight to the death between ourselves than to have you for a mediator.'

Similarly, certain nobodies think they are somebody when they interfere in a public row.

The Stag at the Spring and the Lion

A stag, oppressed by thirst, came to a spring to drink. After having a drink, he saw the shadowy figure of himself in the water. He much admired his fine antlers, their grandeur and extent. But he was discontented with his legs, which he thought looked thin and feeble. He remained there deep in reverie when suddenly a lion sprang out at him and chased him. The stag fled rapidly and ran a great distance, for the stag's advantage is his legs, whereas a lion's is his heart. As long as they were in open ground, the stag easily outdistanced the lion. But they entered a wooded area and the stag's antlers became entangled in the branches, bringing him to a halt so that he was caught by the lion.

As he was on the point of death, the stag said:

'How unfortunate I am! My feet, which I had denigrated, could have saved me, whereas my antlers, on which I prided myself, have caused my death!'

And thus, in dangerous situations it is often the friends whom we suspect who save us, while those on whom we rely betray us.

The Kid on the Roof of the House, and the Wolf

A kid who had wandered on to the roof of a house saw a wolf pass by and he began to insult and jeer at it. The wolf replied:

'Hey, you there! It's not you who mock me but the place on which you are standing.'

This fable shows that often it is the place and the occasion which give one the daring to defy the powerful.

The Two Enemies

Two men who loathed each other were sailing in the same boat. One took up his position at the stern and the other at the prow. A storm blew up and the boat was on the point of sinking. The man at the stern asked the helmsman which part of the vessel would go down first. 'The prow,' he said. 'Then,' replied the man, 'death will no longer be sad for me, if I can see my enemy die first.'

This fable shows that many people are not in the least disturbed at the harm that befalls them, provided they can see their enemies' downfall first.

The Sun and the Frogs

It was summer, and people were celebrating the wedding feast of the Sun. All the animals were rejoicing at the event, and only the frogs were left to join in the gaiety. But a protesting frog called out:

'Fools! How can you rejoice? The Sun dries out all the marshland. If he takes a wife and has a child similar to himself, imagine how much more we would suffer!'

Plenty of empty-headed people are jubilant about things which they have no cause to celebrate.

The Mule

A mule who had grown fat on barley began to get frisky, saying to herself: 'My father is a fast-running horse, and I take after him in every way.' But, one day, she was forced to run a race. At the end of the race she looked glum and remembered that her father was really an ass.

This fable shows that even if circumstances put a man on show, he ought never to forget his origins, for life is full of uncertainty.

The Old Horse

An old horse had been sold to a miller to turn the millstone. When he was harnessed to the mill-wheel he groaned and exclaimed:

'From the turn of the race course I am reduced to such a turn as this!'

Don't be too proud of youthful strength, for many a man's old age is spent in hard work.

The Camel Seen for the First Time

When they first set eyes on a camel, men were afraid. Awed by its huge size, they ran away. But when, in time, they realized its gentleness, they plucked up enough courage to approach it. Then, gradually realizing that it had no temper, they went up to it and grew to hold it in such contempt that they put a bridle on it and gave it to the children to lead.

This fable shows that habit can overcome the fear which awesome things inspire.

The Walnut Tree

A walnut tree which grew on the edge of a path was constantly hit by a volley of stones. It said to itself with a sigh:
 'How unlucky I am that year after year I attract insults and suffering.'

This fable is aimed at people who don't withdraw from a source of annoyance for their own good.

The Gardener Watering the Vegetables

A man passed a gardener who was watering his vegetables and he stopped to ask him why the wild vegetables were flourishing and vigorous while the cultivated ones were sickly and puny.

The gardener replied: 'It's because the Earth is a mother to the one and a stepmother to the others.'

Similarly, the children fed by a stepmother are not nourished like those who have their true mother.

The Kithara-player

A kithara-player, devoid of talent, sang from morning to night in a house with thickly plastered walls. As the walls echoed with his own sounds he imagined that he had a very beautiful voice. He so overestimated his own voice from then on that he decided to perform in a theatre. But he sang so badly on the stage that he was driven off it by people throwing stones.

Thus, certain orators who, at school, seem to have some talent, reveal their incompetence as soon as they enter the political arena.

The Gnat and the Bull

A gnat had settled on a bull's horn. After he had been there for a while and was about to fly off, he asked the bull whether he would, after all, like him to go away. The bull replied:

'When you came, I didn't feel you. And when you go I won't feel you either.'

One could apply this fable to the feeble person whose presence or absence is neither helpful nor harmful.

The Ageing Lion and the Fox

A lion who was getting old and could no longer obtain his food by force decided that he must resort to trickery instead. So he retired to a cave and lay down pretending to be ill. Thus, whenever any animals came to his cave to visit him, he ate them all as they appeared.

When many animals had disappeared, a fox figured out what was happening. He went to see the lion but stood at a safe distance outside the cave and asked him how he was.

'Oh, not very well,' said the lion. 'But why don't you come in?'

But the fox said:

'I would come inside if I hadn't seen that a lot of footprints are pointing inwards towards your cave but none are pointing out.'

Wise men note the indications of dangers and thus avoid them.

The Snake, the House-ferret and the Mice

A snake and a house-ferret were fighting each other in a certain house where they lived. The mice of the house, who were forever being eaten by one or the other of them, came quietly out of their holes when they heard them fighting. At the sight of the mice, the two combatants gave up their battle and turned on the mice.

It is the same in the city-states [poleōn]; *people who interfere in the quarrels of the demagogues become, without suspecting it, the victims of both sides.*

The Snake and the Crab

A snake and a crab frequented the same place. The crab continually behaved towards the snake in all simplicity and kindness. But the snake was always cunning and perverse. The crab ceaselessly urged the snake to behave towards him with honesty and to imitate his own manner towards him; he did not listen. So, indignant, the crab waited for an occasion when the snake was asleep, grabbed it and killed it. Seeing it stretched out dead, the crab called out:

'Hey, friend! It's no use being straight now that you are dead, you should have done that when I was urging you to before; then you wouldn't have had to be put to death!'

One could rightly tell this fable with regard to people who, during their life, are wicked towards their friends and do them a service after their death.

The Trodden-on Snake and Zeus

The snake, heavily trodden on so often by men's feet, went to Zeus to complain. Zeus said to it:
 'If you had bitten the first one who trod on you, the second one would not have tried to do so.'

This fable shows that those who hold their own against the first people who attack them make themselves formidable to others who do so.

The Child Catching Locusts, and the Scorpion

A child was catching locusts in front of the city wall. After having caught a certain number of them, he saw a scorpion. He took it for a locust and, cupping his hand, was about to put it in his palm when the scorpion, rearing his spike, said to the child:

'Would that you had done that! For then you would have lost the locusts that you have already caught!'

This fable shows us that we should not behave in the same way towards good and wicked people.

The Child and the Raven

A woman consulted the diviners about her infant son. They predicted that he would be killed by a raven [*korax*]. Terror-stricken by this prediction, she had a huge chest constructed and shut the boy up inside it to prevent him from being killed by a raven. And every day, at a given time, she opened it and gave the child as much food as he needed. Then, one day when she had opened the chest and was putting back the lid, the child foolishly stuck his head out. So it happened that the *korax* [hooked handle] on the chest fell down on to the top of his head and killed him.

The Flea and the Man

Once, a flea was irritating a man relentlessly. So he caught it and said to it:

'Who are you, who makes a meal of all my limbs, biting me all over at random?'

The flea answered:

'That's the way we live. Don't kill me, for I can't do much harm.'

The man started to laugh and said:

'You're going to die now, and at my hands, for however great or small the harm it is imperative to stop you breeding.'

This fable shows that it is not necessary to take pity on the wicked, however strong or feeble he may be.

The Jackdaw and the Ravens

A jackdaw who grew larger in size than the other jackdaws disdained their company. So he took himself off to the ravens and asked if he could share his life with them. But the ravens, unfamiliar with his shape and his voice, mobbed him and chased him away. So, rejected by them, he went back to be with the jackdaws. But the jackdaws, outraged at his defection, refused to have him back. And thus he was an outcast from the society of both jackdaws and ravens.

It is similar with people. Those who abandon their own country in preference for another are in low esteem there for being foreigners, but despised by their compatriots because they have scorned them.

The Man Bitten by a Dog

A man who had been bitten by a dog roamed far and wide, looking for someone to heal his wound. Someone told him all he had to do was wipe the blood from his wound with some bread and throw the bread to the dog which had bitten him. To this the injured man replied:

'But if I did that, every dog in the city would bite me.'

Similarly, if you indulge someone's wickedness, you provoke him to do even more harm.

The Sleeping Dog and the Wolf

A dog lay asleep in front of a farm building. A wolf pounced on him and was going to make a meal of him, when the dog begged him not to eat him straight away:

'At the moment,' he said, 'I am thin and lean. But wait a little while; my masters will be celebrating a wedding feast. I will get some good mouthfuls and will fatten up and will be a much better meal for you.'

The wolf believed him and went on his way. A little while later he came back and found the dog asleep on top of the house. He stopped below and shouted up to him, reminding him of their agreement. Then the dog said:

'Oh, wolf! If you ever see me asleep in front of the farm again, don't wait for the wedding banquet!'

This fable shows that wise people, when they get out of a fix, take care of themselves all the rest of their life.

The Dog with a Bell

A dog furtively bit people, so his master hung a bell on him to warn everyone he was coming. Then the dog, shaking his bell, swaggered about in the agora. An old bitch said to him:

'What have you got to strut about? You don't wear the bell as a result of any virtue, but to advertise your secret ill nature.'

The secret spitefulness of boastful people is exposed by their vainglorious behaviour.

The Wolf and the Lamb

A wolf saw a lamb drinking at a stream and wanted to devise a suitable pretext for devouring it. So, although he was himself upstream, he accused the lamb of muddying the water and preventing him from drinking. The lamb replied that he only drank with the tip of his tongue and that, besides, being downstream he couldn't muddy the water upstream. The wolf's stratagem having collapsed, he replied:

'But last year you insulted my father.'

'I wasn't even born then,' replied the lamb.

So the wolf resumed:

'Whatever you say to justify yourself, I will eat you all the same.'

This fable shows that when some people decide upon doing harm, the fairest defence has no effect whatever.

The Wolf and the Young Lamb Taking Refuge in a Temple

A wolf pursued a young lamb, who took refuge in a temple. The wolf called out to it and said that the sacrificer would offer it up to the god if he found the lamb there. But the lamb replied:

'Ah well! I would prefer to be a victim of a god than to die by your hand.'

This fable shows that if one is being driven towards death, it is better to die with honour.

The Diviner

A diviner was sitting plying his trade in the agora. Suddenly, someone rushed up to him and said that the front door of his house was wide open and the contents gone. The diviner leapt up in consternation and ran home, gasping to see what had happened. A passer-by who saw him running called out:

'Hey there! You who pride yourself on foretelling the future for others! Can't you foresee what will happen to yourself?'

One could apply this fable to people who order their own lives woefully but who dabble in controlling affairs which are not their concern.

The Field Mouse and the Town Mouse

A field mouse had a town mouse for a friend. The field mouse invited the town mouse to dinner in the country. When he saw that there was only barley and corn to eat, the town mouse said:

'Do you know, my friend, that you live like an ant? I, on the other hand, have an abundance of good things. Come home with me and I will share it all with you.'

So they set off together. The house mouse showed his friend some beans and bread-flour, together with some dates, a cheese, honey and fruit. And the field mouse was filled with wonder and blessed him with all his heart, cursing his own lot. Just as they were preparing to start their meal, a man suddenly opened the door. Alarmed by the noise, the mice rushed fearfully into the crevices. Then, as they crept out again to taste some dried figs, someone else came into the room and started looking for something. So they again rushed down the holes to hide. Then the field mouse, forgetting his hunger, sighed, and said to his friend:

'Farewell, my friend. You can eat your fill and be glad of heart, but at the price of a thousand fears and dangers. I, poor little thing, will go on living by nibbling barley and corn without fear or suspicion of anyone.'

*

This fable shows that one should:

> *Live simply and free from passion*
> *Instead of luxuriously in fear and dread.*

The Bat, the Bramble and the Gull

The bat, the bramble and the gull met up with the intention of doing a bit of trading together. The bat went out and borrowed some money to fund the enterprise, the bramble contributed a lot of cloth to be sold and the gull brought a large supply of copper to sell. Then they set sail to go trading, but a violent storm arose which capsized their ship and all the cargo was lost. They were able to save nothing but themselves from the shipwreck.

Ever since that time, the gull has searched the seashore to see if any of his copper might be washed up somewhere, the bat, fearing his creditors, dare not go out by day and only feeds at night, and the bramble clutches the clothes of all those who pass by, hoping to recognize a familiar piece of material.

This fable shows that we always return to those things in which we have a stake.

The Woodcutter and Hermes

A woodcutter who was chopping wood on the banks of a river had lost his axe. Not knowing what to do, he sat himself down on the bank and wept. The god Hermes, learning the cause of his distress, took pity on him. Hermes plunged into the river, brought out a golden axe and asked the woodcutter if this were the one which he had lost. The man said, no, that wasn't the one. So Hermes dived back in again and this time he produced a silver axe. But the woodcutter said, no, that wasn't his axe either.

Hermes plunged in a third time and brought him his own axe. The man said, yes, indeed, this was the very axe which he had lost.

Then Hermes, charmed by his honesty, gave him all three.

Returning to his friends, the woodcutter told them about his adventure. One of them took it into his head to get himself some axes as well. So he set off for the riverbank, threw his axe into the current deliberately and then sat down in tears. Then Hermes appeared to him also and, learning the cause of his tears, he dived in and brought him too a golden axe, asking if it were the one which he had lost.

The man, all joyful, cried out: 'Yes! It is indeed the one!'

But the god, horrified at such effrontery, not only withheld the golden axe but didn't return the man's own.

This fable shows that the gods favour honest people but are hostile to the dishonest.

The Ass Carrying Salt

An ass with a load of salt was crossing a stream. He slipped and fell into the water. Then the salt dissolved, and when he got up his load was lighter than before, so he was delighted. Another time, when he arrived at the bank of a stream with a load of sponges, he thought that if he fell into the water again when he got up the load would be lighter. So he slipped on purpose. But, of course, the sponges swelled up with the water and the ass was unable to get up again, so he drowned and perished.

Thus it is sometimes that people don't suspect that it is their own tricks which land them in disaster.

The Ass, the Cock and the Lion

One day, an ass and a cockerel were feeding together when a lion attacked the ass. The cockerel let out a loud crow and the lion fled, for lions are afraid of the sound of a cock crowing.

The ass, imagining that the lion was fleeing because of him, did not hesitate to rush after him. When he had pursued the lion for about the distance where a cock's crow can no longer be heard, the lion turned round and devoured him. As he was dying, the ass brayed:

'What an unfortunate and stupid fellow I am! Why did I, who was not born to warlike parents, set out to fight?'

This fable shows that the enemy is often portrayed as of no consequence, but when we attack him he destroys us.

The Ass and the Lap-dog or *The Dog and Its Master*

There was a man who owned a Maltese lap-dog and an ass. He was always playing with the dog. When he dined out, he would bring back titbits and throw them to the dog when it rushed up, wagging its tail. The ass was jealous of this and, one day, trotted up and started frisking around his master. But this resulted in the man getting a kick on the foot, and he grew very angry. So he drove the ass with a stick back to its manger, where he tied it up.

This fable shows that we are not all made to do the same things.

The Ass Who Was Taken for a Lion

An ass, clothed in the skin of a lion, passed himself off in the eyes of everyone as a lion, and made everyone flee from him, both men and animals. But the wind came along and blew off the lion's skin, leaving him naked and exposed. Everyone then fell upon him when they saw this, and beat him with sticks and clubs.

Be poor and ordinary. Don't have pretensions to wealth or you will be exposed to ridicule and danger. For we cannot adapt ourselves to that which is alien to us.

The Bird-catcher and the Wild and Domesticated Pigeons

A bird-catcher spread his nets and tied his domesticated pigeons to them. Then he withdrew and watched from a distance what would happen. Some wild pigeons approached the captive birds and became entangled in the snares. The bird-catcher ran back and started to grab them. As he did so, they reproached the domesticated pigeons because, being of the same race, they should have warned them of the trap. But the domesticated pigeons replied:

'We are more concerned with preventing our master's displeasure than with pleasing our kindred.'

Thus it is with domestic slaves: you can't blame them when, for love of their masters, they fail to show love towards their own kind.

The Hen and the Swallow

A hen found the eggs of a snake and carefully hatched them by sitting upon them and keeping them warm. A swallow, who had seen her doing this, said to her:

'What a fool you are! Why are you rearing these creatures who, once grown, will make you the first victim of their evildoing?'

Perversity cannot be tamed even by the kindest treatment.

The Partridge and the Man

A man caught a partridge while hunting and was about to kill it. She pleaded with him:

'Let me live! In my place I would bring you lots of partridges.'

'All the more reason to kill you,' replied the man, 'since you wish to ensnare your friends and comrades.'

This shows that the man who weaves a plot against his friends will himself fall into danger and ambushes.

The Monkey and the Camel

At an assembly of the beasts, a monkey got up and danced. He was enthusiastically applauded by everyone present. A jealous camel wanted to earn the same praise. He got up and also tried to dance, but he did such absurd things that the other animals became disgusted and beat him out of their sight with sticks.

This fable is suitable for those people who, through envy, compete with those who are their betters.

The Mole and His Mother

A mole – the mole is a blind creature – said to his mother that he could see. To put him to the test, his mother gave him a grain of frankincense [*libanōtos*] and asked him what it was.

'It's a pebble,' he said.

'My child,' replied the mother, 'not only are you bereft of sight, but you have also lost your sense of smell.'

Similarly, boastful people promise the impossible and are proved powerless in the most simple affairs.

1. BOCCACCIO · *Mrs Rosie and the Priest*
2. GERARD MANLEY HOPKINS · *As kingfishers catch fire*
3. *The Saga of Gunnlaug Serpent-tongue*
4. THOMAS DE QUINCEY · *On Murder Considered as One of the Fine Arts*
5. FRIEDRICH NIETZSCHE · *Aphorisms on Love and Hate*
6. JOHN RUSKIN · *Traffic*
7. PU SONGLING · *Wailing Ghosts*
8. JONATHAN SWIFT · *A Modest Proposal*
9. *Three Tang Dynasty Poets*
10. WALT WHITMAN · *On the Beach at Night Alone*
11. KENKŌ · *A Cup of Sake Beneath the Cherry Trees*
12. BALTASAR GRACIÁN · *How to Use Your Enemies*
13. JOHN KEATS · *The Eve of St Agnes*
14. THOMAS HARDY · *Woman much missed*
15. GUY DE MAUPASSANT · *Femme Fatale*
16. MARCO POLO · *Travels in the Land of Serpents and Pearls*
17. SUETONIUS · *Caligula*
18. APOLLONIUS OF RHODES · *Jason and Medea*
19. ROBERT LOUIS STEVENSON · *Olalla*
20. KARL MARX AND FRIEDRICH ENGELS · *The Communist Manifesto*
21. PETRONIUS · *Trimalchio's Feast*
22. JOHANN PETER HEBEL · *How a Ghastly Story Was Brought to Light by a Common or Garden Butcher's Dog*
23. HANS CHRISTIAN ANDERSEN · *The Tinder Box*
24. RUDYARD KIPLING · *The Gate of the Hundred Sorrows*
25. DANTE · *Circles of Hell*
26. HENRY MAYHEW · *Of Street Piemen*
27. HAFEZ · *The nightingales are drunk*
28. GEOFFREY CHAUCER · *The Wife of Bath*
29. MICHEL DE MONTAIGNE · *How We Weep and Laugh at the Same Thing*
30. THOMAS NASHE · *The Terrors of the Night*
31. EDGAR ALLAN POE · *The Tell-Tale Heart*
32. MARY KINGSLEY · *A Hippo Banquet*
33. JANE AUSTEN · *The Beautifull Cassandra*
34. ANTON CHEKHOV · *Gooseberries*
35. SAMUEL TAYLOR COLERIDGE · *Well, they are gone, and here must I remain*
36. JOHANN WOLFGANG VON GOETHE · *Sketchy, Doubtful, Incomplete Jottings*
37. CHARLES DICKENS · *The Great Winglebury Duel*
38. HERMAN MELVILLE · *The Maldive Shark*
39. ELIZABETH GASKELL · *The Old Nurse's Story*
40. NIKOLAY LESKOV · *The Steel Flea*

41. HONORÉ DE BALZAC · *The Atheist's Mass*
42. CHARLOTTE PERKINS GILMAN · *The Yellow Wall-Paper*
43. C.P. CAVAFY · *Remember, Body . . .*
44. FYODOR DOSTOEVSKY · *The Meek One*
45. GUSTAVE FLAUBERT · *A Simple Heart*
46. NIKOLAI GOGOL · *The Nose*
47. SAMUEL PEPYS · *The Great Fire of London*
48. EDITH WHARTON · *The Reckoning*
49. HENRY JAMES · *The Figure in the Carpet*
50. WILFRED OWEN · *Anthem For Doomed Youth*
51. WOLFGANG AMADEUS MOZART · *My Dearest Father*
52. PLATO · *Socrates' Defence*
53. CHRISTINA ROSSETTI · *Goblin Market*
54. *Sindbad the Sailor*
55. SOPHOCLES · *Antigone*
56. RYŪNOSUKE AKUTAGAWA · *The Life of a Stupid Man*
57. LEO TOLSTOY · *How Much Land Does A Man Need?*
58. GIORGIO VASARI · *Leonardo da Vinci*
59. OSCAR WILDE · *Lord Arthur Savile's Crime*
60. SHEN FU · *The Old Man of the Moon*
61. AESOP · *The Dolphins, the Whales and the Gudgeon*
62. MATSUO BASHŌ · *Lips too Chilled*
63. EMILY BRONTË · *The Night is Darkening Round Me*
64. JOSEPH CONRAD · *To-morrow*
65. RICHARD HAKLUYT · *The Voyage of Sir Francis Drake Around the Whole Globe*
66. KATE CHOPIN · *A Pair of Silk Stockings*
67. CHARLES DARWIN · *It was snowing butterflies*
68. BROTHERS GRIMM · *The Robber Bridegroom*
69. CATULLUS · *I Hate and I Love*
70. HOMER · *Circe and the Cyclops*
71. D. H. LAWRENCE · *Il Duro*
72. KATHERINE MANSFIELD · *Miss Brill*
73. OVID · *The Fall of Icarus*
74. SAPPHO · *Come Close*
75. IVAN TURGENEV · *Kasyan from the Beautiful Lands*
76. VIRGIL · *O Cruel Alexis*
77. H. G. WELLS · *A Slip under the Microscope*
78. HERODOTUS · *The Madness of Cambyses*
79. *Speaking of Siva*
80. *The Dhammapada*

'Wake,
butterfly —'

MATSUO BASHŌ
Born 1644, near Ueno, Japan
Died 1694, Osaka, Japan

This selection taken from *On Love and Barley: Haiku of Bashō*,
translated with an introduction by Lucien Stryk and
published in 1985.

MATSUO BASHŌ IN PENGUIN CLASSICS
On Love and Barley
The Narrow Road to the Deep North and Other Travel Sketches

MATSUO BASHŌ

Lips too chilled

Translated by
Lucien Stryk

PENGUIN BOOKS

PENGUIN CLASSICS

UK | USA | Canada | Ireland | Australia
India | New Zealand | South Africa

Penguin Books is part of the Penguin Random House group of companies
whose addresses can be found at global.penguinrandomhouse.com.

This selection published in Penguin Classics 2015

010

Copyright © Lucien Stryk, 1985

The moral right of the translator has been asserted

Set in 10/14.5 pt Baskerville 10 Pro
Typeset by Jouve (UK), Milton Keynes
Printed and bound in Great Britain by Clays Ltd, Elcograf S.p.A.

A CIP catalogue record for this book is available from the British Library

ISBN: 978-0-141-39845-7

www.greenpenguin.co.uk

Penguin Random House is committed to a
sustainable future for our business, our readers
and our planet. This book is made from Forest
Stewardship Council® certified paper.

In my new robe
this morning –
someone else.

Fields, mountains
of Hubaku, in
nine days – spring.

Matsuo Bashō

Year by year,
the monkey's mask
reveals the monkey.

New Year – the Basho-Tosei
hermitage
a-buzz with haiku.

Lips too chilled

New Year –
feeling broody
from late autumn.

Spring come – New Year's
gourd stuffed, five quarts
of last year's rice.

Matsuo Bashō

Plunging hoofs stir
Futami sand – divine white
horse greets New Year.

Spring night,
cherry-
blossom dawn.

Lips too chilled

Wearing straw cloaks,
with spring
saints greet each other.

Spring's exodus –
birds shriek,
fish eyes blink tears.

Matsuo Bashō

Ploughing the field
for cherry-hemp –
storm echoes.

Spring rain –
under trees
a crystal stream.

Lips too chilled

Monks' feet clomping
through icy dark,
drawing sweet water.

Spring moon –
flower face
in mist.

Matsuo Bashō

Spring rain –
they rouse me,
old sluggard.

Ebb tide –
willows
dip to mud.

Sparrows in eaves,
mice in ceiling –
celestial music.

Dark night –
plover crying
for its nest.

Matsuo Bashō

Over skylark's song
Noh cry
of pheasant.

How terrible
the pheasant's call –
snake-eater.

Lips too chilled

Hozo mountain-pass
soars
higher than the skylark.

Bush-warbler dots
the rice-ball
drying on the porch.

Matsuo Bashō

Bucking the oven
gap – cat
yowls in heat.

Now cat's done
mewing, bedroom's
touched by moonlight.

Lips too chilled

Do not forget the plum,
blooming
in the thicket.

Spring air –
woven moon
and plum scent.

Matsuo Bashō

Mountain path –
sun rising
through plum scent.

Another haiku?
Yet more cherry blossoms –
not my face.

Sleeping willow –
soul of
the nightingale.

Behind the virgins'
quarters,
one blossoming plum.

Matsuo Bashō

First cherry
budding
by peach blossoms.

Red plum blossoms:
where behind the
bead-screen's love?

Lips too chilled

Pretending to drink
sake from my fan,
sprinkled with cherry petals.

If I'd the knack
I'd sing like
cherry flakes falling.

Matsuo Bashō

Striding ten, twelve
miles in search of
cherry wreaths – how glorious.

Under the cherry –
blossom soup,
blossom salad.

Reeling with *sake*
and cherry blossoms,
a sworded woman in *haori*.

Boozy on blossoms –
dark rice,
white *sake*.

Matsuo Bashō

Come out, bat –
birds, earth itself
hauled off by flowers.

                        Waterfall garlands –
                        tell
                        that to revellers.

Spraying in wind,
through blossoms,
waves of Lake Grebe.

Be careful where
you aim,
peaches of Fushimi.

Matsuo Bashō

Sparrows
in rape-field,
blossom-viewing.

Cold white azalea –
lone nun
under thatched roof.

Draining the *sake*
cask – behold,
a gallon flower-vase.

On my knees, hugging
roots, I grieve
for Priest Tando.

Matsuo Bashō

Taros sprouting
at the gate,
young creepers.

Search carefully –
in the hedge,
a shepherd's purse.

Aged – eating
laver, my teeth
grind sand.

Cherry blossoms –
lights
of years past.

Matsuo Bashō

Squalls shake the Basho
tree – all
night my basin echoes rain.

On the dead limb
squats a crow –
autumn night.

Lips too chilled

Kiyotaki river –
pine needles wildfire
on the crest.

Parting,
straw-clutching
for support.

Matsuo Bashō

Yellow rose petals
thunder –
a waterfall.

Whiter than stones
of Stone Mountain –
autumn wind.

Sparrow, spare
the horsefly
dallying in flowers.

Drizzly June –
long hair, face
sickly white.

Matsuo Bashō

Nara's Buddhas,
one by one –
essence of asters.

Darkening waves –
cry of wild ducks,
faintly white.

Faceless – bones
scattered in the field,
wind cuts my flesh.

Where cuckoo
vanishes –
an island.

Matsuo Bashō

Winter downpour –
even the monkey
needs a raincoat.

June clouds,
at ease on
Arashiyama peak.

Lips too chilled

Butterfly –
wings curve into
white poppy.

Summer wraps –
is there no end
to lice?

Matsuo Bashō

First winter rain –
I plod on,
Traveller, my name.

How quiet –
locust-shrill
pierces rock.

Wild mallow fringing
the wood,
plucked by my horse.

Futami friends, farewell –
clam torn from shell,
I follow autumn.

Matsuo Bashō

Traveller sleeps –
a sick wild duck reels
through cold night.

When I bend low
enough, purseweed
beneath my fence.

Poet grieving over shivering
monkeys, what of this child
cast out in autumn wind?

Poor boy – leaves
moon-viewing
for rice-grinding.

Matsuo Bashō

Wake, butterfly –
it's late, we've miles
to go together.

Violets –
how precious on
a mountain path.

Gulping June
rains, swollen
Mogami river.

Early autumn –
rice field, ocean,
one green.

Matsuo Bashō

Bright moon: I
stroll around the pond –
hey, dawn has come.

Storming over
Lake Nio, whirlwinds
of cherry blossoms.

From moon-wreathed
bamboo grove,
cuckoo song.

Visiting tombs,
white-hairs bow
over canes.

Matsuo Bashō

Skylark on moor –
sweet song
of non-attachment.

Clouds –
a chance to dodge
moon-viewing.

Birth of art –
song of rice planters,
chorus from nowhere.

Cresting Lake Omi's
seven misted views,
Miidera's bells.

Matsuo Bashō

Over Benkei's temple,
flashing Yoshitune's
sword – May carp.

Cormorant fishing:
how stirring,
how saddening.

Skylark sings all
day, and day
not long enough.

Year's end –
still in straw hat
and sandals.

Matsuo Bashō

Moonlit plum tree –
wait,
spring will come.

Snowy morning –
one crow
after another.

Come, see real
flowers
of this painful world.

Morning-glory –
it, too,
turns from me.

Matsuo Bashō

Travel-weary,
I seek lodging –
ah, wisteria.

Come, let's go
snow-viewing
till we're buried.

Chrysanthemum
silence – monk
sips his morning tea.

Crow's
abandoned nest,
a plum tree.

Matsuo Bashō

Melon
in morning dew,
mud-fresh.

Wintry day,
on my horse
a frozen shadow.

Summer moon –
clapping hands,
I herald dawn.

Drenched bush-clover,
passers-by –
both beautiful.

Matsuo Bashō

Harsh sound –
hail spattering
my traveller's hat.

Lips too chilled
for prattle –
autumn wind.

Not one traveller
braves this road –
autumn night.

Withered grass,
under piling
heat-waves.

Matsuo Bashō

Phew –
dace-guts scent
waterweed.

June rain,
hollyhocks turning
where sun should be.

Lips too chilled

Journey's end –
still alive, this
autumn evening.

How cold –
leek tips
washed white.

Matsuo Bashō

Firefly-viewing –
drunken steersman,
drunken boat.

Dewy shoulders
of my paper robe –
heat-waves.

1. BOCCACCIO · *Mrs Rosie and the Priest*
2. GERARD MANLEY HOPKINS · *As kingfishers catch fire*
3. *The Saga of Gunnlaug Serpent-tongue*
4. THOMAS DE QUINCEY · *On Murder Considered as One of the Fine Arts*
5. FRIEDRICH NIETZSCHE · *Aphorisms on Love and Hate*
6. JOHN RUSKIN · *Traffic*
7. PU SONGLING · *Wailing Ghosts*
8. JONATHAN SWIFT · *A Modest Proposal*
9. *Three Tang Dynasty Poets*
10. WALT WHITMAN · *On the Beach at Night Alone*
11. KENKŌ · *A Cup of Sake Beneath the Cherry Trees*
12. BALTASAR GRACIÁN · *How to Use Your Enemies*
13. JOHN KEATS · *The Eve of St Agnes*
14. THOMAS HARDY · *Woman much missed*
15. GUY DE MAUPASSANT · *Femme Fatale*
16. MARCO POLO · *Travels in the Land of Serpents and Pearls*
17. SUETONIUS · *Caligula*
18. APOLLONIUS OF RHODES · *Jason and Medea*
19. ROBERT LOUIS STEVENSON · *Olalla*
20. KARL MARX AND FRIEDRICH ENGELS · *The Communist Manifesto*
21. PETRONIUS · *Trimalchio's Feast*
22. JOHANN PETER HEBEL · *How a Ghastly Story Was Brought to Light by a Common or Garden Butcher's Dog*
23. HANS CHRISTIAN ANDERSEN · *The Tinder Box*
24. RUDYARD KIPLING · *The Gate of the Hundred Sorrows*
25. DANTE · *Circles of Hell*
26. HENRY MAYHEW · *Of Street Piemen*
27. HAFEZ · *The nightingales are drunk*
28. GEOFFREY CHAUCER · *The Wife of Bath*
29. MICHEL DE MONTAIGNE · *How We Weep and Laugh at the Same Thing*
30. THOMAS NASHE · *The Terrors of the Night*
31. EDGAR ALLAN POE · *The Tell-Tale Heart*
32. MARY KINGSLEY · *A Hippo Banquet*
33. JANE AUSTEN · *The Beautifull Cassandra*
34. ANTON CHEKHOV · *Gooseberries*
35. SAMUEL TAYLOR COLERIDGE · *Well, they are gone, and here must I remain*
36. JOHANN WOLFGANG VON GOETHE · *Sketchy, Doubtful, Incomplete Jottings*
37. CHARLES DICKENS · *The Great Winglebury Duel*
38. HERMAN MELVILLE · *The Maldive Shark*
39. ELIZABETH GASKELL · *The Old Nurse's Story*
40. NIKOLAY LESKOV · *The Steel Flea*

41. HONORÉ DE BALZAC · *The Atheist's Mass*
42. CHARLOTTE PERKINS GILMAN · *The Yellow Wall-Paper*
43. C.P. CAVAFY · *Remember, Body . . .*
44. FYODOR DOSTOYEVSKY · *The Meek One*
45. GUSTAVE FLAUBERT · *A Simple Heart*
46. NIKOLAI GOGOL · *The Nose*
47. SAMUEL PEPYS · *The Great Fire of London*
48. EDITH WHARTON · *The Reckoning*
49. HENRY JAMES · *The Figure in the Carpet*
50. WILFRED OWEN · *Anthem For Doomed Youth*
51. WOLFGANG AMADEUS MOZART · *My Dearest Father*
52. PLATO · *Socrates' Defence*
53. CHRISTINA ROSSETTI · *Goblin Market*
54. *Sindbad the Sailor*
55. SOPHOCLES · *Antigone*
56. RYŪNOSUKE AKUTAGAWA · *The Life of a Stupid Man*
57. LEO TOLSTOY · *How Much Land Does A Man Need?*
58. GIORGIO VASARI · *Leonardo da Vinci*
59. OSCAR WILDE · *Lord Arthur Savile's Crime*
60. SHEN FU · *The Old Man of the Moon*
61. AESOP · *The Dolphins, the Whales and the Gudgeon*
62. MATSUO BASHŌ · *Lips too Chilled*
63. EMILY BRONTË · *The Night is Darkening Round Me*
64. JOSEPH CONRAD · *To-morrow*
65. RICHARD HAKLUYT · *The Voyage of Sir Francis Drake Around the Whole Globe*
66. KATE CHOPIN · *A Pair of Silk Stockings*
67. CHARLES DARWIN · *It was snowing butterflies*
68. BROTHERS GRIMM · *The Robber Bridegroom*
69. CATULLUS · *I Hate and I Love*
70. HOMER · *Circe and the Cyclops*
71. D. H. LAWRENCE · *Il Duro*
72. KATHERINE MANSFIELD · *Miss Brill*
73. OVID · *The Fall of Icarus*
74. SAPPHO · *Come Close*
75. IVAN TURGENEV · *Kasyan from the Beautiful Lands*
76. VIRGIL · *O Cruel Alexis*
77. H. G. WELLS · *A Slip under the Microscope*
78. HERODOTUS · *The Madness of Cambyses*
79. *Speaking of Siva*
80. *The Dhammapada*

'. . . ever-present, phantom thing; My slave, my comrade, and my king'

EMILY BRONTË
Born 1818, Thornton, England
Died 1848, Haworth, England

Poems in this book taken from Janet Gezari's edition of
The Complete Poems, first published by Penguin Books in 1992.
The poem 'Often rebuked, yet always back returning' is
now widely felt to be by Charlotte Brontë, but is too
wonderful to be excluded.

BRONTË IN PENGUIN CLASSICS
The Complete Poems
Wuthering Heights

EMILY BRONTË

The Night is Darkening Round Me

PENGUIN BOOKS

PENGUIN CLASSICS

UK | USA | Canada | Ireland | Australia
India | New Zealand | South Africa

Penguin Books is part of the Penguin Random House group of companies whose addresses can be found at global.penguinrandomhouse.com.

This selection published in Penguin Classics 2015

011

Set in 9/12.4 pt Baskerville 10 Pro
Typeset by Jouve (UK), Milton Keynes
Printed and bound in Great Britain by Clays Ltd, Elcograf S.p.A.

A CIP catalogue record for this book is available from the British Library

ISBN: 978-0-141-39847-1

www.greenpenguin.co.uk

MIX
Paper from
responsible sources
FSC® C018179

Penguin Random House is committed to a sustainable future for our business, our readers and our planet. This book is made from Forest Stewardship Council® certified paper.

Contents

Faith and Despondency: '"The winter wind is loud and wild"'	1
Stars: 'Ah! why, because the dazzling sun'	4
The Philosopher: '"Enough of thought, philosopher!"'	6
Remembrance: 'Cold in the earth – and the deep snow piled above thee'	8
A Death-Scene: '"O Day! he cannot die"'	10
Song: 'The linnet in the rocky dells'	12
Anticipation: 'How beautiful the earth is still'	14
The Prisoner (A Fragment): 'In the dungeon-crypts, idly did I stray'	16
Hope: 'Hope was but a timid friend'	19
A Day Dream: 'On a sunny brae, alone I lay'	20
To Imagination: 'When weary with the long day's care'	23
How Clear She Shines: 'How clear she shines! How quietly'	25
Sympathy: 'There should be no despair for you'	27

Plead for Me: 'Oh, thy bright eyes must answer now'	28
Self-Interrogation: '"The evening passes fast away"'	30
Death: 'Death! that struck when I was most confiding'	32
Stanzas to —: 'Well, some may hate, and some may scorn'	34
Honour's Martyr: 'The moon is full this winter night'	35
Stanzas: 'I'll not weep that thou art going to leave me'	38
My Comforter: 'Well hast thou spoken, and yet, not taught'	39
The Old Stoic: 'Riches I hold in light esteem'	41
'Woods you need not frown on me'	42
'The blue bell is the sweetest flower'	43
The Night-Wind: 'In summer's mellow midnight'	45
'The night is darkening round me'	47
'Shall Earth no more inspire thee'	49
'No coward soul is mine'	51
'All hushed and still within the house'	53
'Often rebuked, yet always back returning'	54
'Why ask to know what date what clime'	55

1. *Faith and Despondency*

'The winter wind is loud and wild,
Come close to me, my darling child;
Forsake thy books, and mateless play;
And, while the night is gathering grey,
We'll talk its pensive hours away; –

'Iernë, round our sheltered hall
November's gusts unheeded call;
Not one faint breath can enter here
Enough to wave my daughter's hair,
And I am glad to watch the blaze
Glance from her eyes, with mimic rays;
To feel her cheek so softly pressed,
In happy quiet on my breast.

'But, yet, even this tranquillity
Brings bitter, restless thoughts to me;
And, in the red fire's cheerful glow,
I think of deep glens, blocked with snow;
I dream of moor, and misty hill,
Where evening closes dark and chill;
For, lone, among the mountains cold,
Lie those that I have loved of old.
And my heart aches, in hopeless pain
Exhausted with repinings vain,
That I shall greet them ne'er again!'

'Father, in early infancy,
When you were far beyond the sea,
Such thoughts were tyrants over me!
I often sat, for hours together,
Through the long nights of angry weather,
Raised on my pillow, to descry
The dim moon struggling in the sky;
Or, with strained ear, to catch the shock,
Of rock with wave, and wave with rock;
So would I fearful vigil keep,
And, all for listening, never sleep.
But this world's life has much to dread,
Not so, my Father, with the dead.

'Oh! not for them, should we despair,
The grave is drear, but they are not there;
Their dust is mingled with the sod,
Their happy souls are gone to God!
You told me this, and yet you sigh,
And murmur that your friends must die.
Ah! my dear father, tell me why?
For, if your former words were true,
How useless would such sorrow be;
As wise, to mourn the seed which grew
Unnoticed on its parent tree,
Because it fell in fertile earth,
And sprang up to a glorious birth –
Struck deep its root, and lifted high
Its green boughs, in the breezy sky.

'But, I'll not fear, I will not weep
For those whose bodies rest in sleep, –
I know there is a blessed shore,
    Opening its ports for me, and mine;
And, gazing Time's wide waters o'er,
    I weary for that land divine,
Where we were born, where you and I
Shall meet our Dearest, when we die;
From suffering and corruption free,
Restored into the Deity.'

'Well hast thou spoken, sweet, trustful child!
    And wiser than thy sire;
And worldly tempests, raging wild,
    Shall strengthen thy desire –
Thy fervent hope, through storm and foam,
    Through wind and ocean's roar,
To reach, at last, the eternal home,
    The steadfast, changeless, shore!'

2. Stars

Ah! why, because the dazzling sun
    Restored our Earth to joy,
Have you departed, every one,
    And left a desert sky?

All through the night, your glorious eyes
    Were gazing down in mine,
And with a full heart's thankful sighs,
    I blessed that watch divine.

I was at peace, and drank your beams
    As they were life to me;
And revelled in my changeful dreams,
    Like petrel on the sea.

Thought followed thought, star followed star,
    Through boundless regions, on;
While one sweet influence, near and far,
    Thrilled through, and proved us one!

Why did the morning dawn to break
    So great, so pure, a spell;
And scorch with fire, the tranquil cheek,
    Where your cool radiance fell?

Blood-red, he rose, and, arrow-straight,
    His fierce beams struck my brow;
The soul of nature, sprang, elate,
    But *mine* sank sad and low!

My lids closed down, yet through their veil,
    I saw him, blazing, still,
And steep in gold the misty dale,
    And flash upon the hill.

I turned me to the pillow, then,
    To call back night, and see
Your worlds of solemn light, again,
    Throb with my heart, and me!

It would not do – the pillow glowed,
    And glowed both roof and floor;
And birds sang loudly in the wood,
    And fresh winds shook the door;

The curtains waved, the wakened flies
    Were murmuring round my room,
Imprisoned there, till I should rise,
    And give them leave to roam.

Oh, stars, and dreams, and gentle night;
    Oh, night and stars return!
And hide me from the hostile light,
    That does not warm, but burn;

That drains the blood of suffering men;
    Drinks tears, instead of dew;
Let me sleep through his blinding reign,
    And only wake with you!

3. The Philosopher

'Enough of thought, philosopher!
    Too long hast thou been dreaming
Unenlightened, in this chamber drear,
    While summer's sun is beaming!
Space-sweeping soul, what sad refrain
Concludes thy musings once again?

    '"Oh, for the time when I shall sleep
        Without identity,
    And never care how rain may steep,
        Or snow may cover me!
    No promised heaven, these wild desires,
        Could all, or half fulfil;
    No threatened hell, with quenchless fires,
        Subdue this quenchless will!"'

'So said I, and still say the same;
    Still, to my death, will say –
Three gods, within this little frame,
    Are warring night and day;
Heaven could not hold them all, and yet
    They all are held in me;
And must be mine till I forget
    My present entity!
Oh, for the time, when in my breast
    Their struggles will be o'er!
Oh, for the day, when I shall rest,
    And never suffer more!'

'I saw a spirit, standing, man,
    Where thou doth stand – an hour ago,
And round his feet three rivers ran,
    Of equal depth, and equal flow –
A golden stream – and one like blood;
    And one like sapphire seemed to be;
But, where they joined their triple flood
    It tumbled in an inky sea.

The spirit sent his dazzling gaze
    Down through that ocean's gloomy night
Then, kindling all, with sudden blaze,
    The glad deep sparkled wide and bright –
White as the sun, far, far more fair
    Than its divided sources were!'

'And even for that spirit, seer,
    I've watched and sought my life-time long;
Sought him in heaven, hell, earth, and air –
    An endless search, and always wrong!
Had I but seen his glorious eye
    Once light the clouds that wilder me,
I ne'er had raised this coward cry
    To cease to think, and cease to be;
I ne'er had called oblivion blest,
    Nor, stretching eager hands to death,
Implored to change for senseless rest
    This sentient soul, this living breath –
Oh, let me die – that power and will
    Their cruel strife may close;
And conquered good, and conquering ill
    Be lost in one repose!'

4. Remembrance

Cold in the earth – and the deep snow piled above thee,
Far, far, removed, cold in the dreary grave!
Have I forgot, my only Love, to love thee,
Severed at last by Time's all-severing wave?

Now, when alone, do my thoughts no longer hover
Over the mountains, on that northern shore,
Resting their wings where heath and fern-leaves cover
Thy noble heart for ever, ever more?

Cold in the earth – and fifteen wild Decembers,
From those brown hills, have melted into spring:
Faithful, indeed, is the spirit that remembers
After such years of change and suffering!

Sweet Love of youth, forgive, if I forget thee,
While the world's tide is bearing me along;
Other desires and other hopes beset me,
Hopes which obscure, but cannot do thee wrong!

No later light has lightened up my heaven,
No second morn has ever shone for me;
All my life's bliss from thy dear life was given,
All my life's bliss is in the grave with thee.

But, when the days of golden dreams had perished,
And even Despair was powerless to destroy;
Then did I learn how existence could be cherished,
Strengthened, and fed without the aid of joy.

Then did I check the tears of useless passion –
Weaned my young soul from yearning after thine;
Sternly denied its burning wish to hasten
Down to that tomb already more than mine.

And, even yet, I dare not let it languish,
Dare not indulge in memory's rapturous pain;
Once drinking deep of that divinest anguish,
How could I seek the empty world again?

5. A Death-Scene

'O Day! he cannot die
When thou so fair art shining!
O Sun, in such a glorious sky,
So tranquilly declining;

'He cannot leave thee now,
While fresh west winds are blowing,
And all around his youthful brow
Thy cheerful light is glowing!

'Edward, awake, awake –
The golden evening gleams
Warm and bright on Arden's lake –
Arouse thee from thy dreams!

'Beside thee, on my knee,
My dearest friend! I pray
That thou, to cross the eternal sea,
Wouldst yet one hour delay:

'I hear its billows roar –
I see them foaming high;
But no glimpse of a further shore
Has blest my straining eye.

'Believe not what they urge
Of Eden isles beyond;
Turn back, from that tempestuous surge,
To thy own native land.

'It is not death, but pain
That struggles in thy breast –
Nay, rally, Edward, rouse again;
I cannot let thee rest!'

One long look, that sore reproved me
For the woe I could not bear –
One mute look of suffering moved me
To repent my useless prayer:

And, with sudden check, the heaving
Of distraction passed away;
Not a sign of further grieving
Stirred my soul that awful day.

Paled, at length, the sweet sun setting;
Sunk to peace the twilight breeze:
Summer dews fell softly, wetting
Glen, and glade, and silent trees.

Then his eyes began to weary,
Weighed beneath a mortal sleep;
And their orbs grew strangely dreary,
Clouded, even as they would weep.

But they wept not, but they changed not,
Never moved, and never closed;
Troubled still, and still they ranged not –
Wandered not, nor yet reposed!

So I knew that he was dying –
Stooped, and raised his languid head;
Felt no breath, and heard no sighing,
So I knew that he was dead.

6. Song

The linnet in the rocky dells,
    The moor-lark in the air,
The bee among the heather bells,
    That hide my lady fair:

The wild deer browse above her breast;
    The wild birds raise their brood;
And they, her smiles of love caressed,
    Have left her solitude!

I ween, that when the grave's dark wall
    Did first her form retain;
They thought their hearts could ne'er recall
    The light of joy again.

They thought the tide of grief would flow
    Unchecked through future years;
But where is all their anguish now,
    And where are all their tears?

Well, let them fight for honour's breath,
    Or pleasure's shade pursue –
The dweller in the land of death
    Is changed and careless too.

And, if their eyes should watch and weep
    Till sorrow's source were dry,
She would not, in her tranquil sleep,
    Return a single sigh!

Blow, west-wind, by the lonely mound,
    And murmur, summer-streams –
There is no need of other sound
    To soothe my lady's dreams.

7. Anticipation

How beautiful the earth is still,
To thee – how full of happiness!
How little fraught with real ill,
Or unreal phantoms of distress!
How spring can bring thee glory, yet,
And summer win thee to forget
December's sullen time!
Why dost thou hold the treasure fast,
Of youth's delight, when youth is past,
    And thou art near thy prime?

When those who were thy own compeers,
Equals in fortune and in years,
Have seen their morning melt in tears,
    To clouded, smileless day;
Blest, had they died untried and young,
Before their hearts went wandering wrong,
Poor slaves, subdued by passions strong,
    A weak and helpless prey!

'Because, I hoped while they enjoyed,
And, by fulfilment, hope destroyed;
As children hope, with trustful breast,
I waited bliss – and cherished rest.
A thoughtful spirit taught me, soon,
That we must long till life be done;
  That every phase of earthly joy
  Must always fade, and always cloy:

'This I foresaw – and would not chase
    The fleeting treacheries;
But, with firm foot and tranquil face,
Held backward from that tempting race,
Gazed o'er the sands the waves efface,
    To the enduring seas –
There cast my anchor of desire
Deep in unknown eternity;
Nor ever let my spirit tire,
With looking for *what is to be!*

'It is hope's spell that glorifies,
Like youth, to my maturer eyes,
All Nature's million mysteries,
    The fearful and the fair –
Hope soothes me in the griefs I know;
She lulls my pain for others' woe,
And makes me strong to undergo
    What I am born to bear.

'Glad comforter! will I not brave,
Unawed, the darkness of the grave?
Nay, smile to hear Death's billows rave –
    Sustained, my guide, by thee?
The more unjust seems present fate,
The more my spirit swells elate,
Strong, in thy strength, to anticipate
    Rewarding destiny!'

8. The Prisoner (A Fragment)

In the dungeon-crypts, idly did I stray,
Reckless of the lives wasting there away;
'Draw the ponderous bars! open, Warder stern!'
He dared not say me nay – the hinges harshly turn.

'Our guests are darkly lodged,' I whisper'd, gazing through
The vault, whose grated eye showed heaven more grey than blue;
(This was when glad spring laughed in awaking pride;)
'Aye, darkly lodged enough!' returned my sullen guide.

Then, God forgive my youth; forgive my careless tongue;
I scoffed, as chill chains on the damp flag-stones rung:
'Confined in triple walls, art thou so much to fear,
That we must bind thee down and clench thy fetters here?'

The captive raised her face, it was as soft and mild
As sculptured marble saint, or slumbering unwean'd child;
It was so soft and mild, it was so sweet and fair,
Pain could not trace a line, nor grief a shadow there!

The captive raised her hand and pressed it to her brow;
'I have been struck,' she said, 'and I am suffering now;
Yet these are little worth, your bolts and irons strong,
And, were they forged in steel, they could not hold me long.'

Hoarse laughed the jailer grim: 'Shall I be won to hear;
Dost think, fond, dreaming wretch, that *I* shall grant thy prayer?
Or, better still, wilt melt my master's heart with groans?
Ah! sooner might the sun thaw down these granite stones.

'My master's voice is low, his aspect bland and kind,
But hard as hardest flint, the soul that lurks behind;
And I am rough and rude, yet not more rough to see
Than is the hidden ghost that has its home in me.'

About her lips there played a smile of almost scorn,
'My friend,' she gently said, 'you have not heard me mourn;
When you my kindred's lives, *my* lost life, can restore,
Then may I weep and sue, – but never, friend, before!

'Still, let my tyrants know, I am not doomed to wear
Year after year in gloom, and desolate despair;
A messenger of Hope, comes every night to me,
And offers for short life, eternal liberty.

'He comes with western winds, with evening's wandering airs,
With that clear dusk of heaven that brings the thickest stars.
Winds take a pensive tone, and stars a tender fire,
And visions rise, and change, that kill me with desire.

'Desire for nothing known in my maturer years,
When Joy grew mad with awe, at counting future tears.
When, if my spirit's sky was full of flashes warm,
I knew not whence they came, from sun, or thunder storm.

'But, first, a hush of peace – a soundless calm descends;
The struggle of distress, and fierce impatience ends.
Mute music soothes my breast, unuttered harmony,
That I could never dream, till Earth was lost to me.

'Then dawns the Invisible; the Unseen its truth reveals;
My outward sense is gone, my inward essence feels:
Its wings are almost free – its home, its harbour found,
Measuring the gulf, it stoops, and dares the final bound.

'Oh, dreadful is the check – intense the agony –
When the ear begins to hear, and the eye begins to see;
When the pulse begins to throb, the brain to think again,
The soul to feel the flesh, and the flesh to feel the chain.

'Yet I would lose no sting, would wish no torture less,
The more that anguish racks, the earlier it will bless;
And robed in fires of hell, or bright with heavenly shine,
If it but herald death, the vision is divine!'

She ceased to speak, and we, unanswering, turned to go –
We had no further power to work the captive woe:
Her cheek, her gleaming eye, declared that man had given
A sentence, unapproved, and overruled by Heaven.

9. Hope

Hope was but a timid friend;
    She sat without the grated den,
Watching how my fate would tend,
    Even as selfish-hearted men.

She was cruel in her fear;
    Through the bars, one dreary day,
I looked out to see her there,
    And she turned her face away!

Like a false guard, false watch keeping,
    Still in strife, she whispered peace;
She would sing while I was weeping;
    If I listened, she would cease.

False she was, and unrelenting;
    When my last joys strewed the ground,
Even Sorrow saw, repenting,
    Those sad relics scattered round;

Hope, whose whisper would have given
    Balm to all my frenzied pain,
Stretched her wings, and soared to heaven,
    Went, and ne'er returned again!

10. A Day Dream

On a sunny brae, alone I lay
    One summer afternoon;
It was the marriage-time of May
    With her young lover, June.

From her mother's heart, seemed loath to part
    That queen of bridal charms,
But her father smiled on the fairest child
    He ever held in his arms.

The trees did wave their plumy crests,
    The glad birds carolled clear;
And I, of all the wedding guests,
    Was only sullen there!

There was not one, but wished to shun
    My aspect void of cheer;
The very grey rocks, looking on,
    Asked, 'What do you here?'

And I could utter no reply;
    In sooth, I did not know
Why I had brought a clouded eye
    To greet the general glow.

So, resting on a heathy bank,
    I took my heart to me;
And we together sadly sank
    Into a reverie.

We thought, 'When winter comes again,
    Where will these bright things be?
All vanished, like a vision vain,
    An unreal mockery!

'The birds that now so blithely sing,
    Through deserts, frozen dry,
Poor spectres of the perished spring,
    In famished troops, will fly.

'And why should we be glad at all?
    The leaf is hardly green,
Before a token of its fall
    Is on the surface seen!'

Now, whether it were really so,
    I never could be sure;
But as in fit of peevish woe,
    I stretched me on the moor,

A thousand thousand gleaming fires
    Seemed kindling in the air;
A thousand thousand silvery lyres
    Resounded far and near:

Methought, the very breath I breathed
    Was full of sparks divine,
And all my heather-couch was wreathed
    By that celestial shine!

And, while the wide earth echoing rung
    To their strange minstrelsy,
The little glittering spirits sung,
    Or seemed to sing, to me.

'O mortal! mortal! let them die;
    Let time and tears destroy,
That we may overflow the sky
    With universal joy!

'Let grief distract the sufferer's breast,
    And night obscure his way;
They hasten him to endless rest,
    And everlasting day.

'To thee the world is like a tomb,
    A desert's naked shore;
To us, in unimagined bloom,
    It brightens more and more!

'And could we lift the veil, and give
    One brief glimpse to thine eye,
Thou wouldst rejoice for those that live,
    Because they live to die.'

The music ceased; the noonday dream,
    Like dream of night, withdrew;
But Fancy, still, will sometimes deem
    Her fond creation true.

11. *To Imagination*

When weary with the long day's care,
    And earthly change from pain to pain,
And lost and ready to despair,
    Thy kind voice calls me back again:
Oh, my true friend! I am not lone,
While thou canst speak with such a tone!

So hopeless is the world without;
    The world within I doubly prize;
Thy world, where guile, and hate, and doubt,
    And cold suspicion never rise;
Where thou, and I, and Liberty,
Have undisputed sovereignty.

What matters it, that, all around,
    Danger, and guilt, and darkness lie,
If but within our bosom's bound
    We hold a bright, untroubled sky,
Warm with ten thousand mingled rays
Of suns that know no winter days?

Reason, indeed, may oft complain
    For Nature's sad reality,
And tell the suffering heart how vain
    Its cherished dreams must always be;
And Truth may rudely trample down
The flowers of Fancy, newly-blown:

But, thou art ever there, to bring
    The hovering vision back, and breathe
New glories o'er the blighted spring,
    And call a lovelier Life from Death,
And whisper, with a voice divine,
Of real worlds, as bright as thine.

I trust not to thy phantom bliss,
    Yet, still, in evening's quiet hour,
With never-failing thankfulness,
    I welcome thee, Benignant Power;
Sure solacer of human cares,
And sweeter hope, when hope despairs!

12. *How Clear She Shines*

How clear she shines! How quietly
    I lie beneath her guardian light;
While heaven and earth are whispering me,
    'Tomorrow, wake, but, dream tonight.'
Yes, Fancy, come, my Fairy love!
    These throbbing temples softly kiss;
And bend my lonely couch above
    And bring me rest, and bring me bliss.

The world is going; dark world, adieu!
    Grim world, conceal thee till the day;
The heart, thou canst not all subdue,
    Must still resist, if thou delay!

Thy love I will not, will not share;
    Thy hatred only wakes a smile;
Thy griefs may wound – thy wrongs may tear,
    But, oh, thy lies shall ne'er beguile!
While gazing on the stars that glow
    Above me, in that stormless sea,
I long to hope that all the woe
    Creation knows, is held in thee!

And this shall be my dream tonight;
    I'll think the heaven of glorious spheres
Is rolling on its course of light
    In endless bliss, through endless years;

I'll think, there's not one world above,
    Far as these straining eyes can see,
Where wisdom ever laughed at Love,
    Or Virtue crouched to Infamy;

Where, writhing 'neath the strokes of Fate,
    The mangled wretch was forced to smile;
To match his patience 'gainst her hate,
    His heart rebellious all the while.
Where Pleasure still will lead to wrong,
    And helpless Reason warn in vain;
And Truth is weak, and Treachery strong;
    And Joy the surest path to Pain;
And Peace, the lethargy of Grief;
    And Hope, a phantom of the soul;
And Life, a labour, void and brief;
    And Death, the despot of the whole!

13. Sympathy

There should be no despair for you
    While nightly stars are burning;
While evening pours its silent dew
    And sunshine gilds the morning.
There should be no despair – though tears
    May flow down like a river:
Are not the best beloved of years
    Around your heart for ever?

They weep, you weep, it must be so;
    Winds sigh as you are sighing,
And Winter sheds his grief in snow
    Where Autumn's leaves are lying:
Yet, these revive, and from their fate
    Your fate cannot be parted:
Then, journey on, if not elate,
    Still, *never* broken-hearted!

14. Plead for Me

Oh, thy bright eyes must answer now,
When Reason, with a scornful brow,
Is mocking at my overthrow!
Oh, thy sweet tongue must plead for me
And tell, why I have chosen thee!

Stern Reason is to judgment come,
Arrayed in all her forms of gloom:
Wilt thou, my advocate, be dumb?
No, radiant angel, speak and say,
Why I did cast the world away.

Why I have persevered to shun
The common paths that others run,
And on a strange road journeyed on,
Heedless, alike, of wealth and power –
Of glory's wreath and pleasure's flower.

These, once, indeed, seemed Beings Divine;
And they, perchance, heard vows of mine,
And saw my offerings on their shrine;
But, careless gifts are seldom prized,
And *mine* were worthily despised.

So, with a ready heart I swore
To seek their altar-stone no more;
And gave my spirit to adore
Thee, ever-present, phantom thing;
My slave, my comrade, and my king,

A slave, because I rule thee still;
Incline thee to my changeful will,
And make thy influence good or ill:
A comrade, for by day and night
Thou art my intimate delight, –

My darling pain that wounds and sears
And wrings a blessing out from tears
By deadening me to earthly cares;
And yet, a king, though Prudence well
Have taught thy subject to rebel.

And am I wrong to worship, where
Faith cannot doubt, nor hope despair,
Since my own soul can grant my prayer?
Speak, God of visions, plead for me,
And tell why I have chosen thee!

15. Self-Interrogation

'The evening passes fast away,
    'Tis almost time to rest;
What thoughts has left the vanished day,
    What feelings, in thy breast?'

'The vanished day? It leaves a sense
    Of labour hardly done;
Of little, gained with vast expense, –
    A sense of grief alone!

'Time stands before the door of Death,
    Upbraiding bitterly;
And Conscience, with exhaustless breath,
    Pours black reproach on me:

'And though I've said that Conscience lies,
    And Time should Fate condemn;
Still, sad Repentance clouds my eyes,
    And makes me yield to them!'

'Then art thou glad to seek repose?
    Art glad to leave the sea,
And anchor all thy weary woes
    In calm Eternity?

'Nothing regrets to see thee go –
    Not one voice sobs "farewell",
And where thy heart has suffered so,
    Canst thou desire to dwell?'

'Alas! The countless links are strong
    That bind us to our clay;
The loving spirit lingers long,
    And would not pass away!

'And rest is sweet, when laurelled fame
    Will crown the soldier's crest;
But, a brave heart, with a tarnished name,
    Would rather fight than rest.'

'Well, thou hast fought for many a year,
    Hast fought thy whole life through,
Hast humbled Falsehood, trampled Fear;
    What is there left to do?'

''Tis true, this arm has hotly striven,
    Has dared what few would dare;
Much have I done, and freely given,
    But little learnt to bear!'

'Look on the grave, where thou must sleep,
    Thy last, and strongest foe;
It is endurance not to weep,
    If that repose seem woe.

'The long war closing in defeat,
    Defeat serenely borne,
Thy midnight rest may still be sweet,
    And break in glorious morn!'

16. Death

Death! that struck when I was most confiding
In my certain faith of joy to be –
Strike again, Time's withered branch dividing
From the fresh root of Eternity!

Leaves, upon Time's branch, were growing brightly,
Full of sap, and full of silver dew;
Birds beneath its shelter gathered nightly;
Daily round its flowers the wild bees flew.

Sorrow passed, and plucked the golden blossom;
Guilt stripped off the foliage in its pride;
But, within its parent's kindly bosom,
Flowed for ever Life's restoring tide.

Little mourned I for the parted gladness,
For the vacant nest and silent song –
Hope was there, and laughed me out of sadness;
Whispering, 'Winter will not linger long!'

And, behold! with tenfold increase blessing,
Spring adorned the beauty-burdened spray;
Wind and rain and fervent heat, caressing,
Lavished glory on that second May!

High it rose – no winged grief could sweep it;
Sin was scared to distance with its shine;
Love, and its own life, had power to keep it
From all wrong – from every blight but thine!

Cruel Death! The young leaves droop and languish;
Evening's gentle air may still restore –
No! the morning sunshine mocks my anguish –
Time, for me, must never blossom more!

Strike it down, that other boughs may flourish
Where that perished sapling used to be;
Thus, at least, its mouldering corpse will nourish
That from which it sprung – Eternity.

17. Stanzas to —

Well, some may hate, and some may scorn,
And some may quite forget thy name;
But my sad heart must ever mourn
Thy ruined hopes, thy blighted fame!
'Twas thus I thought, an hour ago,
Even weeping o'er that wretch's woe;
One word turned back my gushing tears,
And lit my altered eye with sneers.
Then 'Bless the friendly dust,' I said,
'That hides thy unlamented head!
Vain as thou wert, and weak as vain,
The slave of Falsehood, Pride, and Pain, –
My heart has nought akin to thine;
Thy soul is powerless over mine.'

But these were thoughts that vanished too;
Unwise, unholy, and untrue:
Do I despise the timid deer,
Because his limbs are fleet with fear?
Or, would I mock the wolf's death-howl,
Because his form is gaunt and foul?
Or, hear with joy the leveret's cry,
Because it cannot bravely die?
No! Then above his memory
Let Pity's heart as tender be;
Say, 'Earth, lie lightly on that breast
And, kind Heaven, grant that spirit rest!'

18. Honour's Martyr

The moon is full this winter night;
    The stars are clear, though few;
And every window glistens bright,
    With leaves of frozen dew.

The sweet moon through your lattice gleams
    And lights your room like day;
And there you pass, in happy dreams,
    The peaceful hours away!

While I, with effort hardly quelling
    The anguish in my breast,
Wander about the silent dwelling,
    And cannot think of rest.

The old clock in the gloomy hall
    Ticks on, from hour to hour;
And every time its measured call
    Seems lingering slow and slower:

And oh, how slow that keen-eyed star
    Has tracked the chilly grey!
What, watching yet! how very far
    The morning lies away!

Without your chamber door I stand;
    Love, are you slumbering still?
My cold heart, underneath my hand,
    Has almost ceased to thrill.

Bleak, bleak the east wind sobs and sighs,
    And drowns the turret bell,
Whose sad note, undistinguished, dies
    Unheard, like my farewell!

Tomorrow, Scorn will blight my name,
    And Hate will trample me,
Will load me with a coward's shame –
    A traitor's perjury.

False friends will launch their covert sneers;
    True friends will wish me dead;
And I shall cause the bitterest tears
    That you have ever shed.

The dark deeds of my outlawed race
    Will then like virtues shine;
And men will pardon their disgrace,
    Beside the guilt of mine.

For, who forgives the accursed crime
    Of dastard treachery?
Rebellion, in its chosen time,
    May Freedom's champion be;

Revenge may stain a righteous sword,
    It may be just to slay;
But, traitor, traitor, – from *that* word
    All true breasts shrink away!

Oh, I would give my heart to death,
  To keep my honour fair;
Yet, I'll not give my inward faith
  My honour's *name* to spare!

Not even to keep your priceless love,
  Dare I, Beloved, deceive;
This treason should the future prove,
  Then, only then, believe!

I know the path I ought to go;
  I follow fearlessly,
Inquiring not what deeper woe
  Stern duty stores for me.

So foes pursue, and cold allies
  Mistrust me, every one:
Let me be false in others' eyes,
  If faithful in my own.

19. Stanzas

I'll not weep that thou art going to leave me,
    There's nothing lovely here;
And doubly will the dark world grieve me,
    While thy heart suffers there.

I'll not weep, because the summer's glory
    Must always end in gloom;
And, follow out the happiest story –
    It closes with a tomb!

And I am weary of the anguish
    Increasing winters bear;
Weary to watch the spirit languish
    Through years of dead despair.

So, if a tear, when thou art dying,
    Should haply fall from me,
It is but that my soul is sighing,
    To go and rest with thee.

20. My Comforter

Well hast thou spoken, and yet, not taught
    A feeling strange or new;
Thou hast but roused a latent thought,
A cloud-closed beam of sunshine, brought
    To gleam in open view.

Deep down, concealed within my soul,
    That light lies hid from men;
Yet, glows unquenched – though shadows roll,
Its gentle ray cannot control,
    About the sullen den.

Was I not vexed, in these gloomy ways
    To walk alone so long?
Around me, wretches uttering praise,
Or howling o'er their hopeless days,
    And each with Frenzy's tongue; –

A brotherhood of misery,
    Their smiles as sad as sighs;
Whose madness daily maddened me,
Distorting into agony
    The bliss before my eyes!

So stood I, in Heaven's glorious sun,
    And in the glare of Hell;
My spirit drank a mingled tone,
Of seraph's song, and demon's moan;
What my soul bore, my soul alone
    Within itself may tell!

Like a soft air, above a sea,
    Tossed by the tempest's stir;
A thaw-wind, melting quietly
The snow-drift, on some wintry lea;
No: what sweet thing resembles thee,
    My thoughtful Comforter?

And yet a little longer speak,
    Calm this resentful mood;
And while the savage heart grows meek,
For other token do not seek,
But let the tear upon my cheek
    Evince my gratitude!

21. The Old Stoic

Riches I hold in light esteem;
    And Love I laugh to scorn;
And lust of fame was but a dream
    That vanished with the morn:

And if I pray, the only prayer
    That moves my lips for me
Is, 'Leave the heart that now I bear,
    And give me liberty!'

Yes, as my swift days near their goal,
    'Tis all that I implore;
In life and death, a chainless soul,
    With courage to endure.

22.

Woods you need not frown on me
Spectral trees that so dolefully
Shake your heads in the dreary sky
You need not mock so bitterly

23.

The blue bell is the sweetest flower
That waves in summer air
Its blossoms have the mightiest power
To soothe my spirit's care

There is a spell in purple heath
Too wildly, sadly drear
The violet has a fragrant breath
But fragrance will not cheer

The trees are bare, the sun is cold
And seldom, seldom seen –
The heavens have lost their zone of gold
The earth its robe of green

And ice upon the glancing stream
Has cast its sombre shade
And distant hills and valleys seem
In frozen mist arrayed –

The blue bell cannot charm me now
The heath has lost its bloom
The violets in the glen below
They yield no sweet perfume

But though I mourn the heather-bell
'Tis better far, away
I know how fast my tears would swell
To see it smile today

And that wood flower that hides so shy
Beneath the mossy stone
Its balmy scent and dewy eye
'Tis not for them I moan

It is the slight and stately stem
The blossom's silvery blue
The buds hid like a sapphire gem
In sheaths of emerald hue

'Tis these that breathe upon my heart
A calm and softening spell
That if it makes the tear-drop start
Has power to soothe as well

For these I weep, so long divided
Through winter's dreary day
In longing weep – but most when guided
On withered banks to stray

If chilly then the light should fall
Adown the dreary sky
And gild the dank and darkened wall
With transient brilliancy

How do I yearn, how do I pine
For the time of flowers to come
And turn me from that fading shine
To mourn the fields of home –

24. The Night-Wind

In summer's mellow midnight
A cloudless moon shone through
Our open parlour window
And rosetrees wet with dew

I sat in silent musing –
The soft wind waved my hair
It told me Heaven was glorious
And sleeping Earth was fair –

I needed not its breathing
To bring such thoughts to me
But still it whispered lowly
'How dark the woods will be! –

'The thick leaves in my murmur
Are rustling like a dream,
And all their myriad voices
Instinct with spirit seem'

I said, 'Go gentle singer,
Thy wooing voice is kind
But do not think its music
Has power to reach my mind –

'Play with the scented flower,
The young tree's supple bough –
And leave my human feelings
In their own course to flow'

The Wanderer would not leave me
Its kiss grew warmer still –
'O come,' it sighed so sweetly
'I'll win thee 'gainst thy will –

'Have we not been from childhood friends?
Have I not loved thee long?
As long as thou hast loved the night
Whose silence wakes my song?

'And when thy heart is laid at rest
Beneath the church-yard stone
I shall have time enough to mourn
And thou to be alone' –

25.

The night is darkening round me
The wild winds coldly blow
But a tyrant spell has bound me
And I cannot cannot go

The giant trees are bending
Their bare boughs weighed with snow
And the storm is fast descending
And yet I cannot go

Clouds beyond clouds above me
Wastes beyond wastes below
But nothing drear can move me
I will not cannot go

——————

I'll come when thou art saddest
Laid alone in the darkened room
When the mad day's mirth has vanished
And the smile of joy is banished
From evening's chilly gloom

I'll come when the heart's [real] feeling
Has entire unbiased sway
And my influence o'er thee stealing
Grief deepening joy congealing
Shall bear thy soul away

Listen 'tis just the hour
The awful time for thee
Dost thou not feel upon thy soul
A flood of strange sensations roll
Forerunners of a sterner power
Heralds of me

— — — — — —

I would have touched the heavenly key
That spoke alike of bliss and thee
I would have woke the entrancing song
But its words died upon my tongue
And then I knew that hallowed strain
Could never speak of joy again
And then I felt

26.

Shall Earth no more inspire thee,
Thou lonely dreamer now?
Since passion may not fire thee
Shall Nature cease to bow?

Thy mind is ever moving
In regions dark to thee;
Recall its useless roving –
Come back and dwell with me –

I know my mountain breezes
Enchant and soothe thee still –
I know my sunshine pleases
Despite thy wayward will –

When day with evening blending
Sinks from the summer sky,
I've seen thy spirit bending
In fond idolatry –

I've watched thee every hour –
I know my mighty sway –
I know my magic power
To drive thy griefs away –

Few hearts to mortals given
On earth so wildly pine
Yet none would ask a Heaven
More like this Earth than thine –

Then let my winds caress thee –
Thy comrade let me be –
Since nought beside can bless thee
Return and dwell with me –

27.

No coward soul is mine
No trembler in the world's storm-troubled sphere
I see Heaven's glories shine
And Faith shines equal arming me from Fear

O God within my breast
Almighty ever-present Deity
Life, that in me hast rest
As I Undying Life, have power in thee

Vain are the thousand creeds
That move men's hearts, unutterably vain,
Worthless as withered weeds
Or idlest froth amid the boundless main

To waken doubt in one
Holding so fast by thy infinity
So surely anchored on
The steadfast rock of Immortality

With wide-embracing love
Thy spirit animates eternal years
Pervades and broods above,
Changes, sustains, dissolves, creates and rears

Though Earth and moon were gone
And suns and universes ceased to be
And thou wert left alone
Every Existence would exist in thee

There is not room for Death
Nor atom that his might could render void
Since thou art Being and Breath
And what thou art may never be destroyed

28.

All hushed and still within the house
Without – all wind and driving rain
But something whispers to my mind
Through rain and [through the] wailing wind
        – Never again
Never again? Why not again?
Memory has power as real as thine

29.

Often rebuked, yet always back returning
    To those first feelings that were born with me,
And leaving busy chase of wealth and learning
    For idle dreams of things which cannot be:

Today, I will seek not the shadowy region;
    Its unsustaining vastness waxes drear;
And visions rising, legion after legion,
    Bring the unreal world too strangely near.

I'll walk, but not in old heroic traces,
    And not in paths of high morality,
And not among the half-distinguished faces,
    The clouded forms of long-past history.

I'll walk where my own nature would be leading:
    It vexes me to choose another guide:
Where the grey flocks in ferny glens are feeding;
    Where the wild wind blows on the mountain side.

What have those lonely mountains worth revealing?
    More glory and more grief than I can tell:
The earth that wakes *one* human heart to feeling
    Can centre both the worlds of Heaven and Hell.

30.

Why ask to know what date what clime
There dwelt our own humanity
Power-worshippers from earliest time
Foot-kissers of triumphant crime
Crushers of helpless misery
Crushing down Justice honouring Wrong
If that be feeble this be strong

Shedders of blood shedders of tears
Self-cursers avid of distress
Yet Mocking heaven with senseless prayers
For mercy on the merciless

It was the autumn of the year
When grain grows yellow in the ear
Day after day from noon to noon,
That August's sun blazed bright as June

But we with unregarding eyes
Saw panting earth and glowing skies
No hand the reaper's sickle held
Nor bound the ripe sheaves in the field

Our corn was garnered months before,
Threshed out and kneaded-up with gore
Ground when the ears were milky sweet
With furious toil of hoofs and feet
I doubly cursed on foreign sod
Fought neither for my home nor God

1. BOCCACCIO · *Mrs Rosie and the Priest*
2. GERARD MANLEY HOPKINS · *As kingfishers catch fire*
3. *The Saga of Gunnlaug Serpent-tongue*
4. THOMAS DE QUINCEY · *On Murder Considered as One of the Fine Arts*
5. FRIEDRICH NIETZSCHE · *Aphorisms on Love and Hate*
6. JOHN RUSKIN · *Traffic*
7. PU SONGLING · *Wailing Ghosts*
8. JONATHAN SWIFT · *A Modest Proposal*
9. *Three Tang Dynasty Poets*
10. WALT WHITMAN · *On the Beach at Night Alone*
11. KENKŌ · *A Cup of Sake Beneath the Cherry Trees*
12. BALTASAR GRACIÁN · *How to Use Your Enemies*
13. JOHN KEATS · *The Eve of St Agnes*
14. THOMAS HARDY · *Woman much missed*
15. GUY DE MAUPASSANT · *Femme Fatale*
16. MARCO POLO · *Travels in the Land of Serpents and Pearls*
17. SUETONIUS · *Caligula*
18. APOLLONIUS OF RHODES · *Jason and Medea*
19. ROBERT LOUIS STEVENSON · *Olalla*
20. KARL MARX AND FRIEDRICH ENGELS · *The Communist Manifesto*
21. PETRONIUS · *Trimalchio's Feast*
22. JOHANN PETER HEBEL · *How a Ghastly Story Was Brought to Light by a Common or Garden Butcher's Dog*
23. HANS CHRISTIAN ANDERSEN · *The Tinder Box*
24. RUDYARD KIPLING · *The Gate of the Hundred Sorrows*
25. DANTE · *Circles of Hell*
26. HENRY MAYHEW · *Of Street Piemen*
27. HAFEZ · *The nightingales are drunk*
28. GEOFFREY CHAUCER · *The Wife of Bath*
29. MICHEL DE MONTAIGNE · *How We Weep and Laugh at the Same Thing*
30. THOMAS NASHE · *The Terrors of the Night*
31. EDGAR ALLAN POE · *The Tell-Tale Heart*
32. MARY KINGSLEY · *A Hippo Banquet*
33. JANE AUSTEN · *The Beautifull Cassandra*
34. ANTON CHEKHOV · *Gooseberries*
35. SAMUEL TAYLOR COLERIDGE · *Well, they are gone, and here must I remain*
36. JOHANN WOLFGANG VON GOETHE · *Sketchy, Doubtful, Incomplete Jottings*
37. CHARLES DICKENS · *The Great Winglebury Duel*
38. HERMAN MELVILLE · *The Maldive Shark*
39. ELIZABETH GASKELL · *The Old Nurse's Story*
40. NIKOLAY LESKOV · *The Steel Flea*

41. HONORÉ DE BALZAC · *The Atheist's Mass*
42. CHARLOTTE PERKINS GILMAN · *The Yellow Wall-Paper*
43. C.P. CAVAFY · *Remember, Body...*
44. FYODOR DOSTOEVSKY · *The Meek One*
45. GUSTAVE FLAUBERT · *A Simple Heart*
46. NIKOLAI GOGOL · *The Nose*
47. SAMUEL PEPYS · *The Great Fire of London*
48. EDITH WHARTON · *The Reckoning*
49. HENRY JAMES · *The Figure in the Carpet*
50. WILFRED OWEN · *Anthem For Doomed Youth*
51. WOLFGANG AMADEUS MOZART · *My Dearest Father*
52. PLATO · *Socrates' Defence*
53. CHRISTINA ROSSETTI · *Goblin Market*
54. *Sindbad the Sailor*
55. SOPHOCLES · *Antigone*
56. RYŪNOSUKE AKUTAGAWA · *The Life of a Stupid Man*
57. LEO TOLSTOY · *How Much Land Does A Man Need?*
58. GIORGIO VASARI · *Leonardo da Vinci*
59. OSCAR WILDE · *Lord Arthur Savile's Crime*
60. SHEN FU · *The Old Man of the Moon*
61. AESOP · *The Dolphins, the Whales and the Gudgeon*
62. MATSUO BASHŌ · *Lips too Chilled*
63. EMILY BRONTË · *The Night is Darkening Round Me*
64. JOSEPH CONRAD · *To-morrow*
65. RICHARD HAKLUYT · *The Voyage of Sir Francis Drake Around the Whole Globe*
66. KATE CHOPIN · *A Pair of Silk Stockings*
67. CHARLES DARWIN · *It was snowing butterflies*
68. BROTHERS GRIMM · *The Robber Bridegroom*
69. CATULLUS · *I Hate and I Love*
70. HOMER · *Circe and the Cyclops*
71. D. H. LAWRENCE · *Il Duro*
72. KATHERINE MANSFIELD · *Miss Brill*
73. OVID · *The Fall of Icarus*
74. SAPPHO · *Come Close*
75. IVAN TURGENEV · *Kasyan from the Beautiful Lands*
76. VIRGIL · *O Cruel Alexis*
77. H. G. WELLS · *A Slip under the Microscope*
78. HERODOTUS · *The Madness of Cambyses*
79. *Speaking of Siva*
80. *The Dhammapada*

'It was as if the sea, breaking down the wall protecting all the homes of the town, had sent a wave over her head' . . .

JOSEPH CONRAD

Born 1857, Berdychiv, Russia

Died 1924, Bishopsbourne, England

'To-morrow' was first published in 1902.

CONRAD IN PENGUIN CLASSICS

Heart of Darkness

Lord Jim

Nostromo

The Secret Agent

The Secret Sharer and Other Stories

Typhoon and Other Stories

Under Western Eyes

JOSEPH CONRAD

To-morrow

PENGUIN BOOKS

PENGUIN CLASSICS

UK | USA | Canada | Ireland | Australia
India | New Zealand | South Africa

Penguin Books is part of the Penguin Random House group of companies whose addresses can be found at global.penguinrandomhouse.com.

This edition published in Penguin Classics 2015

009

Set in 10/14.5 pt Baskerville 10 Pro
Typeset by Jouve (UK), Milton Keynes
Printed and bound in Great Britain by Clays Ltd, Elcograf S.p.A.

A CIP catalogue record for this book is available from the British Library

ISBN: 978-0-141-39849-5

www.greenpenguin.co.uk

Penguin Random House is committed to a sustainable future for our business, our readers and our planet. This book is made from Forest Stewardship Council® certified paper.

To-morrow

What was known of Captain Hagberd in the little seaport of Colebrook was not exactly in his favour. He did not belong to the place. He had come to settle there under circumstances not at all mysterious – he used to be very communicative about them at the time – but extremely morbid and unreasonable. He was possessed of some little money evidently, because he bought a plot of ground, and had a pair of ugly yellow brick cottages run up very cheaply. He occupied one of them himself and let the other to Josiah Carvil – blind Carvil, the retired boat-builder – a man of evil repute as a domestic tyrant.

These cottages had one wall in common, shared in a line of iron railing dividing their front gardens; a wooden fence separated their back gardens. Miss Bessie Carvil was allowed, as it were of right, to throw over it the tea-cloths, blue rags, or an apron that wanted drying.

'It rots the wood, Bessie my girl,' the captain would remark mildly, from his side of the fence, each time he saw her exercising that privilege.

She was a tall girl; the fence was low, and she could spread her elbows on the top. Her hands would be red with the bit of washing she had done, but her forearms were white and shapely, and she would look at her father's landlord in silence – in an informed silence which had an air of knowledge, expectation, and desire.

'It rots the wood,' repeated Captain Hagberd. 'It is the only unthrifty, careless habit I know in you. Why don't you have a clothes-line out in your back yard?'

Miss Carvil would say nothing to this – she only shook her head negatively. The tiny back yard on her side had a few stone-bordered little beds of black earth, in which the simple flowers she found time to cultivate appeared somehow extravagantly overgrown, as if belonging to an exotic clime; and Captain Hagberd's upright, hale person, clad in No. 1 sail-cloth from head to foot, would be emerging knee-deep

To-morrow

out of rank grass and the tall weeds on his side of the fence. He appeared, with the colour and uncouth stiffness of the extraordinary material in which he chose to clothe himself – 'for the time being,' would be his mumbled remark to any observation on the subject – like a man roughened out of granite, standing in a wilderness not big enough for a decent billiard-room. A heavy figure of a man of stone, with a red handsome face, a blue wandering eye, and a great white beard flowing to his waist and never trimmed as far as Colebrook knew.

Seven years before, he had seriously answered, 'Next month, I think,' to the chaffing attempt to secure his custom made by that distinguished local wit, the Colebrook barber, who happened to be sitting insolently in the tap-room of the New Inn near the harbour, where the captain had entered to buy an ounce of tobacco. After paying for his purchase with three half-pence extracted from the corner of a handkerchief which he carried in the cuff of his sleeve, Captain Hagberd went out. As soon as the door was shut the barber laughed. 'The old one and the young one will be strolling arm in arm to get shaved in my place presently. The tailor shall be set to work, and

Joseph Conrad

the barber, and the candlestick maker; high old times are coming for Colebrook; they are coming, to be sure. It used to be "next week," now it has come to "next month," and so on – soon it will be next spring, for all I know.'

Noticing a stranger listening to him with a vacant grin, he explained, stretching out his legs cynically, that this queer old Hagberd, a retired coasting-skipper, was waiting for the return of a son of his. The boy had been driven away from home, he shouldn't wonder; had run away to sea and had never been heard of since. Put to rest in Davy Jones's locker this many a day, as likely as not. That old man came flying to Colebrook three years ago all in black broadcloth (had lost his wife lately then), getting out of a third-class smoker as if the devil had been at his heels; and the only thing that brought him down was a letter – a hoax probably. Some joker had written to him about a seafaring man with some such name who was supposed to be hanging about some girl or other, either in Colebrook or in the neighbourhood. 'Funny, ain't it?' The old chap had been advertising in the London papers for Harry Hagberd, and offering rewards for any sort of likely information. And the barber would go on to describe, with sardonic gusto, how that stranger in mourning had been seen exploring the country, in carts, on foot, taking everybody into his confidence, visiting all the inns and alehouses for miles around, stopping people on the road with his questions, looking into the very ditches almost; first in the greatest excitement, then with a plodding sort of perseverance, growing slower and slower; and he could not even tell you plainly how his son looked. The sailor was supposed to be one of two that had left a timber ship, and to have been seen dangling after some girl; but the old man described a boy of fourteen or so – 'a clever-looking, high-spirited boy.' And when people only smiled at this he would rub his forehead in a confused sort of way before he slunk off, looking offended. He found nobody, of course; not a trace of anybody – never heard of anything worth belief, at any rate; but he had not been able somehow to tear himself away from Colebrook.

'It was the shock of this disappointment, perhaps, coming soon after the loss of his wife, that had driven him crazy on that point,' the barber suggested, with an air of great psychological insight. After a time the old man abandoned the active search. His son had evidently gone away; but he settled himself to wait. His son had been once at least in Colebrook in preference to his native place. There must have been some reason for it, he seemed to think, some very powerful inducement, that would bring him back to Colebrook again.

'Ha, ha, ha! Why, of course, Colebrook. Where else? That's the only place in the United Kingdom for your long-lost sons. So he sold up his old home in Colchester, and down he comes here. Well, it's a craze, like any other. Wouldn't catch me going crazy over any of my youngsters clearing out. I've got eight of them at home.' The barber was showing off his strength of mind in the midst of a laughter that shook the tap-room.

Strange, though, that sort of thing, he would confess, with the frankness of a superior intelligence, seemed to be catching. His establishment, for instance, was near the harbour, and whenever a sailorman came in for a hair-cut or a shave – if it was a strange face he couldn't help thinking directly, 'Suppose he's the son of old Hagberd!' He laughed at himself for it. It was a strong craze. He could remember the time when the whole town was full of it. But he had his hopes of the old chap yet. He would cure him by a course of judicious chaffing. He was watching the progress of the treatment. Next week – next month – next year! When the old skipper had put off the date of that return till next year, he would be well on his way to not saying any more about it. In other matters he was quite rational, so this, too, was bound to come. Such was the barber's firm opinion.

Nobody had ever contradicted him; his own hair had gone grey since that time, and Captain Hagberd's beard had turned quite white, and had acquired a majestic flow over the No. 1 canvas suit, which he had made for himself secretly with tarred twine, and had assumed suddenly, coming out in it one fine morning, whereas the evening before he had been seen going home in his mourning of broadcloth. It caused a sensation in the High Street – shopkeepers coming to their doors, people in the houses snatching up their hats to run out – a stir at which he seemed strangely surprised at first, and then scared; but his only answer to the wondering questions was that startled and evasive, 'For the present.'

That sensation had been forgotten long ago; and

Captain Hagberd himself, if not forgotten, had come to be disregarded – the penalty of dailiness – as the sun itself is disregarded unless it makes its power felt heavily. Captain Hagberd's movements showed no infirmity: he walked stiffly in his suit of canvas, a quaint and remarkable figure; only his eyes wandered more furtively perhaps than of yore. His manner abroad had lost its excitable watchfulness; it had become puzzled and diffident, as though he had suspected that there was somewhere about him something slightly compromising, some embarrassing oddity; and yet had remained unable to discover what on earth this something wrong could be.

He was unwilling now to talk with the townsfolk. He had earned for himself the reputation of an awful skinflint, of a miser, in the matter of living. He mumbled regretfully in the shops, bought inferior scraps of meat after long hesitations; and discouraged all allusions to his costume. It was as the barber had foretold. For all one could tell, he had recovered already from the disease of hope; and only Miss Bessie Carvil knew that he said nothing about his son's return because with him it was no longer 'next week,' 'next month,' or even 'next year.' It was 'to-morrow.'

In their intimacy of back yard and front garden he talked with her paternally, reasonably, and dogmatically, with a touch of arbitrariness. They met on the ground of unreserved confidence, which was authenticated by an affectionate wink now and then. Miss Carvil had come to look forward rather to these winks. At first they had discomposed her: the poor fellow was mad. Afterwards she had learned to laugh at them: there was no harm in him. Now she was aware of an unacknowledged, pleasurable, incredulous emotion, expressed by a faint blush. He winked not in the least vulgarly; his thin red face, with a well-modelled curved nose, had a sort of distinction – the more so that when he talked to her he looked with a steadier and more intelligent glance. A handsome, hale, upright, capable man, with a white beard. You did not think of his age. His son, he affirmed, had resembled him amazingly from his earliest babyhood.

Harry would be one-and-thirty next July, he declared. Proper age to get married with a nice, sensible girl that could appreciate a good home. He was a very high-spirited boy. High-spirited husbands were the easiest to manage. These mean, soft chaps, that you would think butter wouldn't melt in their mouths, were the ones to make a woman thoroughly miserable. And there was nothing like home – a fireside – a good roof: no turning out of your warm bed in all sorts of weather. 'Eh, my dear?'

Captain Hagberd had been one of those sailors that pursue their calling within sight of land. One of the many children of a bankrupt farmer, he had been apprenticed hurriedly to a coasting-skipper, and had remained on the coast all his sea life. It must have been a hard one at first: he had never taken to it; his affection turned to the land, with its innumerable houses, with its quiet lives gathered round its firesides. Many sailors feel and profess a rational dislike for the sea, but his was a profound and emotional animosity, as if the love of the stabler element had been bred into him through many generations.

'People did not know what they let their boys in for when they let them go to sea,' he expounded to Bessie. 'As soon make convicts of them at once.' He did not believe you ever got used to it. The weariness of such a life got worse as you got older. What sort of trade was it in which more than half your time you did not put your foot inside your house? Directly you got out to sea you had no means of knowing what went on at home. One might have thought him weary of distant voyages; and the longest he had ever made had lasted a fortnight, of which the most part had been spent at anchor, sheltering from the weather. As soon as his wife had inherited a house and enough to live on (from a bachelor uncle who had made some money in the coal business) he threw up his command of an East-coast collier with a feeling as though he had escaped from the galleys. After all these years he might have counted on the fingers of his two hands all the days he had been out of sight of England. He had never known what it was to be out of soundings. 'I have never been further than eighty fathoms from the land' was one of his boasts.

Bessie Carvil heard all these things. In front of their cottage grew an under-sized ash; and on summer afternoons she would bring out a chair on the grass-plot and sit down with her sewing. Captain Hagberd, in his canvas suit, leaned on a spade. He dug every day in his front plot. He turned it over and over several times every year, but was not going to plant anything 'just at present.'

To Bessie Carvil he would state more explicitly: 'Not till our Harry comes home to-morrow.' And she had heard this formula of hope so often that it only awakened the vaguest pity in her heart for that hopeful old man.

Everything was put off in that way, and everything was being prepared likewise for to-morrow. There was a boxful of packets of various flower-seeds to choose from, for the front garden. 'He will doubtless let you have your say about that, my dear,' Captain Hagberd intimated to her across the railing.

Miss Bessie's head remained bowed over her work. She had heard all this so many times. But now and then she would rise, lay down her sewing, and come slowly to the fence. There was a charm in these gentle ravings. He was determined that his son should not go away again for the want of a home all ready for him. He had been filling the other cottage with all sorts of furniture. She imagined it all new, fresh with varnish, piled up as in a warehouse. There would be tables wrapped up in sacking; rolls of carpets thick and vertical like fragments of columns; the gleam of white marble tops in the dimness of the drawn blinds. Captain Hagberd always described his purchases to her carefully, as to a person having a legitimate interest in them. The overgrown yard of his cottage could be laid over with concrete . . . after to-morrow.

'We may just as well do away with the fence. You could have your drying-line out, quite clear of your flowers.' He winked, and she would blush faintly.

This madness that had entered her life through the kind impulses of her heart had reasonable details. What if some day his son returned? But she could not even be quite sure that he ever had a son; and if he existed anywhere, he had been too long away. When Captain Hagberd got excited in his talk she would steady him by a pretence of belief, laughing a little to salve her conscience.

Only once she had tried pityingly to throw some doubt on that hope doomed to disappointment, but the effect of her attempt had scared her very much. All at once over that man's face there came an expression of horror and incredulity, as though he had seen a crack open out in the firmament.

'You – you – you don't think he's drowned!'

For a moment he seemed to her ready to go out of his mind, for in his ordinary state she thought him more sane than people gave him credit for. On that occasion the violence of the emotion was followed by a most paternal and complacent recovery.

'Don't alarm yourself, my dear,' he said a little cunningly. 'The sea can't keep him. He does not belong to it. None of us Hagberds ever did belong to it. Look at me; I didn't get drowned. Moreover, he isn't a sailor at all; and if he is not a sailor, he's bound to come back. There's nothing to prevent him coming back . . .'

His eyes began to wander.

'To-morrow.'

She never tried again, for fear the man should go out of his mind on the spot. He depended on her. She seemed the only sensible person in the town; and he would congratulate himself frankly before her face on having secured such a level-headed wife for his son. The rest of the town, he confided to her once, in a fit of temper, was certainly queer. The way they looked at you – the way they talked to you! He had never got on with any one in the place. Didn't like the people. He would not have left his own country

To-morrow

if it had not been clear that his son had taken a fancy to Colebrook.

She humoured him in silence, listening patiently by the fence; crocheting with downcast eyes. Blushes came with difficulty on her dead-white complexion, under the negligently twisted opulence of mahogany-coloured hair. Her father was frankly carroty.

She had a full figure; a tired, unrefreshed face. When Captain Hagberd vaunted the necessity and propriety of a home and the delights of one's own fireside, she smiled a little, with her lips only. Her home delights had been confined to the nursing of her father during the ten best years of her life.

A bestial roaring coming out of an upstairs window would interrupt their talk. She would begin at once to roll up her crochet-work or fold her sewing, without the slightest sign of haste. Meanwhile the howls and roars of her name would go on, making the fishermen strolling upon the sea-wall on the other side of the road turn their heads towards the cottages. She would go in slowly at the front door, and a moment afterwards there would fall a profound silence. Presently she would reappear, leading by the hand a man, gross and unwieldy like a hippopotamus, with a bad-tempered, surly face.

He was a widowed boat-builder, whom blindness had overtaken years before in the full flush of business. He behaved to his daughter as if she had been responsible for its incurable character. He had been heard to bellow at the top of his voice, as if to defy Heaven, that he did not care: he had made enough money to have ham and eggs for his breakfast every morning. He thanked God for it, in a fiendish tone as though he were cursing.

Captain Hagberd had been so unfavourably impressed by his tenant that once he told Miss Bessie, 'He is a very extravagant fellow, my dear.'

She was knitting that day, finishing a pair of socks for her father, who expected her to keep up the supply dutifully. She hated knitting, and, as she was just at the heel part, she had to keep her eyes on her needles.

'Of course it isn't as if he had a son to provide for,' Captain Hagberd went on a little vacantly. 'Girls, of course, don't require so much – h'm – h'm. They don't run away from home, my dear.'

'No,' said Miss Bessie, quietly.

To-morrow

Captain Hagberd, amongst the mounds of turned-up earth, chuckled. With his maritime rig, his weather-beaten face, his beard of Father Neptune, he resembled a deposed sea-god who had exchanged the trident for the spade.

'And he must look upon you as already provided for, in a manner. That's the best of it with the girls. The husbands . . .' He winked. Miss Bessie, absorbed in her knitting, coloured faintly.

'Bessie! my hat!' old Carvil bellowed out suddenly. He had been sitting under the tree mute and motionless, like an idol of some remarkably monstrous superstition. He never opened his mouth but to howl for her, at her, sometimes about her; and then he did not moderate the terms of his abuse. Her system was never to answer him at all; and he kept up his shouting till he got attended to – till she shook him by the arm, or thrust the mouthpiece of his pipe between his teeth. He was one of the few blind people who smoke. When he felt the hat being put on his head he stopped his noise at once. Then he rose, and they passed together through the gate.

He weighed heavily on her arm. During their slow, toilful walks she appeared to be dragging with her for a penance the burden of that infirm bulk. Usually they crossed the road at once (the cottages stood in the fields near the harbour, two hundred yards away from the end of the street), and for a long, long time they would remain in view, ascending imperceptibly the flight of wooden steps that led to the top of the sea-wall. It ran on from east to west, shutting out the Channel like a neglected railway embankment, on which no train had ever rolled within memory of man. Groups of sturdy fishermen would emerge upon the sky, walk along for a bit, and sink without haste. Their brown nets, like the cobwebs of gigantic spiders, lay on the shabby grass of the slope; and, looking up from the end of the street, the people of the town would recognise the two Carvils by the creeping slowness of their gait. Captain Hagberd, pottering aimlessly about his cottages, would raise his head to see how they got on in their promenade.

He advertised still in the Sunday papers for Harry Hagberd. These sheets were read in foreign parts to the end of the world, he informed Bessie. At the same time he seemed to think that his son was in England – so near to Colebrook that he would of course turn up 'to-morrow.' Bessie, without committing herself

To-morrow

to that opinion in so many words, argued that in that case the expense of advertising was unnecessary; Captain Hagberd had better spend that weekly half-crown on himself. She declared she did not know what he lived on. Her argumentation would puzzle him and cast him down for a time. 'They all do it,' he pointed out. There was a whole column devoted to appeals after missing relatives. He would bring the newspaper to show her. He and his wife had advertised for years; only she was an impatient woman. The news from Colebrook had arrived the very day after her funeral; if she had not been so impatient she might have been here now, with no more than one day more to wait. 'You are not an impatient woman, my dear.'

'I've no patience with you sometimes,' she would say.

If he still advertised for his son he did not offer rewards for information any more; for, with the muddled lucidity of a mental derangement, he had reasoned himself into a conviction as clear as daylight that he had already attained all that could be expected in that way. What more could he want? Colebrook was the place, and there was no need to ask for more. Miss Carvil praised him for his good sense, and he was soothed by the part she took in his hope, which had become his delusion; in that idea which blinded his mind to truth and probability, just as the other old man in the other cottage had been made blind, by another disease, to the light and beauty of the world.

But anything he could interpret as a doubt – any coldness of assent, or even a simple inattention to the development of his projects of a home with his returned son and his son's wife – would irritate him into flings and jerks and wicked side-glances. He would dash his spade into the ground and walk to and fro before it. Miss Bessie called it his tantrums. She shook her finger at him. Then, when she came out again, after he had parted with her in anger, he would watch out of the corner of his eyes for the least sign of encouragement to approach the iron railings and resume his fatherly and patronising relations.

For all their intimacy, which had lasted some years now, they had never talked without a fence or a railing between them. He described to her all the splendours accumulated for the setting-up of their housekeeping, but had never invited her to an inspection. No human eye was to behold them till Harry had his first look.

To-morrow

In fact, nobody had ever been inside his cottage; he did his own housework, and he guarded his son's privilege so jealously that the small objects of domestic use he bought sometimes in the town were smuggled rapidly across the front garden under his canvas coat. Then, coming out, he would remark apologetically, 'It was only a small kettle, my dear.'

And, if not too tired with her drudgery, or worried beyond endurance by her father, she would laugh at him with a blush, and say: 'That's all right, Captain Hagberd; I am not impatient.'

'Well, my dear, you haven't long to wait now,' he would answer with a sudden bashfulness, and looking uneasily, as though he had suspected that there was something wrong somewhere.

Every Monday she paid him his rent over the railings. He clutched the shillings greedily. He grudged every penny he had to spend on his maintenance, and when he left her to make his purchases his bearing changed as soon as he got into the street. Away from the sanction of her pity, he felt himself exposed without defence. He brushed the walls with his shoulder. He mistrusted the queerness of the people; yet, by then, even the town children had left off calling after him, and the tradesmen served him without a word. The slightest allusion to his clothing had the power to puzzle and frighten especially, as if it were something utterly unwarranted and incomprehensible.

In the autumn, the driving rain drummed on his sail-cloth suit saturated almost to the stiffness of sheet-iron, with its surface flowing with water. When the weather was too bad, he retreated under the tiny porch, and, standing close against the door, looked at his spade left planted in the middle of the yard. The ground was so much dug up all over, that as the season advanced it turned to a quagmire. When it froze hard, he was disconsolate. What would Harry say? And as he could not have so much of Bessie's company at that time of the year, the roars of old Carvil, that came muffled through the closed windows, calling her indoors, exasperated him greatly.

'Why don't that extravagant fellow get you a servant?' he asked impatiently one mild afternoon. She had thrown something over her head to run out for a while.

'I don't know,' said the pale Bessie, wearily, staring away with her heavy-lidded, grey, and unexpectant glance. There were always smudgy shadows under her eyes, and she did not seem able to see any change or any end to her life.

'You wait till you get married, my dear,' said her only friend, drawing closer to the fence. 'Harry will get you one.'

His hopeful craze seemed to mock her own want of hope with so bitter an aptness that in her nervous irritation she could have screamed at him outright. But she only said in self-mockery, and speaking to him as though he had been sane, 'Why, Captain Hagberd, your son may not even want to look at me.'

He flung his head back and laughed his throaty affected cackle of anger.

'What! That boy? Not want to look at the only sensible girl for miles around? What do you think I am here for, my dear – my dear – my dear?... What? You wait. You just wait. You'll see to-morrow. I'll soon –'

'Bessie! Bessie! Bessie!' howled old Carvil inside. 'Bessie! – my pipe!' That fat blind man had given himself up to a very lust of laziness. He would not lift his hand to reach for the things she took care to leave at his very elbow. He would not move a limb; he would not rise from his chair; he would not put one foot before another, in that parlour (where he knew his way as well as if he had his sight), without calling her to his side and hanging all his atrocious weight on her shoulder. He would not eat one single mouthful of food without her close attendance. He had made himself helpless beyond his affliction, to enslave her better. She stood still for a moment, setting her teeth in the dusk, then turned and walked slowly indoors.

Captain Hagberd went back to his spade. The shouting in Carvil's cottage stopped, and after a while the window of the parlour downstairs was lit up. A man coming from the end of the street with a firm leisurely step passed on, but seemed to have caught sight of Captain Hagberd, because he turned back a pace or two. A cold white light lingered in the western sky. The man leaned over the gate in an interested manner.

'You must be Captain Hagberd,' he said, with easy assurance.

The old man spun round, pulling out his spade, startled by the strange voice.

'Yes, I am,' he answered nervously.

The other, smiling straight at him, uttered very

To-morrow

slowly: 'You've been advertising for your son, I believe?'

'My son Harry,' mumbled Captain Hagberd, off his guard for once. 'He's coming home to-morrow.'

'The devil he is!' The stranger marvelled greatly, and then went on, with only a slight change of tone: 'You've grown a beard like Father Christmas himself.'

Captain Hagberd drew a little nearer, and leaned forward over his spade. 'Go your way,' he said, resentfully and timidly at the same time, because he was always afraid of being laughed at. Every mental state, even madness, has its equilibrium based upon self-esteem. Its disturbance causes unhappiness; and Captain Hagberd lived amongst a scheme of settled notions which it pained him to feel disturbed by people's grins. Yes, people's grins were awful. They hinted at something wrong: but what? He could not tell; and that stranger was obviously grinning – had come on purpose to grin. It was bad enough on the streets, but he had never before been outraged like this.

The stranger, unaware how near he was of having his head laid open with a spade, said seriously: 'I am not trespassing where I stand, am I? I fancy there's something wrong about your news. Suppose you let me come in.'

'*You* come in!' murmured old Hagberd, with inexpressible horror.

'I could give you some real information about your son – the very latest tip, if you care to hear.'

'No,' shouted Hagberd. He began to pace wildly to and fro, he shouldered his spade, he gesticulated with his other arm. 'Here's a fellow – a grinning fellow, who says there's something wrong. I've got more information than you're aware of. I've all the information I want. I've had it for years – for years – for years – enough to last me till to-morrow. Let you come in, indeed! What would Harry say?'

Bessie Carvil's figure appeared in black silhouette on the parlour window; then, with the sound of an opening door, flitted out before the other cottage, all black, but with something white over her head. These two voices beginning to talk suddenly outside (she had heard them indoors) had given her such an emotion that she could not utter a sound.

Captain Hagberd seemed to be trying to find his way out of a cage. His feet squelched in the puddles

To-morrow

left by his industry. He stumbled in the holes of the ruined grass-plot. He ran blindly against the fence.

'Here, steady a bit!' said the man at the gate, gravely stretching his arm over and catching him by the sleeve. 'Somebody's been trying to get at you. Hallo! what's this rig you've got on? Storm canvas, by George!' He had a big laugh. 'Well, you *are* a character!'

Captain Hagberd jerked himself free, and began to back away shrinkingly. 'For the present,' he muttered, in a crestfallen tone.

'What's the matter with him?' The stranger addressed Bessie with the utmost familiarity, in a deliberate, explanatory tone. 'I didn't want to startle the old man.' He lowered his voice as though he had known her for years. 'I dropped into a barber's on my way, to get a twopenny shave, and they told me there he was something of a character. The old man has been a character all his life.'

Captain Hagberd, daunted by the allusion to his clothing, had retreated inside, taking his spade with him; and the two at the gate, startled by the unexpected slamming of the door, heard the bolts being shot, the snapping of the lock, and the echo of an affected gurgling laugh within.

'I didn't want to upset him,' the man said, after a short silence. 'What's the meaning of all this? He isn't quite crazy.'

'He has been worrying a long time about his lost son,' said Bessie, in a low apologetic tone.

'Well, I am his son.'

'Harry!' she cried – and was profoundly silent.

'Know my name? Friends with the old man, eh?'

'He's our landlord,' Bessie faltered out, catching hold of the iron railing.

'Owns both them rabbit-hutches, does he?' commented young Hagberd, scornfully. 'Just the thing he would be proud of. Can you tell me who's that chap coming to-morrow? You must know something of it. I tell you, it's a swindle on the old man – nothing else.'

She did not answer, helpless before an insurmountable difficulty, appalled before the necessity, the impossibility and the dread of an explanation in which she and madness seemed involved together.

'Oh – I am so sorry,' she murmured.

'What's the matter?' he said, with serenity. 'You

To-morrow

needn't be afraid of upsetting me. It's the other fellow that'll be upset when he least expects it. I don't care a hang; but there will be some fun when he shows his mug to-morrow. I don't care *that* for the old man's pieces, but right is right. You shall see me put a head on that coon – whoever he is!'

He had come nearer, and towered above her on the other side of the railings. He glanced at her hands. He fancied she was trembling, and it occurred to him that she had her part perhaps in that little game that was to be sprung on his old man to-morrow. He had come just in time to spoil their sport. He was entertained by the idea – scornful of the baffled plot. But all his life he had been full of indulgence for all sorts of women's tricks. She really was trembling very much; her wrap had slipped off her head. 'Poor devil!' he thought. 'Never mind about that chap. I daresay he'll change his mind before to-morrow. But what about me? I can't loaf about the gate till the morning.'

She burst out: 'It is *you* – you yourself that he's waiting for. It is *you* who come to-morrow.'

He murmured 'Oh! It's me!' blankly, and they seemed to become breathless together. Apparently he was pondering over what he had heard; then, without irritation, but evidently perplexed, he said: 'I don't understand. I hadn't written or anything. It's my chum who saw the paper and told me – this very morning . . . Eh? what?'

He bent his ear; she whispered rapidly, and he listened for a while, muttering the words 'yes' and 'I see' at times. Then, 'But why won't to-day do?' he queried at last.

'You didn't understand me!' she exclaimed, impatiently. The clear streak of light under the clouds died out in the west. Again he stooped slightly to hear better; and the deep night buried everything of the whispering woman and the attentive man, except the familiar contiguity of their faces, with its air of secrecy and caress.

He squared his shoulders; the broad-brimmed shadow of a hat sat cavalierly on his head. 'Awkward this, eh?' he appealed to her. 'To-morrow? Well, well! Never heard tell of anything like this. It's all to-morrow, then, without any sort of to-day, as far as I can see.'

She remained still and mute.

'And you have been encouraging this funny notion,' he said.

'I never contradicted him.'

'Why didn't you?'

'What for should I?' she defended herself. 'It would only have made him miserable. He would have gone out of his mind.'

'His mind!' he muttered, and heard a short nervous laugh from her.

'Where was the harm? Was I to quarrel with the poor old man? It was easier to half believe it myself.'

'Aye, aye,' he meditated, intelligently. 'I suppose the old chap got around you somehow with his soft talk. You are good-hearted.'

Her hands moved up in the dark nervously. 'And it might have been true. It was true. It has come. Here it is. This is the to-morrow we have been waiting for.'

She drew a breath, and he said, good-humouredly: 'Aye, with the door shut. I wouldn't care if . . . And you think he could be brought round to recognise me . . . Eh? What? . . . You could do it? In a week you say? H'm, I daresay you could – but do you think I could hold out a week in this dead-alive place? Not me! I want either hard work, or an all-fired racket, or more space than there is in the whole of England. I have been in this place, though, once before, and for more than a week. The old man was advertising for me then, and a chum I had with me had a notion of getting a couple of quid out of him by writing a lot of silly nonsense in a letter. That lark did not come off, though. We had to clear out – and none too soon. But this time I've a chum waiting for me in London, and besides . . .'

Bessie Carvil was breathing quickly.

'What if I tried a knock at the door?' he suggested.

'Try,' she said.

Captain Hagberd's gate squeaked, and the shadow of the son moved on, then stopped with another deep laugh in the throat, like the father's, only soft and gentle, thrilling to the woman's heart, awakening to her ears.

'He isn't frisky – is he? I would be afraid to lay hold of him. The chaps are always telling me I don't know my own strength.'

'He's the most harmless creature that ever lived,' she interrupted.

'You wouldn't say so if you had seen him chasing me upstairs with a hard leather strap,' he said. 'I haven't forgotten it in sixteen years.'

To-morrow

She got warm from head to foot under another soft, subdued laugh. At the rat-tat-tat of the knocker her heart flew into her mouth.

'Hey, dad! Let me in. I am Harry, I am. Straight! Come back home a day too soon.'

One of the windows upstairs ran up.

'A grinning information fellow,' said the voice of old Hagberd, up in the darkness. 'Don't you have anything to do with him. It will spoil everything.'

She heard Harry Hagberd say, 'Hallo, dad,' then a clanging clatter. The window rumbled down, and he stood before her again.

'It's just like old times. Nearly walloped the life out of me to stop me going away, and now I come back he throws a confounded shovel at my head to keep me out. It grazed my shoulder.'

She shuddered.

'I wouldn't care,' he began, 'only I spent my last shillings on the railway fare and my last twopence on a shave – out of respect for the old man.'

'Are you really Harry Hagberd?' she asked swiftly. 'Can you prove it?'

'Can I prove it? Can any one else prove it?' he said jovially. 'Prove with what? What do I want to prove?

There isn't a single corner in the world, barring England, perhaps, where you could not find some man, or more likely a woman, that would remember me for Harry Hagberd. I am more like Harry Hagberd than any man alive; and I can prove it to you in a minute, if you will let me step inside your gate.'

'Come in,' she said.

He entered then the front garden of the Carvils. His tall shadow strode with a swagger; she turned her back on the window and waited, watching the shape, of which the footfalls seemed the most material part. The light fell on a tilted hat; a powerful shoulder that seemed to cleave the darkness; on a leg stepping out. He swung about and stood still, facing the illuminated parlour window at her back, turning his head from side to side, laughing softly to himself.

'Just fancy, for a minute, the old man's beard stuck on to my chin. Hey? Now say. I was the very spit of him from a boy.'

'It's true,' she murmured to herself.

'And that's about as far as it goes. He was always one of your domestic characters. Why, I remember how he used to go about looking very sick for three days before he had to leave home on one of his trips to South Shields for coal. He had a standing charter from the gas-works. You would think he was off on a whaling cruise – three years and a tail. Ha, ha! Not a bit of it. Ten days on the outside. The *Skimmer of the Seas* was a smart craft. Fine name, wasn't it? Mother's uncle owned her . . .'

He interrupted himself, and in a lowered voice, 'Did he ever tell you what mother died of?' he asked.

'Yes,' said Miss Bessie, bitterly: 'from impatience.'

He made no sound for a while; then brusquely: 'They were so afraid I would turn out badly that they fairly drove me away. Mother nagged at me for being idle, and the old man said he would cut my soul out of my body rather than let me go to sea. Well, it looked as if he would do it too – so I went. It looks to me sometimes as if I had been born to them by a mistake – in that other hutch of a house.'

'Where ought you to have been born by rights?' Bessie Carvil interrupted him, defiantly.

'In the open, upon a beach, on a windy night,' he said, quick as lightning. Then he mused slowly. 'They were characters, both of them, by George; and the old man keeps it up well – don't he? A damned shovel on the – Hark! who's that making that row? "Bessie, Bessie." It's in your house.'

'It's for me,' she said with indifference.

He stepped aside, out of the streak of light. 'Your husband?' he inquired, with the tone of a man accustomed to unlawful trysts. 'Fine voice for a ship's deck in a thundering squall.'

'No; my father. I am not married.'

'You seem a fine girl, Miss Bessie, dear,' he said at once. She turned her face away.

'Oh, I say, what's up? Who's murdering him?'

'He wants his tea.' She faced him, still and tall, with averted head, with her hands hanging clasped before her.

'Hadn't you better go in?' he suggested, after watching for a while the nape of her neck, a patch of dazzling white skin and soft shadow above the sombre line of her shoulders. Her wrap had slipped down to her elbows. 'You'll have all the town coming out presently. I'll wait here a bit.'

Her wrap fell to the ground, and he stooped to pick it up; she had vanished. He threw it over his arm, and approaching the window squarely he saw a monstrous form of a fat man in an arm-chair, an unshaded lamp, the yawning of an enormous mouth in a big flat face encircled by a ragged halo of hair, Miss Bessie's head and bust. The shouting stopped; the blind ran down. He lost himself in thinking how awkward it was. Father mad; no getting into the house. No money to get back; a hungry chum in London who would begin to think he had been given the go-by. 'Damn!' he muttered. He could break the door in, certainly; but they would perhaps bundle him into chokey for that without asking questions – no great matter, only he was confoundedly afraid of being locked up, even in mistake. He turned cold at the thought. He stamped his feet on the sodden grass.

'What are you? A sailor?' said an agitated voice.

She had flitted out, a shadow herself, attracted by the reckless shadow waiting under the wall of her home.

'Anything. Enough of a sailor to be worth my salt before the mast. Came home that way this time.'

'Where do you come from?' she asked.

'Right away from a jolly good spree,' he said, 'by

the London train – see? Ough! I hate being shut up in a train. I don't mind a house so much.'

'Ah,' she said, 'that's lucky.'

'Because in a house you can at any time open the blamed door and walk away straight before you.'

'And never come back?'

'Not for sixteen years at least,' he laughed. 'To a rabbit-hutch, and get a confounded old shovel . . .'

'A ship is not so very big,' she taunted.

'No, but the sea is great.'

She dropped her head, and as if her ears had been opened to the voices of the world, she heard, beyond the rampart of sea-wall, the swell of yesterday's gale breaking on the beach with monotonous and solemn vibrations, as if all the earth had been a tolling bell.

'And then, why, a ship's a ship. You love her and leave her; and a voyage isn't a marriage.' He quoted the sailor's saying lightly.

'It is not a marriage,' she whispered.

'I never took a false name, and I've never yet told a lie to a woman. What lie? Why, *the* lie –. Take me or leave me, I say: and if you take me, then it is . . .' He hummed a snatch very low, leaning against the wall.

> Oh, ho, ho Rio!
> And fare thee well,
> My bonnie young girl,
> We're bound to Rio Grande.

'Capstan song,' he explained. Her teeth chattered.

'You are cold,' he said. 'Here's that affair of yours I picked up.' She felt his hands about her, wrapping her closely. 'Hold the ends together in front,' he commanded.

'What did you come here for?' she asked, repressing a shudder.

'Five quid,' he answered, promptly. 'We let our spree go on a little too long and got hard up.'

'You've been drinking?' she said.

'Blind three days; on purpose. I am not given that way – don't you think. There's nothing and nobody that can get over me unless I like. I can be as steady as a rock. My chum sees the paper this morning, and says he to me: "Go on, Harry: loving parent. That's five quid sure." So we scraped all our pockets for the fare. Devil of a lark!'

'You have a hard heart, I am afraid,' she sighed.

'What for? For running away? Why! he wanted to

make a lawyer's clerk of me – just to please himself. Master in his own house; and my poor mother egged him on – for my good, I suppose. Well, then – so long; and I went. No, I tell you: the day I cleared out, I was all black and blue from his great fondness for me. Ah! he was always a bit of a character. Look at that shovel now. Off his chump? Not much. That's just exactly like my dad. He wants me here just to have somebody to order about. However, we two were hard up; and what's five quid to him – once in sixteen hard years?'

'Oh, but I am sorry for you. Did you never want to come back home?'

'Be a lawyer's clerk and rot here – in some such place as this?' he cried in contempt. 'What! if the old man set me up in a home to-day, I would kick it down about my ears – or else die there before the third day was out.'

'And where else is it that you hope to die?'

'In the bush somewhere; in the sea; on a blamed mountaintop for choice. At home? Yes! the world's my home; but I expect I'll die in a hospital some day. What of that? Any place is good enough, as long as I've lived; and I've been everything you can think of almost but a tailor or a soldier. I've been a boundary rider; I've sheared sheep; and humped my swag; and harpooned a whale. I've rigged ships, and prospected for gold, and skinned dead bullocks – and turned my back on more money than the old man would have scraped in his whole life. Ha, ha!'

He overwhelmed her. She pulled herself together and managed to utter, 'Time to rest now.'

He straightened himself up, away from the wall, and in a severe voice said, 'Time to go.'

But he did not move. He leaned back again, and hummed thoughtfully a bar or two of an outlandish tune.

She felt as if she were about to cry. 'That's another of your cruel songs,' she said.

'Learned it in Mexico – in Sonora.' He talked easily. 'It is the song of the Gambusinos. You don't know? The song of restless men. Nothing could hold them in one place – not even a woman. You used to meet one of them now and again, in the old days, on the edge of the gold country, away north there beyond the Rio Gila. I've seen it. A prospecting engineer in Mazatlan took me along with him to help look after the waggons. A sailor's a handy chap to have about you anyhow. It's all a desert: cracks in the earth that you can't see the bottom of; and mountains – sheer rocks standing up high like walls and church spires, only a hundred times bigger. The valleys are full of boulders and black stones. There's not a blade of grass to see; and the sun sets more red over that country than I have seen it anywhere – blood-red and angry. It *is* fine.'

'You do not want to go back there again?' she stammered out.

He laughed a little. 'No. That's the blamed gold country. It gave me the shivers sometimes to look at it – and we were a big lot of men together, mind; but these Gambusinos wandered alone. They knew that country before anybody had ever heard of it. They had a sort of gift for prospecting, and the fever of it was on them too; and they did not seem to want the gold very much. They would find some rich spot, and then turn their backs on it; pick up perhaps a little – enough for a spree – and then be off again, looking for more. They never stopped long where there were houses; they had no wife, no chick, no home, never a chum. You couldn't be friends with a Gambusino; they were too restless – here to-day, and gone, God knows where, to-morrow. They told no one of their finds, and there has never been a Gambusino well off. It was not for the gold they cared; it was the wandering about looking for it in the stony country that got into them and wouldn't let them rest; so that no woman yet born could hold a Gambusino for more than a week. That's what the song says. It's all about a pretty girl that tried hard to keep hold of a Gambusino lover, so that he should bring her lots of gold. No fear! Off he went, and she never saw him again.'

'What became of her?' she breathed out.

'The song don't tell. Cried a bit, I daresay. They were the fellows: kiss and go. But it's the looking for a thing – a something . . . Sometimes I think I am a sort of Gambusino myself.'

'No woman can hold you, then,' she began in a brazen voice, which quavered suddenly before the end.

'No longer than a week,' he joked, playing upon her very heartstrings with the gay, tender note of his laugh, 'and yet I am fond of them all. Anything for a woman of the right sort. The scrapes they got me into, and the scrapes they got me out of! I love them at first sight. I've fallen in love with you already, Miss – Bessie's your name – eh?'

She backed away a little, and with a trembling laugh: 'You haven't seen my face yet.'

He bent forward gallantly. 'A little pale: it suits some. But you are a fine figure of a girl, Miss Bessie.'

She was all in a flutter. Nobody had ever said so much to her before.

His tone changed. 'I am getting middling hungry, though. Had no breakfast to-day. Couldn't you scare up some bread from that tea for me, or –'

She was gone already. He had been on the point of asking her to let him come inside. No matter. Anywhere would do. Devil of a fix! What would his chum think?

'I didn't ask you as a beggar,' he said, jestingly, taking a piece of bread-and-butter from the plate she held before him. 'I asked as a friend. My dad is rich, you know.'

'He starves himself for your sake.'

'And I have starved for his whim,' he said, taking up another piece.

'All he has in the world is for you,' she pleaded.

'Yes, if I come here to sit on it like a dam' toad in

To-morrow

a hole. Thank you; and what about the shovel, eh? He always had a queer way of showing his love.'

'I could bring him round in a week,' she suggested timidly.

He was too hungry to answer her; and, holding the plate submissively to his hand, she began to whisper up to him in a quick, panting voice. He listened, amazed, eating slower and slower, till at last his jaws stopped altogether. 'That's his game, is it?' he said, in a rising tone of scathing contempt. An ungovernable movement of his arm sent the plate flying out of her fingers. He shot out a violent curse.

She shrank from him, putting her hand against the wall.

'No!' he raged. 'He expects! Expects *me* – for his rotten money! . . . Who wants his home? Mad – not he! Don't you think? He wants his own way. He wanted to turn me into a miserable lawyer's clerk, and now he wants to make of me a blamed tame rabbit in a cage. Of me! Of me!' His subdued angry laugh frightened her now.

'The whole world ain't a bit too big for me to spread my elbows in, I can tell you – what's your name – Bessie – let alone a dam' parlour in a hutch. Marry! He wants me to marry and settle! And as likely as not he has looked out the girl too – dash my soul! And do you know the Judy, may I ask?'

She shook all over with noiseless dry sobs; but he was fuming and fretting too much to notice her distress. He bit his thumb with rage at the mere idea. A window rattled up.

'A grinning information fellow,' pronounced old Hagberd dogmatically, in measured tones. And the sound of his voice seemed to Bessie to make the night itself mad – to pour insanity and disaster on the earth. 'Now I know what's wrong with the people here, my dear. Why, of course! With this mad chap going about. Don't you have anything to do with him, Bessie. Bessie, I say!'

They stood as if dumb. The old man fidgeted and mumbled to himself at the window. Suddenly he cried, piercingly: 'Bessie – I see you. I'll tell Harry.'

She made a movement as if to run away, but stopped and raised her hands to her temples. Young Hagberd, shadowy and big, stirred no more than a man of bronze. Over their heads the crazy night whimpered and scolded in an old man's voice.

'Send him away, my dear. He's only a vagabond. What you want is a good home of your own. That chap has no home – he's not like Harry. He can't be Harry. Harry is coming to-morrow. Do you hear? One day more,' he babbled more excitedly. 'Never you fear – Harry shall marry you.'

His voice rose very shrill and mad against the regular deep soughing of the swell coiling heavily about the outer face of the sea-wall.

'He will have to. I shall make him, or if not' – he swore a great oath – 'I'll cut him off with a shilling to-morrow, and leave everything to you. I shall. To you. Let him starve.'

The window rattled down.

Harry drew a deep breath, and took one step towards Bessie. 'So it's you – the girl,' he said, in a lowered voice. She had not moved, and she remained half turned away from him, pressing her head in the palms of her hands. 'My world!' he continued, with an invisible half-smile on his lips. 'I have a great mind to stop . . .'

Her elbows were trembling violently.

'For a week,' he finished without a pause.

She clapped her hands to her face.

He came up quite close, and took hold of her wrists gently. She felt his breath on her ear.

'It's a scrape I am in – this, and it is you that must see me through.' He was trying to uncover her face. She resisted. He let her go then, and stepping back a little, 'Have you got any money?' he asked. 'I must be off now.'

She nodded quickly her shamefaced head, and he waited, looking away from her, while, trembling all over and bowing her neck, she tried to find the pocket of her dress.

'Here it is!' she whispered. 'Oh, go away! Go away for God's sake! If I had more – more – I would give it all to forget – to make you forget.'

He extended his hand. 'No fear! I haven't forgotten a single one of you in the world. Some gave me more than money – but I am a beggar now – and you women always had to get me out of my scrapes.'

He swaggered up to the parlour window, and in the dim light filtering through the blind, looked at the coin lying in his palm. It was a half-sovereign. He slipped it into his pocket. She stood a little on one side, with her head drooping, as if wounded; with her arms hanging passive by her side, as if dead.

To-morrow

'You can't buy me in,' he said, 'and you can't buy yourself out.'

He set his hat firmly with a little tap, and next moment she felt herself lifted up in the powerful embrace of his arms. Her feet lost the ground; her head hung back; he showered kisses on her face with a silent and overmastering ardour, as if in haste to get at her very soul. He kissed her pale cheeks, her hard forehead, her heavy eyelids, her faded lips; and the measured blows and sighs of the rising tide accompanied the enfolding power of his arms, the overwhelming might of his caresses. It was as if the sea, breaking down the wall protecting all the homes of the town, had sent a wave over her head. It passed on; she staggered backwards, with her shoulders against the wall, exhausted, as if she had been stranded there after a storm and a shipwreck.

She opened her eyes after a while; and, listening to the firm, leisurely footsteps going away with their conquest, began to gather her skirts, staring all the time before her. Suddenly she darted through the open gate into the dark and deserted street.

'Stop!' she shouted. 'Don't go!'

And listening with an attentive poise of the head,

she could not tell whether it was the beat of the swell or his fateful tread that seemed to fall cruelly upon her heart. Presently every sound grew fainter, as though she were slowly turning into stone. A fear of this awful silence came to her – worse than the fear of death. She called upon her ebbing strength for the final appeal:

'Harry!'

Not even the dying echo of a footstep. Nothing. The thundering of the surf, the voice of the restless sea itself, seemed stopped. There was not a sound – no whisper of life, as though she were alone and lost in that stony country of which she had heard, where madmen go looking for gold and spurn the find.

Captain Hagberd, inside his dark house, had kept on the alert. A window ran up; and in the silence of the stony country a voice spoke above her head, high up in the black air – the voice of madness, lies and despair – the voice of inextinguishable hope. 'Is he gone yet – that information fellow? Do you hear him about, my dear?'

She burst into tears. 'No! no! no! I don't hear him any more,' she sobbed.

He began to chuckle up there triumphantly. 'You

frightened him away. Good girl. Now we shall be all right. Don't you be impatient, my dear. One day more.'

In the other house old Carvil, wallowing regally in his arm-chair, with a globe-lamp burning by his side on the table, yelled for her, in a fiendish voice: 'Bessie! Bessie! You, Bessie!'

She heard him at last, and, as if overcome by fate, began to totter silently back towards her stuffy little inferno of a cottage. It had no lofty portal, no terrific inscription of forfeited hopes – she did not understand wherein she had sinned.

Captain Hagberd had gradually worked himself into a state of noisy happiness up there.

'Go in! Keep quiet!' she turned upon him tearfully, from the doorstep below.

He rebelled against her authority in his great joy at having got rid at last of that 'something wrong.' It was as if all the hopeful madness of the world had broken out to bring terror upon her heart, with the voice of that old man shouting of his trust in an everlasting to-morrow.

1. BOCCACCIO · *Mrs Rosie and the Priest*
2. GERARD MANLEY HOPKINS · *As kingfishers catch fire*
3. *The Saga of Gunnlaug Serpent-tongue*
4. THOMAS DE QUINCEY · *On Murder Considered as One of the Fine Arts*
5. FRIEDRICH NIETZSCHE · *Aphorisms on Love and Hate*
6. JOHN RUSKIN · *Traffic*
7. PU SONGLING · *Wailing Ghosts*
8. JONATHAN SWIFT · *A Modest Proposal*
9. *Three Tang Dynasty Poets*
10. WALT WHITMAN · *On the Beach at Night Alone*
11. KENKŌ · *A Cup of Sake Beneath the Cherry Trees*
12. BALTASAR GRACIÁN · *How to Use Your Enemies*
13. JOHN KEATS · *The Eve of St Agnes*
14. THOMAS HARDY · *Woman much missed*
15. GUY DE MAUPASSANT · *Femme Fatale*
16. MARCO POLO · *Travels in the Land of Serpents and Pearls*
17. SUETONIUS · *Caligula*
18. APOLLONIUS OF RHODES · *Jason and Medea*
19. ROBERT LOUIS STEVENSON · *Olalla*
20. KARL MARX AND FRIEDRICH ENGELS · *The Communist Manifesto*
21. PETRONIUS · *Trimalchio's Feast*
22. JOHANN PETER HEBEL · *How a Ghastly Story Was Brought to Light by a Common or Garden Butcher's Dog*
23. HANS CHRISTIAN ANDERSEN · *The Tinder Box*
24. RUDYARD KIPLING · *The Gate of the Hundred Sorrows*
25. DANTE · *Circles of Hell*
26. HENRY MAYHEW · *Of Street Piemen*
27. HAFEZ · *The nightingales are drunk*
28. GEOFFREY CHAUCER · *The Wife of Bath*
29. MICHEL DE MONTAIGNE · *How We Weep and Laugh at the Same Thing*
30. THOMAS NASHE · *The Terrors of the Night*
31. EDGAR ALLAN POE · *The Tell-Tale Heart*
32. MARY KINGSLEY · *A Hippo Banquet*
33. JANE AUSTEN · *The Beautifull Cassandra*
34. ANTON CHEKHOV · *Gooseberries*
35. SAMUEL TAYLOR COLERIDGE · *Well, they are gone, and here must I remain*
36. JOHANN WOLFGANG VON GOETHE · *Sketchy, Doubtful, Incomplete Jottings*
37. CHARLES DICKENS · *The Great Winglebury Duel*
38. HERMAN MELVILLE · *The Maldive Shark*
39. ELIZABETH GASKELL · *The Old Nurse's Story*
40. NIKOLAY LESKOV · *The Steel Flea*

41. HONORÉ DE BALZAC · *The Atheist's Mass*
42. CHARLOTTE PERKINS GILMAN · *The Yellow Wall-Paper*
43. C.P. CAVAFY · *Remember, Body . . .*
44. FYODOR DOSTOEVSKY · *The Meek One*
45. GUSTAVE FLAUBERT · *A Simple Heart*
46. NIKOLAI GOGOL · *The Nose*
47. SAMUEL PEPYS · *The Great Fire of London*
48. EDITH WHARTON · *The Reckoning*
49. HENRY JAMES · *The Figure in the Carpet*
50. WILFRED OWEN · *Anthem For Doomed Youth*
51. WOLFGANG AMADEUS MOZART · *My Dearest Father*
52. PLATO · *Socrates' Defence*
53. CHRISTINA ROSSETTI · *Goblin Market*
54. *Sindbad the Sailor*
55. SOPHOCLES · *Antigone*
56. RYŪNOSUKE AKUTAGAWA · *The Life of a Stupid Man*
57. LEO TOLSTOY · *How Much Land Does A Man Need?*
58. GIORGIO VASARI · *Leonardo da Vinci*
59. OSCAR WILDE · *Lord Arthur Savile's Crime*
60. SHEN FU · *The Old Man of the Moon*
61. AESOP · *The Dolphins, the Whales and the Gudgeon*
62. MATSUO BASHŌ · *Lips too Chilled*
63. EMILY BRONTË · *The Night is Darkening Round Me*
64. JOSEPH CONRAD · *To-morrow*
65. RICHARD HAKLUYT · *The Voyage of Sir Francis Drake Around the Whole Globe*
66. KATE CHOPIN · *A Pair of Silk Stockings*
67. CHARLES DARWIN · *It was snowing butterflies*
68. BROTHERS GRIMM · *The Robber Bridegroom*
69. CATULLUS · *I Hate and I Love*
70. HOMER · *Circe and the Cyclops*
71. D. H. LAWRENCE · *Il Duro*
72. KATHERINE MANSFIELD · *Miss Brill*
73. OVID · *The Fall of Icarus*
74. SAPPHO · *Come Close*
75. IVAN TURGENEV · *Kasyan from the Beautiful Lands*
76. VIRGIL · *O Cruel Alexis*
77. H. G. WELLS · *A Slip under the Microscope*
78. HERODOTUS · *The Madness of Cambyses*
79. *Speaking of Siva*
80. *The Dhammapada*

'Their fruits be diverse and plentiful, as nutmegs, ginger, long pepper, lemons, cucumbers, cocos, sago, with divers other sorts . . .'

RICHARD HAKLUYT
Born *c.* 1552, Hereford
Died 1616, London

HAKLUYT IN PENGUIN CLASSICS
Voyages and Discoveries

RICHARD HAKLUYT

The Voyage of Sir Francis Drake Around the Whole Globe

PENGUIN BOOKS

PENGUIN CLASSICS

UK | USA | Canada | Ireland | Australia
India | New Zealand | South Africa

Penguin Books is part of the Penguin Random House group of companies whose addresses can be found at global.penguinrandomhouse.com.

This selection published in Penguin Classics 2015

008

Set in 9/12.4 pt Baskerville 10 Pro
Typeset by Jouve (UK), Milton Keynes
Printed and bound in Great Britain by Clays Ltd, Elcograf S.p.A.

A CIP catalogue record for this book is available from the British Library

ISBN: 978–0–141–39851–8

www.greenpenguin.co.uk

Penguin Random House is committed to a sustainable future for our business, our readers and our planet. This book is made from Forest Stewardship Council® certified paper.

Contents

1. The famous voyage of Sir Francis Drake into the South Sea, and there hence about the whole globe of the earth, begun in the year of our Lord 1577. 1

2. The prosperous voyage of the worshipful Thomas Candish of Trimley in the County of Suffolk Esquire, into the South Sea, and from thence round about the circumference of the whole earth, begun in the year of our Lord 1586, and finished 1588. 23

The famous voyage of Sir Francis Drake into the South Sea, and there hence about the whole globe of the earth, begun in the year of our Lord, 1577.

The 15 day of November, in 1577, Mr Francis Drake, with a fleet of five ships and barks, and 164 men, gentlemen and sailors, departed from Plymouth, giving out his pretended voyage for Alexandria.

Upon the coast of Barbary, the 27 day we found an island called Mogador, between which island and the main, we found a very good and safe harbour for our ships to ride in.

On this island our general erected a pinnace, whereof he brought out of England with him four already framed.

We departed from this place the last day of December, and coasting along the shore, we did descry certain Spanish fishermen to whom we gave chase and took three of them, and proceeding further we met with three caravels and took them also.

The 17 day of January we arrived at Cabo Blanco, where we remained 4 days, and in that space our general mustered, and trained his men on land in warlike manner, to make them fit for all occasions.

We departed this harbour the 22 of January, carrying along with us one of the Portuguese caravels which was bound to the islands of Cape Verde for salt.

Richard Hakluyt

Upon one of those islands called Maio, we gave ourselves a little refreshing. The island is wonderfully stored with goats and wild hens, and it hath salt also without labour, the people gather it into heaps, which continually in great quantity is increased upon the sands by the flowing of the sea, and the receiving heat of the sun.

Amongst other things we found here a kind of fruit called cocos, which because it is not commonly known with us in England, I thought good to make some description of it.

The tree beareth no leaves nor branches, but at the very top the fruit groweth in clusters, hard at the top of the stem of the tree, as big every several fruit as a man's head: but having taken off the uttermost bark, which you shall find to be very full of strings or sinews, as I may term them, you shall come to a hard shell which may hold of quantity in liquor a pint commonly, or some a quart, and some less: within that shell of the thickness of half an inch good, you shall have a kind of hard substance and very white, no less good and sweet than almonds: within that again a certain clear liquor, which being drunk, you shall not only find it very delicate and sweet, but most comfortable and cordial.

Our general departed hence the 31 of this month, and sailed by the island of San Tiago, but far enough from the danger of the inhabitants, who shot and discharged at us three pieces, but they all fell short of us, and did us no harm. The mountains and high places of the island are said to be possessed by the Moors, who having been slaves to the Portuguese, made escape to the desert places of the island, where they abide with great strength.

We espied two ships under sail, to the one of which we

gave chase, and in the end boarded her with a ship-boat without resistance, and she yielded unto us good store of wine.

Being departed from these islands, we drew towards the line, where we were becalmed the space of 3 weeks, but yet subject to diverse great storms, terrible lightnings and much thunder: but with this misery we had the commodity of great store of fish, as dolphins, bonitos, and flying fishes, whereof some fell into our ships, where hence they could not rise again for want of moisture, for when their wings are dry, they cannot fly.

The first land that we fell with was the coast of Brazil, which we saw the fifth of April in the height of 33 degrees towards the pole Antarctic, and being discovered at sea by the inhabitants of the country, they made upon the coast great fires for a sacrifice (as we learned) to the devils, about which they use conjurations, making heaps of sand and other ceremonies, that when any ship shall go about to stay upon their coast, not only sands may be gathered together into shoals in every place, but also that storms and tempests may arise, to the casting away of ships and men.

The place where we met, our general called the Cape of Joy, where every ship took in some water. Here we found a good temperature and sweet air, a very fair and pleasant country with an exceedingly fruitful soil, where were great store of large and mighty deer, but we came not to the sight of any people: but travelling further into the country, we perceived the footing of people in the clay-ground, showing that they were men of great stature. Being returned to our ships, we weighed anchor, and harboured ourselves between a rock and the main, where by means of the rock that broke the force of the sea, we rode very safe, and upon this rock we killed for our provision certain sea-wolves, commonly called with us seals.

From hence we went our course to 36 degrees, and entered the great river of Plate, and ran into 54 and 55 fathoms and a half of fresh water, but our general finding here no good harbour, as he thought he should, bare out again to sea the 27 of April, but we sailing along, found a fair and reasonable good bay wherein were many, and the same profitable islands, one whereof had so many seals, as would at the least have laden all our ships.

Our general being on shore in an island, the people of the country showed themselves unto him, leaping and dancing, and entered into traffic with him, but they would not receive any things at any man's hands, but the same must be cast upon the ground. They are of clean, comely, and strong bodies, swift on foot, and seem to be very active.

We watered and made new provision of victuals, as by seals, whereof we slew to the number of 200 or 300 in the space of an hour.

The next day, we harboured ourselves again in a very good harbour, called by Magellan Puerto San Julián, where we found a gibbet standing upon the main, which we supposed to be the place where Magellan did execution upon some of his disobedient and rebellious company.

In this port our general began to enquire diligently of the actions of Mr Thomas Doughty, and found them not to be such as he looked for, but tending rather to contention or mutiny, whereby (without redress) the success of the voyage

The famous voyage of Sir Francis Drake into the South Sea

might greatly have been hazarded: whereupon the company was called together and made acquainted with the particulars of the cause, which were found partly by Master Doughty's own confession, and partly by the evidence of the fact, to be true: which when our general saw, although his private affection to Mr Doughty (as he then in the presence of us all sacredly protested) was great, yet the care he had of the state of the voyage, of the expectation of Her Majesty, and of the honour of his country did more touch him (as indeed it ought), than the private respect of one man: so that the cause being thoroughly heard, and all things done in good order as near as might be to the course of our laws in England, it was concluded that Mr Doughty should receive punishment according to the quality of the offence: he seeing no remedy but patience for himself, desired before his death to receive the communion, which he did at the hands of Mr Fletcher our minister, and our general himself accompanied him in that holy action: which being done, and the place of execution made ready, he having embraced our general and taken his leave of all the company, with prayer for the Queen's Majesty and our realm, in quiet sort laid his head to the block, where he ended his life. This being done, our general made divers speeches to the whole company, persuading us to unity, obedience, love, and regard of our voyage; and for the better confirmation thereof, willed every man the next Sunday following to prepare himself to receive the communion, as Christian brethren and friends ought to do, which was done in very reverent sort, and so with good contentment every man went about his business.

The 20 day we fell with the Strait of Magellan going into

the South Sea, at the cape or headland whereof we found the body of a dead man, whose flesh was clean consumed.

In this strait there be many fair harbours, with store of fresh water, but yet they lack their best commodity: for the water is there of such depth, that no man shall find ground to anchor in, except it be in some narrow river or corner, or between some rocks, so that if any extreme blasts or contrary winds do come (whereunto the place is much subject) it carrieth with it no small danger.

The land on both sides is very huge and mountainous, covered with snow. This strait is extremely cold, with frost and snow continually; the trees seem to stoop with the burden of the weather, and yet are green continually, and many good and sweet herbs do very plentifully grow and increase under them.

The 24 of August we arrived at an island in the straits, where we found great store of fowl which could not fly, of the bigness of geese, whereof we killed in less than one day 3,000 and victualled ourselves thoroughly therewith.

The seventh day we were driven by a great storm from the entering into the South Sea two hundred leagues and odd in longitude, and one degree to the southward of the Strait: in which height, and so many leagues to the westward, the fifteenth day of September fell out the eclipse of the moon at the hour of six of the clock at night: But neither did the ecliptical conflict of the moon impair our state, nor her clearing again amend us a whit, but the accustomed eclipse of the sea continued in his force, we being darkened more than the moon seven fold.

From the bay (which we called the Bay of Severing of

Friends) we were driven back to the southward of the straits in 57 degrees and a tierce: in which height we came to an anchor among the islands, having there fresh and very good water, with herbs of singular virtue. Not far from hence we entered another bay, where we found people both men and women in their canoes, naked, and ranging from one island to another to seek their meat, who entered traffic with us for such things as they had.

We returning hence northward again, found the 3 of October three islands, in one of which was such plenty of birds as is scant credible to report.

We ran, supposing the coast of Chile to lie as the general maps have described it, namely northwest, which we found to lie and trend to the northeast and eastwards, whereby it appeareth that this part of Chile hath not been truly hitherto discovered, or at least not truly reported for the space of 12 degrees at the least, being set down either of purpose to deceive, or of ignorant conjecture.

The 29 of November we cast anchor, and our general hoisting out our boat, went with ten of our company to shore, where we found people, whom the cruel and extreme dealings of the Spaniards have forced for their own safety and liberty to flee from the main, and to fortify themselves in this island. The people came down to us to the waterside with show of great courtesy, bringing to us potatoes, roots, and two very fat sheep, which our general received and gave them other things for them, and had promise to have water there: but the next day repairing again to the shore, and sending two men a land with barrels to fill water, the people taking them for Spaniards (to whom they use to show no favour if they take them) laid violent hands on them, and as we think, slew them.

Our general seeing this, stayed here no longer, but weighed anchor, and set sail towards the coast of Chile, and drawing towards it, we met near to the shore an Indian in a canoe, who thinking us to have been Spaniards, came to us and told us, that at a place called Santiago, there was a great Spanish ship laden from the kingdom of Peru: for which good news our general gave him divers trifles, whereof he was glad, and went along with us and brought us to the place, which is called the port of Valparaíso.

We found indeed the ship riding at anchor, having in her eight Spaniards and three negroes, who thinking us to have been Spaniards and their friends, welcomed us with a drum: as soon as we were entered, one of our company called Thomas Moon began to lay about him, and struck one of the Spaniards, and said unto him, *abajo perro*, that is in English, go down dog. One of these Spaniards seeing persons of that quality in those seas, crossed and blessed himself: but to be short, we stowed them under hatches all save one Spaniard, who suddenly and desperately leapt overboard into the sea, and swam ashore to the town of Santiago, to give them warning.

They of the town being not above nine households, presently fled away and abandoned the town. Our general manned his boat, and the Spanish ship's boat, and went to the town, we rifled it, and came to a small chapel which we entered, and found therein a silver chalice, two cruets, and one altar-cloth, the spoil whereof our general gave to Mr Fletcher his minister.

The famous voyage of Sir Francis Drake into the South Sea

We found also in this town a warehouse stored with wine of Chile, and many boards of cedar-wood, all which wine we brought away with us, and certain of the boards to burn for fire-wood: we departed the haven, having first set all the Spaniards on land, saving one John Griego a Greek born, whom our general carried with him for his pilot to bring him into the haven of Lima.

At sea, our general rifled the ship, and found in her good store of the wine of Chile, and 25,000 pesos of very pure and fine gold of Valdivia, amounting in value to 37,000 ducats of Spanish money, we arrived next at a place called Coquimbo, where our general sent 14 of his men on land to fetch water: but they were espied by the Spaniards, who came with 300 horsemen and 200 footmen, and slew one of our men with a piece, the rest came aboard in safety, and the Spaniards departed: we went ashore again, and buried our man, and the Spaniards came down again with a flag of truce, but we set sail and would not trust them.

From hence we went to a certain port called Tarapaca, where being landed, we found by the sea side a Spaniard lying asleep, who had lying by him 13 bars of silver, which weighed 4000 ducats Spanish; we took the silver, and left the man.

Not far from hence going on land for fresh water, we met with a Spaniard and an Indian boy driving 8 llamas or sheep of Peru which are as big as asses: every one of which sheep had on his back 2 bags of leather, each bag containing 50 lbs. weight of fine silver: so that bringing both the sheep and their burthen to the ships, we found in all the bags 800 weight of silver.

Richard Hakluyt

Here hence we sailed to a place called Arica, and being entered the port, we found there three small barks which we rifled, and found in one of them 57 wedges of silver, each of them weighing about 20 pound weight, and every of these wedges were of the fashion and bigness of a brickbat. Our general contented with the spoil of the ships, left the town and put off again to sea and set sail for Lima.

To Lima we came the 13 day of February, and being entered the haven, we found there about twelve sail of ships lying fast moored at an anchor; for the masters and merchants were here most secure, having never been assaulted by enemies. Our general rifled these ships, and found in one of them a chest full of royals of plate, and good store of silks and linen cloth. In which ship he had news of another ship called the *Cacafuego* which was gone towards Paita, and that the same ship was laded with treasure: whereupon we stayed no longer here, but cutting all the cables of the ships in the haven, we let them drive whither they would, either to sea or to the shore, and with all speed we followed the *Cacafuego*: but she was gone from thence towards Panama, whom our general still pursued, and by the way met with a bark laden with ropes and tackle for ships, which he boarded and searched, and found in her 80 lbs. weight of gold, and a crucifix of gold with goodly great emeralds set in it which he took, and some of the cordage also for his own ship.

We departed, still following the *Cacafuego*, and our general promised our company that whosoever could first descry her, should have his chain of gold for his good news. It fortuned that John Drake going up into the top, descried her about three of the clock, and about six of the clock we

The famous voyage of Sir Francis Drake into the South Sea

came to her and boarded her, and shot at her three pieces of ordnance, and struck down her mizzen, and being entered, we found in her great riches, as jewels and precious stones, thirteen chests full of royals of plate, fourscore pound weight of gold, and six and twenty ton of silver. The place where we took this prize, was called Cape de San Francisco, about 150 leagues from Panama.

We went on our course still towards the west, and not long after met with a ship laden with linen cloth and fine China-dishes of white earth, and great store of China-silks, of all which things we took as we listed.

The owner himself of this ship was in her, who was a Spanish gentleman, from whom our general took a falcon of gold, with a great emerald in the breast thereof, and the pilot of the ship he took also with him, and so cast the ship off.

This pilot brought us to the haven of Guatulco. We landed, and went presently to the town, and to the townhouse, where we found a judge sitting in judgement, being associate with three other officers, upon three negroes that had conspired the burning of the town: both which judges and prisoners we took, and brought them a shipboard, and caused the chief judge to write his letter to the town, to command all the townsmen to avoid that we might safely water there. Which being done, and they departed, we ransacked the town, and in one house we found a pot of the quantity of a bushel, full of reals of plate, which we brought to our ship.

And here one Thomas Moon one of our company, took a Spanish gentleman as he was flying out of the town, and searching him, he found a chain of gold about him, and other jewels, which he took, and so let him go.

Richard Hakluyt

Our general thinking himself both in respect of his private injuries received from the Spaniards, as also of their contempts and indignities offered to our country and prince in general, sufficiently satisfied and revenged: and supposing that Her Majesty at his return would rest content with this service, purposed to continue no longer upon the Spanish coasts, but began to consider and to consult the best way for his country.

He thought it not good to return by the Straits, for two special causes: the one, lest the Spaniards should there wait and attend for him in great strength, whose hands, he being left but one ship, could not possibly escape. The other cause was the dangerous situation of the mouth of the Straits in the South Sea, where continual storms blustering, as he found by experience, besides the shoals and sands upon the coast, he thought it not a good course to adventure that way: he resolved therefore to avoid these hazards, to go forward to the islands of the Moluccas, and there hence to sail the course of the Portuguese by the Cape of Buena Esperanza.

Upon this resolution, he began to think of his best way to the Moluccas, and finding himself where he now was becalmed, he saw that of necessity he must sail somewhat northerly to get a wind. We therefore set sail, and sailed 600 leagues at the least for a good wind.

The 5 day of June, being in 43 degrees towards the pole Arctic, we found the air so cold, that our men being grievously pinched with the same, complained of the extremity thereof, and the further we went, the more the cold increased upon us. Whereupon we thought it best for that time to seek the land, and did so, finding it not mountainous, but low

The famous voyage of Sir Francis Drake into the South Sea

plain land, till we came within 38 degrees, it pleased God to send us into a fair and good bay, with a good wind to enter the same.

In this bay we anchored, and the people of the country having their houses close by the water's side, showed themselves unto us, and sent a present to our general.

When they came unto us, they greatly wondered at the things that we brought, but our general (according to his natural and accustomed humanity) courteously entreated them, and liberally bestowed on them necessary things to cover their nakedness, whereupon they supposed us to be gods, and would not be persuaded to the contrary.

Their houses are digged round about with earth, and have clefts of wood set upon them, joining close together at the top like a spire steeple, which by reason of that closeness are very warm.

Their beds is the ground with rushes strewed on it, and lying about the house, have the fire in the midst. The men go naked, the women take bulrushes, and comb them after the manner of hemp, and thereof make their loose garments, which being knit about their middles, hang down about their hips, having also about their shoulders a skin of deer, with the hair upon it. These women are very obedient and serviceable to their husbands.

After they were departed from us, they came and visited us the second time, and brought with them feathers and bags of tobacco for presents: and when they came to the top of the hill (at the bottom whereof we had pitched our tents) they stayed themselves: where one appointed for speaker wearied himself with making a long oration, which done, they left their bows upon the hill, and came down with their presents.

In the meantime the women remaining on the hill, tormented themselves lamentably, tearing their flesh from their cheeks, whereby we perceived that they were about a sacrifice. In the meantime our general with his company went to prayer, and to reading of the Scriptures, at which exercise they were attentive, and seemed greatly to be affected with it.

The news of our being there spread through the country, the people that inhabited round about came down, and amongst them the king himself, a man of a goodly stature, and comely personage.

In the forefront was a man, who bore the sceptre or mace before the king, whereupon hanged two crowns, a lesser and a bigger, with three chains of a marvellous length: the crowns were made of knit work wrought artificially with feathers of divers colours: the chains were made of a bony substance, and few be the persons among them that are admitted to wear them. Next unto him, was the king himself, with his guard about his person, clad with coney skins, and other skins: after them followed the naked common sort of people, every one having his face painted, some with white, some with black, and other colours.

In the meantime our general gathered his men together, and marched within his fenced place, making against their approaching a very war-like show.

In coming towards our bulwarks and tents, the sceptre-bearer began a song observing his measures in a dance, and that with a stately countenance, whom the king with his guard, and every degree of persons following, did

The famous voyage of Sir Francis Drake into the South Sea

in like manner sing and dance, saving only the women, which danced and kept silence. The general permitted them to enter within our bulwark, where they continued their song and dance a reasonable time. They made signs to our general to sit down, to whom the king, and divers others made supplications, that he would take their province into his hand, and become their king, making signs that they would resign unto him their right and title of the whole land, and become his subjects. In which, to persuade us the better, the king and the rest, with one consent, and with great reverence, joyfully singing a song, did set the crown upon his head, enriched his neck with all their chains: which thing our general thought not meet to reject, because he knew not what honour and profit it might be to our country. Wherefore in the name, and to the use of Her Majesty he took the sceptre, crown, and dignity of the said country into his hands.

Our necessary business being ended, our general with his company travelled up into the country to their villages, where we found herds of deer by 1,000 in a company, being most large, and fat of body.

Our general called this country Nova Albion, and that for two causes: the one in respect of the white cliffs, which lie towards the sea: and the other, because it might have some affinity with our country in name, which sometime was so called.

There is no part of earth here to be taken up, wherein there is not some probable show of gold or silver.

At our departure hence our general set up a monument of our being there, as also of Her Majesty's right and title to the same, namely a plate, nailed upon a fair great post, whereupon was engraved Her Majesty's name, the day and year of our arrival there, with the free giving up of the province and people into Her Majesty's hands, together with Her Highness' picture and arms, in a piece of six pence of current English money under the plate, whereunder was also written the name of our general.

It seemeth that the Spaniards hitherto had never been in this part of the country, neither did ever discover the land by many degrees, to the southwards.

After we had set sail from hence, we continued without sight of land till the 13 day of October, which day we fell with certain islands 8 degrees to the northward of the line, from which came a great number of canoes, having in some of them 4 in some 6 and in some also 14 men, bringing with them cocos, and other fruits. Their canoes were hollow within, and cut with great art and cunning, being very smooth within and without, having a prow, and a stern of one sort, yielding inward circle-wise, being of a great height, and full of certain white shells for a bravery, and on each side of them lie out two pieces of timber about a yard and a half long, more or less.

This people have the nether part of their ears cut into a round circle, hanging down very low upon their cheeks, whereon they hang things of a reasonable weight. The nails of their hands are an inch long, their teeth are as black as pitch.

We continued our course by the islands of Tagulada, Zelon, and Zewarra, being friends to the Portuguese, the first whereof hath growing in it great store of cinnamon.

The 14 of November we fell with the islands of Molucca,

The famous voyage of Sir Francis Drake into the South Sea

next morning early we came to anchor, at which time our general sent a messenger to the king with a velvet cloak for a present, and token of his coming to be in peace, and that he required nothing but traffic and exchange of merchandise, whereof he had good store.

The king was moved with great liking towards us, and sent to our general, that he should have what things he needed. In token whereof he sent to our general a signet, and within short time after came in his own person to our ship, to bring her into a better and safer road than she was in at present.

The king sent before 4 great and large canoes, in every one whereof were certain of his greatest, attired in white lawn of cloth of Calicut, having over their heads from the one end of the canoe to the other, a covering of thin perfumed mats, borne up with a frame made of reeds for the same use, under which every one did sit in his order according to his dignity, to keep him from the heat of the sun, divers of whom being of good age and gravity, did make an ancient and fatherly show. There were also divers young and comely men attired in white, as were the others: the rest were soldiers.

These canoes were furnished with war-like munition, every man for the most part having his sword and target, with his dagger, besides other weapons, as lances, calivers, darts, bows and arrows.

They rowed about us, one after another, and passing by, did their homage with great solemnity.

The king was a man of tall stature and seemed to be much delighted with the sound of our music, to whom as also to his nobility, our general gave presents.

At length the king craved leave of our general to depart,

promising the next day to come aboard, and in the meantime to send us such victuals, as were necessary for our provision: so that the same night we received of them meal, which they call sago, made of the tops of certain trees, tasting in the mouth like sour curds, but melteth like sugar, whereof they make certain cakes, which may be kept the space of ten years, and yet then good to be eaten. We had of them store of rice, hens, unperfect and liquid sugar, sugar canes, with store of cloves.

The king having promised to come aboard, brake his promise, but sent his brother to make his excuse, and to entreat our general to come on shore, offering himself pawn aboard for his safe return. Whereunto the general consented not, upon mislike conceived of the breach of his promise. But to satisfy him, our general sent certain of his gentlemen to the court.

The king at last came in guarded with 12 lances covered over with a rich canopy, with embossed gold. Our men rising to meet him, he graciously did welcome, and entertain them. He was attired after the manner of the country, but more sumptuously than the rest. From his waist down to the ground, was all cloth of gold, and the same very rich: his legs were bare, but on his feet were a pair of shoes made of Cordovan skin. In the attire of his head were finely wreathed hooped rings of gold, and about his neck he had a chain of perfect gold, the links whereof were great, and one fold double. On his fingers he had six very fair jewels, and sitting in his chair of estate, at his right hand stood a page with a fan in his hand, breathing and gathering the air to the king. The fan was in length two foot, and in breadth one foot, set with

The famous voyage of Sir Francis Drake into the South Sea

8 sapphires, richly embroidered, and knit to a staff 3 foot in length, by which the page did hold, and move it.

This island is the chiefest of all the islands of Molucca. The king with his people are Moors in religion, observing certain new moons, with fasting: during which fasts, they neither eat nor drink in the day, but in the night.

Our general considering the great distance, and how far he was yet off from his country, thought it not best here to linger the time any longer, but weighing his anchors, set out, and sailed to a certain little island to the southwards of Celebes, where we graved our ship, and continued there in that and other businesses 26 days. This island is thoroughly grown with wood of a large and high growth, very straight and without boughs, save only in the head or top, whose leaves are not much differing from our broom in England. Amongst these trees night by night, through the whole land, did show themselves an infinite swarm of fiery worms flying in the air, whose bodies being no bigger than our common English flies, make such a show and light, as if every twig or tree had been a burning candle.

When we had ended our business here, we weighed, and set sail: but having at that time a bad wind, with much difficulty we recovered to the northward of the island of Celebes, where by reason of contrary winds, we were enforced to alter to the southward again, finding that course also to be very hard and dangerous for us, by reason of infinite shoals which lie off, and among the islands. Upon the 9 of January in the year 1579 we ran suddenly upon a rock, where we stuck fast from 8 of the clock at night till 4 of the clock in the afternoon the next day, being indeed out of all hope to escape the danger: but our general showed himself courageous, and of a good confidence in the mercy and protection of God: and we did our best endeavour to save ourselves, which it pleased God so to bless, that in the end we cleared ourselves most happily of the danger.

We lighted our ship upon the rocks of 3 ton of cloves, 8 pieces of ordnance, and certain meal and beans: and then the wind (as it were in a moment by the special grace of God) changing from the starboard to the larboard of the ship, we hoisted our sails, and the happy gale drove our ship off the rock into the sea again, to the no little comfort of all our hearts, for which we gave God such praise and thanks, as so great a benefit required.

The 8 of February following, we fell with the fruitful island of Barateve. The people of this island are comely in body and stature, and of a civil behaviour, just in dealing, and courteous to strangers. The men go naked, saving their heads and privities, every man having something or other hanging at their ears. The women are covered from the middle down to the foot, wearing a great number of bracelets upon their arms, being made some of bone, some of horn, and some of brass, the lightest whereof by our estimation weighed two ounces apiece.

With this people linen cloth is good merchandise, whereof they make rolls for their heads, and girdles to wear about them.

Their island is both rich and beautiful: rich in gold, silver, copper, and sulphur, wherein they seem skilful and expert.

Their fruits be diverse and plentiful, as nutmegs, ginger, long pepper, lemons, cucumbers, cocos, sago, with divers

The famous voyage of Sir Francis Drake into the South Sea

other sorts: since the time that we first set out of our own country of England, we happened on no place, wherein we found more comforts and better means of refreshing.

We set our course for Java, where arriving, we found great courtesy, and honourable entertainment. This island is governed by 5 kings, whom they call Rajah.

Of these five we had four a shipboard at once, and two or three often. They are wonderfully delighted in coloured clothes, as red and green: their upper parts of their bodies are naked save their heads, whereupon they wear a Turkish roll, as do the Moluccans: from the middle downward they wear a pintado of silk, trailing upon the ground, in colour as best they like.

They have an house in every village for their common assembly: every day they meet twice, men, women, and children, bringing with them such victuals as they think good, some fruits, some rice boiled, some hens roasted, some sago, having a table made 3 foot from the ground, whereon they set their meat, that every person sitting at the table may eat, one rejoicing in the company of another.

They boil their rice in an earthen pot, made in form of a sugar loaf being full of holes, as our pots which we water our gardens withal, and it is open at the great end, wherein they put their rice dry, without any moisture. In the meantime they have ready another great earthen pot, set fast in a furnace, boiling full of water, whereinto they put their pot with rice, by such measure, that they swelling become soft at the first, and by their swelling stopping the holes of the pot, admit no more water to enter, but the more they are boiled, the harder and more firm substance they become, so that in the end they are a firm and good bread, of the which with oil, butter, sugar, and other spices, they make diverse sorts of meats very pleasant of taste, and nourishing to nature.

The French pox is here very common to all, and they help themselves, sitting naked from ten to two in the sun, whereby the venomous humour is drawn out. Not long before our departure, they told us, that not far off there were such great ships as ours, wishing us to beware: upon this our captain would stay no longer.

From Java we sailed for the Cape of Good Hope, which was the first land we fell withal: neither did we touch with it, or any other land, until we came to Sierra Leone, upon the coast of Guinea: we ran hard aboard the Cape, finding the report of the Portuguese to be most false, who affirm, that it is the most dangerous cape of the world, never without intolerable storms and present dangers to travellers.

This cape is a most stately thing, and the fairest cape we saw in the whole circumference of the earth, and we passed by it the 18 of June.

From thence we continued our course to Sierra Leone, on the coast of Guinea, where we arrived the 22 of July, and found necessary provisions, great store of elephants, oysters upon trees of one kind, spawning and increasing infinitely.

We arrived in England the third of November 1580 being the third year of our departure.

The prosperous voyage of the worshipful Thomas Candish of Trimley in the County of Suffolk Esquire, into the South Sea, and from thence round about the circumference of the whole earth, begun in the year of our Lord 1586, and finished 1588.

We departed out of Plymouth on Thursday the 21 of July 1586 with 3 sails, to wit, the *Desire* a ship of 120 tons, the *Content* of 60 tons, and the *Hugh Gallant* a bark of 40 tons: in which small fleet were 123 persons and victuals sufficient for the space of two years, Thomas Candish being our general.

The first of August we came in sight of Fuerteventura, one of the isles of the Canaries, about ten of the clock in the morning.

The 25 day we fell with the point on the south side of Sierra Leone.

On Sunday the 28 the general sent some of his company on shore, and there they played and danced all the forenoon among the negroes.

On Monday morning being the 29 day, our general landed with 70 men or thereabout, and went up to their town, where we burnt 2 or 3 houses, and took what spoil we would, which was but little, but all the people fled: and in our retiring aboard in a very little plain at their town's end they shot their arrows at us out of the woods, and hurt three or four of our men; their arrows were poisoned, but yet none of our men miscarried at that time, thanked be God. Their town is marvellous artificially builded with mud walls, and built round, with their yards paled in and kept very clean as well in their streets as in their houses. These negroes use good obedience to their king. There were in their town by estimation about one hundred houses.

The first of September there went many of our men on shore at the watering place, and did wash shirts very quietly all the day: and the second day they went again, and the negroes were in ambush round about the place: the negroes rushed out upon our men so suddenly, that in retiring to our boats, many of them were hurt: among whom one William Pickman a soldier was shot into the thigh, who plucking the arrow out, broke it, and left the head behind: the poison wrought so that night, that he was marvellously swollen, and all his belly and privy parts were as black as ink, and the next morning he died.

The last of October running west southwest about 24 leagues from Cape Frio in Brazil, we fell with a great mountain which had an high round knop on the top of it standing from it like a town, with two little islands from it.

The first of November we went in between the Ilha de São Sebastião and the mainland, and had our things on shore, and set up a forge, and had our cask on shore: our coopers made hoops, and so we remained there until the 23 day of the same month: in which time we fitted our things, built our pinnace, and filled our fresh water.

The prosperous voyage of the worshipful Thomas Candish

The 17 day of December in the afternoon we entered into an harbour, where there is a wonderful great store of seals, and another island of birds which are grey gulls. These seals are of a wonderful great bigness, huge, and monstrous of shape, and for the fore-part of their bodies cannot be compared to any thing better than to a lion: their head, and neck, and fore-parts of their bodies are full of rough hair: their feet are in manner of a fin, and in form like unto a man's hand: they breed and cast every month, giving their young milk, yet continually get they their living in the sea, and live altogether upon fish: their young are marvellous good meat, and being boiled or roasted, are hardly to be known from lamb or mutton. The old ones be of such bigness and force, that it is as much as 4 men are able to do to kill one of them with great cowlstaves: and he must be beaten down with striking on the head of him: for his body is of that bigness that four men could never kill him, but only on the head. For being shot through the body with an arquebus or a musket, yet he will go his way into the sea, and never care for it at the present.

This harbour is a very good place to trim ships in, and bring them on ground, and grave them in: for there ebbeth and floweth much water: therefore we graved and trimmed all our ships there.

The 24 of December being Christmas Eve, a man and a boy went into a very fair green valley at the foot of the mountains, where was a little pit or well which our men had digged and made some 2 or 3 days before to get fresh water: this man and boy came thither to wash their linen: there were a great store of Indians which were come down and found the man and boy in washing. These Indians being divided on each side of the rocks, shot at them with their arrows and hurt them both, but they fled presently, being about fifty or threescore, though our general followed them but with 16 or 20 men. The man's name which was hurt was John Garge, the boy's name was Lutch: the man was shot clean through the knee, the boy into the shoulder: either of them having very sore wounds. Their arrows are made of little canes, and their heads are of a flint stone, set into the cane very artificially: they seldom or never see any Christians: they are as wild as ever was a buck or any other wild beast: for we followed them, and they ran from us as it had been the wildest thing in the world. We took the measure of one of their feet, and it was 18 inches long. Their use is when any of them die, to bring him or them to the cliffs by the sea side, and upon the top of them they bury them, and in their graves are buried with them their bows and arrows, and all their jewels which they have in their lifetime, which are fine shells which they find by the sea side, which they cut and square after an artificial manner: and all is laid under their heads. The grave is made all with great stones of great length and bigness, being set all along full of the dead man's darts which he used when he was living. And they colour both their darts and their graves with a red colour which they use in colouring of themselves.

The 6 day [of January] we put in for the Straits.

The 7 day between the mouth of the Straits and the narrowest place thereof, we took a Spaniard whose name was Hernando, who was there with 23 Spaniards more, which were all that remained of four hundred, which were left there

The prosperous voyage of the worshipful Thomas Candish

three years before in these Straits of Magellan, all the rest being dead with famine. And the same day we passed through the narrowest of the Straits.

The ninth day we departed from Penguin Island, and ran south southwest to King Philip's city which the Spaniards had built: which town or city had four forts, and every fort had in it one cast piece, which pieces were buried in the ground, the carriages were standing in their places unburied: we digged for them and had them all. They had contrived their city very well, and seated it in the best place of the Straits for wood and water: they had built up their churches by themselves: they had laws very severe among themselves, for they had erected a gibbet, whereon they had done execution upon some of their company. It seemed unto us that their whole living for a great space was altogether upon mussels and limpets: for there was not anything else to be had, except some deer which came out of the mountains down to the fresh rivers to drink. These Spaniards which were there, were only come to fortify the Straits, to the end that no other nation should have passage through into the South Sea saving only their own: but as it appeared, it was not God's will so to have it. For during the time that they were there, which was two years at the least, they could never have anything to grow or in any wise prosper. And on the other side the Indians oftentimes preyed upon them, until their victuals grew so short, that they died like dogs in their houses, and in their clothes, wherein we found them still at our coming, until that in the end the town being wonderfully tainted with the smell and the savour of the dead people, the rest which remained alive were driven to bury such things as they had there in their town either for provision or for furniture, and so to forsake the town, and to go along the sea side, and seek their victuals to preserve them from starving, taking nothing with them, but every man his arquebus (some were not able to carry them for weakness) and so lived for the space of a year and more with roots, leaves, and sometimes a fowl which they might kill with their piece. To conclude, they were determined to have travelled towards the river of Plate, only being left alive 23 persons, whereof two were women, which were the remainder of 4 hundred. In this place we watered and wooded well and quietly.

There was a fresh water river, where our general went up with the ship-boat about three miles, which river hath very good and pleasant ground about it, and it is low and champaign soil, and so we saw none other ground else in all the Straits but that was craggy rocks and monstrous high hills and mountains. In this river are great store of savages which we saw, and had conference with them: they were men eaters, and fed altogether upon raw flesh, and other filthy food: which people had preyed upon some of the Spaniards before spoken of. For they had gotten knives and pieces of rapiers to make darts of. They used all the means they could possibly to have allured us up farther into the river, of purpose to have betrayed us, which being espied by our general, he caused us to shoot at them with our arquebuses, whereby we killed many of them.

During this time, which was a full month, we fed almost altogether upon mussels and limpets, and birds, or such as we could get on shore, seeking every day for them, as the fowls of the air do, where they can find food, in continual rainy weather.

The prosperous voyage of the worshipful Thomas Candish

The 24 day of February we entered into the South Sea: the first of March a storm took us. This storm continued 3 or 4 days, and for that time we in the *Hugh Gallant* being separated from the other 2 ships looked every hour to sink, our bark was so leak, and ourselves so weakened with freeing it of water, that we slept not in three days and three nights.

The 15 of March in the morning the *Hugh Gallant* came in between the island of Santa Maria and the main where she met with the admiral and the *Content* which had rid at the island called La Mocha 2 days: at which place some of our men went on shore with the vice-admiral's boat, where the Indians fought with them with their bows and arrows, and were marvellous wary of their calivers. These Indians were enemies to the Spaniards, and belonged to a great place called Arauco, and took us for Spaniards, as afterwards we learned.

This place which is called Arauco is wonderfully rich, and full of gold mines, and yet it could not be subdued at any time by the Spaniards, but they always returned with the greatest loss of men. For these Indians are marvellous desperate and careless of their lives to live at their own liberty and freedom.

We weighed anchor, and ran under the west side of Santa Maria island, where we rode very well in six fathoms of water.

There came down to us certain Indians with two which were the principals of the island to welcome us on shore, thinking we had been Spaniards, for it is subdued by them: who brought us up to a place where the Spaniards had erected a church with crosses and altars in it. And there were about this church 2 or 3 store-houses, which were full of wheat and barley ready threshed. The wheat and barley was as fair, as clean, and every way as good as any we have in England. There were also cades full of potato roots, which were very good to eat, ready made up in the store-houses for the Spaniards against they should come for their tribute. This island also yieldeth many sorts of fruits, hogs, and hens. These Indians are held in such slavery by them, that they dare not eat a hen or an hog themselves. Thus we fitted ourselves here with corn as much as we would have, and as many hogs as we had salt to powder them withal, and great store of hens, with a number of bags of potato roots, and about 500 dried dogfishes, and Guinea wheat, which is called maize.

The fifteenth [of April, 1587] we came thwart of a place called Morro Moreno, an excellent harbour: here we went with our general on shore to the number of 30 men: and at our going on shore upon our landing, the Indians of the place came down from the rocks to meet with us, with fresh water and wood on their backs. They are in marvellous awe of the Spaniards, and very simple people, and live marvellously savagely: for they brought us to their bidings about two miles from the harbour, where we saw their women and lodging, which is nothing but the skin of some beast laid upon the ground: and over them instead of houses, is nothing but five or six sticks laid across, which stand upon two forks with sticks on the ground and a few boughs laid on it. Their diet is raw fish, which stinketh most vilely. And when any of them die, they bury their bows and arrows with them, with their canoe and all that they have: for we opened one

The prosperous voyage of the worshipful Thomas Candish

of their graves, and saw the order of them. Their canoes or boats are marvellous artificially made of two skins like unto bladders, and are blown full at one end with quills: they have two of these bladders blown full, which are sewn together and made fast with a sinew of some wild beast; which when they are in the water swell, so that they are as tight as may be. They go to sea in these boats, and catch very much fish with them, and pay much of it for tribute unto the Spaniards: but they use it marvellous beastly.

The 27 day we took a small bark, which came from Santiago. In this bark was one George a Greek, a reasonable pilot for all the coast of Chile. There were also in the said bark one Fleming and three Spaniards: and they were all sworn and received the sacrament before they came to sea by three or four friars, that if we should chance to meet them, they should throw those letters over board: which (as we were giving them chase with our pinnace) before we could fetch them up, they had accordingly thrown away. Yet our general wrought so with them, that they did confess it: but he was fain to cause them to be tormented with their thumbs in a wrench, and to continue them at several times with extreme pain. Also he made the old Fleming believe that he would hang him; and the rope being about his neck he was pulled up a little from the hatches, and yet he would not confess, choosing rather to die, than he would be perjured. In the end it was confessed by one of the Spaniards, whereupon we burnt the bark, and carried the men with us.

The tenth day [of May] the *Hugh Gallant* in which bark I Francis Pretty was lost company with our admiral.

The 17 of May we met with our admiral again, and all the

rest of our fleet. They had taken two ships, the one laden with sugar, molasses, maize, Cordovan skins, montego de porco, many packs of pintados, many Indian coats, and some marmalade, and 1000 hens: and the other ship was laden with wheat meal, and boxes of marmalade. One of these ships which had the chief merchandise in it, was worth twenty thousand pounds, if it had been in England or in any other place of Christendom where we might have sold it. We filled all our ships with as much as we could bestow of these goods: the rest we burnt and the ships also; and set the men and women that were not killed on shore.

The 20 day in the morning we came into the road of Paita, and being at an anchor, our general landed with sixty or seventy men, skirmished with them of the town, and drove them all to flight to the top of the hill which is over the town. We found the quantity of 25 pounds weight in silver in pieces of eight reals, and abundance of household stuff and storehouses full of all kind of wares: but our general would not suffer any man to carry much cloth or apparel away, because they should not cloy themselves with burthens: for they were five men to one of us: and we had an English mile and a half to our ships. Thus we came down in safety to the town, which was very well builded, and marvellous clean kept in every street, with a town-house or guild hall in the midst, and had to the number of two hundred houses at the least in it. We set it on fire to the ground, and goods to the value of five or six thousand pounds: there was also a bark riding in the road which we set on fire and departed.

The 25 day of May we arrived at the island of Puna, where is a very good harbour, where we found a great ship of the

The prosperous voyage of the worshipful Thomas Candish

burthen of 250 tons riding at an anchor with all her furniture, which was ready to be hauled on ground: for there is a special good place for that purpose. We sunk it, and went on shore where the lord of the island dwelt, who had a sumptuous house marvellous well contrived: and out of every chamber was framed a gallery with a stately prospect into the sea on one side, and into the island on the other side, with a marvellous great hall below, and a very great storehouse at the one end of the hall: the most part of the cables in the South Sea are made upon that island. This great cacique doth make all the Indians upon the island to work and to drudge for him: and he himself is an Indian born, but is married to a marvellous fair woman which is a Spaniard.

This Spanish woman his wife is honoured as a queen in the island, and never goeth on the ground upon her feet: but when her pleasure is to take the air, she is always carried in a shadow like unto an horse-litter upon four men's shoulders, with a veil or canopy over her for the sun or the wind, having her gentlewomen still attending about her with a great troop of the best men of the island with her. But both she and the lord of the island with all the Indians in the town were newly fled out of the island before we could get to an anchor, by reason we were becalmed before we could get in, and were gone over unto the mainland, having carried away with them to the sum of 100,000 crowns.

This island is very pleasant: but there are no mines of gold nor silver in it. There are at least 200 houses in the town about the cacique's palace, and as many in one or two towns more upon the island, which is almost as big as the Isle of Wight. There is planted on the one side of the cacique's house a fair garden, with all herbs growing in it, and at the lower end a well of fresh water, and round about it are trees set, whereon bombazine cotton groweth after this manner: the tops of the trees grow full of cods, out of which the cotton groweth, and in the cotton is a seed of the bigness of a pea, and in every cod there are seven or eight of these seeds: and if the cotton be not gathered when it is ripe, then these seeds fall from it, and spring again.

There are also in this garden fig trees which bear continually, also pompions, melons, cucumbers, radishes, rosemary and thyme, with many other herbs and fruits. At the other end of the house there is also another orchard, where grow oranges sweet and sour, lemons, pomegranates and limes, with divers other fruits.

There is very good pasture ground in this island; and withal many horses, oxen, bullocks, sheep very fat and fair, great store of goats which be very tame, and are used continually to be milked. They have moreover abundance of pigeons, turkeys, and ducks of a marvellous bigness.

There was also a very large and great church hard by the cacique's house, whither he caused all the Indians in the island to come and hear mass: for he himself was made a Christian when he was married to the Spanish woman before spoken of, and upon his conversion he caused the rest of his subjects to be christened. In this church was an high altar with a crucifix, and five bells hanging in the nether end thereof. We burnt the church and brought the bells away.

The second day of June in the morning, by and by after break of day, every one of the watch being gone abroad to seek to fetch in victuals, some one way, some another, upon

The prosperous voyage of the worshipful Thomas Candish

the sudden there came down upon us an hundred Spanish soldiers with muskets and an ensign, which were landed on the other side of the island that night, and all the Indians of the island with them, every one with weapons. Thus being taken at advantage we had the worst: for our company was not past sixteen or twenty; whereof they had slain one or two before they were come to the houses: yet we skirmished with them an hour and a half: at the last being sore overcharged with multitudes, we were driven down from the hill to the water's side, and there kept them play a while, until in the end Zachary Saxie, who with his halberd had kept the way of the hill, and slain a couple of them, as he breathed himself being somewhat tired, had an honourable death and a short; for a shot struck him to the heart: who feeling himself mortally wounded cried to God for mercy, and fell down presently dead. But soon after the enemy was driven somewhat to retire from the bank's side to the green: and in the end our boat came and carried as many of our men away as could go in her, which was in hazard of sinking while they hastened into it: and one of our men whose name was Robert Maddocke was shot through the head with his own piece, being a snap-hance, as he was hasting into the boat. But four of us were left behind which the boat could not carry: to wit, myself Francis Pretty, Thomas Andrewes, Stephen Gunner, and Richard Rose: which had our shot ready and retired ourselves unto a cliff, until the boat came again, which was presently after they had carried the rest aboard. There were six and forty of the enemy's slain by us, whereof they had dragged some into bushes, and some into old houses, which we found afterwards. We lost twelve men.

The self same day, we went on shore again with seventy men, and had a fresh skirmish with the enemies, and drove them to retire, being an hundred Spaniards serving with muskets, and two hundred Indians with bows, arrows and darts. This done, we set fire on the town and burnt it to the ground, having in it to the number of three hundred houses: and shortly after made havoc of their fields, orchards and gardens, and burnt four great ships more which were in building on the stocks.

The fifth day of June we departed, and turned up for a place which is called Rio Dolce, where we watered: at which place also we sunk the *Hugh Gallant* for want of men, being a bark of forty tons.

The 27 in the morning by the break of day we came into the road of Aguatulco, where we found a bark of 50 tons, laden with cacaos and anil which they had there landed: and the men were all fled on shore. We landed there, and burnt their town, with the church and custom-house which was very fair and large: in which house were 600 bags of anil to dye cloth; every bag whereof was worth 40 crowns, and 400 bags of cacaos: every bag whereof is worth ten crowns. These cacaos go among them for meat and money. For 150 of them are in value one real of plate in ready payment. They are very like unto an almond, but are nothing so pleasant in taste: they eat them, and make drink of them. This the owner of the ship told us.

[The 8 we came to the road of Chaccalla.] Our general sent up Captain Havers with forty men of us before day, we went unto a place about two leagues up into the country in a most villainous desert path through the woods and wilderness:

The prosperous voyage of the worshipful Thomas Candish

and in the end we came to a place where we took three householders with their wives and children and some Indians, we bound them all and made them come to the sea side with us.

Our general made their wives to fetch us plantains, lemons, and oranges, pine-apples and other fruits whereof they had abundance, and so let their husbands depart.

The 4 of November the *Desire* and the *Content*, beating up and down upon the headland of California, between seven and 8 of the clock in the morning one of the company which was the trumpeter of the ship going up into the top espied a sail bearing in from the sea with the cape, whereupon he cried out with no small joy, a sail, a sail: we gave them chase some 3 or 4 hours, standing with our best advantage and working for the wind. In the afternoon we got up unto them, giving them the broadside with our great ordnance and a volley of small shot, and presently laid the ship aboard, whereof the King of Spain was owner, called the *Santa Anna* and thought to be 700 tons in burthen. As we were ready on their shipside to enter her, being not past 50 or 60 men at the uttermost, we perceived that the captain had made fights fore and after, and having not one man to be seen, stood close under their fights, with lances, javelins, rapiers, and targets, and an innumerable sort of great stones, which they threw overboard upon our heads being so many of them, they put us off the ship again, with the loss of 2 of our men which were slain, and with the hurting of 4 or 5. We new trimmed our sails, and gave them a fresh encounter with our great ordnance and also with our small shot, raking them through and through, to the killing and maiming of many of their men. Their captain still like a valiant man with his company stood very stoutly not yielding as yet: our general encouraging his men afresh with the whole noise of trumpets gave them the third encounter with our great ordnance. They being thus discomforted and spoiled, and their ship being in hazard of sinking by reason of the great shot, whereof some were under water, within 5 or 6 hours fight set out a flag of truce, desiring our general to save their lives and to take their goods, and that they would presently yield. Our general of his goodness promised them mercy, and willed them to strike their sails, and to hoist out their boat and to come aboard: one of their chief merchants came aboard unto our general: and falling down upon his knees, offered to have kissed our general's feet, and craved mercy. The general of his great humanity, promised their lives and good usage. The said pilot and captain presently certified the general what goods they had within board, to wit, an hundred and 22 thousand pesos of gold: with silks, satins, damasks, with musk and divers other merchandise, and great store of all manner of victuals with the choice of many conserves for to eat, and of sundry sorts of very good wines. On the 6 day of November following we went into an harbour which is called by the Spaniards, Puerto Seguro.

Here the whole company of the Spaniards, to the number of 190 persons were set on shore: where they had a fair river of fresh water, with great store of fresh fish, fowl and wood, and also many hares and coneys upon the mainland. Our general also gave them great store of victuals, of garbanzos, pease, and some wine. Also they had all the sails of their ship to make them tents on shore, with licence to take such store of planks as should be sufficients to make them a bark. Then we fell to hoisting in of our goods, sharing of the treasure, and allotting to every man his portion. In division whereof the eighth of this month, many of the company fell into a mutiny against our general, which nevertheless were after a sort pacified for the time.

Our general discharged the captain, with provision for his defence against the Indians, both of swords, targets, pieces, shot and powder to his great contentment: but before his departure, he took out of this great ship two young lads born in Japan, which could both write and read their own language. He took also with him out of their ship, 3 boys born in the isle of Manila, the one about 15, the other about 13, and the youngest about 9 years old. The third remaineth with the right honourable the Countess of Essex.

He took also from them a Spaniard, which was a very good pilot unto the islands of Ladrones, where the Spaniards do put in to water, sailing between Acapulco and the Philippines: in which isles of Ladrones, they find fresh water, plantains, and potato roots: howbeit the people be very rude and heathens. The 19 day of November about 3 of the clock in the afternoon, our general caused the King's ship to be set on fire, which having to the quantity of 500 tons of goods in her we saw burnt into the water, and then set sail joyfully homewards towards England with fair wind: we left the *Content* astern of us. Thinking she would have overtaken us, we lost her company and never saw her after. We were sailing unto the isles of Ladrones the rest of November, and all December, and so forth until the 3 of January 1588, with a fair wind for the space of 45 days: and we esteemed it to be between 17 and 18 hundred leagues. We were coming up within 2 leagues of the island, where we met with 60 or 70 sails of canoes full of savages, who came off to sea unto us, and brought with them in their boats plantains, cocos, potato roots, and fresh fish, which they had caught at sea, and held them up unto us for to exchange with us; we made fast little pieces of old iron upon small cords and fishing lines, and so veered the iron into their canoes, and they caught hold of them and took off the iron, and in exchange of it they would make fast unto the same line either a potato root, or a bundle of plantains, which we hauled in: and thus our company exchanged with them until they had satisfied themselves with as much as did content them: yet we could not be rid of them. For afterward they were so thick about the ship, that it stemmed and broke 1 or 2 of their canoes: but the men saved themselves being in every canoe 4, 6, or 8 persons all naked and excellent swimmers and divers. They are of a tawny colour and marvellous fat, and bigger ordinarily of stature than the most part of our men in England, wearing their hair long: their canoes were as artificially made as any that ever we had seen: considering they were made and contrived without any edge-tool. They are not above half a yard in breadth and in length some seven or eight yards, and their heads and sterns are both alike: their sail is made of mats of sedges, square or triangle wise: and they sail as well right against the wind, as before the wind: these savages followed us so long, that we could not be rid of them: until in the end our general commanded some half dozen arquebuses to be made ready; and himself struck one of them and the rest shot at them: but they were so nimble,

The prosperous voyage of the worshipful Thomas Candish

that we could not discern whether they were killed or not, because they would fall back into the sea and prevent us by diving.

The 14 day of January, by the break of day we fell with a headland of the isles of the Philippines. Manila is well planted and inhabited with Spaniards to the number of six or seven hundred persons: which dwell in a town unwalled, which hath 3 or 4 small block houses, part made of wood, and part of stone being indeed of no great strength: they have one or two small galleys belong to the town. It is a very rich place of gold and many other commodities; and they have yearly traffic from Acapulco in Nueva España, and also 20 or 30 ships from China, which bring them many sorts of merchandise. They bring great store of gold with them, which they traffic and exchange for silver, and give weight for weight.

The fifteenth of January we fell with an island called Capul. Our ship was no sooner come to an anchor, but presently there came a canoe rowing aboard us, wherein was one of the chief caciques of the island, who supposing that we were Spaniards, brought us potato roots, and green cocos, in exchange whereof we gave his company pieces of linen to the quantity of a yard for four cocos, and as much linen for a basket of potato roots of a quart in quantity; which roots are very good meat, and excellent sweet either roasted or boiled.

This cacique's skin was carved and cut with sundry and many strokes and devices all over his body. Presently the people of the island came down with their cocos and potato roots, and brought with them hens and hogs. Thus we rode at anchor all day, doing nothing but buying roots, cocos, hens, hogs, refreshing ourselves marvellously well.

The same day at night being the fifteenth of January 1588, Nicholas Roderigo the Portuguese, whom we took out of the great *Santa Anna* at the cape of California, desired to speak with our general in secret: our general understood, and asked him what he had to say. The Portuguese made him this answer. That the Spaniard which was taken out of the great *Santa Anna* for a pilot, had written a letter, and secretly sealed it and locked it up in his chest, meaning to convey it by the inhabitants of this island to Manila, the contents whereof were: that there had been two English ships along the coast of Chile, Peru, [and] Nueva España, and that they had taken many ships and merchandise in them, and burnt divers towns, and spoiled all that ever they could come unto, and that they had taken the King's ship which came from Manila and all his treasure, with all the merchandise that was therein: and had set the people on shore. Therefore he willed them that they should make strong their bulwarks with their two galleys. He further signified, that we were riding at an island called Capul at the end of the island of Manila, being but one ship with small force in it: if they could use any means to surprise us being there at an anchor, they should dispatch it: for our force was but small, and our men but weak, and that the place where we rode was but 50 leagues from them. Our general called for him, and charged him with these things, which at the first he utterly denied: but in the end, the matter being made manifest, the next morning our general willed that he should be hanged.

The prosperous voyage of the worshipful Thomas Candish

The people of this island go almost all naked and are tawny of colour. The men wear only a strop about their waists, of some kind of linen of their own weaving, which is made of plantain leaves, and another strop coming from their back under their twists, which covers their privy parts, and is made fast to their girdles at their navels.

Every man and man-child among them hath a nail of tin thrust quite through the head of his privy part, being split in the lower end and rivetted, and on the head of the nail is as it were a crown: which is driven through their privities when they be young, and the place groweth up again, without any great pain to the child: and they take this nail out and in, as occasion serveth: and for the truth whereof we ourselves have taken one of these nails from a son of one of the kings which was of the age of 10 years, who did wear the same in his privy member.

This custom was granted at the request of the women of the country, who finding their men to be given to the foul sin of sodomy, desired some remedy against that mischief. Moreover all the males are circumcised, having the foreskin of their flesh cut away. These people wholly worship the devil, and often times have conference with him, which appeareth unto them in most ugly and monstrous shape.

On the 23 day of January, our general Mr Thomas Candish caused all the principals of this island, and of an hundred islands more, which he had made to pay tribute unto him (in hogs, hens, potatoes and cocos) to appear before him, and made himself and his company known unto them, that they were English men, and enemies to the Spaniards: and thereupon spread his ensign and sounded up the drums, which they much marvelled at: they promised both themselves and all the islands thereabout to aid him, whensoever he should come again to overcome the Spaniards. Also our general gave them, in token that we were enemies to the Spaniards, money back again for all their tribute which they had paid: which they took marvellous friendly, and rowed about our ship to show us pleasure: at the last our general caused a saker to be shot off, whereat they wondered, and with great contentment took their leaves of us.

On the 21 day of February, being Ash Wednesday Captain Havers died of a most fervent and pestilent ague, to the no small grief of our general, who caused two falcons and one saker to be shot off, who after he was shrouded in a sheet and a prayer said, was heaved overboard with great lamentation of us all. After his death myself with divers others in the ship fell marvellously sick, and so continued in very great pain for the space of three weeks or a month by reason of the extreme heat of the climate.

The first day of March having passed through the straits of Java, we came to an anchor under the southwest parts of Java: where we espied certain of the people fishing by the sea side. Our general taking into the ship-boat certain of his company, and a negro which could speak the tongue, made towards those fishers, which having espied our boat ran on shore into the wood for fear: but our general caused his negro to call unto them: presently one of them came out to the shore side and made answer. Our general by the negro enquired of him for fresh water, which they found, and caused the fisher to go to the king and to certify him of a ship that was come to have traffic for victuals, and for

The prosperous voyage of the worshipful Thomas Candish

diamonds, pearls, or any other rich jewels that he had: for which he should have either gold or other merchandise in exchange.

Two or three canoes came from the town unto us with eggs, hens, fresh fish, oranges, and limes. Our general weighed anchor and stood in nearer for the town: and as we were under sail we met with one of the king's canoes coming toward us. In this canoe was the king's secretary, who had on his head a piece of dyed linen cloth folded up like a Turk's turban: he was all naked saving about his waist, his breast was carved with the broad arrow upon it: he went barefooted: he had an interpreter with him, which was a mestizo, that is, half an Indian and half a Portuguese, who could speak very good Portuguese. This secretary signified unto our general that he had brought him an hog, hens, eggs, fresh fish, sugar-canes and wine: (which wine was as strong as any aquavitae, and as clear as any rock water). Our general used him singularly well, banqueted him most royally with the choice of many and sundry conserves, wines both sweet and other, and caused his musicians to make him music. This done our general told him that he and his company were Englishmen; and that we had been at China and had had traffic there with them, and that we were come thither to discover, and purposed to go to Malacca. The people of Java told our general that there were certain Portuguese in the island which lay there as factors continually to traffic with them, to buy negroes, cloves, pepper, sugar, and many other commodities. This secretary of the king with his interpreter lay one night aboard our ship. In the evening at the setting of the watch, our general commanded every

Richard Hakluyt

man in the ship to provide his arquebus and his shot, and so with shooting off 40 or 50 small shot and one saker, himself set the watch with them. This was no small marvel unto these heathen people, who had not commonly seen any ship so furnished with men and ordnance.

After the break of day there came to the number of 9 or 10 of the king's canoes so deeply laden with victuals as they could swim with two great live oxen, half a score of wonderful great and fat hogs, a number of hens which were alive, drakes, geese, eggs, plantains, sugar canes, sugar in plates, cocos, sweet oranges and sour, limes, great store of wine and aquavitae, salt to season victuals withal, and almost all manner of victuals else. Among all the rest came two Portuguese of middle stature, and men of marvellous proper personage; they were each of them in a loose jerkin and hose, which came down from the waist to the ankle, because of the use of the country, and partly because it was Lent, and a time for doing of their penance: they had on each of them a very fair and a white lawn shirt, very decently, only their bare legs excepted. These Portuguese were no small joy unto our general and all the rest of our company: for we had not seen any Christian that was our friend of a year and a half before. Our general used and entreated them singularly well, with banquets and music: they told us that they were no less glad to see us, than we to see them, and enquired of the estate of their country, and what was become of Dom Antonio their King, and whether he be living or no: for the Spaniards had always brought them word that he was dead. Then our general satisfied them in every demand: assuring them, that their King was alive, and in England, and had honourable allowance of our Queen, and that there was war between Spain and England, and that we were come under the King of Portugal into the South Sea, and had warred upon the Spaniards there, and had fired, spoiled and sunk all the ships along the coast that we could meet withal, to the number of eighteen or twenty sails. With this report they were sufficiently satisfied.

On the other side they declared unto us the state of the island of Java. First the plentifulness and great choice and store of victuals of all sorts, and of all manner of fruits as before is set down: then the great and rich merchandise which are there to be had. The name of the king of that island was Raja Bolamboam, who was a man had in great majesty and fear among them. The common people may not bargain, sell or exchange any thing with any other nation without special licence from their king: and if any so do, it is present death for him. The king himself is a man of great years, and hath an hundred wives, his son hath fifty. The custom of the country is, that whensoever the king doth die, they take the body so dead and burn it and preserve the ashes, and within five days next after, the wives go together to a place appointed, and the chief of the women, hath a ball in her hand, and throweth it from her, and to the place where the ball resteth, thither they go all, and turn their faces to the eastward, and every one with a dagger in their hand, (which dagger they call a kris, and is as sharp as a razor) stab themselves to the heart, and falling grovelling on their faces so end their days. This thing is as true as it seemeth to any hearer to be strange.

The men of themselves be very politic and subtile, and

singularly valiant, and wonderfully at commandment and fear of their king. For example: if their king command them to undertake any exploit, be it never so dangerous or desperate, they dare not nor will refuse it, though they die every man in the execution of the same. For he will cut off the heads of every one of them which return alive without bringing of their purpose to pass: they never fear any death. If any of them feeleth himself hurt with lance or sword, he will willingly run himself upon the weapon quite through his body to procure his death more speedily, and in this desperate sort end his days, or overcome his enemy. Moreover, although the men be tawny of colour and go continually naked, yet their women be fair of complexion and go more apparelled.

They told us further, that if their King, Dom Antonio would come unto them, they would warrant him to have all the Moluccas at commandment, besides, China, and the isles of the Philippines, and that he might be assured to have all the Indians on his side that are in the country. The next day being the 16 of March we set sail towards the Cape of Good Hope, on the southernmost coast of Africa.

The rest of March and all the month of April we spent in traversing that mighty and vast sea, between the isle of Java and the main of Africa, observing the stars, the fowls, which are marks unto the seamen of fair weather, approaching lands or islands, the winds, the tempests, the rains and thunders, with the alterations of the tides and currents.

The 11 of May in the morning one of the company went into the top, and espied land. This cape is very easy to be known. For there are right over it three very high hills standing but a small way one off another, and the highest standeth in the midst and the ground is much lower by the seaside.

This cape of Buena Esperanza is set down and accompted for two thousand leagues from the island of Java in the Portuguese sea charts: but it is not so much almost by an hundred and fifty leagues, as we found by the running of our ship. We were in running of these eighteen hundred and fifty leagues just nine weeks.

The eighth day of June by break of day we fell in sight of the island of Saint Helena.

This island is very high land, and lieth in the main sea standing as it were in the midst of the sea between the main land of Africa, and the main of Brazil and the coast of Guinea.

The same day about two or three of the clock in the afternoon we went on shore, where we found a marvellous fair and pleasant valley, wherein divers handsome buildings and houses were set up, and especially one which was a church, which was tiled and whited on the outside very fair, and made with a porch, and within the church at the upper end was set an altar, whereon stood a very large table set in a frame having in it the picture of Our Saviour Christ upon the Cross and the image of Our Lady praying.

There are two houses adjoining to the church, which serve for kitchens to dress meat in: the coverings of the said houses are made flat, whereon is planted a very fair vine, and through both the said houses runneth a very good and wholesome stream of fresh water.

There is also right over against the said church a fair

causeway made up with stones reaching unto a valley by the seaside, in which valley is planted a garden, wherein grow great store of pompions and melons: and upon the said causeway is a frame erected whereon hang two bells wherewith they ring to mass; and hard unto it is a cross set up, which is squared, framed and made very artificially of free stone, whereon is carved in ciphers what time it was builded, which was in the year of our Lord 1571.

This valley is the fairest and largest low plot in all the island, and it is marvellous sweet and pleasant, and planted in every place either with fruit trees, or with herbs. There are fig trees, which bear fruit continually, and marvellous plentifully: for on every tree you shall have blossoms, green figs, and ripe figs, all at once: and it is so all the year long. There be also great store of lemon trees, orange trees, pomegranate trees, pomecitron trees, date trees, which bear fruit as the fig trees do, and are planted carefully and very artificially with very pleasant walks under and between them, and the said walks be overshadowed with the leaves of the trees: and in every void place is planted parsley, sorrel, basil, fennel, aniseed, mustard seed, radishes, and many special good herbs: and the fresh water brook runneth through divers places of this orchard, and may with very small pains be made to water any one tree in the valley.

This fresh water stream cometh from the tops of the mountains, and falleth from the cliff into the valley the height of a cable, and hath many arms out of it, which refresh the whole island, and almost every tree in it. The island is altogether high mountains and steep valleys, except it be in the tops of some hills, and down below in some of the valleys, where marvellous store of all these kind of fruits before spoken of do grow: there is greater store growing in the tops of the mountains than below in the valleys: but it is wonderful laboursome and also dangerous travelling up unto them and down again by reason of the height and steepness of the hills.

There is also upon this island great store of partridges, which are very tame, not making any great haste to fly away though one come very near them, but only to run away, and get up into the steep cliffs: we killed some of them with a fowling piece. They differ very much from our partridges which are in England both in bigness and also in colour. For they be within a little as big as an hen, and are of an ash colour, and live in coveys twelve, sixteen, and twenty together.

There are likewise no less store of pheasants in the island, which are also marvellous big and fat, surpassing those which are in our country in bigness.

There are in this island thousands of goats, which the Spaniards call cabritos, which are very wild: you shall see one or two hundred of them together: they will climb up the cliffs which are so steep that a man would think it a thing unpossible for any living thing to go here. We took and killed many of them for all their swiftness.

Here are in like manner great store of swine which be very wild and very fat, and of a marvellous bigness: they keep altogether upon the mountains, and will very seldom abide any man to come near them.

We found in the houses at our coming 3 slaves which were negroes, which told us that the East Indian fleet, which were in number 5 sails, the least whereof were in burthen of 8 or 900 tons, all laden with spices and Calicut cloth, with store of treasure and very rich stones and pearls, were gone from the said island of Saint Helena but 20 days before we came thither.

This island hath been found of a long time by the Portuguese, and hath been altogether planted by them, for their refreshing as they come from the East Indies.

The 20 day of June having taken in wood and water and refreshed ourselves with such things as we found there, and made clean our ship, we set sail about 8 of the clock in the night toward England.

The third of September we met with a Flemish hulk which came from Lisbon, and declared unto us the overthrowing of the Spanish fleet, to the singular rejoicing and comfort of us all.

The 9 of September, after a terrible tempest which carried away most part of our sails, by the merciful favour of the Almighty we recovered our long wished port of Plymouth in England, from whence we set forth at the beginning of our voyage.

1. BOCCACCIO · *Mrs Rosie and the Priest*
2. GERARD MANLEY HOPKINS · *As kingfishers catch fire*
3. *The Saga of Gunnlaug Serpent-tongue*
4. THOMAS DE QUINCEY · *On Murder Considered as One of the Fine Arts*
5. FRIEDRICH NIETZSCHE · *Aphorisms on Love and Hate*
6. JOHN RUSKIN · *Traffic*
7. PU SONGLING · *Wailing Ghosts*
8. JONATHAN SWIFT · *A Modest Proposal*
9. *Three Tang Dynasty Poets*
10. WALT WHITMAN · *On the Beach at Night Alone*
11. KENKŌ · *A Cup of Sake Beneath the Cherry Trees*
12. BALTASAR GRACIÁN · *How to Use Your Enemies*
13. JOHN KEATS · *The Eve of St Agnes*
14. THOMAS HARDY · *Woman much missed*
15. GUY DE MAUPASSANT · *Femme Fatale*
16. MARCO POLO · *Travels in the Land of Serpents and Pearls*
17. SUETONIUS · *Caligula*
18. APOLLONIUS OF RHODES · *Jason and Medea*
19. ROBERT LOUIS STEVENSON · *Olalla*
20. KARL MARX AND FRIEDRICH ENGELS · *The Communist Manifesto*
21. PETRONIUS · *Trimalchio's Feast*
22. JOHANN PETER HEBEL · *How a Ghastly Story Was Brought to Light by a Common or Garden Butcher's Dog*
23. HANS CHRISTIAN ANDERSEN · *The Tinder Box*
24. RUDYARD KIPLING · *The Gate of the Hundred Sorrows*
25. DANTE · *Circles of Hell*
26. HENRY MAYHEW · *Of Street Piemen*
27. HAFEZ · *The nightingales are drunk*
28. GEOFFREY CHAUCER · *The Wife of Bath*
29. MICHEL DE MONTAIGNE · *How We Weep and Laugh at the Same Thing*
30. THOMAS NASHE · *The Terrors of the Night*
31. EDGAR ALLAN POE · *The Tell-Tale Heart*
32. MARY KINGSLEY · *A Hippo Banquet*
33. JANE AUSTEN · *The Beautifull Cassandra*
34. ANTON CHEKHOV · *Gooseberries*
35. SAMUEL TAYLOR COLERIDGE · *Well, they are gone, and here must I remain*
36. JOHANN WOLFGANG VON GOETHE · *Sketchy, Doubtful, Incomplete Jottings*
37. CHARLES DICKENS · *The Great Winglebury Duel*
38. HERMAN MELVILLE · *The Maldive Shark*
39. ELIZABETH GASKELL · *The Old Nurse's Story*
40. NIKOLAY LESKOV · *The Steel Flea*

41. HONORÉ DE BALZAC · *The Atheist's Mass*
42. CHARLOTTE PERKINS GILMAN · *The Yellow Wall-Paper*
43. C.P. CAVAFY · *Remember, Body . . .*
44. FYODOR DOSTOEVSKY · *The Meek One*
45. GUSTAVE FLAUBERT · *A Simple Heart*
46. NIKOLAI GOGOL · *The Nose*
47. SAMUEL PEPYS · *The Great Fire of London*
48. EDITH WHARTON · *The Reckoning*
49. HENRY JAMES · *The Figure in the Carpet*
50. WILFRED OWEN · *Anthem For Doomed Youth*
51. WOLFGANG AMADEUS MOZART · *My Dearest Father*
52. PLATO · *Socrates' Defence*
53. CHRISTINA ROSSETTI · *Goblin Market*
54. *Sindbad the Sailor*
55. SOPHOCLES · *Antigone*
56. RYŪNOSUKE AKUTAGAWA · *The Life of a Stupid Man*
57. LEO TOLSTOY · *How Much Land Does A Man Need?*
58. GIORGIO VASARI · *Leonardo da Vinci*
59. OSCAR WILDE · *Lord Arthur Savile's Crime*
60. SHEN FU · *The Old Man of the Moon*
61. AESOP · *The Dolphins, the Whales and the Gudgeon*
62. MATSUO BASHŌ · *Lips too Chilled*
63. EMILY BRONTË · *The Night is Darkening Round Me*
64. JOSEPH CONRAD · *To-morrow*
65. RICHARD HAKLUYT · *The Voyage of Sir Francis Drake Around the Whole Globe*
66. KATE CHOPIN · *A Pair of Silk Stockings*
67. CHARLES DARWIN · *It was snowing butterflies*
68. BROTHERS GRIMM · *The Robber Bridegroom*
69. CATULLUS · *I Hate and I Love*
70. HOMER · *Circe and the Cyclops*
71. D. H. LAWRENCE · *Il Duro*
72. KATHERINE MANSFIELD · *Miss Brill*
73. OVID · *The Fall of Icarus*
74. SAPPHO · *Come Close*
75. IVAN TURGENEV · *Kasyan from the Beautiful Lands*
76. VIRGIL · *O Cruel Alexis*
77. H. G. WELLS · *A Slip under the Microscope*
78. HERODOTUS · *The Madness of Cambyses*
79. *Speaking of Siva*
80. *The Dhammapada*

KATE CHOPIN

A Pair of Silk Stockings

PENGUIN BOOKS

PENGUIN CLASSICS

UK | USA | Canada | Ireland | Australia
India | New Zealand | South Africa

Penguin Books is part of the Penguin Random House group of companies
whose addresses can be found at global.penguinrandomhouse.com.

This selection published in Penguin Classics 2015

009

Set in 10/14.5 pt Baskerville 10 Pro
Typeset by Jouve (UK), Milton Keynes
Printed and bound in Great Britain by Clays Ltd, Elcograf S.p.A.

A CIP catalogue record for this book is available from the British Library

ISBN: 978-0-141-39853-2

www.greenpenguin.co.uk

MIX
Paper from
responsible sources
FSC® C018179

Penguin Random House is committed to a
sustainable future for our business, our readers
and our planet. This book is made from Forest
Stewardship Council® certified paper.

Contents

Désirée's Baby	1
Miss McEnders	12
The Story of an Hour	28
Nég Créol	34
A Pair of Silk Stockings	47

Désirée's Baby

As the day was pleasant, Madame Valmondé drove over to L'Abri to see Désirée and the baby.

It made her laugh to think of Désirée with a baby. Why, it seemed but yesterday that Désirée was little more than a baby herself; when Monsieur in riding through the gateway of Valmondé had found her lying asleep in the shadow of the big stone pillar.

The little one awoke in his arms and began to cry for 'Dada'. That was as much as she could do or say. Some people thought she might have strayed there of her own accord, for she was of the toddling age. The prevailing belief was that she had been purposely left by a party of Texans, whose canvas-covered wagon, late in the day, had crossed the ferry that Coton Maïs kept, just below the plantation. In time Madame Valmondé abandoned every speculation but the one that Désirée had been sent to her by a beneficent Providence to be the child of her affection, seeing that she was without child of the flesh. For the girl grew to be beautiful and gentle, affectionate and sincere, – the idol of Valmondé.

It was no wonder, when she stood one day against the stone pillar in whose shadow she had lain asleep, eighteen years before, that Armand Aubigny riding by and seeing her there, had fallen in love with her. That was the way all the Aubignys fell in love, as if struck by a pistol shot. The wonder was that he had not loved her before; for he had known her since his father brought him home from Paris, a boy of eight, after his mother died there. The passion that awoke in him that day, when he saw her at the gate, swept along like an avalanche, or like a prairie fire, or like anything that drives headlong over all obstacles.

Monsieur Valmondé grew practical and wanted things well considered: that is, the girl's obscure origin. Armand looked into her eyes and did not care. He was reminded that she was nameless. What did it matter about a name when he could give her one of the oldest and proudest in Louisiana? He ordered the *corbeille* from Paris, and contained himself with what patience he could until it arrived; then they were married.

Madame Valmondé had not seen Désirée and the baby for four weeks. When she reached L'Abri she shuddered at the first sight of it, as she always did. It was a sad looking place, which for many years had not known the gentle presence of a mistress, old Monsieur Aubigny having married and buried his wife in France, and she having loved her own land too well ever to leave it. The roof came down steep and black like a cowl, reaching out beyond the wide galleries that encircled the yellow stuccoed house. Big, solemn oaks grew close to it, and their thick-leaved, far-reaching branches shadowed it like a pall. Young Aubigny's rule was a strict one, too, and under it his negroes had forgotten how to be gay, as they had been during the old master's easy-going and indulgent lifetime.

The young mother was recovering slowly, and lay full length, in her soft white muslins and laces, upon a couch. The baby was beside her, upon her arm, where he had fallen asleep, at her breast. The yellow nurse woman sat beside a window fanning herself.

Madame Valmondé bent her portly figure over

Désirée and kissed her, holding her an instant tenderly in her arms. Then she turned to the child.

'This is not the baby!' she exclaimed, in startled tones. French was the language spoken at Valmondé in those days.

'I knew you would be astonished,' laughed Désirée, 'at the way he has grown. The little *cochon de lait!* Look at his legs, mamma, and his hands and finger-nails, – real finger-nails. Zandrine had to cut them this morning. Isn't it true, Zandrine?'

The woman bowed her turbaned head majestically, 'Mais si, Madame.'

'And the way he cries,' went on Désirée, 'is deafening. Armand heard him the other day as far away as La Blanche's cabin.'

Madame Valmondé had never removed her eyes from the child. She lifted it and walked with it over to the window that was lightest. She scanned the baby narrowly, then looked as searchingly at Zandrine, whose face was turned to gaze across the fields.

'Yes, the child has grown, has changed,' said Madame Valmondé, slowly, as she replaced it beside its mother. 'What does Armand say?'

Désirée's Baby

Désirée's face became suffused with a glow that was happiness itself.

'Oh, Armand is the proudest father in the parish, I believe, chiefly because it is a boy, to bear his name; though he says not, – that he would have loved a girl as well. But I know it isn't true. I know he says that to please me. And mamma,' she added, drawing Madame Valmondé's head down to her and speaking in a whisper, 'he hasn't punished one of them – not one of them – since baby is born. Even Négrillon, who pretended to have burnt his leg that he might rest from work – he only laughed, and said Négrillon was a great scamp. Oh, mamma, I'm so happy; it frightens me.'

What Désirée said was true. Marriage, and later the birth of his son had softened Armand Aubigny's imperious and exacting nature greatly. This was what made the gentle Désirée so happy, for she loved him desperately. When he frowned she trembled, but loved him. When he smiled, she asked no greater blessing of God. But Armand's dark, handsome face had not often been disfigured by frowns since the day he fell in love with her.

When the baby was about three months old, Désirée

awoke one day to the conviction that there was something in the air menacing her peace. It was at first too subtle to grasp. It had only been a disquieting suggestion; an air of mystery among the blacks; unexpected visits from far-off neighbours who could hardly account for their coming. Then a strange, an awful change in her husband's manner, which she dared not ask him to explain. When he spoke to her, it was with averted eyes, from which the old love-light seemed to have gone out. He absented himself from home; and when there, avoided her presence and that of her child, without excuse. And the very spirit of Satan seemed suddenly to take hold of him in his dealings with the slaves. Désirée was miserable enough to die.

She sat in her room, one hot afternoon, in her *peignoir,* listlessly drawing through her fingers the strands of her long, silky brown hair that hung about her shoulders. The baby, half naked, lay asleep upon her own great mahogany bed, that was like a sumptuous throne, with its satin-lined half-canopy. One of La Blanche's little quadroon boys – half naked too – stood fanning the child slowly with a fan of peacock feathers. Désirée's eyes had been fixed absently and sadly upon the baby, while she was striving to penetrate the threatening mist that she felt closing about her. She looked from her child to the boy who stood beside him, and back again; over and over. 'Ah!' It was a cry that she could not help; which she was not conscious of having uttered. The blood turned like ice in her veins, and a clammy moisture gathered upon her face.

She tried to speak to the little quadroon boy; but no sound would come, at first. When he heard his name uttered, he looked up, and his mistress was pointing to the door. He laid aside the great, soft fan, and obediently stole away, over the polished floor, on his bare tiptoes.

She stayed motionless, with gaze riveted upon her child, and her face the picture of fright.

Presently her husband entered the room, and without noticing her, went to a table and began to search among some papers which covered it.

'Armand,' she called to him, in a voice which must have stabbed him, if he was human. But he did not notice. 'Armand,' she said again. Then she rose and tottered towards him. 'Armand,' she panted once more, clutching his arm, 'look at our child. What does it mean? tell me.'

He coldly but gently loosened her fingers from about his arm and thrust the hand away from him. 'Tell me what it means!' she cried despairingly.

'It means,' he answered lightly, 'that the child is not white; it means that you are not white.'

A quick conception of all that this accusation meant for her nerved her with unwonted courage to deny it. 'It is a lie; it is not true, I am white! Look at my hair, it is brown; and my eyes are grey, Armand, you know they are grey. And my skin is fair,' seizing his wrist. 'Look at my hand; whiter than yours, Armand,' she laughed hysterically.

'As white as La Blanche's,' he returned cruelly; and went away leaving her alone with their child.

When she could hold a pen in her hand, she sent a despairing letter to Madame Valmondé.

'My mother, they tell me I am not white. Armand has told me I am not white. For God's sake tell them it is not true. You must know it is not true. I shall die. I must die. I cannot be so unhappy, and live.'

The answer that came was as brief:

'My own Désirée: Come home to Valmondé; back to your mother who loves you. Come with your child.'

When the letter reached Désirée she went with it

Désirée's Baby

to her husband's study, and laid it open upon the desk before which he sat. She was like a stone image: silent, white, motionless after she placed it there.

In silence he ran his cold eyes over the written words. He said nothing. 'Shall I go, Armand?' she asked in tones sharp with agonized suspense.

'Yes, go.'

'Do you want me to go?'

'Yes, I want you to go.'

He thought Almighty God had dealt cruelly and unjustly with him; and felt, somehow, that he was paying Him back in kind when he stabbed thus into his wife's soul. Moreover he no longer loved her, because of the unconscious injury she had brought upon his home and his name.

She turned away like one stunned by a blow, and walked slowly towards the door, hoping he would call her back.

'Good-by, Armand,' she moaned.

He did not answer her. That was his last blow at fate.

Désirée went in search of her child. Zandrine was pacing the sombre gallery with it. She took the little one from the nurse's arms with no word of explanation, and descending the steps, walked away, under the live-oak branches.

It was an October afternoon; the sun was just sinking. Out in the still fields the negroes were picking cotton.

Désirée had not changed the thin white garment nor the slippers which she wore. Her hair was uncovered and the sun's rays brought a golden gleam from its brown meshes. She did not take the broad, beaten road which led to the far-off plantation of Valmondé. She walked across a deserted field, where the stubble bruised her tender feet, so delicately shod, and tore her thin gown to shreds.

She disappeared among the reeds and willows that grew thick along the banks of the deep, sluggish bayou; and she did not come back again.

Some weeks later there was a curious scene enacted at L'Abri. In the centre of the smoothly swept back yard was a great bonfire. Armand Aubigny sat in the wide hallway that commanded a view of the spectacle; and it was he who dealt out to a half dozen negroes the material which kept this fire ablaze.

A graceful cradle of willow, with all its dainty

furbishings, was laid upon the pyre, which had already been fed with the richness of a priceless *layette*. Then there were silk gowns, and velvet and satin ones added to these; laces, too, and embroideries; bonnets and gloves; for the *corbeille* had been of rare quality.

The last thing to go was a tiny bundle of letters; innocent little scribblings that Désirée had sent to him during the days of their espousal. There was the remnant of one back in the drawer from which he took them. But it was not Désirée's; it was part of an old letter from his mother to his father. He read it. She was thanking God for the blessing of her husband's love: –

'But, above all,' she wrote, 'night and day, I thank the good God for having so arranged our lives that our dear Armand will never know that his mother, who adores him, belongs to the race that is cursed with the brand of slavery.'

Miss McEnders

1

When Miss Georgie McEnders had finished an elaborately simple toilet of grey and black, she divested herself completely of rings, bangles, brooches – everything to suggest that she stood in friendly relations with fortune. For Georgie was going to read a paper upon 'The Dignity of Labour' before the Woman's Reform Club; and if she was blessed with an abundance of wealth, she possessed a no less amount of good taste.

Before entering the neat victoria that stood at her father's too-sumptuous door – and that was her special property – she turned to give certain directions to the coachman. First upon the list from which she read was inscribed: 'Look up Mademoiselle Salambre.'

Miss McEnders

'James,' said Georgie, flushing a pretty pink, as she always did with the slightest effort of speech, 'we want to look up a person named Mademoiselle Salambre, in the southern part of town, on Arsenal street,' indicating a certain number and locality. Then she seated herself in the carriage, and as it drove away proceeded to study her engagement list further and to knit her pretty brows in deep and complex thought.

'Two o'clock – look up M. Salambre,' said the list. 'Three-thirty – read paper before Woman's Ref. Club. Four-thirty – ' and here followed cabalistic abbreviations which meant: 'Join committee of ladies to investigate moral condition of St Louis factory-girls. Six o'clock – dine with papa. Eight o'clock – hear Henry George's lecture on Single Tax.'

So far, Mademoiselle Salambre was only a name to Georgie McEnders, one of several submitted to her at her own request by her furnishers, Push and Prodem, an enterprising firm charged with the construction of Miss McEnders' very elaborate trousseau. Georgie liked to know the people who worked for her, as far as she could.

She was a charming young woman of twenty-five, though almost too white-souled for a creature of flesh and blood. She possessed ample wealth and time to squander, and a burning desire to do good – to elevate the human race, and start the world over again on a comfortable footing for everybody.

When Georgie had pushed open the very high gate of a very small yard she stood confronting a robust German woman, who, with dress tucked carefully between her knees, was in the act of noisily 'redding' the bricks.

'Does M'selle Salambre live here?' Georgie's tall, slim figure was very erect. Her face suggested a sweet peach blossom, and she held a severely simple lorgnon up to her short-sighted blue eyes.

'Ya! ya! aber oop stairs!' cried the woman brusquely and impatiently. But Georgie did not mind. She was used to greetings that lacked the ring of cordiality.

When she had ascended the stairs that led to an upper porch she knocked at the first door that presented itself, and was told to enter by Mlle Salambre herself.

The woman sat at an opposite window, bending over a bundle of misty white goods that lay in a fluffy heap in her lap. She was not young. She might have been thirty, or she might have been forty. There were lines about her round, piquante face that denoted close acquaintance with struggles, hardships and all manner of unkind experiences.

Georgie had heard a whisper here and there touching the private character of Mlle Salambre which had determined her to go in person and make the acquaintance of the woman and her surroundings; which latter were poor and simple enough, and not too neat. There was a little child at play upon the floor.

Mlle Salambre had not expected so unlooked-for an apparition as Miss McEnders, and seeing the girl standing there in the door she removed the eyeglasses that had assisted her in the delicate work, and stood up also.

'Mlle Salambre, I suppose?' said Georgie, with a courteous inclination.

'Ah! Mees McEndairs! What an agree'ble surprise! Will you be so kind to take a chair.' Mademoiselle had lived many years in the city, in various capacities, which brought her in touch with the fashionable set. There were few people in polite society whom Mademoiselle did not know – by sight, at least; and their private histories were as familiar to her as her own.

'You 'ave come to see your – the work?' the woman

went on with a smile that quite brightened her face. 'It is a pleasure to handle such fine, such delicate quality of goods, Mees,' and she went and laid several pieces of her handiwork upon the table beside Georgie, at the same time indicating such details as she hoped would call forth her visitor's approval.

There was something about the woman and her surroundings, and the atmosphere of the place, that affected the girl unpleasantly. She shrank instinctively, drawing her invisible mantle of chastity closely about her. Mademoiselle saw that her visitor's attention was divided between the lingerie and the child upon the floor, who was engaged in battering a doll's unyielding head against the unyielding floor.

'The child of my neighbour downstairs,' said Mademoiselle, with a wave of the hand which expressed volumes of unutterable ennui. But at that instant the little one, with instinctive mistrust, and in seeming defiance of the repudiation, climbed to her feet and went rolling and toddling towards her mother, clasping the woman about the knees, and calling her by the endearing title which was her own small right.

A spasm of annoyance passed over Mademoiselle's face, but still she called the child *'Chene,'* as she grasped its arm to keep it from falling. Miss McEnders turned every shade of carmine.

'Why did you tell me an untruth?' she asked, looking indignantly into the woman's lowered face. 'Why do you call yourself "Mademoiselle" if this child is yours?'

'For the reason that it is more easy to obtain employment. For reasons that you would not understand,' she continued, with a shrug of the shoulders that expressed some defiance and a sudden disregard for consequences. 'Life is not all *couleur de rose,* Mees McEndairs; you do not know what life is, you!' And drawing a handkerchief from an apron pocket she mopped an imaginary tear from the corner of her eye, and blew her nose till it glowed again.

Georgie could hardly recall the words or actions with which she quitted Mademoiselle's presence. As much as she wanted to, it had been impossible to stand and read the woman a moral lecture. She had simply thrown what disapproval she could into her hasty leave-taking, and that was all for the moment. But as she drove away, a more practical form of rebuke suggested itself to her not too nimble intelligence – one that she promised herself to act upon as soon as her home was reached.

When she was alone in her room, during an interval between her many engagements, she then attended to the affair of Mlle Salambre.

Georgie believed in discipline. She hated unrighteousness. When it pleased God to place the lash in her hand she did not hesitate to apply it. Here was this Mlle Salambre living in her sin. Not as one who is young and blinded by the glamour of pleasure, but with cool and deliberate intention. Since she chose to transgress, she ought to suffer, and be made to feel that her ways were iniquitous and invited rebuke. It lay in Georgie's power to mete out a small dose of that chastisement which the woman deserved, and she was glad that the opportunity was hers.

She seated herself forthwith at her writing table, and penned the following note to her furnishers:

MESSRS. PUSH & PRODEM.

Gentlemen – Please withdraw from Mademoiselle Salambre all work of mine, and return same to me at once – finished or unfinished.

Yours truly,
GEORGIE McENDERS.

Miss McEnders

2

On the second day following this summary proceeding, Georgie sat at her writing table, looking prettier and pinker than ever, in a luxurious and soft-toned robe de chambre that suited her own delicate colouring, and fitted the pale amber tints of her room decorations.

There were books, pamphlets and writing material set neatly upon the table before her. In the midst of them were two framed photographs, which she polished one after another with a silken scarf that was near.

One of these was a picture of her father, who looked like an Englishman, with his clean-shaved mouth and chin, and closely-cropped side whiskers, just turning grey. A good-humoured shrewdness shone in his eyes. From the set of his thin, firm lips one might guess that he was in the foremost rank in the interesting game of 'push' that occupies mankind. One might further guess that his cleverness in using opportunities had brought him there, and that a dexterous management of elbows had served him no less. The other picture was that of Georgie's fiancé, Mr Meredith Holt, approaching more closely than he liked to his forty-fifth year and an unbecoming corpulence. Only one who knew beforehand that he was a *viveur* could have detected evidence of such in his face, which told little more than that he was a good-looking and amiable man of the world, who might be counted on to do the gentlemanly thing always. Georgie was going to marry him because his personality pleased her; because his easy knowledge of life – such as she apprehended it – commended itself to her approval; because he was likely to interfere in no way with her 'work'. Yet she might not have given any of these reasons if asked for one. Mr Meredith Holt was simply an eligible man, whom almost any girl in her set would have accepted for a husband.

Georgie had just discovered that she had yet an hour to spare before starting out with the committee of four to further investigate the moral condition of the factory-girl, when a maid appeared with the announcement that a person was below who wished to see her.

'A person? Surely not a visitor at this hour?'

Miss McEnders

'I left her in the hall, miss, and she says her name is Mademoiselle Sal-Sal – '

'Oh, yes! Ask her to kindly walk up to my room, and show her the way, please, Hannah.'

Mademoiselle Salambre came in with a sweep of skirts that bristled defiance, and a poise of the head that was aggressive in its backward tilt. She seated herself, and with an air of challenge waited to be questioned or addressed.

Georgie felt at ease amid her own familiar surroundings. While she made some idle tracings with a pencil upon a discarded envelope, she half turned to say:

'This visit of yours is very surprising, madam, and wholly useless. I suppose you guess my motive in recalling my work, as I have done.'

'Maybe I do, and maybe I do not, Mees McEndairs,' replied the woman, with an impertinent uplifting of the eyebrows.

Georgie felt the same shrinking which had overtaken her before in the woman's presence. But she knew her duty, and from that there was no shrinking.

'You must be made to understand, madam, that there is a right way to live, and that there is a wrong way,' said Georgie with more condescension than she knew. 'We cannot defy God's laws with impunity, and without incurring His displeasure. But in His infinite justice and mercy He offers forgiveness, love and protection to those who turn away from evil and repent. It is for each of us to follow the divine way as well as may be. And I am only humbly striving to do His will.'

'A most charming sermon, Mees McEndairs!' mademoiselle interrupted with a nervous laugh; 'it seems a great pity to waste it upon so small an audience. And it grieves me, I cannot express, that I have not the time to remain and listen to its close.'

She arose and began to talk volubly, swiftly, in a jumble of French and English, and with a wealth of expression and gesture which Georgie could hardly believe was natural, and not something acquired and rehearsed.

She had come to inform Miss McEnders that she did not want her work; that she would not touch it with the tips of her fingers. And her little, gloved hands recoiled from an imaginary pile of lingerie with unspeakable disgust. Her eyes had travelled nimbly over the room, and had been arrested by the two photographs on the table. Very small, indeed, were

Miss McEnders

her worldly possessions, she informed the young lady; but as Heaven was her witness – not a mouthful of bread that she had not earned. And her parents over yonder in France! As honest as the sunlight! Poor, ah! for that – poor as rats. God only knew how poor; and God only knew how honest. Her eyes remained fixed upon the picture of Horace McEnders. Some people might like fine houses, and servants, and horses, and all the luxury which dishonest wealth brings. Some people might enjoy such surroundings. As for her! – and she drew up her skirts ever so carefully and daintily, as though she feared contamination to her petticoats from the touch of the rich rug upon which she stood.

Georgie's blue eyes were filled with astonishment as they followed the woman's gestures. Her face showed aversion and perplexity.

'Please let this interview come to an end at once,' spoke the girl. She would not deign to ask an explanation of the mysterious allusions to ill-gotten wealth. But mademoiselle had not yet said all that she had come there to say.

'If it was only me to say so,' she went on, still looking at the likeness, 'but, *cher maître!* Go, yourself,

Mees McEndairs, and stand for a while on the street and ask the people passing by how your dear papa has made his money, and see what they will say.'

Then shifting her glance to the photograph of Meredith Holt, she stood in an attitude of amused contemplation, with a smile of commiseration playing about her lips.

'Mr Meredith Holt!' she pronounced with quiet, supressed emphasis – 'ah! *c'est un propre, celui là!* You know him very well, no doubt, Mees McEndairs. You would not care to have my opinion of Mr Meredith Holt. It would make no difference to you, Mees McEndairs, to know that he is not fit to be the husband of a self-respecting barmaid. Oh! you know a good deal, my dear young lady. You can preach sermons in *merveille!*'

When Georgie was finally alone, there came to her, through all her disgust and indignation, an indefinable uneasiness. There was no misunderstanding the intention of the woman's utterances in regard to the girl's fiancé and her father. A sudden, wild, defiant desire came to her to test the suggestion which Mademoiselle Salambre had let fall.

Yes, she would go stand there on the corner and

Miss McEnders

ask the passers-by how Horace McEnders made his money. She could not yet collect her thoughts for calm reflection; and the house stifled her. It was fully time for her to join her committee of four, but she would meddle no further with morals till her own were adjusted, she thought. Then she quitted the house, very pale, even to her lips that were tightly set.

Georgie stationed herself on the opposite side of the street, on the corner, and waited there as though she had appointed to meet some one.

The first to approach her was a kind-looking old gentleman, very much muffled for the pleasant spring day. Georgie did not hesitate an instant to accost him:

'I beg pardon, sir. Will you kindly tell me whose house that is?' pointing to her own domicile across the way.

'That is Mr Horace McEnders' residence, Madame,' replied the old gentleman, lifting his hat politely.

'Could you tell me how he made the money with which to build so magnificent a home?'

'You should not ask indiscreet questions, my dear young lady,' answered the mystified old gentleman, as he bowed and walked away.

The girl let one or two persons pass her. Then she stopped a plumber, who was going cheerily along with his bag of tools on his shoulder.

'I beg pardon,' began Georgie again; 'but may I ask whose residence that is across the street?'

'Yes'um. That's the McEnderses.'

'Thank you; and can you tell me how Mr McEnders made such an immense fortune?'

'Oh, that ain't my business; but they say he made the biggest pile of it in the Whisky Ring.'

So the truth would come to her somehow! These were the people from whom to seek it – who had not learned to veil their thoughts and opinions in polite subterfuge.

When a careless little newsboy came strolling along, she stopped him with the apparent intention of buying a paper from him.

'Do you know whose house that is?' she asked him, handing him a piece of money and nodding over the way.

'W'y, dats ole MicAndrus' house.'

'I wonder where he got the money to build such a fine house.'

'He stole it; dats w'ere he got it. Thank you,'

pocketing the change which Georgie declined to take, and he whistled a popular air as he disappeared around the corner.

Georgie had heard enough. Her heart was beating violently now, and her cheeks were flaming. So everybody knew it; even to the street gamins! The men and women who visited her and broke bread at her father's table, knew it. Her co-workers, who strove with her in Christian endeavour, knew. The very servants who waited upon her doubtless knew this, and had their jests about it.

She shrank within herself as she climbed the stairway to her room.

Upon the table there she found a box of exquisite white spring blossoms that a messenger had brought from Meredith Holt, during her absence. Without an instant's hesitation, Georgie cast the spotless things into the wide, sooty fireplace. Then she sank into a chair and wept bitterly.

The Story of an Hour

Knowing that Mrs Mallard was afflicted with a heart trouble, great care was taken to break to her as gently as possible the news of her husband's death.

It was her sister Josephine who told her, in broken sentences; veiled hints that revealed in half concealing. Her husband's friend Richards was there, too, near her. It was he who had been in the newspaper office when intelligence of the railroad disaster was received, with Brently Mallard's name leading the list of 'killed.' He had only taken the time to assure himself of its truth by a second telegram, and had hastened to forestall any less careful, less tender friend in bearing the sad message.

She did not hear the story as many women have heard the same, with a paralysed inability to accept its significance. She wept at once, with sudden, wild abandonment, in her sister's arms. When the storm of grief had spent itself she went away to her room alone. She would have no one follow her.

There stood, facing the open window, a comfortable, roomy armchair. Into this she sank, pressed down by a physical exhaustion that haunted her body and seemed to reach into her soul.

She could see in the open square before her house the tops of trees that were all aquiver with the new spring life. The delicious breath of rain was in the air. In the street below a peddler was crying his wares. The notes of a distant song which some one was singing reached her faintly, and countless sparrows were twittering in the eaves.

There were patches of blue sky showing here and there through the clouds that had met and piled one above the other in the west facing her window.

She sat with her head thrown back upon the cushion of the chair, quite motionless, except when a sob came up into her throat and shook her, as a child who has cried itself to sleep continues to sob in its dreams.

She was young, with a fair, calm face, whose lines bespoke repression and even a certain strength. But now there was a dull stare in her eyes, whose gaze was fixed away off yonder on one of those patches of blue sky. It was not a glance of reflection, but rather indicated a suspension of intelligent thought.

There was something coming to her and she was waiting for it, fearfully. What was it? She did not know; it was too subtle and elusive to name. But she felt it, creeping out of the sky, reaching toward her through the sounds, the scents, the colour that filled the air.

Now her bosom rose and fell tumultuously. She was beginning to recognize this thing that was approaching to possess her, and she was striving to beat it back with her will – as powerless as her two white slender hands would have been.

When she abandoned herself a little whispered word escaped her slightly parted lips. She said it over and over under her breath: 'free, free, free!' The vacant stare and the look of terror that had followed it went from her eyes. They stayed keen and bright. Her pulses beat fast, and the coursing blood warmed and relaxed every inch of her body.

She did not stop to ask if it were or were not a monstrous joy that held her. A clear and exalted perception enabled her to dismiss the suggestion as trivial.

The Story of an Hour

She knew that she would weep again when she saw the kind, tender hands folded in death; the face that had never looked save with love upon her, fixed and grey and dead. But she saw beyond that bitter moment a long procession of years to come that would belong to her absolutely. And she opened and spread her arms out to them in welcome.

There would be no one to live for her during those coming years; she would live for herself. There would be no powerful will bending hers in that blind persistence with which men and women believe they have a right to impose a private will upon a fellow-creature. A kind intention or a cruel intention made the act seem no less a crime as she looked upon it in that brief moment of illumination.

And yet she had loved him – sometimes. Often she had not. What did it matter! What could love, the unsolved mystery, count for in face of this possession of self-assertion which she suddenly recognized as the strongest impulse of her being!

'Free! Body and soul free!' she kept whispering.

Josephine was kneeling before the closed door with her lips to the keyhole, imploring for admission. 'Louise, open the door! I beg; open the door – you will make yourself ill. What are you doing, Louise? For heaven's sake open the door.'

'Go away. I am not making myself ill.' No; she was drinking in a very elixir of life through that open window.

Her fancy was running riot along those days ahead of her. Spring days, and summer days, and all sorts of days that would be her own. She breathed a quick prayer that life might be long. It was only yesterday she had thought with a shudder that life might be long.

She arose at length and opened the door to her sister's importunities. There was a feverish triumph in her eyes, and she carried herself unwittingly like a goddess of Victory. She clasped her sister's waist, and together they descended the stairs. Richards stood waiting for them at the bottom.

Some one was opening the front door with a latchkey. It was Brently Mallard who entered, a little travel-stained, composedly carrying his grip-sack and umbrella. He had been far from the scene of accident, and did not even know there had been one. He stood amazed at Josephine's piercing cry; at

Richards' quick motion to screen him from the view of his wife.

But Richards was too late.

When the doctors came they said she had died of heart disease – of joy that kills.

Nég Créol

At the remote period of his birth he had been named César François Xavier, but no one ever thought of calling him anything but Chicot, or Nég, or Maringouin. Down at the French market, where he worked among the fishmongers, they called him Chicot, when they were not calling him names that are written less freely than they are spoken. But one felt privileged to call him almost anything, he was so black, lean, lame, and shrivelled. He wore a headkerchief, and whatever other rags the fishermen and their wives chose to bestow upon him. Throughout one whole winter he wore a woman's discarded jacket with puffed sleeves.

Among some startling beliefs entertained by Chicot was one that '*Michié St Pierre et Michié St Paul*' had created him. Of '*Michié bon Dieu*' he held his own

Nég Créol

private opinion, and not a too flattering one at that. This fantastic notion concerning the origin of his being he owed to the early teaching of his young master, a lax believer, and a great *farceur* in his day. Chicot had once been thrashed by a robust young Irish priest for expressing his religious views, and at another time knifed by a Sicilian. So he had come to hold his peace upon that subject.

Upon another theme he talked freely and harped continuously. For years he had tried to convince his associates that his master had left a progeny, rich, cultured, powerful, and numerous beyond belief. This prosperous race of beings inhabited the most imposing mansions in the city of New Orleans. Men of note and position, whose names were familiar to the public, he swore were grandchildren, great-grandchildren, or, less frequently, distant relatives of his master, long deceased. Ladies who came to the market in carriages, or whose elegance of attire attracted the attention and admiration of the fishwomen, were all *des 'tites cousines* to his former master, Jean Boisduré. He never looked for recognition from any of these superior beings, but delighted to discourse by the hour upon their dignity and pride of birth and wealth.

Chicot always carried an old gunny-sack, and into this went his earnings. He cleaned stalls at the market, scaled fish, and did many odd offices for the itinerant merchants, who usually paid in trade for his service. Occasionally he saw the colour of silver and got his clutch upon a coin, but he accepted anything, and seldom made terms. He was glad to get a handkerchief from the Hebrew, and grateful if the Choctaws would trade him a bottle of *filé* for it. The butcher flung him a soup bone, and the fishmonger a few crabs or a paper bag of shrimps. It was the big *mulatresse, vendeuse de café,* who cared for his inner man.

Once Chicot was accused by a shoe-vender of attempting to steal a pair of ladies' shoes. He declared he was only examining them. The clamour raised in the market was terrific. Young Dagoes assembled and squealed like rats; a couple of Gascon butchers bellowed like bulls. Matteo's wife shook her fist in the accuser's face and called him incomprehensible names. The Choctaw women, where they squatted, turned their slow eyes in the direction of the fray, taking no further notice; while a policeman jerked Chicot around by the puffed sleeve and brandished a club. It was a narrow escape.

Nég Créol

Nobody knew where Chicot lived. A man – even a *nég créol* – who lives among the reeds and willows of Bayou St John, in a deserted chicken-coop constructed chiefly of tarred paper, is not going to boast of his habitation or to invite attention to his domestic appointments. When, after market hours, he vanished in the direction of St Philip street, limping, seemingly bent under the weight of his gunny-bag, it was like the disappearance from the stage of some petty actor whom the audience does not follow in imagination beyond the wings, or think of till his return in another scene.

There was one to whom Chicot's coming or going meant more than this. In *la maison grise* they called her La Chouette, for no earthly reason unless that she perched high under the roof of the old rookery and scolded in shrill sudden outbursts. Forty or fifty years before, when for a little while she acted minor parts with a company of French players (an escapade that had brought her grandmother to the grave), she was known as Mademoiselle de Montallaine. Seventy-five years before she had been christened Aglaé Boisduré.

No matter at what hour the old negro appeared at

her threshold, Mamzelle Aglaé always kept him waiting till she finished her prayers. She opened the door for him and silently motioned him to a seat, returning to prostrate herself upon her knees before a crucifix, and a shell filled with holy water that stood on a small table; it represented in her imagination an altar. Chicot knew that she did it to aggravate him; he was convinced that she timed her devotions to begin when she heard his footsteps on the stairs. He would sit with sullen eyes contemplating her long, spare, poorly clad figure as she knelt and read from her book or finished her prayers. Bitter was the religious warfare that had raged for years between them, and Mamzelle Aglaé had grown, on her side, as intolerant as Chicot. She had come to hold St Peter and St Paul in such utter detestation that she had cut their pictures out of her prayer-book.

Then Mamzelle Aglaé pretended not to care what Chicot had in his bag. He drew forth a small hunk of beef and laid it in her basket that stood on the bare floor. She looked from the corner of her eye, and went on dusting the table. He brought out a handful of potatoes, some pieces of sliced fish, a few herbs, a yard of calico, and a small pat of butter wrapped in

Nég Créol

lettuce leaves. He was proud of the butter, and wanted her to notice it. He held it out and asked her for something to put it on. She handed him a saucer, and looked indifferent and resigned, with lifted eyebrows.

'*Pas d' sucre*, Nég?'

Chicot shook his head and scratched it, and looked like a black picture of distress and mortification. No sugar! But tomorrow he would get a pinch here and a pinch there, and would bring as much as a cupful.

Mamzelle Aglaé then sat down, and talked to Chicot uninterruptedly and confidentially. She complained bitterly, and it was all about a pain that lodged in her leg; that crept and acted like a live, stinging serpent, twining about her waist and up her spine, and coiling round the shoulder-blade. And then *les rheumatismes* in her fingers! He could see for himself how they were knotted. She could not bend them; she could hold nothing in her hands, and had let a saucer fall that morning and broken it in pieces. And if she were to tell him that she had slept a wink through the night, she would be a liar, deserving of perdition. She had sat at the window *la nuit blanche,* hearing the hours strike and the market-wagons rumble. Chicot nodded, and kept up a running fire of sympathetic comment and suggestive remedies for rheumatism and insomnia: herbs, or *tisanes,* or *grigris,* or all three. As if he knew! There was Purgatory Mary, a perambulating soul whose office in life was to pray for the shades in purgatory, – she had brought Mamzelle Aglaé a bottle of *eau de Lourdes,* but so little of it! She might have kept her water of Lourdes, for all the good it did, – a drop! Not so much as would cure a fly or a mosquito! Mamzelle Aglaé was going to show Purgatory Mary the door when she came again, not only because of her avarice with the Lourdes water, but, beside that, she brought in on her feet dirt that could only be removed with a shovel after she left.

And Mamzelle Aglaé wanted to inform Chicot that there would be slaughter and bloodshed in *la maison grise* if the people below stairs did not mend their ways. She was convinced that they lived for no other purpose than to torture and molest her. The woman kept a bucket of dirty water constantly on the landing with the hope of Mamzelle Aglaé falling over it or into it. And she knew that the children were instructed to gather in the hall and on the stairway, and scream and make a noise and jump up and down like galloping horses, with the intention of driving her to suicide. Chicot should notify the policeman on the beat, and have them arrested, if possible, and thrust into the parish prison, where they belonged.

Chicot would have been extremely alarmed if he had ever chanced to find Mamzelle Aglaé in an uncomplaining mood. It never occurred to him that she might be otherwise. He felt that she had a right to quarrel with fate, if ever mortal had. Her poverty was a disgrace, and he hung his head before it and felt ashamed.

One day he found Mamzelle Aglaé stretched on the bed, with her head tied up in a handkerchief. Her sole complaint that day was, '*Aïe – aïe – aïe! Aïe – aïe – aïe!*' uttered with every breath. He had seen her so before, especially when the weather was damp.

'*Vous pas bézouin tisane*, Mamzelle Aglaé? *Vous pas veux mo cri gagni docteur?*'

She desired nothing. '*Aïe – aïe – aïe!*'

He emptied his bag very quietly, so as not to disturb her; and he wanted to stay there with her and lie down on the floor in case she needed him, but the woman from below had come up. She was an Irishwoman with rolled sleeves.

'It's a shtout shtick I'm afther giving her, Nég, and she do but knock on the flure it's me or Janie or wan of us that'll be hearing her.'

'You too good, Brigitte. *Aïe – aïe – aïe! Une goutte d'eau sucré*, Nég! That Purg'tory Marie, – you see hair, *ma bonne* Brigitte, you tell hair go say li'le prayer *là-bas au Cathédral. Aïe – aïe – aïe!*'

Nég could hear her lamentation as he descended the stairs. It followed him as he limped his way through the city streets, and seemed part of the city's noise; he could hear it in the rumble of wheels and jangle of car-bells, and in the voices of those passing by.

He stopped at Mimotte the Voudou's shanty and bought a *grigri* – a cheap one for fifteen cents. Mimotte held her charms at all prices. This he intended to introduce next day into Mamzelle Aglaé's room, – somewhere about the altar, – to the confusion and discomfort of '*Michié bon Dieu,*' who persistently declined to concern himself with the welfare of a Boisduré.

Nég Créol

At night, among the reeds on the bayou, Chicot could still hear the woman's wail, mingled now with the croaking of the frogs. If he could have been convinced that giving up his life down there in the water would in any way have bettered her condition, he would not have hesitated to sacrifice the remnant of his existence that was wholly devoted to her. He lived but to serve her. He did not know it himself; but Chicot knew so little, and that little in such a distorted way! He could scarcely have been expected, even in his most lucid moments, to give himself over to self-analysis.

Chicot gathered an uncommon amount of dainties at market the following day. He had to work hard, and scheme and whine a little; but he got hold of an orange and a lump of ice and a *choufleur.* He did not drink his cup of *café au lait,* but asked Mimi Lambeau to put it in the little new tin pail that the Hebrew notion-vender had just given him in exchange for a mess of shrimps. This time, however, Chicot had his trouble for nothing. When he reached the upper room of *la maison grise,* it was to find that Mamzelle Aglaé had died during the night. He set his bag down in the middle of the floor, and stood shaking, and whined low like a dog in pain.

Everything had been done. The Irishwoman had gone for the doctor, and Purgatory Mary had summoned a priest. Furthermore, the woman had arranged Mamzelle Aglaé decently. She had covered the table with a white cloth, and had placed it at the head of the bed, with the crucifix and two lighted candles in silver candlesticks upon it; the little bit of ornamentation brightened and embellished the poor room. Purgatory Mary, dressed in shabby black, fat and breathing hard, sat reading half audibly from a prayerbook. She was watching the dead and the silver candlesticks, which she had borrowed from a benevolent society, and for which she held herself responsible. A young man was just leaving, – a reporter snuffing the air for items, who had scented one up there in the top room of *la maison grise*.

All the morning Janie had been escorting a procession of street Arabs up and down the stairs to view the remains. One of them – a little girl, who had had her face washed and had made a species of toilet for the occasion – refused to be dragged away. She stayed seated as if at an entertainment, fascinated alternately by the long, still figure of Mamzelle Aglaé, the

Nég Créol

mumbling lips of Purgatory Mary, and the silver candlesticks.

'Will ye get down on yer knees, man, and say a prayer for the dead!' commanded the woman.

But Chicot only shook his head, and refused to obey. He approached the bed, and laid a little black paw for a moment on the stiffened body of Mamzelle Aglaé. There was nothing for him to do here. He picked up his old ragged hat and his bag and went away.

'The black h'athen!' the woman muttered. 'Shut the dure, child.'

The little girl slid down from her chair, and went on tiptoe to shut the door which Chicot had left open. Having resumed her seat, she fastened her eyes upon Purgatory Mary's heaving chest.

'You, Chicot!' cried Matteo's wife the next morning. 'My man, he read in paper 'bout woman name' Boisduré, use' b'long to big-a famny. She die roun' on St Philip – po', same-a like church rat. It's any them Boisdurés you alla talk 'bout?'

Chicot shook his head in slow but emphatic denial. No, indeed, the woman was not of kin to his

Boisdurés. He surely had told Matteo's wife often enough – how many times did he have to repeat it! – of their wealth, their social standing. It was doubtless some Boisduré of *les Attakapas;* it was none of his.

The next day there was a small funeral procession passing a little distance away, – a hearse and a carriage or two. There was the priest who had attended Mamzelle Aglaé, and a benevolent Creole gentleman whose father had known the Boisdurés in his youth. There was a couple of player-folk, who, having got wind of the story, had thrust their hands into their pockets.

'Look, Chicot!' cried Matteo's wife. 'Yonda go the fune'al. Mus-a be that-a Boisduré woman we talken 'bout yesaday.'

But Chicot paid no heed. What was to him the funeral of a woman who had died in St Philip street? He did not even turn his head in the direction of the moving procession. He went on scaling his red-snapper.

A Pair of Silk Stockings

Little Mrs Sommers one day found herself the unexpected possessor of fifteen dollars. It seemed to her a very large amount of money, and the way in which it stuffed and bulged her worn old *porte-monnaie* gave her a feeling of importance such as she had not enjoyed for years.

The question of investment was one that occupied her greatly. For a day or two she walked about apparently in a dreamy state, but really absorbed in speculation and calculation. She did not wish to act hastily, to do anything she might afterward regret. But it was during the still hours of the night when she lay awake revolving plans in her mind that she seemed to see her way clearly toward a proper and judicious use of the money.

A dollar or two should be added to the price

usually paid for Janie's shoes, which would insure their lasting an appreciable time longer than they usually did. She would buy so and so many yards of percale for new shirt-waists for the boys and Janie and Mag. She had intended to make the old ones do by skilful patching. Mag should have another gown. She had seen some beautiful patterns, veritable bargains in the shop windows. And still there would be left enough for new stockings – two pairs apiece – and what darning that would save for a while! She would get caps for the boys and sailor-hats for the girls. The vision of her little brood looking fresh and dainty and new for once in their lives excited her and made her restless and wakeful with anticipation.

The neighbours sometimes talked of certain 'better days' that little Mrs Sommers had known before she had ever thought of being Mrs Sommers. She herself indulged in no such morbid retrospection. She had no time – no second of time to devote to the past. The needs of the present absorbed her every faculty. A vision of the future like some dim, gaunt monster sometimes appalled her, but luckily to-morrow never comes.

Mrs Sommers was one who knew the value of

A Pair of Silk Stockings

bargains; who could stand for hours making her way inch by inch toward the desired object that was selling below cost. She could elbow her way if need be; she had learned to clutch a piece of goods and hold it and stick to it with persistence and determination till her turn came to be served, no matter when it came.

But that day she was a little faint and tired. She had swallowed a light luncheon – no! when she came to think of it, between getting the children fed and the place righted, and preparing herself for the shopping bout, she had actually forgotten to eat any luncheon at all!

She sat herself upon a revolving stool before a counter that was comparatively deserted, trying to gather strength and courage to charge through an eager multitude that was besieging breast-works of shirting and figured lawn. An all-gone limp feeling had come over her and she rested her hand aimlessly upon the counter. She wore no gloves. By degrees she grew aware that her hand had encountered something very soothing, very pleasant to touch. She looked down to see that her hand lay upon a pile of silk stockings. A placard near by announced that they had been reduced in price from two dollars and fifty cents to one dollar and ninety-eight cents; and a young girl who stood behind the counter asked her if she wished to examine their line of silk hosiery. She smiled, just as if she had been asked to inspect a tiara of diamonds with the ultimate view of purchasing it. But she went on feeling the soft, sheeny luxurious things – with both hands now, holding them up to see them glisten, and to feel them glide serpent-like through her fingers.

Two hectic blotches came suddenly into her pale cheeks. She looked up at the girl.

'Do you think there are any eights-and-a-half among these?'

There were any number of eights-and-a-half. In fact, there were more of that size than any other. Here was a light-blue pair; there were some lavender, some all black and various shades of tan and grey. Mrs Sommers selected a black pair and looked at them very long and closely. She pretended to be examining their texture, which the clerk assured her was excellent.

'A dollar and ninety-eight cents,' she mused aloud. 'Well, I'll take this pair.' She handed the girl a five-dollar bill and waited for her change and for her

A Pair of Silk Stockings

parcel. What a very small parcel it was! It seemed lost in the depths of her shabby old shopping-bag.

Mrs Sommers after that did not move in the direction of the bargain counter. She took the elevator, which carried her to an upper floor into the region of the ladies' waiting-rooms. Here, in a retired corner, she exchanged her cotton stockings for the new silk ones which she had just bought. She was not going through any acute mental process or reasoning with herself, nor was she striving to explain to her satisfaction the motive of her action. She was not thinking at all. She seemed for the time to be taking a rest from that laborious and fatiguing function and to have abandoned herself to some mechanical impulse that directed her actions and freed her of responsibility.

How good was the touch of the raw silk to her flesh! She felt like lying back in the cushioned chair and revelling for a while in the luxury of it. She did for a little while. Then she replaced her shoes, rolled the cotton stockings together and thrust them into her bag. After doing this she crossed straight over to the shoe department and took her seat to be fitted.

She was fastidious. The clerk could not make her

out; he could not reconcile her shoes with her stockings, and she was not too easily pleased. She held back her skirts and turned her feet one way and her head another way as she glanced down at the polished, pointed-tipped boots. Her foot and ankle looked very pretty. She could not realize that they belonged to her and were a part of herself. She wanted an excellent and stylish fit, she told the young fellow who served her, and she did not mind the difference of a dollar or two more in the price so long as she got what she desired.

It was a long time since Mrs Sommers had been fitted with gloves. On rare occasions when she had bought a pair they were always 'bargains', so cheap that it would have been preposterous and unreasonable to have expected them to be fitted to the hand.

Now she rested her elbow on the cushion of the glove counter, and a pretty, pleasant young creature, delicate and deft of touch, drew a long-wristed 'kid' over Mrs Sommers's hand. She smoothed it down over the wrist and buttoned it neatly, and both lost themselves for a second or two in admiring contemplation of the little symmetrical gloved hand. But there were other places where money might be spent.

A Pair of Silk Stockings

There were books and magazines piled up in the window of a stall a few paces down the street. Mrs Sommers bought two high-priced magazines such as she had been accustomed to read in the days when she had been accustomed to other pleasant things. She carried them without wrapping. As well as she could she lifted her skirts at the crossings. Her stockings and boots and well fitting gloves had worked marvels in her bearing – had given her a feeling of assurance, a sense of belonging to the well-dressed multitude.

She was very hungry. Another time she would have stilled the cravings for food until reaching her own home, where she would have brewed herself a cup of tea and taken a snack of anything that was available. But the impulse that was guiding her would not suffer her to entertain any such thought.

There was a restaurant at the corner. She had never entered its doors; from the outside she had sometimes caught glimpses of spotless damask and shining crystal, and soft-stepping waiters serving people of fashion.

When she entered her appearance created no surprise, no consternation, as she had half feared it might. She seated herself at a small table alone, and an attentive waiter at once approached to take her order. She did not want a profusion; she craved a nice and tasty bite – a half dozen blue-points, a plump chop with cress, a something sweet – a crème-frappée, for instance; a glass of Rhine wine, and after all a small cup of black coffee.

While waiting to be served she removed her gloves very leisurely and laid them beside her. Then she picked up a magazine and glanced through it, cutting the pages with the blunt edge of her knife. It was all very agreeable. The damask was even more spotless than it had seemed through the window, and the crystal more sparkling. There were quiet ladies and gentlemen, who did not notice her, lunching at the small tables like her own. A soft, pleasing strain of music could be heard, and a gentle breeze was blowing through the window. She tasted a bite, and she read a word or two, and she sipped the amber wine and wiggled her toes in the silk stockings. The price of it made no difference. She counted the money out to the waiter and left an extra coin on his tray, whereupon he bowed before her as before a princess of royal blood.

A Pair of Silk Stockings

There was still money in her purse, and her next temptation presented itself in the shape of a matinée poster.

It was a little later when she entered the theatre, the play had begun and the house seemed to her to be packed. But there were vacant seats here and there, and into one of them she was ushered, between brilliantly dressed women who had gone there to kill time and eat candy and display their gaudy attire. There were many others who were there solely for the play and acting. It is safe to say there was no one present who bore quite the attitude which Mrs Sommers did to her surroundings. She gathered in the whole – stage and players and people in one wide impression, and absorbed it and enjoyed it. She laughed at the comedy and wept – she and the gaudy woman next to her wept over the tragedy. And they talked a little together over it. And the gaudy woman wiped her eyes and sniffled on a tiny square of filmy, perfumed lace and passed little Mrs Sommers her box of candy.

The play was over, the music ceased, the crowd filed out. It was like a dream ended. People scattered in all directions. Mrs Sommers went to the corner and waited for the cable car.

Kate Chopin

A man with keen eyes, who sat opposite to her, seemed to like the study of her small, pale face. It puzzled him to decipher what he saw there. In truth, he saw nothing – unless he were wizard enough to detect a poignant wish, a powerful longing that the cable car would never stop anywhere, but go on and on with her forever.

1. BOCCACCIO · *Mrs Rosie and the Priest*
2. GERARD MANLEY HOPKINS · *As kingfishers catch fire*
3. *The Saga of Gunnlaug Serpent-tongue*
4. THOMAS DE QUINCEY · *On Murder Considered as One of the Fine Arts*
5. FRIEDRICH NIETZSCHE · *Aphorisms on Love and Hate*
6. JOHN RUSKIN · *Traffic*
7. PU SONGLING · *Wailing Ghosts*
8. JONATHAN SWIFT · *A Modest Proposal*
9. *Three Tang Dynasty Poets*
10. WALT WHITMAN · *On the Beach at Night Alone*
11. KENKŌ · *A Cup of Sake Beneath the Cherry Trees*
12. BALTASAR GRACIÁN · *How to Use Your Enemies*
13. JOHN KEATS · *The Eve of St Agnes*
14. THOMAS HARDY · *Woman much missed*
15. GUY DE MAUPASSANT · *Femme Fatale*
16. MARCO POLO · *Travels in the Land of Serpents and Pearls*
17. SUETONIUS · *Caligula*
18. APOLLONIUS OF RHODES · *Jason and Medea*
19. ROBERT LOUIS STEVENSON · *Olalla*
20. KARL MARX AND FRIEDRICH ENGELS · *The Communist Manifesto*
21. PETRONIUS · *Trimalchio's Feast*
22. JOHANN PETER HEBEL · *How a Ghastly Story Was Brought to Light by a Common or Garden Butcher's Dog*
23. HANS CHRISTIAN ANDERSEN · *The Tinder Box*
24. RUDYARD KIPLING · *The Gate of the Hundred Sorrows*
25. DANTE · *Circles of Hell*
26. HENRY MAYHEW · *Of Street Piemen*
27. HAFEZ · *The nightingales are drunk*
28. GEOFFREY CHAUCER · *The Wife of Bath*
29. MICHEL DE MONTAIGNE · *How We Weep and Laugh at the Same Thing*
30. THOMAS NASHE · *The Terrors of the Night*
31. EDGAR ALLAN POE · *The Tell-Tale Heart*
32. MARY KINGSLEY · *A Hippo Banquet*
33. JANE AUSTEN · *The Beautifull Cassandra*
34. ANTON CHEKHOV · *Gooseberries*
35. SAMUEL TAYLOR COLERIDGE · *Well, they are gone, and here must I remain*
36. JOHANN WOLFGANG VON GOETHE · *Sketchy, Doubtful, Incomplete Jottings*
37. CHARLES DICKENS · *The Great Winglebury Duel*
38. HERMAN MELVILLE · *The Maldive Shark*
39. ELIZABETH GASKELL · *The Old Nurse's Story*
40. NIKOLAY LESKOV · *The Steel Flea*

41. HONORÉ DE BALZAC · *The Atheist's Mass*
42. CHARLOTTE PERKINS GILMAN · *The Yellow Wall-Paper*
43. C.P. CAVAFY · *Remember, Body...*
44. FYODOR DOSTOEVSKY · *The Meek One*
45. GUSTAVE FLAUBERT · *A Simple Heart*
46. NIKOLAI GOGOL · *The Nose*
47. SAMUEL PEPYS · *The Great Fire of London*
48. EDITH WHARTON · *The Reckoning*
49. HENRY JAMES · *The Figure in the Carpet*
50. WILFRED OWEN · *Anthem For Doomed Youth*
51. WOLFGANG AMADEUS MOZART · *My Dearest Father*
52. PLATO · *Socrates' Defence*
53. CHRISTINA ROSSETTI · *Goblin Market*
54. *Sindbad the Sailor*
55. SOPHOCLES · *Antigone*
56. RYŪNOSUKE AKUTAGAWA · *The Life of a Stupid Man*
57. LEO TOLSTOY · *How Much Land Does A Man Need?*
58. GIORGIO VASARI · *Leonardo da Vinci*
59. OSCAR WILDE · *Lord Arthur Savile's Crime*
60. SHEN FU · *The Old Man of the Moon*
61. AESOP · *The Dolphins, the Whales and the Gudgeon*
62. MATSUO BASHŌ · *Lips too Chilled*
63. EMILY BRONTË · *The Night is Darkening Round Me*
64. JOSEPH CONRAD · *To-morrow*
65. RICHARD HAKLUYT · *The Voyage of Sir Francis Drake Around the Whole Globe*
66. KATE CHOPIN · *A Pair of Silk Stockings*
67. CHARLES DARWIN · *It was snowing butterflies*
68. BROTHERS GRIMM · *The Robber Bridegroom*
69. CATULLUS · *I Hate and I Love*
70. HOMER · *Circe and the Cyclops*
71. D. H. LAWRENCE · *Il Duro*
72. KATHERINE MANSFIELD · *Miss Brill*
73. OVID · *The Fall of Icarus*
74. SAPPHO · *Come Close*
75. IVAN TURGENEV · *Kasyan from the Beautiful Lands*
76. VIRGIL · *O Cruel Alexis*
77. H. G. WELLS · *A Slip under the Microscope*
78. HERODOTUS · *The Madness of Cambyses*
79. *Speaking of Siva*
80. *The Dhammapada*

'The vessel drove before her bows two billows of liquid phosphorus...'

CHARLES DARWIN
Born 1809, Shrewsbury, Shropshire
Died 1882, Downe, Kent

Extracts taken from *The Voyage of the Beagle*,
first published in 1839.

CHARLES DARWIN IN PENGUIN CLASSICS
Autobiographies
On the Origin of Species
The Descent of Man
The Expression of the Emotions in Man and Animals
The Voyage of the Beagle

CHARLES DARWIN

It was snowing butterflies

PENGUIN BOOKS

PENGUIN CLASSICS

UK | USA | Canada | Ireland | Australia
India | New Zealand | South Africa

Penguin Books is part of the Penguin Random House group of companies
whose addresses can be found at global.penguinrandomhouse.com.

This selection published in Penguin Classics 2015

013

Set in 9.5/13 pt Baskerville 10 Pro
Typeset by Jouve (UK), Milton Keynes
Printed and bound in Great Britain by Clays Ltd, Elcograf S.p.A.

A CIP catalogue record for this book is available from the British Library

ISBN: 978-0-141-39855-6

www.greenpenguin.co.uk

Penguin Random House is committed to a
sustainable future for our business, our readers
and our planet. This book is made from Forest
Stewardship Council® certified paper.

Contents

Patagonia	1
Tierra del Fuego	33
Strait of Magellan	40

Patagonia

DECEMBER 6TH, 1833 – The *Beagle* sailed from the Rio Plata, never again to enter its muddy stream. Our course was directed to Port Desire, on the coast of Patagonia. Before proceeding any further, I will here put together a few observations made at sea.

Several times when the ship has been some miles off the mouth of the Plata, and at other times when off the shores of Northern Patagonia, we have been surrounded by insects. One evening, when we were about ten miles from the Bay of San Blas, vast numbers of butterflies, in bands or flocks of countless myriads, extended as far as the eye could range. Even by the aid of a glass it was not possible to see a space free from butterflies. The seamen cried out 'it was snowing butterflies', and such in fact was the appearance. More species than one were present, but the main part belonged to a kind very similar to, but not identical with, the common English *Colias edusa*. Some moths and hymenoptera accompanied the butterflies; and a fine Calosoma flew on board. Other instances are known of this beetle having been caught far out at sea; and this is the more remarkable, as the greater number of the Carabidæ seldom or never take wing. The day had been fine and calm, and the one previous to it equally so, with light and variable airs. Hence we cannot suppose that the insects were blown off the land, but we must conclude that they voluntarily took flight. The great bands of the Colias seem at first to afford an instance like those on record of the migrations of *Vanessa cardui*; but the presence of other insects makes the case distinct, and not so easily intelligible. Before sunset, a strong breeze sprung up from the north, and this must have been the cause of tens of thousands of the butterflies and other insects having perished.

On another occasion, when 17 miles off Cape Corrientes, I had a net overboard to catch pelagic animals. Upon drawing it up, to my surprise I found a considerable number of beetles in it, and although in the open sea, they did not appear much injured by the salt water. I lost some of the specimens, but those which I preserved, belonged to the genera, colymbetes, hydroporus, hydrobius (two species), notaphus, cynucus, adimonia, and scarabæus. At first, I thought that these insects had been blown from the shore; but upon reflecting that out of the eight species, four were aquatic, and two others partly so in their habits, it appeared to me most probable that they were floated into the sea, by a small stream which drains a lake near Cape Corrientes. On any supposition, it is an interesting circumstance to find insects, quite alive, swimming in the open ocean, 17 miles from the nearest point of land. There are several accounts of insects having been blown off the Patagonian shore. Captain Cook observed it, as did more lately Captain King in the *Adventure*. The cause probably is due to the want of shelter, both of trees and hills, so that an insect on the wing with an off-shore breeze, would be very apt to be blown out to sea. The most remarkable instance I ever knew of an insect being caught far from the land, was that of a large grasshopper (*Acrydium*), which flew on board, when the *Beagle* was to windward of the Cape de Verd Islands, and when the nearest point of land, not directly opposed to the trade-wind, was Cape Blanco on the coast of Africa, 370 miles distant.

On several occasions, when the vessel has been within the mouth of the Plata, the rigging has been coated with the web of the Gossamer Spider. One day (November 1st, 1832) I paid particular attention to the phenomenon. The weather had been fine and clear, and in the morning the air was full of patches of the flocculent web, as on an autumnal day in England. The ship was sixty miles distant from the land, in the direction of a steady though light breeze. Vast numbers of a small spider, about one-tenth of an inch in length, and of a dusky red colour were attached to the webs. There must have been, I should suppose, some thousands on the ship. The little spider when first coming in contact with the rigging, was always seated on a single thread, and not on the flocculent mass.

This latter seems merely to be produced by the entanglement of the single threads. The spiders were all of one species, but of both sexes, together with young ones. These latter were distinguished by their smaller size, and more dusky colour. I will not give the description of this spider, but merely state that it does not appear to me to be included in any of Latreille's genera. The little aeronaut as soon as it arrived on board, was very active, running about; sometimes letting itself fall, and then reascending the same thread; sometimes employing itself in making a small and very irregular mesh in the corners between the ropes. It could run with facility on the surface of water. When disturbed it lifted up its front legs, in the attitude of attention. On its first arrival it appeared very thirsty, and with exserted maxillæ drank eagerly of the fluid; this same circumstance has been observed by Strack: may it not be in consequence of the little insect having passed through a dry and rarefied atmosphere? Its stock of web seemed inexhaustible. While watching some that were suspended by a single thread, I several times observed that the slightest breath of air bore them away out of sight, in a horizontal line. On another occasion (25th) under similar circumstances, I repeatedly observed the same kind of small spider, either when placed, or having crawled, on some little eminence, elevate its abdomen, send forth a thread, and then sail away in a lateral course, but with a rapidity which was quite unaccountable. I thought I could perceive that the spider before performing the above preparatory steps, connected its legs together with the most delicate threads, but I am not sure, whether this observation is correct.

One day, at St Fe, I had a better opportunity of observing some similar facts. A spider which about three-tenths of an inch in length, and which in its general appearance resembled a Citigrade (therefore quite different from the gossamer), while standing on the summit of a post, darted forth four or five threads from its spinners. These glittering in the sunshine, might be compared to rays of light; they were not, however, straight, but in undulations like a film of silk blown by the wind. They were more than a yard in length, and diverged in an ascending direction from the orifices. The spider then suddenly let go its hold, and was quickly borne out of sight. The day was hot and apparently quite calm; yet under such circumstances the atmosphere can never be so tranquil, as not to affect a vane so delicate as the thread of a spider's web. If during a warm day we look either at the shadow of any object cast on a bank, or over a level plain at a distant landmark, the effect of an ascending current of heated air will almost always be evident. And this probably would be sufficient to carry with it so light an object as the little spider on its thread. The circumstance of spiders of the same species but of different sexes and ages, being found on several occasions at the distance of many leagues from the land, attached in vast numbers to the lines, proves that they are the manufacturers of the mesh, and that the habit of sailing through the air, is probably as characteristic of some tribe, as that of diving is of the Argyroneta. We may then reject Latreille's supposition, that the gossamer owes its origin to the webs of the young of several genera, as Epeira or Thomisa: although, as we have seen that the young of other spiders do possess the power of performing aerial voyages.

During our different passages south of the Plata, I often towed astern a net made of bunting, and thus caught many curious animals. The structure of the Beroe (a kind of jelly fish) is most extraordinary, with its rows of vibratory ciliæ, and complicated though irregular system of circulation. Of Crustacea, there were many strange and undescribed genera. One, which in some respects is allied to the Notopods (or those crabs which have their posterior legs placed almost on their backs, for the purpose of adhering to the under side of ledges), is very remarkable from the structure of its hind pair of legs. The penultimate joint, instead of being terminated by a simple claw, ends in three bristle-like appendages of dissimilar lengths, the longest equalling that of the entire leg. These claws are very thin, and are serrated with teeth of an excessive fineness, which are directed towards the base. The curved extremities are flattened, and on this part five most minute cups are placed, which seem to act in the same manner as the suckers on the arms of the cuttle-fish. As the animal lives in the open sea, and probably wants a place of rest, I suppose this beautiful structure is adapted to take hold of the globular bodies of the Medusæ, and other floating marine animals.

In deep water, far from the land, the number of living creatures is extremely small: south of the latitude 35°, I never succeeded in catching any thing besides some beroe, and a few species of minute crustacea belonging to the Entomostraca. In shoaler water, at the distance of a few miles from the coast, very many kinds of crustacea and some other animals were numerous, but only during the night. Between latitudes 56° and 57° south of Cape Horn the net was put astern several times; it never, however, brought up any thing besides a few of two extremely minute species of Entomostraca. Yet whales and seals, petrels and albatross, are exceedingly abundant throughout this part of the ocean. It has always been a source of mystery to me, on what the latter, which live far from the shore, can subsist. I presume the albatross, like the condor, is able to fast long; and that one good feast on the carcass of a putrid whale lasts for a long siege of hunger. It does not lessen the difficulty to say, they feed on fish; for on what can the fish feed? It often occurred to me, when observing how the waters of the central and intertropical parts of the Atlantic, swarmed with Pteropoda, Crustacea, and Radiata, and with their devourers the flying-fish, and again with *their* devourers the bonitos and albicores, that the lowest of these pelagic animals perhaps possess the power of decomposing carbonic acid gas, like the members of the vegetable kingdom.

While sailing in these latitudes on one very dark night, the sea presented a wonderful and most beautiful spectacle. There was a fresh breeze, and every part of the surface, which during the day is seen as foam, now glowed with a pale light. The vessel drove before her bows two billows of liquid phosphorus, and in her wake she was followed by a milky train. As far as the eye reached, the crest of every wave was bright, and the sky above the horizon, from the reflected glare of these livid flames, was not so utterly obscure, as over the rest of the heavens.

As we proceed further southward, the sea is seldom phosphorescent; and off Cape Horn, I do not recollect more than once having seen it so, and then it was far from being brilliant. This circumstance probably has a close connexion with the scarcity of organic beings in that part of the ocean. After the elaborate paper by Ehrenberg, on the phosphorescence of the sea, it is almost superfluous on my part to make any observations on the subject. I may however add, that the same torn and irregular particles of gelatinous matter, described by Ehrenberg, seem in the southern as well as in the northern hemisphere, to be the common cause of this phenomenon. The particles were so minute as easily to pass through fine gauze; yet many were distinctly visible by the naked eye. The water when placed in a tumbler and agitated gave out sparks, but a small portion in a watch-glass, scarcely ever was luminous. Ehrenberg states, that these particles all retain a certain degree of irritability. My observations, some of which were made directly after taking up the water, would give a different result. I may also mention, that having used the net during one night I allowed it to become partially dry, and having occasion twelve hours afterwards, to employ it again, I found the whole surface sparkled as brightly as when first taken out of the water. It does not appear probable in this case, that the particles could have remained so long alive. I remark also in my notes, that having kept a Medusa of the genus Dianæa, till it was dead, the water in which it was placed became luminous. When the waves scintillate with bright green sparks, I believe it is generally owing to minute crustacea. But there can be no doubt that very many other pelagic animals, when alive, are phosphorescent.

On two occasions I have observed the sea luminous at considerable depths beneath the surface. Near the mouth of the Plata some circular and oval patches, from 2 to 4 yards in diameter, and with defined outlines, shone with a steady, but pale light; while the surrounding water only gave out a few sparks. The appearance resembled the reflection of the moon, or some luminous body; for the edges were sinuous from the undulation of the surface. The ship, which drew thirteen feet water, passed over, without disturbing, these patches. Therefore we must suppose that some animals were congregated together at a greater depth than the bottom of the vessel.

Near Fernando Noronha the sea gave out light in flashes. The appearance was very similar to that which might be expected from a large fish moving rapidly through a luminous fluid. To this cause the sailors attributed it; at the time, however, I entertained some doubts, on account of the frequency and rapidity of the flashes. With respect to any general observations, I have already stated that the display is very much more common in warm than in cold countries. I have sometimes imagined that a disturbed electrical condition of the atmosphere was most favourable to its production. Certainly I think the sea is most luminous after a few days of more calm weather than ordinary, during which time it has swarmed with various animals. Observing that the water charged with gelatinous particles is in an impure state, and that the luminous appearance in all common cases is produced by the agitation of the fluid in contact with the atmosphere, I have always been inclined to consider that the phosphorescence was the result of the decomposition of the organic particles, by which process (one is tempted almost to call it a kind of respiration) the ocean becomes purified.

DECEMBER 23RD – We arrived at Port Desire, situated in lat. 47°, on the coast of Patagonia. The creek runs for about twenty miles inland, with an irregular width. The *Beagle* anchored a few miles within the entrance in front of the ruins of an old Spanish settlement.

The same evening I went on shore. The first landing in any new country is very interesting, and especially when, as in this case, the whole aspect bears the stamp of a marked and individual character. At the height of between 200 and 300 feet, above some masses of porphyry, a wide plain extends, which is truly characteristic of Patagonia. The surface is quite level, and is composed of well-rounded shingle mixed with a whitish earth. Here and there scattered tufts of brown wiry grass are supported, and still more rarely some low thorny bushes. The weather is dry and pleasant, for the fine blue sky is but seldom obscured. When standing in the middle of one of these desert plains, the view on one side is generally bounded by the escarpment of another plain, rather higher, but equally level and desolate; and on the other side it becomes indistinct from the trembling mirage which seems to rise from the heated surface.

The plains are traversed by many broad, flat-bottomed valleys, and in these the bushes grow rather more abundantly. The present drainage of the country is quite insufficient to excavate such large channels. In some of the valleys ancient stunted trees, growing in the very centre of the dry watercourse, seem as if placed to prove how long a time had elapsed, since any flood had passed that way. We have evidence, from shells lying on the surface, that the plains of gravel have been elevated within a recent epoch above the level of the sea; and we must look to that period for the excavation of the valleys by the slowly retiring waters. From the dryness of the climate, a man may walk for days together over these plains without finding a single drop of water. Even at the base of the porphyry hills, there are only a few small wells containing but little water, and that rather saline and half putrid.

In such a country the fate of the Spanish settlement was soon decided; the dryness of the climate during the greater part of the year, and the occasional hostile attacks of the wandering Indians, compelled the colonists to desert their half-finished buildings. The style, however, in which they were commenced, showed the strong and liberal hand of Spain in the old time. The end of all the attempts to colonize this side of America south of 41°, have been miserable. At Port Famine, the name expresses the lingering and extreme sufferings of several hundred wretched people, of whom one alone survived to relate their misfortunes. At St Joseph's bay, on the coast of Patagonia, a small settlement was made; but during one Sunday the Indians made an attack and massacred the whole party, excepting two men, who were led captive many years among the wandering tribes. At the Rio Negro I conversed with one of these men, now in extreme old age.

The zoology of Patagonia is as limited as its Flora. On the arid plains a few black beetles (Heteromera) might be seen slowly crawling about, and occasionally a lizard darting from side to side. Of birds we have three carrion hawks, and in the valleys a few finches and insect feeders. The *Ibis malanops* (a species said to be found in central Africa) is not uncommon on the most desert parts. In the stomachs of these birds I found grasshoppers, cicadæ, small lizards, and even scorpions. At one time of the year they go in flocks, at another in pairs: their cry is very loud and singular, and resembles the neighing of the guanaco.

I will here give an account of this latter animal, which is very common, and is the characteristic quadruped of the plains of Patagonia. The Guanaco, which by some naturalists is considered as the same animal with the Llama, but in its wild state, is the South American representative of the camel of the East. In size it may be compared to an ass, mounted on taller legs, and with a very long neck. The guanaco abounds over the whole of the temperate parts of South America, from the wooded islands of Tierra del Fuego, through Patagonia, the hilly parts of La Plata, Chile, even to the Cordillera of Peru. Although preferring an elevated site, it yields in this respect to its near relative the Vicuna. On the plains of Southern Patagonia, we saw them in greater numbers than in any other part. Generally they go in small herds, from half a dozen to thirty together; but on the banks of the St Cruz we saw one herd which must have contained at least 500. On the northern shores of the Strait of Magellan they are also very numerous.

Generally the guanacoes are wild and extremely wary. Mr Stokes told me, that he one day saw through a glass a herd of these beasts, which evidently had been frightened, running away at full speed, although their distance was so great that they could not be distinguished by the naked eye. The sportsman frequently receives the first intimation of their presence, by hearing, from a long distance, the peculiar shrill neighing note of alarm. If he then looks attentively, he will perhaps see the herd standing in a line on the side of some distant hill. On approaching them, a few more squeals are given, and then off they set at an apparently slow, but really quick canter, along some narrow beaten track to a neighbouring hill. If, however, by chance he should abruptly meet a single animal, or several together, they will generally stand motionless, and intently gaze at him; then perhaps move on a few yards, turn round, and look again. What is the cause of this difference in their shyness? Do they mistake a man in the distance for their chief enemy the puma? Or does curiosity overcome their timidity? That they are curious is certain; for if a person lies on the ground, and plays strange antics, such as throwing up his feet in the air, they will almost always approach by degrees to reconnoitre him. It was an artifice that was repeatedly practised by our sportsmen with success, and it had moreover the advantage of allowing several shots to be fired, which were all taken as parts of the performance. On the mountains of Tierra del Fuego, and in other places, I have more than once seen a guanaco, on being approached, not only neigh and squeal, but prance and leap about in the most ridiculous manner, apparently in defiance as a challenge. These animals are very easily domesticated, and I have seen some thus kept near the houses, although at large on their native plains. They are in this state very bold, and readily attack a man, by striking him from behind with both knees. It is asserted, that the motive for these attacks is jealousy on account of their females. The wild guanacoes, however, have no idea of defence; even a single dog will secure one of these large animals, till the huntsman can come up. In many of their habits they are like sheep in a flock. Thus when they see men approaching in several directions on horseback, they soon became bewildered and know not which way to run. This greatly facilitates the Indian method of hunting, for they are thus easily driven to a central point, and are encompassed.

The guanacoes readily take to the water: several times at Port Valdes they were seen swimming from island to island. Byron, in his voyage, says he saw them drinking salt water. Some of our officers likewise saw a herd apparently drinking the briny fluid from a salina near Cape Blanco. I imagine in several parts of the country, if they do not drink salt water, they drink none at all. In the middle of the day, they frequently roll in the dust, in saucer-shaped hollows. The males fight together; two one day passed quite close to me, squealing and trying to bite each other; and several were shot with their hides deeply scored. Herds sometimes appear to set out on exploring-parties: at Bahia Blanca, where, within 30 miles of the coast, these animals are extremely unfrequent, I one day saw the tracks of thirty or forty, which had come in a direct line to a muddy salt-water creek. They then must have perceived that they were approaching the sea, for they had wheeled with the regularity of cavalry, and had returned back in as straight a line as they had advanced. The guanacoes have one singular habit, which is to me quite inexplicable; namely, that on successive days they drop their dung in the same defined heap. I saw one of these heaps which was eight feet in diameter, and necessarily was composed of a large quantity. Frezier remarks on this habit as common to the guanaco as well as to the llama; he says it is very useful to the Indians, who use the dung for fuel, and are thus saved the trouble of collecting it.

The guanacoes appear to have favourite spots for dying in. On the banks of the St Cruz, the ground was actually white with bones, in certain circumscribed spaces, which were generally bushy and all near the river. On one such spot I counted between ten and twenty heads. I particularly examined the bones; they did not appear, as some scattered ones which I had seen, gnawed or broken, as if dragged together by beasts of prey. The animals in most cases, must have crawled, before dying, beneath and amongst the bushes. Mr Bynoe informs me that during the last voyage, he observed the same circumstance on the banks of the Rio Gallegos. I do not at all understand the reason of this, but I may observe, that the wounded guanacoes at the St Cruz, invariably walked towards the river. At St Jago in the Cape de Verd islands I remember having

Patagonia

seen in a retired ravine a corner under a cliff, where numerous goats' bones were collected: we at the time exclaimed, that it was the burial-ground of all the goats in the island. I mention these trifling circumstances, because in certain cases they might explain the occurrence of a number of uninjured bones in a cave, or buried under alluvial accumulations; and likewise the cause, why certain mammalia are more commonly embedded than others in sedimentary deposits. Any great flood of the St Cruz, would wash down many bones of the guanaco, but probably not a single one of the puma, ostrich, or fox. I may also observe, that almost every kind of water-fowl when wounded takes to the shore to die; so that the remains of birds, from this cause alone and independently of other reasons, would but rarely be preserved in a fossil state.

* * *

JANUARY 9TH, 1834 – Before it was dark the *Beagle* anchored in the fine spacious harbour of Port St Julian, situated about 110 miles to the south of Port Desire. On the south side of the harbour, a cliff of about 90 feet in height intersects a plain constituted of the formations above described; and its surface is strewed over with recent marine shells. The gravel, however, differently from that in every other locality, is covered by a very irregular and thin bed of a reddish loam, containing a few small calcareous concretions. The matter somewhat resembles that of the Pampas, and probably owes its origin either to a small stream having formerly entered the sea at that spot, or to a mud-bank similar to those now existing at the head of the harbour. In one spot this earthy matter filled up a hollow, or gully, worn quite through the gravel, and in this mass a group of large bones was embedded. The animal to which they belonged, must have lived, as in the case at Bahia Blanca, at a period long subsequent to the existence of the shells now inhabiting the coast. We may feel sure of this, because the formation of the lower terrace or plain, must necessarily have been posterior to those above it, and on the surface of the two higher ones, sea-shells of recent species are scattered. From the small physical change, which the last 100 feet elevation of the continent could have produced, the climate, as well as the general condition of Patagonia, probably was nearly the same, at the time when the animal was embedded, as it now is. This conclusion is moreover supported by the identity of the shells belonging to the two ages. Then immediately occurred the difficulty, how could any large quadruped have subsisted on these wretched deserts in lat. 49° 15'? I had no idea at the time, to what kind of animal these remains belonged. The puzzle, however, was soon solved when Mr Owen examined them; for he considers that they formed part of an animal allied to the guanaco or llama, but fully as large as the true camel. As all the existing members of the family of Camelidæ are inhabitants of the most sterile countries, so may we suppose was this extinct kind. The structure of the cervical vertebræ, the transverse processes not being perforated for the vertebral artery, indicates its affinity: some other parts, however, of its structure, probably are anomalous.

The most important result of this discovery, is the confirmation of the law that existing animals have a close relation in form with extinct species. As the guanaco is the characteristic quadruped of Patagonia, and the vicuna of the snow-clad summits of the Cordillera, so in bygone days, this gigantic species of the same family must have been conspicuous on the southern plains. We see this same relation of type between the existing and fossil Ctenomys, between the capybara (but less plainly, as shown by Mr Owen) and the gigantic Toxodon; and lastly, between the living and extinct Edentata. At the present day, in South America, there exist probably nineteen species of this order, distributed into several genera; while throughout the rest of the world there are but five. If, then, there is a relation between the living and the dead, we should expect that the Edentata would be numerous in the fossil state. I need only reply by enumerating the megatherium, and the three or four other great species, discovered at Bahia Blanca; the remains of some of which are also abundant over the whole immense territory of La Plata. I have already pointed out the singular relation between the armadilloes and their great prototypes, even in a point apparently of so little importance as their external covering.

The order of rodents at the present day, is most conspicuous in South America, on account of the vast number and size of the species, and the multitude of individuals: according to the same law, we should expect to find their representatives in a fossil state. Mr Owen has shown how far the Toxodon is thus related; and it is moreover not improbable that another large animal has likewise a similar affinity.

The teeth of the rodent nearly equalling in size those of the Capybara, which were discovered near Bahia Blanca, must also be remembered.

The law of the succession of types, although subject to some remarkable exceptions, must possess the highest interest to every philosophical naturalist, and was first clearly observed in regard to Australia, where fossil remains of a large and extinct species of Kangaroo and other marsupial animals were discovered buried in a cave. In America the most marked change among the mammalia has been the loss of several species of Mastodon, of an elephant, and of the horse. These Pachydermata appear formerly to have had a range over the world, like that which deer and antelopes now hold. If Buffon had known of these gigantic armadilloes, llamas, great rodents, and lost pachydermata, he would have said with a greater semblance of truth, that the creative force in

Patagonia

America had lost its vigour, rather than that it had never possessed such powers.

It is impossible to reflect without the deepest astonishment, on the changed state of this continent. Formerly it must have swarmed with great monsters, like the southern parts of Africa, but now we find only the tapir, guanaco, armadillo, and capybara; mere pigmies compared to the antecedent races. The greater number, if not all, of these extinct quadrupeds lived at a very recent period; and many of them were contemporaries of the existing molluscs. Since their loss, no very great physical changes can have taken place in the nature of the country. What then has exterminated so many living creatures? In the Pampas, the great sepulchre of such remains, there are no signs of violence, but on the contrary, of the most quiet and scarcely sensible changes. At Bahia Blanca I endeavoured to show the probability that the ancient Edentata, like the present species, lived in a dry and sterile country, such as now is found in that neighbourhood. With respect to the camel-like llama of Patagonia, the same grounds which, before knowing more than the size of the remains, perplexed me, by not allowing any great change of climate, now that we can guess the habits of the animal, are strangely confirmed. What shall we say of the death of the fossil horse? Did those plains fail in pasture, which afterwards were overrun by thousands and tens of thousands of the successors of the fresh stock introduced with the Spanish colonist? In some countries, we may believe, that a number of species subsequently introduced, by consuming the food of the antecedent races, may have caused their extermination; but we can scarcely credit that the armadillo has devoured the food of the immense Megatherium, the capybara of the Toxodon, or the guanaco of the camel-like kind. But granting that all such changes have been small, yet we are so profoundly ignorant concerning the physiological relations, on which the life, and even health (as shown by epidemics) of any existing species depends, that we argue with still less safety about either the life or death of any extinct kind.

One is tempted to believe in such simple relations, as variation of climate and food, or introduction of enemies, or the increased numbers of other species, as the cause of the succession of races. But it may be asked whether it is probable that any such cause should have been in action during the same epoch over the whole northern hemisphere, so as to destroy the *Elephas primigenus*, on the shores of Spain, on the plains of Siberia, and in Northern America; and in a like manner, the *Bos urus*, over a range of scarcely less extent? Did such changes put a period to the life of *Mastodon angustidens*, and of the fossil horse, both in Europe and on the Eastern slope of the Cordillera in Southern America? If they did, they must have been changes common to the whole world; such as gradual refrigeration, whether from modifications of physical geography, or from central cooling. But on this assumption, we have to struggle with the difficulty that these supposed changes, although scarcely sufficient to affect molluscous animals either in Europe or South America, yet destroyed many quadrupeds in regions now characterized by *frigid, temperate*, and *warm* climates! These cases of extinction forcibly recall the idea (I do not wish to draw any close analogy) of certain fruit-trees, which, it has been asserted, though grafted on young stems, planted in varied situations, and fertilized by the richest manures, yet at one period, have all withered away and perished. A fixed and determined length of life has in such cases been given to thousands and thousands of buds (or individual germs), although produced in long succession. Among the greater number of animals, each individual appears nearly independent of its kind; yet all of one kind may be bound together by common laws, as well as a certain number of individual buds in the tree, or polypi in the Zoophyte.

I will add one other remark. We see that whole series of animals, which have been created with peculiar kinds of organization, are confined to certain areas; and we can hardly suppose these structures are only adaptations to peculiarities of climate or country; for otherwise, animals belonging to a distinct type, and introduced by man, would not succeed so admirably, even to the extermination of the aborigines. On such grounds it does not seem a necessary conclusion, that the extinction of species, more than their creation, should exclusively depend on the nature (altered by physical changes) of their country. All that at present can be said with certainty, is that, as with the individual, so with the species, the hour of life has run its course, and is spent.

* * *

APRIL 13TH – The *Beagle* anchored within the mouth of the Santa Cruz. This river is situated about 60 miles south of Port St Julian. During the last voyage, Captain Stokes proceeded 30 miles up, but then, from the want of provisions, was obliged to return. Excepting what was discovered at that time, scarcely any thing was known about this large river. Captain FitzRoy now determined to follow its course as far as time would allow. On the 18th, three whale-boats started, carrying three weeks' provisions; and the party consisted of twenty-five souls – a force which would have been sufficient to have defied a host of Indians. With a strong flood-tide, and a fine day, we made a good run, soon drank some of the fresh water, and were at night nearly above the tidal influence.

The river here assumed a size and appearance, which, even at the highest point we ultimately reached, was scarcely diminished. It was generally from 300 to 400 yards broad, and in the middle about 17 feet deep. The rapidity of the current, which in its whole course runs at the rate of from 4 to 6 knots an hour, is perhaps its most remarkable feature. The water is of a fine blue colour, but with a slight milky tinge, and not so transparent as at first sight would have been expected. It flows over a bed of pebbles, like those which compose the beach and surrounding plains. Although its course is winding, it runs through a valley which extends in a direct line to the westward. This valley varies from 5 to 10 miles in breadth; it is bounded by step-formed terraces, which rise in most parts one above the other to the height of 500 feet, and have on the opposite sides a remarkable correspondence.

APRIL 19TH – Against so strong a current, it was of course quite impossible to row or sail. Consequently the three boats were fastened together head and stern, two hands left in each, and the rest came on shore to track. As the general arrangements, made by Captain FitzRoy, were very good for facilitating the work of all, and as all had a share of it, I will describe the system. The party, including everyone, was divided into two spells, each of which hauled at the tracking line alternately for an hour and a half. The officers of each boat lived with, ate the same food, and slept in the same tent with their crew, so that each boat was quite independent of the others. After sunset, the first level spot where any bushes were growing, was chosen for our night's lodging. Each of the crew took it in turns to be cook. Immediately the boat was hauled up, the cook made his fire; two others pitched the tent; the coxswain handed the things out of the boat; the rest carried them up to the tents, and collected firewood. By this order, in half an hour, every thing was ready for the night. A watch of two men and an officer was always kept, whose duty it was to look after the boats, keep up the fire, and guard against Indians. Each in the party had his one hour every night.

During this day we tracked but a short distance, for there were many islets, covered by thorny bushes, and the channels between them were shallow.

APRIL 20TH – We passed the islands and set to work. Our regular day's march, although it was hard enough, carried us on an average only 10 miles in a straight line, and perhaps 15 or 20 altogether. Beyond the place where we slept last night the country is completely *terra incognita*, for it was there that Captain Stokes turned back. We saw in the distance a great smoke, and found the skeleton of a horse, so we knew that Indians were in the neighbourhood. On the next morning (21st) tracks of a party of horse, and marks left by the trailing of the *chuzos* were observed on the ground. It was generally thought they must have reconnoitred us during the night. Shortly afterwards we came to a spot, where from the fresh footsteps of men, children, and horses, it was evident the party had crossed the river.

* * *

APRIL 29TH – From some high land we hailed with joy the white summits of the Cordillera, as they were seen occasionally peeping through their dusky envelope of clouds. During the few succeeding days, we continued to get on slowly, for we found the river-course very tortuous, and strewed with immense fragments of various ancient slaty rocks, and of granite. The plain bordering the valley had here attained an elevation of about 1,100 feet, and its character was much altered. The well-rounded pebbles of porphyry were in this part mingled with many immense angular fragments of basalt and of the rocks above mentioned. The first of these erratic blocks which I noticed, was 67 miles distant from the nearest mountain; another which had been transported to rather a less distance, measured 5 yards square, and projected 5 feet above the gravel. Its edges were so angular, and its size so great, that I at first mistook it for a rock *in situ*, and took out my compass to observe the direction of its cleavage. The plains here were not quite so level as those nearer the coast, but yet, they betrayed little signs of any violent action. Under these circumstances, it would be difficult, as it appears to me, to explain this phenomenon on any theory, excepting through that of transport by ice while the country was under water. But this is a subject to which I shall again recur.

During the two last days we met with signs of horses, and with several small articles which had belonged to the Indians, – such as parts of a mantle and a bunch of ostrich feathers – but they appeared to have been lying long on the ground. Between the place where the Indians had so lately crossed the river and this neighbourhood, though so many miles apart, the country appears to be quite unfrequented. At first, considering the abundance of the guanacoes, I was surprised at this; but it is explained by the stony nature of the plains, which would soon disable an unshod horse from taking part in the chase. Nevertheless, in two places in this very central region, I found small heaps of stones, which I do not think could have been accidentally thrown together. They were placed on points, projecting over the edge of the highest lava cliff, and they resembled, but on a small scale, those near Port Desire.

MAY 4TH – Captain FitzRoy determined to take the boats no higher. The river had a winding course, and was very rapid; and the appearance of the country offered no temptation to proceed any further. Every where we met with the same productions, and the same dreary landscape. We were now 140 miles distant from the Atlantic, and about 60 from the nearest arm of the Pacific. The valley in this upper part expanded into a wide basin, bounded on the north and south by the basaltic platforms, and fronted by the long range of the snow-clad Cordillera. But we viewed these grand mountains with regret, for we were obliged to imagine their form and nature, instead of standing, as we had hoped, on their crest, and looking down on the plain below. Besides the useless loss of time which an attempt to ascend any higher would have cost us, we had already been for some days on half allowance of bread. This, although really enough for any reasonable men, was, after our hard day's march, rather scanty food. Let those alone who have never tried it, exclaim about the comfort of a light stomach and an easy digestion.

5TH – Before sunrise we commenced our descent. We shot down the stream with great rapidity, generally at the rate of 10 knots an hour. In this one day we effected what had cost us five-and-a-half hard days' labour in ascending. On the 8th, we reached the *Beagle* after our twenty-one days' expedition. Every one excepting myself had cause to be dissatisfied; but to me the ascent afforded a most interesting section of the great tertiary formation of Patagonia.

Tierra del Fuego

DECEMBER 17TH, 1832 – Having now finished with Patagonia, I will describe our first arrival in Tierra del Fuego. A little after noon we doubled Cape St Diego, and entered the famous strait of Le Maire. We kept close to the Fuegian shore, but the outline of the rugged, inhospitable Staten land was visible amidst the clouds. In the afternoon we anchored in the Bay of Good Success. While entering we were saluted in a manner becoming the inhabitants of this savage land. A group of Fuegians partly concealed by the entangled forest, were perched on a wild point overhanging the sea; and as we passed by, they sprang up, and waving their tattered cloaks sent forth a loud and sonorous shout. The savages followed the ship, and just before dark we saw their fire, and again heard their wild cry. The harbour consists of a fine piece of water half surrounded by low rounded mountains of clay-slate, which are covered to the water's edge by one dense gloomy forest. A single glance at the landscape was sufficient to show me, how widely different it was from any thing I had ever beheld. At night it blew a gale of wind, and heavy squalls from the mountains swept past us. It would have been a bad time out at sea, and we, as well as others, may call this Good Success Bay.

In the morning, the Captain sent a party to communicate with the Fuegians. When we came within hail, one of the four natives who were present advanced to receive us, and began to shout most vehemently, wishing to direct us where to land. When we were on shore the party looked rather alarmed, but continued talking and making gestures with great rapidity. It was without exception the most curious and interesting spectacle I had ever beheld. I could not have believed how wide was the difference, between savage and civilized man. It is greater than between a wild and domesticated animal, in as much as in man there is a greater power of improvement. The chief spokesman was old, and appeared to be the head of the family; the three others were powerful young men, about 6 feet high. The women and children had been sent away. These Fuegians are a very different race from the stunted miserable wretches further to the westward. They are much superior in person, and seem closely allied to the famous Patagonians of the Strait of Magellan. Their only garment consists of a mantle made of guanaco skin, with the wool outside; this they wear just thrown over their shoulders, as often leaving their persons exposed as covered. Their skin is of a dirty coppery red colour.

The old man had a fillet of white feathers tied round his head, which partly confined his black, coarse, and

Tierra del Fuego

entangled hair. His face was crossed by two broad transverse bars; one painted bright red reached from ear to ear, and included the upper lip; the other, white like chalk, extended parallel and above the first, so that even his eyelids were thus coloured. Some of the other men were ornamented by streaks of black powder, made of charcoal. The party altogether closely resembled the devils which come on the stage in such plays as Der Freischutz.

Their very attitudes were abject, and the expression of their countenances distrustful, surprised, and startled. After we had presented them with some scarlet cloth, which they immediately tied round their necks, they became good friends. This was shown by the old man patting our breasts, and making a chuckling kind of noise, as people do when feeding chickens. I walked with the old man, and this demonstration of friendship was repeated several times; it was concluded by three hard slaps, which were given me on the breast and back at the same time. He then bared his bosom for me to return the compliment, which being done, he seemed highly pleased. The language of these people, according to our notions, scarcely deserves to be called articulate. Captain Cook has compared it to a man clearing his throat, but certainly no European ever cleared his throat with so many hoarse, guttural, and clicking sounds.

They are excellent mimics: as often as we coughed or yawned, or made any odd motion, they immediately imitated us. Some of our party began to squint and look awry; but one of the young Fuegians (whose whole face was painted black, excepting a white band across his eyes) succeeded in making far more hideous grimaces. They could repeat with perfect correctness, each word in any sentence we addressed them, and they remembered such words for some time. Yet we Europeans all know how difficult it is to distinguish apart the sounds in a foreign language. Which of us, for instance, could follow an American Indian through a sentence of more than three words? All savages appear to possess, to an uncommon degree, this power of mimicry. I was told almost in the same words, of the same ludicrous habits among the Caffres: the Australians, likewise, have long been notorious for being able to imitate and describe the gait of any man, so that he may be recognized. How can this faculty be explained? is it a consequence of the more practised habits of perception and keener senses, common to all men in a savage state, as compared to those long civilized?

When a song was struck up by our party, I thought the Fuegians would have fallen down with astonishment. With equal surprise they viewed our dancing; but one of the young men, when asked, had no objection to a little waltzing. Little accustomed to Europeans as they appeared to be, yet they knew, and dreaded our fire-arms; nothing would tempt them to take a gun in their hands. They begged for knives, calling them by the Spanish word 'cuchilla'. They explained also what they wanted, by acting as if they had a piece of blubber in their mouth, and then pretending to cut instead of tear it.

It was interesting to watch the conduct of these people towards Jemmy Button (one of the Fuegians who had been taken, during the former voyage, to England): they immediately perceived the difference between him and the rest, and held much conversation between themselves on the subject. The old man addressed a long harangue to Jemmy, which it seems was to invite him to stay with them. But Jemmy understood very little of their language, and was, moreover, thoroughly ashamed of his countrymen. When York Minster (another of these men) came on shore, they noticed him in the same way, and told him he ought to shave; yet he had not twenty dwarf hairs on his face, whilst we all wore our untrimmed beards. They examined the colour of his skin, and compared it with ours. One of our arms being bared, they expressed the liveliest surprise and admiration at its whiteness. We thought that they mistook two or three of the officers, who were rather shorter and fairer (though adorned with large beards), for the ladies of our party. The tallest amongst the Fuegians was evidently much pleased at his height being noticed. When placed back to back with the tallest of the boat's crew, he tried his best to edge on higher ground, and to stand on tiptoe. He opened his mouth to show his teeth, and turned his face for a side view; and all this was done with such alacrity, that I dare say he thought himself the handsomest man in Tierra del

Fuego. After the first feeling on our part of grave astonishment was over, nothing could be more ludicrous or interesting than the odd mixture of surprise and imitation which these savages every moment exhibited.

The next day I attempted to penetrate some way into the country. Tierra del Fuego may be described as a mountainous country, partly submerged in the sea, so that deep islets and bays occupy the place where valleys should exist. The mountain sides (except on the exposed western coast) are covered from the water's edge upwards by one great forest. The trees reach to an elevation of between 1,000 and 1,500 feet; and are succeeded by a band of peat, with minute alpine plants; and this again is succeeded by the line of perpetual snow, which, according to Captain King, in the Strait of Magellan descends to between 3,000 and 4,000 feet. To find an acre of level land in any part of the country is most rare. I recollect only one little flat near Port Famine, and another of rather larger extent near Goeree Road. In both these cases, and in all others, the surface was covered by a thick bed of swampy peat. Even within the forest the ground is concealed by a mass of slowly putrefying vegetable matter, which, from being soaked with water, yields to the foot.

Finding it nearly hopeless to push my way through the wood, I followed the course of a mountain torrent. At first, from the waterfalls and number of dead trees, I could hardly crawl along; but the bed of the stream soon became a little more open, from the floods having swept the sides. I continued slowly to advance for an hour along the broken and rocky banks; and was amply repaid by the grandeur of the scene. The gloomy depth of the ravine well accorded with the universal signs of violence. On every side were lying irregular masses of rock and up-torn trees; other trees, though still erect, were decayed to the heart and ready to fall. The entangled mass of the thriving and the fallen reminded me of the forests within the tropics; – yet there was a difference; for in these still solitudes, Death, instead of Life, seemed the predominant spirit. I followed the water-course till I came to a spot where a great slip had cleared a straight space down the mountain side. By this road I ascended to a considerable elevation, and obtained a good view of the surrounding woods. The trees all belong to one kind, the *Fagus betuloides*, for the number of the other species of beech, and of the Winter's bark, is quite inconsiderable. This tree keeps its leaves throughout the year; but its foliage is of a peculiar brownish-green colour, with a tinge of yellow. As the whole landscape is thus coloured, it has a sombre, dull appearance; nor is it often enlivened by the rays of the sun.

Strait of Magellan

DECEMBER 21ST – The *Beagle* got under way: and on the succeeding day, favoured to an uncommon degree by a fine easterly breeze, we closed in with the Barnevelts, and, running past Cape Deceit with its stony peaks, about three o'clock doubled the weather beaten Cape Horn! The evening was calm and bright and means of judging of the distance, how the mountain appeared to rise in height.

The Fuegians twice came and plagued us. As there were many instruments, clothes, and men on shore, it was thought necessary to frighten them away. The first time, a few great guns were fired, when they were far distant. It was most ludicrous to watch through a glass the Indians, as often as the shot struck the water, take up stones, and as a bold defiance, throw them towards the ship, though about a mile and a half distant! A boat was then sent with orders to fire a few musket-shot wide of them. The Fuegians hid themselves behind the trees; and for every discharge of the musket they fired their arrows: all, however, fell short of the boat, and the officer as he pointed at them laughed. This made the Fuegians frantic with passion, and they shook their mantles in vain rage. At last seeing the balls cut and strike the trees, they ran away; and we were left in peace and quietness.

On a former occasion, when the *Beagle* was here in the month of February, I started one morning at four o'clock to ascend Mount Tarn, which is 2,600 feet high, and is the most elevated point in this immediate neighbourhood. We went in a boat to the foot of the mountain (but not to the best part), and then began our ascent. The forest commences at the line of high-water mark, and during the two first hours I gave over all hopes of reaching the summit. So thick was the wood, that it was necessary to have constant recourse to the compass; for every landmark, though in a mountainous country, was completely shut out. In the deep ravines, the death-like scene of desolation exceeded all description; outside it was blowing a gale, but in these hollows, not even a breath of wind stirred the leaves of the tallest trees. So gloomy, cold, and wet was every part, that not even the fungi, mosses, or ferns, could flourish. In the valleys it was scarcely possible to crawl along, they were so completely barricaded by the great mouldering trunks, which had fallen down in every direction. When passing over these natural bridges, one's course was often arrested by sinking knee deep into the rotten wood; at other times, when attempting to lean against a firm tree, one was startled by finding a mass of decayed matter ready to fall at the slightest touch. We at last found ourselves among the stunted trees, and then soon reached the bare ridge, which conducted us to the summit. Here was a view characteristic of Tierra del Fuego; – irregular chains of hills, mottled with patches of snow, deep yellowish-green valleys, and arms of the sea intersecting the land in many directions. The strong wind was piercingly cold, and the atmosphere rather hazy, so that we did not stay long on the top of the mountain. Our descent was not quite so laborious as our ascent; for the weight of the body forced a passage, and all the slips and falls were in the right direction.

* * *

The perfect preservation of the Siberian animals, perhaps presented, till within a few years, one of the most difficult problems which geology ever attempted to solve. On the one hand it was granted, that the carcasses had not been drifted from any great distance by any tumultuous deluge, and on the other it was assumed as certain, that when the animals lived, the climate must have been so totally different, that the presence of ice in the vicinity was as incredible, as would be the freezing of the Ganges. Mr Lyell in his *Principles of Geology* has thrown the greatest light on this subject, by indicating the northerly course of the existing rivers with the probability that they formerly carried carcasses in the same direction; by showing (from Humboldt) how far the inhabitants of the hottest countries sometimes wander; by insisting on the caution necessary in judging of habits between animals of the same genus, when the species are not identical; and especially by bringing forward in the clearest manner the probable change from an insular to an extreme climate, as the consequence of the elevation of the land, of which proofs have lately been brought to light.

In a former part of this volume, I have endeavoured to prove, that as far as regards the *quantity* of food, there is no difficulty in supposing that these large quadrupeds inhabited sterile regions, producing but a scanty vegetation. With respect to temperature, the woolly covering both of the elephant and the rhinoceros seems at once to render it at least probable (although it has been argued that some animals living in the hottest regions are thickly clothed) that they were fitted for a cold climate. I suppose no reason can be assigned why, during a former epoch, when the pachydermata abounded over the greater part of the world, some species should not have been fitted for the northern regions, precisely as now happens with deer and several other animals. If, then, we believe that the climate of Siberia, anteriorly to the physical changes above alluded to, had some resemblance with that of the southern hemisphere at the present day – a circumstance which harmonizes well with other facts, as I think has been shown by the imaginary case, when we transported existing phenomena from one to the other hemisphere – the following conclusions may be deduced as probable: first, that the degree of cold formerly was not excessive; secondly, that snow did not for a long time together cover the ground (such not being the case at the extreme parts 55°–56° of S. America); thirdly, that the vegetation partook of a more tropical character than it now does in the same latitudes; and lastly, that at but a short distance to the northward of the country thus circumstanced (even not so far as where Pallas found the entire rhinoceros), the soil might be perpetually congealed: so that if the carcass of any animal should once be buried a few feet beneath the surface, it would be preserved for centuries.

Both Humboldt and Lyell have remarked, that at the present day, the bodies of any animals, wandering beyond the line of perpetual congelation which extends as far south as 62°, if once embedded by any accident a few feet beneath the surface, would be preserved for an indefinite length of time: the same would happen with carcasses drifted by the rivers; and by such means the extinct mammalia may have been entombed. There is only one small step wanting, as it appears to me, and the whole problem would be solved with a degree of simplicity very striking, compared with the several theories first invented. From the account given by Mr Lyell of the Siberian plains, with their innumerable fossil bones, the relics of many successive generations, there can be little doubt that the beds were accumulated either in a shallow sea, or in an estuary. From the description given in Beechey's voyage of

Strait of Magellan

Eschscholtz Bay, the same remark is applicable to the north-west coast of America: the formation there appears identical with the common littoral deposits recently elevated, which I have seen on the shores of the southern part of the same continent. It seems also well established, that the Siberian remains are only exposed where the rivers intersect the plain. With this fact, and the proofs of recent elevation, the whole case appears to be precisely similar to that of the Pampas: namely, that the carcasses were formerly floated into the sea, and the remains covered up in the deposits which were then accumulating. These beds have since been elevated; and as the rivers excavate their channels the entombed skeletons are exposed.

Here then, is the difficulty: how were the carcasses preserved at the bottom of the sea? I do not think it has been sufficiently noticed, that the preservation of the animal with its flesh was an occasional event, and not directly consequent on its position far northward. Cuvier refers to the voyage of Billing as showing that the *bones* of the elephant, buffalo, and rhinoceros, are nowhere so abundant as on the islands between the mouths of the Lena and Indigirska. It is even said that excepting some hills of rock, the whole is composed of sand, ice, and bones. These islands lie to the northward of the place where Adams found the mammoth with its flesh preserved, and even 10° north of the Wiljui, where the rhinoceros was discovered in a like condition. In the case of the *bones* we may suppose that the carcasses were drifted into a deeper sea, and there remaining at the bottom, the flesh decomposed. But in the second and more extraordinary case, where putrefaction seems to have been arrested, the body probably was soon covered up by deposits which were then accumulating. It may be asked, whether the mud a few feet deep, at the bottom of a shallow sea which is annually frozen, has a temperature higher than 32°? It must be remembered how intense a degree of cold is required to freeze salt water; and that the mud at some depth below the surface, would have a low mean temperature, precisely in the same manner as the subsoil on the land is frozen in countries which enjoy a short but hot summer. If this be possible, the entombment of these extinct quadrupeds is rendered very simple; and with regard to the conditions of their former existence, the principal difficulties have, I think, already been removed.

* * *

There is one marine production, which from its importance is worthy of a particular history. It is the kelp or *Fucus giganteus* of Solander. This plant grows on every rock from low-water mark to a great depth, both on the outer coast and within the channels. I believe, during the voyages of the *Adventure* and *Beagle*, not one rock near the surface was discovered, which was not buoyed by this floating weed. The good service it thus affords to vessels

Strait of Magellan

navigating near this stormy land is evident; and it certainly has saved many a one from being wrecked. I know few things more surprising than to see this plant growing and flourishing amidst those great breakers of the western ocean, which no mass of rock, let it be ever so hard, can long resist. The stem is round, slimy, and smooth, and seldom has a diameter of so much as an inch. A few taken together are sufficiently strong to support the weight of the large loose stones to which in the inland channels they grow attached; and some of these stones are so heavy, that when drawn to the surface they can scarcely be lifted into a boat by one person.

Captain Cook, in his second voyage, says, that at Kerguelen Land 'some of this weed is of a most enormous length, though the stem is not much thicker than a man's thumb. I have mentioned, that on some of the shoals upon which it grows, we did not strike ground with a line of 24 fathoms. The depth of water, therefore, must have been greater. And as this weed does not grow in a perpendicular direction, but makes a very acute angle with the bottom, and much of it afterwards spreads many fathoms on the surface of the sea, I am well warranted to say that some of it grows to the length of sixty fathoms and upwards.' Certainly at the Falkland Islands, and about Tierra del Fuego, extensive beds frequently spring up from 10- and 15-fathom water. I do not suppose the stem of any other plant attains so great a length as 360 feet, as stated by Captain Cook. Its geographical range is very considerable; it is found from the extreme southern islets near Cape Horn, as far north, on the eastern coast (according to information given me by Mr Stokes), as lat. 43° – and on the western it was tolerably abundant, but far from luxuriant, at Chiloe, in lat. 42°. It may possibly extend a little further northward, but is soon succeeded by a different species. We thus have a range of 15° in latitude; and as Cook, who must have been well acquainted with the species, found it at Kerguelen Land, no less than 140° in longitude.

The number of living creatures of all orders, whose existence intimately depends on the kelp, is wonderful. A great volume might be written, describing the inhabitants of one of these beds of sea-weed. Almost every leaf, excepting those that float on the surface, is so thickly incrusted with coral-lines, as to be of a white colour. We find exquisitely-delicate structures, some inhabited by simple hydra-like polypi, others by more organized kinds, and beautiful compound Ascidiæ. On the flat surfaces of the leaves various patelliform shells, Trochi, uncovered molluscs, and some bivalves are attached. Innumerable crustacea frequent every part of the plant. On shaking the great entangled roots, a pile of small fish, shells, cuttle-fish, crabs of all orders, sea-eggs, star-fish, beautiful Holuthuriæ (some taking the external form of the nudibranch molluscs), Planariæ, and crawling nereidous animals of a multitude of forms, all fall out together. Often as I recurred to a branch of the kelp, I never failed

Strait of Magellan

to discover animals of new and curious structures. In Chiloe, where, as I have said, the kelp did not thrive very well, the numerous shells, coral-lines, and crustacea were absent; but there yet remained a few of the flustraceæ, and some compound Ascidiæ; the latter, however, were of different species from those in Tierra del Fuego. We here see the fucus possessing a wider range than the animals which use it as an abode.

I can only compare these great aquatic forests of the southern hemisphere with the terrestrial ones in the intertropical regions. Yet if the latter should be destroyed in any country, I do not believe nearly so many species of animals would perish, as, under similar circumstances, would happen with the kelp. Amidst the leaves of this plant numerous species of fish live, which nowhere else would find food or shelter; with their destruction the many cormorants, divers, and other fishing birds, the otters, seals, and porpoises, would soon perish also; and lastly, the Fuegian savage, the miserable lord of this miserable land, would redouble his cannibal feast, decrease in numbers, and perhaps cease to exist.

June 8th – We weighed anchor early in the morning, and left Port Famine. Captain FitzRoy determined to leave the Strait of Magellan by the Magdalen channel, which had not long been discovered. Our course lay due south, down that gloomy passage which I have before alluded to, as appearing to lead to another and worse world. The wind was fair, but the atmosphere was very thick; so that we missed much curious scenery. The dark ragged clouds were rapidly driven over the mountains, from their summits nearly to their bases. The glimpses which we caught through the dusky mass were highly interesting: jagged points, cones of snow, blue glaciers, strong outlines marked on a lurid sky, were seen at different distances and heights. In the midst of such scenery we anchored at Cape Turn, close to Mount Sarmiento, which was then hidden in the clouds. At the base of the lofty and almost perpendicular sides of our little cove, there was one deserted wigwam, and it alone reminded us that man sometimes wandered in these desolate regions. But it would be difficult to imagine a scene where he seemed to have less claims, or less authority. The inanimate works of nature – rock, ice, snow, wind, and water – all warring with each other, yet combined against man – here reigned in absolute sovereignty.

JUNE 9TH – In the morning we were delighted by seeing the veil of mist gradually rise from Sarmiento, and display it to our view. This mountain, which is one of the highest in Tierra del Fuego, has an elevation of 6,800 feet. Its base, for about an eighth of its total height, is clothed by dusky woods, and above this a field of snow extends to the summit. These vast piles of snow, which never melt, and seem destined to last as long as the world holds together, present a noble and even sublime spectacle. The outline of the mountain was admirably clear and defined. Owing to the abundance of light reflected from the white and glittering surface, no shadows are cast on any part; and those lines which intersect the sky can alone be distinguished: hence the mass stood out in the boldest relief. Several glaciers descended in a winding course, from the snow to the sea-coast: they may be likened to great frozen Niagaras; and perhaps these cataracts of blue ice are to the full as beautiful as the moving ones of water. By night we reached the western part of the channel; but the water was so deep that no anchorage could be found. We were in consequence obliged to stand off and on, in this narrow arm of the sea, during a pitch-dark night of fourteen hours long.

JUNE 10TH – In the morning we made the best of our way into the open Pacific. The Western coast generally consists of low, rounded, quite barren, hills of granite and greenstone. Sir John Narborough called one part South Desolation, because it is 'so desolate a land to behold'; and well indeed might he say so. Outside the main islands there are numberless scattered rocks, on which the long swell of the open ocean incessantly rages. We passed out between the East and West Furies, and a little further northward there are so many breakers that the sea is called the Milky Way. One sight of such a coast is enough to make a landsman dream for a week about shipwreck, peril, and death; and with this sight, we bade farewell for ever to Tierra del Fuego.

1. BOCCACCIO · *Mrs Rosie and the Priest*
2. GERARD MANLEY HOPKINS · *As kingfishers catch fire*
3. *The Saga of Gunnlaug Serpent-tongue*
4. THOMAS DE QUINCEY · *On Murder Considered as One of the Fine Arts*
5. FRIEDRICH NIETZSCHE · *Aphorisms on Love and Hate*
6. JOHN RUSKIN · *Traffic*
7. PU SONGLING · *Wailing Ghosts*
8. JONATHAN SWIFT · *A Modest Proposal*
9. *Three Tang Dynasty Poets*
10. WALT WHITMAN · *On the Beach at Night Alone*
11. KENKŌ · *A Cup of Sake Beneath the Cherry Trees*
12. BALTASAR GRACIÁN · *How to Use Your Enemies*
13. JOHN KEATS · *The Eve of St Agnes*
14. THOMAS HARDY · *Woman much missed*
15. GUY DE MAUPASSANT · *Femme Fatale*
16. MARCO POLO · *Travels in the Land of Serpents and Pearls*
17. SUETONIUS · *Caligula*
18. APOLLONIUS OF RHODES · *Jason and Medea*
19. ROBERT LOUIS STEVENSON · *Olalla*
20. KARL MARX AND FRIEDRICH ENGELS · *The Communist Manifesto*
21. PETRONIUS · *Trimalchio's Feast*
22. JOHANN PETER HEBEL · *How a Ghastly Story Was Brought to Light by a Common or Garden Butcher's Dog*
23. HANS CHRISTIAN ANDERSEN · *The Tinder Box*
24. RUDYARD KIPLING · *The Gate of the Hundred Sorrows*
25. DANTE · *Circles of Hell*
26. HENRY MAYHEW · *Of Street Piemen*
27. HAFEZ · *The nightingales are drunk*
28. GEOFFREY CHAUCER · *The Wife of Bath*
29. MICHEL DE MONTAIGNE · *How We Weep and Laugh at the Same Thing*
30. THOMAS NASHE · *The Terrors of the Night*
31. EDGAR ALLAN POE · *The Tell-Tale Heart*
32. MARY KINGSLEY · *A Hippo Banquet*
33. JANE AUSTEN · *The Beautifull Cassandra*
34. ANTON CHEKHOV · *Gooseberries*
35. SAMUEL TAYLOR COLERIDGE · *Well, they are gone, and here must I remain*
36. JOHANN WOLFGANG VON GOETHE · *Sketchy, Doubtful, Incomplete Jottings*
37. CHARLES DICKENS · *The Great Winglebury Duel*
38. HERMAN MELVILLE · *The Maldive Shark*
39. ELIZABETH GASKELL · *The Old Nurse's Story*
40. NIKOLAY LESKOV · *The Steel Flea*

41. HONORÉ DE BALZAC · *The Atheist's Mass*
42. CHARLOTTE PERKINS GILMAN · *The Yellow Wall-Paper*
43. C.P. CAVAFY · *Remember, Body...*
44. FYODOR DOSTOYEVSKY · *The Meek One*
45. GUSTAVE FLAUBERT · *A Simple Heart*
46. NIKOLAI GOGOL · *The Nose*
47. SAMUEL PEPYS · *The Great Fire of London*
48. EDITH WHARTON · *The Reckoning*
49. HENRY JAMES · *The Figure in the Carpet*
50. WILFRED OWEN · *Anthem For Doomed Youth*
51. WOLFGANG AMADEUS MOZART · *My Dearest Father*
52. PLATO · *Socrates' Defence*
53. CHRISTINA ROSSETTI · *Goblin Market*
54. *Sindbad the Sailor*
55. SOPHOCLES · *Antigone*
56. RYŪNOSUKE AKUTAGAWA · *The Life of a Stupid Man*
57. LEO TOLSTOY · *How Much Land Does A Man Need?*
58. GIORGIO VASARI · *Leonardo da Vinci*
59. OSCAR WILDE · *Lord Arthur Savile's Crime*
60. SHEN FU · *The Old Man of the Moon*
61. AESOP · *The Dolphins, the Whales and the Gudgeon*
62. MATSUO BASHŌ · *Lips too Chilled*
63. EMILY BRONTË · *The Night is Darkening Round Me*
64. JOSEPH CONRAD · *To-morrow*
65. RICHARD HAKLUYT · *The Voyage of Sir Francis Drake Around the Whole Globe*
66. KATE CHOPIN · *A Pair of Silk Stockings*
67. CHARLES DARWIN · *It was snowing butterflies*
68. BROTHERS GRIMM · *The Robber Bridegroom*
69. CATULLUS · *I Hate and I Love*
70. HOMER · *Circe and the Cyclops*
71. D. H. LAWRENCE · *Il Duro*
72. KATHERINE MANSFIELD · *Miss Brill*
73. OVID · *The Fall of Icarus*
74. SAPPHO · *Come Close*
75. IVAN TURGENEV · *Kasyan from the Beautiful Lands*
76. VIRGIL · *O Cruel Alexis*
77. H. G. WELLS · *A Slip under the Microscope*
78. HERODOTUS · *The Madness of Cambyses*
79. *Speaking of Siva*
80. *The Dhammapada*

'Then she began to run, and she ran over the sharp stones and through the thorns, and the wild animals bounded past her . . .'

JACOB LUDWIG KARL GRIMM
Born 1785 in Hanau, Hesse-Kassel
Died 1863 in Berlin, Germany

WILLIAM KARL GRIMM
Born 1786 in Hanau, Hesse-Kassel
Died 1859 in Berlin, Germany

Taken from David Luke's translation of *Selected Tales*, first published in 1982.

BROTHERS GRIMM IN PENGUIN CLASSICS
Selected Tales

BROTHERS GRIMM

The Robber Bridegroom

Translated by
David Luke

PENGUIN BOOKS

PENGUIN CLASSICS

UK | USA | Canada | Ireland | Australia
India | New Zealand | South Africa

Penguin Books is part of the Penguin Random House group of companies whose addresses can be found at global.penguinrandomhouse.com.

This selection published in Penguin Classics 2015

010

Translation copyright © 1982 by David Luke

The moral right of the translator has been asserted

Set in 9.5/13 pt Baskerville 10 Pro
Typeset by Jouve (UK), Milton Keynes
Printed in Great Britain by Clays Ltd, Elcograf S.p.A.

A CIP catalogue record for this book is available from the British Library

ISBN: 978–0–141–39857–0

www.greenpenguin.co.uk

Penguin Random House is committed to a sustainable future for our business, our readers and our planet. This book is made from Forest Stewardship Council® certified paper.

Contents

The Master Huntsman	1
The Robber Bridegroom	9
The Devil's Three Golden Hairs	15
The Six Servants	25
The Bremen Town Band	35
Snowwhite	40
Lazy Harry	52

The Master Huntsman

Once upon a time there was a young fellow who had learnt the locksmith's trade, and he told his father that he would like to go out into the world now and try his luck. 'Yes,' said his father, 'that suits me,' and he gave him some money to take with him. So he travelled around looking for work. After a time he began to find that the locksmith's trade was not to his liking and no longer suited him, but he fancied the idea of hunting. On his wanderings he met a huntsman in a green coat, who asked him where he had come from and where he was going. The lad replied that he was a journeyman locksmith, but that he no longer cared for the trade and would like to learn hunting instead; would the huntsman take him on as an apprentice? 'Oh yes, if you'll come along with me.' So the young lad went with him, signed on with him for several years and learnt hunting. After that he wanted to go out and try his luck again, and the huntsman gave him an air-gun instead of wages, but it was a special kind of gun: if he shot with it he would never miss. So he set off and presently came to a very large forest. There was no reaching the end of it in one day, so when evening fell he perched on a tall tree to be out of reach of the wild beasts. At about midnight he thought he saw a faint light gleaming some way off; he peered at it through the branches and noted carefully where it was; then he took off his hat and threw it down in the direction of the light, to mark which way he should walk when he got down from the tree. Then he climbed down, walked towards his hat, put it on again and continued in the same direction. The further he walked the bigger the light grew, and when he got near it he saw that it was an enormous fire, and round it sat three giants who had spitted an ox and were roasting it. And one of them said: 'Let me just taste whether the meat's done yet.' And he tore off a piece and was about to put it in his mouth when the huntsman shot it out of his hand. 'Well, look at that,' said the giant, 'the wind blew the meat right out of my hand.' And he pulled off another piece, but just as he was going to take a bite the huntsman shot it away too. At this the giant slapped his neighbour's face and exclaimed angrily: 'Will you stop snatching my food!' 'I didn't snatch it,' said the other, 'I think it was shot down by a sniper.' The giant took a third piece, but the moment he had it in his hand the huntsman shot it down too. The giants said to each other: 'That must be a good marksman if he can shoot the meat right out of our mouths; he'd be useful to us.' And they shouted: 'Come on over here, sharpshooter, sit down at the fire with us and eat your fill, we won't touch you; but if you

The Master Huntsman

don't come and we fetch you by force, that'll be the end of you.' So the lad came over to them and told them he was a trained huntsman, and that whatever he took aim at with his gun he would hit it without fail. Then they said that if he would go along with them he would be well looked after. They told him that on the far side of the forest there was a wide river, and beyond it stood a tower, and in the tower lived a beautiful princess whom they intended to carry off. 'All right,' he said, 'I'll soon get hold of her for you.' 'But there's a snag in it,' they added. 'There's a little dog there, and it starts barking as soon as anyone comes near the place, and as soon as it barks everyone at the king's court wakes up, and that's why we can't get in. Will you undertake to shoot the dog?' 'Yes,' he answered, 'that's child's play to me.' Then he took a boat and crossed the water, and when he was about to land the little dog came running towards him and was just going to bark when he seized his gun and shot it dead. When the giants saw this they were delighted, thinking the princess was as good as theirs; but the huntsman first wanted to see how things stood, and told them to wait outside till he called them. Then he went into the castle; there was not a sound to be heard and everyone was asleep. In the first room he entered there was a sword hanging on the wall: it was made of pure silver, and on it was a golden star and the king's name, and beside it on a table lay a sealed letter. He opened the letter, which said that whoever had the sword would be able to kill any enemy he met. So he took the sword from the wall, buckled it on and went further till he came to the room where the princess was lying asleep: and she was so beautiful that he stopped and gazed at her and held his breath. He said to himself: 'It would be wrong to let those savage giants get an innocent maiden into their power: they have wicked intentions.' He looked round again and saw a pair of slippers under her bed: on the right slipper was her father's name and a star and on the left her own name and a star. And she was wearing a long silk kerchief embroidered in gold, with her father's name on the right side and on the left her own name, all embroidered in golden letters. Then the huntsman took a pair of scissors and cut off the right-hand end of the kerchief and put it in his knapsack, into which he also put her right slipper with the king's name on it. Now the maiden was still lying there asleep, and she was all sewn into her nightgown: so he cut off a small piece of her nightgown and put it with the other things, but all this he did without touching her. Then he left her to sleep on in peace, and when he got back to the gate the giants were still out there waiting for him, thinking he would bring the princess to them. But he called out to them to come in, saying that the princess was already in his power, and that he couldn't open the door for them but that there was a hole they must crawl through. So when the first of them came to the hole the huntsman wound the giant's hair round his hand, pulled his head through, drew his sword and cut it off with one

The Master Huntsman

blow; then he pulled the whole body in. After this he called to the second giant and cut his head off too, and finally he did the same to the third. Feeling glad to have saved the beautiful princess from her enemies, he cut out the giants' tongues and put them in his knapsack. After that he thought: I'll go home to my father and show him what I've done already, then I'll travel about in the world; if God has good fortune in store for me, it'll come to me sooner or later.

But in the castle the king woke up and saw the three giants lying there dead. He went to his daughter's bedchamber, woke her up and asked her who it could have been that had killed the giants. She said: 'Father dear, I don't know, I was asleep.' Then when she got up and was going to put on her slippers she found the right slipper missing, and when she looked at her kerchief she found that the right-hand end of it was missing, and when she looked at her nightgown a piece had been cut out of that too. The king ordered the whole court to be assembled, including his soldiers and everyone who was there, and asked who had saved his daughter and killed the giants. Now in his army he had a captain, an ugly one-eyed fellow, and he claimed to have done it. Then the old king said that if he had done such a deed he must also marry his daughter. But the princess said: 'Dear father, rather than marry that man I will go as far away into the world as my legs will carry me.' The king said that if she refused to marry him she must take off her royal garments and put on peasant's clothes and leave the court; and he ordered her to go to a potter and set herself up selling earthenware pots and plates. So she took off her royal garments and went to a potter and borrowed a lot of earthenware crockery from him, promising that if she had sold it by evening she would pay him for it. The king also ordered her to sit down at a street corner and offer it for sale there, and then he arranged with some carters to drive right through the middle of it and break it into a thousand pieces. So when the princess had put out her wares on the street, the carts came and smashed them to smithereens. She began to cry and said: 'Oh God help me, how shall I pay the potter now!' The king had done this in order to force her to marry the captain; but instead she went back to the potter and asked if he would lend her some more things. He refused to do so until she had paid for the first lot. So she went to her father and wept and lamented and said she would go away into the world. So he said: 'I'll have a hut built for you out there in the forest, and you shall live in it for the rest of your life and cook meals for everyone, but you are to accept no payment for them.' When the hut was ready a sign was hung out over the door, and on it was written: 'Free meals today, tomorrow you pay.' She lived in the hut for a long time, and word went round in the world that here was a young lady who cooked free meals and that this was written up over the door. The huntsman heard this story too and thought: This is a chance for me; after all, I'm poor

The Master Huntsman

and I've no money. So he took his air-gun and his knapsack, which still had in it all the things he had once taken away from the castle as proofs, and went into the forest; and sure enough he found the hut with the sign: 'Free meals today, tomorrow you pay.' Wearing the sword with which he had cut off the heads of the three giants, he went in and asked for something to eat. He was delighted to see the beautiful girl; and beautiful she certainly was. She asked where he came from and where he was going and he told her that he was travelling about in the world. Then she asked him where he had got the sword, because it had her father's name on it. He asked if she was the king's daughter. 'Yes,' she answered. 'With this sword,' he said, 'I cut off the heads of three giants.' And as proof he fetched their tongues out of his knapsack, then he showed her the slipper and the pieces he had cut from her kerchief and her nightgown. At this she was overjoyed and said he was the man who had saved her. So they went together to the castle and asked to speak to the old king, and she took him to her bedchamber and told him that it was the huntsman who had really rescued her from the giants. And when the old king saw all the proofs he could no longer doubt it, and said that he was glad to have found out what had happened, and that he would now give his daughter in marriage to the huntsman. The princess consented to this very gladly. Then they gave him fine clothes as if he were a visiting lord, and the king ordered a banquet. At table the captain sat down on the princess's left and the huntsman on her right, and the captain supposed that he was a gentleman from abroad who was visiting them. When they had eaten and drunk, the old king told the captain that he would like to set him a riddle to guess. 'If a man,' said the king, 'were to claim to have killed three giants, and were to be asked where the giants' tongues were, and were to be shown their heads and see that the tongues were missing, what would be the reason for that?' The captain replied: 'I suppose the giants had no tongues.' 'Not so,' said the king, 'every creature has a tongue.' And then he asked the captain what fate such a man would deserve. The captain answered: 'He would deserve to be torn to pieces.' Then the king said: 'You have passed sentence on yourself.' So the captain was arrested and torn apart by four horses; and the princess was married to the huntsman. After the wedding he went and fetched his mother and father, and they lived happily with their son, and after the old king's death he inherited the kingdom.

The Robber Bridegroom

Once upon a time there was a miller who had a beautiful daughter, and when she grew up he was anxious to see her well married and provided for. He thought: If a proper suitor comes along and asks for her hand, he shall have her. Before long a suitor turned up who seemed to be very rich, and since the miller could find nothing against him he promised him his daughter. But the girl didn't really take to him as a girl should to her betrothed bridegroom: she didn't trust him, and her heart contracted with horror every time she looked at him or thought of him. One day he said to her: 'You're my betrothed bride and yet you never even come to visit me.' The girl replied: 'I don't know, sir, where your house is.' And the bridegroom said: 'My house is out there in the dark forest.' She tried to think of excuses and said she wouldn't be able to find the way there. The bridegroom said: 'Next Sunday you must come out to visit me. I've invited the guests already, and to help you find your way through the forest I'll put down a trail of ashes for you.' When Sunday came and she had to set out, she felt afraid without really knowing why, and filled both her pockets with peas and lentils to mark the path. When she came to the edge of the forest, she found that ashes had been scattered and she followed the trail, but at every step, left and right, she threw a few peas on the ground. She walked nearly all day till she came to the middle of the forest, where it was darkest of all, and here she found an isolated house. She didn't like the look of it, it seemed gloomy and sinister. She went in, but there was no one there and everything was very silent. Suddenly a voice called out:

> 'Go home, go home, my lady bride,
> This is a house where murderers hide.'

Looking up, she saw that the voice was that of a bird hanging in a cage on the wall. It called out again:

> 'Go home, go home, my lady bride,
> This is a house where murderers hide.'

Then the fair bride walked on from room to room and explored the whole house, but it was all empty and not a soul was to be seen. Finally she reached the cellar, and there a very old woman was sitting wagging her head. 'Can you not tell me, good woman,' asked the girl, 'whether my bridegroom lives here?' 'Oh, you poor child,' answered the old woman, 'what a place you have strayed to! This is a den of murderers. You think you're a bride

The Robber Bridegroom

soon to be wedded, but it's death you're going to wed. Look, I've had to fill that great cauldron with water and put it on the fire; once they have you in their power, they'll chop you up without mercy and cook you and eat you, for they're eaters of human flesh. If I don't take pity on you and save you, you're lost.'

So saying, the old woman hid the girl behind a huge barrel where she couldn't be seen. 'Be as quiet as a mouse,' she said, 'don't move and don't stir, or it'll be the end of you. In the night, when the robbers are asleep, we'll escape; I've waited long enough for a chance myself.' Scarcely had she said this when the godless crew returned home. They were dragging another young maiden with them; they were drunk, and paid no heed to her screams and lamentations. They gave her some wine to drink, three glasses full, one of white and one of red and one of yellow, and that made her heart burst. Then they tore off her pretty clothes, laid her out on a table, hacked her fair body to pieces and sprinkled them with salt. The poor bride hidden behind the barrel trembled and shuddered, for she saw clearly what a fate the robbers had had in store for her. One of them noticed a gold ring on the murdered girl's little finger, and as it didn't come off at once when he pulled, he took an axe and chopped the finger off. But the finger jumped up into the air and jumped right over the barrel and fell straight into the bride's lap. The robber took a candle and began looking for it, but he couldn't find it. Then another of them said: 'Did you look behind the big barrel as well?' But the old woman exclaimed: 'Come along and eat, and leave searching till tomorrow; the finger won't run away.'

The robbers said: 'The old woman's right,' and stopped looking for it and sat down to their supper; and the old woman poured a sleeping draught into their wine, so that they were soon lying down in the cellar asleep and snoring. When the bride heard this, she came out from behind the barrel. She had to step over the sleeping men, who were lying on the ground in rows, and she was terrified that she might wake one up. But God helped her and she got past them safely. The old woman came upstairs with her and opened the door, and they hurried away from that murderers' den as fast as they could. The wind had blown away the ash trail, but the peas and lentils had sprouted up and showed them the way in the moonlight. They walked all night and reached the mill in the morning, and the girl told her father everything that had happened.

When the day came on which the wedding was to take place the bridegroom appeared, and the miller had had all his friends and relatives invited. As they sat at dinner, everyone in turn was asked to tell a story. The bride sat silent and didn't speak a word. Then the bridegroom said to her: 'Well, my love, can you think of nothing? Why don't you tell us a story too?' She answered: 'I will tell

The Robber Bridegroom

you a dream I had. I was walking alone through a forest and finally came to a house with not a living soul in it, but on a wall there was a bird in a cage that called out:

> "Go home, go home, my lady bride,
> This is a house where murderers hide."

It said these words to me twice. My dear, it was only a dream. Then I explored all the rooms, and they were all empty and it was all so uncanny; finally I went down to the cellar and found a very old woman sitting there wagging her head. I asked her: "Does my bridegroom live in this house?" She answered: "Oh, you poor child, you have come to a den of murderers; your bridegroom lives here, but he intends to chop you up and kill you and then cook you and eat you." My dear, it was only a dream. But the old woman hid me behind a big barrel, and no sooner was I hidden there than the robbers came home dragging a girl with them. They gave her three kinds of wine to drink, white and red and yellow, and that made her heart burst. My dear, it was only a dream. Then they pulled off her pretty clothes, chopped her fair body in pieces on a table and sprinkled them with salt. My dear, it was only a dream. And one of the robbers saw that on her ring-finger there was still a gold ring, and because it was hard to get off he took an axe and chopped it off; but the finger jumped up into the air and jumped right over the big barrel and fell into my lap. And here is the finger with the ring on it.' So saying, she took it out and showed it to the company.

The robber, who had turned white as a sheet as she told her story, jumped up and tried to escape, but the guests seized him and handed him over to the authorities. Then he and his whole band were brought to justice for their foul deeds.

The Devil's Three Golden Hairs

Once upon a time there was a poor woman who gave birth to a little son, and because he came into the world with a caul it was prophesied that in his fourteenth year he would marry the king's daughter. Soon after this it happened that the king came to that village and no one knew it was the king, and when he asked the people what had been happening recently, they answered: 'There was a child born the other day with a caul, and that'll bring him luck in everything he does. It's even been prophesied that in his fourteenth year he'll marry the king's daughter.' The king, who had a wicked heart and was angered by this prophecy, went to the parents, pretended to be very friendly and said: 'You poor folk, let me have your child, I'll look after him well.' At first they refused, but the stranger offered to pay a lot of money for the boy, and they thought: He's a fortune-child, so it's bound to turn out all right for him anyway. So in the end they consented and handed him over.

The king put the child in a box and rode off with him till he came to a deep river; and here he threw the box into the water, thinking: Well, I've rid my daughter of that unexpected suitor. But the box didn't sink, it floated like a little boat, and not a drop of water got into it. It drifted downstream as far as a mill within two leagues of the king's capital, and here it got caught against the dam. Luckily a miller's boy was standing there and noticed it, and he pulled it ashore with a hook, thinking he had found a treasure chest; but when he opened it, there lay a fine little boy looking as fresh as a daisy. He took him to the miller and his wife, and as they had no children of their own they were delighted and said: 'He's a gift from God.' They took good care of the foundling, and he grew up as good as gold.

It so happened that one day the king came into the mill to shelter from a storm, and he asked the miller and his wife whether the big sturdy boy was their son. 'No,' they answered, 'he's a foundling. Fourteen years ago he came floating down to the mill dam in a box, and our servant pulled him out of the water.' Then the king realized this was the very same fortune-child he had thrown into the river, and he said: 'Good people, could the lad not take a letter for me to the queen? I'll pay him two gold pieces.' 'As my lord the king commands,' they replied, and told the boy to be ready to leave. Then the king wrote a letter to the queen which said: 'As soon as the boy carrying this letter arrives, he is to be killed and buried, and all that is to be over and done with before I get back.'

The boy set out with this letter, but lost his way and in

The Devil's Three Golden Hairs

the evening found himself in a great forest. In the darkness he saw a faint light, made his way towards it and came to a small house. When he entered, an old woman was sitting by the fire all by herself. She was startled to see the lad and said: 'Where are you from and where are you going?' 'I'm from the mill,' he answered, 'and I'm on my way to the queen with a letter I have to take to her; but I've lost my way in the forest, so I'd like to stay the night here.' 'You poor boy,' said the woman, 'this house belongs to a gang of robbers, and when they get home they'll kill you.' 'I don't mind who comes,' said the boy, 'I'm not afraid; but I'm so tired that I can't go any further.' And he lay down on a bench and went to sleep. Presently the robbers came in and asked angrily what strange boy this was lying there. The old woman said: 'Oh, he's just an innocent child, he's got lost in the wood, so I felt sorry for him and let him stay. He's been told to take a letter to the queen.' The robbers opened the letter and read it, and found that it said that as soon as the boy arrived he was to be put to death. At this the hard-hearted robbers took pity on him, and their leader tore up the letter and wrote another which said that as soon as the boy arrived he was to be married to the king's daughter. Then they let him lie there in peace till the next morning, and when he woke up they gave him the letter and showed him the right way. But when the queen had received the letter and read it, she did what it told her to do: she ordered a magnificent wedding feast and the princess was married to the fortune-child. And since he was a handsome and good-natured young man, she was quite happy and content to live with him.

After a time the king came back to his palace and saw that the prophecy had been fulfilled and that the fortune-child was married to his daughter. 'How did this come about?' he demanded. 'I gave quite different orders in my letter.' So the queen handed him the letter and invited him to see for himself what was in it. The king read the letter and saw at once that it had been exchanged for the other one. He asked the young man what had happened to the letter he had been given, and why he had brought a different one instead. 'I know nothing about it,' the boy answered. 'It must have been exchanged during the night, when I was sleeping in the forest.' The king said in a rage: 'You shan't get away with it as easily as that. Anyone who wants my daughter for his wife has got to go down into Hell and fetch me three golden hairs from the Devil's head. That's what I want, and if you bring them to me you shall keep my daughter.' The king hoped in this way to be rid of him for ever. But the fortune-child answered: 'I'll fetch the golden hairs, I'm not afraid of the Devil.' With that he took his leave and began his journey.

His road took him to a great city, where the watchman at the gate questioned him about his trade and about what he knew. 'I know everything,' replied the fortune-child. 'In that case you can do us a favour,' said the

The Devil's Three Golden Hairs

watchman. 'You can tell us why the fountain in our market place that used to have wine running out of it has dried up, so that we don't even get water from it now.' 'I'll tell you that,' he answered, 'but you must wait till I return.' Then he went on and came to another city, and again the watchman at the gate asked him what his trade was and what he knew. 'I know everything,' he answered. 'Then you can do us a favour and tell us why a tree in our city that used to bear golden apples doesn't even grow leaves any more.' 'I'll tell you that,' he answered, 'but you must wait till I return.' Then he went on and came to a wide river that he had to cross. The ferryman asked him what his trade was and what he knew. 'I know everything,' he answered. 'Then you can do me a favour,' said the ferryman, 'and tell me why I have to keep on pushing this boat to and fro and no one ever takes over the job from me.' 'I'll tell you that,' he answered, 'but you must wait till I return.'

When he had crossed the river he found the entrance to Hell. Everything inside was black and sooty, and the Devil wasn't at home, but there sat his grandmother in a big armchair. 'What do you want?' she asked him, and she didn't look all that fierce. 'I'd like three golden hairs, please, from the Devil's head,' he answered, 'otherwise I won't be allowed to keep my wife.' 'That's a bold request,' said she. 'If the Devil comes home and finds you here, you'll be for it; but I'm sorry for you, so I'll see if I can help you.' She changed him into an ant and said: 'Crawl into the fold of my skirt, you'll be safe there.' 'Yes,' he answered, 'that's all right, but there are three things I'd like to know as well: why has a fountain that used to flow with wine dried up, so that it doesn't even give water now? And why has a tree that used to bear golden apples even stopped growing leaves? And why is it that a ferryman has to keep on crossing the river and no one ever takes over the job from him?' 'Those are hard questions,' she answered, 'but just keep quiet and stay still and pay attention to what the Devil says when I pull his three golden hairs out.'

When evening fell the Devil came home, and he'd no sooner entered than he noticed that things were not as usual. 'I smell human flesh, I smell it,' he said. 'There's something going on here.' Then he searched in every corner but couldn't find anything. His grandmother scolded him. 'I've only just done the sweeping,' she said, 'and tidied the whole place, and now you're messing it all up again. You're forever smelling human flesh! Sit down and eat your supper.' When he had eaten and drunk, he felt tired and lay down with his head in his grandmother's lap and told her to pick some of the lice out of his hair. It wasn't long before he fell asleep and started puffing and snoring. Then the old woman seized a golden hair, tweaked it out and laid it down beside her. 'Ow!' shrieked the Devil, 'what do you think you're doing?' 'I had a bad dream,' his grandmother answered, 'so I grabbed at your hair.' 'Well, what were you dreaming about?' asked the

The Devil's Three Golden Hairs

Devil. 'I dreamt there was a fountain in a market place, and wine used to come from it, but now it's dried up and won't even give them water; what can be the reason for that?' 'Ho, ho, if only they knew!' answered the Devil. 'There's a toad sitting under a stone in the well; if they kill it the wine will flow again all right.' His grandmother picked out some more of his lice till he fell asleep and started snoring fit to shake the windows. Then she tweaked out the second golden hair. 'Ow-wow! What are you doing?' shrieked the Devil in a rage. 'Never mind, never mind,' she said. 'I did it in my sleep, I was dreaming.' 'What were you dreaming about this time?' he asked. 'I dreamt about a kingdom where there was a fruit-tree that used to bear golden apples, and now it won't even grow leaves. I wonder what can have caused that?' 'Ho ho, if only they knew!' answered the Devil. 'There's a mouse gnawing at its root; if they kill the mouse the golden apples will soon grow again, but if it goes on gnawing the whole tree will wither. And now leave me in a peace, you and your dreams; if you wake me up again I'll box your ears.' His grandmother spoke to him soothingly and picked out some more lice till he was asleep and snoring. Then she seized the third golden hair and tweaked it out. The Devil jumped up with a yell and began to set about her, but she calmed him down again and said: 'How can one help having bad dreams!' 'What have you been dreaming now?' he asked, his curiosity getting the better of him. 'I dreamt there was a ferryman complaining that he has to keep on crossing the river and no one takes over the job from him. What can be the cause of that?' 'Ho ho, the stupid lout!' answered the Devil. 'When someone comes and wants to cross, he must just put the oar into his hand, and then the other man will have to do the ferrying and he'll be free.' So now that his grandmother had plucked out the three golden hairs and the three questions had been answered, she left the old dragon in peace, and he slept till daybreak.

When the Devil had gone out again, the old woman took the ant from the fold in her skirt and gave the fortune-child his human form back. 'Here are the three golden hairs,' she said, 'and I expect you heard what the Devil said about your three questions.' 'Yes,' he answered, 'I heard it all and I'll remember it well.' 'So that's your problem solved,' she said, 'and now you can be off.' He thanked the old woman for her much needed help and climbed up out of Hell, feeling very pleased with his success. When he came to the ferryman, he was asked for his promised answer. 'First take me across,' said the fortune-child, 'and then I'll tell you how you can be released.' And when he had got to the opposite bank, he gave him the Devil's advice: 'Next time someone comes to be ferried across, just put the oar into his hand.' He went on and came to the city where the barren tree was, and there too the watchman demanded his answer. So he told him what he had heard from the Devil: 'Kill the

The Devil's Three Golden Hairs

mouse that's gnawing at its root, and it'll bear golden apples again.' The watchman thanked him, and as a reward gave him two donkeys laden with gold and told them to follow him. Finally he came to the city where the fountain had dried up. So he told the watchman as the Devil had said: 'There's a toad sitting in it under a stone; you must look for it and kill it, and then you'll get plenty of wine from the fountain again.' The watchman thanked him, and he gave him two donkeys laden with gold as well.

Then at last the fortune-child got home to his wife, who was delighted to see him again and to hear how well everything had gone. He took the king what he had asked for, the Devil's three golden hairs, and when the king saw the four donkey-loads of gold he was very pleased indeed and said: 'Now that you have fulfilled all the conditions you can keep my daughter. But, my dear son-in-law, won't you tell me how you came by all that gold? You have brought back very great treasure!' 'I crossed a river,' he answered, 'and that's where I got it from; it's lying all along the bank instead of sand.' 'Could I fetch some for myself as well?' asked the king with great eagerness. 'As much as you want, sir,' replied the young man. 'There's a ferryman on the river, get him to ferry you over and you'll be able to fill your sacks at the other side.' The king, his heart filled with greed, set off in great haste, and when he came to the river he beckoned to the ferryman to take him across. The ferryman came and told him to get into the boat, and when they reached the opposite bank he handed him the oar and jumped out. And after that the king had to go on ferrying as a punishment for his sins.

'Is he still doing it?' 'Why not? I don't suppose anyone has taken the oar from him.'

The Six Servants

Long ago there lived an old queen who was a sorceress and her daughter was the most beautiful maiden under the sun. But the old queen's one idea was to lure people to their destruction, and when a suitor came she would say that any man wanting to marry her daughter must first perform a task, or his life would be forfeit. Many were dazzled by the maiden's beauty and did try their luck, but they failed to perform the task the queen set them, and then they were shown no mercy: they had to kneel at the block and have their heads cut off. Now there was a prince who had also heard of the maiden's beauty, and he said to his father: 'Let me go and try to win her hand.' 'No, no!' said the king, 'if you go, you will be going to your death.' Then his son took to his bed and became mortally ill and lay there for seven years, and no doctor could help him. When his father saw that there was no more hope, he said to him very sorrowfully: 'Go and try your fortune, for I know no other way to help you.' When his son heard that, he rose from his bed fully restored to health, and joyfully set out on his journey.

It happened that as he was riding over open country he saw something on the ground some way off that looked like a huge haystack, and when he got nearer he could see that it was the belly of a man lying on his back, a paunch the size of a small mountain. When the Fat Man saw the traveller he sat up and said: 'If you need someone, sir, then take me into your service.' The prince answered: 'What use can I make of a great unwieldy fellow like you?' 'Oh,' said the Fat Man, 'that's a mere trifle: when I feel really expansive, I'm three thousand times this size.' 'If that's so,' said the prince, 'then I can use you, come along with me.' So the Fat Man came along with the prince, and after a while they found another man lying on the ground with one ear pressed against the grass. 'What are you doing there?' asked the prince. 'I'm listening,' answered the man. 'What are you listening for so attentively?' 'I'm listening to what's going on in the world at this moment, for nothing escapes my ears, I can even hear the grass growing.' The prince asked: 'Tell me, what do you hear at the court of the old queen who has the beautiful daughter?' The man answered: 'I can hear the whistling of a sword through the air as it strikes off a suitor's head.' The prince said: 'I can use you, come along with me.' So they travelled on, and presently they saw a pair of feet lying on the ground, and part of the legs as well, but they couldn't see the other end of whoever they belonged to. When they had gone on quite some distance they came to the body, and finally to the head. 'Well!' said the

The Six Servants

prince. 'What a tall whopper you are!' 'Oh,' said the Tall Man, 'this is nothing: when I really stretch my limbs I'm three thousand times this height, taller than the highest mountain on earth. I'll be glad to serve you, sir, if you'll take me on.' 'Come with us,' said the prince, 'I can use you.' They travelled on and found a man sitting at the roadside with his eyes blindfolded. The prince asked him: 'Have you got such weak eyes that you can't look at the daylight?' 'No,' answered the man, 'I can't take off the blindfold because my eyes are so powerful that when they look at anything it explodes. If that's any use to you, sir, I'll gladly serve you.' 'Come with us,' answered the prince, 'I can use you.' They travelled on and found a man lying in the full heat of the sun shivering with cold and shaking in every limb. 'How can you be shivering in this hot sunshine?' asked the prince. 'Oh dear me,' replied the man, 'I have a quite different constitution: the hotter it is, the colder I get and my bones freeze to the very marrow, but the colder it is the hotter I get. If there's ice all round me I can't bear the heat, and if it's fire I can't stand the cold.' 'You're a strange fellow,' said the prince, 'but if you'd like to serve me, come along with us.' They travelled on and saw a man standing and craning his neck, gazing in all directions and away into the distance. The prince asked: 'What are you so busy looking for?' The man replied: 'I've got such sharp eyes that I can see right beyond all the forests and fields and valleys and mountains and right through the whole world.' The prince said: 'If you'd like to, then come along with me, because you're just what I still needed.'

The prince with his six servants now entered the city where the old queen lived. He didn't tell her who he was, but said: 'Madam, if you will give me your beautiful daughter, I will perform whatever you command me.' The sorceress was glad to have such a handsome youth falling into her snares again, and she said: 'I will set you three tasks, and if you succeed in each of them you shall become my daughter's lord and husband.' 'What is the first task to be?' he asked. 'I want you to fetch me back a ring I dropped into the Red Sea.' So the prince went home to his servants and said: 'The first task's not easy, I'm to fetch a ring out of the Red Sea; now tell me how to do that.' The Sharpsighted Man said: 'I'll find out where it is,' and after looking down into the sea he told them: 'There it is, caught on a jagged piece of rock.' The Tall Man carried them to the shore of the Red Sea and said: 'I could fetch it out all right if I could only see it.' 'Well, if that's the only problem!' exclaimed the Fat Man, and he lay down and put his mouth to the water. The waves poured into it as if into a bottomless pit, and he drank up the whole sea till it was as dry as a field. The Tall Man stooped down slightly and picked up the ring. The prince was delighted once he had it, and he took it to the old queen, who was astonished and said: 'Yes, that's the right ring. You've been successful with your first task, but now here is the second. You see there on the field in front of my castle,

The Six Servants

there are three hundred fat oxen grazing, and these you must devour, skin and bone and hair and horns and all; and down in my cellar there are three hundred casks of wine, which you must drink with the meat; and if you leave so much as one single ox-hair or one little drop of the wine, your life will be forfeit.' The prince said: 'And may I invite no guests? No meal is tasty without company.' The old woman laughed maliciously and replied: 'You may invite one guest to keep you company, but not more than one.'

So the prince went to his servants and said to the Fat Man: 'Today you are to be my guest and eat your fill for once.' So the Fat Man expanded and ate up the three hundred oxen, leaving not so much as a hair, then asked if breakfast was all he was to get. The wine he drank straight from the barrels without needing a glass, and finished it right to the last drop. When the meal was over, the prince went to the old queen and told her that he had performed the second task. She was amazed and said: 'You have done better than any of the others; but there's still one task left.' And she thought: You'll not escape me, you'll not keep your head on your shoulders. 'Tonight,' she said, 'I shall bring my daughter to you in your room, and you shall put your arm round her; but as you sit there with her beware of falling asleep, for I shall come at exactly twelve o'clock, and if she's no longer in your arms then, you will have lost.' The prince thought: This task is easy, I'm sure I'll be able to keep my eyes open; but he called his servants and told them what the old queen had said, adding: 'Who knows what tricks she may be up to? We had better be cautious, and you must keep watch and see to it that once the maiden is in my room she doesn't get out of it again.' When night fell the old woman came with her daughter and left her in the prince's arms; then the Tall Man made a ring of himself and lay down round both of them, and the Fat Man stood in front of the door so that no living soul could get in. So there they both sat, and the maiden didn't speak a word, but the moon shone through the window on to her face so that he could see her wonderful beauty. He did nothing but gaze at her, full of joy and love, and his eyes never once felt weary. That lasted till eleven o'clock; and then the old queen cast a spell on all of them that made them fall asleep, and at the same moment the maiden vanished.

They remained fast asleep till a quarter to twelve, and then the spell lost its power and they all woke up again. 'Alack and alas!' cried the prince, 'now I am lost!' And his faithful servants began to lament as well, but the Listener said: 'Be quiet, let me listen.' And he listened for a moment, then said: 'She's sitting inside a rock three hundred hours journey from here, bewailing her fate. Only you can help her, Tall Man; if you stretch yourself you'll be there in a couple of steps.' 'Yes,' answered the Tall Man, 'but our friend with the powerful eyes must come along as well, so that we can get rid of the rock.' So the

The Six Servants

Tall Man hoisted the Blindfolded Man on to his back, and in an instant, before you could snap your fingers, they had arrived in front of the enchanted rock. At once the Tall Man unbound the eyes of his companion, who merely had to look about him and the rock exploded into smithereens. The Tall Man picked up the princess and carried her back to the palace in no time, then he fetched his companion with equal speed, and before the clock struck twelve they were all sitting there as before, wide awake and in high spirits. When twelve struck, the old sorceress came creeping in with a mocking expression on her face, as if to say: 'Now I've got him.' For she thought her daughter was sitting inside the rock three hundred hours away. But when she saw her daughter in the prince's arms, she was dumbfounded and exclaimed: 'This is a man with more power than I have.' But there was nothing she could say, and she had to consent to let him marry the maiden. But she whispered into her daughter's ear: 'What a disgrace for you to have to obey a common man, and not to be able to take a husband of your own choice.'

At this the maiden's proud heart was filled with anger and she began to plan revenge. Next morning she had three hundred cords of wood piled up, and said to the prince: 'You have performed the three tasks, but I'll not become your wife until one of you is willing to sit in the middle of a fire made of that pile of wood.' She thought: None of his servants will burn himself to death, and for love of me he will sit in it himself, and then I shall be free.' But the servants said: 'We've all done something now except the Freezer, so it's his turn to help.' And they seated him in the middle of the pile of faggots and set it alight. The fire began to burn, and it burnt for three days till it had burnt up all the wood; and when the flames died down, there was the Freezer standing among the ashes trembling like an aspen leaf and saying: 'I've never endured such cold in all my life, I'd have frozen to death if it had gone on longer.'

After this no further excuse could be found, and the beautiful maiden had to accept the unknown young man as her husband. But as they were driving to the church the old queen said: 'I'll not bear the disgrace of it,' and she sent troops after the bride with orders to shoot down all opposition and bring her daughter back to her. But the Listener had pricked up his ears and heard these secret instructions. 'What shall we do?' he asked the Fat Man. The Fat Man knew what to do: he gave one or two belches and spewed out behind the carriage some of the sea water he had drunk. The result was a huge lake in which the troops got stuck and drowned. When the sorceress heard this she sent out her armoured cavalry, but the Listener heard the clanking of their armour and uncovered the eyes of the Blindfolded Man, who gave the enemy a rather sharp look that made them disintegrate like glass. After that they drove on without further interference, and after

The Six Servants

the pair had been wedded in the church the six servants took leave of their master, saying: 'You've got what you wanted, sir, and you no longer need us: we'll travel on and try our luck.'

Half an hour's distance before the royal palace was a village, and outside it a swineherd was tending his pigs. When they arrived here, the prince said to his wife: 'Do you actually know who I am? I am not a prince but a swineherd, and that man there with the pigs is my father. The two of us will have to do our share of the work too and help him to look after them.' Then he stopped with her at an inn, and secretly told the innkeeper and his wife that during the night they were to take her royal clothes away from her. When she woke next morning she had nothing to put on, and the landlady gave her an old skirt and a pair of old woollen stockings, even acting as if this were a great favour and saying: 'If it weren't for your husband, you'd have got nothing from me at all.' Then she believed that he really was a swineherd and kept the pigs with him, and thought: I've deserved this by my pride and arrogance. That lasted a week and she couldn't bear it any longer, for her feet were all covered with sores. Then some servants came and asked if she knew who her husband was. 'Yes,' she answered, 'he's a swineherd and he's just gone out to try and sell some ribbons and laces.' But they said: 'Come with us, we'll take you to him.' And they took her up into the palace, and when she entered the hall her husband was standing there in royal clothing. But she didn't recognize him till he fell on her neck, kissed her and said: 'I suffered so much for you, so I wanted you to suffer a bit for me.' And now the wedding was really celebrated, and your storyteller wishes he'd been there too.

The Bremen Town Band

A man had a donkey who had been patiently hauling sacks of grain to the mill for many a long year, but now his strength was failing and he was becoming less and less fit for work. His master was thinking of sparing his feed and getting rid of him; but the donkey sensed that there was trouble afoot, so he ran away and set out towards Bremen, reckoning that he might get a job there in the town band. When he'd been on his way for a little while, he came across a hound lying by the roadside and panting as if he'd been running very hard. 'Well now, Buster,' asked the donkey, 'what are you puffing and blowing like that for?' 'Oh,' said the dog, 'I'm old and getting weaker day by day, and I'm no good at hunting any more, so my master was going to kill me: and so I ran away, but how shall I earn my living now?' 'I'll tell you what,' said the donkey, 'I'm on my way to Bremen to join the town band: come with me and let them sign you up in it too. I'll play the lute and you can bang the drums.' The dog accepted this invitation, and on they went. Before long they found a cat sitting by the roadside making a face like three rainy days in a row. 'Now then, Mr Whiskerwiper, what's happened to make you look so sour?' asked the donkey. 'How do you expect me to look when my life's in danger?' answered the cat. 'Just because I'm not so young as I was and my teeth aren't as sharp as they used to be and I'd sooner sit by the fire and purr than chase about after mice, my mistress tried to drown me. I managed to escape of course, but now what's to be done and where am I to go?' 'Come with us to Bremen: you sing very good serenades, so they'll take you on in the town band.' The cat thought this a good idea and joined them. Next our three refugees passed a farm, and there was the cock sitting on the gate crowing its head off. 'What a horrible noise you're making,' said the donkey, 'what's it all about?' 'I've been forecasting fine weather,' said the cock, 'because it's today Our Lady does her washing and wants to hang the Christ Child's shirts out to dry; and yet, just because tomorrow's Sunday and guests are coming, my hard-hearted mistress has told the cook that she wants to have me in tomorrow's soup, so I'm to have my head cut off this evening. So now I'm having a good crow while I still can.' 'Nonsense, Redcrest,' said the donkey, 'come along with us instead: we're going to Bremen, and any place'll suit you better than a stewpot. You've got a great voice, and when we all make music together, let me tell you, it'll certainly sound like something.' The cock thought this a sensible proposal, and all four of them went on their way together.

The Bremen Town Band

But they couldn't reach Bremen in one day, and in the evening they came to a forest and decided to spend the night there. The donkey and the dog lay down under a big tree, and the cat and the cock took to its branches, but the cock flew right to the top where he would be safest. Before going to sleep, he took one more look round in all directions and thought he saw a spark of light in the distance, so he called out to his companions that there must be a house not far away because he could see a light burning. The donkey said: 'Then we must get on our feet and go to it, because we've got a pretty poor lodging here.' The dog said he wouldn't mind either if he could have a bone or two, with some meat on them. So they set off in the direction of the light, and soon enough it was getting brighter, and it got bigger and bigger till they came to a well-lit house where a band of robbers lived. The donkey, being the tallest, went up to the window and looked in. 'What do you see, Greyskin?' asked the cock. 'What do I see?' exclaimed the donkey. 'I see a table laid with fine food and drink, and a pack of robbers sitting round it enjoying themselves.' 'That would be something for us,' said the cock. 'Yes, yes, my goodness, I wish we were there!' said the donkey. So the animals put their heads together to decide what would be the best way of driving the robbers out of the house, and at last they thought of a plan. The donkey had to stand with its front feet against the window, the dog had to jump onto the donkey's back and the cat climb onto the dog, and finally the cock flew up and perched on the cat's head. When they had done that, one of them gave a signal, and all together they began making their music: the donkey brayed, the dog barked, the cat mewed and the cock crowed, and then they all crashed into the room through the window, smashing the panes to smithereens. At this bloodcurdling din the robbers started to their feet, thinking some hobgoblin had broken into the house, and rushed out into the wood in a panic. Whereupon our four friends sat down at the table, made the best of what was left, and ate as if they had a month's fast ahead of them.

When our four minstrels had finished their meal, they put out the light and looked for sleeping quarters, each according to his natural needs and preferences. The donkey lay down on the dung-heap, the dog behind the door and the cat near the warm ashes on the hearth, while the cock went to its roost among the rafters; and being tired after their long journey, they soon fell asleep. When midnight was past and the robbers, watching from a safe distance, noticed that the house was now dark and that all seemed quiet, their captain said: 'Well now, we shouldn't have let ourselves be frightened off like that,' and he ordered one of his men to go back to the house and investigate. The man found the whole place lying silent, went into the kitchen to fetch a light, mistook the cat's fiery red eyes for live coals and tried to light a match at them. But the cat wasn't to be trifled with like this, and leapt at his face spitting and scratching. At this he

The Bremen Town Band

panicked, took to his heels and tried to leave by the back door, but the dog was lying there and jumped up and bit him in the leg. He ran for his life across the yard, and just as he was passing the dung-heap he got a mighty kick in the backside from the donkey; meanwhile the cock, perching on its roost and wakened by the noise, began screeching: 'Kikiriki-kee! Kikiriki-kee!' The robber ran back as fast as he could to his captain and said: 'Oh my God, there's some horrible witch sitting in the house who hissed at me and scratched my face with her long nails, and there's a man with a knife standing by the door who stabbed me in the leg, and a black monster in the yard who started beating me with a wooden club, and up in the roof there's the judge sitting, and he called out: "Bring the thief to me! Bring the thief to me!" So I got away while the going was good.' After that the robbers didn't dare enter the house again, but the four members of the Bremen town band so much enjoyed living there that they just stayed on.

> And for many a year this tale has been told;
> The last tongue to tell it's not yet cold.

Snowwhite

Once upon a time, in the middle of winter when the snowflakes were falling from the sky like feathers, a queen sat sewing at a window with a frame of black ebony. And as she sewed and looked up at the falling snow, she pricked her finger with her needle, and into the snow there fell three drops of blood. The red looked so beautiful against the white that she thought to herself: If only I had a child as white as snow, as red as blood and as black as the wood of this window frame! Soon after this she gave birth to a little daughter who was as white as snow, as red as blood and had hair as black as ebony, and for this reason was called 'little Snowwhite'. And when the child was born the queen died.

A year later the king took another wife. She was a beautiful woman, but proud and haughty, and could not bear that anyone else's beauty should excel her own. She possessed a magic mirror, and when she stood in front of it and looked at herself she would say:

> 'Mirror, mirror on the wall,
> Who is the fairest of us all?'

Snowwhite

The mirror would answer:

> 'My lady queen is the fairest of all.'

And this satisfied her, for she knew that the mirror spoke the truth.

But Snowwhite was growing up and becoming more and more beautiful, and by the age of seven she was as lovely as the bright day and more beautiful even than the queen. One day when the queen asked her mirror:

> 'Mirror, mirror on the wall,
> Who is the fairest of us all?'

it answered:

> 'My lady queen is fair to see,
> But Snowwhite is fairer far than she.'

At this the queen took fright and turned yellow and green with envy. From now on, whenever she saw Snowwhite, her heart turned over inside her, she hated the girl so. And envy and pride took root like weeds in her heart and grew higher and higher, giving her no peace by day or night. So she sent for a huntsman and said: 'Take that child out into the forest, I'm sick of the sight of her. You are to kill her and bring me her lungs and liver as proof.' The huntsman obeyed and took Snowwhite with him, but when he had drawn his hunting-knife and was about to thrust it into her innocent heart she began to cry and said: 'Oh, dear huntsman, let me live; I will run away into the wild forest and never come home again.' And because she was so beautiful the huntsman took pity on her and said: 'Run away then, you poor child.' The wild beasts will soon have eaten you, he thought, and yet it was as if a stone had been rolled from his heart because he did not have to kill her. And when a young boar happened to come bounding up he slaughtered it, cut out its lungs and liver and took them to the queen as the proof she wanted. The cook was ordered to stew them in salt, and the wicked woman devoured them, thinking she had eaten the liver and lungs of Snowwhite.

And now the poor child was utterly alone in the huge forest, and so terrified that she gazed at every leaf on the trees, trying to think what to do to save herself. Then she began to run, and she ran over the sharp stones and through the thorns, and the wild animals bounded past her but did not harm her. She ran on as far as her feet would carry her, until it was nearly evening: then she saw a little cottage and went into it to rest. Inside the cottage everything was tiny, but more dainty and neat than you can imagine. There stood a little table with a white tablecloth and seven little plates, every plate with its little spoon, and seven little knives and forks and cups as well. In a row along the wall stood seven little beds all made up with sheets as white as snow. Because she was so hungry and thirsty, Snowwhite ate a little of the vegetables and bread from each plate and drank a sip of wine from each of the cups; for she didn't want to take the whole of

Snowwhite

anyone's supper. Then, because she was so tired, she lay down on one of the little beds – but none of them fitted her: one was too long, the next too short, till finally the seventh was the right size. So in it she stayed, and said her prayers and went to sleep.

When it had got quite dark, the owners of the little house came home: they were the seven dwarfs who worked in the hills, hacking and digging out precious metal. They lit their seven lamps, and as soon as there was light in the cottage they saw that someone had been there, because not everything was exactly as they had left it. The first said: 'Who's been sitting on my chair?' The second said: 'Who's been eating from my plate?' The third said: 'Who's taken some of my bread?' The fourth said: 'Who's eaten some of my vegetables?' The fifth said: 'Who's been poking with my fork?' The sixth said: 'Who's been cutting with my knife?' The seventh said: 'Who's been drinking out of my cup?' Then the first of them looked round and saw that there was a little hollow on his bed, and he said: 'Who's stepped on my bed?' The others came running up and exclaimed: 'Someone's been in mine too.' But when the seventh looked at his bed he saw Snowwhite lying there asleep. And he called the others, who came running up and cried out in amazement; they fetched their seven little lamps and shone them on Snowwhite. 'Oh goodness me! Oh goodness me!' they cried. 'What a lovely girl!' And they were so delighted that they didn't wake her, but let her go on sleeping in the little bed. But the seventh dwarf slept with his companions, one hour with each of them, and so the night passed.

When it was morning Snowwhite woke up, and when she saw the seven dwarfs she was scared. But they spoke to her kindly and asked her what her name was. 'I'm called Snowwhite,' she replied. 'How did you get into our house?' asked the dwarfs. So she told them how her stepmother had tried to have her killed, but that the huntsman had spared her life, and then she had wandered all day till finally she found their cottage. The dwarfs said: 'If you will keep house for us, and do the cooking and the beds and the washing and the sewing and the knitting, and keep everything neat and tidy, you can stay with us and you shan't want for anything.' 'Yes,' said Snowwhite, 'I'd like that very much.' So she stayed with them, and looked after their cottage. In the morning they went into the hills and dug for ore and gold, in the evening they came back and their supper had to be ready. The young girl was by herself all day, and the kind dwarfs warned her and said: 'Beware of your stepmother, she will soon find out that you are here; don't on any account let anyone in.'

But after the queen, as she supposed, had eaten Snowwhite's liver and lungs, her first thought was she was again the most beautiful of all women, and she stood before her mirror and said:

> 'Mirror, mirror on the wall,
> Who is the fairest of us all?'

Snowwhite

And the mirror answered:

> 'My lady queen is fair to see:
> But Snowwhite lives beyond the hills,
> With the seven dwarfs she dwells,
> And fairer far than the queen is she.'

Then the queen took fright, for she knew that the mirror never told a lie, and she realized that the huntsman had deceived her and that Snowwhite was still alive. So she began plotting and planning again how to kill her; for so long as she was not the fairest of all, her envy never left her in peace. And having finally thought of a plan, she painted her face and disguised herself as an old pedlar-woman, and no one could have recognized her. In this disguise she went over the seven hills to the house of the seven dwarfs, knocked at the door and called out: 'Fine wares for sale, for sale!' Snowwhite peeped out of the window and called to her: 'Good day, old lady, what have you got to sell?' 'Fine wares, lovely things,' she answered, 'laces of all colours' – and she fetched out one that was made of many-coloured silk. I can let in this honest woman, thought Snowwhite, and she unbolted the door and bought the pretty lace. 'My child,' said the old woman, 'how untidy you look! Come, I'll lace you up properly.' Snowwhite suspected nothing, stood in front of the old woman and let herself be laced with the new lace; but the old woman laced her up very fast and pulled the lace so tight that Snowwhite's breath was stopped and she fell down as if dead. 'Now you're no longer the fairest of us all,' said the queen and hurried out.

Not long after, when evening fell, the seven dwarfs came home: but what a fright they got when they saw their dear little Snowwhite lying on the ground, not moving or stirring, as if she were dead! They lifted her up, and seeing that she was laced too tightly they cut the laces – then she began to breathe a little, and gradually she came back to life. When the dwarfs heard what had happened they said: 'That old pedlar-woman was the godless queen and no one else – be on your guard and let no one in here when we're not with you.'

But when the evil woman got home, she went to her mirror and asked:

> 'Mirror, mirror on the wall,
> Who is the fairest of us all?'

And the mirror answered as before:

> 'My lady queen is fair to see:
> But Snowwhite lives beyond the hills,
> With the seven dwarfs she dwells,
> And fairer far than the queen is she.'

When the queen heard that, she was so startled that all the blood rushed to her heart, for she saw very well that Snowwhite had come to life again. 'But now,' she said, 'I'll think out something that will deal with you once and for all.' And by the witchcraft she knew she made a

Snowwhite

poisoned comb. Then she disguised herself and took the form of another old woman. And again she went over the seven hills to the house of the seven dwarfs, knocked at the door and called out: 'Fine wares for sale, for sale!' Snowwhite peeped out and said: 'Go away, I'm not allowed to let anyone in.' 'Surely they'll allow you to take a look,' said the old woman, and pulled out the poisoned comb and held it up. The young girl liked it so much that she let herself be fooled and opened the door. When they had agreed on a price the old woman said: 'Now I'll comb your hair properly for you.' Poor Snowwhite suspected nothing and let the old woman have her way; but she had hardly stuck the comb into her hair when its poison worked and the young girl fell senseless to the ground. 'That's done for you now, my beauty queen,' said the wicked woman, and off she went. But fortunately it was nearly evening and the seven little dwarfs were coming home. When they saw Snowwhite lying on the floor as good as dead, they suspected her stepmother at once, and searched and found the poisoned comb, and as soon as they had pulled it out of her hair Snowwhite revived and told them what had happened. Then they warned her again to be on her guard and not to open the door to anyone.

Back home the queen stood before her mirror and said:

> 'Mirror, mirror on the wall,
> Who is the fairest of us all?'

And it answered as before:

> 'My lady queen is fair to see:
> But Snowwhite lives beyond the hills,
> With the seven dwarfs she dwells,
> And fairer far than the queen is she.'

When she heard the mirror say this, she trembled and shook with fury. 'Snowwhite shall die,' she cried, 'even if it costs me my own life.' With that she went to a completely secret remote room which no one else ever entered, and there she made an apple filled with deadly poison. Outwardly it looked like a beautiful white-and-red-cheeked apple which made everyone who saw it want to take a bite out of it, but anyone who did so was doomed. When the apple was ready, she painted her face and disguised herself as a peasant woman, and then she went over the seven hills to the house of the seven dwarfs. When she knocked, Snowwhite put her head out of the window and said: 'I can't let anyone in, the seven dwarfs have told me I mustn't.' 'That's all right,' answered the peasant woman, 'I'll have no difficulty selling my apples. Here, I'll make you a present of one.' 'No,' said Snowwhite, 'I'm not allowed to take anything.' 'Are you afraid it's poisoned?' said the old woman. 'Look here, I'll cut the apple in two: you eat the red cheek and I'll eat the white one.' But the apple was so cunningly made that only the red cheek was poisoned. Snowwhite was longing to eat this lovely apple, and when she saw the peasant woman doing so she could resist no longer, put her hand out and took the poisoned half. But no sooner did she have a bite in her mouth than she fell to the floor dead. Then the queen gazed at her gloatingly and laughed a dreadful laugh and said: 'White as snow, red as blood, black as ebony! This time the dwarfs won't wake you.' And when she got home and asked the mirror:

> 'Mirror, mirror on the wall,
> Who is the fairest of us all?'

it at last answered:

> 'My lady queen is the fairest of all.'

And then her envious heart was at rest, if an envious heart ever can be.

When the dwarfs came home in the evening, they found Snowwhite lying on the ground, and not a breath stirring from her mouth, and she was dead. They lifted her up, looked all over her for something poisonous, unlaced her, combed her hair, washed her with water and wine, but it was all no good: the sweet girl was dead and dead she stayed. They laid her on a bier, and all seven sat by it and mourned her and wept for her for three days. Then they were going to bury her, but she still looked as fresh as a living person and still had her lovely red cheeks. They said: 'This is something we can't bury in the black earth,' and they had a transparent glass coffin made so that she could be seen from all sides; they laid her in it, and on it in letters of gold they wrote her name, and that she was a princess. Then they put the coffin out on the hill, and one of them always sat by it keeping watch. And the animals came too and mourned Snowwhite, first an owl, then a raven, and then a little dove.

So Snowwhite lay in her coffin for a long, long time; she didn't go bad, but just looked as if she were asleep, for she was still as white as snow, as red as blood and her hair was as black as ebony. Then it happened that a prince strayed into the forest and arrived at the dwarfs' house to spend the night there. He saw the coffin on the hill with the lovely Snowwhite inside, and read what was written on it in letters of gold. And he said to the dwarfs: 'Let me have that coffin, I'll pay you whatever you ask for it,' but the dwarfs answered: 'We wouldn't sell it for all the gold in the world.' So he said: 'Then give it to me, for I can't live without seeing Snowwhite, and I will honour her and treasure her as my dearest possession.' When he said that, the kind little dwarfs took pity on him and gave him the coffin. So the prince told his servants to carry it away on their shoulders. And it happened that they stumbled against a shrub and gave the coffin such a jolt that the lump of poisoned apple which Snowwhite had bitten off was jerked out of her throat. And presently she opened her eyes, pushed up the lid of the coffin and sat up and was alive again. 'Oh goodness, where am I?' she exclaimed. The prince's heart leapt with joy and he said: 'You are with me.' And he told her what had happened and said: 'I love you more than anything in the world: come with me to my father's palace, and you shall be my wife.' And Snowwhite liked him and went with him, and their wedding was prepared with great splendour and magnificence.

But Snowwhite's godless stepmother was asked to the feast too. So when she had put on beautiful clothes, she stood before the mirror and said:

> 'Mirror, mirror on the wall,
> Who is the fairest of us all?'

And the mirror answered:

> 'My lady queen is fair to see:
> But the young queen is fairer far than she.'

At this the evil woman shrieked out a curse and was beside herself with fear. At first she decided not to go to the wedding at all, but the thing preyed on her mind and she just had to go to see the young queen. And when she entered she recognized Snowwhite and stood rooted to the spot with fright and terror. But already a pair of iron slippers had been heated over glowing coals and they were brought in with tongs and placed before her. Then she had to put her feet into the red-hot shoes and dance till she dropped dead.

Lazy Harry

Harry was so lazy that although he had nothing else to do but drive his goat out to graze every day, he still heaved many a sigh when he got back home in the evening after completing his day's labours. 'What a weary job it is,' he would say, 'what a terrible burden, year after year, driving that goat out into the fields every day till Michaelmas! If I could even lie down and take a nap while she feeds! But no, I've got to keep my eyes open or she'll damage the young trees, or squeeze through a hedge into someone's garden, or even run away altogether. What sort of a life is that? No peace of mind, no relaxation.' He sat down and collected his thoughts and tried to work out some way of getting this burden off his back. For a long time all his ponderings were in vain, then suddenly the scales seemed to fall from his eyes. 'I know what I'll do!' he exclaimed. 'I'll marry Fat Katie; she's got a goat as well, so she can take mine out with hers and I won't have to go on wearing myself to a shadow like this.'

So Harry got up, set his weary limbs in motion and walked right across the street, for it was no further than

Lazy Harry

that to where Fat Katie's parents lived; and there he asked for the hand of their hard-working, virtuous daughter. Her parents didn't stop to think twice; 'Like to like makes a good match,' they remarked, and gave their consent. So now Fat Katie became Harry's wife and drove both the goats out to graze. Harry spent his days very pleasantly, with nothing more strenuous to recover from than his own idleness. He only went out with her now and then, saying: 'I'm just doing this so that I'll enjoy my bit of a rest afterwards all the more; you lose all your appreciation of it otherwise.'

But Fat Katie was no less idle than Harry. 'Harry dear,' she said one day, 'why should we needlessly make our lives a misery like this and spoil the best years of our youth? Those two goats wake us out of our best morning sleep anyway with their bleating: wouldn't it be better to give them both to our neighbour and get a beehive from him in exchange? We'll put up the beehive in a sunny place behind the house and just leave it to look after itself. Bees don't need to be minded and taken out to graze: they'll fly out and find their own way home and make honey, without our having to raise a finger.' 'You're a very sensible girl,' answered Harry, 'and we'll do as you suggest right away. What's more, honey's tastier than goat's milk and it does you more good and you can store it for longer.'

The neighbour willingly gave them a beehive in exchange for their two goats. The bees flew in and out tirelessly from early in the morning till late in the evening and filled the hive with the finest honey, so that in the autumn Harry was able to collect a whole jar of it.

They stood the jar on a shelf that was fixed to the wall above their bed; and fearing that someone might steal it or the mice might get at it, Katie fetched in a sturdy hazel rod and put it at the bedside, so that she wouldn't have to bestir herself unnecessarily but just reach for it and drive away any unwelcome visitors without having to get up.

Lazy Harry didn't like to rise before midday: 'Too soon out of bed and you'll soon be dead,' he would remark. So there he was one morning, still lolling among the feathers in broad daylight, having a good rest after his long sleep, and he said to his wife: 'Women have a sweet tooth, and you've been at that honey again: I think our best plan, before it all gets eaten up by you, would be to give it in exchange for a goose and a young gander.' 'But not till we have a child to mind them!' replied Fat Katie. 'You don't suppose I'd want to be bothered with young goslings, needlessly wearing out my strength?' 'And do you suppose,' said Harry, 'that the boy will look after geese? Nowadays children don't do what they're told any more, they do just as they please, because they think they're cleverer than their parents, just like that farmhand who was sent to fetch a cow and started chasing three blackbirds.' 'Well then,' answered Katie, 'this one had better look out if he doesn't do as I tell him. I'll take a

Lazy Harry

stick to him and give his hide a real good tanning. Watch me, Harry!' she exclaimed in her excitement, seizing the stick she kept to drive away the mice, 'watch me beat the backside off him!' She lifted the stick, but unfortunately struck the honey-jar above the bed. The jar was knocked against the wall and fell to smithereens, and all that fine honey went trickling over the floor. 'Well, so much for the goose and the young gander,' said Harry, 'we shan't have to mind them now. But it's a bit of luck that the jar didn't fall on my head; we've every cause to be content with our lot.' And seeing that some honey was still left in one of the fragments, he reached out and picked it up and said cheerfully: 'Wife, let's enjoy the little that's left over here, and then take a bit of a rest after the fright we've had. What does it matter if we get up a little later than usual, the day's still long enough.' 'Oh yes,' answered Katie, 'better late than never. You know the one about the snail that was invited to the wedding? It set out and got there in time for the christening. And just outside the house it fell from the top of a fence, and said to itself: "More haste, less speed."'

1. BOCCACCIO · *Mrs Rosie and the Priest*
2. GERARD MANLEY HOPKINS · *As kingfishers catch fire*
3. *The Saga of Gunnlaug Serpent-tongue*
4. THOMAS DE QUINCEY · *On Murder Considered as One of the Fine Arts*
5. FRIEDRICH NIETZSCHE · *Aphorisms on Love and Hate*
6. JOHN RUSKIN · *Traffic*
7. PU SONGLING · *Wailing Ghosts*
8. JONATHAN SWIFT · *A Modest Proposal*
9. *Three Tang Dynasty Poets*
10. WALT WHITMAN · *On the Beach at Night Alone*
11. KENKŌ · *A Cup of Sake Beneath the Cherry Trees*
12. BALTASAR GRACIÁN · *How to Use Your Enemies*
13. JOHN KEATS · *The Eve of St Agnes*
14. THOMAS HARDY · *Woman much missed*
15. GUY DE MAUPASSANT · *Femme Fatale*
16. MARCO POLO · *Travels in the Land of Serpents and Pearls*
17. SUETONIUS · *Caligula*
18. APOLLONIUS OF RHODES · *Jason and Medea*
19. ROBERT LOUIS STEVENSON · *Olalla*
20. KARL MARX AND FRIEDRICH ENGELS · *The Communist Manifesto*
21. PETRONIUS · *Trimalchio's Feast*
22. JOHANN PETER HEBEL · *How a Ghastly Story Was Brought to Light by a Common or Garden Butcher's Dog*
23. HANS CHRISTIAN ANDERSEN · *The Tinder Box*
24. RUDYARD KIPLING · *The Gate of the Hundred Sorrows*
25. DANTE · *Circles of Hell*
26. HENRY MAYHEW · *Of Street Piemen*
27. HAFEZ · *The nightingales are drunk*
28. GEOFFREY CHAUCER · *The Wife of Bath*
29. MICHEL DE MONTAIGNE · *How We Weep and Laugh at the Same Thing*
30. THOMAS NASHE · *The Terrors of the Night*
31. EDGAR ALLAN POE · *The Tell-Tale Heart*
32. MARY KINGSLEY · *A Hippo Banquet*
33. JANE AUSTEN · *The Beautifull Cassandra*
34. ANTON CHEKHOV · *Gooseberries*
35. SAMUEL TAYLOR COLERIDGE · *Well, they are gone, and here must I remain*
36. JOHANN WOLFGANG VON GOETHE · *Sketchy, Doubtful, Incomplete Jottings*
37. CHARLES DICKENS · *The Great Winglebury Duel*
38. HERMAN MELVILLE · *The Maldive Shark*
39. ELIZABETH GASKELL · *The Old Nurse's Story*
40. NIKOLAY LESKOV · *The Steel Flea*

41. HONORÉ DE BALZAC · *The Atheist's Mass*
42. CHARLOTTE PERKINS GILMAN · *The Yellow Wall-Paper*
43. C.P. CAVAFY · *Remember, Body . . .*
44. FYODOR DOSTOEVSKY · *The Meek One*
45. GUSTAVE FLAUBERT · *A Simple Heart*
46. NIKOLAI GOGOL · *The Nose*
47. SAMUEL PEPYS · *The Great Fire of London*
48. EDITH WHARTON · *The Reckoning*
49. HENRY JAMES · *The Figure in the Carpet*
50. WILFRED OWEN · *Anthem For Doomed Youth*
51. WOLFGANG AMADEUS MOZART · *My Dearest Father*
52. PLATO · *Socrates' Defence*
53. CHRISTINA ROSSETTI · *Goblin Market*
54. *Sindbad the Sailor*
55. SOPHOCLES · *Antigone*
56. RYŪNOSUKE AKUTAGAWA · *The Life of a Stupid Man*
57. LEO TOLSTOY · *How Much Land Does A Man Need?*
58. GIORGIO VASARI · *Leonardo da Vinci*
59. OSCAR WILDE · *Lord Arthur Savile's Crime*
60. SHEN FU · *The Old Man of the Moon*
61. AESOP · *The Dolphins, the Whales and the Gudgeon*
62. MATSUO BASHŌ · *Lips too Chilled*
63. EMILY BRONTË · *The Night is Darkening Round Me*
64. JOSEPH CONRAD · *To-morrow*
65. RICHARD HAKLUYT · *The Voyage of Sir Francis Drake Around the Whole Globe*
66. KATE CHOPIN · *A Pair of Silk Stockings*
67. CHARLES DARWIN · *It was snowing butterflies*
68. BROTHERS GRIMM · *The Robber Bridegroom*
69. CATULLUS · *I Hate and I Love*
70. HOMER · *Circe and the Cyclops*
71. D. H. LAWRENCE · *Il Duro*
72. KATHERINE MANSFIELD · *Miss Brill*
73. OVID · *The Fall of Icarus*
74. SAPPHO · *Come Close*
75. IVAN TURGENEV · *Kasyan from the Beautiful Lands*
76. VIRGIL · *O Cruel Alexis*
77. H. G. WELLS · *A Slip under the Microscope*
78. HERODOTUS · *The Madness of Cambyses*
79. *Speaking of Siva*
80. *The Dhammapada*

'I hate and I love. And if you ask me how, I do not know: I only feel it, and I'm torn in two.'

GAIUS VALERIUS CATULLUS
Born *c.* 84 BCE
Died *c.* 54 BCE

Taken from Peter Whigham's translation of *The Poems*,
first published in 1966.

CATULLUS IN PENGUIN CLASSICS
The Poems

CATULLUS

I Hate and I Love

Translated by
Peter Whigham

PENGUIN BOOKS

PENGUIN CLASSICS

UK | USA | Canada | Ireland | Australia
India | New Zealand | South Africa

Penguin Books is part of the Penguin Random House group of companies
whose addresses can be found at global.penguinrandomhouse.com.

This selection published in Penguin Classics 2015
011

Translation copyright © Peter Whigham, 1966

The moral right of the translator has been asserted

Set in 9/12.4 pt Baskerville 10 Pro
Typeset by Jouve (UK), Milton Keynes
Printed and bound in Great Britain by Clays Ltd, Elcograf S.p.A.

A CIP catalogue record for this book is available from the British Library

ISBN: 978-0-141-39859-4

www.greenpenguin.co.uk

Penguin Random House is committed to a
sustainable future for our business, our readers
and our planet. This book is made from Forest
Stewardship Council® certified paper.

1

To whom should I present this
little book so carefully polished
but to you, Cornelius, who have always
been so tolerant of my verses,
                              you
who of us all has dared
to take the whole of human history
as his field
            – three doctoral and weighty volumes!
Accept my book, then, Cornelius
for what it's worth,
            and may the Muse herself
turn as tolerant an eye upon these songs
            in days to come.

5

Lesbia
    live with me
& love me so
we'll laugh at all
the sour-faced strict-
ures of the wise.
This sun once set
will rise again,
when our sun sets
follows night &
an endless sleep.
Kiss me now a
thousand times &
now a hundred
more & then a
hundred & a
thousand more again
till with so many
hundred thousand
kisses you & I
shall both lose count
nor any can
from envy of
so much of kissing
put his finger
on the number

I Hate and I Love

of sweet kisses
you of me &
I of you,
  darling, have had.

6

Your most recent acquisition, Flavius,
must be as unattractive as
                       (doubtless) she is unacceptable
or you would surely have told us about her.
You are wrapped up with a whore to end all whores
and ashamed to confess it.
                       You do not spend bachelor nights.
Your divan, reeking of Syrian unguents,
draped with bouquets & blossoms etc.
                       proclaims it,
the pillows & bedclothes indented in several places,
a ceaseless jolting & straining of the framework
the shaky accompaniment to your sex parade.
Without more discretion your silence is pointless.
Attenuated thighs betray your preoccupation.
Whoever, whatever she is, good or bad,
                       tell us, my friend –
Catullus will lift the two of you & your love-acts into the heavens
in the happiest of his hendecasyllables.

7

Curious to learn
how many kiss-
es of your lips
might satisfy
my lust for you,
Lesbia, know
as many as
are grains of sand
between the oracle
of sweltering Jove
at Ammon &
the tomb of old
Battiades the First,
in Libya
where the silphium grows;
alternatively,
as many as
the sky has stars
at night shining
in quiet upon
the furtive loves
of mortal men,
as many kiss-
es of your lips
as these might slake
your own obsessed
Catullus, dear,

Catullus

        so many that
        no prying eye
        can keep the count
        nor spiteful tongue fix
        their total in
        a fatal formula.

8

Break off
>> fallen Catullus
>>>> time to cut losses,
bright days shone once,
>> you followed a girl
>>>> here & there
loved as no other
>> perhaps
>>>> shall be loved,
then was the time
>> of love's *insouciance*,
>>>> your lust as her will
matching.
>> Bright days shone
>>>> on both of you.
Now,
>> a woman is unwilling.
>>>> Follow suit
weak as you are
>> no chasing of mirages
>>>> no fallen love,
a clean break
>> hard against the past.
>>>> Not again, Lesbia.
No more.
>> Catullus is clear.
>>>> He won't miss you.

Catullus

    He won't crave it.
        It is cold.
             But you will whine.
    You are ruined.
        What will your life be?
             Who will 'visit' your room?
    Who uncover that beauty?
        Whom will you love?
             Whose girl will you be?
    Whom kiss?
        Whose lips bite?
             Enough. Break.
    Catullus.
        Against the past.

9

Veraniolus,
first of friends,
have you returned
to your own roof
your close brothers
& your mother
still alive? In-
deed it's true you're
back again &
safe & sound
among us all.
So now I'll watch
& listen to your
anecdotes of
Spanish men &
Spanish places
told as only
you can tell them.
I shall embrace
your neck & kiss
you on the mouth
& on the eyes,
Veraniolus . . .

Catullus

> Of all light-hearted
> men & women
> none is lighter-
> hearted than Cat-
> ullus is to-day.

11

Furius, Aurelius, friends of my youth,
whether I land up in the Far East,
where the long-drawn roll of the Indian Ocean
        thumps on the beach,
or whether I find myself surrounded by Hyrcanians,
the supple Arabs, Sacians, Parthian bowmen,
or in the land where the seven-tongued Nile
        colours the Middle Sea,
whether I scale the pinnacles of the Alps
viewing the monuments of Caesar triumphant,
the Rhine, the outlandish seas of
        the ultimate Britons,
whatever Fate has in store for me,
equally ready for anything,
I send Lesbia this valediction,
        succinctly discourteous:
live with your three hundred lovers,
open your legs to them all (simultaneously)
lovelessly dragging the guts out of each of them
        each time you do it,
blind to the love that I had for you
once, and that you, tart, wantonly crushed
as the passing plough-blade slashes the flower
        at the field's edge.

13

I shall expect
you in to dine
a few days hence
Fabullus mine,
and we'll eat well
enough, my friend,
if you provide
the food & wine
& the girl, too,
pretty & willing.
I, Catullus,
promise you
wine & wit &
all the laughter
of the table
should you provide
whatever food
or wine you're able.
For, charmed Fabullus,
your old friend's purse
is empty now
of all but cobwebs!

In return, the
distillation
of Love's essence
take from me, or

I Hate and I Love

whatever's more
attractive or
seductive than
Love's essence. For
Venus & her
Cupids gave my
girl an unguent,
this I'll give to
you, Fabullus, and
when you've smelt it
all you'll want the
gods to do is
*make you one
gigantic nose
to smell it, always, with.*

14

If, my irrepressible Calvus, I didn't
happen to love you more than my eyes
this hoax gift of yours would have made me
as cross as Vatinius . . .

    What have I done to deserve
such (& so many) poets?

    I am utterly demoralised.
May the gods scowl on whoever
sent you this clutch of offenders
in the first place.

    – A grateful client?
I smell Sulla, the pedagogue.
A *recherché* & freshly culled volume,
such as this, could well come from his hands.
And that's as it should be – a meet &
acceptable sign that your efforts
(on his behalf) are not wasted.
But the collection itself is implacably bad.
And you, naturally, sent it along to Catullus
– your Saturnalian *bonne-bouche* –
so that Gaius, on this of all days,
might suffer the refinements of tedium.
No. Little Calvus. You won't run away
with this – for tomorrow, when the shops open,
I shall comb the bookstalls for Caesius, Aquinus,
Suffenus – all who excel in unpleasantness –

and compound your present with interest.
Until then, hence from my home, hence
by the ill-footed porter who brought you.
Parasites of our generation. Poets I blush for.

32

Call me to you
at siesta
we'll make love
my gold & jewels
my treasure trove
my sweet Ipsíthilla,
when you invite
me lock no doors
nor change your mind
& step outside
but stay at home
& in your room
prepare yourself
to come nine times
straight off together,
in fact if you
should want it now
I'll come at once
for lolling on
the sofa here
with jutting cock
and stuffed with food
I'm ripe for stuffing
                              you,
my sweet Ipsíthilla.

34

Moving in her radiant care
chaste men and girls moving
wholly in Diana's care
    hymn her in this.

Latona's daughter, greatest
of the Olympian race, dropped
at birth beneath the olive trees
    on Delian hills,

alive over mountain passes,
over green glades and
sequestered glens,
    – in the talkative burn,

Juno Lucina in the groans
of parturition, Hecat, fearful at crossed ways, the nymph
    of false moonlight.

You whose menstrual course
divides our year, stuff
the farmer's harvest barn
    with harvesting.

Sacred, by whatever name invoked
in whatever phase you wear, turn
upon our Roman brood, of old
    your shielding look.

37

Nine posts, five doors, up the Clivus
        Victoriae, stands an
unsavoury resort . . . unsavoury
        habitués inside,
who think that only they have cocks,
        that only they can ruffle
a pudendum, the rest of us
        as apt as goats. I could
cheerfully bugger you all while
        you wait, kicking your heels.
Your numbers, a hundred or so,
        leave me undaunted. Think
of the man-power involved! And
        think of me now, scribbling
each of your names in black letters
        on the house-front. For she
whom once I loved as no other
        girl has been loved lives here.
Who has fled from my touch & sight.
        Whom I fought for & could
not keep . . . A mixed bunch – successful,
        respectable men swap
places with dregs from the back-streets.
        She is open to all.
And one, who outdoes his home-grown
        rabbits – Egnatius,

I Hate and I Love

the Spaniard with the beard, known for
        his wild dundrearies &
glistening teeth, assiduously
        (with native urine) scrubbed.

38

Angst,
>ennui & angst

consume my days & weeks,
and you have not written
or done anything to soothe my illness.
I am piqued.
>So much for our friendship.

Ah! Cornificius,
>a word from you would cure everything,

though more full of tears
>than a line from Simonides.

39

Because he has bright white teeth, Eg-
        natius whips out a
tooth-flash on all possible
        (& impossible) occasions.
You're in court. Counsel for defence
        concludes a moving per-
oration. (Grin.) At a funeral,
        on all sides heart-broken
mothers weep for only sons. (Grin.)
        Where, when, whatever the
place or time – grin. It could be a
        sort of 'tic'. If so, it's
a very *vulgar* tic, Egnatius,
        & one to be rid of.
A Roman, a Tiburtine or
        Sabine, washes his teeth.
Well-fed Umbrians & over-
        fed Etruscans wash theirs
daily. The dark Lanuvians
        (who don't need to), & we
Veronese, all wash our teeth . . .
        But we keep them tucked in.
We spare ourselves the nadir of
        inanity – inane
laughter. You come from Spain. Spaniards
        use their morning urine

Catullus

>   for tooth-wash. To us that blinding
>   mouthful means one thing &
>   one only – the quantity of
>   urine you have swallowed.

40

Whatever could have possessed you
to impale yourself on my iambics?
What ill-disposed deity inveigled you
Ravidus, into this one-sided contest?
Was it a letch for celebrity,
at no matter what cost?
                      – then you shall have it:
'Ravidus, loving in the place Catullus loves,
is lastingly nailed in this lampoon.'

43

O elegant whore!
>   with the remarkably long nose
unshapely feet
>   lack lustre eyes
fat fingers
>   wet mouth
and language not of the choicest,
you are I believe the mistress
of the hell-rake Formianus.

And the Province calls you beautiful;
they set you up beside my Lesbia.
O generation witless and uncouth!

45

Phyllis Corydon clutched to him
her head at rest beneath his chin.
He said, 'If I don't love you more
than ever maid was loved before
I shall (if this the years not prove)
in Afric or the Indian grove
some green-eyed lion serve for food.'
> *Amor, to show that he was pleased,*
> *approvingly (in silence) sneezed.*

Then Phyllis slightly raised her head
(her lips were full & wet & red)
to kiss the sweet eyes full of her:
'Corydon mine, with me prefer
always to serve unique Amor:
my softer flesh the fire licks
more greedily and deeper sticks.'
> *Amor, to show that he was pleased,*
> *approvingly (in silence) sneezed.*

So loving & loved so, they rove
between twin auspices of Love.
Corydon sets in his eye-lust
Phyllis before all other dust;
Phyllis on Corydon expends
her nubile toys, Love's dividends.
Could Venus yield more love-delight
than here she grants in Love's requite?

46

Now spring bursts
        with warm airs
now the *furor* of March skies
        retreats under Zephyrus . . .
and Catullus will forsake
        these Phrygian fields
the sun-drenched farm-lands of Nicaea
& make for the resorts of Asia Minor,
        the famous cities.
Now, the trepidation of departure
        now lust of travel,
feet impatiently urging him to be gone.
Good friends, good-bye,
        we, met in this distant place,
far from our Italy
        who by divergent paths
must find our separate ways home.

48

Iuventius,
were I allowed
to kiss your eyes
as sweet as honey
on & on, three
thousand kisses
would not seem
too much for me,
as many as
ripe harvest ears
of sheaves of corn
would still not be
too much of kiss-
ing you, for me.

50

The other day we spent,
Calvus, at a loose end
flexing our poetics.
Delectable twin poets,
swapping verses, testing
form & cadence, fishing
for images in wine
& wit. I left you late,
came home still burning with
your brilliance, your invention.
Restless, I could not eat,
nor think of sleep. Under
my eyelids you appeared
& talked. I twitched, feverishly,
looked for morning . . . at last,
debilitated, limbs
awry across the bed
I made this poem of
my ardour & for our
gaiety, Calvus . . . Don't
look peremptory, or
contemn my apple. Think.
The Goddess is ill-bred
exacts her hubris-meed:
lure not her venom.

51

Godlike the man who
sits at her side, who
watches and catches
    that laughter
which (softly) tears me
to tatters: nothing is
left of me, each time
    I see her,
. . . tongue numbed; arms, legs
melting, on fire; drum
drumming in ears; head-
    lights gone black.

Coda

Her ease is your sloth, Catullus
you itch & roll in her ease:

former kings and cities
lost in the valley of her arm.

58

Lesbia, our Lesbia, the same old Lesbia,
Caelius, she whom Catullus loved once
more than himself and more than all his own,
loiters at the cross-roads
                        and in the backstreets
ready to toss-off the 'magnanimous' sons of Rome.

65

Although entangled in prolonged grief
severed from the company of the Muses
and far from Pieria
>   my brain children still-born
myself among Stygian eddies
the eddies plucking at the pallid foot
of a brother
>   who lies under Dardanian soil
stretched by the coastland
>   whom none may now hear
none touch
>   shuttered from sight
whom I treasured more than this life
and shall –
>   in elegies of loss
plaintive as Procne crying under the shadow of the cypress
for lost Itylus,
>   I send, Hortalus, mixed with misery
Berenice's Lock –
>   clipped from Callimachus
for you might think my promise
had slipped like vague wind through my head
or was like the apple
>   unavowed
the girl takes from her lover
>   thrusts into her soft bodice

Catullus

and forgets there . . .
        till her mother takes her off guard –
she is startled,
        the love-fruit trundles ponderously across the
                floor
and the girl, blushing, stoops gingerly
                        to pick it up.

68

Borne down by bitter misfortune
you send me this letter, Manlius,
blotted with tears,
> it comes like flotsam
from a spumy sea –
> from the shipwreck of your affairs –
a cry from the undertow . . .
and that you,
> whom Venus deprives
of soft sleep,
> whom the Greek Muse
no longer tempts,
> who turn restlessly
in an empty bed,
> call me 'my friend',
that you look to Catullus
> for love-gifts of Venus
& of the Holy Muses,
> is a gift in itself,
but your own tears blind you to mine.
I am not neglectful of friendship,
but we two squat in the same coracle,
we are both swamped by the same stormy waters,
I have not the gifts of a happy man . . .
Often enough,
> when a man's toga first sat on my shoulders

Catullus

I chased love & the Muses,
> in the onset of youth
the tart mixture of Venus
> seeming sweet,
but a brother's death
> drove a young man's kickshaws
into limbo –
> I have lost you, my brother
and your death has ended
> the spring season
of my happiness,
> our house is buried with you
& buried the laughter that you taught me.
There are no thoughts of love nor of poems
in my head
> since you died.
Hence, Manlius
> the reproach in your Roman letter
leaves me unmoved:
> 'Why loiter in Verona,
Catullus, where
> for men of our circle
cold limbs in an empty bed
> are the rule –
not the exception?'
> Forgive me, my friend
but the dalliance of love
> that you look for
has been soured by mourning.
> As for a poem . . .

I Hate and I Love

our tastes call for my Greek books,
        and those are at home
where we both live
        and where our years pile up,
in Rome . . .
        I have few copies of anything by me.
One case only has followed me North.
There is nothing curmudgeonly here –
on whom do you think
        I would sooner lavish
love-gifts of Venus
        & gifts of the Holy Muses
than you?
        You have turned to a friend
& the friend's hands are empty . . .
How can I give what I have not got?
        [. . .]
        [Abridged.]

70

Lesbia says she'd rather marry me
than anyone,
       though Jupiter himself came asking
or so she says,
       but what a woman tells her lover in desire
should be written out on air & running water.

72

There was a time, Lesbia, when
you confessed only to Catullus in love:
you would set me above Jupiter himself.
I loved you then
         not as men love their women
but as a father his children – his family.
To-day I know you too well
         and desire burns deeper in me
and you are more coarse
         more frivolous in my thought.
'How,' you may ask, 'can this be?'
Such actions as yours excite
         increased violence of love,
Lesbia, but with friendless intention.

73

Cancel, Catullus, the expectancies of friendship
cancel the kindnesses deemed to accrue there:
kindness is barren, friendship breeds nothing,
only the weight of past deeds growing oppressive
as Catullus has discovered, bitter & troubled,
in one he had once accounted a unique friend.

75

Reason blinded by sin, Lesbia,
a mind drowned in its own devotion:
come clothed in your excellences –
I cannot think tenderly of you,
sink to what acts you dare –
I can never cut this love.

76

If evocations of past kindness shed
ease in the mind of one of rectitude,
of bond inviolate, who never in abuse of God
led men intentionally to harm,
such, as life lasts, must in Catullus shed
effect of joy from disregarded love.
For what by man can well in act or word
be done to others has by me been done
sunk in the credit of an unregarding heart.
Why protract this pain? why not resist
yourself in mind; from this point inclining
yourself back, breaking this fallen love
counter to what the gods desire of men?
Hard suddenly to lose love of long use,
hard precondition of your sanity
regained. Possible or not, this last
conquest is for you to make, Catullus.
May the pitying gods who bring
help to the needy at the point of death
look towards me and, if my life were clean,
tear this malign pest out from my body
where, a paralysis, it creeps from limb to limb
driving all former laughter from the heart.
I do not now expect – or want – my love returned,
nor cry to the moon for Lesbia to be chaste:
only that the gods cure me of this disease
and, as I once was whole, make me now whole again.

77

Whom I have trusted to no end (Rufus)
other than expense of evil knowledge
has come to the ambush,
        inflamed viscera,
raped all that was precious.
Here was poison in rape of life
        here was disease of love.
Witness the chaste mouth of a chaste woman
soiled by loathsome saliva –
        not with impunity:
your acts shall to succeeding ages
be by the bent Sibyl broadcast, in accents of infamy.

79

They nickname Lesbia's brother 'pulcher',
        naturally
since she prefers him to Catullus & the Catulli;
but let him dispose as he will of Catullus
        (& the Catulli)
when he finds three men of distinction
        willing to greet him in public.

83

Lesbia is extraordinarily vindictive
about me in front of her husband
who is thereby moved to fatuous laughter –
a man mulishly insensitive, failing to grasp
that a mindless silence (about me) spells safety
while to spit out my name in curses, baring
her white teeth, means she remembers me, and
what is more pungent still, is scratching the wound
ripening herself while she talks.

84

'*H*advantageous' breathes Arrius heavily
              when he means 'advantageous',
intending 'artificial' he labours '*h*artificial',
convinced he is speaking impeccably while
he blows his 'h's about most '*h*artificially'.
One understands that his mother – his uncle –
his family, in fact, on the distaff side
spoke so.
         Fortunately he was posted to Syria
and our ears grew accustomed to normal speech again,
unapprehensive for a while of such words
until suddenly the grotesque news reaches us
that the Ionian Sea has become
                      since the advent of Arrius
no longer Ionian
        but (inevitably) *H*ionian.

85

I hate and I love. And if you ask me how,
I do not know: I only feel it, and I'm torn in two.

86

We have heard of Quintia's beauty. To me she is tall, slender
and of a white 'beauty'. Such things I freely admit;
but such things do not constitute beauty.
    In her there is nothing of Venus,
not a pinch of love spice in her long body.
While Lesbia, Lesbia is loveliness indeed.
    Herself of particular beauty
has she not plundered womanhead of all its graces,
    flaunting them as her adornment?

87

No woman loved, in truth, Lesbia
    as you by me;
no love-faith found so true
    as mine in you.

91

In this hopeless & wasting love of mine
I trusted you for one reason, Gellius:
not because I knew you well
        nor respected your constancy
nor thought you able (or willing) to rinse out your mind
but merely because the woman for whom
this compulsive desire is eating me
happens to be neither your mother
        nor sister
nor any other close female relative.
In spite of our intimacy I did not believe
you would find here incentive for action.
– You did,
        in the overwhelming attraction
pure sin holds for you, Gellius,
        or anything smacking of sin.

96

If, Calvus, effects of grief
        affect
those enigmatic sepulchres
        of former love
& spent friendships,
        lamented & evoked in our desire,
reflect, her early death
        will never grieve Quintilia
half so much
        as your long love must make her gay.

99

Purloining while you played in honeyed youth
a kiss, sweeter than one suspects ambrosia tastes,
I paid, Iuventius, in full:
                      an hour or more
you racked me with my own self-exculpations
your loathing left untouched by tears.
No sooner had I kissed you
                      than with every finger
in every corner of your mouth
                      you washed & rubbed
all contact of my lips
                like the slaver of some syphilitic whore
away. More:
        you gave me, fallen, to an enemy
                      – Amor
who has not since ceased to rack me in his own usage,
so that a purloined kiss
                once ambrosial,
is changed to one more acid than acid hellbane tastes.
Met with such strong despite of love
                      my fallen love
shall from this day no kisses more purloin.

101

Journeying over many seas & through many countries
I come dear brother to this pitiful leave-taking
the last gestures by your graveside
the futility of words over your quiet ashes.
Life cleft us from each other
pointlessly depriving brother of brother.
Accept then, in our parents' custom
these offerings, this leave-taking
echoing for ever, brother, through a brother's tears.
                              – 'Hail & Farewell'.

104

Do you really believe I could blacken my life,
the woman dearer to me than my two eyes?
If I could
      I should not be sunk in this way in my love for her –

who performs a zoo of two-backed beasts,
daily with Tappo.

107

If ever anyone anywhere, Lesbia, is looking
               for what he knows will not happen
and then unexpectedly it happens –
                       the soul is astonished,
as we are now in each other,
               an event dearer than gold,
for you have restored yourself, Lesbia, desired
restored yourself, longed for, unlooked for,
                    brought yourself back
to me. White day in the calendar!
               Who happier than I?
What more can life offer
   than the longed for unlooked for event when it happens?

109

Joy of my life! you tell me this –
that nothing can possibly break this love of ours for each
    other.

God let her mean what she says,
                              from a candid heart,
that our two lives may be linked in their length
day to day,
        each to each,
in a bond of sacred fidelity.

1. BOCCACCIO · *Mrs Rosie and the Priest*
2. GERARD MANLEY HOPKINS · *As kingfishers catch fire*
3. *The Saga of Gunnlaug Serpent-tongue*
4. THOMAS DE QUINCEY · *On Murder Considered as One of the Fine Arts*
5. FRIEDRICH NIETZSCHE · *Aphorisms on Love and Hate*
6. JOHN RUSKIN · *Traffic*
7. PU SONGLING · *Wailing Ghosts*
8. JONATHAN SWIFT · *A Modest Proposal*
9. *Three Tang Dynasty Poets*
10. WALT WHITMAN · *On the Beach at Night Alone*
11. KENKŌ · *A Cup of Sake Beneath the Cherry Trees*
12. BALTASAR GRACIÁN · *How to Use Your Enemies*
13. JOHN KEATS · *The Eve of St Agnes*
14. THOMAS HARDY · *Woman much missed*
15. GUY DE MAUPASSANT · *Femme Fatale*
16. MARCO POLO · *Travels in the Land of Serpents and Pearls*
17. SUETONIUS · *Caligula*
18. APOLLONIUS OF RHODES · *Jason and Medea*
19. ROBERT LOUIS STEVENSON · *Olalla*
20. KARL MARX AND FRIEDRICH ENGELS · *The Communist Manifesto*
21. PETRONIUS · *Trimalchio's Feast*
22. JOHANN PETER HEBEL · *How a Ghastly Story Was Brought to Light by a Common or Garden Butcher's Dog*
23. HANS CHRISTIAN ANDERSEN · *The Tinder Box*
24. RUDYARD KIPLING · *The Gate of the Hundred Sorrows*
25. DANTE · *Circles of Hell*
26. HENRY MAYHEW · *Of Street Piemen*
27. HAFEZ · *The nightingales are drunk*
28. GEOFFREY CHAUCER · *The Wife of Bath*
29. MICHEL DE MONTAIGNE · *How We Weep and Laugh at the Same Thing*
30. THOMAS NASHE · *The Terrors of the Night*
31. EDGAR ALLAN POE · *The Tell-Tale Heart*
32. MARY KINGSLEY · *A Hippo Banquet*
33. JANE AUSTEN · *The Beautifull Cassandra*
34. ANTON CHEKHOV · *Gooseberries*
35. SAMUEL TAYLOR COLERIDGE · *Well, they are gone, and here must I remain*
36. JOHANN WOLFGANG VON GOETHE · *Sketchy, Doubtful, Incomplete Jottings*
37. CHARLES DICKENS · *The Great Winglebury Duel*
38. HERMAN MELVILLE · *The Maldive Shark*
39. ELIZABETH GASKELL · *The Old Nurse's Story*
40. NIKOLAY LESKOV · *The Steel Flea*

41. HONORÉ DE BALZAC · *The Atheist's Mass*
42. CHARLOTTE PERKINS GILMAN · *The Yellow Wall-Paper*
43. C.P. CAVAFY · *Remember, Body . . .*
44. FYODOR DOSTOEVSKY · *The Meek One*
45. GUSTAVE FLAUBERT · *A Simple Heart*
46. NIKOLAI GOGOL · *The Nose*
47. SAMUEL PEPYS · *The Great Fire of London*
48. EDITH WHARTON · *The Reckoning*
49. HENRY JAMES · *The Figure in the Carpet*
50. WILFRED OWEN · *Anthem For Doomed Youth*
51. WOLFGANG AMADEUS MOZART · *My Dearest Father*
52. PLATO · *Socrates' Defence*
53. CHRISTINA ROSSETTI · *Goblin Market*
54. *Sindbad the Sailor*
55. SOPHOCLES · *Antigone*
56. RYŪNOSUKE AKUTAGAWA · *The Life of a Stupid Man*
57. LEO TOLSTOY · *How Much Land Does A Man Need?*
58. GIORGIO VASARI · *Leonardo da Vinci*
59. OSCAR WILDE · *Lord Arthur Savile's Crime*
60. SHEN FU · *The Old Man of the Moon*
61. AESOP · *The Dolphins, the Whales and the Gudgeon*
62. MATSUO BASHŌ · *Lips too Chilled*
63. EMILY BRONTË · *The Night is Darkening Round Me*
64. JOSEPH CONRAD · *To-morrow*
65. RICHARD HAKLUYT · *The Voyage of Sir Francis Drake Around the Whole Globe*
66. KATE CHOPIN · *A Pair of Silk Stockings*
67. CHARLES DARWIN · *It was snowing butterflies*
68. BROTHERS GRIMM · *The Robber Bridegroom*
69. CATULLUS · *I Hate and I Love*
70. HOMER · *Circe and the Cyclops*
71. D. H. LAWRENCE · *Il Duro*
72. KATHERINE MANSFIELD · *Miss Brill*
73. OVID · *The Fall of Icarus*
74. SAPPHO · *Come Close*
75. IVAN TURGENEV · *Kasyan from the Beautiful Lands*
76. VIRGIL · *O Cruel Alexis*
77. H. G. WELLS · *A Slip under the Microscope*
78. HERODOTUS · *The Madness of Cambyses*
79. *Speaking of Siva*
80. *The Dhammapada*

'You must be Odysseus, man of twists and turns . . .'

HOMER
Date and location of birth and death unknown

HOMER IN PENGUIN CLASSICS
The Homeric Hymns
The Iliad
The Odyssey

HOMER

Circe and the Cyclops

Translated by
Robert Fagles

PENGUIN BOOKS

PENGUIN CLASSICS

UK | USA | Canada | Ireland | Australia
India | New Zealand | South Africa

Penguin Books is part of the Penguin Random House group of companies
whose addresses can be found at global.penguinrandomhouse.com.

This selection published in Penguin Classics 2015
009

Copyright © 1996 by Robert Fagles

The moral right of the translator has been asserted

Set in 9.5/13 pt Baskerville 10 Pro
Typeset by Jouve (UK), Milton Keynes
Printed and bound in Great Britain by Clays Ltd, Elcograf S.p.A.

A CIP catalogue record for this book is available from the British Library

ISBN: 978-0-141-39861-7

www.greenpenguin.co.uk

Penguin Random House is committed to a
sustainable future for our business, our readers
and our planet. This book is made from Forest
Stewardship Council® certified paper.

Contents

In the One-Eyed Giant's Cave   1

The Bewitching Queen
   of Aeaea   27

In the One-Eyed Giant's Cave

Odysseus, the great teller of tales, launched out on
>his story:
'Alcinous, majesty, shining among your island people,
what a fine thing it is to listen to such a bard
as we have here – the man sings like a god.
The crown of life, I'd say. There's nothing better
than when deep joy holds sway throughout the realm
and banqueters up and down the palace sit in ranks,
enthralled to hear the bard, and before them all,
>the tables
heaped with bread and meats, and drawing wine from
>a mixing-bowl
the steward makes his rounds and keeps the winecups
>flowing.
This, to my mind, is the best that life can offer.

>But now
you're set on probing the bitter pains I've borne,
so I'm to weep and grieve, it seems, still more.
Well then, what shall I go through first,
what shall I save for last?
What pains – the gods have given me my share.
Now let me begin by telling you my name . . .
so you may know it well and I in times to come,
if I can escape the fatal day, will be your host,
your sworn friend, though my home is far from here.

Homer

I am Odysseus, son of Laertes, known to the world
for every kind of craft – my fame has reached the skies.
Sunny Ithaca is my home. Atop her stands our seamark,
Mount Neriton's leafy ridges shimmering in the wind.
Around her a ring of islands circle side-by-side,
Dulichion, Same, wooded Zacynthus too, but mine
lies low and away, the farthest out to sea,
rearing into the western dusk
while the others face the east and breaking day.
Mine is a rugged land but good for raising sons –
and I myself, I know no sweeter sight on earth
than a man's own native country.

                            True enough,
Calypso the lustrous goddess tried to hold me back,
deep in her arching caverns, craving me for a husband.
So did Circe, holding me just as warmly in her halls,
the bewitching queen of Aeaea keen to have me too.
But they never won the heart inside me, never.
So nothing is as sweet as a man's own country,
his own parents, even though he's settled down
in some luxurious house, off in a foreign land
and far from those who bore him.

                             No more. Come,
let me tell you about the voyage fraught with hardship
Zeus inflicted on me, homeward bound from Troy . . .

   The wind drove me out of Ilium on to Ismarus,
the Cicones' stronghold. There I sacked the city,

In the One-Eyed Giant's Cave

killed the men, but as for the wives and plunder,
that rich haul we dragged away from the place –
we shared it round so no one, not on my account,
would go deprived of his fair share of spoils.
Then I urged them to cut and run, set sail,
but would they listen? Not those mutinous fools;
there was too much wine to swill, too many sheep
    to slaughter
down along the beach, and shambling longhorn
    cattle.
And all the while the Cicones sought out other
    Cicones,
called for help from their neighbors living inland:
a larger force, and stronger soldiers too,
skilled hands at fighting men from chariots,
skilled, when a crisis broke, to fight on foot.
Out of the morning mist they came against us –
packed as the leaves and spears that flower forth
    in spring –
and Zeus presented us with disaster, me and my
    comrades
doomed to suffer blow on mortal blow. Lining up,
both armies battled it out against our swift ships,
both raked each other with hurtling bronze lances.
Long as morning rose and the blessed day grew stronger
we stood and fought them off, massed as they were,
    but then,
when the sun wheeled past the hour for unyoking oxen,

the Cicones broke our lines and beat us down at last.
Out of each ship, six men-at-arms were killed;
the rest of us rowed away from certain doom.

   From there we sailed on, glad to escape our death
yet sick at heart for the dear companions we had lost.
But I would not let our rolling ships set sail until the
     crews
had raised the triple cry, saluting each poor comrade
cut down by the fierce Cicones on that plain.
Now Zeus who masses the stormclouds hit the fleet
with the North Wind –
              a howling, demonic gale, shrouding over
in thunderheads the earth and sea at once –
                      and night swept down
from the sky and the ships went plunging headlong on,
our sails slashed to rags by the hurricane's blast!
We struck them – cringing at death we rowed our ships
to the nearest shoreline, pulled with all our power.
There, for two nights, two days, we lay by, no letup,
eating our hearts out, bent with pain and bone-tired.
When Dawn with her lovely locks brought on the
     third day,
then stepping the masts and hoisting white sails high,
we lounged at the oarlocks, letting wind and helmsmen
keep us true on course . . .
                    And now, at long last,
I might have reached my native land unscathed,

In the One-Eyed Giant's Cave

but just as I doubled Malea's cape, a tide-rip
and the North Wind drove me way off course
careering past Cythera.
                      Nine whole days
I was borne along by rough, deadly winds
on the fish-infested sea. Then on the tenth
our squadron reached the land of the Lotus-eaters,
people who eat the lotus, mellow fruit and flower.
We disembarked on the coast, drew water there
and crewmen snatched a meal by the swift ships.
Once we'd had our fill of food and drink I sent
a detail ahead, two picked men and a third, a runner,
to scout out who might live there – men like us perhaps,
who live on bread? So off they went and soon enough
they mingled among the natives, Lotus-eaters,
      Lotus-eaters
who had no notion of killing my companions, not at all,
they simply gave them the lotus to taste instead . . .
Any crewmen who ate the lotus, the honey-sweet fruit,
lost all desire to send a message back, much less return,
their only wish to linger there with the Lotus-eaters,
grazing on lotus, all memory of the journey home
dissolved forever. But *I* brought them back, back
to the hollow ships, and streaming tears – I forced them,
hauled them under the rowing benches, lashed them fast
and shouted out commands to my other, steady comrades:
"Quick, no time to lose, embark in the racing ships!" –
so none could eat the lotus, forget the voyage home.

They swung aboard at once, they sat to the oars in ranks
and in rhythm churned the water white with stroke on
 stroke.

   From there we sailed on, our spirits now at a low ebb,
and reached the land of the high and mighty Cyclops,
lawless brutes, who trust so to the everlasting gods
they never plant with their own hands or plow the soil.
Unsown, unplowed, the earth teems with all they need,
wheat, barley and vines, swelled by the rains of Zeus
to yield a big full-bodied wine from clustered grapes.
They have no meeting place for council, no laws either,
no, up on the mountain peaks they live in arching caverns –
each a law to himself, ruling his wives and children,
not a care in the world for any neighbor.
                                                                Now,
a level island stretches flat across the harbor,
not close inshore to the Cyclops' coast, not too far out,
thick with woods where the wild goats breed by
 hundreds.
No trampling of men to start them from their lairs,
no hunters roughing it out on the woody ridges,
stalking quarry, ever raid their haven.
No flocks browse, no plowlands roll with wheat;
unplowed, unsown forever – empty of humankind –
the island just feeds droves of bleating goats.
For the Cyclops have no ships with crimson prows,

In the One-Eyed Giant's Cave

no shipwrights there to build them good trim craft
that could sail them out to foreign ports of call
as most men risk the seas to trade with other men.
Such artisans would have made this island too
a decent place to live in . . . No mean spot,
it could bear you any crop you like in season.
The water-meadows along the low foaming shore
run soft and moist, and your vines would never flag.
The land's clear for plowing. Harvest on harvest,
a man could reap a healthy stand of grain –
the subsoil's dark and rich.
There's a snug deep-water harbor there, what's more,
no need for mooring-gear, no anchor-stones to heave,
no cables to make fast. Just beach your keels, ride out
the days till your shipmates' spirit stirs for open sea
and a fair wind blows. And last, at the harbor's head
there's a spring that rushes fresh from beneath a cave
and black poplars flourish round its mouth.
                                                    Well,
here we landed, and surely a god steered us in
through the pitch-black night.
Not that he ever showed himself, with thick fog
swirling around the ships, the moon wrapped in clouds
and not a glimmer stealing through that gloom.
Not one of us glimpsed the island – scanning hard –
or the long combers rolling us slowly toward the coast,
not till our ships had run their keels ashore.

Homer

Beaching our vessels smoothly, striking sail,
the crews swung out on the low shelving sand
and there we fell asleep, awaiting Dawn's first light.

>When young Dawn with her rose-red fingers shone once more

we all turned out, intrigued to tour the island.
The local nymphs, the daughters of Zeus himself,
flushed mountain-goats so the crews could make their meal.
Quickly we fetched our curved bows and hunting spears
from the ships and, splitting up into three bands,
we started shooting, and soon enough some god
had sent us bags of game to warm our hearts.
A dozen vessels sailed in my command
and to each crew nine goats were shared out
and mine alone took ten. Then all day long
till the sun went down we sat and feasted well
on sides of meat and rounds of heady wine.
The good red stock in our vessels' holds
had not run out, there was still plenty left;
the men had carried off a generous store in jars
when we stormed and sacked the Cicones' holy city.
Now we stared across at the Cyclops' shore, so near
we could even see their smoke, hear their voices,
their bleating sheep and goats . . .
And then when the sun had set and night came on
we lay down and slept at the water's shelving edge.

In the One-Eyed Giant's Cave

When young Dawn with her rose-red fingers shone
    once more
I called a muster briskly, commanding all the hands,
"The rest of you stay here, my friends-in-arms.
I'll go across with my own ship and crew
and probe the natives living over there.
What *are* they – violent, savage, lawless?
or friendly to strangers, god-fearing men?"

    With that I boarded ship and told the crew
to embark at once and cast off cables quickly.
They swung aboard, they sat to the oars in ranks
and in rhythm churned the water white with stroke
    on stroke.
But as soon as we reached the coast I mentioned –
    no long trip –
we spied a cavern just at the shore, gaping above
    the surf,
towering, overgrown with laurel. And here big flocks,
sheep and goats, were stalled to spend the nights,
and around its mouth a yard was walled up
with quarried boulders sunk deep in the earth
and enormous pines and oak-trees looming darkly . . .
Here was a giant's lair, in fact, who always pastured
his sheepflocks far afield and never mixed with others.
A grim loner, dead set in his own lawless ways.
Here was a piece of work, by god, a monster
built like no mortal who ever supped on bread,

no, like a shaggy peak, I'd say – a man-mountain
rearing head and shoulders over the world.

                        Now then,
I told most of my good trusty crew to wait,
to sit tight by the ship and guard her well
while I picked out my dozen finest fighters
and off I went. But I took a skin of wine along,
the ruddy, irresistible wine that Maron gave me once,
Euanthes' son, a priest of Apollo, lord of Ismarus,
because we'd rescued him, his wife and children,
reverent as we were;
he lived, you see, in Apollo's holy grove.
And so in return he gave me splendid gifts,
he handed me seven bars of well-wrought gold,
a mixing-bowl of solid silver, then this wine . . .
He drew it off in generous wine-jars, twelve in all,
all unmixed – and such a bouquet, a drink fit for
     the gods!
No maid or man of his household knew that secret store,
only himself, his loving wife and a single servant.
Whenever they'd drink the deep-red mellow vintage,
twenty cups of water he'd stir in one of wine
and what an aroma wafted from the bowl –
what magic, what a godsend –
no joy in holding back when *that* was poured!
Filling a great goatskin now, I took this wine,
provisions too in a leather sack. A sudden foreboding
told my fighting spirit I'd soon come up against

In the One-Eyed Giant's Cave

some giant clad in power like armor-plate –
a savage deaf to justice, blind to law.

    Our party quickly made its way to his cave
but we failed to find our host himself inside;
he was off in his pasture, ranging his sleek flocks.
So we explored his den, gazing wide-eyed at it all,
the large flat racks loaded with drying cheeses,
the folds crowded with young lambs and kids,
split into three groups – here the spring-born,
here mid-yearlings, here the fresh sucklings
off to the side – each sort was penned apart.
And all his vessels, pails and hammered buckets
he used for milking, were brimming full with whey.
From the start my comrades pressed me, pleading hard,
"Let's make away with the cheeses, then come back –
hurry, drive the lambs and kids from the pens
to our swift ship, put out to sea at once!"
But I would not give way –
and how much better it would have been –
not till I saw him, saw what gifts he'd give.
But he proved no lovely sight to my companions.

    There we built a fire, set our hands on the cheeses,
offered some to the gods and ate the bulk ourselves
and settled down inside, awaiting his return . . .
And back he came from pasture, late in the day,
herding his flocks home, and lugging a huge load

of good dry logs to fuel his fire at supper.
He flung them down in the cave – a jolting crash –
we scuttled in panic into the deepest dark recess.
And next he drove his sleek flocks into the open vault,
all he'd milk at least, but he left the males outside,
rams and billy goats out in the high-walled yard.
Then to close his door he hoisted overhead
a tremendous, massive slab –
no twenty-two wagons, rugged and four-wheeled,
could budge that boulder off the ground, I tell you,
such an immense stone the monster wedged to block
    his cave!
Then down he squatted to milk his sheep and bleating
    goats,
each in order, and put a suckling underneath each dam.
And half of the fresh white milk he curdled quickly,
set it aside in wicker racks to press for cheese,
the other half let stand in pails and buckets,
ready at hand to wash his supper down.
As soon as he'd briskly finished all his chores
he lit his fire and spied us in the blaze and
"Strangers!" he thundered out, "now who are you?
Where did you sail from, over the running sea-lanes?
Out on a trading spree or roving the waves like pirates,
sea-wolves raiding at will, who risk their lives
to plunder other men?"
                      The hearts inside us shook,
terrified by his rumbling voice and monstrous hulk.

In the One-Eyed Giant's Cave

Nevertheless I found the nerve to answer, firmly,
"Men of Achaea we are and bound now from Troy!
Driven far off course by the warring winds,
over the vast gulf of the sea – battling home
on a strange tack, a route that's off the map,
and so we've come to you . . .
so it must please King Zeus's plotting heart.
We're glad to say we're men of Atrides Agamemnon,
whose fame is the proudest thing on earth these days,
so great a city he sacked, such multitudes he killed!
But since we've chanced on you, we're at your knees
in hopes of a warm welcome, even a guest-gift,
the sort that hosts give strangers. That's the custom.
Respect the gods, my friend. We're suppliants – at your
    mercy!
Zeus of the Strangers guards all guests and suppliants:
strangers are sacred – Zeus will avenge their rights!"

"Stranger," he grumbled back from his brutal heart,
"you must be a fool, stranger, or come from nowhere,
telling *me* to fear the gods or avoid their wrath!
We Cyclops never blink at Zeus and Zeus's shield
of storm and thunder, or any other blessed god –
we've got more force by far.
I'd never spare you in fear of Zeus's hatred,
you or your comrades here, unless I had the urge.
But tell me, where did you moor your sturdy ship
when you arrived? Up the coast or close in?

Homer

I'd just like to know."
                          So he laid his trap
but he never caught me, no, wise to the world
I shot back in my crafty way, "My ship?
Poseidon god of the earthquake smashed my ship,
he drove it against the rocks at your island's far cape,
he dashed it against a cliff as the winds rode us in.
I and the men you see escaped a sudden death."

Not a word in reply to that, the ruthless brute.
Lurching up, he lunged out with his hands toward
          my men
and snatching two at once, rapping them on the ground
he knocked them dead like pups –
their brains gushed out all over, soaked the floor –
and ripping them limb from limb to fix his meal
he bolted them down like a mountain-lion, left no scrap,
devoured entrails, flesh and bones, marrow and all!
We flung our arms to Zeus, we wept and cried aloud,
looking on at his grisly work – paralyzed, appalled.
But once the Cyclops had stuffed his enormous gut
with human flesh, washing it down with raw milk,
he slept in his cave, stretched out along his flocks.
And I with my fighting heart, I thought at first
to steal up to him, draw the sharp sword at my hip
and stab his chest where the midriff packs the liver –
I groped for the fatal spot but a fresh thought held
          me back.

In the One-Eyed Giant's Cave

There at a stroke we'd finish off ourselves as well —
how could *we* with our bare hands heave back
that slab he set to block his cavern's gaping maw?
So we lay there groaning, waiting Dawn's first light.

    When young Dawn with her rose-red fingers shone
        once more
the monster relit his fire and milked his handsome ewes,
each in order, putting a suckling underneath each dam,
and as soon as he'd briskly finished all his chores
he snatched up two more men and fixed his meal.
Well-fed, he drove his fat sheep from the cave,
lightly lifting the huge doorslab up and away,
then slipped it back in place
as a hunter flips the lid of his quiver shut.
Piercing whistles — turning his flocks to the hills
he left me there, the heart inside me brooding on revenge:
how could I pay him back? would Athena give me glory?
Here was the plan that struck my mind as best . . .
the Cyclops' great club: there it lay by the pens,
olivewood, full of sap. He'd lopped it off to brandish
once it dried. Looking it over, we judged it big enough
to be the mast of a pitch-black ship with her twenty oars,
a freighter broad in the beam that plows through
        miles of sea —
so long, so thick it bulked before our eyes. Well,
flanking it now, I chopped off a fathom's length,
rolled it to comrades, told them to plane it down,

and they made the club smooth as I bent and shaved
the tip to a stabbing point. I turned it over
the blazing fire to char it good and hard,
then hid it well, buried deep under the dung
that littered the cavern's floor in thick wet clumps.
And now I ordered my shipmates all to cast lots –
who'd brave it out with me
to hoist our stake and grind it into his eye
when sleep had overcome him? Luck of the draw:
I got the very ones I would have picked myself,
four good men, and I in the lead made five . . .

    Nightfall brought him back, herding his woolly sheep
and he quickly drove the sleek flock into the vaulted cavern,
rams and all – none left outside in the walled yard –
his own idea, perhaps, or a god led him on.
Then he hoisted the huge slab to block the door
and squatted to milk his sheep and bleating goats,
each in order, putting a suckling underneath each dam,
and as soon as he'd briskly finished all his chores
he snatched up two more men and fixed his meal.
But this time I lifted a carved wooden bowl,
brimful of my ruddy wine,
and went right up to the Cyclops, enticing,
"Here, Cyclops, try this wine – to top off
the banquet of human flesh you've bolted down!
Judge for yourself what stock our ship had stored.

In the One-Eyed Giant's Cave

I brought it here to make you a fine libation,
hoping you would pity me, Cyclops, send me home,
but your rages are insufferable. You barbarian –
how can any man on earth come visit you after *this*?
What you've done outrages all that's right!"

At that he seized the bowl and tossed it off
and the heady wine pleased him immensely – "More" –
he demanded a second bowl – "a hearty helping!
And tell me your name now, quickly,
so I can hand my guest a gift to warm *his* heart.
Our soil yields the Cyclops powerful, full-bodied wine
and the rains from Zeus build its strength. But this,
this is nectar, ambrosia – this flows from heaven!"

So he declared. I poured him another fiery bowl –
three bowls I brimmed and three he drank to the last
    drop,
the fool, and then, when the wine was swirling round
    his brain,
I approached my host with a cordial, winning word:
"So, you ask me the name I'm known by, Cyclops?
I will tell you. But you must give me a guest-gift
as you've promised. Nobody – that's my name. Nobody –
so my mother and father call me, all my friends."

But he boomed back at me from his ruthless heart,
"*Nobody?* I'll eat Nobody last of all his friends –

Homer

I'll eat the others first! That's my gift to *you*!"

                                                With that
he toppled over, sprawled full-length, flat on his back
and lay there, his massive neck slumping to one side,
and sleep that conquers all overwhelmed him now
as wine came spurting, flooding up from his gullet
with chunks of human flesh – he vomited, blind drunk.
Now, at last, I thrust our stake in a bed of embers
to get it red-hot and rallied all my comrades:
"Courage – no panic, no one hang back now!"
And green as it was, just as the olive stake
was about to catch fire – the glow terrific, yes –
I dragged it from the flames, my men clustering round
as some god breathed enormous courage through us all.
Hoisting high that olive stake with its stabbing point,
straight into the monster's eye they rammed it hard –
I drove my weight on it from above and bored it home
as a shipwright bores his beam with a shipwright's drill
that men below, whipping the strap back and forth,
      whirl
and the drill keeps twisting faster, never stopping –
So we seized our stake with its fiery tip
and bored it round and round in the giant's eye
till blood came boiling up around that smoking shaft
and the hot blast singed his brow and eyelids round
      the core
and the broiling eyeball burst –

                                    its crackling roots blazed

In the One-Eyed Giant's Cave

and hissed –
        as a blacksmith plunges a glowing ax or adze
in an ice-cold bath and the metal screeches steam
and its temper hardens – that's the iron's strength –
so the eye of the Cyclops sizzled round that stake!
He loosed a hideous roar, the rock walls echoed round
and we scuttled back in terror. The monster wrenched
    the spike
from his eye and out it came with a red geyser of blood –
he flung it aside with frantic hands, and mad with pain
he bellowed out for help from his neighbor Cyclops
living round about in caves on windswept crags.
Hearing his cries, they lumbered up from every side
and hulking round his cavern, asked what ailed him;
"What, Polyphemus, what in the world's the trouble?
Roaring out in the godsent night to rob us of our
    sleep.
Surely no one's rustling your flocks against your will –
surely no one's trying to kill you now by fraud or
    force!"

"*Nobody,* friends" – Polyphemus bellowed back from
    his cave –
"Nobody's killing me now by fraud and not by force!"

"If you're alone," his friends boomed back at once,
"and nobody's trying to overpower you now – look,
it must be a plague sent here by mighty Zeus

and there's no escape from *that*.
You'd better pray to your father, Lord Poseidon.

They lumbered off, but laughter filled my heart
to think how nobody's name – my great cunning stroke –
had duped them one and all. But the Cyclops there,
still groaning, racked with agony, groped around
for the huge slab, and heaving it from the doorway,
down he sat in the cave's mouth, his arms spread wide,
hoping to catch a comrade stealing out with sheep –
such a blithering fool he took me for!
But I was already plotting . . .
what was the best way out? how could I find
escape from death for my crew, myself as well?
My wits kept weaving, weaving cunning schemes –
life at stake, monstrous death staring us in the face –
till this plan struck my mind as best. That flock,
those well-fed rams with their splendid thick fleece,
sturdy, handsome beasts sporting their dark weight
      of wool:
I lashed them abreast, quietly, twisting the willow-twigs
the Cyclops slept on – giant, lawless brute – I took them
three by three; each ram in the middle bore a man
while the two rams either side would shield him well.
So three beasts to bear each man, but as for myself?
There was one bellwether ram, the prize of all the flock,
and clutching him by his back, tucked up under
His shaggy belly, there I hung, face upward,

In the One-Eyed Giant's Cave

both hands locked in his marvelous deep fleece,
clinging for dear life, my spirit steeled, enduring . . .
So we held on, desperate, waiting Dawn's first light.

                                        As soon
as young Dawn with her rose-red fingers shone
      once more
the rams went rumbling out of the cave toward pasture,
the ewes kept bleating round the pens, unmilked.
their udders about to burst. Their master now,
heaving in torment, felt the back of each animal
halting before him here, but the idiot never sensed
my men were trussed up under their thick fleecy ribs.
And last of them all came my great ram now, striding out,
weighed down with his dense wool and my deep plots.
Stroking him gently, powerful Polyphemus murmured.
"Dear old ram, why last of the flock to quit the cave?
In the good old days you'd never lag behind the rest –
you with your long marching strides, first by far
of the flock to graze the fresh young grasses,
first by far to reach the rippling streams,
first to turn back home, keen for your fold
when night comes on – but now you're last of all.
And why? Sick at heart for your master's eye
that coward gouged out with his wicked crew? –
only after he'd stunned my wits with wine –
that, that Nobody . . .
who's not escaped his death, I swear, not yet.

Homer

Oh if only you thought like *me,* had words like *me*
to tell me where that scoundrel is cringing from my rage!
I'd smash him against the ground, I'd spill his brains –
flooding across my cave – and that would ease my heart
of the pains that good-for-nothing Nobody made me
      suffer!"

And with that threat he let my ram go free outside.
But soon as we'd got one foot past cave and courtyard,
first I loosed myself from the ram, then loosed my men,
then quickly, glancing back again and again we drove
our flock, good plump beasts with their long shanks,
straight to the ship, and a welcome sight we were
to loyal comrades – we who'd escaped our deaths –
but for all the rest they broke down and wailed.
I cut it short, I stopped each shipmate's cries,
my head tossing, brows frowning, silent signals
to hurry, tumble our fleecy herd on board,
launch out on the open sea!
They swung aboard, they sat to the oars in ranks
and in rhythm churned the water white with stroke on
      stroke.
But once offshore as far as a man's shout can carry,
I called back to the Cyclops, stinging taunts:
"So, Cyclops, no weak coward it was whose crew
you bent to devour there in your vaulted cave –
you with your brute force! Your filthy crimes
came down on your own head, you shameless cannibal,

In the One-Eyed Giant's Cave

daring to eat your guests in your own house –
so Zeus and the other gods have paid you back!"

That made the rage of the monster boil over.
Ripping off the peak of a towering crag, he heaved it
so hard the boulder landed just in front of our dark prow
and a huge swell reared up as the rock went plunging under –
a tidal wave from the open sea. The sudden backwash
drove us landward again, forcing us close inshore
but grabbing a long pole, I thrust us off and away,
tossing my head for dear life, signaling crews
to put their backs in the oars, escape grim death.
They threw themselves in the labor, rowed on fast
but once we'd plowed the breakers twice as far,
again I began to taunt the Cyclops – men around me
trying to check me, calm me, left and right:
"So headstrong – why? Why rile the beast again?"

"That rock he flung in the sea just now, hurling our ship
to shore once more – we thought we'd die on the spot!"

"If he'd caught a sound from one of us, just a moan,
he would have crushed our heads and ship timbers
with one heave of another flashing, jagged rock!"

"Good god, the brute can throw!"
                                    So they begged
but they could not bring my fighting spirit round.

Homer

I called back with another burst of anger, "Cyclops –
if any man on the face of the earth should ask you
who blinded you, shamed you so – say Odysseus,
raider of cities, *he* gouged out your eye,
Laertes' son who makes his home in Ithaca!"

So I vaunted and he groaned back in answer,
"Oh no, no – that prophecy years ago . . .
it all comes home to me with a vengeance now!
We once had a prophet here, a great tall man,
Telemus, Eurymus' son, a master at reading signs,
who grew old in his trade among his fellow-Cyclops.
All this, he warned me, would come to pass someday –
that I'd be blinded here at the hands of one Odysseus.
But I always looked for a handsome giant man to cross
     my path,
some fighter clad in power like armor-plate, but now,
look what a dwarf, a spineless good-for-nothing,
stuns me with wine, then gouges out my eye!
Come here, Odysseus, let me give you a guest-gift
and urge Poseidon the earthquake god to speed
     you home.
I am his son and he claims to be my father, true,
and he himself will heal me if he pleases –
no other blessed god, no man can do the work!"

                                         "Heal you!" –
here was my parting shot – "Would to god I could
     strip you

In the One-Eyed Giant's Cave

of life and breath and ship you down to the House
    of Death
as surely as no one will ever heal your eye,
not even your earthquake god himself!"

   But at that he bellowed out to lord Poseidon,
thrusting his arms to the starry skies, and prayed, "Hear me –
Poseidon, god of the sea-blue mane who rocks the earth!
If I really am your son and you claim to be my father –
come, grant that Odysseus, raider of cities,
Laertes' son who makes his home in Ithaca,
never reaches home. Or if he's fated to see
his people once again and reach his well-built house
and his own native country, let him come home late
and come a broken man – all shipmates lost,
alone in a stranger's ship –
and let him find a world of pain at home!"

                              So he prayed
and the god of the sea-blue mane, Poseidon, heard his
    prayer.
The monster suddenly hoisted a boulder – far larger –
wheeled and heaved it, putting his weight behind it,
massive strength, and the boulder crashed close,
landing just in the wake of our dark stern,
just failing to graze the rudder's bladed edge.
A huge swell reared up as the rock went plunging under,
yes, and the tidal breaker drove us out to our island's
far shore where all my well-decked ships lay moored,

clustered, waiting, and huddled round them, crewmen
sat in anguish, waiting, chafing for our return.
We beached our vessel hard ashore on the sand,
we swung out in the frothing surf ourselves,
and herding Cyclops' sheep from our deep holds
we shared them round so no one, not on my account,
would go deprived of his fair share of spoils.
But the splendid ram – as we meted out the flocks
my friends-in-arms made him my prize of honor,
mine alone, and I slaughtered him on the beach
and burnt his thighs to Cronus' mighty son,
Zeus of the thundercloud who rules the world.
But my sacrifices failed to move the god:
Zeus was still obsessed with plans to destroy
my entire oarswept fleet and loyal crew of comrades.
Now all day long till the sun went down we sat
and feasted on sides of meat and heady wine.
Then when the sun had set and night came on
we lay down and slept at the water's shelving edge.
When young Dawn with her rose-red fingers shone
    once more
I roused the men straightway, ordering all crews
to man the ships and cast off cables quickly.
They swung aboard at once, they sat to the oars in ranks
and in rhythm churned the water white with stroke
    on stroke.
And from there we sailed on, glad to escape our death
yet sick at heart for the comrades we had lost."

The Bewitching Queen of Aeaea

'We reached the Aeolian island next, the home of Aeolus,
Hippotas' son, beloved by the gods who never die –
a great floating island it was, and round it all
huge ramparts rise of indestructible bronze
and sheer rock cliffs shoot up from sea to sky.
The king had sired twelve children within his halls,
six daughters and six sons in the lusty prime of youth,
so he gave his daughters as wives to his six sons.
Seated beside their dear father and doting mother,
with delicacies aplenty spread before them,
they feast on forever . . . All day long
the halls breathe the savor of roasted meats
and echo round to the low moan of blowing pipes,
and all night long, each one by his faithful mate,
they sleep under soft-piled rugs on corded bedsteads.
To this city of theirs we came, their splendid palace,
and Aeolus hosted me one entire month, he pressed me for news
of Troy and the Argive ships and how we sailed for home,
and I told him the whole long story, first to last.
And then, when I begged him to send me on my way,
he denied me nothing, he went about my passage.
He gave me a sack, the skin of a full-grown ox,
binding inside the winds that howl from every quarter,

Homer

for Zeus had made that king the master of all the winds,
with power to calm them down or rouse them as he
    pleased.
Aeolus stowed the sack inside my holds, lashed so fast
with a burnished silver cord
not even a slight puff could slip past that knot.
Yet he set the West Wind free to blow us on our way
and waft our squadron home. But his plan was bound
    to fail,
yes, our own reckless folly swept us on to ruin . . .

    Nine whole days we sailed, nine nights, nonstop.
On the tenth our own land hove into sight at last –
we were so close we could see men tending fires.
But now an enticing sleep came on me, bone-weary
from working the vessel's sheet myself, no letup,
never trusting the ropes to any other mate,
the faster to journey back to native land.
But the crews began to mutter among themselves,
sure I was hauling troves of gold and silver home,
the gifts of open-hearted Aeolus, Hippotas' son.
"The old story!" One man glanced at another,
    grumbling.
"Look at our captain's luck – so loved by the world,
so prized at every landfall, every port of call."

    "Heaps of lovely plunder he hauls home from Troy,
while we who went through slogging just as hard,

we go home empty-handed."

                      "Now this Aeolus loads him
down with treasure. Favoritism, friend to friend!"

"Hurry, let's see what loot is in that sack,
how much gold and silver. Break it open – now!"

A fatal plan, but it won my shipmates over.
They loosed the sack and all the winds burst out
and a sudden squall struck and swept us back to sea,
wailing, in tears, far from our own native land.
And I woke up with a start, my spirit churning –
should I leap over the side and drown at once or
grit my teeth and bear it, stay among the living?
I bore it all, held firm, hiding my face,
clinging tight to the decks
while heavy squalls blasted our squadron back
again to Aeolus' island, shipmates groaning hard.

We disembarked on the coast, drew water there
and crewmen snatched a meal by the swift ships.
Once we'd had our fill of food and drink
I took a shipmate along with me, a herald too,
and approached King Aeolus' famous halls and here
we found him feasting beside his wife and many
        children.
Reaching the doorposts at the threshold, down we sat
but our hosts, amazed to see us, only shouted questions:

Homer

"Back again, Odysseus – why? Some blustering god
    attacked you?
Surely we launched you well, we sped you on your way
to your own land and house, or any place you pleased."

So they taunted, and I replied in deep despair,
"A mutinous crew undid me – that and a cruel sleep.
Set it to rights, my friends. You have the power!"

So I pleaded – gentle, humble appeals –
but our hosts turned silent, hushed . . .
and the father broke forth with an ultimatum:
"Away from my island – fast – most cursed man alive!
It's a crime to host a man or speed him on his way
when the blessed deathless gods despise him so.
Crawling back like this –
it proves the immortals hate you! Out – get out!"

Groan as I did, his curses drove me from his halls
and from there we pulled away with heavy hearts,
with the crews' spirit broken under the oars' labor,
thanks to our own folly . . . no favoring wind in sight.

Six whole days we rowed, six nights, nonstop.
On the seventh day we raised the Laestrygonian land,
Telepylus heights where the craggy fort of Lamus rises.
Where shepherd calls to shepherd as one drives in his
    flocks

The Bewitching Queen of Aeaea

and the other drives his out and he calls back in answer,
where a man who never sleeps could rake in double wages,
one for herding cattle, one for pasturing fleecy sheep,
the nightfall and the sunrise march so close together.
We entered a fine harbor there, all walled around
by a great unbroken sweep of sky-scraping cliff
and two steep headlands, fronting each other, close
around the mouth so the passage in is cramped.
Here the rest of my rolling squadron steered,
right into the gaping cove and moored tightly,
prow by prow. Never a swell there, big or small;
a milk-white calm spreads all around the place.
But I alone anchored my black ship outside,
well clear of the harbor's jaws
I tied her fast to a cliffside with a cable.
I scaled its rock face to a lookout on its crest
but glimpsed no trace of the work of man or beast
  from there;
all I spied was a plume of smoke, drifting off the land.
So I sent some crew ahead to learn who lived there –
men like us perhaps, who live on bread?
Two good mates I chose and a third to run the news.
They disembarked and set out on a beaten trail
the wagons used for hauling timber down to town
from the mountain heights above . . .
and before the walls they met a girl, drawing water,
Antiphates' strapping daughter – king of the
  Laestrygonians.

She'd come down to a clear running spring, Artacia,
where the local people came to fill their pails.
My shipmates clustered round her, asking questions:
who was king of the realm? who ruled the natives here?
She waved at once to her father's high-roofed halls.
They entered the sumptuous palace, found his wife inside –
a woman huge as a mountain crag who filled them all
    with horror.
Straightaway she summoned royal Antiphates from
    assembly,
her husband, who prepared my crew a barbarous
    welcome.
Snatching one of my men, he tore him up for dinner –
the other two sprang free and reached the ships.
But the king let loose a howling through the town
that brought tremendous Laestrygonians swarming up
from every side – hundreds, not like men, like Giants!
Down from the cliffs they flung great rocks a man could
    hardly hoist
and a ghastly shattering din rose up from all the ships –
men in their death-cries, hulls smashed to splinters –
They speared the crews like fish
and whisked them home to make their grisly meal.
But while they killed them off in the harbor depths
I pulled the sword from beside my hip and hacked away
at the ropes that moored my blue-prowed ship of war
and shouted rapid orders at my shipmates:
"Put your backs in the oars – now row or die!"

The Bewitching Queen of Aeaea

In terror of death they ripped the swells – all as one –
and what a joy as we darted out toward open sea,
clear of those beetling cliffs . . . my ship alone.
But the rest went down en masse. Our squadron sank.

From there we sailed on, glad to escape our death
yet sick at heart for the dear companions we had lost.
We reached the Aeaean island next, the home of Circe
the nymph with lovely braids, an awesome power too
who can speak with human voice,
the true sister of murderous-minded Aeetes.
Both were bred by the Sun who lights our lives;
their mother was Perse, a child the Ocean bore.
We brought our ship to port without a sound
as a god eased her into a harbor safe and snug,
and for two days and two nights we lay by there,
eating our hearts out, bent with pain and bone-tired.
When Dawn with her lovely locks brought on the
    third day,
at last I took my spear and my sharp sword again,
rushed up from the ship to find a lookout point,
hoping to glimpse some sign of human labor,
catch some human voices . . .
I scaled a commanding crag and, scanning hard,
I could just make out some smoke from Circe's halls,
drifting up from the broad terrain through brush
    and woods.
Mulling it over, I thought I'd scout the ground –

Homer

that fire aglow in the smoke, I saw it, true,
but soon enough this seemed the better plan:
I'd go back to shore and the swift ship first,
feed the men, then send *them* out for scouting.
I was well on my way down, nearing our ship
when a god took pity on me, wandering all alone;
he sent me a big stag with high branching antlers,
right across my path – the sun's heat forced him down
from his forest range to drink at a river's banks –
just bounding out of the timber when I hit him
square in the backbone, halfway down the spine
and my bronze spear went punching clean through –
he dropped in the dust, groaning, gasping out his breath.
Treading on him, I wrenched my bronze spear from
    the wound,
left it there on the ground, and snapping off some twigs
and creepers, twisted a rope about a fathom long,
I braided it tight, hand over hand, then lashed
the four hocks of that magnificent beast.
Loaded round my neck I lugged him toward the ship,
trudging, propped on my spear – no way to sling him
over a shoulder, steadying him with one free arm –
the kill was so immense!
I flung him down by the hull and roused the men,
going up to them all with a word to lift their spirits:
"Listen to me, my comrades, brothers in hardship –
we won't go down to the House of Death, not yet,

The Bewitching Queen of Aeaea

not till our day arrives. Up with you, look,
there's still some meat and drink in our good ship.
Put our minds on food – why die of hunger here?"

    My hardy urging brought them round at once.
Heads came up from cloaks and there by the barren sea
they gazed at the stag, their eyes wide – my noble trophy.
But once they'd looked their fill and warmed their hearts,
they washed their hands and prepared a splendid meal.
Now all day long till the sun went down we sat
and feasted on sides of meat and seasoned wine.
Then when the sun had set and night came on
we lay down and slept at the water's shelving edge.
When young Dawn with her rose-red fingers shone once more
I called a muster quickly, informing all the crew,
"Listen to me, my comrades, brothers in hardship,
we can't tell east from west, the dawn from the dusk,
nor where the sun that lights our lives goes under earth
nor where it rises. We must think of a plan at once,
some cunning stroke. I doubt there's one still left.
I scaled a commanding crag and from that height
surveyed an entire island

ringed like a crown by endless wastes of sea.
But the land itself lies low, and I did see smoke
drifting up from its heart through thick brush and
> woods."

My message broke their spirit as they recalled
the gruesome work of the Laestrygonian king Antiphates
and the hearty cannibal Cyclops thirsting for our blood.
They burst into cries, wailing, streaming live tears
that gained us nothing – what good can come of grief?

And so, numbering off my band of men-at-arms
into two platoons, I assigned them each a leader:
I took one and lord Eurylochus the other.
We quickly shook lots in a bronze helmet –
the lot of brave Eurylochus leapt out first.
So he moved off with his two and twenty comrades,
weeping, leaving us behind in tears as well . . .
Deep in the wooded glens they came on Circe's palace
built of dressed stone on a cleared rise of land.
Mountain wolves and lions were roaming round the grounds –
she'd bewitched them herself, she gave them magic drugs.
But they wouldn't attack my men; they just came pawing
up around them, fawning, swishing their long tails –
eager as hounds that fawn around their master,
coming home from a feast,
who always brings back scraps to calm them down.
So they came nuzzling round my men – lions, wolves

The Bewitching Queen of Aeaea

with big powerful claws – and the men cringed in fear
at the sight of those strange, ferocious beasts... But still
they paused at her doors, the nymph with lovely braids,
Circe – and deep inside they heard her singing, lifting
her spellbinding voice as she glided back and forth
at her great immortal loom, her enchanting web
a shimmering glory only goddesses can weave.
Polites, captain of armies, took command,
the closest, most devoted man I had: "Friends,
there's someone inside, plying a great loom,
and how she sings – enthralling!
The whole house is echoing to her song.
Goddess or woman – let's call out to her now!"

So he urged and the men called out and hailed her.
She opened her gleaming doors at once and stepped
    forth,
inviting them all in, and in they went, all innocence.
Only Eurylochus stayed behind – he sensed a trap...
She ushered them in to sit on high-backed chairs,
then she mixed them a potion – cheese, barley
and pale honey mulled in Pramnian wine –
but into the brew she stirred her wicked drugs
to wipe from their memories any thought of home.
Once they'd drained the bowls she filled, suddenly
she struck with her wand, drove them into her pigsties,
all of them bristling into swine – with grunts,
snouts – even their bodies, yes, and only

the men's minds stayed steadfast as before.
So off they went to their pens, sobbing, squealing
as Circe flung them acorns, cornel nuts and mast,
common fodder for hogs that root and roll in mud.

Back Eurylochus ran to our swift black ship
to tell the disaster our poor friends had faced.
But try as he might, he couldn't get a word out.
Numbing sorrow had stunned the man to silence –
tears welled in his eyes, his heart possessed by grief.
We assailed him with questions – all at our wits' end –
till at last he could recount the fate our friends had met:
"Off we went through the brush, captain, as you commanded.
Deep in the wooded glens we came on Circe's palace
built of dressed stone on a cleared rise of land.
Someone inside was plying a great loom,
and how she sang – in a high clear voice!
Goddess or woman – we called out and hailed her . . .
She opened her gleaming doors at once and stepped forth,
inviting us all in, and in we went, all innocence.
But *I* stayed behind – I sensed a trap. Suddenly
all vanished – blotted out – not one face showed again,
though I sat there keeping watch a good long time."

At that report I slung the hefty bronze blade
of my silver-studded sword around my shoulder,

The Bewitching Queen of Aeaea

slung my bow on too and told our comrade,
"Lead me back by the same way that you came."
But he flung both arms around my knees and pleaded,
begging me with his tears and winging words:
"Don't force me back there, captain, king –
leave me here on the spot.
You will never return yourself, I swear,
you'll never bring back a single man alive.
Quick, cut and run with the rest of us here –
we can still escape the fatal day!"

    But I shot back, "Eurylochus, stay right here,
eating, drinking, safe by the black ship.
I must be off. Necessity drives me on."

    Leaving the ship and shore, I headed inland,
clambering up through hushed, entrancing glades until,
as I was nearing the halls of Circe skilled in spells,
approaching her palace – Hermes god of the
        golden wand
crossed my path, and he looked for all the world
like a young man sporting his first beard,
just in the prime and warm pride of youth,
and grasped me by the hand and asked me kindly,
"Where are you going now, my unlucky friend –
trekking over the hills alone in unfamiliar country?
And your men are all in there, in Circe's palace,
cooped like swine, hock by jowl in the sties.

Homer

Have you come to set them free?
Well, I warn you, you won't get home yourself,
you'll stay right there, trapped with all the rest.
But wait, I can save you, free you from that great danger.
Look, here is a potent drug. Take it to Circe's halls –
its power alone will shield you from the fatal day.
Let me tell you of all the witch's subtle craft . . .
She'll mix you a potion, lace the brew with drugs
but she'll be powerless to bewitch you, even so –
this magic herb I give will fight her spells.
Now here's your plan of action, step by step.
The moment Circe strikes with her long thin wand,
you draw your sharp sword sheathed at your hip
and rush her fast as if to run her through!
She'll cower in fear and coax you to her bed –
but don't refuse the goddess' bed, not then, not if
she's to release your friends and treat you well yourself.
But have her swear the binding oath of the blessed gods
she'll never plot some new intrigue to harm you,
once you lie there naked –
never unman you, strip away your courage!"

        With that
the giant-killer handed over the magic herb,
pulling it from the earth,
and Hermes showed me all its name and nature.
Its root is black and its flower white as milk
and the gods call it moly. Dangerous for a mortal man
to pluck from the soil but not for deathless gods.

The Bewitching Queen of Aeaea

All lies within their power.
                        Now Hermes went his way
to the steep heights of Olympus, over the island's woods
while I, just approaching the halls of Circe,
my heart a heaving storm at every step,
paused at her doors, the nymph with lovely braids –
I stood and shouted to her there. She heard my voice,
she opened her gleaming doors at once and stepped
        forth,
inviting me in, and in I went, all anguish now . . .
She led me in to sit on a silver-studded chair,
ornately carved, with a stool to rest my feet.
In a golden bowl she mixed a potion for me to drink,
stirring her poison in, her heart aswirl with evil.
And then she passed it on, I drank it down
but it never worked its spell –
she struck with her wand and "Now," she cried,
"off to your sty, you swine, and wallow with your friends!"
But I, I drew my sharp sword sheathed at my hip
and rushed her fast as if to run her through –
She screamed, slid under my blade, hugged my knees
with a flood of warm tears and a burst of winging words:
"Who are you? where are you from? your city?
        your parents?
I'm wonderstruck – you drank my drugs, you're
        not bewitched!
Never has any other man withstood my potion, never,
once it's past his lips and he has drunk it down.

Homer

You have a mind in *you* no magic can enchant!
You must be Odysseus, man of twists and turns –
Hermes the giant-killer, god of the golden wand,
he always said you'd come,
homeward bound from Troy in your swift black ship.
Come, sheathe your sword, let's go to bed together,
mount my bed and mix in the magic work of love –
we'll breed deep trust between us."

                                          So she enticed
but I fought back, still wary. "Circe, Circe,
how dare you tell me to treat you with any warmth?
You who turned my men to swine in your own house
        and now
you hold me here as well – teeming with treachery
you lure me to your room to mount your bed,
so once I lie there naked
you'll unman me, strip away my courage!
Mount your bed? Not for all the world. Not
until you consent to swear, goddess, a binding oath
you'll never plot some new intrigue to harm me!"

                                              Straightaway
she began to swear the oath that I required – never,
she'd never do me harm – and when she'd finished,
then, at last, I mounted Circe's gorgeous bed . . .

    At the same time her handmaids bustled through
        the halls,
four in all who perform the goddess' household tasks:

The Bewitching Queen of Aeaea

nymphs, daughters born of the springs and groves
and the sacred rivers running down to open sea.
One draped the chairs with fine crimson covers
over the seats she'd spread with linen cloths below.
A second drew up silver tables before the chairs
and laid out golden trays to hold the bread.
A third mulled heady, heart-warming wine
in a silver bowl and set out golden cups.
A fourth brought water and lit a blazing fire
beneath a massive cauldron. The water heated soon,
and once it reached the boil in the glowing bronze
she eased me into a tub and bathed me from
    the cauldron,
mixing the hot and cold to suit my taste, showering
head and shoulders down until she'd washed away
the spirit-numbing exhaustion from my body.
The bathing finished, rubbing me sleek with oil,
throwing warm fleece and a shirt around my shoulders,
she led me in to sit on a silver-studded chair,
ornately carved, with a stool to rest my feet.
A maid brought water soon in a graceful golden pitcher
and over a silver basin tipped it out
so I might rinse my hands,
then pulled a gleaming table to my side.
A staid housekeeper brought on bread to serve me,
appetizers aplenty too, lavish with her bounty.
She pressed me to eat. I had no taste for food.
I just sat there, mind wandering, far away . . .

lost in grim forebodings.
                              As soon as Circe saw me,
huddled, not touching my food, immersed in sorrow,
she sidled near with a coaxing, winged word:
"Odysseus, why just sit there, struck dumb,
eating your heart out, not touching food or drink?
Suspect me of still more treachery? Nothing to fear.
Haven't I just sworn my solemn, binding oath?"

   So she asked, but I protested, "Circe –
how could any man in his right mind endure
the taste of food and drink before he'd freed
his comrades-in-arms and looked them in the eyes?
If you, you really want me to eat and drink,
set them free, all my beloved comrades –
let me feast my eyes."
                      So I demanded.
Circe strode on through the halls and out,
her wand held high in hand and, flinging open the
       pens,
drove forth my men, who looked like full-grown swine.
Facing her, there they stood as she went along
       the ranks,
anointing them one by one with some new magic oil –
and look, the bristles grown by the first wicked drug
that Circe gave them slipped away from their limbs
and they turned men again: younger than ever,
taller by far, more handsome to the eye, and yes,

they knew me at once and each man grasped my hands
and a painful longing for tears overcame us all,
a terrible sobbing echoed through the house . . .
The goddess herself was moved and, standing by me,
warmly urged me on – a lustrous goddess now:
"Royal son of Laertes, Odysseus, tried and true,
go at once to your ship at the water's edge,
haul her straight up on the shore first
and stow your cargo and running gear in caves,
then back you come and bring your trusty crew."

   Her urging won my stubborn spirit over.
Down I went to the swift ship at the water's edge,
and there on the decks I found my loyal crew
consumed with grief and weeping live warm tears.
But now, as calves in stalls when cows come home,
droves of them herded back from field to farmyard
once they've grazed their fill – as all their young calves
come frisking out to meet them, bucking out of
      their pens,
lowing nonstop, jostling, rushing round their mothers –
so my shipmates there at the sight of my return
came pressing round me now, streaming tears,
so deeply moved in their hearts they felt as if
they'd made it back to their own land, their city,
Ithaca's rocky soil where they were bred and reared.
And through their tears their words went winging
      home:

"You're back again, my king! How thrilled we are –
as if we'd reached our country, Ithaca, at last!
But come, tell us about the fate our comrades met."

Still I replied with a timely word of comfort:
"Let's haul our ship straight up on the shore first
and stow our cargo and running gear in caves.
Then hurry, all of you, come along with me
to see our friends in the magic halls of Circe,
eating and drinking – the feast flows on forever."

So I said and they jumped to do my bidding.
Only Eurylochus tried to hold my shipmates back,
his mutinous outburst aimed at one and all:
"Poor fools, where are we running now?
Why are we tempting fate? –
why stumble blindly down to Circe's halls?
She'll turn us all into pigs or wolves or lions
made to guard that palace of hers – by force, I tell you –
just as the Cyclops trapped our comrades in his lair
with hotheaded Odysseus right beside them all –
thanks to this man's rashness they died too!'

So he declared and I had half a mind
to draw the sharp sword from beside my hip
and slice his head off, tumbling down in the dust,
close kin that he was. But comrades checked me,
each man trying to calm me, left and right:

The Bewitching Queen of Aeaea

"Captain, we'll leave him here if you command,
just where he is, to sit and guard the ship.
Lead us on to the magic halls of Circe."

                                                With that,
up from the ship and shore they headed inland.
Nor did Eurylochus malinger by the hull;
he straggled behind the rest,
dreading the sharp blast of my rebuke.

                                                  All the while
Circe had bathed my other comrades in her palace,
caring and kindly, rubbed them sleek with oil
and decked them out in fleecy cloaks and shirts.
We found them all together, feasting in her halls.
Once we had recognized each other, gazing face-to-face,
we all broke down and wept – and the house
      resounded now
and Circe the lustrous one came toward me, pleading,
"Royal son of Laertes, Odysseus, man of action,
no more tears now, calm these tides of sorrow.
Well I know what pains you bore on the swarming sea,
what punishment you endured from hostile men
      on land.
But come now, eat your food and drink your wine
till the same courage fills your chests, now as then,
when you first set sail from native land, from rocky
      Ithaca!
Now you are burnt-out husks, your spirits haggard, sere,
always brooding over your wanderings long and hard,

your hearts never lifting with any joy –
you've suffered far too much."

                              So she enticed
and won our battle-hardened spirits over.
And there we sat at ease,
day in, day out, till a year had run its course,
feasting on sides of meat and drafts of heady wine . . .
But then, when the year was gone and the seasons
    wheeled by
and the months waned and the long days came round
    again,
my loyal comrades took me aside and prodded,
"Captain, this is madness!
High time you thought of your own home at last,
if it really is your fate to make it back alive
and reach your well-built house and native land."

    Their urging brought my stubborn spirit round.
So all that day till the sun went down we sat
and feasted on sides of meat and heady wine.
Then when the sun had set and night came on
the men lay down to sleep in the shadowed halls
but I went up to that luxurious bed of Circe's,
hugged her by the knees
and the goddess heard my winging supplication:
"Circe, now make good a promise you gave me once –
it's time to help me home. My heart longs to be home,
my comrades' hearts as well. They wear me down,

The Bewitching Queen of Aeaea

pleading with me whenever you're away."

So I pressed
and the lustrous goddess answered me in turn:
"Royal son of Laertes, Odysseus, old campaigner,
stay on no more in my house against your will.
But first another journey calls. You must travel down
to the House of Death and the awesome one,
      Persephone,
there to consult the ghost of Tiresias, seer of Thebes,
the great blind prophet whose mind remains unshaken.
Even in death – Persephone has given him wisdom,
everlasting vision to him and him alone . . .
the rest of the dead are empty, flitting shades."

So she said and crushed the heart inside me.
I knelt in her bed and wept. I'd no desire
to go on living and see the rising light of day.
But once I'd had my fill of tears and writhing there,
at last I found the words to venture, "Circe, Circe,
who can pilot us on that journey? Who has ever
reached the House of Death in a black ship?"

The lustrous goddess answered, never pausing,
"Royal son of Laertes, Odysseus, born for exploits,
let no lack of a pilot at the helm concern you, no,
just step your mast and spread your white sail wide –
sit back and the North Wind will speed you on your way.
But once your vessel has cut across the Ocean River

you will raise a desolate coast and Persephone's Grove,
her tall black poplars, willows whose fruit dies young.
Beach your vessel hard by the Ocean's churning shore
and make your own way down to the moldering House
    of Death.
And there into Acheron, the Flood of Grief, two
    rivers flow,
the torrent River of Fire, the wailing River of Tears
that branches off from Styx, the Stream of Hate,
and a stark crag looms
where the two rivers thunder down and meet.
Once there, go forward, hero. Do as I say now.
Dig a trench of about a forearm's depth and length
and around it pour libations out to all the dead –
first with milk and honey, and then with mellow wine,
then water third and last, and sprinkle glistening
    barley
over it all, and vow again and again to all the dead,
to the drifting, listless spirits of their ghosts,
that once you return to Ithaca you will slaughter
a barren heifer in your halls, the best you have,
and load a pyre with treasures – and to Tiresias,
alone, apart, you will offer a sleek black ram,
the pride of all your herds. And once your prayers
have invoked the nations of the dead in their
    dim glory,
slaughter a ram and a black ewe, turning both
    their heads

The Bewitching Queen of Aeaea

toward Erebus, but turn your head away, looking
> toward

the Ocean River. Suddenly then the countless shades
of the dead and gone will surge around you there.
But order your men at once to flay the sheep
that lie before you, killed by your ruthless blade,
and burn them both, and then say prayers to the gods,
to the almighty god of death and dread Persephone.
But you – draw your sharp sword from beside
> your hip,

sit down on alert there, and never let the ghosts
of the shambling, shiftless dead come near that blood
till you have questioned Tiresias yourself. Soon, soon
the great seer will appear before you, captain of armies:
he will tell you the way to go, the stages of your voyage,
how you can cross the swarming sea and reach home
> at last."

And with those words Dawn rose on her golden
> throne

and Circe dressed me quickly in sea-cloak and shirt
while the queen slipped on a loose, glistening robe,
filmy, a joy to the eye, and round her waist
she ran a brocaded golden belt
and over her head a scarf to shield her brow.
And I strode on through the halls to stir my men,
hovering over each with a winning word: "Up now!
No more lazing away in sleep, we must set sail –

Queen Circe has shown the way."

                        I brought them round,
my hardy friends-in-arms, but not even from there
could I get them safely off without a loss . . .
There was a man, Elpenor, the youngest in our ranks,
none too brave in battle, none too sound in mind.
He'd strayed from his mates in Circe's magic halls
and keen for the cool night air,
sodden with wine he'd bedded down on her roofs.
But roused by the shouts and tread of marching men,
he leapt up with a start at dawn but still so dazed
he forgot to climb back down again by the long
       ladder –
headfirst from the roof he plunged, his neck snapped
from the backbone, his soul flew down to Death.

    Once on our way, I gave the men their orders:
"You think we are headed home, our own dear land?
Well, Circe sets us a rather different course . . .
down to the House of Death and the awesome one,
       Persephone,
there to consult the ghost of Tiresias, seer of Thebes."

    So I said, and it broke my shipmates' hearts.
They sank down on the ground, moaning, tore their
       hair.
But it gained us nothing – what good can come of
       grief?

The Bewitching Queen of Aeaea

    Back to the swift ship at the water's edge we went,
our spirits deep in anguish, faces wet with tears.
But Circe got to the dark hull before us,
tethered a ram and black ewe close by –
slipping past unseen. Who can glimpse a god
who wants to be invisible gliding here and there?"

1. BOCCACCIO · *Mrs Rosie and the Priest*
2. GERARD MANLEY HOPKINS · *As kingfishers catch fire*
3. *The Saga of Gunnlaug Serpent-tongue*
4. THOMAS DE QUINCEY · *On Murder Considered as One of the Fine Arts*
5. FRIEDRICH NIETZSCHE · *Aphorisms on Love and Hate*
6. JOHN RUSKIN · *Traffic*
7. PU SONGLING · *Wailing Ghosts*
8. JONATHAN SWIFT · *A Modest Proposal*
9. *Three Tang Dynasty Poets*
10. WALT WHITMAN · *On the Beach at Night Alone*
11. KENKŌ · *A Cup of Sake Beneath the Cherry Trees*
12. BALTASAR GRACIÁN · *How to Use Your Enemies*
13. JOHN KEATS · *The Eve of St Agnes*
14. THOMAS HARDY · *Woman much missed*
15. GUY DE MAUPASSANT · *Femme Fatale*
16. MARCO POLO · *Travels in the Land of Serpents and Pearls*
17. SUETONIUS · *Caligula*
18. APOLLONIUS OF RHODES · *Jason and Medea*
19. ROBERT LOUIS STEVENSON · *Olalla*
20. KARL MARX AND FRIEDRICH ENGELS · *The Communist Manifesto*
21. PETRONIUS · *Trimalchio's Feast*
22. JOHANN PETER HEBEL · *How a Ghastly Story Was Brought to Light by a Common or Garden Butcher's Dog*
23. HANS CHRISTIAN ANDERSEN · *The Tinder Box*
24. RUDYARD KIPLING · *The Gate of the Hundred Sorrows*
25. DANTE · *Circles of Hell*
26. HENRY MAYHEW · *Of Street Piemen*
27. HAFEZ · *The nightingales are drunk*
28. GEOFFREY CHAUCER · *The Wife of Bath*
29. MICHEL DE MONTAIGNE · *How We Weep and Laugh at the Same Thing*
30. THOMAS NASHE · *The Terrors of the Night*
31. EDGAR ALLAN POE · *The Tell-Tale Heart*
32. MARY KINGSLEY · *A Hippo Banquet*
33. JANE AUSTEN · *The Beautifull Cassandra*
34. ANTON CHEKHOV · *Gooseberries*
35. SAMUEL TAYLOR COLERIDGE · *Well, they are gone, and here must I remain*
36. JOHANN WOLFGANG VON GOETHE · *Sketchy, Doubtful, Incomplete Jottings*
37. CHARLES DICKENS · *The Great Winglebury Duel*
38. HERMAN MELVILLE · *The Maldive Shark*
39. ELIZABETH GASKELL · *The Old Nurse's Story*
40. NIKOLAY LESKOV · *The Steel Flea*

41. HONORÉ DE BALZAC · *The Atheist's Mass*
42. CHARLOTTE PERKINS GILMAN · *The Yellow Wall-Paper*
43. C.P. CAVAFY · *Remember, Body . . .*
44. FYODOR DOSTOEVSKY · *The Meek One*
45. GUSTAVE FLAUBERT · *A Simple Heart*
46. NIKOLAI GOGOL · *The Nose*
47. SAMUEL PEPYS · *The Great Fire of London*
48. EDITH WHARTON · *The Reckoning*
49. HENRY JAMES · *The Figure in the Carpet*
50. WILFRED OWEN · *Anthem For Doomed Youth*
51. WOLFGANG AMADEUS MOZART · *My Dearest Father*
52. PLATO · *Socrates' Defence*
53. CHRISTINA ROSSETTI · *Goblin Market*
54. *Sindbad the Sailor*
55. SOPHOCLES · *Antigone*
56. RYŪNOSUKE AKUTAGAWA · *The Life of a Stupid Man*
57. LEO TOLSTOY · *How Much Land Does A Man Need?*
58. GIORGIO VASARI · *Leonardo da Vinci*
59. OSCAR WILDE · *Lord Arthur Savile's Crime*
60. SHEN FU · *The Old Man of the Moon*
61. AESOP · *The Dolphins, the Whales and the Gudgeon*
62. MATSUO BASHŌ · *Lips too Chilled*
63. EMILY BRONTË · *The Night is Darkening Round Me*
64. JOSEPH CONRAD · *To-morrow*
65. RICHARD HAKLUYT · *The Voyage of Sir Francis Drake Around the Whole Globe*
66. KATE CHOPIN · *A Pair of Silk Stockings*
67. CHARLES DARWIN · *It was snowing butterflies*
68. BROTHERS GRIMM · *The Robber Bridegroom*
69. CATULLUS · *I Hate and I Love*
70. HOMER · *Circe and the Cyclops*
71. D. H. LAWRENCE · *Il Duro*
72. KATHERINE MANSFIELD · *Miss Brill*
73. OVID · *The Fall of Icarus*
74. SAPPHO · *Come Close*
75. IVAN TURGENEV · *Kasyan from the Beautiful Lands*
76. VIRGIL · *O Cruel Alexis*
77. H. G. WELLS · *A Slip under the Microscope*
78. HERODOTUS · *The Madness of Cambyses*
79. *Speaking of Siva*
80. *The Dhammapada*

'But I ran up the broken stairway, and came out suddenly, as by a miracle, clean on the platform of my San Tommaso, in the tremendous sunshine.'

D. H. LAWRENCE

Born 1885, Eastwood, England

Died 1930, Vence, France

'The Spinner and the Monks', 'Il Duro' and 'John' are taken from *Twilight in Italy*, first published in 1916.
'The Florence Museum' is taken from *Etruscan Places*, first published in 1932.

D. H. LAWRENCE IN PENGUIN CLASSICS

Apocalypse
D. H. Lawrence and Italy
The Fox, the Captain's Doll, the Ladybird
Lady Chatterley's Lover
The Prussian Officer and Other Stories
The Rainbow
Sea and Sardinia
Selected Poems

D. H. LAWRENCE

Il Duro

PENGUIN BOOKS

PENGUIN CLASSICS

UK | USA | Canada | Ireland | Australia
India | New Zealand | South Africa

Penguin Books is part of the Penguin Random House group of companies
whose addresses can be found at global.penguinrandomhouse.com.

This selection published in Penguin Classics 2015

008

Set in 9.5/13 pt Baskerville 10 Pro
Typeset by Jouve (UK), Milton Keynes
Printed and bound in Great Britain by Clays Ltd, Elcograf S.p.A.

A CIP catalogue record for this book is available from the British Library

ISBN: 978-0-141-39863-1

www.greenpenguin.co.uk

MIX
Paper from
responsible sources
FSC® C018179

Penguin Random House is committed to a
sustainable future for our business, our readers
and our planet. This book is made from Forest
Stewardship Council® certified paper.

Contents

The Spinner and the Monks   1

Il Duro   20

John   30

The Florence Museum   49

The Spinner and the Monks

The Holy Spirit is a Dove, or an Eagle. In the Old Testament it was an Eagle; in the New Testament it is a Dove.

And there are, standing over the Christian world, the Churches of the Dove and the Churches of the Eagle. There are, moreover, the Churches which do not belong to the Holy Spirit at all, but which are built to pure fancy and logic; such as the Wren Churches in London.

The Churches of the Dove are shy and hidden: they nestle among trees, and their bells sound in the mellowness of Sunday; or they are gathered into a silence of their own in the very midst of the town, so that one passes them by without observing them; they are as if invisible, offering no resistance to the storming of the traffic.

But the Churches of the Eagle stand high, with their heads to the skies, as if they challenged the world below. They are the Churches of the Spirit of David, and their bells ring passionately, imperiously, falling on the subservient world below.

The Church of San Francesco was a Church of the Dove. I passed it several times, in the dark, silent little square, without knowing it was a church. Its pink walls were blind, windowless, unnoticeable, it gave no sign, unless one caught sight of the tan curtain hanging in the door, and the slit of darkness beneath. Yet it was the chief church of the village.

But the Church of San Tommaso perched over the village. Coming down the cobbled, submerged street, many a time I looked up between the houses and saw the thin old church standing above in the light, as if it perched on the house-roofs. Its thin grey neck was held up stiffly, beyond was a vision of dark foliage, and the high hillside.

I saw it often, and yet for a long time it never occurred to me that it actually existed. It was like a vision, a thing one does not expect to come close to. It was there standing away upon the house-tops, against a glamour of foliaged hillside. I was submerged in the village, on the uneven, cobbled street, between old high walls and cavernous shops and the houses with flights of steps.

For a long time I knew how the day went, by the imperious clangour of midday and evening bells striking down upon the houses and the edge of the lake. Yet it did not occur to me to ask where these bells rang. Till at last my everyday trance was broken in upon, and I knew the ringing of the Church of San Tommaso. The church became a living connection with me.

So I set out to find it, I wanted to go to it. It was very near. I could see it from the piazza by the lake. And the

The Spinner and the Monks

village itself had only a few hundreds of inhabitants. The church must be within a stone's throw.

Yet I could not find it. I went out of the back door of the house, into the narrow gulley of the back street. Women glanced down at me from the top of the flights of steps, old men stood, half-turning, half-crouching under the dark shadow of the walls, to stare. It was as if the strange creatures of the under-shadow were looking at me. I was of another element.

The Italian people are called 'Children of the Sun.' They might better be called 'Children of the Shadow.' Their souls are dark and nocturnal. If they are to be easy, they must be able to hide, to be hidden in lairs and caves of darkness. Going through these tiny, chaotic back-ways of the village was like venturing through the labyrinth made by furtive creatures, who watched from out of another element. And I was pale, and clear, and evanescent, like the light, and they were dark, and close, and constant, like the shadow.

So I was quite baffled by the tortuous, tiny, deep passages of the village. I could not find my way. I hurried towards the broken end of a street, where the sunshine and the olive trees looked like a mirage before me. And there above me I saw the thin, stiff neck of old San Tommaso, grey and pale in the sun. Yet I could not get up to the church, I found myself again on the piazza.

Another day, however, I found a broken staircase, where weeds grew in the gaps the steps had made in falling, and maidenhair hung on the darker side of the wall. I went up unwillingly, because the Italians used this old staircase as a privy, as they will any deep side-passage.

But I ran up the broken stairway, and came out suddenly, as by a miracle, clean on the platform of my San Tommaso, in the tremendous sunshine.

It was another world, the world of the eagle, the world of fierce abstraction. It was all clear, overwhelming sunshine, a platform hung in the light. Just below were the confused, tiled roofs of the village, and beyond them the pale blue water, down below; and opposite, opposite my face and breast, the clear, luminous snow of the mountain across the lake, level with me apparently, though really much above.

I was in the skies now, looking down from my square terrace of cobbled pavement, that was worn like the threshold of the ancient church. Round the terrace ran a low, broad wall, the coping of the upper heaven where I had climbed.

There was a blood-red sail like a butterfly breathing down on the blue water, whilst the earth on the near side gave off a green-silver smoke of olive trees, coming up and around the earth-coloured roofs.

It always remains to me that San Tommaso and its terrace hang suspended above the village, like the lowest step of heaven, of Jacob's ladder. Behind, the land rises in a high sweep. But the terrace of San Tommaso is let down from heaven, and does not touch the earth.

The Spinner and the Monks

I went into the church. It was very dark, and impregnated with centuries of incense. It affected me like the lair of some enormous creature. My senses were roused, they sprang awake in the hot, spiced darkness. My skin was expectant, as if it expected some contact, some embrace, as if it were aware of the contiguity of the physical world, the physical contact with the darkness and the heavy, suggestive substance of the enclosure. It was a thick, fierce darkness of the senses. But my soul shrank.

I went out again. The pavemented threshold was clear as a jewel, the marvellous clarity of sunshine that becomes blue in the height seemed to distil me into itself.

Across, the heavy mountain crouched along the side of the lake, the upper half brilliantly white, belonging to the sky, the lower half dark and grim. So then, that is where heaven and earth are divided. From behind me, on the left, the headland swept down out of a great, pale-grey, arid height, through a rush of russet and crimson, to the olive smoke and the water of the level earth. And between, like a blade of the sky cleaving the earth asunder, went the pale-blue lake, cleaving mountain from mountain with the triumph of the sky.

Then I noticed that a big, blue-checked cloth was spread on the parapet before me, over the parapet of heaven. I wondered why it hung there.

Turning round, on the other side of the terrace, under a caper-bush that hung like a blood-stain from the grey wall above her, stood a little grey woman whose fingers were busy. Like the grey church, she made me feel as if I were not in existence. I was wandering by the parapet of heaven, looking down. But she stood back against the solid wall, under the caper-bush, unobserved and unobserving. She was like a fragment of earth, she was a living stone of the terrace, sun-bleached. She took no notice of me, who was hesitating looking down at the earth beneath. She stood back under the sun-bleached solid wall, like a stone rolled down and stayed in a crevice.

Her head was tied in a dark-red kerchief, but pieces of hair, like dirty snow, quite short, stuck out over her ears. And she was spinning. I wondered so much, that I could not cross towards her. She was grey, and her apron, and her dress, and her kerchief, and her hands and her face were all sun-bleached and sun-stained, greyey, bluey, browny, like stones and half-coloured leaves, sunny in their colourlessness. In my black coat, I felt myself wrong, false, an outsider.

She was spinning, spontaneously, like a little wind. Under her arm she held a distaff of dark, ripe wood, just a straight stick with a clutch at the end, like a grasp of brown fingers full of a fluff of blackish, rusty fleece, held up near her shoulder. And her fingers were plucking spontaneously at the strands of wool drawn down from it. And hanging near her feet, spinning round upon a black thread, spinning busily, like a thing in a gay wind, was her shuttle, her bobbin wound fat with the coarse, blackish worsted she was making.

The Spinner and the Monks

All the time, like motion without thought her fingers teased out the fleece, drawing it down to a fairly uniform thickness: brown, old, natural fingers that worked as in a sleep, the thumb having a long grey nail; and from moment to moment there was a quick, downward rub, between thumb and forefinger, of the thread that hung in front of her apron, the heavy bobbin spun more briskly, and she felt again at the fleece as she drew it down, and she gave a twist to the thread that issued, and the bobbin spun swiftly.

Her eyes were clear as the sky, blue, empyrean, transcendent. They were clear, but they had no looking in them. Her face was like a sun-worn stone.

'You are spinning,' I said to her.

Her eyes glanced over me, making no effort of attention.

'Yes,' she said.

She saw merely a man's figure, a stranger, standing near. I was a bit of the outside, negligible. She remained as she was, clear and sustained like an old stone upon the hillside. She stood short and sturdy, looking for the most part straight in front, unseeing, but glancing from time to time, with a little, unconscious attention, at the thread. She was slightly more animated than the sunshine and the stone and the motionless caper-bush above her. Still her fingers went along the strand of fleece near her breast.

'That is an old way of spinning,' I said.

'What?'

She looked up at me with eyes clear and transcendent as the heavens. But she was slightly roused. There was the slight motion of the eagle in her turning to look at me, a faint gleam of rapt light in her eyes. It was my unaccustomed Italian.

'That is an old way of spinning,' I repeated.

'Yes – an old way,' she repeated, as if to say the words so that they should be natural to her. And I became to her merely a transient circumstance, a man, part of the surroundings. We divided the gift of speech, that was all.

She glanced at me again, with her wonderful, unchanging eyes, that were like the visible heavens, unthinking, or like two flowers that are open in pure clear unconsciousness. To her I was a piece of the environment. That was all. Her world was clear and absolute, without consciousness of self. She was not self-conscious, because she was not aware that there was anything in the universe except *her* universe. In her universe I was a stranger, a foreign *signore*. That I had a world of my own, other than her own, was not conceived by her. She did not care.

So we conceive the stars. We are told that they are other worlds. But the stars are the clustered and single gleaming lights in the night-sky of our world. When I come home at night, there are the stars. When I cease to exist as the microcosm, when I begin to think of the cosmos, then the stars are other worlds. Then the macrocosm absorbs

The Spinner and the Monks

me. But the macrocosm is not me. It is something which I, the microcosm, am not.

So that there is something which is unknown to me and which nevertheless exists. I am finite, and my understanding has limits. The universe is bigger than I shall ever see, in mind or spirit. There is that which is not me.

If I say 'The planet Mars is inhabited,' I do not know what I mean by 'inhabited,' with reference to the planet Mars. I can only mean that that world is not my world. I can only know there is that which is not me. I am the microcosm, but the macrocosm is that also which I am not.

The old woman on the terrace in the sun did not know this. She was herself the core and centre to the world, the sun, and the single firmament. She knew that I was an inhabitant of lands which she had never seen: But what of that! There were parts of her own body which she had never seen, which physiologically she could never see. They were none the less her own because she had never seen them. The lands she had not seen were corporate parts of her own living body, the knowledge she had not attained was only the hidden knowledge of her own self. She *was* the substance of the knowledge, whether she had the knowledge in her mind or not. There was nothing which was not herself, ultimately. Even the man, the male, was part of herself. He was the mobile, separate part, but he was none the less herself because he was sometimes severed from her. If every apple in the world were cut in two, the apple would not be changed. The reality is the apple, which is just the same in the half apple as in the whole.

And she; the old spinning-woman, was the apple, eternal, unchangeable, whole even in her partiality. It was this which gave the wonderful clear unconsciousness to her eyes. How could she be conscious of herself, when all was herself?

She was talking to me of a sheep that had died, but I could not understand, because of her dialect. It never occurred to her that I could not understand. She only thought me different, stupid. And she talked on. The ewes had lived under the house, and a part was divided off for the he-goat, because the other people brought their she-goats to be covered by the he-goat. But how the ewe came to die I could not make out.

Her fingers worked away all the time in a little, half-fretful movement, yet spontaneous as butterflies leaping here and there. She chattered rapidly on in her Italian that I could not understand, looking meanwhile into my face, because the story roused her somewhat. Yet not a feature moved. Her eyes remained candid and open and unconscious as the skies. Only a sharp will in them now and then seemed to gleam at me, as if to dominate me.

Her shuttle had caught in a dead chicory plant, and spun no more. She did not notice. I stooped and broke

The Spinner and the Monks

off the twigs. There was a glint of blue on them yet. Seeing what I was doing, she merely withdrew a few inches from the plant. Her bobbin hung free.

She went on with her tale, looking at me wonderfully. She seemed like the Creation, like the beginning of the world, the first morning. Her eyes were like the first morning of the world, so ageless.

Her thread broke. She seemed to take no notice, but mechanically picked up the shuttle, wound up a length of worsted, connected the ends from her wool strand, set the bobbin spinning again, and went on talking, in her half-intimate, half-unconscious fashion, as if she were talking to her own world in me.

So she stood in the sunshine on the little platform, old and yet like the morning, erect and solitary, sun-coloured, sun-discoloured, whilst I at her elbow, like a piece of night and moonshine, stood smiling into her eyes, afraid lest she should deny me existence.

Which she did. She had stopped talking, did not look at me any more, but went on with her spinning, the brown shuttle twisting gaily. So she stood, belonging to the sunshine and the weather, taking no more notice of me than of the dark-stained caper-bush which hung from the wall above her head, whilst I, waiting at her side, was like the moon in the daytime sky, over-shone, obliterated, in spite of my black clothes.

'How long has it taken you to do that much?' I asked.

She waited a minute, glanced at her bobbin.

'This much? I don't know. A day or two.'

'But you do it quickly.'

She looked at me, as if suspiciously and derisively. Then, quite suddenly, she started forward and went across the terrace to the great blue-and-white checked cloth that was drying on the wall. I hesitated. She had cut off her consciousness from me. So I turned and ran away, taking the steps two at a time, to get away from her. In a moment I was between the walls, climbing upwards, hidden.

The school-mistress had told me I should find snowdrops behind San Tommaso. If she had not asserted such confident knowledge I should have doubted her translation of *perce-neige*. She meant Christmas roses all the while.

However, I went looking for snowdrops. The walls broke down suddenly, and I was out in a grassy olive orchard, following a track beside pieces of fallen overgrown masonry. So I came to skirt the brink of a steep little gorge, at the bottom of which a stream was rushing down its steep slant to the lake. Here I stood to look for my snowdrops. The grassy, rocky bank went down steep from my feet. I heard water tittle-tattling away in deep shadow below. There were pale flecks in the dimness, but these, I knew, were primroses. So I scrambled down.

Looking up, out of the heavy shadow that lay in the cleft, I could see, right in the sky, grey rocks shining transcendent in the pure empyrean. 'Are they so far up?' I

The Spinner and the Monks

thought. I did not dare to say, 'Am I so far down?' But I was uneasy. Nevertheless it was a lovely place, in the cold shadow, complete; when one forgot the shining rocks far above, it was a complete, shadowless world of shadow. Primroses were everywhere in nests of pale bloom upon the dark, steep face of the cleft, and tongues of fern hanging out, and here and there under the rods and twigs of bushes were tufts of wrecked Christmas roses, nearly over, but still, in the coldest corners, the lovely buds like handfuls of snow. There had been such crowded sumptuous tufts of Christmas roses everywhere in the stream-gullies, during the shadow of winter, that these few remaining flowers were hardly noticeable.

I gathered instead the primroses, that smelled of earth and of the weather. There were no snowdrops. I had found the day before a bank of crocuses, pale, fragile, lilac-coloured flowers with dark veins, pricking up keenly like myriad little lilac-coloured flames among the grass, under the olive trees. And I wanted very much to find the snowdrops hanging in the gloom. But there were not any.

I gathered a handful of primroses, then I climbed suddenly, quickly out of the deep watercourse, anxious to get back to the sunshine before the evening fell. Up above I saw the olive trees in their sunny golden grass, and sunlit grey rocks immensely high up. I was afraid lest the evening would fall whilst I was groping about like an otter in the damp and the darkness, that the day of sunshine would be over.

Soon I was up in the sunshine again, on the turf under the olive trees, reassured. It was the upper world of glowing light, and I was safe again.

All the olives were gathered, and the mills were going night and day, making a great, acrid scent of olive oil in preparation, by the lake. The little stream rattled down. A mule driver 'Hued!' to his mules on the Strada Vecchia. High up, on the Strada Nuova, the beautiful, new, military high-road, which winds with beautiful curves up the mountain-side, crossing the same stream several times in clear-leaping bridges, travelling cut out of sheer slope high above the lake, winding beautifully and gracefully forward to the Austrian frontier, where it ends: high up on the lovely swinging road, in the strong evening sunshine, I saw a bullock wagon moving like a vision, though the clanking of the wagon and the crack of the bullock whip resounded close in my ears.

Everything was clear and sun-coloured up there, clear-grey rocks partaking of the sky, tawny grass and scrub, browny-green spires of cypresses, and then the mist of grey-green olives fuming down to the lake-side. There was no shadow, only clear sun-substance built up to the sky, a bullock wagon moving slowly in the high sunlight, along the uppermost terrace of the military road. I sat in the warm stillness of the transcendent afternoon.

The four o'clock steamer was creeping down the lake from the Austrian end, creeping under the cliffs. Far away, the Verona side, beyond the Island, lay fused in dim gold.

The Spinner and the Monks

The mountain opposite was so still, that my heart seemed to fade in its beating, as if it too would be still. All was perfectly still, pure substance. The little steamer on the floor of the world below, the mules down the road cast no shadow. They too were pure sun-substance travelling on the surface of the sun-made world.

A cricket hopped near me. Then I remembered that it was Saturday afternoon, when a strange suspension comes over the world. And then, just below me, I saw two monks walking in their garden between the naked, bony vines, walking in their wintry garden of bony vines and olive trees, their brown cassocks passing between the brown vine-stocks, their heads bare to the sunshine, sometimes a glint of light as their feet strode from under their skirts.

It was so still, everything so perfectly suspended, that I felt them talking. They marched with the peculiar march of monks, a long, loping stride, their heads together, their skirts swaying slowly, two brown monks with hidden hands, sliding under the bony vines and beside the cabbages, their heads always together in hidden converse. It was as if I were attending with my dark soul to their inaudible undertone. All the time I sat still in silence, I was one with them, a partaker, though I could hear no sound of their voices. I went with the long stride of their skirted feet, that slid springless and noiseless from end to end of the garden, and back again. Their hands were kept down at their sides, hidden in the long sleeves and the skirts of their robes. They did not touch each other, nor gesticulate as they walked. There was no motion save the long, furtive stride and the heads leaning together. Yet there was an eagerness in their conversation. Almost like shadow-creatures ventured out of their cold, obscure element, they went backwards and forwards in their wintry garden, thinking nobody could see them.

Across, above them, was the faint, rousing dazzle of snow. They never looked up. But the dazzle of snow began to glow as they walked, the wonderful, faint, ethereal flush of the long range of snow in the heavens, at evening, began to kindle. Another world was coming to pass, the cold, rare night. It was dawning in exquisite, icy rose upon the long mountain-summit opposite. The monks walked backwards and forwards, talking, in the first undershadow.

And I noticed that up above the snow, frail in the bluish sky, a frail moon had put forth, like a thin, scalloped film of ice floated out on the slow current of the coming night. And a bell sounded.

And still the monks were pacing backwards and forwards, backwards and forwards, with a strange, neutral regularity.

The shadows were coming across everything, because of the mountains in the West. Already the olive wood where I sat was extinguished. This was the world of the monks, the rim of pallor between night and day. Here

The Spinner and the Monks

they paced, backwards and forwards, backwards and forwards, in the neutral, shadowless light of shadow.

Neither the flare of day nor the completeness of night reached them, they paced the narrow path of the twilight, treading in the neutrality of the law. Neither the blood nor the spirit spoke in them, only the law, the abstraction of the average. The infinite is positive and negative. But the average is only neutral. And the monks trod backward and forward down the line of neutrality.

Meanwhile, on the length of mountain-ridge, the snow grew rosy-incandescent, like heaven breaking into blossom. After all, eternal not-being and eternal being are the same. In the rosy snow that shone in heaven over a darkened earth was the ecstasy of consummation. Night and day are one, light and dark are one, both the same in the origin and in the issue, both the same in the moment of ecstasy, light fused in darkness and darkness fused in light, as in the rosy snow above the twilight.

But in the monks it was not ecstasy, in them it was neutrality, the under earth. Transcendent, above the shadowed, twilit earth was the rosy snow of ecstasy. But spreading far over us, down below, was the neutrality of the twilight, of the monks. The flesh neutralising the spirit, the spirit neutralising the flesh, the law of the average asserted, this was the monks as they paced backward and forward.

The moon climbed higher, away from the snowy, fading

ridge, she became gradually herself. Between the roots of the olive tree was a rosy-tipped daisy just going to sleep. I gathered it and put it among the frail, moony little bunch of primroses, so that its sleep should warm the rest. Also I put in some little periwinkles, that were very blue, reminding me of the eyes of the old woman.

The day was gone, the twilight was gone, and the snow was invisible as I came down to the side of the lake. Only the moon, white and shining, was in the sky, like a woman glorying in her own loveliness as she loiters superbly to the gaze of all the world, looking sometimes through the fringe of dark olive leaves, sometimes looking at her own superb, quivering body, wholly naked in the water of the lake.

My little old woman was gone. She, all day-sunshine, would have none of the moon. Always she must live like a bird, looking down on all the world at once, so that it lay all subsidiary to herself, herself the wakeful consciousness hovering over the world like a hawk, like a sleep of wakefulness. And, like a bird, she went to sleep as the shadows came.

She did not know the yielding up of the senses and the possession of the unknown, through the senses, which happens under a superb moon. The all-glorious sun knows none of these yieldings up. He takes his way. And the daisies at once go to sleep. And the soul of the old spinning-woman also closed up at sunset, the rest was a sleep, a cessation.

The Spinner and the Monks

It is all so strange and varied: the dark-skinned Italians ecstatic in the night and the moon, the blue-eyed old woman ecstatic in the busy sunshine, the monks in the garden below, who are supposed to unite both, passing only in the neutrality of the average. Where, then, is the meeting-point: where in mankind is the ecstasy of light and dark together, the supreme transcendence of the afterglow, day hovering in the embrace of the coming night like two angels embracing in the heavens, like Eurydice in the arms of Orpheus, or Persephone embraced by Pluto?

Where is the supreme ecstasy in mankind, which makes day a delight and night a delight, purpose an ecstasy and a concourse in ecstasy, and single abandon of the single body and soul also an ecstasy under the moon? Where is the transcendent knowledge in our hearts, uniting sun and darkness, day and night, spirit and senses? Why do we not know that the two in consummation are one; that each is only part; partial and alone for ever; but that the two in consummation are perfect, beyond the range of loneliness or solitude?

Il Duro

The first time I saw Il Duro was on a sunny day when there came up a party of pleasure-makers to San Gaudenzio. They were three women and three men. The women were in cotton frocks, one a large, dark, florid woman in pink, the other two rather insignificant. The men I scarcely noticed at first, except that two were young and one elderly.

They were a queer party, even on a feast day, coming up purely for pleasure, in the morning, strange, and slightly uncertain, advancing between the vines. They greeted Maria and Paolo in loud, coarse voices. There was something blowsy and uncertain and hesitating about the women in particular, which made one at once notice them.

Then a picnic was arranged for them out of doors, on the grass. They sat just in front of the house, under the olive tree, beyond the well. It should have been pretty, the women in their cotton frocks and their friends, sitting with wine and food in the spring sunshine. But somehow it was not: it was hard and slightly ugly.

Il Duro

But since they were picnicking out of doors, we must do so too. We were at once envious. But Maria was a little unwilling, and then she set a table for us.

The strange party did not speak to us, they seemed slightly uneasy and angry at our presence. I asked Maria who they were. She lifted her shoulders, and, after a second's cold pause, said they were people from down below, and then, in her rather strident, shrill, slightly bitter, slightly derogatory voice, she added:

'They are not people for you, Signore. You don't know them.'

She spoke slightly angrily and contemptuously of them, rather protectively of me. So that vaguely I gathered that they were not quite 'respectable.'

Only one man came into the house. He was very handsome, beautiful rather, a man of thirty-two or -three, with a clear golden skin, and perfectly turned face, something godlike. But the expression was strange. His hair was jet black and fine and smooth, glossy as a bird's wing, his brows were beautifully drawn, calm above his grey eyes, that had long, dark lashes.

His eyes, however, had a sinister light in them, a pale, slightly repelling gleam, very much like a god's pale-gleaming eyes, with the same vivid pallor. And all his face had the slightly malignant, suffering look of a satyr. Yet he was very beautiful.

He walked quickly and surely, with his head rather down, passing from his desire to his object, absorbed, yet curiously indifferent, as if the transit were in a strange world, as if none of what he was doing were worth the while. Yet he did it for his own pleasure, and the light on his face, a pale, strange gleam through his clear skin, remained like a translucent smile, unchanging as time.

He seemed familiar with the household, he came and fetched wine at his will. Maria was angry with him. She railed loudly and violently. He was unchanged. He went out with the wine to the party on the grass. Maria regarded them all with some hostility.

They drank a good deal out there in the sunshine. The women and the older man talked floridly. Il Duro crouched at the feast in his curious fashion – he had strangely flexible loins, upon which he seemed to crouch forward. But he was separate, like an animal that remains quite single, no matter where it is.

The party remained until about two o'clock. Then, slightly flushed, it moved on in a ragged group up to the village beyond. I do not know if they went to one of the inns of the stony village, or to the large strange house which belonged to the rich young grocer of the village below, a house kept only for feasts and riots, uninhabited for the most part. Maria would tell me nothing about them. Only the young well-to-do grocer, who had lived in Vienna, the Bertolotti, came later in the afternoon enquiring for the party.

And towards sunset I saw the elderly man of the group stumbling home very drunk down the path, after the two

Il Duro

women, who had gone on in front. Then Paolo sent Giovanni to see the drunken one safely past the landslip, which was dangerous. Altogether it was an unsatisfactory business, very much like any other such party in any other country.

Then in the evening Il Duro came in. His name is Faustino, but everybody in the village has a nickname, which is almost invariably used. He came in and asked for supper. We had all eaten. So he ate a little food alone at the table, whilst we sat round the fire.

Afterwards we played 'Up, Jenkins.' That was the one game we played with the peasants, except that exciting one of theirs, which consists in shouting in rapid succession your guesses at the number of fingers rapidly spread out and shut into the hands again upon the table.

Il Duro joined in the game. And that was because he had been in America, and now was rich. He felt he could come near to the strange Signori. But he was always inscrutable.

It was queer to look at the hands spread on the table: the Englishwomen, having rings on their soft fingers; the large fresh hands of the elder boy, the brown paws of the younger; Paolo's distorted great hard hands of a peasant; and the big, dark brown, animal, shapely hands of Faustino.

He had been in America first for two years and then for five years – seven years altogether – but he only spoke a very little English. He was always with Italians. He had served chiefly in a flag factory, and had had very little to do save to push a trolley with flags from the dyeing-room to the drying-room – I believe it was this.

Then he had come home from America with a fair amount of money, he had taken his uncle's garden, had inherited his uncle's little house, and he lived quite alone.

He was rich, Maria said, shouting in her strident voice. He at once disclaimed it, peasant-wise. But before the Signori he was glad also to appear rich. He was mean, that was more, Maria cried, half-teasing, half getting at him.

He attended to his garden, grew vegetables all the year round, lived in his little house, and in spring made good money as a vine-grafter: he was an expert vine-grafter.

After the boys had gone to bed he sat and talked to me. He was curiously attractive and curiously beautiful, but somehow like stone in his clear colouring and his clear-cut face. His temples, with the black hair, were distinct and fine as a work of art.

But always his eyes had this strange, half-diabolic, half-tortured pale gleam, like a goat's, and his mouth was shut almost uglily, his cheeks stern. His moustache was brown, his teeth strong and spaced. The women said it was a pity his moustache was brown.

'Peccato! – sa, per bellezza, i baffi neri – ah-h!'

Then a long-drawn exclamation of voluptuous appreciation.

'You live quite alone?' I said to him.

Il Duro

He did. And even when he had been ill he was alone. He had been ill two years before. His cheeks seemed to harden like marble, and to become pale at the thought. He was afraid, like marble with fear.

'But why?' I said, 'why do you live alone? You are sad – è triste.'

He looked at me with his queer, pale eyes.

I felt a great static misery in him, something very strange.

'Triste!' he repeated, stiffening up, hostile. I could not understand.

'Vuol' dire che hai l'aria dolorosa,' cried Maria, like a chorus interpreting. And there was always a sort of loud ring of challenge somewhere in her voice.

'Sad,' I said, in English.

'Sad!' he repeated, also in English. And he did not smile or change, only his face seemed to become more stone-like. And he only looked at me, into my eyes, with the long, pale, steady, inscrutable look of a goat, I can only repeat, something stone-like.

'Why,' I said, 'don't you marry? Man doesn't live alone.'

'I don't marry,' he said to me, in his emphatic, deliberate, cold fashion, 'because I've seen too much. Ho visto troppo.'

'I don't understand,' I said.

Yet I could feel that Paolo, sitting silent, like a monolith also, in the chimney opening, he understood: Maria also understood.

Il Duro looked again steadily into my eyes.

'Ho visto troppo,' he repeated, and the words seemed engraved on stone. 'I've seen too much.'

'But you can marry,' I said, 'however much you have seen, if you have seen all the world.'

He watched me steadily, like a strange creature looking at me.

'What woman?' he said to me.

'You can find a woman – there are plenty of women,' I said.

'Not for me,' he said. 'I have known too many. I've known too much, I can marry nobody.'

'Do you dislike women?' I said.

'No – quite otherwise. I don't think ill of them.'

'Then why can't you marry? Why must you live alone?'

'Why live with a woman?' he said to me, and he looked mockingly. 'Which woman is it to be?'

'You can find her,' I said. 'There are many women.'

Again he shook his head in the stony, final fashion.

'Not for me. I have known too much.'

'But does that prevent you from marrying?'

He looked at me steadily, finally. And I could see it was impossible for us to understand each other, or for me to understand him. I could not understand the strange white gleam of his eyes, where it came from.

Also I knew he liked me very much, almost loved me, which again was strange and puzzling. It was as if he were a fairy, a faun, and had no soul. But he gave me a feeling of vivid sadness, a sadness that gleamed like phosphorescence. He himself was not sad. There was a completeness about him, about the pallid otherworld he inhabited, which excluded sadness. It was too complete, too final, too defined. There was no yearning, no vague merging off into mistiness ... He was as clear and fine as semi-transparent rock, as a substance in moonlight. He seemed like a crystal that has achieved its final shape and has nothing more to achieve.

That night he slept on the floor of the sitting-room. In the morning he was gone. But a week after he came again, to graft the vines.

All the morning and the afternoon he was among the vines, crouching before them, cutting them back with his sharp, bright knife, amazingly swift and sure, like a god. It filled me with a sort of panic to see him crouched flexibly, like some strange animal god, doubled on his haunches, before the young vines, and swiftly, vividly, without thought, cut, cut, cut at the young budding shoots, which fell unheeded on to the earth. Then again he strode with his curious, half goat-like movement across the garden, to prepare the lime.

He mixed the messy stuff, cow-dung and lime and water and earth, carefully with his hands, as if he understood that too. He was not a worker. He was a creature in intimate communion with the sensible world, knowing purely by touch the limey mess he mixed amongst, knowing as if by relation between that soft matter and the matter of himself.

Then again he strode over the earth, a gleaming piece of earth himself, moving to the young vines. Quickly, with a few clean cuts of the knife, he prepared the new shoot, which he had picked out of a handful which lay beside him on the ground, he went finely to the quick of the plant, inserted the graft, then bound it up, fast, hard.

It was like God grafting the life of man upon the body of the earth, intimately, conjuring with his own flesh.

All the while Paolo stood by, somehow excluded from the mystery, talking to me, to Faustino. And Il Duro answered easily, as if his mind were disengaged. It was his senses that were absorbed in the sensible life of the plant and the lime and the cow-dung he handled.

Watching him, watching his absorbed, bestial, and yet god-like crouching before the plant, as if he were the god of lower life, I somehow understood his isolation, why he did not marry. Pan and the ministers of Pan do not marry, the sylvan gods. They are single and isolated in their being.

It is in the spirit that marriage takes place. In the flesh there is connection; but only in the spirit is there a new thing created out of two different antithetic things. In the body I am conjoined with the woman. But in the spirit my conjunction with her creates a third thing, an absolute, a Word, which is neither me nor her, nor of me nor of her, but which is absolute.

Il Duro

And Faustino had none of this spirit. In him sensation itself was absolute – not spiritual consummation, but physical sensation. So he could not marry, it was not for him. He belonged to the god Pan, to the absolute of the senses.

All the while his beauty, so perfect and so defined, fascinated me, a strange static perfection about him. But his movements, whilst they fascinated, also repelled. I can always see him crouched before the vines on his haunches, his haunches doubled together in a complete animal unconsciousness, his face seeming in its strange golden pallor and its hardness of line, with the gleaming black of the fine hair on the brow and temples, like something reflective, like the reflecting surface of a stone that gleams out of the depths of night. It was like darkness revealed in its steady, unchanging pallor.

Again he stayed through the evening, having quarrelled once more with the Maria about money. He quarrelled violently, yet coldly. There was something terrifying in it. And as soon as the matter of dispute was settled, all trace of interest or feeling vanished from him.

Yet he liked, above all things, to be near the English Signori. They seemed to exercise a sort of magnetic attraction over him. It was something of the purely physical world, as a magnetised needle swings towards soft iron. He was quite helpless in the relation. Only by mechanical attraction he gravitated into line with us.

But there was nothing between us except our complete difference. It was like night and day flowing together.

John

Besides Il Duro, we found another Italian who could speak English, this time quite well. We had walked about four or five miles up the lake, getting higher and higher. Then quite suddenly, on the shoulder of a bluff far up, we came on a village, icy cold, and as if forgotten.

We went into the inn to drink something hot. The fire of olive sticks was burning in the open chimney, one or two men were talking at a table, a young woman with a baby stood by the fire watching something boil in a large pot. Another woman was seen in the house-place beyond.

In the chimney-seats sat a young mule-driver, who had left his two mules at the door of the inn, and opposite him an elderly stout man. They got down and offered us the seats of honour, which we accepted with due courtesy.

The chimneys are like the wide open chimney-places of old English cottages, but the hearth is raised about a foot and a half or two feet from the floor, so that the fire is almost level with the hands, and those who sit in the chimney-seats are raised above the audience in the room, something like two gods flanking the fire, looking out of

John

the cave of ruddy darkness into the open, lower world of the room.

We asked for coffee with milk and rum. The stout landlord took a seat near us below. The comely young woman with the baby took the tin coffee-pot that stood among the grey ashes, put in fresh coffee among the old bottoms, filled it with water, then pushed it more into the fire.

The landlord turned to us with the usual naïve, curious deference, and the usual question:

'You are Germans?'

'English.'

'Ah – Inglesi.'

Then there is a new note of cordiality – or so I always imagine – and the rather rough, cattle-like men who are sitting with their wine round the table look up more amicably. They do not like being intruded upon. Only the landlord is always affable.

'I have a son who speaks English,' he says: he is a handsome, courtly old man, of the Falstaff sort.

'Oh!'

'He has been in America.'

'And where is he now?'

'He is at home. O – Nicoletta, where is the Giovann'?'

The comely young woman with the baby came in.

'He is with the band,' she said.

The old landlord looked at her with pride.

'This is my daughter-in-law,' he said.

She smiled readily to the Signora.

'And the baby?' we asked.

'Mio figlio,' cried the young woman, in the strong, penetrating voice of these women. And she came forward to show the child to the Signora.

It was a bonny baby: the whole company was united in adoration and service of the bambino. There was a moment of suspension, when religious submission seemed to come over the inn-room.

Then the Signora began to talk, and it broke upon the Italian child-reverence.

'What is he called?'

'Oscare,' came the ringing note of pride. And the mother talked to the baby in dialect. All, men and women alike, felt themselves glorified by the presence of the child.

At last the coffee in the tin coffee-pot was boiling and frothing out of spout and lid. The milk in the little copper pan was also hot, among the ashes. So we had our drink at last.

The landlord was anxious for us to see Giovanni, his son. There was a village band performing up the street, in front of the house of a colonel who had come home wounded from Tripoli. Everybody in the village was wildly proud about the colonel and about the brass band, the music of which was execrable.

We just looked into the street. The band of uncouth fellows was playing the same tune over and over again before a desolate, newish house. A crowd of desolate, forgotten villagers stood round, in the cold upper air. It seemed altogether that the place was forgotten by God and man.

But the landlord, burly, courteous, handsome, pointed out with a flourish the Giovanni, standing in the band playing a cornet. The band itself consisted only of five men, rather like beggars in the street. But Giovanni was the strangest! He was tall and thin and somewhat German-looking, wearing shabby American clothes and a very high double collar and a small American crush hat. He looked entirely like a ne'er-do-well who plays a violin in the street, dressed in the most down-at-heel, sordid respectability.

'That is he – you see, Signore – the young one under the balcony.'

The father spoke with love and pride, and the father was a gentleman, like Falstaff, a pure gentleman. The daughter-in-law also peered out to look at Il Giovann', who was evidently a figure of repute, in his sordid, degenerate American respectability. Meanwhile, this figure of repute blew himself red in the face, producing staccato strains on his cornet. And the crowd stood desolate and forsaken in the cold, upper afternoon.

Then there was a sudden rugged 'Evviva, Evviva!' from the people, the band stopped playing, somebody valiantly broke into a line of the song:

> Tripoli, sarà italiana,
> Sarà italiana al rombo del cannon'.

The colonel had appeared on the balcony, a smallish man, very yellow in the face, with grizzled black hair and very shabby legs. They all seemed so sordidly, hopelessly shabby.

He suddenly began to speak, leaning forward, hot and feverish and yellow, upon the iron rail of the balcony. There was something hot and marshy and sick about him, slightly repulsive, less than human. He told his fellow-villagers how he loved them, how, when he lay uncovered on the sands of Tripoli, week after week, he had known they were watching him from the Alpine height of the village, he could feel that where he was they were all looking. When the Arabs came rushing like things gone mad, and he had received his wound, he had known that in his own village, among his own dear ones, there was recovery. Love would heal the wounds, the home country was a lover who would heal all her sons' wounds with love.

Among the grey, desolate crowd were sharp, rending 'Bravos!' – the people were in tears – the landlord at my side was repeating softly, abstractedly: 'Caro – caro – Ettore, caro colonello—' and when it was finished, and the little colonel with shabby, humiliated legs was gone in, he turned to me, and said, with challenge that almost frightened me:

'Un brav' uomo.'

'Bravissimo,' I said.

Then we, too, went indoors.

John

It was all, somehow, grey and hopeless and acrid, unendurable.

The colonel, poor devil – we knew him afterwards – is now dead. It is strange that he is dead. There is something repulsive to me in the thought of his lying dead: such a humiliating, somehow degraded corpse. Death has no beauty in Italy, unless it be violent. The death of man or woman through sickness is an occasion of horror, repulsive. They belong entirely to life, they are so limited to life, these people.

Soon the Giovanni came home, and took his cornet upstairs. Then he came to see us. He was an ingenuous youth, sordidly shabby and dirty. His fair hair was long and uneven, his very high starched collar made one aware that his neck and his ears were not clean, his American crimson tie was ugly, his clothes looked as if they had been kicking about on the floor for a year.

Yet his blue eyes were warm and his manner and speech very gentle.

'You will speak English with us,' I said.

'Oh,' he said, smiling and shaking his head, 'I could speak English very well. But it is two years that I don't speak it now, over two years now, so I don't speak it.'

'But you speak it very well.'

'No. It is two years that I have not spoke, not a word – so, you see, I have –'

'You have forgotten it? No, you haven't. It will quickly come back.'

'If I hear it – when I go to America – then I shall – I shall –'

'You will soon pick it up.'

'Yes – I shall pick it up.'

The landlord, who had been watching with pride, now went away. The wife also went away, and we were left with the shy, gentle, dirty, and frowsily-dressed Giovanni.

He laughed in his sensitive, quick fashion.

'The women in America, when they came into the store, they said, "Where is John, where is John?" Yes, they liked me.'

And he laughed again, glancing with vague, warm, blue eyes, very shy, very coiled upon himself with sensitiveness.

He had managed a store in America, in a smallish town. I glanced at his reddish, smooth, rather knuckly hands, and thin wrists in the frayed cuff. They were real shopman's hands.

The landlord brought some special feast-day cake, so overjoyed he was to have his Giovanni speaking English with the Signoria.

When we went away, we asked 'John' to come down to our villa to see us. We scarcely expected him to turn up.

Yet one morning he appeared, at about half-past nine, just as we were finishing breakfast. It was sunny and warm and beautiful, so we asked him please to come with us picnicking.

He was a queer shoot, again, in his unkempt longish

hair and slovenly clothes, a sort of very vulgar down-at-heel American in appearance. And he was transported with shyness. Yet ours was the world he had chosen as his own, so he took his place bravely and simply, a hanger-on.

We climbed up the water-course in the mountain-side, up to a smooth little lawn under the olive trees, where daisies were flowering and gladioli were in bud. It was a tiny little lawn of grass in a level crevice, and sitting there we had the world below us, the lake, the distant island, the far-off, low Verona shore.

Then 'John' began to talk, and he talked continuously, like a foreigner, not saying the things he would have said in Italian, but following the suggestion and scope of his limited English.

In the first place, he loved his father – it was 'my father, my father' always. His father had a little shop as well as the inn in the village above. So John had had some education. He had been sent to Brescia and then to Verona to school, and there had taken his examinations to become a civil engineer. He was clever, and could pass his examinations. But he never finished his course. His mother died, and his father, disconsolate, had wanted him at home. Then he had gone back, when he was sixteen or seventeen, to the village beyond the lake, to be with his father and to look after the shop.

'But didn't you mind giving up all your work?' I said.

He did not quite understand.

'My father wanted me to come back,' he said.

It was evident that Giovanni had had no definite conception of what he was doing or what he wanted to do. His father, wishing to make a gentleman of him, had sent him to school in Verona. By accident he had been moved on into the engineering course. When it all fizzled to an end, and he returned half-baked to the remote, desolate village of the mountain-side, he was not disappointed or chagrined. He had never conceived of a coherent purposive life. Either one stayed in the village, like a lodged stone, or one made random excursions into the world, across the world. It was all aimless and purposeless.

So he had stayed a while with his father, then he had gone, just as aimlessly, with a party of men who were emigrating to America. He had taken some money, had drifted about, living in the most comfortless, wretched fashion, then he had found a place somewhere in Pennsylvania, in a dry goods store. This was when he was seventeen or eighteen years old.

All this seemed to have happened to him without his being very much affected, at least consciously. His nature was simple and self-complete. Yet not so self-complete as that of Il Duro or Paolo. They had passed through the foreign world and been quite untouched. Their souls were static, it was the world that had flowed unstable by.

But John was more sensitive, he had come more into contact with his new surroundings. He had attended night classes almost every evening, and had been taught English like a child. He had loved the American free school, the teachers, the work.

But he had suffered very much in America. With his curious, over-sensitive, wincing laugh, he told us how the boys had followed him and jeered at him, calling after him, 'You damn Dago, you damn Dago.' They had stopped him and his friend in the street and taken away their hats, and spat into them, and made water into them. So that at last he had gone mad. They were youths and men who always tortured him, using bad language which startled us very much as he repeated it, there on the little lawn under the olive trees, above the perfect lake: English obscenities and abuse so coarse and startling that we bit our lips, shocked almost into laughter, whilst John, simple and natural, and somehow, for all his long hair and dirty appearance, flower-like in soul, repeated to us these things which may never be repeated in decent company.

'Oh,' he said, 'at last, I get mad. When they come one day, shouting, "You damn Dago, dirty dog," and will take my hat again, oh, I get mad, and I would kill them. I would kill them, I am so mad. I run to them, and throw one to the floor, and I tread on him while I go upon another, the biggest. Though they hit me and kick me all over, I feel nothing, I am mad. I throw the biggest to the floor, a man, he is older than I am, and I hit him, so hard I would kill him. When the others see it they are afraid, they throw stones and hit me on the face. But I don't feel it – I don't know nothing. I hit the man on the floor, I almost kill him. I forget everything except I will kill him –'

'But you didn't?'

'No – I don't know –' and he laughed his queer, shaken laugh. 'The other man, what was with me, my friend, he came to me and we went away. Oh, I was mad, I completely mad. I would have killed them.'

He was trembling slightly, and his eyes were dilated with a strange, greyish-blue fire that was very painful and elemental. He looked beside himself. But he was by no means mad.

We were shaken by the vivid, lambent excitement of the youth, we wished him to forget. We were shocked, too, in our souls to see the pure elemental flame shaken out of his gentle, sensitive nature. By his slight, crinkled laugh we could see how much he had suffered. He had gone out and faced the world, and he had kept his place, stranger and Dago though he was.

'They never came after me no more, not all the while I was there.'

Then he said he became the foreman in the store – at first he was only assistant. It was the best store in the town, and many English ladies came, and some Germans. He liked the English ladies very much: they always wanted him to be in the store. He wore white clothes there, and they would say:

'You look very nice in the white coat, John,' or else:
'Let John come, he can find it,' or else they said:
'John speaks like a born American.'
This pleased him very much.

In the end, he said, he earned a hundred dollars a month. He lived with the extraordinary frugality of the Italians, and had quite a lot of money.

He was not like Il Duro. Faustino had lived in a state of miserliness almost in America, but then he had had his debauches of shows and wine and carousals. John went chiefly to the schools, in one of which he was even asked to teach Italian. His knowledge of his own language was remarkable and most unusual!

'But what,' I asked, 'brought you back?'

'It was my father. You see, if I did not come to have my military service, I must stay till I am forty. So I think perhaps my father will be dead, I shall never see him. So I came.'

He had come home when he was twenty to fulfil his military duties. At home he had married. He was very fond of his wife, but he had no conception of love in the old sense. His wife was like the past, to which he was wedded. Out of her he begot his child, as out of the past. But the future was all beyond her, apart from her. He was going away again, now, to America. He had been some nine months at home after his military service was over. He had no more to do. Now he was leaving his wife and child and his father to go to America.

'But why,' I said, 'Why? You are not poor, you can manage the shop in your village.'

'Yes,' he said. 'But I will go to America. Perhaps I shall go into the store again, the same.'

'But is it not just the same as managing the shop at home?'

'No – no – it is quite different.'

Then he told us how he bought goods in Brescia and in Salò for the shop at home, how he had rigged up a funicular with the assistance of the village, an overhead wire by which you could haul the goods up the face of the cliffs right high up, to within a mile of the village. He was very proud of this. And sometimes he himself went down the funicular to the water's edge, to the boat, when he was in a hurry. This also pleased him.

But he was going to Brescia this day to see about going again to America. Perhaps in another month he would be gone.

It was a great puzzle to me why he would go. He could not say himself. He would stay four or five years, then he would come home again to see his father – and his wife and child.

There was a strange, almost frightening destiny upon him, which seemed to take him away, always away from home, from the past, to that great, raw America. He seemed scarcely like a person with individual choice, more like a creature under the influence of fate which was disintegrating the old life and precipitating him, a fragment inconclusive, into the new chaos.

He submitted to it all with a perfect unquestioning simplicity, never even knowing that he suffered, that he must suffer disintegration from the old life. He was moved entirely from within, he never questioned his inevitable impulse.

'They say to me, "Don't go – don't go" –' he shook his head. 'But I say I will go.'

And at that it was finished.

So we saw him off at the little quay, going down the lake. He would return at evening, and be pulled up in his funicular basket. And in a month's time he would be standing on the same lake steamer going to America.

Nothing was more painful than to see him standing there in his degraded, sordid American clothes, on the deck of the steamer, waving us good-bye, belonging in his final desire to our world, the world of consciousness and deliberate action. With his candid, open, unquestioning face, he seemed like a prisoner being conveyed from one form of life to another, or like a soul in trajectory, that has not yet found a resting-place.

What were wife and child to him: they were the last steps of the past. His father was the continent behind him; his wife and child the foreshore of the past; but his face was set outwards, away from it all – whither, neither he nor anybody knew, but he called it America.

*

D. H. Lawrence

When I was in Constance the weather was misty and enervating and depressing, it was no pleasure to travel on the big, flat, desolate lake.

When I went from Constance, it was on a small steamer down the Rhine to Schaffhausen. That was beautiful. Still, the mist hung over the waters, over the wide shallows of the river, and the sun, coming through the morning, made lovely yellow lights beneath the bluish haze, so that it seemed like the beginning of the world. And there was a hawk in the upper air fighting with two crows, or two rooks. Ever they rose higher and higher, the crow flickering above the attacking hawk, the fight going on like some strange symbol in the sky, the Germans on deck watching with pleasure.

Then we passed out of sight, between wooded banks and under bridges where quaint villages of old romance piled their red and coloured pointed roofs beside the water, very still, remote, lost in the vagueness of the past. It could not be that they were real. Even when the boat put in to shore, and the customs officials came to look, the village remained remote in the romantic past of High Germany, the Germany of fairy tales and minstrels and craftsmen. The poignancy of the past was almost unbearable, floating there in colour upon the haze of the river.

We went by some swimmers, whose white, shadowy bodies trembled near the side of the steamer, under water. One man with a round, fair head, lifted his face and one arm from the water and shouted a greeting to us, as if he

John

were a Niebelung, saluting with bright arm lifted from the water, his face laughing, the fair moustache hanging over his mouth. Then his white body swirled in the water, and he was gone, swimming with the side stroke.

Schaffhausen the town, half old and bygone, half modern, with breweries and industries, that is not very real. Schaffhausen Falls, with their factory in the midst and their hotel at the bottom, and the general cinematograph effect, they are ugly.

It was afternoon when I set out to walk from the Falls to Italy, across Switzerland. I remember the big, fat, rather gloomy fields of this part of Baden, damp and unliving. I remember I found some apples under a tree in a field near a railway embankment, then some mushrooms, and I ate both. Then I came on to a long, desolate high road, with dreary, withered trees on either side, and flanked by great fields where groups of men and women were working. They looked at me as I went by down the long, long road, alone and exposed and out of the world.

I remember nobody came at the border village to examine my pack, I passed through unchallenged. All was quiet and lifeless and hopeless, with big stretches of heavy land.

Till sunset came, very red and purple, and suddenly, from the heavy spacious open land I dropped sharply into the Rhine valley again, suddenly, as if into another glamorous world.

There was the river rushing along between its high,

mysterious, romantic banks, which were high as hills, and covered with vine. And there was the village of tall, quaint houses flickering its lights on to the deep-flowing river, and quite silent, save for the rushing of water.

There was a fine covered bridge, very dark. I went to the middle, and looked through the opening at the dark water below, at the façade of square lights, the tall village-front towering remote and silent above the river. The hill rose on either side the flood, down here was a small, forgotten, wonderful world, that belonged to the date of isolated village communities and wandering minstrels.

So I went back to the inn of 'The Golden Stag,' and, climbing some steps, I made a loud noise. A woman came, and I asked for food. She led me through a room where were enormous barrels, ten feet in diameter, lying fatly on their sides; then through a large stone-clean kitchen, with bright pans, ancient as the Meistersinger; then up some steps and into the long guest-room, where a few tables were laid for supper.

A few people were eating. I asked for Abendessen, and sat by the window looking at the darkness of the river below, the covered bridge, the dark hill opposite, crested with its few lights.

Then I ate a very large quantity of knoedel soup, and bread, and drank beer, and was very sleepy. Only one or two village men came in, and these soon went again, the place was dead still. Only at a long table on the opposite side of the room were seated seven or eight men, ragged, disreputable, some impudent – another came in late – the landlady gave them all thick soup with dumplings and bread and meat, serving them in a sort of brief disapprobation. They sat at the long table, eight or nine tramps and beggars and wanderers out of work, and they ate with a sort of cheerful callousness and brutality for the most part, and as if ravenously, looking round and grinning sometimes, subdued, cowed, like prisoners, and yet impudent. At the end one shouted to know where he was to sleep. The landlady called to the young serving-woman, and in a classic German severity of disapprobation, they were led up the stone stairs to their room. They tramped off in threes and twos, making a bad, mean, humiliated exit. It was not yet eight o'clock. The landlady sat talking to one bearded man, staid and severe, whilst, with her work on the table, she sewed steadily.

As the beggars and wanderers went slinking out of the room, some called impudently, cheerfully:

'Nacht, Frau Wirtin – G'Nacht, Wirtin –'te Nacht, Frau,' to all of which the hostess answered a stereotyped 'Gute Nacht,' never turning her head from her sewing or indicating by the faintest movement that she was addressing the men who were filing raggedly to the doorway.

So the room was empty, save for the landlady and her sewing, the staid, elderly villager to whom she was talking in the unbeautiful dialect, and the young serving-woman who was clearing away the plates and basins of the tramps and beggars.

Then the villager also went.

'Gute Nacht, Frau Seidl,' to the landlady; 'Gute Nacht,' at random, to me.

So I looked at the newspaper. Then I asked the landlady for a cigarette, not knowing how else to begin. So she came to my table, and we talked.

It pleased me to take upon myself a sort of romantic, wandering character; she said my German was 'schön'; a little goes a long way.

So I asked her who were the men who had sat at the long table. She became rather stiff and curt.

'They are the men looking for work,' she said, as if the subject were disagreeable.

'But why do they come here, so many?' I asked.

Then she told me that they were going out of the country: this was almost the last village of the border: that the relieving officer in each village was empowered to give to every vagrant a ticket entitling the holder to an evening meal, bed, and bread in the morning, at a certain inn. This was the inn for the vagrants coming to this village. The landlady received fourpence per head, I believe it was, for each of these wanderers.

'Little enough,' I said.

'Nothing,' she replied.

She did not like the subject at all. Only her respect for me made her answer.

The Florence Museum

It would perhaps be easier to go to the Archaeological Museum in Florence, to look at the etruscan collection, if we decided once and for all that there never were any Etruscans. Because, in the cut-and-dried museum sense, there never were.

The Etruscans were not a race, that is obvious. And they were not a nation. They were not even as much of a people as the Romans of the Augustan age were: and a Roman of the Augustan age might be a Latin, an Etruscan, a Sabine, a Samnite, an Umbrian, a Celt, a Greek, a Jew, or almost anything else of the world of that day. He might come from any tribe or race, almost, and still be first and foremost a Roman. 'I am a Roman.'

What makes a civilised people is not blood, but some dominant culture-principle. Certain blood-streams give rise to, or are sympathetic to, certain culture principles. The handful of original Romans in Latium contained the germ of the civilising principle of Rome, that was all.

But there was not even an original handful of original Etruscans. In Etruria there is no starting-point. Just as there is no starting-point for England, once we have the courage to look beyond Julius Caesar and 55 BC Britain was active and awake and alive long before Caesar saw it. Nor was it a country of blue-painted savages in bear-skins. It had an old culture of its own, older than the little hill of Romulus.

But then the historical invasions started. Romans, Jutes, Angles, Saxons, Danes, Normans, Jews, French: after all, what is England? What does the word England mean, even? What clue would it give to the rise of the English, should all our history be lost? About as good a clue as Tusci or Tyrrheni give to the make-up of the Etruscan.

Etruria is a parallel case to England. In the dim British days before Julius Caesar, there were dim Italian days too, and endless restless Italian tribes and peoples with their own speech and customs and religious practices. They were not just brutes, nor cave-men, because they lived in the days before Homer. They were men, alive and alert, having their own complex forms of expression.

And in those dim days where history does not exist – not because men, intelligent men did not then exist, but because one culture wipes out another as completely as possible; in those dim days, there were invasions, invasion after invasion no doubt, from the wild north on foot, from the old, cultured Aegean basin, in ships. Men kept on coming, and kept on coming: strangers.

But there were two deep emotions or culture-rhythms

The Florence Museum

which persisted in all the confusion: and one was some old, old Italian rhythm of life, belonging to the soil, which invaded every invader; and the other was the old cosmic consciousness, or culture principle, of the prehistoric Mediterranean, particularly of the eastern Mediterranean. Man is *always* trying to be conscious of the cosmos, the cosmos of life and passion and feeling, desire and death and despair, as well as of physical phenomena. And there are still millions of undreamed-of ways of becoming aware of the cosmos. Which is to say, there are millions of worlds, whole cosmic worlds, to us yet unborn.

Every religion, every philosophy, and science itself, each has a clue to the cosmos, to the becoming aware of the cosmos. Each clue leads to its own goal of consciousness, then is exhausted. So religions exhaust themselves, so science exhausts itself, once the human consciousness reaches its own limit. The infinite of the human consciousness lies in an infinite number of different starts to an infinite number of different goals; which somehow, we know when we get there, is one goal. But the new start is from a point in the hitherto unknown.

What we have to realise in looking at etruscan things is that they reveal the last glimpses of a human cosmic consciousness – or human attempt at cosmic consciousness – different from our own. The idea that our history emerged out of caves and savage lake-dwellings is puerile. Our history emerges out of the closing of a previous great phase of human history, a phase as great as our own. It is much more likely the monkey is descended from us, than we from the monkey.

What we see, in the etruscan remains, is the fag end of the revelation of another form of cosmic consciousness: and also, that salt of the earth, the revelation of the human existence of people who lived and who *were*, in a way somewhat different from our way of living and being. There are two separate things: the artistic or impulsive or culture-expression, and the religious or scientific or civilisation expression of a group of people. The first is based on emotion; the second on concepts.

The Etruscans consisted of all sorts of tribes and distinct peoples: that is obvious: and they did not intermingle. Velathri (Volterra) and Tarquinii were two quite distinct peoples, racially. No doubt they spoke different languages, vulgarly. The thing they had in common was the remains of an old cosmic consciousness, an old religion, an old attempt on man's part to understand, or at least to interpret to himself, the cosmos as he knew it. That was the civilising principle.

Civilisations rise in waves, and pass away in waves. And not till science, or art, tries to catch the ultimate meaning of the symbols that float on the last waves of the prehistoric period; that is, the period before our own; shall we be able to get ourselves into right relation with man as man is and has been and will always be.

In the days before Homer, men in Europe were *not* mere brutes and savages and prognathous monsters: neither

The Florence Museum

were they simple-minded children. Men are always men, and though intelligence takes different forms, men are always intelligent: they are not empty brutes, or dumbbells *en masse*.

The symbols that come down to us on the last waves of prehistoric culture are the remnants of a vast old attempt made by humanity to form a conception of the universe. The conception was shattered and diminished even by the time it rose to new life, in Egypt. It rose up again, in ancient China and India, in Babylonia and in Asia Minor, in the Druid, in the Teuton, in the Aztec and in the Maya of America, in the very negroes. But each time it rose in a smaller, dying wave, as one tide of consciousness slowly changed to another tide, full of cross-currents. Now our own tide of consciousness is on the ebb, so we can catch the ripples of the tide that ebbed as we arose, and we may read their meaning.

There is no unified and homogeneous etruscan people. There is no Etruscan, pure and simple, and never was: any more than, today, there is one absolute American. There are etruscan characteristics, that is all.

And the real *etruscan* characteristics are the religious symbols. As far as *art* goes, there is no etruscan art. It is an art of all sorts, dominated by an old religious idea.

The religious idea came presumably from the Aegean, the ancient eastern Mediterranean. It was an ebb from an old wider consciousness. If we look at our world today, as far as *culture* goes, it has one culture: the christian-scientific. Whether it be Pekin or Dahomey or New York or Paris, it is more or less the same conception of life and the cosmos, nowadays.

And so it must have been before. The pyramid builders of America must have had some old idea, remnant of an idea, in common with the Egyptian and the Etruscan. And the Celt, the Gaul, the Druid, must have had some lingering idea of the ancient cosmic meaning of the waters, of the leaping fish, of the undying, ever re-born dead, shadowily sharing it with the ancient Italic peoples, as well as with the Hittites or the Lydians.

There are no Etruscans out-and-out, and there never were any. There were different prehistoric tribes stimulated by contact with different peoples from the eastern Mediterranean, and lifted on the last wave of a dying conception of the living cosmos.

That is what one feels. If it is wrong it is wrong. But few things, *that are felt*, are either absolutely wrong or absolutely right. Things absolutely wrong are not felt, they do not arise from contact. They arise from prejudice and pre-conceived notions. As for things absolutely right, they too cannot be felt. Whatever can be felt is capable of many different forms of expression, forms often contradictory, as far as logic or reason goes.

But in the bewildering experience of searching for the Etruscans there is the one steady clue that we can follow:

or rather, there are two clues. The first is the peculiar physical or *bodily*, lively quality of all the art. And this, I take it, is Italian, the result of the Italian soil itself. The Romans got a great deal of their power from *resisting* this curious Italian physical expressiveness: and for the same reason, in the Roman the salt soon lost its savour, in the true Etruscan, never.

The second clue is the more concrete, because more ideal presence of the symbols. Symbols are at least *half* ideas: and so they are half fixed. Emotion and the robust physical gesture are always fluid and changing, never fixed.

So we have the two clues, that of the dominant idea, or half-idea, in the religious symbols; and that of the dominant *feeling*, in the peculiar physical freeness and exuberance and spontaneity. It is the spontaneity of the flesh itself.

These are the two clues to the Etruscan. And they lead from beginning to end, from the point where the Etruscan emerges out of the Oriental, Lydian or Hittite or whatever he may be, till the last days when he is swamped by the Roman and the Greek.

1. BOCCACCIO · *Mrs Rosie and the Priest*
2. GERARD MANLEY HOPKINS · *As kingfishers catch fire*
3. *The Saga of Gunnlaug Serpent-tongue*
4. THOMAS DE QUINCEY · *On Murder Considered as One of the Fine Arts*
5. FRIEDRICH NIETZSCHE · *Aphorisms on Love and Hate*
6. JOHN RUSKIN · *Traffic*
7. PU SONGLING · *Wailing Ghosts*
8. JONATHAN SWIFT · *A Modest Proposal*
9. *Three Tang Dynasty Poets*
10. WALT WHITMAN · *On the Beach at Night Alone*
11. KENKŌ · *A Cup of Sake Beneath the Cherry Trees*
12. BALTASAR GRACIÁN · *How to Use Your Enemies*
13. JOHN KEATS · *The Eve of St Agnes*
14. THOMAS HARDY · *Woman much missed*
15. GUY DE MAUPASSANT · *Femme Fatale*
16. MARCO POLO · *Travels in the Land of Serpents and Pearls*
17. SUETONIUS · *Caligula*
18. APOLLONIUS OF RHODES · *Jason and Medea*
19. ROBERT LOUIS STEVENSON · *Olalla*
20. KARL MARX AND FRIEDRICH ENGELS · *The Communist Manifesto*
21. PETRONIUS · *Trimalchio's Feast*
22. JOHANN PETER HEBEL · *How a Ghastly Story Was Brought to Light by a Common or Garden Butcher's Dog*
23. HANS CHRISTIAN ANDERSEN · *The Tinder Box*
24. RUDYARD KIPLING · *The Gate of the Hundred Sorrows*
25. DANTE · *Circles of Hell*
26. HENRY MAYHEW · *Of Street Piemen*
27. HAFEZ · *The nightingales are drunk*
28. GEOFFREY CHAUCER · *The Wife of Bath*
29. MICHEL DE MONTAIGNE · *How We Weep and Laugh at the Same Thing*
30. THOMAS NASHE · *The Terrors of the Night*
31. EDGAR ALLAN POE · *The Tell-Tale Heart*
32. MARY KINGSLEY · *A Hippo Banquet*
33. JANE AUSTEN · *The Beautifull Cassandra*
34. ANTON CHEKHOV · *Gooseberries*
35. SAMUEL TAYLOR COLERIDGE · *Well, they are gone, and here must I remain*
36. JOHANN WOLFGANG VON GOETHE · *Sketchy, Doubtful, Incomplete Jottings*
37. CHARLES DICKENS · *The Great Winglebury Duel*
38. HERMAN MELVILLE · *The Maldive Shark*
39. ELIZABETH GASKELL · *The Old Nurse's Story*
40. NIKOLAY LESKOV · *The Steel Flea*

41. HONORÉ DE BALZAC · *The Atheist's Mass*
42. CHARLOTTE PERKINS GILMAN · *The Yellow Wall-Paper*
43. C.P. CAVAFY · *Remember, Body . . .*
44. FYODOR DOSTOEVSKY · *The Meek One*
45. GUSTAVE FLAUBERT · *A Simple Heart*
46. NIKOLAI GOGOL · *The Nose*
47. SAMUEL PEPYS · *The Great Fire of London*
48. EDITH WHARTON · *The Reckoning*
49. HENRY JAMES · *The Figure in the Carpet*
50. WILFRED OWEN · *Anthem For Doomed Youth*
51. WOLFGANG AMADEUS MOZART · *My Dearest Father*
52. PLATO · *Socrates' Defence*
53. CHRISTINA ROSSETTI · *Goblin Market*
54. *Sindbad the Sailor*
55. SOPHOCLES · *Antigone*
56. RYŪNOSUKE AKUTAGAWA · *The Life of a Stupid Man*
57. LEO TOLSTOY · *How Much Land Does A Man Need?*
58. GIORGIO VASARI · *Leonardo da Vinci*
59. OSCAR WILDE · *Lord Arthur Savile's Crime*
60. SHEN FU · *The Old Man of the Moon*
61. AESOP · *The Dolphins, the Whales and the Gudgeon*
62. MATSUO BASHŌ · *Lips too Chilled*
63. EMILY BRONTË · *The Night is Darkening Round Me*
64. JOSEPH CONRAD · *To-morrow*
65. RICHARD HAKLUYT · *The Voyage of Sir Francis Drake Around the Whole Globe*
66. KATE CHOPIN · *A Pair of Silk Stockings*
67. CHARLES DARWIN · *It was snowing butterflies*
68. BROTHERS GRIMM · *The Robber Bridegroom*
69. CATULLUS · *I Hate and I Love*
70. HOMER · *Circe and the Cyclops*
71. D. H. LAWRENCE · *Il Duro*
72. KATHERINE MANSFIELD · *Miss Brill*
73. OVID · *The Fall of Icarus*
74. SAPPHO · *Come Close*
75. IVAN TURGENEV · *Kasyan from the Beautiful Lands*
76. VIRGIL · *O Cruel Alexis*
77. H. G. WELLS · *A Slip under the Microscope*
78. HERODOTUS · *The Madness of Cambyses*
79. *Speaking of Siva*
80. *The Dhammapada*

'And again, as always, he had the feeling he was holding something that never was quite his – his. Something too delicate, too precious, that would fly away once he let go.'

KATHERINE MANSFIELD
Born 1888, Wellington, New Zealand
Died 1923, Fontainebleau, France

All stories taken from *The Garden Party and Other Stories*,
first published 1922.

KATHERINE MANSFIELD IN PENGUIN CLASSICS
The Collected Stories of Katherine Mansfield
The Garden Party and Other Stories

KATHERINE MANSFIELD

Miss Brill

PENGUIN BOOKS

PENGUIN CLASSICS

UK | USA | Canada | Ireland | Australia
India | New Zealand | South Africa

Penguin Books is part of the Penguin Random House group of companies
whose addresses can be found at global.penguinrandomhouse.com.

This selection published in Penguin Classics 2015
009

Set in 10/14.5 pt Baskerville 10 Pro
Typeset by Jouve (UK), Milton Keynes
Printed and bound in Great Britain by Clays Ltd, Elcograf S.p.A.

A CIP catalogue record for this book is available from the British Library

ISBN: 978–0–141–39865–5

www.greenpenguin.co.uk

Penguin Random House is committed to a
sustainable future for our business, our readers
and our planet. This book is made from Forest
Stewardship Council® certified paper.

Contents

Marriage à la Mode 1

Miss Brill 21

The Stranger 31

Marriage à la Mode

On his way to the station William remembered with a fresh pang of disappointment that he was taking nothing down to the kiddies. Poor little chaps! It was hard lines on them. Their first words always were as they ran to greet him, 'What have you got for me, daddy?' and he had nothing. He would have to buy them some sweets at the station. But that was what he had done for the past four Saturdays; their faces had fallen last time when they saw the same old boxes produced again.

And Paddy had said, 'I had red ribbing on mine *bee*-fore!'

And Johnny had said, 'It's always pink on mine. I hate pink.'

But what was William to do? The affair wasn't so easily settled. In the old days, of course, he would have taken a taxi off to a decent toyshop and chosen them something in five minutes. But nowadays they had Russian toys, French toys, Serbian toys – toys from God knows where. It was over a year since Isabel had scrapped the old donkeys and engines and so on because they were so 'dreadfully sentimental' and 'so appallingly bad for the babies' sense of form.'

'It's so important,' the new Isabel had explained, 'that they should like the right things from the very beginning. It saves so much time later on. Really, if the poor pets have to spend their infant years staring at these horrors, one can imagine them growing up and asking to be taken to the Royal Academy.'

And she spoke as though a visit to the Royal Academy was certain immediate death to anyone . . .

'Well, I don't know,' said William slowly. 'When I was their age I used to go to bed hugging an old towel with a knot in it.'

The new Isabel looked at him, her eyes narrowed, her lips apart.

'*Dear* William! I'm sure you did!' She laughed in the new way.

Sweets it would have to be, however, thought William gloomily, fishing in his pocket for change for the taxi-man. And he saw the kiddies handing the

Marriage à la Mode

boxes round – they were awfully generous little chaps – while Isabel's precious friends didn't hesitate to help themselves . . .

What about fruit? William hovered before a stall just inside the station. What about a melon each? Would they have to share that, too? Or a pineapple for Pad, and a melon for Johnny? Isabel's friends could hardly go sneaking up to the nursery at the children's meal-times. All the same, as he bought the melon William had a horrible vision of one of Isabel's young poets lapping up a slice, for some reason, behind the nursery door.

With his two very awkward parcels he strode off to his train. The platform was crowded, the train was in. Doors banged open and shut. There came such a loud hissing from the engine that people looked dazed as they scurried to and fro. William made straight for a first-class smoker, stowed away his suitcase and parcels, and taking a huge wad of papers out of his inner pocket, he flung down in the corner and began to read.

'Our client moreover is positive . . . We are inclined to reconsider . . . in the event of –' Ah, that was better. William pressed back his flattened hair and stretched his legs across the carriage floor. The familiar dull gnawing in his breast quietened down. 'With regard to our decision –' He took out a blue pencil and scored a paragraph slowly.

Two men came in, stepped across him, and made for the farther corner. A young fellow swung his golf clubs into the rack and sat down opposite. The train gave a gentle lurch, they were off. William glanced up and saw the hot, bright station slipping away. A red-faced girl raced along by the carriages, there was something strained and almost desperate in the way she waved and called. 'Hysterical!' thought William dully. Then a greasy, black-faced workman at the end of the platform grinned at the passing train. And William thought, 'A filthy life!' and went back to his papers.

When he looked up again there were fields, and beasts standing for shelter under the dark trees. A wide river, with naked children splashing in the shallows, glided into sight and was gone again. The sky shone pale, and one bird drifted high like a dark fleck in a jewel.

'We have examined our client's correspondence files . . .' The last sentence he had read echoed in his

Marriage à la Mode

mind. 'We have examined . . .' William hung on to that sentence, but it was no good; it snapped in the middle, and the fields, the sky, the sailing bird, the water, all said, 'Isabel.' The same thing happened every Saturday afternoon. When he was on his way to meet Isabel there began those countless imaginary meetings. She was at the station, standing just a little apart from everybody else; she was sitting in the open taxi outside; she was at the garden gate; walking across the parched grass; at the door, or just inside the hall.

And her clear, light voice said, 'It's William,' or 'Hillo, William!' or 'So William has come!' He touched her cool hand, her cool cheek.

The exquisite freshness of Isabel! When he had been a little boy, it was his delight to run into the garden after a shower of rain and shake the rose-bush over him. Isabel was that rose-bush, petal-soft, sparkling and cool. And he was still that little boy. But there was no running into the garden now, no laughing and shaking. The dull, persistent gnawing in his breast started again. He drew up his legs, tossed the papers aside, and shut his eyes.

'What is it, Isabel? What is it?' he said tenderly.

They were in their bedroom in the new house. Isabel sat on a painted stool before the dressing-table that was strewn with little black and green boxes.

'What is what, William?' And she bent forward, and her fine light hair fell over her cheeks.

'Ah, you know!' He stood in the middle of the strange room and he felt a stranger. At that Isabel wheeled round quickly and faced him.

'Oh, William!' she cried imploringly, and she held up the hairbrush. 'Please! Please don't be so dreadfully stuffy and – tragic. You're always saying or looking or hinting that I've changed. Just because I've got to know really congenial people, and go about more, and am frightfully keen on – on everything, you behave as though I'd –' Isabel tossed back her hair and laughed – 'killed our love or something. It's so awfully absurd' – she bit her lip – 'and it's so maddening, William. Even this new house and the servants you grudge me.'

'Isabel!'

'Yes, yes, it's true in a way,' said Isabel quickly. 'You think they are another bad sign. Oh, I know you do. I feel it,' she said softly, 'every time you come up the stairs. But we couldn't have gone on living in that other poky little hole, William. Be practical, at least! Why, there wasn't enough room for the babies even.'

No, it was true. Every morning when he came back from chambers it was to find the babies with Isabel in the back drawing-room. They were having rides on the leopard skin thrown over the sofa back, or they were playing shops with Isabel's desk for a counter, or Pad was sitting on the hearthrug rowing away for dear life with a little brass fire-shovel, while Johnny shot at pirates with the tongs. Every evening they each had a pick-a-back up the narrow stairs to their fat old Nanny.

Yes, he supposed it was a poky little house. A little white house with blue curtains and a window-box of petunias. William met their friends at the door with 'Seen our petunias? Pretty terrific for London, don't you think?'

But the imbecile thing, the absolutely extraordinary thing was that he hadn't the slightest idea that Isabel wasn't as happy as he. God, what blindness! He hadn't the remotest notion in those days that she really hated that inconvenient little house, that she thought the fat Nanny was ruining the babies, that she was desperately lonely, pining for new people and new music and pictures and so on. If they hadn't gone to that studio party at Moira Morrison's – If Moira Morrison hadn't said as they were leaving, 'I'm going to rescue your wife, selfish man. She's like an exquisite little Titania' – if Isabel hadn't gone with Moira to Paris – if – if . . .

The train stopped at another station. Bettingford. Good heavens! They'd be there in ten minutes. William stuffed the papers back into his pockets; the young man opposite had long since disappeared. Now the other two got out. The late afternoon sun shone on women in cotton frocks and little sunburnt, barefoot children. It blazed on a silky yellow flower with coarse leaves which sprawled over a bank of rock. The air ruffling through the window smelled of the sea. Had Isabel the same crowd with her this weekend, wondered William?

And he remembered the holidays they used to have, the four of them, with a little farm girl, Rose, to look after the babies. Isabel wore a jersey and her hair in a plait; she looked about fourteen. Lord! how his nose used to peel! And the amount they ate, and the amount they slept in that immense feather bed with their feet locked together . . . William couldn't help a grim smile as he thought of Isabel's horror if she knew the full extent of his sentimentality.

'Hillo, William!' She was at the station after all, standing just as he had imagined, apart from the others, and – William's heart leapt – she was alone.

'Hallo, Isabel!' William stared. He thought she looked so beautiful that he had to say something, 'You look very cool.'

'Do I?' said Isabel. 'I don't feel very cool. Come along, your horrid old train is late. The taxi's outside.' She put her hand lightly on his arm as they passed the ticket collector. 'We've all come to meet you,' she said. 'But we've left Bobby Kane at the sweet shop, to be called for.'

'Oh!' said William. It was all he could say for the moment.

There in the glare waited the taxi, with Bill Hunt and Dennis Green sprawling on one side, their hats tilted over their faces, while on the other, Moira Morrison, in a bonnet like a huge strawberry, jumped up and down.

'No ice! No ice! No ice!' she shouted gaily.

And Dennis chimed in from under his hat. '*Only* to be had from the fishmonger's.'

And Bill Hunt, emerging, added, 'With *whole* fish in it.'

'Oh, what a bore!' wailed Isabel. And she explained to William how they had been chasing round the town for ice while she waited for him. 'Simply everything is running down the steep cliffs into the sea, beginning with the butter.'

'We shall have to anoint ourselves with the butter,' said Dennis. 'May thy head, William, lack not ointment.'

'Look here,' said William, 'how are we going to sit? I'd better get up by the driver.'

'No, Bobby Kane's by the driver,' said Isabel. 'You're to sit between Moira and me.' The taxi started. 'What have you got in those mysterious parcels?'

'De-cap-it-ated heads!' said Bill Hunt, shuddering beneath his hat.

'Oh, fruit!' Isabel sounded very pleased. 'Wise William! A melon and a pineapple. How too nice!'

'No, wait a bit,' said William, smiling. But he really was anxious. 'I brought them down for the kiddies.'

'Oh, my dear!' Isabel laughed, and slipped her

Marriage à la Mode

hand through his arm. 'They'd be rolling in agonies if they were to eat them. No' – she patted his hand – 'you must bring them something next time. I refuse to part with my pineapple.'

'Cruel Isabel! Do let me smell it!' said Moira. She flung her arms across William appealingly. 'Oh!' The strawberry bonnet fell forward: she sounded quite faint.

'A Lady in Love with a Pineapple,' said Dennis, as the taxi drew up before a little shop with a striped blind. Out came Bobby Kane, his arms full of little packets.

'I do hope they'll be good. I've chosen them because of the colours. There are some round things which really look too divine. And just look at this nougat,' he cried ecstatically, 'just look at it! It's a perfect little ballet!'

But at that moment the shopman appeared. 'Oh, I forgot. They're none of them paid for,' said Bobby, looking frightened. Isabel gave the shopman a note, and Bobby was radiant again. 'Hallo, William! I'm sitting by the driver.' And bare-headed, all in white, with his sleeves rolled up to the shoulders, he leapt into his place. 'Avanti!' he cried . . .

After tea the others went off to bathe, while William stayed and made his peace with the kiddies. But Johnny and Paddy were asleep, the rose-red glow had paled, bats were flying, and still the bathers had not returned. As William wandered downstairs, the maid crossed the hall carrying a lamp. He followed her into the sitting-room. It was a long room, coloured yellow. On the wall opposite William someone had painted a young man, over life-size, with very wobbly legs, offering a wide-eyed daisy to a young woman who had one very short arm and one very long, thin one. Over the chairs and sofa there hung strips of black material, covered with big splashes like broken eggs, and everywhere one looked there seemed to be an ashtray full of cigarette ends. William sat down in one of the armchairs. Nowadays, when one felt with one hand down the sides, it wasn't to come upon a sheep with three legs or a cow that had lost one horn, or a very fat dove out of the Noah's Ark. One fished up yet another little paper-covered book of smudged-looking poems . . . He thought of the wad of papers in his pocket, but he was too hungry and tired to read. The door was open; sounds came from the kitchen. The servants were talking as if they were

Marriage à la Mode

alone in the house. Suddenly there came a loud screech of laughter and an equally loud 'Sh!' They had remembered him. William got up and went through the french windows into the garden, and as he stood there in the shadow he heard the bathers coming up the sandy road; their voices rang through the quiet.

'I think it's up to Moira to use her little arts and wiles.'

A tragic moan from Moira.

'We ought to have a gramophone for the weekends that played "The Maid of the Mountains."'

'Oh no! Oh no!' cried Isabel's voice. 'That's not fair to William. Be nice to him, my children! He's only staying until tomorrow evening.'

'Leave him to me,' cried Bobby Kane. 'I'm awfully good at looking after people.'

The gate swung open and shut. William moved on the terrace; they had seen him. 'Hallo, William!' And Bobby Kane, flapping his towel, began to leap and pirouette on the parched lawn. 'Pity you didn't come, William. The water was divine. And we all went to a little pub afterwards and had sloe gin.'

The others had reached the house. 'I say, Isabel,'

called Bobby, 'would you like me to wear my Nijinsky dress tonight?'

'No,' said Isabel, 'nobody's going to dress. We're all starving. William's starving, too. Come along, *mes amis*, let's begin with sardines.'

'I've found the sardines,' said Moira, and she ran into the hall, holding a box high in the air.

'A Lady with a Box of Sardines,' said Dennis gravely.

'Well, William, and how's London?' asked Bill Hunt, drawing the cork out of a bottle of whisky.

'Oh, London's not much changed,' answered William.

'Good old London,' said Bobby, very hearty, spearing a sardine.

But a moment later William was forgotten. Moira Morrison began wondering what colour one's legs really were under water.

'Mine are the palest, palest mushroom colour.'

Bill and Dennis ate enormously. And Isabel filled glasses, and changed plates, and found matches, smiling blissfully. At one moment she said, 'I do wish, Bill, you'd paint it.'

'Paint what?' said Bill loudly, stuffing his mouth with bread.

Marriage à la Mode

'Us,' said Isabel, 'round the table. It would be so fascinating in twenty years' time.'

Bill screwed up his eyes and chewed. 'Light's wrong,' he said rudely, 'far too much yellow'; and went on eating. And that seemed to charm Isabel, too.

But after supper they were all so tired they could do nothing but yawn until it was late enough to go to bed . . .

It was not until William was waiting for his taxi the next afternoon that he found himself alone with Isabel. When he brought his suitcase down into the hall, Isabel left the others and went over to him. She stooped down and picked up the suitcase. 'What a weight!' she said, and she gave a little awkward laugh. 'Let me carry it! To the gate.'

'No, why should you?' said William. 'Of course not. Give it to me.'

'Oh, please do let me,' said Isabel. 'I want to, really.' They walked together silently. William felt there was nothing to say now.

'There,' said Isabel triumphantly, setting the suitcase down, and she looked anxiously along the sandy road. 'I hardly seem to have seen you this time,' she said breathlessly. 'It's so short, isn't it? I feel you've only just come. Next time –' The taxi came into sight. 'I hope they look after you properly in London. I'm so sorry the babies have been out all day, but Miss Neil had arranged it. They'll hate missing you. Poor William, going back to London.' The taxi turned. 'Goodbye!' She gave him a little hurried kiss; she was gone.

Fields, trees, hedges streamed by. They shook through the empty, blind-looking little town, ground up the steep pull to the station. The train was in. William made straight for a first-class smoker, flung back into the corner, but this time he let the papers alone. He folded his arms against the dull, persistent gnawing, and began in his mind to write a letter to Isabel.

The post was late as usual. They sat outside the house in long chairs under coloured parasols. Only Bobby Kane lay on the turf at Isabel's feet. It was dull, stifling; the day drooped like a flag.

'Do you think there will be Mondays in Heaven?' asked Bobby childishly.

And Dennis murmured, 'Heaven will be one long Monday.'

But Isabel couldn't help wondering what had happened to the salmon they had for supper last night. She had meant to have fish mayonnaise for lunch and now...

Moira was asleep. Sleeping was her latest discovery. 'It's *so* wonderful. One simply shuts one's eyes, that's all. It's *so* delicious.'

When the old ruddy postman came beating along the sandy road on his tricycle one felt the handle-bars ought to have been oars.

Bill Hunt put down his book. 'Letters,' he said complacently, and they all waited. But, heartless postman – O malignant world! There was only one, a fat one for Isabel. Not even a paper.

'And mine's only from William,' said Isabel mournfully.

'From William – already?'

'He's sending you back your marriage lines as a gentle reminder.'

'Does everybody have marriage lines? I thought they were only for servants.'

'Pages and pages! Look at her! A Lady reading a Letter,' said Dennis.

My darling, precious Isabel. Pages and pages there

were. As Isabel read on her feeling of astonishment changed to a stifled feeling. What on earth had induced William . . . ? How extraordinary it was . . . What could have made him . . . ? She felt confused, more and more excited, even frightened. It was just like William. Was it? It was absurd, of course, it must be absurd, ridiculous. 'Ha, ha, ha! Oh dear!' What was she to do? Isabel flung back in her chair and laughed till she couldn't stop laughing.

'Do, do tell us,' said the others. 'You must tell us.'

'I'm longing to,' gurgled Isabel. She sat up, gathered the letter, and waved it at them. 'Gather round,' she said. 'Listen, it's too marvellous. A love-letter!'

'A love-letter! But how divine!' *Darling precious Isabel.* But she had hardly begun before their laughter interrupted her.

'Go on, Isabel, it's perfect.'

'It's the most marvellous find.'

'Oh, do go on, Isabel!'

God forbid, my darling, that I should be a drag on your happiness.

'Oh! oh! oh!'

'Sh! sh! sh!'

And Isabel went on. When she reached the end

Marriage à la Mode

they were hysterical: Bobby rolled on the turf and almost sobbed.

'You must let me have it just as it is, entire, for my new book,' said Dennis firmly. 'I shall give it a whole chapter.'

'Oh, Isabel,' moaned Moira, 'that wonderful bit about holding you in his arms!'

'I always thought those letters in divorce cases were made up. But they pale before this.'

'Let me hold it. Let me read it, mine own self,' said Bobby Kane.

But, to their surprise, Isabel crushed the letter in her hand. She was laughing no longer. She glanced quickly at them all; she looked exhausted. 'No, not just now. Not just now,' she stammered.

And before they could recover she had run into the house, through the hall, up the stairs into her bedroom. Down she sat on the side of the bed. 'How vile, odious, abominable, vulgar,' muttered Isabel. She pressed her eyes with her knuckles, and rocked to and fro. And again she saw them, but not four, more like forty, laughing, sneering, jeering, stretching out their hands while she read them William's letter. Oh, what a loathsome thing to have done. How could she have done it! *God forbid, my darling, that I should be a drag on your happiness.* William! Isabel pressed her face into the pillow. But she felt that even the grave bedroom knew her for what she was, shallow, tinkling, vain . . .

Presently from the garden below there came voices.

'Isabel, we're all going for a bathe. Do come!'

'Come, thou wife of William!'

'Call her once before you go, call once yet!'

Isabel sat up. Now was the moment, now she must decide. Would she go with them, or stay here and write to William. Which, which should it be? 'I must make up my mind.' Oh, but how could there be any question? Of course she would stay here and write.

'Titania!' piped Moira.

'Isa-bel?'

No, it was too difficult. 'I'll – I'll go with them, and write to William later. Some other time. Later. Not now. But I shall *certainly* write,' thought Isabel hurriedly.

And, laughing in the new way, she ran down the stairs.

Miss Brill

Although it was so brilliantly fine – the blue sky powdered with gold and great spots of light like white wine splashed over the Jardins Publiques – Miss Brill was glad that she had decided on her fur. The air was motionless, but when you opened your mouth there was just a faint chill, like a chill from a glass of iced water before you sip, and now and again a leaf came drifting – from nowhere, from the sky. Miss Brill put up her hand and touched her fur. Dear little thing! It was nice to feel it again. She had taken it out of its box that afternoon, shaken out the moth-powder, given it a good brush, and rubbed the life back into the dim little eyes. 'What has been happening to me?' said the sad little eyes. Oh, how sweet it was to see them snap at her again from the red eiderdown! . . . But the nose, which was of some black composition, wasn't at all firm. It must have had a knock, somehow.

Never mind – a little dab of black sealing-wax when the time came – when it was absolutely necessary... Little rogue! Yes, she really felt like that about it. Little rogue biting its tail just by her left ear. She could have taken it off and laid it on her lap and stroked it. She felt a tingling in her hands and arms, but that came from walking, she supposed. And when she breathed, something light and sad – no, not sad, exactly – something gentle seemed to move in her bosom.

There were a number of people out this afternoon, far more than last Sunday. And the band sounded louder and gayer. That was because the Season had begun. For although the band played all the year round on Sundays, out of season it was never the same. It was like someone playing with only the family to listen; it didn't care how it played if there weren't any strangers present. Wasn't the conductor wearing a new coat, too? She was sure it was new. He scraped with his foot and flapped his arms like a rooster about to crow, and the bandsmen sitting in the green rotunda blew out their cheeks and glared at the music. Now there came a little 'flutey' bit – very pretty! – a little chain of bright drops. She was sure it would be repeated. It was; she lifted her head and smiled.

Only two people shared her 'special' seat: a fine old man in a velvet coat, his hands clasped over a huge carved walking-stick, and a big old woman, sitting upright, with a roll of knitting on her embroidered apron. They did not speak. This was disappointing, for Miss Brill always looked forward to the conversation. She had become really quite expert, she thought, at listening as though she didn't listen, at sitting in other people's lives for just a minute while they talked round her.

She glanced, sideways, at the old couple. Perhaps they would go soon. Last Sunday, too, hadn't been as interesting as usual. An Englishman and his wife, he wearing a dreadful Panama hat and she button boots. And she'd gone on the whole time about how she ought to wear spectacles; she knew she needed them; but that it was no good getting any; they'd be sure to break and they'd never keep on. And he'd been so patient. He'd suggested everything – gold rims, the kind that curved round your ears, little pads inside the bridge. No, nothing would please her.

'They'll always be sliding down my nose!' Miss Brill had wanted to shake her.

The old people sat on the bench, still as statues. Never mind, there was always the crowd to watch. To and fro, in front of the flower-beds and the band rotunda, the couples and groups paraded, stopped to talk, to greet, to buy a handful of flowers from the old beggar who had his tray fixed to the railings. Little children ran among them, swooping and laughing; little boys with big white silk bows under their chins, little girls, little French dolls, dressed up in velvet and lace. And sometimes a tiny staggerer came suddenly rocking into the open from under the trees, stopped, stared, as suddenly sat down 'flop,' until its small high-stepping mother, like a young hen, rushed scolding to its rescue. Other people sat on the benches and green chairs, but they were nearly always the same, Sunday after Sunday, and – Miss Brill had often noticed – there was something funny about nearly all of them. They were odd, silent, nearly all old, and from the way they stared they looked as though they'd just come from dark little rooms or even – even cupboards!

Behind the rotunda the slender trees with yellow

Miss Brill

leaves down drooping, and through them just a line of sea, and beyond the blue sky with gold-veined clouds.

Tum-tum-tum tiddle-um! tiddle-um! tum tiddley-um tum ta! blew the band.

Two young girls in red came by and two young soldiers in blue met them, and they laughed and paired and went off arm-in-arm. Two peasant women with funny straw hats passed, gravely, leading beautiful smoke-coloured donkeys. A cold, pale nun hurried by. A beautiful woman came along and dropped her bunch of violets, and a little boy ran after to hand them to her, and she took them and threw them away as if they'd been poisoned. Dear me! Miss Brill didn't know whether to admire that or not! And now an ermine toque and a gentleman in grey met just in front of her. He was tall, stiff, dignified, and she was wearing the ermine toque she'd bought when her hair was yellow. Now everything, her hair, her face, even her eyes, was the same colour as the shabby ermine, and her hand, in its cleaned glove, lifted to dab her lips, was a tiny yellowish paw. Oh, she was so pleased to see him – delighted! She rather thought they were going to meet that afternoon. She described where she'd been – everywhere, here, there, along by the sea. The day was so charming – didn't he agree? And wouldn't he, perhaps? . . . But he shook his head, lighted a cigarette, slowly breathed a great deep puff into her face, and, even while she was still talking and laughing, flicked the match away and walked on. The ermine toque was alone; she smiled more brightly than ever. But even the band seemed to know what she was feeling and played more softly, played tenderly, and the drum beat, 'The Brute! The Brute!' over and over. What would she do? What was going to happen now? But as Miss Brill wondered, the ermine toque turned, raised her hand as though she'd seen someone else, much nicer, just over there, and pattered away. And the band changed again and played more quickly, more gaily than ever, and the old couple on Miss Brill's seat got up and marched away, and such a funny old man with long whiskers hobbled along in time to the music and was nearly knocked over by four girls walking abreast.

Oh, how fascinating it was! How she enjoyed it! How she loved sitting here, watching it all! It was like a play. It was exactly like a play. Who could

Miss Brill

believe the sky at the back wasn't painted? But it wasn't till a little brown dog trotted on solemn and then slowly trotted off, like a little 'theatre' dog, a little dog that had been drugged, that Miss Brill discovered what it was that made it so exciting. They were all on the stage. They weren't only the audience, not only looking on; they were acting. Even she had a part and came every Sunday. No doubt somebody would have noticed if she hadn't been there; she was part of the performance after all. How strange she'd never thought of it like that before! And yet it explained why she made such a point of starting from home at just the same time each week – so as not to be late for the performance – and it also explained why she had quite a queer, shy feeling at telling her English pupils how she spent her Sunday afternoons. No wonder! Miss Brill nearly laughed out loud. She was on the stage. She thought of the old invalid gentleman to whom she read the newspaper four afternoons a week while he slept in the garden. She had got quite used to the frail head on the cotton pillow, the hollowed eyes, the open mouth and the high pinched nose. If he'd been dead she mightn't have noticed for weeks; she wouldn't have minded.

But suddenly he knew he was having the paper read to him by an actress! 'An actress!' The old head lifted; two points of light quivered in the old eyes. 'An actress – are ye?' And Miss Brill smoothed the newspaper as though it was the manuscript of her part and said gently: 'Yes, I have been an actress for a long time.'

The band had been having a rest. Now they started again. And what they played was warm, sunny, yet there was just a faint chill – a something what was it? – not sadness – no, not sadness – a something that made you want to sing. The tune lifted, lifted, the light shone; and it seemed to Miss Brill that in another moment all of them, all the whole company, would begin singing. The young ones, the laughing ones who were moving together, they would begin, and the men's voices, very resolute and brave, would join them. And then she too, she too, and the others on the benches – they would come in with a kind of accompaniment – something low, that scarcely rose or fell, something so beautiful – moving . . . And Miss Brill's eyes filled with tears and she looked smiling at all the other members of the company. Yes, we understand, we understand, she thought – though what they understood she didn't know.

Just at that moment a boy and a girl came and sat down where the old couple had been. They were beautifully dressed; they were in love. The hero and heroine, of course, just arrived from his father's yacht. And still soundlessly singing, still with that trembling smile, Miss Brill prepared to listen.

'No, not now,' said the girl. 'Not here, I can't.'

'But why? Because of that stupid old thing at the end there?' asked the boy. 'Why does she come here at all – who wants her? Why doesn't she keep her silly old mug at home?'

'It's her fu-fur which is so funny,' giggled the girl. 'It's exactly like a fried whiting.'

'Ah, be off with you!' said the boy in an angry whisper. Then: 'Tell me, ma petite chère –'

'No, not here,' said the girl. 'Not *yet*.'

On her way home she usually bought a slice of honey-cake at the baker's. It was her Sunday treat. Sometimes there was an almond in her slice, sometimes not. It made a great difference. If there was an almond it was like carrying home a tiny present – a surprise – something that might very well not have been there. She hurried on the almond Sundays and struck the match for the kettle in quite a dashing way.

But today she passed the baker's by, climbed the stairs, went into the little dark room – her room like a cupboard – and sat down on the red eiderdown. She sat there for a long time. The box that the fur came out of was on the bed. She unclasped the necklet quickly; quickly, without looking, laid it inside. But when she put the lid on she thought she heard something crying.

The Stranger

It seemed to the little crowd on the wharf that she was never going to move again. There she lay, immense, motionless on the grey crinkled water, a loop of smoke above her, an immense flock of gulls screaming and diving after the galley droppings at the stern. You could just see little couples parading – little flies walking up and down the dish on the grey crinkled tablecloth. Other flies clustered and swarmed at the edge. Now there was a gleam of white on the lower deck – the cook's apron or the stewardess perhaps. Now a tiny black spider raced up the ladder on to the bridge.

In the front of the crowd a strong-looking, middle-aged man, dressed very well, very snugly in a grey overcoat, grey silk scarf, thick gloves and dark felt hat, marched up and down, twirling his folded umbrella. He seemed to be the leader of the little crowd on the wharf and at the same time to keep them together. He was something between the sheep-dog and the shepherd.

But what a fool – what a fool he had been not to bring any glasses! There wasn't a pair of glasses between the whole lot of them.

'Curious thing, Mr Scott, that none of us thought of glasses. We might have been able to stir 'em up a bit. We might have managed a little signalling. *Don't hesitate to land. Natives harmless.* Or: *A welcome awaits you. All is forgiven.* What? Eh?'

Mr Hammond's quick, eager glance, so nervous and yet so friendly and confiding, took in everybody on the wharf, roped in even those old chaps lounging against the gangways. They knew, every man-jack of them, that Mrs Hammond was on that boat, and he was so tremendously excited it never entered his head not to believe that this marvellous fact meant something to them too. It warmed his heart towards them. They were, he decided, as decent a crowd of people – those old chaps over by the gangways, too – fine, solid old chaps. What chests – by Jove! And he squared his own, plunged his thick-gloved hands into his pockets, rocked from heel to toe.

The Stranger

'Yes, my wife's been in Europe for the last ten months. On a visit to our eldest girl, who was married last year. I brought her up here, as far as Crawford, myself. So I thought I'd better come and fetch her back. Yes, yes, yes.' The shrewd grey eyes narrowed again and searched anxiously, quickly, the motionless liner. Again his overcoat was unbuttoned. Out came the thin, butter-yellow watch again, and for the twentieth – fiftieth – hundredth time he made the calculation.

'Let me see, now. It was two fifteen when the doctor's launch went off. Two fifteen. It is now exactly twenty-eight minutes past four. That is to say, the doctor's been gone two hours and thirteen minutes. Two hours and thirteen minutes! Whee-ooh!' He gave a queer little half-whistle and snapped his watch to again. 'But I think we should have been told if there was anything up – don't you, Mr Gaven?'

'Oh, yes, Mr Hammond! I don't think there's anything to – anything to worry about,' said Mr Gaven, knocking out his pipe against the heel of his shoe. 'At the same time –'

'Quite so! Quite so!' cried Mr Hammond. 'Dashed annoying!' He paced quickly up and down and came back again to his stand between Mr and Mrs Scott and Mr Gaven. 'It's getting quite dark, too,' and he waved his folded umbrella as though the dusk at least might have had the decency to keep off for a bit. But the dusk came slowly, spreading like a slow stain over the water. Little Jean Scott dragged at her mother's hand.

'I wan' my tea, mammy!' she wailed.

'I expect you do,' said Mr Hammond. 'I expect all these ladies want their tea.' And his kind, flushed, almost pitiful glance roped them all in again. He wondered whether Janey was having a final cup of tea in the saloon out there. He hoped so; he thought not. It would be just like her not to leave the deck. In that case perhaps the deck steward would bring her up a cup. If he'd been there he'd have got it for her – somehow. And for a moment he was on deck, standing over her, watching her little hand fold round the cup in the way she had, while she drank the only cup of tea to be got on board . . . But now he was back here, and the Lord only knew when that cursed Captain would stop hanging about in the stream. He took another turn, up and down, up and down. He walked as far as the cab-stand to make sure his driver hadn't disappeared; back he swerved again to the little flock huddled in the shelter of the banana crates. Little Jean Scott was still wanting her tea. Poor little beggar! He wished he had a bit of chocolate on him.

'Here, Jean!' he said. 'Like a lift up?' And easily, gently, he swung the little girl on to a higher barrel. The movement of holding her, steadying her, relieved him wonderfully, lightened his heart.

'Hold on,' he said, keeping an arm round her.

'Oh, don't worry about *Jean*, Mr Hammond!' said Mrs Scott.

'That's all right, Mrs Scott. No trouble. It's a pleasure. Jean's a little pal of mine, aren't you, Jean?'

'Yes, Mr Hammond,' said Jean, and she ran her finger down the dent of his felt hat.

But suddenly she caught him by the ear and gave a loud scream. 'Lo-ok, Mr Hammond! She's moving! Look, she's coming in!'

By Jove! So she was. At last! She was slowly, slowly turning round. A bell sounded far over the water and a great spout of steam gushed into the air. The gulls rose; they fluttered away like bits of white paper. And whether that deep throbbing was her engines or his heart Mr Hammond couldn't say. He had to nerve himself to bear it, whatever it was. At that moment old Captain Johnson, the harbour-master, came striding down the wharf, a leather portfolio under his arm.

'Jean'll be all right,' said Mr Scott. 'I'll hold her.' He was just in time. Mr Hammond had forgotten about Jean. He sprang away to greet old Captain Johnson.

'Well, Captain,' the eager, nervous voice rang out again, 'you've taken pity on us at last.'

'It's no good blaming me, Mr Hammond,' wheezed old Captain Johnson, staring at the liner. 'You got Mrs Hammond on board, ain't yer?'

'Yes, yes!' said Hammond, and he kept by the harbour-master's side. 'Mrs Hammond's there. Hul-lo! We shan't be long now!'

With her telephone ring-ringing, the thrum of her screw filling the air, the big liner bore down on them, cutting sharp through the dark water so that big white shavings curled to either side. Hammond and the harbour-master kept in front of the rest. Hammond took off his hat; he raked the decks – they were crammed with passengers; he waved his hat and bawled a loud, strange 'Hul-lo!' across the water, and

The Stranger

then turned round and burst out laughing and said something – nothing – to old Captain Johnson.

'Seen her?' asked the harbour-master.

'No, not yet. Steady – wait a bit!' And suddenly, between two great clumsy idiots – 'Get out of the way there!' he signed with his umbrella – he saw a hand raised – a white glove shaking a handkerchief. Another moment, and – thank God, thank God! – there she was. There was Janey. There was Mrs Hammond, yes, yes, yes – standing by the rail and smiling and nodding and waving her handkerchief.

'Well, that's first class – first class! Well, well, well!' He positively stamped. Like lightning he drew out his cigar-case and offered it to old Captain Johnson. 'Have a cigar, Captain! They're pretty good. Have a couple! Here' – and he pressed all the cigars in the case on the harbour-master – 'I've a couple of boxes up at the hotel.'

'Thenks, Mr Hammond!' wheezed old Captain Johnson.

Hammond stuffed the cigar-case back. His hands were shaking, but he'd got hold of himself again. He was able to face Janey. There she was, leaning on the rail, talking to some woman and at the same time watching him, ready for him. It struck him, as the gulf of water closed, how small she looked on that huge ship. His heart was wrung with such a spasm that he could have cried out. How little she looked to have come all that long way and back by herself! Just like her, though. Just like Janey. She had the courage of a – And now the crew had come forward and parted the passengers; they had lowered the rails for the gangways.

The voices on shore and the voices on board flew to greet each other.

'All well?'

'All well.'

'How's mother?'

'Much better.'

'Hullo, Jean!'

'Hillo, Aun' Emily!'

'Had a good voyage?'

'Splendid!'

'Shan't be long now!'

'Not long now.'

The engines stopped. Slowly she edged to the wharf-side.

'Make way there – make way – make way!' And

The Stranger

the wharf hands brought the heavy gangways along at a sweeping run. Hammond signed to Janey to stay where she was. The old harbour-master stepped forward; he followed. As to 'ladies first,' or any rot like that, it never entered his head.

'After you, Captain!' he cried genially. And, treading on the old man's heels, he strode up the gangway on to the deck in a bee-line to Janey, and Janey was clasped in his arms.

'Well, well, well! Yes, yes! Here we are at last!' he stammered. It was all he could say. And Janey emerged, and her cool little voice – the only voice in the world for him – said,

'Well, darling! Have you been waiting long?'

No; not long. Or, at any rate, it didn't matter. It was over now. But the point was, he had a cab waiting at the end of the wharf. Was she ready to go off? Was her luggage ready? In that case they could cut off sharp with her cabin luggage and let the rest go hang until tomorrow. He bent over her and she looked up with her familiar half-smile. She was just the same. Not a day changed. Just as he'd always known her. She laid her small hand on his sleeve.

'How are the children, John?' she asked.

(Hang the children!) 'Perfectly well. Never better in their lives.'

'Haven't they sent me letters?'

'Yes, yes – of course! I've left them at the hotel for you to digest later on.'

'We can't go quite so fast,' said she. 'I've got people to say goodbye to – and then there's the Captain.' As his face fell she gave his arm a small understanding squeeze. 'If the Captain comes off the bridge I want you to thank him for having looked after your wife so beautifully.' Well, he'd got her. If she wanted another ten minutes – As he gave way she was surrounded. The whole first-class seemed to want to say goodbye to Janey.

'Goodbye, *dear* Mrs Hammond! And next time you're in Sydney I'll *expect* you.'

'Darling Mrs Hammond! You won't forget to write to me, will you?'

'Well, Mrs Hammond, what this boat would have been without you!'

It was as plain as a pikestaff that she was by far the most popular woman on board. And she took it all – just as usual. Absolutely composed. Just her little self – just Janey all over; standing there with her veil

The Stranger

thrown back. Hammond never noticed what his wife had on. It was all the same to him whatever she wore. But today he did notice that she wore a black 'costume' – didn't they call it? – with white frills, trimmings he supposed they were, at the neck and sleeves. All this while Janey handed him round.

'John, dear!' And then: 'I want to introduce you to –'

Finally they did escape, and she led the way to her state-room. To follow Janey down the passage that she knew so well – that was so strange to him; to part the green curtains after her and to step into the cabin that had been hers gave him exquisite happiness. But – confound it! – the stewardess was there on the floor, strapping up the rugs.

'That's the last, Mrs Hammond,' said the stewardess, rising and pulling down her cuffs.

He was introduced again, and then Janey and the stewardess disappeared into the passage. He heard whisperings. She was getting the tipping business over, he supposed. He sat down on the striped sofa and took his hat off. There were the rugs she had taken with her; they looked good as new. All her luggage looked fresh, perfect. The labels were written in her beautiful little clear hand – 'Mrs John Hammond.'

'Mrs John Hammond!' He gave a long sigh of content and leaned back, crossing his arms. The strain was over. He felt he could have sat there for ever sighing his relief – the relief at being rid of that horrible tug, pull, grip on his heart. The danger was over. That was the feeling. They were on dry land again.

But at that moment Janey's head came round the corner.

'Darling – do you mind? I just want to go and say goodbye to the doctor.'

Hammond started up. 'I'll come with you.'

'No, no!' she said. 'Don't bother. I'd rather not. I'll not be a minute.'

And before he could answer she was gone. He had half a mind to run after her; but instead he sat down again.

Would she really not be long? What was the time now? Out came the watch; he stared at nothing. That was rather queer of Janey, wasn't it? Why couldn't she have told the stewardess to say goodbye for her? Why did she have to go chasing after the ship's doctor? She could have sent a note from the hotel even

The Stranger

if the affair had been urgent. Urgent? Did it – could it mean that she had been ill on the voyage – she was keeping something from him? That was it! He seized his hat. He was going off to find that fellow and to wring the truth out of him at all costs. He thought he'd noticed just something. She was just a touch too calm – too steady. From the very first moment –

The curtains rang. Janey was back. He jumped to his feet.

'Janey, have you been ill on this voyage? You have!'

'Ill?' Her airy little voice mocked him. She stepped over the rugs, came up close, touched his breast, and looked up at him.

'Darling,' she said, 'don't frighten me. Of course I haven't! Whatever makes you think I have? Do I look ill?'

But Hammond didn't see her. He only felt that she was looking at him and that there was no need to worry about anything. She was here to look after things. It was all right. Everything was.

The gentle pressure of her hand was so calming that he put his over hers to hold it there. And she said:

'Stand still. I want to look at you. I haven't seen you yet. You've had your beard beautifully trimmed, and you look – younger, I think, and decidedly thinner! Bachelor life agrees with you.'

'Agrees with me!' He groaned for love and caught her close again. And again, as always, he had the feeling he was holding something that never was quite his – his. Something too delicate, too precious, that would fly away once he let go.

'For God's sake let's get off to the hotel so that we can be by ourselves!' And he rang the bell hard for some one to look sharp with the luggage.

Walking down the wharf together she took his arm. He had her on his arm again. And the difference it made to get into the cab after Janey – to throw the red-and-yellow striped blanket round them both – to tell the driver to hurry because neither of them had had any tea. No more going without his tea or pouring out his own. She was back. He turned to her, squeezed her hand, and said gently, teasingly, in the 'special' voice he had for her: 'Glad to be home again, dearie?' She smiled; she didn't even bother to answer, but gently she drew his hand away as they came to the brighter streets.

'We've got the best room in the hotel,' he said.

The Stranger

'I wouldn't be put off with another. And I asked the chambermaid to put in a bit of a fire in case you felt chilly. She's a nice, attentive girl. And I thought now we were here we wouldn't bother to go home tomorrow, but spend the day looking round and leave the morning after. Does that suit you? There's no hurry, is there? The children will have you soon enough . . . I thought a day's sightseeing might make a nice break in your journey – eh, Janey?'

'Have you taken the tickets for the day after?' she asked.

'I should think I have!' He unbuttoned his overcoat and took out his bulging pocket-book. 'Here we are! I reserved a first-class carriage to Salisbury. There it is – "Mr *and* Mrs John Hammond." I thought we might as well do ourselves comfortably, and we don't want other people butting in, do we? But if you'd like to stop here a bit longer –?'

'Oh, no!' said Janey quickly. 'Not for the world! The day after tomorrow, then. And the children –'

But they had reached the hotel. The manager was standing in the broad, brilliantly-lighted porch. He came down to greet them. A porter ran from the hall for their boxes.

'Well, Mr Arnold, here's Mrs Hammond at last!'

The manager led them through the hall himself and pressed the elevator-bell. Hammond knew there were business pals of his sitting at the little hall tables having a drink before dinner. But he wasn't going to risk interruption; he looked neither to the right nor the left. They could think what they pleased. If they didn't understand, the more fools they – and he stepped out of the lift, unlocked the door of their room, and shepherded Janey in. The door shut. Now, at last, they were alone together. He turned up the light. The curtains were drawn; the fire blazed. He flung his hat on to the huge bed and went towards her.

But – would you believe it! – again they were interrupted. This time it was the porter with the luggage. He made two journeys of it, leaving the door open in between, taking his time, whistling through his teeth in the corridor. Hammond paced up and down the room, tearing off his gloves, tearing off his scarf. Finally he flung his overcoat on the bedside.

At last the fool was gone. The door clicked. Now they *were* alone. Said Hammond: 'I feel I'll never have you to myself again. These cursed people!

The Stranger

Janey' – and he bent his flushed, eager gaze upon her – 'let's have dinner up here. If we go down to the restaurant we'll be interrupted, and then there's the confounded music' (the music he'd praised so highly, applauded so loudly last night!). 'We shan't be able to hear each other speak. Let's have something up here in front of the fire. It's too late for tea. I'll order a little supper, shall I? How does the idea strike you?'

'Do, darling!' said Janey. 'And while you're away – the children's letters –'

'Oh, later on will do!' said Hammond.

'But then we'd get it over,' said Janey. 'And I'd first have time to –'

'Oh, I needn't go down!' explained Hammond. 'I'll just ring and give the order . . . you don't want to send me away, do you?'

Janey shook her head and smiled.

'But you're thinking of something else. You're worrying about something,' said Hammond. 'What is it? Come and sit here – come and sit on my knee before the fire.'

'I'll just unpin my hat,' said Janey, and she went over to the dressing-table. 'A-ah!' She gave a little cry.

'What is it?'

'Nothing, darling. I've just found the children's letters. That's all right! They will keep. No hurry now!' She turned to him, clasping them. She tucked them into her frilled blouse. She cried quickly, gaily: 'Oh, how typical this dressing-table is of you!'

'Why? What's the matter with it?' said Hammond.

'If it were floating in eternity I should say "John!"' laughed Janey, staring at the big bottle of hair tonic, the wicker bottle of eau-de-Cologne, the two hair-brushes, and a dozen new collars tied with pink tape. 'Is this all your luggage?'

'Hang my luggage!' said Hammond; but all the same he liked being laughed at by Janey. 'Let's talk. Let's get down to things. Tell me' – and as Janey perched on his knees he leaned back and drew her into the deep, ugly chair – 'tell me you're really glad to be back, Janey.'

'Yes, darling, I am glad,' she said.

But just as when he embraced her he felt she would fly away, so Hammond never knew – never knew for dead certain that she was as glad as he was. How could he know? Would he ever know? Would he always have this craving – this pang like hunger

The Stranger

somehow, to make Janey so much part of him that there wasn't any of her to escape? He wanted to blot out everybody, everything. He wished now he'd turned off the light. That might have brought her nearer. And now those letters from the children rustled in her blouse. He could have chucked them into the fire.

'Janey,' he whispered.

'Yes, dear?' She lay on his breast, but so lightly, so remotely. Their breathing rose and fell together.

'Janey!'

'What is it?'

'Turn to me,' he whispered. A slow, deep flush flowed into his forehead. 'Kiss me, Janey! You kiss me!'

It seemed to him there was a tiny pause – but long enough for him to suffer torture – before her lips touched his, firmly, lightly – kissing them as she always kissed him, as though the kiss – how could he describe it? – confirmed what they were saying, signed the contract. But that wasn't what he wanted; that wasn't at all what he thirsted for. He felt suddenly horribly tired.

'If you knew,' he said, opening his eyes, 'what it's

been like – waiting today. I thought the boat never would come in. There we were, hanging about. What kept you so long?'

She made no answer. She was looking away from him at the fire. The flames hurried – hurried over the coals, flickered, fell.

'Not asleep, are you?' said Hammond, and he jumped her up and down.

'No,' she said. And then: 'Don't do that, dear. No, I was thinking. As a matter of fact,' she said, 'one of the passengers died last night – a man. That's what held us up. We brought him in – I mean, he wasn't buried at sea. So, of course, the ship's doctor and the shore doctor –'

'What was it?' asked Hammond uneasily. He hated to hear of death. He hated this to have happened. It was, in some queer way, as though he and Janey had met a funeral on their way to the hotel.

'Oh, it wasn't anything in the least infectious!' said Janey. She was speaking scarcely above her breath. 'It was *heart*.' A pause. 'Poor fellow!' she said. 'Quite young.' And she watched the fire flicker and fall. 'He died in my arms,' said Janey.

The Stranger

The blow was so sudden that Hammond thought he would faint. He couldn't move; he couldn't breathe. He felt all his strength flowing – flowing into the big dark chair, and the big dark chair held him fast, gripped him, forced him to bear it.

'What?' he said dully. 'What's that you say?'

'The end was quite peaceful,' said the small voice. 'He just' – and Hammond saw her lift her gentle hand – 'breathed his life away at the end.' And her hand fell.

'Who – else was there?' Hammond managed to ask.

'Nobody. I was alone with him.'

Ah, my God, what was she saying! What was she doing to him! This would kill him! And all the while she spoke:

'I saw the change coming and I sent the steward for the doctor, but the doctor was too late. He couldn't have done anything, anyway.'

'But – why *you*, why *you?*' moaned Hammond.

At that Janey turned quickly, quickly searched his face.

'You don't *mind*, John, do you?' she asked. 'You don't – It's nothing to do with you and me.'

Somehow or other he managed to shake some sort of smile at her. Somehow or other he stammered: 'No – go – on, go on! I want you to tell me.'

'But, John darling. –'

'Tell me, Janey!'

'There's nothing to tell,' she said, wondering. 'He was one of the first-class passengers. I saw he was very ill when he came on board . . . But he seemed to be so much better until yesterday. He had a severe attack in the afternoon – excitement – nervousness, I think, about arriving. And after that he never recovered.'

'But why didn't the stewardess –'

'Oh, my dear – the stewardess!' said Janey. 'What would he have felt? And besides . . . he might have wanted to leave a message . . . to –'

'Didn't he?' muttered Hammond. 'Didn't he say anything?'

'No, darling, not a word!' She shook her head softly. 'All the time I was with him he was too weak . . . he was too weak even to move a finger . . .'

Janey was silent. But her words, so light, so soft, so chill, seemed to hover in the air, to rain into his breast like snow.

The fire had gone red. Now it fell in with a sharp sound and the room was colder. Cold crept up his arms. The room was huge, immense, glittering. It filled his whole world. There was the great blind bed, with his coat flung across it like some headless man saying his prayers. There was the luggage, ready to be carried away again, anywhere, tossed into trains, carted on to boats.

. . . 'He was too weak. He was too weak to move a finger.' And yet he died in Janey's arms. She – who'd never – never once in all these years – never on one single solitary occasion –

No; he mustn't think of it. Madness lay in thinking of it. No, he wouldn't face it. He couldn't stand it. It was too much to bear!

And now Janey touched his tie with her fingers. She pinched the edges of the tie together.

'You're not – sorry I told you, John darling? It hasn't made you sad? It hasn't spoilt our evening – our being alone together?'

But at that he had to hide his face. He put his face into her bosom and his arms enfolded her.

Spoilt their evening! Spoilt their being alone together! They would never be alone together again.

1. BOCCACCIO · *Mrs Rosie and the Priest*
2. GERARD MANLEY HOPKINS · *As kingfishers catch fire*
3. *The Saga of Gunnlaug Serpent-tongue*
4. THOMAS DE QUINCEY · *On Murder Considered as One of the Fine Arts*
5. FRIEDRICH NIETZSCHE · *Aphorisms on Love and Hate*
6. JOHN RUSKIN · *Traffic*
7. PU SONGLING · *Wailing Ghosts*
8. JONATHAN SWIFT · *A Modest Proposal*
9. *Three Tang Dynasty Poets*
10. WALT WHITMAN · *On the Beach at Night Alone*
11. KENKŌ · *A Cup of Sake Beneath the Cherry Trees*
12. BALTASAR GRACIÁN · *How to Use Your Enemies*
13. JOHN KEATS · *The Eve of St Agnes*
14. THOMAS HARDY · *Woman much missed*
15. GUY DE MAUPASSANT · *Femme Fatale*
16. MARCO POLO · *Travels in the Land of Serpents and Pearls*
17. SUETONIUS · *Caligula*
18. APOLLONIUS OF RHODES · *Jason and Medea*
19. ROBERT LOUIS STEVENSON · *Olalla*
20. KARL MARX AND FRIEDRICH ENGELS · *The Communist Manifesto*
21. PETRONIUS · *Trimalchio's Feast*
22. JOHANN PETER HEBEL · *How a Ghastly Story Was Brought to Light by a Common or Garden Butcher's Dog*
23. HANS CHRISTIAN ANDERSEN · *The Tinder Box*
24. RUDYARD KIPLING · *The Gate of the Hundred Sorrows*
25. DANTE · *Circles of Hell*
26. HENRY MAYHEW · *Of Street Piemen*
27. HAFEZ · *The nightingales are drunk*
28. GEOFFREY CHAUCER · *The Wife of Bath*
29. MICHEL DE MONTAIGNE · *How We Weep and Laugh at the Same Thing*
30. THOMAS NASHE · *The Terrors of the Night*
31. EDGAR ALLAN POE · *The Tell-Tale Heart*
32. MARY KINGSLEY · *A Hippo Banquet*
33. JANE AUSTEN · *The Beautifull Cassandra*
34. ANTON CHEKHOV · *Gooseberries*
35. SAMUEL TAYLOR COLERIDGE · *Well, they are gone, and here must I remain*
36. JOHANN WOLFGANG VON GOETHE · *Sketchy, Doubtful, Incomplete Jottings*
37. CHARLES DICKENS · *The Great Winglebury Duel*
38. HERMAN MELVILLE · *The Maldive Shark*
39. ELIZABETH GASKELL · *The Old Nurse's Story*
40. NIKOLAY LESKOV · *The Steel Flea*

41. HONORÉ DE BALZAC · *The Atheist's Mass*
42. CHARLOTTE PERKINS GILMAN · *The Yellow Wall-Paper*
43. C.P. CAVAFY · *Remember, Body . . .*
44. FYODOR DOSTOEVSKY · *The Meek One*
45. GUSTAVE FLAUBERT · *A Simple Heart*
46. NIKOLAI GOGOL · *The Nose*
47. SAMUEL PEPYS · *The Great Fire of London*
48. EDITH WHARTON · *The Reckoning*
49. HENRY JAMES · *The Figure in the Carpet*
50. WILFRED OWEN · *Anthem For Doomed Youth*
51. WOLFGANG AMADEUS MOZART · *My Dearest Father*
52. PLATO · *Socrates' Defence*
53. CHRISTINA ROSSETTI · *Goblin Market*
54. *Sindbad the Sailor*
55. SOPHOCLES · *Antigone*
56. RYŪNOSUKE AKUTAGAWA · *The Life of a Stupid Man*
57. LEO TOLSTOY · *How Much Land Does A Man Need?*
58. GIORGIO VASARI · *Leonardo da Vinci*
59. OSCAR WILDE · *Lord Arthur Savile's Crime*
60. SHEN FU · *The Old Man of the Moon*
61. AESOP · *The Dolphins, the Whales and the Gudgeon*
62. MATSUO BASHŌ · *Lips too Chilled*
63. EMILY BRONTË · *The Night is Darkening Round Me*
64. JOSEPH CONRAD · *To-morrow*
65. RICHARD HAKLUYT · *The Voyage of Sir Francis Drake Around the Whole Globe*
66. KATE CHOPIN · *A Pair of Silk Stockings*
67. CHARLES DARWIN · *It was snowing butterflies*
68. BROTHERS GRIMM · *The Robber Bridegroom*
69. CATULLUS · *I Hate and I Love*
70. HOMER · *Circe and the Cyclops*
71. D. H. LAWRENCE · *Il Duro*
72. KATHERINE MANSFIELD · *Miss Brill*
73. OVID · *The Fall of Icarus*
74. SAPPHO · *Come Close*
75. IVAN TURGENEV · *Kasyan from the Beautiful Lands*
76. VIRGIL · *O Cruel Alexis*
77. H. G. WELLS · *A Slip under the Microscope*
78. HERODOTUS · *The Madness of Cambyses*
79. *Speaking of Siva*
80. *The Dhammapada*

'Drawn on by his eagerness for the open sky, he left his guide and soared upwards . . .'

PUBLIUS OVIDIUS NASO
Born 43 BC, Sulmo, Italy
Died AD 17, in exile

Taken from Books VIII and IX of Mary M. Innes's
translation of *Metamorphoses*.

OVID IN PENGUIN CLASSICS
The Erotic Poems
Fasti
Heroides
Metamorphoses

OVID

The Fall of Icarus

Translated by
Mary M. Innes

PENGUIN BOOKS

PENGUIN CLASSICS

UK | USA | Canada | Ireland | Australia
India | New Zealand | South Africa

Penguin Books is part of the Penguin Random House group of companies
whose addresses can be found at global.penguinrandomhouse.com.

This selection published in Penguin Classics 2015
013

Copyright © Mary M. Innes, 1955

Set in 10/14.5 pt Baskerville 10 Pro
Typeset by Jouve (UK), Milton Keynes
Printed and bound in Great Britain by Clays Ltd, Elcograf S.p.A.

A CIP catalogue record for this book is available from the British Library

ISBN: 978-0-141-39867-9

www.greenpenguin.co.uk

Penguin Random House is committed to a
sustainable future for our business, our readers
and our planet. This book is made from Forest
Stewardship Council® certified paper.

When the morning star had banished the night, unveiling the brightness of the day, the East wind fell, and rainclouds gathered in the sky. Sped on his way by the mild South wind, Cephalus returned home, accompanied by the sons of Aeacus. After a prosperous voyage they reached the harbour they were making for, sooner than they had dared to hope.

Meanwhile Minos was plundering the shores of Megara, and trying out his military strength against the town of Alcathous, where Nisus ruled. This venerable white-haired king had one bright purple tress right in the middle of his head. On its safety depended the safety of his kingdom.

The rising moon was now displaying her horns for the sixth time, and still the outcome of the struggle hung in the balance. Winged victory had long been hovering between the two sides, undecided. There was a tower belonging to the king, built on to those tuneful city walls where Leto's son, they say, laid down his golden lyre, so that its music was imparted to the masonry. Often in the days of peace Nisus' daughter had been in the habit of climbing up there, and flinging pebbles against the stones to make them ring. During the war, too, she used often to watch the grim struggle from that vantage point and, as the conflict dragged on, she had come to know the names of the leaders and to recognize their arms and their horses, their attire and their Cretan quivers. Better than any of the others, she knew their general, Europa's son; indeed she knew him better than she should have done. In her eyes, Minos was perfect. When he wore his helmet with its plumed crest, she thought how handsome he looked in a helmet; if he was carrying his shield of shining bronze, the shield became him well; when, with straining muscles, he hurled his pliant spear, the princess praised his strength and skill: when he fitted an arrow to his bowstring and bent the bow in a wide arc, she swore that Apollo looked just like that when he stood with his arrows in his hand. But when Minos laid aside his helmet and revealed his features, when, decked

The Fall of Icarus

in purple, he bestrode his white horse with its embroidered trappings and pulled on its foam-flecked bit, Nisus' daughter was almost driven out of her senses, and was all but out of her mind with love. Happy the javelin he touched, she declared, and happy the reins he gathered in his hands. Had it but been possible, her impulse was to rush to him, braving the enemy's lines, though she was only a girl. She wanted to throw herself from the top of some tower, into the Cretan camp, or to open to the enemy the gates that brazen bolts held fast, or to do anything else to please Minos. As she sat gazing at the shining canvas of the Cretan king's tent, 'I do not know,' she mused, 'whether to be glad or sorry that this miserable war is being fought. I am sorry that Minos is my enemy, when I love him so: but if there had been no war, I should never have known him! Now, if he were to take me as a hostage, he could abandon the war, and have me as his companion, as a pledge of peace. O my handsome hero, if your mother was herself as beautiful as you, it is no wonder that a god fell in love with her! Thrice blessed would I be, if I could take wing and, gliding through the air, light down in the camp of the Cretan king, there to confess my feelings and my love, and ask what dowry would make Minos take me for his wife: anything, short of my father's kingdom! For I would rather lose the marriage I dream of, than obtain it by treachery: though indeed many people have found it profit them to be defeated, when their victor has been reasonable and kindly. There is no doubt that Minos is justified in waging war to avenge his murdered son: he is strong in the cause for which he fights, strong in the arms that defend it. We shall be conquered, I feel sure, and if that is the fate that awaits our city, why should not I, in my love, open up these gates to him, instead of waiting for his military strength to breach the walls? It is better that he should be able to win without delay, without slaughter, without the cost of his own blood. At any rate, I should not then have to fear lest someone unwittingly wound your breast, my Minos. Unwittingly, I say, for there is no one so hard-hearted that he would dare to aim his cruel spear against you, if he knew who you were.'

The plan she had begun to make appealed to her, and she resolved to give herself up to Minos, with her father's kingdom as a dowry, and so put an end to the war. But the will to do this was not enough.

The Fall of Icarus

'There is a garrison on sentry duty at the entrance to the city,' she said to herself, 'and my father has the keys to the gates. Wretched girl that I am, he is the only one I have to fear: he alone prevents me from accomplishing what I desire. Would to the gods I were rid of my father! But surely every man is his own god: Fortune refuses her aid to those who merely pray, and take no action. Anyone else, fired with a desire as great as mine, would long ago have destroyed anything that stood in the way of her love, and have been glad to do so. Why should I be less brave than another? I would make my way boldly through fire and sword, and in this case there is no need of either, but only of a lock of my father's hair. That lock is more precious to me than gold, for the purple tress will make me happy, and bring me that for which I pray!' As she was musing thus, night, the mighty healer of men's cares, came on, and with the darkness she grew bolder. During those first peaceful hours, when sleep enfolds the hearts of mortals whom day's anxieties have wearied, she silently entered her father's bedroom, and performed her awful deed. His own daughter robbed her father of the hair on which his whole destiny depended. When she had obtained her horrible prize, she made her way through the very midst of the enemy – so confident was she in the service she had done them – till she came to the king. He was startled by her arrival, but she addressed him in these words: 'Love has driven me to crime. I, Scylla, daughter of King Nisus, hand over to you the gods of my country and my home. I ask nothing in return except yourself. Take this pledge of my love, this purple tress of hair, and believe that it is not my father's hair but his head which I deliver up to you!' She held out her gift in her guilty hand, but Minos shrank back from what she offered him. Shaken at the thought of so unnatural a deed, he cried: 'You are a disgrace to our times! I pray that the gods may rid the earth of you, that land and sea may deny you any refuge! Certainly I shall not allow my world, the island of Crete which was the cradle of Jupiter, to come in contact with such a monster!' This was his reply. Then he imposed his own conditions, which were eminently just, upon his captured enemies and, when he had done so, ordered the mooring cables to be unloosed, and told the rowers to take their places in the bronze-beaked ships.

Scylla watched the ships being dragged down to

The Fall of Icarus

the sea and, when she saw them already afloat upon the waves, realized that the enemy leader was not going to reward her for her crime. She had no more prayers to utter; her mood changed to one of violent rage instead. In a fury, she tore her hair and shook her fists at Minos. 'Where are you going?' she cried. 'You whom I have preferred to my country and to my own father? Where are you going, leaving behind the one who made your recent conquest possible? Where are you off to, hard-hearted man, after gaining a victory for which I deserve all the credit and all the blame? Does the gift I have made you move you not at all? Does my love mean nothing, or the fact that all my hopes are centred on you alone? For, if you leave me, where shall I go? My own country lies vanquished and, even supposing it still survived, it is closed to me since I betrayed it. Shall I go to my father, after delivering him up to you? The citizens hate me, as they have every right to do, and neighbouring peoples are afraid of the example I have set. All the world is shut against me, so that Crete is my only refuge. If you prevent me from finding shelter there, if you are so lost to all sense of gratitude as to abandon me, then you are the son, not of Europa, but rather of the inhospitable Syrtis, of an Armenian tigress, or of Charybdis' pool, which the South wind lashes to fury: you are no child of Jove, and the story of your birth is a lie! It was not a god disguised as a bull who lured your mother away, but a real bull, a wild beast that had never known love for any heifer. O Nisus, my father, punish me! You walls that I lately betrayed, rejoice in my misfortunes! For I freely confess that I have earned your hatred, and that I deserve to die. But let it be one of those whom I have treacherously wronged who destroys me; why do you, Minos, punish my crime, when it has brought you victory? What my father and my country regard as guilt should be to you a proof of devotion. In very truth, that unfaithful wife who tricked a fierce bull by means of a wooden model, and bore a child half animal, half human, was a fit mate for you! Tell me, do my words reach your ears, or do those same winds that speed your ships carry away my pleas, you ungrateful wretch, and make them vain? Now, indeed, I am not surprised that Pasiphae preferred her bull to you: of the two, you were the more savage. Alas, he is ordering his crews to make haste: the wave roars under the beat of the oarblades, and I and my country together fade into the distance. But it is no use! You need not try to forget the service I have done you. I shall follow you, even against your will. I shall seize hold of your vessel's curving stern, and be carried with you far across the seas!'

No sooner had she said this, than she jumped into the water, and swam after the ships; her violent passion lending her strength, she grasped and clung to the Cretan vessel, an unwelcome companion. Her father caught sight of her (for he had been newly changed into a sea eagle, with tawny feathers, and was now hovering in the air) and attacked her, as she clung there, intending to rend her flesh with his hooked beak. In her terror she let go her hold on the boat, but as she fell the light breeze seemed to bear her up, and prevent her from touching the waters. She found herself all feathers: and when downy plumage had changed her into a bird she was called Ciris, or Shearer, a name she owes to the cutting off of her father's hair.

When Minos had returned safely to Crete, he disembarked, and sacrificed a hundred oxen to Jupiter in payment of his vows. The trophies he had won were hung up to adorn the palace. In his absence the monstrous child which the queen had borne, to the disgrace of the king's family, had grown up, and the strange hybrid creature had revealed his wife's disgusting love affair to everyone. Minos determined to rid his home of this shameful sight, by shutting the monster away in an enclosure of elaborate and involved design, where it could not be seen. Daedalus, an architect famous for his skill, constructed the maze, confusing the usual marks of direction, and leading the eye of the beholder astray by devious paths winding in different directions. Just as the playful waters of the Macander in Phrygia flow this way and that, without any consistency, as the river, turning to meet itself, sees its own advancing waves, flowing now towards its source and now towards the open sea, always changing its direction, so Daedalus constructed countless wandering paths and was himself scarcely able to find his way back to the entrance, so confusing was the maze.

There Minos imprisoned the monster, half-bull, half-man, and twice feasted him on Athenian blood; but when, after a further interval of nine years, a third band of victims was demanded, this brought about the creature's downfall. For, thanks to the help of the

The Fall of Icarus

princess Ariadne, Theseus rewound the thread he had laid, retraced his steps, and found the elusive gateway as none of his predecessors had managed to do. Immediately he set sail for Dia, carrying with him the daughter of Minos; but on the shore of that island he cruelly abandoned his companion. Ariadne, left all alone, was sadly lamenting her fate, when Bacchus put his arms around her, and brought her his aid. He took the crown from her forehead and set it as a constellation in the sky, to bring her eternal glory. Up through the thin air it soared and, as it flew, its jewels were changed into shining fires. They settled in position, still keeping the appearance of a crown, midway between the kneeling Hercules and Ophiuchus, who grasps the snake.

Meanwhile Daedalus, tired of Crete and of his long absence from home, was filled with longing for his own country, but he was shut in by the sea. Then he said: 'The king may block my way by land or across the ocean, but the sky, surely, is open, and that is how we shall go. Minos may possess all the rest, but he does not possess the air.' With these words, he set his mind to sciences never explored before, and altered the laws of nature. He laid down a row of feathers, beginning with tiny ones, and gradually increasing their length, so that the edge seemed to slope upwards. In the same way, the pipe which shepherds used to play is built up from reeds, each slightly longer than the last. Then he fastened the feathers together in the middle with thread, and at the bottom with wax; when he had arranged them in this way, he bent them round into a gentle curve, to look like real birds' wings. His son Icarus stood beside him and, not knowing that the materials he was handling were to endanger his life, laughingly captured the feathers which blew away in the wind, or softened the yellow wax with his thumb, and by his pranks hindered the marvellous work on which his father was engaged.

When Daedalus had put the finishing touches to his invention, he raised himself into the air, balancing his body on his two wings, and there he hovered, moving his feathers up and down. Then he prepared his son to fly too. 'I warn you, Icarus,' he said, 'you must follow a course midway between earth and heaven, in case the sun should scorch your feathers, if you go too high, or the water make them heavy if you are too low. Fly halfway between the two. And

The Fall of Icarus

pay no attention to the stars, to Bootes, or Helice or Orion with his drawn sword: take me as your guide, and follow me!'

While he was giving Icarus these instructions on how to fly, Daedalus was at the same time fastening the novel wings on his son's shoulders. As he worked and talked the old man's cheeks were wet with tears, and his fatherly affection made his hands tremble. He kissed his son, whom he was never to kiss again: then, raising himself on his wings, flew in front, showing anxious concern for his companion, just like a bird who has brought her tender fledgelings out of their nest in the tree-tops, and launched them into the air. He urged Icarus to follow close, and instructed him in the art that was to be his ruin, moving his own wings and keeping a watchful eye on those of his son behind him. Some fisher, perhaps, playing his quivering rod, some shepherd leaning on his staff, or a peasant bent over his plough handle caught sight of them as they flew past and stood stock still in astonishment, believing that these creatures who could fly through the air must be gods.

Now Juno's sacred isle of Samos lay on the left, Delos and Paros were already behind them, and

Lebinthus was on their right hand, along with Calymne, rich in honey, when the boy Icarus began to enjoy the thrill of swooping boldly through the air. Drawn on by his eagerness for the open sky, he left his guide and soared upwards, till he came too close to the blazing sun, and it softened the sweet-smelling wax that bound his wings together. The wax melted. Icarus moved his bare arms up and down, but without their feathers they had no purchase on the air. Even as his lips were crying his father's name, they were swallowed up in the deep blue waters which are called after him. The unhappy father, a father no longer, cried out: 'Icarus!' 'Icarus,' he called. 'Where are you? Where am I to look for you?' As he was still calling 'Icarus' he saw the feathers on the water, and cursed his inventive skill. He laid his son to rest in a tomb, and the land took its name from that of the boy who was buried there.

As Daedalus was burying the body of his ill-fated son, a chattering lapwing popped its head out of a muddy ditch, flapped its wings and crowed with joy. At that time it was the only bird of its kind, and none like it had ever been seen before. The transformation had been a recent one, and was a lasting reproach to

The Fall of Icarus

Daedalus: for his sister, knowing nothing of fate's intention, had sent her son, an intelligent boy of twelve, to learn what Daedalus could teach him. This lad, observing the backbone of a fish, and taking it as a pattern, notched a series of teeth in a sharp iron blade, thus inventing the saw. He was the first, too, to fasten two iron arms together into one joint, so that, while remaining equidistant, one arm might stand still, and the other describe a circle round it. Daedalus was jealous, and flung his nephew headlong down from Minerva's sacred citadel. Then he spread a false report that the boy had fallen over. But Pallas, who looks favourably upon clever men, caught the lad as he fell and changed him into a bird, clothing him with feathers in mid-air. The swiftness of intellect he once displayed was replaced by swiftness of wing and foot. His name remained the same as before. However, this bird does not soar high into the air, nor does it build its nest on branches in the tree-tops: rather it flutters along the ground, and lays its eggs in the hedgerows, for it is afraid of heights, remembering its fall in the days of long ago.

Daedalus, weary with wandering, had now found refuge in Etna's land and Cocalus, who had taken up arms in answer to his request for aid, had won a reputation for clemency. Athens had now ceased to pay her mournful tribute, thanks to Theseus' victory. The temples were decked with garlands of flowers, and the people were singing hymns to the warrior Minerva, to Jove, and to the other gods, honouring them with gifts, with offerings of incense, and with the sacrifices which they had promised. Rumour, swiftly travelling, had spread Theseus' fame through the various cities of Argos, and the peoples of rich Achaea sought his help in their hour of peril. Among the rest, Calydon begged and besought him to come to its aid, though it had its own hero, Meleager. The request was occasioned by a boar, which was at once the servant and the avenging minister of Diana. The goddess was angry with the people: for, according to the tale, King Oeneus, out of the bountiful harvests of a good year, made offering of the first fruits of corn to Ceres, poured a libation of wine in honour of Bacchus, and one of olive oil in honour of Minerva. First the gods of the farmers, and then all the gods in heaven, received the honours they desired – except Leto's daughter. She alone was neglected, and her altars were the only ones left without an offering of incense.

The Fall of Icarus

Now the gods feel anger, too. 'I shall not submit to this without protest: men may say that I went unhonoured, but they will not say I went unavenged!' cried Diana; and she let loose a wild boar in Oeneus' land, to punish him for having scorned her. This boar was as big as the bulls found in grassy Epirus, bigger than the Sicilian ones. There was a fiery gleam in its bloodshot eyes, it held its neck high and stiff, its hide bristled with hairs that stuck straight out like spears. It bellowed harshly, the hot foam flecking its broad shoulders, and its teeth were like elephants' tusks: fire issued from its jaws, the leaves were set alight by its breath.

This monster trampled down the tender shoots of the growing crops, or again, when the harvest had fulfilled the farmers' hopes, it turned their joy to tears by ravaging the fields and breaking down the corn in the ear. The threshing floor and barns waited in vain for the promised harvests. Heavy vine clusters with their trailing leaves were strewn on the ground among berries and branches from the evergreen olive. The boar launched furious attacks on the flocks also: neither shepherds nor dogs could save them, nor could the fierce bulls defend the herds. People fled in all directions, thinking themselves safe only when protected by the walls of the city: till Meleager and a handful of picked men banded themselves together in a desire to win fame and glory.

There were the twin sons of Tyndareus, one renowned as a boxer, and the other as a horseman: Jason who had built the first ship, Theseus and Pirithous, inseparable companions, and the two sons of Thestius. Aphareus' sons were there, Lynceus and swift Idas; Caeneus too, who had once been a woman, the warrior Leucippus, Acastus, noted for his javelin-throwing, Hippothous and Dryas, along with Phoenix, Amyntor's son, the two sons of Actor, and Phyleus who had come from Elis. Telamon joined them, and Peleus, the father of great Achilles, as well as the son of Pheres, and Iolaus from Boeotia. Eurytion was with them too, a man full of vigour, and Echion, whom none could surpass in running, the Locrian Lelex, and Panopeus and Hyleus, fierce Hippasus and Nestor, then still in the prime of life. There was also the contingent which Hippocoon had sent from ancient Amyclae, and Penelope's father-in-law Laertes came, accompanied by the Arcadian Ancaeus. The wise seer, Ampycus' son, was there, and

Amphiaraus, who had not yet fallen a victim to his wife's treachery. The girl warrior from Tegea, the pride of the Lycaean grove, came too; a polished buckle fastened the neck of her garment, and her hair was simply done, gathered into a single knot. An ivory quiver, containing her arrows, hung from her left shoulder, and rattled as she moved, while she carried her bow as well, in her left hand. Such was her attire – she had features which in a boy would have been called girlish, but in a girl they were like a boy's.

As soon as the hero of Calydon saw her, he fell in love, though the gods would not sanction it, and was fired with secret desire. 'Happy indeed, the man whom she thinks worthy of her hand!' he sighed. He was too modest, and had no time, to say more; for there was a matter of greater urgency on hand, the mighty battle with the boar.

A dense forest of trees, which had never felt the woodman's axe, rose up from the level plain, affording a wide view over the sloping fields. When the warriors reached this wood, some of them spread out their hunting nets, some unleashed the dogs, while others, looking for danger, followed the trail of the boar's footprints. In the depths of a sunken hollow into which rainwater drained from above, grew pliant willows and thin sedge, marsh grasses and osiers and tall bullrushes, rising from a carpet of short reeds. The boar was driven out from this retreat, and rushed furiously into the midst of its foes, like a lightning flash struck out from the clouds as they are dashed together. Trees were brought down by its charge, and there was a sound of crashing as the animal blundered against their trunks. The young heroes raised a shout, and grasped their weapons in their strong hands, holding them poised for the throw, with broad iron tips thrust forward. The boar rushed on, scattering the dogs as they tried to block its furious onset, tossing the yapping beasts out of the way with side-long blows from its tusks. Echion hurled the first spear: but it missed its mark, and merely scarred the bark of a maple tree. The next missile looked as if it would lodge in the boar's back, but Jason of Pagasae, who threw it, put too much force behind the blow, and his spear overshot the mark. Then Mopsus, son of Ampycus, cried out: 'O Apollo, as I have worshipped you in the past, and do so still, grant that my spear may reach its mark: let there be no mistake!' The god granted his prophet's prayer as far as possible, for Mopsus struck the boar, but failed to wound it. As the weapon flew through the air, Diana had stolen away its iron tip, and only the wooden shaft, robbed of its point, reached its destination. But the boar's fury was roused, and blazed up as fiercely as the fire of a thunderbolt. Sparks flashed from its eyes, and it breathed out flames from its breast. Then, with unswerving attack, the murderous brute charged straight down on the band of young warriors, just as a massive rock, shot from the sling of a catapult, goes hurtling through the air towards enemy walls, or towers packed with soldiers. Eupalamus and Pelagon, who were keeping guard on the right, were flung to the ground, but their friends snatched them up from where they lay. Enaesimus, the son of Hippocoon, was not so lucky: he did not escape the boar's deadly tusks. Trembling with fear, he was preparing to run away, when the sinews behind his knees were slashed, and his muscles gave way beneath him. Nestor of Pylos, too, might well have perished before the time of the Trojan war, had he not used his spear as a vaulting pole, and leaped into the branches of a nearby tree, whence he looked down, from a safe height, on the foe he had escaped. The boar fiercely sharpened its tusks on the bark of an oak: then, confident in its newly whetted weapons, returned to its disastrous attacks, ripping open the thigh of the warrior Hippasus with its curved teeth. But now the twin brothers, Castor and Pollux, not yet raised to be stars in the heavens, rode up together, a striking pair on their horses whiter than snow, and both together sent their sharp javelins quivering through the air. They would have wounded the bristling brute, had it not retreated into the dark woods, where neither horse nor javelin could penetrate. Telamon went after it but, in his eagerness, he was careless of where he was going, tripped over the root of a tree, and fell headlong. While Peleus was helping him to his feet, the girl from Tegea fitted an arrow to her bowstring: then, bending the bow, she sent the shaft speeding through the air. It grazed the top of the boar's back, and stuck just below its ear, staining the bristles with a thin trickle of blood. Meleager was as pleased at the girl's success as she was herself. He was the first, so it is thought, to see the blood and, having seen it, was the first to point it out to his friends. 'You will be

The Fall of Icarus

honoured for your prowess as you deserve,' he told Atalanta.

The men flushed with shame, and urged each other on, shouting words of encouragement, and hurling their weapons without any concerted plan of attack. But just because they were so numerous, the missiles were rendered ineffective and prevented from reaching their mark. Then the Arcadian Ancaeus, armed with his two-headed axe, rushed furiously upon his fate, crying: 'See how far superior to a woman's weapons are those of a man! Make way for me! Even though Leto's daughter herself protect this boar with her own arrows, none the less, in spite of Diana, my hand will destroy it.' With these proud and boastful words, he raised his two-headed axe in both hands, and stood on tip-toe, bending forward, poised to strike. The boar charged down upon this daring foe and, aiming its tusks at the upper part of his loins, gored him in that most vital spot. Ancaeus collapsed: his inner organs slipped and trailed from his body in a mass of blood – the earth was soaked with the crimson stream. Pirithous, Ixion's son, rushed against the brute, brandishing his spears in his strong hand. But

Ovid

Theseus, son of Aegeus, called to him: 'Heart of my heart, dearer than myself to me, stop at a safe distance! We can show our courage from afar: his hot-headed valour did Ancaeus no good!' As he spoke, he hurled his cornel spear with its heavy bronze tip: but though it was well thrown and would have reached its mark, it was stopped by the leafy branch of an oak. Jason, too, threw his javelin; but by bad luck his aim swerved, and the weapon killed an innocent hound, passing through its thighs, and pinning it to the ground. Meleager, son of Oeneus, threw two spears, with very different effect: for the first stuck in the ground, but the other lodged right in the middle of the boar's back. Without loss of time, while the beast was furiously twisting its body round and round, its jaws slavering with a mixture of foam and fresh blood, the hero who had dealt the wound came up close to the animal, and roused his foe to fury, before finally burying his shining spear in its shoulder. His friends cheered with delight, and made a rush to shake the victor by the hand. They gazed with wonder at the huge beast that covered so much ground as it lay and, convinced that it was still unsafe

The Fall of Icarus

to go near, each one of them stained his own weapon in the blood of the boar.

Meleager himself set his foot on its monstrous head: then, turning to Atalanta, 'Take the spoil I have secured, lady of Nonacris,' he said, 'and let me share my glory with you.' Thereupon he gave her as a trophy the bristling hide, and the boar's head, with its magnificent tusks. She was as pleased with the giver of the gift as with the gift itself: but the others were jealous, and a murmur ran through the whole company. Then the two sons of Thestius shook their fists and shouted: 'Come now, put down these spoils, woman, and do not interfere with our claims to honour! Do not let confidence in your beauty mislead you, either, in case your love-sick benefactor should prove unable to help you.' Then they took away the spoils from Atalanta, and deprived Meleager of the right to present them to her. The son of Mars could not endure this; bursting with rage, gnashing his teeth, he cried: 'You robbers, stealing another man's glory! I shall teach you the difference between threats and action!' and he ran his sword through the heart of Plexippus who was standing by, all unsuspecting.

It was an abominable deed. Toxeus hesitated as to what he should do, for he wished to avenge his brother, but at the same time was afraid of sharing his fate: Meleager did not suffer him to hesitate for long, for he plunged his weapon, still reeking with the murder of one brother, into the warm blood of the other.

Althaea had been told of her son's victory, and was already carrying offerings to the temple of the gods, when she saw her brothers being brought home dead. The city was filled with her wailing, as she gave vent to her clamorous grief: she beat her breast, and changed the gold-embroidered robes she wore for black clothing. However, when she heard who had killed her brothers, she forgot her grief, and turned from tears to concentrate on revenge.

There was a log, which the three sister goddesses had placed on the fire, at the time when this Althaea, Thestius' daughter, was lying in bed with her baby newly born. As they spun the threads of destiny, holding them firmly under their thumbs, they said: 'To the log and to the new-born child we assign the same span of years.' As soon as the goddesses had recited their verses and left the house, the mother snatched

The Fall of Icarus

the blazing log from the fire, and flung cold water on it. For long it had been hidden away in the depths of the house, and its preservation had kept the young hero safe too. Now his mother brought it out, called for chips of pine wood and shavings, and when these had been piled up, kindled the flames that were to be her son's undoing. Then four times she tried to throw the log on the flames, and four times she stopped herself. Her affection for her son fought against her feelings for her brothers, and divided loyalty tore her heart in opposite directions. Often her face grew pale with fear at the thought of such a crime, often blazing anger made her eyes sparkle with fire. At times her expression was cruel and threatening, at others it could have been thought to be full of compassion. The heat of her fierce rage dried up her tears, yet still the tears welled up, and like a ship which feels the double pull as wind and tides draw it in different directions, as it sways uncertainly with both, so Thestius' daughter was swayed by her shifting emotions, and her anger alternately died away and flared up again. However, her sisterly affection began to get the better of her feelings as a mother, and in order to satisfy her brothers' ghosts with blood, by a guilty deed she saved herself from guilt. When the deadly flames were burning steadily: 'Let this funeral pyre consume the child I bore!' she cried. Then, taking the fateful log in her murderous hands, the wretched woman stood before the funeral altars and prayed: 'Goddesses three, who preside over punishments, Furies, behold this unnatural sacrifice, by which I am at once avenging and committing crime. Death must atone for death, wickedness be piled on wickedness, slaughter upon slaughter, till this accursed household perish under its accumulation of woe. Shall Oeneus continue to enjoy the company of his victorious son, while Thestius is deprived of his? Better that both should have cause to mourn! Only do you, my brothers, ghosts but recently descended to the shades, recognize my devotion, and welcome this offering provided at such a cost, the child of my womb, born to my sorrow!

'Alas, where do I rush so fast? O my brothers, forgive a mother! My hands cannot carry out their purpose: I confess my son has deserved to die, but I cannot bear that I should be the author of his death. Will he then go unpunished? Will he live, a victorious hero, exulting in this very exploit, ruling the kingdom

The Fall of Icarus

of Calydon, while you lie dead, nothing but chill ghosts and a few ashes? No, that I cannot endure. Let the guilty wretch perish too, and carry with him to the grave his father's hopes, his kingdom, and his ruined country. But where is the affection a mother should feel for her son? Where are the loving ties that ought to bind parents to their children. Where the anguish I endured through ten long months? O my son, how much better had I allowed you to burn in those flames, when you were a baby! You received your life from my hands, but now you will die the death you have deserved! Accept the reward for what you have done: give me back the life I have twice bestowed on you, once when you were born, and again when I snatched the log from the fire. Either that, or send me to join my brothers in the tomb!

'I want to, yet I cannot! What am I to do? At one moment I see before my eyes my brothers' wounds, and a vision of their dreadful murder: the next, my love for my son, the name of mother, break my resolution. Poor wretch that I am! It will be an evil thing, my brothers, if you triumph – yet triumph, none the less, provided that I too may follow you to the shades, you and the son I sacrifice to solace you!' With these words she flung the fatal log, with unsteady hands, into the heart of the flames, turning her face away as she did so. The very wood groaned, or seemed to groan, as it was kindled and set alight by the unwilling fire.

Meleager, though he knew nothing of what was happening, and was not even present, was scorched by that flame, and felt a hidden fire consuming his vitals. He endured his agony with indomitable courage; but still, he grieved that he should meet so inglorious an end, that his death involved no bloodshed, and declared Ancaeus lucky to have suffered the wounds he did. For the last time he called upon his aged father, his brothers and loving sisters, cried out his wife's name, groaning as he did so, and perhaps his mother's too. As the fire blazed up, so did his agony: then both died down again, and were extinguished together. Gradually his breath dispersed into the thin air, as the white ash gradually settled over the glowing embers.

The highlands of Calydon were prostrate with grief. Young men and old were in mourning, the common people and the leaders of the country all lamented. The women who dwelt by Evenus' stream tore their hair and beat their breasts. Meleager's father lay prone upon the ground, his white hair and age-worn face begrimed with dust, complaining bitterly that he had lived too long. As for his mother, knowing full well the dreadful thing she had done, with her own guilty hand she exacted punishment from herself, driving a sword through her own body.

Though the gods had given me a hundred mouths and a hundred tongues, poetic genius and all Helicon for my province, still I could not adequately express the sad laments of Meleager's unhappy sisters. Heedless of what was seemly, they beat their bruised breasts and, while their brother's body remained, fondled and cherished it, kissing the poor corpse, and the bier on which it lay. When his limbs had been reduced to ashes, they gathered these together, and clasped them to their breasts: then they flung themselves on the ground by his grave and, embracing the tombstone, bathed the name inscribed there with their tears. At last Diana was content with the disasters which had befallen the house of Parthaon; she raised the girls into the air, all except Gorge and great Alcmene's daughter-in-law, causing feathers to sprout from their bodies, and stretching wings along their arms. She gave them horny beaks and, when she had so changed them, dispatched them into the sky.

Meanwhile Theseus, having played his part in the joint enterprise, was making his way back to Athena's city where Erechtheus once ruled, when Achelous, swollen with rain, blocked his path, and forced him to delay. 'Come into my house, great Athenian,' said the river god, 'and do not trust yourself to my greedy flood. These waters, as they roar in their slanting channel, are wont to sweep away massive tree trunks, and hurl rocks along. I have seen great stables, cattle and all, swept from their sites upon my banks: and then the oxen could make no use of their sturdy strength, nor could the horses use their speed. Many a young man, too, has been drowned in these turbulent waters, when melting snows from the mountains have swollen my torrent. It is safer to wait quietly, till my river runs within its usual limits and, reduced to a slender stream, is contained in its own channel.' Aegeus' son agreed with the river, and replied: 'I shall take your advice, Achelous, and seek shelter in your home.' He did as he said, and entered the caves built of porous pumice and rough tufa stone. The ground was damp with soft moss, the ceiling roofed with

The Fall of Icarus

alternate bands of conch shells and shells of purple fish.

Now the sun had travelled two thirds of the way across the sky, when Theseus and his companions took their places on the couches. On one side of Theseus was the son of Ixion, on the other the hero Lelex from Troezen, whose hair was already streaked with white at the temples. Others too, were there, whom the Acarnanian river god had deemed worthy of sharing the honour of Theseus' company, for Achelous was highly delighted to have so distinguished a guest. The nymphs, bare-footed, at once set out the tables and loaded them with good things: afterwards, when the banquet had been cleared away, they served wine in jewelled cups. Then Theseus, bravest of heroes, looked out over the waters that stretched before his eyes, and pointing with his finger, said: 'Tell me, what place is that? What is the name of that island? Though it looks like more than one.' 'What you see is not one island,' answered the river. 'There are five there, but the distance prevents your seeing that they are separate. Do not be too astonished at what Diana did to Calydon when she was scorned: for these used to be naiads! But on one occasion, after they had made a sacrifice of ten bullocks, they invited all the other rural deities to their festival, and proceeded with their festival dances, quite forgetting me! I swelled with rage, till my waters were as full as they are when at their fullest. Then, with heart and flood equally ruthless, I tore apart forest from forest, field from field, and in my swirling tide swept down to the sea the nymphs and their dancing floor. Then, at last, too late, did they remember me. My waves and those of the ocean split that piece of land apart and divided it into as many portions as you see islands, dotted over the ocean. They are called the Echinades. But there is one, look, which you see for yourself lies far apart from the others, and it is dear to me. The sailors call it Perimele. I fell in love with that girl, and robbed her of her maidenhood, a thing which outraged her father Hippodamas so much that he hurled his daughter from a cliff into the sea, intending to kill her. But I caught her up, and supported her as she swam. As I did so, I prayed to Neptune: "You to whose lot has fallen the kingdom of the restless sea, next in importance to that of heaven, lend us your aid, great god of the trident, and grant a place, I pray you, to one drowned by her

The Fall of Icarus

father's cruelty: or else let her become herself a place." While I was still speaking land, newly formed, embraced her floating limbs, and a massive island materialized on top of her changed body.'

His story finished, the river god fell silent. The whole company was stirred by the miracle he had related, but Ixion's son laughed at them for believing the tale. Arrogant and contemptuous of the gods as he was, he challenged his host. 'Your story is pure invention, Achelous,' he said. 'You put too much faith in the power of the gods, if you think they can give and take away the shapes of things.' All were dumbfounded, and disapproved of such words, but before anyone else could speak Lelex, ripe in years and wisdom, broke in: 'The power of heaven is measureless, and knows no bounds; whatever the gods wish is at once achieved. Here is a story which will convince you.

'In the hill-country of Phrygia there is an oak, growing close beside a linden tree, and a low wall surrounds them both. I have seen the spot myself, for Pittheus sent me on a mission to that land, where his father Pelops once was king. Not far off is a stagnant pool: once it was habitable country, but now it has become a stretch of water, haunted by marsh birds, divers and coots. Jupiter visited this place, disguised as a mortal, and Mercury, the god who carries the magic wand, laid aside his wings and accompanied his father. The two gods went to a thousand homes, looking for somewhere to rest, and found a thousand homes bolted and barred against them. However, one house took them in: it was, indeed, a humble dwelling roofed with thatch and reeds from the marsh, but a good-hearted old woman, Baucis by name, and her husband Philemon, who was the same age as his wife, had been married in that cottage in their youth, and had grown grey in it together. By confessing their poverty and accepting it contentedly, they had eased the hardship of their lot. It made no difference in that house whether you asked for master or servant – the two of them were the entire household: the same people gave the orders and carried them out. So, when the heaven-dwellers reached this humble home and, stooping down, entered its low doorway, the old man set chairs for them, and invited them to rest their weary limbs; Baucis bustled up anxiously to throw a rough piece of cloth over the chairs, and stirred up the warm ashes

The Fall of Icarus

on the hearth, fanning the remains of yesterday's fire, feeding it with leaves and chips of dried bark, and blowing on it till it burst into flames. Then the old woman took down finely split sticks and dry twigs which were hanging from the roof, broke them into small pieces, and pushed them under her little pot. Her husband had brought in some vegetables from his carefully watered garden, and these she stripped of their outer leaves. Philemon took a two-pronged fork and lifted down a side of smoked bacon that was hanging from the blackened rafters; then he cut off a small piece of their long-cherished meat, and boiled it till it was tender in the bubbling water. Meanwhile the old couple chattered on, to pass the time, and kept their guests from noticing the delay. There was a beech-wood bowl there, hanging from a nail by its curved handle, which was filled with warm water, and the visitors washed in this, to refresh themselves. On a couch with frame and legs of willow-wood lay a mattress, stuffed with soft sedge grass. Baucis and Philemon covered this with the cloths which they used to put out only on solemn holidays – even so, the stuff was old and cheap, a good match for the willow couch. Then the gods took their places for the meal. Old Baucis tucked up her dress and, with shaky hands, set the table down in front of them. One of its three legs was shorter than the others, but she pushed a tile in below, to make it the same height. When she had inserted this, and so levelled the sloping surface, she wiped over the table with some stalks of fresh mint. Then she placed upon the board the mottled berry which honest Minerva loves, wild cherries picked in the autumn and preserved in lees of wine, endives and radishes and a piece of cheese, and eggs lightly roasted in ashes not too hot; all these were set out in clay dishes and, after they had been served, a flagon with a raised pattern, just as much silver as their dinner service, was set on the table, and beech-wood cups, lined inside with yellow wax. After a short while, the hearth provided them with food piping hot and the wine, which was of no great age, was sent round again. Then it was set aside for a little, to make way for dessert, which consisted of nuts, a mixture of figs and wrinkled dates, plums and fragrant apples in shallow baskets, and black grapes, just gathered. A shining honey-comb was set in the midst of these good things and, above all, there was cheerful company, and bustling hospitality, far beyond their means.

'As the dinner went on, the old man and woman saw that the flagon, as often as it was emptied, refilled itself of its own accord, and that the wine was automatically replenished. At the sight of this miracle, Baucis and Philemon were awed and afraid. Timidly stretching out their hands in prayer, they begged the gods' indulgence for a poor meal, without any elaborate preparations. They had a single goose, which acted as guardian of their little croft: in honour of their divine visitors, they were making ready to kill the bird, but with the help of its swift wings it eluded its owners for a long time, and tired them out, for age made them slow. At last it seemed to take refuge with the gods themselves, who declared that it should not be killed. 'We are gods,' they said, 'and this wicked neighbourhood is going to be punished as it richly deserves; but you will be allowed to escape this disaster. All you have to do is to leave your home, and climb up the steep mountainside with us.' The two old people both did as they were told and, leaning on their sticks, struggled up the long slope.

'When they were a bowshot distant from the top, they looked round and saw all the rest of their country drowned in marshy waters, only their own home left standing. As they gazed in astonishment, and wept for the fate of their people, their old cottage, which had been small, even for two, was changed into a temple: marble columns took the place of its wooden supports, the thatch grew yellow, till the roof seemed to be made of gold, the doors appeared magnificently adorned with carvings, and marble paved the earthen floor. Then Saturn's son spoke in majestic tones: "Tell me, my good old man, and you, who are a worthy wife for your good husband, what would you like from me?' Philemon and Baucis consulted together for a little, and then the old man told the gods what they both wished. 'We ask to be your priests, to serve your shrine; and since we have lived in happy companionship all our lives, we pray that death may carry us off together at the same instant, so that I may never see my wife's funeral, and she may never have to bury me.' Their prayer was granted. They looked after the temple as long as they lived.

'Then, one day, bowed down with their weight of years, they were standing before the sacred steps, talking of all that had happened there, when Baucis saw Philemon beginning to put forth leaves, and old Philemon saw Baucis growing leafy too. When the tree-tops were already growing over their two faces, they exchanged their last words while they could, and cried simultaneously: "Good-bye, my dear one!" As they spoke, the bark grew over and concealed their lips. The Bithynian peasant still points out the trees growing there side by side, trees that were once two bodies. This tale was told me by responsible old men, who had nothing to gain by deceiving me. Indeed, I myself have seen the wreaths hanging on the branches, and have hung up fresh ones, saying: "Whom the gods love are gods themselves, and those who have worshipped should be worshipped too."'

That was the end of his story. Both the story-teller and the tale he told excited the whole company, but Theseus most of all. As he was clamouring to hear more of the wonderful deeds of the gods, the river god of Calydon raised himself on his elbow, and addressed the hero in these words: 'There are some, bravest Theseus, whose shape has been changed just once, and has then remained permanently altered. Others again have power to change into several forms. Take, for instance, Proteus, the god who dwells in the sea that encircles the earth. People have seen him at one time in the shape of a young man, at another transformed into a lion; sometimes he used to appear to them as a raging wild boar, or again as a snake, which they shrank from touching; or else horns transformed him into a bull. Often he could be seen as a stone, or a tree, sometimes he presented the appearance of running water, and became a river, sometimes he was the very opposite, when he turned into fire.

'The wife of Autolycus, who was Erysichthon's daughter, had the same power. Her father was a man who scorned the gods, and never made any offering of incense on the altars. He is even reported to have used his sacrilegious axe on the trees of Ceres' grove, violating the ancient woodlands with its blade. Among these trees there stood a huge oak, which had grown sturdy and strong in the course of years, a forest in itself, hung round with wreaths and garlands and votive tablets, tributes for prayers that had been granted. Under this tree the dryads often held their festive dances, often they joined hands in a circle and embraced its trunk, whose circumference measured fifteen cubits. In height, too, it towered above the other trees, as much as they did above the grassy sward. Yet this did not deter Erysichthon from wielding his axe against it. He ordered his servants to cut down the sacred tree and, when he saw them hesitate to carry out his commands, the scoundrel snatched an axe from one of the men, and shouted: 'Should this tree be itself a goddess, and not just a tree the goddess loves, still its leafy top will be brought down to earth!' As he uttered these words, he held his weapon poised, ready to strike the trunk obliquely. The oak tree of Ceres trembled and groaned: at the same time, the leaves and acorns began to turn white, and the long branches lost their colour. Then, when his impious hand had made a gash in its trunk, blood flowed out where the bark was split open, just as it pours from the severed neck of some mighty bull, slain before the altars as an offering. Everyone stood still in horrified amazement: out of all the company, one man dared to try to prevent the sacrilege, to stop the cruel axe. Thessalian Erysichthon glared at him: 'Take that as a reward for your pious thoughts!' he stormed, and swung his axe against the man instead of the tree, lopping off his head. Then he turned again to the oak, and dealt it blow after blow.

'Meanwhile, from the heart of the tree, a voice was heard saying: "I who dwell within this tree am a nymph, whom Ceres dearly loves. I warn you with my dying breath, that punishment for your wickedness is at hand: that thought comforts me in death." But Erysichthon persisted in his criminal action. When the tree had at length been weakened by innumerable blows, ropes were attached to the trunk, and it was brought crashing down, creating havoc in the wood as it fell, by reason of its great weight. All her sister dryads, sorely distressed at the loss which the grove and they themselves had suffered, dressed themselves in black garments, and mournfully approached Ceres, begging that Erysichthon should be punished. That most beautiful goddess consented; nodding her head, she made the fields, laden with heavy harvests, tremble, as she devised a punishment which would have made its victim an object of pity indeed, if he had not forfeited all men's pity by his deeds. She planned to torment him with deadly Hunger.

'Since destiny does not allow Ceres and Hunger to meet, she could not approach this creature herself, but she gave orders to a rustic oread, one of the mountain spirits. "There is a place," she said, "which lies far off, in the icy land of Scythia, a gloomy barren spot where the earth knows nothing of crops or trees. It is the home of sluggish Chill, of Pallor and Ague, and ravening Hunger lives there too. Go, then, bid Hunger bury herself in the wicked stomach of this impious wretch: tell her to fight and overcome my powers of nourishment, and to let no amount of food defeat her. Do not be frightened at the length of the journey; take my chariot and my dragons and drive them through the air." Ceres then handed over her car, and the oread was borne through the skies in the borrowed chariot.

'She alighted in Scythia, and there unyoked her dragons on the summit of a rocky mountain, which the inhabitants call Caucasus. She went to look for Hunger, whom she found in a stony field, tearing up a few scant grasses with her nails and her teeth. The creature's face was colourless, hollow-eyed, her hair uncared for, her lips bleached and cracked. Scabrous sores encrusted her throat, her skin was hard and transparent, revealing her inner organs. The brittle bones stuck out beneath her hollow loins, and instead of a stomach she had only a place for one. Her breast, hanging loose, looked as if it were held in position only by the framework of her spine. Her joints seemed large in contrast to her skinny limbs, the curve of her knees made a real swelling, and her ankle-bones formed protuberances that were out of all proportion. When the oread saw her, she did not venture to go up close, but delivered the goddess's orders from a distance and, in a very short time, though she had only just come, and though she remained a good way off, she seemed herself to feel the pangs of hunger. Turning her team, she drove the dragons back through the air to Haemonia.

'Although she is always opposed to Ceres' activities, Hunger obeyed the goddess's instructions. The wind carried her through the air till she came to the house she had been told to visit. Immediately she entered the bedroom of the scoundrel Erysichthon. Finding him sound asleep (for it was night-time) she flung both her arms around him, insinuated herself into her victim, breathing into his lips, his throat, his heart, and spread famishing hunger through his hollow veins. When she had carried out her orders, she left the fertile world again, and returned to her poverty-stricken home and her accustomed haunts.

'Erysichthon was still slumbering peacefully, soothed by the wings of the gentle god of sleep, but he dreamed that he was feasting, and chewed uselessly at nothing, grinding his teeth together, and cheating himself by swallowing a mere pretence of food. Instead of a banquet he gulped down insubstantial air, all to no purpose. When he awoke, he was furiously hungry: his famished jaws and burning stomach were utterly at the mercy of his craving. Without delay, he gave orders for all the foodstuffs that earth and air and sea provide to be brought to him, complained of hunger when the laden tables were set before him, and in the midst of feasting sought still more feasts. Supplies which would have satisfied whole cities or an entire nation were not enough for him, and the more he ate, the more he desired. As the sea receives rivers from all over the earth and yet has always room for more, and drinks up the waters from distant lands, or as greedy flames never refuse nourishment, but burn up countless faggots, made hungrier by the very abundance of supplies and requiring more, the more they are given: so the jaws of the scoundrel Erysichthon welcomed all the provisions that were offered, and at the same

Ovid

time asked for more. All the food he consumed only excited his desire for food, and by eating he continually produced an aching void.

'Now, thanks to this hunger, to the bottomless pit that was his stomach, his family fortunes had dwindled away: but still his dreadful hunger remained, not diminished in the slightest. His burning appetite was unabated. At length, when he had eaten up all his wealth, he was left with only his daughter, a girl who deserved to have had a better parent. In his penniless state, he sold her too: but she was a girl of spirit, and rebelled against having a master. Stretching out her hands over the nearby waters, she cried: "You who robbed me of my maidenhood, and have your reward, rescue me from slavery!" Neptune was the one who had the reward of which she spoke, and he did not scorn her prayer. Although her owner, coming along behind, had seen the girl only a moment before, the god changed her shape, gave her the face of a man, and dressed her in fisherman's clothes. Her master came up and, looking straight at her, said: "You there, concealing your dangling hooks with tiny bits of bait, you with the rod in your hands, I wish you a calm sea, and gullible fishes that never notice

The Fall of Icarus

the hook till they are caught, if you will tell me where the girl is, who was standing on the shore just now, with her hair all disordered, dressed in cheap clothes. I saw her on the sands: but tell me, where is she? For her footprints go no further."

'The other, realizing that what the god had done for her had been successful, was delighted that she herself should be asked where she was. In reply to her master's question, she said: "Excuse me, whoever you are. I have never taken my eyes off this pool, and have been entirely occupied with my fishing. To remove any doubts you may have, I swear, so may the god of the sea assist me in my livelihood, that no one but myself has been on this shore for a long time, and no woman has set foot here." The man believed her and, turning round, walked away over the sand, cheated of his slave. Then the girl's true shape was restored to her.

'Her father, when he perceived that his daughter could undergo such transformations, often sold her to different masters, and she escaped in the form of a horse, or a bird, or again as an ox or a stag, thus obtaining provisions, dishonestly, for her gluttonous father. However, when in the violence of his malady he had consumed all that was offered and had thus merely aggravated his grievous sickness, the wretch began to bite and gnaw at his own limbs, and fed his body by eating it away.

'But why do I waste time over tales of other people? I myself, my young friend, have the power to alter my body, though the number of shapes I can assume is limited. Sometimes I appear as you see me now, sometimes I change into a snake, or again I become a bull, the leader of the herd, whose strength lies in his horns – horns, I say, for I had two while I could. But now, as you see for yourself, one side of my forehead has lost its weapon' ... and his words gave place to groans.

Then Neptune's son, brave Theseus, asked Achelous why he was groaning, and how his forehead had come by this injury. The river of Calydon, who wore a circlet of reeds on his tangled locks, answered him in these words: 'It is a painful thing you ask of me: who would want to speak of battles in which he had been defeated? However, I shall tell you what happened: for the glory of having fought is greater than the disgrace of having been beaten, and I am much consoled in my defeat by the thought that my opponent was so great a hero.

'Perhaps you have heard tell of Deianira? She was a most lovely girl who, in days gone by, roused jealous hopes in the hearts of many suitors and I, along with the rest, went to the house of the man I hoped would be my father-in-law. "Son of Parthaon," I said, "take me as your daughter's husband." My words were echoed by Hercules, whereupon the other suitors left the field to us two. My rival declared that he would give his bride Jupiter as a father-in-law, and called to mind his own famous Labours, and the fact that he had succeeded in carrying out his stepmother's commands. I countered his claims, saying: "It is disgraceful that a god should yield place to mortal." – for in those days Hercules was not yet a god – "In me you see the king of the waters which flow through your country in their slanting channels. As a son-in-law I shall not be a stranger, sent from foreign shores, but one of your own people, and a part of your kingdom. Only do not hold it against me that Juno, queen of heaven, does not hate me, that I have never been punished by having labours imposed upon me!

Ovid

'"As to your other point, son of Alcmene, Jupiter whom you boastfully declare to be your father, is either not your father at all, or if he is, it was guilt that made him so! When you claim him as father, you convict your mother of adultery. Choose whether you prefer to say that Jove is not really your father, or to admit that you were born as a result of a piece of disgraceful behaviour."

'Hercules had long been glowering at me as I spoke. Instead of controlling his flaring rage, as a hero should, he retorted: "I am better with my hands than with my tongue: provided I can defeat you in the fight, you can have your verbal victory!" and he rushed fiercely upon me. I was ashamed to draw back, after my recent boasting. Flinging off my garments, I raised my arms, held them crooked before my chest in a position of defence, and prepared myself to fight. My opponent sprinkled me with dust that he had gathered in his cupped palms, and in his turn was covered with yellow sand, till he was all golden. Then he clutched at my neck, and again at my rapidly shifting legs, or seemed to clutch, attacking me from every angle. But my weight was my salvation. I was impervious to his assaults, just as a massive rock,

The Fall of Icarus

besieged by the roaring waves, stands fast and is kept safe by its very bulk.

'We drew a little apart, and then rushed to join battle again, each holding his ground, determined not to yield, foot pressed against foot. Leaning forward from the waist, I thrust my fingers against his fingers, my head against his head. I have seen sturdy bulls rush upon one another, in just the same way, when they are fighting to win the sleekest cow in all the meadows for their prize. The herds look on, trembling, not knowing which will be the victor, and gain such mastery. Three times Hercules tried, without avail, to thrust away my breast that was locked against his own; at the fourth attempt he shook off my grip, and loosened my straining arms. Then, striking me a blow that whirled me about (for I am resolved to tell the truth), he flung himself, with all his weight, upon my back, and clung there. Believe me, I am not just trying to enhance your respect for me – it is no exaggeration to say that I really seemed to be crushed down by a mountain on top of me. However, I barely managed to insert my arms, streaming with sweat, beneath his body, and so with difficulty was able to loosen his cruel grip on my breast. Still he pressed me hard, and prevented me, panting and breathless as I was, from recovering my strength. In this way he got control of my neck and then, at last, I was forced to my knees, and bit the dust.

'Proved inferior to him in valour, I had resort to stratagems, and slipped from the hero's grasp by turning myself into a long snake. But when I had coiled my body into sinuous spirals, and was flickering my forked tongue, hissing fiercely, Hercules of Tiryns laughed, and mocked my tricks. "I was defeating snakes in my cradle!" he cried, "and though you may be more terrible than any other, Achelous, yet you are only one solitary serpent, and how small a part of the Lernaean hydra that will be! The hydra throve on its wounds, and none of its hundred heads could be cut off with impunity, without being replaced by two new ones which made its neck stronger than ever. Yet, in spite of its branching snakes, reborn as they were cut down, in spite of the strength it derived from attempts to harm it, still I got the upper hand of the hydra, vanquished the monster, and ripped its body open. Imagine, then, what will happen to you, who have changed yourself into a mere semblance of a snake, employing weapons

The Fall of Icarus

that are not natural to you, and concealing yourself under a borrowed shape!" With these words, he fastened his fingers tightly round the upper part of my throat. I was being throttled, as if my neck were caught in a vice, and struggled to wrest my jaws out of the grip of his thumbs.

'So he overcame me in this guise too; but there remained my third shape, that of a fierce bull. I therefore transformed myself into a bull, and as such renewed the fight. My adversary, attacking from the left, flung his arms round the bulging muscles of my neck. As I charged away, he followed close beside me, dragging at my head, till he forced my horns into the hard ground, and laid me prostrate in the deep dust. Nor was this enough: as he grasped my stiff horn in his cruel hand, he broke and tore it off, mutilating my brow. But the naiads filled it with fruits and fragrant flowers, and sanctified it, and now my horn enriches the Goddess of Plenty.' When he had finished speaking, one of his attendants, a nymph dressed in the style of Diana, came forward, her hair streaming over her shoulders, and brought all autumn's harvest in the rich horn, with delicious apples for their dessert.

Ovid

Dawn came, and when the first rays of the sun struck the mountaintops, the young men went on their way; for they did not wait till the river was flowing peacefully and smoothly, nor even till all the floods had subsided. Achelous hid his rustic features and the head that had lost its horn in the depths of his waters.

1. BOCCACCIO · *Mrs Rosie and the Priest*
2. GERARD MANLEY HOPKINS · *As kingfishers catch fire*
3. *The Saga of Gunnlaug Serpent-tongue*
4. THOMAS DE QUINCEY · *On Murder Considered as One of the Fine Arts*
5. FRIEDRICH NIETZSCHE · *Aphorisms on Love and Hate*
6. JOHN RUSKIN · *Traffic*
7. PU SONGLING · *Wailing Ghosts*
8. JONATHAN SWIFT · *A Modest Proposal*
9. *Three Tang Dynasty Poets*
10. WALT WHITMAN · *On the Beach at Night Alone*
11. KENKŌ · *A Cup of Sake Beneath the Cherry Trees*
12. BALTASAR GRACIÁN · *How to Use Your Enemies*
13. JOHN KEATS · *The Eve of St Agnes*
14. THOMAS HARDY · *Woman much missed*
15. GUY DE MAUPASSANT · *Femme Fatale*
16. MARCO POLO · *Travels in the Land of Serpents and Pearls*
17. SUETONIUS · *Caligula*
18. APOLLONIUS OF RHODES · *Jason and Medea*
19. ROBERT LOUIS STEVENSON · *Olalla*
20. KARL MARX AND FRIEDRICH ENGELS · *The Communist Manifesto*
21. PETRONIUS · *Trimalchio's Feast*
22. JOHANN PETER HEBEL · *How a Ghastly Story Was Brought to Light by a Common or Garden Butcher's Dog*
23. HANS CHRISTIAN ANDERSEN · *The Tinder Box*
24. RUDYARD KIPLING · *The Gate of the Hundred Sorrows*
25. DANTE · *Circles of Hell*
26. HENRY MAYHEW · *Of Street Piemen*
27. HAFEZ · *The nightingales are drunk*
28. GEOFFREY CHAUCER · *The Wife of Bath*
29. MICHEL DE MONTAIGNE · *How We Weep and Laugh at the Same Thing*
30. THOMAS NASHE · *The Terrors of the Night*
31. EDGAR ALLAN POE · *The Tell-Tale Heart*
32. MARY KINGSLEY · *A Hippo Banquet*
33. JANE AUSTEN · *The Beautifull Cassandra*
34. ANTON CHEKHOV · *Gooseberries*
35. SAMUEL TAYLOR COLERIDGE · *Well, they are gone, and here must I remain*
36. JOHANN WOLFGANG VON GOETHE · *Sketchy, Doubtful, Incomplete Jottings*
37. CHARLES DICKENS · *The Great Winglebury Duel*
38. HERMAN MELVILLE · *The Maldive Shark*
39. ELIZABETH GASKELL · *The Old Nurse's Story*
40. NIKOLAY LESKOV · *The Steel Flea*

41. HONORÉ DE BALZAC · *The Atheist's Mass*
42. CHARLOTTE PERKINS GILMAN · *The Yellow Wall-Paper*
43. C.P. CAVAFY · *Remember, Body . . .*
44. FYODOR DOSTOEVSKY · *The Meek One*
45. GUSTAVE FLAUBERT · *A Simple Heart*
46. NIKOLAI GOGOL · *The Nose*
47. SAMUEL PEPYS · *The Great Fire of London*
48. EDITH WHARTON · *The Reckoning*
49. HENRY JAMES · *The Figure in the Carpet*
50. WILFRED OWEN · *Anthem For Doomed Youth*
51. WOLFGANG AMADEUS MOZART · *My Dearest Father*
52. PLATO · *Socrates' Defence*
53. CHRISTINA ROSSETTI · *Goblin Market*
54. *Sindbad the Sailor*
55. SOPHOCLES · *Antigone*
56. RYŪNOSUKE AKUTAGAWA · *The Life of a Stupid Man*
57. LEO TOLSTOY · *How Much Land Does A Man Need?*
58. GIORGIO VASARI · *Leonardo da Vinci*
59. OSCAR WILDE · *Lord Arthur Savile's Crime*
60. SHEN FU · *The Old Man of the Moon*
61. AESOP · *The Dolphins, the Whales and the Gudgeon*
62. MATSUO BASHŌ · *Lips too Chilled*
63. EMILY BRONTË · *The Night is Darkening Round Me*
64. JOSEPH CONRAD · *To-morrow*
65. RICHARD HAKLUYT · *The Voyage of Sir Francis Drake Around the Whole Globe*
66. KATE CHOPIN · *A Pair of Silk Stockings*
67. CHARLES DARWIN · *It was snowing butterflies*
68. BROTHERS GRIMM · *The Robber Bridegroom*
69. CATULLUS · *I Hate and I Love*
70. HOMER · *Circe and the Cyclops*
71. D. H. LAWRENCE · *Il Duro*
72. KATHERINE MANSFIELD · *Miss Brill*
73. OVID · *The Fall of Icarus*
74. SAPPHO · *Come Close*
75. IVAN TURGENEV · *Kasyan from the Beautiful Lands*
76. VIRGIL · *O Cruel Alexis*
77. H. G. WELLS · *A Slip under the Microscope*
78. HERODOTUS · *The Madness of Cambyses*
79. *Speaking of Siva*
80. *The Dhammapada*

'Yes, we did many things, then – all Beautiful . . .'

SAPPHO
Born *c.* 630 BCE, Mytilene, Lesbos
Died *c.* 570 BCE, Mytilene, Lesbos

Taken from Aaron Poochigian's translation of
Stung with Love: Poems and Fragments, first published in 2009.

SAPPHO IN PENGUIN CLASSICS
Stung with Love: Poems and Fragments

SAPPHO

Come Close

Translated by
Aaron Poochigian

PENGUIN BOOKS

PENGUIN CLASSICS

UK | USA | Canada | Ireland | Australia
India | New Zealand | South Africa

Penguin Books is part of the Penguin Random House group of companies
whose addresses can be found at global.penguinrandomhouse.com.

This selection published in Penguin Classics 2015

012

Translation copyright © Aaron Poochigian, 2009

The moral right of the translator has been asserted

Set in 9.5/13 pt Baskerville 10 Pro
Typeset by Jouve (UK), Milton Keynes

Printed and bound in Great Britain by Clays Ltd, Elcograf S.p.A.

A CIP catalogue record for this book is available from the British Library

ISBN: 978-0-141-39869-3

www.greenpenguin.co.uk

Penguin Random House is committed to a sustainable future for our business, our readers and our planet. This book is made from Forest Stewardship Council® certified paper.

Contents

Goddesses	1
Desire and Death-Longing	11
Her Girls and Family	19
Troy	35
Maidens and Marriages	41
The Wisdom of Sappho	51

GODDESSES

Sappho

Leave Crete and sweep to this blest temple
Where apple-orchard's elegance
Is yours, and smouldering altars, ample
Frankincense.

Here under boughs a bracing spring
Percolates, roses without number
Umber the earth and, rustling,
The leaves drip slumber.

Here budding flowers possess a sunny
Pasture where steeds could graze their fill,
And the breeze feels as gentle as honey . . .

Kypris, here in the present blend
Your nectar with pure festal glee.
Fill gilded bowls and pass them round
Lavishly.

Come Close

Sweet mother, I can't take shuttle in hand.
There is a boy, and lust
Has crushed my spirit – just
As gentle Aphrodite planned.

Since I have cast my lot, please, golden-crowned
Aphrodite, let me win this round!

Sappho

Subtly bedizened Aphrodite,
Deathless daughter of Zeus, Wile-weaver,
I beg you, Empress, do not smite me
With anguish and fever

But come as often, on request,
(Hearing me, heeding from afar,)
You left your father's gleaming feast,
Yoked team to car,

And came. Fair sparrows in compact
Flurries of winged rapidity
Cleft sky and over a gloomy tract
Brought you to me –

And there they were, and you, sublime
And smiling with immortal mirth,
Asked what was wrong? why I, this time,
Called you to earth?

What was my mad heart dreaming of? –
'Who, Sappho, at a word, must grow
Again receptive to your love?
Who wronged you so?

'She who shuns love soon will pursue it,
She who scorns gifts will send them still:
That girl will learn love, though she do it
Against her will.'

Come to me now. Drive off this brutal
Distress. Accomplish what my pride
Demands. Come, please, and in this battle
Stand at my side.

Sappho

'Kytherea, precious
Adonis is nearly dead.
How should we proceed?'

'Come, girls, beat your fists
Down upon your breasts
And shred your dresses.'

A full moon shone,
And around the shrine
Stood devotees
Poised and in place.

Come Close

>   Untainted Graces
>   With wrists like roses,
>   Please come close,
>   You daughters of Zeus.

Now, Dika, weave the aniseed together, flower and stem,
With your soft hands, crown yourself with a lovely diadem
Because the blessèd Graces grant gifts to the garlanded
And snub the worshipper with no flowers on her head.

Sappho

Come close, you precious
Graces and Muses
With beautiful tresses.

Here is the reason: it is wrong
To play a funeral song
In the Musicians' House –
It simply would not be decorous.

Come Close

God-crafted product of the tortoise shell,
Come to me; Lyre, be voluble.

He is unrivalled, like a Lesbian
Musician matched with other men.

Sappho

But when you lie dead
No one will notice later or feel sad
Because you gathered no sprays from the roses
Of the Pierian Muses.

Once lost in Hades' hall
You will be homeless and invisible –
Another shadow flittering back and forth
With shadows of no worth.

DESIRE AND DEATH-LONGING

Sappho

That impossible predator,
Eros the Limb-Loosener,
Bitter-sweetly and afresh
Savages my flesh.

Like a gale smiting an oak
On mountainous terrain,
Eros, with a stroke,
Shattered my brain.

But a strange longing to pass on
Seizes me, and I need to see
Lotuses on the dewy banks of Acheron.

Come Close

That fellow strikes me as god's double,
Couched with you face to face, delighting
In your warm manner, your amiable
Talk and inviting

Laughter – the revelation flutters
My ventricles, my sternum and stomach.
The least glimpse, and my lost voice stutters,
Refuses to come back

Because my tongue is shattered. Gauzy
Flame runs radiating under
My skin; all that I see is hazy,
My ears all thunder.

Sweat comes quickly, and a shiver
Vibrates my frame. I am more sallow
Than grass and suffer such a fever
As death should follow.

But I must suffer further, worthless
As I am . . .

Sappho

'In all honesty, I want to die.'

Leaving for good after a good long cry,
She said: 'We both have suffered terribly,
But, Sappho, it is hard to say goodbye.'

I said: 'Go with my blessing if you go
Always remembering what we did. To me
You have meant everything, as you well know.

'Yet, lest it slip your mind, I shall review
Everything we have shared – the good times, too:

'You culled violets and roses, bloom and stem,
Often in spring and I looked on as you
Wove a bouquet into a diadem.

'Time and again we plucked lush flowers, wed
Spray after spray in strands and fastened them
Around your soft neck; you perfumed your head

'Of glossy curls with myrrh – lavish infusions
In queenly quantities – then on a bed
Prepared with fleecy sheets and yielding cushions,

'Sated your craving . . .'

Come Close

May gales and anguish sweep elsewhere
The killer of my character.

But I am hardly some backbiter bent
On vengeance; no, my heart is lenient.

Sappho

You were at hand,
And I broke down raving –
My craving a fire
That singed my mind,
A brand you quenched.

Cold grew
The spirits of the ladies;
They drew
Their wings close to their bodies.

Come Close

Moon and the Pleiades go down.
Midnight and tryst pass by.
I, though, lie
Alone.

Peace, you never seemed so tedious
As now – no, never quite like this.

Over eyelids dark night fell
Invisible.

HER GIRLS AND FAMILY

Sappho

But I love extravagance,
And wanting it has handed down
The glitter and glamour of the sun
As my inheritance.

I truly do believe no maiden that will live
To look upon the brilliance of the sun
Ever will be contemplative
Like this one.

Come Close

Stand and face me, dear; release
That fineness in your irises.

May you bed down,
Head to breast, upon
The flesh
Of a plush
Companion.

Sappho

As for you girls, the gorgeous ones,
There will be no change in my plans.

What farm girl, garbed in fashions from the farm
And witless of the way
A hiked hem would display
Her ankles, captivates you with her charm?

Come Close

      . . . off in Sardis
And often turns her thoughts back to our shores.

The girl adored you more than anything,
As if you were a goddess –
But most of all she loved to hear you sing.

Now she outshines those dames with Lydian faces
Just as, when the sun
Has set, the rosy-fingered Moon surpasses

The stars surrounding her. With equal grace
She casts her lustre on
The flower-rich fallows and the sterile seas.

Dew is poured out in handsome fashion; lissome
Chervil unfurls; Rose
And Sweet Clover with heady flowers blossom.

Often on long walks she commemorates
How tender Atthis was.
Her fortune eats at her inconstant thoughts . . .

Sappho

You will have memories
Because of what we did back then
When we were new at this,

Yes, we did many things, then – all
Beautiful . . .

Come Close

I loved you once, years ago, Atthis,
When your flower was in place.
You seemed a gawky girl then, artless,
Without grace.

Atthis, you looked at what I was
And hated what you saw
And now, all in a flutter, chase
After Andromeda.

Sappho

> . . . because
> The people I most strive to please
> Do me the worst injuries . . .

By giving me creations of their own
My girls have handed me renown.

And this next charming ditty I –
In honour of my girls –
Shall sing out prettily.

Come Close

Abanthis, please pick up your lyre,
Praise Gongyla. Your need to sing
Flutters about you in the air –
You gorgeous thing.

Her garment (when you stole a glance)
Roused you, and I'm in ecstasy.
Likewise, the goddess Kypris once
Disciplined me

Blaming the way I prayed . . .

Sappho

As you are dear to me, go claim a younger
Bed as your due.
I can't stand being the old one any longer,
Living with you.

Girls, chase the violet-bosomed Muses' bright
Gifts and the plangent lyre, lover of hymns:

Stiffness has seized on these once supple limbs,
And black braids with the passing years turned white.

Age weighs heavily on me, and the knees
Buckle that long ago, like fawns, pranced nimbly.

I groan much but to what end? Humans simply
Cannot be ageless like divinities.

They say that rosy-forearmed Dawn, when stung
With love, swept a sweet youth to the earth's rim –

Tithonous. Even there age withered him,
Bound still to a wife forever young.

Sappho

Kypris, may Doricha discover
You are the bitterest thing of all
And not keep boasting that a lover
Twice came to call.

Nereids, Kypris, please restore
My brother to this port, unkilled.
May all his heart most wishes for
Now be fulfilled.

Excuse the misdeeds in his past,
Make him his friends' boon and foes' bane,
And may we never find the least
Cause to complain.

May he choose to give his sister
Her share of honour but my gloomy
Misgivings . . .

Come Close

I have a daughter who reminds me of
A marigold in bloom.
Kleïs is her name,
And I adore her.
I would refuse all Lydia's glitter for her
And all other love.

I do not have an
Ornately woven
Bandeau to hand you,
Kleïs. From
Where would it come?

Sappho

. . . You see, my mother,

Back when she was young,
Thought it was fancy for a girl to wear
A purple fillet, a headband –

Yes, this was quite the thing.
Now, though, we have seen a girl with hair
More orange than a firebrand

Sport all the flowers of spring
Woven together, garlands upon garlands –
And only lately, fresh from Sardis,

A spangled headband . . .

Mnasis sent you from Phocaia
Purple kerchiefs you can tie
Around your brow to serve
As headscarves, too –
Rich gifts which you,
With your fine cheeks, deserve.

A handkerchief
Dripping with . . .

TROY

Sappho

Idaos, then, the panting emissary,
Reported:
       'Out of Asia deathless glory:
From holy Thebe and the stream-fed port
Of Plakia, Hector and his men escort
The bright-eyed, delicate Andromache
On shipboard over the infertile sea –
With sweet red garments, bracelets made of gold,
Beautiful baubles, ivory and untold
Chalices chased in silver.' So he spoke.

Dear Priam rose at once, and the news broke,
Spreading to friends throughout the city's wide
Expanse. And soon the sons of Ilos tied
Pack mules to smooth-wheeled carts, and whole
    parades
Clambered aboard the transports – wives and maids
With slim-tapering ankles. Some way off,
The daughters of King Priam stood aloof,
And youthful stewards harnessed teams of horses
To chariots . . .

Come Close

. . . And sweetly then the double-oboe's cadence
Mingled with rhythmic rattles as the maidens
Sang sacred songs. A fine sound strode the air.
Cups on the roadside, vessels everywhere,
Cassia and frankincense were mixed with myrrh.
Old women (venerable as they were)
Warbled and trilled. The men all in a choir
Summoned first that lover of the lyre,
The long-range archer, Paeon, then extolled
Andromache and Hector, godlike to behold.

Sappho

Some call ships, infantry or horsemen
The greatest beauty earth can offer;
I say it is whatever a person
Most lusts after.

Showing you all will be no trouble:
Helen surpassed all humankind
In looks but left the world's most noble
Husband behind,

Coasting off to Troy where she
Thought nothing of her loving parents
And only child but, led astray . . .

. . . and I think of Anaktoria
Far away, . . .

And I would rather watch her body
Sway, her glistening face flash dalliance
Than Lydian war cars at the ready
And armed battalions.

Come Close

Yes, you have all heard
That Leda, long ago, one day
Noticed an egg, hyacinth-coloured,
Hidden away.

Reveal your graceful figure here,
Close to me, Hera. I make entreaty
Just as the kings once made their prayer,
The famous Atreidai –

Winning victories by the score
At Troy first, then at sea, they sailed
The channel to this very shore,
Tried leaving but failed

Until they prayed to you, the Saviour
Zeus and Thyone's charming son.
Like long ago, then, grant this favour,
As you have done . . .

MAIDENS AND MARRIAGES

Sappho

Once as a too, too lissome
Maiden was plucking a blossom . . .

Artemis made the pledge no god can break:
'Upon my head and all that I hold dear,
I shall remain a maid, a mountaineer
Hunting on summits – grant this for my sake.'

The Father of the Blessèd gave the nod – yes;
And all the gods pronounced her Frontier Goddess
And Slayer of Stags, and Eros never crosses
Her path . . .

(I)

A ripe red apple grows, the highest of them all,
Over the treetop, way up on a tapering spray,
But apple-gatherers never see it – no,
Rather, they *do* see it is far away,
Beyond their reach, impossible.
This matter stands just so.

(II)

A hillside hyacinth shepherds treaded flat,
A red bloom in the dust – it is like that.

'Maidenhead, maidenhead, where have you gone?'

'I shall never, ever join you again.'

Sappho

Hesperus, you are
The most fetching star.
What Dawn flings afield
You bring back together –
Sheep to the fold, goats to the pen,
And the child to his mother again.

Nightingale,
All you sing
Is desire;
You are the crier
Of coming spring.

Come Close

Because once on a time you were
Young, sing of what is taking place,
Talk to us for a spell, confer
Your special grace.

For we march to a wedding – yes,
You know it well. So pack the maids off
Quickly, and may the gods possess . . .

Sappho

Groomsmen, kings with bastions
In strong positions,
Keep this bride
Well fortified.

It would take seven fathoms to span
The feet of the doorkeeper (the best man);
His sandals are five cows' worth of leather
And ten shoemakers stitched them together.

'What do you resemble, dear husband-to-be?'

'You resemble a supple seedling, a green tree.'

> Carpenters, raise the rafter-beam
> (For Hymen's wedding hymn)
> A little higher to make room
> (For Hymen's wedding hymn)
> Because here comes the groom –
> An Ares more imposing than
> A giant, a terribly big man.

Sappho

Blest bridegroom, this day of matrimony,
Just as you wished it, has come true:
The bride is whom you wished for . . .
                                        'You
Move gracefully; your eyes are honey;
Charm was showered on your radiant face –
Yes, Aphrodite granted you outstanding praise.'

Come Close

The ambrosial mixture
Ready in the mixing bowl,
Hermes went round with a pitcher
And served the gods. When all
Had tipped their goblets and poured offerings,
They prayed that the groom suffer only the good
    things.

Because there is no other girl than she,
Bridegroom – a child still, of such quality.

Star clusters near the fair moon dim
Their shapely shimmering whenever
She rises, lucent to the brim
And flowing over.

Sappho

And may the maidens all night long
Celebrate your shared love in song
And the bride's bosom,
A violet-blossom.

Get up, now! Rouse that gang of fellows –
Your boys – and we shall sleep as well as
The bird that intones
Piercing moans.

THE WISDOM OF SAPPHO

The gorgeous man presents a gorgeous view;
The good man will in time be gorgeous, too.

>Wealth without real worthiness
Is no good for the neighbourhood;
But their proper mixture is
The summit of beatitude.

Neither the honey nor the bee
For me . . .

'I want to tell you something but good taste
Restrains me.'
               'If you wanted to express
Some noble or gorgeous thought – that is, unless
Your tongue were keen to utter in hot haste
Some shameful slur, "good taste" would not have
    dressed
Your face in red, no, you would have professed
Whatever you would say upfront and straightaway.'

Sappho

Either I have slipped out of your head
Or you adore some fellow more, instead.

I don't know what the right course is;
Twofold are my purposes.

Come Close

I declare
That later on,
Even in an age unlike our own,
Someone will remember who we are.

1. BOCCACCIO · *Mrs Rosie and the Priest*
2. GERARD MANLEY HOPKINS · *As kingfishers catch fire*
3. *The Saga of Gunnlaug Serpent-tongue*
4. THOMAS DE QUINCEY · *On Murder Considered as One of the Fine Arts*
5. FRIEDRICH NIETZSCHE · *Aphorisms on Love and Hate*
6. JOHN RUSKIN · *Traffic*
7. PU SONGLING · *Wailing Ghosts*
8. JONATHAN SWIFT · *A Modest Proposal*
9. *Three Tang Dynasty Poets*
10. WALT WHITMAN · *On the Beach at Night Alone*
11. KENKŌ · *A Cup of Sake Beneath the Cherry Trees*
12. BALTASAR GRACIÁN · *How to Use Your Enemies*
13. JOHN KEATS · *The Eve of St Agnes*
14. THOMAS HARDY · *Woman much missed*
15. GUY DE MAUPASSANT · *Femme Fatale*
16. MARCO POLO · *Travels in the Land of Serpents and Pearls*
17. SUETONIUS · *Caligula*
18. APOLLONIUS OF RHODES · *Jason and Medea*
19. ROBERT LOUIS STEVENSON · *Olalla*
20. KARL MARX AND FRIEDRICH ENGELS · *The Communist Manifesto*
21. PETRONIUS · *Trimalchio's Feast*
22. JOHANN PETER HEBEL · *How a Ghastly Story Was Brought to Light by a Common or Garden Butcher's Dog*
23. HANS CHRISTIAN ANDERSEN · *The Tinder Box*
24. RUDYARD KIPLING · *The Gate of the Hundred Sorrows*
25. DANTE · *Circles of Hell*
26. HENRY MAYHEW · *Of Street Piemen*
27. HAFEZ · *The nightingales are drunk*
28. GEOFFREY CHAUCER · *The Wife of Bath*
29. MICHEL DE MONTAIGNE · *How We Weep and Laugh at the Same Thing*
30. THOMAS NASHE · *The Terrors of the Night*
31. EDGAR ALLAN POE · *The Tell-Tale Heart*
32. MARY KINGSLEY · *A Hippo Banquet*
33. JANE AUSTEN · *The Beautifull Cassandra*
34. ANTON CHEKHOV · *Gooseberries*
35. SAMUEL TAYLOR COLERIDGE · *Well, they are gone, and here must I remain*
36. JOHANN WOLFGANG VON GOETHE · *Sketchy, Doubtful, Incomplete Jottings*
37. CHARLES DICKENS · *The Great Winglebury Duel*
38. HERMAN MELVILLE · *The Maldive Shark*
39. ELIZABETH GASKELL · *The Old Nurse's Story*
40. NIKOLAY LESKOV · *The Steel Flea*

41. HONORÉ DE BALZAC · *The Atheist's Mass*
42. CHARLOTTE PERKINS GILMAN · *The Yellow Wall-Paper*
43. C.P. CAVAFY · *Remember, Body . . .*
44. FYODOR DOSTOEVSKY · *The Meek One*
45. GUSTAVE FLAUBERT · *A Simple Heart*
46. NIKOLAI GOGOL · *The Nose*
47. SAMUEL PEPYS · *The Great Fire of London*
48. EDITH WHARTON · *The Reckoning*
49. HENRY JAMES · *The Figure in the Carpet*
50. WILFRED OWEN · *Anthem For Doomed Youth*
51. WOLFGANG AMADEUS MOZART · *My Dearest Father*
52. PLATO · *Socrates' Defence*
53. CHRISTINA ROSSETTI · *Goblin Market*
54. *Sindbad the Sailor*
55. SOPHOCLES · *Antigone*
56. RYŪNOSUKE AKUTAGAWA · *The Life of a Stupid Man*
57. LEO TOLSTOY · *How Much Land Does A Man Need?*
58. GIORGIO VASARI · *Leonardo da Vinci*
59. OSCAR WILDE · *Lord Arthur Savile's Crime*
60. SHEN FU · *The Old Man of the Moon*
61. AESOP · *The Dolphins, the Whales and the Gudgeon*
62. MATSUO BASHŌ · *Lips too Chilled*
63. EMILY BRONTË · *The Night is Darkening Round Me*
64. JOSEPH CONRAD · *To-morrow*
65. RICHARD HAKLUYT · *The Voyage of Sir Francis Drake Around the Whole Globe*
66. KATE CHOPIN · *A Pair of Silk Stockings*
67. CHARLES DARWIN · *It was snowing butterflies*
68. BROTHERS GRIMM · *The Robber Bridegroom*
69. CATULLUS · *I Hate and I Love*
70. HOMER · *Circe and the Cyclops*
71. D. H. LAWRENCE · *Il Duro*
72. KATHERINE MANSFIELD · *Miss Brill*
73. OVID · *The Fall of Icarus*
74. SAPPHO · *Come Close*
75. IVAN TURGENEV · *Kasyan from the Beautiful Lands*
76. VIRGIL · *O Cruel Alexis*
77. H. G. WELLS · *A Slip under the Microscope*
78. HERODOTUS · *The Madness of Cambyses*
79. *Speaking of Siva*
80. *The Dhammapada*

'No, no, I've got your word for it, I've got to die . . . you promised me . . . you told me . . .'

IVAN TURGENEV
Born 1818, Oryol, Russia
Died 1883, Bougival, France

Kasyan from the Beautiful Lands is taken from
Richard Freeborn's first translation of *Sketches from a
Hunter's Album*, first published in 1967.

District Doctor is taken from Richard Freeborn's
second translation of *Sketches from a Hunter's Album*, 1990.

IVAN TURGENEV IN PENGUIN CLASSICS
Fathers and Sons
First Love
Home of the Gentry
On the Eve
Rudin
Sketches from a Hunter's Album
Spring Torrents
Three Sketches from a Hunter's Album

IVAN TURGENEV

Kasyan from the Beautiful Lands

Translated by
Richard Freeborn

PENGUIN BOOKS

PENGUIN CLASSICS

UK | USA | Canada | Ireland | Australia
India | New Zealand | South Africa

Penguin Books is part of the Penguin Random House group of companies whose addresses can be found at global.penguinrandomhouse.com.

This selection published in Penguin Classics 2015
008

Translation copyright © Richard Freeborn, 1967, 1990

The moral right of the translator has been asserted

Set in 10/14.5 pt Baskerville 10 Pro
Typeset by Jouve (UK), Milton Keynes
Printed and bound in Great Britain by Clays Ltd, Elcograf S.p.A.

A CIP catalogue record for this book is available from the British Library

ISBN: 978-0-141-39871-6

www.greenpenguin.co.uk

MIX
Paper from
responsible sources
FSC® C018179

Penguin Random House is committed to a sustainable future for our business, our readers and our planet. This book is made from Forest Stewardship Council® certified paper.

Contents

District Doctor   1

Kasyan from the Beautiful
    Lands   19

District Doctor

One time in the autumn, on coming back from a long trip, I caught a cold and had to go to bed. Luckily the fever struck me in a provincial town, in a hotel, and I sent for a doctor. In half an hour the district doctor appeared, a man of small stature, thinnish and black-haired. He wrote out the usual prescription for something to make me sweat, ordered the application of a mustard plaster and very skilfully slipped his five-rouble payment into his coat cuff, all the while drily coughing and glancing to one side, and was just on the point of leaving when a conversation was struck up and he remained. The fever tormented me. I foresaw a sleepless night and was glad to chatter with the good fellow. Tea was served. My good doctor started talking. He was no fool and expressed himself vivaciously and rather entertainingly. Strange things happen on this earth: you can live a long while with someone and be on the friendliest of terms, and yet you'll never once talk openly with him, from the depths of your soul; while with someone else you may scarcely have met, at one glance, whether you to him or he to you, just as in a confessional, you'll blurt out the story of your life. I don't know what made me deserve the confidence of my new friend, save that, on the spur of the moment, he 'took to me', as they say, and recounted to me a fairly remarkable episode, and it is his story I now wish to relate to the well-disposed reader. I will try to express myself in the doctor's own words.

'You don't happen to know, do you,' he began in a weak and quavering voice (the result of unadulterated birch snuff), 'you don't happen to know the local judge, Mylov, Pavel Lukich? . . . You don't? . . . Well, it doesn't matter.' (He coughed and wiped his eyes.) 'So you see it was like this, as you might say, so as not to tell a lie – during Lent, just when everything was thawing. I was sitting with him, at our judge's house, and I was playing whist. Our judge was a good chap and very fond of playing whist. Suddenly' (my doctor friend frequently used the word 'suddenly') 'they tell me someone's asking for me. I ask what he wants.

District Doctor

He's brought a note – it must be from a patient. Let me see it, I say. Yes, it's from a patient . . . Well, that's all right, it's our bread and butter, you know . . . It's like this: the note's from a lady, a landowner and widow, who says her daughter's dying, come for God's sake, horses've been sent to fetch you. Well, that's not so bad so far, except that she's twenty miles away and it's dark outside and the roads are bloody awful! What's more, she herself's poorly off, there's no more'n couple of silver coins in it for me, and that's doubtful, probably I'll have to make do with a bit of cloth and a few crumbs of this and that. But duty comes first, you know, when someone's dying. Suddenly I transfer my cards to an inveterate member of our group, Kalliopin, and set off home. I see a little cart standing by my porch harnessed with peasant horses – big-bellied, huge-bellied, and woolly coats on 'em thick as felt – and a coachman's sitting there without his hat, as a mark of respect. Well, I think, it's clear as daylight, my good fellow, that your lords and masters don't eat off gold plate . . . You may laugh at that, but I'll tell you one thing, those of us who're poor, we notice these things . . . If a coachman sits there like a prince, for instance, and doesn't take his cap off and even grins to himself under his beard and twirls his whip, you can bet you'll get a couple of real big banknotes! But I see there's not a whiff of that in this case. However, I tell myself, you can't do a thing about it – duty comes first. I grab hold of the most obvious medicines and set off. Believe it or not, I scarcely manage to get there. The road's absolutely hellish – streams, snow, mud, gullies, and then suddenly it turns out a dam's burst – one disaster after another! Still, I get there. The house is small, with a straw roof. There's light in the windows, meaning that they're waiting. I go in. I'm met by an old woman, very dignified, in a bonnet. "Please help," she says, "she's dying." I tell her: "Don't worry. Where's the patient?" "This way please." I find myself in a small, clean room, with a lamp burning in the corner and a girl of about twenty lying on the bed unconscious. She's literally blazing hot and breathing heavily in a fever. There are two other girls there, her sisters, frightened and tearful. "Yesterday evening," they tell me, "she was in perfect health and had a hearty appetite. This morning she complained of having a headache, but towards evening she suddenly became like this . . ." I tell them again: "Don't worry" – a doctor's obligation, you know – and I set to work. I bled her, ordered mustard plasters to be applied and wrote out a prescription. Meantime I'm looking at her, can't take my eyes off her, you know – well, my God, I've never seen such a face before – in a word, she's beautiful! Pity for her literally tears me apart. Such delightful features, such eyes . . . Then, thank God, she got a bit better, started sweating and realized where she was, looked around her, smiled, ran her hand across her face . . . Her sisters bent over her and asked her how she was. "All right," she says and turns over. I see she's gone to sleep. Well, I say, we must let her rest now. So we all go out of the room on tiptoe. Only a maid remains behind to watch over her. In the sitting-room the samovar's ready, along with a bottle of Jamaican – in my business, you know, you can't get by without a tot of rum. They offer me some tea and beg me to stay overnight. I say yes – after all, where could I go at that time of night? The old woman goes on groaning and sighing. "What for?" I ask. "She'll live, don't you worry. It'd be better if you got some rest yourself. It's two o'clock in the morning." "You'll be sure and rouse me if anything happens?" "I'll do that, I'll do that." The old lady went off to her room and the sisters went off to theirs. A bed was set up for me in the sitting-room. So I lay down, but I couldn't sleep. Hardly surprising, though you'd have thought I'd be worn out. I simply couldn't get the sick girl off my mind. Finally I couldn't stand it any more and suddenly got up, thinking I'd go and see what was happening to my patient. Her bedroom was just off the sitting-room. Well, I rose and opened her door softly, my heart beating like mad. I see the maid's asleep, her mouth wide open and snoring, the wretch! But the sick girl's lying with her face towards me and moving her arms about, poor thing. I'd no sooner approached than she suddenly opens her eyes and stares at me. "Who is it? Who's there?" I got confused. "All right, don't be frightened, my dear," I say. "I'm the doctor and I've come to see how you are." "You're the doctor?" "Yes. Your mother sent into the town for me. I've bled you, my dear, and now you must rest and in a couple of days, God grant, we'll have you on your feet again." "Oh, yes, doctor, you mustn't let me die . . . please, please." "Don't say such things, God be with you!" But her fever'd returned, I thought. I felt her pulse and found her feverish. She looked at me and then suddenly seized me by the hand. "I'll tell you why I don't want to die,

District Doctor

I'll tell you, I'll tell you . . . now we're alone. Only, please, don't tell anyone else. Just listen." I bent down to her and she strained her lips toward my ear and her hair touched my cheek – I can tell you, my head was spinning from being so close to her – and she started whispering . . . I couldn't understand a word . . . Of course, she was delirious . . . She went on whispering and whispering, so fast it didn't sound like Russian, and then she stopped, shuddered, dropped her head on the pillow and shook her finger at me. "See you don't tell anyone, doctor." I calmed her somehow or other, gave her a drink, roused the maid and left.'

At this point, sighing bitterly once again, the district doctor took some snuff and paused for a moment.

'However,' he went on, 'the next day the sick girl, contrary to my expectations, was no better. I thought and thought about her and suddenly decided to stay, although other patients were waiting for me . . . And, you know, you mustn't neglect your patients: a practice can suffer from that sort of thing. But, in the first place, the sick girl was in a desperate state; and, secondly, to tell the truth, I had a strong personal attachment to her. What's more, I liked the whole family. Although they didn't have much in the way of possessions, they were extraordinarily well educated, one might say. Their father'd been a man of learning, a writer. He'd died, of course, in poverty, but he'd succeeded in giving his children an excellent education and he'd also left many books behind. Because I looked after the sick girl so zealously, or for some other reason, I have to say that they grew very fond of me in that household and treated me as one of the family . . . Meantime, the state of the roads became frightful. All communications, so to speak, were completely severed. Even medicine was only obtainable from the town with difficulty . . . The sick girl didn't get any better . . . Day after day, day after day . . . Well, you see, sir, you see . . .' (The doctor fell silent.) '. . . I don't rightly know how to put it, sir . . .' (He again took some snuff, wheezed and drank some tea.) 'I'll tell you straight out, my sick patient . . . how can I put it? . . . well, fell in love with me . . . or no, she didn't so much fall in love as . . . well, besides . . . I can't rightly say, sir . . .' (The doctor hung his head and went red.)

'No,' he went on vivaciously, 'it wasn't love! When all's said and done, you've got to know your own worth. She was an educated girl, intelligent, well-read, while I'd completely forgotten, one might say, all the Latin I'd ever learned. As for my figure' (the doctor glanced at himself with a smile) 'I didn't have all that much to boast about. But the Lord God hadn't made a complete fool out of me – I can tell black from white, you know, and I can make sense of things as well. For instance, I understood very well that Alexandra Andreyevna – she was called Alexandra Andreyevna – felt for me not love so much as what might be called a friendly disposition and a kind of respect. Although she may perhaps have been mistaken in her attitude, her state was, well, you can judge for yourself . . . Besides,' added the doctor, who'd spoken so brokenly and scarcely without drawing breath, in evident confusion, 'I've probably let my tongue run away with me, so you won't understand a thing . . . So, look, if you don't mind, I'll tell it all just as it happened.'

He finished his glass of tea and started speaking in a quieter voice.

'So it was like this. My patient grew worse – worse and worse. You're not a medical man, my good sir, so you can't understand what happens in the soul of someone like me, particularly at the beginning, when he starts to realize that the illness is getting the better of him. Your self-confidence flies out the window! You suddenly feel so small it's hard to describe. It seems to you you've forgotten everything you've ever learned, and your patient no longer trusts you, and others round you start noticing you're at a loss and start telling you the symptoms and looking at you from under their brows and whispering . . . oh, it's bloody awful! Surely, you think, there's got to be a medicine for this illness, it's just a case of finding it. Is this it? You try it – no, it's not that! You don't give the medicine time to work but try another, then another. You pick up your book of prescriptions and study it – ah, that's the one! Sometimes you just open the book at random and think, what the hell . . . But all the time the patient's dying, while another doctor might've saved him. You say you need a second opinion, because you can't take all the responsibility on yourself. And what a fool you look in such circumstances! Well, as time goes by you get used to it, it's nothing. Your patient's died, but it's not your fault, you followed the rules. But what's much worse is when you can see the blind trust they place in you, yet you feel you're not in any position to help. It was precisely such trust that Alexandra Andreyevna's family placed in me, while forgetting that their daughter was in danger. I was also, for my own part, assuring them it was all right, while my heart was right down in my boots. To cap all my misfortunes, the weather got so bad that the coachman couldn't go for the medicines for whole days at a time. And I never left the sick girl's room, couldn't tear myself away, told her silly jokes and played cards with her. At nights I sat beside her bed. The old lady thanked me with tears in her eyes and I thought to myself: "I don't deserve your thanks." I confess to you quite openly – there's nothing left to hide now – I fell in love with my patient. And Alexandra Andreyevna grew very fond of me and wouldn't allow anyone else into her room. She began talking to me, asking me where I'd done my training, what my life was like, who my parents were, who'd I go visiting? I felt I shouldn't let her talk, but I couldn't really stop her, definitely stop her, you know. I'd seize myself by the head and tell myself, "What're you doing, you blackguard?" But she'd take my hand and hold it, look at me, gaze at me, gaze and gaze at me and turn away and sigh and say, "How good you are!" Her hands were so hot, her eyes so round and longing. She'd say: "Yes, you're good, you're a good man, you're not like our neighbours . . . No, you're not like them at all, not at all . . . How is it we haven't met before?" And I'd say: "Alexandra Andreyevna, don't fret . . . Believe me, I don't feel, I've no idea why I should deserve this, only just don't fret, for God's sake, don't fret . . . everything'll be all right, you'll get well." But I ought to tell you, by the way,' the doctor added, bending forward and raising his eyebrows, 'that they didn't have much to do with the neighbours, because the small fry weren't really up to them and they were too proud to curry favour with the rich. I'm telling you they were an extremely well-educated family, so for me, you know, it was a privilege to be there. She'd only accept medicine from me . . . she'd raise herself, the poor girl, with my help, and have the medicine and look at me and my heart'd literally beat faster and faster. But all the while she was getting worse, worse and worse, and I thought she's bound to die, bound to. Believe me, I was ready to lie down in the coffin myself, what with the mother and the sisters seeing it all and looking me straight in the eyes, their confidence gradually slipping away: "What's wrong? How is she?" "Oh, it's nothing, nothing at all!" And how could it be nothing at all when her mind was already being affected? So there I am one night, sitting once again beside the sick girl. The maid's also there, snoring her head off . . . you couldn't blame her really, she'd been chivvied from pillar to post. Alexandra Andreyevna'd felt bad all evening; the fever'd tormented her. Right up until midnight she'd been tossing and turning and then she'd finally gone to sleep; or at least she lay there quietly. The lamp in the corner was burning before the icon and I sat there, you know, bent up, also snoozing. Suddenly, as if someone'd given me a shove in the side, I turned round and there – good God! – was Alexandra Andreyevna looking me straight in the eyes, with her lips apart and her cheeks literally on fire. "What's wrong?" "Doctor, I'm going to die, aren't I?" "God forbid!" "No, doctor, no, please, don't tell me I'll live . . . don't say that . . . Oh, if only you knew! . . . Listen, for God's sake don't hide from me what my condition is really!" She spoke, taking such quick breaths. "If I know for sure I'm going to die, then I'll tell you everything, everything!" "Please, Alexandra Andreyevna, please!" "Listen, I've not slept at all and I've been watching you . . . for God's sake . . . I trust you, you're a good man, you're an honest man, I beg you in the name of all that's holy, tell me the truth! If only you knew how important it is for me . . . Doctor, for God's sake tell me, am I in danger?" "What can I tell you, Alexandra Andreyevna? Please don't . . ." "For God's sake I implore you!" "I can't hide from you, Alexandra Andreyevna, that you *are* in danger, but God is merciful . . ." "I'll die, I'll die . . ." And she was literally overjoyed. Her face became so happy I was frightened. "Don't be frightened, don't be frightened, death doesn't worry me at all." She suddenly raised herself and leant on one elbow. "Now . . . well, now I can tell you that I'm grateful to you from the bottom of my heart, that you're a good, kind man and I love you . . ." I started at her like an idiot and I felt real fright, you know . . . "Do you hear what I'm saying, I love you . . ." "Alexandra Andreyevna, I'm not worth it!" "No, no, you don't understand me, you don't understand . . ." And suddenly she stretched out her arms and seized me by the head and kissed me. Believe you me, I almost cried out. I flung myself on to my knees and buried my head in the pillows. She fell silent, her fingers quivering in my hair. I could hear her crying. I began comforting her, trying to assure her – oh, I don't know what it was I said to her! I said: "You'll wake up the maid, Alexandra Andreyevna . . . Thank

District Doctor

you, thank you, believe me . . . now be quiet." "That's enough of that, enough," she went on saying. "God be with them, let them all wake up, let them all come in here, I don't care, after all I'm going to die . . . What's wrong with you, why d'you look so scared? Lift your head up . . . Or maybe you don't love me, maybe I've made a mistake? . . . In that case forgive me." "Alexandra Andreyevna, what're you saying? . . . I love you, Alexandra Andreyevna." She looked me straight in the eyes and opened her arms. "Hold me, then." I'll tell you in all honesty I don't know how I didn't go mad that night. I felt that my sick girl was driving herself crazy. I could see she wasn't in her right mind and I realized that if she hadn't thought herself about to die she wouldn't have given me a single thought. You know, like it or not, it's horrible to be dying at twenty-five years of age without ever having loved someone – and that's what was driving her crazy, that's why, out of desperation, she'd chosen me . . . Do you see now what I mean? Well, she wouldn't let me out of her arms. "Have pity on me, Alexandra Andreyevna, and have pity on yourself," I said. "Why?" she said. "What's pity got to do with it? After all I'm going to die." She repeated this again and again. "If

I knew I'd be alive and again be a proper young lady, I'd be ashamed, really ashamed . . . but it's not like that, is it?" "But who said you're going to die?" "Oh, no, enough's enough, you can't fool me, you're a poor liar, you've only got to look at yourself to see that.' 'You will live, Alexandra Andreyevna, I'll cure you. We'll ask your mother's permission . . . and we'll get married and live happily ever after." "No, no, I've got your word for it, I've got to die . . . you promised me . . . you told me . . ." It was a bitter thing for me, bitter for many reasons. You know how it is, sometimes little things happen which seem nothing at all, but they hurt. It occurred to her to ask me my name, not my surname but my forename. As bad luck would have it, I'd been given the name Tripthong. Yes, yes, Tripthong, Tripthong Ivanych. In that household they all called me "doctor". There was nothing to be done about it, so I said: "Tripthong, milady." She screwed up her eyes, shook her head and whispered something in French – oh, something impolite – and then laughed, which was also bad. So that's how I spent practically the whole night with her. In the morning I left her room half out of my mind. I went back to her room in the afternoon, after tea. Oh, my God, oh, my God! I couldn't recognize her. I've seen better-looking corpses. In all honesty I swear to you I don't understand now, I really don't understand how I survived that torture. Three days and three nights my sick girl scraped by . . . and what nights! The things she said to me! And on the last night, just imagine, there I sat beside her and prayed to God that she'd be taken quickly, and me as well. Suddenly the old lady, her mother, came rushing in. I'd already told her, the mother, the day before that there was little hope, things were bad and it might be an idea to fetch the priest. The sick girl, on seeing her mother, said: "Oh, what a good thing you've come . . . Look at us, we love each other, we've given each other our word . . ." "Doctor, what's wrong, what's she saying?" I was stunned. "She's delirious," I said. "It's the fever." But she said: "Enough's enough, you were saying something quite different just now, and you accepted the ring from me . . . Why pretend now? My mother's kind, she'll forgive, she'll understand, and I'm dying, why should I tell a lie? Give me your hand . . ." I jumped up and ran out. The old lady, of course, guessed what'd happened.

'I won't weary you any longer, and in any case I find

it painful to remember. My sick patient died the following day. The Kingdom of Heaven be hers!' (The doctor added this rapidly and with a sigh.) 'Before she died she asked that the rest of the family should go and I should stay with her alone. "Forgive me," she said. "Perhaps I'm to blame in your eyes . . . it's the illness . . . but believe me, I never loved anyone more than you . . . don't forget me . . . take care of my ring . . ."'

The district doctor turned away. I took his hand.

'Oh,' he cried, 'let's talk about something else! Or perhaps you'd like a little game of whist? Chaps like us, you know, shouldn't give way to such highfalutin' feelings. Chaps like us should only bother with things like stopping the children crying or the wife scolding. Since then I've contracted a legal marriage, as they say . . . Well, you know . . . I found a merchant's daughter. Dowry of seven thousand roubles. She's called Akulina, which is about right for a Tripthong. She's a woman with a fierce tongue, but thankfully she's asleep all day . . . What d'you say to some whist?'

We sat down to whist for copeck stakes. Tripthong Ivanych won two and a half roubles off me and went home late, very content with his victory.

Kasyan from the Beautiful Lands

I was returning from a hunting trip in a shaky little cart and, under the oppressive effects of an overcast summer day's stifling heat (it is notorious that on such days the heat can be even more insufferable than on clear days, especially when there is no wind), I was dozing as I rocked to and fro, in gloomy patience, allowing my skin to be eaten out by the fine white dust which rose incessantly from beneath the heat-cracked and juddering wheels on the hard earth track, when suddenly my attention was aroused by the unusual agitation and anxious body movements of my driver, who until that instant had been in an even deeper doze than I was. He pulled at the reins, fidgeted on his seat and began shouting at the horses, all the time glancing somewhere off to the side. I looked around. We were driving through a broad, flat area of ploughed land into which low hills, also ploughed up, ran down like unusually gentle, rolling undulations. My gaze encompassed in all about three miles of open, deserted country; all that broke the almost straight line of the horizon were distant, small groves of birch trees with their rounded, tooth-shaped tips. Narrow paths stretched through the fields, dipped into hollows and wound over knolls, and on one of these, which was due to cross our track about five hundred yards from us, I could distinguish a procession. It was at this that my driver had been glancing.

It was a funeral. At the front, in a cart drawn only by one small horse, the priest was riding at walking pace; the deacon sat next to him and was driving; behind the cart, four peasants with bared heads were carrying the coffin, draped in a white cloth; two women were walking behind the coffin. The fragile, plaintive voice of one of the women suddenly reached my ears; I listened: she was singing a lament. Pitifully this ululant, monotonous and helplessly grieving melody floated in the emptiness of the fields. My driver whipped up the horses in the desire to forestall the procession. It is a bad omen to meet up with a corpse on the road. He did, in fact, succeed in galloping along the track just in time before the procession reached it.

Kasyan from the Beautiful Lands

But we had hardly gone a hundred yards farther on when our cart gave a severe lurch, keeled over and almost capsized. The driver stopped the wildly racing horses, leaned over from his seat to see what had happened, gave a wave of the hand and spat.

'What's wrong there?' I asked.

The driver got down without answering and with no sign of hurry.

'Well, what is it?'

'The axle's broken ... burned through,' he answered gloomily, and, in a sudden fit of temper, tugged so sharply at the breech-band of the trace-horse that the animal almost toppled over on her side. However, she regained her balance, snorted, shook her mane and proceeded with the utmost calmness to scratch the lower part of her front leg with her teeth.

I got down and stood for a short while on the road, resigning myself to a vague and unpleasant sense of bewilderment. The right wheel had almost completely turned inwards under the cart and seemed to lift its hub in the air in dumb resignation.

'What's to be done now?' I asked eventually.

'That's to blame!' said my driver, directing his whip towards the procession which by this time succeeded in turning on to the track and was beginning to approach us. 'I've always noticed it,' he continued. 'It's always a bad omen to meet up with a corpse, that's for sure.'

Again he took it out on the trace-horse who, seeing how irritable and severe he was, decided to stand stock-still and only occasionally gave a few modest flicks with her tail. I took a few steps to and fro along the track and stopped again in front of the wheel.

In the meantime, the procession had caught up with us. Turning aside from the track on to the grass, the sad cortège passed by our cart. My driver and I removed our caps, exchanged bows with the priest and looks with the pall-bearers. They progressed with difficulty, their broad chests heaving under the weight. Of the two women who walked behind the coffin, one was extremely old and pale of face; her motionless features, cruelly contorted with grief, preserved an expression of stern and solemn dignity. She walked in silence, now and then raising a frail hand to her thin, sunken lips. The other woman, of about twenty-five, had eyes that were red and moist with tears, and her whole face had become swollen from crying. As she drew level with us, she ceased her lament and covered her face with her sleeve. Then the procession went past us, turning back on to the track once more, and her piteous, heart-rending lament was resumed. After following with his eyes the regular to-and-fro motion of the coffin without uttering a sound, my driver turned to me.

'It's Martin, the carpenter, the one from Ryabovo, that they're taking to be buried,' he said.

'How do you know that?'

'I could tell from the women. The old one's his mother and the young one's his wife.'

'Had he been ill, then?'

'Aye ... the fever ... The manager sent for the doctor three days back, but the doctor wasn't home. He was a good carpenter, he was. Liked his drink a bit, but he was a real good carpenter. You see how his wife's grieving for him. It's like they say, though – a woman's tears don't cost nothin', they just flow like water, that's for sure.'

And he bent down, crawled under the rein of the trace-horse and seized hold of the shaft with both hands.

'Well,' I remarked, 'what can we do now?'

My driver first of all leaned his knees against the shoulder of the other horse and giving the shaft a couple of shakes, set the shaft-pad back in its place, crawled back once again under the rein of the trace-horse and, after giving her a shove on the nose while doing so, walked up to the wheel – walked up to it and, without taking his eyes off it, slowly extracted a snuff-box from beneath the skirt of his long tunic, slowly pulled open the lid by a little strap, slowly inserted two thick fingers (the tips of them could hardly fit into the snuff-box at once), kneaded the tobacco, wrinkled up his nose in readiness, gave several measured sniffs, accompanied at each inhalation of the snuff with prolonged snorting and grunting, and, after painfully screwing up and blinking his tear-filled eyes, settled into deep thoughtfulness.

'So, what do you think?' I asked when all this was over.

My driver carefully replaced the snuff-box in his pocket, brought his hat down over his brows without touching it, simply by a movement of his head, and climbed thoughtfully up on to the seat.

'Where are you off to?' I asked, not a little amazed.

'Please be seated,' he answered calmly and picked up the reins.

'But how are we going to go?'

'We'll go all right.'

'But the axle . . .'

'Please be seated.'

'But the axle's broken . . .'

'It's broken, yes, it's broken all right, but we'll make it to the new village – at walking pace, that is. It's over there to the right, beyond the wood, that's where the new village is, what they call the Yudin village.'

'But d'you think we'll get there?'

My driver did not even deign to answer me.

'I'd better go on foot,' I said.

'As you please . . .'

He waved his whip and the horses set off.

We did, in fact, reach the new village, even though the right front wheel hardly held in place and wobbled in a most unusual fashion. It almost flew off as we negotiated a small knoll, but my driver shouted at it angrily and we successfully descended the far slope.

Yudin village consisted of six small, low-roofed huts which had already begun to lean to one side or the other despite the fact that they had no doubt been put up quite recently, and not even all the yards had wattle fencing. As we entered the village, we did not meet a living soul; there were not even any chickens to be seen in the village street; there were not even any dogs, save for one black, stubby-tailed animal that jumped hastily from a completely dried-up ditch, where it must have been driven by thirst, only to dash headlong under a gate without so much as giving a bark. I turned into the first hut, opened the porch door and called for the owners: no one answered me. I called again: a hungry miaowing came from behind the inner door. I shoved it with my foot and an emaciated cat flashed past me, its green eyes glittering in the dark. I stuck my head into the room and looked around: it was dark, smoky and empty. I went into the backyard and there was no one there. A calf gave a plaintive moo in the enclosure, and a crippled grey goose took a few waddling steps off to one side. I crossed to the second hut – and there was no one there either. So I went out into the backyard.

In the very middle of the brilliantly lit yard, right out in the middle of the sun, as they say, there was lying, face downward and with his head covered with a cloth coat, someone I took to be a boy. A few paces from him, beside a wretched little cart, a miserable little horse, all skin and bones, stood in a tattered harness under a straw overhang. Its thick reddish-brown coat was dappled with small bright splashes

Kasyan from the Beautiful Lands

of sunlight that streamed through narrow openings in the dilapidated thatchwork. There also, high up in their little bird-houses, starlings chattered, looking down upon the world with placid inquisitiveness from their airy home. I walked up to the sleeping figure and began to rouse it.

The sleeper raised his head, saw me and at once jumped to his feet.

'What is it? What's happened?' he started muttering in bewilderment.

I did not answer him at once because I was so astonished by his appearance. Imagine, if you please, a dwarf of about fifty years old, with a small, swarthy, wrinkled face, a little pointed nose, barely discernible little brown eyes and abundant curly black hair which sat upon his tiny head just as broadly as the cap sits on the stalk of a mushroom. His entire body was extraordinarily frail and thin, and it is quite impossible to convey in words how unusual and strange was the look in his eyes.

'What is it?' he asked me again.

I explained the position to him and he listened to me without lowering his slowly blinking eyes.

'Is it not possible then for us to obtain a new axle?' I asked finally. 'I would gladly pay.'

'But who are you? Are you out hunting?' he asked, encompassing me with his glance from head to foot.

'I'm out hunting.'

'You shoot the birds of the air, eh? . . . And the wild animals of the forest? . . . Isn't it sinful you are to be killing God's own wee birds and spilling innocent blood?'

The strange little old man spoke with a very pronounced dwelling on each word. The sound of his voice also astonished me. Not only was there nothing decrepit about it but it was surprisingly sweet, youthful and almost feminine in its gentleness.

'I have no axle,' he added after a short interval of silence. 'This one won't do' – he pointed to his own little cart – 'because, after all, yours is a big cart.'

'But would it be possible to find one in the village?'

'What sort of village is it we have here! Here, there's not anyone of us has a single thing. And there's no one at home – aren't they all out at work for sure. Be off with you!' he said, suddenly, and lay down again on the ground.

I had certainly not expected an outcome of this kind.

'Listen, old man,' I started to say, touching him on the shoulder, 'have a heart, help me.'

'Be off with you in the name o' God! It's tired out I am, an' me having gone into town and back,' he told me and pulled his cloth coat over his head.

'Please do me a favour,' I went on, 'I . . . I'll pay you . . .'

'I'm not needin' your money.'

'Please, old man . . .'

He raised himself half-way and sat himself upright, crossing his delicate, spindly legs.

'It's takin' you I might be to where they've been cutting down the trees. 'Tis a place where some local merchants have bought a piece o' woodland, the Lord be the judge of 'em, an' they're getting rid of all the trees and putting up an office they are, the Lord judge 'em for it. That's where you might order an axle from 'em or buy one ready-made.'

'Excellent!' I exclaimed delightedly. 'Excellent! Let's go.'

'An oak axle, mind you, a good one,' he continued without rising from where he was sitting.

'Is it far to where they're cutting down the trees?'

'A couple o' miles.'

'Well, then, we can get there on your little cart.'

'Oh, but wait a moment . . .'

'Now come along,' I said. 'Come on, old man! My driver's waiting for us in the street.'

The old man got up reluctantly and followed me out into the street. My driver was in a thoroughly vexed state of mind: he had wanted to water the horses, but it had turned out that there was very little water in the well and what there was had an unpleasant taste; and that was putting first things first, as drivers are accustomed to say . . . However, as soon as he saw the old man he grinned broadly, nodded his head and cried out:

'If it's not little Kasyan! Good to see you!'

''Tis good to see you, Yerofey, righteous man that you are!' answered Kasyan in a despondent voice.

I at once told my driver about the old man's suggestion; Yerofey expressed his assent and drove into the yard. While Yerofey was quite deliberately making a great display of briskness in unharnessing the horses, the old man stood with one shoulder leaning against the gates and glanced unhappily either at him or me. He appeared to be at a loss and, so far as I could see, he was not unduly delighted by our sudden visit.

Kasyan from the Beautiful Lands

'Have they resettled you as well?' Yerofey suddenly asked him as he removed the shaft-bow.

'Me as well.'

'Yuck!' said my driver through his teeth. 'You know Martin, the carpenter . . . Martin of Ryabovo, don't you?'

'That I do.'

'Well, he's dead. We just met up with his coffin.'

Kasyan gave a shudder.

'Dead?' he muttered, and stared at the ground.

'Yes, he's dead. Why didn't you cure him, eh? People say you do cures, that you've got the power of healing.'

My driver was obviously taunting and making fun of the old man.

'And that's your cart, is it?' he added, shrugging a shoulder in its direction.

''Tis mine.'

'A cart, is it, a cart!' he repeated and, taking it by the shafts, almost turned it upside down. 'A cart, indeed! But what'll you be using to get to the clearings? You won't be able to harness our horse into those shafts. Our horses are big, but what's this meant to be?'

'I wouldn't be knowing,' answered Kasyan, 'what

you'll be using. For sure there's that poor creature,' he added with a sigh.

'D'you mean this?' asked Yerofey, seizing on what Kasyan had been saying, and, going up to Kasyan's miserable little horse, contemptuously stuck the third finger of his right hand in its neck. 'See,' he added reproachfully, 'gone to sleep, it has, the useless thing!'

I asked Yerofey to harness it up as quickly as possible. I wanted to go myself with Kasyan to the place where they were clearing the woodland, for those are the places where grouse are often found. When the little cart was finally ready, I somehow or other settled myself along with my dog on its warped, bast floor, and Kasyan, hunching himself up into a ball, also sat on the front support with the same despondent expression on his face – then it was that Yerofey approached me and, giving me a mysterious look, whispered:

'And it's a good thing, sir, that you're going with him. He's one of those holy men, you know, sir, and he's nicknamed The Flea. I don't know how you were able to understand him . . .'

I was about to comment to Yerofey that so far Kasyan had seemed to me to be a man of very good sense, but my driver at once continued in the same tone of voice:

'You just watch out and see that he takes you where he should. And make sure you yourself choose the axle, the stouter the better... What about it, Flea,' he added loudly, 'is there anywhere here to find a bite to eat?'

'Seek and it shall be found,' answered Kasyan, giving the reins a jerk, and we rolled away.

His little horse, to my genuine surprise, went far from badly. Throughout the entire journey Kasyan maintained a stubborn silence and answered all my questions peremptorily and unwillingly. We quickly reached the clearings, and once there we made our way to the office, a tall hut standing by itself above a small ravine which had been haphazardly dammed and turned into a pond. I found in this office two young clerks working for the merchants, both of them with teeth as white as snow, sugary sweet eyes, sugary sweet, boisterous chatter and sugary sweet, clever little smiles, did a deal with them for an axle and set off for the clearings. I thought that Kasyan would stay by the horse and wait, but he suddenly approached me.

'And is it that you're after shooting the wee birds?' he ventured. 'Is that it?'

'Yes, if I find them.'

'I'll go along with you. D'you mind?'

'Please do, please do.'

And we walked off. The area of felled trees extended for less than a mile. I confess that I looked at Kasyan more than at my dog. He had been aptly nicknamed the Flea. His black and hatless little head (his hair, by the way, was a substitute for any cap) bobbed up and down among the bushes. He walked with an extraordinarily sprightly step and literally took little jumps as he went, ceaselessly bending down, plucking herbs, stuffing them under his shirt, muttering words through his nose and shooting glances at me and my dog, giving us such keen and unusual looks. In the low bushes, the 'underbush' and in the clearings there are often little grey birds which all the time switch from sapling to sapling and emit short whistling sounds as they dive suddenly in their flight. Kasyan used to tease them, exchanging calls with them; a young quail would fly up shrilly from under his feet and he would call shrilly after it; a lark might start rising above him, fluttering its wings and pouring out its song – Kasyan would at once catch up its refrain. But to me he said not a word.

The weather was beautiful, still more beautiful than

Kasyan from the Beautiful Lands

it had been before; yet there was still no lessening of the heat. Across the clear sky drifted, with scarcely a movement, a few distant clouds, yellowish-white, the colour of a late snowfall in the spring, flat in shape and elongated like furled sails. Their feathered edges, light and wispy as cotton, altered slowly but obviously with each passing instant; they were as if melting, these clouds were, and they cast no shadow. For a long while Kasyan and I wandered through the clearings. Young shoots which had not yet succeeded in growing more than a couple of feet high spread their thin, smooth stems round the blackened and squat stumps of trees; round, spongy fungoid growths with grey edges, the kind which they boil down to make tinder, adhered to these tree-stumps; wild strawberries spread their wispy pink runners over them; mushrooms were also ensconced there in tight family clusters. One's feet were continually becoming entangled and caught by the tall grass, drenched in the sun's heat; in all directions one's eyes were dazzled by the sharp, metallic flashes of light from the young, reddish leaves on the saplings; everywhere in gay abundance appeared sky-blue clusters of vetch, the little golden chalices of buttercups, the partly mauve, partly yellow flowers of

St John and Mary daisies; here and there, beside overgrown tracks, in which the traces of cart-wheels were marked by strips of short-stemmed red grass rose piles of firewood, stacked in six-foot lengths and darkened by the wind and rain; slight shadows extended from them in slanting rectangles – otherwise there was no shade of any kind. A light breeze sprang up occasionally and then died. It would blow suddenly straight into one's face and caper around, as it were, setting everything happily rustling, nodding and swaying about, making the supple tips of the fern bow gracefully, so that one was delighted at it; but then it would again fade away, and everything would once more be still. Only the grasshoppers made a combined whirring, as if infuriated – such an oppressive, unceasing, insipid, dry sound. It was appropriate to the unabating, midday heat, as if literally engendered by it, literally summoned by it out of the sun-smelted earth.

Without coming across a single covey, we finally reached some new clearings. Here, recently felled aspens were stretched sadly on the ground, pressing down both grass and undergrowth beneath their weight; on some of them the leaves, still green but already dead, hung feebly from the stiff branches; on others they had already withered and curled up. A special, extraordinarily pleasant acrid scent came from the fresh, golden-white chips of wood which lay in heaps about the moistly bright tree-stumps. Far off, closer to the wood, there could be heard the faint clatter of axes and from time to time, solemnly and quietly, as if in the act of bowing and spreading out its arms, a curly-headed tree would fall.

For a long while I could find no game; finally, a landrail flew out of an extensive oak thicket which was completely overgrown with wormwood. I fired: the bird turned over in the air and fell. Hearing the shot, Kasyan quickly covered his face with his hand and remained stock-still until I had reloaded my gun and picked up the shot bird. Just as I was preparing to move farther on, he came up to the place where the bird had fallen, bent down to the grass which had been sprinkled with several drops of blood, gave a shake of the head and looked at me in fright. Afterwards I heard him whispering: 'A sin! 'Tis a sin, it is, a sin!'

Eventually the heat forced us to find shelter in the wood. I threw myself down beneath a tall hazel bush, above which a young and graceful maple had made a beautiful spread of its airy branches. Kasyan seated himself on the thick end of a felled birch. I looked at him. Leaves fluttered slightly high above, and their liquid, greenish shadows glided calmly to and fro over his puny figure, clad somehow or other in a dark cloth coat, and over his small face. He did not raise his head. Bored by his silence, I lay down on my back and began admiringly to watch the peaceful play of the entwined leaves against the high, clear sky. It is a remarkably pleasant occupation, to lie on one's back in a forest and look upwards! It seems that you are looking into a bottomless sea, that it is stretching out far and wide *below* you, that the trees are not rising from the earth but, as if they were the roots of enormous plants, are descending or falling steeply into those lucid, grassy waves, while the leaves on the trees glimmer like emeralds or thicken into a gold-tinted, almost jet-black greenery. Somewhere high, high up, at the very end of a delicate branch, a single leaf stands out motionless against a blue patch of translucent sky, and, beside it, another sways, resembling in its movements the ripplings upon the surface of a fishing reach, as if the movement were of its own making and not caused by the wind. Like magical underwater islands, round white clouds gently float into view and pass by, and then suddenly the whole of this sea, this radiant air, these branches and leaves suffused with sunlight, all of it suddenly begins to stream in the wind, shimmers with a fugitive brilliance, and a fresh, tremulous murmuration arises which is like the endless shallow splashing of oncoming ripples. You lie still and you go on watching: words cannot express the delight and quiet, and how sweet is the feeling that creeps over your heart. You go on watching, and that deep, clear azure brings a smile to your lips as innocent as the azure itself, as innocent as the clouds passing across it, and as if in company with them there passes through your mind a slow cavalcade of happy recollections, and it seems to you that all the while your gaze is travelling farther and farther away and drawing all of you with it into that calm, shining infinity, making it impossible for you to tear yourself away from those distant heights, from those distant depths . . .

'Master, eh, master!' Kasyan suddenly said in his resonant voice.

I raised myself up in surprise; until that moment he had hardly answered any of my questions and now he had suddenly started talking of his own accord.

'What do you want?' I asked.

'Why is it now that you should be killing that wee bird?' he began, looking me directly in the face.

'How do you mean: why? A landrail is a game bird. You can eat it.'

'No, it wasn't for that you were killing it, master. You won't be eating it! You were killing it for your own pleasure.'

'But surely you yourself are used to eating a goose or a chicken, for example, aren't you?'

'Such birds are ordained by God for man to eat, but a landrail – that's a bird of the free air, a forest bird. And he's not the only one; aren't there many of them, every kind of beast of the forest and of the field, and river creature, and creature of the marsh and meadow and the heights and the depths – and a sin it is to be killing such a one, it should be let to live on the earth until its natural end . . . But for man there is another food laid down; another food and another drink; bread is God's gift to man, and the waters from the heavens, and the tame creatures handed down from our fathers of old.'

I looked at Kasyan in astonishment. His words flowed freely; he did not cast around for them, but spoke with quiet animation and a modest dignity, occasionally closing his eyes.

'So according to you it's also sinful to be killing fish?' I asked.

'A fish has cold blood,' he protested with certainty, 'it's a dumb creature. A fish doesn't know fear, doesn't know happiness: a fish is a creature without a tongue. A fish doesn't have feelings, it has no living blood in it . . . Blood,' he continued after a pause, 'blood is holy! Blood does not see the light of God's sun, blood is hidden from the light . . . And a great sin it is to show blood to the light of day, a great sin and cause to be fearful, oh, a great one it is!'

He gave a sigh and lowered his eyes. I must admit that I looked at the strange old man in complete amazement. His speech did not sound like the speech of a peasant: simple people did not talk like this, nor did ranters. This language, thoughtfully solemn and unusual as it was, I had never heard before.

'Tell me, please, Kasyan,' I began, without lowering my eyes from his slightly flushed face, 'what is your occupation?'

He did not answer my question immediately. His gaze shifted uneasily for a moment.

'I live as the Lord ordains I should,' he said eventually, 'but as for an occupation, no, I don't have an occupation of any kind. 'Tis a poor mentality I have, right from when I was small. I work so long as I can, but it's a poor worker I'm being. There's nothing for me to do! My health's gone and my hands're all foolish. In the springtime, though, I catch nightingales.'

'You catch nightingales? Then why were you talking about not touching the beast of the forest and the field and other creatures?'

'Not to be killing 'em, that's the point; death will take what's due to it. Now there's Martin the carpenter: he lived his life, Martin the carpenter did, and he didn't have long and he died; and now his wife's grieving over her husband and her little ones . . . It's not for man nor beast to get the better of death. Death doesn't come running, but you can't run away from it, neither; nor must you be helping it along. I don't kill the nightingales, Good Lord preserve us! I don't catch them to cause them pain, nor to put their lives in any peril, but for man's enjoyment, for his consolation and happiness.'

'Do you go into the Kursk region to catch them?'

'I go into Kursk and I go farther, depending how things are. I sleep in the swamplands, and also I sleep in the woodlands, and I sleep all alone in the fields and in the wild places: that's where snipe do their whistling, where you can hear the hares crying, where the drakes go hissing . . . At eventide I take note where they are, and come morning I listen out for them, at dawn I spread my net over the bushes. There's a kind of nightingale sings real piteously, sweetly and piteously, it does . . .'

'Do you sell them?'

'I give 'em away to good people.'

'What d'you do apart from this?'

'What do I do?'

'What keeps you busy?'

The old man was silent for a moment.

'Nothing keeps me busy. 'Tis a poor worker I am. But I understand how to read and write.'

'So you're literate?'

'I understand how to read and write. The Lord God helped me, and some kind people.'

'Are you a family man?'

'No, I've got no family.'

'Why's that? They've all died, have they?'

'No, it's just like it wasn't my task in life, that's all. Everything's according to the will of God, we all live our lives according to the will of God; but a man's got to be righteous – that's what! That means he must live a fitting life in God's eyes.'

'And you haven't any relatives?'

'I have ... I have, yes.' The old man became confused.

'Tell me, please,' I began. 'I heard my driver asking you, so to speak, why you hadn't cured Martin the carpenter? Is it true you can heal people?'

'Your driver's a just man,' Kasyan answered me thoughtfully, 'but he's also not without sin. He says I have the power of healing. What power have I got! And who is there has such power? It all comes from God. But there ... there are herbs, there are flowers: they help, it's true. There's marigold, there's one, a kindly herb for curing human beings; there's the plantains, too; there's nothing to be ashamed of in talking about them – good clean herbs are of God's making. But others aren't. Maybe they help, but they're a sin and it's a sin to talk about them. Perhaps they might be used with the help of prayer ... Well, of course, there are special words ... But only he who has faith shall be saved,' he added, lowering his voice.

'Did you give anything to Martin?' I asked.

'I learned about him too late,' answered the old man. 'And what would've been the good! It is all ordained for man from his birth. He was not a dweller, was Martin the carpenter, not a dweller on this earth: and that's how it turned out. No, when a man's not ordained to live on this earth, the sweet sunlight doesn't warm him like it warms the others, and the produce of the earth profits him nothing, as if all the time he's being called away . . . Aye, God rest his soul!'

'Have you been resettled here among us for long?' I asked after a short silence.

Kasyan stirred.

'No, not long: 'bout four years. Under the old master we lived all the time where we were, but it was the custodians of the estate who resettled us. The old master we had was a meek soul, a humble man he was – God grant he enter the Kingdom of Heaven! But the custodians, of course, decided justly. It looks like this is how it was meant to be.'

'But where did you live before this?'

'We came from the Beautiful Lands.'

'Is that far from here?'

''Bout sixty miles.'

'Was it better there?'

'It was better . . . much better. The land's free and open there, with plenty of rivers, a real home for us; but here it's all enclosed and dried up. We've become orphans here. There where we were, on the Beautiful Lands, I mean, you'd go up a hill, you'd go up – and, Good Lord, what wouldn't you see from there? Eh? There'd be a river there, a meadow there and there a forest, and then there'd be a church, and again more meadows going far, far off, as far as anything. Just as far as far, that's how you'd go on looking and looking and wonderin' at it, that's for sure! As for here, true – the land's better: loamy soil it is, real good loam, so the peasants say. But so far as I'm concerned, there's sufficient food everywhere to keep me going.'

'But if you were to tell the truth, old fellow, you'd want to be where you were born, wouldn't you?'

'For sure I'd like to take a look at it. Still, it doesn't matter where I am. I'm not a family man, not tied to anywhere. And what would I be doing sittin' at home a lot? It's when I'm off on my way, off on my travels,' he began saying in a louder voice, 'that everything's surely easier. Then the sweet sunlight shines on you, and you're clearer to God, and you sing in better tune. Then you look-see what herbs is growing there, and

Kasyan from the Beautiful Lands

you take note of 'em and collect the ones you want. Maybe there's water runnin' there, water from a spring, so you have a drink of it and take note of that as well. The birds of the air'll be singing . . . And then on t'other side of Kursk there'll be the steppes, O such steppelands, there's a wonder for you, a real joy to mankind they are, such wide expanses, a sign of God's bounty. And they go on and on, people do say, right to the warm seas where Gamayun lives, the bird of the sweet voice, to the place where no leaves fall from the trees in winter, nor in the autumn neither, and golden apples do grow on silver branches and each man lives in contentment and justice with another . . . That's where I'd like to be going . . . Though I've been about a bit in my time! I've been in Romyon and in Sinbirsk, that fine city, and in Moscow herself, dressed in her golden crowns. And to Oka, river of mother's milk, I've been, and to Tsna, fair as a dove, and to our mother, the Volga, and many's the people. I've seen, good Chrestians all, and many's the honest towns I've been in . . . But I'd still like to be going to that place . . . and that's it . . . and soon-like . . . And it's not only I, sinner that I am, but many other Chrestians that go walking and wandering through the wide world with nothin' but bast on their feet and seekin' for the truth . . . Sure they are! . . . But as for what's at home, eh? There's no justice in the way men live – that's what . . .'

Kasyan uttered these last words with great speed and almost inaudibly: afterwards he said something else, which I was unable even to hear, and his face took on such a strange expression that I was spontaneously reminded of the title 'holy man' which Yerofey had given him. He stared down at the ground, gave a phlegmy cough and appeared to collect his senses.

'O the sweet sun!' he uttered almost under his breath. 'O such a blessing, Good Lord! O such warmth here in the forest!'

He shrugged his shoulders, fell silent, glanced round distractedly and started singing in a quiet voice. I could not catch all the words of his protracted little song, but I heard the following words:

> But Kasyan's what they call me,
> And by nickname I'm the Flea . . .

'Ha!' I thought, 'he's making it up . . .'

Suddenly he shuddered and stopped his singing, gazing intently into the forest thicket. I turned and saw a little peasant girl of about eight years of age, dressed in a little blue coat, with a chequered handkerchief tied over her head and a small wattle basket on her bare, sunburnt arm. She had obviously not expected to come across us here at all; she had stumbled on us, as they say, and now stood stock-still on a shady patch of grass in a green thicket of nut trees, glancing fearfully at me out of her jet-black eyes. I had scarcely had time to notice her when she at once plunged out of sight behind a tree.

'Annushka! Annushka! Come here, don't be frightened,' the old man called to her in a gentle voice.

'I'm frightened,' a thin little voice answered.

'Don't be frightened, don't be frightened, come to me.'

Annushka silently left her hiding-place, quietly made her way round – her child's feet scarcely made any noise in the thick grass – and emerged from the thicket beside the old man. She was not a girl of about eight years of age, as it had seemed to me at first judging by her lack of inches, but of thirteen or fourteen. Her whole body was small and thin, but very well-made and supple, and her beautiful little face was strikingly similar to Kasyan's, although Kasyan was no beauty. The same sharp features, the same unusual look, which was both cunning and trustful, meditative and penetrating, and exactly the same gestures ... Kasyan took her in at a glance as she stood sideways to him.

'You've been out picking mushrooms, have you?' he asked.

'Yes,' she answered with a shy smile.

'Did you find many?'

'Yes.' (She directed a quick glance at him and again smiled.)

'Are there any white ones?'

'There are white ones as well.'

'Come on, show them ...' (She lowered the basket from her arm and partly raised the broad dock leaf with which the mushrooms were covered.) 'Ah!' said Kasyan, bending over the basket, 'they're real beauties! That's really something, Annushka!'

'Is she your daughter, Kasyan?' I asked. (Annushka's face crimsoned faintly.)

'No, she's just a relative,' Kasyan said with pretended indifference. 'Well, Annushka, you be off,' he added at once, 'and God be with you! Watch where you go ...'

Kasyan from the Beautiful Lands

'But why should she go on foot?' I interrupted. 'We could take her home in the cart.'

Annushka blushed red as a poppy, seized hold of the basket by its string handle and glanced at the old man in alarm.

'No, she'll walk home,' he objected in the same indifferent tone of voice. 'Why shouldn't she? She'll get home all right . . . Off with you now!'

Annushka walked off briskly into the forest. Kasyan followed her with his eyes, then looked down at the ground and grinned to himself. In this protracted grin, in the few words which he had spoken to Annushka and in the sound of his voice as he was talking to her there had been ineffable, passionate love and tenderness. He again glanced in the direction that she had gone, again smiled and, wiping his face, gave several nods of the head.

'Why did you send her away so soon?' I asked him. 'I would have bought some mushrooms from her . . .'

'You can buy them there at home whenever you like, it's no matter,' he answered, addressing me with the formal 'You' for the first time.

'She's very pretty, that girl of yours.'

'No . . . how so? . . . she's just as they come,' he

answered with apparent unwillingness, and from that very moment dropped back into his former taciturnity.

Seeing that all my efforts to make him start talking again were fruitless, I set off for the clearings. The heat had meanwhile dissipated a little; but my bad luck or, as they say in our parts, my 'nothing doing' continued the same and I returned to the village with no more than a single landrail and a new axle. As we were driving up to the yard, Kasyan suddenly turned to me.

'Master, sir,' he began, 'sure I'm the one you should blame, sure it was I who drove all the game away from you.'

'How so?'

'It's just something I know. There's that dog of yours, a good dog and trained to hunt, but he couldn't do anything. When you think of it, people are people, aren't they? Then there's this animal here, but what've they been able to make out of him?'

It would have been useless for me to start persuading Kasyan that it was impossible to 'cast a spell' over game and therefore I did not answer him. At that moment we turned in through the gates of the yard.

Annushka was not in the hut; she had already arrived and left behind her basket of mushrooms.

Kasyan from the Beautiful Lands

Yerofey fixed the new axle, having first subjected it to a severe and biased evaluation; and an hour later I drove away, leaving Kasyan a little money, which at first he did not wish to accept but which later, having thought about it and having held it in the palm of his hand, he placed inside the front of his shirt. During this whole hour he hardly uttered a single word; as previously, he stood leaning against the gates, made no response to my driver's reproachful remarks and was extremely cold to me in saying goodbye.

As soon as I had returned I had noticed that my Yerofey was once again sunk in gloom. And in fact he had found nothing edible in the village and the water for the horses had been of poor quality. So we drove out. With a dissatisfaction that expressed itself even in the nape of his neck, he sat on the box and dearly longed to strike up a conversation with me, but in anticipation of my initial question he limited himself to faint grumblings under his breath and edifying, occasionally caustic, speeches directed at the horses.

'A village!' he muttered. 'Call it a village! I asked for some *kvas* and they didn't even have any *kvas* . . . Good God! And as for water, it was simply muck!' (He spat loudly.) 'No cucumbers, no *kvas*, not a bloody thing. As for you,' he added thunderously, turning to the right-hand horse, 'I know you, you dissemblin' female, you! You're a right one for pretendin', you are . . .' (And he struck her with the whip.) 'That horse has gone dead cunnin', she has, and before it was a nice, easy creature . . . Gee-up there, look-see about it.'

'Tell me, please, Yerofey,' I began, 'what sort of a person is that Kasyan?'

Yerofey did not reply immediately: in general he was thoughtful and slow in his ways, but I could guess at once that my question had cheered and calmed him.

'The Flea, you mean?' he said eventually, jerking at the reins. 'A strange and wonderful man he is, truly a holy man, and you'd not find another one like him all that quick. He's, so to speak, as like as like our grey horse there: he's got out of hand just the same . . . that's to say, he's got out of the way of workin'. Well, of course, he's no worker. Just keeps himself going, but still . . . For sure he's always been like that. To start with he used to be a carrier along with his uncles: there were three of 'em; but after a time, well, you know, he got bored and gave it up. Started living at home, he did, but couldn't feel settled – he's restless as a flea. Thanks be to God, it happened he had a kind master who didn't force him to work. So from that time on he's been wanderin' here, there and everywhere, like a roaming sheep. And God knows, he's remarkable enough, with his being silent as a tree-stump one moment and then talking away all of a sudden the next – and as for what he says, God alone knows what that is. Maybe you think it's his manner? It's not his manner, because he's too ungainly. But he sings well – a bit pompous-like, but not too bad really.'

'Is it true he has the power of healing?'

'A power of healing! What would he be doing with that? Just ordinary he is. But he did cure me of scrofula . . . A lot of good it does him! He's just as stupid as they come, he is,' he added, after a pause.

'Have you known him long?'

'Long enough. We were neighbours of his in Sychovka, on the Beautiful Lands.'

'And that girl we came across in the wood – Annushka – is she a blood relation of his?'

Yerofey glanced at me over his shoulder and bared his teeth in a wide grin.

'Huh . . . Yes, they're relations. She's an orphan, got no mother and nobody knows who her mother was. But it's likely she's related to him: she's the spittin' image of him . . . And she lives with him. A smart girl, she is, no denying that; and a good girl, and the old man, he dotes on her: she's a good girl. And likely he'll – you may not believe it – but likely he'll take it into his head to teach his Annushka readin' and writin'. You never know, it's just the sort of thing he'd start: he's as extrardin'ry as that, changeable-like he is, even untellable . . . Hey, hey, hey!' My driver suddenly interrupted himself and, bringing the horses to a stop, leaned over the side and started sniffing. 'Isn't there a smell of burning? There is an' all! These new axles'll be the end of me. It seemed I'd put enough grease on. I'll have to get some water. There's a little pond over there.'

And Yerofey got down slowly from the box, untied a bucket, walked to the pond and, when he returned, listened with considerable pleasure to the way the axle-hole hissed as it was suddenly doused with water. About six times in the course of seven or so miles he had to douse the overheated axle, and evening had long since fallen by the time we returned home.

1. BOCCACCIO · *Mrs Rosie and the Priest*
2. GERARD MANLEY HOPKINS · *As kingfishers catch fire*
3. *The Saga of Gunnlaug Serpent-tongue*
4. THOMAS DE QUINCEY · *On Murder Considered as One of the Fine Arts*
5. FRIEDRICH NIETZSCHE · *Aphorisms on Love and Hate*
6. JOHN RUSKIN · *Traffic*
7. PU SONGLING · *Wailing Ghosts*
8. JONATHAN SWIFT · *A Modest Proposal*
9. *Three Tang Dynasty Poets*
10. WALT WHITMAN · *On the Beach at Night Alone*
11. KENKŌ · *A Cup of Sake Beneath the Cherry Trees*
12. BALTASAR GRACIÁN · *How to Use Your Enemies*
13. JOHN KEATS · *The Eve of St Agnes*
14. THOMAS HARDY · *Woman much missed*
15. GUY DE MAUPASSANT · *Femme Fatale*
16. MARCO POLO · *Travels in the Land of Serpents and Pearls*
17. SUETONIUS · *Caligula*
18. APOLLONIUS OF RHODES · *Jason and Medea*
19. ROBERT LOUIS STEVENSON · *Olalla*
20. KARL MARX AND FRIEDRICH ENGELS · *The Communist Manifesto*
21. PETRONIUS · *Trimalchio's Feast*
22. JOHANN PETER HEBEL · *How a Ghastly Story Was Brought to Light by a Common or Garden Butcher's Dog*
23. HANS CHRISTIAN ANDERSEN · *The Tinder Box*
24. RUDYARD KIPLING · *The Gate of the Hundred Sorrows*
25. DANTE · *Circles of Hell*
26. HENRY MAYHEW · *Of Street Piemen*
27. HAFEZ · *The nightingales are drunk*
28. GEOFFREY CHAUCER · *The Wife of Bath*
29. MICHEL DE MONTAIGNE · *How We Weep and Laugh at the Same Thing*
30. THOMAS NASHE · *The Terrors of the Night*
31. EDGAR ALLAN POE · *The Tell-Tale Heart*
32. MARY KINGSLEY · *A Hippo Banquet*
33. JANE AUSTEN · *The Beautifull Cassandra*
34. ANTON CHEKHOV · *Gooseberries*
35. SAMUEL TAYLOR COLERIDGE · *Well, they are gone, and here must I remain*
36. JOHANN WOLFGANG VON GOETHE · *Sketchy, Doubtful, Incomplete Jottings*
37. CHARLES DICKENS · *The Great Winglebury Duel*
38. HERMAN MELVILLE · *The Maldive Shark*
39. ELIZABETH GASKELL · *The Old Nurse's Story*
40. NIKOLAY LESKOV · *The Steel Flea*

41. HONORÉ DE BALZAC · *The Atheist's Mass*
42. CHARLOTTE PERKINS GILMAN · *The Yellow Wall-Paper*
43. C.P. CAVAFY · *Remember, Body . . .*
44. FYODOR DOSTOEVSKY · *The Meek One*
45. GUSTAVE FLAUBERT · *A Simple Heart*
46. NIKOLAI GOGOL · *The Nose*
47. SAMUEL PEPYS · *The Great Fire of London*
48. EDITH WHARTON · *The Reckoning*
49. HENRY JAMES · *The Figure in the Carpet*
50. WILFRED OWEN · *Anthem For Doomed Youth*
51. WOLFGANG AMADEUS MOZART · *My Dearest Father*
52. PLATO · *Socrates' Defence*
53. CHRISTINA ROSSETTI · *Goblin Market*
54. *Sindbad the Sailor*
55. SOPHOCLES · *Antigone*
56. RYŪNOSUKE AKUTAGAWA · *The Life of a Stupid Man*
57. LEO TOLSTOY · *How Much Land Does A Man Need?*
58. GIORGIO VASARI · *Leonardo da Vinci*
59. OSCAR WILDE · *Lord Arthur Savile's Crime*
60. SHEN FU · *The Old Man of the Moon*
61. AESOP · *The Dolphins, the Whales and the Gudgeon*
62. MATSUO BASHŌ · *Lips too Chilled*
63. EMILY BRONTË · *The Night is Darkening Round Me*
64. JOSEPH CONRAD · *To-morrow*
65. RICHARD HAKLUYT · *The Voyage of Sir Francis Drake Around the Whole Globe*
66. KATE CHOPIN · *A Pair of Silk Stockings*
67. CHARLES DARWIN · *It was snowing butterflies*
68. BROTHERS GRIMM · *The Robber Bridegroom*
69. CATULLUS · *I Hate and I Love*
70. HOMER · *Circe and the Cyclops*
71. D. H. LAWRENCE · *Il Duro*
72. KATHERINE MANSFIELD · *Miss Brill*
73. OVID · *The Fall of Icarus*
74. SAPPHO · *Come Close*
75. IVAN TURGENEV · *Kasyan from the Beautiful Lands*
76. VIRGIL · *O Cruel Alexis*
77. H. G. WELLS · *A Slip under the Microscope*
78. HERODOTUS · *The Madness of Cambyses*
79. *Speaking of Siva*
80. *The Dhammapada*

'But I, while vineyards ring with the cicadas' scream, Retrace your steps, alone, beneath the burning sun.'

PUBLIUS VERGILIUS MARO
Born 70 BCE, Mantua, Italy
Died 19 BCE, Brindisi, Italy

This selection is taken from Guy Lee's translation of *The Eclogues*,
first published in 1980, and Kimberly Johnson's translation of
The Georgics, first published in 2009.

VIRGIL IN PENGUIN CLASSICS
The Aeneid
The Eclogues
The Georgics

VIRGIL

O Cruel Alexis

Translated by
Guy Lee and Kimberly Johnson

PENGUIN BOOKS

PENGUIN CLASSICS

UK | USA | Canada | Ireland | Australia
India | New Zealand | South Africa

Penguin Books is part of the Penguin Random House group of companies
whose addresses can be found at global.penguinrandomhouse.com.

This selection published in Penguin Classics 2015

008

Translation copyright © Guy Lee, 1980, 1984
Translation copyright © Kimberly Johnson, 2009

Set in 9/12.4 pt Baskerville 10 Pro
Typeset by Jouve (UK), Milton Keynes
Printed and bound in Great Britain by Clays Ltd, Elcograf S.p.A.

A CIP catalogue record for this book is available from the British Library

ISBN: 978-0-141-39873-0

www.greenpenguin.co.uk

Penguin Random House is committed to a
sustainable future for our business, our readers
and our planet. This book is made from Forest
Stewardship Council® certified paper.

Contents

The Eclogues   1

The Georgics: Book Four   29

Eclogue I

MELIBOEUS   TITYRUS

M. Tityrus, lying back beneath wide beechen cover,
  You meditate the woodland Muse on slender oat;
  We leave the boundaries and sweet ploughlands of
      home.
  We flee our homeland; you, Tityrus, cool in shade,
  Are teaching woods to echo *Lovely Amaryllis.*
T. Oh, Melibóeus, a god has made this leisure ours.
  Yes, he will always be a god for me; his altar
  A tender ram-lamb from our folds will often stain.
  He has allowed, as you can see, my cows to range
  And me to play what tune I please on the wild reed.
M. I am not envious, more amazed: the countryside's
  All in such turmoil. Sick myself, look, Tityrus,
  I drive goats forward; this one I can hardly lead.
  For here in the hazel thicket just now dropping twins,
  Ah, the flock's hope, on naked flint, she abandoned
      them.
  I keep remembering how the oak-trees touched of
      heaven,
  If we had been right-minded, foretold this evil time.
  But give us that god of yours: who is he, Tityrus?
T. The city men call Rome I reckoned, Melibóeus,
  Fool that I was, like this of ours, to which we
      shepherds

      Are often wont to drive the weanlings of the ewes.
      So puppies are like dogs, I knew, so kids are like
      Their mother goats, so I'd compare big things to small.
      But she has raised her head among the other cities
      High as a cypress-tree above the guelder-rose.

M. And what was your great reason, then, for seeing Rome?

T. Liberty, which, though late, looked kindly on the indolent,
    After my beard fell whiter to the barber's trim,
    Looked kindly, though, and after a long while arrived,
    After Amaryllis had us and Galatéa left.
    For (yes, I will confess) while Galatea held me,
    There was no hope of liberty nor thought of thrift.
    Though many a sacrificial victim left my pens,
    And much cream cheese was pressed for the ungrateful city,
    My right hand never came back home heavy with bronze.

M. I wondered, Amaryllis, why you wept and called
    To the gods – for whom you left fruit hanging on the tree;
    Tityrus was away. The very pines, Tityrus,
    The very springs, these very orchards called to you.

T. What could I do? For nowhere else could I escape
    From slavery or meet divinities so present.
    It was here I saw him, Meliboeus, the young man
    For whom twice six days every year our altar smokes.

Eclogue I

    It was here to my petition he first gave reply:
    'Graze cattle as before, my children, and yoke bulls.'
M. Lucky old man, the land then will remain your own,
    And large enough for you, although bare rock and bog
    With muddy rushes covers all the pasturage:
    No unaccustomed feed will try your breeding ewes,
    And no infection harm them from a neighbour's flock.
    Lucky old man, among familiar rivers here
    And sacred springs you'll angle for the cooling shade;
    The hedge this side, along your neighbour's boundary,
    Its willow flowers as ever feeding Hybla bees,
    Will often whisper you persuasively to sleep;
    The pruner under that high bluff will sing to the breeze,
    Nor yet meanwhile will cooing pigeons, your own brood,
    Nor turtledove be slow to moan from the airy elm.
T. Then sooner will light-footed stags feed in the sky
    And ocean tides leave fishes naked on the shore,
    Sooner in exile, wandering through each other's land,
    Will Parthian drink the Arar, or Germany the Tigris,
    Than from our memory will his face ever fade.
M. But *we* must leave here, some for thirsty Africa,
    Others for Scythia and Oäxes' chalky flood
    And the Britanni quite cut off from the whole world.
    Look, shall I ever, seeing after a long while
    My fathers' bounds and my poor cabin's turf-heaped roof,

Virgil

    Hereafter marvel at my kingdom – a few corn-ears?
    Some godless veteran will own this fallow tilth,
    These cornfields a barbarian. Look where strife
        has led
    Rome's wretched citizens: we have sown fields for
        these!
    Graft pear-trees, Meliboeus, now, set vines in rows.
    Go, little she-goats, go, once happy flock of mine.
    Not I hereafter, stretched full length in some green
        cave,
    Shall watch you far off hanging on a thorny crag;
    I'll sing no songs; not in my keeping, little goats,
    You'll crop the flowering lucerne and bitter willow.

T. However, for tonight you could rest here with me
    Upon green leafage: I can offer you ripe fruit
    And mealy chestnuts and abundance of milk cheese.
    Far off the roof-tops of the farms already smoke
    And down from the high mountains taller
        shadows fall.

Eclogue II

For beautiful Alexis, the master's favourite,
Shepherd Córydon burned, and knew he had no hope.
Only, he used to walk each day among the dense
Shady-topped beeches. There, alone, in empty longing,
He hurled this artless monologue at hills and woods:
    'O cruel Alexis, have you no time for my tunes?
No pity for us? You'll be the death of me at last.
Now, even the cattle cast about for cool and shade,
Now even green lizards hide among the hawthorn brakes,
And Thestylis, for reapers faint from the fierce heat,
Is crushing pungent pot-herbs, garlic and wild thyme.
But I, while vineyards ring with the cicadas' scream,
Retrace your steps, alone, beneath the burning sun.
Had I not better bide the wrath of Amaryllis,
Her high-and-mighty moods? Better endure Menalcas,
However black he were and you however blond?
O lovely boy, don't trust complexion overmuch:
White privet flowers fall, black bilberries are picked.
You scorn me, Alexis, never asking who I am,
How rich in flocks, how affluent in snowy milk.
My thousand ewe-lambs range the hills of Sicily;
Come frost, come summer, never do I lack fresh milk.
I play the tunes Amphíon used, when he called cattle,
Dircéan Amphion on Actéan Aracýnthus.
I'm not that ugly: on the beach I saw myself
Lately, when sea stood wind-becalmed. With you as judge
I'd not be scared of Daphnis, if mirrors tell the truth.

Virgil

O if you'd only fancy life with me in country
Squalor, in a humble hut, and shooting fallow deer,
And shepherding a flock of kids with green hibiscus!
Piping beside me in the woods you'll mimic Pan
(Pan pioneered the fixing fast of several reeds
With bees-wax; sheep are in Pan's care, head-shepherds
    too);
You'd not be sorry when the reed callused your lip:
What pains Amyntas took to master this same art!
I have a pipe composed of seven unequal stems
Of hemlock, which Damoetas gave me when he died,
A while ago, and said, "Now she owns you, the second,"
Damoetas said; Amyntas envied me, the fool.
Two chamois kids, besides, I found in a sheer coomb.
Their hides are dappled even now with white; they drain
One ewe's dugs each a day; I'm keeping them for you,
Though Thestylis has long desired to take them from me;
She'll do it too, since you regard our gifts as crude.
Come here, O lovely boy: for you the Nymphs bring lilies,
Look, in baskets full; for you the Naiad fair,
Plucking pale violets and poppy heads, combines
Narcissus with them, and the flower of fragrant dill;
Then, weaving marjoram in, and other pleasant herbs,
Colours soft bilberries with yellow marigold.
Myself, I'll pick the grey-white apples with tender down,
And chestnuts, which my Amaryllis used to love;
I'll add the waxy plum (this fruit too shall be honoured),
And I'll pluck you, O laurels, and you, neighbour myrtle,
For so arranged you mingle pleasant fragrances.
Corydon, you're a yokel; Alexis scorns your gifts,

Nor could you beat Iollas in a giving-match.
Alas, what have I done, poor lunatic, unleashing
Auster on flower-beds and wild boar on clear springs!
Ah, you are mad to leave me. Gods have dwelt in woods,
Dardanian Paris too. Pallas can keep her cities,
But let the woods beyond all else please you and me.
Grim lions pursue the wolf, wolves in their turn the goat,
Mischievous goats pursue the flowering lucerne,
And Corydon you, Alexis – each at pleasure's pull.
Look, oxen now bring home their yoke-suspended ploughs,
And the sun, going down, doubles growing shadows;
But I burn in love's fire: can one set bounds to love?
Ah, Corydon, Corydon, what madness mastered you!
You've left a vine half-pruned upon a leafy elm:
Why not at least prepare to weave of osiers
And supple rushes something practical you need?
If this Alexis sneers at you, you'll find another.'

Eclogue IV

Sicilian Muses, grant me a slightly grander song.
Not all delight in trees and lowly tamarisks;
Let woods, if woods we sing, be worthy of a consul.
    Now the last age of Cumae's prophecy has come;
The great succession of centuries is born afresh.
Now too returns the Virgin; Saturn's rule returns;
A new begetting now descends from heaven's height.
O chaste Lucina, look with blessing on the boy
Whose birth will end the iron race at last and raise
A golden through the world: now your Apollo rules.
And, Pollio, this glory enters time with you;
Your consulship begins the march of the great months;
With you to guide, if traces of our sin remain,
They, nullified, will free the lands from lasting fear.
He will receive the life divine, and see the gods
Mingling with heroes, and himself be seen of them,
And rule a world made peaceful by his father's virtues.
    But first, as little gifts for you, child, Earth untilled
Will pour the straying ivy rife, and baccaris,
And colocasia mixing with acanthus' smile.
She-goats unshepherded will bring home udders plumped
With milk, and cattle will not fear the lion's might.
Your very cradle will pour forth caressing flowers.
The snake will perish, and the treacherous poison-herb
Perish; Assyrian spikenard commonly will grow.
And then, so soon as you can read of heroes' praise

Eclogue IV

And of your father's deeds, and know what manhood
    means,
Soft spikes of grain will gradually gild the fields,
And reddening grapes will hang in clusters on wild brier,
And dewy honey sweat from tough Italian oaks.
Traces, though few, will linger yet of the old deceit,
Commanding men to tempt Thetis with ships, to encircle
Towns with walls, to inflict deep furrows on the Earth.
There'll be a second Tiphys then, a second Argo
To carry chosen heroes; there'll even be second wars,
And once more great Achilles will be sent to Troy.
Later, when strength of years has made a man of you,
The carrier too will quit the sea, no naval pines
Barter their goods, but every land bear everything.
The soil will suffer hoes no more, nor vines the hook.
The sturdy ploughman too will now unyoke his team,
And wool unlearn the lies of variable dye,
But in the fields the ram himself will change his fleece,
Now to sweet-blushing murex, now to saffron yellow,
And natural vermilion clothe the grazing lambs.
  'Speed on those centuries', said the Parcae to their
    spindles,
Concordant with the steadfast nod of Destiny.
O enter (for the time approaches) your great glory,
Dear scion of gods, great aftergrowth of Jupiter!
Look at the cosmos trembling in its massive round,
Lands and the expanse of ocean and the sky profound;
Look how they all are full of joy at the age to come!
O then for me may long life's latest part remain
And spirit great enough to celebrate your deeds!

Virgil

Linus will not defeat me in song, nor Thracian Orpheûs,
Though one should have his father's aid and one his
    mother's,
Orpheus Callíopë and Linus fair Apollo.
If Pan too challenged me, with Arcady as judge,
Pan too, with Arcady as judge, would own defeat.
    Begin, small boy, to know your mother with a smile
(Ten lunar months have brought your mother long
    discomfort)
Begin, small boy: him who for parent have not smiled
No god invites to table nor goddess to bed.

Eclogue V

MENALCAS   MOPSUS

Me. Why don't we, Mopsus, meeting like this, good men both,
    You to blow the light reeds, I to versify,
    Sit down together here where hazels mix with elms?
Mo. You're senior, Menalcas; I owe you deference,
    Whether we go where fitful Zephyrs make uncertain
    Shade, or into the cave instead. See how the cave
    Is dappled by a woodland vine's rare grape-clusters.
Me. Only Amyntas in our hills competes with you.
Mo. What? He might just as well compete to outplay Phoebus.
Me. Then, Mopsus, you start first – with Phyllis' flames perhaps
    Or Alcon's praises or a flyting against Codrus.
    You start, and Tityrus will watch the grazing kids.
Mo. No, I'll try out the song I wrote down recently
    On green beech bark, noting the tune between the lines:
    Then you can tell Amyntas to compete with me.
Me. As surely as tough willow yields to the pale olive,
    Or humble red valerian to the crimson rose,
    So does Amyntas in our judgement yield to you.
    But no more talk, lad: we have come into the cave.
Mo. The Nymphs for Daphnis, cut off by a cruel death,

Virgil

    Shed tears (you streams and hazels witness for the
        Nymphs),
    When, clasping her own son's poor body in her arms,
    A mother called both gods and stars alike cruel.
    In those days there were none who drove their
        pastured cattle
    To the cool rivers, Daphnis; no four-footed beast
    Would either lap the stream or touch a blade of grass.
    The wild hills, Daphnis, and the forests even tell
    How Punic lions roared in grief at your destruction.
    Daphnis ordained to yoke Armenian tigresses
    To chariots, Daphnis to lead on the Bacchic rout
    And twine tough javelins with gentle foliage.
    As vines are glorious for trees, as grapes for vines,
    As bulls for herds, and standing crops for fertile
        fields,
    You are all glory to your folk. But since fate took you,
    Apollo's self and Pales' self have left the land.
    From furrows we have often trusted with large barleys
    Are born unlucky darnel and the barren oat.
    For the soft violet, for radiant narcissus,
    Thistles spring up and paliurus with sharpened
        spines.
    Scatter the ground with petals, cast shade on the
        springs,
    Shepherds, (that such be done for him is Daphnis'
        will),
    And make a mound and add above the mound a song:
    Daphnis am I in woodland, known hence far as the stars,
    Herd of a handsome flock, myself the handsomer.

Eclogue V

Me. For us your song, inspired poet, is like sleep
    On meadow grass for the fatigued, or in the heat
    Quenching one's thirst from a leaping stream of sweet water.
    You equal both your master's piping and his voice.
    Lucky lad! From now on you'll be second to him.
    Yet we, no matter how, will in return recite
    This thing of ours, and praise your Daphnis to the stars –
    Yes, to the stars raise Daphnis, for Daphnis loved us too.
Mo. What greater service could you render us than that?
    The lad himself deserved singing, and Stimichon
    Some time ago spoke highly of your song to us.
Me. Daphnis in white admires Olympus' strange threshold,
    And sees the planets and the clouds beneath his feet.
    Therefore keen pleasure grips forest and countryside,
    Pan also, and the shepherds, and the Dryad maids.
    The wolf intends no ambush to the flock, the nets
    No trickery to deer: Daphnis the good loves peace.
    For gladness even the unshorn mountains fling their voices
    Toward the stars; now even the orchards, even the rocks
    Echo the song: 'A god, a god is he, Menalcas!'
    O bless your folk and prosper them! Here are four altars:
    Look, Daphnis, two for you and two high ones for Phoebus.
    Two goblets each, frothing with fresh milk, every year

>   And two large bowls of olive oil I'll set for you;
>   And best of all, gladdening the feast with Bacchus' store
>   (In winter, by the hearth; at harvest, in the shade),
>   I'll pour Ariusian wine, fresh nectar, from big stoups.
>   Damoetas and the Lyctian Aegon will sing for me;
>   Alphesiboeus imitate the Satyrs' dance.
>   These offerings ever shall be yours, both when we pay
>   The Nymphs our solemn vows and when we purge the fields.
>   So long as fish love rivers, wild boar mountain heights,
>   So long as bees eat thyme, and the cicada dew,
>   Always your honour, name and praises will endure.
>   As farmers every year to Bacchus and to Ceres,
>   So they will vow to you; you too will claim their vows.
> *Mo.* What can I give you, what return make for such song?
>   For neither does the whistling of Auster coming
>   Sound so pleasant to me, nor beaches beaten by waves,
>   Nor rivers rushing down the valleys among rocks.
> *Me.* We shall present you first with this frail hemlock pipe.
>   This taught us 'Corydon burned for beautiful Alexis';
>   This also taught us 'Whose flock? Meliboeus his?'
> *Mo.* You take the crook, then, which Antígenes failed to get
>   For all his asking (lovable as then he was),
>   A handsome thing, with matching knobs and brass,
>   Menalcas.

Eclogue VI

With Syracusan verses our Thaléa first
Thought fit to play, nor blushed to live among the woods.
When I was singing kings and battles, Cynthius pulled
My ear in admonition: 'A shepherd, Tityrus,
Should feed his flock fat, but recite a thin-spun song.'
I now (for you'll have many eager to recite
Your praises, Varus, and compose unhappy wars)
Will meditate the rustic Muse on slender reed.
I sing to order. Yet if any read this too,
If any love-beguiled, Varus, our tamarisks
Will sing of you, each grove of you, nor any page
Please Phoebus more than that headed by Varus' name.
    Proceed, Piéridës. Young Chromis and Mnasyllos
Once saw Silenus lying in a cave asleep,
His veins, as ever, swollen with yesterday's Iacchus;
Only, the garlands lay apart, fallen from his head,
And from its well-worn handle a heavy tankard hung.
Attacking (for the old man had often cheated both
With hope of song) they bind him with his own garlands.
Aeglë joins in, arriving as they grow alarmed,
Aeglë of Naiads loveliest, and, now he's looking,
With blood-red mulberries paints his temples and his brow.
The trick amuses him, but 'Why the bonds?' he asks;
'Release me, lads; it is enough to have shown your power.
Now hear the song you want; your payment shall be song,
Hers of another kind.' And with that he begins.
Then truly you could see Fauns and wild animals

Virgil

Playing in rhythm, then stubborn oaks rocking their
  crowns.
Not so much joy does Phoebus bring Parnassus' crag,
Nor Orpheûs so astonish Rhódopë and Ísmarus.

  For he was singing how through a great emptiness
The seeds of earth and breath and sea and liquid fire
Were forced together; how from these first things all else,
All, and the cosmos' tender globe grew of itself;
Then land began to harden and in the deep shut off
Nereûs and gradually assume the shapes of things;
And now the dawn of the new sun amazes earth,
And showers fall from clouds moved higher overhead,
When first the forest trees begin to rise, and when
Rare creatures wander over unfamiliar hills.
Here he recounts the stones by Pyrrha thrown, Saturnian
Kingship, Caucasian eagles and Prometheus' theft;
Adds at what fountain mariners for Hylas lost
Shouted till all the shore re-echoed *Hylas, Hylas*;
And (fortunate if herds of kine had never been)
Consoles Pasíphaë for love of a white steer.
Unlucky maiden, ah, what madness mastered you!
The Proetides with mimic lowing filled the fields,
But yet not one pursued so base an intercourse
With beasts, although she feared the plough's yoke for her
  neck
And many a time would feel on her smooth brow for horns.
Unlucky maiden, ah, you wander now on mountains,
But he, with snow-white flank pressing soft hyacinth,
Beneath black ilex ruminates the sallow grass,

Eclogue VI

Or tracks some female in a great herd. 'Close, you Nymphs,
Dictéan Nymphs, now close the clearings in the woods.
Somewhere, perhaps, the wandering hoof-prints of a bull
Will find their own way to our eyes; possibly he,
Attracted by green grass, or following the herd,
Is led on by some cow to Gortyn's cattle-sheds.'
Then sings he the maid who admired Hesperidéan apples;
Then with the moss of bitter bark surrounds and lifts
The Phaëthóntiads from earth as alders tall;
Then sings of Gallus wandering by Permessus' stream,
How one of the Sisters led him to Aonia's mountains,
And how all Phoebus' choir stood up to greet a man;
How Linus there, the shepherd of inspired song,
His locks adorned with flowers and bitter celery,
Told him: 'The Muses give you this reed pipe (there,
    take it)
Which once they gave the old Ascréan, whose melody
Could draw the stubborn rowans down the mountainside.
Tell you with this the origin of Grynia's grove,
Lest any sacred wood be more Apollo's pride.'
    Why should I speak of Nisus' Scylla, who (so runs
The rumour), white groin girdled round with barking
    monsters,
Tossed the Dulichian ships and in her deep whirlpool
With sea-hounds, ah, would savage frightened mariners?
Or how he told the tale of Tereûs' limbs transformed,
What feast, what present Philomel prepared for him,
By what route sought the wilderness, and on what wings
Before that swooped unhappy over her own roof?

Virgil

    All, that from Phoebus' meditation, in old days, blest
    Eurotas heard and bade his laurels memorize,
    He sings (the smitten valleys tell it to the stars),
    Till Vesper came to view in a reluctant sky
    And bade the flock be folded and their number told.

Eclogue VII

MELIBOEUS

M. Daphnis was seated once beneath a rustling ilex,
And Corydon and Thyrsis had combined their flocks,
Corydon she-goats milk-distended, Thyrsis ewes,
Both in the flower of their ages, Arcadians both,
Well-paired at singing and prepared to cap a verse.
Here, while I shielded tender myrtles from the cold,
My herd's old man, the he-goat, had wandered off; and then
I notice Daphnis. 'Quick,' he says, at sight of me,
'Come here, Meliboeus, (your he-goat and the kids are safe)
And rest in shade, if you can take time off. The steers
Will find their own way through the meadows here to drink.
Here Mincius fringes his green banks with tender reeds,
And swarms of bees are humming from the sacred oak.'
So what was I to do? I had no Phyllis, no
Alcippë at home to pen the lambs I'd lately weaned,
And a great match was promised – Corydon v. Thyrsis;
However, I postponed my business for their play.
They therefore both began competing in alternate
Verses; the Muses wished alternatives recalled.

Virgil

> These Corydon delivered, Thyrsis those, in turn.

C. Nymphs, our belov'd, Libethrians, either grant me song
Such as you grant my Codrus (he is second best
At verse to Phoebus), or, if we can't all succeed,
Here on the sacred pine shall hang a tuneful pipe.

T. Shepherds, with ivy decorate the rising poet,
Arcadians, so that Codrus burst his guts with envy;
Or, if he praise beyond what pleases, bind my brow
With baccar, lest an ill tongue harm the bard to be.

C. For you this bristling boar's head, Delia, from little
Mico, and the branching antlers of a long-lived stag.
If this good luck be lasting, you shall stand full-length
In smoothest marble, calves enlaced in scarlet boots.

T. A bowl of milk each year, Priapus, and these cakes
Are all you need expect; you guard a poor man's patch.
Our present means have made you marble; none the less,
If lambing-time recruit the flock, you shall be gold.

C. Nerínë Galatéa, sweeter than Hyblan thyme,
Whiter to me than swans, more shapely than pale ivy,
Soon as the bulls return from pasture to the byre,
If you have any care for your Corydon, come to him.

T. Nay, you can think me sourer than Sardinia's herb,
Rougher than broom, cheaper than seaweed tossed ashore,
If this day's light's not longer than twelve months to me.

Eclogue VII

    Go home from pasture, shame upon you, bull-
        calves, go.

C.   You mossy springs, and meadow-grass softer than
       sleep,
    And that arbutus green whose rare shade covers you,
    Fend off the solstice from the flock: now summer
       comes
    Scorching; now buds are bursting on the tough
       vine-branch.

T. Here's hearth and pitch-pine billets, here's a roaring
       fire
    Ever alight, and doorposts black with ingrained soot.
    We mind the freezing cold of Boreas here no more
    Than the wolf numbers, or torrential streams their
       banks.

C.   Still are the junipers, and the prickly Spanish
       chestnuts;
    Beneath each tree her fruit is lying strewn around;
    Now everything is laughing: but if fair Alexis
    Should leave these hills, you'd even see the streams
       run dry.

T. Parched fields and thirsty grass, dying of tainted air;
    Liber begrudges tendrilled shade to these hillsides:
    But when our Phyllis comes, each coppice will be
       green,
    And Jove descend abundantly in merry rain.

C.   Dearest the poplar to Alcídes, vines to Bacchus,
    Myrtle to lovely Venus, to Phoebus his own bay.
    Phyllis loves hazels, and, while those are Phyllis' love,
    Hazels will never lose to myrtle, or Phoebus' bay.

Virgil

T. Fairest the ash in forest, in pleasure-gardens pine,
    Poplars by streams, and on high mountains silver fir:
    But visit me more often, lovely Lycidas,
    And forest ash and garden pine will honour you.
M. This I remember, and how Thyrsis lost the match.
    For us, from that day, Corydon's been Corydon.

Eclogue IX

LYCIDAS   MOERIS

L. Where do feet lead you, Moeris? Like the road, to
     town?
M. Oh, Lycidas, we've lived to reach this – that a stranger
     (Something we never feared) should seize our little
         farm
     And say: 'This property is mine; old tenants, out!'
     Defeated now, sad that the world is Fortune's wheel,
     We take these kids (and may they bring bad luck)
         to him.
L. Surely I'd heard that everything, from where the hills
     Begin to drop down, sloping gently from the ridge,
     Right to the water and the old beeches' broken crowns –
     That all this your Menalcas salvaged with his songs?
M. You had, and so the rumour ran; but songs of ours
     Avail among the War-God's weapons, Lycidas,
     As much as Chaonian doves, they say, when the eagle
         comes.
     Had not a raven on the left from the hollow ilex
     Warned me at all costs to cut short these new disputes,
     Your Moeris here would now be dead – Menalcas too.
L. Alas, who'd dream of such a crime? Alas, Menalcas,
     Your solace and yourself so nearly snatched from us!
     Then, who would sing *The Nymphs*? And who 'scatter
         the ground

Virgil

    With flowering herbs' or 'cast green shadows on the springs'?
    Or there's the song I lately overheard from you,
    The day you made your way to our darling Amaryllis:
    'Tityrus, till I come (the way's short), feed the goats,
    And drive them fed to water, Tityrus, and take care
    While driving not to cross the he-goat – that one butts.'

M. Yes, and the song (still incomplete) he made for Varus:
    'Varus, your name, if only Mantua be spared
    (Ah, Mantua, too near, alas, to poor Cremona!),
    Shall be uplifted to the stars by singing swans.'

L. As you would wish your swarms to shun Cyrnéan yews,
    And clover-feed to swell the udders of your cows,
    Begin, if you've anything. The Pierians have made
    Me too a poet; I too have my songs; the shepherds
    Even call me bard, but I do not believe them.
    As yet I cannot rival Varius or Cinna,
    But gabble like a gander among articulate swans.

M. I mean to, Lycidas; I'm thinking it out now,
    Jogging my memory, for it's a famous song.
    'Come here, O Galatéa. What sport is there in water?
    Here it is radiant springtime; here by the riverside
    Earth pours forth the pied flowers; here the white poplar leans
    Over a cave, and limber vines weave tents of shade.
    Come here, and leave the crazy waves to beat the beach.'

Eclogue IX

L. What of that song I heard you sing one cloudless night
   Alone? I know the tune, if I could find the words:
   'Daphnis, why watch the ancient risings of the Signs?
   See where the star of Dionéan Caesar passes,
   The star when cornfields should rejoice in crops and
       when
   Grape-clusters on the sunny slopes should colour up.
   Graft pear-trees, Daphnis. Grandchildren will pick
       your fruit.'

M. The years take all, one's wits included. I remember
   Often in boyhood singing the long suns asleep.
   So many songs I've now forgotten; even his voice
   Is failing Moeris now: the wolves saw Moeris first.
   Menalcas, though, will sing them for you often enough.

L. You try our love too long with these apologies.
   And now the level sea's all hushed for you, and look
   How all the airs of the wind's murmuring have
       dropped.
   Here too we're halfway on our journey, for Bianor's
   Monument can just be seen. Here, where the farmers
   Strip the thick-grown leaves, here, Moeris, let us sing.
   Set down the kids here. We shall reach town just the
       same.
   Or, if afraid lest night, before then, turn to rain,
   We're free to walk on singing (the road will seem less
       hard).
   I'll take this load of yours, so we can walk and sing.

M. No more of that, lad, and let's do what's urgent now;
   Then, when himself has come, the better we'll sing
   songs.

Eclogue X

Permit me, Arethusa, this last desperate task.
For Gallus mine (but may Lycóris read it too)
A brief song must be told; who'd deny Gallus song?
So, when you slide along below Sicanian waves,
May bitter Doris never taint you with her brine.
Begin then: let us tell of Gallus' troubled love,
While snub-nosed she-goats nibble at the tender shoots.
Not to the deaf we sing; the forests answer all.
    What woodlands or what rides detained you, Naiad
        maids,
When Gallus pined away of an unworthy love?
For not the summits of Parnassus, for not Pindus'
Delayed your presence, nor Aonian Aganippë.
The laurels even, even the tamarisks wept for him
Lying beneath a lonely cliff; even Maenalus'
Pine-forests wept for him, and cold Lycaeus' rocks.
And the sheep stand around; they think no shame of us,
Nor be you shamed, inspired poet, by the flock:
Lovely Adonis too fed sheep beside a stream.
The shepherd also came, the heavy swineherds came,
Menalcas came, wet through from steeping winter mast.
All ask him 'Whence that love of yours?' Apollo came;
'Gallus, you're mad!' he cried. 'Lycoris your beloved
Pursues another man through snows and horrid camps.'
Silvanus also came, with rustic honour crowned,
Tossing tall lilies on his head and fennel flowers.
Pan came, Arcadia's god, whom we ourselves have seen

Eclogue X

Ruddled with elderberry blood and cinnabar.
'When will it end?' he said. 'Love cares not for such things;
You'll never glut cruel Love with tears, nor grass with
    streams,
Nor worker-bees with clover, nor she-goats with leaves.'
But sadly he replied: 'Arcadians, will you sing, though,
Of these things to your hills? You are supreme in song,
Arcadians. O how softly then my bones would rest,
If only your reed pipe hereafter told my love!
And how I wish that I'd been one of you, and either
Guarded your flock or harvested the ripened grapes!
For surely, were I mad on Phyllis or Amyntas
Or anyone (what if Amyntas is dark-skinned?
Dark too are violets, and bilberries are dark),
They'd lie with me among willows, under a limber vine;
Phyllis would gather garlands for me, Amyntas sing.
Here, Lycoris, are cool fountains, here soft fields,
Here woodland, here with you I'd be Time's casualty.
But now, demented love detains me under arms
Of callous Mars, amid weapons and opposing foes.
You, far from fatherland, (could I but disbelieve it!)
Gaze – ah, callous – on Alpine snows and frozen Rhine,
Alone, without me. Ah, may the frosts not injure *you*!
Ah, may the rough ice never cut *your* tender feet!
I'll go and tune to the Sicilian shepherd's oat
The songs I put together in Chalcidic verse.
The choice is made – to suffer in the woods among
The wild beasts' dens, and carve my love into the bark
Of tender trees: as they grow, so my love will grow.
But meanwhile with the Nymphs I'll range on Maenala

Or hunt the savage boar. No frosts will hinder me
From drawing coverts on Parthenium with hounds.
Already I see myself explore the sounding rocks
And groves, already long to shoot Cydonian darts
From Parthian horn – as if this remedied our madness,
Or that god learnt from human hardship to grow mild!
Now, once again, we take no joy in Hamadryads,
Nor even in song – again wish even the woods away.
No alteration can our labours make in him,
Not if we drank of Hebrus in the middle frosts
Of watery winter and endured Sithonian snows,
Nor if, when dying bark shrivels on the lofty elm,
Beneath the Crab we herded Ethiopian sheep.
Love conquers all: we also must submit to Love.'

    To have sung of these things, goddesses, while he sat and wove
A frail of slim hibiscus, will suffice your poet.
Pierians, you will make them very great, for Gallus –
Gallus, whose love so grows upon me hour by hour
As the green alder pushes upward in new spring.
Let us arise: for singers heavy is the shade,
Heavy the shade of juniper; and shade harms fruit.
Go, little she-goats, Hesper comes, go home replete.

The Georgics: Book Four

Onward. The celestial gifts of honey from the sky
I will sound. Attend this part as well, O Maecenas.
The wondrous spectacle of a tiny world –
bold-hearted princes, a whole nation's customs
and passions and citizens and wars will I describe for you.
In miniature my labour, but no miniature glory, if adverse
divinities allow it, if Apollo hears my prayer.

First, a settled site for your bees must be sought,
where no winds may access (for winds prevent them
bringing home their food), nor sheep or tussling kids
romp upon the flowers, nor rambling heifer in the
    meadows
to shake off the dew and erode the plantlife.
Keep gaudy lizards with their scaly backs
from the rich cells, and the bee-eater and other birds,
and Procne, breast stained with bloody hands.
For these devastate completely, far and wide, snatching
in their mouths bees on the wing, sweet snacks for their
    rough nestlings.
But let pure springs and pools greening with moss
be near, and a trickling stream slipping through the grass,
and let a palm or spreading oleaster overshade the
    vestibule,
so that when new kings lead out the first swarms
in dear spring and the youth frolic free of the honeycomb,
a nearby bank may woo them to dodge the heat

and a wayside tree may charm with its leafy welcome.
In mid-water, whether it tranquil pools or flows along,
pile willows and enormous rocks across
that upon bridges aplenty they may rest and open
wings to the summer sun, if perforce the eastwind
has sprinkled upon the slowpokes, or dunked them
      headfirst into the deep.
Hereabout let flourish green cassia and far-fragrant
thyme and a garland of savory with its heady exhalations,
and let violet beds drink from the gurgling spring.
As for the hives: whether you have one stitched
from hollow bark or woven of limber wicker
let it have narrow entrances, for winter with its chill
congeals honey, and heat streams it away runny.
Either offence against the bees must be feared the same:
not for nothing do they striving smear with wax
fine cracks in their rooms, and with flower-paste fill up
seams, and store up glue collected for this very purpose,
stickier than birdlime or the pitch of Phrygian Ida.
Often, if rumour's true, in dug-out burrows
underground they snug their home, or deep within
      pumice-pores
are found, or in the cavity of a rotting tree.
Either way, do slick with smooth mud their crazed chambers,
cosying them up, and toss a few leaves on top.
Neither allow a yew too near the hive, nor fire
the redding crab at your hearth, nor trust a sunken bog
or where the stench of swamp is strong, or where hollow
the struck rocks ring and the voice's echo ricochets back.

*

The Georgics: Book Four

When in rout the golden sun has driven winter
beneath the earth and unveiled with summer light the sky,
O then they wing the glades and forests,
harvest purple blooms and lightly sip
the river's surface. For this, cheered with an unfamiliar glee,
they nestle nests and larvae, for this they skilful mould
fresh wax and fashion sticky honey.
Thus when you look up at their legion just unloosed
from the hive, up to the starred sky floating through liquid
    summer air,
and wonder at their cloud dark on the trailing wind,
take note: for sweet waters and sheltering leaves
they always beeline. Here scatter my prescribed delicacies:
rubbed balm, and tendrils of lowly waxflower,
and thrill up a tinkling sound, shaking Mother Cybele's
    cymbals all around.
On their own they'll settle upon the scented places, on
    their own
they'll burrow themselves by instinct in inmost chambers.

But if for battle they've burst forth – for often
between two kings strife with great riot swoops:
at once the rancour of the throng, the hearts churning
for war you can sense from afar. For a martial reveille
of raucous brass rattles the laggards, and a buzz
is heard like the broken blast of bugles.
Then all hopped-up they muster themselves, flash wings,
whet stingers with jaws and cinch up muscles,
and round the king right up to his battle-post thronged
they swarm and with great ruckus call out the foe.

Virgil

Thus when they find a rainless spring day and open field
they charge from their coverts: *Clash!* Noise through
highest air, massed and bunched into a great ball
then headlong they crash! Not thicker hail from vast heaven
nor acorns hail so from the shaken oak.
The princes themselves among the battle lines with striking wings:
great hearts thump inside their tiny breasts,
ever so steadfast not to surrender till severe the victor
drives this side or that to turn tail in flight.
These tremors of passion, these battles so dire
with a little dust tossed are quelled and come to rest.

But when from the front you have recalled both commanders,
he who looks shabbier, lest he be a waste and a burden,
consign to extinction: let the better reign singly in his court.
He will glow with spots shagged in gold.
For two kinds there are: the nobler, distinguished in mien
and bright in burnished scales, the other unkempt
in his sloth, inglorious, dragging his fat paunch.
Just as the mould of kings is twofold, so too the commoners' bodies.
Some look rough and slovenly, as when out of thick dust
comes a wayfarer, parched, and spits dirt from his thirsty
mouth. Others gleam and fulgent flash
blazing in bodies trimmed with uniform flecks of gold:
this is the better breed, from these at the sky's appointed season

you will strain sweeter honey – so sweet, but more clear,
and fit to mellow the harsh taste of wine.

But when aimless flits the swarm, and gads about the sky,
and scorns the honeycombs, and leaves the hive to chill
you must curb their fickle spirits from these pointless antics.
It's no great task to curb them: you rip the kings' wings off –
while they cool their heels, no one will dare
take to the air or snatch up the banner from the encampment.
Let gardens breathing saffron flowers beckon,
and let the watchman against thieves and birds, guardian
Priapus of the Hellespont, protect with his willow-hook.
Let him whose care they are himself fetch thyme and pines
from mountain peaks, and plant them round about their lodge,
himself callous his hand with rugged work, himself plant
fruitful slips in the soil and water them with kind sprinklings.

Indeed, were I not fast upon the very end of my labours
furling sails, and rushing to nose my prow shoreward,
perhaps how care in tillage bedizens the lush garden
I'd sing, and the rosebeds of twice-blooming Paestum,
how the chicory exults in the brook it drinks,
and the banks green in celery, and how twining through its vines
the cucumber swells into corpulence; nor should I keep silent
on late-blooming narcissus or the stalk of supple acanthus,
pale ivies and shore-loving myrtles.

Virgil

For I remember how, beneath the towers of Tarentum's citadel
where dark Galaesus waters the golden fields,
I saw an old Corycian, who had a few acres
of godforsaken land – a patch not fertile for the plough-ox
nor fit for flocks nor favourable for the vine.
Yet here, planting well-spaced vegetables among the scrub,
white lilies and verbena, and the flimsy poppy,
in cheer he matched the wealth of kings, and late returning
home at night he loaded his table with banquets unbought.
First in spring to pluck roses, first in fall to pick apples,
and when lowering winter was still cracking rocks
with cold, and with ice bridling the coursing stream,
he was already cutting back the soft hyacinth's old growth,
chiding tardy summer and the westwind's delay.
Therefore this man was first to luxuriate in brood-bees
and an abundant swarm, first to collect foamy honey
from the squeezed comb, his lindens and pines most lush
and as many buds as his lavish tree bedecks itself
in early bloom, so many fruits it holds in ripe autumn.
What's more, mature the elms he set in widespread rows,
hard-barked the pear trees, blackthorns already bearing sloes,
the plane tree already providing shade for carouses.
But I prevented by my too-slight space
pass silent on and leave that tale for others after me.

Now come: I will unfold what nature
Jupiter himself bestowed on bees, for which reward
following the ringing chants and clashing bronzes of the Curetes

they had fed the king of heaven deep within a Dictaean
        cave.
They alone in common rear their young, in partnership
        they hold
their city's habitations, and live out their lives under
        sovereign laws,
they alone recognize a fatherland and constant home,
and mindful of the coming winter endure summer toil
and in common store lay in their gleanings.
For some have charge of provisions, and by settled compact
busy in the fields; some within their houses' walls
lay down tears of the narcissus and sticky sap
from tree-bark as the first foundation of the hive, then
        drape up
viscous wax. Others train out the nation's hope,
the full-grown hatch; others pack in purest
honey, swelling the cells with liquid nectar.
There are those to whom guard duty at the gates falls
        by lot;
in turn they eye heaven's showers and overcast,
or receive loads from incomers, or in mustered squads
blockade the drones (that shiftless ruck) from the stalls.
The industry glows, and the fragrant honey breathes of
        thyme.
As when the Cyclopes from malleable ore
work lightning bolts, some with ox-hide bellows
suck and blow the air, others dunk the screaming bronze
in a cistern; Aetna groans beneath its anvilled charge;
they heave their arms with mighty force in alternating
rhythm, and turn the metal with pincing tongs:

Virgil

just so, if one may small compare with great,
an innate love of gain pricks on Athenian bees
each in his own capacity. The elders warden the towns,
fortify the hives and fashion daedal chambers.
Worn out, the young ones drag themselves home far into night,
legs thick with thyme. They feast on arbutes all around,
on grey-green willows, on cassia and red-flecked crocus,
on the sappy linden and dusky hyacinths.
Together their rest from labour, together their labour:
at dawn they rush out their gates, no dilly-dally; and when at last
the evening star exhorts them quit their forage
afield, then they head for their hutches, then restore their bodies.
A buzzing: they murmur around the doors and on the doorsteps.
Later, when they've tucked themselves into their chambers, hushed
is the night, well-earned sleep overtakes their tuckered limbs.
But truly, rain threatening, they don't venture far from their stalls
nor trust the sky when the eastwind advances,
but on all sides, safe beneath the city's ramparts, siphon up water
and attempt short sorties, and often take up pebbles, with which,
as a skiff unsteady on the tossing wave takes on ballast,
they balance themselves through the flimsy cloud.

*

The Georgics: Book Four

You will marvel *this* custom has found favour among bees:
they indulge not in lovemaking, nor slacken their sinews
sluggish in venery, nor birth young in travail,
but alone the females gather up their children in their mouths
from leaves and herbs delectable, unmated they provide a king
and tiny citizens, and remodel their courts and waxy realms.
Often too, wandering among jagged flint they scrape
their wings, and freely give their lives under their load:
so great their love of flowers and the glory of
    honey-making.
Thus although the limit of a slender age awaits each one
(for never more than seven summers it's unskeined)
yet the race endures immortal, through unnumbered years
    stands fast
the fortune of the house, and their pedigree records
    ancestors of ancestors.

What's more, not Egypt nor great Lydia, nor the Parthian
    peoples,
nor the Hydaspean Medes so venerate their king.
Their king unharmed, the swarm has a single mind;
if lost, they break faith, tear down their stockpiled honey
and themselves dismantle the trellises of the hive.
He is protector of their works, him they revere and all
surround him with crowded noise and pack him in
    thronging,
and often lift him to their shoulders, and throw their bodies
into battle seeking among the wounds a beautiful death.

*

Virgil

Following such signs and such habits, some
have said that bees enjoy a share of the divine mind
and ethereal draughts. For God moves through all things –
lands and the sea's expanse and deepest heaven.
Flocks, herds, men, all breeds of beasts . . .
from Him each at birth draws its fine-spun life,
it seems, and to Him all return at last: all things undone
restored, no place for death, but alive they fly
into the station of a star and mount to heaven's zenith.

If ever you want to breach the bees' tight courts, and uncache
hoarded honey from their treasuries, first with a handful of water
spritz and freshen your mouth, and hold out penetrating smoke.
Their rage surpasses measure: hurt, they breathe venom
into their stings, leave their stingers unseen
stuck in the vein, and lay down their lives in the wound.
Twice men gather the lavish yield, two seasons the harvest:
soon as Pleiad Taygete has shown her heavenly face
to earth and with her foot scorns the spurned flood of Ocean,
and when that same star fleeing rainy Pisces
more sadly sinks down from the sky into the wintry waves.
But if you fear a harsh winter, and would spare their future
and pity their crushed spirits and shattered fortunes, –
yet who to fumigate with thyme and prune off disused cells
would hesitate? For often unnoticed the newt has nibbled
the honeycombs, or whole dens of light-fleeing cockroaches,
or the no-account drone bellies up to another's ration,

The Georgics: Book Four

or the vicious hornet has engaged their unequal arms
or the malevolent race of moths, or the spider spited by
    Minerva
has hung in the aisles her loose webs.
The more they're plundered, the more doggedly they'll
    press
to repair the wrack of their fallen race:
they'll cram the galleries and weave their garners about
    with nectar.

But if (since life has brought to bees our calamities too)
their bodies droop under grim disease –
which instantly you can discern by no vague signs:
sick, their colour changes at once, ragged leanness
disfigures their looks, then the bodies of those deprived of
    life
they bear out from their homes and lead the funeral march,
or linked by their feet they hang from the doorways,
or shut within chambers they linger, all
listless with starvation and numb with pinching cold.
Then a sound is heard, lower, a drawn-out mutter,
as sometimes cold the southwind hushes through the trees,
as the sea hisses roiling in its outflowing swell,
as seethes in shut furnaces the furious blaze.
Now I suggest you burn fragrant galbanum
and run in honey through straws of reed
heartening them, calling the weary to familiar food.
It will help, too, to mix the flavour of pounded gall-nuts
with dried roses, or must made concentrate
over a good fire, or raisin-wine from the Psithian vine,

Virgil

and Athenian thyme with heady-smelling centaury.
There also is a flower in the meadows, to which the name
> *amellus*

farmers gave, an easy plant to ferret out,
for from one clump it lifts a massy spray –
itself golden, but in its petals which splay thickly around
crimson sheens beneath dark violet;
often the gods' altars are garlanded with its woven wreaths,
bitter on the tongue its taste, in grazed vales
shepherds gather it, and near the winding waters of Mella.
Boil its roots in fragrant wine
and set it at their doors for food in heaping baskets.

But if a man's whole hive suddenly has failed
and he knows not whence to revive the breed in a new line,
time to unfold the famed discovery of the Arcadian master
and by what means the spoiled blood from slain bullocks
has often engendered bees. I'll unspool
the whole account, retracing from its earliest source.
For where the blessed race of Pellaean Canopus
dwell near the Nile pooling in its sprawling stream
and ride their acres in painted skiffs,
where quivered Persia's territory hedges, and the river
onrushing, spilled unbroken down from the swart Indians,
branches into seven separate mouths
and with its black silt fertilizes Egypt green,
the whole region rests its sure well-being on this art.
First a spot – narrow and secluded for this very purpose –
is chosen: this with a narrow tile roof
and cramped walls they enclose, and add four windows

The Georgics: Book Four

with slant light to front the four winds.
Then a calf with horns just arched upon his two-year brow
is fetched, with both his nostrils and the breath of his mouth,
despite great struggling, stopped up. After he's beaten to death
his carcass is pulped up, pounded through the unbroken hide.
They leave him lying thus in his pen, and stuff beneath his flanks
broken twigs, thyme and fresh cassia.
This is accomplished when first the Zephyrs drive the waves,
before the meadows blush so in new colour, before
chattering the swallow hangs her nest among the rafters.
Meanwhile, fluid warmed in the softening bones
stews, and creatures with ways wondrous to behold,
devoid of foot at first but soon buzzing at the wing,
brew up, and more and more take to the narrow air
until, like a shower poured from summer clouds
they burst forth, or like arrows from the plucked string
when light-armed Parthians engage the opening volley.

What god, O Muses, forged for us this art?
Whence did man's strange practice take its start?
The shepherd Aristaeus, flying Tempe on the Peneus
when his bees were lost (the story goes) to sickness and starvation,
lamenting stopped by the sacred spring at the stream's headwaters

Virgil

much complaining, and prayed aloud his mother thus:
'Mother, O mother Cyrene, who commands these waters'
     depths,
why me? – why from the glorious line of gods
(if truly, as you claim, my father is Thymbraean Apollo)
did you bear me, hated by the Fates? Or where is your love
     of me
banished? Why did you enjoin me hope for heaven?
Look: even this very trophy of mortal life
which the skilful care of crops and herds had hardly
     hammered out
for me, for all my efforts, though you're my mother, I
     resign.
Nay – go and with your own hand uproot my fruitful
     orchards,
put hostile fire to my stables, destroy my harvest,
burn my crops and heft the stout axe against my vines,
if such spite for my glory has seized you!'

But his mother in her bedchamber beneath the river's
     depths
felt his clamour. Around her, nymphs spun Milesian fleeces
dyed with the deep colour of glass –
Drymo and Xantho and Ligea and Phyllodoce,
their hair poured shimmering upon their radiant necks,
Cydippe and golden Lycorias, one a maid,
the other having just suffered her first birth-pangs,
Clio and Beroe her sister, Ocean's daughters both,
both in gold, both in rainbowed hides arrayed,
and Ephyre and Opis and Asian Deiopea,

and last swift Arethusa with her arrows laid aside.
Among these Clymene gossiped of the frustrate vigilance
of Vulcan, of Mars' wiles and stolen pleasures,
and from Chaos on recounted the myriad loves of the gods.
While by this ballad captivated from the spindle they twisted
their soft work, again the grief of Aristaeus struck
his mother's ears, and upon their glassy chairs all
startled. But before the other sisters Arethusa
far surveying raised her golden head above the surface stream
and from afar: 'Your fright at so loud howling's not amiss,
O sister Cyrene! Himself, your dearest care,
Aristaeus heartsick by the waters of Father Peneus
stands weeping, and you he calls by name of *Cruelty*.'
To whom his mother, struck to the quick with sudden dread, cries:
'Go! Lead him! Lead him to us! He may tread this porch divine.'
And so she commanded the deep river to yawn
apart, that the youth might enter on foot. Hunched up
into mountain-shape the waters stood around him,
and welcomed him into a vast chasm, inviting him beneath the current.
Now wondering at his mother's home, a watery realm,
at lakes closed in caves and echoing groves,
he went on, astonished by the mighty rush of waters –
every river gliding beneath the wide earth
he descried, distinct in their courses: Phasis and Lycus,
the spring from which deep Enipeus first jets forth,

Virgil

from which Father Tiber, from which the Anian stream
and rocky raucous Hypanis, and Mysian Caicus,
and Eridanus, both horns on his bullish front gilt,
than which no other stream more violent flows
out over fertile farmland into the purple sea.
When he's come into her chamber, its ceiling hung with pumice,
and Cyrene understands her son's vain tears,
her sisters timely minister to his hands
with clear spring water, and bring close-shorn napkins.
Some lade the table with a banquet and set down brimming
cups. The altars burn with Panchaian flame.
His mother declared: 'Lift your goblets of Maeonian wine:
we offer to Ocean.' With that she prayed
to Ocean, father of all, and the sister nymphs
who a hundred woods, a hundred rivers guard.
Thrice with liquid nectar she sprinkled the blazing hearth,
thrice the flame flared up anew, shooting to the rooftop.
With this omen bolstering his spirits, she thus began:

'There is in Neptune's Carpathian depths a seer,
aquamarine Proteus, who paces out the wide ocean
on a chariot yoked with fish and hippocampi.
Just now the ports of Thessaly and his native Pallene
he revisits; him the nymphs venerate and ancient
Nereus himself, for the seer has seen all –
what is, what has been, what's spun out soon to come,
for such seemed good to Neptune, whose herds immense
of squalid seals he pastures beneath the swell.
Him, son, you first must clap in shackles, so that the whole

The Georgics: Book Four

cause of malaise he may unriddle and rally your fortunes.
Without duress no counsel will he give, nor will you bend him
by imploring; turn stern force and chains upon your captive:
only against these his wiles will crash themselves to froth.
I myself, when the sun stokes up its midday heat,
when plants thirst and shade is more delightful to the flock,
will guide you to the old man's retreat, where weary from the waves
he withdraws, that you may come at him sprawled in easy sleep.
But when you hold him fast gripped in hands and shackles
then his multiform shapes will bamboozle you, and his wild-beast looks.
For suddenly he'll be a bristled boar, a deadly tigress,
a scaly dragon, a tawny-necked lioness,
or blast out the piercing hiss of flame and thus slip out
from his bonds, or melt into mere water and spill away.
But the more he turns himself into all shapes
the more, O son, hold firm his chains
until after his body's changing he is such
as you saw him when he lidded his eyes at the start of sleep.'

She spoke, and radiated ambrosia's pure perfume,
in which her son's whole body she enwrapped;
from his sleeked locks a sweet scent breathed,
and vigour came upon his nimble limbs. There is a spacious cavern

worn in a mountain's side, where by the wind many a wave
is driven and splits itself into secluded lagoons,
at times a safest anchorage for swamped mariners.
Inside, Proteus screens himself in the covert of a massive boulder.
Here the nymph stations the youth in ambush
away from the light; she herself waits far off, veiled in mist.
Soon the ravaging Dog Star which scorches the thirsty Indians
blazed in the firmament, and the fiery sun had devoured half
his wheel: the grasses parched, and sunken streams
baked in their dry throats, boiled down to slime by its rays,
when Proteus, seeking his usual cove came down
from the waves. Around him the race of the vast sea
revelled, sprayed briny droplets far and wide.
The seals stretched themselves out for sleep scattered along the shore.
He himself – just as at times the caretaker of cotes upon a hill
when the evening star leads home the calves from pasture
and with their bleating din the lambs whet the wolves –
sat on a rock in their midst and counted their number.
Now that Aristaeus gets his chance,
scarce he lets the old man settle his tired limbs
when with a mighty yell he rushes him, and claps him in shackles
where he lies. Proteus for his part not forgetful of his art
transforms himself into all wondrous things of the earth:
a flame, a horrible beast, a stream flowing.

The Georgics: Book Four

But when no design wins deliverance, defeated
he returns to himself, and speaking at last with the mouth
    of a man
he asked, 'Now, sauciest youth, who charged you
to invade our home? What seek you here?' But Aristaeus:
'*You* know, Proteus – you above all know, nor can anything
    deceive you,
so *you* give up deceiving! Following the gods' behest
we come here, seeking an oracle for my flagging fortunes.'
So he intoned. At this the seer finally under sturdy force
rolled his eyes blazing with grey-green light
and savagely gnashing teeth thus unsealed his mouth with
    the fates:

'The wrath of no mean deity hounds you.
You do penance for a sore offence. Heartbroken Orpheus
    stirs up
these punishments against you (did not Fate intervene) –
far less than your deserving! – and rages tormented for his
    wife reft away.
Just so: headlong along the river that she might escape you,
doomed girl, she didn't see the monstrous snake
before her feet hugging the banks in tall grass.
The chorus of her companion dryads with wailing rimmed
the mountain's peaks, the crags of Rhodope mourned,
and alpen Pangaea, the martial land of Rhesus and the
    Getae,
the Hebrus mourned, and Orithyia the northwind's Attic
    bride.
But *he*, consoling love's agony with his hollow-shell lyre,

Virgil

sang you, sweet wife, you to himself on the lonely shore,
you with the rising day, you at the day's decline.
Even the jaws of Taenarus, the steep gates of Dis,
the grove shrouded in black dread
he entered, and approached the dead, and their terrible
    king,
and the hearts unversed in gentling to human prayers.
But by his monody shaken from the deepest pits of Erebus
came wispy shades, and ghosts of those deprived of light,
as many as the birds that by the thousand hide themselves
    in leaves
when evening's star or winter sleet drives them from the
    mountains . . .
mothers and men and, emptied of life, the bodies
of bold-hearted heroes, boys and unwed maidens
and youths lain on the pyres before their parents' stares.
Around them the black mire and grotesque cattails
of Cocytus, revolting swamp that binds them with sluggish
    water
and Styx winding nine times around imprisons them.
Why, the very halls were astonished, and Death's inmost
Tartarus, and the Furies with livid snakes braided
in their hair, and Cerberus held agape his three mouths,
and the spin of Ixion's wheel halted with the wind.
And soon his steps retracing he had dodged every pitfall
and Eurydice restored was coming to the upper air
following behind (for that stipulation had Proserpina
    made)
when a sudden madness seized him, reckless loving –
truly forgivable, if Hell knew to forgive:

The Georgics: Book Four

he stopped, and upon his own Eurydice, already at the very
    edge of light,
forgetful, alas! and his judgement overthrown . . . he
    looked back. Instantly
all his labour fell apart, broken the pitiless tyrant's pact,
and thrice thunder sounded over the pools of Avernus.
She cried, "O Orpheus, what has ruined wretched me
    and you,
what utter madness? Behold – again the cruel Fates
call me back, and darkness shrouds my swimming eyes!
And now, farewell – I am carried off cloaked in endless
    night,
stretching toward you helpless hands, O! yours no more!"
She cried, and sudden from his sight, like smoke mingling
into thin air, vanished away, and – as he clutched vainly
at shadows, longing to say so much . . . she never
saw him more, nor did the ferryman of Orcus
let him cross that swampy obstacle again.
What could he do? Where take himself, his wife twice
    snatched away?
With what sobs could he move Hades, with what word its
    powers?
Even now she was floating cold as death in the Stygian raft.
For seven whole months, month on month, they say,
beneath a skyscraping cliff by desolate Strymon's wave
he wept, and under the frozen stars spun out this song,
soothing tigers and enticing oaks with his dirge,
as mourning beneath the poplar shade the nightingale
laments her lost brood, which a rude ploughman
spying ripped unfledged from their nest, she sobs

nightlong, and on a branch perched her doleful song
renews, and fills full the sphere with dreary plaints.
No love, nor any wedding-song could bend his soul.
Lonely he would wander the Hyperborean ice, the
    snow-crusted Tanais,
the steppes ever widowed by Rhipaean frosts,
wailing Eurydice wrested away and the gift of Dis
annulled – by which devotion spurned, the Thracian
    dames
amid their consecrated rites and midnight bacchant orgies
tore the youth apart and scattered him across the field's
    expanse.
Even then, while down the middle of its rapids
the Hebrus, river of his father's realm, swept and rolled
his head ripped from its marble neck,
Eurydice his mere voice and cold tongue were calling,
O poor Eurydice as his spirit fled,
Eurydice the banks replied the whole river long.'

So said Proteus, and threw himself into the deep sea,
and where he dived the water whirled to foam beneath his
    vortex.
But Cyrene stayed. Unsought she addressed him, shaken:
'Son, you may lay down your soul's heavy care.
Here the whole cause of sickness, for this the nymphs
with whose troupe she used to trip through ancient groves
woeful brought this woeful blight upon your bees.
    Suppliant, you must extend
an offering, praying peace, and do homage to the lenient
    wood nymphs,

The Georgics: Book Four

for they will grant pardon for your orisons, and ease their
 anger.
But first I will explain how you should supplicate in
 sequence:
select four choice bulls, outstanding in form,
who now with your herd graze the green ridge of Lycaeus,
and as many heifers with necks unworked.
For these erect four altars at the goddesses' high shrines,
and from their throats cascade the hallowed blood,
and leave their oxen carcasses in a leafy grove.
Later, when the ninth dawn flaunts her rising,
you will send Lethean poppies to Orpheus as a funeral
 offering
and sacrifice a black ewe, and return to the grove.
There honour Eurydice, now appeased, with a slaughtered
 calf.'
No delay – like a shot he performs his mother's
 instructions:
to the shrines he comes, rears the altars assigned,
leads in four choice bulls, outstanding in form
and as many heifers with necks unworked.
Later, when the ninth dawn had paraded her rising,
he sends a funeral offering to Orpheus and returns to the
 grove.
Here – . . . They spot a wonder, sudden and marvellous
to tell: in the oxens' liquified guts and through the whole
belly, bees buzz and swarm through the split flanks
and trail in unending clouds, and now surge
to a treetop and dangle in clusters from the limber boughs.

*

Virgil

This I sang, about the care of fields and flocks
and about trees, while Caesar the great thundered in war
beside the deep Euphrates, and conqueror dealt out
laws to ready nations and pursued his course to heaven.
I, Virgil, at that time by sweet Parthenope
nurtured, flourishing in the study of inglorious leisure,
I who toyed with shepherd songs, and bold with youth,
sang you, Tityrus, beneath a vault of spreading beech.

1. BOCCACCIO · *Mrs Rosie and the Priest*
2. GERARD MANLEY HOPKINS · *As kingfishers catch fire*
3. *The Saga of Gunnlaug Serpent-tongue*
4. THOMAS DE QUINCEY · *On Murder Considered as One of the Fine Arts*
5. FRIEDRICH NIETZSCHE · *Aphorisms on Love and Hate*
6. JOHN RUSKIN · *Traffic*
7. PU SONGLING · *Wailing Ghosts*
8. JONATHAN SWIFT · *A Modest Proposal*
9. *Three Tang Dynasty Poets*
10. WALT WHITMAN · *On the Beach at Night Alone*
11. KENKŌ · *A Cup of Sake Beneath the Cherry Trees*
12. BALTASAR GRACIÁN · *How to Use Your Enemies*
13. JOHN KEATS · *The Eve of St Agnes*
14. THOMAS HARDY · *Woman much missed*
15. GUY DE MAUPASSANT · *Femme Fatale*
16. MARCO POLO · *Travels in the Land of Serpents and Pearls*
17. SUETONIUS · *Caligula*
18. APOLLONIUS OF RHODES · *Jason and Medea*
19. ROBERT LOUIS STEVENSON · *Olalla*
20. KARL MARX AND FRIEDRICH ENGELS · *The Communist Manifesto*
21. PETRONIUS · *Trimalchio's Feast*
22. JOHANN PETER HEBEL · *How a Ghastly Story Was Brought to Light by a Common or Garden Butcher's Dog*
23. HANS CHRISTIAN ANDERSEN · *The Tinder Box*
24. RUDYARD KIPLING · *The Gate of the Hundred Sorrows*
25. DANTE · *Circles of Hell*
26. HENRY MAYHEW · *Of Street Piemen*
27. HAFEZ · *The nightingales are drunk*
28. GEOFFREY CHAUCER · *The Wife of Bath*
29. MICHEL DE MONTAIGNE · *How We Weep and Laugh at the Same Thing*
30. THOMAS NASHE · *The Terrors of the Night*
31. EDGAR ALLAN POE · *The Tell-Tale Heart*
32. MARY KINGSLEY · *A Hippo Banquet*
33. JANE AUSTEN · *The Beautifull Cassandra*
34. ANTON CHEKHOV · *Gooseberries*
35. SAMUEL TAYLOR COLERIDGE · *Well, they are gone, and here must I remain*
36. JOHANN WOLFGANG VON GOETHE · *Sketchy, Doubtful, Incomplete Jottings*
37. CHARLES DICKENS · *The Great Winglebury Duel*
38. HERMAN MELVILLE · *The Maldive Shark*
39. ELIZABETH GASKELL · *The Old Nurse's Story*
40. NIKOLAY LESKOV · *The Steel Flea*

41. HONORÉ DE BALZAC · *The Atheist's Mass*
42. CHARLOTTE PERKINS GILMAN · *The Yellow Wall-Paper*
43. C.P. CAVAFY · *Remember, Body . . .*
44. FYODOR DOSTOEVSKY · *The Meek One*
45. GUSTAVE FLAUBERT · *A Simple Heart*
46. NIKOLAI GOGOL · *The Nose*
47. SAMUEL PEPYS · *The Great Fire of London*
48. EDITH WHARTON · *The Reckoning*
49. HENRY JAMES · *The Figure in the Carpet*
50. WILFRED OWEN · *Anthem For Doomed Youth*
51. WOLFGANG AMADEUS MOZART · *My Dearest Father*
52. PLATO · *Socrates' Defence*
53. CHRISTINA ROSSETTI · *Goblin Market*
54. *Sindbad the Sailor*
55. SOPHOCLES · *Antigone*
56. RYŪNOSUKE AKUTAGAWA · *The Life of a Stupid Man*
57. LEO TOLSTOY · *How Much Land Does A Man Need?*
58. GIORGIO VASARI · *Leonardo da Vinci*
59. OSCAR WILDE · *Lord Arthur Savile's Crime*
60. SHEN FU · *The Old Man of the Moon*
61. AESOP · *The Dolphins, the Whales and the Gudgeon*
62. MATSUO BASHŌ · *Lips too Chilled*
63. EMILY BRONTË · *The Night is Darkening Round Me*
64. JOSEPH CONRAD · *To-morrow*
65. RICHARD HAKLUYT · *The Voyage of Sir Francis Drake Around the Whole Globe*
66. KATE CHOPIN · *A Pair of Silk Stockings*
67. CHARLES DARWIN · *It was snowing butterflies*
68. BROTHERS GRIMM · *The Robber Bridegroom*
69. CATULLUS · *I Hate and I Love*
70. HOMER · *Circe and the Cyclops*
71. D. H. LAWRENCE · *Il Duro*
72. KATHERINE MANSFIELD · *Miss Brill*
73. OVID · *The Fall of Icarus*
74. SAPPHO · *Come Close*
75. IVAN TURGENEV · *Kasyan from the Beautiful Lands*
76. VIRGIL · *O Cruel Alexis*
77. H. G. WELLS · *A Slip under the Microscope*
78. HERODOTUS · *The Madness of Cambyses*
79. *Speaking of Siva*
80. *The Dhammapada*

H.G. WELLS

A Slip under the Microscope

PENGUIN BOOKS

PENGUIN CLASSICS

UK | USA | Canada | Ireland | Australia
India | New Zealand | South Africa

Penguin Books is part of the Penguin Random House group of companies
whose addresses can be found at global.penguinrandomhouse.com.

This selection published in Penguin Classics 2015

011

Set in 9.5/13 pt Baskerville 10 Pro
Typeset by Jouve (UK), Milton Keynes

Printed and bound in Great Britain by Clays Ltd, Elcograf S.p.A.

A CIP catalogue record for this book is available from the British Library

ISBN: 978-0-141-39875-4

www.greenpenguin.co.uk

MIX
Paper from
responsible sources
FSC® C018179

Penguin Random House is committed to a
sustainable future for our business, our readers
and our planet. This book is made from Forest
Stewardship Council® certified paper.

Contents

The Door in the Wall   1

A Slip under the Microscope   27

The Door in the Wall

1

One confidential evening, not three months ago, Lionel Wallace told me this story of the Door in the Wall. And at the time I thought that so far as he was concerned it was a true story.

He told it me with such a direct simplicity of conviction that I could not do otherwise than believe in him. But in the morning, in my own flat, I woke to a different atmosphere; and as I lay in bed and recalled the things he had told me, stripped of the glamour of his earnest slow voice, denuded of the focused, shaded table light, the shadowy atmosphere that wrapped about him and me, and the pleasant bright things, the dessert and glasses and napery of the dinner we had shared, making them for the time a bright little world quite cut off from everyday realities, I saw it all as frankly incredible. 'He was mystifying!' I said, and then: 'How well he did it! . . . It isn't quite the thing I should have expected him, of all people, to do well.'

Afterwards as I sat up in bed and sipped my morning tea, I found myself trying to account for the flavour of reality that perplexed me in his impossible reminiscences, by supposing they did in some way suggest, present, convey – I hardly know which word to use – experiences it was otherwise impossible to tell.

Well, I don't resort to that explanation now. I have got over my intervening doubts. I believe now, as I believed at the moment of telling, that Wallace did to the very best of his ability strip the truth of his secret for me. But whether he himself saw, or only thought he saw, whether he himself was the possessor of an inestimable privilege or the victim of a fantastic dream, I cannot pretend to guess. Even the facts of his death, which ended my doubts for ever, throw no light on that.

That much the reader must judge for himself.

I forget now what chance comment or criticism of mine moved so reticent a man to confide in me. He was, I think, defending himself against an imputation of slackness and unreliability I had made in relation to a great public movement, in which he had disappointed me. But he plunged suddenly. 'I have,' he said, 'a preoccupation–

'I know,' he went on, after a pause, 'I have been negligent. The fact is – it isn't a case of ghosts or apparitions – but – it's an odd thing to tell of, Redmond – I am haunted. I am haunted by something – that rather takes the light out of things, that fills me with longings . . .'

He paused, checked by that English shyness that so often overcomes us when we would speak of moving or

The Door in the Wall

grave or beautiful things. 'You were at Saint Althelstan's all through,' he said, and for a moment that seemed to me quite irrelevant. 'Well' – and he paused. Then very haltingly at first, but afterwards more easily, he began to tell of the thing that was hidden in his life, the haunting memory of a beauty and a happiness that filled his heart with insatiable longings, that made all the interests and spectacle of worldly life seem dull and tedious and vain to him.

Now that I have the clue to it, the thing seems written visibly in his face. I have a photograph in which that look of detachment has been caught and intensified. It reminds me of what a woman once said of him – a woman who had loved him greatly. 'Suddenly,' she said, 'the interest goes out of him. He forgets you. He doesn't care a rap for you – under his very nose . . .'

Yet the interest was not always out of him, and when he was holding his attention to a thing Wallace could contrive to be an extremely successful man. His career, indeed, is set with successes. He left me behind him long ago; he soared up over my head, and cut a figure in the world that I couldn't cut – anyhow. He was still a year short of forty, and they say now that he would have been in office and very probably in the new Cabinet if he had lived. At school he always beat me without effort – as it were by nature. We were at school together at Saint Althelstan's College in West Kensington for almost all our school-time. He came into the school as my co-equal, but he left far above me, in a blaze of scholarships and brilliant performance. Yet I think I made a fair average running. And it was at school I heard first of the 'Door in the Wall' – that I was to hear of a second time only a month before his death.

To him at least the Door in the Wall was a real door, leading through a real wall to immortal realities. Of that I am now quite assured.

And it came into his life quite early, when he was a little fellow between five and six. I remember how, as he sat making his confession to me with a slow gravity, he reasoned and reckoned the date of it. 'There was,' he said, 'a crimson Virginia creeper in it – all one bright uniform crimson, in a clear amber sunshine against a white wall. That came into the impression somehow, though I don't clearly remember how, and there were horse-chestnut leaves upon the clean pavement outside the green door. They were blotched yellow and green, you know, not brown nor dirty, so that they must have been new fallen. I take it that means October. I look out for horse-chestnut leaves every year and I ought to know.

'If I'm right in that, I was about five years and four months old.'

He was, he said, rather a precocious little boy – he learnt to talk at an abnormally early age, and he was so sane and 'old-fashioned', as people say, that he was permitted an amount of initiative that most children scarcely

The Door in the Wall

attain by seven or eight. His mother died when he was two, and he was under the less vigilant and authoritative care of a nursery governess. His father was a stern, preoccupied lawyer, who gave him little attention and expected great things of him. For all his brightness he found life grey and dull, I think. And one day he wandered.

He could not recall the particular neglect that enabled him to get away, nor the course he took among the West Kensington roads. All that had faded among the incurable blurs of memory. But the white wall and the green door stood out quite distinctly.

As his memory of that childish experience ran, he did at the very first sight of that door experience a peculiar emotion, an attraction, a desire to get to the door and open it and walk in. And at the same time he had the clearest conviction that either it was unwise or it was wrong of him – he could not tell which – to yield to this attraction. He insisted upon it as a curious thing that he knew from the very beginning – unless memory has played him the queerest trick – that the door was unfastened, and that he could go in as he chose.

I seem to see the figure of that little boy, drawn and repelled. And it was very clear in his mind, too, though why it should be so was never explained, that his father would be very angry if he went in through that door.

Wallace described all these moments of hesitation to

me with the utmost particularity. He went right past the door, and then, with his hands in his pockets and making an infantile attempt to whistle, strolled right along beyond the end of the wall. There he recalls a number of mean dirty shops, and particularly that of a plumber and decorator with a dusty disorder of earthenware pipes, sheet lead, ball taps, pattern books of wallpaper, and tins of enamel. He stood pretending to examine these things, and *coveting*, passionately desiring, the green door.

Then, he said, he had a gust of emotion. He made a run for it, lest hesitation should grip him again; he went plump with outstretched hand through the green door and let it slam behind him. And so, in a trice, he came into the garden that has haunted all his life.

It was very difficult for Wallace to give me his full sense of that garden into which he came.

There was something in the very air of it that exhilarated, that gave one a sense of lightness and good happening and well-being; there was something in the sight of it that made all its colour clean and perfect and subtly luminous. In the instant of coming into it one was exquisitely glad – as only in rare moments, and when one is young and joyful one can be glad in this world. And everything was beautiful there . . .

Wallace mused before he went on telling me. 'You see,' he said, with the doubtful inflection of a man who pauses at incredible things, 'there were two great panthers there . . . Yes, spotted panthers. And I was not afraid.

The Door in the Wall

There was a long wide path with marble-edged flower borders on either side, and these two huge velvety beasts were playing there with a ball. One looked up and came towards me, a little curious as it seemed. It came right up to me, rubbed its soft round ear very gently against the small hand I held out, and purred. It was, I tell you, an enchanted garden. I know. And the size? Oh! it stretched far and wide, this way and that. I believe there were hills far away. Heaven knows where West Kensington had suddenly got to. And somehow it was just like coming home.

'You know, in the very moment the door swung to behind me, I forgot the road with its fallen chestnut leaves, its cabs and tradesmen's carts, I forgot the sort of gravitational pull back to the discipline and obedience of home, I forgot all hesitations and fear, forgot discretion, forgot all the intimate realities of this life. I became in a moment a very glad and wonder-happy little boy – in another world. It was a world with a different quality, a warmer, more penetrating and mellower light, with a faint clear gladness in its air, and wisps of sun-touched cloud in the blueness of its sky. And before me ran this long wide path, invitingly, with weedless beds on either side, rich with untended flowers, and these two great panthers. I put my little hands fearlessly on their soft fur, and caressed their round ears and the sensitive corners under their ears, and played with them, and it was as though they welcomed me home. There was a keen sense of homecoming in my mind, and when presently a tall, fair girl appeared in the pathway and came to meet me, smiling, and said "Well?" to me, and lifted me and kissed me, and put me down and led me by the hand, there was no amazement, but only an impression of delightful rightness, of being reminded of happy things that had in some strange way been overlooked. There were broad red steps, I remember, that came into view between spikes of delphinium, and up these we went to a great avenue between very old and shady dark trees. All down this avenue, you know, between the red chapped stems, were marble seats of honour and statuary, and very tame and friendly white doves . . .

'Along this cool avenue my girl-friend led me, looking down – I recall the pleasant lines, the finely-modelled chin of her sweet kind face – asking me questions in a soft, agreeable voice, and telling me things, pleasant things I know, though what they were I was never able to recall . . . Presently a Capuchin monkey, very clean, with a fur of ruddy brown and kindly hazel eyes, came down a tree to us and ran beside me, looking up at me and grinning, and presently leapt to my shoulder. So we two went on our way in great happiness.'

He paused.

'Go on,' I said.

'I remember little things. We passed an old man musing among laurels, I remember, and a place gay with paroquets, and came through a broad shaded colonnade to a spacious cool palace, full of pleasant fountains, full of beautiful things, full of the quality and promise of heart's desire. And there were many things and many people, some that still seem to stand out clearly and some that are vaguer; but all these people were beautiful and kind. In some way – I don't know how – it was conveyed to me that they all were kind to me, glad to have me there, and filling me with gladness by their gestures, by the touch of their hands, by the welcome and love in their eyes. Yes—'

He mused for a while. 'Playmates I found there. That was very much to me, because I was a lonely little boy. They played delightful games in a grass-covered court where there was a sundial set about with flowers. And as one played one loved . . .

'But – it's odd – there's a gap in my memory. I don't remember the games we played. I never remembered. Afterwards, as a child, I spent long hours trying, even with tears, to recall the form of that happiness. I wanted to play it all over again – in my nursery – by myself. No! All I remember is the happiness and two dear playfellows who were most with me . . . Then presently came a sombre dark woman, with a grave, pale face and dreamy eyes, a sombre woman, wearing a soft long robe of pale purple, who carried a book, and beckoned and took me aside with her into a gallery above a hall – though my playmates were loth to have me go, and ceased their game and stood watching as I was carried away. "Come back to us!" they cried. "Come back to us soon!" I looked up at her face, but she heeded them not at all. Her face was very gentle and grave. She took me to a seat in the gallery, and I stood beside her, ready to look at her book as she opened it upon her knee. The pages fell open. She pointed, and I looked, marvelling, for in the living pages of that book I saw myself; it was a story about myself, and in it were all the things that had happened to me since ever I was born . . .

'It was wonderful to me, because the pages of that book were not pictures, you understand, but realities.'

Wallace paused gravely – looked at me doubtfully.

'Go on,' I said. 'I understand.'

'They were realities – yes, they must have been; people moved and things came and went in them; my dear mother, whom I had near forgotten; then my father, stern and upright, the servants, the nursery, all the familiar things of home. Then the front door and the busy streets, with traffic to and fro. I looked and marvelled, and looked half doubtfully again into the woman's face and turned the pages over, skipping this and that, to see more of this book and more, and so at last I came to myself hovering and hesitating outside the green door in the long white wall, and felt again the conflict and the fear.

'"And next?" I cried, and would have turned on, but the cool hand of the grave woman delayed me.

'"Next?" I insisted, and struggled gently with her hand, pulling up her fingers with all my childish strength, and as she yielded and the page came over she bent down upon me like a shadow and kissed my brow.

'But the page did not show the enchanted garden, nor the panthers, nor the girl who had led me by the hand, nor the playfellows who had been so loth to let me go. It showed a long grey street in West Kensington, in that chill hour of afternoon before the lamps are lit; and I was there, a wretched little figure, weeping aloud, for all that I could do to restrain myself, and I was weeping because I could not return to my dear playfellows who had called after me, "Come back to us! Come back to us soon!" I was there. This was no page in a book, but harsh reality; that enchanted place and the restraining hand of the grave mother at whose knee I stood had gone – whither had they gone?'

He halted again, and remained for a time staring into the fire.

'Oh! the woefulness of that return!' he murmured.

'Well?' I said, after a minute or so.

'Poor little wretch I was! – brought back to this grey world again! As I realized the fullness of what had happened to me, I gave way to quite ungovernable grief. And the shame and humiliation of that public weeping and my disgraceful homecoming remain with me still. I see again the benevolent-looking old gentleman in gold spectacles who stopped and spoke to me – prodding me first with his umbrella. "Poor little chap," said he; "and are you lost then?" – and me a London boy of five and more! And he must needs bring in a kindly young policeman and make a crowd of me, and so march me home. Sobbing, conspicuous, and frightened, I came back from the enchanted garden to the steps of my father's house.

'That is as well as I can remember my vision of that garden – the garden that haunts me still. Of course, I can convey nothing of that indescribable quality of translucent unreality, that *difference* from the common things of experience that hung about it all; but that – that is what happened. If it was a dream, I am sure it was a daytime and altogether extraordinary dream . . . H'm! – naturally there followed a terrible questioning, by my aunt, my father, the nurse, the governess – everyone . . .

'I tried to tell them, and my father gave me my first thrashing for telling lies. When afterwards I tried to tell my aunt, she punished me again for my wicked persistence. Then, as I said, everyone was forbidden to listen to me, to hear a word about it. Even my fairy-tale books were taken away from me for a time – because I was too "imaginative". Eh? Yes, they did that! My father belonged to the old school . . . And my story was driven back upon myself. I whispered it to my pillow – my pillow that was often damp and salt to my whispering lips with childish tears. And I added always to my official and less fervent prayers this one heartfelt request: "Please God I may dream of the garden. Oh! take me back to my garden!" Take me back to my garden! I dreamt often of the garden.

The Door in the Wall

I may have added to it, I may have changed it; I do not know . . . All this, you understand, is an attempt to reconstruct from fragmentary memories a very early experience. Between that and the other consecutive memories of my boyhood there is a gulf. A time came when it seemed impossible I should ever speak of that wonder glimpse again.'

I asked an obvious question.

'No,' he said. 'I don't remember that I ever attempted to find my way back to the garden in those early years. This seems odd to me now, but I think that very probably a closer watch was kept on my movements after this misadventure to prevent my going astray. No, it wasn't till you knew me that I tried for the garden again. And I believe there was a period – incredible as it seems now – when I forgot the garden altogether – when I was about eight or nine it may have been. Do you remember me as a kid at Saint Althelstan's?'

'Rather!'

'I didn't show any signs, did I, in those days of having a secret dream?'

2

He looked up with a sudden smile.

'Did you ever play North-West Passage with me? . . . No, of course you didn't come my way!

'It was the sort of game,' he went on, 'that every imaginative child plays all day. The idea was the discovery of a North-West Passage to school. The way to school was plain enough; the game consisted in finding some way that wasn't plain, starting off ten minutes early in some almost hopeless direction, and working my way round through unaccustomed streets to my goal. And one day I got entangled among some rather low-class streets on the other side of Campden Hill, and I began to think that for once the game would be against me and that I should get to school late. I tried rather desperately a street that seemed a *cul-de-sac*, and found a passage at the end. I hurried through that with renewed hope. "I shall do it yet," I said, and passed a row of frowsy little shops that were inexplicably familiar to me, and behold! there was my long white wall and the green door that led to the enchanted garden!

'The thing whacked upon me suddenly. Then, after all, that garden, that wonderful garden, wasn't a dream!'

He paused.

'I suppose my second experience with the green door marks the world of difference there is between the busy life of a schoolboy and the infinite leisure of a child. Anyhow, this second time I didn't for a moment think of going in straight away. You see—. For one thing, my mind was full of the idea of getting to school in time – set on not breaking my record for punctuality. I must surely have felt *some* little desire at least to try the door – yes. I must have felt that . . . But I seem to remember the attraction of the door mainly as another obstacle to my overmastering determination to get to school. I was immensely interested by this discovery I had made, of course – I went on with my mind full of it – but I went on. It didn't check me. I ran past, tugging out my watch, found I had ten minutes still to spare, and then I was going downhill into familiar surroundings. I got to school, breathless, it is true, and wet with perspiration, but in time. I can remember hanging up my coat and hat . . . Went right by it and left it behind me. Odd, eh?'

He looked at me thoughtfully. 'Of course I didn't know then that it wouldn't always be there. Schoolboys have limited imaginations. I suppose I thought it was an awfully jolly thing to have it there, to know my way back to it; but there was the school tugging at me. I expect I was a good deal distraught and inattentive that morning, recalling what I could of the beautiful strange people I should presently see again. Oddly enough I had no doubt in my mind that they would be glad to see me . . . Yes, I must have thought of the garden that morning just as a jolly sort of place to which one might resort in the interludes of a strenuous scholastic career.

'I didn't go that day at all. The next day was a half-holiday, and that may have weighed with me. Perhaps, too, my state of inattention brought down impositions upon me, and docked the margin of time necessary for the *détour*. I don't know. What I do know is that in the meantime the enchanted garden was so much upon my mind that I could not keep it to myself.

'I told – what was his name? – a ferrety-looking youngster we used to call Squiff.'

'Young Hopkins,' said I.

'Hopkins it was. I did not like telling him. I had a feeling that in some way it was against the rules to tell him, but I did. He was walking part of the way home with me; he was talkative, and if we had not talked about the enchanted garden we should have talked of something else, and it was intolerable to me to think about any other subject. So I blabbed.

'Well, he told my secret. The next day in the play interval I found myself surrounded by half a dozen bigger boys, half teasing, and wholly curious to hear more of the enchanted garden. There was that big Fawcett – you remember him? – and Carnaby and Morley Reynolds. You weren't there by any chance? No, I think I should have remembered if you were . . .

'A boy is a creature of odd feelings. I was, I really believe, in spite of my secret self-disgust, a little flattered to have the attention of these big fellows. I remember particularly a moment of pleasure caused by the praise of Crawshaw – you remember Crawshaw major, the son of Crawshaw the composer? – who said it was the best

The Door in the Wall

lie he had ever heard. But at the same time there was a really painful undertow of shame at telling what I felt was indeed a sacred secret. That beast Fawcett made a joke about the girl in green—'

Wallace's voice sank with the keen memory of that shame. 'I pretended not to hear,' he said. 'Well, then Carnaby suddenly called me a young liar, and disputed with me when I said the thing was true. I said I knew where to find the green door, could lead them all there in ten minutes. Carnaby became outrageously virtuous, and said I'd have to – and bear out my words or suffer. Did you ever have Carnaby twist your arm? Then perhaps you'll understand how it went with me. I swore my story was true. There was nobody in the school then to save a chap from Carnaby, though Crawshaw put in a word or so. Carnaby had got his game. I grew excited and red-eared, and a little frightened. I behaved altogether like a silly little chap, and the outcome of it all was that instead of starting alone for my enchanted garden, I led the way presently – cheeks flushed, ears hot, eyes smarting, and my soul one burning misery and shame – for a party of six mocking, curious, and threatening schoolfellows.

'We never found the white wall and the green door . . .'

'You mean—?'

'I mean I couldn't find it. I would have found it if I could.

'And afterwards when I could go alone I couldn't find

it. I never found it. I seem now to have been always looking for it through my schoolboy days, but I never came upon it – never.'

'Did the fellows – make it disagreeable?'

'Beastly . . . Carnaby held a council over me for wanton lying. I remember how I sneaked home and upstairs to hide the marks of my blubbering. But when I cried myself to sleep at last it wasn't for Carnaby, but for the garden, for the beautiful afternoon I had hoped for, for the sweet friendly women and the waiting playfellows, and the game I had hoped to learn again, that beautiful forgotten game . . .

'I believed firmly that if I had not told— . . . I had bad times after that – crying at night and wool-gathering by day. For two terms I slacked and had bad reports. Do you remember? Of course you would! It was *you* – your beating me in mathematics that brought me back to the grind again.'

3

For a time my friend stared silently into the red heart of the fire. Then he said: 'I never saw it again until I was seventeen.

'It leapt upon me for the third time – as I was driving to Paddington on my way to Oxford and a scholarship. I had just one momentary glimpse. I was leaning over the apron of my hansom smoking a cigarette, and no doubt thinking myself no end of a man of the world, and suddenly there was the door, the wall, the dear sense of unforgettable and still attainable things.

'We clattered by – I too taken by surprise to stop my cab until we were well past and round a corner. Then I had a queer moment, a double and divergent movement of my will: I tapped the little door in the roof of the cab, and brought my arm down to pull out my watch. "Yes, sir!" said the cabman, smartly. "Er – well – it's nothing," I cried. "*My* mistake! We haven't much time! Go on!" And he went on . . .

'I got my scholarship. And the night after I was told of that I sat over my fire in my little upper room, my study, in my father's house, with his praise – his rare praise – and his sound counsels ringing in my ears, and I smoked my favourite pipe – the formidable bulldog of adolescence – and thought of that door in the long white wall. "If I had stopped," I thought, "I should have missed my scholarship, I should have missed Oxford – muddled all the fine career before me! I begin to see things better!" I fell musing deeply, but I did not doubt then this career of mine was a thing that merited sacrifice.

'Those dear friends and that clear atmosphere seemed very sweet to me, very fine but remote. My grip was fixing now upon the world. I saw another door opening – the door of my career.'

He stared again into the fire. Its red light picked out a

stubborn strength in his face for just one flickering moment, and then it vanished again.

'Well,' he said and sighed, 'I have served that career. I have done – much work, much hard work. But I have dreamt of the enchanted garden a thousand dreams, and seen its door, or at least glimpsed its door, four times since then. Yes – four times. For a while this world was so bright and interesting, seemed so full of meaning and opportunity, that the half-effaced charm of the garden was by comparison gentle and remote. Who wants to pat panthers on the way to dinner with pretty women and distinguished men? I came down to London from Oxford, a man of bold promise that I have done something to redeem. Something – and yet there have been disappointments . . .

'Twice I have been in love – I will not dwell on that – but once, as I went to someone who, I knew, doubted whether I dared to come, I took a short cut at a venture through an unfrequented road near Earl's Court, and so happened on a white wall and a familiar green door. "Odd!" said I to myself, "but I thought this place was on Campden Hill. It's the place I never could find somehow – like counting Stonehenge – the place of that queer daydream of mine." And I went by it intent upon my purpose. It had no appeal to me that afternoon.

'I had just a moment's impulse to try the door, three steps aside were needed at the most – though I was sure enough in my heart that it would open to me – and then

I thought that doing so might delay me on the way to that appointment in which my honour was involved. Afterwards I was sorry for my punctuality – I might at least have peeped in and waved a hand to those panthers, but I knew enough by this time not to seek again belatedly that which is not found by seeking. Yes, that time made me very sorry . . .

'Years of hard work after that, and never a sight of the door. It's only recently it has come back to me. With it there has come a sense as though some thin tarnish had spread itself over my world. I began to think of it as a sorrowful and bitter thing that I should never see that door again. Perhaps I was suffering a little from overwork – perhaps it was what I've heard spoken of as the feeling of forty. I don't know. But certainly the keen brightness that makes effort easy has gone out of things recently, and that just at a time – with all these new political developments – when I ought to be working. Odd, isn't it? But I do begin to find life toilsome, its rewards, as I come near them, cheap. I began a little while ago to want the garden quite badly. Yes – and I've seen it three times.'

'The garden?'

'No – the door! And I haven't gone in!'

He leant over the table to me, with an enormous sorrow in his voice as he spoke. 'Thrice I have had my chance – *thrice*! If ever that door offers itself to me again, I swore, I will go in, out of this dust and heat, out of this dry glitter of vanity, out of these toilsome futilities. I will go and never return. This time I will stay . . . I swore it, and when the time came – *I didn't go*.

'Three times in one year have I passed that door and failed to enter. Three times in the last year.

'The first time was on the night of the snatch division on the Tenants' Redemption Bill, on which the Government was saved by a majority of three. You remember? No one on our side – perhaps very few on the opposite side – expected the end that night. Then the debate collapsed like eggshells. I and Hotchkiss were dining with his cousin at Brentford; we were both unpaired, and we were called up by telephone, and set off at once in his cousin's motor. We got in barely in time, and on the way we passed my wall and door – livid in the moonlight, blotched with hot yellow as the glare of our lamps lit it, but unmistakable. "My God!" cried I. "What?" said Hotchkiss. "Nothing!" I answered, and the moment passed.

'"I've made a great sacrifice," I told the whip as I got in. "They all have," he said, and hurried by.

'I do not see how I could have done otherwise then. And the next occasion was as I rushed to my father's bedside to bid that stern old man farewell. Then, too, the claims of life were imperative. But the third time was different; it happened a week ago. It fills me with hot remorse to recall it. I was with Gurker and Ralphs – it's no secret now, you know, that I've had my talk with Gurker. We had been dining at Frobisher's, and the talk had become intimate between us. The question of my place in the reconstructed Ministry lay always just over the boundary of the discussion. Yes – yes. That's all settled. It needn't be talked about yet, but there's no reason to keep a secret from you . . . Yes – thanks! thanks! But let me tell you my story.

'Then, on that night things were very much in the air. My position was a very delicate one. I was keenly anxious to get some definite word from Gurker, but was hampered by Ralphs' presence. I was using the best power of my brain to keep that light and careless talk not too obviously directed to the point that concerned me. I had to. Ralphs' behaviour since has more than justified my caution . . . Ralphs, I knew, would leave us beyond the Kensington High Street, and then I could surprise Gurker by a sudden frankness. One has sometimes to resort to these little devices . . . And then it was that in the margin of my field of vision I became aware once more of the white wall, the green door before us down the road.

'We passed it talking. I passed it. I can still see the shadow of Gurker's marked profile, his opera hat tilted forward over his prominent nose, the many folds of his neck wrap going before my shadow and Ralphs' as we sauntered past.

'I passed within twenty inches of the door. "If I say goodnight to them, and go in," I asked myself, "what will happen?" And I was all a-tingle for that word with Gurker.

'I could not answer that question in the tangle of my other problems. "They will think me mad," I thought. "And suppose I vanish now! – Amazing disappearance of a prominent politician!" That weighed with me. A thousand inconceivably petty worldlinesses weighed with me in that crisis.'

Then he turned on me with a sorrowful smile, and, speaking slowly, 'Here I am!' he said.

'Here I am!' he repeated, 'and my chance has gone from me. Three times in one year the door has been offered me – the door that goes into peace, into delight, into a beauty beyond dreaming, a kindness no man on earth can know. And I have rejected it, Redmond, and it has gone—'

'How do you know?'

'I know. I know. I am left now to work it out, to stick to the tasks that held me so strongly when my moments came. You say I have success – this vulgar, tawdry, irksome, envied thing. I have it.' He had a walnut in his big hand. 'If that was my success,' he said, and crushed it, and held it out for me to see.

'Let me tell you something, Redmond. This loss is destroying me. For two months, for ten weeks nearly now, I have done no work at all, except the most necessary and urgent duties. My soul is full of inappeasable regrets. At nights – when it is less likely I shall be recognized – I go out. I wander. Yes. I wonder what people would think of that if they knew. A Cabinet Minister, the responsible head of that most vital of all departments, wandering alone – grieving – sometimes near audibly lamenting – for a door, for a garden!'

4

I can see now his rather pallid face, and the unfamiliar sombre fire that had come into his eyes. I see him very vividly tonight. I sit recalling his words, his tones, and last evening's *Westminster Gazette* still lies on my sofa, containing the notice of his death. At lunch today the club was busy with his death. We talked of nothing else.

They found his body very early yesterday morning in a deep excavation near East Kensington Station. It is one of two shafts that have been made in connection with an extension of the railway southward. It is protected from the intrusion of the public by a hoarding upon the high road, in which a small doorway has been cut for the convenience of some of the workmen who live in that direction. The doorway was left unfastened through a misunderstanding between two gangers, and through it he made his way.

My mind is darkened with questions and riddles.

It would seem he walked all the way from the House that night – he has frequently walked home during the past Session – and so it is I figure his dark form coming along the late and empty streets, wrapped up, intent. And then did the pale electric lights near the station cheat the rough planking into a semblance of white? Did that fatal unfastened door awaken some memory?

Was there, after all, ever any green door in the wall at all?

I do not know. I have told his story as he told it to me. There are times when I believe that Wallace was no more than the victim of the coincidence between a rare but not unprecedented type of hallucination and a careless trap, but that indeed is not my profoundest belief. You may think me superstitious, if you will, and foolish; but, indeed, I am more than half convinced that he had, in truth, an abnormal gift, and a sense, something – I know not what – that in the guise of wall and door offered him an outlet, a secret and peculiar passage of escape into another and altogether more beautiful world. At any rate, you will say, it betrayed him in the end. But did it betray him? There you touch the inmost mystery of these dreamers, these men of vision and the imagination. We see our world fair and common, the hoarding and the pit. By our daylight standard he walked out of security into darkness, danger, and death.

But did he see like that?

A Slip under the Microscope

Outside the laboratory windows was a watery-grey fog, and within a close warmth and the yellow light of the green-shaded gas lamps that stood two to each table down its narrow length. On each table stood a couple of glass jars containing the mangled vestiges of the crayfish, mussels, frogs, and guineapigs upon which the students had been working, and down the side of the room, facing the windows, were shelves bearing bleached dissections in spirits, surmounted by a row of beautifully executed anatomical drawings in whitewood frames and overhanging a row of cubical lockers. All the doors of the laboratory were panelled with blackboard, and on these were the half-erased diagrams of the previous day's work. The laboratory was empty, save for the demonstrator, who sat near the preparation-room door, and silent, save for a low, continuous murmur, and the clicking of the rocker microtome at which he was working. But scattered about the room were traces of numerous students: handbags, polished boxes of instruments, in one place a large drawing covered by newspaper, and in another a prettily bound copy of *News from Nowhere*, a book oddly at variance with its surroundings. These things had been put down hastily as the students had arrived and hurried at once to secure their seats in the adjacent lecture theatre. Deadened by the closed door, the measured accents of the professor sounded as a featureless muttering.

Presently, faint through the closed windows came the sound of the Oratory clock striking the hour of eleven. The clicking of the microtome ceased, and the demonstrator looked at his watch, rose, thrust his hands into his pockets, and walked slowly down the laboratory towards the lecture- theatre door. He stood listening for a moment, and then his eye fell on the little volume by William Morris. He picked it up, glanced at the title, smiled, opened it, looked at the name on the fly-leaf, ran the leaves through with his hand, and put it down. Almost immediately the even murmur of the lecturer ceased, there was a sudden burst of pencils rattling on the desks in the lecture theatre, a stirring, a scraping of feet, and a number of voices speaking together. Then a firm footfall approached the door, which began to open, and stood ajar as some indistinctly heard question arrested the newcomer.

The demonstrator turned, walked slowly back past the microtome, and left the laboratory by the preparation-room door. As he did so, first one, and then several students carrying notebooks entered the laboratory from the lecture theatre, and distributed themselves among the little tables, or stood in a group about the doorway. They were an exceptionally heterogeneous assembly, for while

A Slip under the Microscope

Oxford and Cambridge still recoil from the blushing prospect of mixed classes, the College of Science anticipated America in the matter years ago – mixed socially too, for the prestige of the College is high, and its scholarships, free of any age limit, dredge deeper even than do those of the Scotch universities. The class numbered one-and-twenty, but some remained in the theatre questioning the professor, copying the blackboard diagrams before they were washed off, or examining the special specimens he had produced to illustrate the day's teaching. Of the nine who had come into the laboratory three were girls, one of whom, a little fair woman wearing spectacles and dressed in greyish-green, was peering out of the window at the fog, while the other two, both wholesome-looking, plain-faced schoolgirls, unrolled and put on the brown holland aprons they wore while dissecting. Of the men, two went down the laboratory to their places, one a pallid, dark-bearded man, who had once been a tailor; the other a pleasant-featured, ruddy young man of twenty, dressed in a well-fitting brown suit; young Wedderburn, the son of Wedderburn the eye specialist. The others formed a little knot near the theatre door. One of these, a dwarfed, spectacled figure with a hunchback, sat on a bent wood stool; two others, one a short, dark youngster and the other a flaxen-haired, reddish-complexioned young man, stood leaning side by side against the slate sink, while the fourth stood facing them, and maintained the larger share of the conversation.

This last person was named Hill. He was a sturdily built young fellow, of the same age as Wedderburn; he had a white face, dark grey eyes, hair of an indeterminate colour, and prominent, irregular features. He talked rather louder than was needful, and thrust his hands deeply into his pockets. His collar was frayed and blue with the starch of a careless laundress, his clothes were evidently ready-made, and there was a patch on the side of his boot near the toe. And as he talked or listened to the others, he glanced now and again towards the lecture-theatre door. They were discussing the depressing peroration of the lecture they had just heard, the last lecture it was in the introductory course in zoology. 'From ovum to ovum is the goal of the higher vertebrata,' the lecturer had said in his melancholy tones, and so had neatly rounded off the sketch of comparative anatomy he had been developing. The spectacled hunchback had repeated it with noisy appreciation, had tossed it towards the fair-haired student with an evident provocation, and had started one of those vague, rambling discussions on generalities so unaccountably dear to the student mind all the world over.

'That is our goal, perhaps – I admit it, as far as science goes,' said the fair-haired student, rising to the challenge. 'But there are things above science.'

'Science,' said Hill confidently, 'is systematic knowledge. Ideas that don't come into the system – must anyhow – be loose ideas.' He was not quite sure whether

A Slip under the Microscope

that was a clever saying or a fatuity until his hearers took it seriously.

'The thing I cannot understand,' said the hunchback, at large, 'is whether Hill is a materialist or not.'

'There is one thing above matter,' said Hill promptly, feeling he made a better point this time, aware, too, of someone in the doorway behind him, and raising his voice a trifle for her benefit, 'and that is, the delusion that there is something above matter.'

'So we have your gospel at last,' said the fair student. 'It's all a delusion, is it? All our aspirations to lead something more than dogs' lives, all our work for anything beyond ourselves. But see how inconsistent you are. Your socialism, for instance. Why do you trouble about the interests of the race? Why do you concern yourself about the beggar in the gutter? Why are you bothering yourself to lend that book' – he indicated William Morris by a movement of the head – 'to everyone in the lab?'

'Girl,' said the hunchback indistinctly, and glanced guiltily over his shoulder.

The girl in brown, with the brown eyes, had come into the laboratory, and stood on the other side of the table behind him, with her rolled-up apron in one hand, looking over her shoulder, listening to the discussion. She did not notice the hunchback, because she was glancing from Hill to his interlocutor. Hill's consciousness of her presence betrayed itself to her only in his studious ignoring of the fact; but she understood that, and it pleased her. 'I see no reason,' said he, 'why a man should live like a brute because he knows of nothing beyond matter, and does not expect to exist a hundred years hence.'

'Why shouldn't he?' said the fair-haired student.

'Why *should* he?' said Hill.

'What inducement has he?'

'That's the way with all you religious people. It's all a business of inducements. Cannot a man seek after righteousness for righteousness' sake?'

There was a pause. The fair man answered, with a kind of vocal padding, 'But – you see – inducement – when I said inducement,' to gain time. And then the hunchback came to his rescue and inserted a question. He was a terrible person in the debating society with his questions, and they invariably took one form – a demand for a definition. 'What's your definition of righteousness?' said the hunchback at this stage.

Hill experienced a sudden loss of complacency at this question, but even as it was asked, relief came in the person of Brooks, the laboratory attendant, who entered by the preparation-room door, carrying a number of freshly killed guineapigs by their hind legs. 'This is the last batch of material this session,' said the youngster who had not previously spoken. Brooks advanced up the laboratory, smacking down a couple of guineapigs at each table. The rest of the class, scenting the prey from afar, came crowding in by the lecture theatre door, and the discussion

A Slip under the Microscope

perished abruptly as the students who were not already in their places hurried to them to secure the choice of a specimen. There was a noise of keys rattling on split rings as lockers were opened and dissecting instruments taken out. Hill was already standing by his table, and his box of scalpels was sticking out of his pocket. The girl in brown came a step towards him, and leaning over his table said softly, 'Did you see that I returned your book, Mr Hill?'

During the whole scene she and the book had been vividly present in his consciousness; but he made a clumsy pretence of looking at the book and seeing it for the first time. 'Oh yes,' he said, taking it up. 'I see. Did you like it?'

'I want to ask you some questions about it – sometime.'

'Certainly,' said Hill. 'I shall be glad.' He stopped awkwardly. 'You liked it?' he said.

'It's a wonderful book. Only some things I don't understand.'

Then suddenly the laboratory was hushed by a curious braying noise. It was the demonstrator. He was at the blackboard ready to begin the day's instruction, and it was his custom to demand silence by a sound midway between the 'Er' of common intercourse and the blast of a trumpet. The girl in brown slipped back to her place: it was immediately in front of Hill's, and Hill, forgetting her forthwith, took a notebook out of the drawer of his table, turned over its leaves hastily, drew a stumpy pencil from his pocket, and prepared to make a copious note of the coming demonstration. For demonstrations and lectures are the sacred text of the College students. Books, saving only the Professor's own, you may – it is even expedient to – ignore.

Hill was the son of a Landport cobbler, and had been hooked by a chance blue paper the authorities had thrown out to the Landport Technical College. He kept himself in London on his allowance of a guinea a week, and found that, with proper care, this also covered his clothing allowance, an occasional waterproof collar, that is; and ink and needles and cotton and such-like necessaries for a man about town. This was his first year and his first session, but the brown old man in Landport had already got himself detested in many public-houses by boasting of his son, 'the Professor'. Hill was a vigorous youngster, with a serene contempt for the clergy of all denominations, and a fine ambition to reconstruct the world. He regarded his scholarship as a brilliant opportunity. He had begun to read at seven, and had read steadily whatever came in his way, good or bad, since then. His worldly experience had been limited to the island of Portsea, and acquired chiefly in the wholesale boot factory in which he had worked by day, after passing the seventh standard of the Board school. He had a considerable gift of speech, as the College Debating Society, which met amidst the crushing machines and mine models in the metallurgical

A Slip under the Microscope

theatre downstairs, already recognized – recognized by a violent battering of desks whenever he rose. And he was just at that fine emotional age when life opens at the end of a narrow pass like a broad valley at one's feet, full of the promise of wonderful discoveries and tremendous achievements. And his own limitations, save that he knew that he knew neither Latin nor French, were all unknown to him.

At first his interest had been divided pretty equally between his biological work at the College and social and theological theorizing, an employment which he took in deadly earnest. Of a night, when the big museum library was not open, he would sit on the bed of his room in Chelsea with his coat and a muffler on, and write out the lecture notes and revise his dissection memoranda until Thorpe called him out by a whistle – the landlady objected to open the door to attic visitors – and then the two would go prowling about the shadowy, shiny, gaslit streets, talking, very much in the fashion of the sample just given, of the God Idea and Righteousness and Carlyle and the Reorganization of Society. And in the midst of it all, Hill, arguing not only for Thorpe but for the casual passer-by, would lose the thread of his argument glancing at some pretty painted face that looked meaningly at him as he passed. Science and Righteousness! But once or twice lately there had been signs that a third interest was creeping into his life, and he had found his attention wandering from the fate of the mesoblastic somites or the probable meaning of the blastopore, to the thought of the girl with the brown eyes who sat at the table before him.

She was a paying student; she descended inconceivable social altitudes to speak to him. At the thought of the education she must have had, and the accomplishments she must possess, the soul of Hill became abject within him. She had spoken to him first over a difficulty about the alisphenoid of a rabbit's skull, and he had found that, in biology at least, he had no reason for self-abasement. And from that, after the manner of young people starting from any starting-point, they got to generalities, and while Hill attacked her upon the question of socialism, – some instinct told him to spare her a direct assault upon her religion – she was gathering resolution to undertake what she told herself was his aesthetic education. She was a year or two older than he, though the thought never occurred to him. The loan of *News from Nowhere* was the beginning of a series of cross loans. Upon some absurd first principle of his, Hill had never 'wasted time' upon poetry, and it seemed an appalling deficiency to her. One day in the lunch hour, when she chanced upon him alone in the little museum where the skeletons were arranged, shamefully eating the bun that constituted his midday meal, she retreated, and returned to lend him, with a slightly furtive air, a volume of Browning. He stood sideways towards her and took the book rather clumsily, because he was holding the bun in the other hand. And

A Slip under the Microscope

in the retrospect his voice lacked the cheerful clearness he could have wished.

That occurred after the examination in comparative anatomy, on the day before the College turned out its students and was carefully locked up by the officials for the Christmas holidays. The excitement of cramming for the first trial of strength had for a little while dominated Hill to the exclusion of his other interests. In the forecasts of the result in which everyone indulged he was surprised to find that no one regarded him as a possible competitor for the Harvey Commemoration Medal, of which this and the two subsequent examinations disposed. It was about this time that Wedderburn, who so far had lived inconspicuously on the uttermost margin of Hill's perceptions, began to take on the appearance of an obstacle. By a mutual agreement, the nocturnal prowlings with Thorpe ceased for the three weeks before the examination, and his landlady pointed out that she really could not supply so much lamp oil at the price. He walked to and fro from the College with little slips of mnemonics in his hand, lists of crayfish appendages, rabbits' skull-bones, and vertebrate nerves, for example, and became a positive nuisance to foot passengers in the opposite direction.

But, by a natural reaction, Poetry and the girl with the brown eyes ruled the Christmas holiday. The pending results of the examination became such a secondary consideration that Hill marvelled at his father's excitement.

Even had he wished it, there was no comparative anatomy to read in Landport, and he was too poor to buy books, but the stock of poets in the library was extensive, and Hill's attack was magnificently sustained. He saturated himself with the fluent numbers of Longfellow and Tennyson, and fortified himself with Shakespeare; found a kindred soul in Pope and a master in Shelley, and heard and fled the siren voices of Eliza Cook and Mrs Hemans. But he read no more Browning, because he hoped for the loan of other volumes from Miss Haysman when he returned to London.

He walked from his lodgings to the College with that volume of Browning in his shiny black bag, and his mind teeming with the finest general propositions about poetry. Indeed, he framed first this little speech and then that with which to grace the return. The morning was an exceptionally pleasant one for London; there was a clear hard frost and undeniable blue in the sky, a thin haze softened every outline, and warm shafts of sunlight struck between the house blocks and turned the sunny side of the street to amber and gold. In the hall of the College he pulled off his glove and signed his name with fingers so stiff with cold that the characteristic dash under the signature he cultivated became a quivering line. He imagined Miss Haysman about him everywhere. He turned at the staircase, and there, below, he saw a crowd struggling at the foot of the noticeboard. This, possibly, was the biology list. He forgot Browning and Miss Haysman for the moment, and joined the scrimmage. And at last, with his cheek flattened against the sleeve of the man on the step above him, he read the list –

CLASS I
H. J. Somers Wedderburn
William Hill

and thereafter followed a second class that is outside our present sympathies. It was characteristic that he did not trouble to look for Thorpe on the physics list, but backed out of the struggle at once, and in a curious emotional state between pride over common second-class humanity and acute disappointment at Wedderburn's success, went on his way upstairs. At the top, as he was hanging up his coat in the passage, the zoological demonstrator, a young man from Oxford who secretly regarded him as a blatant 'mugger' of the very worst type, offered his heartiest congratulations.

At the laboratory door Hill stopped for a second to get his breath, and then entered. He looked straight up the laboratory and saw all five girl students grouped in their places, and Wedderburn, the once retiring Wedderburn, leaning rather gracefully against the window, playing with the blind tassel and talking apparently to the five of them. Now, Hill could talk bravely enough and even overbearingly to one girl, and he could have made a speech to a roomful of girls, but this business of standing at ease and appreciating, fencing, and returning quick remarks round a group was, he knew, altogether beyond him. Coming up the staircase his feelings for Wedderburn had been generous, a certain admiration perhaps, a willingness to shake his hand conspicuously and heartily as one who had fought but the first round. But before Christmas Wedderburn had never gone up to that end of the room to talk. In a flash Hill's mist of vague excitement condensed abruptly to a vivid dislike of Wedderburn. Possibly his expression changed. As he came up to his place, Wedderburn nodded carelessly to him, and the others glanced round. Miss Haysman looked at him and away again, the faintest touch of her eyes. 'I can't agree with you, Mr Wedderburn,' she said.

'I must congratulate you on your first class, Mr Hill,' said the spectacled girl in green, turning round and beaming at him.

'It's nothing,' said Hill, staring at Wedderburn and Miss Haysman talking together, and eager to hear what they talked about.

'We poor folks in the second class don't think so,' said the girl in spectacles.

What was it Wedderburn was saying? Something about William Morris! Hill did not answer the girl in spectacles, and the smile died out of his face. He could not hear, and failed to see how he could 'cut in'. Confound Wedderburn! He sat down, opened his bag, hesitated whether to return the volume of Browning forthwith, in the sight of all, and instead drew out his new notebooks for the short course in elementary botany that was now beginning, and which would terminate in February. As he did so, a fat heavy man with a white face and pale grey eyes – Bindon, the professor of botany, who came up from Kew for January and February – came in by the lecture-theatre door, and passed, rubbing his hands together and smiling, in silent affability down the laboratory.

In the subsequent six weeks Hill experienced some very rapid and curiously complex emotional developments. For the most part he had Wedderburn in focus – a fact that Miss Haysman never suspected. She told Hill (for in the comparative privacy of the museum she talked a good deal to him of socialism and Browning and general propositions) that she had met Wedderburn at the house of some people she knew, and 'he's inherited his cleverness; for his father, you know, is the great eye specialist'.

'*My* father is a cobbler,' said Hill, quite irrelevantly, and perceived the want of dignity even as he said it. But the gleam of jealousy did not offend her. She conceived herself the fundamental source of it. He suffered bitterly from a sense of Wedderburn's unfairness, and a realization of his own handicap. Here was this Wedderburn had picked up a prominent man for a father, and instead of his losing so many marks on the score of that advantage, it was counted to him for righteousness! And while Hill had to introduce himself and talk to Miss Haysman clumsily over mangled guineapigs in the laboratory, this Wedderburn, in some backstairs way, had access to her social altitudes, and could converse in a polished argot that Hill understood perhaps, but felt incapable of speaking. Not, of course, that he wanted to. Then it seemed to Hill that for Wedderburn to come there day after day with cuffs unfrayed, neatly tailored, precisely barbered, quietly perfect, was in itself an ill-bred, sneering sort of proceeding. Moreover, it was a stealthy thing for Wedderburn to behave insignificantly for a space, to mock modesty, to lead Hill to fancy that he himself was beyond dispute the man of the year, and then suddenly to dart in front of him, and incontinently to swell up in this fashion. In addition to these things, Wedderburn displayed an increasing disposition to join in any conversational grouping that included Miss Haysman; and would venture, and indeed seek occasion, to pass opinions derogatory to socialism and atheism. He goaded Hill to incivilities by neat, shallow, and exceedingly effective personalities about the socialist leaders, until Hill hated Bernard Shaw's graceful egotisms, William Morris's limited editions and luxurious wallpapers, and Walter Crane's charmingly absurd ideal working men, about as much as he hated Wedderburn. The dissertations in the laboratory, that had been his glory in the previous term, became a danger, degenerated into inglorious tussles with Wedderburn, and Hill kept to them only out of an obscure perception that his honour was involved. In the debating society Hill knew quite clearly that, to a thunderous accompaniment of banged desks, he could have pulverized Wedderburn. Only Wedderburn never attended the debating society to be pulverized, because – nauseous affectation! – he 'dined late'.

You must not imagine that these things presented themselves in quite such a crude form to Hill's perception. Hill was a born generalizer. Wedderburn to him was not so much an individual obstacle as a type, the salient angle of a class. The economic theories that, after infinite ferment, had shaped themselves in Hill's mind, became abruptly concrete at the contact. The world became full of easy-mannered, graceful, gracefully dressed, conversationally dexterous, finally shallow Wedderburns, Bishops Wedderburn, Wedderburn M.P.s, Professors Wedderburn, Wedderburn landlords, all with finger-bowl shibboleths and epigrammatic cities of refuge from a sturdy debater. And everyone ill-clothed or ill-dressed, from the cobbler to the cab-runner, was, to Hill's imagination, a man and a brother, a fellow-sufferer. So that he became, as it were, a champion of the fallen and oppressed, albeit to outward seeming only a self-assertive, ill-mannered young man, and an unsuccessful champion at that. Again and again a skirmish over the afternoon tea that the girl students had inaugurated left Hill with flushed cheeks and a tattered temper, and the debating society noticed a new quality of sarcastic bitterness in his speeches.

You will understand now how it was necessary, if only in the interests of humanity, that Hill should demolish Wedderburn in the forthcoming examination and outshine him in the eyes of Miss Haysman; and you will perceive, too, how Miss Haysman fell into some common feminine misconceptions. The Hill–Wedderburn quarrel, for in his unostentatious way Wedderburn reciprocated Hill's ill-veiled rivalry, became a tribute to her indefinable charm: she was the Queen of Beauty in a tournament of scalpels and stumpy pencils. To her confidential friend's secret annoyance, it even troubled her conscience, for she was a good girl, and painfully aware, through Ruskin and contemporary fiction, how entirely men's activities are determined by women's attitudes. And if Hill never by any chance mentioned the topic of love to her, she only credited him with the finer modesty for that omission.

So the time came on for the second examination, and Hill's increasing pallor confirmed the general rumour that he was working hard. In the aerated bread shop near South Kensington Station you would see him, breaking his bun and sipping his milk with his eyes intent upon a paper of closely written notes. In his bedroom there were propositions about buds and stems round his looking-glass, a diagram to catch his eye, if soap should chance to spare it, above his washing basin. He missed several meetings of the debating society, but he found the chance encounters with Miss Haysman in the spacious ways of the adjacent art museum, or in the little museum at the top of the College, or in the College corridors, more frequent and very restful. In particular, they used to meet in a little gallery full of wrought-iron chests and gates near the art library, and there Hill used to talk, under the gentle stimulus of her flattering attention, of Browning and his personal ambitions. A characteristic she found remarkable in him was his freedom from avarice. He contemplated quite calmly the prospect of living all his life on an income below a hundred pounds a year. But he was determined to be famous, to make, recognizably in his own proper person, the world a better place to live in. He took Bradlaugh and John Burns for his leaders and models, poor, even impecunious, great men. But Miss Haysman thought that such lives were deficient on the aesthetic side, by which, though she did not know it, she meant good wallpaper and upholstery, pretty books, tasteful clothes, concerts, and meals nicely cooked and respectfully served.

At last came the day of the second examination, and the professor of botany, a fussy, conscientious man, rearranged all the tables in a long narrow laboratory to prevent copying, and put his demonstrator on a chair on a table (where he felt, he said, like a Hindu god), to see all the cheating, and stuck a notice outside the door, 'Door closed', for no earthly reason that any human being could discover. And all the morning from ten till one the quill of Wedderburn shrieked defiance at Hill's, and the quills of the others chased their leaders in a tireless pack, and so also it was in the afternoon. Wedderburn was a little quieter than usual, and Hill's face was hot all day, and his overcoat bulged with textbooks and notebooks against the last moment's revision. And the next day, in the morning and in the afternoon, was the practical examination, when sections had to be cut and slides identified. In the morning Hill was depressed because he knew he had cut a thick section, and in the afternoon came the mysterious slip.

It was just the kind of thing that the botanical professor was always doing. Like the income tax, it offered a premium to the cheat. It was a preparation under the microscope, a little glass slip, held in its place on the stage of the instrument by light steel clips, and the inscription set forth that the slip was not to be moved. Each student was to go in turn to it, sketch it, write in his book of answers what he considered it to be, and return to his place. Now, to move such a slip is a thing one can do by a chance movement of the finger, and in a fraction of a second. The professor's reason for decreeing that the slip should not be moved depended on the fact that the object he wanted identified was characteristic of a certain tree-stem. In the position in which it was placed it was a difficult thing to recognize, but once the slip was moved so as to bring other parts of the preparation into view, its nature was obvious enough.

Hill came to this, flushed from a contest with staining reagents, sat down on the little stool before the

A Slip under the Microscope

microscope, turned the mirror to get the best light, and then, out of sheer habit, shifted the slip. At once he remembered the prohibition, and, with an almost continuous motion of his hands, moved it back, and sat paralysed with astonishment at his action.

Then, slowly, he turned his head. The professor was out of the room; the demonstrator sat aloft on his impromptu rostrum, reading the *Q. Jour. Mi. Sci.*; the rest of the examinees were busy, and with their backs to him. Should he own up to the accident now? He knew quite clearly what the thing was. It was a lenticel, a characteristic preparation from the elder-tree. His eyes roved over his intent fellow-students and Wedderburn suddenly glanced over his shoulder at him with a queer expression in his eyes. The mental excitement that had kept Hill at an abnormal pitch of vigour these two days gave way to a curious nervous tension. His book of answers was beside him. He did not write down what the thing was, but with one eye at the microscope he began making a hasty sketch of it. His mind was full of this grotesque puzzle in ethics that had suddenly been sprung upon him. Should he identify it? or should he leave this question unanswered? In that case Wedderburn would probably come out first in the second result. How could he tell now whether he might not have identified the thing without shifting it? It was possible that Wedderburn had failed to recognize it, of course. Suppose Wedderburn too had shifted the slide? He looked up at the clock. There were fifteen minutes in which to make up his mind. He gathered up his book of answers and the coloured pencils he used in illustrating his replies and walked back to his seat.

He read through his manuscript, and then sat thinking and gnawing his knuckle. It would look queer now if he owned up. He *must* beat Wedderburn. He forgot the examples of those starry gentlemen, John Burns and Bradlaugh. Besides, he reflected, the glimpse of the rest of the slip he had had was after all quite accidental, forced upon him by chance, a kind of providential revelation rather than an unfair advantage. It was not nearly so dishonest to avail himself of that as it was of Broome, who believed in the efficacy of prayer, to pray daily for a first-class. 'Five minutes more,' said the demonstrator, folding up his paper and becoming observant. Hill watched the clock hands until two minutes remained; then he opened the book of answers, and, with hot ears and an affectation of ease, gave his drawing of the lenticel its name.

When the second pass list appeared, the previous positions of Wedderburn and Hill were reversed, and the spectacled girl in green, who knew the demonstrator in private life (where he was practically human), said that in the result of the two examinations taken together Hill had the advantage of a mark – 167 to 166 out of a possible 200. Everyone admired Hill in a way, though the suspicion of 'mugging' clung to him. But Hill was to find congratulations and Miss Haysman's enhanced opinion of him, and even the decided decline in the crest of

A Slip under the Microscope

Wedderburn, tainted by an unhappy memory. He felt a remarkable access of energy at first, and the note of a democracy marching to triumph returned to his debating society speeches; he worked at his comparative anatomy with tremendous zeal and effect, and he went on with his aesthetic education. But through it all, a vivid little picture was continually coming before his mind's eye – of a sneakish person manipulating a slide.

No human being had witnessed the act, and he was cocksure that no higher power existed to see it; but for all that it worried him. Memories are not dead things, but alive; they dwindle in disuse, but they harden and develop in all sorts of queer ways if they are being continually fretted. Curiously enough, though at the time he perceived clearly that the shifting was accidental, as the days wore on his memory became confused about it, until at last he was not sure – although he assured himself that he *was* sure – whether the movement had been absolutely involuntary. Then it is possible that Hill's dietary was conducive to morbid conscientiousness; a breakfast frequently eaten in a hurry, a midday bun, and, at such hours after five as chanced to be convenient, such meat as his means determined, usually in a chop-house in a back street off the Brompton Road. Occasionally he treated himself to threepenny or ninepenny classics, and they usually represented a suppression of potatoes or chops. It is indisputable that outbreaks of self-abasement and emotional revival have a distinct relation to periods of scarcity. But apart from this influence on the feelings, there was in Hill a distinct aversion to falsity that the blasphemous Landport cobbler had inculcated by strap and tongue from his earliest years. Of one fact about professed atheists I am convinced; they may be – they usually are – fools, void of subtlety, revilers of holy institutions, brutal speakers, and mischievous knaves, but they lie with difficulty. If it were not so, if they had the faintest grasp of the idea of compromise, they would simply be liberal churchmen. And, moreover, this memory poisoned his regard for Miss Haysman. For she now so evidently preferred him to Wedderburn that he felt sure he cared for her, and began reciprocating her attentions by timid marks of personal regard; at one time he even bought a bunch of violets, carried it about in his pocket, and produced it with a stumbling explanation, withered and dead, in the gallery of old iron. It poisoned, too, the denunciation of capitalist dishonesty that had been one of his life's pleasures. And, lastly, it poisoned his triumph in Wedderburn. Previously he had been Wedderburn's superior in his own eyes, and had raged simply at a want of recognition. Now he began to fret at the darker suspicion of positive inferiority. He fancied he found justifications for his position in Browning, but they vanished on analysis. At last – moved, curiously enough, by exactly the same motive forces that had resulted in his dishonesty – he went to Professor Bindon, and made a

A Slip under the Microscope

clean breast of the whole affair. As Hill was a paid student, Professor Bindon did not ask him to sit down, and he stood before the professor's desk as he made his confession.

'It's a curious story,' said Professor Bindon, slowly realizing how the thing reflected on himself, and then letting his anger rise, – 'A most remarkable story. I can't understand your doing it, and I can't understand this avowal. You're a type of student – Cambridge men would never dream – I suppose I ought to have thought – Why *did* you cheat?'

'I didn't cheat,' said Hill.

'But you have just been telling me you did.'

'I thought I explained–'

'Either you cheated or you did not cheat.'–

'I said my motion was involuntary.'

'I am not a metaphysician, I am a servant of science – of fact. You were told not to move the slip. You did move the slip. If that is not cheating–'

'If I was a cheat,' said Hill, with the note of hysterics in his voice, 'should I come here and tell you?'

'Your repentance, of course, does you credit,' said Professor Bindon, 'but it does not alter the original facts.'

'No, sir,' said Hill, giving in in utter self-abasement.

'Even now you cause an enormous amount of trouble. The examination list will have to be revised.'

'I suppose so, sir.'

'Suppose so? Of course it must be revised. And I don't see how I can conscientiously pass you.'

'Not pass me?' said Hill. 'Fail me?'

'It's the rule in all examinations. Or where should we be? What else did you expect? You don't want to shirk the consequences of your own acts?'

'I thought, perhaps' – said Hill. And then, 'Fail me? I thought, as I told you, you would simply deduct the marks given for that slip.'

'Impossible!' said Bindon. 'Besides, it would still leave you above Wedderburn. Deduct only the marks – Preposterous! The Departmental Regulations distinctly say–'

'But it's my own admission, sir.'

'The Regulations say nothing whatever of the manner in which the matter comes to light. They simply provide–'

'It will ruin me. If I fail this examination, they won't renew my scholarship.'

'You should have thought of that before.'

'But, sir, consider all my circumstances–'

'I cannot consider anything. Professors in this College are machines. The Regulations will not even let us recommend our students for appointments. I am a machine, and you have worked me. I have to do–'

'It's very hard, sir.'

'Possibly it is.'

A Slip under the Microscope

'If I am to be failed this examination, I might as well go home at once.'

'That is as you think proper.' Bindon's voice softened a little; he perceived he had been unjust, and, provided he did not contradict himself, he was disposed to amelioration. 'As a private person,' he said, 'I think this confession of yours goes far to mitigate your offence. But you have set the machinery in motion, and now it must take its course. I – I am really sorry you gave way.'

A wave of emotion prevented Hill from answering. Suddenly, very vividly, he saw the heavily lined face of the old Landport cobbler, his father. 'Good God! What a fool I have been!' he said hotly and abruptly.

'I hope,' said Bindon, 'that it will be a lesson to you.'

But, curiously enough, they were not thinking of quite the same indiscretion.

There was a pause.

'I would like a day to think, sir, and then I will let you know – about going home, I mean,' said Hill, moving towards the door.

The next day Hill's place was vacant. The spectacled girl in green was, as usual, first with the news. Wedderburn and Miss Haysman were talking of a performance of *The Meistersingers* when she came up to them.

'Have you heard?' she said.

'Heard what?'

'There was cheating in the examination.'

'Cheating!' said Wedderburn, with his face suddenly hot. 'How?'

'That slide'–

'Moved? Never!'

'It was. That slide that we weren't to move'–

'Nonsense!' said Wedderburn. 'Why! How could they find out? Who do they say–?'

'It was Mr Hill.'

'*Hill!*'

'Mr Hill!'

'Not – surely not the immaculate Hill?' said Wedderburn, recovering.

'I don't believe it,' said Miss Haysman. 'How do you know?'

'I *didn't*,' said the girl in spectacles. 'But I know it now for a fact. Mr Hill went and confessed to Professor Bindon himself.'

'By Jove!' said Wedderburn. 'Hill of all people. But I am always inclined to distrust these philanthropists-on-principle' –

'Are you quite sure?' said Miss Haysman, with a catch in her breath.

'Quite. It's dreadful, isn't it? But, you know, what can you expect? His father is a cobbler.'

Then Miss Haysman astonished the girl in spectacles.

'I don't care. I will not believe it,' she said, flushing darkly under her warm-tinted skin. 'I will not believe it until he has told me so himself – face to face. I would scarcely believe it then,' and abruptly she turned her back on the girl in spectacles, and walked to her own place.

'It's true, all the same,' said the girl in spectacles, peering and smiling at Wedderburn.

But Wedderburn did not answer her. She was indeed one of those people who seem destined to make unanswered remarks.

1. BOCCACCIO · *Mrs Rosie and the Priest*
2. GERARD MANLEY HOPKINS · *As kingfishers catch fire*
3. *The Saga of Gunnlaug Serpent-tongue*
4. THOMAS DE QUINCEY · *On Murder Considered as One of the Fine Arts*
5. FRIEDRICH NIETZSCHE · *Aphorisms on Love and Hate*
6. JOHN RUSKIN · *Traffic*
7. PU SONGLING · *Wailing Ghosts*
8. JONATHAN SWIFT · *A Modest Proposal*
9. *Three Tang Dynasty Poets*
10. WALT WHITMAN · *On the Beach at Night Alone*
11. KENKŌ · *A Cup of Sake Beneath the Cherry Trees*
12. BALTASAR GRACIÁN · *How to Use Your Enemies*
13. JOHN KEATS · *The Eve of St Agnes*
14. THOMAS HARDY · *Woman much missed*
15. GUY DE MAUPASSANT · *Femme Fatale*
16. MARCO POLO · *Travels in the Land of Serpents and Pearls*
17. SUETONIUS · *Caligula*
18. APOLLONIUS OF RHODES · *Jason and Medea*
19. ROBERT LOUIS STEVENSON · *Olalla*
20. KARL MARX AND FRIEDRICH ENGELS · *The Communist Manifesto*
21. PETRONIUS · *Trimalchio's Feast*
22. JOHANN PETER HEBEL · *How a Ghastly Story Was Brought to Light by a Common or Garden Butcher's Dog*
23. HANS CHRISTIAN ANDERSEN · *The Tinder Box*
24. RUDYARD KIPLING · *The Gate of the Hundred Sorrows*
25. DANTE · *Circles of Hell*
26. HENRY MAYHEW · *Of Street Piemen*
27. HAFEZ · *The nightingales are drunk*
28. GEOFFREY CHAUCER · *The Wife of Bath*
29. MICHEL DE MONTAIGNE · *How We Weep and Laugh at the Same Thing*
30. THOMAS NASHE · *The Terrors of the Night*
31. EDGAR ALLAN POE · *The Tell-Tale Heart*
32. MARY KINGSLEY · *A Hippo Banquet*
33. JANE AUSTEN · *The Beautifull Cassandra*
34. ANTON CHEKHOV · *Gooseberries*
35. SAMUEL TAYLOR COLERIDGE · *Well, they are gone, and here must I remain*
36. JOHANN WOLFGANG VON GOETHE · *Sketchy, Doubtful, Incomplete Jottings*
37. CHARLES DICKENS · *The Great Winglebury Duel*
38. HERMAN MELVILLE · *The Maldive Shark*
39. ELIZABETH GASKELL · *The Old Nurse's Story*
40. NIKOLAY LESKOV · *The Steel Flea*

41. HONORÉ DE BALZAC · *The Atheist's Mass*
42. CHARLOTTE PERKINS GILMAN · *The Yellow Wall-Paper*
43. C.P. CAVAFY · *Remember, Body...*
44. FYODOR DOSTOYEVSKY · *The Meek One*
45. GUSTAVE FLAUBERT · *A Simple Heart*
46. NIKOLAI GOGOL · *The Nose*
47. SAMUEL PEPYS · *The Great Fire of London*
48. EDITH WHARTON · *The Reckoning*
49. HENRY JAMES · *The Figure in the Carpet*
50. WILFRED OWEN · *Anthem For Doomed Youth*
51. WOLFGANG AMADEUS MOZART · *My Dearest Father*
52. PLATO · *Socrates' Defence*
53. CHRISTINA ROSSETTI · *Goblin Market*
54. *Sindbad the Sailor*
55. SOPHOCLES · *Antigone*
56. RYŪNOSUKE AKUTAGAWA · *The Life of a Stupid Man*
57. LEO TOLSTOY · *How Much Land Does A Man Need?*
58. GIORGIO VASARI · *Leonardo da Vinci*
59. OSCAR WILDE · *Lord Arthur Savile's Crime*
60. SHEN FU · *The Old Man of the Moon*
61. AESOP · *The Dolphins, the Whales and the Gudgeon*
62. MATSUO BASHŌ · *Lips too Chilled*
63. EMILY BRONTË · *The Night is Darkening Round Me*
64. JOSEPH CONRAD · *To-morrow*
65. RICHARD HAKLUYT · *The Voyage of Sir Francis Drake Around the Whole Globe*
66. KATE CHOPIN · *A Pair of Silk Stockings*
67. CHARLES DARWIN · *It was snowing butterflies*
68. BROTHERS GRIMM · *The Robber Bridegroom*
69. CATULLUS · *I Hate and I Love*
70. HOMER · *Circe and the Cyclops*
71. D. H. LAWRENCE · *Il Duro*
72. KATHERINE MANSFIELD · *Miss Brill*
73. OVID · *The Fall of Icarus*
74. SAPPHO · *Come Close*
75. IVAN TURGENEV · *Kasyan from the Beautiful Lands*
76. VIRGIL · *O Cruel Alexis*
77. H. G. WELLS · *A Slip under the Microscope*
78. HERODOTUS · *The Madness of Cambyses*
79. *Speaking of Siva*
80. *The Dhammapada*

'Do you see your son, standing over there, in the antechamber? Well, I am going to shoot him.'

HERODOTUS
Born *c.* 484 BCE, Halicarnassus, Caria
Died *c.* 425 BCE, location unknown

This selection is taken from Tom Holland's translation of
The Histories, first published in 2013.

HERODOTUS IN PENGUIN CLASSICS
The Histories

HERODOTUS

The Madness of Cambyses

Translated by
Tom Holland

PENGUIN BOOKS

PENGUIN CLASSICS

UK | USA | Canada | Ireland | Australia
India | New Zealand | South Africa

Penguin Books is part of the Penguin Random House group of companies
whose addresses can be found at global.penguinrandomhouse.com.

This selection published in Penguin Classics 2015
008

Translation copyright © Tom Holland, 2013

The moral right of the translator has been asserted

Set in 9.5/13 pt Baskerville 10 Pro
Typeset by Jouve (UK), Milton Keynes

Printed and bound in Great Britain by Clays Ltd, Elcograf S.p.A.

A CIP catalogue record for this book is available from the British Library

ISBN: 978-0-141-39877-8

www.greenpenguin.co.uk

Penguin Random House is committed to a sustainable future for our business, our readers and our planet. This book is made from Forest Stewardship Council® certified paper.

[1] This, then, was the Amasis against whom Cambyses, the son of Cyrus, was leading an army drawn from all the peoples subject to him, Greeks included – to be specific, Ionians and Aeolians. What lay behind the invasion? Cambyses had made a demand of Amasis, through a herald dispatched to Egypt, that he hand over one of his daughters to him – a demand which had in turn been made on the prompting of an Egyptian with a grudge against Amasis. This physician, alone among his colleagues, had been torn away by royal edict from his wife and children, and packed off to Persia, after Amasis had received a request from Cyrus for the best eye-doctor in Egypt. No wonder, then, that the Egyptian should have been so filled with resentment that he succeeded in pressing (indeed, almost instructing) Cambyses into asking for a daughter from Amasis – who was then confronted by the choice of surrendering his daughter at the cost of deep personal distress, or of rebuffing the request, and making an enemy of Cambyses. Already vexed by the menace of Persian power, Amasis found himself quite unable to answer yes or no. He knew full well that his

daughter would be taken by Cambyses not as a wife, but as a concubine; and so it was with this in mind that he finally settled on a course of action. It so happened that the one surviving member of the previous royal house was a daughter of Apries, a strikingly statuesque and handsome girl named Nitetis. Amasis duly arrayed her in fine clothes and gold jewellery, and sent her off to Persia, as though she were his own daughter. In due course, however, when Cambyses happened to address the girl by her father's name, she replied, 'You have no idea, my Lord, just how badly Amasis has abused you. Despite the fact that he dispatched me to you decked out in all this finery, as though it were indeed his own daughter that he had gift-wrapped, the truth is that I am the daughter of Apries, the one-time master of Amasis, but lately toppled and murdered by him, him and all the Egyptians.' Such was the declaration (and such the provocation that it served to bring to light) which led Cambyses, son of Cyrus, to descend upon Egypt in a towering fury. Or so, at any rate, the Persians report.

[2] The Egyptians, however, claim Cambyses as one of their own, asserting that he was the son of this same daughter of Apries, and that it was Cyrus, not Cambyses, who sent to Amasis for his daughter. In presenting this version of events, however, they are way off the mark. Indeed, since the Egyptians themselves have a better grasp than anyone of how Persian laws function, it can hardly have escaped their attention, firstly, that it is

The Madness of Cambyses

wholly illegal for a bastard to inherit the Persian throne while there is still a legitimate heir alive, and secondly, that Cambyses was the child of Cassandane, the daughter of Pharnaspes, a man of Achaemenid stock, and not an Egyptian at all. The point of the distorted account given by the Egyptians, of course, is to provide them with a feigned link of kinship to the House of Cyrus.

[3] So that is how the matter stands. There is, however, another story – one that I personally do not find persuasive – which relates how a Persian woman came in to visit the wives of Cyrus, and was so impressed by the sight of Cassandane standing there with her tall and handsome offspring that she began to lavish extravagant praise on them. But Cassandane, who was one of Cyrus' wives, only retorted, 'Yes, and see with what a lack of respect Cyrus treats me, despite the fact that I have borne him such children. The only one he has any respect for is his new acquisition from Egypt.' These comments were prompted by Cassandane's resentment of Nitetis; and they were answered by her eldest child, Cambyses. 'That, Mother,' he told her, 'is why, once I am a man, I will turn all Egypt upon its head.' He was barely ten years old when he made this promise, to the great astonishment of the women. He never forgot it, however; and sure enough, no sooner had he come of age and taken possession of the throne, than he was embarking on his invasion of Egypt.

[4] There was another, quite distinct, episode, however, which also contributed to this expedition. One of the

mercenaries employed by Amasis was a man named Phanes, who originally came from Halicarnassus, and was both sound in judgement and bold in war. For some reason or other, he developed a grudge against Amasis, and fled Egypt by boat, his aim being to secure an audience with Cambyses. Such had been his standing among the mercenaries, however, and so detailed the intelligence he had on Egyptian affairs, that Amasis was frantic to capture him, and duly set about hunting him down. He dispatched in a trireme the most trustworthy of his eunuchs, who duly ran his quarry to ground in Lycia. Despite this success, the eunuch did not manage to transport him back to Egypt – for Phanes ran rings round his captor. First he got his guards roaringly drunk; then off he slipped to Persia. When he arrived, he found that Cambyses, despite his enthusiasm for leading his army against Egypt, was at a loss to know which approach to take, for none of the invasion routes offered any water, and so Phanes, in addition to the intelligence that he provided on Amasis, detailed the course that should be taken. 'Make contact with the king of the Arabians,' he advised. 'Ask him for safe passage.'

[5] Certainly, there is no other obvious way into Egypt. The territory between Phoenicia and the limits of the city of Cadytis belongs to Syrians who are known as 'Palestinians'; then from Cadytis (which I would estimate to be almost on the scale of Sardis), the coastal trading-posts as far as the city of Ienysus are subject to the Arabians;

The Madness of Cambyses

beyond Ienysus, and all the way to the Serbonian marsh, where a spur of Mount Casium extends down to the sea, it reverts to Syrian control; onwards from the Serbonian marsh (in which some say Typhon lies hidden), and the crossing has been made into Egypt. The tract of land between the city of Ienysus and Mount Casium and the Serbonian marsh is no small distance, for it takes some three days to cross, and is so ferociously parched as to be quite without water.

[6] I am now going to point out something which few of those who make the voyage to Egypt have thought to reflect upon. Every year there is a constant flow into Egypt of earthenware jars filled with wine, imported from across the Greek world and from Phoenicia – and yet it is hardly an exaggeration to say that empty earthenware wine-jars are never seen. One might well ask, then, what on earth happens to them? This too I can answer. Every headman of a village is required to collect together all the earthenware from his own community and bring it to Memphis; and the people of Memphis must then fill the jars with water, and convey them to the same waterless stretches of Syria. This is the process by which every piece of earthenware imported into Egypt, once it has been emptied, finds its way to Syria to join all the other jars that have been assembled there over time.

[7] Now, it was the Persians, in the immediate wake of their conquest of Egypt, who provisioned the entry route into Egypt with supplies of water, in the manner I have

just described; but at the time, there was not a drop to be had. So it was that Cambyses, advised of this by his foreign friend from Halicarnassus, sent messengers with a request for safe passage to the king of the Arabians – who duly answered the pledges given him by granting pledges of his own.

[8] The Arabians, to a degree that few other peoples can match, regard the giving of pledges as a sacred business. Should two parties wish to make a compact, then the procedure is for a third man to stand between them and use a sharp piece of stone to score a light incision along the palms of their hands, just below their thumbs; he will then take a strip of cloth from both men's cloaks, and use the material to anoint with their blood seven stones which have been placed between them; as he does this, so will he invoke Dionysus and Urania. Once the ritual is completed, the man who is giving the pledge will commend the foreigner – or fellow-townsman, as the case may be – to his friends, and these friends will then regard it as their solemn duty to honour the pledge themselves. Apart from Urania, the only god whose existence the Arabians acknowledge is Dionysus; his cropped locks, they say, provide them with the inspiration for the way in which they wear their own hair short: that is, cut in a circle, with the temples shaved. Dionysus is called *Orotalt* by the Arabians, and Urania is *Alilat*.

[9] So it was that the king of the Arabians, after he had given his word to the messengers who had come from

The Madness of Cambyses

Cambyses, devised the following plan. First he filled camel-skins with water and loaded them up onto every living camel he had; then, that done, he drove the camels out into the desert, and there awaited Cambyses' army. Such, at any rate, is the more convincing of the accounts that are given; but there is also a less convincing version which nevertheless, since it does have some plausibility, demands to be told. There is a large river in Arabia, the Corys by name, which flows into the Red Sea, as it is called. The story goes that the king of the Arabians had raw ox-hides and the skins of various other animals stitched together so as to make a pipe, sufficient in length to reach from this same river to the desert; and that he then channelled water through the pipe into large reservoirs which had been dug in the desert for the purpose of receiving and storing the water. It is twelve days' journey from the river to this particular desert. There were three pipes, and each one conducted the water to one of three locations.

[10] Psammenitus, the son of Amasis, made camp by what is known as the Pelusiac Mouth of the Nile, there to await Cambyses. Amasis himself was no longer alive by the time Cambyses came to invade Egypt, for he had died after a reign that had lasted forty-four years, and never once known any serious calamity. Following his death and mummification, Amasis was laid to rest in the burial-vault that he himself had had built within the shrine. During the reign of his son, Psammenitus, over

Egypt, a phenomenon was witnessed which utterly stupefied the Egyptians: rain fell on Egyptian Thebes. This was something that had never happened before; nor, according to the Thebans themselves, has it happened since, up to my own lifetime. Rain is simply not a feature of upper Egypt. On this one occasion, however, it did rain in Thebes: a light drizzle.

[11] Once the Persians had crossed the desert, they took up positions close to the Egyptians, aiming to engage them in battle; whereupon the Greeks and the Carians, who were employed as mercenaries by the Egyptian king, felt so outraged by what Phanes had done in leading an army of gibberish-spouting foreigners against Egypt, that they devised their own riposte. Phanes had children whom he had left behind in Egypt; and these children were now brought to the camp, and into the full view of their father. The mercenaries then set up a mixing-bowl midway between their own and the enemy camp, after which they led out the children one by one, and cut their throats over the mixing-bowl. After the final dispatch of all the children, wine and water were poured into the bowl as well; the mercenaries then gulped down the blood and headed off into battle. Fierce though the fighting was, however, and numerous the casualties on both sides, it was the Egyptians who finally turned tail.

[12] I witnessed something truly extraordinary there, which I was tipped off about by the locals. The site is strewn with the bones of men from both sides who fell in

the battle, with those of the Persians quite distinct from those of the Egyptians, just as they were when the fighting originally began; and so brittle are the skulls of the Persians that, should you wish to make a hole in one, you would have only to tap it with a single pebble, whereas those of the Egyptians are so tough that it would be a challenge to smash them through, even if you pounded at them with a rock. Why should this be so? The locals gave a reason which seems to me eminently plausible: namely, that Egyptians are in the habit of shaving their heads from the very earliest days of their childhood, so that the bone ends up thickened by exposure to the sun. (This also explains why Egyptians never go bald – for it is a fact that the incidence of baldness among Egyptians is the lowest anywhere in the world.) This explanation of the toughness of Egyptian skulls also serves to suggest why Persian skulls should be so brittle: the Persians keep their heads out of the sun from birth by wearing conical felt caps, or *tiaras*. So that is how the matter stands. I saw something very similar at Papremis, when I inspected the skulls of those who had perished at the side of Achaemenes, the son of Darius, at the hands of Inaros the Libyan.

[13] When the Egyptians turned tail from the battlefield, they fled in disarray. Once they were all cornered in Memphis, Cambyses sent a Mytilenaean ship upriver, carrying a Persian herald whose mission it was to summon the Egyptians to negotiate. But the Egyptians, when they

saw that the ship had docked in Memphis, came pouring out from behind the fortress in a great mob; they destroyed the ship, butchered and dismembered the crew and carted the remains back inside the walls. They were duly put under siege and eventually brought to surrender. Meanwhile, the Libyans who bordered Egypt were so terrified by what had happened to their neighbour that they surrendered without so much as putting up a fight, accepted tributary status and started to send Cambyses gifts. So too did the people of Cyrene and Barca, whose alarm was no less than that of the Libyans. Although Cambyses looked smilingly upon the gifts he had received from the Libyans, he frowned upon those from the Cyrenaeans – because, I would guess, they were so meagre. All that the Cyrenaeans ever sent was 500 *minae* of silver – which Cambyses scooped up in his hands and tossed out among his troops.

[14] Nine days after taking possession of the fortress of Memphis, Cambyses installed Psammenitus, the king who had reigned over the Egyptians for six months, in the outskirts of the city, with the aim of testing him by offering him insult – Psammenitus and a group of other Egyptians too. First Cambyses had the daughter of the king dressed in the clothes of a slave; then he sent her out with a bucket to fetch water, together with other unmarried girls chosen from among the daughters of Egypt's most prominent men, and dressed in a manner similar to the princess. As the girls went past their fathers,

The Madness of Cambyses

wailing and weeping, so all the other men, when they saw the humiliation inflicted on their children, wailed and wept in answer; but Psammenitus, the moment he had seen and fathomed what was happening, only bowed his head to the ground. Then Cambyses, once the girls with their water-buckets had gone by, sent out the king's son, together with two thousand other Egyptians of the same age, all of them with ropes tied around their necks and bits placed in their mouths. They were being led to the place where they were to pay the penalty for the massacre of the Mytilenaeans in Memphis, and the destruction of the ship, for it was the decree of the royal judges that, for every casualty that had been inflicted, ten Egyptians of the highest rank should die in return. But when Psammenitus saw the young men come out and pass him by, and learned that his son was being led to execution, he did not weep as all the other Egyptians who were sitting down around him did, nor betray any agony, but instead behaved exactly as he had done while watching his daughter. Once this procession too had gone by, it happened that one of his old dining companions, a man well advanced in years but who had fallen so far from his previous estate that he had been left with nothing more than a beggar might have, came asking for alms among the soldiers, and passed by Psammenitus, the son of Amasis, and all the other Egyptians who were sitting there on the city's outskirts. At the sight of this, Psammenitus let out a great wail of misery, and beat his head, and called to his comrade by name. Now there were men, it seems, who had been set to stand guard over him, and who had been keeping Cambyses informed about Psammenitus' response to all the various processions out of the city. His reactions astounded Cambyses; and so he sent a messenger to Psammenitus with a question. 'Psammenitus,' the messenger said, 'your master, the Lord Cambyses, wants to know why you neither cried out nor sobbed at the sight of your daughter being humiliated and your son going to his death, whereas a beggar who is not even a relation of yours, so he has been informed, solicited marks of respect from you.' To this question Psammenitus answered: 'Son of Cyrus, the evils that have afflicted my own household are too great to be wept over. Tears were, however, an appropriate response to the misery of my old companion, who on the very threshold of old age has been toppled from happiness and wealth, and come to beggary.' When these words were reported back by the messenger, they seemed to those who heard them well said. According to the Egyptians, tears rose to the eyes of Croesus (for he too, as luck would have it, had come to Egypt in Cambyses' train), and to the eyes of all the Persians who were gathered there, and even into Cambyses himself there entered some spark of compassion. And straight away, he gave orders that the son of Psammenitus should be spared the fate of all the other condemned men, and that Psammenitus himself should

The Madness of Cambyses

be raised up from where he had been sitting, out on the margins of the city, and brought into his presence.

[15] The men who had gone in pursuit of Psammenitus' son discovered that he had been the very first to be hacked down, and was therefore no longer alive; but Psammenitus himself was raised up and led into the presence of Cambyses. There he passed the rest of his days, and had to endure no further brutal treatment. Indeed, had he only had the good sense to avoid meddling, he would surely have had Egypt restored to him, and been appointed its governor, for it is the habitual policy of the Persians to honour the sons of kings, and even to hand back the rule of a kingdom to the sons of those kings who rebel against them. That it is their custom to do so can readily be deduced from a whole host of other examples. Particularly notable are the cases of Thannyras, the son of Inaros, who had the position of authority that his father had lost given back to him, and of Pausiris, the son of Amyrtaeus, who also had the rulership that his father had lost restored to him – and this despite the fact that there was no one who ever did more damage to the Persians than Inaros and Amyrtaeus. As it was, however, Psammenitus paid the price for all his plots and trouble-making: for he was caught red-handed inciting the Egyptians to rebellion. When all was made known to Cambyses, Psammenitus drank the blood of a bull, and promptly dropped down dead. That was the end of him.

Herodotus

[16] From Memphis, Cambyses proceeded to the city of Sais; he was minded to do something there that he did, sure enough, put into practice. No sooner had he arrived in the palace of Amasis than he gave orders that Amasis' corpse was to be exhumed from its resting place, and brought outside. Once this had been done, he commanded his men to whip it, to pluck out its hairs, to stab it and to inflict on it any number of other insults. The corpse, however, because it had been mummified, stood proof against all this and refused to fall to pieces, so once the efforts of his men had brought them to the point of exhaustion, Cambyses ordered the body to be burned. Such a command was sheer sacrilege, for fire is believed by the Persians to be a god. Indeed, the burning of corpses is contrary to the customs of both peoples: the Persians, following on from what I just said, claim that it is quite wrong to offer up a human corpse to a god, while the Egyptians hold fire to be a living, breathing beast, one that devours everything it gets in its clutches, until it is sated and expires after it has swallowed its final morsel. To give a corpse to any wild beast is absolutely contrary to Egyptian custom – which is why, to make certain that it will not be eaten by worms, they embalm it before laying it to rest. So the orders given by Cambyses broke the laws of both peoples alike. The Egyptians, though, claim that this outrage was inflicted not upon Amasis, but upon some other Egyptian of a similar age – and that it was actually this man whom the Persians were

insulting when they believed themselves to be insulting Amasis. The Egyptians say that Amasis had learned from an oracle what was fated to happen to him after death, and that in an effort to ward off what was coming, he had the man whose corpse had been whipped buried right by the doors inside his own tomb, and at the same time ordered his son to place his own corpse as deep as possible in the furthermost recesses of the tomb. It is my own opinion, however, that these supposed instructions of Amasis about how he and the other man were to be buried did not in fact originate with him but were made up by the Egyptians in an effort to save face.

[17] Cambyses' next step was to consult with his advisers on the viability of three separate military ventures: one against the Carthaginians, one against the Ammonians and one against the long-lived Ethiopians who inhabit Libya, beside the Southern Sea. Cambyses' decision was that he should dispatch his war-fleet against the Carthaginians, and a portion of his land-forces against the Ammonians; but that his first move against the Ethiopians should be a campaign of espionage. Under cover of taking gifts to the Ethiopian king, his spies were to reconnoitre all that they could, and in particular to find out whether the reports of Ethiopia's 'Table of the Sun' had any basis in fact.

[18] This Table of the Sun, the story goes, is a meadow situated on the edge of the city, filled with the roasted cuts of every kind of four-footed animal. All those who

happen to be serving as the city's officials at a given moment painstakingly deposit the meat there under cover of night; and then, come the day, whoever so wishes can go there and tuck in. The natives, however, say that the meat is generated every night by the earth itself. Such, then, are the claims made for the so-called 'Table of the Sun'.

[19] Cambyses' decision to deploy spies prompted him to issue an immediate summons to the city of Elephantine, to those men among the 'Fish-Eaters' who understood the Ethiopian language. His messengers went off to fetch them, and in the meantime Cambyses gave orders that all those in his war-fleet should set sail against Carthage. The Phoenicians, however, refused to do so: they declared themselves bound by the most solemn oaths, and that it would be the height of impiety for them to launch an assault against their own offspring. This reluctance of the Phoenicians to take part left the rest of the fleet quite inadequate to the task. So it was that the Carthaginians escaped being enslaved by the Persians. Cambyses, you see, did not feel himself justified in bringing force to bear on the Phoenicians, since they had freely submitted to the Persians, and because his entire war-fleet was dependent upon them. (The Cypriots had similarly submitted to the Persians of their own accord, and joined the expedition against Egypt.)

[20] Once the Fish-Eaters had arrived from Elephantine and come into the presence of Cambyses, he dispatched

The Madness of Cambyses

them to the Ethiopians, complete with instructions as to what they were to say, and a whole load of gifts: a purple robe, a necklace of twisted gold, bracelets, an alabaster box of myrrh and a jar of palm wine. It is said that these Ethiopians to whom Cambyses was sending his messengers are the tallest and most handsome men in the world. Their customs are reported to be very different from those of other peoples; and none more so than the one which determines who becomes their king. The man in their city who is judged to be the tallest and strongest in proportion to his height – that is the man who is reckoned worthy of the throne.

[21] These, then, were the people visited by the Fish-Eaters, who duly handed over their gifts to the king, and said: 'Cambyses, the king of the Persians, desirous as he is of tying the knot of friendship and mutual hospitality with you, has sent us with orders to come here for talks, and to make a gift to you of these things in which he himself takes most delight.' But the Ethiopian could tell that they were spies; and told them so. 'You are nothing but liars, come here to spy on my realm! As for these gifts that you have been sent by the Persian King to bring me, they suggest no great desire on his part to establish links of friendship with me, but rather that he has no sense of what is right. How otherwise to explain this longing of his for lands that are not his own, and his hauling into slavery peoples that never did him any wrong? You are to give him this bow, and repeat these words to him:

"From the King of the Ethiopians to the King of the Persians, some advice. Only when the Persians can readily draw bows of an equal size should he think to lead an army against the long-lived Ethiopians – and even then, he should be sure to outnumber us. Meanwhile, let him feel proper gratitude to the gods that they have never turned the minds of the sons of Ethiopia to thoughts of adding other lands to their own."'

[22] And with these words, he unstrung the bow and handed it over to his visitors. Then he took the purple robe, and asked them what it was, and how it had been made. The Fish-Eaters gave him a truthful account of the purple-fish and the dyeing process; but the king only told the men that they were as deceitful as their garments. His second question was about the twisted gold necklace and the bracelets. The Fish-Eaters began to explain that the gold was for decoration; but the king, who thought that the bracelets were fetters, burst out laughing, and declared that the fetters in his own land were stronger by far. The third question was about the myrrh. The visitors described how it was manufactured and used to anoint the body; but the king dismissed it as he had similarly dismissed the robe. When he came to the wine, however, and learned how it was made, he had a drink and was delighted by it. 'What does your king eat,' he went on to ask, 'and what is the maximum span of a Persian man's life?' 'He eats bread,' they answered, and then explained to him how wheat is grown. 'As for the span of a man's life, the fullest

measure is set at eighty years.' To this, however, the king declared, 'I do not wonder that your lives should be so short, when all you eat is dung. Indeed, you would not even be able to stay alive for as long as you do, were it not for the restorative powers of this drink.' And so saying, he indicated the wine to the Fish-Eaters. 'For only in this do the Persians leave us trailing.'

[23] Then it was the turn of the Fish-Eaters to ask the king how long his own people lived, and what kind of things they ate. 'The majority', he answered, 'live to be one hundred and twenty, with some living even longer than that. As for our diet – we boil meat and drink milk.' When the spies expressed astonishment at the number of years, the king led them to a spring from which there came a scent like that of violets; and when the spies washed themselves in it, the water left them with a sheen, as though it had been olive oil. So delicate was this spring-water, the spies reported, that nothing could float on its surface: wood, and even things lighter than wood, just sank to the bottom. (Certainly, if the reports of this water are true, and assuming that the Ethiopians use it for everything, then it would indeed explain their longevity.) From the spring the spies were led to a dungeon full of men, where everyone was shackled with fetters of gold. (This because, among the Ethiopians, it is bronze which ranks as the rarest and most precious of metals.) Then, once they had seen the dungeon, they also saw the so-called 'Table of the Sun'.

[24] After this, and last of all, they saw the Ethiopians' coffins, which are said to be made of a translucent material. What the Ethiopians do with a corpse is to dry it out, either after the Egyptian manner or in some other way, and smear it all over with plaster and adorn it with paint, so as to render it as lifelike as possible; they then enclose it within a hollow column of translucent material (which they mine in great quantities, and which is easy to work). The corpse is now quite visible in the middle of the column, but without giving off any noxious stench, or indeed anything unpleasant at all. This column will be kept by the dead person's closest relatives in their home for a year, during which time they will bring him the first fruits of everything, and offer him up burnt sacrifice. Then, once the year has passed, they will carry it out and set it up among all the other columns which are dotted around the city.

[25] Once the spies had seen everything, they left for home. So angry did their report make Cambyses that he immediately launched an attack on the Ethiopians, without having built up any stockpiles of food, or taken into account that the target of his expedition lay at the very ends of the earth. Instead, mad as he was and quite out of his senses, he had no sooner heard from the Fish-Eaters than he went off with his army, the entire body of his land-forces, all except for the Greeks he had with him in Egypt, who were ordered to stay behind. Once the advance of his army had brought him to Thebes, he

The Madness of Cambyses

ordered a detachment of his men, some fifty thousand in all, to bring him back the Ammonians as slaves and to burn down the oracle of Zeus, while he himself led the rest of his forces onwards against the Ethiopians. The army had not even gone a fifth of the way, however, before everything that they had by way of provisions was gone; nor did it take long, once the food had run out, for the pack-animals to disappear as well, for they too were all consumed. If, once he had grasped the situation, Cambyses had only revised his plan and led his army back, then he would have compensated for his original mistake, and shown himself a man of good sense; as it was, he took no account at all of what was happening but pressed on regardless. The soldiers, for as long as there was anything in the earth that could be scavenged, kept themselves alive by eating grass, but in due course, after they arrived in the sands, there were some of them who did a truly terrible thing: they cast lots, and devoured every tenth man among them. When Cambyses learned of this, such was his dread of cannibalism that he abandoned his expedition against the Ethiopians and went back; but by the time that he had returned to Thebes, he had lost a large part of his army. From Thebes he went downriver to Memphis, where he dismissed the Greeks and let them sail home.

[26] Such was the fate of the expedition against the Ethiopians. The invasion force sent against the Ammonians set out from Thebes, and was shown a route by guides

that indisputably saw it arrive in Oasis, a city inhabited by Samians who are said to belong to the Aeschrionian tribe, and who live seven days' travel away across the sand-dunes from Thebes. (The name of the place, in Greek, is 'The Isles of the Blessed'.) That the army made it as far as Oasis is a matter of record; but beyond Oasis we have no certain information about what happened to the Persians, since they failed to reach the Ammonians, and never made it home either. The only evidence derives, either directly or indirectly, from the Ammonians themselves, who have a story to tell. They claim that in the course of launching its attack against them across the desert from Oasis, the army arrived at a point approximately midway between them and Oasis; and as the Persians were taking their breakfast, a south wind of remarkable strength swept down upon them. Such a mass of sand was this wind carrying that when it deposited its load on the Persians, they were utterly engulfed – and so it was that they came to vanish. That, say the Ammonians, is what happened to the army.

[27] The arrival of Cambyses in Memphis coincided with the manifestation in Egypt of Apis, whom the Greeks call *Epaphus*. No sooner had he made his appearance than the Egyptians began to put on their finest clothes, and to hold street parties. When Cambyses saw what was going on, he jumped to the conclusion that they were celebrating his own failures, so he summoned the prefects of Memphis. Once they had all come into his presence,

The Madness of Cambyses

he fixed them with a glare and asked them, 'Why, when the Egyptians never behaved in this manner the last time I was in Memphis, are they doing so now, after I have lost the greater part of my army?' The Egyptians explained that a god had appeared to them, and that because these appearances tended to be separated by lengthy intervals of time, it was the practice of all the Egyptians to celebrate each one with festivities. But Cambyses, having heard them out, told them that they were liars – and that he was condemning them to death.

[28] Once the executions had been carried out, he summoned into his presence the priests, who reiterated the earlier explanation. 'So some pet god has turned up in Egypt!' Cambyses exclaimed. 'Then I want to know all about it.' And with this declaration, he ordered the priests to bring him Apis, and they duly went off to fetch him. This Apis (or *Epaphus*) is a calf born of a cow which, from that moment on, evermore carries a barren womb. The Egyptians say that a beam of light descends from the sky onto this cow, and that it is from this light that Apis is born. The calf, which goes by the god's own name, has distinctive markings: although otherwise black, it has a white diamond upon its forehead and the likeness of an eagle upon its back, the hairs of its tail are double and it has a mark shaped like a beetle under its tongue.

[29] The priests brought in Apis, and Cambyses, who was teetering on the edge of madness, drew a dagger and struck at him, aiming for the belly but hitting the thigh

instead. Cambyses laughed, then spoke to the priests. 'You poor fools! What kind of god is born a thing like this, nothing but flesh and blood, and vulnerable to a touch of iron? The kind of god, no doubt, that you Egyptians deserve! But do not think you will get away with fooling me!' With these words he commanded those of his men who were responsible for such matters to flog the priests without mercy and to seize and kill any other Egyptians whom they found celebrating the festival. So it was that the Egyptians' festivities were broken up and the priests punished. Apis, struck in the thigh, wasted away where he lay in the shrine. Once he had died of his wound, the priests came and buried him without Cambyses knowing.

[30] The immediate consequence of this crime, the Egyptians claim, was that Cambyses went mad – although even before it he had barely been sane. The first victim of his criminal deeds was his brother Smerdis, who shared with Cambyses both parents, and who had already been packed off from Egypt to Persia. Smerdis had been the one Persian capable of drawing the bow brought back by the Fish-Eaters from the Ethiopian king, which he had pulled a distance equivalent to the length of two fingers, when none of the other Persians had managed even that. This had provoked Cambyses to much jealous resentment. Then, after Smerdis had left for Persia, Cambyses had a vision as he slept, in which it seemed to him that a messenger came from Persia, and reported to him that

The Madness of Cambyses

Smerdis was sitting on the royal throne, and that his head was brushing the sky. This dream left Cambyses terrified that his brother might kill him, and rule in his place; and so off to Persia he sent Prexaspes, the man whom he trusted more than any other Persian, with orders to eliminate Smerdis. So Prexaspes went up to Susa, and killed him. Some say that he took Smerdis out hunting, and killed him then; others, that he led him down to the Red Sea, and drowned him.

[31] This, then, or so it is reported, was the first of the atrocities committed by Cambyses. His second victim was his sister, who had accompanied him to Egypt, and who not only shared with him both parents, but was his wife too: he had married her despite the fact that until then it had not remotely been the habit of the Persians to set up house with their sisters. It so happened, however, that Cambyses had passionately lusted after another of his sisters, and longed to marry her, despite the fact that what he had set his heart on was quite without precedent. So he had summoned the Royal Judges, as they are known, and asked them whether there might not be some law which obliged a man who wished to marry his sister to do so. (The men who become these Royal Judges are a select band of Persians; they remain in office until they die or else are convicted of some offence. They preside over all the cases brought by the Persians, and are the interpreters of their ancestral statutes: everything is referred to them.) The ruling they gave in response to Cambyses'

question satisfied justice without compromising their own security: they declared that, although they had failed to find a law which actually obliged a brother to marry his sister, they had discovered one which permitted the King of the Persians to do as he pleased. So it was that they avoided being intimidated by Cambyses into breaking the law, but not to the point of sacrificing themselves in its defence; for what they had found was a quite additional law, supportive of his desire to marry his sisters. The consequence was that Cambyses had married the one he particularly lusted after; but then, after barely any time at all, he had taken another sister as his wife too. It was the younger of these two sisters who had accompanied him to Egypt – and whom he killed.

[32] As with the death of Smerdis, so with hers – alternative stories are told. Greeks say that Cambyses threw a lion's cub into the ring with a young dog, and that this wife of his was one of those watching; the puppy was losing, but its brother [another young dog] managed to break free of its leash and came to its rescue, so that the one puppy became two, and the cub was duly vanquished. Cambyses was delighted by the show; but his wife wept as she sat beside him. When he noticed this, Cambyses asked her, 'Why are you crying?' 'I cried', she answered, 'because when I saw the puppy coming to the rescue of its brother, I was reminded of Smerdis, and it struck me that there is now no one to come to your assistance.' It was because of this comment, so Greeks say,

The Madness of Cambyses

that Cambyses killed her. The Egyptian version is that one day, when everyone was sitting down around the table, Cambyses' wife took a lettuce and plucked off all its leaves, and then asked her husband whether the lettuce was more beautiful stripped bare or as it had been when still thick with leaves. 'When thick with leaves,' he said. 'And yet what have you done,' she answered, 'if not strip bare the House of Cyrus, so that it precisely resembles this lettuce?' So angered was Cambyses by this that he leapt on her; and she, who was carrying his child in her womb, suffered a miscarriage, and died.

[33] Such were the ways in which the House of Cambyses was affected by the madness brought on him by the business with Apis – or perhaps, bearing in mind how many ailments there are to which mankind is prone, his lunacy was caused by something else altogether. Indeed, it has been claimed that Cambyses was afflicted from birth by a particularly terrible ailment, called by some the 'sacred disease'. If so, it would hardly be surprising were a man afflicted by such a serious physical malady to be unsound of mind as well.

[34] His madness also affected other Persians. There is the story, for instance, of what he said to Prexaspes, a man whom he had always honoured above all others, appointing him court chamberlain, and his son as pourer of the royal wine – no small honour in itself. 'Prexaspes,' Cambyses is reported to have said, 'what kind of man do the Persians think I am? When they talk about me, what

do they say?' 'Master,' Prexaspes answered, 'they praise you to the skies, except when it comes to one thing – for they do say that you take your love of wine to excess.' Cambyses, thrown into a rage by this news of the Persians, answered, 'So now the Persians are saying that I am too fond of wine, are they? That it has driven me mad? That I am not in my right mind? Then what they told me before was just a lie!' He was alluding here to a previous occasion, when his Persian advisers, and Croesus too, were sitting in council with him, and Cambyses asked them how they rated him as a man, compared to his father. The Persians answered that he was better than his father, 'For you have everything that he had – but you have also won possession of Egypt and the sea.' That was what the Persians had to say; but Croesus, who was also present, judged this answer inadequate, and said to Cambyses, 'In my opinion, son of Cyrus, you are not alike to your father in all respects. This is because you do not yet have a son fit to compare with the son that he left behind in you.' Cambyses, who was delighted to hear this, lavished praise on Croesus' judgement.

[35] This, then, was the episode that he had called to mind. 'Find out for yourself', he raged at Prexaspes, 'whether what the Persians say about me is true, or whether it is they, when they report such things, who have lost their wits. Do you see your son, standing over there, in the antechamber? Well, I am going to shoot him. Now, if I manage to hit him directly in the heart, then that will

The Madness of Cambyses

make it as clear as can be that the Persians have been talking nonsense. But should I miss him, then, yes, report as the truth what is claimed by the Persians, that I am indeed out of my mind!' So saying, he drew his bow to the full and shot the child – who fell to the ground. 'Cut the boy open,' Cambyses ordered, 'and identify where he was hit!' Then, when the arrow was found in the heart, Cambyses was put into such a good mood that he laughed, and said to the father of the child: 'You see, Prexaspes? It is as clear as clear can be. I am not mad! It is the Persians who have lost their wits! But tell me – have you ever seen anyone, anywhere in the world, hit the mark with a shot like that?' Prexaspes, seeing that the man was quite insane, and afraid for his own skin, answered him: 'Master, I doubt that even the god himself could have hit with such pin-point accuracy.' So much, then, for the behaviour of Cambyses on that occasion; on another, he apprehended twelve Persians who were equal in rank to the best, convicted them on some trifling charge and then buried them alive, head first.

[36] These actions prompted Croesus the Lydian to feel that it was his responsibility to have words with Cambyses. 'My Lord,' he said, 'rather than giving free rein to the passions of your youth, you should be keeping them under a tight control and getting a grip on yourself. Prudence is the best policy, just as forethought is the wisest. You are killing men who are your own fellow-citizens, executing them on the most paltry of charges, even killing

children! If you keep on indulging in such behaviour, watch out that the Persians do not rise in revolt against you. As for me, your father Cyrus repeatedly charged and instructed me to offer you criticism, and to recommend to you whatever course of action I should find the fittest.' Such was his advice; but Cambyses, despite the manifest goodwill with which it had been offered, replied: 'You have a nerve, to think to offer me advice! You – who governed your own country to such brilliant effect! You – who gave my father such excellent advice, when you told him to cross the River Araxes and attack the Massagetans, despite the fact that they were perfectly willing to make the crossing into our own territory! It was your incompetence when you were at the head of your native land which brought about your own downfall – just as it was the confidence that Cyrus put in your advice which brought about his. But do not expect to get away with it now! Indeed, I have been waiting a long time for an excuse to get my hands on you!' So saying, Cambyses grabbed a bow, intending to shoot him down; but Croesus leapt to his feet and ran from the room. Cambyses, frustrated in his attempt to use his bow, gave orders instead to his servants that they were to apprehend Croesus and put him to death. The servants, however, familiar with these swings in the royal mood, kept Croesus hidden; they reasoned that, were Cambyses to repent of what he had done and look to have Croesus back, they would be able to unveil him, and would be rewarded for having saved his life; whereas, if Cambyses did not change his mind, and did not come to miss Croesus, they could always finish off the job they had been given. In the event, Cambyses soon longed to have Croesus back, and the servants, once they had become aware of this, let the king know that he was still alive. Cambyses, however, though he acknowledged himself delighted at the survival of Croesus, declared that those responsible for it should not go unpunished, and sentenced them all to death. And put them to death is precisely what he did.

[37] There were many such acts of lunacy committed by Cambyses against the Persians and their allies; indeed, during his stay in Memphis, he broke into ancient tombs and examined the corpses. Similarly, he went so far as to enter the shrine of Hephaestus, and laughed uproariously at the image of the god. This statue of Hephaestus closely resembles the Phoenician *pataici*, which the Phoenicians carry around on the prows of their triremes. Should anyone never have seen one of these, it is best described, I think, as a likeness of a male pygmy. Cambyses also penetrated the shrine of the Cabiri, which only the priest may lawfully enter. There, he actually had the statues of the gods burned while pouring scorn on them. In appearance, these same statues are very similar to those of Hephaestus; indeed, the Cabiri are said to be his children.

[38] Everywhere you look, it seems to me, the evidence accumulates that Cambyses was utterly deranged, for why

otherwise would he have mocked what to others were hallowed customs? Just suppose that someone proposed to the entirety of mankind that a selection of the very best practices be made from the sum of human custom: each group of people, after carefully sifting through the customs of other peoples, would surely choose its own. Everyone believes his own customs to be far and away the best. From this, it follows that only a madman would think to jeer at such matters. Indeed, there is a huge amount of corroborating evidence to support the conclusion that this attitude to one's own native customs is universal. Take, for example, this story from the reign of Darius. He called together some Greeks who were present and asked them how much money they would wish to be paid to devour the corpses of their fathers – to which the Greeks replied that no amount of money would suffice for that. Next, Darius summoned some Indians called Callantians, who do eat their parents, and asked them in the presence of the Greeks (who were able to follow what was being said by means of an interpreter) how much money it would take to buy their consent to the cremation of their dead fathers – at which the Callantians cried out in horror and told him that his words were a desecration of silence. Such, then, is how custom operates; and how right Pindar is, it seems to me, when he declares in his poetry that 'Custom is the King of all'.

[39] At the same time as Cambyses was invading Egypt, the Lacedaemonians were launching their own campaign

against Samos, specifically against Polycrates, the son of Aeaces, who had toppled the government there and taken possession of the city. Initially, he had divided it up into three, and given shares to his brothers, Pantagnotus and Syloson; but subsequently, he had put the first of these brothers to death, and driven the younger one, Syloson, into exile, so that the whole of Samos became his. Having done this, he tied the knot of friendship and mutual hospitality with Amasis, the king of Egypt, a pledge that the two men sealed by the sending and receiving of gifts. And straightaway, in next to no time, the affairs of Polycrates had prospered to such a degree that they were being bruited throughout Ionia, and across the Greek world. No matter where he directed his campaigns, fortune consistently favoured him. He built up a fleet of one hundred pentecounters and recruited a thousand archers, raiding and plundering without discrimination – indeed, he used to say that he would earn more gratitude from friends by restoring to them what he had taken from them than he would have done by not taking it in the first place. Many were the islands he conquered, and numerous the cities on the mainland too. Among his victories was the defeat that he inflicted at sea upon the men of Lesbos, who had sent their entire force to the assistance of the Milesians, but now became his prisoners; labouring in chains, they dug the whole of the moat which encircles the walls of Samos.

[40] Now, as may well be imagined, Polycrates' astounding good fortune did not go unnoticed by Amasis, who

was unsettled by it. Eventually, with Polycrates' run of luck continuing to bring him ever greater successes, Amasis wrote a letter and sent it off to Samos. 'Here is what Amasis has to say to Polycrates,' it read. 'How pleasant it is to learn that a friend, a man who is bound to one by ties of mutual hospitality, is faring so well. Nevertheless, your astounding good fortune is not a cause of unconfined joy to me – for I well know that the gods are given to envy. What I wish for myself, and for those I care about – if I may put it like this – is a career that blends good fortune with the occasional stumble. Better to go through life experiencing bad as well as good luck than to know nothing but success. I have never yet known nor heard tell of anyone who enjoyed a prosperity so total that he did not ultimately come to a bad end and lose everything that had previously sustained him. That being so, I would advise you, in the face of all your good fortune, to adopt the following policy. Think hard, and identify the object that is most precious to you, the one that it would cause you the most heartache to lose – and then throw it away, some place where there is no chance of its ever coming back into human hands. If, by the time you get to read this, there have still been no disasters to punctuate your run of good fortune, then remedy the situation in the manner that I have here suggested.'

[41] Once Polycrates had read this through, and after reflection had come to appreciate that the advice offered him by Amasis made good sense, he sought to identify

The Madness of Cambyses

which of his treasures it would most pain him to lose. After much soul-searching, he fixed upon the signet-ring that he habitually wore: its stone, an emerald, was set in gold, and had been worked by Theodorus, the son of Telecles, a Samian. Accordingly, once he had decided that this was the treasure he would throw away, what Polycrates did was to man a pentaconter, board it and order it out to the open sea. Next, with the island left far behind, he took off his signet-ring and threw it into the sea, in the full view of everyone on board. Then, that once done, he sailed back to Samos, where he retired to his home and mourned his loss.

[42] It so happened, however, five or six days after this, that a fisherman caught a large and beautiful fish, and thought it only fitting to make a gift of it to Polycrates. He hauled it to the front doors, where he announced that he wished to come into the sight of Polycrates. Permission was granted and the fish handed over. 'My king,' the fisherman said, 'although I am a man who has no living aside from what I catch with my own hands, I knew, when I caught this one, that it would be quite wrong for me to take it to the market-square. Such a fish, it struck me, is really worthy only of you and of your administration – which is why I have brought it here and given it to you.' Polycrates, who was delighted by these words, answered him: 'And excellently well done it is too! I owe you a double debt of gratitude – both for what you have said and for what you have given me. We invite you to come

and dine with us this evening.' The fisherman went back home bursting with pride; but the servants, when they sliced open the fish, found in its stomach the very signet-ring of Polycrates! No sooner had they laid their eyes on it and taken it out than they were carrying it into the presence of Polycrates in a state of high excitement; and as they presented him with the signet-ring, they told him how it had been found. And at this, there came into Polycrates' mind a sense of how touched by the numinous the whole business surely was; so he wrote down in a letter a full account of what he had done and what had happened, and then, when he had finished writing, sent it off to Egypt.

[43] When Amasis read the letter that had come from Polycrates, he realized that it was quite impossible for one man to redeem another from something that is inevitably going to happen, and that Polycrates, a man touched by such unfailing good fortune that even those things he threw away were found again, was certainly not someone destined for a happy end. So Amasis sent a herald to Samos with news that the treaty of mutual friendship between them was dissolved. His motive for doing this was to ensure that when some great and terrible calamity did eventually befall Polycrates, he would not feel in his heart the pain that he would feel for a man who was his friend.

[44] It was against this same Polycrates, the one whose luck knew no bounds, that the Lacedaemonians launched

a military offensive, in answer to an appeal from a faction on Samos that would later go on to found Cydonia in Crete. Now, at the time when Cambyses, the son of Cyrus, had been assembling his army for the invasion of Egypt, Polycrates, going behind the Samians' backs, had sent him a herald. 'Send me a request for troops,' Polycrates had requested, 'back here in Samos.' Cambyses, once he had listened to this message, was more than happy to send a message of his own back to Samos, asking Polycrates to dispatch a naval task-force to help him take on Egypt. The townsmen duly nominated by Polycrates, all of whom were on his list of likely subversives, were sent off in forty warships, together with instructions to Cambyses never to send them back.

[45] There are some who say that these Samians packed off by Polycrates never actually made it to Egypt, but only sailed as far as the waters off Carpathos, where they held a council of war and decided that they did not want to continue any further with their voyage. Others claim that they did make it to Egypt, where they were interned, but managed to slip away. Then, as they were making their voyage back to Samos, Polycrates came out to meet them with his fleet, and engaged them in a battle – which was won by the returning exiles. When they landed on the island, however, they had the worst of an infantry battle and this is why they sailed to Lacedaemon. Yet others, however, claim that the Samians who had come back from Egypt did in fact beat Polycrates – a story which seems

most implausible to me. Why, after all, would they have needed to ask the Lacedaemonians for assistance if they were capable of overthrowing Polycrates on their own? What is more, it goes against all logic to imagine that a man backed up by hired auxiliaries and a vast squad of archers, recruited from among his own people, could conceivably have been defeated by the few returning Samians. As a safeguard, Polycrates also crammed the wives and children of his subjects into the ship-sheds, ready to set fire to them, ship-sheds and all, should his fellow-townsmen decide to desert to the returning exiles.

[46] When the Samians who had been expelled by Polycrates arrived in Sparta, they came into the presence of the authorities, and spoke at great length, commensurate with their need. The response of the authorities to this first audience, however, was to complain that they could not remember the early section of the speech, and had failed to understand what came after. As a consequence, when the Samians gained a second audience, they simply came in with a sack and said nothing at all, except to comment, 'This sack needs barley-meal.' 'There was no need to say "sack",' came back the reply. The Lacedaemonians resolved, nevertheless, that they would indeed give aid.

[47] So they made their preparations for the campaign against Samos and set off. They did this, according to the Samians, because they owed a debt of gratitude for the naval assistance that the Samians had provided some time

The Madness of Cambyses

previously in their war against the Messenians; but the Lacedaemonians themselves say that they were prompted to launch their campaign less out of any desire to assist the Samians in their hour of need than because they wished to be avenged for the theft of the mixing-bowl which they had been taking to Croesus, and of a breast-plate which Amasis, the king of Egypt, had sent them as a gift. It is certainly the case that a year before they stole the bowl the Samians had indeed carried off this same breastplate, which was made of linen, had a large number of figures woven into it and was embroidered with gold and cotton. Most wondrous of all, however, is that each one of the breastplate's threads, fine though it is, consists in turn of three hundred and sixty separate threads, all of them clear to the eye. There is another breastplate, exactly like it, which Amasis presented as an offering to Athena in Lindus.

[48] The Corinthians, because they wished to ensure that the campaign against Samos did go ahead, had enthusiastically joined in: they too, a generation previously, at around the same time as the bowl was stolen, had been grievously insulted by the Samians. Three hundred boys, the sons of the leading men of Corcyra, had been sent by Periander, the son of Cypselus, to Alyattes in Sardis to be castrated. The Corinthians who were escorting the boys put in at Samos; when the whole story came out, and the Samians discovered why the boys were being taken to Sardis, their first step was to instruct the

boys to take sanctuary in the shrine of Artemis; next, they refused to turn a blind eye to the attempts that were being made to drag the suppliants away from the sanctuary; and then, when the Corinthians blocked the boys' food supply, the Samians instituted a festival which they still celebrate to this day just as it was first established. Every nightfall, for the entire time spent by the boys in the sanctuary, the Samians so arranged things that unmarried girls and boys would stage dances; and next, having arranged these dances, they made it a rule that the dancers should carry cakes of sesame and honey, which could then be snatched by the sons of the Corcyrans to provide them with sustenance. This continued until the Corinthians who had been guarding the boys gave up and went away – at which point the Samians took the boys back to Corcyra.

[49] Now had the Corinthians and the Corcyrans been on good terms with one another after Periander died, such an episode would hardly have provided the Corinthians with sufficient motivation to join the campaign. As it was, however, despite their shared kinship, the two peoples had been at odds with one another ever since the first colonization of the island. No wonder, then, that the Corinthians should have kept the wrong done them by the Samians very much in their minds. It was Periander's desire for vengeance that had prompted him to nominate the sons of the leading men of Corcyra for castration, and then to send them to Sardis, for the Corcyrans, by

committing an atrocious crime against him, had been the ones who first began the feud.

[50] It so happened, after Periander had killed his wife Melissa, that a very similar misfortune came hard on the heels of the one that had already befallen him. Melissa had borne him two sons: one of them now seventeen and the other eighteen years old. They were sent for by Procles, the tyrant of Epidaurus, who was their maternal grandfather, and who treated them with great kindness – as was only to be expected, of course, since they were the sons of his daughter. But when Procles came to send them back, he said, as they parted from him, 'Do you know, my boys, who it was killed your mother?' This was a question to which the elder of the two paid not the slightest attention, but which Lycophron, as the younger was called, found so painful to hear that he refused, on his arrival in Corinth, to engage his father – as the murderer of his mother – in conversation; not only that, but he refused to respond to any of Periander's attempts to talk to him, or to ask him questions. Eventually, Periander became so infuriated that he threw Lycophron out of his house.

[51] Then, once he had driven his younger son away, he asked the older one what the father of their mother had said to them. 'He received us with great kindness,' the son answered, 'but as for his parting words, they have quite slipped my mind. No, I cannot recall them.' Periander, however, persisted with his questioning, arguing

that Procles was very unlikely to have made no suggestion to them at all; and then the boy did recall what Procles had said, and repeated it. So it was that Periander grasped what had happened; and, determined not to be swayed by sentiment, he sent a messenger to the people with whom his exiled son had made a new life, and ordered them not to take him in any longer. And so it went on: Lycophron would no sooner find somewhere to stay after he was expelled than he would be kicked out of his new home as well, since all those who opened their doors to him would receive threats from Periander and orders to send him packing. And every time Lycophron was sent packing, he would go to another of his comrades; and they, despite being terrified, would let him in, on the grounds that he was, after all, the son of Periander.

[52] In the end, Periander issued a proclamation, declaring that a fine payable to Apollo, holy in character and set by him at a specific rate, would be imposed upon anyone who might offer shelter to Lycophron or engage him in conversation. Sure enough, as a consequence of this edict, there was no one willing to speak to the boy or to offer him hospitality. Even Lycophron himself thought it wrong to try to defy the prohibitions, and instead, because he still refused to back down, he just hung around the colonnades instead. Three days passed, and on the fourth, seeing how filthy and emaciated his son was, Periander felt such pity that he stifled his anger and approached him. 'My boy,' he said, 'which of these

The Madness of Cambyses

two states is preferable – the one that you are currently in, or the condition of power and plenty that is mine, and which it is yours to inherit if you will only pay the respect that is due your father? You are my son, a prince of this rich and happy city of Corinth – and yet you choose to lead the life of a wandering beggar, and make me, the man who least deserves such treatment, the object of all your hostility and rage. Remember that if something terrible has happened to make you suspicious of me, then I too am caught up in the same business. More so, indeed, than you – for it was I who actually committed the deed. You have learned two lessons both at once: how much better it is to be envied than to be pitied, and what it means to indulge oneself in anger against one's parent and superior. Come, then, return home.' Such was the attempt made by Periander to win back his son; but the only answer that Lycophron gave was to say, 'You owe the god a fine for having come into conversation with me.' It was now that Periander appreciated just how far gone his son was, and how impregnable his condition of misery; so he sent him out of sight by having him shipped off to Corcyra (which was also then subject to Periander's rule). Next, with Lycophron sent on his way, Periander led an army against the man whom he blamed more than any other for what had happened to him: Procles, his father-in-law. Epidaurus fell, and Procles too, who was taken alive.

[53] Time passed, and as Periander grew older, he was

brought to acknowledge that his ability to oversee and manage the affairs of state was no longer what it had been. Accordingly, unable to distinguish any mark of talent in his elder son, who struck him as manifestly lacking in intelligence, Periander sent to Corcyra, summoning Lycophron to take up the reins of supreme power. Even when Lycophron disdained to give the bearer of this message an answer, Periander would still not relinquish his hopes of the young man, but instead, as a second messenger, sent the person whom he calculated would prove more liable to persuade his son than anyone else: his own daughter, the sister of Lycophron. 'Silly boy,' the girl said, on her arrival, 'do you really want supreme power falling into the hands of others? Your patrimony plundered? Would you really rather that than return and have it for yourself? Get back home with you now and stop putting yourself through this torture! Pride is a thing that cripples a man, just as two wrongs do not make a right! Plenty have put pragmatism ahead of the demands of justice. You would hardly be the first to find that the defence of a mother's interests can threaten those dues that are owed him by a father. A tyranny is a precarious thing, much lusted after by others – and besides, he is an old man, long since past his prime. Do not, then, give away to others the good things that are your own!' Nevertheless, despite having been tutored by her father in all these various blandishments, Lycophron's only response to her speech was to declare that he would never come to

The Madness of Cambyses

Corinth so long as he knew that his father was still alive. She duly reported this back. Now Periander dispatched a third emissary, declaring that he himself wished to come to Corcyra, and that Lycophron should come to Corinth and succeed to the tyranny. To these terms his son consented; and Periander duly made ready to leave for Corcyra and his son for Corinth. So anxious, however, were the Corcyrans to stop Periander from coming to their country, once they had got wind of what was afoot, that they put the young man to death. It was this that prompted Periander to take his vengeance on the people of Corcyra.

[54] The force of Lacedaemonians that came to Samos and began to put it under siege was a formidable one. They launched an attack against the city walls, and managed to scale the tower that stood by the sea, on the outer reaches of the town, only to be driven back when Polycrates himself arrived with a large number of reinforcements. Meanwhile, a sally was launched from the upper tower – the one which stands on the ridge of the mountain – by the mercenaries and the Samians themselves; but although they initially succeeded in holding their own against the Lacedaemonians, they were soon put to flight and cut down by their pursuers.

[55] Now, if all the Lacedaemonians who were there that day had proved the peers of Archias and Lycopas, then Samos would have been taken. For Archias and

Lycopas were the only ones to join the Samians as they fled back inside the city walls, and because this left the two of them with their line of retreat blocked off, it saw them perish inside the city of Samos. Once, in his native village of Pitana, I met with another Archias, a man who was the son of Samius and the grandson of the original Archias, and who esteemed the Samians the most of any foreigners; and this Archias told me personally that his father was given the name of 'Samius' because his own father had died a hero's death on Samos. The reason that he so respected the Samians, he explained, was because they had buried his grandfather at public expense.

[56] For forty days Samos was put under siege, until the Lacedaemonians, unable to break the deadlock, returned to the Peloponnese. There is a more far-fetched account, according to which Polycrates used the local mint to strike a large quantity of coins in lead, which he then had covered in gold leaf and gave to the Lacedaemonians, who took them and only then set off. This was the first time that the Lacedaemonians, or indeed any Dorians, had ever launched an expedition against Asia.

[57] Once they realized that the Lacedaemonians were ready to abandon them, the Samians who had joined the campaign against Polycrates sailed off to Siphnos. They were in need of funds, and this was the same period in which Siphnos was at the very peak of her prosperity: the people of Siphnos were the richest of all the islanders, thanks to the gold and silver mines on their island.

Indeed, these mines were so productive that a tenth of the revenue generated from them was sufficient to endow a treasury at Delphi which was the match, in terms of wealth, of any other there. Every year, the people of Siphnos would distribute the proceeds from the mines among themselves; and so it was, as they were building the treasury, that they asked the oracle whether their current prosperity would continue indefinitely. The Pythia replied:

> 'Well, whenever the town-halls on Siphnos turn to white,
> And the market white of brow, then will you need someone shrewd
> To flag for you a battalion of wood, and a herald of red.'

At the time, both the market-square and the town-hall on Siphnos were clad in Parian marble.

[58] The Siphnians were unable to make any sense of this oracle, either at the time or later when the Samians appeared. The point, however, was that the moment the Samians put in at Siphnos, they sent messengers to the city on board one of their ships – and Samian ships, back in ancient times, were always painted red. It was to this that the Pythia had been alluding when she warned the Siphnians to guard against 'a battalion of wood, and a herald of red'. Sure enough, once the messengers had arrived, demanded a loan of 10 talents from the Siphnians

and been rebuffed, the Samians set themselves to stripping the country bare. The Siphnians, the moment they discovered what was happening, went out to the rescue, but were defeated, with many of them being cut off from their city by the Samians, who extorted 100 talents from them.

[59] From the people of Hermione, the Samians took not money but the island of Hydrea off the Peloponnese, which they then entrusted for safe-keeping to the people of Troezen. They themselves, meanwhile, founded Cydonia in Crete, despite the fact that their original purpose in sailing there had not been to colonize it at all, but rather to drive out the Zacynthians from the island. They remained there for five years and prospered to such effect that all the shrines which exist there now, including the temple of Dictynna, were built by them. In the sixth year, however, the Aeginetans combined with the Cretans to defeat the Samians at sea and reduce them to slavery; the boar-shaped prows which the Samians had on their ships were hacked off by the Aeginetans and presented as offerings to the shrine of Athena in Aegina. This the Aeginetans did because they bore a grudge against the Samians, for in the time when Amphicrates had been king of Samos, the Samians had launched a campaign against the Aeginetans, one which had inflicted great damage (although the Samians too had suffered numerous casualties at the hands of the Aeginetans). The entire episode had stemmed from this.

The Madness of Cambyses

[60] If I have gone on at some length about the Samians, it is because they were responsible for three construction projects which no other Greeks have ever rivalled. One is a tunnel which leads upwards through a mountain some 150 fathoms high, and has mouths at both ends. The tunnel is 7 stades long, and 8 feet high and wide. Dug out along its entire course there is another channel, 20 cubits deep and 3 feet wide, along which water is channelled through pipes from a great spring and brought to the city. Its architect was a man from Megara: Eupalinus, the son of Naustrophus. If that ranks as the first of the three wonders, then the second is a mole which encloses the harbour from the sea: it reaches down some 20 fathoms at its deepest, and is over 2 stades in length. Third on the list of Samian wonder-works is a temple, the largest known to man. The first architect to work on it was Rhoecus, the son of Phileas, a native of the island. Such is the case for covering the Samians in detail.

[61] Now, as Cambyses, the son of Cyrus, was whiling away his time in Egypt, quite out of his mind, there rose in rebellion against him two brothers, Magians both, one of whom Cambyses had left behind to serve him as the steward of his household. This Magian had been prompted to his coup by the realization that the death of Smerdis had been kept a secret, so that there were very few Persians who actually knew of it, most being under the impression

that Smerdis was still alive. These were the circumstances that had set the Magian plotting, and aiming to get his hands on the kingdom. His brother, whom I mentioned as being his partner in the rebellion, was very similar in appearance to Smerdis, the son of Cyrus, whose own brother, Cambyses, had had him executed. Indeed, not only was this Magian similar in appearance to Smerdis, but he even had the same name, Smerdis. 'I will take care of everything for you,' Patizeithes, the Magian, had managed to convince him; and the man was then led by his brother, and seated upon the royal throne. Once that was done, Patizeithes sent heralds off in all directions, but he made especially sure to send one to Egypt, to announce to the army that they were to take their orders in the future not from Cambyses, but from Smerdis, the son of Cyrus.

[62] Sure enough, this proclamation was delivered by the various heralds, including the one who had been detailed to go to Egypt – although, as things turned out, he found Cambyses and his army in Syria, at Agbatana, where he duly stood up among the soldiers and publicly repeated what he had been told to repeat by the Magian. Hearing what had been said, Cambyses presumed that the herald was telling the truth, and that Prexaspes, the man he had sent to kill Smerdis, had betrayed him by failing to do as instructed. 'Prexaspes,' Cambyses said, fixing him with a glare, 'is this how you carried out the mission I gave you?' 'Master,' Prexaspes answered, 'it is

The Madness of Cambyses

none of it true. Your brother, Smerdis, cannot possibly have risen in revolt against you. You will never have any trouble, no matter where on the scale of danger, from that particular man. I did precisely as you told me to do, and then I buried him – yes, personally, with my own hands. If it is true that the dead are in revolt, then look for Astyages the Mede to rise against you too. If everything continues as it has always done, however, then there is no need for you to fear any injury in the future from your brother. That is why I think the best policy would be to go after this herald and ask him, under interrogation, who it was sent him with this announcement that we should follow the orders of King Smerdis.'

[63] This advice of Prexaspes struck Cambyses as being very sensible, and so the herald was tracked down straightaway and brought back. On his return, Prexaspes questioned him. 'Now, my man, you say that you have come here as the messenger of Smerdis, the son of Cyrus. Tell us the truth, now, and you can be on your way scot-free. Did your orders come directly from Smerdis, in person, or did they come from some underling?' 'I have never once seen Smerdis, the son of Cyrus,' answered the man, 'not since the day that King Cambyses set off on his invasion of Egypt. It was the Magian, the one appointed by Cambyses to be the steward of his household, who gave me this particular mission – although he did say that the order to deliver the speech I gave you came from Smerdis, the son of Cyrus.' All this, delivered

to Cambyses and Prexaspes, was of course the simple truth. 'Prexaspes,' Cambyses told him, 'I exonerate you of the charge of disobedience. You are a good man, and you did precisely as ordered. But which Persian can it possibly be, then, who has risen in rebellion against me, and usurped the name of Smerdis?' 'My Lord,' Prexaspes answered, 'I think I have worked out what has happened. The rebels are a couple of Magians: Patizeithes, the man you left behind as the steward of your household, and his brother Smerdis.'

[64] And it was then, upon hearing the name of Smerdis, that the truth of what Prexaspes had said, and of his own dream, hit Cambyses: for what had he seen in his sleep, if not someone informing him that Smerdis was sitting upon the royal throne, and that his head was brushing the sky? Cambyses realized now that his killing of his brother had been quite needless; so he wept for Smerdis, and then, brushing away his tears, and in agony at the whole wretched business, leapt onto his horse, fully intending to lead his army as fast as he could on Susa, to attack the Magian. As he leapt onto his horse, however, the tip of his scabbard snapped off, and the naked blade of the dagger struck his thigh, wounding him in the very spot where previously he himself had struck Apis, the god of the Egyptians. The wound, Cambyses sensed, was a mortal one; and so he asked, 'What is the name of this city?' Back came the reply: 'Agbatana.' Now, some time previously, the oracle in Bouto had told Cambyses that

his life would end in Agbatana. He had concluded from this that he would die an old man in the Median Agbatana, the city which served him as the hub of his administration; but the oracle, it turned out, had been alluding to the Syrian Agbatana. And when, in response to his question, Cambyses came to learn the name of the city, such was the trauma of the misfortune that the Magian had brought upon him, and of his wound, that he quite recovered his sanity and fathomed the meaning of the oracle. 'It is here', he declared, 'that Cambyses, the son of Cyrus, is fated to meet his end.'

[65] And that, at the time, was that; but then, some twenty days later, Cambyses sent for the most eminent Persians in his train, and said to them, 'Men of Persia, I am obliged by circumstances to reveal to you the matter which more than any other I had been hoping to keep a secret. While I was in Egypt, I saw something in my sleep – a vision that I wish that I had never seen. I imagined that there came to me from my palace a messenger, who reported to me that Smerdis was sitting upon the royal throne, and that his head was brushing the sky. Nervous that my own brother might seize power from me, I acted speedily – but not sensibly. Indeed, although I can see now that no man has it within himself to turn destiny aside, such was my stupidity that I sent Prexaspes off to Susa to kill Smerdis – a terrible deed. Yet once it had been done, I carried on with my life feeling perfectly secure, nor did it so much as cross my mind that with

Smerdis out of the way some other man might rise against me. On every count, then, I missed the point of what was to happen – with the consequence that I became the killer of my brother, and quite needlessly so, since I have still ended deprived of my kingdom. You see, the Smerdis whose rebellion I was warned about in my dream, by the agency of the heavens, was none other than the Magian. But I have done what I have done – and you must come to terms with the fact that Smerdis, the son of Cyrus, is no longer among you. The men now in power in this, your kingdom, are the Magians: one, the steward whom I left behind to administer my household, and the other his brother, Smerdis. There is one man, more than any other, who should have avenged the disgrace that these Magians have brought on me – and yet he, by a most cruel twist of fate, has met his end at the hands of his nearest kinsman. My next best option, then – my brother no longer being here – is one that I must of necessity take: namely, to command you, men of Persia, to fulfil my dying wishes. I call now as my witnesses the gods of the royal household, and lay upon all of you here, and especially those of you who are Achaemenids, this charge: never to let supremacy pass back to the Medes. Should they obtain it by means of treachery, then by treachery you must take it back; should it be force that brings them their success, then you must recover it through the exercise of brute force. Do that, and I pray that the earth will be fruitful for you, and your women and cattle fecund – for you will be, and will forever be, free men. Should you not regain power, however, nor make any effort to recover it, then I pray that the opposite befalls you – and more, that every man in Persia meets an end such as has overtaken me.' And even as he said this, Cambyses wept for all he had done.

[66] When the Persians saw their king in tears, they all tore the clothes that they had on, and gave themselves over to uninhibited lamentation. Later, when the bone turned gangrenous and the thigh had rotted, the wound fast carried off Cambyses, after a reign that had lasted in all for seven years and five months. He died quite childless, having fathered neither son nor daughter. Meanwhile, the Persians who had been in attendance on him refused to accept that the Magians could possibly have taken power, for they believed all Cambyses' talk about the death of his brother to have been mere disinformation, fed to them with the aim of embroiling the whole of Persia in a war against Smerdis.

1. BOCCACCIO · *Mrs Rosie and the Priest*
2. GERARD MANLEY HOPKINS · *As kingfishers catch fire*
3. *The Saga of Gunnlaug Serpent-tongue*
4. THOMAS DE QUINCEY · *On Murder Considered as One of the Fine Arts*
5. FRIEDRICH NIETZSCHE · *Aphorisms on Love and Hate*
6. JOHN RUSKIN · *Traffic*
7. PU SONGLING · *Wailing Ghosts*
8. JONATHAN SWIFT · *A Modest Proposal*
9. *Three Tang Dynasty Poets*
10. WALT WHITMAN · *On the Beach at Night Alone*
11. KENKŌ · *A Cup of Sake Beneath the Cherry Trees*
12. BALTASAR GRACIÁN · *How to Use Your Enemies*
13. JOHN KEATS · *The Eve of St Agnes*
14. THOMAS HARDY · *Woman much missed*
15. GUY DE MAUPASSANT · *Femme Fatale*
16. MARCO POLO · *Travels in the Land of Serpents and Pearls*
17. SUETONIUS · *Caligula*
18. APOLLONIUS OF RHODES · *Jason and Medea*
19. ROBERT LOUIS STEVENSON · *Olalla*
20. KARL MARX AND FRIEDRICH ENGELS · *The Communist Manifesto*
21. PETRONIUS · *Trimalchio's Feast*
22. JOHANN PETER HEBEL · *How a Ghastly Story Was Brought to Light by a Common or Garden Butcher's Dog*
23. HANS CHRISTIAN ANDERSEN · *The Tinder Box*
24. RUDYARD KIPLING · *The Gate of the Hundred Sorrows*
25. DANTE · *Circles of Hell*
26. HENRY MAYHEW · *Of Street Piemen*
27. HAFEZ · *The nightingales are drunk*
28. GEOFFREY CHAUCER · *The Wife of Bath*
29. MICHEL DE MONTAIGNE · *How We Weep and Laugh at the Same Thing*
30. THOMAS NASHE · *The Terrors of the Night*
31. EDGAR ALLAN POE · *The Tell-Tale Heart*
32. MARY KINGSLEY · *A Hippo Banquet*
33. JANE AUSTEN · *The Beautifull Cassandra*
34. ANTON CHEKHOV · *Gooseberries*
35. SAMUEL TAYLOR COLERIDGE · *Well, they are gone, and here must I remain*
36. JOHANN WOLFGANG VON GOETHE · *Sketchy, Doubtful, Incomplete Jottings*
37. CHARLES DICKENS · *The Great Winglebury Duel*
38. HERMAN MELVILLE · *The Maldive Shark*
39. ELIZABETH GASKELL · *The Old Nurse's Story*
40. NIKOLAY LESKOV · *The Steel Flea*

41. HONORÉ DE BALZAC · *The Atheist's Mass*
42. CHARLOTTE PERKINS GILMAN · *The Yellow Wall-Paper*
43. C.P. CAVAFY · *Remember, Body . . .*
44. FYODOR DOSTOEVSKY · *The Meek One*
45. GUSTAVE FLAUBERT · *A Simple Heart*
46. NIKOLAI GOGOL · *The Nose*
47. SAMUEL PEPYS · *The Great Fire of London*
48. EDITH WHARTON · *The Reckoning*
49. HENRY JAMES · *The Figure in the Carpet*
50. WILFRED OWEN · *Anthem For Doomed Youth*
51. WOLFGANG AMADEUS MOZART · *My Dearest Father*
52. PLATO · *Socrates' Defence*
53. CHRISTINA ROSSETTI · *Goblin Market*
54. *Sindbad the Sailor*
55. SOPHOCLES · *Antigone*
56. RYŪNOSUKE AKUTAGAWA · *The Life of a Stupid Man*
57. LEO TOLSTOY · *How Much Land Does A Man Need?*
58. GIORGIO VASARI · *Leonardo da Vinci*
59. OSCAR WILDE · *Lord Arthur Savile's Crime*
60. SHEN FU · *The Old Man of the Moon*
61. AESOP · *The Dolphins, the Whales and the Gudgeon*
62. MATSUO BASHŌ · *Lips too Chilled*
63. EMILY BRONTË · *The Night is Darkening Round Me*
64. JOSEPH CONRAD · *To-morrow*
65. RICHARD HAKLUYT · *The Voyage of Sir Francis Drake Around the Whole Globe*
66. KATE CHOPIN · *A Pair of Silk Stockings*
67. CHARLES DARWIN · *It was snowing butterflies*
68. BROTHERS GRIMM · *The Robber Bridegroom*
69. CATULLUS · *I Hate and I Love*
70. HOMER · *Circe and the Cyclops*
71. D. H. LAWRENCE · *Il Duro*
72. KATHERINE MANSFIELD · *Miss Brill*
73. OVID · *The Fall of Icarus*
74. SAPPHO · *Come Close*
75. IVAN TURGENEV · *Kasyan from the Beautiful Lands*
76. VIRGIL · *O Cruel Alexis*
77. H. G. WELLS · *A Slip under the Microscope*
78. HERODOTUS · *The Madness of Cambyses*
79. *Speaking of Siva*
80. *The Dhammapada*

'To the utterly at-one with Śiva there's no dawn . . .'

BASAVAṆṆA

MAHĀDĒVIYAKKA

ALLAMA PRABHU

Lived in the 12th century in what is now Karnataka, India

DĒVARA DĀSIMAYYA

Lived in the mid-10th century, probably in Mudanuru, India

Taken from A. K. Ramanujan's translation and edition of *Speaking of Śiva*, first published in 1973.

Speaking of Śiva

Translated by
A. K. Ramanujan

PENGUIN BOOKS

PENGUIN CLASSICS

UK | USA | Canada | Ireland | Australia
India | New Zealand | South Africa

Penguin Books is part of the Penguin Random House group of companies whose addresses can be found at global.penguinrandomhouse.com.

This selection published in Penguin Classics 2015
009

Translation copyright © A. K. Ramanujan 1973

Set in 9.5/13 pt Baskerville 10 Pro
Typeset by Jouve (UK), Milton Keynes
Printed and bound in Great Britain by Clays Ltd, Elcograf S.p.A.

A CIP catalogue record for this book is available from the British Library

ISBN: 978–0–141–39879–2

www.greenpenguin.co.uk

Penguin Random House is committed to a sustainable future for our business, our readers and our planet. This book is made from Forest Stewardship Council® certified paper.

Contents

Basavaṇṇa	1
Dēvara Dāsimayya	15
Mahādēviyakka	25
Allama Prabhu	41

BASAVAṆṆA

Look, the world, in a swell
of waves, is beating upon my face.

Why should it rise to my heart,
tell me.
O tell me, why is it
rising now to my throat?
Lord,
how can I tell you anything
when it is risen high
over my head
lord lord
listen to my cries
O lord of the meeting rivers
listen.

Basavaṇṇa

Cripple me, father,
that I may not go here and there.
Blind me, father,
that I may not look at this and that.
Deafen me, father,
that I may not hear anything else.

> Keep me
> at your men's feet
> looking for nothing else,
> O lord of the meeting rivers.

Speaking of Śiva

Don't make me hear all day
    'Whose man, whose man, whose man is this?'

Let me hear, 'This man is mine, mine,
    this man is mine.'

O lord of the meeting rivers,
    make me feel I'm a son
    of the house.

Basavaṇṇa

Śiva, you have no mercy.
Śiva, you have no heart.

Why why did you bring me to birth,
    wretch in this world,
    exile from the other?

Tell me, lord,
don't you have one more
little tree or plant
made just for me?

Speaking of Śiva

As a mother runs
close behind her child
with his hand on a cobra
or a fire,

> the lord of the meeting rivers
> stays with me
> every step of the way
> and looks after me.

Basavaṇṇa

When a whore with a child
takes on a customer for money,

neither child nor lecher
will get enough of her.

She'll go pat the child once,
then go lie with the man once,

neither here nor there.
Love of money is relentless,

my lord of the meeting rivers.

Speaking of Śiva

A snake-charmer and his noseless wife,
snake in hand, walk carefully
trying to read omens
for a son's wedding,

but they meet head-on
a noseless woman
and her snake-charming husband,
and cry 'The omens are bad!'

His own wife has no nose;
there's a snake in his hand.
What shall I call such fools
who do not know themselves

and see only the others,

> O lord
> of the meeting
> rivers!

Basavaṇṇa

Before
>the grey reaches the cheek,
>the wrinkle the rounded chin
>and the body becomes a cage of bones:

before
>with fallen teeth
>and bent back
>you are someone else's ward:

before
>you drop your hand to the knee
>and clutch a staff:

before
>age corrodes
>your form:

before
>death touches you:

>>worship
>>our lord
>>of the meeting rivers!

Make of my body the beam of a lute
    of my head the sounding gourd
    of my nerves the strings
    of my fingers the plucking rods.

Clutch me close
    and play your thirty-two songs
    O lord of the meeting rivers!

Basavanna

You went riding elephants.
You went riding horses.
You covered yourself
with vermilion and musk.
          O brother,
but you went without the truth,
you went without sowing and reaping
the good.
         Riding rutting elephants
of pride, you turned easy target
to fate.
         You went without knowing
our lord of the meeting rivers.

You qualified for hell.

Look here, dear fellow:
I wear these men's clothes
only for you.

Sometimes I am man,
sometimes I am woman.

O lord of the meeting rivers
I'll make wars for you
but I'll be your devotees' bride.

Basavaṇṇa

The rich
will make temples for Śiva.
What shall I,
a poor man,
do?

My legs are pillars,
the body the shrine,
the head a cupola
of gold.

Listen, O lord of the meeting rivers,
things standing shall fall,
but the moving ever shall stay.

DĒVARA DĀSIMAYYA

You balanced the globe
    on the waters
    and kept it from melting away,

you made the sky stand
    without pillar or prop.

O Rāmanātha,
    which gods could have
    done this?

Dēvara Dāsimayya

A fire
in every act and look and word.
Between man and wife
a fire.
In the plate of food
eaten after much waiting
a fire.
In the loss of gain
a fire.
And in the infatuation
of coupling
a fire.

You have given us
five fires
and poured dirt in our mouths

O Rāmanātha.

The five elements
have become one.

The sun and the moon,
O Rider of the Bull,
aren't they really
your body?

I stand,
look on,
you're filled
with the worlds.

What can I hurt now
after this, Rāmanātha?

Dēvara Dāsimayya

Whatever It was

that made this earth
the base,
the world its life,
the wind its pillar,
arranged the lotus and the moon,
and covered it all with folds
of sky

with Itself inside,

to that Mystery
indifferent to differences,

to It I pray,
O Rāmanātha.

Speaking of Śiva

What does it matter
if the fox roams
all over the Jambu island?
Will he ever stand amazed
in meditation of the Lord?
Does it matter if he wanders
all over the globe
and bathes in a million sacred rivers?

A pilgrim who's not one with you,
Rāmanātha,
roams the world
like a circus man.

Dēvara Dāsimayya

To the utterly at-one with Śiva

there's no dawn,
no new moon,
no noonday,
nor equinoxes,
nor sunsets,
nor full moons;

his front yard
is the true Benares,

O Rāmanātha.

If they see
breasts and long hair coming
they call it woman,

if beard and whiskers
they call it man:

but, look, the self that hovers
in between
is neither man
nor woman

O Rāmanātha.

Dēvara Dāsimayya

Suppose you cut a tall bamboo
in two;
make the bottom piece a woman,
the headpiece a man;
rub them together
till they kindle:
        tell me now,
the fire that's born,
is it male or female,

        O Rāmanātha?

MAHĀDĒVIYAKKA

You're like milk
in water: I cannot tell
what comes before,
what after;
which is the master,
which the slave;
what's big,
what's small.

O lord white as jasmine
if an ant should love you
and praise you,
will he not grow
to demon powers?

Mahādēviyakka

> Illusion has troubled body as shadow
>   troubled life as a heart
>   troubled heart as a memory
>   troubled memory as awareness.
>
> With stick raised high, Illusion herds
>   the worlds.
>   Lord white as jasmine
>   no one can overcome
>   your Illusion.

It was like a stream
    running into the dry bed
    of a lake,
          like rain
pouring on plants
parched to sticks.

It was like this world's pleasure
    and the way to the other,
               both
    walking towards me.

Seeing the feet of the master,
O lord white as jasmine,
    I was made
    worthwhile.

Mahādēviyakka

When I didn't know myself
where were you?

Like the colour in the gold,
you were in me.

I saw in you,
lord white as jasmine,
the paradox of your being
in me
without showing a limb.

Locks of shining red hair
a crown of diamonds
small beautiful teeth
and eyes in a laughing face
that light up fourteen worlds –
    I saw His glory,
and seeing, I quell today
the famine in my eyes.

I saw the haughty Master
for whom men, all men,
are but women, wives.

I saw the Great One
who plays at love
with Śakti,
original to the world,

I saw His stance
and began to live.

Mahādēviyakka

Four parts of the day
I grieve for you.
Four parts of the night
I'm mad for you.

I lie lost
sick for you, night and day,
 O lord white as jasmine.

Since your love
was planted,
I've forgotten hunger,
thirst, and sleep.

Listen, sister, listen.
I had a dream

I saw rice, betel, palmleaf
and coconut.
I saw an ascetic
come to beg,
white teeth and small matted curls.

I followed on his heels
and held his hand,
he who goes breaking
all bounds and beyond.

I saw the lord, white as jasmine,
and woke wide open.

Mahādēviyakka

When one heart touches
    and feels another
won't feeling weigh over all,
can it stand any decencies then?

O mother, you must be crazy,
I fell for my lord
    white as jasmine,
I've given in utterly.

Go, go, I'll have nothing
of your mother-and-daughter stuff.
You go now.

Husband inside,
lover outside.
I can't manage them both.

This world
and that other,
cannot manage them both.

O lord white as jasmine

I cannot hold in one hand
both the round nut
and the long bow.

Mahādēviyakka

Why do I need this dummy
 of a dying world?
 illusion's chamberpot,
 hasty passions' whorehouse,
 this crackpot
 and leaky basement?

Finger may squeeze the fig
 to feel it, yet not choose
 to eat it.

Take me, flaws and all,
O lord

white as jasmine.

I love the Handsome One:
    he has no death
    decay nor form
    no place or side
    no end nor birthmarks.
    I love him O mother. Listen.

I love the Beautiful One
    with no bond nor fear
    no clan no land
    no landmarks
    for his beauty.

So my lord, white as jasmine, is my husband.

Take these husbands who die,
    decay, and feed them
    to your kitchen fires!

Mahādēviyakka

Riding the blue sapphire mountains
wearing moonstone for slippers
blowing long horns
O Śiva
when shall I
crush you on my pitcher breasts

O lord white as jasmine
when do I join you
stripped of body's shame
and heart's modesty?

What do
the barren know
of birthpangs?

Stepmothers,
what do they know
of loving care?

How can the unwounded
know the pain
of the wounded?

O lord white as jasmine
your love's blade stabbed
and broken in my flesh,

I writhe.
O mothers
how can you know me?

Mahādēviyakka

The heart in misery
has turned
upside down.

> The blowing gentle breeze
> is on fire.
> O friend moonlight burns
> like the sun.

Like a tax-collector in a town
I go restlessly here and there.

> Dear girl go tell Him
> bring Him to His senses.
> Bring Him back.

My lord white as jasmine
is angry
that we are two.

ALLAMA PRABHU

I saw:
    heart conceive,
        hand grow big with child;
ear drink up the smell
        of camphor, nose eat up
the dazzle of pearls;
    hungry eyes devour
diamonds.
            In a blue sapphire
I saw the three worlds
    hiding,
        O Lord of Caves.

Allama Prabhu

If mountains shiver in the cold
with what
will they wrap them?

If space goes naked
with what
shall they clothe it?

If the lord's men become worldlings
where will I find the metaphor,

   O Lord of Caves.

Speaking of Śiva

Before anyone calls him, he calls them.
I saw him clamber over the forehead of the wild elephant
born in his womb
and sway in play
in the dust of the winds.

I saw him juggle his body as a ball
in the depth of the sky,
play with a ten-hooded snake
in a basket; saw him blindfold
the eyes of the five virgins.
I saw him trample the forehead
of the lion that wanders in the ten streets,
I saw him raise the lion's eyebrows.
I saw him grow from amazement
to amazement, holding a diamond
in his hand.

      Nothing added,
nothing taken,

          the Lord's stance
          is invisible
          to men untouched
          by the Liṅga of the Breath.

Allama Prabhu

A wilderness grew
in the sky.
In that wilderness
a hunter.
In the hunter's hands
a deer.

> The hunter will not die
> till the beast
> is killed.

Awareness is not easy,
is it,
O Lord of Caves?

For a wedding of dwarfs
rascals beat the drums
and whores
carry on their heads
holy pitchers;

> with hey-ho's and loud hurrahs
> they crowd the wedding party
> and quarrel over flowers and betelnuts;

> all three worlds are at the party;
> what a rumpus this is,
> without our Lord of Caves.

Allama Prabhu

> The fires of the city burned in the forest,
> forest fires burned in the town.
> Listen, listen to the flames
> of the four directions.
> Flapping and crackling in the vision
> a thousand bodies dance in it
> and die countless deaths,
>
> O Lord of Caves.

If it rains fire
   you have to be as the water;

if it is a deluge of water
   you have to be as the wind;

if it is the Great Flood,
   you have to be as the sky;

and if it is the Very Last Flood of all the worlds,
   you have to give up self

and become the Lord.

Allama Prabhu

> Who can know green grass flames
>   seeds of stone
>
>   reflections of water
>   smell of the wind
>
>   the sap of fire
>   the taste of sunshine on the tongue
>
>   and the lights in oneself
>
> except your men?

One dies,
another bears him to the burial ground:
still another takes them both
and burns them.

No one knows the groom
and no one the bride.
Death falls across
the wedding.

Much before the decorations fade
the bridegroom is dead.

Lord, only your men
have no death.

Allama Prabhu

The wind sleeps
to lullabies of sky.

Space drowses,
infinity gives it suck
from her breast.

The sky is silent.
The lullaby is over.

The Lord is
as if He were not.

Light
devoured darkness.

I was alone
inside.

Shedding
the visible dark

I
was Your target

O Lord of Caves.

Allama Prabhu

> Sleep, great goddess sleep,
> heroine of three worlds,
> spins and sucks up
>   all, draws breath
>   and throws them down
>   sapless.
>
> I know of no hero
>   who can stand before her.
>   Struck by her arrows,
>   people rise and fall.

Some say
they saw It.
What is It,
the circular sun,
the circle of the stars?

The Lord of Caves
lives in the town
of the moon mountain.

Allama Prabhu

    Looking for your light,
I went out:

        it was like the sudden dawn
of a million million suns,

        a ganglion of lightnings
for my wonder.

        O Lord of Caves,
if you are light,
there can be no metaphor.

1. BOCCACCIO · *Mrs Rosie and the Priest*
2. GERARD MANLEY HOPKINS · *As kingfishers catch fire*
3. *The Saga of Gunnlaug Serpent-tongue*
4. THOMAS DE QUINCEY · *On Murder Considered as One of the Fine Arts*
5. FRIEDRICH NIETZSCHE · *Aphorisms on Love and Hate*
6. JOHN RUSKIN · *Traffic*
7. PU SONGLING · *Wailing Ghosts*
8. JONATHAN SWIFT · *A Modest Proposal*
9. *Three Tang Dynasty Poets*
10. WALT WHITMAN · *On the Beach at Night Alone*
11. KENKŌ · *A Cup of Sake Beneath the Cherry Trees*
12. BALTASAR GRACIÁN · *How to Use Your Enemies*
13. JOHN KEATS · *The Eve of St Agnes*
14. THOMAS HARDY · *Woman much missed*
15. GUY DE MAUPASSANT · *Femme Fatale*
16. MARCO POLO · *Travels in the Land of Serpents and Pearls*
17. SUETONIUS · *Caligula*
18. APOLLONIUS OF RHODES · *Jason and Medea*
19. ROBERT LOUIS STEVENSON · *Olalla*
20. KARL MARX AND FRIEDRICH ENGELS · *The Communist Manifesto*
21. PETRONIUS · *Trimalchio's Feast*
22. JOHANN PETER HEBEL · *How a Ghastly Story Was Brought to Light by a Common or Garden Butcher's Dog*
23. HANS CHRISTIAN ANDERSEN · *The Tinder Box*
24. RUDYARD KIPLING · *The Gate of the Hundred Sorrows*
25. DANTE · *Circles of Hell*
26. HENRY MAYHEW · *Of Street Piemen*
27. HAFEZ · *The nightingales are drunk*
28. GEOFFREY CHAUCER · *The Wife of Bath*
29. MICHEL DE MONTAIGNE · *How We Weep and Laugh at the Same Thing*
30. THOMAS NASHE · *The Terrors of the Night*
31. EDGAR ALLAN POE · *The Tell-Tale Heart*
32. MARY KINGSLEY · *A Hippo Banquet*
33. JANE AUSTEN · *The Beautifull Cassandra*
34. ANTON CHEKHOV · *Gooseberries*
35. SAMUEL TAYLOR COLERIDGE · *Well, they are gone, and here must I remain*
36. JOHANN WOLFGANG VON GOETHE · *Sketchy, Doubtful, Incomplete Jottings*
37. CHARLES DICKENS · *The Great Winglebury Duel*
38. HERMAN MELVILLE · *The Maldive Shark*
39. ELIZABETH GASKELL · *The Old Nurse's Story*
40. NIKOLAY LESKOV · *The Steel Flea*

41. HONORÉ DE BALZAC · *The Atheist's Mass*
42. CHARLOTTE PERKINS GILMAN · *The Yellow Wall-Paper*
43. C.P. CAVAFY · *Remember, Body . . .*
44. FYODOR DOSTOEVSKY · *The Meek One*
45. GUSTAVE FLAUBERT · *A Simple Heart*
46. NIKOLAI GOGOL · *The Nose*
47. SAMUEL PEPYS · *The Great Fire of London*
48. EDITH WHARTON · *The Reckoning*
49. HENRY JAMES · *The Figure in the Carpet*
50. WILFRED OWEN · *Anthem For Doomed Youth*
51. WOLFGANG AMADEUS MOZART · *My Dearest Father*
52. PLATO · *Socrates' Defence*
53. CHRISTINA ROSSETTI · *Goblin Market*
54. *Sindbad the Sailor*
55. SOPHOCLES · *Antigone*
56. RYŪNOSUKE AKUTAGAWA · *The Life of a Stupid Man*
57. LEO TOLSTOY · *How Much Land Does A Man Need?*
58. GIORGIO VASARI · *Leonardo da Vinci*
59. OSCAR WILDE · *Lord Arthur Savile's Crime*
60. SHEN FU · *The Old Man of the Moon*
61. AESOP · *The Dolphins, the Whales and the Gudgeon*
62. MATSUO BASHŌ · *Lips too Chilled*
63. EMILY BRONTË · *The Night is Darkening Round Me*
64. JOSEPH CONRAD · *To-morrow*
65. RICHARD HAKLUYT · *The Voyage of Sir Francis Drake Around the Whole Globe*
66. KATE CHOPIN · *A Pair of Silk Stockings*
67. CHARLES DARWIN · *It was snowing butterflies*
68. BROTHERS GRIMM · *The Robber Bridegroom*
69. CATULLUS · *I Hate and I Love*
70. HOMER · *Circe and the Cyclops*
71. D. H. LAWRENCE · *Il Duro*
72. KATHERINE MANSFIELD · *Miss Brill*
73. OVID · *The Fall of Icarus*
74. SAPPHO · *Come Close*
75. IVAN TURGENEV · *Kasyan from the Beautiful Lands*
76. VIRGIL · *O Cruel Alexis*
77. H. G. WELLS · *A Slip under the Microscope*
78. HERODOTUS · *The Madness of Cambyses*
79. *Speaking of Siva*
80. *The Dhammapada*

'. . . a most delicious, nourishing, and wholesome food . . .'

JONATHAN SWIFT
Born 1667, Dublin
Died 1745, Dublin

SWIFT IN PENGUIN CLASSICS
A Modest Proposal and Other Writings
Gulliver's Travels

JONATHAN SWIFT

A Modest Proposal

FOR Preventing the Children of poor People in Ireland, *from being a Burden to their Parents or Country; and for making them beneficial to the Publick*

PENGUIN CLASSICS

UK | USA | Canada | Ireland | Australia
India | New Zealand | South Africa

Penguin Books is part of the Penguin Random House group of companies
whose addresses can be found at global.penguinrandomhouse.com.

This selection published in Penguin Classics 2015
011

Set in 9.5/13 pt Baskerville 10 Pro
Typeset by Jouve (UK), Milton Keynes

Printed and bound in Great Britain by Clays Ltd, Elcograf S.p.A.

A CIP catalogue record for this book is available from the British Library

ISBN: 978–0–141–39818–1

www.greenpenguin.co.uk

Penguin Random House is committed to a sustainable future for our business, our readers and our planet. This book is made from Forest Stewardship Council® certified paper.

Contents

A Meditation upon a Broom-Stick — 1

A Description of a City-Shower — 3

A Short View of the State of Ireland — 6

A Modest Proposal — 18

An Examination of Certain Abuses, Corruptions, and Enormities, in the City of Dublin — 32

A Meditation Upon A Broom-Stick

According to

THE STYLE AND MANNER OF THE HONOURABLE ROBERT BOYLE'S MEDITATIONS

This single Stick, which you now behold ingloriously lying in that neglected Corner, I once knew in a flourishing State in a Forest: It was full of Sap, full of Leaves, and full of Boughs: But now, in vain does the busy Art of Man pretend to vye with Nature, by tying that withered Bundle of Twigs to its sapless Trunk: It is now at best but the Reverse of what it was; a Tree turned upside down, the Branches on the Earth, and the Root in the Air: It is now handled by every dirty Wench, condemned to do her Drudgery; and by a capricious Kind of Fate, destined to make other Things clean, and be nasty it self. At length, worn to the Stumps in the Service of the Maids, it is either thrown out of Doors, or condemned to the last Use of kindling a Fire. When I beheld this, I sighed, and said within my self, SURELY MORTAL MAN IS A BROOMSTICK! Nature sent him into the World strong and lusty, in a thriving Condition, wearing his own Hair on his Head, the proper Branches of this reasoning Vegetable; till the Axe of Intemperance has lopped off his Green Boughs, and left him a withered Trunk: He then flies to Art, and puts on a *Perriwig*; valuing himself upon an unnatural Bundle of Hairs, all covered with Powder, that never grew on his Head. But now, should this our *Broom-stick* pretend to enter the Scene, proud of those *Birchen* Spoils it never bore, and all covered with Dust, though the Sweepings of the finest Lady's Chamber, we should be apt to ridicule and despise its Vanity: Partial Judges that we are of our own Excellencies, and other Mens Defaults!

But a *Broom-stick*, perhaps you will say, is an Emblem of a Tree standing on its Head; and pray what is Man but a topsy-turvy Creature? His Animal Faculties perpetually mounted on his Rational; his Head where his Heels should be, groveling on the Earth. And yet, with all his Faults, he sets up to be a universal Reformer and Correcter of Abuses; a Remover of Grievances; rakes into every Slut's Corner of Nature, bringing hidden Corruptions to the Light, and raiseth a mighty Dust where there was none before; sharing deeply all the while in the very same Pollutions he pretends to sweep away. His last Days are spent in Slavery to Women, and generally the least deserving; till worn to the Stumps, like his Brother *Bezom*, he is either kicked out of Doors, or made use of to kindle Flames for others to warm themselves by.

A Description of a City-Shower

    Careful Observers may foretell the Hour
(By sure Prognosticks) when to dread a Shower;
While Rain depends, the pensive Cat gives o'er
Her Frolicks, and pursues her Tail no more.
Returning Home at Night, you'll find the Sink
Strike your offended Sense with double Stink.
If you be wise, then go not for to dine,
You'll spend in Coach-hire more than save in Wine.
A coming Show'r your shooting Corns presage,
Old Aches throb, your hollow Tooth will rage.
Sauntering in Coffee-house is Dulman seen;
He damns the Climate, and complains of Spleen.

    Mean while the South rising with dabbled Wings,
A Sable Cloud athwart the Welkin flings,
That swill'd more Liquor than it could contain,
And like a Drunkard gives it up again.
Brisk Susan whips her Linen from the Rope,
While the first drizzling Show'r is borne aslope.
Such is that Sprinkling which some careless Quean
Flirts on you from her Mop, but not so clean.
You fly, invoke the Gods; then turning, stop
To rail; she singing, still whirls on her mop.
Not yet, the Dust had shunn'd th'unequal Strife,
But aided by the Wind, fought still for Life;

Jonathan Swift

And wafted with its Foe by violent Gust,
'Twas doubtful which was Rain, and which was Dust.
Ah! where must needy Poet seek for Aid,
When Dust and Rain at once his Coat invade;
His only Coat, where Dust confus'd with Rain
Roughen the Nap, and leave a mingled Stain.

    Now in contiguous Drops the Flood comes down,
Threat'ning with Deluge this devoted Town.
To Shops in Crowds the daggled Females fly,
Pretend to cheapen Goods, but nothing buy.
The Templer spruce, while ev'ry Spout's a-broach,
Stays till 'tis fair, yet seems to call a Coach.
The tuck'd-up Sempstress walks with hasty Strides,
While Streams run down her oil'd Umbrella's Sides.
Here various Kinds by various Fortunes led,
Commence Acquaintance underneath a Shed.
Triumphant Tories, and desponding Whigs,
Forget their Fewds and join to save their Wigs.
Box'd in a Chair the Beau impatient sits,
While Spouts run clatt'ring o'er the Roof by Fits;
And ever and anon with frightful Din
The Leather sounds, he trembles from within.
So when Troy chair-men bore the Wooden Steed,
Pregnant with Greeks, impatient to be freed.
(Those Bully Greeks, who, as the Moderns do,
Instead of paying Chair-men, run them thro'.)

A Description of a City-Shower

Laoco'n struck the Outside with his Spear,
And each imprison'd Hero quak'd for Fear.

   Now from all Parts the swelling Kennels flow,
And bear their Trophies with them as they go:
Filth of all Hues and Odours seem to tell
What Street they sail'd from, by their Sight and Smell.
They, as each Torrent drives, with rapid Force,
From Smithfield or St. Pulchre's shape their Course,
And in huge Confluent join'd at Snow-Hill Ridge,
Fall from the Conduit, prone to Holbourn-Bridge.
Sweeping from Butchers Stalls, Dung, Guts, and Blood,
Drown'd Puppies, stinking Sprats, all drench'd in Mud,
Dead Cats and Turnip-Tops come tumbling down the
    Flood.

A Short View of the State of Ireland

I am assured, that it hath, for some Time, been practised as a Method of making Men's Court, when they are asked about the Rate of Lands, the Abilities of Tenants, the State of Trade and Manufacture in this Kingdom, and how their Rents are paid; to answer, that in their Neighbourhood, all Things are in a flourishing Condition, the Rent and Purchase of Land every Day encreasing. And if a Gentleman happen to be a little more sincere in his Representations, besides being looked on as not well affected, he is sure to have a Dozen Contradictors at his Elbow. I think it is no Manner of Secret, why these Questions are so *cordially* asked, or so *obligingly* answered.

But since, with regard to the Affairs of this Kingdom, I have been using all Endeavours to subdue my Indignation; to which, indeed, I am not provoked by any personal Interest, being not the Owner of one Spot of Ground in the whole *Island*; I shall only enumerate by Rules generally known, and never contradicted, what are the true Causes of any Countries flourishing and growing rich,

A Short View of the State of Ireland

and then examine what Effects arise from those Causes in the Kingdom of *Ireland*.

The first Cause of a Kingdom's thriving, is the Fruitfulness of the Soil, to produce the Necessaries and Conveniencies of Life, not only sufficient for the Inhabitants, but for Exportation into other Countries.

The Second, is the Industry of the People in working up all their native Commodities, to the last Degree of Manufacture.

The Third, is the Conveniency of safe Ports and Havens, to carry out their own Goods, as much manufactured, and bring in those of others, as little manufactured, as the Nature of mutual Commerce will allow.

The Fourth is, that the Natives should, as much as possible, export and import their Goods in Vessels of their own Timber, made in their own Country.

The Fifth, is the Priviledge of a free Trade in all foreign Countries which will permit them; except to those who are in War with their own Prince or State.

The Sixth, is, by being governed only by Laws made with their own Consent; for otherwise they are not a free People. And therefore, all Appeals for Justice, or Applications for Favour or Preferment, to another Country, are so many grievous Impoverishments.

The Seventh is, by Improvement of Land, Encouragement of Agriculture, and thereby encreasing the Number of their People; without which, any Country, however blessed by Nature, must continue poor.

The Eighth, is the Residence of the Prince, or chief Administrator of the Civil Power.

The Ninth, is the Concourse of Foreigners for Education, Curiosity, or Pleasure; or as to a general Mart of Trade.

The Tenth, is by disposing all Offices of Honour, Profit, or Trust only to the Natives, or at least with very few Exceptions; where Strangers have long inhabited the Country, and are supposed to understand, and regard the Interest of it as their own.

The Eleventh, is when the Rents of Lands, and Profits of Employments, are spent in the Country which produced them, and not in another; the former of which will certainly happen, where the Love of our native Country prevails.

The Twelfth, is by the publick Revenues being all spent and employed at home; except on the Occasions of a foreign War.

The Thirteenth is, where the People are not obliged, unless they find it for their own Interest or Conveniency, to receive any Monies, except of their own Coinage by a publick Mint, after the Manner of all civilized Nations.

The Fourteenth, is a Disposition of the People of a Country to wear their own Manufactures, and import as few Incitements to Luxury, either in Cloaths, Furniture,

A Short View of the State of Ireland

Food, or Drink, as they possibly can live conveniently without.

There are many other Causes of a Nation's thriving, which I cannot at present recollect; but without Advantage from at least some of these, after turning my Thoughts a long Time, I am not able to discover from whence our Wealth proceeds, and therefore would gladly be better informed. In the mean Time, I will here examine what Share falls to *Ireland* of these Causes, or of the Effects and Consequences.

It is not my Intention to complain, but barely to relate Facts; and the Matter is not of small Importance. For it is allowed, that a Man who lives in a solitary House, far from Help, is not wise in endeavouring to acquire in the Neighbourhood, the Reputation of being rich; because those who come for Gold, will go off with Pewter and Brass, rather than return empty: And in the common Practice of the World, those who possess most Wealth, make the least Parade; which they leave to others, who have nothing else to bear them out, in shewing their Faces on the *Exchange*.

As to the first Cause of a Nation's Riches being the Fertility of the Soil, as well as Temperature of Climate, we have no Reason to complain; for, although the Quantity of unprofitable Land in this Kingdom, reckoning Bogg, and Rock, and barren Mountain, be double in Proportion to what it is in *England*; yet the native Productions which both Kingdoms deal in, are very near on

Equality in Point of Goodness; and might, with the same Encouragement, be as well manufactured. I except Mines and Minerals; in some of which, however, we are only defective in Point of Skill and Industry.

In the Second, which is the Industry of the People; our Misfortune is not altogether owing to our own Fault, but to a Million of Discouragements.

The Conveniency of Ports and Havens, which Nature hath bestowed so liberally on this Kingdom, is of no more Use to us, than a beautiful Prospect to a Man shut up in a Dungeon.

As to shipping of its own, *Ireland* is so utterly unprovided, that of all the excellent Timber cut down within these Fifty or Sixty Years, it can hardly be said, that the Nation hath received the Benefit of one valuable House to dwell in, or one Ship to trade with.

Ireland is the only Kingdom I ever heard or read of, either in ancient or modern Story, which was denied the Liberty of exporting their native Commodities and Manufactures wherever they pleased; except to Countries at War with their own Prince or State: Yet this Privilege, by the Superiority of meer Power, is refused us, in the most momentous Parts of Commerce; besides an Act of Navigation, to which we never consented, pinned down upon us, and rigorously executed; and a Thousand other unexampled Circumstances, as grievous, as they are invidious to mention. To go onto the rest.

It is too well known, that we are forced to obey some

Laws we never consented to; which is a Condition I must not call by its true uncontroverted Name, for fear of Lord Chief Justice *Whitshed*'s Ghost, with his *Libertas & natale Solum*, written as a Motto on his Coach, as it stood at the Door of the Court, while he was perjuring himself to betray both. Thus, we are in the Condition of Patients, who have Physick sent them by Doctors at a Distance, Strangers to their Constitution, and the Nature of their Disease: And thus, we are forced to pay five Hundred *per Cent.* to decide our Properties; in all which, we have likewise the Honour to be distinguished from the whole Race of Mankind.

As to Improvement of Land; those few who attempt that, or Planting, through Covetousness, or Want of Skill, generally leave Things worse than they were; neither succeeding in Trees nor Hedges; and by running into the Fancy of Grazing, after the Manner of the *Scythians*, are every Day depopulating the Country.

We are so far from having a King to reside among us, that even the Viceroy is generally absent four Fifths of his Time in the Government.

No Strangers from other Countries, make this a Part of their Travels; where they can expect to see nothing, but Scenes of Misery and Desolation.

Those who have the Misfortune to be born here, have the least Title to any considerable Employment; to which they are seldom preferred, but upon a political Consideration.

Jonathan Swift

One third Part of the Rents of *Ireland* is spent in *England*; which, with the Profit of Employments, Pensions, Appeals, Journies of Pleasure or Health, Education at the *Inns* of Court, and both Universities, Remittances at Pleasure, the Pay of all Superior Officers in the Army, and other Incidents, will amount to a full half of the Income of the whole Kingdom, all clear Profit to *England*.

We are denied the Liberty of Coining Gold, Silver, or even Copper. In the Isle of *Man*, they coin their own *Silver*; every petty Prince, Vassal to the *Emperor*, can coin what Money he pleaseth. And in this, as in most of the Articles already mentioned, we are an Exception to all other States or Monarchies that were ever known in the World.

As to the last, or Fourteenth, Article, we take special Care to act diametrically contrary to it in the whole Course of our Lives. Both Sexes, but especially the Women, despise and abhor to wear any of their own Manufactures, even those which are better made than in other Countries; particularly a Sort of Silk Plad through which the Workmen are forced to run a Sort of Gold Thread, that it may pass for *Indian*. Even Ale and Potatoes are imported from *England*, as well as Corn: And our foreign Trade is little more than Importation of *French* Wine; for which I am told we pay ready Money.

Now, if all this be true, upon which I could easily enlarge; I would be glad to know by what secret Method

A Short View of the State of Ireland

it is, that we grow a rich and flourishing People, without *Liberty*, *Trade*, *Manufactures*, *Inhabitants*, *Money*, or the *Privilege of Coining*; without *Industry*, *Labour*, or *Improvement of Lands*; and with more than half the Rent and Profits of the whole *Kingdom*, annually exported; for which we receive not a single Farthing: And to make up all this, nothing worth mentioning, except the Linnen of the *North*, a Trade casual, corrupted, and at Mercy; and some Butter from *Cork*. If we do flourish, it must be against every Law of Nature and Reason; like the Thorn at *Glassenbury*, that blossoms in the Midst of Winter.

Let the worthy *Commissioners* who come from *England*, ride round the Kingdom, and observe the Face of Nature, or the Faces of the Natives; the Improvement of the Land; the thriving numerous Plantations; the noble Woods; the Abundance and Vicinity of Country-Seats; the commodious Farmers Houses and Barns; the Towns and Villages, where every Body is busy, and thriving with all Kind of Manufactures; the Shops full of Goods, wrought to Perfection, and filled with Customers; the comfortable Diet and Dress, and Dwellings of the People; the vast Numbers of Ships in our Harbours and Docks, and Ship-wrights in our Seaport-Towns; the Roads crouded with Carriers, laden with rich Manufactures; the perpetual Concourse to and fro of pompous Equipages.

With what Envy and Admiration, would those Gentlemen return from so delightful a Progress? What glorious

Reports would they make, when they went back to *England*?

But my Heart is too heavy to continue this Irony longer; for it is manifest, that whatever Stranger took such a Journey, would be apt to think himself travelling in *Lapland*, or *Ysland*, rather than in a Country so favoured by Nature as ours, both in Fruitfulness of Soil, and Temperature of Climate. The miserable Dress, and Dyet, and Dwelling of the People. The general Desolation in most Parts of the Kingdom. The old Seats of the Nobility and Gentry all in Ruins, and no new ones in their Stead. The Families of Farmers, who pay great Rents, living in Filth and Nastiness upon Butter-milk and Potatoes, without a Shoe or Stocking to their Feet; or a House so convenient as an *English* Hog-sty, to receive them. These, indeed, may be comfortable Sights to an *English* Spectator; who comes for a short Time, only *to learn the Language*, and returns back to his own Country, whither he finds all our Wealth transmitted.

> *Nostrâ miseriâ magna es.*
> [By our misery you are great]

There is not one Argument used to prove the Riches of *Ireland*, which is not a logical Demonstration of its Poverty. The Rise of our Rents is squeezed out of the very Blood, and Vitals, and Cloaths, and Dwellings of the

A Short View of the State of Ireland

Tenants; who live worse than *English* Beggars. The Lowness of Interest, in all other Countries a Sign of Wealth, is in us a Proof of Misery; there being no Trade to employ any Borrower. Hence alone comes the Dearness of Land, since the Savers have no other Way to lay out their Money. Hence the Dearness of Necessaries for life; because the Tenants cannot afford to pay such extravagant Rates for Land, (which they must take, or go a-begging) without raising the Price of Cattle, and of Corn, although themselves should live upon Chaff. Hence our encrease of Buildings in this City; because Workmen have nothing to do, but employ one another; and one Half of them are infallibly undone. Hence the daily Encrease of *Bankers*; who may be a necessary Evil in a trading Country, but so ruinous in ours; who, for their private Advantage, have sent away all our Silver, and one Third of our Gold; so that within three Years past, the running Cash of the Nation, which was about five Hundred Thousand Pounds, is now less than two; and must daily diminish, unless we have Liberty to coin, as well as that important Kingdom the Isle of *Man*, and the meanest Prince in the *German* Empire, as I before observed.

I have sometimes thought, that this Paradox of the Kingdom growing rich, is chiefly owing to those worthy Gentlemen the BANKERS; who, except some Custom-house Officers, Birds of Passage, oppressive thrifty 'Squires, and a few others who shall be nameless, are the only thriving People among us: And I have often wished, that a Law were enacted to hang up half a Dozen *Bankers* every Year; and thereby interpose at least some short Delay, to the further Ruin of *Ireland*.

Ye are idle, ye are idle, answered *Pharoah* to the *Israelites*, when they complained to *his Majesty*, that they were forced to make Bricks without Straw.

England enjoys every one of those Advantages for enriching a Nation, which I have above enumerated; and, into the Bargain, a good Million returned to them every Year, without Labour or Hazard, or one Farthing Value received on our Side. But how long we shall be able to continue the Payment, I am not under the least Concern. One Thing I know, that *when the Hen is starved to Death, there will be no more Golden Eggs*.

I think it a little unhospitable, and others may call it a subtil Piece of Malice; that, because there may be a Dozen Families in this Town, able to entertain their *English* Friends in a generous Manner at their Tables; their Guests, upon their Return to *England*, shall report, that we wallow in Riches and Luxury.

Yet, I confess, I have known an Hospital, where all the Houshold-Officers grew rich; while the Poor, for whose Sake it was built, were almost starving for want of Food and Raiment.

To conclude. If *Ireland* be a rich and flourishing Kingdom; its Wealth and Prosperity must be owing to certain Causes, that are yet concealed from the whole Race of

Mankind; and the Effects are equally invisible. We need not wonder at Strangers, when they deliver such Paradoxes; but a Native and Inhabitant of this Kingdom, who gives the same Verdict, must be either ignorant to Stupidity; or a Man-pleaser, at the Expence of all Honour, Conscience, and Truth.

A Modest Proposal

FOR *PREVENTING THE CHILDREN OF POOR PEOPLE IN* IRELAND, *FROM BEING A BURDEN TO THEIR PARENTS OR COUNTRY; AND FOR MAKING THEM BENEFICIAL TO THE PUBLICK*

Written in the Year 1729

It is a melancholly Object to those who walk through this great Town, or travel in the Country; when they see the *Streets*, the *Roads*, and *Cabbin-doors* crowded with *Beggars* of the Female Sex, followed by three, four, or six Children, *all in Rags*, and importuning every Passenger for an Alms. These *Mothers*, instead of being able to work for their honest Livelyhood, are forced to employ all their Time in stroling to beg Sustenance for their *helpless Infants*; who, as they grow up, either turn *Thieves* for want of Work; or leave their *dear Native Country, to fight for the Pretender in* Spain; or sell themselves to the *Barbadoes*.

I think it is agreed by all Parties, that this prodigious Number of Children in the Arms, or on the Backs, or at the *Heels* of their *Mothers*, and frequently of their *Fathers*, is *in the present deplorable State of the Kingdom*, a very great additional Grievance; and therefore, whoever could find out a fair, cheap, and easy Method of making these Children sound and useful Members of the Commonwealth, would deserve so well of the Publick, as to have his Statue set up for a Preserver of the Nation.

But my Intention is very far from being confined to provide only for the Children of *professed Beggars*: It is of a much greater Extent, and shall take in the whole Number of Infants at a certain Age, who are born of Parents, in effect as little able to support them, as those who demand our Charity in the Streets.

As to my own Part, having turned my Thoughts for many Years, upon this important Subject, and maturely weighed the several *Schemes of other Projectors*, I have always found them grosly mistaken in their Computation. It is true, a Child *just dropt from its Dam*, may be supported by her Milk, for a Solar Year with little other Nourishment; at most not above the Value of two Shillings; which the Mother may certainly get, or the Value in *Scraps*, by her lawful Occupation of *Begging*: And, it is exactly at one Year old, that I propose to provide for them in such a Manner, as, instead of being a Charge upon their *Parents*, or the *Parish*, or *wanting Food and Raiment* for the rest of their Lives; they shall, on the contrary, contribute to the Feeding, and partly to the Cloathing, of many Thousands.

There is likewise another great Advantage in my *Scheme*, that it will prevent those *voluntary Abortions*, and that horrid Practice of *Women murdering their Bastard Children*; alas! too frequent among us; sacrificing the *poor innocent Babes*, I doubt, more to avoid the Expence than the Shame; which would move Tears and Pity in the most Savage and inhuman Breast.

The Number of Souls in *Ireland* being usually reckoned one Million and a half; of these I calculate there may be about Two Hundred Thousand Couple whose Wives are Breeders; from which Number I subtract thirty thousand Couples, who are able to maintain their own Children; although I apprehend there cannot be so many, under *the present Distresses of the Kingdom*; but this being granted, there will remain an Hundred and Seventy Thousand Breeders. I again subtract Fifty Thousand for those Women who miscarry, or whose Children die by Accident, or Disease, within the Year. There only remain an Hundred and Twenty Thousand Children of poor Parents annually born: The Question therefore is, How this Number shall be reared, and provided for? Which, as I have already said, under the present Situation of Affairs, is utterly impossible, by all the Methods hitherto proposed: For we can *neither employ them in Handicraft* or *Agriculture*; we neither build Houses, (I mean in the Country) nor cultivate Land: They can very seldom pick up a Livelyhood *by Stealing* until they arrive at six Years old; except where they are of towardly Parts; although, I confess, they

A Modest Proposal

learn the Rudiments much earlier; during which Time, they can, however, be properly looked upon only as *Probationers*; as I have been informed by a principal Gentleman in the County of *Cavan*, who protested to me, that he never knew above one or two Instances under the Age of six, even in a Part of the Kingdom *so renowned for the quickest Proficiency in that Art*.

I am assured by our Merchants, that a Boy or a Girl before twelve Years old, is no saleable Commodity; and even when they come to this Age, they will not yield above Three Pounds, or Three Pounds and half a Crown at most, on the Exchange; which cannot turn to Account either to the Parents or Kingdom; the Charge of Nutriment and Rags, having been at least four Times that Value.

I shall now therefore humbly propose my own Thoughts; which I hope will not be liable to the least Objection.

I have been assured by a very knowing *American* of my Acquaintance in *London*; that a young healthy Child, well nursed, is, at a Year old, a most delicious, nourishing, and wholesome Food; whether *Stewed*, *Roasted*, *Baked*, or *Boiled*; and, I make no doubt, that it will equally serve in a *Fricasie*, or *Ragout*.

I do therefore humbly offer it to *publick Consideration*, that of the Hundred and Twenty thousand Children, already computed, Twenty thousand may be reserved for Breed; whereof only one Fourth Part to be Males; which is more than we allow to *Sheep*, *black Cattle*, or *Swine*; and my Reason is, that these Children are seldom the Fruits of Marriage, *a Circumstance not much regarded by our Savages*; therefore, *one Male* will be sufficient to serve *four Females*. That the remaining Hundred thousand, may, at a Year old, be offered in Sale to the *Persons of Quality* and *Fortune*, through the Kingdom; always advising the Mother to let them suck plentifully in the last Month, so as to render them plump, and fat for a good Table. A Child will make two Dishes at an Entertainment for Friends; and when the Family dines alone, the fore or hind Quarter will make a reasonable Dish; and seasoned with a little Pepper or Salt, will be very good Boiled on the Fourth Day, especially in *Winter*.

I have reckoned upon a Medium, that a Child just born will weigh Twelve Pounds; and in a solar Year, if tolerably nursed, encreaseth to twenty eight Pounds.

I grant this Food will be somewhat dear, and therefore very *proper for Landlords*; who, as they have already devoured most of the Parents, seem to have the best Title to the Children.

Infants Flesh will be in Season throughout the Year; but more plentiful in *March*, and a little before and after: For we are told by a grave Author, an eminent *French* Physician, that *Fish being a prolifick Dyet*, there are more Children born in *Roman Catholick Countries* about Nine Months after *Lent*, than at any other Season: Therefore reckoning a Year after *Lent*, the Markets will be more glutted than usual; because the Number of *Popish*

A Modest Proposal

Infants, is, at least, three to one in this Kingdom; and therefore it will have one other Collateral Advantage, by lessening the Number of *Papists* among us.

I have already computed the Charge of nursing a Beggar's Child (in which List I reckon all *Cottagers*, *Labourers*, and Four fifths of the *Farmers*) to be about two Shillings *per Annum*, Rags included; and I believe, no Gentleman would repine to give Ten Shillings for the *Carcase of a good fat Child*; which, as I have said, will make four Dishes of excellent nutritive Meat, when he hath only some particular Friend, or his own Family, to dine with him. Thus the Squire will learn to be a good Landlord, and grow popular among his Tenants; the Mother will have Eight Shillings net Profit, and be fit for Work until she produceth another Child.

Those who are more thrifty (*as I must confess the Times require*) may flay the Carcase; the Skin of which, artificially dressed, will make admirable *Gloves for Ladies*, and *Summer Boots for fine Gentlemen*.

As to our City of *Dublin*; Shambles may be appointed for this Purpose, in the most convenient Parts of it; and Butchers we may be assured will not be wanting; although I rather recommend buying the Children alive, and dressing them hot from the Knife, as we do *roasting Pigs*.

A very worthy Person, *a true Lover of his Country*, and whose Virtues I highly esteem, was lately pleased, in discoursing on this Matter, to offer a Refinement upon my Scheme. He said, that many Gentlemen of this Kingdom, having of late destroyed their Deer; he conceived that the Want of Venison might be well supplied by the Bodies of young Lads and Maidens, not exceeding fourteen Years of Age, nor under twelve; so great a Number of both Sexes in every County being now ready to starve, for Want of Work and Service: And these to be disposed of by their Parents, if alive, or otherwise by their nearest Relations. But with due Deference to so excellent a Friend, and so deserving a Patriot, I cannot be altogether in his Sentiments. For as to the Males, my *American* Acquaintance assured me from frequent Experience, that their Flesh was generally tough and lean, like that of our School-boys, by continual Exercise; and their Taste disagreeable; and to fatten them would not answer the Charge. Then, as to the Females, it would, I think, with humble Submission, *be a Loss to the Publick*, because they soon would become Breeders themselves: And besides it is not improbable, that some scrupulous People might be apt to censure such a Practice (although indeed very unjustly) as a little bordering upon Cruelty; which, I confess, hath always been with me the strongest Objection against any Project, how well soever intended.

But in order to justify my Friend; he confessed, that this Expedient was put into his Head by the famous *Salmanaazor*, a Native of the Island *Formosa*, who came from thence to *London*, above twenty Years ago, and in Conversation told my Friend, that in his Country, when any young Person happened to be put to Death, the

Executioner sold the Carcase to *Persons of Quality*, as a prime Dainty; and that, in his Time, the Body of a plump Girl of fifteen, who was crucified for an Attempt to poison the Emperor, was sold to his Imperial *Majesty's prime Minister of State*, and other great *Mandarins* of the Court, *in Joints from the Gibbet*, at Four hundred Crowns. Neither indeed can I deny, that if the same Use were made of several plump young Girls in this Town, who, without one single Groat to their Fortunes, cannot stir Abroad without a Chair, and appear at the *Play-house* and *Assemblies* in foreign Fineries, which they never will pay for; the Kingdom would not be the worse.

Some Persons of a desponding Spirit are in great Concern about that vast Number of poor People, who are Aged, Diseased, or Maimed; and I have been desired to employ my Thoughts what Course may be taken, to ease the Nation of so grievous an Incumbrance. But I am not in the least Pain upon that Matter; because it is very well known, that they are every Day *dying*, and *rotting*, by *Cold* and *Famine*, and *Filth*, and *Vermin*, as fast as can be reasonably expected. And as to the younger Labourers, they are now in almost as hopeful a Condition: They cannot get Work, and consequently pine away for Want of Nourishment, to a Degree, that if at any Time they are accidentally hired to common Labour, they have not Strength to perform it; and thus the Country, and themselves, are in a fair Way of being soon delivered from the Evils to come.

I have too long digressed; and therefore shall return to my Subject. I think the Advantages by the Proposal which I have made, are obvious, and many, as well as of the highest Importance.

For, *First*, as I have already observed, it would greatly lessen *the Number of Papists*, with whom we are yearly over-run; being the principal Breeders of the Nation, as well as our most dangerous Enemies; and who stay at home on Purpose, with a Design *to deliver the Kingdom to the Pretender*; hoping to take their Advantage by the Absence *of so many good Protestants*, who have chosen rather to leave their Country, than stay at home, and pay Tithes against their Conscience, to an idolatrous *Episcopal Curate*.

Secondly, The poorer Tenants will have something valuable of their own, which, by Law, may be made liable to Distress, and help to pay their Landlord's Rent; their Corn and Cattle being already seized, and *Money a Thing unknown*.

Thirdly, Whereas the Maintenance of an Hundred Thousand Children, from two Years old, and upwards, cannot be computed at less than ten Shillings a Piece *per Annum*, the Nation's Stock will be thereby encreased Fifty Thousand Pounds *per Annum*; besides the Profit of a new Dish, introduced to the Tables of all *Gentlemen of Fortune* in the Kingdom, who have any Refinement in Taste; and the Money will circulate among our selves, the Goods being entirely of our own Growth and Manufacture.

A Modest Proposal

Fourthly, The constant Breeders, besides the Gain of Eight Shillings *Sterling per Annum*, by the Sale of their Children, will be rid of the Charge of maintaining them after the first Year.

Fifthly, This Food would likewise bring great *Custom to Taverns*, where the Vintners will certainly be so prudent, as to procure the best Receipts for dressing it to Perfection; and consequently, have their Houses frequented by all the *fine Gentlemen*, who justly value themselves upon their Knowledge in good Eating; and a skilful Cook, who understands how to oblige his Guests, will contrive to make it as expensive as they please.

Sixthly, This would be a great Inducement to Marriage, which all wise Nations have either encouraged by Rewards, or enforced by Laws and Penalties. It would encrease the Care and Tenderness of Mothers towards their Children, when they were sure of a Settlement for Life, to the poor Babes, provided in some Sort by the Publick, to their annual Profit instead of Expence. We should soon see an honest Emulation among the married Women, *which of them could bring the fattest Child to the Market*. Men would become as *fond* of their Wives, during the Time of their Pregnancy, as they are now of their *Mares* in Foal, their *Cows* in Calf, or *Sows* when they are ready to farrow; nor offer to beat or kick them, (as it is too *frequent* a Practice) for fear of a Miscarriage.

Many other Advantages might be enumerated. For Instance, the Addition of some Thousand Carcasses in our Exportation of barrelled Beef: The Propagation of *Swines Flesh*, and Improvement in the Art of making good *Bacon*; so much wanted among us by the great Destruction of *Pigs*, too frequent at our Tables, which are no way comparable in Taste, or Magnificence, to a well-grown fat yearly Child; which, roasted whole, will make a considerable Figure at a *Lord Mayor*'s *Feast*, or any other publick Entertainment. But this, and many others, I omit; being studious of Brevity.

Supposing that one Thousand Families in this City, would be constant Customers for Infants Flesh; besides others who might have it at *merry Meetings*, particularly at *Weddings* and *Christenings*; I compute that *Dublin* would take off annually, about Twenty Thousand Carcasses; and the rest of the Kingdom (where probably they will be sold somewhat cheaper) the remaining Eighty Thousand.

I can think of no one Objection, that will possibly be raised against this Proposal; unless it should be urged, that the Number of People will be thereby much lessened in the Kingdom. This I freely own; and it was indeed one principal Design in offering it to the World. I desire the Reader will observe, that I calculate my Remedy *for this one individual Kingdom of* IRELAND, *and for no other that ever was, is, or I think ever can be upon Earth*. Therefore, let no Man talk to me of other Expedients: *Of taxing our Absentees at five Shillings a Pound: Of using neither Cloaths, nor Houshold Furniture; except what is of our own Growth and*

Manufacture: Of utterly rejecting the Materials and Instruments that promote foreign Luxury: Of curing the Expensiveness of Pride, Vanity, Idleness, and Gaming in our Women: Of introducing a Vein of Parsimony, Prudence and Temperance: Of learning to love our Country; wherein we differ even from LAPLANDERS, *and the Inhabitants of* TOPINAMBOO: *Of quitting our Animosities, and Factions; nor act any longer like the* Jews, *who were murdering one another at the very Moment their City was taken: Of being a little cautious not to sell our Country and Consciences for nothing: Of teaching Landlords to have, at least, one Degree of Mercy towards their Tenants.* Lastly, *Of putting a Spirit of Honesty, Industry, and Skill into our Shop-keepers; who, if a Resolution could now be taken to buy only our native Goods, would immediately unite to cheat and exact upon us in the Price, the Measure, and the Goodness; nor could ever yet be brought to make one fair Proposal of just Dealing, though often and earnestly invited to it.*

Therefore I repeat; let no Man talk to me of these and the like Expedients; till he hath, at least, a Glimpse of Hope, that there will ever be some hearty and sincere Attempt to put *them in Practice.*

But, as to my self; having been wearied out for many Years with offering vain, idle, visionary Thoughts; and at length utterly despairing of Success, I fortunately fell upon this Proposal; which, as it is wholly new, so it hath something *solid* and *real*, of no Expence, and little Trouble, full in our own Power; and whereby we can incur no Danger in *disobliging* ENGLAND: For, this Kind of

Commodity will not bear Exportation; the Flesh being of too tender a Consistence, to admit a long Continuance in Salt; *although, perhaps, I could name a Country, which would be glad to eat up our whole Nation without it.*

After all, I am not so violently bent upon my own Opinion, as to reject any Offer proposed by wise Men, which shall be found equally innocent, cheap, easy, and effectual. But before something of that Kind shall be advanced, in Contradiction to my Scheme, and offering a better; I desire the Author, or Authors, will be pleased maturely to consider two Points. *First*, As Things now stand, how they will be able to find Food and Raiment, for a Hundred Thousand useless Mouths and Backs? And *secondly*, There being a round Million of Creatures in human Figure, throughout this Kingdom; whose whole Subsistence, put into a common Stock, would leave them in Debt two Millions of Pounds Sterling; adding those, who are Beggars by Profession, to the Bulk of Farmers, Cottagers, and Labourers, with their Wives and Children, who are Beggars in Effect; I desire those Politicians, who dislike my Overture, and may perhaps be so bold to attempt an Answer, that they will first ask the Parents of these Mortals, Whether they would not, at this Day, think it a great Happiness to have been sold for Food at a Year old, in the Manner I prescribe; and thereby have avoided such a perpetual Scene of Misfortunes, as they have since gone through; by the *Oppression of Landlords*; the Impossibility of paying Rent, without Money or

Trade; the Want of common Sustenance, with neither House nor Cloaths, to cover them from the Inclemencies of the Weather; and the most inevitable Prospect of intailing the like, or greater Miseries upon their Breed for ever.

I profess, in the Sincerity of my Heart, that I have not the least personal Interest, in endeavouring to promote this necessary Work; having no other Motive than the *publick Good of my Country, by advancing our Trade, providing for Infants, relieving the Poor, and giving some Pleasure to the Rich*. I have no Children, by which I can propose to get a single Penny; the youngest being nine Years old, and my Wife past Child-bearing.

An Examination of Certain Abuses, Corruptions, and Enormities, in the City of Dublin

WRITTEN IN THE YEAR 1732

Nothing is held more commendable in all great Cities, especially the Metropolis of a Kingdom, than what the *French* call the *Police*: By which Word is meant the Government thereof, to prevent the many Disorders occasioned by great Numbers of People and Carriages, especially through narrow Streets. In this Government our famous City of *Dublin* is said to be very defective; and universally complained of. Many wholesome Laws have been enacted to correct those Abuses, but are ill executed; and many more are wanting; which I hope the united Wisdom of the Nation (whereof so many good Effects have already appeared this Session) will soon take into their profound Consideration.

As I have been always watchful over the Good of mine own Country; and particularly for that of our renowned City; where, (*absit invidia*) I had the Honour to draw my first Breath; I cannot have a Minute's Ease or Patience to forbear enumerating some of the greatest Enormities,

An Examination of Certain Abuses, Corruptions, and Enormities

Abuses, and Corruptions spread almost through every Part of *Dublin*; and proposing such Remedies, as, I hope, the Legislature will approve of.

The narrow Compass to which I have confined my self in this Paper, will allow me only to touch the most important Defects; and such as I think seem to require the most speedy Redress.

And first: Perhaps there was never known a wiser Institution than that of allowing certain Persons of both Sexes, in large and populous Cities, to cry through the Streets many Necessaries of Life. It would be endless to recount the Conveniences which our City enjoys by this useful Invention, and particularly Strangers, forced hither by Business, who reside here but a short time: For, these having usually but little Money, and being wholly ignorant of the Town, might at an easy Price purchase a tolerable Dinner, if the several Criers would pronounce the Names of the Goods they have to sell, in any tolerable Language. And therefore, until our Law-makers shall think it proper to interpose so far as to make those Traders pronounce their Words in such Terms, that a plain Christian Hearer may comprehend what is cryed; I would advise all new Comers to look out at their Garret Windows, and there see whether the Thing that is cryed be *Tripes*, or *Flummery*, *Buttermilk*, or *Cowheels*. For, as Things are now managed, how is it possible for an honest Countryman, just arrived, to find out what is meant, for Instance, by the following Words, with which his Ears are

Jonathan Swift

constantly stunned twice a Day, *Muggs, Juggs, and Porringers, up in the Garret, and down in the Cellar*. I say, how is it possible for any Stranger to understand that this Jargon is meant as an Invitation to buy a Farthing's Worth of Milk for his Breakfast or Supper, unless his Curiosity draws him to the Window, or until his Landlady shall inform him? I produce this only as one Instance, among a Hundred much worse; I mean where the Words make a Sound wholly inarticulate, which give so much Disturbance, and so little Information.

The Affirmation solemnly made in the Cry of *Herrings*, is directly against all Truth and Probability; *Herrings alive, alive here*: The very Proverb will convince us of this; for what is more frequent in ordinary Speech, than to say of some Neighbour for whom the Passing-Bell rings, that *he is dead as a Herring*? And, pray, how is it possible, that a *Herring*, which, as *Philosophers* observe, cannot live longer than One Minute, Three Seconds and a half out of Water, should bear a Voyage in open Boats from *Howth* to *Dublin*, be tossed into twenty Hands, and preserve its Life in Sieves for several Hours? Nay, we have Witnesses ready to produce, that many Thousands of these *Herrings*, so impudently asserted to be alive, have been a Day and a Night upon dry Land. But this is not the worst. What can we think of those impious Wretches, who dare in the Face of the Sun, vouch the very same Affirmative of their *Salmon*; and cry, *Salmon alive, alive*; whereas, if you call the Woman who cryes it, she is not ashamed to turn back

An Examination of Certain Abuses, Corruptions, and Enormities

her Mantle, and shew you this individual *Salmon* cut into a dozen Pieces. I have given good Advice to these infamous Disgracers of their Sex and Calling, without the least Appearance of Remorse; and fully against the Conviction of their own Consciences. I have mentioned this Grievance to several of our Parish Ministers; but all in vain: So that it must continue until the Government shall think fit to interpose.

There is another *Cry*, which, from the strictest Observation I can make, appears to be very modern, and it is that of *Sweet-hearts*; and is plainly intended for a Reflection upon the Female Sex; as if there were at present so great a Dearth of Lovers, that the Women instead of receiving Presents from Men, were now forced to offer Money, to purchase *Sweet-hearts*.* Neither am I sure, that this *Cry* doth not glance at some Disaffection against the Government; insinuating, that while so many of our Troops are engaged in foreign Service, and such a great Number of our gallant Officers constantly reside in *England*; the Ladies are forced to take up with *Parsons* and *Attornies*: But this is a most unjust Reflection; as may soon be proved by any Person who frequents the *Castle*, our publick Walks, our Balls and Assemblies; where the Crowds of *Toupees* were never known to swarm as they do at present.

There is a *Cry* peculiar to this City, which I do not remember to have been used in *London*; or at least, not

---

* A kind of sugar-cake.

in the same Terms that it hath been practised by both Parties, during each of their Power; but, very unjustly by the *Tories*. While these were at the Helm, they grew daily more and more impatient to put all true *Whigs* and *Hanoverians* out of Employments. To effect which, they hired certain ordinary Fellows, with large Baskets on their Shoulders, to call aloud at every House, *Dirt to carry out*; giving that Denomination to our whole Party; as if they would signify, that the Kingdom could never be *cleansed*, until we were *swept* from the Earth like *Rubbish*. But since that happy Turn of Times, when we were so *miraculously* preserved by just an *Inch*, from *Popery*, *Slavery*, *Massacre*, and the *Pretender*; I must own it Prudence in us, still to go on with the same *Cry*; which hath ever since been so effectually observed, that the true *political Dirt* is wholly removed and thrown on its proper Dunghills, there to corrupt, and be no more heard of.

But, to proceed to other Enormities: Every Person who walks the Streets, must needs observe an immense Number of human Excrements at the Doors and Steps of waste Houses, and at the Sides of every dead Wall; for which the disaffected Party hath assigned a very false and malicious Cause. They would have it that these Heaps were laid there privately by *British Fundaments*, to make the World believe, that our *Irish* Vulgar do daily eat and drink; and consequently, that the Clamour of Poverty among us, must be false; proceeding only from *Jacobites* and *Papists*. They would confirm this, by pretending to

An Examination of Certain Abuses, Corruptions, and Enormities

observe, that a *British Anus* being more narrowly perforated than one of our own Country; and many of these Excrements, upon a strict View appearing Copple-crowned, with a Point like a Cone or Pyramid, are easily distinguished from the *Hibernian*, which lie much flatter, and with less Continuity. I communicated this Conjecture to an eminent Physician, who is well versed in such profound Speculations; and at my Request was pleased to make Trial with each of his Fingers, by thrusting them into the *Anus* of several Persons of both Nations; and professed he could find no such Difference between them as those ill-disposed People alledge. On the contrary, he assured me, that much the greater Number of narrow Cavities were of *Hibernian* Origin. This I only mention to shew how ready the *Jacobites* are to lay hold of any Handle to express their Malice against the Government. I had almost forgot to add, that my Friend the Physician could, by smelling each Finger, distinguish the *Hibernian* Excrement from the *British*; and was not above twice mistaken in an Hundred Experiments; upon which he intends very soon to publish a learned Dissertation.

There is a Diversion in this City, which usually begins among the *Butchers*; but is often continued by a Succession of other People, through many Streets. It is called the COSSING *of a Dog*: And I may justly number it among our Corruptions. The Ceremony is thus: A strange Dog happens to pass through a Flesh-Market: Whereupon an expert *Butcher* immediately cries in a loud Voice, and the proper Tone, *Coss, Coss,* several Times: The same Word is repeated by the People. The Dog, who perfectly understands the Term of Art, and consequently the Danger he is in, immediately flies. The People, and even his own *Brother Animals,* pursue: The Pursuit and Cry attend him perhaps half a Mile; he is well worried in his Flight; and sometimes hardly escapes. This, our Ill-wishers of the *Jacobite* Kind, are pleased to call a *Persecution*; and affirm, that it always falls upon *Dogs* of the *Tory* Principle. But, we can well defend our selves, by justly alledging, that, when they were uppermost, they treated our *Dogs* full as inhumanly: As to my own Part, who have in former Times often attended these *Processions*; although I can very well distinguish between a *Whig* and a *Tory Dog*; yet I never carried my Resentments very far upon a *Party Principle*, except it were against certain malicious *Dogs*, who most discovered their Enmity against us in the *worst of Times*. And, I remember too well, that in the wicked Ministry of the Earl of *Oxford*; a large Mastiff of our Party being unmercifully *cossed*; ran, without Thinking, between my Legs, as I was coming up *Fishamble-street*; and, as I am of low Stature, with very short Legs, bore me riding backwards down the Hill, for above Two Hundred Yards: And, although I made use of his Tail for a Bridle, holding it fast with both my Hands, and clung my Legs as close to his Sides as I could; yet we both came down together into the Middle of the Kennel; where after rowling three or four Times over each other, I got up with much ado,

An Examination of Certain Abuses, Corruptions, and Enormities

amidst the Shouts and Huzza's of a Thousand malicious *Jacobites*: I cannot, indeed, but gratefully acknowledge, that for this and many other *Services* and *Sufferings*, I have been since more than over-paid.

This Adventure may, perhaps, have put me out of Love with the Diversion of *Cossing*; which I confess myself an Enemy to; unless we could always be sure of distinguishing *Tory Dogs*; whereof great Numbers have since been so prudent, as entirely to change their Principles; and are now justly esteemed the best *Worriers* of their former Friends.

I am assured, and partly know, that all the Chimney-Sweeper Boys, where Members of P[arliamen]t chiefly lodge, are hired by *our Enemies* to sculk in the Tops of Chimneys, with their Heads no higher than will just permit them to look round; and at the usual Hours when Members are going to the House, if they see a Coach stand near the Lodging of any *loyal* Member; they call *Coach*, *Coach*, as loud as they can bawl, just at the Instant when the Footman begins to give the same Call. And this is chiefly done on those Days, when any Point of Importance is to be debated. This Practice may be of very dangerous Consequence. For, these Boys are all hired by Enemies to the Government: And thus, by the Absence of a few Members for a few Minutes, a Question may be carried against the *true Interest* of the Kingdom; and, very probably, not without an Eye towards the *Pretender*.

I have not observed the Wit and Fancy of this Town,

Jonathan Swift

so much employed in any one Article as that of contriving Variety of Signs to hang over Houses, where *Punch* is to be sold. The Bowl is represented full of *Punch*; the Ladle stands erect in the middle; supported sometimes by one, and sometimes by two Animals, whose Feet rest upon the Edge of the Bowl. These Animals are sometimes one black *Lion*, and sometimes a Couple; sometimes a single *Eagle*, and sometimes a spread One; and we often meet a *Crow*, a *Swan*, a *Bear*, or a *Cock*, in the same Posture.

Now, I cannot find how any of these Animals, either separate, or in Conjunction, are, properly speaking, fit Emblems or Embellishments, to advance the Sale of *Punch*. Besides, it is agreed among *Naturalists*, that no Brute can endure the Taste of strong Liquor; except where he hath been used to it from his Infancy: And, consequently, it is against all the Rules of *Hieroglyph*, to assign those Animals as Patrons, or Protectors of *Punch*. For, in that Case, we ought to suppose that the Host keeps always ready the real Bird, or Beast, whereof the Picture hangs over his Door, to entertain his Guests; which, however, to my Knowledge, is not true in Fact: Not one of those Birds being a proper Companion for a *Christian*, as to aiding and assisting in making the *Punch*. For, as they are drawn upon the Sign, they are much more likely to mute, or shed their Feathers into the Liquor. Then, as to the *Bear*, he is too terrible, awkward, and slovenly a Companion to converse with; neither are any of them all *handy* enough to fill Liquor to the Company: I do, therefore,

An Examination of Certain Abuses, Corruptions, and Enormities

vehemently suspect a *Plot* intended against the Government, by these Devices. For, although the *Spread-Eagle* be the Arms of *Germany*, upon which Account it may possibly be a lawful *Protestant* Sign; yet I, who am very suspicious of fair Out-sides, in a Matter which so nearly concerns our Welfare; cannot but call to Mind, that the *Pretender*'s Wife is said to be of *German* Birth: And that many *Popish* Princes, in so vast an Extent of Land, are reported to excel both at making and drinking *Punch*. Besides, it is plain, that the *Spread-Eagle* exhibits to us the perfect Figure of a *Cross*; which is a Badge of *Popery*. Then, as to the *Cock*, he is well known to represent the *French* Nation, our old and dangerous Enemy. The *Swan*, who must of Necessity cover the entire Bowl with his Wings, can be no other than the *Spaniard*; who endeavours to engross all the Treasures of the *Indies* to himself. The *Lion* is indeed the common Emblem of Royal Power, as well as the Arms of *England*: But to paint him black, is perfect *Jacobitism*; and a manifest Type of those who *blacken* the Actions of the best Princes. It is not easy to distinguish whether that other Fowl painted over the *Punch-Bowl*, be a *Crow* or *Raven*? It is true, they have both been held ominous Birds: But I rather take it to be the former; because it is the Disposition of a *Crow*, to pick out the Eyes of other Creatures, and often even of *Christians* after they are dead; and is therefore drawn here, with a Design to put the *Jacobites* in Mind of their old Practice; first to lull us a-sleep, (which is an Emblem of Death) and then to blind our Eyes, that we may not see their dangerous Practices against the State.

To speak my private Opinion; the least offensive Picture in the whole Sett, seems to be the *Bear*; because he represents *Ursa Major*, or the *Great Bear*, who presides over the *North*; where the *Reformation* first began; and which, next to *Britain*, (including *Scotland* and the *North of Ireland*) is the great Protector of the *true Protestant* Religion. But, however, in those Signs where I observe the *Bear* to be *chained*, I cannot help surmising a *Jacobite* Contrivance; by which, these Traytors hint an earnest Desire of using all *true Whigs*, as their Predecessors did the primitive Christians: I mean, to represent us as *Bears*, and then halloo their *Tory-Dogs* to bait us to Death.

Thus I have given a fair Account of what I dislike, in all the Signs set over those Houses that invite us to *Punch*. I own it was a Matter that did not need explaining; being so very obvious to common Understanding: Yet, I know not how it happens, but methinks there seems a fatal Blindness to overspread our corporeal Eyes, as well as our intellectual; and I heartily wish, I may be found a false Prophet. For, these are not bare Suspicions, but manifest Demonstrations.

Therefore, away with these *Popish*, *Jacobite*, and idolatrous Gew-gaws. And I heartily wish a Law were enacted, under severe Penalties, against drinking any *Punch* at all: For, nothing is easier, than to prove it a disaffected Liquor. The chief Ingredients, which are *Brandy*, *Oranges*,

An Examination of Certain Abuses, Corruptions, and Enormities

and *Lemons*, are all sent us from *Popish* Countries; and nothing remains of *Protestant* Growth, but *Sugar* and *Water*. For, as to Biscuit, which formerly was held a necessary Ingredient, and is truly *British*, we find it is entirely rejected.

But I will put the Truth of my Assertion past all Doubt: I mean, that this Liquor is by one important Innovation, grown of ill Example, and dangerous Consequence to the Publick. It is well known, that, by the true original Institution of making *Punch*, left us by Captain *Ratcliff*; the Sharpness is only occasioned by the Juice of *Lemons*; and so continued until after the happy *Revolution*. *Oranges*, alas! are a meer Innovation, and, in a manner, *but of Yesterday*. It was the Politicks of *Jacobites* to introduce them gradually: And to what Intent? The Thing speaks it self. It was cunningly to shew their Virulence against his sacred Majesty King *William, of ever glorious and immortal Memory*. But of late (to shew how fast Disloyalty increaseth) they came from one to two, and then to three *Oranges*; nay, at present, we often find *Punch* made all with *Oranges*; and not one single *Lemon*. For, the *Jacobites*, before the Death of that immortal Prince, had, by a Superstition, formed a private Prayer; that, as they *squeezed* the *Orange*, so might that *Protestant* King be *squeezed* to Death: According to the known *Sorcery* described by *Virgil*; *Limus ut hic durescit, & hæc ut cera liquescit*, &c. And thus the *Romans*, when they sacrificed an Ox, used this Kind of Prayer: *As I knock down this Ox, so may thou,* O Jupiter, *knock down our*

Enemies. In like Manner, after King *William*'s Death, whenever a *Jacobite squeezed* an *Orange*, he had a mental Curse upon the *glorious Memory*; and a hearty Wish for Power to *squeeze* all his Majesty's Friends to Death, as he *squeezed* that *Orange*, which bore one of his Titles, as he was Prince of *Orange*. This I do affirm for Truth; many of that Faction having confessed it to me, under an *Oath of Secrecy*; which, however, I thought it my Duty not to keep, when I saw my dear Country in Danger. But, what better can be expected from an *impious* Set of Men, who never scruple to drink CONFUSION to all *true Protestants*, under the Name of *Whigs*? A most unchristian and inhuman Practice; *which, to our great Honour and Comfort, was never charged upon us, even by our most malicious Detractors*.

The Sign of two *Angels*, hovering in the Air, and with their Right Hands supporting a *Crown*, is met with in several Parts of this City; and hath often given me great Offence: For, whether by the Unskilfulness, or dangerous Principles of the Painters, (although I have good Reasons to suspect the latter) those *Angels* are usually drawn with such horrid, or indeed rather diabolical *Countenances*, that they give great Offence to every loyal Eye; and equal Cause of Triumph to the *Jacobites*; being a most infamous Reflection upon our able and excellent Ministry.

I now return to that great Enormity of City *Cries*; most of which we have borrowed from *London*. I shall consider them only in a *political* View, as they nearly affect the Peace and Safety of both Kingdoms: And having been

An Examination of Certain Abuses, Corruptions, and Enormities

originally contrived by wicked *Machiavels*, to bring in *Popery*, *Slavery*, and *arbitrary Power*, by defeating the *Protestant* Succession, and introducing the *Pretender*; ought, in Justice, to be here laid open to the World.

About two or three Months after the happy *Revolution*, all Persons who possest any Employment or Office, in Church or State, were obliged by an Act of Parliament, to take the Oaths to King *William* and Queen *Mary*: And a great Number of disaffected Persons, refusing to take the said Oaths, from a pretended Scruple of Conscience, but really from a Spirit of *Popery* and Rebellion, they contrived a Plot, to make the swearing to those Princes odious in the Eyes of the People. To this End, they hired certain Women of ill Fame, but loud shrill Voices, under Pretence of selling Fish, to go through the Streets, with Sieves on their Heads, and cry, *buy my Soul, buy my Soul*; plainly insinuating, that all those who swore to King *William*, were just ready to sell their *Souls* for an Employment. This Cry was revived at the Death of Queen *Anne*, and I hear still continues in *London*, with much Offence to all *true Protestants*; but, to our great Happiness, seems to be almost dropt in *Dublin*.

But, because I altogether contemn the Displeasure and Resentment of *High-flyers*, *Tories*, and *Jacobites*, whom I look upon to be *worse even than profest Papists*; I do here declare, that those Evils which I am going to mention, were all brought upon us in the *worst of Times*, under the late Earl of *Oxford*'s Administration, during the four last

Years of Queen *Anne*'s Reign. *That wicked Minister was universally known to be a Papist in his Heart. He was of a most avaricious Nature, and is said to have died worth four Millions,* sterl[ing] *besides his vast Expences in Building, Statues, Plate, Jewels, and other costly Rarities. He was of a mean obscure Birth, from the very Dregs of the People; and so illiterate, that he could hardly read a Paper at the Council Table. I forbear to touch at his open, prophane, profligate Life; because I desire not to rake into the Ashes of the Dead; and therefore I shall observe this wise Maxim:* De mortuis nil nisi bonum.

This flagitious Man, in order to compass his black Designs, employed certain wicked Instruments (which great Statesmen are never without) to adapt several *London* Cries, in such a Manner as would best answer his Ends. And, whereas it was upon good Grounds grievously suspected, that all *Places* at Court were sold to the highest Bidder: Certain Women were employed by his Emissaries, to carry *Fish* in Baskets on their Heads, and bawl through the Streets, *Buy my fresh Places*. I must, indeed, own that other Women used the same Cry, who were innocent of this wicked Design, and really sold their Fish of that Denomination, to get an honest Livelyhood: But the rest, who were in the *Secret*, although they carried *Fish* in their Sieves or Baskets, to save Appearances; yet they had likewise a certain Sign, somewhat resembling that of the *Free-Masons*, which the Purchasers of *Places* knew well enough, and were directed by the Women whither they were to resort, and make their Purchase. And, I remember very well, how oddly it lookt, when we observed many Gentlemen finely drest, about the Court-End of the Town, and as far as *York-Buildings*, where the Lord-Treasurer *Oxford* dwelt; calling the Women who cried *Buy my fresh Places*, and talking to them in the Corner of a Street, until they understood each other's Sign. But we never could observe that any Fish was bought.

Some Years before the Cries last mentioned; the Duke of *Savoy* was reported to have made certain Overtures to the Court of *England*, for admitting his eldest Son, by the Dutchess of *Orleans*'s Daughter, to succeed to the Crown, as next Heir, upon the *Pretender*'s being rejected; and that Son was immediately to turn *Protestant*. It was confidently reported, that great Numbers of People disaffected to the then *Illustrious* but now *Royal* House of *Hanover*, were in those Measures. Whereupon, another Sett of Women were hired by the *Jacobite* Leaders, to cry through the whole Town, *Buy my* Savoys, *dainty* Savoys, *curious* Savoys. But, I cannot directly charge the late Earl of *Oxford* with this *Conspiracy*, because he was not then chief Minister. However, this wicked Cry still continues in *London*, and was brought over hither; where it remains to this Day; and is in my humble Opinion, a very offensive Sound to every true Protestant who is old enough to remember those *dangerous* Times.

During the Ministry of that corrupt and *Jacobite* Earl abovementioned, the secret pernicious Design of those in Power, was to sell *Flanders* to *France*: The Consequence

Jonathan Swift

of which, must have been the infallible Ruin of the *States-General*, and would have opened the Way for *France* to obtain that universal Monarchy, they have so long aimed at; to which the *British* Dominions must next, after *Holland*, have been compelled to submit. Whereby the *Protestant* Religion would be rooted out of the World.

A Design of this vast Importance, after long Consultation among the *Jacobite* Grandees, with the Earl of *Oxford* at their Head; was at last determined to be carried on by the same Method with the former: It was therefore again put in Practice; but the Conduct of it was chiefly left to chosen Men, whose Voices were louder and stronger than those of the other Sex. And upon this Occasion, was first instituted in *London*, that famous Cry of FLOUNDERS. But the Cryers were particularly directed to pronounce the Word *Flaunders*, and not *Flounders*. For, the Country which we now by Corruption call *Flanders*, is in its true Orthography spelt *Flaunders*, as may be obvious to all who read old *English* Books. I say, from hence begun that thundering Cry, which hath ever since stunned the Ears of all *London*, made so many Children fall into Fits, and Women miscarry; *Come buy my fresh* Flaunders, *curious* Flaunders, *charming* Flaunders, *alive, alive, ho*; which last Words can with no Propriety of Speech, be applied to Fish manifestly dead, (as I observed before in *Herrings* and *Salmon*) but very justly to ten Provinces, containing many Millions of living *Christians*. But the Application is still closer, when we consider that all the People were to be taken like *Fishes* in a Net; and, by Assistance of the *Pope*, who sets up to be the *universal Fisher of Men*, the whole innocent Nation was, according to our common Expression, to be *laid as flat as a* Flounder.

I remember, my self, a particular Cryer of *Flounders* in *London*, who arrived at so much Fame for the Loudness of his Voice, as to have the Honour of being mentioned, upon that Account, in a Comedy. He hath disturbed me many a Morning, before he came within Fifty Doors of my Lodging: And although I were not, in those Days, so fully apprized of the Designs which our common Enemy had then in Agitation; yet, I know not how, by a secret Impulse, young as I was, I could not forbear conceiving a strong Dislike against the Fellow; and often said to my self, this Cry seems to be forged in the *Jesuites* School: *Alas, poor* England! *I am grievously mistaken, if there be not some* Popish *Plot at the Bottom*. I communicated my Thoughts to an intimate Friend, who reproached me with being too visionary in my Speculations. But it proved afterwards, that I conjectured right. And I have since reflected, that if the wicked Faction could have procured only a Thousand Men, of as strong Lungs as the Fellow I mentioned, none can tell how terrible the Consequences might have been, not only to these two Kingdoms, but over all *Europe*, by selling *Flanders* to *France*. And yet these Cries continue unpunished, both in *London* and *Dublin*;

Jonathan Swift

although, I confess, not with equal Vehemency or Loudness; because the Reason for contriving this desperate Plot, is, to our great Felicity, wholly ceased.

It is well known, that the Majority of the *British* House of Commons, in the last Years of Queen *Anne*'s Reign, were in their Hearts directly opposite to the Earl of *Oxford*'s pernicious Measures; which put him under the Necessity of bribing them with Sallaries. Whereupon he had again Recourse to his old Politicks. And accordingly, his Emissaries were very busy in employing certain artful Women, of no good Life or Conversation, (as it was fully proved before Justice *Peyton*) to cry that Vegetable commonly called *Sollary*, through the Town. These Women differed from the common Cryers of that Herb, by some private Mark which I could never learn; but the Matter was notorious enough, and sufficiently talked of; and about the same Period was the Cry of *Sollary* brought over into this Kingdom. But since there is not, at this present, the least Occasion to suspect the Loyalty of our Cryers upon that Article, I am content that it may still be tolerated.

I shall mention but one Cry more, which hath any Reference to Politicks; but is, indeed, of all others, the most insolent, as well as treasonable, under our present happy Establishment. I mean that of *Turnups*; not of *Turnips*, according to the best Orthography, but absolutely *Turnups*. Although this Cry be of an older Date than some of the preceding Enormities; for it began soon after the

An Examination of Certain Abuses, Corruptions, and Enormities

Revolution; yet was it never known to arrive at so great an Height, as during the Earl of *Oxford*'s Power. Some People, (whom I take to be private Enemies) are, indeed, as ready as my self to profess their Disapprobation of this Cry, on Pretence that it began by the Contrivance of certain old Procuresses, who kept Houses of ill Fame, where lewd Women met to draw young Men into Vice. And this they pretend to prove by some Words in the Cry; because, after the Cryer had bawled out *Turnups, ho, buy my dainty Turnups*, he would sometimes add the two following Verses.

> *Turn up the Mistress, and turn up the Maid,*
> *And turn up the Daughter, and be not afraid.*

This, say some political Sophists, plainly shews, that there can be nothing further meant in so infamous a Cry, than an Invitation to Lewdness; which, indeed, ought to be severely punished in all well regulated Governments; yet cannot be fairly interpreted as a Crime of State. But, I hope, we are not so weak and blind to be deluded at this Time of Day, with such poor Evasions. I could, if it were proper, demonstrate the very Time when those two Verses were composed, and name the Author, who was no other than the famous Mr. *Swan*, so well known for his Talent at Quibbling; and was as virulent a *Jacobite* as any in *England*. Neither could he deny the Fact, when he was taxed for it in my Presence, by Sir *Harry Dutton-Colt*, and Colonel *Davenport*, at the *Smyrna* Coffee-House, on the

10th of *June*, 1701. Thus it appears to a Demonstration, that those Verses were only a Blind to conceal the most dangerous Designs of the Party; who, from the first Years after the happy Revolution, used a Cant-way of talking in their Clubs, after this Manner: *We hope to see the Cards shuffled once more, and another King* Turn up *Trump*: And, *when shall we meet over a Dish of* Turnups? The same Term of Art was used in their Plots against the Government, and in their treasonable Letters writ in Cyphers, and decyphered by the famous Dr. *Wallis*, as you may read in the Tryals of those Times. This I thought fit to set forth at large, and in so clear a Light; because the *Scotch* and *French* Authors have given a very different Account of the Word Turnup; but whether out of Ignorance or Partiality, I shall not decree; because, I am sure the Reader is convinced by my Discovery. It is to be observed, that this Cry was sung in a particular Manner, by Fellows in Disguise, to give Notice where those Traytors were to meet, in order to concert their villainous Designs.

I have no more to add upon this Article, than an humble Proposal, that those who cry this Root at present in our Streets of *Dublin*, may be compelled by the Justices of the Peace, to pronounce *Turnip*, and not *Turnup*; for, I am afraid, we have still too many Snakes in our Bosom; and it would be well if their Cellars were sometimes searched, when the Owners least expect it; for I am not out of Fear, that *latet anguis in Herba*.

Thus, we are zealous in Matters of small Moment, while

we neglect those of the highest Importance. I have already made it manifest, that all these Cries were contrived in the *worst of Times*, under the Ministry of that desperate Statesman, *Robert* late Earl of *Oxford*; and for that very Reason, ought to be rejected with Horror, as begun in the Reign of *Jacobites*, and may well be numbered among the Rags of *Popery* and *Treason*: Or if it be thought proper, that these Cries must continue, surely they ought to be only trusted in the Hands of *true Protestants* who have given Security to the Government.

1. BOCCACCIO · *Mrs Rosie and the Priest*
2. GERARD MANLEY HOPKINS · *As kingfishers catch fire*
3. *The Saga of Gunnlaug Serpent-tongue*
4. THOMAS DE QUINCEY · *On Murder Considered as One of the Fine Arts*
5. FRIEDRICH NIETZSCHE · *Aphorisms on Love and Hate*
6. JOHN RUSKIN · *Traffic*
7. PU SONGLING · *Wailing Ghosts*
8. JONATHAN SWIFT · *A Modest Proposal*
9. *Three Tang Dynasty Poets*
10. WALT WHITMAN · *On the Beach at Night Alone*
11. KENKŌ · *A Cup of Sake Beneath the Cherry Trees*
12. BALTASAR GRACIÁN · *How to Use Your Enemies*
13. JOHN KEATS · *The Eve of St Agnes*
14. THOMAS HARDY · *Woman much missed*
15. GUY DE MAUPASSANT · *Femme Fatale*
16. MARCO POLO · *Travels in the Land of Serpents and Pearls*
17. SUETONIUS · *Caligula*
18. APOLLONIUS OF RHODES · *Jason and Medea*
19. ROBERT LOUIS STEVENSON · *Olalla*
20. KARL MARX AND FRIEDRICH ENGELS · *The Communist Manifesto*
21. PETRONIUS · *Trimalchio's Feast*
22. JOHANN PETER HEBEL · *How a Ghastly Story Was Brought to Light by a Common or Garden Butcher's Dog*
23. HANS CHRISTIAN ANDERSEN · *The Tinder Box*
24. RUDYARD KIPLING · *The Gate of the Hundred Sorrows*
25. DANTE · *Circles of Hell*
26. HENRY MAYHEW · *Of Street Piemen*
27. HAFEZ · *The nightingales are drunk*
28. GEOFFREY CHAUCER · *The Wife of Bath*
29. MICHEL DE MONTAIGNE · *How We Weep and Laugh at the Same Thing*
30. THOMAS NASHE · *The Terrors of the Night*
31. EDGAR ALLAN POE · *The Tell-Tale Heart*
32. MARY KINGSLEY · *A Hippo Banquet*
33. JANE AUSTEN · *The Beautifull Cassandra*
34. ANTON CHEKHOV · *Gooseberries*
35. SAMUEL TAYLOR COLERIDGE · *Well, they are gone, and here must I remain*
36. JOHANN WOLFGANG VON GOETHE · *Sketchy, Doubtful, Incomplete Jottings*
37. CHARLES DICKENS · *The Great Winglebury Duel*
38. HERMAN MELVILLE · *The Maldive Shark*
39. ELIZABETH GASKELL · *The Old Nurse's Story*
40. NIKOLAY LESKOV · *The Steel Flea*

41. HONORÉ DE BALZAC · *The Atheist's Mass*
42. CHARLOTTE PERKINS GILMAN · *The Yellow Wall-Paper*
43. C.P. CAVAFY · *Remember, Body . . .*
44. FYODOR DOSTOEVSKY · *The Meek One*
45. GUSTAVE FLAUBERT · *A Simple Heart*
46. NIKOLAI GOGOL · *The Nose*
47. SAMUEL PEPYS · *The Great Fire of London*
48. EDITH WHARTON · *The Reckoning*
49. HENRY JAMES · *The Figure in the Carpet*
50. WILFRED OWEN · *Anthem For Doomed Youth*
51. WOLFGANG AMADEUS MOZART · *My Dearest Father*
52. PLATO · *Socrates' Defence*
53. CHRISTINA ROSSETTI · *Goblin Market*
54. *Sindbad the Sailor*
55. SOPHOCLES · *Antigone*
56. RYŪNOSUKE AKUTAGAWA · *The Life of a Stupid Man*
57. LEO TOLSTOY · *How Much Land Does A Man Need?*
58. GIORGIO VASARI · *Leonardo da Vinci*
59. OSCAR WILDE · *Lord Arthur Savile's Crime*
60. SHEN FU · *The Old Man of the Moon*
61. AESOP · *The Dolphins, the Whales and the Gudgeon*
62. MATSUO BASHŌ · *Lips too Chilled*
63. EMILY BRONTË · *The Night is Darkening Round Me*
64. JOSEPH CONRAD · *To-morrow*
65. RICHARD HAKLUYT · *The Voyage of Sir Francis Drake Around the Whole Globe*
66. KATE CHOPIN · *A Pair of Silk Stockings*
67. CHARLES DARWIN · *It was snowing butterflies*
68. BROTHERS GRIMM · *The Robber Bridegroom*
69. CATULLUS · *I Hate and I Love*
70. HOMER · *Circe and the Cyclops*
71. D. H. LAWRENCE · *Il Duro*
72. KATHERINE MANSFIELD · *Miss Brill*
73. OVID · *The Fall of Icarus*
74. SAPPHO · *Come Close*
75. IVAN TURGENEV · *Kasyan from the Beautiful Lands*
76. VIRGIL · *O Cruel Alexis*
77. H. G. WELLS · *A Slip under the Microscope*
78. HERODOTUS · *The Madness of Cambyses*
79. *Speaking of Siva*
80. *The Dhammapada*